The Gift of E̶t̶e̶r̶n̶a̶l̶ ̶L̶i̶f̶e̶

All have sinned.   :23.

The wages of sin.   Ro. 6:23.

Christ died for our sins.   1 Pe. 3:18.

Repent.   Ac. 3:19.

Saved by grace through faith.   Eph. 2:8.

Confess and believe.   Ro. 10:9-10.

Call on the name.   Ro. 10:13.

Children of God.   1 Jn. 3:1-10.; Jn. 1:12

The believer has eternal life.   Jn. 3:16-18.

Salvation; the written word.   Jn. 20:30

Faith comes by hearing the word. Ro. 10:17

One mediator.   1 Tim. 2:5.

New Testament
TransLine

ἰχθύς

New Testament
TransLine

A LITERAL TRANSLATION IN OUTLINE FORMAT

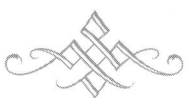

MICHAEL MAGILL

GRAND RAPIDS, MICHIGAN 49530 USA

ZONDERVAN™

New Testament TransLine
Copyright © 2002 by Michael J. Magill

Requests for information should be addressed to:
Zondervan, *Grand Rapids, Michigan 49530*

Library of Congress Cataloging-in-Publication Data

Bible. N.T. English. Magill. 2002.
    New Testament TransLine: a literal translation in outline format / Michael Magill
      p. cm.
    Includes bibliographical references.
    ISBN: 0-310-22803-4
    1. Bible — Outlines, syllabi, etc.   I. Magill, Michael, 1952–.   II. Title.
BS2095 .M26 2002
220'.02'02 — dc21   2001046802
                                                                                                       CIP

This edition printed on acid-free paper.

All rights reserved. No part of this publication may be reproduced, stored in a retrieval system, or transmitted in any form or by any means — electronic, mechanical, photocopy, recording, or any other — except for brief quotations in printed reviews, without the prior permission of the publisher.

Printed in the United States of America

02 03 04 05 06 07 08 /❖ DC/ 10 9 8 7 6 5 4 3 2 1

May the blessing of the Father of Lights rest on all readers and expounders of his inspired Word, and move us all, in these proud and dangerous days, to yield up our high thoughts unto him who 'of God is made unto us wisdom,' and to determine, even as an inspired apostle determined amid the skeptical disputants of his own times, 'not to know anything save Jesus Christ and Him crucified.'

—Charles Ellicott, September 1861, England

The grass withers, the flower fades, but the Word of our God stands forever.

— Isaiah, a prophet of God

All Scripture is God-breathed, and profitable for teaching, for rebuking, for correcting, for training in righteousness, in order that the person of God may be complete, having been equipped for every good work.

— Paul, an apostle of Jesus Christ

Set them apart in the truth. Your Word is truth.

— Jesus Christ, Son of God

Contents

Introduction	ix
Key	xxii
Matthew	1
Mark	108
Luke	177
John	295
Acts	391
Romans	505
1 Corinthians	574
2 Corinthians	634
Galatians	677
Ephesians	697
Philippians	721
Colossians	737
1 Thessalonians	753
2 Thessalonians	765
1 Timothy	775
2 Timothy	795
Titus	807
Philemon	815
Hebrews	820
James	869
1 Peter	887
2 Peter	905
1 John	919
2 John	939
3 John	943
Jude	947
Revelation	955
Maps	1027

Introduction

The New Testament TransLine is a combination of a **TRANS**-lation and an out-**LINE**. It is a literal translation arranged in outline format so as not only to translate the words, but also to visually display the flow of thought contained in the Greek words. The outline format allows the translation to correspond more closely to the Greek forms, grammar, and sentence structure than ever before seen in an English translation, and thus allows the reader to see many things that would have been obvious to Greek readers of the first century, and to see the flow of thought contained in the Greek, as the original writers intended it. The goal of the New Testament TransLine is to enable Bible readers who do not know Greek to gain a depth of insight into the Word formerly available only to those who do. It puts the power to understand God's word at a much deeper level into the hands of all God's people.

The New Testament TransLine features:

1. A literal translation from the Greek corresponding more precisely to the original Greek words and grammar than anything possible in a translation done in prose format. Words not in the Greek are in *italics* or in [brackets]. Words emphasized in the Greek are in **bold**.
2. A visual display of the flow of thought of each book based on the Greek grammar.
3. An overview of each book using the words of the biblical writer.
4. Notes on alternate meanings of a Greek word that help flesh out its meaning.
5. Notes in English listing all the places a Greek word is used in the New Testament for over 3200 words, 59% of the New Testament vocabulary. Thus you can confirm the translation and gain valuable insight into the meaning and usage of a Greek word without knowing any Greek. Abbreviated notes on over 450 additional words (8%) are also included.
6. Notes on interpretation that explain the meaning where needed, or that list the different interpretations made of a particular passage.
7. Notes describing over 3000 textual variations in the Greek manuscripts that lie behind all English translations.
8. The Greek word number (GK number) for each Greek word in the notes. Using this number, readers who do not know any Greek can directly link up to other helpful tools using these word numbers.

Using the New Testament TransLine:

The outline style. When you read, consider the outline numbers as simply a different kind of verse numbering system. Use them to follow the flow of thought. Each outline number is made up of a number and a letter, such as 1A., 1B., 1C., 1D. The letter indicates the outline level (like the traditional I., A., 1., a.). The number indicates the sequential points at that level (as in I., II., III., IV., V.). This style is used because it permits a deeper outline (in one place the outline extends to the "J" level), and is easier to follow over multiple pages. The introduction and conclusion are numbered in the traditional style to separate them from the main flow of thought of the book.

Traditional style	Style used here
I.	1A.

	A.			1B.		
	1.			1C.		
	a.			1D.		
II.			2A.			
	A.		1B.			
	1.		1C.			
	a.		1D.			
	(1).		1E.			
	(a).		1F.			
	B.		2B.			
	C.		3B.			
	1.		1C.			
	2.		2C.			
III.			3A.			

Focus on the New Testament text. Just by reading the translation and following the outline connections, you will understand the flow of thought in most cases. You can read all the "A" points of a book to see the main divisions of the book. You can read all the "B" points under a certain "A" point to see how that point is developed, etc. Using the overview as a guide to the flow of thought, you can follow what is being said at every level throughout the book. This is God's Word. This is where the emphasis of your reading and meditation should be placed. Think about what you do and do not understand, what you want to know and pursue, and what God is calling you to do in response to His Word.

Use only the notes that interest you. The notes are included to assist you, and to be there as a reference when you need them. They speak to many levels of interest, so you will not be interested in all the notes all the time. Just follow your own interests, which will grow as your understanding grows. The notes are not intended to be read all at one time as you are reading the New Testament text. But when you desire, the notes will enable you to study a Greek word by looking up and comparing all its uses, for example.

Use the GK numbers to access other tools. Since the study of the meaning and usage of Greek words is so highly profitable in understanding the New Testament, the Greek word numbers (GK numbers, based on the Goodrick and Kohlenberger numbering system) for each Greek word have been included in the word notes. The reader with no knowledge of Greek can use these word numbers to directly access Kohlenberger's *Greek-English Concordance to the New Testament* (this is often more convenient than looking up the verses one by one), Verbrugge's *The NIV Theological Dictionary of New Testament Words* (this provides a full view of the meaning and usage of significant Greek words), and other tools using this numbering system. The New Testament TransLine will serve you well as the starting point for your studies.

Reference numbers and letters. The small number after a word links you to the corresponding note on the facing page. The small letter after a word links this word to the cross references at the bottom of the facing page. This cross reference links you to the note on this Greek word in the New Testament TransLine. Look for the same English word at the cross reference noted, although the form may be different. For example, if you are looking for "doing" in 1 Jn 3:9, the form at the cross reference may be "doing", "does", "did", "do", or "done". If the English rendering at the cross reference is not the same, then the word to look for is provided after the cross reference. For example, on "appeared" in Mt 1:20, look for a form of "shine" in Phil 2:15.

Verse numbers. The verse numbers down the right hand side of the page indicate that the verse begins on that line, at the left margin. If a verse does not begin at the left margin, or if more than one verse begin on one line, then a raised dot marks the place where the verse begins.

Old Testament references. Unless otherwise noted, all references to words in the Old Testament (such as, "Same word as in Gen 1:1") are to the Greek words in the Septuagint, the ancient Greek translation of the Old Testament (but always using the standard English/Hebrew verse numbers).

How does the outline format contribute to the translation?

Understanding translations. Two general approaches exist for making translations. One is called formal equivalence, or word-for-word translation. It seeks to convey *the words and grammar* used by the writers as much as possible. The NKJV, NASB, RSV, and the New Testament TransLine are examples. The other method is called dynamic equivalence, or thought-for-thought translation. It seeks to convey *the meaning* intended by the writers, using normal and pleasing English terms and grammar that convey the same meaning, rephrasing sentences as needed. This is done to various degrees based on how far the focus is moved from the Greek to the English, and how much "interpretation" is added to the "translation." At one extreme the translation remains close to the Greek, but enhances or clarifies the meaning in English. The NRSV is an example. At the other extreme the translation is a paraphrase completely rewritten into words and phrases chosen by the translator to convey what the translator feels is being said. The Living Bible and The Message are examples. All of these approaches are valid and useful.

Word-for-word translation. Even word-for-word translation, however, cannot follow the Greek absolutely. English is just too different from Greek. Greek does not rely on word order as English does. Long "run on" sentences are normal in Greek, but difficult to follow in English. A strictly word-for-word translation is very difficult for an English reader to follow. To experience this for yourself, just look at an interlinear Greek New Testament, which has the English words printed directly under the Greek words.

The outline format. The outline format permits a translation that corresponds much more precisely to the Greek words and sentence structure. Even the flavor, style and feel of the Greek can be reflected in English. For example, you will see and feel the difference in the writing styles of the four Gospel writers. The outline format serves as a skeleton on which to hang the phrases and sentences, avoiding the need to add words or rephrase in English. For example, Eph 1:3-14 is one long sentence in the Greek. In a prose-format translation, it must be broken up into smaller sentences in order to be understood in English. But this very process, while absolutely necessary and unavoidable, obscures the apostle's flow of thought. The outline format provides a framework that allows you to see Paul's words and his flow of thought as they are in Greek, and the notes help you see the places where people disagree about the flow of thought. Thus the outline format clarifies the meaning intended by the apostle. Commentaries do a wonderful job explaining the New Testament on the Greek or the English level and are essential tools. But often the more words one uses to try to explain the flow of thought, the harder it is to grasp. With the New Testament TransLine, the flow of thought is contained in the outline structure itself. Words of explanation are replaced by the visual presentation, allowing you to focus directly on the words of Scripture.

Comparing translations. Imagine a translation scale of zero to ten, where zero is the Greek New Testament and ten is an exciting English paraphrase such as The Message or The Living Bible. A one would be a Greek-English interlinear. A five would be a translation that seeks to perfectly balance the Greek and English, staying as close to the Greek as possible, but using English sentence structures and phrasing so as to be beautiful and elegant in English. The NASB, KJV, and RSV would be examples of a five. The NRSV would be a six; the NIV a seven. There are many wonderful translations available between five and ten. But none have been able to be more literal than the NASB, for example, because of the limitations of the prose format. The New Testament TransLine would be a three, opening a view into the New Testament never before seen by English readers.

Limitations of the New Testament TransLine:

The translation. Because the New Testament TransLine is more closely equivalent to the Greek, it is also more foreign-sounding to the English ear. Translators call this "translation English," meaning that it reflects the Greek ways of writing rather than the English ways of writing. In good English translations, this is not desirable, since a certain beauty and elegance in English is being sought. But since the goal of the New Testament TransLine is not elegance in English, but to more closely reflect the Greek writings, a more foreign-sounding translation is to be expected. By way of comparison, the NIV expresses the thoughts contained in the Greek using the full breadth and beauty of English, foregoing strict conformity to the Greek phraseology. The New Testament TransLine expresses much more of the breadth and beauty of the Greek phraseology, sacrificing normal English idiom. The RSV, NASB, and NKJV represent the best attempts to strike a pleasing balance between the two languages. There is no perfect translation, only translations that achieve the balance of translation goals they set out to accomplish. The New Testament TransLine is aimed at providing a view of the Greek not currently available to the English reader, even though this results in a translation that from the point of view of English idiom and grammar is inferior to all of the other versions mentioned. But this limitation will not hinder you at all, because if you use the New Testament TransLine together with your regular Bible, you will have the best of both viewpoints! You will be able to clearly see and appreciate the choices made by the translators of your version—how they made short sentences out of long ones, how they smoothed out a foreign-sounding idiom, how they clarified a difficult phrase or sentence, how they phrased the Greek in proper and pleasing English.

Think of it this way. When you hear a foreigner first learning to speak English, you commonly hear such a person rendering the forms and sentence structures of their native language in English words. It sounds foreign to English-speakers. It is improper English. Sometimes it is difficult to understand. As the person learns more English, they adopt the commonly understood English patterns of expression. In a similar way, since the New Testament TransLine is seeking to give the English reader more insight from the Greek point of view, the Greek forms and structures are retained to a greater degree than proper in good English, but not to such a degree that the meaning is obscured. This allows the reader to see and feel more of the Greek. For example, when referring to a man, the Greek form of expression can be "he," "**he**" or "he himself," "the *one*," "this *one*," or "that *one*." All of these are rendered as such in the New Testament TransLine, according to their form in the Greek way of speaking, whereas in the polished English translations mentioned above, they are usually all rendered with the simple "he," according to their function in the normal English way of speaking. In general, the New Testament TransLine seeks to render the actual form of the Greek expressions. When this cannot be consistently done, or when it obscures rather than illuminates, then it is rendered according to its function in normal English, and a note is provided with the more literal rendering.

If the New Testament TransLine, used together with the other versions, permits the English reader to see and feel more of the Greek perspective, to see what the other translations have done to more explicitly render the Greek in better English, and to understand the various ways in which other translations move from the Greek forms of phrasing to normal English patterns of phrasing, and from translating to paraphrasing, then its translation goals will have been attained. The English reader will then be able to evaluate and appreciate the benefits and limitations of each type of translation.

The outline. The outline itself does not come 100% straight from the Greek. No such thing is possible. Said in reverse, the Greek grammar alone does not demand that every point be connected exactly as in the New Testament TransLine. The flow of thought is contained in the events, the ideas, and the grammar. When the flow of thought is contained in the ideas, sometimes it is easy to see and follow, other times it is very difficult. In the places where the reasoning is difficult, meditation on why the thoughts are connected as they are in the New Testament TransLine will result in the reader thinking about the same things Greek scholars and commentary writers think about. In all cases, the outline is based on consideration of every Greek word and the immediate context, with the goal of accurately reflecting what is there. The guiding principle has been that the words themselves must carry the flow of thought. The most natural, simple, clear connection of thought has been sought.

The problem passages. When they exist, the multiple viewpoints on a word or verse are listed. The supporting arguments for the views can be found in the commentaries. The goal of the New Testament TransLine is to alert you to these issues so that you can direct your meditation and study according to your interests. Since the New Testament TransLine is an annotated translation, not a commentary, I do not express my own opinion about which view I prefer (although sometimes it is necessary to reflect a view in the translation). To do so would be of little value without analyzing the issue and all the views, and giving the reasons for my preference, and this would have added considerable length to this volume.

Notes for English readers on the Greek translation:

Vocabulary. In general, the renderings given to the Greek words in the New Testament TransLine are of a broad, simple, standardized nature, and are not as finely nuanced as in other translations. Most translations try to reflect the particular shade or nuance of meaning in each place a certain word is used, minimizing footnotes. The New Testament TransLine tries to use the same rendering in all places a Greek word is used, adding a note containing the other shades of meaning and the other places that word is used so that the reader can compare all the uses of that Greek word. An attempt is made to render different forms of a Greek word (a noun, adjective, adverb, and verb of the same root word, for example) in a way that reflects the relationship between them. For example, see "sound-minded" in 1 Tim 3:2. Words are not independent islands, and by this method the New Testament TransLine seeks to reflect and display more of the interrelationships and connections between the Greek words than is normally done in English. The Greek student can find the more finely-tuned renderings in a lexicon, and English readers can see them in the standard English translations. In addition, the writers often use the same root word in its verb, noun, and adjective form in the same context. For example, "If the salt became tasteless, by what will it be salted?" (Mt 5:13); "the good-news which I announced-as-good-news" (1 Cor 15:1). Or they use the same verb multiple times, as "think" is used three times in Phil 2:2, 5. This repetition is mirrored in the New Testament TransLine whenever possible, allowing the English reader to see the words from the Greek perspective.

Word order. Greek words have different endings that determine the part of speech of each word, so they can be placed almost anywhere in the sentence. English words do not have such endings, so word order is critical. Normal English word order is subject, verb, object, prepositional phrase, as in "Fred hit the ball with the bat." In Greek the word order could be "The ball hit Fred with the bat" or "Hit Fred with the bat the ball." Clearly these must be placed in English word order to be understood in English. Sometimes the Greek word order could be kept in English, but it sounds like poetry to us. For example, "Imitators of me be, brothers," Phil 3:17. Since the writers of the New Testament wrote in the common language of the people, not poetry, the New Testament TransLine in general places words in normal English word order whenever possible, "Brothers, be imitators of me." Thus the word order of the Greek is not retained in the New Testament TransLine, in the interests of understandability. Using English word order in general allows the New Testament TransLine to include other literal aspects of the Greek without overwhelming the English reader with foreignness. But in those cases where the word order is a factor in understanding what is being said, the Greek word order is retained, or an explanation is given in the notes.

Italics. Words in *italics* in the New Testament TransLine are a vital part of the literal translation into English. They are not optional words, but words required or implied by the use in context of various aspects of Greek grammar and sentence construction. Do not skip over them when reading. **Warning:** Italics are used in a different way in the New Testament TransLine and are not directly comparable to their use in other translations! The need to use italics at all illustrates the fact that Greek and English express certain matters in different ways. The Greek can express things through the grammar of the words that the English can express only with additional words. In the New Testament TransLine, the *expressed* Greek words are in plain type; the words *implied by the grammar* of the Greek word, phrase, or sentence structure are in *italic* type. Both together make up a literal translation into English. Using italics to display these words is not a perfect solution, but it does permit more visibility of the Greek word relations than has previously been available to the English reader. Taking this approach, instead of putting all the implied words in plain type as is usually and properly done in English translations, allows the New Testament TransLine to more precisely display the forms of the Greek word relations. This allows the English reader to see things a little more from the Greek perspective. The English reader will understand *that* these words are implied; the reader who knows Greek will understand *why*. In the vast majority of cases, there is no dispute about what word is implied by the grammar, or about the alternate ways to express it accurately in English. It is all quite routine. Where there is uncertainty regarding the intended meaning, the alternatives are given in the notes.

Here are a few examples of the use of italics. Some readers may prefer to skip past these details.

In Greek, the relationship that a noun, pronoun, adjective or article has to the sentence is indicated by the ending on the word, and its use in the context. For example, one ending can imply "of" or "from" or "than"; another, "for" or "to" or "with" or "by" or "in," depending on how the word is used. Thus, the Greek says "the disciples *of* the Pharisees," "*of*" being part of the article "the," so to speak, not an independent word. These implied helping words are in *italics* in the New Testament TransLine, since which one to use is based on the use of the word in context. But Greek also separately expresses these helping words (prepositions), for various reasons. When this is the case, they are in plain type. Thus, the difference in the form of expression chosen by the biblical writer can be clearly seen by the English reader in cases like Luke 1:55, "just as He spoke to [an expressed preposition] our fathers—*to* [implied by the grammar] Abraham and *to* [implied by the grammar] his seed forever."

In Greek, the pronoun "you" has different endings for the singular and the plural. In English, it is not always clear in the context which is being used. So in order to make clear that the "you" is plural, sometimes the word "all" or "people" is added in *italics*. For example, "Do not marvel that I said to you 'You *all* must be born again' " (Jn 3:7). "If I told you *people* earthly things" (Jn 3:12).

In Greek, a writer may deliberately leave routine words out of a phrase or sentence, expecting the reader to supply them from the context. The structure of the phrase or sentence demands that the reader supply the necessary word to make it complete. This is a very common feature of Greek, but not English, which requires more explicitness. For example, the writer may intend that the reader supply the verb, as Peter does in 1 Peter 1:3, "Blessed *be* the God"; "and His ears *are open*" in 3:12; "But if *one suffers*" in 4:16; "Because *it is* time" in 4:17, etc. Or, the reader may be expected to supply the object, as in "I exhort *you*" in 2:11; "blessing *them*" in 3:9; or a possessive pronoun, as in "observing *your* good works" in 2:12; "for *His* possession" in 2:9.

In Greek, the grammar of a participle in context often implies a personal subject, expressed in the New Testament TransLine with the word "one" in *italics*. For example, Peter says "the *One* having caused" in 1:3; "the *ones* being guarded" in 1:5. The "one" is implied by the usage of the participle. These are commonly rephrased in English as "who caused," "who are being guarded."

In Greek, the gender relation of a word is implied by the ending of the word as used in context. For example, Peter says the work of "each *person*" (1:17), the grammar of the adjective "each" in context implying the word "person," or "one" (NASB), or "man" in a generic sense (NIV). The NRSV rephrases "each person" here as "their." Peter's intent is perfectly clear and may be properly expressed in English in these various ways. "Free *ones*" (2:16) and "all *things*" (4:7) are other examples.

In Greek, purpose and result are expressed in several ways, as in English. There are words that are translated "that," "in order that," and "so that." Take for example, "He died in order that He might save us." But many times the word "that" is not stated or is represented by another word. The required words are added in *italics*. For example, "He died *that* He *might* save us," "He died *that He might* save us," "He died *so as* to save us." These all mean the same thing, but represent different grammatical constructions.

In Greek, the usage of the article "the" is not like English. There are many places where Greek includes the article, but it is not needed in English (for example, "I thank God always" would read "I thank the God always"). In these cases, the article is not included in the New Testament TransLine. On the other hand, there are many places where Greek implies an article but does not write it (such as the object of a preposition, "for *the* praise of *the* glory of His grace"). If it is needed in English, it is included in *italics*. Finally, in many places smooth English prefers an article where the Greek does not have one for various reasons ("having taken *the* form of *a* slave"). These are also included in *italics*. Since Greek has no indefinite article, "a" or "an," they are always included in *italics*.

Brackets. When words are added to clarify the meaning of a word, phrase or sentence, they are added in brackets. These words are not implied by the grammar or sentence structure, but by the intended meaning of the biblical writer. If one skips over them, the actual words expressed in Greek may be read. For example, the word "deep feelings" in Mt 9:36 can refer to several specific emotions. The phrase "[of compassion]" is added to clarify the word, but the word is understandable without this clarification. In the phrase "reclining back [to eat]" in Mt 26:20, "[to eat]" is added to the word "reclining back" to bring out its meaning in this context. Others rephrase this idiom as "sat down," since we do not recline to eat in our society as people did in that day. In Mt 9:31, "[the news about]" is added to clarify the meaning. As with words in italics, these words are rarely in dispute. Most are usually in plain type in the other translations; some are in italics. When they are in doubt, the various views are mentioned in a note.

The gender issue. Words such as "sons," "brothers," "man," and the pronoun "he" are often used in the New Testament when both men and women are in view, a custom also followed in English until recent times. Since the New Testament TransLine is reflecting the ancient Greek, these words are rendered as the biblical writers wrote them. Although this is not the modern gender-explicit or gender-neutral way of speaking, it accurately reflects the Greek point of view. The modern reader can easily make the transition between how the Greek states it, and how we in the 21st century prefer to state it. In the case of "brother" and "son," the reader can discern from the context whether physical brothers/sons, fellow-members of Abraham's physical family (Israelites, male and female), or fellow-members of God's spiritual family (fellow-believers, brothers and sisters in the Lord) are in view. In the case of "man," there are Greek words that always refer specifically to a male or a female, and they are translated as such. But there is another Greek word (*anthropos*, from which we get "anthropo"-logy) which means "man" in the sense of "male" and "mankind, a person, whether male or female." In order to clearly reflect the writers' intended meaning in English, this word is translated "man" only when a male person is intended. Otherwise, it is rendered "person, mankind, human." This permits the English reader to see the meaning in places like Jn 6:10, which uses two different words to say that the "people" (*anthropos*) sat down to eat, and the "men" were counted.

Verbs. In English we use helping words to convey the meaning of the verb. For example, consider the verb "walk." We say "to walk," "he has walked," "I have been walking," "having walked," "while walking," "he will walk," "he had walked," "I am walking," "I was walking," etc. The words "to, has, have been, having, while, will, had, am, was," and the pronouns, are helping words. In Greek there are no helping words. Whether the verb means "I am walking," "You will walk," or "They have walked" is indicated by the form of the verb, by the ending on the verb itself (the context indicates whether the third person singular means "he," "she," or "it"). In the New Testament TransLine, the helping words are considered to be part of the verb form itself and are not placed in italics. Special renderings of the tense indicated by the context that overrule the routine meaning of the verb forms are described in the notes. If the pronoun (I, we, you, he, she, they) is separately expressed in Greek, it is done for emphasis. In the New Testament TransLine, such words are in **bold**.

The Greek tenses do not correspond precisely to English tenses. This is especially true of the Perfect tense. For example, consider "It has been written." Put simply, the Greek perfect tense can either lay the stress on a past completed action (as in English, translated as "it has been written"), or on the continuing result of that completed action (translated as "it is written," which sounds like a present tense in English). There is no clear way to bring both senses into English. Most translations choose which emphasis to bring across in each specific case. In general, the New Testament TransLine renders the tenses in an artificially strict fashion. Present tense, "I walk" or "I am walking." Imperfect tense, "I was walking." Future tense, "I will walk." Aorist tense, "I walked" or "I walk." Perfect tense, "I have walked." Pluperfect tense, "I had walked." This method displays the difficult cases in which the meaning of the Greek tense must be interpreted. For example, "I was well pleased" in Mt 17:5.

The Greek participle is one of the rich features of the Greek language and is used in various ways. For example, consider the participle "having come." Based on the context, this could mean "when he came," "after he came," "since he came," "although he came," "if he comes," "because he came," "by his coming," etc. In the New Testament TransLine, however, the participle is translated in an artificially strict fashion in order to communicate to the English reader that a participle is being used and to retain the Greek sentence structure. To illustrate using the word "walk," the verbal use of the participle for the present tense is translated "walking" or "while walking"; for the aorist and perfect tenses, "having walked." The substantive use of the participle for the present tense is translated "The *one* walking" (one is in italics because it is implied in the usage of the participle with the article); for the aorist and perfect tense, "The *one* having walked." The reader can easily discern in most cases which nuance to place on the "while" or "having." When this convention cannot be followed, a note is added to point it out. While the result may not sound like the way we would normally speak in English, it allows the English reader to "hear" the text from the Greek perspective. For example, note Matthew 2:10-12, and Mt 27:48.

>Here is more detail on the verb and participle. Some readers may prefer to skip this section.

>The New Testament TransLine rendering of verbs and participles is deliberately standardized with a non-nuanced, basic significance, reflecting the Greek form of the word. In other words, they are generally rendered in a "raw" form, to which a translator would then normally add a more explicit nuance in English, based on the implications of the context. English simply prefers more explicitness than Greek. In most cases, these nuances from the context are clear and obvious to everyone, and can be supplied by the reader, as intended by the Greek. In some places, there are different opinions about which grammatical nuance the context implies, and these are addressed in the notes. In general, the intent of the New Testament TransLine is to remain one step short of interpreting the grammatical nuance, allowing the reader to see the raw data from which such interpretation proceeds. For example, based on the context, the usage of the participle in "having known God, they did not glorify Him as God" in Rom 1:21 more explicitly means "although they knew"; the verb in "He was teaching them, saying" in Mt 5:2 may mean "He began to teach"; the verb in "I was compelling them to blaspheme" in Act 26:11 may mean "I was trying to compel"; the participle in "how shall we escape, having neglected" in Heb 2:3 more explicitly means "if we neglect."

>This does not mean that the New Testament TransLine's rendering of verbs and participles is "more accurate" or "more literal." Rather, the New Testament TransLine has more simple, more rudimentary, less explicit renderings that follow the Greek forms more closely. The renderings in other translations are fuller, more explicit expressions of the meaning of the word together with its contextual implications, in normal English forms. The one contains the raw data; the other, the finely tuned and polished end-product. But this does mean that the other versions are more interpretive, since they seek to make explicit what is implied by the context, although in the vast majority of cases the interpretation required is minimal, routine, obvious, and undisputed. And this explains, in part, why we see differences of phrasing in the various standard translations. There is more than one way to correctly rephrase these things in English!

The reader who knows Greek will understand the New Testament TransLine renderings for what they are, and will immediately begin considering how to properly nuance them. The English reader can also do this, to some degree. But with English readers, the renderings in the New Testament TransLine face a danger from their "rawness" and standardization, a danger of not being fully understood or perhaps of even being misunderstood. The English reader can avoid such dangers by using the other translations as a guide to the various ways in which the verbs and participles can be properly nuanced.

Linked contrasts. About 90 times in the New Testament, the Greek uses a certain construction (men... de) to link two phrases or sentences together in a contrast, similar to "on the one hand... on the other hand" (but this rendering is too strong in all but a few cases). This idiom is normally not translated into English because we have no equivalent way of saying it. The New Testament TransLine attempts to reflect it by using a bolded word and a dash. For example, "The **harvest** is great— but the workers are few" (Mt 9:37). This idiom does two things: it links the two parts together as one unit of thought, and it alerts the reader at the beginning of the first part that a second part is coming, causing the reader to anticipate the conclusion of the contrast. If while reading you emphasize the bolded word, and pause at the dash, you will approximate the idea of the Greek. When this idiom is used, a note is added saying that the grammar is emphasizing the contrast between the two halves of the sentence.

The Gospels. Because the Gospels each present the details of the life of Christ, there are many parallel accounts of the same events or words. Special care has been taken to ensure that when two Gospels use the same words and grammar, it is translated the same way in both. When they use different words or grammar, the New Testament TransLine reflects it. The cross-references to parallel accounts and verbally similar places are provided in the notes.

The Greek text behind the New Testament TransLine:

The history of the Greek text. The books of the New Testament were written in Greek. In His wisdom, God did not think it necessary to preserve for us the original copy of these books. Instead, we have thousands of handwritten copies—Greek manuscripts and papyrus fragments produced from the second century up to the invention of the printing press. There is far more manuscript evidence for the New Testament documents than for any other document of ancient history. We also have ancient translations of the New Testament, and quotations of New Testament verses in ancient writings, dating from the second to the sixth century and beyond. These and other sources form the raw material from which the Greek New Testament is constructed. Soon after the invention of the printing press, Greek New Testaments began to be printed. Among others were those of Erasmus (1527), Stephanus (1551), and Beza (1598). In fact, it was Robert Stephanus, in his fourth edition of the Greek New Testament published in 1551, who first added the verse numbers which we now use. These Greek texts were the sources used to produce the King James translation in 1611. In 1633, the Greek text behind the KJV began to be called the "Textus Receptus"—the received or standard Greek text. It remained the standard Greek text for 250 years, although other Greek texts continued to be produced. Even today, some still prefer to follow this time-honored text, or one similar to it. The situation changed as a result of the great manuscript discoveries of the 19th and 20th centuries. These resulted in new Greek texts incorporating this important new manuscript evidence. Most modern translations are based upon one of these updated Greek texts. Today's standard Greek text was prepared by a committee of scholars and is used worldwide by Protestants and Catholics, liberals and conservatives, scholars and pastors (though other Greek texts do exist). Except for punctuation, the New Testament TransLine follows this Greek text exactly—not because any (including those who produced it) consider it the final word on the subject, but so that the starting point of this translation is clear to everyone, and so that the variants can be clearly seen and understood.

> This Greek New Testament is printed in two formats, which differ only in the footnotes. The first is published by the United Bible Societies and is called *The Greek New Testament*. The Fourth Revised Edition (UBS4) was published in 1993. The second is published by the German Bible Society and is called the Nestle-Aland *Novum Testamentum Graece*. The 27th edition (NA27) was published in 1993.

Textual variants— the differences between the Greek manuscripts. The handwritten copies which God has left us contain all the types of errors which any honest hand-copier would make. Some were accidental, as when one's eye skips from one line to a similar word in the next line. Some were intentional, as when a difficult idiom or word order or spelling was smoothed out. Sometimes explanatory marginal notes were incorporated into the text by a subsequent copier because he thought the previous copier had accidentally left them out. Each change was then included in all the subsequent copies made from that manuscript. These differences between the Greek manuscripts are called "textual variants." Most of these variances relate to differences of spelling and similar matters of no significance to the meaning of the text. But some are "significant." All the textual variants have been identified and studied by scholars. Many unsung heroes over the centuries have toiled over the thousands of Greek manuscripts and other writings in multiple languages, in a painstaking effort to produce the most accurate Greek text possible. Textual scholars have analyzed every minute detail in all the copies, making the text of the New Testament far more reliable than any other document of antiquity. The result of their work is contained in the Greek New Testament in footnotes listing the significant variants, and detailing the manuscripts that contain them. These textual details may not be important to the average Bible reader. He or she may even ignore the subject and continue to use whatever Bible version is most familiar—a perfectly acceptable choice. But should he or she ever desire to know more about the subject, the laborers have been in the field for centuries, and their work is available for public examination.

> The UBS Greek New Testament lists 1438 sets of variants with a broad description of the manuscripts supporting them. The Nestle-Aland Greek New Testament lists a much larger number of variants with a more brief description of the manuscript support.

Because the New Testament TransLine is a very literal translation, it is able for the first time to allow the English reader to personally examine these variants in detail. As you examine them, you will see that most of them make little if any difference to the meaning of the verse. Some are important, such as Mk 16:8-20, Jn 7:53-8:11. Some will help you understand a difference between English translations such as the NKJV and the NIV. And some will help you in your understanding of the verse. You will also notice the extreme detail and precision reflected in the variants. For example, does it say "Jesus Christ" or "Christ Jesus"; "Spirit" or "Holy Spirit"; "His hands" or "*His* hands"; "He said" or "Jesus said." A substantial but not exhaustive list of variants is included in the New Testament TransLine, providing an accurate picture of the nature of the issue, with particular focus on the variants that are reflected in the major translations and that might be of interest to the English reader.

> Over 1300 textual variants from UBS4 are listed in the notes of the New Testament TransLine in a simplified manner. Over 1300 more variants are provided from NA27. Most of these relate to the KJV. Over 400 more variants are provided that are not listed in either Greek text, but are seen in the KJV. Variants of mainly scholarly interest are not included.

> **Rating the textual variants.** To provide some understanding of the relative certainty of each of the readings in the New Testament TransLine, the ratings given to them by the UBS committee are also given. These ratings represent a thorough analysis of a great deal of detailed and complex manuscript information. Each one is based on manuscript evidence, a theory for weighing that evidence, knowledge of errors common to copyists, and an analysis of the context. These considerations result in a probability as to which reading is most likely to have been the oldest, the one from which the others proceeded. The rating reflects the strength of that probability in the opinion of the UBS committee. The reasoning behind the rating of each variant in UBS4 has been published in Metzger's *A Textual Commentary on the Greek New Testament*. Variants described in the footnotes of UBS4 are identified in the notes of the New Testament TransLine using the letter rating given to them by the UBS4 committee.

{A} means that in the opinion of the committee, the reading is certain.
{B} means that in the opinion of the committee, the reading is almost certain.
{C} means that the committee had difficulty determining which reading was best.
{D} means that the committee had great difficulty arriving at a decision.

The "reading" is the New Testament text. The "variants" or "alternate readings" are in the notes. Variants not listed in UBS4 are identified as follows:

{N} means that the source describing the variant is the 27th edition of the Nestle Aland Greek text. Had these variants been rated by the UBS4 committee, most of them would be {A}, but some were the accepted reading in the 25th edition.

{K} means that the variant comes from the Greek text underlying the KJV but is not listed in UBS4 or NA27, or that the variant is found in the KJV without Greek manuscript support (for example, some readings were included in the KJV based on the Latin translation). Had these variants been rated by the UBS4 committee, most if not all of them would be {A}.

Understanding the ratings. In order to truly understand what lies behind a variant reading and its rating, and to determine whether you agree with the rating, the Greek sources must be studied. Since the English reader cannot do so, he or she will not be able to assess the manuscript evidence for the variants or the theories for weighing it. However, the English reader can understand what the variants are and observe their potential significance to the meaning of the verse. The ratings provide a highly simplified glimpse into the relative strengths of the variants as perceived by the UBS committee. This helps because it will not work to just pick the reading that you think makes best sense. Many variants arose precisely because copyists tried to clarify or simplify a word or phrase that was obscure to them. When utilizing the ratings, however, be aware that other scholars may assess the probabilities differently for a given variant. Even the UBS committee had "majority" and "minority" opinions in a few cases. In addition, some scholars use a different theory to weigh the manuscript evidence, resulting in readings more similar to the KJV. It is not the place of the New Testament TransLine to advocate any theory, to endorse any of these good-faith efforts to produce the best possible Greek text, or to express its own opinion regarding any variant, but simply to present the textual facts for the reader's consideration. The UBS/NA Greek text serves best as the starting point for this purpose.

Primary sources used for this translation:

Greek text:

Aland, Aland, Karavidopoulos, Martini, Metzger, *The Greek New Testament*, Fourth Revised Edition (UBS4), United Bible Societies, 1994.

Aland, *Synopsis of the Four Gospels*, Tenth Edition, German Bible Society, 1993. (A presentation of the parallel accounts and verbally similar portions of the Gospels in parallel columns, with Greek (UBS4) and English (RSV) on facing pages).

Metzger, *A Textual Commentary on the Greek New Testament*, Second Edition, United Bible Societies, 1994. (An explanation of the reasoning of the UBS committee for each textual variant in UBS4).

Nestle, Aland, *Novum Testamentum Graece*, 27th Edition, Deutsche Bibelgesellschaft (German Bible Society), 1993.

Greek-English lexicons:

Danker, *A Greek-English Lexicon of the New Testament and Other Early Christian Literature*, Third Edition of Bauer, Arndt, and Gingrich, The University of Chicago Press, 2000.
Liddell, Scott, Jones, McKenzie, Glare, *A Greek-English Lexicon*, Ninth Edition, Clarendon Press (Oxford University Press), 1996.

Concordances:

Bushell, *BibleWorks 5.0*, Hermeneutika Computer Bible Research Software, 2001. (A computer program linking multiple Greek and Hebrew texts and lexicons, and English and other translations, with a powerful search engine. Based on UBS4).
Kohlenberger, Goodrick, Swanson, *The Greek English Concordance to the New Testament*, Zondervan, 1997. (The Greek word with English excerpts from the NIV, based on UBS4).

All these works are of monumental importance and represent the present culmination of the efforts of hundreds of people over the centuries. They are foundational to our English Bible and to all Bible study. In addition, many commentaries from the last 150 years have been used to define alternate views of problem passages and to double-check the New Testament TransLine. Though I deemed it best not to include source reference details in this volume, I wish to acknowledge my great debt to all these who labored before me with quill and computer. In fact, in a real sense, the New Testament TransLine is a fruit of their labors. It makes available to the English reader a more sizeable and worthy portion of their work.

KEY TO THE TRANSLATION

Italics indicate words that are implied by the grammar of the Greek word, phrase, or sentence structure, or are required in normal English grammar. They are part of the literal translation.

[Brackets] indicate words added to clarify the meaning intended by the biblical writer. Skip over these words if you like, and what remains will be the literal translation.

Bold words are the words actually emphasized in the Greek by the biblical writer. For example, sometimes a subject is emphasized, "But **I** say to you," or, "**they** will be comforted." Sometimes the Greek word order is arranged so as to place emphasis on a word.

Dashed words are single Greek words translated by multiple English words. For example, "announced-as-good-news" represents a single Greek word. Such words are dashed when linked to notes, and on some other occasions. Every occurrence of such words is not dashed.

Small numbers after a word, like Savior^{12}, point to a note on the facing note page.

Small letters after a word, like Savior^{A}, point to the list of cross references at the bottom of the note page. The reference listed for that letter gives the location of the note on that word.

Verse numbers in the right-hand column mark the beginning of each verse. If the verse does not start at the beginning of the line, a raised dot marks the place.

KEY TO THE NOTES

Or, means that alternate translations of that Greek word or phrase are being given.

That is, means that an explanation of what is said is being given.

Some ... Others indicate different views as to the meaning.

Elsewhere only means that all the other places where that Greek word is used are listed.

Same word as means that some of the other uses are listed, but not all.

Related to indicates that another form of the same root word is being given. For example, the noun, verb and adjective forms of the same Greek root word might be listed.

Some manuscripts say indicates that a variant reading is being given.

{A}, {B}, {C}, {D}, {N}, {K} are ratings of the probability that the reading in the text is the oldest. This is explained in the Introduction under "The Greek text behind the New Testament TransLine."

GK *2652* is the Greek word number for that word. Use it to find that Greek word in products that use the GK numbering system.

Overview | # Matthew

1A. The book of the genealogy of Jesus Christ, son of David, son of Abraham	1:1-17
2A. Now the birth of Jesus Christ was as follows— He was fathered in Mary by the Holy Spirit	1:18-25
3A. Now after His birth, magi worshiped Him, Herod tried to kill Him, and God protected Him	2:1-23
4A. Now during those days John the Baptist comes, proclaiming in Judea. Repent, the kingdom is near	3:1-12
5A. Then Jesus comes from Galilee to the Jordan to John to be baptized by him	3:13-17
6A. Then Jesus was led up into the wilderness by the Spirit to be tempted by the devil	4:1-11
7A. And He went back to Galilee. From that time on, He proclaimed the kingdom. He called disciples. He went around all Galilee teaching, proclaiming, and curing. The report went out to all Syria	4:12-24
8A. And large crowds followed Him from Galilee, Decapolis, Jerusalem, and Judea. And having seen the crowds, He went up to the mountain and was teaching them, saying—	4:25-5:2
1B. Blessed are the poor in spirit, the mourners, the gentle, the hungry, the merciful, and others	5:3-12
2B. You are the salt of the earth. If salt becomes tasteless, it no longer has strength for anything	5:13
3B. You are the light of the world. Let your light shine so that people may glorify your Father	5:14-16
4B. I came to fulfill the Law. Unless your righteousness abounds, you will not enter. Murder and anger, adultery and lust, divorce, oaths, eye for an eye, love and hate. Be perfect	5:17-48
5B. But take heed not to do your righteousness before people— almsgiving, praying, fasting	6:1-18
6B. Do not be treasuring up treasures on earth, but seek His kingdom. You cannot be serving both	6:19-34
7B. Do not be judging others. With what judgment you judge, you will be judged. Pearls and pigs	7:1-6
8B. Be asking and you will receive; seeking and you will find; knocking and it will be opened	7:7-11
9B. Therefore, everything you want others to be doing to you, you be doing to them	7:12
10B. Enter through the narrow gate on the narrow road leading to life	7:13-14
11B. Beware of the false prophets. You will know them by their fruits	7:15-20
12B. Not everyone saying "Lord, Lord" will enter the kingdom, but the one doing God's will	7:21-27
9A. And when Jesus finished these words, they were astounded. And having come down from the mountain, large crowds followed Him	7:28-8:1
1B. And a leper said, If You are willing, You are able to cleanse me. I am willing. Be cleansed	8:2-4
2B. And having entered Capernaum, He healed a centurion's paralyzed servant. Great faith	8:5-13
3B. And having come into Peter's house, He healed the fever of Peter's mother-in-law	8:14-15
4B. And having become evening, they brought Him many, and He healed them all	8:16-17
5B. They departed for the other side. On the sea, He calmed the storm	8:18-27
6B. And at the other side of the sea, Jesus cast demons into a herd of pigs	8:28-34
7B. And He crossed back over the sea, and forgave and healed a paralytic. Which is easier?	9:1-8
8B. He called Matthew. While eating at his house, the Pharisees objected. The ill need a physician	9:9-13
9B. Then the disciples of John come and asked why His disciples are not fasting. New wine	9:14-17
10B. While answering, an official asked Him to raise his daughter. Going, He healed a woman	9:18-26
11B. And passing on from there, two blind men followed Him. Jesus healed them	9:27-31
12B. And He healed a mute man. The crowds marveled, the Pharisees called it Satanic	9:32-34
10A. And Jesus was going through all the villages teaching, proclaiming and curing. And having seen the crowds, He had deep feelings for them, for they were like sheep not having a shepherd	9:35-36
1B. Then He says to His disciples, Ask the Lord of the harvest to send out workers	9:37-38
2B. And having summoned the twelve, He gave them authority over demons and diseases	10:1
3B. Now the names of the twelve apostles are these	10:2-4
4B. Jesus sent out these twelve, after instruction, to proclaim the kingdom to Israel and heal	10:5-42
5B. When He finished giving directions to the twelve, He passed on to teach and proclaim	11:1

Matthew
Overview

11A. Now John, having heard in prison of His works, sent his disciples to ask— Are you the One?　　11:2-3

   1B. And Jesus said to them, Report to John what you are hearing and seeing　　11:4-6
   2B. And while they were proceeding, Jesus spoke of John. If you will accept it, John is Elijah　　11:7-19
   3B. Then Jesus began to reproach the cities in which He did miracles for not repenting　　11:20-24
   4B. At that time, Jesus praised God for hiding these things from the wise. Come to Me, all　　11:25-30
   5B. At that time, the Pharisees objected to them picking grain. I am Lord of the Sabbath　　12:1-8
   6B. In their synagogue, Jesus healed on the Sabbath. The Pharisees plotted against Him　　12:9-21
   7B. Then Jesus healed, and the Pharisees said He did it by Beelzebub. It will not be forgiven　　12:22-37
   8B. Then scribes and Pharisees said, We want to see a sign. No sign will be given　　12:38-45
   9B. While still speaking, His family came. He said, My family is whoever does God's will　　12:46-50
   10B. On that day, from a boat, He spoke to the crowds in parables about the kingdom　　13:1-35
   11B. Then having left the crowds, He explained and spoke parables to the disciples　　13:36-52
   12B. When He finished these parables, He went to His hometown. They took offense　　13:53-58
   13B. At that time, Herod said Jesus is John the Baptist, risen from the dead　　14:1-12
   14B. And having heard of it, Jesus withdrew. Crowds followed. He fed 5000　　14:13-21
   15B. And He sent the disciples away in a boat. At night, He walked out to them on water　　14:22-33
   16B. And having crossed, He healed the sick. All who touched His garment were healed　　14:34-36
   17B. Then Pharisees objected to a lack of hand-washing. What comes out of the heart defiles　　15:1-20
   18B. And Jesus withdrew to Tyre and Sidon. He healed the daughter of a Canaanite woman　　15:21-28
   19B. And He went beside the Sea of Galilee, where He healed large crowds and fed 4000　　15:29-38
   20B. And having crossed to Magadan, the Pharisees asked for a sign from heaven　　15:39-16:4
   21B. And having crossed, Jesus said to the disciples, Beware of the leaven of the Pharisees　　16:4-12
   22B. Jesus asks His disciples, Who do you say I am? You are the Christ, the Son of God　　16:13-20

12A. From that time on, Jesus began to show them He must go to Jerusalem, suffer, die, rise again　　16:21

   1B. And having taken Him aside, Peter said, This shall never happen to you. Get behind Me　　16:22-23
   2B. Then He said to them, Deny yourself and follow Me. Some here will see My glory　　16:24-28
   3B. And after six days, Jesus was transfigured before Peter, James and John　　17:1-8
   4B. And coming down from the mountain, Jesus said, Tell no one. They asked about Elijah　　17:9-13
   5B. And having come to the crowd, Jesus healed a person that the disciples could not heal　　17:14-21
   6B. And being gathered in Galilee, Jesus said He would be killed, and raised the third day　　17:22-23
   7B. And having come to Capernaum, Peter got their tax money from the mouth of a fish　　17:24-27
   8B. At that hour, they asked, "Who is greater in the kingdom? He said, the childlike believer　　18:1-35

13A. And when He finished these words, He left Galilee for Judea. He healed large crowds there　　19:1-2

   1B. And Pharisees came to Him, testing Him regarding divorce and the Law of Moses　　19:3-12
   2B. Then children were brought to Him, and He laid His hands upon them　　19:13-15
   3B. And one asked, What should I do to have eternal life? It is hard for the rich to enter. As　　19:16-20:16
      for you, you will sit on twelve thrones. But many first will be last
   4B. And while going up to Jerusalem, He said, I will be crucified, and raised on the third day　　20:17-19
   5B. Then the mother of James and John asked that they sit on His right hand and left　　20:20-28
   6B. And while leaving Jericho, Jesus healed two blind men　　20:29-34
   7B. And near Jerusalem, Jesus sent the disciples to get a donkey. He enters with hosannas　　21:1-9

Overview | **Matthew**

14A. And having entered Jerusalem, the whole city said, Who is this? It is the prophet, Jesus — 21:10-11

  1B. And Jesus entered the temple and threw out those buying and selling. Priests objected — 21:12-17
  2B. Now in the morning, Jesus cursed a barren fig tree. It withered — 21:18-22
  3B. And having come into the temple, the priests asked, By what authority do you do this? He said, Tell me first the source of John's baptism. They refused. He spoke parables — 21:23-22:14
  4B. Then the Pharisees tried to snare Him, saying, Is it lawful to pay a poll tax to Caesar? — 22:15-22
  5B. On that day, the Sadducees asked, Whose wife will she be in the resurrection? — 22:23-33
  6B. And a Pharisee Law-expert asked, Which is the great commandment in the Law? — 22:34-40
  7B. Jesus asked them, If the Christ is the son of David, why does David call him Lord? — 22:41-46
  8B. Then Jesus rebuked the Pharisees. Woe to you. Your house is left to you desolate — 23:1-39
  9B. And having departed from the temple, the disciples showed Jesus the buildings of the temple — 24:1

    1C. He said, Not a stone will be left upon a stone which will not be torn down — 24:2
    2C. They asked Him privately, "When? And what will be the sign of Your coming? — 24:3
    3C. And Jesus said to them— — 24:4

      1D. Watch out that no one deceive you, saying 'I am the Christ'. There will be wars — 24:5-6
      2D. Wars, famines, and earthquakes are the beginning of birth-pains. You will be killed. The good news will be proclaimed to the world. Then the end will come — 24:7-14
      3D. When you see the abomination, flee. For then there will be a great affliction — 24:15-28
      4D. After those days, the sun and moon will be darkened, the stars will fall — 24:29
      5D. Then the Son of Man will appear. He will send forth His angels — 24:30-31
      6D. Now learn the parable of the fig tree. When you see all these things, He is near — 24:32-35
      7D. But no one knows the day or hour. It will be like the days of Noah, like a thief — 24:36-44
      8D. Who then is the faithful slave? The one found doing His will when He comes — 24:45-51
      9D. The kingdom is like ten virgins, five prepared, five unprepared when He comes — 25:1-13
      10D. It is like a man who handed over his belongings to his slaves— 5, 2, and 1 talents — 25:14-30
      11D. When He comes, He will sit on His throne and send people to their destinies — 25:31-46

15A. And when Jesus finished all these words, He said, After two days, I will be crucified — 26:1-2

  1B. Then the priests gathered to plot to seize and kill Jesus. Not during the Feast — 26:3-5
  2B. A woman anoints Jesus with costly perfume. She is preparing me for burial — 26:6-13
  3B. Then Judas asks, What are you willing to give me to betray Jesus? Thirty silver coins — 26:14-16
  4B. They eat the Passover. One of you will betray Me. The bread and the cup — 26:17-29
  5B. On the Mount of Olives, Jesus said, You all will be caused to fall. Peter said, not me! — 26:30-35
  6B. At Gethsemane, He prays, they sleep. Judas arrives. They seize Him. The disciples flee — 26:36-56
  7B. The priests and elders condemn Him to death. Peter denies Him three times — 26:57-75
  8B. Having become morning, they led Him away bound, to Pilate — 27:1-2
  9B. Then Judas, having seen that He was condemned, regretted it. He hanged himself — 27:3-10
  10B. Pilate asked, Are You King of the Jews? Jesus or Barabbas? Crucify Him! — 27:11-26
  11B. Then they mocked Him, crucified Him, blasphemed Him. Jesus let His spirit go — 27:27-56
  12B. Having become evening, Joseph asks for His body and places it in his new tomb — 27:57-61
  13B. On the next day, the priests ask Pilate to guard the tomb. They seal it — 27:62-66

16A. On Sunday, He arose. They met Him and worshiped Him. He said, Go and make disciples — 28:1-20

Matthew 1:1		Verse

1A.[1] *The* book[2] *of the* genealogy[3] *of* Jesus Christ, son *of* David, son *of* Abraham—   1

    1B. Abraham fathered[4] Isaac, and Isaac fathered Jacob, and Jacob fathered Judah and his brothers,°and   2-3
Judah fathered Perez and Zerah by Tamar, and Perez[5] fathered Hezron, and Hezron fathered Ram,
and Ram fathered Aminadab, and Aminadab fathered Nahshon, and Nahshon fathered Salmon,°and   4-5
Salmon fathered Boaz by Rahab, and Boaz fathered Obed by Ruth, and Obed fathered Jesse,°and   6
Jesse fathered David the king

    2B. And David[6] fathered Solomon by the *one of* Uriah,°and Solomon fathered Rehoboam, and   7
Rehoboam fathered Abijah, and Abijah fathered Asaph[7],°and Asaph fathered Jehoshaphat, and   8
Jehoshaphat fathered Joram, and Joram fathered[8] Uzziah,°and Uzziah fathered Jotham, and Jotham   9
fathered Ahaz, and Ahaz fathered Hezekiah,°and Hezekiah fathered Manasseh, and Manasseh   10
fathered Amos[9], and Amos fathered Josiah,°and Josiah fathered[10] Jeconiah and his brothers at the   11
time of the deportation *of* Babylon

    3B. And after the deportation *of* Babylon, Jeconiah fathered Shealtiel, and Shealtiel fathered   12
Zerubbabel,°and Zerubbabel fathered Abihud[11], and Abihud fathered Eliakim, and Eliakim fathered   13
Azor,°and Azor fathered Zadok, and Zadok fathered Achim, and Achim fathered Eliud,°and Eliud   14-15
fathered Eleazar, and Eleazar fathered Matthan, and Matthan fathered Jacob,°and Jacob fathered   16
Joseph[12] the husband *of* Mary— by whom[13] Jesus was born[A], the *One* being called Christ

    4B. So all[14] the generations[B] from Abraham to David *are* fourteen generations, and from David to the   17
deportation *of* Babylon *are* fourteen generations, and from the deportation[15] *of* Babylon to the Christ
are fourteen generations

2A.[16] Now the birth[17] *of* Jesus Christ[18] was as follows   18

    1B. His mother Mary having been promised-in-marriage[19] *to* Joseph— before they came-together[20],
she was found[21] having *a* child in *the* womb[C] by[22] *the* Holy Spirit

    2B. And Joseph her husband[23]— being righteous[24], and not wanting[D] to publicly-expose[25] her—   19
intended[26] to send her away[27] secretly[28]

        1C. And he having pondered[29] these *things,* behold— *an* angel *of the* Lord appeared[E] *to* him in *a*   20
dream[F], saying

            1D. "Joseph, son *of* David, do not fear[30] to take[31] Mary *as* your wife. For the *child* having
been fathered[32] in her is by *the* Holy Spirit. °And she will give-birth[G] to *a* Son. And you   21
shall call[H] His name Jesus. For **He** will save[J] His people[K] from their sins

            2D. And[33] this entire *thing*[34] has taken place in order that the *thing* might be fulfilled[L] having   22
been spoken[35] by *the* Lord through the prophet[M] saying

                1E. "Behold— the virgin[N] will have *a* child in *the* womb[C], and she will give-birth[G] to *a*   23
Son. And they will call[H] His name 'Immanuel' " [Isa 7:14], which being translated[O]
is "God with us"

        2C. And Joseph, having arisen from the sleep, did as the angel *of the* Lord commanded[P] him and   24
took *her as* his wife. °And he was not knowing[36] her until which *time* she gave-birth[G] to *a*   25
Son[37]. And he called[H] His name Jesus

3A. Now Jesus having been born[A] in Bethlehem *of* Judea in *the* days *of* Herod the king[38]—   2:1

1. On the genealogy of Jesus, compare Lk 3:23-38.
2. Or, "record". Same word used in phrases like "the book of Psalms", "the book of life". Used 10 times. GK *1047*.
3. Or, "origin, beginning, birth". Our word "genesis" is a transliteration of this word. Some translate this word "history, account" as in Gen 2:4, taking this verse as a title to the whole book. In Gen 5:1, it means "genealogy". On this word, see "existence" in Jam 3:6.
4. Or, "caused to be born, became the father or progenitor of, begat". On this word, see "born" in 1 Jn 2:29. It is used of a child, and, skipping generations, of more distant descendants, such as a grandchild or great grandchild. "Born" in v 16 and 2:1 is the same word, with different grammar.
5. From Perez to David, Matthew follows the Septuagint (or, LXX, the Greek translation of the Hebrew OT used at that time) at Ruth 4:18-22, including the spelling of names (except for Boaz and Obed). In both places, some generations appear to be omitted between Rahab and David, based on 1 King 6:1.
6. From Solomon to Zerubbabel, Matthew follows 1 Chron 3:5-19, with spelling differences on Solomon, Jotham, and Josiah. He also substitutes "Uzziah" (his name in 2 Chron 26:1) for "Azariah" (his name in 1 Chron 3:12). Some manuscripts say "David the king" {N}.
7. Some manuscripts say "Asa" here and next {B}, as in 1 Chron 3:10. Some think the incorrect "Asaph" was later changed to the correct "Asa". Others think the correct "Asa" was later changed or copied incorrectly as "Asaph". GK *811*.
8. Ahaziah, Joash and Amaziah are omitted.
9. Some manuscripts say "Amon" here and next {B}, as in 1 Chron 3:14. Same issue as "Asaph".
10. Jehoiakim is omitted. His son, Jehoiachin, was also known as Jeconiah.
11. The names from Abihud to Jacob are not otherwise known to us.
12. Some think this is the personal genealogy of Joseph. Others think it is the legal, royal line of succession to David's throne down to Joseph. There are other views. See Luke 3:23.
13. This word is feminine, referring to Mary. Some manuscripts say "Joseph— *to* whom having been promised-in-marriage, the virgin Mary bore Jesus, the *One* being called Christ" {A}.
14. That is, all the ones Matthew names above. Matthew limits his list to fourteen in each group.
15. In order to have fourteen in each group, some think Matthew intends Jeconiah to be counted twice. He is the last son before the deportation and the first father after. Others think that David is to be counted in both group one and two, and Jeconiah only in group three. Others think that the Jeconiah in group two refers to Jehoiakim and the Jeconiah in group three refers to Jehoiachin. Others think that Mary is to be counted in addition to Joseph in group three.
16. On the birth and childhood of Jesus, compare Lk 2:1-52.
17. Same word as "genealogy" in v 1.
18. Some manuscripts say "Christ Jesus"; others, "Jesus" {B}.
19. Or, "betrothed". That is, by her parents, according to their custom. Elsewhere only in Lk 1:27; 2:5. GK *3650*.
20. Some think Matthew means this in a sexual sense. Others think he means "before Joseph brought her into his house", the next step after the betrothal (and which includes the sexual sense). GK *5302*.
21. That is, by Joseph. This would be considered adultery even though they were only betrothed, Deut 22:23-24.
22. That is, she was pregnant by the Holy Spirit. Same word as in "by" Tamar, Rahab, Ruth, etc., v 3, 5, 6, 16, 20. GK *1666*.
23. We would say "her *future* husband". On this word, see "man" in 1 Tim 2:12.
24. Because Joseph was righteous, he was no longer willing to take her— an adulteress— as his wife.
25. Or, "disgrace, make a public example of ". Elsewhere only as "exposed" in Col 2:15. GK *1258*. Related to "publicly disgrace" in Heb 6:6.
26. Or, "wanted, resolved, desired, wished". On this word, see "willed" in Jam 1:18.
27. That is, to divorce her. On this word, "send away", see 5:31. Joseph planned to end their promise to marry by giving her a bill of divorce, without publicly charging her with adultery.
28. Or, "privately, quietly, *in* secret", in a manner unseen, not known, not noticed, not observed, that escapes the notice of others. Elsewhere only in 2:7; Jn 11:28; Act 16:37. GK *3277*. Related to "escape notice" in 2 Pet 3:5.
29. Or, "thought out, considered, reflected on". Elsewhere only as "thinking" in 9:4. GK *1926*. Related to the word in Act 10:19, and "thoughts" in Heb 4:12.
30. Or, "become afraid". On this word, see "respecting" in Eph 5:33.
31. Same word as in v 24; 2:13, 14, 20, 21; 4:5, 8; Jn 14:3. On this word, see Lk 17:34.
32. Same word as was used throughout the genealogy above. See v 2.
33. Some think this is Matthew's comment. Others think it is still the words of the angel.
34. This expression "this entire *thing*" is elsewhere only in 26:56, in a similar statement.
35. Or, "the *word* having been spoken, what *was* spoken". This phrase "the *thing* having been spoken" is unique to Matthew. It occurs only in 1:22; 2:15, 17, 23; 4:14; 8:17; 12:17; 13:35; 21:4; 22:31; 24:15; 27:9. In addition, in each case where it is present, "saying" modifies "prophet" ("God" in 22:31). It is spoken by the Lord, through the prophet who says what follows.
36. That is, Joseph was not having sexual intercourse with Mary. On this word, see Lk 1:34.
37. Some manuscripts say "her firstborn Son" {A}. Compare 13:55-56.
38. That is, Herod the Great, king of Judea from 37 to 4 B.C. He is mentioned only in Mt 2 and Lk 1:5. He built the Temple in Jerusalem, the city and harbor of Caesarea, Masada, etc. Upon his death, his kingdom was divided among three of his sons— Archelaus (v 22) and Antipas (Mt 14:1) from one wife, and Philip II (Lk 3:1) from a second wife. A third wife bore Philip I (Mt 14:3). A fourth wife bore Aristobulus, who became the father of Agrippa (Act 12:1) and Herodias (Mt 14:3). Herodias married Philip I and had a daughter named Salome (Mt 14:6); and later left him and married Antipas, to which John the Baptist objected. Salome later married Philip II. Elsewhere in the Gospels, "Herod" refers to this man's son, Herod Antipas. GK *2476*.

A. 1 Jn 2:29 B. Mt 24:34 C. 1 Thes 5:3 D. Jn 7:17, willing E. Phil 2:15, shine F. Mt 2:12 G. Lk 2:11, born H. Rom 8:30 J. Lk 19:10
K. Rev 21:3 L. Eph 5:18, filled M. 1 Cor 12:28 N. Rev 14:14 O. Act 13:8 P. Act 17:26, appointed

Matthew 2:2	6	Verse

    1B. Behold— magi[1] from *the* east arrived in Jerusalem, saying, "Where is the *One* having been born King *of* the Jews? For we saw His star[A] in the east[2], and came to pay-homage[3] *to* Him"   2

    2B. And having heard *it*, King Herod was disturbed[4], and all Jerusalem with him   3

        1C. And having gathered-together[B] all the chief priests and scribes *of* the people, he was inquiring[C] from them *as to* where the Christ was[5] [to be] born   4

        2C. And the *ones* said *to* him, "In Bethlehem *of* Judea. For thus it has been written through the prophet [in Mic 5:2]—   5

            1D. 'And **you**, Bethlehem, land *of* Judah, are by no means least among the rulers[D] *of* Judah. For *One* ruling[6] will come out of you Who will shepherd[E] My people Israel' "   6

        3C. Then Herod, having called the magi secretly, learned-accurately[7] from them the time *of* the appearing[F] *of the* star[A]   7

        4C. And having sent them to Bethlehem, he said, "Having gone, search-out[G] accurately[8] concerning the Child. And when you find *Him*, report[H] *to* me so that **I** also, having come, may pay-homage[9] *to* Him"   8

    3B. And the *ones,* having heard the king, proceeded. And behold— the star[A] which they saw in the east[10] was going-ahead-of [J] them, until having come, it stood[11] over where the Child was   9

        1C. And having seen the star,[12] they rejoiced *with* extremely great joy[13]   10

        2C. And having come into the house[14], they saw[15] the Child with Mary His mother   11

        3C. And having fallen-*down*, they paid homage *to* Him

        4C. And having opened their treasure-chests[K], they offered[L] gifts *to* Him— gold and frankincense[16] and myrrh[17]

        5C. And having been warned[M] in *a* dream[18] not to return to Herod, they went back to their country by another way   12

    4B. And they having gone away, behold— *an* angel *of the* Lord appears[F] *to* Joseph in *a* dream saying, "Having arisen, take the Child and His mother, and flee into Egypt. And be there until I tell you. For Herod is about to seek-*for* the Child *that* he might destroy[N] Him"   13

        1C. And the *one*, having arisen, took the Child and His mother *by* night and withdrew[O] into Egypt, and was there until the end[19] *of* Herod— in order that the *thing* might be fulfilled having been spoken by *the* Lord through the prophet saying "I called My Son out of Egypt" [Hos 11:1]   14   15

    5B. Then Herod, having seen that he was tricked[20] by the magi, became very furious[21]. And having sent-out *men*, he killed[22] all the boys[P]— the *ones* in Bethlehem and in all its districts from two years old and under— in accordance with the time which he learned-accurately[23] from the magi   16

        1C. Then the *thing* was fulfilled[Q] having been spoken through Jeremiah the prophet saying[24] "*A* voice was heard in Ramah[25], weeping[26] and great mourning— Rachel weeping-*for*[R] her children. And she was not willing to be comforted[S], because they are no *more*[27]" [Jer 31:15]   17-18

    6B. And Herod having come-to-an-end[28], behold— *an* angel *of the* Lord appears[F] *to* Joseph in *a* dream in Egypt saying, "Having arisen, take the Child and His mother, and proceed into *the* land *of* Israel. For the *ones* seeking the life *of* the Child are dead"   19   20

        1C. And the *one*, having arisen, took the Child and His mother and entered into *the* land *of* Israel   21

1. These were wise men-priests-seers, experts in astrology and interpretation of dreams. While their country is not known, they are at least similar to the Babylonian wise men over whom Daniel was made ruler, Dan 2:48. Perhaps their knowledge came from Daniel's prophecies. This word is used in Dan 1:20; 2:2, 10, 27; 5:7, 11, 15, where it is translated "conjurers" (NASB), "astrologers" (NKJV), or "enchanters" (NIV, NRSV). The singular is "magus". The plural is "magi" in Mt 2:1; 7, 16. Elsewhere only as "magician" in Act 13:6, 8. GK *3407*. Related to "practice magic" in Act 8:9.
2. That is, while they were in the east. The star was west of them. Or, "at *its* rising". Same phrase as in v 9. "East" is "from *the* rising *of the* sun" (Rev 7:2; 16:12), where "rising" is the same word as "east" here. Same word as in 2:1, 9; 8:11; 24:27; Mk 16 short ending; Lk 13:29; Rev 21:13. Elsewhere only as "rising" in Lk 1:78. GK *424*.
3. Or, "worship". On this word, see "worship" in 14:33. Same word as in v 8, 11.
4. Or, "troubled, unsettled, stirred up, thrown into confusion". On this word, see Gal 1:7.
5. More literally, "is", as the Greek typically phrases it.
6. Or, "governing, leading". On this word, see "leading" in Heb 13:7.
7. Or, "ascertained exactly". Elsewhere only in v 16. GK *208*. Related to "accurately" in v 8.
8. Or, "carefully". Same word as in Act 18:25, 26; 23:15, 20; 24:22; 1 Thes 5:2. Elsewhere only as "carefully" in Lk 1:3; Eph 5:15. GK *209*.
9. Same word as v 2.
10. Or, "at *its* rising", as in v 2.
11. Or, "was stopped, stood [still]". On this word, see "standing" in Mk 13:14.
12. They "saw" it in the east (v 2, 9), which may imply they had not seen it since. Now they see it again and rejoice. Or, Matthew may mean "having seen the star stop and stand over where the Child was", they rejoiced.
13. More literally, "rejoiced *an* extremely great rejoicing". Similar to the phrase in Jn 3:29, and in 1 Thes 3:9.
14. Joseph has apparently moved his family from the stable (Lk 2:7) to a house, something he would do as quickly as possible.
15. Some manuscripts say "found" {N}.
16. Or, "incense". Elsewhere only in Rev 18:13. This is a white gum used in worship, and used medicinally. GK *3337*.
17. This is a resinous, aromatic gum used with incense. Elsewhere only in Jn 19:39, where it is used to anoint the dead for burial. GK *5043*.
18. Or, "by way of *a* dream", a phrase used only by Matthew. Elsewhere only in Mt 1:20; 2:12, 13, 19, 22; 27:19. GK *3941*.
19. That is, the death of Herod. This is a euphemism for death. Used only here. GK *5463*. Related word in v 19.
20. Or, "made a fool, mocked". Same word used of Christ being "mocked". On this word, see Lk 23:11.
21. Or, "enraged". Used only here. GK *2597*. Related to "fury" in Rev 16:19.
22. Or, "did away with". Some think this might have involved up to twenty infants, given the size of Bethlehem. Used with reference to persons as killing in the sense of "taking" life, whether in battle, by murder, assassination, suicide, or execution. The root word is "to take". Same word as in Lk 22:2; Act 2:23; 5:33, 36; 7:28; 9:23, 24, 29; 10:39; 12:2; 16:27; 22:20; 23:15, 21, 27; 25:3; 26:10; 2 Thes 2:8. Elsewhere only as "execute" in Lk 22:32; Act 13:28; "do away with" in Heb 10:9; and with different grammar, "take up" in Act 7:21. GK *359*.
23. Same word as in v 7. That is, the time since they first saw the star.
24. This word modifies "prophet". That is, spoken by the Lord, through Jeremiah the prophet who says what follows. See 1:22.
25. This is a town about 6 miles or 9 kilometers north of Jerusalem. Bethlehem was about 4.5 miles or 7 kilometers south of Jerusalem. GK *4821*.
26. Some manuscripts say "lamentation and weeping and great mourning" {B}.
27. Or, "not *alive*, not *there*". In Jer 31:15, Rachel, representing the mother of the nation, weeps over the ten tribes killed or carried into captivity by the Assyrians. Matthew sees another fulfillment of this here when some of her children are again taken by violence.
28. That is, having died. Related to "end" in v 15. On this word, see Mk 9:48.

A. Rev 6:13   B. Mt 25:35, brought in   C. Act 23:34, learn   D. Mt 27:2, governor   E. Rev 19:15   F. Phil 2:15, shine   G. Mt 10:11   H. 1 Jn 1:3, announcing   J. 2 Jn 9   K. Mt 12:35, treasure   L. Heb 5:7   M. Lk 2:26, revealed   N. 1 Cor 1:18, perish   O. Mt 4:12, went back   P. Act 3:13, servant   Q. Eph 5:18, filled   R. Jn 11:33   S. Rom 12:8, exhorting

  2C. But having heard that Archelaus[1] was[2] king *of* Judea in place of his father Herod, he feared[A] to go there[3]   22
  3C. And having been warned[B] in *a* dream, he withdrew[C] into the regions[D] *of* Galilee
  4C. And having come, he dwelled in *a* city[4] being called Nazareth— so that the *thing* having been spoken through the prophets might be fulfilled, because[5] He will be called *a* Nazarene[6]   23

4A.[7] Now during those days[8] John the Baptist comes[9], proclaiming[E] in the wilderness[10] *of* Judea,˚and[11] saying, "Repent[12], for the kingdom[13] *of* the heavens has drawn-near[F]"   3:1-2

  1B. For this *one* is the *one* having been spoken *of* through Isaiah the prophet saying[14] [in Isa 40:3], "*A* voice *of one* shouting[15] in the wilderness— 'Prepare[G] the way *of the* Lord, be making His paths straight[H]'"   3
  2B. Now John himself was having[16] his clothing [made] of camel's hair, and *a* belt made-of-leather around his waist[J]. And his food was locusts and wild honey   4
  3B. At that time Jerusalem and all Judea and all the surrounding-region[K] *of* the Jordan was going out to him. ˚And they were being baptized[L] in the Jordan River by him while confessing-out[17] their sins   5 / 6
  4B. But having seen many *of* the Pharisees and Sadducees coming to[18] his baptism[M], he said *to* them, "Brood[19] *of* vipers— who showed[20] you to flee from the coming wrath[N]?   7

    1C. "Therefore produce fruit worthy[O] *of* repentance[P]   8
    2C. "And do not think[21] *that you may* say within[22] yourselves, 'We have Abraham *as our* father'   9

      1D. "For I say *to* you that God is able to raise-up children *for* Abraham from these stones!
      2D. "And the axe is **already** lying[23] at the root *of* the trees. Therefore every tree not producing good fruit is cut down and thrown into *the* fire   10

    3C. "I[24] am baptizing[L] you with[25] water for repentance[P]— but the *One* coming after me is more powerful *than* me, *of* Whom I am not fit[Q] to carry the sandals   11

      1D. "**He** will baptize you with *the* Holy Spirit and fire[26]—˚ Whose winnowing-tool[27] *is* in His hand   12

        1E. "And He will cleanse-out[28] His threshing floor[29], and gather His wheat into the barn
        2E. "But He will burn up the chaff[30] *with an* inextinguishable[R] fire"

5A.[31] Then Jesus comes[32] from Galilee to the Jordan to John *that He might* be baptized[L] by him   13

  1B. But John was preventing Him, saying, "I have *a* need to be baptized by You, and **You** are coming to me?"   14
  2B. But having responded, Jesus said to him, "Permit[S] it at this time. For it is fitting[T] *for* us to fulfill[33] all righteousness in this manner[34]". Then he permits[S] Him   15
  3B. And having been baptized, Jesus immediately ascended[35] from[36] the water   16

    1C. And behold— the heavens were opened *to* Him[37]
    2C. And he[38] saw the Spirit *of* God descending as-if[39] *a* dove, and[40] coming upon Him
    3C. And behold— *a* voice from the heavens, saying, "This is My beloved[41] Son with Whom I was well-pleased[42]"   17

6A.[43] Then Jesus was led-up[44] into the wilderness[U] by the Spirit to be tempted[45] by the devil[V]. ˚And having fasted[W] *for* forty days and forty nights, afterward He was hungry   4:1-2

1. This son of Herod ruled Judea, Idumea, and Samaria from 4 B.C. to A.D. 6. See 2:1. He was worse than his father. The Emperor Augustus deposed and exiled him in A.D. 6, and reorganized his territory as a Roman province under a "prefect" (a military governor), in which capacity Pilate later served. It continued as such until A.D. 41, when the Emperor Claudius added it to the territories ruled by King Agrippa I (see Act 12:1; Lk 3:1). Used only here. GK *793*.
2. More literally, "is", as the Greek typically phrases it.
3. Joseph may have intended to reside in Bethlehem or Jerusalem.
4. Or, "town", of varying sizes. Used 162 times. GK *4484*.
5. Or, "that", introducing a quote. This is not a quote from the OT. Matthew is referring to the "prophets" in general (as in 26:56), who say that the Messiah will be despised and lowly. He sees this as partially fulfilled in the fact that Jesus is called a Nazarene (note Jn 1:46; 7:41). Nazareth was a small and unimportant town in Galilee. Of the 12 places Matthew uses the preceding formula to introduce a reference to the OT (see 1:22), this is the only one followed by this word. GK *4022*. Compare the use of this word in 4:6. There are other views.
6. Elsewhere only in 26:71; Lk 18:37; Jn 18:5, 7; 19:19; Act 2:22; 3:6; 4:10; 6:14; 22:8; 24:5 (Nazarenes); 26:9. GK *3717*. Related to "from Nazareth", on which see Mk 1:24.
7. Parallel account at Mk 1:2; Lk 3:1; Jn 1:19.
8. That is, when Jesus was living with His family in Nazareth.
9. Or, "arrives, appears publicly". GK *4134*. Same word as in 3:13, and as "arrived" in 2:1.
10. Or, "desert", the uninhabited, uncultivated part of Judea. This adjective means "deserted", "desolate" (as in Gal 4:27), and is used of such places, as here. Used 48 times. GK *2245*.
11. Some manuscripts omit this word {C}.
12. On this word, see Act 26:20. Related to "repentance" in v 8.
13. This word can have the sense of the "kingship, reign, royal power" of a king; the act of "reigning, ruling" by a king; and the "realm", the territory or people ruled by a king. Used 162 times. GK *993*. Related to "king" and the verb "reign" (Rev 19:6).
14. This word modifies "prophet", as in 2:17.
15. Or, "crying-out, crying-aloud, calling". Same word as in Mk 1:3; 15:34; Lk 3:4; 9:38; 18:38; Jn 1:23; Act 8:7; 17:6; 25:24; Gal 4:27. Elsewhere only as "cry out" in Lk 18:7. GK *1066*. Related to "shout-out" in Mt 27:46, and "outcry" in Jam 5:4.
16. That is, it was John's habit to wear such a garment.
17. Or, "acknowledging, admitting". On this word, see Jam 5:16.
18. Or, "upon, for". Matthew may mean "for the purpose of" being baptized (compare Lk 3:7); or, "coming to or upon" the place (same word as "to" the Jordan in v 13) to observe John baptizing. Compare Lk 7:30. Some manuscripts omit "his" {N}. GK *2093*.
19. Or, "Offspring, Children". Elsewhere only in 12:34; 23:33; Lk 3:7; all in "brood *of* vipers". GK *1165*.
20. Or, "indicated"; in a negative sense, "warned". Elsewhere only in Lk 3:7; 6:47; 12:5; Act 9:16; 20:35. GK *5683*.
21. Or, "expect, imagine". Do not be of this opinion. On this word, see Lk 19:11.
22. Or, "among". This very thing is said in Jn 8:39.
23. Or, "being laid". John is referring to Israel. The Messiah will winnow the nation, v 12. Same word as in Lk 2:12; Jn 20:5; 1 Cor 3:11; 1 Jn 5:19; as "set" in Rev 4:2; and as "appointed" in Lk 2:34. Used 24 times. GK *3023*.
24. John uses grammar that emphasizes the contrast between himself and the One coming after him.
25. Or, "in". Same word as "in" the Jordan (v 6), and as "with" the Holy Spirit later in this verse. See Mk 1:8.
26. Some think John means that believers will be baptized with the Holy Spirit, unbelievers with fire, as in v 10, 12. Others think the "fire" refers to the "tongues as if of fire" on the day of Pentecost, Act 2:1-3. Others think that it refers to the purifying work of the Holy Spirit, "and *with* [His] fire". Compare Lk 12:49. This word is used 71 times. GK *4786*. Related to "burn" in 2 Cor 11:29; and "fire-red" in Rev 6:4.
27. Oxen threshed the grain by walking on it, breaking it apart. Then this tool was used to throw it into the air so that the wind could blow away the chaff, separating it from the grain, which fell back to the floor. The One coming is ready to begin winnowing His people. Elsewhere only in Lk 3:17. GK *4768*.
28. Used only here. GK *1351*. Related to "clean-out" in Lk 3:17.
29. The grain is on His threshing floor. He will winnow it and take both wheat and chaff to their destination.
30. Elsewhere only in Lk 3:17. That is, the husks and straw remaining after the wheat is removed. GK *949*.
31. Parallel account at Mk 1:9; Lk 3:21. Compare Jn 1:29-34; 3:22-36.
32. Same word as in v 1.
33. Some think Jesus means that as a devout son of Israel, it was fitting that He submit to John's preparatory baptism, even though He had no need to "confess out" or repent. Others think He means that this will serve as His consecration to His work as Messiah, followed by the Father's acceptance of Him in this role in v 17. There are other views. On this word, see "filled" in Eph 5:18.
34. That is, in John baptizing Jesus.
35. Or, "went up, came up". Related to "descending" later in the verse. GK *326*.
36. Or, "away from", in the sense of "up on the shore". GK *608*. See Mk 1:10 on this.
37. Some take "*to* Him" to mean that only Jesus (and John, Jn 1:32) experienced this. Some manuscripts omit "*to* Him" {C}.
38. Or, "He". Matthew could mean John, or Jesus. Compare Lk 3:21-22; Jn 1:32.
39. Or, "like". On this word, see Rom 6:13. It is not the same word as in Mk 1:10; Lk 3:22; Jn 1:32 (GK *6055*), but is related to it. Luke links this to the bodily form.
40. Some manuscripts omit this word {C}.
41. Same word as in Rom 1:7; 1 Cor 4:14; 1 Jn 2:7. Used 61 times, all as "beloved". GK *28*. Related to "*devotedly*-love" in Jn 21:15.
42. On "was well-pleased", see 17:5.
43. Parallel account at Mk 1:12; Lk 4:1.
44. Or, "brought up". Same word as in Lk 4:5; Act 16:34; as "bring up" in Lk 2:22; Rom 10:7; Heb 13:20; and as "put so sea" (lead the ship up on the sea) in Act 20:13. Used 23 times. GK *343*.
45. Or, "tested". On this word, see Heb 2:18.

A. Eph 5:33, respecting   B. Lk 2:26, revealed   C. Mt 4:12, went back   D. Rom 11:25, part   E. 2 Tim 4:2   F. Lk 21:28   G. Mk 14:15   H. Act 8:21   J. Heb 7:5, loins   K. Mk 1:28   L. Mk 1:8   M. Mk 1:4   N. Rev 16:9   O. Rev 16:6   P. 2 Cor 7:10   Q. 2 Cor 3:5, sufficient   R. Mk 9:43   S. Mt 6:12, forgive   T. 1 Cor 11:13   U. Mt 3:1   V. Rev 12:9   W. Mt 6:16

Matthew 4:3	Verse

    1B. And having come to *Him*, the *one* tempting said *to* Him, "If[1] You are God's **Son**, say that these stones should become loaves-of-bread"[2]   3

        1C. But the *One*, having responded, said, "It has been written [in Deut 8:3], 'Mankind[3] shall live not on bread alone, but on every word proceeding out through *the* mouth *of* God' "   4

    2B. Then[4] the devil takes Him into the holy city. And he stood Him on the pinnacle *of* the temple. °And he says *to* Him, "If You are God's **Son**, throw Yourself down. For it has been written, 'Because[5] He will command[A] His angels concerning You, and they will lift You up on *their* hands that You may not ever strike[B] Your foot against *a* stone' " [Ps 91:11-12]   5-6

        1C. Jesus said *to* him, "Again[6], it has been written, 'You shall not put *the* Lord your God to the test[7]' " [Deut 6:16]   7

    3B. Again, the devil takes Him to *a* very high mountain and shows[C] Him all the kingdoms[D] *of* the world, and their glory. °And he said *to* Him, "I will give all these *things to* You if, having fallen-down[E], You give-worship[8] *to* me"   8 / 9

        1C. Then Jesus says *to* him, "Go-away[9], Satan! For it has been written, 'You shall worship *the* Lord your God, and serve[F] Him only[G]' " [Deut 6:13]   10

    4B. Then the devil leaves Him. And behold— angels came to *Him* and were ministering[H] *to* Him   11

7A.[10] And having heard that John was handed-over[11] [to prison], He went-back[12] into Galilee   12

    1B. And having left-behind[J] Nazareth,[13] having come, He dwelled in Capernaum— the *one* by-the-sea in the districts[K] *of* Zebulun and Naphtali— °in order that the *thing* might be fulfilled having been spoken through Isaiah the prophet saying[14]   13 / 14

        1C. "Land *of* Zebulun and land *of* Naphtali, *the* way *of the* sea,[15] beyond the Jordan, Galilee *of* the Gentiles— °the people sitting[16] in darkness saw *a* great Light. And *for* the *ones* sitting in *the* region[L] and shadow *of* death, *a* Light rose *for* them" [Isa 9:1-2]   15 / 16

    2B. From that time on,[17] Jesus began to proclaim and say, "Repent[M], for the kingdom *of* the heavens has drawn-near[N]"   17

3B.[18] And while walking beside the Sea *of* Galilee   18

        1C. He saw two brothers— Simon (the *one* being called Peter) and Andrew, his brother— throwing *a* casting-net[19] into the sea. For they were fishermen

            1D. And He says *to* them, "Come after Me, and I will make you fishermen *of* people"   19
            2D. And immediately the *ones*, having left[O] the nets[20], followed Him   20

        2C. And having gone on from there He saw two other brothers— James (the *son of* Zebedee) and John, his brother— preparing[21] their nets in the boat with Zebedee their father   21

            1D. And He called[P] them
            2D. And immediately the *ones*, having left[O] the boat and their father, followed Him   22

    4B.[22] And He[23] was going around in all Galilee— teaching in their synagogues, and proclaiming[Q] the good-news[R] *of* the kingdom[D], and curing[S] every disease[T] and every infirmity[24] among the people   23

1. As God said in 3:17. Or, "Since". Same word as in v 6. The grammar assumes that the premise is true. Assuming that You are what God said You are, prove it with Your power (v 3) or His power (v 6).
2. Only God creates by speaking it. If Jesus did not have the power to do so, this would not even be a temptation. That He had the power is clear in 14:19. "Loaves-of-bread" is the same word as "bread" in Lk 4:3, where this phrase is singular, and as "bread" next in Mt 4:4. It occurs 97 times. GK *788*.
3. Or, "Man, The human, The person, Humankind". This is the word *anthropos*, from which we get "anthropo"-logy, the study of man. It is used to refer to a "man" (a male), as in 8:9; 9:9; 19:3, 5; 26:24, 72; Mk 14:13; Lk 5:20; 9:44; and in the sense of "person, human", including male and female. There is another word which means "man, husband" (see 1 Tim 2:12), and another meaning "male" (see Mt 19:4). To distinguish this word from those, and to give the correct sense of this word, it is rendered "man" (about 260 times) only when referring to a male, except in the phrase "Son of Man" (see Jn 5:27), which emphasizes Christ's humanity (perhaps meaning "the human One") and His connection with the prophecy of Dan 7:13. Otherwise, it is rendered as "mankind" only in Mt 4:4; Mk 2:27; 11:2; Lk 4:4; 19:30; Jn 1:4; Act 4:17; 15:17; 17:26; 19:35; 2 Cor 4:2; 1 Tim 6:16; Jam 3:8; Rev 9:15, 18, 20; 14:4, 21:3; as "human" about 55 times, as in Mt 9:8; 15:9; 16:23; 19:26; 21:25; Mk 3:28; Jn 5:34; 10:33; Act 5:38; 17:29; Rom 2:1; 3:5; 1 Cor 1:25; 3:3; 13:1; 15:39; Gal 1:1, 10, 11, 12; 3:15; Eph 3:5; Phil 2:7; 1 Thes 2:13; 4:8; Heb 13:6; 2 Pet 1:21; 1 Jn 5:9; Rev 21:17; and as "person, people" about 210 times, as in Mt 10:36; 12:12, 36; 15:11; 16:26; 23:7; Mk 1:17; Jn 1:9; 2:25; 3:19; 6:10; 12:43; Act 4:12; 5:29; 17:30; Rom 2:9; 5:12; Eph 4:22; 1 Thes 2:4; 1 Tim 2:4, 5; 4:10; Tit 2:11; Heb 6:16; Jam 2:24; 1 Pet 2:4; Rev 9:6. Used 550 times. GK *476*.
4. Matthew and Luke reverse the order of the second and third temptations. See Lk 4:5.
5. Or, "written that 'He will command' ", "that" introducing the quotation, as this word is rendered in Lk 4:10. However, Matthew does not use the word this way in any of his other seven quotations that follow "it has been written" (2:5; 4:4, 7, 10; 11:10; 21:13; 26:31). In addition, "because" is part of the verse quoted from Ps 91:11. The devil is saying "Jump, because God said He would protect You".
6. That is, for the second time I say. Or, *Yet*-again, On the other hand", in response to Satan's quotation of Scripture. On this word, see Mk 15:13.
7. This verb, "put to the test, test out" is the same one Paul uses in 1 Cor 10:9. Elsewhere only in Lk 4:12; 10:25. GK *1733*. Related to "tempted" in Heb 2:18, and "trials" in Jam 1:2. To deliberately take such an action in view of a Scriptural promise, and then ask God to save us from its consequences, is to wrongly put God to the test. God's promise in Ps 91 is true, but Satan's suggested test of it is evil. Note also Act 5:9; 15:10.
8. Same word as "worship" in v 10. On this word, see 14:33.
9. Or, "Be going" or simply "Go". Same word as "get" in 16:23; and as "go" in 8:4, 13; 18:15; 19:21; 21:28; 28:10. Used 79 times. GK *5632*. Some manuscripts add "behind Me" {A}, so that it says "Get behind Me" as in 16:23.
10. Parallel to Mk 1:14; Lk 3:19; 4:14. Compare Jn 4:1-3.
11. That is, by Herod Antipas, 14:3. On this word, see Mt 26:21.
12. Or, "withdrew". Same word as in 2:12. Elsewhere only as "go-away" in Mt 2:13; 9:24; Act 26:31; "depart" in Mt 27:5; and "withdraw" in Mt 2:14, 22; 12:15; 14:13; 15:21; Mk 3:7; Jn 6:15; Act 23:19. GK *432*.
13. Luke may give an incident from this time in Nazareth at Lk 4:16.
14. This word modifies "prophet", as in 2:17.
15. That is, toward the sea, west of the Jordan and the Sea of Galilee, the location of the lands of Zebulun and Naphtali.
16. Compare Lk 1:79. On this word, see Rev 14:6.
17. This phrase also occurs in 16:21 and 26:16. Elsewhere only in Lk 16:16.
18. Parallel account at Mk 1:16. Compare Lk 5:1-11; Jn 1:35-51.
19. This is a circular net used in fishing, thrown by hand. Used only here. GK *312*. The related verb is in Mk 1:16. The general word for "net" is in v 20, and the word for the large "drag-net" used in fishing is in Mt 13:47.
20. This is a general word for "nets" used to catch fish, birds, etc. Used 12 times, always of fishing nets. GK *1473*.
21. Or, "putting in order, restoring". It could refer to mending, cleaning, re-folding, etc. On this word, see Rom 9:22.
22. Parallel to Mk 1:39; Lk 4:44.
23. Some manuscripts say "Jesus" {N}.
24. Or, "weakness, ailment, softness". Elsewhere only in 9:35; 10:1, where this same phrase occurs. GK *3433*.

A. Mk 10:3 B. Rom 14:21, stumble C. 1 Tim 6:15 D. Mt 3:2 E. Rom 11:11, fall F. Heb 12:28, worship G. Jam 2:24, alone H. 1 Pet 4:10
J. Act 6:2 K. Mk 10:1 L. Mk 1:5, country M. Act 26:20 N. Lk 21:28 O. Mt 6:12, forgive P. Rom 8:30 Q. 2 Tim 4:2 R. 1 Cor 15:1
S. Mt 8:7 T. Mt 8:17

5B.	And the report¹ *of* Him went into all Syria². And they brought to Him all the *ones* being ill³, being gripped⁴ *with* various diseases^A and torments⁵, and⁶ being demon-possessed^B, and having seizures⁷, and paralytics⁸. And He cured^C them	24
8A.⁹	And large crowds from Galilee and Decapolis^D and Jerusalem and Judea and beyond the Jordan followed Him. ˚And having seen the crowds, He went up on the mountain. And He having sat-*down*, His disciples¹⁰ came to Him. ˚And having opened His mouth He was teaching^E them¹¹, saying—	25 5:1 2
1B.¹²	"Blessed¹³ *are* the poor¹⁴ *in* spirit, because the kingdom *of* the heavens is theirs	3
1C.	"Blessed¹⁵ *are* the *ones* mourning^F, because **they**¹⁶ will be comforted^G	4
2C.	"Blessed *are* the gentle¹⁷ *ones*, because **they** will inherit^H the earth	5
3C.	"Blessed *are* the *ones* hungering and thirsting *as to* righteousness, because **they** will be filled-to-satisfaction^J	6
4C.	"Blessed *are* the merciful *ones*, because **they** will be shown-mercy^K	7
5C.	"Blessed *are* the pure¹⁸ *in* heart, because **they** will see God	8
6C.	"Blessed *are* the peacemakers¹⁹, because **they** will be called sons *of* God²⁰	9
7C.	"Blessed *are* the *ones* having been persecuted^L for the sake of righteousness, because the kingdom *of* the heavens is theirs	10
1D.	"You are blessed *ones* whenever they reproach^M you and persecute *you* and speak every [kind of] evil against you while lying²¹, because-of²² Me. ˚Be rejoicing^N, and be overjoyed²³, because your reward *is* great in the heavens. For in this manner they persecuted the prophets^O before you	11 12
2B.²⁴	"**You** are the salt²⁵ *of* the earth	13
1C.	"But if the salt should become-tasteless²⁶, with what will it be salted²⁷?	
2C.	"It no longer has strength²⁸ for anything except, having²⁹ been thrown outside, to be trampled-underfoot^P by people	
3B.	"**You** are the light³⁰ *of* the world	14
1C.	"*A* city lying^Q on *a* hill is not able to be hidden^R	
2C.³¹	"Nor do they burn³² *a* lamp, and put it under the basket^S, but on the lampstand^T— and it shines^U *on* all the *ones* in the house	15
3C.	"In this manner³³, let your light shine^U in front of people, so that they may see your good works and glorify^V your Father in the heavens	16
4B.	"Do not think^W that I came to abolish³⁴ the Law or the Prophets. I did not come to abolish, but to fulfill³⁵. ˚For truly³⁶ I say *to* you, until heaven and earth pass away, one iota³⁷ or one stroke³⁸ will by no means pass away from the Law until all *things* take-place³⁹	17 18
1C.	"Therefore, whoever breaks⁴⁰ one *of* the least *of* these commandments^X, and in this manner teaches people— he will be called least in the kingdom *of* the heavens	19
1D.	"But whoever does^Y and teaches *them*— this *one* will be called great in the kingdom *of* the heavens	

1. Or, "news". On this word, see "hearing" in Heb 4:2.
2. Syria is the Roman province that included Palestine. It included all the regions mentioned in v 25.
3. This is an idiom, "having it badly". On this idiom, see Mk 1:32.
4. Or, "held under the control of, ruled by". Or, in a negative sense, "afflicted, oppressed". More serious than "being ill", it may imply a loss of control of a function or of one's life. Used in this sense also in Lk 4:38; Act 28:8. On this word, see "control" in 2 Cor 5:14.
5. On this word, see Lk 16:23. Related to "tormented" in Rev 14:10.
6. Some manuscripts omit this word {C}.
7. Or, "being moonstruck, being a lunatic". That is, ones out of control of themselves. Ancient people thought this condition was brought on by the phases of the moon. Elsewhere only in Mt 17:15. GK *4944*. Related to "moon". Based on the descriptions in Mk 9:18; Lk 9:39, some translate it "epileptic".
8. Our word comes from this Greek word, *paralutikos*. Same word as in 9:2, 6; Mk 2:3, 4, 5, 9, 10. Elsewhere only as "paralyzed" in Mt 8:6. GK *4166*. Related to "make feeble" in Heb 12:12.
9. Most think this is the same occasion as Lk 6:12-49.
10. Matthew could mean the twelve (as in 10:1; 11:1), or the larger group of "learners" from whom the twelve were chosen, Lk 6:13, 17, 20. On this word, see Lk 6:40.
11. Some think Matthew means "the crowds" in 4:25 (note 7:28). Others think he means the "disciples" in v 1. Others think it is addressed to both, with a different nuance to each. In addition, some view chapters 5-7 as the attainable standard of righteousness necessary to enter the kingdom of heaven. Others view it as the premier application of the Law, giving the unattainable standards that drive us to Christ (Gal 3:24; 1 Tim 1:8). Others view it as the standard of conduct for those who have entered the kingdom of heaven. There are other views.
12. Compare Lk 6:20-26.
13. Or, "Happy, Fortunate". On this word, see Lk 6:20. This could be rendered "The poor *in* spirit *are* fortunate", and likewise with the beatitudes that follow. Jesus declares blessed the qualities that reveal the character of the heart, not the outer things we humans usually focus on (riches, health, etc.).
14. On this word, see Gal 4:9. That is, like the man in Lk 18:13.
15. The rest of the beatitudes are placed at the "C." level as a subject grouping only, not because they are subordinate to verse 3.
16. Or, "they themselves", and likewise in each case down through v 9. They and no other. Jesus emphasizes this word.
17. Or, "meek". Like Christ, 11:29; 21:5. Not the self-assertive. On this word, see 1 Pet 3:4.
18. Or, "clean", as elsewhere in Matthew (23:26; 27:59), and Tit 1:15.
19. This word is made of the noun "peace", and the verb "to make". Used only here. GK *1648*. The related verb is in Col 1:20.
20. That is, ones characterized by the same trait as God, your Father. God is the ultimate peacemaker, sending His Son to make peace, Rom 5:1. On "sons of God", see Rom 8:14.
21. That is, they speak it falsely. Compare 1 Pet 4:15-16. Some manuscripts omit "while lying" {C}.
22. Or, "for the sake of". It is "because of" from the persecutor's point of view; "for the sake of" from the believer's point of view. Same word as in Lk 6:22, and as "for the sake of" here in v 10. GK *1915*.
23. On this word, see "rejoice greatly" in Lk 10:21.
24. Compare Mk 9:50; Lk 14:34-35.
25. That is, the preservative against moral decay. GK *229*.
26. Same word as in Lk 14:34. Mark says "unsalty" in Mk 9:50.
27. Or, "seasoned". This is the verb related to the word "salt". Elsewhere only in Mk 9:49. GK *245*.
28. That is, it is not potent for anything. It no longer has the power or strength or ability to be used for anything. The Greek actually states this in reverse, "For nothing does it still have strength except...". On this word, see "can do" in Gal 5:6.
29. Some manuscripts say "except to be thrown outside and trampled-underfoot" {N}.
30. That is, the source of spiritual truth, reflected from God, lighting the darkness. Note Phil 2:15.
31. Compare Mk 4:21; Lk 8:16.
32. That is, have a lamp burning, as we would "burn" a kerosene lamp. Same word as Lk 12:35; 24:32; Rev 19:20. Used 11 times. GK *2794*.
33. That is, publicly, like a city on a hill or a lamp on a lampstand, for all to see and benefit from.
34. Or, "destroy, tear down, do away with". On this word, see "tear down" in 24:2.
35. Or, "complete, finish". Some take this to mean that in His life, Jesus perfectly fulfilled the requirements of the Law; others, that in His teaching, He fulfilled or filled out the true meaning and intent of the Law; others, that in His death, He brought the Law to its completion and conclusion. Note Rom 10:4, where similar views arise. On this word, see "filled" in Eph 5:18.
36. The OT prophets said "Thus says the Lord". Jesus is the Lord! So the Son of God says "Truly I say", invoking no higher authority than Himself. This is partially responsible for the crowd's reaction in 7:28. This word is not related to the word "true" (see 14:33). It is the word also translated "amen" (29 times). GK *297*. It is used only by Jesus in this sense (100 times). John has it as "truly, truly". Jesus is asserting the absolute certainty and reality of what He says based on His own authority. He directly speaks God's words on the matter. He alone speaks (and heals, 8:3) in this manner. Compare Jn 14:10. In Lk 12:44, 21:3, Luke says "truly" using the word in Mt 14:33 in place of this word.
37. This is the smallest letter in the Greek alphabet, equivalent to an English "i". Jesus is referring to the smallest letter in the Hebrew alphabet, in which the Law was written. Used only here. GK *2740*.
38. In Greek, this is used of the various accents and marks. Jesus is referring to a small stroke that distinguishes some Hebrew letters from others. In English, it would be like the single stroke that distinguishes an "E" from an "F", or an "O" from a "Q". Elsewhere only in Lk 16:17. GK *3037*.
39. Or, "come about, happen". A common word, used 669 times. GK *1181*. Compare Lk 16:17.
40. Or, "looses, undoes, abolishes, annuls, puts an end to, repeals, does away with". Not "fails to obey" (everyone is guilty of this), but "annuls the authority of". Jesus was accused of this in Jn 5:18. Same word as "loose" in 16:19; "untie" in 21:2; and "break" in Jn 5:18; 7:23; 10:35. Used 42 times, mostly as "untie, release". GK *3395*. Related to "abolish" in v 17.

A. Mt 8:17 B. Mt 8:16 C. Mt 8:7 D. Mk 7:31 E. Rom 12:7 F. Jam 4:9 G. Rom 12:8, exhorting H. Gal 4:30 J. Phil 4:12 K. Rom 12:8
L. 2 Tim 3:12 M. 1 Pet 4:14 N. 2 Cor 13:11 O. 1 Cor 12:28 P. Heb 10:29 Q. Mt 3:10 R. Jn 8:59 S. Mk 4:21 T. Rev 1:12 U. 2 Cor 4:6
V. Rom 8:30 W. Act 14:19 X. Mk 12:28 Y. Rev 13:13

Matthew 5:20   Verse

    2C.   "For I say *to* you that unless your righteousness[A] abounds[1] more *than* [that of] the scribes and Pharisees,[2] you will by-no-means[3] enter into the kingdom[B] *of* the heavens[C]   20

        1D.   "You heard that it was said *to*[4] the ancient[D] *ones*, 'You shall not murder[E]', and 'Whoever murders shall be liable[5] *to* the judgment[6]'   21

            1E.   "But **I** say[7] *to* you that everyone being angry[F] *with* his brother[8] shall be liable *to* judgment   22

                1F.   And whoever says *to* his brother[G], 'Raca[9]', shall be liable *to* the Sanhedrin[10]
                2F.   And whoever says, 'Fool[11]', shall be liable to the Gehenna[12] *of* fire[13]

            2E.   "Therefore if you are offering[H] your gift[14] at the altar[J], and there you remember that your brother has something against you   23

                1F.   "Leave your gift there in front of the altar, and go   24
                2F.   "First be reconciled[15] *to* your brother, and then, having come, be offering your gift

            3E.[16]   "Be settling[17] *with* your adversary[K] quickly[L]— until[18] you are with him on the way[M] [to court]— that *your* adversary[K] might not perhaps hand you over *to* the judge, and the judge[19] *to* the officer[N], and you be thrown into prison[O]   25

                1F.   "Truly[P] I say *to* you, you will by no means come out from there until you pay the last quadrans[20]   26

        2D.   "You heard that it was said[21], 'You shall not commit-adultery[Q]'   27

            1E.   "But **I** say *to* you that everyone looking-*at*[R] a woman so-as[22] to desire[23] her already committed-adultery-*with*[24] her in his heart   28
            2E.[25]   "And if your right eye is causing you to fall[S], tear it out,[26] and throw *it* from you   29

                1F.   "For it is better *for* you that one *of* your body-parts[T] perish[U], and your whole body not be thrown into Gehenna[27]

            3E.   "And if your right hand is causing you to fall, cut it off, and throw *it* from you   30

                1F.   "For it is better *for* you that one *of* your body-parts perish, and your whole body not go[28] into Gehenna

        3D.   "And it was said, 'Whoever sends-away[29] his wife, let him give her *a* divorce[30] *certificate*'   31

1. Jesus explains this by what follows. He means not just not murdering, but not being angry; not just not committing adultery, but not lusting; not just properly executing a divorce, but not divorcing; not just keeping oaths, but not using or needing them; not just limiting revenge to a properly measured response, but not responding in kind at all; not just loving neighbors, but loving enemies. The first item is the Pharisees' righteousness; the second is the abounding He has in mind. It is the true intent of the Law, the true requirement of God. The standard is internal perfection, not merely external conformity, v 48. On this word, see 2 Cor 8:2.
2. This was a shocking statement, and something that would have been thought impossible. It is impossible, if it is based on human achievement. A different kind of righteousness will be required. Note Rom 10:3.
3. Or, "never". This is the strongest negative in Greek. Used by Matthew in 5:18, 20, 26; 10:23, 42; 13:14; 15:6; 16:22, 28; 18:3, 23:39; 24:2, 21, 34, 35; 25:9; 26:29, 35. See Gal 5:16.
4. Or, "*by*". In either case, it was ancient teachers of the Law teaching their interpretation of it.
5. Or, "subject, answerable". Same word as in v 22. On this word, see "guilty" in 1 Cor 11:27.
6. Same word as in v 22. Some think Jesus means the judgment of a local court. Related to "sue" in v 40; and to "go to court" in 1 Cor 6:1. On this word, see Jn 3:19.
7. Jesus is not contradicting the Law, but explaining its true meaning. He applies it to the internal thoughts of the heart, not just to outward actions. Only by limiting it to the external can a person claim to have kept the Law.
8. Some manuscripts add "without-a-cause" {B}.
9. This is a transliterated Aramaic word of verbal abuse meaning "empty one". It is like our "blockhead, numbskull". Used only here. GK *4819*.
10. That is, the ruling body of Israel, the highest of human courts.
11. The distinction intended between "Raca" and "Fool" is uncertain. Some think "fool" is simply the Greek translation of "Raca", no distinction being intended. Others think it is a transliteration of a Hebrew word meaning "rebel". Others think it means "fool" from God's point of view— an obstinate, godless person, so that "Raca" would be insulting one's mental abilities, and "fool" one's character. In addition, some think there is an escalation of offense (anger, Raca, fool) and of punishment (local court, Sanhedrin, Gehenna). Others think the three concepts are equivalent. On this word, see "foolish" in Tit 3:9.
12. Or, "hell", referring to the Valley of Hinnom near Jerusalem, which symbolized to the Jews the place of future torment. Elsewhere only in v 29, 30; 10:28; 18:9; 23:15, 33; Mk 9:43, 45, 47; Lk 12:5; Jam 3:6. GK *1147*.
13. Or, "the fiery hell". The Gehenna characterized by fire. Same phrase as in 18:9. Compare Mk 9:43; Jam 3:6.
14. That is, your offering. Elsewhere only in Mt 2:11; 5:24; 8:4; 15:5; 23:18, 19; Mk 7:11; Lk 21:1, 4; Eph 2:8; Heb 5:1; 8:3, 4; 9:9; 11:4; Rev 11:10. GK *1565*.
15. Used only here. GK *1367*. Related to the word in Rom 5:10.
16. Compare Lk 12:57-59.
17. Or, "Be of good will, Be well disposed" to him, resulting in an agreement. Used only here. GK *2333.* Related to "goodwill" in Eph 6:7.
18. More literally, "up to which *time*". Try to settle before you come before the judge. This idiom is elsewhere only in Lk 12:50; 13:8; 22:16; Jn 9:18; all "until". Or, "as long as which", that is, "while", in which case "[to court]" could be omitted. GK *2401, 4015.*
19. Some manuscripts say "and the judge hand you over *to* the officer" {N}.
20. On this word, see Mk 12:42. It is the smallest denomination of Roman coin. In other words, once you enter the judicial system— this world's or God's— the full penalty must be paid.
21. Some manuscripts add "*to* the ancient *ones*", as in v 21 {N}.
22. Or, "that *he might* desire her", expressing the purpose of looking. Jesus again focuses on the heart, not simply the external action. The same construction occurs in Mt 6:1; 13:30; 23:5; 26:12; Mk 13:22; 1 Thes 2:9; 2 Thes 3:8; and is elsewhere only as "so that" in 2 Cor 3:13; Eph 6:11; and perhaps Lk 18:1. GK *4639.*
23. On this word, see Gal 5:17. It means "to desire", or in a sexual context, it can mean "to lust".
24. Same word as in v 27, on which see v 32a.
25. Compare 18:8-9; Mk 9:43-48.
26. Take whatever action necessary to avoid sinning. Flee or separate yourself from the external inducements. On the word "causing to fall", see 1 Cor 8:13.
27. Maintain an eternal perspective on the matter. Sin is more serious than seeing. On this word, see v 22.
28. Some manuscripts say "be thrown" {N}.
29. Or, "dismisses, releases". "Divorce" in the modern sense includes a physical separation aspect, and a legal aspect. Here, this word refers to the separation aspect, and "give her a divorce *certificate*" to the legal aspect, as also in 19:7; Mk 10:4. Elsewhere in marriage contexts (14 of its 66 uses, GK *668*), this word could be rendered "divorce" in the modern sense, 1:19; 5:32; 19:3, 8, 9; Mk 10:2, 11, 12; Lk 16:18. This word also means "pardon, leave, set free, let go". On this subject, see also the word "separate" in Mt 19:6; Mk 10:9; 1 Cor 7:10, 11, 15; "leave" in 1 Cor 7:11, 12, 13; and "release" in 1 Cor 7:27.
30. Or, "abandonment", a "standing away from". That is, if you are going to force your wife to leave, do it properly according to the Law of Moses. Make it legal, so that you do not disobey the Law of Moses when you send her away. The issue is not whether to send her away (Jewish men believed they had the right) but doing it properly. This was their interpretation of Moses. It is not what the Law says. See Mk 10:4. Elsewhere only in 19:7, Mk 10:4, in the phrase "certificate *of* divorce". The word "certificate" is not used here. GK *687*. Related to "apostasy" in 2 Thes 2:3. Not related to "send away" earlier in this verse.

A. Rom 1:17   B. Mt 3:2   C. 2 Cor 12:2   D. Act 15:7, old   E. Jam 4:2   F. Rev 11:18   G. Act 16:40   H. Heb 5:7   J. Rev 8:3   K. 1 Pet 5:8   L. Rev 22:7   M. Lk 3:4   N. Jn 18:12   O. Act 5:22   P. Mt 5:18   Q. Mt 5:32   R. Rev 1:11, see   S. 1 Cor 8:13   T. Col 3:5   U. 1 Cor 1:18

       1E. "But **I** say *to* you that everyone sending-away[A] his wife except for *a* matter[1] *of* sexual-immorality[2] is causing[B] her to commit-adultery[3]   32

       2E. "And whoever marries[4] *a woman* having been sent-away[A] [from her husband] is committing-adultery[5]

  4D. "Again, you heard that it was said *to* the ancient[C] *ones*, 'You shall not break-*your*-oath[6], but you shall pay[7] your oaths[8] *to* the Lord'   33

       1E. "But **I** say *to* you not to swear-with-an-oath[9] at all—   34

           1F. Neither by heaven, because it is *the* throne *of* God

           2F. Nor by earth, because it is *a* footstool *of* His feet   35

           3F. Nor with reference to Jerusalem, because it is *the* city *of* the great King

           4F. Nor may you swear-with-an-oath by your head, because you are not able to make[B] one hair white or black   36

       2E. "But let your statement[D] be, 'Yes, yes', [or] 'No, no'.[10] And the *thing* beyond[11] these is from the evil[E] *one*[12]   37

  5D. "You heard that it was said, '*An* eye for *an* eye, and *a* tooth for *a* tooth'[13]   38

       1E.[14] "But **I** say *to* you not to resist[15] the evil[E] *person*   39

           1F. "But whoever slaps[16] you on your[17] right cheek, turn the other *to* him also

           2F. "And *to* the *one* wanting[F] to sue[18] you and take your tunic[19], permit[G] him also the cloak[20]   40

           3F. "And whoever will press you into service[21] *for* one mile[22], go with him two   41

       2E. "Give *to* the *one* asking you,[23] and do not turn away from the *one* wanting[F] to borrow[H] from you   42

  6D. "You heard that it was said, 'You shall love[J] your neighbor,[24] and hate[K] your enemy'   43

       1E.[25] "But **I** say *to* you, be loving[J] your enemies,[26] and be praying for the *ones* persecuting[L] you,[27] *so that you may prove-to-be[28] sons[M] *of* your Father[29] in *the* heavens   44, 45

           1F. "Because He causes His sun to rise upon evil and good *ones*, and He sends rain upon righteous and unrighteous *ones*

           2F. "For if you love[J] the *ones* loving you, what reward[N] do you have? Are not even the tax-collectors[O] doing the same?   46

           3F. "And if you greet[P] your brothers only, what extraordinary[30] *thing* are you doing? Are not even the Gentiles[31] doing the same?   47

  3C.[32] "Therefore **you** shall be perfect[33], as your heavenly Father is perfect   48

5B. "But[34] take-heed[Q] not to do[R] your righteousness[35] in-front-of[36] people so-as[37] to be seen *by* them. Otherwise indeed[38], you do not have *a* reward[N] with your Father in the heavens   6:1

1. Or, "word, account". If the husband sends his wife away for anything except sexual immorality, he is responsible for making her an adulteress when she remarries. He is guilty of the sin in this matter. Jesus is saying that the husband should not send away his wife if she has not committed sexual immorality. Beyond this, there are different views on what inferences about divorce may be drawn from this verse. Note that He is not fully addressing the issue of divorce here, but is attacking the commonly held Jewish husband's point of view stated in v 31. On this word, see "word" in 1 Cor 12:8.
2. On this word, see 1 Cor 5:1.
3. Or, "become an adulteress", that is, when she remarries. Some think Jesus means the husband causes her "to suffer from adultery" when he remarries. In any case, Jesus is holding the husband accountable for her. And when he remarries, he also commits adultery (19:9), as does the man marrying her, spoken of next. As lust is a kind of adultery (v 28), divorce and remarriage is a kind of adultery, unless the partner has already committed sexual immorality. This word has this grammar elsewhere only in Jn 8:4, also of the woman. Elsewhere only in v 27, 28; 19:18; and Mk 10:19; Lk 16:18; 18:20; Rom 2:22; 13:9; Jam 2:11; Rev 2:22. GK *3658*.
4. Some manuscripts say "and the *one* having married..." {B}.
5. Or, "is an adulterer". Related to the word above. Elsewhere only in 19:9; Mk 10:11, 12. GK *3656*.
6. Or, "make false oaths, swear falsely". Used only here. GK *2155*. Related to "oath" next, and to "perjurer" in 1 Tim 1:10.
7. Or, "give back, render". If you swear by God to do something, it becomes a debt that you owe to Him in addition to the person to whom you have sworn. You "pay" the oath to God by "keeping, performing" what you swore to the person. On this word, see "render" in 16:27.
8. Some Jews believed oaths "to the Lord" must be kept, but oaths sworn by other things like those mentioned next could be violated. In other words, they were swearing an oath in a way that in their minds was not firmly linked to genuine truthfulness. On this word, see Jam 5:12. Related to "swear with an oath" next.
9. Or, "affirm, confirm with an oath" such as follows; I swear by heaven, by earth, etc. On this word, see Jam 5:12. Do not be one who must swear an oath in order to be believed. Some think this is universal in scope; others, that Jesus is referring to everyday conversations in which one might swear an oath to bolster a claim. Note 26:63. On the scope of this command, compare the verses noted in Jam 5:12.
10. That is, let your yes or no be your firm link to absolute truthfulness, without playing such games with words.
11. Or, "more *than*". GK *4356*.
12. Or, "from evil", of evil origin.
13. That is, retaliate in kind, avenge yourself by doing the same thing back to them. Jews in Bible times took this to mean that they had to right to take personal revenge upon others.
14. Compare Lk 6:27-31.
15. Or, "oppose, stand against". On this word, see Eph 6:13. Leave vengeance to God. Jesus Himself is the prime example. He is speaking of personal retaliation, not of permitting evil to be done to others. For example, it is godly to defend the widow or orphan from the evil person exploiting them, Isa 1:17. In other words, show love to your enemies, not retaliation, not "returning evil for evil", Rom 12:17. Three examples follow.
16. Elsewhere only in 26:67, of Jesus. A slap is a personal affront. Some take this in an absolute sense. GK *4824*. Related to "slap" in Jn 18:22.
17. Some manuscripts omit this word {C}, so that it says, "on the right cheek".
18. Or, "wanting you to be judged". On this word, see "judge" in 7:1.
19. That is, your undergarment worn next to the skin, a sleeveless shirt reaching below the knees. Same word as in 10:10; Mk 6:9; Lk 3:11; 6:29; 9:3; Jn 19:23; Act 9:39; Jude 23. Elsewhere only as "clothes" in Mk 14:63. GK *5945*.
20. That is, the outer garment. This was also their blanket. Jews were not permitted to take it, Ex 22:26-27. On this word, see "garments"in 1 Pet 3:3.
21. This word, "press into service, requisition, compel, force" is used elsewhere only of Simon being "pressed into service" to carry the cross in Mt 27:32; Mk 15:21. Soldiers would "compel" people to carry their things. GK *30*.
22. A Roman mile is 1000 paces (counted on one leg, making it 2000 steps of both legs). More precisely, it is eight stades (see Rev 14:20), which is about 4854 feet or 1.5 kilometers. Used only here. GK *3627*.
23. Not simply family and friends, but the "evil *person*" (v 39), and "enemies" (v 44). This is what God does.
24. The Jews considered only fellow Jews to be their neighbors.
25. Compare Lk 6:32-35.
26. Some manuscripts add "be blessing the *ones* cursing you, be doing good *to* the *ones* hating you" {A}, as in Lk 6:27-28.
27. Some manuscripts say "the *ones* mistreating you and persecuting you" {A}, as in Lk 6:28.
28. Or, "be, become". GK *1181*.
29. That is, characterized by the same things as your Father. He loves His enemies.
30. Or, "uncommon, remarkable; what *thing* more, beyond". Same word as "beyond" in v 37. GK *4356*.
31. That is, the non-believers. On this word, see 3 Jn 7. Some manuscripts say "tax gatherers" {B}, as in v 46.
32. Compare Lk 6:36.
33. On this word, see "complete" in 1 Cor 13:10. Same grammar as the commands in v 21, 27, 33, 43.
34. Some manuscripts omit this word {C}.
35. That is, your righteous deeds, such as almsgiving, prayer, and fasting. Some manuscripts say "almsgiving" {N}, the word in v 2.
36. Or, "before, in the sight of ". Same word as in 5:16, 24; 7:6; 10:32; Mk 2:12; 9:2; Rev 19:10; and as "before" in Mt 6:2; Lk 21:36; 2 Cor 5:10. Used 48 times. GK *1869*.
37. That is, do not do them for this purpose. Same grammar as in 5:28. Compare 5:16, where the purpose is to bring glory to God, not yourself. God sees the heart.
38. On this idiom "otherwise indeed", see 2 Cor 11:16.

A. Mt 5:31 B. Rev 13:13, does C. Act 15:7, old D. 1 Cor 12:8, word E. Act 25:18 F. Jn 7:17, willing G. Mt 6:12, forgive H. Lk 6:34, lend J. Jn 21:15, devotedly-love K. Rom 9:13 L. 2 Tim 3:12 M. Gal 3:7 N. Rev 22:12, recompense O. Mt 18:17 P. Mk 15:18 Q. 1 Tim 3:8, pay attention to R. Rev 13:13

1C. "So whenever you do almsgiving[1], do not trumpet *it* before you as-indeed the hypocrites[2] do in the synagogues and in the lanes[3] so that they may be glorified[A] by people[B]. Truly[C] I say *to* you, they are receiving their reward[D] in full[4] — 2

    1D. "But while **you** *are* doing almsgiving, do not let your left *hand* know what your right — 3
        hand is doing, ˚so that your almsgiving may be in secret[E] — 4
    2D. "And your Father, the *One* seeing in secret[E], will[5] reward[F] you

2C. "And whenever you pray[G], do not be like the hypocrites. Because standing in the synagogues — 5
and on the corners *of* the wide-roads[H], they **love**[J] to pray so that they may make-an-appearance[6] *to* people. Truly[C] I say *to* you, they are receiving their reward[D] in full

    1D. "But whenever **you** pray, enter into your inner-room[7]. And having shut your door, pray — 6
        to your Father, the *One* in secret
    2D. "And your Father, the *One* seeing in secret, will reward[F] you[8]

3C. "And while praying[G], do not babble[9] as-indeed the Gentiles *do*. For they are thinking[10] that — 7
they will they will be heard by means of their many-words[11]

    1D. "So do not be like them, for your Father knows *of the things* which you have *a* need — 8
        before you ask Him
    2D.[12] "Therefore, **you** be praying as follows, 'Our Father in the heavens— — 9

        1E. 'Let[13] Your name be treated-as-holy[14]
        2E. 'Let Your kingdom[K] come — 10
        3E. 'Let Your will[L] be done[15]— as in heaven, also on earth
        4E. 'Give us today our daily[16] bread — 11
        5E. 'And forgive[17] us our debts, as **we** also forgave[18] our debtors — 12
        6E. 'And do not bring[19] us into *a* temptation[20], but deliver[21] us from the evil *one*[22]' — 13

    3D.[23] "For[24] if you forgive people their trespasses[25], your heavenly Father will also forgive — 14
        you. ˚But if you do not forgive people *their trespasses*[26], neither will your Father forgive — 15
        your trespasses

4C. "And whenever you fast[27], do not be like the sad-faced[28] hypocrites[M]. For they disfigure[29] their — 16
faces so that they may appear[N] *to* people *as ones* fasting. Truly I say *to* you, they are receiving their reward in full

    1D. "But while **you** *are* fasting, anoint[O] your head and wash[P] your face ˚so that you may not — 17-18
        appear[N] *to* people *as one* fasting, but *to* your Father, the *One* in secret[30]
    2D. "And your Father, the *One* seeing in secret, will reward you[31]

6B.[32] "Do not be treasuring-up[33] treasures *for* yourselves on earth, where moth and eating[34] destroy[35], — 19
and where thieves break-in[Q] and steal. ˚But be treasuring up treasures *for* yourselves in heaven, — 20
where neither moth nor eating destroys, and where thieves do not break in nor steal

    1C. "For where your treasure is, there your heart also will be[36] — 21

1. Or, "alms". That is, charity, charitable-giving to the poor. Same word as in 6:3, 4. Elsewhere only as "alms" in Lk 11:41; 12:33; Act 3:2, 3, 10; and plural, "acts of almsgiving" in Act 9:36; 10:2, 4, 31; 24:17. The Law commanded it, Deut 15:11. GK *1797*. Related to "merciful" in 5:7. The root word is "have mercy".
2. Or, "pretenders, actors". Our word comes from this Greek word "*hupokrites*". Elsewhere only in Mt 6:5, 16; 7:5; 15:7; 22:18; 23:13, 15, 23, 25, 27, 29; 24:51; Mk 7:6; Lk 6:42; 12:56; 13:15. GK *5695*. Related to "pretend" in Lk 20:20, and "hypocrisy" in Gal 2:13.
3. Or, "narrow streets, alleys". Elsewhere only in Lk 14:21; Act 9:11; 12:10. GK *4860*.
4. This was used as an accounting term, "to receive in full". On this word, see Phil 4:18. Their reward is being glorified by people. They sought this, and they receive it, nothing more. Same word as in v 5, 16.
5. Some manuscripts say "will Himself reward you" {N}. Others add "in the open" {B}.
6. Or, "appear, be visible". Same word as "appear" in v 16, 18. On this word, see "shine" in Phil 2:15. Not the same word as "be seen" in v 1.
7. Or, "storeroom". That is, a room in the interior of a house. Same word as in 24:26; Lk 12:3. Elsewhere only as "storeroom" in Lk 12:24. GK *5421*.
8. Some manuscripts add "in the open" {B}.
9. Some think Jesus is referring to uttering "meaningless words"; others, to "empty repetition", repeating the same words again and again (as in the two-hour incident in Act 19:34). In any case, the emphasis is on the quantity of words. Used only here. GK *1006*.
10. Or, "imagining, expecting, supposing, presuming". On this word, see Lk 19:11.
11. Or, "wordiness, much talking". Used only here. GK *4494*.
12. Compare Lk 11:2-4.
13. Each request is in the form of a command (as normal for a direct request), but the grammar changes with the fourth request.
14. Or, "hallowed, sanctified, consecrated". On this word, see "sanctified" in Heb 10:29. The opposite of "profane" in 12:5.
15. Or, "come about, take place, happen, come to pass, become [reality]". Same word as in 8:13; 9:29; 18:19; 26:42; Lk 23:24; 1 Cor 14:26; Rev 16:17; 21:6. GK *1181*.
16. This word is found only in the phrase "daily bread" here and in Lk 11:3. Its exact nuance is uncertain. Some think it means "necessary for existence"; others, "for today"; others, our "daily ration given out for tomorrow". In any case, the only request for material things in the Lord's prayer does not reach beyond our immediate need. What about tomorrow? Jesus later says not to worry about it, v 34. GK *2157*.
17. This word means "forgive" in the sense of "let go, cancel, pardon, release". This sense of the word is found only in Mt 6:14, 15; 9:2, 5, 6; 12:31, 32; 18:21, 27, 32, 35; Mk 2:5, 7, 9, 10; 3:28; 4:12; 11:25; Lk 5:20, 21, 23, 24; 7:47, 48, 49; 11:4; 12:10; 17:3, 4; 23:34; Jn 20:23; Act 8:22; Rom 4:7; Jam 5:15; 1 Jn 1:9; 2:12. Elsewhere this word mainly means "to leave, permit, allow". Used 143 times. GK *918*. Related to "forgiveness" in Col 1:14.
18. Note the tenses. Forgiveness is assumed to be a characteristic part of a believer's way of life. Jesus explains this in v 14-15. Some manuscripts say "are forgiving" {N}. Note Lk 17:3.
19. This verb "to bring in" is elsewhere only in Lk 5:18, 19; 11:4; 12:11; Act 17:20; 1 Tim 6:7; Heb 13:11. GK *1662*. Some render it "lead" here.
20. Or, "trial, testing". On this word, see "trials" in Jam 1:2. Some prefer "trial" here, since God does not tempt us to do evil, Jam 1:13. Others think Jesus means "do not bring us into a situation in which we will be tempted by the evil one", as God did Jesus in 4:1, and as Jesus said to Peter in Lk 22:40, "Pray that you may not enter into temptation" (using this same word).
21. Or, "rescue, save". On this word, see Col 1:13. Some think this is a separate petition, making it point 7E.
22. Or, "from evil". Some manuscripts add "Because Yours is the kingdom and the power and the glory forever, amen" {A}.
23. Compare Mk 11:25.
24. Of all the petitions above, Jesus felt this one needed further explanation.
25. Or, "false steps, sins". Elsewhere only in 6:15; Mk 11:25; Rom 4:25; 5:15, 16, 17, 18, 20; 11:11, 12; 2 Cor 5:19; Gal 6:1; Eph 1:7; 2:1, 5; Col 2:13. GK *4183*. The root word means "fall". Related to "fall away" in Heb 6:6.
26. Some manuscripts include these words {C}.
27. That is, voluntarily skip meals for spiritual purposes. Elsewhere only in 4:2; 6:17, 18; 9:14, 15; Mk 2:18, 19, 20; Lk 5:33, 34, 35; 18:12; Act 13:2, 3. GK *3764*. Related to "fastings" in 2 Cor 11:27.
28. Or, "sullen-faced, gloomy-faced". Elsewhere only in Lk 24:17. GK *5034*.
29. Or, "render invisible or unrecognizable, ruin, destroy". This is a play on words. This is the word "appear" which follows, with a negative prefix. The hypocrites "mal-appear" or "dis-appear" their faces that they may "appear" to be fasting. They blackened their faces with ashes. Elsewhere only as "destroy" in v 19, 20; "perish" in Act 13:41; and "disappear" in Jam 4:14. GK *906*. Related to "disappearance" in Heb 8:13; "hidden" in Heb 4:13; and "invisible" in Lk 24:31.
30. This word occurs only in this verse. GK *3224*. It is related to the word in v 4 and 6.
31. Some manuscripts add "in the open" {A}.
32. Compare Lk 12:33-34.
33. On this word, see "store up" in 1 Cor 16:2.
34. Or, "consuming, eating-*by-rust*". Jesus may be broadly referring to the "eating" of treasures in general by insects, worms, and all the other natural processes of this world, as this word is normally used. In this case, "eating" refers to the broad category of consumption, of which "moth" eating is but one example. If He specifically has metal treasures in view here, then it could be rendered "eating-by-rust, corroding" (a natural extension of this word, but one not found elsewhere in Greek. The normal word group for "corrode, rust" is in Jam 5:2-3, along with "moth-eaten"). In this case, moth and rust would refer to the consumption of different categories of treasure. This noun is the same word as in v 20; Rom 14:17; 1 Cor 8:4; 2 Cor 9:10; Col 2:16. Elsewhere only as "meal" in Heb 12:16; and "food" in Jn 4:32; 6:27, 55. GK *1111*. Related to "food" in Mk 7:19; "moth-eaten" in Jam 5:2; and "eaten-by-worms" in Act 12:23.
35. They "ruin, destroy", or cause to "disappear, perish". Same word as "disfigure" in v 16.
36. Jesus next uses two illustrations to explain and apply this.

A. Rom 8:30   B. Mt 4:4, mankind   C. Mt 5:18   D. Rev 22:12, recompense   E. 1 Cor 4:5, hidden   F. Mt 16:27, render   G. 1 Tim 2:8   H. Lk 14:2   J. Jn 21:15, affectionately-love   K. Mt 3:2   L. Jn 7:17   M. Mt 6:2   N. Phil 2:15, shine   O. Jam 5:14   P. Mk 7:3   Q. Mt 24:43

Matthew 6:22	20	Verse

       1D.[1] "The lamp[A] *of* the body is the eye[2]   22

           1E. "Therefore if your eye is single[3], your whole body will be full-of-light[4]
           2E. "But if your eye is bad[5], your whole body will be full-of-darkness[B]   23
           3E. "If then the light in you is darkness[6], how great *is* the darkness!

       2D.[7] "No one can be serving[8] two masters[C]   24

           1E. "For either he will hate[D] the one and love[E] the other, or he will be devoted-to[9] one and disregard[10] the other
           2E. "You cannot be serving God and wealth[11]

  2C.[12] "For this reason[13] I say *to* you— do not be anxious[14] *for* your life *as to* what you may eat or what you may drink[15], nor *for* your body *as to* what you may put-on[F]   25

       1D. "Is not life more *than* food, and the body *more than* clothing?
       2D. "Look at the birds *of* the heaven— that they do not sow, nor reap, nor gather into barns. And your heavenly Father feeds them. Are **you** not worth[16] more *than* they?   26
       3D. "And which of you while being anxious is able to add[G] one cubit[17] upon his life-span[18]?   27
       4D. "And why are you anxious about clothing? Observe-closely[19] the lilies *of* the field, how they grow   28

           1E. "They do not labor nor spin. *But I say *to* you that not even Solomon in all his glory clothed *himself* like one *of* these   29
           2E. "But if God dresses[20] in this manner the grass *of* the field existing[H] today and being thrown into *an* oven tomorrow, *will He* not *by* much more *care for* you— ones of-little-faith[21]?   30

       5D. "Therefore, do not be[22] anxious, saying, 'What may we eat?' or 'What may we drink?' or 'What may we put-on?'   31

           1E. "For the Gentiles are seeking-after[J] all[23] these *things*   32
           2E. "For your heavenly Father knows that you have need *of* all these *things*
           3E. "But be seeking[K] first the kingdom *of* God[24] and His righteousness[L], and all these *things* will be added[G] *to* you   33

       6D. "Therefore do not be anxious for tomorrow, for tomorrow will be anxious *for* itself. Sufficient[25] *for* the day *is* the trouble[26] *of* it[27]   34

7B.[28] "Do not be judging[29], in order that you may not be judged. *For with what judgment[M] you judge, you will be judged.[30] And with what measure you measure[N], it will be measured[31] *to* you   7:1-2

    1C. "And why do you look-*at* the speck in the eye *of* your brother[O], but do not consider[32] the log[33] in **your** eye? *Or how will you say *to* your brother, 'Permit[P] me to take out[34] the speck from your eye', and behold— the log *is* in your eye?   3 / 4

       1D. "Hypocrite[Q]! First take out the log from your eye, and then you will see-clearly[R] to take out the speck from the eye *of* your brother   5

    2C. "Do not give the holy *thing* to the dogs[35], nor throw your pearls in front of the pigs, so that they will not perhaps trample[S] them with their feet, and having turned, tear you to pieces[36]   6

1. Compare Lk 11:34-35.
2. That is, your eye is the source or gateway of light for your body, physically and spiritually. Whether it is focused on spiritual or earthly treasures will determine whether you live in light or darkness.
3. Or, "sincere, simple". Some think Jesus is referring to a single focus on treasures in heaven. Where your spiritual eye is focused determines how much spiritual light reaches your heart. Others think He means "healthy"; here, spiritually healthy, without guile. Elsewhere only in Lk 11:34. GK *606*.
4. Or, "illuminated, shining". The light from your eye will shine in on your whole body. Your perceptions will give light to your life. Same word as in Lk 11:34, 36. Elsewhere only as "bright" in Mt 17:5. GK *5893*.
5. Some think Jesus means "double-focused", on earthly wealth and God. Seeing double results in darkness for the whole body. Your perceptions will bring confusion and darkness to your path. Others think He means "damaged, sick", spiritually diseased. On this word, see "evil" in Act 25:18.
6. That is, if the spiritual "light" your eye allows in is in fact "darkness" because of your focus on earthly treasures, your darkness is great indeed. Compare Lk 11:34-35.
7. Compare Lk 16:13.
8. Or, "being a slave *to*, serving as slave *to*". That is, at the same time. On this word, see "are slaves" in Rom 6:6.
9. Or, "hold on to, help, support". On this word, see "hold on to" in 1 Thes 5:14.
10. Or, "despise, treat with contempt, look down on, care nothing for". On this word, see Rom 2:4. Either internally (love vs. hate) or externally (devoted allegiance vs. disregard), a slave will be for one of the two masters. Such slaves will either internally hate the one and what they have to do for him (if they can not escape it), or they will implement in action and time what they feel inside by devoting themselves to the one and ignoring the other (if they can make this choice).
11. Or, "property, money". Their agendas and directives lead down different paths, 1 Tim 6:9, 10. Some transliterate this word into English as "mammon", wealth personified. Elsewhere only in Lk 16:9; 11, 13. GK *3490*.
12. Compare Lk 12:22-34.
13. That is, that you might act in accordance with the location of your treasure and heart in heaven.
14. Or, "be worried-*about*, be concerned-*about*". Same word as in 6:27, 28, 31, 34; Lk 10:41; 12:22, 25, 26. Elsewhere only as "be anxious-*about*" in Mt 10:19; Lk 12:11; Phil 4:6; "be concerned-*about*" in 1 Cor 7:32, 33, 34; Phil 2:20; and "have concern" in 1 Cor 12:25. GK *3534*. Related to "anxiety" in 1 Pet 5:7.
15. Some manuscripts omit "or what you may drink" {C}.
16. Same word as "more-valuable" in Mt 10:31; 12:12; Lk 12:7. Same word as in Lk 12:24, where "more" is separately expressed, as it is here. On this word, see "mattering" in Phil 1:10.
17. That is, about 18 inches or a half meter. On this word, see Rev 21:17.
18. Or, "mature age, adulthood, stature, height". Jesus clearly means "one cubit" to be a trifling amount, a "very little thing", Lk 12:26. Since 18 inches would be a huge and impossible amount to add to one's height, "life-span" seems to be the better choice of meanings here. Though one could say, "add one hour to his life span", perhaps Jesus had in mind "Who can add 18 inches— one step— to his life's path". Same word as in Lk 12:25. Note Ps 39:4. Elsewhere only as "stature" in Lk 2:52; 19:3; Eph 4:13; and "mature age" in Jn 9:21, 23; Heb 11:11. GK *2461*.
19. Used only here. GK *2908*. Not related to the word in Lk 12:27.
20. Elsewhere only in 11:8; Lk 7:25. GK *314*.
21. This adjective is elsewhere only in 8:26; 14:31; 16:8; Lk 12:28. GK *3899*. Related word in 17:20.
22. The grammar here and in v 34 implies "do not become anxious, do not worry" (addressing the issue as a whole). In v 25 the grammar means "do not be worrying", focusing on the habit or pattern of behavior, and implies "do not be in the habit or process of being anxious", or "stop being anxious".
23. The word order of "all these *things*" is different here than in v 32b, 33, and Lk 12:30 (which are literally, "these all"), which may imply some additional emphasis on "all" here.
24. Some manuscripts omit "of God", making it "seek first His kingdom and righteousness" {C}.
25. Or, "enough, adequate". Elsewhere only as "enough" in 10:25, 1 Pet 4:3. GK *757*. The related verb is in 2 Cor 12:9.
26. Or, "evil, misfortune". On this word, see "badness" in 1 Pet 2:1.
27. That is, the trouble of each day is enough for that day. Leave tomorrow to itself.
28. Compare Lk 6:37-42.
29. That is, in the sense of "passing judgment on, criticizing, finding fault with", as this word is used in Jn 8:15; Rom 14:3, 10, 13; 1 Cor 4:5; 10:29; Col 2:16; Jam 4:12, etc. Not in the sense of "distinguishing, determining, administering justice" as this word is used in Lk 7:43; 12:57; Jn 7:24; Act 4:19; 16:15; Rom 14:5; 1 Cor 5:3, 12; 6:2; 10:15; 11:13, etc. This verb covers the entire range of meaning from "evaluate, think, determine" to "decide, prefer" to "express an opinion" to "criticize, find fault with" to "sue, go to court" to "decide in court, administer justice" to "condemn". Used 114 times. GK *3212*. Related to "judgment" in Jn 9:39 and Jn 3:19, and to the noun "judge".
30. You will be held to the standards you enforce on others! Some think Jesus means "by God", as Paul applies it in Rom 2:1-3. Others think He means "by people", who respond to you in kind.
31. Some manuscripts have a prefix on this word {N}, so that it means "measured-back", as in Lk 6:38.
32. Or, "notice, perceive". Same word as in Lk 6:41. On this word, see Heb 10:24.
33. Or, "beam", the main beam used in a floor or roof. Elsewhere only in v 4, 5; Lk 6:41, 42. GK *1512*.
34. More literally, "Permit *that* I may take out".
35. By "dogs", Jesus means unholy and impure persons. On this word, see Rev 22:15. The Jews used this word to refer to Gentiles. Related to "little dogs" in Mt 15:26, 27. Note that this requires "distinguishing, deciding"— judging in the second sense of the word in v 1. Perhaps this is included here to give balance to v 1, 3. We sometimes have a tendency to judge too harshly on little things, and to be too lax about important things.
36. When they see it is not food to their liking, they may turn on you. The word "tear to pieces" is GK *4838*.

A. Lk 11:34 B. Lk 11:34 C. Mt 8:2 D. Rom 9:13 E. Jn 21:15, devotedly-love F. Rom 13:14 G. Lk 17:5, increase H. Rev 22:14 J. Phil 4:17, seek for K. Phil 2:21 L. Rom 1:17 M. Jn 9:39 N. Jn 3:34 O. Act 16:40 P. Mt 6:12, forgive Q. Mt 6:2 R. Mk 8:25, look intently S. Heb 10:29

8B.¹ "Be asking^A, and it will be given *to* you. Be seeking^B, and you will find. Be knocking, and it will be opened *to* you. °For everyone asking receives. And *the one* seeking finds. And *to* the *one* knocking, it will be opened

    1C. "Or what person is there from-*among* you whom

        1D. "His² son will ask-*for* bread— he will not give him *a* stone,³ *will he*?
        2D. "Or indeed he will ask-*for a* fish— he will not give him *a* snake,⁴ *will he*?⁵

    2C. "Therefore if **you**, being evil^C, know-*how* to give good^D gifts *to* your children, how much more will your Father in the heavens give good^D *things to* the *ones* asking Him!

9B.⁶ "Therefore,⁷ everything that you want⁸ people to⁹ be doing *to* you, thus also **you** be doing *to* them. For this is the Law and the Prophets
10B.¹⁰ "Enter through the narrow^E gate

    1C. "Because wide *is* the gate, and broad¹¹ *is* the road^F leading-away to destruction¹²— and many are the *ones* entering through it
    2C. "How¹³ narrow *is* the gate, and constricted¹⁴ *is* the road^F leading-away to life— and few are the *ones* finding it

11B. "Beware of the false-prophets^G— who come to you in *the* clothing *of* sheep, but inside are ravenous¹⁵ wolves. °You will know¹⁶ them by their fruits¹⁷

    1C.¹⁸ "They do not collect grapes from thorns, or figs from thistles, *do they*?¹⁹
    2C. "Thus²⁰, every good²¹ tree produces good²² fruit. But the bad²³ tree produces bad²⁴ fruit

        1D. "*A* good tree is not able to produce bad fruit, nor *is a* bad tree *able* to produce good fruit²⁵
        2D. "Every tree not producing good fruit is cut down and thrown into *the* fire

    3C. "So indeed, you will know them by their fruits

12B.²⁶ "Not everyone saying *to* Me, 'Lord, Lord',²⁷ will enter into the kingdom *of* the heavens, but the *one* doing the will^H *of* My Father in the heavens

    1C. "Many will say *to* Me on that day, 'Lord, Lord, did we not prophesy^J *in* Your name, and cast-out^K demons²⁸ *in* Your name, and do many miracles²⁹ *in* Your name?'

        1D. "And then I will declare³⁰ *to* them that 'I never knew³¹ you. Depart^L from Me, *ones* working^M lawlessness^N'

    2C.³² "Therefore everyone who hears these words *of* Mine, and is doing them, will be like³³ *a* wise³⁴ man who built his house upon the bed-rock³⁵

        1D. "And the rain came down, and the rivers³⁶ came, and the winds blew— and they fell against that house. And it did not fall, for it had been founded^O upon the bed-rock

    3C. "And everyone hearing these words *of* Mine, and not doing them, will be like *a* foolish^P man who built his house upon the sand

1. Compare Lk 11:9-13.
2. Some manuscripts say "If his son asks for bread... or if he asks for *a* fish" {N}.
3. That is, something useless.
4. That is, something harmful.
5. The grammar indicates that a "no" answer is expected to both questions. Compare Lk 11:11-12.
6. Compare Lk 6:31.
7. Jesus is summarizing all the teaching about personal behavior, 5:17-7:11.
8. Or, "wish, desire, intend". On this word, see "willing" in Jn 7:17.
9. More literally, "want that people should be doing". GK *2671*.
10. Compare Lk 13:24.
11. Or, "spacious, roomy". Used only here. GK *2353*. Some take it in a metaphorical sense, "easy, comfortable".
12. Some think the road precedes the gate; others, that it follows it. On this word, see 2 Pet 2:1.
13. Some manuscripts say "because" {B}, as in v 13.
14. Or, "pressed in, compressed" and therefore "narrowed, constricted". This is a participle, "having been constricted". Some take it in a metaphorical sense, "hard, difficult". On this word, see "afflicted" in 2 Cor 4:8.
15. That is, "thieving, violently greedy, vicious". Elsewhere only as "swindler" in Lk 18:11; 1 Cor 5:10, 11; 6:10. GK *774*. Related to "snatch away" in 2 Cor 12:2.
16. Or, "recognize". Same word as in v 20. On this word, see "understood" in Col 1:6.
17. That is, their teachings (Deut 13:1-3; 2 Pet 2:1-3, etc.), and their character as seen in themselves, in their works of faith (see 1 Thes 1:3), and in what they produce in others (Jam 3:13-18), not in their claims alone or their works done without connection to Christ (Mt 7:22). Same word as in 3:8, 10; 21:43; Jn 15:2, 5, 8; Gal 5:22; Phil 1:11; 4:17. Used 66 times. GK *2843*.
18. Compare Lk 6:43-45.
19. The grammar indicates a "no" answer is expected. We do not gather fruit from non-fruit-bearing plants.
20. Or, "So, In this manner". Jesus is stating His intended lesson from the grape/thorn, fig/thistle illustration, with reference to "by their fruits".
21. Or, "useful, beneficial". Same word as in "good tree", v 18. On this word, see 1 Tim 5:10b.
22. Or, "sound, healthy, fit, beautiful, desirable, excellent, pleasant, fine, commendable". Same word as in "good fruit" in v 18, 19. On this word, see 1 Tim 5:10a.
23. Or, "unfit, unusable, rotten, worthless". Same word as in "bad tree" in v 18. Elsewhere only in 12:33; 13:48; Lk 6:43; Eph 4:29. GK *4911*.
24. Or, "useless, harmful, evil". Same word as in "bad fruit" in v 18. The contrast may be between types of trees and the value of their fruits, as in v 16 and Lk 6:44 (grapes/thorns, figs/thistles), and similar to the good and bad fish in Mt 13:48. Thus every "beneficial" type of tree (like a fruit tree) produces fruit "fit" to eat. But the "unusable" type of tree produces "useless" fruit. Or, the contrast may be between the quality of the fruit tree and of its fruit, like the fruitless fig tree in 21:19. Thus the "good" fruit tree produces "healthy" fruit. But the "rotten" fruit tree produces "bad" fruit, or none at all. On this word, see "evil" in Act 25:18.
25. That is, a "beneficial" type tree is not able to produce "useless" fruit, nor is an "unusable" type tree able to produce "fit" fruit to eat. Or, a "good" fruit tree is not able to produce "bad" fruit, nor is a "rotten" fruit tree able to produce "healthy" fruit.
26. Compare Lk 6:46.
27. The demons acknowledge Jesus as Lord, Jam 2:19. Not the hearers, but the doers will be justified, Rom 2:13; Jam 1:22. It is not enough to simply "confess to know God", Tit 1:16. Words alone are worthless, Jam 2:14-26. Though Jesus means "Lord, Lord", many in His audience would have understood these words as "Master, Master" (see 8:2 on this word).
28. Compare Mk 9:38.
29. Or, "*works of* power". On this word, see 1 Cor 12:10. Judas was such a one.
30. Or, "confess". On this word, see "confess" in 1 Tim 6:12.
31. That is, as one of My people, as one of My brothers or sisters, as part of My family. On this word, see Lk 1:34.
32. Compare Lk 6:47-49.
33. Or, "become like". Some manuscripts say "I will compare him *to*" {B}.
34. Or, "sensible, prudent, shrewd", wise in a practical sense. Same word as in 24:45; 25:2, 4, 8, 9; Lk 12:42; Rom 11:25; 12:16; 1 Cor 4:10; 10:15; 2 Cor 11:19. Elsewhere only as "shrewd" in Mt 10:16; Lk 16:8. GK *5861*. Related to "think" in Rom 8:5.
35. Same word as in v 25; 16:18; Lk 6:48; 8:6, 13. Elsewhere only as "rock" in Mt 27:51, 60; Mk 15:46; Rom 9:33; 1 Cor 10:4; 1 Pet 2:8; Rev 6:15, 16. GK *4376*. Related word in 16:18. Compare "stone" in Mk 16:3.
36. That is, rivers of flood waters. Same word as in Lk 6:48, 49.

A. 1 Jn 5:14, request   B. Phil 2:21   C. Act 25:18   D. 1 Tim 5:10b   E. Lk 13:24   F. Lk 3:4, way   G. Rev 16:13   H. Jn 7:17   J. 1 Cor 14:1
K. Jn 12:31   L. Act 13:13   M. Mt 26:10   N. 1 Jn 3:4   O. Eph 3:17   P. Tit 3:9

| Matthew 7:27 | 24 | Verse |

    1D. "And the rain came down, and the rivers came, and the winds blew— and they struck-against[A] that house. And it fell[B], and the falling[1] *of* it was great"   27

9A. And it came about *that* when Jesus finished[2] these words, the crowds were astounded[3] at His teaching.   28
For He was teaching them as *One* having authority[C], and not as their[4] scribes. °And He having come 29-8:1
down from the mountain, large crowds followed Him[5]

  1B.[6] And behold— *a* leper having come to *Him* was prostrating-*himself*[7] *before* Him, saying, "Master[8],   2
    if You are willing[D], You are able to cleanse[9] me"

    1C. And having stretched-out[E] *His* hand, He[10] touched[F] him, saying, "I[11] am willing[D]. Be   3
      cleansed". And immediately his leprosy was cleansed
    2C. And Jesus says *to* him, "See *that* you tell no one. But go[12], show yourself *to* the priest, and offer   4
      the gift[G] which Moses commanded[H], for *a* testimony[J] *to* them[13]"

  2B.[14] And He having entered into Capernaum— *a* centurion[15] came to Him, appealing-to[K] Him °and   5-6
    saying, "Master, my servant[16] has been put[17] in the house paralyzed[L], being terribly tormented[M]"

    1C. And He says *to* him, "Having come, **I** will cure[18] him"[19]   7
    2C. And having responded, the centurion said, "Master, I am not fit[N] that You should come in   8
      under my roof. But only speak *it in a* word,[20] and my servant will be healed[21]

      1D. "For **I** also am *a* man under authority[C], having soldiers[O] under myself. And I say *to* this   9
        one, 'Go!' and he goes; and *to* another, 'Come!' and he comes; and *to* my slave, 'Do
        this!' and he does *it*"[22]

    3C. Now having heard, Jesus marveled[P], and said *to* the *ones* following, "Truly[Q] I say *to* you, with   10
      no one in Israel[23] did I find so-great[24] *a* faith!

      1D.[25] "And I say *to* you that many will come from east and west, and will lie-back [to eat]   11
        with Abraham and Isaac and Jacob in the kingdom *of* the heavens. °But the sons *of* the   12
        kingdom[26] will be thrown out into the outer darkness[27]. In that place, there will be the
        weeping[28] and the grinding[29] *of* teeth"

    4C. And Jesus said *to* the centurion, "Go. Let it be done[R] *for* you as you believed[S]"   13
    5C. And his[30] servant was healed at that hour

  3B.[31] And Jesus, having come into the house *of* Peter, saw his mother-in-law having been put[32] *in bed*,   14
    and being sick-with-fever[T]

    1C. And He touched[F] her hand, and the fever left her   15
    2C. And she arose, and was serving[U] Him[33]

  4B.[34] And having become evening, they brought to Him many being demon-possessed[35]. And He cast-   16
    out[V] the spirits *with a* word, and cured all the *ones* being ill[W]

1. Or, "collapse, downfall". Elsewhere only in Lk 2:34. GK *4774*. Related to the preceding verb.
2. On this phrase, see 13:53.
3. Or, "overwhelmed, amazed, astonished". Literally, "struck out of *their senses*". Elsewhere only in 13:54; 19:25; 22:33; Mk 1:22; 6:2; 7:37; 10:26; 11:18; Lk 2:48; 4:32; 9:43; Act 13:12. GK *1742*. Compare Mk 1:22.
4. Some manuscripts omit this word {N}, so that it says "the scribes".
5. The events of 8:2 to 9:34 are Matthew's next topic— the miracles of the King. They are not in chronological order, but are samples of His miracles from various periods of His ministry. Compare Mark and Luke.
6. Parallel account at Mk 1:40; Lk 5:12.
7. On this word, see "worship" in 14:33.
8. This word is used 717 times, mostly as "Lord", referring to the Father or to the Son of God. It is also used of a "master" or "owner" as opposed to a slave or possession (as in 6:24; Lk 19:33). It is used as a term of respect, "sir", to a husband (1 Pet 3:6), a father (Mt 21:30), Paul and Silas (Act 16:30), a government official (Mt 27:63), the Emperor (Act 25:26), an angel (Act 10:4). In the TransLine, when this word is used in the Gospels to address Jesus, it is translated "Lord" only if the one speaking knows Him to be the Son of God (on the twelve, note 14:30). If the speaker perceives Him to be a teacher or healer or the Messiah, it is translated "Master" (only in Mt 8:2, 6, 8, 21, 25; 9:28; 14:28, 30; 15:22, 25, 27; 17:15; 20:30, 31, 33; Mk 7:28; Lk 5:8, 12; 7:6; 9:59, 61; 13:23; 18:41; 19:8; Jn 4:49; 6:34; 9:38); otherwise, it is translated "Sir" (only in Jn 4:11, 15, 19; 5:7; 8:11; 9:36). GK *3261*.
9. Same word as in v 3; 10:8; 11:5. On this word, see Heb 9:22.
10. Some manuscripts say "Jesus" {N}.
11. Jesus alone heals in His own name, without invoking God or the power of God or the name of God.
12. Some think Jesus means "Go straight to Jerusalem and see the priest, as the Law requires". Others think Jesus was trying to maintain some control on the level of publicity His work raised. There are other views.
13. Some think Jesus means "the priests"; others, the people this man was not to tell. See Mk 1:44.
14. Parallel account at Lk 7:1.
15. That is, a Roman commander of a hundred soldiers. He reported to a "tribune" (see "commander" in Act 21:31). Similar to a modern "captain". Elsewhere only in v 8, 13; 27:54; Lk 7:2, 6; 23:47; Act 10:1, 22; 21:32; 22:25, 26; 23:17, 23; 24:23; 27:1, 6, 11, 31, 43. GK *1672*. Mark uses a different word in 15:39.
16. Same word as in Lk 7:7, where this person is also called his slave, 7:2.
17. And therefore "is lying". Same word as in v 14; 9:2; Mk 7:30. GK *965*.
18. Or, "heal". This word means "to do service to, to care for, to attend to" parents, children, masters, the sick, the gods, animals, plants, belongings, graves, etc. It was used of medical care or treatment. Our word "therapy" comes from this word. In the NT, it is always used of the sick (except in Act 17:25, which refers to "servicing" God), and always of miraculous physical healings (except in Lk 8:43, by physicians; and perhaps in Rev 13:3, 12, of the beast). Elsewhere only of Jesus in Mt 4:23, 24; 8:16; 9:35; 12:10; 15, 22; 14:14; 15:30; 17:18; 19:2; 21:14; Mk 1:34; 3:2, 10; 6:5; Lk 4:23, 40; 5:15; 6:7, 18; 7:21; 8:2; 13:14; 14:3; Jn 5:10; the twelve in Mt 10:1, 8; 17:16; Mk 6:13; Lk 9:1, 6; Act 4:14; 5:16; the 72 in Lk 10:9; Philip in Act 8:7; and Paul in Act 28:9. GK *2543*. Related to "service" in Rev 22:2.
19. Or, "Shall **I**, having come, cure him?" Both knew a Gentile's house was "unclean". Some think Jesus was willing to enter it, and take this as a statement, **I** (surprisingly) will come. Others think Jesus was giving the centurion the opportunity to clarify his request, and take this as a question, Shall **I** come? The man immediately says no.
20. That is, in a word of command that it be so. Jesus also casts out demons "*with a* word", v 16. Same phrase as in Lk 7:7. Some manuscripts say "speak *a* word" {K}.
21. Or, "cured". This word was used specifically of the sick, or of something broken. It means "to heal, remedy, repair, treat". Used of miraculous physical healings also in v 13; 15:28; Mk 5:29; Lk 5:17; 6:18, 19; 7:7; 8:47; 9:2 (by the twelve); 9:11, 42; 14:4; 17:15; 22:51; Jn 4:47; 5:13; Act 9:34 (by Peter); 10:38; 28:8 (by Paul); and of healing by the prayer of others in Jam 5:16. All are done by Jesus except those noted. Elsewhere only of spiritual healing in Mt 13:15; Jn 12:40; Act 28:27; Heb 12:13; 1 Pet 2:24. GK *2615*. Related to "healings" in 1 Cor 12:9 and in Lk 13:32, and to "physician". Not related to "cure" in v 7.
22. The centurion is thus saying with regard to Jesus that disease is likewise under His authority, obedient to His word. His physical presence at the centurion's house is not needed.
23. Some manuscripts say "you, not even in Israel did I find so great *a* faith" {B}, as in Lk 7:9.
24. This word means either "so great in quantity", or, "so great in quality". GK *5537*.
25. Compare Lk 13:28-30.
26. That is, Gentiles (foreigners) from east and west will share in it, but the sons (Jews), the "legal" heirs, the ones who should have inherited it, will not.
27. The phrase "outer darkness", and the word "outer", are elsewhere only in 22:13; 25:30. GK *2035, 5030*.
28. This noun is used 9 times. GK *3088*. The related verb is in Jn 11:33.
29. Or, "gnashing, grating" because of pain. Used only in the phrase "weeping and grinding *of* teeth", which occurs also in 13:42, 50; 22:13; 24:51; 25:30; Lk 13:28. GK *1106*. The related verb is in Act 7:54.
30. Some manuscripts omit this word {C}, so that it says "and the servant".
31. Parallel account at Mk 1:29, Lk 4:38.
32. Same word as in v 6.
33. Some manuscripts say "them" {N}.
34. Parallel account at Mk 1:32; Lk 4:40.
35. Or, "being demonized, being tormented by demons". Elsewhere only in 4:24; 8:28, 33; 9:32; 12:22; 15:22; Mk 1:32; 5:15, 16, 18; Lk 8:36; Jn 10:21. GK *1227*. Related to "demon", which is used 63 times. Equivalent to "having a demon" in Mt 11:18; Lk 4:33; 7:33; 8:27; Jn 7:20; 8:48, 49, 52; 10:20.

A. Rom 14:21, stumble B. Rom 11:11 C. Rev 6:8 D. Jn 7:17 E. Act 27:30 F. 1 Cor 7:1 G. Mt 5:23 H. Act 17:26, appointed J. Act 4:33
K. Rom 12:8, exhorting L. Mt 4:24, paralytic M. Rev 14:10 N. 2 Cor 3:5, sufficient O. Mt 28:12 P. Rev 17:8 Q. Mt 5:18 R. Mt 6:10
S. Jn 3:36 T. Mk 1:30 U. 1 Pet 4:10, ministering V. Jn 12:31 W. Mk 1:32

1C.	So that the *thing* might be fulfilled[A] having been spoken through Isaiah the prophet saying[1] "**He** took[2] our weaknesses[3], and carried[4] *our* diseases[5]" [Isa 53:4]	17
5B.	Now Jesus, having seen *a* crowd[6] around Him, gave-orders[B] to depart to the other side	18
1C.[7]	And having come to *Him*, one scribe said *to* Him, "Teacher, I will follow You wherever You go"	19
1D.	And Jesus says *to* him, "The foxes have holes, and the birds *of* the heaven[C] *have* nests[D], but the Son *of* Man[8] does not have *a* place where He may lay *His* head"[9]	20
2C.	And another *of* His[10] disciples said *to* Him, "Master, permit[E] me first to go and bury my father"[11]	21
1D.	But Jesus says *to* him, "Be following Me, and allow[F] the dead to bury their *own* dead[12]"	22
3C.[13]	And He having gotten into the[14] boat, His disciples followed Him	23
1D.	And behold— *a* great shaking[15] took place in the sea, so that the boat *was* being covered[G] by the waves. But **He** was sleeping	24
2D.	And having gone to *Him*, they[16] woke Him, saying, "Master, save *us*[17]. We are perishing[H]"	25
3D.	And He says *to* them, "Why are you afraid[18], *ones* of-little-faith[J]?" Then having arisen[19], He rebuked[K] the winds and the sea. And there was *a* great calm[L]	26
4D.	And the men marveled[M], saying, "What kind of *man* is this *One*, that[20] even the winds and the sea obey[N] Him?"	27
6B.[21]	And He having come to the other side, to the country *of* the Gadarenes[22]— two *men* being demon-possessed[23] met Him, coming out of the tombs. *They* were very violent[24], so that no one *was* strong-enough[O] to pass through that way	28
1C.	And behold— they cried-out[25], saying, "What do we have to do with You,[26] Son *of* God? Did You come here to torment[P] us before *the* time[27]?"	29
2C.	Now there was *a* herd *of* many pigs feeding[Q] far away from them. °And the demons were begging[R] Him, saying, "If You are casting us out, send *us*[28] out into the herd *of* pigs"	30-31
3C.	And He said *to* them, "Go!"	32
4C.	And the *ones*, having come out, went into the pigs.[29] And behold— the whole herd rushed[S] down the steep-bank[30] into the sea[31] and died in the waters	
5C.	And the *ones* feeding[32] *them* fled. And having gone into the city, they reported[T] everything— even the *things about* the *ones* being demon-possessed	33
6C.	And behold— the whole city came out to meet[33] *with* Jesus. And having seen Him, they begged[R] that He pass on from their districts[34]	34
7B.[35]	And having gotten into *a* boat, He crossed-over and came to *His* own city[36]	9:1
1C.	And behold— they were bringing to Him *a* paralytic[U] having been put[V] on *a* bed	2
2C.	And Jesus, having seen their faith, said *to* the paralytic[U], "Take-courage[W], child. Your sins are forgiven[X]"	
3C.	And behold— some *of* the scribes said within[37] themselves, "This *One* is blaspheming[38]"	3
4C.	And Jesus, having seen[39] their thoughts[Y], said "Why[40] are you thinking[41] evil *things* in your hearts?	4
1D.	"For which is easier— to say, 'Your sins are forgiven', or to say, 'Arise, and walk'?	5
2D.	"But in order that you may know that the Son *of* Man has authority[Z] on earth to forgive sins"— then He says *to* the paralytic, "Having arisen, pick up your bed and go to your house"	6

1. This word modifies "prophet", as in 2:17.
2. Or, "He Himself took". Here, this prophecy of the Messiah is fulfilled in His work of physical healing. His healings point to His identity as the One spoken of in Isa 53. Compare Jn 6:2, and how Jesus answers John in Mt 11:2-6. This prophecy is ultimately fulfilled in His death, referring to sin, our spiritual disease, 1 Pet 2:24; Jn 1:29, etc.
3. Or, "infirmities, sicknesses". Used of physical and spiritual sickness or weakness. Same word as in Rom 6:19; 8:26; 1 Cor 2:3; 15:43; 2 Cor 11:30; 12:5, 9, 10; 13:4; Gal 4:13; Heb 4:15; 5:2; 7:28; 11:34. Elsewhere only as "sickness" in Jn 5:5; 11:4; 1 Tim 5:23; and "infirmity" in Lk 5:15; 8:2; 13:11, 12; Act 28:9. GK *819*. Related to "be sick" in 2 Tim 4:20, and the adjective "weak" in 1 Thes 5:14, which are used in the same manner.
4. Or, "bore, carried away". Same word as in 3:11; Mk 14:13; Lk 10:4; 11:27; 14:27; 22:10; Jn 10:31; 12:6; Act 3:2; 9:15; 21:35; Rom 11:18; 15:1; Gal 6:2, 5; Rev 17:7. Elsewhere only as "bear" in Mt 20:12; Lk 7:14; Jn 16:12; 19:17; Act 15:10; Gal 5:10; 6:17; "carry away" in Jn 20:15; "bear with" in Rev 2:2; and "bear up" in Rev 2:3. GK *1002*.
5. Elsewhere only in 4:23, 24; 9:35; 10:1; Mk 1:34; Lk 4:40; 6:18; 7:21; 9:1; Act 19:12. GK *3798*. Related to "be diseased" in 1 Tim 6:4.
6. Some manuscripts say "*a* great crowd"; others, "crowds"; others, "great crowds" {C}.
7. Compare Lk 9:57-62.
8. On this term, see Jn 5:27.
9. In other words, Jesus is not going to an earthly home or destiny where this man can follow.
10. Some manuscripts omit this word {C}, so that it says "*of* the disciples".
11. Some think this man's father actually just died. Others think he meant, "Let me fulfill my duty to my father. When he dies, then I will follow". Compare 4:22.
12. That is, let the spiritually dead (see Eph 2:1) bury the physically dead. Follow now. Used 128 times, in both senses. GK *3738*.
13. Parallel account at Mk 4:35; Lk 8:22.
14. Some manuscripts say "*a* boat" {N}.
15. The shaking was caused by a windstorm, Mk 4:37; Lk 8:23. On this word, see "earthquake" in Rev 11:19.
16. Some manuscripts say "the disciples"; others, "His disciples" {B}.
17. Some manuscripts include this word "us" {B}.
18. On this adjective and question, see Mk 4:40.
19. Related to "awakened" in Mk 4:39; Lk 8:24, which preceded this.
20. Or, "because". GK *4022*. Or, "that both the winds...".
21. Parallel account at Mk 5:1; Lk 8:26.
22. Some manuscripts say "Gergesenes" {C}. Used only here. GK *1123*. See Mk 5:1.
23. Matthew and Mark mention only one, perhaps the more prominent one. On this word, see 8:16.
24. Or, "difficult to deal with, dangerous, troublesome, savage". On this word, see "difficult" in 2 Tim 3:1.
25. Or, "shouted, screamed, called out". Used 55 times. GK *3189*. Related to "shout" in Act 22:23, and "outcry" in Heb 5:7.
26. This is an idiom, literally "What *is* there *for* us and *for* you?" What business do we share? See Jn 2:4 on this. Some manuscripts add "Jesus" {N}, as in Mk 5:7; Lk 8:28.
27. This word also means "season" in Act 1:7; Gal 4:10; "right time" in Rom 5:6; "proper time" in Lk 12:42; 1 Pet 5:6; "opportune time" in Lk 4:13; "opportunity" in Gal 6:10. Used 85 times. GK *2789*.
28. Some manuscripts say "Permit us to go away into..." {N}.
29. Some manuscripts say "the herd *of* pigs" {N}.
30. Elsewhere only in Mk 5:13; Lk 8:33. GK *3204*.
31. This is the common word for "sea", used 91 times, here of the Sea of Galilee. GK *2498*. Luke calls it a "lake", Lk 5:1.
32. Or, "tending, driving to pasture, grazing". Same word as in v 30. On this word, see Jn 21:15.
33. On this idiom, see "meet" in 25:1.
34. On this incident, see Lk 8:32.
35. Parallel account at Mk 2:1; Lk 5:17.
36. That is, Capernaum, 4:13.
37. Or, "among". GK *1877*.
38. On this word, see 1 Tim 6:1.
39. Some manuscripts say "Jesus, knowing..." {B}, as in 12:25.
40. That is, "for what purpose". On this word, see 27:46.
41. On this word, see "pondered" in 1:20. Related to "thoughts" earlier in this verse.

A. Eph 5:18, filled B. Mt 14:28, order C. 2 Cor 12:2 D. Lk 9:58 E. 1 Tim 2:12 F. Mt 6:12, forgive G. 1 Pet 4:8 H. 1 Cor 1:18 J. Mt 6:30
K. 2 Tim 4:2, warn L. Lk 8:24 M. Rev 17:8 N. Act 6:7 O. Gal 5;6, can do P. Rev 14:10 Q. Jn 21:15 R. Rom 12:8, exhorting S. Act 7:57
T. 1 Jn 1:3, announcing U. Mt 4:24 V. Mt 8:6 W. Act 23:11 X. Mt 6:12 Y. Heb 4:12 Z. Rev 6:8

5C.	And having arisen[A], he went to his house	7
6C.	And having seen *it*, the crowds were awed[1]. And they glorified[B] God, the *One* having given such authority[C] *to* humans[2]	8

8B.[3] And while Jesus *was* passing on from there, He saw *a* man sitting at the tax-office[D], being called Matthew. And He says *to* him, "Be following Me!" And having stood up, he followed Him — 9

    1C. And it came about while He *was* reclining-back [to eat] in the[4] house that[5] behold— many tax-collectors[E] and sinners[6], having come, were reclining-back-with Jesus and His disciples — 10
    2C. And having seen *it*, the Pharisees were saying *to* His disciples, "For what reason is your Teacher eating with the tax-collectors and sinners?" — 11
    3C. And the *One*[7], having heard *it*, said, "The *ones* being strong[F] have no need *of a* physician, but the *ones* being ill[G]. °But having gone, learn what it means [in Hos 6:6]— 'I desire[H] mercy[8], and not *a* sacrifice'. For I did not come to call[J] righteous[K] *ones*, but sinners[9]" — 12, 13

9B.[10] Then the disciples *of* John come to Him, saying "For what reason are we and the Pharisees fasting[L] often[11], but Your disciples are not fasting?" °And Jesus said *to* them— — 14, 15

    1C. "The sons *of* the wedding-hall[12] cannot be mourning[M] as long as the bridegroom is with them, *can they*?[13]

        1D. "But days will come when the bridegroom is taken-away[N] from them.[14] And then they will fast

    2C. "And no one puts *a* patch *of* unshrunk cloth on *an* old garment. For the fullness[O] *of* it takes from the garment,[15] and *a* worse tear takes place — 16
    3C. "Nor do they put new wine into old wineskins. Otherwise indeed[16] the wineskins are burst, and the wine spills out, and the wineskins are ruined[17]. But they put new wine into fresh[18] wineskins, and both are preserved[P]" — 17

10B.[19] While He *was* speaking these *things to* them, behold— one[20] [synagogue] official[21], having come, was prostrating-*himself*[22] before Him, saying that "My daughter just-now came-to-an-end[23]. But having come, lay Your hand on her, and she will live" — 18

    1C. And having arisen[A], Jesus followed him, and [so did] His disciples — 19
    2C. And behold— *a* woman having-a-bloody-discharge[24] *for* twelve years, having approached[Q] from behind, touched[R] the tassel[S] *of* His garment[T]. °For she was saying within herself, "If I only touch[R] His garment, I will be restored[25]" — 20, 21

        1D. But Jesus, having turned and having seen her, said, "Take-courage[U], daughter[V]. Your faith has restored you" — 22
        2D. And the woman was restored from that hour

    3C. And Jesus, having come into the house *of* the official, and having seen the flute-players, and the crowd being thrown-into-a-commotion[26], °was saying "Go away. For the little-girl[W] did not die, but is sleeping[X]" — 23, 24

        1D. And they were laughing-scornfully[Y] *at* Him
        2D. But when the crowd was put out, having gone in, He took-hold-of[Z] her hand, and the little girl arose[A] — 25
        3D. And this news[27] went out into that whole land — 26

1. Or, "afraid". They were struck with fear or awe. On this word, see "respecting" in Eph 5:33. Some manuscripts say "marveled" {A}.
2. Or, "people, men". They are putting Jesus in the class of ones receiving this privilege. They recognize the source of His power. On this word, see "mankind" in 4:4.
3. Parallel account at Mk 2:13; Lk 5:27.
4. Or, "*his* house". That is, in Matthew's house, Mk 2:15; Lk 5:29.
5. On this word within the clause "and it came about... that", see Lk 5:1.
6. That is, ones who fail God's requirements, do wrong, miss the mark. Here it is used in the stronger sense of "irreligious", people living outside of God's laws. Used 47 times. GK *283*. Related to the verb "sin" in Act 25:8, and the noun in Jn 8:46.
7. Some manuscripts say "And Jesus..." {N}.
8. Same word as in 12:7; 23:23; Rom 11:31; 15:9; Heb 4:16; Jam 2:13; Jude 21. Used 27 times. GK *1799*. Related to "show mercy" in Rom 12:8.
9. Some manuscripts add "to repentance" {N}.
10. Parallel account at Mk 2:18; Lk 5:33.
11. John's disciples may have been fasting regarding his imprisonment, or their own repentance and preparation. Some of the Pharisees fasted twice a week (Lk 18:12). Some manuscripts omit this word {C}.
12. This word refers to the place where the wedding occurs (as in the variant in 22:10), or, "the bridal chamber", the bedroom where the marriage is consummated. Used only in this statement, which is also in Mk 2:19; Lk 5:34. GK *3813*. Related to "bride" and "bridegroom". The "sons of the wedding hall" refers to the groomsmen, the attendants of the groom, here representing the disciples.
13. The grammar indicates that a "no" answer is expected.
14. Here Jesus gives the first allusion to His death.
15. That is, when it shrinks during washing. The patch "takes" from the old, tearing the old cloth.
16. On this idiom, "otherwise indeed", see 2 Cor 11:16.
17. Or, "lost, destroyed". On this word, see "perish" in 1 Cor 1:18.
18. On the words "new", "fresh", and "old", and the point of v 16-17, see Mk 2:21-22.
19. Parallel account at Mk 5:21; Lk 8:40.
20. Many simplify this to "a", "a [synagogue] official". It is the numeral "one". On this word, see Eph 4:7.
21. Related to "synagogue-official" in Mk 5:22; Lk 8:49. His name was Jairus. On this word, see "ruler" in Rev 1:5.
22. On this word, see "worship" in 14:33.
23. That is, she died. This is a euphemism for death. On this word, see Mk 9:48.
24. Or, "suffering a loss of blood, hemorrhaging". Used only here. GK *137*.
25. Or, "saved", that is, saved from this disease, healed. Same word as in v 22. On this word, see Jam 5:15.
26. Or, "thrown into an uproar, a disturbance, disorder, confusion". In other words, Jesus came into the house and saw the funeral crowd expressing itself in the customary way. Elsewhere only in Mk 5:39; Act 17:5; 20:10. GK *2572*. Related to "commotion" in Mk 5:38.
27. Or, "report". Elsewhere only in Lk 4:14. GK *5773*. Some manuscripts say the news "*of* her"; others, "*of* Him" {N}.

A. Mt 28:6 B. Rom 8:30 C. Rev 6:8 D. Mk 2:14 E. Mt 18:17 F. Gal 5:6, can do G. Mk 1:32 H. Jn 7:17, willing J. Rom 8:30 K. Rom 1:17
L. Mt 6:16 M. Jam 4:9 N. Mk 2:20 O. Col 1:19 P. Lk 2:19 Q. Heb 10:22 R. 1 Cor 7:1 S. Mt 23:5 T. 1 Pet 3:3 U. Act 23:11 V. Lk 13:16
W. Mk 6:22, girl X. 1 Thes 5:10 Y. Lk 8:53 Z. Heb 4:14, hold on to

| Matthew 9:27 | 30 | Verse |

11B. And while Jesus *was* passing on from there, two blind *men* followed Him[1], crying-out[A] and saying, "Have-mercy-on[B] us, Son *of* David[2]!" — 27

    1C. And *He* having gone into the house, the blind *men* came to Him — 28
    2C. And Jesus says *to* them, "Do you believe[3] that I am able to do this?" They say *to* Him, "Yes, Master[C]"
    3C. Then He touched[D] their eyes, saying, "Let it be done[E] *to* you according-to[4] your faith". *And their eyes were opened — 29-30
    4C. And Jesus sternly-commanded[5] them, saying, "See *that* no one knows *it*"
    5C. But the *ones*, having gone forth, widely-spread[6] [the news about] Him in that whole land — 31

12B.[7] And while they *were* going forth, behold— they brought to Him *a* mute man being demon-possessed[F]. *And the demon having been cast-out[G], the mute *man* spoke — 32 / 33

    1C. And the crowds marveled[H], saying, "It never was visible[8] like this in Israel!"
    2C. But the Pharisees were saying, "He is casting out the demons by the ruler[J] *of* the demons" — 34

10A. And Jesus was going around all the cities and the villages, teaching in their synagogues, and proclaiming[K] the good-news[L] *of* the kingdom, and curing every disease and every infirmity.[9] *And having seen the crowds,[10] He felt-deep-feelings[11] [of compassion] concerning[12] them, because they had been troubled[13] and thrown-forth[14] like sheep not having *a* shepherd[M] — 35 / 36

    1B.[15] Then He says *to* His disciples[16], "The **harvest**[17] *is* great— but the workers *are* few! *Therefore ask the Lord *of* the harvest that He send-out[18] workers into His harvest" — 37-38
    2B.[19] And having summoned His twelve disciples, He gave them authority[N] *over* unclean spirits so as to be casting them out, and to be curing every disease and every infirmity — 10:1
    3B.[20] Now the names *of* the twelve apostles[21] are these— — 2

        1C. First[22], Simon (the *one* being called Peter) and Andrew (his brother)
        2C. And James (the *son of* Zebedee) and John (his brother)
        3C. Philip and Bartholomew — 3
        4C. Thomas and Matthew (the tax-collector)
        5C. James (the *son of* Alphaeus) and Thaddaeus[23]
        6C. Simon (the Cananaean[24]) and Judas the Iscariot[O] (the *one* also having handed Him over) — 4

    4B.[25] Jesus sent out these twelve, having instructed[26] them, saying— — 5

        1C. "Do not go into *the* path[27] *of* Gentiles, and do not enter into *a* city *of* Samaritans. *But be proceeding instead to the lost[28] sheep *of the* house[P] *of* Israel — 6
        2C. "And while proceeding, be proclaiming[K], saying that 'The kingdom *of* the heavens has drawn near'.[29] *Be curing *ones* being sick, raising dead *ones*,[30] cleansing[Q] lepers, casting out demons[31] — 7 / 8
        3C. "You received freely[32]— give freely
        4C. "Do not acquire[33] gold nor silver nor copper[34] [money] for your [money] belts—*not *a* [traveler's] bag[R] for *the* journey, nor two tunics[35], nor sandals[36], nor *a* staff[37]. For the worker *is* worthy[S] *of* his food[38] — 9-10
        5C. "And into whatever city or village you enter, search-out[39] who is worthy[S] in it, and stay there until you go forth[40]. *And while entering into the house[T], greet[U] it[41] — 11 / 12

            1D. "And if the house[T] is **worthy**[42], let your peace come upon it— but if it is not worthy, let your peace return to you — 13

1. Some manuscripts omit this word {C}.
2. This phrase was a name for a descendant of David (as in Mt 1:20); and for the Messiah in particular, 1:1; 12:23; 15:22; 20:30; 31; 21:9, 15; Mk 10:47, 48; 12:35; Lk 18:38, 39; 20:41. Compare Lk 1:32; Rom 1:3.
3. Or, "have faith". On this word, see Jn 3:36. Related to "faith" in the next verse.
4. Or, "in agreement with, corresponding to, based on". GK *2848*.
5. Or, "sternly warned". Jesus commanded with intense emotion. On this word, see "deeply moved" in Jn 11:33.
6. Elsewhere only in 28:15; Mk 1:45. GK *1424*.
7. Compare Mt 12:22-37; Mk 3:22-30; Lk 11:14-26.
8. Or, "appeared, came to light, was revealed, shined" and therefore "was seen". That is, it has never been done like this before, it has never happened like this. On this word, see "shine" in Phil 2:15.
9. This is the same statement as in 4:23. Some manuscripts add "among the people" {N}.
10. This is the King's third response to the crowds. Jesus taught them (5:1), healed them (8:1), and now sends the twelve.
11. This word means "to feel deep feelings" of anger, compassion, mercy, pity, love, affection, sympathy, depending on the context. It refers to feelings or emotions deep in the "bowels" or "heart". Elsewhere only in 14:14; 15:32; 18:27; 20:34; Mk 1:41; 6:34; 8:2; 9:22; Lk 7:13; 10:33; 15:20. GK *5072*. Related to "deep feelings" in Phil 1:8.
12. Only here does the NT say deep feelings "concerning" them (GK *4309*). Elsewhere, it is "for" them, or "toward" them.
13. Or, "harassed, bothered". Elsewhere only in Mk 5:35; Lk 7:6; 8:49. This is a participle, "they were having been troubled and thrown forth". GK *5035*. Some manuscripts say "weary" {N}, using the word in 15:32.
14. That is, "scattered". Or, "thrown down", that is, as wounded or helpless. Elsewhere only as "throw" in 15:30; 27:5; "throw down" in Lk 4:35; and "throw off" in Lk 17:2; Act 27:19, 29. This word means "to throw, cast, hurl, toss, fling". GK *4849*. Related to "throw off" in Act 22:23.
15. Compare Lk 10:2.
16. That is, His followers. This is a larger group than the twelve, who are mentioned next in 10:1.
17. Jesus uses grammar that emphasizes the contrast between the two halves of this sentence.
18. Or, "put out, bring out". On this word, see "cast out" in Jn 12:31.
19. Parallel account at Mk 6:7, Lk 9:1.
20. Compare at Mk 3:16; Lk 6:14; Act 1:13.
21. Or, "sent *ones*", sent with a commission. On this word, see 1 Cor 12:28. On these men, see Lk 6:14-16.
22. That is, first among the apostles, the most prominent one. Peter is always mentioned first.
23. Some manuscripts say "Lebbaeus, the *one* having been called Thaddaeus" {B}.
24. That is, the zealot. On this word, see Mk 3:18. Some manuscripts say "Cananite" {N}, the one from Cana.
25. Parallel account at Mk 6:8; Lk 9:3. Compare Lk 10:1-12.
26. Or, "commanded, given orders *to*". Jesus gave them the following set of orders, directives. On this word, see "command" in 1 Tim 1:3.
27. Or, "road, way". Do not join up with Gentiles while on your way. Do not go to them or with them. On this word, see "way" in Lk 3:4.
28. This is a participle. The grammar indicates that it means "the sheep having gotten lost", or "having become lost", not "having been lost". The same word and grammar is in 15:24; Lk 15:4, 6, 24, 32; 19:10. On this word, see "perish" in 1 Cor 1:18.
29. This is the same message as John (Mt 3:2) and Jesus (Mt 4:17).
30. Some manuscripts omit "be raising dead *ones*"; others move it after "be cleansing lepers"; others move it after "be casting out demons" {N}.
31. In other words, be saying and doing what you have seen Me say and do.
32. Or, "as a gift". Accept no money from anyone. On this word, see "without a reason" in Gal 2:21.
33. Or, "procure, get, obtain". On this word, see 1 Thes 4:4.
34. Same word as "money" in Mk 6:8. Compare Lk 9:3.
35. Or, "shirts", that is, an extra undershirt. Compare Lk 3:11. On this word, see Mt 5:40.
36. That is, beyond the pair you are wearing, which also applies to the staff next. Elsewhere only in 3:11; Mk 1:7; Lk 3:16; 10:4; 15:22; 22:35; Jn 1:27; Act 7:33; 13:25. GK *5687*. The related verb is the word "tie on" in Mk 6:9.
37. That is, a walking stick, meaning that they should not buy a new one or a second one. Compare Mk 6:8, Lk 9:3. Some manuscripts have this plural {N}. Do not obtain nor take along any extra provisions for the journey ahead, nor the means to buy or carry them. Your daily needs will be provided to you daily along the way.
38. In this context, Jesus is applying this principle to all their needed provisions. 1 Tim 5:18 says "wages". On this word, see Mt 24:45.
39. Or, "inquire into". Same word as in 2:8. Elsewhere only as "question" in Jn 21:12. GK *2004*. Related to "interrogate" in Act 22:24.
40. That is, from the city.
41. That is, express good wishes toward the house and the people in it. Compare "Peace to you", Jn 20:19, 26.
42. Jesus uses grammar that emphasizes the contrast between the two halves of this sentence. On this word, see Rev 16:6.

A. Mt 8:29 B. Rom 12:8, showing mercy C. Mt 8:2 D. 1 Cor 7:1 E. Mt 6:10 F. Mt 8:16 G. Jn 12:31 H. Rev 17:8 J. Rev 1:5 K. 2 Tim 4:2
L. 1 Cor 15:1 M. Eph 4:11 N. Rev 6:8 O. Jn 6:71 P. Mk 3:20 Q. Heb 9:22 R. Lk 9:3 S. Rev 16:6 T. Mk 3:25 U. Mk 15:18

6C. "And whoever does not welcome^A you, nor listen-to your words— shake-out^B the dust *from* your feet while going outside *of* that house or city. *Truly^C I say *to* you, it will be more-tolerable[1] *for the* land *of* Sodom and Gomorrah on *the* day *of* judgment^D than *for* that city   14
15

7C.[2] "Behold[3]— **I** am sending you out as sheep in *the* midst *of* wolves. Therefore be shrewd[4] as the snakes, and innocent[5] as the doves. *And beware[6] of people   16
17

    1D. "For[7] they will hand you over to councils[8], and whip[9] you in their synagogues. *And you will even be brought before governors[10] and kings[11] for My sake— for *a* testimony^E *to* them[12] and *to* the Gentiles   18

        1E.[13] "But whenever they hand you over, do not be anxious-*about*^F how or what you should speak. For what you should speak will be given *to* you in that hour   19

            1F. "For **you** are not the *ones* speaking, but the Spirit *of* your Father *is* the *One* speaking in you   20

        2D. "And brother will hand-over^G brother to death, and *a* father *his* child. And children will rise-up-in-rebellion[14] against parents and they[15] will put them to death. *And you will be being hated^H by all because of My name. But the *one* having endured^J to *the* end[16], this *one* will be saved^K   21
22

        1E. "But whenever they persecute^L you in this city, flee^M to another.[17] For truly I say *to* you— you will by no means finish[18] the cities *of* Israel until the Son *of* Man comes[19]   23

    3D.[20] "A disciple[21] is not above the teacher, nor *is a* slave above his master. *It is enough^N *for* the disciple that he become like his teacher, and the slave like his master. If they called the Household-Master[22] Beelzebul[23], how much more His household-members!   24-25

        1E.[24] "So[25] do not fear[26] them. For nothing has been covered[27] which will not be revealed^O, and *is* secret^P which will not be known[28]   26

            1F. "What I am saying *to* you in the darkness^Q, speak in the light   27
            2F. "And what you are hearing in *your* ear, proclaim^R upon the housetops^S

        2E. "And do not be fearing[29] anything from[30] the *ones* killing the body, but not being able to kill the soul^T   28

            1F. "But be fearing instead the *One* being able to destroy^U both soul and body in Gehenna^V

        3E. "Are not two sparrows sold *for an* assarion[31]? And one of them will not fall on the ground apart from your Father[32]   29

            1F. "But even the hairs *of* **your** head have all been numbered[33]!   30
            2F. "So do not be fearing. **You** are more valuable *than* many sparrows   31

8C.[34] "Everyone therefore who will confess[35] Me in front of people, **I** also will confess him in front of My Father in the heavens. *But whoever denies[36] Me in front of people, **I** also will deny him in front of My Father in the heavens   32
33

9C.[37] "Do not suppose^W that I came to cast[38] peace over[39] the earth. I did not come to cast peace, but *a* sword^X   34

1. Or, "more endurable, more bearable". Elsewhere only in 11:22, 24; Lk 10:12, 14. GK *445*.
2. Compare Mt 24:9-14; Mk 13:9-13; Lk 21:12-19; Jn 16:1-4.
3. This section is prophetic, looking beyond their immediate mission to their life ministry and beyond.
4. Or, "prudent, sensible". On this word, see "wise" in 7:24. Some think Jesus means "shrewd at recognizing and avoiding danger". Jesus is a prime example. He avoided it until His hour came.
5. Or, "pure". That is, blameless, so that your own behavior does not bring people down on you unnecessarily. On this word, see Rom 16:19.
6. Same command, "beware of", as in 7:15; 16:6, 11; Lk 20:46. Same word as "take heed" in Lk 12:1. On this word, see "pay attention to" in 1 Tim 3:8.
7. These verses, v 17-22, are also in Mk 13:9-13; Lk 21:12-19.
8. That is, local courts, local sanhedrins (consisting of 23 members). On this word, see "council [chamber]" in Act 5:27.
9. Or, "flog, scourge". On this word, see Heb 12:6.
10. Like Pilate, Felix (Act 23:24) and Festus (Act 24:27).
11. Like Agrippa I (Act 12:1), Agrippa II (Act 25:13), and Caesar.
12. That is, the Jews, in their councils and synagogues.
13. Compare also Lk 12:11-12.
14. Or, "will rebel, revolt, stand up against". Elsewhere only in Mk 13:12. GK *2060*.
15. This may refer to "children", or to "the authorities" in general.
16. Same phrase, "to *the* end", as in 24:13; Mk 13:13. On this phrase, see "to the uttermost" in 1 Thes 2:16. Other phrases using the same word "end" with a different preposition may be found in Heb 3:14; 6:11; 1 Cor 1:8. On "end", see Rom 10:4.
17. Some manuscripts add "and if they persecute you from this *one*, flee to another" {C}. Flee from the wolves, v 16.
18. On this word, see Rev 10:7. Related to "end" in v 22.
19. Some think Jesus means "comes to you at the end of this preaching tour I am sending you on"; others, "comes publicly as Messiah in Jerusalem" in 21:9. Others think the "coming" referred to is His transfiguration, or resurrection, or the Day of Pentecost, or His coming to destroy Jerusalem in judgment, or His second coming. Others translate this verb "goes", that is, goes to the Father after His resurrection. This common word meaning "to come, go" is used 632 times. GK *2262*. Note 16:28.
20. Compare Jn 15:20.
21. Or, "learner, pupil, student". On this word, see Lk 6:40.
22. That is, Jesus. On this word, see 20:1.
23. That is, a devil. On this word, see Mk 3:22. Do not think this coming persecution strange. If Jesus the teacher and master experienced persecution, how much more His students and slaves! Compare 1 Pet 4:12.
24. Compare Lk 12:2-7.
25. Because you are My disciples and slaves (v 24), sent out by Me (v 16).
26. The grammar views the matter as a whole, and implies, Do not start to fear or become fearful of them.
27. Or, "veiled, hidden". This is a participle, nothing "is having been covered". On this word, see 1 Pet 4:8. Related to the word in Lk 12:2.
28. In other words, do not fear, because they will not get away with anything. The motives and actions of both you and them will become known to all. So take what I tell you privately and proclaim it publicly without fear.
29. The grammar views the matter as a process, and implies "stop fearing" or "do not be in the habit or pattern of fearing". Likewise in v 31.
30. Or, "Do not be afraid of the *ones*...". This idiom, "to fear from", is elsewhere only in Lk 12:4.
31. This is a Roman copper coin. Elsewhere only in Lk 12:6. GK *837*. Sixteen assarion made one denarius. See Mk 12:42.
32. That is, apart from His will, without His consent.
33. This is a participle, the hairs "are having been numbered". Not the same grammar as in Lk 12:7.
34. Compare Lk 12:8-9; Mk 8:38; Lk 9:26.
35. Same word as in Rom 10:9. On this word, see 1 Tim 6:12. Here and in Lk 12: 8, it literally says "confess in Me... confess in him". This reflects an Aramaic way of speaking, and is not found with the other 22 uses of this word.
36. Or, "repudiates". Same word as in Act 3:13, 14. On this word, see 1 Tim 2:12. Both Peter (Mt 26:70, 72) and some of those mentioned in Act 3:14-16 repented of their denial and confessed Him.
37. Compare Lk 12:51-53.
38. This is the common word for "throw, put, cast", on which see "throw" in Rev 2:22.
39. Or, "on, across". GK *2093*.

A. Mt 10:40 B. Act 13:51 C. Mt 5:18 D. Jn 3:19 E. Act 4:33 F. Mt 6:25 G. Mt 26:21 H. Rom 9:13 J. Jam 1:12 K. Lk 19:10 L. 2 Tim 3:12 M. 1 Cor 6:18 N. Mt 6:34, sufficient O. 2 Thes 2:3 P. 1 Cor 4:5, hidden Q. Jn 1:5 R. 2 Tim 4:2 S. Lk 5:19 T. Jam 5:20 U. 1 Cor 1:18, perish V. Mt 5:22 W. Act 14:19, think X. Eph 6:17

Matthew 10:35	34	Verse

    1D. "For I came to cause-a-separation[1]— *a* man against[2] his father, and *a* daughter against her mother, and *a* daughter-in-law against her mother-in-law. °And *the* enemies *of* the person *will be* his household-members   35
         36
    2D.[3] "The *one* loving father or mother above Me is not worthy[A] *of* Me. And the *one* loving son or daughter above Me is not worthy *of* Me   37
    3D. "And he who is not taking his cross[4] and following after Me is not worthy *of* Me   38
    4D.[5] "The *one* having found his life[6] will lose it, and the *one* having lost his life for My sake will find it   39

   10C. "The *one* welcoming[7] you is welcoming Me. And the *one* welcoming Me is welcoming the One having sent Me forth[B]   40

    1D. "The *one* welcoming *a* prophet[C] in *the* name *of a* prophet[8] will receive *the* reward[D] *of a* prophet   41
    2D. "And the *one* welcoming *a* righteous[E] *one* in *the* name *of a* righteous *one* will receive *the* reward *of a* righteous *one*
    3D. "And whoever gives one *of* these little *ones* only *a* cup *of* cold *water* to drink in *the* name *of a* disciple— truly[F] I say *to* you he will by no means lose his reward"   42

  5B. And it came about *that* when Jesus finished[G] giving-directions[9] *to* His twelve disciples, He passed-on[H] from there *that* He might teach and proclaim[10] in their cities   11:1

11A. Now John,[11] having in prison[12] heard-*of* the works *of* the Christ, having sent through his[13] disciples, °said *to* Him, "Are **You** the *One* coming[14], or should we be looking-for[15] *a* different[16] *one*?"   2-3

 1B.[17] And having responded, Jesus said *to* them, "Having gone, report[J] *to* John *the things* which you are hearing and seeing[18]—   4

  1C. "Blind *ones* are seeing-again[K], and lame[L] *ones* are walking. Lepers are being cleansed[M], and deaf *ones* are hearing. And dead *ones* are being raised, and poor[N] *ones* are having-good-news-announced[19] *to* them   5
  2C. "And blessed[O] is whoever does not take-offense[20] in Me"   6

 2B. And while these *ones were* proceeding, Jesus began to speak *to* the crowds about John—   7

  1C. "What[21] did you go out into the wilderness[P] to look-*at*? *A* reed being shaken by *the* wind?
  2C. "But what did you go out to see? *A* man having been dressed[Q] in soft *garments*? Behold— the *ones* wearing[R] the soft *garments* are in the houses[S] *of* kings!   8
  3C. "But what did you go out to see? *A* prophet? Yes, I say *to* you, and more[22] *than a* prophet   9

   1D.[23] "This *one* is about whom it has been written [in Mal 3:1], 'Behold— **I** am sending-forth[B] My messenger[T] ahead *of* Your presence[24], who will make Your way ready[25] in front of You'   10
   2D. "Truly[F] I say *to* you, *a* greater[26] *one than* John the Baptist has not arisen[U] among *ones* born *of* women   11

    1E. "But the least[27] *one* in the kingdom[V] *of* the heavens[W] is greater[28] *than* he

     1F. "But the kingdom *of* the heavens is being treated-violently[29] from the days *of* John the Baptist until now. And violent[30] *ones* are snatching[31] it away[32]   12

1. Or, "divide in two, separate, dis-unite". Used only here. GK *1495*.
2. Matthew uses a different word for "against" than Luke.
3. Compare Lk 14:25-27.
4. That is, we must not seek to escape from that which causes us to suffer for Christ. We must accept it, carry it, and follow Him, denying our self-interest. Our "cross" is any personal issue which for us symbolizes our self-death for Him, our denying self for Him, our suffering loss for Him, not suffering in general. Note that it is an ongoing matter, not a one-time thing. In this context, it especially means carrying the cross of rejection by an unbelieving family member, v 37. Compare Mt 16:24. This word is used 27 times. GK *5089*. Related to "crucify" in Mt 27:35.
5. Compare Mt 16:25.
6. That is, having found himself, having defined his life, by choosing his own self-interest over Christ.
7. Or, "receiving hospitably, accepting". Same word as in Mt 10:14, 41; 18:5; Mk 6:11; 9:37; Lk 8:13; 9:5, 48, 53; 10:8, 10; 16:4, 9; Jn 4:45; 2 Cor 8:17; Gal 4:14; Col 4:10; Heb 11:31. Elsewhere only as "receive" in Mk 10:15; Lk 18:17; Act 3:21; 7:38, 59; 17:11; 22:5; 28:21; 2 Cor 6:1; 7:15; 11:16; Phil 4:18; 2 Thes 2:10; Jam 1:21; "accept" in Mt 11:14; Act 8:14; 11:1; 1 Cor 2:14; 2 Cor 11:4; 1 Thes 1:6; 2:13; and "take" in Lk 2:28, 16:6, 7; 22:17; Eph 6:17. GK *1312*.
8. That is, because he is a prophet. Next, because he is a righteous one; then, because he is a disciple, v 42. The same concept is in Mk 9:41.
9. Or, "commanding, giving orders *to*". On this word, see "direct" in 1 Cor 7:17.
10. Same two words as 4:23; 9:35, "teach", "proclaim".
11. Having presented His teaching (8A.), His works (9A.), and His sending of the twelve to proclaim the kingdom to Israel (10A.), Matthew now uses John to "prepare the way" again by asking the key question, "Are You the One?". What follows details how Jesus both hid and revealed (11:25-26; 13:12) the answer to that question as He responded to opposition and continued His words and works of self-revelation. It culminates in the response of Peter. As to why John would ask such a question, some think prison made him doubt or lose patience. Others think he was expecting the kingly, conquering, judging Messiah and was puzzled over Jesus. There are other views.
12. Josephus says John was imprisoned at Machaerus, a palace of Herod Antipas (see 14:1) east of the Dead Sea, in Perea. On this word, see "jailhouse" in Act 5:21.
13. Some manuscripts say "sent two *of* his" {B}, as in Lk 7:18.
14. Or, "the Coming *One*". That is, the Messiah.
15. Or, "or are we looking for" another. Same words as in Lk 7:19.
16. Or, "another" (GK *2283*). Not the same word as in Lk 7:19 (GK *257*).
17. Parallel account at Lk 7:18.
18. Jesus lists things Isaiah prophesied Messiah would do, Isa 35:5-6; 61:1. His works answer John's question.
19. More literally, "are being announced good news, are being evangelized". Same word as in Lk 7:22. On this word, see Act 5:42.
20. Or, "is not caused to fall by Me". On this word, see "cause to fall" 1 Cor 8:13.
21. Or, "Why did you go out into the wilderness? To look at *a* reed...? But why did you go out? To see *a* man...? ... But why did you go out? To see a prophet?". Some manuscripts have a word order in v 9 that would require it to be punctuated as in the footnote {B}.
22. Jesus could mean "*one who is* more than", or, "*something* more than" (like 12:41, which uses a different word).
23. Compare also Mk 1:2; Lk 1:17.
24. Or, "face". On this phrase, "ahead of your presence", see Lk 9:52.
25. On this word, "make ready", see Mk 1:2.
26. Some think Jesus means greater in character, in obedience to God. Others think He means greater in what John would know and do with regard to Messiah. This word means "greater", with the specific sense coming from the context: "larger, louder, more important, more strict, older". Used 48 times. GK *3505*. Related to "great" in Heb 11:24.
27. Or, "lesser". Same word as "smaller" in 13:32; Mk 4:31; and as "least" in Lk 7:28; 9:48. In the one case, Jesus would mean "lesser than John"; in the other, "least of all". This word means "little", with the specific sense coming from the context: "small, short, young, insignificant". Used 46 times. GK *3625*.
28. Not in character, work or reward, but in privilege— as adult family members of God, no longer as children under a tutor (Gal 3:23; 4:1-2). John belongs to the OT order preceding the Messiah, v 13. These in the kingdom will see and hear all about His life, death, and resurrection. They get to see and know the King. Note 13:16-17.
29. This word can mean "to use violence or force, to inflict violence or force, to be treated with violence or force". Elsewhere only as "forcing-*himself*" in Lk 16:16. GK *1041*. In the Septuagint, it is used in the sense of "urge, strongly invite" (that is, use verbal or social force or pressure) as in Gen 33:11; Judg 19:7; and in the sense of "force one's way", as in Ex 19:24; Deut 22:25. Related to "violent" next in v 12; "prevail upon" in Act 16:15; "violence" in Act 5:26; and "violent" in Act 2:2.
30. This word refers to one who uses hostile force or violence to attain his desires. Used only here. GK *1043*.
31. This word means "snatch away, take by force, seize, steal". Elsewhere by Matthew only of the evil one "snatching away" the seed in 13:19, and of "snatching away" the strong man's things in 12:29. Used of taking Jesus away by force to make Him king in Jn 6:15. On this word, see 2 Cor 12:2.
32. Some think Jesus means that the kingdom is being attacked by enemies like Herod (who imprisoned John) and the Pharisees, who "are snatching away" the people and the message of the kingdom. Others think the kingdom is "forcing itself, forcefully advancing" (as seen with demons, 9:32-33), and the "forceful" (in a positive sense, the spiritually bold, daring, aggressive ones) are "taking hold" of it. Others think John and Jesus are "forcing" it on Israel, but violent men are snatching it away. Others think the kingdom is "being forced, pressed into, taken by storm". People were waiting patiently for Messiah before John, but now they are "pressing hard" to get in, to seize it. Others think people like the Zealots or those in Jn 6:15 are trying to establish it by force. There are other views.

A. Rev 16:6 B. Mk 3:14, send out C. 1 Cor 12:28 D. Rev 22:12, recompense E. Rom 1:17 F. Mt 5:18 G. Rev 10:7 H. Jn 5:24, pass J. 1 Jn 1:3, announcing K. Act 22:13, look up L. Heb 12:13 M. Heb 9:22 N. Gal 4:9 O. Lk 6:20 P. Mt 3:1 Q. Mt 6:30 R. 1 Cor 15:49, bear S. Mk 3:20 T. 1 Tim 3:16 U. Mt 28:6 V. Mt 3:2 W. 2 Cor 12:2

        3D. "For all the prophets[A] and the Law prophesied[B] until John.[1] *And if you are willing[C] to 13-14
            accept[D] it, he himself is Elijah— the *one* going-to[E] come[2]
        4D. "Let the *one* having ears[3] hear   15

    4C.[4] "But *to* what will I liken this generation[F]? It is like children sitting in the marketplaces, who, 16
        calling to the others[5], *say 'We played the flute *for* you, and you did not dance'. 'We lamented[6], 17
        and you did not beat-your-breast[7]'

        1D. "For John came neither eating nor drinking,[8] and they say 'He has *a* demon'   18
        2D. "The Son *of* Man came eating and drinking, and they say 'Behold— *a* man *who is a* 19
            glutton and drunkard[9], *a* friend *of* tax-collectors[G] and sinners[H]'"
        3D. "And wisdom[J] was vindicated[10] by her works[11]"

3B.[12] Then He began to reproach[13] the cities in which most-of[14] His miracles[K] took place, because they 20
    did not repent[L]

    1C. "Woe *to* you, Chorazin[15]! Woe *to* you, Bethsaida! Because if the miracles having taken place in 21
        you had taken place in Tyre and Sidon, they would have repented long ago in sackcloth and ashes

        1D. "Nevertheless[16] I say *to* you— it will be more tolerable[17] *for* Tyre and Sidon on *the* day 22
            of judgment[M] than *for* you

    2C. "And you, Capernaum, will you be exalted[N] up to heaven?[18] You will go-down[19] as far as 23
        Hades[O]. Because if the miracles having taken place in you had been done[20] in Sodom, it would
        have remained[P] until today

        1D. "Nevertheless I say *to* you that it will be more tolerable *for* the land *of* Sodom on *the* day 24
            of judgment than *for* you"

4B.[21] At that time,[22] having responded, Jesus said, "I praise[23] You, Father, Lord *of* heaven and earth, 25
    that[24] You hid[25] these *things* from wise *ones* and intelligent[Q] *ones,* and You revealed[R] them *to*
    children[26]. *Yes, Father, because[27] in-this-manner[28] it became[29] well-pleasing[30] in Your sight 26

    1C. "All *things* were handed-over[S] *to* Me by My Father   27
    2C. "And no one knows[31] the Son except the Father. Nor does anyone know the Father except the
        Son, and *anyone to* whom[32] the Son wills[33] to reveal[R] *Him*
    3C. "Come to Me, all the *ones* being weary[34] and having been burdened[35], and **I** will give you rest[36]. 28
        Take My yoke[T] upon you[37] and learn[U] from Me, because I am gentle[38] and humble[39] *in* heart, 29
        and you will find rest[40] *for* your souls[V]. *For My yoke *is* easy[41], and My burden[42] is light" 30

5B.[43] At that time Jesus went through the grainfields *on* the Sabbath. And His disciples were hungry and 12:1
    began to pluck[44] heads[W] [of grain] and eat

    1C. And the Pharisees, having seen *it*, said *to* Him, "Behold—Your disciples are doing what is not 2
        lawful[X] to be doing on *a* Sabbath"[45]
    2C. And the *One* said *to* them—   3

        1D. "Did you not read [in 1 Sam 21:1-6] what David did when he was hungry, and the *ones*
            with him—* how   4

            1E. "He entered into the house[Y] *of* God

1. On this sentence, compare Lk 16:16.
2. That is, the one predicted to come before the day of the Lord in Mal 4:5-6. Note Mt 17:12; Jn 1:21; Lk 1:17.
3. Some manuscripts add "to hear" {B}, "having ears to hear". If John is Elijah, then Jesus is Messiah.
4. Parallel account at Lk 7:31.
5. Some manuscripts say "to *their* friends" {N}, using the word in 20:13.
6. Or, "sang a funeral song". Elsewhere only in Lk 7:32; 23:27; Jn 16:20. Some manuscripts add "*for* you" {B}. GK *2577*.
7. Or, "mourn greatly". On this word, see Rev 1:7. In other words, John and Jesus did not respond to them as they wanted them to do. They wanted John to make merry with them, but he was too ascetic. They wanted Jesus to mourn the things they mourn, but He was too sociable.
8. That is, he did not eat and socialize with them, but lived apart from them in the desert. Jesus did the opposite. Compare Lk 1:15.
9. Or, "*a* wine drinker". Both words are elsewhere only in Lk 7:34. Jesus must be eating too much food and drinking too much wine, because He eats and drinks with people who do so— sinners. GK *3884*. Related to "wine" in 1 Tim 5:23.
10. Or, "justified, declared right". Wisdom is seen in the things it does, the results it produces. The results produced by the life choices of John and Jesus vindicate God's wisdom. This generation's "wisdom" has led it to reject John and Jesus! On this word, see "declare righteous" in Rom 3:24.
11. Some manuscripts say "children" {B}, as in Lk 7:35.
12. Compare Lk 10:12-15.
13. Or, "scold, reprimand". On this word, see 1 Pet 4:14.
14. Or, "His greatest miracles, His very great miracles". Same word as in 21:8.
15. This city is near Capernaum, and is mentioned elsewhere only in Lk 10:13. GK *5960*. Though "most" or "very great" miracles were done there, no account of it is given explicitly in the Gospels. This reveals how much we do not know about the ministry of Jesus. Note Jn 21:25.
16. That is, "in spite of the fact that they did not repent and were judged by God, I say to you by comparison...". Or, "But", "But in contrast to what you may think about them or your own situation...". This word also means "yet, however, except, only". Used 31 times. GK *4440*.
17. On this word, see 10:15. Same word as in v 24. They had far less "light" than you.
18. The grammar requires a "no" answer. Some manuscripts have it as a statement, And you Capernaum, "the *one* having been exalted up to heaven, you will..."; others, "who were exalted up to heaven, you will..." {B}.
19. Some manuscripts say "you will be brought down" {C}.
20. Same word as "taken place" in v 21, but with different grammar. Same word as Lk 10:13. GK *1181*.
21. Compare Lk 10:21-22.
22. This took place when the 70 returned, Lk 10:17, 21.
23. Same word as in Lk 10:21, Rom 15:9. On this word, see "confess out" in Jam 5:16.
24. Or, "because". Same word translated "because" in v 26.
25. On this word, see Jn 8:59. Related to the word in Lk 10:21.
26. Or, "childlike *ones*". Same word as in 21:16; Lk 10:21; Rom 2:20; Eph 4:14. On this word, see "infant" in 1 Cor 3:1. The contrast is between wise ones (in their own eyes) without God's revelation, and simple, childlike ones with it.
27. Or, "that", so that is says, "Yes Father, *I praise You* that in this manner...". GK *4022*.
28. Or, "thus, so". GK *4047*.
29. Or, "was, proved to be, came to be". GK *1181*.
30. On this noun, see "good pleasure" in Eph 1:5.
31. Or, "recognizes, understands, knows exactly". Same word as later in the verse. On this word, see "understood" in Col 1:6. Related to the word in Lk 10:22.
32. Or, "and *to* whomever the Son...".
33. Or, "wishes, desires, wants". Elsewhere by Matthew only as "intend" in 1:19. On this word, see Jam 1:18.
34. Same word as in Jn 4:6; Rev 2:3. This word means "laboring, working hard", and as a result, "being weary". Used 23 times, mostly as "labor". GK *3159*. The related noun "labor" (see 1 Cor 3:8) and the following verb "rest" are used together in Rev 14:13, "rest from their labors".
35. That is, loaded down with burdens to carry. Elsewhere only in Lk 11:46. Compare Mt 23:4. These people are laboring to carry the unbearable yoke (Act 15:10) of legalistic traditions imposed by the Pharisees and scribes. GK *5844*. Related to "burden" in v 30.
36. On "give rest", see "refreshed" in Phm 7. The related noun is used later in this verse.
37. That is, hitch yourself to My plow. Accept My teaching.
38. Same word as in 5:5. On this word, see 1 Pet 3:4.
39. Or, "lowly, poor". On this word, see "lowly" in Jam 1:9. Jesus is completely unlike their present teachers.
40. Or, "refreshment, relief". On this word, see 12:43.
41. Or, "pleasant". On this word, see "good" in 1 Pet 2:3. It is "good" in the sense of what one carrying a load would consider good; that is, easy, pleasant.
42. Or, "load, cargo". On this word, see "load" in Gal 6:5.
43. Parallel account at Mk 2:23; Lk 6:1.
44. The Law permits this plucking of a neighbor's grain, Deut 23:25. Elsewhere only in Mk 2:23; Lk 6:1. GK *5504*.
45. Such plucking was considered "work" by the Rabbis, and so was not permitted by them.

A. 1 Cor 12:28 B. 1 Cor 14:1 C. Jn 7:17 D. Mt 10:40, welcome E. Mk 10:32 F. Mt 24:34 G. Mt 18:17 H. Mt 9:10 J. 1 Cor 12:8 K. 1 Cor 12:10 L. Act 26:20 M. Jn 3:19 N. Jn 8:28, lifted up O. Rev 1:18 P. Jn 15:4, abide Q. 1 Cor 1:19 R. 2 Thes 2:3 S. Mt 26:21 T. Gal 5:1 U. Phil 4:11 V. Jam 5:20 W. Mk 4:28 X. 1 Cor 6:12 Y. Mk 3:20

2E. "And they[1] ate the Bread *of* Presentation[2] which it was not lawful[3] *for* him to eat, nor *for* the *ones* with him, but *for* the priests alone[A]?"

    2D. "Or did you not read in the Law that *on* the Sabbaths, the priests in the temple profane[4] the Sabbath[5] and are guiltless[6]? °But I say *to* you that *a greater-thing*[7] *than* the temple is here

    3D. "But if you had known what it means[B] [in Hos 6:6]— 'I desire[C] mercy, and not *a* sacrifice'— you would not have condemned[D] the guiltless *ones*

    4D. "For the Son *of* Man is **Lord**[E] *of* the[8] Sabbath"

6B.[9] And having passed-on[F] from there, He went into their synagogue. °And behold— *there was a* man having *a* withered[G] hand[10]

    1C. And they questioned Him, saying, 'Is it lawful[H] to cure[J] *on* the Sabbath?'— in order that they might accuse[K] Him

    2C. And the *One* said *to* them, "What person will there be from-*among* you who will have one sheep, and if this *sheep* falls into *a* pit *on* the Sabbath, will not take hold of it and raise[L] *it*? How much then is *a* person more-valuable[M] *than a* sheep! So then, it is lawful to be acting commendably[11] *on* the Sabbath"

    3C. Then He says *to* the man, "Stretch-out[N] your hand". And he stretched *it* out, and it was restored[O], healthy[12] like the other

    4C. And having gone out, the Pharisees took counsel[13] against Him, so that they might destroy[P] Him

    5C. But Jesus, having known *it*, withdrew[Q] from there. And large crowds[14] followed Him, and He cured[J] them all. °And He warned[R] them that they should not make Him known[15], °in order that the *thing* might be fulfilled having been spoken through Isaiah the prophet saying[16]

        1D. "Behold, My servant[S] Whom I chose[17], My Beloved in Whom My soul was well-pleased[18]—

            1E. "I will put My Spirit upon Him
            2E. "And He will announce[19] justice *to* the Gentiles
            3E. "He will not quarrel[20], nor shout[T], nor will anyone hear His voice in the wide-roads[U]
            4E. "He will not break *a* reed having been bruised[21], and He will not quench[V] *a* smoldering wick, until He leads-out[22] justice[23] to victory[W]
            5E. "And *the* Gentiles will put-hope[X] *in* His name" [Isa 42:1-4]

7B.[24] Then *a* blind and mute *man* being demon-possessed[Y] was brought to Him. And He cured him, so that the mute[25] *man was* speaking and seeing

    1C. And all the crowds were astonished[Z], and were saying, "This *One* is not the Son *of* David, *is He*?"[26]
    2C. But the Pharisees, having heard *it*, said, "This *One* is not casting out the demons except by Beelzebul[27], *the* ruler *of* the demons!"
    3C. And knowing their thoughts[28], He[29] said *to* them—

        1D. "Every kingdom having been divided against[30] itself is desolated[AA]. And every city or house having been divided against itself will not stand[31]

            1E. "And if Satan is casting-out[BB] Satan, he was divided against[32] himself. How then will his kingdom stand?

        2D. "And if **I** am casting out the demons by Beelzebul, by whom are **your sons** casting *them* out?[33] For this reason[34] **they** will be your judges

1. Some manuscripts say "he" {C}.
2. On this word, see Mk 2:26. That is, the 12 loaves of "showbread", Lev 24:6-9.
3. Same word as in v 2, 10, 12. This is a participle, it "was not being lawful". On this word, see 1 Cor 6:12.
4. Or, "desecrate". That is, treat as common. Elsewhere only in Act 24:6. GK *1014*. Related to "profane" in 1 Tim 1:9.
5. That is, because the priests work on the Sabbath, performing their temple sacrifices. In other words, the temple ministry is more important than the Sabbath. And Jesus is more important than the temple.
6. Or, "innocent, without a charge, without a ground of accusation". Elsewhere only in v 7. GK *360*.
7. Some manuscripts say "*A greater One*" {N}.
8. Some manuscripts say "even *of* the..." {K}, as in Mk 2:28.
9. Parallel account at Mk 3:1; Lk 6:6.
10. Some manuscripts say "*a* man was having the hand withered" {N}.
11. Or, "appropriately, rightly, well", to do something outwardly good and right. The Pharisees try to frame the question as regarding "work". Jesus says it is about doing good. Who among them would say that God forbids doing good on the Sabbath? He shames them into silence, and anger, v 14. This is the adverb of the word "good". Most simplify this phrase to "to do good", as Mark and Luke give it. On this phrase, see "do well" in Act 10:33.
12. Or, "sound". Same word as in 15:31; Mk 5:34; Jn 5:6, 9, 11, 14, 15; Act 4:10; Tit 2:8. Elsewhere only as "sound" in Jn 7:23. GK *5618*. Related to the word in 1 Tim 1:10.
13. The phrase "to take counsel" is a Latin way of speaking, meaning "to form a plan, plot, decide, consult", and is elsewhere only in 22:15; 27:1, 7; 28:12. On "counsel", see "consultation" in Mk 15:1.
14. Some manuscripts omit this word {C}, so that it says "And many followed Him...".
15. Or, "visible, plainly seen". On this word, see "evident" in Rom 1:19.
16. This word modifies "prophet", as in 2:17.
17. Used only here. GK *147*. Related to the word in 2 Thes 2:13.
18. On "was well pleased", see 17:5. On "soul", see Jam 5:20.
19. Or, "declare, proclaim, report". On this word, see 1 Jn 1:3.
20. Or, "wrangle". Used only here. GK *2248*. Related to the word in 1 Cor 1:11.
21. Same word as in Lk 9:39. Elsewhere only as "broken" in Mk 5:4; 14:3; Jn 19:36; "crush" in Rom 16:20; and "broken to pieces" in Rev 2:27. GK *5341*.
22. Or, "brings out, sends out, takes out, puts out". Used 81 times, but only here in this sense. On this word, see "cast out" in Jn 12:31.
23. Or, "judgment", that is, God's standard of justice or judgment, as seen in the Cross. Same word as in v 18. On this word, see "judgment" in Jn 3:19.
24. Compare Mt 9:32-34; Mk 3:22-30; Lk 11:14-26.
25. Some manuscripts say "blind and mute"; others, "mute and blind" {N}.
26. The grammar indicates a "no" answer is expected, "This can't be..., can it? By "Son of David", the crowds mean "Messiah" (see 9:27). This represents a hesitant move toward acceptance. Their expectations of Messiah lead them to think "No", but His miracles lead them to think "Yes". Maybe it is He. Same grammar as in Jn 4:29.
27. On this word, see Mk 3:22. It is simple logic. It cannot be by the power of Jesus Himself, it is not by God's power (since Jesus violates the Sabbath), so it must be by Satan's power.
28. Or, "reflections", what they were thinking about. On this word, see Heb 4:12.
29. Some manuscripts say "Jesus" {C}.
30. This word is used twice in v 25, v 30, twice in v 32. GK *2848*. Not the same word as in v 26.
31. Or, "be made to stand, be established". Those in it will not be able to make it stand if they are divided. The same idea is in v 26 in Satan's kingdom. On this word, see Mk 13:14.
32. This word is the word used in Mk 3:24, 25, 26; Lk 11:17, 18. GK *2093*.
33. That is, if I do it by Satan's power, how can you prove your sons do not do likewise? How do you know Satan is not empowering them? The reasoning required to answer in their case will also answer in His.
34. That is, since they also are casting them out (in their own way, as in Lk 9:49; Act 19:13), they will be the judges of the validity of your assertion. They will be the source of the reasoning justifying their case, and therefore His.

A. Jam 2:24 B. Mt 26:26, is C. Jn 7:17, willing D. Lk 6:37 E. Mt 8:2, master F. Jn 5:24, pass G. Mk 3:3 H. 1 Cor 6:12 J. Mt 8:7 K. Jn 5:45
L. Mt 28:6, arose M. Phil 1:10, mattering N. Act 27:30 O. Mk 8:25 P. 1 Cor 1:18, perish Q. Mt 4:12, went back R. 2 Tim 4:2 S. Act 3:13
T. Act 22:23 U. Lk 14:21 V. 1 Thes 5:19 W. 1 Cor 15:57 X. Jn 5:45 Y. Mt 8:16 Z. Mk 2:12 AA. Rev 18:17 BB. Jn 12:31

	1E. "But if **I** am casting out the demons by *the* Spirit *of* God, then the kingdom *of* God came[1] upon you	28
	3D. "Or how can anyone enter into the house *of* the strong *man* and snatch-away[2] his things, unless he first binds[A] the strong *man*? And then he will plunder[3] his house	29
	4D. "The *one* not being with Me[4] is against Me. And the *one* not gathering[B] with Me is scattering[C]. °For this reason I say *to* you—	30 31
	1E. "Every sin and blasphemy[D] will be forgiven *to* people. But the blasphemy *against* the Spirit will not be forgiven[5]	
	2E. "And whoever speaks *a* word[E] against the Son *of* Man, it will be forgiven *to* him. But whoever speaks against[6] the Holy Spirit, it will not be forgiven *to* him— neither in this age nor in the *one* coming[7]	32
	5D. "Either make the tree good[F] and its fruit good[F], or make the tree bad[8] and its fruit bad.[9] For the tree is known[10] by the fruit	33
	6D. "Brood[G] *of* vipers! How are you able to speak good[11] *things,* being evil[H]? For the mouth speaks out of the abundance[J] *of* the heart	34
	1E. "The good[K] person brings out good[K] *things* from *his* good[K] treasure[12]	35
	2E. "And the evil[H] person brings out evil[H] *things* from *his* evil[H] treasure	
	3E. "And I say *to* you that every useless[13] word[L] which people will speak— they will render[M] *an* account[N] for it on *the* day *of* judgment[O]. °For by your words you will be declared-righteous[P], and by your words you will be condemned[Q]"	36 37
8B.[14]	Then some *of* the scribes and Pharisees responded *to* Him[15], saying "Teacher, we want to see *a* sign from You". °But the *One*, having responded, said *to* them—	38 39
	1C. "*An* evil[H] and adulterous[16] generation[R] is seeking-for *a* sign. And *a* sign will not be given *to* it, except the sign *of* Jonah the prophet	
	1D. "For just as Jonah was three days and three nights in the belly *of* the sea-creature[17], so the Son *of* Man will be three days and three nights[18] in the heart *of* the earth	40
	2C. "Ninevite men[19] will rise-up[20] at the judgment[O] with this generation, and they will condemn[S] it. Because they repented[T] at the proclamation[U] *of* Jonah, and behold— *a* greater *thing than* Jonah *is* here	41
	3C. "*The* Queen *of the* South will be raised[21] at the judgment with this generation, and she will condemn[S] it. Because she came from the ends[22] *of* the earth to hear the wisdom *of* Solomon, and behold— *a* greater *thing than* Solomon *is* here	42
	4C.[23] "Now when the unclean spirit departs from the person[V], it goes through waterless places seeking rest[24], and does not find *it*	43
	1D. "Then it says, 'I will return to my house from where I came-out[25]'	44
	2D. "And having come, it finds *it* being unoccupied[W], having been swept and put-in-order[26]	
	3D. "Then it proceeds, and takes along with itself seven other spirits more evil *than* itself	45
	4D. "And having gone in, they dwell[X] there	
	5D. "And the last *state*[27] *of* that person becomes worse *than* the first	
	6D. "So it will be also *with* this evil generation"[28]	

1. Or, "arrived". Same word as in Lk 11:20. See 1 Thes 2:16 on it.
2. On this word, see 2 Cor 12:2. Some manuscripts say "plunder" {N}, the same word as later in this verse.
3. Used in both occurrences in Mk 3:27. Related to "snatch away" earlier.
4. That is, not standing with Him, but with His enemy, Satan (like those in v 24). Such people have decided against Jesus, linking Him to evil. Compare Mk 9:40.
5. You have set yourself against His working in Me, and against Me. Compare Mk 3:30. On this word, see Mt 6:12.
6. This is GK *2848*. Not the same word as in Lk 12:10.
7. It is an eternal sin, Mk 3:29.
8. The emphasis is either on "rotten" or "worthless". On this word, used twice in this verse, see "bad" tree in 7:17.
9. Some think Jesus means that they are trying to make the tree (Jesus) bad, and His fruit (casting out demons, healing) good. Jesus says, you cannot have it both ways. Make them both the same, good or bad. Stop riding the fence. Others think the tree is the Pharisees. Either repent and show the fruit (3:8), or carry out your evil desires against Me (23:32).
10. Or, "recognized". On this word, see Lk 1:34.
11. How can you have good fruit since you are bad trees? How can you say that both I and My works are good, since you are evil?
12. Or, "treasury, treasure-house", referring to the person's heart. Same word as in Lk 6:45; and as "treasure-chest" in Mt 2:11. Used 17 times. GK *2565*. Some manuscripts add "*of* his heart" {N}, as in Lk 6:45.
13. Or, "unproductive". On this word, see Jam 2:20. That is, every non-edifying word, every word that does no good.
14. Compare Lk 11:29-32; and Mt 16:1-4; Mk 8:11-12.
15. Some manuscripts omit "*to* Him" {N}.
16. That is, spiritually unfaithful to God. On this word, see Jam 4:4.
17. Or, "huge fish", a generic term used of large sea creatures or sea monsters. Used only here. GK *3063*.
18. This is another way of saying "three days". A day and a night is one day, as in Gen 1:5. It does not mean "72 hours", but simply "three days". Note how Luke says this in Lk 11:30.
19. That is, the men from Nineveh where Jonah went to preach.
20. Or, "stand up". On this word, see Lk 18:33.
21. Or, "will arise". On this word, see "arose" in 28:6.
22. Or, "limits, extremities". On this word, see Heb 6:16. On this queen, see 1 Kings 10:1-13.
23. Compare Lk 11:24-26.
24. Or, "*a* resting place". Elsewhere only in 11:29; Lk 11:24; Rev 4:8; 14:11. GK *398*.
25. Same word as "departs" in v 43.
26. Or, "adorned, decorated". On this word, see "adorn" in 1 Tim 2:9.
27. More literally, "the last *things*" versus "the first *things*".
28. Jesus is casting out demons and putting Israel's house in order. But upon this evil generation's rejection of Him, demons will return and they will be worse off.

A. 1 Cor 7:27 B. Mt 25:35, brought in C. Jn 16:32 D. 1 Tim 6:4 E. 1 Cor 12:8 F. 1 Tim 5:10a G. Mt 3:7 H. Act 25:18 J. 2 Cor 8:14
K. 1 Tim 5:10b L. Rom 10:17 M. Mt 16:27 N. 1 Cor 12:8, word O. Jn 3:19 P. Rom 3:24 Q. Lk 6:37 R. Mt 24:34 S. 1 Cor 11:32
T. Act 26:20 U. 1 Cor 1:21 V. Mt 4:4, mankind W. 1 Cor 7:5, devote yourselves X. Eph 3:17

Matthew 12:46	42	Verse

9B.[1] While He *was* still speaking *to* the crowds, behold— His mother and brothers[2] were standing outside, seeking[A] to speak *to* Him   46

     1C. And[3] someone said *to* Him, "Behold— Your mother and Your brothers are standing outside, seeking to speak *to* You"   47

     2C. But the *One*, having responded, said *to* the *one* speaking *to* Him, "Who is My mother and who are My brothers?"   48

     3C. And having stretched-out[B] His hand toward His disciples, He said "Behold— My mother and My brothers!   49

         1D. "For whoever does the will[C] *of* My Father in *the* heavens[D]— **he** is My brother and sister and mother"   50

10B. On that day Jesus, having gone out *of* the house, sat beside the sea. °And large crowds[E] were gathered-together[F] with Him so that He, having gotten into *a* boat, sits-*down* [to teach]. And the whole crowd was standing on the shore. °And He spoke many *things to* them in parables[4], saying—   13:1-2   3

     1C.[5] "Behold— the *one* sowing went out *that he might* sow. °And during his sowing—   4

         1D. "Some *seeds* fell along the road. And having come, the birds ate them up[G]

         2D. "And others fell on the rocky[6] *places* where they were not having much soil. And immediately[7] they sprang-up, because of not having *a* depth[H] *of* soil[J]. °But *the* sun having risen, they were scorched[K]. And because of not having *a* root, they were dried-up[L]   5   6

         3D. "And others fell on the thorns. And the thorns came up and choked[8] them   7

         4D. "And others fell on the good[M] soil and were giving fruit— one *a* hundred, and another sixty, and another thirty   8

         5D. "Let the *one* having ears[9], hear"   9

     2C.[10] And having come to *Him*, the disciples[11] said *to* Him, "For what reason are You speaking *to* them in parables?" °And the *One*, having responded, said *to* them—   10   11

         1D. "Because[12] it has been given *to* you to know[13] the mysteries[14] *of* the kingdom[N] *of* the heavens. But it has not been given *to* those *ones*

             1E. "For whoever has— it will be given *to* him, and he will be caused to abound[O]   12

             2E. "But whoever does not have— even what he has will be taken-away from him

         2D. "For this reason I am speaking *to* them in parables— because while seeing[P], they are not seeing[P]. And while hearing, they are not hearing, nor understanding[15]. °And the prophecy *of* Isaiah is being fulfilled[Q] *in* them, the *one* saying[16] [in Isa 6:9-10]   13   14

             1E.[17] "*In* hearing[R], you will hear[S] and by no means understand. And while seeing[P], you will see and by no means perceive.[18] °For the heart *of* this people became dull[19], and they hardly[20] heard *with their* ears, and they closed their eyes[21]   15

                 1F. "That they might not[22] ever see[T] *with their* eyes, and hear *with their* ears, and understand *in their* heart, and turn-back[U], and I shall[23] heal[V] them"

1. Parallel account at Mk 3:31. Compare Lk 8:19-21.
2. On the brothers and sisters of Jesus, see 13:55.
3. Some manuscripts omit this verse {C}.
4. Used 46 times in Matthew, Mark, and Luke to refer to a story or comparison used to illustrate a spiritual truth. Used in Lk 4:23 as "proverb"; and in Heb 9:9; 11:19 as "symbol". GK *4130*.
5. Parallel account at Mk 4:1, Lk 8:4.
6. That is, bed-rock or a rocky outcropping without much soil on it; not "soil with stones in it". Elsewhere only in v 20; Mk 4:5, 16. GK *4378*. Related to "bed-rock" in Lk 8:6.
7. Or, "at once". Used 36 times. GK *2311*. Related word in Mk 6:25.
8. Or, "strangled, suffocated". Compare Lk 8:7. Same word as in 18:28. Elsewhere only as "drown" in Mk 5:13. GK *4464*. Related to the word in v 22.
9. Some manuscripts add "to hear" {B}, "ears to hear".
10. Parallel account at Mk 4:10; Lk 8:9.
11. That is, the twelve plus those around Him, Mk 4:10.
12. Or, this word may simply introduce the quotation, so that it says "It has been given...".
13. Or, "understand". On this word, see Lk 1:34.
14. That is, the things formerly hidden, but now revealed by Him. Note v 35. Jesus is revealing things about the kingdom not formerly known by the Jews. Speaking in parables hides these truths from some (the unbelieving Jews) while revealing them to others (His disciples). On this word, see Rom 11:25.
15. Same word as in v 14, 15, 19, 23; and in Rom 3:11; 15:21; Eph 5:17. Used 26 times. GK *5317*.
16. This word modifies "prophecy".
17. Compare also Jn 12:39-40; Act 28:25-27.
18. They will see what Jesus does and hear the words from His lips, but they will not understand their significance. Paul, Luke, Mark, Matthew and John all quote this prophecy with reference to them.
19. Or, "thick, fat, insensitive". Elsewhere only in Act 28:27. GK *4266*.
20. That is, with difficulty. They are spiritually hard of hearing. Elsewhere only in Act 28:27. GK *977*.
21. What Jesus says they did, John says God did in Jn 12:39.
22. The grammar expresses the purpose of the people. They willfully closed their eyes to God in order that they might not ever see what they did not want to see, and never have to change their ways and return to Him. They closed their eyes in order that they might not ever enter into the process described here— see, hear, understand, turn back, be healed. Because of this, Jesus speaks to them in parables, so that they might not understand what they do not want to understand.
23. Or, "would". The healing is the certain conclusion of this process, but they exclude themselves from it.

A. Phil 2:21 B. Act 27:30 C. Jn 7:17 D. 2 Cor 12:2 E. Mk 2:13, multitude F. Mt 25:35, brought in G. Mk 12:40, devouring H. 2 Cor 8:2, deep J. Rev 7:1, land K. Rev 16:9 L. Mk 3:1, became withered M. 1 Tim 5:10a N. Mt 3:2 O. 2 Cor 8:2 P. Rev 1:11 Q. 1 Thes 2:16, fill up R. Heb 4:2 S. Act 22:9 T. Lk 2:26 U. Jam 5:19 V. Mt 8:8

3D.¹ "But blessed^A *are* **your** eyes because they are seeing^B, and your ears, because they are hearing. ˚For truly^C I say *to* you that many prophets and righteous *ones* desired^D to experience² *the things* which you are seeing^B, and they did not experience *them*, and to hear *the things* which you are hearing, and they did not hear *them* 16
17

4D. "**You** therefore, hear the parable^E *of* the *one* having sown³— 18

    1E. "Anyone hearing the word⁴ *of* the kingdom and not understanding^F *it*— the evil *one* comes and snatches-away^G the *thing* having been sown in his heart. This *person* is the *one* having been sown *the seed* along the road 19

    2E. "And the *one* having been sown *the seed* on the rocky *places*— this *person* is the *one* hearing the word and immediately receiving^H it with joy. ˚And he does not have *a* root in himself, but is temporary⁵. And affliction^J or persecution^K having come about because of the word— immediately he is caused-to-fall^L 20
21

    3E. "And the *one* having been sown *the seed* into the thorns— this *person* is the *one* hearing the word, and the anxiety⁶ *of the* age⁷ and the deceitfulness⁸ *of* riches is choking^M the word, and it becomes unfruitful⁹ 22

    4E. "And the *one* having been sown *the seed* on the good soil— this *person* is the *one* hearing the word and understanding¹⁰ *it,* who indeed¹¹ is bearing-fruit¹² and producing: one *a* hundred, and another sixty, and another thirty" 23

3C. He put-before^N them another parable, saying, "The kingdom *of* the heavens became-like¹³ *a* man having sown good seed in his field. ˚But during the men's sleeping, his enemy came and re-sowed¹⁴ darnel¹⁵ between the wheat, and went away 24
25

    1D. "Now when the grass budded¹⁶ and produced fruit¹⁷, then the darnel appeared^O also 26
    2D. "And having come to *him*, the slaves^P *of* the house-master^Q said *to* him, 'Master^R, did you not sow good seed in your field?¹⁸ Then from where does it have *the* darnel?' 27
    3D. "And the *one* said *to* them, '*A* hostile¹⁹ man did this' 28
    4D. "And the slaves say *to* him, 'Then do you want us, having gone, to collect²⁰ them?'
    5D. "But the *one* says, 'No, that while collecting the darnel, you may not perhaps uproot the wheat together with them. ˚Permit^S both to grow together until the harvest^T. And at *the* time *of* the harvest I will say *to* the harvesters, "Collect first the darnel, and bind^U them into bundles so-as to burn them up. But gather the wheat into my barn" ' " 29
30

4C.²¹ He put-before^N them another parable, saying, "The kingdom *of* the heavens is like *a* seed²² *of a* mustard-plant²³, which having taken, *a* man²⁴ sowed in his field²⁵ 31

    1D. "Which is **smaller**²⁶ *than* all the seeds— but when it grows is larger *than* the garden-plants²⁷. And it becomes *a* tree,²⁸ so that²⁹ the birds *of* the heaven^V come and are nesting³⁰ in its branches" 32

5C.³¹ He spoke another parable *to* them, "The kingdom *of* the heavens is like leaven³², which having taken, *a* woman³³ concealed³⁴ into three measures³⁵ *of* wheat-flour³⁶ until which *time the* whole *thing* was leavened³⁷" 33

6C.³⁸ Jesus spoke all *things to* the crowds in parables. And He was speaking nothing *to* them apart from *a* parable, ˚so that the *thing* might be fulfilled^W having been spoken through the prophet³⁹ saying⁴⁰ 34
35

    1D. "I will open My mouth in parables. I will utter⁴¹ *things* having been hidden^X since *the* foundation *of the* world⁴²" [Ps 78:2]

1. Compare Lk 10:23-24.
2. Or, "see", but not the same word as next. On this word, see Lk 10:24.
3. The one sowing is the Son of Man, as in v 37.
4. Or, "message", and likewise down through v 23. The seed is the word, Mk 4:14; Lk 8:11. On this word, see "word" in 1 Cor 12:8.
5. Or, "transitory", lasting only for a time. Same word as in Mk 4:17. Elsewhere only in 2 Cor 4:18; Heb 11:25. GK *4672*.
6. Or, "worry, care, concern". On this word, see 1 Pet 5:7. Related to "be anxious" in Mt 6:25.
7. Or, "world". GK *172*. Some manuscripts say "this age" {N}.
8. Or, "deception". On this word, see "deceptions" in 2 Pet 2:13.
9. Fruit-bearing is the evidence of life. Lack of good fruit results in being culled out (like the trees in 3:10) and burned, like the darnel, v 30.
10. This is in contrast with the first "soil", who do not understand (v 19, same word). Same word as in v 13.
11. Or, "certainly, surely", the intent being to provide emphasis. Or, "now, at this point", if the emphasis is on time. Or, "therefore", emphasizing a conclusion. Elsewhere only as "now" in Lk 2:15; Act 13:2; 15:36; and "therefore" in 1 Cor 6:20. GK *1314*.
12. This is in contrast with the second two "soils", who are unfruitful.
13. Or, "was like, was likened to". Same word and grammar as in 18:23; 22:2. Some think Jesus means it in a timeless sense, "is like". Others think He is speaking in a prophetic sense from the point of view of the end of the age. Same word as in Act 14:11; Heb 2:17. Elsewhere only as "be like" in Mt 6:8; 7:24, 26; 25:1; "liken" (compare) in Mt 11:16; Mk 4:30; Lk 7:31; 13:18, 20; Rom 9:29. GK *3929*. Related to "likeness" in Heb 4:15; Phil 2:7, and Jam 3:9.
14. Or, "over-sowed, sowed upon". Used only here. GK *2178*.
15. This is a weed that is indistinguishable from wheat in its earlier stages. Used only in v 25-40. GK *2429*.
16. Or, "sprouted". Same word as in Mk 4:27; Heb 9:4. Elsewhere only as "produced" in Jam 5:18. GK *1056*.
17. That is, heads of grain. Once the heads of grain appeared, they could be distinguished.
18. The grammar indicates a "yes" answer is expected.
19. Same word as "enemy" in v 25. GK *2398*. Here it modifies "man".
20. More literally, "do You want *that*, having gone, we should collect them?"
21. Parallel account at Mk 4:30. Compare Lk 13:18-19.
22. Or, "kernel, berry, grain". That is, a single seed (unlike v 4, 24). Not the same word as in v 32. Elsewhere only in 17:20; Mk 4:31; Lk 13:19; 17:6; Jn 12:24; 1 Cor 15:37. All but the last two are in the phrase "seed *of a* mustard-plant". GK *3133*. Some think the grain is "the kingdom of heaven", or the work of the Messiah, in the sense that it starts small in the world but grows large. Others apply this to individuals. There are other views of the details of the parable.
23. This plant can grow 9-12 feet high (3 to 4 meters). Elsewhere only in 17:20; Mk 4:31; Lk 13:19; 17:6. GK *4983*.
24. In Mark, the man is not mentioned, Mk 4:31. Some think the man is Christ; others, the Father.
25. Some think the field is the world, as in v 38; others, an individual's life. It is "his own garden" in Lk 13:19.
26. Jesus uses grammar that emphasizes the contrast between the two halves of this sentence.
27. Same word as in Mk 4:32; Lk 11:32. Elsewhere only as "vegetables" in Rom 14:2. GK *3303*.
28. That is, in relative size. The emphasis is on starting very small and growing huge in relation to the size of the original grain. The Jews, by contrast, expected a full-grown kingdom established immediately by the Messiah by force.
29. This word "so that" indicates the result. It becomes a tree with the result that the birds nest in it.
30. Some think the birds nesting are added to show how large the grain becomes. Others think this represents the evil one (as in v 4, 19) coming to live and work from within the visible kingdom that Christ grows in the world.
31. Compare Lk 13:20.
32. Leaven was used to make bread rise. It was a piece of fermented dough saved from a previous batch of bread. It was not fresh "yeast", but it functioned like it. Some think the leaven symbolizes the gospel, as in v 19; others, evil, like the darnel in v 25. Elsewhere only in 16:6, 11, 12; Mk 8:15; Lk 12:1; 13:21; 1 Cor 5:6, 7, 8; Gal 5:9. GK *2434*.
33. Some think the woman is God or Christ or the church; others, the devil.
34. Or, "hid-in". Elsewhere only in Lk 13:21. Normally we would say "mixed", but that places emphasis on the mixer and the mixing. Jesus is emphasizing the "hiddenness" of the leaven within the flour, and its transformation of the whole from within. This hidden, slow, inner transforming power of the kingdom is in direct contrast to the Jewish expectation of a violent, forced imposition of God's kingdom on the Romans by the Messiah. GK *1606*. The root word is "hide" in Jn 8:59.
35. Or, "seah", a Hebrew measure equal to about 1.5 Roman modius-measures, on which see Mk 4:21. That makes this about six gallons or 25 liters, a batch size seen in Gen 18:6. Some think "three" symbolizes the Jews, Samaritans, and Gentiles, Act 1:8. Elsewhere only in Lk 13:21. GK *4929*.
36. Some think this symbolizes the world; others, the visible church; others, an individual. God hides the gospel in the world or an individual and it permeates and transforms from within. Or, Satan hides evil in the visible church until it is transformed. Elsewhere only in Lk 13:21. GK *236*.
37. This is the verb related to "leaven" earlier. Elsewhere only in Lk 13:21; 1 Cor 5:6; Gal 5:9. GK *2435*.
38. Parallel account at Mk 4:33.
39. Some manuscripts say "Isaiah the prophet" {C}. Some think "Isaiah" was inserted later. Others think Matthew wrote "Asaph", but it was changed later to the more familiar "Isaiah". "Asaph" is the correct source, Ps 78:2.
40. This word modifies "prophet", as in 1:22.
41. Used only here. GK *2243*.
42. On this phrase, see Heb 9:26. Some manuscripts omit this word {C}, in which case it would be "since *the* beginning".

A. Lk 6:20 B. Rev 1:11 C. Mt 5:18 D. Gal 5:17 E. Mt 13:3 F. Mt 13:13 G. Mt 11:12 H. Rom 7:8, taken J. Rev 7:14 K. Mk 10:30 L. 1 Cor 8:13 M. Mk 4:7 N. Act 17:3 O. Phil 2:15, shine P. Rom 6:17 Q. Mt 20:1 R. Mt 8:2 S. Mt 6:12, forgive T. Mk 4:29 U. 1 Cor 7:27 V. 2 Cor 12:2 W. Eph 5:18, filled X. Jn 8:59

| Matthew 13:36 | 46 | Verse |

11B. Then, having left the crowds, He[1] went into the house. And His disciples came to Him, saying, "Make-clear[2] *to* us the parable *of* the darnel *of* the field" — 36

    1C. And the *One*, having responded, said[3]— 37

        1D. "The *one* sowing the good[A] seed[B] is the Son *of* Man. °And the field is the world[4]. And the good seed— these are the sons *of* the kingdom[5]. And the darnel are the sons *of* the evil *one*. °And the enemy having sown them is the devil[C]. And the harvest is *the* conclusion[6] *of the* age. And the harvesters are angels. °Therefore, just as the darnel is collected and burned up[7] *with* fire, so it will be at the conclusion *of* the[8] age — 38 / 39 / 40

            1E. "The Son *of* Man will send out His angels, and they will collect out of His kingdom[9] all the causes-of-falling[10] and the *ones* doing lawlessness[D]. °And they will throw them into the furnace *of* fire[11]. In that place, there will be the weeping and the grinding[12] *of* teeth — 41 / 42

            2E. "Then the righteous *ones* will shine-forth[13] like the sun in the kingdom *of* their Father — 43

            3E. "Let the *one* having ears[14], hear

        2D. "The[15] kingdom *of* the heavens is like *a* treasure[16] having been hidden[E] in the field, which having found, *a* man hid[E]. And from his joy,[17] he goes and sells all that he has[18] and buys that field — 44

        3D. "Again, the kingdom *of* the heavens is like *a* man *who is a* merchant seeking[19] fine pearls[20]. °And[21] having found one very-valuable[22] pearl, having gone, he has sold all that he was having[23], and he bought it — 45 / 46

        4D. "Again, the kingdom *of* the heavens is like *a* drag-net[24] having been cast[F] into the sea and having gathered[G] *fish* of every kind[H]— °which, when it was filled[J], having pulled *it* up on the shore, and having sat-*down*, they collected the good[25] *ones* into containers and threw[F] the bad[26] *ones* outside — 47 / 48

            1E. "So it will be at the conclusion[K] *of* the age. The angels will go forth and separate[27] the evil *ones* out of *the* midst[28] *of* the righteous *ones*. °And they will throw them into the furnace *of* fire. In that place, there will be the weeping and the grinding *of* teeth — 49 / 50

        5D. "Did[29] you understand[L] all these *things*?" — 51

    2C. They say *to* Him, "Yes"[30]

    3C. And the *One* said *to* them, "For this reason,[31] every scribe[32] having become-a-disciple[33] *in*[34] the kingdom *of* the heavens is like *a* man *who is a* house-master[M], who brings out new[N] *things* and old[O] *things* from his treasure[35]" — 52

12B.[36] And it came about *that* when Jesus finished[37] these parables, He went-away[38] from there. °And having come into His hometown[39], He was teaching them in their synagogue, so that they were astounded[P] and saying "From where *did* this wisdom and the miracles[Q] *come to* this *One*? °Is not this *One* the son *of* the carpenter[40]? Is not His mother called Mary, and His brothers, James[41] and Joseph[42] and Simon[43] and Jude[44]? °And His sisters,[45] are they not all with us? From where then *did* all these *things* come *to* this *One*?" — 53-54 / 55 / 56

    1C. And they were taking-offense[46] at Him — 57

    2C. But Jesus said *to* them, "*A* prophet is not without-honor[R] except in *his* hometown[S] and in his house"

    3C. And He did not do many[47] miracles[Q] there because of their unbelief[T] — 58

1. Some manuscripts say "Jesus" {N}.
2. Or, "Explain". Elsewhere only in 18:31. GK *1397.*
3. Some manuscripts add "*to* them" {N}.
4. Some think Jesus means "the church in the world", the "visible church", based on the view that in v 41 He calls it "His kingdom". Others think He means "the world" as the term is normally used.
5. That is, believers, actual inheritors of the kingdom. Compare 8:12. On "sons", see Gal 3:7.
6. Same word as in v 40, 49. On this word, see 24:3. In others words, believers and non-believers will co-exist in the "world" until the end of the age. By contrast, the Jews expected the Messiah to immediately destroy all the enemies of Israel and fulfill v 43.
7. Some manuscripts omit this word {N}.
8. Some manuscripts say "this" {N}.
9. Some think Jesus means the kingdom He establishes when He comes, looking to the future, as in v 43. Others think He means the kingdom in which they grew together until the harvest, looking to the past.
10. That is, the things that cause others to fall into sin. On this word, see Rom 11:9.
11. That is, a furnace characterized by fire, a fiery furnace. Same phrase as in v 50. It is a metaphor for hell, like "outer darkness" in 8:12.
12. On this word and phrase, see 8:12.
13. Or, "shine out". Presently, they and their light are dimmed or hidden by the evil around them. Used only here. GK *1719.* Related to "shine" in 5:16; 17:2.
14. Some manuscripts add "to hear" {B}, "ears to hear".
15. Some manuscripts say "Again, the kingdom..." {N}, as in v 45, 47.
16. Some think the treasure in both v 44 and v 45 symbolizes the blessings of the kingdom. There are other views.
17. Or, "And from the joy *of* it".
18. By contrast, the Jews expected the kingdom to come upon them by an act of God, without personal sacrifice.
19. The person in v 44 "finds" or stumbles upon the treasure. This person is diligently seeking. By contrast, the Jews did not view the kingdom as something to be "found" by them, but as something given to them by God.
20. Elsewhere only in 7:6; 13:46; 1 Tim 2:9; Rev 17:4; 18:12, 16; 21:21. GK *3449.*
21. Some manuscripts say "...pearls, who, having found..." {N}.
22. Or, "very costly, very expensive". Same word as in Jn 12:3. Elsewhere only as "more valuable" in 1 Pet 1:7. GK *4501.*
23. That is, all his possessions. He does what the man in 19:21 is not willing to do.
24. That is, a large fishing net deployed from a boat. Used only here. GK *4880.* On nets, see 4:18.
25. That is, "fit" for eating. Same word as "good" fruit in 7:17.
26. That is, unusable. Same word as "bad" tree in 7:17.
27. Same word as in 25:32. On this word, see Rom 1:1.
28. On the phrase "out of the midst", see 2 Thes 2:7.
29. Some manuscripts say "Jesus says *to* them, 'Did...' " {N}.
30. Some manuscripts add "Lord" {N}, so that it says "Yes, Lord".
31. That is, because the disciples now understand these truths about the kingdom, the following parable is true of them. Since they understand, they now have added new, previously hidden things (v 35) about the kingdom to their treasure-chest of knowledge about the kingdom. They can now bring forth both old and new truths.
32. That is, every expert or instructor regarding what the OT teaches about Messiah. They already have many OT truths about the kingdom in their treasure chest. Now they have the words of Jesus. This is the word used of Jewish "scribes" (experts in the Law). Here and in 23:34, it is used in an extended sense to refer to experts from Jesus' point of view, believers having the word of prophecy made more firm (2 Pet 1:19). Used 63 times. GK *1208.*
33. Or, "having been discipled, instructed, trained, made a disciple". Same word as in 27:57. Elsewhere only as "make disciples" in Mt 28:19; Act 14:21. GK *3411.* This is the verb related to the word "disciple" in Lk 6:40.
34. That is, in the truths of the kingdom. Or, "*for* the kingdom".
35. Or, "treasure house, treasury". Same word as in 12:35.
36. Parallel account at Mk 6:1. Compare Lk 4:16-20; Jn 4:43-44.
37. This phrase, "And it came about *that* when Jesus finished" is also in 7:28; 11:1; 19:1; 26:1. It forms the conclusion of what precedes, and a transition to what follows. When He finished giving the parables from the boat, He went into the house, v 2, 36. When He finished giving the parables in the house, He went away from there. Some organize the book so that these five statements form the major divisions. On "finish", see Rev 10:7.
38. Elsewhere only in 19:1. GK *3558.* He picked up and left. By 14:13, He has returned.
39. That is, Nazareth.
40. Same word used of Jesus Himself in Mk 6:3. The grammar indicates that a "yes" answer is expected to this question and to the next two.
41. James became the head of the church in Jerusalem, and wrote the book of James. He is mentioned in Mk 6:3; Act 12:17; 15:13; 21:18; 1 Cor 15:7; Gal 1:19; 2:9, 12; Jam 1:1; Jude 1:1. In A.D. 62, after the death of Festus (the procurator of Judea, Act 24:27), the high priest had James killed before a new procurator could be appointed by Rome. This was illegal, and Agrippa II (see Act 25:13) deposed him for it. GK *2610.*
42. Some manuscripts say "Joses" {B}, as in Mk 6:3.
43. Mentioned also in Mk 6:3.
44. Or, "Judas, Judah". The writer of the book of Jude. He is referred to in Mk 6:3; Jude 1. GK *2683.*
45. Some take "brothers and sisters" in its natural sense, as children born to Joseph and Mary after Jesus was born (note 1:25). Others think they were half brothers and sisters, children of Joseph by a former wife. Others take them to be cousins, children of Mary's sister (see the note on Jn 19:25).
46. Or, "being caused to fall". On this word, see "cause to fall" in 1 Cor 8:13.
47. Or, "great". This word means "many, great", with a more specific sense coming from the context. It is also used in an adverbial sense, taking its meaning from the context, as in "greatly" in Mt 27:19; "strictly" in Mk 5:43; "sternly" in Mk 3:12; "solemnly" in Mk 6:23. Used 416 times. GK *4498.*

A. 1 Tim 5:10a B. Heb 11:11 C. Rev 12:9 D. 1 Jn 3:4 E. Jn 8:59 F. Rev 2:22, throw G. Mt 25:35, brought in H. 1 Cor 12:28 J. Eph 5:18 K. Mt 24:3 L. Mt 13:13 M. Mt 20:1 N. Heb 8:13 O. Mk 2:21 P. Mt 7:28 Q. 1 Cor 12:10 R. 1 Cor 12:23 S. Heb 11:14, homeland T. 1 Tim 1:13

13B.¹	At that time, Herod the tetrarch² heard the report^A *about* Jesus, and said *to* his servants^B, "This One is John the Baptist. He himself arose^C from the dead, and for this reason the *miraculous-powers*³ are at-work⁴ in him"	14:1-2
1C.⁵	For⁶ Herod, having seized^D John, bound^E him and put *him* away in prison⁷ because of Herodias⁸, the wife *of* Philip⁹ his brother¹⁰	3
1D.	For John was saying *to* him, "It is not lawful^F *for* you to have¹¹ her"	4
2C.	And while wanting^G to kill him, he feared the crowd, because they were holding^H him as *a* prophet	5
3C.	But *at* Herod's birthday-celebrations^J having come about, the daughter¹² *of* Herodias danced¹³ in *their* midst	6
1D.	And she pleased^K Herod	
2D.	Hence, he declared^L with *an* oath^M to give her whatever she asked	7
3D.	And the *one,* having been prompted¹⁴ by her mother, says, "Give me here on *a* platter^N the head *of* John the Baptist"¹⁵	8
4D.	And [although] having been grieved^O, the¹⁶ king ordered^P *that it* be given, because of the oaths and the *ones* reclining-back-with *him* [to eat]	9
5D.	And having sent, he beheaded John in the prison. And his head was brought on *a* platter and given *to* the girl^Q, and she brought *it to* her mother	10-11
4C.	And having come to *him*, his disciples took away the corpse¹⁷ and buried him¹⁸. And having gone¹⁹, they reported^R *it to* Jesus	12
14B.²⁰	And having heard-*of it,*²¹ Jesus withdrew^S from there privately²² in *a* boat to *a* desolate^T place. And having heard-*of it*, the crowds followed Him *on* foot from the cities	13
1C.	And having gone-out²³, He²⁴ saw *a* large crowd, and felt-deep-feelings^U [of compassion] for them. And He cured their sick *ones*	14
2C.	And having become evening²⁵, the²⁶ disciples came to Him saying, "*This* place is desolate and the hour already passed. Send-away^V the crowds in order that having gone away into the villages, they may buy themselves food"	15
3C.	But Jesus²⁷ said *to* them, "They have no need to go away— **you** give them *something* to eat"	16
4C.	But the *ones* say *to* Him, "We do not have *anything* here except five loaves and two fish!"	17
5C.	But the *One* said, "Bring them here *to* Me"	18
6C.	And having ordered^P the crowds to lie-back on the grass²⁸, having taken the five loaves and the two fish, having looked up to heaven, He blessed *them*²⁹. And having broken^W *them*, He gave the loaves *to* the disciples, and the disciples *gave them to* the crowds	19
7C.	And they all ate and were filled-to-satisfaction^X	20
8C.	And they picked up the *amount of* the fragments^Y being left over— twelve full³⁰ baskets	
9C.	And the *ones* eating were about five-thousand men, apart from women and children	21
15B.³¹	And immediately He³² compelled³³ the disciples to get into the boat and to be going ahead of Him to the other side while³⁴ He sent-away^V the crowds	22
1C.	And having sent-away^V the crowds, He went up on the mountain privately to pray. And having become³⁵ evening, He was there alone	23
2C.	And the boat was already many stades³⁶ distant^Z from the land³⁷, being tormented³⁸ by the waves. For the wind was contrary^AA	24
3C.	And He³⁹ came to them *in the* fourth watch *of* the night⁴⁰, walking across⁴¹ the sea	25

1. Parallel account at Mk 6:14; Lk 9:7.
2. Or, "governor". That is, Herod Antipas (Lk 3:1), a son of Herod the Great (see 2:1), who was given Galilee and Perea when his father died. He built Tiberius (Jn 6:1) on the west shore of the Sea of Galilee and made it his capital. He ruled from 4 B.C. to A.D. 39, when he was exiled and his territory turned over to Herod Agrippa I (see Act 12:1). He divorced the daughter of Aretas (see 2 Cor 11:32) to marry Herodias, v 3. He mocked Jesus, Lk 23:8-11. On this word, see Lk 3:19.
3. Or, "the Powers", the supernatural beings who were the source of the miracles in Herod's mind. On this, see Act 8:10. Same word as in Mk 6:14. It is also the same word as "miracles" in Mt 13:54.
4. On this word, see "works" in 1 Cor 12:11.
5. Parallel account at Mk 6:16. Compare Lk 3:19-20.
6. Matthew explains what happened to John at some time previous to this, then continues in v 13.
7. He was "put away" back in 4:12. He may have remained there over a year before he was executed.
8. She was the grand-daughter of Herod the Great, the daughter of Aristobulus, the sister of Agrippa I. See 2:1. She married Herod Philip I, a paternal brother of her father. Later, she left him and married Herod Antipas, also a paternal brother of her father by a different wife. She chose to go into exile with Antipas when he was exiled in A.D. 39. Elsewhere only in v 6; Mk 6:17, 19, 22; Lk 3:19. GK *2478*.
9. That is, Philip I, who was a private citizen in Rome, the paternal brother of Herod Antipas. See 2:1.
10. This was not so much because Herod took personal offense at John's statement, but because he feared John would successfully turn the people against him over the issue, leading to rebellion, according to Josephus.
11. That is, to have her as your wife. Same phrase as in 1 Cor 5:1.
12. Herodias had a daughter named Salome when she was married to Philip I. See 2:1. Some think this is the daughter mentioned here and in Mk 6:22, where she may also be called Herodias.
13. Elsewhere only in Mk 6:22; Mt 11:17; Lk 7:32. GK *4004*.
14. Or, "put forward, coached, instructed". Used only here. GK *4586*. Used in Deut 6:7 of "teaching" one's children, and in Ex 35:34.
15. This is the Greek word order of her request, "John the Baptist" being saved to the end of the sentence.
16. Some manuscripts say "And the king was grieved. But he commanded..." {B}.
17. Some manuscripts say "body" {N}.
18. Some manuscripts say "it" {C}.
19. Or, "having come". On this word, see "come" in Mk 16:2.
20. Parallel account at Mk 6:32; Lk 9:10; Jn 6:1.
21. That is, having heard that Herod thought Jesus was John the Baptist raised from the dead, v 1. Perhaps Jesus also heard of John's death at this time. It is unclear whether Matthew means that John's death occurred at this time.
22. This idiom is elsewhere only in 14:23; 17:1, 19; 20:17; 24:3; Mk 4:34; 6:31, 32; 7:33; 9:2, 28; 13:3; Lk 9:10; 10:23; Act 23:19; Gal 2:2. GK *2625*.
23. Or, "come out". See Mk 6:34 on this.
24. Some manuscripts say "Jesus" {N}.
25. Here Matthew means "late in the day, before sundown, between 3 and 6 P.M.". Note the same phrase in v 23. This word is used 14 times. GK *4068*.
26. Some manuscripts say "His" {N}.
27. Some manuscripts omit this word {C}, so that it says "But the *One* said...".
28. There was grass because it occurred in spring, near Passover, Jn 6:4.
29. Some think Matthew means "He blessed *God*", or "spoke a blessing", as in Lk 1:64; 2:28; 24:53, perhaps saying "Blessed are You O Lord, King of the World, who brings forth bread from the earth", a common Jewish prayer at meals. Others think "He blessed *the food*", meaning He consecrated or dedicated it to God's use, as in Mk 8:7; Lk 9:16; 1 Cor 10:16. The same issue arises in Mt 26:26; Mk 6:41, 14:22; Lk 24:30. On "blessed", see Lk 6:28. Elsewhere by Matthew only in 21:9; 23:39; 25:34: 26:26. John 6:11 says He "gave thanks", using the word in Mt 26:27.
30. Same word as in Lk 4:1; Jn 1:14; Act 6:3, 5; 9:36; 13:10; 19:28; 3 Jn 8. Used 16 times. GK *4441*. Related to "filled" in Eph 5:18.
31. Parallel account at Mk 6:45; Jn 6:16.
32. Some manuscripts say "Jesus" {K}.
33. John 6:15 explains why Jesus compelled them to go. On this word, see Gal 6:12.
34. Or, "until", "until which *time* He sent away the crowds" and joined them. He will depart after He has sent them away. GK *2401*.
35. Same phrase as v 15, but referring to a point further on that evening, between 6 and 9 P.M.
36. On this word, see Rev 14:20. Jn 6:19 says it was 25 or 30 stades, about halfway across.
37. Instead of "many stades distant from the land", some manuscripts say "*as far as* the middle *of* the sea" {C}, similar to Mk 6:47.
38. Same word as in Mk 6:48. On this word, see Rev 14:10.
39. Some manuscripts say "Jesus" {K}.
40. That is, between 3 and 6 A.M. Jesus apparently had been praying for several hours, since early evening, v 23. On the four watches, see Mk 13:35.
41. Or, "over". Same word as in v 29. GK *2093*. This word is used in v 26 (and in Mk 6:48; Jn 6:19) with different grammar, meaning "on" the sea.

A. Heb 4:2, hearing B. Act 3:13 C. Mt 28:6 D. Heb 4:14, hold on to E. 1 Cor 7:27 F. 1 Cor 6:12 G. Jn 7:17, willing H. Mk 11:32 J. Mk 6:21 K. 1 Thes 2:4 L. 1 Tim 6:12, confess M. Jam 5:12 N. Lk 11:39 O. 2 Cor 7:9 P. Mt 14:28 Q. Mk 6:22 R. 1 Jn 1:3, announcing S. Mt 4:12, went back T. Mt 3:1, wilderness U. Mt 9:36 V. Mt 5:31 W. Act 2:46 X. Phil 4:12 Y. Mt 15:37 Z. Mt 15:8 AA. 1 Thes 2:15

Matthew 14:26	50	Verse

    4C. But the disciples, having seen Him walking on the sea, were frightened[1], saying that "It is *a* phantom[A]". And they cried-out[B] from the fear[C]   26

    5C. But immediately Jesus[2] spoke *to* them, saying, "Take-courage[D], **I** am *the One*[3]. Do not be afraid"[4]   27

    6C. But having responded *to* Him, Peter said, "Master[E], if **You** are *the One*[5], order[6] me to come to You across the waters"   28

        1D. And the *One* said, "Come"   29

        2D. And having gone down from the boat, Peter walked across the waters and came[7] to[8] Jesus. But seeing the strong[9] wind, he became afraid. And having begun to sink[10], he cried-out[B], saying, "Master[11], save me!"   30

        3D. And immediately Jesus, having stretched-out[F] *His* hand, took-hold-of[G] him. And He says to him, "One of-little-faith[H], for what *purpose*[12] did you doubt[J]?"   31

    7C. And they having gone-up[13] into the boat, the wind stopped[K]   32

    8C. And the *ones* in the boat[14] gave-worship[15] *to* Him, saying, "Truly[16] You are God's Son"   33

16B.[17] And having crossed-over, they came on land in[18] Gennesaret[L]. °And having recognized[M] Him, the men *of* that place sent out into that whole surrounding-region[N]. And they brought to Him all the *ones* being ill[O]. °And they were begging[P] Him that they might only touch the tassel[Q] *of* His garment. And all-who touched *it* were restored[19]   34-35   36

17B.[20] Then Pharisees and scribes come to Jesus from Jerusalem, saying, °"For what reason are Your disciples transgressing the tradition[R] *of* the elders[S]? For they are not washing their hands when they eat bread"[21]   15:1-2

    1C. But the *One*, having responded, said *to* them   3

        1D. "For what reason indeed are **you** transgressing the commandment[T] *of* God for the sake of your tradition[R]?

            1E. "For God said[22] [in Ex 20:12], 'Be honoring *your* father and *your* mother', and [in Ex 21:17], 'Let the *one* speaking-evil-of father or mother come-to-an-end[23] *by a* death[24]'   4

            2E. "But **you** say, 'Whoever says *to his* father or *his* mother— "Whatever you might be benefitted[U] from me *is a* gift[25] [to God]"— °shall[26] by-no-means[27] honor[28] his father[29]'   5   6

            3E. "And you nullified[30] the word[31] *of* God for the sake of your tradition

        2D. "Hypocrites[V]! Isaiah prophesied[W] rightly[X] concerning you, saying [in Isa 29:13] °'This people[32] honors Me *with their* lips, but their heart is far distant[33] from Me. °But they are worshiping[Y] Me in-vain[34]— teaching *as* teachings[35] the commandments[Z] *of* humans[AA]'"   7-8   9

    2C. And having summoned the crowd, He said *to* them, "Listen and understand.[36] °The *thing* entering into the mouth does **not** defile[37] the person. But the *thing* proceeding out of the mouth— this defiles the person"   10-11

    3C. Then having come to *Him*, the disciples say *to* Him, "Do You know that the Pharisees, having heard *Your* statement[BB], took-offense[38]?   12

        1D. But the *One*, having responded, said, "Every plant which My heavenly Father did not plant will be uprooted. °Leave them *alone*. They are blind guides *of* blind[39] *ones*. And if *a* blind *one* guides *a* blind *one*, both will fall into *a* pit"   13   14

    4C. And having responded, Peter said *to* Him, "Explain[40] this[41] parable *to* us"   15

1. Or, "disturbed, thrown into confusion, troubled". On this word, see "disturbed" in Gal 1:7. Same word as in Mk 6:50.
2. Some manuscripts omit this word {C}, so that it says "He spoke".
3. That is, "It is I". Note v 28. On this phrase, see Jn 8:58.
4. The grammar implies "stop being afraid, stop fearing".
5. That is, "if it is You".
6. Or, "command". Same word as in v 9, 19; 18:25; Lk 18:40; Act 12:19; and as "give orders" in Mt 8:18; 27:64. Used 25 times. GK *3027*.
7. Or, "went". Instead of "and came", some manuscripts say "to go" {B} (or "to come"; it is the same word).
8. Or, "toward". GK *4639*.
9. Some manuscripts omit this word {C}.
10. Or, "to be sinking". The grammar means "having started the process of sinking", "beginning to sink".
11. Based on v 33, when this word is used by the twelve after this event, it is translated "Lord". On this word, see 8:2.
12. Not "for what *reason*" (looking to the waves), but, "To what *end*?". What was the point of doubting? On this phrase, see Mk 15:34.
13. Or, "come up". Some manuscripts say "gotten into" {N}, the same word as in v 22.
14. Some manuscripts say "boat, having come, gave-worship {N}.
15. Or, "prostrated-*themselves before* Him". Physically, this verb refers to prostrating oneself before someone or kneeling before someone with the forehead touching the ground or the person's feet. This is done before idols, angels, powerful people (like a master, a king, a prophet), and before God. Depending on the context, this act may be done in order to express worship (as in Mt 4:10; Rev 11:16), or to pay homage or respect (as in Mt 2:2, 8, 11; Mk 15:19), or to plead (as in Mt 15:25). It is used in the Gospels in all these senses with regard to those approaching Jesus. It is not related to "kneeling" in 17:14. In the TransLine, this word is translated (depending on the grammar) "worship" (27 times), or "give worship" (21 times) when the person involved would perceive himself as worshiping God, or a supposed deity (as in Rev 9:20; 13:4, 8). What did those approaching Jesus in the Gospels perceive Him to be? Early, He was perceived as a king (2:2), or a prophet (16:13-14; Jn 6:14), or the Messiah (as they understood the term). Since the Jews would not have "worshiped" (as we use this word with reference to God) a king or prophet or the Messiah, it is translated "pay homage" (only in Mt 2:2, 8, 11; Mk 15:19; Act 10:25) or, "prostrate-*oneself*" (only in Mt 8:2; 9:18; 15:25; 18:26; 20:20; Mk 5:6; Jn 9:38). Beginning here (compare Mk 6:52; Mt 16:17), the disciples perceived Him to be the Son of God, and so it is translated "worship". Used 60 times in the NT, it is also in Mt 28:9, 17; Jn 4:20; 12:20; Act 7:43; 8:27; 1 Cor 14:25; Heb 1:6; Rev 4:10. GK *4686*.
16. Or, "really, actually". Related to the "truth" in Jn 4:23. Elsewhere by Matthew only in 26:73; 27:54. Jesus uses this word in Lk 9:27; 12:44; 21:3; Jn 1:47; 8:31; 17:8. Same word as in Mk 14:70; 15:39; Jn 4:42; 6:14; 7:40; Act 12:11; 1 Thes 2:13; 1 Jn 2:5. Elsewhere only as "really" in Jn 7:26. GK *242*.
17. Parallel account at Mk 6:53. Compare Jn 6:22-25.
18. Instead of "on land in", some manuscripts say "to the land *of*" {N}.
19. Or, "brought safely through". Same word as in Lk 7:3.
20. Parallel account at Mk 7:1.
21. Note Mark's explanation of this in Mk 7:3-4.
22. Some manuscripts say "For God commanded, saying" {B}.
23. That is, die. On this word, see Mk 9:48.
24. That is, let him die by execution. This imitates a Hebrew idiom meaning, "let him surely die".
25. Or, "offering". I have made it a gift devoted to God. Same word as in 5:23. Mk 7:11 says "Corban", then translates it with this same word. It is like saying "I have vowed to give my estate to God when I die, so under no circumstances can I use any of it to help you".
26. Some manuscripts add a word meaning "and, indeed" {N}, so that it says "he indeed shall". Or, it could then be rendered "... gift [to God]" *shall be free*. And he shall by no means...".
27. On this emphatic negative, see 5:20.
28. You say that whoever makes this vow must not honor the request of his parents. The vow, according to their traditions, supersedes God's direct command because the vow pertains to God, but the honor pertains only to humans. On this word, see 1 Tim 5:3.
29. Some manuscripts add "or his mother" {C}.
30. Or, "made void, made of no effect, canceled the force of, invalidated, annulled". Same word as in Mk 7:13. Elsewhere only as "unratified" in Gal 3:17. GK *218*.
31. Some manuscripts say "commandment"; others, "law" {B}.
32. Some manuscripts say "This people draws near to Me with their mouth, and honors..." {N}.
33. The verb "is distant" is also in 14:24; Mk 7:6; Lk 7:6: 15:20; 24:13. GK *600*.
34. Or, "to no end, pointlessly, futilely". Elsewhere only in Mk 7:7. GK *3472*. Related to "futile" in 1 Cor 15:17.
35. That is, doctrines. On this word, see 1 Tim 5:17. Same word as in Mk 7:7.
36. Or, "Be listening and understanding". The grammar is different in Mk 7:14. On this word, see Mt 13:13.
37. Or, "make unclean or impure, profane". Jesus is not contradicting the Law of Moses (5:17). For a Jew at that time to knowingly defy the dietary Laws of Moses would be an example of evil from the heart. But their rules of ritual defilement (such as handwashing here) were not part of God's Law at all. In one sentence, their system of traditions built up around being "clean" and "unclean"— a major part of their life— is rejected. Note Mk 7:19.
38. Or, "were offended, were caused to fall". That is, because v 3-11 are a direct attack on them as teachers, and on their traditions. On this word, see "cause to fall" in 1 Cor 8:13.
39. Some manuscripts omit this word {C}, so that it says, "they are blind guides". Note Lk 6:39.
40. Or, "Declare, Interpret". Used only here. GK *5851*.
41. Some manuscripts omit this word {C}, so that it says "explain the parable". Peter is referring to v 10-11.

A. Mk 6:49 B. Mt 8:29 C. Eph 5:21 D. Act 23:11 E. Mt 8:2 F. Act 27:30 G. Lk 20:20 H. Mt 6:30 J. Mt 28:17 K. Mk 4:39 L. Mk 6:53 M. Col 1:6, understood N. Mk 1:28 O. Mk 1:32 P. Rom 12:8, exhorting Q. Mt 23:5 R. 1 Cor 11:2 S. 1 Tim 5:17 T. Mk 12:28 U. Rom 2:25, profits V. Mt 6:2 W. 1 Cor 14:1 X. Act 10:33, well Y. Act 13:50 Z. Col 2:22 AA. Mt 4:4, mankind BB. 1 Cor 12:8, word

    1D. And the *One* said, "Are **you** even yet also without-understanding¹? ˚Do you not² perceive^A 16-17
      that everything proceeding into the mouth advances^B into the stomach^C, and is expelled
      into *a* latrine³? ˚But the *things* proceeding out of the mouth come out of the heart. And 18
      those *things* defile^D the person^E

      1E. "For out of the heart come evil thoughts⁴, murders^F, adulteries, sexual-immoralities^G, 19
        thefts, false-testimonies⁵, blasphemies^H
      2E. "These are the *things* defiling the person. But the eating *with* unwashed^J hands does 20
        not defile the person^E"

18B.⁶ And having gone out from there, Jesus withdrew^K into the regions^L *of* Tyre and Sidon 21

  1C. And behold— *a* Canaanite⁷ woman having come out from those districts⁸ was crying out, 22
    saying, "Have mercy on me, Master^M, Son *of* David⁹. My daughter is badly demon-possessed^N"

    1D. But the *One* did not respond *a* word *to* her 23

  2C. And having come to *Him*, His disciples were asking Him, saying, "Send her away, because she
    is crying-out^O after us"

    1D. But the *One*, having responded, said, "I was not sent-forth^P except for¹⁰ the lost¹¹ sheep 24
      of the house *of* Israel"

  3C. But the *one*, having come, was prostrating-*herself*¹² *before* Him, saying, "Master^M, help^Q me" 25

    1D. And the *One*, having responded, said, "It is not good to take the bread *of* the children 26
      and throw *it to* the little-dogs¹³"
    2D. But the *one* said, "Yes, Master^M. For indeed¹⁴ the little-dogs eat from the crumbs falling 27
      from the table *of* their masters^M!"
    3D. Then, having responded, Jesus said *to* her, "O woman, your faith *is* great. Let it be done^R 28
      for you as you wish^S"
    4D. And her daughter was healed^T from that hour

19B.¹⁵ And having passed on from there, Jesus went beside the Sea *of* Galilee. And having gone up on 29
  the mountain, He was sitting there

  1C. And large crowds came to Him, having with them lame¹⁶ *ones*, blind *ones*, crippled *ones*, mute 30
    ones, and many others. And they threw¹⁷ them at His feet¹⁸
  2C. And He cured them, ˚so that the crowd marveled— seeing mute *ones* speaking¹⁹, crippled *ones* 31
    healthy^U, and lame *ones* walking, and blind *ones* seeing. And they glorified^V the God *of* Israel
  3C. And Jesus, having summoned His disciples, said, "I feel-deep-feelings^W [of compassion] 32
    toward the crowd, because *it is* already three days they are remaining-with^X Me, and they do
    not have anything they may eat. And I do not want to send them away hungry, so that they may
    not perhaps become-exhausted²⁰ on the way"

    1D. And the disciples say *to* Him, "From where *are there* so many loaves *for* us in *a* desolate 33
      place so as to fill-to-satisfaction^Y so large *a* crowd?"²¹
    2D. And Jesus says *to* them, "How many loaves^Z do you have?" And the *ones* said, "Seven, 34
      and *a* few small-fish²²"

1. On this word, see Rom 10:19. Same word as in Mk 7:18.
2. Some manuscripts say "not yet" {N}.
3. Elsewhere only in Mk 7:19, in this same statement. GK *909*.
4. Or, "reasonings". On this word, see Jam 2:4.
5. Or, "perjuries", if in a courtroom setting. Elsewhere only in 26:59. GK *6019*. Related to "give false testimony" in Mk 14:56.
6. Parallel account at Mk 7:24.
7. That is, from the land of Canaan. Used only here. GK *5914*. Mk 7:26 says "a Greek, a Syro-Phoenician".
8. Or, "boundaries". Same word as in v 39. On this word, see Mk 10:1.
9. That is, "Messiah". See 9:27.
10. Or, "to". GK *1650*. Not the same word as in 10:6 (GK *4639*).
11. That is, the sheep having gotten lost or become lost. On this word, see 10:6.
12. On this word, see "worship" in 14:33.
13. Or, "house dogs, lap dogs". Jesus answers here with a proverbial-type statement. The woman responds with the same kind of statement in v 27. Elsewhere only in v 27; Mk 7:27, 28. GK *3249*. Related to "dogs" in Mt 7:6.
14. This is the same word as "even" in Mk 7:28. GK *2779*.
15. Parallel account at Mk 8:1.
16. The manuscripts vary as to the order of these four terms {N}.
17. Or, "hurled, flung, tossed" them, indicating here not violence, but haste and urgency. On this word, see "throw forth" in 9:36.
18. Some manuscripts say "the feet *of* Jesus" {N}.
19. Some manuscripts add "and" ("and crippled..."); others omit "crippled *ones* healthy"; others say "deaf *ones* hearing" instead of "mute *ones* speaking" {C}.
20. Or, "faint, give out". Jesus does not want to allow this possibility to occur. On this word, see "lose heart" in Gal 6:9.
21. Some fault the disciples for not remembering 14:14-21. But after being "summoned" and hearing v 32, they would naturally think that Jesus was asking them to do something about it, as He did in 14:16. Why should their first thought be to assume that He intended to repeat the miracle? Jesus does not fault them, v 34.
22. Elsewhere only in Mk 8:7. GK *2715*.

A. Eph 3:20, think B. 2 Pet 3:9, make room C. Lk 1:15, womb D. Mk 7:15 E. Mt 4:4, mankind F. Act 9:1 G. 1 Cor 5:1 H. 1 Tim 6:4
J. Mk 7:2 K. Mt 4:12, went back L. Rom 11:25, part M. Mt 8:2 N. Mt 8:16 O. Mt 8:29 P. Mk 3:14, send out Q. Rev 12:16 R. Mt 6:10
S. Jn 7:17, willing T. Mt 8:8 U. Mt 12:13 V. Rom 8:30 W. Mt 9:36 X. Act 11:23, continue in Y. Phil 4:12 Z. Mt 4:3, loaves of bread

	3D. And having ordered[A] the crowd to fall-back[1] on the ground [to eat], °He took the seven loaves and the fish. And having given-thanks[B], He broke *them,* and was giving *them to* the[2] disciples, and the disciples *to* the crowds	35-36
	4D. And they all ate and were filled-to-satisfaction[C]	37
	5D. And they picked up the *amount of* the fragments[3] being left-over[D]— seven full large-baskets[4]	
	6D. And the *ones* eating were four-thousand men, apart from women and children[5]	38
20B.[6]	And having sent away the crowds, He got into the boat and went to the districts[E] *of* Magadan[7]. And having come to *Him,* the Pharisees and Sadducees— testing[F] *Him*— asked Him to show[G] them *a* sign out-of[8] heaven[9]	39 16:1
	1C. But the *One*, having responded, said *to* them[10]—	2
	1D.[11] "Having become evening, you say, 'Fair weather!— for the heaven[12] is red'. °And early-in-the-morning[H], 'Stormy-weather today!— for the lowering[13] heaven is red'	3
	1E. "You[14] know-*how* to discern[15] **the appearance**[J] **of the heaven**[16]— but cannot discern the signs *of* the times!	
	2D. "*An* evil and adulterous[17] generation is seeking-for[K] *a* sign[L]. And *a* sign will not be given *to* it, except the sign *of* Jonah[18]"	4
21B.[19]	And having left them behind, He went away. °And the[20] disciples, having come to the other side, forgot to take bread	5
	1C. And Jesus said *to* them, "Watch-out[M] and beware of[21] the leaven[N] *of* the Pharisees and Sadducees"	6
	2C. And the *ones* were discussing[22] among[23] themselves, saying that[24] "We did not take bread"	7
	3C. But having known *it,* Jesus said, "Why are you discussing among yourselves, *ones* of-little-faith[O], that you do not have[25] bread?	8
	1D. "Do you not yet perceive[26]?	9
	2D. "Do you not even remember[27] the five loaves *of* the five-thousand, and how many baskets[P] you received? °Not even the seven loaves *of* the four-thousand, and how many large-baskets[Q] you received?	10
	3D. "How *is it* you do not perceive that I did not speak *to* you concerning bread?	11
	4D. "But beware[28] of the leaven *of* the Pharisees and Sadducees"	
	4C. Then they understood[R] that He did not say to beware of the leaven *of* bread[29], but of the teaching[30] *of* the Pharisees and Sadducees	12
22B.[31]	And Jesus, having come into the regions *of* Philip's[32] Caesarea, was asking His disciples[S], saying, "Who do people[T] say *that* the[33] Son *of* Man is?"	13
	1C. And the *ones* said, "Some, John the Baptist. And others, Elijah. And different[U] *ones*, Jeremiah or one *of* the prophets"	14
	2C. He says *to* them, "But who do **you** say *that* I am?"	15
	3C. And having responded, Simon Peter said "**You** are the Christ, the Son *of* the living God"	16
	4C. And having responded, Jesus said *to* him—	17
	1D. "You are blessed[34], Simon Bar-Jonah[35], because flesh and blood did not reveal[V] *it* to you, but My Father in the heavens	

1. Or, "recline, lean back". GK *404*.
2. Some manuscripts say "His" {N}, as in Mk 8:6.
3. Or, "pieces". Used 9 times. GK *3083*. Related to "broke" in Act 2:46, and "breaking" in Act 2:42.
4. Used only in this incident, Mt 16:10; Mk 8:8, 20, and of the basket that held Paul, Act 9:25. GK *5083*.
5. Some manuscripts say "children and women" {N}.
6. Parallel account at Mk 8:10-12. Compare Mt 12:38-42; Lk 11:29-32.
7. Some manuscripts say "Magdala" {C}. Used only here. GK *3400*. Compare Mk 8:10.
8. Or, "from". GK *1666*. Not the same word as "from" in Mk 8:11 (GK *608*).
9. That is, not a healing about which the source can be debated (God or Satan), but something indisputably from God, like the plagues Egypt. Jesus did such miracles (feeding 5000, calming the storm), but not for them.
10. Some manuscripts omit the rest of v 2-3 {C}, so that it says "...said *to* them, *"An* evil and adulterous...".
11. Compare Lk 12:54-56.
12. That is, the "sky", as this word is sometimes used. On this word, see 2 Cor 12:2.
13. Or, "gloomy, overcast". Elsewhere only as "become downcast" in Mk 10:22. GK *5145*. We have the saying, "Red sky at night, sailor's delight. Red sky in the morning, sailor take warning".
14. Or, this may be a question, "Do you indeed know...?". Some manuscripts say "Hypocrites! You..." {K}.
15. The signs from heaven (v 1) are plain to see, but you can discern only the physical ones, not the spiritual ones; the ones from the physical heaven, not the ones from God's heaven. On this word, see "doubt" in Jam 1:6.
16. Jesus uses grammar that emphasizes the contrast between the two halves of this sentence.
17. That is, spiritually unfaithful to God. On this word, see Jam 4:4.
18. Some manuscripts add "the prophet" {N}, as in 12:39.
19. Parallel account at Mk 8:13.
20. Some manuscripts say "His" {N}.
21. On "beware of ", see 10:17.
22. Or, "reasoning". On this word, see "reasoning" in Lk 5:21.
23. Or, "within" (GK *1877*). Matthew uses this phrase "among [or, within] themselves" only in 3:9; 9:3, 21; 16:7, 8; 21:25, 38.
24. Or, "saying, '*It is* because we...". Jesus is still thinking of the incident in v 1-4. But the disciples think He is talking about literal bread, and start to discuss the fact that they forgot it.
25. Some manuscripts say "did not take" {N}.
26. Or, "understand", but not the same word as in v 12. Do you not yet perceive spiritual truth? Same word as in 15:17; 16:11. On this word, see "think" in Eph 3:20.
27. Or, "Do you not yet understand nor remember the five..., nor the seven...".
28. Some manuscripts include this in the previous sentence "...bread, but *that you should* beware..." {N}.
29. Some manuscripts say "leaven *of* bread *of* the Pharisees and Sadducees"; others simply "leaven" {C}.
30. That is, teaching that can permeate their thinking with leftover ideas from the past. Teaching that refused to believe unless Jesus did a sign from heaven, v 1. In Lk 12:1, the leaven of the Pharisees is "hypocrisy".
31. Parallel account at Mk 8:27; Lk 9:18.
32. That is, Herod Philip's capital city, about 25 miles or 40 kilometers north of the Sea of Galilee. Mentioned elsewhere only in Mk 8:27. On Philip, see Lk 3:1. It was called this to distinguish it from the seaport called "Caesarea" (see Act 8:40).
33. Some manuscripts say "*that* I, the Son *of* Man, am" {B}.
34. Same adjective as in 5:3. God has shown His favor toward you. "You are *a* blessed *one*".
35. This is transliterated from Hebrew, meaning "son of Jonah". Used only here. GK *980*. See "John" in Jn 1:42.

A. 1 Tim 1:3, command   B. Mt 26:27   C. Phil 4:12   D. 2 Cor 8:2, abound   E. Mk 10:1   F. Heb 2:18, tempted   G. Act 18:28   H. Mk 13:35
J. Lk 9:52, presence   K. Phil 4:17   L. 2 Thes 2:9   M. Lk 2:26, see   N. Mt 13:33   O. Mt 6:30   P. Jn 6:13   Q. Mt 15:37   R. Mt 13:13   S. Lk 6:40
T. Mt 4:4, mankind   U. 1 Cor 12:9   V. 2 Thes 2:3

Matthew 16:18 — 56 — Verse

    2D. "And **I** also[1] say *to* you that **you** are *a* rock[2], and upon this bed-rock[3] I will build[A] My church[B]— and *the* gates *of* Hades[4] will not prevail-against[5] it   18

        1E. "I will give you the keys *of* the kingdom *of* the heavens[6]   19
        2E. "And whatever you bind[7] on earth will have been bound[8] in the heavens
        3E. "And whatever you loose[9] on earth will have been loosed[10] in the heavens"

    5C. Then He gave-orders[11] *to* the[12] disciples that they should tell no one that **He** is the Christ[13]   20

12A.[14] From that time *on*,[15] Jesus began to show[C] His disciples that He must[16] go to Jerusalem, and suffer[D] many *things* from the elders and chief priests and scribes, and be killed, and be raised *on* the third day   21

  1B. And having taken Him aside, Peter began to rebuke[E] Him, saying, "*God be* merciful[17] *to* You, Lord! This shall never happen[18] *to* You"   22

    1C. But the *One*, having turned, said *to* Peter, "Get[19] behind Me, Satan! You are *a* cause-of-falling[20] *to* Me, because you are not thinking[F] the *things of* God, but the *things of* humans[G]"   23

  2B.[21] Then Jesus said *to* His disciples, "If anyone wants[H] to come after Me, let him deny[22] himself, and take up his cross[23], and be following Me   24

    1C. "For whoever wants[H] to save[J] his life[24] will lose[K] it. But whoever loses his life for My sake will find it   25

    1D. "For what will *a* person[G] be profited[25] if he gains[L] the whole world, but forfeits[26] his life[27]?   26

1. Jesus may mean "in addition to what the Father revealed, I also reveal...", or, "in addition to you being blessed".
2. Or, "Peter". Used 156 times in the NT, all other times as Peter's name. GK *4377*. The Greek word means "a piece of rock, a stone", and is related to the word "bed-rock" that follows. Jesus is not giving Peter the name here, for He has already done so in Jn 1:42. It is natural for Him to call Peter a "rock" here, after the confession he just made on behalf of all of them. "You are blessed" and "You are a rock". There is a play on words here, with the emphasis being on the meaning of his name rather than on the proper name itself. However, either way of translating is imperfect. "Rock" shows the flow of thought. "Peter" shows the connection to the apostle. The Greek reader would immediately see both. Perhaps it should be rendered "Peter *(a rock)*, and...". "Peter" is Greek, "Cephas" is Aramaic, both meaning "rock", Jn 1:42.
3. On this word, see 7:24, the bed-rock on which the house is built. It means "a mass of rock, a cliff, bed-rock, rock, *a* rock". It can be a synonym of the word "rock" preceding. Here, there is a play on the two words, since Matthew uses two different Greek words to bring out what Jesus meant when He used the same Aramaic (the language Jesus spoke) word in both places. On what rock does Jesus build His church? Some think He means Peter himself, the leader of the apostles, the sense in which He intends it being described in v 19. He is a foundation rock in a house built of living stones, 1 Pet 2:5; Eph 2:20. Others think Christ is pointing to Himself. He Himself is both the builder and the cornerstone, 1 Cor 3:11; Eph 2:20. Others think it is Peter's confession. The church is built on the human confession of Christ as the Son of God. Others think it is the Father's revelation of Christ's identity to humans, v 17, starting with Peter.
4. On Hades, see Rev 1:18. Some think Jesus means the gates all humans pass through at death. Death will not be able to defeat the church in the world, nor hold the Christian dead within its gates. Others think these gates are the entrances for the forces of darkness into the world. The forces of Hades will not be victorious over His church.
5. Or, "win the victory over, be strong against". Elsewhere only as "prevail" in Lk 23:23; and "have strength" in Lk 21:36. GK *2996*. Related to "prevail" in Act 19:16.
6. Having keys means having the power to open and lock doors. The use of these keys may be seen in Acts, where Peter is the one to "open" the kingdom for the Jews (2:22-41), the Samaritans (8:14-17, Peter and John), and the Gentiles (10:34-48; 15:7).
7. Or, "tie up". On this word, see 1 Cor 7:27.
8. This is a participle, it "will be having been bound" or, "it will be standing as bound". This is the rare future perfect passive tense, used twice in this verse, and elsewhere only in Mt 18:18, and perhaps Lk 12:52. Jesus is promising Peter divine guidance, so that whatever Peter "binds" will correspond to what has been "bound" in heaven. He is not saying that whatever Peter binds will be seconded by God, but that Peter will speak with God's authority, under His guidance.
9. Or, "unbind, untie, release, abolish". Same word as in 18:18, and as "break" in 5:19. Some think "binding and loosing" means "forbidding and permitting" things, as the Rabbis used the terms (note 5:19). Others think they are explained by Jn 20:23 as "forgiving and retaining sins". Others think Jesus is referring to the powers of excommunication (compare the same phrases in 18:18). In addition, some think Peter held these powers exclusively; others, that he passed them on to a successor; others, that they passed from him to all the other apostles; others, that they passed to all believers.
10. This is a participle, it "will be having been loosed". Same grammar as "bound" above.
11. Some manuscripts say "warned" {N}.
12. Some manuscripts say "His" {N}.
13. That is, the Messiah. Some manuscripts say "Jesus, the Christ" {B}. Why? To avoid a repeat of what people tried to do in Jn 6:15. "Messiah" had political overtones that Jesus did not want to fan.
14. Parallel account at Mk 8:31; Lk 9:22.
15. Matthew reaches a turning point, as in 4:17. For the first time, Jesus speaks directly about His coming death and resurrection. After this, Jesus concentrates on preparing the twelve for this event, and for their life and mission after it, as He moves toward it.
16. Or, "He has to". More literally, "that it is necessary *that* He go" or "that it is necessary *for* Him to go". The root word means "it is binding" upon Him. This frequent idiom is used of that which must necessarily take place, the necessity or compulsion proceeding from various sources (based on the context), whether internal (like duty) or external (like the will of God, law, custom, or the circumstances themselves). Here, it is necessary in the will of God. Same idiom as in 17:10; 26:54; Mk 13:10; Lk 2:49; 24:26; Jn 3:7; 4:24; Act 1:16; 4:12; 14:22; 17:3; 2 Cor 5:10; 1 Tim 3:2; Heb 11:6; Rev 1:1; etc. GK *1256*. Same word as in the idiom "should have" in Mt 25:27, and "ought to" in Act 25:10.
17. This idiom means "May God mercifully spare You from this". On this word, see Heb 8:12.
18. Or, "be *for* You". The word "be" sometimes means "happen", as in Mk 11:23, 24; 13:4; Lk 21:7; 22:49, etc. GK *1639*.
19. Or, "Be going behind Me". Jesus recognizes that Satan is using Peter. The grammar means "Be engaging in the process of going behind Me". Same command as in Mk 8:33. On this word, see "go away" in Mt 4:10.
20. Or, "offense, trap". On this word, see Rom 11:9.
21. Parallel account at Mk 8:34; Lk 9:23. Compare Mt 10:39; Lk 17:33; Jn 12:25.
22. That is, disown and refuse to follow the impulses of self. This is a stronger form of the root word "deny" (both are in Lk 12:9). Used only in this statement, Mk 8:34; of being denied before angels, Lk 12:9; and of Peter denying the Lord, Mt 26:34, 35, 75; Mk 14:30, 31, 72; Lk 22:34, 61. GK *565*. Here it means to no longer own one's life, but to serve the Master, Jesus, having been bought with a price, 1 Cor 6:19; Gal 2:20.
23. That is, the instrument of suffering and death, a symbol of our death to self for Christ. Compare 10:38.
24. That is, by avoiding his "cross" and refusing to "deny himself". Compare Jn 12:25.
25. On this word, see Rom 2:25. Some manuscripts say "What is *a* person profited" {N}.
26. Same word as in Mk 8:36.
27. Or, "soul". The same Greek word is used four times in v 25-26. In v 25, Jesus means "life" in an earthly, temporal sense. In v 26, He means "life" in a spiritual and eternal sense. Lk 9:25 says "himself". On this word, see "soul" in Jam 5:20.

A. 1 Cor 14:4, edify B. Rev 22:16 C. 1 Tim 6:15 D. Gal 3:4 E. 2 Tim 4:2, warn F. Rom 8:5 G. Mt 4:4, mankind H. Jn 7:17, willing J. Lk 19:10 K. 1 Cor 1:18, perish L. Mk 8:36

	2D. "Or what will *a* person give in-exchange-for[1] his life?	
	2C. "For the Son *of* Man is going to come in the glory *of* His Father with His angels. And then He will render[2] *to* each *one* according to his practice[3]	27
	3C. "Truly[A] I say *to* you that there are some[4] *of* the *ones* standing here who will by no means taste death[5] until they see the Son *of* Man coming[B] in His kingdom[C]"	28
3B.[6] And after six days, Jesus takes-along[D] Peter and James and John his brother, and brings them up on *a* high mountain privately[E]		17:1
	1C. And He was transfigured[7] in front of them. And His face shined[F] like the sun, and His garments became white as the light	2
	2C. And behold— Moses and Elijah appeared[G] *to* them, talking[H] with Him	3
	3C. And having responded, Peter said *to* Jesus, "Lord, it is good *that* we are here. If You wish, I will[8] make three dwellings[9] here— one *for* You, and one *for* Moses, and one *for* Elijah"	4
	4C. While he *was* still speaking	5
	1D. Behold— *a* bright[10] cloud overshadowed[11] them[12]	
	2D. And behold— *a* voice out of the cloud saying "This is My beloved[J] Son, with[13] Whom I was well-pleased[14]. Be listening-to Him"	
	5C. And having heard[15] *it*, the disciples fell on their face and became extremely afraid[K]	6
	1D. And Jesus came to *them*, and having touched them, said, "Arise, and do not be afraid[16]"	7
	2D. And having lifted up their eyes, they saw no one except Jesus Himself alone	8
4B.[17] And while they *were* coming down from the mountain, Jesus commanded[L] them, saying, "Tell the sight[18] *to* no one until which *time* the Son *of* Man is raised[M] from *the* dead"		9
	1C. And the[19] disciples questioned[N] Him, saying, "Why then[20] do the scribes say that Elijah must[21] come first?"	10
	2C.[22] And the *One*,[23] having responded, said[24], "**Elijah**[25] is coming[26] and will restore[27] all *things*— but I say *to* you that Elijah already[O] came[28]	11 12
	1D. "And they did not recognize[P] him, but did with[29] him whatever they wanted[Q]	
	2D. "So also the Son *of* Man is going to suffer[R] by them"	
	3D. Then the disciples understood[S] that He spoke *to* them about John the Baptist	13
5B.[30] And *they* having come to the crowd, *a* man came to Him, kneeling-before[31] Him, °and saying, "Master[T], have mercy on my son, because he has seizures[U] and is suffering[R] badly[32]. For he often falls into the fire, and often into the water. °And I brought him to Your disciples, and they were not able to cure[V] him"		14-15 16
	1C. But having responded, Jesus said, "O unbelieving[33] and perverted[34] generation![35] How long[36] will I be with[37] you? How long will I bear-with[W] you? Bring[38] him here *to* Me". °And Jesus rebuked[X] it, and the demon departed from him, and the boy was cured from that hour	17 18
	2C. Then the disciples, having come to Jesus privately[E], said, "For what reason were **we** not able to cast it out?"	19
	3C.[39] And the *One* says *to* them, "Because of your little-faith[40]. For truly I say *to* you, if you have faith like *a* seed *of a* mustard-plant[41], you will say *to* this mountain, 'Pass[Y] from-here to-there', and it will pass. And nothing will be impossible[Z] *for* you	20 21[42]

1. You may have gained the whole world, but what do you have of equal value which you can exchange with God so as to buy back the soul which He will require from you? Elsewhere only in Mk 8:37. GK *498*.
2. Or, "give back, pay back, pay out"; if good, "reward". Same word as in Rom 2:6; Rev 22:12. Used 48 times. GK *625*.
3. Or, "activity, action, course of action, doing, deed". Same word as in Act 19:18; Rom 8:13; Col 3:9. Elsewhere only as "action" in Lk 23:51; and "function" in Rom 12:4. GK *4552*. Related word in Rom 2:1. Some manuscripts say "works" {B}. Compare Rev 20:12.
4. Some think Jesus is referring to the three with Him at the transfiguration, next. For more views, see Mk 9:1.
5. On the phrase "taste death", see Heb 2:9. It means "experience death, die".
6. Parallel account at Mk 9:2; Lk 9:28. Compare 2 Pet 1:17-18.
7. Or, "transformed", that is, changed in form. Same word as in Mk 9:2.
8. Some manuscripts say "let us", as in Mk 9:5; Lk 9:33; others, "we will" {B}.
9. Or, "tents, tabernacles", assuming they were going to stay. On this word, see Lk 9:33.
10. Or, "full of light", as this word is used in 6:22.
11. Or, "covered, hovered over" them. Same word as in Mk 9:7; Lk 9:34. Elsewhere only in Lk 1:35; Act 5:15. GK *2173*. Perhaps to those outside the cloud, those inside the cloud appeared as if in a shadow or haze or silhouette.
12. Who? Perhaps Jesus, Moses and Elijah, for the disciples hear the voice come "out of" the cloud. Compare Lk 9:34.
13. Or, "in". Same word as in 3:17; Mk 1:11; Lk 3:22. GK *1877*. Mt 12:18 and 2 Pet 1:17 use a different word (GK *1650*).
14. Or, "took pleasure, delighted". Some take this in a timeless sense, rendering it "I am well pleased, I delight". Others think God is speaking with reference to His choice of His Son for this task before the foundation of the world, "I was well pleased, I delighted", as in Isa 42:1. Lk 9:35 says "My Son, the *One* having been chosen". Others take it in a historical sense, "I have become well pleased" in His obedience. There are other views. Same word and form as in 3:17; Mk 1:11; Lk 3:22; 2 Pet 1:17. Same word as in Mt 12:18; Lk 12:32; Rom 15:26, 27; 1 Cor 1:21; 10:5; 2 Cor 12:10; Gal 1:15; Col 1:19; 1 Thes 2:8; Heb 10:6, 8, 38. Elsewhere only as "prefer" in 2 Cor 5:8; 1 Thes 3:1; and as "take pleasure" in 2 Thes 2:12. GK *2305*. Related to "good pleasure" in Eph 1:5.
15. Peter reminds us of what he saw and heard in 2 Pet 1:16-18.
16. The grammar implies "Stop being afraid, stop fearing".
17. Parallel account at Mk 9:9.
18. Or, "vision". That is, what you have seen, as stated in Mk 9:9; Lk 9:36. Same word as in Act 7:31, the "sight" of the burning bush. On this word, see "vision" in Act 10:3.
19. Some manuscripts say "His" {N}.
20. The disciples do not understand the connection between Elijah and Messiah. If Messiah is here, where is Elijah? If Elijah must come before the consummation of the age, where is he? If he came and went, and You say not to tell anyone about it (v 9), why does Mal 4:5 say he comes first? Note 11:14.
21. More literally, "that it is necessary *for* Elijah to come first". On this idiom, see 16:21. The necessity is based on the will of God.
22. Compare Mt 11:14; Lk 1:17; Jn 1:21.
23. Some manuscripts say "And Jesus," {N}.
24. Some manuscripts add "*to* them" {K}.
25. Jesus uses grammar that emphasizes the contrast between the two halves of this sentence.
26. Some manuscripts say "coming first" {N}.
27. On this word, see Mk 8:25. Same word as in Act 1:6. Related to "restoration" in Act 3:21, the future restoration.
28. On Elijah "coming" and "came", see the note on Mk 9:12.
29. Or, "in his case, in connection with him". GK *1877*.
30. Parallel account at Mk 9:14; Lk 9:37.
31. Same word as in Mk 10:17. Elsewhere only as "kneel" in 27:29; Mk 1:40. GK *1206*. Related to "knee".
32. Some manuscripts say "and he is ill" {N}, using the idiom in Mk 1:32.
33. Or, "faithless". Same word as in this statement in Mk 9:19; Lk 9:41. Used of "unbelievers", as in Lk 12:46; 2 Cor 4:4; and of "unbelieving" disciples, as in Jn 20:27. Used 23 times. GK *603*.
34. Or, "crooked". This is a participle, "having been perverted". Same word as in Lk 9:41. On this word, see Phil 2:15.
35. Some think Jesus is referring to "this generation" (see 24:34) of Jews, of which this father and his demon-possessed son are the first He encountered after the glory of His transfiguration. Others think He is referring to the nine disciples who did not have enough faith (v 20) to cast it out; others, to the scribes doubting Him; others, to everyone included here, for they all lacked faith in one sense or another.
36. This is an idiom, literally "until when", where "when" is GK 4536. This idiom is elsewhere only in Mk 9:19; Lk 9:41; Jn 10:24; Rev 6:10.
37. Or, "together with". GK *3552*. Not the same word as Mk 9:19; Lk 9:41 (GK *4639*).
38. Or, "Be bringing". Same word and grammar as in Mk 9:19. The emphasis of the grammar is on carrying out the process necessary to bring him here. On this word, see "carry" in 2 Pet 1:17.
39. Compare Lk 17:6; and Mt 21:21; Mk 11:22-23.
40. Used only here. GK *3898*. Related to "ones of little faith" in 6:30. Some manuscripts say "unbelief " {A}.
41. That is, the tiniest amount can unleash the power of God. But their "little faith" did not issue in them using any faith at all on this occasion. A little faith can be powerful because it is not the faith, but God who moves the mountains. On "seed of a mustard plant", see 13:31. Compare Lk 17:6.
42. Some manuscripts add as v 21 "But this kind does not go out except by prayer and fasting" {A}.

A. Mt 5:18   B. Mk 16:2   C. Mt 3:2   D. Lk 17:34, taken   E. Mt 14:13   F. 2 Cor 4:6   G. Lk 2:26, see   H. Act 25:12   J. Mt 3:17   K. Eph 5:33, respecting   L. Mk 10:3   M. Mt 28:6   N. Lk 9:18   O. Mt 24:32   P. Col 1:6, understood   Q. Jn 7:17, willing   R. Gal 3:4   S. Mt 13:13   T. Mt 8:2   U. Mt 4:24   V. Mt 8:7   W. 2 Cor 11:4   X. 2 Tim 4:2, warn   Y. Jn 5:24   Z. Lk 1:37

Matthew 17:22	60	Verse

6B.[1] And while they *were* being gathered[2] in Galilee, Jesus said *to* them, "The Son *of* Man is going to be handed-over[A] into *the* hands *of* men. *And they will kill Him. And He will be raised[3] *on* the third day". And they were extremely grieved[B] — 22, 23

7B. And they having come to Capernaum, the *ones*[4] taking the double-drachmas[5] came to Peter and said, "Does not your teacher pay[C] the double-drachmas?"[6] *He says, "Yes" — 24, 25

    1C. And *Peter* having come into the house, Jesus anticipated[7] him, saying, "What seems[D] *right to* you, Simon— from whom do the kings *of* the earth take[E] taxes[8] or *a* poll-tax[9], from their sons or from the strangers[10]?"

    2C. And *Peter* having said[11] "from the strangers", Jesus said *to* him, "Then indeed, the sons are free[12]! *But in order that we may not offend[13] them— having gone to *the* sea, cast[F] *a* hook. And take the first fish having come up. And having opened its mouth, you will find *a* stater[14]. Having taken that, give *it to* them for Me and you" — 26, 27

8B.[15] At that hour the disciples came to Jesus, saying, "Who then[16] is greater[17] in the kingdom *of* the heavens?" *And having summoned[G] *a* child, He stood him[18] in *the* middle[H] *of* them,* and said— 18:1, 2-3

    1C. "Truly[J] I say *to* you, unless you are turned-around[19] and become[20] like children[K], you will never enter into the kingdom *of* the heavens. *Therefore whoever will humble[L] himself like this child[K], this *one* is the greater *one* in the kingdom *of* the heavens — 4

    2C. "And whoever welcomes[21] one such[22] child[K] on the basis of My name[23], welcomes Me. *But whoever causes one *of* these little *ones* believing[24] in Me to fall[25]— it *would* be better[26] *for* him that *a* donkey's millstone[27] be hung[M] around his neck and he be sunk[28] in the deep-part *of* the sea[29] — 5-6

        1D. "Woe *to* the world because of the causes-of-falling[N]. For *it is a* necessity[O] *that* causes-of-falling *should* come. Nevertheless, woe *to* the[30] person through whom the cause-of-falling comes — 7

        2D.[31] "But if your[32] hand or your foot is causing you to fall, cut it[33] off and throw *it* from you. It is better[34] *for* you to enter into life crippled or lame[P], than to be thrown into the eternal[Q] fire having two hands or two feet — 8

        3D. "And if your eye is causing you to fall, tear it out and throw *it* from you. It is better *for* you to enter into life one-eyed, than to be thrown into the Gehenna *of* fire[35] having two eyes — 9

    3C. "See *that* you do not look-down-upon[36] one *of* these little *ones* — 10

        1D. "For I say *to* you that their angels[37] in *the* heavens are continually[R] seeing[38] the face *of* My Father in *the* heavens — 11[39]

        2D.[40] "What seems[D] *right to* you?[41] — 12

            1E. "If *a* hundred sheep belong *to* any man, and one of them went-astray[S], will he not leave the ninety nine on the mountains, and having gone, be seeking[T] the *one* going astray?[42]

            2E. "And if it comes about *that he* finds it, truly I say *to* you that he rejoices over it more than over the ninety nine not having gone astray[43] — 13

            3E. "So it is not *the* will[U] in-the-sight-of[44] your[45] Father in *the* heavens that one *of* these little *ones*[46] should be-lost[47] — 14

1. Parallel account at Mk 9:30; Lk 9:43.
2. Or, "gathering *themselves*". Elsewhere only in Act 28:3. GK *5370*. Related to "gathering" in Act 23:12. Some manuscripts say "*were staying*" {B}.
3. Or, "will arise". On this word, see "arose" in 28:6.
4. These would be Jews commissioned by the Temple, not the hated "tax collectors" who collected for Rome.
5. That is, the yearly half-shekel (two drachma) temple tax required of all male Jews 20 to 50 years old, Ex 30:11-16. It was collected from Jews throughout the world. A drachma (see Lk 15:8) was a silver coin equivalent to a denarius (see Mt 20:2), and to one fourth of a Jewish shekel. Used only in this verse. GK *1440*.
6. The grammar indicates a "yes" answer is expected.
7. That is, Jesus began to answer before Peter could ask. Perhaps He had overheard them talking. Used only here. GK *4740*.
8. That is, local taxes. Same word as in Rom 13:7.
9. That is, the tax based on the census and paid to the Emperor. Elsewhere only in 22:17, 19; Mk 12:14. GK *3056*.
10. Sons belonging to the royal household are contrasted to those belonging to the other households (the citizens). The King's family pays no taxes. On this word, see "foreigners" in Heb 11:34.
11. Some manuscripts say "And Peter says *to* Him" {B}.
12. That is, not bound by the tax, exempt from the tax. In other words, the sons of the Father (Jesus and the disciples) are exempt from His Father's temple tax. This is the logical deduction, but Jesus next gives a more practical answer. Used 23 times. GK *1801*. Related to "set free" in Rom 8:2.
13. Or, "cause them to fall", on which see 1 Cor 8:13.
14. This is a Greek silver coin worth one shekel or two double-drachmas, enough to pay for both Jesus and Peter. Used only here. GK *5088*.
15. Parallel account at Mk 9:33; Lk 9:46.
16. Since You are Messiah, how will we rank in your kingdom?
17. Though the form of this word means "greater", some think the sense of it here is "greatest". Likewise in v 4. On this word, see 11:11.
18. Or, "her". The grammar is not specific.
19. Or, "changed, converted" inwardly, "turned [from your ways to God]". Similar in meaning to Jn 3:2, "unless you are born again". Same word as "turned" in Jn 12:40. This is the common word for "turn", used 21 times. GK *5138*.
20. That is, humble yourself to become dependent and helpless before God, as this child is before adults and God. What the child does naturally, the adult must purposefully choose. If you think "I can do it myself", you will not enter.
21. Having answered their question, Jesus now goes on to draw another lesson from this child. On this word, see 10:40.
22. Some think Jesus means one child like this child before them, one "little one believing in Me" (v 6), as in Mk 9:37; others, a child like the one who "humbles himself" in v 4, meaning one of His spiritual children regardless of age. In any case, Jesus is referring to welcoming one who is least associated with "greatness". Compare 10:40; 25:40.
23. On "on the basis of My name", see Act 2:38.
24. Or, "these little *ones who are* believing in Me", or more literally, "these little *ones*, the *ones* believing in Me".
25. On "causes to fall", see 1 Cor 8:13. The same word is used in v 8, 9, and a related word is used three times in v 7.
26. Same word as in 5:29, 30; Jn 11:50; 16:7; 18:14. On this word, see "beneficial" in 1 Cor 6:12. It is not the same word as in the similar statements in Lk 17:2, Mk 9:42, or as in v 8, 9.
27. On this phrase, "donkey's millstone", see Mk 9:42.
28. It is better to be killed than face the consequences of this. The death is a one-time event; the consequences are an eternal loss. The grammar is different in Mk 9:42; Lk 17:2. Elsewhere only in 14:30, of Peter sinking. GK *2931*.
29. This is an idiom, literally "in the open-sea *of* the sea", "in the high-sea *of* the sea". The first word is elsewhere only as "open-sea" in Act 27:5. GK *4283*.
30. Some manuscripts say "that" {N}.
31. Compare Mt 5:29-30; Mk 9:43-48.
32. Woe to "the person" (v 7) who causes God's children to fall. But as for you (v 8), if your hand causes you to fall in this area, cut it off (as Jesus also said in 5:29-30). Better to be maimed or to die in the sea (v 6) than to fall in this area.
33. Some manuscripts have this word plural, "them" {N}.
34. Though the form of this word means "good", it is sometimes used in the first part of a comparison (as here with "than"), giving it the meaning "better". On this word, see "good" in 1 Tim 5:10a.
35. On "Gehenna of fire", see 5:22.
36. Or, "despise, disregard, treat with contempt". On this word, see "disregard" in Rom 2:4. It is the opposite of "welcome" in v 5. That is, because of their age; and with reference to spiritual children, for their differences of opinion (as in Rom 14), or behavior (as in 1 Cor 8), or social status (as in Eph 6:9; 1 Cor 1:26), etc. Do not rank yourself as "greater" (v 1) than others and treat them with contempt. Rather, rescue them, if they are lost, v 12-14.
37. Some find the concept of "guardian angels" here. Others think that while angels do have a ministering role (Heb 1:14), it may be going beyond what this verse says to say that every individual person has an angel assigned to them. In any case, this verse affirms the great value and priority God places on all His children. Note Lk 15:10; 16:22.
38. That is, they have continual access to God. On this word, see Rev 1:11.
39. Some manuscripts add as v 11, "For the Son *of* Man came to save the lost" {B}, similar to Lk 19:10.
40. Compare Lk 15:3-7.
41. This is a second reason not to look down on "these little ones", v 10. Not only do the angels minister to them, but God rescues them.
42. The grammar indicates that a "yes" answer is expected.
43. Luke follows this parable (and its companion parable of the lost coin) with the parable of the prodigal son, in which the father illustrates this finding and rejoicing, Lk 15:20-24, 31-32.
44. Or, "before, in the presence of". This is a reverential way of saying it is not God's will. Same word as 11:26. GK *1869*.
45. Some manuscripts say "My" {C}.
46. God is not a respecter of persons. He values His "little" people as much as His apostles, His slaves as much as His masters (Eph 6:9), His poor as much as His rich (Jam 2:1).
47. Or, "perish". On this word, see "perish" in 1 Cor 1:18.

A. Mt 26:21 B. 2 Cor 7:9 C. Rev 10:7, finished D. Lk 19:11, thinking E. Rom 7:8 F. Rev 2:22, throw G. Act 2:39, call to H. 2 Thes 2:7, midst J. Mt 5:18 K. 1 Jn 2:14 L. Phil 4:12 M. Act 10:39 N. Rom 11:9 O. 1 Cor 7:26 P. Heb 12:13 Q. Mt 25:46 R. 2 Thes 3:16 S. Jam 5:19, err T. Phil 2:21 U. Jn 7:17

4C.¹ "But if your brother^A sins² against you³, go, expose⁴ him between you and him alone^B   15

    1D. "If he listens-to you, you gained⁵ your brother
    2D. "But if he does not listen, take-along^C with you one or two more, in order that every   16
        word^D may be established^E based-on⁶ *the* mouth *of* two or three witnesses
    3D. "And if he refuses-to-listen-to^F them, tell *it* to the church⁷   17
    4D. "And if he even refuses to listen to the church, let him be *to* you just like the Gentile⁸
        and the tax-collector⁹

        1E. "Truly^G I say *to* you, whatever you bind¹⁰ on earth will have been bound¹¹ in heaven.   18
            And whatever you loose on earth will have been loosed in heaven
        2E. "Again,¹² truly¹³ I say *to* you that if two of you on earth agree¹⁴ concerning any   19
            matter¹⁵ which they may ask, it will be done^H *for* them by My Father in *the* heavens

            1F. For¹⁶ where two or three have been gathered-together¹⁷ in¹⁸ My name, I am   20
                there in *the* midst^J *of* them"

5C.¹⁹ Then having come to *Him*, Peter²⁰ said *to* Him, "Lord, how often will my brother^A sin^K against   21
    me and I will forgive^L him? Up to seven-times?"
6C. Jesus says *to* him, "I do not say *to* you up to seven-times²¹, but up to seventy-times²² [and]   22
    seven. °For this reason, the kingdom *of* the heavens became-like²³ *a* man *who was a* king, who   23
    wished^M to settle *the* account^N with his slaves^O

    1D. "And he having begun to settle²⁴ *it*, one debtor^P *of* ten-thousand talents²⁵ was brought to him   24

        1E. "But he not having *the means* to pay^Q, the master ordered *that* he be sold— and *his*   25
            wife and *his* children and all that he has— and *that it* be paid
        2E. "Then the slave, having fallen, was prostrating-himself²⁶ *before* him, saying, 'Be²⁷   26
            patient²⁸ with me and I will pay everything *to* you'
        3E. "And having felt-deep feelings^R [of compassion], the master *of* that slave released^S   27
            him and forgave^L him the loan²⁹

    2D. "But having gone out, that slave found one *of* his fellow-slaves^T who owed^U him *a*   28
    hundred denarii³⁰

        1E. "And having seized him, he was choking^V *him*, saying, 'Pay^Q me³¹, since³² you are
            owing^U *me* something'
        2E. "Then his fellow slave, having fallen³³, was begging^W him, saying, 'Be patient with   29
            me and I will pay *it*³⁴ *to* you'
        3E. "And the *one* was not willing^M, but having gone, he threw him into prison until he   30
            should pay the *amount* being owed

    3D. "Then his fellow slaves, having seen the *things* having taken place, were extremely grieved^X.   31
        And having come, they made-clear^Y *to* their master all the *things* having taken place
    4D. "Then, having summoned him, his master says *to* him, 'Evil^Z slave! I forgave^L you all that   32
        debt because you begged^W me. °Should not you also have³⁵ had mercy on your fellow   33
        slave, as I also had mercy on you?'
    5D. "And having become angry³⁶, his master handed him over *to* the tormenters³⁷ until which   34
        time he should pay^Q all the *amount* being owed³⁸
    6D. "So also My heavenly Father will do *to* you if you do not forgive³⁹— each *one* his   35
        brother— from your hearts"

1. Compare Lk 17:3.
2. This is a different case. What should be done when you are suffering an injury, not inflicting one?
3. Some manuscripts omit "against you" {C}.
4. Or, "reprove, rebuke, convict". On this word, see Eph 5:11. Note the two separate commands, "Go, expose", not as so often in Matthew "Having gone, expose". This also occurs in 8:4, 19:21; 21:28; 28:10, etc.
5. That is, gained him for the benefit of the kingdom. On this word, see Mk 8:36. Compare 1 Pet 3:1.
6. Or, "on the basis of". Same phrase as in 2 Cor 13:1, and similar to 1 Tim 5:19; Heb 10:28. It refers to Deut 19:15.
7. The church, through its leaders, speaks as one with the voice of Christ, focusing the individual on the impact of this sin upon his relationship with God, and with the Christian community. He must choose between them.
8. Or, "pagan, non-believer". On this word, see 3 Jn 7.
9. A tax collector was viewed as a traitor to Israel, a servant of the enemy (Rome). They were not allowed in the synagogue, and no one ate or socialized with them. They were outcasts. Used 21 times. GK *5467*. On the tax system, see the note on Lk 3:13.
10. On "bind" and "loose", see 16:19. Here, the "you" in "you bind" and "you loose" is plural. Some think it refers to "the church" in v 17. Others think it refers to the apostles. In 16:19, it was singular, referring to Peter.
11. This is a participle, it "will be having been bound". Likewise with "loose", it "will be having been loosed". Same tense as in 16:19. Whatever you as a church "bind" will correspond to what has already been "bound" in heaven. Some think Jesus means "whatever you as a church permit or forbid with regard to his behavior...". If so, this verse is in regard to the church's behavioral decision—whether what the brother did was sin or not. Since the Jewish "traditions of the elders" which had guided their lives were rejected, new decisions would have to be made by the church based on the OT Scripture under the guidance of God. This divine guidance is what is promised here. On the other views, see 16:19.
12. Some think that Jesus now speaks with regard to the church's disciplinary decision in v 17. Even if the "church" is only two or three, if they are in agreement about what they want to ask of God (v 19), then God will do it (as in 1 Cor 5:5). Others think this refers to the apostles. Others think that v 19-20 are not connected to v 15-18 at all, but form a separate point regarding prayer in general (5C.).
13. Some manuscripts omit this word {C}. See 5:18 on it.
14. Same word as in Lk 5:36; Act 5:9; 15:15. Elsewhere only as "make an agreement" in Mt 20:2, 13. GK *5244*. Related to "harmony" in 2 Cor 6:15. Some manuscripts say "shall agree" {N}.
15. Or, "thing". Same word as in Rom 16:2; 1 Cor 6:1; 2 Cor 7:11; 1 Thes 4:6. Elsewhere only as "thing" in Lk 1:1; Act 5:4; Heb 6:18; 10:1; 11:1, Jam 3:16. GK *4547*.
16. The divine guidance promised is made explicit here.
17. This is a participle, "are having been gathered-together". GK *5251*.
18. Or, "with reference to". GK *1650*. Not the same word as in v 5.
19. Compare Lk 17:4.
20. Peter is responding to v 15, "if he listens to you...". The rabbis taught that one should forgive three times.
21. Elsewhere only in v 21; Lk 17:4. GK *2232*.
22. That is, seventy occasions, as with "seven-times" in v 21, 22. Some think Jesus means "seventy-times [and] seven" (77 times, as this exact phrase is used in Gen 4:24). Others think He means "seventy-times [times] seven" (490 times). In either case, it is more times than one can keep track of. It is like asking how often we should "love one another". Used only here. GK *1574*.
23. Or, "was like". Same word and grammar as in 13:24. It is like this in that our own forgiveness gives us a standing obligation to forgive others.
24. Or, "to be settling". The grammar means "having started the process of settling it". On this word, see Mt 25:19.
25. This is a huge amount of money. One silver talent was 6000 denarii (see 20:2), that is, 6000 day's wages for a laborer, the wages for twenty years of work. So 10,000 talents is 60 million denarii, which is 600,000 times more than the slave in verse 28 owed. Such is our debt to God versus others' debt to us. A gold talent was worth much more, a copper talent less. Elsewhere only in 25:15, 16, 20, 22, 24, 25, 28. GK *5419*.
26. On this word, see "worship" in 14:33.
27. Some manuscripts say "Master, be..." {A}.
28. Or, "Have patience". On this word, see 1 Cor 13:4. Same word as in v 29.
29. Used only here. GK *1245*. Related to "lend" in Lk 6:34.
30. On this word, see 20:2. A hundred day's wages.
31. Some manuscripts include "me" {N}.
32. Or, "if". The grammar implies that the lender accepted this as the fact of the matter, so for clarity it is rendered "since" here.
33. Some manuscripts add "at his feet" {N}.
34. Some manuscripts say "everything" {K}.
35. On the idiom "should have", see 25:27. The grammar of this question expects a "yes" answer.
36. Or, "wrathful". On this word, see Rev 11:18.
37. Or, "torturers", the ones in the prison. Used only here. GK *991*. Related to "torment" in Rev 14:10.
38. Some manuscripts add *to* him" {N}. Of course, he would never be able to repay it.
39. On this word, see 6:12. Some manuscripts add "their trespasses" {N}.

A. Act 16:40 B. Jam 2:24 C. Lk 17:34, taken D. Rom 10:17 E. Mk 13:14, standing F. Mk 5:36, ignore G. Mt 5:18 H. Mt 6:10 J. 2 Thes 2:7 K. Act 25:8 L. Mt 6:12 M. Jn 7:17, willing N. 1 Cor 12:8, word O. Rom 6:17 P. Rom 1:14 Q. Mt 16:27, render R. Mt 9:36 S. Mt 5:31, sends away T. Rev 19:10 U. 1 Jn 4:11, ought V. Mt 13:7 W. Rom 12:8, exhorting X. 2 Cor 7:9 Y. Mt 13:36 Z. Act 25:18

Matthew 19:1   64   Verse

13A.[1] And it came about *that* when Jesus finished these[2] words, He went-away[A] from Galilee and came into the districts[3] *of* Judea, beyond the Jordan. °And large crowds followed Him, and He cured[B] them there   19:1

     2

   1B. And Pharisees[4] came to Him— testing[C] Him, and saying[5], "Is it lawful[D] *for a* man[6] to send-away[7] his wife for[8] any reason[9]?"   3

     1C. And the *One*, having responded, said[10], "Did you not read[11] [in Gen 1:27] that the *One* having created[12] from *the* beginning[13] 'made[E] them male[14] and female[15]'? °And He said [in Gen 2:24], 'For this reason[16] *a* man will leave-behind[F] *his* father and *his* mother and will be joined[17] *to* his wife. And the two will be[18] one flesh'—   4

     5

       1D. "So then, they are no longer two, but one flesh   6

       2D. "Therefore what God paired-together[19], let *a* person[20] not separate[21]"

     2C. They say *to* Him, "Why then did Moses command[G] *us* to give *a* certificate[22] *of* divorce[23] and send her[24] away?"   7

     3C. He says *to* them that "Moses permitted[25] you to send away your wives because of your hardness-of-heart[H]. But from the beginning it has not been so[26]   8

       1D.[27] "And I say *to* you that whoever sends away his wife not[28] based on sexual-immorality[29], and[30] marries[J] another, is committing-adultery[31]"   9

     4C. His[32] disciples[K] say *to* Him, "If the case[33] *of* the man with the wife is like this, it is not expedient[34] to marry!"   10

     5C. But the *One* said *to* them, "Not all give-way-to[35] this[36] statement[L], but [only] *ones to* whom it has been given[37]   11

       1D. "For there are eunuchs[38] who were born[M] thus[N] from *a* mother's womb[O]. And there are eunuchs who were made-eunuchs by people[P]. And there are eunuchs who made themselves eunuchs[39] for the sake of the kingdom *of* the heavens   12

       2D. "Let the *one* being able to give way, give way"[40]

Matthew 19:12

1. Parallel account at Mk 10:1.
2. That is, chapter 18. On this phrase, see 13:53. This ends the ministry of Jesus in Galilee.
3. Or, "boundaries". On this word, see Mk 10:1.
4. Some manuscripts say "the Pharisees" {N}.
5. Some manuscripts add "*to* Him" {N}.
6. Note that as in Mt 5:31, this question is asked from the Jewish man's perspective. Jesus is not fully addressing the question of divorce here, but is refuting the commonly held Jewish husband's point of view.
7. That is, divorce. On this word, see Mt 5:31. Same word as in v 7, 8, 9. Not related to "divorce" in v 7.
8. Or, "based on, according to, with respect to, because of ". GK *2848*.
9. Or, "for all grounds, for every charge, for every cause". That is, for any fault he might accuse her. This was the Pharisees' understanding of "some uncleanness" in Deut 24:1, and their accepted practice, though some taught a stricter standard. They all thought divorce was the husband's right, debating only over the grounds. Jesus rejects this, causing the reaction in v 10. Same word as "case" in v 10. On this word, see "charge" in Jn 18:38.
10. Some manuscripts add "*to* them" {N}.
11. The answer is not found in Deut 24, the exception, but in Gen 1-2, the rule, the intention of God.
12. Instead of "created", some manuscripts say "made" {B}, "the *One* having made *them*".
13. That is, God made them as a pair from the beginning. This phrase, "from *the* beginning", is elsewhere only in v 8; 24:21; Mk 10:6; 13:19; Lk 1:2; Jn 8:44; 15:27; Act 26:4; 2 Pet 3:4; 1 Jn 1:1; 2:7, 13, 14, 24; 3:8, 11; 2 Jn 5, 6. This is the Greek word order. Some take this phrase with what precedes, and render it "at the beginning".
14. These two words refer to the man and the woman as different biological creations. This word is elsewhere only in Mk 10:6; Lk 2:23; Rom 1:27; Gal 3:28; Rev 12:5, 13. GK *781*.
15. Elsewhere only in Mk 10:6; Rom 1:26, 27; Gal 3:28. GK *2559*. Related to the word "nipple" (not in NT), and "nursing" in 21:16. That is, God made "man" (Gen 1:27, referring to humankind) as "male and female", a complimentary pair.
16. That is, because God made them to be a pair.
17. Or, "join *himself*". On this word, see 1 Cor 6:16. Related word in Mk 10:7.
18. This is an idiom reflecting a Hebrew way of speaking. Literally, "will be for one flesh".
19. Or, "yoked-together", joined as a pair. Elsewhere only in Mk 10:9. GK *5183*. Related to "pair" in Lk 14:19.
20. Or, "*a* man, *a* human, man". That Jesus meant this in the broader sense is clear in Mk 10:9-12, but the Pharisees here would have taken Him to mean "a man, a husband". See the note on Mk 10:9. On this word, see "mankind" in Mt 4:4.
21. In other words, God made the two to be permanently one. This is His plan for a man and a woman. Do not send her away. Same word as in Mk 10:9; 1 Cor 7:10, 11, 15; and Rom 8:35, 39; Phm 15; Heb 7:26. Elsewhere only as "depart" in Act 1:4; 18:1, 2. GK *6004*.
22. Or, "writing". Same word as in Mk 10:4, on which see "scroll" in Rev 5:1.
23. The certificate was to protect the wife, so that she could remarry. On this word, see 5:31.
24. Some manuscripts omit this word {C}, leaving it implied. "Send away" is used exactly as in 5:31.
25. On Moses' command in Deut 24:1, see Mk 10:4. He did not command it, nor does Jesus command it here.
26. That is, since creation it has never been God's desire that a man should divorce his wife. It comes from hardness of heart. The hardness of heart by the husbands under discussion here is a sin. The sending her away with the legal protection of the divorce certificate was permitted but not endorsed by Moses, and it results in another sin, as Jesus says next.
27. Compare also Mt 5:32; Lk 16:18.
28. This implies that whoever sends his wife away based on sexual immorality, and marries another, is not committing adultery. Some think this means that Jesus is permitting divorce for this cause. He is permitting what He says Moses permitted, but further defining the grounds. Others think it means only that he is not committing adultery because she has already done so, and that it does not address the question of what the husband should do if she has done this. All agree that Jesus is not endorsing the view that a husband must divorce his wife for this cause, as some in that day taught.
29. Some manuscripts say "except for *a* matter *of* sexual immorality" {B}, as in 5:32.
30. Instead of "and...adultery", some manuscripts say "makes her commit adultery" {B}, as in 5:32.
31. Or, "is an adulterer". The main point Jesus is making is, Do not send her away. It is not lawful for a husband to send his wife away for every reason, v 3. On this word, see 5:32b. Some manuscripts add "And the *one* marrying *a* woman having been sent away from *her* husband is committing adultery" {B}, similar to 5:32.
32. Some manuscripts say "the disciples" {C}.
33. Or, "charge, cause". Same word as "reason" in v 3. Some think the disciples mean "if this is the only valid reason a man can use to divorce his wife"; others, more generally, "if this is the condition or status of the husband". In either case, this direct attack on male authority is shocking even to the disciples.
34. Or, "advantageous, profitable". Or, "it is better not to marry". On this word, see "beneficial" in 1 Cor 6:12.
35. Or, "make room for, accept". Same word as twice in v 12. On this word, see "make room" in 2 Pet 3:9. Jesus does not deny what the disciples say, but adds to it that not all have the ability to live this way, as unmarried ones. This is clearly an understatement, because God made them as a pair from the beginning. Marriage is for most people. But Jesus states that remaining single is also a gift, validating this choice in contradiction of the views of many in His day.
36. Some manuscripts say "the statement" {C}.
37. Both remaining single and being married are gifts of God, 1 Cor 7:7.
38. That is, celibate or castrated males. On this word, see Act 8:27. Here Jesus refers to a person born with a disposition to remain unmarried. Next, to one who is forced into that condition by castration. Last, to one who chooses that path for the sake of the kingdom (who is unmarried by choice for this purpose).
39. That is, by abstaining from marriage, not by castrating themselves.
40. Why? To serve God without distraction (1 Cor 7: 29-35), a course Paul recommended (1 Cor 7:8).

A. Mt 13:53 B. Mt 8:7 C. Heb 2:18, tempted D. 1 Cor 6:12 E. Rev 13:13, does F. Act 6:2 G. Mk 10:3 H. Mk 16:14 J. 1 Cor 7:9
K. Lk 6:40 L. 1 Cor 12:8, word M. 1 Jn 2:29 N. Jn 3:16, so O. Lk 1:15 P. Mt 4:4, mankind

2B.[1] Then children[A] were brought to Him in order that He might lay[B] *His* hands on them and pray. But the disciples rebuked[2] them[3] 13

    1C. But Jesus said, "Permit[4] the children, and do not be forbidding[5] them to come to Me. For the kingdom *of* the heavens is *of* such[6] ones" 14
    2C. And having laid *His* hands on them, He proceeded from there 15

3B.[7] And behold— one having come to Him said, "Teacher[8], what good *thing* should[9] I do in order that I may have[10] eternal[C] life?" 16

    1C. And the *One* said *to* him, "Why do you ask Me about *what is* good? There is One *Who is* good.[11] But if you wish to enter into life, keep the commandments[D]" 17

        1D. He says *to* Him, "Which *ones*?" 18
        2D. And Jesus said, "You shall not murder[E]. You shall not commit-adultery[F] You shall not steal. You shall not give-false-testimony[G]. *Be honoring[H] your* father and *your* mother. And, You shall love your neighbor as[12] yourself" 19
        3D. The young man says *to* Him, "I kept[J] all these *things*[13]. What am I still lacking[K]?" 20
        4D. Jesus said *to* him, "If you wish to be perfect[14], go, sell your possessions[15] and give *it to* the poor[L], and you will have treasure in *the* heavens. And come, be following Me" 21
        5D. But having heard the[16] statement, the young man went away grieving[M]. For he was having[17] many properties[18] 22

    2C. And Jesus said *to* His disciples, "Truly I say *to* you that *a* rich *one* will enter with-difficulty[19] into the kingdom *of* the heavens. *And again I say *to* you, it is easier *that a* camel go through *a* hole[20] *of a* needle[21], than *that a* rich *one* enter into the kingdom *of* God" 23-24
    3C. And having heard *it*, the[22] disciples were extremely astounded[N], saying, "Who then can be saved[O]?" 25
    4C. And having looked at *them*, Jesus said *to* them, "With humans, this is impossible[P]. But with God, all *things are* possible[23]" 26
    5C. Then Peter, having responded, said *to* Him, "Behold— **we** left everything and followed You. What then will there be[24] *for* us?" 27
    6C. And Jesus said *to* them 28

        1D.[25] "Truly I say *to* you that you, the *ones* having followed Me— at the regeneration[26] when the Son *of* Man sits on *the* throne *of* His glory[27], **you** also will sit on twelve thrones, judging[28] the twelve tribes[Q] *of* Israel[29]
        2D. "And everyone who left houses or brothers or sisters or father or mother[30] or children or fields for the sake of My name will receive[31] *a* hundred-fold[32], and will inherit[R] eternal life 29
        3D.[33] "But many[34] first[35] *ones* will be last[S], and last *ones,* first.[36] *For the kingdom *of* the heavens is like *a* man *who is a* house-master[37], who went out together with early-morning[38] to hire workers into his vineyard 30-20:1

            1E. "And having made-an-agreement[39] with the workers for *a* denarius[40] *for* the day, he sent them out into his vineyard 2

                1F. "And having gone out around *the* third[41] hour, he saw others standing idle[42] in the marketplace. *And *to* those he said, '**You** also go into the vineyard, and I will give you whatever may be right[T]'. *And the *ones* went 3-5

1. Parallel account at Mk 10:13; Lk 18:15.
2. Or, "warned them [to stay away]". Same word as used by Matthew in 8:26; 16:22; 17:18; 20:31; and as "warned" in 12:16. On this word, see "warn" in 1 Tim 4:2.
3. That is, those who brought them. Luke calls the children "babies", Lk 18:15. See Mk 10:13.
4. Or, "Leave the children *alone*", taking this as a stand-alone command, as in 27:49. This is the Greek word order of this sentence. Some arrange it "Permit the children to come to Me, and do not be forbidding them", as in the Greek word order of Mk 10:14 and Lk 18:16. Here, "to come to Me" goes with both commands.
5. Or, "hindering, preventing, trying to stop". On this word, see 1 Cor 14:39.
6. It is "*made up of* such *ones*", or it "*belongs to* such *ones*". That is, to "childlike persons" (see 18:3), whether physically a child or an adult, as Mk 10:15 and Lk 18:17 go on to state.
7. Parallel account at Mk 10:17; Lk 18:18.
8. Some manuscripts say "Good teacher" {A}, as in Mk 10:17; Lk 18:18.
9. Or, "shall", as also in Mk 10:17. Compare Lk 18:18.
10. On this question, compare Mk 10:17; Lk 10:25.
11. Instead of "Why... good", some manuscripts say "Why do you call Me good? No one *is* good except One— God" {A}, as in Mk 10:18; Lk 18:19. On "good", see 1 Tim 5:10b.
12. Or, "like". Love your neighbor in the same manner as you love yourself. See Lev 19:18. This command is repeated in 22:39; Mk 12:31; Lk 10:27; Rom 13:9; Gal 5:14; Jam 2:8. See also Mt 5:43; Mk 12:33; Rom 15:2; Eph 4:25; Jam 4:12. This word is used 504 times. GK *6055*. On "love", see "*devoutly*-love" in Jn 21:15.
13. Some manuscripts add "from my youth" {A}, as in Mk 10:20.
14. Or, "complete", so as to "lack" nothing. On this word, see "complete" in 1 Cor 13:10.
15. Or, "belongings, property", like the ones in 13:45-46 and Act 4:34-35 did. This is a participle, on which see Heb 10:34. Compare Lk 12:33; 14:33.
16. Some manuscripts say "this"; others say "having heard *it*" {N}.
17. The grammar places emphasis on this man's continuing possession of his things.
18. Or, "possessions, acquisitions". Elsewhere only in Mk 10:22; Act 2:45; 5:1. GK *3228*. Related to "acquire" in 1 Thes 4:4.
19. Or, "difficultly". Elsewhere only as "difficultly" in Mk 10:23; Lk 18:24. GK *1552*. Related to "difficult" in Mk 10:24. This is another shocking statement. Wealth was considered to be a clear sign of the blessing of God.
20. Or, "bored-hole". Used only here. GK *5585*. The related verb (not used in the NT) means "to bore, pierce". Matthew, Mark and Luke each use a different word. See Mk 10:25. In other words, it is humanly impossible, as they understood (v 25), and Jesus says (v 26).
21. That is, a sewing needle. Elsewhere only in Mk 10:25. GK *4827*. Related to "to sew" in Mk 2:21 and to "seamless" (un-sewn) in Jn 19:23. Luke uses a different word, Lk 18:25.
22. Some manuscripts say "His" {N}.
23. Both "impossible" and "possible" are related to "can" in v 25, which could be rendered "who can-possibly be saved?".
24. Or, "What then will happen *to* us?". The word "be" sometimes means "happen", as in 16:22.
25. Compare Lk 22:28-30.
26. Or, "rebirth [of the world]". It is explained by what follows. P-M (see Rev 20:1 on P-M and A-M) thinks Jesus is referring to the millennial kingdom on earth (see Rev 20:1-4 on this); A-M, to the new heavens and earth where there will also be twelve foundations with their names on them, Rev 21. On this word, see Tit 3:5.
27. Or, "His throne *of* glory", or, "His glorious throne". Same phrase as in 25:31, when Jesus comes in glory.
28. That is, administering justice, serving as judge over. On this word, see 7:1.
29. P-M (see Rev 20:1) takes this literally; A-M, as symbolic of all believers.
30. Some manuscripts add "or wife" {C}, as in Lk 18:29.
31. Some think Jesus means "at the regeneration", like the apostles, v 28. Others think He means "in this age", as in Mk 10:30; Lk 18:30. If so, those who make such sacrifices will receive "a hundred houses, fields", "a hundred brothers, sisters, fathers, mothers, children", within the family of believers of which the person is now a part.
32. That is, a hundred times as much. Elsewhere only in Mk 10:30; Lk 8:8. GK *1671*. This may simply be a hyperbole meaning "many times as much", as Lk 18:30 renders it. And here, some manuscripts say "many times as much" {B}.
33. Compare Mk 10:31; Lk 13:30.
34. Note that Jesus says "many", that is, some of the first ones, but not all of them (the whole class).
35. Or, "foremost, chief, prominent, leading *ones*". Jesus could mean first in time, or first in status. On this word, see 1Cor 15:3.
36. The parable that follows is intended to explain this statement. Jesus is continuing to address their question of 19:27, "what will there be for us?". That is, what is the reward for our sacrifices? This is still on the disciples' mind in 20:20. The point of the parable seems to be not to envy others, for His rewards will not be as we might predict based on what we know. On this statement, compare 20:16; Mk 10:31; Lk 13:30.
37. Or, "a master of a house, a house owner". Same word as in 13:27, 52; 20:11; 21:33; 24:43; Mk 14:14; Lk 12:39; 13:25; 14:21. Elsewhere only as "household-master" in Mt 10:25; and "master" in Lk 22:11. GK *3867*. Related to "manage the house" in 1 Tim 5:14.
38. That is, the house-master went out with daybreak, with sunrise. On this word, see Mk 13:35.
39. Based on the fact that the master enters a contract with this group and not with the others, some think the thrust of the parable is that Jews (who have a "contract") and Gentiles (who do not, and who come later) will both receive the same reward of salvation. Note Lk 13:30. Others think this detail points to self-seeking people who say "what is there for me?" like Peter in 19:27. This attitude shows itself again in their grumbling, v 11. The other three groups represent people who serve God without thought of a reward, simply trusting Him to be fair. God rewards both sovereignly.
40. The agreement was "One denarius for a day's work", the standard pay. A denarius was a Roman silver coin, a day's wage for a laborer or a soldier. Today, compare it to the minimum wage times eight hours. Elsewhere only in 18:28; 20:9, 10, 13; 22:19; Mk 6:37; 12:15; 14:5; Lk 7:41; 10:35; 20:24; Jn 6:7; 12:5; Rev 6:6. GK *1324*.
41. That is, 9 A.M. The sixth hour would be noon, the ninth, 3 P.M., the eleventh, 5 P.M. They worked until 6 P.M.
42. Or, "not working, unemployed". Same word as in v 6. On this word, see "useless" in Jam 2:20.

A. 1 Jn 2:14 B. Lk 10:30, laid on C. Mt 25:46 D. Mk 12:28 E. Jam 4:2 F. Mt 5:32 G. Mk 14:56 H. 1 Tim 5:3 J. Jn 12:25 K. Lk 15:14, be in need L. Gal 4:9 M. 2 Cor 7:9 N. Mt 7:28 O. Lk 19:10 P. Heb 6:4 Q. Rev 1:7 R. Gal 4:30 S. Heb 1:2 T. Rom 1:17, righteous

	2F.	"And[1] again having gone out around *the* sixth and *the* ninth hour, he did similarly	
	3F.	"And having gone out around the eleventh *hour,* he found others standing there[2]. And he says *to* them, 'Why are you standing here idle[A] the whole day? They say *to* him, 'Because no one hired us'. He says *to* them, '**You** also go into the vineyard[3]'	6 7

    2E. "And having become evening, the master[B] *of* the vineyard says *to* his manager[4], 'Call the workers, and pay[C] them the wages[D]— beginning from[5] the last *ones*, up to the first *ones*'   8

    3E. "And having come, the *ones hired* around the eleventh hour received *a* denarius apiece   9

    4E. "And having come, the first *ones* thought[E] that they would[6] receive more. And they also themselves received the[7] denarius[8] apiece. *And having received *it,* they were grumbling[F] against the house-master, saying, 'These last *ones* did[G] one hour, and you made[G] them equal[H] *to* us— the *ones* having borne[J] the burden[K] *of* the day and the burning-heat[L]'[9]   10
11
12

    5E. "But the *one,* having responded, said *to* one *of* them, 'Friend[10], I am not wronging[M] you. Did you not make-an-agreement[N] *with* me *for a* denarius? *Take what *is* yours and go. But I want to give *to* this last *one* as *I* also *gave to* you   13
14

        1F. 'Or[11] is it not lawful[O] *for* me to do what I want[P] with my *things*?   15
        2F. 'Or is your eye[12] evil because **I** am good?'[13]

    6E. "Thus the last *ones* will be first, and the first *ones,* last"[14]   16

4B.[15] And while going up to Jerusalem, Jesus took aside the twelve disciples[16] privately[Q], and said *to* them on the road[17], *"Behold— we are going up to Jerusalem. And the Son *of* Man will be handed-over[R] *to* the chief priests and scribes. And they will condemn[S] Him *to* death, and will hand Him over *to* the Gentiles so that *they might* mock[T] and whip[U] and crucify[V] *Him.* And He will be raised[18] *on* the third day"   17
18
19

5B.[19] Then the mother *of* the sons *of* Zebedee came to Him with her sons[20], prostrating-*herself*[21] and asking something from Him   20

    1C. And the *One* said *to* her, "What do you want?"   21
    2C. She says *to* Him, "Say[22] that these two sons *of* mine may sit one on Your right *side* and one on Your left *side* in Your kingdom"[23]
    3C. But having responded, Jesus said, "You[24] do not know what you are asking. Are you able to drink the cup which **I** am about to drink[25]?"   22

        1D. They say *to* Him, "We are able"
        2D. He says *to* them, "You will drink **My cup**[26]— but the sitting on My right *side* and on *the* left *side,* this[27] is not Mine to give, but *it is for* whom it has been prepared[W] by My Father"   23

    4C.[28] And having heard-*of it,* the ten were indignant[29] about the two brothers. *But Jesus, having summoned them, said, "You know that the rulers[X] *of* the Gentiles are lording-over[30] them, and the great *ones* are exercising-authority-over[31] them. *It shall not be[32] so among you   24-25
26

        1D. "But whoever wants to become great among you shall be your servant[33], *and whoever wants to be first among you shall be your slave[Y]   27

            1E. "Just as the Son *of* Man did not come to be served[Z], but to serve, and to give His life *as a* ransom[34] for many"   28

1. Some manuscripts omit this word {C}.
2. Some manuscripts add "idle" {N}.
3. Some manuscripts add "and you will receive whatever may be right" {N}.
4. Or, "foreman". On this word, see "steward" in Lk 8:3.
5. Or, "having begun from". In English, we prefer to say "beginning with" or "starting with". This idiom makes reference to the point or place from (at) which, or the person from (with) which the action in the context begins (or began). Thus here, the paying begins with the last ones. This idiom is elsewhere only in Lk 23:5; 24:27, 47; Jn 8:9; Act 1:22; 8:35; 10:37.
6. More literally, "they will receive", as the Greek typically phrases it.
7. Some manuscripts omit this word {C}, so that it says "*a* denarius".
8. Some think the denarius represents "eternal life", 19:29. Others think it represents the "hundred-fold" reward for our sacrifices, 19:29. It is a hundred times whatever one has "left".
9. Thus the last are paid first; all receive the same; the first expected more, more than was promised.
10. This word also means "comrade, companion, mate, fellow, associate, partner, colleague". It is used of a crewmate, comrade-in-arms, fellow partisan, fellow member of a group, etc. Elsewhere only in 22:12; 26:50. GK *2279*.
11. Some manuscripts omit this word {C}.
12. This is the common word for "eye", used 100 times. GK *4057*.
13. That is, are you envious because I am generous to them? "Evil eye" is also in Mk 7:22.
14. Clearly, some who appear to deserve the most will receive the same as others who appear to deserve the least, and vice versa. Beyond this, some think Jesus means "first" in the sense of time or seniority, and identify this group with the Jews (see v 2) or those who have been Christians longer. Those who come later in calendar time (the Gentiles, or Christians after the apostles) or who are Christians for a shorter amount of their lifetime, will receive the same reward— eternal life. Thus, the first and last on earth are equal in heaven. Others think He means "foremost", and identify this group with those who appear to be first in this world (because of their labor, position, sacrifice, or riches). Those less prominent will receive the same reward— a hundredfold— based on God's sovereign choice and values, not earthly appearances. Thus, the hundredfold reward of some who are first on earth will result in them being last in heaven, behind some who were considered last on earth. Consult the commentaries on these and other views. Some manuscripts add "For many are called *ones*, but few are chosen *ones*" {A}, as in 22:14.
15. Parallel account at Mk 10:32; Lk 18:31.
16. Some manuscripts omit this word {C}.
17. Some manuscripts say "privately on the road, and said *to* them" {N}.
18. Or, "will arise". On this word, see "arose" in 28:6.
19. Parallel account at Mk 10:35.
20. That is, James and John, Mk 10:35.
21. On this word, see "worship" in 14:33.
22. Or, "Speak *it*", say the word. This is the common word for say or speak, on which see Jn 12:49. Some render it "command" here.
23. When the apostles sit upon their twelve thrones (19:28), let my sons sit next to you.
24. This word is plural. Jesus answers all three.
25. Some manuscripts add "or be baptized the baptism which I am baptized" {A}, as in Mk 10:38.
26. Jesus uses grammar that emphasizes the contrast between the two halves of this sentence. Some manuscripts add "and you will be baptized the baptism which I am baptized" {N}, as in Mk 10:39. James was killed with a sword in Act 12:2. John was banished to Patmos, Rev 1:9.
27. Some manuscripts omit this word {C}
28. Compare Lk 22:24-27.
29. Or, "aroused, angry, displeased". Elsewhere only in 21:15; 26:8; Mk 10:14, 41; 14:4; Lk 13:14. GK *24*.
30. Or, "domineering over, ruling over". The rulers reign as masters over their subjects. On this word, see 1 Pet 5:3.
31. They rule by directive, by vested authority. Elsewhere only in Mk 10:42. GK *2980*. Related to the word in Lk 22:25.
32. Some manuscripts say "But it is not so among you" {B}.
33. On this word, see 1 Cor 3:5. Compare Mt 23:11; Mk 9:35.
34. Elsewhere only in Mk 10:45. GK *3389*. Related to "redemption" in Rom 3:24 and Heb 9:12; and "redeem" in 1 Pet 1:18. This is the first time Jesus mentions the reason for His death.

A. Jam 2:20, useless B. Mt 8:2 C. Mt 16:27, render D. Rev 22:12, recompense E. Act 14:19 F. Lk 5:30 G. Rev 13:13, does H. Phil 2:6
J. Mt 8:17, carry K. 1 Thes 2:7, weight L. Jam 1:11 M. Act 7:24 N. Mt 18:19, agree O. 1 Cor 6:12 P. Jn 7:17, willing Q. Mt 14:13
R. Mt 26:21 S. 1 Cor 11:32 T. Lk 23:11 U. Heb 12:6 V. Mt 27:35 W. Mk 14:15 X. Rev 1:5 Y. Rom 6:17 Z. 1 Pet 4:10, ministering

6B.¹ And while they *were* proceeding out from Jericho, *a* large crowd followed Him. °And behold— 29-30
two² blind *men* sitting beside the road, having heard that Jesus was³ going by, cried-out^A saying,
"Have-mercy-on^B us, Master⁴, Son *of* David⁵"

    1C. But the crowd rebuked⁶ them in order that they might keep-silent^C. But the *ones* cried out   31
        louder, saying, "Have mercy on us, Master, Son *of* David"
    2C. And having stopped⁷, Jesus called them, and said, "What do you want Me to do⁸ *for* you?"   32

        1D. They say *to* Him, "Master— that our eyes might be opened!"   33
        2D. And having felt-deep-feelings^D [of compassion], Jesus touched^E their eyes⁹   34
        3D. And they¹⁰ immediately saw-again^F. And they followed Him

7B.¹¹ And when they drew-near^G to Jerusalem, and came to Bethphage, to the Mount *of* Olives, then   21:1
Jesus sent forth two disciples, °saying *to* them, "Proceed to the village before you, and immediately   2
you will find *a* donkey having been tied^H, and *a* colt¹² with her. Having untied^J *them,* bring *them*
to Me. °And if someone says something *to* you, you shall say that 'The Lord¹³ has need^K *of* them',   3
and immediately he will send them forth"

    1C. Now this¹⁴ has taken place in order that the *thing* might be fulfilled having been spoken through   4
        the prophet saying¹⁵ °"Say *to* the daughter^L *of* Zion^M, 'Behold, your King is coming *to* you—   5
        gentle¹⁶, and mounted¹⁷ upon *a* donkey, even upon *a* colt, *a* foal¹⁸ *of a* beast-of-burden¹⁹ "
        [Zech 9:9]
    2C. And the disciples— having proceeded, and having done just as Jesus directed^N them—   6
        brought the donkey and the colt. And they put *their* cloaks on them. And He sat on them²⁰   7
    3C. And most-of²¹ the crowd spread^O their cloaks in the road   8
    4C. And others were cutting branches from the trees and spreading^O *them* in the road
    5C. And the crowds going ahead of Him²², and the *ones* following *Him,* were crying out, saying,   9
        "Hosanna²³ *to* the Son *of* David²⁴. Blessed²⁵ *is* the One coming in *the* name *of the* Lord.
        Hosanna in the highest²⁶ [heavens]"

14A.²⁷ And He having entered into Jerusalem, the whole city was shaken²⁸, saying, "Who is this?" °And the   10-11
crowds were saying, "This is the prophet^P Jesus²⁹ from Nazareth *of* Galilee"

  1B.³⁰ And Jesus entered into the temple³¹   12

    1C. And He threw-out^Q all the *ones* selling and buying in the temple, and overturned the tables *of*
        the money-changers³² and the seats *of* the *ones* selling the doves³³

        1D. And He says *to* them, "It has been written [in Isa 56:7], 'My house shall be called^R *a*   13
            house^S *of* prayer'. But **you** are making³⁴ it *a* den³⁵ *of* robbers³⁶"

    2C. And blind *ones* and lame *ones* came to Him in the temple, and He cured^T them   14
    3C. But the chief priests and the scribes— having seen the marvelous *things* which He did, and   15
        the boys³⁷ crying-out^A in the temple and saying "Hosanna *to* the Son *of* David"— were
        indignant^U °and said *to* Him, "Do You hear what these *boys* are saying?"   16

        1D. And Jesus says *to* them, "Yes— did you never read [in Ps 8:2] that 'You prepared-
            Yourself^V praise³⁸ out of *the* mouth *of* children³⁹ and nursing⁴⁰ *ones*'?"
        2D.⁴¹ And having left them behind^W, He went outside *of* the city to Bethany, and spent-the-   17
            night⁴² there

1. Parallel account at Mk 10:46; Lk 18:35. Compare Mt 9:27-31.
2. Mk 10:46 and Lk 18:35 mention one blind man. Some think they are referring to the prominent speaker.
3. More literally, "is", as the Greek typically phrases it.
4. Some manuscripts omit this word; others say instead "Jesus" {C}. On this word, see 8:2.
5. That is, Messiah. See 9:27.
6. Same word as in 19:13.
7. Or, "stood [still]". On this word, see "standing" in Mk 13:14.
8. This is an idiom, more literally, "What do you want *that* I should do?"
9. Elsewhere only in Mk 8:23. GK *3921*.
10. Some manuscripts say "their eyes" {N}.
11. Parallel account at Mk 11:1; Lk 19:29; Jn 12:12.
12. Or, "foal". That is, you will find a young donkey and its mother. Mk 11:2 and Lk 19:30 mention only the colt Jesus rode.
13. Instead of this referring to Jesus Himself, some think it refers to the "owner", who was with Jesus.
14. Some manuscripts say "Now all this" {N}.
15. This word modifies "prophet", as in 1:22.
16. Same word as in 5:5. This is seen in the King's riding a donkey, not a war stallion.
17. This is a participle, more literally, "having mounted, having gotten upon". On this word, see "set foot" in Act 21:4.
18. Same word as "son" in Gal 3:7.
19. Or, "a yoked animal". This word was used of donkeys, but is not the same word as earlier in the verse.
20. That is, on the garments, on the colt. Perhaps the mother was led along to quiet the colt. Some manuscripts say "cloaks on them, and sat *Him* on them" {K}. The verb "sat on" is used only here. GK *2125*.
21. Or, "the very-large crowd". Same word and grammar as in 11:20. This superlative is elsewhere only as "very-large" in Mk 4:1, and "most" in 1 Cor 14:27. GK *4498*.
22. Some manuscripts omit this word {N}, so that it says, "the crowds going ahead, and the *ones* following".
23. This is a transliterated Hebrew word meaning "Save *us*, we pray" or "help *us*, we pray", as in Ps 118:25, from which the next sentence is also taken. It was used in worship as a shout of praise. They are calling out to Jesus as their Messiah, as the Pharisees understood, v 15. Elsewhere only in v 15; Mk 11:9, 10; Jn 12:13. GK *6057*. Luke 19:38 says "glory".
24. That is, the Messiah. See 9:27.
25. This is a participle, "having been blessed". On this word, see Lk 6:28.
26. That is, in God's presence. Same phrase as in Mk 11:10; Lk 2:14; 19:38. Elsewhere only as a name or description of God, "the Most High", Mk 5:7; Lk 1:32, 35, 76; 6:35; 8:28; Act 7:48; 16:17; Heb 7:1. GK *5736*. Related to "on high" in Lk 1:78; "lifted up" in Jn 8:28; and "highly-*valued*" in Lk 16:15.
27. Parallel account at Mk 11:11.
28. Or, "agitated, stirred up". Related to "earthquake". Elsewhere only in 27:51; 28:4; Heb 12:26; Rev 6:13. GK *4940*.
29. Some manuscripts say "Jesus the prophet" {N}. It can be rendered either way with either Greek word order.
30. Parallel account at Mk 11:15; Lk 19:45. Compare Jn 2:13-22.
31. Some manuscripts add "*of* God" {B}.
32. The money-changers changed foreign currency into Jewish currency. Elsewhere only in Mk 11:15; Jn 2:15. GK *3142*. This word comes from the word for "small coin".
33. These were used for sacrifices, as Joseph and Mary did for Jesus, Lk 2:24.
34. Some manuscripts say "you made" {N}. Compare Mk 11:17.
35. Or, "hideout". Same word as in Mk 11:17; Lk 19:46. Elsewhere only as "cave" in Jn 11:38; Heb 11:38; Rev 6:15. GK *5068*.
36. Or, "bandits, pirates, plunderers". Also used of a political insurrectionist, revolutionary. Elsewhere only in this phrase in Mk 11:17; Lk 19:46; of the two crucified with Jesus in Mt 27:38, 44; Mk 15:27; of Barabbas in Jn 18:40; of one distinguished from a "thief" in Jn 10:1, 8; of Jesus in Mt 26:55; Mk 14:48; Lk 22:52; and in Lk 10:30, 36; 2 Cor 11:26. GK *3334*.
37. Or, "male children". Perhaps these were twelve-year-olds, like Jesus in Lk 2:43 (same word). Same word as in Mt 2:16. GK *4090*. This could also mean "children" (boys and girls), however Matthew uses a different but related word (GK *4086*) nine times to mean this, as in 11:16; 14:21; 18:2; 19:13.
38. Elsewhere only in Lk 18:43. GK *142*. Related word in Rom 15:11.
39. Same word as in 11:25. On this word, see "infants" in 1 Cor 3:1.
40. Or, "sucking *ones*", that is, nursing babies, as also in Lk 11:27. Some nursed up to three years old (2 Macc 7:27). The point is, "In the first words of the smallest children". If God accepts praise from these little ones in Ps 8, why not these boys now? He will bring it from the stones if necessary, Lk 19:40. Elsewhere only meaning "nursing mothers" (ones giving suck) in Mt 24:19; Mk 13:17; Lk 21:23. GK *2558*. Related to "female" in Mt 19:4.
41. Compare Jn 12:1 and Mk 11:11-12, which may indicate this is Monday night (as we call it).
42. Or, "lodged, camped outside". Elsewhere only in Lk 21:37. GK *887*.

A. Mt 8:29 B. Rom 12:8, showing mercy C. Mt 4:39, be still D. Mt 9:36 E. 1 Cor 7:1 F. Act 22:13, look up G. Lk 21:28 H. 1 Cor 7:27, bound J. Mt 5:19, break K. Tit 3:14 L. Lk 13:16 M. Jn 12:15 N. Mt 27:10 O. Mk 14:15 P. 1 Cor 12:28 Q. Jn 12:31, cast out R. Rom 8:30 S. Mk 3:20 T. Mt 8:7 U. Mt 20:24 V. Rom 9:22 W. Act 6:2, left behind

2B.[1] Now early-in-the-morning[2], while returning to the city, He was hungry. °And having seen one fig 18-19
tree near the road, He went to it, and found nothing on it except leaves only[3]

    1C. And He says *to* it, "May fruit no longer come[4] from you— forever[5]"
    2C. And the fig tree was dried-up[A] at-once[6]
    3C. And having seen *it*, the disciples marveled[B], saying, "How was the fig tree dried up at once?"   20
    4C. And having responded, Jesus said *to* them, "Truly I say *to* you— if you have faith and do not   21
doubt[C], you will not only do the *thing of* the fig tree, but even if you say *to* this mountain, 'Be taken up and be thrown into the sea', it will be done[7]

        1D. "And you will receive all that you ask in prayer, believing[D]"   22

3B.[8] And He having come into the temple, the chief priests and the elders *of* the people came-to Him   23
while *He was* teaching, saying, "By what-kind-of[9] authority[E] are You doing these *things*, and who gave You this authority?"

    1C. And having responded, Jesus said *to* them, "**I** also will ask you one thing[F], which if you tell   24
Me, **I** also will tell you by what-kind-of authority I am doing these *things*— °From where was   25
the baptism[G] *of* John, from heaven or from humans[H]?"
    2C. And the *ones* were discussing[J] among[10] themselves, saying

        1D. "If we say, 'From heaven', He will say *to* us, 'Then for what reason did you not believe him?'
        2D. "But if we say, 'From humans', we fear the crowd[11]. For they all are holding[12] John as   26
a prophet"
        3D. And having responded *to* Jesus, they said, "We do not know"   27

    3C. **He** also said *to* them, "Nor am **I** telling you by what-kind-of authority I am doing these *things*.
But what seems[K] *right* to you?—   28

        1D. "*A* man had two children[L]

            1E. "And having gone to the first he said, 'Child[L], go, work today in the[13] vineyard'. °And   29
the *one*, having responded, said, 'I will not'. But having regretted[14] *it* later, he went[15]
            2E. "And having gone to the other[16], he spoke similarly. And the *one*, having responded,   30
said, 'I *will*, sir[M]', and he did not go[17]
            3E. "Which of the two did the will[N] *of* the father?"   31
            4E. They say, "The first"[18]
            5E. Jesus says *to* them, "Truly I say *to* you that the tax-collectors[O] and the prostitutes[P]
are going-ahead-of[19] you into the kingdom *of* God

                1F. "For John came to you in[20] *the* way *of* righteousness and you did not believe   32
him. But the tax collectors and the prostitutes believed him. And **you**, having seen *it*, did not-even[21] regret *it* later, *that You might* believe him

        2D.[22] "Listen-to another parable[Q]. There was *a* man *who was a* house-master[R], who planted   33
a vineyard, and put *a* fence around it, and dug *a* winepress in it, and built *a* tower. And he rented it *to* farmers[S], and went-on-a-journey[23]

1. Parallel account at Mk 11:12, 20.
2. Treating this from a topical point of view (as he has done throughout this book), Matthew combines a two-part event into one, placing it all on Tuesday morning. Mark gives the chronological perspective. On this word, see "early morning" in Mk 13:35.
3. This is a parable of Israel and its judgment. It had the appearance of life, but no fruit. See Mk 11:13.
4. Or, "come to pass, be, arise". GK *1181*.
5. This is an idiom, "into the age". See Rev 20:10.
6. Or, "immediately". Compare Mk 11:20. Elsewhere only in v 20; Lk 1:64; 4:39; 5:25; 8:44, 47, 55; 13:13; 18:43; 19:11; 22:60; Act 3:7; 5:10; 12:23; 13:11; 16:26, 33. GK *4202*.
7. Or, "it will come about", as this word is rendered in Mk 11:23. On this word, see 6:10.
8. Parallel account at Mk 11:27; Lk 20:1.
9. Or, "what". That is, a prophet's authority? Messiah's? Authority from heaven or humans? This word means "what kind of, what manner of", and simply "what, which". Used 33 times. GK *4481*.
10. Some manuscripts say "with" {N}.
11. That is, that they might stone us, Lk 20:6. Neither answer was politically expedient.
12. Same word as in v 46. See Mk 11:32.
13. Some manuscripts say "my" {N}.
14. Or, "changed *his* mind". Same word as in v 32; 27:3; 2 Cor 7:8. Elsewhere only as "change the mind" in Heb 7:21. GK *3564*.
15. This son represents the tax collectors and prostitutes, v 31.
16. Some manuscripts say "the second" {N}.
17. This son represents the chief priests and elders, v 23.
18. Some manuscripts have the two sons in reverse order, and then say here, "the last" or "the second". Other manuscripts say "the last" here {C}, referring to the son who said yes and did nothing—which is either a copyist's blunder, or it means that the Pharisees deliberately gave the wrong answer to spoil the point.
19. Or, "going before, preceding". On this word, see 2 Jn 9.
20. Or, "in connection with". GK *1877*.
21. That is, the chief priests and elders did not regret their initial refusal to believe John. Some manuscripts say "did not regret" {N}.
22. Parallel account at Mk 12:1; Lk 20:9.
23. Elsewhere only in 25:14, 15; Mk 12:1; Lk 15:13; 20:9. GK *623*. Related to "away from home" in 2 Cor 5:6; and "away on a journey" in Mk 13:34.

A. Mk 3:1, became withered B. Rev 17:8 C. Jam 1:6 D. Jn 3:36 E. Rev 6:8 F. 1 Cor 12:8, word G. Mk 1:4 H. Mt 4:4, mankind J. Lk 5:21, reasoning K. Lk 19:11, thinking L. 1 Jn 3:1 M. Mt 8:2, master N. Jn 7:17 O. Mt 18:17 P. 1 Cor 6:15 Q. Mt 13:3 R. Mt 20:1 S. Jn 15:1

Matthew 21:34	74	Verse

      1E. "And when the time *of* the fruits drew-near[A], he sent forth his slaves[B] to the farmers to receive[C] his fruits. °And the farmers, having taken[C] his slaves, beat[D] one, and killed another, and stoned another   34 / 35

      2E. "Again he sent-forth[E] other slaves— more *than* the first. And they did similarly *to* them   36

      3E. "But finally he sent forth his son to them, saying, 'They will have-regard-for[F] my son'   37

          1F. "But the farmers, having seen the son, said among themselves, 'This is the heir[G]. Come, let us kill him and let us have[1] his inheritance[H]'   38

          2F. "And having taken him, they threw *him* outside *of* the vineyard and killed *him*   39

      4E. "Therefore when the owner *of* the vineyard comes, what will he do *to* those farmers?"   40

      5E. They say *to* Him, "He will miserably destroy[J] *the* miserable[2] *ones* themselves! And he will rent the vineyard *to* other farmers who will give-back[K] the fruits *to* him in their seasons"   41

      6E. Jesus says *to* them, "Did you never read in the Scriptures, '*The* stone which the *ones* building rejected[L], this became[3] *the* head *of the* corner[4]. This came about from *the* Lord, and it is marvelous[M] in our eyes'? [in Ps 118:22-23]   42

          1F. "For this reason[5] I say *to* you that the kingdom *of* God will be taken-away from you, and will be given *to a* nation[6] producing its fruits   43

          2F. "And[7] the *one* having fallen upon this stone will be broken-to-pieces[8]. And[9] upon whomever it may fall, it will crush[10] him"   44

4C. And having heard His parables, the chief priests and the Pharisees knew that He was[11] speaking about them. °And while seeking to seize[N] Him, they feared the crowds, because they were holding[O] Him for *a* prophet[12]   45 / 46

5C.[13] And having responded, Jesus again spoke in parables *to* them, saying, "The kingdom *of the* heavens became-like[14] *a* man *who was a* king, who made wedding-celebrations[P] *for* his son[15]   22:1-2

    1D. "And he sent out his slaves to call the *ones* having been invited[16] to the wedding-celebrations   3

      1E. "And they were not willing[Q] to come

    2D. "Again he sent out other slaves saying, 'Say *to* the *ones* having been invited, "Behold— I have prepared my luncheon[17], my bulls and fatted-cattle having been slaughtered[R], and everything *is* prepared. Come to the wedding-celebrations"'   4

      1E. "But the *ones*, having paid-no-concern[18], departed— one to *his* own field, and another on his business. °And the rest, having seized[N] his slaves, mistreated[S] *them* and killed *them*   5 / 6

    3D. "And the king became angry[19]. And having sent his troops[T], he destroyed[J] those murderers and set their city on fire.[20] °Then he says *to* his slaves, '**The wedding-celebration**[21] is prepared— but the *ones* having been invited were not worthy[U]! °Therefore go to the outlets[22] *of* the roads, and invite all-that you find to the wedding-celebrations'   7 / 8 / 9

      1E. "And having gone out into the roads, those slaves gathered-together[V] all whom they found, both evil[23] and good[24]. And the wedding-hall was filled[W] *with ones* reclining-back [to eat]   10

1. Or, "hold". If we kill him, we can hold on to his inheritance— this vineyard. We can keep it for ourselves. Some manuscripts say "seize" {N}.
2. There is a play on words here. The owner will put the wretches themselves to a wretched death. He will bring the bad ones themselves to a bad end. It would normally be translated, "He will severely destroy *the* evil *ones* themselves". On this word, see "evil" in 3 Jn 11.
3. This is an idiom based on a Hebrew way of speaking. Literally, it "came-to-be for *the* head...". GK *1181*.
4. On this word and phrase, see Mk 12:10.
5. That is, because you rejected Me (v 42), and killed Me (v 39).
6. Or, "people". It will be taken from the nation of Israel and given to a spiritual "nation" (1 Pet 2:9), made up of Jews and Gentiles (Eph 2:11-22). On this word, see "Gentile" in Act 15:23.
7. Some manuscripts omit this verse {C}, which is found in Lk 20:18.
8. Or, "crushed, shattered". Elsewhere only in this statement in Lk 20:18. GK *5314*.
9. Or, "But". GK *1254*.
10. Or, "winnow" him, "scatter" him like chaff. Some take these statements to mean that whether they fall over Christ, or whether He falls on them in their ignorance of Him, the result is the same. Others, that if they fall over Him, they will be broken, but can be healed. But if He falls on them, they will be crushed. Elsewhere only in Lk 20:18. GK *3347*.
11. More literally, "is speaking", as the Greek typically phrases it.
12. Because the crowd held Jesus (v 11) as a prophet (and John, v 26), and understood that Jesus was speaking of the Pharisees, the Pharisees feared the crowd. Compare Mk 12:12; Lk 20:19.
13. Compare Lk 14:15-24.
14. Or, "was like". Same word and grammar as in 13:24.
15. The king is the Father; Jesus is the Son.
16. Or, "called". Same word as just used, so it could be rendered "to call the... called", that is, the Jews. Same word as in v 4, 8, 9, and related to "called" in 14. On this word, see "called" in Rom 8:30.
17. Or, "meal". That is, the main morning meal, usually eaten before noon. With this meal, the celebrations began. They often lasted a week. On this word, see "morning meal" in Lk 14:12.
18. Or, "neglected, disregarded". On this word, see "having neglected" salvation in Heb 2:3.
19. Or, "wrathful". On this word, see Rev 11:18.
20. Some think this city represents Jerusalem, the city of the chief priests and Pharisees. Some then think in addition that the first slaves in v 3 are the OT prophets; the second group in v 4 are the NT prophets; and that this is the destruction of Jerusalem in A.D. 70; and that the others gathered are the Gentiles, the other nation in 21:43. Others think the city is not intended to represent Jerusalem, and do not give a specific meaning to each detail (the gathering of the others in v 9 does not await the fall of Jerusalem nearly 40 years later). In either case, the main point of the parable is clear.
21. Jesus uses grammar that emphasizes the contrast between the two halves of this sentence.
22. That is, the points where the city streets join the country roads. All those coming in from the country (the world) could be approached there, since those in the city (Jerusalem) refused to come. Used only here. GK *1447*.
23. Like the tax collectors and prostitutes, 21:31.
24. Like Nicodemus and Joseph of Arimathea, etc.

A. Lk 21:28   B. Rom 6:17   C. Rom 7:8, taken   D. Jn 18:23   E. Mk 3:14, send out   F. Lk 18:2   G. Rom 8:17   H. Eph 1:14   J. 1 Cor 1:18, perish   K. Mt 16:27, render   L. Heb 12:17   M. Jn 9:30, marvel   N. Heb 4:14, hold on to   O. Mk 11:32   P. Mt 22:11, wedding   Q. Jn 7:17   R. Act 10:13   S. 1 Thes 2:2   T. Act 23:10   U. Rev 16:6   V. Mt 25:35, brought in   W. Act 2:4

4D. "And the king, having come in to see[1] the *ones* reclining-back [to eat], saw there *a* person not having dressed-in[2] *the* clothing *of a* wedding[3]   11

    1E. "And he says *to* him, 'Friend[A], how did you come in here, not having *the* clothing *of a* wedding[4]?'   12
    2E. "But the *one* was silenced[5]

5D. "Then the king said *to* the servants[B], 'Having bound[C] his feet and hands, throw[6] him out, into the outer darkness'   13

    1E. "In that place, there will be the weeping and the grinding[7] *of* teeth
    2E. "For many are called[8] *ones*, but few *are* chosen[9] *ones*"   14

4B.[10] Then the Pharisees, having gone, took counsel[11] so that they might snare[12] Him in *a* statement[D].   15
And they send-forth[E] their disciples[F] *to* Him, with the Herodians[13], saying, "Teacher, we know   16
that You are truthful[G], and You teach the way *of* God in truth[H]. And You are not concerned[14] about [pleasing] any one, for You do not look[J] at *the* face *of* people[15]. °Tell us then, what seems[K] *right*   17
to You? Is it lawful[L] to give *a* poll-tax[M] *to* Caesar[N], or not?"

    1C. But having known their evilness[16], Jesus said, "Why are you testing[O] Me, hypocrites[P]? °Show   18-19
    Me the coin *for* the poll-tax". And the *ones* brought to Him *a* denarius[17]
    2C. And He says *to* them, "Whose *is* this image[18] and inscription?" °They say *to* Him, "Caesar's"   20-21
    3C. Then He says *to* them, "Then give-back[19] the *things of* Caesar[20] *to* Caesar, and the *things of* God *to* God"
    4C. And having heard *it*, they marveled[Q]. And having left Him, they went away   22

5B.[21] On that day, Sadducees came to Him— *ones* saying[22] *that* there is not *a* resurrection[R]   23

    1C. And they questioned Him, °saying, "Teacher, Moses said [in Deut 25:5], 'If someone dies not   24
    having children, his brother shall as-next-of-kin-marry[23] his wife[S] and raise-up[T] *a* seed[24] *for* his brother'

        1D. "Now there were seven brothers with us. And the first, having married[U], came-to-an-end[25]. And not having *a* seed, he left his wife *to* his brother. °Likewise also the second,   25
        and the third, up to the seventh. °And last[26] *of* all, the woman died   26
           27
        2D. "In the resurrection, therefore, *of* which *of* the seven will she be *the* wife? For they all had her"   28

    2C. But having responded, Jesus said *to* them, "You are mistaken[27], not knowing the Scriptures[V],   29
    nor the power *of* God

        1D. "For in the resurrection, they neither marry[U] nor are given-in-marriage[W], but are like angels[28] in heaven   30
        2D. "And concerning the resurrection *of* the dead, did you not read the *thing* having been   31
        spoken *to* you by the God saying[29] °'I am the God *of* Abraham, and the God *of* Isaac, and   32
        the God *of* Jacob'? [Ex 3:15] He is not the[30] God *of* dead *ones*, but *of* living *ones*"

    3C. And having heard *it*, the crowds were astounded[X] at His teaching[Y]   33

1. That is, in the sense of "visit, greet, come to see", as this word is used in Rom 15:24. GK *2517*. Not the same word as "saw" next.
2. Or, "not having been dressed in". On this word, see "put on" in Rom 13:14.
3. The same word is used to mean "wedding" in v 11, 12; Jn 2:1; Rev 19:7, 9; "wedding celebration" in v 2, 3, 4, 8, 9; 25:10; Lk 12:36; 14:8; Jn 2:2; and "wedding hall" in Mt 22:10. Elsewhere only as "marriage" in Heb 13:4. GK *1141*. Related to "marry" in 1 Cor 7:9; and "give in marriage" in 1 Cor 7:38. Some manuscripts have the word "wedding-hall" used in Mt 9:15 {B}.
4. That is, belonging to a wedding. This scene pictures the separation at the end of the age. The clothing represents faith-righteousness, as in Rev 19:8. This man thought his own clothes (his works) were good enough. Given the nature of who was gathered in v 10, some think Jesus means that this one refused the wedding garment which the King provided for all his guests; others, that he did not prepare himself properly, like those of 25:10.
5. Same word as in v 34. This person was made speechless by the question. He knew what was proper and that he had no excuse. On this word, see Mk 4:39.
6. Some manuscripts say "take him away and throw..." {N}.
7. On this word and sentence, and on "outer darkness", see 8:12.
8. Related to the verb "invited" used in this parable. On this word, see Rom 8:28.
9. On this word, see Rom 8:33.
10. Parallel account at Mk 12:13; Lk 20:20.
11. On the phrase "took counsel", see 12:14.
12. Or, "trap". This is a hunting term. Used only here. GK *4074*. Related to "snare" in Rom 11:9.
13. That is, those politically linked to Herod and his family. Elsewhere only in Mk 3:6; 12:13. GK *2477*.
14. This is an idiom, more literally, "It is not *a* concern *to* You about anyone". Your teaching is not influenced by what people think. Same idiom as in Mk 12:14. On this word, see "concerned" in 1 Cor 7:21.
15. That is, You do not show partiality. Luke says "receive the face", 20:21. On this idiom, compare "respect of persons" in Jam 2:1.
16. Or, "wickedness, maliciousness". That is, their evil intentions. Same word as in Lk 11:39; Rom 1:29; 1 Cor 5:8; Eph 6:12. Elsewhere only as "evil" in Mk 7:22; Act 3:26. GK *4504*. Related to "evil" in Act 25:18.
17. On this word, see 20:2. This is a Roman silver coin.
18. Or, "likeness". On this word, see Col 1:15.
19. Or, "render, pay". They ask should we "give" it (as a gift); Jesus says, "give back, pay" what is due him. On this word see "render" in 16:27.
20. That is, the *things belonging to* Caesar, the *things belonging to* God.
21. Parallel account at Mk 12:18; Lk 20:27.
22. Some manuscripts say "the *ones* saying" {B}. Compare Act 23:8.
23. This word, "marry as next of kin" is used only here. GK *2102*. This is called the levirate (from a Latin word meaning "brother-in-law") marriage. See Deut 25:5-10.
24. Or, "offspring, a posterity". On this word, see Heb 11:11.
25. That is, died. On this word, see Mk 9:48.
26. Same word as in Lk 20:32. GK *5731*.
27. Or, "deceived, going astray". Or, it may mean "deceiving *yourselves*". On this word, see "err" in Jam 5:19.
28. Some manuscripts add "*of* God" {B}.
29. This word modifies "God". In saying what follows, God spoke to them about the resurrection. On this phrase, see 1:22.
30. Scripture does not say, "I was the God of Abraham", but "I am". Abraham lives! And it does not say "I am the God of Abraham's spirit", but of Abraham (who is body and spirit). His status as a spirit is temporary. He will be raised! Some manuscripts omit this word, as in Mk 12:27. Others say "God is not God *of* dead..." {C}. Compare Lk 20:37.

A. Mt 20:13   B. 1 Cor 3:5   C. 1 Cor 7:27   D. 1 Cor 12:8, word   E. Mk 3:14, send out   F. Lk 6:40   G. Jn 6:55, true   H. Jn 4:23   J. Rev 1:11, see   K. Lk 19:11, thinking   L. 1 Cor 6:12   M. Mt 17:25   N. Lk 3:1   O. Heb 2:18, tempted   P. Mt 6:2   Q. Rev 17:8   R. Act 24:15   S. 1 Cor 11:3   T. Lk 18:33, rise up   U. 1 Cor 7:9   V. 2 Per 3:16   W. 1 Cor 7:38   X. Mt 7:28   Y. 1 Cor 14:6

| Matthew 22:34 | 78 | Verse |

6B.¹ And the Pharisees, having heard that He silenced^A the Sadducees, were gathered-together at the same *place*². *And one of them, *a* Law-expert³, asked *Him*— testing^B Him⁴—*"Teacher, which *is* the great⁵ commandment^C in the Law?" *And the *One* said⁶ *to* him— 34
 35-36
 37

    1C. " 'You shall love^D the Lord your God with your whole heart, and with your whole soul^E, and with your whole mind^F' [Deut 6:5]—*this is the great and foremost⁷ commandment 38
    2C. "And *the* second *is* like it, 'You shall love^D your neighbor as⁸ yourself' [Lev 19:18] 39
    3C. "The whole Law and the Prophets hang⁹ on these two commandments^C" 40

7B.¹⁰ Now the Pharisees having been gathered-together¹¹, Jesus questioned^G them, *saying, "What seems *right to* you concerning the Christ— Whose son is He?" 41-42

    1C. They say *to* Him, "David's"
    2C. He says *to* them, "How then does David by¹² *the* Spirit call Him 'Lord', saying [in Ps 110:1], *'The Lord said *to* my Lord, "Be sitting on My right *side*, until I put Your enemies under¹³ Your feet" '? 43-44

        1D. "Therefore if David calls Him 'Lord', how¹⁴ is He his son?" 45

    3C. And no one was able to answer Him *a* word, nor did anyone dare^H from that day to question Him any more 46

8B.¹⁵ Then Jesus spoke *to* the crowds and *to* His disciples, *saying— 23:1-2

    1C. "The scribes and the Pharisees sat-down¹⁶ on *the* seat *of* Moses. *Therefore, do^J and be keeping¹⁷ all that they tell you¹⁸ 3
    2C. "But do not be acting¹⁹ in accordance with their works

        1D. "For they say *things* and do not do^J *them*
        2D.²⁰ "And²¹ they bind-up²² heavy^K and hard-to-bear²³ burdens²⁴, and lay them on the shoulders *of* people. But **they** are not willing^L to move^M them *with* their finger²⁵ 4
        3D. "And they do all their works so-as to be seen²⁶ *by* people. For they widen^N their phylacteries²⁷ and lengthen^O *their* tassels²⁸ 5
        4D.²⁹ "And they love^P the place-of-honor³⁰ at the banquets^Q, and the seats-of-honor³¹ in the synagogues, *and the greetings in the marketplaces, and to be called 'Rabbi³²' by people 6
 7

            1E. "But you— 8

                1F. "Do not be called 'Rabbi'³³. For One is your Teacher³⁴, and **you** are all brothers^R
                2F. "And do not call^S *one* on earth your³⁵ father. For One is your Father— the heavenly *One* 9
                3F. "Nor be called master-teachers³⁶, because your master-teacher is One— the Christ 10

            2E. "But the greater *of* you shall be your servant^T 11
            3E. "And whoever will exalt himself will be humbled, and whoever will humble himself will be exalted³⁷ 12

    3C.³⁸ "But woe *to* you, scribes and Pharisees, hypocrites, because you are shutting^U the kingdom *of* the heavens in-front-of³⁹ people^V. For **you** are not entering, nor are you permitting^W the *ones* entering to enter 13
 14⁴⁰

1. Parallel account at Mk 12:28. Compare Lk 10:25-28.
2. Or, simply "gathered together". On this idiom "at the same *place*", see Act 2:47. Same phrase as in Act 4:26.
3. On this word, see Lk 7:30. Some manuscripts omit this word; others say "*a* certain Law-expert" {C}.
4. Some manuscripts add "and saying" {N}.
5. Though the form of this word is "great", some give it the sense of "greatest" here and in v 38. GK *3489*. Mk 12:28 says "foremost". Both words are here in v 38.
6. Some manuscripts say "And Jesus said" {N}.
7. Or, "first". On this word, see "first" in 1 Cor 15:3. Some manuscripts reverse the two words {K}, so that it says "first and great".
8. Or, "like". On this word, see Mt 19:19.
9. That is, like a door on its hinges. On this word, see Act 10:39.
10. Parallel account at Mk 12:35; Lk 20:41.
11. Same word as in v 34. Since these leaders had gathered, Jesus asks them a question. GK *5251*.
12. Or, "in". That is, under the inspiration of the Holy Spirit. GK *1877*.
13. Instead of "under Your feet", some manuscripts say "*as a* footstool *of* Your feet" {N}, as in the Septuagint.
14. On this question, see Mk 12:37.
15. Parallel account at Mk 12:38; Lk 20:45.
16. That is, they sit as official teachers of the Law.
17. Some manuscripts say "be keeping and doing" {N}. On this word, see 1 Jn 5:18.
18. Some manuscripts add "to keep" {N}.
19. Same word as "do" in the previous sentence. Act in accordance with what they teach you from the Law, but not in accordance with their actions. Do not follow their example.
20. Compare Lk 11:46.
21. Some manuscripts say "For" {K}.
22. That is, they tie them up in bundles. Elsewhere only as "bind" in Lk 8:29; Act 22:4. GK *1297*. Related to "bundle" in 13:30.
23. Elsewhere only in Lk 11:46. GK *1546*. Some manuscripts omit "and hard to bear" {C}.
24. That is, their traditions. On this word, see "load" in Gal 6:5.
25. Jesus may mean the scribes and Pharisees would not even lift a finger to help those on whom they had placed heavy burdens. Or, He may mean this to further v 3— they do not do what they say, or what they impose on others. They could avoid defilement in ways the common people could not. Thus, they did not have to bear the burden resulting from their rules, and the people could not bear it, Act 15:10. Compare Lk 11:46.
26. Same phrase as "*so as* to be seen" in 6:1.
27. These are small leather boxes worn on the forehead and the arm, containing Ex 13:1-10; 11-16; Deut 6:4-9; 11:13-21. Used only here. GK *5873*. Related to "guard". They were guarding themselves to keep the commandments, in a literal obedience to Ex 13:9, 16; Deut 6:8; 11:18. But they liked bigger ones, for show.
28. That is, the tassels the Jews wore on the four corners of their garment in obedience to Num 15:38-41. Jesus also wore them, 9:20; 14:36. But the Pharisees liked longer ones, for show. Elsewhere only in Mk 6:56; Lk 8:44. GK *3192*. Some manuscripts add "*of* their garments" {N}.
29. Compare Lk 11:43.
30. Or, "first [or, foremost] places to eat". Literally, the "first reclining place". People in that day reclined to eat. Elsewhere only in Mk 12:39; Lk 14:7, 8; 20:46. GK *4752*.
31. Or, "first seats, foremost seats". Elsewhere only in Mk 12:39; Lk 11:43; 20:46. GK *4751*.
32. Same word as in v 8. It is translated "teacher" by John in Jn 1:38, the same word Jesus uses next. Used of John the Baptist in Jn 3:26, and elsewhere only of Jesus in Mt 26:25, 49; Mk 9:5; 11:21; 14:45; Jn 1:38, 49; 3:2; 4:31; 6:25; 9:2; 11:8. GK *4806*. Some manuscripts say "Rabbi, Rabbi" {N}.
33. That is, do not accept human titles of honor that elevate you above your brothers and sisters, exalting yourself, v 12.
34. God is your teacher, the human speaker is His servant, and yours, v 11. On this word, see 1 Cor 12:28. Some manuscripts add "the Christ" {N}, as in v 10. Some manuscripts say "Master-teacher" {N}, using the word in v 10.
35. Some manuscripts omit "your" {B}. That is, elevating a person as a leader or originator. Jesus is not referring to one's actual father—physical (even as in Lk 16:24; Act 7:2) or spiritual (1 Cor 4:15-16). This kind of fatherhood is simply a fact of life. He is referring to titles elevating one brother over another. He just told the teachers not to accept such distinctions, now He tells the learners not to give them. At the same time, leaders are to be "esteemed superabundantly in love because of their work", 1 Thes 5:13.
36. Or, "teachers, masters, doctors, leaders, guides", elevating you as a leading teacher. Used only in this verse. GK *2762*. This is not the normal word for "teacher" (in v 8), or the normal word for "master". Related to the verb "to lead the way, guide, to show the way in doing a thing" (not used in the NT), and to "leading" in Heb 13:7.
37. These same words "humble, exalt" are also in Lk 14:11; 18:14; 2 Cor 11:7; Jam 4:10; 1 Pet 5:6. On them, see Phil 4:12, and "lifted up" in Jn 8:28.
38. Compare Lk 11:52.
39. Or, "before, ahead of ". You shut the door from the outside before they can enter. Note 11:12.
40. Some manuscripts add as v 14, or before v 13, "And woe *to* you, scribes and Pharisees, hypocrites, because you devour the houses *of* the widows, and *are* praying long *for a* pretense. Because of this, you will receive *a* greater condemnation" {A}, similar to Mk 12:40.

A. Mk 4:39   B. Heb 2:18, tempted   C. Mk 12:28   D. Jn 21:15, devotedly love   E. Jam 5:20   F. Lk 1:51, thought   G. Lk 9:18   H. 2 Cor 11:21   J. Rev 13:13   K. Act 25:7, weighty   L. Jn 7:17   M. Rev 2:5   N. 2 Cor 6:11, open wide   O. 2 Cor 10:15, enlarge   P. Jn 21:15, affectionately love   Q. Lk 14:12, dinner   R. Act 16:40   S. Rom 8:30   T. 1 Cor 3:5   U. Jn 20:19, lock   V. Mt 4:4, mankind   W. Mt 6:12, forgive

| Matthew 23:15 | 80 | Verse |

4C. "Woe *to* you, scribes and Pharisees, hypocrites[A], because you go-around[1] the sea and the dry[2] *land* to make one proselyte[3]. And when he becomes *one*, you make him *a* son *of* Gehenna[4] double-more[5] *than* you   15

5C. "Woe *to* you, blind guides— the *ones* saying   16

     1D. 'Whoever swears-an-oath[B] by the temple, it is nothing. But whoever swears-an-oath by the gold *of* the temple, he is obligated[C]'

         1E. "Foolish[D] and blind *ones*! For which is greater, the gold, or the temple having sanctified[6] the gold?   17

     2D. "And, 'Whoever swears-an-oath by the altar, it is nothing. But whoever swears-an-oath by the gift[7] on it, he is obligated'   18

         1E. "Blind[8] *ones*! For which *is* greater, the gift, or the altar sanctifying the gift?   19
         2E. "Therefore, the *one* having sworn[B] by the altar is swearing by it and by all the *things* on it. °And the *one* having sworn by the temple, is swearing by it and by the *One* dwelling-in[9] it. °And the *one* having sworn by heaven, is swearing by the throne *of* God and by the *One* sitting on it   20 / 21 / 22

6C.[10] "Woe *to* you, scribes and Pharisees, hypocrites, because you are giving-a-tenth-of[11] the mint and the dill and the cummin[12], and you neglected[13] the weightier[E] *things of* the Law— the justice[F], and the mercy[G], and the faithfulness[14]   23

     1D. "But[15] *you* ought-to-have[16] done these[17] *things*, and not be neglecting[18] those[19] *things*. Blind guides— the *ones* straining-out[20] the gnat, but swallowing[H] the camel!   24

7C.[21] "Woe *to* you, scribes and Pharisees, hypocrites, because you cleanse[J] the outside *of* the cup and the dish, but inside they are full from[22] [your] plundering[23] and self-indulgence[24]   25

     1D. Blind Pharisee— first cleanse the inside *of* the cup[25], in order that the outside *of* it may also become clean![26]   26

8C.[27] "Woe *to* you, scribes and Pharisees, hypocrites, because you are similar[28] *to* burial-places having been whitewashed[29], which **outside**[30] appear beautiful— but inside are full *of* bones *of* dead *ones* and all impurity[K]!   27

     1D. So also **you outside** appear righteous[L] *to* people[M]— but inside you are full[31] *of* hypocrisy[N] and lawlessness[O]!   28

9C.[32] "Woe *to* you, scribes and Pharisees, hypocrites, because you build the burial-places[33] *of* the prophets and adorn[34] the tombs[35] *of* the righteous[L] *ones*, °and say, 'If we had been in the days *of* our fathers, we would not have been their partners[P] in the blood[Q] *of* the prophets'   29 / 30

     1D. "So then, you are testifying[R] *concerning* yourselves that you are sons[S] *of* the *ones* having murdered the prophets[36]   31
     2D. "And **you**— fill-up[37] the measure[T] *of* your fathers!   32

10C. "Snakes, brood[U] *of* vipers, how may you escape from the condemnation[38] *of* Gehenna[V]?   33

1. Same word as in 4:23; 9:35. GK *4310*.
2. On this word, see "withered" in Mk 3:3. In Heb 11:29, "land" is expressed with this word.
3. Or, "convert". Our English word "proselyte" comes from this Greek word. It means "one having come to" your view. Elsewhere only in Act 2:11; 6:5; 13:43. GK *4670*. The Jews used it of those who became full Jews, accepting circumcision. Jesus says, you make proselytes to Phariseeism, not to God.
4. That is, ones destined to Gehenna. On this word, see 5:22.
5. Or, "twofold-more". This form of this word is used only here. On this word, see "double" in 1 Tim 5:17.
6. Or, "having made holy, having consecrated", set apart to God. Some manuscripts say "sanctifying" {N}, as in v 19. On this word, see Heb 10:29.
7. Same word as in 5:23.
8. Some manuscripts say "Fools and blind *ones*" {B}, as in v 17.
9. Or, "inhabiting". Same word and grammar as in Lk 13:4; Act 1:19; 2:9, 14; 4:16; 9:32, 35; 19:10, 17; Rev 17:2. God dwells in it in the same sense as in the rest of the universe, not in a local sense, as said in Act 7:48; 17:24. Yet He also dwells in it as the place where He chooses to be worshiped by His people Israel in accordance with the Law He gave them, a choice that ended with the death of His Son. Elsewhere of God only in Col 1:19; 2:9, of "dwelling" in Christ. GK *2997*.
10. Compare Lk 11:42.
11. On this word, see "collect a tenth from" in Heb 7:5.
12. These are three spices. Jesus does not fault the scribes and Pharisees for their over-attention to micro matters (gnats), but for their lack of attention to macro matters (camels). The Law only commanded a tithe for certain crops. They went beyond what the Law required.
13. Or, "left, left behind, let go". Same word as in Mk 7:8. On this word, see "forgive" in 6:12.
14. That is, fidelity, being trustworthy. Or, "faith". On this word, see "faith" in Eph 2:8.
15. Some manuscripts omit this word {C}.
16. Or, "should-have". Or, "But it was necessary to have...". On this idiom, see "should have" in 25:27.
17. That is, the "latter" things mentioned, the justice, etc., which the Law commands.
18. Some manuscripts say "and not to leave-behind" {C}.
19. That is, the "former" things mentioned, the tithing which you chose as an expression of your devotion.
20. Or, "filtering". The Pharisees actually strained their drinks so as not to drink an unclean gnat (Lev 11:41), but figuratively swallowed the unclean camel (Lev 11:4). Used only here. GK *1494*.
21. Compare Lk 11:39-41.
22. Or, "of ". The cup is filled with the things resulting from your greedy and self-indulgent actions. GK *1666*.
23. Or, "plunder, greed". On this word, see Heb 10:34. Related to "ravenous" in 7:15, and "snatch away" in 11:12. Note Mk 12:40.
24. Or, "lack of self-control", as in 1 Cor 7:5.
25. Instead of "cup... outside *of* it", some manuscripts say "cup and the dish... outside *of* it"; others, "cup and the dish... outside *of* them"; others, "cup... inside *of* it" {D}.
26. Since the outside is dirtied from within (the heart), the inside must be cleansed first. On "clean", see Tit 1:15.
27. Compare Lk 11:44.
28. Or, "are like, resemble". Used only here. GK *4234*. Related to "similar" in Mk 7:13.
29. Burial places were whitewashed to prevent Jewish pilgrims unfamiliar with the area from accidentally coming in contact with them, and becoming "unclean". This was done a month before Passover. Elsewhere only in Act 23:3. GK *3154*.
30. Both here and in v 28, Jesus uses grammar that emphasizes the contrast between the "outside" and "inside" statements.
31. On this adjective, see Rom 15:14. Not the same word as the verb in v 25, 27 (GK *1154*).
32. Compare Lk 11:47-48.
33. Or, "graves, tombs". Same word as in v 27; 27:61, 64, 66; 28:1. Elsewhere only as "grave" in Rom 3:13. GK *5439*. This word puts the emphasis on "burial". Related to "burial" and "dig a trench" (not in the NT), and to "prepare for burial" in Mt 26:12.
34. Or, "decorate, put in order". On this word, see 1 Tim 2:9.
35. Or, "monuments, graves". Same word as in Lk 11:47. Used 40 times, 27 referring to the tomb of Jesus. GK *3646*. It means "tomb" in the sense of "memorial place". Related to "tomb" in Lk 23:53; "memorial" in Mt 26:13; "memory" in 2 Pet 1:15; and "remember" in Jn 16:21.
36. Compare Lk 11:48.
37. This is a command, a direct challenge to them— Do what is in your hearts, do what your fathers did.
38. Or, "judgment, sentence of judgment, punishment". That is, the sentence consisting of Gehenna. On this word, see "judgment" in Jn 3:19.

A. Mt 6:2 B. Jam 5:12, swearing C. 1 Jn 4:11, ought D. Tit 3:9 E. Act 25:7 F. Jn 3:19, judgment G. Mt 9:13 H. Heb 11:29, swallowed up J. Heb 9:22 K. 1 Thes 2:3 L. Rom 1:17 M. Mt 4:4, mankind N. Gal 2:13 O. 1 Jn 3:4 P. 2 Pet 1:4, sharer Q. 1 Jn 1:7 R. Jn 1:7 S. Gal 3:7 T. Jn 3:34 U. Mt 3:7 V. Mt 5:22

Matthew 23:34	82	Verse

    11C.[1] "For this reason[2] behold— **I** am sending-forth[A] prophets[B] and wise *ones* and scribes[3] to you.   34
Some of them you will kill and crucify[C]. And *some* of them you will whip[D] in your synagogues and persecute[E] from city to city

        1D. "So that all *the* righteous blood being shed[F] on the earth[4] may come upon you[5]—   35

            1E. "From the blood *of* Abel, the righteous *one*, up to the blood *of* Zechariah, son *of* Berechiah[6], whom you murdered[G] between the temple and the altar

        2D. "Truly[H] I say *to* you, all these *things* will come upon this generation[J]   36

    12C.[7] "Jerusalem, Jerusalem, the *one* killing the prophets and stoning the *ones* having been sent forth to her   37

        1D. "How often I wanted to gather together your children the way[K] *a* hen gathers together her chicks under *her* wings, and you did not want[8] *it*
        2D. "Behold— your house[L] is being left *to* you desolate[9]. °For I say *to* you, you will by no means see Me[10] from now *on* until you say, 'Blessed[11] *is* the One coming in *the* name *of the* Lord' "[12]   38-39

9B.[13] And having departed from the temple, Jesus was proceeding. And His disciples came to *Him* to show[M] Him the buildings *of* the temple[14]   24:1

    1C. But the[15] *One*, having responded, said *to* them, "Do you see all these *things*?[16] Truly[H] I say *to* you— *a* stone upon *a* stone[17] will by no means be left here which will not be torn-down[18]"   2
    2C. And while He *was* sitting on the Mount *of* Olives, the disciples came to Him privately[N], saying, "Tell us—   3

        1D. "When will these[19] *things* happen[20]?
        2D. "And what *will be* the sign[21] *of* Your coming[22] and *the* conclusion[23] *of* the age?"

    3C. And having responded, Jesus said *to* them—   4

        1D. "Be watching out *that* no one may deceive[O] you[24]

            1E. "For many will come on the basis of My name[25], saying, '**I** am the Christ'. And they will deceive[O] many   5
            2E. "And you will-certainly[26] hear-*of* wars[27] and rumors[P] *of* wars. See *that* you are not alarmed[28]! For *they* must[29] take place, but it is not yet the end[30]   6

        2D. "For[31] nation will arise[32] against nation, and kingdom against kingdom. And there will be famines[33] and earthquakes in various places[34]. °But all these *things are*[35] *a* beginning *of* birth-pains[36]   7
               8

            1E.[37] "Then[38] they will hand you over[39] to affliction[40], and they will kill you. And you will be being hated[41] by all the nations because of My name   9
            2E. "And then[42] many will be caused-to-fall[Q], and will hand one another over, and will hate one another. °And many false-prophets will arise and deceive[O] many. °And the love *of* the majority will grow cold because of lawlessness[R] being multiplied[S]   10
               11-12
            3E. "But the *one* having endured[43] to *the* end[44]— this *one* will be saved   13

1. Compare Lk 11:49-51.
2. That is, in response to you and your evil hearts.
3. Or, "experts in the Law". Jesus is referring to the apostles and others whom He will send after His death, 10:16-18. Same word as in 13:52. GK *1208*.
4. Or, "land, ground". Used of the whole earth (as in 5:18, 35; 6:10), and of the "land" of Israel, etc. (as in 2:6, 20; 4:15). On this word, see "land" in Rev 7:1. Not "the blood of all the righteous", but "all the righteous blood" shed by you and your fathers.
5. That is, that the bloodguilt of your fathers may be avenged upon you, as you repeat their crimes on those I send. Compare Lk 11:50.
6. That is, the first (Gen 4:8) and last (2 Chron 24:21) murders recorded in the OT, in the Hebrew order of books. 2 Chron 24:20-21 calls Zechariah the son of Jehoiada. Some think Jehoiada was actually his grandfather, just as Iddo was the grandfather of another Zechariah (compare Zech 1:1 with Ezra 6:14). Others think he had two names. Others think there was an early copyist's error.
7. Compare Lk 13:34-35.
8. Same word as "I wanted" earlier in the verse, on which see "willing" in Jn 7:17.
9. Or, "deserted, empty". On this adjective, see "wilderness" in 3:1. Related to "desolation" in Lk 21:20. Some manuscripts omit this word {B}, as in Lk 13:35.
10. That is, as Messiah, Son of God.
11. This is a participle, "having been blessed". On this word, see Lk 6:28.
12. In Matthew, these words represent the end of the public ministry of Jesus to Israel. Luke quotes them earlier, in 13:34-35.
13. Parallel account at Mk 13:1; Lk 21:5.
14. This temple was built by Herod the Great (the one who killed the babies, see 2:1), but was not yet finished.
15. Some manuscripts say "But Jesus" {K}.
16. The grammar indicates that a "yes" answer is expected.
17. Compare Mk 13:2; Lk 19:44; 21:6.
18. Or, "destroyed, demolished, thrown down, done away with". Same word used of "tearing down" this temple in 26:61; 27:40; Mk 13:2; 14:58; 15:29; Lk 21:6; Act 6:14; and in Rom 14:20; 2 Cor 5:1; Gal 2:18; "abolish" in Mt 5:17; and "overthrow" in Act 5:38, 39. Elsewhere only as "take up lodging" (see Lk 9:12). GK *2907*.
19. That is, the tearing down of the temple (24:2), the things coming upon this generation (23:34-36), the house being left desolate (23:38), His coming ("until", 23:39).
20. Or, "be". Same word as in 16:22.
21. Same word as in v 24, 30. Jesus answers this in v 30. But before that, there will be false signs, v 24. On this word, see 2 Thes 2:9.
22. On this word, see 2 Thes 2:8. Same word as in v 27, 37, 39.
23. Or, "consummation, completion, finish, close, end". Related to "end" in v 6, 14. Same word as in 13:39, 40, 49 (which also refer to the event in 24:30-31), and 28:20. Elsewhere only in Heb 9:26. GK *5333*. The related verb is "accomplished" in Mk 13:4.
24. As to the chronology of v 5-14, some think they refer to events prior to the destruction of Jerusalem in A.D. 70. Others, to the birth-pains that started in the apostles' day, and continue through this age. The end time begins in v 14b. This means they are not signs of the end, but things about which we are not to be deceived or alarmed. Others think that Jesus intended a double meaning, one for the apostles in the first century, and one describing what will happen when the "birth pains" of the end time begin, until the end when Christ returns (v 14b). There are other views on this and the other details of this chapter. Consult the commentaries.
25. On this phrase, "on the basis of " the name, see Act 2:38.
26. Or, "you must" hear, "you will be destined" to hear, or "you **will**" hear. This word is used 109 times in the NT, but is future tense only here and in 2 Pet 1:12 ("I will certainly"). The same word is in a similar idiom in Act 24:15. On this word, see "going to" in Mk 10:32.
27. Or, "battles". On this word, see Rev 12:7.
28. Or, this word may be a command (as it is in Mk 13:7), making two commands here, "Watch out! Do not be alarmed!". This is the same word Paul uses in 2 Thes 2:2, where the Thessalonians may have been "alarmed" by such things as these.
29. Or, "*it* must", that is, all this. On this idiom, see 16:21. Some manuscripts say "For all *things* must take place" {B}.
30. Or, "but the end is not yet". Same word as in v 13, 14. On this word, see Mk 13:7. Some think Jesus means "the end of Jerusalem"; others, "the beginning of the end time", meaning they are not signs; others, "the end of the end time when Jesus returns" (v 30-31), meaning they are the first signs of the beginning of the end-time period.
31. In connecting this verse to the context, Luke 21:10 has been followed. Luke separates it from the preceding statements, and makes it the beginning of what follows.
32. Or, "be raised". Same word as in v 11, 24. See "arose" in 28:6 on it.
33. Some manuscripts say "famines and plagues" as in Lk 21:11; others "plagues and famines and" {B}.
34. Or, "according to *their* places, from place to place". Same idiom as in Mk 13:8; Lk 21:11. Those who see this verse as a sign of the end time take Jesus to mean these things will be "more frequent" or "more intense". Others take it as a general description of the course of this age up to A.D. 70, and/or up to the end time.
35. Or, "*will be*".
36. Same word as in Mk 13:8; 1 Thes 5:3. Some think this refers to the birth-pains of the Second Coming, and so to events at the beginning of the end time; others, to the birth-pains of the time of the end, and so to events during this age which precede the end time; others, to birth-pains of the events of A.D. 70.
37. Compare also Mt 10:17-23; Jn 16:1-4.
38. Or, "At that time". Matthew uses this word 90 of its 160 occurrences, both to introduce that which is next in time (as in 4:10), or next in sequence (with no specific reference to time, as in 19:13; 23:1; 26:3), and to mean "at that time" (as in 3:5; 27:16). In this chapter, one's interpretation will be influenced by which of these three meanings is adopted. It is used in 24:9, 10, 14, 16, 21, 23, 30, 40; 25:1, 7, 31, 34, 37, 41, 44, 45. Thus here Jesus could mean "At the time of the birth-pains...", or, "Next, as the birth pains continue...", or, "Then (some amount of time after v 6-8)...". GK *5538*.
39. Some think Jesus is referring to the persecution experienced by the early church. Others think persecutions of the entire age are included. Others think it also refers to persecutions arising in the end time.
40. Same word as in v 21, though not necessarily the same event.
41. Same sentence as in 10:22; Mk 13:13; Lk 21:17. Same word as in Jn 15:18, 19; 1 Jn 3:13. On this word, see Rom 9:13.
42. Or, "at that time". On this word, see v 9.
43. Same sentence as in 10:22; Mk 13:13. On this word, see Jam 1:12.
44. On "to *the* end", see 10:22.

A. Mk 3:14, send out   B. 1 Cor 12:28   C. Mt 27:35   D. Heb 12:6   E. 2 Tim 3:12   F. Mt 26:28, poured out   G. Jam 4:2   H. Mt 5:18   J. Mt 24:34
K. Act 27:25   L. Mk 3:20   M. Act 18:28   N. Mt 14:13   O. Jam 5:19, err   P. Heb 4:2, hearing   Q. 1 Cor 8:13   R. 1 Jn 3:4   S. Act 7:17

>   4E. "And this good-news^A *of* the kingdom¹ will be proclaimed^B in the whole world^C for *a* testimony^D *to* all the nations² 14
>   5E. "And then the end³ will come
>
> 3D.⁴ "Therefore when you see⁵ the abomination^E *of* desolation⁶— the *thing* having been spoken through Daniel⁷ the prophet— standing⁸ in *the* holy place⁹ (let the *one* reading understand¹⁰) 15
>
>   1E. "Then¹¹ let the *ones* in Judea be fleeing^F to the mountains 16
>
>   1F.¹² "Let the *one* upon the housetop^G not go down to take¹³ the *things*¹⁴ out of his house 17
>   2F. "And let the *one* in the field not turn^H behind to take his cloak¹⁵ 18
>   3F. "And woe *to* the *ones* having *a* child in *the* womb^J, and *to* the *ones* nursing^K in those days 19
>   4F. "And be praying that your flight may not take place *in* winter, nor *on a* Sabbath 20
>
>   2E. "For then¹⁶ there will be *a* great affliction¹⁷ such as has not taken place since *the* beginning *of the* world^L until now, nor ever¹⁸ will take place 21
>
>   1F "And if those days had not been shortened¹⁹, no flesh would have been saved²⁰ 22
>   2F. "But those days will be shortened for the sake of the chosen²¹ *ones*
>
>   3E.²² "Then²³ if someone says *to* you, 'Behold— here *is* the Christ,' or 'Here', do not believe *it* 23
>
>   1F. "For false-christs and false-prophets^M will arise²⁴ and give great signs and wonders,²⁵ so as to deceive^N, if possible, even the chosen *ones* 24
>   2F. "Behold— I have told you beforehand.²⁶ *Therefore, if they say *to* you 25-26
>
>   1G. "'Behold— He is in the wilderness^O', do not go out
>   2G. "'Behold— *He is* in the inner-rooms^P', do not believe *it*
>   3G. "For just as the lightning comes out from *the* east and is visible²⁷ as far as *the* west, so²⁸ will the coming *of* the Son *of* Man be 27
>   4G.²⁹ "Wherever³⁰ the corpse^Q may be, there the vultures^R will be gathered³¹ 28
>
> 4D.³² "And immediately³³ after the affliction³⁴ *of* those days, the sun will be darkened^S, and the moon will not give its glow^T, and the stars will fall from the heaven^U, and the powers^V *of* the heavens^U will be shaken^W 29
> 5D. "And then³⁵ the sign³⁶ *of* the Son *of* Man will appear^X in *the* heaven^U 30
>
>   1E. "And at-that-time³⁷ all the tribes^Y *of* the earth will beat-their-breasts³⁸. And they will see the Son *of* man coming on the clouds *of* heaven^U with power^V and great glory
>   2E. "And He will send-out^Z His angels with *a* loud trumpet³⁹. And they will gather together His chosen *ones* from the four winds, from *the* ends⁴⁰ *of the* heavens to their [other] ends 31
>
> 6D.⁴¹ "Now learn^AA the parable^BB from the fig-tree⁴²— when its branch already⁴³ becomes tender and grows-out⁴⁴ *its* leaves, you know that the summer *is* near 32

1. Same phrase as in 4:23; 9:35.
2. Some think this was accomplished in Paul's lifetime, Col 1:23; others, that it is accomplished in this age, before the end time begins; others, that is accomplished during the end time, but before Christ returns.
3. Some think Jesus means "the end time will suddenly begin", as in v 39; others, "Christ will return" as in v 30.
4. Parallel account at Mk 13:14; Lk 21:20.
5. Some think this is the sign of "these things coming upon this generation" (23:36) and the destruction of Jerusalem, as clearly in Lk 21:20-24. Others think it is a sign of the beginning of the end time, or of the time of wrath, as in 2 Thes 2:3-4. Others think Jesus meant both, the first-century event being a type of the end-time event.
6. The "abomination of desolation" refers to an act of sacrilege, an abomination to God consisting in or resulting in or characterized by desolation. Some think it is the end-time act of a person (2 Thes 2:3, Rev 13); others, the desolation of the temple in A.D. 70, (Lk 21:20). Others think the event in A.D. 70 is a type or picture of a similar end-time event. Elsewhere only in Mk 13:14; Lk 21:20. GK 2247. Related to "desolate" in 23:38.
7. See Dan 9:27, "an abomination that causes desolation", and Dan 8:13; 11:31; 12:11. It could be rendered "the desolating abomination", the abomination characterized by desolation.
8. Grammatically, this word refers back to "abomination".
9. Or, "in *a* holy place". Some think Jesus means the A.D. 70 temple; others Jerusalem; others Judea; others an end-time "temple of God", 2 Thes 2:4. Note Lk 21:20. In September of A.D. 66, Florus, the Roman procurator, raided the temple treasury, which the Jews saw as the "abomination" fulfilling Dan 9:27. They revolted against Rome, thinking God intended to fight for them and establish His kingdom on earth. The Romans destroyed Jerusalem and the temple in A.D. 70 after a five month siege.
10. In other words, this concept is capable of misunderstanding. It may imply "it is not as you usually think". For example, "it is not as the Jews understand Daniel's prophecy". Or, it may imply "it is the reader in that day who will understand exactly what this means, not the writer (Matthew) in his day". On this word, see "think" in Eph 3:20.
11. Or, "At that time". See v 9.
12. Compare Lk 17:31-32.
13. Or, "pick up, remove". That is, go down to flee, and flee without your belongings. GK *149*.
14. Some manuscripts say "take anything" {N}.
15. Or, "coat, outer garment". Do not even get your jacket. Leave immediately. On this word, see "garments" in 1 Pet 3:3. Some manuscripts have this word plural, "garments" {N}. Compare Lk 21:21.
16. Or, "at that time" (see v 9). Mark says "those days will be", 13:19.
17. Or, "distress, trouble, tribulation". Same word as in v 9, 29; 13:21; Mk 13:19. Lk 21:23 uses a different word, "distress". On "the great affliction", see Rev 7:14. Some think Jesus means this occurs "in Judea" (v 16), and refers to the events of A.D. 70. Others think He means it occurs "in the world", an event still future. Some think both.
18. This is an emphatic negative, the strongest in Greek. It will "never, by no means" occur. See 5:20 on it.
19. Or, "cut off, cut short, curtailed". Elsewhere only in Mk 13:20. GK *3143*.
20. Literally, "All flesh would not have been saved", a Hebrew way of speaking. Here and in Mk 13:20, some think Jesus means "all humanity"; others, the Jews in Judea where this takes place, v 16. "All flesh" is elsewhere only in Lk 3:6; Jn 17:2; Act 2:17; Rom 3:20; 1 Cor 1:29; 15:39; Gal 2:16; 1 Pet 1:24. On "flesh", see Col 2:23.
21. Same word as in v 24, 31. On this word, see Rom 8:33.
22. Compare Lk 17:23-24.
23. Or, "At that time" (see v 9). Compare Lk 17:20-21.
24. Same word as in v 7.
25. Some think this has a final fulfillment in the events described in 2 Thes 2:8-10; Rev 13. On "wonders", see 2 Thes 2:9.
26. Or, "I have foretold *it to* you". Same word as in Mk 13:23.
27. Or, "shines". On this word, see "shine" in Phil 2:15.
28. Some manuscripts say "so also" {K}.
29. Compare Lk 17:37.
30. Some manuscripts say "For wherever" {N}.
31. Linked as here with v 27, this refers to the vultures gathering upon the corpses of those judged and killed by Jesus at His return, 2 Thes 1:8-9; Rev 19:18, 21. Both His coming, and its catastrophic aftermath, will be unmistakable. Others link this with v 24 (making it point 3F.), meaning that the false prophets (the vultures) will gather upon the spiritually dead (the corpses). Others link this with v 15-26 (making it point 4E.), meaning that Jerusalem is the corpse attracting the Roman eagles. Others see it as a general rule— as the dead carcass attracts vultures, so the spiritually dead will attract judgment. There are other views. Consult the commentaries. GK *5251*.
32. Parallel account at Mk 13:24, Lk 21:25.
33. Some think this verse is symbolic of events in A.D. 70, such as the falling of political rulers. Compare Act 2:19-20. Others think this jumps in time to the events at the end of the final tribulation. Compare Mk 13:24.
34. Same word as in v 21. The "affliction of those days" refers back to v 15-28.
35. Or, "at that time" (see v 9).
36. Some think Jesus is referring to some sign preceding His coming; others, to His coming itself, as in Mk 13:26.
37. Or, "then" (see "then" in v 9).
38. On this word and statement, see Rev 1:7. See also Zech 12:10-12.
39. Some manuscripts add "sound" {B}. Note 1 Cor 15:52; 1 Thes 4:16.
40. Or, "extremities". Same word as in Mk 13:27. Elsewhere only of the "tip" of a finger in Lk 16:24; and the "top" of a staff in Heb 11:21. GK *216*. If "heaven" means "sky" here, as it sometimes does, then it means "from horizon to horizon". Otherwise, it means all on the earth (the four winds) and all in heaven. Compare Mk 13:27.
41. Parallel account at Mk 13:28; Lk 21:29.
42. This is used as an illustration in 21:19 (Mk 11:13); Lk 13:6-7; Rev 6:13. Some think Jesus is referring to Israel. Others think it simply refers to an ordinary fig tree, as in Lk 21:29, where Luke adds "and all the trees". Used 16 times. GK *5190*.
43. Or, "now, presently, by this time". By the time when its branch becomes tender..., you know. Used 61 times. GK *2453*.
44. Or, "generates, produces, puts forth". Elsewhere only in Mk 13:28. GK *1770*. Related to "grow" in Lk 8:6. Luke 21:30 uses a different word.

A. 1 Cor 15:1 B. 2 Tim 4:2 C. Heb 2:5 D. Act 4:33 E. Rev 17:4 F. 1 Cor 6:18 G. Lk 5:19 H. Jam 5:19, turn back J. 1 Thes 5:3 K. Mt 21:16 L. 1 Jn 2:15 M. Rev 16:13 N. Jam 5:19, err O. Mt 3:1 P. Mt 6:6 Q. Mk 15:45 R. Rev 8:13, eagle S. Rom 1:21 T. Mk 13:24 U. 2 Cor 12:2 V. Mk 5:30 W. Act 17:13 X. Phil 2:15, shine Y. Rev 1:7 Z. Mk 3:14 AA. Phil 4:11 BB. Mt 13:3

1E. "So also you— when you see all these *things*,¹ you know² that He³ is near^A, at *the* doors. °Truly^B I say *to* you that this generation⁴ will by no means pass away until all these *things* take place 33
34

1F. "Heaven and earth will pass away, but My words^C will by-no-means⁵ pass away 35

7D. "But no one knows^D about that day and hour— not even the angels *of* the heavens, nor the Son⁶— except the⁷ Father alone 36

1E.⁸ "For just as the days *of* Noah *were*, so⁹ will the coming^E *of* the Son *of* Man be 37

1F. "For as in those¹⁰ days before the flood^F 38

1G. "They were eating¹¹ and drinking, marrying and giving-in-marriage^G, until which day Noah entered into the ark
2G. "And they did not know^H until the flood came and took-away¹² everyone 39

2F.¹³ "So also¹⁴ will the coming¹⁵ *of* the Son *of* Man be. °At-that-time¹⁶ there will be 40

1G. "Two *men* in the field— one is taken¹⁷, and one is left¹⁸
2G. "Two *women* grinding at the mill— one is taken, and one is left 41

3F. "Therefore keep-watching¹⁹, because you do not know^D *on* which day²⁰ your Lord is coming 42

2E.²¹ And you know²² that *saying*, that if the house-master^J had known *on* which watch²³ the thief was coming, he would have kept-watch and would not have allowed^K his house to be broken-into²⁴ 43

1F. "For this reason **you** also be²⁵ prepared²⁶ *ones*— because the Son *of* Man is coming *at an* hour which you do not expect²⁷ 44

8D.²⁸ "Who then²⁹ is the faithful^L and wise³⁰ slave^M whom *his* master^N put-in-charge³¹ over his body-of-servants³² *that he might* give them *their* food³³ at *the* proper-time?³⁴ 45

1E. "Blessed³⁵ *is* that slave whom his master, having come, will find so³⁶ doing 46

1F. "Truly I say *to* you that he will put him in charge over all his possessions^O 47

2E. "But if that bad^P slave says in his heart, 'My master is delaying³⁷', °and begins to strike^Q his fellow-slaves^R, and is eating and drinking³⁸ with the *ones* being drunk^S— 48-49

1F. "The master *of* that slave will come on *a* day which he does not expect³⁹, and at *an* hour which he does not know 50
2F. And he will cut him in two⁴⁰, and assign⁴¹ *him* his part⁴² with the hypocrites^T. In that place, there will be the weeping and the grinding *of* teeth⁴³ 51

1. Seeing all the things of v 5-29 or 15-29 is seeing the tree leafed out. When you see it all, the coming of Jesus is near.
2. Or, "know", a command. Same word and form as in v 32. On this word, see Lk 1:34.
3. That is, the Son of Man, v 27, 30. Or, "it", His coming.
4. Some think Jesus means the generation at the destruction of Jerusalem, foreshadowing His coming; others, the generation alive to "see all these things", v 33. Others take "generation" to mean a "kind of person" (as in Lk 16:8), and think He is referring to unbelieving Israel. This kind of Jew— ones rejecting Christ— will continue until He comes. In this view, He is predicting the continuance of the Jewish people until the end. "This generation" is also in 11:16; 12:41, 42, 45; 23:36; Mk 8:12, 38; 13:30; Lk 7:31; 11:29, 30, 31, 32, 50, 51; 17:25; 21:32; Act 2:40; Heb 3:10. This word is elsewhere only in Mt 1:17; 12:39; 16:4; 17:17; Mk 9:19; Lk 1:48, 50; 9:41; Act 8:33; 13:36; 14:16; 15:21; Eph 3:5, 21; Phil 2:15; Col 1:26; and as "kind" in Lk 16:8. GK *1155*.
5. Or, "never". Same strong negative as in v 34, 21. See 5:20 on it.
6. On this, see Mk 13:32. Some manuscripts omit "nor the Son" {B}.
7. Some manuscripts say "My" {N}.
8. Compare Lk 17:26-27.
9. Some manuscripts say "so also" {N}.
10. Some manuscripts say "in the days" {C}.
11. Or, "chewing, munching, crunching". Not the same word as in v 49. That is, life was going on as normal. It was not the culmination of human events. It came upon the world from the outside. On this word, see Jn 6:54.
12. Not the same word as in v 40-41. It was an intervention into human history. GK *149*.
13. Compare Lk 17:34-37.
14. Some manuscripts omit this word {C}.
15. Note the unexpectedness. It comes upon people suddenly while they are carrying on their normal lives. It comes like a thief, while they feel at peace, 1 Thes 5:2-3. Some think Jesus is referring to the beginning of the end time, the time of His coming; others, to His physical coming in v 30.
16. Or, "then" (see v 9).
17. Or, "taken along, taken with". On this word, see Lk 17:34. Some think this refers to believers, just as Noah was taken aside and protected through the affliction of those days, while the others were left behind for judgment. The chosen (v 31), the wise virgins (25:10), the two slaves (25:20, 22) and the sheep (25:34) are all "taken" first. In addition, some think this will be done on earth, in the midst of the events. Others think it will be in heaven, through what Paul calls "the rapture", 1 Thes 4:17. Now compare the view in the next note.
18. Or, "left behind, abandoned". Same word as in Lk 17:34. GK *918*. Others think this action refers to believers, just as Noah was "left" on earth after the flood "took away" (v 39) the others. In 13:41, 49, the evil ones are taken. Compare Lk 17:34.
19. Or, "be staying alert". Same word as in v 43; 25:13; 26:38, 40, 41. On this word, see 1 Thes 5:6.
20. Some manuscripts say "*at* which hour" {B}.
21. Compare Lk 12:39-40.
22. Or, "know", "understand", a command. Same word and form as in v 33.
23. That is, which watch of the night. On the four watches of the night, see Mk 13:35. On "watch" see Lk 2:8.
24. That is, if the house-master knew that a thief was coming, and when, he would be prepared for him at that time. Since he does not, he must be prepared at all times. Literally, "dug through", broken into by digging through a wall. Elsewhere only in Mt 6:19, 20; Lk 12:39. GK *1482*. Related to "to dig" in Mt 21:33; 25:18; Mk 12:1, and "dug out" in Mk 2:4.
25. Or, "prove to be, become". GK *1181*.
26. Or, "ready". Used by Matthew also in 22:4, 8; 25:10. Same sentence as in Lk 12:40. On this word, see Mk 14:15.
27. Or, "think *it will be*, suppose, presume, imagine". We know that Jesus will come, but not when. So we must be prepared at all times. Same word as in Lk 12:40, on which see "thinking" in Lk 19:11.
28. Compare Lk 12:41-49.
29. In view of the sudden nature of the return of Jesus, who is the wise one whom He put in charge of a task when He left? The wise slave is the one doing His will while waiting for Him. He will be rewarded. Jesus puts this in the form of a question so that each person will ask, "Am I a wise and faithful slave?"
30. Same word as in 25:2.
31. Or, "appointed, set". Same word as in v 47. On this word, see Act 6:3. Compare Lk 12:42.
32. That is, the group of servants that belong to and serve the master in whatever capacity he assigns them. Used only here. GK *3859*. Related to "household-servant" in Rom 14:4. The root word is "house". Lk 12:42 has an unrelated word meaning "body-of-servants", which some manuscripts have here {N}.
33. Or, "nourishment, provision, sustenance". Used 16 times. GK *5575*. Lk 12:42 uses a different word.
34. Because of the leadership picture in this parable, some think Jesus is referring to the leaders— the "apostles, prophets, evangelists, pastors and teachers", Eph 4:11. Others think this is simply a picture of whatever task each person has been given. It represents all Christians doing whatever task the Master gave them to do.
35. On this adjective, see Lk 6:20.
36. Some take this narrowly of the leaders "giving out [spiritual] food". Others take it broadly as "doing as the master directed". Others link it to what precedes this parable, watching for Him and being prepared for Him in work and heart.
37. Some manuscripts add "to come" {N}, as in Lk 12:45.
38. Some manuscripts say "and to eat and drink" {K}.
39. Or, "anticipate, look for". On this word, see "wait in expectation" in Lk 3:15.
40. This word "cut in two" is elsewhere only in Lk 12:46. GK *1497*.
41. Or, "put, make, appoint". On this word, see "put" in Act 19:21.
42. Or, "share, place". Same word as in Lk 12:46; Jn 13:8; Rev 20:6; 21:8; 22:19. On this word, see Rom 11:25.
43. On this sentence, see 8:12.

A. Lk 21:30 B. Mt 5:18 C. 1 Cor 12:8 D. 1 Jn 2:29 E. 2 Thes 2:8 F. 2 Pet 2:5 G. 1 Cor 7:38 H. Lk 1:34 J. Mt 20:1 K. 1 Cor 10:13 L. Col 1:2 M. Rom 6:17 N. Mt 8:2 O. Mt 19:21 P. 3 Jn 11, evil Q. Lk 6:29 R. Rev 19:10 S. 1 Cor 11:21 T. Mt 6:2

9D. "At-that-time[1], the kingdom *of* the heavens will be-like[A] ten virgins[B], who, having taken their lamps[2], went out to meet[3] the bridegroom[4] 25:1

    1E. "Now five of them were foolish[5], and five *were* wise[6] 2

        1F. "For[7] the foolish *ones*, having taken their lamps, did not take oil[8] with them[9] 3
        2F. "But the wise *ones* took oil in jars[10] with their lamps 4

    2E. "And while the bridegroom *was* delaying, they all became drowsy and were sleeping[11] 5
    3E. "And *in the* middle *of the* night,[12] *a* shout[C] has come[13]— 'Behold, the bridegroom[14]! Come out to meet[15] him!' 6
    4E. "Then all those virgins arose and put their lamps in-order[D] 7
    5E. "And the foolish *ones* said *to* the wise *ones*, 'Give us from your oil, because our lamps are going-out[16]'. *But the wise *ones* responded, saying, 'There will not by any means ever[17] be enough[E] *for* us and *for* you. Go instead to the *ones* selling and buy *for* yourselves' 8 9
    6E. "And while they *were* going away to buy, the bridegroom came. And the prepared[F] *ones* entered with him into the wedding-celebrations[G]. And the door was shut[H] 10
    7E. "And later, the other virgins also come, saying, 'Sir, sir[18], open *for* us' 11
    8E. "But the *one*, having responded, said, 'Truly I say *to* you, I do not know[J] you' 12
    9E. "Therefore, keep-watching[K], because you do not know the day nor the hour[19] 13

10D.[20] "For *it*[21] is just like *a* man going-on-a-journey[L]— 14

    1E. "He called *his* own slaves[M] and handed over his possessions[N] *to* them. *And he gave five talents[22] *to* one, and two *to* another, and one *to* another— *to* each according to *his* own ability[O]. And he went on *his* journey 15

        1F. "Immediately[23] having gone, the *one* having received the five talents worked[24] with them and gained[25] another five[26] 16
        2F. "Similarly[27], the *one having received* the two *talents* gained[28] another two 17
        3F. "But the *one* having received the one *talent*, having gone, dug [a hole in] *the* ground[P] and hid[Q] his master's silver[29] *talent* 18

    2E. "Now after much time, the master *of* those slaves comes and settles[30] *the* account[R] with them 19

        1F. "And having come to *him*, the *one* having received the five talents brought another five talents, saying, 'Master[S], you handed-over[T] five talents *to* me. Look, I gained another five talents[31]' 20

            1G. "His master said *to* him, 'Well[32] done, good[U] and faithful[V] slave. You were faithful[V] over *a* few *things*. I will put you in charge[33] over many *things*. Enter into the joy *of* your master[S]' 21

        2F. "And[34] also having come to *him*, the *one having received* the two talents said, 'Master, you handed over two talents *to* me. Look, I gained another two talents' 22

            1G. "His master said *to* him, 'Well done, good and faithful slave. You were faithful over *a* few *things*. I will put you in charge over many *things*. Enter into the joy *of* your master' 23

1. Or, "Then". On this word, see "then" in 24:9. That is, when Jesus comes unexpectedly, as described in 24:36-51.
2. Or, "torches". That is, oil lamps with wicks. Same word as in v 3, 4, 7, 8; Act 20:8. Elsewhere only as "torch" in Jn 18:3; Rev 4:5; 8:10. GK *3286*. Torches were sticks with a cloth wrapped around one end which was soaked in oil. Torches were often used in processions, and some think this is meant here.
3. This is a noun, referring to a meeting event. Literally, they went out "for *a* coming-to-meet" the bridegroom. Elsewhere only in 8:34; Jn 12:13. GK *5637*. Related to "meet" in 25:6 and Lk 14:31.
4. Some manuscripts add "and the bride" {B}. The groom and groomsmen went to the bride's house and then brought her, her attendants, family and friends in a procession to his family's house, where wedding celebrations often lasting a week took place. Some think that they are meeting him here on his way to the bride's house. Others think it is on the way to his father's house, where the celebrations are, v 10.
5. These represent those who think of themselves as friends of Jesus, but whom He does not know, v 12. Some manuscripts have "wise" first and "foolish" second {K}.
6. Or, "sensible". Same word as v 4, 8, 9; 24:45. On this word, see 7:24. These represent the true Christians. Note that His people are not referred to as the "bride" in this parable. The bride is not mentioned at all.
7. Some manuscripts say "The *ones* who *were* foolish" {K}.
8. That is, olive oil, as in v 4, 8. On this word, see Jam 5:14.
9. Some suggest that the lamp is the outward profession of Christianity and the oil is the inner reality.
10. Or, "flasks, vessels, containers". Used only here. GK *31*. Some manuscripts say "their jars" {N}.
11. This is not an issue in the parable. All ten slept. The issue is lack of oil— lack of preparedness.
12. That is, unexpectedly. Similar to the idiom in Act 26:13.
13. Or, "has come about, taken place, happened". GK *1181*.
14. Some manuscripts add "is coming" {K}.
15. This is a noun, referring to a meeting event. Literally, come out "for *a* meeting" *of* him. Elsewhere only in Act 28:15; 1 Thes 4:17. GK *561*. Related to the word in v 1. The related verb, "to meet", is in Mk 14:13; Lk 17:12. Some manuscripts omit "him" {C}.
16. Or, "being quenched". On this word, see "quench" in 1 Thes 5:19.
17. Or, this word "not ever" (GK *3607*), which is the first word in the Greek sentence, may be taken as an exclamation, so that it says "No! There will by no means be enough...". There are three negatives here, making it quite emphatic. Some manuscripts omit one of the negatives, so that the remark may be rendered "No! There may not be enough...", or "Perhaps there may not be enough..." {N}.
18. Same word as "Lord, Lord" in 7:21, 22; Lk 6:46. These are the only places it is repeated this way. On this word, see "Master" in 8:2.
19. Some manuscripts add "in which the Son *of* Man is coming" {A}.
20. Compare Lk 19:11-27.
21. That is, the kingdom of the heavens, as in v 1. Others think Jesus means to imply "*He is*", referring to the Son of Man.
22. This is a large sum of money, representing our individual gifts and abilities, both spiritual and natural. A silver talent was 6000 denarii (see 20:2), that is, 6000 days wages for a laborer. On this word, see 18:24.
23. Or, it may be punctuated "journey immediately. Having gone". Some manuscripts say "And immediately having gone" {B}. Elsewhere in Matthew, this word is always connected with "and" ("And immediately..."), and always goes with what follows. GK *2311*.
24. That is, he did business with them. On this word, see 26:10.
25. Some manuscripts say "made" {N}.
26. Some manuscripts add "talents" {N}.
27. Some manuscripts say "And similarly" {N}, or "Similarly also".
28. Some manuscripts say "**He** also gained" {N}.
29. Or, "money". This word is singular only here in Matthew, agreeing with the one talent. On this word, see "money" in v 27.
30. Elsewhere only in 18:23, 24. GK *5256*.
31. Some manuscripts add "beside them" {N} here and in v 22.
32. Or, "*It is* good", or, "Excellent!". Same word as in v 23. GK *2292*. Related to the word in Lk 19:17.
33. Same word as "put in charge" in v 23; 24:45.
34. Some manuscripts omit this word {C}.

A. Mt 13:24 B. Rev 14:4 C. Heb 5:7, outcry D. 1 Tim 2:9, adorn E. 2 Cor 12:9, be sufficient F. Mk 14:15 G. Mt 22:11, wedding H. Jn 20:19, lock J. 1 Jn 2:29 K. 1 Thes 5:6 L. Mt 21:33 M. Rom 6:17 N. Mt 19:21 O. Mk 5:30, power P. Rev 7:1, land Q. Jn 8:59 R. 1 Cor 12:8, word S. Mt 8:2 T. Mt 26:21 U. 1 Tim 5:10b V. Col 1:2

    3F. "And also having come to *him*, the *one* having received[1] the one talent said, 24
     'Master, I knew you— that you are *a* hard[A] man, reaping where you did not
     sow and gathering[B] from where you did not scatter[2] [threshings]. °And having 25
     become afraid, having gone, I hid your talent in the ground.[3] Look, you have
     what *is* yours'

      1G. "But having responded, his master said *to* him 'Evil[C] and lazy[D] slave! You 26
       knew that I reap where I did not sow and gather from where I did not scatter![4]
       Therefore you should-have[5] put my money[6] *with* the bankers[7]. And having 27
       come, **I** would have received-back[E] what *was* mine with interest[8]
      2G. 'Therefore take the talent away from him, and give *it to* the *one* having the 28
       ten talents. °For *to* everyone having, it will be given, and he will be 29
       caused-to-abound[9]. But *from* the *one* not having, even what he has will
       be taken away from him
      3G. 'And throw-out[F] the unprofitable[10] slave into the outer darkness' 30
      4G. "In that place, there will be the weeping and the grinding *of* teeth[11]

  11D. "Now when the Son *of* Man comes in His glory, and all the angels[12] with Him, at-that- 31
   time[13] He will sit on *the* throne *of* His glory[14]

    1E. "And all the nations[15] will be gathered[B] in front of Him 32
    2E. "And He will separate[16] them[17] from one another, just as the shepherd[G] separates
     the sheep from the goats. °And He will make the **sheep**[18] stand[19] on His right *side*— 33
     and the goats on *the* left *side*
    3E. "Then the King[20] will say *to* the *ones* on His right *side*, 'Come, the *ones* having been 34
     blessed[H] *of* My Father[21]— inherit[J] the kingdom having been prepared[K] *for* you since
     the foundation *of the* world[22]

     1F. 'For I was hungry, and you gave Me *something* to eat[23]. I thirsted, and you 35
      gave-a-drink-*to* Me. I was *a* stranger[L], and you brought Me in[24]; °naked[M], and 36
      you clothed Me. I was sick, and you looked-after[N] Me. I was in prison, and
      you came to Me'
     2F. "Then the righteous[O] *ones* will respond *to* Him, saying, 'Lord, when did we see 37
      You hungering and we fed *You*, or thirsting and we gave-a-drink? °And when 38
      did we see You *a* stranger and we brought *You* in, or naked and we clothed *You*?
      And when did we see You being sick or in prison and we came to You?' 39
     3F. "And having responded, the King will say *to* them, 'Truly I say *to* you, in-as- 40
      much-as[25] you did *it to* one *of* the least *of* these My brothers[26], you did *it to* Me'

    4E. "Then He will also say *to* the *ones* on *the* left *side*, 'Depart from Me— the[27] *ones* having 41
     been cursed[P]— into the eternal fire having been prepared[28] *for* the devil and his angels

     1F. 'For I was hungry, and you did not give Me *something* to eat. I thirsted, and you 42
      did not give-a-drink-*to* Me. °I was *a* stranger, and you did not bring Me in; naked, 43
      and you did not clothe Me; sick, and in prison, and you did not look after Me'
     2F. "Then **they** also will respond, saying, 'Lord, when did we see You hungering, or 44
      thirsting, or *a* stranger, or naked, or sick, or in prison, and we did not serve[Q] You?'
     3F. "Then He will respond *to* them, saying, 'Truly I say *to* you, in as much as you 45
      did not do *it to* one *of* the least *of* these, neither did you do *it to* Me'

    5E.[29] "And these will go to eternal[30] punishment[R], but the righteous *ones* to eternal life" 46

1. This is the same word as in v 20, but a different tense, implying "having received and still having".
2. That is, "winnow" threshings, so as to gather the grain from the threshing floor. Or, "scatter [seed]", repeating the previous statement. Same word as in v 26. Elsewhere only of "scattering" sheep in Mt 26:31; Mk 14:27, and people in Lk 1:51; Jn 11:52; Act 5:37; and of "squandering" property in Lk 15:13; 16:1. GK *1399*.
3. This one did nothing with what he was given, and here seeks to excuse his inaction by blaming the master— because you are the way you are, I did not invest or work with what you gave me. He bore no fruit. The others worked with what the master gave them as with a trust to be invested.
4. Others take this as a question, "You knew... scatter? Then you should have...".
5. Or, "ought to have". More literally, "it was necessary *for* you to have" put. This idiom refers to what should or ought to have happened by necessity (but didn't), the compulsion being based on what was fitting or proper or required by the circumstances. "It was necessary to have" done so, it was "binding" (the root word), but it was not done. Here, the necessity was created by the knowledge the man just revealed that he had at the time. Same idiom as in 18:33; 23:23; Lk 13:16; Act 24:19; 27:21; 2 Cor 2:3; Heb 9:26. GK *1256*. Same word as in the idiom "must" in Mt 16:21, and "ought to" in Act 25:10.
6. Same word as in Mt 28:12, 15; Mk 14:11; Lk 9:3; 19:15, 23; 22:5. Elsewhere only as "silver coins" in Mt 26:15; 27:3, 5, 6, 9; Act 19:19; and "silver" in Mt 25:18; Act 3:6; 7:16; 8:20; 20:33; 1 Pet 1:18. GK *736*.
7. Or, the "table-men", referring to the money table. Used only here. GK *5545*. Related to "table" in Lk 19:23.
8. That is, compound interest, the "produce, offspring" of the money. Elsewhere only in Lk 19:23. GK *5527*.
9. Or, "he will have an abundance". Same word as in 13:12. On this word, see "abound" in 2 Cor 8:2.
10. Or, "worthless, useless, good for nothing", and therefore "unworthy, miserable". He brought no gain to the master. Elsewhere only in Lk 17:10. GK *945*. Related to "became-useless" in Rom 3:12; and "useless" in Phm 11.
11. On this sentence, and on "outer darkness", see 8:12.
12. Some manuscripts say "holy angels" {N}.
13. Or, "then" (see "then" in 24:9). Jesus returns to where He left off in 24:31.
14. Or, "on His throne *of* glory", "His glorious throne". This phrase is elsewhere only in 19:28. On "throne", see Rev 20:11.
15. This phrase "all the nations" is also in 24:9, 14; 28:19; Mk 11:17; 13:10; Lk 21:24; 24:47; Act 14:16, etc. On "nations", see "Gentiles" in Act 15:23.
16. Same word as in 13:49.
17. Grammatically, this word does not refer to "nations" or to "sheep", but to the people in the nations.
18. Jesus uses grammar that emphasizes the contrast between the two halves of this sentence.
19. Or, "He will put, set" instead of "make stand". On this word, see Mk 13:14.
20. That is, the Son of Man, v 31, 40.
21. That is, blessed by My Father, "My Father's blessed ones".
22. On the phrase "since *the* foundation *of the* world", see Heb 9:26.
23. Same phrase as in 14:16. Some render the verbal idea as a noun, "you gave Me food".
24. Or, "brought Me with *you*; took Me in with *you*", that is, into your house, or with you on your way. Or, "you gathered Me in with *yourself*" to help Me. Same word as in v 38, 43, and as in Deut 22:2; Judg 19:18; 2 Sam 11:27; and as "gathered" here in v 32. Used 56 other times as "gather, gather together". GK *5251*. The root words mean "to bring with, to bring together".
25. Or, "to the extent, in so far as". On this idiom, which is also in v 45, see "to the extent" in Rom 11:13.
26. That is, family members of Christ, fellow Christians. Your actions indicate a family relationship to Christ. On this word, see Act 16:40.
27. Some manuscripts omit this word {C}, so that it says "Depart from Me having been cursed", under a curse, or, "Depart from Me, accursed *ones*".
28. Same word as in v 34. On this word, see Mk 14:15. Some manuscripts say "which My Father prepared" {N}.
29. Compare Jn 5:29.
30. Same word used of "life" next; Jn 3:16; of "fire" in Mt 18:8; 25:41; of "destruction" in 2 Thes 1:9; of "salvation" in Heb 5:9; of "judgment" in Heb 6:2; of "redemption" in Heb 9:12; of the "Spirit" in Heb 9:14; of the "covenant" in Heb 13:20; of "glory" in 1 Pet 5:10; of "kingdom" in 2 Pet 1:11. Used 71 times. GK *173*. Related to "forever" in Rev 20:10. Compare Mk 9:48.

A. Jn 6:60   B. Mt 25:35, brought in   C. Act 25:18   D. Rom 12:11, hesitation   E. 2 Cor 5:10   F. Jn 12:31, cast out   G. Eph 4:11   H. Lk 6:28
J. Gal 4:30   K. Mk 14:15   L. Rom 16:23, host   M. Jam 2:15   N. Heb 2:6   O. Rom 1:17   P. Rom 12:14   Q. 1 Pet 4:10, ministering   R. 1 Jn 4:18

Matthew 26:1   92   Verse

15A.[1] And it came about *that* when Jesus finished all[2] these words, He said *to* His disciples, "You know that   26:1-2
after two days the Passover[A] [Feast] comes[3], and the Son *of* Man is handed-over[B] so as to be crucified[C]"

    1B. Then the chief priests[4] and the elders *of* the people were gathered together in the courtyard[5] *of* the   3
        high priest, the *one* being called Caiaphas[D]. And they plotted[E] in order that they might seize[F] Jesus   4
        by deceit[6] and kill *Him*. But they were saying, "Not during the Feast, in order that no uproar[7] may   5
        take place among the people"
    2B.[8] Now Jesus having come-to-be in Bethany[9] at *the* house *of* Simon the leper, *a* woman[10] came to Him   6-7
        having *an* alabaster-jar[G] *of* very-expensive[11] perfume[12]. And she poured *it* down upon His head while
        He was reclining-back [to eat]

        1C. But having seen *it*, the[13] disciples were indignant[H], saying, "For what *purpose is* this waste[J]?   8
            For this[14] could have been sold *for* much and given *to* poor[K] *ones*"   9
        2C. But having known *it*, Jesus said *to* them, "Why are you causing troubles[15] *for* the woman? For   10
            she worked[16] *a* good[17] work[18] for[19] Me

            1D. "For you **always** have the poor with you, but you do not always have **Me**   11
            2D. "For this *one* having put this perfume on My body did *it* so as to prepare Me for burial[20]   12
            3D. "Truly[L] I say *to* you, wherever this good-news[M] is proclaimed[N] in the whole world[O], what   13
                this *one* did will also be spoken for *a* memorial[21] *of* her"

    3B.[22] Then one *of* the twelve, the *one* being called Judas Iscariot, having gone to the chief priests,[23]   14
        said, "What are you willing[P] to give me, and **I** will hand Him over *to* you?"   15

        1C. And the *ones* set[24] thirty silver-coins[25] *for* him
        2C. And from that time on,[26] he was seeking *a* favorable-opportunity[27] in order that he might hand   16
            Him over

    4B.[28] Now *on* the first *day of* the *Feast of* Unleavened-Bread[Q], the disciples came to Jesus, saying,   17
        "Where do You want us to prepare[29] *for* You to eat the Passover[A] [meal]?"

        1C. And the *One* said, "Go into the city[30] to so-and-so[31], and say *to* him, 'The Teacher says, "My   18
            time is near[R]. I am doing[32] the Passover [meal] with you[33], along-with My disciples" ' "
        2C. And the disciples did as Jesus directed[S] them. And they prepared[T] the Passover [meal]   19
        3C.[34] And having become evening, He was reclining back [to eat] with the twelve[35]   20

            1D. And while they *were* eating, He said, "Truly I say *to* you that one of you will hand Me over[36]"   21

                1E. And while being extremely grieved[U], each one[37] began to say *to* Him, "**I** am not *the*   22
                    one, am I, Lord?"[38]
                2E. And the *One*, having responded, said, "The *one* having dipped[V] *his* hand[39] with Me   23
                    in the bowl[40]— this *one* will hand Me over

                    1F. "**The Son *of* Man**[41] is going just as it has been written about Him— but woe   24
                        to that man by whom the Son *of* Man is being handed-over[B]! It *would have*
                        been better *for* him if that man had not been born"[42]

                3E. And having responded, Judas— the *one* handing Him over— said, "**I** am not *the*   25
                    one, am I, Rabbi?"[43]

                    1F. He says *to* him, "**You** said *it*"[44]

1. Parallel account at Mk 14:1; Lk 22:1.
2. This is the fifth use of this phrase (see 13:53), but the only place where Matthew adds "all". He may be referring strictly to chapters 24-25; or to "all" His words that day (21:23-25:46); or to "all" the words of His ministry (4:17-25:46).
3. Or, "comes about, takes place, happens". GK *1181*.
4. Some manuscripts add "and the scribes" {N}.
5. Or, "palace". Elsewhere by Matthew only in 26:58, 69. Used 12 times. It also means "fold" in Jn 10:1. GK *885*.
6. Or, "treachery, cunning". Elsewhere only in Mk 7:22; 14:1; Jn 1:47; Act 13:10; Rom 1:29; 2 Cor 12:16; 1 Thes 2:3; 1 Pet 2:1, 22; 3:10. GK *1515*. Related to "deceitful" in 2 Cor 11:13; "deceive" in Rom 3:13; and "handle deceitfully" in 2 Cor 4:2.
7. Same word as in 27:24, where an uproar did occur— against Jesus! On this word, see "commotion" in Mk 5:38.
8. Parallel account at Mk 14:3; Jn 12:3. Compare Lk 7:37-50.
9. Chronologically, this took place six days before Passover, Jn 12:1, which would place it at the end of Matthew 20. Matthew's arrangement is topical, so he places it here, where it fits smoothly.
10. That is, Mary, Jn 11:2; 12:3.
11. Used only here. GK *988*. Related to "very valuable" in Jn 12:3.
12. Or, "ointment" (but pourable), "fragrant oil". Made from plants. Elsewhere only in 26:12; Mk 14:3, 4, 5; Lk 7:37, 38, 46; 23:56; Jn 11:2; 12:3, 5; Rev 18:13. GK *3693*. The related verb is in Mk 14:8.
13. Some manuscripts say "His" {N}.
14. Some manuscripts add "perfume" {N}, the word in v 7.
15. On "causing troubles", see Lk 18:5.
16. This word, "to work, do, carry out, accomplish, perform", is used 41 times. GK *2237*.
17. Or, "fitting, useful, praiseworthy, beautiful". On this word, see 1 Tim 5:10a.
18. Or, "did a good deed". The verb and noun of the same root word are used, as in Jn 3:21; 6:28; 9:4; Act 13:41; 1 Cor 16:10. This noun, "work, deed, act", is used 169 times. GK *2240*. Related to "worker" in 1 Tim 5:18. On "good work", see Rom 2:7 and Tit 2:14.
19. Or, "to, with reference to". That is, for Me in My present situation. GK *1650*. Compare Mk 14:6.
20. This word, "to prepare for burial" is elsewhere only in Jn 19:40. GK *1946*. Related to the "preparation for burial" in Mk 14:8. Some think Mary knowingly did it for this purpose. Same grammar as in 5:28. She understood what was going to happen better than the apostles. She believed what He said in v 2. Others think she did it without realizing that this was its ultimate purpose.
21. Elsewhere only in Mk 14:9; Act 10:4. GK *3649*. Related to the word "tomb", and the verb "to remember", and the word "remembrance" in 1 Cor 11:24. Her memorial is not a tombstone, but the telling of this story. Same word as in Ex 17:14; 28:29.
22. Parallel account at Mk 14:10; Lk 22:3.
23. The opportunity brought by Judas leads the Jewish leaders to move up their timetable, v 5, to God's timetable, Act 2:23.
24. This common word can mean "set on a scale", and thus "weigh out" as in Zech 11:12, where this same word is used. It may imply the Jewish leaders paid Judas at this time. But it could also mean they "set" the price here and paid him later. Note Lk 22:5. On this word, see "standing" in Mk 13:14.
25. This word was used of the "shekel" (a Jewish silver coin worth four denarii, see 20:2), and some think this is the coin in view here. In this case, the price was 120 days pay for a laborer. It was the price that must be paid the owner of a slave gored by an ox, Ex 21:32. Same word as 27:3, 5, 6, 9; and as "money" in Mk 14:11; Lk 22:5. On this word, see "money" in Mt 25:27.
26. On this phrase, see 4:17.
27. Elsewhere only in Lk 22:6. GK *2321*. Related to "conveniently" in Mk 14:11, and to "find an opportunity" in Act 17:21.
28. Parallel account at Mk 14:12; Lk 22:7.
29. More literally, "Where do You want *that* we should prepare".
30. Passover could only be celebrated within the city of Jerusalem, Deut 16:5-7.
31. Some think Jesus did not want to name His host so that Judas would not know the location in advance. Others think Matthew omitted the name to protect this person from the Jews. Used only here. GK *1265*. Compare Mk 14:13-14.
32. Or, "observing". On this word, see Rev 13:13.
33. That is, at your house.
34. Parallel account at Mk 14:17; Lk 22:14; Jn 13:2.
35. Some manuscripts add "disciples" {C}
36. The word "hand over" is the same word Judas used in v 15, 16, and Jesus used in v 2. It means "to hand over, deliver, give over". When the context implies the unjust nature of it, it can be rendered "betray". Elsewhere by Matthew only in 4:12; 5:25; 10:4, 17, 19, 21; 11:27; 17:22; 18:34; 20:18, 19; 24:9, 10; 25:14, 20, 22; 26:2, 15, 16, 23, 24, 25, 45, 46, 48; 27:2, 3, 4, 18, 26. It is also used in a positive sense, as in Act 14:26; 15:40; and of "handing down, delivering" teachings, as in Lk 1:2; Act 6:14; 1 Cor 11:2, 23; 15:3; Jude 3. Used 119 times. GK *4140*. Related to "tradition" in 1 Cor 11:2.
37. Or, "each individual". This phrase "each one" is elsewhere only in Lk 4:40; 16:5; Act 2:3, 6; 17:27; 20:31; 21:26; 1 Cor 12:18; Eph 4:7, 16 ("each individual"); Col 4:6; 1 Thes 2:11; 2 Thes 1:3; Rev 21:21. Some manuscripts say "each *of* them" {N}. GK *1667, 1651*.
38. The grammar indicates a "no" response is expected. The disciples each expect Jesus to say "no, you are not the one".
39. That is, what is held in his hand. "Dip" is the same word as in Mk 14:20.
40. This is another way of saying "One of you", one of the ones eating with Me.
41. Jesus uses grammar that emphasizes the contrast between the two halves of this sentence.
42. Non-existence would have been better for Judas than to have lived and committed this deed. On "born", see 1 Jn 2:29.
43. The grammar indicates that Judas expects a "no" answer, just like the others. This is the same exact question as in v 22, except Judas calls Jesus "Rabbi" instead of "Lord".
44. Some think this means "Yes". Others think it is an intentionally ambiguous answer, since Jesus does not specify whether He means "you said *it* [rightly]" (No, you are not the one, the answer Judas's question expects), or, "you said *it* [falsely]" (Yes, you are the one). Note that the adverb is included in Lk 20:39; Jn 4:17, "You spoke well", or "You said rightly". Which He means must be determined from the context. Here, we know and Judas knew that Jesus meant the latter. But the other disciples assumed He meant the former. They did not suspect Judas, as seen in Jn 13:28. See the same phrase in v 64. See Lk 22:21 on when Judas left.

A. Jn 18:28 B. Mt 26:21 C. Mt 27:35 D. Lk 3:2 E. Act 9:23 F. Heb 4:14, hold on to G. Mk 14:3 H. Mt 20:24 J. 2 Pet 2:1, destruction K. Gal 4:9 L. Mt 5:18 M. 1 Cor 15:1 N. 2 Tim 4:2 O. 1 Jn 2:15 P. Jn 7:17 Q. Mk 14:12 R. Lk 21:30 S. Mt 27:10 T. Mk 14:15 U. 2 Cor 7:9 V. Mk 14:20

  2D.¹ And while they *were* eating, having taken bread² and having blessed³ *it*⁴, Jesus broke^A   26
    it. And having given *it to* the disciples, He said, "Take, eat. This is⁵ My body"
  3D. And having taken *a* cup⁶ and given-thanks⁷, He gave *it to* them, saying, "Drink from it,   27
    everyone

    1E. "For this is My blood^B *of* the covenant⁸— the *blood* being poured-out⁹ for many for   28
      forgiveness^C *of* sins^D
    2E. "And I say *to* you, I will by-no-means¹⁰ drink of this fruit¹¹ *of* the grapevine from   29
      now *on* until that day when I drink it new¹² with you in the kingdom *of* My Father"

5B.¹³ And having sung-a-hymn¹⁴, they went out to the Mount *of* Olives   30

 1C. Then¹⁵ Jesus says *to* them, "**You** all will be caused-to-fall¹⁶ in-connection-with¹⁷ Me during this   31
   night. For it has been written [in Zech 13:7], 'I will strike the Shepherd^E, and the sheep *of* the
   flock^F will be scattered^G'. *But¹⁸ after I am raised^H, I will go ahead of you to Galilee"   32
 2C. But having responded, Peter said *to* Him, "If all will be caused-to-fall¹⁹ in connection with   33
   You, **I** will never be caused to fall"
 3C. Jesus said *to* him, "Truly I say *to* you that during this night, before *a* rooster crows, you will   34
   deny²⁰ Me three-times"
 4C. Peter says *to* Him, "Even if I have-to²¹ die with You, I will never deny You"   35
 5C. All²² the disciples also spoke likewise

6B.²³ Then Jesus comes with them to *a* place being called Gethsemane²⁴. And He says *to* the disciples,   36
 "Sit here²⁵ while²⁶ I pray, having gone there"

 1C. And having taken-along^J Peter and the two sons²⁷ *of* Zebedee, He began to be grieved^K and   37
   distressed^L. *Then He says *to* them, "My soul is deeply-grieved²⁸, to the point of death. Stay^M   38
   here and keep-watching²⁹ with Me"
 2C. And having gone ahead *a* little, He fell on His face while praying and saying, "My Father, if   39
   it is possible, let this cup pass from Me. Yet not as **I** want³⁰, but as You *want* "

  1D. And He comes to the disciples and finds them sleeping^N. And He says *to* Peter, "So were   40
    you³¹ [three] not strong-*enough*³² to keep watch with Me *for* one hour? *Keep watching,   41
    and be praying that³³ you may not enter into temptation³⁴. The **spirit**³⁵ *is* willing³⁶— but
    the flesh *is* weak^O"

 3C. Again, having gone away for *a* second *time,* He prayed^P, saying, "My Father, if this³⁷ cannot   42
   pass³⁸ unless I drink it, let Your will be done^Q"

  1D. And having come, He again found them sleeping^N. For their eyes had been weighed-down³⁹   43

 4C. And having left them again⁴⁰, having gone away, He prayed for *a* third *time*, having spoken   44
   the same thing⁴¹ again

  1D. Then He comes to the disciples and says *to* them, "Are you sleeping^N and resting⁴² from-   45
    now-on⁴³? Behold— the hour has drawn-near^R, and the Son *of* Man is being handed-over^S
    into *the* hands *of* sinners^T. *Arise^U, let us be going^V. Behold— the *one* handing Me over   46
    has drawn near"

 5C. And while He *was* still speaking, behold— Judas, one *of* the twelve, came. And with him *was*   47
   a large crowd from the chief priests and elders *of* the people with swords^W and clubs^X

1. Compare also 1 Cor 11:23-25.
2. Some manuscripts say "the bread" {N}.
3. On this word, see Lk 6:28. Some manuscripts say "given thanks" {N}.
4. Or, "having blessed *God*". See 14:19.
5. This is the common verb "to be", used 2462 times in the NT. GK *1639*. Some take this as a literal correspondence, so that the bread "becomes" or "contains" His body. Others take it as a figurative correspondence, so that the bread "means" or represents or symbolizes His body, as with the symbolic elements of the Passover meal. Likewise with "blood". Compare Jn 6:48-58. This word is rendered "means" in 9:13; 12:7; Mk 3:17; 7:11; Lk 8:9, 11; Act 2:12; 10:17; 17:20; Eph 4:9, etc. It also means "be" in the sense of "happen" (see Mt 16:22) and "exist" (see Rev 22:14).
6. Some manuscripts say "the cup" {B}.
7. Same word as in 15:36; Mk 8:6, 14:23; Lk 22:17, 19; Jn 6:11, 23; Act 27:35; Rom 14:6; 1 Cor 11:24. Used 38 times. GK *2373*. Related to "thanksgiving" in 1 Tim 4:3.
8. Some manuscripts say "new covenant" {B}, as in Lk 22:20. It is the blood inaugurating the new covenant, Heb 9:14-15. On this word, see Heb 8:6.
9. Or, "shed". Same word as in Mk 14:24; Lk 22:20. Elsewhere only as "shed" in Mt 23:35; Act 22:20. GK *1773*. Related to the word in Act 2:17. Jesus is pouring it out; others are shedding it.
10. Or, "never". This is an emphatic negative. Same idiom as in v 35. See 5:20 on it.
11. Or, "product, produce". Used of the "produce" of the earth as opposed to "offspring" animals. Elsewhere only in Mk 14:25; Lk 22:18; 2 Cor 9:10. GK *1163*.
12. That is, until I drink new wine with you. Compare Mk 14:25. On this word, see Heb 8:13.
13. Parallel account at Mk 14:26. Compare at Lk 22:31; Jn 13:38; and Lk 22:39.
14. On this word, see "sing praise" in Act 16:25. Some think Matthew is referring to the second part of the Hallel, Ps 115-118, sung at the end of the Passover meal.
15. Or, "At that time" (see 24:9).
16. Same word as in v 33. On this word, see 1 Cor 8:13.
17. That is, in connection with what is going to happen to Me tonight. GK *1877*.
18. This (GK *1254*) is not the same word as in Mk 14:28 (GK *247*).
19. The grammar of this phrase means "assuming that all will be caused to fall...". Compare Mk 14:29.
20. Same word as in v 35, 75. On this word, see 16:24.
21. On this idiom, see "must" in 16:21.
22. Some manuscripts say "And all" or "But all" {N}.
23. Parallel account at Mk 14:32; Lk 22:39; Jn 18:1.
24. This is a transliterated Hebrew word meaning "olive press". It is the name of an olive orchard on the Mount of Olives, east of Jerusalem. Elsewhere only in Mk 14:32. GK *1149*.
25. On this word, see Lk 9:27. Not the same word as in Mk 14:32 (GK *6045*).
26. More literally, "as long as which". Or, "until", "until which *time* I pray" and return. GK *2401*.
27. That is, James and John, Mt 4:21; Mk 14:33.
28. Or, "very sad". Elsewhere only in Mk 6:26; 14:34; Lk 18:23, 24. GK *4337*. Related to "grieved" in v 37, on which see 2 Cor 7:9.
29. Same word as in v 40, 41. On this word, see 1 Thes 5:6.
30. Or, "wish, will". Compare Jn 12:27. On this word, see "willing" in Jn 7:17.
31. Though Jesus speaks to Peter, the verb "were you strong" is plural, referring to all three of them.
32. Or, "did you not have strength, were you not able". On this word, see "can do" in Gal 5:6.
33. Or, "Keep watching and praying, in order that...", depending on whether this is the content or the purpose of the prayer.
34. Some think Jesus is referring to the temptation to deny Him because of what is about to happen, as He said they would, v 30-35. Others think He means the temptation to sleep. Compare 6:13.
35. Jesus uses grammar that emphasizes the contrast between the two halves of this sentence.
36. Or, "eager, ready", as seen in their promise in v 35. The disciples' heart is right. But their weak flesh needs strength if they are to stand firm. They must pray for strength so that the upcoming trial does not become a cause of falling for them (v 30), a temptation to deny Jesus. Instead, they slept. Their fear turned the "trial" of His arrest into a "temptation" to put self above Him. They fled to protect themselves. Others think Jesus is referring to sleep and bodily weakness— they want to stay awake, but their body is tired. Same word as in Mk 14:38. Elsewhere only as "eager" in Rom 1:15. GK *4609*. Related to "eagerness" in 2 Cor 8:19.
37. Some manuscripts add "cup" {N}.
38. Some manuscripts add "from Me" {N}, as in v 39.
39. A similar idiom is in Lk 9:32. This is a participle, their eyes "were having been weighed down" with sleep. They became so heavy that they could not hold them open any longer.
40. Or, "having left them, again having gone away". This is the Greek word order, "again" standing between the two participles. Some take it with the first; others, with the second.
41. Or, "statement, word [of prayer]", singular. Not the same "words", but the same request. On this word, see "word" in 1 Cor 12:8.
42. Others take these as commands, "Sleep and rest from now on", either as a reproach, or as fatherly sympathy; others, assuming some time elapsed before the next statement, as a concession, "Go ahead and sleep".
43. Or, "henceforth, for the remaining time, in the future". That is, "Are you going to continue sleeping?" Some take it to mean "still", "are you still sleeping", which makes it refer to the past up to the present, rather than from the present out into the future. This word means "the rest, the remaining, the other". Same word as "henceforth" in 1 Cor 7:29; Gal 6:17; 2 Tim 4:8; Heb 10:13. On this word, see "other" in 2 Pet 3:16. Not the same word as "still" in v 47 (which is the normal word for "still", GK *2285*).

A. Act 2:46 B. 1 Jn 1:7 C. Col 1:14 D. Jn 8:46 E. Eph 4:11 F. Jn 10:16 G. Mt 25:24 H. Mt 28:6, arose J. Lk 17:34, taken K. 2 Cor 7:9 L. Phil 2:26 M. Jn 15:4, abide N. 1 Thes 5:10 O. 1 Thes 5:14 P. 1 Tim 2:8 Q. Mt 6:10 R. Lk 21:28 S. Mt 26:21 T. Mt 9:10 U. Mt 28:6 V. Mk 1:38 W. Eph 6:17 X. 1 Pet 2:24, cross

6C. Now the *one* handing Him over gave them *a* sign[A], saying, "Whomever I kiss[1] is He. Seize Him". °And immediately having gone to Jesus, he said, "Greetings[B], Rabbi", and kissed[2] Him. And Jesus said *to* him, "Friend[3], *it is*[4] for what you are here[5]" — 48, 49, 50

7C. Then, having come to *Him*, they put *their* hands on Jesus and seized Him — 51

8C. And behold— one *of* the *ones* with Jesus, having stretched-out[C] *his* hand, withdrew[6] his sword. And having struck the slave[7] *of* the high priest, he took-off[D] his ear[8] — 51

9C. Then Jesus says *to* him, "Return[9] your sword into its place — 52

    1D. "For all the *ones* having taken[E] *the* sword will perish[F] by *the* sword

    2D. "Or do you think[10] that I am not able to appeal-to[G] My Father, and He will provide[11] Me right-now[H] more *than* twelve legions[12] *of* angels? — 53

    3D. "How then would the Scriptures *saying* that it must[13] take place in this manner be fulfilled[J]?" — 54

10C. At that hour, Jesus said *to* the crowds, "Did you come out to arrest[K] Me with swords and clubs as-*if* against *a* robber[L]? Daily I was sitting in the temple teaching, and you did not seize[M] Me. °But this entire *thing*[14] has taken place in order that the Scriptures *of* the prophets might be fulfilled" — 55, 56

11C. Then all the disciples, having left[15] Him, fled[N]

7B.[16] Now the *ones*[17] having seized Jesus led *Him* away to Caiaphas[O] the high priest, where the scribes and the elders were gathered together. °And Peter was following Him at *a* distance, as far as the courtyard[P] *of* the high priest. And having entered inside, he was sitting with the officers[18] to see the outcome[Q] — 57, 58

    1C. Now the chief priests[19] and the whole Sanhedrin were seeking false-testimony[R] against Jesus, so that they might put Him to death.[20] °And they did not find *it*, many false-witnesses[21] having come-forward[22] — 59, 60

        1D. But finally, two[23] having come-forward[S] °said, "This *One* said, 'I am able to tear-down[24] the temple[T] *of* God, and to build *it* in three days' " — 61

        2D. And having stood up, the high priest said *to* Him, "Are You answering nothing? What *is it* these[25] *ones* are testifying against You?" — 62

            1E. But Jesus was being silent[U] — 63

        3D. And[26] the high priest said *to* Him, "I am putting You under oath[27] by the living God that You tell us if **You** are the Christ, the Son *of* God"

            1E. Jesus says *to* him, "**You**[28] said *it*.[29] Nevertheless[30], I say *to* you— from-now-*on*[31] you will see the Son *of* Man sitting on *the* right side *of* the Power[32], and coming on the clouds *of* heaven"[33] — 64

        4D. Then the high priest tore[V] his garments, saying, "He blasphemed[34]! What further need do we have *of* witnesses? See— now you heard the blasphemy[W]. °What seems *right to* you?" — 65, 66

        5D. And the *ones*, having responded, said, "He is subject-to[35] death!"

        6D. Then they spat in His face and beat[36] Him. And the *ones*[37] slapped[38] *Him*, °saying, "Prophesy[39] *to* us, Christ— who is the *one* having hit You?" — 67-68

    2C. Now Peter was sitting outside in the courtyard[P] — 69

        1D. And one servant-girl[X] came to him, saying, "**You** also were with Jesus the Galilean"

            1E. But the *one* denied *it* in front of everyone[40], saying, "I do not know what you are saying" — 70

1. This word means "to love" and then "to show outward signs of affection", and thus, "to kiss". On this word, see *"affectionately-love"* in Jn 21:15. Related to the noun "kiss" in Rom 16:16.
2. That is, as a greeting. This word means specifically, "to kiss". Elsewhere only in Mk 14:45; Lk 7:38, 45; 15:20; Act 20:37. GK *2968*. Related to "kiss" in v 48
3. Or, "comrade, companion, associate". On this word, see 20:13.
4. The precise meaning of this reply by Jesus is uncertain because the key word that gives it meaning must be supplied. Compare Lk 22:48, which was spoken before the kiss. This was spoken after the kiss. Some take it as a question, *"Is this* for what are you here?". Others take it as a command, *"Do that* for which you are here". Others take it as a statement, *"This is* for what you are here", just as it has been written, v 24, 56.
5. Or, "are present, are come". On this word, see "be present" in Rev 17:8.
6. On this word, see Act 21:1. Related to "drawn" in Mk 14:47.
7. That is, Peter struck Malchus, Jn 18:10. On this word, see Rom 6:17.
8. Elsewhere only in Lk 22:51; Jn 18:26. GK *6065*. Related to the word in Mk 14:47.
9. Or, "Turn away". On this word, see "turn away from" in Heb 12:25.
10. Or, "presume, imagine, suppose". On this word, see Lk 19:11.
11. Or, "put at My disposal", "place beside" Me. Having the power to prevent this is not the issue. On this word, see "present" in Rom 12:1.
12. At the time of Augustus, a Roman legion had about 6000 soldiers, plus horsemen and auxiliaries. Perhaps Jesus simply means "a huge overwhelming force". Elsewhere only of a "legion" of demons in a man, Mk 5:9, 15; Lk 8:30. GK *3305*.
13. Or, "has to". On this idiom, see 16:21.
14. Or, "this whole *thing*". This idiom is elsewhere only in 1:22. Some think this is Matthew's comment, not part of what Jesus said to them.
15. Or, more strongly based on the context, "abandoned, deserted". On this word, see "forgive" in 6:12.
16. Parallel account at Mk 14:53; Lk 22:54; Jn 18:12.
17. Or, "Now the *ones*, having seized Jesus, led *Him* away...".
18. That is, the temple guards. On this word, see Jn 18:12.
19. Some manuscripts add "and the elders" {N}.
20. Note that the Jewish leaders had their man, their verdict, and their sentence. All they needed was the evidence.
21. Elsewhere only in 1 Cor 15:15. GK *6020*. Related to "false testimony" in v 59, and "give false testimony" in Mk 14:56.
22. Starting back at the end of v 59, some manuscripts say "to death, and they did not find *it*. Even many false witnesses having come forward, they did not find *it*" {N}.
23. Some manuscripts add "false witnesses" {N}.
24. On this word, see 24:2. Compare Mk 14:57. This statement is similar to the one in Jn 2:19.
25. Or, this could be one question, "Do You answer nothing *as to* what these *ones*...". Compare Mk 14:60.
26. Some manuscripts say "And having responded, the high priest" {N}.
27. This word, "put under oath, adjure, cause to swear" is used only here. GK *2019*. Related to "make swear" in Act 19:13; "adjure" in 1 Thes 5:27; and "oath" in Jam 5:12. In other words, "Tell us under oath if You are the Christ". Anything Jesus now says in response is "under oath".
28. This word is singular here, answering the high priest. In Lk 22:70, it is plural, answering "all of them".
29. Some think this means "Yes". Others think the meaning depends on the context. See the same phrase in v 25. Here, Jesus clearly means "yes" because He follows this reply with His own direct confirmation of their statement, "Nevertheless, I say to you...". Jesus did not wish to simply answer the question. He wanted to directly state that He is exactly the Messiah coming in power and glory to carry out judgment that they were expecting. And they understood Him. Mk 14:62 says "I am", giving the intent of what Jesus says here. See Mt 27:11 on a similar phrase, "you are saying".
30. Or, "But, Yet, However". On this word, see 11:22.
31. Or, "henceforth". Same phrase as in 23:39 and 26:29. Elsewhere only in Jn 13:19; 14:7; Rev 14:13. GK *608*, *785*. This will be how you see Me from now on— as Messiah, executing the power of God. This will be your next view of Me after the events of this day.
32. That is, of God. Or, "*of* power", God's power. Same phrase as in Mk 14:62. Same word as in Lk 22:69, on which see Mk 5:30. Related to the word in Lk 1:49.
33. Jesus is referring to the Messianic prophecies (Ps 110:1; Dan 7:13), applying them to Himself— I am the One spoken of by the prophets. This is a clear and explicit sworn statement to these Jews who knew the Scripture. Note 24:30.
34. That is, spoke against God. In claiming to be God's Son, Jesus was claiming to have the same nature as God, and therefore was claiming deity, as seen in Jn 5:18; 10:33. On this word, see 1 Tim 6:1.
35. Or, "deserving of". Same word as "liable to" in 5:21-22. Jesus is liable to the penalty of death. On this word, see "guilty" in 1 Cor 11:27.
36. Members of the Sanhedrin struck Jesus with their fists. On this word, see 1 Cor 4:11.
37. This is the literal rendering. This idiom introduces a second class of individuals alongside those mentioned in the previous sentence. Who are the ones doing this thing? The idiom can mean "And others", referring to a different component of the group holding Jesus; or, "And some", referring to a sub-group of those who were spitting on and beating Jesus. Compare Mk 14:65; Lk 22:63-65. This idiom is also in 28:17, Jn 7:41.
38. On this word, see 5:39. Related to the word in Jn 18:22.
39. On this word, see 1 Cor 14:1. They expected supernatural knowledge.
40. Some manuscripts add "them" {N}, so that it says "them all", where "all" is the same plural word as "everyone".

A. 2 Thes 2:9   B. 2 Cor 13:11, rejoice   C. Act 27:30   D. Mk 14:47   E. Rom 7:8   F. 1 Cor 1:18   G. Rom 12:8, exhorting   H. Rev 12:10, now   J. Eph 5:18, filled   K. Lk 2:21, conceived   L. Mt 21:13   M. Heb 4:14, hold on to   N. 1 Cor 6:18   O. Lk 3:2   P. Mt 26:3   Q. Rom 10:4, end   R. Mt 15:19   S. Heb 10:22, approach   T. Rev 11:1   U. Mk 4:39, be still   V. Lk 8:29   W. 1 Tim 6:4   X. Jn 18:17

	2D. And *he* having gone out to the gate¹, another² saw him. And she says *to* the *ones* there³, "This *one*⁴ was with Jesus the Nazarene^A"	71
	1E. And again he denied^B *it* with *an* oath^C that "I do not know the man"	72
	3D. And having come to *him* after *a* little *while*, the *ones* standing *there* said *to* Peter, "Truly⁵ **you** also are *one* of them, for even your speaking⁶ makes you evident⁷"	73
	1E. Then he began to curse⁸, and to swear-with-an-oath⁹ that "I do not know the man"	74
	4D. And immediately *a* rooster crowed. °And Peter remembered¹⁰ the word Jesus *had* spoken¹¹— that "Before *a* rooster crows, you will deny^D Me three-times". And having gone outside, he wept^E bitterly^F	75

8B.¹² Now having become early-morning, all the chief priests and the elders *of* the people took counsel¹³ against Jesus so as to put Him to death.¹⁴ °And having bound^G Him, they led *Him* away and handed *Him* over *to* Pilate¹⁵ the governor¹⁶   27:1 / 2

9B.¹⁷ Then Judas (the *one* handing Him over)— having seen that He was condemned¹⁸, having regretted^H *it*— returned the thirty silver-coins¹⁹ *to* the chief priests and elders, °saying, "I sinned, having handed-over^J innocent²⁰ blood"   3 / 4

    1C. But the *ones* said, "What *is it* to us? **You** shall see *to it*"
    2C. And having thrown^K the silver-coins into²¹ the temple, he departed. And having gone away, he hanged *himself*   5
    3C. But the chief priests, having taken the silver-coins, said, "It is not lawful^L to put them into the temple-treasury, since it is *the* price^M *of* blood".²² °And having taken counsel, they bought the field *of* the potter with them²³, for *a* burial-place *for* strangers^N. °For this reason, that field was called *the* Field *of* Blood²⁴ up to today   6 / 7 / 8

        1D. Then the *thing* was fulfilled having been spoken through Jeremiah²⁵ the prophet saying²⁶ "And they took²⁷ the thirty silver-coins— the price^M *of* the *One* having been priced, Whom they from *the* sons^O *of* Israel priced²⁸— °and they gave them for the field *of* the potter, just as *the* Lord directed²⁹ me"   9 / 10

10B.³⁰ Now Jesus was stood³¹ in front of the governor   11

    1C. And the governor questioned^P Him, saying, "Are **You** the King *of* the Jews?"

        1D. And Jesus said, "**You** are saying *it*"³²

    2C. And during His being accused^Q by the chief priests and elders, He answered nothing   12

        1D. Then Pilate says *to* Him, "Do You not hear how many *things* they are testifying against You?"   13
        2D. And He did not answer him with-regard-to even one charge³³, so that the governor *was* marveling^R greatly^S   14

    3C. Now at *the* Feast^T, the governor was accustomed^U to release^V *for* the crowd one prisoner^W whom they were wanting^X. °And at that time they were holding *a* notorious^Y prisoner being called Jesus³⁴ Barabbas   15 / 16

1. Or, "gateway". That is, the gateway from the street into the courtyard of the house. Used 18 times. GK *4784*. Or, "And another saw him *who had* gone out to the gate".
2. That is, another servant girl.
3. Some manuscripts say "*to* them there" {N}.
4. Some manuscripts say "This *one* also" {B}.
5. Or, "Really". On this word, see 14:33.
6. That is, Peter's manner of speaking, or his Galilean accent or dialectical differences. His speaking gave him away as a Galilean. On this word, see Jn 8:43.
7. Or, "clear, plain". On this word, see Gal 3:11.
8. Used only here. It means "to put under a curse", as in "May God curse me if I know the man". GK *2874*.
9. Perhaps Peter said, "By the temple, I do not know the man". Same word as in 5:34. On this word, see "swear" in Jam 5:12.
10. This word (GK *3630*) is related to the word in Mk 14:72 (GK *389*). Luke uses another related word.
11. Or, "the word *of* Jesus, *who had* said that". This is a participle modifying "Jesus".
12. Parallel account at Mk 15:1; Lk 22:66; 23:1; Jn 18:28.
13. On the phrase "took counsel", see 12:14. The same phrase is in v 7.
14. Having condemned Jesus for blasphemy, they now had to devise a charge that would be acceptable to Pilate.
15. Some manuscripts say "Pontius Pilate" {B}. See Lk 3:1 on him.
16. Used 20 times. GK *2450*. The related verb is in Lk 2:2.
17. Compare Act 1:18-19.
18. Same word as in 20:18, where Jesus predicted it. On this word, see 1 Cor 11:32.
19. On this word, see "money" in 25:27. The same word is in v 5, 6, 9.
20. Elsewhere only of Pilate, in 27:24. GK *127*.
21. This word means either somewhere "in" the temple area, or, "into" the Holy Place. GK *1650*. Some manuscripts say "in" the temple {N}, using GK *1877*.
22. That is, Christ's blood, v 9. The Jewish leaders had no scruples about paying it, but now that the price paid to Judas for Jesus has accomplished its purpose, they have scruples about taking it back.
23. This is an idiom, literally, "for [the value of] them".
24. Because it was bought with blood money.
25. This paraphrase comes from Jeremiah 18:2-12; 19:1-11; 32:6-9; and Zechariah 11:12-13. It is mainly from Zechariah. Some think Matthew attributes it to Jeremiah because he is the better known prophet, as also occurs in Mk 1:2.
26. This word modifies "prophet". See 1:22.
27. Same word as "taken" in v 6. GK *3284*.
28. That is, the price of the One having had a price set for Him by these sons of Israel. On this word, see "honoring" in 1 Tim 5:3.
29. Or, "ordered, commanded". Elsewhere only in 21:6; 26:19. GK *5332*.
30. Parallel account at Mk 15:2; Lk 23:2; Jn 18:29.
31. Or, "made to stand". On this word, see "standing" in Mk 13:14. Some manuscripts say "Now Jesus stood" {N}.
32. Same phrase as in Mk 15:2; Lk 23:3. Compare Jn 18:37. Some think it means "Yes". Others think its meaning comes from the context. Though Jesus means "You are saying *it* [correctly]", He leaves the adverb unexpressed, leaving Pilate to supply it, which Pilate does based on His Jewish accusers (note v 12, 37). Jesus answers this way because "King of the Jews" means something different to Pilate than to Jesus. Similar to the phrase in 26:64. The full phrase can be seen in Jn 13:13, "You speak rightly". Both "wrongly" and "rightly" occur in Jn 18:23.
33. Or, "up-to even one word". On this word, see "word" in Rom 10:17.
34. Some manuscripts omit this word {C}. See Mk 15:7 on Barabbas.

A. Mt 2:23 B. 2 Tim 2:12 C. Jam 5:12 D. Mt 16:24 E. Jn 11:33 F. Lk 22:62 G. 1 Cor 7:27 H. Mt 21:29 J. Mt 26:21 K. Mt 9:36, thrown forth L. 1 Cor 6:12 M. 1 Tim 5:17, honor N. Rom 16:23, host O. Gal 3:7 P. Lk 9:18 Q. Jn 5:45 R. Rev 17:8 S. Mk 1:35, very T. Jn 13:29 U. Lk 4:16, become a custom V. Mt 5:31, sends away W. Eph 3:1 X. Jn 7:17, willing Y. Rom 16:7, notable

Matthew 27:17 — 100 — Verse

    1D. So they[1] having been gathered together, Pilate said *to* them, "Whom do you want me to release[2] *for* you? Jesus[3] Barabbas, or Jesus, the *One* being called Christ?" — 17

        1E. For he knew[4] that they[5] handed Him over because of envy[A] — 18
        2E. And while he *was* sitting on the judgment-seat[B], his wife sent out *a message* to him, saying, "Have nothing to do with that righteous *One*.[6] For I suffered[C] greatly today in *a* dream[D] because of Him" — 19
        3E. But the chief priests and the elders persuaded[E] the crowds that they should ask-*for* Barabbas and destroy[F] Jesus — 20

    2D. Now having responded, the governor said *to* them, "Which of the two do you want me to release[7] *for* you?" — 21

        1E. And the *ones* said, "Barabbas"

    3D. Pilate says *to* them, "Then what should I do *as to* Jesus, the *One* being called Christ?" — 22

        1E. They all say[8], "Let Him be crucified[G]!"

    4D. But the *one*[9] said, "What indeed[10] did He do wrong[11]?" — 23

        1E. But the *ones* were crying out even more, saying, "Let Him be crucified!"

    5D. And Pilate— having seen that he[12] is profiting nothing[13], but rather *an* uproar[H] is taking place— having taken water, washed-off[14] *his* hands in front of the crowd, saying, "I am innocent[J] of the blood *of* this[15] *One*. **You** shall see *to it*[16] — 24

        1E. And having responded, all the people said, "His blood *be* upon us and upon our children" — 25

    4C. Then he released Barabbas *to* them. But having flogged[17] Jesus, he handed *Him* over in order that He might be crucified — 26

11B.[18] Then the soldiers[K] *of* the governor, having taken Jesus into the Praetorium[19], gathered the whole [Roman] cohort[20] to[21] Him — 27

    1C. And having stripped[L] Him, they put *a* scarlet cloak[22] on Him. °And having woven *a* crown[M] out of thorns[N], they put *it* on His head, and *they put* a staff[23] in His right *hand* — 28-29

        1D. And having knelt[O] in front of Him, they mocked[24] Him, saying, "Hail[25], King *of* the Jews!"
        2D. And having spat[P] on Him, they took the staff and were striking[Q] *Him* on His head — 30
        3D. And when they mocked Him, they stripped the cloak off Him and put His garments on Him — 31

    2C.[26] And they led Him away so as to crucify *Him*. °And while going forth, they found *a* Cyrenian[27] man, Simon *by* name. They pressed this *one* into service[28] in order that he might take-up His cross[R] — 32

    3C. And having come to *a* place being called Golgotha[29] (which is meaning "*The* Place *of a* Skull[30]"), °they gave Him wine[31] having been mixed with gall[32] to drink. And having tasted[S] *it*, He did not want[T] to drink[33] — 33, 34

    4C. And having crucified[34] Him, they divided[U] His garments among *themselves*[35], casting[V] *a* lot[36]. And sitting-*down*, they were guarding[W] Him there — 35, 36

1. That is, the crowds, v 15, 20.
2. This is an idiom, literally, "Whom do you want *that* I should release...". The same idiom is in v 21.
3. Some manuscripts omit this word {C}.
4. This word (see 1 Jn 2:29 on it) is not related to the word in Mk 15:10 (see Lk 1:34 on it).
5. That is, the chief priests and elders, v 12, 20.
6. This is an idiom, literally, "Nothing *for* you and *for* that righteous *One*". See a similar idiom in Jn 2:4.
7. More literally, "want *that* I should release".
8. Some manuscripts add "*to* him" {N}.
9. Some manuscripts say "the governor" {N}.
10. Or, "Why, what evil did He do?". It is an incredulous question. The word "indeed" is also used in this way in Mk 15:14; Lk 23:22; Jn 7:41; Act 8:31; 16:37; 19:35; Rom 3:3; 1 Cor 11:22; Phil 1:18. GK *1142*.
11. Or, "evil". What did He do that is criminally wrong? What crime did He commit? Same word as in Jn 18:30, on which see "evil" in 3 Jn 11.
12. Or, "it".
13. Pilate is getting nothing for his efforts. On "profit nothing", see Jn 6:63.
14. Used only here. GK *672*. This is Jewish symbolism.
15. Or, "of this blood". Some manuscripts say "of the blood *of* this righteous *One*" {B}.
16. That is, to the responsibility for the taking of this life. This is the same thing the priests told Judas, v 4. They accept it.
17. Or, "scourged", that is, whipped with a whip. Elsewhere only in Mk 15:15. GK *5849*. This was common Roman practice before a person was crucified. Related to "lash" in Jn 2:15. Not related to "whip" in Mt 20:19; Jn 19:1.
18. Parallel account at Mk 15:16. Compare Jn 19:2-3.
19. That is, the Roman palace or fortress. On this word, see Phil 1:13.
20. This word was used of a Roman battalion (one tenth of a legion, and thus about 600 soldiers), and of a "tactical unit" or "detachment" of soldiers. Here, Matthew seems to mean that the portion of the cohort then on duty in the fortress came to watch. Elsewhere only in Mk 15:16; Jn 18:3, 12; Act 10:1; 21:31; 27:1. GK *5061*.
21. As this word is used with "gathered" in Mk 5:21, meaning that the cohort physically gathered together around Jesus. Or, "against", as it is used in Act 4:27, in which case it would refer to their intent to harm Jesus. GK *2093*.
22. Used only here and in v 31, this refers to a short cloak worn by soldiers, officers, and officials. GK *5948*.
23. Or, "walking stick", in imitation of a kingly scepter. Same word as in v 30, and as "stick" in v 48.
24. Some manuscripts say "they were mocking" {B}. Same word as in 20:19; 27:31, 41. On this word, see Lk 23:11.
25. Or, "Greetings, Hello, Welcome". It is a common word of greeting, not associated with worship or paying homage, though they did this also in Mk 15:19. Same word as "greetings" in 26:49; 28:9; and Act 15:23; 23:26. On this word, see "rejoice" in 2 Cor 13:11.
26. Parallel account at Mk 15:20; Lk 23:26; Jn 19:16.
27. That is, from Cyrene, a city on the coast of Africa, west of Egypt. On this word, see Act 6:9.
28. On the word "press into service", see 5:41. The Roman officer had this authority under Roman law.
29. This is a transliterated Hebrew word meaning "skull". Elsewhere only in Mk 15:22; Jn 19:17. GK *1201*.
30. The Greek word is *kranion*, from which we get "cranium". Elsewhere only in Mk 15:22; Lk 23:33; Jn 19:17. GK *3191*. This word in Latin is *Calvariae*, from which we get "Calvary".
31. Some manuscripts say "sour-wine" {N}, as in v 48.
32. Some think the soldiers added gall to make it taste bitter, another insult. Others think that this drink was provided by noble Jewish women to all victims of crucifixion in order to dull the senses. On this word, see Act 8:23.
33. That is, Jesus refused the drink. He was unwilling to drink it.
34. Used 46 times. GK *5090*. Related to "cross" in 10:38.
35. The grammar of the verb "divided among" implies "*themselves*". Likewise in Mk 15:24; Lk 23:34. In Jn 19:24, which actually quotes from Ps 22:18, "themselves" is expressed.
36. Some manuscripts add "in order that the *thing* might be fulfilled having been spoken through the prophet — they divided up My garments *among* themselves, and they cast *a* lot upon my clothing" {A}, as in Jn 19:24. On "lot", see "share" in Col 1:12.

A. Mk 15:10 B. Rom 14:10 C. Gal 3:4 D. Mt 2:12 E. 1 Jn 3:3:19 F. 1 Cor 1:18, perish G. Mt 27:35 H. Mk 5:38, commotion J. Mt 27:4 K. Mt 28:12 L. 2 Cor 5:3, take off M. Rev 4:4 N. Lk 6:44 O. Mt 17:14 P. Mk 14:65 Q. Lk 6:29 R. Mt 10:38 S. Heb 6:4 T. Jn 7:17, willing U. Act 2:3 V. Rev 2:22, throw W. 1 Jn 5:18, keeping

5C.	And above His head they put on His charge[A], having been written, "This is Jesus, the King *of* the Jews"	37
6C.	Then two robbers[1] are crucified[B] with Him, one on *the* right *side* and one on *the* left *side*	38
7C.	And the *ones* passing by were blaspheming[C] Him while shaking[D] their heads°and saying, "The *One* tearing-down[E] the temple and building *it* in three days, save[F] Yourself— if[2] You are God's **Son**— and[3] come down from the cross"	39-40
8C.	Likewise also the chief priests, mocking[G] *Him* with the scribes and elders, were saying	41

    1D. "He saved[F] others— Himself He is not able to save[F]!" — 42
    2D. "He[4] is King *of* Israel— let Him come down now from the cross and we will put-faith[5] upon Him"
    3D. "He trusts[H] in God— let Him deliver[6] *Him*[7] now, if He wants[8] Him. For He said that 'I am **God's** Son'" — 43

9C.	And even the robbers[9]— the *ones* having been crucified[B] with Him— were reproaching[J] Him the same	44
10C.[10]	And from *the* sixth hour, *a* darkness[K] came[11] over all the land[12] until *the* ninth hour[13]	45

    1D. And around the ninth hour Jesus shouted-out[14] *with a* loud voice, saying, "Eli, Eli[15], lema sabachthani?", that is, "My God, My God, why[16] did you forsake[17] Me?" — 46

        1E. And some *of* the *ones* standing there, having heard, were saying that "This *One* is calling Elijah" — 47
        2E. And immediately one of them— having run, and having taken *a* sponge, and having filled *it with* sour-wine[18], and having put *it* on *a* stick[19]— was giving-a-drink-*to* Him — 48
        3E. But the others[L] were saying, "Leave[20] *Him alone*. Let us see if Elijah comes *to* save[21] Him"[22] — 49

    2D. And Jesus, again having cried-out[M] *with a* loud voice,[23] let *His* spirit go[24] — 50
    3D. And behold— the curtain[25] *of* the temple[N] was torn[26] in two from top to bottom — 51
    4D. And the earth was shaken[O] and the rocks were split
    5D. And the tombs were opened. And many bodies *of* the saints[P] having fallen-asleep[Q] were raised[27]. °And having come out from the tombs[R] after His resurrection[28], they entered into the holy city and appeared *to* many — 52 / 53
    6D. And the centurion[29] and the *ones* with him guarding[S] Jesus— having seen the earthquake and the *things* having taken place— became extremely afraid, saying[30], "Truly[T] this *One* was God's Son!" — 54

11C.	And many women were there watching at *a* distance, who followed Jesus from Galilee while serving[U] Him	55

    1D. Among whom was Mary the Magdalene[31], and Mary[32] the mother *of* James and Joseph[33], and the mother[34] *of* the sons[35] *of* Zebedee — 56

12B.[36]	Now having become evening[37], *a* rich man from Arimathea[38] came, Joseph *as to* the-name[39], who also himself became-a-disciple[V] *to* Jesus. °This *one*, having gone to Pilate, asked-*for* the body *of* Jesus	57 / 58

    1C. Then Pilate ordered[W] that *it*[40] be given-back[X]
    2C. And having taken the body, Joseph wrapped[41] it in clean linen-cloth,°and laid it in his new tomb[R] which he hewed[Y] in the rock. And having rolled[42] *a* large stone to the door *of* the tomb, he departed — 59-60

1. Or, "insurrectionists". On this word, see 21:13. Same word as in Mk 15:27. Luke uses a different word in 23:32. Used of Barabbas in Jn 18:40. Some think these were two of his men.
2. Or, "since". The grammar assumes the reality of it, as in 4:3. The context indicates it is mockingly assumed. Assuming You are what You say, prove it by saving Yourself.
3. Some manuscripts omit this word {C}, so that there are two sentences, "... save Yourself. If You are... come down".
4. Some manuscripts say "If He is..." {B}.
5. Or, "believe in". Same word as "believe" in Mk 15:32. Some manuscripts say "we will believe Him" {N}. On "put faith upon", see Rom 4:5.
6. Same word as in 6:13, "deliver us from the evil one", Matthew's only other use of this word. On this word, see Col 1:13.
7. Some manuscripts include this word {N}. Or, "Let Him deliver Him now, if He wants".
8. Or, "if He delights *in* Him", in conformity to Ps 22:8 (where this same word is used), a reference Matthew may intend his readers to recognize here. Both make good sense here. On this meaning of this word, see Col 2:18.
9. Or, "And the robbers also".
10. Parallel account at Mk 15:33; Lk 23:44; Jn 19:28.
11. Or, "took place, occurred". GK *1181*.
12. Or, "earth". Or, "the whole land". Same word as in Rev 7:1.
13. That is, from noon to 3 P.M.
14. Or, "cried out". Used only here. GK *331*. Related to "shout" in Mk 15:34.
15. The word "Eli" is transliterated from Hebrew. "Lema" and "sabachthani" are transliterated from Aramaic. Some manuscripts say "lama", which is transliterated from Hebrew {N}. Note Mk 15:34.
16. Or, "for what purpose", "to what end". It is shorthand for "in order that what might happen?". Elsewhere only in 9:4; Lk 13:7; Act 4:25; 7:26; 1 Cor 10:29. GK *2672*. Jesus is quoting Ps 22:1. See Mk 15:34 on this.
17. Or, "abandon, desert". On this word, see 2 Cor 4:9.
18. Or, "wine vinegar" watered down. This was a favorite beverage of the soldiers and common people, and cheaper than wine. Elsewhere only in Mk 15:36; Lk 23:36; Jn 19:29, 30. GK *3954*. Related to "sharp", not the word "wine". This bit of refreshment occurs just before Jesus makes His final shout in v 50; Jn 19:30.
19. Or, "rod, staff". Compare Jn 19:29. On this word, see Mk 15:36.
20. This command, "Leave *alone*", is singular, spoken by the unnamed ones in v 47, to the one giving the drink. The majority try to stop the one from giving Jesus anything. Compare Mk 15:36 on this. Same word as in Mk 14:6, 15:36. GK *918*.
21. On the grammar of this word, see "to do" in Act 24:17.
22. Some manuscripts add "And another, having taken *a* spear, pierced His side. And water and blood came out" {B}, as in Jn 19:34. The scribes who added this failed to notice that Jesus had not died yet!
23. The words Jesus spoke are recorded in Jn 19:30 and Lk 23:46.
24. Or, "sent away *His* spirit". On the word "let go", see "forgive" in 6:12. Compare Mk 15:37; Jn 19:30.
25. Some think Matthew means the curtain before the Holy Place; others, the one before Holy of Holies. In the OT, the word was used of both curtains (see for example Ex 26:33 and 38:18). Either way, it is symbolic of the fact that the way into the presence of God is now opened to all, Heb 9:8. On this word, see Heb 9:3.
26. Or, "split, divided". The same word is used later in the verse of the rocks being "split". Same word as in Mk 15:38; Lk 5:36; 23:45; Jn 19:24; 21:11. Elsewhere only as "divide" in Mk 1:10; Act 14:4; 23:7. GK *5387*. Related to "division" in 1 Cor 1:10.
27. Or, "arose". Clearly the tombs were opened at this time (Friday afternoon), and those raised went into the city after the resurrection of Jesus on Sunday morning. It is unclear whether Matthew means they were raised on Sunday (along with Him), or raised at this time (but did not enter the city). This is symbolic of the fact that Jesus conquered death for all believers. On this word, see "arose" in 28:6.
28. Or, "raising, awakening". Used only here. GK *1587*. Related to "raised" in v 52, and "arose" in 28:6, 7.
29. That is, the Roman soldier in charge. On this word, see 8:5.
30. The verbs "seen", "afraid", and "saying" are all plural, referring to all of them, not just the centurion.
31. That is, the one from Magdala, on the Sea of Galilee. Mentioned also in v 61; 28:1. See Lk 8:2 on her.
32. This woman is mentioned also in 27:61 and 28:1 as "the other Mary"; Mk 15:40, 47; 16:1; Lk 24:10. Compare Jn 19:25.
33. Some manuscripts say "Joses" {N}, as in Mk 15:40.
34. If Mark is referring to the same person, then her name was Salome, Mk 15:40; 16:1. Compare Jn 19:25.
35. That is, James and John, 10:2.
36. Parallel account at Mk 15:42; Lk 23:50; Jn 19:38.
37. That is, first evening, between 3 and 6 P.M., as in 14:15, before sunset when the Sabbath began. Note Mk 15:42; Lk 23:54.
38. This was a town in Judea. Elsewhere only in Mk 15:43; Lk 23:51; Jn 19:38. GK *751*.
39. This method of referring to a person's name, "*as to* the-name", or "*with respect to* the-name", is used only here in the NT. GK *5540*.
40. Some manuscripts say "the body" {N}.
41. Same word as in Lk 23:53. Elsewhere only as "wrapped up" in Jn 20:7. GK *1962*.
42. Elsewhere only in Mk 15:46. GK *4685*.

A. Jn 18:38   B. Mt 27:35   C. 1 Tim 6:1   D. Rev 2:5, move   E. Mt 24:2   F. Lk 19:10   G. Lk 23:11   H. 1 Jn 3:19, persuade   J. 1 Pet 4:14
K. Jn 3:19   L. 2 Pet 3:16   M. Mt 8:29   N. Rev 11:1   O. Mt 21:10   P. 1 Pet 1:16, holy   Q. 1 Thes 4:13   R. Mt 23:29   S. 1 Jn 5:18, keeping
T. Mt 14:33   U. 1 Pet 4:10, ministering   V. Mt 13:52   W. Mt 14:28   X. Mt 16:27, render   Y. Mk 15:46

	3C. And Mary the Magdalene was there, and the other Mary¹, sitting in front of the burial-place^A	61
13B.	Now *on* the next-day² which is after the Preparation³ *day*, the chief priests and the Pharisees were gathered together with Pilate,°saying, "Sir^B, we remembered that that deceiver^C said while still alive, 'I am arising⁴ after three days'. °Therefore, give-orders^D *that* the burial-place^A be made-secure^E until the third day, so that His disciples, having come⁵, might not at any time steal Him and say *to* the people, 'He arose from the dead', and the last deception^F will be worse *than* the first"	62 63 64
	1C. Pilate said *to* them, "Have⁶ a guard⁷. Go, make *it* secure as you know-*how*^G"	65
	2C. And the *ones*, having gone, made the burial-place secure, having sealed^H the stone^J along-with⁸ the guard	66
16A.⁹	Now after¹⁰ *the* Sabbath, *in* the dawning¹¹ toward *the* first *day of the* week¹², Mary the Magdalene and the other Mary went to see the burial-place¹³	28:1
1B.	And behold— *a* great earthquake took place. For *an* angel *of the* Lord— having come down from heaven, and having gone to *it*— rolled away the stone¹⁴ and was sitting on it	2
	1C. And his appearance¹⁵ was like lightning^K, and his clothing *was* white^L as snow	3
	2C. And the *ones* guarding^M were shaken^N from the fear^O *of* him, and became like dead *men*	4
	3C. And having responded,¹⁶ the angel said *to* the women, "Don't **you**¹⁷ be fearing¹⁸, for I know that you are seeking^P **Jesus**, the *One* having been crucified. °He is not here, for He arose¹⁹, just as He said	5 6
	1D. "Come, see the place where He²⁰ was lying^Q	
	2D. "And having gone quickly^R, tell His disciples that 'He arose from the dead. And behold— He is going-ahead-of²¹ you to Galilee. You will see Him there'	7
	3D. "Behold— I told you"	
2B.	And having quickly^R departed²² from the tomb^S with fear and great joy²³, they ran to report^T *it* to His disciples. °And²⁴ behold— Jesus met them, saying "Greetings^U"	8 9
	1C. And the *ones*, having gone to *Him*, took-hold-of^V His feet and gave-worship^W *to* Him	
	2C. Then Jesus says *to* them, "Do not be fearing. Go, report²⁵ *to* My brothers that²⁶ they should go to Galilee. And there they will see Me"	10
3B.	And while they *were* going, behold— some *of* the guard²⁷, having come into the city, reported²⁸ all the *things* having taken place *to* the chief priests	11
	1C. And having been gathered together with the elders, and having taken counsel²⁹, they gave sufficient³⁰ money *to* the soldiers³¹,°saying, "Say that 'His disciples, having come *by* night, stole Him while we *were* sleeping^X'. °And if this should be heard³² before³³ the governor, **we** will persuade³⁴ him. And we will make **you** free-from-concern³⁵"	12 13 14
	2C. And the *ones*, having taken the money, did as they were instructed^Y	15
	3C. And this statement was spread-widely^Z among Jews, until this very day³⁶	
4B.³⁷	And the eleven disciples proceeded to Galilee, to the mountain where Jesus ordered^AA them	16
	1C. And having seen³⁸ Him, they worshiped³⁹ *Him*⁴⁰. But the *ones*⁴¹ doubted⁴²	17

1. See v 56.
2. That is, Saturday. Used 17 times. GK *2069*.
3. That is, Friday. On this word, see Jn 19:31.
4. Or, "I am being raised", that is, I will be raised. On this word, see "arose" in 28:6.
5. Some manuscripts add "*by* night" {N}.
6. The form of this word could either be a command, "Have *a* guard", or a statement, "You have *a* guard". In either case, Pilate is responding favorably to their request. GK *2400*.
7. This is a transliterated Latin word referring to a detachment of Roman soldiers doing guard duty. Elsewhere only in 27:66; 28:11 (where its plurality is clear). GK *3184*. Compare the terms in Jn 18:12.
8. This is the Greek word order. Matthew may mean that the chief priests and Pharisees went "along with" the Roman guard and they sealed the stone together, using a Temple seal, a Roman seal, or both. Or he may mean that the priests sealed the stone "by means of " the Roman guard, the Romans placing a Roman seal on the tomb. Or he may mean that the priests made it secure by sealing the stone "along with" posting the Roman guard. GK *3552*. The seal carries the authority of the state. On "seal", see Eph 1:13.
9. Parallel account at Mk 16:1; Lk 24:1; Jn 20:1.
10. This word means "after" or "late". Some think Matthew means "after *the* Sabbath", that is, sometime after sunset on Saturday. Others think he means "late *on the* Sabbath", that is, sometime Saturday evening before sunset. In other words, these women visit the grave here before the Sabbath was over, then go and buy spices Saturday evening after the Sabbath was over (Mk 16:1), then return to the grave on Sunday morning (Mk 16:2), where Mt 28:2 resumes. Elsewhere only as "evening" in Mk 11:19; 13:35. GK *4067*. These two views correspond with two views on the next word.
11. This word is used in two ways. Some think Matthew means "near sunrise on Sunday morning", the dawning of daytime, its normal Greek meaning, and so, "after the Sabbath". Others think he means "near sunset on Saturday night", the dawning of the Jewish day (as in its only other use in Lk 23:54, "the Sabbath was dawning"), and so, "late on the Sabbath". GK *2216*.
12. The words "Sabbath" and "week" are the same Greek word. It means "week" 9 times and "Sabbath" 59 times. GK *4879*.
13. Note that here the women come "to see the burial-place". In Lk 24:1; Mk 16:2, they come to anoint Him. This suggests two visits to some, and corresponds with the "late on the Sabbath as the Jewish day was dawning" view above. On this word, see 23:29.
14. Some manuscripts add "from the door" {N}.
15. Or, "form, outward appearance". Used only here. GK *1624*. Related to "appearance" in 2 Cor 5:7.
16. That is, to the arrival of the women.
17. The emphasis may mean "you in contrast with the guards"; or, "you of all people, you who love Him".
18. The grammar implies "stop fearing, stop being afraid".
19. Or, "was raised". Same word as in v 7. This verb means "to raise, to arise" in several senses. It can mean "to wake up" from sleep, "to get up" from sitting down, "to rise, arise, raise, be raised" from the dead, etc. Used 144 times. GK *1586*. Related to "resurrection" in Mt 27:53.
20. Some manuscripts say "the Lord" {A}.
21. Same word as in 26:32. On this word, see 2 Jn 9.
22. Some manuscripts say "having gone out" {B}, as in Mk 16:8.
23. The life of Jesus life began with "great joy" in 2:10 (same words); here it begins again with "great joy". This phrase is found in Matthew only in these two places. Compare Lk 24:52, where the same thing occurs!
24. Some manuscripts say "Now as they were going to report *to* His disciples— and behold, ..." {A}.
25. This same word is used in v 8, 11; Mk 16:10, 13; Lk 24:9. On this word, see "announce" in 1 Jn 1:3.
26. Or, "Go, report *it to* My brothers, so that they will go to Galilee", based on the command Jesus had previously given them. Compare Mk 16:7. The one case gives a kind of command, the other gives the purpose of the reporting.
27. That is, the Roman guard, the soldiers, v 12. On this word, see 27:65.
28. Some manuscripts say "informed" {B}.
29. On the phrase "take counsel", see 12:14.
30. Or, "considerable, enough". On this word, see 2 Cor 3:5.
31. Other than the metaphorical use in 2 Tim 2:3, this word is used 25 times in the NT— always of Roman soldiers. Matthew uses it three times, 8:9; 27:27; 28:12. GK *5132*. On the temple "officers", see Jn 18:12.
32. That is, in a judicial sense. If you are put on trial before Pilate for losing the body, we will persuade him.
33. Some manuscripts say "by" {N}.
34. The chief priests probably mean "with a bribe". The Roman governors commonly accepted money for favors.
35. Or, "free from worry". On this word, see 1 Cor 7:32. The soldiers had much to worry about. If Pilate heard that they were sleeping on duty and allowed the body of Jesus to be stolen (as this lie purports), they would be executed. Without this assurance (and the money), they would not have agreed to the lie.
36. This is an idiom, literally "until the today day", on which see Rom 11:8. Some manuscripts omit "day", so that it says "until today" {C}.
37. Compare Mk 16:15-18; Lk 24:46-49; Jn 20:21-23.
38. Some think that this is the appearance to 500 people that Paul mentions in 1 Cor 15:6.
39. As in Lk 24:52. Or, "prostrated-*themselves*", as this word is used in Mt 20:20. On this word, see 14:33.
40. Some manuscripts include this word with grammar so that it means "gave worship *to* Him" or "prostrated-*themselves before* Him" {N}.
41. This is the literal rendering. This idiom introduces a second class of individuals alongside the eleven mentioned in the previous sentence (see 26:67 on it). Who is being referred to? The idiom can mean "But others", referring to a group of disciples other than the eleven disciples. Or it can mean "But some", referring to a sub-group of those just mentioned. In this case, Matthew is referring to some of the eleven, who perhaps were not sure it was really Jesus because He was at a distance. Then He "came to them" and spoke to them, v 18.
42. Or, "hesitated". Elsewhere only in 14:31. GK *1491*.

A. Mt 23:29 B. Mt 8:2, master C. 1 Tim 4:1, deceitful D. Mt 14:28, order E. Act 16:24, secure F. 1 Thes 2:3, error G. 1 Jn 2:29, know H. Eph 1:13 J. Mk 16:3 K. Rev 4:5 L. Jn 4:35 M. 1 Jn 5:18, keeping N. Mt 21:10 O. Eph 5:21 P. Phil 2:21 Q. Mt 3:10 R. Rev 22:7 S. Mt 23:29 T. 1 Jn 1:3, announcing U. 2 Cor 13:11, rejoice V. Heb 4:14, hold on to W. Mt 14:33 X. 1 Thes 4:13, falling asleep Y. Rom 12:7, teaching Z. Mt 9:31 AA. Rom 13:1, established

Matthew 28:18	106	Verse

    2C. And having come to *them*, Jesus spoke *to* them, saying   18

        1D. "All authority[A] in heaven and on earth was given *to* Me
        2D. "Therefore[1] having gone[2], make-disciples-of[3] all the nations[B]   19

            1E. "Baptizing[C] them in[4] the name[5] *of* the Father and the Son and the Holy Spirit
            2E. "Teaching[D] them to keep[E] all that I commanded[F] you   20

        3D. "And behold— **I** am with you all the days until the conclusion[6] *of* the age"[7]

1. Some manuscripts omit this word {N}.
2. This participle gives an attendant circumstance to the command that follows. The command is to make disciples of all nations, but this cannot be done without having gone to all nations. Therefore both are required. This word could be rendered as a subordinate command, "Go, make disciples", but this rendering makes them appear to be commands of equal weight. This word is used this way in 2:8; 9:13; 11:4; 22:15; 27:66; etc. Compare 18:15, where two commands of equal weight are given. Using different words in these same two ways, compare 28:7 and 10. This word is used as a command in 2:20; 8:9; 10:6; etc. It means "to go, proceed, walk, travel. Used 153 times. GK *4513*.
3. On this word, see "become a disciple" in 13:52.
4. Or, "into". This is the same word as "in the Jordan" in Mk 1:9. See the note there.
5. This word is singular.
6. That is, when Jesus visibly returns. On this word, see 24:3.
7. Some manuscripts add "amen" {A}.

A. Rev 6:8   B. Act 15:23, Gentiles   C. Mk 1:8   D. Rom 12:7   E. 1 Jn 5:18   F. Mk 10:3

Mark

Overview

The beginning of the good news of Jesus Christ, the Son of God	1:1

1A.	Just as Isaiah wrote, John came— making ready the way, proclaiming a baptism of repentance	1:2-8
2A.	In those days, Jesus came and was baptized by John. Then He was tempted in the wilderness	1:9-13
3A.	Now after John was handed over, Jesus went to Galilee proclaiming the good news of God	1:14-15

1B.	While passing beside the Sea of Galilee, He called Simon, Andrew, James, John	1:16-20
2B.	They go into Capernaum. He teaches and heals. They are astounded. Peter's mother-in-law	1:21-38
3B.	He went proclaiming in their synagogues in all Galilee. He heals a leper	1:39-45
4B.	He came to Capernaum and forgave and healed a paralytic on the Sabbath. Some objected	2:1-12
5B.	He went out by the sea and taught. He called Levi and ate at his house. Some objected	2:13-17
6B.	Why are Your disciples not fasting? The bridegroom is here. New wine and wineskins	2:18-22
7B.	The disciples picked grain on the Sabbath. Some objected. I am Lord of the Sabbath	2:23-28
8B.	He healed a man on the Sabbath. Pharisees and Herodians plotted to destroy Him	3:1-6
9B.	Jesus withdrew to the sea. A great multitude followed. He cured many	3:7-12
10B.	He goes up into the mountain, and appoints twelve to be with Him and to proclaim	3:13-19
11B.	He goes into a house. Some say He cast out demons by Satan. His family comes	3:20-35
12B.	He was teaching in parables. The sower. The lamp. The mustard seed. He explains	4:1-34
13B.	That evening, they left in a boat, and He calmed the sea. They said, Who is this One?	4:35-41
14B.	At the other side, He cast demons into a herd of pigs, and sent the man to proclaim it	5:1-20
15B.	He crossed back over and healed a woman and raised Jairus's daughter from the dead	5:21-6:1
16B.	He comes to His hometown and taught in the synagogue. They took offense at Him	6:1-6
17B.	He was going around the villages, teaching. And He sent out the twelve, two by two	6:6-13
18B.	King Herod heard of Him and said He was John the Baptist risen from the dead	6:14-29
19B.	The apostles gather and report all that they did. They go to rest. Jesus feeds 5000	6:30-44
20B.	He sends the disciples away in a boat. Later, He comes to them walking on the sea	6:45-52
21B.	Having crossed over to Gennesaret, He healed people wherever He went	6:53-56
22B.	Pharisees accuse His disciples. He says, It is what comes out of the heart that defiles	7:1-23
23B.	Jesus departed to Tyre, and healed a Gentile's daughter— crumbs from the table	7:24-30
24B.	He went to the Sea of Galilee in Decapolis and healed a deaf mute	7:31-37
25B.	In those days, there again being large crowd, Jesus fed about 4000	8:1-9
26B.	He left for Dalmanutha. The Pharisees asked for a sign. None will be given	8:10-12
27B.	He left for the other side. They forgot bread. Jesus said, Do you not yet understand?	8:13-21
28B.	They come to Bethsaida. Jesus heals a blind man in two steps	8:22-26
29B.	On the way to Caesarea, Jesus asked, Who do you say I am? You are the Christ	8:27-30

4A.	And He began to teach His disciples that He must suffer, be rejected, be killed, and rise up	8:31-32

1B.	Peter rebuked Him. Jesus said, You are not thinking the things of God, but of humans	8:32-33
2B.	Jesus said, If any want to follow Me, let him deny himself, take up his cross, and follow	8:34-9:1
3B.	After six days, Jesus takes Peter, James, and John up on a mountain, and is transfigured	9:2-8
4B.	While coming down from the mountain, they asked about Elijah	9:9-13
5B.	Having come back to the disciples, Jesus healed one the disciples could not	9:14-29
6B.	Passing through Galilee, Jesus was teaching them that He must be killed, and arise	9:30-32
7B.	At Capernaum, they were discussing who was greater. Jesus said, the servant, the child	9:33-50

5A. And He went from there into the districts of Judea. Crowds gathered and He was teaching them   10:1

    1B. Pharisees asked, Is lawful for a man to divorce a wife— testing Him   10:2-12
    2B. They were bringing children to Him. You must welcome the kingdom like a child   10:13-16
    3B. What should I do to inherit eternal life? Sell, follow me. It is not easy for a rich man   10:17-31
    4B. On the road, Jesus took aside the twelve and said He would be killed, and will rise again   10:32-34
    5B. James and John ask to sit next to Him in the kingdom. He said, It is not mine to give   10:35-45
    6B. At Jericho, Jesus healed Bartimaeus, a blind beggar   10:46-52
    7B. At Bethany, He sent two disciples to get a colt. He road it, and they cried out Hosanna!   11:1-10

6A. And Jesus entered into Jerusalem, into the temple   11:11

    1B. Having looked around, He went out to Bethany, since it was late   11:11
    2B. On the next day, He cursed a fig tree   11:12-14
    3B. He entered the temple and drove out those buying and selling. The priests plotted   11:15-19
    4B. Passing by the next morning, they saw the fig tree withered. Be having faith in God   11:20-26
    5B. In the temple, the chief priests say, By what authority are you doing these things? The parable of the vineyard   11:27-12:12
    6B. They sent some Pharisees to trap Him. Is it lawful to give a poll-tax to Caesar?   12:13-17
    7B. Sadducees come to Him, questioning Him about the resurrection. Whose wife is she?   12:18-27
    8B. A scribe asked, What is the foremost commandment? Love God. Love your neighbor   12:28-34
    9B. Jesus asked them, David calls the Christ "Lord". In what way is He his son?   12:35-37
    10B. In His teaching, He was saying, Beware of the scribes seeking honor and money   12:37-40
    11B. He was observing those giving to the temple, and praised a widow who gave all she had   12:41-44
    12B. Jesus prophesies regarding the future of the temple and the signs of the end   13:1-37

7A. Now the Passover was two days away and the priests planned how to seize and kill Him   14:1-2

    1B. At Bethany, a woman poured perfume on Him. Jesus said, She has anointed Me for burial   14:3-9
    2B. Judas went to the priests in order that He might hand Him over to them   14:10-11
    3B. They ate the Passover meal together. One will betray Me. This is My body, My blood   14:12-25
    4B. They went to the Mount of Olives. Jesus said they would fall away. Peter said, Not me   14:26-31
    5B. They come to Gethsemane. Jesus prayed, they slept. Judas comes, Jesus is taken   14:32-52
    6B. They lead Him to the high priest. They condemn Him for blasphemy. Peter denies Him   14:53-72
    7B. The Jews lead Him to Pilate. Pilate offers to free Jesus or Barabbas. Crucify Him!   15:1-15
    8B. The soldiers mock Him, and crucify Him. The Jews blaspheme Him. He expires   15:16-41
    9B. Joseph of Arimathea asked Pilate for the body, and placed it in a tomb   15:42-47

8A. After the Sabbath, three women bought spices that they might anoint Him. He was raised. They flee, afraid. He appears to the disciples, commissions them, and ascends   16:1-20

Mark 1:1	110	Verse

The beginning[1] *of* the good-news[A] *of* Jesus[2] Christ, God's Son[3]   1

1A.[4] Just as it has been written in Isaiah the prophet[5]— "Behold, I am sending-forth[B] My messenger[C] ahead   2
of Your presence[6], who will make Your way ready[7]: °*a* voice *of one* shouting[D] in the wilderness[E],   3
'Prepare[8] the way *of the* Lord, be making His paths straight' "—°John came[9], the[10] *one* baptizing in the   4
wilderness and[11] proclaiming[F] *a* baptism[12] *of* repentance[G] for *the* forgiveness[H] *of* sins[J]

    1B. And the whole Judean country[13] was going out to him, and all the people-of-Jerusalem[K]. And they   5
were being baptized by him in the Jordan River while confessing-out[14] their sins

    2B. And John was dressed-in[15] camel's hair[16] and *a* belt made-of-leather around his waist[L], and *was*   6
eating locusts and wild honey

    3B. And he was proclaiming[F], saying, "The *One* more powerful[M] *than* me is coming after me— *of*   7
Whom I am not fit[N], having stooped[O], to untie[P] the strap[Q] *of* His sandals. °**I** baptized you *with*[17]   8
water, but **He** will baptize[18] you with[19] *the* Holy Spirit"

2A.[20] And it came about during those days *that* Jesus came from Nazareth *of* Galilee, and was baptized in[21]   9
the Jordan by[22] John

    1B. And immediately[23] while ascending[24] out-of [25] the water, He saw the heavens being divided[26], and   10
the Spirit like *a* dove descending to[27] Him. °And *a* voice came from the heavens— "**You** are My   11
beloved[R] Son. With[28] You I was[29] well-pleased"

    2B.[30] And immediately the Spirit sends Him out[31] into the wilderness   12

        1C. And He was in the wilderness forty days being tempted[S] by Satan[T]   13
        2C. And He was with the wild-beasts[32]
        3C. And the angels were ministering[33] *to* Him

3A.[34] Now after John *was* handed-over[U] [to prison],[35] Jesus came to Galilee proclaiming[F] the good-news[A] *of*   14
God[36], °and saying that "The time has been fulfilled[V], and the kingdom *of* God has drawn-near[W].   15
Repent[X], and put-faith in[37] the good-news[A]"

    1B.[38] And while passing-by beside the Sea *of* Galilee   16

        1C. He saw Simon[39] and Andrew (the brother *of* Simon[40]), casting-a-net[41] in the sea. For they were
fishermen

            1D. And Jesus said *to* them, "Come after Me, and I will make you become fishermen *of*   17
people[Y]"
            2D. And immediately, having left the[42] nets, they followed Him   18

        2C. And having gone on *a* little[43], He saw James (the *son of* Zebedee) and John (his brother)— they   19
also in *their* boat, preparing[44] the nets

            1D. And immediately, He called[Z] them   20
            2D. And having left their father Zebedee in the boat with the hired[45] *ones*, they went after Him

    2B.[46] And they proceed into Capernaum   21

        1C. And immediately, having entered into the synagogue *on* the Sabbath, He was teaching

1. Some think this is a title to the whole book, which covers the life of Christ from John the Baptist to the resurrection. Others think it is a heading for v 2-8, or 2-13.
2. Some think Mark means the good news about Jesus; others, the good news proclaimed by Jesus.
3. Some manuscripts omit "God's Son" {C}.
4. Parallel account at Mt 3:1; Lk 3:1; Jn 1:19.
5. Some manuscripts say "written in the prophets" {A}. The quotation is from Mal 3:1 (see also Mt 11:10; Lk 7:27) and Isa 40:3 (see also Mt 3:3; Lk 3:4; Jn 1:23). Mark only names the better known prophet, a common practice. The main sentence is "Just as it has been written... John came". Compare Lk 1:17.
6. Or, "face". That is, in advance of the personal presence of Jesus. On "ahead of Your presence", see Lk 9:52.
7. This word "make ready" is the same word as in Mt 11:10; Lk 1:17; 7:27. On this word, see "prepare" in Heb 9:2. Not the same word as "prepare" next, although it has that meaning. Some manuscripts add "before You" {N}.
8. John is a voice shouting to Israel to prepare for the Messiah. Moral and spiritual preparation is in view, repentance. On this word, see 14:15.
9. Or, "arose". GK *1181*. Related to the word in Mt 3:1.
10. Some manuscripts omit this word, so that it says "John came baptizing..." {C}. Some treat the participle as a noun, "John the Baptist came".
11. Some manuscripts omit this word {N}.
12. Elsewhere only in Mt 3:7; 21:25; Mk 10:38, 39; 11:30; Lk 3:3; 7:29; 12:50; 20:4; Act 1:22; 10:37; 13:24; 18:25; 19:3, 4; Rom 6:4; Eph 4:5; 1 Pet 3:21. GK *967*. Related to "baptize" in Mk 1:8; "cleansings" in Heb 6:2; "dip" in Rev 19:13; "dip-into" in Mk 14:20; and "Baptist" in Mk 6:25.
13. Mark could mean the people of the country of Judea as opposed to its capital Jerusalem; or of the countryside as opposed to that city. It also means "region, field, land". Used 28 times. GK *6001*.
14. Or, "openly admitting". On this word, see Jam 5:16.
15. Or, "had dressed in". This is a participle, he "was having been dressed-in". John was habitually dressed this way. On this word, see "put on" in Rom 13:14. "Dressed in" is related to "clothing" in Mt 3:4.
16. John's outer garment was made of camel's hair, more literally, "hairs *of a* camel".
17. This grammatical construction means "in" or "with", and is used with "baptize" only as "*in*" or "*with*" water in Mk 1:8; Lk 3:16; Act 1:5; 11:16. Some manuscripts include the preposition used in the next phrase {B}.
18. Or, "dip, immerse, wash, cleanse". The word "baptize" is used only as listed in the previous note and the following three notes; and with "on the basis of" in Act 2:38; with "on behalf of" in 1 Cor 15:29; with "baptism" in Mk 10:38, 39; Lk 7:29; 12:50; Act 19:4; and standing alone in Mt 3:16; Mk 6:14, 24; 16:16; Lk 3:12, 21; Jn 1:25, 28; 3:22, 23, 26; 4:1, 2; 10:40; Act 2:41; 8:12, 13, 36, 38; 9:18; 10:47; 16:15, 33; 18:8; 22:16; 1 Cor 1:14, 16, 17; and as "cleanse" in Mk 7:4; Lk 11:38. GK *966*.
19. This preposition (*en*) can mean "in, with, by". It is used with "baptize" only as "in the wilderness" in Mk 1:4; "in the Jordan" in Mt 3:6; Mk 1:5; "in Aenon" in Jn 3:23; "in" or "with" water in Mt 3:11; Jn 1:26, 31, 33; "in" or "with" the Spirit in Mt 3:11; Mk 1:8; Lk 3:16; Jn 1:33; Act 1:5; 11:16; 1 Cor 12:13; "in" or "with" fire in Mt 3:11; Lk 3:16; "in the name" in Act 10:48; and "in the cloud and sea" in 1 Cor 10:2. GK *1877*.
20. Parallel account at Mt 3:13; Lk 3:21. Compare Jn 1:29-34; 3:22-36.
21. Or, "into". This preposition (*eis*) can mean "to, into, in, for", etc. It is used with "baptize" only as "in" or "into" the Jordan in Mk 1:9; "in" or "into" the name in Mt 28:19; Act 8:16; 19:5; 1 Cor 1:13, 15; "into the baptism" in Act 19:3; "into Christ" in Rom 6:3; Gal 3:27; "into His death" in Rom 6:3; "into Moses" in 1 Cor 10:2; "into one body" in 1 Cor 12:13; "for forgiveness" in Mk 1:4; Lk 3:3; Act 2:38; and "for repentance" in Mt 3:11. Note also "into" or "to" the water in Act 8:38. GK *1650*.
22. This preposition (*hupo*) is used with "baptize" only as "by John" in Mt 3:6, 13; Mk 1:5, 9; Lk 3:7; 7:30; and "by Jesus" in Mt 3:14. GK *5679*. Thus, using these three different prepositions, Jesus was baptized "in" or "into" the Jordan (v 9), "by" John (v 9), and "in" or "with" water (Mt 3:11). See 1 Cor 12:13.
23. This is a keyword for Mark. See 6:25 on it.
24. Or, "coming up, going up". This is a common word, used 82 times. GK *326*. Same word as in Mt 3:16, and "came up" in Act 8:39.
25. Matthew uses a different word, "from" (Mt 3:16). Some think both mean "coming up out of the water" (implying immersion). Others think they mean coming up the river bank, "out of" and "away from" the water, implying nothing as to the mode of baptism. GK *1666*.
26. Or, "split". On this word, see Mt 27:51, where the curtain of the temple is "torn" in two.
27. Or, "on". GK *1650*. Mt 3:16 and Lk 3:22 use the normal word for "upon" (GK *2093*).
28. Or, "In". On this word, see Mt 17:5.
29. On "was well-pleased", see Mt 17:5.
30. Parallel account at Mt 4:1; Lk 4:1.
31. Or, "puts out, drives out". Same word as in v 43; Mt 9:38. On this word, see "cast out" in Jn 12:31.
32. Some think this is added to emphasize just how "in the wild" Jesus was, and how alone He was. On this word, see "beast" in Rev 13:1.
33. Or, "serving Him". On this word, see 1 Pet 4:10.
34. Parallel account at Mt 4:12; Lk 3:19; 4:14. Compare Jn 4:1-3.
35. That is, by Herod Antipas, 6:17.
36. Some manuscripts say "good news *of* the kingdom *of* God" {A}. Some think Mark means the good news "*from* God"; others, "*about* God".
37. Or, "believe in". On this phrase, "put faith in", see Jn 3:15.
38. Parallel account at Mt 4:18. Compare Lk 5:1-11; Jn 1:35-51.
39. On all four of the men called here, see Lk 6:14.
40. Some manuscripts say "Andrew, his brother" {N}.
41. That is, throwing out a circular net. Used only here. GK *311*. Related to "casting-net" in Mt 4:18.
42. Some manuscripts say "their" {N}.
43. Some manuscripts add "from there" {K}, as in Mt 4:21.
44. On this word, see Mt 4:21.
45. That is, the employees, those hired for a wage. Elsewhere only in Jn 10:12, 13. GK *3638*.
46. Parallel account at Lk 4:31.

A. 1 Cor 15:1 B. Mk 3:14, send out C. 1 Tim 3:16 D. Mt 3:3 E. Mt 3:1 F. 2 Tim 4:2 G. 2 Cor 7:10 H. Col 1:14 J. Jn 8:46 K. Jn 7:25 L. Heb 7:5, loins M. Rev 18:8, strong N. 2 Cor 3:5, sufficient O. Jn 8:6 P. Mt 5:19, break Q. Act 22:25 R. Mt 3:17 S. Heb 2:18 T. Rev 12:9 U. Mt 26:21 V. Eph 5:18, filled W. Lk 21:28 X. Act 26:20 Y. Mt 4:4, mankind Z. Rom 8:30

1D. And they were astounded[A] at His teaching,[1] for He was teaching them as *one* having authority[B], and not as the scribes — 22

2C. And immediately[C] there was *a* man in their synagogue with[2] *an* unclean spirit. And he cried-out[D], °saying, "What[3] do we have to do with You,[4] Jesus from-Nazareth[5]? Did You come[6] to destroy[E] us? I know You, Who You are— the Holy[F] One *of* God!" — 23, 24

   1D. And Jesus rebuked[G] him, saying, "Be silenced[H], and come out of him" — 25
   2D. And the unclean spirit— having convulsed[7] him, and having called-out[8] *with a* loud voice[9]— came out of him — 26
   3D. And they were all astonished[10], so that *they were* discussing[J] with themselves, saying, What is this? *A* new teaching based-on[11] authority[12]! He commands[K] even[13] the unclean spirits, and they obey[L] Him!" — 27
   4D. And the report[14] *about* Him immediately went out everywhere into the whole surrounding-region[15] *of* Galilee — 28

3C.[16] And immediately, having gone out of the synagogue, they[17] came into the house *of* Simon and Andrew, with James and John — 29

   1D. Now the mother-in-law *of* Simon was lying-down, being sick-with-fever[18] — 30

     1E. And immediately, they speak *to* Him concerning her
     2E. And having gone to *her*, He raised[M] her, having taken-hold-of[N] *her* hand. And the fever left her — 31
     3E. And she was serving[O] them

   2D. And having become evening, when the sun set[19], they were bringing to Him all the *ones* being ill[20], and the *ones* being demon-possessed[P]. °And the whole city was gathered-together[21] at the door — 32, 33

     1E. And He cured[Q] many being ill *with* various diseases[R] — 34
     2E. And He cast-out[S] many demons, and was not permitting[T] the demons to speak, because they knew Him

4C. And having arisen[U] early-in-the-morning[22], very[23] *late* at-night[24], He went out, and went away to *a* desolate[25] place, and was praying there — 35

   1D. And Simon and the *ones* with him hunted-for[26] Him, °and found Him. And they say *to* Him that "Everyone is seeking[V] You"[27] — 36-37
   2D. And He says *to* them, "Let us be going[28] elsewhere[29], into the next[30] towns[31], in order that I may proclaim[W] there also. For I came-forth[32] for this *purpose*" — 38

3B.[33] And He went[34] proclaiming[W] in their synagogues in all Galilee, and casting out the demons — 39

   1C.[35] And *a* leper comes to Him, appealing-to[X] Him, and kneeling[36], and saying *to* Him that "If You are willing[Y], You are able to cleanse[Z] me" — 40
   2C. And[37] having felt-deep-feelings[AA] [of compassion], having stretched-out His hand, He touched *him* — 41

     1D. And He says *to* him, "I am willing[Y]. Be cleansed[Z]"
     2D. And[38] immediately the leprosy departed from him, and he was cleansed[Z] — 42

1. Both the manner of it, and the content of it.
2. Or, "in", that is, in the sphere of, in the power of. Same phrase in 5:2. Same word as with "in the Spirit". GK *1877*.
3. Some manuscripts say "Let *us* alone! What do we..." {N}, as in Lk 4:34.
4. This is an idiom, literally "What [is there] *for* us and *for* you". On this phrase, see Jn 2:4.
5. That is, the inhabitant of Nazareth. Elsewhere only in 10:47; 14:67; 16:6; Lk 4:34; 24:19. GK *3716*. Using a related word, Jesus is also called "the Nazarene" (see Mt 2:23), though not by Mark.
6. Or, this could be a statement, "You came to destroy us!".
7. Or, "thrown him into convulsions". Used of dogs tearing meat from a dead animal, throwing their head back and forth as they pull. Elsewhere only in 9:26; Lk 9:39. GK *5057*.
8. This is the verb related to "voice" next, "he voiced *with a* loud voice". The same phrase is also in Lk 23:46; Act 16:28; Rev 14:18. This word means "to call, call out", and is also used of rooster "crowing". Used 43 times. GK *5888*.
9. This word means "sound", with the specific sense coming from the context. It mostly refers to the speaking "voice" as here; but also the "blast" of a trumpet in Rev 8:13; a "shout" in Mk 15:37; Act 24:21; a "tone" of speaking in Gal 4:20. Used 139 times. GK *5889*. Related to "called out" earlier.
10. Or, "astounded, amazed". Elsewhere only in 10:24, 32. GK *2501*. Related to "struck with wonder" in 9:15; and "wonder" in Act 3:10.
11. Or, "according to, by way of ". GK *2848*.
12. Note v 22. Or, "authority" may go with what follows, "... teaching! With authority He commands...".
13. Some manuscripts say "What is this? What new teaching *is* this? Because with authority He even commands" {B}.
14. Or, "news". On this word, see "hearing" in Heb 4:2.
15. Elsewhere only in Mt 3:5; 14:35; Lk 3:3; 4:14, 37; 7:17; 8:37; Act 14:6. GK *4369*.
16. Parallel account at Mt 8:14, 16; Lk 4:38.
17. That is, Jesus, Simon and Andrew. Some manuscripts say "He" {B}.
18. Elsewhere only in Mt 8:14. GK *4789*. Related to "fever" in Act 28:8.
19. In other words, after the Sabbath was over. Same word as in Lk 4:40.
20. This is an idiom, literally, "having *it* badly". Elsewhere only in 1:34; 2:17; 6:55; Mt 4:24; 8:16; 9:12; 14:35; Lk 5:31; 7:2. GK *2400, 2809*. The opposite idiom is in 16:18, "be well" ("have *it* well"). Also related to "at the point of death" in 5:23, ("have it at the extremity"), and "got better" in Jn 4:52 ("had it better"). The generic phrase is in Act 15:36, "how they are having *things*".
21. This is a participle, it "was having been gathered-together".
22. This word refers to the time between 3 and 6 A.M. On this word, see "early morning" in 13:35.
23. This is an idiom, more literally, "very much" at night. Jesus arose early in the morning, but very late into the night. In other words, while it was still dark. Same word as in 6:51; 9:3; 16:2, Mark's only other uses of it. Used 12 times. GK *3336*.
24. This word, "at night" is used only here. GK *1939*.
25. Or, "deserted, solitary, lonely". On this word, see "wilderness" in Mt 3:1.
26. Or, "searched for". Used only here. GK *2870*. Not related to "seeking" in the next verse.
27. That is, seeking Jesus because of v 27, 28, 34. Everyone was not "hunting for" Him in the sense of v 36.
28. Or, "leading forth, leading on". That is, let us be on our way. Same word as in Mt 26:46; Mk 14:42; Jn 11:7, 15, 16; 14:31. On this word, see "led" in Lk 4:1.
29. Used only here. GK *250*. Some manuscripts omit this word {K}.
30. That is, the upcoming towns, the neighboring towns. More literally, the towns "holding [next]". Same idiom as in "next day" in Lk 13:33.
31. This word may refer to towns associated with a city versus villages or country towns; or to larger country towns not recognized as a city. Used only here. GK *3268*.
32. That is, from the Father, as in Jn 8:42. Compare Lk 4:43.
33. Parallel to Mt 4:23; Lk 4:44.
34. Some manuscripts say "He was" {B}.
35. Parallel account at Mt 8:2; Lk 5:12.
36. Some manuscripts say "and kneeling before Him"; others omit "and kneeling" {C}.
37. Some manuscripts say "And Jesus" {N}.
38. Some manuscripts say "And He having spoken, immediately..." {N}.

A. Mt 7:28 B. Rev 6:8 C. Mk 6:25 D. Lk 23:18 E. 1 Cor 1:18, perish F. 1 Pet 1:16 G. 2 Tim 4:2, warn H. Mk 4:39 J. Mk 8:11, debate K. Lk 8:25 L. Act 6:7 M. Mt 28:6, arose N. Heb 4:14, hold on to O. 1 Pet 4:10, ministering P. Mt 8:16 Q. Mt 8:7 R. Mt 8:17 S. Jn 12:31 T. Mt 6:12, forgive U. Lk 18:33, rise up V. Phil 2:21 W. 2 Tim 4:2 X. Rom 12:8, exhorting Y. Jn 7:17 Z. Heb 9:22 AA. Mt 9:36

Mark 1:43	114	Verse

    3C. And having sternly-commanded[1] him, He immediately[A] sent him out   43

        1D. And He says *to* him, "See *that* you tell no one anything. But go, show[B] yourself *to* the priest,[2] and offer for your cleansing[C] *the things* which Moses commanded[D], for *a* testimony[3] *to* them[4]"   44

    4C. But the *one,* having gone forth, began to proclaim[E] greatly, and to widely-spread[5] the word, so that He *was* no longer able to enter openly[F] into *a* city, but was outside at desolate[G] places. And they were coming to Him from-all-directions   45

4B.[6] And having entered again into Capernaum after *some* days, it was heard that He was[7] at home[8]   2:1

    1C. And[9] many were gathered together, so that *the house was* no longer having-room[H], not even the *places* at the door[10]. And He was speaking the word *to* them   2

    2C. And they come bringing to Him *a* paralytic[J] being picked-up by four *men*   3

        1D. And not being able to bring *him* to Him[11] because of the crowd, they unroofed[12] the roof where He was   4

        2D. And having dug out *an opening,* they lower[K] the cot on-which[13] the paralytic was lying-down

    3C. And Jesus, having seen their faith, says *to* the paralytic[J], "Child[L], your sins are forgiven[14]"   5

    4C. Now some *of* the scribes were sitting there and reasoning[M] in their hearts, "Why is this *One* speaking in this manner? He is blaspheming[15]. Who is able to forgive sins except One— God?"   6-7

    5C. And immediately Jesus— having known[16] *in* His spirit that they were[17] reasoning[M] in this manner within themselves— says *to* them, "Why are you reasoning[M] these *things* in your hearts?   8

        1D. "Which is easier— "To say *to* the paralytic, 'Your sins are forgiven[18]', or to say, 'Arise[N], and pick-up your cot, and walk'?   9

        2D. "But in order that you may know that the Son *of* Man has authority[O] to forgive sins on earth"— He says *to* the paralytic, "I say *to* you, arise, pick up your cot, and go to your house"   10 / 11

    6C. And he arose[N], and immediately having picked-up[19] the cot, went out in front of everyone, so that everyone *was* astonished[20] and glorifying[P] God, saying that "We never saw *anything* like this"   12

5B.[21] And He went out again beside the sea.[22] And all the multitude[23] was coming to Him. And He was teaching them. And while passing on, He saw Levi[24], the *son of* Alphaeus[25], sitting at the tax-office[26]. And He says *to* him, "Be following Me!" And having stood-up[Q], he followed Him   13 / 14

    1C. And it comes about *that* He *was* reclining [to eat] in his[27] house. And many tax-collectors[R] and sinners[S] were reclining-back-with Jesus and His disciples. For there were many[28], and they were following Him   15

    2C. And the scribes *of* the Pharisees[29], having seen that He was[30] eating with the sinners and tax collectors, were saying *to* His disciples, "Why is it that[31] He is eating[32] with the tax collectors and sinners?"   16

    3C. And having heard, Jesus says *to* them that[33] "The *ones* being strong[T] have no need *of a* physician, but the *ones* being ill[U]. I did not come to call righteous[V] *ones,* but sinners[34]"   17

6B.[35] And the disciples *of* John and the Pharisees[36] were fasting[W]. And they come and say *to* Him, "For what reason are the disciples[X] *of* John and the disciples *of* the Pharisees fasting,[37] but **Your** disciples are not fasting?" And Jesus said *to* them—   18 / 19

1. Or, "sternly warned". Same word as in Mt 9:30. The command is in v 44. On this word, see "deeply moved" in Jn 11:33.
2. That is, in Jerusalem, at the temple.
3. Or, "evidence". Some think Jesus means a testimony as to the healing; others, a testimony that a prophet has arisen; others, a testimony that He adheres to the Law. "For a testimony" is also in Mt 8:4; 10:18; 24:14; Mk 6:11; 13:9; Lk 5:14; 9:5; 21:13; Heb 3:5; Jam 5:3. On this word, see Act 4:33.
4. Some think Jesus means to the priests; others, to the ones he was not to be telling at this time.
5. On this word, see Mt 9:31. Not related to the word in Lk 5:15.
6. Parallel account at Mt 9:1; Lk 5:17.
7. More literally, "is", as the Greek typically phrases it.
8. Or, "in *the* house".
9. Some manuscripts say "And immediately" {N}.
10. In other words, no one could even get in the door. It was jammed inside and outside. The phrase "at the door" is also in 1:33; Jn 18:16, and in Mk 11:4 ("at *a* door"), and elsewhere only in Act 3:2 ("at the gate").
11. Some manuscripts instead say "able to come near Him" {B}.
12. Used only here. GK *689*. Related to "roof" next.
13. Or, "where". Same word as "where" earlier in the verse. GK *3963*.
14. As in Mt 9:2. Some manuscripts say "have been forgiven" {B}, as in Lk 5:20. On this word, see Mt 6:12.
15. On this word, see 1 Tim 6:1. Some manuscripts say "... speaking blasphemies in this manner?" {N}.
16. Or, "understood, recognized, perceived". Same word as in Lk 5:22. Mt 9:4 says "seen". On this word, see "understood" in Col 1:6.
17. More literally, "are", as the Greek typically phrases it.
18. As in Mt 9:5. Some manuscripts say "have been forgiven" {B}, as in Lk 5:23.
19. Same word as in v 3.
20. Or, "amazed, beside *themselves*". It literally means "to stand outside of oneself". Same word as in Mt 12:23; Mk 5:42; 6:51; Lk 2:47; 8:56; 24:22; Act 2:7, 12; 8:9, 11, 13; 9:21; 10:45; 12:16. Elsewhere only as "lost one's senses" in Mk 3:21 and 2 Cor 5:13. GK *2014*.
21. Parallel account at Mt 9:9; Lk 5:27.
22. Capernaum (2:1) is on the northern shore of the Sea of Galilee.
23. Or, "the whole crowd" which was following Jesus at the time. This phrase is elsewhere only as "the whole crowd" in Mt 13:2; Mk 11:18; Lk 13:17; Act 21:27; and with a plural verb following as "all the multitude" in Mk 4:1; 9:15; Lk 6:19. The plural "all the crowds" is in Mt 12:23; Lk 23:48. This word, "crowd, multitude", is used 175 times. GK *4063*.
24. This name for Matthew is also used in Lk 5:27, 29. GK *3322*. On Matthew, see Lk 6:15.
25. This is the same name as the father of James. See Lk 6:15. Some think Levi and James were brothers, although this is never stated in the NT. Others think both of their fathers had the same name.
26. Or, "tax booth". Levi was on the job, collecting for Herod Antipas. Elsewhere only in Mt 9:9; Lk 5:27. GK *5468*.
27. That is, Levi's house, Lk 5:29.
28. Some think Mark means "many tax collectors and sinners"; others, "many disciples".
29. Some manuscripts say "And the scribes and the Pharisees" {C}.
30. More literally, "is", as the Greek typically phrases it.
31. Mark uses this grammar for asking a question also in 9:11, 28. Or, it may be rendered as an exclamation implying a question, "were saying *to* His disciples that 'He is eating with... sinners!'".
32. Some manuscripts add "and drinking" {B}.
33. Some manuscripts omit this word, which serves to introduce the quotation {C}.
34. Some manuscripts add "to repentance" {K}, as in Lk 5:32.
35. Parallel account at Mt 9:14; Lk 5:33.
36. That is, the disciples... and the Pharisees, these two groups. Some manuscripts say "*of* the Pharisees" {N}, as in the next sentence.
37. On why each group might have been fasting, see Mt 9:14.

A. Mk 6:25 B. 1 Tim 6:15 C. 2 Pet 1:9, purification D. Act 17:26, appointed E. 2 Tim 4:2 F. Act 10:3, clearly G. Mt 3:1, wilderness H. 2 Pet 3:9, make room J. Mt 4:24 K. Act 27:17 L. 1 Jn 3:1 M. Lk 5:21 N. Mt 28:6, arose O. Rev 6:8 P. Rom 8:30 Q. Lk 18:33, rise up R. Mt 18:17 S. Mt 9:10 T. Gal 5:6, can do U. Mk 1:32 V. Rom 1:17 W. Mt 6:16 X. Lk 6:40

| Mark 2:20 | 116 | Verse |

    1C. "The sons *of* the wedding-hall[1] cannot **be fasting**[A] while the bridegroom is with them, *can they*?[2] As long *a* time as they have the bridegroom with them, they cannot be fasting

        1D. "But days will come when the bridegroom is taken-away[3] from them, and then they will fast in that day[4]   20

    2C. "No one sews *a* patch *of* unshrunk cloth on *an* old garment[B]. Otherwise the fullness[C] [of the patch] takes from it[5]— the new[6] *from* the old[7]— and *a* worse tear[D] takes place[8]   21

    3C. "And no one puts new[9] wine into old wineskins. Otherwise the wine will burst[10] the wineskins, and the wine is lost[11], and the wineskins[12]. But *one puts* new[13] wine into fresh[14] wineskins"   22

7B.[15] And it came about *that* He *was* passing through the grainfields on the Sabbath. And His disciples began to make *their* way while plucking[E] the heads[F] [of grain]   23

    1C. And the Pharisees were saying *to* Him, "Look! Why are they doing *on* the Sabbath what is not lawful?"[16]   24

    2C. And He says *to* them, "Did you never read [in 1 Sam 21:1-6] what David did when he had *a* need[G] and was hungry, he and the *ones* with him— °how[17]   25 / 26

        1D. "He entered into the house[H] *of* God in the time of Abiathar[18] *the* high-priest[19]
        2D. "And he ate the Bread *of* Presentation[20], which is not lawful[J] *for anyone* to eat but the priests
        3D. "And he gave *it* also *to* the *ones* being with him?"

    3C. And He was saying *to* them, "The Sabbath was made[21] for the sake of mankind[K], and not mankind for the sake of the Sabbath. °So then,[22] the Son *of* Man is **Lord**[23] even[24] *of* the Sabbath"   27 / 28

8B.[25] And He entered again into the synagogue. And there was *a* man there having *his* hand having become-withered[26]   3:1

    1C. And they were closely-watching[L] Him *to see* if He would cure[M] him *on* the Sabbath, in order that they might accuse[N] Him   2

    2C. And He says *to* the man having the withered[27] hand, "Arise[O] into the middle"   3

    3C. And He says *to* them, "Is it lawful[J] *on* the Sabbath to do[P] good[Q], or to do-harm[28], to save *a* life, or to kill?" But the *ones* were being silent[R]   4

    4C. And having looked-around-at[29] them with anger, while being deeply-grieved[30] at the hardness[S] *of* their heart, He says *to* the man, "Stretch out the[31] hand". And he stretched *it* out, and his hand was restored[32]   5

    5C. And having gone out, the Pharisees immediately were giving counsel[T] against Him with the Herodians[33] so that they might destroy[34] Him   6

9B. And Jesus withdrew[35] to the sea with His disciples, and *a* great multitude from Galilee followed[36]. And from Judea, °and from Jerusalem, and from Idumea and beyond the Jordan and around Tyre and Sidon— *a* great multitude hearing all that He was doing came to Him   7 / 8

    1C. And He said *to* His disciples that *a* small-boat[37] should be standing-ready-for[38] Him because of the crowd— in order that they might not be pressing[39] Him   9

        1D. For He cured[M] many, so that *they were* falling-upon[U] Him in order that all who were having scourges[40] might touch Him   10

1. That is, the groomsmen, the groom's attendants, referring to the disciples. See Mt 9:15.
2. The grammar indicates that a "no" answer is expected.
3. Elsewhere only in this statement, Mt 9:15; Lk 5:35. GK *554*. This is the first allusion Jesus makes to His death.
4. Some manuscripts say "in those days" {K}.
5. That is, when the garment shrinks during washing, the patch "takes" from the old, tearing the old cloth.
6. This word means new in the sense of "fresh, recently made, unused". Same word as in "fresh" wineskins, v 22. On this word, see Heb 8:13.
7. This word means old in the sense of "worn-out, obsolete". Same word as in "old" wineskins, v 22. So the intent of these words is "the recently made *patch* from the worn out *garment*". Used 19 times. GK *4094*. Related to "made old" in Heb 8:13.
8. Jesus is not a patch on the Jewish system of that day, sewn on to the old ways to make repairs. He is a new garment. So His disciples act in a new way, not as would be expected under the old way. That is why they are not fasting.
9. This word means "new" in the sense of "young". Jesus is referring to undeveloped wine, not yet fermented. So the intent is that no one puts unfermented wine into "worn out" wineskins. Such skins are hard and inflexible. Same word as "new" later in this verse; Col 3:10; Heb 12:24; "young" in Tit 2:4; and "younger" in Lk 15:12; Act 5:6; 1 Tim 5:1; Tit 2:6. Used 23 times. GK *3742*...
10. Some manuscripts say "Otherwise, the new wine bursts..." {N}.
11. Or, "perishes". Same word as "ruined" in Mt 9:17; Lk 5:37. On this word, see "perish" in 1 Cor 1:18.
12. Some manuscripts say "and the wine spills out and the wineskins are ruined" {C}, as in Mt 9:17.
13. Some manuscripts say "new wine must be put into" {C}, as in Lk 5:38.
14. Jesus, the new and fresh, cannot be contained within the old and worn out Jewish system of that day. The "new" (Heb 12:24; 2 Cor 3:6) covenant makes the "old" (2 Cor 3:14) covenant obsolete (Heb 8:13). On this word, see "new" in v 21.
15. Parallel account at Mt 12:1; Lk 6:1.
16. According to the Pharisees' traditions, the disciples were working, in that they were "reaping". See Mt 12:1.
17. Some manuscripts omit this word {N}.
18. This took place when Ahimelech was serving as high priest, in the time of Abiathar whom we know as the pivotal high priest associated with David at this period of David's life. Ahimelech, the father of Abiathar, was the high priest David spoke to 1 Sam 21:1-6, but he was killed in 22:16. Abiathar became high priest after Saul killed all the other priests, 1 Sam 22:16-20. On the phrase "in the time of...", see Lk 3:2.
19. Or, "chief priest", as this word is used in Act 19:14. GK *797*.
20. Or, "*of* the setting before". That is, the bread set before God, the consecrated bread; the twelve loaves of "show-bread", Lev 24:6-9; Ex 25:30. The loaves were changed each Sabbath, and eaten by the priests. Same word as in Mt 12:4; Lk 6:4; Heb 9:2. On this word, see "purpose" in Rom 8:28.
21. Or, "came into being, came about". Mankind was not created for the purpose of keeping Sabbath laws. In the creation order, mankind was created on the sixth day, and the seventh day was blessed and sanctified by God (Gen 2:3) for the benefit of all mankind. Later, in the Law given to Moses, God used this creation order as the basis of the fourth commandment, Ex 20:9-11, Deut 5:12-15. Jesus may be referring to the creation order in general, or to the Jewish Sabbath law in particular. In either case, the Sabbath was for their benefit, not their enslavement. Normally, the benefit God intended was gained by Sabbath observance, but in some cases, like David's, at the expense of the Sabbath rules. GK *1181*.
22. That is, because Jesus is Lord of mankind, He is also Lord of mankind's Sabbath.
23. Or, "master". On this word, see "master" in Mt 8:2.
24. Or, "also", "is also **Lord** *of* the Sabbath".
25. Parallel account at Mt 12:9; Lk 6:6.
26. Or, "become stiff, become rigid" (as in 9:18). Elsewhere only as "dried up", as in Mt 13:6; 21:19; Mk 5:29; 11:20; Jn 15:6; 1 Pet 1:24; Rev 14:15, 16:12, etc. Used 15 times. GK *3830*. Mark uses the related adjective in v 3. Some think the use of the participle here indicates it was not congenital. Others do not think this is necessarily implied.
27. Same word as in Mt 12:10; Lk 6:6, 8; Jn 5:3. Elsewhere only as "dry" in Mt 23:15; Lk 23:31; Heb 11:29. GK *3831*. Related to the word in v 1.
28. Or, "do evil, do wrong" against another person. The answer is that the day of the week makes no difference. It is wrong to do harm on all seven days. It is right to do good on all seven days. These reach far beyond one's daily work, from which one is to rest. God made the Sabbath as a day of rest from work, not from doing good. The Pharisees' tradition is wrong. Mt 12:11 gives an example. Same word as in Lk 6:9. Elsewhere only as "do evil" in 1 Pet 3:17; 3 Jn 11. GK *2803*. Related to "evil" in 3 Jn 11.
29. Elsewhere only in Mk 3:34; 5:32; 9:8; 10:23; 11:11; Lk 6:10. GK *4315*.
30. Used only here. GK *5200*. The root word is "grieve" in 2 Cor 7:9.
31. Some manuscripts say "your" {N}.
32. Same word as in Mt 12:13; Lk 6:10, on which, see Mk 8:25. Some manuscripts add "healthy like the other" {K}, as in Mt 12:13.
33. On this group, see Mt 22:16.
34. These men want to destroy Jesus because He is obviously a false prophet, being a Sabbath-breaker. As a false prophet, He is a religious and political problem which they must work together to eliminate. On this word, see "perish" in 1 Cor 1:18.
35. Or, "went back". Jesus continues to teach all around Galilee (as in 1:39), but only once more is it said to be in a synagogue (6:2). He is always on the move, teaching in the villages (6:6) and desolate areas, with crowds coming to Him, encountering various responses. Some start a new "A." point here. This is Mark's only use of this word. On this word, see "went back" in Mt 4:12.
36. Some manuscripts add "Him" {C}.
37. Elsewhere only in Jn 6:22, 23, 24; 21:8. GK *4449*.
38. Or, "remaining with, staying by". On this word, see "devoting themselves to" in Act 2:42.
39. Or, "crowding, squeezing" Him. On this word, see "afflict" in 2 Cor 4:8. Related to "press upon" in Mk 5:24.
40. Same word as in 5:29, 34, Lk 7:21. Used of ailments perceived as a "scourge" from God. Elsewhere only as "whips" in Act 22:24; and "whippings" in Heb 11:36. GK *3465*. Related to the verb "whip" in Heb 12:6, and in Act 22:25.

A. Mt 6:16 B. 1 Pet 3:3 C. Col 1:19 D. 1 Cor 1:10, division E. Mt 12:1 F. Mk 4:28 G. Tit 3:14 H. Mk 3:20 J. 1 Cor 6:12 K. Mt 4:4 L. Lk 6:7 M. Mt 8:7 N. Jn 5:45 O. Mt 28:6 P. Rev 13:13 Q. 1 Tim 5:10b R. Mk 4:39, be still S. Rom 11:25 T. Mk 15:1, consultation U. Act 8:16

        2D. And the unclean spirits, whenever they were seeing Him, were falling-before Him, and crying-out[A], saying that "**You** are the Son *of* God". °And He was sternly[B] rebuking[C] them, in order that they might not make Him known[D]

10B.[1] And He goes up on the mountain, and summons[E] whom **He** was wanting[F]. And they went to Him

    1C. And He appointed[2] twelve, whom He also named[G] apostles[3]—

        1D. In order that they might be with Him
        2D. And in order that He might send them out[4] to proclaim[H], °and to have authority[J] to cast[5] out the demons

    2C.[6] And He appointed the twelve,[7] even

        1D. Peter— He put *the* name on Simon
        2D. And James, the *son of* Zebedee, and John, the brother *of* James. And He put on them *the* name Boanerges[8], which means "sons *of* thunder"
        3D. And Andrew
        4D. And Philip
        5D. And Bartholomew
        6D. And Matthew
        7D. And Thomas
        8D. And James, the *son of* Alphaeus
        9D. And Thaddaeus
        10D. And Simon, the Cananaean[9]
        11D. And Judas Iscariot[K], who also handed Him over

11B. And He goes[10] into *a* house[11]

    1C. And the crowd comes-together again, so that they *were* not even able to eat bread

        1D. And having heard-*of it*[12], the *ones* from Him[13] went-forth[14] to take-hold-of[15] Him. For they were saying[16] that "He lost-*His*-senses[17]"

    2C.[18] And the scribes having come down from Jerusalem were saying that "He has Beelzebul[19]", and that "He is casting-out[L] the demons by the ruler[M] *of* the demons". °And having summoned them, He was speaking *to* them in parables—

        1D. "How is Satan able to be casting-out[L] Satan?

            1E. "And if *a* kingdom is divided[N] against itself, that kingdom is not able to stand[20]
            2E. "And if *a* house[21] is divided against itself, that house will not be able to stand
            3E. "And if Satan stood-up[O] against himself and was divided, he is not able to stand, but he has *an* end[22]

        2D. "But no one, having entered into the house *of* the strong[P] *man,* can plunder[23] his things[Q] unless he first binds[R] the strong *man*. And then he will plunder his house
        3D.[24] "Truly[S] I say *to* you that all sins and blasphemies[T] will be forgiven[U] *to* the sons *of* humans[25]— whatever they may blaspheme[V]. °But whoever blasphemes against the Holy Spirit does not have forgiveness[W] forever[X], but is[26] guilty[Y] *of an* eternal[Z] sin[27]"—

1. Parallel account at Lk 6:12. Compare Mt 10:1-4.
2. Same word as in v 16; Heb 3:2. On this word, see "does" in Rev 13:13.
3. Some manuscripts omit "whom He also named apostles" {C}, which appears in Lk 6:13. On "apostles", see 1 Cor 12:28.
4. This verb "to send out, send forth" is the verb related to "apostles", which means "sent ones". Used 132 times. GK *690*.
5. Some manuscripts say "authority to cure diseases and to cast" {N}.
6. Compare at Mt 10:2; Lk 6:14; Act 1:13.
7. Some manuscripts omit "And He appointed the twelve" {C}. On these men, see Lk 6:14.
8. This is an Aramaic word transliterated into Greek. Used only here. GK *1065*. Its meaning is given by Mark.
9. This is an Aramaic word transliterated into Greek, but not explained by Mark. It means "zealot". Elsewhere only in Mt 10:4. GK *2831*. In Lk 6:15; Act 1:13, the Greek word "Zealot" is used of this man.
10. Or, "comes". Some manuscripts say "they go" {B}. On this word, see "come" in 16:2.
11. Some think it is Jesus' house, connecting this with the coming of His family in v 31. Others think it is some unidentified house, as Mark uses "into *a* house" elsewhere, 7:17; 9:28. Elsewhere, Mark always identifies the house as "their house", 8:3; "his house", 8:26; "your house", 2:11; 5:19; "her house", 7:30. Verses 20-21 are found only in Mark. This word is used 114 times of a single family "house, home, household", and of those terms in the broadest sense (for example, of the nation Israel). GK *3875*. Related word in v 25.
12. Mark may mean "that Jesus was unable even to eat a meal"; or, "that Jesus was at the house".
13. This idiom, "the *ones* from Him", could refer to some of the disciples or friends of Jesus, or to His relatives. These people outside the house "heard" the problem and "went forth" to solve it. Some think Mark means that the family of Jesus heard it, and came to rescue Him, arriving outside in v 31.
14. Or, "went out, came out". GK *2002*.
15. Or, "to take charge of, seize, take custody of ". On this word, see "hold on to" in Heb 4:14.
16. This could be the statement of a well-intentioned mother or disciple who felt the need to "rescue" Jesus— "You're crazy to keep speaking this way. You must come and eat. Have some sense!" Or, it could be the misinformed statement of brothers who did not understand His mission or believe in Him (Jn 7:5). Others think it is impersonal, "people were saying" this to the ones from Him.
17. Or, "is beside Himself, out of His mind". Same word as in 2 Cor 5:13, of Paul. On this word, see "astonished" in 2:12. The same thing was said about Paul, using a different word, in Act 26:24.
18. Compare Mt 9:32-34; 12:22-37; Lk 11:14-26.
19. That is, the devil, the "ruler of demons", Mt 12:24; Lk 11:15. "Beelzebub" was the name of a Philistine deity, meaning "lord of flies" or "lord of the house". Some think the Jews deliberately mispronounced it "Beelzebul", meaning, "lord of dung". Others think this is just an alternate spelling. Elsewhere only in Mt 10:25; 12:24, 27; Lk 11:15, 18, 19, always "Beelzebul". GK *1015*. Some manuscripts always spell it "Beelzebub" {N}.
20. Or, "to be made to stand, to be established". GK *2705*.
21. This word is used of the physical building, and the family or "household" living there, including servants (as in Jn 4:53; 1 Cor 16:15; Phil 4:22). Used 93 times. GK *3864*.
22. That is, he is finished. Same words as in Heb 7:3, "having... *an* end *of* life". On this word, see Rom 10:4.
23. Jesus has bound Satan and is plundering his house by casting out demons. Elsewhere only in Mt 12:29. GK *1395*.
24. Compare Mt 12:31-32; Lk 12:10.
25. That is, the human race. Same phrase as in Eph 3:5. On "sons", see Gal 3:7. On "humans", see "mankind" in Mt 4:4.
26. Some manuscripts say "will be" {N}.
27. Some manuscripts say "condemnation" {B}, so that it says "But he is subject to eternal condemnation".

A. Mt 8:29 B. Mt 13:52, many C. 2 Tim 4:2, warn D. Rom 1:19, evident E. Act 2:39, call to F. Jn 7:17, willing G. 2 Tim 2:19 H. 2 Tim 4:2 J. Rev 6:8 K. Jn 6:71 L. Jn 12:31 M. Rev 1:5 N. 1 Cor 7:17, apportioned O. Lk 18:33, rise up P. Rev 18:8 Q. 1 Thes 4:4, vessel R. 1 Cor 7:27 S. Mt 5:18 T. 1 Tim 6:4 U. Mt 6:12 V. 1 Tim 6:1 W. Col 1:14 X. Rev 20:10 Y. 1 Cor 11:27 Z. Mt 25:46

| Mark 3:30 | 120 | Verse |

        1E. Because[1] they were saying, "He has *an* unclean spirit"   30

  3C.[2] And His mother and His brothers[3] come. And while standing outside[4], they sent-forth[A] *a message* to Him, calling Him   31

      1D. And *a* crowd was sitting around Him. And they say *to* Him, "Behold— Your mother and Your brothers and Your sisters[5] are outside seeking[B] You"   32

      2D. And having responded *to* them, He says, "Who is My mother and[6] My[7] brothers?"   33

      3D. And having looked-around-at[C] the *ones* sitting *in a* circle around Him, He says, "Look— My mother and My brothers! °For[8] whoever does the will[D] *of* God— this *one* is My brother and sister[9] and mother"   34 / 35

12B.[10] And again He began to teach beside the sea. And *a* very large crowd is gathered-together[11] with Him, so that He, having gotten into *a* boat, sits-*down* in the sea [to teach]. And all the multitude[12] were near[13] the sea on the land. °And He was teaching[E] them many *things* in parables[F]   4:1 / 2

  1C. And He was saying *to* them in His teaching[G], °"Listen! Behold— the *one* sowing went out to sow. °And it came about during the sowing *that*   3 / 4

      1D. "Some *seed* fell along the road. And the birds[14] came and ate it up[H]

      2D. "And other[15] *seed* fell on the rocky[J] *place* where it was not having much soil.[16] And immediately it sprang-up because of not having *a* depth[K] *of* soil. °And when the sun rose, it was scorched[L]. And because of not having *a* root, it was dried-up[M]   5 / 6

      3D. "And other *seed* fell into the thorns. And the thorns came up and choked[17] it, and it did not give fruit   7

      4D. "And others[18] fell into the good[N] soil[O], and were giving fruit while coming up and growing[19]. And they were bearing[P] thirty fold[20], and sixty fold, and *a* hundred fold"   8

      5D. And He was saying, "He who has ears to hear, let him hear"   9

  2C. And when He came-to-be alone[21], the *ones* around Him with the twelve were questioning[Q] Him *as* to the parables[22]   10

      1D. And He was saying *to* them, "The mystery[23] *of* the kingdom *of* God has been given *to* you[24]. But all *things* come[25] in parables *to* those outside,°in order that[26]   11 / 12

        1E. "While seeing[R], they may be seeing and not perceive[S]

        2E. "And while hearing, they may be hearing and not understanding[T]

        3E. "That they may not ever turn-back[U] and it be forgiven[V] them"[27]

      2D. And He says *to* them, "Do you not know this parable? And how will you understand[W] all the parables?   13

        1E. "The *one* sowing sows the word   14

        2E. "Now these *people* are the *ones* along the road, where the word is sown. And when they hear, immediately Satan comes and takes away the word having been sown into them[28]   15

        3E. "And these[29] *people* are the *ones* being sown *the seed* on the rocky[30] *places*— who, when they hear the word, immediately are receiving it with joy. °And they do not have *a* root in themselves, but are temporary[X]. Then, affliction[Y] or persecution[Z] having come about because of the word, immediately they are caused-to-fall[AA]   16 / 17

1. This phrase explains why Jesus said this. If He does a miracle in your presence which you fully acknowledge, but attribute to Satan, what more can be done? You have seen the Spirit of God work, and called Him Satan. You have taken your stand against Him in the face of evidence that is clear and convincing even to you. You have cut yourself off from the source of forgiveness. Some think this is the "sin leading to death" in 1 Jn 5:16.
2. Parallel account at Mt 12:46. Compare Lk 8:19-21.
3. On the brothers and sisters of Jesus, see Mt 13:55-56.
4. Some think Mark means "outside the house", v 20. Others think he means "outside the crowd". Compare Mt 12:46; Lk 8:19.
5. Some manuscripts omit "and Your sisters" {C}.
6. Some manuscripts say "or" {N}.
7. Some manuscripts omit this word {C}.
8. Some manuscripts omit this word {C}.
9. Some manuscripts say "My sister" {N}.
10. Parallel account at Mt 13:1; Lk 8:4.
11. Some manuscripts say "was gathered" {K}.
12. Same word as "crowd" earlier in the verse. Same words as "the whole crowd" in Mt 13:2, but followed by a plural verb here. On this word, see 2:13.
13. Or, "[facing] toward, before, at". GK *4639*.
14. Some manuscripts add "*of* the heaven" {K}.
15. That is, another portion of seed, viewed as a group.
16. Not soil with stones in it, but rock covered with not much soil. Compare Lk 8:6.
17. Compare Lk 8:7. Same word as in v 19, and as in Mt 13:22; Lk 8:14. Elsewhere only as "throng" in Lk 8:42. GK *5231*.
18. That is, other seeds, viewed as individuals. Jesus changes to the plural here.
19. Both "coming up" and "growing" are plural, agreeing with "others". Some manuscripts have a different grammar that would mean these words go with "fruit" {C}, "they were giving fruit [that was] coming up and growing. And they were bearing...".
20. Or, "times thirty". This word "times, fold" may represent the Aramaic sign of multiplication. It is the numeral "one" (see Eph 4:7), and some prefer to translate it "one, thirty; and one, sixty; and one, *a* hundred". Likewise in v 20. Matthew and Luke say it differently in Mt 13:8, 23; Lk 8:8.
21. This idiom is elsewhere only in Lk 9:18. Literally, "in only *them places*". That is, away from the crowds.
22. Some manuscripts have this singular {N}.
23. On this word, see Rom 11:25. That is, truth about Jesus and His kingdom known only by His revelation.
24. Some manuscripts add "to know" {K}.
25. Or, "take place, are". GK *1181*.
26. Here Jesus says the purpose of His speaking in parables is "in order that" they may remain spiritually blind. Mt 13:13-15 says He did so "because" they were blind with a blindness of their own choosing. So He speaks in parables both "because" they are spiritually blind, and "in order that" they might remain so.
27. Jesus is quoting from Isa 6:9-10, as does Mt 13:14-15; Lk 8:10; Jn 12:40; Act 28:26-27. A key prophecy.
28. Some manuscripts say "in their hearts" {C}, similar to Mt 13:19.
29. Some manuscripts say "and likewise these" {N}. The grammar of this word refers to people, not "seed".
30. Note that Jesus mixes the illustration and the application in order to abbreviate the statement. The full statement would be "These people are the ones having the word sown into them like the seed was sown into the rocky places". Likewise with verse 18 and 20.

A. Mk 3:14, send out B. Phil 2:21 C. Mk 3:5 D. Jn 7:17 E. Rom 12:7 F. Mt 13:3 G. 1 Cor 14:6 H. Mk 12:40, devouring J. Mt 13:5
K. 2 Cor 8:2, deep L. Rev 16:9 M. Mk 3:1, became withered N. 1 Tim 5:10a O. Rev 7:1, land P. 2 Pet 1:17, carried Q. Jn 17:9, pray
R. Rev 1:11 S. Lk 2:26, see T. Mt 13:13 U. Jam 5:19 V. Mt 6:12 W. 1 Jn 2:29, know X. Mt 13:21 Y. Rev 7:14 Z. Mk 10:30 AA. 1 Cor 8:13

4E. "And other[1] *people* are the *ones* being sown *the seed* into the thorns. These are the *ones* having heard the word[A]—*and coming-in,[2] the anxieties[3] *of* the age[4] and the deceitfulness[5] *of* riches and the desires[B] with respect to the other *things* are choking the word, and it becomes unfruitful[C]   18, 19

5E. "And those[6] *people* are the *ones* having been sown[7] *the seed* on the good soil, who are hearing[8] the word, and accepting[9] *it*, and bearing-fruit[D]— thirty fold[10], and sixty fold, and *a* hundred fold"   20

3C.[11] And He was saying *to* them,[12] "The lamp[13] does not come in order that it may be put under the basket[14], or under the bed, *does it*?[15] Is it not in order that it may be put on the lampstand[E]?   21

1D. "For it[16] is not hidden[F], except in order that it may be made-visible[17]. Nor did it become hidden-away[18], but in order that it may come into visibility[19]   22

2D. "If anyone has ears to hear, let him hear"   23

4C.[20] And He was saying *to* them, "Be watching[G] what you listen-to[21]. With what measure[H] you measure, it will be measured *to* you[22]— and it will be added[J] *to* you[23]   24

1D. "For he who has— it will be given *to* him[24]   25

2D. "And he who does not have— even what he has will be taken-away[25] from him"

5C. And He was saying, "The kingdom *of* God is like[K] this— as-*if a* person would throw the seed upon the soil[L],*and would be sleeping and arising night and day, and the seed would be budding[M] and growing-long[26]— how[K], **he** does not know[27]   26, 27

1D. "The[28] soil bears-fruit[D] by-itself[29]— first grass, then *a* head[30], then *a* full grain[31] in the head   28

2D. "And whenever the fruit permits[32], immediately he[33] sends-forth[N] the sickle[34], because the harvest[35] has come[36]"   29

6C.[37] And He was saying, "How should we liken[O] the kingdom[P] *of* God, or with what parable[Q] may we present[38] it?—*as a* seed *of a* mustard-plant,[39] which   30, 31

1D. "When it is sown upon the soil, *is* being smaller *than* all[40] the seeds upon the soil

2D. "And when it is sown, it goes-up, and becomes larger[41] *than* all the garden-plants[R]. And it makes large branches so that the birds *of* the heaven[S] are able to be nesting[T] under the shade *of* it"   32

7C.[42] And *with* many such parables He was speaking the word *to* them, as[43] they were able to hear *it*   33

1D. And He was not speaking *to* them apart from *a* parable   34

2D. But He was explaining[44] everything privately[U] *to* His own disciples

13B.[45] And on that day, having become evening, He says *to* them, "Let us go to the other side". *And having left the crowd, they take Him along as He was[46], in the boat. And other boats were with Him   35-36

1C. And *a* great storm[47] *of* wind takes place. And the waves were throwing-over[V] into the boat so that the boat *was* already being filled[48]. *And **He** was in the stern on the cushion, sleeping[W]   37, 38

2C. And they wake[X] Him, and say *to* Him, "Teacher, do You not care[49] that we are perishing[Y]?"

1. Some manuscripts say "these" {N}, as in v 16.
2. Worries come into the person's life alongside the word and choke it.
3. Or, "worries, cares, concerns". On this word, see 1 Pet 5:7. Related to "be anxious" in Mt 6:25.
4. Or, "world". GK *172*. Some manuscripts say "*of* this age" {K}. Instead of "age", some manuscripts say "life" {N}.
5. Same word as in Mt 13:22.
6. Some manuscripts say "these" {K}.
7. Note the change in tense. The second two soils are in the process of "being sown", in hope that a fruitful crop can be grown. The last soil is the ones "having been sown". The sowing is accomplished, and the bearing is in progress. Only Mark conveys this distinction in the words of Jesus, as with the distinction in "hearing" next.
8. Or, "listening to" in the sense of "obeying", as in v 24. Note the change in tense. There is continuous action here, but not in the word "hear" in the first three soils.
9. Or, "welcoming". Same word as in Act 16:21; 22:18; 1 Tim 5:19, Heb 12:6. Elsewhere only as "welcome" in Act 15:4. GK *4138*.
10. On this word, see v 8.
11. Parallel account at Lk 8:16. Compare Mt 5:15.
12. Jesus spoke the parables to the crowd, and explained them to the disciples, v 33-34.
13. Some think the lamp is Jesus, or the message He brought. He came to be the light, Jn 12:46. No one brings a light into the house to hide it. Yet Jesus is "hiding" the truth in parables. Jesus, His kingdom, and His message are hidden or concealed at this point of His ministry in a certain sense. But this is for a purpose. Others think the lamp is the word in a believer's life. It was not given to you to be hidden, but to shine forth. See Lk 8:16.
14. Literally, a "modius measure", the basket or container used to measure one modius of grain. The basket is named for the amount it holds. A modius was a Roman dry measure equal to about two gallons, 8.5 liters, one peck. Elsewhere only in Mt 5:15; Lk 11:33. GK *3654*.
15. The grammar indicates a "no" answer is expected here, and a "yes" answer for the next question.
16. That is, the lamp. One would only hide a lamp for the purpose of shining it at the proper time. Jesus came that He might be put on the lampstand and light the world. But His light is hidden from Israel now, so that it may be revealed after His resurrection. He did not come to remain hidden. In the other view, the light is in you for the purpose of shining forth from your life. Let it shine. Most translations paraphrase this verse.
17. Or, "revealed". On this word, see "made evident" in 1 Jn 2:19.
18. Or, "hidden-from *view*, secret, concealed". Related to "hidden" earlier in the verse, with the prefix "from, away" added. Same two words as in Lk 8:17. Elsewhere only in Col 2:3. GK *649*.
19. On this idiom, "come into visibility", see Lk 8:17. Related to "made visible" earlier.
20. Parallel account at Lk 8:18.
21. Or, "hear", and follow. Lk 8:18 says "how" you listen. Compare Lk 6:40.
22. The measure you use reflects your spiritual capacity. What you listen to and follow will be the measure of what you can receive. For example, if you listen to and follow the traditions of the Pharisees, it will limit your ability to receive spiritual truth. The "system" you follow will impact your ability to hear and receive truth and blessing.
23. Some manuscripts say "*to* you, the *ones* hearing" {A}.
24. Those receiving and obeying truth will receive more truth.
25. Same word as in Mt 13:12; 21:43; 25:29; Lk 8:18; 19:26, in statements similar to this. GK *149*.
26. Used only here. GK *3602*. Related to "length" in Eph 3:18; Rev 21:16.
27. The seed has life in it, and it grows without the assistance or knowledge of the sower. The person sows. God causes the growth, 1 Cor 3:6, in ways beyond his knowledge. Then the person harvests what God has grown, v 29.
28. Some manuscripts say "For the" {N}.
29. Or, "on its own". Our word "automatic" comes from this word, *automatos*. Elsewhere only in Act 12:10. GK *897*.
30. Same word as later in the verse. Elsewhere only as "heads [of grain] in 2:23; Mt 12:1; Lk 6:1. Here, the grain has not yet appeared. GK *5092*.
31. Or, "grain-of-wheat". This word means "wheat", or "grain" in general. Used 14 times. GK *4992*.
32. Or, "allows". That is, when it has ripened itself. Literally, when it "hands *itself* over" for harvesting. On this word, see "hand over" in Mt 26:21.
33. That is, the person who sowed the seed.
34. Elsewhere only in Rev 14:14, 15, 16, 17, 18, 19. GK *1535*.
35. Same word as in Mt 13:30, 39; Rev 14:15, where it refers to the end of the age. Note Mt 24:14. Elsewhere only in Mt 9:37, 38; Lk 10:2; Jn 4:35, where it refers to the harvest of people ripe for the gospel. GK *2546*.
36. Or, "is here, is present". On this word, see "present" in Rom 12:1.
37. Parallel account at Mt 13:31. Compare Lk 13:18-19.
38. Or, "put". Same word as "put" in v 21. On this word, see "put" in Act 19:21. GK *5502*. Related to "put before" in Mt 13:24, 31.
39. On this phrase, see Mt 13:31.
40. That is, than all the seeds people in that day sowed.
41. It has a small and insignificant beginning, but grows larger than all. This is not how the Jews conceived of the kingdom. It was to arrive from God, conquer their enemies, and immediately establish itself in the world.
42. Parallel account at Mt 13:34.
43. That is, "to the degree that" they were able to hear it. GK *2777*.
44. Or, "interpreting". GK *2147*. Related to "interpretation" in 2 Pet 1:20.
45. Parallel account at Mt 8:23; Lk 8:23.
46. Or, "along, as He was [still] in the boat". This is the Greek word order. This may be describing the condition of Jesus. The disciples took Him straight from His speaking without any rest, explaining why He slept. Or it may be describing His location. The disciples left the crowd and joined Him in the boat after He called to them "Let us go...". They left the crowd and took Him, since He was still in the boat.
47. Same word as Lk 8:23. On this word, see 2 Pet 2:17.
48. Elsewhere only in 15:36; Lk 14:23; Jn 2:7; 6:13; Rev 8:5; 15:8. GK *1153*. Not related to the word in Lk 8:23 (GK *5230*). Related to "are full" in Rev 4:6.
49. This is an idiom, more literally, "Is it not a concern *to* You?". On this word, see "concerned" in 1 Cor 7:21.

A. 1 Cor 12:8 B. Gal 5:16 C. 1 Cor 14:14 D. Rom 7:4 E. Rev 1:12 F. 1 Cor 4:5 G. Rev 1:11, see H. Jn 3:34 J. Lk 17:5, increase K. Mt 19:19, as L. Rev 7:1, land M. Mt 13:26 N. Mk 3:14, send out O. Mt 13:24, became like P. Mt 3:2 Q. Mt 13:3 R. Mt 13:32 S. 2 Cor 12:2 T. Act 2:26, dwell U. Mt 14:13 V. Mk 14:72, put upon W. 1 Thes 5:10 X. Mt 28:6, arose Y. 1 Cor 1:18

	3C. And having awakened[A], He rebuked[B] the wind, and said *to* the sea, "Be still[1], be silenced[2]". And the wind stopped[3]. And there was *a* great calm[C]. °And He said *to* them, "Why are you afraid[4]? Do you not yet have faith?"[5]	39 40
	4C. And they feared *a* great fear.[6] And they were saying to one another, "Who then is this *One*, that even the wind and the sea obey[D] Him?"	41
14B.[7]	And they came to the other side *of* the sea, to the country[E] *of* the Gerasenes[8]	5:1
	1C. And He having gone out of the boat, immediately[9] *a* man with[10] *an* unclean spirit met Him, out of the tombs—	2
	1D. Who was having *his* dwelling-place in the tombs[11]	3
	2D. And no one was able to bind[F] him any-more[12], not even *with a* chain[13]—°because he often *had* been bound *with* shackles[14] and chains, and the chains *had* been torn-apart[15] by him, and the shackles broken[G]	4
	3D. And no one was strong-*enough*[H] to subdue[16] him	
	4D. And continually[J], *by* night and *by* day[17], in the tombs[18] and in the mountains, he was crying-out[K] and cutting himself *with* stones	5
	2C. And having seen Jesus from *a* distance, he ran and prostrated-*himself*[19] *before* Him. °And having cried-out[K] *with a* loud voice, he says, "What do I have to do with You,[20] Jesus, Son *of* the Most-High[L] God? I make You swear[21] *by* God, do not torment[M] me"	6-7
	1D. For He was saying *to* him, "Come out of the man, unclean spirit"	8
	3C. And He was asking him, "What *is the* name *for* you?"	9
	1D. And he says *to* Him,[22] "*The* name *for* me is Legion[N], because we are many"	
	2D. And he was begging[O] Him greatly that He not send them outside *of* the country[E]	10
	4C. Now there was *a* large herd *of* pigs feeding[P] there at the mountain. °And they[23] begged[O] Him, saying, "Send us to the pigs, in order that we may enter into them"	11-12
	5C. And He[24] permitted[Q] them	13
	6C. And the unclean spirits, having come out, entered into the pigs. And the herd— about[25] two-thousand— rushed[R] down the steep-bank[S] into the sea. And they were drowning[T] in the sea	
	7C. And the *ones* feeding[P] them fled, and reported[U] *it* in the city and in the fields. And they came to see what the *thing* having happened was[26]	14
	1D. And they come to Jesus, and see the *one* being demon-possessed[V] sitting, having been clothed, and being sound-minded[W]— the *one* having had the "legion"	15
	2D. And they became afraid	
	3D. And the *ones* having seen *it* related[X] *to* them how it happened *to* the *one* being demon-possessed, and about the pigs	16
	8C. And they began to beg[O] Him to depart from their districts[27]	17
	9C. And while He *was* getting into[28] the boat, the *one* having been demon-possessed was begging[O] Him that he might be with Him	18
	1D. And He[29] did not permit[Y] him, but says *to* him, "Go to your house, to your *people*, and report[U] *to* them all-that the Lord has done *for* you, and *that* He had mercy on you"	19
	2D. And he departed, and began to proclaim[Z] in Decapolis[AA] all-that Jesus did *for* him	20

1. Or, "Be silent, Hush". Used of bees, "be still!". Elsewhere only as "be silent" in Mt 26:63; Mk 3:4; 9:34; 14:61; Lk 1:20; 19:40; Act 18:9; and as "keep silent" in Mt 20:31; Mk 10:48. GK *4995*.
2. The tense is unusual for a command, implying "Be silenced and stay silent". Related to the word for "muzzle". Same word as in Mt 22:12, 34; Mk 1:25; Lk 4:35; 1 Pet 2:15. Elsewhere only as "muzzle" in 1 Tim 5:18. GK *5821*.
3. Or, "abated, ceased". Elsewhere only in Mt 14:32; Mk 6:51, all of wind. GK *3156*.
4. Or, "fearful, cowardly, timid". Same word as in Mt 8:26. Elsewhere only as "cowardly" in Rev 21:8. GK *1264*. It means "fearful" as a result of cowardice or lack of moral courage. Related to "afraid" in Jn 14:27, and "fearfulness" in 2 Tim 1:7.
5. Some manuscripts say "Why are you so afraid? How *is it* you do not have faith?" {A}.
6. That is, they were extremely afraid. Same phrase as in Lk 2:9.
7. Parallel account at Mt 8:28; Lk 8:26.
8. Some manuscripts say "Gadarenes", as in Mt 8:28; others, "Gergesenes" {C}. Note Mt 8:28; Lk 8:26. The region called Decapolis (v 20) included the cities of Gerasa, Gadara, and Gergesa. Elsewhere only in Lk 8:26, 37. GK *1170*.
9. Some manuscripts omit this word {N}.
10. Or, "in". Same word as in 1:23.
11. This word is also in v 5 and Lk 8:27 (see Lk 23:53 on it). It is related to the word in v 2, which is also in Mt 8:28 (see Mt 23:29 on it).
12. Some manuscripts omit this word {K}.
13. On this word, see Act 28:20 Some manuscripts have this plural {K}.
14. That is, bindings for the feet. On this word, see Lk 8:29.
15. On this word, see "torn to pieces" in Act 23:10. Not related to the word in Lk 8:29.
16. Or, "tame". Elsewhere only as "tame" in Jam 3:7, 8. GK *1238*.
17. On this phrase, see Rev 7:15.
18. Some manuscripts reverse the order of "tombs" and "mountains" {K}.
19. On this word, see "worship" in Mt 14:33.
20. This is an idiom, literally, "What [is there] *for* me and *for* you". On this phrase, see Jn 2:4.
21. Or, "I adjure You, I put you on oath". Note that Jesus does not answer this challenge. On this word, see Act 19:13.
22. Some manuscripts say "And he responded, saying" {N}.
23. Some manuscripts say "And all the demons..." {N}.
24. Some manuscripts say "And immediately Jesus" permitted them {N}.
25. Some manuscripts say "and there were about..." {K}.
26. More literally, "is", as the Greek typically phrases it.
27. The people accept what happened as an "act of God", but they do not want anything else to happen to them. On this incident, see Lk 8:32.
28. Some manuscripts say "And He having gotten into" {K}.
29. Some manuscripts say "Jesus" {K}.

A. Jn 6:18, become aroused   B. 2 Tim 4:2, warn   C. Lk 8:24   D. Act 6:7   E. Mk 1:5   F. 1 Cor 7:27   G. Mt 12:20, bruised   H. Gal 5:6, can do
J. 2 Thes 3:16   K. Mt 8:29   L. Mt 21:9, highest   M. Rev 14:10   N. Mt 26:53   O. Rom 12:8, exhorting   P. Jn 21:15   Q. 1 Tim 2:12   R. Act 7:57
S. Mt 8:32   T. Mt 13:7, choked   U. 1 Jn 1:3, announcing   V. Mt 8:16   W. Rom 12:3   X. Lk 8:39   Y. Mt 6:12, forgive   Z. 2 Tim 4:2   AA. Mk 7:31

	3D. And they all were marveling	
15B.[1]	And Jesus having crossed-over again in the boat[2] to the other side, *a* large crowd was gathered to[3] Him. And He was beside the sea	21
1C.	And one *of* the synagogue-officials[4] comes, Jairus *by* name. And having seen Him, he falls at[5] His feet, and begs[A] Him greatly[6], saying that "My little-daughter is at the point of death[7]. *I beg* that having come, You lay *Your* hands on her in order that she may be restored[8] and live"	22 23
2C.	And He departed with him. And *a* large crowd was following Him, and they were pressing-upon[9] Him	24
3C.	And *there was a* woman[10] being in *a* flow *of* blood *for* twelve years, and having suffered[B] many *things* by many physicians, and having spent[C] everything of hers[11], and not having been benefitted[D] at all, but rather having come to the worse	25-26
1D.	Having heard about[12] Jesus, having come in the crowd from behind, she touched[E] His garment[F]. For she was saying that "If I touch[E] even His garments[F], I will be restored"	27 28
2D.	And immediately the fountain[13] *of* her blood was dried-up[G], and she knew[H] *in her* body that she had[14] been healed[J] from the scourge[K]	29
3D.	And immediately Jesus— having known[L] in Himself the power[15] having gone forth from Him, having turned around in the crowd— was saying, "Who[16] touched[E] My garments[F]?"	30
4D.	And His disciples were saying *to* Him, "You see the crowd pressing-upon You, and You say 'Who touched Me?'"	31
5D.	And He was looking around to see the *one* having done[17] this	32
6D.	And the woman— having become afraid, and while trembling[18], knowing[M] what had[19] happened *to* her[20]— came and fell-before Him, and told Him the whole truth[N]	33
7D.	And the *One* said *to* her, "Daughter[O], your faith has restored you. Go in peace, and be healthy[21] from your scourge[K]"	34
4C.	While He *is* still speaking, they come from [the house of] the synagogue-official, saying that "Your daughter[O] died[P]. Why are you troubling[22] the Teacher further?"	35
1D.	But Jesus, having ignored[23] the statement[Q] being spoken, says *to* the synagogue-official, "Do not be fearing, only be believing[24]"	36
2D.	And He did not permit[R] anyone to follow[S] with Him except Peter and James and John (the brother *of* James)	37
3D.	And they come[25] to the house *of* the synagogue official. And He sees *a* commotion[26], and *ones* weeping[T] and wailing loudly	38
4D.	And having gone in, He says *to* them, "Why are you being thrown-into-a-commotion[U], and weeping[T]? The child did not die[P], but is sleeping[V]". And they were laughing-scornfully[27] *at* Him	39 40
5D.	But **He**, having put everyone out, takes along the father *of* the child, and the mother, and the *ones* with Him, and proceeds in where the child was[28]. And having taken hold of the hand *of* the child, He says *to* her, "Talitha koum[29]" (which being translated[W] is "Little-girl[X], I say *to* you, arise[Y]")	41
6D.	And immediately the little girl stood-up[Z], and was walking around (for she was twelve years *old*)	42
1E.	And immediately[30] they were astonished[31] *with* great astonishment[32]	
2E.	And He gave-orders *to* them strictly[AA] that no one should know[H] this	43
3E.	And He said *that something should* be given *to* her to eat	

1. Parallel account at Mt 9:18; Lk 8:40.
2. Some manuscripts omit "in the boat" {C}.
3. Or, "up to, upon". GK *2093*.
4. On this word, see Act 18:8. Some manuscripts say "And behold, one..." {N}.
5. Or, "toward, to". GK *4639*.
6. Or, "loudly, earnestly". Same word as "loudly" in v 38. On this word, see "many" in Mt 13:52.
7. This is an idiom, literally, she "has *it* extremely", "has *it* at the extremity". This idiom is like "has *it* badly", meaning "being ill" (see Mk 1:32), but means "is at the extreme point of illness, at the point of death".
8. Or, "saved". Same word as in v 28, 34. On this word, see Jam 5:15.
9. Or, "pressing in on, pressing together on". Elsewhere only in v 31. GK *5315*. Related to "press" in 3:9.
10. Some manuscripts say "*a* certain woman" {N}. Note this vivid Greek statement in v 25-27. The main sentence is "And *a* woman... touched His garment". In between, there are seven participle phrases setting the circumstances. The main verb is held until the end. "*There was*" is added and the sentence is split only to make it a little easier in English.
11. This is an idiom, literally, "all the *things* from her", that is, all her resources. Similar to Lk 10:7, "the *things* from them", and Phil 4:18, "the *things* from you". Compare Lk 8:43.
12. Some manuscripts say "heard the *things* about Jesus" {N}.
13. Or, "spring". That is, the source of the flow of blood, whatever it was. On this word, see "spring" in Jn 4:6.
14. More literally, "has", as the Greek typically phrases it.
15. Or, "the miracle". This word means "power, capability". When the power comes from God, it also means the "miracle" (see 1 Cor 12:10) or the "work of power" done. Used 119 times. GK *1539*. Related to "be able" in 1 Jn 3:9.
16. Jesus wishes to acknowledge the woman's faith, and make the miracle public.
17. This word is feminine. It could be rendered, to see "*her* having done" this. Jesus knew who it was, but waited for her to respond.
18. Elsewhere only in Lk 8:47; 2 Pet 2:10. GK *5554*. Related to the word in Phil 2:12.
19. More literally, "has", as the Greek typically phrases it.
20. Some manuscripts say "in her" {N}.
21. On this adjective, see Mt 12:13. The command here is the verb "to be" (GK *1639*), meaning "continue to be" healthy.
22. Or, "bothering, annoying". On this word, see Mt 9:36. Same word as in Lk 8:49.
23. Or, "overheard", and then ignored. Elsewhere only as "refuses-to-listen" in Mt 18:17. GK *4159*. Related to "disobedience" in 2 Cor 10:6. Some manuscripts say "having heard", as in Lk 8:50; others, "But immediately Jesus, having heard..." {B}.
24. The grammar implies, "continue believing". Compare Lk 8:50.
25. Some manuscripts say "He comes" {K}.
26. Or, "uproar, confusion, disorder, unrest". Same word as in Act 24:18. Elsewhere only as "uproar" in Mt 26:5; 27:24; Mk 14:2; Act 20:1; 21:34. GK *2573*. Related to "throw into a commotion" next.
27. The ones there know she is dead. On this word, see Lk 8:53.
28. Some manuscripts add "lying" {N}.
29. Some manuscripts say "koumi" {N}. This is a transliterated Aramaic phrase. This variant reflects a grammatical difference in the underlying Aramaic command.
30. Some manuscripts omit this word {C}. See 6:25 on it.
31. On this word, see 2:12. A related word follows.
32. Our word "ecstasy" comes from this Greek word, *ekstasis*. It is a "standing outside" of oneself. Same word as 16:8; Lk 5:26; Act 3:10. Elsewhere only as "trance" in Act 10:10; 11:5; 22:17. GK *1749*.

A. Rom 12:8, exhorting B. Gal 3:4 C. Act 21:24 D. Rom 2:25, profits E. 1 Cor 7:1 F. 1 Pet 3:3 G. Mk 3:1, became withered H. Lk 1:34
J. Mt 8:8 K. Mk 3:10 L. Col 1:6 M. 1 Jn 2:29 N. Jn 4:23 O. Lk 13:16 P. Rom 7:10 Q. 1 Cor 12:8, word R. Mt 6:12, forgive S. Mk 14:51
T. Jn 11:33 U. Mt 9:23 V. 1 Thes 5:10 W. Act 13:8 X. Mk 6:22, girl Y. Mt 28:6 Z. Lk 18:33, rise up AA. Mt 13:52, many

| Mark 6:1 | 128 | Verse |

  7D. And He went out from there   6:1

16B.[1] And He comes[2] into His hometown[3]. And His disciples are following Him

  1C. And having become Sabbath, He began to teach in the synagogue   2

    1D. And while listening, many were astounded[A], saying, "From where *did* these *things come to* this *One*? And what *is* the wisdom[B] having been given *to* this *One*? And[4] such miracles[C] taking place by His hands! °Is this *One* not the carpenter[5], the son *of* Mary, and brother *of* James and Joses and Jude and Simon? And are not His sisters[6] here with us?"   3
    2D. And they were taking-offense[7] at Him
    3D. And Jesus was saying *to* them that "*A* prophet[D] is not without-honor[E] except in his hometown[F], and among his relatives[G], and in his house[H]"   4

  2C. And He was not able[8] to do any miracle[C] there except, having laid *His* hands on *a* few sick[J] ones, He cured[K] them   5
  3C. And He was marveling[L] because of their unbelief[9]   6

17B.[10] And He was going-around the villages *in a* circle, teaching. °And He summons the twelve, and began to send them out two *by* two[11]   7

  1C. And He was giving them authority[M] *over* the unclean spirits
  2C. And He instructed[N] them that   8

    1D. They should be taking nothing for *the* journey except *a* staff[12] only— no bread, no [traveler's] bag[O], no money[13] for the [money] belt
    2D. But *should go* having [merely] tied-on[14] sandals[15]   9
    3D. "And do not put on two tunics[16]"

  3C. And He was saying *to* them, "Wherever you enter into *a* house, be staying[P] there until you go forth from-that-place.[17] °And whatever place[18] does not welcome[Q] you, nor do they listen-to you— while proceeding out from-that-place, shake-out[19] the dirt[20] under your feet for *a* testimony[R] *against* them"[21]   10, 11
  4C. And having gone forth, they proclaimed[S] that they should repent[22]. °And they were casting out many demons. And they were anointing[23] many sick *ones with* oil[24] and curing[K] *them*   12-13

18B.[25] And King Herod[26] heard [of Him], for His name became known[T]   14

  1C. And they[27] were saying that "John, the *one* baptizing[U], has arisen[V] from *the* dead. And for this reason the *miraculous*-powers[28] are at-work[29] in Him"

    1D. And others were saying that "He is Elijah"   15
    2D. And others were saying that "*He is a* prophet like one *of* the [former] prophets"

  2C.[30] But having heard, Herod was saying, "John, whom **I** beheaded— this[31] *one* arose[V]"   16

    1D. For Herod himself, having sent out *men*, seized[W] John and bound[X] him in prison because of Herodias[32], the wife *of* Philip his brother— because he married[Y] her   17

      1E. For John was saying *to* Herod that "It is not lawful[Z] *for* you to have the wife *of* your brother"   18

1. Parallel account at Mt 13:53. Compare Lk 4:16-30; Jn 4:43-44.
2. Some manuscripts say "came" {N}.
3. That is, Nazareth. On this word, see "homeland" in Heb 11:14.
4. Some manuscripts say "that indeed such miracles should take place..."; others, "And such miracles are taking place..." {C}.
5. This is the only place Jesus is called a carpenter. Elsewhere only in Mt 13:55. GK *5454*. Some manuscripts say "the son *of* the carpenter and Mary" {A}.
6. On His brothers and sisters, see Mt 13:55-56.
7. Or, "being caused to fall" by Him. On this word, see "caused to fall" in 1 Cor 8:13.
8. The reason is not stated. If Lk 4:16-30 is referring to this incident, it was because they drove Jesus out. If not, it may have been because He refused to do "signs" for those who knowingly rejected Him, as these people did. Note 8:12.
9. It is a marvel. They acknowledged His wisdom and miracles (v 2), yet rejected Him! On this word, see 1 Tim 1:13.
10. Parallel account at Mt 10:1; Lk 9:1.
11. This is an idiom, literally "two, two".
12. Or, "walking stick". Mt 10:10 and Lk 9:3 say "not a staff ". Some think they quote Jesus as meaning not to acquire a new one or a second one, whereas Mark quotes Him as meaning the disciples should take whatever one they already have.
13. Like a leptos or a quadran, see 12:42. Compare Mt 10:9; Lk 9:3. Same word as in 12:41, and as "copper" in Mt 10:9. GK *5910*.
14. This word is related to "sandal" in Mt 10:10; Lk 10:4, but not to "sandals" next. On this word, see "sandaled" in Eph 6:15.
15. Not the same word as Mt 10:10; Lk 10:4. A synonym. Elsewhere only in Act 12:8. GK *4908*.
16. That is, "undershirts", worn next to the skin. In other words, make no preparations for the journey. Go as you are, without doing the normal planning and preparation any traveler would do. Do not even take an extra pair of underwear. Just put your shoes on and go. God will provide all you need through those welcoming you. Compare Lk 3:11. On this word, see Mt 5:40. Some manuscripts make this part of what precedes, instead of a direct quote {N}, "sandals—and not to put on two tunics".
17. That is, remain in that house until you depart from that city. Do not move around.
18. Some manuscripts instead say "And whoever..." {N}.
19. On this word, see Act 13:51. Same word as in Mt 10:14. Lk 9:5 uses a related word.
20. Mark uses a different word than Mt 10:14 or Lk 9:5. Elsewhere only in Rev 18:19. GK *5967*.
21. Some manuscripts add "Truly I say *to* you, it will be more tolerable *for* Sodom or Gomorrah on *the* day *of* judgment than *for* that city" {N}, as in Mt 10:15.
22. Same word as in 1:15, Mark's only other use of it. On this word, see Act 26:20.
23. Or, "putting on, rubbing on". The "anointing with oil" associated with healing occurs only here and Jam 5:14. Oil was medicinal, as seen in Lk 10:34. Here its purpose is unclear. Some think it is symbolic, perhaps of the Spirit, or that the healing is through the power of Another. There are other views. On this word, see Jam 5:14.
24. That is, olive oil. On this word, see Jam 5:14.
25. Parallel account at Mt 14:1; Lk 9:7.
26. That is, Herod Antipas. On this man, see Mt 14:1.
27. That is, the ones making Jesus known, repeated by Herod and his servants. Compare Mt 14:1; Lk 9:7. Some manuscripts say "he was saying" {B}.
28. Or, "the Powers" (see Mt 14:2). Same word as "miracle" in v 2, 5.
29. Same word as in Mt 14:2.
30. Parallel account at Mt 14:3. Compare Lk 3:19-20.
31. Some manuscripts say "This is John whom I beheaded. **He** arose from *the* dead" {N}.
32. On Herodias and Philip, see Mt 14:3. This occurred in 1:14.

A. Mt 7:28 B. 1 Cor 12:8 C. 1 Cor 12:10 D. 1 Cor 12:28 E. 1 Cor 12:23 F. Heb 11:14, homeland G. Rom 16:7, kinsmen H. Mk 3:25
J. Mk 16:18 K. Mt 8:7 L. Rev 17:8 M. Rev 6:8 N. 1 Tim 1:3, command O. Lk 9:3 P. Jn 15:4, abide Q. Mt 10:40 R. Act 4:33 S. 2 Tim 4:2
T. Rom 1:19, evident U. Mk 1:8 V. Mt 28:6 W. Heb 4:14, hold on to X. 1 Cor 7:27 Y. 1 Cor 7:9 Z. 1 Cor 6:12

2D.	And Herodias was hostile[1] *to* him, and was wanting[A] to kill him, and was not being able	19
	1E. For Herod was fearing[B] John, knowing *that* he *was a* righteous[C] and holy[D] man. And he was protecting[E] him	20
	2E. And having heard him, he was greatly perplexed[2]	
	3E. And-*yet* he was listening-to him with-pleasure[3]	
	3D. And *an* opportune[4] day having come about when Herod, *for* his birthday-celebrations[5], made *a* banquet[F] *for* his princes[6] and the commanders[7] and the leading[8] ones *of* Galilee, and his[9] daughter Herodias having come in and danced[10]—	21
		22
	1E. She pleased[G] Herod, and the *ones* reclining-back-with *him* [to eat]	
	2E. The king said *to* the girl[11], "Ask me whatever you wish[A], and I will give *it to* you". And he swore-with-an-oath[H] *to* her solemnly[12], "Whatever thing[13] you[14] ask me, I will give *it to* you— up to half *of* my kingdom[J]"	23
	3E. And having gone out, she said *to* her mother, "What should I ask-*for*?" And the *one* said, "The head *of* John, the *one* baptizing[15]"	24
	4E. And having immediately[16] gone in with haste[K] to the king, she asked, saying, "I want you to[17] give me at-once[18], on *a* platter[L], the head *of* John the Baptist[19]"	25
	5E. And the king, having become deeply-grieved[M], did not want to reject[N] her, because of the oaths[O] and the *ones* reclining-back [to eat]. °And immediately having sent-out *an* executioner[20], the king commanded[P] *him* to bring his head[21]	26
		27
	6E. And having gone, he beheaded him in the prison. °And he brought his head on *a* platter, and gave it *to* the girl. And the girl gave it *to* her mother	28
	4D. And his disciples, having heard-*of it*, came and took away his corpse[Q], and laid it in *a* tomb	29
19B.[22]	And the apostles[23] are gathered-together with Jesus. And they reported[R] *to* Him all[24] that they did and that they taught	30
	1C. And He says *to* them, "Come, you yourselves privately[S], to *a* desolate[25] place, and rest *a* little". For the *ones* coming and the *ones* going were many, and they were not even finding *an* opportunity[26] to eat	31
	2C.[27] And they went away privately[S] in the boat to *a* desolate place	32
	3C. And they[28] saw them going, and many knew[29] *where*. And they ran there together *on* foot from all the cities. And they came-ahead-of [30] them[31]	33
	4C. And having gone out[32], He saw *a* large crowd, and felt-deep-feelings[T] [of compassion] toward them because they were like sheep not having *a* shepherd[U]. And He began to teach them many *things*	34
	5C. And already having become *a* late hour, having come to Him, His disciples were saying that "*This* place is desolate, and *it is* already *a* late hour. °Send them away in order that having gone away into the surrounding farms and villages, they may buy themselves what they may eat"	35
		36
	1D. But the *One*, having responded, said *to* them, "**You** give them *something* to eat"	37
	2D. And they say *to* Him, "Should we, having gone away, buy loaves *worth* two-hundred denarii[33], and give them *something* to eat?"	
	3D. And the *One* says *to* them, "How many loaves do you have? Go[34], see!" And having come-to-know[V], they say, "Five, and two fish"	38
	4D. And He commanded[P] them to make everyone lie-back[35] party *by* party[36] on the green[37] grass. °And they fell-back grouping *by* grouping[38], by hundreds and by fifties	39
		40

1. More literally, Herodias was "having *it* in" for John, "holding in" anger and retaliation against him. She was internally setting herself against him, plotting how to destroy him without angering Herod. Same word as in Lk 11:53. Elsewhere only as "held in" in Gal 5:1. GK *1923*.
2. On this word, see 2 Cor 4:8. Herod "was at a loss" about what to do. Some manuscripts instead say "he was doing many *things*" {C}.
3. Same word as in 12:37; 2 Cor 11:19. Elsewhere only as "gladly" in 2 Cor 12:9, 15. GK *2452*. Related to "pleasure" in Lk 8:14.
4. That is, for Herodias. Elsewhere only as "well-timed" in Heb 4:16. GK *2322*. Related to "find an opportunity" in v 31.
5. Elsewhere only in Mt 14:6. GK *1160*.
6. That is, Herod's government officials; officials of his administration. On this word, see Rev 6:15.
7. That is, the Roman officers. On this word, see Act 21:31.
8. Or, "prominent *ones*, first *ones*". That is, the local dignitaries. GK *4755*.
9. The girl was this Herod's daughter by virtue of his marriage to her mother, mentioned in v 17 (Philip was her physical father). Some manuscripts say "the daughter *of* Herodias herself" {C}. Josephus calls her Salome, but she may have also been known as Herodias, her mother's name. Herod's children took on the name Herod almost like a title. See Mt 14:6 on her.
10. Three participles set the stage for the main sentence. A day having come about, and Herodias having come in and danced, "she pleased Herod".
11. Or, "maiden, young woman". Same word as in v 28; Mt 14:11. This word was used of "little girls" and girls of marriageable age. Used of Esther in Est 2:7, and Ruth in Ruth 2:22. Some think Salome was about 13 to 15 years old at this time. Elsewhere only as "little girl" in Mt 9:24, 25; Mk 5:41, 42 (where she is said to be twelve). GK *3166*.
12. Some manuscripts omit this word {C}.
13. On "whatever thing", see Col 3:17.
14. Some manuscripts say "solemnly that 'Whatever you ask...'" {C}.
15. Note that a participle is used here (as in 1:4; 6:14; only in Mark is John referred to this way), and the noun is used in v 25 (as in 8:28). On this word see 1:8.
16. This word is used 51 times, 41 by Mark. GK *2317*. It is a key word for Mark. There is a related word in Mt 13:5. The KJV renders them both "straightway", the root word being "straight" in Act 8:21.
17. More literally, "I want that you should give me". GK *2671*.
18. Same word as in Act 10:33; 21:32; 23:30; Phil 2:23. Elsewhere only as "immediately" in Act 11:11. GK *1994*. Not related to "immediately" earlier in the verse.
19. Elsewhere only in Mt 3:1; 11:11, 12; 14:2, 8; 16:14; 17:13; Mk 8:28; Lk 7:20, 33; 9:19. GK *969*. Related to "baptism" in Mk 1:4.
20. Or, "courier, bodyguard". Herod said to this man "Bring me his head". Used only here. GK *5063*.
21. Some manuscripts say "commanded his head to be brought" {N}.
22. Parallel account at Lk 9:10.
23. Or, "sent *ones*". The twelve were "sent out" in v 7, where the verb related to this word was used. On this word, see 1 Cor 12:28.
24. Some manuscripts say "both all that..." {K}. Some manuscripts omit the next "that" {N}, so that it says "all that they did and taught".
25. Same word as in v 32, 35, and as 1:35.
26. Or, "having a favorable time". Related to "opportune" in v 21. On this word, see Act 17:21.
27. Parallel account at Mt 14:13; Lk 9:10; Jn 6:1.
28. That is, "people" saw. The word "many" is the last word in this sentence. Some make it the subject of both verbs, "And many saw... and knew". Some manuscripts say "And the crowds saw" {K}, as in Mt 14:13.
29. Or, "recognized, learned". Or, "knew, recognized *them*". Same word as "recognized" in v 54. On this word, see "understood" in Col 1:6.
30. Some think this means these people arrived first; others, that this group who knew them "went before, preceded, went ahead of" or led the other people to them. Whether this "many" arrived ahead of the boat or led the crowd from all the cities there sometime after the boat had arrived is related to the meaning of "gone out" in v 34. Elsewhere only as "go ahead" in Mt 26:39; 14:35; Lk 1:17; Act 12:10; 20:5, 13; 2 Cor 9:5; and "precede" in Lk 22:47. GK *4601*.
31. Some manuscripts say instead "and came together to them". Others say both, "and came ahead of them and came together to Him" {B}.
32. Or, "having come out". Some think Mark means "[of the boat]", as in v 54; 5:2. Others think he means "[from their private place where they had gone]", as may be implied in Lk 9:10; Jn 6:3. Same word as Mt 14:14. GK *2002*.
33. That is, 200 days wages for a laborer. On this word, see Mt 20:2.
34. Some manuscripts say "Go and see" {N}.
35. Some manuscripts say "them *that* everyone should lie back..." {N}.
36. That is, in eating groups. Our word "symposium" comes from this word, *sumposion*. It meant "drinking parties", and then "a party of guests". Used only here. GK *5235*.
37. This word marks this as a springtime event. It was near Passover, Jn 6:4.
38. This word implies that the people were divided up like "garden-plots". Some think this refers to their orderly arrangement in rows; others, to their colorful clothing, like flowers. Used only here. GK *4555*.

A. Jn 7:17, willing B. Eph 5:33, respecting C. Rom 1:17 D. 1 Pet 1:16 E. Lk 2:19, preserving F. Lk 14:12, dinner G. 1 Thes 2:4 H. Jam 5:12, swearing J. Mt 3:2 K. 2 Cor 8:16, earnestness L. Lk 11:39 M. Mt 26:38 N. Gal 2:21, set aside O. Jam 5:12 P. Lk 8:25 Q. Mk 15:45 R. 1 Jn 1:3, announcing S. Mt 14:13 T. Mt 9:36 U. Eph 4:11 V. Lk 1:34, know

	5D. And having taken the five loaves and the two fish, having looked up to heaven, He blessed[A] *them*[1], and broke the loaves in pieces[2], and was giving *them to* His[3] disciples in order that they might be setting *it* before[B] them. And He divided[C] the two fish *to* everyone	41
	6D. And they all ate and were filled-to-satisfaction[D]	42
	7D. And they picked up fragments[E]— *the* fillings[4] *of* twelve baskets[F], and from the fish[5]	43
	8D. And the *ones* having eaten the loaves[6] were five-thousand men[7]	44
20B.[8]	And immediately, He compelled[9] His disciples to get into the boat, and to be going ahead to the other side[10], toward[11] Bethsaida, while **He** sends-away[G] the crowd	45
	1C. And having said-good-bye[H] *to* them[12], He went away on the mountain to pray	46
	2C. And having become evening, the boat was in *the* middle *of* the sea, and He *was* alone on the land	47
	3C. And having seen[13] them being tormented[14] in the rowing[J]— for the wind was contrary[K] *to* them— He[15] comes to them around *the* fourth watch *of* the night[16], walking on the sea. And He was intending[17] to pass-by them	48
	4C. But the *ones,* having seen Him walking on the sea, thought that "It is *a* phantom[18]", and cried-out[19]. °For they all saw Him and were frightened[20]	49 50
	5C. But immediately the *One* spoke with them. And He says *to* them, "Take-courage[L], **I am** *the One*[21]. Do not be afraid"	
	6C. And He went up with them in the boat. And the wind stopped[M]	51
	7C. And they were very exceedingly[22] astonished[23] in themselves. °For they did not understand[24] on the basis of the loaves-of-bread, but their heart had been hardened[25]	52
21B.[26]	And having crossed-over, they came on land in Gennesaret[27], and moored[28]	53
	1C. And they having gone out of the boat— immediately having recognized[N] Him, °*the people* ran around that whole region. And they began to carry around the *ones* being ill[O] on *their* cots *to*-where they were hearing that He was[29]	54-55
	2C. And wherever He was entering— into villages, or into cities, or into fields— they were laying the *ones* being sick[P] in the marketplaces, and were begging[Q] Him that they might touch even[30] the tassel[R] *of* His garment. And all who touched[S] it were being restored[31]	56
22B.[32]	And the Pharisees and some *of* the scribes are gathered-together with Him, having come from Jerusalem	7:1
	1C. And having seen some *of* His disciples, that they are eating *their* bread *with* defiled[33] hands, that is, unwashed[34]—	2
	1D. For the Pharisees and all the Jews do not eat unless they wash[35] *their* hands *with a* fist[36]— holding-on-to[T] the tradition[U] *of* the elders	3
	2D. And they do not eat [when they return][37] from *the* marketplace unless they cleanse[38] [themselves][39]	4
	3D. And there are many other *traditions*[40] which they received[V] to hold-on-to[T]— *the* cleansing[41] *of* cups and pitchers and copper-pots and couches[42]	
	2C. And[43] the Pharisees and the scribes ask Him— "For what reason are Your disciples not walking according to the tradition[U] *of* the elders, but are eating *their* bread *with* defiled[44] hands?"	5
	3C. And the *One* said *to* them	6

1. That is, the food. Or, "*God*". See Mt 14:19 on this.
2. On the word "broke in pieces", see Lk 9:16.
3. Some manuscripts omit this word {C}, so that it says "the disciples".
4. Or, "contents, full-measures". This word is plural only here and in 8:20. On this word, see "fullness" in Col 1:19. Mark uses a different word and grammar in 8:8, 19.
5. That is, the fragments of bread and fish filled up twelve baskets.
6. Some manuscripts omit "the loaves" {C}.
7. This word means males. Compare Mt 14:21.
8. Parallel account at Mt 14:22; Jn 6:16.
9. Same word as in Mt 14:22. The reason why is seen in Jn 6:15.
10. Some manuscripts omit "to the other side" {A}.
11. Or, "to Bethsaida". They were already near Bethsaida (Lk 9:10), which is near the northeast shore of the Sea of Galilee, east of Capernaum. Perhaps Jesus sent them back toward there, and beyond it to the other side (to Capernaum, Jn 6:17), and they were blown off course to the south, to Gennesaret (Mk 6:53). There are other views.
12. That is, to the crowd.
13. Some manuscripts say "And He saw..." {N}.
14. Or, "harassed, tortured". Or, "tormenting *themselves* at the rowing". That is, because of the wind and waves, Mt 14:24. On this word, see Rev 14:10.
15. Some manuscripts say "them. And He comes..." {N}.
16. The fourth watch was from 3-6 A.M. On the four watches, see 13:35. On "watch", see Lk 2:8.
17. Or, "wishing, wanting". On this word, see "willing" in Jn 7:17.
18. Or, "ghost". Our English word comes from this Greek word, *phantasma*. Elsewhere only in Mt 14:26. GK *5753*.
19. On this word, see Lk 23:18. Related to the word in Mt 14:26 (GK *3189*).
20. Same word as in Mt 14:26. On this word, see "disturbed" in Gal 1:7.
21. That is, "It is I". On this phrase, see Jn 8:58.
22. Some manuscripts omit this word {C}.
23. On this word, see 2:12. Some manuscripts add "and they were marveling" {B} (these two verbs appear together in Act 2:7).
24. Same word as in 4:12. The disciples saw and heard, but did not understand. They thought He was just a prophet. On this word, see Mt 13:23.
25. This is a participle, their heart "was having been hardened". On this word, see Rom 11:7. The disciples did not understand the person and power of Jesus when He fed the 5000. But now they understand. Compare 8:17; Mt 14:33.
26. Parallel account at Mt 14:34. Compare Jn 6:22-25.
27. This plain was on the west side of the Sea of Galilee, south of Capernaum. Elsewhere only in Mt 14:34; Lk 5:1. GK *1166*.
28. Or, "were brought to anchor". Used only here. GK *4694*.
29. More literally, "is", as the Greek typically phrases it.
30. Or, "at least". Same word as in 5:28. GK *2829*.
31. Same word as in 5:23. Related to the word in Mt 14:36.
32. Parallel account at Mt 15:1.
33. Or, "common, unconsecrated, unclean". Same word as in v 5. Mark does not mean "dirty", but "not ceremonially washed according to their traditions", "not ritually purified" from any contact with unclean things or people. On this word, see Heb 10:29. The related verb is in v 15.
34. Mark breaks off the sentence here and explains this concept to his readers, and then begins again in v 5. Elsewhere only in Mt 15:20. GK *481*. Some manuscripts add "they found fault" {N}, completing the sentence, using the same word as in Rom 9:19.
35. Related to "unwashed" in v 2. Also used of the face in Mt 6:17, the eyes in Jn 9:7, the feet in Jn 13:5; 1 Tim 5:10. Used 17 times. GK *3782*. Related to "wash-basin" in Jn 13:5. It is differentiated from "bathe" (the whole body) in Jn 13:10.
36. The procedure in view here is uncertain. Some think Mark means rubbing one hand and forearm with the other hand clenched in a fist. Others think it is a fist washed in the hollow of the other hand. Others think it means "with a handful of water". Water for this custom is seen in Jn 2:6. The NKJV paraphrases "in a special way"; the NIV, a "ceremonial washing", both of which give the correct idea without reference to the exact procedure. Used only here. GK *4778*. Instead of "*with a* fist", some manuscripts have a word that means "often" or "thoroughly" {A}.
37. Or, "[food]".
38. Or, "dip, immerse, wash, baptize". Same word as in Lk 11:38. Except for these two places, it is always translated "baptize". On this word, see "baptize" in Mk 1:8. This word is not related to "wash" in v 3. It refers to a ritual "washing" or "cleansing" of the body and of vessels (as in Lev 11:31, 32; 15:11, etc.), in case anything "unclean" was touched.
39. Or, "[it]", the food.
40. This word is supplied from v 3.
41. Related to "cleanse" earlier in the verse. On this word, see Heb 6:2.
42. That is, the dining couches on which people of that day reclined to eat. GK *3109*. Some manuscripts omit "and couches" {C}.
43. Some manuscripts say "Then" {N}, making the connection with v 2 clearer.
44. Some manuscripts say "unwashed" {N}, as in v 2.

A. Lk 6:28 B. Act 17:3, put before C. 1 Cor 7:17, apportioned D. Phil 4:12 E. Mt 15:37 F. Jn 6:13 G. Mt 5:31 H. 2 Cor 2:13 J. Lk 8:29, driven K. 1 Thes 2:15 L. Act 23:11 M. Mk 4:39 N. Col 1:6, understood O. Mk 1:32 P. 2 Tim 4:20 Q. Rom 12:8, exhorting R. Mt 23:5 S. 1 Cor 7:1 T. Heb 4:14 U. 1 Cor 11:2 V. Lk 17:34, taken

1D. "Isaiah prophesied^A rightly^B concerning you hypocrites^C, as it has been written [in Isa 29:13], that¹ 'This people honors^D Me *with their* lips, but their heart is far distant^E from Me. ˚But they are worshiping^F Me in-vain^G, teaching *as* teachings² *the* commandments³ *of* humans^H'   7

2D. "Having neglected⁴ the commandment^J *of* God, you are holding on to the tradition *of* humans⁵!"   8

4C. And He was saying *to* them, "You are nicely⁶ setting-aside⁷ the commandment^J *of* God in order that you may establish⁸ your tradition!   9

  1D. "For Moses said [in Ex 20:12], 'Be honoring your father and your mother', and [in Ex 21:17], 'Let the *one* speaking-evil-of^K father or mother come-to-an-end⁹ *by a* death¹⁰'   10

  2D. "But **you** say if *a* person says *to his* father or mother, 'Whatever you might be benefitted^L from me *is* Corban¹¹ (which means, "Gift¹²")', ˚you¹³ no longer permit^M him to do anything *for his* father or mother— ˚nullifying¹⁴ the word *of* God *by* your tradition which you handed-down^N   11, 12, 13

  3D. "And you are doing many similar¹⁵ such *things*"

5C. And having summoned the crowd again¹⁶, He was saying *to* them, "Everyone listen-to Me and understand^O—   14

  1D. "There is nothing outside *of* the person proceeding into him which is able to defile¹⁷ him   15

  2D. "But the *things* proceeding out of the person are the *things* defiling the person   16¹⁸

6C. And when He entered into *a* house away-from the crowd, His disciples were questioning Him *as to* the parable   17

  1D. And He says *to* them, "So are even **you** without-understanding^P? Do you not perceive^Q that everything outside proceeding into the person is not able to defile him ˚because it does not proceed into his heart, but into *his* stomach, and it proceeds out into the latrine?"   18, 19

    1E. *He was* making all foods¹⁹ clean²⁰

  2D. And He was saying that "The *thing* proceeding out of the person— that defiles the person   20

    1E. "For from within, out of the heart *of* people, proceed the evil²¹ thoughts^R, sexual-immoralities^S, thefts, murders, ˚adulteries, greeds^T, evils^U, deceit^V, sensuality^W, *an* evil eye,²² blasphemy^X, arrogance²³, foolishness^Y   21, 22

    2E. "All these evil *things* proceed out from within, and defile the person"   23

23B.²⁴ And having arisen, He went from there to the districts *of* Tyre²⁵. And having entered into *a* house, He was wanting²⁶ no one to know²⁷ *it*. And-*yet* He was not able to escape-notice^Z   24

1C. But immediately, *a* woman having heard about Him²⁸— *of* whom her little daughter was having *an* unclean spirit— having come, fell at His feet   25

2C. Now the woman was *a* Greek²⁹, *a* Syro-Phoenician³⁰ *by* nationality^AA. And she was asking Him that He cast out the demon from her daughter   26

  1D. And He was saying³¹ *to* her, "First allow^BB the children³² to be filled-to-satisfaction^CC. For it is not good^DD to take the bread *of* the children and throw *it* to the little-dogs³³"   27

  2D. But the *one* responded and says *to* Him, "Master³⁴, even the little dogs under the table eat from the crumbs *of* the children!"   28

1. Some manuscripts omit this word {C}, which serves to introduce the quotation.
2. Or, "doctrines". That is, teaching them as if they were God's teachings. Same root word as the verb just used. On this word, see 1 Tim 5:17.
3. Same word as in Mt 15:9, on which see Col 2:22.
4. Same word as in Mt 23:23.
5. Some manuscripts say "humans— *the* washings *of* pitchers and cups, and many other very similar such *things* you do" {A}.
6. Or, "splendidly, beautifully". This is the adverb of the word "good", used here sarcastically. On this word, see "well" in Act 10:33.
7. Or, "rejecting". On this word, see Gal 2:21.
8. Or, "that you may make your tradition stand". GK *2705*. Some manuscripts say "keep" {D}.
9. That is, die. On this word, see 9:48.
10. On this phrase, see Mt 15:4.
11. This is a transliterated Hebrew word meaning "a gift or offering to God". In other words, the child tells the needy parent, "I have set this aside as an offering to God, and therefore I cannot use it to help you". Used only here. GK *3167*.
12. Same word as in Mt 15:5.
13. Some manuscripts add the word meaning "and" or "indeed" {N}. With this word, the rendering given above would become "you indeed no longer". Or, the sentence could be rendered "... if a person says.. Gift")', *he shall be free*. And you no longer permit...".
14. Same word as in Mt 15:6.
15. Used only here. GK *4235*. Related word in Mt 23:27.
16. Some think this indicates the Pharisees were speaking to Jesus privately. Some manuscripts say "summoned the whole crowd" {N}.
17. Or, "make ceremonially unclean". Same word as in Mt 15:11, 18, 20; Mk 7:18, 20, 23; Act 21:28; Heb 9:13. Elsewhere only as "make defiled" in Act 10:15; 11:9. GK *3124*. Related to the adjective "defiled" in v 2.
18. Some manuscripts add as v 16, "If anyone has ears to hear, let him hear" {A}.
19. Elsewhere only in Mt 14:15; Lk 3:11; 9:13; Jn 4:34; Rom 14:15, 20; 1 Cor 3:2; 6:13; 8:8, 13; 10:3; 1 Tim 4:3; Heb 9:10; 13:9. GK *1109*. Related to "eating" in Mt 6:19.
20. This word "making clean" can also be rendered "cleansing, declaring clean, treating clean". Some think this is Mark's comment (similar to what he did in 3:30; 7:3-4), agreeing grammatically with the subject ("He" in "He says", v 18). Mark is making explicit what Jesus implied. Peter learned this in Act 10:15, where this same word is used. Foods are not inherently clean or unclean. Apart from God's Law, they have no moral effect. It is not the food going in that defiles, but the disobedience to God going out. See Mt 15:11. Others think these are Jesus' words, "into the latrine, cleansing all foods", meaning that the latrine proves they are clean because they pass through the body without affecting the heart. Others render it, "latrine, purging all foods", simply completing the physical description. On this word, see "cleansed" in Heb 9:22.
21. This is GK *2805*. The word in Mt 15:19 is the word Mark uses in v 22, 23 (GK *4505*).
22. Same words as Mt 20:15, where it refers to envy. GK *4505*, *4057*.
23. Or, "haughtiness, pride". Used only here. GK *5661*. Related to "arrogant" in Jam 4:6.
24. Parallel account at Mt 15:21.
25. Some manuscripts add "and Sidon" {B}, as in Mt 15:21. Note v 31.
26. Or, "wishing, intending". On this word, see "willing" in Jn 7:17.
27. Or, "come to know, learn". On this word, see Lk 1:34.
28. Instead of this, some manuscripts say "For *a* woman having heard about Him" {N}.
29. That is, Greek speaking, Greek in culture. A Gentile.
30. That is, from Phoenicia, a region of which Tyre is a town, in the Roman province of Syria. Used only here. GK *5355*. She is also known as a "Canaanite" in Mt 15:22, from the Jewish point of view.
31. Some manuscripts say "But Jesus said" {K}.
32. That is, the children of Israel.
33. Or, "house dogs". On this word, see Mt 15:26. Jesus responds with a proverbial-type statement. The woman answers with the same type of statement in v 28.
34. Some manuscripts say "Yes, Master" {B}, as in Mt 15:27. On this word, see Mt 8:2.

A. 1 Cor 14:1 B. Act 10:33, well C. Mt 6:2 D. 1 Tim 5:3 E. Mt 15:8 F. Act 13:50 G. Mt 15:9 H. Mt 4:4, mankind J. Mk 12:28 K. Act 19:9 L. Rom 2:25, profits M. Mt 6:12, forgive N. Mt 26:21, hand over O. Mt 13:13 P. Rom 10:19 Q. Eph 3:20, think R. Jam 2:4 S. 1 Cor 5:1 T. Eph 4:19 U. Mt 22:18, evilness V. Mt 26:4 W. 2 Pet 2:2 X. 1 Tim 6:4 Y. 2 Cor 11:17 Z. 2 Pet 3:5 AA. 1 Cor 12:28, kind BB. Mt 6:12, forgive CC. Phil 4:12 DD. 1 Tim 5:10a

	3D. And He said *to* her, "Because of this statement,¹ go— the demon has gone out of your daughter"	29
	4D. And having gone to her house, she found the child having been put² on the bed, and the demon having gone out	30
24B.	And again having gone out of the districts^A *of* Tyre, He went through Sidon³ to the Sea *of* Galilee in the midst^B *of* the districts *of* Decapolis⁴	31
	1C. And they bring *to* Him *a* deaf and speech-impaired⁵ *one,* and are begging^C Him that He lay *His* hand on him	32
	2C. And having taken him away from the crowd privately^D, He put His fingers into his⁶ ears. And having spit⁷, He touched^E his⁶ tongue. *And having looked up to heaven, He sighed⁸. And He says *to* him, "Ephphatha⁹", which means, "Be opened"	33 34
	3C. And immediately¹⁰ his ears were opened, and the binding¹¹ *of* his tongue was released^F, and he was speaking correctly¹²	35
	4C. And He gave-orders *to* them that they should be telling no one. But as much as He was giving orders *to* them, **they** even more abundantly were proclaiming^G *it*	36
	5C. And they were being super-abundantly¹³ astounded^H, saying, "He has done all *things* well¹⁴. He even makes the deaf to hear, and the¹⁵ mute to speak"	37
25B.¹⁶	In those days, *there* again being *a* large crowd, and¹⁷ *they* not having anything they might eat— having summoned the¹⁸ disciples, He¹⁹ says *to* them, *"I feel-deep-feelings^J [of compassion] toward the crowd, because *it is* already three days they are remaining-with^K Me, and they do not have anything they may eat. *And if I send them away to their house hungry, they will become-exhausted²⁰ on the way. And some *of* them have come^L from *a* distance"	8:1 2 3
	1C. And His disciples responded *to* Him that "From where will anyone be able to fill these *ones* to satisfaction *with* bread²¹ here in *a* desolate-place?"²²	4
	2C. And He was asking them, "How many loaves do you have?" And the *ones* said, "Seven"	5
	3C. And He orders²³ the crowd to fall-back on the ground [to eat]	6
	4C. And having taken the seven loaves, having given-thanks^M, He broke^N *them,* and was giving *them to* His disciples in order that they might be setting *them* before^O *them*. And they set *them* before the crowd	
	5C. And they had *a* few small-fish. And having blessed^P them, He said to be setting these also before *them*	7
	6C. And they ate, and were filled-to-satisfaction^Q	8
	7C. And they picked up *the* leftovers^R *of* fragments^S— seven large-baskets^T	
	8C. And there were²⁴ about four-thousand *men*	9
	9C. And He sent them away	
26B.²⁵	And immediately^U, having gotten into the boat with His disciples, He went to the regions^V *of* Dalmanutha²⁶	10
	1C. And the Pharisees came out, and began to debate²⁷ *with* Him, seeking from Him *a* sign from heaven, testing^W Him	11
	2C. And having sighed-deeply²⁸ in His spirit, He says, "Why is this generation^X seeking *a* sign? Truly^Y I say *to* you, *a* sign will *never*²⁹ be given *to* this generation"	12
27B.³⁰	And having left them, having again gotten *into the boat*³¹, He went to the other side. *And they forgot to take bread. And except one loaf, they were not having *any* with them in the boat	13-14

1. That is, because of what the woman said in v 28 and what it revealed about her.
2. And therefore, "lying". Same word as in Mt 8:6. Some manuscripts say "the demon having gone out and *her* daughter having been put on the bed" {N}.
3. Some manuscripts instead say "the districts *of* Tyre and Sidon, He went to the Sea *of* Galilee..." {A}.
4. This word means "ten cities". That is, to the east side of the sea, where this region of "ten cities" was found. Elsewhere only in 5:20; Mt 4:25. GK *1279*.
5. Used of one with a speech impediment, or who speaks with difficulty. Used only here. GK *3652*.
6. Or, "His". In both cases noted in this verse, the "his" can be understood either way. The significance of these actions is not clear. Some think it was a kind of sign language, by which Jesus was telling the man what He was going to heal.
7. Jesus spit, but it is unclear where. Some suggest He spit on His finger and touched the man's tongue. In 8:23 Jesus spits in the man's eyes. Elsewhere only in Jn 9:6, where Jesus also uses saliva. GK *4772*. Related word in 14:65.
8. Or, "groaned". On this word, see "groan" in Jam 5:9.
9. This is a transliterated Aramaic word which Mark next translates into Greek. Used only here. GK *2395*.
10. Some manuscripts omit this word {C}.
11. Or, "bond, fetter". That is, the binding that held the mute man's tongue; that which impeded his speaking. On this word, see "imprisonment" in Phil 1:7.
12. Or, "rightly, straightly", that is, normally. Elsewhere only in Lk 7:43; 10:28; 20:21. GK *3987*.
13. Or, "beyond all measure". Used only here. GK *5669*. Related to "super-abounded" in Rom 5:20, and to "more abundantly" in v 36.
14. Or, "commendably". On this phrase, see Act 10:33.
15. Some manuscripts omit this word {C}, so that it says "and mute *ones* to speak".
16. Parallel account at Mt 15:29.
17. Some manuscripts say "In those days, *the* crowd being very-great, and not having anything..." {N}.
18. Some manuscripts say "His" {N}.
19. Some manuscripts say "Jesus" {K}.
20. Same word as in Mt 15:32.
21. Same word as "loaves" in Mt 15:33; and here in v 5, 6. On this word, see "loaves of bread" in Mt 4:3.
22. On this response, see Mt 15:33.
23. On this word, see "command" in 1 Tim 1:3. Some manuscripts say "ordered" {K}.
24. Some manuscripts say "And the *ones* having eaten were" {N}.
25. Parallel account at Mt 16:1-4. Compare Mt 12:38-42; Lk 11:29-32.
26. This may be the same place as "Magadan" in Mt 15:39, or near it. The location of both is uncertain. Used only here. GK *1236*. Some manuscripts say "Magdala" {B}.
27. Or, "discuss, dispute, argue". Same word as in 9:14, 16; 12:28; Act 6:9; 9:29. Elsewhere only as "discuss" in Mk 1:27; 9:10; Lk 22:23; 24:15. GK *5184*. Related to "debater" in 1 Cor 1:20.
28. Or, "groaned deeply". Used only here. GK *417*. Related to "sighed" in 7:34.
29. Literally, "Truly I say *to* you, if *a* sign will be given...". This is the conclusion of a Hebrew oath, "May [?] happen to me if a sign will be given". Same idiom as in Heb 3:11, used by God. It is a very strong negation. Mt 16:4 has different grammar.
30. Parallel account at Mt 16:5.
31. Some manuscripts include this phrase "into the boat" {N}, which is supplied from v 10.

A. Mk 10:1 B. 2 Thes 2:7 C. Rom 12:8, exhorting D. Mt 14:13 E. 1 Cor 7:1 F. Mt 5:19, break G. 2 Tim 4:2 H. Mt 7:28 J. Mt 9:36 K. Act 11:23, continue L. Jn 8:42, am here M. Mt 26:27 N. Act 2:46 O. Act 17:3, put before P. Lk 6:28 Q. Phil 4:12 R. 2 Cor 8:14, abundance S. Mt 15:37 T. Mt 15:37 U. Mk 6:25 V. Rom 11:25, part W. Heb 2:18, tempted X. Mt 24:34 Y. Mt 5:18

	1C. And He was giving orders *to* them, saying, "Watch out! Beware[1] of the leaven[2] *of* the Pharisees, and the leaven *of* Herod[3]"	15
	2C. And they were discussing[A] with one another that[4] they[5] do[6] not have bread[7]	16
	3C. And having known[B] *it*, He[8] says *to* them, "Why are you discussing that you do not have bread?	17
	1D. "Do you not yet perceive[C], nor understand[D]?	
	2D. "Do you have your heart hardened[9]? ˚Having eyes, are you not seeing[E]? And having ears, are you not hearing?	18
	3D. "And do you not remember?—	
	1E. "When I broke[F] the five loaves for the five-thousand, how many full[G] baskets[H] *of* fragments[J] did you pick up?" They say *to* Him, "Twelve"	19
	2E. "When[10] *I broke* the seven *loaves* for the four-thousand, *the* fillings[11] *of* how many large-baskets[12] *of* fragments did you pick up?" And they say *to* Him[13], "Seven"	20
	4C. And He was saying *to* them, "Do[14] you not yet understand[D]?"	21
28B.	And they come[15] to Bethsaida[16]. And they bring Him *a* blind *man,* and are begging[K] Him that He touch him	22
	1C. And having taken-hold-of[L] the hand *of* the blind *man,* He brought him outside *of* the village[17]	23
	2C. And having spit[M] in his eyes[18], having laid[N] *His* hands on him, He was asking him, "Do you see[E] anything?"[19]	
	1D. And having looked-up[O], he was saying, "I am seeing[E] people, because[20] I am looking-at[P] *something* like trees[21] walking around"	24
	3C. Then again[22] He laid *His* hands on his eyes, and looked-intently[23], and restored[24] *them*	25
	1D. And he was seeing[25] everything clearly[26]	
	4C. And He sent him away to his house, saying, "Do not even enter into the village[27]"	26
29B.[28]	And Jesus and His disciples went forth into the villages *of* Philip's[29] Caesarea. And on the way, He was questioning[Q] His disciples, saying *to* them, "Who do people say *that* I am?"	27
	1C. And the *ones* spoke *to* Him, saying,[30] "That[31] *You are* John the Baptist. And others, Elijah. But others, that *You are* one *of* the prophets"	28
	2C. And **He** was questioning[Q] them,[32] "But who do **you** say *that* I am?"	29
	3C. Having responded, Peter says *to* Him, "**You** are the Christ"	
	4C. And He warned[R] them that they should be telling no one about Him	30
4A.[33]	And He began[34] to teach them that the Son *of* Man must[S] suffer[T] many *things,* and be rejected[U] by the elders and the chief priests and the scribes, and be killed, and rise-up[V] after three days. ˚And He was stating the matter[W] *with* openness[X]	31 32
1B.	And Peter, having taken Him aside, began to rebuke[R] Him. ˚But the *One*, having turned around, and having looked-at[35] His disciples, rebuked[R] Peter. And He says, "Get behind Me, Satan— because you are not thinking[Y] the *things of* God, but the *things of* humans[Z]"	33
2B.[36]	And having summoned the crowd with His disciples, He said *to* them, "If anyone wants[37] to be following[38] after Me, let him deny[AA] himself, and take up his cross,[39] and be following Me	34

1. This idiom "beware of " is elsewhere only in 12:38. "Beware" is GK *1063*. It is not the same word as in Mt 16:6. Some manuscripts say "Watch out and beware"; others omit one or the other verb {N}.
2. On this word, see Mt 13:33. On the leaven of the Pharisees, see Mt 16:12.
3. On Herod, see Mt 14:1. Some manuscripts say "*of* the Herodians" {A}.
4. Or, "because". Some manuscripts say "saying that" {N}, as in Mt 16:7.
5. Some manuscripts say "we" {N}, as in Mt 16:7.
6. In English, we usually change this to "did". Compare Mt 16:7.
7. The disciples' focus is on their belly instead of on what Jesus is telling them. Something far more important than where their next meal is coming from is happening in their presence, and they are missing the point of it. They are responding to Him just like the crowd.
8. Some manuscripts say "Jesus" {N}.
9. This is a participle, "having been hardened". Some manuscripts say "still hardened" {N}. Sometimes a failure to understand is really a refusal to understand, proceeding from a hard heart. Same word as in 6:52.
10. Some manuscripts say "And when" {N}.
11. Same word as in 6:43.
12. Same word as in 8:8.
13. Some manuscripts omit "*to* Him" {C}.
14. Some manuscripts say "How do you..." {N}.
15. Some manuscripts say "And He comes" {K}.
16. This city was on the north side of the Sea of Galilee.
17. The reason is not given. Perhaps Jesus did not want to draw a crowd (note v 26), so He led him out of the village and healed him on His way to the next village.
18. On this word, see Mt 20:34. Not related to the word in v 25 (GK *4057*).
19. Some manuscripts say "was asking him if he saw anything" {N}.
20. Some manuscripts say, "I am seeing people like trees, walking" {K}.
21. Some think this indicates the man was not born blind. He knew what trees looked like.
22. It is unclear why Jesus healed him in two steps. The details are not given. This is the only example of a two-step healing.
23. Elsewhere only as "see clearly" in Mt 7:5; Lk 6:42. GK *1332*.
24. Same word and grammar as in Mt 17:11; Mk 9:12; Act 1:6. Elsewhere only as a passive, "was restored", in Mt 12:13; Mk 3:5; Lk 6:10; Heb 13:19. It is not passive here. But since "them" is not expressed, some take this to mean "he restored, he changed back, he recovered", and render it "he was restored". In this case, the man is the subject of the last two verbs, "And he looked intently, and recovered, and was seeing everything clearly". GK *635*. Related to "restoration" in Act 3:21. Not related to "restore" in Jam 5:15.
25. Same word as in Act 22:11, where Paul was not seeing. Or, "looking at", as in Mk 10:21, 27; 14:67. Used 12 times. GK *1838*. Some manuscripts say "saw" {K}.
26. Or, "brightly, beaming, plainly". Used only here. GK *5495*.
27. Some manuscripts add "Nor speak *to* anyone in the village" {B}.
28. Parallel account at Mt 16:13; Lk 9:18.
29. On this city, see Mt 16:13. On Philip, see Lk 3:1.
30. The idiom "speak... saying" is also in Mt 22:1; Mk 12:26; Lk 7:39; 12:16; 13:27; 14:3; 20:2. Some manuscripts say "And the *ones* responded, 'That...'" {N}.
31. Some manuscripts omit this word {C}. This same word is in the third answer, "that" you are one of the prophets.
32. Some manuscripts say "And **He** says *to* them" {K}.
33. Parallel account at Mt 16:21; Lk 9:22.
34. This is the first time the suffering of Jesus is directly stated. It is a new stage in His relationship with the disciples.
35. Or, "seen". Same word as in 12:34; Jn 21:21. GK *3972*. Some think this means Jesus turned His back on Peter, and looked at the disciples. Others think He turned around to face Peter, looking at the disciples behind him.
36. Parallel account at Mt 16:24; Lk 9:23.
37. Some manuscripts say "Whoever wants" {N}.
38. Some manuscripts say "to come" {N}, as in Mt 16:24. Compare Lk 9:23.
39. On "take up his cross", see Mt 10:38; 16:24. Note that the cross as the means of the death of Jesus has not yet been mentioned in Mark.

A. Lk 5:21, reasoning B. Lk 1:34 C. Eph 3:20, think D. Mt 13:13 E. Rev 1:11 F. Act 2:46 G. Mt 14:20 H. Jn 6:13 J. Mt 15:37 K. Rom 12:8, exhorting L. Lk 20:20 M. Mk 7:33 N. Lk 10:30, laid on O. Act 22:13 P. Lk 2:26 Q. Lk 9:18 R. 2 Tim 4:2, warn S. Mt 16:21 T. Gal 3:4 U. Heb 12:17 V. Lk 18:33 W. 1 Cor 12:8, word X. Heb 4:16, confidence Y. Rom 8:5 Z. Mt 4:4, mankind AA. Mt 16:24

Mark 8:35	140	Verse

    1C.[1] "For whoever wants to save[A] his life[B] will lose[C] it. But whoever will lose his life for the sake *of* Me and the good-news[2] will save it   35

        1D. "For what does it profit[D] *a* person to gain[3] the whole world, and forfeit[4] his life[5]?   36
        2D. "For[6] what might *a* person give in-exchange-for[E] his life?   37

    2C. "For whoever *is* ashamed-of[F] Me and My words in this adulterous[7] and sinful[G] generation[H], the Son *of* Man will also be ashamed of him when He comes in the glory *of* His Father with the holy angels"   38
    3C. And[8] He was saying *to* them, "Truly[J] I say *to* you that there are some[9] *of* the *ones* standing here who will by-no-means[10] taste death[11] until they see the kingdom[K] *of* God having come in power[L]"   9:1

3B.[12] And after six days, Jesus takes along Peter and James and John, and brings them up on *a* high mountain privately[M], alone[N]   2

    1C. And He was transfigured[13] in front of them. °And His garments became shining[14], very white[15], such as *a* bleacher[16] on earth is not able to make so white[17]   3
    2C. And Elijah appeared[O] *to* them, with Moses. And they were talking-with[P] Jesus   4
    3C. And having responded, Peter says *to* Jesus, "Rabbi[Q], it is good *that* we are here. And let us make three dwellings[18]— one *for* You, and one *for* Moses, and one *for* Elijah"   5

        1D. For he did not know what he should respond[19], for they became terrified[20]   6

    4C. And there came-to-be *a* cloud overshadowing[R] them[21]. And *a* voice came out of the cloud— "This is My beloved[S] Son. Be listening-to Him"   7
    5C. And suddenly[22], having looked around, they no longer saw anyone with themselves but[23] Jesus alone[N]   8

4B.[24] And while they *were* coming down from the mountain, He gave orders *to* them that they should relate[T] *to* no one *the things* which they saw, except when the Son *of* Man rises-up[25] from *the* dead   9

    1C. And they held[U] the matter[26] to themselves, discussing[V] what the 'rising-up from *the* dead' meant[27]   10
    2C. And they were questioning Him, saying "*Why is it* that the scribes say that Elijah must[W] come first?"[28]   11
    3C.[29] And the *One* said[30] *to* them   12

        1D. "**Elijah**[31], having come first, restores[32] all *things*—

            1E. "And-*yet* how has it been written for[33] the Son *of* Man that He *would* suffer[X] many *things* and be treated-with-contempt[34]?

        2D. "But[35] I say *to* you that Elijah indeed[36] has come, and they did *to* him whatever they were wanting[Y], just as it has been written for him"   13

5B.[37] And having come to the disciples, they[38] saw *a* large crowd around them, and scribes[39] debating[40] with them. °And immediately, all the multitude, having seen Him, were struck-with-wonder[41]. And running-up, they were greeting[Z] Him   14 / 15

    1C. And He asked them[42], "What are you[43] debating with them?"   16

1. Compare Mk 10:39; Lk 17:33; Jn 12:25.
2. Or, "gospel". Elsewhere by Mark only in 1:1, 14, 15; 10:29; 13:10; 14:9; 16:15. On this word, see 1 Cor 15:1.
3. Same word as in Mt 16:26; Lk 9:25, and as Mt 18:15; 25:16, 17, 20, 22; Act 27:21; 1 Cor 9:19, 20, 21, 22; Phil 3:8; 1 Pet 3:1. Elsewhere only as "make a gain" in Jam 4:13. GK *3045*. Related to "gains" in Phil 3:7.
4. Or, "suffer loss of ". On this word, see "suffer loss" in 1 Cor 3:15.
5. Or, "soul". The same word is used four times in v 35-37. On this word, see "soul" in Jam 5:20.
6. Some manuscripts say "Or" {K}.
7. That is, spiritually unfaithful to God. On this word, see Jam 4:4.
8. In contrast to the shame of His death in v 31, which led to the words in v 33-38, Jesus now speaks of His power.
9. Some will see the kingdom, but not all. There is another sense in which none of them saw the "kingdom of God" in their lifetimes, Act 1:6-7. Some think Jesus is referring to the three with Him at the transfiguration (v 2), where they saw the King in His glory, 2 Pet 1:16; Jn 1:14. Others think He is referring to the eleven (and any of the "crowd", 8:34) who saw Him after His resurrection (Act 1:3), or who experienced the coming of the Spirit on Pentecost (Acts 2). Others think He is referring to those present to see the destruction of Jerusalem in A.D. 70, the judgment of the King on Israel. There are other views.
10. On this idiom, see 13:2.
11. On "taste death", see Heb 2:9.
12. Parallel account at Mt 17:1; Lk 9:28. Compare 2 Pet 1:17-18.
13. Or, "transformed, changed". On this word, see "transformed" in Rom 12:2.
14. Or, "radiant, gleaming, glistening". Used of bright polished surfaces, of stars, of the "flash" of lightning. Used only here. GK *5118*.
15. Some manuscripts add "like snow" {K}.
16. Or, "fuller, launderer, cloth refiner". That is, one who bleaches cloth white. Used only here. GK *1187*.
17. This word, "to make white, to whiten", is elsewhere only in Rev 7:14. GK *3326*.
18. Or, "tents". On this word, see Lk 9:33.
19. Peter did not know what his response should be. This just came out without thinking. Some manuscripts say "what he is saying"; others, "what he was saying"; others, "what he will say" {N}. Luke says "not knowing what he is saying", 9:33. Same words and grammar as "They did not know what they should answer Him" in Mk 14:40, except there is no "Him" here.
20. On this adjective, see Heb 12:21, where Moses reacted the same way. Related to "afraid" in Lk 9:34.
21. Perhaps Mark means Jesus, Moses, and Elijah. See Mt 17:5 on this.
22. Or, "all of a sudden". Used only here. GK *1988*.
23. Some manuscripts say "except" {N}, as in Mt 17:8.
24. Parallel account at Mt 17:9.
25. Or, "stands up". See Lk 18:33 on this.
26. Or, "And they seized the statement, discussing with themselves...". Compare v 32.
27. More literally, "means", as the Greek typically phrases it. On this word, see "is" in Mt 26:26.
28. On why the disciples ask this question, see Mt 17:10. Same grammar as the question in v 28. Or, this may be a statement implying a question, "questioning Him, saying that the scribes say... first".
29. Compare Mt 11:4; Lk 1:17; Jn 1:21.
30. Some manuscripts say "And the *One*, having responded, said" {N}, like v 19.
31. Jesus uses grammar that emphasizes the contrast between the two "Elijah" statements (1D. and 2D.).
32. Same word as in Act 1:6. On this word, see Mk 8:25. Related to "restoration" in Act 3:21. In other words, the scribes are right.
33. On this idiom in v 12, 13, "written for" Him, see Jn 12:16.
34. Or, "despised". Used only here. If Elijah simply comes first and restores all things and Messiah comes in glory, then how can this be true also? It is because there are two comings, one in suffering (which they did not expect) and one in glory. Some think Jesus means Elijah also has two comings, a future one (perhaps Rev 11:3), and a past one in John the Baptist, v 13; Mt 11:14; 17:13. Others think He means that just as His own coming was in an unexpected way, so was Elijah's. He is John, who did not do what they expected Elijah to do any more than Jesus did what they expected Messiah to do. Note that Jesus does not refer to Elijah's recent appearance at the transfiguration as a fulfillment of Mal 4:5-6. GK *2022*. Related to the word in 1 Thes 5:20.
35. Or, "Yet, However, Nevertheless". GK *247*. A stronger word, not related to the one in Mt 17:12 (GK *1254*).
36. Or, "also". GK *2779*.
37. Parallel account at Mt 17:14; Lk 9:37.
38. That is, Jesus, Peter, James, and John. Some manuscripts say "He" {B}.
39. Some think the scribes were gathering evidence against Jesus from this failure by His disciples.
40. Or, "arguing, discussing". Same word as in v 16. On this word, see 8:11.
41. This word refers to emotions ranging from astonishment to wonder to fear upon seeing some sight. Here, some think the very presence of Jesus sparked wonder in them. Others think they were filled with wonder and fear and excitement and awe about the situation He was now coming into— could Jesus do anything for this one the disciples could not heal? Would He prove the scribes wrong? Elsewhere only as "alarmed" (the "fear and alertness" end of the emotions) in 14:33; 16:5, 6. GK *1701*. Related to "astonished" in 1:27; "wonder" in Act 3:10; and "struck with wonder" in Act 3:11.
42. Some manuscripts say "the scribes" {K}.
43. That is, you scribes, v 14.

A. Lk 19:10 B. Jam 5:20, soul C. 1 Cor 1:18, perish D. Rom 2:25 E. Mt 16:26 F. Rom 1:16 G. Mt 19:10, sinner H. Mt 24:34 J. Mt 5:18 K. Mt 3:2 L. Mk 5:30 M. Mt 14:13 N. Jam 2:24 O. Lk 2:26, see P. Act 25:12 Q. Mt 23:7 R. Mt 17:5 S. Mt 3:17 T. Lk 8:39 U. Heb 4:14, hold on to V. Mk 8:11, debate W. Mt 16:21 X. Gal 3:4 Y. Jn 7:17, willing Z. Mk 15:18

2C. And one from the crowd answered Him,[1] "Teacher, I brought my son having *a* mute spirit to 17
You. °And wherever it overcomes[2] him, it throws-him-to-the-ground[3], and he foams-at-the- 18
mouth[4], and grinds[5] *his* teeth, and becomes-stiff[A]. And I spoke *to* Your disciples in order that
they might cast[6] it out, and they were not strong-*enough*[7]"

3C. And the *One*, having responded *to* them[8], says, "O unbelieving generation,[9] how long[10] will I 19
be with you? How long will I bear-with[B] you? Bring him to Me"

4C. And they brought him to Him. And having seen Him, the spirit immediately convulsed[11] him. 20
And having fallen on the ground, he was rolling-*himself* while foaming-at-the-mouth

5C. And He asked his father, "How long[12] is it since this has happened *to* him?" 21

    1D. And the *one* said, "From childhood. °And it often threw him even into fire and into 22
waters[C] in order that it might destroy[D] him. But if You are able *to do* anything[13], help[14]
us, having felt-deep-feelings[15] [of pity] toward us"

    2D. And Jesus said *to* him, " 'If You are able[16]?' All *things are* possible *for* the *one* believing[E]" 23

    3D. Immediately, having cried-out[F], the father *of* the child was saying[17], "I[18] believe. Help 24
my unbelief [19]"

6C. And Jesus, having seen that *a* crowd is running-together-upon[20] *them*, rebuked[G] the unclean 25
spirit, saying *to* it, "Mute and deaf spirit, **I** command[H] you— come out of him, and enter into
him no longer"

    1D. And having cried-out[F], and having convulsed[J] *him* greatly, it came out. And he became 26
as if dead, so that the majority *were* saying that "He died"

    2D. But Jesus, having taken hold of his hand, raised[K] him. And he stood-up[L] 27

7C. And He having entered into *a* house, His disciples were questioning Him privately[M], "*Why is* 28
it that[21] **we** were not able to cast it out?" °And He said *to* them, "This kind[N] can come out by 29
nothing except by prayer[22]"

6B.[23] And having gone forth from there, they were passing through Galilee. And He was not wanting 30
anyone to[24] know *it*

    1C. For He was teaching His disciples, and saying *to* them that "The Son *of* Man is being handed- 31
over[25] into *the* hands *of* men. And they will kill Him. And having been killed, He will rise-up[L]
after[26] three days"

    2C. But the *ones* were not-understanding[O] the statement,[27] and they were fearing to question Him 32

7B.[28] And they came[29] to Capernaum. And having come-to-be in the house, He was questioning them, 33
"What were you discussing[30] on the way?"

    1C. But the *ones* were being silent[P]. For on the way they argued[Q] with one another who *was* greater[31] 34

    2C. And having sat-*down*, He called the twelve. And He says *to* them, "If anyone wants[R] to be 35
first[S], he shall[32] be last *of* all, and servant[T] *of* all"

    3C. And having taken *a* child[U], He stood him[33] in *the* middle *of* them. And having taken him in *His* 36
arms, He said *to* them

        1D. "Whoever welcomes[V] one such-as-these[34] children[U] on the basis of My name[35], welcomes 37
Me. And whoever welcomes Me does not [merely] welcome Me, but the *One* having sent
Me forth[W]"

1. Some manuscripts say "And having responded, one from the crowd said..." {N}.
2. Or, "seizes". On this word, see Jn 1:5. Related to "seize" in Lk 9:39 (GK *3284*).
3. Same word as in Lk 9:42, "to throw to the ground". GK *4838*.
4. Elsewhere only in v 20. GK *930*. Related to "foam" in Lk 9:39; and "foam up" in Jude 13.
5. Used only here. GK *5563*.
6. Or, "And I told Your disciples to cast". Compare Lk 9:40.
7. Or, "they were not able, did not have the power". On this word, see "can do" in Gal 5:6.
8. Some manuscripts say "him" {K}.
9. See Mt 17:17 on the meaning of this.
10. On this idiom, "how long", see Mt 17:17.
11. Or, "convulsed-greatly". Elsewhere only in Lk 9:42. GK *5360*. Related to the word in v 26.
12. More literally, "How much time", an idiom used only here.
13. Since His disciples could do nothing, this father is unsure whether Jesus can help. The grammar does not indicate strong doubt (if, and You probably cannot), but implies "Assuming You are able to do something".
14. Or, "come to our aid". Same word as in v 24. On this word, see Rev 12:16.
15. On this word, see Mt 9:36. The father thought he must suggest this motive in light of the words of rebuke in v 19. "Jesus, turn from Your frustration with this generation to pity on our case. Help us out of pity for us".
16. Jesus repeats the father's words from v 22 back to him, "If you are able". There is both faith and doubt in his statement in v 22. Jesus focuses first on the doubt. Some manuscripts say instead, "If you [the father] are able to believe, all *things are* possible *for*..." {B}.
17. Some manuscripts add "with tears" {A}.
18. Some manuscripts say "Master, I believe..." {K}.
19. That is, "Help me where I am wavering and starting to doubt". On this word, see 1 Tim 1:13.
20. This is another of Mark's vivid words, used only here. GK *2192*. Related to "ran together" in 6:33.
21. Same grammar, "*Why is it* that", as the question in v 11 and 2:16.
22. On this word, see 1 Tim 2:1. Some manuscripts add "and fasting" {A}.
23. Parallel account at Mt 17:22; Lk 9:43.
24. More literally, "He was not wanting that anyone should know *it*". GK *2671*.
25. That is, "is *going to* be handed over", the future sense coming from the context. Matthew and Luke include the word "going to". On this word, see Mt 26:21.
26. Some manuscripts say "*on* the third day" {N}. Both mean the same thing.
27. Compare Lk 9:45.
28. Parallel account at Mt 18:1; Lk 9:46.
29. Some manuscripts say "He came" {N}.
30. On this word, see "reasoning" in Lk 5:21. Some manuscripts add "with yourselves" {K}.
31. Though the form of this word means "greater", some think that here it has the sense of "greatest". GK *3505*.
32. Or, "will". Some think Jesus means "he will be last", this is what he will do, this is the choice he will make. Others take this as a type of command, "he shall be last", he must be last, let him be last. Both are true of course.
33. Or, "her". The Greek is not specific here.
34. Jesus generalizes from the child before them to "these children". That is, one of these most needy, most dependent, most needing to be served ones; one of these who are least associated with greatness in this world. Serving them is serving Christ. Welcoming them is welcoming the King, and is the opposite of striving to be reckoned as the greatest. He does not value worldly status. This is true of physical children "believing in Me" (v 42); and of spiritual children of any age. This is the same word (GK *5525*) as "such" in Mt 18:5, but is plural here to match "children".
35. On this phrase, "on the basis of My name", see Act 2:38.

A. Mk 3:1, become withered B. 2 Cor 11:4 C. Jn 3:23 D. 1 Cor 1:18, perish E. Jn 3:36 F. Mt 8:29 G. 2 Tim 4:2, warn H. Lk 8:25 J. Mk 1:26 K. Mt 28:6, arose L. Lk 18:33, rise up M. Mt 14:13 N. 1 Cor 12:28 O. Rom 10:3, being ignorant of P. Mk 4:39, be still Q. Act 17:2, reasoned R. Jn 7:17, willing S. 1 Cor 15:3 T. 1 Cor 3:5 U. 1 Jn 2:14 V. Mt 10:40 W. Mk 3:14, send out

	1E. John[1] said *to* Him,[2] "Teacher, we saw someone casting-out[A] demons in Your name[3]. And we were forbidding[4] him, because he was not following us"	38
	2E. But Jesus said, "Do not be forbidding him"	39
	1F. "For there is no one who will do *a* miracle[5] on the basis of My name, and soon be able to speak-evil-of[B] Me	
	2F. "For he who is not against us, is for us[6]	40
	3F. "For whoever gives you *a* cup *of* water to drink in *the* name that you are Christ's[7]— truly[C] I say *to* you that he will by no means lose his reward[D]	41
	2D. "And[8] whoever causes one *of* these little *ones* believing[E] in Me[9] to fall[10]— it *would* be better[11] *for* him if instead *a* donkey's[12] millstone[13] were lying[14] around his neck, and he had been thrown into the sea	42
	1E.[15] "And[16] if your hand should be causing you to fall, cut it off[17]. It is better *that* you enter into life crippled than go into Gehenna[F] having two hands— into the inextinguishable[18] fire	43 44[19]
	2E. "And if your foot should be causing you to fall, cut it off. It is better *that* you enter into life lame than be thrown into Gehenna having two feet[20]	45 46[21]
	3E. "And if your eye should be causing you to fall, throw it out[A]. It is better *that* you enter into the kingdom *of* God[22] one-eyed than be thrown into Gehenna[23] having two eyes—	47
	1F. "Where their worm[24] does not come-to-an-end[25]	48
	2F. "And the fire is not quenched[26]	
	4E. "For everyone will be salted[27] *with* fire[28]	49
	3D.[29] "Salt[30] *is* good. But if the salt should become unsalty[31], with what will you season[32] it? Be having salt in yourselves,[33] and be living-in-peace[G] with one another"	50
5A.[34] And having arisen[H], He goes from there into the districts[35] *of* Judea and[36] beyond the Jordan. And crowds again are coming-together to Him. And as He was accustomed[37], He again was teaching them		10:1
	1B. And Pharisees[38] having come to *Him* were asking Him if it is lawful[J] *for a* husband[K] to send-away[39] *a* wife[L]— testing[M] Him	2
	1C. And the *One*, having responded, said *to* them, "What did Moses command[40] you?"	3

1. John interrupts with an incident where they did not "welcome" one who claimed to serve Him.
2. Some manuscripts say "And John responded *to* Him, saying...{N}.
3. Some manuscripts add "who is not following us" {N}.
4. Or, "hindering, preventing, trying to stop". On this word, see 1 Cor 14:39.
5. Or, "*a work of* power". Whether Jesus in fact "knows" this person is not stated (even ones He does not "know" will do such things "in His name", Mt 7:22). The focus is not on his case, but on the disciples' response. On this word, see 1 Cor 12:10.
6. Some manuscripts say "... against you, is for you" {N}, as in Lk 9:50. That is, whoever has not decided against us, and so is not actively opposing us, is for us. Compare Mt 12:30.
7. That is, because you belong to Christ, because you are followers of Christ. This is the same idea as "in the name of a disciple" in Mt 10:41-42. Some manuscripts say "in My name, because you are Christ's" {A}.
8. Now Jesus turns to the other case, as in Mt 18:6, to any who would harm His children.
9. Some manuscripts omit "in Me" {C}.
10. On the verb "cause to fall", see 1 Cor 8:13. The same word follows in v 43, 45, 47.
11. Not the same word as in the similar statements in Mt 18:6 or Lk 17:2. On this word, see "good" in 1 Tim 5:10a.
12. Literally, *a* millstone "pertaining-to-a-donkey", that is, a large one that a donkey would turn. Some paraphrase it as "large". Elsewhere only in Mt 18:6. GK *3948*. Some manuscripts omit this word {K}.
13. Same word as in Mt 18:6. Elsewhere only as the smaller "mill" that would be turned manually by two women, in Mt 24:41; Rev 18:22. GK *3685*. Related to the word in Lk 17:2, and in Rev 18:21.
14. Same word as in Lk 17:2. The grammar is unusually vivid. Such a person would be better off to already be dead at the bottom of the sea with a millstone lying around his neck than to commit this sin. He would be better to have been violently killed before he did this than to face the consequences of it. In Matthew 18:6, the word and grammar is different.
15. Compare Mt 5:29-30; 18:8-9.
16. These verses amplify the seriousness with which Christ views sin, the sin in v 42, and all other sin. They are spoken with reference all humans, as is v 42. Compare Mt 18:7. It is better not to allow anything in your life to cause you or a fellow-believer to fall. The consequences are frightening.
17. On the word "cut off", which is also in v 45, see Gal 5:12. Related to the word in Mt 18:8. In other words, take whatever measures necessary to eliminate causes of falling in your life.
18. Or, "unquenchable". Elsewhere only in Mt 3:12; Lk 3:17. GK *812*. Not related to the word in v 48.
19. Some manuscripts add as v 44 "where their worm does not come to an end, and the fire is not quenched" {A}, as in v 48.
20. Some manuscripts add "into the inextinguishable fire" {A}, as in v 43.
21. Some manuscripts add as v 46 "where their worm does not come to and end, and the fire is not quenched" {A}, as in v 48.
22. Note that entering "life" (v 43, 45) is now entering "the kingdom of God".
23. Some manuscripts say "the Gehenna *of* fire" {N}, as in Mt 18:9.
24. Or, "larva, maggot". Used only here. GK *5038*. Related to "eaten by worms" in Act 12:23. Jesus is quoting Isa 66:24.
25. That is, "die". This is a euphemism for death. In other words, the maggots eating their flesh never come to an end, a striking picture. Elsewhere only in Mt 2:19; 9:18; 15:4; 22:25; Mk 7:10; Lk 7:2; Jn 11:39; Act 2:29; 7:15; Heb 11:22. GK *5462*. Related to "end" in Mt 2:15.
26. Or, "extinguished, put out". On this word, see 1 Thes 5:19.
27. Some think this refers to future judgment. The imagery comes from Lev 2:13, where salt was added to a sacrifice. Thus, Jesus will make an offering of humans to God, to which He will add a purifying fire. Everyone will be tested by fire. Some will be purified and saved through the fire. Others will remain in the fire, Gehenna. This concept is similar to 1 Cor 3:13-15. Others think it refers to a separation in this life. Through the seasoning of fiery trials, all will move toward life or Gehenna. Others think it refers to the purification of believers in this life. The fire is His purifying work in us, the discipline of our Father, Heb 12:6. Others add this on to point 2F., further emphasizing the ongoing nature of that fire. Such ones are preserved (as salt preserves) by fire, for fire. There are other views. Consult the commentaries. On this word, see Mt 5:13. Compare "baptized with fire" in Mt 3:11.
28. Some manuscripts add "and every sacrifice will be salted *with* salt" {B}, a reference to Lev 2:13.
29. Compare Mt 5:13; Lk 14:34-35.
30. Jesus returns to His main point and concludes it in this verse, keying off the word "salt". He turns from fire being applied like salt, to salt itself, functioning as it was created to function, as a picture of believer's lives. GK *229*.
31. Or, "saltless". Used only here. GK *383*.
32. Same word as in Lk 14:34. Elsewhere only in Col 4:6. GK *789*.
33. God created you to season those around you. If your life loses its seasoning power, as it surely will if you are squabbling over who is greater, how can it be regained? Jesus does not answer this, but instead says, Do not lose it. Have salt in yourselves. Be what God made you to be, servants of all, at peace.
34. Parallel account at Mt 19:1.
35. Or, "boundaries". This word means the "borders, boundaries", or the "districts, regions" marked or enclosed by them. Same word as 5:17; 7:24, 31. Elsewhere only in Mt 2:16; 4:13; 8:34; 15:22, 39; 19:1; Act 13:50. GK *3990*. Our word "horizon" comes from this word. Some think Jesus was in Judea near the Jordan; others, out of Judea, beyond the Jordan.
36. Some manuscripts omit this word, as in Mt 19:1; others say "through *the* other side *of* the Jordan" {C}.
37. On this word, see "become a custom" in Lk 4:16.
38. Some manuscripts say "the Pharisees" {B}.
39. That is, divorce her. Same word as in v 4, 11, 12. Not related to "divorce" in v 4. On this word, see Mt 5:31. Compare Mt 19:1-12 to this passage.
40. Same word as in Mt 19:7; and in Mt 4:6; 17:9; 28:20; Mk 13:34; Lk 4:10; Jn 8:5; 14:31; 15:14, 17; Act 13:47; Heb 9:20. Elsewhere only as "give commands" in Act 1:2; Heb 11:22. GK *1948*. Related to "commandment" in Col 2:22 and in Mk 12:28.

A. Jn 12:31, cast out   B. Act 19:9   C. Mt 5:18   D. Rev 22:12, recompense   E. Jn 3:36   F. Mt 5:22   G. Rom 12:18   H. Lk 18:33, rise up
J. 1 Cor 6:12   K. 1 Cor 11:3   L. 1 Cor 11:3   M. Heb 2:18, tempted

	2C. And the *ones* said, "Moses permitted¹ *us* to write *a* certificate^A *of* divorce² and send *her* away"	4
	3C. But Jesus said *to* them, "He wrote this commandment^B *to* you because-of³ your hardness-of-heart⁴	5
	1D. "But from *the* beginning *of* creation^C, 'He⁵ made them male^D and female^E' [Gen 1:27]. 'For this reason,⁶ *a* man will leave-behind^F his father and mother, and will be joined⁷ to his wife⁸. ˚And the two will be⁹ one flesh' [Gen 2:24]	6 7 8
	2D. "So then, they are no longer two, but one flesh	
	3D. "Therefore what God paired-together^G, let *a* person¹⁰ not separate¹¹"	9
	4C. And the disciples were questioning Him again about this in the house	10
	1D.¹² And He says *to* them, "Whoever sends-away^H his wife and marries another is committing-adultery against her.¹³ ˚And if she¹⁴, having sent-away^H her husband, marries another,¹⁵ she is committing-adultery¹⁶"	11 12
2B.¹⁷ And they¹⁸ were bringing children¹⁹ to Him in order that He might touch^J them. But the disciples rebuked^K them²⁰		13
	1C. But Jesus, having seen *it*, was indignant²¹, and said *to* them, "Permit^L the children to be coming to Me. Do²² not be forbidding^M them. For the kingdom *of* God is *of* such²³ *ones*. ˚Truly I say *to* you, whoever does not receive^N the kingdom *of* God like *a* child²⁴ will never²⁵ enter into it"	14 15
	2C. And having taken them in *His* arms, He was blessing²⁶ *them*, while laying^O *His* hands on them²⁷	16
3B.²⁸ And while He *was* proceeding out on²⁹ *the* road³⁰, one having run up and knelt-before^P Him was asking Him, "Good^Q Teacher, what should I do in order that I may inherit^R eternal life?"		17
	1C. And Jesus said *to* him, "Why do you call Me good^Q? No one *is* good except One— God.³¹ You know the commandments^S— 'Do not murder^T, do not commit-adultery^U, do not steal, do not give-false-testimony^V, do not defraud³², be honoring your father and mother' "	18 19
	1D. And the *one* said *to* Him, "Teacher, I kept³³ these all from my youth"³⁴	20
	2D. And Jesus, having looked at him, loved³⁵ him. And He said *to* him, "One *thing* is lacking³⁶ *as to* you³⁷— go, sell all-that you have and give *it to* the³⁸ poor^W, and you will have treasure^X in heaven. And come, be following Me³⁹"	21
	3D. But the *one*, having become downcast⁴⁰ at *His* word, went away grieving^Y. For he was having⁴¹ many properties^Z	22
	2C. And having looked around, Jesus says *to* His disciples, "How difficultly⁴² the *ones* having wealth⁴³ will enter into the kingdom *of* God"	23
	3C. And the disciples were astonished⁴⁴ at His words	24

1. Writing to Gentiles, Mark does not include the distinction between "command" and "permit" in Mt 19:7-8, nor the issue of proper grounds. He gives a more general summary of the words of Jesus. He also includes the application to wives in v 12, bringing out this aspect which Matthew omitted (because Matthew was writing to Jews, whose wives were not permitted to divorce their husbands, although they could ask to be divorced by their husbands). On this word, see 1 Tim 2:12.
2. On this word, see Mt 5:31. Moses "permitted" divorce with a certificate of divorce, which was to protect the woman and allow her to remarry. Moses implied this permission when he referred to the certificate of divorce while commanding something else. He "commanded" that the first husband could not remarry his former wife if she married and was divorced by a second husband. See Deut 24:1-4.
3. Or, "with regard to, with reference to". GK *4639*.
4. On this word, see 16:14. Same word as Mt 19:8.
5. Some manuscripts say "God" {B}. God made "man" as "male and female", a pair, Gen 1:26-27.
6. That is, because God made them to be a complimentary pair.
7. Or, "united, adhered, glued". Elsewhere only in Eph 5:31. GK *4681*. Related to the word in Mt 19:5; 1 Cor 6:16.
8. Some manuscripts omit "and will be joined to his wife" {C}.
9. This is an idiom, literally, "the two will be for one flesh". It reflects a Hebrew way of speaking.
10. Or, "*a* human". This is not the word for "husband". It means "man" (any person, male or female), or, "*a* man" (a male, as in v 7). The command applies to both the man and the woman in v 11-12. So Jesus means "*a* person", though the Pharisees would have taken Him to mean "*a* man". On this word, see "mankind" in Mt 4:4.
11. On this word, see Mt 19:6. Jesus is not fully addressing the question of divorce here, but is giving the meaning of marriage from God's point of view. God made them to be joined in pairs, and it is not His will that the husband send away his wife. This is His plan and intention. God made marriage, not divorce. In specific cases, other factors must be considered, and other principles of God, as Paul does in the case in 1 Cor 7:12-15.
12. Compare also Lk 16:18; Mt 5:32.
13. Mt 5:32 adds that this husband makes his wife commit adultery also, and the man marrying her.
14. Some think Jesus had Herodias (see Mt 14:3 on her) in mind here.
15. Some manuscripts say, "And if *a* wife sends away her husband, and is married *to* another"; others, "And if *a* wife goes out from *her* husband and marries another" {N}.
16. On this word in v 11, 12, see Mt 5:32b. Related to the word in v 19.
17. Parallel account at Mt 19:13; Lk 18:15.
18. That is, "people", a general reference.
19. This is the same word used of the twelve-year-old in 5:41. It has as broad a meaning as the English word "child". On this word, see 1 Jn 2:14. Luke uses the word "babies" in Lk 18:15, and this word in 18:16. Since this was not an organized event, perhaps there was a range of ages.
20. That is, the ones bringing them. Some manuscripts say "were rebuking the *ones* bringing *them*" {A}.
21. Used only here of Jesus. See Mt 20:24 on this word, and compare what provoked this in others.
22. Some manuscripts say "And do not..." {K}.
23. That is, it belongs to such ones as these, childlike ones, whether physically children or adults. Children and their faith are the model of the kind of faith all believers— children and adults— must have to enter. See Mt 19:14.
24. Some think Jesus means "like one would receive a child", with open arms, joyfully; others, "like a child would receive it", humbly, dependently, trustingly, as in Mt 18:3-4. Children readily accept gifts.
25. Or, "by no means". On this idiom, see 13:2.
26. Or, "calling down blessings on" them, "blessing them one after another". Used only here, and a rare word. GK *2986*. Some manuscripts have the normal word {N}, the related word in Lk 6:28.
27. Some manuscripts say "He was laying *His* hands on them and blessing them" {N}.
28. Parallel account at Mt 19:16; Lk 18:18.
29. Or, "to, into". GK *1650*.
30. Or, "journey, way". Mark may mean it in a more specific sense, "to *the* road" from wherever Jesus was staying; or in a more general sense, "on *the* journey". GK *3847*. Using a different word, he says "on the road" in v 32.
31. On this answer, see Lk 18:19.
32. On this word, see 1 Cor 6:7. Some manuscripts omit "do not defraud" {A}.
33. Same word, but different grammar than Mt 19:20 and Lk 18:21. On this word, see 12:25. This word is in the OT with this grammar in Num 9:23; Josh 22:3; and with the grammar used in Matthew and Luke in Gen 26:5; 2 Sam 22:22; 2 King 18:6; Job 23:11; Ps 119:55, 168.
34. This is an honest and truthful statement from this man's point of view, defining the commands as the Jews did (as external requirements). Yet it is not enough. He still felt he had a lack, a need. Note what Paul says in Phil 3:6.
35. Some think this means Jesus embraced the man, or "kissed" him (as this word is used in Mt 26:48); others, that He was fond of him. In any case, He expressed His love to him by speaking the following words to him in an attempt to draw him closer.
36. On this word, see "be in need" in Lk 15:14. Same word as in Mt 19:20.
37. Based on what is said, this one thing appears to be a single-minded devotion to God.
38. Some manuscripts omit this word {C}, so that it says "*to* poor *ones*". An example of this is in Act 4:34-35.
39. Some manuscripts add "having taken up the cross" {A}.
40. Or, "gloomy, sad". On this word, see "lowering" in Mt 16:3. The man's appearance took on a gloomy, lowering look.
41. On this word, see Mt 19:22. Compare Lk 18:23.
42. On this word, see "with difficulty" in Mt 19:23.
43. Or, "money, means". Same word as in Lk 18:24. Elsewhere only as "money" in Act 4:37; 8:18, 20; 24:26. GK *5975*.
44. Wealth was considered to be a sign of blessing from God. Jesus says it is a hindrance to entering the kingdom, a shocking statement to the disciples. On this word, see 1:27.

A. Rev 5:1, scroll   B. Mk 12:28   C. Rom 8:39   D. Mt 19:4   E. Mt 19:4   F. Act 6:2   G. Mt 19:6   H. Mt 5:31   J. 1 Cor 7:1   K. 2 Tim 4:2, warn   L. Mt 6:12, forgive   M. 1 Cor 14:39   N. Mt 10:40, welcome   O. Act 19:21, put   P. Mt 17:14   Q. 1 Tim 5:10b   R. Gal 4:30   S. Mk 12:28   T. Jam 4:2   U. Mt 5:32   V. Mk 14:56   W. Gal 4:9   X. Mt 12:35   Y. 2 Cor 7:9   Z. Mt 19:22

4C. But Jesus, having responded again, says *to* them, "Children^A, how difficult¹ it is² to enter into the kingdom^B *of* God. *It is easier that a* camel go through the hole³ *of* the needle⁴ than *that a* rich *one* enter into the kingdom *of* God"⁵   25

5C. And the *ones* were even more astounded^C, saying to themselves⁶, "Who indeed can be saved^D?"   26

6C. Having looked at them, Jesus says, "With humans^E *it is* impossible^F, but not with God. For all *things are* possible with God"   27

7C. Peter began to say *to* Him, "Behold— **we** left everything, and have followed You"   28

8C. Jesus said, "Truly^G I say *to* you, there is no one who left house or brothers or sisters or mother or father⁷ or children or fields for the sake *of* Me and for the sake *of* the good-news^H *except he receive⁸   29 / 30

    1D. *A* hundred-fold^J now in this time⁹— houses and brothers and sisters and mothers¹⁰ and children and fields, along-with persecutions¹¹
    2D. "And in the coming age— eternal life
    3D.¹² "But many first *ones* will be last, and the¹³ last *ones*, first"   31

4B.¹⁴ And they were on the road going up to Jerusalem, and Jesus was going-ahead-of^K them. And they were astonished¹⁵. And¹⁶ the *ones* following were fearing^L. And having again taken aside the twelve, He began to tell them the *things* going-to¹⁷ happen *to* Him—*that   32 / 33

    1C. "Behold— we are going up to Jerusalem. And the Son *of* Man will be handed-over^M *to* the chief priests and the scribes. And they will condemn^N Him *to* death, and will hand Him over *to* the Gentiles. *And they will mock^O Him, and spit-on^P Him, and whip¹⁸ Him, and kill *Him*. And after three days,¹⁹ He will rise-up^Q"   34

5B.²⁰ And James and John,²¹ the sons *of* Zebedee, approach²² Him, saying *to* Him, "Teacher, we want You to²³ do *for* us whatever we ask You"   35

    1C. And the *One* said *to* them, "What do you want Me to do²⁴ *for* you?"   36
    2C. And the *ones* said *to* Him, "Grant *to* us that we may sit²⁵ one on Your right *side* and one on *the* left²⁶ *side* in Your glory"   37
    3C. But Jesus said *to* them, "You do not know what you are asking. Are you able to drink the cup which **I** drink, or²⁷ to be baptized^R the baptism^S which **I** am baptized?"   38

        1D. And the *ones* said *to* Him, "We are able"   39
        2D. And Jesus said *to* them, "You will drink the cup which **I** drink. And you will be baptized the baptism which **I** am baptized. *But the sitting on My right *side* or²⁸ on *the* left²⁹ *side* is not Mine to give, but *it is for* whom³⁰ it has been prepared^T"   40

4C.³¹ And having heard-*of it*, the ten began to be indignant^U about James and John. *And having summoned^V them, Jesus says³² *to* them, "You know that the *ones* having-the-reputation-of³³ being rulers³⁴ *of* the Gentiles are lording-over³⁵ them, and their great *ones* are exercising-authority-over³⁶ them. *But it is not³⁷ so among you   41-42 / 43

    1D. "But whoever wants to become great among you shall be your servant^W, *and whoever wants to be first among you shall be slave³⁸ *of* all   44

        1E. "For even the Son *of* Man did not come to be served^X, but to serve, and to give His life^Y *as a* ransom³⁹ for many"   45

1. Used only here. GK *1551*. Related to "difficultly" in v 23.
2. Some manuscripts say "it is *that* the *ones* having trusted on wealth should enter into..." {B}.
3. Or, "perforation". Used only here. GK *5584*. Matthew (19:24), Mark and Luke (18:25) each use a different word, none of which are related to our English idiom "eye".
4. That is, a sewing needle. Same word as in Mt 19:24. Some manuscripts say "*a hole of a* needle" {C}.
5. That is, it is impossible, as they understood (v 26), and as Jesus says in v 27. It is humanly impossible.
6. Some manuscripts say "Him" {B}.
7. Some manuscripts next add "or wife" {N}. Some reverse "mother or father" {K}.
8. This idiom means "who will not receive". Lk 18:30 has it more strongly. Mt 19:29 states it positively.
9. Or, "season". That is, in this lifetime. Same word as in Lk 18:30. On this word, see Mt 8:29.
10. That is, a hundred houses, brothers, mothers, or whatever one left for Jesus, is gained within one's new spiritual family. Compare 3:35; Act 4:32-35; Rom 16:13; 1 Cor 4:15; Phm 10; 1 Tim 5:1-2.
11. Elsewhere only in Mt 13:21; Mk 4:17; Act 8:1; 13:50; Rom 8:35; 2 Cor 12:10; 2 Thes 1:4; 2 Tim 3:11. GK *1501*. Related to "persecute" in 2 Tim 3:12.
12. Compare Mt 19:30; Lk 13:30.
13. Some manuscripts omit this word {C}. Rewards and eternal life will not be granted based on outward appearance. Some have applied the comparison to rich vs. poor, or Jew vs. Gentile, or Pharisee vs. sinner.
14. Parallel account at Mt 20:17; Lk 18:31.
15. Same word as in v 24. It describes emotions ranging from astonishment to fear. Mark states the "fear" side next, separately. The reactions of those going to Jerusalem with Jesus filled the whole range of emotion.
16. Or, "But". Some think there are two groups here; others, one.
17. This word means "going to, about to, destined to, will certainly" and "intending to", depending on the grammar and the context. Used 109 times. GK *3516*.
18. Same word as in Mt 20:19; Lk 18:33; Jn 19:1. On this word, see Heb 12:6.
19. Some manuscripts say "*on* the third day" {A}.
20. Parallel account at Mt 20:20.
21. Mark does not mention their mother with them, as does Mt 20:20.
22. Or, "come to". Used only here. GK *4702*. Not related to the word in Mt 20:20 (GK *4665*).
23. More literally, "we want that You should do *for* us". GK *2671*.
24. More literally, "what do you want *as to* Me *that* I should do *for* you". Some manuscripts say "what do you want *that* I should do *for* you" {C}.
25. That is, when the twelve sit on their thrones with Jesus, as He promised (Mt 19:28). Note that they are continuing to think as they did in 9:34.
26. Elsewhere only in Mt 6:3; Lk 23:33; 2 Cor 6:7. GK *754*. Matthew uses the word in v 40.
27. On the following phrase, compare Lk 12:50. Some manuscripts say "and" {K}.
28. Some manuscripts say "and" {K}.
29. Same word as in Mt 20:21, 23. Used 9 times. GK *2381*. Not related to the word in v 37.
30. That is, the sitting in these places belongs to those for whom it has been prepared.
31. Compare also Lk 22:24-27.
32. Some manuscripts say "But Jesus summoned them, and says *to* them" {K}.
33. Or, "being recognized as". They "seem [to people in general] to be", and thus "are recognized as being", "have the reputation of being", "are deemed to be" rulers by those over whom they rule. They are the acknowledged rulers. Same word as in Gal 2:2; and as "seems" in Lk 22:24. On this word, see "thinking" in Lk 19:11.
34. Used also in Rom 15:12 in the sense of "ruling". GK *806*. Mt 20:25 uses the related noun.
35. Or, "domineering, ruling over". On this word, see 1 Pet 5:3.
36. Same word as in Mt 20:25.
37. Some manuscripts say "it shall not be" {A}, making this a kind of command, as in the next two sentences.
38. Compare Lk 9:48. On this word, see Rom 6:17.
39. Same word as in Mt 20:28.

A. 1 Jn 3:1 B. Mt 3:2 C. Mt 7:28 D. Lk 19:10 E. Mt 4:4, mankind F. Heb 6:4 G. Mt 5:18 H. Mk 8:35 J. Mt 19:29 K. 2 Jn 9 L. Eph 5:33, respecting M. Mt 26:21 N. 1 Cor 11:32 O. Lk 23:11 P. Mk 14:65 Q. Lk 18:33 R. Mk 1:8 S. Mk 1:4 T. Mk 14:15 U. Mt 20:24 V. Act 2:39, call to W. 1 Cor 3:5 X. 1 Pet 4:10, ministering Y. Jam 5:20, soul

| Mark 10:46 | 150 | Verse |

- 6B.[1] And they come to Jericho. And while He and His disciples and *a* considerable[A] crowd *are* proceeding-out[B] from Jericho, Bartimaeus, the son *of* Timaeus[2], *a* blind beggar[3], was sitting beside the road — 46

    - 1C. And having heard that it was[4] Jesus from-Nazareth[5], he began to cry-out[C] and say, "Son *of* David[6], Jesus, have-mercy-on[D] me" — 47
    - 2C. And many were rebuking[E] him in order that he might keep-silent[7]. But the *one* was crying-out *by* much more, "Son *of* David, have mercy on me" — 48
    - 3C. And having stopped[8], Jesus said, "Call him"[9] — 49

        - 1D. And they call the blind *one*, saying *to* him, "Take-courage[F], arise[G], He is calling you!"
        - 2D. And the *one*, having thrown-off his cloak, having jumped-up[10], came to Jesus — 50

    - 4C. And having responded *to* him, Jesus said, "What do you want Me to do[11] *for* you?" — 51

        - 1D. And the blind *one* said *to* Him, "Rabboni[12]— that I may see-again[H]!"
        - 2D. And Jesus said *to* him, "Go. Your faith has restored[J] you" — 52
        - 3D. And immediately he saw-again[H]. And he was following Him[13] on the road

- 7B.[14] And when they draw-near[K] to Jerusalem— to Bethphage and Bethany, near the Mount *of* Olives— He sends-forth[L] two *of* His disciples, ˚and says *to* them, "Go to the village before you. And immediately while proceeding into it, you will find *a* colt having been tied[M], on which none *of* mankind[15] yet sat. Untie[N] it, and be bringing *it*. ˚And if someone says *to* you, 'Why are you doing this?', say, 'The Lord[16] has need *of* it, and immediately[O] He sends[17] it back[18] here' " — 11:1, 2, 3

    - 1C. And they went and found *a* colt[19] having been tied at *a* door[P], outside on the street. And they untie it — 4

        - 1D. And some *of* the *ones* standing there were saying *to* them, "What are you doing untying the colt?" — 5
        - 2D. But the *ones* spoke *to* them just as Jesus spoke, and they permitted[Q] them — 6

    - 2C. And they bring[20] the colt to Jesus. And they throw their cloaks on it, and He sat on it — 7
    - 3C. And many spread[R] their cloaks[S] on the road — 8
    - 4C. And others *spread* leafy-branches[21], having cut *them* from the fields[22]
    - 5C. And the *ones* going ahead and the *ones* following were crying-out[23] "Hosanna[T]! Blessed[24] *is* the *One* coming in *the* name *of the* Lord. ˚Blessed *is* the coming kingdom[25] *of* our father David[26]. Hosanna in the highest[27] [heavens]!" — 9, 10

- 6A.[28] And He[29] entered into Jerusalem, into the temple — 11

    - 1B. And having looked-around-at[U] everything, the hour being already late[30], He went out to Bethany with the twelve[31]
    - 2B.[32] And *on* the next day,[33] they having departed from Bethany, He was hungry. ˚And having seen from *a* distance *a* fig-tree[V] having leaves, He went *to see* if perhaps He would[34] find anything on it — 12-13

        - 1C. And having come to it, He found nothing except leaves— for it was not the season[W] *for* figs[35]
        - 2C. And having responded, He[36] said *to* it, "May no one eat fruit from you any longer— forever[37]!" — 14
        - 3C. And His disciples were listening

1. Parallel account at Mt 20:29; Lk 18:35. Compare Mt 9:27-31.
2. Outside of Jesus and the apostles, only Simon (15:21) is so explicitly named in Mark. This man is only named in Mark. He may have been or become known to Mark. Some think this may be why Mark mentions only one of the blind men. Mt 20:30 mentions two; Lk 18:35, one. The fact that only one is detailed in Mark and Luke does not mean only one was healed. GK *5505*.
3. Some manuscripts say "*a* blind *one*, was sitting beside the road, begging" {N}.
4. More literally, "is", as the Greek typically phrases it.
5. On this word, see 1:24. Some manuscripts say "the Nazarene" {N}, on which see Mt 2:23.
6. This is a name for Messiah. See Mt 9:27 on it.
7. On this word, see "be still" in 4:39. Same word as in Mt 20:31.
8. Or, "stood [still]". GK *2705*.
9. Some manuscripts say "Jesus said *that* he *should* be called" {N}.
10. Used only here. GK *403*. Some manuscripts say "having arisen" {K}, using the common word in 10:1.
11. More literally, "what do you want *that* I should do".
12. Or, "My rabbi, My master". This is a transliterated Hebrew word elsewhere only in Jn 20:16, where John translates it, "teacher". GK *4808*. Related to "Rabbi" in Mt 23:7.
13. Some manuscripts say "Jesus" {N}.
14. Parallel account at Mt 21:1; Lk 19:29; Jn 12:12.
15. Or, "no one *from* mankind, none *of* humanity". That is, no human. This idiom is elsewhere only in Lk 19:30; 1 Tim 6:16; Jam 3:8. Related to "any of mankind" in Act 4:17. In all cases, "mankind" is plural, on which see Mt 4:4.
16. Instead of this referring to Jesus Himself, some think Jesus means "the lord", that is, the owner of the animal.
17. Or, "*will* send, is *going to* send". The present tense verb is given a future sense by the context. Some manuscripts say "will send it here" {B}.
18. Or, "again". Some take this phrase "and... here" as part of what they are to say, assuring the owner that the animal will be returned. Others take it as the comment of Jesus, as in Mt 21:3 (which does not have this word), "say 'The Lord has need *of* it'. And immediately...". The one questioning you "immediately sends it back here" with you. Some manuscripts omit this word {B}, so that it says "sends it here".
19. Some manuscripts say "the" colt, and "the" door {N}.
20. Some manuscripts say "brought" {N}.
21. Or, "leaves, straw". Used of the kind of material stuffed into a mattress. Used only here. GK *5115*.
22. Some manuscripts instead say "And others were cutting leafy-branches from the trees, and spreading *them* in the road" {N}, similar to Mt 21:8.
23. On this word, see Mt 8:29. Some manuscripts add, "saying" {N}.
24. This is a participle, "having been blessed", as also in v 10. On this word, see Lk 6:28.
25. These people viewed Jesus as the prophesied King (as in Lk 19:38) who would establish His kingdom on earth.
26. Some manuscripts say "the kingdom *of* our father David coming in *the* name *of the* Lord" {K}.
27. On this phrase, see Mt 21:9.
28. Parallel account at Mt 21:10.
29. Some manuscripts say "Jesus" {K}.
30. Or, "evening", that is, either before or after sundown. Used only here. GK *4070*.
31. In the time scheme noted in Jn 12:1, this would be Sunday night (as we call it).
32. Parallel account at Mt 21:18.
33. This would then be Monday morning.
34. More literally, "will", as the Greek typically phrases it.
35. This is symbolic of Israel in that day. Jesus finds no figs because it was not the season for figs. The King comes to His people Israel and finds them not ready, not ripe, not in season. They have the appearance of life, but they have no fruit, which is seen in their rejection of Him. To Israel, this was not the "season" for Messiah. But if now was not the season for Messiah, with their King standing in their presence, when would it be? Jesus faults the tree— that is, Israel— and curses it.
36. Some manuscripts say "Jesus" {K}.
37. Compare Mt 21:19. This cursing is symbolic of what was coming. The kingdom was taken from them and given to others, Mk 12:9; Mt 21:43. Their nation was destroyed. Thus the last miracle of Jesus in Mark before His death is one of destruction, a kind of parable of what was coming upon those about to kill Him. This is an idiom, "into the age", on which see Rev 20:10.

A. 2 Cor 3:5, sufficient   B. Rev 1:16, coming out   C. Mt 8:29   D. Rev 12:8, showing mercy   E. 2 Tim 4:2, warn   F. Act 23:11   G. Mt 28:6
H. Act 22:13, look up   J. Jam 5:15   K. Lk 21:28   L. Mk 3:14, send out   M. 1 Cor 7:27, bound   N. Mt 5:19, break   O. Mk 6:25   P. Col 4:3
Q. Mt 6:12, forgive   R. Mk 14:15   S. 1 Pet 3:3, garments   T. Mt 21:9   U. Mk 3:5   V. Mt 24:32   W. Mt 8:29, time

3B.[1] And they come into Jerusalem. And having entered into the temple, He began to throw-out[A] the *ones* selling and the *ones* buying in the temple. And He overturned the tables *of* the money-changers[2], and the seats *of* the *ones* selling doves[3]. °And He was not permitting[B] that anyone carry *an* object[4] through the temple 15

16

- 1C. And He was teaching and saying *to* them, "Has it not been written [in Isa 56:7] that 'My house will be called *a* house *of* prayer *for* all the nations[C]'? But **you** have made[5] it *a* den[D] *of* robbers[E]" 17
- 2C. And the chief priests and the scribes heard *it*. And they were seeking[F] how they might destroy[G] Him. For they were fearing Him, for the whole crowd was astounded[H] at His teaching 18
- 3C. And when it became evening[6], they were going[7] outside *of* the city 19

4B.[8] And while passing by early-in-the-morning[9], they saw the fig tree having dried-up from *the* roots 20

- 1C. And having remembered,[10] Peter says *to* Him, "Rabbi, look! The fig tree which You cursed[J] has dried-up[11]" 21
- 2C. And having responded, Jesus says *to* them, "Be[12] having faith *in* God. °Truly[13] I say *to* you that whoever says *to* this mountain, 'Be taken up and be thrown into the sea', and does not doubt[K] in his heart, but is believing[L] that what he is speaking is coming-about[14], it[15] will happen[16] *for* him 22-23

    - 1D. "For this reason I say *to* you, be believing[17] that you received[18] all that you are praying and asking, and it will happen[M] *for* you 24
    - 2D.[19] "And[20] whenever you stand praying, forgive[B]— if you have anything against anyone— in order that your Father in the heavens also may forgive you your trespasses[N]" 25

26[21]

5B.[22] And they come again into Jerusalem. And while He *is* walking around in the temple, the chief priests and the scribes and the elders come to Him. °And they were saying *to* Him, "By what-kind-of[23] authority[O] are You doing these *things,* or[24] who gave You this authority that you may be doing these *things*?" 27

28

- 1C. And[25] Jesus said *to* them, "I will ask[26] you one thing[P], and you answer Me, and I will tell you by what kind of authority I am doing these *things*— °Was the baptism[Q] *of* John from heaven, or from humans[R]? Answer Me!" 29

30

- 2C. And they were discussing[S] it with themselves, saying 31

    - 1D. "If we say, 'From heaven', He will say, 'Then[27] for what reason did you not believe him?'
    - 2D. "But should[28] we say, 'From humans'?" They were fearing[T] the crowd, for they all were holding[29] as to John that he **really**[U] was *a* prophet 32
    - 3D. And having responded *to* Jesus, they say "We do not know" 33

- 3C. And[30] Jesus says *to* them, "Nor am **I** telling you by what kind of authority I am doing these *things*"
- 4C.[31] And He began to speak *to* them in parables— "*A* man planted *a* vineyard and put *a* fence around *it*, and dug *a* pit[32] [for a wine press], and built *a* tower. And he rented it *to* farmers[V], and went-on-a-journey[W] 12:1

    - 1D. "And he sent forth *a* slave[X] to the farmers *at* the *harvest* time in order that he might receive from the fruits *of* the vineyard from the farmers. °And having taken him, they beat[Y] *him,* and sent *him* away empty-*handed*[Z] 2

3

    - 2D. "And again he sent-forth another[33] slave to them. And[34] that *one* they struck-on-the-head, and dishonored[AA] 4
    - 3D. "And[35] he sent forth another— and that *one* they killed— and many others, *they* beating some and killing others 5

1. Parallel account at Mt 21:12; Lk 19:45. Compare Jn 2:13-22.
2. On this word, see Mt 21:12. These men changed foreign coin for Jewish coin.
3. These were used in sacrifices, Joseph and Mary being an example, Lk 2:24.
4. Or, "vessel, jar, dish, equipment". This is a very general word used 23 times. Some limit it to "merchandise" based on the context. Some think people were using the temple as a shortcut. Jesus demands a higher respect for the temple. On this word, see "vessel" in 1 Thes 4:4.
5. Some manuscripts say "you made" {N}, as in Lk 19:46. Mt 21:13 says "are making".
6. Or, "late", the first watch, 6 to 9 P.M. That is, Monday evening (as we call it). On this word, see "after" in Mt 28:1. Related to "late" in v 11.
7. Some manuscripts say "He was going" {C}.
8. Parallel account at Mt 21:18.
9. Perhaps before 6 A.M. This would now be Tuesday morning. On this word, see "early morning" in 13:35.
10. That is, what Jesus said the previous morning, v 14.
11. Peter only notes what has happened, the miracle itself. In what follows, Jesus responds to this comment with regard to the work of power. The disciples do not ask why it happened, so the meaning of it with regard to Israel is left unstated. Same word as in Mt 21:19, 20. On this word, see "become withered" in Mk 3:1.
12. In place of this sentence, some manuscripts say "If you have faith *in* God, truly..." {B}.
13. Some manuscripts say "For truly" {N}. On "truly", see Mt 5:18.
14. Or, "taking place, happening, coming to pass". GK *1181*. It is present tense. Some give it a future sense, "that it *will* come about", based on the context.
15. Some manuscripts say "whatever he says" {N}.
16. Same word as in v 24. The word "be" sometimes means "happen", as in Mt 16:22.
17. Another prerequisite to answered prayer is "if it be Your will", as seen in Jesus Himself, 14:36. But Jesus here is exhorting them to faith, to believing God.
18. Some manuscripts say "you are receiving"; others, "you will receive" {A}.
19. Compare Mt 6:14-15.
20. Some think Jesus added this to remind them there are other prerequisites to answered prayer.
21. Some manuscripts add as v 26, "But if you do not forgive, neither will your Father in the heavens forgive your trespasses" {A}, as in Mt 6:15.
22. Parallel account at Mt 21:23; Lk 20:1.
23. Or, "what". Same word as in v 29 and 33. A prophet's authority? Messiah's? From heaven or humans? On this word, see Mt 21:23.
24. Some manuscripts say "and" {K}.
25. Some manuscripts say "And having responded, Jesus said to them" {K}.
26. This word (GK *2089*) is related to the word in Mt 21:24; Lk 20:3 (GK *2263*).
27. Some manuscripts omit this word {C}.
28. Some manuscripts say "if" {K}, "But if we say 'From humans'?".
29. Or, "regarding, looking upon". Same word as in the similar statement in Mt 14:5; 21:26, 46; and as Phil 2:29. On this word, see "have" in 1 Jn 1:8.
30. Some manuscripts say "And having responded, Jesus says *to* them" {N}.
31. Parallel account at Mt 21:33; Lk 20:9.
32. Used only here. GK *5700*. Related to "winepress" in Mt 21:33 (GK *3332*).
33. Same word as "other" in Mt 21:36. GK *257*.
34. Some manuscripts say "And having stoned that *one*, they struck *him* on the head and sent *him* away, having dishonored *him*" {N}.
35. Some manuscripts say "And again..." {K}.

A. Jn 12:31, cast out   B. Mt 6:12, forgive   C. Act 15:23, Gentiles   D. Mt 21:13   E. Mt 21:13   F. Phil 2:21   G. 1 Cor 1:18, perish   H. Mt 7:28   J. Rom 12:14   K. Jam 1:6   L. Jn 3:36   M. Mt 16:22   N. Mt 6:14   O. Rev 6:8   P. 1 Cor 12:8, word   Q. Mk 1:4   R. Mt 4:4, mankind   S. Lk 5:21, reasoning   T. Eph 5:33, respecting   U. Jn 8:36   V. Jn 15:1   W. Mt 21:33   X. Rom 6:17   Y. Jn 18:23   Z. 1 Thes 2:1, empty   AA. Act 5:41

      4D. "He was still having one *to send*— *a* beloved[1] son. He sent him forth to them last, saying   6
           that 'They will have-regard-for[2] my son'

          1E. "But those farmers said to themselves that 'This *one* is the heir[A]. Come, let us kill[B]   7
              him, and the inheritance[C] will be ours'
          2E. And having taken *him*, they killed[B] him and threw him outside *of* the vineyard   8

      5D. "Therefore[3] what will the owner[4] *of* the vineyard do? He will come and destroy[D] the   9
           farmers, and give the vineyard *to* others[5]
      6D. "Did you not even read this Scripture[E] [in Ps 118:22-23]— '*The* stone which the *ones*   10
           building rejected[F], this became[6] *the* head[7] *of the* corner[8]. *This came about from *the* Lord,   11
           and it is marvelous[G] in our eyes'?"

  5C. And they were seeking to seize[H] Him. And[9] they feared the crowd. For[10] they[11] knew that He   12
      spoke the parable[J] against[12] them
  6C. And having left Him, they went away

6B.[13] And they send forth some *of* the Pharisees and the Herodians[K] to Him in order that they might   13
catch[14] Him *in a* statement[L]. *And[15] having come, they say *to* Him, "Teacher, we know that You   14
are truthful[M]. And You are not concerned about [pleasing] anyone,[16] for You do not look at *the* face
of people,[17] but You teach the way *of* God in accordance with truth[18]. Is it lawful[N] to give *a* poll-
tax[19] *to* Caesar, or not? Should we give *it,* or should we not give *it*?"

  1C. But the *One*, knowing[20] their hypocrisy[O], said *to* them, "Why are you testing[P] Me? Bring Me   15
      a denarius[21] in order that I may see *it*". *And the *ones* brought *it*   16
  2C. And He says *to* them, "Whose *is* this image[22] and inscription?" And the *ones* said *to* Him,
      "Caesar's"
  3C. And Jesus said *to* them, "Give back the *things of* Caesar[23] *to* Caesar, and the *things of* God *to* God"   17
  4C. And they were marveling-greatly[24] at Him

7B.[25] And Sadducees come to Him, who say *that* there is not *a* resurrection[26]   18

  1C. And they were questioning[Q] Him, saying, *"Teacher, Moses wrote *to* us [in Deut 25:5] that if   19
      a brother *of* someone dies and leaves-behind[R] *a* wife and does not leave[S] *a* child, that his
      brother should take the wife, and raise-up-from[27] her *a* seed[28] *for* his brother

      1D. "There were seven brothers. And the first took *a* wife, and dying, did not leave *a* seed.   20
           And the second took her, and died, not having left-behind[29] *a* seed. And the third similarly.   21
           And the seven[30] did not leave *a* seed. Last[31] *of* all, the woman also died   22
      2D. "In[32] the resurrection when they rise up[33], *of* which *of* them will she be *the* wife? For the   23
           seven had her *as* wife"

  2C. Jesus said[34] *to* them, "Are you not mistaken[35] because of this— not knowing the Scriptures,   24
      nor the power *of* God?[36]

      1D. "For when they rise-up[T] from *the* dead, they neither marry[U] nor are they given-in-   25
           marriage[V], but they are like angels in the heavens
      2D. "And concerning the dead, that they are raised[W], did you not read in the book *of* Moses   26
           at the [place about the burning] bush, how God spoke *to* him, saying [in Ex 3:15], 'I *am*
           the[37] God *of* Abraham, and the God *of* Isaac, and the God *of* Jacob'? *He is not God *of*   27
           dead *ones*,[38] but[39] *of* living *ones*. You[40] are greatly mistaken"

1. On this adjective, see Mt 3:17.
2. Same word as in Mt 21:37, on which see Lk 18:2.
3. Some manuscripts omit this word {C}.
4. On this word, see "master" in Mt 8:2. The owner represents God the Father.
5. Compare Mt 21:43.
6. Literally, "came-to-be for the head", reflecting a Hebrew way of speaking.
7. Same word as in Mt 5:36; 14:8; Act 18:6; 1 Cor 11:3, 4, 5; Eph 1:22; Col 1:18; Rev 13:3. Used 75 times. GK *3051*.
8. That is, the head-stone belonging to the corner. Some take this to mean the "cornerstone" of a foundation; others, the "capstone" of an arched doorway. Elsewhere only in this phrase in Mt 21:42; Lk 20:17; Act 4:11; 1 Pet 2:7; and in Mt 6:5; Act 26:26; Rev 7:1; 20:8. GK *1224*.
9. This is the Greek word order. Or, "And-*yet*", giving the reason they did not seize Jesus, rather than a second statement.
10. Mark may be giving the reason for the seeking and the fear. Or, "crowd, for...", giving the reason they feared the crowd. Or, "Him, and-*yet* they feared the crowd. For they...", giving the reason they were seeking to seize Him. Lk 20:19 is a parallel statement with similar issues.
11. Mark may mean that the crowd knew this. Or, he may mean that the priests and scribes and elders (11:27) knew this, "they" referring to these people throughout the verse. See Lk 20:19 on this.
12. Or, "to, with reference to". GK *4639*. Same word as Lk 20:19.
13. Parallel account at Mt 22:15; Lk 20:20.
14. Used figuratively here, this word means "to take by hunting or fishing". Used only here. GK *65*. Related to "hunter" and "prey".
15. Some manuscripts say "And the *ones*, having come, say..." {N}.
16. That is, You are not concerned about pleasing any constituency. On this idiom, see Mt 22:16.
17. That is, You are not partial to anyone. See also "respect of persons" in Jam 2:1.
18. On this phrase, see Lk 4:25.
19. Same word as in Mt 22:17. On this word, see Mt 17:25.
20. Mt 22:18 (GK *1182*), Mk 12:15 (GK *3857*), and Lk 20:23 (GK *2917*) each use a different word for "know", and for what Jesus knew— here, their "hypocrisy".
21. This is a Roman silver coin. On this word, see Mt 20:2.
22. Or, "likeness". On this word, see Col 1:15.
23. That is, the things belonging to Caesar, the things belonging to God.
24. Used only here. GK *1703*. Related to the word in Mt 22:22; Lk 20:26 (GK *2513*).
25. Parallel account at Mt 22:23; Lk 20:27.
26. Compare Act 23:8 on this.
27. Same word as in Lk 20:28. Elsewhere only as "stand up out of" in Act 15:5. GK *1985*. Related to the word in Mt 22:24.
28. That is, descendants, offspring.
29. Some manuscripts say "and neither did **he** leave-behind" {N}.
30. Some manuscripts add "took her and" {N}.
31. This is GK *2274*. Not the same word as in Mt 22:27.
32. Some manuscripts say "Therefore, in..." {C}.
33. Some manuscripts omit "when they rise up" {C}.
34. Some manuscripts say "And having responded, Jesus said..." {N}.
35. Same word as in Mt 22:29, where it is not a question. On this word, see "err" in Jam 5:19.
36. The grammar indicates that a "yes" answer is expected; they are mistaken.
37. Some manuscripts say "I am God *of* Abraham, God *of* Isaac, and God *of* Jacob..." {C}, as in Lk 20:37.
38. See Mt 22:32 on this.
39. Some manuscripts add "God" {N}, "but God *of* living...".
40. Some manuscripts say "Therefore **you** are..." {N}.

A. Rom 8:17 B. Rom 7:11 C. Eph 1:14 D. 1 Cor 1:18, perish E. 2 Pet 3:16 F. Heb 12:17 G. Jn 9:30, marvel H. Heb 4:14, hold on to J. Mt 13:3 K. Mt 22:16 L. 1 Cor 12:8, word M. Jn 6:55, true N. 1 Cor 6:12 O. Gal 2:13 P. Heb 2:18, tempted Q. Lk 9:18 R. Act 6:2 S. Mt 6:12, forgive T. Lk 18:33 U. 1 Cor 7:9 V. 1 Cor 7:38 W. Mt 28:6, arose

| Mark 12:28 | 156 | Verse |

8B.[1] And having come to *Him*, one *of* the scribes— having heard them debating[A], having seen[2] that He answered them well— asked Him, "Which is *the* foremost[3] commandment[4] *of* all?" — 28

   1C. Jesus answered that — 29

      1D. "Foremost[5] is, 'Hear, Israel. *The* Lord our God is one Lord.[6] °And you shall love[B] *the* Lord your God from your whole heart, and from your whole soul[C], and from your whole mind[D], and from your whole strength'[7] [Deut 6:4-5] — 30
      2D. "Second *is* this,[8] 'You shall love[B] your neighbor as[9] yourself' [Lev 19:18] — 31
      3D. "There is not another commandment greater *than* these"

   2C. And the scribe said *to* Him, "Well[E] *said*, Teacher! In accordance with [God's] truth[10], You said that[11] He is one[12]. And there is not another except Him. °And the *statement* 'to love Him from the whole heart, and from the whole understanding[F], and from the whole[13] strength', and the *statement* 'to love the neighbor as himself', are more [important] *than* all the whole-burnt-offerings[14] and sacrifices" — 32, 33

   3C. And Jesus, having looked-at[15] him[16] because he responded thoughtfully[17], said *to* him, "You are not far from the kingdom *of* God" — 34

9B.[18] And no one was daring[G] to question[H] Him any more. °And having responded, Jesus was saying while teaching in the temple, "How *is it that* the scribes say that the Christ is *the* son *of* David? — 35

   1C. "David himself said by the Holy Spirit [in Ps 110:1], '*The* Lord[J] said *to* my Lord, "Be sitting on My right *side* until I put Your enemies under[19] Your feet" ' — 36

      1D. "David[20] himself calls Him 'Lord'. And in what way is He his son?"[21] — 37

10B.[22] And the large crowd was listening-to Him with-pleasure[23]. °And in His teaching He was saying, "Beware[K] of the scribes— — 38

   1C. "The *ones* delighting[24] to walk around in robes, and *to receive* greetings in the marketplaces, and seats-of-honor[L] in the synagogues, and places-of-honor[M] at the banquets[N] — 39
   2C. "*They are* the[25] ones devouring[26] the houses *of* the widows,[27] and praying long *for a* pretense[28] — 40
   3C. "These *ones* will receive greater condemnation[O]"

11B.[29] And having sat-*down* opposite the treasury[30], He[31] was observing how the crowd throws money[32] into the treasury. And many rich[P] *ones* were throwing much *money* — 41

   1C. And one poor[Q] widow having come threw two leptos[33], which is *a* quadrans[34] — 42
   2C. And having summoned His disciples, He said *to* them, "Truly[R] I say *to* you that this poor widow threw[35] more *than* all[36] the *ones* throwing into the treasury. °For they all threw out of the *money* abounding[37] *to* them. But this *one*, out of her need[38], threw all that she was having— her whole living[39]" — 43, 44

12B.[40] And while He *is* proceeding out of the temple, one *of* His disciples says *to* Him, "Teacher, look! What[41] stones and what buildings!" — 13:1

   1C. And[42] Jesus said *to* him, "Do you see these great buildings? *A* stone upon *a* stone will by no means be left here[43] which will by-any-means[44] not be torn-down[S]" — 2
   2C. And while He *was* sitting on the Mount *of* Olives opposite the temple, Peter and James and John and Andrew were questioning Him privately[T], °"Tell us— — 3, 4

1. Parallel account at Mt 22:34. Compare Lk 10:25-28.
2. Instead of "having seen", some manuscripts say "knowing" {N}.
3. Or, "first". GK *4755*. Mt 22:36 says "great".
4. Same word as in Mt 5:19; 15:3; Jn 13:34; 1 Tim 6:14; 1 Jn 5:3; and "command" in Col 4:10. Used 67 times. GK *1953*. Related to the verb in Mk 10:3.
5. Some manuscripts add "*of* all the commandments" {N}.
6. Or, "our Lord God is one Lord", or, "*the* Lord our God, *the* Lord is one".
7. Some manuscripts add "This *is the* foremost commandment" {N}.
8. Some manuscripts say "And *the* second like *it is* this— " {N}.
9. Or, "like". On this, see Mt 19:19.
10. On this phrase, see Lk 4:25.
11. Or, "... truth you spoke, because He is one". This is the Greek word order of this sentence.
12. Some manuscripts say "because there is one God" {K}.
13. Some manuscripts say "and from *the* whole soul, and from *the* whole strength" {N}.
14. That is, sacrificial animals wholly consumed by fire. Elsewhere only in Heb 10:6, 8. GK *3906*.
15. Same word as in 8:33.
16. Some manuscripts omit this word {C}, so that it says "having seen that he responded thoughtfully".
17. Or, "wisely". Used only here. GK *3807*. Related to "mind".
18. Parallel account at Mt 22:41; Lk 20:41.
19. As in Mt 22:44. Some manuscripts say "*as a* footstool *of* your feet" {C}, as in Lk 20:43; Act 2:35; Heb 1:13.
20. Some manuscripts say "Therefore, David..." {N}.
21. Jesus wants His listeners to reconsider their understanding of this matter, because there is something contained in this paradox about David that they have not fully understood. If the Messiah is David's Lord, how can He be his distant physical descendant? If He is David's superior, how can He be his son? Jesus is God's Son (David's Lord); and Mary's Son (David's descendant).
22. Parallel account at Mt 23:1; Lk 20:45.
23. Same phrase as 6:20, where Herod listened to John with pleasure, before he killed him.
24. On this word, see Col 2:18. Same word as in Lk 20:46. Mt 3:6 uses the word "love".
25. The grammar is unusual. Instead of two parallel descriptions of these scribes, Jesus may intend these to be two independent statements. In this case, point 1C. would be "Beware of the scribes— the *ones* delighting... banquets". Point 2C. would be rendered "The *ones* devouring the houses *of* the widows and praying long *for a* pretense— these *ones* will receive greater condemnation".
26. Or, "consuming, eating up". Same word as in Lk 15:30; 20:47; 2 Cor 11:20; Gal 5:15; Rev 11:5; 12:4; 20:9. Elsewhere only as "eat up" in Mt 13:4; Mk 4:4; Lk 8:5; Rev 10:9, 10; and "consume" in Jn 2:17. GK *2983*.
27. That is, taking financial advantage of widows based on "spiritual" pretexts. Same phrase as in Lk 20:47.
28. That is, for a falsely alleged motive. On this word, see Phil 1:18. These scribes use prayer to gain favor with people.
29. Parallel account at Lk 21:1.
30. Same word as later in the verse and in v 43. It can refer generally to the temple treasury, or more specifically to the receptacles into which offerings were thrown. There were thirteen such receptacles in the temple, shaped like trumpets. Elsewhere only in Lk 21:1; Jn 8:20. GK *1126*. Related to the word in Act 8:27.
31. Some manuscripts say "Jesus" {B}.
32. That is, Jesus was observing this category of behavior, the manner in which the crowd gives offerings when they throw their money into the treasury. His focus is on how they give, not how they physically threw the money. Note the three different tenses of "throw" in v 41-42.
33. That is, two thin copper Jewish coins. This is the smallest denomination of Jewish coinage. Elsewhere only in Lk 12:59; 21:2. GK *3321*. Two leptos made a quadrans, four quadrans made an assarion (see Mt 10:29). Sixteen assarion made a denarius (see Mt 20:2). So a leptos is 128th of a denarius, of one day's wages for a laborer.
34. This is the smallest denomination of Roman coin. Elsewhere only in Mt 5:26. GK *3119*.
35. Some manuscripts say "has thrown" {N}, making this the fourth tense used with this word in v 41-43.
36. Some think Jesus means more than any one of them; others, more than all of them together.
37. Or, "overflowing, being left over". These people gave from their excess. On this word, see 2 Cor 8:2.
38. Or, "lack, want". The widow gave out of what was already not enough for her. Elsewhere only in Phil 4:11. GK *5730*. Related to "be in need" in Lk 15:14.
39. Same word as in Lk 21:4.
40. Parallel account at Mt 24:1; Lk 21:5.
41. On this word, see "what kind of " in 1 Jn 3:1. Based on the context, it means here "how great" or "how wonderful". Compare Lk 21:5.
42. Some manuscripts say "And having responded, Jesus..." {N}.
43. Some manuscripts omit this word {B}.
44. This phrase "by no means, by any means, never" is an emphatic negative, the strongest in Greek. Jesus uses it twice in this verse. Used by Mark in 9:1, 41; 10:15; 13:2, 19, 30, 31; 14:25, 31; 16:18. See "never" in Gal 5:16.

A. Mk 8:11   B. Jn 21:15, devotedly love   C. Jam 5:20   D. Lk 1:51, thought   E. Act 10:33   F. Eph 3:4   G. 2 Cor 11:21   H. Lk 9:18   J. Mt 8:2, master   K. Mk 8:15   L. Mt 23:6   M. Mt 23:6   N. Lk 14:12, dinner   O. Jn 9:39, judgment   P. 1 Tim 6:17   Q. Gal 4:9   R. Mt 5:18   S. Mt 24:2   T. Mt 14:13

                1D. "When will these *things* happen¹?
                2D. "And what *will be* the sign^A when all these *things* are about to be accomplished²?"

        3C. And Jesus began to say *to* them   5

                1D. "Be watching out *that* no one may deceive^B you

                        1E. "Many will come on the basis of My name³, saying that '**I** am *the One*⁴'. And they   6
                              will deceive many
                        2E. "And whenever you hear-*of* wars^C and rumors^D *of* wars, do not be alarmed⁵. *They*   7
                              must⁶ take place, but *it is* not yet the end⁷

                2D. "For⁸ nation will arise⁹ against nation, and kingdom against kingdom. There will be   8
                      earthquakes in various places¹⁰. There will be famines¹¹. These *things are*¹² a beginning
                      of birth-pains¹³
                3D.¹⁴ "But you— be watching¹⁵ yourselves   9

                        1E. "They will hand you over to councils¹⁶. And you will be beaten¹⁷ in synagogues.
                              And you will be stood before governors^E and kings for My sake, for *a* testimony^F
                              to them—ᵃ and the good-news^G must^H first¹⁸ be proclaimed^J to all the nations   10

                                1F.¹⁹ "And whenever they lead^K you while handing *you* over, do not be anxious-   11
                                        beforehand²⁰ *as* to what you should speak.²¹ But whatever is given *to* you in
                                        that hour, speak this

                                        1G. "For **you** are not the *ones* speaking, but the Holy Spirit

                        2E. "And brother^L will hand-over^M brother to death, and *a* father *his* child. And children 12
                              will rise-up-in-rebellion^N against parents, and they²² will put them to death
                        3E. "And you will be being hated^O by all because of My name²³   13
                        4E. "But the *one* having endured^P to *the* end²⁴— this *one* will be saved^Q

                4D.²⁵ "But when you see the abomination^R *of* desolation²⁶ standing²⁷ where *he*²⁸ should²⁹ not³⁰ 14
                      (let the *one* reading understand³¹)—

                        1E. "Then³² let the *ones* in Judea be fleeing^S to the mountains

                                1F.³³ "And³⁴ let the *one* upon the housetop^T not go down³⁵ nor go in to take³⁶ anything 15
                                        out of his house
                                2F. "And let the *one* in the field not turn-back^U to the *things* behind³⁷ to take his cloak 16
                                3F. "And woe *to* the *ones* having *a child* in *the* womb^V, and *to* the *ones* nursing^W 17
                                        in those days
                                4F. "And be praying that it may not take place *in* winter   18

                        2E. "For those days will be *an* affliction³⁸ such-as³⁹ has not taken place such-as-this⁴⁰   19
                              since *the* beginning *of the* creation which God created until now, and never⁴¹ will
                              take place [again]

                                1F. "And if *the* Lord had not shortened⁴² the days, no flesh would have been saved⁴³ 20
                                2F. "But⁴⁴ He shortened the days for the sake of the chosen⁴⁵ *ones* whom He chose⁴⁶

1. Or, "be". On this word, see Mt 16:22.
2. Or, "carried out, fulfilled, completed, consummated, brought to an end, concluded". Related to "conclusion" in Mt 24:3. Some think "these things" refers to the prophecy in v 2, and "all these things" is a physical reference to "all these buildings". In this case, this is rendered "about to be brought to an end". Others think "these things" refers to v 2, and "all these things" refers to the totality of events surrounding the one mentioned in v 2. In this case, it is rendered "accomplished, fulfilled, carried out", and refers to the same thing as "conclusion of the age" in Mt 24:3. Elsewhere only as "complete" in Lk 4:2, 13; Act 21:27; Rom 9:28; and "consummate" in Heb 8:8. GK *5334*.
3. On this phrase, "on the basis of My name", see Act 2:38.
4. Or, "I am *He*". That is, the Christ, Mt 24:5.
5. Same word as in Mt 24:6, on which see 2 Thes 2:2.
6. Or, "It must", that is, all this. On this idiom, see Mt 16:21.
7. Or, "conclusion, termination". On the meaning of this, see Mt 24:6. Used with reference to prophetic events in Mt 24:6, 13, 14; Mk 13:7, 13; Lk 21:9; 1 Cor 15:24; 1 Pet 4:7. On this word, see Rom 10:4.
8. In connecting this verse with the context, Lk 21:10 has been followed. Luke separates it from the preceding statements, and makes it the beginning of what follows.
9. Or, "be raised". Same word as in v 22 and Mt 24:7.
10. Same phrase as in Mt 24:7.
11. Some manuscripts add "and disturbances" {B}, using the word in Act 12:18.
12. Or, "*will be*".
13. On this word, see Mt 24:8. It implies there are worse things, and a glorious thing, to follow.
14. Compare also Mt 10:17-23; Jn 16:1-4.
15. Same word as "watch out" in v 5, 23, 33. GK *1063*.
16. Same word as in Mt 10:17. Local Jewish courts.
17. Same word as in 12:3, 5. On this word, see Jn 18:23. Not the same word as Mt 10:17.
18. That is, "first", before the "end" comes, as in Mt 24:14.
19. Compare also Lk 12:11-12.
20. Used only here. GK *4628*. Related to "be anxious" in Mt 10:19, on which see Mt 6:25.
21. Some manuscripts add "nor meditate-upon *it*" {K}, using the word "plot" in Act 4:25, which also means "think about, practice, prepare" (it is related to "prepare-beforehand" in Lk 21:14).
22. This may refer back to the "children", or it may refer in general to the "authorities".
23. On this sentence, see Mt 24:9.
24. On "to *the* end", see Mt 10:22. This sentence is also in Mt 10:22; 24:13.
25. Parallel account at Mt 24:15; Lk 21:20.
26. On this word and phrase, see Mt 24:15. Compare Lk 21:20. Some manuscripts add "the *thing* having been spoken by Daniel the prophet" {K}, as in Mt 24:15.
27. This is the common word for "stand", used 155 times. It also means stand *there*; stand [firm]; stand [still], stop; make stand, establish. GK *2705*.
28. Or, "*it*". The grammar of "standing" implies "he" here, and does not agree with "abomination" (as it does in Mt 24:15). Some think this implies this is referring to a person. Others think the grammar is according to sense, and implies nothing about whether the abomination is a person. On the meaning of this, see Mt 24:15.
29. Or, "ought not to". On this idiom, see "ought to" in Act 25:10.
30. Mt 24:15 says, "in *the* holy place".
31. On this command, see Mt 24:15.
32. Or, "At that time". Same word as in v 21, 26, 27. On this word, see Mt 24:9.
33. Compare also Lk 17:31-32.
34. Some manuscripts omit this word {C}.
35. Some manuscripts add "into the house" {N}.
36. That is, do not go down or enter your house for the purpose of taking your belongings. Go down to flee!
37. On "to *the things* behind", see "back" in Jn 6:66.
38. Same word as in v 24. On this word, see Mt 24:21.
39. Or, "of such a kind as, of such sort as". Same word as in Mt 24:21; Rev 16:18; Mk 9:3. GK *3888*.
40. Note that in Mark this concept is repeated with two different words. GK *5525*. In Mt 24:21, it is said once. Lk 21 omits it.
41. This is the strongest negative in Greek. See 13:2 on it.
42. Same word as later in the verse. On this word, see Mt 24:22.
43. That is, from physical death. Literally, "all flesh would not have been saved", a Hebrew way of speaking. On this phrase, see Mt 24:22.
44. This is GK *247*. Not the same word as Mt 24:22 (GK *1254*).
45. Same word as as v 22 and Mt 24:22. On this word, see Rom 8:33.
46. Related to the previous word. On this word, see 1 Cor 1:27.

A. 2 Thes 2:9   B. Jam 5:19, err   C. Rev 12:7   D. Heb 4:2, hearing   E. Mt 27:2   F. Act 4:33   G. Mk 8:35   H. Mt 16:21   J. 2 Tim 4:2   K. Lk 4:1   L. Act 16:40   M. Mt 26:21, hand over   N. Mt 10:21   O. Rom 9:13   P. Jam 1:12   Q. Lk 19:10   R. Rev 17:4   S. 1 Cor 6:18   T. Lk 5:19   U. Jam 5:19   V. 1 Thes 5:3   W. Mt 21:16

3E.[1] "And then[2] if someone says *to* you, 'Look— here *is* the Christ', 'Look— there *He is*', do not be believing *it* — 21

    1F. "For false-christs and false-prophets[A] will arise[B], and will give[3] signs and wonders[C] so-as to be leading-astray[4], if possible, the chosen[D] *ones* — 22

    2F. "But **you** be watching out. I have told you everything beforehand[5] — 23

5D.[6] "But in those days after that affliction[7], the sun will be darkened[E], and the moon will not give its glow[8], °and the stars will be falling from the heaven[9], and the powers[F] in the heavens will be shaken[G] — 24, 25

6D. "And then they will see the Son *of* Man coming in *the* clouds with great power[F] and glory — 26

    1E. "And at that time He will send out the angels, and He will gather together His[10] chosen[D] *ones* from the four winds, from *the* end[H] *of the* earth to *the* end *of the* heaven — 27

7D.[11] "Now learn[J] the parable from the fig tree[12]— when its branch already[K] becomes tender and grows-out[L] *its* leaves, you know that the summer is near — 28

    1E. "So also you— when you see these[13] *things* taking place, you know[14] that He[15] is near, at *the* doors. °Truly[M] I say *to* you that this generation[16] will by no means pass away until[17] which *time* these *things* all take place — 29, 30

        1F. "Heaven and earth will pass away, but My words will by-no-means[18] pass away — 31

8D. "But no one knows[N] about that day or the hour— not even the angels in heaven, nor the Son[19]— except the Father — 32

    1E. "Be watching out, be keeping-alert[20], for you do not know when the time is — 33

    2E. "*It is* like *a* man away-on-a-journey[21]— — 34

        1F. "Having left his house and having given authority[O] *to* his slaves[P]— *to* each *as to* his work[22]— he also commanded[Q] the doorkeeper that he should be keeping-watch[23]

        2F. "Therefore, keep watching— for you do not know when the master[R] *of the* house is coming, whether evening or midnight or rooster-crowing or early-morning[24]— °that having come suddenly[S], he may not find you sleeping[T] — 35, 36

    3E. "And what I say *to* you I say *to* everyone— 'Keep watching' " — 37

7A.[25] Now the Passover[U] [Feast] and the *Feast of* Unleavened-Bread[V] was after two days. And the chief priests and the scribes were seeking how, having seized Him by deceit[W], they might kill[X] *Him*. °For[26] they were saying, "Not during the Feast[Y], so that there will not perhaps be *an* uproar[27] *of* the people" — 14:1, 2

    1B.[28] And He being in Bethany at the house *of* Simon the leper, while He *is* reclining [to eat], *a* woman[29] came having *an* alabaster-jar[30] *of* very-precious[Z] genuine[31] nard[32] perfume[33]. Having broken the alabaster-jar, she poured *it* down *over* His head — 3

        1C. But some were being indignant[34] to themselves[35]— "For what *purpose* has this waste *of* perfume taken place? °For this perfume could have been sold *for* over three-hundred denarii[36] and given *to* the poor[AA]". And they were sternly-scolding[BB] her — 4, 5

1. Compare also Lk 17:23-24.
2. Or, "at that time". On this word, see Mt 24:9. Compare Lk 17:20-21.
3. Some manuscripts say "do" {N}.
4. Or, "misleading". On this word, see 1 Tim 6:10. Related to "deceive" in Mt 24:24. On the grammar of "so as to", see Mt 5:28 (it is not the same as in Mt 24:24).
5. On the word "told beforehand", see "spoken beforehand" in Jude 17.
6. Parallel account at Mt 24:29; Lk 21:25.
7. Compare Mt 24:29; Lk 21:25. Same word as in v 19.
8. Or, "light". Elsewhere only in Mt 24:29, in this same phrase. GK *5766.*
9. Some manuscripts say "And the stars *of* the heaven will fall" {N}. Compare Rev 6:13.
10. Some manuscripts omit this word {C}, so that it says "the chosen ones".
11. Parallel account at Mt 24:32; Lk 21:29.
12. On the meaning of this parable, see Mt 24:32.
13. That is, verses 5 to 23 or 25, or verses 14 to 23 or 25. Seeing this is seeing the tree leafed out.
14. Or, "know", a command. Same word and grammar as in v 28. GK *1182.*
15. That is, the Son of Man, v 26. Or, "it", His coming.
16. On "this generation", see Mt 24:34.
17. This is a different word than in Mt 24:34 and Lk 21:32, but with the same meaning. GK *3588.*
18. Or, "never". Same word as in v 30. On this word, see 13:2.
19. This information regarding the Second Coming was not relevant to the mission of Jesus at His first coming, and therefore was part of what He "emptied" when He took on the form of a man, Phil 2:7.
20. Same word as in Lk 21:36. On this word, see Eph 6:18. Some manuscripts add, "and be praying" {B}.
21. Used only here. GK *624.* Related to the word in Mt 21:33.
22. Or, "*to* each *with reference to* his work". Or, "[and] *to* each *one* his work".
23. Same word as in v 35, 37, and in Mt 24:42. On this word, see 1 Thes 5:6.
24. These four terms represent the 1st (6-9 P.M.), 2nd (9-12 A.M.), 3rd (12-3 A.M.), and 4th (3-6 A.M.) watches (see Lk 2:8) of the night. Same word as in Mt 20:1; Jn 18:28. Elsewhere only as "early in the morning" in Mt 16:3; 21:18; Mk 1:35; 11:20; 15:1; 16:2, 9; Jn 20:1; Act 28:23. GK *4745.* Related to the word in Mt 27:1; Jn 21:4; and to "morning" in Rev 2:28.
25. Parallel account at Mt 26:1; Lk 22:1.
26. Some manuscripts say "But" {K}.
27. Same word as in Mt 26:5.
28. Parallel account at Mt 26:6; Jn 12:3. Compare Lk 7:37-50.
29. It was Mary, the sister of Lazarus and Martha (Jn 11:2; 12:3), who sat at His feet in Lk 10:39. Chronologically, this took place six days before Passover (Jn 12:1), which would place it at the end of Mk 10. Mark's arrangement here is topical.
30. This word is transliterated into English. It refers to a special and expensive container with a long neck which was broken off in order to use the contents. Elsewhere only in Mt 26:7; Lk 7:37. GK *223.*
31. Or, "pure". Elsewhere only in Jn 12:3. GK *4410.* Related to "faithful, trustworthy".
32. Or, "spikenard". That is, oil extracted from the nard plant. Elsewhere only in Jn 12:3. GK *3726.*
33. Or, "fragrant oil". On this word, see Mt 26:7.
34. On this word, see Mt 20:24. That is, the disciples were expressing their indignation to each other.
35. Some manuscripts add "and saying" {N}.
36. That is, 300 day's wages for a laborer. A year's wages. On this word, see Mt 20:2. Some think this may have been a family heirloom.

A. Rev 16:13 B. Mt 28:6 C. 2 Thes 2:9 D. Rom 8:33 E. Rom 1:21 F. Mk 5:30 G. Act 17:13 H. Mt 24:31 J. Phil 4:11 K. Mt 24:32
L. Mt 24:32 M. Mt 5:18 N. 1 Jn 2:29 O. Rev 6:8 P. Rom 6:17 Q. Mk 10:3 R. Mt 8:2 S. Lk 2:13 T. 1 Thes 5:10 U. Jn 18:28 V. Mk 14:12
W. Mt 26:4 X. Rom 7:11 Y. Jn 13:29 Z. 1 Pet 3:4 AA. Gal 4:9 BB. Jn 11:33, deeply moved

| Mark 14:6 | 162 | Verse |

    2C. But Jesus said, "Leave[1] her *alone*. Why are you causing troubles[A] *for* her? She worked *a* good[2] work in[3] Me   6

        1D. "For you **always** have the poor with you. And whenever you want, you are able to do good *for* them. But you do not always have **Me**   7

        2D. "She did what she had[4]. She anticipated[5] to perfume[6] My body for *its* preparation-for-burial[7]   8

        3D. "And truly[B] I say *to* you, wherever the[8] good-news[C] is proclaimed[D] in the whole world, what this *one* did will also be spoken for *a* memorial[E] *of* her"   9

2B.[9] And Judas Iscariot[F], the one *from* the twelve, went to the chief priests in order that he might hand Him over[G] *to* them   10

    1C. And the *ones,* having heard, rejoiced[H], and promised[J] to give him money[K]   11

    2C. And he was seeking[L] how he might conveniently[10] hand Him over

3B.[11] And *on* the first day *of* the *Feast of* Unleavened-Bread[12], when they were sacrificing[13] the Passover[M] [lamb], His disciples say *to* Him, "Where do You want us, having gone, to prepare[14] in order that You may eat the Passover [meal]?"   12

    1C. And He sends-forth[N] two of His disciples. And He says *to* them, "Go into the city,[15] and *a* man will meet you carrying *a* jar[16] *of* water. Follow him. °And wherever he enters, say *to* the house-master[O] that 'The Teacher says, "Where is My guest-room[17] where I may eat the Passover[M] [meal] with My disciples?"' °And **he** will show[P] you *a* large upstairs room having been spread[18] [with furnishings], prepared[19]. And prepare *for* us there"   13, 14, 15

    2C. And the disciples went forth and came to the city, and found *it* just as He told them. And they prepared the Passover[M] [meal]   16

    3C.[20] And having become evening, He comes with the twelve   17

        1D. And while they *were* reclining-back and eating, Jesus said, "Truly[B] I say *to* you that one of you will hand Me over— the *one* eating with Me[21]!"   18

            1E. They began to be grieved[Q], and to say *to* Him one by one[22], "It is not I, is it ?"[23]   19

            2E. And the *One* said[24] *to* them, "It is one *of* the twelve, the *one* dipping[25] with Me into the bowl   20

                1F. "Because **the Son *of* Man**[26] is going just as it has been written about Him— but woe *to* that man by whom the Son *of* Man is being handed-over[G]! It would have been better[R] *for* him if that man had not been born[S]"   21

        2D.[27] And while they *were* eating, having[28] taken bread, having blessed[T] *it*[29], He broke[U] *it* and gave *it to* them and said, "Take[30] *it*. This is[31] My body"   22

        3D. And having taken *a* cup, having given-thanks[V], He gave *it to* them. And they all drank from it. °And He said *to* them   23, 24

            1E. "This is My blood[32] *of* the covenant[33]— the *blood* being poured-out[W] for many

            2E. "Truly I say *to* you that I will no longer[34] by any means drink of the fruit[35] *of* the grapevine until that day when I drink it new[X] in the kingdom[36] *of* God"   25

4B.[37] And having sung-a-hymn[38], they went out to the Mount *of* Olives   26

1. This command "Leave *alone*" is plural, addressing them all. Compare Jn 12:7.
2. On this answer, see Mt 26:10.
3. That is, in My case, in connection with Me. GK *1877.* Compare Mt 26:10.
4. That is, in doing this good work, she took action with what was available to her. She did what she could do.
5. Or, combining with the next word, "took beforehand to anoint", and thus "anointed beforehand". She anticipated My death and acted beforehand to perfume My body. GK *4624.*
6. Or, "to anoint with perfume". Related to "perfume" in v 3. Used only here. GK *3690.*
7. Elsewhere only in Jn 12:7. GK *1947.* Related to the verb in Mt 26:12. The root word is "burial-place" in Mt 23:29.
8. Some manuscripts say "this" {N}.
9. Parallel account at Mt 26:14; Lk 22:3.
10. Or, "opportune-ly". On this word, see "in season" in 2 Tim 4:2. Related to "favorable opportunity" in Mt 26:16.
11. Parallel account at Mt 26:17; Lk 22:7.
12. This Feast is mentioned elsewhere only in Mt 26:17; Mk 14:1; Lk 22:1, 7; Act 12:3; 20:6. It was established by God at the time of the Exodus. This eight-day Feast was sometimes simply called "Passover", as in Lk 22:1; Act 12:2, 4. The Law says God's people were to eat unleavened bread from the evening of the 14th of Nisan to the evening of the 21st (Ex 12:18; Lev 23:5); that the Passover lamb was to be sacrificed between 3 P.M. and dark on the 14th of Nisan (Ex 12:6); and that the meal was to be eaten that evening (Ex 12:8, on the 15th of Nisan, which began at sunset). Here in this verse, it is now Thursday. Mark says Jesus was removed from the cross before the Sabbath began (15:42) at sundown on Friday night (as we call it). He was crucified on Friday, the Preparation day (Mk 15:42; Lk 23:54, Jn 19:31) at the third hour (15:25), and died at the ninth hour (15:34). He had been delivered to Pilate "early in the morning" (15:1) on Friday, having been betrayed the night before, Thursday night (as we call it). He "ate the Passover with His disciples" (14:14) that Thursday "evening" (14:17, as we call it), just before His betrayal. Thus here, Thursday afternoon, "they were sacrificing the Passover [lamb]" in preparation for the evening meal. Compare Jn 18:28; 19:31. On the chronological issues regarding this week, consult the commentaries. Elsewhere only as "unleavened" in 1 Cor 5:7, 8. GK *109.*
13. Mark could mean "when they were actually making the sacrifices", placing this after 3 P.M.; or, "when they customarily were making the sacrifices", placing this question any time on "the first day" just mentioned, as in Lk 22:7. On this word, see "slaughter" in Act 10:13.
14. This is an idiom, more literally, "where do You want *that*, having gone, we should prepare".
15. Passover could only be celebrated within the city of Jerusalem, based on Deut 16:5-7.
16. That is, a jar or jug made of clay. These were normally carried by women. Elsewhere only in Lk 22:10. GK *3040.*
17. Same word as in Lk 22:11.
18. Same word as in Mt 21:8; Mk 11:8; Lk 22:12. Elsewhere only as "making-a-bed" in Act 9:34. GK *5143.*
19. This adjective means "prepared, ready". Used 17 times. GK *2289.* Related to the verb next, which is used 40 times, GK *2286.*
20. Parallel account at Mt 26:20; Lk 22:14; Jn 13:2.
21. That is, one of the very ones eating with Me. Jesus is alluding to Ps 41:9. Compare Lk 22:21.
22. This idiom, "one by one" is also in Jn 8:9, and elsewhere only as "each one" in Rev 4:8. Related to "individually" in Eph 5:33.
23. The grammar indicates a "no" answer is expected. Some manuscripts add "And another *said*, '*It is* not I, *is it?*'" {N}, perhaps referring to Judas as in Mt 26:25.
24. Some manuscripts say "And the *One*, having responded, said" {K}.
25. This does not identify Judas individually, but one of the twelve. It restates v 18. Elsewhere only in Mt 26:23. GK *1835.*
26. Jesus uses grammar that emphasizes the contrast between the two halves of this sentence.
27. Compare also 1 Cor 11:23-25.
28. Some manuscripts say "Jesus having taken" {N}.
29. Or, "*God*". See Mt 14:19 on this.
30. Some manuscripts add "eat" {N}, so that it says, "Take, eat", as in Mt 26:26.
31. On this word, see Mt 26:26.
32. On this word, see 1 Jn 1:7. That is, the sacrificial blood offered to inaugurate the covenant. The phrase "blood of the covenant" is also in Mt 26:28; Heb 9:20; 10:29; 13:20. Note also Lk 22:20; 1 Cor 11:25.
33. On this word, see Heb 8:6. Some manuscripts say "new covenant" {A}.
34. Some manuscripts omit "no longer", so that it says "I will never drink..." {C}.
35. Or, "product". On this word, see Mt 26:29.
36. Some think Jesus means the still future Messianic kingdom. Others think He means the time between the resurrection and ascension.
37. Parallel account at Mt 26:30. Compare Lk 22:31, 39; Jn 13:38.
38. Same word as in Mt 26:30.

A. Lk 18:5 B. Mt 5:18 C. 1 Cor 15:1 D. 2 Tim 4:2 E. Mt 26:13 F. Jn 6:71 G. Mt 26:21, hand over H. 2 Cor 13:11 J. 1 Jn 2:25 K. Mt 25:27 L. Phil 2:21 M. Jn 18:28 N. Mk 3:14, send out O. Mt 20:1 P. 1 Tim 6:15 Q. 2 Cor 7:9 R. 1 Tim 5:10a, good S. 1 Jn 2:29 T. Lk 6:28 U. Act 2:46 V. Mt 26:27 W. Mt 26:28 X. Heb 8:13

1C. And Jesus says *to* them that "You will all be caused-to-fall[1], because it has been written [in 27
Zech 13:7], 'I will strike the Shepherd[A], and the sheep will be scattered[B]'. °But after I am 28
raised[C], I will go ahead of you to Galilee"
2C. But Peter said *to* Him, "Even though[2] all will be caused to fall, nevertheless, I *will* not" 29
3C. And Jesus says *to* him[3], "Truly I say *to* you, that you, today, *on* this night, before *a* rooster 30
crows twice[4]— you will deny[D] Me three-times"
4C. But the *one* was saying emphatically[5], "If I have-to[6] die-with[E] You, I will never deny You" 31
5C. And they all were also speaking similarly

5B.[7] And they come to *a* place *of* which the name *is* Gethsemane[8]. And He says *to* His disciples, "Sit 32
here while[9] I pray"

1C. And He takes along Peter and James and John with Him. And He began to be alarmed[10] and 33
distressed[F]. °And He says *to* them, "My soul is deeply-grieved[G], to the point of death. Stay[H] 34
here and keep-watching[11]"
2C. And having gone ahead *a* little, He was falling on the ground, and praying[J] that if it is possible, 35
the hour might pass from Him. °And He was saying, "Abba[12]! Father! All *things are* possible 36
for You. Remove[13] this cup from Me. But not what **I** want[K], but what You *want*"

1D. And He comes and finds them sleeping[L]. And He says *to* Peter, "Simon, are you sleeping? 37
Were you[14] not strong-*enough*[15] to keep watch *for* one hour? °Keep watching, and be praying 38
that[16] you may not come into temptation[17]. The **spirit**[18] *is* willing[M]— but the flesh *is* weak"[19]

3C. And having gone away again, He prayed, having spoken the same thing[20] 39

1D. And again having come, He found them sleeping. For their eyes were being very- 40
weighed-down[21]. And they did not know what they should answer Him

4C. And He comes the third-*time*, and says *to* them, "Are you sleeping[L] and resting[N] from now on?[22] 41
It is enough[23]. The hour came. Behold— the Son *of* Man is being handed-over[O] into the hands
of the sinners. °Arise, let us be going[P]. Behold— the *one* handing Me over has drawn-near[Q]" 42
5C. And immediately[R], while He *is* still speaking, Judas— one *of* the twelve— arrives. And with 43
him *is a* crowd from[24] the chief priests and the scribes and the elders with swords[S] and clubs[T]
6C. Now the *one* handing Him over had given *a* signal *to* them, saying, "Whomever I kiss is He. 44
Seize Him, and lead *Him* away securely[25]". °And having come, having immediately gone to 45
Him, He says "Rabbi[26]". And he kissed[27] Him
7C. And the *ones* put *their* hands on Him and seized[U] Him 46
8C. And *a* certain[28] one *of* the *ones* standing near, having drawn[29] *his* sword, hit the slave[V] *of* the 47
high priest, and took-off[30] his ear[31]
9C. And having responded, Jesus said *to* them, "Did you come out to arrest[W] Me with swords and 48
clubs as-*if* against *a* robber[X]? °Daily I was with you in the temple teaching, and you did not 49
seize[U] Me. But *this is* in order that the Scriptures might be fulfilled"
10C. And having left[32] Him, they all fled 50
11C. And *a* certain young-man[33] was following[34] Him, having put-on *a* linen-cloth[35] over *his* naked[Y] 51
body. And they[36] seize[U] him. °But the *one*, having left-behind[Z] the linen-cloth, fled[37] naked 52

6B.[38] And they led Jesus away to the high priest. And all the chief priests and the elders and the scribes 53
come together. °And Peter followed Him at *a* distance, as far as inside in the courtyard *of* the high 54
priest. And he was sitting-together with the officers[39], and warming *himself* toward the light [of
the fire]

1. Same word as in v 29. On this word, see 1 Cor 8:13. Some manuscripts add "in connection with Me during this night" {N}, as in Mt 26:31.
2. More literally, "If even all will...". Peter is not questioning whether they will fall (as in "even if" they fall). The grammar of this idiom (see 1 Cor 7:21) means "Assuming that even all will fall as You say, nevertheless, I will not".
3. This is the second warning given to Peter, as in Mt 26:34. The first warning was given in the upper room, Lk 22:34; Jn 13:38.
4. Some manuscripts omit this word {C}, as in Mt 26:34; Lk 22:34; Jn 13:38.
5. Or, "insistently". Used only here. GK *1735*. Some manuscripts say "more emphatically" {K}.
6. On this idiom, see "must" in Mt 16:21.
7. Parallel account at Mt 26:36; Lk 22:40; Jn 18:1.
8. On this word, see Mt 26:36.
9. Or, "until". GK *2401*.
10. Or, "anxious, troubled". Compare Ps 22. On this word, see "struck with wonder" in 9:15.
11. Same word as in v 37, 38; Mt 26:38. On this word, see 1 Thes 5:6.
12. This is a transliteration of the Aramaic word for "father". The translation into Greek is given next. Elsewhere only in Rom 8:15; Gal 4:6. GK *5*.
13. Same word as in Lk 22:42. Compare Jn 12:27.
14. This is singular, referring to Peter. In Mt 26:40, it is plural.
15. Same word as in Mt 26:40.
16. Or, "keep watching and praying, in order that...", depending on whether this is the content or the purpose of the prayer.
17. Or, "testing". On the meaning of this, see Mt 26:41.
18. Jesus uses grammar that emphasizes the contrast between the two halves of this sentence.
19. On the meaning of this, see Mt 26:44.
20. See Mt 26:49 on the meaning of this.
21. They were "very heavy". Used only here. GK *2852*. Related to the word in Mt 26:43.
22. Or, "Sleep and rest...". On this response by Jesus, see Mt 26:45.
23. The exact nuance of this exclamation is uncertain. Some think it means "Enough of this sleeping!"; others, "I am finished praying", v 32; others, "This is a sufficient rebuke"; others, "The time is up". There are other views. GK *600*.
24. This word (GK *4123*) is not the same word as Mt 26:47 (GK *608*).
25. Or, "safely". On this word, see Act 16:23.
26. Some manuscripts say "Rabbi, Rabbi" {N}. On this word, see Mt 23:7.
27. On "kiss" in v 44 and "kissed" here, see Mt 26:48-49.
28. Some manuscripts omit "*a* certain" {C}. That is, Peter, Jn 18:10.
29. Elsewhere only in Act 16:27. GK *5060*. Related to "withdraw" in Mt 26:51.
30. That is, he cut it off. Same word as in Mt 26:51; Lk 22:50. Elsewhere only as "take away" in Lk 1:25; 10:42; 16:3; Rom 11:27; Heb 10:4; and "take" in Rev 22:19. GK *904*.
31. Elsewhere only in Jn 18:10. GK *6064*. Related to the word in Mt 26:51.
32. Same word as in Mt 26:56.
33. This one is distinguished from "they all" who fled (v 49), so he is not one of the eleven. This incident is mentioned only in Mark, and some think he is referring to himself here, or to an eyewitness known to him. Some think this person came from a nearby house upon hearing the commotion.
34. Or, "following with, accompanying, following closely". Same word as in 5:37. Elsewhere only as "accompany" in Lk 23:49. GK *5258*.
35. Some think Mark means a linen garment; others, a sheet. Elsewhere only in v 52, and of the "linen cloth" used to wrap the body of Christ, Mt 27:59; Mk 15:46; Lk 23:53. GK *4984*.
36. Some manuscripts say "the young men" {N}.
37. Some manuscripts add "from them" {N}.
38. Parallel account at Mt 26:57; Lk 22:54; Jn 18:12.
39. Same word as in v 65.

A. Eph 4:11   B. Mt 25:24   C. Mt 28:6   D. Mt 16:24   E. 2 Cor 7:3, die together   F. Phil 2:26   G. Mt 26:38   H. Jn 15:4, abide   J. 1 Tim 2:8   K. Jn 7:17, willing   L. 1 Thes 5:10   M. Rom 1:15, eager   N. Phm 7, refreshed   O. Mt 26:21   P. Mk 1:38   Q. Lk 21:28   R. Mk 6:25   S. Eph 6:17   T. 1 Pet 2:24, cross   U. Heb 4:14, hold on to   V. Rom 6:17   W. Lk 2:21, conceived   X. Mt 21:13   Y. Jam 2:15   Z. Act 6:2

Mark 14:55		Verse

1C. Now the chief priests and the whole Sanhedrin were seeking^A testimony^B against Jesus, so that *they might* put Him to death^C. And they were not finding *it* — 55

    1D. For many were giving-false-testimony¹ against Him. And the testimonies^B were not identical² — 56

    2D. And some, having stood up, were giving false testimony against Him, saying °that "**We** heard Him saying that '**I** will tear down^D this temple made-by-*human*-hands^E, and in three days I will build another not-made-by-*human*-hands³' ". °And not even thus⁴ was their testimony^B identical — 57-58, 59

    3D. And the high priest, having stood up into *the* middle^F, questioned^G Jesus, saying, "Are You not answering anything? What *is it* these *ones* are testifying against You?"⁵ — 60

        1E. But the *One* was being silent^H. And He did not answer anything — 61

    4D. Again the high priest was questioning^G Him. And he says *to* Him, "Are **You** the Christ, the Son *of* the Blessed^J *One*?"

        1E. And Jesus said, "**I** am. And you will see the Son *of* Man sitting on *the* right *side of* the Power⁶, and coming with the clouds *of* heaven"⁷ — 62

    5D. And the high priest, having torn^K his clothes, says "What further need do we have *of* witnesses? °You heard the blasphemy^L. What appears^M right *to* you?" — 63, 64

    6D. And the *ones* all condemned^N Him to be subject-to-death^O

    7D. And some⁸ began to spit-on⁹ Him, and to cover¹⁰ His face and beat¹¹ Him and say *to* Him, "Prophesy!" And the officers¹² received¹³ Him *with* slaps^P — 65

2C. And Peter being below in the courtyard^Q— — 66

    1D. One *of* the servant-girls^R *of* the high priest comes. °And having seen Peter warming *himself*, having looked at him, she says, "**You** also were with the *One* from-Nazareth^S, Jesus" — 67

        1E. But the *one* denied^T *it*, saying, "I neither know^U nor understand^V what **you** are saying" — 68

    2D. And he went outside to the entryway¹⁴. And *a* rooster crowed¹⁵. °And the¹⁶ servant-girl^R having seen him began again¹⁷ to say *to* the *ones* standing near that "This *one* is *one* of them" — 69

        1E. But the *one* was again denying^T *it* — 70

    3D. And after *a* little *while*, again the *ones* standing near were saying *to* Peter, "Truly¹⁸ you are *one* of them, for you also are *a* Galilean"¹⁹

        1E. But the *one* began to curse²⁰, and to swear-with-an-oath²¹ that "I do not know^U this man Whom you are saying" — 71

    4D. And immediately²² *a* rooster crowed for *a* second-*time*²³. And Peter remembered the word, how Jesus said *to* him that "Before *a* rooster crows twice²⁴, you will deny^W Me three-times". And having put *his* mind upon²⁵ *it*, he was weeping²⁶ — 72

7B.²⁷ And immediately, early-in-the-morning²⁸, the chief priests (with the elders and scribes) and the whole Sanhedrin having made *a* consultation²⁹, having bound^X Jesus, took *Him* away³⁰, and handed *Him* over *to* Pilate^Y — 15:1

1. Elsewhere only in v 57; Mt 19:18; Mk 10:19; Lk 18:20. GK *6018*. Related to "false testimony" in Mt 26:60.
2. Or, "equal". Same word as in v 59. On this word, see "equal" in Phil 2:6.
3. Same word as in 2 Cor 5:1. Elsewhere only as "not done by human hands" in Col 2:11. GK *942*. Related to the previous word.
4. That is, not even in their false accusations. Compare Mt 26:61; Jn 2:19.
5. Or, this could be a single question, "Are you not answering anything *as to* what these *ones* are testifying against You?" Compare Mt 26:62.
6. That is, of God. Same word as in Mt 26:64.
7. Jesus is claiming to be the fulfillment of the Messianic prophecies in Ps 110:1; Dan 7:13.
8. Compare Lk 22:63. Some think the "some" is some of the leaders, the Sanhedrin; others, some of the ones holding Jesus, who handed Him over to the officers.
9. Same word as in Mk 10:34; 15:19; Lk 18:32. Elsewhere only as "spit" in Mt 26:67; 27:30. GK *1870*. Related word in Mk 7:33.
10. Same word as in Lk 22:64, where "His face" is not stated as here.
11. That is, to strike or box with the fist. On this word, see 1 Cor 4:11.
12. That is, the temple police. On this word, see Jn 18:12.
13. Or, "took". Some manuscripts have a different word, rendered "struck" by the KJV {N}.
14. Or, "gateway, forecourt". Used only here. GK *4580*.
15. Some manuscripts omit "And *a* rooster crowed" {C}.
16. Some think Mark means "the same one" as in v 67; others, the one who was there in that area.
17. The "again" goes with what follows, "she again (for the second time) began to say", just as in v 70 the ones there "again (for the third time) were saying".
18. Or, "really". On this word, see Mt 14:33.
19. Some manuscripts add "And your speech is like *one*" {N}.
20. That is, to bind himself under a curse, "May I be under a curse if I know the man". Elsewhere only as "bind under a curse" in Act 23:12, 14, 21. GK *354*. Related to "accursed" in Rom 9:3; and to "curse" in Mt 26:74.
21. Same word as in Mt 26:74.
22. Some manuscripts omit this word {N}.
23. Some manuscripts omit "for a second-*time*" {B}.
24. Some manuscripts omit this word {B}.
25. That is, having thought about it. The exact nuance of this verb "to put on" is not clear here. Or, "And having begun", that is, having put *himself* on it. Or, "And having put *his hands* on *his face*". Or, "And having put on *his cloak*". Or, "having pulled *his cloak* over *his head*". Or, "having thrown *himself* over". Same verb as "put on" in v 46; Mt 9:16; Jn 7:30; "throw on" in 1 Cor 7:35; and "throw over" in Mk 4:37. Used 18 times. GK *2095*. There are other views.
26. Some manuscripts say "he wept". Others replace the whole sentence with "And he began to weep" {B}. On this word, see Jn 11:33.
27. Parallel account at Mt 27:1, 11; Lk 22:66; 23:1; Jn 18:28.
28. Perhaps before 6 A.M. Same word as in Jn 18:28. On this word, see "early morning" in 13:35.
29. This phrase "made *a* consultation" is used only here. Or, it may refer to the result of a deliberation, a "plan, decision, plot". Matthew uses this word five times in the phrase "took counsel" (see Mt 12:14). Luke uses this word to mean "council" in Act 25:12. Elsewhere only in Mk 3:6 in the phrase "give counsel". GK *5206*. Here, some think Mark means "held a council meeting", a second meeting early the next morning; others, "passed a resolution" condemning Jesus at such a meeting. Related to "counselor" in Rom 11:34, and "counseled" in Jn 18:14.
30. Or, "led *Him* away". On this word, "took away", see "carry forth" in 1 Cor 16:3. Mt 27:2 says "led away", using the word Mark uses in v 16 (GK *552*).

A. Phil 2:21 B. Jn 1:7 C. Rom 7:4, put to death D. Mt 24:2 E. Act 17:24 F. 2 Thes 2:7, midst G. Lk 9:18 H. Mk 4:39, be still J. Rom 9:5 K. Lk 8:29 L. 1 Tim 6:4 M. Phil 2:15, shine N. 1 Cor 11:32 O. Mt 26:66 P. Jn 18:22 Q. Mt 26:3 R. Jn 18:17 S. Mk 1:24 T. 2 Tim 2:12 U. 1 Jn 2:29 V. Act 18:25, know about W. Mt 16:24 X. 1 Cor 7:27 Y. Lk 3:1

| Mark 15:2 | 168 | Verse |

- 1C. And Pilate questioned[A] Him, "Are **You** the King *of* the Jews?" — 2
    - 1D. And the *One*, having responded *to* him, says "**You** are saying *it*"[1]
- 2C. And the chief priests were accusing[B] Him *as to* many *things* — 3
    - 1D. And Pilate again was questioning Him, saying, "Are You not answering anything? Look how many *things* they are accusing[B] You" — 4
    - 2D. But Jesus no longer answered anything, so that Pilate *was* marveling[C] — 5
- 3C. Now at *the* Feast[D], he was [in the habit of] releasing[2] *for* them one prisoner[E] whom they were requesting[F]. °And the *one* being called Barabbas[3] had been bound[4] with the rebels[5] who[6] had committed[G] murder[H] in the rebellion[7] — 6, 7
    - 1D. And having come up[8], the crowd began to ask *him to do* as he was [in the habit of] doing[9] *for* them — 8
    - 2D. And Pilate responded *to* them, saying "Do you want me to release[10] the King *of* the Jews *for* you?" — 9
        - 1E. For he knew that the chief priests had handed Him over because of envy[11] — 10
    - 3D. But the chief priests stirred-up[12] the crowd in order that he might release Barabbas *for* them instead — 11
    - 4D. And Pilate, again having responded, was saying *to* them "Then what do you want me to do[13] *as to* the *One* whom you call[14] the King *of* the Jews?" — 12
        - 1E. And the *ones* cried-out[J] again[15], "Crucify[K] Him!" — 13
    - 5D. But Pilate was saying *to* them, "What indeed[16] did He do wrong?"[17] — 14
        - 1E. But the *ones* cried out even more, "Crucify Him!"
- 4C. And Pilate, wanting[L] to do enough[18] *for* the crowd, released Barabbas *for* them, and handed-over[M] Jesus, having flogged[N] *Him*, in order that He might be crucified — 15

- 8B.[19] And the soldiers[O] led Him away inside the palace[P] (that is, *the* Praetorium[Q]). And they call together the whole [Roman] cohort[R] — 16
    - 1C. And they dress Him in *a* purple[20] *cloak*. And having woven *a* crown[S] made-of-thorns[21], they set *it* on Him — 17
        - 1D. And they began to greet[22] Him, "Hail[23], King *of* the Jews!" — 18
        - 2D. And they were striking[T] His head *with a* staff[U], and spitting-on[V] Him — 19
        - 3D. And while putting-down[W] *their* knees, they were paying-homage[X] *to* Him
        - 4D. And when they mocked[Y] Him, they stripped[Z] the purple *cloak* off Him, and put His[24] garments on Him — 20
    - 2C.[25] And they lead Him out in order that they might crucify Him. °And they press-into-service[26] *a* certain *one* passing by, coming from *the* country[27]— Simon,[28] *a* Cyrenian, the father *of* Alexander and Rufus[29]— in order that he might take up His cross — 21

1. On this answer, see Mt 27:11.
2. The grammar of this verb in this context refers to what Pilate was in the habit of doing, what was his custom to do. Note how Matthew says it in 27:15.
3. Barabbas is mentioned elsewhere only in Mt 27:16, 17, 20, 21, 26; Mk 15:11, 15; Lk 23:18; Jn 18:40. GK 972. Note also Act 3:14.
4. This is a participle, he "was having been bound". On this word, see 1 Cor 7:27.
5. Or, "revolutionaries, insurrectionists, rioters". Used only here. GK 5086. Related to "rebellion" later in the verse. Luke indicates that Barabbas was part of this group, Lk 23:19. Matthew calls him "notorious", 27:16. Some think he was their leader. Some manuscripts have the related verb "the *ones* having rebelled" {N}.
6. This word is plural, referring to all these rebels.
7. Or, "insurrection, revolt, uprising, sedition, riot". Same word as in Lk 23:19, 25. We do not know the details of the rebellion to which Mark refers. On this word, see "dispute" in Act 23:7.
8. Some manuscripts say "having cried out" {B}.
9. This picks up from v 6.
10. This is an idiom, more literally, "do you want *that* I should release...". On this word, see "sends away" in Mt 5:31.
11. Or, "jealousy". Same word as in Mt 27:18; Rom 1:29; Gal 5:21; Phil 1:15; 1 Tim 6:4; Tit 3:3. Elsewhere only as "jealousy" in Jam 4:5; 1 Pet 2:1. GK 5784.
12. Or, "shook up". Elsewhere only in Lk 23:5, where the Jewish leaders accused Jesus of it. GK 411. Related to "earthquake".
13. This is an idiom, literally, "what do you want *that* I should do". Some manuscripts omit "do you want", so that it says "What then should I do..." {C}.
14. Some manuscripts omit "*the one* whom you call" {C}, so that it says "do *as to* the King...".
15. Or, cried "back", as this word is used in Jn 18:40. If Mark means "again", then the first cry is implied in v 11. It would have been "Barabbas!", as in Mt 27:21. This word means "again, back, anew", and is used 141 times. GK 4099.
16. On this word, see Mt 27:23.
17. What crime did He commit? On this question, see Mt 27:23.
18. Or, "sufficient". This phrase, "to do enough", is an idiom meaning "to please, to satisfy, to content the crowd, to do what is sufficient to placate the crowd". It is used only here. On this word, see "sufficient" in 2 Cor 3:5.
19. Parallel account at Mt 27:27. Compare Jn 19:2-3.
20. Same word as in v 20. Used of the Roman soldier's cloak, and of fine purple clothing, Lk 16:19. Elsewhere only of purple cloth, Rev 18:12. GK 4525.
21. Elsewhere only in Jn 19:5. GK 181.
22. This word is used of giving appropriate greetings, salutations, words of welcome upon arrival, and farewells upon leaving. Here, the soldiers mockingly greet Jesus as a king. Same word as in Act 25:13; and as in Mt 5:47; 9:15; 10:12; Lk 1:40; 10:4, its only other uses in the Gospels. It is used 59 times in the NT, all rendered "greet" except for "say farewell" in Act 20:1. GK 832.
23. Or, "Greetings, Welcome". On this word, see Mt 27:29. Not related to the previous word.
24. Some manuscripts say "*His* own" {N}.
25. Parallel account at Mt 27:31; Lk 23:26; Jn 19:16.
26. Same word as in Mt 27:32.
27. Or, "field". GK 69.
28. Because Simon is so explicitly named, which is unusual for Mark (see 10:46), some think that he or his sons were or became known to Mark.
29. Some think this is the same person mentioned in Rom 16:13.

A. Lk 9:18 B. Jn 5:45 C. Rev 17:8 D. Jn 13:29 E. Eph 3:1 F. Heb 12:25, refuse G. Rev 13:13, does H. Act 9:1 J. Mt 8:29 K. Mt 27:35 L. Jam 1:18, willed M. Mt 26:21 N. Mt 27:26 O. Mt 28:12 P. Mt 26:3, courtyard Q. Phil 1:13 R. Mt 27:27 S. Rev 4:4 T. Lk 6:29 U. Mk 15:36, stick V. Mk 14:65 W. Act 19:21, put X. Mt 14:33, worship Y. Lk 23:11 Z. 2 Cor 5:3, take off

	3C. And they bring Him to the Golgotha[1] place, which being translated[A] is "*The* Place *of a* Skull[B]".	22
	And they were giving wine having been mixed-with-myrrh[2] *to* Him[3], but *the* One[4] did not take *it*	23
	4C. And they crucify[C] Him, and divide[D] His garments among *themselves*[5], casting *a* lot[E] for them *to decide* who should take what. °And it was *the* third[6] hour, and they crucified Him	24 25
	5C. And the inscription *of* His charge[F] had been inscribed[7]— "The King *of* the Jews"	26
	6C. And they crucify two robbers[8] with Him— one on *the* right *side* and one on His left *side*	27 28[9]
	7C. And the *ones* passing by were blaspheming[G] Him while shaking[H] their heads and saying, "Ha! The *One* tearing-down[J] the temple and building *it* in three days— °save[K] Yourself, having come down[10] from the cross"	29 30
	8C. Likewise also the chief priests, mocking[L] *Him* to one another with the scribes, were saying	31
	1D. "He saved others— Himself He is not able to save!	
	2D. "Let the Christ, the King *of* Israel, come down now from the cross, that we may see and believe"	32
	9C. And the *ones* having been crucified with Him were reproaching[M] Him	
	10C.[11] And having become *the* sixth[12] hour, *a* darkness[N] came over the whole land[O] until *the* ninth hour	33
	1D. And *at* the ninth hour Jesus shouted[13] *with a* loud voice, "Eloi, Eloi, lema[14] sabachthani?", which being translated[A] is "My God, My God, for what *purpose*[15] did You forsake[P] Me?"	34
	1E. And some *of* the *ones* standing near, having heard, were saying, "Look— He is calling Elijah"	35
	2E. And someone— having run, and[16] having filled[17] *a* sponge *of* sour-wine[Q], having put *it* on *a* stick[18]— was giving-a-drink *to* Him, saying, "Leave *Him alone*[19]. Let us see if Elijah comes to take Him down"	36
	2D. And Jesus, having let-go[20] *a* loud shout[21], expired[22]	37
	3D. And the curtain[23] *of* the temple was torn[R] in two from top to bottom	38
	4D. And the centurion[24] standing-by from opposite Him, having seen that[25] He expired in this manner, said, "Truly[26] this man was God's Son[27]!"	39
	11C. And women were also watching at *a* distance, among whom *were*	40
	1D. Both Mary the Magdalene[28] and Mary[29] the mother *of* James the little[30] and Joses, and Salome[31]— °who[32], when He was in Galilee, were following Him and serving[S] Him	41
	2D. And many other *women* having come up with Him to Jerusalem	
9B.[33]	And having already become evening[34], because it was Preparation[35] *day* (that is, the-day-before-the-Sabbath[36]), °Joseph from Arimathea[T] having come— *a* prominent council-member[37] who also himself was waiting-for[U] the kingdom[V] *of* God— having become daring[38], went in to Pilate and asked-*for* the body *of* Jesus	42 43
	1C. But Pilate wondered[W] whether He was[39] dead by-this-time[X]. And having summoned the centurion, he asked him whether He died already[40]. °And having come-to-know[Y] *it* from the centurion, he granted[41] the corpse[42] *to* Joseph	44 45
	2C. And having bought linen-cloth[Z], having taken Him down, he wrapped *Him* in[43] the linen cloth, and laid Him in *a* tomb which had been hewn[44] out of rock[AA]. And he rolled[45] *a* stone against[46] the door *of* the tomb	46

1. This is a transliterated Aramaic word, whose Greek equivalent is next given. On this word, see Mt 27:33.
2. This was to dull the senses. Used only here. GK *5046*.
3. Some manuscripts add "to drink" {N}.
4. This idiom is used only here, and in a variant of Jn 5:11. Some manuscripts say "but the *One*" {N}, as often in Mark, and as in Jn 5:11. GK *4005*.
5. On "divide among *themselves*", see Mt 27:35.
6. That is, 9 A.M., Jewish time. Compare Jn 19:14.
7. This is a participle, it "was having been inscribed".
8. Not the same word used of the "rebels" in v 7. However, some think these two were part of that group. Same word as in Mt 27:38. On this word, see Mt 21:13.
9. Some manuscripts add as v 28, "And the Scripture saying 'And He was counted with lawless *ones*' was fulfilled" {A}, as in Lk 22:37.
10. Some manuscripts have this as a command, "come down" {K}.
11. Parallel account at Mt 27:45; Lk 23:44; Jn 19:28.
12. The sixth hour would be noon, the ninth, 3 P.M.
13. On this word, see Mt 3:3. Related to "shouted-out" in Mt 27:46.
14. This entire phrase is transliterated from Aramaic, whereas Mt 27:46 is a mix of Hebrew and Aramaic. However, some manuscripts say "lama" here, which is transliterated from Hebrew {N}.
15. This idiom "for what *purpose*" is elsewhere only in 14:4; Mt 14:31; 26:8. Not the same word as in Mt 27:46, but the same idea. Jesus is quoting Ps 22:1. In some unfathomable way, the One receiving judgment for our sin experiences a previously unknown kind of separation from the Father, and cries out to Him.
16. Some manuscripts omit this word {C}.
17. On this word, see 4:37. Not the same word as in Mt 27:48 (GK *4398*).
18. Or, "branch". This word means "reed, branch" and anything made from it. Same word as in Mt 27:48. Elsewhere only as "reed" in Mt 11:7; 12:20; Lk 7:24; "staff" (walking stick) in Mt 27:29, 30; Mk 15:19; "reed-pen" in 3 Jn 13; and measuring "rod" in Rev 11:1; 21:15, 16. GK *2812*.
19. This command, "Leave *alone*", is plural, spoken by the one giving Jesus the drink to unnamed ones around him. Compare the similar command in Mt 27:49. In both places, others render this as an exclamation, "Hold off", or, "Wait". Others combine this and "Let us see" into one expression, "Let us see". Here, some think a bystander giving Jesus a drink is telling the other mocking bystanders to leave Him alone and see what happens. Others think it is spoken to the soldiers by a bystander, "Permit [me to give Him a drink]. Let us see...". There are other views.
20. Same word as in Mt 27:50, "let go His spirit". GK *918*.
21. Or, "voice". Same word as "voice" in Mt 27:50; Lk 23:46. GK *5889*. Jesus did not unconsciously succumb to death, He gave up His life after a strong shout. On what Jesus shouted, see Jn 19:30; Lk 23:46.
22. Or, "breathed out *His last*". That is, He died. Elsewhere only in v 39 and Lk 23:46. GK *1743*. Related to "breath". Compare the word in Act 5:5.
23. On which curtain, see Mt 27:51.
24. This is transliterated from the Latin. Our word "centurion" comes from this word, *kenturion*. Elsewhere only in v 44, 45. GK *3035*. The usual Greek word for "centurion" (not used by Mark) is in Mt 27:54.
25. Some manuscripts say "having seen that having cried out, He expired..." {C}. Compare Mt 27:54.
26. Or, "really". On this word, see Mt 14:33.
27. The centurion could mean "a divine person", as the Romans used this phrase. Or, he could be expressing a genuine faith. The words do not make explicit what was in his heart.
28. She was from the town of Magdala, on the Sea of Galilee. See Lk 8:2 on her.
29. Some think this is Mary the wife of Clopas. See Jn 19:25.
30. Mark could mean "the small" (physically), or "the young". This nickname only occurs here. Compare Mt 27:56; Jn 19:25. GK *3625*.
31. If this is the same person as in Mt 27:56, then this is the name of the mother of the sons of Zebedee, James and John. See Jn 19:25. Mentioned elsewhere only in 16:1. GK *4897*.
32. That is, the two Marys and Salome.
33. Parallel account at Mt 27:57; Lk 23:50; Jn 19:38.
34. That is, the first evening, between 3 and 6 P.M., as seen also in Mt 14:15.
35. That is, Friday, the day to prepare for the Sabbath when no work could be done. On this word, see Jn 19:31.
36. Or, "Sabbath-eve". Used only here. GK *4640*.
37. That is, a member of the Sanhedrin. Elsewhere only in Lk 23:50. GK *1085*.
38. Or, "having dared, having become courageous, having become bold". The secret disciple (Jn 19:38), "summons the courage" to do this. On this word, see "dare" in 2 Cor 11:21.
39. More literally, "is", as the Greek typically phrases it.
40. Or, "some time ago, in the past, formerly". On this word, see "formerly" in Jude 4. Some manuscripts instead have the same word used earlier in the verse, "by this time" {B}, in which case both would be rendered "already".
41. Or, "bestowed". Related to "gift". Pilate gave it as a gift, not requiring any money as governors often did for such favors. On this word, see 2 Pet 1:3.
42. Elsewhere only in Mt 14:12; 24:28; Mk 6:29; Rev 11:8, 9. GK *4773*. Some manuscripts say "body" {N}.
43. This word, "to wrap in" something, is used only here. GK *1912*. Related to "wrapping, bandaging" (not in NT).
44. This is a participle, it "was having been hewn". Elsewhere only in Mt 27:60. GK *3300*.
45. Same word as in Mt 27:60.
46. Or, "to, over, across, upon". GK *2093*.

A. Act 13:8 B. Mt 27:33 C. Mt 27:35 D. Act 2:3 E. Col 1:12, share F. Jn 18:38 G. 1 Tim 6:1 H. Rev 2:5, move J. Mt 24:2 K. Lk 19:10 L. Lk 23:11 M. 1 Pet 4:14 N. Jn 3:19 O. Rev 7:1 P. 2 Cor 4:9 Q. Mt 27:48 R. Mt 27:51 S. 1 Pet 4:10, ministering T. Mt 27:57 U. Act 24:15 V. Mt 3:2 W. Rev 17:8, caused to marvel X. Mt 24:32, already Y. Lk 1:34 Z. Mk 14:51 AA. Mt 7:24, bed-rock

| Mark 15:47 | 172 | Verse |

      3C. And Mary the Magdalene and Mary the *mother of* Joses were observing where He had[1] been laid   47

8A.[2] And the Sabbath having passed[3], Mary the Magdalene, and Mary the *mother of* James, and Salome, bought[A] spices[4] in order that having come, they might anoint[5] Him   16:1

    1B. And very early-in-the-morning[6] *on* the first *day of* the week, they come[7] to the tomb[B]— the sun having risen[8]   2

        1C. And they were saying to themselves, "Who will roll-away the stone[9] from the door[C] *of* the tomb *for* us?" *And having looked-up[D], they see that the stone has been rolled-away   3 / 4

            1D. For it was extremely large

        2C. And having entered into the tomb, they saw *a* young-man[E] sitting at the right, having been clothed-with *a* white[F] robe[G]   5
        3C. And they were alarmed[H]. *But the *one* says *to* them, "Do not be alarmed. You are seeking[J] Jesus from-Nazareth[K], the *One* having been crucified. He arose[L], He is not here   6

            1D. "Look— the place where they laid Him!
            2D. "But go, tell His disciples and Peter that 'He is going-ahead-of[M] you to Galilee. You will see Him there, just as He told[10] you' "   7

        4C. And having gone out, they fled[N] from the tomb[11]   8

            1D. For trembling[O] and astonishment[P] was holding them
            2D. And they said nothing *to* anyone, for they were fearing[12]

[Most Greek manuscripts[13] have this "long ending" after verse 8]

    2B. And [Jesus] having risen-up[Q] early-in-the-morning[14] *on* the first[15] *day of the* week   9

        1C.[16] He appeared[R] first[17] *to* Mary the Magdalene, from whom He had cast-out[S] seven demons[18]

            1D. That *one*[19], having gone, reported[T] *it to* the *ones* having been with Him, while *they were* mourning[U] and weeping[V]   10
            2D. And-those-*ones*[20], having heard that He was[21] alive[W] and was seen by her, did not-believe[22] *her*   11

        2C. And after these *things*, He appeared[X] in *a* different[Y] form[23] *to* two of them walking, while *they were* proceeding into *the* country   12

            1D. And those *ones*, having gone, reported[T] *it to* the rest   13
            2D. They did not even believe[Z] those *ones*

        3C.[24] And[25] later He appeared[X] *to* the eleven themselves while *they were* reclining-back [to eat]   14

            1D. And He reproached[26] their unbelief[AA] and hardness-of-heart[27] because they did not believe[Z] the *ones* having seen Him arisen[28]

1. More literally, "has", as the Greek typically phrases it.
2. Parallel account at Mt 28:1; Lk 24:1; Jn 20:1.
3. That is, after sunset on Saturday night (as we call it).
4. Or, "aromatic oils". Elsewhere only in Lk 23:56; 24:1; Jn 19:40; all of this event. GK *808*. Our word "aroma" comes from this Greek word, *aroma*.
5. Used only here of the dead body of Jesus. Same word as in Jn 12:3. On this word, see Jam 5:14.
6. That is, before 6 A.M. On this word, see "early morning" in 13:35.
7. Or, "go". This is the common word meaning "come, go". Same word as v 1, and as "went" in Mt 28:1; Lk 24:1; and "goes" in Jn 20:1. Used 632 times. GK *2262*.
8. That is, when they arrived at the tomb, the sun had risen. GK *422*.
9. This word is used of large stones which it took several or many men to move (such as building stones, millstones and tomb entrance stones like this one); precious stones, jewels; and rocks a person might pick up and throw (as in Jn 8:59). Used 59 times. GK *3345*. Compare "bed-rock" in Mt 7:24.
10. He told them in 14:28.
11. This verse is parallel to Mt 28:8; Lk 24:9.
12. This word is used in this tense only in 10:32, and 6:20; 9:32; 11:18, 32; Lk 9:45; 19:21; 22:2; Jn 9:22; Act 5:26; 9:26. GK *5828*. The word is used 95 times.
13. Some think that this ending was written by Mark, based on the fact that most manuscripts have this ending and on other evidence. Others think the two oldest manuscripts, which omit verses 9-20, along with other evidence, indicate that this ending is not original. This is the view taken by UBS4, which marks this ending as not an original part of Mark's text, but as very ancient. This view suggests that either Mark intended to end at v 8, or he never finished his Gospel, or the last page was lost. Then this ending was composed by someone else and added to Mark's work.
14. That is, before 6 A.M. Same word as in v 2.
15. Used only here with "week". Not the same word as in v 2. Same word as in "first" day of Unleavened Bread, 14:12. GK *4754*. The word "first" in verse 2 (GK *1651*) is the one used in the other six occurrences of "first day of the week" in the NT.
16. Parallel account at Jn 20:11.
17. Some think Mark means "first" in this sequence of three appearances in this book. Others think he means "first" before appearing to anyone else.
18. This fact is also mentioned in Lk 8:2. This is the fourth time Mark has mentioned her, 15:40, 47; 16:1.
19. This word is used in this way only in v 10, 13 and 20 in Mark. It has not been Mark's way of referring to people. John uses it frequently in this way. GK *1697*.
20. This word, which is also in v 13, is used by Jesus in the parable in Mk 12:4, 5. It is used 22 times in the NT. Same word as "that *one*" in v 10, with "and" added as a prefix. GK *2797*. It has not been Mark's normal way of referring to people.
21. More literally, "is", as the Greek typically phrases it.
22. Or, "refused to believe". Same word as in v 16, and Lk 24:11. On this word, see "are faithless" in 2 Tim 2:13. Related to "unbelief" in v 14.
23. Some think Mark means a different form than Jesus had while alive with them. Others think he means a different form than He appeared to Mary— a traveler vs. a gardener. On this word, see Phil 2:6.
24. Parallel account at Lk 24:36; Jn 20:19.
25. Some manuscripts omit this word {C}.
26. Or, "reprimanded". Same word as in 15:32. On this word, see 1 Pet 4:14.
27. Same word as in 10:5. Elsewhere only in Mt 19:8. GK *5016*.
28. Or, "raised, having arisen". This is a participle, "having been raised". That is, after He arose. On this word, see Mt 28:6.

A. Rev 5:9 B. Mt 23:29 C. Col 4:3 D. Act 22:13 E. 1 Jn 2:13 F. Jn 4:35 G. Rev 6:11 H. Mk 9:15, struck with wonder J. Phil 2:21 K. Mk 1:24 L. Mt 28:6 M. 2 Jn 9 N. 1 Cor 6:18 O. Phil 2:12 P. Mk 5:42 Q. Lk 18:33 R. Phil 2:15, shine S. Jn 12:31 T. 1 Jn 1:3, announcing U. Jam 4:9 V. Jn 11:33 W. Rev 20:4, came to life X. 1 Jn 2:19, made evident Y. 1 Cor 12:9 Z. Jn 3:36 AA. 1 Tim 1:13

3B.[1] And[2] He said *to* them, "Having gone into all the world, proclaim[A] the good-news[3] *to* all creation[4] 15

    1C. "The *one* having believed[B] and having been baptized[5] will be saved[C]. But the *one* having not-believed[D] will be condemned[E] 16

    2C. "And these signs[F] will accompany[6] the *ones* having believed[B]. In My name— 17

        1D. "They will cast-out[G] demons
        2D. "They will speak[H] *in*[7] new[8] tongues[J]
        3D. "And they will pick up snakes[9] with *their* hands[10] 18
        4D. "And if they drink any deadly[11] *thing*, it will by-no-means[12] hurt[13] them
        5D. "They will lay[K] hands on sick[14] *ones*, and they will be well[15]"

4B.[16] So indeed the Lord Jesus[17], after *He* spoke *to* them, was taken-up[18] into heaven and sat-*down* on the right *side of* God—*and those *ones*, having gone-forth, proclaimed[L] it everywhere 19
   20

    1C. The Lord working-with[19] *them* and confirming[20] the word[21] by the signs[F] following-after[22] *them*[23]

[A few Greek manuscripts[24] have this "short ending" after verse 8]

    5C. And they promptly[25] reported[26] all the *things* having been commanded[27] them *to* the *ones* around Peter

2B. And after these *things*, Jesus Himself also sent-forth[28] the sacred[M] and imperishable[N] proclamation[O] *of* eternal[P] salvation[29] through them, from *the* east[30] and as-far-as *the* west[31]. Amen

1. Compare Mt 28:16-20; Lk 24:46-49; Jn 20:21-23.
2. Or, this may have been spoken on the first Sunday night, making this point 2D.
3. Or, "gospel". In the four Gospels, the term "the good news" is used alone like this only in Mark. On this word, see 8:35.
4. Or, "*in* all creation, *to* every creature". In any case, this emphasizes the global nature of the command. "All creation" is also in Col 1:15, 23. That is, to every human being. On this word, see Rom 8:39.
5. The words "believe" and "baptize" are used together in this way only here in the NT. In Act 2:38, there is "repent and be baptized" (see also Mk 1:4; Lk 3:3; Act 13:24). Note Jn 4:1, "making and baptizing disciples".
6. Or, "closely follow, follow beside". Elsewhere only as "closely follow" in Lk 1:3; 1 Tim 4:6; 2 Tim 3:10. GK *4158*. The purpose of these signs is seen in v 20, and in Act 14:3; Heb 2:3-4.
7. Or, "*with*". On "tongues", see 1 Cor 12:10. On "in" or "with" tongues, see 1 Cor 14:2.
8. Some manuscripts omit this word {B}. Used with "tongues" only here. On this word, see Heb 8:13.
9. Same word as in Lk 10:19. Compare Act 28:3-6.
10. Some manuscripts say only "They will pick up snakes" {C}.
11. Used only here. GK *2503*. Related to "death".
12. Or, "never", the strongest negative in Greek. On this idiom, see "by any means" in 13:2.
13. Or, "harm, injure". Elsewhere only in Lk 4:35. GK *1055*. Related to "harmful" in 1 Tim 6:9.
14. Same word as in 6:5, 13. Elsewhere only in Mt 14:14; 1 Cor 11:30. GK *779*.
15. This is an idiom, literally, "they will have *it* well". The opposite idiom is in 1:32, "being ill".
16. Parallel account at Lk 24:50; Act 1:9.
17. Some manuscripts omit this word {C}.
18. Same word as in Act 1:2, 11, 22; 1 Tim 3:16. GK *377*.
19. On this word, see "work together" in Rom 8:28.
20. Same word as in Heb 2:3. On this word, see 1 Cor 1:6.
21. Or, "the message". On this word, see 1 Cor 12:8.
22. Or, "authenticating, confirming, concurring". Elsewhere only in 1 Tim 5:10, 24; 1 Pet 2:21. GK *2051*.
23. Some manuscripts add "Amen" {B}.
24. Those Greek manuscripts having this short ending also include verses 9-20 after it. In other words, if they have the short ending, they have both endings. This ending is marked in UBS4 as not an original part of Mark's text, but as very ancient. None consider this ending to be an original part of Mark's Gospel.
25. Or, "briefly, quickly". Elsewhere only as "briefly" in Act 24:4. GK *5339*.
26. Or, "proclaimed, told out". Related to "commanded" later in the verse— they "told out" all the things "having been told" to them. On this word, see 1 Pet 2:9.
27. This word is used 32 times in the NT, but is passive only here. On this word, see 1 Tim 1:3.
28. Same word as in Gal 4:4, 6.
29. The phrase "eternal salvation" is also in Heb 5:9.
30. Or, the "rising" of the sun. On this word, see Mt 2:2.
31. Or, the "setting" of the sun. Used only here in the NT. GK *1550*. Related to "west" in Lk 12:54.

A. 2 Tim 4:2   B. Jn 3:36   C. Lk 19:10   D. 2 Tim 2:13, are faithless   E. 1 Cor 11:32   F. 2 Thes 2:9   G. Jn 12:31   H. Jn 12:49   J. 1 Cor 12:10
K. Lk 10:30, laid on   L. 2 Tim 4:2   M. 2 Tim 3:15   N. 1 Cor 15:52, undecayable   O. 1 Cor 1:21   P. Mt 25:46

Overview	**Luke**

Introduction	1:1-4
1A. In the days of Herod, king of Judea	1:5
1B. Zechariah was told by an angel that Elizabeth would bear a son— John	1:5-25
2B. Mary was told by an angel that she would bear a Son by the Holy Spirit— Jesus	1:26-38
3B. Mary went to Elizabeth and stayed three months. They both praised God	1:39-56
4B. Elizabeth gave birth. Zechariah praised God. John lived in the desolate places	1:57-80
5B. Mary gave birth in Bethlehem. Shepherds rejoiced. Jesus was circumcised	2:1-21
6B. They brought Him to Jerusalem. Simeon and Anna praised God. They return to Nazareth	2:22-39
7B. And the Child was growing and becoming strong. The grace of God was upon Him	2:40
2A. And when He was twelve, they found Him in His Father's temple, listening and questioning	2:41-52
3A. In the fifteenth year of Tiberius, John began to preach and baptize. Jesus came and was baptized	3:1-22
4A. Jesus was about thirty when He began His ministry. His genealogy and temptation	3:23-4:13
5A. Jesus returned to Galilee in the power of the Spirit and began teaching in their synagogues	4:14-15
1B. At Nazareth, He read Isaiah and said, Today this Scripture is fulfilled, enraging them	4:16-30
2B. He went to Capernaum and cast out a demon. At Simon's house, He healed many	4:31-43
3B. At the lake of Gennesaret, He taught from a boat, and directed Simon to a great catch	4:44-5:11
4B. In one of the cities, He healed a leper. News spread more. Large crowds came	5:12-16
5B. On one day He healed a paralytic and forgave him. Pharisees objected. Which is easier?	5:17-26
6B. He called Levi, a tax collector, and ate at his house. Pharisees objected. New wine	5:27-39
7B. Passing through some grainfields, His disciples violated a Sabbath rule of the Pharisees	6:1-5
8B. On another Sabbath, He healed a man. Pharisees were enraged, and discussed what to do	6:6-11
9B. He spent the night in prayer, then chose the twelve, healed and taught	6:12-49
10B. After He finished, He entered Capernaum and healed a centurion's slave	7:1-10
11B. Afterward, He proceeded to Nain and raised a widow's son from his coffin	7:11-17
12B. John the Baptist asked, Are You the One? Tell him what you see. He spoke of John	7:18-35
13B. While eating with some Pharisees, a sinful woman anointed Him. They objected	7:36-50
14B. Afterward, He traveled from city to city. He spoke of the sower. His mother and brother	8:1-21
15B. Crossing the sea, Jesus calmed the winds and the water	8:22-25
16B. In the country of the Gerasenes, Jesus cast demons into a herd of pigs	8:26-39
17B. Returning, He raised Jairus's daughter, healing a woman along the way	8:40-56
18B. He empowered the twelve, and sent them out. Herod hears. On their return, He fed 5000	9:1-17
19B. Who do the crowds say that I am? Who do you say? Take up your cross and follow Me	9:18-27
20B. About eight days later, on a mountain with Peter, John and James, He was transfigured	9:28-36
21B. On the next day, He cast out a demon the disciples could not	9:37-43
22B. He said to His disciples that He must be killed and raised. They did not understand	9:44-45
23B. His disciples argued over who was greatest. He said, the one who is least among you	9:46-50
6A. Now while the days were being fulfilled for His ascension, He set His face to go to Jerusalem	9:51
1B. And He sent ahead messengers, who were not welcomed by a village in Samaria	9:52-56
2B. While they were proceeding, Jesus responded to some wanting to follow Him	9:57-62
3B. The Lord appointed, instructed, and sent out 72. They returned with joy. He praised God	10:1-24
4B. A Law-expert said, What must I do to inherit eternal life? The good Samaritan parable	10:25-37

Luke

Overview

5B. While proceeding, He stayed with Martha. Mary preferred to sit and listen, the good part — 10:38-42
6B. And after He prayed, the disciples asked Him how to pray. He instructed them — 11:1-13
7B. And some said He cast out demons by Beelzebul. Others asked for a sign. He responds — 11:14-36
8B. And at lunch, He did not wash. They objected. He rebuked the Pharisees and lawyers — 11:37-52
9B. And they plotted against Him, and myriads flocked to Him, in which circumstances — 11:53-12:1

    1C. He taught His disciples. Beware of the Pharisees. Do not fear them. Confess Me — 12:1-12
    2C. Someone said to settle a dispute. Who made Me your judge? Be rich toward God — 12:13-21
    3C. He said to His disciples, Do not be anxious about life. Seek his kingdom. Be ready — 12:22-53
    4C. He said to the crowds, Judge the right thing for yourselves. Repent or perish — 12:54-13:9

10B. Jesus healed a woman on the Sabbath. The official objected. Jesus rebuked him — 13:10-21
11B. And one asked, Are there few being saved? He said, Strive to enter by the narrow door — 13:22-30
12B. Some Pharisees said, Herod wants to kill You. Jesus mourned the fate of Jerusalem — 13:31-35
13B. Jesus healed a man on the Sabbath at a Pharisee's house. He spoke parables to them — 14:1-24
14B. And He said to the crowds, Whoever does not carry his own cross cannot be My disciple — 14:25-35
15B. Now tax collectors and sinners drew near to hear, and Pharisees grumbled about them — 15:1-2

    1C. He told them of the lost sheep and coin. God seeks the lost, rejoices in repentance — 15:3-10
    2C. He spoke the parable of the two sons— the wild living son and his unloving brother — 15:11-32
    3C. And He spoke to the disciples about money. Invest it in your eternal dwellings — 16:1-13
    4C. The Pharisees sneered at all this. He said, You are self righteous, and told of Lazarus — 16:14-31
    5C. And He warned the disciples about causes of falling. Rebuke and forgive your brother — 17:1-4
    6C. The apostles ask for more faith. The smallest amount is enough. Estimating yourself — 17:5-10

16B. And while proceeding, He healed ten lepers. One came back to thank Him — 17:11-19
17B. He said the kingdom is within you. Days will come when you will desire to see it, and you will not. It will be like the days of Noah and Lot. Pray, do not lose heart — 17:20-18:8
18B. And He told a parable to ones trusting in themselves— the Pharisee and the tax collector — 18:9-14
19B. And they were bringing Him babies. You must receive the kingdom like a child — 18:15-17
20B. And a rich ruler said, What shall I do to inherit eternal life? Sell all, be following Me — 18:18-30
21B. And He said to the twelve, I will be killed and raised again. They did not understand — 18:31-34
22B. And drawing near to Jericho, He healed a blind man — 18:35-43
23B. And He stayed in Jericho with Zacchaeus. Because they supposed the kingdom would come immediately, He told a parable about servants investing the master's resources — 19:1-27

7A. And having said these things, He was proceeding ahead, going up to Jerusalem — 19:28

    1B. And He sent disciples to get a colt. The crowds said, Blessed is the King. The Pharisees objected. Jesus wept over Jerusalem. You did not recognize your time of visitation — 19:29-44
    2B. And Jesus entered the temple and drove out the sellers. And He was teaching daily — 19:45-48
    3B. And on one day, the priests asked, By what authority do you do these things? The parable of the vine-growers who killed the owner's son. The vineyard will be taken away — 20:1-19
    4B. And they sent spies to try to trap Him. Is it lawful to pay tributes to Caesar? — 20:20-26
    5B. And some Sadducees questioned Him. In the resurrection, whose wife is she? — 20:27-40
    6B. And He said to them, How is it that they say the Christ is David's son? — 20:41-44
    7B. And while all were listening, He warned His disciples to beware of the scribes — 20:45-47

8B. And He saw a widow giving her offering. She gave more than all	21:1-4
9B. And while some were admiring the temple, Jesus says the temple will be destroyed	21:5-6
1C. And they questioned Him, When will this happen, and what will be the sign	21:7
2C. And He said, Watch out that you may not be deceived. Many will come in My name	21:8-9
3C. Then He was saying to them	21:10
1D. There will be wars, famines, plagues. There will be great signs from heaven	21:10-11
2D. But before all these things, they will persecute you	21:12-19
3D. But when you see Jerusalem surrounded, flee. These are days of vengeance	21:20-24
4D. And Jerusalem will be trampled until the times of the Gentiles are fulfilled	21:24
5D. And there will be signs in the sun, moon and stars, and anguish on earth	21:25-26
6D. And then they will see the Son of Man coming in a cloud with power and glory	21:27
7D. When these things are beginning to take place, look up! Your redemption is near	21:28
4C. And He spoke a parable. When the tree puts out leaves, summer is near. So, when you see these things, it is near. Take heed to yourselves. Keep alert in every season	21:29-36
10B. Now He taught during the day, but would go out to at night to the Mount of Olives	21:37-38
8A. Now Passover was drawing near. And the priests sought how to kill Him	22:1-2
1B. And Satan entered Judas, and he plotted with the priests to betray Him	22:3-6
2B. And they ate the Passover together. The bread and cup. The betrayer. The greatest	22:7-38
3B. And they went to the Mount of Olives. Jesus prayed. Judas kissed Him. He is arrested	22:39-53
4B. And they led Him to the house of the high priest. Peter followed, and denied Him	22:54-65
5B. And when it became day, the elders assembled and condemned Him	22:66-71
6B. And they all led Him before Pilate, who found no guilt in Him. He sent Him to Herod	23:1-7
7B. Herod questioned Him, but He did not answer. He mocked Him and returned Him	22:8-12
8B. Pilate tried to release Him three times, and then handed Him over to their will	22:13-25
9B. They led Him away and crucified Him. They mocked Him. Jesus expired	23:26-49
10B. And Joseph of Arimathea asked for the body, and placed it in a tomb	23:50-54
9A. Now having closely followed, the women looked at the tomb and how His body was laid	23:55
1B. And having returned, they prepared spices and perfumes	23:56
2B. And they rested on the Sabbath, but then went to the tomb. Angels said He was raised	23:56-24:8
3B. And they reported these things to the eleven. They did not believe. Peter ran to see	24:9-12
4B. That day, two were on the road to Emmaus. Jesus spoke with them and revealed Himself	24:13-32
5B. That night, the two returned to the eleven in Jerusalem. The Lord appeared to them all	24:33-45
6B. And He said, You are witnesses. Wait in Jerusalem for power	24:46-49
7B. And He led them outside near Bethany. He blessed them, and was carried up into heaven	24:50-52
8B. And they were continually in the temple, blessing God	24:53

Luke 1:1	180	Verse

- A. In-as-much-as[1] many undertook[2] to compile[3] *a* narrative[4] about the things having been fulfilled[5] among us, *just as the eyewitnesses from *the* first[6] and *ones* having become servants[7] *of* the word[A] handed-down[B] *to* us   1, 2
- B. It seemed *good to* me also, having closely-followed[8] everything carefully[9] from-the-beginning[10], to write *it for* you in-order[11], most-excellent[12] Theophilus[13], *in order that you may fully-know[C] the certainty[14] *of the* things[15] about which[16] you were instructed[D]   3, 4

1A. In the days *of* Herod[E], king *of* Judea   5

   1B. There was[17] *a* certain priest— Zechariah *by* name, from *the* division[18] *of* Abijah— and *a* wife *for* him from the daughters[19] *of* Aaron[20]. And her name *was* Elizabeth

      1C. And they were both righteous[F] *ones* in the sight of God, walking[21] in all the commandments[G] and regulations[H] *of the* Lord *as* blameless[22] *ones*   6

      2C. And there was not *a* child *for* them, because Elizabeth was barren[J]. And they were both advanced[23] in their days   7

      3C. And it came about during his serving-as-priest[24] before God in the order *of* his division, *that according to the custom[25] *of* the priestly-office[26], he obtained-by-lot[27] *that* he might offer-incense[28], [after] having entered into the temple *of* the Lord   8-9

         1D. And *the* whole assembly[K] *of the* people was praying outside *at the* hour *of the offering of* incense   10

         2D. And *an* angel *of the* Lord appeared[L] *to* him, standing on *the* right *side of the* altar *of* incense   11

         3D. And having seen *him*, Zechariah was frightened[M], and fear[N] fell upon him   12

         4D. But the angel said to him, "Do not be fearing, Zechariah, because your prayer[29] was heard. And your wife Elizabeth will bear[O] you *a* son, and you shall call his name John. And there will be joy and gladness[P] *for* you. And many will rejoice over his birth[Q]   13, 14

            1E. "For he will be great in the sight of the Lord   15

            2E. "And he will never drink wine[R] and fermented-drink[30]

            3E. "And he will be filled[S] *with the* Holy Spirit *while* still *of*[31] his mother's womb[32]

            4E. "And he will turn-back[T] many *of the* sons[U] *of* Israel to *the* Lord their God   16

            5E.[33] "And **he** will go-ahead before Him[34] in *the* spirit and power *of* Elijah   17

               1F. "To turn-back[T] *the* hearts *of* fathers to *their* children,[35] and *to* turn back disobedient[36] *ones* with[37] *the* understanding[38] *of* righteous[F] *ones*

               2F. "To prepare[39] *a* people having been made-ready[40] *for the* Lord"

         5D. And Zechariah said to the angel, "Based-on[41] what shall I know[42] this? For **I** am *an* old-man[V], and my wife *is* advanced[43] in her days"   18

         6D. And having responded, the angel said *to* him, "**I** am Gabriel[44], the *one* standing in the presence of God. And I was sent forth to speak to you, and to announce these *things* as-good-news[W] *to* you. *And behold— you shall be silent[X] and not able to speak[45] until which day these *things* take place, because[46] you did not believe my words, which will be fulfilled in their proper-time[Y]"   19, 20

         7D. And the people were waiting for Zechariah. And they were wondering[Z] during his delaying in the temple   21

         8D. And having come out, he was not able to speak *to* them   22

            1E. And they realized[C] that he had[47] seen *a* vision[AA] in the temple

            2E. And **he** was motioning[48] *to* them and continuing[BB] *to be* mute

1. Or, "Since, Seeing that", referring to a well known fact. Used only here. It is a literary word. GK *2077*.
2. Or, "took in hand, set their hand to, attempted". Elsewhere only as "attempt" in Act 9:29; 19:13. GK *2217*. Related to "hand".
3. Or, "arrange in order, draw up". Used only here. GK *421*.
4. Or, "account", giving details in sequence. Used only here. GK *1456*. Related to "relate" in 8:39.
5. Or, "accomplished". Same word as in 2 Tim 4:5, 17, of "fulfilling" a ministry. Elsewhere only of people, as "fully convinced" in Rom 4:21; 14:5; "fully assured" in Col 4:12. GK *4442*. Related to "fullness of conviction" in 1 Thes 1:5.
6. That is, from when Jesus began His ministry. Luke is referring to the apostles and others. On this word, see "beginning" in Col 1:18.
7. This is a second description of this group. They were eyewitnesses... and became servants. On this word, see "attendants" in 1 Cor 4:1, where Paul uses it of himself.
8. Or, "traced accurately, followed with the mind, investigated". On this word, see "accompany" in Mk 16:17.
9. Or, "accurately". On this word, see Mt 2:8. While in Judea during Paul's imprisonment there, Luke had two years in which to interview everyone still available, Act 24:27.
10. Or, "from the first", but not the same word as in v 2. Luke means from before Christ's birth, as seen in v 5. On this word, see "again" in Jn 3:3.
11. That is, in a logical, orderly, consecutive sequence. On this word, see "successive" in 8:1.
12. Elsewhere only in Act 23:26; 24:3; 26:25. GK *3196*.
13. On this person, see Act 1:1.
14. Or, "security, reliability, safety". Elsewhere only as "security" in Act 5:23; 1 Thes 5:3. GK *854*.
15. Or, "statements, words, sayings, teachings, doctrines". GK *3364*. Not the same word as in v 1 (GK *4547*).
16. Or, "you may know the certainty about *the* words which".
17. Or, "came to be, arose". GK *1181*.
18. The "division" of Abijah was the eighth of 24 divisions of priests (1 Chron 24:10; 2 Chron 8:14). Each division served eight days in the temple, Sabbath to Sabbath, twice per year. Elsewhere only in v 8. GK *2389*.
19. That is, descendants, as in 13:16.
20. Thus, this priest married a priest's daughter.
21. Or, "going, proceeding, living". On this word, see "gone" in Mt 28:19.
22. On this adjective, see Phil 3:6.
23. This is a participle, they were "having advanced", or, "having gotten on". Same word as in 1:18; 2:36. Elsewhere only as "gone on" in Mt 4:21; Mk 1:19. GK *4581*.
24. Or, "performing his priestly duties". Used only here. GK *2634*. This idiom "during his..." is a mark of Luke's style.
25. Same word as in 2:42; 22:39; Jn 19:40; Act 6:14; 15:1; 16:21; 21:21; 25:16; 26:3; 28:17. Elsewhere only as "habit" in Heb 10:25. GK *1621*. Related to the word in Lk 2:27, and the word in Lk 4:16.
26. That is, the custom of casting lots to see who would perform this duty. Their custom was to cast lots twice a day, for the morning and the evening service. On this word, see Heb 7:5.
27. On this word, see "received" in 2 Pet 1:1.
28. That is, to offer it inside the Holy Place, on the Altar of Incense. This was a once in a lifetime event for a priest. A priest could only do it once, and many never got to do it. Used only here. GK *2594*.
29. Some think this refers to Zechariah's prayer at this temple service on behalf of Israel for the Messiah to come, for salvation for Israel; others, to his prayer for a son made years prior to this day.
30. Or, "liquor, beer, alcoholic beverage". That is, intoxicating drinks made from things other than grapes, whether stronger than wine or not. A transliterated Hebrew word. Used only here. GK *4975*.
31. This word means "of, from", and is found in the phrase "from his mother's womb" in Mt 19:12; Act 3:2; 14:8; Gal 1:15. Because of the word "still" here, some think the angel means "while still originating from the womb", that is, "in the womb". John will be filled before his birth, perhaps referring to v 41. Others think the angel means "while still from his mother's womb", that is, while still a newborn baby. John will be filled from birth. GK *1666*.
32. This word means "womb", "belly" (in Mt 12:40; Jn 7:38), and "stomach" (as in Mt 15:17; Rom 16:18; 1 Cor 6:13; Phil 3:19). Used 22 times. GK *3120*.
33. Compare Mt 17:11.
34. Some think this is referring to "the Lord their God", v 16; others, to the Messiah, in fulfillment of Mal 4.
35. Compare Mal 4:5-6, to which the angel is referring. Family harmony follows spiritual harmony with God.
36. Elsewhere only in Act 26:19; Rom 1:30; 2 Tim 3:2; Tit 1:16; 3:3. GK *579*. Related to "disobey" in Rom 11:30.
37. Or, "by means of, in, in connection with". GK *1877*.
38. Or, "way of thinking". On this word, see Eph 1:8.
39. Same word as in 1:76; 3:4; Mt 3:3, etc. GK *2286*.
40. Same word as in Mk 1:2.
41. Or, "According to, By way of". GK *2848*. Zechariah does not ask "how", but "on what grounds".
42. That is, "be sure of" this. Zechariah is asking for a sign so he can know that it is true. On this word, see v 34.
43. This is a participle, as in v 7.
44. Gabriel is mentioned only here and v 26 in the NT. GK *1120*. There is also a Gabriel in Dan 8:16; 9:21.
45. Both "silent" and "able" are participles, meaning "You shall continue being silent and unable to speak".
46. Or, "in return for". On this phrase, see 2 Thes 2:10.
47. More literally, "has", as the Greek typically phrases it.
48. Or, "nodding". Zechariah was "nodding" with his head or "gesturing" with his hands. Used only here. GK *1377*. Related to "motioning" in v 62.

A. 1 Cor 12:8 B. Act 16:4, delivering C. Col 1:6, understood D. Gal 6:6 E. Mt 2:1 F. Rom 1:17 G. Mk 12:28 H. Rom 1:32 J. Heb 11:11 K. Act 6:2, multitude L. Lk 2:26, see M. Gal 1:7, disturbed N. Eph 5:21 O. 1 Jn 2:29, born P. Jude 24 Q. Jam 3:6, existence R. 1 Tim 5:23 S. Act 2:4 T. Jam 5:19 U. Gal 3:7 V. Tit 2:2 W. Act 5:42, announce the good news X. Mk 4:39, be still Y. Mt 8:29, time Z. Rev 17:8, caused to marvel AA. 2 Cor 12:1 BB. Lk 22:28

4C.	And it came about *that* when the days *of* his service[1] were fulfilled[A], he went to his house	23
5C.	And after these days, Elizabeth his wife conceived[B]. And she was concealing[2] herself *for* five months, saying ˚that "Thus *the* Lord has done *for* me in *the* days *in* which He looked-upon[C] *me* to take-away[D] my reproach[3] among people"	24 25

2B. Now in the sixth month,[4] the angel Gabriel was sent-forth[E] from God to *a* city *of* Galilee *for* which *the* name *was* Nazareth,˚ to *a* virgin[F] having been promised-in-marriage[G] to *a* man *for* whom *the* name *was* Joseph, from[5] *the* house[H] *of* David. And the name *of* the virgin *was* Mary | 26
27

1C.	And having come-in to[6] her, he said, "Greetings[J], favored *one*[7]! The Lord *is* with you[8]"	28
2C.	But *the one* was[9] very-troubled[10] at the statement[K], and was pondering[L] what-kind-of[11] greeting this might be	29
3C.	And the angel said *to* her, "Do not be fearing, Mary. For you found favor[12] with God. ˚And behold— you will conceive[B] in *your* womb[M] and give-birth[N] to *a* son. And you shall call His name Jesus	30-31

1D.	"This *One* will be great, and will be called 'Son *of the* Most-High[O]'	32
2D.	"And *the* Lord God will give Him the throne *of* David, His father. ˚And He will reign[13] over the house[H] *of* Jacob forever[14]. And there will not be *an* end[P] *of* His kingdom"	33

4C.	And Mary said to the angel, "How[15] will this happen[16], since I am not knowing[17] *a* man[18]?"	34
5C.	And having responded, the angel said *to* her, "*The* Holy Spirit will come[Q] upon you, and *the* power *of the* Most-High will overshadow[R] you. For this reason[19] also the Holy *Child* being born[20] will be called God's Son[21]	35

1D.	"And behold— Elizabeth your relative also herself has conceived *a* son in her old age. And this is *the* sixth month *for* her, the *one* being called barren,˚ because no word from God will be impossible[22]"	36 37

6C.	And Mary said, "Behold the slave[23] *of the* Lord. May it be done[S] *to* me according to your word[T]"	38
7C.	And the angel departed from her	

3B. And having arisen during these days, Mary proceeded to the hill country with haste[U], to *a* city *of* Judah,˚ and entered into the house *of* Zechariah, and greeted[V] Elizabeth | 39
40

1C.	And it came about *that* when Elizabeth heard the greeting *of* Mary, the baby[24] leaped[25] in her womb[W]	41
2C.	And Elizabeth was filled[A] with *the* Holy Spirit[26],˚ and exclaimed[27] *with a* loud shout[X] and said	42

1D.	"You *are* blessed[28] among women, and blessed *is* the fruit *of* your womb[W]	
2D.	"And why[29] has this happened *to* me— that the mother *of* my Lord[Y] should come to me?	43

1E.	"For[30] behold— when the sound *of* your greeting came-to-be in my ears, the baby leaped with gladness[31] in my womb[W]	44

3D.	"And blessed[32] *is she* having believed that[33] there will be *a* fulfillment[34] to the *things* having been spoken *to* her from *the* Lord"	45

3C.	And Mary said, "My soul magnifies[35] the Lord,˚ and my spirit rejoiced-greatly[36] over God my Savior[37]	46-47

1. That is, his week of priestly service. On this word, see 2 Cor 9:12.
2. Elizabeth kept her joy to herself, exulting in the fact that God had truly blessed her. Some think Luke means she secluded herself from others; others, that she withheld this fact from others. Used only here. GK *4332*. The root word means "hide, conceal, cover, keep secret".
3. Or, "disgrace". That is, for being barren. Used only here. GK *3945*. Related to the word in Heb 10:33.
4. That is, of Elizabeth's pregnancy, v 24, 36.
5. Some take this phrase with "virgin"; others, with Joseph; others, with both.
6. That is, come in to Mary's house. On this idiom "come-in to", see Act 16:40.
7. This is a participle, "*one* having been bestowed favor" or "grace". Related to "favor" in v 30. On this word, see "graciously-bestowed-on" in Eph 1:6.
8. Some manuscripts add "You *are* blessed among women" {A}, as in v 42.
9. Some manuscripts say "*one*, having seen *him*, was..." {N}.
10. Or, "very disturbed, agitated, confused, perplexed" Used only here. GK *1410*.
11. Or, "what sort of ". More literally, "of-what-kind this greeting might be". On this word, see 1 Jn 3:1.
12. Or, "grace". Same word as in 2:52, and as "grace" in 2:40. On this word, see "grace" in Eph 2:8. Related to the word in v 28.
13. Or, "be king". On this word, see Rev 19:6. Related to the word "kingdom" in this verse.
14. This is an idiom, "into the age". See Rev 20:10.
15. Mary does not ask for a sign, as in v 18. She asks the practical question, since she is not yet married.
16. Or, "be". On this word, see Mt 16:22.
17. Same word as in Mt 1:25. In the OT (and in Greek), "know" is sometimes used as a euphemism for sexual relations. See Gen 4:1, 17; 1 Sam 1:19. This word means "know, come to know, understand, recognize, acknowledge". Used 222 times. GK *1182*.
18. Or, "husband". That is, I am not having sexual relations with a man. How will this come to pass, since I am not presently married and able to conceive?
19. That is, because God will be His Father.
20. Some manuscripts add "from you" {A}.
21. Some punctuate this "the *Child* being born will be called holy, *the* Son *of* God".
22. Literally, "every word from God will not be impossible", a Hebrew way of speaking. Some manuscripts say "every word will not be impossible with God" {N}, the only difference being in the grammar of the word "with, from". "Word" (same word as in v 38) can also mean "thing, matter" (as in v 4), so that it says "every thing from God will not be impossible", or as we would say it, "Nothing from God will be impossible". Elsewhere only in Mt 17:20. GK *104*.
23. Same word as in v 48. Elsewhere only as "*female* slaves" in Act 2:18. GK *1527*. It is the feminine form of "slave" in Rom 6:17.
24. Or, "fetus, infant". Same word as in v 44; 2:12, 16; 18:15; Act 7:19; 1 Pet 2:2. Elsewhere only as "babyhood" in 2 Tim 3:15. GK *1100*.
25. Or, "leaped for joy". Same word as in v 44, where "gladness" is added. Elsewhere only as "leap for joy" in 6:23. GK *5015*.
26. This is how Elizabeth knew the things she says next. The Spirit revealed them to her.
27. Or, "called out". Used only here. GK *430*.
28. This is a participle, "having been blessed, having received a blessing", both times in this verse. The root word means "spoken well of ", but here it means blessed by God. On this word, see 6:28.
29. Or, "from where, how". GK *4470*.
30. Elizabeth is explaining how she knew that Mary was "the mother of my Lord". The Spirit caused the baby to leap, and revealed to her the reason why the baby leaped. Note that she called Mary's unborn baby her Lord.
31. Same word as in v 14. On this word, see Jude 24.
32. Or, "happy, fortunate". Not related to the word in v 42. On this word, see 6:20.
33. Or, "because". Some think Elizabeth blesses Mary, who "believed that" it will happen (in contrast with Zechariah in v 18); whose response was belief. Others, think Elizabeth is prophesying that these things will come to pass, "... having believed, because there will be *a* fulfillment...", giving further assurance from God to Mary. GK *4022*.
34. Or, "completion". On this word, see "perfection" in Heb 7:11.
35. Or, "makes great". On this word, see "enlarge" in 2 Cor 10:15. In Latin, this word is *Magnificat*, which has become a name for this "magnification" of God by Mary.
36. This word is related to "gladness" in v 44. On this word, see 10:21. Some think the change to a past tense in this verb means Mary is referring specifically here to the angel's visit and announcement. Others think this verb has a timeless sense, and means "rejoices greatly", parallel with "magnifies".
37. Used 24 times. GK *5400*. Related to "save" in Lk 19:10.

A. Act 2:4, filled B. Lk 2:21 C. Act 4:29 D. Mk 14:47, took off E. Mk 3:14, send out F. Rev 14:4 G. Mt 1:18 H. Mk 3:20 J. 2 Cor 13:11, rejoice K. 1 Cor 12:8, word L. Lk 5:21, reasoning M. 1 Thes 5:3 N. Lk 2:11, born O. Mt 21:9, highest P. Rom 10:4 Q. Lk 21:26, coming upon R. Mt 17:5 S. Mt 6:10 T. Rom 10:17 U. 2 Cor 8:16, earnestness V. Mk 15:18 W. Lk 1:15 X. Heb 5:7, outcry Y. Mt 8:2, master

	1D. "Because He looked-upon[A] the lowliness[1] *of* His slave[B]	48
	1E. "For behold— from now *on*, all generations will consider me blessed[2], *because[3] the Powerful[4] One did great *things for* me	49
	2D. "And His name *is* holy. *And His mercy to[5] generations and generations[6] *is on* the *ones* fearing Him	50
	3D. "He did *a* mighty-deed[7] with His arm[8]	51
	1E. "He scattered[C] *ones* arrogant[9] *in the* thought[10] *of* their heart	
	2E. "He brought-down[D] rulers[11] from *their* thrones, and lifted-up[E] lowly[12] *ones*	52
	3E. "He filled[F] *ones* being hungry with good *things,* and sent *ones* being rich away empty[G]	53
	4E. "He[13] helped[H] Israel His servant[J] *so that* He might remember[14] mercy, *just as He spoke to our fathers— *to* Abraham, and *to his* seed forever[15]"	54-55
4C.	And Mary stayed[K] with her about three[16] months, and returned to her house	56
4B. Now *for* Elizabeth, the time was fulfilled[L] *that* she might give-birth[M], and she bore[N] *a* son		57
1C.	And the neighbors[17] and her relatives heard that *the* Lord magnified[18] His mercy with her, and they were rejoicing-with her	58
2C.	And it came about *that* on the eighth day they came to circumcise[O] the child[P]. And they were calling[19] him Zechariah, on the basis of the name *of* his father	59
	1D. And having responded, his mother said, "No! Instead he will be called John"	60
	2D. And they said to her that "There is no one from your relatives who is called *by* this name"	61
	3D. And they were motioning[20] to his father *as to* what he would wish[Q] him to be called	62
	4D. And having asked-*for a* tablet, he wrote, saying "John is his name". And they all marveled[R]	63
	5D. And at-once[S] his mouth **was opened**, and his tongue *loosed*. And he was speaking, blessing[21] God	64
3C.	And awe[22] came[23] over all the *ones* living around them. And all these things were being talked-over[24] in the whole hill country *of* Judea	65
	1D. And all the *ones* having heard *it* put[T] *these matters* in their heart, saying, "What then will this child be?" For[25] indeed, *the* hand *of the* Lord was with him	66
4C.	And Zechariah, his father, was filled[L] with *the* Holy Spirit and prophesied[26], saying	67
	1D. "Blessed[27] *be the* Lord God *of* Israel[28], because He visited[29] *us,* and accomplished[30] redemption[31] *for* His people, *and raised-up[U]	68 69
	1E. "*A* horn[32] *of* salvation[V] *for us in the* house *of* David His servant[J]—*just as He spoke through *the* mouth *of* His holy prophets from *the* past age[33]	70
	2E. "*A* salvation from our enemies and from *the* hand *of* all the *ones* hating[W] us	71
	3E. "*So as to* show mercy to[34] our fathers, and remember[X] His holy covenant[Y]—*the* oath which He swore[35] to Abraham our father	72-73
	4E. "*That He might* grant *to* us *that*	
	1F. "*Having been delivered*[36] from *the* hand *of our*[37] enemies	74

1. God looked with favor upon Mary in her humble status as a carpenter's bride. On this word, see Jam 1:10.
2. This verb, "to consider blessed, fortunate", is elsewhere only in Jam 5:11. GK *3420*. Related to "blessed" in v 45. People will no longer consider Mary as a lowly one, but as a most fortunate recipient of God's favor.
3. Others make this "because" phrase point 2D., parallel with the first "because" phrase.
4. Or, "Strong, Mighty". On this word, see 24:19. Related to the word Jesus used of God in Mt 26:64, "Power".
5. Or, "toward, for, in". GK *1650*. Same words as in "mercy to" thousands, Ex 20:6; 34:7; Deut 5:10; Jer 32:18.
6. Some manuscripts say "to generations *of* generations"; others, "to generation and generation" {N}. On this word, see Mt 24:34.
7. Not related to "Powerful" in v 49. This noun is singular. Rendered as here, this refers to this mighty deed God did in Mary and through Mary, moving from a self view in 1D., to a God view in 2D., to a deed view here. Others render it in more general terms, "He exercised strength", "He showed strength", "He performed mighty deeds", detailed in the phrases following. This phrase "to do a mighty deed, to show strength", does not occur elsewhere in the Greek Bible, but is similar to "show mercy" in v 72. On this word, see "might" in Eph 6:10.
8. Some think that in what follows Mary is speaking of what God has accomplished in the past, detailing His mercy to the generations, v 50 (making this point 1E.); others, of what He did in choosing her, speaking in generalized terms; others, of what He will do through the Messiah, of the far reaching future meaning of what He did to her, of the mighty thing which has only begun in her. In this view, she is speaking of what she knows will happen through Him as if it has already happened (some view this as speaking prophetically, like v 68; others, in this case, as speaking out and claiming the Messianic hope she cherished with others based on Scripture).
9. Or, "proud, haughty". On this word, see Jam 4:6.
10. Or, "understanding, mind, way of thinking, disposition". Same word as in Eph 2:3. Elsewhere only as "mind" in Mt 22:37; Mk 12:30; Lk 10:27; Col 1:21; Heb 8:10; 10:16; 1 Pet 1:13; 2 Pet 3:1; and "understanding" in Eph 4:18; 1 Jn 5:20. GK *1379*. Related to "mind" in Rom 7:23.
11. On this word, see "court official" in Act 8:27.
12. Or, "humble". On this word, see Jam 1:9. Related to "lowliness" in v 48.
13. Others would make this point 4D.
14. That is, "keep in mind" (not forget) mercy, in keeping with His promise to bless Abraham and his descendants forever. This God has done by now sending the Messiah. This word is used elsewhere of the Father only in v 72; Act 10:31; Heb 2:6; 8:12; 10:17; Rev 16:19. Same word as in Lk 23:42; 1 Cor 11:2; Heb 13:3; 2 Pet 3:2; Jude 17. Elsewhere this word has the sense of "recall to mind", as in Lk 16:25; 24:6, 8. Used 23 times. GK *3630*. A related word is used of God in Rev 18:5.
15. This is the Greek word order of v 54-55. It could also be punctuated "remember mercy *for* Abraham and his seed forever, just as He spoke to our fathers". In either case, "spoke" has the sense of "promised". This word is an idiom, "into the age". See Rev 20:10.
16. One would naturally presume Luke means that she remained until the birth of the baby (six months in v 36 plus three here), but he holds the announcement of the birth until his next unit of thought in v 57.
17. Or, "*ones* living around" her. Used only here. GK *4341*. The related verb "live around" is in v 65.
18. Same word as in v 46.
19. Or, "were *going to* call him". Either the people at the ceremony were referring to the baby by this name (that is, prior to or during the ceremony), or they expressed their intention to call him by this name as part of the ceremony. In any case, Elizabeth stopped them. On this word, which is also in v 60, 61, and 62, see Rom 8:30.
20. That is, with their hands. Used only here. GK *1935*. Related to the word in v 22.
21. Or, "speaking well of, praising". On this word, see 6:28.
22. Or, "fear". On this word, see "fear" in Eph 5:21.
23. Or, "came-about, came-to-be". GK *1181*.
24. Or, "talked through, talked about, discussed". Elsewhere only in 6:11. GK *1362*.
25. Some think this sentence is part of the quotation of what people were saying, and refers to the circumstances of John's birth (1:8-25). What will this baby become, for God's hand was certainly with him in his birth. Others think this is Luke's comment. Some manuscripts say "And *the* hand *of the* Lord..." {N}.
26. On this word, see 1 Cor 14:1. Zechariah spoke revelation from God.
27. This is an adjective, related to the verb in v 64. On this word, see Rom 9:5.
28. Or, "*the* Lord, the God *of* Israel".
29. Same word as in v 78; 7:16. On this word, see "look after" in Heb 2:6.
30. Or, "made, brought about". Zechariah is speaking prophetically, as if the future were already past. On this word, see "does" in Rev 13:13.
31. Same word as in 2:38. On this noun, see Heb 9:12.
32. Zechariah is referring to Jesus as a horn of salvation, a strong one bringing salvation. "Horn" represents strength or power in an OT metaphor, Ps 132:17, 2 Sam 22:3; Ps 18:2. Used 11 times. GK *3043*.
33. Or, "from long ago, from *of* old". There had not been a prophet in centuries. Same phrase as in Act 3:21; 15:18. Some take "age" in an absolute sense, and paraphrase this "since the world began". Elsewhere only plural, "from the *past* ages", in Eph 3:9; Col 1:26. GK *172*.
34. Or, "deal mercifully with, show kindness to". This phrase "show mercy to" is an idiom, literally "do mercy with", and is found in Lk 10:37; Jam 2:13; and in Gen 24:12; Jdg 1:24; Ruth 1:8; 1 Sam 15:6; 20:8; 2 Sam 3:8; 9:1; 10:2; 1 King 3:6; Jer 32:18, etc. This implies the fathers are living. God raised up a horn of salvation so as to show mercy to the fathers by at last carrying out His promises to them, and so as to be mindful of the covenant He swore to them.
35. That is, in Gen 22:16-18. God swore that all the nations of the earth will be blessed in Abraham. On this word, see Jam 5:12.
36. Or, "rescued". On this word, see Col 1:13.
37. Some manuscripts include this word {B}.

A. Jam 2:3 B. Lk 1:38 C. Mt 25:24 D. 2 Cor 10:4, tearing down E. Jn 8:28 F. Rom 15:24 G. 1 Thes 2:1 H. 1 Tim 6:2 J. Act 3:13 K. Jn 15:4, abide L. Act 2:4, filled M. Lk 2:11, born N. 1 Jn 2:29, born O. Lk 2:21 P. 1 Jn 2:14 Q. Jn 7:17, willing R. Rev 17:8 S. Mt 21:19 T. Act 19:21 U. Mt 28:6, arose V. Lk 19:9 W. Rom 9:13 X. Lk 1:54 Y. Heb 8:6

Luke 1:75	186	Verse

      2F. "*We might* be serving[1] Him **fearlessly**,*in holiness[A] and righteousness[B] before Him, *for* all our days[2]   75

  2D. "And indeed[3] **you**, child, will be called *a* prophet[C] *of the* Most-High[D]. For you will go before *the* Lord[4]   76

      1E. S*o as* prepare[E] His ways[5]
      2E. *That you might* give His people *the* knowledge[F] *of* salvation[6]   77

          1F. "By *the* forgiveness[G] *of* their sins
          2F. "Because of *the* deep-feelings-*of*[H] mercy *of* our God, with[7] which[8] *the* rising[9] Sun[10] from on-high[11] will visit[12] us   78

              1G. "*So as* to shine-upon[J] the *ones* sitting[K] in darkness and *a* shadow *of* death[13]   79
              2G. "*That He might* direct[14] our feet into *the* way *of* peace[15]"

    5C. And the child was growing and becoming-strong[16] *in* spirit. And he was in the desolate[L] *places* until *the* day *of* his public-appearance[17] to Israel   80

5B.[18] Now it came about during those days *that a* decree[M] went out from Caesar Augustus[19] *that* all the world[20] *should* be registered[21]. *This first[22] registration[23] took place while Quirinius[24] *was* being-governor[25] *of* Syria   2:1 / 2

  1C. And they were all going to register-*themselves*[26]— each *one* to his *own* city[27]   3
  2C. And Joseph also went up   4

      1D. From Galilee, out of *the* city *of* Nazareth
      2D. To Judea, to *the* city *of* David,[28] which is called Bethlehem— because of his being from *the* house[N] and family[29] *of* David
      3D. *So as* to register *himself* with Mary[30]— the *one*[31] having been promised-in-marriage[32] to him, being pregnant[33]   5

  3C. And it came about during their being there[34] *that* the days were fulfilled[O] *that* she *might* give-birth[P]. *And she gave birth to her firstborn[Q] son   6 / 7

      1D. And she wrapped Him in swaddling-cloths[35], and laid Him in *a* manger[36], because there was not *a* place *for* them in the inn[37]

  4C. And shepherds[R] were in the same region[S], living-in-the-fields[38], and watching[T] over their flock[U] *for* watches[39] *of* the night   8

      1D. And[40] *an* angel *of the* Lord stood near them, and *the* glory *of the* Lord shined[V] around them   9
      2D. And they feared *a* great fear[41]
      3D. And the angel said *to* them, "Do not be fearing.[42] For behold— I am announcing-as-good-news[W] *to* you *a* great joy which will be *for* all the people   10

          1E. "Because[43] *a* Savior[X] was born[44] *for* you today in *the* city *of* David, Who is Christ *the* Lord   11
          2E. "And this *will be* the sign *for* you— you will find *a* baby[Y] having been wrapped in swaddling cloths and[45] lying[Z] in *a* manger"   12

1. Or, "worshiping". On this word, see "worship" in Heb 12:28.
2. Some think v 71-75 mean Zechariah was expecting the earthy Messianic kingdom promised to Israel in which the Messiah comes with salvation and conquers the enemies of Israel, thus bringing spiritual and national salvation. Others think it refers only to spiritual salvation. Some manuscripts say "all the days *of* our life" {N}.
3. Some manuscripts omit this word {K}.
4. Some think Zechariah means the Most High, v 76; others, the Messiah, the rising Sun, v 78. Compare v 17.
5. Or, "paths". Same words as in 3:4, "Prepare the way of the Lord".
6. John will go before the Lord for the purpose of giving the knowledge of salvation to His people, a salvation which the Lord will bring (the One for whom he was preparing), a salvation by forgiveness based on the mercy of God.
7. Or, "in connection with, because of which, by". GK *1877*.
8. This is plural, referring back to "deep feelings of mercy". Others think it refers to the knowledge of salvation, the forgiveness, and the mercy, making this point 3F.
9. Same word as in "rising" of the sun in Rev 7:2; 16:12. On this word, see "east" in Mt 2:2.
10. Or, "rising *Star*, Dawn". That is, the Messiah. Compare Mal 4:2, the "Sun of righteousness will rise" (where "rise" is related to this word).
11. Or, "the high [heaven]". Same word as in 24:49; Eph 4:8. Elsewhere only as "height" in Eph 3:18; Jam 1:9; Rev 21:16. GK *5737*. Related to "Most High" in v 76.
12. Some manuscripts say "visited" {B}. Same word as in v 68.
13. Compare Mt 4:16.
14. Or, "lead, guide, cause to go straight". Elsewhere only in 1 Thes 3:11; 2 Thes 3:5. GK *2985*.
15. That is, peace with God— salvation, forgiveness.
16. Same phrase used of Jesus in 2:40. On this word, see "be strengthened" in Eph 3:16.
17. Or, "manifestation, public showing forth". Used only here. GK *345*. Related to "appoint" in Act 1:24.
18. On the birth and childhood of Jesus, compare Mt 1:18-2:23.
19. This Roman Emperor, also know as Octavian, ruled from 27 B.C. to A.D. 14. Used only here. GK *880*.
20. Or, "inhabited earth". That is, from the Roman perspective, referring to the Roman Empire. On this word, see Heb 2:5.
21. Or, "enrolled, listed" on a census roll. Same word as in v 3, 5. Elsewhere only in Heb 12:23. GK *616*.
22. Or, "This registration, *a* first, took place", the Greek word order. Or, "This was *the* first registration while...". This seems to have been around 4-5 B.C., and administered by King Herod at the insistence of Rome. Its purpose was to determine how much tribute Judea would pay to Rome. Luke mentions a census again in Act 5:37. That one was in A.D. 6 after Archelaus (see Mt 2:22) had been deposed and Judea was put directly under Roman rule. Some think that was a second census; others, Rome taking over what Herod had begun. Consult the commentaries.
23. Or, "enrollment, listing, census". Elsewhere only in Act 5:37. GK *615*. Related to "register" in v 1.
24. It is uncertain what specific post Quirinius held at this time. In A.D. 6 he was the Roman legate of the province of Syria, which included Judea. He had authority over the Roman prefects (see Pilate in 3:1) in Judea. GK *3256*.
25. Or, "being leader, ruler". The verb refers to a position of leadership, not a specific office. The root word is "to lead". Elsewhere only in 3:1, of the prefect of Judea. GK *2448*. Related to "government" in 3:1; "governor" in Mt 27:2; and "leading" in Heb 13:7.
26. Or, "to be registered". Same word as in v 1.
27. This indicates that Herod carried out this registration according to Jewish customs.
28. David was born there, the eighth son of Jesse, 1 Sam 17:12, 58.
29. On this word, see Eph 3:15. It emphasizes Joseph's link to David, his ancestor.
30. It is uncertain whether Mary was required to go in Herod's arrangement. Some think she went because she and Joseph knew the prophecy, and saw the census as God's hand directing her to go. Others think she went without respect to the prophecy, in the providence of God.
31. Some manuscripts say "wife" {N}.
32. Luke refers to Mary this way because although Joseph had taken her as his wife, they had not consummated the marriage, Mt 1:24-25. He is alluding to the fact that her child was not Joseph's child. On this word, see Mt 1:18.
33. Used only here. GK *1607*. The related verb (not in the NT) means "to impregnate" (for the male); "to conceive" (for the female). The root word means "to swell".
34. No more than a week is needed to cover the time between leaving Nazareth and having the baby in Bethlehem. But the words also allow for a longer period of time in Bethlehem before the birth. Luke is not specific.
35. This verb, "to wrap in swaddling cloths" is elsewhere only in v 12. These are bands of cloth. GK *5058*.
36. That is, an animal feeding trough in a stall or stable. Elsewhere only in v 12, 16; 13:15. GK *5764*.
37. Or, "lodging place, guest-room". Elsewhere only as "guest room" in Mk 14:14; Lk 22:11. GK *2906*. The normal word for "inn" is in Lk 10:34.
38. Used only here. GK *64*.
39. There were four watches of the night, three hours each, on which see Mk 13:35. Used in this sense elsewhere only in Mt 14:25; 24:43; Mk 6:48; Lk 12:38. This is a general statement, they were "watching their watches". Verse 9 then refers to specific shepherds on a specific watch. On this word, see "prison" in Act 5:22.
40. Some manuscripts say "And behold" {B}.
41. That is, they were extremely afraid. Same phrase as in Mk 4:41.
42. Or, "Do not be afraid". The grammar implies "Stop fearing".
43. Or, "That". GK *4022*.
44. Or, "was given birth". Same word as in Mt 2:2, and as "give birth" here in v 6, 7. Used 18 times. GK *5503*.
45. Some manuscripts omit this word {N}.

A. Eph 4:24 B. Rom 1:17 C. 1 Cor 12:28 D. Mt 21:9, highest E. Mk 14:15 F. 1 Cor 12:8 G. Col 1:14 H. Phil 1:8 J. Tit 2:11, appeared K. Rev 14:6 L. Mt 3:1, wilderness M. Eph 2:15 N. Mk 3:20 O. Act 2:4, filled P. Lk 2:11, born Q. Col 1:15 R. Eph 4:11 S. Mk 1:5, country T. Jn 12:25, keep U. Jn 10:16 V. Act 26:13 W. Act 5:42 X. Lk 1:47 Y. Lk 1:41 Z. Mt 3:10

	4D. And suddenly[1] *a* multitude[A] *of the* heavenly host[2] was[3] with the angel, praising[B] God and saying, "Glory *to* God in *the* highest[C] [heavens]. And peace on earth among[4] people *of* [His] good-will[5]"	13 14
	5D. And it came about *that* when the angels departed from them into heaven, the shepherds[6] were saying to one another, "Let us go[7] now[8] to Bethlehem and see this thing having taken place which the Lord made-known[D] *to* us"	15
	6D. And they came, having hurried[E], and found[9] both Mary and Joseph, and the baby lying in the manger	16

    1E. And having seen *Him*, they made-known[D] about the thing having been spoken *to* them about this Child   17

    2E. And all the *ones* having heard *it* marveled[F] about the *things* having been spoken to them by the shepherds   18

    3E. But Mary was preserving[10] all these things, pondering *them* in her heart   19

7D. And the shepherds returned, glorifying[G] and praising[B] God for everything which they heard and saw, just as it was spoken to them   20

5C. And when eight days were fulfilled[H] *that they might* circumcise[11] Him[12], His name was indeed called Jesus— the *name* having been named[13] by the angel before He was conceived[14] in the womb[J]   21

6B. And when the days *of* their[15] purification[K] according to the Law *of* Moses were fulfilled[16]—   22

  1C. They brought Him up to Jerusalem

    1D. So *as* to present[L] *Him* to the Lord, just as it has been written in *the* Law *of the* Lord [in Ex 13:2]— that "every male opening[M] *the* womb[17] shall be called holy[N] *to* the Lord"   23

    2D. And *that she might* give *a* sacrifice[18] in accordance with the *thing* having been said in the Law *of the* Lord [in Lev 12:8]— "*a* pair *of* turtledoves or two young *ones of* pigeons"   24

  2C. And behold— *a* man was in Jerusalem *for* whom *the* name *was* Simeon. And this man *was* righteous and reverent[19], waiting-for[20] *the* consolation *of* Israel[21]. And *the* Holy Spirit was upon him   25

    1D. And it had been revealed[22] *to* him by the Holy Spirit *that he would* not see[23] death before he would see the Christ *of the* Lord   26

    2D. And he came in the Spirit into the temple   27

    3D. And at the parents bringing-in the child[24] Jesus *that they might* do[25] for Him according to the *thing* having become-a-custom[26] *from* the Law, **he** also took Him into *his* arms. And he blessed[27] God, and said   28

      1E. "Now You are releasing[28] Your slave[O] in peace in accordance with Your word, Master[P], because my eyes saw Your salvation[29] which You prepared[Q] in the presence[30] *of* all the peoples—   29
30-31

        1F. "*The* light for *the* revelation[R] *of the* Gentiles[31]   32

        2F. "And *the* glory *of* Your people Israel"

    3D. And His father and mother[32] were marveling[F] at the *things* being spoken about Him[33]   33

    4D. And Simeon blessed them, and said to Mary His mother, "Behold— this *One* is appointed[34]   34

1. Elsewhere only in Mk 13:36; Lk 9:39; Act 9:3; 22:6. GK *1978*. Related to "unexpected" in Lk 21:34.
2. Or, "army". Elsewhere only in Act 7:42. GK *5131*.
3. Or, "came-to-be". GK *1181*.
4. Or, "in, within, in connection with, in the case of, in the sphere of". GK *1877*.
5. Or, "favor, good pleasure". On this word, see "good pleasure" in Eph 1:5. Some think the angels mean "among people *who are recipients of His* good will", that is, who are objects of God's favor, whom His good will has blessed. This is a Hebrew way of speaking. There is a sense in which this could mean "His chosen ones" (compare 10:21 where this same word is used), and another sense in which it could mean "all people" (Jn 3:16). Others think it means "among people *characterized by* good will" toward God. Some manuscripts say "peace on earth, good will among people" {A}.
6. Some manuscripts say "the men, the shepherds" {N}.
7. Or, "go through" the fields. GK *1451*.
8. In this context, this word emphasizes an urgency regarding time. On this word, see "indeed" in Mt 13:23.
9. Or, "found out, sought out, discovered". Elsewhere only in Act 21:4. GK *461*. Related to "find" in v 12.
10. Or, "keeping *in mind*, holding *in memory*, treasuring up". Mary did not allow the memories to fade away. Same word as in Mt 9:17. Elsewhere only as "protect" in Mk 6:20. GK *5337*.
11. Same word as in Jn 7:22; Act 15:1; Col 2:11; and as "receive-circumcision" in Gal 5:2; 6:12. Used 17 times. GK *4362*. Related to "circumcised" in Eph 2:11.
12. Some manuscripts say "the Child" {N}.
13. More literally, "called". That is, spoken. In other words, the baby's heavenly Father chose the name, not His earthly parents. Same word as "called" earlier, and not related to "name" earlier.
14. Same word as 1:24, 31, 36; Jam 1:15. Elsewhere only as "arrest, seize" (see Lk 22:54); "help" (take hold with, see Phil 4:3); and "took" in Lk 5:9. GK *5197*. The root word is "take".
15. Some manuscripts say "her" {K}; others, "His" {N}. It was Mary's purification and Jesus' presentation, as seen next.
16. That is, after 33 more days, Lev 12:1-8.
17. That is, opening it for the first time. Every firstborn male belonged to the Lord, in memory of the fact that their firstborns were spared when those of Egypt were killed, Ex 13:11-15. This is the third word Luke has used for "womb" (see 1:15 and 1:31). Elsewhere only in Rom 4:19. GK *3616*. Related to "mother".
18. The sacrifices were for Mary, to end her period of ritual uncleanness.
19. Or, "God-fearing, devout". The root word means "taking hold well" with reference to the commands of God. Elsewhere only in Act 2:5; 8:2; 22:12. GK *2327*. Related to "reverence" in Heb 5:7.
20. Same word as in v 38. On this word, see Act 24:15.
21. That is, for the kingdom of God established by Messiah, Mk 15:43; Lk 2:38; 23:51. Note Tit 2:13; Jude 21. On "consolation", see "encouragement" in Act 4:36.
22. This is a participle, "it was having been revealed". Or, "divinely communicated". Elsewhere only as "warned" in Mt 2:12, 22; Heb 8:5; 11:7; 12:25; "directed" in Act 10:22; "called" in Act 11:26; Rom 7:3. GK *5976*. Related to "divine response" in Rom 11:4.
23. That is, "experience", as this word is rendered in 10:24. This word means "see, look at; perceive; be seen, appear". Used 449 times. GK *3972*.
24. That is, at the event of bringing Him in. We would say "When the parents brought in the child Jesus".
25. That is, for the purpose of carrying out their duties according to the custom. On this idiom "*that* they *might* do", see Gal 3:10.
26. Luke is referring to v 23, their customary practice in obedience to Ex 13:2. Used only here. GK *1616*. Related to "custom" in 1:9.
27. Same word as in v 34. On this word, see 6:28.
28. Or, "letting go, dismissing, sending away, freeing". Some think Simeon means he is freed to die in peace, because he saw what God promised him, v 26 implying death was near. Others think he was freed from his long-held expectation, implying nothing as to death. On this word, see "send away" in Mt 5:31.
29. Elsewhere only in 3:6; Act 28:28; Eph 6:17. GK *5402*. Related word in Lk 19:9.
30. Or, "face", for all to see. Same idiom as in Act 3:13. This Child comes for all peoples, not just the Jews. GK *4725*.
31. Or, "nations". That is, a light bringing God's revelation to them; a light that they may know God's revelation. On this word, see Act 15:23.
32. Instead of "His father and mother", some manuscripts say "Joseph and His mother" {B}.
33. Such things! And strangers speaking them!
34. Or, "destined". Same word as in Phil 1:16.

A. Act 6:2 B. Rom 15:11 C. Mt 21:9 D. Phil 1:22, know E. 2 Pet 3:12, hasten F. Rev 17:8 G. Rom 8:30 H. Act 2:4, filled J. Lk 1:15 K. 2 Pet 1:9 L. Rom 12:1 M. Act 17:3 N. 1 Pet 1:16 O. Rom 6:17 P. Jude 4 Q. Mk 14:15 R. 2 Thes 2:7

Luke 2:35   190   Verse

        1E. "For[1] the falling[A] and rising[B] of many in Israel
        2E. "And for[2] a sign[C] being spoken-against[3]—°and indeed[4] a sword[5] will pierce[6] the   35
            soul[D] of you yourself
        3E. "So that the thoughts[7] of many hearts may be revealed[E]"

    3C. And there was Anna— a prophet[8], a daughter of Phanuel, from the tribe[F] of Asher   36

        1D. This one was advanced[9] in her many days—

            1E. Having lived with a husband seven years from her virginity
            2E. And herself being a widow up-to[10] eighty four years   37
            3E. Who was not departing[11] from the temple, serving[12] night and day[13] with fastings[G]
                and prayers[14]

        2D. And[15] having come-upon[16] them at the very hour[17], she was returning-thanks[18] to God[19],   38
            and was speaking about Him to all the ones waiting for the redemption[20] of Jerusalem[21]

    4C. And when they finished[H] all the things according to the Law of the Lord,[22] they returned to   39
        Galilee— to their own city, Nazareth

  7B. And the Child was growing and becoming strong,[23] while being filled[J] with wisdom. And the grace   40
    of God was upon Him

2A. And His parents were going to Jerusalem yearly for the Feast[K] of the Passover[L]. °And when He became   41-42
twelve years old— they going up in accordance with the custom[M] of the Feast, °and having completed[N]   43
the days— during their returning, the boy Jesus stayed-behind[O] in Jerusalem

  1B. And His parents[24] did not know it

    1C. But having thought[P] that He was[25] in the caravan[26], they went a day's journey   44
    2C. And they were searching-for[Q] Him among the relatives[R] and the acquaintances[S]
    3C. And not having found Him, they returned to Jerusalem, searching-for[Q] Him   45

  2B. And it came about after three days[27] that they found Him in the temple, sitting in the midst[T] of the   46
    teachers, both listening-to them and questioning[U] them. °And all the ones listening-to Him were   47
    astonished[V] at His understanding[W] and His answers

    1C. And having seen Him, they were astounded[X]   48
    2C. And His mother said to Him, "Child, why did you do[28] us like this? Behold— Your father and
        I were looking-for[Y] You, while suffering-pain[29]"
    3C. And He said to them, "Why[30] is it that you were looking-for[Y] Me? Did you not know that I   49
        must[31] be in the things[32] of My Father[33]?
    4C. And **they** did not understand[Z] the thing which He spoke to them[34]   50

  3B. And He went down with them, and came to Nazareth, and was being subject[35] to them[36]   51
  4B. And His mother was keeping[37] all these things in her heart
  5B. And Jesus was advancing[AA] in wisdom and stature[38], and in favor with God and people   52

1. That is, for the purpose of causing the fall of some and the rising of others. GK *1650*.
2. That is, for the purpose of becoming a sign from God that will be opposed by many. GK *1650*.
3. Or, "opposed, contradicted". On this word, see "contradict" in Rom 10:21.
4. Some manuscripts omit this word {C}.
5. That is, a sword of grief, as a result of the opposition just mentioned.
6. Or, "go through". GK *1451*.
7. Or, "reasonings". On this word, see Jam 2:4. Jesus is the catalyst that exposes what is inside everyone.
8. This word is the feminine form of "prophet" in 1 Cor 12:28. Same word as in Rev 2:20.
9. This is a participle, as in 1:7.
10. Or, "until". Some think Luke means "until *she was* 84 years *old*". Others think he means Anna was a widow for "up to 84 years", making her about 105 years old if it is assumed that she married at age 14. Some manuscripts say "about" instead of "up to" {N}.
11. Or, "withdrawing". This may imply that Anna lived there, or simply that she was always there. On this word, see 1 Tim 4:1.
12. Or, "worshiping". That is, serving God. On this word, see "worship" in Heb 12:28.
13. This phrase "night and day" means "continually". Note the different grammar in 1 Tim 5:5, "*by* night and *by* day", meaning "both during the night and during the day". See Rev 7:15 on these two phrases.
14. Anna was a prophet serving day and night in the temple. How long she had been there is not specified.
15. Some manuscripts say "And **she**, having... hour, was giving" {N}.
16. Or, "stood near". On this word, see "suddenly come upon" in 21:34.
17. That is, the hour Simeon spoke to them, v 27-35. This phrase, "at the very hour", is elsewhere only in Lk 10:21; 12:12; 13:31; 20:19; 24:33; Act 16:18; 22:13. The word "hour" is used 106 times. See also 1 Jn 2:18. GK *6052*.
18. Or, "praising-back". Used only here. GK *469*. Related to "praise" in 10:21.
19. Some manuscripts say "*to* the Lord" {K}.
20. Same word as in 1:68.
21. Some manuscripts say "in Jerusalem" {A}.
22. That is, all the things the Law required.
23. This is the same phrase used of John in 1:80. Some manuscripts add "*in* spirit" {N}, as in 1:80.
24. Instead of "His parents", some manuscripts say "Joseph and His mother" {N}.
25. More literally, "is", as the Greek typically phrases it.
26. Or, "group of travelers". Used only here. GK *5322*. Related to "travel with" in Act 9:7.
27. Some think Luke means that having gone a day's journey out and back, His parents found Jesus on the third day; others, that they searched for three days, two of them in Jerusalem; others, that they searched three days in Jerusalem.
28. Or, "Why did You act *toward* us in this manner". On this word, see Rev 13:13.
29. This word is used here and in Act 20:38 of mental pain. Elsewhere only in Lk 16:24, 25, of physical pain. GK *3849*. Related to "pain" in 1 Tim 6:10.
30. Jesus is surprised His parents did not know where He was, or where He would be.
31. Or, "have to". More literally, "that it is necessary *that* I be...". On this idiom, see Mt 16:21.
32. If Jesus is answering their "why" question, "Why did You do this? (v 48), then this means "at the *interests*" or "*business*" of My Father. If He is answering the "where" question implied in "why were you looking for Me" (v 49), then this means "in the *possessions*", or more narrowly, "in the *house*" of My Father. The grammar of the question indicates that a "yes" answer is expected. Note that Jesus says "My" not "our" Father.
33. Note the contrast between "Your father" in v 48, and "My Father" here.
34. That is, Joseph and Mary did not fully understand the implications of the fact the God was His Father.
35. That is, Jesus was continuing to live in submission to His parents in Nazareth. On this word, see Eph 5:21.
36. This is the last mention of Joseph. It is assumed that he died before 3:1.
37. Luke may be emphasizing this because Mary was his source for the information in chapters 1:5-2:52. Elsewhere only in Act 15:29. GK *1413*. Related to "preserving" in v 19. The Greek grammar of this section is different than the rest of the book, having a more "Hebrew" flavor.
38. This could mean "height" or "age, span of years". On this word, see "life span" in Mt 6:27.

A. Mt 7:27 B. Act 24:15, resurrection C. 2 Thes 2:9 D. Jam 5:20 E. 2 Thes 2:3 F. Rev 1:7 G. 2 Cor 11:27 H. Rev 10:7 J. Eph 5:18
K. Jn 13:29 L. Jn 18:28 M. Lk 1:9 N. Heb 2:10, perfect O. Jam 1:12, endure P. Act 14:19 Q. Act 11:25 R. Rom 16:7, kinsmen S. Lk 23:49
T. 2 Thes 2:7 U. Lk 9:18 V. Mk 2:12 W. Eph 3:4 X. Mt 7:28 Y. Phil 2:21, seeking Z. Mt 13:13 AA. 2 Tim 2:16

3A.[1] Now in *the* fifteenth year *of* the government[2] *of* Tiberius[3] Caesar[4]— Pontius Pilate[5] being-governor[A] *of* Judea, and Herod[6] being-tetrarch[7] *of* Galilee, and Philip[8] his brother being tetrarch *of* the region *of* Ituraea[9] and Trachonitis[10], and Lysanias being tetrarch *of* Abilene[11], ⸀in-the-time-of[12] *the* high priest Annas[13] and Caiaphas[14]—   3:1 / 2

    1B. *The* word *of* God came to[15] John, the son *of* Zechariah, in the wilderness[B]

        1C. And he went into all the surrounding-region[C] *of* the Jordan, proclaiming[D] *a* baptism[E] *of* repentance[F] for *the* forgiveness[G] *of* sins, ⸀as it has been written in *the* book *of the* words *of* Isaiah the prophet[16] [in Isa 40:3-5]—   3 / 4

            1D. "*A* voice *of one* shouting[H] in the wilderness— 'Prepare[J] the way[17] *of the* Lord, be making His paths straight[K]. ⸀Every valley will be filled[L], and every mountain and hill will be made-low[M]. And the crooked[N] *paths* will become[18] straight[K], and the rough *will become* smooth paths. ⸀And all flesh[19] will see the salvation[O] *of* God' "   5 / 6

        2C. Therefore[20] he was saying *to* the crowds coming out to be baptized[P] by him, "Brood[Q] *of* vipers— who showed[R] you to flee from the coming wrath[S]?   7

            1D. "Therefore produce fruits worthy[T] *of* repentance[F]   8
            2D. "And do not begin to say within[21] yourselves, 'We have Abraham *as our* father'

                1E. "For I say *to* you that God is able to raise-up[U] children *for* Abraham from these stones!
                2E. "And indeed the axe is **already** lying[22] at the root *of* the trees. Therefore every tree not producing good fruit is cut down and thrown into *the* fire"   9

        3C. And the crowds were questioning him, saying, "What then should we do?"   10

            1D. And having responded, he was saying *to* them, "Let the *one* having two tunics[23] give[24] *to* the *one* not having, and let the *one* having food be doing likewise"   11

        4C. And tax collectors also came to be baptized. And they said to him, "Teacher, what should we do?"   12

            1D. And the *one* said to them, "Be collecting[25] nothing more than the *amount* having been commanded[V]"   13

        5C. And *ones* serving-as-soldiers[W] also were questioning him, saying, "And us, what should we do?"   14

            1D. And he said *to* them, "Do not violently-extort[26] anyone, nor extort-with-false-charges[27]. And be content[X] *with* your wages[28]"

    2B. And while the populace[Y] *was* waiting-in-expectation[29] and all *were* pondering[Z] in their hearts about John— if perhaps **he** might be the Christ— ⸀John responded, saying *to* everyone   15 / 16

        1C. "**I**[30] am baptizing you *with* water— but the *One* more powerful *than* me is coming, *of* Whom I am not fit[AA] to untie the strap *of* His sandals

            1D. "**He** will baptize you with[31] *the* Holy Spirit and fire[32]—

1. Parallel account at Mt 3:1; Mk 1:2; Jn 1:19.
2. Or, "governorship". Used only here. GK *2449*. Related to "being governor" next, not to "king, kingdom".
3. Tiberius was the Roman Emperor from A.D. 14 to 37, after Augustus (2:1). GK *5501*. However, he became co-ruler with Augustus in A.D. 11 or 12, with authority over the provinces. So the beginning point of the fifteen years here is debated. In any case, a year between A.D. 26 and 29 is indicated. Consult the commentaries.
4. Caesar is the emperor's title. Used 29 times. GK *2790*.
5. Pilate was the fifth Roman prefect (a military officer put in charge of a district to maintain order) of Judea since the province was established in A.D. 6 (see "Archelaus", Mt 2:22). Used 55 times. GK *4397*. Pilate served from A.D. 26 to 36, when he was ordered to go to Rome to account for his actions by Vitellius, legate of Syria.
6. That is, Herod Antipas, on whom see Mt 14:1. His father Herod the Great gave him this territory, Mt 2:1. This Herod and his wife Herodias are the ones mentioned in Lk 3:19. Jesus was tried before this Herod, Lk 23:6-12.
7. Or, "being governor, being provincial ruler". This position was lower than a king, and under the authority of Rome. This verb is used only in this verse. GK *5489*. Related to the noun in 3:19.
8. That is, Philip II, the half-brother of Antipas, Mt 2:1. His capital was Philip's Caesarea (see Mt 16:13). He reigned from 4 B.C. (the death of his father Herod the Great) until his death in A.D. 34. He married Salome (see Mt 14:6, the one who danced), who was the daughter of his half-brother Philip I and Herodias (see Mt 14:3). In A.D. 37, his territory was given to Agrippa I (see Act 12:1; Mt 2:1) by Emperor Caligula. GK *5805*.
9. This was a region southwest of Damascus. Its capital was Chalcis. Used only here. GK *2714*.
10. This was a region south of Damascus. Used only here. GK *5551*.
11. This was a region northwest of Damascus. Used only here. GK *9*.
12. Same word as in Mt 1:11; Mk 2:26; Lk 4:27; Act 11:28. GK *2093*. Or, "during *the* high-priest*hood of* Annas...", the word "high priest" (GK *797*, used 122 times) being used this way only here.
13. When Archelaus (Mt 2:22) was deposed in A.D. 6 and Judea became a Roman province, the Romans took over the appointing of the high priests. Annas was the first, appointed by Quirinius (Lk 2:1). He served from A.D. 6 to 15, when he was deposed by Valerius Gratus. Elsewhere only in Jn 18:13, 24; Act 4:6. GK *484*. However, he dominated the high priesthood for years from behind the scenes. Seven others from his family were appointed as high priest.
14. Caiaphas was the son-in-law of Annas. He was appointed by Valerius Gratus (the prefect before Pilate) and served from A.D. 18 to 36. He was deposed by Vitellius, legate of Syria, after Vitellius ordered Pilate to go to Rome. Elsewhere only in Mt 26:3, 57; Jn 11:49; 18:13, 14, 24, 28; Act 4:6. GK *2780*.
15. Or, "upon". GK *2093*.
16. Some manuscripts add "saying" {K}.
17. This word means a physical "path, road, way", and a "journey". It is also used of God's "ways", and of a "way of life". Christianity is called "the Way" in Act 9:2. Used 101 times. GK *3847*.
18. This is an idiom, literally "will be for straight", a Hebrew way of speaking. Likewise with "the rough for smooth paths".
19. On "all flesh", see "no flesh" in Mt 24:22.
20. That is, because the word of God came upon John to prepare the Lord's way, v 3-4.
21. Or, "among". The Jews in Jn 8:39 say this very thing.
22. Or, "being laid". Same word as in Mt 3:10.
23. That is, the inner garment worn next to the skin. On this word, see Mt 5:40.
24. This word means "give a share", a part of what you have. On this word, see Rom 12:8.
25. Or, "carrying out". Used in this sense also in 19:23. The whole tax system was built on not doing this. A "publican" contracted with Rome to deliver a specified amount from the "tax farm" for which he was responsible. Everything above that he kept for himself. He then hired subordinates, down to the actual "tax-collectors" (see Mt 18:17) like Matthew, who did the same. On this word, see "practice" in Rom 2:1.
26. Or, "intimidate, oppress, extort using violence". Used only here. GK *1398*. Related to "shake". Do not "shake down" anyone, threatening or using violence unless they give you money. Related to "abuse of power" (not in NT).
27. Or, "extort using false accusations". Elsewhere only as "extort" in Lk 19:8, of one repenting of doing so. GK *5193*.
28. Or, "rations, allowances, pay". A military term. On this word, see Rom 6:23.
29. Same word as in Act 27:33; 28:6. Elsewhere only as "expect" in Mt 24:50; Lk 8:40; 12:46; Act 3:5; 10:24; 28:6; "look for" in Mt 11:3; Lk 7:19, 20; 2 Pet 3:12, 13, 14; and "wait for" in Lk 1:21. GK *4659*. Related to "expectation" in 21:26.
30. John uses grammar that emphasizes the contrast between the two halves of this sentence.
31. Or, "in". On this word, see Mk 1:8.
32. On this, see Mt 3:12.

A. Lk 2:2 B. Mt 3:1 C. Mk 1:28 D. 2 Tim 4:2 E. Mk 1:4 F. 2 Cor 7:10 G. Col 1:14 H. Mt 3:3 J. Mk 14:15 K. Act 8:21 L. Eph 5:18 M. Phil 4:12, humbled N. 1 Pet 2:18 O. Lk 2:30 P. Mk 1:8 Q. Mt 3:7 R. Mt 3:7 S. Rev 16:19 T. Rev 16:6 U. Mt 28:6, arose V. 1 Cor 7:17, directing W. 1 Tim 1:18, fight X. 2 Cor 12:9, sufficient Y. Rev 21:3, peoples Z. Lk 5:21, reasoning AA. 2 Cor 3:5, sufficient

	1E. "Whose winnowing-tool[1] *is* in His hand *so as* to clean-out[2] His threshing floor, and gather the wheat into His barn	17
	2E. "But He will burn up the chaff[3] *with an* inextinguishable[A] fire"	
3B.	So indeed, while also exhorting[B] many other *things*, he was announcing-good-news-to[C] the people	18
4B.[4]	But Herod[5] the tetrarch[6]—	19
	1C. While being rebuked[7] by him	
	1D. Concerning Herodias, the wife *of* his brother[8]	
	2D. And concerning all *the* evil[D] *things* which Herod did	
	2C. Also added[E] this to everything— he also[9] locked-up[F] John in prison[G]	20
5B.[10]	And it came about when all the people were baptized[11], Jesus also having been baptized and praying[H], *that*	21
	1C. The heaven was opened	
	2C. And the Holy Spirit descended upon Him *in a* bodily[12] form[13] like *a* dove	22
	3C. And *a* voice came from heaven[14]— "**You** are My beloved[J] Son. With You I was[15] well-pleased"	
4A. And Jesus Himself was, [when] beginning *His ministry,* about thirty years old, being *a* son, as it was being supposed[16], *of* Joseph		23
1B.[17] The *son of* Heli, the *son of* Matthat, the *son of* Levi, the *son of* Melchi, the *son of* Jannai, the *son of* Joseph, the *son of* Mattathias, the *son of* Amos, the *son of* Nahum, the *son of* Hesli, the *son of* Naggai, the *son of* Maath, the *son of* Mattathias, the *son of* Semein, the *son of* Josech, the *son of* Joda, the *son of* Joanan, the *son of* Rhesa, the *son of* Zerubbabel, the *son of* Shealtiel, the *son of* Neri, the *son of* Melchi, the *son of* Addi, the *son of* Cosam, the *son of* Elmadam, the *son of* Er, the *son of* Joshua, the *son of* Eliezer, the *son of* Jorim, the *son of* Matthat, the *son of* Levi, the *son of* Simeon, the *son of* Judah, the *son of* Joseph, the *son of* Jonam, the *son of* Eliakim, the *son of* Melea, the *son of* Menna, the *son of* Mattatha, the *son of* Nathan, the *son of* David, the *son of* Jesse, the *son of* Obed, the *son of* Boaz, the *son of* Sala[18], the *son of* Nahshon, the *son of* Aminadab, the *son of* Admin, the *son of* Arni[19], the *son of* Hezron, the *son of* Perez, the *son of* Judah, the *son of* Jacob, the *son of* Isaac, the *son of* Abraham, the *son of* Terah, the *son of* Nahor, the *son of* Serug, the *son of* Reu, the *son of* Peleg, the *son of* Heber, the *son of* Shelah, the *son of* Cainan, the *son of* Arphaxad, the *son of* Shem, the *son of* Noah, the *son of* Lamech, the *son of* Methuselah, the *son of* Enoch, the *son of* Jared, the *son of* Mahalaleel, the *son of* Cainan, the *son of* Enosh, the *son of* Seth, the *son of* Adam, the *son of* God		24 25 26 27 28-29 30 31 32 33 34 35 36 37 38
2B.[20] And Jesus, full[K] *of the* Holy Spirit, returned from the Jordan. And He was being led[21] in[22] the Spirit in[23] the wilderness *for* forty days while being tempted[24] by the devil[L]. And He did not eat anything during those days. And they[25] having been completed[26], He was hungry		4:1 2
	1C. And the devil said *to* Him, "If[27] You are God's **Son**, say *to* this stone that it should become bread"	3
	1D. And Jesus responded to him, "It has been written [in Deut 8:3] that 'Mankind[28] shall not live on bread alone[29]' "	4

1. On this word, see Mt 3:12. This tool was used to throw the threshings into the air so the wind could separate the grain from the chaff.
2. That is, cleanse it of threshings by first separating them into wheat and chaff, and then taking each to their destinations. Used only here. GK *1350*. Related to "cleanse out" in Mt 3:12.
3. Same word as in Mt 3:12. That is, the husks and straw left after the wheat is removed.
4. Parallel account at Mt 4:12; Mk 1:14. Compare Mt 14:3-4; Mk 6:17-18; Jn 4:1-3.
5. That is, Herod Antipas, on whom see Mt 14:1. On his wife Herodias, see Mt 14:3.
6. Or, "governor". Elsewhere only in Mt 14:1; Lk 9:7; Act 13:1. GK *5490*. Related to the verb in v 1.
7. On this word, see "exposed" in Eph 5:11.
8. Some manuscripts add "Philip" {N}, as in Mt 14:3; Mk 6:17.
9. Some manuscripts omit this word, {C}.
10. Parallel account at Mt 3:13; Mk 1:9. Compare Jn 1:29-34.
11. More literally, "at the being baptized *as to* all the people". That is, at the time when John baptized all the people. It is a general reference to that period of time. Some think Luke means that Jesus came last on this day, "*after* all the people *were* baptized". On this word, see Mk 1:8.
12. That is, having a body with an outward appearance similar to a dove. Elsewhere only in 1 Tim 4:8. GK *5394*. Related to "body" in Eph 1:23.
13. Or, "outward appearance". On this word, see "appearance" in 2 Cor 5:7.
14. Some manuscripts add "saying" {K}.
15. On "I was well pleased", see Mt 17:5.
16. Compare the genealogy at Mt 1:1.
17. But actually the son of Mary. This is the Greek word order. Some think this is Mary's genealogy, Heli being her father. Others think this is Joseph's personal genealogy, as opposed to his legal, royal genealogy in Mt 1. See Mt 1:16. There are other views. On this word, see "think" in Act 14:19.
18. Some manuscripts say "Salmon" {B}.
19. Some manuscripts have the last three names as "Adam, Admin, Arni"; others, as "Aminadab, Admin, Aram"; others, as "Aminadab, Aram, Joram"; others as two names, "Aminadab, Aram" (as in Mt 1:3-4) {C}.
20. Parallel account at Mt 4:1; Mk 1:12.
21. This word means "to lead, bring", and "to go" (see Mk 1:38). Used 69 times. GK *72*.
22. Or, "by, in union with". GK *1877*. Same word as in v 14. Not the same word as "by" the devil in v 2, or as "by" the Spirit in Mt 4:1.
23. GK *1877*. Some manuscripts say "into" {N}, as in Mt 4:1 (GK *1650*).
24. Or, "tested". On this word, see Heb 2:18. Some think this means Jesus endured temptations throughout the forty days, in addition to the ones mentioned next, which Luke and Matthew say were afterward.
25. That is, the forty days.
26. Or, "concluded, finished, ended". On this word, see "accomplished" in Mk 13:4. Some manuscripts add "afterward" {K}, as in Mt 4:2.
27. Or, "Since". The grammar assumes the truth of this premise. Same in v 9. Assuming that You are what God said You are (3:22), prove it with Your power (v 3), or His power (v 9). See Mt 4:3 on this.
28. Or, "The man, The person". On this word, see Mt 4:4.
29. Some manuscripts add "but on every word *of* God" {B}, similar to Mt 4:4.

A. Mk 9:43 B. Rom 12:8 C. Act 5:42 D. Act 25:18 E. Lk 17:5, increase F. Act 26:10 G. Act 5:22 H. 1 Tim 2:8 J. Mt 3:17 K. Mt 14:20 L. Rev 12:9

2C. And[1] having led Him up, he showed Him all the kingdoms *of* the world[2] in *a* moment[3] *of* time. And the devil said *to* Him, "I will give You all this authority[A] and their glory, because it has been handed-over[B] *to* me, and I give it *to* whomever I wish. °Therefore if **You** worship[4] before me, it will all be Yours"

    1D. And having responded, Jesus said *to* him "It[5] has been written [in Deut 6:13], 'You shall worship *the* Lord your God, and serve[C] Him only'"

3C. And he led Him into Jerusalem and stood *Him* on the pinnacle *of* the temple. And he said *to* Him, "If You are God's **Son**, throw Yourself down from here. °For it has been written [in Ps 91:11] that 'He will command[D] His angels concerning You *that they might* protect[6] You', °and [in Ps 91:12] that[7] 'They will lift You up on *their* hands that You may not ever strike Your foot against *a* stone'"

    1D. And having responded, Jesus said *to* him that "It has been said [in Deut 6:16], 'You shall not put *the* Lord your God to the test[8]'"

4C. And having completed[9] every temptation[10], the devil departed from Him until *an* opportune-time[E]

5A.[11] And Jesus returned to Galilee in the power *of* the Spirit. And news[12] about Him went out throughout the whole surrounding-region. °And **He** was teaching in their synagogues, while being glorified[13] by all

  1B.[14] And He came to Nazareth,[15] where He had been brought-up[16]. And in accordance with the *thing* having become-a-custom[17] *with* him, He entered into the synagogue on the day *of* the Sabbath, and stood up to read

    1C. And *the* scroll[F] *of* the prophet Isaiah was given *to* Him. And having unrolled[18] the scroll, He found the place where it had been written[19] [in Isa 61:1-2]—

      1D. "*The* Spirit *of the* Lord *is* upon Me, because of which He anointed[20] Me to[21] announce-good-news[G] *to* poor[H] ones. He has sent me out[22]

        1E. "To proclaim[J] *a* release[23] *to* captives[24], and recovery-of-sight *to* blind *ones*
        2E. "To send-out[25] with *a* release *ones* having been broken[26]
        3E. "To proclaim *the* acceptable[27] year *of the* Lord"

    2C. And having rolled up the scroll, having given *it* back *to* the attendant[K], He sat-*down*[28]. And the eyes *of* everyone in the synagogue were looking-intently[29] *at* Him
    3C. And He began[30] to say *to* them that "Today this Scripture[L] has been fulfilled[M] in your ears"[31]

      1D. And they all were testifying[32] *concerning* Him, and marveling[N] at the words *of* grace[33] proceeding from His mouth[34]
      2D. And they were saying, "Is not this *One* Joseph's son?"[35]

    4C. And He said to them, "You will surely[36] speak this proverb[37] *to* Me— 'Physician[38], cure[O] yourself'[39]. Do also here in your hometown[40] all-that we heard having taken place in Capernaum"
    5C. But He said, "Truly[41] I say *to* you that no prophet[P] is acceptable[42] in his hometown[Q]. °And I say *to* you in accordance with [God's] truth[43]—

      1D. "There were many widows in Israel in the days *of* Elijah, when the heaven[R] was shut for three years and six months, when *a* great famine[S] took place over all the land[44]

1. Matthew and Luke reverse the order of the second and third temptations. Luke progresses geographically up to a climax in Jerusalem. Matthew may progress chronologically. Some manuscripts say "And the devil, having led Him up to *a* high mountain, showed..." {N}, similar to Mt 4:8.
2. On this word, see Heb 2:5. Mt 4:8 uses GK *3180*.
3. Or, "instant". Used only here. GK *5117*.
4. Or, "pay homage". Same word as in v 8. On this word, see Mt 14:33.
5. Some manuscripts say "Get behind Me Satan. It..." {N}.
6. Or, "guard carefully". Used only here. GK *1428*.
7. In Luke, Satan quotes Ps 91:11 and 12 separately. Mt 4:6 combines them into a single quote
8. On the verb "put to the test", and the meaning of this, see Mt 4:7.
9. Same word as in v 2.
10. The three temptations mentioned are just samples. On this word, see "trials" in Jam 1:2.
11. Parallel account at Mt 4:12; Mk 1:14. Compare Jn 4:1-3.
12. Same word as in Mt 9:26.
13. Same word as in Lk 2:20; 5:25, 26; 7:16; 13:13; 17:15; 18:43; 23:47. On this word, see Rom 8:30.
14. Compare Mt 13:53-58; Mk 6:1-6; Jn 4:43-44.
15. Some think this is the same visit described at Mt 13:53; Mk 6:1, topically placed first by Luke to highlight the key issue of the ministry of Jesus (faith in Him and His message) and His rejection. Note that the second main section of the book also begins with a rejection, 9:52-56. Others think there were two separate visits to Nazareth, and that this one occurred before Jesus left Nazareth in Mt 4:13.
16. Or, "had grown up". This is a participle, "He was having been brought up". On this word, see "feed" in 23:29.
17. Same phrase as in Act 17:2. Elsewhere only as "be accustomed" in Mt 27:15; Mk 10:1. GK *1665*. Related to "custom" in Lk 1:9. Some think Luke is referring to the lifelong custom of Jesus attending on the Sabbath; others, to His custom at this time in His ministry of standing to read and speak out to the people in their synagogues, v 15, 31.
18. Some manuscripts say "opened" {B}. Used only here, as is "roll up" in v 20. Scrolls were "unrolled". Books in leaf form like our books (they are called a "codex") were "opened". The synagogue would have had a scroll. GK *408*.
19. This is a participle, where "it was having been written".
20. This is the verb related to "Christ", "the anointed *One*". Elsewhere only in Act 4:27; 10:38; 2 Cor 1:21; Heb 1:9. GK *5987*. Related to "smear on" in Jn 9:6; and "rub in" in Rev 3:18. Compare "Messiah" in Jn 1:41.
21. This is the Greek word order. Some punctuate this "anointed Me. He has sent me out to announce good news *to* poor *ones*", making "to announce good news *to* poor *ones*" point 1E., parallel with the three that follow.
22. Some manuscripts add "to heal the *ones* having been broken *as to* the heart" {A}, as in Isa 61:1.
23. On this word, see "forgiveness" in Col 1:14.
24. Or, "prisoners". Used only here. GK *171*. Related to the two words in Eph 4:8.
25. Same word as earlier in the verse. Jesus was sent out to send out others. On this word, see Mk 3:14.
26. Or, "shattered", whether in spirit or body. Used only here. GK *2575*. Used of "breaking" pottery. Compare Mt 5:3-4.
27. Or, "favorable, welcome". It is the Lord's favored year for them at last. Same word as in v 24. Elsewhere only in Act 10:35; 2 Cor 6:2; Phil 4:18. GK *1283*.
28. That is, sat down to teach, facing them all from the front. In that day, teachers stood to read, sat to teach.
29. Elsewhere only in Lk 22:56; Act 1:10; 3:4, 12; 6:15; 7:55; 10:4; 11:6; 13:9; 14:9; 23:1; 2 Cor 3:7, 13. GK *867*.
30. This may indicate that Jesus spoke at length, this verse giving only a summary of what He said.
31. That is, Jesus is there, sent by God to proclaim and do these things. He is the answer to this prophecy.
32. That is, bearing witness to the good things Jesus had said and done, particularly to the miracles.
33. Or, "gracious words", words characterized by grace. Some think Luke is referring to the winsome and attractive words of Jesus in general; others, more specifically, to the words of healing and forgiveness referred to in v 18. In any case, they were words not expected from one such as Joseph's son, and are in contrast to the words of rejection Jesus speaks next in v 24-27.
34. The first response of the people in Nazareth to Jesus is positive. They initially praise Him, and marvel at His speaking and at what He has become, but they do not believe Him.
35. Some take this as another statement of the initial positive response. Luke gives no indication it is negative. This question indicates a hometown pride that Jesus was one of them. The famous prophet from Capernaum was their local boy. The grammar indicates that a "yes" answer is expected. In this case, the fuller negative response quoted in Matthew and Mark comes a little later. Others take this as Luke's summary of the negative response quoted more fully in Matthew and Mark. This is their justification for rejecting Him.
36. Or, "by all means, certainly, doubtless". On this word, see 1 Cor 9:10.
37. On this word, see "parable" in Mt 13:3. Here it means "figurative saying, proverb".
38. Since this is related to "heal" (in Mt 8:8), it could be rendered "Healer, cure Yourself". GK *2620*.
39. Some think Jesus means "Repair your own status with us" by doing these things here. Prove You are what You just claimed to be in v 18-19. Others think it is explained by what follows, "Give Your medicine to Your own people". You will surely ask Me to heal you as I did them.
40. Same word as in v 24. On this word, see "homeland" in Heb 11:14.
41. On this word, see Mt 5:18. Not related to "truth". It is usually translated "amen". Elsewhere by Luke only in 12:37; 18:17, 29; 21:32; 23:43. Compare "truly" in 9:27.
42. Or, "welcome". On this word, see v 19. Therefore, even if Jesus did the same miracles He did in Capernaum, He would still not be acceptable to them, due to their unbelief.
43. This phrase, "in accordance with truth" (either God's truth, or true reality) is elsewhere only in Mk 12:14, 32; Lk 20:21; 22:59; Act 4:27; 10:34. As the OT shows, a prophet is not a miracle worker sent to heal everyone having a need. The miracle is not the message, but a sign pointing to the source of the message, God. Jesus was not sent to do miracles for them simply because they are His hometown folk, but to announce the good news, v 43. His miracles are intended to produce the reaction seen next in v 36, but this was not possible here, due to their unbelief.
44. See 1 King 17:9.

A. Rev 6:8 B. Mt 26:21 C. Heb 12:28, worship D. Mk 10:3 E. Mt 8:29, time F. Rev 5:1 G. Act 5:42 H. Gal 4:9 J. 2 Tim 4:2 K. 1 Cor 4:1 L. 2 Pet 3:16 M. Eph 5:18, filled N. Rev 17:8 O. Mt 8:7 P. 1 Cor 12:28 Q. Heb 11:14, homeland R. 2 Cor 2:2 S. Lk 21:11

        1E. "And Elijah was sent to none *of* them— except to [the village of] Zarephath of-Sidon, to *a* widow woman"   26

    2D. "And there were many lepers in Israel in the time of Elisha the prophet   27

        1E. "And none *of* them was cleansed[A]— except Naaman the Syrian"[1]

  6C. And[2] they were all filled[B] *with* fury[3] in the synagogue while hearing these *things*   28

    1D. And having arisen, they drove[C] Him outside *of* the city, and led Him up to *the* brow *of the* hill on which their city had been built so as to throw Him down the cliff [4]   29
    2D. But **He**, having gone[5] through *the* middle[D] *of* them, was proceeding   30

2B.[6] And He went down to Capernaum, *a* city *of* Galilee   31

  1C. And He was teaching them on the Sabbath

    1D. And they were astounded[E] at His teaching, because His message[7] was with authority[F]   32

  2C. And in the synagogue there was *a* man having *a* spirit *of an* unclean demon[8]. And he cried-out[G] *with a* loud voice,[9] *"Let us* alone[10]! What do we have to do with You,[11] Jesus from-Nazareth[H]? Did You come to destroy[J] us? I know You, Who You are— the Holy[K] *One of* God!"   33, 34

    1D. And Jesus rebuked[L] him, saying, "Be silenced[M] and come out from him"   35
    2D. And the demon, having thrown him down[12] into *their* midst[D], came out from him, not having hurt[N] him at all
    3D. And astonishment[O] came over everyone. And they were talking-with[P] one another, saying, "What *is* this message[13]? Because He commands[Q] the unclean spirits with authority and power, and they come out!"   36
    4D. And *the* news[14] about Him was going out into every place *of* the surrounding-region[R]   37

  3C.[15] And having arisen from the synagogue, He entered into the house *of* Simon   38

    1D. Now *the* mother-in-law *of* Simon was being gripped[16] *with a* high fever[S]

        1E. And they asked Him concerning her
        2E. And having stood over her, He rebuked[L] the fever, and it left her   39
        3E. And having stood up at-once[T], she was serving[U] them

    2D. And while the sun *was* setting[17], all who were having *ones* being sick[V] *with* various diseases[W] brought them to Him   40

        1E. And the *One*, laying[X] *His* hands on each one *of* them, was curing[Y] them
        2E. And demons also were coming out from many, shouting[18], and saying that "**You** are the Son[19] *of* God!" And rebuking[L] *them,* He was not allowing them to speak, because they knew *that* He was[20] the Christ   41

  4C.[21] And having become day, having gone out, He went to *a* desolate[Z] place   42

    1D. And the crowds were seeking-for[22] Him. And they came to Him and were holding Him back[23] *that He might* not proceed from them

1. See 2 King 5:1-14.
2. The two OT examples are both cases of doing a miracle for a Gentile, rather than for unbelieving Israel. Jesus is classing these Jews of His hometown with unbelieving Israel in the days of Elijah and Elisha.
3. Jesus rebuffs His hometown people, and their heart is exposed in their actions, proving that He was right about them.
4. This verb, "to throw down the cliff" is used only here. GK *2889*.
5. Luke gives no indication of how this happened. Perhaps Jesus rebuked them. Perhaps the Spirit restrained them. Jesus walked through the crowd and went on His way. GK *1451*.
6. Parallel account at Mk 1:21.
7. Or, "word". Same word as in v 36. On this word, see "word" in 1 Cor 12:8.
8. Mark calls it an "unclean spirit" (Mk 1:23), a phrase used 23 times in the NT. "Demon" occurs 62 times in the NT (see 1 Cor 10:20). The phrases "spirit *of an* unclean demon" and "unclean demon" are used only here. "Spirit" and "demon" are used together in a phrase elsewhere only in Rev 16:14, "spirits *of* demons". Since pagans used this word to refer to gods and deities (as in Act 17:18), "unclean" is added to make the meaning clear.
9. Some manuscripts add "saying" {K}.
10. Some think this is the word "Ah", a scream, a word used only here (GK *1568*). Others think it is the command "let *us* alone", from the word "permit" in 1 Cor 10:13.
11. This is an idiom, literally, "What [is there] *for* us and *for* You". On this idiom, see Jn 2:4.
12. On the verb "to throw down", see "throw forth" in Mt 9:36.
13. Or, "word". Same word as in v 32. It could be referring broadly to the message Jesus was proclaiming, or narrowly to the word spoken to cast out this demon.
14. Or, "report". This word refers to the "sound" coming from whatever is in the context; here, from the people reacting to Jesus. Elsewhere only as "noise" in Act 2:2; and "blast" in Heb 12:19. GK *2491*. Our word "echo" comes from this word. Related to "roar" in 21:25.
15. Parallel account at Mt 8:14, 16; Mk 1:29.
16. Or, "held under the control of, ruled", in a negative sense, "afflicted". Same word as in Mt 4:24.
17. That is, after the sun went down, ending the Sabbath, but before dark. Elsewhere only in Mk 1:32. GK *1544*.
18. On this word, see Act 22:23. Some manuscripts say "crying-out" {C}.
19. Some manuscripts say "... are the Christ, the Son..." {N}.
20. More literally, "is", as the Greek typically phrases it.
21. Parallel account at Mk 1:35.
22. On this word, see Phil 4:17. Related to "seeking" in Mk 1:37.
23. Or, "detaining Him". On this word, see "hold down" in Rom 1:18.

A. Heb 9:22 B. Act 2:4 C. Jn 12:31, cast out D. 2 Thes 2:7, midst E. Mt 7:28 F. Rev 6:8 G. Lk 23:18 H. Mk 1:24 J. 1 Cor 1:18, perish
K. 1 Pet 1:16 L. 2 Tim 4:2, warn M. Mk 4:39 N. Mk 16:18 O. Act 3:10, wonder P. Act 25:12 Q. Lk 8:25 R. Mk 1:28 S. Act 28:8
T. Mt 21:19 U. 1 Pet 4:10, ministering V. 2 Tim 4:20 W. Mt 8:17 X. Lk 10:30, laid on Y. Mt 8:7 Z. Mt 3:1, wilderness

2D. And the *One* said to them that "I must[1] **also** announce the kingdom[A] *of* God as good news[2] *to* the other cities, because I was sent-forth[B] for[3] this *purpose*" — 43

3B. And He was proclaiming[C] in the synagogues *of* Judea.[4] *And it came about during the crowd's pressing-upon[D] Him and listening-to[5] the word *of* God, that[6] **He** was standing beside the lake[7] *of* Gennesaret[8] — 44-5:1

    1C. And[9] He saw two boats standing beside[10] the lake. And the fishermen, having gotten-out of them, were washing[E] *their* nets — 2

    2C. And having gotten into one *of* the boats, which was Simon's, He asked him to put-out *a* little from the land. And having sat-*down*, He was teaching the crowds from the boat — 3

    3C. And when He ceased[F] speaking, He said to Simon, "Put-out into the deep[G] [water] and lower[11] your nets for *a* catch" — 4

        1D. And having responded, Simon said, "Master[12], having labored[H] through *the* whole night, we took nothing. But at[13] Your word, I will lower the nets — 5

        2D. And having done this, they enclosed[J] *a* large number *of* fish. And their nets were being torn[K]. *And they signaled[14] *to their* companions[15] in the other boat *that,* having come, *they might* help[L] them. And they came. And they filled[M] both the boats so that they[16] *were* sinking — 6, 7

        3D. And having seen *it*, Simon Peter fell at the knees *of* Jesus, saying, "Depart from me, because I am *a* sinful man, Master[17]" — 8

            1E. For astonishment[18] at the catch *of* fish which they took[19] seized him, and all the *ones* with him. *And likewise also James and John, sons *of* Zebedee, who were partners[20] *with* Simon — 9, 10

        4D. And Jesus said to Simon, "Do not be fearing. From now *on* you will be catching[21] people[N]!"

    4C. And having brought[22] *their* boats on land, having left[O] everything, they followed Him — 11

4B.[23] And it came about during His being in one *of* the cities that[24] behold— *there was a* man full[P] *of* leprosy — 12

    1C. And having seen Jesus, having fallen on *his* face, he begged[Q] Him, saying, "Master, if You are willing[R], You are able to cleanse[S] me"

    2C. And having stretched-out[T] *His* hand, He touched him, saying, "I am willing. Be cleansed". And immediately the leprosy departed from him — 13

    3C. And **He** ordered[U] him to tell no one, "But having gone, show yourself *to* the priest and offer[25] *the things* for your cleansing just as Moses commanded[V], for *a* testimony[W] *to* them" — 14

    4C. But the word about Him was spreading[26] more, and large crowds were coming together to hear, and to be cured[27] from their infirmities[X] — 15

    5C. But **He** was retreating[28] within the desolate *places* and praying — 16

5B.[29] And it came about on one *of* the days, that[30] **He** was teaching. And Pharisees and Law-teachers[31] were sitting *there* who had come[32] from every village *of* Galilee and Judea and Jerusalem. And *the* power *of the* Lord was *present* that He *might* be healing[33] — 17

    1C. And behold— men bringing on *a* bed *a* man who had been paralyzed[34]. And they were seeking[Y] to bring him in, and to place him[35] before Him — 18

        1D. And not having found by what *way* they might bring him in because of the crowd, having gone up on the housetop[36], they let him down through the tiles, with the little-bed[37], into *their* midst, in front of Jesus — 19

1. Or, "have to". On this idiom, see Mt 16:21.
2. The phrase "announcing the kingdom of God as good news" is similar to that in 8:1; 16:16; and Act 8:12. On the verb "announce as good news", see Act 5:42.
3. This idiom is used only here. GK *2093*. Not the same word as Mk 1:38 (GK *1650*).
4. This sentence is parallel to Mt 4:23; Mk 1:39. Some manuscripts say "Galilee" {B}.
5. Some manuscripts say "Him *that they might* listen to the word *of* God" {N}.
6. This word is the usual word "and", GK *2779*. This construction, "and it came about... that", with this word meaning "that" in imitation of a Hebrew way of speaking, occurs only in Luke (Lk 5:1, 12, 17; 8:1, 22; 9:28, 51; 14:1; 17:11; 19:15; 24:4, 15; Act 11:26). Mt 9:10 is similar.
7. Luke always calls it a lake, never a "sea". Used 11 times. GK *3349*.
8. That is, the Sea of Galilee. It is called such only here, the only place Luke names it. On this word, see Mk 6:53. See also "Tiberias" in Jn 6:1.
9. Some think v 2-11 is the same incident as in Mt 4:18-22; Mk 1:16-20; others, a different incident.
10. Same word as in v 1. Jesus stood "beside the lake" (on shore), the boats stood "beside the lake" (in the water).
11. This command is plural, for Simon's crew must help do this.
12. The root word means "to be set over, to stand over", and this word means "master, superintendent, captain, chief, commander, boss, supervisor, president, chairman, governor, etc". Elsewhere only in Luke 8:24, 45; 9:33, 49; 17:13, all addressing Jesus as here. GK *2181*. Related to "know about" in Act 18:25. In parallel passages, Matthew says "Lord", and Mark says "Teacher" or "Rabbi". Not related to "master, lord" in v 8, or to "master, ruler" in 2:29.
13. Or, "upon, on the basis of ". GK *2093*.
14. The other boat was still on the shore. Used only here. GK *2916*. "Waved down" is the idea here.
15. Some think Luke is referring to James and John, as in v 10; others, to hired hands. On this word, see "partakers" in Heb 3:1.
16. The grammar indicates that this refers to the boats.
17. On this word, which Luke uses over 200 times, see Mt 8:2. Same word as in v 12.
18. Same word as in 4:36.
19. Or, "caught, seized". On this word, see "conceived" in 2:21. Related to "took" in v 5.
20. Or, "sharers". Not the same word as in v 7. On this word, see "sharers" in 2 Pet 1:4.
21. Or, "catching alive, capturing". Related to "catch" in v 4, 9, with "alive" added. On this word, see 2 Tim 2:26.
22. This is the same word as "put in" in Act 27:3 and 28:12, but with different grammar. GK *2864*.
23. Parallel account at Mt 8:2; Mk 1:40.
24. Same word as in v 1.
25. Same word as in Mk 1:44; Mt 8:4. See there on this verse.
26. Or, "going through [the region]". GK *1451*.
27. On this word, see Mt 8:7. Some manuscripts add "by Him" {N}.
28. Or, "going back, withdrawing, retiring". Elsewhere only in 9:10. GK *5723*.
29. Parallel account at Mt 9:1; Mk 2:1.
30. Same word as in v 1.
31. That is, scribes, emphasizing them as teachers of the Law. On this word, see 1 Tim 1:7. Related to "Law-experts" in 7:30.
32. This is a participle, "who were having come".
33. Or, "[present] for Him to be healing". Some manuscripts say "that *He might* be healing them" {A}. On this word, see Mt 8:8.
34. This is a participle, a man who "was having been paralyzed". On this word, see "made feeble" in Heb 12:12.
35. Some manuscripts omit this word, leaving it implied {C}.
36. The flat housetops were reached by outside stairs. Elsewhere only in Mt 10:27; 24:17; Mk 13:15; Lk 12:3; 17:31; and Act 10:9, where Peter was praying there. GK *1560*.
37. Elsewhere only in v 24. GK *3110*. Related to "bed" in v 18.

A. Mt 3:2 B. Mk 3:14, send out C. 2 Tim 4:2 D. Lk 23:23 E. Rev 7:14 F. 1 Cor 13:8 G. 2 Cor 8:2 H. Mt 11:28, being weary J. Gal 3:22, confine K. Lk 8:29 L. Lk 2:21, conceived M. Act 2:4 N. Mt 4:4, mankind O. Mt 6:12, forgive P. Mt 14:20 Q. 2 Cor 8:4 R. Jn 7:17 S. Heb 9:22 T. Act 27:30 U. 1 Tim 1:3, command V. Act 17:26, appointed W. Act 4:33 X. Mt 8:17, weakness Y. Phil 2:21

2C. And having seen their faith[A], He said[1], "Man,[2] your sins have been forgiven[B] you" 20
3C. And the scribes and the Pharisees began to reason[3], saying, "Who is this *One* Who is speaking blasphemies[C]? Who is able to forgive sins except God alone?"[4] 21
4C. But Jesus, having known[D] their reasonings[5], having responded, said to them, "Why are you reasoning in your hearts? 22

    1D. "Which is easier— to say, 'Your sins have been forgiven you', or to say, 'Arise and walk'? 23
    2D. "But in order that you may know that the Son *of* Man has authority[E] on earth to forgive sins"— He said *to* the *one* having been paralyzed, "I say *to* you, arise[F], and having picked up your little-bed, proceed to your house" 24

5C. And having stood-up[G] at once in their presence, having picked up *the thing* upon which he was lying-down, he went to his house glorifying[H] God 25
6C. And astonishment[J] seized[K] everyone. And they were glorifying[H] God. And they were filled[L] *with* awe[M], saying that "We saw incredible[6] *things* today" 26

6B.[7] And after these *things*, He went out and saw[8] *a* tax-collector[N], Levi[9] *by* name, sitting at the tax-office[10]. And He said *to* him, "Be following Me!" ˚And having left-behind[O] everything, having stood up, he was following Him 27, 28

  1C. And Levi made *a* great reception[11] *for* Him in his house. And there was *a* large crowd *of* tax collectors and others who were reclining [to eat] with them 29
  2C. And the Pharisees and their scribes[12] were grumbling[13] to His disciples, saying, "For what reason are you[14] eating and drinking with the tax collectors and sinners?" 30

    1D. And having responded, Jesus said to them, "The *ones* being healthy[P] have no need[Q] *of a* physician, but the *ones* being ill[R]. ˚I have not come to call righteous *ones* to repentance[S], but sinners" 31, 32

  3C.[15] And the *ones* said to Him, "The disciples[16] *of* John are fasting[T] frequently[17] and making[U] prayers. Likewise also the *ones of* the Pharisees.[18] But **Yours** are eating and drinking" 33

    1D. And Jesus said to them, "You cannot make the sons *of* the wedding-hall[19] **fast** while the bridegroom is with them, *can you*?[20] 34

      1E. "But days will come. And[21] when the bridegroom is taken-away[V] from them,[22] then they will fast in those days" 35

    2D. And He was also speaking *a* parable[W] to them, that 36

      1E. "No one having torn[X] *a* patch from *a* new garment puts *it* on *an* old[23] garment. Otherwise indeed[24] he[25] will both tear[X] the new[26], and the patch from the new will not agree[27] *with* the old
      2E. "And no one puts new[28] wine into old wineskins. Otherwise indeed the new wine will burst the wineskins, and **it** will spill-out[Y], and the wineskins will be ruined[29]. But new wine must-be-put[30] into fresh wineskins[31] 37, 38
      3E. "And[32] no one having drunk old *wine* desires[33] new. For he says, 'The old is good[34]' " 39

7B.[35] And it came about on *a* Sabbath[36] that He *was* proceeding through grainfields. And His disciples were plucking[37] and eating the heads[Z] [of grain], rubbing *them in their* hands 6:1

1. Some manuscripts add "*to* him" {K}.
2. Same form of address as in 12:14.
3. Same word as in Mk 2:6, 8; Lk 5:22; 12:17; 20:14. Elsewhere only as "ponder" in Lk 1:29; 3:15; and "discuss" in Mt 16:7, 8; 21:25; Mk 8:16, 17; 9:33; 11:31. GK *1368*. Related to "reasonings" in v 22.
4. This is correct reasoning by the scribes and Pharisees. But they were not open to considering the implications of Jesus' actions upon the question of who He was. Since He cannot be God, He must be blaspheming.
5. Related to the verb in v 21. On this word, see "thoughts" in Jam 2:4.
6. Or, "contrary to expectation", and so "wonderful, remarkable, extraordinary". Used only here. GK *4141*. Our word "paradox" comes from this Greek word, *paradoxos*.
7. Parallel account at Mt 9:9; Mk 2:13.
8. This is GK *2517*. Mt 9:9 and Mk 2:14 use a different word, GK *3972*.
9. He is listed as "Matthew" in 6:15. Compare Mt 9:9; 10:3.
10. On this word, see Mk 2:14. On the system of tax collection, see Lk 3:13.
11. Or, "banquet". Elsewhere only in Lk 14:13. GK *1531*. Related to "welcome" in Mt 10:40.
12. Some manuscripts say "and their scribes and the Pharisees" {N}.
13. Or, "complaining". Same word as in Mt 20:11; Jn 6:41, 43, 61; 1 Cor 10:10. Elsewhere only as "murmur" in Jn 7:32. GK *1197*. Related to the word in Phil 2:14.
14. This word is plural, referring to Jesus and His disciples. Mt 9:11 and Mk 2:16 refer to Jesus Himself.
15. Parallel account at Mt 9:14; Mk 2:18.
16. Some manuscripts make this verse a question, "Why do the disciples..." {B}, as in Mk 2:18. Perhaps John's disciples fasted regarding John's imprisonment or regarding their own repentance and preparation for the One coming.
17. Elsewhere only as "very frequently" in Act 24:26; and "frequent" in 1 Tim 5:23. GK *4781*.
18. Some Pharisees fasted twice a week (18:12), on Monday and Thursday.
19. That is, the attendants of the bridegroom, the groomsmen. On this word, see Mt 9:15.
20. The grammar indicates that a "no" answer is expected.
21. Some manuscripts omit this word {K}, so that it says "But days will come when...".
22. Jesus gives the first allusion to His death.
23. On the word "old" in v 36-39, see Mk 2:21.
24. On this idiom, "otherwise indeed", which is also in v 37, see 2 Cor 11:16.
25. Or, "it", such an action as just described.
26. That is, the new garment (Jesus and His message) will be damaged by tearing the patch from it. And the patch will not fit with the old garment (the Jewish system). Jesus is not a patch for the old system. He is a new garment, and this is why His disciples do not fast. The word "new" used three times in this verse is the same word as "fresh" in v 38. See Heb 8:13 on it.
27. Or, "fit, match". On this word, see Mt 18:19.
28. The word "new" used four times in v 37-39 is the same word as in Mk 2:22. See there on "new", "old", and "fresh".
29. Or, "lost". On this word, see "perish" in 1 Cor 1:18.
30. Used only here. GK *1064*. Related to "they put" in Mt 9:17.
31. Some manuscripts add "and both are preserved" {B}, as in Mt 9:17. Jesus, the new and fresh, cannot be contained in the old Jewish system. See Mk 2:22.
32. Some manuscripts omit this word {C}.
33. Some manuscripts say "immediately desires" {N}. On this word, see "willing" in Jn 7:17.
34. Or, "pleasant, suitable". Some manuscripts say "better" {A}. A person does not naturally desire to leave what is comfortable and known (the rabbinic system and culture) for what is so young and unknown (Jesus and His kingdom). On this word, see 1 Pet 2:3.
35. Parallel account at Mt 12:1; Mk 2:23.
36. Some manuscripts say "*a* second-first" Sabbath, a word used only here in all Greek literature {C}. GK *1310*. It may be translated "second after the first", or, "next to the first"— the "first" being some significant "first" Sabbath. Some suggest the "first" Sabbath is the Sabbath during Passover week, so that this means "the second Sabbath after Passover". Others conjecture that Luke originally wrote two words, the "second First" Sabbath, meaning the second Passover Sabbath of the ministry of Jesus, but that later scribes combined them into one word. Others think this word was not written by Luke, but is a blunder made by scribes copying the manuscript of Luke. There are other views.
37. The Law permitted this, Deut 23:25. On this word, see Mt 12:1.

A. Eph 2:8   B. Mt 6:12   C. 1 Tim 6:4   D. Col 1:6, understood   E. Rev 6:8   F. Mt 28:6   G. Lk 18:33, rise up   H. Rom 8:30   J. Mk 5:42
K. Rom 7:8, taken   L. Act 2:4   M. Eph 5:21, fear   N. Mt 18:17   O. Act 6:2   P. 1 Tim 1:10   Q. Tit 3:14   R. Mk 1:32   S. 2 Cor 7:10   T. Mt 6:16
U. Rev 13:13, does   V. Mk 2:20   W. Mt 13:3   X. Mt 27:51   Y. Act 2:17, pour out   Z. Mk 4:28

| Luke 6:2 | 204 | Verse |

    1C. And some *of* the Pharisees said¹, "Why are you² doing what is not lawful³ *on* the Sabbath?"   2

    2C. And having responded to them, Jesus said, "Did you not even read [in 1 Sam 21:1-6] this   3
which David did when he was hungry, he and the *ones* being⁴ with him?—˚how⁵   4

        1D. "He entered into the house^A *of* God

        2D. "And having taken the Bread *of* Presentation⁶, he ate *it* and gave⁷ *it to* the *ones* with him—
which is not lawful^B *for anyone* to eat but the priests alone^C?

    3C. And He was saying *to* them, "The Son *of* Man is **Lord**^D *of* the⁸ Sabbath"   5

8B.⁹ And it came about on another Sabbath *that* He entered into the synagogue and *was* teaching. And   6
there was *a* man there, and his right hand was withered^E

    1C. And the scribes and the Pharisees were closely-watching¹⁰ Him *to see* if He cured¹¹ on the   7
Sabbath, in order that they might find *a reason* to be accusing^F Him¹²

    2C. But **He** knew^G their reasonings¹³. And He said *to* the man having the withered^E hand, "Arise,   8
and stand into the middle^H". And having stood-up, he stood *there*

    3C. And Jesus said to them, "I am asking you¹⁴ if it is lawful¹⁵ *on* the Sabbath to do-good^J or to   9
do-harm¹⁶, to save^K *a* life or to destroy^L *it*?"

    4C. And having looked-around^M *at* them all, He said *to* him, "Stretch-out^N your hand". And the   10
one did *it*, and his hand was restored¹⁷

    5C. And **they** were filled^O *with* rage¹⁸, and were talking-over^P with one another what they might   11
do *to* Jesus

9B.¹⁹ And it came about during these days *that* He went out to the mountain to pray^Q. And He was   12
spending the night in prayer^R *to* God

    1C. And when it became day, He called to His disciples   13

        1D.²⁰ And²¹ having chosen^S twelve from them, whom He also named^T apostles²²—

            1E. Simon²³, whom He also named^T Peter²⁴   14

            2E. And Andrew²⁵, his brother

            3E. And²⁶ James²⁷

            4E. And John²⁸

            5E. And Philip²⁹

            6E. And Bartholomew³⁰

            7E. And Matthew³¹   15

            8E. And Thomas³²

            9E. And James³³, *the son of* Alphaeus³⁴

            10E. And Simon³⁵, the *one* being called *a* Zealot³⁶

            11E. And Judas³⁷, *the son of* James   16

            12E. And Judas Iscariot³⁸, who³⁹ became *a* traitor

        2D. And having come down with them⁴⁰   17

        3D. He stood on *a* level place

    2C.⁴¹ And *there was a* large crowd *of* His disciples, and *a* great multitude *of* the people from all
Judea and Jerusalem and the coastal-region *of* Tyre and Sidon,˚ who came to hear Him and   18
to be healed^U from their diseases^V

1. Some manuscripts add "to them" {K}.
2. This is plural.
3. In the traditions of the Pharisees, they considered this prohibited "work". Some manuscripts add "to do" {N}.
4. Some manuscripts omit this word {C}.
5. Some manuscripts omit this word {C}.
6. That is, the twelve loaves of "showbread". See Mk 2:26.
7. Some manuscripts add "also" {A}.
8. Some manuscripts add "even" {B}, so that it says "even *of* the Sabbath", as in Mk 2:28.
9. Parallel account at Mt 12:9; Mk 3:1.
10. Same word as in Mk 3:2; Lk 14:1; 20:20; Act 9:24. Elsewhere only as "observe" in Gal 4:10. GK *4190*. Related to "observation" in Lk 17:20.
11. Literally, "cures", as the Greek typically phrases it. On this word, see Mt 8:7. Some manuscripts say "would cure" {N}, as in Mk 3:2.
12. Some manuscripts say "find *an* accusation *against* Him" {N}.
13. Same word as in 5:22.
14. This word is plural, referring to the scribes and Pharisees.
15. Some manuscripts say "I will ask you something. Is it lawful..." {N}.
16. On this word, and on the meaning of this, see Mk 3:4.
17. On this word, see Mk 8:25. Some manuscripts add "healthy like the other" {N}, as in Mt 12:13.
18. Senseless anger, irrational anger is the idea. The sensible thing to say would have been what was said in 7:16 or Jn 3:2. Note that even by the Pharisees' definitions, Jesus did no work. He did not touch the man, nor even speak a word of healing. No created being has such power, so God must have done the work. Jesus does good, and they discuss how to do evil to Him! Elsewhere only as "folly" in 2 Tim 3:9. GK *486*.
19. Parallel account at Mk 3:13. Compare Mt 10:1-4.
20. Compare at Mt 10:2; Mk 3:16; Act 1:13.
21. Note the progression of the main sentence. And having chosen (v 13), and having come down (v 17), He stood.
22. Or, "sent *ones*". On this word, see 1 Cor 12:28.
23. He is called "Simon" 51 times, all in the Gospels and Acts. GK *4981*. He is called "Simeon", the Aramaic spelling of his name, only in Act 15:14 and 2 Pet 1:1 (GK *5208*).
24. He is called "Peter" 156 times, all in the Gospels and Acts except Gal 2:7, 8; 1 Pet 1:1; 2 Pet 1:1. GK *4377*. Peter means "rock" in Greek, as does "Cephas" in Aramaic. He is called "Cephas" in Jn 1:42, and by Paul (see Gal 1:18).
25. Andrew is mentioned elsewhere only in Mt 4:18; 10:2; Mk 1:16, 29; 3:18; 13:3; Jn 1:40, 44; 6:8; 12:22; Act 1:13. GK *436*.
26. Some manuscripts omit this word {N}, so that it says "James and John", and likewise down the list so that all the names are grouped in pairs, as in Mt 10.
27. James is mentioned also in Mt 4:21; 10:2; 17:1; Mk 1:19, 29; 3:17; 5:37; 9:2; 10:35, 41; 13:3; 14:33; Lk 5:10; 8:51; 9:28, 54; Act 1:13; 12:2 (where he was killed by Herod Agrippa I). GK *2610*. On James the brother of Jesus, see Mt 13:55.
28. John is mentioned 34 times. He is the brother of James, and the writer of John, 1, 2, 3 John, and Revelation. GK *2722*.
29. Philip is mentioned also in Mt 10:3; Mk 3:18; Jn 1:43, 44, 45, 46, 48; 6:5, 7; 12:21, 22; 14:8, 9; Act 1:13. GK *5805*.
30. Bartholomew is mentioned elsewhere only in Mt 10:3; Mk 3:18; Act 1:13. GK *978*. Some think this is the Nathanael of Jn 1:44-49; 21:2, who was the friend or brother of Philip.
31. He is called Matthew in Mt 9:9; 10:3; Mk 3:18; Act 1:13. GK *3414*. He is called "Levi" in Mk 2:14; Lk 5:27, 29 (GK *3322*).
32. Thomas is mentioned in Mt 10:3; Mk 3:18; Jn 14:5; 20:26, 27, 28; Act 1:13; and in Jn 11:16; 20:24; 21:2, where John says he was also called "Didymus". GK *2605*.
33. James is mentioned also in Mt 10:3; Mk 3:18; Act 1:13. Some think he is the James mentioned as the son of Mary in Mt 27:56; Mk 15:40 (James the less); 16:1; Lk 24:10. GK *2610*. Some also think that this Mary is the one mentioned in Jn 19:25 as the wife of Clopas.
34. Alphaeus is mentioned also in Mt 10:3; Mk 3:18; Act 1:13. Elsewhere this name is only used of Matthew's father in Mk 2:14. GK *271*.
35. Simon is mentioned also in Mt 10:4; Mk 3:18; Act 1:13. GK *4981*.
36. Simon is called this also in Act 1:13. The Aramaic equivalent is "Cananaean", used in Mt 10:4; Mk 3:18. The Zealots were a Jewish nationalist group seeking independence from Rome. On this word, see 1 Cor 14:12.
37. Judas is mentioned also in Act 1:13; and in Jn 14:22, "Judas, not Iscariot". GK *2683*. He is called "Thaddaeus" in Mt 10:3 and Mk 3:18. Some render this "the *brother of* James".
38. See Jn 6:71 on him.
39. Some manuscripts add "also" {K}.
40. Luke could mean with the twelve chosen from among those Jesus summoned in v 13; or, with the larger group of disciples in v 13.
41. Most think this is the same occasion as in Mt 4:25.

A. Mk 3:20 B. 1 Cor 6:12 C. Jam 2:24 D. Mt 8:2, master E. Mk 3:3 F. Jn 5:45 G. 1 Jn 2:29 H. 2 Thes 2:7, midst J. Lk 6:33 K. Lk 19:10 L. 1 Cor 1:18, perish M. Mk 3:5 N. Act 27:30 O. Act 2:4 P. Lk 1:65 Q. 1 Tim 2:8 R. 1 Tim 2:1 S. 1 Cor 1:27 T. 2 Tim 2:19 U. Mt 8:8 V. Mt 8:17

1D. And the *ones* being troubled[1] by unclean spirits[2] were being cured[A]
2D. And all the multitude[B] were seeking to touch[C] Him because power was going forth from Him and healing[3] everyone   19

3C.[4] And **He**, having lifted-up[D] His eyes toward His disciples[5], was saying—   20

1D.[6] "Blessed[7] *are* the poor[8] ones, because the kingdom[E] *of* God is yours[9]

    1E. "Blessed[10] *are* the *ones* hungering now, because you will be filled-to-satisfaction[11]   21
    2E. "Blessed *are* the *ones* weeping[F] now, because you will laugh
    3E. "You are blessed whenever people hate[G] you, and whenever they separate[12] you,   22
    and reproach[H] *you*, and throw-out[J] your name as evil[K] because-of[13] the Son *of* Man.
    Rejoice[L] on that day and leap-for-joy[M], for behold— your reward[N] *is* great in heaven   23

        1F. "For their fathers were doing *it* in the same *way*[14] *to* the prophets

2D. "But[15] woe *to* you rich *ones*, because you are receiving your comfort[16] in full[17]   24

    1E. "Woe *to* you, the *ones* having been filled[18] now[19], because you will hunger   25
    2E. "Woe[20]— the *ones* laughing now, because you will mourn[O] and weep[F]
    3E. "Woe— when all people speak well[P] *of* you[21]   26

        1F. "For their fathers were doing *it* in the same *way* *to* the false-prophets[Q]

3D. "But[22] I say *to* you, the *ones* hearing[23]—   27

    1E.[24] "Be loving[R] your enemies[25]

        1F. "Be acting commendably[26] *to* the *ones* hating[G] you. °Be blessing[27] the *ones*   28
        cursing[28] you. Be praying[29] for the *ones* mistreating[30] you
        2F. "*To* the *one* striking[31] you on the cheek[32]— be offering[S] also the other. And   29
        from the *one* taking away your cloak— also do not withhold[33] the tunic[34]
        3F. "*To* everyone asking you— be giving. And from the *one* taking away your   30
        things— do not be demanding *them* back
        4F.[35] "And just as you want people[36] to[37] be doing *to* you, be doing[38] *to* them likewise   31

    2E.[39] "If indeed you are loving the *ones* loving you,[40] what-kind-of[T] credit[U] is it *to* you?   32
    For even the sinners[V] are loving the *ones* loving them

        1F. "For[41] if indeed you are doing-good-*to*[42] the *ones* doing-good-*to* you,[43] what   33
        kind of credit is it *to* you? Even[44] the sinners are doing the same

1. Elsewhere only as "causing trouble" in Heb 12:15. GK *1943*. Related to the word in Act 5:16.
2. Or, "... troubled were being cured from unclean spirits". Some manuscripts add "and" {K}, so that point 2C. says "diseases, and the *ones* being troubled by unclean spirits"), and this point says only "And they were being cured".
3. Or, "from Him. And He was healing everyone".
4. Most think this is Luke's telling of the sermon in Mt 5-7. Consult the commentaries on their relationship.
5. Luke could mean the large crowd of His disciples, v 17. Or, this may refer to the smaller group whom He summoned and from whom He chose the twelve, v 13.
6. Compare Mt 5:3-12.
7. Or, "Happy, Fortunate", from God's point of view; privileged recipients of God's favor and goodness. Compare the word in v 28. This adjective is also in Mt 5:3-11; 11:6; 13:16; 16:17; 24:46; Lk 1:45; 6:21, 22; 7:23; 10:23; 11:27, 28; 12:37, 38, 43; 14:14, 15; 23:29; Jn 13:17; 20:29; Act 20:35; Rom 4:7, 8; 14:22; Tit 2:13; Jam 1:12, 25; 1 Pet 3:14; 4:14; Rev 1:3; 14:13; 16:15; 19:9; 20:6; 22:7, 14. Used of God, the source of grace and goodness, in 1 Tim 1:11; 6:15. Elsewhere only as "fortunate" in Act 26:2; and "happy" in 1 Cor 7:40. GK *3421*. Related to "consider blessed" in Lk 1:48; and "blessedness" in Gal 4:15.
8. Same word as in Mt 5:3. Some think Jesus means that disciples who physically have nothing are spiritual possessors of everything, and truly blessed. Non-disciples who are physically rich (v 24), are spiritually bankrupt, and truly woeful. Others think He means "poor in spirit" as in Mt 5:3, versus falsely thinking one is spiritually rich, as in Rev 3:17.
9. That is, it belongs to you, it is your own.
10. The rest of the beatitudes are placed at the "E." level as a subject grouping only, not because they are subordinate to the first one. Likewise with the woes in v 25-26.
11. Both "hungering" and "filled-to-satisfaction" are the same words as in Mt 5:6.
12. That is, exclude you. On this word, see Rom 1:1.
13. It is "because of " from the persecutor's point of view; "for the sake of " from the believer's point of view. GK *1915*.
14. Or, "in accordance with the same *things*". This phrase is elsewhere only in v 26; 17:30. Related to the phrase in Act 14:1.
15. Note that these four woes correspond to the four blessings in v 20-23. GK *4440*.
16. Or, "consolation", as in 2:25, the only other use in Luke. On this word, see "encouragement" in Act 4:36.
17. This word, "receive in full" is the same word as in Mt 6:2, on which see Phil 4:18. Such people already have received all the blessing they will ever have. They have satisfied themselves with so little.
18. Or, "filled full". Same word as in 1:53. On this word, see Rom 15:24.
19. Some manuscripts omit this word {N}.
20. Some manuscripts add "*to* you" here and in v 26, as in the previous woe {N}.
21. Or, "*as to* you, *with reference to* you". Everyone must either be deceived, or they are seeing only what they want to see in you for some other motive. Believers and unbelievers do not value the same things.
22. In contrast to what you have heard or thought. Not the same word as in v 24. GK *247*.
23. That is, hearing and obeying, taking to heart, having an ear to hear.
24. Compare Mt 5:39-42.
25. These verses speak of active love toward them, even when resistance or retaliation seems natural.
26. Or, "beautifully, well". Same word as "well" in v 26, 48. Same phrase as Mt 12:12.
27. That is, calling down God's blessing upon them, giving a blessing to them. This verb means "to speak well of, praise; to call down God's blessings on; to give a blessing or benefit to" (as when God "blesses" us). On blessing food, see Mt 14:19. Elsewhere only in Mt 14:19; 21:9; 23:39; 25:34; 26:26; Mk 6:41; 8:7; 11:9, 10; 14:22; Lk 1:42, 64; 2:28, 34; 9:16; 13:35; 19:38; 24:30, 50, 51, 53; Jn 12:13; Act 3:26; Rom 12:14; 1 Cor 4:12; 10:16; 14:16; Gal 3:9; Eph 1:3; Heb 6:14; 7:1, 6, 7; 11:20, 21; Jam 3:9; 1 Pet 3:9. GK *2328*. Related to the adjective "blessed" in Rom 9:5, and the noun "blessing" in 2 Cor 9:5. All three words are used in Eph 1:3. Not related to "blessed" in v 20.
28. Same word as in Rom 12:14, where Paul repeats this saying.
29. Some manuscripts say "And be praying..." {K}.
30. Or, "abusing". On this word, see "maligning" in 1 Pet 3:16.
31. Same word as used of Christ in Mt 27:30, and Sosthenes in Act 18:17, and Paul in Act 23:2, 3. Elsewhere only in Mt 24:49; Mk 15:19; Lk 12:45; 18:13; 23:48; Act 18:17; 21:32; 1 Cor 8:12. GK *5597*.
32. Elsewhere only in Mt 5:39. GK *4965*.
33. Or, "forbid [him], try to stop [him from taking]". On this word, see "forbidding" in 1 Cor 14:39.
34. That is, the inner garment worn next to the skin. In Mt 5:40, in a Jewish court setting, the order is reversed. The Jews sued for the tunic because they could not take the coat. Here, the setting is of a physical taking. If someone takes the more valuable outer coat, do not refuse to give them the inner tunic.
35. Compare Mt 7:12.
36. This command refers especially to enemies, as the context before and after shows, but generalizes to include all people.
37. More literally, "just as you want that people should be doing". GK *2671*. For example, to love you, v 32; to do good to you, v 33; to lend to you, v 34; to be compassionate toward you, v 36.
38. Some manuscripts say "you also be doing" {B}.
39. Compare Mt 5:44-47.
40. The grammar of this statement assumes its reality— "assuming it is true that...". Jesus is explaining "love your enemies", v 27. Loving your friends is good, and human. But it does not make you like God, v 35.
41. Some manuscripts omit this word {C}, so that it says "And if you...". Jesus is explaining v 27b. There is human-like good doing, and there is God-like good doing.
42. Elsewhere only in Lk 6:9, 35; 1 Pet 2:15, 20; 3:6, 17; 3 Jn 11. GK *16*. Related to "good-doing" in 1 Pet 4:19.
43. The grammar of this statement indicates that this is something you probably would do. Likewise with v 34.
44. Some manuscripts say "For even..." {N}.

A. Mt 8:7 B. Mk 2:13 C. 1 Cor 7:1 D. 2 Cor 11:20 E. Mt 3:2 F. Jn 11:33 G. Rom 9:13 H. 1 Pet 4:14 J. Jn 12:31, cast out K. Act 25:18 L. 2 Cor 13:11 M. Lk 1:41, leap N. Rev 22:12, recompense O. Jam 4:9 P. Act 10:33 Q. Rev 16:13 R. Jn 21:15, devotedly love S. Act 17:31, grant T. Mt 21:23 U. Eph 2:8, grace V. Mt 9:10

2F. "And if you lend-*to*¹ *ones* from whom you are expecting² to receiveᴬ, what kind of credit is it *to* you? Even³ sinners are lending *to* sinners to⁴ receive-backᴮ the equal⁵ *amounts*	34
3F. "But be loving your enemies, and be doing good, and be lending, expecting-back⁶ nothing⁷	35

        1G. "And your reward will be great
        2G. "And you will be sons⁸ *of the* Most-Highᶜ, because **He** is good⁹ to the ungrateful¹⁰ and evilᴰ *ones*

4F.¹¹ "Be¹² compassionate¹³, just-as¹⁴ your Father also¹⁵ is compassionate	36
3E.¹⁶ "And¹⁷ do not be judging¹⁸, and you will never be judged	37

    1F. "And do not be condemning¹⁹, and you will never be condemned

2F. "Be pardoning²⁰, and you will be pardoned. *Be giving, and it will be given *to* you	38

        1G. "They²¹ will give *a* good measure²²— having been pressed down, having been shakenᴱ, running over— into your fold²³ [of the garment]. For *with* what measure²⁴ you measure, it will be measured-back *to* you"

4C. And²⁵ He also spoke *a* parableᶠ *to* them— ²⁶	39
1D. "*A* blind *one* is not able to guide²⁷ *a* blind one, *is he*?²⁸ Will they not both fall into *a* pit?²⁹	
2D. "*A* disciple³⁰ is not above the³¹ teacher. But³² everyone having been fully-trained³³ will be like³⁴ his teacher³⁵	40
3D. "And why³⁶ do you look-*at* the speck in the eye *of* your brotherᴳ, but do not consider³⁷ the log in *your* own eye? *How³⁸ can you say *to* your brother, 'Brother, permitᴴ me to³⁹ take-outʲ the speck in your eye', while yourself not seeing *the* log in your eye?	41 42

    1E. "Hypocriteᴷ! First take out the log from your eye. And then you will see-clearlyᴸ to take out the speck in the eye *of* your brother

1. Jesus is explaining "to everyone asking you— give", v 30. If you lend expecting repayment— with or without interest— do not expect a reward from God. It is simply a human business transaction. Same word as in v 35. Elsewhere only with different grammar as "borrow" in Mt 5:42. GK *1247*. Related to "lender" in 7:41; and "loan" in Mt 18:27.
2. Or, "hoping". This word is normally translated "hope". On this word, see "put hope" in Jn 5:45. Related to the word in v 35.
3. Some manuscripts say "For even sinners..." {N}.
4. More literally, "*to* sinners [with the expectation] that they should receive-back...". GK *2671*.
5. That is, receive back payment in full. This word is plural. On this word, see Phil 2:6.
6. Or, "hoping for nothing back", in contrast to the related word in v 34. The loving, doing good, and lending of v 32-34 all represent normal human behavior. Jesus is not condemning these things. He wants us as individuals to go beyond them, to do these things for His kingdom without thought of human reciprocation, looking only to Him for a reward. Note Lk 14:12-14. This can also be rendered "despairing nothing", not despairing about getting it back. Used only here. GK *594*.
7. Some manuscripts have this word in a form that can mean "no one" {B}, "despairing *as to* no one".
8. That is, you will be like your heavenly Father because you will be doing what He does. You will bear a family resemblance to Him, as a son to a father. On this word, see Gal 3:7.
9. Or, "kind". On this word, see 1 Pet 2:3.
10. Or, "unthankful". Elsewhere only in 2 Tim 3:2. GK *940*.
11. Compare Mt 5:48.
12. Or, "Become, Prove to be". GK *1181*.
13. This is the general principle, and like v 31, it applies especially to enemies. It is assumed that one would do this for friends. On this adjective, see Jam 5:11. Some manuscripts say "Therefore become compassionate..." {K}.
14. That is, in the same manner as your Father in heaven.
15. Some manuscripts omit this word {C}.
16. Compare Mt 7:1-5.
17. Some manuscripts omit this word {K}.
18. Though these are general principles, the emphasis of the context is still on enemies. Do not judge or condemn them, but pardon and give to them. Same word as in Mt 7:1. Do not pass judgment on, criticize, find fault with.
19. Or, "pronouncing guilty". Same word as in Mt 12:7, where the Pharisees did it, and as Jam 5:6, where the rich did it. Elsewhere only in Mt 12:37, where "by your words you will be condemned". GK *2868*. Related to "sentence of condemnation" in Act 25:15.
20. Or, "releasing, setting free, letting go". Pardon your debtors. On this word, see "send away" in Mt 5:31.
21. That is, God's agents— whether human or angelic— for disbursing His rewards, v 35.
22. That is, an overflowing measure of what you gave out will be returned to you. Your own measuring cup will be filled to overflowing with what you gave, and dumped back in your lap. The "good measure" is defined next.
23. Or, "bosom, lap". That is, into your garment pulled up at the waist to form a pocket. On this word, see "bosom" in Jn 1:18.
24. On this word, see Jn 3:34. Some manuscripts say "For *with* the same measure which" {N}.
25. Luke seems to begin here a second part or aspect of the sermon, not directly connected with what precedes. He seems to intend that v 39-49 be grouped together, as were v 20-38. However, some group v 37-42 together.
26. Some think Luke now gives the words Jesus spoke to those "not hearing", in contrast to v 27. Jesus speaks to the self-delusion of ones like the Pharisees, who do not follow Him. Others think what follows is addressed to the disciples as future leaders, correcting them. There are other views. Consult the commentaries on the flow of v 39-49.
27. Same word as in Mt 15:14. Elsewhere only in Jn 16:13; Act 8:31; Rev 7:17. GK *3842*.
28. The grammar indicates a "no" answer is expected to this question, and a "yes" answer to the next one.
29. Some think Jesus means that the disciples are blind without Him, and cannot lead others unless they know the truth; others, that He is referring to spiritually blind teachers, like the Pharisees. Not seeing the truth themselves, they can only lead their unseeing disciples to the errors into which they themselves have blindly fallen. Compare Mt 23:16 for examples.
30. Or, "learner, pupil, student, follower". Some think this explains v 39. Both will fall because the disciple is like the teacher. Others think this moves on from v 39 to a new point. Compare Mt 10:24. This word is used 261 times, all in the Gospels and Acts. GK *3412*. The related verb is in Mt 13:52.
31. Some manuscripts say "his" {N}.
32. Or, "And".
33. Or, "made complete, put into proper condition". On this word, see "prepared" in Rom 9:22.
34. This true whether one's teacher is Jesus, or a spiritually blind one. On this word, see "as" in Mt 19:19. Compare Mk 4:24.
35. Some think Jesus means the disciples can and must become like Him, submitting to His teaching; others, that if people continue following blind guides (like the Pharisees), they will remain blind.
36. Some think Jesus means that the disciples must not judge others, but themselves. You can only correct in others what you have corrected in yourself. Others think He means that ones like the Pharisees cannot attempt to judge others like Jesus or His disciples, because they are blinded by the falsehoods in their own eyes. They must clear their eyes of what is blocking the truth before they can correct the perception of another.
37. Or, "notice". Both "consider" and "log" are also in Mt 7:3.
38. Some manuscripts say "Or how..."; others, "And how..." {N}.
39. More literally, "permit *that* I may take out".

A. Rom 7:8, taken   B. Lk 16:25, receive   C. Mt 21:9, highest   D. Act 25:18   E. Act 17:13   F. Mt 13:3   G. Act 16:40   H. Mt 6:12, forgive   J. Jn 12:31, cast out   K. Mt 6:2   L. Mk 8:25, look intently

       4D.¹ "For² there is no good³ tree producing bad fruit, nor again⁴, *a* bad tree producing good fruit   43

            1E. "For each tree is known⁵ by *its* own fruit. For they do not collect figs from thorns⁶,   44
               nor do they gather⁷ *a* grape-bunch⁸ from *a* bramble-bush⁹
            2E. "The good¹⁰ person brings forth the good *thing* out of the good treasure¹¹ *of his* heart.   45
               And the evil¹² *person* brings forth the evil *thing* out of *his* evil *treasure*¹³. For his
               mouth speaks out of *the* abundance^A *of the* heart^B

       5D.¹⁴ "And why are you calling^C Me, 'Lord, Lord¹⁵', and you are not doing *the things* which   46
         I say?¹⁶

            1E.¹⁷ "Everyone coming to Me and hearing My words and doing them— I will show^D   47
               you *to* whom he is like^E. ˚He is like^E *a* man building^F *a* house who dug, and went   48
               down deep, and laid^G *a* foundation^H on the bed-rock¹⁸

                  1F. "And *a* flood¹⁹ having come about, the river broke-against²⁰ that house. And it
                     was not strong-*enough*^J to shake^K it, because it *had* been built^F well²¹

            2E. "But the *one* having heard and not having done *My* words is like *a* man having built   49
               a house on the ground^L without *a* foundation, which the river broke-against

                  1F. "And immediately it collapsed²², and the breakage²³ *of* that house became great"

10B.²⁴ After He completed^M all His words in the hearing *of* the people, He entered into Capernaum   7:1

   1C. And *a* certain centurion's^N slave^O, who was precious²⁵ *to* him, being ill^P, was about to come-   2
      to-an-end²⁶. ˚But having heard about Jesus, he sent-forth^Q elders *of* the Jews to Him, asking   3
      Him so that having come, He might restore²⁷ his slave
   2C. And the *ones* having come to Jesus were appealing-to^R Him earnestly^S, saying that "He *for* whom   4
      You will grant^T this is worthy²⁸. ˚For he loves our nation, and **he** built^F the synagogue *for* us"   5
   3C. Now Jesus was proceeding with them. And He already being not far distant from the house,   6
      the centurion sent friends, saying *to* Him, "Master^U, do not be troubling^V *Yourself*

       1D. "For I am not fit^W that You should come in under my roof. ˚For this reason I did not even   7
          consider myself worthy^X to come to You
       2D. "But speak *it in a* word,²⁹ and let my servant be healed³⁰

            1E. "For **I** also am *a* man being placed³¹ under authority, having soldiers under myself.   8
               And I say *to* this *one*, 'Go!', and he goes; and *to* another, 'Come!', and he comes;
               and *to* my slave, 'Do this!', and he does *it*"

   4C. And having heard these *things*, Jesus marveled-at^Y him. And having turned *to* the crowd   9
      following Him, He said, "I say *to* you, not even in Israel did I find so great *a* faith"
   5C. And having returned to the house, the *ones* having been sent found the slave³² being healthy³³   10

11B. And it came about afterwards³⁴ *that* He proceeded to *a* city being called Nain. And His disciples³⁵   11
   and *a* large crowd were proceeding-with Him

   1C. Now when He drew-near^Z *to* the gate *of* the city, and behold— *one* having died was being   12
      carried out, *an* only-born^AA son *to* his mother. And she was *a* widow. And *a* considerable^W
      crowd *from* the city was with her

1. Compare Mt 7:16-20.
2. Some think Jesus means the disciples must have a change of heart, because their effect on others will match their heart; others, that ones like the Pharisees are incapable of producing good fruit and need a change of heart.
3. Both occurrences of "good" here are the same word as in "good fruit" in Mt 7:17 (see 1 Tim 5:10a on it). Both occurrences of "bad" here are the same word as in "bad tree" in Mt 7:17. Thus, Jesus could mean no "fit, pleasing, desirable" type of tree (like a fruit tree) produces "unusable" fruit; no "unusable" type of tree produces "fit" fruit to eat. Or, He could mean no "healthy" tree produces "rotten" fruit; no "rotten" tree produces "fit" fruit to eat. If the next verse is intended to explain this one, then the contrast of types of trees is in view here. See Mt 7:17-18 on this.
4. Or, "on the other hand". GK *4099*. Some manuscripts omit this word {N}.
5. Or, "recognized". On this word, see 1:34.
6. That is, from thorny branches such as were used in the crown of thorns, Mt 27:29. Same word as in Lk 8:7; Mt 7:16; Heb 6:8. Used 14 times. GK *180*.
7. Elsewhere only in Rev 14:18, 19. GK *5582*.
8. Same word as "grapes" in Mt 7:16, but singular here. Elsewhere only in Rev 14:18. GK *5091*.
9. Or, "thorn-bush". Elsewhere only of the burning "bush" seen by Moses, Mk 12:26; Lk 20:37; Act 7:30, 35. GK *1003*.
10. This word, used three times here, is the same word as in "good tree" in Mt 7:17. See 1 Tim 5:10b on it.
11. Or, "treasure-house, treasury". On this word, see Mt 12:35.
12. Used three times here, this is the same word as in "bad fruit" in Mt 7:17. On this word, see Act 25:18.
13. The grammar implies "treasure", not "heart". Some manuscripts add here "treasure *of* his heart" {N}.
14. Compare Mt 7:21.
15. Or, "Master, Master". See Mt 7:21 on "Lord, Lord".
16. Treating Jesus respectfully but not doing what He says is fruitless. What one does with His words is what makes the difference, not what one merely says about Him or them.
17. Compare Mt 7:24-27.
18. Same word as in Mt 7:24.
19. Or, "high water". Used only here. GK *4439*.
20. Or, "burst against, dashed against". Elsewhere only in v 49. GK *4703*. Related to "breakage" in v 49.
21. More literally, "because of it having been built well". Some manuscripts instead say "for it had been founded upon the bed-rock" {A}, as in Mt 7:25.
22. Or, "fell together, fell in". Used only here. GK *5229*. Some manuscripts say "fell" {N}, the related word in Mt 7:27.
23. Or, the "bursting, dashing" and so "wreck, ruin". Used only here. GK *4837*. Related to "broke against" in v 48, 49.
24. Parallel account at Mt 8:5.
25. Or, "esteemed, respected, honored *by* him". On this word, see Phil 2:29.
26. That is, die. This is a euphemism for death. On this word, see Mk 9:48.
27. On this word, see "bring safely through" in Act 27:43. Related to "restore" in Jam 5:15.
28. That is, in the eyes of the Jewish community, for the reasons given next.
29. On this phrase, see Mt 8:8.
30. Some manuscripts say "and my servant will be healed" {B}, as in Mt 8:8.
31. Or, "classed, stationed". I also serve in a command structure, taking orders and giving them. On this word, see "established" in Rom 13:1.
32. Some manuscripts say "the slave being sick being healthy" {A}, that is, they found the sick slave healthy.
33. Same word as 5:31; 15:27. On this word, see 1 Tim 1:10.
34. Or, "next". On this word, see "next" in Act 21:1. Some manuscripts say "*on* the next *day*" {B}.
35. Some manuscripts say "many disciples *of* His" {B}, a phrase found only here.

A. 2 Cor 8:14 B. Rev 2:23 C. Rom 8:30 D. Mt 3:7 E. Rev 1:13, resembling F. 1 Cor 14:4, edify G. Act 19:21, put H. 1 Tim 6:19 J. Gal 5:6, can do K. Act 17:13 L. Rev 7:1, land M. Eph 5:18, filled N. Mt 8:5 O. Rom 6:17 P. Mk 1:32 Q. Mk 3:14, send out R. Rom 12:8, exhorting S. Tit 3:13, diligently T. Act 17:31 U. Mt 8:2 V. Mt 9:36 W. 2 Cor 3:5, sufficient X. 2 Thes 1:11, consider worthy Y. Rev 17:8 Z. Lk 21:28 AA. Jn 1:18

2C. And having seen her, the Lord felt-deep-feelings^A [of compassion] for her 13

    1D. And He said *to* her, "Do not be weeping^B"
    2D. And having come to *it*, He touched^C the funeral-bed[1]. And the *ones* bearing^D *it* stopped[2] 14
    3D. And He said, "Young-man^E, I say *to* you, arise^F!" °And the dead *one* sat up and began to speak 15
    4D. And He gave him *to* his mother

    3C. And awe^G seized^H everyone. And they were glorifying^J God, saying that "*A* great prophet arose^F among us", and that "God visited[3] His people" 16
    4C. And this statement[4] concerning Him went out in all Judea and *in* all the surrounding-region^K 17

12B.[5] And his[6] disciples reported^L *to* John about all these *things*. And having summoned^M *a* certain two *of* his disciples, John°sent *them* to the Lord[7], saying, "Are **You** the *One* coming, or should we be looking-for[8] another *one*?" 18, 19

    1C. And having come to Him, the men said, "John the Baptist sent us forth to You, saying, 'Are **You** the *One* coming, or should we be looking for another *one*?' " 20
    2C. At that hour[9], He cured^N many from diseases^O and scourges^P and evil spirits. And He granted^Q seeing^R *to* many blind *ones* 21
    3C. And having responded, He[10] said *to* them, "Having gone, report^L *to* John *the things* which you saw and heard— 22

        1D. "Blind *ones* are seeing-again^S, lame *ones* are walking, lepers are being cleansed^T. And deaf *ones* are hearing, dead *ones* are being raised^F, poor *ones* are having-good-news-announced[11] *to them*
        2D. "And blessed^U is whoever does not take-offense[12] in Me" 23

    4C. And the messengers *of* John having departed, He began to speak to the crowds about John 24

        1D. "What[13] did you go out into the wilderness to look-*at*? *A* reed being shaken^V by *the* wind?
        2D. "But what did you go out to see? *A* man having been dressed^W in soft garments? Behold— the *ones* being[14] in glorious[15] clothing and luxury^X are in the royal[16] *palaces* 25
        3D. But what did you go out to see? *A* prophet? Yes, I say *to* you, and more[17] *than a* prophet. 26

            1E.[18] "This *one* is about whom it has been written [in Mal 3:1], 'Behold— I am sending forth My messenger ahead *of* Your presence[19], who will make Your way ready in front of You' 27
            2E. "I[20] say *to* you— no one is greater among *ones* born *of* women *than* John[21] 28

                1F. "But the least[22] *one* in the kingdom *of* God is greater *than* he

        4D. "And all the people having heard *him*[23]— even the tax collectors— vindicated[24] God, having been baptized^Y *with* the baptism^Z *of* John. °But the Pharisees and the Law-experts[25] rejected[26] the purpose[27] *of* God for themselves, not having been baptized by him 29, 30
        5D.[28] "*To* what[29] then[30] will I liken^AA the people *of* this generation, and *to* what are they like^BB? 31

            1E. "They are like^BB children sitting in *the* marketplace and calling to one another, who say 'We played the flute *for* you, and you did not dance. We lamented[31], and you did not weep'[32] 32

1. Or, "bier". That is, the stretcher on which the dead were carried to the grave. Used only here. GK *5049*.
2. Or, "stood [still]". GK *2705*.
3. Same word as in 1:68.
4. Or, "word, message, report". That is, that a great prophet arose among us, v 16. On this word, see 1 Cor 12:8.
5. Parallel account at Mt 11:2.
6. That is, John's.
7. Some manuscripts say "to Jesus" {C}.
8. Or, "are we looking for". The form of this word permits either translation.
9. Some manuscripts say "And at the same hour" {N}.
10. Some manuscripts say "Jesus" {K}.
11. These are things Isaiah prophesied Messiah would do, 35:5-6; 61:1. Compare Lk 4:18. The works answer John's question. Note that this last phrase is the climax, the thing of eternal consequence. On this word, see Mt 11:5.
12. Or, "is not caused to fall". On this word, see 1 Cor 8:13.
13. Or, "Why", with a different punctuation of these questions. See Mt 11:7 on this.
14. Or, "existing, living". On this word, see Phil 2:6.
15. Or, "splendid, distinguished, honored". Same word as in 13:17; Eph 5:27. Elsewhere only as "distinguished" in 1 Cor 4:10. GK *1902*. Related to "glorify" in 2 Thes 1:10, 12.
16. Related to "king". Elsewhere only in 1 Pet 2:9. GK *994*. Matthew says, "houses *of* kings" in Mt 11:8.
17. Jesus could mean "*one who is* more than", or "*something* more than", as in Mt 11:9. John is more because he is also the one sent to prepare for Messiah, as Jesus says next.
18. Compare also Mk 1:2; Lk 1:17.
19. Or, "face". On this phrase, see 9:52.
20. Some manuscripts say "For I say..."; others, "And I say"; others, "Truly I say" {N}.
21. Some manuscripts say "No one is *a* greater prophet *than* John the Baptist..." {B}.
22. Or, "lesser". See Mt 11:11 on this.
23. Some think Jesus means John, making v 29-30 the comment of Jesus about the reception of John's message of preparation by these two groups. Compare Mt 21:31-32. Others think Luke means Jesus, making v 29-30 a comment by Luke about their response to the words of Jesus in v 27-28. See also note 29.
24. Or, "justified, declared right". On this word, see "declared righteous" in Rom 3:24. That is, the hearers declared and acknowledged the justice and rightness of what God required of them through John, as seen in their acceptance of his baptism for themselves. If it is Luke's comment, then they acknowledged the justice of God in the words of Jesus about John, because they had been baptized by John. Reflecting the latter interpretation, some render the following participle ("having been baptized") as "because they had been baptized".
25. That is, the experts in Jewish law, who both interpreted and taught it. Also known as scribes, this word emphasizes their knowledge of the Law. Same word as in Mt 22:35; Lk 10:25; 11:45, 46, 52; 14:3. Elsewhere only as "pertaining to the Law" in Tit 3:9; and "lawyer" in Tit 3:13. GK *3788*. Related to "law-teacher" in 5:17.
26. Or, "set aside". Same word as in 10:16.
27. That is, the leaders rejected John's work of preparation, as seen in their refusal of his baptism. If this is Luke's comment, then they rejected the words of Jesus about John, because they had refused John's baptism. On this word, see "counsel" in Eph 1:11.
28. Parallel account at Mt 11:16.
29. Some manuscripts say "And the Lord said, '*To* what..." {K}. Because it is so unnatural to switch from quoting Jesus to Luke's comment and back to quoting Jesus without any indication of it, some who considered verses 29-30 to be Luke's comment added "and the Lord said" here to make it clearer, and the KJV included it. Other translations following this view put v 29-30 in a parenthesis, or use their quotation marks to indicate that they think these are Luke's words.
30. That is, in view of the fact that you rejected John and are rejecting Me.
31. Some manuscripts add "*for* you" {B}. On this word, see Mt 11:17.
32. In other words, John and Jesus did not respond to them as they expected. On "weep", see Jn 11:33.

A. Mt 9:36 B. Jn 11:33 C. 1 Cor 7:1 D. Mt 8:17, carry E. 1 Jn 2:13 F. Mt 28:6, arose G. Eph 5:21, fear H. Rom 7:8, taken J. Rom 8:30 K. Mk 1:28 L. 1 Jn 1:3, announcing M. Act 2:39, call to N. Mt 8:7 O. Mt 8:17 P. Mk 3:10 Q. 1 Cor 2:12, freely give R. Rev 1:11 S. Act 22:13, look up T. Heb 9:22 U. Lk 6:20 V. Act 17:13 W. Mt 6:30 X. 2 Pet 2:13, reveling Y. Mk 1:8 Z. Mk 1:4 AA. Mk 13:24, become like BB. Rev 1:13, resembling

1F. "For John the Baptist has come not eating bread nor drinking wine,¹ and you say 'He has *a* demon'"	33
2F. "The Son *of* Man has come eating and drinking, and you say 'Behold— *a* man who *is a* glutton and drunkard², *a* friend *of* tax-collectors^A and sinners^B'"	34
3F. "And wisdom was vindicated³ by all her children"	35

13B. And one *of* the Pharisees was asking Him to⁴ eat with him. And having entered into the house *of* the Pharisee, He laid-down [to eat] — 36

    1C.⁵ And behold— *there was a* woman⁶ in the city who *was a* sinner⁷. And having learned^C that He is reclining [to eat] at the house *of* the Pharisee, having brought *an* alabaster-jar^D *of* perfume^E, *and having stood behind *Him* at His feet⁸ weeping^F— 37 / 38

        1D. She began to wet His feet *with* the tears, and was wiping *them with* the hair *of* her head
        2D. And she was kissing^G His feet, and anointing⁹ *them with* the perfume

    2C. And having seen *it*, the Pharisee having invited^H Him spoke within himself, saying, "If **this** One were¹⁰ *a* prophet, He would know^J who and what-kind-of^K *person* the woman *is* who is touching^L Him— that she is *a* sinner^B" — 39

    3C. And having responded, Jesus said to him, "Simon, I have something to speak *to* you". And the *one* says, "Teacher, speak" — 40

        1D. "There were two debtors¹¹ *to a* certain lender¹². The one was owing^M five-hundred denarii¹³, and the other, fifty. *They¹⁴ not having *the means* to pay^N, he forgave¹⁵ both. So which *of* them will love¹⁶ him more?" — 41 / 42
        2D. And having responded, Simon said, "I assume¹⁷ that *it is to* whom he forgave the more" — 43
        3D. And the *One* said *to* him, "You judged^O correctly^P"

    4C. And having turned toward the woman, He said *to* Simon, "Do you see this woman? I entered into your house—¹⁸ — 44

        1D. "You did not give Me water for *My* feet. But this *one* wet My feet *with her* tears and wiped *them with* her hair¹⁹
        2D. "You did not give Me *a* kiss^Q. But this *one* did not stop kissing^G My feet since²⁰ I came-in — 45
        3D. "You did not anoint My head *with* oil²¹. But this *one* anointed My feet *with* perfume — 46
        4D. "For which reason I say *to* you— her many sins have been forgiven, because she loved²² much. But he *to* whom little is forgiven²³, loves little" — 47

    5C. And He said *to* her, "Your sins have been forgiven" — 48
    6C. And the *ones* reclining-back-with *Him* [to eat] began to say among themselves, "Who is this *One*, Who even forgives sins?" — 49
    7C. And He said to the woman, "Your faith^R has saved^S you. Go in peace" — 50

14B. And it came about during the successive²⁴ *days* that **He** was traveling-through²⁵ according to city and village²⁶, proclaiming^T, and announcing the kingdom *of* God as good news²⁷ — 8:1

    1C. And the twelve *were* with Him, *and some women who had been cured²⁸ from evil spirits and infirmities^U— — 2

        1D. Mary, the *one* being called Magdalene²⁹, from whom seven demons had come out³⁰
        2D. And Joanna³¹, *the* wife *of* Chuza, Herod's³² steward³³ — 3

1. John came as an ascetic, living alone in the desert, not socializing with them. Compare 1:15.
2. Jesus socialized with them. And He must be guilty of this because He eats and drinks with sinners. This is no more true of Him than that John had a demon, v 33. On this word, see Mt 11:19.
3. Same word as in v 29. On this statement, see Mt 11:19. Matthew refers to wisdom's "works"; Luke, to the "children" following wisdom and producing the works, that is, to believers like those in v 29. Some take this in a timeless sense, "is vindicated"; others, as referring to those who have responded to John and to Jesus.
4. More literally, "in order that He might eat". GK *2671*.
5. Compare the anointing at Mt 26:6; Mk 14:3; Jn 12:3.
6. Some have identified this woman as Mary the Magdalene (8:2), but Luke does not do so. Some think this is the same incident as in Mt 26:6; Mk 14:3; Jn 12:2; others, a different incident occurring much earlier.
7. This is the woman's public reputation. Many assume Luke means she was a prostitute or adulteress, but Luke does not say this. She could have simply been one living her life in rebellion to God, apart from the religious community, as "sinner" means in v 34.
8. People in that day reclined to eat by laying on their left side with their head at the table and their feet away from it. So the woman was both "behind" Jesus and "at, beside" His feet.
9. Same word as twice in v 46. On this word, see Jam 5:14.
10. The grammar indicates that the Pharisee is assuming this is not true, that Jesus is not a prophet. Compare the case in Jn 4:18-19.
11. Elsewhere only in 16:5. GK *5971*.
12. Used only here. GK *1250*. Related to the verb "lend" in 6:34.
13. One denarius was one day's wages for a laborer. On this word, see Mt 20:2.
14. Some manuscripts say "And they..." {N}.
15. Or, "granted *it to*, freely gave *it to*, gave it as a gift *to*". Both debtors had their debts canceled by grace. Related to "grace", this word refers to forgiveness as a act of grace by the giver. Same word as in v 43; 2 Cor 2:7, 10; 12:13; Eph 4:32; Col 2:13; 3:13. Same word as "freely gave" (see 1 Cor 2:12). GK *5919*.
16. The love is expressed in gratitude for the forgiveness.
17. Or, "suppose". Same word as in Act 2:15. It is used of a thought or opinion "taken up". Same word as "taken up" in Lk 10:30. Elsewhere only as "received" in Act 1:9; and "support" in 3 Jn 8. GK *5696*.
18. Jesus applies the parable of v 41-42 directly to Simon and the woman. She loved more, he less.
19. Some manuscripts say "the hair *of* her head" {K}, as in v 38.
20. This is an idiom, "from which *hour*". See Rev 16:18 on it.
21. That is, olive oil. On this word, see Jam 5:14.
22. The woman's love is a manifestation of her faith, v 50. It reflects her perception of the depth of her sin (her debt) and the greatness of her forgiveness (like the man owing the 500 denarii). She still deeply felt the reality of both. Like the man in the parable, she loves much because she experienced the forgiveness of much (prior to this event). Her love is the evidence of her feeling of forgiveness, not the cause of it.
23. Jesus leaves it to Simon to apply this to himself. Has he been forgiven little, or nothing at all? What is the evidence of his actions and thoughts? On this word, used four times in v 47-49, see Mt 6:12.
24. Or, "afterward". That is, the ones following in order. Elsewhere only as "in order" in Lk 1:3; Act 11:4; "successively" in Act 18:23; and "successors" in Act 3:24. GK *2759*.
25. Elsewhere only in Act 17:1. GK *1476*.
26. That is, city by city and village by village, from one city or village to the next. Similar to the phrase in 13:22.
27. On "announcing the kingdom *of* God as good news", see 4:43.
28. This is a participle, they "were having been cured". On this word, see Mt 8:7.
29. That is, "from Magdala", a city on the west side of the Sea of Galilee. Elsewhere only in Mt 27:56, 61; 28:1; Mk 15:40, 47; 16:1, 9; Lk 24:10; Jn 19:25; 20:1, 18; all of which say "Mary the Magdalene" except Lk 24:10. GK *3402*.
30. This does not mean Mary was immoral (as some suggest), as a review of the others from whom demons were cast out shows. For example, she may have been very sick, paralyzed, or driven to madness like the man in v 27. The NT does not say how this manifested itself in her. But she clearly did become one who "loved much", like the woman in 7:47. She should be remembered for this, not for conjectures about her former life.
31. She is mentioned again only in 24:10.
32. That is, Herod Antipas, Mt 14:1; Lk 3:1.
33. Or, "manager, foreman, administrator, trustee, guardian, governor". This term was also used of a procurator. It is not known what Chuza did, so the exact meaning intended here is not known. Elsewhere only as "manager" in Mt 20:8; and "guardian" in Gal 4:2. GK *2208*. Related to "commission" in Act 26:12.

A. Mt 18:17   B. Mt 9:10   C. Col 1:6, understood   D. Mk 14:3   E. Mt 26:7   F. Jn 11:33   G. Mt 26:49   H. Rom 8:30, called   J. Lk 1:34
K. 1 Jn 3:1   L. 1 Cor 7:1   M. 1 Jn 4:11, ought   N. Mt 16:27, render   O. Mt 7:1   P. Mk 7:35   Q. Rom 16:16   R. Eph 2:8   S. Lk 19:10   T. 2 Tim 4:2
U. Mt 8:17, weakness

   3D. And Susanna
   4D. And many others
   5D. Who were serving[A] them[1] out of their possessions[2]

 2C.[3] And while *a* large crowd *was* gathering, and the *ones* from every city[4] *were* coming to Him, He spoke with[5] *a* parable[B]— *"The one* sowing went out *that he might* sow his seed. And during his sowing

   1D. "Some *seed* fell along the road. And it was trampled-underfoot[C]. And the birds *of* the heaven ate it up[D]
   2D. "And other[6] *seed* fell-down on the bed-rock[7]. And having grown[8], it was dried-up[E], because of not having moisture
   3D. "And other *seed* fell in *the* middle *of* the thorns[F]. And the thorns, having grown-with *it*, choked[9] it
   4D. "And other *seed* fell into the fertile[10] soil[G]. And having grown, it produced[H] fruit, *a* hundred-fold"
   5D. While saying these *things*, He was calling, "Let the *one* having ears to hear, hear"

 3C.[11] And His disciples were asking Him[12] what this parable might mean. *And the One* said—

   1D. "It has been given *to* you to know the mysteries[K] *of* the kingdom[L] *of* God. But *I* speak in parables *to* the others in order that while seeing[M] they may not be seeing[M], and while hearing, they may not be understanding[13]
   2D. "Now the parable means[14] this—

     1E. "The seed is the word[N] *of* God[15]
     2E. "And the[16] *people*[17] along the road are the *ones* having heard. Then the devil comes and takes away the word from their heart[O], in order that they may not be saved[P], having believed[18]
     3E. "And the *people* on the bed-rock *are* ones who are welcoming[19] the word with joy when they hear *it*. And these do not have *a* root[Q]— *they are* ones who are believing for *a* time[R], and are departing[20] in *a* time *of* testing[21]
     4E. "And the[22] *seed* having fallen into the thorns— these *people* are the *ones* having heard, and while proceeding are being choked[23] by *the* anxieties[24] and riches and pleasures[25] *of* life[26]. And they are not bringing-*fruit*-to-maturity[27]
     5E. "And the *seed* in the good[28] soil[G]— these *people* are *ones* who, having heard the word in *a* good[29] and fertile heart[30], are holding-on-to[31] *it*, and bearing-fruit[S] with endurance[32]

 4C.[33] "And no one having lit *a* lamp covers it *with a* container[T], or puts *it* under *a* bed. But he puts *it* on *a* lampstand[U], in order that the *ones* coming in may see the light[34]

   1D. "For[35] there is not *a* hidden[V] *thing* which will not become visible[36], nor *a* hidden-away[37] *thing* which will never be known[W] and come into visibility[38]

 5C.[39] "Therefore be watching[X] how[40] you listen—

   1D. "For whoever has[41]— it will be given *to* him
   2D. "And whoever does not have— even what he thinks[42] *that he* has will be taken-away from him"

1. That is, Jesus and the twelve. Some manuscripts say "Him" {B}.
2. Or, "belongings". This is a participle, on which see Heb 10:34. The women used their personal resources to provide for the needs of Jesus and the disciples.
3. Parallel account at Mt 13:1; Mk 4:1.
4. This is an idiom, literally "according to city", as in v 1. The people came in groups by city.
5. Or, "through, by means of". GK *1328*.
6. Or, "different". Luke uses a different word here and in v 7, 8 (GK *2283*) than Matthew and Mark (GK *257*), with the same meaning. He is referring to another portion of seed, viewed as a group. That Luke does not mean four "different" seeds is clear from v 11, where he identifies the seed as "the" word of God.
7. Or, "rock". That is, bed-rock thinly covered with soil, not soil with rocks in it. Same word as in v 13 and in 6:48. On this word, see Mt 7:24. Related to "rocky *places*" in Mt 13:5.
8. Same word as in v 8. Elsewhere only in Heb 12:15. GK *5886*. Related to "grow with" in v 7, which is used only there (GK *5243*).
9. Elsewhere only as "drowned" in v 33. GK *678*. Matthew (13:7), Mark (4:7) and Luke (8:7) use the same root word with different prefixes, but the same basic meaning. The thorns killed it, choked it off.
10. That is, "good" in the sense of "generous, useful, beneficial". On this word, see 1 Tim 5:10b. Mt 13:8 and Mk 4:8 have a different word, the same word Luke uses in v 15. Luke uses both words to describe the heart in v 15.
11. Parallel account at Mt 13:10; Mk 4:10.
12. Some manuscripts add "saying" {N}, so that it says "saying, 'What might this parable mean?'".
13. This is the purpose of speaking in parables, in fulfillment of Isa 6:9-10. On this word, see Mt 13:13. Compare Mk 4:12; Mt 13:14-15.
14. Or, "is". Same word as in v 9, where it could be rendered "might be". On this word, see "is" in Mt 26:26.
15. The soil pictures the response to the word of God by the person.
16. The grammar of this word here and in v 13 agrees with "people". The grammar changes in v 14.
17. That is, the people represented by the road, on whom the seed of the word of God fell. Same idea in v 13.
18. That is, by believing. The seed is immediately taken away, gaining no significant reception. On this word, which is also in v 13, see Jn 3:36.
19. Or, "receiving, accepting", but not the same word as in Mt 13:20; Mk 4:16. On this word, see Mt 10:40.
20. Or, "withdrawing", one after the other. Same word as in 2:37; 4:13; 13:27. On this word, see 1 Tim 4:1. These people show some signs of life and grow for a while, but depart at the first stress.
21. Or, "trial, temptation". On this word, see "trials" in Jam 1:2.
22. The grammar of this word here and in v 15 agrees with "seed", as in v 5-8.
23. On this word, see Mk 4:7. Related to the word in v 7. These people show signs of life for a longer period, co-existing with the thorns. But they never reach the goal, they never bear fruit, the word is crowded out of their lives.
24. Or, "worries, concerns, cares". On this word, see 1 Pet 5:7. Related to "be anxious" in Mt 6:25.
25. Elsewhere only in Tit 3:3; Jam 4:1, 3; 2 Pet 2:13. GK *2454*. Our word "hedonist" comes from this word. Related to "with pleasure" in Mk 6:20.
26. This word refers to the externals of life, the means of life, the possessions. On this word, see 1 Jn 2:16.
27. This word, "bring to maturity, bring to completion" was also used of women "bringing to completion" the baby in their womb. For these people, life was "conceived", but never "born". Used only here. GK *5461*.
28. That is, "good" in the sense of "beautiful, free from defects". Same word as used by Matthew and Mark. On this word, see 1 Tim 5:10a.
29. Same word as "good" soil in this verse. On "fertile", see v 8.
30. These people do not just hear the word, they hear it in the heart, and in a heart that is true and responsive.
31. Or, "retaining, holding fast". On this word, see "hold down" in Rom 1:18.
32. On this word, see Jam 1:3. Holding on (endurance), and fruit bearing, are the marks of genuine believers.
33. Parallel account at Mk 4:21. Compare Mt 5:15; 10:26; Lk 11:33; 12:2.
34. Some think the lamp is Jesus; others, His word in the believer's life. See Mk 4:21 on this.
35. Some think Jesus means that His light will not remain hidden. What He now conceals in parables will become visible and known to all. Nothing will remain hidden or secret. Others think He means that God's light will make everything visible to all. All hearts will be exposed. Let the light in you shine, for it will expose the secrets of people's hearts. See Mk 4:22.
36. Or, "evident, known, clear, plain, open". On this word, see "evident" in Rom 1:19.
37. Or, "secret, concealed". Related to "hidden" earlier in the verse, and having the same basic meaning. On this word, see Mk 4:22.
38. Same word as "visible" earlier. "Come into visibility" is an idiom meaning "become widely known, come to light". The same phrase occurs in a similar verse in Mk 4:22.
39. Parallel account at Mk 4:24. Compare Mt 25:29; Lk 19:26.
40. Listen with an open, receptive, and obedient heart; listen like the man in 6:48.
41. That is, has a growing spiritual life and spiritual understanding. Compare Mk 4:24-25.
42. Or, "imagines", in which case this person's own opinion is in error. Or, "seems to have", in which case the opinion of others is in error. On this word, see Lk 19:11.

A. 1 Pet 4:10, ministering B. Mt 13:3 C. Heb 10:29 D. Mk 12:40, devouring E. Mk 3:1, became withered F. Lk 6:44 G. Rev 7:1, land H. Rev 13:13, does J. Mt 19:29 K. Rom 11:25 L. Mt 3:2 M. Rev 1:11 N. 1 Cor 12:8 O. Rev 2:23 P. Lk 19:10 Q. Heb 12:15 R. Mt 8:29 S. Rom 7:4 T. 1 Thes 4:4, vessel U. Rev 1:12 V. 1 Cor 4:5 W. Lk 1:34 X. Rev 1:11

	6C.[1] And His mother and brothers[2] came to Him, and they were not able to meet[3] *with* Him because of the crowd[4]	19
	1D. And it was reported[A] *to* Him, "Your mother and Your brothers are standing outside, wishing[B] to see You"	20
	2D. But the *One*, having responded, said to them, "My mother and My brothers are these— the *ones* hearing and doing the word[C] *of* God"	21
15B.[5]	And it came about on one *of* the days that[D] **He** got into *a* boat, and His disciples. And He said to them, "Let us go to the other side *of* the lake[6]". And they put-to-sea[E]	22
	1C. Now while they *were* sailing, He fell-asleep[7]. And *a* storm[8] *of* wind came down on the lake, and they were being filled-with[F] *water* and were being-in-danger[G]	23
	2C. And having gone to *Him*, they woke Him up[9], saying, "Master[H], Master, we are perishing[J]!"	24
	3C. And the *One*, having awakened, rebuked[K] the wind and the surge[10] *of* the water. And they ceased[L], and there was calm[11]. *And He said *to* them, "Where *is* your faith?"	25
	4C. But having feared[12], they marveled[13], saying to one another, "Who then is this *One*, that[14] He commands[15] even the winds and the water, and they obey[M] Him?"	
16B.[16]	And they sailed-down to the country[N] *of* the Gerasenes[17], which is opposite Galilee[18]	26
	1C. And He having gone out[19] on the land, *a* certain man from the city met *Him,* having[20] demons	27
	1D. And *for a* considerable[O] time,[21] he did not put-on[P] *a* garment[Q], and was not staying in *a* house, but in the tombs[R]	
	2C. And having seen Jesus, having cried out, he fell before Him and said *with a* loud voice, "What do I have to do with you,[22] Jesus, Son *of* the Most-High[S] God? I beg[T] You, do not torment[U] me"	28
	1D. For He ordered[23] the unclean spirit to come out from the man	29
	1E. For it had seized[24] him many times	
	2E. And he was being bound *with* chains[V] and shackles[25], while being guarded[W]. And tearing[26] the bonds[27], he was being driven[28] by the demon into the desolate *places*	
	3C. And Jesus asked him, "What is *the* name *for* you?"	30
	1D. And the *one* said, "Legion[X]", because many demons entered into him	
	2D. And they were begging[Y] Him that He not command them to go into the abyss[Z]	31
	4C. Now there was *a* herd *of* many[29] pigs there feeding on the mountain. And they begged[Y] Him that He permit[AA] them to enter into those *pigs*[30]	32
	5C. And He permitted[AA] them	
	6C. And the demons, having come out from the man, entered into the pigs. And the herd rushed[BB] down the steep-bank[CC] into the lake, and was drowned[DD]	33
	7C. And the *ones* feeding[31] *them,* having seen the *thing* having happened, fled and reported[A] *it* in the city and in the fields. *And they came out to see the *thing* having happened	34 35
	1D. And they came to Jesus and found the man from whom the demons went out sitting— having been clothed, and being sound-minded[EE]— at the feet *of* Jesus	
	2D. And they became afraid	

1. Compare Mt 12:46-50; Mk 3:31-35.
2. On the brothers and sisters of Jesus, see Mt 13:55-56.
3. Or, "join". Used only here. GK *5344*.
4. That is, the crowd mentioned in v 4. Matthew puts this "on that day", 12:46-50 with 13:1.
5. Parallel account at Mt 8:23; Mk 4:35.
6. That is, the Sea of Galilee. On this word, see 5:1.
7. Used only here. GK *934*.
8. Same word as in Mk 4:37.
9. On this word, "woke up", see "aroused" in Jn 6:18. Same word as "awakened" next, with different grammar. This word is related to "woke" in Mt 8:25; Mk 4:38.
10. Same word as in Jam 1:6.
11. Same words as in Mt 8:26; Mk 4:39, without "great". "Calm" is GK *1132*, and is used only in these three places.
12. Or, "been afraid". Same word as in Mk 4:41. On this word, see "respecting" in Eph 5:33.
13. Same word as in Mt 8:27. On this word, see "caused to marvel" in Rev 17:8.
14. Or, "because". GK *4022*.
15. Or, "orders". Same word as in v 31. Elsewhere only in Mk 1:27; 6:27, 39; 9:35; Lk 4:36; 14:22; Act 23:2; Phm 8. GK *2199*. Related to the noun in Rom 16:26.
16. Parallel account at Mt 8:28; Mk 5:1.
17. Some manuscripts say "Gadarenes" (as in Mt 8:28); others, "Gergesenes" {C}. See Mk 5:1.
18. That is, on the opposite side of the lake from the district of Galilee; on the east side.
19. On the grammar of this phrase, which is not the same as in the parallel passages, compare also Mt 9:28.
20. Some manuscripts say "who had" {N}.
21. Some manuscripts have this phrase in the previous sentence, so that it says "having demons for *a* considerable time met *Him*. And he did not..." {N}. Instead of "he did not put on *a* garment", some manuscripts say "he was not dressed" {N}, using the word in 16:19.
22. This is an idiom, literally, "What [is there] *for* me and *for* You". On this idiom, see Jn 2:4.
23. Some manuscripts say "was ordering" {N}. On this word, see "command" in 1 Tim 1:3.
24. This word is used of a violent seizing and carrying away. Elsewhere only of a ship being seized by the wind and driven off course, Act 27:15; and of people being violently seized and taken somewhere, Act 6:12; 19:29. GK *5275*. Related to "snatch away" in 2 Cor 12:2.
25. That is, bindings for the feet. Elsewhere only in Mk 5:4. GK *4267*.
26. Or, "breaking". This man used a tearing action to break the bonds. Elsewhere only of clothes in Mt 26:65; Mk 14:63; Act 14:14; and of nets in Lk 5:6. GK *1396*.
27. This word is related to "bound" earlier. On this word, see "imprisonment" in Phil 1:7.
28. Same word as in Jam 3:4; 2 Pet 2:17, where a ship or a mist is "driven" by wind or a storm. Elsewhere only of men driving a boat forward by "rowing" Mk 6:48; Jn 6:19. GK *1785*.
29. Or, "*a* considerable-number". Mt 8:30, Mk 5:11, and Lk 8:32 each use a different word here. GK *2653*.
30. The demons wish to remain in an active role in the area. They immediately do so by killing the pigs. Whether or not this was the intention of Jesus is not stated. In any case, this great sign becomes a test of the people. They could be drawn to Jesus by it, or push Him away. They choose the latter response to His unquestioned work of power. Thus Jesus helps the man by casting out the demons. Perhaps then the demons force an immediate test, and turn the people against Jesus through fear (this is one conjecture). Jesus leaves, but sends the man to proclaim to his people.
31. Or, "tending". Same word as in v 32. On this word, see Jn 21:15.

A. 1 Jn 1:3, announcing B. Jn 7:17, willing C. 1 Cor 12:8 D. Lk 5:1 E. Act 20:13 F. Act 2:1, fulfilled G. 1 Cor 15:30 H. Lk 5:5 J. 1 Cor 1:18 K. 2 Tim 4:2, warn L. 1 Cor 13:8 M. Act 6:7 N. Mk 1:5 O. 2 Cor 3:5, sufficient P. Rom 13:14 Q. 1 Pet 3:3 R. Lk 23:53 S. Mt 21:9, highest T. 2 Cor 8:4 U. Rev 14:10 V. Act 28:20 W. Jn 12:25, keep X. Mt 26:53 Y. Rom 12:8, exhorting Z. Rev 9:1 AA. 1 Tim 2:12 BB. Act 7:57 CC. Mt 8:32 DD. Lk 8:7, choked EE. Rom 12:3

    3D. And the *ones* having seen reported *to* them how the *one* having been demon-possessed[A] was restored[B]   36

  8C. And the whole crowd *from* the surrounding-region[C] *of* the Gerasenes[1] asked Him to depart from them because they were being gripped[2] *with* great fear[D]   37
  9C. And **He**, having gotten into *a* boat, returned. °But the man from whom the demons had gone out was begging[3] Him to be *with* Him   38

    1D. But He[4] sent him away, saying, °"Return[E] to your house and be relating[5] all-that God did *for* you"   39
    2D. And he departed, proclaiming[F] throughout the whole city all-that Jesus did *for* him

17B.[6] And during Jesus' returning[E], the crowd welcomed[G] Him, for they were all expecting[H] Him   40

  1C. And behold— *a* man came, *for* whom *the* name *was* Jairus. And this *one* was *an* official[7] *of* the synagogue. And having fallen at[8] the feet *of* Jesus, he was begging Him to enter into his house, because there was *an* only-born[J] daughter *to* him, about twelve years *old*, and **she** was dying   41, 42
  2C. Now during His going, the crowds were thronging[9] Him. °And *a* woman being in *a* flow *of* blood for twelve years— who, having expended[10] her whole living[11] *on* physicians[12], was not able to be cured[K] by anyone— °having approached from behind, touched the tassel[L] *of* His garment   43, 44

    1D. And at once her flow *of* blood stopped[M]
    2D. And Jesus said, "Who *is* the *one* having touched[N] Me?"[13]   45
    3D. And while all *were* denying[O] *it*, Peter[14] said, "Master[P], the crowds are enclosing[15] You and pressing-against[16] You[17]"
    4D. But Jesus said, "Someone touched Me, for **I** recognized[18] power having gone forth from Me"   46
    5D. And the woman, having seen that she did not escape-notice[Q], came trembling[R]. And having fallen before Him, she declared[19] in the presence of all the people for what reason she touched Him, and how she was healed[S] at-once[T]   47
    6D. And the *One* said *to* her, "Daughter[20], your faith has restored[B] you. Go in peace"   48

  3C. While He *is* still speaking, someone comes from [the house of] the synagogue-official[21], saying[22] that "Your daughter is dead. Be troubling[23] the Teacher no longer[24]"   49

    1D. But Jesus, having heard, responded *to* him, "Do not be fearing. Only believe[25], and she will be restored[B]"   50
    2D. And having come to the house, He did not permit[U] anyone to go in with Him[26] except Peter and John and[27] James, and the father *of* the child, and the mother   51
    3D. Now they[28] were all weeping[V] and beating-their-breasts[W] *for* her. But the *One* said, "Do not be weeping,[29] for[30] she did not die, but she is sleeping". °And they were laughing-scornfully[31] *at* Him, knowing that she died   52, 53
    4D. But **He**, having[32] taken hold of her hand, called, saying, "Child, arise[X]!"   54
    5D. And her spirit returned, and she stood up at-once[T]   55

      1E. And He directed[Y] *that* something should be given *to* her to eat
      2E. And her parents were astonished[Z]   56
      3E. And the *One* ordered[AA] them to tell no one the *thing* having taken place[33]

18B.[34] Now having called together the twelve[35], He gave them power and authority over all the demons, and to cure diseases. °And He sent them out to proclaim the kingdom *of* God, and to heal the sick *ones*[36]   9:1, 2

1. See v 26. The same variants occur here.
2. Or, "held under the control of, ruled, governed, overcome". On this word, see "control" in 2 Cor 5:14.
3. Same word as in v 28. Not related to the word in v 31, 32, which is the word used throughout the story by Matthew and Mark.
4. Some manuscripts say "Jesus" {K}.
5. Or, "narrating, describing, leading through". In this predominately Gentile area next to Israel, Jesus has no need to restrain this man. Same word as in Mk 5:16; 9:9; Lk 9:10; Act 9:27; 12:17. Elsewhere only as "describe" in Act 8:33; "tell" in Heb 11:32. GK *1455*. Related to "narrative" in Lk 1:1; "tell in detail" in Act 13:41; and "expound" in Jn 1:18.
6. Parallel account at Mt 9:18; Mk 5:21.
7. Or, "leader". On this word, see "ruler" in Rev 1:5. Compare the word in v 49.
8. Or, "near, beside". GK *4123*.
9. Or, "pressing, crowding". A vivid word to use here. Elsewhere it means "choked", as in v 14.
10. Used only here. GK *4649*. Related to "consumed" in Gal 5:15.
11. Or, "means of living". On this word, see "life" in 1 Jn 2:16. She spent everything she had on this.
12. Some manuscripts omit "having expended *her* whole living *on* physicians" {C}. GK *2620*.
13. This sign reveals something about the power and knowledge of Jesus, and the power of faith in Him, but it cannot be known to others unless the woman tells what happened.
14. Some manuscripts add "and the *ones* with him" {B}.
15. Or, "confining, holding in". Same word as "gripped" in v 37.
16. Used only here. GK *632*. Related to the word in Mk 5:31.
17. Some manuscripts add "and You say, 'Who *is* the *one* having touched Me?" {B}, similar to Mk 5:31.
18. Or, "perceived, noticed". On this word, see "know" in 1:34. Jesus "knew" it. Related to "known" in Mk 5:30 (GK *2105*).
19. Some manuscripts add "*to* Him" {K}. On this word, see "announcing" in 1 Jn 1:3.
20. Some manuscripts say "Take courage, daughter. Your..." {N}, as in Mt 9:22.
21. Or, "synagogue-leader". On this word, see Act 18:8. The two separate words are in v 41.
22. Some manuscripts add "*to* him" {N}.
23. Same word as in 7:6 and Mk 5:35. On this word, see Mt 9:36.
24. Some manuscripts say "Do not be troubling the Teacher" {B}.
25. The grammar implies "believe now as an act of faith". Some manuscripts have the same grammar as Mk 5:36 {N}.
26. Some manuscripts omit "with Him" {N}.
27. Some manuscripts reverse these names, "James and John" {N}.
28. That is, the ones in the house when Jesus and the others entered.
29. The grammar implies "stop weeping".
30. Some manuscripts omit this word {N}.
31. Or, "laughing-against, laughing-mockingly, laughing down, ridiculing". Elsewhere only in this story, Mt 9:24; Mk 5:40. GK *2860*. The root word is "laugh" in 6:21 (GK *1151*).
32. Some manuscripts say "having put everyone outside and having taken..." {N}
33. That is, the thing Jesus did. Leave the crowd in uncertainty about the details. Do not become heralds of it. Note that this is the opposite of v 39. This is Israel, and Jesus is trying to control the pace of the public response to Him.
34. Parallel account at Mt 10:1; Mk 6:7.
35. Some manuscripts say "His twelve disciples"; others, "the twelve apostles" {B}.
36. Some manuscripts omit "the sick *ones*"; others say, "the *ones* being sick" {C}.

A. Mt 8:16   B. Jam 5:15   C. Mk 1:28   D. Eph 5:21   E. 2 Pet 2:21, turn back   F. 2 Tim 4:2   G. Act 2:41   H. Lk 3:15, waiting in expectation
J. Jn 1:18   K. Mt 8:7   L. Mt 23:5   M. Mk 13:14, standing   N. 1 Cor 7:1   O. 2 Tim 2:12   P. Lk 5:5   Q. 2 Pet 3:5   R. Mk 5:33   S. Mt 8:8
T. Mt 21:19   U. Mt 6:12, forgive   V. Jn 11:33   W. Rev 1:7   X. Mt 28:6   Y. 1 Cor 7:17   Z. Mk 2:12   AA. 1 Tim 1:3, command

| Luke 9:3 | 222 | Verse |

1C. And He said to them, "Be taking nothing for the journey— neither *a* staff[1], nor *a* [traveler's] bag[2], nor bread, nor money[3], nor *are you* to have two tunics[4] each[5] — 3

    1D. "And into whatever house you enter, be staying[A] there, and going forth from there[6] — 4
    2D. "And all who do not welcome[B] you— while going out from that city, be shaking-off[7] the dust from your feet for *a* testimony[C] against them" — 5

2C. And going forth, they were going from village-to-village[8] announcing-the-good-news[D] and curing[E] everywhere — 6
3C.[9] And Herod the tetrarch[10] heard-*of* all the *things* taking place[11] — 7

    1D. And he was greatly-perplexed[12] because of *it* being said by some that John arose[F] from *the* dead, ˚and by some that Elijah appeared[G], and *by* others that some prophet *of* the ancients[13] rose-up[H] — 8
    2D. And Herod said, "**I** beheaded John. But who is this *One* about Whom I am hearing such *things*?" — 9
    3D. And he was seeking to see Him

4C.[14] And having returned[J], the apostles related[K] to Him all that they did. And having taken them along, He retreated[L] privately[M] toward[15] *a* city[16] being called Bethsaida. ˚But the crowds, having known[17] *it*, followed Him — 10, 11

    1D. And having welcomed[N] them, He was speaking *to* them about the kingdom *of* God and healing[O] the *ones* having *a* need[P] *of a* cure[18]
    2D. And the day began to decline[19]. And having come to *Him*, the twelve said *to* Him, "Send-away[Q] the crowd in order that having gone into the surrounding villages and farms, they may take-up-lodging[20] and find provisions[21], because here we are in *a* desolate[R] place" — 12
    3D. But He said to them, "**You** give them *something* to eat" — 13
    4D. And the *ones* said, "There are not more than five loaves and two fish *with* us[22]— unless perhaps, having gone, **we** should buy food for this whole *group-of*-people[23]". ˚For there were about five-thousand men[24] — 14
    5D. And He said to His disciples, "Make them lie-down [to eat] *in* eating-groups[25]— about[26] fifty each". ˚And they did so, and made everyone lie down — 15
    6D. And having taken the five loaves and the two fish, having looked up to heaven, He blessed[S] them, and broke *them* in pieces[27], and was giving *them to* the disciples to set-before the crowd — 16
    7D. And they ate and were all filled-to-satisfaction[T] — 17
    8D. And the *amount of* fragments[U] left-over[28] *by* them was picked up— twelve baskets

19B.[29] And it came about during His being alone[30] praying,[31] *that* the disciples were with Him. And He questioned[32] them, saying, "Who do the crowds say *that* I am?" — 18

    1C. And the *ones*, having responded, said, "John the Baptist; and others, Elijah; and others, that some prophet *of* the ancients[33] rose-up[H]" — 19
    2C. And He said *to* them, "But who do **you** say *that* I am?" — 20
    3C. And Peter, having responded, said, "The Christ *of* God"
    4C. But the *One*, having warned[34] them, ordered[V] *them* to be telling this *to* no one— ˚having said that "The Son *of* Man must[W] suffer[X] many *things*, and be rejected[Y] by[35] the elders and chief priests and scribes, and be killed, and be raised[Z] on the third day" — 21-22
    5C.[36] And He was saying to everyone, "If anyone wants to be coming after Me, let him deny[37] himself, and let him take up his cross[38] daily, and let him be following Me — 23

1. Or, "walking stick". Compare Mk 6:8; Mt 10:10. Some think Jesus means "a second staff". On this word, see "rod" in 1 Cor 4:21.
2. Or, "knapsack", a bag used to carry provisions. Elsewhere only in the same story in Mt 10:10; Mk 6:8; in Lk 10:4; and in Lk 22:35, 36, which refers back to this event. GK *4385*.
3. That is, like a denarius (see Mt 20:2) or a drachma (see Lk 15:8). Same word as "silver" in Mt 10:9. On this word, see "money" in Mt 25:27.
4. Or, "undergarments". Do not take a spare. Compare 3:11. On this word, see Mt 5:40.
5. Some manuscripts omit this word {C}. In other words, make no preparations for the journey.
6. That is, do not move from house to house in one town.
7. Elsewhere only in Act 28:5. GK *701*. Related to "shake out" in Mk 6:11.
8. This is an idiom, literally, "according to the villages". Similar to 8:1, 4; 13:22.
9. Parallel account at Mt 14:1; Mk 6:14.
10. That is, Herod Antipas, tetrarch of Galilee. See Mt 14:1 and Lk 3:1 on him, and Lk 3:19 on "tetrarch".
11. Some manuscripts add "by Him" {N}, so that it says "all the *things* being done by Him".
12. Elsewhere only in Act 2:12; 5:24; 10:17. GK *1389*. Related to "perplexed" in 2 Cor 4:8.
13. Luke could mean "*of* the ancient *ones*", or, "*of* the ancient *times*". On this word, see "old" in Act 15:7.
14. Parallel account at Mt 14:13; Mk 6:30; Jn 6:1.
15. Note v 12. Jesus and the apostles were in a desolate place, not the city itself. GK *1650*.
16. Instead of "*a* city being called Bethsaida", some manuscripts say "*a* desolate place *belonging to a* city being called Bethsaida" {B}. Compare Mk 6:45.
17. Or, "come-to-know, learned, recognized". On this word, see 1:34.
18. Or, "medical treatment, care, service". Related to the verb "cure" in Mt 8:7. On this word, see "service" in Rev 22:2.
19. This idiom is used again in 24:29. GK *3111*. Mt 14:15 calls it evening; Mk 6:35 calls it a late hour.
20. This idiom is used also in 19:7. The root meaning is that the people "tear down, break down, unharness [the animals]" for the night. On this word, see "tear down" in Mt 24:2.
21. Used only here. GK *2169*.
22. That is, we do not have more than five loaves and two fish.
23. Or, "all this people" (singular), an expression found only here. Same word as in Act 5:37. GK *3295*. The grammar indicates the disciples expect a negative answer to their doubtfully expressed suggestion. Their response amounts to "How can **we** do so?" Next, Jesus tells them how.
24. That is, males. On this word, see 1 Tim 2:12.
25. Used only here. GK *3112*. Related to "lie down" earlier. This could be rendered "Make them recline in reclining groups".
26. Some manuscripts omit this word {C}.
27. This word, "broke in pieces", is elsewhere only in Mk 6:41. GK *2880*. Related to the word in Mt 14:19.
28. This is a participle, the amount "having left over, having abounded, having surpassed [the need] *for* them".
29. Parallel account at Mt 16:13; Mk 8:27.
30. That is, in a private place, away from the crowds. This idiom is elsewhere only in Mk 4:10.
31. ThSame idiom as the similar phrase in 11:1, "during His being in a certain place praying", and 2:6; 5:12.
32. Or, "asked". This word is used 56 times. GK *2089*.
33. Same word as in v 8.
34. The warning is given next, in v 22.
35. Same word as "from" in Mt 16:21. GK *608*. Mk 8:31 uses GK *5679*.
36. Parallel account at Mt 16:24; Mk 8:34. Compare Mt 10:39; Lk 17:33; Jn 12:25.
37. On this word, see 2 Tim 2:12. Related to the word in Mt 16:24; Mk 8:34.
38. On "take up his cross", see Mt 16:24; 10:38.

A. Jn 15:4, abide   B. Mt 10:40   C. Act 4:33   D. Act 5:42   E. Mt 8:7   F. Mt 28:6   G. Phil 2:15, shine   H. Lk 18:33   J. 2 Pet 2:21, turn back
K. Lk 8:39   L. Lk 5:16   M. Mt 14:13   N. Act 2:41   O. Mt 8:8   P. Tit 3:14   Q. Mt 5:31   R. Mt 3:1, wilderness   S. Lk 6:28   T. Phil 4:12
U. Mt 15:37   V. 1 Tim 1:3, command   W. Mt 16:21   X. Gal 3:4   Y. Heb 12:17   Z. Mt 28:6, arose

1D. "For whoever wants to save^A his life^B will lose^C it. But whoever loses his life[1] for My sake— this *one* will save it	24
1E. "For what is *a* person profited[2]— having gained^D the whole world, but having lost or having forfeited[3] himself?	25
2D. "For whoever *is* ashamed-of^E Me and My words, the Son *of* Man will be ashamed-of **this *one*** when He comes in the glory[4] *of* Himself and the Father and the holy angels	26
3D. "And I say *to* you truly[5], there are some[6] *of* the *ones* standing here[7] who will by-no-means[8] taste death[9] until they see the kingdom^F *of* God"	27
20B.[10] And it came about, about eight days after these words, that[11] having taken-along^G Peter and John and[12] James, He went up on the mountain to pray	28
1C. And during His praying the appearance[13] *of* His face became different^H, and His clothing *became* white, while gleaming-out[14]	29
2C. And behold, two men were talking-with^J Him, who were Moses and Elijah—˚who, having appeared^K in glory^L, were speaking *of* His departure[15] which He was about to bring-to-fulfillment[16] in Jerusalem	30-31
3C. Now Peter and the *ones* with him had been weighed-down[17] *with* sleep. But having fully-awakened[18], they saw His glory and the two men standing-with Him	32
4C. And it came about during their parting[19] from Him, *that* Peter said to Jesus, "Master^M, it is good *that* we are here. And let us make three dwellings[20], one *for* You, and one *for* Moses, and one *for* Elijah"— not knowing what he was[21] saying	33
5C. And while he *was* saying these *things*, there came-to-be *a* cloud. And it was overshadowing^N them. And they became afraid at their[22] entering[23] into the cloud	34
6C. And *a* voice came out of the cloud, saying, "This is My chosen[24] Son. Be listening-to Him"	35
7C. And at the voice coming,[25] Jesus was found alone^O	36
8C. And **they** kept-silent^P, and reported *to* no one during those days anything *of the things* which they had[26] seen	
21B.[27] And it came about *on* the next day, they having come down from the mountain, *that a* large crowd met Him	37
1C. And behold— *a* man from the crowd shouted^Q, saying, "Teacher, I beg^R You to look^S upon my son, because he is *an* only-born^T *son to* me. ˚And behold— *a* spirit seizes^U him and he[28] suddenly cries-out^V. And it convulses^W him, along with foam [at the mouth]. And it departs from him with difficulty, while bruising[29] him. ˚And I begged^R Your disciples to[30] cast it out, and they were not able"	38 39 40
2C. And having responded, Jesus said, "O unbelieving and perverted[31] generation, how long[32] will I be with you, and bear-with^X you? Bring your son to[33] *Me* here"	41
3C. And while he *was* still approaching, the demon threw him to the ground[34] and convulsed[35] *him*	42
4C. And Jesus rebuked^Y the unclean spirit, and healed the boy, and gave him back *to* his father	
5C. And they were all astounded^Z at the majesty[36] *of* God	43
22B.[37] But while all *were* marveling^{AA} at everything which He was doing[38], He said to His disciples,˚"**You** put[39] these[40] words into your ears— for the Son *of* Man is going to be handed-over^{BB} into *the* hands *of* men"	44
1C. But the *ones* were not understanding[41] this statement. And it had been concealed[42] from them, so that[43] they did not perceive[44] it. And they were fearing to ask[45] Him about this statement[46]	45

1. Or, "soul" both times in this verse. On this word, see "soul" in Jam 5:20. Note that Luke says "himself" in v 25.
2. Note how Matthew, Mark, and Luke have different grammar for this word. On this word, see Rom 2:25.
3. Or, "suffered loss of". Same word as in Mk 8:36.
4. Jesus refers here to the glory of all three, His and the Father's and the holy angels' glory. Compare Mk 8:38.
5. Or, "truthfully". On this word, see Mt 14:33.
6. Some think Jesus is referring to the three with Him at the transfiguration next. For other views, see Mk 9:1.
7. Elsewhere in this sense only in Mt 26:36, and as "there" in Act 15:34; 18:19; 21:4. GK *899*. Mt 16:28 and Mk 9:1 use GK *6045*.
8. Or, "never". It is an emphatic negative, the strongest in Greek. Elsewhere by Luke only in 1:15; 6:37; 8:17; 10:19; 12:59; 13:35; 18:17, 30; 21:18, 32, 33; 22:16, 18, 67, 68; Act 13:41; 28:26. On this idiom, see Gal 5:16.
9. On "taste death", see Heb 2:9.
10. Parallel account at Mt 17:1; Mk 9:2. Compare 2 Pet 1:17-18.
11. On this word, see 5:1. Some manuscripts omit this word {C}.
12. Some manuscripts reverse the names to "James and John" {N}.
13. Or, "outward appearance". On this word, see 2 Cor 5:7.
14. Used only here. GK *1993*. Related to the "gleaming" clothes of the angels in Lk 24:4; the "flash" of lightning in Lk 17:24; and to the light that "flashed around" Paul in Act 9:3. The root word is "lightning".
15. This is the word "exodus", "a way out", referring to the coming death of Jesus. Elsewhere only in Heb 11:22; 2 Pet 1:15. GK *2016*. The Greek word is *exodos*.
16. Or, "fulfill", viewing it as something prophesied for Jesus in the OT, Lk 24:44. Or, "complete, finish", viewing it as a task yet to be completed. On this word, see "filled" in Eph 5:18.
17. This is a participle, they "were having been weighed down". Same word as in Mt 26:43 and Lk 21:34. On this word, see "burdened" in 2 Cor 1:8.
18. Used only here. GK *1340*. It could also mean "having kept awake", meaning the three were very sleepy, but still awake when they first saw them. Related to "keep watch" in 1 Thes 5:6.
19. Or, "being separated, going away". Used only here. GK *1431*. Related to "separate" in Mt 19:6.
20. Or, "tents, tabernacles". Same word as in 16:9; Mt 17:4; Mk 9:5; Rev 13:6; 21:3. Used of the "tabernacle" in Heb 8:2; and as "tent" in Act 15:16; Heb 11:9. Used 20 times. GK *5008*. Related to "tent" in 2 Cor 5:4 and 2 Pet 1:13; and to "dwell" in Rev 7:15.
21. More literally "is", as the Greek typically phrases it.
22. This may refer to Jesus, Moses, and Elijah; or, to the three apostles. Perhaps the former, since the disciples hear God speak "out of" the cloud. Compare Mt 17:5.
23. That is, "when they entered".
24. More literally, "My Son, the *One* having been chosen". Some manuscripts say "My beloved Son" {B}, as in Mk 9:7. On this word, see 1 Cor 1:27.
25. That is, upon the completion of the statement by God.
26. More literally "have", as the Greek typically phrases it.
27. Parallel account at Mt 17:14; Mk 9:14.
28. Or, this may refer to the spirit, which "seizes him and suddenly cries out, and convulses him".
29. Luke may mean physically "bruising" him; or, "breaking, shattering, crushing" him emotionally. On this word, see Mt 12:20.
30. More literally, "in order that they might cast it out", as in Mk 9:18. GK *2671*.
31. Or, "crooked". This is a participle, "having been perverted". On the meaning of this sentence, see Mt 17:17.
32. This is an idiom, "until when" will I be with you? See Mt 17:17 on it.
33. This word, "bring to" (GK *4642*) is not related to "bring" in Mt 17:17; Mk 9:19. The grammar does not place emphasis on the process, as in Mt 17:17.
34. This word "to throw to the ground" is the same word as in Mk 9:18. GK *4838*.
35. Related to the word in v 39. On this word, see Mk 9:20.
36. Or, "grandeur, greatness, magnificence". Elsewhere only in Act 19:27; 2 Pet 1:16. GK *3484*. Related to "great" in Act 2:11.
37. Parallel account at Mt 17:22; Mk 9:30.
38. Some manuscripts say "which Jesus did" {N}.
39. This is a command, made more emphatic by separately expressing the subject, "you". Same word as in 1:66; 21:14; Act 5:4. On this word, see Act 19:21.
40. That is, the words following. Or, Jesus may be referring more broadly to all His words the disciples are hearing, "into your ears. For the Son...". Remember them. In either case, it is the statement about being handed over that they do not understand.
41. Or, "were being ignorant of, were not knowing" the meaning of it. On this word, see "be ignorant of" in Rom 10:3.
42. This is a participle, it "was having been concealed", or "hidden". Some think Luke means "by God"; others, "by their own mind-set". Used only here. GK *4152*.
43. Or, "in order that they might not". GK *2671*.
44. Or, "understand". Used only here. GK *150*. Related to "perception" in Phil 1:9, and "faculties" in Heb 5:14.
45. GK *2263*. Related to the word in Mk 9:32.
46. The disciples do not seem to have wanted to understand it, because it did not fit into their way of thinking. Their mind was focused on their own glory in the earthly kingdom they expected Jesus to inaugurate, as seen next. On this word, see "word" in Rom 10:17.

A. Lk 19:10   B. Jam 5:20, soul   C. 1 Cor 1:18, perish   D. Mk 8:36   E. Rom 1:16   F. Mt 3:2   G. Lk 17:34, taken   H. 1 Cor 12:9   J. Act 25:12
K. Lk 2:26, see   L. 2 Pet 2:10   M. Lk 5:5   N. Mt 17:5   O. Jam 2:24   P. 1 Cor 14:34   Q. Mt 3:3   R. 2 Cor 8:4   S. Jam 2:3, look upon   T. Jn 1:18
U. Rom 7:8, taken   V. Mt 8:29   W. Mk 1:26   X. 2 Cor 11:4   Y. 2 Tim 4:2, warn   Z. Mt 7:28   AA. Rev 17:8   BB. Mt 26:21

23B.[1] And *an* argument[2] came-in[3] among them *as to* which *of* them might be greater[4] 46

    1C. But Jesus, knowing[5] the reasoning[6] *of* their heart, having taken-hold-of[A] *a* child, stood him[7] beside Himself, *and said *to* them, "Whoever welcomes[B] this child on the basis of My name[8], welcomes Me.[9] And whoever welcomes Me, welcomes the *One* having sent Me forth. For the *one* being least[10] among you all, this *one* is[11] great[12]" 47, 48

    2C. And having responded, John[13] said, "Master[C], we saw someone casting-out[D] demons in Your name. And we were forbidding[14] him because he is not following with us" 49

    3C. And Jesus said to him, "Do not be forbidding[15] *him*. For he who is not against you[16], is for you" 50

6A. Now it came about during[17] the days *of* His ascension[18] being fulfilled[19], that[E] **He** set[20] *His* face *that He might* proceed to Jerusalem[21] 51

    1B. And He sent out messengers ahead *of* His presence[22]. And having gone, they entered into *a* village *of* Samaritans so-as[23] to prepare[F] *for* Him. *And they did not welcome[B] Him, because His face was going toward Jerusalem[24] 52, 53

        1C. And the disciples having seen *it*, James and John said, "Lord, do You want us to call[25] fire to come down from heaven and consume[G] them[26]?" 54

        2C. But having turned, He rebuked[H] them[27] 55

        3C. And they proceeded to another village 56

    2B. And while they *were* proceeding on the road 57

        1C. Someone said to Him, "I will follow You wherever You go"

            1D. And Jesus said to him, "The foxes have holes, and the birds *of* the heaven *have* nests[28], but the Son *of* Man does not have *a* place where He may lay *His* head"[29] 58

        2C.[30] And He said to another, "Be following Me". But the *one* said, "Master[31], permit[J] me, having gone, to first bury my father"[32] 59

            1D. But He said *to* him, "Allow[K] the dead to bury their *own* dead.[33] But **you**, having gone, be proclaiming the kingdom *of* God" 60

        3C. And another also said, "I will follow You, Master. But first permit[J] me to say-good-bye[34] *to* the *ones* in my house" 61

            1D. But Jesus said to him[35], "No one having put *his*[36] hand on *the* plow and looking to the *things* behind[37] is fit[38] *for* the kingdom *of* God" 62

    3B. And after these *things*, the Lord appointed[L] seventy two[39] others[40], and sent them out[M] ahead *of* His presence[41] two by two, to every city and place where He Himself was going to go 10:1

        1C.[42] And[43] He was saying to them— 2

            1D. "The **harvest**[44] *is* great— but the workers *are* few! Therefore ask the Lord[N] *of* the harvest that He send-out[O] workers into His harvest

            2D. "Go! Behold— I am sending you out[M] as lambs[45] in *the* midst[P] *of* wolves 3

            3D. "Do not be carrying *a* money-bag[46]— not *a* [traveler's] bag[Q], not sandals.[47] And greet[R] no one along the road.[48] *And into whatever house you enter, first say, 'Peace *on* this house' 4, 5

1. Parallel account at Mt 18:1; Mk 9:33.
2. Or, "reasoning, thought". On this word, see "thought" in Jam 2:4. Related to "argued" in Mk 9:34.
3. Luke states this as if it came in from the outside. This word "to enter, come in" is used 194 times, mostly with a physical subject. Only here and in Rom 5:12 (sin entered) does it have an abstract subject. GK *1656*.
4. The disciples were ranking themselves. Though the form of this word means "greater", some think the sense of it in this context is "greatest".
5. Some manuscripts say "seeing" {C}.
6. Same word as "argument" in v 46. An external "reasoning" started, but Jesus knew their internal "reasoning".
7. Or, "her". The Greek is not specific here.
8. On this phrase, "on the basis of My name", see Act 2:38.
9. Welcoming this child is welcoming the King. Earthly status is not relevant in His kingdom.
10. Or, "lesser". On this word, see Mt 11:11.
11. The child is great in the kingdom, and the one who becomes as a child. Some manuscripts say "shall be" {N}.
12. Though the form of this word is "great", some think the sense of it in this context is "greatest".
13. John responds with a case where they did not "welcome" one serving in the name of Jesus.
14. Same word as in Mk 9:38, on which see 1 Cor 14:39. Some manuscripts say "we forbade" {B}.
15. This verb, and "you" in the next sentence, is plural. Jesus is addressing all of the disciples through John.
16. Some manuscripts say "us, is for us" {N}, as in Mk 9:40. Compare Mk 9:39-40 on this.
17. Or, "while the days *of* His ascension *were* being fulfilled". Compare the similar phrase in Act 2:1.
18. That is, the days remaining until His "ascension" or "taking up", and so to His "death, decease". Used only here. GK *378*. Related to "taken up" in Act 1:2.
19. On this word, see Act 2:1.
20. Or, "established, fixed firmly". Same word as "fixed" in 16:26. On this word, see "established" in 1 Thes 3:2.
21. That is, Jesus set His course for Jerusalem. He firmly established His purpose and direction.
22. That is, ahead of Him. Same phrase as in 10:1; 7:27; Mt 11:10; Mk 1:2; and as Act 13:24, "before the presence of His coming". Same word as "face" in v 51, 53. This word means "face, presence, appearance", and is used 76 times. GK *4725*.
23. This word is used elsewhere in this sense only in Act 20:24, and an idiom in Heb 7:9. On this word, see "as" in Mt 19:19.
24. The Samaritans were hostile to Jews, especially to ones going to Jerusalem. They spurned Jesus because He was a Jew.
25. This is an idiom, literally, "Do You want *that* we should call". The disciples want to retaliate for the personal affront, precisely the thing Jesus taught them not to do in 6:28. This impulse is not from God.
26. Some manuscripts add "as also Elijah did" {B}.
27. Some manuscripts add after this, "and He said, "You do not know *of* what kind *of* spirit you are. For the Son *of* Man did not come to destroy the lives *of* people, but to save" {A}.
28. Elsewhere only in Mt 8:20. GK *2943*. Related to "nested" in 13:19, and to "dwelling" in 9:33.
29. In others words, Jesus has no permanent place on earth to which He is going, to which you might follow Him. And the glorious place on earth to which you may think He is going is not at all where He is going.
30. Compare Mt 8:18-22.
31. Some manuscripts omit this word {C}. On this word, see Mt 8:2. Same word as in v 61.
32. His father may have just died, or this man may mean "When he dies and I fulfill my family duties, I will follow".
33. That is, let the spiritually dead bury the physically dead. Put Me before family immediately.
34. Same word as in 14:33. On this word, see 2 Cor 2:13.
35. Some manuscripts omit "to him" {C}.
36. Some manuscripts include this word {C}.
37. Or, "and looking back". On this idiom, "to the *things* behind", see Jn 6:66.
38. Or, "useful, suitable". Same word as in 14:35. Elsewhere only as "useful" in Heb 6:7. GK *2310*.
39. Some manuscripts omit this word, making it "seventy" others {C}.
40. Some manuscripts add "also" {N}.
41. Or, "face". See 9:52 on this phrase.
42. Compare Mt 9:37-10:16.
43. Some manuscripts say "Therefore" {K}.
44. Jesus uses grammar that emphasizes the contrast between the two halves of this sentence. He also made this same statement when He appointed the twelve in Mt 9:37-10:1. On this word, see Mk 4:29.
45. That is, as defenseless ones, meek ones responding to what you find; not as conquerors.
46. Elsewhere only in 12:33; 22:35, 36. GK *964*.
47. Take no extra provisions, nor the means to purchase what you might need. Go with the shirt on your back and the power and message I give you.
48. Travel quickly from place to place with no socializing along the way. Your mission is in the cities, not on the roads. It is a mission of proclamation and announcement, not relationship building.

A. Lk 20:20 B. Mt 10:40 C. Lk 5:5 D. Jn 12:31 E. Lk 5:1 F. Mk 14:15 G. Gal 5:15 H. 2 Tim 4:2, warn J. 1 Tim 2:12 K. Mt 6:12, forgive L. Act 1:24 M. Mk 3:14, send out N. Mt 8:2, master O. Jn 12:31, cast out P. 2 Thes 2:7 Q. Lk 9:3 R. Mk 15:18

| Luke 10:6 | 228 | Verse |

1E. "And if *a son of* peace¹ is there, your peace will rest on him. Otherwise indeed,² it will return to you — 6

2E. "And be staying^A in the very house, eating and drinking the *things* from them.³ For the worker *is* worthy^B *of* his wages^C. Do not be passing^D from house to house — 7

    4D. "And into whatever city you enter and they welcome^E you— be eating the *things* being set-before^F you.⁴ °And be curing^G the sick *ones* in it. And be saying *to* them, 'The kingdom^H *of* God has drawn-near^J to you' — 8, 9

    5D. "But into whatever city you enter and they do not welcome^E you— having gone out into its wide-roads⁵, say, °'We are wiping-off⁶ *against* you even the dust having clung^K *to* us from your city— to *our* feet⁷. Nevertheless know this— that the kingdom *of* God has drawn near⁸'. °I⁹ say *to* you that it will be more-tolerable¹⁰ on that day *for* Sodom than *for* that city! — 10, 11, 12

        1E.¹¹ "Woe *to* you, Chorazin! Woe *to* you, Bethsaida! Because if the miracles^L having taken place in you had been done¹² in Tyre and Sidon, they would have repented^M long-ago^N, sitting in sackcloth and ashes. °Nevertheless¹³ it will be more tolerable *for* Tyre and Sidon at the judgment^O than *for* you — 13, 14

        2E. "And you, Capernaum, will you be exalted^P up to heaven?¹⁴ You will go-down¹⁵ as far as Hades^Q — 15

    6D. "The *one* listening-to you is listening-to Me. And the *one* rejecting^R you is rejecting Me. And the *one* rejecting Me is rejecting the *One* having sent Me forth^S" — 16

2C. And the seventy two¹⁶ returned with joy, saying, "Lord, even the demons are subject¹⁷ *to* us in Your name". °And He said *to* them, "I was seeing¹⁸ Satan having fallen¹⁹ like lightning from heaven²⁰ — 17, 18

    1D. "Behold²¹— I have given²² you the authority^T to trample²³ on snakes and scorpions, and over all the power *of* the enemy.²⁴ And nothing will by-any-means²⁵ harm^U you — 19

    2D. "Nevertheless, do not be rejoicing^V in this— that the spirits are subject *to* you. But²⁶ be rejoicing that your names have been recorded²⁷ in the heavens" — 20

3C.²⁸ At the very hour, He rejoiced-greatly²⁹ in the Holy Spirit³⁰, and said, "I praise^W You, Father, Lord *of* heaven and earth, that³¹ You hid³² these³³ *things* from wise *ones* and intelligent^X *ones*, and You revealed^Y them *to* children³⁴. Yes, Father, because³⁵ in this manner it became well-pleasing³⁶ in Your sight — 21

    1D. "All³⁷ *things* were handed-over^Z *to* Me by My Father — 22

    2D. "And no one knows³⁸ Who the Son is except the Father, and Who the Father is except the Son— and *anyone to* whom³⁹ the Son wills⁴⁰ to reveal *Him*"

4C.⁴¹ And having turned to the disciples,⁴² He said privately^AA, "Blessed⁴³ *are* the eyes seeing^BB *the things* which you are seeing. °For I say *to* you that many prophets and kings wanted to experience⁴⁴ *the things* which **you** are seeing, and they did not experience *them*; and to hear *the things* which you are hearing, and they did not hear *them*"⁴⁵ — 23, 24

4B.⁴⁶ And behold— *a* certain Law-expert^CC stood up, putting Him to the test⁴⁷, saying, "Teacher, [by] having done⁴⁸ what shall I inherit^DD eternal life?" — 25

    1C. And the *One* said to him, "What has been written in the Law? How do you read *it*?" — 26

1. That is, a person characterized by peace toward you and your message. On "son", see Gal 3:7.
2. On this idiom, "otherwise indeed", see 2 Cor 11:16.
3. That is, accepting the food provided by them as the provision from God, as wages from God.
4. That is, eat what they eat, without complaint.
5. On this word, see 14:21. Go on the main streets, not the small lanes.
6. Used only here. GK *669*. Related to the word in 7:38, 44.
7. Jesus may mean "[from our head down] to *our* feet". Or, "[even] to *our* feet". Some manuscripts omit "to *our* feet" {N}.
8. Some manuscripts add "to you" {N}.
9. Some manuscripts say "But I" {N}.
10. Same word as in v 14. On this word, see Mt 10:15.
11. Compare Mt 11:20-24.
12. Same word and grammar as in Mt 11:23.
13. On the meaning of this sentence, see Mt 11:22.
14. The grammar indicates a "no" answer is expected. Some manuscripts have this as one statement, "And you, Capernaum, the *one* having been exalted up to heaven, you will go down..." {N}.
15. Some manuscripts say "be brought down" {C}.
16. Some manuscripts omit this word {C}, as in v 1.
17. Same word as in v 20. On this word, see Eph 5:21.
18. Or, "perceiving, watching, observing". Some think Jesus means He was seeing it with the sending out of the seventy-two; others, each time they cast out a demon; others, at His own victory at His temptation. There are other views. Used 58 times. GK *2555*.
19. Some think Jesus means He was prophetically seeing Satan's final downfall; others, that He was repeatedly seeing his actual defeat as demons were cast out. There are other views.
20. Or, "from heaven like lightning". Jesus could mean "clearly and unmistakably", as in 17:24; or, "suddenly, instantly", and according to one view above, "repeatedly".
21. Are you surprised at having power over demons? Behold, I have given you more power than you realize, power to overcome all the attacks of the enemy.
22. Some manuscripts say "I give" {N}.
23. Or, "tread on". Elsewhere only in Lk 21:24; Rev 11:2 of Gentiles "trampling" Jerusalem; and in Rev 14:20 and 19:15 of "treading" the winepress of the wrath of God. GK *4251*.
24. Some take this literally; others, figuratively, of the fraud, deception, treachery and falsehood of the enemy. Compare Mk 16:18; Ps 91:13-14. Jesus has given these lambs (v 3) power over the enemy, and protection from the enemy. Nothing can stop them from carrying out this mission He gave them. The message of v 9 will by all means be proclaimed to Israel. Nothing can stop the coming of the Messiah to His people from building to the crescendo He intends. Some think this refers specifically to the seventy-two and this mission, like the command in v 4 (compare the command to the twelve in 9:3 and 22:35-36); others take it in a broader sense.
25. Or, "ever". The strongest negative in Greek. See "by no means" in 9:27.
26. Some manuscripts say "But rather" {K}.
27. Or, "written-in". On this word, see "inscribed" in 2 Cor 3:2. Some manuscripts say "were written" {N}.
28. Compare Mt 11:25-27.
29. Or, "exulted". Same word as in 1:47; Jn 8:56; Act 2:26; 16:34; 1 Pet 1:6, 8. Elsewhere only as "be overjoyed" in Mt 5:12; Jn 5:35; 1 Pet 4:13; Rev 19:7. GK *22*. Related to "gladness" in Jude 24.
30. That is, in the power of the Spirit, filled with the Spirit. Some manuscripts say "Jesus rejoiced greatly in the Spirit", meaning the Holy Spirit or *His* spirit {C}.
31. Or, "because". Same word as "because" in the next sentence.
32. On this word, see 1 Cor 2:7. Related to the word in Mt 11:25.
33. That is, the good news of the kingdom, which the seventy-two were proclaiming, v 9.
34. Or, "childlike *ones*". On this word, see Mt 11:25.
35. Or, "that", so that it says "Yes Father, [I praise you] that...". On this sentence, see Mt 11:26.
36. On this noun, see "good-pleasure" in Eph 1:5.
37. Some manuscripts say "And having turned to the disciples, He said, 'All...'" {A}.
38. Related to the word used in Mt 11:27. On this word, see 1:34.
39. More literally, "and *to* whomever".
40. Or, "desires, wants, wishes, intends". Same word as in 22:42. On this word, see Jam 1:18.
41. Compare Mt 13:16-17.
42. Luke could mean Jesus turned to the seventy-two (v 17) from others assumed to be present; or, to the twelve from the seventy-two.
43. Or, "Fortunate". Same word as in 6:20.
44. Or, "see", but not the same word as the other three times here. This word is used twice here, and an unrelated word is used three times. Many render both words as "see", taking them as synonyms. If Jesus intended a distinction between the two words here, this word may be rendered "see" in the sense of "experience", as in "see death", 2:26; "see mourning", Rev 18:7; "see decay", Act 2:27, etc. Same word as in Mt 13:17, on which see "see" in Lk 2:26.
45. Truly the disciples enjoyed a unique privilege, not repeated before or since, until Jesus comes. Jesus also said this to the twelve in Mt 13:16-17. They got to see it all fulfilled, right before their eyes! We enjoy the fruit of that fulfillment.
46. Compare Mt 22:34-40; Mk 12:28-34.
47. On this word, "put to the test", see Mt 4:7.
48. The same exact question appears in 18:18, Luke's phrasing of the question in Mt 19:16; Mk 10:17. What is there, after I have done it, that will cause me to inherit eternal life. What act of devotion or sacrifice will do it for me?

A. Jn 15:4, abide B. Rev 16:6 C. Rev 22:12, recompense D. Jn 5:24 E. Mt 10:40 F. Act 17:3, put before G. Mt 8:7 H. Mt 3:2 J. Lk 21:28
K. 1 Cor 6:16, join L. 1 Cor 12:10 M. Act 26:20 N. Jude 4, formerly O. Jn 3:19 P. Jn 8:28, lifted up Q. Rev 1:18 R. Gal 2:21, set aside
S. Mk 3:14, send out T. Rev 6:8 U. Act 7:24, wronged V. 2 Cor 13:11 W. Jam 5:16, confess out X. 1 Cor 1:19 Y. 2 Thes 2:3 Z. Mt 26:21
AA. Mt 14:13 BB. Rev 1:11 CC. Lk 7:30 DD. Gal 4:30

2C. And the *one*, having responded, said, "You shall love[A] *the* Lord your God from your whole heart, and with your whole soul[B], and with your whole strength, and with your whole mind[C], and your neighbor[D] as[1] yourself"   27

3C. And He said *to* him, "You answered correctly[E]. Be doing this and you will live"   28

4C. But the *one*, wanting to vindicate[2] himself, said to Jesus, "And who is my neighbor?"   29

5C. Having taken-up[F] *the question*, Jesus said, "A certain man was going down from Jerusalem to Jericho. And he fell-into[3] robbers[G], who, both having stripped[H] him and having laid-on[4] blows[5], went away— having left *him* half-dead   30

    1D. "And by coincidence[6], *a* certain priest was going down on that road. And having seen him, he passed-by-on-the-other-side[7]   31

    2D. "And likewise also *a* Levite[J] having come-to-be upon[8] the place, having come[9] and having seen, passed by on the other side   32

    3D. "But *a* certain Samaritan[10], while traveling, came upon him. And having seen, he felt-deep-feelings[K] [of compassion]   33

        1E. "And having gone to *him*, he bound his wounds[11], pouring on oil[12] and wine   34

        2E. "And having put him on *his* own mount[13], he brought him to *an* inn and took-care-of[14] him

        3E. "And on the next day[15], having taken out two denarii[16], he gave *them to* the innkeeper[17] and said, 'Take-care-of him. And whatever thing[18] you spend-further **I** will give-back[L] *to* you during my returning[19]'   35

    4D. "Which *of* these three seems[M] *to* you to have become[20] *a* neighbor[D] *of* the *one* having fallen into the robbers[G]?"   36

    5D. And the *one* said, "The *one* having shown mercy[N] to[21] him"   37

    6D. And[22] Jesus said *to* him, "Go, and **You** be doing likewise"

5B. And during their proceeding, **He** entered into *a* certain[23] village. And *a* certain woman, Martha *by* name, received[24] Him   38

    1C. And *to* this *one* there was *a* sister being called Mary, who[25] also[26] was listening-to His word[O], having sat near to the feet *of* the Lord[27]   39

    2C. But Martha was being distracted[28] with much service[29]. And having stood-near[P], she said "Lord, do You not care[30] that my sister left me to be serving[Q] alone? Tell her then, that she should help[R] me"   40

    3C. But having responded, the Lord said *to* her[31], "Martha, Martha, you are anxious[32] and troubled[33] about many *things*. °But there is *a* need[34] *of* one[35] *thing*. For Mary chose[S] the good[36] part[37], which will not be taken-away[T] *from* her"   41   42

6B. And it came about during His being in *a* certain place praying, *that* when He ceased[U], *a* certain *one* *of* His disciples said to Him, "Lord, teach us to pray, just as John also taught his disciples"   11:1

    1C.[38] And He said *to* them, "Whenever you pray, say, 'Father[39]—   2

        1D. 'Let Your name be treated-as-holy[40]

        2D. 'Let Your kingdom[V] come[41]

        3D. 'Be giving us each day[42] our daily[W] bread   3

        4D. 'And forgive[X] us our sins, for **we** also are forgiving everyone being indebted[43] *to* us   4

        5D. 'And do not bring[Y] us into *a* temptation[44]' "

1. Or, "like". On this command, see Mt 19:19. The man quotes from Deut 6:5; Lev 19:18.
2. Or, "justify". Some think Luke means "to justify his question" which the man himself answered in v 27; to vindicate his asking a question to which he already knew the answer. The man now asks what he considers to be the hard question. The Jews believed only fellow Jews were their neighbors for purposes of this law. Others think the man is asserting his own righteousness. On this word, see "declare righteous" in Rom 3:24.
3. Or, "encountered". On this word, see Jam 1:2.
4. This word means "to put on, lay on". It is used of "laying on" hands for various purposes (see Heb 6:2), and as "put on" in Mt 21:7; 27:29, 37; Lk 15:15; Jn 9:15. Used 39 times. GK *2202*.
5. Luke uses this idiom "to lay on blows" again in Act 16:23, a beating which resulted in "wounds" (16:33, same word). On this word, see "wound" in Rev 13:3. Same word as "beatings" in 2 Cor 6:5; 11:23.
6. Or, "chance". Used only here. GK *5175*. The related verb (not in the NT) means "come together by chance, meet by accident".
7. Elsewhere only in v 32. GK *524*.
8. Or, "along, opposite, before, in relation to". GK *2848*. Same word as in v 33.
9. That is, having come by. Some manuscripts omit "having come-to-be", so that it says "Levite having come to the place and having seen". Others omit "having come", so that it says "Levite having come-to-be upon the place and having seen" {C}.
10. The Jews would not have considered this person a "neighbor".
11. The Greek word is *trauma*, from which we get our word. Used only here. GK *5546*. Related to the word in 20:12.
12. That it, olive oil. On this word, see Jam 5:14.
13. That is, the Samaritan's mount, referring to whatever kind of animal he was riding. On this word, see "livestock" in 1 Cor 15:39.
14. Same word as in v 35. On this word, see 1 Tim 3:5.
15. Some manuscripts say "day, having gone out, having taken out two..." {N}.
16. That is, two day's wages. This was enough to pay for several days of food and lodging, perhaps as much as a month. On this word, see Mt 20:2.
17. Related to "inn" in v 34. Both words are used only here. GK *4106, 4107*.
18. On this idiom, see Col 3:17.
19. Or, "while *I am* returning". That is, his returning to his destination, on the way to which this inn was a stopping point. Elsewhere only in 19:15, with different grammar. GK *2059*.
20. Or, "proved to be". The important question is not "who is my neighbor whom I am responsible to love", but rather, "to whom have I become a neighbor by loving them". The law commands love, and the love is due to everyone who crosses my path. GK *1181*.
21. On this phrase "show mercy to", see 1:72.
22. Some manuscripts say "Then" {N}.
23. Mary and Martha live in Bethany in Jn 11:1.
24. Or, "received as a guest, welcomed into *her* house, entertained as a guest". Elsewhere only in Lk 19:6; Act 17:7; Jam 2:25. GK *5685*. Some manuscripts add "into her house" {B}.
25. Some manuscripts omit this word, so that it says "Mary. And she was listening..." {C}.
26. Luke could mean "also" along with Martha; or, "also" along with the others who were listening.
27. Some manuscripts instead say "*of* Jesus" {N}.
28. Or, "pulled away, drawn off, diverted". Used only here. GK *4352*. Related to "undistracted" in 1 Cor 7:35.
29. That is, the preparations for the meal. On this word, see "ministry" in 1 Cor 12:5.
30. More literally, "is it not *a* concern *to* You". The grammar indicates a "yes" answer is expected, "yes, I care". On this word, see "concerned" in 1 Cor 7:21.
31. Instead of what precedes, some manuscripts say "Jesus said *to* her" {N}.
32. On this verb, see Mt 6:25, where Jesus says not to be anxious about what to eat because life is more than food.
33. Or, "upset". Used only here. GK *2571*. The related words mean "disorder, turmoil, confusion". Related to "throw into a commotion" in Mt 9:23. Martha was troubled by the confusion of things to do and the disorder of her situation.
34. Or, "necessity". On this word, see Tit 3:14.
35. Some think this refers to the meal— you are worried about many dishes, many things to eat. Only one dish is really necessary for the meal. In other words, Martha is overreacting. Some manuscripts say "*a few things* or one *thing*" {C}, taking this view. Others think it refers to a spiritual truth. In the light of eternity, there is only one real need— to know God. Mary chose to listen to Jesus while He was there speaking, rather than to prepare and serve food. Listening to God is the "good part" of life. The eating can be arranged later. In other words, Mary is focusing on higher priorities.
36. Though the form of this word is "good", some think the sense of it here is "better" or "best".
37. Or, "share, portion". Mary is the one who responds with such great love for Jesus in Jn 12:3. On this word, see Col 1:12.
38. Compare Mt 6:9-15.
39. Each of the following is in the form of a command, with a change in grammar at point 3D. Some manuscripts say "Our Father in the heavens" {A}, as in Mt 6:9.
40. On this phrase, see Mt 6:9.
41. Some manuscripts add "Let Your will be done— as in heaven, also on earth" {A}, as in Mt 6:10.
42. Or, "day by day, every day, according to *the* day". Same idiom as "daily" in 9:23; 19:47, etc.
43. Or, "owing us". On this word, see "ought" in 1 Jn 4:11. This the verb related to "debts" and "debtors" in Mt 6:12.
44. On this word, see Mt 6:13. Some manuscripts add "but deliver us from the evil *one*" {A}, as in Mt 6:13.

A. Jn 21:15, devotedly love B. Jam 5:20 C. Lk 1:51, thought D. Act 7:27 E. Mk 7:35 F. Lk 7:43, assume G. Mt 21:13 H. 2 Cor 5:3, take off J. Jn 1:19 K. Mt 9:36 L. Mt 16:27, render M. Lk 19:11, thinking N. Lk 1:72 O. 1 Cor 12:8 P. Lk 21:34, suddenly come upon Q. 1 Pet 4:10, ministering R. Rom 8:26 S. 1 Cor 1:27 T. Mk 14:47, took off U. 1 Cor 13:8 V. Mt 3:2 W. Mt 6:11 X. Mt 6:12 Y. Mt 6:13

2C. And He said to them— 5

    1D. "Which of you will have *a* friend[A], and will go to him *at* midnight, and say *to* him, 'Friend, lend[1] me three loaves-of-bread, °because my friend came to me from *a* journey, and I do not have what I will set-before[B] him'? °And that *one,* having responded from inside, says, 'Do not be causing[2] me troubles. The door has already been locked[C], and my children are with me in bed.[3] I am not able, having arisen[D], to give *it to* you' 6 7

        1E. "I say *to* you— 8

            1F. "Even though[4] he will not, having arisen, give *to* him because of being his friend
            2F. "Yet because of his shamelessness[5], he[6] will, having been raised[7], give *to* him as much as he needs

        2E.[8] "And **I** say *to* you— be asking, and it will be given *to* you. Be seeking, and you will find. Be knocking, and it will be opened *to* you 9

            1F. "For everyone asking receives. And the *one* seeking finds. And *to* the *one* knocking, it will be opened[9] 10

    2D.[10] "And what father from-*among* you will his son ask-*for a* fish[E], and he will give him *a* snake instead of *a* fish? °Or indeed he will ask-*for an* egg— will he give him *a* scorpion?[11] 11 12

        1E. "Therefore if **you**, being[12] evil[F], know-*how*[G] to give good gifts *to* your children, how much more will *your* Father from heaven give[13] *the* Holy Spirit *to* the *ones* asking Him!" 13

7B.[14] And He was casting-out[H] *a* demon, and **it** was[15] mute. And it came about, the demon having gone out, *that* the mute *man* spoke. And the crowds marveled[J]. °But some of them said, "He is casting out the demons by[16] Beelzebul[K], the ruler[L] *of* the demons[M]". °And others, testing[N] *Him*, were seeking[O] from Him *a* sign out of heaven[17] 14 15 16

    1C. But **He**, knowing[G] their thoughts[18], said *to* them— 17

        1D. "Every kingdom having been divided[19] against itself is desolated[P]. And *a* house *divided* against *a* house falls[20]

            1E. "And if indeed[21] Satan was divided against himself, how will his kingdom stand[22]?— because you are saying *that* I *am* casting out the demons by Beelzebul 18

        2D. "And if **I** am casting out the demons by Beelzebul, by whom are **your sons** casting *them* out?[23] For this reason, **they** will be your judges 19

            1E. "But if **I**[24] am casting out the demons by *the* finger *of* God, then the kingdom *of* God came[25] upon you 20

        3D. "Whenever the strong *man* having fully-armed-*himself*[26] is guarding[Q] his *own* courtyard[27], his possessions[28] are in peace[R]. °But when *one* stronger *than* he, having come against *him*, overcomes[29] him— he takes away his full-armor[30] upon which he trusted[S], and distributes[T] his spoils 21 22

        4D. "The *one* not being with Me is against Me. And the *one* not gathering[31] with Me, is scattering[32] 23

1. This word is used of informal lending between friends, expecting a payback in kind. Used only here. GK *3079*. Related to "use".
2. The grammar implies "Stop causing me troubles". On this phrase, see Lk 18:5.
3. The family all slept in one room. The friend is imposing on the whole family.
4. More literally, "If he even will not... give to him...". This idiom means "accepting that he will even not give to him because he is a friend, yet...". On this idiom, see 1 Cor 7:21. Compare 18:4, where this same point is made.
5. Or, "impudence". That is, because of the shameless persistence of the one asking. From the point of view of the friend in bed, the one asking is shameless, refusing to bow to propriety. From the point of view of the one asking, he is persistent and insistent until he gets his answer. Persistent asking is the point. Keep asking as long as you continue to have a need. Jesus is not implying that God is like the man in bed, as also in 18:2-5. Used only here. GK *357*.
6. That is, the friend in bed.
7. This word (see v 31) is not the same word as "arisen" in v 7, 8 (see 18:33). The man will not voluntarily raise himself and give it to his friend. But when he has been raised— forced to get up— by the continued asking of his friend, he will do so.
8. Compare Mt 7:7-8.
9. Some manuscripts say "it is opened" {C}.
10. Compare Mt 7:9-11.
11. Some manuscripts add a third example, and phrase the three questions like Mt 7:9-10. They say "father from-*among* you will *his* son ask-*for a* loaf— he will not give him *a* stone, *will he*? Or indeed *a* fish— he will not give him *a* snake instead *of a* fish, *will he*? Or indeed he will ask-*for an* egg— he will not give him *a* scorpion, *will he*?" {C}.
12. GK *5639*. Not the same word as Mt 7:11.
13. Some manuscripts say "will *your* Father give from heaven *the* Holy Spirit" {C}.
14. Compare Mt 9:32-34; 12:22-37; Mk 3:22-30.
15. Some manuscripts omit "and **it** was" {C}, so that it says "casting out *a* mute demon". The demon made the man mute.
16. Or, "in connection with, in union with, by means of ". GK *1877*. The same word is in v 18, 19, 20.
17. Jesus takes up this second issue in v 29.
18. Not the same word as Mt 12:25. Used only here. GK *1378*. Related to "thought" in 1:51.
19. On this word, see Act 2:3. Related to "divide" in Mt 12:25 and Mk 3:24, (on which see "apportioned" in 1 Cor 7:17).
20. Or, "is desolated, and house falls upon house", the latter phrase expanding upon the desolation, or meaning "and house attacks house".
21. Or, "If Satan also...". This idiom (see 1 Cor 7:21) means "Assuming that Satan indeed was..., how".
22. Or, "be made to stand, be established". How will Satan be able to make it stand if he is divided against himself? GK *2705*.
23. On this statement, see Mt 12:27.
24. Some manuscripts do not emphasize this word, in which case it would not be bold {C}.
25. Or, "arrived". On this word, see 1 Thes 2:16.
26. Or, "being fully armed", "in full armor", putting the emphasis on the man's armed state. Used only here. GK *2774*. Related to "arm" in 1 Pet 4:1.
27. That is, the courtyard of his house. On this word, see Mt 26:3.
28. Or, "belongings". This is a participle, on which see Heb 10:34.
29. Or, "conquers". On this word see Rev 2:7. It is because Jesus is stronger and has overcome Satan that He is casting out demons. This is the lesson they should be drawing from it.
30. Elsewhere only in Eph 6:11, 13, where the individual pieces are mentioned. GK *4110*. Related to "fully armed", v 21.
31. That is, gathering the flock of sheep. The shepherd gathers; the wolf scatters.
32. Neutrality is impossible. Those not siding with the Victor are aiding the enemy. On this word, see Jn 16:32.

A. Lk 14:10   B. Act 17:3, put before   C. Jn 20:19   D. Lk 18:33, rise up   E. Jn 21:6   F. Act 25:18   G. 1 Jn 2:29, know   H. Jn 12:31   J. Rev 17:8   K. Mk 3:22   L. Rev 1:5   M. 1 Cor 10:20   N. Heb 2:18, tempted   O. Phil 2:21   P. Rev 18:17   Q. Jn 12:25, keep   R. Act 15:33   S. 1 Jn 3:19, persuade   T. Act 4:35

5D.¹ "When the unclean spirit departs from the person, it goes-through^A waterless places seeking^B rest^C. And not finding *it*— 24

    1E. "Then² it says, 'I will return³ to my house from where I came out'
    2E. "And having come, it finds *it* having⁴ been swept and put-in-order⁵ 25
    3E. "Then it proceeds, and takes along **seven** other spirits more evil *than* itself 26
    4E. "And having gone in, they dwell^D there
    5E. "And the last *state of* that person becomes worse *than* the first"⁶

2C. And it came about during His saying these *things that a* certain woman from the crowd, having raised^E *her* voice, said *to* Him, "Blessed⁷ *is* the womb^F having carried^G You, and *the* breasts^H which You sucked^J" 27

    1D. But **He** said, "More-than-that⁸, blessed *are* the *ones* hearing the word *of* God and keeping^K *it*" 28

3C.⁹ And while the crowds *were* assembling-more¹⁰, He began to say "This generation¹¹ is *an* evil generation. It is seeking^B *a* sign¹² 29

    1D. "And *a* sign will not be given *to* it except the sign *of* Jonah¹³. ˚For as Jonah became *a* sign *to* the Ninevites, so the Son *of* Man also will be *to* this generation 30
    2D. "*The* Queen *of the* South will be raised¹⁴ at the judgment^L with the men *of* this generation, and she will condemn^M them. Because she came from the ends¹⁵ *of* the earth to hear the wisdom *of* Solomon, and behold— *a* greater *thing than* Solomon *is* here 31
    3D. "Ninevite men¹⁶ will rise-up¹⁷ at the judgment^L with this generation, and they will condemn^M it. Because they repented^N at the proclamation^O *of* Jonah, and behold— *a* greater *thing than* Jonah *is* here 32
    4D. "No one having lit^P *a* lamp, puts *it* in *a* crypt¹⁸, nor under the basket¹⁹, but on the lampstand^Q, in order that the *ones* coming in may see²⁰ the light 33

        1E.²¹ "The lamp²² *of* the body is your²³ eye²⁴. When²⁵ your eye is single²⁶, your whole body is also full-of-light²⁷. But when²⁸ it is bad²⁹, your body *is* also full-of-darkness³⁰ 34

            1F. "So be watching-out³¹ *that* the light in you is not darkness^R! 35

        2E. "Therefore if your whole body *is* full-of-light, not having any part full-of-darkness, [then] *the* whole *body* will be full-of-light³² as when the lamp gives-light-to^S you *with its* bright-light³³" 36

8B. Now at the speaking³⁴, *a* Pharisee asks Him so that He might eat-the-morning-meal³⁵ with him. And having gone in, He fell-back [to eat] 37

    1C. And the Pharisee, having seen *it*, marveled^T that He was not first cleansed³⁶ before the morning-meal³⁷ 38

        1D.³⁸ But the Lord said to him, "Now³⁹ **you** Pharisees cleanse^U the outside *of* the cup and the platter⁴⁰, but the inside *of* you is full^V *of* plundering^W and evilness^X 39

            1E. "Foolish^Y *ones*— did not the *One* having made^Z the outside, also make the inside? 40
            2E. "But give the *things* being-within⁴¹ *as* alms⁴², and behold— all *things* are clean *for* you 41

1. Compare Mt 12:43-45.
2. Some manuscripts omit this word {C}.
3. This word (GK *5715*) is related to the word in Mt 12:44 (GK *2188*).
4. Some manuscripts say "finds *it* being unoccupied, having been swept and put in order" {B}, as in Mt 12:44.
5. Same word as in Mt 12:44.
6. And so it happened in Israel, Mt 12:45. Israel's state after Jesus became worse than before. Note Lk 23:31.
7. Or, "Fortunate", Same word as in 6:20.
8. Or, "Rather". Jesus confirms and corrects, "Yes, but rather...". Used only here. GK *3528*. Related to "on the contrary" in Rom 9:20; 10:18; and "more than that" in Phil 3:8. Mary truly is blessed and favored, 1:28, 42, 45. This woman is saying what Mary said all generations would say, 1:48.
9. Compare Mt 12:38-42; 16:1-4; Mk 8:10-12.
10. Or, "increasing". Used only here. GK *2044*. Related to the word in 24:33.
11. On "this generation", see Mt 24:34. Some manuscripts omit this word {N}.
12. Jesus now answers the question of v 16. On this word, see 2 Thes 2:9.
13. Some manuscripts add "the prophet" {N}, as in Mt 12:39. Compare Mt 16:4.
14. Or, "will arise". On this word, see "arose" in Mt 28:6.
15. Or, "extremities, limits". On this word, see Heb 6:16. On this queen, see 1 Kings 10:1-13.
16. That is, men from Nineveh where Jonah went to preach.
17. Or, "stand up". On this word, see 18:33.
18. Or, "vault, hidden place", like a cellar. Our word "crypt" comes from this word. Used only here. GK *3219*. Related to "hidden" in 1 Cor 4:5. On this saying, compare 8:16.
19. On this word, see Mk 4:21. Some manuscripts omit "nor under the basket" {C}. The purpose of a lamp is to illuminate. Jesus is the light, providing illumination for all who are entering the kingdom. He is shining for all to see. To see, one only needs the light, assuming one can see.
20. Verses 34-36 expand on this generation's ability to see the light on the lampstand.
21. Compare Mt 6:22-24.
22. That is, the source of light. Used 14 times. GK *3394*.
23. Some manuscripts say "the" {K}, as in Mt 6:22.
24. The bodily source of physical light for the body, the light giver to the body, is the eye. So also in the spiritual realm. Whether or not you are illuminated by the light of Jesus depends on the state of your spiritual eye (that is, your heart).
25. Or, "Whenever". GK *4020*. Some manuscripts say "Therefore when..." {N}.
26. On this word, see Mt 6:22. Some think Jesus means "healthy"; others, "single-focused". When your eye has a single focus on God's truth, your whole life will be full of the light of Christ.
27. Same word as twice in v 36. On this word, see Mt 6:22.
28. Or, "as soon as". Elsewhere only in Mt 2:8; Lk 11:22. GK *2054*.
29. Some think Jesus means "double-focused"; others, "damaged, sick". Same word as in Mt 6:23. On this word, see "evil" in Act 25:18.
30. It will not allow the light to come into the body. Elsewhere only in v 36; Mt 6:23. GK *5027*.
31. On this word, see "looking for" in 2 Cor 4:18. Watch out that the "illumination" in your life is not actually darkness. A striking paradox. Jesus moves from a bad eye to the distorted light it admits. An eye focused on signs and traditions will not allow God's lamp— Christ— to shine into your life. This generation is evil because its eye is darkened by the falsehoods it considers light. Compare Mt 6:23.
32. Jesus applies the lamp illustrations to His hearers. If you and your spiritual eye-lamp are such that your whole life is full of light without restriction (as described in v 34), then your whole life will be full of light from God's lamp as from the physical lamp on a lampstand (v 33). If your spiritual sight allows God's light into your whole life, then your whole life will be full of light from His lamp. You will clearly see the light from God's Lamp (Jesus) and come to it, and have no need for signs. Rephrased in negative terms, if you are only partially receptive to God's light, your life will only be partially lit up by His Lamp, resulting in a continual asking for more light, more signs. This generation seeks signs because of its bad spiritual sight, not because God's Lamp (Jesus) is insufficiently bright. There are other views of this verse. Consult the commentaries.
33. Elsewhere this word means "lightning" (see Rev 4:5 on it).
34. This idiom means "At the event of His speaking". This phrase itself says nothing about the timing of the request. It could have been before, during (in v 29), or after. Note the different grammar of the phrase in v 27.
35. Or, "eat lunch". Elsewhere only as "eat breakfast" in Jn 21:12, 15. GK *753*.
36. That is, Jesus did not ceremonially wash His hands according to their custom. On this word, see Mk 7:4.
37. On this word, see 14:12. Related to the word in v 37.
38. Compare Mt 23:25-26.
39. This word is used in a temporal and in a logical sense. Thus, some think Jesus means "at the present time", "right now" in your washing; others, "As it is, as a matter of fact". GK *3814*.
40. Elsewhere only of the platter for John's head, Mt 14:8, 11; Mk 6:25, 28. GK *4402*.
41. Some think Jesus means "Give what is in your cup and on your platter (that is, your possessions) as alms". Since the cup represents their lives, others think He means the Pharisees must give what should be found inside their hearts; that is, love of God and justice (v 42), mercy and faithfulness (Mt 23:23), etc.. It is the love of God and of neighbor proceeding from the heart that will make you "clean" inside and out, not ceremonial washings alone apart from a work in the heart. Used only here. GK *1913*.
42. That is, as charitable giving to the poor. On this word, see "almsgiving" in Mt 6:2

A. Rom 5:12 B. Phil 2:21 C. Mt 12:43 D. Eph 3:17 E. 2 Cor 11:2, lifts up F. Lk 1:15 G. Mt 8:17 H. Rev 1:13 J. Mt 21:16, nursing K. Jn 12:25 L. Jn 3:19 M. 1 Cor 11:32 N. Act 26:20 O. 1 Cor 1:21 P. 1 Cor 7:1, touch Q. Rev 1:12 R. Jn 3:19 S. Heb 6:4, enlightened T. Rev 17:8 U. Heb 9:22 V. Rev 4:6 W. Heb 10:34 X. Mt 22:18 Y. 2 Cor 11:16 Z. Rev 13:13, does

2D.[1] "But woe *to* you Pharisees, because you are giving-a-tenth-of[2] the mint and the rue and every garden-plant[A], and are disregarding[3] the justice[B] and the love[C] *of* God[4]	42

              1E. "But *you* ought-to-have[5] done these[6] *things,* and not be slackening[7] those *things*[8]

        3D.[9] "Woe *to* you Pharisees, because you love[D] the seat-of-honor[E] in the synagogues and the greetings in the marketplaces   43

        4D.[10] "Woe *to* you[11], because you are like unmarked[12] graves[F], and the people walking over them do not know *it*"[13]   44

    2C. And having responded, one *of* the Law-experts[G] says to Him, "Teacher, while saying these *things*, You also are insulting[H] us"   45

        1D.[14] And the *One* said, "Woe *to* you Law-experts also, because you burden[J] people *with* hard-to-bear[K] burdens[15], and **you** do not touch[16] the burdens *with* one *of* your fingers   46

        2D.[17] "Woe *to* you, because you build the tombs[18] *of* the prophets, and your fathers killed them!   47

            1E. "Therefore you are witnesses and are giving-approval[19] *to* the works *of* your fathers, because **they**[20] killed them— and **you** build *their* tombs[21]   48

            2E. "For this reason[22] the wisdom *of* God[23] also said, 'I will send-forth[L] prophets[M] and apostles[24] to them. And *some* of them they will kill and persecute[N]   49

                1F. 'In order that the blood *of* all the prophets having been shed[O] since *the* foundation[P] *of the* world may be required[25] from this generation[Q]—   50

                    1G. 'From *the* blood *of* Abel up to *the* blood *of* Zechariah[26], the *one* having perished[R] between the altar and the house[S] [of God]   51

                2F. 'Yes, I say *to* you, it shall be required from this generation'

        3D.[27] "Woe *to* you Law-experts, because you took away the key *of* knowledge[28]. **You** did not enter, and you hindered[29] the *ones* entering"   52

9B. And He having gone out from there,[30] the scribes and the Pharisees began to be terribly[31] hostile[32], and to question[33] Him concerning more *things* ˚while lying-in-wait-for[34] Him to catch[35] something from His mouth[36]—˚in which[37] *circumstances*, the myriads[38] *of* the crowd having been gathered-together so that *they were* trampling[39] one another,   53   54   12:1

    1C. He began to speak to His disciples[40] first[41]—

1. Compare Mt 23:23-24.
2. Jesus turns to the outside things the Pharisees give, the tithing of external things. Same word as in 18:12.
3. Or, "passing by" without obedience or attention. Same word as in 15:29. GK *4216*.
4. That is, you fail to give out justice and your love for God from within (because it is not there).
5. Or, "should have". On this idiom, see "should have" in Mt 25:27.
6. That is, the latter things, the justice and love, as in Mt 23:23.
7. Or, "relaxing, disregarding". Compare Mt 23:23. On this word, see Heb 12:12.
8. Jesus does not fault the Pharisees for personally going beyond the Law in the matter of tithing (though He does fault them for imposing this on others in v 46). He faults them for attending to the externals like tithing with a heart that is far from God, Mk 7:6. This is worthless and pointless religion, Mt 15:9.
9. Compare Mt 23:6-7.
10. Compare Mt 23:27-28.
11. Some manuscripts add "scribes and Pharisees, hypocrites" {N}.
12. More literally, "not plain, unclear, not evident; unseen". Elsewhere only as "uncertain" in 1 Cor 14:8. GK *83*. Related to "evident" in Gal 3:11 (same word without the negative prefix).
13. You are containers of death, defiling all who come in contact with you. People become "unclean" by contact with you without even knowing it. Compare Mt 23:27.
14. Compare Mt 23:4.
15. On this word, see "load" in Gal 6:5. Related to the verb earlier in the verse.
16. Some think this means "touch in order to help the people with this burden". Others think Jesus means "touch so as to obey yourself". You yourselves do not do what you require others to do. The scribes could avoid things bringing defilement, something the common working people could not do. Thus they did not have to carry the burden that the people could not avoid, and could not bear, Act 15:10. Compare Mt 23:4. Used only here. GK *4718*.
17. Compare Mt 23:29-36.
18. Same word as in Mt 23:29.
19. Or, "giving-consent". On this word, see Rom 1:32.
20. Jesus uses grammar that emphasizes the linkage between the two groups.
21. Some manuscripts include these words {C}. You are building the prophet's tombs while failing to obey them! You are really just like your fathers. God will send more prophets to you so you can even repeat their murders.
22. That is, because of your spiritual union in spirit with your prophet-killing fathers. Compare Mt 23:34.
23. That is, God in His wisdom. This phrase is used in this way only here.
24. Or, "messengers". That is, the NT prophets and apostles who went forth after the resurrection. Compare Mt 23:34-35. On this word, see 1 Cor 12:28.
25. It is a debt to justice that this generation will pay. Israel paid with the total destruction of A.D. 70. On this word, see "seek out" in Heb 11:6.
26. That is, the first (Gen 4:8) and last (2 Chron 24:21) murders of the OT, in the Hebrew order of the OT books.
27. Compare Mt 23:13.
28. Some think Jesus means the key "consisting of knowledge"; others, "opening the door to knowledge". In either case, the knowledge leading to salvation is in view. The scribes did not use this key to enter into the kingdom of God for themselves, and they hindered those trying to use it to enter. They locked up the Scriptures with their traditions.
29. Or, "forbade, tried to stop". Compare Mt 23:13. On this word, see "forbidding" in 1 Cor 14:39.
30. Instead of "He having gone out from there", some manuscripts say "while He *was* saying these *things* to them" {N}.
31. Or, "fearfully, fiercely". Elsewhere only in Mt 8:6. GK *1267*.
32. That is, internally hostile. More literally, to terribly "have *it* in" for Jesus, or "hold in" retaliation against Him. It is the calculating hostility of one prevented from outwardly retaliating by others— here, by the crowds. It is an internal "setting oneself against" someone, planning their demise in a way that does not harm one's relationship with those preventing an immediate outward attack. Same word as in Mk 6:19, of Herodias toward John.
33. The exact nuance of this word is uncertain. It was used of teaching orally, where the teacher dictates a question and the student answers from memory— "to catechize". Some put the emphasis on the questioning, "question closely, interrogate, quiz". Others put it on checking the answer, "watch His words closely". Including both ideas, they began to "question and test" Him on theological issues. Used only here. GK *694*.
34. Or, "lying in ambush for". Elsewhere only in Act 23:21. GK *1910*. Related to "ambush" in Act 23:16.
35. This is a hunting term also meaning "to hunt after, chase". Used only here. GK *2561*. Related to "trap" in Rom 11:9; and "wild-animal". Some manuscripts say "seeking to catch" {N}.
36. Some manuscripts add "in order that they might accuse Him" {N}.
37. This idiom can mean here "during which", as in 21:6; 23:29; Act 24:18; 26:12; Heb 10:32; or, "in which *circumstances*", as in Phil 4:11; or, "among whom", as in Act 17:34; 20:25; Rom 1:6; Eph 2:3; Phil 2:15. In any case, it closely links chapter 12 to chapter 11. Jesus is vividly portrayed as speaking in the midst of myriads of people thronging to hear Him, and opponents burning with hostility lying in wait to ambush Him.
38. A large but unspecified number. On this word, see Act 21:20.
39. Or, "treading on". On this word, see "trample-underfoot" in Heb 10:29.
40. Luke seems to mean that 12:1-13:9 was spoken on one occasion, though this is not certain (a similar question arises in 15:1-17:10). He gives no change of scene, only of the hearers. Jesus speaks to the disciples in v 1-12, the crowds in v 13-21, the disciples in v 22-53, and the crowds in 12:54-13:9.
41. Some think Jesus spoke "first" to them, not the Pharisees or the crowds just mentioned. Others think He spoke what follows "first of all"; that it was the first thing He spoke to them after the confrontation with the Pharisees. Others think it means first in sequence, in a discourse that alternates back and forth from the disciples to the crowd.

A. Mt 13:32   B. Jn 3:19, judgment   C. 1 Jn 4:16   D. Jn 21:15, devotedly love   E. Mt 23:6   F. Mt 23:29, tomb   G. Lk 7:30   H. 1 Thes 2:2, mistreat   J. Mt 11:28   K. Mt 23:4   L. Mk 3:14, send out   M. 1 Cor 12:28   N. 2 Tim 3:12   O. Act 2:17, pour out   P. Heb 9:26   Q. Mt 24:34   R. 1 Cor 1:18   S. Mk 3:20

1D.[1] "Take heed to yourselves[2] because of the leaven[3] of the Pharisees, which is hypocrisy[4]

    1E. "But[5] nothing has been covered-up[6] which will not be revealed[A], and *is* secret[B] which will not be known[C]—   2

        1F. "Because[7] whatever you said in the darkness will be heard in the light   3
        2F. "And what you spoke to the ear in the inner-rooms[D] will be proclaimed[E] on the housetops[F]

  2D. "And I say *to* you My friends[G]— do not fear[8] *anything* from[9] the *ones* killing the body, and after these *things* not having anything more to do   4

    1E. "But I will show[H] you Whom you should fear— fear the *One* having *the* authority[J] to throw into Gehenna[K] after the killing. Yes, I say *to* you, fear this *One*   5
    2E. "Are not five sparrows sold *for* two assarion[10]? And one of them has not been forgotten[11] before God. °Yet even the hairs *of* your head have all been numbered. Do not be fearing,[12] you are more valuable[L] *than* many sparrows   6 / 7

  3D. "And I say *to* you, everyone who confesses[M] Me[13] in front of people, the Son *of* Man also will confess him in front of the angels *of* God. °But the *one* having denied[14] Me before people will be denied[15] before the angels *of* God   8 / 9
  4D.[16] "And everyone who shall speak *a* word against[17] the Son *of* Man— it will be forgiven[N] *to* him. But *to* the *one* having blasphemed[18] against the Holy Spirit— it will not be forgiven   10
  5D.[19] "And whenever they bring you in before the synagogues and the rulers[O] and the authorities[J], do not be anxious-*about*[20] how or what you should speak-in-defense[P], or what you should say   11

    1E. "For the Holy Spirit will teach you at the very hour *the things* which *you* ought-to[21] say"   12

2C. And someone from the crowd said *to* Him, "Teacher, tell my brother to divide[Q] the inheritance[R] with me"   13

  1D. But the *One* said *to* him, "Man[22], who appointed[S] Me judge or arbitrator[23] over you?"   14
  2D. And He said to them[24], "Watch out and guard[T] *yourselves* from all[25] greed[U], because one's life[26] is not in[27] *what* abounds[V] *to* him out of his possessions[28]"   15
  3D. And He spoke *a* parable to them, saying, "The land *of a* certain rich man was productive[29]   16

    1E. "And he was reasoning[W] within himself, saying, 'What should I do, because I do not have *a place* where I will gather[30] my fruits?'   17
    2E. "And he said, 'I will do this—   18

        1F. 'I will tear-down[X] my barns and build larger *ones*, and there I will gather all my grain and good *things*
        2F. 'And I will say *to* my soul, "Soul[31], you have many good *things* lying-in-store[Y] for many years— Be resting[Z]. Eat, drink. Be enjoying-yourself[32]" '   19

    3E. "But God said *to* him, 'Foolish *one*! *On* this night they are demanding[33] your life[34] from you. And *the things* which you prepared[35]— *for* whom will they be?'   20
    4E. "So *is* the *one* storing-up[36] *for* himself, and not being rich[AA] toward[37] God"   21

  3C. And He said to His[38] disciples, "For this reason[39], I say *to* you—   22

1. Compare Mt 10:26-32.
2. Or, "Be on your guard". This phrase "take heed to yourselves" is used only by Luke, in Lk 17:3; 21:34; Act 5:35; 20:28. Same word as "beware of" in Mt 10:17. On the word "take heed to", see "pay attention to" in 1 Tim 3:8. GK *4668*. Not the same word as in v 15.
3. On this word, see Mt 13:33. Note Mt 16:12, where the leaven is their teaching.
4. Certainly 11:53-54 ranks as a classic example of hypocrisy, prompting this warning. On this word, see Gal 2:13.
5. These hypocrites will be exposed. Some manuscripts say "For" {N}.
6. Or, "concealed". This is a participle, "nothing is having been covered up". Used only here. GK *5158*. Related to "covered" in Mt 10:26.
7. Or, "In return for everything that you said... it will be heard". On this idiom, see 2 Thes 2:10.
8. The grammar implies "start to fear, become fearful".
9. Or, "do not be afraid of the *ones*...". Jesus has in mind the coming persecutions mentioned in v 11. This idiom "to fear from" is also in Mt 10:28. "Fear" is the same word as in v 5, on which see "respecting" in Eph 5:33.
10. On this coin, see Mt 10:29. It is one sixteenth of a denarius.
11. This is a participle, one of them "is not having been forgotten".
12. The grammar implies "Stop fearing" or "do not be in the habit of fearing".
13. More literally, "confesses in Me", on which see Mt 10:32. Likewise later in the verse, "confess in him".
14. That is, permanently. Peter denied (same word, 22:57) Jesus, but repented and confessed Him. On this word, see 2 Tim 2:12.
15. On this word, see Mt 16:24. Related to the previous word.
16. Compare Mt 12:31-32; Mk 3:28-30.
17. Same word as later in the verse, and in Mk 3:29. GK *1650*. Mt 12:32 uses a different word (GK *2848*).
18. This is another way of saying "speak against". On this word, see 1 Tim 6:1.
19. Compare Mt 10:19-20; Mk 13:11; Lk 21:14-15.
20. Same word as in Mt 10:19, in a similar statement. On this word, see Mt 6:25.
21. Or, "should". Or, "which it is necessary" to say. On this idiom, see Act 25:10.
22. This is used as a form of address also in 5:20; 22:58, 60. On this word, see "mankind" in Mt 4:4.
23. Or, "divider". Used only here. GK *3537*. Related to "divide" in v 13. Some manuscripts reverse these two words {B}.
24. That is, to the crowd, in response to the question of the man in v 13.
25. That is, every kind of. Some manuscripts omit this word {K}.
26. More literally, "because not in the abounding *to* someone out of the *things* belonging *to* him is his life".
27. Or, "in connection with, located in". GK *1877*.
28. Or, "belongings". This is a participle, on which see Heb 10:34.
29. Or, "bore well, yielded well". Used only here. GK *2369*.
30. This rich man has so much, such abundance, he has nowhere to put it.
31. Only here in the NT is the "soul" addressed in this way. On this word, see Jam 5:20.
32. On this word, see "celebrate" in Rev 12:12. Note the different tense of the first and fourth term.
33. That is, they are going to demand it, they will demand it. The verb is not passive, but some prefer to render impersonal verbs like this as a passive, "it will be required". "They" are apparently the angels God sends for this purpose. Note 16:22. Elsewhere only as "demand back" in 6:30. GK *555*. Some manuscripts say "ask" {N}.
34. Or, "soul". Same word as in v 22, 23, and as "soul" in v 19. In this context, it means life in an earthly sense.
35. Your earthly abundance will not be for you, proving that this is not what life is, v 15. Note Ps 17:13-15.
36. Or, "treasuring up". Same word as "treasure up" in Mt 6:19, 20. On this word, see 1 Cor 16:2.
37. Or, "in relation to, regarding, with reference to", as in 16:8. GK *1650*.
38. Some manuscripts omit this word {C}, so that it says "to the disciples". Jesus returns to speaking to them as He was in v 1-12. He first applies to them what He just said to the crowd in v 15-21.
39. That is, because of the true nature of life and possessions, as just discussed.

A. 2 Thes 2:3   B. 1 Cor 4:5, hidden   C. Lk 1:34   D. Mt 6:6   E. 2 Tim 4:2   F. Lk 5:19   G. Lk 14:10   H. Mt 3:7   J. Rev 6:8   K. Mt 5:22   L. Phil 1:10, mattering   M. 1 Tim 6:12   N. Mt 6:12   O. Col 1:18, beginning   P. Lk 21:14   Q. 1 Cor 7:17, apportioned   R. Eph 1:14   S. Act 6:3, put in charge   T. Jn 12:25, keep   U. Eph 4:19   V. 2 Cor 8:2   W. Lk 5:21   X. 2 Cor 10:4   Y. Mt 3:10, lying   Z. Phm 7, refreshed   AA. 1 Tim 6:18

1D.[1] "Do not be anxious[2] *for your* life[A] *as to* what you may eat, nor *for your* body *as to* what you may put-on[B]

    1E. "For life is more *than* food, and the body *is more than* clothing — 23

    2E. "Consider[C] the ravens— that they do not sow nor reap, *for* which there is not *a* storeroom nor *a* barn. And God feeds them. How much more are **you** worth[D] *than* the birds! — 24

    3E. "And which of you while being anxious is able to add[E] *a* cubit[3] upon his life-span[4]? ˚If then you are not even able *to do a* very little *thing*, why are you anxious about the rest[F]? — 25-26

    4E. "Consider[C] the lilies, how they grow— — 27

        1F. "They do not labor nor spin. But I say *to* you— not even Solomon in all his glory clothed *himself* like one *of* these

        2F. "But if God dresses[5] in this manner the grass in *a* field existing[G] today and being thrown into *an* oven tomorrow, how much more *will He care for* you— *ones*-of-little-faith[H]? — 28

2D. "And don't **you** be seeking[6] what you may eat and[7] what you may drink. And do not be unsettled[8] — 29

    1E. "For the nations[9] *of* the world are seeking-after[J] all[10] these *things* — 30

    2E. "And your Father knows that you have need *of* these *things*

    3E. "But[11] be seeking[K] His kingdom[12], and these *things* will be added[E] *to* you — 31

3D.[13] "Do[14] not be fearing, little flock[L], because your Father was well-pleased[15] to give you the kingdom[M]. ˚Sell[16] your possessions[17], and give *it as* alms[18] — 32 / 33

    1E. "Make yourselves money-bags not becoming-old[N]— *an* unfailing[19] treasure[O] in the heavens, where *a* thief does not draw-near[P], nor does *a* moth destroy[Q]

    2E. "For where your treasure is, there also your heart[R] will be — 34

4D. "Let your waists[S] be girded[20] and *your* lamps burning, ˚and you *be* like people waiting-for[T] their master[U] when he departs[21] from the wedding-celebrations[V]— in order that *he* having come and having knocked, they may immediately open [the door] *for* him — 35-36

    1E. "Blessed[22] *are* those slaves[W] whom the master, having come, will find keeping-watch[23] — 37

    2E. "Truly[X] I say *to* you that he will gird[Y] *himself*, and have them lie back [to eat]. And having come-to[24] the table, he will serve[25] them

    3E. "Even if in the second[26], even if he comes in the third watch[27] and finds *them* so, blessed are those[28] *ones* — 38

5D.[29] "And you know[30] this *saying*— that if the house-master[Z] had known *at* which hour the thief was coming, he would not[31] have permitted[AA] his house to be broken-into[BB] — 39

    1E. "**You** also be[32] prepared[CC] *ones*, because the Son *of* Man is coming *at an* hour which you do not expect[DD]" — 40

6D. And Peter said[33], "Lord, are You speaking this parable to us, or also to everyone?"[34] — 41

7D.[35] And the Lord said, "Who then[36] is the faithful[EE], wise[37] steward[38] whom *his* master will put-in-charge[FF] over his body-of-servants[39], *that he might* be giving *them their* food-allowance[40] at *the* proper-time[GG]? — 42

1. Compare Mt 6:25-34.
2. Same word as in Mt 6:25.
3. That is, about 18 inches, or one half meter. On this word, see Rev 21:17. Some manuscripts say "one cubit" {N}, as in Mt 6:27.
4. On this word, and the meaning of this statement, see Mt 6:27.
5. Used only here. GK *313*. Related to the word in Mt 6:30.
6. Same word as in v 31. Compare Mt 6:31. Or, "And you, do not be seeking". Jesus expresses "you" separately from the command, for emphasis and in contrast to the nations. On this word, see Phil 2:21.
7. Some manuscripts say "or" {N}.
8. Or, "up in the air, suspended, worrying, doubting, anxious". Our word "meteor" comes from this word, which means "in mid air, high in the air". Some think Jesus means do not be "anxious, in an unsettled mental state, worrying, up in the air, in suspense" about things. Others think He means do not be "lifted up, buoyed up, presumptuous, exalted" by your possessions, as this word is used in the OT. Used only here. GK *3577*.
9. Same word as "Gentiles" in Mt 6:32. On this word, see "Gentiles" in Act 15:23.
10. The word order, which is different than Mt 6:32, also permits this to be rendered "For all the nations *of* the world are seeking after these *things*".
11. This word (GK *4440*) is not the same as in Mt 6:33 (GK *1254*).
12. Some manuscripts say "the kingdom *of* God" {B}.
13. Compare Mt 6:19-21.
14. Placed here, v 32 is assuring the disciples in view of the following command. Do not be anxious, v 22. Rather, be fearless about investing your possessions in the kingdom He gave you. Others take v 32 with what precedes, making it point 4E., and making v 33 point 3D. In this case, Jesus is assuring them in their seeking of His kingdom.
15. On this word, see Mt 17:5. Some give this a timeless sense here, "is well pleased".
16. Note the progression. Do not be anxious about your possessions, do not be seeking them, sell them. Jesus does not mean we should impoverish ourselves so that we become ones needing alms, but that we should transfer our earthly treasures to our unfailing heavenly account. The tense here does not mean "be selling them" as a habit of life (compare 14:33), but to "sell them" in an act of faith, like the man in 19:8, and those in Act 4:34. Same tense as Lk 18:22. GK *4797*.
17. Or, "belongings, property, the *things* being present, the *things* being at hand". This is a participle, on which see Heb 10:34. Compare 8:43, where that woman spent all her "living" on an illness.
18. That is, as charitable giving to the poor. Give it to ones who can give you no return (14:13-14), and your Father will reward you. On this word, see "almsgiving" in Mt 6:2.
19. Or, "inexhaustible". That is, unable to run out. Used only here. GK *444*. Related to "fails" in 16:9.
20. Or, "tied around". This is a participle, "be having been girded". The grammar means "having been and continuing to be girded", "in a state of being girded". That is, remain prepared for action, be ready for work. On this word and metaphor, see Eph 6:14. Same word as in v 37.
21. Elsewhere only in Phil 1:23. GK *386*. Literally, "to unloose, undo",

as a boat from its moorings. The servants are anticipating their master's "departing" from the celebrations, his "coming", and his "knocking" at home. Some render this "return", which combines all three ideas. The point here is "watching" in preparedness, v 37. Related to "departure" in 2 Tim 4:6.
22. Or, "Happy, Fortunate". Same word as in v 38, 43. On this word, see 6:20.
23. Or, "staying alert". On this word, see 1 Thes 5:6.
24. This verb is used in this sense elsewhere only in 17:7. GK *4216*.
25. An unusual thing for a master to do! The servants are to wait expectantly, prepared to serve the master as soon as he knocks. But when he returns, behold— he serves them! On this word, see "ministering" in 1 Pet 4:10.
26. The wedding celebrations in v 36 are envisioned as continuing through the first watch, 6 to 9 P.M.
27. The second watch was from 9 P.M. to midnight, the third from midnight to 3 A.M. See Mk 13:35.
28. Some manuscripts add "slaves" {N}, as in v 37.
29. Compare Mt 24:43-44.
30. Or, "know this", a command. Jesus is stating this as a saying or proverb, as in Mt 24:43. On this word, see 1:34.
31. Some manuscripts say "he would have kept watch and would not..." {B}, as in Mt 24:43.
32. Or, "prove to be, become". GK *1181*. Same sentence as Mt 24:44.
33. Some manuscripts add "*to* Him" {N}.
34. Some think Peter means, "Are all Your disciples to 'watch' and be 'prepared' for a sudden coming, when they will be 'served' by You, or is this message just for the twelve?" Compare Mk 13:37. Others think Peter is referring to v 37 in particular, "Is this future honor and reward You mentioned for all, or only for the twelve?" The content sounds like it is for the disciples, yet it is spoken in a parable as if to the crowds.
35. Compare Mt 24:45-51.
36. In view of the sudden return of Jesus (v 37, 40), who is the wise one who will be entrusted a task when his master goes away? Jesus does not answer this directly, leaving each person to fill in his or her own name. Thus He answers Peter's question indirectly by giving a parable that applies to all. All are to watch for Him, serving faithfully.
37. Or, "sensible". On this word, see Mt 7:24. Some manuscripts say "faithful and wise" {K}.
38. On this word, see 1 Pet 4:10. Based on the description that follows, some think Jesus is referring to the leaders in the church being faithful to their calling. Others think this parable pictures whatever is entrusted to each individual believer. Thus He is referring to all believers being faithful to whatever He has given them.
39. Used only here in this sense, which is similar to "body-of-household-servants" in Mt 24:45. Related to "servant" in Heb 3:5. On this word, see "service" in Rev 22:2. Related to "cure" in Mt 8:7. It was used of "service, care, attendance upon" parents, children, masters, the sick, the gods, animals, plants, buildings, graves, etc. In this verse, it means the "group of servants" who do these various things.
40. Or, "food ration", the measure of grain. Used only here. GK *4991*. This is the task of the one in the parable.

A. Jam 5:20, soul   B. Rom 13:14   C. Heb 10:24   D. Phil 1:10, mattering   E. Lk 17:5, increase   F. 2 Pet 3:16, other   G. Rev 22:14   H. Mt 6:30
J. Phil 4:17, seek for   K. Phil 2:21   L. 1 Pet 5:2   M. Mt 3:2   N. Heb 8:13, make old   O. Mt 12:35   P. Lk 21:28   Q. 2 Cor 4:16   R. Rev 2:23
S. Heb 7:5, loins   T. Act 24:15   U. Mt 8:2   V. Mt 22:11, wedding   W. Rom 6:17   X. Mt 5:18   Y. Eph 6:14   Z. Mt 20:1   AA. Mt 6:12, forgive
BB. Mt 24:43   CC. Mk 14:15   DD. Lk 19:11, thinking   EE. Col 1:2   FF. Act 6:3   GG. Mt 8:29, time

1E. "Blessed[A] *is* that slave[B] whom his master, having come, will find so[1] doing — 43

    1F. "Truly[2] I say *to* you that he will put him in charge over all his possessions[3] — 44

2E. "But[4] if that slave says in his heart, 'My master is delaying to come', and he begins to strike[C] the male-servants[D] and the female-servants[E], and to eat and drink and get-drunk[5]— 45

    1F. "The master *of* that slave will come on *a* day which he does not expect[F], and at *an* hour which he does not know[G] 46
    2F. "And he will cut him in two[H], and assign *him* his part[6] with the unbelievers[7]

3E. "But that slave[8] having known[G] the will[J] *of* his master, and not having prepared[K] or acted[L] in accordance with his will, will be beaten[M] many *blows*. ˚But the *one* not having known[G], and having done[L] *things* worthy[N] *of* blows[9], will be beaten[M] *a* few *blows* 47 48

4E. "And *to* everyone whom much was given, much will be sought[O] from him.[10] And *to* whom they entrusted[11] much, they will ask him even more

8D. "I[12] came to cast[P] **fire**[13] upon the earth— and how I wish[14] that[15] it were already kindled[16]! But I have *a* **baptism**[Q] to be baptized[17]— and how I am held[18] *by it* until[19] it is accomplished[20]! 49 50

9D.[21] "Do you think[R] that I came[22] to grant[S] peace[23] on[24] earth? No, I say *to* you, but rather division! 51

    1E. "For from now *on*,[25] there will be five in one house having been divided[26]— three against two, and two against three 52
    2E. "They will be divided[27]— father against son and son against father, mother against daughter and daughter against mother, mother-in-law against her daughter-in-law and daughter-in-law against mother-in-law" 53

4C. And He was also saying *to* the crowds— 54

1D.[28] "Whenever you see the[29] cloud rising in *the* west[30], immediately you say that '*A* rainstorm is coming', and so it happens. ˚And whenever *a* south *wind is* blowing,[31] you say that 'There will be burning-heat[T]', and it happens 55

    1E. "Hypocrites[U]! You know-*how*[32] to test the appearance[V] *of* the earth and the heaven[W], but how *is it* you do not know-*how* to test[33] this time[34]? 56

2D.[35] "And why also are you not judging[X] the right[36] *thing* from yourselves[37]? 57

    1E. "For as you are going with your adversary[Y] to the magistrate[38], make *an* effort[39] on the way to be released[40] from him, so that he may not perhaps drag you before the judge, and the judge will hand you over *to* the bailiff[41], and the bailiff will throw you into prison 58

        1F. "I say *to* you, you will by no means come out from there until you pay[Z] even the last leptos[42]" 59

3D. And some were present at the very time, reporting[AA] *to* Him about the Galileans whose blood Pilate[BB] mixed with their sacrifices.[43] ˚And having responded, He said *to* them 13:1 2

1. That is, faithfully doing what the master gave him to do when he departed.
2. Or, "Truthfully". On this word, see Mt 14:33.
3. Same word as in v 33. Such ones will be rewarded with a greater stewardship when the master returns.
4. Now Jesus gives the opposite case, the unfaithful servant, like the one in 19:20 or Mt 25:24.
5. This slave turns away in his heart, and then it shows in his behavior. He lives in disobedience to his master's will, doing things he has forbidden. On this word, see Jn 2:10. Related to the word in Mt 24:49.
6. On "assign his part", see Mt 24:51. That is, he will share the lot of unbelievers.
7. Or, "unfaithful *ones,* faithless *ones*". Mt 24:51 calls them "hypocrites", and refers to hell. This person suffers a violent death, and an inheritance with the unbelievers.
8. Some think v 47-48 further explains the case of v 46. When that person receives his lot with the unbelievers (hell), his suffering will be in proportion to his knowledge. In this case, this should be point 1G. Others think Jesus is giving two additional cases, willful, and unintentional neglect of the master's will by believers. Their punishment will be proportional to their knowledge. In this case, Jesus is speaking of what Paul later describes in 1 Cor 3:12-15, etc.
9. Or, "lashes, strokes". Same word as in 10:30.
10. For every gift given, an appropriate response is expected.
11. Or, "deposited". For every deposit made, a greater return is expected— the deposit plus interest, as in 19:22-23. On this word, see "put before" in Act 17:3.
12. Having answered Peter's question, Jesus now continues.
13. Compare Mt 3:12.
14. Or, "want, desire". On this word, see "willing" in Jn 7:17.
15. Or, "if ", "and how I wish [to cast it] if it were...!". Or, "and what I wish [to do] if it were...!". In other words, Jesus wishes He could do it right then and there, but He cannot do so. GK *1623*.
16. Or, "set on fire, lit". Some think Jesus means the fire of judgment, which will burn up the chaff, the unbelievers; the judgment following the winnowing of His people, 3:9, 17; 13:7. Others think He is referring to the spiritual fire that sets His people ablaze for Him; the fire of the Holy Spirit; the fire which results in the divisions mentioned in v 51 because of the offense of the Cross. He will set the world on fire with His gospel. Elsewhere only in Jam 3:5. GK *409.*
17. That is, a baptism of blood. Jesus is referring to His violent death on the cross, as also in Mk 10:38.
18. Or, "occupied, gripped, distressed". Some think Jesus means this in a positive sense, "how I am under the control of this mission, how My life is gripped by it, how occupied I am with it", as Paul "was occupied with the word" in Act 18:5. Others think He means it in a negative sense, "how distressed I am by it". On this word, see "control" in 2 Cor 5:14.
19. More literally, "up to which *time*". On this idiom, see Mt 5:25.
20. Or, "finished, fulfilled, completed". On this word, see "finish" in Rev 10:7. Same word as "finished" in Jn 19:30.
21. Compare Mt 10:34-36.
22. Or, "appeared, arrived". Same word as Mt 3:1, 13. GK *4134*.
23. That is, harmony between people. This is what the Jews thought Messiah would do.
24. Or, "in, in the sphere of ". GK *1877.*
25. That is, in view of My coming and fulfilling My mission on earth. Jesus brings peace within His family, but division within human families! On this phrase, see Jn 8:11.
26. Or, "For from now *on*, five in one house will have been divided" ("will be having been divided").
27. Some manuscripts have this verb singular {K}, so that it says "Father will be divided against son...".
28. Compare Mt 16:2-3.
29. Some manuscripts omit this word, so that it says "*a* cloud" {C}.
30. That is, coming in off the Mediterranean Sea. Elsewhere only in Mt 8:11; 24:27; Lk 13:29; Rev 21:13. GK *1553.* Related to "setting" in 4:40, and "west" in Mark's short ending.
31. That is, coming in off the desert to the south.
32. This word (GK *3857*) is not related to the word in Mt 16:3 (GK *1182*).
33. Some manuscripts say "how *is it* you do not test" {B}. On this word used twice in this verse, see "approve" in Rom 12:2.
34. That is, this time we live in. Compare Mt 16:3.
35. Compare Mt 5:25-26.
36. Or, "just, righteous". On this word, see "righteous" in Rom 1:17.
37. That is, from your own knowledge, apart from other people (the Pharisees and scribes). For example, you do not need a judge to settle your disputes. Why not settle them yourselves? If you go before the judge, you will pay the full penalty of the law. In this parable, Jesus is exhorting the crowd to make their own decision about Him, for if they postpone the issue until they stand before God, they will pay His full penalty. Same phrase as 21:30.
38. Or, "ruler, official", referring to a member of the local court or Sanhedrin. On this word, see "ruler" in Rev 1:5.
39. This phrase "make an effort" is an idiom of Latin origin. Literally, "give *a* working, give *a* pursuit".
40. Or, "freed", "to have been released". That is, to come to terms with your adversary, and so be permanently released from his complaint against you. On this word, see Act 19:12.
41. Used only in this verse. GK *4551.*
42. On this word, see Mk 12:42. It is the smallest Jewish coin, 1/128 of a denarius.
43. Perhaps when Jesus spoke of settling disputes on the way, some gave this case of some Galileans who did not do so and paid with their lives while making their sacrifices. The nature of their dispute with Pilate is not known.

A. Lk 6:20   B. Rom 6:17   C. Lk 6:26   D. Act 3:13, servant   E. Jn 18:17, servant girl   F. Lk 3:15, waiting in expectation   G. Lk 1:34   H. Mt 24:51, cut in two   J. Jn 7:17   K. Mk 14:15   L. Rev 13:13, does   M. Jn 18:23   N. Rev 16:6   O. Phil 2:21   P. Rev 2:22, throw   Q. Mk 1:4   R. Lk 19:11   S. Eph 1:22, give   T. Jam 1:11   U. Mt 6:2   V. Lk 9:52, presence   W. 2 Cor 12:2   X. Mt 7:1   Y. 1 Pet 5:8   Z. Mt 16:27, render   AA. 1 Jn 1:3, announcing   BB. Lk 3:1

        1E. "Do you think[A] that these Galileans were[1] sinners[B] more than all the Galileans, because they have suffered[C] these *things*? °No, I say *to* you. But unless you repent[D], you will all likewise perish[E]   3

        2E. "Or those eighteen on whom the tower in Siloam fell and killed them— do you think that **they** were debtors[2] more than all the people dwelling in Jerusalem? °No, I say *to* you. But unless you repent, you will all similarly perish"   4
                                                                                                                                                 5

    4D. And He was telling this parable— "*A* certain *one* had *a* fig tree having been planted in his vineyard.[3] And he came seeking[F] fruit on it, and did not find *it*   6

        1E. "And he said to the vine-keeper[4], 'Behold— *it is* three years[5] since[6] I am coming, seeking[7] fruit on this fig tree, and I am not finding *it*. Therefore[8], cut it down[9]! Why[G] is it even using-up[10] the soil[H]?'   7

        2E. "But the *one*, having responded, says *to* him, 'Master, leave it also this year, until[11] I dig around it and throw manure. °And **if it produces fruit**[12] in the future[13]— otherwise indeed,[14] cut it down' "   8
                                                                                                                                                 9

10B. Now He was teaching in one *of* the synagogues on the Sabbath   10

  1C. And behold— *there was a* woman[15] having *a* spirit *of* infirmity[16] eighteen years. And she was bending-over, and not being able to bend-up[17] completely[18]   11

    1D. And having seen her, Jesus called *to* her and said *to* her, "Woman, you have been released[J] *from* your infirmity". °And He laid[K] His hands on her   12
                                                                                                                                      13
    2D. And at-once[L] she was made-straight[M]. And she was glorifying[N] God

  2C. But having responded, the synagogue official— being indignant[O] because Jesus cured[P] *on* the Sabbath— was saying *to* the crowd that "There are six days on which *one* ought-to[Q] work. So be cured while coming on **them**, and not *on* the day *of* the Sabbath"   14

    1D. But the Lord responded *to* him and said, "Hypocrites[19]! Does not each *of* you *on* the Sabbath release[20] his ox or donkey from the manger[21], and having led *it* away, water *it*? °But this *one*, being *a* daughter[22] *of* Abraham whom Satan bound[R] *for* behold, ten and eight[23] years— ought *she* not to have[24] been released from this bond[S] *on* the day *of* the Sabbath?"[25]   15
                                                                                                                               16

  3C. And while He *was* saying these *things*, all the *ones* being opposed[T] *to* Him were being put-to-shame[26]   17
  4C. And the whole crowd was rejoicing[U] over all the glorious[27] *things* being done by Him

    1D.[28] Therefore,[29] He was saying, "*To* what is the kingdom *of* God like, and *to* what shall I liken[30] it?   18

        1E. "It is like *a* seed *of a* mustard-plant[V] which, having taken, *a* man threw into his *own* garden. And it grew and became[31] *a* tree[32]. And the birds *of* the heaven nested[W] in its branches"   19

    2D.[33] And again He said, "*To* what shall I liken the kingdom *of* God?   20

        1E. "It is like leaven[X], which having taken, *a* woman concealed[34] into three measures[Y] *of* wheat-flour until which *time* the whole *thing* was leavened[Z]"   21

1. Or, "proved to be". GK *1181*. Same word as in v 4.
2. That is, sinners, as in v 2. Jesus describes sin as a debt to God, as in Mt 6:12, "forgive us our debts".
3. Some think the fig tree represents Israel and the vineyard represents the world. Others think the vineyard is Israel and the fig tree is Jerusalem. In any case, Jesus came seeking fruit on this tree, but found none.
4. Or, "vineworker". Used only here. Related to "vineyard" in v 6. GK *307*.
5. Some think this implies that Christ's ministry to Israel had been going on for three years by now, and that v 8-9 implies it will now extend to a fourth year. Others think it refers to the combined ministries of John the Baptist and Jesus. Others think the numbers are merely a part of the parable. The length of His ministry is nowhere given, but can only be inferred from a sequential harmonization of the four Gospel accounts.
6. Literally, "from which *time*". On this idiom, see Rev 16:18.
7. Note that the owner has been seeking fruit for three years, implying nothing as to how long the tree has been there.
8. Some manuscripts omit this word {C}.
9. This word, "cut down", is the same word as in 3:9. It also means "cut off", as in Mt 5:30; Rom 11:22. Used 10 times. GK *1716*.
10. Or, "making useless, wasting". On this word, see "done away with" in Rom 6:6.
11. More literally, "up to which *time*". On this idiom, see Mt 5:25.
12. Jesus uses grammar that emphasizes the contrast between the two halves of this sentence.
13. The vine-keeper does not state the response, which could be "fine" or "good", or "then we have saved it".
14. On this idiom, "otherwise indeed", see 2 Cor 11:16. Some manuscripts say "produces fruit— otherwise indeed, cut it down in the future" {B}.
15. Some manuscripts say "there was *a* woman..." {K}.
16. That is, a spirit causing her infirmity. On this word, see "weakness" in Mt 8:17.
17. Or, "raise up, stand erect". On this word, see "straighten up" in 21:28. Same root word as "bending-over". The woman was bending over, but not able to bend back up.
18. This is an idiom, literally "to the full", on which see "completely" in Heb 7:25. This is the Greek word order. Some take this with "able", so that it has the idea of her "being completely unable to bend up".
19. Some manuscripts have this word singular {N}.
20. Or, "untie, loose". Same word as in v 16. On this word, see "break" in Mt 5:19. Related to "released" in v 12.
21. On this word, see 2:7. After you feed it, you lead it to water.
22. That is, a descendant. This word is used of the female physical offspring of parents; of female "descendants, children" in a broader sense, as here and 1:5; and figuratively, as in 23:38; Mt 21:5; Jn 12:15. Used 28 times. GK *2588*. Compare "son" in Gal 3:7.
23. Note that Luke used the word "eighteen" in v 11. Jesus emphasizes the duration by stating it this way.
24. Or, "was it not necessary *for her* to have". On the idiom "ought to have", see "should have" in Mt 25:27.
25. The grammar indicates a "yes" answer is expected. Yes, the woman ought to have been released.
26. Or, "humiliated". On this word, see Rom 5:5.
27. Or, "splendid". On this word, see 7:25.
28. Compare Mt 13:31-32; Mk 4:30-32.
29. Jesus puts "all the glorious things" in proper perspective for the crowd. His kingdom starts small, but grows large. It will transform from within.
30. Or, "compare". Related to "like" earlier and next (GK *3927*). On this word, see "become like" in Mt 13:24.
31. More literally, it "came to be for" a tree, reflecting a Hebrew way of speaking.
32. Some manuscripts say "*a* large tree" {B}.
33. Compare Mt 13:33.
34. On this word, see Mt 13:33. Some manuscripts have a related word meaning "hid" {C}.

A. Lk 19:11 B. Mt 9:10 C. Gal 3:4 D. Act 26:20 E. 1 Cor 1:18 F. Phil 2:21 G. Mt 27:46 H. Rev 7:1, land J. Mt 5:31, sends away K. Lk 10:30, laid on L. Mt 21:19 M. Heb 12:12, straighten up N. Rom 8:30 O. Mt 20:24 P. Mt 8:7 Q. Act 25:10 R. 1 Cor 7:27 S. Phil 1:7, imprisonment T. Phil 1:28 U. 2 Cor 13:11 V. Mt 13:31 W. Act 2:26, dwell X. Mt 13:33 Y. Mt 13:33 Z. Mt 13:33

11B. And He was journeying-through[1] according to cities and villages[2], teaching and making *the* journey to Jerusalem. °And someone said *to* Him, "Master[A], *are* the *ones* being saved[B] few?"   22, 23

   1C.[3] And the *One* said to them,°"Be striving[4] to enter through the narrow[5] door[6], because many, I say *to* you, will seek to enter, and will not be able[7]   24

      1D. "From whatever *time*   25

         1E. "The house-master[C] arises and shuts the door
         2E. "And you[8] begin to stand outside and to be knocking on the door saying, 'Master, open *for* us'
         3E. "And having responded, he will say *to* you, 'I do not know[D] you— where you are from'

      2D. "Then[9] you will begin to say, 'We ate and drank in your presence, and you taught on our wide-roads[E]'   26
      3D. "And he will speak, saying[10] *to* you, 'I do not know you[11]— where you are from. Depart from me, all *you*[12] workers *of* unrighteousness[F]'   27
      4D.[13] "In that place[14], there will be the weeping and the grinding *of* teeth when you shall see Abraham and Isaac and Jacob and all the prophets in the kingdom *of* God, but you being thrown outside   28

         1E. "And they will come from east and west, and from north and south, and lie back [to eat] in the kingdom *of* God   29
         2E.[15] "And behold— there are last *ones* who will be first, and there are first *ones* who will be last[16]"   30

12B. At the very hour[17], some Pharisees came to *Him*, saying *to* Him, "Go out, and proceed[18] from here, because Herod[19] wants to kill You". °And He said *to* them—   31, 32

   1C. "Having gone, tell this fox[20], 'Behold— I am casting-out[G] demons[H] and performing[21] healings[22] today and tomorrow, and *on* the third[23] *day* I come-to-the-end[24]'
   2C. "Nevertheless, I must[J] proceed[25] today and tomorrow and the next[26] *day*, because it cannot-be[27] *that a* prophet[K] *should* perish[L] outside *of* Jerusalem   33
   3C.[28] "Jerusalem, Jerusalem, the *one* killing the prophets and stoning the *ones* having been sent to her   34

      1D. "How often I wanted to gather-together your children the way[M] *a* hen *does her own* brood[29] under *her* wings, and you did not want[30] it
      2D. "Behold— your house is being left *to* you[31]   35
      3D. "And[32] I say *to* you, you will by no means see Me[33] until *the time* will come[34] when you say, 'Blessed[35] *is* the *One* coming in *the* name *of the* Lord' "

13B. And it came about at His going into *the* house *of* one *of* the leaders[N] *of* the Pharisees *on a* Sabbath to eat bread, that[O] **they** were closely-watching[P] Him   14:1

   1C. And behold— *a* certain man in front of Him was suffering-from-dropsy[36]   2

      1D. And having responded, Jesus spoke to the Law-experts[Q] and Pharisees, saying, "Is it lawful[R] to cure *on* the Sabbath, or not[37]?" °But the *ones* were quiet[S]   3, 4
      2D. And having taken-hold-of[T] *him*, He healed[U] him, and sent *him* away
      3D. And He said to them,[38] "Whose son[39] or ox *of* yours will fall into *a* well[V], and he[40] will not immediately pull him up[W] on *the* day *of* the Sabbath?"   5

1. Or, "proceeding through". Related to "journey" later in the verse, and rendered this way to reflect this. Elsewhere only as "proceed through" in Lk 6:1; 18:36; Act 16:4; Rom 15:24. GK *1388*.
2. From one city and village to the next. Similar to the phrase in 8:1.
3. Compare Mt 7:13-14.
4. Or, "fighting, struggling, straining, exerting effort". On this word, see "struggle" in 1 Tim 4:10.
5. Elsewhere only in Mt 7:13, 14. GK *5101*.
6. Some manuscripts say "gate" {N}, as in Mt 7:13.
7. That is, many will seek to enter after the time of salvation is past, when the door is shut. To the question "Are there few?" and the question "When will the door be shut?", Jesus would say, "Be striving now!".
8. This word is plural, as throughout this parable.
9. In other words, once you find yourself excluded by the master, you will not be "able" to get in, even though you "will seek to enter", v 24. First, the master closes the door. Second, you arrive and knock. Third, he denies you. "Then", v 26, you will begin to "seek to enter" by giving your reasons. But you will remain outside. Some begin the conclusion with the master's first denial (3E.) by adding "then", "[Then] also having responded, he will say...", making it 2D.
10. On the idiom "speak... saying", see Mk 8:28. Some manuscripts say "He will say, "I tell you I do not know you..." {C}.
11. Some manuscripts omit this word {C}, so that it says "know where you are from".
12. The master is addressing those outside as "workers of unrighteousness".
13. Compare Mt 8:11-12.
14. That is, the place "outside" the shut door, v 25. On weeping and grinding of teeth, see Mt 8:12.
15. Compare Mt 19:30; Mk 10:31.
16. Some considered last on this earth— like Gentiles, tax collectors and prostitutes— will be first. Some considered to be first on this earth— like the Jews Jesus is speaking to— will be last, excluded from God's presence. Put another way, some considered farthest from the kingdom will enter it; some considered closest will be the farthest from it.
17. On this phrase, see 2:38. Some manuscripts instead say "day" {N}.
18. That is, go out from this village, and proceed on from this region. Go to Judea, out of Herod's jurisdiction.
19. That is, Herod Antipas, who killed John. On Herod, see 3:1.
20. From this, some infer that these Pharisees came from Herod with this threat, perhaps sent by him to scare Jesus away. Others think they were truly concerned about Jesus and came to warn Him. Luke does not make their motives clear.
21. Or, "completing, bringing to completion, finishing". Related to "come to the end" next. Elsewhere only as "fully formed" in Jam 1:15. GK *699*.
22. Elsewhere only in Act 4:22, 30. GK *2617*. Related to "heal" in Mt 8:8.
23. Some think Jesus is referring to His divinely ordained time schedule. That is, His course will continue day by day to its predetermined end, and will not be altered by Herod. Others think He means His work will continue for a brief time, and then cease (that is, with His death); others, that He will be finished there on the third literal day.
24. Some think Jesus means "come to *My* goal, reach *My* goal"; others, "come to the finish, the completion" of My work; others, "come to the end" of My life, "I am perfected" (note v 33). On this word, see "perfect" in Heb 2:10.
25. Same word as in v 31. Jesus indeed must go on, not because of Herod, but because His destiny is in Jerusalem.
26. This is an idiom, literally, "*on the day* holding" to the previous one. Same idiom in Act 20:15; 21:26; and Mk 1:38.
27. Or, "it is inadmissible, it is not allowable, it is not permitted, it is impossible". Used only here. GK *1896*. Related to "impossible" in 17:1.
28. Compare Mt 23:37-39.
29. Used only here. GK *3799*. Related to "chicks" in Mt 23:37.
30. Same word as "wanted" earlier in the verse. On this word, see "willing" in Jn 7:17.
31. Some manuscripts add "desolate" {B}, as in Mt 23:38.
32. Some manuscripts omit this word {C}.
33. That is, as Messiah.
34. Some manuscripts omit "*the time* will come when" {C}.
35. This is a participle, "Having been blessed". On this word, see 6:28.
36. Dropsy is an accumulation of fluid and swelling of the tissues. Used only here. GK *5622*. The root word is "water".
37. Some manuscripts omit "or not" {N}.
38. Some manuscripts say "And having responded, He said to them..." {N}.
39. Some manuscripts say "donkey" {B}.
40. That is, the father of the son, or the owner of the ox.

A. Mt 8:2   B. Lk 19:10   C. Mt 20:1   D. 1 Jn 2:29   E. Lk 14:21   F. Rom 1:18   G. Jn 12:31   H. 1 Cor 10:20   J. Mt 16:21   K. 1 Cor 12:28   L. 1 Cor 1:18   M. Act 27:25   N. Rev 1:5, ruler   O. Lk 5:1   P. Lk 6:7   Q. Lk 7:30   R. 1 Cor 6:12   S. 1 Thes 4:11   T. Lk 20:20   U. Mt 8:8   V. Rev 9:1, shaft   W. Act 11:10, pull up

4D. And they were not able to answer-back[1] to these *things*   6

2C. And He was speaking *a* parable[2] to the *ones* having been invited[A], fixing-*His*-attention-on[3] how they were choosing[B] the places-of-honor[C], saying to them—   7

   1D. "Whenever you are invited by someone to wedding-celebrations[D], do not lie down [to eat] in the place-of-honor— lest   8

      1E. "*A* more distinguished[4] *one than* you may have been invited[5] by him
      2E. "And having come, the *one* having invited you and him will say *to* you, 'Give *your* place *to* this *one*'   9
      3E. "And then you will begin to hold the last place with shame[E]

   2D. "But whenever you are invited, having gone, fall back [to eat] in the last place, so that when the *one* having invited you comes, he will say *to* you, 'Friend[6], move up higher'. Then there will be glory *for* you in the presence of all the *ones* reclining back with you [to eat]   10
   3D. "Because everyone exalting[F] himself will be humbled[G]. And the *one* humbling himself will be exalted"   11

3C. And He was also saying to the *one* having invited[A] Him—   12

   1D. "Whenever you make *a* morning-meal[7] or *a* dinner[8], do not be calling your friends, nor your brothers, nor your relatives, nor rich neighbors[9]— that **they** also might not perhaps invite you in return, and it become *a* repayment[10] *to* you
   2D. "But whenever you make *a* reception[11], be inviting poor[H] *ones*, crippled *ones*, lame[J] *ones*, blind *ones*, and you will be blessed[K] because they do not have *the* means to repay[12] you. For it will be repaid *to* you at the resurrection *of* the righteous"   13   14

4C.[13] And one *of* the *ones* reclining back with *Him* [to eat], having heard these *things,* said *to* Him, "Blessed[K] *is* whoever will eat bread in the kingdom *of* God!" °But[14] the One said *to* him—   15   16

   1D. "*A* certain man was making *a* great dinner, and he invited[A] many. °And he sent-out[L] his slave[M] *at* the hour *of* the dinner to say *to* the *ones* having been invited, 'Come, because it is[15] already prepared[N]'   17
   2D. "And they all alike[16] began to excuse-*themselves*[17]   18

      1E. "The first said *to* him, 'I bought *a* field. And I have *a* necessity[O], having gone out, to see it. I ask you, have me excused[18]'
      2E. "And another said, 'I bought five pair[19] *of* oxen, and I am proceeding to test[20] them. I ask you, have me excused'   19
      3E. "And another said, 'I married[P] *a* woman, and for this reason I am not able to come'   20

   3D. "And having come, the slave reported[Q] these *things to* his master[R]   21
   4D. "Then, having become-angry[21], the house-master[S] said *to* his slave, 'Go out quickly[T] into the wide-roads[22] and lanes[23] *of* the city, and bring in here the poor *ones* and crippled *ones* and blind *ones* and lame *ones*'
   5D. "And the slave said, 'Master, what you commanded[U] has been done[24], and there is still room[V]'   22
   6D. "And the master said to the slave, 'Go out to the roads[25] and fences[26], and compel[27] *them* to come in, in order that my house may be filled[W]. °For I say *to* you all[28] that none *of* those men having been invited will taste[X] my dinner' "   23   24

1. Elsewhere only in Rom 9:20. GK *503*. Some manuscripts add "*to Him*" {N}.
2. This is not a lesson on manners, but a parable. Jesus is referring to their attitude toward the kingdom of God. The Pharisees are assuming they have the place of privilege, but are truly heading toward an unexpected humiliation. These ones who think they are first, will end up last. They need to humble themselves before God.
3. Or, "focusing on". Or, more mildly, "noting". On this word, see 1 Tim 4:16.
4. Or, "esteemed, honored". On this word, see "precious" in Phil 2:29.
5. This is a participle, "may be having been invited".
6. Same word as in Mt 11:19; Lk 11:5; 12:4; Jn 11:11; 15:13. Used 29 times. GK *5813*. Related to "*affectionately*-love" in Jn 21:15.
7. This word refers to the main morning meal, usually eaten before noon. Same word as in 11:38. Elsewhere only as "luncheon" in Mt 22:4. GK *756*. Related to the verb in 11:37.
8. Or, "banquet, supper", the evening meal which was eaten late in the day, often after dark. Same word as in Lk 14:16, 17, 24; Jn 12:2; 13:2, 4; 21:20; 1 Cor 11:21. Elsewhere only as "supper" in 1 Cor 11:20; and "banquet" in Mt 23:6; Mk 6:21; 12:39; Lk 20:46; Rev 19:9, 17. GK *1270*. Related to "dining" in 1 Cor 11:25.
9. Do not look at these things as the world looks at them.
10. In such a case, "you have your reward in full". No reward from God is due. Do not confuse being "friendly" or "neighborly" in this way (which is appropriate in its place) with serving God. God serves those who cannot repay.
11. Or, "banquet, a meal for guests", like the one Jesus was attending here. On this word, see 5:29.
12. On this word, see 2 Thes 1:6. Related to "repayment" in v 12.
13. Compare Mt 22:1-14.
14. The man's statement is true, but the ones eating in the kingdom will not be the ones he thinks.
15. Instead of "it is", some manuscripts say "all *things* are" {C}.
16. This is an idiom, used only here. Literally, "from one" voice, tongue, consent, and so, "alike, unanimously".
17. Or, "to beg off, decline, reject, refuse". On this word, see "refuse" in Heb 12:25.
18. Or, "have me *as* having been excused". Same word as earlier.
19. Or, "yoke, team". That is, pairs or teams yoked together. Elsewhere only in 2:24. GK *2414*.
20. Or, "examine, prove by testing, put to the test". On this word, see "approve" in Rom 12:2.
21. Or, "become wrathful". On this word, see Rev 11:18.
22. Or, "main streets, broad-ways". Elsewhere only in Mt 6:5; 12:19; Lk 10:10; 13:26; Act 5:15; Rev 11:8; 21:21; 22:2. GK *4423*. Related to "wide" in Mt 7:13.
23. Or, "narrow streets, alleys". On this word, see Mt 6:2. Both of these terms refer to city streets.
24. Or, "has taken place". GK *1181*.
25. Or, "paths". That is, the roads outside of the city, out in the country.
26. Or, "hedges, walls". This word refers to the fences or hedges put around fields and vineyards, as in Mt 21:33; Mk 12:1. Vagabonds and beggars could be found there. Elsewhere only as "partition" in Eph 2:14. GK *5850*.
27. On this word, see Gal 6:12. It is related to "necessity" in v 18. Persuade them it is a serious offer.
28. The word "you" is plural, and this is added to reflect this. Some think Jesus makes this sudden change in order to directly include His listeners in the application of parable. Others think He is including the originally invited guests, who now show up late.

A. Rom 8:30, called   B. 1 Cor 1:27   C. Mt 23:6   D. Mt 22:11, wedding   E. Heb 12:2   F. Jn 8:28, lifted up   G. Phil 4:12   H. Gal 4:9   J. Heb 12:13
K. Lk 6:20   L. Mk 3:14   M. Rom 6:17   N. Mk 14:15   O. 1 Cor 7:26   P. 1 Cor 7:9   Q. 1 Jn 1:3, announcing   R. Mt 8:2   S. Mt 20:1   T. Gal 1:6
U. Lk 8:25   V. Eph 4:27, place   W. Mk 4:37   X. Heb 6:4

14B.	And large crowds were proceeding-with Him. And having turned, He said to them—	25
1C.[1]	"If anyone comes to Me, and does not hate[2] his *own* father and mother and wife and children and brothers and sisters, and furthermore, even his *own* life[3], he cannot be My disciple[A]. Whoever is not carrying[B] his *own* cross[4] and coming after Me, cannot be My disciple	26 27
1D.	"For which of you wanting to build *a* tower, does not first, having sat-*down*, calculate[5] the cost *to see* whether he has *enough* for *the* completion?	28
1E.	"In order that he having laid *a* foundation[C] and not being able to finish *it* out[6]— all the *ones* observing[D] may not perhaps begin to mock[E] him, ˚saying that 'This man began to build and was not able to finish *it* out!'	29 30
2D.	"Or what king going to engage another king in battle[F] will not, having sat-*down* first, deliberate[7] whether he is able with ten thousand *men* to meet[8] the *one* coming against him with twenty thousand?	31
1E.	"Otherwise indeed[9], *the one coming* still being far away— *the king*[10], having sent-forth[G] *a* delegation, asks the *things* for peace[H]	32
3D.	"So therefore,[11] any of you who is not saying-goodbye[12] *to* all his possessions[13] cannot be My disciple	33
2C.[14]	"Therefore[15], salt *is* good. But if indeed[16] the salt should become-tasteless[17], with what will it be seasoned[J]? ˚It is fit[K] neither for soil[L] nor for *the* manure-pile[18]. They throw it outside	34 35
3C.	"Let the *one* having ears to hear, hear"	
15B.	Now all the tax-collectors[M] and the sinners[N] were drawing-near[O] *to* Him to hear Him.[19] ˚And both the Pharisees and the scribes were grumbling[20], saying that "This *One* is welcoming[P] sinners and eating with them"	15:1-2
1C.	And He spoke this parable to them,[21] saying—	3
1D.[22]	"What man from-*among* you having *a* hundred sheep and having lost one of them, does not leave-behind[Q] the ninety nine in the wilderness[R] and proceed after the *one* having become-lost[23] until he finds it? ˚And having found *it*, he puts *it* on his shoulders, rejoicing[S]. ˚And having come to the house, he calls-together *his* friends[24] and neighbors[T], saying *to* them, 'Rejoice-with me, because I found my lost[25] sheep!'	4 5 6
1E.	"I say *to* you that in this manner there will be joy in heaven over one sinner repenting[U] more-than[26] over ninety nine righteous *ones* who have no need[V] *of* repentance[W]	7
2D.	"Or what woman having ten[27] drachmas[28], if she loses one drachma, does not light[X] *a* lamp and sweep the house and seek[Y] carefully until which *time* she finds *it*? ˚And having found *it*, she calls together *her* women friends and neighbors, saying, 'Rejoice-with me, because I found the drachma which I lost!'	8 9
1E.	"In this manner, I say *to* you, joy comes-about[29] in the presence of the angels *of* God over one sinner repenting"	10
2C.	And[30] He said, "*A* certain man had two sons	11

1. Compare Mt 10:37-39.
2. This refers to the same issue as the "division" in 12:52-53. Compare Mt 10:37. On this word, see Rom 9:13.
3. Compare Jn 12:25. On this word, see "soul" in Jam 5:20.
4. You must turn from your human allegiances, bear the loss, and follow Me. On this, see Mt 10:38; 16:24.
5. That is, count the cost of success, of achieving your goal. On this word, see Rev 13:18.
6. This is the word "finish" in Rev 10:7, with a prefix meaning "out", "to finish out, complete". Elsewhere only in v 30. GK *1754*.
7. Or, "take counsel, decide". On this word, see "plan" in Jn 11:53.
8. That is, successfully meet in battle. Elsewhere only in Mt 8:28; 28:9; Mk 5:2; Lk 8:27; Jn 4:51; 11:20, 30; 12:18; Act 16:16. GK *5636*. Related to the word in Mt 25:1.
9. On this idiom, "otherwise indeed", see 2 Cor 11:16.
10. The grammar indicates that the king with 10,000 sends to the king coming with 20,000 to ask for peace.
11. So applying this to you then, here is the cost you must count and bear— a restatement of "hating his own life" in v 26.
12. Or, "taking leave of, bidding farewell". This has a figurative sense here, "renouncing". Your habit of life must be one of separating yourself from possessions to "taking hold of real life", 1 Tim 6:19. Compare the different tense of "sell" in 12:33. On this word, see 2 Cor 2:13.
13. Same word as in 12:33.
14. Compare Mt 5:13; Mk 9:50.
15. Jesus concludes with an illustration. Some manuscripts omit this word {N}.
16. Or, "But if even salt becomes-tasteless...".
17. Or, "become insipid, lose its savor". Same word as in Mt 5:13. That is, if it is not usable for its purpose, like a "disciple" who does not carry his cross and follow after Him as just discussed. GK *3701*.
18. Used only here. GK *3161*. Related to "manure" in 13:8.
19. Some think Luke means it was the habit of all this class of sinners to draw near wherever Jesus might be; others, that all this group (in the sense of "everyone" in 16:16) in this particular place where He has arrived came out on this occasion. What follows is spoken in this mixed group of outcast sinners and Pharisees, of hearers and disciples.
20. This is a more emphatic form of the word in 5:30. Elsewhere only in 19:7. GK *1339*.
21. Note that these words apply to both groups in v 1-2, in different ways. Jesus primarily rebukes the Pharisees, while at the same time also expressing God's joy at the repentance of the tax collectors and sinners He is seeking.
22. Compare Mt 18:12-14.
23. Or, "to the lost *one*". Note the two perspectives here using the same word. The man "lost" a sheep. The sheep "got lost" or "became lost". Same word as in v 6, 8, 9, 17 ("perish"), 24, 32. This word is a link between the three parables in this chapter. On this word, see "lost" in Mt 10:6.
24. Or, Jesus may mean "*men* friends and neighbors" in particular, since He follows this with a case of a woman and her friends.
25. This is a participle, my sheep "having become-lost", as in v 4. Matthew says "gone astray", 18:12, 13.
26. Or, "*rather*-than". See the example in v 32. Some think there is joy over the ninety-nine who never got lost, but more joy over the one who repented. It is also a different kind of joy, the brief joy of celebration over finding what was lost versus the abiding joy of always having. Both are seen in the father in v 31-32. Others think the ninety-nine represents the Pharisees who need no repentance in their own eyes (like in 5:31-32), and that there is no joy over them until they also repent. There are none having no need of repentance, only ones who repented and ones who did not.
27. Note the change from one lost of a hundred, to one of ten, to one of two in v 11.
28. A drachma was a Greek silver coin, equivalent to the Roman "denarius" (see Mt 20:2). One drachma would be one day's wages for a laborer. Used only here and v 9. GK *1534*. This woman would be living in a one room house with a dirt floor.
29. Or, "arises, takes place, occurs, happens". GK *1181*.
30. Note that in this parable, Jesus again speaks to both the sinners in 15:1 (the younger brother), and the Pharisees in 15:2 (the older brother). Both wanted to spend the father's resources on themselves. The older brother did not share the father's view of the younger brother, or of himself. Both needed to repent. The father loves both and goes out to them. The younger son repented and was joyfully accepted back by the father. Whether the older son repented is left unstated.

A. Lk 6:40 B. Mt 8:17 C. 1 Tim 6:19 D. Lk 10:18, seeing E. Lk 23:11 F. Rev 12:7, war G. Mk 3:14, send out H. Act 15:33 J. Mk 9:50 K. Lk 9:62 L. Rev 7:1, land M. Mt 18:17 N. Mt 9:10 O. Lk 21:28 P. Act 24:15, wait for Q. Act 6:2 R. Mt 3:1 S. 2 Cor 13:11 T. Jn 9:8 U. Act 26:20 V. Tit 3:14 W. 2 Cor 7:10 X. 1 Cor 7:1, touch Y. Phil 2:21

1D. "And the younger *of* them said *to his* father, 'Father, give me the part[A] *of your* substance[1] falling[2] to *me*'. And the *one* distributed[3] *his* property[4] *to* them   12

2D. "And after not many days, having gathered together everything, the younger son went-on-a-journey[B] to *a* distant country[C]. And there he squandered[5] his substance living[D] wildly[6]   13

3D. "And **he** having spent[E] everything, *a* severe famine[F] came about in relation to that country, and **he** began to be-in-need[7]   14

    1E. "And having gone, he joined[G] *himself to* one *of* the citizens[H] *of* that country. And he sent him into his fields to feed[J] pigs   15

    2E. "And he was desiring[K] to be filled-to-satisfaction[8] with the carob-pods which the pigs were eating. And no one was giving *anything to* him   16

    3E. "But having come to himself, he said, 'How many hired-workers *of* my father *are* abounding[9] *with* bread, but **I** am perishing[10] here[11] *in a* famine[12]!   17

        1F. 'Having arisen[L], I will proceed to my father and say *to* him, "Father, I sinned against heaven, and in your sight. °I[13] am no longer worthy[M] to be called your son. Make me as one *of* your hired-workers" '   18   19

4D. "And having arisen, he went to his father. But he still being far distant[N], his father saw him and felt-deep-feelings[O] [of love]. And having run, he fell upon his neck and kissed him[14]   20

    1E. "And the son said *to* him, 'Father, I sinned[P] against heaven and in your sight. I am no longer worthy to be called your son[15]'   21

    2E. "But the father[16] said to his slaves[Q], 'Quickly[17], bring-out the best[18] robe and put *it* on him. And give *him a* ring for his hand and sandals for the feet. °And bring the fatted calf. Slaughter[R] *it*. And having eaten, let us celebrate[S]!   22   23

        1F. 'Because **this** son *of* mine[19] was dead, and he became-alive-again[20]. He had become-lost[21], and he was found'   24

    3E. "And they began to celebrate

5D. "Now his older son was in *the* field. And when, while coming[22], he drew-near[T] *to* the house, he heard music[23] and dancing   25

    1E. "And having summoned[U] one *of* the servants[V], he was inquiring[W] *as to* what these *things* might be   26

        1F. "And the *one* said *to* him that 'Your brother has come. And your father slaughtered the fatted calf because he received him back[24] being healthy[25]'   27

    2E. "And he became-angry[X], and was not willing[Y] to go in   28

    3E. "And his father, having come out, was appealing-to[Z] him

    4E. "But the *one*, having responded, said *to* his father, 'Behold— I am slaving[26] *for* you *for* so many years, and I never disregarded[27] your command.[28] And you never gave **me** *a* goat in order that I might celebrate[S] with my friends[29]   29

        1F. 'But when this **son *of* yours** came— the *one* having devoured[AA] your property[30] with prostitutes— you slaughtered the fatted calf *for* him!'   30

1. Or, "property, estate", your physical "substance". Related to what "is, exists". Elsewhere only in v 13. GK *4045*.
2. Or, "belonging". More literally, "put upon, thrown upon". On this word, see "put upon" in Mk 14:72. That is, give me my future inheritance. The younger son got one third, the elder son two thirds, Deut 21:17.
3. Or, "divided". On this word, see 1 Cor 12:11.
4. Or, "life, living, livelihood, means of living", the externals of "life". On this word, see "life" in 1 Jn 2:16.
5. Or, "scattered". Same word as in 16:1. On this word, see "scatter" in Mt 25:24.
6. Or, "recklessly, riotously, loosely". This adverb is used only here. GK *862*. Related to "wild-living" in Eph 5:18.
7. Or, "to lack, come short, be deficient". Same word as in 2 Cor 11:9; Phil 4:12; Heb 11:37. Elsewhere only as "lack" in Mt 19:20; Mk 10:21; Lk 22:35; 1 Cor 1:7; 8:8; 12:24; and "come short" in Jn 2:3; Rom 3:23; 2 Cor 11:5; 12:11; Heb 4:1; 12:15. GK *5728*. Related to "need" in Mk 12:44; and "lack" in Phil 2:30.
8. On this word, see Phil 4:12. Some manuscripts say, "to fill his belly" {B}, using the word in Mk 4:37.
9. Or, are "having more than enough, having leftovers *of*". Same word as "left over" in 9:17. On this word, see 2 Cor 8:2.
10. Same word as "become lost" in v 4, but different grammar. It could be rendered "losing-*myself*".
11. Some manuscripts omit this word {N}.
12. Or, "*with* hunger". Same word as in v 14. See 21:11 on it.
13. Some manuscripts say "And I" {K}. The same variant occurs in v 21.
14. Same phrase as in Act 20:37, where people fell upon Paul's neck and kissed him.
15. Some manuscripts add "Make me as one *of* your hired-workers" {A}, as in v 19.
16. The father bursts in with joy before the son can even finish his speech.
17. Some manuscripts omit this word {N}, on which see Rev 22:7.
18. Or, "the first, foremost". That is, the first in value, the finest. On this word, see "first" in 1 Cor 15:3.
19. Compare how the brother says this in v 30.
20. Or, "lived-again, came to life again". On this word, see Rom 7:9. Related word in v 32.
21. This is a participle, he "was having become lost". Same word as in v 4.
22. In other words, while coming in the course of his work, not because he heard about his brother.
23. Or, "*an* instrument, *a* band". Our word "symphony" comes from this word, *sumphonia*. Used only here. GK *5246*.
24. On the word "receive back", see "receive" in 16:25.
25. That is, as opposed to receiving back news of his death. On this word, see 1 Tim 1:10.
26. Or, "serving as a slave *to* you". How dramatic of this son who inherited two thirds of the estate! On this word, see Rom 6:6.
27. Or, "passed by" in disobedience or neglect. Elsewhere in this sense only in 11:42.
28. The older brother represents the Pharisees, exaggerating their own obedience, not sharing the father's love for the sinner, and jealous of the father's celebration over their repentance. To him, it is so unfair!
29. Neither did the father ever do this for the younger brother! This is the father's celebration of joy, not the son's.
30. Same word as in v 12.

A. Rom 11:25 B. Mt 21:33 C. Mk 1:5 D. Rev 20:4, came to life E. Act 21:24 F. Lk 21:11 G. 1 Cor 6:16 H. Heb 8:11 fellow citizen
J. Jn 21:15 K. Gal 5:17 L. Lk 18:33, rise up M. Rev 16:6 N. Mt 15:8 O. Mt 9:36 P. Act 25:8 Q. Rom 6:17 R. Act 10:13 S. Rev 12:12
T. Lk 21:28 U. Act 2:39, call to V. Act 3:13 W. Act 23:34, learned X. Rev 11:18 Y. Jn 7:17 Z. Rom 12:8, exhorting AA. Mk 12:40

	5E.	"And the *one* said *to* him, 'Child^A, **you** are always with me, and all my *things* are yours¹. *But it-was-necessary² to celebrate and rejoice^B, because this **brother *of* yours** was dead, and he became-alive³. And *he had* become-lost⁴, and he was found' "	31 32
3C.		And⁵ He was also saying to the⁶ disciples, "There was *a* certain rich man who had *a* steward⁷. And this *one* was accused⁸ *to* him as squandering⁹ his possessions¹⁰	16:1
	1D.	"And having called him, he said *to* him, 'What *is* this I am hearing¹¹ about you? Render^C the account^D *of* your stewardship¹², for you can no longer be steward'	2
	2D.	"And the steward said within himself, 'What should I do, because my master^E is taking-away^F the stewardship¹³ from me? I am not strong-*enough*^G to dig. I am ashamed^H to beg. I know¹⁴ what I will do so that they will¹⁵ welcome^J me into their houses when I am removed^K from the stewardship'. *And having summoned^L each one *of* the debtors¹⁶ *of* his master—	3 4 5
		1E. "He was saying *to* the first, 'How much do you owe^M *to* my master?' *And the *one* said, '*A* hundred baths¹⁷ *of* olive-oil^N'. And the *one* said *to* him, 'Take^J your writings¹⁸, and having sat-*down* quickly^O, write fifty'	6
		2E. "Then he said *to* another, 'And you, how much do you owe?' And the *one* said, '*A* hundred cor¹⁹ *of* wheat'. He²⁰ says *to* him, 'Take your writings, and write eighty'	7
	3D.	"And the master²¹ praised^P the unrighteous^Q steward²² because he acted^R shrewdly²³. Because²⁴ the sons *of* this age²⁵ are more shrewd in-relation-to²⁶ their *own* kind²⁷ than the sons^S *of* the light²⁸	8
	4D.	"And **I** say *to* you—	9
		1E. "Make friends^T *for* yourselves by means of unrighteous^Q wealth²⁹, so that when it fails³⁰, they³¹ will welcome^J you into the eternal dwellings^U	
		2E. "The *one* trustworthy in *a* very-little³² *thing* is also trustworthy in much³³. And the *one* unrighteous^V in *a* very little *thing* is also unrighteous in much³⁴	10
			1F. "Therefore if you did not prove-to-be³⁵ trustworthy³⁶ with unrighteous^V wealth, who will entrust^W the true³⁷ *thing to* you?	11
			2F. "And if you did not prove-to-be trustworthy with the *thing* belonging to another³⁸, who will give you your *own thing*?³⁹	12
		3E.⁴⁰ "No household-servant^X can be serving⁴¹ two masters	13
			1F. "For either he will hate the one and love the other, or he will be devoted to one and disregard⁴² the other	
			2F. "You cannot be serving God and wealth"	

1. More literally, "all *that is* mine, is yours". The totality of what is mine is yours. The younger brother had received his share, so everything remaining belonged to the older brother as his inheritance.
2. Or, "*we* had to". On this idiom, see "must" in Mt 16:21.
3. Or, "he lived, he came to life". On this word, see "came to life" in Rev 20:4. Related to the word in v 24, but without the prefix meaning "again". Some manuscripts have the same word as v 24 {N}.
4. This is a participle, "*he was* having become lost". Same word as in v 4.
5. Some think Luke means that 15:1-17:10 occurred on the same occasion (a similar question arises in 12:1). There is no change of scene, only of the hearers. Jesus continues to speak words that apply to all present, in different ways. The previous parable transitions between concern for the lost one and the proper use of money. The wrong view of money (that it is for our earthly benefit) seen in both brothers in 15:11-32 is now addressed. The present parable speaks primarily to the disciples (ones who have repented), while at the same time rebuking the Pharisees (the reverse of 15:3). Others think this introduces a new occasion not linked to chapter 15, making this point 16B. In either case, this is also spoken in the hearing of the Pharisees, v 14.
6. Some manuscripts say "His" {N}.
7. Or, "manager, household administrator". Same word as in v 3, 8. On this word, see 1 Pet 4:10.
8. This is the verb related to "devil", which means "accuser, slanderer". Used only here. GK *1330*.
9. Same word as in 15:13.
10. Same word as in 12:15.
11. Or, "How *is it* I am hearing this...", "Why am I hearing this...".
12. Or, "management, mode of operation, administration". On this word, see Eph 1:10.
13. That is, my position of management responsibility, as in v 4. Same word as in v 2.
14. The grammar indicates this is a sudden inspiration. "I've got it! I know what I will do".
15. Or, "in order that they might". Likewise in v 9. GK *2671*.
16. While producing the accounts for the master (v 2), the steward quickly forgave part of their debt so that they would be indebted to him after he was removed. The point is that he used his master's resources to create a new life for himself. We are to use our money, the things entrusted to us (God's resources), for the same purpose, v 9.
17. Or, "measures". This is a transliterated Hebrew word. It is a liquid measure. There were different measuring systems in different times and places. Some estimate one bath at about 5-7 gallons (21-26 liters); others, at 8-10 gallons (32-39 liters). It depends on which ancient source one follows. Used only here. GK *1004*.
18. That is, your written records, receipts, bills, accounts. On this word, see Jn 7:15.
19. This is a transliterated Hebrew word. It is a dry measure. Some estimate one cor at about 11 bushels or 90 gallons or 393 liters; others, at six bushels or 50 gallons or 220 liters. Used only here. GK *3174*.
20. Some manuscripts say "And the *one* says..." {N}.
21. Or, "And the Lord". Some think this is referring to the master in the parable; others, to the Lord Jesus, making this Luke's comment.
22. More literally, "the steward *of* unrighteousness", the steward characterized by unrighteousness. This is a Hebrew way of speaking.
23. Or, "wisely, prudently". Used only here. GK *5862*. Related to "shrewd" next, on which see "wise" in Mt 7:24.
24. Jesus adds this to make clear the point He wishes us to draw from the parable. He is not praising the steward for his unrighteousness, but for his shrewd use of another's resources for his own future good.
25. That is, "*belonging to* this age", or "*characterized by* this age", versus the sons of the light. GK *172*.
26. Or, "with reference to, regarding, toward". GK *1650*.
27. Or, "generation, clan". On this word, see "generation" in Mt 24:34.
28. That is, than believers in relation to their own kind. Unbelievers act more shrewdly in this world with regard to their future welfare in earthly "houses" (v 4), than believers do with regard to their future welfare in heavenly "dwellings" (v 9).
29. Same word as in v 11, 13. On this word, see Mt 6:24. Literally, "the wealth *of* unrighteousness", the wealth characterized by unrighteousness. It is the wealth of this age, the wealth you are not to serve as slave, v 13. In other words, use your money (your Master's resources) in this age so that in the next, it will return a dividend to you. 14:13 is an example. Be as adept and creative at using your resources from God righteously for eternal rewards as this one was unrighteously for earthly ones. This is the point Jesus makes from the parable. Beyond this, there are many views about what other points might be made from the details of the parable. Consult the commentaries.
30. Or, "leaves off, ceases, gives out, comes to an end". That is, when the money comes to an end, when you die. Same word as in 22:32; 23:45. Elsewhere only as "end" in Heb 1:12. GK *1722*. Related to "unfailing" in 12:33. Some manuscripts say "you fail" {K}.
31. Some think this refers to God's agents, and God Himself; others, to the friends, assuming they also died.
32. Or, "*the* least *thing*". However, the contrast is between very-little and much, not least and most. GK *1788*.
33. Or, "in *a* great *thing*, in *a* large *thing*".
34. The same character is seen in one's handling of the small things and the big things. Inner character is not created by the task, but demonstrated by it. So if a small thing like money has shown one to be untrustworthy, who is going to entrust a larger thing to that person?
35. Or, "did not become, were not". Same word as in v 12. GK *1181*.
36. Or, "faithful". This word is related to "entrust" next, and is rendered this way to reflect this. Same word as in v 12 and twice in v 10. On this word, see "faithful" in Col 1:2.
37. Or, "genuine, real". That is, the truly valuable thing, true spiritual, eternal wealth. Jesus contrasts what in eternal reality is not important or valuable with what in eternal reality is important and valuable. On this word, see Jn 7:28.
38. Earthly wealth belongs to God. We are merely stewards of it.
39. We often think of money as our "own", and the future blessing as God's. Jesus views our present things as God's resources entrusted to us, and His future blessings as what will be our "own".
40. Compare Mt 6:24.
41. That is, "serving as a slave *to*, being a slave *to*". On this word, see "are slaves" in Rom 6:6.
42. On "devoted to" and "disregard", see Mt 6:24.

A. 1 Jn 3:1 B. 2 Cor 13:11 C. Mt 16:27 D. 1 Cor 12:8, word E. Mt 8:2 F. Mk 14:47, took off G. Gal 5:6, can do H. 1 Jn 2:28, put to shame J. Mt 10:40, welcome K. Act 19:26, turn away L. Act 2:39, call to M. 1 Jn 4:11, ought N. Jam 5:14, oil O. Gal 1:6 P. Rom 15:11 Q. Rom 1:18, unrighteousness R. Rev 13:13, does S. Gal 3:7 T. Lk 14:10 U. Lk 9:33 V. 1 Cor 6:9, wrong-doers W. Jn 3:36, believe X. Rom 14:4

4C. Now the Pharisees, being money-lovers[1], were listening-to all[2] these *things,* and they were sneering-at[3] Him. °And He said *to* them— 14
15

    1D. "**You** are the *ones* declaring yourselves righteous[4] in the sight of people, but God knows[A] your hearts[B]— because the highly-*valued*[5] *thing* among people *is an* abomination[6] in the sight of God

        1E. "The Law and the Prophets *were* until[7] John. From that time *on,*[8] the kingdom *of* God is being announced-as-good-news[C], and everyone[9] is forcing-*himself*[10] into it 16

        2E. "But[11] it is easier *that* the heaven and the earth *should* pass away than *that* one stroke[D] *of* the Law *should* fail[12] 17

            1F. "Everyone sending-away[13] his wife and marrying[E] another is committing-adultery[F]. And the *one* marrying[14] *one* having been sent-away from *her* husband is committing-adultery 18

    2D. "Now[15] there was *a* certain rich[G] man. And he was dressing *himself* in purple and fine-linen[16], radiantly[17] enjoying-*himself*[18] daily[19]. °And *a* certain poor[H] *man,* Lazarus[20] *by* name, had been put at his gate— having been covered-with-sores, °and desiring[J] to be fill-to-satisfaction[21] by the *things* falling[22] from the table *of* the rich *man*. Even indeed[23] the dogs coming were licking his sores 19
20
21

        1E. "And it came about *that* the poor *man* died and he was carried-away[K] by the angels to the bosom *of* Abraham[24] 22

        2E. "And the rich *man* also died and was buried

            1F. "And having lifted-up[L] his eyes in Hades[M] while being in torments[25], he sees Abraham from a-distance[26], and Lazarus in his bosoms[27] 23

            2F. "And **he**, having called, said, 'Father Abraham, have-mercy-on[N] me and send Lazarus in order that he may dip[O] the tip[P] *of* his finger *in* water and cool-off my tongue, because I am suffering-pain[28] in this flame[Q]' 24

            3F. "But Abraham said, 'Child[R], remember[S] that during your life[T] you received[29] your good *things*, and likewise Lazarus the bad *things* 25

                1G. "But now, here[30], he is being comforted[U] and **you** are suffering-pain

                2G. "And in all these *regions*[31], *a* great chasm[32] has been fixed[33] between us and you[34], so that the *ones* wanting to cross[V] from here to you are not able, nor may they cross-over from there to us' 26

            4F. "And he said, 'Then I ask[W] you, father, that you send him to the house *of* my father— °for I have five brothers— so that he may solemnly-warn[35] them in order that **they** also might not come to this place *of* torment' 27
28

            5F. "But Abraham says, 'They have Moses and the Prophets. Let them listen-to them' 29

            6F. "But the *one* said, 'No[36], father Abraham. But if someone goes to them from *the* dead, they will repent[X]' 30

            7F. "But he said *to* him, 'If they do not listen-to Moses and the Prophets, neither will they be persuaded[Y] if someone[37] rises-up[Z] from *the* dead' " 31

5C. And[38] He said to His[39] disciples— 17:1

1. The Pharisees equated wealth with the blessing of God, and proof of His favor. On this word, see 2 Tim 3:2.
2. Some think "all" means 15:1-16:13. Jesus responds to their reaction, v 15-18 being addressed to the heart issue seen in 15:2, and v 19-31 to the heart issue of 16:1-13. Others think "all" refers only to 16:1-13, v 15-18 going to their hearts, v 19-31 to the consequences.
3. Or, "turning up the nose at, ridiculing, mocking". The idea of spending now to build up treasures then always seems foolish to people outside God's family. Elsewhere only in 23:35. GK *1727*. Related to "mock" in Gal 6:7.
4. On "declare righteous", see Rom 3:24. And by contrast, the Pharisees are also passing judgment on the ones in 15:1.
5. Or, "highly-*esteemed,* high*,* exalted". God knows you Pharisees are not righteous, because the things you value and base your opinion on, He hates. And the things He values, you do not value, as seen in your attitude toward these tax collectors and sinners, and your views on money, and on divorce (v 18). This word means "high" in various senses. Same word as "lofty" in Rom 11:20; 12:16. Used 11 times. GK *5734*. Related to "lifted up" in Jn 8:28.
6. Or, "detestable". On this word, see Rev 17:4.
7. Or, "as far as", GK *3588*. Some manuscripts have the same word as in Mt 11:13 {N} (GK *2401*).
8. On this phrase "from that time *on*", see Mt 4:17. Compare Mt 11:12.
9. This is like saying "all Jerusalem" in Mt 2:3, or "all Israel" in Act 13:24. This is why tax collectors and sinners also are drawing near to hear (Lk 15:1), and repenting. Failing to understand this, you Pharisees continue condemning and excluding them.
10. Same word as "treated-violently" in Mt 11:12. Some think Jesus means everyone is "*trying to* force his way, press" into it. The crowds press to see Jesus, and experience the blessings of the kingdom, and enter it. But the Pharisees are rejecting it and trying to force their views on Jesus. Others think He means "everyone is forced into it", "is strongly urged into it", similar to Lk 14:23, as this word is used in Judg 19:7 where a guest is "urged" to stay. Everyone is being urged to enter it, including tax collectors. Others think He means "everyone forces against it", exerts force or violence against it. Compare Mt 11:12.
11. Though the Pharisees try to force themselves in on their own terms, God's Law will not be set aside. Not one Law will be set aside when granting entrance to His kingdom, Mt 5:17-19; not for tax collectors, and not for Pharisees. No one will enter it without repenting of their version of Law-breaking.
12. Or, "fall, fall *down*". Same word as in 1 Cor 13:8.
13. That is, divorcing. Jesus is giving another example of their Law-breaking. The Pharisees condemn the tax collectors and sinners, but they themselves are violating God's Law in this area, and teaching others to do so. Jesus is charging them with adultery, an adultery which they legalized with their traditions. The self-justifying sinners like them are the ones rejected by God, not the repentant sinners. On this word, see Mt 5:31.
14. Some manuscripts say "And everyone marrying..." {N}.
15. This parable is spoken to all "money lovers", whether sinners or Pharisees.
16. That is, a fine-linen undergarment and a purple outer garment. Used only here. GK *1116*. Related to the word in Rev 19:8.
17. Or, "brilliantly, brightly". That is, in their bright clothing and shining things. Used only here. GK *3289*. Related to "shining" in Rev 18:14; 22:1; and "shine" in 2 Cor 4:6.
18. Same word as "celebrate" in 15:23.
19. Not at festivals or weddings like others, but every day.
20. This is the only place Jesus gives a name to a person in a parable.
21. Same phrase as in 15:16, "desiring to be filled to satisfaction".
22. Some manuscripts say "the crumbs falling" {B}, as in Mt 15:27. Lazarus wished he could be filled, but he was not. Some think he was given such table scraps, but that they were not enough to fill him. Others think he was not given anything, but lived off begging from passers-by, visitors to the rich man.
23. Or, "But even". Some think Jesus means Lazarus received help only from those passing by, "even indeed" from dogs who cleaned his sores. Others think He means Lazarus desired to be filled, "but even" the dogs tormented him.
24. That is, to be with Abraham in paradise.
25. Same word as in v 28. Elsewhere only in Mt 4:24. GK *992*. Related to "torment" in Rev 14:10.
26. Or, "from far-away". GK *3427*.
27. Or, "at his bosoms, at his side". It is plural only here, and may have the same meaning as the singular. Same word as in v 22, on which see Jn 1:18. Some think Jesus means Lazarus is under Abraham's arm with his head against his chest, hugged and loved like the son come home at last. Others think he is at the side of Abraham at a great banquet, reclining in the place of honor, as in Jn 13:23.
28. Same word as in v 25. On this word, see 2:48.
29. Same word as in Gal 4:5; Col 3:24; 2 Jn 8; and as "receive-back" in Lk 6:34; 15:27; 18:30; 23:41; Rom 1:27. Elsewhere only as "take away" in Mk 7:33. GK *655*.
30. Some manuscripts omit this word {K}.
31. Or, "in connection with all these *things*". Some manuscripts say "And in addition to all these *things*" {N}.
32. Or, "wide opening, yawning, gulf, gaping expanse". Used only here. GK *5926*. We get "chasm" from this word *chasma*.
33. Or, "set, established". On this word, see "establish" in 1 Thes 3:2.
34. This word is plural, referring to all those on the other side.
35. On this word, see "solemnly-charge" in 1 Tim 5:21.
36. After all, I did not take them seriously, and neither do my brothers.
37. In fact, another Lazarus did rise from the dead, and the chief priests wanted to kill him! (Jn 11:43; 12:10).
38. Some think this introduces a new occasion, a new "B" level point after 16:1; others, a further response to the issues raised in chapters 15-16. As in 16:1, Jesus speaks to the disciples with words that also rebuke the Pharisees. In addition, some think v 1-2; 3-4; 5-6; and 7-10 are unconnected sayings; others think there is a flow of thought.
39. Some manuscripts say "the" {K}.

A. Lk 1:34 B. Rev 2:23 C. Act 5:42 D. Mt 5:18 E. 1 Cor 7:9 F. Mt 5:32 G. 1 Tim 6:17 H. Gal 4:9 J. Gal 5:17 K. 1 Cor 16:3, carry forth L. 2 Cor 11:2 M. Rev 1:18 N. Rom 12:8, showing mercy O. Rev 19:13 P. Mt 24:31, end Q. 2 Thes 1:8 R. 1 Jn 3:1 S. Lk 1:54 T. Rom 8:10 U. Rom 12:8, exhorting V. Heb 11:29 W. Jn 17:9, pray X. Act 26:20 Y. 1 Jn 3:19 Z. Lk 18:33

1D. "It is impossible¹ *that* the causes-of-falling² *should* not come.³ Nevertheless, woe *to the one* through whom they come

    1E. "It *would* be better⁴ *for* him if *a* mill's⁵ stone were lying-around^A his neck and he had been thrown-off⁶ into the sea,⁷ than that he should cause one *of* these⁸ little *ones* to fall⁹   2

2D.¹⁰ "Take heed to yourselves¹¹— If your brother^B sins¹², rebuke^C him. And if he repents^D,   3
forgive^E him.¹³ °And if he sins against you seven times *in* the day, and returns to you   4
seven times¹⁴ saying 'I repent', forgive him"

6C. The apostles said *to* the Lord¹⁵, "Increase¹⁶ faith *for* us". °And the Lord said—   5-6

    1D.¹⁷ "If you have faith¹⁸ like *a* seed *of a* mustard-plant^F, you would say *to* this¹⁹ mulberry-tree, 'Be uprooted and be planted in the sea', and it would have obeyed^G you²⁰
    2D. "And²¹ who from-*among* you *is there* who, having *a* slave^H plowing or shepherding²²,   7
will say *to* him having come in from the field, 'Immediately^J having come-to²³ *the table*, fall back [to eat]!'?

        1E. "But will he not say *to* him, 'Prepare^K something I may have-for-dinner^L. And   8
having girded-*yourself*^M, be serving^N me until I eat and drink. And after these *things*, **you** will eat and drink'?
        2E. "He does not have gratitude²⁴ *for* the²⁵ slave because he did the *things* having been   9
commanded²⁶, *does he*?²⁷
        3E. "So also you,²⁸ when you do²⁹ all the *things* having been commanded^O *to* you, be saying   10
that 'We are unprofitable³⁰ slaves^H. We have done what we were obligated^P to do' "

16B. And it came about during the proceeding to Jerusalem that^Q **He** was going through *the* midst³¹ *of*   11
Samaria and Galilee. °And while He *was* entering into *a* certain village, ten leprous men met Him,   12
who stood at-a-distance. °And **they** lifted *their* voice³², saying, "Jesus, Master^R, have-mercy-on^S us!"   13

    1C. And having seen *them*, He said *to* them, "Having gone, show^T yourselves *to* the priests".³³   14
And it came about during their going *that* they were cleansed^U
    2C. And one of them, having seen that he was healed^V, returned glorifying^W God with *a* loud voice.   15
And he fell on *his* face at His feet while giving-thanks^X *to* Him. And **he** was *a* Samaritan   16
    3C. And having responded, Jesus said, "*Were* not ten cleansed^U? But where *are* the nine? °Were   17-18
none found having returned to give glory^Y *to* God except this foreigner?"³⁴
    4C. And He said *to* him, "Having arisen, go. Your faith has restored^Z you"   19

17B. And having been asked by the Pharisees when the kingdom *of* God is coming   20

    1C. He responded *to* them and said— "The kingdom *of* God is not coming with observation³⁵, °nor   21
will they say, 'Behold— here *it is*', or, 'There *it is*'. For behold— the kingdom *of* God is within³⁶ you"
    2C.³⁷ And He said to the disciples, "Days will come when you will desire^AA to see one *of* the days³⁸   22
of the Son *of* Man, and you will not see *it*. °And they will say *to* you, 'Behold— there *He is*',   23
or³⁹, 'Behold— here *He is*'. Do not go, nor pursue *them*

1. Used only here. GK *450*. Related to "cannot be" in 13:33.
2. On this word, see Rom 11:9. In this context, Jesus is referring to things such as the Pharisees were just described as doing in chapters 15-16— rejecting the repentant, teaching traditions that set aside God's laws, loving and living for money, etc. But any behavior or teaching that causes others to fall is included.
3. This is stated positively in Mt 18:7, negatively here. Causes of falling are bound to come.
4. Used only here. GK *3387*. Luke, Mt 18:6, and Mk 9:42 each use a different word to express this.
5. Or, a stone "belonging-to-a-mill". Used only here. GK *3683*. Related to "millstone" in Mk 9:42.
6. Or, "cast, hurled, tossed". On this word, see "thrown forth" in Mt 9:36. Mk 9:42 uses an unrelated word (GK *965*).
7. Same vivid grammar as in Mk 9:42. A person would be better off to already be dead at the bottom of the sea with a mill's stone lying around his neck than to do this. Compare Mt 18:6.
8. Some think Jesus is referring to the tax collectors and sinners in 15:1, as well as to the insignificant believers like Lazarus, these little disciples the Pharisees or rich ones disdain. Others think this is not connected with chapters 15-16, and that it refers to these beloved little disciples against whom such ones in v 1 bring a cause of falling.
9. On this verb, "cause to fall", see 1 Cor 8:13. Related to the word in v 1.
10. Compare Mt 18:15-21.
11. On this phrase, see 12:1. That is, be on guard to treat one another properly as follows, not as described in v 1-2. Some take "Take heed to yourselves" only with what precedes, making it point 2E.
12. Some manuscripts add "against you" {A}. Apply God's laws to your brothers and sisters to help them where needed.
13. This is in direct contrast to what the Pharisees did regarding the tax collectors, 15:2; 17:1.
14. Some manuscripts add "*in* the day" {N}.
15. Some think this introduces a different occasion, unrelated to v 4, a new "B" level point. Others think this is the apostles' response 15:1-17:4, or to 17:1-4 in particular.
16. Or, "Add faith *to* us, Grant us faith". That is, "Increase *our* faith for us". Perhaps the apostles think that if they are going to forgive seven times a day, they need more faith. Perhaps after all the Lord's words about properly handling money, not causing others to fall, rebuking and forgiving others, etc., they were overwhelmed and felt they needed more faith to obey. But this is not so. The smallest amount is enough. Elsewhere only as "add" in Mt 6:27, 33; Mk 4:24; Lk 3:20; 12:25, 31; Act 2:41, 47; 5:14; 11:24; Gal 3:19; Heb 12:19; "put with" in Act 13:36; and "proceed" (see 19:11). GK *4707*.
17. Compare Mt 17:20; 21:21; Mk 11:22-23.
18. The grammar means "Assuming you have faith" of even this tiny amount.
19. Some manuscripts omit this word {C}.
20. It is not the quantity of our faith that accomplishes great things, but God. With a tiny bit of faith in Him, God can do great things through us. Jesus is telling the apostles that they already have enough to do far more than they realize. They just need to utilize it.
21. Some think this parable is not related to the request of v 5, but to the preceding context. Jesus is warning them against taking an attitude like the Pharisees, who thought they merited God's favor, and that God was obligated to reward them because of their obedience. Others think He is warning the disciples against a prideful attitude that could result from the future great deeds of faith they will do, to which He alluded in v 6.
22. That is, shepherding sheep. On this word, see Rev 19:15.
23. Same verb as in 12:37.
24. Or, "thankfulness, gratefulness", an attitude of favor. This phrase is elsewhere only in 1 Tim 1:12; 2 Tim 1:3; Heb 12:28; "have favor" in Act 2:47; and as "have a benefit" in 2 Cor 1:15. GK *5921*. "Gratitude" is the word "grace" (see Eph 2:8 on it).
25. Some manuscripts say "that" {K}.
26. Some manuscripts add "*to him*" {B}.
27. The grammar indicates a "no" answer is expected. Some manuscripts add "I think not" {B}.
28. This is what Jesus means by this parable. It is intended to teach us what we should think about ourselves. When we finish everything commanded, we have only fulfilled our obligation, our duty, what we owe our Master. However far our faith extends in action, we can never earn or merit anything from Him. Whatever rewards come to us will be by God's grace, not any obligation on His part.
29. Or, "accomplish, perform". Had Jesus said "only do", the parable would have a very different meaning.
30. On this word, see Mt 25:30. We are unable to bring the Master any gain exceeding His investment in us, for which He would be obligated to reward us.
31. Or, "between". Luke could mean "through the middle of them", or, "between them", on their borders. This use of "through" (GK *1328*) in this idiom is found only here in the Greek Bible.
32. This word is singular. The ten shouted together as one voice. This phrase is elsewhere only in Act 4:24.
33. That is, go obtain a ritual cleansing in accordance with the Law, implying that they would be healed.
34. Thanksgiving to the Healer for the healing should come first, then the obtaining of the ritual cleansing.
35. Or, "*a* close-watching, *a* looking-closely". That is, in such a way that it can be physically observed. Jesus will later say, "My kingdom is not of this world", Jn 18:36. Used only here. GK *4191*. Related to "closely watch" in 6:7. Medical writers used this word of closely watching for symptoms of a disease. Compare v 24 and 21:31.
36. Or, "inside". Elsewhere only in Mt 23:26, "inside" of the cup. GK *1955*. This preposition is the opposite of "outside". Some take this in an individual sense, meaning "in the hearts of people"; others, in a national sense, "in your midst, among you" (it is all around you in Me and in those who believe in Me). In either case, it is spiritual in nature.
37. Compare Mt 24:23-27.
38. This phrase "one *of* the days" is elsewhere only in 5:17; 8:22; 20:1. Some think Jesus means one of the days after He returns in glory. There are other views.
39. Some manuscripts omit this word {C}. Some manuscripts reverse it, so that it says " ' Behold— here He is', or, 'Behold— there He is' " {C}, as in Mk 13:21.

A. Heb 5:2, surrounded   B. Act 16:40   C. 2 Tim 4:2, warn   D. Act 26:20   E. Mt 6:12   F. Mt 13:31   G. Act 6:7   H. Rom 6:17   J. Mt 13:5
K. Mk 14:15   L. 1 Cor 11:25, dining   M. Eph 6:14   N. 1 Pet 4:10, ministering   O. 1 Cor 7:17, directing   P. 1 Jn 4:11, ought   Q. Lk 5:1   R. Lk 5:5
S. Rom 12:8, showing mercy   T. Act 18:28   U. Heb 9:22   V. Mt 8:8   W. Rom 8:30   X. Mt 26:27   Y. 2 Pet 2:10   Z. Jam 5:15   AA. Gal 5:17

Luke 17:24	260	Verse

    1D. For just like the lightning[A] flashing[B] out of the *one part* under heaven shines[C] to the *other* 24
part under heaven, so[1] will the Son *of* Man be in His day[2]

        1E. "But first He must[D] suffer[E] many *things* and be rejected[F] by this generation[G] 25

    2D.[3] "And as it happened in the days *of* Noah [in Gen 6-7], so it will be also in the days *of* 26
the Son *of* Man—

        1E. "They were eating, drinking, marrying[H], being given-in-marriage[4], until which day 27
Noah entered into the ark, and the flood[J] came and destroyed[K] everyone

    3D. "Likewise, just as it happened in the days *of* Lot [in Gen 19]— 28

        1E. "They were eating, drinking, buying, selling, planting, building. °But *on* the day Lot 29
departed from Sodom, it rained fire and sulphur[L] from heaven and destroyed[K] everyone

        2E. "It will be[5] the same *way*[6] on the day the Son *of* Man is revealed 30

    4D.[7] "On that day, let he who will be on the housetop[M] and his things in the house not go 31
down to take them. And let the *one* in *a* field likewise not turn-back[N] to the *things* behind[8].
Remember[9] Lot's wife 32

        1E.[10] "Whoever seeks[O] to preserve[11] his life[12] will lose[K] it. But whoever loses *it* will 33
keep it alive[13]

    5D.[14] "I say *to* you— 34

        1E. "*On* this night there will be two *people*[15] on one bed— the one will be taken[16], and
the other will be left[17]

        2E. "There will be two *women* grinding at the same *place*[18]— the one will be taken, and 35
the other will be left 36[19]

    6D.[20] And having responded, they say *to* Him, "Where, Lord?"[21] And the *One* said *to* them, 37
"Where the body[22] *is*, there also[23] the vultures[P] will be gathered-together[24]"

3C. And He was speaking *a* parable[Q] *to* them[25] with-regard-to[26] *it* being necessary[27] *that* they 18:1
always be praying and not losing-heart[28], °saying 2

    1D. "There was in *a* certain city *a* certain judge not fearing God and not having-regard-for[29]
the person[R]

    2D. "And there was *a* widow in that city. And she was coming to him, saying, 'Avenge[30] me 3
from my adversary[S]'

    3D. "And he was not willing[T] for *a* time. But after these[31] *things*, he said within himself, 'Even 4
though[32] I do not fear God nor have regard for *the* person,°yet because of this widow's 5
causing me trouble[33], I will avenge her— in order that she, while continually[34] coming,
may not be wearing me out[35]' "

    4D. And the Lord said— 6

        1E. "Listen-to what the unrighteous judge[36] is saying[37]

1. Some manuscripts add "also" {K}. All will see it, as unmistakably as a light turned on in a dark room.
2. Some manuscripts omit "in His day" {C}.
3. Compare Mt 24:37-39.
4. That is, life will be going on as normal. It will be unexpected, like a thief at night. On this word, see 1 Cor 7:38.
5. Or, "happen", as in Mt 16:22. Same word as "be" in v 24, 26 (GK *1639*), not as "happened" in v 26, 28 (GK *1181*).
6. Or, "in accordance with the same *things,* in the same *manner*". On this phrase, see 6:23.
7. Compare Mt 24:17-18; Mk 13:15-16.
8. Or, "likewise not return back". On "to the *things* behind", see "back" in Jn 6:66.
9. That is, be keeping in mind what happened in her case.
10. Compare Mt 16:25.
11. Or, "secure, keep safe, gain *for himself*". On this word, see "obtain" in 1 Tim 3:13. Some manuscripts say "to save" {B}.
12. Same word as in 9:24.
13. Or, "preserve it". On this word, "keep alive", see "give life to" in 1 Tim 6:13.
14. Compare Mt 24:40-41.
15. The sense is most general. Or, "*men*", since Jesus refers to women in the next verse. Note v 36, and Mt 24:40-41.
16. This word means "take (with)", as in Mt 1:20; "take along", as in Lk 9:10; 11:26; "take aside", as in Lk 18:31. It implies nothing as to whether the taking is for blessing, as in Lk 9:28; Jn 14:3; Act 16:33; or for judgment, as in Jn 19:16. It also means "receive" in a positive sense, as in Col 2:6; Heb 12:28; and "accept" in Jn 1:11. Compare Mt 24:40. Used 49 times. GK *4161*.
17. Or, "left behind, abandoned". Some think Jesus means that as Noah and Lot were "taken" for their protection and the others "left" for judgment, so some will be "taken into the kingdom, away from destruction", or, "taken in the rapture" (1 Thes 4:17). Others think that as the others were "taken" in judgment, and Noah and Lot were "left" living on earth after the judgment, so some are "left" to enter His kingdom on earth, as in Mt 13:41-43.
18. This is a daytime activity. On this idiom, "at the same *place*", see Act 2:47.
19. Some manuscripts add as v 36, "Two *men will be* in *a* field— one will be taken and the other will be left" {A}, as in Mt 24:40.
20. Compare Mt 24:28.
21. Some think this question applies to v 34-35, taking it to mean "Where will they be taken or left?"; or, "Where will this separation, this taking and leaving, take place?" Others think it applies to v 22-35 (making it point 3C.), and means "Where will You come back?" There are other views.
22. Matthew says "corpse", Mt 24:28. Some think Jesus means "where the body of those judged is taken or left, there the vultures will have them", similar to Rev 19:18, 21. Others think Jesus answers their question of locality with a universal principle. Wherever the spiritually dead are, there judgment will fall. Others taking this as point 3C. think He means that His coming will be as clearly accompanied by obvious signs as dead bodies are by vultures. Consult the commentaries on these and other views.
23. Or, "indeed". Some manuscripts omit this word {N}.
24. This word (GK *2190*) is related to the word in Mt 24:28.
25. That is, to the disciples in 17:22. This is what they must do while waiting and desiring to see the days of the Son of Man.
26. Or, "so as" (see Mt 5:28 on this). The literal grammar may be conveyed in two ways. Some think Luke is giving the purpose of the parable— Jesus spoke "*to* them so as [to show them] *that* they must always pray and...". Others think he is pointing to the subject to be addressed with the parable, as when we speak "to" an issue— Jesus spoke "with regard to" (same word as in 19:9) the necessity of praying always. The end result is virtually the same. GK *4639*.
27. On this idiom, see "must" in Mt 16:21.
28. Or, "growing weary, growing tired". On this word, see 2 Cor 4:1. We must keep praying, for God will answer.
29. Or, "respecting", literally, "turning himself to". Same word as in Mt 21:37; Mk 12:6; Lk 18:4; 20:13; and as "respect" in Heb 12:9. That is, this man's judgments were not influenced by God's justice or the person before him, but solely by his own reasoning. Elsewhere only as "to shame" (literally, turn one on himself) in 1 Cor 4:14; and "to be ashamed" (literally, turned on oneself) in 2 Thes 3:14; Tit 2:8. GK *1956*. Related to "shame" in 1 Cor 6:5.
30. Or, "grant me justice". That is, "Give me a just return from my adversary". Since the offense is not stated, the widow could mean "Punish him for his crime", or "Make him fulfill his legal obligation to me", or "Protect me from his attacks", all bringing an end to the situation. Same word as in v 5. On this word, see "punish" in 2 Cor 10:6. Related to "vengeance" in v 7-8, and to "avenger" in Rom 13:4.
31. That is, after the widow repeatedly came to him, v 3.
32. More literally, "If I even do not fear...". This idiom (see 1 Cor 7:21) means "accepting that I even do not fear God..., yet I will answer her request because of her persistent asking". This is the same point made in 11:8.
33. This phrase "causing trouble" is also in Mt 26:10; Mk 14:6; Lk 11:7; Gal 6:17. On "trouble", see "labor" in 1 Cor 3:8. On "cause", see "grant" in Act 17:31.
34. Or, "to *the* end, perpetually". On this phrase, see 1 Thes 2:16, "to the uttermost". Some put this with "wear out", so that it says "that she, while coming" may not "completely, fully" or "finally, at last" wear me out.
35. This word "wear out" has a physical sense "to give a black eye, bruise"; a moral sense, "to give a black eye, disgrace"; and a figurative sense, "to browbeat, wear out, annoy greatly". Here, the judge fears repeated harassment, not a one time physical attack or anything people might think. Elsewhere only as "bruise" in 1 Cor 9:27. GK *5724*.
36. More literally, "the judge *of* unrighteousness"; that is, the judge characterized by unrighteousness.
37. The judge is saying that he will answer her request because of her continual coming and persistent asking.

A. Rev 4:5 B. Lk 24:4, gleam C. 2 Cor 4:6 D. Mt 16:21 E. Gal 3:4 F. Heb 12:17 G. Mt 24:34 H. 1 Cor 7:9 J. 2 Pet 2:5 K. 1 Cor 1:18, perish L. Rev 14:10 M. Lk 5:19 N. Jam 5:19 O. Phil 2:21 P. Rev 8:13, eagle Q. Mt 13:3 R. Mt 4:4, mankind S. 1 Pet 5:8 T. Jn 7:17

2E. "And shall not God execute[1] vengeance[2] *for* His chosen[A] *ones*— the *ones* crying-out[3] *to* Him *by* day and *by* night and He is being patient[4] with them?   7

    1F. "I say *to* you that He will execute vengeance *for* them quickly[5]   8
    2F. "However, the Son *of* Man having come, will[6] He find faith[7] on the earth?"

18B. And He also spoke this parable to some putting-confidence[B] upon themselves that they were[8] righteous[C], and treating the rest[9] with contempt[10]—   9

  1C. "Two men went up to the temple to pray— the one *a* Pharisee, and the other *a* tax-collector[D]   10
  2C. "The Pharisee, having stood, was praying these *things* to himself[11]— 'God, I thank[E] You that I am not just-like the rest *of* the people[12]— swindlers[F], unrighteous[G] *ones*, adulterers, or even like this tax collector. °I fast[H] twice *a* week.[13] I give-a-tenth-of[14] all[15] that I get[16]'   11, 12
  3C. "But the tax collector, standing at-a-distance, was not willing[J] even to lift-up[K] *his* eyes to heaven, but was striking[L] his chest[M], saying, 'God, be merciful[17] *to* me, the[18] sinner[N]!'   13
  4C. "I say *to* you, this *one* went-down[19] to his house having been declared-righteous[O], rather-than that *one*— because everyone exalting[P] himself will be humbled[Q], but the *one* humbling himself will be exalted"   14

19B.[20] And they were also[21] bringing babies[22] to Him in order that He might touch[R] them. But having seen *it*, the disciples were rebuking[S] them[23]   15

  1C. But Jesus summoned them[24], saying, "Permit[T] the children[U] to be coming to Me, and do not be forbidding[V] them. For the kingdom *of* God is *of* such[25] *ones*. °Truly[W] I say *to* you, whoever does not receive[X] the kingdom *of* God like *a* child[26] will never enter into it"   16, 17

20B.[27] And *a* certain ruler questioned Him, saying, "Good[Y] Teacher, [by] having done what shall I inherit[Z] eternal life?"[28]   18

  1C. And Jesus said *to* him, "Why do you call Me good? No one *is* good except One— God.[29] °You know the commandments[AA]— 'Do not commit-adultery[BB], do not murder[CC], do not steal, do not give-false-testimony[DD], be honoring your father and mother' "   19-20

    1D. And the *one* said, "I kept[EE] these all from *my* youth"   21
    2D. And having heard *it*, Jesus said *to* him, "One *thing* is still lacking[30] *for* you— Sell all that you have and distribute[31] *it* to poor *ones*, and you will have treasure in the heavens. And come, be following Me"   22
    3D. But the *one*, having heard these *things*, became deeply-grieved[32]. For he was extremely rich   23

  2C. And having seen him having become deeply grieved,[33] Jesus said, "How difficultly[FF] the *ones* having wealth[34] come into the kingdom *of* God. °For it is easier *that a* camel enter through *an* opening[35] *of a* needle[36] than *that a* rich *one* enter into the kingdom *of* God"   24, 25
  3C. And the *ones* having heard *it* said, "Who indeed can be saved[GG]?"   26
  4C. And the *One* said, "The *things* impossible[HH] with humans are possible with God"   27
  5C. And Peter said, "Behold— **we**, having left *our* own *things*[37], followed[38] You"   28
  6C. And the *One* said *to* them, "Truly[W] I say *to* you[39] that there is no one who left house or wife or brothers or parents or children for the sake *of* the kingdom *of* God, °who will by any means not[40] receive back[41]   29, 30

    1D. "Many-times-as-much[42] in this time[43]
    2D. "And in the coming age— eternal life"

1. Or, "do, bring about, accomplish". The grammar expects a "yes" answer, "Yes he will do it". On this word, see "does" in Rev 13:13.
2. Or "punishment". On this word, see "punishment" in 2 Thes 1:8. Same word as in Rom 12:19, "Vengeance is Mine". The phrase "execute vengeance" is elsewhere only in v 8; Act 7:24; and in Ex 12:12; Num 33:4; Judg 11:36; Ps 149:7; Ezek 16:41; 25:11, 17; 30:14; Mic 5:15. Compare "execute judgment" in Jn 5:27.
3. On this word, see "shout" in Mt 3:3. Related to "outcry" in Jam 5:4.
4. On this word, see 1 Cor 13:4. This phrase "be patient with" is elsewhere only in Mt 18:26, 29; Jam 5:7. Unlike the unrighteous judge, who refused to help the widow and who only answered because of his impatience with her, God will answer the ones crying out to Him, and He is patient with them, never tiring of hearing from them. Both His action and attitude are the opposite of this judge. Our part is to "always pray and not lose heart". Others take this word as meaning "delay". Thus some suggest Jesus means, "And He is delaying [to act] for them" from their point of view. Others make it a separate question, "night? And is He delaying over them?" Others link it to the previous question and force the tenses to agree, "will not God execute vengeance..., and [will] He delay long over them?" In these last two views, some take "them" as the chosen ones; others, as the enemies. Consult the commentaries on these and other views.
5. Or, "with haste", by God's clock. On this idiom, see Rev 1:1. That is, when the Son of Man comes, to which He next refers. Note 2 Thes 1:7-10.
6. Jesus will come and answer, but will He find those faithfully asking, like the widow? The grammar is deliberately chosen so as not to imply an answer (same grammar as in Act 8:30). Some think He asks the question to encourage us to have faith, leaving each to answer for himself. Note how this question points to the necessity of v 1. Others think He means that this will not be the case.
7. Or, "faithfulness". Literally, "the faith". Some think this means "the faith being spoken of in this parable", the faith that prays always and does not lose heart. Others think it means "faith in God", believing people. On this word, see "faith" in Eph 2:8.
8. More literally, "are", as the Greek typically phrases it.
9. Or, "the others". Same word as in v 11. On this word, see "other" in 2 Pet 3:16.
10. On this word, "treat with contempt", see 1 Thes 5:20.
11. Or, "with reference to himself". On the phrase "to himself", see 24:12. Some punctuate it, "having stood to himself, was praying...", that is, having stood apart from others.
12. This Pharisee puts himself in a class by himself.
13. Some Pharisees fasted on Thursday (the day Moses ascended the mountain) and Monday (the day he came down). They went beyond the Law, which only commanded a fast on the Day of Atonement.
14. On this word, see "collect a tenth from" in Heb 7:5.
15. Pharisees went beyond the Law, which only commanded a tithe on certain crops. They tithed even spices, Mt 23:23.
16. Or, "acquire, procure, gain". Some think this Pharisee means "all my income". Others think he means "all I buy", again going beyond the Law. On this word, see "acquire" in 1 Thes 4:4.
17. Or, "forgive, pardon". Grammatically, this word is passive, and means "be satisfied, be propitiated to me [as to Your wrath]". But from the human point of view, what this man is asking God to do is "be merciful, forgive me, accept me" as a result of being satisfied, and so the word is used in the OT. Same word as "relent" in Ex 32:14; "be atoned for" in Deut 21:8; "pardon" in 2 King 5:18; 24:4; Ps 25:11; Lam 3:42; "forgive" in 2 Chron 6:30; Ps 65:3; 78:38; 79:9. On this word, see "make-an-offering-for-satisfaction" in Heb 2:17. GK *2661*. Related to "merciful" in Heb 8:12.
18. This man thinks of himself as "the" sinner. The Pharisee thinks of others as sinners.
19. The temple was "up", v 10.
20. Parallel account at Mt 19:13; Mk 10:13.
21. Or, "even". That is, in addition to their sick ones.
22. Or, "infants". On this word, see 1:41. Luke uses "children" in v 16, the same word Mt 19:13 and Mk 10:13 have here also.
23. That is, the ones bringing them.
24. The grammar indicates Luke is referring to the babies. Jesus summoned the babies and spoke to the disciples.
25. That is, it belongs to childlike ones such as these, whether children or adults. See Mt 19:14.
26. See Mk 10:15 on this.
27. Parallel account at Mt 19:16; Mk 10:17.
28. Same exact question as in 10:25.
29. Only God is good in an absolute sense, and Jesus is good in this sense. But unless this ruler is intending to address Jesus as God, he should not be calling Him good. If Jesus is not God, He is certainly not good. He is a deceiver, just as the Pharisees said. This man's superficial use of the word "good" mirrors his superficial concept of what God required of him. He is looking at both from his own human perspective, not God's perspective. Jesus points him to God.
30. On this word, see Jam 1:5. Not the same word as in Mk 10:21.
31. As the ones in Act 4:35 did, where this same word is used.
32. Same word as in v 24. On this word, see Mt 26:38.
33. That is, Jesus saw the man become grieved. Some manuscripts omit "having become deeply grieved" {C}.
34. Or, "money". On this word, see Mk 10:23.
35. Or, "aperture, orifice". Used only here. GK *5557*. Matthew and Mark and Luke each use a different word. Jesus means that it is impossible, as is clear from v 26 and 27. Compare Mt 19:24; Mk 10:25.
36. Used only here. GK *1017*. Used of a missile, dart, arrow, the "point" of a spear. Related to "arrows" in Eph 6:16. Matthew and Mark use a different word.
37. On "*our* own *things*", see Jn 19:27.
38. Some manuscripts say instead "**we** have left everything and followed..." {N}.
39. This word is plural, addressing them all.
40. The phrase "by any means not" is the strongest negative in Greek. See 9:27.
41. Some manuscripts omit this word {C}.
42. Or, "Many times more". That is, more houses, wives, brothers, parents, children, etc., as in Mk 10:30. This person is now part of a much larger family, the family of God. Used only here. GK *4491*.
43. Or, "season". That is, during this life on earth. Same word as in Mk 10:30.

A. Rom 8:33 B. 1 Jn 3:19, persuade C. Rom 1:17 D. Mt 18:17 E. Mt 26:27, given thanks F. Mt 7:15, ravenous G. 1 Cor 6:9, wrong-doers H. Mt 6:16 J. Jn 7:17 K. 2 Cor 11:20 L. Lk 6:29 M. Jn 13:25 N. Mt 9:10 O. Rom 3:24 P. Jn 8:28, lifted up Q. Phil 4:12 R. 1 Cor 7:1 S. 2 Tim 4:2, warn T. Mt 6:12, forgive U. 1 Jn 2:14 V. 1 Cor 14:39 W. Mt 5:18 X. Mt 10:40, welcome Y. 1 Tim 5:10b Z. Gal 4:30 AA. Mk 12:28 BB. Mt 5:32 CC. Jam 4:2 DD. Mk 14:56 EE. Jn 12:25 FF. Mt 19:23, with difficulty GG. Lk 19:10 HH. Heb 6:4

21B.[1] And having taken aside the twelve, He said to them, "Behold— we are going up to Jerusalem. 31
And all the *things* having been written by the prophets *for* the Son *of* Man will be fulfilled[A]. °For 32
He will be handed-over[B] *to* the Gentiles. And He will be mocked[C] and mistreated[D] and spit-on[E].
And having whipped[F] *Him*, they will kill Him. And *on* the third day, He will rise-up²" 33

   1C. And **they** understood[G] none *of* these *things*. Indeed this statement[H] had been hidden[3] from 34
them, and they were not coming-to-know[4] the *things* being said

22B.[5] And it came about during His drawing-near[6] to Jericho, *that a* certain blind *one*[7] was sitting beside 35
the road, begging

   1C. And having heard *a* crowd proceeding through, he was inquiring[J] *as to* what this might be. 36
And they reported[K] *to* him that "Jesus the Nazarene[8] is passing by" 37
   2C. And he shouted[L], saying, "Jesus, Son *of* David,[9] have-mercy-on[M] me!" 38
   3C. And the *ones* preceding *Him* were rebuking[N] him in order that he might be silent[10]. But **he** 39
was crying out *by* much more, "Son *of* David, have mercy on me!"
   4C. And having stood [still][11], Jesus ordered[O] *that* he be brought to Him. And he having drawn 40
near, He asked him,[12] °"What do you want Me to do[13] *for* you?" 41

      1D. And the *one* said, "Master[P]— that I may see-again[Q]!"
      2D. And Jesus said *to* him, "See-again[Q]! Your faith has restored[R] you" 42
      3D. And at once he saw-again[Q]. And he was following Him, glorifying[S] God 43
      4D. And all the people, having seen *it,* gave praise[T] *to* God

23B. And having entered, he was going through Jericho. °And behold— *there was a* man being called 19:1-2
by *the* name Zacchaeus. And **he** was *a* chief-tax-collector[14]. And **he** *was* rich[U]

   1C. And he was seeking[V] to see Who Jesus was[15]. And he was not able because of the crowd, 3
because he was short *in* stature[W]
   2C. And having run ahead to the *place* in front, he went up on *a* sycamore-tree[16] in order that he 4
might see Him, because He was going to come through that *way*
   3C. And when He came upon the place, having looked-up[Q], Jesus[17] said to him, "Zacchaeus, 5
having hurried[X], come down. For today I must[Y] stay[18] at your house"
   4C. And having hurried[X], he came down and received[19] Him, rejoicing[Z] 6

      1D. And having seen *it*, they all were grumbling[AA], saying that "He went in to take-up- 7
lodging[20] with *a* sinful[BB] man"

   5C. And having stood[21], Zacchaeus said to the Lord, "Behold, Master[22]— I am giving **half *of* my** 8
possessions[CC] *to* the poor. And if I extorted[23] anything *from* anyone, I am giving *it* back fourfold"
   6C. And Jesus said with-regard-to[24] him that "Today salvation[25] came[26] *to* this house, because even 9
he[27] is *a* son *of* Abraham. °For the Son *of* Man came to seek[V] and to save[28] the lost[29]" 10
   7C.[30] And while they *were* listening-to these[31] *things*, having proceeded[32] [to speak further], He 11
spoke *a* parable because of His being near Jerusalem and their thinking[33] that the kingdom
of God was[34] about to appear[35] at-once[DD]. °Therefore He said— 12

      1D. "*A* certain well-born[36] man traveled to *a* distant country to receive *a* kingdom *for* himself,
and to return[37]
      2D. "And having called ten *of* his *own* slaves, he gave them ten minas[38], and said to them, 'Do 13
business while I am coming[39]'. °But his citizens[40] were hating[EE] him, and they sent-forth[FF] 14
a delegation after him[41], saying, 'We do not want[GG] this *one* to be-king[42] over us'

1. Parallel account at Mt 20:17; Mk 10:32.
2. Or, "stand up, get up", as in 17:19; 22:45. This word is used 108 times, usually as "stand up, arise". It is used of resurrection less than one third of the time, of which only 18 are of Christ. Will Jesus rise up in the sense of 16:31, or Jn 6:39, or Act 3:22, or Act 20:30? All of these use this same word. Note the same confusion in Jn 11:23-24; Act 13:33. This word both reveals and conceals, like "lift up" in Jn 8:28. The disciples wondered (Mk 9:10), but did not understand (Lk 18:34). GK *482*. Related to "resurrection" in Act 24:15.
3. This is a participle. It "was having been hidden". Compare 9:45. Same word as in 19:42.
4. Or, "understanding". On this word, see "know" in 1:34.
5. Parallel account at Mt 20:29; Mk 10:46. Compare Mt 9:27-31.
6. Mt 20:29 and Mk 10:46 say "going out". Some think this man was sitting on the way in, began following Jesus, was joined by a second blind man, began shouting, and both were healed on the way out. Others think Luke is referring to the new Roman Jericho (which Antony gave to Cleopatra, and Herod the Great and Archelaus enlarged) which they were entering; Matthew and Mark to the old OT Jericho which they were leaving. There are other views. On this word, see Lk 21:28. "Jericho" is GK *2637*.
7. Mt 20:30 mentions two blind men. Mark and Luke tell the story of one of them, perhaps the prominent speaker, or the one that became known to the church (Mark names him in detail).
8. Used only here in Luke. On this word, see Mt 2:23.
9. That is, Messiah. On this phrase, see Mt 9:27.
10. On this word, see 1 Cor 14:34. Not the same word as in Mk 10:48.
11. Same word as "stopped" in Mt 20:32 and Mk 10:49, but different grammar. GK *2705*.
12. Some manuscripts add "saying" {N}.
13. More literally, "want that I should do *for* you?"
14. This man was one to whom someone like Matthew (Mt 10:3) would have reported. Used only here. GK *803*.
15. More literally, "is", as the Greek typically phrases it.
16. Or, "fig-mulberry tree, sycamore-fig tree". Used only here. GK *5191*.
17. Some manuscripts say "Jesus saw him and said..." {N}.
18. Or, "remain, abide". On this word, see "abide" in Jn 15:4.
19. That is, "received Him as a guest, received Him into his house". On this word, see 10:38.
20. Same word as in 9:12.
21. Or, "stopped". The setting for this statement and the response of Jesus in v 9 and v 11 could be inside the house of Zacchaeus, perhaps at a meal, in which case he "stood [up]" to say this. Or, the setting could be on the road, after leaving his house, in which case Zacchaeus "stopped" or "stood [still]" to say this. GK *2705*.
22. Same word as "Lord" earlier. See Mt 8:2 on it.
23. On this word, see "extort with false charges" in 3:14. The grammar indicates that Zacchaeus is assuming that he had done so. Note the contrast with the man in 18:23.
24. Or, "to", as in v 5, 8, 13. GK *4639*.
25. This word means "deliverance" (Act 7:25; Phil 1:19), and "preservation" (Act 27:34), from danger or death. Elsewhere only as "salvation" (43 times), mostly in a spiritual sense (being saved from eternal death, and all that this means positively). GK *5401*. Related to "save" in v 10.
26. Or, "came about *in*, took place *in*". GK *1181*. Not the same word as in v 10.
27. Or, "because **he** also".
28. This verb means "to save, deliver, rescue". It is often used of saving from death, and from eternal death, but also of saving from disease (see "restore" in Jam 5:15), and of "saving" the people out of Egypt (Jude 5). Used 106 times. GK *5392*. Related to "salvation" in v 9, and 2:30, and Tit 2:11; and to "savior" in Lk 1:47.
29. This is a participle addressing this group as a collective whole, "that which is lost", "the [group] having become lost". On this word, see Mt 10:6.
30. Compare Mt 25:14-30.
31. That is, to the statements about salvation coming today, v 9-10. Jesus adds this parable to clarify that the salvation He was referring to was not the immediate establishment of the kingdom for Israel which the Jews expected. He will be going away to receive His kingdom, and they must do business while He is gone.
32. Or, "having added [to them]". Paraphrasing, "He went on to speak a parable". Same word as in 20:11, 12; Act 12:3. This reflects a Hebrew way of speaking. On this word, see "increase" in 17:5.
33. Or, "supposing, imagining, presuming, expecting". This word is used of "thinking, supposing, considering" something to be true; of how something "seems" to be to a person, or "has the reputation of " (see Gal 2:2) being. Whether or not the thing in view is in fact the true reality is apparent in the context. Used 62 times. GK *1506*.
34. More literally, "is", as the Greek typically phrases it.
35. Or, "appear plainly, come to light, come into sight". Elsewhere only as "sighted" in Act 21:3. GK *428*.
36. Or, "noble, socially important". On this word, see 1 Cor 1:26.
37. Jesus is referring to Himself. This is a well-understood concept, since all rulers received their kingdom (the territory and people over which they reigned) from Rome, and some went there to secure it (as Archelaus did, Mt 2:22)
38. This is a Greek unit of money worth 100 denarii (Mt 20:2). 60 minas equals one talent (see Mt 25:15). Note that each receives the same amount, one mina each. Elsewhere only in v 16, 18, 20, 24, 25. GK *3641*.
39. Or, "going". More literally, "during which *time* I am coming". Both the going *away* and the coming *back* are included. But from the viewpoint of importance to the slaves, he is "coming". On this word, see Mk 16:2.
40. The man's slaves represent the disciples; the citizens represent the Jews rejecting Jesus.
41. That is, to the one from whom this man was going to receive his kingdom. Note v 27.
42. Or, "to reign, to have a kingdom". Same word as in v 27. On this word, see "reign" in Rev 19:6. Related to "kingdom" in v 12. This very thing happened to Archelaus (see Mt 2:22 on him) when he went to Rome.

A. Rev 10:7, finished B. Mt 26:21 C. Lk 23:11 D. 1 Thes 2:2 E. Mk 14:65 F. Heb 12:6 G. Mt 13:13 H. Rom 10:17, word J. Act 23:34, learned K. 1 Jn 1:3, announcing L. Mt 3:3 M. Rom 12:8, showing mercy N. 2 Tim 4:2, warn O. Mt 14:28 P. Mt 8:2 Q. Act 22:13, look up R. Jam 5:15 S. Rom 8:30 T. Mt 21:16 U. 1 Tim 6:17 V. Phil 2:21 W. Mt 6:27, life span X. 2 Pet 3:12, hasten Y. Mt 16:21 Z. 2 Cor 13:11 AA. Lk 15:2 BB. Mt 9:10, sinner CC. Heb 10:34 DD. Mt 21:19 EE. Rom 9:13 FF. Mk 3:14, send out GG. Jn 7:17, willing

3D. "And it came about at his return[A], having received the kingdom, that[B] he said *that* these slaves[C] *to* whom he had given the money[D] *should* be called *to* him in order that he might come-to-know[E] what they[1] gained-through-doing-business[2] 15

    1E. "And the first *one* arrived, saying, 'Master[F], your mina earned[3] ten minas'. *And he said *to* him, 'Very-well[4] *done*, good slave[C]. Because you proved-to-be[5] faithful[6] in *a* very-little[7] *thing*— be[8] having authority[G] over ten cities[9]' 16-17

    2E. "And the second *one* came, saying, 'Your mina, master, made five minas'. *And he said also *to* this *one*, 'And **you**— be[10] over five cities' 18-19

    3E. "And the other[11] *one* came, saying, 'Master, behold— your mina, which I was holding, laying-away[12] in *a* handkerchief[H]. *For I was fearing you, because you are *a* harsh[13] man. You take up what you did not lay-*down*[14], and you reap what you did not sow' 20 / 21

        1F. "He[15] says *to* him, 'I will judge[J] you out of your *own* mouth, evil[K] slave. You knew that **I** am *a* harsh man, taking up what I did not lay-*down* and reaping what I did not sow![16] *And for what reason did you not give my money[D] *to be* on *a* [banker's] table[17], and **I**, having come, would have collected[18] it with interest[L]?' 22 / 23

        2F. "And he said *to* the *ones* standing-near, 'Take the mina away from him and give *it to* the *one* having the ten minas' 24

        3F. "And they said *to* him,[19] 'Master, he has ten minas [already]' 25

        4F. "'I[20] say *to* you that *to* everyone having, it will be given. But from the *one* not having, even what he has will be taken away'[21] 26

        5F. "However[22], bring here these enemies *of* mine— the *ones* not having wanted me to be king over them— and slay them in front of me" 27

7A. And having said these *things*, He was proceeding ahead, going up to Jerusalem 28

    1B.[23] And it came about when He drew-near[M] to Bethphage and Bethany— near the mountain being called '*of* Olives'— *that* He sent-forth[N] two *of* the[24] disciples, *saying, "Go to the village before *you*, in which you, while proceeding, will find *a* colt having been tied[O], on which none *of* mankind[25] ever sat. And[26] having untied[P] it, bring *it*. *And if someone asks you, 'For what reason are you untying *it*?', thus you shall say[27]— that[28] 'The Lord has need *of* it' " 29 / 30 / 31

        1C. And having gone, the *ones* having been sent-forth[N] found *it* just as He said *to* them 32

            1D. And while they *were* untying[P] the colt, its owners[29] said to them, "Why are you untying the colt?" 33

            2D. And the *ones* said that[30] "The Lord has need *of* it" 34

        2C. And they brought it to Jesus. And having cast[Q] their cloaks[R] upon the colt, they put Jesus on *it* 35

        3C. And while He *was* proceeding, they were spreading their cloaks under[31] *Him* in the road 36

        4C. And while He *was* drawing-near[M] now[32], at the descent *of* the Mount *of* Olives, the whole crowd *of* the disciples began to praise[S] God, rejoicing[33] *with a* loud voice, for all *the* miracles[T] which they saw, *saying, "Blessed[34] *is* the King[35] coming[36] in *the* name *of the* Lord. Peace in heaven and glory in *the* highest[U] [heavens]!" 37 / 38

        5C. And some *of* the Pharisees from the crowd said to Him, "Teacher, rebuke[V] Your disciples" 39

            1D. And having responded, He said, "I say *to* you, if these will be silent[W], the stones will cry out!" 40

1. Some manuscripts say "someone" {B}.
2. Used only here. GK *1390*. Same word as "do business" in v 13 (GK *4549*), with a prefix added.
3. This word, "to work besides, to earn in addition", is used only here. GK *4664*.
4. Used only here. GK *2301*. Related to the word in Mt 25:21, 23.
5. Or, "became, were". GK *1181*.
6. Or, "trustworthy". Same word as in Mt 25:21, 23; and as "trustworthy" in Lk 16:10-12. On this word, see Col 1:2.
7. Same word as in 16:10; 12:26. GK *1788*.
8. This is a command. GK *1639*.
9. Note that the reward is in proportion to what the slave earned, yet all out of proportion to it.
10. This is a command. GK *1181*.
11. Or, "the different *one*". That is, the one unlike the other nine, of whom two are given as examples. On this word, see "different" in 1 Cor 12:9. Some manuscripts omit "the" {N}, so that it says "And another came".
12. On this word, see "reserved" in Col 1:5. This slave did nothing with what he was given. What he was entrusted remained inactive.
13. Or, "strict, rigid, rigorous, exacting, austere". The slave blames his inaction on the master! "It's because of the way you are that I acted as I did". Elsewhere only in v 22. GK *893*. Our word "austere" come from this Greek word, *austeros*.
14. Literally, "you take what you did not put". It can also be rendered "take away... lay *away*", "remove... put *aside*". In a banking sense, "You withdraw what you did not deposit". You take the profits of the work of others.
15. Some manuscripts say "And he..." {K}.
16. Others take this as a question, "You knew that...?".
17. The word "banker" in Mt 25:27 is related to this word "table", which is used 15 times. GK *5544*.
18. Same word as in 3:13.
19. Some think this is a continuation of the parable, "they (the ones told to take it away in v 24) said *to* him (the master)". Others think it is a parenthetical statement, "they (the listeners) said *to* Him (Jesus)". Some manuscripts omit this verse {A}.
20. Some manuscripts say "For I..." {K}.
21. The fate of this slave is not given. He has his allotment taken away, but he is not explicitly classed as an enemy. Here, the treatment of his slaves and his enemies is contrasted. This may illustrate 1 Cor 3:15. But if it is correct to use the similar parable spoken later to the disciples in Mt 25 to clarify this point, then this slave represents the nominal believer who is cast out with the enemies in Mt 25:30, illustrating Mt 7:21-23; Lk 13:28.
22. Or, "Nevertheless, But". In contrast with the master's treatment of his own slaves, his enemies are killed. On this word, see "nevertheless" in Mt 11:22.
23. Parallel account at Mt 21:1; Mk 11:1; Jn 12:12.
24. Some manuscripts say "His" {K}.
25. On this idiom, see Mk 11:2.
26. Some manuscripts omit this word {N}.
27. Some manuscripts add "*to* him" {N}.
28. Or, "say— 'Because the Lord has...' ". This word may be rendered "that", introducing the quote, or "because", as part of the quote. Same word as in v 34. Mk 11:3 omits it. GK *4022*.
29. Or, "masters". On this word, see "master" in Mt 8:2.
30. Or, "said, "Because the Lord...". See the note in v 31.
31. This word "spread under" is used only here. GK *5716*. Related to the word in Mt 21:8; Mk 11:8.
32. Or, this may be punctuated "drawing near, now at the descent". This word means "already, now". Same word as in 23:44. On this word, see "already" in Mt 24:32.
33. Some render this participle in an adverbial sense, "joyfully", "began to joyfully praise God *with a* loud...".
34. This is a participle, "Having been blessed". On this word, see 6:28.
35. Luke has already noted their expectations, v 11.
36. Some manuscripts say "*is* the *One* coming *as* King in..." {C}.

A. Lk 10:35 B. Lk 5:1 C. Rom 6:17 D. Mt 25:27 E. Lk 1:34, know F. Mt 8:2 G. Rev 6:8 H. Jn 11:44, face cloth J. Mt 7:1 K. Act 25:18
L. Mt 25:27 M. Lk 21:28 N. Mk 3:14, send out O. 1 Cor 7:27, bound P. Mt 5:19, break Q. 1 Pet 5:7 R. 1 Pet 3:3, garments S. Rom 15:11
T. 1 Cor 12:10 U. Mt 21:9 V. 2 Tim 4:2, warn W. Mk 4:39, be still

	6C. And when He drew-near[A], having seen the city, He wept[B] over it,°saying that "If you, even you, had known on this day[1] the *things* for peace[2]! But now[3] they were hidden[C] from your eyes. Because days will come[D] upon you—	41-42

43 |

      1D. "And your enemies will throw-up *a* palisade[4] *against* you, and encircle[5] you, and confine[6] you from all sides[7]

      2D. "And they will dash you to the ground[8], and your children[E] within you[9]   44

      3D. "And they will not leave *a* stone upon *a* stone within you

      4D. "Because[10] you did not recognize[11] the time *of* your visitation[12]"

2B.[13] And having entered into the temple, He began to throw-out[F] the *ones* selling[14],°saying *to* them, "It has been written [in Isa 56:7], 'And My house[G] shall be[15] *a* house *of* prayer'. But **you** made it *a* den[16] *of* robbers[H]"   45-46

    1C. And He was teaching daily in the temple   47

    2C. And the chief priests and the scribes and the leading[J] *ones of* the people were seeking to destroy[K] Him. °And they were not finding what they might do, for all the people hung-on[17] Him[18], listening   48

3B.[19] And it came about on one *of* the[20] days while He *was* teaching the people in the temple and announcing-the-good-news[L], *that* the chief priests and the scribes with the elders stood-near[21]. And they spoke, saying to Him, "Tell us, by what-kind-of[22] authority[M] are You doing these *things*, or who is the *one* having given You this authority?"   20:1

  2

    1C. And having responded, He said to them, "**I** also will ask you *a*[23] thing[24], and you tell Me— Was the baptism[N] *of* John from heaven, or from humans[O]?"   3

  4

    2C. And the *ones* reasoned[25] with themselves, saying that   5

      1D. "If we say, 'From heaven', He will say, 'For[26] what reason did you not believe[P] him?'

      2D. "But if we say, 'From humans', all the people will stone us to death[27]. For they are convinced[28] *that* John is[29] *a* prophet[Q]"   6

      3D. And they answered *that they did* not know from where *it was*   7

    3C. And Jesus said *to* them, "Nor am **I** telling you by what-kind-of authority I am doing these *things*"   8

    4C.[30] And He began to tell this parable to the people— "*A* certain[31] man planted *a* vineyard and rented it *to* farmers[R], and went-on-a-journey[S] *for* considerable[T] periods-of-time[32]   9

      1D. "And *at harvest* time, he sent-forth[U] *a* slave[V] to the farmers so that they would[33] give *to* him from the fruit *of* the vineyard. But the farmers sent him out empty-*handed*[W], having beaten[X] *him*   10

      2D. "And he proceeded[34] to send[Y] another[35] slave. But the *ones*, having beaten[X] and dishonored[Z] that *one* also, sent *him* out empty-*handed*   11

      3D. "And he proceeded to send *a* third. But the *ones* also threw out this *one*, having wounded[36] *him*   12

      4D. "And the owner[37] *of* the vineyard said, 'What shall I do? I will send my beloved[AA] son. Perhaps[38] they will have-regard-for[BB] this *one*'   13

        1E. "But having seen him, the farmers were reasoning[CC] with one another, saying, 'This *one* is the heir[DD]. Let[39] us kill him in order that the inheritance[EE] may become ours'   14

        2E. "And having thrown him outside *of* the vineyard, they killed *him*   15

1. Some manuscripts say "known, even indeed on this your day, the *things*..." {B}.
2. That is, the things that would result in or lead to peace, as this same phrase is used in 14:32. Some manuscripts say "your peace" {B}.
3. Or, "But as it is". GK *3814*.
4. Or, "siege-work". That is, a fence of stakes or timbers fortifying the embankments or ramparts of an attacking army. In a nonmilitary sense, it means "stake, pole", and is used of the stakes in a grape vineyard. Used only here. GK *5918*. Same word as in Deut 20:19, where Israel was commanded not to cut down trees for such a thing; and in Eccl 9:14; Isa 29:3; 37:33; Ezek 4:2; 21:22; 26:8. The Romans built one during their attack in A.D. 70. The Jews burned it.
5. Or, "surround". Used only here. GK *4333*. Related to "surround" in 21:20.
6. Or, "hold you in, enclose, control". On this word, see "control" in 2 Cor 5:14.
7. The three things mentioned here were a standard military strategy against a walled city for centuries. Jesus is predicting that Jerusalem would be attacked. Next, He predicts the outcome of the attack.
8. This word, "dash to the ground" is used of buildings or cities, meaning "level to the ground, raze to the ground", and of people (as in Ps 137:9; Hos 10:14; 14:1; Nah 3:10). Here it is used of both. Used only here. GK *1610*. Related to "ground" in Act 22:7.
9. That is, the children of Israel within Jerusalem.
10. This is an idiom meaning "in return for". See 2 Thes 2:10 on it.
11. Or, "know, come to know". On this word, see "know" in 1:34.
12. Same word as in 1 Pet 2:12. That is, the time when God visited them in the ministry of Jesus.
13. Parallel account at Mt 21:12; Mk 11:15. Compare Jn 2:13-22.
14. Some manuscripts say "the *ones* selling and buying in it" {N}.
15. Some manuscripts say "written that "My house is..." {N}.
16. Or, "hideout". On this word, and on "robbers", see Mt 21:13.
17. Used only here. GK *1717*. Related to "hang" in Act 10:39.
18. Or, "hung-on, listening-to Him". This could mean the people paid close attention to Jesus while listening to Him, or that they persisted or kept on listening to Him. In either case, the physical presence of the people listening to Jesus prevented the Jewish leaders from acting against Him.
19. Parallel account at Mt 21:23; Mk 11:27.
20. This appears to be Tuesday morning (see Mt 21:17, 18). Some manuscripts say "those" {N}.
21. On this word, see "suddenly came upon" in 21:34.
22. Or, "what". That of a Prophet? That of Messiah? From heaven or from humans? On this word, see Mt 21:23.
23. Some manuscripts say "one" {N}, as in Mt 21:24; Mk 11:29.
24. Or, "question". Same word as in Mt and Mk. On this word, see "word" in 1 Cor 12:8.
25. Or, the leaders "inferred from premises". Used only here. GK *5199*. Related to "discussing" in Mt 21:25; Mk 11:31. In Aristotle it means "to infer by way of syllogism". In other words, they reasoned "if this, then this", as is seen next.
26. Some manuscripts say "Then for what reason..." {N}, as in Mt 21:25; Mk 11:31.
27. This verb "stone to death" is used only here. GK *2902*. Related to "to stone" in Jn 8:5; 10:31; Act 14:19, etc.
28. This is a participle, they "are having been persuaded" and therefore "are convinced". On this word, see "persuade" in 1 Jn 3:19.
29. That is, they are convinced that John holds this status. They are holding John as a prophet, as Mt 21:26 says. Or, if Luke intends this in a historical sense, we English speakers would change the tense to "was" a prophet.
30. Parallel account at Mt 21:33; Mk 12:1.
31. Some manuscripts omit this word {C}.
32. Or, "considerable times", plural. This is one of Luke's idioms. Here, it refers to years. In 23:8, it probably means "months". Elsewhere the idiom is only singular, "considerable time", in Lk 8:27; Act 8:11; 14:3; 27:9. The word "considerable" is GK *2653*.
33. More literally, "will".
34. This idiom, he "proceeded" to do something, is a Hebrew way of speaking. It is also in v 12; 19:11.
35. This word (on which, see "different" in 1 Cor 12:9) is not the same word as in Mk 12:4.
36. Elsewhere only in Act 19:16. GK *5547*. Our word "traumatize" comes from this word *traumatizo*. Related to "wound" in 10:34.
37. Or, "master". On this word, see "master" in Mt 8:2.
38. Or, "probably". Used only here. GK *2711*. Same word as in Gen 32:21; Jer 26:3; 36:3, 7.
39. Some manuscripts say "Come, let us..." {N}.

A. Lk 21:28 B. Jn 11:33 C. Jn 8:59 D. Jn 8:42, am here E. 1 Jn 3:1 F. Jn 12:31, cast out G. Mk 3:20 H. Mt 21:13 J. 1 Cor 15:3, first K. 1 Cor 1:18, perish L. Act 5:42 M. Rev 6:8 N. Mk 1:4 O. Mt 4:4, mankind P. Jn 3:36 Q. 1 Cor 12:28 R. Jn 15:1 S. Mt 21:33 T. 2 Cor 3:5, sufficient U. Mk 3:14, send out V. Rom 6:17 W. 1 Thes 2:1, empty X. Jn 18:23 Y. Jn 20:21 Z. Act 5:41 AA. Mt 3:17 BB. Lk 18:2 CC. Lk 5:21 DD. Rom 8:17 EE. Eph 1:14

5D. "Therefore, what will the owner^A *of* the vineyard do *to* them? °He will come and destroy^B these farmers, and give the vineyard *to* others" 16
6D. And having heard *it*, they¹ said, "May it never be²!"
7D. But the *One*, having looked-at^C them, said, "Then what is³ this having been written [in Ps 118:22]— '*The* stone which the *ones* building rejected^D, this became⁴ *the* head *of the* corner⁵'? 17

    1E. "Everyone having fallen upon that stone will be broken-to-pieces^E. And⁶ upon whomever it may fall, it will crush^F him" 18

5C. And the scribes and the chief priests⁷ sought to put *their* hands on Him at the very hour. And⁸ they feared the people. For⁹ they¹⁰ knew that He spoke this parable against them 19

4B.¹¹ And having closely-watched^G Him, they sent forth spies¹² pretending¹³ themselves to be righteous¹⁴, in order that they might take-hold-of¹⁵ *a* statement^H *of* His, so as to hand Him over *to* the rule^J and the authority^K *of* the governor^L. °And they questioned^M Him, saying, "Teacher, we know that You speak and teach correctly¹⁶. And You do not receive *the* face¹⁷, but You teach the way *of* God in accordance with truth¹⁸. °Is it lawful^N *that* we *should* give *a* tribute¹⁹ ***to*** **Caesar**, or not?" 20 21 22

1C. But having perceived their craftiness^O, He said to them, °"Show²⁰ Me *a* denarius²¹. *Of* whom does it have *an* image²² and inscription?" And the *ones* said, "*Of* Caesar^P" 23-24
2C. And the *One* said to them, "Well-then²³, give-back^Q the *things of* Caesar *to* Caesar, and the *things of* God *to* God" 25
3C. And they were not able to take-hold-of *a* word²⁴ *of* His in the presence *of* the people. And having marveled^R at His answer, they became silent^S 26

5B.²⁵ And having come to *Him*, some *of* the Sadducees— the *ones* denying²⁶ *that there* is *a* resurrection^T— questioned^M Him, °saying 27 28

1C. "Teacher, Moses wrote *to* us [in Deut 25:5] *that* if *a* brother *of* someone dies having *a* wife, and this²⁷ *one* is²⁸ childless, that his brother should take the wife and raise-up-from^U her *a* seed²⁹ *for* his brother

    1D. "So there were seven brothers. And the first, having taken *a* wife, died childless. °And the second.³⁰ °And the third took her. And similarly, the seven also did not leave-behind^V children, and died. °Last³¹, the woman also died 29-30 31 32
    2D. "The woman, therefore, at the resurrection— *of* which *of* them does she become *the* wife? For the seven had her *as* wife" 33

2C. And Jesus said³² *to* them, "The sons *of* this age³³ marry^W and are given-in-marriage 34

    1D. "But the *ones* having been considered-worthy³⁴ to attain³⁵ that age and the resurrection from *the* dead³⁶ neither marry, nor are they given-in-marriage^X 35

        1E. "For they are not even still able to die,³⁷ for they are angel-like³⁸ 36
        2E. "And they are sons *of* God,³⁹ being sons *of* the resurrection⁴⁰

    2D. "But that the dead are raised^Y, even Moses showed⁴¹ at the bush⁴² [in Ex 3:16]— when he calls^Z *the* Lord the 'God *of* Abraham and God *of* Isaac and God *of* Jacob'. °Now He is not God *of* dead *ones*, but *of* living *ones*. For *to* Him⁴³ all are alive" 37 38

1. That is, the people, v 9.
2. Or, "happen, come about, take place". GK *1181*.
3. That is, what does this mean? GK *1639*.
4. This is an idiom, literally, "came-to-be for", a Hebrew way of speaking.
5. On this phrase, see Mk 12:10.
6. Or, "But". On the meaning of this verse, see Mt 21:44.
7. Some manuscripts say "the chief priests and the scribes" {N}.
8. This is the Greek word order. This may be separate and additional from what precedes. Or, "And-*yet* they feared...", giving the reason they failed to seize Him.
9. Luke may be giving the reason for the seeking and the fear. Or it may be punctuated, "people, for they knew...", giving the reason for their fear; or, "hour, and-*yet* they feared the people. For they knew...", giving the reason they sought Him.
10. Luke could mean "the people" knew this. In this case, Luke moves from "the people" (singular) to "they knew" (plural), reflecting common grammar found also in Lk 1:21; 9:12; 13: 14; 20:6; etc. Or, "they" may continue to refer to the scribes and priests, so that the subject stays the same throughout the verse. The scribes and priests "sought... and feared... for they knew...". In any case, they fear the effect Jesus might have on the people. Everyone understood Him— people (v 16), and priests— and the priests feared how the people would respond, and sought to get rid of Jesus. Mk 12:12 is a parallel verse with the same issues. Compare also Lk 22:2; Mt 21:46.
11. Parallel account at Mt 22:15; Mk 12:13.
12. This word means "one secretly put in as an agent, hired to lie in wait". Used only here. GK *1588*.
13. Or, "acting the part". Used only here. GK *5693*. Related to "hypocrite" in Mt 6:2; "hypocrisy" in Gal 2:13.
14. That is, the spies pretended that they were sincerely struggling with this matter of conscience in v 21.
15. Or, "grasp, seize, catch, get, obtain". Same word as in v 26. Elsewhere only in Mt 14:31; Mk 8:23; Lk 9:47; 14:4; 23:26; Act 9:27; 16:19; 17:19; 18:17; 21:30, 33; 23:19; 1 Tim 6:12, 19; Heb 2:16; 8:9. GK *2138*.
16. Same word as in 7:43; 10:28. On this word, see Mk 7:35.
17. This phrase "to receive the face" is a Hebrew way of speaking, meaning "to show partiality, respect of persons". It is also in Gal 2:6. See the related word "respect of persons" in Jam 2:1.
18. On "in accordance with truth", see 4:25.
19. That is, a tax to a foreign state. On this word, see Rom 13:6.
20. Some manuscripts say "Why are you testing Me? Show..." {N}. This word (on which, see 1 Tim 6:15) is related to the word in Mt 22:19 (on which see Act 18:28).
21. This is a Roman silver coin. On this word, see Mt 20:2.
22. Or, "likeness". On this word, see Col 1:15.
23. Or, "So indeed". On this word, see "so indeed" in 1 Cor 9:26.
24. Or, "saying". On this word, see Rom 10:17.
25. Parallel account at Mt 22:23; Mk 12:18.
26. Or, "speaking-out-against". On this word, see "contradict" in Rom 10:21. Some manuscripts say "saying" {C}, so that it says "the *ones* saying *that there* is no resurrection". Compare Act 23:8.
27. That is, this dead brother.
28. Some manuscripts say "dies" {N}.
29. That is, offspring, descendants. On this word, see Heb 11:11.
30. Some manuscripts say "And the second took the wife, and this *one* died childless" {N}.
31. Same word as in Mt 22:27. Mark 12:22 uses a different word.
32. Some manuscripts say "And having responded, Jesus said..." {N}.
33. On this phrase, see 16:8.
34. On this word, see 2 Thes 1:5. Compare Paul's statement in Act 26:7.
35. Or, "obtain, gain, find, reach". That is, considered worthy by God. How we view ourselves will not be relevant, Mt 7:22-23. The grounds of this worthiness are not given here. Same word as in Act 24:2; and as "obtain" in Act 26:22; 27:3; 2 Tim 2:10; Heb 8:6; 11:35. Used 12 times. GK *5593*. Related to "obtain" in Heb 11:33.
36. That is, the age entered by means of the resurrection of the righteous, the age to come. All not "considered worthy" obtain the other resurrection, Rev 20:5, 15; Jn 5:29.
37. If such people cannot die, there is no need to procreate; hence, no need for marriage and families.
38. That is, not subject to death. This adjective is used only here. GK *2694*. Mt 22:30 and Mk 12:25 say "like angels".
39. That is, such people live as members of God's family, in direct relation to Him, not in separate families. Heavenly society will not be organized on the basis of humanly generated families. On "sons of God", see Rom 8:14.
40. They are physically "born" into His family through the resurrection. They are sons "proceeding from" or "originating in" the resurrection. Their new life (in this full sense) as God's family members begins with the resurrection. By "sons", Jesus means "family members", "offspring", not "males". On "sons", see Gal 3:7.
41. Or, "indicated, disclosed, made known, revealed". Elsewhere only as "disclose" in Jn 11:57; Act 23:30; 1 Cor 10:28. GK *3606*.
42. That is, in the passage about the burning bush.
43. To us they seem to no longer exist, but to God they continue to be alive.

A. Mt 8:2, master   B. 1 Cor 1:18, perish   C. Mk 8:25, seeing   D. Heb 12:17   E. Mt 21:44   F. Mt 21:44   G. Lk 6:7   H. 1 Cor 12:8, word
J. Col 1:18, beginning   K. Rev 6:8   L. Mt 27:2   M. Lk 9:18   N. 1 Cor 6:12   O. 1 Cor 3:19   P. Lk 3:1   Q. Mt 16:27, render   R. Rev 17:8
S. 1 Cor 14:34   T. Act 24:15   U. Mk 12:19   V. Act 6:2   W. 1 Cor 7:9   X. 1 Cor 7:38   Y. Mt 28:6, arose   Z. Jn 12:49, say

3C. And having responded, some *of* the scribes said, "Teacher, You spoke well". °For¹ they were no longer daring^A to ask Him anything	39-40
6B.² And He said to them, "How *is it that* they say *that* the Christ is David's son?	41
1C. "For³ David himself says in *the* book *of* Psalms [110:1], '*The* Lord said *to* my Lord^B, "Be sitting on My right *side* °until I put Your enemies *as a* footstool *of* Your feet" '	42 / 43
1D. "Therefore David calls^C Him 'Lord'. And how is He his son?"⁴	44
7B.⁵ And while all the people *were* listening, He said *to* His⁶ disciples, °"Beware^D of the scribes—	45-46
1C. "The *ones* delighting⁷ to walk around in robes, and loving^E greetings in the marketplaces, and seats-of-honor^F in the synagogues, and places-of-honor^G at the banquets^H	
2C. "Who are devouring⁸ the houses *of* the widows, and praying long *for a* pretense⁹	47
3C. "These *ones* will receive greater condemnation'"	
8B.¹⁰ And having looked-up^K, He saw the rich^L *ones* throwing their gifts into the treasury^M	21:1
1C. And He saw¹¹ *a* certain needy¹² widow throwing two leptos¹³ there	2
2C. And He said, "Truly¹⁴ I say *to* you that this poor^N widow threw more *than* all.¹⁵ °For all these *ones* threw into the gifts¹⁶ out of the *money* abounding¹⁷ *to* them. But this *one*, out of her lack¹⁸, threw all the living¹⁹ which she was having²⁰	3-4
9B.²¹ And while some *were* talking about the temple— that it has been adorned^O *with* beautiful^P stones and gifts-dedicated-to-God²²— He said, °"*As to* these *things* which you are observing^Q— days²³ will come during which *a* stone on *a* stone will not be left which will not be torn-down^R"	5 / 6
1C. And they questioned^S Him, saying, "Teacher—	7
1D. "When therefore will these *things* happen²⁴?	
2D. "And what *will be* the sign^T when these *things* are about to take place?"	
2C. And the *One* said, "Be watching-out^U *that* you may not be deceived^V	8
1D. "For many will come on the basis of My name²⁵, saying, '**I** am *the One*²⁶', and, 'The time has drawn-near^W'. Do not²⁷ go after them	
2D. "And whenever you hear-*of* wars and disturbances²⁸, do not be frightened²⁹. For these *things* must^X take place first, but *it is* not immediately^Y the end³⁰"	9
3C. Then He was saying *to* them³¹—	10
1D. "Nation will arise³² against nation, and kingdom against kingdom. °There will be both great earthquakes, and famines³³ and plagues³⁴ in various places³⁵. There will be both fearful³⁶ *things* and great signs^T from heaven³⁷	11
2D.³⁸ "But before all these³⁹ *things*—	12
1E. "They will put their hands on you and persecute^Z *you*— *they* handing *you* over to the synagogues and prisons, *you* being led-away before kings and governors, for the sake of⁴⁰ My name	

1. The scribes complimented Jesus, for they no longer dared to test Him. Some manuscripts say "And" {N}.
2. Parallel account at Mt 22:41; Mk 12:35.
3. Some manuscripts say "And" {N}.
4. On this question, see Mk 12:37.
5. Parallel account at Mt 23:1; Mk 12:38.
6. Some manuscripts omit this word {C}, so that it says "the disciples".
7. Same word as Mk 12:38, on which see Col 2:18.
8. That is, these scribes take financial advantage of widows. On this word, see Mk 12:40.
9. That is, for a falsely alleged motive. On this word, see Phil 1:18.
10. Parallel account at Mk 12:41.
11. Some manuscripts add "also" {K}.
12. Or, "poor". Used only here. GK *4293*. Related to the word in 2 Cor 9:9. Used of the working poor.
13. On this word, see Mk 12:42. That is, two small coins. One leptos was 128th of a denarius.
14. Or, "Truthfully". On this word, see Mt 14:33.
15. Some think Jesus means more than any one of them; others, more than all of them combined.
16. Same word as in v 1. That is, in among the other gifts or offerings in the treasury box containing them. On this word, see Mt 5:23. Some manuscripts add "*of* God" {B}, that is "the gifts *belonging to* God".
17. Or, "overflowing, left over". On this word, see 2 Cor 8:2.
18. Or, "shortcoming, deficiency". On this word see Phil 2:30. Related to "need" in Mk 12:44, and "be in need" in Lk 15:14. The rich gave from their overflow, their excess, their having more than enough; the widow gave from her shortfall, her not having enough.
19. Or, "livelihood, means of living". On this word, see "life" in 1 Jn 2:16.
20. Jesus is not criticizing the former. He is showing that God sees (and rewards) the realities, not the appearances.
21. Parallel account at Mt 24:1; Mk 13:1.
22. Or, "sacred gifts, consecrated offerings, votive offerings". Used only here. GK *356*.
23. In v 24, Luke calls these days, "the times of the Gentiles".
24. Or, "be". On this word, see Mt 16:22.
25. On "on the basis of My name", see Act 2:38.
26. Or, "I am *He*". That is, the Christ, Mt 24:5.
27. Some manuscripts say "Therefore do not..." {N}.
28. Or, "insurrections, disorders, anarchies, instabilities". On this word, see "disorder" in Jam 3:16.
29. Or, "scared, terrified". Elsewhere only in 24:37. GK *4765*. Related to "terror" in 1 Pet 3:6.
30. On this word, see Mt 24:6; Mk 13:7.
31. Some think this phrase indicates the beginning of a new subject (perhaps jumping to the end time), or a new treatment of the subject of v 8-9. Others think this phrase is intended to place emphasis on v 10-11, which continues on from v 8-9 with the non-signs about which they should not be disturbed or frightened. In this case, all of v 10-11 would be point 3D.
32. Or, "be raised". Same word as in Mt 24:7; Mk 13:8.
33. Same word as in Mt 24:7; Mk 13:8; Lk 4:25; 15:14, 17; Act 7:11; 11:28; Rom 8:35; Rev 6:8; 18:8. Elsewhere only as "hunger" in 2 Cor 11:27. GK *3350*.
34. Or, "pestilences". That is, epidemic diseases. On this word, see Act 24:5.
35. Same phrase as in Mt 24:7. Mt 24:8 and Mk 13:8 call these "birthpains". Some manuscripts say "great earthquakes in various places, and famines and plagues" {N}.
36. Or, "terrors, horrors", fearful sights or events. Used only here. Related to "fear" in Eph 5:21.
37. This sentence is only in Luke. Some think it refers to the things mentioned in v 25, from which Jesus steps back in time in v 12. In this case, v 10-11, or this sentence only, jumps to His coming in the end time. Others think v 10-11 all belongs to A.D. 70, from which He steps back in time in v 12.
38. Compare also Mt 10:17-23; Jn 16:1-4.
39. Some think Jesus is stepping back in time from the things of v 10-11, or v 11, and that He means "before they all occur". Others take "before" in the sense of "above, higher in rank", meaning that the following things are the "foremost" of all the things about which they should not be deceived or frightened, continuing on from v 8-11.
40. Or, "because of ". It is "because of " from the persecutor's point of view; "for the sake of " from the believer's point of view, as in Mt 10:18; Mk 13:9. GK *1915*.

A. 2 Cor 11:21 B. Mt 8:2, master C. Rom 8:30 D. Mt 10:17 E. Jn 21:15, affectionately love F. Mt 23:6 G. Mt 23:6 H. Lk 14:12, dinner J. Jn 9:39, judgment K. Act 22:13 L. 1 Tim 6:17 M. Mk 12:41 N. Gal 4:9 O. 1 Tim 2:9 P. 1 Tim 5:10a, good Q. Lk 10:18, seeing R. Mt 24:2 S. Lk 9:18 T. 2 Thes 2:9 U. Rev 1:11, see V. Jam 5:19, err W. Lk 21:28 X. Mt 16:21 Y. Mt 13:5 Z. 2 Tim 3:12

| Luke 21:13 | 274 | Verse |

    1F. "It will turn-out[1] *for* you *to be* for *a* testimony[2] 13
    2F.[3] "So put[4] in your hearts not to prepare-beforehand[5] to speak-a-defense[6] 14

      1G. "For **I**[7] will give you *a* mouth[8], and wisdom, which all the *ones* being 15
        opposed[A] *to* you will not be able to resist[9] or to speak-against[10]

   2E. "And you will be handed-over[B] even by parents and brothers and relatives and 16
     friends. And they will put *some* of you to death
   3E. "And you will be being hated[C] by all because of My name 17
   4E. "And *a* hair of your head will by no means be lost[11]. *Gain[12] your souls[13] by your 18-19
     endurance[14]

 3D.[15] "But when you see Jerusalem being surrounded[16] by army-encampments[17], then 20
   recognize[18] that her desolation[19] has drawn-near[D]

   1E. "Then[20] let the *ones* in Judea be fleeing[E] to the mountains 21

     1F.[21] "And let the *ones* in *the* midst[F] *of* her[22] be going-out[23]
     2F. "And let the *ones* in the fields not be entering into her
     3F. "Because these are days *of* vengeance[G], *that* all the *things* having been written 22
       may be fulfilled[H]
     4F. "Woe *to* the *ones* having *a* child in *the* womb[J], and *to* the *ones* nursing[K] in 23
       those days

   2E. "For there will be *a* great distress[24] upon the land[25], and wrath[L] *against* this people[26]

     1F. "And they will fall *by the* edge[M] *of the* sword 24
     2F. "And they will be taken-captive[N] to all the nations

 4D. "And Jerusalem will be being trampled[27] by *the* Gentiles[28] until[29] which *time the* times *of*
   the Gentiles[30] are fulfilled[O]
 5D.[31] "And[32] there will be signs in *the* sun and moon and stars, and on earth[P], *the* anguish[33] *of* 25
   nations in perplexity[34] *about the* roar[35] *of the* sea and *wave*-tossing[36]—

   1E. "People fainting[37] from fear[Q] and *the* expectation[38] *of the things* coming-upon[39] the 26
     world[R], for the powers[S] *of* the heavens will be shaken[T]

 6D. "And then[40] they will see the Son *of* Man coming in *a* cloud with power[S] and great glory 27
 7D. "Now [when] these *things*[41] [are] beginning to take place, straighten-up[42] and lift-up[U] 28
   your heads, because your redemption[V] is drawing-near[43]"

4C.[44] And He spoke *a* parable *to* them— "Look at the fig-tree[W], and all the trees[45]. *When they 29-30
   already[46] put-forth[47] *leaves*, seeing *it*, you know from yourselves[48] that summer is already near[49]

   1D. "So also you— when you see these *things* taking place, you know[50] that the kingdom *of* 31
     God is near.[51] *Truly[X] I say *to* you that this generation[52] will by no means pass away 32
     until all *things* take place

     1E. "Heaven and earth will pass away, but My words will by-no-means[53] pass away 33

1. Or, "lead to". Same word as in Phil 1:19. Elsewhere only as "get out" in Lk 5:2; Jn 21:9. GK *609*.
2. That is, it will become an opportunity to bear witness to Jesus before them. Compare Mt 10:18.
3. Compare also Lk 12:11-12.
4. Same word as in 9:44.
5. Or, "premeditate, practice beforehand". Used only here. GK *4627*. Related to "take care with" in 1 Tim 4:15.
6. Or, "to defend *yourself*, to make *a* defense". Compare 12:11, where this same word occurs. Same word as in Act 19:33; 24:10; 25:8; 26:1, 2, 24. Elsewhere only as "defend" in Rom 2:15; 2 Cor 12:19. GK *664*. Related to "defense" in 1 Pet 3:15.
7. Compare 12:12; Mk 13:11; Mt 10:20.
8. That is, a mouth speaking words, the ability to speak.
9. Or, "stand against". On this word, see Eph 6:13.
10. On this word, see "contradict" in Rom 10:21. Act 4:14 is an example of this very thing, using this word.
11. Or, "perish". Some think Jesus means "eternally", since "some" will be put to death, v 16. Others think He means "without God's permission". On this word see "perish" in 1 Cor 1:18.
12. Or, "Acquire, Get, Obtain". On this word, see "acquire" in 1 Thes 4:4. Instead of a command, some manuscripts say "you will gain your souls..." {C}. Compare Mt 24:13.
13. Or, "lives". Jesus is speaking of their eternal lives, since they will put "some" to death, v 16. On this word see Jam 5:20.
14. On this word, see Jam 1:3. That is, endurance in faith while suffering to the point of death.
15. Parallel account at Mt 24:15; Mk 13:14. Compare Lk 19:43-44.
16. On this word, see Jn 10:24. Related to "encircle" in 19:43.
17. This word is also used to refer simply to the "armies, legions". That is, when you see armies preparing to attack the city. Used only here. GK *5136*. Jesus is referring to the destruction of Jerusalem in A.D. 70, as seen clearly in v 24.
18. Or, "know". On this word see "know" in 1:34.
19. On this word, see Mt 24:15. Related to "desolate" in Mt 23:38.
20. Or, "At that time". On this word, see Mt 24:9. Same word as in v 20, 27. The following three things are the opposite of what people in ancient times normally did, and the opposite of what the Jews did in A.D. 70. The local people normally ran into a city, hoping to find safety and protection there, and to defend themselves.
21. Compare also Lk 17:31-32.
22. That is, Jerusalem.
23. Or, "leaving, departing". Used only here. GK *1774*.
24. On this word, see "necessity" in 1 Cor 7:26. Not related to "affliction" in Mt 24:21.
25. Or, "earth". That is, the land of Israel. On this word, see Rev 7:1.
26. On "this people", see 1 Cor 14:21.
27. Or, "tread on". On this word, see 10:19.
28. Or, "nations", as in v 24, 25. On this word see Act 15:23.
29. Since this begins the times of the Gentiles, the description of v 20-24 must refer to the destruction of Jerusalem in A.D. 70, and v 12-19 to the things preceding it. Compare Mt 24:29; Mk 13:24.
30. Some think Jesus means the times of their ascendancy over Israel; others, the times during which God uses them for the execution of His judgment upon Israel; others, the times during which they will be saved by the gospel. There are other views. Compare Rom 11:25.
31. Parallel account at Mt 24:29; Mk 13:24.
32. Jesus is now giving the things following or concluding the times of the Gentiles, the global events occurring at His return.
33. Or, "distress". This word refers to the anguish that comes from being held or constrained or confined or controlled by circumstances beyond one's control. Elsewhere only in 2 Cor 2:4. GK *5330*. Related to "control" in 2 Cor 5:14.
34. Or, "uncertainty". That is, the nations are uncertain, at a loss, seeing no way out, perplexed about what to do. Used only here. GK *680*. Related to the verb "to be perplexed" in 2 Cor 4:8.
35. Or, "sound, noise". It means the sound of whatever is referred to in the context; here, of the sea. Used only here. GK *2492*. Related to "news" in 4:37. Some manuscripts have this word as a verb {N}, making this phrase point 1E., "... perplexity— *The* sea and waves roaring".
36. Or, "shaking". This noun refers to a tossing motion, and is used of earthquakes and sea waves. Used only here. GK *4893*. Related to "shaken" in v 26. Some render it "waves", "roar *of* the sea and waves".
37. Or, "expiring". This word means "breathe out, stop breathing", and is used to mean both "faint, swoon" and "expire, die". Used only here. GK *715*.
38. Or, "anticipation". Elsewhere only in Act 12:11. GK *4660*. Related to "wait in expectation" in 3:15.
39. Or, "coming against", as in 11:22. Used 9 times. GK *2088*.
40. Or, "at that time". Same word as in v 21.
41. Some think Jesus is referring back to v 25; others, to v 20; others, to v 10.
42. Or, "stand erect". Same word as in Jn 8:7, 10. Elsewhere only as "bend-up" in Lk 13:11. GK *376*.
43. Same word as in v 20; Mt 4:17; Lk 10:9; 18:35; Rom 13:12; Jam 4:8; 1 Pet 4:7. Used 42 times. GK *1581*. Related to "near" in v 30.
44. Parallel account at Mt 24:32; Mk 13:28.
45. This is the common word for "tree", used 25 times. GK *1285*.
46. On this word, used twice in this verse, see Mt 24:32.
47. Elsewhere only as "put forward" in Act 19:33. GK *4582*.
48. That is, from your own knowledge and experience. "From yourselves" is the same phrase as in 12:57, and as "from ourselves" in 2 Cor 3:5.
49. Used 31 times. GK *1584*. Related to "draw near" in v 28.
50. Or, "know", a command. Same word and grammar as in v 30. On this word see 1:34.
51. With this visible coming of the "kingdom of God", compare 17:20-21.
52. On "this generation", see Mt 24:34.
53. Or, "never". Same strong negative as in v 32. See 9:27 on it.

A. Phil 1:28   B. Mt 26:21   C. Rom 9:13   D. Lk 21:28   E. 1 Cor 6:18   F. 2 Thes 2:7   G. 2 Thes 1:8, punishment   H. Act 2:4, filled   J. 1 Thes 5:3   K. Mt 21:16   L. Rev 16:19   M. Heb 11:34   N. 2 Cor 10:5   O. Eph 5:18, filled   P. Rev 7:1, land   Q. Eph 5:21   R. Heb 2:5   S. Mk 5:30   T. Act 17:13   U. 2 Cor 11:20   V. Rom 3:24   W. Mt 24:32   X. Mt 5:18

2D. "But take heed to yourselves¹ that your hearts^A may not at any time be weighed-down^B 34
with carousing² and drunkenness^C and anxieties³ pertaining-to-life⁴, and that unexpected⁵
day suddenly-come-upon⁶ you ˚like *a* snare⁷ 35

    1E. "For it⁸ will come-in-upon⁹ all the *ones* sitting¹⁰ on *the* face *of* all the earth

  3D. "And¹¹ be keeping-alert¹² in every season¹³, praying that you may have strength¹⁴ to 36
escape¹⁵ all these *things* being about to take place, and to stand before the Son *of* Man"

10B. Now *as to* the days¹⁶, He was teaching in the temple. But *as to* the nights, going out [of Jerusalem], 37
He was spending-the-night¹⁷ on the mountain being called '*of* Olives'. ˚And all the people were 38
arising-very-early¹⁸ *to come* to Him in the temple, to hear Him

8A.¹⁹ Now the Feast *of* Unleavened-Bread²⁰, the *one* being called Passover²¹, was drawing-near^D. ˚And the chief 22:1-2
priests and the scribes were seeking^E *as to* how they might kill²² Him, for they were fearing the people²³

  1B.²⁴ And Satan entered into Judas²⁵, the *one* being called "Iscariot^F", being *one* of the number^G *of* the 3
twelve. ˚And having gone, he talked-with^H the chief priests and [temple] captains²⁶ *as to* how he 4
might hand Him over *to* them

    1C. And they rejoiced²⁷ and agreed²⁸ to give him money²⁹ 5
    2C. And he consented^J, and was seeking^E *a* favorable-opportunity^K *that he might* hand Him over^L 6
without *a* crowd *with* them³⁰

  2B.³¹ And the [first] day³² *of* the *Feast of* Unleavened-Bread came— on which it-was-necessary³³ *that* 7
the Passover [lamb] be sacrificed^M. ˚And He sent-forth^N Peter and John, having said, "Having 8
gone³⁴, prepare^O the Passover [meal] *for* us, in order that we may eat *it*"

    1C. And the *ones* said *to* Him, "Where do You want us to prepare³⁵ *it*?" 9
    2C. And the *One* said *to* them, "Behold— you having entered into the city, *a* man will meet^P you 10
carrying^Q *a* jar^R *of* water. Follow him to the house into which he proceeds. ˚And you will say 11
to the master³⁶ *of* the house, 'The Teacher says *to* you, "Where is the guest-room³⁷ where I may
eat the Passover [meal] with My disciples?" ' ˚And that *one* will show you *a* large upstairs- 12
room having been spread^S [with furnishings]. Prepare *it* there"
    3C. And having gone, they found *it* just as He had told them. And they prepared the Passover [meal] 13
    4C.³⁸ And when the hour came, He fell back [to eat], and the apostles³⁹ with Him 14

      1D. And He said to them, "I greatly desired⁴⁰ to eat this Passover [meal] with you before I suffer^T 15

        1E. "For I say *to* you that I will by no means eat⁴¹ it⁴² until⁴³ it is fulfilled^U in the 16
kingdom^V *of* God"

      2D. And having taken⁴⁴ *a* cup⁴⁵, having given-thanks^W, He said, "Take this and distribute⁴⁶ *it* 17
to yourselves⁴⁷

1. Same phrase as in 12:1, "take heed to yourselves".
2. Or, "reveling, dissipation, excessive drinking". This word means "intoxication", and its result, "hangover, drunken nausea, drunken headache, dizziness". Used only here. GK *3190*.
3. Or, "worries, cares". Same word as in 8:14.
4. Elsewhere only in 1 Cor 6:3, 4. GK *1053*. Related to the word "life" in 1 Jn 2:16.
5. Or, "unforeseen, sudden". This adjective modifies "day". It is a "day *which may be described as* unexpected". It is unexpected in its very nature, and by such people in particular (since they are distracted). Part of the very nature of this day is that it comes on the world with sudden unexpectedness, although Christians know it is coming. But Christians whose hearts are weighed down as described here say "I know it is coming some day, but I do not expect it soon. My master delays (Mt 24:48)". For these, that day will in fact be a "sudden, unexpected" day that "comes upon" them. Christians "taking heed" to their spiritual lives live in expectation of it at all times, keeping watch, Mt 24:42, 44. Many render this as an adverb, "suddenly", "and that day come upon you suddenly". Elsewhere only in 1 Thes 5:3. GK *167*. Related to "suddenly" in 2:13.
6. Used here and in 1 Thes 5:3 in the sense of "come upon suddenly or by surprise, spring upon", as also in Act 4:1; 6:12; 17:5; 23:27. Elsewhere only as "come upon" in Lk 2:38; "stand near" in Lk 2:9; 10:40; 20:1; 24:4; Act 12:7; 22:13, 20; 23:11; 2 Tim 4:6; "stand over" in Lk 4:39; "stand at" in Act 10:17; 11:11; 2 Tim 4:2; and "set upon" in Act 28:2. GK *2392*.
7. Or, "trap". The point of comparison is the sudden unexpectedness with which the snare comes upon its victim. On this word, see Rom 11:9. Some manuscripts place "like *a* snare" with what follows and drop the "in" from the verb in v 35 {B}, so that it says "For like *a* snare it will come-upon...".
8. That is, "that day" (v 34), the day when these things begin to happen (v 31, 28), when the kingdom of God is near (v 31). The events of "that day" will be worldwide in scope. Compare Mt 24:21-22; Mk 13:19-20.
9. This verb "come in on" is used only here. GK *2082*. It not related to the word in v 34. It is the verb "to come" with prefixes added meaning "in" and "upon". That day comes in on them from outside their world. Used in 1 Macc 16:16.
10. That is, on all humanity. "Sitting on the earth" also occurs in Rev 14:6.
11. Some manuscripts say "Therefore" {N}.
12. Same word as in Mk 13:33.
13. That is, all the time, always, at all times (although it is singular here). This phrase is elsewhere only in Eph 6:18. Some take this with what follows, "Keep alert, praying in every season that...". On "season", see "time" in Mt 8:29.
14. Or, "may prevail". On this word, see "prevail-against" in Mt 16:18. Instead of "may have strength", some manuscripts say "may be considered worthy" {N}, using the word in 20:35.
15. Or, "flee from". On this word see Rom 2:3.
16. That is, for the duration of the daytime.
17. On this word, see Mt 21:17. Some think this means Jesus camped outside there; others, that He stayed with friends there.
18. That is, before dawn, in the early dawn. Luke seems to imply that it was earlier than normal. Used only here. GK *3983*. Related to "very early" in 24:22.
19. Parallel account at Mt 26:1; Mk 14:1.
20. On this feast, see Mk 14:12.
21. Note that "Passover" is used to refer to entire eight-day Feast. On "Passover", see Jn 18:28.
22. Or, "do away with, execute". Same word as "execute" in 23:32. On this word, see Mt 2:16.
23. This may be explaining why the leaders were "seeking how" to do this. Since they feared the people, they had to find a way to covertly or justifiably kill Him. Or, it may be explaining why they wanted to "kill" Him. Since they feared the people would accept Jesus and therefore reject them, they had to eliminate Him.
24. Parallel account at Mt 26:14; Mk 14:10.
25. Compare Jn 6:70-71; 13:2, 27.
26. That is, the captains of the temple police or officers. On this word, see Act 5:26.
27. Or, "they were delighted". On this word see 2 Cor 13:11.
28. Elsewhere only in Jn 9:22; Act 23:20. GK *5338*.
29. Same word as "silver-coins" in Mt 26:15. On this word see Mt 25:27.
30. That is, with Jesus and the disciples. Or, "hand Him over *to* them without *a* crowd".
31. Parallel account at Mt 26:17; Mk 14:12.
32. This year, it was Thursday, the day before the Preparation day (Friday). See Mk 14:12. This day began at sundown on what we call Wednesday evening, and was followed by daytime on Thursday.
33. On this idiom, see "must" in Mt 16:21.
34. This word (GK *4513*) is not the same word as in Mk 14:12 (GK *599*) or 14:13 (GK *5632*).
35. This idiom is more literally, "Where do you want *that* we should prepare *it*?".
36. More literally, the "house-master *of* the house". Same word as in Mk 14:14, but here "*of* the house" is also expressed separately.
37. Same word as in Mk 14:14. On this word, see "inn" in 2:7.
38. Parallel account at Mt 26:20; Mk 14:17; Jn 13:2.
39. Some manuscripts say "the twelve apostles" {N}.
40. More literally, "I desired *with* desire", a Hebrew way of speaking. On "desire", see Gal 5:16, 17.
41. Some manuscripts add "no longer" {B}, so that it says "that no longer by any means will I eat...".
42. That is, the Passover meal. Some think this means Jesus did not eat this meal, though He desired to do so; others, that He will not eat it after this meal. Some manuscripts say "of it" {N}.
43. More literally, "up to which *time*". On this idiom, see Mt 5:25.
44. Or, "received, accepted". Not the same word as "take" later in the verse and in v 19. On this word, see "welcome" in Mt 10:40.
45. Some manuscripts say "the cup" {N}.
46. Or, "divide". Some think this means the disciples poured some wine from this cup into their cups; others, that they drank from the single cup passed around. Some think this is in preparation for v 20; others, that this is the initial cup of the Passover meal, and is not related to the cup in v 20. In this case, this verse is equivalent to "while they were eating" in Mt 26:26. There are other views. On this word, see "dividing" in Act 2:3.
47. Some think this implies Jesus did not drink it at this meal; others, that He had just drank from it, having drunk first in accordance with the custom at the Passover.

A. Rev 2:23 B. Lk 9:32 C. Rom 13:13 D. Lk 21:28 E. Phil 2:21 F. Jn 6:71 G. Rev 13:17 H. Act 25:12 J. Jam 5:16, confess out K. Mt 26:16 L. Mt 26:21, hand over M. Act 10:13, slaughter N. Mk 3:14, send out O. Mk 14:15 P. Act 20:22 Q. Mt 8:17 R. Mk 14:13 S. Mk 14:15 T. Gal 3:4 U. Eph 5:18, filled V. Mt 3:2 W. Mt 26:27

| Luke 22:18 | 278 | Verse |

    1E. "For I say *to* you that[1] I will by no means drink from the fruit[2] *of* the grapevine from now on[3] until which *time* the kingdom *of* God comes[4]"   18

3D.[5] And having taken[A] bread, having given-thanks[B], He broke[C] *it* and gave *it to* them, saying, "This is[6] My body, the[7] *one* being given for you. Be doing this for My remembrance[D]"   19

  4D. And similarly the cup after the dining[8], saying, "This cup *is* the new[E] covenant[F] in My blood[G]— the *blood* being poured-out[H] for you. °Yet behold— the hand *of* the *one* handing Me over *is* with Mine on the table!⁹   20   21

    1E. "Because[10] **the Son *of* Man**[11] is proceeding according-to[12] the *thing* having been determined[13]— nevertheless, woe *to* that man by whom He is being handed-over[J]!"   22

5D. And **they** began to discuss[K] with themselves *as to* which of them then the *one* going to do this *thing* might be   23

6D.[14] And *a* contention[15] also took place among them *as to* which *of* them seems[16] to be greater[17]. °And the *One* said *to* them—   24   25

    1E. "The kings *of* the Gentiles are lording-over[18] them. And the *ones* having-authority[19] over them are calling-*themselves*[20] 'Benefactors[21]'. °But you *shall* not *be* so. But let the greater[22] *one* among you be[23] like the younger *one*; and the *one* leading[24] like the *one* serving[L]   26

        1F. "For who *is* greater, the *one* reclining-back [to eat] or the *one* serving? Is it not the *one* reclining-back?[25] But **I** am in your midst[M] as the *One* serving!   27

    2E.[26] "But[27] **you** are the *ones* having continued[28] with Me in My trials[N]   28

        1F. "And **I** am conferring[29] you *a* kingdom[O], just as My Father conferred Me° so that you may eat and drink at My table in My kingdom   29-30

        2F. "And you will sit on thrones judging[30] the twelve tribes[P] *of* Israel

    3E.[31] "Simon[32], Simon. Behold— Satan asked-for[33] you all[34] that he might sift[35] *you* like wheat. °But **I** prayed for you[36], that your faith may not fail[37]. And when **you** have turned-back[38], establish[39] your brothers"   31   32

        1F. But the *one* said *to* Him, "Lord, I am prepared[Q] to go **with You** even[40] to prison[R] and to death!"   33

        2F. And the *One* said, "I say *to* you, Peter[41], *a* rooster will not crow today until[42] you deny[S] three-times *that you* know Me"   34

7D. And He said *to* them, "When I sent you out without money-bag and [traveler's] bag[T] and sandals,[43] you did not lack anything, *did you*?"[44]   35

    1E. And the *ones* said, "Nothing"

    2E. And He said *to* them, "But now[45] let the *one* having *a* money-bag take *it*. Likewise also *a* [traveler's] bag. And let the *one* not having *one* sell his cloak[U] and buy *a* sword[46]   36

        1F. "For I say *to* you that this [saying] having been written [in Isa 53:12] must[47] be fulfilled[48] in Me— 'And He was counted[49] with lawless[V] *ones*'. For indeed the *thing* concerning Me has *a* fulfillment[50]"   37

1. Some manuscripts omit this word {C}.
2. Or, "product". On this word, see Mt 26:29.
3. Some think this means Jesus did not drink it at this meal; others, that He would not drink it after this meal. Some manuscripts omit "from now *on*" {N}. On this phrase, see Jn 8:11.
4. Compare 21:31; 17:20-21.
5. Compare also 1 Cor 11:23-25.
6. On this word, see Mt 26:26.
7. Some manuscripts omit from here through v 20 {B}, so that it says "body. Yet behold...". There are other variations. These variants regard the first cup in v 17 as part of the Lord's Supper, and eliminate the cup in v 20.
8. That is, the eating of supper. On this word, see 1 Cor 11:25.
9. That is, it is one of the ones eating with Me. This could mean Judas is still there, and was revealed after the supper. Judas's statement in Mt 26:25 takes place after Lk 22:22, but Matthew and Mark reverse the order of these two events at the Passover meal. While the Gospels say that both events occurred "while they were eating" (Mt 26:21, 26; Mk 14:18, 22; Lk 22:14, 20), none claim to give the exact order of the two events. In other words, the Gospels do not clearly indicate when Judas left in relation to bread and cup. Jn 13:30 says he left after eating a morsel of bread, but John does not mention the bread and cup at all.
10. Some manuscripts instead have a word that can be rendered "And" or "Indeed" {N}.
11. Jesus uses grammar that emphasizes the contrast between the two halves of this sentence.
12. Or, "in accordance with, in keeping with, based on". GK *2848*.
13. That is, by God. On this word, see "designated" in Rom 1:4.
14. Compare Mt 20:24-28; Mk 10:41-45.
15. In the actual sequence of events, some think this happened at the beginning of the meal, prior to Jn 13:4. Used only here. GK *5808*. Related to "contentious" in 1 Cor 11:16.
16. Or, "has the reputation of" being greater, as this word is used in Mk 10:42. "Seems" could indicate the disciples are arguing about their potential rank or reputation in the eyes of others in the coming kingdom. "Have the reputation" would mean they are debating their present actual rank or reputation in the eyes of others. In any case, they disputed over their reputations, over how others would rank them.
17. Though the form of this word means "greater", many think the sense of it is "greatest" here and in v 26. Same word as in v 27. GK *3505*.
18. Or, "are lords, are masters" of them. Same word as "be lord" in Rom 14:9. On this word, see Rom 7:1. Related to the word in Mt 20:25; Mk 10:42.
19. Or, "exercising authority". On this word, see "mastered" in 1 Cor 6:12. Related to the word in Mt 20:25.
20. Or, "are called". On this word see Rom 8:30.
21. That is, ones doing what is good for the people, benefitting the people. Used only here. GK *2309*. Related to "doing good" in Act 10:38.
22. Or, "older", in specific contrast with "younger" next. Same word as in v 24.
23. Or, "become". Gk *1181*.
24. Or, "ruling, governing". On this word, see Heb 13:7.
25. The grammar indicates that a "yes" answer is expected.
26. Compare Mt 19:28.
27. From a present honor He has not given them and they are not to assume, Jesus turns to a future honor He will grant them.
28. Or, "remained continually". Elsewhere only in 1:22; Gal 2:5; Heb 1:11; 2 Pet 3:4. GK *1373*.
29. Or, "ordaining, decreeing, assigning, appointing, covenanting". On this verb, see "covenant" in Heb 8:10.
30. That is, administering justice. On this word, see Mt 19:28.
31. Compare Jn 13:38; Mt 26:30; Mk 14:26.
32. From future honor and glory for the eleven, Jesus turns back to the major failure to occur that night on the part of one of them. Some manuscripts say "And the Lord said, 'Simon..." {B}, making this point 7D.
33. Or, "demanded". Used only here. GK *1977*. Compare Job 1:6-12.
34. The word "you" is plural, referring to all of them, and this is added to reflect this.
35. Or, "winnow". Satan wants to shake you all through a sieve and see if he can keep and toss aside or destroy any of you. He wants to throw you all up in the air and see if he can blow any of you away like chaff. They all prove to be wheat. Used only here. GK *4985*.
36. This (and the rest of the verse) is singular, referring to Peter, the one who would fail to the greatest extent. He was the one most in danger of being sifted out.
37. Or, "leave off, cease". On this word, see 16:9.
38. This is a participle, "*are* having turned back" On this word see Jam 5:19.
39. Or, "stabilize, support". On this word, see 1 Thes 3:2.
40. Or, "both". GK *2779*.
41. This and Mt 16:18 are the only places in the Gospels where Jesus calls him "Peter".
42. Some manuscripts say "before" {N}, as in Mt 26:34; Mk 14:30; and Lk 22:61.
43. These are the same three items are mentioned in 10:4. Compare 9:3.
44. The grammar indicates that a "no" answer is expected.
45. Now the situation is changing. The disciples must plan and make provisions for themselves as one normally would.
46. Some take this literally; others, figuratively. Prudently provide for your protection. Perhaps Jesus says this in contrast to Himself, for He now proceeds to the place where He knows He will be found and arrested.
47. On this idiom, see Mt 16:21. Some manuscripts add "still" {N}.
48. Same word as "accomplished" in 12:50.
49. That is, classed, considered to be one of. On this word, see "consider" in Rom 3:28.
50. Or, "the *thing* concerning Me has *an* end", which some take to mean "My life is at its end". On this word, see "end" in Rom 10:4. Related to "fulfilled" earlier.

A. Rom 7:8 B. Mt 26:27 C. Act 2:46 D. 1 Cor 11:24 E. Heb 8:13 F. Heb 8:6 G. 1 Jn 1:7 H. Mt 26:28 J. Mt 26:21 K. Mk 8:11, debate L. 1 Pet 4:10, ministering M. 2 Thes 2:7 N. Jam 1:2 O. Mt 3:2 P. Rev 1:7 Q. Mk 14:15 R. Act 5:22 S. Mt 16:24 T. Lk 9:3 U. 1 Pet 3:3, garment V. 1 Cor 9:21, without the Law

3E. And the *ones* said, "Lord, behold— here¹ *are* two swords^A" 38
4E. And the *One* said *to* them, "It is enough"²

3B.³ And having gone out,⁴ He went in accordance with *His* custom⁵ to the Mount *of* Olives. And the⁶ 39
disciples also⁷, they followed Him. °And having come-to-be at the place, He said *to* them, "Be 40
praying *that you may* not enter into temptation⁸"

   1C. And **He** withdrew⁹ from them about *a* stone's throw. And having put *down His* knees, He was 41
praying,°saying, "Father, if You are willing^B, remove¹⁰ this cup from Me. Yet let not My will^C, 42
but Yours be done^D"

      1D. And¹¹ *an* angel from heaven appeared^E *to* Him, strengthening¹² Him 43
      2D. And having come-to-be in agony¹³, He was praying more-fervently^F. And His sweat 44
became like¹⁴ drops¹⁵ *of* blood going down upon the ground¹⁶

   2C. And having arisen^G from prayer, having come to the disciples, He found them being asleep^H 45
because of grief¹⁷. °And He said *to* them, "Why are you sleeping^J? Having stood-up^G, be 46
praying that¹⁸ you may not enter into temptation"
   3C. While He *was* still speaking, behold— *a* crowd. And the *one* being called Judas, one *of* the 47
twelve, was preceding¹⁹ them. And he drew-near^K *to* Jesus to kiss^L Him. °And Jesus said *to* 48
him, "Judas, are you handing-over^M the Son *of* Man **with *a* kiss^N**?"
   4C. And the *ones* around Him, having seen the *thing which* will happen²⁰, said²¹, "Lord, shall we 49
strike with *a* sword?" °And *a* certain one of them struck the slave *of* the high priest and took- 50
off^O his right ear²²
   5C. But having responded, Jesus said, "Allow²³ up to this". And having touched *his* ear^P, He 51
healed^Q him
   6C. And Jesus said to *the* chief priests and captains^R *of* the temple and elders having come against²⁴ 52
Him, "Did you come out with swords^A and clubs^S as-*if* against *a* robber^T? °Daily while I *was* 53
being with you in the temple, you did not stretch-out^U *your* hands against Me.²⁵ But this is your
hour, and the authority^V *of* darkness"

4B.²⁶ And having arrested²⁷ Him, they led *Him,* and brought *Him* into the house *of* the high priest. And 54
Peter was following at-a-distance

   1C. And *they* having kindled *a* fire in *the* middle^W *of* the courtyard^X, and having sat-down-together, 55
Peter was sitting amidst^W them

      1D. And *a* certain servant-girl^Y, having seen him sitting toward the light, and having looked- 56
intently^Z *at* him, said, "This *one* also was with Him"

         1E. But the *one* denied^AA *it*²⁸, saying, "I do not know^BB Him, woman" 57

      2D. And after *a* short *time*, another *man*²⁹ having seen him said, "**You** also are *one* of them" 58

         1E. But Peter said, "Man, I am not!"

      3D. And about one hour having passed³⁰, *a* certain other *man*³¹ was insisting³², saying, "In 59
accordance with truth,³³ this *one* also was with Him, for he also is *a* Galilean"

         1E. But Peter said, "Man, I do not know^BB what you are saying" 60

1. Some think the disciples mean here in this room. Some think this is where Peter got the sword in v 50.
2. Some think Jesus is closing this conversation, "That's enough!", with a tone of rebuke or irony; others, that He means these two swords will be enough for tonight.
3. Parallel account at Mt 26:36; Mk 14:32; Jn 18:1.
4. Compare Mt 26:30; Mk 14:26; Jn 14:31; 18:1
5. Or, "habit". On this word, see 1:9. Judas was aware of this custom, and led the authorities there.
6. Some manuscripts say "His" {K}.
7. In the Greek, the "also" goes with "disciples" rather than "followed" ("also followed" in English gives the impression that others were following, which is not Luke's intent). Luke is abbreviating "And the disciples went also, following Him".
8. Same word as in v 46. On this word, see "trials" in Jam 1:2. Compare Mt 26:41; 6:13.
9. Or, "was parted". On this word, see Act 21:1.
10. Or, "carry away, take away". Same word as in Mk 14:36. Elsewhere only as "carry away" in Heb 13:9; and "carry along" in Jude 12. GK *4195*.
11. Some manuscripts omit v 43-44. These verses are marked in UBS4 as not being an original part of Luke's Gospel, but as very ancient.
12. Elsewhere only in Act 9:19. GK *1932*.
13. Or, "anguish". Used only here. GK *75*. Our word "agony" comes from this word *agonia*. Related to "struggle" in 1 Tim 4:10.
14. Or, "as if". On this word, see "as if" in Rom 6:13.
15. Used only here. GK *2584*.
16. Some think Luke means sweat was dripping off of Jesus like drops of blood dripping from an open wound; others, that this was a bloody sweat, a blood-colored sweat, a sweat containing some blood.
17. Or, "from grief". On "grief", see 2 Cor 7:10. Same word as in Jn 16:6.
18. Or, "Be praying, in order that you may not enter", depending on whether this is the content or the purpose of the prayer.
19. Or, "going before", that is, leading them. On this word, see "came ahead of" in Mk 6:33.
20. Or, "be", as in Mt 16:22. That is, that Jesus would be arrested.
21. Some manuscripts add "*to* Him" {N}.
22. This is GK *4044*. Used 36 times. Matthew, Mark, and Luke each use a different word.
23. Or, "Permit". If addressed to the disciples, some think this means "allow this arrest to take place"; others, that it is an exclamation meaning something like "Leave it alone, stop it, no more of this, let it go". If addressed to the crowd, some think it means "allow this striking out by Peter", excuse it; others, "permit Me to heal him". On this word, see 1 Cor 10:13.
24. Same word as in following question. Some manuscripts say "to" here {N}.
25. If you have a legitimate cause to arrest Me, why did you not do so then?
26. Parallel account at Mt 26:57; Mk 14:53; Jn 18:12.
27. Or, "seized". Same word as in Mt 26:55; Mk 14:48; Jn 18:12; Act 1:16; 12:3; and "seized" in Act 23:27; 26:21. On this word, see "conceived" in Lk 2:21.
28. Some manuscripts say "Him" {N}.
29. This man, and probably others, joined in with the servant girl in saying this, Mk 14:69; Mt 26:71.
30. Or, "separated, divided, intervened" from the previous point of time. After an interval of about one hour. On this word, see "separated" in 24:51.
31. This man also was one of several saying this, Mt 26:73; Mk 14:70.
32. Elsewhere only in Act 12:15. GK *1462*.
33. On this phrase, see 4:25.

A. Eph 6:17 B. Jam 1:18 C. Jn 7:17 D. Mt 6:10 E. Lk 2:26, see F. 1 Pet 1:22 G. Lk 18:33, rise up H. 1 Thes 4:13, falling asleep J. 1 Thes 5:10 K. Lk 21:28 L. Mt 26:48 M. Mt 26:21 N. Rom 16:16 O. Mk 14:47 P. Mt 26:51 Q. Mt 8:8 R. Act 5:26 S. 1 Pet 2:24, cross T. Mt 21:13 U. Act 27:30 V. Rev 6:8 W. Mt 26:3 X. 2 Thes 2:7, midst Y. Jn 18:17 Z. Lk 4:20 AA. 2 Tim 2:12 BB. 1 Jn 2:29

4D. And at-once^A, while he *was* still speaking, *a* rooster crowed 61
   5D. And having turned, the Lord looked-at^B Peter¹
   6D. And Peter was reminded^C *of* the word *of* the Lord— how He said *to* him that "Before *a* rooster crows today², you will deny^D Me three-times". *And having gone outside, he³ wept^E bitterly⁴ 62

  2C. And the men holding⁵ Him were mocking^F Him while beating^G *Him*. *And having covered⁶ Him, they⁷ were asking *Him*, saying, "Prophesy⁸— who is the *one* having hit You?" *And blaspheming^H, they were saying many other *things* against Him 63-64 / 65

5B.⁹ And when it became day, the Council-of-elders^J *of* the people was gathered together— both chief priests and scribes. And they led Him away to their council¹⁰ [chamber], *saying, "If **You** are the Christ, tell us" 66 / 67

  1C. But He said *to* them, "If I tell you, you will by no means believe. *And if I question¹¹ *you*, you will by no means answer.¹² *But¹³ from now *on*, the Son *of* Man will be sitting on *the* right *side of* the power *of* God" 68 / 69
  2C. And they all said, "Are **You** then¹⁴ the Son *of* God?" 70
  3C. And the *One* said to them, "**You**¹⁵ are saying that **I** am"¹⁶
  4C. And the *ones* said, "What further need do we have *of* testimony^K? For we ourselves heard *it* from His mouth" 71

6B.¹⁷ And having arisen^L, the whole assembly *of* them¹⁸ led Him before Pilate^M 23:1

  1C. And they began to accuse^N Him, saying, "We found this *One* perverting^O our¹⁹ nation, and forbidding^P to give tributes²⁰ *to* Caesar, and saying *that* He is²¹ Christ, *a* King" 2
  2C. And Pilate asked Him, saying, "Are **You** the King *of* the Jews?" 3

    1D. And the *One*, having responded *to* him, said, "**You** are saying *it*"²²

  3C. And Pilate said to the chief priests and the crowds, "I find no guilt²³ in this man" 4
  4C. But the *ones* were insisting²⁴, saying that "He is stirring-up²⁵ the people, teaching throughout all Judea— having indeed²⁶ begun from²⁷ Galilee, as far as here" 5
  5C. And Pilate, having heard *it*²⁸, asked if the man was²⁹ *a* Galilean. *And having learned^Q that He was from the authority^R *of* Herod³⁰, he sent Him up³¹ to Herod— he also being in Jerusalem during these days 6-7

7B. Now Herod, having seen Jesus, rejoiced greatly³². For he was wanting^S to see Him for considerable^T periods-of-time³³ because of hearing³⁴ about Him. And he was hoping to see some sign being done by Him 8

  1C. And he was questioning^U Him with many words, but **He** answered him nothing 9
  2C. And the chief priests and the scribes were standing *there*, accusing^N Him vigorously³⁵ 10
  3C. And Herod also³⁶— with his troops³⁷— 11

    1D. Having treated Him with contempt³⁸
    2D. And having mocked³⁹ *Him*, having clothed *Him* with shining^V clothing⁴⁰
    3D. Sent⁴¹ Him back *to* Pilate

  4C. Now both Herod and Pilate became friends^W with one another on the very day. For they were-previously⁴² existing⁴³ with hostility^X toward them⁴⁴ 12

1. Perhaps Jesus looked through a door or window, or while He was being taken through the courtyard where Peter was.
2. Some manuscripts omit this word {N}.
3. Some manuscripts say "Peter" {A}.
4. Elsewhere only in Mt 26:75. GK *4396*. Related word in Col 3:19.
5. That is, "holding in custody, confining". On this word, see "control" in 2 Cor 5:14.
6. Based on the context and English idiom, some render this "blindfolded". While this could be what the men did, it may convey a more specific idea than intended here. They may have just thrown something over His head. Elsewhere only in Mk 14:65; Heb 9:4. GK *4328*. The root word is "to cover" in 1 Pet 4:8.
7. Some manuscripts say "they were striking His face and were asking..." {N}.
8. On this word, see 1 Cor 14:1. Tell us based on a revelation from God.
9. Parallel account at Mt 27:1; Mk 15:1.
10. Or, "to their Sanhedrin", naming the judicial body for his readers. On this word, see Act 5:27. Used only here in Luke. Not related to "council of elders".
11. Some manuscripts say "also question" {N}.
12. The leaders will not discuss it honestly. Some manuscripts say "answer Me, or release *Me*" {B}.
13. Jesus answers them in terms of His relation to God. This is a perfectly clear answer, and avoids the use of the term "Christ, Messiah", which they defined in political terms. Jesus is claiming to be the fulfillment of Ps 110. Some manuscripts omit this word {K}.
14. Or, "therefore". If You will sit on God's right side, are You then claiming to be His Son?
15. This word is plural, answering all of them. Compare Mt 26:64.
16. On this answer, see Mt 27:11 and 26:64. Clearly, the leaders understood Jesus to mean "You are [rightly] saying that I am". Mk 14:62 says "I am", giving the intent of this.
17. Parallel account at Mt 27:2, 11; Mk 15:1; Jn 18:28.
18. That is, the Council in v 66, the Sanhedrin.
19. Some manuscripts omit this word, so that it says "the nation" {N}.
20. Same word as in 20:22. On this word, see Rom 13:6.
21. This idiom, "saying *that* he is", is also in Act 5:36; 8:9; Rev 2:9; 3:9; all of false claims from the speaker's point of view.
22. On this answer, see Mt 27:11.
23. Or, "cause, source, basis" of guilt or accusation. Same word as in v 14, 22, where Pilate repeats this. Elsewhere only as "cause" in Act 19:40; Heb 5:9. GK *165*. Related to "charge" in Mt 27:37; Jn 18:38; 19:4; and "charge" in Act 25:7.
24. Or, "growing strong, urgent, emphatic". Used only here. GK *2196*.
25. Or, "shaking up". On this word, see Mk 15:11.
26. Some manuscripts omit this word {N}.
27. Or, "indeed beginning from". On this idiom, see "beginning from" in Mt 20:8.
28. Some manuscripts say "having heard 'Galilean', asked..." {N}.
29. More literally, "is", as the Greek typically phrases it. Same with the "was" in the next sentence.
30. Herod Antipas was governor (tetrarch) of Galilee, so Jesus was his subject. See Mt 14:1 on him.
31. This verb "sent up" is the same word as in Act 25:21. Elsewhere only as "sent back" in Lk 23:11, 15; Phm 12. GK *402*.
32. Or, "was very delighted". "Rejoiced" is the same word as in 22:5.
33. Or, "considerable times", plural. On this idiom, see 20:9. Here, it probably means "months".
34. Some manuscripts add "many *things*" {N}.
35. Or, "powerfully, forcefully, vehemently". Elsewhere only in Act 18:28. GK *2364*.
36. That is, like those in 22:63-65. Some manuscripts omit this word {C}.
37. That is, Herod's armed guards, his bodyguards. On this word, see Act 23:10.
38. On "treat with contempt", see 1 Thes 5:20.
39. Same word as in 18:32; 22:63; 23:36; Mt 20:19; 27:29, 31, 41; Mk 10:34; 15:20, 31; and Lk 14:29. Elsewhere only as "tricked" in Mt 2:16. GK *1850*. Related to "mockers" in 2 Pet 3:3.
40. This phrase "shining clothing" is elsewhere only of an angel in Act 10:30, and a rich man in Jam 2:2, 3. "Shining" is also used of the clothing of the wife of the Lamb, Rev 19:8. Putting on this clothing was clearly part of the mocking just mentioned. It is unclear whether Luke means this clothing was still on Jesus when Herod sent Him back.
41. All the verbs— treated, mocked, put, sent-back— are singular, referring to Herod. He personally mocked and disgraced this pretend prophet who would not perform for him or answer him. The main sentence is "And Herod... sent Him back to Pilate".
42. The verb "were previously, were formerly" is elsewhere only in Act 8:9. GK *4732*.
43. Or, "being". That is, these two were living with hostility toward them. GK *1639*.
44. That is, each felt the other was hostile toward him. The cause of this is not known. Through this incident, this was cleared up.

A. Mt 21:19 B. Mk 8:25, seeing C. Jn 14:26 D. Mt 16:24 E. Jn 11:33 F. Lk 23:11 G. Jn 18:23 H. 1 Tim 6:1 J. 1 Tim 4:14 K. Jn 1:7 L. Lk 18:33, rise up M. Lk 3:1 N. Jn 5:45 O. Phil 2:15 P. 1 Cor 14:39 Q. Col 1:6, understood R. Rev 6:8 S. Jn 7:17, willing T. 2 Cor 3:5, sufficient U. Lk 9:18 V. Rev 22:1 W. Lk 14:10 X. Eph 2:14

| Luke 23:13 | 284 | Verse |

8B. Now Pilate, having called-together the chief priests and the rulers^A and the people, *said to them—   13-14

  1C. "You brought me this man as *One* turning-away¹ the people

    1D. "And behold— **I**, having examined^B *Him* in your presence, found **no** guilt² in this man *of the things* which you are accusing^C against Him
    2D. "But neither *did* Herod, for he sent Him back to us³. And behold— nothing worthy^D *of* death has been committed⁴ *by* Him   15
    3D. "Therefore, having disciplined⁵ Him, I will release^E *Him*"   16
                                                                 17⁶
    4D. But they cried-out⁷ all-together⁸, saying, "Take away this *One*, and release Barabbas^F *for* us"— *who had been thrown⁹ in prison because of *a* certain rebellion¹⁰ having taken place in the city, and murder^G   18 19

  2C. And¹¹ again Pilate addressed them, wanting^H to release Jesus   20

    1D. But the *ones* were calling-out^J, saying, "Crucify^K, crucify Him!"   21

  3C. And *a* third *time* the *one* said to them, "What indeed¹² did this *One* do wrong? I found no guilt¹³ *worthy of* death in Him. Therefore, having disciplined Him, I will release *Him*"   22

    1D. But the *ones* were pressing-upon¹⁴ *him with* loud voices, asking *that* He be crucified. And their voices¹⁵ were prevailing¹⁶   23

  4C. And Pilate decided¹⁷ *that* their request^L *should* be done^M   24

    1D. And he released¹⁸ the *one* having been thrown into prison because of rebellion and murder, whom they were asking-*for*   25
    2D. And he handed-over^N Jesus *to* their will^O

9B.¹⁹ And when they led Him away, having taken-hold-of^P *a* certain Simon, *a* Cyrenian coming from *the* country, they laid the cross^Q on him to carry behind Jesus   26

  1C. And *a* large crowd *of* the people, and *of* women²⁰ who²¹ were beating-their-breasts^R and lamenting^S Him, was following Him. *But having turned to them²², Jesus said—   27 28

    1D. "Daughters^T *of* Jerusalem, do not be weeping^U for Me. But weep for yourselves and for your children

      1E. "Because behold— days are coming²³ during which they will say, 'Blessed²⁴ *are* the barren^V, and²⁵ the wombs^W which did not bear^X and breasts^Y which did not feed²⁶'. At-that-time²⁷ they will begin to say *to* the mountains, 'Fall on us', and *to* the hills, 'Cover^Z us'   29 30
      2E. "Because if they are doing these *things* in-the-case-of²⁸ the wet²⁹ wood³⁰, what will happen in-the-case-of the dry?"³¹   31

  2C. And two other³² criminals³³ were also being led to be executed³⁴ with Him   32
  3C. And when they came to the place being called "*The* Skull^AA", there they crucified Him and the criminals— one on *the* right *side*, and the other on *the* left³⁵ *side*   33

    1D. But³⁶ Jesus was saying, "Father, forgive^BB them, for they do not know what they are doing"   34

1. That is, misleading or turning the people away from their duties to Rome (Pilate would not be concerned about their religious duty). On this word, see Heb 12:25.
2. Same word as in v 4.
3. Some manuscripts say "for I sent you [people] up to him" {A}.
4. Or, "done". This is a participle, "is having been committed". On this word, see "practicing" in Rom 2:1.
5. Same word as in v 22. On this word, see 1 Cor 11:32.
6. Some manuscripts add as v 17, "Now he was having *an* obligation to release one [prisoner] *to* them at the feast" {A}.
7. Elsewhere only of demons crying out in Mk 1:23; Lk 4:33; 8:28; and of crying out in terror in Mk 6:49. GK *371*.
8. Or, "all at once". Used only here. GK *4101*.
9. This is a participle, "who was having been thrown".
10. Same word as in v 25. On this word, see Mk 15:7.
11. Some manuscripts say "Therefore" {K}.
12. On this word and question, see Mt 27:23.
13. Same word as in v 4.
14. Or, "being urgent". Same word as in 5:1. Luke could mean they were physically pressing around Pilate, as in 5:1. Or, he could mean they were "pressing" their demands. Elsewhere only as "lie upon" in Jn 11:38; 21:9; Act 27:20; 1 Cor 9:16; and "imposed" in Heb 9:10. GK *2130*. The root word is "to lie".
15. Some manuscripts say "and the voices *of* them and *of* the chief priests" {B}.
16. Or, "winning". On this word, see "prevail against" in Mt 16:18.
17. Or, "adjudged, determined". Pilate rendered his judicial decision in the matter. Used only here. GK *2137*.
18. Some manuscripts add "*to* them" {K}.
19. Parallel account at Mt 27:31; Mk 15:20; Jn 19:16.
20. These are local women of Jerusalem, not the women following Him from Galilee, v 49, 55.
21. Some manuscripts add "also" {K}.
22. That is, the women.
23. Jesus is referring to A.D. 70 and the destruction of Jerusalem.
24. Or, "Fortunate". On this word, see 6:20.
25. Or, "even". GK *2779*.
26. Or, "nourish". Same word as in Mt 6:26; 25:37; Lk 12:24. Elsewhere only as "nourish" in Rev 12:6, 14; "bring up" in Lk 4:16; "provide for" in Act 12:20; "fatten" in Jam 5:5. GK *5555*. Not related to "nurse" in Mt 21:16. Some manuscripts say "nurse" {N}, using the word in Mt 21:16.
27. Or, "Then". On this word, see "then" in Mt 24:9.
28. Or, "in connection with". GK *1877*.
29. Or, "moist". Jesus may mean "wet", the basic meaning of this word, versus dry. Or, He may mean "wet" in the sense of "green, living, pliant", versus dead, brittle. Used only here. GK *5619*.
30. Or, "tree". This is not the normal word for "tree". It is used for "cut wood, firewood, timber", and anything made of wood. But it is also used of live trees. On this word, see "cross" in 1 Pet 2:24.
31. That is, if the Gentile rulers do this to God's innocent Son, what will happen to unrepentant Israel? If even wet wood is made to burn (referring to His own undeserved death), what will happen to the dry (referring to guilty Israel). So weep for yourselves, for what is coming upon you.
32. That is, others of a different kind. On this word, see "different" in 1 Cor 12:9. They were "robbers", Mt 27:38. In the Romans' eyes, all three were criminals. Some punctuate this so as not to class Jesus as a criminal, thinking that Luke would not have intended to say this, "And others were also being led, two criminals, to be...". But Luke may be stating this in fulfillment of 22:37. The Greek word order is "other criminals two". Some manuscripts say "other two criminals" {N}, which may be rendered in the same two ways mentioned, or as "two others, criminals".
33. On this word, see 2 Tim 2:9. Same word as in v 33, 39.
34. Or, "killed, put to death". On this word, see "kill" in Mt 2:16.
35. On this word, see Mk 10:37. Mt 27:38 and Mk 15:27 use a different word (on which, see Mk 10:40).
36. Some manuscripts omit this sentence, "But Jesus... are doing". It is marked in UBS4 as not being an original part of Luke's Gospel, but as very ancient.

A. Rev 1:5   B. 1 Cor 2:14   C. Jn 5:45   D. Rev 16:6   E. Mt 5:31, sends away   F. Mk 15:7   G. Act 9:1   H. Jn 7:17, willing   J. Act 12:22
K. Mt 27:35   L. 1 Jn 5:15   M. Mt 6:10   N. Mt 26:21   O. Jn 7:17   P. Lk 20:20   Q. Mt 10:38   R. Rev 1:7   S. Mt 11:17   T. Lk 13:16   U. Jn 11:33
V. Heb 11:11   W. Lk 1:15   X. 1 Jn 2:29, born   Y. Rev 1:13   Z. 1 Pet 4:8   AA. Mt 27:33   BB. Mt 6:12

4C. And they cast lots[A], dividing[B] His garments among *themselves*[1]	
5C. And the people were standing *there* watching[2]	35
6C. And the rulers[3] were also sneering-at[C] *Him*, saying, "He saved[D] others. Let Him save Himself if this *One* is[4] the Christ *of* God, the Chosen[5] *One*"	
7C. And the soldiers[E] also mocked[F] Him, coming to *Him*, offering Him sour-wine[G], •and saying, "If **You** are[6] the King *of* the Jews, save Yourself"	36-37
8C. And there was also *an* inscription over Him[7]— "This *is* the King *of* the Jews"	38
9C. And one[8] *of* the criminals[H] having been hung[9] was blaspheming[J] Him, saying, "Are **You** not the Christ?[10] Save Yourself and us"	39
1D. But having responded, the other, rebuking him, said, "Do **you** not even fear God? Because you are under[11] the same condemnation[12]! •And **we**[13] are *suffering* justly[K], for we are receiving-back[L] *things* worthy[M] *of the things* which we did— but this *One* did nothing out-of-place[14]"	40 41
2D. And he was saying, "Jesus[15], remember[16] me when You come into[17] Your kingdom"	42
3D. And He said *to* him, "Truly[N] I say *to* you, you will be with Me **today** in paradise[O]"	43
10C.[18] And it was now[19] about *the* sixth hour[20]. And *a* darkness[P] came over the whole land[21] until *the* ninth hour, •the sun having failed[22]. And the curtain[23] *of* the temple was torn in-the-middle[24]	44 45
1D. And having called-out *with a* loud voice, Jesus said, "Father, I commend[25] My spirit into Your hands"	46
2D. And having said this, He expired[26]	
3D. And having seen the *thing* having taken place[27], the centurion[Q] was glorifying[R] God, saying, "This man **really**[28] was righteous[S]"	47
11C. And all the crowds having come together for this sight[29], having watched the *things* having taken place, were returning, striking[T] *their* chests[30]	48
12C. But all His acquaintances[31], and the women accompanying[32] Him from Galilee, were standing at *a* distance while seeing[33] these *things*	49
10B.[34] And behold— *there was a* man, Joseph *by* name	50
1C. Being *a* council-member[U], and[35] *a* good[V] and righteous[S] man—•this *one* had not consented[36] *to* the plan[37] and their action[38]	51
2C. From Arimathea[W], *a* city *of* the Jews	
3C. Who[39] was waiting-for[40] the kingdom *of* God	
4C. This *one*, having gone to Pilate, asked-*for* the body *of* Jesus	52
1D. And having taken *it* down, he wrapped[X] it in linen-cloth[41], and laid Him in *a* tomb[42] cut-in-the-rock[43] where **no one**[44] was yet lying[Y]	53
2D. And it was *the* day *of* Preparation[45], and *the* Sabbath was dawning[46]	54
9A.[47] Now having closely-followed[48], the women who had come-with[49] Him from Galilee saw the tomb and how His body was laid	55
1B. And having returned, they prepared spices[50] and perfumes[Z]	56
2B. And **on the Sabbath**[51] they rested[52] in-accordance-with[53] the commandment—•but *on the* first *day of* the week *at* deep[54] dawn[55], they went to the tomb bringing *the* spices which they prepared[56]	24:1
1C. And they found the stone having been rolled-away from the tomb[57]	2

1. On the verb "divide-among *themselves*", see Mt 27:35.
2. Or, "observing". Same word as in v 48; Mt 27:55; Mk 15:40. On this word, see "seeing" in Lk 10:18.
3. On this word, see Rev 1:5. Some manuscripts add "with them" {N}.
4. The grammar means "Assuming that He is the Christ (as He claims), let Him save Himself ".
5. On this word, see Rom 8:33. This is the Greek word order. Some manuscripts say "the Christ, the Chosen *One of* God" {K}.
6. The grammar means "Assuming that You are the King (as You claim), save Yourself ".
7. Some manuscripts say "*an* inscription having been written over Him *in* Greek and Latin and Hebrew letters" {A}, like Jn 19:20.
8. Mt 27:44 and Mk 15:32 say both criminals were reproaching Jesus. Some think both did this at first, but one repented on the cross. Others think both reproached Him, but one blasphemed Him. There are other views.
9. That is, hung on a cross. On this word, see Act 10:39.
10. The grammar indicates a "yes" answer is expected. The mocking nature of it is seen in what is said next. Some manuscripts say "If **You** are the Christ, save Yourself and us" {N}.
11. Or, "in the sphere of ". Same word as in Rom 2:12; 3:19. GK *1877*.
12. Or, "sentence, verdict, judgment, punishment". That is, the condemnation to death. On this word, see "judgment" in Jn 9:39.
13. This man uses grammar that emphasizes the contrast between the two halves of this sentence.
14. Or, "wrong" morally. On this word, see 2 Thes 3:2.
15. In v 42-43, some manuscripts say "And he was saying *to* Jesus, "Remember me, Lord, when You come in Your kingdom". And Jesus said *to* him, "Truly..." {N}.
16. That is, keep me in mind, do not forget me. On this word, see 1:54.
17. Some manuscripts say "in" {B}, which can mean "in connection with".
18. Parallel account at Mt 27:45; Mk 15:33; Jn 19:28.
19. Or, "already, by this time". Same word as in 19:37. Some manuscripts omit this word {N}.
20. That is, noon.
21. Or, "earth". On this word, see Rev 7:1.
22. That is, its light grew dark. On this word, see 16:9. Some manuscripts say instead "And the sun was darkened" {B}.
23. On this word, and on "torn", see Mt 27:51.
24. Same idiom as in Jn 19:18, of Jesus being "in the middle". That is, torn in two, down the middle. GK *3545*.
25. Or, "entrust, deposit". Same word as in Act 14:23; 20:32. On this word, see "put before" in Act 17:3.
26. That is, He died. On this word, see Mk 15:37.
27. That is, that Jesus died in this way, Mt 27:54; Mk 15:39.
28. Or, "certainly, in truth". Jesus really was righteous, just as people said. On this word, see Jn 8:36.
29. Or, "spectacle". Related to "watched" next. GK *2556*. Or, "for this spectacle, having spectated the *things*...".
30. This phrase "striking the chest" is also in 18:13. On this word, see Jn 13:25.
31. More literally, "the known *ones to* Him". Same word as in 2:44. On this adjective, see "known" in Rom 1:19.
32. Or, "following with". On this word, see "follow" in Mk 14:51.
33. On this common word for "seeing", see 2:26. Not the same word as in v 48.
34. Parallel account at Mt 27:57; Mk 15:42; Jn 19:38.
35. Some manuscripts omit this word {C}.
36. Or, "agreed". This is a participle, he "was having not consented". It literally means he had not "put down [his vote] with" them. It is unclear whether this means that he voted "no", or that he was not there to cast his vote. Used only here. GK *5163*. Related to "agreement" in 2 Cor 6:16.
37. Or, "resolution, purpose, decision, plot". Luke could mean their long-standing plan, or, their final decision. On this word, see "counsel" in Eph 1:11. Related to "council-member", and to "plan" in Jn 11:53.
38. Or, "deed, act". On this word, see "practice" in Mt 16:27.
39. Some manuscripts say "Who also himself was also waiting for..." {N}.
40. Same word as in Lk 2:25, 38. On this word, see Act 24:15.
41. On this word, see Mk 14:51. Same word as in Mt 27:59; Mk 15:46.
42. Same word as in 24:1. Elsewhere only in Mk 5:3, 5; Lk 8:27; Act 2:29; 7:16; Rev 11:9. GK *3645*. Related to the word in Mt 27:60; Mk 15:46; Jn 19:41; which is also in Lk 24:2. Related to "remembrance".
43. This adjective is used only here. GK *3292*. It is unrelated to the verb "hew" in Mt 27:60; Mk 15:46.
44. There are three negatives in this phrase. It is very emphatic.
45. That is, Friday, the preparation day for the Sabbath. On this word, see Jn 19:31.
46. That is, the sun was going down. The new day, the Sabbath, "dawned" at dark. On this word, see Mt 28:1.
47. Parallel account at Mt 28:1; Mk 16:1; Jn 20:1.
48. That is, the women closely followed Joseph and the body. Elsewhere only in Act 16:17. GK *2887*.
49. This is a participle, who "were having come with".
50. On this word, see Mk 16:1. The women prepared these things before the sun went down Friday night. They also bought and prepared more on Saturday night, Mk 16:1.
51. Luke uses grammar that closely links the two halves of this sentence.
52. Or, "were quiet". On this word, see "quiet" in 1 Thes 4:11.
53. Or, "in keeping with, according to". GK *2848*. That is, as the Law required.
54. Elsewhere only in Jn 4:11; Act 20:9; Rev 2:24. GK *960*. Related to "deep" in 2 Cor 8:2.
55. That is, very early, while it was still dark, Jn 20:1. Elsewhere only in Jn 8:2; Act 5:21. GK *3986*. Related to "very early" in v 22.
56. Some manuscripts add, "and certain *women* [came] with them" {N}.
57. Same word as in v 9, 12, 22, 24, on which see Mt 23:29. Related to the word in 23:53.

A. Col 1:12, share B. Act 2:3 C. Lk 16:14 D. Lk 19:10 E. Mt 28:12 F. Lk 23:11 G. Mt 27:48 H. 2 Tim 2:9 J. 1 Tim 6:1 K. 1 Cor 15:34, righteously L. Lk 16:25, receive M. Rev 16:6 N. Mt 5:18 O. 2 Cor 12:4 P. Jn 3:19 Q. Mt 8:5 R. Rom 8:30 S. Rom 1:17 T. Lk 6:29 U. Mk 15:43 V. 1 Tim 5:10b W. Mt 27:57 X. Mt 27:59 Y. Mt 3:10 Z. Mt 26:7

2C. But having gone in, they did not find the body *of* the Lord Jesus¹. °And it came about during their being perplexed² about this, that^A behold— two men³ stood-near^B them in gleaming⁴ clothing — 3-4

3C. And they⁵ having become terrified⁶ and bowing *their* faces to the ground, they⁷ said to them, "Why are you seeking^C the Living *One* among the dead? °He⁸ is not here, but He arose^D — 5, 6

    1D. "Remember⁹ how He spoke *to* you while still being in Galilee, °saying *as to* the Son *of* Man that *He* must¹⁰ be handed-over^E into *the* hands *of* sinful^F men, and be crucified, and rise-up^G *on* the third day" — 7

    2D. And they remembered His words — 8

3B. And having returned from the tomb, they reported^H all these *things to* the eleven and *to* all the rest — 9

    1C. Now *the* women were¹¹ the Magdalene Mary¹², and Joanna^J, and Mary¹³ the *mother of* James, and the other *women* with them. They were saying¹⁴ these *things* to the apostles — 10

    2C. And these¹⁵ words appeared^K in their sight as if nonsense¹⁶, and they were not-believing¹⁷ them¹⁸ — 11

    3C. But¹⁹ Peter, having arisen^G, ran to the tomb. And having stooped-to-look²⁰, he sees the linen-cloths²¹ only²². And he went away marveling²³ to himself²⁴ *as to* the *thing* having taken place — 12

4B. And behold— two of them²⁵ were going on the very day²⁶ to *a* village being sixty stades²⁷ distant^L from Jerusalem, *for* which *the* name *was* Emmaus. °And **they** were conversing²⁸ with one another about all these *things* having happened — 13, 14

    1C. And it came about during their conversing and discussing^M, that^N Jesus Himself, having drawn-near^O, was going with them — 15

    2C. But their eyes were being held-back²⁹ *that* they might not³⁰ recognize^P Him — 16

    3C. And He said to them, "What *are* these words which you are exchanging³¹ with one another while walking?" — 17

    4C. And they stood [still], sad-faced³². °And having responded, one³³— Cleopas *by* name— said to Him, "Are **You** alone^Q staying³⁴ *in* Jerusalem and did not know^R the *things* having taken place in it in these days?" — 18

    5C. And He said *to* them, "What *things*?" — 19

    6C. And the *ones* said *to* Him—

        1D. "The *things* concerning Jesus from-Nazareth³⁵

            1E. "Who became³⁶ *a* man³⁷ *who was a* prophet^S, powerful³⁸ in deed and word before God and all the people

            2E. "And how the chief priests and our rulers^T handed Him over for condemnation³⁹ *to* death, and they crucified Him — 20

        2D. "But **we** were hoping^U that **He** was⁴⁰ the *One* going to redeem⁴¹ Israel — 21

        3D. "Yet indeed also in-addition-to⁴² all these⁴³ *things*, it is the third day⁴⁴ since^V these *things* took place

        4D. "Yet some women from-*among* us also astonished^W us. Having come-to-be at the tomb very-early⁴⁵, °and not having found His body, they came saying also to have seen *a* vision⁴⁶ *of* angels who say *that* He *is* alive^X — 22, 23

            1E. "And some *of* the *ones* with us went to the tomb and found *it* so— just as the women indeed said — 24

            2E. "But they did not see Him"

1. Some manuscripts omit "*of* the Lord Jesus" {B}.
2. On this word, see 2 Cor 4:8. Some manuscripts instead have a related word "greatly perplexed" {N}, on which see Lk 9:7.
3. That is, angels, v 23. Angels in the form of men.
4. Or, "brightly shining". Elsewhere only in 17:24, of lightning "flashing". GK *848*. Related to "gleaming out" in 9:29.
5. That is, the women.
6. On this word, see v 37.
7. That is, the two men. The grammar is clear that "them" next refers to the women.
8. Some manuscripts omit this sentence {B}.
9. This is a command. On this word, see Lk 1:54.
10. On this idiom, see Mt 16:21. Some manuscripts say "saying that the Son *of* Man must..." {N}.
11. Some manuscripts omit this word, so that it says "Now the Magdalene... James and the other *women* with them were saying these *things*...". Others say "Now it was... saying these *things*" {B}.
12. She is referred to this way only here. See Lk 8:2 on her.
13. See Mt 27:56 on her.
14. Some manuscripts say, "who were saying..." {N}.
15. Note the disciples' summary of the women's words in v 23. Some manuscripts say "their" {N}.
16. Or, "idle talk, trumpery (showy but useless talk), delirious talk, raving". Used only here. GK *3333*.
17. Or, "refusing to believe". Same word as in v 41; Mk 16:11. On this word, see "are faithless" in 2 Tim 2:13.
18. That is, the women, as the grammar of this word indicates. The apostles did not believe the women.
19. Some manuscripts omit v 12 {B}.
20. This word is used of this action also in Jn 20:5, 11. Luke may mean Peter "bent over to look into *it*". Or, he may simply mean "having looked" into it, as this word is elsewhere only used in Jam 1:25; 1 Pet 1:12. GK *4160*. The root word is "stoop" in Jn 8:6.
21. That is, those used to wrap the body. On this word, see Jn 19:40.
22. Or, "alone". That is, without the body. Some manuscripts say "lying alone" {N}.
23. Or, "wondering", as in Mk 15:44. Peter either marveled that Jesus had returned to heaven in this way, or wondered what had happened to the body. On this word, see "caused to marvel" in Rev 17:8.
24. Same phrase as in 18:11, of the Pharisee praying "to himself". This phrase is elsewhere only plural, discussing "with themselves" in Mk 1:27; 11:31; Lk 20:5; 22:23; saying "to themselves" in Mk 10:26; 12:7; 14:4; 16:3; Jn 7:35; 12:19 (and in Mk 9:10). Some manuscripts say "he went away to his [house], marveling..." {N}.
25. That is, two of "the rest" in v 9. One is named Cleopas, v 18.
26. That is, Sunday, the same day begun in v 1.
27. That is, 6.9 miles or 11.1 kilometers. On "stade", see Rev 14:20.
28. Same word as in v 15. On this word, see Act 24:26.
29. Or, "held fast", held in God's power. On this word, see "hold on to" in Heb 4:14.
30. Or, "*so that they* did not recognize".
31. Literally, "throwing back and forth". Used only here. GK *506*.
32. On this word, see Mt 6:16. Some manuscripts say "you are" instead of "they stood [still]", so that this becomes part of the words of Jesus, "... while walking? And you are sad-faced" {B}.
33. Some manuscripts add "of them" {N}.
34. Or, "living as a pilgrim or stranger, sojourning". On this word, see Heb 11:9. This is the Greek word order. It means "Are You the only one who does not know about this?" Or, "Are **You** living-as-a-stranger alone in Jerusalem...", meaning, "Have You been so isolated that you do not know about this?"
35. On this word, see Mk 1:24. Some manuscripts say "the Nazarene" {B}, the word in Lk 18:37.
36. Or, "proved to be, was ". GK *1181*.
37. This idiom "*a man who was a* prophet" is like "*a man who is a* glutton", Mt 11:19; "*a man who is a* merchant", Mt 13:45; "*a man who is a* house-master", Mt 20:1; "*a man who was a* king", Mt 18:23; "*a man who was a* murderer", Act 3:14; "*a certain man who was a* magician", Act 13:6. These examples use two different words for "man". This idiom links "man" with another noun in a way that is redundant in English. In each of these cases, English translations usually omit "man", so that it just says "*a* prophet, *a* glutton, *a* merchant", etc.
38. Same word as in 1:49; Act 7:22; 18:24; 25:5; 1 Cor 1:26, 2 Cor 12:10. It mainly means "powerful, capable, able", and "possible". Used 32 times. GK *1543*. Related to "be able" in 1 Jn 3:9.
39. Or, "for *a sentence of* death". Same word as in 23:40.
40. More literally, "is", as the Greek typically phrases it.
41. On this word, see 1 Pet 1:18. Note 2:38, where people were waiting for the "redemption of Jerusalem"; and 1:68.
42. Or, "besides, together with". GK *5250*.
43. That is, the things about Jesus, His life and death, and their hopes for Him, v 19-20. Yet on top of everything, Jesus has been dead three days now, so we must get on with our lives.
44. This is a difficult idiom. No subject is expressed. Some think Jesus is the subject, so that it is literally, "He is spending this third day [dead] since...". Others take it as an impersonal reference to time, literally "*one* is spending this third day since...", which is simplified to "it is the third day since...". Some manuscripts supply "today" {N}, so that it says "today is spending this third day since...", which is simplified to "today is the third day since...". The word "spending" in this idiom (or it may be rendered "leading", GK *72*), is related to "spend" in 1 Tim 2:2.
45. Used only here. GK *3984*. Related to "dawn" in v 1; and to "arising very early" in 21:38.
46. Same word as in 1:22. On this word, see 2 Cor 12:1.

A. Lk 5:1   B. Lk 21:34, suddenly come upon   C. Phil 2:21   D. Mt 28:6   E. Mt 26:21   F. Mt 9:10, sinner   G. Lk 18:33, rise up   H. 1 Jn 1:3, announcing   J. Lk 8:3   K. Phil 2:15, shine   L. Mt 15:8   M. Mk 8:11, debate   N. Lk 5:1   O. Lk 21:28   P. Col 1:6, understood   Q. Jam 2:24   R. Lk 1:34   S. 1 Cor 12:28   T. Rev 1:5   U. Jn 5:45, put hope   V. Rev 16:18   W. Mk 2:12   X. Rev 20:4, came to life

7C.	And **He** said to them, "O foolish[A] *ones,* and slow *in* the heart to be putting-faith upon[1] all[2] that the prophets spoke! °Did not the Christ have-to[3] suffer[B] these *things,* and enter into His glory?"	25 26
	1D. And beginning from[4] Moses and from all the prophets, He interpreted[5] *to* them the *things* concerning Himself in all the Scriptures[C]	27
8C.	And they drew-near[D] to the village where they were going. And **He** made-as-if[6] to be proceeding farther. °And they strongly-urged[E] Him, saying, "Stay[F] with us, because it is toward evening, and the day has already[7] declined[G]". And He went in *that He might* stay with them	28 29
	1D. And it came about at His lying down [to eat] with them *that* having taken the bread, He blessed[H] it[J]. And having broken[J] *it,* He was giving *it to* them	30
	2D. And their eyes were opened[K], and they recognized[L] Him[9]. And **He** became invisible[10] from them	31
	3D. And they said to one another, "Was not our heart burning[M] within us[11] as He was speaking *to* us on the road, as[12] He was opening[K] the Scriptures *to* us?"	32

5B.[13] And having arisen[N] *at* the very hour, they returned[14] to Jerusalem. And they found the eleven[15] and the *ones* with them having been assembled[16], °saying[17] that "The Lord really[O] arose[18]! And He appeared[P] *to* Simon"

1C.	And **they** were describing[19] the *things* on the road, and how He was recognized[Q] *by* them in[20] the breaking[R] *of* the bread	35
2C.	And while they *were* speaking these *things,* He[21] Himself stood in *the* midst[S] *of* them	36
	1D. And[22] He says *to* them, "Peace *to* you"	
3C.	But having been frightened[T] and having become terrified[23], they were thinking[U] *that they were* seeing *a* spirit	37
	1D. And He said *to* them, "Why are you troubled[24]? And for what reason are doubts[25] coming-up[26] in your heart[27]? °Look at My hands and My feet[28], that **I** am Myself. Touch[29] Me and see, because *a* spirit does not have flesh and bones as you observe[V] Me having"	38 39
	2D. And[30] having said this, He showed them *His* hands and *His* feet	40
4C.	But while they *were* still not-believing[31] *it* because of the joy, and marveling[W], He said *to* them, "Do you have something edible here?"	41
	1D. And the *ones* gave Him *a* part *of a* broiled fish[32]	42
	2D. And having taken *it,* He ate *it* in their presence	43
5C.	And[33] He said to them, "These *are* My[34] words which I spoke to you while still being with you— that all the *things* having been written about Me in the Law *of* Moses and the Prophets and *the* Psalms must[X] be fulfilled[Y]"	44
	1D. Then He opened[35] their mind[Z] *that they might* understand[AA] the Scriptures[36]	45

6B.[37] And[38] He said *to* them that 46

    1C. "Thus it has been written[39]—

1. Or, "believing in". On "putting faith upon", see Rom 4:5.
2. Many Jews believed the things about the Messiah entering His glory, but ignored the things about His suffering.
3. Or, "Was it not necessary that the Christ suffer". On this idiom, "have to", see "must" in Mt 16:21.
4. On "beginning from", see Mt 20:8.
5. Or, "explained, gave the meaning of". On this word, see 1 Cor 12:30.
6. Or, "made as though, acted as if". Used only here. GK *4701*. Jesus prepared to, or actually began to leave.
7. Some manuscripts omit this word {N}.
8. Or, "*God*". See Mt 14:19 on this.
9. Not because Jesus broke bread with them, but because He who held back their eyes in v 16 opened them now. The breaking of bread was the occasion, not the cause. These men would not have been in the upper room on Passover.
10. That is, Jesus vanished. This adjective is used only here. GK *908*. Related to "disfigure" in Mt 6:16.
11. Some manuscripts omit "within us" {C}.
12. Some manuscripts say "and as..." {N}.
13. Parallel account at Mk 16:14; Jn 20:19.
14. One can be sure that this trip took far less time than the earlier one! Did these two run the whole way?
15. This is used here as a title, not a count. Only ten were actually present, because Thomas was not there, Jn 20:19, 24. Compare "the twelve" in 1 Cor 15:5.
16. Or, "collected, gathered". Used only here. GK *125*. Related to the words in 11:29 and Act 12:12.
17. The grammar indicates that the eleven and the ones with them were saying this.
18. Or, "was raised". On this word, see Mt 28:6.
19. Or, "expounding". On this word, see "expound" in Jn 1:18.
20. That is, "in connection with, at". GK *1877*.
21. Some manuscripts say "Jesus" {N}.
22. Some manuscripts omit this sentence {B}.
23. Or, "afraid". Same word as in v 5; Act 10:4; Rev 11:13. Elsewhere only as "afraid" in Act 24:25. GK *1873*.
24. This is a participle, "why are you having been troubled". On this word, see "disturbed" in Gal 1:7.
25. Or, "disputes, arguments, reasonings". The disciples' minds were tossing up arguments as to why this could not really be Jesus. On this word, see "thoughts" in Jam 2:4.
26. Or, "arising". Same phrase as in Act 7:23; 1 Cor 2:9. GK *326*.
27. Some manuscripts have this word plural {N}.
28. Some think this implies that both were nailed to the cross. Compare Jn 20:25.
29. Or, "Handle". Same word as in 1 Jn 1:1; Heb 12:18. Elsewhere only as "grope for" in Act 17:27. GK *6027*.
30. Some manuscripts omit this verse {B}.
31. That is, "not-believing" in the sense of being astonished, saying "I can't believe it! Unbelievable!". Same word as in v 11, where it has its normal connotation.
32. Some manuscripts add "and *a* honeycomb from *a* beehive" {B}.
33. Others start point 6B. here, grouping these words with what follows instead of with resurrection Sunday.
34. Some manuscripts omit this word {K}, so that it says "the words".
35. Same word as in v 31, 32. On this word, see Act 17:3.
36. Some think this was in conjunction with their reception of the Spirit in Jn 20:22.
37. Compare Mt 28:16-20; Mk 16:15-18; Jn 20:21-23.
38. Some think v 46-49 were also spoken on that first Sunday, making this point 6C. Compare Jn 20:21-23. Others think Luke jumps to the day of the final ascension. Note that Luke does not include the appearances of Jesus in Galilee at all. The command to sit in Jerusalem (v 49; compare Act 1:4) may imply the Galilee appearances were past. Others think v 44-49 summarize the things Jesus said to them during the days prior to His ascension.
39. Some manuscripts add "and thus it was necessary" {N}.

A. Tit 3:3 B. Gal 3:4 C. 2 Pet 3:16 D. Lk 21:28 E. Act 16:15, prevail upon F. Jn 15:4, abide G. Lk 9:12 H. Lk 6:28 J. Act 2:46 K. Act 17:3 L. Col 1:6, understood M. Mt 5:15 N. Lk 18:33, rise up O. Jn 8:36 P. Lk 2:26, see Q. Lk 1:34, know R. Act 2:42 S. 2 Thes 2:7 T. Lk 21:9 U. Lk 19:11 V. Lk 10:18, seeing W. Rev 17:8 X. Mt 16:21 Y. Eph 5:18, filled Z. Rom 7:23 AA. Mt 13:13

| Luke 24:47 | 292 | Verse |

      1D. "*That* the Christ suffers[A] and rises-up[B] from *the* dead *on* the third day 47
      2D. "And *that* repentance[C] for[1] *the* forgiveness[D] *of* sins is proclaimed[E] on the basis of His name[2] to all the nations— beginning[3] from Jerusalem

  2C. "You[4] *are* witnesses[F] *of* these[5] *things* 48
  3C. "And behold[6]— **I** am sending-forth[G] the promise *of* My Father[7] upon you 49
  4C. "But **you** sit in the city[8] until which *time* you put-on[9] power[10] from on-high[11]"

7B.[12] And He led them outside[13] until near[14] Bethany. And having lifted-up[H] His hands, He blessed[J] them 50

  1C. And it came about during His blessing[J] them *that* He separated[15] from them, and was being carried-up[16] into heaven 51
  2C. And **they**, having worshiped[17] Him, returned to Jerusalem with great joy[18] 52

8B. And they were continually[K] in the temple blessing[19] God[20] 53

1. Some manuscripts say "and" {B}. The phrase "repentance for forgiveness of sins" is also in Mk 1:4 and Lk 3:3, where it is the message of John the Baptist. Repentance "and" forgiveness is in Act 5:31.
2. On the phrase "on the basis of His name", see Act 2:38.
3. The grammar refers back to the unexpressed subject of "is proclaimed". That is, "*The proclaimers* beginning from Jerusalem". Or, this phrase may go with what follows, "Beginning from Jerusalem, you *are* witnesses...". On the idiom "beginning from", see Mt 20:8.
4. Some manuscripts say "And **you** are witnesses..." {N}.
5. Note that the two points of v 46-47 are the very two points that Paul debated and proclaimed in his ministry, according to his testimony in Act 26:23.
6. Some manuscripts omit this word {C}.
7. That is, the Spirit.
8. Some manuscripts add "*of* Jerusalem" {N}.
9. Or, "clothe *yourselves* with". On this word, see Rom 13:14. This is expanded in Act 1:4-8.
10. Same word as in Act 1:8.
11. Or, "from *the* high [heaven]". On this word, see 1:78.
12. Parallel account at Mk 16:19; Act 1:9.
13. That is, outside of Jerusalem. Note Mt 21:17. Some manuscripts omit this word {C}, so that it says "And He led them out as far as near Bethany".
14. The phrase "until near, as far as near" is used only here, but is similar to "as far as outside" in Act 21:5. "Near" is the same word used in 19:29, where Luke says Bethany is "near" the Mount of Olives. GK *4639*. So anywhere on the Mount of Olives (see Act 1:12) qualifies as "near" Bethany.
15. Or, "parted, stood apart". It means "to set an interval of space or time from a former position". Elsewhere only as "passed" in 22:59; and "set an interval" in Act 27:28. GK *1460*. Here, the "days of His ascension" (9:51) are fulfilled. In Act 1:2, Luke refers to the ascension as part of his Gospel.
16. Or, "taken up". That is, by a cloud, Act 1:9. On this word, see "bear" in Heb 9:28. Some manuscripts omit "and was being carried up into heaven" {B}.
17. On this word, see Mt 14:33. Some manuscripts omit "having worshiped Him" {B}.
18. The life of Jesus began in "great joy" in Lk 2:10; and begins again in "great joy" here. As in Matthew (see 28:8), these are the only two places "great joy" occurs in Luke. It is elsewhere only in Act 15:3; 3 Jn 4. The word "joy" is used 59 times. GK *5915*. The related verb is "rejoice" in 2 Cor 13:11.
19. Some manuscripts say "praising and blessing"; others have one or the other word {B}. Same word as in v 50, 51.
20. Some manuscripts add "Amen" {A}.

A. Gal 3:4 B. Lk 18:33 C. 2 Cor 7:10 D. Col 1:14 E. 2 Tim 4:2 F. Act 1:8 G. Mk 3:12, send out H. 2 Cor 11:20 J. Lk 6:28 K. 2 Thes 3:16

John

Overview

1A.	The Word was with God and was God. The Word became flesh and we beheld His glory. John testifies to Him. We all received of His fullness. He expounded God to us	1:1-18
2A.	And this is the testimony of John— I am not the Christ. Jesus is the Lamb of God, Son of God	1:19-34
3A.	Two of John's disciples follow Jesus. He makes the water wine. They go to Capernaum	1:35-2:12
4A.	At Passover, Jesus went up to Jerusalem. He drove out the sellers. He spoke to Nicodemus	2:13-3:21
5A.	After these things, Jesus went into Judea. John the Baptist said, He must grow, I must diminish	3:22-36
6A.	Jesus left Judea and went to Galilee. And He had to go through Samaria	4:1-4
1B.	At a well in Samaria, He spoke to a woman— I will give you living water. I am Messiah	4:5-44
2B.	He came to Galilee and they welcomed Him. He healed the son of a royal one	4:45-54
7A.	After these things, there was a Feast of the Jews, and Jesus went up to Jerusalem	5:1
1B.	Now at a pool near the Sheep gate lay many sick ones. There was a man there sick 38 years	5:2-5
2B.	Jesus healed the man, and he picked up his cot and was walking	5:6-9
3B.	It was a Sabbath on that day. So the Jews objected. The man told them Jesus healed him	5:9-15
4B.	Since Jesus did it on a Sabbath, and claimed God was His Father, they wanted to kill Him	5:16-18
5B.	Therefore Jesus said to them	5:19
1C.	The Son does what He sees the Father doing. He will give life and judge	5:19-30
2C.	The Father testifies about the Son— in His works, His voice, and the Scriptures	5:31-47
8A.	After these things, Jesus went to the other side of the Sea of Galilee	6:1
1B.	And a large crowd followed because of the signs He did. Jesus fed the 5000	6:2-15
2B.	That evening, His disciples left by boat for Capernaum. Jesus walked on the water	6:16-21
3B.	The next day, the crowd went to Capernaum seeking Jesus	6:22-24
1C.	Jesus said to them, Work for food remaining for eternal life. I am the Bread of life	6:25-40
2C.	The Jews grumbled at this. Jesus said, The bread I give for the world is My flesh	6:41-51
3C.	The Jews were fighting over this. Jesus said, The one eating My flesh and drinking My blood has eternal life	6:52-59
4C.	Many disciples said, This statement is hard. Jesus said, My words are spirit and life	6:60-65
5C.	From this time, many withdrew. The twelve said, You have the words of eternal life	6:66-71
4B.	After these things, Jesus was walking in Galilee, for the Jews in Judea were seeking to kill Him	7:1
9A.	Now the Tent-pitching Feast of the Jews was near	7:2
1B.	His brothers asked Him to go and reveal Himself. Jesus said no, and went secretly	7:3-13
2B.	At the middle of the Feast, Jesus went up to the temple and was teaching	7:14
1C.	My teaching is not Mine, but from the One having sent Me. You want to kill Me	7:15-24
2C.	You know Me, but I have not come of Myself. I know Him who sent Me forth	7:25-30
3C.	Many from the crowd believed in Jesus and said, Will the Christ do more signs? The Pharisees sent officers to seize Him. I am with you a short time longer	7:31-36

John — Overview

3B.	On the last day, Jesus said, If any one is thirsting, let him come to Me and drink. Some believed. The officers returned without Him	7:37-8:1
4B.	They brought Jesus a woman caught in adultery. He said, Let the sinless one throw first	8:2-11
5B.	Then Jesus said, I am the light of the world. My testimony is true. My Father is testifying	8:12-20
6B.	Then Jesus said, I am going, and unless you believe that I am the One, you will die in your sins. When you lift up the Son of Man, then you will know I am the One	8:21-30
7B.	Then Jesus said to those who believed in Him, If you remain in My word, then you are truly My disciples, and the truth will set you free. You are slaves of sin. Your father is the devil. If anyone keeps My word, he will never see death. Before Abraham was, I am	8:31-59
8B.	While passing on, Jesus saw a man blind from birth	9:1
1C.	This man was born blind that the works of God might be made visible in him	9:2-5
2C.	Jesus made mud, smeared it on his eyes, and healed him	9:6-7
3C.	The neighbors say, How were your eyes opened? The man says Jesus did it	9:8-12
4C.	They bring him to the Pharisees, who object because it was the Sabbath. He testifies	9:13-34
5C.	Jesus finds him and says, Do you believe in the Son of Man? I am He	9:35-38
6C.	He said, I came that the ones not seeing may see, and the ones seeing may become blind	9:39
7C.	Some Pharisees said, We are not blind ones, are we?	9:40
8C.	Jesus said, You are thieves and robbers in the fold. The sheep will follow Me out	9:41-10:6
9C.	I am the door to life, the good shepherd who lays down his life for the sheep	10:7-18
10C.	A division occurred among them because of these words	10:19-21
10A.	Then the Feast of Dedication took place. Are You the Christ? Jesus said, I told you. The works testify. I and the Father are One. They tried to stone Him because He made Himself God	10:22-42
11A.	Mary and Martha sent to Him. Jesus came back and raised Lazarus. Many believed in Him. Caiaphas said, one Man should die for the people. Jesus went away	11:1-54
12A.	Now the Passover was near	11:55
1B.	Many were seeking Jesus, wondering if He would come to the feast at all	11:55-57
2B.	Jesus came to Bethany, and Mary anointed Him with perfume. He said, for My burial	12:1-11
3B.	The next day, the crowd laid palm branches before Him and shouted Hosanna	12:12-19
4B.	Some Greeks came to see Him. Jesus said, The hour has come for Me to be glorified. Follow Me. Believe in the Light	12:20-36
5B.	He having done so many signs, Israel did not believe Him, that Scripture might be fulfilled	12:37-43
6B.	Jesus said, He who believes in Me, believes in Him who sent Me. I am the Light. My words will judge those who reject Me. I speak the Father's words	12:44-50
13A.	Jesus loved His own to the end	13:1
1B.	At dinner, Jesus washed the disciples' feet, then explained it to them. Follow My example	13:2-20
2B.	Jesus was troubled in spirit and said, One of you will hand Me over. Judas leaves	13:21-30
3B.	When Judas went out, Jesus says	13:31
1C.	Now the Son of Man was glorified. God will glorify Him immediately	13:32
2C.	Little children, I am going, you cannot come. Love one another as I loved you	13:33-35
3C.	Peter says, Where are you going? Why can't I follow, I will die for You	13:36-38
4C.	Do not be troubled. I am going to prepare a place for you in My Father's house. You know the way. I am the way. You will know My Father. I am in the Father	14:1-11

Overview	297	**John**

      5C. The one believing will do greater works than Me, because I am going to the Father. The Helper will be with you forever, the Spirit of truth — 14:12-17

      6C. I will not leave you as orphans. I am coming to you. I will reveal Myself to you — 14:18-26

      7C. I leave you peace, My peace. Do not be troubled or afraid. I will no longer speak many things with you, for the ruler of the world is coming — 14:27-31

   4B. Arise, let us be going from here — 14:31

      1C. I am the true grapevine. Abide in Me and bear much fruit, and glorify My Father — 15:1-17

      2C. If the world hates you, it hated Me first. It hates you because I chose you. It hated Me without a cause. The Helper will testify concerning Me. They will persecute you — 15:18-16:4

      3C. I say these things now because I am going. It is better that I go, for I will send you the Helper. He will convict the world, guide you in all truth, disclose the future, glorify Me — 16:5-15

      4C. I am leaving the world, going to the Father. I will see you again, you will rejoice — 16:16-32

      5C. I spoke these things that you may have peace. Take courage, I have overcome the world — 16:33

   5B. Jesus lifted up His eyes to heaven and said — 17:1

      1C. Father, the hour has come. Glorify Your Son. I glorified You. Glorify Me — 17:1-5

      2C. I revealed Your name to the men You gave Me. Keep them in Your name — 17:6-13

      3C. I have given them Your word. Keep them from the evil one. Set them apart in the truth — 17:14-19

      4C. I ask also for those who believe through their word, that they may be one in Us — 17:20-23

      5C. Father, I desire that they be with Me where I am, and see My glory — 17:24

      6C. Father, I knew You, and these knew You sent Me. I will make You known to them — 17:25-26

14A. Having said these things, they went to the garden — 18:1

   1B. Judas came to the garden with the Roman soldiers and temple officers — 18:2-3

   2B. Jesus said, Whom are you seeking? They said, Jesus. He said, I am He. Let these go — 18:4-11

   3B. They arrested Jesus and took Him to Annas and Caiaphas. Peter denied Him — 18:12-27

   4B. They lead Him to Pilate, who found no fault in Him, but condemned Him — 18:28-19:16

   5B. Pilate handed Him over to be crucified. Jesus said, It has been accomplished, and died — 19:16-30

   6B. The Jews requested the legs to be broken. Jesus was already dead, but was pierced — 19:31-37

   7B. Joseph asked for His body and with Nicodemus, placed it in his tomb — 19:38-42

15A. On the first day of the week, Mary came to the tomb and saw the stone rolled away — 20:1

   1B. She runs and tells Peter and John. They ran and saw the tomb and the graveclothes — 20:2-10

   2B. Mary was weeping by the tomb. Jesus appeared to her. She told the disciples — 20:11-18

   3B. Jesus appeared to the disciples in a room and sends them. Thomas was not there — 20:19-23

   4B. After eight days, Jesus appeared again to them, including Thomas. My Lord and My God — 20:24-29

   5B. Jesus did many other signs not written here. These are written that you may believe — 20:30-31

16A. After these things, Jesus manifested Himself to them in Galilee. He fed them. He asked Peter, Do you love Me? Feed My sheep. Peter will die a martyr. John will remain as He pleases — 21:1-24

Conclusion — 21:25

1A. In *the* beginning[1] was the Word[2], and the Word was with God, and the Word was God[3]   1

    1B. This *One* was in *the* beginning[A] with God   2

        1C. All *things* came-into-being[4] through Him, and apart from Him not even one[5] *thing* came into being which has come-into-being[6]   3

        2C. In Him was life[B], and the life[7] was the light *of* mankind[C]   4

        3C. And the light[8] is shining[D] in the darkness[9], and the darkness did not overcome[10] it   5

    2B. There came-to-be[11] *a* man, having been sent-forth[E] from God. *The* name *for* him *was* John   6

        1C. This *one* came[12] for *a* testimony[13]— in order that he might testify[14] concerning the Light, in order that all might believe[F] through him   7

        2C. That *one* was not the Light, but *came* in order that he might testify concerning the Light— *the true[G] Light which gives-light-to[15] every person was coming[16] into the world[17]   8-9

            1D. He was in the world,[18] and the world came-into-being through Him, and the world did not know[19] Him   10

            2D. He came to *His* own *things*[20], and *His* own *ones* did not accept[21] Him   11

            3D. But all who did receive[22] Him, He gave them— the *ones* believing in His name[23]— *the* right[24] to become children[H] *of* God[25]   12

                1E. Who **were born**[26] not of bloods[27], nor of *the* will[J] *of the* flesh,[28] nor of *the* will *of a* husband[29], but of God[30]   13

  3B. And the Word became[31] flesh and dwelt[32] among us, and we saw[33] His glory— glory as *of the* only-born[34] from *the* Father,[35] full *of* grace[K] and truth[36]   14

        1C. John[37] testifies concerning Him. And he has cried-out[L], saying, "This *One* was the *One of* Whom I said, 'The *One* coming after me[38] has become ahead of me,[39] because He was before[40] me' "   15

        2C. Because[41] **we** all received from His fullness[42]— even grace upon[43] grace   16

            1D. Because the Law was given through Moses; grace and truth came through Jesus Christ   17

1. That is, at the first moment of creation, as in Gen 1:1. The Word preexists all creation, Col 1:17; Jn 17:5.
2. This word is used of Jesus also in v 14. Compare 1 Jn 1:1, "the Word of Life"; and Rev 19:13, "the Word of God". GK *3364*.
3. John directly states what Jesus Himself claimed and His enemies understood, 5:18; 10:33; and for which they killed Him, 19:7.
4. Or, "came-to-be, became existent, originated, were made". This word is used three times in this verse, and in v 6, 10. On this word, see "comes" in 2 Pet 1:20. GK *1181*.
5. Instead of "not even one", some manuscripts say "nothing" {N}.
6. Some punctuate this "came into being. What has come into being in Him was life..." (for His creation).
7. That is, the life just spoken of, the life of God, spiritual life. Life "was" in the Word from eternity. The light proceeding from this life "was" lighting mankind since creation, and "is shining" even now. God's life shines forth in God's light, lighting the way to Him. Compare 5:26. There are other views. Consult the commentaries.
8. In John, this word is used in 1:4, 5, 7, 8, 9; 3:19, 20, 21; 5:35; 8:12; 9:5; 11:9, 10; 12:35, 36, 46. Used 73 times. GK *5890*.
9. Darkness is something one "walks in" (8:12), or "remains in" (12:46), and something which "blinds" (1 Jn 2:11). Elsewhere only in Mt 10:27; Lk 12:3; Jn 6:17; 8:12; 12:35, 46; 20:1; 1 Jn 1:5; 2:8, 9, 11. GK *5028*. Related word in 3:19.
10. Or, "overtake, master, overpower, suppress; grasp, comprehend". Some think John means darkness (all the forces of darkness in the broadest sense) did not overcome the light— not in the Garden, and not at the cross. Others think he means darkness (unbelieving people) did not understand the Light, making this thought parallel with v 10b and 11b. Same word as in Mk 9:18. Elsewhere only as "overtake" in Jn 12:35; 1 Thes 5:4; "caught" (seized, overtaken) in Jn 8:3, 4; "take hold of " in Rom 9:30; 1 Cor 9:24; Phil 3:12, 13; "understand" in Act 4:13; 10:34; "find out" in Act 25:25; and "grasp" in Eph 3:18. GK *2898*.
11. Or, "arose". The appearance on the scene of John the Baptist initiated the coming of the Light. GK *1181*.
12. John's purpose in God's plan is now stated. This is the common word for coming and going. On this word, see Mk 16:2.
13. The Baptist came as a witness, to give "testimony" about the Light. His testimony is in v 15, 19-34; 3:27-36. Used 37 times, all as "testimony", 30 being by John. GK *3456*. Related to the noun "witness" (not used in this book; see Act 1:8), and to the verb next.
14. Or, "bear witness". Used 76 times, 47 being by John. GK *3455*.
15. Or, "illuminates". On this word, see "enlighten" in Heb 6:4.
16. The Light was in the act of coming, or was about to come, on the scene. Compare 3:19; 12:46. Others render this phrase "He [the Light, v 8] was the true Light which gives light to every person, coming into the world"; others, "There was the true Light which, coming into the world, gives light to every person". Some punctuate the last phrase as "every person coming into the world", so that "coming" refers to "person" instead of "the true Light".
17. The mixed result of this true Light coming into the world to give light is given next in v 10-13, and is explained in 3:19-21.
18. Some think this is referring to the preincarnate Word as the light of mankind, expanding on v 4-5; others, to the incarnate Light before He began His ministry, or as a summary of His whole life.
19. Or, "recognize, acknowledge". On this word, see Lk 1:34.
20. On "*His* own *things*", see 19:27.
21. Or, "receive, take-to" themselves. Same word as "receive" in 1 Cor 15:1; Phil 4:9; Col 2:6; Heb 12:28. On this word, see "taken" in Lk 17:34. The Messiah was not accepted by His own people.
22. This is the common word for "take, receive", used 258 times. On this word, see "taken" in Rom 7:8. Related to "accept" in v 11.
23. This phrase defines "receive Him" earlier. "Believe in His name" also occurs in 2:23; 3:18; 1 Jn 5:13.
24. Or, "authority, capability". On this word, see 1 Cor 8:9.
25. The phrase "children of God" is also in 11:52; Rom 8:16, 21; 9:8; Phil 2:15; 1 Jn 3:1, 2, 10; 5:2. The emphasis of being called "children" is on the birth from above, and on sharing the nature of our Father, 2 Pet 1:4. The emphasis of being called "sons" is on being heirs (see Rom 8:14).
26. Or, "fathered, begotten". In the Greek, this is the last word in the sentence, for emphasis. On this word, see 1 Jn 2:29.
27. Though used 97 times in the NT, this word is plural only here. That is, not from a blending of human bloodlines, not descended from the genealogical lines of a human father and mother, not born from human blood relatives. On this word, see 1 Jn 1:7.
28. That is, not born out of the body's sexual drives.
29. This word means "man, husband", a male specifically. Not born out of a man's desire to procreate. On this word, see "man" in 1 Tim 2:12.
30. Such people were born directly of God in a second birth.
31. The Word "was" with God (v 1), and "became" a human being. He was existing in the form of God, but emptied Himself and took the form of a slave, Phil 2:6-7.
32. Or, "lived". Note that John is referring in summary form to Jesus Christ's whole life. On this word, see Rev 7:15.
33. The apostles were eyewitnesses, 2 Pet 1:16-18. They saw and heard.
34. On this word, see v 18.
35. That is, a unique glory, glory as of the one and only Son of His one and only Father. Both are unique.
36. Jesus was full of the grace He brought (v 16, 17), and the truth about God He expounded (v 17, 18). On this word, see 4:23.
37. John now gives the Baptist's testimony regarding Jesus, since this was the purpose for which the Baptist came (v 7).
38. Jesus "came after" the Baptist historically— both in His physical birth, and in beginning His ministry.
39. That is, in worthiness (see 1:27), in spiritual strength and power (see Mt 3:11), in His rank and authority.
40. That is, Jesus preexisted me. Same word as in v 30; 15:18. GK *4755*.
41. Some think John is adding his testimony to the Baptist's. We apostles know the Word became flesh and was full of grace and truth because we all received from His fullness. We directly experienced it. We received the truth He expounded about God, v 18. Others think John is adding the testimony of all Christians to his own witness in v 14. Jesus truly was full of grace and truth because all we Christians received it from Him. Some manuscripts say "And we all..." {N}.
42. Same word as in Col 1:19; 2:9, the fullness of Deity. On this word, see Col 1:19.
43. Or, "for, after, in place of ". Some think John means "grace after grace", repeated gifts of grace, a continual flow of grace; others, the grace of Christ "in place of " the grace contained in the Law of Moses, as explained in v 17; others, grace "corresponding to" His grace. This preposition is used only here by John. GK *505*.

A. Col 1:18 B. Rom 8:10 C. Mt 4:4 D. Phil 2:15 E. Mk 3:14, send out F. Jn 3:36 G. Jn 7:28 H. 1 Jn 3:1 J. Jn 7:17 K. Eph 2:8 L. Mt 8:29

John 1:18	300	Verse

    4B. No one has ever[1] seen God; *the* only-born[2] God[3], the *One* being[4] in the bosom[5] *of* the Father— that *One* expounded[6] *Him*   18

2A.[7] And this is the testimony[A] *of* John, when the Jews[8] from Jerusalem sent-out[B] priests[9] and Levites[10] to him[11] in order that they might ask him, "Who are **you**?", ˚and he confessed[12] and did not deny[C]   19   20

    1B. And he confessed that "**I** am not the Christ"

        1C. And they asked him, "What then?   21

            1D. "Are **you** Elijah?" And he says, "I am not"[13]
            2D. "Are **you** the Prophet[14]?" And he answered, "No"

        2C. Then they said *to* him, "Who are you— in order that we may give *an* answer *to* the *ones* having sent[D] us? What do you say about yourself?"   22

            1D. He said, "I *am the* 'voice *of one* shouting[E] in the wilderness[F]— "Make-straight[15] the way *of the* Lord"', just as Isaiah the prophet said [in Isa 40:3]"   23
            2D. And they had been sent-out[16] from the Pharisees   24

        3C. And they asked him, and said *to* him, "Why then are you baptizing[G] if **you** are not the Christ, nor Elijah, nor the Prophet?"   25

            1D. John responded *to* them saying, "**I** am baptizing with[17] water. Amidst[18] you stands[19] *One* Whom **you** do not know— ˚the *One* coming after me,[20] *of* Whom **I**[21] am not worthy[H] that I may untie[22] the strap[J] *of* **His** sandal"   26   27

        4C. These *things* took place in Bethany[23] beyond the Jordan, where John was baptizing   28

    2B. *On* the next day he[24] sees Jesus coming toward him[25]   29

        1C. And he says, "Look— the Lamb[26] *of* God[27], the *One* taking-away the sin [K]*of* the world[L]

            1D. "This *One* is *the One* about Whom **I** said, '*A* man is coming after me Who has become ahead of me, because He was before[M] me'   30
            2D. "And **I** did not know Him. But **I** came baptizing with water for this reason— that He might be revealed[28] *to* Israel   31

        2C.[29] And John testified[N], saying that   32

            1D. "I have seen the Spirit descending like *a* dove out of heaven. And He remained[O] upon Him
            2D. "And **I** did not know Him.[30] But the *One* having sent[D] me to baptize with water, that *One* said *to* me, 'Upon whomever you see the Spirit descending and remaining upon Him— this *One* is *the One* baptizing with[31] the Holy Spirit'   33
            3D. "And **I** have seen, and have testified that this *One* is the Son[32] *of* God"   34

3A.[33] *On* the next day John was again standing *there*, and two of his disciples. ˚And having looked at Jesus walking, he says, "Look— the Lamb *of* God". ˚And the two disciples heard him speaking, and followed Jesus   35-36   37

    1B. And Jesus, having turned, and having seen them following, says *to* them, "What are you seeking[P]?"   38

1. Or, "at any time". Same word as in 1 Jn 4:12. On this word, see 6:35.
2. Or, "unique, one and only". This word means "only-born, only-child, one-and-only, only begotten, unique (the only example of its kind)". Some think John is referring to Jesus as incarnate. The "only born God" is the Word who "was God" (v 1) who "became" flesh (v 14), capturing all this in one phrase. Others think he is speaking of His eternal relationship to the Father as His unique, one and only Son. This word is used of Jesus also in 1:14; 3:16, 18; 1 Jn 4:9. Elsewhere only of an only child in Lk 7:12; 8:42; 9:38; Heb 11:17. GK *3666*. Compare "fathered" in 1 Jn 5:18, and "firstborn" in Col 1:15.
3. Some manuscripts say "Son" {B}, as in 3:16, 18; 1 Jn 4:9. The meaning is the same in either case, "God the Son".
4. Some think John is referring to the present exaltation of Jesus. He "was" with God (v 1), and after the cross, He is again in His bosom. Others think he is referring to His eternal place in His bosom as the Son, the Word "with God".
5. Or, "chest, breast, side". That is, in close communion, in the place of honor. Same word as in Jn 13:23; Lk 16:22, 23. Elsewhere only as "fold" in Lk 6:38; and as "bay" in Act 27:39. GK *3146*.
6. Or, "described, explained". In one sense, the word means to "lead out" the details of a thing, whether as dictating, expounding, interpreting, explaining, telling at length, relating, etc. Jesus expounded God to us; He showed us who God is. He did this in Himself, because when we see Him, we see the Father, 14:7, 9. In another sense, it means "to lead the way, to show the way". Jesus "led the way [to Him]", as He says in 14:6. The Word, who was in the beginning with God, who is God, who is the only-born God, who is in the bosom of the Father— That One expounded Him and led the way to Him. What He expounded in word and deed, we "received" (v 16), and we proclaim to the world in this book. Elsewhere only as "describe" in Lk 24:35; Act 10:8; 15:12, 14; 21:19. GK *2007*. Related to "lead" in Heb 13:7 (the root word); "relate" in Lk 8:39; and "tell in detail" in Act 13:41.
7. Parallel account at Mt 3:1; Mk 1:2; Lk 3:1.
8. That is, the Jewish leaders. Where the other Gospels would say "the Pharisees" or "the scribes and the Pharisees", John simply says "the Jews". Matthew, Mark and Luke do not use this word in this sense. Those three Gospels combined use this word 17 times, 12 of those in the phrase "King of the Jews". Used 195 times in the NT, John uses this word 71 times, Acts 79 times. Note 2:18; 5:10, 16, 18; 7:13; 9:22; 18:36; 19:7, 38. GK *2681*.
9. Priests were descendants of the family of Aaron within the tribe of Levi, Ex 28:1.
10. Or, "when the Jews sent priests and Levites from Jerusalem...". Levites were descendants of other families in the tribe of Levi. They performed various roles supporting the priests, Num 3:6-9. The temple police, and its musicians, were Levites. Here, they may have come as the "police escort" of the priests. Elsewhere only in Lk 10:32; Act 4:36. GK *3324*.
11. Some manuscripts omit "to him" {C}.
12. Or, "acknowledged, publicly declared". On this word, see 1 Tim 6:12.
13. Compare Mt 11:14; 17:11-13; Mk 9:12-13; Lk 1:17.
14. That is, the prophet like Moses, whom God promised in Deut 18:15, 18-19. Note Jn 6:14; 7:40; Act 3:22-23, 7:37.
15. This verb is related to the adjective "straight" in Mt 3:3; Mk 1:3; Lk 3:4 (on which, see Act 8:21). GK *2316*.
16. This is a participle, they "were having been sent out". Some think John is defining "the *ones* having sent us" in v 22, and further defining the "Jews" of v 19. Others think he is referring to a sub-group of the ones sent in v 19, or to an additional group, which now asks the next question, making this sentence part of point 3C. It would be rendered "And [some] having been sent out were from the Pharisees. And they asked...", or, "And [some] had been sent out from the Pharisees. And they asked...". Some manuscripts say "And the *ones* having been sent out were from..." {N}, making this a group of Pharisees (a religious party in Israel). Same word as in v 19. On this word, see Mk 3:14. Not related to "sent" in v 22.
17. Or, "in". On this word, see Mk 1:8. Same word as in v 31, 33.
18. Or, "In your midst, among you". On this word, see 2 Thes 2:7. Some manuscripts say "But amidst you" {N}.
19. Or, "is standing". The Baptist has apparently already baptized Jesus. Some manuscripts say "was standing" {B}.
20. Some manuscripts say instead "... know. **He** is the *One* coming after me Who has become ahead of me, *of* Whom..." {N}, like v 30, 15.
21. Some manuscripts do not emphasize "I" {C}, meaning it would not be bolded here.
22. Not the same grammar as in Mk 1:7; Lk 3:16. Compare Mt 3:11.
23. Not Bethany near Jerusalem. Some manuscripts say "Bethabara" {C}.
24. Some manuscripts say "John" {K}.
25. This may have been when Jesus was returning from His forty days of temptation in the wilderness.
26. Elsewhere only in v 36; Act 8:32 (referring to Isa 53), and 1 Pet 1:19. GK *303*. This word refers to a sacrificial lamb, 1 year old. There is another word for lamb used in Jn 21:15; Rev 13:11; and 28 times of Christ in Revelation 5-22. (GK *768*)
27. Or, "God's Lamb", the Lamb from God, belonging to Him, provided by Him; His sacrificial Lamb.
28. Or, "manifested, made evident, made known". On this word, see "made evident" in 1 Jn 2:19.
29. Compare Mt 3:16; Mk 1:10; Lk 3:22.
30. That is, the Baptist did not officially know directly from God that Jesus was the Coming One, as seen in what follows. That he knew Him privately, and knew what God had told Elizabeth and Mary, seems reasonable to assume. Compare Mt 3:14.
31. Or, "in". Same word as in v 31, 26. On baptize "in" or "with" water or the Spirit, see Mk 1:8.
32. Some manuscripts say "chosen *One*" {B}.
33. Compare Mt 4:18-22; Mk 1:16-20; Lk 5:1-11.

A. Jn 1:7 B. Mk 3:14 C. 2 Tim 2:12 D. Jn 20:21 E. Mt 3:3 F. Mt 3:1 G. Mk 1:8 H. Rev 16:6 J. Act 22:25 K. Jn 8:46 L. 1 Jn 2:15 M. Jn 1:15 N. Jn 1:7 O. Jn 15:4, abide P. Phil 2:21

    1C. And the *ones* said *to* Him, "Rabbi[A] (which being translated[B] means "Teacher"), where are You staying[C]?"

    2C. He says *to* them, "Come, and you will see"[1]   39

    3C. So[2] they went, and saw where He was[3] staying, and stayed with Him that day.[4] *The* hour[5] was about *the* tenth[6]

    4C. Andrew[D], the brother *of* Simon Peter, was one of the two[7] having heard *it* from John, and having followed Him. °This *one* first[8] finds *his* own brother Simon, and says *to* him, "We have found the Messiah[9]" (which being translated[B] is "Christ")   40 / 41

        1D. He brought him to Jesus   42

        2D. Having looked-at[E] him, Jesus said, "**You** are Simon, the son *of* John[10]. **You** will be called[F] Cephas[11]" (which is translated[12] "Peter")

 2B. *On* the next day[13] He[14] wanted[15] to go forth to Galilee. And He finds Philip[16]. And Jesus says *to* him, "Be following Me"   43

    1C. Now Philip was from Bethsaida, of the city *of* Andrew and Peter[17]. °Philip finds Nathanael[18] and says *to* him, "We have found *the One of* whom Moses wrote in the Law, and the Prophets *wrote*— Jesus, son *of* Joseph, from Nazareth"[19]   44-45

        1D. And Nathanael said *to* him, "Is anything good[G] able[20] to be **out of Nazareth**?"   46

        2D. Philip says *to* him, "Come and see"

    2C. Jesus saw Nathanael coming to Him, and says about him, "Look— truly[H] *an* Israelite in whom there is no deceit[J]"   47

        1D. Nathanael says *to* Him, "From where do You know me?"   48

        2D. Jesus responded and said *to* him, "Before Philip called you, while being[21] under the fig tree, I saw you"

        3D. Nathanael responded *to* Him, "Rabbi, **You** are the Son *of* God. **You** are *the* King *of* Israel"   49

        4D. Jesus responded and said *to* him, "Do you[22] believe because I said *to* you that I saw you under the fig tree? You will see greater *things than* these!"   50

        5D. And He says *to* him, "Truly, truly[23], I say *to* you *all*[24], you[25] will see heaven opened[26] and the angels *of* God ascending and descending upon the Son *of* Man"[27]   51

 3B. And *on* the third[28] day *a* wedding took place in Cana *of* Galilee. And the mother *of* Jesus was there. And both Jesus and His disciples were invited[29] to the wedding-celebration[30]   2:1 / 2

    1C. And *it*[31] having come-short-of[K] wine, the mother *of* Jesus says to Him, "They do not have wine"[32]   3

    2C. And[33] Jesus says *to* her, "What do I have to do with you[34], woman[35]? My hour has not yet come"[36]   4

    3C. His mother says *to* the servants, "Do whatever thing[37] He says *to* you"[38]   5

1. Some manuscripts say "Come and see" {N}.
2. Some manuscripts omit this word {N}.
3. More literally, "is", as the Greek typically phrases it.
4. This is the first encounter with Jesus for these two. Later, Jesus calls them to be His disciples (Mt 4:18; Mk 1:16); and later, His apostles (Mt 10:1; Mk 3:14; Lk 6:13). Here, they choose to follow Him; later He chooses them, 6:70.
5. Some manuscripts say "Now the hour..." {K}.
6. Some think John means 4 P.M., counted from sunrise, 6 A.M. Others think he means 10 A.M., Roman time. Had he said "and stayed with Him that evening", 4 P.M. would be certain. See 19:14 on why the issue arises.
7. Some think the other was John himself, the apostle and writer of this book (not the Baptist, mentioned next).
8. This may mean that this was the "first" thing Andrew did after Jesus accepted their company; or, that Simon was the "first" one that Andrew found and told about Jesus. Some manuscripts say "This first *one* finds..." {B}, meaning that Andrew was the first one to find and tell another about Jesus. In this case, John may be implying that Philip was second, v 44; or, that the unnamed second disciple of v 40 was the second (that is, that John found James).
9. This is a transliterated Hebrew word meaning "Anointed One". Elsewhere only in 4:25. GK *3549*. "Christ" is the Greek translation of this Hebrew word, and is related to the verb "to anoint" in Lk 4:18.
10. Same name as in 21:15, 16, 17. GK *2722*. In Mt 16:17, this man is called "Jonah", and some manuscripts say that here {B}. "Jonah" and "John" may be alternate Greek spellings of the same Hebrew name, like "Simon" and "Simeon" (see Lk 6:14).
11. Cephas (see Gal 1:18) is Aramaic, Peter (see Lk 6:14) is Greek. Both mean "rock".
12. Elsewhere only in 9:7; Heb 7:2. GK *2257*. Related to the word in v 38 and 41, and to the word in 1 Cor 12:10.
13. This is the fourth day mentioned, 19-28; 29-34; 35-42. Some find a fourth day in v 41.
14. Some manuscripts say "Jesus" {K}.
15. Or, "intended, desired". Jesus resolved to do so, and went to Cana of Galilee in 2:1. On this word, see "willing" in 7:17.
16. Where Jesus found Philip between Judea and Galilee is not stated. See Lk 6:14 on him.
17. These two lived in Capernaum, Mk 1:21, 29, but apparently were reared in Bethsaida. In the same way, Jesus was reared in Nazareth, but lived in Capernaum, Mt 4:13.
18. Nathanael is mentioned elsewhere only in v 46-49, and in 21:2 as "Nathanael of Cana". GK *3720*. He was Philip's relative or friend. Some think Nathanael is the Bartholomew in Lk 6:14.
19. Philip speaks what he heard from Jesus directly or through one of the other disciples. Jesus was Joseph's legal son, and was from Nazareth, even though He was not Joseph's physical son, and was born in Bethlehem.
20. This is an honest question. Is it able, based on the prophecies? Compare the confident statement in 7:52.
21. The grammar means while Nathanael was under the fig tree.
22. Or, this may be an exclamation, "You believe because... tree!".
23. On this word, see Mt 5:18. It is doubled like this always, and only, in this Gospel, 25 times.
24. This and the next "you" are plural, and this word is added to reflect this. Jesus is speaking to Nathanael, yet to all of them.
25. Some manuscripts say "from now *on,* you will..." {N}, using the same idiom as in Mt 26:64.
26. This is a participle, "having opened".
27. Some think Jesus means the disciples would see angels doing His bidding, responding to His directives, in confirmation of what Nathanael said in v 49. In His deeds, they will see Jesus as a conduit to God. Compare Gen 28:12.
28. That is, on the third day after the departure for Galilee in v 43. Cana was near Nazareth, about 70 miles or 112 kilometers from Jerusalem.
29. John does not indicate whether this invitation occurred upon the arrival of Jesus, or is the reason Jesus left for Galilee in 1:43.
30. Same word as "wedding" in v 1. On this word, see "wedding" in Mt 22:11.
31. That is, the wedding celebration. It is an impersonal reference to the hosts, the parents.
32. Some think Mary is asking Jesus to help, perhaps to go and get some, but she is not asking for His first miracle. She seems to feel it is her responsibility to do something, and she gives orders to the servants in v 5, so perhaps she was in charge. Perhaps the bridegroom was a relative. Others think she is asking Jesus to reveal Himself with a miracle.
33. Some manuscripts omit this word {C}.
34. This is an idiom, literally, "What [is there] *for* me and *for* you". That is, what business do we share as to this matter? What common interest do we have with one another as to this matter? What claim do you have on Me in this matter? Jesus separates Himself from Mary as her son. His ministry has begun. This same idiom is found in Mt 8:29; Mk 1:24; 5:7; Lk 4:34; 8:28. It can also be seen in another form in the comment of Pilate's wife in Mt 27:19, and in 1 Cor 5:12. Some take it here to mean "what [is it] *to* Me and *to* you", that is, what business is it of ours?
35. Jesus does not address Mary as "mother", but as any other woman. This is the same word He addresses her with in 19:26, and other women in Mt 15:28; Lk 13:12; Jn 4:21; 8:10; 20:15. It is a respectful term of address. On this word, see 1 Tim 2:11.
36. Or, "is not yet present". This "hour" is referred to in 7:30; 8:20; and it comes in 12:23, 27; 13:1; 17:1, where it is clear that it refers to the time of Jesus' sacrificial death. See also 7:6, 8. During His period of ministry, He no longer relates to Mary in a family, son-mother way, fulfilling her requests. And the time for "asking in His name" has not yet come, 16:23-24. He is doing His Father's work, not her family business. Others think Jesus means "the time for Me to publicly reveal Myself has not yet arrived". He does a private miracle for His disciples. Same word as "am here" in 8:42.
37. On this idiom, see Col 3:17.
38. Mary's response reveals that she thinks Jesus is going to do something, though she does not know what. She takes His response in v 4 to mean "I will not answer you on your terms, but on My own". He chooses to do a miracle as the Son of God, not an errand as the son of Mary. He acts for His own purposes (v 11), not for hers.

A. Mt 23:7   B. Act 13:8   C. Jn 15:4, abide   D. Lk 6:14   E. Mk 8:25, seeing   F. Rom 8:30   G. 1 Tim 5:10b   H. Mt 14:33   J. Mt 26:4   K. Lk 15:14, be in need

	4C. Now six stone waterpots^A were setting there for^1 the purification^2 [rite] *of* the Jews, each having-room-for^B two or three measures^3. °Jesus says *to* them, "Fill^C the waterpots *with* water". And they filled them up to *the* top	6 7
	5C. And He says *to* them, "Draw *some* now, and carry^D *it to* the headwaiter^4". And the *ones* carried *it*	8
	6C. And when the headwaiter tasted^E the water having become wine— and he did not know where it was^5 from, but the servants having drawn the water^6 knew— the headwaiter calls the bridegroom,°and says *to* him	9 10
	1D. "Every person^F first puts^G *out* the fine^H wine, and when they get-drunk^7, the^8 lesser^9. **You** have kept^J the fine wine until now"	
	7C. Jesus did this beginning^K *of* signs^10 in Cana *of* Galilee, and revealed^11 His glory. And His disciples believed in Him	11
	4B. After this He went down to Capernaum^12— He and His mother and His^13 brothers^14 and His disciples. And they stayed there not many days	12
4A. And the Passover^L [Feast] *of* the Jews was near, and Jesus went up to Jerusalem		13
	1B.^15 And in the temple,^16 He found the *ones* selling oxen and sheep and doves, and the changers-of-money^17 sitting [at their tables]	14
	1C. And having made *a* lash^18 from ropes^19, He drove *them* all out^M of the temple, and^20 the sheep and the oxen	15
	2C. And He poured-out^N the coins^21 *of* the money-changers^O	
	3C. And He overturned the tables	
	4C. And He said *to* the *ones* selling the doves, "Take these *things* from here.^22 Do not be making^23 the house^P *of* My Father^24 *a* house *of a* market^25"	16
	5C. His disciples remembered^Q that it has been written^26 [in Ps 69:9], "Zeal^R *for* Your house will consume^27 Me"	17
	6C. Then the Jews^28 responded and said *to* Him, "What sign do You show us, that you are doing^29 these *things*?"	18
	1D. Jesus responded and said *to* them, "Destroy^S this temple^T, and in three days I will raise^30 it"	19
	2D. Then the Jews said, "This temple was built *for* forty and six years,^31 and **You** will raise it in three days?" °But that *One* was speaking about the temple^T *of* His body	20 21
	3D. So when He was raised^32 from *the* dead, His disciples remembered^33 that He was saying this^34, and believed the Scripture, and the word which Jesus spoke	22
	2B. Now while He was in Jerusalem at the Passover^L during the Feast^U, many believed in His name^35— seeing His signs^36 which He was doing	23
	1C. But Jesus Himself was not entrusting^37 Himself *to* them	24
	1D. Because of His knowing^38 all *people*	
	2D. And because He was having no need^V that someone should testify about the person^F, for He Himself was knowing what was in the person^39	25
	3B. Now there was *a* man from the Pharisees— the name *for* him *was* Nicodemus^40— *a* ruler^W *of* the Jews. °This *one* came to Him^41 *by* night^42 and said *to* Him, "Rabbi^X, we know that You have come from God *as a* teacher. For no one is able to be doing these signs which **You** are doing unless God is with him"	3:1 2

1. Or, "in accordance with". GK *2848*.
2. On this, see Mk 7:3. On this word, see 2 Pet 1:9.
3. One measure was 39 liters, or 10 gallons. So this was 80-120 liters or 20 to 30 gallons. The large quantity is surprising, assuming John means it was all turned to wine (some do not think so, suggesting other scenarios). Jesus did much more than supply the current need. Used only here. GK *3583*.
4. Some think Jesus means the slave responsible for the banquet; others, based on the context here, the guest who was in charge of the banquet, "the president, governor, ruler, master" of it. Elsewhere only in v 9. GK *804*.
5. More literally, "is", as the Greek typically phrases it.
6. This may imply that when the servants drew it, it was still water. It became wine on the way. Or, this may simply be an abbreviation of "the water having become wine".
7. In making this proverbial statement, the man is not saying the guests are now drunk, or that they will become drunk; only that he would have expected this fine wine first. It is a comment about the quality of the wine, not the state of the guests. Elsewhere only in Lk 12:45; Eph 5:18; 1 Thes 5:7; Rev 17:2. GK *3499*. Related to "be drunk" in 1 Cor 11:21; "drunkard" in 1 Cor 5:11; and "drunkenness" in Rom 13:13.
8. Some manuscripts say "then the lesser" {N}.
9. That is, the inferior, lower quality, and therefore cheaper wine. On this word, see "younger" in Rom 9:12.
10. Or, "Jesus did this *as a* beginning *of* signs". Compare 4:54.
11. Or, "manifested". Same word as in 1:31. This is primarily why Jesus did this miracle, and all miracles. They are signs or revelations, revealing His glory, "attesting" or "proving" who He is, Act 2:22. See Jn 6:2. Thus, He did His first miracle for His disciples, to reveal Himself to them. They are the primary beneficiaries of this miracle.
12. Some think Jesus moved to Capernaum at this time, Mt 4:13; others, either before or after this occasion.
13. Some manuscripts omit this word; others omit "and His disciples" {C}.
14. On the "brothers" of Jesus, see Mt 13:55-56.
15. Compare Mt 21:12-13; Mk 11:15-17; Lk 19:45-46.
16. That is, in the outer court, the court of the Gentiles. Jesus did not object to what these merchants were doing, but where. Their service was needed by the worshipers, because Jewish foreign visitors needed to buy animals for the sacrifices and change their currency into shekels.
17. Used only here. GK *3048*. From a root word meaning "to cut into pieces", this word is used of one who "changes into smaller coins". Related to the word "coin" in v 15. Not related to "money changers" in v 15.
18. Or, "whip". Used only here. GK *5848*. Related to "flog" in Mt 27:26. Some manuscripts say "made [something] like *a* lash..." {B}.
19. Or, "cords". Elsewhere only in Act 27:32. GK *5389*.
20. Or, "both". Jesus expelled the people and the animals.
21. More literally, "coin", referring to all their money. Used only here. GK *3047*. Some manuscripts say "coins" {N}.
22. The doves in their cages had to be carried out. Jesus did not destroy the merchants' property, or free the birds.
23. The grammar implies, "Stop making...".
24. At the beginning of the ministry of Jesus, it is "My Father's house"; at the end, it is "your house", Mt 23:38.
25. Or, "market-center, commerce center, trading place". Used only here. GK *1866*. Related to "business" in Mt 22:5, and "merchant" in Mt 13:45, and "do business" in Jam 4:13. Our word "emporium" comes from this word, *emporion*.
26. This is a participle, "it is having been written", it stands written. Same phrase as in 6:31, 45; 10:34; 12:14; 20:30. GK *1211*.
27. Or, "devour, eat up". On this word, see "devour" in Mk 12:40. Some manuscripts say "consumed" {K}.
28. That is, the Jewish leaders. See 1:19.
29. That is, to prove Your authority to be doing these things.
30. The Jews remembered this statement in part, as seen in Mt 26:61; Mk 14:58. The sign Jesus offers them is the same sign He later calls the sign of Jonah, Mt 12:39-40; 16:4. On this word, see Mt 28:6.
31. That is, this temple as they now see it, for it was not finished yet. The grammar refers merely to the fact that 46 years had been expended thus far, not to the process ("has been being built *for* 46 years") or to the completion ("was built *in* 46 years"). Herod the Great began to rebuild it in 20-19 B.C. It was finished by Herod Agrippa II (see Act 25:13) in A.D. 64. It was destroyed by the Romans in A.D. 70.
32. Or, "arose". On this word, see "arose" in Mt 28:6.
33. The disciples did not understand this saying of Jesus at this time, but they recalled it to mind when Jesus was actually raised.
34. Some manuscripts add "*to* them" {K}.
35. On "believe in His name", see 1:12.
36. See Jn 6:2.
37. This is the same word as "believe" in v 23 and 3:36. Many believed in Jesus, but He did not believe in them; they trusted in His name, but He did not trust in them.
38. That is, because Jesus knew all people. John uses this grammar only here. "Because of His knowing" has the same grammar as Lk 2:4; 19:11; Act 4:2; 12:20; 27:4; Phil 1:7; Heb 10:2; Jam 4:2, etc.
39. This is clearly seen next in the case of Nicodemus, and in 4:18.
40. Other than in v 1-9, Nicodemus is mentioned elsewhere only in 7:50; 19:39. GK *3773*.
41. Some manuscripts say "Jesus" {K}.
42. This is repeated in 19:39. Some think it is mentioned because it symbolizes coming out of darkness into the light; others, that Nicodemus feared what others would think; others, that this was the only time Jesus would be alone.

A. Jn 4:28 B. 2 Pet 3:9, make room for C. Mk 4:37 D. 2 Pet 1:17 E. Heb 6:4 F. Mt 4:4, mankind G. Act 19:21 H. 1 Tim 5:10a, good J. 1 Jn 5:18 K. Col 1:18 L. Jn 18:28 M. Jn 12:31, cast out N. Act 2:17 O. Mt 21:12 P. Mk 3:20 Q. Lk 1:54 R. 2 Cor 11:2, jealousy S. Mt 5:19, break T. Rev 11:1 U. Jn 13:29 V. Tit 3:14 W. Rev 1:5 X. Mt 23:7

John 3:3	306	Verse

1C. Jesus responded and said *to* him, "Truly, truly[1], I say *to* you— unless one is born[2] again[3], he is not able to see the kingdom[A] *of* God"   3

2C. Nicodemus says to Him, "How is *a* person able to be born while being *an* old-man[4]? He is not able to enter *a* second *time* into the womb[B] *of* his mother and be born, *is he*?"[5]   4

3C. Jesus responded[6]—   5

    1D. "Truly, truly, I say *to* you, unless one is born of water and *the* Spirit,[7] he is not able to enter into the kingdom *of* God

        1E. "The *thing* having been born of the flesh is flesh,[8] and the *thing* having been born of the Spirit is spirit[9]   6

    2D. "Do not marvel[C] that I said *to* you, 'You[10] *all* must[D] be born again'   7

        1E. "The wind[11] blows where it wants[E], and you hear the sound *of* it. But you do not know from where it comes, and[12] where it is going. So[13] is everyone having been born of the Spirit"   8

4C. Nicodemus responded and said *to* Him, "How are these[14] *things* able to happen[15]?"   9

5C. Jesus responded and said *to* him, "Are **you** the teacher *of* Israel and you do not understand[16] these *things*?   10

    1D. "Truly, truly, I say *to* you that we[17] are speaking what we know, and we are testifying[F] what we have seen,[18] and you[19] *people* are not receiving our testimony[G]. °If I told you *people* earthly[20] *things* and you do not believe, how will you believe if I tell you heavenly *things*?   11, 12

    2D. "And[21] no one has gone up into heaven[22] except the *One* having come down from heaven— the Son *of* Man[23]   13

    3D. "And[24] just as Moses lifted-up[25] the serpent[H] in the wilderness[J], so the Son *of* Man must[D] be lifted up °in order that everyone putting-faith in[26] Him[27] may have eternal[K] life[28]   14, 15

        1E. "For[29] God so[30] loved[L] the world[M] that He gave *His* only-born[N] Son, in order that everyone believing in Him may[31] not perish[O], but may have eternal life   16

        2E. "For God did not send-forth[P] the Son into the world in order that He might judge[32] the world, but in order that the world might be saved[Q] through Him[33]   17

            1F. "The *one* believing in Him is not judged[34]   18

1. Before Nicodemus can ask his question, which may have been something like "But are You the Messiah bringing God's kingdom?", Jesus responds. On this idiom, see 1:51.
2. Same word as in 1:13; 3:4-8; 1 Jn 2:29; 3:9; 4:7; 5:1, 4, 18. On this word, see 1 Jn 2:29.
3. Or, "from above". Same word as in v 7. Note "born of God" in 1:13. Here, Jesus means "from the Spirit", as explained in v 5, 8, which is both "from above" and "again". But Nicodemus clearly understands Him— wrongly— to mean born physically "again", a second time, v 4. Elsewhere only as "anew" in Gal 4:9; from the "top" in Mt 27:51; Mk 15:38; Jn 19:23; "from the beginning" in Lk 1:3; Act 26:5; and "from above" in Jn 3:31; 19:11; Jam 1:17; 3:15, 17. GK *1173*.
4. Nicodemus combines a broadly stated principle with his own case in particular. Used only here. GK *1173*.
5. The grammar indicates that a "no" answer is expected. It implies "Surely this cannot be what You mean".
6. Jesus is responding to Nicodemus's taking His statement as relating to physical birth.
7. Some think Jesus explains both in the next verse. "Of water" is "of the flesh", referring to physical birth, the birth Nicodemus mentioned in v 4. "Water" refers to semen, or amniotic fluid. "Of *the* Spirit" refers to spiritual birth, the birth mentioned in v 3. A second birth is indeed needed to enter, but not a physical one. Others think "of water" refers to water baptism. In this case, "of water and *the* Spirit" is equivalent to "of the Spirit" in v 6, and to "born again" in v 3, the water referring the outward act, the Spirit's birth to the inner reality. Some think "water" refers to John's baptism in Nicodemus's case, but is also prophetic of Christian baptism. It symbolizes repentance and cleansing from the old life. There are other views. Consult the commentaries.
8. In v 6 and 8, Jesus uses a physical illustration to explain the spiritual truths in v 5 and 7.
9. Flesh fathers flesh, Spirit fathers spirit. They reproduce "after their kind". The child shares the parent's nature, physically, and spiritually.
10. This word is plural, and "all" is added to reflect this. It is equivalent to "one" in v 3, 5; and "everyone" in v 8. It is a general truth.
11. This is the same word as "Spirit". GK *4460*. Related to "blows" next.
12. Some manuscripts say "or" {K}.
13. We do not know the source or destination of the wind. We only see its effects— the sound and movement it causes. So in the spiritual realm. We do not understand physically "how" (the question in v 4). We only see the effect in the person's life after the person has been born of the Spirit. The spiritual wind blows, one is drawn to Him (6:44), and born from above. The seed is sown, and it grows— how, we do not know, Mk 4:27.
14. That is, being born again and entering the kingdom.
15. Or, how can these things "come about, take place, be"? GK *1181*. The first question by Nicodemus was "How can one be physically born a second time?", v 4. Now he asks "How can one be spiritually born from above?" Jesus chides his ability to understand such spiritual realities (v 10), and then tells him in v 14-15— believe in Me. This answer is then explained in v 16-21.
16. Or, "know". On this word, see "know" in Lk 1:34.
17. Some think Jesus is including the Baptist; others, the prophets; others, the disciples; others, the Father; others, that He is referring to Himself, as in 9:4.
18. Jesus asserts His authority, then chastises Israel for not accepting it.
19. This word is plural here and in all four places in v 12. "People" is added to reflect this. Some think Jesus is referring to the Pharisees, v 1; or more broadly, to the Jewish leaders in general; others, even more broadly, to "people like you". These are general statements reaching beyond Nicodemus.
20. That is, things relating to physical reality, to this human existence; things proceeding from an earthly point of view versus a heavenly one; things reaching from earth to heaven versus from heaven to earth. Even things like 2:16, relating to the earthly temple. If the Jews do not accept that kind of statement, and the authority of Jesus to speak it, why would they believe Him if He spoke of spiritual, unseen realities?
21. Now Jesus gives the source of His authority, of what "we know" and "we have seen" (v 11); and of the Pharisees' lack of authority for passing judgment on what He says. He has "come from God" (v 2) in a much deeper sense than Nicodemus realizes, in a unique sense.
22. Some take this to mean "has personal communion with God".
23. Some manuscripts add "the *One* being in heaven" {B}, which some think refers to Jesus as God. He has descended, and yet His eternal being is also in heaven. He is everywhere, yet in this body.
24. Jesus now gives the answer to the question in v 9.
25. On this, see Num 21:8-9. Jesus too will be lifted up, and all putting faith in Him will live. Same word as in 8:28. While Jesus was referring to the cross, this would not be clear to Nicodemus at this time.
26. Or, "believing in". This grammar for "believe in, put faith in" is elsewhere only in Mk 1:15 ("in the gospel") and Eph 1:13 ("in which gospel", or, "in Whom"). On this word, see "believe" in 3:36. Compare 2 Thes 2:12. It is not the preposition "in" normally used to say "believe in Him" (as in v 16). Compare Rom 4:5, "put faith upon". Some manuscripts do have the normal preposition here, and say "believing in Him may not perish but may have eternal life" {B}.
27. Or, "it", the Son of Man lifted up.
28. This is the Greek word order. It may also be punctuated "everyone believing may have eternal life in Him".
29. Some think v 16-21 are John's words of explanation for us; others, Jesus' explanation for Nicodemus.
30. This word means "so, thus, in this manner, like this, as follows, so much", and is used 208 times. GK *4048*. Here, some think John means "in this manner", as it is used in 7:46; 11:48; 18:22; others, "so much, to such an extent, so very", as it is used in Gal 1:6, "so quickly"; Gal 3:3, "so foolish"; Heb 12:21, "so fearful"; and Rev 16:18, "so great".
31. Or, "so that everyone believing in Him shall not perish, but shall have...", depending on whether this is expressing God's purpose, or the result. GK *2671*.
32. Or, "pass judgment on, execute judgment against, condemn". Yet Jesus has the authority to judge, and will exercise it later, 5:27. Compare 9:39; 12:47. Same word as in v 18; 5:22, 30; 7:24; 8:15, 16, 26; 12:47, 48; 16:11; 18:31. On this word, see Mt 7:1.
33. Jesus came to save, but this salvation results in judgment for those who reject it.
34. This one does not come into judgment, but has passed from death to life, 5:24. On this word, see Mt 7:1.

A. Mt 3:2   B. Lk 1:15   C. Rev 17:8   D. Mt 16:21   E. Jn 7:17, willing   F. Jn 1:7   G. Jn 1:7   H. Rev 12:9   J. Mt 3:1   K. Mt 25:46   L. Jn 21:15, devotedly love   M. 1 Jn 2:15   N. Jn 1:18   O. 1 Cor 1:18   P. Mk 3:14, send out   Q. Lk 19:10

2F. "But the *one* not believing has been judged^A already, because he has not believed in the name *of* the only-born^B Son *of* God

    1G. "And this is the judgment[1]— that the Light has come into the world, and people loved^C the darkness[2] rather than the Light, for their works were evil^D   19

        1H. "For everyone practicing^E bad^F *things* hates^G the Light, and does not come to the Light, in order that his works may not be exposed[3]   20

        2H. "But the *one* doing the truth[4] comes to the Light, in order that his works may become-visible[5]— that[6] they have been worked[7] **in**[8] **God**"   21

5A. After these *things* Jesus and His disciples went into the Judean land[9], and there He was spending-time^H with them and baptizing[10]   22

    1B. Now John also was baptizing in Aenon near Salim, because there were many waters[11] there. And they were coming and being baptized. °For John had not yet been thrown[12] into prison   23 / 24

    2B. Then *a* debate[13] arose[14] from[15] the disciples *of* John with *a* Jew[16] about purification[17]   25

    3B. And they came to John and said *to* him, "Rabbi^J, He who was with you beyond the Jordan, *concerning* Whom **you** have testified, look— this *One* is baptizing, and all[18] are going to Him!"   26

    4B. John responded and said—   27

        1C. "*A* person^K cannot receive even one *thing* unless it has been given[19] *to* him from heaven. °**You** yourselves are testifying *concerning* me that I said that[20] '**I** am not the Christ', but that 'I am *one* having been sent-forth^L ahead of that *One*'[21]   28

        2C. "The *one* having the bride is *the* bridegroom. And the friend[22] *of* the bridegroom, the *one* standing *there* and hearing him, rejoices *with* joy[23] because of the voice *of* the bridegroom.[24] So this, my joy,[25] has been made-full[26]   29

        3C. "It-is-necessary^M *for* that *One* to grow[27], and *for* me to diminish[28]   30

            1D. "The[29] *One* coming from-above^N is above[30] all   31

                1E. "The *one*[31] being from the earth is from the earth and is speaking from the earth

            2D. "The *One* coming from heaven is above all. °What[32] He has seen and did hear— this He is testifying   32

                1E. "And no one is receiving His testimony[33]

                2E. "The *one*[34] having received His testimony certified[35] that God is truthful,[36] °for He Whom God sent forth is speaking the words *of* God   33-34

                    1F. "For He[37] does not give *Him* the Spirit from *a* measure[38]

                    2F. "The[39] Father loves^C the Son[40], and has given all *things* in His hand[41]   35

                        1G. "The *one* believing[42] in the Son has eternal life   36

                        2G. "But the *one* disobeying[43] the Son will not see life, but the wrath^O *of* God remains^P on him"

1. Or, "verdict, decision". This is how God presently judges the ones not believing— they loved the darkness because their deeds are evil. This is His present verdict. Terrifying consequences await those who end their life with this judgment still true of them. Same word as in 5:22, 24, 27, 29, 30; 7:24; 8:16; 12:31; 16:8, 11; Heb 9:27; 10:27; 2 Pet 3:7; Rev 16:7; and as "justice" in Mt 12:18, 20; 23:23. Used 47 times. GK *3213*. Related to "judge" in Mt 7:1.
2. Same word as in Mt 4:16; Lk 1:79; Act 26:18; Rom 13:12; Eph 5:8, 11; Col 1:13; 1 Pet 2:9. Used 31 times. GK *5030*. Related to the word in Jn 1:5, and "darkened" in Rom 1:21 and Eph 4:18.
3. Thus the reason such people reject the Light lies with them. On this word, see Eph 5:11.
4. On "doing the truth", compare "doing sin" in 8:34.
5. Or, "be revealed". On this word, see "made evident" in 1 Jn 2:19.
6. Or, "because". GK *4022*.
7. Or, "done, wrought, performed". This is a participle, they "are having been worked". On this word, see Mt 26:10. Related to "works" in v 20.
8. Or, "in union with, in connection with, by means of ". Or, "under" God, in His sphere of influence, as this word is used in Rom 2:12. GK *1877*.
9. That is, Jesus left Jerusalem and went into Judea. This idiom, "the Judean land", is used only here. Compare Mk 1:5.
10. Note John's clarification of this in 4:2. On this word, see Mk 1:8.
11. That is, many sources of water. Or, "much water", large quantities of water. On "many waters", see Rev 14:2. "Water" (used 76 times. GK *5623*) is plural elsewhere only in Mt 8:32; 14:28, 29; Mk 9:22; and Rev 7:17; 8:10, 11; 11:6; 14:7; 16:4, 5; 17:15.
12. This is a participle, he "was not yet having been thrown" into prison. In Mt 4:12 and Mk 1:14, this future imprisonment is where their description of the ministry of Jesus begins. In John, this imprisonment occurs before 5:1, and may have occurred in conjunction with the departure from Judea in 4:1-3.
13. Or, "controversy". On this word, see "controversy" in 1 Tim 6:4.
14. Or, "took place, came about". GK *1181*.
15. The debate was between these disciples and this Jew, but this preposition indicates it originated with these disciples.
16. Some manuscripts have this plural, "with *the* Jews" {B}.
17. On this word, see 2 Pet 1:9. Perhaps John's disciples debated the place or effect of his baptism in view of that of Jesus.
18. This hyperbole betrays the hearts of these men.
19. This is a participle, unless it "is having been given" to him.
20. Some manuscripts omit this word {C}.
21. That is, John can only receive what God gives him. And God gave him the task of preparing the Lord's way, as these disciples very well know.
22. Christ is the bridegroom, John is the friend of the bridegroom.
23. The phrase "rejoices with joy" is a Hebrew way of saying "rejoices greatly".
24. As the groomsman standing and listening to the bridegroom with his bride rejoices to hear him, so John rejoices to hear of Jesus' words and actions. Jesus is the center of attention, and John is His friend.
25. That is, this rejoicing with 'friend of the bridegroom joy', which is my joy, has been made full (or, fulfilled) in my case.
26. Same word as in 15:11; 17:13. Compare 16:24.
27. Or, "increase". That is, grow in brightness as the Light in the darkness, grow in His effect on Israel, grow in His following, spread in His influence. Same word as the gospel "growing" in Col 1:6 (see also Act 6:7; 12:24; 19:20), and Israel "increasing" in Act 7:17. Used of plants, children, the church, faith, and Christians "growing". Used 23 times. GK *889*.
28. Or, "reduce, decrease, be made lower". Elsewhere only as "made lower" in Heb 2:7, 9. GK *1783*. Related to "lesser" in Jn 2:10.
29. Some think that v 31-36 are the apostle John's comments; others, a continuation of the Baptist's words.
30. Or, "over". Not related to "from-above". Same word as later in the verse. GK *2062*. Jesus is preeminent. Paul says Jesus is "over all" in Rom 9:5, using a different word.
31. This contrast is true of the Baptist, but is stated in a form that is true of all. Jesus comes from above, and is above all in rank and authority. The Baptist is from the earth, like all humans, and speaks the things of God from an earthly perspective. As a prophet, he speaks what God reveals to him, but knows nothing more, as in 1 Pet 1:10-12. All humans speak of heaven from an earthly source of knowledge, not from firsthand knowledge (like Jesus).
32. Jesus speaks from personal knowledge— not what was revealed to Him, but what He has personally seen and heard in heaven. Compare 1 Jn 1:1. Some manuscripts say "And what...". Others combine this with v 31, omitting "is above all" and "this", so that it says "The *One* coming from heaven is testifying what He has seen and did hear" {C}.
33. The Baptist may be referring primarily to the Jewish leadership in Jerusalem— the same ones rejecting him or giving him no more than lip service. Compare v 11, 26. Or, the apostle John may be referring to people in general.
34. This is true of the Baptist and the special certification he gave (1:32-34), but is stated in a form that is true of all who have received Jesus. The contrast here between 1E. and 2E. is like that in 1:11-12.
35. Or, "set his seal, sealed, attested". Same word as in 6:27. On this word, see "sealed" in Eph 1:13.
36. To accept what Jesus says is to set your personal seal of approval on the truthfulness of God's words, for His words are God's words. The reverse is in 1 Jn 5:10— to reject Jesus is to make God a liar.
37. Note that this is a negative statement, the Greek word order being, "Not from *a* measure does He give *Him* the Spirit". Some rephrase this as a positive statement, "He gives *Him* the Spirit without measure". Some manuscripts say "God" {B}.
38. Or, "by means of *a* measure, out of *a* measure". This idiom is used only here. Jesus is not like the Baptist, or any other prophet to whom God gives a measured gift of His Spirit. God "is not giving" Him a measured-out portion, as with the other prophets. All the fullness dwells in Jesus, Col 1:19; 2:9. There are other views. Consult the commentaries. Same word as in Eph 4:7, where we all have a "measure" of grace. Same noun as in Mt 7:2; 23:32; Mk 4:24; Lk 6:38; Rom 12:3; 2 Cor 10:13; Eph 4:13, 16; Rev 21:17. Elsewhere only as "measuring" rod in Rev 21:15. GK *3586*.
39. Having stated the negative, the positive is now given.
40. The Baptist called Jesus "the Son of God" in 1:34.
41. Compare Jn 13:3.
42. This word means "believe, put faith in, trust". It is also rendered "put faith" (see Rom 4:5 and Jn 3:15); and "entrust" in Lk 16:11; Jn 2:24; Rom 3:2; 1 Cor 9:17; Gal 2:7; 1 Thes 2:4; 1 Tim 1:11; Tit 1:3. Used 241 times. GK *4409*. Related to "faith" in Eph 2:8; and "faithful" in Col 1:2.
43. Or, "refusing to believe". On this word, see Rom 11:30.

A. Mt 7:1 B. Jn 1:18 C. Jn 21:15, devotedly love D. Act 25:18 E. Rom 2:1 F. Jam 3:16 G. Rom 9:13 H. Act 12:19 J. Mt 23:7 K. Mt 4:4, mankind L. Mk 3:14, send out M. Mt 16:21, must N. Jn 3:3, again O. Rev 16:19 P. Jn 15:4, abide

6A. So when Jesus[1] knew[2] that the Pharisees heard that Jesus was[3] making and baptizing more disciples[A]   4:1
than John °(although[4] Jesus Himself was not baptizing, but His disciples), °He left[5] Judea and went again[6]   2-3
toward Galilee. °And He had-to[7] go through Samaria   4

    1B. So He comes into *a* city *of* Samaria being called Sychar, near the place which Jacob gave *to* his son   5
son Joseph. °Now *a* spring[8] *of* Jacob was there. So Jesus, having become weary[B] from the journey, was   6
sitting thus[9] at the spring. *The* hour was about *the* sixth[10]

        1C. *A* woman of Samaria comes to draw water—   7

            1D. Jesus says *to* her, "Give Me *water* to drink"

                1E. For His disciples had gone into the city in order that they might buy food[11]   8

            2D. So the Samaritan woman says *to* Him, "How *is it* **You**, being *a* Jew, are asking *something*   9
to drink from me, being *a* Samaritan woman?"

                1E. For Jews do not use-*things*-together-with[12] Samaritans[13]

            3D. Jesus responded and said *to* her, "If you knew[C] the gift[D] *of* God[14], and Who the *One* saying   10
to you 'Give Me *water* to drink' is— **you** would have asked Him, and He would have
given you living[E] water"

            4D. The woman[15] says *to* Him, "Sir[F], You have no bucket[16], and the well[17] is deep. From where   11
then do You have the living water? °**You** are not greater *than* our father Jacob, *are You*[18],   12
who gave us the well, and himself drank from it, and his sons, and his animals[19]?"

            5D. Jesus responded and said *to* her, "Everyone drinking from this water will thirst again.   13
But whoever should drink[20] from the water which **I** will give him— he will never[21] thirst,   14
ever[22]. On the contrary, the water which I will give him will become *a* spring *of* water in
him, bubbling-up[23] to eternal life"

            6D. The woman says to Him, "Sir, give me this water, in order that I may not[24] be thirsting,   15
nor coming here to draw *it*"

            7D. He[25] says *to* her, "Go, call your husband, and come here"   16

            8D. The woman responded and said *to* Him, "I do **not** have *a* husband"   17

            9D. Jesus says *to* her, "You said rightly[G] that 'I do not have *a* **husband**[26]'. °For you had five   18
husbands. And now he whom you have is not your husband. You have spoken this *as a*
true[H] *thing*"

            10D. The woman says *to* Him, "Sir, I perceive[J] that **You** are *a* prophet.[27] °Our fathers   19-20
worshiped on this mountain,[28] and **you**[29] *Jews* say that the place where one must[30]
worship is in Jerusalem"

            11D. Jesus says *to* her, "Believe Me, woman,[31] that *an* hour is coming when **you**[32] *Samaritans*   21
will give-worship *to* the Father neither on this mountain nor in Jerusalem

                1E. "**You** *Samaritans* worship what you do not know[C]. **We** *Jews* worship what we know,   22
because salvation[K] is from the Jews

                2E. "But *an* hour is coming, and now is, when the true[L] worshipers will give-worship   23
to the Father in spirit and truth[33]

                    1F. "For indeed the Father is seeking[M] such *ones to be* the *ones* worshiping Him
                    2F. "God *is* spirit, and the *ones* worshiping Him must[N] worship[34] in spirit and truth"   24

1. Some manuscripts say "the Lord" {C}.
2. Or, "came to know, learned". On this word, see Lk 1:34.
3. More literally, "is", as the Greek typically phrases it.
4. Or, "and yet". Used only here. GK *2793*. John is correcting the information that the Pharisees heard.
5. Perhaps Jesus left so the Pharisees could not try to play Him against the Baptist. John could correct his own disciples (3:25-26), but the Pharisees might attempt to exploit such questions among the people. This may also have been when John was imprisoned. See 3:24. Compare Mt 4:12; Mk 1:14; Lk 3:20; 4:14.
6. Or, "back". Jesus was there in 1:43-2:12. On this word, see Mk 15:13. Some manuscripts omit this word {A}.
7. Or, "it was necessary *that* He go". On this idiom, see "must" in Mt 16:21.
8. Same word as in v 14; Jam 3:11; 2 Pet 2:17; Rev 7:17; 8:10; 14:7; 16:4; 21:6. Elsewhere only as "fountain" in Mk 5:29. GK *4380*. Not related to "well" in v 11, which is the "shaft" in which the "spring" of water is located, but used to refer to both. "Spring" puts emphasis on the water; "well" on the shaft dug down to the water.
9. Some think John means "wearied, tired"; others, "as He was", without any preparation. On this word, see "so" in 3:16. Compare 13:25, where this same word is used.
10. Some think John means noon, counting from sunrise, 6 A.M. Others think he means 6 P.M., counting from noon, Roman time. See 19:14 on this.
11. Or, "provisions". It is plural here. On this word, see Mt 24:45.
12. Or, "make use of *vessels* with", or more broadly, "associate with" as friends and equals. A Jew would not share water from the same bucket or cup as this Samaritan woman. Jews had business dealings with Samaritans, as seen even in v 8, but avoided becoming "unclean" by contact with them. Used only here. GK *5178*. Related to "make use of" in 1 Cor 7:21.
13. Some include this in the woman's statement. Some manuscripts omit "For Jews... Samaritans" {A}.
14. The gift is the living water, eternal life, v 14.
15. Some manuscripts omit "the woman" {C}, so that it says "She says...".
16. Or, "drawing *thing*". Used only here. GK *534*. Related to the verb "draw" in v 7, 15.
17. Same word as in v 12. See "spring" in v 6. On this word, see "shaft" in Rev 9:1.
18. The grammar indicates a "no" answer is expected.
19. This word was used of animals fed by humans, especially sheep and goats. Used only here. GK *2576*.
20. Jesus contrasts the continual drinking of physical water, and the one-time drink of His spiritual water.
21. This is an emphatic negative (see 8:51), further strengthened by adding "ever".
22. Or, "forever, into *the* age". GK *172*. This combination of "never" and "ever" is elsewhere only in Jn 8:51, 52; 10:28; 11:26; 13:8; 1 Cor 8:13.
23. Or, "springing up, welling up", but not related to "spring" or "well". Elsewhere only as "leap" in Act 3:8; 14:10. GK *256*. Related to "leap on" in Act 19:16.
24. Or, "so that I will not". GK *2671*.
25. Some manuscripts say "Jesus" {N}.
26. Jesus changes the word order of the woman's claim, giving it His own emphasis.
27. That is, because Jesus had supernatural knowledge about this woman's past. Compare the case in Lk 7:39. On "prophet", see 1 Cor 12:28. Since He was clearly a prophet, she asks Him an appropriate question.
28. Mount Gerizim is where the Samaritans worshiped, and this well was at the foot of it.
29. The "you" here is plural, to reflect which, "Jews" is added.
30. Or, where "it is necessary to". On this idiom, see Mt 16:21. Or, where "one ought to". On this idiom, see Act 25:10.
31. Some manuscripts say "Woman, believe Me" {K}.
32. The "you" here and in v 22 is also plural.
33. Truth is that which corresponds to reality, from God's point of view. Same word as in Lk 4:25; Jn 1:17; 8:32; 17:17; Rom 1:18, 25; Eph 1:13; 4:25; Phil 1:18; 2 Thes 2:10; 1 Tim 2:4, 7; 1 Jn 2:4; 3:18. Used 109 times. GK *237*. Related to "true" in Jn 6:55 and 7:28, and "truly" in Mt 14:33.
34. On "give worship" and "worship" (same word, different grammar) in v 20, 21, 22, 23, 24, see Mt 14:33.

A. Lk 6:40   B. Mt 11:28   C. 1 Jn 2:29   D. Rom 5:15   E. Rev 20:4, came to life   F. Mt 8:2, master   G. Act 10:33, well   H. Jn 6:55   J. Lk 10:18, seeing   K. Lk 19:9   L. Jn 7:28   M. Phil 2:21   N. Mt 16:21

	12D. The woman says *to* Him, "I know that Messiah[A] is coming— the *One* being called Christ. When that *One* comes, He will declare[B] all *things to* us"	25
	13D. Jesus says *to* her, "**I**, the *One* speaking *to* you, am *He*'"	26
2C.	And at this *point* His disciples came, and they were marveling[C] that He was speaking with *a* woman. Yet no one said, "What are you seeking?[2]" or, "Why are You speaking with her?"	27
3C.	So the woman left her waterpot[3], and went into the city. And she says *to* the people, °"Come, see *a* man Who told me everything that I did. This *One* is not the Christ, *is He*?"[4] °They[5] went out of the city, and were coming to Him	28-29 30
4C.	In the meantime the disciples were asking Him, saying, "Rabbi[D], eat"	31
	1D. But the *One* said *to* them, "**I** have food[E] to eat that **you** do not know *about*"	32
	2D. So the disciples were saying to one another, "Someone did not bring Him *something* to eat, *did he*?"[6]	33
	3D. Jesus says *to* them, "My food[F] is that[7] I may do the will[8] *of* the *One* having sent Me, and accomplish[9] His work	34
		1E. "Do **you** not say that 'There are still four months, and the harvest comes'?[10]	35
		2E. "Behold, I say *to* you— lift-up[G] your eyes and look-*at* the fields, that[11] they are white[12] for harvest[13]. Already[14] °the *one* reaping is receiving wages,[15] and is gathering fruit for life eternal, so that the *one* sowing and the *one* reaping may rejoice[H] together	36
			1F. "For in this *case*, the saying[J] is true[K], that 'One is the *one* sowing and another *is* the *one* reaping[16]	37
			2F. "**I** sent[17] you out to be reaping what **you** have not labored-*for*.[18] Others have labored[L], and **you** have entered into their labor"	38
5C.	And many *of* the Samaritans from that city believed in Him because of the word *of* the woman testifying[19] that "He told me everything which I did"	39
6C.	Therefore when the Samaritans came to Him, they were asking Him to stay[M] with them. And He stayed there *for* two days	40
7C.	And many more[20] believed because of His word. °And they were saying *to* the woman that "We are no longer believing because of your speaking[21]. For we ourselves have heard, and we know that this *One* is truly[N] the Savior[O] *of* the world[22]"	41-42
8C.	And after the two days, He went forth from there to[23] Galilee. °For Jesus Himself testified[P] that *a* prophet does not have honor[Q] in *his* own homeland[24]	43-44
2B. So when He came to Galilee,[25] the Galileans welcomed[R] Him, having seen all that He did in Jerusalem at the Feast. For **they** also went to the Feast.[26] °So He[27] came again to Cana *of* Galilee, where He made the water wine	45 46
	1C. And there was *a* certain royal[28] *one* whose son was sick[S] in Capernaum. °This *one*— having heard that Jesus had[29] come from Judea to Galilee— went to Him, and was asking that He come down and heal[T] his son. For he was about to die	47
	2C. So Jesus said to him, "Unless you[30] *people* see signs and wonders, you will by no means believe"[31]	48
	3C. The royal *one* says to Him, "Master[U], come down before my child dies"	49
	4C. Jesus says *to* him, "Go, your son lives"[32]	50
	5C. The man believed the word which Jesus spoke *to* him, and was going	
		1D. Now while he *was* already going down, his slaves[V] met him[33], saying that his boy[W] lives[34]	51
		2D. So he inquired[X] from them the hour at which he got better[35]	52

1. On the phrase "I am *He*", see 8:58.
2. Some think John means "What are you seeking [from Him]?"; others, "What are You seeking [from her]?". On "seeking", see Phil 2:21.
3. With the "bucket" (v 11), the woman drew from the well; with the "waterpot", she carried it home. Elsewhere only in 2:6, 7. GK *5620*.
4. The grammar indicates that the woman expects the people to say "no" at this point. But the question calls upon them to examine the possibility. The same type of question occurs in v 33; Mt 12:23. "You don't think this might be the Messiah, do you?" She clearly believes Jesus is the Messiah, v 39.
5. Some manuscripts say "So they..." {N}, using the same word as in v 28.
6. The grammar indicates a "no" answer is expected.
7. Or, "to do". GK *2671*.
8. Jesus hungers to do God's will, and doing it satisfies His soul as food does the body.
9. Or, "complete, finish". Same word as in 5:36; 17:4, on which see "perfect" in Heb 2:10.
10. The grammar indicates a "yes" answer is expected. Do you not expect a delay between sowing and harvesting? Some think Jesus is appealing to the common experience of people. Others think that in addition, it implies there were actually four months remaining at that moment until harvest that year.
11. Or, "because". GK *4022*.
12. Some think Jesus is referring to the people coming to Him from the city (v 30) in their white garments, not to any agricultural crop. In any case, He is referring to the spiritual harvest. Used 25 times. GK *3328*.
13. The spiritual harvest is here, as seen with this woman. Jesus just reaped the woman, and she is now reaping others, without any delay. Others have already sown, as seen in her statement in v 25, so the fields are ready.
14. Or, this word may be joined to what precedes, "are already white for harvest". Some manuscripts add "and", so that it says, "are already white for harvest. And the *one* reaping..." {B}.
15. In other words, the reapers are already working the harvest. Both Jesus and the woman, as seen in v 39, are reaping. The "wages" are the "food" He has now (v 32), enjoyed while bringing in the harvest. The fruit gathered will be enjoyed in eternal life. There, all who had a part in sowing and reaping will rejoice over it forever.
16. Someone else is the sower. Jesus and the woman are the reapers. They entered into a harvest already prepared by others.
17. Now Jesus applies this to the disciples with Him. The past tense may refer to the work they entered in 4:2.
18. Israel was already prepared, anticipating the Messiah. The world was prepared for reaping. The disciples will reap the harvest for which many others have labored (extending from Jesus back to Moses).
19. This shows the powerful effect of the woman's testimony in v 29. Some Samaritans believe before they see Jesus.
20. More literally, "more *by* much". That is, more than believed because of the woman's word, v 39.
21. That is, what this woman said. Some believed because of her testimony, v 39. Many more were tentatively convinced by her, but fully believed when they heard Jesus for themselves. On this noun, see 8:43.
22. The Samaritans must have heard this from Jesus, who would have explained why He, the Jewish Messiah, did not treat them as the Jews did. Some manuscripts say "...world, the Christ" {N}. John calls Him "Savior of the world" also in 1 Jn 4:14.
23. Some manuscripts say "there, and went to Galilee" {N}.
24. Some think the homeland in view is Judea. Jesus went to Galilee because He would have been dishonored in Judea by the Pharisees, as began to happen in 4:1-3. Others think the homeland is Galilee. Jesus went to Galilee because He knew He would not be honored there in a way that would bring Him into premature conflict with the Pharisees, as began to happen in 4:1-3. Others think the homeland is Israel. Jesus deliberately went from where He was being honored (Samaria), back to Israel where He knew this would not be the case, where they would seek Him for His miracles, not His message. In Samaria, they were convinced by His word (v 42), without signs (none are recorded). In Israel they sought Him for His signs, but did not believe His word. His popularity in Judea (v 1) and Galilee (v 44) was for the wrong reasons, and He was returning to Israel to bring this to its inevitable conclusion. There are other views. Consult the commentaries. Same word as "hometown" in Mt 13:57; Mk 6:4; Lk 4:24; where Jesus says this after He is dishonored in Nazareth. On this word, see Heb 11:14.
25. That is, when Jesus came to where He was going in v 2 when He passed through Samaria.
26. That is, unlike the Samaritans, who for this reason did not know Jesus.
27. Some manuscripts say "Jesus" {N}.
28. John probably means a royal official in the service of Herod Antipas (see Mt 14:1 on him), though he could mean a member of Herod's family. On this word, see Act 12:20.
29. More literally, "has", as the Greek typically phrases it.
30. This word is plural, as is the next "you" in this sentence. "People" is added to reflect this.
31. This is in contrast to the Samaritans, who believed "because of His word", v 41. The Jews come to Jesus as a miracle worker, not as "the Savior of the world", v 42. Jesus is expressing His disappointment that this is the case.
32. Note that Jesus heals with a word, over a distance of some 20 miles or 32 kilometers (from Cana to Capernaum).
33. Some manuscripts add "and reported" {N}.
34. Some manuscripts say "saying that 'your boy lives' "; others, "saying that 'your son lives' " {B}.
35. This is an idiom, literally "he had *it* better", that is, recovered. On this idiom, compare "being ill" in Mk 1:32.

A. Jn 1:41 B. Jn 16:13 C. Rev 17:8 D. Mt 23:7 E. Mt 6:19, eating F. Mk 7:19 G. 2 Cor 11:20 H. 2 Cor 13:11 J. 1 Cor 12:8, word
K. Jn 7:28 L. Mt 11:28, being weary M. Jn 15:4, abide N. Mt 14:33 O. Lk 1:47 P. Jn 1:7 Q. 1 Tim 5:17 R. Mt 10:40 S. 2 Tim 4:20
T. Mt 8:8 U. Mt 8:2 V. Rom 6:17 W. Act 3:13, servant X. Act 23:34, learned

       3D. So[1] they said *to* him that "The fever[A] left him yesterday *at the* seventh[2] hour"

       4D. Then the father knew that *it was* at that hour at which Jesus said *to* him, "Your son lives"   53

       5D. And he believed[3], he and his whole household[B]

    6C. Now[4] this again[5] *was a* second[6] sign Jesus did, having come from Judea to Galilee   54

7A. After these *things* there was *a* Feast[7] *of* the Jews, and Jesus went up to Jerusalem   5:1

  1B. Now in Jerusalem near the Sheep[8] *gate*, there is *a* pool— the *one* being called Bethzatha[9] *in* Hebrew,   2

      having five porticos[10]. *In these *porticos*, a* multitude[11] *of* the *ones* being sick[C] were lying-down—   3

      blind *ones*, lame[D] *ones*, withered[12] *ones*. *And there was *a* certain man there having[14] thirty and[15]   4[13]-5

      eight years in his sickness[16]

  2B. Jesus— having seen this *one* lying down, and having known[17] that he already had[18] *a* long time [in   6

      his sickness]— says *to* him, "Do you want to become healthy[19]?"

    1C. The *one* being sick[C] answered Him, "Sir[E], I do not have *a* man to[20] put[F] me into the pool when   7

        the water is stirred-up[G]. But while **I** am going, another goes down before me"

    2C. Jesus says *to* him, "Arise, pick up your cot, and walk!"   8

    3C. And immediately the man became healthy, and picked up his cot, and was walking   9

  3B. Now it was *a* Sabbath on that day. *So the Jews were saying *to* the *one* having been cured[H], "It is   10

      the Sabbath, and it is not lawful[J] *for* you to pick up your cot"

    1C. But the *one* answered them, "The One having made me healthy, that One said *to* me, 'Pick up   11

        your cot and walk' "

    2C. They[21] asked him, "Who is the man having said *to* you, 'Pick up[22] and walk'?"   12

    3C. But the *one* having been healed[K] did not know who He was[23]. For Jesus withdrew[24], *a* crowd[25]   13

        being in the place

    4C. After these *things*, Jesus finds him in the temple. And He said *to* him, "See— you have become   14

        healthy! Do not be sinning[26] any longer, in order that something worse may not happen *to* you"

    5C. The man went away, and reported[27] *to* the Jews that Jesus was[28] the *One* having made him healthy   15

  4B. And for this reason, the Jews[29] were persecuting[L] Jesus[30]— because He was doing[31] these *things* on   16

      a Sabbath

    1C. But Jesus[32] answered them, "My Father is working[M] until now, and **I** am working"[33]   17

    2C. Therefore, for this reason the Jews were seeking[N] more to kill[O] Him— because   18

      1D. He was not only breaking[34] the Sabbath

      2D. But He was also calling[P] God *His* own[35] Father, making Himself equal[36] *to* God!

  5B. Therefore Jesus responded and was saying *to* them—   19

    1C. "Truly[Q], truly, I say *to* you— the Son can do[37] nothing from[38] Himself except something He

        sees the Father doing[39]

      1D. "For[40] whatever *things* that *One* is doing, these *things* the Son is also likewise doing

        1E. "For[41] the Father loves[R] the Son, and shows[S] Him all *things* that He Himself is doing   20

1. Some manuscripts say "And" {N}.
2. Some think the slaves mean 1 P.M., counted from sunrise. In this case, "yesterday" is from the Jewish point of view. They met that evening, which to them was the next day (it began at sundown). Others think they mean 7 P.M., counted from noon. See 19:14. In this case, the late hour explains why the official was returning the next day.
3. In v 50, the man believed in the word of healing. Now he believes in Jesus. Though wonderful for him, it proves what Jesus said in v 48, and stands in contrast to v 41-42.
4. Some manuscripts omit this word {C}.
5. That is, continuing from what John said in 2:11.
6. Jesus had done other signs in Judea, 2:23. This is the second (see 2:11) sign John mentions that was done in Cana, Galilee, after He had returned from Judea. John could mean the second in Galilee, the second in Cana, or the second manifesting His glory (due to the special nature of both). John may also mean the second of the seven He records (see 11:1), although he does not number the rest.
7. Some manuscripts say "the Feast" {A}. There are several views on which Feast this was.
8. Or, "sheep *place*, sheep *pool*". "Gate" is supplied based on Neh 3:1, 32; 12:39. The KJV supplies "market". This can also be rendered "Now in Jerusalem near the sheep pool is the *pool* being called...". Used only here. GK *4583*.
9. Used only here. GK *1032*. Some manuscripts say "Bethsaida" (as in 1:44, etc.); others, "Bethesda" (only here in the NT) {C}.
10. That is, covered colonnades or cloisters where people gathered. Elsewhere only in 10:23; Act 3:11; 5:12. GK *5119*.
11. Some manuscripts say "*a great multitude*" {N}.
12. Same word as in Mk 3:3. Some manuscripts add "awaiting the moving *of* the water" {A}. Note v 7.
13. Some manuscripts (with several variations) add as verse 4, "For *an* angel in due season was going down in the pool and stirring up the water. Then the *one* first having stepped in after the stirring up *of* the water was becoming healthy *for* whatever disease he was indeed being afflicted" {A}. Whether this explanation is based in fact, or correctly represents the beliefs of this sick man, is uncertain. But it is clear that John did not write it.
14. The idiom of "having" time is also in v 6; 8:57; 9:21, 23; 11:17.
15. Some manuscripts omit this word {C}.
16. That is, the man had been lame or withered for 38 years. On this word, see "weakness" in Mt 8:17.
17. Or, "having come to know, having learned". John could mean Jesus knew it supernaturally, or that someone told Him. Perhaps Jesus inquired as to who had been sick the longest, and chose this one for healing. On this word, see Lk 1:34.
18. More literally, "has", as the Greek typically phrases it.
19. On this word, see Mt 12:13. Same word as in v 9, 11, 14, 15.
20. More literally, "in order that he might" put. GK *2671*.
21. Some manuscripts say "So they asked..." {N}.
22. To the Jews, any significance the healing might have had is canceled by the violation of their Sabbath traditions. Compare the man's viewpoint in v 15. Some manuscripts add "your cot" {N}.
23. More literally, "is", as the Greek typically phrases it.
24. Or, "turned aside". Used only here. GK *1728*. Jesus turned His head in another direction and went away.
25. John could mean Jesus turned aside because there was a crowd; or, that He turned aside into the crowd, the crowd giving Him the means to withdraw unnoticed. Both are true.
26. That is, do not go on sinning any longer. Repent. Same command as in 8:11. Some think Jesus is implying that the man's 38 year sickness was the result of sin; others do not. Jesus is speaking of the future, of what might happen if he continues in sin. "Something worse" could be a more severe ailment, death, or hell.
27. The man's motive is not stated. Jesus may have told him to do so. Some manuscripts say "said" {N}.
28. More literally, "is", as the Greek typically phrases it.
29. That is, the Jewish leaders, as in v 10, 18. See 1:19 on this.
30. Some manuscripts add "and seeking to kill Him" {N}.
31. The grammar implies the Jews were responding to Jesus' pattern of behavior, not just this one incident.
32. Some manuscripts omit this word {C}, so that it says "But the *One* answered...".
33. Jesus claims a unique relationship to the Father ("My", not "our" Father), and a divine justification to work on the Sabbath. He places His work on the Sabbath on an equal plane with God's working on the Sabbath.
34. Or, "loosing". That is, annulling its authority. Same word as in Mt 5:19, and as in Jn 7:23.
35. Jesus was claiming a special relationship, a direct relationship, as seen in Lk 1:35.
36. On this word, see Phil 2:6, where Paul says Jesus was equal with God. Compare 10:33. If God is the father of Jesus, then Jesus has the same essence and nature as God, as do all fathers and sons. Claiming to be God's Son in this sense is claiming to be God, or as John says, equal to God. This "equality" is seen clearly in what He says to them beginning in v 19.
37. The focus of this part of Jesus' answer is on His authority for His actions, for His working on the Sabbath, v 17, 18. In summary, He always acts in submission to His Father, and He does all things the Father does. Thus, He has the Father's authority.
38. Or, "of ". That is, of His own initiative, originating in Himself. Same phrase as in 7:18; 11:51 (the high priest); 15:4; 16:13. Related to "from yourself " in 18:34, and "from Myself " in 5:30; 7:17; 8:28; 14:10; and "of Myself" in 7:28; 8:42; 10:18. A different word is used in "out of Myself " in 12:49.
39. That is, the Son's self-initiated acts are always in harmony with what He sees the Father doing.
40. Not only can the Son not do something out of harmony with the Father, He does do what the Father is doing. Thus there is no transgression, and no falling short. Negatively, He cannot do something unless the Father is doing it. Positively, He is doing everything the Father is doing. He is in perfect harmony with the Father.
41. How does the Son see what the Father is doing? The Father shows Him, because He loves Him. How much of what the Father is doing does He see? All things. Here Jesus makes explicit the infinite extent of what He is claiming. Only One "making Himself equal to God" could claim such a thing.

A. Act 28:8 B. Mk 3:25, house C. 2 Tim 4:20 D. Heb 12:13 E. Mt 8:2, master F. Rev 2:22, throw G. Gal 1:7, disturb H. Mt 8:7 J. 1 Cor 6:12
K. Mt 8:8 L. 2 Tim 3:12 M. Mt 26:10 N. Phil 2:21 O. Rom 7:11 P. Jn 12:49, say Q. Jn 1:51 R. Jn 21:15, affectionately love S. 1 Tim 6:15

2E. "And He will show Him **greater** works *than* these[1], in order that[2] **you** may marvel[A]	
2D. "For[3] just as the Father raises[B] the dead and gives-life-to[4] *them*, so also the Son gives-life-to[5] *the ones* whom He wishes[6]	21
1E. "For the Father does not even judge[7] anyone, but He has given all judgment[C] *to* the Son,*in order that[8] all[9] may honor[D] the Son just-as[10] they are honoring the Father	22 23
1F. "The *one* not honoring the Son is not honoring the Father having sent Him	
2E. "Truly[E], truly, I say *to* you[11] that the *one* hearing My word and believing the *One* having sent Me, has eternal life. And he does not come into judgment[C], but has passed[12] from death to life	24
3D. "Truly, truly, I say *to* you that *an* hour is coming, and now is,[13] when the dead[14] will hear the voice *of* the Son *of* God, and the *ones* having heard[15] will live[F]	25
1E. "For just as the Father has life[G] in Himself, so also He gave[16] *to* the Son to have life in Himself[17]	26
2E. "And He gave Him authority to execute[18] judgment[19], because He is *a* son *of* man[20]	27
4D. "Do not be marveling-*at*[A] this,[21] because *an* hour is coming in which all the *ones* in the graves[H] will hear His voice,*and will come out—	28 29
1E.[22] "The *ones* having done[J] the good[K] *things*— to *a* resurrection[L] *of* life 2E. "The *ones* having practiced[M] the bad[23] *things*— to *a* resurrection *of* judgment[C]	
5D. "**I** can do nothing from Myself.[24] Just as I am hearing, I am judging.[25] And **My** judgment[C] is righteous[26], because I am not seeking[N] **My** will, but the will *of* the *One*[27] having sent Me	30
2C. "If[28] am **I** testifying[O] about Myself, My testimony[P] is not true.[29] *There is Another— the *One* testifying about Me— and I know that the testimony which He is testifying about Me is true[Q]	31-32
1D. "**You** have sent out *messengers* to John, and he has testified *to* the truth[30]	33
1E. "But **I** do not receive[31] testimony from *a* human.[32] Nevertheless, I am saying these *things* in order that **you** may be saved[33]	34
2E. "That *one* was[34] the burning[R] and shining[S] lamp, and **you** were willing to be overjoyed[T] in his light for *an* hour[35]	35

1. That is, than works like healing this man. First of all, Jesus means greater works on earth, in His lifetime. The greater miracles of chapters 9 and 11 are included, but the greatest of all was the cross and resurrection! At these the Jews will marvel. In the future, He will also carry out the resurrection and the judgment mentioned in what follows, but their response to that will not be "marveling". Believers will marvel when Jesus returns (2 Thes 1:10), but the rest will suffer affliction.
2. Or, "so that you will marvel". GK *2671*. The marveling by these Jews will be in fulfillment of prophecy, Act 13:41. They will marvel and perish, unless they repent.
3. Jesus now gives the ultimate examples of the "whatever things" God is doing— the granting of eternal life, the resurrection, and the judgment. Note how He answers the specific issue by putting it in the context of much larger issues, with which the Jews would disagree even more! "My authority for healing on the Sabbath was that of God Himself, and it extends far beyond this. I have the ultimate authority over life and judgment, over your eternal destiny".
4. Or, "makes alive". Same word as in 6:63; Rom 4:17; 8:11; 1 Cor 15:22, 36; 2 Cor 3:6; Gal 3:21. Elsewhere only as "made alive" in 1 Pet 3:18; and "life-giving" in 1 Cor 15:45. GK *2443*. It is used of giving physical life, spiritual life, and resurrection life.
5. Note the tense. This is something Jesus "is doing", continuing the main argument. "Raising the dead and giving life" includes both the eternal life He "is giving" now (as in v 25), and the resurrection He "will give" later (as in v 28). The present tense informs us He is thinking of both aspects, not the latter only. Had Jesus said "will give life", this would become point 1F., developing what the Father "will show Him", v 20.
6. Or, "wills, wants, desires". On this word, see "willing" in 7:17. Same word as "want" in Rom 9:18.
7. Giving life and judging are two sides of the coin, and are seen together again in v 24, 26-27, 29.
8. Or, "so that everyone will honor", depending on whether Jesus is expressing God's purpose or the future result. GK *2671*.
9. Those to whom Jesus gives life honor Him by believing; the rest will bow the knee at His judgment.
10. That is, in the same manner, to the same degree; that the Father and the Son might be treated equally (v 18) as to honor. Only one "making Himself equal to God" would say such a thing. GK *2777*.
11. Jesus now makes clear who the ones are to whom He "wishes" to give life, v 21.
12. Same word as in 1 Jn 3:14; Jn 13:1; and as "pass on" in Mt 8:34; 11:1; Jn 7:3. Used 12 times. GK *3553*.
13. This hour is present now, in the Son Himself. It is not the same as the hour yet to come in v 28.
14. That is, the spiritually dead, Eph 2:1. Those who hear this voice will have eternal life.
15. This is a subgroup of "the dead". The spiritually dead will hear, the ones who hear and believe will live.
16. Some think Jesus is referring to what the Father gave to be in the incarnate Son; others, to an eternal giving within their eternal relationship as Father and Son, 1:4. Same word and tense as in v 27. Compare the tense "has given" in v 22, 36. On this word, see Eph 1:22.
17. Jesus is the source of life for the dead who hear and believe, 1 Jn 5:11. He gives them life out of Himself.
18. Or, "do, accomplish, perform". This phrase "execute judgment" is also in Jude 15. Same word as in Lk 18:7, 8. On this word, see "does" in Rev 13:13.
19. Some manuscripts add "also" {N}.
20. That is, because He is a human. Or, "*the* Son *of* Man". In either case, as the incarnate Son, He has this authority. Compare Act 10:42; 17:31. This phrase "son *of* man" (without "the") is elsewhere only in Heb 2:6; Rev 1:13; 14:14 (and in Num 23:19; Job 16:21; 25:6; 35:8; Ps 8:5; 80:17; 144:3; Isa 51:12; Jer 49:18, 33; 50:40; 51:43; Dan 7:13); the plural "sons *of* men" is only in Mk 3:28; Eph 3:5 (and over a dozen times in the OT). The phrase "the Son *of* Man" (with "the") is used 82 times in the NT. Some think no difference in meaning between the two phrases is intended, both identifying Christ as the one in Dan 7:13. Others think the former refers to a quality of existence Christ shares with all humans; the latter to Christ alone, as His self-chosen title while on earth, pointing to Dan 7:13 (where as part of a larger description, this phrase in itself means "like a human"). Compare Rev 1:13. On "man", see "mankind" in Mt 4:4.
21. Do not marvel that Jesus is granting eternal life to those who hear His voice, for His voice will also raise the physically dead on that day, and direct them to their destinies.
22. Compare Mt 25:46.
23. On this word, see Jam 3:16. On this subject, note Rom 2:6-10.
24. Some think this point is the conclusion of what precedes; others, the beginning of what follows, making this point 2C. On "from Myself ", see "from Himself " in v 19.
25. That is, as I hear the Father judging, so I am judging. This complements v 19. As Jesus sees the Father doing as to actions, and as He hears Him judging as to thoughts, He does the same. This includes His present judgments regarding Himself being God's Son, regarding His own actions, regarding others, and regarding them (as seen in what follows); and His future judgment on that day. His judgments are a just reflection of the Father's will.
26. Or, "right, just". On this word, see Rom 1:17. Same word as in 7:24.
27. Some manuscripts say "Father" {N}.
28. The focus of this part of Jesus' answer is on His being God's Son, v 17, 18, and their response to it.
29. That is, if I alone were to testify that I am His Son, it would not be true. What Jesus is claiming can only be accepted as true if the Father Himself also testifies in agreement. And He has done so, as explained next. Compare 8:13-14.
30. Jesus is referring to 1:19, and John's testimony in 1:19-34.
31. Or, "take, accept". On this word, see "taken" in Rom 7:8.
32. The testimony Jesus receives and offers as to who He is does not come from a human source, but from the sources mentioned next. Jesus is not rejecting John's testimony, as He says next. After all, John "came for a testimony", 1:7. Jesus is pointing to greater testimony than John's, under which John's is subsumed.
33. Jesus is reminding the Jews of John's testimony in order that they might believe it. It was spoken for their benefit.
34. The tense may indicate that John's testimony was finished; that he had been imprisoned.
35. The Jewish leaders rejoiced that perhaps Messiah was coming as John said. But this joy was short-lived, because they rejected his testimony and refused his baptism, Lk 7:30.

A. Rev 17:8 B. Mt 28:6, arose C. Jn 3:19 D. 1 Tim 5:3 E. Jn 1:51 F. Rev 20:4, came to life G. Rom 8:10 H. Mt 23:29, tomb J. Rev 13:9
K. 1 Tim 5:10b L. Act 24:15 M. Rom 2:1 N. Phil 2:21 O. Jn 1:7 P. Jn 1:7 Q. Jn 6:55 R. Mt 5:15 S. Phil 2:15 T. Lk 10:21, rejoice greatly

2D. "But **I** have testimony greater *than* John's[1] 36

    1E. "For the works[A] which the Father has given *to* Me that I should accomplish[2] them[3]— the works themselves which I am doing are testifying[4] about Me, that the Father has sent Me forth

    2E. "And the Father having sent[B] Me— that *One* has[5] testified[6] about Me 37

        1F. "Neither His voice have you ever heard, nor His form[7] have you seen

        2F. "And you do not have His word abiding[C] in you, because *the One* Whom that *One* sent-forth[D]— this *One* **you** are not believing! 38

    3E. "You search[8] the Scriptures[E] because **you** think[F] *that* in them *you* have eternal life— and those *Scriptures* are the *ones* testifying about Me! °And you are not willing[G] to come to Me in order that you may have life 39 / 40

3D. "I do not receive glory from people[H], °but I know[9] you— that you do not have the love[J] *of* God in yourselves[10] 41-42

    1E. "**I** have come in the name *of* My Father, and you are not receiving[K] Me. If another comes in *his* own name, you will receive that *one*[11] 43

    2E. "How are **you** able to believe while receiving glory from one another, and you are not seeking[L] the glory from the only God? 44

4D. "Do not be thinking[F] that **I** will accuse[12] you before the Father. The *one* accusing you is Moses, in whom **you** have put-hope[13] 45

    1E. "For if you were believing Moses, you would be believing Me, for that *one* wrote about Me 46

    2E. "But if you do not believe the writings *of* that *one*, how will you believe My words?" 47

8A.[14] After these *things*, Jesus went away to the other side *of* the Sea *of* Galilee— *of* Tiberias[15] 6:1

    1B. And *a* large crowd was following Him, because they were seeing the[16] signs[17] which He was doing on the *ones* being sick[M]. °And Jesus went up on the mountain, and was sitting there with His disciples. °And the Passover[18], the Feast[N] *of* the Jews, was near 2 / 3 / 4

        1C. Then Jesus— having lifted-up[O] *His* eyes and seen that *a* large crowd was[19] coming to Him— says to Philip, "From where may we buy bread, in order that these *ones* may eat?" 5

            1D. Now He was saying this testing[P] him. For He Himself knew what He was going to do 6

        2C. Philip answered Him, "Loaves *worth* two-hundred denarii[20] are not enough *for* them, in order that each *one*[21] may receive *a* little bit[22]" 7

        3C. One of His disciples— Andrew, the brother *of* Simon Peter— says *to* Him, °"There is *a* boy[23] here who has five barley loaves and two fish[24], but what are these for so many?" 8-9

        4C. Jesus[25] said, "Make the people fall-back [to eat]". And there was much grass in the place 10

        5C. So the men[26]— about five-thousand *as to* the number— fell back [to eat]

        6C. Then Jesus took the loaves. And having given-thanks[Q], He distributed[R] them *to* the *ones*[27] reclining-back [to eat]— likewise also from the fish— as much as they were wanting[S] 11

        7C. And when they were filled[28], He says *to* His disciples, "Gather the left-over[29] fragments[T] so that nothing may be lost" 12

1. Jesus mentions three witnesses: His works, the Father, and the Scriptures.
2. This is the same word as in 4:34.
3. Compare 17:4; 4:34. Others omit this word, and render it "given *to* Me to accomplish", simplifying it.
4. The miracles of Jesus are signs pointing to who He is, 2:11. They are God's testimony, confirming what Jesus says.
5. Some manuscripts say "And the Father Himself having sent Me has..." {N}.
6. Note the change in tense. The works "are testifying"; the Father "has testified". He has done so "in many portions and in many ways", Heb 1:1. Some think Jesus is referring to all that the Father has spoken regarding the Messiah, including at His baptism and transfiguration (which Peter also points to in 2 Pet 1:17-18). He refers to it here as something spoken by the Father. Then He refers to the Scriptures as a separate witness in v 39, the place where the Father's words are recorded. Others think Jesus is referring to the Scriptures here, making v 37-40 one witness, and making v 39-40 point 3F.
7. Or, "outward appearance". This is the same word used of the dove in Lk 3:22. On this word, see "appearance" in 2 Cor 5:7.
8. Or, this may be a command "Search...". Same word as in 7:52. On this word, see 1 Cor 2:10.
9. Or, "have known, have come to know". The grammar implies "I have known and continue to know". Same word as in 2:24. On this word, see Lk 1:34.
10. Jesus is not looking for glory from humans (outside of God's will), revealing that His motive is to please God. But He knows the motive of these Jews is not love for God. They love the praise of people, not God, and thus not the One He sent. Compare 12:43.
11. The Jewish leaders will receive a human teacher or rabbi who does not claim to be sent by God. With a human teacher, they are in a reciprocal relationship of peers, exchanging glory on an equal basis. With a prophet sent from God, they must be in a subordinate position, hearing and obeying. This has always been at the root of why God's prophets were rejected.
12. Or, "bring charges against". Same word as in Mt 12:10; Lk 23:14; Act 24:2; 28:19; Rom 2:15; Rev 12:10. Used 23 times. GK *2989*. Related to "accusation" in Tit 1:6.
13. Same word as in Mt 12:21; Rom 15:12; 2 Cor 1:10; 1 Tim 4:10; 5:5; 6:17; 1 Pet 1:13; 3:5. This verb means "hope, hope for, put hope, expect". Used 31 times. GK *1827*. Related to the noun in Col 1:5.
14. Parallel account at Mt 14:13; Mk 6:32; Lk 9:10.
15. This Roman name for this sea is also used in 21:1. The city of Tiberias (v 23) was the capital city of Herod Antipas (see Mt 14:1), which he built on the western shore of this sea. GK *5500*. It was also known as the lake of Gennesaret, Lk 5:1.
16. Some manuscripts say "His" {K}.
17. The healings were signs pointing to who Jesus is, 5:36; 2:11, 23; 7:31; 12:37. This was their primary purpose.
18. This is the second Passover explicitly named. Some think this is two years after the one in 2:13; others, one year. Jesus did not attend this Passover for the reason stated in 7:1. On this word, see 18:28.
19. More literally, "is", as the Greek typically phrases it.
20. A denarius was one day's wages for a laborer. On this word, see Mt 20:2.
21. Some manuscripts add "*of* them" {K}.
22. Or, "something". Some manuscripts omit this word {C}. GK *5516*.
23. Or, "youth, lad, little boy". Used only here. GK *4081*.
24. This word was used of pieces of cooked fish, but also of fish just caught, as in 21:10. Elsewhere only in 6:11; 21:9, 13. GK *4066*. It is not the same word as in Mt 14:17; Mk 6:38; Lk 9:13; Jn 21:6; which is the word for fish as an animal.
25. Some manuscripts say "And Jesus..." {N}.
26. This word refers to the males. Note Mt 14:21.
27. Some manuscripts say "distributed *to* the disciples, and the disciples *to* the *ones*" {N}, like Mt 14:19.
28. Or, "filled full". On this word, see Rom 15:24. Not the same word as in Mt 14:20; Mk 6:42; Lk 9:17; which John uses in v 26.
29. This is a participle, the fragments having left over, having abounded, having surpassed the need.

A. Mt 26:10 B. Jn 20:21 C. Jn 15:4 D. Mk 3:14, send out E. 2 Pet 3:16 F. Lk 19:11 G. Jn 7:17 H. Mt 4:4, mankind J. 1 Jn 4:16 K. Jn 1:12 L. Phil 2:21 M. 2 Tim 4:20 N. Jn 13:29 O. 2 Cor 11:20 P. Heb 2:18, tempted Q. Mt 26:27 R. Act 4:35 S. Jn 7:17, willing T. Mt 15:37

8C. So they gathered, and filled^A twelve baskets¹ *of* fragments from the five barley loaves, which² were left over *by* the *ones* having eaten — 13
9C. Therefore the people, having seen *the* sign³ which He⁴ did, were saying that "This *One* is truly^B the Prophet⁵ coming into the world" — 14
10C. Then Jesus— having known that they were⁶ about to come and take Him away-by-force⁷ in order that they might make Him king— withdrew⁸ again to the mountain, Himself alone^C — 15

2B.⁹ Now when it became evening, His disciples went down to the sea. °And having gotten into *a* boat, they were going to the other side *of* the sea, to Capernaum — 16-17

    1C. And darkness already had come, and Jesus had not-yet¹⁰ come to them
    2C. And the sea was becoming aroused¹¹ *from a* great wind blowing — 18
    3C. So having rowed¹² about twenty five or thirty stades¹³, they see¹⁴ Jesus walking on the sea and becoming near the boat. And they became afraid — 19
    4C. But the *One* says *to* them, "**I** am *the One*¹⁵. Do not be afraid".¹⁶ °So they were willing^D to take Him into the boat — 20-21
    5C. And immediately^E the boat came-to-be at the land to which they were going¹⁷

3B.¹⁸ *On* the next day the crowd standing on the other side *of* the sea saw that there had not been¹⁹ another small boat there except [the] one²⁰, and that Jesus had not entered²¹ into the boat with His disciples, but His disciples had gone²² away alone^C. °Other²³ small-boats²⁴ came from Tiberias near the place where they ate the bread, the Lord having given-thanks^F. °So when the crowd saw that Jesus was²⁵ not there, nor His disciples, **they**²⁶ got into the small boats, and went to Capernaum seeking^G Jesus — 22, 23, 24

    1C. And having found Him on the other side *of* the sea, they said *to* Him, "Rabbi^H, when²⁷ have You come here?" — 25

        1D. Jesus responded *to* them and said, "Truly^J, truly, I say *to* you— — 26

            1E. "You are seeking^G Me

                1F. "Not because you saw signs²⁸
                2F. "But because you ate of the loaves-of-bread and were filled-to-satisfaction²⁹

            2E. "Do not be working^K *for* the food^L *which is* perishing^M, but *for* the food *which is* remaining^N to³⁰ eternal life— which the Son *of* Man will give *to* you — 27

                1F. "For God the Father certified³¹ this *One*"

        2D. So they said to Him, "What may we be doing in order that we may be working^K the works^O *of* God³²?" — 28
        3D. Jesus responded and said *to* them, "This is the work *of* God— that you be believing^P in *the One* Whom that *One* sent-forth^Q" — 29
        4D. So they said *to* Him, "What then do **You** do *as a* sign,³³ in order that we may see *it* and believe You? What *thing* do you work? — 30

            1E. "Our³⁴ fathers³⁵ ate the manna³⁶ in the wilderness^R, just as it has been written³⁷ [in Ps 78:24], 'He gave them bread from heaven to eat' " — 31

        5D. So Jesus said *to* them, "Truly, truly, I say *to* you, Moses has not given you the bread from heaven, but My Father is giving you the true^S Bread from heaven³⁸ — 32

1. Elsewhere only in Mt 14:20; 16:9; Mk 6:43; 8:19; Lk 9:17; all with reference to this incident. GK *3186*.
2. This word refers to "fragments".
3. Some manuscripts say "signs" {B}.
4. Some manuscripts say "Jesus" {B}.
5. That is, the one Moses spoke of, referred to also in 1:21.
6. More literally, "are", as the Greek typically phrases it.
7. On this word, "take away by force, snatch away, seize", see "snatch away" in 2 Cor 12:2. The people were going to take Jesus against His will to make Him king.
8. Or, "went back". This is John's only use of this word. On this word, see "went back" in Mt 4:12.
9. Parallel account at Mt 14:22; Mk 6:45.
10. Some manuscripts say "not" {N}.
11. Same word as in 2 Pet 1:13; 3:1. Elsewhere only as "woke up" in Lk 8:24; and "awakened" in Mk 4:39; Lk 8:24. GK *1444*.
12. Or, "having driven forward [by rowing]". Same word as in Mk 6:48. On this word, see "driven" in Lk 8:29.
13. On this measure of distance, see Rev 14:20. Here it amounts to 2.9 to 3.5 miles, or 4.6 to 5.6 kilometers, about halfway across. The Sea of Galilee is about six miles or ten kilometers wide.
14. Or, "observe". GK *2555*. Not related to the word in Mt 14:26; Mk 6:49 (GK *3972*).
15. That is, it is I. On this phrase, see Jn 8:58.
16. The grammar implies "Stop being afraid".
17. This is not mentioned in Mt 14:32; Mk 6:51, which only say the wind stopped. John may intend this in a miraculous sense. Or, he may mean it in a relative sense, in comparison to the 8 to 10 hours (note Mt 14:25) it took to get halfway. The boat arrived at once, right away, without any further hindrance.
18. Compare at Mt 14:34; Mk 6:53.
19. More literally, "was not", as the Greek typically phrases it.
20. Some manuscripts say, "except that one into which His disciples entered" {A}. The crowd looked back on the previous day and realized that there had only been one boat there, and that Jesus had not entered it with His disciples. He must still be there! When they could not find Him, they followed after the disciples.
21. More literally, "did not enter", as the Greek typically phrases it.
22. More literally, "went away", as the Greek typically phrases it.
23. Or, "However, small boats". The form of this word could be either the word "but, however" (GK *247*), or the word "other" (GK *257*), and both fit here. Boats arrived, which they used to follow.
24. Some manuscripts say "boats" {C}.
25. More literally, "is", as the Greek typically phrases it.
26. Some manuscripts add "also" {N}.
27. Or, "at what time". The crowd followed the disciples to find out where Jesus went, and are surprised to find Him with them. John's point is that they recognized that they last saw Jesus on the other side, and that they did not know when or how He got across the sea. GK *4536*.
28. Jesus passes by the crowd's superficial question and speaks to their hearts and motives. They were not seeking the meaning of His signs, only a personal earthly benefit from them. They were not seeking Him for spiritual motives.
29. Same word as in Mt 14:20. On this word, see Phil 4:12.
30. Or, "into, for". Work for food that satisfies an eternal hunger, not a temporary physical hunger. GK *1650*.
31. Or, "attested, set His seal on". Same word as in 3:33. The Father attested to Jesus in the miracle itself, as Jesus said in 5:36. And Jesus is the One with authority over eternal life, 5:21-23. This is the question the crowd should have been asking (v 26), "Who is God certifying You to be with this sign?"
32. That is, works pleasing to God, the works God desires. The crowd takes up the command to work in v 27.
33. Here the crowd's unbelief becomes clear. God had just attested to Jesus with a sign, the very miracle because of which they were now seeking Him, v 26, 14, and 2. Jesus responds in parabolic language.
34. The crowd gives this as an example of the type of sign they want to see.
35. This word means "father" in the sense of "parent", and in the sense of "forefather, ancestor", as here. Used 413 times. GK *4252*.
36. Same word as in v 49. On this word, see Rev 2:17.
37. This is a participle, as "it is having been written", it stands written, as in 2:17.
38. The manna was earthly, perishing bread, given to sustain the earthly lives of the Israelites, Ex 16. Through Moses God gave them earthly bread that came from heaven, not "the true bread from heaven". The Father is now giving these Jews the real Bread of eternal life—Jesus Himself.

A. Mk 4:37   B. Mt 14:33   C. Jam 2:24   D. Jn 7:17   E. Mt 13:5   F. Mt 26:27   G. Phil 2:21   H. Mt 23:7   J. Jn 1:51   K. Mt 26:10   L. Mt 6:19, eating   M. 1 Cor 1:18   N. Jn 15:4, abide   O. Mt 26:10   P. Jn 3:36   Q. Mk 3:14, send out   R. Mt 3:1   S. Jn 7:28

	1E. "For the bread *of* God¹ is the *One* coming² down from heaven and giving life *to* the world"	33
6D.	So they said to Him, "Master³, give us this bread always⁴"	34
7D.	Jesus⁵ said *to* them, "I am the bread *of* life	35
	1E. "The *one* coming to Me will never hunger, and the *one* believing^A in Me will never ever⁶ thirst. ˚But I said *to* you⁷ that you have indeed⁸ seen Me⁹, and you are not believing	36
	2E. "All that the Father gives *to* Me will come to Me, and I will never¹⁰ throw¹¹ outside the *one* coming to Me	37
	1F. "Because I have come down from heaven not in order that I may be doing **My** will^B, but the will of the *One* having sent^C Me	38
	2F. "And this is the will *of* the *One*¹² having sent Me— that *as to* all that He has given *to* Me, I will not lose^D *anything* from it¹³, but I will raise it up^E on the last day	39
	1G. "For¹⁴ this is the will *of* My Father¹⁵— that everyone seeing the Son and believing in Him may have eternal^F life, and **I** will raise him up on the last day"	40
2C.	Then the Jews were grumbling^G about Him because He said, "**I** am the bread having come down from heaven". ˚And they were saying, "Is this *One* not Jesus, the son *of* Joseph, whose father and mother **we** know?¹⁶ How does He now¹⁷ say that 'I have come down from heaven'?"	41 42
1D.	Jesus responded and said *to* them, "Do not be grumbling with one another. ˚No one is able to come¹⁸ to Me unless the Father having sent Me draws¹⁹ him. And **I** will raise him up on the last day	43-44
	1E. "It has been written²⁰ in the prophets [in Isa 54:13]— 'and they shall all be taught²¹ ones *of* God'	45
	2E. "Everyone²² having heard from the Father, and having learned^H, comes to Me—	
	1F. "Not that anyone has seen the Father²³, except the *One* being from God— this *One* has seen the Father	46
	3E. "Truly^J, truly, I say *to* you— the *one* believing²⁴ has eternal life	47
	1F. "**I** am the bread *of* life	48
	1G. "Your fathers ate the manna in the wilderness and died²⁵	49
	2G. "This is the bread coming down from heaven in order that anyone may eat of it and not die	50
	2F. "**I** am the living bread having come down from heaven. If anyone eats of this bread, he will live forever^K	51
	3F. "And²⁶ indeed the bread which **I** will give²⁷ for the life *of* the world is My flesh²⁸"	
3C.	Then the Jews were fighting²⁹ with one another, saying, "How can this *One* give us His³⁰ flesh³¹ to eat?"	52

1. That is, the bread God is giving.
2. Grammatically, this refers to "bread", and could be rendered "the *bread* coming", which is how the crowd took it, as seen in their response next, v 34. But Jesus was referring to Himself, as seen in v 35.
3. On this word, see Mt 8:2. Based on v 14, it is rendered "Master" here.
4. Or, "at all times". The crowd may be thinking of physical bread, as the woman was thinking of physical water in 4:15. Moses gave them manna for forty years. So You give us this true bread from heaven from now on, all the time. Or, they may even be asking for true spiritual bread. But they fail to understand that Jesus said He Himself is the bread. On this word, see 1 Thes 5:16.
5. Some manuscripts say "And Jesus"; others, "Then Jesus" {N}.
6. Or, "at any time". Elsewhere only in Lk 19:30; Jn 1:18; 5:37; 8:33; 1 Jn 4:12. GK *4799*. Not the same word as in 4:14.
7. Jesus "said" it, using different words, in v 26-27.
8. Or, "even, also, both". The ones believing will receive the bread of life that you ask for, v 34. But I have already said that your problem is unbelief. You have seen Me do a sign in which God certified Me, but you do not believe, v 26-27. You have indeed seen what you ask for in v 30. You are refusing the very bread you ask for in v 34.
9. Some manuscripts omit this word {C}.
10. Or, "by no means". On this phrase, see 8:51.
11. Or, "put, send, cast". Said in reverse, I will always keep inside, hold on to, the one coming. "Throw outside" is also in 9:34; Lk 13:28. On this word, see "cast out" in Jn 12:31.
12. Some manuscripts say "Father" {N}.
13. That is, from the total quantity the Father has given to Jesus. Jesus is not speaking of individuals here, but of the total number of individuals; the "all that" of v 37, 39; 17:2; the whole mass. Next, in v 40, He speaks individually.
14. Some manuscripts say "And" {K}.
15. The Father's will for people (v 40) is that everyone believing in the Son will have eternal life. Therefore, the Father's will for the Son (v 39) is that He will lose none from the group of believers the Father gives Him. Some manuscripts say "*of* the *One* having sent Me" {K}.
16. The grammar indicates a "yes" answer is expected. Note that the Jews correctly understood the implication of His "coming down from heaven", but rejected it.
17. Some manuscripts say "then" {N}, so that it says "How then does He say...".
18. This verse is the flip-side of v 37. All that the Father gives will come to Me; none can come to Me unless drawn by the Father. Compare v 65; 8:43; 12:39.
19. The unbelief of these Jews makes further explanation of His Sonship pointless. Jesus instead declares why they do not believe Him, and points them again to the truth in v 47-50. Same word as in 12:32, and as in 18:10; 21:6, 11. Elsewhere only as "dragged" in Act 16:19; 21:30; Jam 2:6. GK *1816*.
20. This is a participle, it "is having been written", as in 2:17.
21. This adjective is elsewhere only in 1 Cor 2:13. That is, ones whom God Himself has taught will be the ones who come to Jesus. GK *1435*. Paul combines this into one word, "God-taught", in 1 Thes 4:9.
22. Some manuscripts say "Therefore everyone..." {N}.
23. Jesus clarifies that the hearing He has in mind with regard to such ones is of a different kind than His own.
24. Some manuscripts add "in Me" {A}.
25. The manna only sustained their physical lives temporarily. The Israelites all eventually died.
26. Jesus now explains how the life He will give is connected to Himself. His words explain for those with an ear to hear (mainly after the cross), and are a stumbling stone for the rest. He adds these words to deepen the mystery for the Jews, not to simplify it. Like parables, this statement was intended to both explain and hide the truth. Hearing this, they will not hear, Mt 13:14-15. Some manuscripts say "... which I will give is My flesh, which I will give for the life *of* the world" {N}.
27. That is, on the cross. Those hearing this would not have understood the sense in which Jesus "will give" it. Nevertheless, Jesus intimately links life with Himself personally, and it is this personal link He now makes even more explicit.
28. The Word became flesh, 1:14, and He "will give" His flesh for the world, as the Lamb of God. On this word, see Col 2:23.
29. Obviously Jesus was speaking symbolically, not of literal cannibalism. But the Jews fought over what this meaning might be. This is an escalation from "grumbling" in v 41. On this word, see "battle" in 2 Tim 2:24.
30. Some manuscripts omit this word {C}, either leaving it implied "*His* flesh", or meaning "give us flesh to eat".
31. The Jews properly make the connection between "flesh" and "eat this bread". But they have no concept of the spiritual meaning of these words, and are stumbling on the physical meaning of them.

A. Jn 3:36 B. Jn 7:17 C. Jn 20:21 D. 1 Cor 1:18, perish E. Lk 18:33, rise up F. Mt 25:46 G. Lk 5:30 H. Phil 4:11 J. Jn 1:51 K. Rev 20:10

1D.	So Jesus said *to* them, "Truly, truly, I say *to* you, unless you eat the flesh *of* the Son *of* Man and drink[1] His blood[A], you do not have life in yourselves[2]	53
1E.	"The *one* eating[3] My flesh and drinking My blood has eternal life, and **I** will raise him up *on* the last day[4]	54
1F.	"For My flesh is true[5] food[6], and My blood is true drink[7]	55
2E.	"The *one* eating My flesh and drinking My blood abides[B] in Me, and I in him. °Just as the living Father sent Me forth[C], and **I** live because of the Father, indeed the *one* eating Me— that *one* also will live because of Me[8]	56-57
3E.	"This is the bread having come down from heaven— not as *the manna* the fathers ate[9] and died. The *one* eating this bread will live forever[D]"	58
2D.	He said these *things* in *a* synagogue while teaching in Capernaum[10]	59
4C.	Then many of His disciples,[11] having heard, said, "This statement[12] is hard[13]. Who can hear[14] it?"	60
1D.	But Jesus, knowing in Himself that His disciples are grumbling[E] about this, said *to* them, "Does this offend[15] you? °Then *what* if you see the Son *of* Man going up where He was formerly[16]?	61 62
1E.	"The Spirit is the *One* giving-life[F]. The flesh profits[17] nothing. The words which **I** have spoken *to* you are spirit, and are life[18]	63
2E.	"But there are some of you who do not believe"	64
1F.	For Jesus knew from *the* beginning who the *ones* not[19] believing were[20], and who the *one who* will hand Him over[G] was	
2F.	And He was saying, "For this reason[21] I have said *to* you that no one is able to come to Me unless it has been granted[22] *to* him from the Father"	65
5C.	From this *time*[23], many of His disciples went back[24], and were no longer walking[H] with Him. So Jesus said *to* the twelve,[25] "**You** also are not wanting[J] to go-away[K], *are you*?"[26]	66 67
1D.	Simon[27] Peter answered Him, "Lord, to whom shall we go? You have *the* words *of* eternal life. °And **we** have believed, and have come-to-know[L] that **You** are the Holy[M] One *of* God[28]"	68 69
2D.	Jesus answered them, "Did **I** not choose[N] you, the twelve, and one of you is *the* devil[29]?	70
1E.	Now He was speaking-*of* Judas[30], son *of* Simon[31] Iscariot[32]. For this *one*, one[33] of the twelve, was going to hand Him over[G]	71
4B.	And[34] after these *things* Jesus was walking[35] in Galilee. For He was not willing[J] to be walking[H] in Judea, because the Jews were seeking[O] to kill[P] Him	7:1
9A.	Now the Tent-pitching[36] Feast *of* the Jews was near[37]	2

1. As food must be taken into the body in order to be transformed into life-giving energy, so Jesus must be taken into the heart, so that He becomes the source and cause of spiritual life, from the inside out. This is the converse of faith. Faith is the heart reaching out to Him; this eating and drinking is the heart bringing Him inside, incorporating Him within. Note how Jesus characterizes these words in v 63. Beyond this, some think Jesus has the future bread and wine of the Lord's Supper in mind (as similarly in 7:39).
2. A more shocking, repugnant, and Law-violating phrase can hardly be imagined for a Jew than drinking human blood. Rather than soften or explain v 51b, Jesus enlarges and emboldens the stumbling stone for these Jews. He makes no attempt to resolve their fighting, but inflames it even more, pushing it to a crescendo. In response to their desire to make Him king (v 15), He is deliberately forcing them to a decision over Him. He is forcing a division among His "disciples", which occurs in v 66. With a shocking presentation of the truth, He quashes the uprising to make Him king.
3. Or, "chewing, munching, crunching, gnawing". Not the same word as v 53. This word is in v 54, 56, 57, 58. It was used of audibly eating fruits and vegetables, and then simply of "eating". This is eating with pleasure! It is an even more graphic word, pushing the bread of life metaphor to its limit. Instead of giving the "spiritual" explanation of this eating, Jesus gives an even more physical one! Elsewhere only in Jn 13:18; Mt 24:38. GK *5592*.
4. This sentence parallels v 40, making "believing" parallel to this eating and drinking.
5. Or, "genuine, real". Same word as in 5:31; 8:17; Phil 4:8; 1 Jn 2:8; and as "real" in Act 12:9. Used 26 times. GK *239*. Related to "truth" in Jn 4:23. Some manuscripts say "truly" both times in this verse {N}.
6. Same word as v 27. On this word, see "eating" in Mt 6:19.
7. This is because it produces true life, eternal life, not just temporary physical life.
8. How such a person will live "because of Me" will not be clear until after the cross, but an intimate abiding is needed.
9. Some manuscripts say "not as your fathers ate the manna and died" {A}.
10. When the synagogue was entered is not clear. Perhaps it was in v 52-53, or in v 41-43.
11. Now the response is from Jesus' disciples, His learners, not from "the Jews" as in v 41, 52.
12. Or, "saying, word, message". On this word, see "word" in 1 Cor 12:8.
13. Or, "harsh". It does not mean hard to understand, but offensive, objectionable, hard to accept. How can Jesus claim to be the bread of life descended from heaven, whose flesh we must eat and blood drink for eternal life? Elsewhere only as "hard" in Mt 25:24; Act 26:14; Jam 3:4; and "harsh" in Jude 15. GK *5017*.
14. Or, "listen to *it*". Who can hear it with acceptance, or listen to and obey it? On this word, see Act 22:9.
15. Or, "cause you to fall". On this word, see "cause to fall" in 1 Cor 8:13.
16. Or, "earlier, before". In other words, if these words offend these disciples, what will happen when they see Jesus returning to heaven, His mission completed? Would this cause them to believe (because they see the spiritual nature of the kingdom and His words), or to fall (because He again does not turn out to be what they expected, an earthly king reigning from Jerusalem)? On this word, see "first" in 2 Cor 1:15.
17. Or, "helps, aids, benefits" nothing. On this word, see Rom 2:25. This phrase "profit nothing" is also in Mt 27:24; Jn 12:19.
18. Jesus is explaining the intent of His words in v 53-58. The Spirit gives life. Eating His physical flesh and drinking His physical blood would profit nothing. His words have a spiritual, life-giving meaning. They are aimed at the spirit, in order to produce life.
19. Some manuscripts omit this word; others omit "who the *ones* not believing were, and" {B}.
20. More literally "are", as the Greek typically phrases it. Likewise with "was" at the end of the verse.
21. That is, because Jesus knew that some among His disciples did not believe in Him.
22. Or, "given". Compare v 44. This is a participle, it "is having been granted". On this word, see Eph 1:22.
23. Or, "*teaching, event* ". Same phrase as in 19:12; 1 Jn 4:6.
24. The idiom rendered "back" is also in 18:6; 20:14. It is a phrase meaning "to the *things* behind", and is found as such in Mk 13:16; Lk 9:62; 17:31. More literally here, they "went away to the *things* behind".
25. Note how the flow of this event has moved from the crowd, v 24; to the Jews, v 41, 52; to the disciples, v 60, 66; and now to the twelve.
26. The grammar indicates Jesus expected a "no" answer.
27. Some manuscripts say "So Simon..." {N}.
28. Some manuscripts say "the Christ, the Holy *One of* God"; others, "the Christ, the Son *of* God"; others, "the Christ, the Son *of* the living God" {A}.
29. This is similar to when Jesus called Peter "Satan" in Mt 16:23. "*The* devil" has the same grammar as in 1 Pet 5:8, Rev 20:2. The grammar of the question indicates that a "yes" answer is expected.
30. Judas is mentioned by name elsewhere only in Mt 10:4; 26:14, 25, 47; 27:3; Mk 3:19; 14:10, 43; Lk 6:16; 22:3, 47, 48; Jn 12:4; 13:2, 26, 29; 18:2, 3, 5; Act 1:16, 25. GK *2683*. Some manuscripts say "Judas Iscariot, [son] *of* Simon" {N}.
31. This Simon is also mentioned in Jn 13:2, 26.
32. Elsewhere only in Mt 10:4; 26:14; Mk 3:19; 14:10; Lk 6:16; 22:3; Jn 12:4; 13:2, 26; 14:22 ("not Iscariot"). Judas is called "Judas the Iscariot" only in Mt 10:4; Jn 12:4. GK *2697*. Some manuscripts say "from Kerioth", a town in southern Judea, or in Moab, thus interpreting "Iscariot" {N}.
33. Some manuscripts say "being one..." {N}.
34. Some manuscripts omit this word {N}.
35. This walking in Galilee extended from near Passover (6:4) to near Tabernacles (7:2); April to October.
36. Or, "Booth-building, Tabernacle-building". This is made from the word "tent, tabernacle" and the word "pitch" in Heb 8:2. This was an eight-day feast in Jerusalem in October, celebrating that "I had the sons of Israel live in tents when I brought them out from the land of Egypt", Lev 23:43. See Lev 23:34-43; Deut 16:13-17. Used only here. GK *5009*.
37. The events of this section (7:2-10:22) begin before this Feast of Tents in October, and extend to the Feast of Dedication in December. The next Passover (in April) mentioned by John (11:55, 13:1) was when Jesus was crucified. So almost 70% of John (chapters 7-21), focuses on the last seven months of His life, and His resurrection.

A. 1 Jn 1:7   B. Jn 15:4   C. Mk 3:14, send out   D. Rev 20:10   E. Lk 5:30   F. Jn 5:21   G. Mt 26:21, hand over   H. Heb 13:9   J. Jn 7:17, willing   K. Mt 4:10   L. Lk 1:34, know   M. 1 Pet 1:16   N. 1 Cor 1:27   O. Phil 2:21   P. Rom 7:11

1B. So His brothers[1] said to Him, "Pass-on[A] from here and go to Judea, so that Your disciples [there] also will see Your works which You are doing. *For no one does something in secret[B] and himself seeks to be in public[2]. If[3] You are doing these *things*, make Yourself known[4] *to* the world". *(For not even His brothers were believing[5] in Him) 3
4
5

    1C. So Jesus says *to* them, "**My** time[6] is not yet here,[7] but your time is always ready[8] 6

        1D. "The world cannot hate[C] you,[9] but it is hating Me because **I** am testifying[D] about it that its works are evil 7
        2D. "**You** go up to the[10] Feast 8
        3D. "**I** am not[11] going up to this Feast, because My time has not yet been fulfilled[E]"

    2C. And having said these *things,* **He**[12] remained[F] in Galilee 9
    3C. But when His brothers went up to the Feast[13], then **He** also went up— not openly[14], but as[15] in secret[B] 10
    4C. Then[16] the Jews[17] were seeking-*for*[G] Him at the Feast, and saying, "Where is that *One*?" 11
    5C. And there was much grumbling[H] about Him among the crowds 12

        1D. Some were saying that "He is good[J]"
        2D. But[18] others were saying, "No, but He is deceiving[K] the crowd"
        3D. Yet no one was speaking *with* openness[19] about Him because of fear[L] *of* the Jews[20] 13

2B. Now the Feast already being-at-the-middle[21], Jesus went up to the temple, and was teaching 14

    1C. Then[22] the Jews[23] were marveling[M], saying, "How does this *One* know writings[24], not having learned[25]?" 15

        1D. So[26] Jesus responded *to* them[27] and said— 16

            1E. "My teaching[N] is not Mine, but the *One's* having sent Me[28]

                1F. "If anyone is willing[29] to be doing His will[30], he will know[31] about the teaching— whether it is from God, or **I** am speaking from Myself[32] 17

            2E. "The *one* speaking from himself is seeking *his* own glory 18

                1F. "But the *One* seeking[G] the glory *of* the *One* having sent Him— this *One* is true[O], and there is no unrighteousness[33] in Him

            3E. "Has not Moses given you the Law? And none of you is doing the Law! Why are you seeking[G] to kill[34] Me?" 19

        2D. The crowd answered,[35] "You have *a* demon![36] Who is seeking to kill You?" 20
        3D. Jesus responded and said *to* them[37], "I did one work,[38] and you all marvel[M]! 21

            1E. "For this reason[39] Moses has given you circumcision (not that it is from Moses, but *it is* from the fathers[40]), and you circumcise *a* man **on *a* Sabbath** 22

1. On the brothers of Jesus, see Mt 13:55-56.
2. If You wish to be known to Israel, go to Judea! Do not stay in the obscurity of Galilee. The brothers of Jesus do not understand His mission. Same word as in v 26; and as "openness" in v 13. On this word, see "confidence" in Heb 4:16.
3. Or, "Since". The grammar means "Assuming that You are doing these things...". Same grammar as in Mt 4:3. Jesus' brothers are not doubting His miracles; they want Him to do them at the Feast in Judea for maximum public exposure.
4. Or, "reveal Yourself". Same word as "reveal" in 1:31; 2:11.
5. His brothers related to Jesus like the ones in 6:26. They were impressed by the signs, but did not grasp their meaning.
6. Or, "favorable-time, opportunity, right-time". Some think Jesus means it is not the right time for Him to be revealed to the world; others, to go up to the Feast. Used twice in v 6, once in v 8, the only uses in John. On this word, see Mt 8:29.
7. The suggestions and reasoning in v 3-4 are not wrong, just premature. The timing is critical for Jesus because the response when He reveals Himself will not be what His brothers think.
8. There is nothing to stop these brothers from going, and from believing. On this word, see "prepared" in Mk 14:15.
9. Because these men are part of the world.
10. Some manuscripts say "this" {K}.
11. Some think that Jesus is not going up in the way His brothers are suggesting— to make Himself known to the world, v 4; others, that it will not be until the time is right, which occurs in the middle of the Feast, v 14. Some manuscripts say "not yet" {C}.
12. Some manuscripts say "... said these *things to* them, He remained..." {B}.
13. Some manuscripts say "... went up, then **He** also went up to the Feast" {N}. On this word, see 13:29.
14. Related to "make known" in v 4. On this word, see "clearly" in Act 10:3.
15. Jesus went up privately, not in a public caravan of pilgrims, staying out of public view. He did not go up to the temple, and may not have entered Jerusalem, until the middle of the Feast. Some manuscripts omit this word {C}.
16. That is, when the Feast began.
17. That is, the Jewish leaders, as opposed to the "crowds" in v 12, who feared them, v 13. See 1:19.
18. Some manuscripts omit this word {C}.
19. Or, "*in* public". Same word as "public" in v 4.
20. That is, the Jewish leaders. See 1:19.
21. That is, about halfway through the feast. Used only here. GK *3548*.
22. Some manuscripts say "And" {K}.
23. That is, the Jewish leaders, as in v 11. They seek to discredit Jesus, and lower Him beneath themselves by implying He is merely speaking His own opinions as a self-taught layman.
24. Or, "learning". This word is used of alphabetic "letters", 2 Cor 3:7; Gal 6:11; "letters" of correspondence, Act 28:21; "writings" (books of Scripture), Jn 5:47; 2 Tim 3:15; and of the "learning" that comes from these things, Act 26:24. Elsewhere only of "writings" (written records) in Lk 16:6, 7; and the "letter" (written code of the Law), Rom 2:27, 29; 7:6; 2 Cor 3:6. GK *1207*. Not related to the word "learned" that follows. Related to "uneducated" in Act 4:13; to the verb "to write"; and to "scribe".
25. That is, how can Jesus be educated in these matters, not having learned in the schools of these leaders? On this word, see Phil 4:11.
26. Some manuscripts omit this word {K}.
27. Jesus responds publicly to their public comment.
28. In other words, Jesus' teaching is not based on His learning or their schools. It is the Father's teaching.
29. Or, "wishing, wanting, resolving, intending". If your purpose is to do God's will, you will know. He will show you. This common word is used 208 times. GK *2527*. The related noun is next.
30. Same word as in Mt 6:10; 7:21; 12:50; Jn 5:30, 6:38; Eph 1:9; 1 Thes 4:3; 5:18; Heb 13:21; 1 Pet 4:19. Used 62 times. GK *2525*.
21. Or, "come to know". On this word, see Lk 1:34.
32. On "from Myself" and "from himself" v 18, see 5:19.
33. Jesus moves from His teaching being true, to His character being righteous, to these Jews being unrighteous, v 19.
34. As stated in 5:18; 7:1. Jesus goes beyond answering them, and aggressively confronts the Law-violating intentions of these leaders. They are not willing or intending to do God's will, but are intending to violate His Law by killing Jesus.
35. The crowd of pilgrim worshipers responds ignorantly, not knowing of the intentions of the Jewish leaders. Compare v 25.
36. On having a demon, see 10:20.
37. By responding to the crowd, and referring to their response as "marveling", Jesus seems to imply that the crowd was aware of the healing incident that took place a year or more earlier to which He now refers, and shared in the marveling that it had been done on a Sabbath (though not in the anger of the leaders). If so, Jesus is correcting the reasoning of both the leaders and the crowd. If not, He is still speaking to the leaders in v 15. In any case, He does not answer the crowds "who" question, but answers the leaders' reasoning as to "why" they wanted to kill Him.
38. That is, one healing on the Sabbath, as seen in v 23. Note that Jesus calls it a "work", not a "healing" or "sign". The Jews wanted to kill Him because of the "work" on the Sabbath aspect of it. Their marveling was not at the healing, but at the fact that it was done on the Sabbath, as seen in 5:10, 12.
39. The relation of this phrase to the context is uncertain. Some think Jesus means "For healing". Moses gave circumcision to Israel for the "healing" or making "sound" of one member. This sets the stage for the comparison in v 23. Others think He means "This is why Moses commanded that you circumcise on the Sabbath— to establish a precedent for working on the Sabbath as I have just done". Others render this "For this reason [I say]". That is, because you marvel at this healing on the Sabbath, I respond as follows. Others place this phrase at the end of what precedes, "marvel **because of this**? Moses...". This would be the only time it comes at the end of a sentence (it is used 64 times), making it emphatic. There are other views. Consult the commentaries.
40. Circumcision was given by God to Abraham as a sign of the covenant (Gen 17:10-14), and later incorporated into the Law of Moses (Lev 12:3).

A. Jn 5:24, pass B. 1 Cor 4:5, hidden C. Rom 9:13 D. Jn 1:7 E. Eph 5:18, filled F. Jn 15:4, abide G. Phil 2:21 H. Phil 2:14 J. 1 Tim 5:10b K. Jam 5:19, err L. Eph 5:21 M. Rev 17:8 N. 1 Cor 14:6 O. Jn 6:55

2E. "If *a* man receives **circumcision** on *a* Sabbath in order that the Law *of* Moses may not be broken[A], are you angry[1] *at* Me because I made *an* **entire man**[2] sound[3] on *a* Sabbath?[4] 23

3E. "Do not be judging[B] according to appearance[5], but be judging[6] the righteous judgment[C]" 24

   2C. Then some of the people-of-Jerusalem[7] were saying, "Is not this *the One* Whom they are seeking to kill?[8] *And look— He is speaking *in* public[9], and they are saying nothing *to* Him. The rulers[D] did not perhaps really[10] know[11] that this *One* is[12] the Christ, *did they*?[13] *However,[14] we know where this *One* is from. But when the Christ is coming,[15] no one knows where He is from" 25 26 27

      1D. So Jesus cried-out[16] while teaching in the temple and saying, "You both know Me and You know where I am from.[17] And[18] I have not come of Myself[19] 28

         1E. "However,[20] the *One* having sent Me is true[21]— Whom **you** do not know. *I know[22] Him, because I am from Him. And that *One* sent Me forth" 29

      2D. Therefore they were seeking to seize[E] Him 30
      3D. And no one put[F] *his* hand on Him, because His hour had not yet come

   2C. But many from the crowd[23] believed in Him. And they were saying, "When the Christ comes, He will not do more[24] signs[G] *than the ones* which this *One* did, *will He*?[25] *The Pharisees heard the crowd murmuring[H] these *things* about Him. And the chief priests and the Pharisees[26] sent out officers[27] in order that they might seize[E] Him 31 32

      1D. So Jesus said,[28] "I am with you *a* short time longer, and [then] I am going to the *One* having sent Me. *You will seek Me, and will not find Me. And where **I** am, **you** are not able to come" 33 34

      2D. Then the Jews said to themselves[29], "Where is this *One* going to go that **we** will not find Him? 35

         1E. "He is not going to go to the Dispersion[30] *of* the Greeks and teach the Greeks[31], *is He*?[32]
         2E. "What is this statement[33] that He said— 'You will seek Me and will not find Me. And where **I** am, **you** are not able to come'?" 36

3B. Now on the last day,[34] the great *day of* the Feast[J], Jesus was standing[35] *there* 37

   1C. And He cried-out, saying, "If anyone is thirsting, let him come to Me[36] and drink. *The *one* believing in Me,[37] just as the Scripture[38] said— Rivers *of* living water will flow from his[39] belly[40]" 38

      1D. Now He said this concerning the Spirit, Whom the *ones* having believed[41] in Him were going to receive. For *the* Spirit[42] was not yet *given*[43], because Jesus was not yet glorified[44] 39

   2C. Then *some* from the crowd,[45] having heard these words[46], were saying, "This *One* is truly[K] the Prophet[47]" 40

      1D. Others were saying, "This *One* is the Christ" 41
      2D. But the *ones*[48] were saying, "The Christ is not indeed[49] coming from Galilee, *is He*?[50] Did not the Scripture say that the Christ comes from the seed *of* David, and from Bethlehem, the village where David was?"[51] 42

1. This word implies a bitter, venomous anger. Used only here. GK *5957*. Related to "gall" in Act 8:23. Perhaps is should be "galled".
2. That is, as opposed to one member of his body, as with circumcision.
3. Or, "healthy". Jesus is referring to the man in 5:8, the recipient of the "one work" in v 21. Same word as "healthy" in 5:6. It is rendered "sound" here because this is the sense it would have with circumcision, the other half of His comparison.
4. If you confer a bodily blessing on a man on the Sabbath as Moses commanded, why are you angry if I confer a greater bodily blessing? If the Law requires the making sound of this one member on the Sabbath, surely making sound a whole body is permitted. The Jews used similar logic in the case of one whose life was in danger on a Sabbath— If one overrides the Sabbath for one of his members, should he not override it if his whole body is in danger? Compare Mt 12:11-12; Lk 13:15-16; Mt 12:5.
5. On this word, see "face" in Rev 1:16.
6. Some manuscripts have a different tense here {N}, so that Jesus means "Do not be judging according to appearance, but make-the-judgment [which is] the righteous judgment".
7. Or, "the Jerusalemites". The locals knew of the leaders' plans. Elsewhere only in Mk 1:5. GK *2643*.
8. The grammar indicates a "yes" answer is expected.
9. Or, "openly, boldly". Same word as in v 4.
10. Or, "truly". On this word, see "truly" in Mt 14:33.
11. Or, "come to know, learn, recognize". On this word, see Lk 1:34.
12. Some manuscripts add "really" {K}, repeating it from earlier.
13. The grammar indicates a "no" answer is expected.
14. As quickly as the people raise the possibility, they dismiss it.
15. That is, at the time of the Christ's coming on the scene. The grammar in v 31 is different. The people do not mean this as to the Messiah's place of birth, which they knew was Bethlehem, v 42. They expected the Messiah to arrive suddenly and unexpectedly and decisively in power, anointed by Elijah, not as one whose ministry grew gradually over time. After the Messiah comes on the scene, then his origins would become known.
16. Same word as in 7:37; 12:44. On this word, see Mt 8:29.
17. Some think this is a statement; others, an ironic exclamation or question.
18. Or, "And-*yet*", as it means in v 30. What the people know in this regard is not wrong, just incomplete. Jesus does not correct them on this point, but adds the main point that they need to know. In addition to what you know about Me, know this— I have not come of Myself. The Word (1:14) did come suddenly on the scene from above, and they do not know where He is from. This is true right along side of the fact that they knew where Jesus was from. GK *2779*.
19. On "of Myself", see "from Himself" in 5:19.
20. In spite of the fact that you do not know this latter fact, or reject it, My sender is real.
21. That is, real, genuine, objectively true, corresponding to reality from God's point of view, as in 1:9; 4:23; 6:32; 15:1; 17:3; 1 Thes 1:9; 1 Jn 2:8. Used 28 times. GK *240*. Related to "truth" in Jn 4:23, and "true" in 6:55.
22. Some manuscripts say "But **I** know..." {N}.
23. That is, in contrast with the leaders of the Jews, v 30.
24. Or, "greater". It may mean more in quantity, or more in quality. On this word, see "many" in Mt 13:52.
25. The grammar indicates a "no" answer is expected.
26. Some manuscripts reverse these two {N}, so that it says "the Pharisees and chief priests".
27. That is, the temple guards, who were Levites. On this word, see 18:12.
28. As in v 16, and v 28, Jesus responds to what is going on around Him. In each of these instances, He is not responding to a direct question put to Him, but to what people were saying to one another about Him. Here He speaks to the crowd of pilgrims, the Jewish leaders, and the officers.
29. Or, "to each other".
30. That is, the Dispersion of the Jews among the Gentile nations. On this word, see 1 Pet 1:1.
31. The Jews may mean the Gentiles; or, the Jewish proselytes; or, the Greek-speaking foreign Jews. See 12:20.
32. The grammar indicates a "no" answer is expected.
33. Or, "thing, saying, word". On this word, see "word" in 1 Cor 12:8.
34. Some think John means the seventh day, Friday; others, the eighth day, the Sabbath. The choice may have a bearing on which aspect of the symbolism of the Feast Jesus might be alluding to. Consult the commentaries.
35. Or, "stood". GK *2705*.
36. Some manuscripts omit "to Me" {B}.
37. Or, this may be punctuated "... let him come to Me. And let the *one* believing in Me drink. Just as...".
38. Perhaps Jesus is referring in general terms to verses like Joel 3:18; Zech 13:1; 14:8; Ezek 47:1; Isa 58:11.
39. Or, "His". Some think this refers to believers, so that the rivers represent the life-giving Spirit flowing out to eternal life (note 4:14), and flowing through believers to others. Others think it refers to Christ, so that the rivers represent the Spirit flowing from Christ to believers. In this case, the punctuation in the note above (which allows either view) is followed.
40. That is, his heart, his innermost being. On this word, see "womb" in Lk 1:15.
41. Some manuscripts say "the *ones* believing" {B}.
42. Some manuscripts say "Holy Spirit" {A}.
43. Or, "For there was not yet *a* Spirit". Compare Act 19:2. Some manuscripts include this word. Others say "upon them" {A}.
44. Same word as in 12:16, 23; 17:1, 5. It refers to Jesus' death, resurrection, and return to the Father. On this word, see Rom 8:30.
45. Some manuscripts say "Then many from the crowd" {N}, as in v 31.
46. Some manuscripts say "these words *of* His" {N}; others, "this saying" {K}.
47. On "the prophet", see 1:21.
48. This is the literal rendering of this idiom, which introduces another class of individuals alongside those already mentioned. Who is being referred to? This idiom can mean "But others" or "But some" from the crowd, referring to a third group not sympathetic with the two groups mentioned. Or it can mean "But the *ones*", referring to the first group in v 40 correcting the second. In any case, they respond to the previous suggestion. Instead of "But the *ones*", some manuscripts say "Others" were saying {N}, as in the previous sentence. On this idiom, see Mt 26:67.
49. This is the same word as in the same tone of question in Mt 27:23.
50. The grammar indicates a "no" answer is expected.
51. The grammar indicates a "yes" answer is expected.

A. Mt 5:19 B. Mt 7:1 C. Jn 3:19 D. Rev 1:5 E. Jn 11:57 F. Mk 14:72, put upon G. 2 Thes 2:9 H. Lk 5:30, grumble J. Jn 13:29 K. Mt 14:33

	3D. So *a* division^A took place in the crowd because of Him	43
	4D. And some of them were wanting to seize^B Him, but no one put *his* hands on Him	44
	3C. Then the officers¹ went to the chief priests and Pharisees. And those *ones* said *to* them, "For what reason did you not bring Him?"	45
	1D. The officers answered, "Never did *a* man speak in this manner²"	46
	2D. Then the Pharisees responded *to* them, "**You** also have not been deceived^C, *have you*?³ Someone from the rulers^D did not believe in Him, *did he,* or from the Pharisees? But this crowd not knowing the Law— they are accursed⁴ *ones*"	47 48-49
	3D. Nicodemus— the *one* having come to Him formerly⁵, being one of them⁶— says to them, "Our Law does not judge^E the person^F unless it first hears from him, and knows what he is doing, *does it*⁷?"	50 51
	4D. They responded and said *to* him, "**You** also are not from Galilee, *are you*? Search^G and see that *a* prophet^H does not arise⁸ from Galilee"	52
	4C. And⁹ each *one* went to his house, but Jesus went to the Mount *of* Olives¹⁰	7:53-8:1
4B. Now *at* dawn,¹¹ He again arrived in the temple. And all the people were coming to Him. And having sat-*down*, He was teaching them		2
	1C. And the scribes¹² and the Pharisees bring *a* woman having been caught¹³ in adultery. And having stood her in *the* middle^J, they say *to* Him, "Teacher, this woman has been caught in the-act¹⁴, while committing-adultery^K. Now in the Law, Moses commanded^L us to be stoning such *women*.¹⁵ What then do **You** say?"	3 4 5
	1D. Now they were saying this testing^M Him, in order that they might have *grounds* to be accusing^N Him¹⁶	6
	2C. But Jesus, having stooped¹⁷ down, was writing¹⁸ in the ground^O *with His* finger¹⁹	
	3C. But as they were continuing-on²⁰ asking Him, He straightened-up²¹ and said *to* them, "Let the sinless²² *one* among you throw *a* stone at her first"²³	7
	4C. And again having stooped-down²⁴, He was writing in the ground	8
	5C. And the *ones,* having heard²⁵ *it,* were going out one by one²⁶, beginning from²⁷ the older *ones*²⁸. And He was left-behind^P alone^Q, and the woman being in *the* middle^J	9
	6C. And Jesus, having straightened up²⁹, said *to* her, "Woman, where are they³⁰? Did no one condemn^R you?"	10
	1D. And the *one* said, "No one, Sir"	11
	2D. And Jesus said, "Neither do **I** condemn^R you.³¹ Go. And³² from now on³³, do not be sinning any longer³⁴"	
5B. Then Jesus again³⁵ spoke *to* them, saying, "**I** am the light *of* the world. The *one* following Me will never walk^S in the darkness^T, but will have the light *of* life³⁶"		12
	1C. So the Pharisees said *to* Him, "**You** are testifying about Yourself— Your testimony is not true"	13
	2C. Jesus responded and said *to* them	14
	1D. "Even if **I** am testifying about Myself, My testimony is true,³⁷ because I know from where I came, and where I am going³⁸	

1. That is, the ones sent in v 32, who were waiting for a favorable opportunity to seize Jesus. As Levites themselves, they would have combined a personal interest in Jesus with their official duty.
2. Some manuscripts add to this "like this man"; others, "like this man speaks" {B}.
3. The grammar indicates a "no" answer is expected, as with the next question.
4. That is, the crowd has a curse upon them. Used only here. GK *2063*.
5. Or, "earlier, before". On this word, see "first" in 2 Cor 1:15. Instead of this word, some manuscripts say "*by* night" {N}.
6. That is, being a Pharisee and a ruler. Nicodemus responds to the taunt in v 48, but does not declare his position.
7. The grammar indicates a "no" answer is expected, as with the next question.
8. Some manuscripts say "has not arisen" {K}.
9. Some think that this story, from 7:53 to 8:11, is an original part of John's Gospel, based on the fact that many manuscripts have it, and on other evidence. Others think that because the oldest manuscripts omit these verses, and because of other evidence, they are not original. This is the view taken by UBS4, which marks these verses as not an original part of John's Gospel, but as very ancient. This view suggests that this is a genuine incident from the life of Christ added at a later date to the Gospel of John. In some manuscripts, this story is found after 7:36; in others, after 7:44; in others, after 21:25; in others, after Lk 21:38. In most that have it, it is here.
10. This is the only time this mountain is mentioned by name in John.
11. If this section is genuine, then this is the day after the Feast ended, 7:37. See 8:12. On "dawn", see Lk 24:1.
12. This is the only place the scribes are mentioned by name in John.
13. Or, "overtaken, seized, taken down". On this word, see "overcome" in 1:5.
14. Used only here. GK *900*.
15. Some manuscripts say "commanded us *that* such *women* should be stoned" {N}. See Deut 22:22-24; Lev 20:10. These verses say the man and the woman are to die, but the Pharisees do not bring the man forth. Their interest was not in upholding Moses.
16. If Jesus said that the Jewish leaders should stone her, it would violate the Roman law under which they were forbidden to execute anyone, 18:31. They could then charge Him before the Romans with sedition. If He said they should not stone her, they could discredit Him among the people of Israel. They think they have Jesus boxed in.
17. Elsewhere only in Mk 1:7. GK *3252*.
18. Or, "drawing, writing down". Some think Jesus was writing specific words. Several suggestions have been made as to what they were. Others think He was simply ignoring them, waiting for them to leave. When they did not (v 7), He responded. Used only here. GK *2863*. "Writing" in v 8 is the same word without the prefix "down".
19. Some manuscripts add "not taking notice" {N}.
20. Or, "persisting". Same word and grammar as in Act 12:16, where Peter "was continuing-on knocking".
21. On this word, see Lk 21:28. Same word as in v 10.
22. That is, the one who has not sinned, who has done no wrong. Used only here. GK *387*. Related to "sin".
23. The real question was not what the Law of Moses said, but who had the authority to carry it out. As a nation, Israel had lost that authority to the Romans. The Jews all knew it. Jesus confronts them with another issue about which they all knew the answer! He is not saying proper authorities must be sinless to enforce the Law, or that proper governments cannot execute punishment. But this was not an official court action. He is forcing the would-be executioners to affirm that they are sinless, and in particular, sinless in this execution they would carry out on God's behalf. If they are going to appoint themselves as God's private executioners, outside of the governmental system, they had better be sinless! The Pharisees all knew that justice was not their real motive.
24. Related to "stooped" in v 6. Used only here. GK *2893*.
25. Some manuscripts add "and being convicted by *their* conscience" {A}.
26. On this idiom "one by one", see Mk 14:19.
27. On the idiom "beginning from", see Mt 20:8.
28. Or, "the elders". On this word, see 1 Tim 5:1. Some manuscripts add "until the last *ones*" {A}.
29. Some manuscripts add "and having seen no one except the woman" {A}.
30. Some manuscripts say "Where are those accusers *of* yours"; others, "Where are your accusers" {A}.
31. That is, neither am I executing sentence against you at this time. Jesus did not come to judge, but to save, 3:17. Jesus will judge on that still future day, 5:22, 29. These are not words of forgiveness, but of an earthly reprieve. Whether the woman later found forgiveness is not stated. As with all humans in this age, Jesus shows mercy and calls for repentance.
32. Some manuscripts omit this word {C}.
33. Some manuscripts omit "from now *on*" {N}. "From now *on*" is elsewhere only in Lk 1:48; 5:10; 12:52; 22:18, 69; Act 18:6; 2 Cor 5:16.
34. That is, do not continue sinning any longer. Repent. This is the same command as in 5:14.
35. If 7:53-8:11 is not genuine but was added later (see 7:53), then John may mean that 8:12-10:21 also took place on the last day of the Feast, 7:37. Otherwise, the next note of time is in 10:22, two months later, and the events from 8:12 to 10:21 occur sometime between the two feasts, between October and December.
36. This may mean the light which proceeds from life (1:4); or, leads the way to life and gives life; or, belongs to life.
37. Compare 5:31. There, if Jesus were to testify apart from His Father's co-witness, it would not be true. Here, what He is testifying is true because it is spoken in agreement with His Father.
38. Jesus knows Himself and His mission, and that His testimony is true. Other witnesses do not make it true, they only confirm that it is true. He has already given the Pharisees other witnesses, but mentions one again in v 18.

A. 1 Cor 1:10   B. Jn 11:57   C. Jam 5:19, err   D. Rev 1:5   E. Mt 7:1   F. Mt 4:4, mankind   G. 1 Cor 2:10   H. 1 Cor 12:28   J. 2 Thes 2:7, midst
K. Mt 5:32   L. Mk 10:3   M. Heb 2:18, tempted   N. Jn 5:45   O. Rev 7:1, land   P. Act 6:2   Q. Jam 2:24   R. 1 Cor 11:32   S. Heb 13:9   T. Jn 1:5

    1E. "But **you** do not know from where I come, or¹ where I am going

   2D. "**You** are judging^A according to the flesh.² **I** am not judging^A anyone³   15

    1E. "But even if **I** am judging^A, My judgment^B is true^C, because I am not alone^D— but *it is* I and the Father having sent Me⁴   16

   3D. "But even in your Law, it has been written that the testimony *of* two people is true   17

    1E. "**I** am the *One* testifying about Myself   18
    2E. "And the **Father** having sent Me is testifying about Me"

  3C. So they were saying *to* Him, "Where is Your Father?"   19

   1D. Jesus answered, "You know neither Me nor My Father. If you knew Me, you would also know My Father"

  4C. These words He⁵ spoke in the treasury^E, while teaching in the temple   20
  5C. And no one seized^F Him, because His hour had not yet come

 6B. Then He said again⁶ *to* them, "I am going away. And you will seek Me⁷. And in your sin, you will die.⁸ Where **I** am going, **you** are not able to come"   21

  1C. So the Jews were saying, "He will not kill Himself, *will He*⁹— because He says, 'Where **I** am going, **you** are not able to come'?"   22
  2C. And¹⁰ He was saying *to* them— "**You** are from below, **I** am from above¹¹. **You** are from **this** world^G, **I** am not from this world¹². *Therefore I said *to* you that you will die^H in your sins. For unless you believe that **I** am *the One*¹³, you will die in your sins"   23 24
  3C. So they were saying *to* Him, "Who are **You**?"¹⁴   25
  4C. Jesus said *to* them, "What thing¹⁵ *from* the beginning¹⁶ I am indeed telling¹⁷ you!

   1D. "I¹⁸ have many *things* to speak and to judge^A concerning you¹⁹   26
   2D. "However,²⁰ the *One* having sent Me is true^J. And what *things* I heard from Him— these *things* **I** am speaking to the world"

    1E. They did not know that He was speaking *to* them *about* the Father²¹   27

  5C. Then²² Jesus said *to* them²³, "When you lift-up²⁴ the Son *of* Man, then you²⁵ will know that   28

   1D. "**I** am *the One*²⁶
   2D. "And²⁷ I am doing nothing from Myself²⁸, but I am speaking these²⁹ *things* just as the³⁰ Father taught^K Me
   3D. "And³¹ the *One* having sent Me is with Me. He³² did not leave Me alone³³, because **I** am always doing the *things* pleasing³⁴ *to* Him"   29

  6C. While He *was* speaking these *things*, many believed in Him   30

 7B. Then Jesus was saying to the Jews having believed Him³⁵, "If **you** remain³⁶ in My word^L, you are truly^M My disciples^N, *and you will know the truth^O, and the truth will set you free³⁷"   31 32

1. Jesus possesses, and these leaders lack, the crucial facts in the matter. Some manuscripts say "and" {N}.
2. That is, the Pharisees are passing judgment on Jesus and condemning Him by wrong criteria.
3. Some think Jesus means "the way you are", according to appearances. Others think He means that He is not engaged in judging anyone. It is not His mission or habit to do so. His mission is to save, 3:17.
4. Even though it is not His mission, if Jesus does judge while carrying out His mission, His judgment is true (unlike theirs). This is because it is in concert with the Father's judgment. It is a wholly different kind of judgment than that of the Pharisees. And Jesus does have many things to judge concerning them, v 26.
5. Some manuscripts say "Jesus" {K}.
6. This may mean "at a later time or occasion", as in v 12. But it may also refer to 7:34, which Jesus expands here.
7. That is, the Messiah.
8. This is the Greek word order here, and in the two places in v 24, reflecting a difference of emphasis.
9. The grammar indicates a "no" answer is expected.
10. Note how the Jews respond with sarcastic mockery in v 22, but Jesus responds solemnly here, as if He must say these words whether or not they want to hear them.
11. More literally, from "the *places* below", "the *places* above". That is, from earth, from heaven.
12. Jesus is asserting His authority for what He says next.
13. Or, "I am He, I am *Who I say I am*". Or simply "I am". On this idiom, see 8:58.
14. The Jews are trying to get Jesus to explicitly say "I am the Christ, the Son of God", so they can charge Him with blasphemy. He does not allow them to hear such a direct statement until His hour is come, Mt 26:63-64.
15. The phrase "what thing" is elsewhere only in Act 9:6, "what thing you must do". It is similar to "whatever thing" in Jn 2:5; 14:13; 15:16; on which see Col 3:17. These are usually simplified to "what" and "whatever", respectively. Instead of "what thing", some manuscripts say "that" {B}. See the next note.
16. Or, "Exactly what thing I am indeed telling you!" Jesus clearly does not want to give them a direct answer. It is not yet His hour. The exact meaning of this word is unclear here. He is using an idiom for which there are not enough examples in Greek literature for scholars to reach a consensus as to its meaning. This word means "beginning", and is used 55 times in the NT (see Col 1:18 on it). But it is used only here in this grammatical relationship to the sentence (more literally, "*as to* the beginning, *with reference to* the beginning"). Others render it as a question, "What thing am I indeed telling you *from* the beginning?" Others, using the reading "that" mentioned in the previous note, render it "*How is it* that I am even speaking *to* you at all?" There are several other views. In any case, the main point of His answer is crystal clear— You ought to know by now who I am!
17. Jesus is the Son of God, 5:18; the life-giver and judge, 5:21-22; the One sent by the Father, 5:37; the bread from heaven, 6:51; the light of the world, 8:12; the One in whom you must believe to have eternal life, 8:24; etc.
18. Probably after a pause and a look, Jesus now continues with what He was saying in v 24.
19. That is, negative things, condemnations, like v 23-24. These things must be spoken. Some come in v 31-58.
20. Some think Jesus means that in spite of the fact that these leaders do not accept Him or the words He has to speak concerning them, His source is real and what He says comes straight from the Father. Others think Jesus means He has words of judgment to speak to them, but He is not speaking them. Rather, He is speaking what the Father gave Him to speak in accordance with His mission. Compare 7:28; 8:16.
21. John seems to mean the Jews did not know that Jesus meant that the One who sent Him was the Father sending His Son. They did not understand He was claiming equality with the Father as the Son, only that He was claiming God sent Him. Had they understood this, they would have reacted as in 5:18; 8:59; and 10:33; where this claim is clear.
22. Jesus says this with reference to the failure to know Him in v 25.
23. Some manuscripts omit "to them" {C}.
24. Or, "raise high, exalt". Same word as in 3:14; 12:32, 34; and as "exalt" in Act 2:33; 5:31. Used 20 times. GK *5738*. Like "rise up" (Lk 18:33), it is a word that reveals, yet conceals the truth. Jesus means these leaders will lift Him up on the cross. They probably took Him to mean "exalt". This is not a word normally associated with death on a cross. Related to "highest" in Mt 21:9.
25. Those among these leaders who will believe (like Nicodemus and Joseph) will not do so until after the cross. Only then will they be sure. Perhaps after the cross, the Spirit opened their eyes to Isa 53, and what is now so confusing became clear to them. The others will also come to know this after the cross, when they stand before God. Some think Jesus is only referring to the latter, much larger group. Others think the words are broad enough to include both groups.
26. Or, "I am *Who I say I am*". Or, simply "I am". On this idiom, see 8:58. Others make this the sole conclusion of the previous sentence, and make what follows separate points (1D. and 2D.), not additional things these leaders "will know".
27. Secondly, you will know that everything I am doing and speaking originated with the Father.
28. On "from Myself", see "from Himself" in 5:19.
29. That is, all of the things Jesus is speaking and teaching.
30. Some manuscripts say "My" {N}.
31. Thirdly, you will know that the Father is with Me, and never left Me alone, because I am doing His will.
32. Some manuscripts say "The Father" {N}.
33. This is especially true of the Cross. The Jews will think God has abandoned Jesus. But afterward, they will know that God did not at all do so, but that this too was His will. Same word as 16:32, on which see Jam 2:24.
34. Same word as in 1 Jn 3:22. Elsewhere only in Act 6:2; 12:3. GK *744*. Related to the verb "pleasing" in 1 Thes 2:4.
35. Some think that whatever the sense may be in which these Jews "believed" Jesus, His word did not "advance" in their hearts (v 37), and it quickly becomes clear that they did not "remain in My word". These are like the ones in 2:23; 6:66. Others think that those responding in v 33 are a different group, responding to this statement Jesus makes to those who truly believe in Him. Consult the commentaries.
36. Or, "continue, abide, stay". On this word, see "abide" in 15:4.
37. On this verb "to set free", see Rom 8:2. Same word as in v 36.

A. Mt 7:1 B. Jn 3:19 C. Jn 7:28 D. Jam 2:24 E. Mk 12:41 F. Jn 11:57 G. 1 Jn 2:15 H. Rom 7:10 J. Jn 6:55 K. Rom 12:7 L. 1 Cor 12:8 M. Mt 14:33 N. Lk 6:40 O. Jn 4:23

| John 8:33 | 334 | Verse |

1C. They responded to Him, "We are *the* seed[1] *of* Abraham, and *to* no one have we ever been slaves[2]. How *is it* **You** say that 'You will become free[A]'?"   33
2C. Jesus answered them, "Truly[B], truly, I say *to* you that everyone doing sin[3] is *a* slave[4] *of* sin. Now the slave[C] does not remain[D] in the house forever[5]. The son remains forever. °Therefore if the Son sets you free, you will really[6] be free[A]   34   35-36

    1D. "I know that you are *the* seed *of* Abraham.[7] But you are seeking[E] to kill[F] Me, because My word is not advancing[8] in you   37
    2D. "I am speaking *the things* which **I** have seen with *My* Father   38
    3D. "And **you** therefore[9] are doing[10] *the things* which you heard[11] from *your* father"

3C. They responded and said *to* Him, "Our father[12] is Abraham"   39
4C. Jesus says *to* them, "If you are[13] children *of* Abraham, you *would* be doing[14] the works *of* Abraham

    1D. "But now[15] you are seeking to kill Me— *a* man Who has told you the truth[G], which I heard from God   40
    2D. "Abraham did not do this
    3D. "**You** are doing the works[H] *of* your father[16]"   41

5C. So they said *to* Him, "**We** have not been born[J] out of sexuality-immorality[17]. We have one Father— God"
6C. Jesus said *to* them, "If God were your Father, you would be loving[K] Me, for **I** came-forth and am-here[18] from God. For I have not even come[L] of Myself[19], but that *One* sent Me forth[M]   42

    1D. "For what reason are you not understanding[N] My speaking[20]?   43

        1E. "*It is* because you are not able to hear My word
        2E. "**You** are of *your* father the devil. And you are wanting[21] to do the desires[O] *of* your father[22]   44

            1F. "That *one* was *a* murderer[P] from *the* beginning, and was not standing[23] in the truth[G], because there is no truth in him
            2F. "Whenever he speaks the lie[24], he speaks from *his* own *things,* because he is *a* liar, and the father *of* it

        3E. "And because **I** am speaking the truth[G], you are not believing Me   45

    2D. "Which of you convicts[25] Me concerning sin[26]? If[27] I am speaking truth, for what reason are **you** not believing Me?   46
    3D. "The *one* being of[28] God hears the words *of* God. For this reason **you** are not hearing— because you are not of God"   47

7C. The Jews responded and said *to* Him, "Do **we** not rightly[Q] say[29] that **You** are *a* Samaritan[30] and have *a* demon?"[31]   48
8C. Jesus answered, "**I** do not have *a* demon, but I am honoring[R] My Father, and **you** are dishonoring[32] Me. °But **I** am not seeking[E] My glory   49   50

    1D. "There is the *One* seeking *it,* and judging[33]
    2D. "Truly, truly, I say *to* you— if anyone keeps[S] My word, he will never[34] see[T] death, ever[35]"   51

1. That is, descendants. On this word, see Heb 11:11.
2. That is, in a religious sense (not a political sense). We have always worshiped the true God as Abraham's offspring, so how can You set us free? On this verb, see "are slaves" in Rom 6:6.
3. Or, "committing sin". On "doing sin", compare 1 Jn 3:4, 8, 9. Compare also "doing the truth" in Jn 3:21; 1 Jn 1:6; and "doing righteousness" in 1 Jn 2:29; 3:7, 10.
4. The freedom Jesus has in mind is a personal, spiritual freedom from sin so as to be full and free family members in God's family, not just Abraham's.
5. Slaves do not permanently live in the house. They go out to their own place. On "forever", see Rev 20:10.
6. Or, "in truth, in reality, certainly". The Son will set you free to live and remain in the Master's house, not as a slave, but as a family member. You will no longer be slaves to sin. Same word as in Mk 11:32; Lk 23:47; 24:34; 1 Cor 14:25; Gal 3:21. Elsewhere only as "real" in 1 Tim 5:3, 5, 16; 6:19. GK *3953*.
7. That is, physically. The conduct of these Jews proves it is not true spiritually.
8. Or, "going forward, making progress". Same word as in Mt 15:17. Or, "making room, making a place, having a place". On this word, see "make room" in 2 Pet 3:9. Said in reverse, "because you are refusing the advance of My word in you".
9. Some manuscripts omit this word {K}, so that it says "And **you** are doing...".
10. Or, this may be a command, "**You** also therefore be doing *the things* which you heard from *your* father" (meaning, "Carry out your plans against Me", as in Mt 23:32); or, "... from the Father" (meaning, "Obey God and stop seeking to kill Me"). The Greek says "the father" in both places in this verse. The contrast between fathers, which is stated explicitly in v 40 and 44, may be implied in this verse. Some manuscripts add the words "My" and "your" {B}, making it explicit here.
11. Some manuscripts say "have seen" {B}.
12. That is, our physical and spiritual father. What we heard has been passed down to us since Abraham.
13. Some manuscripts say "If you were" {N}.
14. Some manuscripts have this as a command {B}, so that it says "if you are children *of* Abraham, be doing the works...".
15. Jesus may mean "But at the present time", or, "But as it is", as things stand. GK *3814*.
16. Jesus is implying that their father is someone other than Abraham.
17. Jesus has called into question their spiritual relationship to Abraham, so the Jews respond by asserting they have an even higher relationship. They are not illegitimate spiritual children, born of spiritual adultery. They have no other spiritual Father but God. They are God's people. Whatever they are doing is borne out of their relationship to Him. Some also find here a mocking of the circumstances of the birth of Jesus. On this word, see 1 Cor 5:1.
18. Or, "am present, have come". Some think "came forth" refers to the incarnation of Jesus; "am here" to His public ministry in Israel. Same word as "have come" in 2:4; 4:47; Mk 8:3; Lk 15:27; Heb 10:7, 9; 1 Jn 5:20. Used 26 times. GK *2457*.
19. On "of Myself", see "from Himself" in 5:19.
20. That is, what Jesus is saying, the content of His speaking. This noun is elsewhere only in Mt 26:73; Jn 4:42. GK *3282*.
21. Or, "intending, wishing, desiring". Your desire to do his will makes you unable to hear My words. On this word, see "willing" in 7:17.
22. That is, to kill Jesus (v 37), and to promote lies based on self-interest. These are the devil's desires.
23. On this word, see "standing-*firm*" in 1 Cor 16:13. GK *5112*. Some manuscripts say "does not stand" {C}, using GK *2705*. The difference is a kind of accent mark.
24. Or, speaks "falsehood". On this word, see "falsehood" in Rev 14:5.
25. Or, "exposes, rebukes". Same word as in 16:8. On this word, see "expose" in Eph 5:11.
26. This word refers to an offense against human or divine requirements, a failing to hit the mark, a wrong. Used 173 times. GK *281*. Related to the verb in Act 25:8, and "sinner" in Mt 9:10.
27. Some manuscripts say "And if" {K}.
28. That is, belonging to, originating in.
29. This is what these leaders were in the habit of saying about Jesus.
30. This is a racial and religious slur. You are a religious half-breed, proclaiming Your own religion in contradiction to the Scriptures and the traditions handed down from our forefathers.
31. On having a demon, see 10:20. The grammar indicates that a "yes" answer is expected.
32. Same word as in Rom 2:23.
33. The Father is in fact seeking the glory of the Son. He is the One discerning your hearts. Jesus will pass judgment based on what He hears from Him, 5:30. These understated words of terror are followed by the gospel of hope.
34. Or, "by no means". This is an emphatic negative, the strongest in Greek. John uses it in 4:14, 48; 6:35, 37; 8:12, 51, 52; 10:5, 28; 11:26, 56; 13:8, 38; 20:25. On this idiom, see Gal 5:16.
35. On "ever", which is also in the next verse, see 4:14.

A. Mt 17:26   B. Jn 1:51   C. Rom 6:17   D. Jn 15:4, abide   E. Phil 2:21   F. Rom 7:11   G. Jn 4:23   H. Mt 26:10   J. 1 Jn 2:29   K. Jn 21:15, devotedly love   L. Mk 16:2   M. Mk 3:14, send out   N. Lk 1:34, know   O. Gal 5:16   P. 1 Jn 3:15   Q. Act 10:33, well   R. 1 Tim 5:3   S. 1 Jn 5:18   T. Lk 10:18

| John 8:52 | 336 | Verse |

9C. So[1] the Jews said *to* Him, "Now we have come-to-know[A] that You have *a* demon[B]. Abraham died, and the prophets! And **You** say, 'If anyone keeps My word, he will never taste death[2], ever!'   52

    1D. "**You** are not greater *than* our father Abraham who died, *are you*?[3]   53
    2D. "The prophets died also
    3D. "Whom do You make Yourself ?"

10C. Jesus answered, "If **I** glorify[C] Myself, My glory is nothing   54

    1D. "The *One* glorifying Me is My Father— Whom **you** say that 'He is our[4] God'
    2D. "And you have not come-to-know[A] Him,[5] but **I** know[D] Him   55
    3D. "And if I say that I do not know Him, I will be *a* liar like you. But I know Him, and I am keeping[E] His word
    4D. "Abraham your father rejoiced-greatly[F] to[6] see My day.[7] And he saw *it*[8], and was glad[G]"   56

11C. So the Jews said to Him, "You do not yet have fifty years[9], and You have seen[10] Abraham?"   57
12C. Jesus said *to* them, "Truly[H], truly, I say *to* you— before Abraham came-into-being[11], **I** am[12]"   58
13C. Therefore[13] they picked up stones in order that they might throw *them* at Him. But Jesus was hidden[14], and went out of the temple[15]   59

8B. And while passing on,[16] He saw *a* man blind from birth   9:1

    1C. And His disciples asked Him, saying, "Rabbi[J], who sinned[K]— this *one* or his parents, that he should be born[L] blind?" °Jesus answered, "Neither this *one* sinned nor his parents, but *it was* in order that the works *of* God might be made-visible[17] in him   2 / 3

        1D. "We[18] must[M] be working[N] the works[O] *of* the *One* having sent Me while it is day. Night is coming, when no one can work   4
        2D. "When[19] I am in the world, I am *the* light *of* the world"   5

    2C. Having said these *things*, He spat[P] on the ground, and made mud from the saliva,[20] and smeared[21] its[22] mud on the eyes[23], °and said *to* him, "Go, wash[Q] in the pool *of* Siloam" (which is translated[R], "Sent[24]")   6 / 7

        1D. So he went away and washed, and came [back] seeing[25]

1. Some manuscripts omit this word {C}.
2. Jesus is referring to eternal death, but the Jews take it as physical death. This does not seem to be serious and sincere argumentation. They appear to be deliberately misinterpreting what He says in order to try to prove Him to be a self-deceived exaggerator. On "taste death", see Heb 2:9.
3. The grammar indicates a "no" answer is expected.
4. Some manuscripts say "Whom **you** say that He is your God" {B}.
5. Some place this phrase with the previous sentence (" '...God', and you have..."), and join the next phrase with what follows ("But **I** know Him. And if I say...").
6. Or, "that he might see". GK *2671*.
7. Abraham looked forward to this day with eyes of faith, seeing and greeting the promises from afar, Heb 11:13. He rejoiced to see the day when the whole world would be blessed through his descendant, as God promised.
8. Abraham saw this day by faith, and rejoiced in it. These Jews, seeing it with their eyes, refuse to believe.
9. Perhaps the Jews mean "you are not even as old as we are". Jesus was about thirty when He began His ministry, Lk 3:23. On "having" years, see 5:5.
10. Again the Jews seem to be deliberately misinterpreting Jesus, pressing the literal physical meaning of "saw", trying to make Him appear to be claiming something all out of proportion to the obvious truth. If Abraham physically saw Your day, then You must have seen Abraham! They think they have Him trapped and will force Him to back down, but He surprises them by claiming much more! Some manuscripts say, "and Abraham has seen You?" {B}.
11. Or, "came-to-be", and in this sense, "was" or "was born". Same word as in 1:2.
12. Used over 70 times, the phrase "I am" is usually followed by a defining word or phrase, as in "I am a man, I am good, I am a Jew, I am from above, I am with you, etc. Jesus says "I am" the bread, the light, the door, the way, the vine, etc. This phrase stands alone like this only in the 17 places noted below, and means "I am *the one*", or "I am *he*", the defining word being implied, but not stated. In Mt 26:22, 25, it means "I am not *the one*", the betrayer; in Mk 13:6 and Lk 21:8 some falsely say "I am *the One*", the Christ; in Act 13:25 the Baptist says "I am not *the One*", the Christ (this is fully stated in Jn 1:20, 3:28); and in Jn 9:9 the blind man says "I am *he*". This phrase is used by Jesus in Mt 14:27; Mk 6:50; Jn 6:20, where He says "I am *the One*", meaning "It is Me", not a phantom (this idea is fully stated in Lk 24:39, "I am myself". Note also Mt 14:28. In Jn 18:5, 6, 8, Jesus says "I am *He*", meaning "Jesus"; and in Jn 4:26 He says "I am *He*", meaning the Messiah. In Jn 8:24, 28; 13:19, He says "I am *the One*", meaning the One from God in the fullest sense. Here in Jn 8:58, notice that "I am *the One*" does not fit the context. No defining word is implied. It is used in an absolute sense. Abraham had a beginning point when he came into existence; Jesus has none. Jesus is not merely claiming to preexist Abraham, so He does not say "I was" or "I have been". He says "Before Abraham came into existence, **I** exist". Since only God simply "exists", or would use such language to describe Himself, Jesus is claiming to be God, as John said in 1:1. Some think Jesus is referring to what God said in Ex 3:14 (LXX), "I am *the One* being" (or, "existing", or, "who is"), or to the same phrase "I am *He*" in Isa 41:4; 43:10,
13; 48:12, etc. Some think this is also the meaning of this phrase in 8:24, 28; 13:19.
13. Understanding this claim, as in 5:18 and 10:33, the Jews try to kill Jesus for blasphemy.
14. Same word and grammar as in Lk 19:42; Jn 12:36; Heb 11:23. This word means "to hide, conceal, keep secret". Elsewhere only in Mt 5:14; 11:25; 13:35, 44; 25:18, 25; Lk 18:34; Jn 19:38; Col 3:3; 1 Tim 5:25; Rev 2:17; 6:15, 16. GK *3221*. Related to "hidden" in 1 Cor 4:5, and in 1 Cor 2:7. Since the word does not necessarily imply that someone else hid Jesus, some render it "hid *Himself*"; others leave it as normal, "was hidden", and leave it unexplained. It could simply mean that Jesus "was hidden" amidst the crowds as He went out of the temple. Compare 5:13.
15. Some manuscripts add "having gone through the midst *of* them. And thus He was going along" {A}.
16. John may mean this took place immediately after 8:59, outside of the temple. If so, Jesus immediately diverts the Jews' anger in v 59 by doing a great public miracle with which they must now contend. Or, it may have been later during this period (see 8:12). Some take "then" in 10:22 to mean that 9:1-10:21 took place nearer that event than to 8:59. This event was on a Sabbath (v 14), and near the pool of Siloam (v 7), which was near the temple area.
17. On this word, see "made evident" in 1 Jn 2:19. This man was blind that others might see— see that Jesus is the light of the world, v 5. This is a most striking depiction of the Jews' lack of sight on the backdrop of this man's reception of sight.
18. Some think Jesus is including the disciples; others, that He is referring to Himself. Compare 3:11. Some manuscripts say "I"; others, "We must work... having sent us" {C}.
19. Or, "Whenever, At the time that". Some think Jesus means "when" in the sense of "while, as longs as", referring to His present incarnation. "During the time that" I am physically present in the world, I am personally the light of the world. In this view, "when I am in the world" is equivalent to "while it is day" in v 4. Others think Jesus means "whenever, as often as, every time that", and is referring to all His visitations in OT times, in this present incarnation, and in the appearances and revelations coming after His death. In this view, He is stating the significance of His presence, whenever it occurs. GK *4020*.
20. To make mud was work ("kneading") in the eyes of these Pharisees, a violation of their Sabbath rules. Jesus deliberately chooses a method of healing that also offends them. He confronts their unbelief head-on. Note that both "offenses" are specified in v 14. In addition, several symbolic meanings are suggested for this. Consult the commentaries.
21. Or, "spread, anointed". Elsewhere only in v 11. GK *2222*. Related to "to anoint" in Lk 4:18
22. Or, "His". That is, the saliva's mud, "the mud *of* it".
23. Some manuscripts add "*of* the blind *one*" {N}.
24. This is a participle, "Having been sent forth". The water was "sent forth" through an underground tunnel built by King Hezekiah to bring water from a source outside the wall to this pool inside the wall.
25. Or, "went [home] seeing". Perhaps the man came back seeking somehow to find Jesus, then went home. On the other hand, perhaps he was sitting outside his home when Jesus came along.

A. Lk 1:34, know B. 1 Cor 10:20 C. Rom 8:30 D. 1 Jn 2:29 E. 1 Jn 5:18 F. Lk 10:21 G. 2 Cor 13:11, rejoice H. Jn 1:51 J. Mt 23:7 K. Act 25:8 L. 1 Jn 2:29 M. Mt 16:21 N. Mt 26:10 O. Mt 26:10 P. Mk 7:33 Q. Mk 7:3 R. Jn 1:42

3C.	Then the neighbors[1], and the *ones* seeing him formerly[A]— because[2] he was *a* beggar[3]— were saying, "Is not this the *one* sitting and begging?"[4]	8
	1D. Others were saying that "This is he"	9
	2D. Others were saying, "No, but he is like him"[5]	
	3D. That *one* was saying that "**I am** *he*"	
	4D. So they were saying *to* him, "How then[6] were your eyes opened?"	10
	5D. That *one* answered, "The man being called Jesus made mud, and smeared *it* on my eyes, and said *to* me 'Go to Siloam[7] and wash'. So having gone away and washed, I received-sight[B]"	11
	6D. And they said *to* him, "Where is that *One*?"	12
	7D. He says, "I do not know"	
4C.	They[8] bring him to the Pharisees— the formerly[C] blind *one*	13
	1D. Now it was *a* Sabbath on the day[9] Jesus made the mud and opened his eyes	14
	2D. Therefore the Pharisees also were asking him again[10] how he received-sight[B]	15
	1E. And the *one* said *to* them, "He put mud on my eyes, and I washed, and I see"	
	3D. Then some of the Pharisees were saying, "This man is not from God, because He does not keep[D] the Sabbath"[11]. But[12] others were saying, "How is *a* sinful[E] man able to do such signs[F]?" And there was *a* division[13] among them. °So[14] they say *to* the blind *one* again, "What do **you** say about Him, *seeing*-that[15] He opened your eyes?"	16 17
	1E. And the *one* said that "He is *a* prophet[G]"	
	4D. Then the Jews did not believe concerning him that he was blind and received-sight[B]— until[16] they called the parents *of* him having received-sight	18
	1E. And they asked them, saying, "Is this your son whom **you** are saying[17] that he was born[H] blind? How then does he see now?"	19
	2E. So[18] his parents responded and said, "We know that this is our son, and that he was born blind. °But how he now sees— we do not know. Or who opened his eyes— **we** do not know.[19] Ask[J] him.[20] He has *a* mature-age[21]. **He** will speak about himself"	20 21
	1F. His parents said these *things* because they were fearing the Jews[22]	22
	1G. For the Jews already had agreed[K] that if anyone confessed[23] Him *as the* Christ, he should become put-out-of-the-synagogue[24]	
	2G. For this reason his parents said that "He has *a* mature-age, question[L] him"	23
	5D. Then they called for *a* second[25] *time* the man who was blind, and said *to* him, "Give glory *to* God.[26] **We** know that this man is *a* sinner"[27]	24
	1E. So[28] that *one* responded[29], "Whether He is *a* sinner[E], I do not know. I know one *thing*— that being *a* blind *one*, now I see"	25
	2E. So they said *to* him[30], "What did He do *to* you? How did He open your eyes?"	26
	3E. He answered them, "I told you already and you did not listen. Why do you want to hear *it* again? **You** also[31] do not want to become His disciples, *do you*?"[32]	27

1. That is, the ones who lived near this man. Elsewhere only in Lk 14:12; 15:6, 9. GK *1150*.
2. Or, "that". GK *4022*.
3. Some manuscripts say "blind" {N}, so that it says "that he was blind".
4. The grammar indicates a "yes" answer is expected.
5. Some manuscripts say instead "And others [were saying] that 'he is like him' " {N}.
6. Some manuscripts omit this word {C}.
7. Some manuscripts say "the pool *of* Siloam" {N}.
8. Some think John means the neighbors, v 8; others, an impersonal "they", certain ones hearing him speak. The man may have been brought as one needing correction; or, as a prime example proving who Jesus is.
9. This may imply that one or more days had passed since the healing; or, it may simply be adding this piece of information which we need to know. Instead of "on the day", some manuscripts say "when" {N}.
10. That is, in addition to all the people who had already asked this question.
11. The Pharisees are correct that no matter what Jesus says or does, He cannot be from God if He breaks God's laws. But their key premise is in error— their Sabbath regulations are not in fact God's laws.
12. Some manuscripts omit this word {C}.
13. The Pharisees are divided over how to interpret this sign in light of their previous conclusions about Jesus. On this word, see 1 Cor 1:10.
14. Some manuscripts omit this word {K}.
15. Or, "because, that". GK *4022*.
16. More literally, "up to which *time*". On this idiom, see Mt 5:25.
17. The parents were speaking publicly of this, as one would expect.
18. Some manuscripts say "And his parents responded *to* them and said" {N}.
19. That is, we have no firsthand knowledge on these two questions.
20. Some manuscripts say "**He** has *a* mature age, ask him. **He** will speak..." {N}.
21. On "having" time, see 5:5. On this word, see "life-span" in Mt 6:27.
22. That is, the Jewish leaders. See 1:19.
23. Or, "declared, acknowledged". On this word, see 1 Tim 6:12.
24. Or, "excluded from the synagogue". This adjective is elsewhere only in 12:42 and 16:2. GK *697*. Related to "synagogue". Such a person would become ex-synagogued, an outcast. Some leaders "believed" but did not "confess" Him for this very reason, 12:42.
25. This may imply that the Pharisees questioned the parents outside of the man's presence; or, that some time elapsed between v 21 and v 24, during which the man and his parents went away. Since the Pharisees could not escape the fact of it, perhaps by their authority they could induce this man to join their view of the One who did it.
26. Some think the Pharisees mean to give God glory by now telling the truth, as in Josh 7:19. Others think they mean to glorify the God who healed you, not this sinner!
27. The Pharisees know this because Jesus does not keep the Sabbath, v 16.
28. Some manuscripts omit this word {K}.
29. Some manuscripts add "and said" {K}.
30. Some manuscripts add "again" {N}.
31. That is, in addition to me. The formerly blind man wanted to become one as soon as possible.
32. The grammar indicates that a "no" answer is expected.

A. 2 Cor 1:15, first   B. Act 22:13, look up   C. Gal 2:6, ever   D. 1 Jn 5:18   E. Mt 9:10, sinner   F. 2 Thes 2:9   G. 1 Cor 12:28   H. 1 Jn 2:29   J. Jn 17:9, pray   K. Lk 22:5   L. Lk 9:18

4E.	And¹ they reviled² him and said, "**You** are *a* disciple^A *of* that *One*, but **we** are disciples *of* Moses. °**We** know that God has spoken *to* Moses. But we do not know where **this** *One* is from"	28 29
5E.	The man responded and said *to* them, "Why³, in this is the marvel⁴— that **you** do not know where He is from, and He opened my eyes!	30

    1F. "We know that God does not hear⁵ sinners. But if anyone is *a* God-fearing⁶ *one,* and is doing His will^B— He hears this *one*   31

    2F. "It was not ever⁷ heard that someone opened *the* eyes *of one* having been born blind   32

    3F. "If this *One* were not from God, He *would* be able to do nothing"   33

6E. They responded and said *to* him, "**You** were born entirely^C in sins⁸, and **you** are teaching us?"   34

7E. And they threw him outside⁹

5C. Jesus heard that they threw him outside, and having found him, said, "Do **you** believe in the Son *of* Man¹⁰?"   35

  1D. That *one* responded and said, "Who indeed is He, Sir, in order that I may believe in Him?"   36
  2D. Jesus said *to* him, "You have both seen Him, and that *One* is the *One* speaking with you"   37
  3D. And the *one* said, "Master¹¹, I believe", and prostrated-*himself*¹² *before* Him   38

6C. And Jesus said,¹³ "**I** came into this world for judgment¹⁴— so that the *ones* not seeing¹⁵ may be seeing, and the *ones* seeing¹⁶ may become blind"   39

7C. *Some* of the¹⁷ Pharisees heard these *things*— the *ones* being with him— and said *to* Him, "**We** indeed are not blind¹⁸ *ones, are we?*"¹⁹   40

8C. Jesus said *to* them, "If you were blind *ones*, you would not have sin.²⁰ But you are saying now that 'We see'— your²¹ sin remains^D   41

  1D. "Truly^E, truly, I say *to* you,²² the *one* not entering into the fold²³ *of* the sheep through the door, but going-up from-another-place²⁴— that *one* is *a* thief^F and *a* robber²⁵   10:1

  2D. "But the *One* entering through the door is *the* shepherd^G *of* the sheep   2

    1E. "The doorkeeper^H opens *to* this *One*   3
    2E. "And the sheep hear²⁶ His voice
    3E. "And He calls *His* own sheep by name,²⁷ and leads them out²⁸

  3D. "When²⁹ He brings out all *His* own³⁰, He proceeds in front of them   4

    1E. "And the sheep are following Him— because they know His voice
    2E. "But they will never follow *a* stranger^J, but will flee^K from him— because they do not know the voice *of* strangers"   5

  4D. Jesus spoke this figure-of-speech³¹ *to* them, but those *ones* did not understand³² what *the things* were which He was speaking *to* them   6

9C. Then³³ Jesus said again³⁴, "Truly, truly, I say *to* you that³⁵—   7

  1D. "**I** am the door³⁶ *of* the sheep³⁷

1. Some manuscripts omit this word; others say "Then"; others say "But the *ones*..." {N}.
2. Or, "insulted, spoke abusively to". The content of it follows. On this word, see 1 Cor 4:12.
3. This same word introduces an incredulous question in 7:41 ("indeed"); here, an incredulous statement. GK *1142*.
4. Or, "the amazing *thing*". Elsewhere only as "marvelous" in Mt 21:42; Mk 12:11; 1 Pet 2:9; Rev 15:1, 3. GK *2515*.
5. Or, "listen to". God does not answer the requests of sinners. On this word, see Act 22:9.
6. Or, "devout, God-worshiper". Used only here. GK *2538*. The root word is "God". Related to "godliness" in 1 Tim 2:10.
7. This is an idiom, literally, "from the age". It is similar to the idiom for "forever, into the age" (see Rev 20:10), but pointed into the past. Used only here. GK *172*. Never in the past experience of the world has anything like this been reported.
8. Like the disciples (v 2), the Pharisees simply assume this since the man was born blind.
9. Some think John means physically, out of their presence; others, that the Pharisees put the man out of the synagogue, v 22. Same phrase as in v 35; 6:37.
10. Some manuscripts say "*of* God" {A}.
11. On this word, which is the same word as "sir" in v 36, see Mt 8:2.
12. Or, "gave-worship *to* Him". On this word, see "worship" in Mt 14:33.
13. Some think this is said later, some time elapsing since v 38; others, that Jesus says it right then, reflecting upon the two responses just seen. Some manuscripts omit v 38 and "And Jesus said" {B}, continuing with the words of Jesus directly from v 37.
14. That is, Jesus came to make a separation, to divide— not to condemn, pronounce judgment, 3:17. His mission is not to execute judgment, but judgment results from His mission. The world separates itself into two groups based on how it responds to Him, 3:18-19. He came to save, which forces this division. Compare Mt 13:13. This noun is used of the judging action of a judge; the "judgment, decision, verdict" given; a judgment against, "condemnation"; and a "lawsuit" (1 Cor 6:7). Used 27 times. GK *3210*. Related to the verb "judge" in Jn 3:17; to "judgment" in 3:19; to the noun "judge"; and to "condemned" in 1 Cor 11:32.
15. That is, that the ones without spiritual sight may receive it in believing in Jesus— like the blind man, who received both physical and spiritual sight, v 38.
16. That is, that the ones claiming to possess spiritual sight may be blinded in rejecting Jesus, like the Pharisees.
17. Some manuscripts say "And [some] of the" {N}.
18. That is, spiritually blind.
19. The grammar indicates a "no" answer is expected.
20. If these Pharisees were blind— lost, and not claiming to possess spiritual sight— they would not be guilty of sin in their response to Jesus (because they would not be treating Him as they are). Since they are even now continuing to claim to see while rejecting Him, their sin remains. On "have sin", see 1 Jn 1:8.
21. Some manuscripts say "therefore your..." {N}.
22. John links the story of the blind man to these words in chapter 10, concluding it with the comment about the blind man in v 21. Since the Jewish leaders/shepherds threw out the blind man (9:34), and Jesus responded with the voice of the Shepherd (9:35-37), to which the man immediately responded (9:38), Jesus now speaks an allegory giving the meaning of this incident for all. The Pharisees claim to "see" and know the way as shepherds of Israel, but they are false shepherds, thieves and robbers in His fold.
23. That is, the fenced or walled enclosure, open to the sky; the corral; the nighttime dwelling place of the sheep. On this word, see "courtyard" in Mt 26:3.
24. That is, climbing over the wall from another location, entering the sheepfold some way other than the gate provided by the owner of the sheep. Used only here. GK *249*.
25. Such a person is not entering to care for the sheep, but to profit from them. On this word, see Mt 21:13.
26. That is, listen to and obey. Same word as in v 16, 27, and as "listen-to in v 8, 20. On this word, see Act 22:9.
27. This picture is a common one. A large sheep pen or fold holding the flocks of several shepherds for the night is watched over by a gatekeeper. In the morning, the shepherd calls out to his flock, and his sheep respond to his voice and come out to him. He leads them to pasture.
28. So by application, Jesus is calling His people out of the fold of Israel. His people hear the call to repent and come to their Shepherd and follow Him. The blind man is an example.
29. Some manuscripts say "And when..." {K}.
30. Instead of "all *His* own", some manuscripts say "*His* own sheep" {N}.
31. Or, "allegory". Same word as in 16:25, 29. Elsewhere only as "proverb" in 2 Pet 2:22. GK *4231*.
32. The Pharisees claim to "see" (9:41), but they do not see at all. The words of Jesus are just madness to them (10:20). They do not understand the application of these words to themselves, to Him, or to Israel.
33. Or, "Therefore, So". John may mean this was spoken on a later occasion; or, that is was spoken because the Pharisees did not understand, v 6.
34. Some manuscripts add "*to* them" {N}.
35. Jesus expands key aspects of the sheep-shepherd metaphor. He sharpens some truths from v 1-5, and brings out other truths. Some manuscripts omit this word {N}.
36. That is, the point of access, of entry and exit to the fold and the pasture. Jesus is making a new point here. In v 2 He was the shepherd entering the door, and was known to the doorkeeper. Here, He is the door, the entryway.
37. Some think Jesus means the door "*to* the sheep", through which all true shepherds pass to get to the sheep. He protects His sheep from the robbers. They gain entry another way (v 1), but the sheep do not follow them out. Others think He means the door "*for* the sheep", through which they enter into the fold, as is more fully brought out in v 9.

A. Lk 6:40 B. Jn 7:17 C. Rev 3:10, whole D. Jn 15:4, abide E. Jn 1:51 F. 1 Thes 5:2 G. Eph 4:11 H. Jn 18:17 J. Heb 11:34, foreigner K. 1 Cor 6:18

1E. "All[1] who came before Me[2] are thieves[A] and robbers[B], but the sheep did not listen-to them	8
2D. "**I am the door.** If anyone enters **through Me**, he will be saved[C]. And he will go in and go out, and he will find pasture	9
1E. "The thief does not come except that he may steal and kill[D] and destroy[E]	10
2E. "**I came** that they may have life[F], and have abundance[3]	
3D. "**I am the good[G] shepherd[H].** The good shepherd lays-*down*[4] His life for the sheep[5]	11
1E. "The *one* being *a* hired[6] *one* and not *a* shepherd[7], *of* whom the sheep are not *his* own—	12
1F. "He sees the wolf coming and leaves[8] the sheep and flees[J], and the wolf snatches[9] them and scatters[K] *them*[10]	
2F. "Because[11] he is *a* hired *one,* and he is not concerned[12] about the sheep	13
4D. "**I am the good shepherd**	14
1E. "And I know[L] My *sheep,* and My *sheep* know Me[13]—*just as the Father knows Me, and **I** know the Father	15
2E. "And I lay-*down*[14] My life for the sheep	
3E. "And I have other sheep, which are not of this fold[15]. I must[M] bring those also	16
4E. "And they[16] will hear[17] My voice. And they will become[18] one flock[19], [with] one Shepherd[20]	
5D. "For this reason the Father loves[N] Me— because **I** lay *down* My life so that I may take it *up*[21] again[22]	17
1E. "No one takes[23] it away from Me, but **I** lay it *down* of Myself[24]	18
1F. "I have authority[O] to lay it *down,* and I have authority to take it *up* again	
2E. "I received this commandment[25] from My Father"	
10C. A[26] division[P] again[27] took place among the Jews because of these words	19
1D. And many of them were saying, "He has *a* demon[28], and He is mad[29]. Why are you listening-to Him?"	20
2D. Others were saying, "These words are not *from one* being demon-possessed[Q]. *A* demon is not able to open *the* eyes *of* blind *ones, is he*?"[30]	21
10A. Then[31] the Festival-of-Dedication[32] took place in Jerusalem. It was winter. *And Jesus was walking in the temple, in the portico[R] *of* Solomon	22-23
1B. Then the Jews surrounded[33] Him. And they were saying *to* Him, "How long[34] are You keeping us in suspense?[35] If **You** are the Christ, tell us *with* plainness[36]"	24
2B. Jesus answered them, "I told you, and you do not believe[37]	25
1C. "The works[S] which **I** am doing in the name *of* My Father— these are testifying[T] about Me	
2C. "However, **you** do not believe, because you are not of My sheep[38]	26

1. That is, all you self-appointed, self-serving leaders of the flock who tried to get the sheep to follow you to a false sheepfold, or out of the true one.
2. That is, in time. Some manuscripts omit "before Me" {C}.
3. Or, "overflow, excess, surplus". That is, have life exceeding their own needs, a surplus abounding and flowing from them as in 7:38, bubbling up as in 4:14. Jesus did not come to give existence, but life, an overflowing life. He is referring to eternal life (v 9, 28), and the spiritual dimension of life. He brings an abundance of "real" life (1 Tim 6:19). GK *4356*.
4. Instead of "lays *down*", some manuscripts say "gives" {B} both here and in v 15.
5. The good shepherd devotes himself to the sheep, even risking his own life to protect them. He might unintentionally even be killed defending them. Jesus, of course, means more than this with regard to Himself. He voluntarily gives up His life for the sheep. But those listening to Jesus would not have understood this deeper meaning.
6. That is, the one working with the sheep for wages. This one puts his own personal interests, his own life, ahead of the flock. Same word as in v 13. On this word, see Mk 1:20.
7. More literally, "The hired *one* and not being *a* shepherd", two descriptions of this one person. Compare the phrase in 1 Tim 4:3.
8. Or, more strongly, based on the context, "abandons". On this word, see "forgive" in Mt 6:12.
9. Same word as in v 28.
10. Some manuscripts say "the sheep" {N}.
11. Some manuscripts say "Now the hired *one* flees because he is *a* hired *one*, ..." {N}, starting a new sentence here.
12. This is an idiom, more literally, "it is not a concern *to* him". On this word, see 1 Cor 7:21.
13. Some manuscripts say "and I am known by My *sheep*" {N}.
14. Some manuscripts say "give" {B}.
15. Same word as in v 1. Jesus may mean the Jewish fold (out of which He is calling the believers, v 3), making the other sheep the Gentiles. He came only to the lost sheep of the house of Israel, Mt 15:24. Or He may mean the nation-of-Israel fold, making the other sheep all the "children of God scattered" outside Israel (Jews and Gentiles), as in 11:52. In either case, believing Jews and Gentiles will be united into one flock, 11:52; Eph 2:15.
16. That is, all His sheep.
17. Same word as in v 3.
18. Or, "be". Some manuscripts say, "And there will be" {C}, using the same word with different grammar. GK *1181*.
19. Not the same word as "fold" earlier in the verse. Elsewhere only in Mt 26:31; Lk 2:8; 1 Cor 9:7. GK *4479*. Related word in 1 Pet 5:2.
20. These are related words in the Greek, somewhat like "one sheepherd, [with] one Sheep-herder".
21. This word, meaning "take *up*" in this context opposite of "lay *down*", occurs again in v 18 (as "take *up*" and as "received"). On this word, see "taken" in Rom 7:8. It is not the same word as "take-away" in v 18.
22. Jesus lays it down in death for the purpose of raising Himself to the life and glory also commanded by the Father.
23. Some manuscripts say "took it away" {B}.
24. This action is completely voluntary and unforced. On "of Myself", see "from Himself" in 5:19.
25. That is, the commandment to lay down and take up His earthly life. This is the Father's will for the Son, which the Son is carrying out by His own choice. The Father loves Him because He does His will. On this word, see Mk 12:28.
26. Some manuscripts say "Then *a* division..." {B}.
27. As in 9:16.
28. Note that this is defined in v 21 as "being demon possessed". See Mt 8:16 on this.
29. Or, "out of His mind, raving". On this word, see 1 Cor 14:23.
30. The grammar indicates that a "no" answer is expected. So the case of the healing of the man born blind, 9:1-10:21, comes down to this— Is Jesus empowered by Satan or God?
31. Or, "At that time". It can mean next in time, or next in sequence. On this word, see Mt 24:9. Some manuscripts say "And" {B}.
32. That is, Hanukkah, the Feast of Lights, an eight-day celebration commemorating the rededication of the temple by Judas Maccabaeus in 165 B.C., after it had been desecrated by Antiochus Epiphanes. It could be observed anywhere, so John specifies Jerusalem. Used only here. GK *1589*. This is the first note of time since 8:2 (see 8:12).
33. Or, "encircled". Same word as in Lk 21:20; Act 14:20. Elsewhere only as "encircled" in Heb 11:30. GK *3240*.
34. On this idiom, see Mt 17:17.
35. This idiom is literally, how long "are you lifting up our soul?", in suspense, anticipation (or, in annoyance, anger, giving it a negative sense).
36. Or, "openness". Same word as in 11:14. On this word, see "confidence" in Heb 4:16.
37. Some manuscripts say "did not believe" {N}.
38. Some manuscripts add "just as I said *to* you" {B}. These Jews are not part of God's flock.

A. 1 Thes 5:2   B. Mt 21:13   C. Lk 19:10   D. Act 10:13, slaughter   E. 1 Cor 1:18, perish   F. Rom 8:10   G. 1 Tim 5:10a   H. Eph 4:11   J. 1 Cor 6:18
K. Jn 16:32   L. Lk 1:34   M. Mt 16:21   N. Jn 21:15, devotedly love   O. Rev 6:8   P. 1 Cor 1:10   Q. Mt 8:16   R. Jn 5:2   S. Mt 26:10   T. Jn 1:7

3C. "My sheep hear[1] My voice[2]   27

    1D. "And **I** know them, and they follow Me
    2D. "And **I** give them eternal life, and they will never perish[A], ever[B]   28

        1E. "And someone will not snatch[3] them out of My hand. °What[4] My Father has given   29
            to Me is greater *than* all
        2E. "And no one is able to snatch *them* out of the hand *of* the[5] Father[6]
        3E. "I and the Father are one"[7]   30

3B. The Jews again[8] carried[9] stones in order that they might stone Him   31
4B. Jesus responded *to* them, "I showed[10] you many good[11] works from the[12] Father. For which work   32
    of them[13] do you stone Me?"
5B. The Jews answered Him[14], "We do not stone You for *a* good work, but for blasphemy[C]— even   33
    because **You**, being *a* human[D], are making[E] Yourself God"[15]
6B. Jesus responded *to* them, "Has it not been written[16] in your Law that 'I said, you are gods'?"[17]   34

    1C. "If He[18] called[F] those *ones* to whom the word *of* God came gods— and the Scripture cannot   35
        be broken[19]— °do **you** say *as to the One* Whom the Father set-apart[20] and sent-forth[G] into the   36
        world that 'You are blaspheming[H]' because I said, 'I am God's Son'?"[21]
    2C. "If I am not doing the works *of* My Father, do not be believing Me   37
    3C. "But if I am doing *them*— even if you do not believe Me, be believing the works, in order that   38
        you may come-to-know and be understanding[22] that the Father *is* in Me, and I in the Father"[23]

7B. Then[24] they were seeking again to seize[J] Him, and He went out of their hand   39
8B. And He went away again beyond the Jordan, to the place where John was first baptizing[K]. And He   40
    was staying[L] there

    1C. And many came to Him, and were saying that "**John**[25] did no sign[M]— but all that John said   41
        about this *One* was true[N]". °And many believed in Him there[26]   42

11A. Now[27] there was *a* certain *one* being sick[O]— Lazarus[28], from Bethany, of the village *of* Mary and   11:1
    Martha[29], her sister. °And it was Mary— the *one* having anointed[P] the Lord *with* perfume[Q] and having   2
    wiped His feet *with* her hair[30]— whose brother Lazarus was sick

    1B. So the sisters sent out *a message* to Him, saying, "Lord, look— *the one* whom You love[31] is sick"   3
    2B. And having heard, Jesus said "This sickness[R] is not *leading* to death[32], but for the glory *of* God—   4
        in order that the Son *of* God may be glorified[S] through it"

        1C. Now Jesus was loving[33] Martha, and her sister, and Lazarus. °So[34] when He heard that he was[35]   5-6
            sick, at that time **He remained**[36] *for* two days in which place He was— °then[37] after this, says   7
        to the disciples, "Let us be going[38] to Judea again"

            1D. The disciples say *to* Him, "Rabbi[T], the Jews were *just*-now seeking[U] to stone[39] You, and   8
                You are going there again?"
            2D. Jesus answered, "Are there not twelve hours *of* the day?[40] If one walks during the day,   9
                he does not stumble[V], because he sees the light *of* this world.[41] °But[42] if one walks during   10
                the night, he stumbles, because the light is not in him"

        2C. He said these *things,* and after this[43] He says *to* them, "Our friend Lazarus has fallen-asleep[W],   11
            but I am going in order that I may awaken[44] him"

1. Same word as in v 3.
2. Or, this may be punctuated "My sheep hear My voice, and I know them". 1D. "And they follow Me, and I give them eternal life". 2D. "And they will never perish, ever, and someone will not snatch them out of My hand".
3. Or, "take away by force, seize". No thief, robber, or wolf will get these sheep, because none is able to do so, v 29. Same word as in v 12. On this word, see 2 Cor 12:2.
4. Or, "*That* which". Jesus may be abstractly referring to His "authority over all flesh to give eternal life" (17:2), with grammar similar to "it had been given" in 19:11. Others think "what My Father has given *to* Me" is the same concept as in 17:24, and as "all that" He gave Him in 6:37, 39; 17:2; that is, the flock viewed as an abstract whole. In this case, this sentence is the beginning of point 2E., and the next sentence would say "able to snatch *it*". The gift that the Father gave Christ (the flock) is of greater importance than any and all who would oppose. The Father will not permit this gift to be diminished in any way. Some manuscripts say "My Father who has given *them to* Me is greater than all. And no one is able to snatch *them*..." {D}.
5. Some manuscripts say "My" {N}.
6. In all the views noted above, the point Jesus is making is that both the Father who gives the flock, and the Son who holds them and gives them eternal life, ensure the eternal safety of the entire flock.
7. That is, one in will and action, thus making Jesus God, v 33, 36. His previous claims (5:17-18, 8:58) leave no doubt about what He is claiming here— a oneness of will and action which He is shares with the Father because He is God's Son (v 36), and therefore shares the essence or substance of His Father. The Jews react accordingly, v 33.
8. The last time was in 8:59.
9. The Jews had to bring the stones from a distance to Solomon's portico (v 23) for this purpose. On this word, see Mt 8:17. Not the same word as in 8:59.
10. That is, as signs to be studied to determine their significance.
11. Or, "commendable, praiseworthy". On this word, see 1 Tim 5:10a.
12. Some manuscripts say "My" {N}.
13. That is, which of the works from My Father. Jesus is emphasizing the source.
14. Some manuscripts add "saying" {N}.
15. Compare 5:18. In claiming to be "one" with God (v 30), Jesus is claiming to be God's Son (v 36), to be one in essence and will.
16. This is a participle, "Is it not having been written", does it not stand written? On this, see 2:17.
17. Jesus is quoting Ps 82:6, where the psalmist calls the judges of Israel gods (in authority over the people), because they carried out divine justice.
18. That is, God, the ultimate author of Scripture. Or, "it", Scripture. Or, "he", the psalmist.
19. That is, its authority cannot be annulled. Same word as in Mt 5:19
20. Or, "consecrated". On this word, see "sanctify" in Heb 10:29. The Father set Jesus apart for His own purposes.
21. Jesus is doing something greater than those in the psalm did, so may He not use the term of Himself? It is an argument from the lesser to the greater. He is not limiting the meaning of "Son of God" to what "gods" meant in their case. He is saying that everything that "gods" meant in their case— and more— is true in His case. Therefore may He not properly use the term of Himself? He is establishing the minimum justification for using this term in a way that even these unbelievers cannot get around without "breaking" the force of the Scripture they claimed to follow.
22. Or, "acknowledging". The words "come-to-know" and "be understanding" are the same word, repeated with a change in tense. On this word, see "know" in Lk 1:34. Instead of "be understanding", some manuscripts say "believe" {B}.
23. Some manuscripts say "and I in Him" {N}.
24. Or, "Therefore". Some manuscripts omit this word {C}.
25. The grammar closely links the two halves of this sentence.
26. As in the allegory, God's sheep were going out of the fold (Judea) to their Shepherd.
27. This occurs at some point between Jesus leaving the Festival of Dedication in December (10:22, 40) and Passover being near in April (11:55), probably closer to the latter.
28. This is the seventh miracle John records: the water to wine, 2:1-11; healing the royal one's son, 4:46-54; healing the lame man, 5:1-9; feeding the 5000, 6:5-13; walking on water, 6:16-21; healing the blind man, 9:1-7.
29. Another incident with these two is recorded in Lk 10:38-42.
30. This well-known incident is described in 12:3-8. John mentions it here to clarify which Mary he means.
31. That is, have affection for, or a family or friend kind of love. Same word as in v 36. On this word, see "*affectionately*-love" in 21:15.
32. That is, death will not be the final result. Same idiom as "*leading* to death" in 1 Jn 5:16.
33. That is, Jesus was committing Himself to this family in love. On this word, see "*devotedly*-love" in 21:15. No distinction may be intended in using these two words.
34. Or, "Therefore". Because Jesus loved them, therefore He remained two days.
35. More literally, "is", as the Greek typically phrases it.
36. John uses grammar that closely links the two halves of this sentence.
37. Or, "next, later". Used only here by John. On this word, see "after that" in 1 Cor 15:23.
38. Or, "be leading forth, be on our way". Same word as in v 15, 16; 14:31; Mk 1:38.
39. The disciples are referring back to 10:31.
40. The grammar indicates a "yes" answer is expected.
41. In other words, Jesus is not going to stumble in going back to Judea, because He is walking in the light of the day God has given Him.
42. The physical reference of this is clear. "The light is not in him" may mean "the sun does not provide illumination into his eyes", but may also have a metaphorical meaning. Jesus may be referring here to the Jews. They are the ones stumbling, because they have no spiritual light in them. Compare 12:35. Others think He is referring to death, after which we no longer have the light of this world in us.
43. This may imply that some time passed, during which the disciples failed to respond. Jesus changes from "Let us go" in v 7 to "I am going" (see Mt 28:19 on this word) here.
44. Or, "rouse out of sleep". Used only here. GK *2030*. Related to "awaken" in Act 16:27. There are two different words groups used for "sleep" in v 11-13. Both are used of physical sleep and as a euphemism for death.

A. 1 Cor 1:18   B. Jn 4:14   C. 1 Tim 6:4   D. Mt 4:4, mankind   E. Rev 13:13, does   F. Jn 12:49, say   G. Mk 3:14, send out   H. 1 Tim 6:1
J. Jn 11:57   K. Mk 1:8   L. Jn 15:4, abide   M. 2 Thes 2:9   N. Jn 6:55   O. 2 Tim 4:20   P. Jam 5:14   Q. Mt 26:7   R. Mt 8:17, weakness   S. Rom 8:30
T. Mt 23:7   U. Phil 2:21   V. Rom 14:21   W. 1 Thes 4:13

	1D. So the disciples said *to* Him,[1] "Lord, if he has fallen asleep, he will be restored[2]"	12
	2D. Now Jesus had spoken concerning his death, but those *ones* thought that He was[3] speaking concerning the sleep[4] *of* slumber[5]. °So at-that-time[6] Jesus said *to* them *with* plainness[A], "Lazarus died. °And I am glad[B] for your sakes that I was not there[7], so that you may believe. But let us be going to him"	13 14 15
	3D. Then Thomas, the *one* being called Didymus[8], said *to his* fellow-disciples, "Let **us** indeed be going, so that we may die with Him[9]"	16

3B. So having come, Jesus found him already having[10] four days in the tomb — 17

    1C. Now Bethany was near Jerusalem, about fifteen stades[11] away. °And many of the Jews[12] had come to Martha and Mary,[13] in order that they might console[C] them concerning *their* brother. °So Martha, when she heard that Jesus was[14] coming, met Him. But Mary was sitting in the house — 18-19, 20

        1D. Then Martha said to Jesus, "Lord, if You had been here, my brother would not have died. But[15] even now I know that whatever You ask God, God will give You" — 21, 22

        2D. Jesus says *to* her, "Your brother will rise-up" — 23

        3D. Martha says *to* Him, "I know that he will rise-up[16] in the resurrection[D] at the last day" — 24

        4D. Jesus said *to* her, "**I** am the resurrection and the life[E]. The *one* believing[F] in Me— even though he dies,[17] he will live. °And everyone living and believing in Me will never die,[18] ever. Do you believe this?" — 25, 26

        5D. She says *to* Him, "Yes, Lord. **I** have believed[19] that **You** are the Christ, the Son *of* God, the *One* coming into the world" — 27

    2C. And having said this, she went away[20] and called Mary her sister secretly[21], having said, "The Teacher is here and is calling you" — 28

        1D. And that *one,* when she heard, arose[22] quickly[G] and was going to Him — 29

            1E. Now Jesus had not yet come into the village, but was still[23] in the place where Martha met Him. °So the Jews— the *ones* being with her in the house and consoling[C] her— having seen that **Mary** stood up quickly and went out, followed her, having supposed[24] that she was[25] going to the tomb[H] in order that she might weep[J] there — 30, 31

        2D. Then Mary— when she came where Jesus was, having seen Him— fell at His feet, saying *to* Him, "Lord, if You had been here, my brother would not have died" — 32

    3C. Then Jesus— when He saw her weeping[26], and the Jews having come with her weeping— was deeply-moved[27] in *His* spirit, and troubled[28] Himself[29] — 33

        1D. And He said, "Where have you laid him?" — 34

        2D. They say *to* Him, "Lord, come and see" — 35

        3D. Jesus wept[30] — 35

        4D. So the Jews were saying, "Look— how He was loving[K] him!" — 36

        5D. And[31] some of them said, "Was not this *One*— the *One* having opened the eyes *of* the blind *one*— able[32] to cause[L] that this *one* also[33] should not die?" — 37

4B. Then Jesus, again being deeply-moved[34] in Himself, comes to the tomb. Now it was *a* cave[M], and *a* stone was lying upon[35] it — 38

    1C. Jesus says, "Take away the stone" — 39

1. Some manuscripts say "So His disciples said, "Lord..." {N}.
2. That is, Lazarus will heal from his sickness. Let him sleep, he will get better. On this word, see Jam 5:15.
3. More literally, "is", as the Greek typically phrases it.
4. Used only here. GK *3122*. Related to "fallen asleep" in v 11 and 12. The disciples thought Jesus meant "asleep", not "dead".
5. This could be rendered "the rest *of* sleep", or "the sleeping *of* sleep" (but the words are not related). Elsewhere only as "sleep" in Mt 1:24; Lk 9:32; Act 20:9; Rom 13:11. GK *5678*. Related to "awaken" in v 11, and to "fell-asleep" in Lk 8:23.
6. Or, "then", meaning "next". Same word as in v 6 (its only other use in this chapter) and as "then" in 10:22.
7. Had Jesus been there, He would have healed Lazarus. Now, He will raise him, that the disciples might believe.
8. The name "Thomas" is a Greek rendering of the Aramaic word for "twin". "Didymus" is the Greek word meaning "twin". On Thomas, see Lk 6:15. He is called Didymus also in 20:24; 21:2. GK *1441*.
9. Some think Thomas means "him", Lazarus.
10. On the idiom of "having" time, see 5:5.
11. On this measure, see Rev 14:20. Here, it amounts to 1.7 miles or 2.8 kilometers.
12. That is, many of the Jews in Jerusalem and Bethany. Same phrase as in v 45.
13. Some manuscripts say "had come to the *women* around Martha and Mary, in order..." {N}.
14. More literally, "is", as the Greek typically phrases it.
15. Some think these are words of hope. Martha's faith is based on the statement in v 4, sent back to her. She struggles to hold on to this hope in what follows. Others think they are words of confidence in Jesus, in spite of the fact that He was too late. Some manuscripts omit this word {C}, so that it says "And now" or "Even now".
16. The word "will rise up" could be taken in two ways. Some think Martha is expressing the least assuming view of what Jesus said, taking His statement as the normal words of comfort believers receive in such circumstances. If Jesus means more, He will say more. Others think she in no way understood or expected His statement to mean that He would raise Lazarus immediately. On this word, see Lk 18:33.
17. That is, physically.
18. That is, spiritually, eternally. Our real life, which is in Jesus, will never end.
19. Some manuscripts say "I believe" {K}.
20. Apparently, Jesus sent her to get Mary.
21. Or, "called Mary her sister, having said secretly". On this word, see Mt 1:19.
22. Some manuscripts say "arises" {N}.
23. Some manuscripts omit this word {N}.
24. On this word, see "thinking" in Lk 19:11. Instead of "having supposed", some manuscripts say "saying" {B}.
25. More literally, "is", as the Greek typically phrases it.
26. Same word as v 31; 16:20; Mk 5:38; 14:72; Lk 6:21; Act 9:39; Rom 12:15; Phil 3:18. Used of Jesus in Lk 19:41. Used 40 times. GK *3081*. Related word in Mt 8:12.
27. Same word as in v 38. This word is used of expressing something with intense emotion, whether indignation (as in "sternly scold", Mk 14:5), or serious purpose (as in "sternly command", Mt 9:30; Mk 1:43), its only other uses. GK *1839*. It was used of horses "snorting" in anger. As seen in its usage, the word itself does not define the emotion, or the form of expression. These come from the context. Here, some think John means the emotion was not expressed. It was "in His spirit", "in Himself" (v 38), but seen on His face. Others think it was audibly expressed, and render this "He groaned". As to the emotion itself, anger and indignation are often associated with this word, and some see anger against the triumph of death over His friends here. Others think the context here points to genuine sorrow and sympathy flowing from His love for them and leading to tears in v 35. There are other views. Consult the commentaries on v 33-35.
28. Or, "stirred up, unsettled". Same word as in Jn 12:27 and 13:21, but it is not passive here. Used only here with reference to what someone does to himself. John does not say that Jesus "was troubled" by the outward circumstances, but that His response came from within Himself. In other words, it was a chosen response, not a reaction. Some think Jesus "stirred Himself" in sympathy for them out of His love for this family, culminating in tears, v 35. John says it this way because knowing what He was about to do, He would not "react" to the circumstances, He would "choose" His expression of love and sympathy for them. Others think John means Jesus agitated Himself over His anger and indignation at death and their misplaced grief over it. On this word, see "disturbed" in Gal 1:7. There are other views.
29. Note that this comes in response to the weeping. This occurs again when Jesus arrives at the tomb in v 38.
30. Or, "shed tears, cried". Not the same word as in v 33. Used only here. GK *1233*. Related to "tears" in Heb 5:7, where Jesus prayed with tears regarding His own death (see Act 20:19 on "tears"). John seems to mean Jesus wept on the way to the tomb, arriving there in v 38. Some think that even though Jesus knew what He was going to do (v 11), and was glad for the disciples (v 15), He genuinely shared in the human emotions associated with the death of a loved one. He shared this moment and the bereaved perspective with Martha and Mary, knowing what the next moment would bring. Take note that Jesus continues to share both perspectives every time one of His children dies— the grief of those left behind, the joy of the one with Him. Others think the tears were from sorrow over their misconception of death. There are other views.
31. Or, "But". GK *1254*.
32. The grammar indicates a "yes" answer is expected. Yes, Jesus was able— if He had only been here, Lazarus would not have died, v 21, 32. Thus, this may be friends making a sincere comment like that of Martha and Mary. Or, this may be spoken in mockery by ones not His friends, perhaps the ones in v 46.
33. That is, that this one also, like the blind man, should have been healed, and therefore not die.
34. On this word, see v 33.
35. Or, "against, over". That is, upon the entrance. GK *2093*.

A. Jn 10:24 B. 2 Cor 13:11, rejoice C. 1 Thes 5:14, encourage D. Act 24:15 E. Rom 8:10 F. Jn 3:36 G. Rev 22:7 H. Mt 23:29 J. Jn 11:33 K. Jn 21:15, affectionately love L. Col 4:16 M. Mt 21:13, den

1D. Martha, the sister *of* the *one* having come-to-an-end¹, says *to* Him, "Lord, he already stinks, for it is *the* fourth-day"	
2D. Jesus says *to* her, "Did I not say *to* you that if you believe, you will see the glory *of* God?"²	40
3D. So they took away the stone³	41

2C. And Jesus lifted *His* eyes upward^A, and said, "Father, I thank^B You that You heard⁴ Me

1D. "Now **I** knew that You always hear Me	42
2D. "But I said *this* for the sake of the crowd having stood around— in order that they may believe that **You** sent Me forth"	

3C. And having said these *things,* He shouted^C *with a* loud voice, "Lazarus, come outside!" 43

1D. The⁵ *one* having died came out, having been bound^D *as to* the feet and the hands *with* grave-cloths⁶. And his face had been bound-around *with a* face-cloth⁷	44
2D. Jesus says *to* them, "Unbind^E him, and allow^F him to go"	

5B. Therefore many of the Jews— the *ones* having come to Mary,⁸ and having seen *the things* which⁹ He did— believed^G in Him 45

6B. But some of them¹⁰ went to the Pharisees and told them *the things* which Jesus did. °So the chief priests and the Pharisees gathered together *a* council¹¹ 46-47

1C. And they were saying, "What are we doing? Because this man is doing many signs^H. °If we tolerate¹² Him in this manner, everyone will believe in Him, and the Romans will come and take away both **our** place¹³ and nation^J" 48

2C. But *a* certain one of them, Caiaphas^K, being *the* high priest *of* that year, said *to* them, "**You** do not know anything— °nor do you consider¹⁴ that it is better *for* you¹⁵ that one Man die for the people, and the whole nation not perish^L" 49 / 50

1D. Now he did not say this from himself¹⁶, but being *the* high priest *of* that year, he prophesied¹⁷ that Jesus was going to die for the nation 51

1E. And not for the nation only,¹⁸ but in order that He might also gather together into one the children^M *of* God having been scattered^N [in the world] 52

3C. Therefore from that day, they planned¹⁹ to²⁰ kill^O Him 53

4C. Therefore Jesus was no longer walking *in* public²¹ among the Jews, but went away from there to the region^P near the wilderness^Q, to *a* city being called Ephraim. And He stayed²² there with the disciples 54

12A. Now the Passover²³ [Feast] *of* the Jews was near 55

1B. And many went up to Jerusalem from the country²⁴ before the Passover [Feast], in order that they might purify²⁵ themselves

1C. So they were seeking^R Jesus, and saying, standing with one another in the temple, "What seems^S *right to* you— that He will by no means come to the Feast?"²⁶ 56

2C. And²⁷ the chief priests and the Pharisees had given commands²⁸ that if anyone came-to-know where He was²⁹, he should disclose^T *it*— so that they might seize³⁰ Him 57

1. That is, having died. This is a euphemism for death. On this word, see Mk 9:48.
2. Martha's faith wavers, and Jesus reminds her of His promise. The grammar indicates a "yes" answer is expected.
3. Some manuscripts add "where the *one* having died was lying" {N}.
4. Note the tense. This may mean that Jesus raised Lazarus already, without a spoken word. Lazarus only awaits the command to come out. Note 12:17. There is no command to rise, as in Mk 5:41 or Lk 7:14. For the benefit of the crowd, He now gives thanks for what has already happened, in order to explicitly link this to the Father who sent Him. Or, Jesus may raise him with the command to come out. In any case, Jesus is now thanking the Father for giving Him this work, 5:20.
5. Some manuscripts say "And the" {N}.
6. Or, "swathings, wrappings, strips of cloth". Used only here. GK *3024*.
7. Same word as in 20:7, of Jesus. Elsewhere only as "handkerchief" in Lk 19:20; Act 19:12. GK *5051*.
8. That is, the ones who came following Mary in v 31, and who came to her in v 19.
9. Some manuscripts have this singular, "having seen what He did" {N}.
10. Some think John means "some" in distinction from the "many" just mentioned (v 45). If so, their motive may be a personal rejection and hostility toward Jesus, or, an uncertainty about what this might mean. Others think he means some of the ones having believed (v 45), who may have gone to present this evidence on behalf of Jesus.
11. Or, "*the* Sanhedrin". Some think John means a meeting of the entire seventy-member Jewish governing body, presided over by the high priest; others, an informal meeting of part of this council. This is the only place John uses this word. On this word, see "council [chamber]" in Act 5:27.
12. Or, "if we let Him go *on*". Same word as in Rev 2:20.
13. Some think these leaders mean this in the sense of "our position as leaders", as in Act 1:25; others, "our holy place", Jerusalem and its temple, as in Act 21:28. Note that they are assuming that Jesus is not the Messiah, for the Messiah would not allow the Romans to take away anything. Jesus is simply a zealous teacher doing many signs, and leading the ignorant masses into a confrontation with Rome. It is up to these leaders to protect the nation from Him! On this word, see Eph 4:27.
14. Or, "calculate, take into account". On this word, see Rom 3:28.
15. Some manuscripts say "us" {B}.
16. On "from himself", see 5:19.
17. That is, the high priest spoke a revelation from God, without knowing it. On this word, see 1 Cor 14:1.
18. As Caiaphas prophesied. Next John gives another reason why Jesus was going to die, extending the remark of Caiaphas to those outside of the nation of Israel— to the "other sheep" Jesus mentioned in 10:16.
19. Or, "took counsel, deliberated". Or, both here and in 12:10, "they resolved to kill Him". Same word as in 12:10; 2 Cor 1:17. Elsewhere only as "deliberate" in Lk 14:31; Act 27:39. GK *1086*. Related to "counsel" in Eph 1:11.
20. Or, "in order that they might", depending on whether John is giving the content or the purpose of the plan. GK *2671*.
21. Or, "*with* openness". Same word as in 7:4.
22. Some manuscripts say "was spending time" {N}, using the word in 3:22.
23. This is the third Passover explicitly named. On this word, see 18:28.
24. That is, the country or land of Israel, in contrast to the city of Jerusalem. Passover could only be celebrated inside the city of Jerusalem. Same word as "region" in v 54.
25. Same word as in Act 21:24, 26; 24:18. On this word, see 1 Jn 3:3.
26. That is, that Jesus surely will not come under these circumstances. Does this seem right to you, or do you think He might come?
27. Some manuscripts add "both" {N}.
28. Some manuscripts have this singular {N}, so that it says "*a* command".
29. More literally, "is", as the Greek typically phrases it.
30. Same word as 7:30, 32, 44; 8:20; 10:39. Used 12 times. GK *4389*.

A. Phil 3:14 B. Mt 26:27, given thanks C. Act 22:23 D. 1 Cor 7:27 E. Mt 5:19, break F. Mt 6:12, forgive G. Jn 3:36 H. 2 Thes 2:9 J. Act 15:23, Gentiles K. Lk 3:2 L. 1 Cor 1:18 M. 1 Jn 3:1 N. Mt 25:24 O. Rom 7:11 P. Mk 1:5, country Q. Mt 3:1 R. Phil 2:21 S. Lk 19:11, thinking T. Lk 20:37, showed

2B. Therefore[1] Jesus, six days[2] before the Passover [Feast], came to Bethany where Lazarus was, *the one* whom[3] Jesus[4] raised[A] from *the* dead 12:1

   1C. So they[5] made *a* dinner[6] *for* Him there. And Martha was serving[7]. And Lazarus was one of the *ones* reclining-back [to eat] with Him 2

   2C.[8] Then Mary, having taken *a* pound[9] *of* very-valuable[B] genuine[C] nard[D] perfume[E], anointed[F] the feet *of* Jesus, and wiped His feet *with* her hair.[10] And the house was filled[G] from the aroma[H] *of* the perfume 3

      1D. But Judas the Iscariot[11]— one of His disciples, the *one* going to hand Him over— says, "For what reason was this perfume not sold *for* three-hundred denarii[12] and given *to* poor[J] *ones*?" 4-5

         1E. Now he said this, not because he was concerned[13] about the poor, but because he was *a* thief[K]. And having the *money*-box[14], he was carrying[15] the *things* being put *there* 6

      2D. So Jesus said, "Leave[16] her *alone* 7

         1E. "*It was* in order that[17] she might keep[L] it for the day *of* My preparation-for-burial[M]

         2E. "For you[18] always have **the poor** with you,[19] but you do not always have **Me**" 8

   3C. Then the[20] large crowd[21] of the Jews came-to-know[N] that He was[22] there. And they came— not because of Jesus only, but in order that they might also see Lazarus, whom He raised from *the* dead 9

   4C. And the chief priests planned[23] to[24] kill[O] Lazarus also, *because many *of* the Jews were going-away[P] and were believing in Jesus because of him 10-11

3B.[25] *On* the next day the large crowd[26]— the *one* having come to the Feast[Q]— having heard[27] that Jesus was[28] coming to Jerusalem, *took the branches *of* palm-trees[29] and came out to meet[30] Him 12 / 13

   1C. And they were shouting[R], "Hosanna[S]! Blessed[31] *is* the *One* coming in *the* name *of the* Lord, even[32] the King *of* Israel". *And Jesus, having found *a* young-donkey[33], sat on it, just as it has been written[34] [in Zech 9:9], *"Do not be fearing, daughter *of* Zion[35]. Behold— your King is coming, sitting on *a* colt *of a* donkey" 14 / 15

      1D. His disciples did not understand[N] these *things* at first. But when Jesus was glorified[36], then they remembered that these *things* had been written[37] for[38] Him, and *that* they did these *things* to Him 16

   2C. Then the crowd[39] was testifying[T]— the *one* being with Him when[40] He called Lazarus out of the tomb and raised[A] him from *the* dead 17

      1D. For this reason also[41] the crowd[42] met[43] Him— because they heard *that* He had[44] done **this** sign 18

   3C. Then the Pharisees said to themselves, "You see[45] that you are profiting nothing[46]! Look— the world[47] went after Him!" 19

4B. Now some of the *ones* going up in order that they might worship[U] at the Feast were Greeks[48]. *So these *ones* came to Philip— the *one* from Bethsaida *of* Galilee— and were asking him, saying, "Sir, we wish to see Jesus" 20-21

   1C. Philip comes and tells Andrew. Andrew[49] and Philip come, and they tell Jesus 22

1. That is, because the Passover was near (11:55), and Jesus' hour was at hand. Or, "Then".
2. If John means six days before the slaughter of the Passover lambs (see Mk 14:12), then this may mean Friday . Some think Jesus arrived Friday from Jericho (Lk 19:5), enjoyed this dinner with Lazarus Friday or Saturday night (as we call it), and entered Jerusalem Sunday morning. There are other views.
3. Some manuscripts say "the *one* having died, whom Jesus raised..." {A}.
4. Some manuscripts say "He" {N}.
5. This is undefined. Some think it means "people in Bethany".
6. Or, "banquet". On this word, see Lk 14:12.
7. It was at Simon the leper's house, Mt 26:6; Mk 14:3. On this word, see "ministering" in 1 Pet 4:10.
8. Parallel account at Mt 26:6; Mk 14:3. Compare Lk 7:37-50.
9. That is, a Roman pound, consisting of 327 grams or 11.5 ounces. Elsewhere only in 19:39. GK *3354*.
10. This was Mary's pure expression of love, and of gratitude for raising her brother.
11. On Judas, see Jn 6:71. Some manuscripts add "[son] *of* Simon" {N}.
12. That is, 300 day's wages of a laborer. A year's wages. On this word, see Mt 20:2.
13. More literally, "because it was a concern *to* him". Same idiom as in 10:13.
14. Elsewhere only in 13:29. GK *1186*.
15. Or, "pilfering". This word means "carry away, remove" (as in 20:15), and with the dishonest sense of it coming from the context, "steal, pilfer". Judas was a thief, he carried the money box for the group, and he pilfered from it. On this word, see Mt 8:17.
16. This command is singular here, aimed at Judas. It is plural in Mk 14:6.
17. Or, "[She had it] in order that...", meaning that this is the purpose for which Mary kept it up to now. In this rendering, it is assumed she poured it all out, and that she had kept it for this moment. The grammar is like 13:18; 14:31; etc. Others render it "Leave her *alone* in order that...". In this view, it is assumed that Mary did not pour it all out after she broke the neck of the alabaster jar (Mk 14:3), and that she is to keep the remainder of it until after the death of Jesus. Some manuscripts say "She has kept it for the day..." {N}, which fits either view.
18. This "you" is plural, addressed to them all.
19. That opportunity will always exist, but this one will never occur again.
20. Some manuscripts omit this word, so that it says "*a* large crowd" {C}.
21. John is referring to the crowd that was at the funeral, 11:19, 45, the friends of Lazarus, Mary, and Martha, and others they had told. They now hear that a dinner is being given for Jesus, and come to see Jesus and Lazarus. This "Lazarus crowd" testifies the next day in v 17.
22. More literally, "is", as the Greek typically phrases it.
23. Same word as in 11:53.
24. Same idiom as in 11:53.
25. Parallel account at Mt 21:1; Mk 11:1; Lk 19:29.
26. This is a different "large crowd", defined next by John as the people of 11:55-56. The "Feast crowd".
27. How did the crowd hear? Probably from the Lazarus crowd of v 9, who heard it the night before.
28. More literally, "is", as the Greek typically phrases it.
29. Or, "date palms". This common tree at that time is often seen on the coins of that day. Elsewhere only as "palm branches" in Rev 7:9. GK *5836*.
30. This is an idiom, literally, came out from Jerusalem "for *a* coming-to-meet" Him. On this word, see Mt 25:1.
31. This is a participle, "Having been blessed". On this word, see Lk 6:28.
32. Some manuscripts omit this word {C}.
33. Used only here. GK *3942*. Related to "donkey" in v 15, and in Mt 21:2, where it refers to the mother of the colt.
34. This is a participle, it "is having been written", as in 2:17.
35. This is a transliterated Hebrew word referring to Jerusalem, its inhabitants, or the people of Israel whose capital is Jerusalem. Elsewhere only in Mt 21:5; Rom 9:33; 11:26; Heb 12:22; 1 Pet 2:6; Rev 14:1. GK *4994*.
36. Same word as in 7:39.
37. This is a participle, "were having been written".
38. Or, "about". That is, written as something destined to occur to Jesus. Same idiom as in Mk 9:12, 13; Rev 10:11. GK *2093*.
39. The Lazarus crowd begins testifying to the Feast crowd (v 12) who came out to meet Jesus.
40. Some manuscripts say "that" {B}, so that it says "Then the crowd being with Him was testifying that...".
41. Some manuscripts omit this word {C}. John explains that the Feast crowd also came out because they had heard about the sign. The Lazarus crowd had spread the word and the Feast crowd wanted to see both Jesus and Lazarus. The Lazarus crowd is now testifying to them as they proceed— Yes, we saw it. This is what He did.
42. That is, the Feast crowd of v 12.
43. That is, had come out to meet Jesus. On this word, see Lk 14:31. Related to "meet" in v 13.
44. More literally "has", as the Greek typically phrases it. They heard "Jesus has raised Lazarus!"
45. Or, this may be a command, "Observe, notice" that you are accomplishing nothing; or, a question. On this word, see Lk 10:18.
46. On the phrase "profit nothing", see 6:63.
47. Some manuscripts say "the whole world" {N}.
48. That is, Gentiles who were Jewish proselytes or God-fearers, coming to worship at Passover. Cornelius (Acts 10) and the Ethiopian (Acts 8) are examples of such ones. John does not use the term "Gentile", and uses "Greek" elsewhere only in 7:35. Same word as in Gal 3:28.
49. Some manuscripts say "And again, Andrew..." {N}. On Philip and Andrew, see Lk 6:14.

A. Mt 28:6, arose B. Mt 13:46 C. Mk 14:3 D. Mk 14:3 E. Mt 26:7 F. Jam 5:14 G. Eph 5:18 H. 2 Cor 2:14 J. Gal 4:9 K. 1 Thes 5:2 L. 1 Jn 5:18 M. Mk 14:8 N. Lk 1:34, know O. Rom 7:11 P. Mt 4:10 Q. Jn 13:29 R. Act 22:23 S. Mt 21:9 T. Jn 1:7 U. Mt 14:33

| John 12:23 | 352 | Verse |

    2C. And Jesus responds *to* them,[1] saying   23

        1D. "The[2] hour has come for[3] the Son *of* Man to be glorified[A]

            1E. "Truly[B], truly, I say *to* you, unless the seed[4] *of* wheat having fallen to the earth[5] dies,   24
it remains alone[C]. But if it dies, it bears much fruit

        2D.[6] "The[7] *one* loving[D] his life loses[E] it, and the *one* hating[F] his life[8] in this world will keep[9]   25
it for eternal life

            1E. "If anyone serves[G] **Me**, let him be following Me. And where **I** am, there also My   26
servant[10] will be
            2E. "If **anyone** serves Me, the Father will honor[H] him

        3D. "Now My soul[11] has been troubled[12]. And what should I say— 'Father[13], save[J] Me from   27
this hour'? But for this reason[14] I came to this hour! °Father, glorify[A] Your name!"   28
        4D. Then *a* voice came from heaven— "I both glorified *it*, and will again glorify *it*"
        5D. Then the crowd— the *one* standing *there* and having heard— was saying *that* thunder[K]   29
had[15] taken place. Others were saying, "*An* angel has spoken *to* Him"
        6D. Jesus responded and said, "This voice has taken place not for My sake, but for your   30
sakes. °Now is *the* judgment[L] *of* this world[M]! Now the ruler[16] *of* this world will be cast[17]   31
out! °And if **I** am lifted-up[18] from the earth, I will draw[N] all[19] *people* to Myself"   32

            1E. Now He was saying this signifying[20] *by* what-kind-of death He was going to die   33

        7D. Then the crowd responded *to* Him, "**We** heard from the Law that the Christ remains   34
forever[O]. How indeed do **You** say that 'The Son *of* Man[21] must[P] be lifted-up[22]'? Who is
this Son *of* Man?"[23]
        8D. Then Jesus said *to* them, "The[24] Light is among[25] you *for a* short time longer   35

            1E. "Be walking[Q] while you have the Light,[26] in order that darkness[R] may not overtake[S]
you. Indeed the *one* walking in the darkness does not know where he is going
            2E. "While you have the Light, be believing in the Light, in order that you may become   36
sons[27] *of* Light"

    3C. Jesus spoke these *things*, and having gone away, was hidden[28] from them[29]

5B. Now He having done so-many[30] signs[T] in front of them[31]— they were not believing[U] in Him   37

    1C. In order that the word *of* Isaiah the prophet might be fulfilled[V] which he spoke [in Isa 53:1],   38
"Lord, who believed[U] our report[W]? And *to* whom was the arm *of the* Lord revealed[X]?"

        1D. For this reason[32] they were not able to believe[U]— because again Isaiah said [in Isa 6:10],   39
"He has blinded their eyes, and He hardened[33] their heart[34]   40

            1E. "In order that they might not[35] see[Y] *with their* eyes, and comprehend[36] *in their* heart,
and be turned, and I shall heal[Z] them"

        2D. Isaiah said these *things* because[37] he saw His glory and spoke about Him[38]   41

1. That is, Philip and Andrew, and the crowd standing near, v 29, 34. Some think the Greeks were also there; others, that Philip and Andrew were to relay the message to them.
2. Before the disciples even ask, Jesus gives them the answer they need to hear, spoken from His perspective. Here, He speaks of Himself in relation to them.
3. More literally, "has come in order that the Son *of* Man may be glorified". The hour has come having this as its purpose in the plan of God. On this idiom, see 16:32. In other words, the time of Jesus' earthly ministry is over, the time of His death and resurrection has arrived. On "glorified", see 7:39. On the "hour" having come, see 2:4.
4. This refers to an individual seed. On this word, see Mt 13:31.
5. Or, "ground, soil". "Soil" fits best for the physical seed, but Jesus is also referring to Himself. On this word, see "land" in Rev 7:1.
6. Compare Mt 16:25.
7. Here, Jesus speaks of His followers in relation to Himself.
8. Or, "soul", as in v 27. On this word, see "soul" in Jam 5:20. That is, this natural life. On "hating" it, compare Lk 14:26. Jesus exemplifies hating His life in this world. Eternal "life" next is the normal word for "life" (see Rom 8:10 on it).
9. Or, "guard, protect, preserve". Such a person will keep his or her life safe. Same word as in v 47; Jude 24; as "protect" in 2 Thes 3:3; and as "guard" in 2 Tim 1:14; 1 Jn 5:21; 17:12; 2 Pet 3:17. It also means "keep" in the sense of "observe, obey". Used 31 times. GK *5875*. Related to "prison" in Act 5:22.
10. On this word, see 1 Cor 3:5. Related to "serve" earlier.
11. Here, Jesus speaks of His own thoughts at the moment, the thoughts pressing on His own mind.
12. That is, by the thought of what this hour will bring. Same word as in 11:33.
13. Others take this as a genuine prayer, "...say? Father, save me from this hour". Some think this prayer means "bring Me safely through it"; others, "keep Me out of it" (let this cup pass from Me, Mt 26:39).
14. Because of the very aspect of this hour now troubling Jesus— His impending death— He came to earth.
15. More literally, "has", as the Greek typically phrases it.
16. That is, Satan. Jesus is lifted up, Satan thrown down. Jesus conquers on the cross, and reigns until He puts all His enemies under His feet, including death, 1 Cor 15:25; Heb 1:13; 10:13.
17. Or, "thrown out, driven out, put out". This is the same word often used of "casting out" demons. Used 81 times. GK *1675*.
18. Same word as in 3:14 and 8:28. This is the third time Jesus has used it of Himself.
19. Some think Jesus means all people without distinction, Jews and Gentiles, people from every nation; others, "all that the Father has given Me".
20. On this word, see Rev 1:1. Its fulfillment is in 18:32.
21. This verse is the only place in the Gospels where this term is used by someone other than Jesus. See 5:27 on it.
22. The crowd probably understood the words of Jesus in v 32 to mean "exalted" into heaven. See 8:28 on this subject.
23. These questions refer to what Jesus has said in v 23-24 and 30-32. If Messiah is to remain forever, then who is this Son of Man in relation to the Messiah?
24. Jesus does not answer the crowd, but exhorts them to act on what they know before it is too late.
25. Jesus has only hours or days before His death. Some manuscripts say "with" {N}.
26. Keep walking while you can see at all by My light. Compare 11:9.
27. That is, ones belonging to the Light, characterized by light. On "sons", see Gal 3:7.
28. Same word as in 8:59.
29. Some make this point 5B., referring to the end of the public ministry of Jesus rather than the end of this incident.
30. Or, "such great". That is, although Jesus had done so many signs. John records seven (see 11:1 for the list). Note also 20:30; 21:25. GK *5537*.
31. That is, Israel. John now summarizes the reception of Jesus by Israel.
32. That is, the fulfillment of prophecy. Compare 6:44.
33. Some manuscripts say "has hardened"; others, "blinded" {C}. On this word, see Rom 11:7.
34. What John says God did, Matthew and Paul say the people themselves did, Mt 13:15; Act 28:27.
35. That is, that the people might not enter into the following process— see, comprehend, be turned, be healed. The healing is the certain conclusion of this process, but they do not even begin the process, because God blinded them. Note that "see-comprehend-be turned" correlates to "believe" in v 39.
36. Or, "understand, perceive", but not the same as either of the words in Mt 13:14; Act 28:26. On this word, see "think" in Eph 3:20.
37. Some manuscripts say "when" {B}.
38. That is, the Christ, the Messiah.

A. Rom 8:30 B. Jn 1:51 C. Jam 2:24 D. Jn 21:15, affectionately love E. 1 Cor 1:18, perish F. Rom 9:13 G. 1 Pet 4:10, ministering H. 1 Tim 5:3 J. Lk 19:10 K. Rev 4:5 L. Jn 3:19 M. 1 Jn 2:15 N. Jn 6:44 O. Rev 20:10 P. Mt 16:21 Q. Heb 13:9 R. Jn 1:5 S. Jn 1:5, overcome T. 2 Thes 2:9 U. Jn 3:36 V. Eph 5:18, filled W. Heb 4:2, hearing X. 2 Thes 2:3 Y. Lk 2:26 Z. Mt 8:8

| John 12:42 | 354 | Verse |

  2C. Yet indeed, even many of the rulers[A] believed in Him. But because of the Pharisees, they were not confessing[1] *it* in order that they might not become put-out-of-the-synagogue[2]. °For they loved[B] the glory *of* people more[3] than the glory *of* God   42
                                  43

6B. And[4] Jesus cried-out[C] and said—   44

  1C. "The *one* believing in Me is not believing in Me, but in the *One* having sent Me. °And the *one* seeing Me is seeing the *One* having sent Me   45

    1D. "**I** have come into the world *as a* **light**, so that everyone believing in Me should not remain in the darkness   46

  2C. "And if anyone hears My words and does not keep[5] *them*, **I** do not judge[D] him   47

    1D. "For I did not come in order that I might judge[D] the world,[6] but in order that I might save[E] the world
    2D. "The *one* rejecting[7] Me and not receiving[F] My words has *that which* judges[D] him— the word which I spoke, that will judge[D] him at the last day   48

  3C. "Because[8] **I** did not speak out of Myself[9], but the Father having sent Me— **He** has given Me *a* commandment[G] *as to* what I should say[10] and what I should speak[11]   49
  4C. "And I know that His commandment[G] is eternal life. Therefore[12] *the things* which **I** speak— just as the Father has told Me, so I speak"   50

13A. Now[13] before[14] the Feast[15] *of* the Passover, Jesus— knowing[16] that His hour came for[17] Him to pass[H] from this world to the Father— having loved[18] *His* own *ones* in the world, loved[19] them to *the* end[20]   13:1

  1B.[21] And dinner[22] taking-place[23], the devil having already put[J] into *his*[24] heart that Judas *son of* Simon Iscariot[25] should hand Him over— °*Jesus*[26], knowing[27] that the Father gave Him all *things* into *His* hands[28], and that He came forth from God and is going to God, °arises from the dinner and lays-down *His* [outer] garments   2
                                3
                                4

    1C. And having taken *a* towel, He tied *it* around Himself.[29] °Then He puts[J] water into the wash-basin[30]. And He began to wash[K] the feet *of* the disciples, and to wipe *them with* the towel which had been tied-around[31] Himself   5

      1D. Then He comes to Simon Peter. He says *to* Him, "Lord, do **You** wash my feet?"   6

        1E. Jesus responded and said *to* him, "**You** do not know what **I** am doing now, but you will understand[32] after these *things*"   7
        2E. Peter says *to* Him, "You will never wash my feet, ever[L]!"   8
        3E. Jesus responded *to* him, "If I do not wash you, you have no part[33] with Me"
        4E. Simon Peter says *to* Him, "Lord, *wash* not my feet only, but also the hands and the head!"   9
        5E. Jesus says *to* him, "The *one* having bathed[34] has no need[M] except to wash[35] *his* feet,[36] but is entirely[37] clean[N]. And **you**[38] are clean— but not all *of you*"   10

          1F. For He knew the *one* handing Him over[O]. For this reason He said that "You are not all clean"   11

1. Or, "declaring, acknowledging". On this word, see 1 Tim 6:12.
2. On this adjective, see 9:22.
3. Or, "rather". This word means "more, rather, instead". Used 81 times. GK *3437*.
4. John does not state when or where Jesus said this. He chooses to close the public ministry of Jesus with this clearly stated message, rather than with his own summary of His reception in v 37-43.
5. Some manuscripts say "believe" {N}. On this word, see 12:25.
6. This was also said in 3:17. When He comes back, He will judge.
7. Or, "refusing, setting aside". On this word, see "set aside" in Gal 2:21.
8. Note that this is the reason for both points above, the positive in v 44 and the negative in v 48.
9. On "out of Myself", see "from Himself" in 5:19. Jesus uses a different preposition here than in all the others listed there, but the idea is the same. His words did not originate out of His own heart or mind.
10. Used 2353 times as "to say, call, mean, claim, tell". GK *3306*.
11. Used 296 times as "to speak, state, tell". GK *3281*.
12. That is, because Jesus knows they are the words of eternal life, He has accurately delivered them, 17:8.
13. There are chronological issues associated with this verse, on which compare 13:29; 18:28; 19:14, 31. Some think these verses indicate that the meal here in chapters 13-16 was not the Passover meal, but a meal "before the Feast of Passover". Others think that the meal here was the Passover. Compare Mk 14:12. This is the Greek order of phrases in v 1. Consult the commentaries.
14. When before the Passover? Some think John means "the evening before" it; others, that it is an indefinite reference to the past time Jesus spent with the disciples; others, that he means "immediately before" the Passover meal taking place in v 2.
15. What occurred before the Passover? Some think John means "Jesus knowing before the Feast that His hour came"; others, "Jesus having loved them before the Feast"; others, that Jesus "loved them to the uttermost at this meal before the Passover meal".
16. Some think John means "although He knew... He loved them", Jesus nevertheless focused on the disciples, not on Himself. Others think he means "because He knew... He loved them", He gave them His final gift of love in what follows. Greek grammar permits either view.
17. More literally, "came in order that He might pass". See 16:32.
18. Some think John means "although He loved them" all along, Jesus loved them now to the uttermost. Others, "because He loved them" so deeply, He now gave them His final gift of love. Greek grammar permits either view.
19. How did He love them? Some think John is referring to the foot-washing that follows, linking v 1-2. Not linking v 1 to v 2, others think he is referring to all of chapters 13-17; others, chapters 13-19, including His death.
20. Or, "to *the* uttermost". Some think John means "to the end of His life"; others, "to the uttermost, to the extreme of His love, fully, decisively", in a final and perfect display of love. On the phrase "to the end", see "to the uttermost" in 1 Thes 2:16.
21. Parallel account at Mt 26:20; Mk 14:17; Lk 22:14.
22. Or, "supper". On this word, see Lk 14:12. It is used of the Lord's "Supper" in 1 Cor 11:20. John does not mention the Lord's Supper at all. Where it best fits in between verse 1 and 31 is debated. See Lk 22:21.
23. Or, "coming about". John may mean that "during the eating of the dinner", Jesus rose; or, that "while dinner was coming", He rose. The dinner appears to still be in progress in v 26. If after reclining to eat, while the dinner was coming about, but before the eating actually began in v 12, Jesus rises from the dinner and washes the disciples' feet, then one view linking v 1 to v 2 (see the notes on v 1) could mean "before the Passover meal began, He loved them to the uttermost by humbling Himself to wash their feet". Some manuscripts have this word in a different tense, meaning "having come about" or "having taken place" {B}, the latter of which is rendered "being ended" in the KJV. GK *1181*.
24. Some think John means the devil had put it into his own heart that Judas will betray Jesus. Others, that the devil put it into the heart of Judas to betray Him. Note v 27. Some manuscripts say, "having already put into the heart *of* Judas, *son of* Simon Iscariot, that he should..." {C}.
25. See 6:71 on him. Compare Lk 22:3.
26. Some manuscripts include this word {N}.
27. Some think John means "although He knew" this is who He was, Jesus rose and washed their feet; others, "because He knew". Greek grammar permits either view.
28. In spite of knowing all about Judas, and having all power to stop him, Jesus rises and washes his feet!
29. Jesus dressed as a slave would, then served the disciples as a slave would. He took the place of a nameless slave.
30. Related to "wash" next. Used only here. GK *3781*.
31. This is a participle, which "was having been tied around". Elsewhere only in v 4; 21:7. GK *1346*. The root word is "gird" in Act 12:8.
32. The foot-washing symbolizes Christ's humble service to believers, cleansing them from sin (see v 10). The voluntary self-humiliation of this act symbolizes His greater voluntary humiliation on the cross. Jesus makes the humble service aspect of this an example for His disciples to follow in v 12-17, but the pinnacle of His humble service comes later. Thus this act becomes partially understood when He explains it in v 12, but not fully understood until after His death.
33. Or, "share". This is because Jesus has in mind the spiritual meaning of His act. If He does not perform His humble service for Peter, cleansing him from sin, Peter does not belong to Christ. On this word, see Rom 11:25.
34. On this word, see "washed" in 2 Pet 2:22. Not related to "wash" next.
35. Same word as in v 5, 6, 8, 12, 14. On this word, see Mk 7:3.
36. In v 7 and 8b, this act symbolizes something about Jesus, the giver. In v 10 Jesus brings out its symbolism for believers, the recipients. When He washes them in v 5-8, He symbolizes His own humiliation on the cross in order to cleanse us from sin. Here, washing only the feet communicates that they are clean, but still need His cleansing as they walk through life, symbolizing the cleansing of believers' sins as they grow in holiness, as John speaks of in 1 Jn 1:9. Some manuscripts say "has no need except to wash the feet only"; others, "has no need other-than to wash the feet"; others, "has no need to wash-*himself*" {B}. Some, accepting the last variant, think the foot-washing symbolizes the bath referred to here, salvation. No further washing is needed.
37. Or, "completely, wholly". Same word as in 9:34. Because such a person had bathed, he is clean, except his feet. It is the difference between the washing (bath) of salvation (Tit 3:5), and the daily cleansing from sin (1 Jn 1:9). Since Jesus is washing believers here (except the one), they have "no need" for the former. GK *3910*.
38. This word is plural, referring to the eleven, not just Peter.

A. Rev 1:5   B. Jn 21:15, devotedly love   C. Mt 8:29   D. Mt 7:1   E. Lk 19:10   F. Jn 1:12   G. Mk 12:28   H. Jn 5:24   J. Rev 2:22, throw
K. Mk 7:3   L. Jn 4:14   M. Tit 3:14   N. Tit 1:15   O. Mt 26:21, hand over

2C.	Then when He washed[A] their feet, and[1] took His garments, and fell back again [to eat], He said *to* them	12
	1D. "Do you understand[2] what I have done[3] *for* you?	
	2D. "**You** call Me 'Teacher' and 'Lord'[4]— and you speak rightly[B], for I am. °Therefore if **I**— the Lord and the Teacher— washed your feet, **you** also ought to be washing the feet *of* one another	13-14
	1E. "For I gave[5] you *an* example[6], in order that **you** also should be doing just as **I** did *for* you[7]	15
	3D. "Truly[8], truly, I say *to* you, *a* slave[C] is not greater *than* his master, nor *is a* messenger[9] greater *than* the *one* having sent[D] him. °If you know[E] these *things*[10], you are blessed[11] if you are doing them	16 17
	1E. "I am not speaking with-reference-to[12] all *of* you. **I** know *the ones* whom I chose[13]. But *it is taking place* in order that[14] the Scripture [in Ps 41:9] might be fulfilled[F]— 'The *one* eating My bread[15] lifted-up[16] his heel against Me'	18
	2E. "From now *on,*[17] I am telling you ahead *of it* taking place[18], in order that when it takes place you may believe that I am *the One*[19]	19
	4D. "Truly, truly, I say *to* you, the *one* receiving[G] whomever I send is receiving Me.[20] And the *one* receiving Me is receiving the *One* having sent[D] Me"	20
2B.[21]	Having said these *things*, Jesus was troubled[22] *in His* spirit. And He testified[23] and said, "Truly, truly, I say *to* you that one of you will hand Me over[H]"	21
	1C. The[24] disciples were looking[J] at one another, being perplexed[25] about whom He was[26] speaking	22
	2C. One[27] of His disciples was reclining-back at the bosom[K] *of* Jesus— *the one* whom Jesus was loving[28]. °So Simon Peter nods[29] *to* this *one* to inquire[L] *as to* who it might be about whom He is speaking[30]	23 24
	1D. So that *one*, having leaned back thus[31] on the chest[32] *of* Jesus, says *to* Him, "Lord, who is it?"	25
	2D. Jesus answers, "It is that *one for* whom **I** will dip[M] the piece-of-bread[33] and give *it to* him"[34]	26
	3D. Then having dipped the piece-of-bread, He takes and[35] gives *it to* Judas, *son of* Simon Iscariot[36]	
	4D. And after the piece-of-bread, at that time Satan entered[37] into that *one*	27
	5D. Then Jesus says *to* him, "What you are doing, do quicker[38]"	
	1E. Now[39] none *of* the *ones* reclining-back [to eat] understood[N] this— for what *purpose* He said *it to* him[40]	28
	1F. For some were thinking[O], since Judas had the *money*-box[P], that Jesus was[41] telling him, "Buy *the things of* which we have *a* need[Q] for the Feast[42]", or that he should give something *to* the poor[43]	29
	6D. So having received the piece-of-bread, that *one* went out immediately.[44] And it was night	30
3B.	Then when he went out, Jesus says	31

1. Some manuscripts omit this word {C}.
2. Or, "know". Same word as in v 7, on which see "know" in Lk 1:34.
3. What Jesus has done is this— the Master has served His slaves, giving them an example to follow, v 15.
4. Or, "the Teacher", "the Lord". On "Lord", see "master" in Mt 8:2.
5. Some manuscripts say "have given" {N}.
6. Same word as in Heb 4:11; Jam 5:10; 2 Pet 2:6. Elsewhere only as "copy" in Heb 8:5; 9:23. GK *5682*.
7. Some think Jesus is referring to the thing He asks the disciples if they understand in v 12— His example of humility and service. Others think that He is referring to actual foot washing, instituting a church ordinance to be followed. "Wash" in this section is the same word as in 1 Tim 5:10, where it is a good work attesting widows. See Mk 7:3 on it.
8. If it is not below the Master's dignity, it is not below His slaves' dignity. On this word, see Mt 5:18.
9. Or, "apostle, sent *one*", but not related to the verb that follows. Used only here in John. On this word, see "apostle" in 1 Cor 12:28.
10. That is, that you ought to serve others as I served you, because a slave is not greater than the master.
11. Or, "happy, fortunate", from God's point of view. On this word, see Lk 6:20.
12. Or, "about, concerning". As in v 10, Jesus refers to Judas. Those who are not "clean" (saved) will not be blessed by doing these things. The blessing is only for believers who conduct themselves this way. GK *4309*.
13. Jesus chose all twelve to be apostles, and knows them all. On this word, see 1 Cor 1:27.
14. The fact that there is one among them to whom these words do not apply (a false one among His chosen twelve, 6:70) is not an accident, but is in order that the Scripture regarding the betrayer might be fulfilled.
15. Some manuscripts say "eating bread with Me" {C}.
16. Some manuscripts say "has lifted up" {N}.
17. Or, "Henceforth". Same phrase as in 14:7, on which see Mt 26:64.
18. Literally, "ahead *of* the taking place", before it happens. Jesus is explaining why He is now speaking repeatedly about this matter. He tells them in v 10 and 18, and explicitly in v 21, 26. He continues to speak explicitly about future matters in chapters 13-16. Note 14:29 and 16:4, where He makes a similar statement. GK *1181*.
19. On "I am *the One*", see 8:58. Only God knows the future.
20. This is the converse of v 16. The disciples are not greater than Jesus, and must humble themselves like He has, v 16-17. But as His representatives, sent by Him, receiving them will be equivalent to receiving Jesus and the Father. Thus they have a certain greatness because they are sent by Jesus, but they must conduct themselves as servants, like Him.
21. Parallel account at Mt 26:21; Mk 14:18; Lk 22:21.
22. Same word as in 11:33.
23. This word is added because Jesus is testifying in advance (v 19) to His future betrayal. On this word, see 1:7.
24. Some manuscripts say "Then the..." {N}.
25. Or, "being uncertain, being at a loss". On this word, see 2 Cor 4:8.
26. More literally, "is", as the Greek typically phrases it.
27. Some manuscripts say "Now one..." {N}.
28. John is thought by most to be referring to himself, as he does again in 19:26; 21:7, 20, and, using a different word for "love", 20:2. This is the writer of the book, 21:20, 24.
29. Or, "gestures". Elsewhere only in Act 24:10. GK *3748*.
30. Some manuscripts instead say "nods *to* this *one*, and says *to* him, "Tell *me* who it is about whom He is speaking" {N}. In this case, Peter either assumes John knows, or he means "find out who Jesus means and tell me".
31. Some manuscripts omit this word {N}. One can imagine John's ear being right below Jesus' mouth. Perhaps they all sat up in v 22, and now John leans back again. Same word as in 4:6.
32. Or, "breast". Elsewhere only in Lk 18:13; 23:48; Jn 21:20; Rev 15:6. GK *5111*.
33. Elsewhere only in v 27, 30. GK *6040*.
34. Some manuscripts say "It is that *one to* whom I will give the piece of bread, having dipped *it*" {C}.
35. Some manuscripts omit "takes and" {C}.
36. Some manuscripts say "*to* Judas Iscariot, *son of* Simon" {N}. See 6:71 on him.
37. Compare 13:2; 6:70-71; Lk 22:3.
38. Or, "sooner, faster". That is, sooner than Judas had intended. This command enables Judas to leave immediately and carry out his plot. The comparative form of the word found here is elsewhere only as "faster" in Jn 20:4; "sooner" in Heb 13:19; and "quicker" in Heb 13:23. It may be rendered "quickly", dropping the comparative aspect. On this word, see "quickly" in Gal 1:6.
39. Some manuscripts omit this word {C}.
40. Some think the disciples understood that Jesus had now identified Judas as the one, but did not understand that Jesus was sending him out to betray Him at that moment. Had they understood this, perhaps they would have tried to prevent it. Thus "none" includes John. Others think they still did not understand that Judas was the one (except for John), and so did not understand the meaning of this command (including John).
41. More literally, "is", as the Greek typically phrases it.
42. Or, "Festival". Elsewhere only of the eight-day Passover/Unleavened Bread Feast, Mt 26:5; 27:15; Mk 14:2; 15:6; Lk 2:41, 42; 22:1; Jn 2:23; 4:45; 6:4; 11:56; 12:12, 20; 13:1; the eight-day Feast of Tabernacles, Jn 7:2, 8, 10, 11, 14, 37; an unnamed Feast in Jn 5:1; and in Col 2:16. GK *2038*. Some think the disciples mean the Passover meal on the next day, taking this to mean that the meal they were now eating was not Passover, but a meal "before" it, 13:1. Others think they mean things for the events or meals on the next day of the Feast, after the Passover meal which they were then eating. Others think they mean additional things for the Passover meal they were then eating. See 13:1; 18:28. Consult the commentaries.
43. It was customary to give to the poor on Passover night. The temple opened at midnight.
44. On when Judas left in relation to the Lord's Supper, see Lk 22:21.

A. Mk 7:3   B. Act 10:33, well   C. Rom 6:17   D. Jn 20:21   E. 1 Jn 2:29   F. Eph 5:18, filled   G. Jn 1:12   H. Mt 26:21, hand over   J. Rev 1:11, see   K. Jn 1:18   L. Act 23:34, learn   M. Rev 19:13   N. Lk 1:34, know   O. Lk 19:11   P. Jn 12:6   Q. Tit 3:14

1C.	"Now the Son *of* Man was glorified,[1] and God was glorified in Him. °If God was glorified in Him,[2] God will also glorify[3] Him in Himself— and will glorify Him immediately[A]	32
2C.	"Little-children[4], I am with you *a* little longer. You will seek[B] Me, and just as I told the Jews that where **I** am going, **you** are not able to come, I also tell you now[5]	33
1D.	"I am giving you *a* new[6] commandment[7]— that you be loving[C] one another; just as I loved you, that **you** also be loving one another. °By this everyone will know that you are disciples *to* Me[8]— if you are having love in-the-case-of[9] one another"	34 35
3C.	Simon Peter says *to* Him, "Lord, where are You going?"[10]	36
1D.	Jesus answered him[11], "Where I am going, you are not able to follow Me now. But you will follow[12] later"	
2D.	Peter says *to* Him, "Lord, for what reason am I not able to follow You right-now[13]? I will lay-*down* my life[D] for You"	37
3D.	[14] Jesus responds[15], "Will you lay-*down* your life for Me? Truly[E], truly, I say *to* you, *a* rooster will by no means crow until which *time* you deny[F] Me three-times!	38
4C.	"Do not let your[16] heart be troubled[17]. Be believing[18] in God. Be believing also[19] **in Me**	14:1
1D.	"There are many places-to-stay[20] in the house[G] *of* My Father— otherwise[21], I would have told you	2
2D.	"For[22] I am going to prepare[H] *a* place[J] *for* you	
3D.	"And if I go and prepare *a* place *for* you, I am coming back[23]	3
4D.	"And I will take[24] you to Myself— in order that where **I** am, **you** also may be	
5D.	"And you know[K] the way where **I**[25] am going"[26]	4
6D.	Thomas says *to* Him, "Lord, we do not know[K] where You are going. How[27] are we able to know[K] the way?"	5
7D.	Jesus says *to* him, "**I** am the way,[28] and the truth, and the life.[29] No one comes to the Father except through Me.[30] °If you[31] have known[L] Me, you will know[32] My Father also. And[33] from now on,[34] you know[L] Him, and you have seen[M] Him"	6 7
8D.	Philip says *to* Him, "Lord, show[N] us the Father, and it is enough[35] *for* us"	8
1E.	Jesus says *to* him, "Am I with you[36] *all for* so long *a* time, and you have not known[37] Me, Philip?—	9
1F.	"The *one* having seen[M] Me has seen[M] the Father. How[38] *is it* **you** say, 'Show us the Father'?	
2F.	"Do you not believe that I *am* in the Father, and the Father is in Me?"[39]	10
2E.	"I am not speaking the words which **I** am saying *to* you[40] from Myself,[41] but[42] the Father abiding[O] in Me is doing His works[43]	
1F.	"Be believing Me[44]— that I *am* in the Father and the Father *is* in Me	11
2F.	"Otherwise, be believing[45] because of the works themselves	

1. Some think Jesus means that now, in sending out Judas as He did, He was glorified by not holding on to His life, but setting in motion His own death. In one sense, His life has come to an end now that Judas has left to betray Him. He has entered His "hour". His death is contained in this seed. Others think He is referring to His coming death as if it were past.
2. Some manuscripts omit "If God was glorified in Him" {C}.
3. Some think Jesus means that since God was glorified in this act of Jesus, God will also glorify Jesus in His death, which is coming immediately, the next day. Others think that since God was glorified in His death (looking at the future event as if it were past), He will glorify Him in His resurrection.
4. This word is used only by John, and only here in John. On this word, see 1 Jn 2:1.
5. Or, "at this moment". He said it to the Jews in 7:33-34; 8:21. On this word, see Rev 12:10.
6. The commandment was old (Lev 19:18), but the example and motive was new, "as I loved you". In addition, it was never given as that which defined the community of believers. It is family love, proceeding from the family love believers have received from God. On this word, see Heb 8:13.
7. This is the first thing Jesus says to the disciples in view of His leaving, because this will be of first importance for them while they remain on earth. He returns to this later.
8. On this phrase, see 15:8.
9. Or, "among", as in Rom 15:5. Or, "in the sphere of, in connection with". GK *1877*.
10. Peter is not prepared to hear v 34 until he understands v 33.
11. Some manuscripts omit this word {C}. Each "you" in this verse is singular. Jesus is answering Peter himself.
12. Some manuscripts add "Me" {N}.
13. Or, "at this moment". Jesus used this word in v 33 ("now"), not in v 36 (which is GK *3814*).
14. Compare Lk 22:31; Mt 26:30; Mk 14:26.
15. Some manuscripts add "*to* him" {N}.
16. Both "your" and "be believing" are plural. Jesus turns from Peter, and speaks to the whole group, answering the question in v 36.
17. That is, about Jesus going away. The grammar implies, "stop letting" or "do not be letting your heart be troubled". Jesus now begins to comfort the disciples regarding His leaving them. His comfort may be summarized as "You will be with Me some day where I am going", v 1-11; "It will be good for you that I go", v 12-17; "I will come to you where you are and reveal Myself to you", v 18-26; "I leave you my peace now", v 27-31. There are other views of the flow of thought of this chapter. Consult the commentaries. On this word, see "disturb" in Gal 1:7.
18. Or, "You are believing in God. Be believing also **in Me**". In both places, "believe" may be a command or a statement.
19. Or, "And be believing **in Me**". Next, Jesus explains where He is going.
20. Or, "dwellings, abodes, rooms, homes". Related to the verb "to stay, abide". Elsewhere only in v 23. GK *3665*.
21. Literally, "But if [this were] not [the case]". This idiom is elsewhere only in Mk 2:21, 22; Jn 14:11; Rev 2:5, 16, and in the related "otherwise indeed" in 2 Cor 11:16.
22. Or, "Because". Be believing in Me... because I am going to My Father's house to prepare for you. Or, this may be answering the unexpressed question "Why are You leaving?". Or, "that", with this as a question, "otherwise would I have told you that I am going to prepare *a* place *for* you?" Some manuscripts omit this word {B}. GK *4022*.
23. Or, "again". Some think Jesus is referring to the Second Coming, the counterpart of His going. On this word, see "again" in Mk 15:13.
24. Or, "receive". Same word as in Mt 1:20.
25. In some manuscripts, the word emphasizing this word is omitted, meaning it would not be bolded {C}.
26. Some manuscripts say "And you know where **I** am going, and you know the way" {B}.
27. Some manuscripts add a word meaning "and, indeed" {N}, so that it says "How indeed...", or, "And how...".
28. From this, Christianity came to be called "the Way" (see Act 9:2). Jesus does not merely show the way, He is the way.
29. Jesus is the way, the path, the means to our heavenly abodes in the Father's house where He is, and to the Father Himself. He is the embodiment of absolute truth, straight from the Father, regarding all these matters. He is the source and fountain of the true eternal life which we will fully experience when we are with Him there.
30. Or, "by means of Me". Thus, Jesus says He is the way, and that there is no other way.
31. Each "you" in this verse is plural. Jesus continues addressing all the disciples.
32. This is a promise. The grammar means "Assuming that [or, since] you have known Me, you will also know My Father". The disciples will know the Father when Jesus takes them where He is going. Yet in another sense, they now know the Father and have seen Him—in Jesus. Some manuscripts have this as a rebuke, "If you had known Me, you would have known **My Father** also" {C}.
33. Some manuscripts omit this word {N}.
34. Same phrase as in 13:19. From the "expounding" (1:18) that Jesus has done, which enters its most significant phase on this night, the disciples do truly know the Father through Jesus, and have seen Him in Jesus. And they will know Him when Jesus receives them to Himself.
35. John's other use of this word is also by Philip, 6:7. On this word, see "sufficient" in 2 Cor 12:9.
36. This "you" is plural, to reflect which, "all" is added. The next three are singular, answering Philip himself.
37. Or, "come to know". Same word as three times in v 7. On this word, see Lk 1:34.
38. Some manuscripts add the word "And, indeed", as in v 5 {N}.
39. The grammar expects a "yes" answer. Yes, Philip believes.
40. This is plural. Both verbs "believe" are plural. Jesus turns from Philip to address His answer to all the disciples.
41. The Father is speaking through Jesus, so these words have His authority. Jesus says this again in v 24. On "from Myself", see "from Himself" in 5:19. Compare 8:28; 12:49.
42. Or, "... Myself. And the Father...".
43. The words of Jesus are among the works the Father is doing in Him. Some manuscripts say "in Me, **He** is doing the works {N}.
44. That is, His words which are not from Himself. Or, believe His works, which the Father is doing in Him.
45. Some manuscripts add "Me" {B}.

A. Mk 6:25   B. Phil 2:21   C. Jn 21:15, devotedly love   D. Jam 5:20, soul   E. Jn 1:51   F. 2 Tim 2:12   G. Mk 3:25   H. Mk 14:15   J. Eph 4:27
K. 1 Jn 2:29   L. Lk 1:34   M. Lk 2:26   N. 1 Tim 6:15   O. Jn 15:4

5C. "Truly[1], truly, I say *to* you— the *one* believing in Me, that *one* also will do the works[A] which 12
I am doing.[2] And he will do greater[3] *works than* these, because **I** am going to the[4] Father

    1D. "And[5] whatever thing[6] you ask[B] in My name, this I will[7] do, in order that the Father may 13
        be glorified[C] in the Son. °If you ask Me[8] anything in My name, **I** will do *it* 14
    2D. "If you love[D] Me, you will keep[9] My commandments[10]. °And[11] **I** will request[12] the Father, 15-16
        and He will give you another Helper[13] to[14] be[15] with[16] you forever[E]—°the Spirit *of* truth[17] 17

        1E. "Whom the world is not able to receive[F] because it does not see nor know Him
        2E. "**You**[18] know Him because He abides[19] with[20] you, and will be[21] in[22] you

6C. "I[23] will not leave[G] you *as* orphans.[24] I am *going to* come[25] to you[26] 18

    1D. "*A* little longer,[27] and the world is no longer *going to* see Me, but **you** are *going to* see[28] 19
        Me.[29] Because **I** live, **you** also will live[30]

        1E. "On that day,[31] **you** will know that I *am* in My Father, and you *are* in Me, and I *am* 20
            in you

    2D. "The *one* having My commandments[H] and keeping[J] them[32]— that *one* is the *one* loving[D] 21
        Me. And the *one* loving Me will be loved by My Father. And **I** will love him and reveal[33]
        Myself *to* him"
    3D. Judas (not the Iscariot[34]) says *to* Him, "Lord, what indeed[35] has taken place that You are 22
        going to reveal Yourself *to* **us** and not *to* the world?"[36]
    4D. Jesus responded and said *to* him[37] 23

        1E. "If anyone loves[38] Me, he will keep My word. And My Father will love him. And
        We will come to him. And We will make *a* place-to-stay[39] with him

            1F. "The *one* not loving Me does not keep[J] My words[40] 24

1. Continuing to comfort the disciples, Jesus turns from what His going means with regard to them being with Him again where He is going, to what His going to the Father will mean to them while they remain behind.
2. That is, works granted by the Father.
3. That is, works producing greater (more extensive) results than the works Jesus did. The conversion of 3000 on Pentecost (Act 2:41) is an example. The disciples also did great miracles in Acts, but these were not in themselves greater than His miracles. But they were greater in the spiritual results produced.
4. Some manuscripts say "My" {K}.
5. Some think the connection is "And toward the doing of these greater works, whatever you ask..."; others, that believers will do greater works "because I am going to the Father, and whatever you ask, I will do..."; others see this as a separate promise alongside that of v 12.
6. On "whatever thing", see Col 3:17.
7. The works "I am doing" on earth (v 12) will be replaced by the works "I will do" after I go to the Father. Jesus will be working through His people, producing greater works.
8. Some manuscripts omit this word {B}.
9. Or, "shall keep", a command. Some manuscripts say "... Me, keep My commandments" {C}. Note 15:10.
10. That is, love one another, 13:34; believe God, believe Me, 14:1, 11.
11. This is another thing Jesus will do to help believers when He goes to the Father, as part of a reciprocal relationship with them. He will ask the Father to give them the Spirit of truth to help them. Since it is a reciprocal relationship, He states both sides of it, as also in v 21, 23— both how we will express our love to Him (v 15), and He to us (v 16).
12. Or, "ask", but not the same word as "ask" in v 13, 14. On this word, see "pray" in 17:9.
13. Or, "Comforter, Counselor, Advocate", one called alongside to help. Some transliterate this Greek word as "Paraclete". Same word as in 14:26; 15:26; 16:7. "Another" implies that Jesus is also a Helper. John uses this word of Him in 1 Jn 2:1 ("Advocate"), its only other use. GK *4156*. Jesus advocates for us to God; the Spirit gives us help from the Father and the Son. The Spirit will help us to do, v 12; to ask, v 13; and to know the truth, v 17. Related to "exhort" in Rom 12:8; and "encouragement" in Act 4:36.
14. More literally, "in order that He may be". GK *2671*.
15. Some manuscripts say "abide" {N}, as in v 17.
16. Or, "in your midst". Not the same word as in v 17. GK *3552*.
17. That is, the Spirit who communicates truth from Jesus, 16:13-14; 15:26.
18. Some manuscripts say "But you..." {N}.
19. Or, "will abide". On this word, see 15:4.
20. Or, "beside, among". GK *4123*.
21. Some manuscripts say "and is" {C}.
22. Or, "within". GK *1877*. Thus three different prepositions are used of the Spirit in v 16-17.
23. Now Jesus turns from what the disciples will do and the help He will give them when He goes to the Father, to what He personally will do for them where they are. He is going to come and reveal Himself to them only, not to the world.
24. Jesus will not abandon the disciples, leave them permanently alone, or go away never to return.
25. Or, "I *will* come". Literally, "I am coming", the future sense coming from the preceding sentence.
26. Some think Jesus means He will visibly come to the disciples after His resurrection, the word "see" being used in the same sense in both halves of v 19; others, that He Himself will spiritually come to them; others, that He will come to them in and through the Spirit, this being a further explanation of v 16-17. Compare v 21, 23; and 16:16-23.
27. That is, tomorrow (Friday) for the world, and Sunday or Pentecost for the disciples (see the views noted above).
28. The world will not see Jesus physically. The disciples will see Him physically or spiritually (see the views noted above).
29. Or, "the world *will* no longer see Me, but **You** *will* see Me". Literally, the world "is no longer seeing", the disciples "are seeing". The present tense verbs are given a future sense by "a little while longer". Note that "going to" is in v 22.
30. That is, the disciples will share in the life of Jesus. His life results in theirs.
31. Some think Jesus means Sunday, when the disciples physically see Him alive again, they will know. Others think they will know on the day of seeing Him spiritually in the coming of the Spirit promised in v 16-17, Pentecost.
32. Jesus broadens His promise from "you", to all who love Him, as seen in their obedience to Him; that is, to all who are in a reciprocal relationship of love with Him. As in v 15-16, the promise is only for those in this reciprocal relationship, both sides of which Jesus again links together.
33. Or, "make known, make clear, make visible". In this broader promise, Jesus is certainly referring to a spiritual presence, not a physical one. Historically, both were true of the apostles. Some think Jesus means He personally will reveal Himself and dwell in His followers (Eph 3:17); others, that this occurs through the coming Spirit (15:26). Same word as in v 22, John's only other use. GK *1872*.
34. On this word, see 6:71. On this Judas, see Lk 6:16.
35. Or, "Lord, and what has happened...". Some manuscripts omit this word {C}. Others say "Lord, why is it that You are going..." {N}.
36. Judas asks this question because the disciples expected the Messiah-King to reveal Himself publicly to the world, and establish His kingdom on earth. What has caused You to change and reveal Yourself only to us who love You?
37. As the plural pronouns ("you") in v 24-26 indicate, the answer is addressed to all the disciples, through Judas.
38. What has happened is that in God's plan, "the world did not know Him", 1:10. Jesus will reveal Himself only to those who do, who love and obey Him. He and the Father will come and dwell with them, revealing themselves to them.
39. That is, the Father and the Son will come to live with such disciples, lodge with them. This is similar to "come in and have dinner with him", Rev 3:20. Some think this means the Father (1 Jn 4:12, 16), the Son (Eph 3:17), and the Spirit (v 17), will dwell in them; others, that this dwelling takes place in and through the Spirit. Same word as v 1. Note the reciprocal relationship again.
40. And for this reason, I will not reveal Myself to such a one. Jesus is explaining the opposite case.

A. Mt 26:10   B. 1 Jn 5:14, request   C. Rom 8:30   D. Jn 21:15, devotedly love   E. Rev 20:10   F. Rom 7:8, taken   G. Mt 6:12, forgive   H. Mk 12:28   J. 1 Jn 5:18

| John 14:25 | 362 | Verse |

        2E. "And the word which you[1] are hearing is not Mine, but the Father's having sent Me

    5D. "I have spoken these[2] *things to* you while staying[3] with you. *But the Helper[4]— the Holy Spirit, Whom the Father will send in My name— that *One* will teach you all *things,* and remind[5] you of everything which **I**[6] said *to* you[7]   25-26

  7C. "I leave[A] you peace.[8] I give you My peace. **I** do not give *to* you as the world gives.[9] Do not let your heart be troubled[10], nor let it be afraid[11]   27

    1D. "You heard that **I** said *to* you, 'I am going, and I am coming to you'.[12] If you were loving Me,[13] you would have rejoiced[B] that[14] I am going to the Father, because the[15] Father is greater *than* Me[16]   28

    2D. "And now I have told you before *it* takes place,[17] in order that when it takes place, you may believe   29

    3D. "I will no longer speak many *things* with you, for the ruler[C] *of* the[18] world is coming. And he does not have anything in Me[19], *but *it is taking place*[20] in order that the world may know[21] that I love[22] the Father, and *that* just as the Father commanded[D] Me, so I am doing[23]   30   31

4B. "Arise, let us be going from here[24]

  1C. "**I** am the true[25] grapevine, and My Father is the farmer[26]. *Every branch in Me not bearing[E] fruit[27]— He takes it away. And every *branch* bearing[E] fruit— He cleans[28] it in order that it may bear[E] more fruit   15:1-2

    1D. "**You** are already clean[29], because of the word[F] which I have spoken *to* you   3
    2D. "Abide[30] in Me, and I in you[31]   4

        1E. "Just as the branch is not able to bear[E] fruit from itself unless it is abiding[32] in the grapevine, so neither *are* you *able* unless you are abiding in Me

    3D. "**I** am the grapevine, you *are* the branches   5

        1E. "The *one* abiding[33] in Me and I in him— this *one* bears[E] much fruit.[34] Because apart from Me, you can do nothing

1. If the "you" is taken as referring to the apostles Jesus is speaking to, then this means that what He is saying to them now comes straight from the Father and has His authority, as in v 10-11. What you apostles are hearing about Our revealing Ourselves (v 23) is the Father's plan. If the "you" is taken as an impersonal reference to "people", then this completes the previous thought. The one not loving Me does not keep My words, and the word which "people" hear from Me is My Father's, so such a one is rejecting both Me and My Father. For this reason, We will not reveal Ourselves to him.
2. As with the previous point (v 12-17), Jesus ends by linking the disciples to the Spirit whom the Father will give to them to help them. Others make this point 7C., beginning His conclusion.
3. Or, "remaining, abiding". On this word, see "abiding" in 15:4. Related to the "place to stay" in v 23, which by contrast the Father and the Son "will make".
4. On this word, see v 16.
5. The disciples cannot absorb more now. The Spirit will guide them later. The grammar of "remind you of everything" is like 2 Tim 2:14, where this same word is used. Same word as in Lk 22:61; Tit 3:1; 2 Pet 1:12; Jude 5. Elsewhere only as "call to mind" in 3 Jn 10. GK 5703. Related to "reminder" in 2 Tim 1:5.
6. In some manuscripts, the word emphasizing this word is omitted, meaning it would not be bolded {C}.
7. This is primarily true for the apostles. It is secondarily true for the following generations who did not directly hear Jesus speak, but hear Him spiritually and through the apostles' written word. We too have the Anointing, 1 Jn 2:27.
8. Now Jesus turns from viewing the future in light of His going away (14:1-26), back to the present, and gives His personal farewell and comfort to them.
9. That is, a false, transient peace; peace promised but never realized; peace dependent on circumstances.
10. Same word as in v 1.
11. Or, "fearful, cowardly, timid". It refers to being afraid to act, rather than to being afraid of the circumstances. Used only here. GK 1262. Related to "afraid" in Mk 4:40; and "fearlessness" in 2 Tim 1:7.
12. Jesus said He was going in 13:33; 14:2; and coming in 14:3, 18.
13. That is, if you were able to express your love to Me right now, instead of worrying about yourselves and being distracted by a multitude of questions, you would be glad for Me.
14. Or, "because". Some manuscripts say "because I said" {N}
15. Some manuscripts say "My" {N}.
16. If the disciples had fully known this One who emptied Himself and took on the form of a slave and became obedient to the point of death on a cross (Phil 2:7-8), they would have rejoiced that He was going to the Father— because Jesus was returning to the greatness of glory He shares with the Father (17:4-5), having accomplished all that He came to do. The Father is greater than the Incarnate Son, the humbled One. In addition, He is functionally greater than the Son, who always obeys His Father's will. As persons, as to Their essence, They are equal.
17. That is, Jesus has told the disciples of His coming departure, and some of its meaning for Him and them. Literally, "before the taking place". Similar grammar to 13:19, with a different preposition used here.
18. Some manuscripts say "this" {K}.
19. Or, "in My case". GK 1877. Satan has no claim on Jesus, no point under his authority or rule. What Jesus does, He does voluntarily.
20. Note the similar grammar in 13:18; 15:25. "Taking place" is supplied from 13:19.
21. Or, "come to know". On this word, see Lk 1:34.
22. Since Jesus loves the Father perfectly, He obeys Him completely. He perfectly exemplifies what will also be true in our relationship with Him, v 15. Note 15:10. Submission and obedience are at the heart of our relationship.
23. This is the Greek word order. Others think Jesus means "but in order that the world may know that I love the Father— even as the Father commanded Me, thus I am doing", which may be more smoothly rendered "but even as the Father commanded Me, thus I am doing, in order that the world may know that I love the Father". Others connect this with what follows, "But that the world may know that I love the Father, and *that* just as the Father commanded Me, so I am doing— arise, let us go from here [to meet this ruler and his forces]".
24. Some think this means Jesus and the disciples left the upper room (making this parallel to Mt 26:30; Mk 14:26), and that what follows was spoken along the way, after which they crossed to the garden, Jn 18:1. Others think these words were spoken in the same room, before they actually left in 18:1. In any case, this indicates a breaking point in His words.
25. Jesus is the real, genuine vine which the earthly vine pictures or illustrates. On this word, see 7:28.
26. Or, "vine-grower", but not related to "vine" (GK 306), "vineyard" (GK 308), or "grape" (GK 5091). It is the one who works the earth; here, tends the vines. Related to "farm", the root words mean "earth-worker". Elsewhere only in Mt 21:33-41; Mk 12:1-9; Lk 20:9-16; 2 Tim 2:6; Jam 5:7. GK 1177. The word "vine-keeper" (related to "grapevine") is used only in Lk 13:7.
27. Judas is an example of this from this very night.
28. Instead of using an agricultural word, Jesus uses the word from the human application of this picture. See the next note. This word means "to clean, make clean, to purify". The picture is of moral and spiritual cleaning, purifying, training, pruning. The Father purifies behavior and heart, and renews the mind (Rom 12:2). Used only here. GK 2748.
29. Related to the word in v 2. They could be rendered "prunes" and "pruned", respectively. Same word as in 13:10, "You are clean, but not all". Neither English nor Greek normally speaks of "cleaning" a branch, or "pruning" a person. So most translations render the first "prunes" (with reference to the branch), and the second "clean" (with reference to the apostles). This is correct, but then the intentional play on words is obscured. On this word, see Tit 1:15.
30. Or, "Remain, Stay, Continue". Same word as in 14:10, 17; 15:4, 5, 6, 7, 9, 10; and as "stay" in 14:25, and "remain" in 15:16. Used 118 times, 68 being by John. GK 3531.
31. Some take this to mean "and I [will abide] in you"; others, "[as] I also [abide] in you"; others, "and [let] Me [abide] in you". Compare v 5, 7, where both sides are again mentioned.
32. Some manuscripts say "abides" here and "abide" next {N}, the different grammar emphasizing the fact of it rather than the continuing nature of it.
33. That is, the one having a continual living connection to Jesus, a living reciprocal relationship with Jesus.
34. Fruit includes all the products of a living relationship with the Vine.

A. Mt 6:12, forgive   B. 2 Cor 13:11   C. Rev 1:5   D. Mk 10:3   E. 2 Pet 1:17, carried   F. 1 Cor 12:8

2E. "If anyone is not abiding¹ in Me— he was thrown² outside³ like the branch⁴, and was dried-upᴬ. And they gather them⁵ together, and throw *them* into the fire. And they are burnedᴮ — 6

3E. "If you abide⁶ in Me, and My wordsᶜ abide in you, ask⁷ whatever you wantᴰ, and it will be doneᴱ *for* you — 7

4E. "By this My Father is glorified⁸— that you be bearingᶠ much fruit, and be⁹ disciplesᴳ *to* Me¹⁰ — 8

4D. "Just as the Father lovedᴴ Me, **I** also¹¹ loved you. Abide in My love.¹² °If you keepᴶ My commandmentsᴷ, you will abide in My love¹³— just as **I** have kept the commandments *of* My Father and am abiding in **His** love — 9-10

5D. "I have spoken these *things to* you in order that My joyᴸ may be¹⁴ in you, and your joy may be made full¹⁵ — 11

1E. "This¹⁶ is My commandmentᴷ— that you be lovingᴴ one another just as I loved you — 12

1F. "No one has greater love *than* this— that one lay-*down* his life for his friends¹⁷ — 13

2E. "**You**¹⁸ are My friendsᴹ if you are doing *the things* which¹⁹ **I** commandᴺ you — 14

1F. "I no longer call you slavesᴼ, because the slave does not know what his master is doing — 15
2F. "But I have called you friends, because I made-knownᴾ *to* you everything which I heard from My Father²⁰

3E. "**You** did not choose²¹ Me, but **I** chose you and appointedᵠ you — 16

1F. "In order that **you** may go and bearᶠ fruit,²² and your fruit may remain²³
2F. "In order that He may give you whatever thing²⁴ you askᴿ the Father in My name²⁵

4E. "I²⁶ am commandingᴺ these²⁷ *things to* you so-that²⁸ you will love one another²⁹ — 17

2C. "If the world hatesˢ you,³⁰ you know³¹ that it has hated Me before you³² — 18

1D. "If you were of the world, the world would be lovingᵀ *its* own. But because you are not of the world, but **I** choseᵁ you out of the world— for this reason the world hates you — 19

2D.³³ "Remember³⁴ the word that **I** said³⁵ *to* you, '*A* slaveᴼ is not greater *than* his master' — 20

1E. "If they persecutedⱽ Me, they will also persecute you
2E. "If they keptᴶ My wordᵂ, they will also keep yours³⁶

3D. "But they will do all these *things to* you because of My name,³⁷ because they do not know the *One* having sent Me — 21

1E. "If I had not come and spoken *to* them, they *would* not be having sin³⁸ — 22

1F. "But now they do not have *an* excuse³⁹ for their sin
2F. "The *one* hatingˢ **Me** is also hating My Father — 23

2E. "If I had not done among them the worksˣ which no other one did, they *would* not be having sin — 24

1. That is, is not in a continuing living connection with Christ, the vine.
2. The grammar ("was thrown") views the branch as thrown out and dried up outside the vineyard, summing up all that this means into a single fact, without reference to the process that led to this state. It emphasizes the fact (his "thrown-out-ness"), not the process (his "being taken and thrown"). Compare "takes away" in v 2, where the emphasis is that the Father is engaged in this process. Here, some think Jesus is speaking vividly from the perspective of the final judgment, "There he is— thrown out and dried up. And the process of gathering and burning is being carried out". Others think He is stating a timeless principle, "he is found to be thrown out and dried up", as is always true with such branches, picturing the future judgment. In any case, He only refers to the final end, skipping all the intermediate details, because this person is not His subject here. His focus is on abiding.
3. That is, outside the vineyard.
4. That is, like the fruitless branch, v 2.
5. That is, all such thrown-out branches.
6. That is, are connected to Me, summing up all that this means into a single fact.
7. Some manuscripts say "you will ask" {N}.
8. Literally, "was glorified". The grammar is stating this as a timeless principle. The Father "is glorified" when disciples are bearing fruit, that is, when such ones are truly His disciples (unlike the branches He takes away, v 2). On this word, see Rom 8:30.
9. Or, "become, prove to be". In these two phrases, Jesus links together the vine metaphor (bearing fruit) and the human reality (being genuine disciples). GK *1181*. Some manuscripts have this as a separate phrase in the future tense, "fruit. And you will be disciples *to* Me" {C}.
10. Jesus uses grammar here and in 13:35 that puts more emphasis on their being "**disciples** to Me" than "**My** disciples".
11. Or, "and", so that it says "As the Father loved Me and **I** loved you, abide in My love".
12. Jesus plainly states the key concept of the vine allegory. Abide in My love by doing as I command.
13. Keeping His commands does not make Jesus love us. His love came first. Keeping them is our loving response (14:15) to His love.
14. Some manuscripts say "abide" {N}.
15. Joy comes in the doing, the keeping the Father's commands, the bearing fruit, the glorifying the Father, the abiding in His love. His joy comes from this. Jesus has spoken all this that we may fully share in this joy by doing the same.
16. In v 12-17, Jesus states in more specific terms the key aspects of what He has said in v 1-11. First, He names the key command referred to in v 10a.
17. This is the height of love Jesus commands us (1 Jn 3:16), and reflects what He was about to do.
18. Next Jesus restates what He said in v 10a in an even more simple and direct way. Doing what He says does not make Him your friend, but is your response as His friends. He chose His disciples as friends first. "If you keep My command to love one another, you are being My friends and abiding in My love".
19. Some manuscripts say "what" (singular), "do what I command"; others, "whatever" I command {N}.
20. Jesus commands us as friends, not slaves. As friends, He has included us in all that He has heard from His Father. Our obedience flows from relationship, from the knowledge of God, not from command alone.
21. Next Jesus makes explicit what He implied in v 9-10, that He first loved them. He initiated the friendship, the love relationship, the fruit-bearing relationship. He initiated the assignment of work and the fruit to come from it. On this word, see 1 Cor 1:27.
22. Just as between Jesus and the Father, our relationship with Jesus involves a fruit-bearing mission.
23. This glorifies the Father, v 8.
24. On this idiom, see Col 3:17.
25. This glorifies the Son (14:13), and is part of an abiding reciprocal relationship (15:7). I chose you to go and bear fruit in a living reciprocal relationship with God, where He answers your prayers.
26. Others make v 17-18 point 2C., v 17 being the contrast leading into v 18.
27. That is, abide in Me, v 4; abide in My love, v 9.
28. Or, "in order that you may". GK *2671*.
29. This is the heart of the abiding, fruit-bearing, reciprocal relationship with God. Jesus commands us to abide in Him because loving one another flows from this living relationship, bringing glory to the Father and the Son.
30. The grammar assumes that this will be the case.
31. Or, this may be a command, "Know, be aware, recognize, understand". On this word, see Lk 1:34.
32. Some manuscripts omit this word {N}, so that it says "hated Me first". On "before", see 1:15.
33. Compare Mt 10:24-25.
34. Instead of a command, this may be a question "Do you remember... master'?".
35. That is, in 13:16. Here Jesus makes a different application of this proverbial statement.
36. Some think Jesus means "If they persecuted Me (and they did)... If they kept My word (and they did not)". They will respond negatively to you as they did to Me. Others think He means "If they persecuted Me (and some did)... If they kept My word (and some did)". They will respond to you as they did to Me, both negatively and positively.
37. The world will persecute you because of their sin, their ignorance of God, their rejection of Me, not any failure in you. Jesus details the world's sin next. They rejected His words (v 22) and His works (v 24), making them rejecters of the Father, guilty before Him. This rejection will continue in the same ways against the disciples, based on their testimony about Jesus, v 27.
38. That is, the world would not be guilty of this sin of rejecting Jesus, of failing to repent in light of the revelation He brought from the Father. On "have sin", see 1 Jn 1:8.
39. Or, "plea". Now, in light of the revelation Jesus brought in words and works, the world has no valid excuse for their failure to repent from the sin they had before He came. On this word, see "pretense" in Phil 1:18.

A. Mk 3:1, become withered B. Mt 5:15 C. Rom 10:17 D. Jn 7:17, willing E. Mt 6:10 F. 2 Pet 1:17, carried G. Lk 6:40 H. Jn 21:15, devotedly love J. 1 Jn 5:18 K. Mk 12:28 L. Lk 24:52 M. Lk 14:10 N. Mk 10:3 O. Rom 6:17 P. Phil 1:22, know Q. 1 Thes 5:9 R. 1 Jn 5:14, request S. Rom 9:13 T. Jn 21:15, affectionately love U. 1 Cor 1:27 V. 2 Tim 3:12 W. 1 Cor 12:8 X. Mt 26:10

	1F. "But now they have both seen and have hated both Me and My Father¹	
3E.	"But *it has taken place* in order that the word having been written in their Law [in Ps 69:4] might be fulfilled^A— that 'They hated^B Me without-a-reason²'	25
4E.	"When³ the Helper⁴ comes Whom **I** will send *to* you from the Father— the Spirit *of* truth, Who proceeds⁵ from the Father—	26
	1F. "That *One* will testify^C about Me	
	2F. "And **you** also are *going to be* testifying⁶— because you are [the ones] with Me from *the* beginning⁷	27
4D.	"I have spoken these *things to* you in order that you may not be caused-to-fall^D	16:1
	1E. "They will make you put-out-of-the-synagogue ones^E	2
	2E. "Indeed⁸, *an* hour is coming for⁹ everyone having killed^F you to think^G *that he* is offering^H service¹⁰ *to* God	
	3E. "And they will do these *things*¹¹ because they did not know the Father nor Me	3
	4E. "But I have spoken these *things to* you so that when their¹² hour comes, you may remember^J that **I** told you ***of* them**	4
3C.	"Now I did not say these¹³ *things to* you from *the* beginning, because I was with you. °But now I am going to the *One* having sent Me	5
1D.	"And none of you is asking Me, 'Where¹⁴ are You going?', °but grief¹⁵ has filled^A your heart because I have spoken these *things to* you	6
2D.	"But **I** tell you the truth^K— it is better¹⁶ *for* you that **I** go away	7
	1E. "For if I do not go away, the Helper¹⁷ will not come to you	
	2E. "But if I go, I will send Him to you	
	3E. "And having come,¹⁸ that *One* will convict¹⁹ the world concerning sin, and concerning righteousness, and concerning judgment	8
	1F. "Concerning sin^L— because²⁰ they are not believing in Me²¹	9
	2F. "And concerning righteousness^M— because I am going to the Father and you are no longer *going to* see²² Me²³	10
	3F. "And concerning judgment^N— because the ruler^O *of* this world has been judged²⁴	11
	4E. "I²⁵ still have many *things* to say *to* you, but you are not able to bear^P *them* now. But when that *One,* the Spirit *of* truth, comes—	12 13
	1F. "He will guide^Q you in²⁶ all the truth. For He will not speak from Himself,²⁷ but He will speak whatever He will hear²⁸	
	2F. "And He will declare²⁹ *to* you the *things* coming	
	3F. "That *One* will glorify^R Me,³⁰ because He will take from *what is* Mine and declare *it to* you	14
	1G. "All that the Father has is Mine.³¹ For this reason I said that He takes from *what is* Mine and will declare *it to* you³²	15
4C.	"*A* little *while* and you are no-longer³³ *going to* see³⁴ Me. And again *a* little *while*, and you will see³⁵ Me"³⁶	16

1. And thus the world does now "have sin" in this matter as a consequence.
2. This hatred was not caused by Jesus, but came from within. On this word, see Gal 2:21.
3. Some manuscripts begin this sentence with a word meaning either "Now", "And", or "But" {N}.
4. On this word, see 14:16. Compare 14:26.
5. Or, "comes out, goes out". Some think Jesus means "goes out eternally", describing the eternal relationship of the Father and the Spirit; others, "is *going to* go out", the present tense verb getting a future sense from "I will send", referring to Pentecost. On this word, see "coming out" in Rev 1:16.
6. Or, "*will* testify". Or, this may be a command, "also be testifying". In either case, the present tense verb gets a future sense from the preceding sentence, since it is when the Spirit "will testify" that the disciples' testifying also takes place.
7. That is, the disciples have been with Jesus since the beginning of His ministry. They are His witnesses.
8. Or, "But". A Jewish disciple might think that being put out of the synagogue is the pinnacle of rejection to be faced, but it is not. GK *247*.
9. More literally, "in order that everyone having killed you may think...". That is, an hour is coming having as its purpose that this will happen. On this idiom, see 16:32. In the purpose of God, an hour is coming for the disciples of Jesus, just as the hour has come for Jesus, 12:23.
10. Or, "worship", divine service. On this word, see "worship" in Rom 12:1.
11. Some manuscripts add "*to* you" {N}.
12. Some manuscripts omit this word {B}, so that it says "when the hour comes".
13. That is, 15:18-16:4, about the fact that after Jesus is gone, the disciples will be hated and persecuted in His place by their own people, who will think they are doing a service to God by killing them.
14. In other words, the disciples' grief has overwhelmed their desire to know more about what this going means and will mean. They are not pursuing such questions. Nevertheless, Jesus now goes on to explain some of it, v 8-15. Note that in 13:36 and 14:5, they asked regarding what He told them they could not do— follow Him where He is going.
15. Same word as in Lk 22:45, where Luke says this is what caused the disciples to sleep in the Garden.
16. Or, "profitable, advantageous". On this word, see Mt 18:6.
17. On this word, see 14:16.
18. What follows is what the Helper will do with regard to the world, v 8-11.
19. Or, "expose". The Helper will do this through the testimony of the disciples and the followers of Jesus. He will expose the world's guilt and their need, and call them to respond. Some will respond, others will reject. Compare the same words in 8:46, "convict concerning". On this word, see "expose" in Eph 5:11.
20. Or "that, in that". Same word as in v 10, 11. GK *4022*.
21. Some think Jesus means the Helper will convict the world of their sin "because they are not believing in Me", which is the ultimate sin, or which is the classic manifestation of their sinfulness; others, "that they are not believing in Me", defining the sin He has in view. There are other views. Consult the commentaries.
22. Same idiom as in v 16, 14:19. Literally, "are seeing", the future sense coming from the previous phrase.
23. Some think Jesus means the Helper will convict the world that Jesus is personally righteous, not unrighteous as His killers supposed; others, that Jesus is the only source of the righteousness God requires, the answer to their need in v 9; others, of their lack of (or, false) righteousness (which is like filthy rags, Isa 64:6). In any case, the Helper does this "because" Jesus is returning to God, approved and vindicated, by virtue of His resurrection. One who understands why Jesus returned to the Father will also understand what true righteousness is.
24. Some think Jesus means the Helper will convict the world of God's coming judgment upon them "because" Satan has now been judged in His victory; others, of their bad judgment, their spiritual blindness (since they thought they were properly judging Him), "because" Satan has been defeated at the cross, not Jesus.
25. Now Jesus turns to what the Spirit will do with regard to the disciples, v 12-15. He will do then what cannot be done now.
26. Or, "with, in connection with, by means of". GK *1877*. Some manuscripts say "into" {B}.
27. Like Jesus, the Spirit will not originate the truth. The truth comes from the Father, through Jesus. On "from Himself", see 5:19.
28. Some manuscripts say "He hears"; others, "He may hear" {N}. Jesus did the same, 12:49; 14:24.
29. Or, "disclose, report, announce, tell, inform". Same word as in v 14, 15; 4:25; Act 19:18; 20:20, 27; Rom 15:21; 1 Pet 1:12; 1 Jn 1:5. Elsewhere only as "report" in Jn 5:15; Act 14:27; 15:4; 2 Cor 7:7. GK *334*.
30. The Spirit will do for Jesus what Jesus did for the Father. He will place Him before the world, resulting in conviction (v 8-11), and before believers.
31. Only One equal to God (5:18) could make such a statement. Compare 17:10.
32. In other words, Jesus does not mean "Mine" in v 14 in an exclusive sense. The Father and the Son are one in this matter, and the Spirit will declare the one truth of God to us. Some manuscripts say "will take" {K}.
33. Some manuscripts say "not" {N}, as in v 17.
34. Same word and idiom as in 14:19. Literally, "are no longer seeing Me". Same word as in v 17a, 19a. On this word, see Lk 10:18.
35. This is a different word for "see" than in the first phrase, and occurs also in v 17, 19, 22. On this word, see Lk 2:26. Both words are used in the same senses, so it is difficult to discern a distinction from the words themselves. But the change may be intended to convey two different senses in which the disciples will see Jesus. They will no longer "observe" Him as Jesus, but they will "see" Him after His resurrection as their risen Lord, or spiritually "see" Him after Pentecost. Compare 14:19, where there is no change of word (both being the same as the word in the first phrase here), and the same views of the meaning.
36. Some manuscripts add "because I am going to the Father" {A}, as in v 17.

A. Eph 5:18, filled B. Rom 9:13 C. Jn 1:7 D. 1 Cor 8:13 E. Jn 9:22 F. Rom 7:11 G. Lk 19:11 H. Heb 5:7 J. Jn 16:21 K. Jn 4:23 L. Jn 8:46 M. Rom 1:17 N. Jn 3:19 O. Rev 1:5 P. Mt 8:17, carry Q. Lk 6:39 R. Rom 8:30

| John 16:17 | 368 | Verse |

    1D. Then *some* of His disciples said to one another   17

        1E. "What is this which He is saying *to* us— '*A* little *while*, and you are not *going to* see Me. And again *a* little *while*, and you will see Me'
        2E. "And— 'Because[1] I am going to the Father'?"

    2D. Then they were saying, "What is this which He is saying[2]— '*A* little *while*'? We do not know what He is speaking *about*   18

    3D. Jesus[3] knew that they were wanting[A] to question[B] Him, and He said *to* them, "Are you seeking[4] with one another concerning this, that I said, '*A* little *while*, and you are not *going to* see Me. And again *a* little *while*, and you will see Me'?   19

        1E. "Truly[C], truly, I say *to* you that **you** will weep[D] and lament[5], but the world will rejoice[E]. **You**[6] will be grieved[F], but your grief[G] will become joy[7]   20

            1F. "The woman has grief[G] when she gives-birth[H], because her hour came. But when she bears[J] the child[K], she no longer remembers[8] the affliction[L] because of the joy that *a* person[M] was born[J] into the world   21
            2F. "**You** then also **now**[9] have[10] grief— but I will see you again,[11] and your heart will rejoice[E]. And no one is *going to* take away[12] your joy from you   22

        2E. "And in that day[13] you will not question[14] Me *as to* anything[15]   23

            1F. "Truly, truly, I say *to* you, if you ask[16] the Father anything[17] in My name, He will give *it to* you[18]
            2F. "Until now you did not ask anything in My name. Be asking and you will receive, in order that your joy may be full[19]   24

        3E. "I have spoken these[20] *things* to you in figures-of-speech[21]   25

            1F. "*An* hour[22] is coming when I will no longer speak *to* you in figures-of-speech, but I will tell[23] you about the Father *with* plainness[N]
            2F. "In that day you will ask in My name. And I am not saying *to* you that **I** will request[24] the Father on your behalf[25]   26

                1G. "For the Father Himself loves[O] you, because **you** have loved[O] Me, and have believed that **I** came forth from God[26]   27

        4E. "I came forth from the Father,[27] and I have come into the world. Again[28], I am leaving[P] the world and going to the Father"   28

    4D. His disciples say[29], "Look—   29

        1E. "Now You are speaking with plainness[N], and You are speaking no figure-of-speech
        2E. "Now we know[Q] that You know[Q] all *things*, and You have no need[R] that anyone question[30] You. By this we believe that You came forth from God"   30

    5D. Jesus responded *to* them, "Now[31] you[32] believe! °Behold, *an* hour is coming, and has come,[33] for[34] you to be scattered[35]— each to *his* own *things*[36]— and leave[P] Me alone   31-32

        1E. "And-*yet* I am not alone[37], because the Father is with Me

1. The disciples are referring to v 10, where these same words are used. Similar words are in 14:12, 28; 16:5.
2. Some manuscripts omit "which He is saying" {C}, so that it says "What is this 'little *while*' ".
3. Some manuscripts say "Then Jesus" {N}.
4. That is, "seeking [to understand], looking-for [My meaning]". On this word, see Phil 2:21.
5. These two words were used of the mourning at funerals. On this word, see Mt 11:17.
6. Some manuscripts say "And **you**..." {N}.
7. This is an idiom based on a Hebrew way of speaking. Literally, it "will come-to-be for joy".
8. That is, "keeps in mind, thinks of ". Used 21 times. GK *3648*. Related word in Lk 1:54.
9. Jesus uses grammar that emphasizes the contrast between the two halves of this sentence.
10. Some manuscripts say "will have" {B}.
11. Some think Jesus is referring to His resurrection day; others, to Pentecost.
12. Or, "*will* take away". Literally, "is taking away". The present tense verb gets its future sense from the previous phrase. "Joy" is related to "rejoice" in the previous sentence. Some manuscripts say "will take away" {B}.
13. That is, in the days of their joy, v 20, 22; after the resurrection of Jesus, and continuing after He ascends and the Spirit comes on Pentecost.
14. That is, ask for information. You will have no need to question Me in order to understand what I have told you. Or, "ask Me anything" in prayer. Same word as in v 19, and as "request" in v 26. On this word, see "praying" in 17:9.
15. The disciples do not ask now from grief, v 6. They will not ask then from joy! Everything will be clear then.
16. Same word as in v 24, 26a. On this word, see "request" in 1 Jn 5:14.
17. Instead of "if you ask the Father anything", some manuscripts say "that whatever you ask the Father" {B}.
18. Some manuscripts say "... anything, He will give *it to* you in My name" {C}.
19. This is a participle, "having been made full". Same phrase as in 1 Jn 1:4, 2 Jn 12. Same word with different grammar in 3:29; 15:11; 17:13. On this word, see "filled" in Eph 5:18.
20. That is, the things Jesus has told the disciples this night, including v 16.
21. Or, in an enigmatic, indirect, somewhat obscure manner. Same word as in v 29. On this word, see 10:6.
22. Some manuscripts say "But *an* hour" {N}. It is the same period as "that day" in v 23, 26.
23. Or, "declare, report, announce". Same word as "announce" in 1 Jn 1:2, 3, John's only other uses.
24. Same word as in 14:16, where Jesus does ask the Father for us, and as "question" in v 23.
25. Or, "for you, with regard to you, in relation to you". GK *4309*. That is, Jesus will not ask in their place, as an intermediary. He does not mean the disciples will ask Him and He will ask the Father for them. They will have direct access. Jesus does intercede on our behalf (Rom 8:34; Heb 7:25; 1 Jn 2:1), as does the Spirit (Rom 8:26), but our prayers are heard directly by the Father. The Father loves His children, and needs no convincing, no higher authority to intervene, before He will hear them. In other words, "His name" gains us direct access to the Father who loves us.
26. Some manuscripts say "the Father" {C}.
27. Some manuscripts omit this phrase {C}, so that what follows continues on directly from v 27.
28. This is the first word in the Greek sentence. Some think Jesus means "Again [I say], I am...", introducing the second saying. Others think it is placed first for emphasis, "I am leaving... and going **again**...". On this word, see Mk 15:13.
29. Some manuscripts add "*to* Him" {N}.
30. Or, "ask You a question". The disciples say this because Jesus has just answered their question of v 17-18 without them asking it. Same word as in v 19, 23.
31. Or, "Right now, at this moment". On this word, see Rev 12:10.
32. Or, "Do you now believe?" The disciples did believe, v 27; 17:8; but did not understand as much as they thought.
33. Similar to "is coming and now is", 4:23, 5:25. Note 17:1. Some manuscripts say "has now come" {N}.
34. More literally, "has come, in order that you may be scattered". The hour having this as its purpose has come. It is in fulfillment of prophecy, Mt 26:31. Same idiom as in 12:23; 13:1; 16:2. GK *2671*. Each is referring to a still future part of God's purpose and plan. It is not the same as "an hour is coming when" in 4:21, 23; 5:25; 16:25.
35. Or, "dispersed". Elsewhere only in Mt 12:30; Lk 11:23; Jn 10:12; 2 Cor 9:9. GK *5025*.
36. That is, his own pursuits, or, "*his* own [home]". On this phrase, see 19:27.
37. Same word earlier, and as in 8:29. On this word, see Jam 2:24.

A. Jn 7:17, willing B. Jn 17:9, pray C. Jn 1:51 D. Jn 11:33 E. 2 Cor 13:11 F. 2 Cor 7:9 G. 2 Cor 7:10 H. Lk 2:11, born J. 1 Jn 2:29, born
K. 1 Jn 2:14 L. Rev 7:14 M. Mt 4:4, mankind N. Jn 10:24 O. Jn 21:15, affectionately love P. Mt 6:12, forgive Q. 1 Jn 2:29 R. Tit 3:14

	5C. "I have spoken these[1] *things to* you in order that you may have peace[A] in Me. You have[2] affliction[B] in the world, but take-courage[C]— **I** have overcome[3] the world"	33
5B.	Jesus spoke these *things,* and having lifted-up[D] His eyes to heaven, said[4]	17:1
	1C. "Father, the hour has come[5]—	
	1D. "Glorify[E] Your Son, so that the Son may[6] glorify You—˚just as You gave Him authority[7] *over* all flesh[8] in order that *as to* all that[9] You have given Him, He may give eternal life *to* them	2
	1E. "And this is eternal life— that they may be knowing[F] You, the only true[G] God, and Jesus Christ Whom You sent-forth[10]	3
	2D. "**I** glorified You on the earth, having accomplished[11] the work which You have given *to* Me that[12] I should do. ˚And now Father, **You** glorify[13] Me[14] with Yourself *with* the glory which I was having with You before the world was[15]	4 5
	2C. "I revealed[16] Your name *to* the men[17] whom You gave *to* Me out of the world	6
	1D. "They were Yours, and You gave them *to* Me	
	2D. "And they have kept[H] Your word[J]. ˚They have now come-to-know that all *things* that You have given *to* Me are from You[18]—	7
	1E. "Because I have given them the words[19] which You gave *to* Me	8
	2E. "And **they** received[K] *them,* and truly[L] understood[20] that I came forth from You, and believed that **You** sent Me forth	
	3D. "**I** am praying[21] for them. I am not praying for the world, but for *the ones* whom You have given *to* Me—	9
	1E. "Because they are Yours—˚indeed all My *things* are Yours;[22] and Yours, Mine[23]	10
	2E. "And I have been glorified[E] in them	
	3E. "And I am no longer in the world, and **they**[24] are in the world, and **I** am coming to You[25]	11
	4D. "Holy Father, keep[26] them in[27] Your name[28] which[29] You have given *to* Me, in order that[30] they may be one,[31] just as We *are*	
	1E. "When I was with them[32], **I** was keeping them in Your name which You have given *to* Me.[33] And I guarded[34] *them,* and none of them perished[M]—	12
	1F. "Except the son *of* destruction[35], in order that the Scripture[N] might be fulfilled[36]	
	2E. "But now I am coming[37] to You[38]	13
	3E. "And I am speaking these[39] *things* in the world[40] so that they may have My joy[41] made-full[42] in themselves	
	3C. "**I** have given them Your word[J], and the world hated[O] them— because they are not of the world, just as **I** am not of the world	14

1. That is, the things on this night.
2. Some manuscripts say "you will have" {N}.
3. Or, "conquered". On this word, see Rev 2:7. 24 of its 28 uses are in John's books. Used only here in the Gospel.
4. Some manuscripts say "and lifted up His eyes to heaven, and said" {N}.
5. On this hour, see 2:4.
6. When the Father glorifies the Son through His death and resurrection, when the Son goes to His Father, the Son will bring further glory to the Father as He continues His works through believers, 14:12-14. Glorify the Son in view of what He still must do. Some manuscripts say "Your Son also may" {B}.
7. Just as the Father gave Jesus authority to give eternal life to His people (His mission in coming to earth), now give Jesus glory that He may glorify the Father. Both sides of this are emphasized again in v 4-5, in reverse order.
8. On "all flesh", see "no flesh" in Mt 24:22.
9. The idiom "all that" is the same as in 6:37, 39. It views all believers as an abstract whole. Compare v 24.
10. Some think this is John's comment. Others think Jesus refers to Himself in the third person. On this word, see "send out" in Mk 3:14.
11. Or, "completed, finished". Jesus views His entire earthly mission, from incarnation to ascension, as complete. Same word as in 4:34; 5:36. Some manuscripts say "earth. I accomplished" {N}.
12. Or, "given Me to do". GK *2671*.
13. This is a command.
14. Glorify the Son in view of what He has done, the opposite viewpoint of v 1.
15. That is, the glory of which Jesus emptied Himself to take on the form of a slave, Phil 2:6-7. Literally, "before the being [or, existing] *as to* the world".
16. Or, "manifested, made known". On this word, see "made evident" in 1 Jn 2:19.
17. That is, the eleven. The twelfth is mentioned in v 12. Compare v 18, 20.
18. That is, that all the words and works of Jesus are from the Father.
19. Or "utterances" (see Rom 10:17 on it). All the "words" of Jesus make up the Father's "word, message" which the disciples have kept.
20. Or, "knew". Same word as "have come to know" in v 7, but different grammar. On this word, see "know" in Lk 1:34.
21. Or, "asking" on behalf of, with reference to; "making a request" concerning, with respect to. The same word is used again in this verse, and in v 15, 20, and as "request" in 14:16; 16:26. These are the only places it is used of Jesus asking the Father. It is used elsewhere of prayer only in 1 Jn 5:16, and perhaps Jn 16:23 ("question"). Elsewhere, this word is used 55 times of asking a question or requesting something from another person. GK *2263*.
22. Or, "All *that is* Mine is Yours". The grammar is emphasizing the totality. In other words, the emphasis is not "Every individual thing that is Mine is Yours" (though this is true), but, "The totality of everything that is Mine is Yours".
23. A human could say the first part in relation to God or another human (as this same idiom is used in Lk 15:31); but only one "equal to God" (5:18) could say the second part in relation to God. Compare 16:15. Only an equal or a superior can say "All that is yours is mine". An inferior can at best say "Most of what is yours is mine".
24. Some manuscripts say "and these are..." {N}.
25. Some think Jesus means "My public ministry is over, and the disciples' work in the world is now upon them, and I am now coming back to You"; others, "I am coming back to You, and their public work in the world is now upon them, and I am now coming to You in prayer with this request".
26. Or, "preserve, protect, keep intact, keep safe, guard". This is the content of Jesus' prayer, His request for the disciples, v 9. Note that He says "I revealed Your name to them (v 6)... keep them in Your name". Same word as in v 12, 15. Note that they "kept" Your word (v 6), so You "keep" them (the same word is used in both places, in different senses). On this word, see 1 Jn 5:18.
27. That is, "in the sphere of ". Or, "by, by means of ". GK *1877*.
28. Some think Jesus means "Keep the disciples in all that Your name means, includes and stands for. Protect and preserve them in their living relationship with You"; others, "Protect them from evil and the evil one by means of Your name, by the power of Your name".
29. This refers to "name". Some manuscripts link it to "them" {B}, "keep in Your name them that You have given *to* Me".
30. This expresses the purpose of it. Keep them in Your name so that they may be continuing in oneness.
31. On the meaning of this, see v 21, where Jesus more fully states it.
32. Some manuscripts add "in the world" {N}.
33. Same phrase as in v 11. Omitting the following "and", and reading "whom" instead of "which", some manuscripts say "I was keeping in Your name they whom You have given *to* Me. I guarded *them*...", which could also be arranged "I was keeping them in Your name. I guarded whom You have given *to* Me" {B}.
34. Or, "protected", as in 2 Thes 3:3. This is a synonym of "keeping" in v 11, 12, with the similar meanings. On this word, see "keep" in 12:25. Perhaps Jesus means "I was preserving them... and I protected them".
35. On this word, see 2 Pet 2:1. Related to "perish". None perished (or, was lost) except the son of perishing, the one characterized by or belonging to this destiny. His character and actions belong to this destiny. The Antichrist is also called this in 2 Thes 2:3. The eleven were sons of light, sons of righteousness, sons of the kingdom, sons of God, etc.
36. Note 13:18.
37. As in v 11, some think Jesus means "ascending back to You"; others, "coming to You now in prayer".
38. Therefore, Father, do now for them what I was doing for them. Keep them.
39. Some think Jesus means "I am speaking this prayer out loud", as in 11:42; others, "I am speaking all the things I have spoken tonight, including this prayer".
40. This is the Greek word order, and means "I am speaking while still on earth, before I leave". Others render it "I am speaking these *things* so that **in the world** they may have", meaning "that they may have My joy in the world where they will remain when I leave". In this case the Greek word order is used to emphasize "in the world".
41. That is, the joy of a holy, fruit-bearing, obedient-to-the-end, relationship with the Father, as in 15:11. It is this joy that the disciples are hearing tonight and in this prayer, and that Jesus desires for them in its fullness.
42. This is a participle, "having been made full" or complete. Same word as in 16:24.

A. Act 15:33 B. Rev 7:14 C. Act 23:11 D. 2 Cor 11:20 E. Rom 8:30 F. Lk 1:34 G. Jn 7:28 H. 1 Jn 5:18 J. 1 Cor 12:8 K. Jn 1:12
L. Mt 14:33 M. 1 Cor 1:18 N. 2 Pet 3:16 O. Rom 9:13

1D. "I am not praying^A that You take them out of the world, but that You keep^B them from the evil *one*[1] — 15

2D. "They are not of the world, just as **I** am not of the world—*set them apart[2] in[3] the[4] truth. Your word[5] is truth^C — 16-17

    1E. "Just as You sent Me forth^D into the world,[6] **I** also sent them forth into the world — 18

    2E. "And **I** am setting apart Myself for them,[7] in order that **they** may also be set apart[8] in truth[9] — 19

4C. "And **I** am not praying^A for these *ones* only, but also for the *ones* believing[10] in Me through their word[11] — 20

    1D. "That[12] they[13] may all be[14] one[15]— just as[16] You, Father, *are* in Me and I *am* in You, that[17] **they** also may be[18] in[19] Us — 21

        1E. "In order that the world may be believing^E that **You** sent Me forth[20]

    2D. "And **I** have given them the glory which You have given *to* Me[21] — 22

        1E. "In order that they may be one[22] just as We *are* one—*I in them and You in Me[23] — 23

        2E. "In order that they may be perfected[24] into one

            1F. "In order that[25] the world may be knowing^F that **You** sent Me forth, and loved^G them[26] just as You loved Me

1. Or, "from evil". This is the negative statement of what is positively asked in v 11.
2. Or, "sanctify, consecrate". Set the disciples apart from the world to You in the sphere of the truth, or by means of the truth, which is Your word. Some think Jesus means "make them morally holy", in which case this word has a different sense in v 19; others, "set them apart for Your service", for the mission on which I sent them, v 18. On this word, see "sanctify" in Heb 10:29.
3. That is, "in the sphere of". Or, "by, with, by means of". GK *1877*.
4. Some manuscripts say "Your" {N}.
5. Note that Jesus says "I have given them Your word (v 14)... set them apart in the truth (Your word)".
6. Compare 10:36, where the Father "set Jesus apart" to His mission and "sent Him forth" into the world, using the same two words as here in v 16-19. On "sent forth", see "send out" in Mk 3:14.
7. That is, Jesus is setting Himself apart to God in His own mission, His work and death for the disciples' sake.
8. This is a participle, be "having been set apart". Jesus sets Himself apart to God in the completing of His mission for the purpose that the disciples may be set apart to God in their mission. Their mission proceeds from His, and from Him.
9. Some think Jesus means "in *Your* truth"; others, "truly". On this word, see 4:23.
10. Some manuscripts say "the *ones who* will believe" {N}.
11. That is, through the mission on which Jesus sent them (v 18), the mission centered in His truth and word (v 17). The entire church is viewed as proceeding from the word of these eleven; as built on their foundation, Eph 2:20.
12. Some think Jesus is stating the content of His request, as this word is used in v 15. Others think He is stating the purpose of His prayer for them all, and render this "in order that", as it is used in v 11. In this case, Jesus means that He is not praying "Keep them" and "Set them apart" for the eleven alone, but for all believers, "in order that they may all be one". GK *2671*. Consult the commentaries on v 21-23.
13. Some think "they all" means all believers including the eleven (that all believers may be one); others, that Jesus is praying separately for the future believers (that such ones all may be one).
14. Same grammar as in "be one" in v 11, 22; "be in us" in v 21, and "be with Me" in v 24. The grammar implies "be continuously being, be being, be in a state of being" with reference to a state entered in the future (as in v 24), or a state continuing in existence from the present ("keep on being"). If the oneness is dependent on the coming Spirit, then the former is in view here. The word and grammar does not mean "become, get to be". GK *1639*.
15. Jesus could mean "one with Us" or "one with each other". Some think He defines this with the following phrase, "that they may be in Us". In this case, He is praying for a spiritual oneness with the Father and Son; a living, fruit-bearing relationship with God; an "abiding in Me and I in You" (15:4), which is the fountainhead of behaviors that result in the world believing. From this oneness, the love of God in us (v 26) flows outward in word and deed. Others think Jesus is praying for a oneness or unity with each other, which is based on our faith in Christ, and results in the world believing. Some holding this view think He is praying for an ethical oneness or likeness shared by His people, a oneness of love (13:34), character, purpose, and action; others, for a living unity of believers, a mystical body or unit of believers standing versus the world, which expresses itself in this ethical behavior.
16. Jesus compares this oneness to Their oneness. It is like Their oneness in some respects, but not equivalent to it. Ours is a oneness based on adoption and grace; Theirs, on essence, on likeness of nature and character.
17. Some think Jesus means "in order that they may be one with Us in a similar way to how we are one with each other". The Father does His works in the Son (14:10), and the Son is in the Father. They are one (10:30), yet distinct. In a similar but not identical way, the Father and Son work in believers (14:12, 15:7), and we are in Them, and one with Them. Others think Jesus means "in order that they may be one with each another in a mystical spiritual oneness that is similar to how we are one with each other". Others view this as a second request, parallel to the first, making it point 2D.
18. Some manuscripts add "one" {B}, so that it says "be one in us".
19. That is, in union with Us, abiding in Us (15:4), having Our life in them. GK *1877*.
20. Some think Jesus means this will occur by means of our oneness with God, as we share His Name, His word, and His love; others, by means of our oneness with one another, our compelling unity.
21. Some think Jesus means the glory He made known as the Incarnate Son (v 6, 8, 14, 26); the glory of Your Name, Your word; the glory the disciples saw and heard in Him (1:14; 2:11); the glory revealed in His life and death, the glory of His person, full of grace and truth. We are still being transformed by this glory, 2 Cor 3:18. Others think Jesus is referring ahead to His exalted glory after His ascension, the glory of His exalted Person working through them, 14:13-14. Others think He means the glory of humble service to God, of taking up your cross and serving God; others, the glory of the divine nature indwelling them (2 Pet 1:4), of "I in them", v 23.
22. Thus the oneness is based on the glory Jesus has given to His followers. He gave the glory to bring about the oneness.
23. This is an abbreviated statement of "I in them and them in Me, Me in You and You in Me", defining the oneness.
24. Jesus gave the glory in order that His disciples might be made perfect or complete in the oneness, brought completely into the oneness, a purpose that will be fully reached after this life. Thus He gave the glory both that they "may be being one" (may be in a state of oneness), and that they "may be perfected into one" (may grow to completeness in that state). This means the oneness is a growing thing, growing with faith. Some think Jesus is referring to a growing experience of the Father and Son, a growing relationship to them with all its results; others, to a growing unity among believers. This is a participle, be "having been perfected". On this word, see Heb 2:10.
25. The growing oneness as possessors and proclaimers of the glory Jesus gave will bring about this result. Some manuscripts say "And in order that the world..." {N}.
26. That is, believers, the "them" in v 22.

A. Jn 17:9 B. 1 Jn 5:18 C. Jn 4:23 D. Mk 3:14, send out E. Jn 3:36 F. Lk 1:34 G. Jn 21:15, devotedly love

John 17:24	374	Verse

      5C. "Father, *as to* what[1] You have given[2] *to* Me, I desire[3] that those *ones* also may be with Me where **I** am,[4] in order that they may be seeing My glory[5] which You have given *to* Me because You loved Me before *the* foundation *of the* world[6]   24

      6C. "Righteous Father, indeed the world did not know You— but **I** knew You   25

          1D. "And these[7] *ones* knew that **You** sent Me forth

          2D. "And I made Your name known *to* them, and will make *it* known, in order that the love[A]   26
with which You loved Me may be in[8] them, and I *may be* in them"

14A.[9] Having said these *things*, Jesus went-out[10] with His disciples to the other side *of* the ravine[11] *of* Kidron where there was *a* garden[B], into which He entered, He and His disciples   18:1

   1B.[12] Now Judas, the *one* handing Him over[C], also knew the place— because Jesus often was gathered there with His disciples. ˚So Judas— having received[13] the [Roman] cohort[14], and officers[15] from the chief priests and from the Pharisees— comes there with lanterns[16] and torches[D] and weapons[E]   2
                                                                                                 3

   2B. Then Jesus, knowing all the *things* coming upon Him, went forth   4

      1C. And He says *to* them, "Whom are you seeking[F]?"

          1D. They answered Him, "Jesus the Nazarene[G]"   5
          2D. He[17] says *to* them, "**I** am[18] *He*"
          3D. Now Judas,[19] the *one* handing Him over, was also standing *there* with them

      2C. So when He said *to* them, "**I** am *He*", they went back,[20] and fell on the ground. ˚Then He again asked them, "Whom are you seeking?"   6-7

          1D. And the *ones* said, "Jesus the Nazarene"
          2D. Jesus responded, "I told you that **I** am *He*. If then you are seeking Me, permit[H] these *ones* to go"   8

                1E. In order that the word which He spoke[21] might be fulfilled[J], that "*The ones* whom You have given Me— I did not lose any of them"   9

      3C. Then Simon Peter, having *a* sword[K], drew[22] it and hit the slave[L] *of* the high priest, and cut-off[M] his right ear[N]. And *the* name *for* the slave was Malchus   10
      4C. Then Jesus said *to* Peter, "Put[O] the[23] sword into the sheath. The cup which the[24] Father has given Me— shall not I drink it?"[25]   11

   3B.[26] Then the [Roman] cohort[P] and *its* commander[27], and the officers[28] *of* the Jews, arrested[29] Jesus, and bound[Q] Him. ˚And they led[30] *Him* to Annas[R] first   12
                                                                                                 13

      1C. For he was *the* father-in-law *of* Caiaphas[S], who was *the* high priest *of* that year. ˚And Caiaphas was the *one* having counseled[31] the Jews that it was[32] better *that* one Man die for the people[33]   14
      2C. Now Simon Peter and another disciple[34] were following Jesus   15

          1D. And that disciple was known[T] *to* the high priest, and he entered with Jesus into the courtyard[U] *of* the high priest.[35] ˚But Peter was standing at the door outside   16
          2D. So the other disciple— the *one* known[T] *by* the high priest— went out and spoke *to* the doorkeeper, and brought in Peter
          3D. Then the doorkeeper[36] servant-girl[37] says *to* Peter, "**You** are not also *one* of the disciples *of* this man, *are you*?"[38] That *one* says, "I am not"   17

1. That is, the totality of believers, viewed as an abstract whole, as in "all that" in v 2. Compare 10:29. It is made personal and individual by "those *ones*" in the next phrase. Some manuscripts say, "whom" {B}, which may be arranged as "Father, I desire that those also whom You have given *to* Me may be...".
2. Jesus refers to the disciples with this word also in v 2, 6, 9, 11.
3. Or, "want, will, wish". On this word, see "willing" in 7:17.
4. Thus Jesus refers back to the point He first made with them, 13:33. Note that all of v 6-23 concerns the disciples while they remain in the world; this concerns them after they leave this world.
5. This is the glory to which Jesus is returning (v 5), His unveiled glory as Jesus the Son of God. Thus there are three kinds or aspects of glory: His glory as the eternal Word with God (1:1; 17:5), His glory on earth as the Incarnate Son (1:14), and His glory as the exalted Son, crowned with glory and honor, sitting at the right hand of God, King of kings, Lord of lords (17:24). The latter two were "given" to Jesus, the Son of God; the first is His eternally, by nature.
6. On the phrase "before the foundation of the world", see 1 Pet 1:20.
7. That is, the eleven.
8. Both here and next, Jesus may mean "within" (as in 14:20), or "among", or both, since one implies the other. GK *1877*.
9. Parallel account at Mt 26:36; Mk 14:32; Lk 22:39.
10. In conjunction with one's view of 14:31, this either means "from the upper room" (making this leaving parallel to Mt 26:30; Mk 14:26); or, "from the city".
11. Or, "brook". This word was used of a ravine, and of the stream that flowed through it in the winter. Used only here. GK *5929*.
12. Parallel account at Mt 26:47; Mk 14:43; Lk 22:47.
13. Or, "taken". On this word, see "taken" in Rom 7:8.
14. On this word, see Mt 27:27. Same word as in v 12. How many were in this detachment is not stated.
15. Same word as in v 12.
16. Used only here. GK *5749*.
17. Some manuscripts say "Jesus" {C}.
18. On this phrase, which is repeated in v 6 and 8, see "I am" in 8:58.
19. Some think Judas kissed Jesus before the question in v 4; others, after v 6 or 9.
20. On the phrase "went back", see 6:66. John does not say how many fell, or what was in their hearts. Some think it was because Judas and the religious leaders in front were stepping back to allow the officers to come forward and seize Him. Others think they were fearful, perhaps fearful Jesus would do some work of power. Others think this was a work of power and glory, emphasizing again that He was voluntarily surrendering.
21. That is, in 17:12. "Lose" here is the same word as "perish" there, the grammar being different. On this word, see "perish" in 1 Cor 1:18.
22. On this word, see 6:44. Mt 26:51, Mk 14:47, and Jn 18:10 each use a different word.
23. Some manuscripts say "your" {K}.
24. Some manuscripts say "My" {N}.
25. The grammar indicates a "yes" answer is expected. Yes, He will drink it.
26. Parallel account at Mt 26:57; Mk 14:53; Lk 22:54.
27. Or, "tribune", the Roman commander of the cohort. On this word, see Act 21:31, where another such commander rescues Paul.
28. That is, the temple police, as also in Mt 26:28; Mk 14:54, 65; Jn 7:32, 45, 46; 18:3, 18, 22; 19:6; Act 5:22, 26. They were Levites. On this word, see "attendants" in 1 Cor 4:1. GK *5677*. Their leader is called a "captain", Act 5:26.
29. Or, "seized". Same word as in Lk 22:54.
30. Some manuscripts say "led *Him* away..." {N}.
31. Same word as in Rev 3:18. Elsewhere only as "plotted" in Mt 26:4; Act 9:23. GK *5205*. Related to "consultation" in Mk 15:1; and "counselor" in Rom 11:34.
32. More literally, "is", as the Greek typically phrases it.
33. This advice is recorded in 11:50.
34. Some think this is John himself; others, perhaps a non-apostle. John is the "other disciple" in 20:2-8.
35. Some think this is the courtyard of the palace of Annas, at which Caiaphas also lived. In any case, the scene does not change, for Peter is still standing there warming himself from v 18 to v 25.
36. Elsewhere only in v 16; Mk 13:34; Jn 10:3. GK *2601*. Related to "door" in Col 4:3.
37. That is, the person the disciple spoke to in v 16. The doorkeeper was a servant girl. Same word as in Mt 26:69; Mk 14:66, 69; Lk 22:56, and as "female servants" in Lk 12:45; and "slave woman" in Gal 4:22. Used 13 times. GK *4087*.
38. The grammar indicates that a "no" answer is expected.

A. 1 Jn 4:16   B. Jn 19:41   C. Mt 26:21, hand over   D. Mt 25:1, lamps   E. Rom 13:12   F. Phil 2:21   G. Mt 2:23   H. Mt 6:12, forgive   J. Eph 5:18, filled   K. Eph 6:17   L. Rom 6:17   M. Gal 5:12   N. Mk 14:47   O. Rev 2:2, throw   P. Mt 27:27   Q. 1 Cor 7:27   R. Lk 3:2   S. Lk 3:2   T. Rom 1:19   U. Mt 26:3

| John 18:18 | 376 | Verse |

        4D. And the slaves[A] and the officers,[1] having made *a* charcoal-fire[B] because it was cold, were standing *there* and warming *themselves*. And Peter was also with them, standing *there* and warming *himself*   18

    3C. So the high priest[2] questioned[C] Jesus about His disciples, and about His teaching[D]   19

        1D. Jesus answered him, "**I** have spoken[3] *in* public[4] *to* the world. **I** always taught at synagogue, and in the temple, where all[5] the Jews come together. And I spoke nothing in secret[E]. °Why are you questioning Me? Question the *ones* having heard what I spoke *to* them. Look, these *ones* know *the things* which **I** said"   20, 21

        2D. And He having said these *things*, one *of* the officers standing near gave Jesus *a* slap[6], having said, "In this manner do you answer the high priest?"   22

            1E. Jesus answered him, "If I spoke wrongly, testify about the *thing* wrong. But if *I spoke* rightly, why do you beat[7] Me?"   23

    4C. Then Annas[F] sent Him forth, having been bound[G], to Caiaphas[H] the high priest   24

    5C. And Simon Peter is standing *there* and warming *himself*   25

        1D. So they said *to* him, "**You** are not also *one* of His disciples, *are you*?"[8] That *one* denied[J] *it* and said, "I am not"

        2D. One of the slaves[A] *of* the high priest— being *a* relative[K] *of the one of* whom Peter cut-off[L] the ear— says, "Did **I** not see you in the garden[M] with Him?"[9] °Then again Peter denied[J] *it*   26, 27

        3D. And immediately[N] *a* rooster crowed

  4B.[10] Then they lead Jesus from Caiaphas to the Praetorium[11]. And it was early-morning[12]. And they themselves did not enter into the Praetorium, in order that they might not be defiled[13], but might eat[14] the Passover[15] [Feast[16]]   28

    1C. So Pilate[O] went outside to them   29

        1D. And he says, "What accusation[P] do you bring against this man?"

        2D. They responded and said *to* him, "If this *One* were not doing wrong[17], we would not have handed Him over *to* you"   30

        3D. So Pilate said *to* them, "**You** take Him, and judge[Q] Him according to[18] your Law"   31

        4D. The[19] Jews said *to* him, "It is not lawful[20] *for* **us** to execute[R] anyone"

            1E. In order that the word *of* Jesus might be fulfilled, which He spoke signifying[21] *by* what kind of death He was going to die   32

    2C. So Pilate entered again into the Praetorium, and called Jesus   33

        1D. And he said *to* Him, "Are **You** the King *of* the Jews?"

        2D. Jesus answered[22], "Are **you** saying this from yourself,[23] or did others tell you about Me?"   34

        3D. Pilate answered, "**I** am not *a* Jew, *am I*?[24] **Your** nation[S] and the chief priests handed You over *to* me. What did You do?"   35

        4D. Jesus answered, "My kingdom[25] is not of this world. If My kingdom were of this world, My servants[26] would be fighting[T] in order that I might not be handed-over[U] *to* the Jews[27]. But as-it-is[28], My kingdom is not from here"   36

        5D. Therefore Pilate said *to* Him, "So-then **You** are *a* king?"[29]   37

1. That is, the slaves of the high priest, and the officers of the temple (the Levites). The Romans are gone.
2. Some think John means Annas, who is also called high priest in Lk 3:2; Act 4:6 (just as we continue to call ex-officials by their former titles); others, Caiaphas, in an informal meeting in Annas's quarters before the official one in v 24.
3. Some manuscripts say "I spoke" {N}.
4. Or, "*with* openness". Same word as in 7:4.
5. Some manuscripts say "where the Jews always" {N}.
6. Or, "blow". This word means a blow with a club or rod, or a slap with an open hand. Jesus calls it a "beating" in v 23. Elsewhere only as "slap" in 19:3; Mk 14:65. GK *4825*. The related verb is in Mt 5:39.
7. Elsewhere only in Mt 21:35; Mk 12:3, 5; 13:9; Lk 12:47, 48; 20:10, 11; 22:63; Act 5:40; 16:37; 22:19; 1 Cor 9:26; 2 Cor 11:20. GK *1296*.
8. The grammar indicates a "no" answer is expected.
9. The grammar indicates a "yes" answer is expected.
10. Parallel account at Mt 27:1, 11; Mk 15:1; Lk 23:1.
11. That is, the Roman palace or fortress, Pilate's residence while in Jerusalem. On this word, see Phil 1:13.
12. Same word as "early in the morning" in Mk 15:1, and related to the word in Mt 27:1. Same word as "early in the morning" in Jn 20:1 where "while still being dark" is added. On this word, see Mk 13:35. John may mean in the hour before or after 6 A.M.
13. On this word, see Tit 1:15. Here it means "made ceremonially unclean". Some think John is referring to a seven-day defilement; others, to a one-day defilement.
14. All the other uses of the phrase "eat the Passover" refer to the final meal Jesus ate with His disciples on the previous night, Mt 26:17; Mk 14:12, 14; Lk 22:8, 11, 15. Note 2 Chron 30:22.
15. Elsewhere only with reference to the Passover [lamb] in Mk 14:12; Lk 22:7; 1 Cor 5:7; the Passover [meal] in Mt 26:17, 18, 19; Mk 14:12, 14, 16; Lk 22:8, 11, 13, 15; Heb 11:28; and the Passover [Feast] in Mt 26:2; Mk 14:1; Lk 2:41; 22:1; Jn 2:13, 23; 6:4; 11:55; 12:1; 13:1; 18:39; 19:14; Act 12:4. The Feast of Unleavened Bread (see Mk 14:12) was also called Passover, Lk 22:1; Act 12:4; Jn 2:23. Three Passovers are explicitly named in John (2:13; 6:4; 11:55), and some think 5:1 refers to a fourth. GK *4247*.
16. Or, "[meal]". Some think John means "celebrate the Feast", and is referring to these leaders' continuing participation in the meals of the Passover Feast. Others think he means "eat the Passover meal", indicating they had not yet eaten it. Of those holding this view, some think it implies that the meal in Jn 13:1 was not the Passover meal, but a meal "before" it. Others think the Passover meal may have been eaten by the Jews on two different evenings based on two different calendars, so that both meals were Passover meals. See 13:1, 29; 19:14, 31. Consult the commentaries on these and other views.
17. Or, "causing harm", specifically implying "committing a crime". That is, doing a civil wrong, a criminal wrong. Same word as in Mt 27:23. On this word, see "evil" in 3 Jn 11. Some manuscripts say "was not *an* evildoer" {B}, using the related word found in 1 Pet 2:12, which also means "criminal".
18. That is, as your Law requires. I give you permission to judge Jesus as you see fit.
19. Some manuscripts say "So the..." {N}, which can also be rendered "Therefore the...".
20. That is, under Roman law. Execution is what Jewish Law would require, but Rome did not permit the Sanhedrin to execute.
21. Same word as in 12:33, where this statement is also found. Since the Romans executed using the cross, when the Jews handed Jesus over to them it sealed the fulfillment of the words of Jesus that He would be lifted up (not stoned).
22. Some manuscripts add "him" {N}.
23. The Jews were charging Jesus with a crime against Rome, with claiming to be a king in a political sense of interest to Pilate. Jesus asks if this is Pilate's meaning, or some other. On "from yourself ", see "from Himself " in 5:19.
24. The grammar indicates a "no" answer is expected.
25. Pilate indicates that he is repeating the Jews' accusation, so Jesus affirms that His kingdom is not earthly and political.
26. More literally, "the servants *to* Me". Same grammar as in "disciples *to* Me" in 15:8. On this word, see "attendants" in 1 Cor 4:1.
27. That is, the Jewish leaders. See 1:19.
28. Or, "But now". Jesus may mean this in a logical sense, "as it is"; or, in a temporal sense, "at the present time". GK *3814*.
29. The grammar indicates that a "yes" answer is expected. Some render this as an exclamation.

A. Rom 6:17　B. Jn 21:9　C. Jn 17:9, pray　D. 1 Cor 14:6　E. 1 Cor 4:5, hidden　F. Lk 3:2　G. 1 Cor 7:27　H. Lk 3:2　J. 2 Tim 2:12　K. Rom 16:7, kinsmen　L. Gal 5:12　M. Jn 19:41　N. Mt 13:5　O. Lk 3:1　P. Tit 1:6　Q. Mt 7:1　R. Rom 7:11, killed　S. Act 15:23, Gentiles　T. 1 Tim 4:10, struggle　U. Mt 26:21

| John 18:38 | 378 | Verse |

6D. Jesus answered, "**You** are saying that¹ I am *a* king. **I** have been born^A for this². And I have come into the world for this— that I might testify^B *to* the truth^C. Everyone being of the truth hears³ My voice"

7D. Pilate says *to* Him, "What is truth?" — 38

3C. And having said this, he again went out to the Jews

    1D. And he says *to* them, "**I** find **no** charge⁴ in⁵ Him. °But it is *a* custom^D *for* you that I release^E one *prisoner for* you at the Passover [Feast]. So do you wish me to release⁶ the King *of* the Jews *for* you?" — 39

    2D. Then they⁷ shouted^F back⁸, saying, "Not this *One*, but Barabbas^G!" — 40

        1E. Now Barabbas was *a* robber⁹

4C. So at that time¹⁰ Pilate¹¹ took Jesus and whipped¹² Him — 19:1

    1D.¹³ And the soldiers^H, having woven *a* crown^J out of thorns^K, put *it* on His head. And they clothed Him with *a* purple garment. °And they were coming to Him and saying¹⁴, "Hail^L, King *of* the Jews!" And they were giving Him slaps^M — 2, 3

5C. And¹⁵ Pilate again went outside — 4

    1D. And he says *to* them, "Look— I am bringing Him outside *to* you in order that you may know that I find no charge in Him"

    2D. Then Jesus came outside, wearing the crown made-of-thorns^N and the purple garment — 5

    3D. And he says *to* them, "Behold, the man!"

    4D. Then when they saw Him, the chief priests and the officers^O shouted^F, saying, "Crucify^P, crucify¹⁶!" — 6

    5D. Pilate says *to* them, "**You** take Him and crucify *Him*, for **I** do not find *a* charge in Him"

    6D. The Jews¹⁷ responded *to* him, "**We** have *a* law.¹⁸ And according to the¹⁹ law He ought to die, because He made Himself *to be* God's Son" — 7

6C. Then when Pilate heard this statement^Q, he became more afraid. °And he entered into the Praetorium again — 8-9

    1D. And he says *to* Jesus, "Where are **You** from?"

    2D. But Jesus did not give him *an* answer

    3D. So Pilate says *to* Him, "You do not speak *to* me? Do You not know that I have authority^R to release^E You, and I have authority to crucify You?"²⁰ — 10

    4D. Jesus answered him²¹, "You *would* not have any authority against²² Me unless it²³ had been given²⁴ *to* you from above. For this reason the *one*²⁵ having handed Me over *to* you has *a* greater²⁶ sin" — 11

7C. From this *time*²⁷, Pilate was seeking²⁸ to release^E Him — 12

    1D. But the Jews shouted²⁹ saying, "If you release^E this *One*, you are not *a* friend^S *of* Caesar^T. Everyone making himself the king is speaking-against^U Caesar"

8C. Therefore Pilate, having heard these words³⁰, brought Jesus outside, and sat on *a* judgment-seat^V in *a* place being called '*The* Pavement³¹' (but *in* Hebrew, 'Gabbatha') — 13

1. Some think this idiom means "Yes". Others think that the meaning comes from the context. Here, Jesus means "you are saying [correctly] that I am a king", as He states directly next. Some render this word "because", that is, "you are saying it [correctly], because I am *a* king". GK *4022*. On this phrase, see Mt 27:11.
2. That is, to be a king.
3. That is, listens to and obeys. On this word, see Act 22:9.
4. Or, "guilt, blame, fault, cause, reason, ground of accusation, case". It is used of a "charge, accusation" and the "guilt, blame, reason" underlying it. Same word as in 19:4, 6; as the "charge" posted above Jesus' head in Mt 27:37; Mk 15:26; as the "charge" worthy of death in Act 13:28; and as "reason" in Mt 19:3. Used 20 times. GK *162*. Related to "guilt" in Lk 23:4, 14, 22.
5. That is, in His case, in connection with Him. GK *1877*. I am finding no guilt or basis of a charge; no case or charge (from the Roman law point of view) in connection with Jesus. From the answer Jesus gave, Pilate clearly sees that He is not a political revolutionary, or a threat to Rome. The case is religious, not political or criminal.
6. This is an idiom, literally, "do you wish *that* I should release...".
7. Some manuscripts add "all"; others add "all" and omit "back" {N}.
8. Or, "again". This is the first shout. On this word, see "again" in Mk 15:13.
9. Or, "insurrectionist". Compare Mk 15:7; Lk 23:19. On this word, see Mt 21:13.
10. This phrase "So at-that-time" is elsewhere only in 11:14; 19:16; 20:8.
11. Implied in this is a trip back inside the Praetorium.
12. This is not the same word as in Mt 27:26; Mk 15:15. Lk 23:16 uses a third word. Some think all these verses refer to the same beating, making this parallel to Mt 27:27. Others think the one in John and Luke was a milder whipping, and the one in Matthew and Mark was the much more serious flogging or scourging that preceded Roman crucifixions. On this word, see Heb 12:6.
13. Compare Mt 27:27-31; Mk 15:16-20.
14. Some manuscripts omit "And they were coming to Him" {N}, so that it says "And they were saying".
15. Some manuscripts say "Then" {N}.
16. Some manuscripts add "Him" {N}.
17. That is, the Jewish leaders. See 1:19.
18. That is, a law regarding this case in the Law of Moses.
19. Some manuscripts say "our" {N}.
20. The grammar indicates a "yes" answer is expected. Some manuscripts reverse the two questions {N}.
21. Some manuscripts omit this word {C}.
22. Or, "in relation to". Same word as in 18:29. GK *2848*.
23. Grammatically, this does not refer to "authority" itself, but to a more abstract concept. Some think Jesus means "unless this situation, this handing over of Me to you"; others, "unless your exercising of authority over Me".
24. This is a participle, unless it "was having been given".
25. That is, Caiaphas, the high priest, the head of the nation.
26. Pilate was acting legally (within his judicial authority), though not morally (from God's viewpoint), in his treatment of Jesus. The high priest and the Sanhedrin who handed Jesus over to Pilate were acting immorally, unfairly, illegally, and in violation of their responsibility as God's priests.
27. Or, "*statement*". That is, from this point on; or, as a result of this statement. Same phrase as in 6:66.
28. Up to this point, Pilate has been trying to get the Jews to drop their demand for execution. Now he seeks a way to release Jesus unilaterally. But the Jews effectively prevent it. Another trip outside is implied here.
29. On this word, see Act 22:23. Some manuscripts say "were shouting"; others, "were crying out" {N}.
30. Some manuscripts have this singular {K}, so that it says "this statement" as in v 8.
31. Or, "the Mosaic", a place paved with stones. Used only here. GK *3346*.

A. 1 Jn 2:29   B. Jn 1:7   C. Jn 4:23   D. 1 Cor 11:16   E. Mt 5:31, sends away   F. Act 22:23   G. Mk 15:7   H. Mt 28:12   J. Rev 4:4   K. Lk 6:44
L. Mt 27:29   M. Jn 18:22   N. Mk 15:17   O. Jn 18:12   P. Mt 27:35   Q. 1 Cor 12:8, word   R. Rev 6:8   S. Lk 14:10   T. Lk 3:1   U. Rom 10:21, contradict   V. Rom 14:10

| John 19:14 | 380 | Verse |

       1D. Now it was Preparation[1] *day of* the Passover [Feast[2]]. *The* hour was about[3] *the* sixth[4]   14
       2D. And he says *to* the Jews, "Look— your King!"
       3D. Then those *ones* shouted[A], "Take *Him* away, take *Him* away, crucify Him!"   15
       4D. Pilate says *to* them, "Shall I crucify your King?"
       5D. The chief priests answered, "We do not have *a* king except Caesar"

    9C. So at that time he handed Him over *to* them[5] in order that He might be crucified   16

5B.[6] "So they took Jesus[7]. ˚And bearing[B] the cross *for* Himself[8], He went out to the *place* being called   17
"The Place *of a* Skull[C]" (which is called *in* Hebrew, "Golgotha"), ˚where they crucified[D] Him and   18
two others with Him— on this *side* and on this *side*[9], and Jesus in the middle[E]

    1C. And Pilate also wrote *a* title[10] and put *it* on the cross[F]. And it had been written[11], "Jesus the   19
Nazarene[G], the King *of* the Jews"

       1D. Therefore many *of* the Jews read this title, because the place where Jesus was crucified   20
was near the city.[12] And it had been written *in* Hebrew[13], Latin, Greek[14]
       2D. So the chief priests *of* the Jews were saying *to* Pilate, "Do not write, 'The King *of* the   21
Jews', but that that *One* said, 'I am King *of* the Jews'"
       3D. Pilate responded, "What I have written, I have written"   22

    2C. Then the soldiers[H], when they crucified Jesus, took His garments[J] and made four parts— *a*   23
part *for* each soldier— and the tunic[K]. Now the tunic was seamless, woven from the top
through *the* whole. ˚So they said to one another, "Let us not tear[15] it, but let us cast-lots[L] for   24
it *to decide* whose it will be"

       1D. In order that the Scripture [in Ps 22:18] might be fulfilled[M], the *one* saying,[16] "They
divided[N] My garments[J] among themselves, and they cast[O] *a* lot[P] for My clothing"
       2D. So indeed, the soldiers did these *things*

    3C. Now His mother, and the sister[17] *of* His mother, Mary[18] the *wife*[19] *of* Clopas, and Mary the   25
Magdalene[Q], were standing beside the cross *of* Jesus

       1D. So Jesus, having seen *His* mother and the disciple whom He was loving[20] standing near,   26
says *to His* mother, "Woman, look— your son!" ˚Then He says *to* the disciple, "Look—   27
your mother!" And from that hour the disciple took her into *his* own *things*[21]

    4C.[22] After this, Jesus— knowing that all *things* have already[23] been finished[24], in[25] order that the   28
Scripture [in Ps 69:21] might be accomplished[26]— says, "I am thirsty"

       1D. *A* jar[27] full *of* sour-wine[R] was setting[S] *there*. So having put *a* sponge full *of* the sour wine   29
on *a* hyssop *branch*,[28] they brought *it* to His mouth
       2D. Then when He received[T] the sour wine, Jesus said, "It has been finished[29]!"   30
       3D. And having bowed *His* head, He gave-over[30] *His* spirit

6B. Then the Jews— because it was Preparation[31] *day*, in order that the bodies might not remain[U] on   31
the cross during the Sabbath (for the day *of* that Sabbath[32] was *a* great[33] *day*)— asked Pilate that
their legs be broken[V], and they be taken away

    1C. So the soldiers came and broke the legs *of* the first *one,* and *of* the other *one* having been   32
crucified-with[W] Him

1. On this word, see v 31.
2. Or, "[meal]". Some think John means "the Friday of the Passover Feast", the preparation day for the Sabbath, as the word is normally used. This would allow the meal of the previous night in 13:1 to have been Passover. Others think he means "the day of preparation for the Passover [meal]" coming that night, a Passover which coincided with the Sabbath that year, v 31, 42. This would mean that the meal in 13:1 was a meal "before" the Passover, and that Jesus died while the Passover lambs were being sacrificed. See 13:1; 19:31; 18:28.
3. Some manuscripts say "[Feast], and about *the* sixth hour" {N}.
4. Mark 15:25 says Jesus was crucified at the third hour, counted from sunrise, 9 A.M. Mt 27:45, Mk 15:33, and Lk 23:44 say that darkness fell at the sixth hour, noon. Some think John means noon. Others think he uses Roman time, counted from noon, as also in 1:39; 4:6, 52; making this 6 A.M. In other words, around 6 A.M., shortly after the beginning of the day, Jesus was about to be sentenced by Pilate. Others think the times are both correct, being approximate only since people in that day had no precise means of timekeeping. In our terms, the end of the third hour is 9 A.M. The beginning of the sixth hour is 11 A.M. If "about" is allowed to mean "within an hour or two of ", then both Mark and John could mean about 10 A.M. Some manuscripts say "third", agreeing with Mk 15:25 {N}.
5. Some think John means to the chief priests last mentioned, that is, to their will; others, to the soldiers who would carry this out.
6. Parallel account at Mt 27:31; Mk 15:20; Lk 23:26.
7. Some manuscripts add "and led *Him*"; others say "and the *ones* having taken Jesus led *Him* away" {B}.
8. Or, "*by* Himself ". Same word as "His *own*" in Lk 14:27, but different grammar. It was Roman custom to make the condemned carry it to the place of execution. Some manuscripts say "bearing His cross, He went..." {N}.
9. This is an idiom, literally, "from here and from here", John pointing out with the right hand and the left as he stood facing Jesus on the cross. Compare Rev 22:2.
10. Or, "notice, inscription". Elsewhere only in v 20. GK *5518*.
11. This is a participle, it "was having been written". Same word as in v 20.
12. Or, "because the place *of* the city where Jesus was crucified was near", which means the same thing.
13. That is, the language of the Hebrews at that time, which modern linguists call Aramaic. Elsewhere only in 5:2; 19:13, 17; 20:16; Rev 9:11; 16:16. GK *1580*. Related to the word in Act 6:1, and in Act 21:40.
14. Some manuscripts say "Hebrew, Greek, Latin" {N}.
15. Or, "split, divide". Same word as in 21:11. On this word, see Mt 27:51.
16. Some manuscripts omit "the *one* saying" {C}.
17. Some think that the three women mentioned in Mt 27:56 and Mk 15:40 are also mentioned here, with the addition of Mary His mother, making four women here. Under this suggestion, this sister would be the Salome mentioned in Mk 15:40, and the mother of the sons of Zebedee in Mt 27:56, making the apostles James and John (Mt 10:2) the cousins of Jesus. Mary of Clopas here would be the mother of James and Joseph mentioned in Mt 27:56; Mk 15:40. Others do not attempt to link the names, since "many other" women were there also, Mt 27:55; Mk 15:41.
18. Some think there are four women here, punctuating it "His mother and the sister *of* His mother, Mary the *wife of* Clopas and Mary the Magdalene", grouping family and friends. Others think three are named, "His mother, and the sister *of* His mother (Mary the *wife of* Clopas), and Mary Magdalene", meaning the sisters had the same name.
19. Or, "*daughter, sister*".
20. See 13:23 on this disciple. It is John himself.
21. That is, into his own interests and pursuits, into his own household, under his care. Same phrase in 1:11; 16:32; Act 21:6. "Own *things*" is also in Lk 18:28; Jn 8:44; 1 Thes 4:11.
22. Parallel account at Mt 27:45; Mk 15:33; Lk 23:44.
23. Or, "now, by this time". On this word, see Mt 24:32.
24. Same word as in v 30.
25. This may refer to what precedes, "finished in order that... fulfilled, says", instead of what follows.
26. Or, "fulfilled". This word is related to "finished", and is used only here with regard to the Scripture being fulfilled. Same word as in 4:34; 17:4.
27. Some manuscripts say "Therefore *a* jar..." {N}, which can also be rendered "Now *a* jar...".
28. Some manuscripts say instead "And the *ones*, having filled *a* sponge *with* sour wine and having put *it* on *a* hyssop *branch*, brought..." {N}.
29. Or, "fulfilled, completed". Same word as in v 28. On this word, see Rev 10:7.
30. Or, "delivered, handed over". It is the same word used of Judas and the priests "handing over" Jesus (see Mt 26:21 on it).
31. That is, Friday, the day before the Sabbath, as seen here and in Mk 15:42; Lk 23:54. Elsewhere only in Mt 27:62; Jn 19:14, 42. GK *4187*. It was called such because all preparations for the Sabbath had to be made by sunset, when the Sabbath began and no work was permitted. Some think this Friday afternoon was the afternoon after the Passover meal. Others think it was the afternoon before it. See 13:1; 19:14; Mk 14:12. Consult the commentaries.
32. A similar phrase, "the day *of* the Sabbath", is in Lk 4:16; 13:14, 16; 14:5; Act 13:14; 16:13.
33. Same word as in 7:37. That is, this Sabbath was a special Sabbath. Some think it coincided with the Passover meal and the first day of the Feast of Unleavened Bread, which was a great day of that Feast (a "holy convocation", Ex 12:16; Lev 23:7). This would mean the Passover lambs were beginning to be sacrificed at the time when Jesus died, and that the Passover meal would be eaten that night, on the Sabbath. Others think it was special because of a sheaf offering made on it (Lev 23:11), or simply because it was the Sabbath that came during this holy Feast week. This would mean the meal of the previous night in 13:1 was the normal Passover meal. See also 18:28; 19:14; Mk 14:12. On this word, see Heb 11:24.

A. Act 22:23 B. Mt 8:17, carry C. Mt 27:33 D. Mt 27:35 E. 2 Thes 2:7, midst F. Mt 10:38 G. Mt 2:23 H. Mt 28:12 J. 1 Pet 3:3 K. Mt 5:40 L. 2 Pet 1:1, receive M. Eph 5:18, filled N. Act 2:3 O. Rev 2:22, throw P. Col 1:12, share Q. Lk 8:2 R. Mt 27:48 S. Mt 3:10, lying T. Rom 7:8, taken U. Jn 15:4, abide V. Jn 19:33 W. Rom 6:6

2C.	But having come to Jesus, when they saw Him already dead[1], they did not break[2] His legs. °But one *of* the soldiers stabbed[3] His side *with a* spear, and immediately[A] blood and water came out[4]	33-34

    1D. And the one having seen[5] *it* has testified[B], and his testimony[C] is true[D]. And that *one*[6] knows that he is speaking true[7] *things*, so that **you** also may believe[8]   35

        1E. For these *things* took place in order that the Scripture [in Ex 12:46] might be fulfilled, "*A* bone *of* His will not be broken[9]". °And again another Scripture [Zech 12:10] says, "They will look at *the One* Whom they pierced[10]"   36 / 37

7B.[11] Now after these *things* Joseph from Arimathea[E]— being *a* disciple[F] *of* Jesus, but having been hidden[12] because of the fear[G] *of* the Jews— asked Pilate in order that he might take away the body *of* Jesus   38

    1C. And Pilate permitted[H] *it*
    2C. So he came and took away His[13] body. °And Nicodemus also came— the *one* having first come to Him *by* night— bringing *a* mixture *of* myrrh[J] and aloes[14], about *a* hundred pounds[15]   39

        1D. So they took the body *of* Jesus and bound[K] *it in* linen-cloths[16] with the spices[L], as is *the* custom[M] *for* the Jews to prepare-for-burial[N]   40
        2D. Now there was *a* garden[17] in the place where He was crucified. And in the garden *was a* new tomb[O] in which no one yet had been laid[18]. °So there— because of the Preparation[P] day *of* the Jews, because the tomb was near— they laid Jesus   41 / 42

15A.[19] Now *on* the first day *of* the week, Mary the Magdalene[20] goes to the tomb early-in-the-morning[Q]— *there* still being darkness[R]— and sees the stone having been taken away from the tomb   20:1

    1B. So she runs[S] and comes to Simon Peter, and to the other disciple whom Jesus was loving[21]. And she says *to* them, "They took the Lord out of the tomb, and we do not know where they put Him"   2
    2B. So Peter and the other disciple went forth, and were going to the tomb. °And the two were running together   3-4

        1C. And the other disciple ran ahead faster[T] *than* Peter, and came to the tomb first. °And having stooped-to-look[22], he sees the linen-cloths lying[U] *there*, but he did not enter   5
        2C. Then Simon Peter also[23] comes, following him. And he entered into the tomb. And he sees the linen-cloths lying *there*,[24] °and the face-cloth[V] which was on His head— not lying[U] with the linen-cloths, but apart-from *them*, having been wrapped-up[25] in one place   6 / 7
        3C. So at that time the other disciple also entered— the *one* having come to the tomb first— and saw and believed.[26] °For they did not yet understand[W] the Scripture[27]— that He must[X] rise-up[Y] from *the* dead   8 / 9
        4C. Then the disciples went away again to them[28]   10

    3B.[29] Now Mary[30] was standing outside at the tomb, weeping[Z]   11

        1C. Then as she was weeping, she stooped-to-look into the tomb. °And she sees two angels in white, sitting— one at the head and one at the feet where the body *of* Jesus was lying[U]   12
        2C. And those *ones* say *to* her, "Woman, why are you weeping?"   13
        3C. She says *to* them, "Because[31] they took my Lord[AA], and I do not know[W] where they put Him"
        4C. Having[32] said these *things*, she turned back[33], and sees Jesus[34] standing *there*. And she did not know[W] that it was[35] Jesus   14

            1D. Jesus says *to* her, "Woman[BB], why are you weeping? Whom are you seeking[CC]?"   15

1. This is a participle, "having died, being dead". GK *2569*.
2. Same word as in v 31, 32. Elsewhere only in Mt 12:20. GK *2862*.
3. Or, "pierced, pricked". Used only here. GK *3817*. Related to "pierced" in Act 2:37.
4. Thus verifying the reality of the physical death of Jesus. On the various symbolic meanings given to this, consult the commentaries. John mentions "blood and water" again in 1 Jn 5:6, 8.
5. John seems to be referring to himself. He was an eyewitness of the fact that no bone was broken, and that the soldiers pierced the side of Jesus. He states this because both these things are fulfillments of prophecies, as he says next. Others think John is referring to some other disciple.
6. Or, "that *One*". Some think John is referring to himself; others, to God; others, to Jesus.
7. This word is plural here. On this word, see 6:55.
8. Some manuscripts say "may be believing" {C}, meaning, "may continue believing". See 20:31.
9. On this word, see "bruised" in Mt 12:20. Same word as in Ex 12:46, which refers to the Passover lamb. Not the same word as in v 33.
10. Or, "thrust through, killed". Elsewhere only in Rev 1:7. GK *1708*. Not the same word as in v 34. Zech 12:10 is being quoted from the Hebrew. This word is used in the LXX in Num 22:29; Judg 9:54; Isa 14:19, etc.
11. Parallel account at Mt 27:57; Mk 15:42; Lk 23:50.
12. Or, "concealed, secret". On this word, see 8:59.
13. Some manuscripts say "the body *of* Jesus" {N}.
14. This is a transliterated Greek word referring to the aromatic sap of a tree. Used only here. GK *264*.
15. That is, Roman pounds. On this word, see 12:3. Equivalent to 33 kilograms or 72 sixteen-ounce pounds. This is a large amount, such as would be done for a king.
16. Elsewhere only in 20:5, 6, 7; and Lk 24:12. GK *3856*. Not related to the word in Lk 23:53. Related to "sheet" in Act 10:11.
17. Elsewhere only in 18:1, 26; Lk 13:19. GK 3057. Related to "gardener" in 20:15.
18. This is a participle, "was having been laid". On this word, see "put" in Act 19:21. Not related to the word in Lk 23:53 (GK *3023*). Some manuscripts say "was laid" {N}.
19. Parallel account at Mt 28:1; Mk 16:1; Lk 24:1.
20. On Mary, see Lk 8:2.
21. This is the word "*affectionately*-love" in 21:15. Elsewhere in this phrase (see 13:23), John uses the word "*devotedly*-love" in 21:15. Some think no difference in meaning is intended.
22. Or, "having looked". Same word as in v 11. On this word, see Lk 24:12.
23. Some manuscripts omit this word {N}.
24. John may mean the cloths were lying collapsed in the form of the body, but he does not state this. The point of all the detail in this verse is that the graveclothes were not missing, or strewn all over, as would be the case if the body had been stolen.
25. Or, "rolled up, folded up". On this word, see "wrapped" in Mt 27:59.
26. Some think John believed in the resurrection, even though he did not yet understand that all along the Scripture had said it must be this way; others, that he believed Jesus, in reference to His going to the Father (13:33; 14:2), but did not yet understand that He was raised back to life on earth.
27. Among others, John is referring to Ps 16, which Peter quotes on Pentecost, Act 2:25-32. Here, John says that Jesus "must" rise; there, Peter says that it was "not possible" that He be held by death.
28. By "them", some think John means the other disciples, Lk 24:9; others, their homes.
29. Parallel account at Mk 16:9.
30. That is, Mary Magdalene, v 18.
31. Or, this word may simply introduce the quotation, "She says *to* them that "They took...".
32. Some manuscripts say "And having" {N}.
33. On this word, see 6:66. More literally, Mary "turned to the *things* behind". She turned away from the tomb. Some think that she heard Jesus behind her, or that the angels looked or pointed to Him when He appeared.
34. It is nowhere stated why Jesus appeared first to the women. But it is fitting that the One who said the greatest ones will be servants (Mt 20:26), appeared first to those who served Him (Lk 8:3).
35. More literally, "is", as the Greek typically phrases it.

A. Mk 6:25 B. Jn 1:7 C. Jn 1:7 D. Jn 7:28 E. Mt 27:57 F. Lk 6:40 G. Eph 5:21 H. 1 Tim 2:12 J. Mt 2:11 K. 1 Cor 7:27 L. Mk 16:1 M. Lk 1:9 N. Mt 26:12 O. Mt 23:29 P. Jn 19:31 Q. Mk 13:35 R. Jn 1:5 S. 2 Thes 3:1 T. Gal 1:6, quickly U. Mt 3:10 V. Jn 11:44 W. 1 Jn 2:29, know X. Mt 16:21 Y. Lk 18:33 Z. Jn 11:33 AA. Mt 8:2, master BB. Jn 2:4 CC. Phil 2:21

|John 20:16|384|Verse|

      2D. That *one*, thinking[A] that He is the gardener[1], says *to* Him, "Sir[B], if **you** carried Him away[C], tell me where you put Him, and **I** will take Him"

      3D. Jesus says *to* her, "Mary"   16

      4D. That *one*, having turned[2], says *to* Him *in* Hebrew[3], "Rabboni[D]!" (which means, Teacher)

      5D. Jesus says *to* her, "Do not be clinging-to[4] Me, for I have not yet gone-up[5] to the Father.[6] But go to My brothers and say *to* them, 'I am going-up[7] to My Father and your Father, and My God[8] and your God'"   17

  5C. Mary the Magdalene comes[9], announcing *to* the disciples that "I have seen[10] the Lord", and *that* He said these *things to* her   18

4B.[11] Then— being evening *on* that first day *of* the week,[12] and the doors having been locked[13] where the disciples[14] were[15] because of the fear[E] *of* the Jews— Jesus came and stood in *their* midst[F]   19

  1C. And He says *to* them, "Peace *to* you"

      1D. And having said this, He showed[G] them[16] *His* hands and *His* side   20

      2D. Then the disciples rejoiced[17], having seen the Lord

  2C. Then Jesus[18] said *to* them again, "Peace *to* you. Just as the Father has sent Me forth, **I** also am sending[19] you[20]"   21

      1D. And having said this, He breathed-on[21] *them*   22

      2D. And He says *to* them, "Receive[H] *the* Holy Spirit.[22] *If you[23] forgive[J] the sins *of* any, they have been forgiven[24] *for* them. If you retain[25] *the* sins *of* any, they have been retained"   23

5B. Now Thomas, one of the twelve, the *one* being called Didymus[K], was not with them when Jesus came   24

  1C. So the other disciples were saying *to* him, "We have seen the Lord!"   25

  2C. But the *one* said *to* them, "Unless I see the mark[26] *of* the nails[27] in His hands, and put my finger into the mark[28] *of* the nails, and put my hand into His side, I will by no means believe"

  3C. And after eight days, His disciples were again inside, and Thomas *was* with them. Jesus comes— the doors having been locked   26

      1D. And He stood in *their* midst and said, "Peace *to* you"

      2D. Then He says *to* Thomas, "Bring[29] your finger here and see My hands. And bring your hand and put *it* into My side. And do not be[30] unbelieving[L], but believing[31]"   27

      3D. Thomas[32] responded and said *to* Him,[33] "My Lord[B] and my God!"   28

      4D. Jesus says *to* him, "You have[34] believed because you have seen Me. Blessed[M] *are* the *ones* not having seen and having believed"   29

6B. Then indeed[35] Jesus also did many other signs[36] in the presence of His[37] disciples, which have not been written[38] in this book. *But these *things* have been written   30, 31

  1C. So that you may believe[39] that Jesus is the Christ, the Son *of* God

  2C. And so that believing, you may have life[N] in His name[O]

1. Used only here. GK *3058*. Related to "garden" in 19:41.
2. Mary has walked by Jesus, or turned back to the tomb, for now she must turn back (v 14) to Him again.
3. Some manuscripts omit this word {K}.
4. This word means "to touch", with the nuance coming from the context. Here, it means "take hold of, hang on to, cling to". The grammar implies, "Stop clinging". There is a similar case in Greek literature of people "taking hold" (same word), in astonishment and delight, of the hands, knees and clothing of a friend who had been presumed dead. Here, Mary needs to "stop clinging" and "be going". GK *721*. Same word as "touch" in 1 Cor 7:1. In Mt 28:9, they "take hold of" His feet (different word).
5. Or, "ascended". Same word as in 3:13; 6:62; Act 2:34; Rom 10:6; and as "ascended" in Eph 4:8, 9, 10. GK *326*.
6. Some think Jesus means that He will not be staying with Mary now, but must depart and ascend to the Father (for reasons of which we are ignorant); others, that there is no need for Mary to cling to Him, because He is not yet ascending to the Father (which He does not do for 40 days), and He has an urgent mission for her. There are other views. Some manuscripts say "My Father" {N}.
7. That is, I am alive, and in the process of ascending to My Father (meaning either an immediate, or a forty-day process).
8. Compare Eph 1:17.
9. Or, "goes". On this word, see Mk 16:2.
10. Some manuscripts say "that she has seen the Lord, and" {N}.
11. Parallel account at Mk 16:14; Lk 24:36.
12. That is, Sunday evening. This is a Roman way of speaking. In Jewish terms, this is the evening of the second day of the week. Saturday night is the evening of the first day.
13. Or, "shut". Same word as in v 26; Lk 11:7; Act 5:23. Elsewhere only as "shut" 12 times. GK *3091*. Related to "key".
14. There were others present in addition to the apostles, Lk 24:33. Some think John is referring to them all; others, to the apostles.
15. Some manuscripts say "had gathered together" {A}, a participle, "were having been gathered together".
16. Some manuscripts add "both" {N}.
17. This fulfills 16:22, where Jesus used this same word.
18. Some manuscripts say "Then He said..." {C}.
19. Not the same word as "send forth" earlier. Jesus has used both words of Himself (Jn 20:21; 5:37), and of them (Jn 17:18; 20:21). He mentioned this sending in His prayer for them in 17:18. This word is used 79 times. GK *4287*. On the unrelated word "send forth", see "send out" in Mk 3:14. Some think no difference in meaning is intended.
20. Some think Jesus is referring to the apostles, His witnesses from the beginning (15:27). In this case, He is specifically commissioning them (17:18), and by application, all who believe through their word (17:20). Others think He is referring to all present there (compare Lk 24:33-36) as representatives of all the church, which is composed of witnesses in a broader sense.
21. Or, "blew on". This is done to indicate that the Spirit comes from Jesus to these disciples. Used only here. GK *1874*. Same word as when God "breathed" life into Adam, Gen 2:7; and in Ezek 21:31 (wrath), 37:9 (life). It was also used of "blowing in" a musical instrument, and of "inflating" something.
22. Some think this is symbolic of the coming that actually occurs on Pentecost; others, of Jesus giving the Spirit here not to individuals, but to the church as a whole. Others think this is a partial reception by the disciples of the Spirit or a gift of the Spirit, the fullness coming on Pentecost. For example, some think they receive spiritual life here, and gifts of power in Acts 2. Others think this is in regard to their commission for the mission just mentioned, while Acts 2 brings the power for it (Lk 24:49). Others link this specifically with the authority given next. Others think the Spirit was given here to lead them into the truth, and that this complements Lk 24:45. There are other views.
23. Some think this authority is given to the apostles and those who carried on their office, ministers; others, to all individual Christians; others, to the church as a whole, represented by all the disciples present on this night.
24. On this word, see Mt 6:12. Some manuscripts say "they are forgiven" {B}.
25. Or, "hold firm, hold on to, hold fast, hold back". On forgiving and retaining sins, compare Mt 16:19; 18:18. Some think Jesus is giving authority to His ministers to absolve sins. Others think this refers to the authority of believers to speak for Jesus, based on His word; to say with His authority based on a person's confession that God forgives them or God does not forgive them, as in 8:24, 47; 9:41 (your sin remains); Act 2:38; etc. On this word, see "hold on to" in Heb 4:14.
26. Or, "imprint". On this word, see "pattern" in 1 Pet 5:3.
27. Used only in this verse. GK *2464*. Related to the verb in Col 2:14.
28. Some manuscripts say "place" {N}.
29. Jesus commands Thomas to do what he said he must do. Some think he did so, as did the others the week before, Lk 24:39. Others think Thomas no longer felt the need to do so.
30. This is a command. The grammar implies, "Stop being...".
31. Or, "faithless, but faithful". Both are adjectives. On this word see "faithful" in Col 1:2.
32. Some manuscripts say "And Thomas..." {N}.
33. Note that this is spoken to Jesus, not as an exclamation. Now believing, Thomas addresses Jesus as God. He "honors the Son just as he honors the Father", 5:23. If Jesus is not God, Thomas is blaspheming.
34. Jesus characterizes Thomas's comment as "believing". After seeing what the ten others saw, he also believes. Some manuscripts say "Thomas, you have..." {K}. Some punctuate this as a question, "Have you... Me?"
35. Or, "So indeed, Now indeed". Same idiom as "so indeed" in 19:24, John's only other use of it.
36. Some take this narrowly in this context as referring to signs of the resurrection of Jesus, authenticating His resurrection, such as eating broiled fish with them (Lk 24:43). In this case, it is the conclusion of the resurrection event. Others take it broadly as referring to the signs (miracles) done throughout His ministry. In this case, it is the conclusion to chapters 1-20. In either case, John's point is the same.
37. Some manuscripts say "the" {C}.
38. This is a participle, "are not having been written". On this expression, see 2:17. John has written of seven, 11:1.
39. Some manuscripts have this word in a different tense, "may be believing" {C}; that is, "may continue believing". Same word and variant as in 19:35. Some narrow John's purpose for writing this book to evangelism ("believe") or edification ("continue believing") based on the tense of this word. Consult the commentaries.

A. Lk 19:11   B. Mt 8:2, master   C. Mt 8:17, carry   D. Mk 10:51   E. Eph 5:21   F. 2 Thes 2:7   G. 1 Tim 6:15   H. Rom 7:8, taken   J. Mt 6:12   K. Jn 11:16   L. Mt 17:17   M. Lk 6:20   N. Rom 8:10   O. 2 Tim 2:19

| John 21:1 | | Verse |

16A. After¹ these *things* Jesus manifested² Himself again *to* the disciples at the Sea *of* Tiberias³. And He manifested *Himself* as follows—   21:1

    1B. Simon Peter, and Thomas (the *one* being called Didymus^A), and Nathanael^B (the *one* from Cana *of* Galilee), and the *sons of* Zebedee,⁴ and two other of His disciples were together   2

        1C. Simon Peter says *to* them, "I am going⁵ to fish". They say *to* him, "**We** are also coming with you". They went out and got into the boat⁶   3
        2C. And during that night they caught^C nothing

    2B. Now having already become⁷ early-morning, Jesus stood at the shore. But the disciples did not know that it was⁸ Jesus   4

        1C. So Jesus says *to* them, "Children⁹, you do not have any fish-to-eat¹⁰, *do you*?"¹¹   5
        2C. They answered Him, "No"
        3C. And the *One* said *to* them, "Cast^D the net^E to the right side *of* the boat and you will find *them*"   6
        4C. So they cast *it*, and they were no longer strong-*enough*^F to draw^G it [into the boat] because *of* the multitude^H *of* the fish¹²
        5C. Then that disciple whom Jesus was loving¹³ says *to* Peter, "It is the Lord"   7

            1D. So Simon Peter— having heard that it was¹⁴ the Lord— tied *his* outer-garment¹⁵ around^J *himself* (for he was naked¹⁶), and threw^D himself into the sea
            2D. But the other disciples came in the small-boat¹⁷ (for they were not far from the land, but about two-hundred cubits¹⁸ away)— dragging^K the net *of* fish   8

        6C. Then when they got out to the land, they see *a* charcoal-fire¹⁹ lying *there*, and fish²⁰ lying upon *it*, and bread   9

            1D. Jesus says *to* them, "Bring from the fish which you now caught^C"   10

                1E. So²¹ Simon Peter went up and drew^G the net to²² land, full^L *of* large fish— *a* hundred fifty three   11
                2E. And *though* being so many, the net was not torn^M

            2D. Jesus says *to* them, "Come, eat-breakfast²³"   12

                1E. And²⁴ none *of* the disciples was daring^N to question²⁵ Him, "Who are **You**?", knowing that it was²⁶ the Lord
                2E. Jesus²⁷ comes and takes the bread and gives *it to* them, and the fish likewise   13

        7C. This *is* now²⁸ *the* third *time* Jesus was manifested²⁹ *to* the disciples³⁰ *after* having arisen³¹ from *the* dead   14

    3B. Then when they ate-breakfast, Jesus says *to* Simon Peter   15

        1C. "Simon, *son of* John³², do you *devotedly*-love³³ Me more *than* these³⁴?"

            1D. He says *to* Him, "Yes, Lord. **You** know that I *affectionately*-love³⁵ You"
            2D. He says *to* him, "Be feeding³⁶ My lambs"

        2C. He says *to* him again *a* second *time*, "Simon, *son of* John, do you *devotedly*-love Me³⁷?"   16

1. Chapter 21 relates the next appearance of Jesus, the third (v 14), and the lessons taught in it. John may simply be continuing on with what actually happened in historical sequence. Others think the book culminates in 20:30-31, and that chapter 21 is an appendix added by John to explain what happened to Peter and to clear up a misunderstanding (v 23). Others think it was not written by John (see 21:24), but was added at a later date. There is no manuscript evidence lacking chapter 21.
2. Or, "revealed, showed". On this word, see "made evident" in 1 Jn 2:19.
3. This is the Roman name for the Sea of Galilee. See 6:1.
4. That is, James and John (the one writing this Gospel), Mt 10:2. This is the closest John comes to naming himself in this book.
5. Some think this implies a turning away from Christ; others, a nervous waiting for Him— "Let's stop sitting around waiting for His next appearance. Let's do something. I'm going fishing!".
6. Some manuscripts add "immediately" {N}.
7. Some manuscripts say "already becoming morning", meaning it was still dark {N}.
8. More literally, "is", as the Greek typically phrases it.
9. Or, "Boys, Lads". On this word, see 1 Jn 2:14.
10. Or, "fish". This word refers to fish as something to eat, rather than as an animal (the word in v 6). John uses a synonym in v 9. Thus he uses three different words for "fish" in v 5-13. Used only here. GK *4709*. Related to "eat".
11. The grammar indicates a "no" answer is expected.
12. This is the word for fish as an animal, also in v 8, 11. Used 20 times. GK *2716*.
13. This is John's self-designation, 13:23.
14. More literally, "is", as the Greek typically phrases it.
15. Used only here. GK *2087*. Related to "put on over" in 2 Cor 5:2.
16. That is, wearing only his underclothes, stripped for work. On this word, see Jam 2:15.
17. This may be another word for the fishing boat, or it may refer to a small boat tied to it.
18. On this measure, see Rev 21:17. Here it amounts to about 100 yards or 92 meters.
19. Elsewhere only in 18:18. GK *471*. Related to "coal" in Rom 12:20.
20. On this word, which is also in v 10, 13, see 6:9.
21. Some manuscripts omit this word {N}.
22. Some manuscripts say "on" {N}.
23. Same word as in v 15. On this word, see "eat the morning meal" in Lk 11:37.
24. Some manuscripts omit this word {N}.
25. Or, "examine, inquire of ". On this word, see "search out" in Mt 10:11.
26. More literally, "is", as the Greek typically phrases it.
27. Some manuscripts say "Then Jesus" {N}. Jesus serves them.
28. Or, "already, by this time". On this word, see "already" in Mt 24:32.
29. Or, "appeared". Same word as in v 1, but different grammar.
30. That is, to a group of the disciples, the other two being in 20:19 and 26.
31. Or, "having been raised". On this word, see "arose" in Mt 28:6.
32. Some manuscripts say "Jonah" {B} here and in v 16, 17. See Jn 1:42.
33. Or, "love". Compare the synonym below. This is the verb related to "agape". It can refer to a volitional love, a love rooted in the one loving rather than elicited by the one loved. Same word as in Mt 5:43; 22:37; Mk 10:21; Lk 6:32; Jn 3:16; 11:5; 14:15; Rom 9:13; 13:8; Gal 2:20; Eph 5:25; 1 Jn 2:15; 4:7, 19; Rev 1:5; 12:11. Used 143 times, all except here in v 15-16 being rendered "love". GK *26*. Related to the noun "love" in 1 Jn 4:16, and "beloved" in Mt 3:17.
34. Some think Jesus means "these other disciples", since Peter had said "Though all fall, I will not", Mt 26:33; Mk 14:29. Other think He means "these fish", your former life. The grammar permits either.
35. Or, "love". Peter uses a different word for "love". Some do not think any distinction between these words is intended (as in 13:23, 20:2), but that it is a stylistic variation (as with lambs/sheep, feed/shepherd, know/recognize here. See also "fish-to-eat" in v 5; send forth/send in 20:21). The use of synonyms in this way is a mark of John's writing style. Others think that while there is not always a distinction between them, a distinction is intended here. Jesus says *agapao* in v 15, 16, a volitional love given based on decision and choice. It is a love based on the commitment of the one loving. Peter may be reluctant to use this word because he had made a different choice— he denied Jesus three times. So Peter says *phileo* in v 15, 16, 17, a love coming in response to something favorable in the other person. It is a friendship kind of love; a love based on the affectionate feelings one has for the other. This word is used 25 times, three times as "kiss" (see Mt 26:48), the rest (outside of v 15-17 here) as "love". GK *5797*. Related to "friend" in Lk 14:10; "kiss" in Rom 16:16; and words such as "love of money" (1 Tim 6:10), "love for mankind" (Tit 3:4), and "brotherly love" (Heb 13:1).
36. Or, "tending, grazing, leading to pasture". Same word as in v 17. Elsewhere only in Mt 8:30, 33; Mk 5:11, 14; Lk 8:32, 34, 15:15. GK *1081*.
37. Note that this time Jesus drops the idea of comparison, "more than these".

A. Jn 11:16   B. Jn 1:45   C. Jn 11:57, seize   D. Rev 2:22, throw   E. Mt 4:20   F. Gal 5:6, can do   G. Jn 6:44   H. Act 6:2   J. Jn 13:5, tied around   K. Rev 12:4, sweeps away   L. Rom 15:14   M. Mt 27:51   N. 2 Cor 11:21

	1D. He says *to* Him, "Yes, Lord. **You** know that I *affectionately*-love You"	
	2D. He says *to* him, "Be shepherding¹ My sheep²"	
3C.	He says *to* him the third³ *time*, "Simon, *son of* John, do you *affectionately*-love Me?"	17
	1D. Peter was grieved^A because⁴ He said *to* him the third *time*, "Do you *affectionately*-love Me?". And he says *to* Him, "Lord, **You** know all *things*. **You** recognize⁵ that I *affectionately*-love You"	
	2D. Jesus⁶ says *to* him, "Be feeding^B My sheep	
	1E. "Truly^C, truly, I say *to* you, when you were younger, you were girding⁷ yourself, and walking where you were wanting *to go*. But when you become-old⁸, you will stretch-out^D your hands, and another will gird you, and bring⁹ *you* where you are not wanting^E *to go*"	18
	2E. Now this He said, signifying¹⁰ *by* what kind¹¹ of death he will glorify^F God	19
4C.	And having said this, He says *to* him, "Be following Me!"	
5C.	Peter,¹² having turned around, sees the disciple following *them* whom Jesus was loving¹³— *the one* who also leaned back on His chest¹⁴ during dinner and said, "Lord, who is the *one* handing You over?"	20
	1D. So¹⁵ Peter, having looked-at this *one*, says *to* Jesus, "Lord, and what *of*¹⁶ this *one*?	21
	1E. Jesus says *to* him, "If I want^E him to remain^G until I come, what *is it* to you? **You** be following Me!"	22
	2E. Therefore this statement^H went out to the brothers^J, that "that disciple does not die"¹⁷	23
	3E. But Jesus did not say *to* him that he does not die, but "If I want him to remain until I come, what *is it* to you¹⁸?"	

This¹⁹ *one* is the disciple^K testifying^L about these *things,* and²⁰ the *one* having written these²¹ *things*, and we²² know that his testimony^M is true^N. *And there are also many other *things* which Jesus did, which if they should be written individually^O, I suppose^P *that* not even the world itself *would* have-room-for^Q the books being written²³.   24 25

1. Same word as in Act 20:28; 1 Pet 5:2. On this verb, see Rev 19:15.
2. Both here and in v 17, some manuscripts say "little-sheep" {N}, using a related word.
3. Some think Jesus asks Peter three times because Peter denied Him three times.
4. Or, "that". Some think John means Peter was grieved because Jesus asked him a third time. The fact that Jesus now substitutes the other word for "love" only proves there is no distinction between them. Others think that it was because on this third time, His question refers to the exact same kind of love Peter had just claimed twice. Whether Peter thought he was claiming a different (lower, less volitional and God-like; or higher, more personal and tender) kind of love or not, it would surely grieve him that the Lord questioned precisely what he was claiming. GK *4022*.
5. Or, "know, understand". On this word, see "know" in Lk 1:34. This is a different word than previously in v 15, 16, and 17 (on which see 1 Jn 2:29). No distinction may be intended. These two words occur together also in Mt 24:43; Mk 4:13; Lk 12:39; Jn 7:27; 8:55; 13:7; Rom 7:7; 1 Cor 2:11; 2 Cor 5:16; Eph 5:5; Heb 8:11; 1 Jn 2:29; 5:20.
6. Some manuscripts say "He says..." {C}.
7. That is, tying on your belt. On this word, see Act 12:8.
8. Elsewhere only as "grow aged" in Heb 8:13. GK *1180*. Related to "old age" in Lk 1:36.
9. Or, "carry, lead". On this word, see "carried" in 2 Pet 1:17.
10. On this word, see Rev 1:1. "Signifying *by* what kind of death" is also in 12:33; 18:32. That is, others will have control over Peter and lead him away to his death.
11. Some think John means "a martyr's death"; others, crucifixion. Peter was crucified by Nero in about A.D. 64-65.
12. Some manuscripts say "Now Peter..." {N}.
13. On this self-designation, see 13:23.
14. Same word as in 13:25.
15. Some manuscripts omit this word {N}.
16. Or, "*as to, with reference to*". Same grammar as in Act 12:18, "what became *of* Peter".
17. That is, prior to the second coming of Jesus.
18. Some manuscripts omit "what *is it* to you" {C}.
19. That is, the one defined by the two descriptions in v 20, the subject of v 20-23. With the reference to himself still in his mind, John now transitions to the conclusion the book, putting the emphasis back on Jesus.
20. Or, "even".
21. Note the comparison between "these things written" and "other things not written" next. John is giving his attestation to the whole book.
22. Some think John is referring to himself, as in 3 Jn 12. Others think this was added by others (perhaps the elders at Ephesus), adding their testimony to John's. Some holding this view think this indicates that all of chapter 21 was added by these other witnesses.
23. Some manuscripts add "amen" {N}.

A. 2 Cor 7:9   B. Jn 21:15   C. Jn 1:51   D. Act 27:30   E. Jn 7:17, willing   F. Rom 8:30   G. Jn 15:4, abide   H. 1 Cor 12:8, word   J. Act 16:40
K. Lk 6:40   L. Jn 1:7   M. Jn 1:7   N. Jn 6:55   O. Eph 5:33   P. Phil 1:17   Q. 2 Pet 3:9, make room for

Overview		**Acts**

1A. I made the first account, Theophilus, about all Jesus began to do and teach. He commanded the apostles to wait for the promise of the Father, and was lifted up. They returned to Jerusalem — 1:1-14

2A. And during these days, the brothers chose Matthias to take Judas's place of ministry and apostleship — 1:15-26

3A. And on the day of Pentecost, they were all together at the same place — 2:1

    1B. And a noise like wind, and tongues like fire came. They began to speak in other tongues — 2:2-4

    2B. The Jews marveled that they heard their native languages. Others said they were drunk — 2:5-13

    3B. And Peter said, God raised Jesus whom you killed, and He has poured forth what you see. Know for certain, God made Him both Lord and Christ— this Jesus whom you crucified — 2:14-36

    4B. And they said, What shall we do? Peter said, repent and be saved from this generation — 2:37-40

    5B. So indeed, about three thousand were added on that day — 2:41

4A. Now they were devoting themselves to teaching, fellowship, breaking bread, and prayers. Many signs and wonders were taking place through the apostles. They were sharing with one another — 2:42-47

5A. Now Peter and John were going up to the temple at the hour of prayer — 3:1

    1B. And a man lame from birth was begging to receive alms — 3:2-3

    2B. And Peter healed him, and he walked into the temple. The people were astonished — 3:4-10

    3B. And Peter said, God glorified Jesus, whom you denied. On the basis of faith in His name, this man was healed. And now, repent and return — 3:11-26

    4B. And while they were speaking, the priests came upon them and jailed them — 4:1-4

    5B. Peter told them it was by the name of Jesus whom you crucified that this man was healed. There is salvation in no other. They warned, threatened, and released them — 4:5-22

    6B. And they all praised God, prayed to speak with boldness, and were filled with the Spirit — 4:23-31

6A. Now the heart and soul of the believers was one. And they sold their belongings to help those among them in need. Ananias did so deceitfully and died. Great fear came upon all — 4:32-5:11

7A. Now many signs and wonders were taking place through the apostles. Many were coming to them. The priests, filled with jealousy, arrested them. Peter said, We must obey God, not man. He raised Jesus, and we are witnesses. Gamaliel advised caution. They beat and released them — 5:12-42

8A. Now a complaint arose over the serving of food. They selected seven men to be put in charge of it — 6:1-7

9A. Now Stephen was doing great wonders and signs among the people — 6:8

    1B. Some argued with him, but they were unable to resist his wisdom. They stirred up others — 6:9-12

    2B. And they seized him, and dragged him before the Sanhedrin, and accused him — 6:12-7:1

    3B. And Stephen said, Your Fathers killed the Prophets who announced the Messiah, whom you also betrayed and murdered. You received the Law, but do not keep it — 7:2-53

    4B. And they were infuriated in their hearts, and grinding their teeth at him — 7:54

    5B. But full of the Spirit, Stephen said, I see Jesus standing on the right side of God — 7:55-56

    6B. And they cried out, and rushed upon him, and stoned him to death, Saul approving — 7:57-8:1

    7B. And a great persecution arose, and they were dispersed to the regions of Judea and Samaria — 8:1-3

    8B. So indeed, the ones having been dispersed went about announcing the word as good news — 8:4

10A. Now Philip, having gone to Samaria, was proclaiming Christ to them — 8:5

    1B. And the crowds paid attention to his word, and the signs he was doing, including Simon — 8:6-11

    2B. And when they believed, they were being baptized, both men and women. Simon also — 8:12-13

Acts
Overview

3B. And the apostles in Jerusalem, having heard, sent Peter and John, who prayed so that they might receive the Spirit. Simon tried to buy this power, and was rebuked by Peter	8:14-25
4B. Now an angel directed Philip to an Ethiopian court official reading Isa 53. He was saved	8:26-39
5B. And Philip was evangelizing all the cities from Azotus to Caesarea	8:40

11A. Now Saul requested letters to Damascus authorizing him to imprison any belonging to the Way — 9:1-2

    1B. And drawing near Damascus, Jesus appeared and said, Why are you persecuting Me? — 9:3-9
    2B. Ananias was sent to him. Saul regained his sight and was baptized — 9:10-19
    3B. Now Saul proclaimed Jesus in Damascus. They plotted against him, but he escaped — 9:19-25
    4B. And having arrived in Jerusalem, Barnabas led him to the apostles — 9:26-30
    5B. So indeed the church in Judea, Galilee and Samaria was having peace and increasing — 9:31

12A. Now Peter, passing through all the regions, came down to Lydda — 9:32

    1B. And he healed a man in Lydda, and all who lived there turned to the Lord — 9:33-35
    2B. Called to Joppa, Peter raised Tabitha (Dorcas). He stayed with Simon, the tanner — 9:36-43
    3B. God told Cornelius to call for Peter. He believed and God poured out the Spirit on him — 10:1-48
    4B. Now those in Jerusalem objected to this at first, but then perceived it as the work of God — 11:1-18

13A. Those dispersed to Antioch saw many Gentiles turn to the Lord. The church at Jerusalem sent Barnabas. He got Saul, and they taught there for a year. Agabus predicted a famine. The Antioch church sent Barnabas and Saul to Jerusalem with an offering to help. Herod had James put to death and imprisoned Peter, but the Lord freed him. Barnabas and Saul returned — 11:19-12:25

14A. The Spirit spoke through prophets in the church at Antioch, sending out Barnabas and Saul — 13:1-3

    1B. So indeed, having sailed to Cyprus, Paul blinded Elymas. The proconsul believed — 13:4-12
    2B. In Pisidian Antioch, Paul proclaimed Jesus. Some believed, others drove him out — 13:13-52
    3B. In Iconium, the same thing occurred — 14:1-7
    4B. In Lystra, Paul was declared to be a god. After Jews came, he was stoned — 14:8-20
    5B. In Derbe, Paul proclaimed the gospel, then returned to the churches, strengthening them — 14:21-23
    6B. And they returned to Syrian Antioch, and reported to the church all that God did — 14:24-27

15A. Now while spending some time in Antioch, some came from Judea saying, You must be circumcised. Paul and Barnabas disputed this. The church sent them to Jerusalem, where Peter and James said, God has accepted the Gentiles. They returned to Antioch with a letter — 14:28-15:34

16A. Now after spending some days in Antioch, Paul wanted to return with Barnabas to the cities — 15:35-36

    1B. And Barnabas was wanting to take John Mark. Paul disagreed, and they split up — 15:37-39
    2B. Paul chose Silas and departed, having been handed over to the grace of God by the brothers. They went through Syria, Cilicia, Derbe and Lystra, where he found Timothy — 15:40-16:5
    3B. And they passed through to Troas, where in a vision, God called them to Macedonia — 16:6-10
    4B. In Philippi, Paul cast out a demon and was jailed by a mob. The jailer was saved — 16:11-40
    5B. In Thessalonica, the Jews dragged Jason before the authorities and forced Paul to leave — 17:1-9
    6B. In Berea, they searched the Scriptures. The Jews from Thessalonica came to agitate — 17:10-14
    7B. In Athens, Paul was alone. He spoke in the synagogues, the market, and the Areopagus — 17:15-34
    8B. In Corinth, Paul found Aquila and Priscilla. The Lord told him in a vision not to fear, that he would not be harmed, but to speak. He taught there for 18 months — 18:1-17

Overview		Acts

    9B. And Paul sailed off to Syria. He stopped in Ephesus, and promised to return, leaving Priscilla and Aquila there. From Caesarea, he went up to the church, and back to Antioch   18:18-22

17A. After some time, Paul departed, passing through Galatia and Phrygia, strengthening the disciples   18:23

    1B. Apollos came to Ephesus, was instructed by Priscilla and Aquila, and went to Corinth   18:24-28
    2B. Paul came to Ephesus. He laid hands on some to receive the Spirit. He spoke in the synagogue, then in the school of Tyrannus for two years. The word was prevailing   19:1-20

18A. Now when these things were completed, Paul put in his spirit to be going to Jerusalem, having passed through Macedonia and Achaia, and then to go to Rome   19:21

    1B. And Paul sent Timothy and Erastus ahead to Macedonia, and held on in Asia for a time   19:22
    2B. Now at this time in Ephesus, Demetrius caused no small disturbance concerning the Way   19:23-40
    3B. And after the uproar ceased, Paul proceeded to Macedonia, and through to Greece   20:1-2
    4B. After three months, Paul returned to Philippi, while the others sailed to Troas   20:3-5
    5B. Paul sailed from Philippi to Troas, where Eutychus fell from the window   20:6-12
    6B. In Miletus, Paul summoned the elders from Ephesus, and exhorted them   20:13-38
    7B. In Tyre, the disciples were telling Paul not to go to Jerusalem   21:1-6
    8B. In Caesarea, at the house of Philip, Agabus said Paul would be bound in Jerusalem   21:7-14
    9B. In Jerusalem, Paul was welcomed by the brothers   21:15-17

        1C. On the following day, James suggested a plan to quiet the Jews   21:18-25
        2C. Then Paul was going to the temple, carrying out this plan   21:26
        3C. But Jews from Asia saw Paul, and stirred up the crowd, and dragged him out   21:27-30
        4C. And the Roman commander rescued him, chained him, and was taking him in   21:31-36
        5C. And Paul asked permission to speak to the crowd   21:37-39
        6C. And he having permitted it, Paul testified to the Jews about his mission   21:40-22:21
        7C. And they were listening until he spoke of going to the Gentiles   22:22
        8C. And the commander jailed him, and discovered Paul was a Roman   22:22-29
        9C. On the next day, the commander took Paul before the Sanhedrin   22:30-23:10
        10C. On the following night, the Lord said, Take courage. You must witness also in Rome   23:11
        11C. The commander discovered a plot to kill Paul, and sent him to Caesarea   23:12-30

    10B. The soldiers delivered Paul and the commander's letter to Felix in Caesarea   23:31-33

        1C. Having read the letter, Felix ordered Paul held until the Jews arrived   23:34-35
        2C. After five days, the Jews came to accuse him, Paul responded, Felix adjourned them   24:1-23
        3C. After some days, Paul spoke to Felix and Drusilla about the gospel   24:24-26
        4C. After two years, the Jews accused Paul before Festus. Paul appealed to Caesar   24:27-25:12
        5C. Some days later, Paul defended himself before King Agrippa and Bernice   25:13-26:32

    11B. Paul was taken to Rome by ship, and suffered a shipwreck along the way   27:1-28:15
    12B. In Rome, Paul was kept under house arrest with a soldier guarding him for two years. And he was preaching the kingdom of God and teaching about the Lord Jesus Christ   28:16-31

1A. I made the **first**[1] account[2] about everything, O Theophilus[3], which Jesus began[4] both to do and teach until which day He was taken-up[5] [after] having given-commands[6] through *the* Holy Spirit *to* the apostles whom He chose[A]— *to* whom He indeed presented[B] Himself alive[7] after His suffering by[8] many convincing-proofs[9], appearing[10] *to* them during[11] forty days, and speaking the *things* concerning the kingdom[C] *of* God

   1B. And being assembled-with[12] *them*

      1C. He ordered[D] them not to depart from Jerusalem, but to wait-for the promise *of* the Father[13] "which you heard *from* Me. °Because **John**[14] baptized[E] *with* water— but **you** will be baptized with[15] *the* Holy **Spirit** after these not many[16] days!"

      2C. So indeed the *ones* having come together were asking Him, saying, "Lord, are You restoring[17] the kingdom[C] *to* Israel at this time?"[18] °And He said to them[19]—

         1D. "It is not yours to know *the* times or seasons[20] which the Father appointed[21] by *His* own authority[F]
         2D. "But you will receive power[22]— the Holy Spirit having come[G] upon you
         3D. "And you will be My witnesses[23]— both in Jerusalem and in all Judea and Samaria, and as far as *the* last place *of* the earth[24]"

      3C. And having said[25] these *things*, while they *were* looking, He was lifted-up[H]. And *a* cloud received[26] Him from their eyes

      4C. And as they were looking-intently[J] into heaven, while He *was* going— and behold, two men in white[K] clothing were standing near them, °who also said

         1D. "Galilean men, why do you stand looking into heaven? This Jesus having been taken-up from you into heaven will come in this manner— the way you saw Him going into heaven"

   2B. Then they returned to Jerusalem[27] from *the* mountain being called '*of* Olives', which is near Jerusalem (having *a* journey *of a* Sabbath)[28]

      1C. And when they went in *the* city, they went up to the upper-room[29] where they were staying—

         1D. Both Peter and John[30], and James[31] and Andrew
         2D. Philip and Thomas
         3D. Bartholomew and Matthew
         4D. James *the* son *of* Alphaeus, and Simon the Zealot[L], and Judas *the* son *of* James

      2C. These all were devoting-themselves[M] with-one-accord[32] *to* prayer,[33] along with women, and Mary the mother *of* Jesus, and His[34] brothers

2A. And during these days[35], Peter, having stood up in *the* midst[N] *of* the brothers[36] (and *the* crowd[O] *of* names[37] at the same *place*[38] was about one-hundred twenty), said

   1B. "Men[P], brothers[Q]—

      1C. "The Scripture[R] had-to[39] be fulfilled[S] which the Holy Spirit spoke-beforehand[40] through *the* mouth *of* David concerning Judas, the *one* having become *a* guide *for* the *ones* having arrested[T] Jesus, °because[41] he was numbered[42] among[43] us, and received[44] *his* share[45] *of* this[46] ministry[U]"

1. Luke's grammar implies a second, this book of Acts.
2. Or, "treatise". Luke and Acts are two parts of one work. Each filled one papyrus scroll. On this word, see "word" in 1 Cor 12:8.
3. Some think this was an actual person of prominence. It was a name used by both Jews and Gentiles. Since the name means "lover of God" or "loved by God", others think it might be a symbolic name for all such people. Elsewhere only in Lk 1:1. GK *2541*.
4. What Jesus began Himself to do in Luke, He continues to do in Acts through His apostles.
5. Same word as in v 11, 22; 10:16; Mk 16:19; 1 Tim 3:16. Used 13 times. GK *377*. Related to "ascension" in Lk 9:51.
6. Or, "commanded". Same word as "command" in 13:47. One of these commands is in v 4. On this word, see Mk 10:3.
7. Or, "living". This is a participle. On this word, see "came to life" in Rev 20:4.
8. Or, "in, with, by means of". GK *1877*.
9. Or, "positive proofs, sure signs". Used only here. GK *5447*.
10. Or, "being seen *by* them". Used only here. GK *3964*. Related to "vision" in 2 Cor 12:1.
11. Not continuously, but periodically during this period. This verse summarizes Lk 24:13-45.
12. Or, And "coming together". Verses 4-8 expand the "having given orders" of v 2, and "speaking" of v 3, and coincide with the meetings in Lk 24:46-49 and 24:50. The meaning of this word is not certain. Others think it means "while eating with"; others, that it is an alternate spelling of a word meaning "while staying with". Used only here. GK *5259*.
13. That is, the promise given by the Father, consisting of the Helper, the Holy Spirit, Jn 14:16, 26. Compare Act 2:33.
14. Jesus uses grammar that emphasizes the contrast between the two halves of this sentence.
15. Or, "in". See Mk 1:8 on this, and Mk 1:4, 8, 9 on baptism.
16. That is, after these few days. Jesus ascended 40 days after Passover, v 3. The apostles waited 10 more days until Pentecost, Act 2:1. On this idiom, see "no small" in 12:18.
17. Same word used of what Elijah would do, Mt 17:11; Mk 9:12. On this word, see Mk 8:25. Related to "restoration" in Act 3:21. God took away the kingdom, Mt 21:43; 23:38.
18. Some think this question is inappropriate— a reflection of the apostles' faulty understanding of the spiritual kingdom Jesus was establishing, and a yearning for the political kingdom on earth centered in Israel which they had expected the Messiah to bring. Others think the question is appropriate, and that His answer implies that the restoration of such a kingdom to Israel will take place in the future, in the Father's own time. Note Lk 21:31.
19. That is, to the eleven apostles, v 2, 13; and by application, to all.
20. The phrase "times and seasons" also occurs in 1 Thes 5:1. Seasons are divisions of times.
21. Or, "established, fixed, set". Or, "put within *His* own authority". On this word, see "put" in 19:21.
22. That is, power for works (miracles) and words (proclamation) to fulfill their mission, as seen in this book. Same word as "miracle" in 1 Cor 12:10.
23. Same word as in Lk 24:48; Act 1:22; 2:32; 3:15; 5:32; 10:39, 41; 13:31; 1 Pet 5:1. Used 35 times. GK *3459*. Related to "testimony" in Jn 1:7 and Act 4:33; "testify" in Jn 1:7 and 1 Thes 2:12. Some manuscripts say "be witnesses *to* Me" {K}.
24. This phrase "as far as *the* last *place of* the earth" is also in 13:47. That is, from the nearest city and country to the farthest.
25. Verses 9-11 expand the "taken up" in v 2, and coincide with Lk 24:51.
26. Or, "took Him up". This word could mean the cloud lifted Jesus up from underneath, as when a dolphin takes up a performer; or, that the cloud enveloped Him from below, removing Him from their sight. Luke uses four different words to describe this, "carried up" in Lk 24:51; "taken up" in Act 1:2, 11; "lifted up" earlier in 1:9; and "received" here. GK *5696*.
27. Verses 12-13 expand on Lk 24:52.
28. That is, the mountain was within a distance allowable for a journey on a Sabbath, which the rabbis determined to be 2000 cubits or 5 stades, that is, about 1000 yards (.57 miles) or 914 meters. Luke does not say here where the apostles were on the mountain, but Lk 24:50 says "near Bethany", which probably means the Bethany side of the mountain. Bethany was about 15 stades from Jerusalem, Jn 11:18.
29. Or, "upstairs room". Elsewhere only in 9:37, 39; 20:8. GK *5673*.
30. Luke joins the two more prominent brothers of each family, then the other two brothers. Note Mt 10:2. On these apostles, see Lk 6:14.
31. Some manuscripts reverse the order of these two names to the more familiar "James and John" {N}.
32. Or, "with one mind, with one purpose". Elsewhere only in 2:46; 4:24; 5:12; 7:57; 8:6; 12:20; 15:25; 18:12; 19:29; Rom 15:6. GK *3924*.
33. This verse expands upon Lk 24:53, bringing the reader up to where Luke left off in that book, and completing the introduction to this book. Some manuscripts add "and supplication" {N}.
34. Some manuscripts add "with", "and with His brothers" {N}. On the brothers and sisters of Jesus, see Mt 13:55-56.
35. This implies some number of days elapsed since the preceding event, though the number not given.
36. Some manuscripts say "disciples" {N}.
37. People are referred to as "names" also in Rev 3:4; 11:13.
38. Or, "together". On "at the same *place*", see 2:47. The location of this meeting is not given. Perhaps it was at the temple, or somewhere outdoors, given the number of people involved.
39. Or, "It was necessary *that* the Scripture be fulfilled". On this idiom, see "must" in Mt 16:21.
40. Or, "foretold". On this word, see Jude 17.
41. The present situation with Judas is in fulfillment of the Scriptures about his death and replacement (v 20), because he— as the predicted traitor— was counted as one of the twelve to make this fulfillment possible.
42. Or, "counted". Or, "had been numbered". This is a participle, Judas was "having been numbered". Used only here. GK *2935*. Related to the word in Lk 22:3, and the word in Lk 12:7.
43. Some manuscripts say "with" {K}.
44. On this word, see 2 Pet 1:1. Judas obtained his apostleship by divine will. The divine lot, so to speak, fell to him.
45. Or, "the lot". Same word as "lot" in v 26. On this word, see Col 1:12.
46. That is, his share of the ministry of the apostles (which was to be witnesses of Christ's resurrection, v 22, and ministry), from which he turned aside (v 25). Judas filled a spot that God created, and that must now be re-filled.

A. 1 Cor 1:27 B. Rom 12:1 C. Mt 3:2 D. 1 Tim 1:3, command E. Mk 1:8 F. Rev 6:8 G. Lk 21:26, coming upon H. 2 Cor 11:20 J. Lk 4:20 K. Rev 4:4 L. Lk 6:15 M. Act 2:42 N. 2 Thes 2:7 O. Mk 2:13, multitude P. 1 Tim 2:12 Q. Act 16:40 R. 2 Pet 3:16 S. Eph 5:18, filled T. Lk 22:54 U. 1 Cor 12:5

	1D. Now indeed this *one* acquired[A] *a* field with *the* wages[B] *of* unrighteousness[1]. And having become prostrate[2], he burst-open in the middle,[3] and all his inward-parts[C] spilled-out[D]. And it became known[E] *to* all the *ones* dwelling-in[F] Jerusalem, so that that field was called 'Hakeldama' *in* their own[4] language, that is, 'Field *of* Blood'[5]	18 19
	2C. "For it has been written in *the* book *of* Psalms—	20
	1D. 'Let his residence become desolate[6], and let there not be the *one* dwelling[F] in it'[7] [Ps 69:25] 2D. And, 'let another take his office[8]' [Ps 109:8]	
	3C. "Therefore, *from* the men having accompanied us during all *the* time that the Lord Jesus went in and went out among us—*beginning from[9] the baptism[G] *of* John, until the day that He was taken-up[H] from us— **one *of* these must**[10] become *a* witness[J] *of* His resurrection with us"	21 22
2B. And they put-*forward*[11] two— Joseph (the *one* being called Barsabbas, who was called Justus), and Matthias		23
	1C. And having prayed, they said, "**You**, Lord, heart-knower[K] *of* all— appoint[12] *the* one whom You chose[13] from these two* to take the place[14] *of* this ministry[L] and apostleship[M] from which Judas turned-aside to go to *his* own place"	24 25
	2C. And they gave lots[N] *for* them[15]	26
	3C. And the lot fell upon Matthias, and he was added[16] with the eleven apostles[O]	
3A. And during the day *of* Pentecost[17] being fulfilled[18], they[19] were all together[20] at the same *place*[21]		2:1
	1B. And suddenly *a* noise[22] from heaven like *of a* violent rushing[P] wind took place, and filled[Q] the whole house where they were sitting. *And dividing[23] tongues[R] as-if[24] *of* fire appeared[S] *to* them. And it[25] sat on each one *of* them	2 3
	1C. And they were all filled[26] *with the* Holy Spirit, and began to speak *in* other[27] tongues[28] as the Spirit was giving *the* uttering[29] *to* them	4
	2B. Now there were Jews[30] dwelling in Jerusalem, reverent[T] men, from every nation under heaven. And this sound[U] having taken place, the crowd came together, and was confounded[31] because they were each one hearing them speaking[32] *in his* own language[33]!	5 6
	1C. And they were astonished[34], and were marveling[V], saying[35], "Behold— are not all these *ones* speaking Galileans?[36] *And how *is it* **we** are each *one* hearing *in* our own language in which we were born[W]?—	7 8
	1D. "Parthians[37] and Medes[38] and Elamites[39], and the *ones* dwelling-in Mesopotamia[40] 2D. "And Judea[41] and Cappadocia, Pontus and Asia, *and Phrygia and Pamphylia[42]	9 10

1. This may mean "the unrighteous wage", the wage characterized by unrighteousness; or, "the wage [he received] *for his* unrighteousness". The priests bought this parcel in Judas's name, Mt 27:6-8.
2. Or, "prone". That is, flat on his face, head down. Used only here. GK *4568*. Some think this word means "swollen, distended". Whether Judas fell down after he hung himself (Mt 27:5), or was cut down, is not stated. The Greek only says "having become". A "fall" is implied, not stated.
3. Luke may mean the bursting was caused by the fall. Or he may mean that it was caused by swelling due to exposure— the body abandoned, unburied, and unwanted by anyone. Both ideas are supported by early translations.
4. Some manuscripts omit this word {N}.
5. The field was called this either because it was acquired with blood money, as in Mt 27:8, or because Judas spilled his blood there, or both.
6. Or, "deserted, abandoned". On this word, see "wilderness" in Mt 3:1.
7. This is nicely rephrased "let there not be one to dwell in it". This was fulfilled when Judas died, as described in v 18-19.
8. That is, Judas's position of oversight, his responsibility. Same word as "office of overseer" in 1 Tim 3:1. The fulfillment of this is addressed next by Peter, v 21-22.
9. On the idiom "beginning from", see Mt 20:8.
10. In the Greek word order, "must" is the first word of v 21, and "one *of* these" are the last words of v 22. This is done for emphasis. Peter's point is, it must be so in order to fulfill the verse he quoted. Some think Peter was correct. Others think he was acting impulsively, God having chosen Paul for this purpose. On "must", see Mt 16:21.
11. More literally, "they stood" two. GK *2705*.
12. Or, "show forth, reveal". Elsewhere only in Lk 10:1, where Jesus appointed the seventy-two. GK *344*. The root word is "show".
13. Same word as v 2, where Jesus "chose" the apostles.
14. Same word as later in the verse, on which see Eph 4:27. Some manuscripts say "share, lot" {B}, using the word in v 17, 26.
15. Some manuscripts say "they gave their lots" {B}.
16. Matthias was included among the twelve. Used only here. GK *5164*. Related to "calculate" in Rev 13:18, and "calculate up" in Act 19:19.
17. This word means "fiftieth". Elsewhere only in Act 20:16; 1 Cor 16:8. GK *4300*. This harvest celebration was held on the 50th day after the sheaf offering at Passover. Also known as the Feast of Harvest (Ex 23:16), and the Feast of Weeks (Ex 34:22, it is the day after seven weeks after Passover). See Lev 23:15-22; Num 28:26-31; Deut 16:9-12.
18. Or, "filled up". Some think Luke means "while the day was in progress"; others, "while the fifty day interval was being brought to completion on this last day of it". Same word and idiom as in Lk 9:51. This word is elsewhere only in Lk 8:23, of the boat being "filled-with" water. GK *5230*. Similar to the idiom in Lk 1:23, 57; 2:6, 21, 22; Act 7:23, 30; 9:23; 24:27. There is no indication of how many days passed after the incident in 1:15-26.
19. Luke does not define this further, except that they were all Galileans, v 7. It may refer to the apostles only, 1:13; to all those in 1:14; or to the 120 in the previous incident (1:15). Being in a house, a smaller number may be indicated.
20. Some manuscripts say "with one accord" {N}.
21. The location is not identified, except as a house, v 2. Some link it to the room entered 10 days ago in 1:13.
22. Or, "sound", but not the same word as in v 6. A wind-like noise filled the whole house. On this word, see "news" in Lk 4:37.
23. This is a participle modifying "tongues". Some think Luke means "tongues being divided" or split, cloven, describing the tongue itself. Others think he means "tongues dividing-up" to the people— either "distributing *themselves*", or, "being distributed". Same word as in Lk 11:17, 18; 12:52, 53. Elsewhere only as "divide among" in Mt 27:35; Mk 15:24; Lk 23:34; Jn 19:24; and "distribute" in Lk 22:17; Act 2:45. GK *1374*.
24. Or, "like" fire. On this word, see Rom 6:13.
25. That is, a tongue.
26. The phrase "filled with the Spirit" using this word is elsewhere only in Lk 1:15, 41, 67; Act 4:8, 31; 9:17; 13:9. It leads to a divine empowerment to speak. Same word as in Lk 4:28; 5:26; 6:11; Act 3:10; 5:17; 13:45; 19:29. Used 24 times. GK *4398*.
27. Or, "different". That is, other than Hebrew (Aramaic)— in the languages of other nations.
28. That is, languages, as seen in v 8. Same word as in v 10. On this word, see 1 Cor 12:10. On "*in*" tongues, see 1 Cor 14:2.
29. Or, "speaking out, declaring". Or, "as the Spirit was giving *it to* them to be uttering". These disciples spoke in foreign languages understood by the unbelievers described in v 8-11. The content of the utterances is described by the hearers in v 11. The twofold result of this miracle is seen in v 12-13. Elsewhere only as "declare" in Act 2:14; 26:25. GK *710*. Related to "utter" in 2 Pet 2:18. Compare 1 Cor 14:21-22.
30. That is, non-Judean Jews, non-native speaking Jews from every nation under heaven, as seen in v 9-11. Some manuscripts omit "Jews" {B}, so that it says "there were reverent men dwelling...".
31. Or, "bewildered, confused". On this word, see 9:22.
32. The details are not given. Did each speak one time in one other language, or one time after another to different people as the Spirit gave the uttering of their language? Did it occur only at this event prior to Peter's speech in v 14, or did it continue throughout the day or beyond that day? What is the relationship of this to what is discussed in 1 Cor 14? Opinions vary about these questions, and about what inferences may be drawn from this event.
33. Elsewhere only in 1:19; 2:8; 21:40; 22:2; 26:14. GK *1365*. Our word "dialect" comes from this word, *dialektos*.
34. Some manuscripts add "all", "they were all astonished...", as in v 12 {N}. On this word, see Mk 2:12.
35. Some manuscripts add "to one another" {N}.
36. The grammar indicates that a "yes" answer is expected.
37. Parthians were from the Empire of Parthia, which stretched from the Euphrates to India. Their empire was a great rival of the Roman Empire at this time. Used only here. GK *4222*.
38. Medes were from the territory near the Persian Gulf (in the Parthian Empire). Used only here. GK *3597*.
39. Elam is also near the Persian Gulf, further east (in the Parthian Empire). Used only here. GK *1780*.
40. Mesopotamia is the land around and between the Tigris and Euphrates Rivers, mostly in modern day Iraq. Thus all four of these names refer to peoples living to the northeast of Israel.
41. Used 43 times. GK *2677*.
42. These refer to Roman provinces or regions, from Judea, north and west into what is modern Turkey.

A. 1 Thes 4:4 B. Rev 22:12, recompense C. Phil 1:8, deep feelings D. Act 2:17, pour out E. Rom 1:19 F. Eph 3:17, dwell G. Mk 1:4 H. Act 1:2 J. Act 1:8 K. Act 15:8 L. 1 Cor 12:5 M. Rom 1:5 N. Col 1:12, share O. 1 Cor 12:28 P. 2 Pet 1:17, carried Q. Eph 5:18 R. 1 Cor 12:10 S. Lk 2:26, see T. Lk 2:25 U. Mk 1:26, voice V. Rev 17:8 W. 1 Jn 2:29

	3D. "Egypt and the regions *of* Libya[1] toward Cyrene[2]	
	3D. "And the Romans residing[3] *here*	
	4D. "Both Jews and proselytes[4]	11
	5D. "Cretans[5] and Arabs[6]	
	6D. "We are hearing them speaking the great[7] *things of* God *in* our *own* tongues"	

   2C. And they were all astonished[A] and greatly-perplexed[B], saying one to another, "What does this mean[8]?"   12

   3C. But others, while scoffing[9], were saying that "They have been filled[10] *with* sweet-new-wine[11]"   13

3B. And Peter, having stood with the eleven, raised his voice and declared[12] *to* them[13]—   14

   1C. "Men[C], Jews[14], and all the *ones* dwelling-in Jerusalem— let this[15] be known[D] *to* you, and pay-attention-to[16] my words

      1D. "For these *ones* are not drunk[E], as **you** are assuming[17]. For it is *the* third hour[18] *of* the day   15

      2D. "But this is the *thing* having been spoken through the prophet Joel [in Joel 2:28-32]— 'And it shall be in the last[F] days, God says, *that*   16 / 17

         1E. 'I will pour-out[19] from[20] My Spirit upon all flesh[21]— and your sons and your daughters will prophesy[G], and your young men will see visions[H], and your older[J] men will dream[K] *with* dreams

         2E. 'And indeed[22] I will pour-out from My Spirit in those days upon My *male*-slaves[L] and upon My *female*-slaves[M]— and they will prophesy   18

         3E. 'And I will give wonders[N] in the heaven above, and signs[O] on the earth below— blood, and fire and *a* vapor *of* smoke. °The sun will be changed[P] into darkness, and the moon into blood[Q], before the great and glorious[23] day *of the* Lord comes[24]   19 / 20

         4E. 'And it shall be *that* everyone who calls-upon[R] the name *of the* Lord will be saved[S]'   21

   2C. "Men[C], Israelites, listen-to these words   22

      1D. "*As to* Jesus the Nazarene[T]— *a* man having been attested[25] by God to you *with* miracles[U] and wonders[N] and signs[O] which God did through Him in your midst, just as you yourselves[26] know

      2D. "This *One*— given-over[27] by the determined[28] purpose[29] and foreknowledge[V] *of* God— you killed[W], having fastened[30] *Him to a cross* by *the* hand *of* Lawless[31] *ones*   23

      3D. "Whom God raised-up[X], having put-an-end-to[32] the pains[33] *of* death, because it was not possible *that* He be held-on-to[34] by it[35]   24

         1E. "For David says with reference to Him [in Ps 16:8-11], 'I was seeing[36] the Lord in my presence continually[Y], because He is on my right *side* so that[37] I may not be shaken[Z]   25

            1F. 'For this reason my heart was cheered[38] and my tongue rejoiced-greatly[AA]   26

            2F. 'And furthermore, my flesh will also dwell[39] in hope, °because You will not abandon[BB] my soul[CC] to Hades[DD], nor give[40] Your holy[EE] *One* to see[41] decay[42]   27

            3F. 'You made *the* ways *of* life known *to* me. You will make me full *of* gladness[43] with Your presence'   28

         2E. "Men, brothers[FF], *it is* proper[44] to say to you with confidence[GG] about the patriarch[HH] David that he both came-to-an-end[45] and was buried. And his tomb is with us to this day   29

1. Libya was a nation west of Egypt, on the North African Coast. Used only here. GK *3340*.
2. Cyrene is a city on the North African coast, west of Libya. Used only here. GK *3255*. "Cyrenian" is in 6:9.
3. Or, "visiting". Used of foreigners temporarily staying in a place. Elsewhere only of Athens, 17:21. GK *2111*. Related to "go on a journey" in Mt 21:33.
4. That is, Gentile converts to Judaism. On this word, see Mt 23:15.
5. From the island of Crete. Elsewhere only in Tit 1:12. GK *3205*.
6. From Arabia, east and south of Israel. Used only here. GK *732*. Related to "Arabia" in Gal 1:17.
7. Or, "magnificent, mighty, splendid, grand". Used only here. GK *3483*. Related to "majesty" in Lk 9:43.
8. Literally, "what does this intend to be?", an idiom elsewhere only in 17:20. These people are looking for the answer. The next group has already decided, v 13. This is the "sign from heaven" the Jews had sought from Jesus.
9. Or, "sneering, mocking, jeering". Used only here. GK *1430*. Related to the word in 17:32.
10. This is a participle, "they are having been filled". That is, they are full. Used only here. GK *3551*. Related to "full" in Rom 15:14.
11. Causing drunkenness, v 15. Some think this means these mockers did not understand the words. Others think they understood the words, but considered the people to be excessively exuberant, as with David in 2 Sam 6:16. The twofold result in v 12-13 is a reflection of the hearts of the hearers, not the utterance of the speaker. Used only here. GK *1183*.
12. Same word as "uttering" in v 4. This utterance also was from the Spirit.
13. On the location of this speech, and the size of this crowd, see v 41.
14. Same word as in v 11. On this word, see Jn 1:19. Not the same word as "Judea" in v 9.
15. That is, v 16— that the explanation for what is being seen and heard is found in the prophecy of Joel 2:28. It is a gift poured out from God's Spirit.
16. Or, "give ear to". Used only here. GK *1969*. Related to "ear".
17. Or, "supposing". Same word as in Lk 7:43.
18. That is, 9 A.M.
19. Same word as in v 18, 33; and in 10:45, where "the gift *of* the Holy Spirit" is poured out, referring again to the tongues, v 46. This word is used of pouring out the Spirit in Tit 3:6; the love of God in Rom 5:5; coins in Jn 2:15; and bowls in Rev 16:1, 2, 3, 4, 8, 10, 12, 17. Elsewhere only as "spill out" in Mt 9:17; Lk 5:37; Act 1:18; "shed" blood in Lk 11:50; Rom 3:15; Rev 16:6; and "poured forth" in Jude 11. GK *1772*. Related word in Mt 26:28.
20. Or, "of ". That is, God will pour out gifts "from, of " His Spirit— prophecies, dreams, visions, but here specifically, "what you both see and hear" (v 33), the tongues. Only here and in v 18 is the word "pour out" followed by the preposition "from, of ". When the Spirit was given (Jn 7:39) to be "in" them (Jn 14:17), He was seen in the gifts of power (Act 1:8) given "from" Him, seen here in the tongues.
21. On "all flesh", see "no flesh" in Mt 24:22.
22. Or, "Yes, and", or, "Even upon My... I will pour out". The promise is repeated from a different viewpoint. The previous statement is from the human viewpoint, "your sons and daughters, etc"; this one is from God's viewpoint, "My slaves".
23. Or, "remarkable, notable, conspicuous, famous, renowned, prominent, visible". Used only here. GK *2212*. Related to "appearance" in 2 Thes 2:8, and "appeared" in Tit 2:11. The root word is "to shine".
24. Some think Peter means that this was all symbolically fulfilled here, indicating that such prophecies are not to be taken literally. Others think Joel's prophecy, including the pouring out from His Spirit, was only partially fulfilled here, and that it awaits a full and literal fulfillment upon all flesh and all the cosmos when Christ returns. In this view, Joel speaks with reference to both the first and second comings, without distinguishing them.
25. Or, "proved, shown". Same word as "prove" in 25:7. On this word, see "display" in 2 Thes 2:4.
26. Some manuscripts add "also" {K}.
27. Or, "given up, surrendered, delivered up". The root word is "give". Used only here. GK *1692*.
28. Or, "decided, appointed". This is a participle, "the having been determined" purpose. Same word as in Lk 22:22.
29. Or, "plan, counsel". Same word as in 4:28. On this word, see "counsel" in Eph 1:11.
30. Or, "fixed, affixed". Used only here. GK *4699*. Not related to "nailed" in Col 2:14. Some manuscripts say "having taken *Him*, having fastened..." {N}.
31. That is, ones without God's Law, although operating under Roman law. On this word, see "without the Law" in 1 Cor 9:21.
32. Or, "loosed, brought to an end, annulled, broken [the authority of]". On this word, see "break" in Mt 5:19.
33. On this word, see "birth-pains" in 1 Thes 5:3. The intent of Peter's metaphor may be that when Jesus died, death was thrown into birth-pains until He was delivered, raised from the dead. God raised Him, releasing death from its role. Or, it may be used figuratively here, without specific reference to "birth" pains.
34. Or, "held fast, held back". That is, held under its control, prevented from leaving. On this word, see Heb 4:14.
35. That is, by death. It was not possible because of the prophecy of David given next.
36. Same word as "foresee" in v 31. Here, it means "seeing-before *me*" in my presence continually.
37. Or, "so that I will not", giving the result. GK *2671*.
38. On this word, see "celebrate" in Rev 12:12. Related to "gladness" in v 28.
39. Or, "settle down, make its dwelling upon". Elsewhere only as "nests" in Mt 13:32; Mk 4:32; Lk 13:19. GK *2942*. Related to "nest" in Lk 9:58.
40. That is, permit. On this word, see Eph 1:22.
41. That is, experience. On this word, see Lk 2:26.
42. Or, "corruption, destruction". Elsewhere only in v 31, and in 13:34, 35, 36, 37, where Paul makes this same argument. GK *1426*.
43. Or, "good cheer", the joy of celebration. Elsewhere only in 14:17. GK *2372*. Related to "cheer" in v 26.
44. Or, "permitted, possible, allowable". This is a participle, it "*is* being proper". On this word, see "lawful" in 1 Cor 6:12.
45. That is, died. On this word, see Mk 9:48.

A. Mk 2:12 B. Lk 9:7 C. 1 Tim 2:12 D. Rom 1:19 E. 1 Cor 11:21 F. Heb 1:2 G. 1 Cor 14:1 H. Rev 9:17 J. 1 Tim 5:1 K. Jude 8 L. Rom 6:17, slave M. Lk 1:38, slave N. 2 Thes 2:9 O. 2 Thes 2:9 P. Gal 1:7 Q. 1 Jn 1:7 R. 1 Pet 1:17 S. Lk 19:10 T. Mt 2:23 U. 1 Cor 12:10 V. 1 Pet 1:2 W. Mt 2:16 X. Lk 18:33 Y. 2 Thes 3:16 Z. Act 17:13 AA. Lk 10:21 BB. 2 Cor 4:9, forsaken CC. Jam 5:20 DD. Rev 1:18 EE. Heb 7:26 FF. Act 16:40 GG. Heb 4:16 HH. Heb 7:4

	3E. "Therefore, being *a* prophet[A], and knowing that God swore[B] *to* him *with an* oath[C] to seat[D] *One* from *the* fruit *of* his loins[1] upon his throne, °having foreseen[2] *it*, he spoke concerning the resurrection *of* the Christ— that He[3] was neither abandoned to Hades, nor did His flesh see decay	30 31
	4D. "God raised up this Jesus, *of* which **we** are all witnesses[E]	32
	5D. "Therefore having been exalted[F] *to*[4] the right *hand of* God, and having received the promise *of* the Holy Spirit[5] from the Father, He poured-out this which **you** are both[6] seeing and hearing	33
	1E. "For[7] David did not go up into the heavens, but he himself says [in Ps 110:1], 'The Lord said *to* my Lord, "Be sitting on My right *side* °until I put Your enemies *as a* footstool *of* Your feet'	34 35
	6D. "Therefore let all *the* house[G] *of* Israel know with-certainty[8] that God made Him both Lord and Christ— this Jesus Whom **you** crucified"	36
4B.	And having heard *it*, they were pierced[9] *in* the heart, and said to Peter and the other apostles, "Men, brothers, what should we do?"	37
	1C. And Peter says[10] to them, "Repent[H], and let each *of* you be baptized[J] on-the-basis-of[11] the name *of* Jesus Christ for *the* forgiveness[K] *of* your[12] sins, and you will receive the gift[L] *of* the Holy Spirit	38
	1D. "For the promise is *for* you, and *for* your children, and *for* all the *ones* far-away[13]— all-whom *the* Lord our God will call-to[14] *Himself*"	39
	2C. And he solemnly-testified[M] *with* many other words, and was exhorting[N] them, saying, "Be saved[O] from this crooked[15] generation[P]"	40
5B.	So indeed, the *ones* having welcomed[16] his word were baptized. And about three-thousand souls were added[Q] on that day[17]	41
4A. Now[18] they were devoting-themselves[19] to the teaching[R] *of* the apostles[20] and *to* fellowship[S], *to* the[21] breaking[22] *of* the bread and *to* prayers		42
	1B. And awe[23] was taking place *in* every soul[T]	43
	2B. And many wonders[U] and signs were taking place through the apostles[24]	
	3B. And all the *ones* believing were at the same *place*[25], and were having all *things* common[26]. °And they were selling properties[27] and possessions[28], and distributing[V] them *to* all— as[29] anyone was having *a* need[W]	44-45
	4B. And while continuing[X] daily with-one-accord[Y] in the temple and breaking[30] bread house by house[31], they were sharing-in[Z] food with gladness[AA] and simplicity[32] *of* heart, °while praising[BB] God, and having favor[CC] with the whole people	46 47
	5B. And the Lord was adding[Q] the *ones* being saved[O] daily at-the-same-*place*[33]	
5A. Now Peter and John were going up to the temple at the hour *of* prayer, the ninth *hour*[34]		3:1
	1B. And *a* certain man being lame from his mother's womb[DD] was being carried	2
	1C. Whom they were putting daily at the gate *of* the temple being called "Beautiful", *that* he might be asking-*for* alms[35] from the *ones* coming into the temple	

1. That is, from David's offspring. On this word, see Heb 7:5. Some manuscripts say "to raise up the Christ from *the* fruit *of* his loins according to *the* flesh to sit upon His throne" {B}.
2. Same word as in Gal 3:8. Elsewhere only as "seeing" in Act 2:25, and "previously seen" in Act 21:29. GK *4632*.
3. Some manuscripts say "His soul" {N}.
4. Or, "*by*".
5. That is, the promise consisting of the Helper, the Holy Spirit. Compare 1:4.
6. That is, the speaking in languages not learned which they are seeing and hearing. Some manuscripts omit this word {C}. Some manuscripts add "now" {N}, "which **you** are now both...".
7. This verse is quoted with regard to the exaltation mentioned in v 33.
8. On this word, see "securely" in 16:23. Related to "certainty" in Lk 1:4.
9. Or, "stabbed, pricked, stunned". Used only here. GK *2920*. Related to "stabbed" in Jn 19:34.
10. Some manuscripts omit this word, leaving it implied {C}; others say "said" {N}.
11. Or, "in reference to, by use of, in, for". This is the only place where this preposition is used with "baptize". GK *2093*. Some manuscripts have the more normal "in" {N}. Luke uses the phrase "on the basis of the name" ten of its fourteen occurrences, Mt 18:5; 24:5; Mk 9:37, 39; 13:6; Lk 1:59; 9:48; 21:8; 24:47; Act 2:38; 4:17, 18; 5:28, 40. See also Act 3:16.
12. Some manuscripts omit this word {N}.
13. Peter may mean physically distant— the Jews in the dispersion. He may mean spiritually distant— the Gentiles, as this word is used in 22:21; Eph 2:13, 17. He may mean distant in time—future generations. Or, he may have all of this in mind, intending it in the broadest sense. GK *3426* and *3431*.
14. Or, "will summon". Same word as in 13:2, and "call" in 16:10. Elsewhere 26 times as "summon". GK *4673*.
15. On this word, see 1 Pet 2:18. This generation is no longer straight with the truth.
16. Or, "received, accepted". Elsewhere only in Lk 8:40; 9:11; Act 18:27; 21:17; 24:3; 28:30. GK *622*. Some manuscripts add "gladly" {N}, as in 21:17.
17. This may mean Peter spoke to over 3000 at one time, the transition from the house in v 2 to the place this occurred (perhaps the temple) not being given. Or, it may mean that at the end of the day, from those who heard this speech at the house and all those who subsequently heard of this event and spoke with the apostles and disciples, 3000 were added.
18. Having seen the proclamation of the church and its response, Luke now gives an internal view of the church. He repeats this cycle two more times in chapters 3-6.
19. Or, "persisting, persevering *in*; attending *to*; engaging *in*; busying, occupying themselves *with*; continuing *in*". Same word as in 1:14; 6:4; Rom 12:12; 13:6; Col 4:2. Elsewhere only as "continuing" in Act 2:46; "attach oneself *to*" in Act 8:13; 10:7; and "stand ready for" in Mk 3:9. GK *4674*. Related to "persevere" in Heb 11:27, and "perseverance" in Eph 6:18.
20. The learners (the disciples) are now the teachers!
21. Some manuscripts say "and to the..." {N}.
22. Some think Luke is referring to eating together, as in the only other use of this word, Lk 24:35. Others think that he is referring to the Lord's Supper, perhaps eaten in conjunction with a meal. GK *3082*. The related verb is in v 46. Related to "fragments" in Mt 15:37.
23. Or, "fear". On this word, see "fear" in Eph 5:21.
24. Some manuscripts add "in Jerusalem. And *a* great awe was upon all" {C}.
25. Or, were "together". See v 47.
26. This is explained in 4:32, where this same word is used. The believers were sharing everything with their new "family" having God as Father. They were sharing their things which God provided and owns, regarding everything as being for God's use.
27. On this word, see Mt 19:22. Same word as in Act 5:1, where Ananias sold a property. Related to "owner" in 4:34.
28. Elsewhere only in Heb 10:34. GK *5638*.
29. Or, "in proportion as, to the degree that, according as". Same word as in 4:35. The believers were repeatedly selling their extra things to help as needs arose. GK *2776*.
30. Elsewhere only of miraculous bread, Mt 14:19; 15:36; Mk 8:6, 19; of the Lord's Supper, Mt 26:26; Mk 14:22; Lk 22:19; 1 Cor 10:16; 11:24; of an ordinary meal, Lk 24:30; Act 27:35; and in Act 20:7, 11, where as here, opinions differ as to whether Luke means the Lord's Supper or an ordinary meal. GK *3089*. Some think "sharing in food" which follows explains this phrase. Others think it is in addition to this phrase. It was the Jewish custom for the father to break the bread at the start of a meal. So this term can simply mean "eating their meals". Or, it could refer to the special Christian celebration, the Lord's Supper. Related to the word in v 42.
31. On this idiom, see 5:42.
32. Used only here. GK *911*.
33. Or, added "together". This idiom is elsewhere only in Mt 22:34; Lk 17:35; Act 1:15; 2:1, 44; 4:26; 1 Cor 7:5 ("together"); 11:20; 14:23. Some take it here to mean "on the same *number*", that is, adding to their total, or to their number. Others take is as a technical phrase meaning "into church fellowship". Some manuscripts add "*to* the church" and take this phrase with 3:1 {B}, so that it says "daily *to* the church. Now together, Peter and John...".
34. That is, 3 P.M. How many days passed since Pentecost is not stated. 2:42-47 describes events in the interim.
35. That is, charitable giving to the poor. On this word, see "almsgiving" in Mt 6:2. Same word as in v 3, 10.

A. 1 Cor 12:28   B. Jam 5:12   C. Jam 5:12   D. Rev 20:4, sat down   E. Act 1:8   F. Jn 8:28, lifted up   G. Mk 3:20   H. Act 26:20   J. Mk 1:8
K. Col 1:14   L. Rom 5:15   M. 1 Tim 5:21, solemnly charge   N. Rom 12:8   O. Lk 19:10   P. Mt 24:34   Q. Lk 17:5, increase   R. 1 Cor 14:6
S. 1 Cor 1:9   T. Jam 5:20   U. 2 Thes 2:9   V. Act 2:3, dividing   W. Tit 3:14   X. Act 2:42, devoting themselves to   Y. Act 1:14   Z. Heb 12:10
AA. Jude 24   BB. Rom 15:11   CC. Eph 2:8, grace   DD. Lk 1:15

2C.	Who, having seen Peter and John being about to go into the temple, was asking to receive[1] alms	3
2B.	And Peter, along with John, having looked-intently[A] at him, said, "Look at us!"	4
1C.	And the *one* was fixing-*his*-attention-on[B] them, expecting[C] to receive something from them	5
2C.	And Peter said, "There is[2] no silver and gold *with* me. But what I have, this I give *to* you— in the name *of* Jesus Christ the Nazarene[D], arise[3] and walk"	6
1D.	And having seized[E] him *by* the right hand, he raised[F] him	7
2D.	And at once his feet and ankles were made-strong[4]	
3D.	And leaping-up[5], he stood and was walking-around	8
3C.	And he entered with them into the temple, walking and leaping[6] and praising[G] God	
4C.	And all the people saw him walking and praising[G] God	9
1D.	And they were recognizing[H] him— that **he**[7] was the *one* sitting for alms at the Beautiful Gate *of* the temple	10
2D.	And they were filled *with* wonder[8] and astonishment[J] at the *thing* having happened *to* him	
3B.	And while he[9] *was* holding-on-to[K] Peter and John, all the people ran-together[10] to them at the portico[L] being called "Solomon's", struck-with-wonder[11]. *And having seen *it*, Peter responded to the people	11 12
1C.	"Men[M], Israelites, why are you marveling[N] at this? Or why are you looking-intently[A] *at* **us** as-*if* **we** caused[12] him to walk *by* **our** own power[O] or godliness[P]?	
1D.	"The God *of* Abraham and the God[13] *of* Isaac and the God *of* Jacob, the God *of* our fathers— He glorified[14] His servant[15] Jesus	13
1E.	"Whom **you** indeed handed-over[Q] and denied[R] in the presence *of* Pilate[S]— that *one* having determined[16] to release[T] *Him*	
1F.	"But **you** denied[R] the Holy[U] and Righteous *One*, and asked *that a* man who was[17] *a* murderer be granted *to* you	14
2E.	"And you killed[V] the Author[18] *of* life, Whom God raised[F] from *the* dead— *of* which **we** are witnesses	15
2D.	"And on-the-basis-of[19] [our] faith[20] *in* His name, His name made this *one* strong whom you see and know. And the faith *that comes* through Him gave him this wholeness[21] in front of all *of* you	16
2C.	"And now, brothers, I know that you acted[W] in-accordance-with[22] ignorance[23], just as also your rulers[X]. *But God fulfilled[Y] in this manner *the things* which He announced-beforehand[24] through *the* mouth *of* all the prophets— *that* His[25] Christ *would* suffer[Z]	17 18
1D.	"Therefore repent[AA] and turn-back[BB] so that your sins *may* be wiped-out[26]	19
1E.	"So that times *of* refreshing[27] may come from *the* presence *of* the Lord, and He may send-forth[28] the Christ having been appointed[29] *for* you— Jesus[30]	20

1. Some manuscripts omit this word, so that it says "was asking for alms" {N}.
2. Or, in a more specific sense, silver and gold "is not possessed *by* me; is not present *with* me; is not at my disposal; is not in my possession; does not belong *to* me". Luke uses this word to mean "is" in 23 of its 25 occurrences in Acts. On this word, see "being" in Phil 2:6. Many simplify this by rephrasing it as "I do not have silver...".
3. Some manuscripts omit "arise and", so that it simply says "walk" {C}. Same word as "raised" in v 7.
4. Or, "made firm". Same word as in v 16. On this word, see "became firm" in 16:5.
5. Used only here. GK *1982*.
6. Same word as in 14:10. On this word, see "bubble up" in Jn 4:14. The man was "springing". Related to "leaping up" earlier.
7. Some manuscripts say "that this *one*" {N}.
8. Or, "amazement". Elsewhere only as "astonishment" in Lk 4:36; 5:9. GK *2502*. Related to "astonish" in Mk 1:27.
9. Some manuscripts say "while the lame *one* having been healed *was* holding-on-to Peter..." {K}.
10. Same word as in Mk 6:33. Elsewhere only as "run with" in 1 Pet 4:4. GK *5340*. Related word in 21:30.
11. This adjective is used only here. GK *1702*. Related to "wonder" in v 10. The related verb is in Mk 9:15.
12. This is a participle, more literally, "as if *it is we* having caused him to walk". Jesus never made such a disclaimer. On this word, see "does" in Rev 13:13.
13. Some manuscripts say "the God *of* Abraham and Isaac and Jacob" {C}.
14. Peter may mean "by healing this man" (as in v 16), or, "by raising Jesus from the dead" (as in v 15).
15. This word is used of Jesus also in v 26; 4:27, 30; Mt 12:18. It was used of Messiah, based on Isa 42:1; 52:13, etc., and points to Jesus as the suffering servant of Isa 53. It means "boy, girl" (with different grammar), and "child, servant". Used 24 times. GK *4090*. Related to "children" in 1 Jn 2:14.
16. Or, "judged, resolved, decided". That is, having made a judicial decision to release Jesus. On this word, see "judge" in Mt 7:1.
17. On the idiom "*a man who was...*", see Lk 24:19.
18. Or, "Originator, Pioneer, Leader". Same word as "leader" in 5:31. On this word, see Heb 2:10.
19. Some manuscripts omit this word {N}, so that it says "And *by* faith...".
20. Same phrase as in Phil 3:9. Same grammar as "on the basis of His name" in Act 2:38.
21. Or, "completeness", that is, complete in all its parts. Used only here. GK *3907*. Related to "whole" in 1 Thes 5:23.
22. Or, "based on, by way of, according to". GK *2848*.
23. The point of this is not that they are therefore excused, but that forgiveness is therefore possible. On this word, see Eph 4:18.
24. Or, "foretold". Elsewhere only in 7:52. GK *4615*.
25. Some manuscripts have this word with prophets {K}, "... all His prophets— *that* the Christ...".
26. Or, "wiped away, rubbed out". On this word, see Col 2:14.
27. Or, "relief, a breathing space, relaxation". Used only here. GK *433*. Related to "refresh" in 2 Tim 1:16.
28. Peter is referring to the Second Coming, v 21. God sent Jesus forth now for your salvation, v 26 (same word, on which see "sent out" in Mk 3:14).
29. Or, "selected, chosen". On this word, see 22:14. Some manuscripts say "preached before" {K}.
30. Or, "send forth the *One* having been appointed *for* you— Christ Jesus". Some manuscripts say "send forth the *One* having been appointed for you— Jesus Christ" {N}.

A. Lk 4:20   B. 1 Tim 4:16   C. Lk 3:15, waiting in expectation   D. Mt 2:23   E. Jn 11:57   F. Mt 28:6, arose   G. Rom 15:11   H. Col 1:6, understood   J. Mk 5:42   K. Heb 4:14   L. Jn 5:2   M. 1 Tim 2:12   N. Rev 17:8   O. 1 Cor 12:10, miracle   P. 1 Tim 2:2   Q. Mt 26:21   R. 2 Tim 2:12   S. Lk 3:1   T. Mt 5:31, sends way   U. 1 Pet 1:16   V. Rom 7:11   W. Rom 2:1, practicing   X. Rev 1:5   Y. Eph 5:18, filled   Z. Gal 3:4   AA. Act 26:20   BB. Jam 5:19

| Acts 3:21 | 404 | Verse |

        1F. "Whom it-is-necessary[1] *that* **heaven**[2] receive[A] until *the* times *of* restoration[3] *of* all *things, of* which God spoke through *the* mouth *of* His[4] holy[5] prophets from *the past* age[6]   21

    2D. "Moses[7] said[8] [in Deut 18:15-19] that '*The* Lord your[9] God will raise-up[B] *a* prophet *for* you from your brothers like me. You shall listen-to[10] Him in relation to all that He says to you. ⸰And it will be *that* every soul[C] who does not listen-to that prophet will be utterly-destroyed[11] out of the people'   22 23

    3D. "And indeed all the prophets from Samuel and *his* successors[12] who spoke[13] also announced[14] these days   24

    4D. "**You** are the sons[D] *of* the prophets, and *of* the covenant[E] which God covenanted[15] with your[16] fathers, saying to Abraham [in Gen 22:18], "And all the families *of* the earth will be blessed[F] in your seed[G]"   25

    5D. "God, having raised-up[B] His Servant[17], sent Him forth ***to you first***— blessing[H] you in[18] turning-away[19] each *of you* from your evil-*ways*"   26

4B. And while they *were* speaking to the people, the priests[20] and the captain[J] *of* the temple [guard] and the Sadducees suddenly-came-upon[K] them, ⸰being greatly-disturbed[21] because of their teaching the people and proclaiming[L] in[22] Jesus the resurrection[M] from *the* dead   4:1 2

    1C. And they put *their* hands on them, and put *them* in jail[23] until the next day. For it was already evening   3

    2C. But many of the *ones* having heard the word believed. And the number *of* the men became about[24] five thousand   4

5B. And it came about on the next *day that* their rulers and elders and scribes were gathered together in Jerusalem— ⸰and Annas[25] the high priest, and Caiaphas, and John, and Alexander, and all who were of *the* high-priestly family[N]   5 6

    1C. And having stood them in the middle, they were inquiring[O], "By what power or by what name did **you** do this?"   7

    2C. Then Peter, having been filled[P] *with the* Holy Spirit, said to them, "Rulers *of* the people, and elders[26]— ⸰If **we** are being examined[Q] today for *a* good-deed[R] *to a* weak[27] man, by what means[28] this *one* has been restored[S]   8 9

        1D. "Let it be known[T] *to* you all and *to* all the people *of* Israel   10

            1E. "That by the name *of* Jesus Christ the Nazarene[U]— Whom **you** crucified, Whom God raised[V] from *the* dead— by this One[29] this *one* stands before you healthy[W]

            2E. "This *One* is the stone—   11

                1F. The *One* having been treated-with-contempt[30] by you, the builders

                2F. The *One* having become[31] *the* head *of the* corner[32]

            3E. "And there is no salvation[X] in[33] any other, for neither is there another name under heaven having been given among people by which we must[Y] be saved[Z]"   12

    3C. Now observing[AA] the boldness[BB] *of* Peter and John, and having understood[34] that they were[35] uneducated[36] and untrained[37] men, they were marveling[CC]. And they were recognizing[DD] them, that they had been[38] with Jesus. ⸰And seeing the man standing *there* with them, the *one* having been cured[EE], they were having nothing to speak-against[39] *it*   13 14

1. Or, "Whom **heaven** must receive". On this idiom, see "must" in Mt 16:21.
2. Peter uses grammar that implies a correlating statement at the end of this sentence, but is left unsaid, something like "And then He will return".
3. Used only here. GK *640*. Related to "restoring" in 1:6.
4. Some manuscripts say "all His" {N}.
5. Some manuscripts say "the mouth *of* the Holy *Ones*— His prophets from *the past* age" {B}.
6. On this phrase, "from *the past* age", see Lk 1:70.
7. Some manuscripts say "For Moses..." {N}. Peter uses grammar that expects a second witness to follow, which comes in v 24.
8. Some manuscripts add "to the fathers" {B}.
9. Some manuscripts say "our"; others omit this word {C}.
10. That is, listen and obey.
11. Used only here. GK *2017*. Same word as "cut off" in Gen 17:14; Ex 12:15; and "destroy" in Deut 1:27, 2:34. Used over 200 times in the Greek OT. Related to "destruction" in 1 Cor 5:5.
12. That is, to the ones coming after him in succession, one by one. On this word, see "successive" in Lk 8:1.
13. Or, "And all the prophets also, from Samuel and *his* successors— as many as spoke also announced these days".
14. On this word, see "proclaim" in Phil 1:18. Some manuscripts say "announced-beforehand" {K}, using the related word in v 18.
15. Peter uses the verb and noun of the same root word. On this word, see Heb 8:10.
16. Some manuscripts say "our" {C}.
17. Some manuscripts add "Jesus" {K}, as in v 13.
18. Or, "by". That is, "in connection with" or "by means of". GK *1877*.
19. God is blessing this generation in seeking to turn them away from their sin of rejecting His Messiah instead of judging them for it— assuming they now listen to Him. On this word, see Heb 12:25.
20. Some manuscripts say "the chief priests" {B}.
21. Elsewhere only as "greatly annoyed" in 16:18. GK *1387*. The root word is "pain" in Col 4:13.
22. This may mean "in the case of Jesus" or "by means of Jesus". This phrase may have Luke's emphasis in the word order, and mean "the resurrection from the dead **in the case of Jesus**". Or, Luke may mean the apostles were teaching that the resurrection of the dead is real— a doctrine which the Sadducees denied— and proclaiming it to be available through faith in Jesus. GK *1877*.
23. Or, "custody, safekeeping", the "keeping" place. Same word as in 5:18, where "public" is added. Luke may mean in the public jail here, or he may mean somewhere in the temple, under guard. The root word is "to keep".
24. Some manuscripts omit this word {C}.
25. On Annas and Caiaphas, see Lk 3:2. John may be the son of Annas named Jonathan, who replaced Caiaphas as high priest in A.D. 36. Alexander is unknown to us.
26. Some manuscripts add "*of* Israel" {B}.
27. Or, "feeble, sick", physically weak and powerless. On this word, see 1 Thes 5:14.
28. This includes both the power and name of v 7. Or, "*name*", agreeing grammatically with "name" in v 7, 10.
29. Or, "this *name*". Note the repetition of "this one" three times in v 10-11. GK *4047*.
30. Or, "despised". Same word as in Lk 23:11, and related to the word in Mk 9:12. On this word, see 1 Thes 5:20. Peter does not say "rejected" (as in Mt 21:42; Mk 12:10; Lk 20:17; 1 Pet 2:7; which are all quoting Ps 118:22). This may be because he is hoping these leaders will not reject Jesus now.
31. More literally, "having come-to-be for *the* head...", a Hebrew way of speaking.
32. On this phrase, see Mk 12:10.
33. Or, "by means of". GK *1877*.
34. Or, "comprehended, grasped". On this word, see "overcome" in Jn 1:5.
35. More literally, "are", as the Greek typically phrases it.
36. Or, "unlearned, unschooled". The apostles were not trained in the Jewish schools. They had no formal rabbinic training. Used only here. GK *63*. Related to "writings" in Jn 7:15, where a similar comment is made of Jesus.
37. That is, "laymen" in theological matters. On this word, see "uninstructed" in 1 Cor 14:16.
38. More literally, "they were", as the Greek typically phrases it.
39. Same word as used by Jesus in Lk 21:15.

A. Mt 10:40, welcome   B. Lk 18:33   C. Jam 5:20   D. Gal 3:7   E. Heb 8:6   F. Gal 3:8   G. Heb 11:11   H. Lk 6:28   J. Act 5:26   K. Lk 21:34   L. Phil 1:18   M. Act 24:15   N. 1 Cor 12:28, kind   O. Act 23:34, learned   P. Act 2:4   Q. 1 Cor 2:14   R. 1 Tim 6:2, good work   S. Jam 5:15   T. Rom 1:19   U. Mt 2:23   V. Mt 28:6, arose   W. Mt 12:13   X. Lk 19:9   Y. Mt 16:21   Z. Lk 19:10   AA. Lk 10:18, seeing   BB. Heb 4:16, confidence   CC. Rev 17:8   DD. Col 1:6, understood   EE. Mt 8:7

    4C. But having ordered[A] them to go outside *of* the council[1] [chamber], they were conferring with one another,* saying, "What should we do[2] *with* these men?   15
16

        1D. "For **that**[3] *a* known[B] sign[C] has taken place through them *is* evident[D] *to* all the *ones* dwelling-in Jerusalem, and we cannot deny[E] it—*but in order that it may not spread further[4] to the people, let us threaten[5] them to no longer be speaking on the basis of this name *to* any *of* mankind[6]"   17

    5C. And having called them, they commanded[F] *them* not to be speaking[7] nor teaching at all on the basis of the name[8] *of* Jesus   18

    6C. But having responded, Peter and John said to them, "Whether it is right[G] in the sight of God to listen-to you rather than God, you judge[9]. *For **we** are not able to not be speaking *the things* which we saw and heard"   19
20

    7C. And the *ones*, having threatened further, released[H] them   21

        1D. Finding nothing *as to* how they might punish[J] them

        2D. Because of the people— because they were all glorifying[K] God for the *thing* having taken place

            1E. For the man was more *than* forty years *old* upon whom this sign[C] *of* healing[L] had taken place   22

  6B. And having been released[H], they went to *their* own *people* and reported[M] all-that the chief priests and the elders said to them   23

    1C. And the *ones* having heard *it* lifted *their* voice to God with-one-accord[N] and said   24

        1D. "Master[O], **You** *are*[10]

            1E. "The *One* having made the heaven and the earth and the sea, and all the *things* in them

            2E. "The *One* having said by *the* Holy Spirit, *from the* mouth *of* our father David, Your servant[11] [in Ps 2:1-2], 'Why[P] did *the* Gentiles[12] rage[13], and *the* peoples plot[14] futile[15] *things*? *The kings *of* the earth took-their-stand[16], and the rulers[Q] were gathered-together at the same *place*[17] against the Lord, and against His Anointed-*One*[18]'   25
26

                1F. "For in accordance with [Your] truth[19], both Herod[R] and Pontius Pilate[S] together with *the* Gentiles and *the* peoples[20] *of* Israel were gathered-together in this city[21] against Your holy servant[T] Jesus Whom You anointed[22]—*to do all-that Your hand and Your[23] purpose[24] predestined[25] to take place   27
28

        2D. "And *as to* the *things* now, Lord—   29

            1E. "Look-upon[26] their threats[U]

            2E. "And grant *to* Your slaves[V] to speak Your word with all boldness[W] *while[27] You *are* stretching-out[X] Your hand for healing[L], and[28] signs[C] and wonders[Y] *are* taking place through the name *of* Your holy servant[T] Jesus"   30

    2C. And they having prayed, the place in which they had been gathered-together[29] was shaken[Z]. And they were all filled[30] *with* the Holy Spirit. And they were speaking the word *of* God with boldness[W]   31

6A. Now[31] *the* heart[AA] and soul[BB] *of* the multitude *of* the *ones* having believed was one   32

1. Or, "Sanhedrin". Luke may be referring to the room, or to the council meeting in it. Same word as in 5:27.
2. Some manuscripts say "will we do" {K}.
3. The grammar emphasizes the contrast between the two halves of this sentence. We cannot deny this known sign, but we can hinder the spread of the teaching based on this name.
4. Thois is an idiom, "to *the* more". On this idiom, see 2 Tim 2:16.
5. Or, "forbid them with threats". Elsewhere only in 1 Pet 2:23. GK *580*. Related to "threaten further" in v 21, and to "threats" in v 29. Some manuscripts say "threaten *with* threats" {N}, imitating a Hebrew way of speaking.
6. That is, to any human. This idiom (used only here) is related to "none of mankind" in Mk 11:2.
7. Or, "uttering a word, producing a sound". On this word, see "utter" in 2 Pet 2:18.
8. On this phrase, see 2:38.
9. This is a command. On this word, see Mt 7:1.
10. Some manuscripts say "You *are* God— the *One*..." {B}.
11. Some manuscripts say instead, "The *One* having said through *the* mouth *of* David Your servant" {C}.
12. Or, "nations". Same word as in v 27. On this word, see 15:23.
13. Or, "behave arrogantly, act haughtily". Used of horses snorting and stomping, and cocks crowing. Used only here. GK *5865*.
14. This word means "think on, meditate on"— here in a negative sense, "conspire, plot". On this word, see its use in a positive sense in 1 Tim 4:15, "take care with".
15. Or, "vain, empty", things without result or effect. On this word, see "empty" in 1 Thes 2:1.
16. Or, "stood near, appeared, presented themselves" with hostile intent. On this word, see "present" in Rom 12:1.
17. This same phrase occurs in Mt 22:34. The verb itself means "gathered together", as it is used here and in v 27 (and in v 5, 31). GK *5251*. The idiom "at the same *place*" corresponds to "in this city" in the next verse. Others render the whole phrase "gathered together", taking the idiom "at the same" to mean "together" here (see 2:47 on this).
18. Or, "Christ". It is rendered this way to show its relationship to "anointed" in v 27.
19. On "in accordance with truth", see Lk 4:25.
20. This word is plural with reference to Israel only here. Some think these disciples mean "the people of Israel", as the singular is used; others, the people groups within Israel, Israel as an aggregate of the peoples attending Passover from various nations. On the plural use of this word, see Rev 21:3.
21. Some manuscripts omit "in this city" {K}.
22. This is the verb related to "Christ", the "Anointed *One*" in v 26. On this word, see Lk 4:18.
23. Some manuscripts omit this word {C}.
24. Same word as in 2:23, God's determined "purpose".
25. On this word, see Rom 8:29. The opposition of the leaders and peoples against Jesus was in fulfillment of the prophecy spoken by David. And they are still opposing Him— as seen in v 5-22.
26. That is, "concern Yourself with". Elsewhere only in Lk 1:25. GK *2078*. The root word is "to see".
27. Or, "during Your stretching out...". This idiom, "during" followed by a verb in this way, is a mark of Luke's style, Lk 1:8, 21; 2:6, 43; 5:1, 12; Act 2:1; 8:6; etc. Others think that here it means "by You stretching out....".
28. On the relationship of this phrase to what precedes, this may mean "for healing and *for* signs and wonders to take place", giving two objects to "stretching out for"; or, "while You *are* stretching out Your hand for healing, and signs and wonders *are* taking place...", giving two components to the "while" phrase; or, "*that they might* speak Your word... healing, and *that* signs and wonders *might* take place...", giving two components to this request.
29. This is a participle, "they were having been gathered together".
30. Same word as in 2:4.
31. As in 2:42, Luke again turns to an internal view of the church.

A. Mt 14:28 B. Rom 1:19 C. 2 Thes 2:9 D. Rom 1:19 E. 2 Tim 2:12 F. 1 Tim 1:3 G. Rom 1:17, righteous H. Mt 5:31, sends away J. 2 Pet 2:9 K. Rom 8:30 L. Lk 13:32 M. 1 Jn 1:3, announcing N. Act 1:14 O. Jude 4 P. Mt 27:46 Q. Rev 1:5 R. Mt 14:1 S. Lk 3:1 T. Act 3:13 U. Eph 6:9, threatening V. Rom 6:17 W. Heb 4:16, confidence X. Act 27:30 Y. 2 Thes 2:9 Z. Act 17:13 AA. Rev 2:23 BB. Jam 5:20

	1B. And not even one *of them* was saying *that* any *of* the *things* belonging[A] *to* him were *his* own, but all *things* were common[1] *to* them	
	2B. And *with* great power[2], the apostles were rendering[3] *their* testimony[4] *of* the resurrection *of* the Lord Jesus[5]	33
	3B. And great grace[B] was upon them all—*for there was not even someone in-need[6] among them	34
	1C. For all-who were owners[7] *of* lands or houses, selling *them,* were bringing[8] the proceeds[C] *of* the *things* being sold[9] *and laying *it* at the feet *of* the apostles. And it was being distributed[10] *to* each *one* as[11] anyone was having *a* need[D]	35
	2C. Now Joseph[12], the *one* having been called Barnabas[13] by the apostles (which being translated[E] is "son *of* encouragement[14]"), *a* Levite[F], *a* Cyprian[15] *by* nationality[G]—*a field belonging[A] *to* him— having made-a sale, brought the money and laid *it* at[16] the feet *of* the apostles	36 37
	4B. But *a* certain man, Ananias *by* name, along with his wife Sapphira, sold property[17]. *And he kept-back[18] *some* of the proceeds[19], *his* wife also having shared-the-knowledge[20]	5:1-2
	1C. And having brought *a* certain part *of it*, he laid *it* at the feet *of* the apostles	
	1D. But Peter said, "Ananias, for what reason did Satan fill[21] your heart *that* you *should* lie-to[22] the Holy Spirit and keep-back *some* of the proceeds *of* the land?	3
	1E. "While remaining[H] *unsold,* was it not remaining[H] yours?[23] And having been sold, was it *not* within your authority[24]?	4
	2E. "Why *is it* that you put[25] this thing in your heart? You did not lie *to* people, but *to* God"[26]	
	2D. And Ananias, hearing these words, having fallen-*down,* expired[27]	5
	3D. And great fear[J] came upon all the *ones* hearing *it*[28]	
	4D. And having arisen, the younger[K] *men* wrapped him up[29]. And having carried *him* out, they buried *him*	6
	2C. Now *an* interval *of* about three hours took place, and his wife came in— not knowing the *thing* having happened	7
	1D. And Peter responded to her, "Tell me whether you[30] *two* sold[31] the land *for* so much?"	8
	2D. And the *one* said, "Yes, *for* so much"	
	3D. And Peter *said* to her, "Why *is it* that it was agreed[32] *by* you *two* to test[33] the Spirit *of the* Lord? Behold— the feet *of* the *ones* having buried your husband *are* at the door. And they will carry you out"	9
	4D. And she fell at-once[L] at his feet, and expired	10
	5D. And having come in, the young-men[M] found her dead. And having carried *her* out, they buried *her* with her husband	
	3C. And great fear[J] came upon the whole church, and upon all the *ones* hearing-*of* these *things*	11
7A.	Now[34] many signs[N] and wonders[O] were taking place through the hands *of* the apostles[P] among the people. And they[35] were all with-one-accord[Q] in the portico[36] *of* Solomon	12
	1B. But none *of* the rest[37] was daring[R] to join[38] them, yet the people were magnifying[39] them	13
	2B. And more *people* believing *in* the Lord were being added[40]— multitudes *of* both men and women	14

1. Or, "shared". The multitude shared everything. Same word as in 2:44; Jude 3. On this word, see "defiled" (which is "common" in another sense) in Heb 10:29. Related to "share" in 2 Jn 11.
2. Luke may mean "powerful speech" (the boldness of v 31); or, "powerful works" (miracles); or, both.
3. Or, "giving back, duly-giving". The word implies the apostles were fulfilling an obligation, paying what was owed. On this word, see Mt 16:27.
4. Same word as in 1 Cor 1:6; 2 Cor 1:12; 2 Thes 1:10; 1 Tim 2:6; 2 Tim 1:8. Used 19 times, 11 of which are in the phrase "for *a* testimony" (see Mk 1:44). GK *3457*. Related to "testimony" in Jn 1:7; and "witness" in Act 1:8.
5. Some manuscripts say "*of Jesus Christ the Lord*"; others, "*of the Lord Jesus Christ*" {C}.
6. Or, "impoverished, needy". Used only here. GK *1890*. Related to the verb "to beg". The reason this was true is explained next.
7. Used only here. GK *3230*. Related to "property" in 5:1.
8. That is, the owners were selling things from time to time and bringing in the proceeds.
9. Same word as in 5:4. On this word, see Rom 7:14. Not the same word as "selling" earlier in v 34, which is also in 4:37 ("made a sale") and 5:1 (GK *4797*). There is no apparent difference in meaning. A third word is used in 5:8.
10. Or, "given-through". Same word as in Lk 18:22, where Jesus commanded one to do this. Elsewhere only in Lk 11:22; Jn 6:11. GK *1344*. The root word is "give".
11. This phrase, "as... need" is exactly the same as in 2:45.
12. Some manuscripts say "Joses" {N}.
13. This is the one in 9:27; 11:22, 30; 12:25; who went with Paul on his first missionary journey (13:1-14:28), and to the Jerusalem council (15:1-29), and split with Paul in 15:35-39. Barnabas was the cousin of Mark, Col 4:10. He is also mentioned in 1 Cor 9:6; Gal 2:1, 9, 13. GK *982*.
14. Or, "exhortation". Some think this means Barnabas was known as an encourager; others, as a preacher, exhorter. Same word as in 15:31; Rom 15:4; Phil 2:1; Heb 6:18; and as "comfort" in Lk 6:24; Act 9:31; 2 Cor 1:3-7; "consolation" in Lk 2:25; "exhortation" in Act 13:15; Rom 12:8; 1 Cor 14:3; 1 Thes 2:3; Heb 12:5; "appeal" in 2 Cor 8:4; "urging" in 2 Cor 8:17. Used 29 times. GK *4155*. Related to "exhort" in Rom 12:8; and "Helper" in Jn 14:16.
15. That is, Barnabas was from the island of Cyprus. This was the first place he went with Paul (13:4), and after he split from Paul (15:39). Elsewhere only in 11:20; 21:16. GK *3250*. On "Cyprus", see 13:4.
16. Or, "to, toward". GK *4639*. Not the same word as in 4:35 and 5:2 ("at, beside, near", GK *4123*), though some manuscripts have that word here {N}.
17. Same word as in 2:45.
18. Or, "removed *for himself*, embezzled, stole". Same word as in v 3. Elsewhere only as "pilfer" in Tit 2:10. GK *3802*.
19. Or, "price", the price received. Same word as in v 3; 4:34. On this word, see "honor" in 1 Tim 5:17.
20. Or, "having co-knowledge". Elsewhere only as "conscious of" in 1 Cor 4:4. GK *5323*. This verb is related to "conscience" in 23:1.
21. Some think this is a Hebrew way of speaking meaning "For what reason did Satan cause you to dare to lie...", Esther 7:5; Eccl 8:11. Some manuscripts say instead "tempt" {B}. On this word, see Eph 5:18.
22. Same word as "lie" in v 4. Used 12 times. GK *6017*. Related to "falsehood" in Rev 14:5, and "liar" in Rom 3:4.
23. Ananias did not have to sell at all. The grammar indicates a "yes" answer is expected to this and the next question.
24. Ananias was under no obligation to give. After selling, the money was still his, to do with as he pleased. On this word, see Rev 6:8.
25. Same word as in Lk 21:14.
26. Ananias lied about the selling price, claiming his gift represented all of it. He could have given any part of it. But he wanted his gift to seem like a greater sacrifice than it actually was. He wanted to be seen as one who gave it all. He attempted to deceive his fellow believers. Luke does not say whether Peter had heard the price from someone else, or the Spirit revealed it to him.
27. That is, died. Elsewhere only in 5:10; 12:23. GK *1775*. This word is based on the word "life, soul". Ananias breathed out his life. A similar word based on the word "breath" is used of Jesus in Mk 15:37.
28. Some manuscripts say "these *things*" {K}, as in v 11.
29. That is, in a burial shroud. Or, "packed him up, removed him". On this word, see "shortened" in 1 Cor 7:29.
30. This word is plural, referring to both of them. To reflect this, "two" is added. Likewise in v 9.
31. Or, "gave up, gave away". Same word as in 7:9; Heb 12:16. This is the third different word Luke uses for "sell" in 4:34-5:8 (see the note on 4:34). This one may put the emphasis on what this couple gave up when they sold the land, or gave away from their possessions. Or, perhaps no difference in meaning is intended. On this word, see "render" in Mt 16:27.
32. Or, "that an-agreement-was-made *by* you *two*". On this word, see Mt 18:19.
33. Or, "tempt". Of course, this is not what these two thought they were doing. Like them, people often prefer to view their actions as if they were independent of God's scrutiny and judgment. On this word, see "tempt" in Heb 2:18.
34. This is Luke's third external view of the church. As in chapters 3-4, the proclaiming and miracle working of the apostles, v 12-16, leads to a confrontation with the Sanhedrin, v 17.
35. That is, the apostles.
36. The apostles were publicly violating the command of the Jewish leadership, 4:18. On this word, see Jn 5:2.
37. Or, "the others". Some think Luke is referring to the Jewish leaders and priests, in contrast with "the people" next; others, to the other believers, who did not dare to publicly defy the Jewish leaders in this way; others, to the non-believers, who (unless they became believers, as in v 14; or were seeking a miracle, as in v 15-17) did not dare to associate with the Christians because of the Ananias and Sapphira event and the Sanhedrin's command, making "the rest" equivalent to "the people" next (they did not join them, but they honored them). On this word, see "other" in 2 Pet 3:16.
38. Or, "unite *with*, associate *with*". That is, in the portico. Same word as in 8:29; 9:26; 10:28; 17:34. On this word, see 1 Cor 6:16.
39. Same word as in 10:46; 19:17. On this word, see "enlarge" in 2 Cor 10:15.
40. Or, "... believing were being added *to* the Lord". Compare 11:24, which has different grammar.

A. Heb 10:34, possessions B. Eph 2:8 C. Act 5:2 D. Tit 3:14 E. Act 13:8 F. Jn 1:19 G. 1 Cor 12:28, kind H. Jn 15:4, abide J. Eph 5:21
K. Tit 2:6 L. Mt 21:19 M. 1 Jn 2:13 N. 2 Thes 2:9 O. 2 Thes 2:9 P. 1 Cor 12:28 Q. Act 1:14 R. 2 Cor 11:21

	1C. So¹ that *they were* even bringing-out the sick^A into the wide-roads^B and putting *them* on little-beds and cots, in order that while Peter *was* coming, if-even² *his* shadow might overshadow³ one *of* them	15
	2C. And the multitude *from* the cities around Jerusalem⁴ was also coming-together⁵, bringing sick^A ones and *ones* being troubled by unclean spirits	16
	3C. Who all were being cured^C	
3B.	And having arisen, the high priest and all the *ones* with him— the sect⁶ *of* the Sadducees existing⁷ *there*— were filled^D *with* jealousy^E. *And they put *their* hands on the apostles and put them in *the* public^F jail⁸	17 18
	1C. But *an* angel *of the* Lord— having opened⁹ the doors *of* the prison during *the* night, and having led them out— said,* "Go! And having stood, be speaking in the temple *to* the people all the words *of* this¹⁰ life^G"	19 20
	2C. And having heard, they entered into the temple at¹¹ dawn¹² and were teaching	21
4B.	And having arrived¹³, the high priest and the *ones* with him called together the Sanhedrin— even the whole council-of-elders¹⁴ *of* the sons^H *of* Israel. And they sent-out^J officers to the jailhouse¹⁵ *that* they *might* be brought	
	1C. But having arrived, the officers^K did not find them in the prison¹⁶	22
	2C. And having returned, they reported^L,* saying that "We found the jailhouse having been locked^M with all security^N, and the guards¹⁷ standing¹⁸ at the doors. But having opened, we found no one inside"	23
	3C. And when both¹⁹ the captain *of* the temple [guard] and the chief priests heard these words, they were greatly-perplexed²⁰ about them *as to* what this would become	24
	4C. But having arrived, someone reported^L *to* them²¹ that "Behold— the men whom you put in the prison are standing in the temple and teaching the people"	25
	5C. Then the captain²², having gone away with the officers²³, was bringing them— not with violence²⁴ (for they were fearing the people, that²⁵ they might be stoned)	26
5B.	And having brought them, they stood *them* in the council²⁶ [chamber]	27
	1C. And the high priest questioned^O them,* saying, "Did we not²⁷ command^P you *with a* command²⁸ not to be teaching on the basis of this name? And behold— you have filled^Q Jerusalem *with* your teaching. And you intend²⁹ to bring the blood *of* this man³⁰ upon us"	28
	2C. But having responded, Peter and the apostles said, "It-is-necessary³¹ to obey³² God rather than people^R	29
	1D. "The God *of* our fathers raised^S Jesus— Whom **you** murdered³³, having hung^T *Him* on *a* cross^U	30
	2D. "God exalted^V this *One* to His right hand³⁴ *as* Leader³⁵ and Savior^W, *that He might* grant repentance³⁶ *to* Israel and forgiveness^X *of* sins	31
	3D. "And **we** are witnesses³⁷ *of* these things³⁸. And *so is* the Holy Spirit, Whom God gave *to* the *ones* obeying Him"	32
	3C. And the *ones* having heard *it* were infuriated³⁹, and were intending⁴⁰ to kill^Y them	33
	4C. But having stood up, *a* certain Pharisee in the Sanhedrin— Gamaliel *by* name, *a* Law-teacher^Z honored⁴¹ *by* all the people— gave-orders^{AA} to make the men⁴² *be* outside *for a* little *while*. And he said to them	34 35
	1D. "Men^{BB}, Israelites, take heed to yourselves⁴³ *as to* what you are about to do to these men	

1. Some consider v 14 a parenthesis, so that this follows directly from v 13.
2. Or, "at least". This word expresses these people's hope of healing. It is the same word used by the woman in Mk 5:28, and as "even" in Mk 6:56. GK *2829*. Compare Act 19:12.
3. On this word, see Mt 17:5. Related to "shadow".
4. Some manuscripts add "to", making it "the surrounding cities to Jerusalem" {B}.
5. Or, "gathering, assembling". Same word used of those who came together to hear and be healed by Jesus in Lk 5:15. GK *5302*.
6. Or, "faction, party". The same group as in 4:1. This "sect" (as opposed to the Pharisee "sect", 15:5) was closely associated with the high priest and his family. On this word, see "faction" in 1 Cor 11:19.
7. Or, "the existing sect", meaning "the local sect". It is the same idiom as in 13:1.
8. Same word as in 4:3. Luke uses three different words here for this place. Based on the root words, it is the place they were "kept" (v 18, jail, GK *5499*); "bound" (v 21, jailhouse); and "guarded" (v 22, prison).
9. Some manuscripts say "... Lord opened the doors... night. And having led them out, he said" {N}.
10. That is, the life which the Sadducees deny (23:8)— eternal life, resurrection life, in Jesus Christ.
11. More literally, "under the dawn", that is, near dawn. GK *5679*.
12. The gates of the temple were closed at night, but the apostles were there when they opened that morning. This phrase reveals their excitement and their urgency to obey. On this word, see Lk 24:1.
13. That is, the next morning after v 18.
14. Or, "Senate". Used only here. GK *1172*. Related to the word "old man" in Jn 3:4.
15. Same word as in v 23; 16:26. Elsewhere only as "prison" in Mt 11:2. GK *1303*. The root word is "to bind" in 1 Cor 7:27.
16. Same word as v 19, 25. Used 47 times. It also means "watch" of the night (see Lk 2:8). GK *5871*. The root word is "to guard", on which see "keep" in Jn 12:25. Related to "guards" in v 23.
17. Elsewhere only in 12:6, 19. GK *5874*.
18. Some manuscripts add "outside" {K}.
19. Some manuscripts say "both the [high] priest and the captain..., and the chief priests" {N}.
20. Same word as in 2:12, the response to the tongues. On this word, see Lk 9:7.
21. Some manuscripts add "saying" {K}.
22. That is, the leader of the Jewish temple police, the "officers" mentioned next. Same word as in v 24; 4:1; Lk 22:4, 52. Elsewhere only of Roman city "magistrates" in Act 16:20, 22, 35, 36, 38. GK *5130*.
23. Same word as in v 22. On this word, see Jn 18:12.
24. Or, "force". Same word as in 21:35. Elsewhere only as "force" in 27:41. GK *1040*. This implies the apostles came with the captain willingly.
25. This idiom, expressing fear of a potential negative consequence, is also in 23:10; 27:17, 29; 2 Cor 11:3; 12:20; Gal 4:11. This word is GK *3590*.
26. Or, "among the Sanhedrin". Same word as "Sanhedrin" in v 21, 34, 41. Luke may be referring to the room where the Sanhedrin met (as in 4:15; Lk 22:66), or to the council meeting there. This word most often means "Sanhedrin" (the Jewish ruling council), but is also used of "councils" in a broader sense (as in Mt 10:17; Mk 13:9). Used 22 times. GK *5284*.
27. The grammar indicates a "yes" answer is expected. Some manuscripts omit this word, making it a statement, "we commanded you..." {C}. The command is in 4:18.
28. This idiom reflects a Hebrew way of speaking.
29. Or, "you are determined, you wish, want, desire". Same word as in v 33. On this word, see "willed" in Jam 1:18.
30. That is, the responsibility for the death of Jesus. The Jews had already accepted it, Mt 27:25.
31. Or, "*We* must obey". On this idiom, see "must" in Mt 16:21.
32. Same word as in v 32. On this word, see 27:21.
33. Or, "killed, slayed"; literally, "laid hands on violently", bringing about death. Elsewhere only in 26:21. GK *1429*.
34. Same phrase as in 2:33.
35. Or, "Prince", not in the sense of royalty, but in the sense of "Leader". Same word as "Author" in 3:15.
36. On this word, see 2 Cor 7:10. God grants repentance to the Gentiles also, 11:18.
37. Some manuscripts add "His" {B}, "His witnesses...".
38. Or, "matters". The apostles witness with bold words. The Spirit witnesses with the works of power about which these Jews were jealous, v 14-16. Compare 14:3.
39. The root word means these leaders were "sawn through", cut through the heart. Elsewhere only in 7:54. GK *1391*. This word is also used outside the NT of "grinding, gnashing" the teeth, often in rage. Related to "sawn in two" in Heb 11:37.
40. Same word as in v 28. Some manuscripts say instead "deliberating"{B}, using the word in 27:39.
41. Or, "respected *by*, precious *to* all...". On this adjective, see "precious" in 2 Pet 1:4.
42. Some manuscripts say "apostles" {N}.
43. On "take heed to yourselves", see Lk 12:1.

A. 1 Thes 5:14, weak B. Lk 14:21 C. Mt 8:7 D. Act 2:4 E. 2 Cor 11:2 F. Act 16:37 G. Rom 8:10 H. Gal 3:7 J. Mk 3:14 K. Jn 18:12
L. 1 Jn 1:3, announcing M. Jn 20:19 N. Lk 1:4, certainty O. Lk 9:18 P. 1 Tim 1:3 Q. Eph 5:18 R. Mt 4:4, mankind S. Mt 28:6, arose
T. Act 10:39 U. 1 Pet 2:24 V. Jn 8:28, lifted up W. Lk 1:47 X. Col 1:14 Y. Mt 2:16 Z. 1 Tim 1:7 AA. Mt 14:28, order BB. 1 Tim 2:12

	1E. "For before these days, Theudas arose^A, saying *that* he was¹ somebody	36

	1F. "*With* whom *a* number *of* men joined-up², about four-hundred
	    2F. "Who was killed³
	    3F. "And all who were being persuaded⁴ *by* him were dispersed, and they became nothing⁵	

	2E. "After this *one*, Judas the Galilean arose^A in the days *of* the registration⁶ and drew-away⁷ *a group-of*-people⁸ after him	37
	1F. "That *one* also perished^B 2F. "And all who were being persuaded *by* him were scattered^C	
	2D. "And *as to* the *things* now, I say *to* you	38
	1E. "Draw-away⁹ from these men, and leave^D them *alone*	
	1F. "Because if this plan^E or this work^F should be from humans¹⁰, it will be overthrown¹¹ 2F. "But if it is from God, you will not be able¹² to overthrow them¹³	39
	2E. "That you indeed may not perhaps be found *to be* fighting-against-God"	
	3D. And they were persuaded¹⁴ *by* him	
	5C. And having summoned^G the apostles, having beaten¹⁵ *them*, they commanded^H *them* not to be speaking on the basis of the name *of* Jesus,¹⁶ and released^J *them*	40
	6B. So indeed the *ones* were going from *the* presence *of* the Sanhedrin rejoicing^K that they were considered-worthy^L to be dishonored¹⁷ for the name¹⁸. ˚And every day, in the temple and house by house¹⁹, they were not ceasing^M teaching and announcing-the-good-news²⁰ *as to* Jesus, the Christ²¹	41 42
8A.	Now²² during these days, while the disciples *were* multiplying^N, grumbling²³ arose²⁴ *from* the Hellenists^O against the Hebrews²⁵ because their widows were being overlooked²⁶ in the daily ministry²⁷ [of food]	6:1
	1B. And the twelve, having summoned^G the multitude²⁸ *of* the disciples, said	2
	1C. "It is not pleasing²⁹ *that* we, having left-behind³⁰ the word^P *of* God, *should* be serving³¹ tables³² 2C. "But³³ brothers^Q, look-for³⁴ seven men from-*among* you being attested³⁵, full^R *of the* Spirit³⁶ and wisdom^S, whom we will put-in-charge³⁷ over this need³⁸	3
	3C. "And **we** will devote-ourselves^T *to* prayer^U and the ministry³⁹ *of the* word^P"	4
	2B. And the statement^P was pleasing^V in the sight of the whole multitude. And they chose⁴⁰ Stephen⁴¹ (*a* man full^R *of* faith and *of the* Holy Spirit), and Philip⁴², and Prochorus, and Nicanor, and Timon, and Parmenas, and Nicolas (*a* proselyte^W *from* Antioch), ˚whom they stood before the apostles	5 6
	1C. And having prayed, they laid *their* hands⁴³ on^X them	
	3B. And the word *of* God⁴⁴ was growing^Y. And the number^Z *of* the disciples in Jerusalem was being multiplied^N greatly. And *a* large crowd^{AA} *of* the priests were obeying⁴⁵ the faith⁴⁶	7

1. More literally, "is", as the Greek typically phrases it.
2. Or, to whom a number of men "attached *themselves*, inclined *themselves*". Used only here. GK *4679*. Related to "partiality" in 1 Tim 5:21.
3. Same word as in v 33, on which see Mt 2:16.
4. Or, "convinced". Or, "were following, obeying" him. Same word as in v 37, 40. On this word, see 1 Jn 3:19.
5. This is a Hebrew way of speaking. More literally, "they came-to-be for nothing".
6. Or, "census". On this word, see Lk 2:2. Some think this refers to a census in A.D. 6 after Archelaus (see Mt 2:22) was deposed and Judea was put under Roman rule. It caused a rebellion, and the rise of the Zealots.
7. Or, "caused to depart". That is, in a rebellion. On this word, see "depart" in 1 Tim 4:1.
8. Same word as in Lk 9:13. On this word, see "peoples" in Rev 21:3. Some manuscripts say "many people" {A}.
9. Or, "Withdraw". Same word as "drew-away" in v 37.
10. That is, if it turns out to be from humans.
11. Or, "thrown down, destroyed, put down". Same word as in the next verse. That is, since Jesus, the leader of these men, has been killed like Theudas and Judas, His followers will soon be scattered as theirs were. There is no reason to take the drastic action of killing these men. On this word, see "tear down" in Mt 24:2.
12. Some manuscripts say "you are not able" {K}.
13. Some manuscripts say "it" {A}, referring to the "work".
14. Luke uses the same word of these leaders that Gamaliel used twice with reference to rebels following a lost cause!
15. Same word as in Mk 13:9, where Jesus predicted it. On this word, see Jn 18:23.
16. As these leaders also commanded in 4:18.
17. Elsewhere only in Mk 12:4; Lk 20:11; Jn 8:49; Rom 1:24; 2:23; Jam 2:6. GK *869*. Related to "dishonor" in 2 Tim 2:20.
18. Or, "*His* name". Some manuscripts say "His name"; others, "the name *of* Jesus" {N}.
19. More literally, "according to house (singular)", here meaning divided up by house, at their house, in every house, in relation to their house. Same phrase as in 2:46, and as "at *the* house" in Rom 16:5; 1 Cor 16:19; Col 4:15; Phm 2. Elsewhere only with "houses" plural, meaning "from house to house", in Act 8:3; 20:20.
20. This verb, "to announce the good news, announce as good news, proclaim the gospel", is used 54 times. GK *2294*. Same word as in Lk 2:10; 4:18; 7:22; 9:6; Act 8:12, 25, 35; 10:36; 14:7, 15; Rom 1:15; 1 Cor 1:17; Gal 1:8, 16; Eph 2:17; Heb 4:2; 1 Pet 1:12; 4:6; Rev 10:7; 14:6. On the noun "good news, gospel", see 1 Cor 15:1.
21. Or, "*as to* Christ Jesus". Or, "announcing-the-good-news-of Jesus *as* the Christ".
22. This is Luke's third internal view of the church, 2:42; 4:32. He has alternated between external and internal views.
23. Or, "complaining". On this word, see Phil 2:14.
24. Or, "came about, took place". GK *1181*.
25. That is, from the Greek-speaking Jewish Christians against the native Hebrew Jewish Christians. Elsewhere only in 2 Cor 11:22; Phil 3:5. GK *1578*. Related to "Hebrew" (language) in 21:40.
26. Or, "neglected". Used only here. GK *4145*. Related to "to see, look".
27. Or, "service". Apparently the ones serving were favoring their own, the locals, no doubt unintentionally. This kind of thing naturally occurs in the absence of explicit planning and organization. On this word, see 1 Cor 12:5. Same word as in v 4. Related to "serve" in v 2.
28. Or, "crowd, assembly, number". Used 31 times. GK *4436*.
29. Or, "it is not *a* pleasing *thing*". On this word, see Jn 8:29.
30. Or, "left to the side", and so, "neglected". There is only so much time. The apostles would have to leave the one to do the other. This would not be pleasing to anyone. Used 24 times meaning "leave, leave behind, leave remaining". GK *2901*.
31. On this word, see "ministering" in 1 Pet 4:10. Related to "deacon" in Phil 1:1.
32. This may mean the apostles had been the ones doing so. Or, it may mean they felt they would have to do so in order to solve the problem. To "serve tables" could mean "to disperse food", or, "to disperse money" (the money of 4:34-35). The word "table" is used of a banker's table in Mt 21:12; Lk 19:23. It is related to "banker" in Mt 25:27.
33. Some manuscripts say "Therefore" {C}.
34. Or, "examine, look at" and thus, "select". On this word, see "look after" in Heb 2:6.
35. That is, attested in the faith. Or, "being borne witness" in a positive sense, "approved, well spoken of". Same word as Act 10:22; 16:2; 22:12; Rom 3:21; 1 Tim 5:10; Heb 7:8, 17; 11:2, 4, 5, 39; 3 Jn 12. On this word, see "testify" in Jn 1:7.
36. Some manuscripts say "Holy Spirit" {N}.
37. Or, "appoint, set". Same word as in Mt 24:45, 47; 25:21, 23; Lk 12:42, 44. Elsewhere only as "appoint" in Lk 12:14; Act 7:10, 27, 35; Tit 1:5; Heb 5:1; 7:28; 8:3; "made" in Rom 5:19; Jam 3:6; 4:4; 2 Pet 1:8; and "conducted" in Act 17:15. GK *2770*. Some manuscripts say "may put in charge" {K}.
38. Or, the "function, business, task, responsibility" addressing the need. On this word, see Tit 3:14.
39. Same word as in v 1.
40. The multitude chose these seven. The mix of Hebrews and Hellenists is unstated. The names are all Greek, so it is possible that all seven were Hellenists. However, the names alone are insufficient to prove this, since Greek names were common in Israel. Some of the apostles have Greek names. On this word, see 1 Cor 1:27.
41. Stephen's story is told in 6:8-8:2. He was the first martyr. Mentioned also in 11:19; 22:20. GK *5108*.
42. Philip's story is told in 8:5-40. In 21:8 he is called an evangelist.
43. On the laying on of hands, see Heb 6:2. It occurs in this sense in Act 13:3; 1 Tim 4:14; 5:22; 2 Tim 1:6.
44. Some manuscripts say "the word *of* the Lord" {B}.
45. Same word as in Act 8:27; Mk 1:27; 4:41; Lk 8:25; 17:6; Rom 6:12, 16, 17; 10:16; Eph 6:1, 5; Phil 2:12; Col 3:20, 22; 2 Thes 1:8; 3:14; Heb 5:9; 11:8; 1 Pet 3:6. Elsewhere only as "answer" in Act 12:13. GK *5634*. Related to "obedience" in Rom 16:26.
46. The phrase "obeying the faith" is found only here, but is related to "obedience of faith" in Rom 1:5; 16:26.

A. Lk 18:33, rise up B. 1 Cor 1:18 C. Mt 25:24 D. Mt 6:12, forgive E. Eph 1:11, counsel F. Mt 26:10 G. Act 2:39, call to H. 1 Tim 1:3 J. Mt 5:31, sends away K. 2 Cor 13:11 L. 2 Thes 1:5 M. 1 Cor 13:8 N. Act 7:17 O. Act 11:20 P. 1 Cor 12:8, word Q. Act 16:40 R. Mt 14:20 S. 1 Cor 12:8 T. Act 2:42 U. 1 Tim 2:1 V. 1 Thes 2:4 W. Mt 23:15 X. Lk 10:30, laid on Y. Jn 3:30 Z. Rev 13:17 AA. Mk 2:13, multitude

Acts 6:8		414	Verse

9A. Now Stephen, full[A] *of* grace[1] and power[B], was doing great wonders[C] and signs among the people — 8

   1B. But some *of* the *ones* from the synagogue[D] being called "*of* Freedmen"[2]— both Cyrenians[3] and Alexandrians[4], and the *ones* from Cilicia[5] and Asia— rose-up[E], debating[6] *with* Stephen — 9

      1C. And they were not able to resist[7] the wisdom[F] and the Spirit *with* which he was speaking — 10
      2C. Then they secretly-induced[8] men [to begin] saying that "We have heard him speaking blasphemous[G] words against Moses and God" — 11
      3C. And they stirred-up[9] the people and the elders and the scribes — 12

   2B. And having suddenly-come-upon[H] *him*, they seized[10] him, and brought *him* to the Sanhedrin

      1C. And they put-*forward*[11] false witnesses, saying, "This man does not cease[J] speaking words[12] against this[13] holy place and the Law. °For we have heard him saying that this Jesus the Nazarene[K] will tear-down[14] this place, and change[L] the customs[M] which Moses handed-down[N] *to* us"[15] — 13, 14
      2C. And having looked-intently[O] at him, all the *ones* sitting in the council[16] [chamber] saw his face *was* like[17] *a* face *of a* angel — 15
      3C. And the high priest said, "Do these *things* hold so?"[18] — 7:1

   3B. And the *one* said, "Men, brothers, and fathers, listen— — 2

      1C. "The God *of* glory[19] appeared[P] *to* our father Abraham while being in Mesopotamia, before he dwelled[Q] in Haran, °and said to him [in Gen 12:1], 'Go out from your land and from[20] your relatives, and come to the land which[21] I will show you'[22] — 3

         1D. "Then having gone out from *the* land *of the* Chaldeans, he dwelled[Q] in Haran — 4
         2D. "And from there, after his father died,[23] He removed[24] him to this land in which **you** are now dwelling[Q]
         3D. "And He did not give him *an* inheritance[R] in it, not even *the* step *of a* foot — 5
         4D. "And He promised to give it *to* him for *a* possession[S], and *to* his seed[T] after him— *there* not being *a* child *for* him!
         5D. "But God spoke as follows [in Gen 15:13-14]— that his seed[T] will be *a* foreigner[25] in *a* land belonging-to-another[26] — 6

            1E. "'And they will enslave[U] it[27] and mistreat[28] *it for* four-hundred years
            2E. "'And **I** will judge[V] the nation *in* whichever they will serve-as-slaves[W], said God — 7
            3E. "'And after these *things*, they will come out and worship[29] Me' in this place

         6D. "And He gave him *the* covenant[X] *of* circumcision[Y] — 8

      2C. "And so he fathered[30] Isaac, and circumcised him *on* the eighth day; and Isaac, Jacob; and Jacob, the twelve patriarchs[Z]. °And the patriarchs, having become-jealous-of[AA] Joseph, sold *him* into Egypt — 9

         1D. "And God was with him, °and rescued[BB] him from all his afflictions[CC], and gave him favor[DD] and wisdom in the sight of Pharaoh, king *of* Egypt. And he appointed[31] him *to be* ruling[EE] over Egypt, and over[32] his whole house — 10
         2D. "And *a* famine[FF] came over all Egypt[33] and Canaan, and *a* great affliction[CC]. And our fathers were not finding food[34] — 11
         3D. "But Jacob, having heard-*of* grain being in Egypt, sent-forth[GG] our fathers first — 12

1. This grace refers to the divine gifts given to Stephen, gifts of speaking and power, as seen in what follows. Some manuscripts say "faith" {N}, as in v 5.
2. That is, Hellenistic Jewish slaves who were freed, and returned to Israel. Some think Luke names one synagogue made up of the four nationalities. Others think he names two synagogues, "*of* Freedmen and Cyrenians and Alexandrians, and, the *ones* from Cilicia and Asia". Others think he names five separate synagogues.
3. That is, from the city of Cyrene on the African coast. Elsewhere only of Simon who carried the cross (Mt 27:32; Mk 15:21; Lk 23:26), and in Act 11:20; 13:1. GK *3254*. "Cyrene" is in Act 2:10.
4. From the city of Alexandria in Egypt.
5. Cilicia (used 8 times. GK *3070*) and Asia (used 18 times. GK *823*) are Roman provinces in what is now known as Turkey.
6. Or, "arguing, disputing". On this word, see Mk 8:11.
7. Same word as in Lk 21:15.
8. Or, "suborned". That is, the debaters secretly instigated false testimony. Used only here. GK *5680*.
9. Or, "set in motion, aroused". Used only here. GK *5167*. Related to "move" in Rev 2:5.
10. That is, seized with violence and took Stephen with them. On this word, see Lk 8:29.
11. Or, "they stood". These debaters controlled it all from behind the scenes. Same word as in 1:23. GK *2705*.
12. Some manuscripts say "blasphemous words" {N}, as in v 11.
13. Some manuscripts say "the" holy place {C}.
14. Same word as in Mt 24:2.
15. Jesus did say these things would happen, and they did happen in A.D. 70. But that this was against this place or the Law is false. It was a fulfillment of God's word. The false witnesses left out Stephen's explanation of this event.
16. Or, "Sanhedrin", as in v 12. On this word, see 5:27.
17. Or, "as if". On this word, see "as if" in Rom 6:13.
18. In other words, are these things true? On this idiom, see 12:15.
19. That is, the God characterized by glory; the glorious God.
20. Some manuscripts omit this word {C}.
21. More literally, "whichever". The land— whichever it may be— I will show you. There is an indefiniteness about it which is difficult to reproduce in English. Heb 11:8 states it clearly.
22. Stephen is saying that the call of Gen 12:1-3 was first given in Chaldea (as implied in Gen 15:7), and provides the explanation for Abraham leaving for Canaan and settling in Haran (Gen 11:31). Gen 12:1-3 then records the repetition of this call in Haran. In other words, Stephen is giving his interpretation of the full Genesis record.
23. Some think Genesis indicates Abraham's father was still living when he left. Gen 11:32 says that his father died at age 205. Abraham left at age 75 (Gen 12:4). Gen 11:26 may indicate Terah was 70 when Abraham was born (assuming they are named in order of birth, and that Abraham is not named first because of his prominence in what follows), making Terah 145 (75 plus 70) when Abraham left Haran. This would mean Terah lived 60 more years after Abraham left Haran. Perhaps Stephen simply means "after he died in the progression of Genesis", since his death is recorded in 11:32, prior to Abraham leaving Haran in Gen 12:4. Some ancient OT manuscripts say in Gen 11:32 that Terah died at age 145, and this was a commonly held view among the Jews in that day.
24. Or, "resettled, changed his dwelling over to". Same word as in v 43. God caused Abraham to resettle through the call of Gen 12:1-3.
25. Or, "resident alien". On this word, see 1 Pet 2:11.
26. Or, "*a* foreign land", but not related to "foreigner" earlier. On this word, see "foreigners" in Heb 11:34.
27. That is, Abraham's seed, viewed as a collective whole. Stephen changes to the plural "they" in v 7.
28. Same word as in v 19. On this word, see "do evil" in 1 Pet 3:13.
29. Or, "serve". Same word as in Ex 3:12, to which this alludes. On this word, see Heb 12:28.
30. On this word, see "born" in 1 Jn 2:29. Same word as in v 29; Mt 1:2.
31. Or, "put him in charge". Same word as in v 27.
32. Some manuscripts omit this word {C}.
33. Some manuscripts say "the land *of* Egypt" {N}.
34. Used only here. GK *5964*. Used of "forage, fodder" for cattle, "food" for people. Related to "grass, hay".

A. Mt 14:20 B. Mk 5:30 C. 2 Thes 2:9 D. Act 13:43, gathering E. Lk 18:33 F. 1 Cor 12:8 G. 1 Tim 1:13 H. Lk 21:34 J. 1 Cor 13:8
K. Mt 2:23 L. Rom 1:23, exchanged M. Lk 1:9 N. Act 16:4, delivering O. Lk 4:20 P. Lk 2:26, see Q. Eph 3:17 R. Eph 1:14 S. Act 7:45, taking possession T. Heb 11:11 U. Rom 6:18 V. Mt 7:1 W. Rom 6:6, are slaves X. Heb 8:6 Y. Eph 2:11, circumcised Z. Heb 7:4
AA. 2 Cor 11:2, jealous for BB. Gal 1:4 CC. Rev 7:14 DD. Eph 2:8, grace EE. Heb 13:7, leading FF. Lk 21:11 GG. Gal 4:4

    4D. "And during the second *visit*, Joseph was made-known-again[1] *to* his brothers, and the family[A] *of* Joseph became known[2] *to* Pharaoh   13
    5D. "And having sent-forth[B] *his brothers*, Joseph summoned Jacob his father and all *his* relatives, amounting-to[3] seventy five[4] souls[C]   14
    6D. "And Jacob went down to Egypt. And **he** came-to-an-end[5], and our fathers. •And they were transferred[D] to Shechem, and placed in the tomb[E] which Abraham[6] bought[7] *for a price*[F] *of* silver from the sons *of* Hamor in[8] Shechem   15-16

  3C. "Now as the time *of* the promise which God declared[9] *to* Abraham was drawing-near[G], *our* people grew and were multiplied[10] in Egypt, •until which *time* another king arose[H] over Egypt[11] who did not know Joseph   17
      18

    1D. "This *one*, having dealt-shrewdly-with[12] our nation[13], mistreated[14] our fathers, *so that he*[15] caused[16] their babies[17] *to be* exposed[18], that *they might* not be kept-alive[19]   19
    2D. "At which time, Moses was born[J]— and he was beautiful[20] *to* God   20

      1E. "Who was brought-up *for* three months in the house *of his* father
      2E. "And he having been exposed, the daughter *of* Pharaoh took him up[21], and brought him up *for* herself for *a* son   21
      3E. "And Moses was trained[K] in all *the* wisdom *of the* Egyptians. And he was powerful[L] in his[22] words[23] and deeds   22

    3D. "And as *a* forty-year[24] period was being fulfilled[M] *for* him,[25] it came-up[26] on his heart to visit[27] his brothers, the sons[N] *of* Israel   23

      1E. "And having seen someone being wronged[28], he defended *him,* and executed vengeance[29] *for* the *one* being oppressed[30], having struck the Egyptian   24
      2E. "Now he was thinking[O] *that* his brothers *were* understanding[P] that God was[31] granting them deliverance[Q] by his hand. But the *ones* did not understand   25
      3E. "And *on* the following day, he appeared[R] *to* them while *they were* fighting[S]   26

        1F. "And he was reconciling[32] them to peace, having said, 'Men, you are brothers. Why are you wronging one another?' [Ex 2:13]
        2F. "But the *one* wronging *his* neighbor[33] rejected[34] him, having said, 'Who appointed[35] **you** ruler[T] and judge over us? •**You** do not intend[36] to kill me the way you killed the Egyptian yesterday, *do you*?'[37] [Ex 2:14]   27
          28
        3F. "And Moses fled[U] at this word   29

    4D. "And he became *a* foreigner[38] in *the* land *of* Midian, where he fathered[J] two sons. •And forty years having been fulfilled[M], an angel[39] appeared[R] *to* him in the wilderness[V] *of* Mount Sinai, in *the* flame[40] *of* fire *of a* bush   30

      1E. "And having seen *it*, Moses was marveling-at[41] the sight   31
      2E. "And while he *was* approaching[W] to look-closely[X], *the* voice *of the* Lord came[42]— 'I *am* the God *of* your fathers, the God *of* Abraham and Isaac and Jacob[43]'   32
      3E. "And having become trembling[Y], Moses was not daring[Z] to look-closely[X]
      4E. "And the Lord said *to* him, 'Untie[AA] the sandal *from* your feet, for the place upon which you stand is holy[BB] ground[CC]. •Having seen, I saw[44] the mistreatment[45] *of* My people in Egypt, and I heard their groaning[DD], and I came down to rescue[46] them. And now, come, I will send[47] you forth[B] to Egypt'   33
         34

1. Or, "reacquainted *to*, recognized *by*". Used only here. GK *341*. Same word as in Gen 45:1, which has different grammar, "made *himself* known".
2. Or, "visible". On this word, see "evident" in Rom 1:19. Not related to "make known" earlier.
3. Or, "consisting in". GK *1877*.
4. Gen 46:27 (and Ex 1:5; Deut 10:22) says 70 persons, and that Joseph had "two sons". Stephen is quoting the Septuagint of Gen 46:27, which (along with Ex 1:5) says 75 persons, including 66 plus Joseph's "nine sons". On who might be included in the two counts, consult the commentaries.
5. That is, died. On this word, see Mk 9:48.
6. Jacob purchased this land in Shechem (Gen 33:19), and Joseph and his sons were buried there (Josh 24:32). Abraham purchased land in Machpelah (Gen 23:14-20), and Jacob was buried there (Gen 49:29-32; 50:13). Stephen has abbreviated all this. In substituting Abraham for Jacob as the purchaser here, some think Stephen confused the two and Luke recorded what he actually said. Others think an early error was made copying the manuscript of Acts (for which there is no evidence at present). For other views, consult the commentaries.
7. Used only here. GK *6050*.
8. Some manuscripts say "the *one of* Shechem", or, "the *father of* Shechem"; others, "the *one* in Shechem" {C}.
9. On this word, see "confess" in 1 Tim 6:12. Some manuscripts say "swore"; others, "promised" {B}.
10. Same word as in 6:6, 7; 9:31; 12:24. Used 12 times. GK *4437*.
11. Some manuscripts omit "over Egypt" {C}.
12. Or, "outwitted, taken advantage of". Used only here. GK *2947*. Same word as in Ex 1:9.
13. Or, "people, race". Same word as "family" in v 13. On this word, see "kind" in 1 Cor 12:28.
14. Same word as in v 6, and as "afflict, oppress" in Ex 1:11. Related word in v 34.
15. That is, the new Pharaoh. Or, "*they*", the Israelites. The subject is not expressed. Both are true. Pharaoh "caused" the Israelites do it; they "caused" their infants to be exposed.
16. Or, "made, forced". Rendered this way, it gives the culmination of Pharaoh's mistreatment, as described in Ex 1:11-22. Or, "*that he might* cause...", giving the purpose of his mistreatment, which was to control the size of the Hebrew population, Ex 1:9-10. On this word, see "does" in Rev 13:13.
17. That is, the newborn male infants, Ex 1:22. On this word, see Lk 1:41.
18. Or, "put out, abandoned". This adjective is used only here. GK *1704*. Related to the verb in v 21 (GK *1758*).
19. Or, "preserved". On this word, see "give life to" in 1 Tim 6:13.
20. Or, "well-bred", in contrast to what the Egyptians thought of the Hebrews. Elsewhere only in Heb 11:23, also of Moses. GK *842*. Same word as in Ex 2:2.
21. This word "took up" is used only here with this grammar. Same word as in Ex 2:5, 10. Some think it means "accepted". On this word, see "kill" in Mt 2:16.
22. Some manuscripts omit this word {K}.
23. Some think Stephen means Moses' written words.
24. Elsewhere only in 13:18. GK *5478*.
25. That is, when Moses was nearly forty years old.
26. Or, "arose". GK *326*. This idiom of a thought "arising on the heart" is also in Lk 24:38; 1 Cor 2:9.
27. Or, "look after, care for". On this word, see "look after" in Heb 2:6.
28. Or, "harmed, injured". This word means "to do wrong (physically or morally), do unrighteousness", as in 1 Cor 6:7; Gal 4:12; Rev 22:11; and "to harm, injure, mistreat as here, Rev 2:11. Used 28 times. GK *92*. Related to "crime" in 18:14, "wrongdoers" in 1 Cor 6:9, "unrighteousness" in Rom 1:18, and "declare righteous" in Rom 3:24.
29. On "execute vengeance", see Lk 18:7.
30. Or, "mistreated, subdued, worn out". On this word, see 2 Pet 2:7.
31. More literally, "is", as the Greek typically phrases it.
32. That is, stopping these Jews from fighting. Used only here. GK *5261*. Related word in Rom 5:10. Some manuscripts say "and he reconciled them..." {N}.
33. Same word as in Mt 19:19. Used 17 times. GK *4446*.
34. Or, "pushed aside". Same word as in v 39. On this word, see "reject" in Rom 11:1.
35. Same word as v 10, 35. On this word, see "put in charge" in 6:3.
36. Or, "want, wish, desire". On this word, see "willing" in Jn 7:17.
37. The grammar indicates that a "no" answer is expected.
38. Same word as in v 6.
39. Some manuscripts say "*an angel of the* Lord" {N}.
40. That is, in the flame belonging to a fire in the bush. On this word, see "flaming" in 2 Thes 1:8.
41. Some manuscripts say "marveled-*at*" {N}.
42. Some manuscripts add "to him" {K}.
43. Some manuscripts say "the God *of* Abraham and the God *of* Isaac and the God *of* Jacob" {N}. In v 31-34, Stephen summarizes Ex 3:4-10.
44. This phrase, "having seen, I saw" is a Hebrew way of speaking, meaning "I have surely seen".
45. Used only here. GK *2810*. Same word as rendered "affliction" or "oppression" in Ex 3:7. Related to the verb in v 19.
46. Same word as in v 10.
47. More literally, "let Me send you forth", a command to Himself, an expression of His own resolve. Since this would sound in English like God was asking permission from Moses, most clarify it by changing it to "I will send you forth". Same word and form as in Ex 3:10. Some manuscripts say "I will send forth" {N}. Same word as "sent forth" in v 35. On this word, see "sent out" in Mk 3:14.

A. 1 Cor 12:28, kind B. Mk 3:14, send out C. Jam 5:20 D. Heb 11:5, removed E. Lk 23:53 F. 1 Tim 5:17, honor G. Lk 21:28 H. Lk 18:33, rise up J. 1 Jn 2:29, born K. 1 Cor 11:32, discipline L. Lk 24:19 M. Eph 5:18, filled N. Gal 3:7 O. Act 14:19 P. Mt 13:13 Q. Lk 19:9, salvation R. Lk 2:26, see S. 2 Tim 2:24, battle T. Rev 1:5 U. 1 Cor 6:18 V. Mt 3:1 W. Heb 10:22 X. Heb 10:24, consider Y. Heb 12:21 Z. 2 Cor 11:21 AA. Mt 5:19, break BB. 1 Pet 1:16 CC. Rev 7:1, land DD. Rom 8:26

5D. "This Moses[1] whom they denied[A], having said, 'Who appointed[B] **you** ruler and judge?' [Ex 2:14]— 35

  1E. "This *one* God has sent-forth[2] *to be* both[3] ruler and deliverer[4], with[5] *the* hand *of the* angel having appeared[C] *to* him in the bush[D]
  2E. "This *one* led them out, having done wonders[E] and signs in Egypt land[6], and in *the* Red[F] Sea, and in the wilderness[G] *for* forty years 36
  3E. "This *one* is the Moses having said *to* the sons *of* Israel, 'God[7] will raise-up[H] *a* prophet[J] like me *for* you from your brothers'[8] [Deut 18:15] 37
  4E. "This *one* is the *one* having been in the congregation[K] in the wilderness, with the angel speaking *to* him at Mount Sinai, and *with* our fathers 38

    1F. "Who received living oracles[9] to give *to* us[10]
    2F. "*To* whom our fathers were not willing[L] to become obedient[M], but they rejected[11] him, and turned-away[N] in their hearts to Egypt 39

      1G. "Having said to Aaron, 'Make gods *for* us who will go before us. For this Moses who led us out *of the* land *of* Egypt— we do not know what happened *to* him' [Ex 32:1] 40
      2G. "And they made-a-calf in those days, and brought-up *a* sacrifice[O] *to* the idol. And they were celebrating[P] in[12] the works *of* their hands 41

    3F. "And God turned-away[N], and handed them over[13] to worship[14] the host[15] *of* heaven, just as it has been written in *the* book *of* the prophets [in Amos 5:25-27]— 42

      1G. 'House *of* Israel, you did not offer[Q] victims[16] and sacrifices[O] *to* Me *for* forty years in the wilderness, *did you*?[17] °Indeed you took-up[R] the tabernacle[18] *of* Moloch[19] and the star *of* your[20] god Rephan[21]— the images[S] which you made to give-worship[T] *to* them. Indeed I will remove[22] you beyond Babylon!' 43

4C. "The tabernacle[23] *of* testimony[24] was *with* our fathers in the wilderness[G], just as the *One* speaking *to* Moses directed[U] him to make it according to the pattern[S] which he had seen 44

  1D. "Which[25] our fathers, having received-*it*-in-succession[26], also brought in with Joshua during the taking-possession[27] *of* the nations whom God drove-out[V] from *the* presence *of* our fathers— until[28] the days *of* David, °who found favor[W] before God 45
  46
  2D. "And he asked *that* he might find *a* dwelling-place[29] *for* the house[30] *of* Jacob, °but Solomon built[X] *a* house *for* Him[31] 47
  3D. "But the Most-High[Y] does not dwell[Z] in *things*[32] made-by-*human*-hands[33], just as the prophet says [in Isa 66:1-2]— 48

    1E. 'The heaven *is a* throne[AA] *for* Me, and the earth *is a* footstool *of* My feet. What kind of house will you build[X] *for* Me?' says *the* Lord, 'or what *will be the* place *of* My rest[BB]? °Did not My hand make all these *things*?[34]' 49
    50

5C. "Stiff-necked *ones*, and uncircumcised *in your* hearts[35] and ears— **you** are always resisting[36] the Holy Spirit. As your fathers *did*, you also *are doing*[37] 51

  1D. "Which *of* the prophets did your fathers not persecute[CC]? 52
  2D. "And they killed[DD] the *ones* having announced-beforehand[EE] about the coming[38] *of* the righteous[FF] *One*—

1. Now Stephen finishes the foundation for his answer to the first charge against him. Stephen is not speaking against Moses, 6:11, and the Law, 6:13. But the fathers of these Jews rejected this Moses sent to them, this one who did signs and wonders, just as they are rejecting Jesus now. Moses gave them the Law, the word of God, which they also rejected, just as they were rejecting His words now. Stephen makes the point with Moses here, and applies it to his hearers in v 51-52.
2. Instead of "has sent forth", some manuscripts say "sent forth" {K}.
3. Some manuscripts omit this word {C}.
4. Or, "redeemer". Used only here. GK *3392*. Related to "redemption" in Rom 3:24.
5. Or, "together with, along with, accompanied by". GK *5250*. Some manuscripts say "by", meaning "by means of " {K}.
6. Some manuscripts say "in *the* land *of* Egypt"; others, "in Egypt" {N}.
7. Some manuscripts say "the Lord your God" {K}.
8. God did so, and these Jews are rejecting Him, as their fathers did Moses. Some manuscripts add "You shall listen-to Him" {N}, as in 3:22.
9. Or, "sayings, declarations". On this word, see Heb 5:12.
10. Some manuscripts say "you" {B}.
11. Same word as in v 27.
12. Or, "in connection with". GK *1877*.
13. The word "hand over" is the same word Paul uses in Rom 1:24, 26, 28 of God handing over the Gentiles.
14. Same word as in v 7. God brought Israel out to worship Him, but handed them over to worship idols. On worshiping the host of heaven, see Deut 17:3; 2 King 17:16; 21:3; Jer 8:2.
15. That is, the sun, moon, and stars. On this word, see Lk 2:13, where it refers to angels.
16. That is, slaughtered animals as offerings. Used only here. GK *5376*. Related to "slaughter" in 8:32, and "slay" in 1 Jn 3:12.
17. The grammar indicates a "no"answer is expected to this question.
18. Or, "tent". That is, the dwelling place. Same word as in v 44. On this word, see "dwelling" in Lk 9:33.
19. Used only here. GK *3661*. Mentioned also in 2 King 23:10; Jer 32:35. A Canaanite god.
20. Some manuscripts omit this word, so that it says, "*of* the god Rephan" {C}.
21. Stephen is quoting the Septuagint of Amos 5:25-27, which gives the names Moloch and Rephan. The manuscripts have several spellings of the name of this god, including Rephan, Rompha, and Remphan {N}. GK *4818*.
22. Or, "deport, resettle". Elsewhere only in v 4, where it is a positive removal for blessing. Here, it is a negative removal for judgment. GK *3579*. Related to "deportation" in Mt 1:17.
23. This phrase "tabernacle *of* testimony" is also in Rev 15:5.
24. Stephen now lays the foundation to answer the second charge, that he spoke against this holy place, 6:13. God does not dwell in any man-made place. This place is only holy to the degree it is set apart to Him. If the Jews killed the Messiah, and God chose to destroy this place as Jesus said, Stephen does no wrong in saying so.
25. This refers to "tabernacle".
26. Or, "received in turn". Used only here. GK *1342*. It is used of something received from a former holder. Related to "successor" in 24:27.
27. Elsewhere only as "possession" in v 5, where it means a "holding-in-possession". GK *2959*. Same word as in Gen 17:8.
28. The "receiving in succession" continued until the days of David.
29. That is, a permanent building, a temple. On this word, see "tent" in 2 Pet 1:13. Related to "tabernacle".
30. That is, a permanent temple of God for the people of Israel. Some manuscripts say "God" {B}.
31. Solomon's temple which he built for God was destroyed by God. It was later rebuilt by Herod, God's enemy.
32. Some manuscripts say "temples" {K}.
33. Using this same word, Paul makes the same point in 17:24.
34. The grammar indicates that a "yes" answer is expected.
35. Some manuscripts have this word singular, "heart" {N}.
36. Or, "opposing", literally, "falling against". Used only here. GK *528*. Same word as in Num 27:14.
37. These Jews are rejecting God's messengers, and putting an improper value on a man-made temple.
38. Or, "arrival". Used only here. GK *1803*. Related to "come" in Mk 16:2.

A. 2 Tim 2:12   B. Act 7:27   C. Lk 2:26, see   D. Lk 6:44, bramble bush   E. 2 Thes 2:9   F. Heb 11:29   G. Mt 3:1   H. Lk 18:33, rise up   J. 1 Cor 12:28   K. Rev 22:16, church   L. Jn 7:17   M. 2 Cor 2:9   N. Mt 18:3, turn around   O. Heb 9:26   P. Rev 12:12   Q. Heb 5:7   R. Act 1:2   S. 1 Pet 5:3, pattern   T. Mt 14:33   U. 1 Cor 7:17   V. Act 27:39   W. Eph 2:8, grace   X. 1 Cor 14:4, edify   Y. Mt 21:9, highest   Z. Eph 3:17   AA. Rev 20:11   BB. Heb 3:11   CC. 2 Tim 3:12   DD. Rom 7:11   EE. Act 3:18   FF. Rom 1:17

	1E. *Of* Whom **you** now became¹ betrayers² and murderers³—˚you who received the Law by⁴ *the* directions⁵ *of* angels, and did not keep^A *it*!"	53
4B.	And hearing these *things*, they were infuriated⁶ *in* their hearts, and were grinding *their* teeth at him	54
5B.	But being full^B *of the* Holy Spirit, having looked-intently^C into heaven, he saw *the* glory *of* God, and Jesus standing⁷ on *the* right *side of* God. ˚And he said, "Behold— I see the heavens opened⁸, and the Son *of* Man standing on *the* right *side of* God!"	55 56
6B.	And having cried-out^D *with a* loud voice, they held-shut⁹ their ears, and rushed¹⁰ against him with-one-accord^E	57
	1C. And having driven^F *him* outside *of* the city, they were stoning *him*	58
	1D. And the witnesses^G laid-aside^H their garments at the feet *of a* young-man¹¹ being called Saul	
	2C. And they were stoning Stephen while *he was* calling-upon^J *Jesus* and saying, "Lord Jesus, receive^K my spirit". ˚And having put *down his* knees, he cried-out^D *with a* loud voice, "Lord, do not set¹² this sin *against* them". And having said this, he fell-asleep^L	59 60
	1D. And Saul was giving-approval^M *to* his killing¹³	8:1
7B.	And *a* great persecution¹⁴ came about on that day against the church in Jerusalem, and they were all dispersed¹⁵ throughout the regions^N *of* Judea and Samaria, except the apostles¹⁶	
	1C. And reverent^O men carried-in¹⁷ Stephen [for burial], and made *a* loud lamentation¹⁸ over him	2
	2C. And Saul¹⁹ was destroying²⁰ the church. Entering from house to house, dragging-away²¹ both men and women, he was handing *them* over to prison^P	3
8B.	So indeed, the *ones* having been dispersed went about announcing the word as good news^Q	4
10A.	Now Philip²², having gone down to the²³ city *of* Samaria, was proclaiming^R the Christ *to* them	5
1B.	And the crowds were with-one-accord^E paying-attention-to²⁴ the *things* being said by Philip, during their hearing and seeing the signs^S which he was doing	6
	1C. For many *of* the *ones* having unclean spirits— they²⁵ were coming out while shouting^T *with a* loud voice. And many paralyzed²⁶ *ones* and lame *ones* were cured^U	7
	2C. And there was great joy in that city	8
	3C. Now *a* certain man, Simon *by* name, was-previously^V in the city practicing-magic²⁷ and astonishing²⁸ the nation²⁹ *of* Samaria, saying *that* he was³⁰ someone great	9
	1D. *To* whom they all, from *the* small up to *the* great, were paying attention, saying, "This *one* is the Power³¹ *of* God being called 'Great' "	10
	2D. And they were paying attention to him because *he had* astonished them *for a* considerable time *with* the magic-arts	11
2B.	And when they believed^W Philip announcing-the-good-news^Q about³² the kingdom^X *of* God³³ and the name *of* Jesus Christ, they were being baptized^Y— both men and women	12
	1C. Now Simon himself also believed^W. And having been baptized^Y, he was attaching-himself^Z *to* Philip. He was astonished, seeing both signs and great miracles³⁴ taking place	13

1. Or, "proved to be, came to be". GK *1181*. Some manuscripts say "have become" {K}.
2. Or, "traitors". Elsewhere only as "traitor" in Lk 6:16; 2 Tim 3:4. GK *4595*. Your fathers killed the announcers; you killed the announced One!
3. Same word as in 3:14; 28:4. Elsewhere only in Mt 22:7; 1 Pet 4:15; Rev 21:8; 22:15. GK *5839*. Related word in Act 9:1.
4. Or, "in, at". GK *1650*.
5. Or, "decrees, ordinances, commanded things". It is plural here. Stephen could mean the directions given to angels by God, or the directions given by angels to Moses. On this word, see "ordinance" in Rom 13:2.
6. Same word as in 5:33.
7. Some think Jesus is standing to welcome Stephen to heaven; others, to call him home to Him; others, as an advocate in Stephen's defense; others, as a witness against his murderers. There are other views. Note that it is this vision Jesus granted to Stephen (which these Jews considered blasphemy) which pushed them over the edge and resulted in Stephen's death.
8. This is a participle, "having been opened", that is, "standing open".
9. These Jews did not want to hear any more "blasphemy" from Stephen. On this word, see "control" in 2 Cor 5:14.
10. Same word as used of the pigs "rushing" down the hill, Mt 8:32; Mk 5:13; Lk 8:33. These leaders stampeded upon Stephen in a violent attack. Elsewhere only in Act 19:29. GK *3994*. Related to "attempt" in 14:5, and "violence" in Rev 18:21.
11. This word is used of someone about 24-40 years old, in the prime of life. Prior to that is one's "youth". Elsewhere only in 20:9; 23:17. GK *3733*.
12. Or, "put, make stand". GK *2705*.
13. Used only here. GK 358. Related to "kill" in Mt 2:16.
14. In other words, the Jewish leaders did not stop with killing Stephen. They went after all the believers.
15. Or, "scattered". That is, scattered like seed, the root word being "to sow". Elsewhere only in v 4; 11:19. GK *1401*. Related to "dispersion" in 1 Pet 1:1.
16. Perhaps the apostles were left alone because of the earlier decision of the Sanhedrin, 5:38-39.
17. Or, "brought-in". That is, helped in burying. Used only here. GK *5172*.
18. Used only here. GK *3157*. Related to "beat the breast" in Rev 1:7.
19. Note how Saul is intertwined three times in 7:58-8:3. Luke returns to him in 9:1.
20. Or, "harming, damaging, ruining, spoiling; inflicting outrages, indignities, and personal injuries upon". Used only here. GK *3381*. Related words not in the NT mean "spoiler, destroyer"; "injurious, destructive"; "outrage, maltreatment".
21. Same word as "drag" in 14:19; 17:6. On this word, see "sweep away" in Rev 12:4.
22. That is, the one in 6:5. Philip is distinguished from the apostles in v 14.
23. Some think Luke means its main city, known as Samaria in the OT, and as Sebaste in NT times, but called Samaria here to link this to Act 1:8; others, "the" main religious city of Samaria, a city named Neapolis (Shechem in the OT). Some manuscripts omit this word, so that it reads "*a* city *of* Samaria" {C}.
24. Or, "giving heed to". Same word as in v 10, 11. On this word, see 1 Tim 3:8.
25. Luke changes subjects from "many" people, to "they", the spirits. Some manuscripts smooth it out, "For unclean spirits shouting *with* a loud voice were coming out *of* many having *them*" {N}.
26. This is a participle, "having been paralyzed". On this word, see "made feeble" in Heb 12:12.
27. Used only here. GK *3405*. Related to "magic-arts" in v 11, and to "magician" in 13:6. This man is known as Simon Magus, "Magus" being the Greek word for "magician" found in 13:6.
28. Same word as in v 11, 13. On this word, see Mk 2:12.
29. Or, "people", in the sense of the people as a whole. GK *1620*. This word is usually rendered "Gentile, nation" (see 15:23 on it).
30. More literally, "is", as the Greek typically phrases it.
31. That is, the supernatural spirit, angel or demon, the divine being. Simon is one of God's "Powers", the one being called "Great". He is the Power named "Great". "Power" may be used in this sense also in Mt 14:2; 24:29; Mk 6:14; 13:25; Lk 21:26; Rom 8:38; 1 Pet 3:22. On this word, see Mk 5:30. Some manuscripts omit "being called", so that it says "This *one* is the Great Power *of* God" {A}.
32. Some manuscripts add "the *things*" {K}, so that it says "announcing-as-good-news the *things* about...".
33. The phrase "announcing the good news about the kingdom of God" is similar to Lk 4:43; 8:1; 16:16.
34. On this word, see 1 Cor 12:10. Some manuscripts say "miracles and signs" {K}.

A. Jn 12:25 B. Mt 14:20 C. Lk 4:20 D. Mt 8:29 E. Act 1:14 F. Jn 12:31, cast out G. Act 1:8 H. Rom 13:12 J. 1 Pet 1:17 K. Mt 10:40, welcome L. 1 Thes 4:13 M. Rom 1:32 N. Mk 1:5, country O. Lk 2:25 P. Act 5:22 Q. Act 5:42, announcing the good news R. 2 Tim 4:2 S. 2 Thes 2:9 T. Mt 3:3 U. Mt 8:7 V. Lk 23:12 W. Jn 3:36 X. Mt 3:2 Y. Mk 1:8 Z. Act 2:42, devoting themselves to

3B. And the apostles in Jerusalem, having heard that "Samaria has accepted[A] the word *of* God"[1], sent- 14
forth[B] Peter and John to them— °who, having come down, prayed for them so that they might 15
receive *the* Holy Spirit[2]

    1C. For He had not yet fallen[3] upon any *of* them, but they had only been baptized[4] in the name *of* 16
        the Lord Jesus[5]
    2C. Then they were laying[C] *their* hands[6] on them, and they were receiving *the* Holy Spirit 17
    3C. Now Simon— having seen that the Spirit[7] was[8] given[9] through the laying-on[D] *of* the hands *of* 18
        the apostles— offered[E] them money[F], °saying, "Give this authority[G] *to* me also, so-that[10] *on* 19
        whomever I lay on *my* hands, he may receive *the* Holy Spirit"

        1D. But Peter said to him, "May your silver be with you for destruction[11], because you thought 20
            to acquire[H] the gift[J] *of* God with money. °There is no part[K] nor share[L] *for* you in this matter[12] 21

            1E. "For your heart is not straight[13] before God[14]
            2E. "Therefore repent[M] from this evilness[N] *of* yours, and pray *to* the Lord[15], if perhaps[16] 22
                the intention *of* your heart will be forgiven[O] you. °For[17] I see you being in *the* gall[18] 23
                of bitterness[19] and *the* bond[20] *of* unrighteousness"

        2D. And having responded, Simon said, "**You**[21] pray to the Lord for me, so that nothing *of* 24
            the things which you have spoken may come upon me"

    4C. So indeed the *ones*— having solemnly-testified[22], and having spoken the word *of* the Lord— were 25
        returning[23] to Jerusalem and announcing-the-good-news-to[P] many villages *of* the Samaritans

4B. Now *an* angel *of the* Lord spoke to Philip saying, "Arise and go toward *the* south[24] on the road going 26
down from Jerusalem to Gaza[25]". This is *a* wilderness[Q] [road].[26] °And having arisen, he proceeded 27

    1C. And behold— *there was an* Ethiopian[27] man

        1D. *A* eunuch[28]
        2D. *A* court-official[29] *of* Candace[30] (queen *of the* Ethiopians), who was over all her treasury[31]
        3D. Who[32] had come to Jerusalem *to* worship[33], °and was returning, and sitting on his chariot[34] 28
        4D. And he was reading the prophet Isaiah

    2C. And the Spirit said *to* Philip, "Approach[R] and join[35] this chariot" 29

        1D. And having run up, Philip heard him reading Isaiah the prophet[36], and said, "Do you 30
            indeed understand[S] *the things* which you are reading?"[37]
        2D. And the *one* said, "How indeed[T] might I be able, unless someone will guide[U] me?" 31
        3D. And he invited[V] Philip to sit with him, having come up

    3C. Now the passage *of* Scripture which he was reading was this— "He was led like *a* sheep to 32
        slaughter[38]. And as *a* lamb before the *one* having sheared[W] it *is* silent[X], so He does not open
        His mouth. °In His[39] humiliation[Y], His justice[40] was taken-away[41]. Who will describe[42] His 33
        generation[43]? Because His life[Z] is taken-away from the earth" [Isa 53:7-8]

        1D. And having responded, the eunuch said *to* Philip, "I ask you, about whom is the prophet 34
            saying this— about himself or about some other?"

1. Same phrase as in 11:1, where the apostles heard the Gentiles accepted the Word of God.
2. That is, the visible manifestation of the Spirit, proving that God accepted the Samaritans just as He had the Jews in chapter 2. Compare the case of the Gentiles in 10:44, and the disciples of John in 19:2. Though the gift of tongues is not specified as the manifestation, it is reasonable to assume this is intended. On "receive the Spirit", see Jn 7:39; 14:17; 20:22; Act 1:8; 2:33, 38; 8:17, 19; 10:47; 19:2; Rom 8:15; 1 Cor 2:12; 2 Cor 11:4; Gal 3:2, 14.
3. This is a participle, "he was not yet having fallen". This word "fall upon" is used of the Spirit also in 10:44; 11:15. Used 11 times. GK *2158*.
4. This is a participle, "they were having been baptized". Here, the Spirit comes after water baptism (as in 2:38; 19:5); in 10:47, before it. In both cases, the Spirit only comes to the new category of believers in the presence of Peter. On this word, see Mk 1:8.
5. These Samaritans had believed and been baptized for forgiveness of sins, but they had not visibly received the gift of the Spirit. Peter and John came to bring it about. The rift between Jews and Samaritans was not allowed to continue in the church. These believers are visibly subordinated to the apostles in the one body of Christ.
6. On "laying on hands", see the related word in Heb 6:2. Used of the Spirit only in v 17, 19; 9:17; 19:6.
7. Some manuscripts say "Holy Spirit" {B}.
8. More literally, "is", as the Greek typically phrases it.
9. It is unclear whether this means that Simon had received the Spirit, or that he only saw others receiving Him.
10. Or, "so that... he will receive". GK *2671*.
11. That is, may your silver come to destruction while in your possession. On this word, see 2 Pet 2:1.
12. Peter may be referring to what Simon asked for, the ability to cause others to visibly receive the Spirit, a task only the apostles were able to perform in this case. Even Philip could not do so. Or, he may mean Simon cannot even receive the Spirit, because of his unbelief.
13. Elsewhere only in Mt 3:3; Mk 1:3; Lk 3:4, 5; Act 9:11; 13:10; 2 Pet 2:15. GK *2318*.
14. Some think Peter means that Simon is not yet a true believer, but continues to be a slave of sin needing to repent, v 22-23. Others think Simon is a true believer (v 13), but is in need of instruction and discipline.
15. Some manuscripts say "pray *to* God" {K}.
16. The idiom "if perhaps" is elsewhere only in Mk 11:13; Act 17:27. It means "in the hope that", but expresses some uncertainty about whether it will in fact happen.
17. Peter explains why he is uncertain about whether Simon will do so.
18. Or, "poison, venom", as this word is used in Job 20:14. In Deut 29:18-19, God warns against "a root springing up with gall and bitterness" (same two words as here), referring to an Israelite who turns to other gods while saying "I will have peace even though I follow the stubbornness of my heart". God says He will not spare such a person, but will blot out his name from under heaven. If Peter has this verse in mind, then he means "I see you having the bitter poison of self deception, thinking you can still serve your old gods and claim to believe in the true God". Elsewhere only in Mt 27:34, where it was mixed with wine. GK *5958*.
19. That is, in *a* bitter gall or poison, a gall characterized by bitterness. Elsewhere only in Rom 3:14; Eph 4:31; Heb 12:15. GK *4394*. Related word in Col 3:19.
20. Or, "*an* unrighteous bond", a bond characterized by unrighteousness. This word refers to the thing that binds together, fastens, unites. Elsewhere only in Eph 4:3, "bond" of peace; in Col 3:14, "bond" of perfection; and in Col 2:19, "ligaments". GK *5278*. Here, Simon is bound by his unrighteousness. He is shackled or tied to it, and it is restraining him from genuine repentance. He is in bondage to unrighteousness.
21. That is, Peter and John. The word is plural. Simon's fear is clear; his repentance is not stated.
22. Same word as in 2:40. On this word, see "solemnly charge" in 1 Tim 5:21.
23. Some manuscripts say "returned... and announced..." {K}.
24. Or, "Go at mid-day", noon, as this word is used in 22:6. Used only in these two places. GK *3540*.
25. This coastal town is on the road to Egypt. Used only here. GK *1124*.
26. Instead of being Luke's explanation to his readers, this may be part of the angel's words, explaining which road to take.
27. Ethiopia was the kingdom south of Egypt, along the Red Sea, including parts of modern Sudan. Its capital was Meroe (in the south of modern Sudan). Used only in this verse. GK *134*.
28. That is, a castrated male. Such ones were used as keepers of the harem, and served the government in other positions. Our English word is from this Greek word *eunouchos*, which literally means "to have charge of the bed". Elsewhere only in v 34, 36, 38, 39, and Mt 19:12. GK *2336*.
29. Or, "ruler". Elsewhere only as "ruler" in Lk 1:52; 1 Tim 6:15. GK *1541*.
30. This is a title, like "Pharaoh", not a name. Luke defines it in what follows. Used only here. GK *2833*.
31. Used only here. GK *1125*. Related to the word in Mk 12:41.
32. Some manuscripts omit this word {N}, making it "*an* Ethiopian man... had come".
33. On this word, see Mt 14:33. On the grammar of this word, see "*to* do" in 24:17. This man was at least a God-fearer, and some think he was a Jew.
34. Used of a traveling chariot or carriage, as here, v 29, 38. Elsewhere only of a war chariot in Rev 9:9. Also used outside the NT of a racing chariot. GK *761*.
35. Or, "stick to". On this word, see 1 Cor 6:16.
36. This man may have just purchased the Septuagint (the Greek translation of the OT, also referred to as the LXX), or the scroll from it containing Isaiah. The quote in v 32-33 is from the Septuagint.
37. The grammar of this question implies neither a "yes" nor a "no" answer. It occurs also in Lk 18:8.
38. Elsewhere only in Rom 8:36; Jam 5:5. GK *5375*. Related to "victim" in Act 7:42.
39. Some manuscripts omit this word {C}.
40. Or, "judgment". That is, the judgment or justice due this One was taken away. On this word, see "judgment" in Jn 3:19.
41. Or, "removed". Same word as later in this verse. GK *149*.
42. Or, "narrate, tell". On this word, see "relate" in Lk 8:39.
43. That is, this One's contemporaries who do this to Him. Or, "family", His origin. Or, "descendants", His posterity. On this word, see Mt 24:34.

A. Mt 10:40, welcome B. Mk 3:14, send out C. Lk 10:30, laid on D. Heb 6:2 E. Heb 5:7 F. Mk 10:23, wealth G. Rev 6:8 H. 1 Thes 4:4 J. Rom 5:15 K. Col 1:12 L. Col 1:12 M. Act 26:20 N. 1 Pet 2:1, badness O. Mt 6:12 P. Act 5:42 Q. Mt 3:1 R. Heb 10:22 S. Lk 1:34, know T. Mt 27:23 U. Lk 6:39 V. Rom 12:8, exhorting W. 1 Cor 11:6 X. 1 Cor 14:10, speechless Y. Jam 1:10, lowliness Z. Rom 8:10

	2D. And Philip— having opened his mouth, and beginning from[1] this Scripture— announced Jesus as good news[A] *to* him		35
	4C. And as they were proceeding along the road, they came upon some water. And the eunuch says, "Behold— water. What is preventing[B] me from being baptized[C]?"		36 37[2]
	1D. And he ordered[D] the chariot to stop[3]. And they both went down into[4] the water, both Philip and the eunuch, and he baptized him		38
	2D. And when they came up out-of[5] the water, *the* Spirit *of the* Lord snatched Philip away[6]. And the eunuch did not see him any longer, for[7] he was going *his* way rejoicing[E]		39
5B. And Philip[8] was found at Azotus[9]. And while going through, he was announcing-the-good-news-to[A] all the cities until he came to Caesarea[10]			40
11A. Now Saul, still[11] breathing threat[F] and murder[12] against the disciples *of* the Lord, having gone to the high priest, ˚asked-*for* letters[G] from him to the synagogues at Damascus[13] so that if he found any being *of* the Way[14], both men and women, he might bring *them* bound[15] to Jerusalem			9:1 2
	1B. And during the proceeding[16], it came about *that* he *was* drawing-near[H] *to* Damascus. And suddenly[J] *a* light from heaven flashed-around[17] him		3
	1C. And having fallen on the ground[K], he heard *a* voice saying *to* him, "Saul, Saul, why are you persecuting[L] Me?"		4
	2C. And he said, "Who are You, sir[18]?"		5
	3C. And the *One said*,[19] "**I** am Jesus Whom **you** are persecuting.[20] ˚But arise and enter into the city, and it will be told you what thing you must[M] do"		6
	4C. And the men traveling-with him were standing speechless[21], **hearing**[22] the voice[23]— but seeing no one		7
	5C. And Saul was raised[24] from the ground. And his eyes having been opened, he was seeing nothing[25]. And hand-leading[26] him, they brought *him* into Damascus		8
	6C. And he was not seeing *for* three days. And he did not eat, nor drink		9
	2B. Now *a* certain disciple was in Damascus— Ananias *by* name		10
	1C. And the Lord said to him in *a* vision[N], "Ananias". And the *one* said, "Behold, I *am here*, Lord"		
		1D. And the Lord *said* to him, "Having arisen[O], go on the lane[P] being called 'Straight', and seek *one*-from-Tarsus[27], Saul *by* name, in *the* house *of* Judas. For behold— he is praying. And he saw[28] *a* man in *a* vision[29], Ananias *by* name, having come in and laid[Q] hands[30] on him so that he might see-again[R]"	11 12
		2D. And Ananias responded, "Lord, I heard[31] about this man from many— how many bad[S] *things* he did *to* Your saints[T] in Jerusalem. ˚And here he has authority[U] from the chief priests to bind all the *ones* calling-upon[V] Your name"	13 14
		3D. And the Lord said to him, "Go, because this *one* is *a* chosen[32] instrument[33] *for* Me— *that* he might carry[W] My name before both Gentiles and kings, and sons *of* Israel. ˚For **I** will show him how-many[34] *things* he must[M] suffer[35] for My name"	15 16
	2C. And Ananias departed, and entered into the house. And having laid[Q] *his* hands on him, he said, "Brother Saul, the Lord has sent me forth[X]— Jesus[36], the *One* having appeared[Y] *to* you on the road *on* which you were coming— so that you may see-again and be filled[Z] *with the* Holy Spirit"[37]		17

1. On the idiom "beginning from", see Mt 20:8.
2. Some manuscripts add as v 37, "And Philip said *to* him, 'If you believe from your whole heart, it is permitted'. And having responded, he said, 'I believe *that* Jesus Christ is the Son *of* God' {A}.
3. Or, "stand [still]". GK *2705*.
4. Or, "to". On "baptize", see Mk 1:8.
5. Or, "from". Note that this word is referring to both of them, like "into" in v 38. Same word as in Mk 1:10. GK *1666*.
6. On the word "snatched away", see 2 Cor 12:2. Luke leaves us to imagine how this occurred. Some manuscripts say "water, *the* Holy Spirit fell upon the eunuch. And *an* angel *of the* Lord snatched" {A}.
7. That is, for he was going on, and Philip was no longer with him.
8. The next time we meet Philip is in 21:8, on an occasion when Luke was with Paul (note that "we came"). So perhaps Luke learned of these events directly from Philip.
9. This is a coastal town north of Gaza. Used only here. GK *111*. Known as Ashdod in the OT. Caesarea is still further north.
10. This either was, or became Philip's home, Act 21:8. This was the capital city and chief port of the province of Judea. It was built by Herod the Great. The Roman governors (like Pilate, Felix, Festus), lived here. Elsewhere only in Act 9:30; 10:1, 24; 11:11; 12:19; 18:22; 21:8, 16; 23:23, 33; 25:1, 4, 6, 13. GK *2791*. On Philip's Caesarea, see Mt 16:13.
11. How much time has elapsed since 8:3 is not stated.
12. Elsewhere only in Mt 15:19; Mk 7:21; 15:7; Lk 23:19, 25; Rom 1:29; Heb 11:37; Rev 9:21. GK *5840*. Related word in Jam 4:2.
13. This is a city north of Israel. It was the capital of the Roman province of Syria. Elsewhere only in v 3, 8, 10, 19, 22, 27, and in reference to the events of this chapter in Act 22:5, 6, 10, 11; 26:12, 20; 2 Cor 11:32; Gal 1:17. GK *1242*.
14. That is, belonging to the Way. Same term as in 19:9, 23; 22:4; 24:14, 22. On this word, see Lk 3:4. Compare 16:17; 18:25, 26.
15. This is a participle, "having been bound".
16. Same word as in Act 22:6; 26:12. On this word, see "gone" in Mt 28:19.
17. Elsewhere only in 22:6. GK *4313*. Related to "lightning", and to "flashing" in Lk 17:24.
18. Or, "lord", as in Rev 7:14. Paul does not yet know who is speaking to him. On this word, see "Master" in Mt 8:2.
19. Some manuscripts say "And the Lord said" {K}.
20. Some early translations, but no Greek manuscripts, say " 'persecuting. *It is* hard *for* you to kick against *the* goads'. While both trembling and marveling, he said, 'Lord, what do you want me to do?' And the Lord *said* to him, 'Arise and enter into the city, and it will...' " {N}. Note 26:14 and 22:10. Erasmus (see the Introduction) translated this from the Latin and included it in his Greek text, from which it came into the KJV.
21. Or, "dumbfounded". Used only here. GK *1917*.
22. Luke uses grammar that emphasizes the contrast between the two halves of this sentence.
23. Or, "sound". On this word, see Mk 1:26. Note 22:9.
24. Or, "arose". On this word, see "arose" in Mt 28:6.
25. Some manuscripts say "no one" {N}.
26. Elsewhere only in 22:11. GK *5932*. Related to the word in 13:11.
27. That is, from the city of Tarsus, 9:30.
28. Saul had this vision while blind! The advance information provides further objectification to the event.
29. Some manuscripts omit "in a vision" {C}.
30. Some manuscripts have this singular {N}, "*his* hand". On this concept, see Heb 6:2.
31. Some manuscripts say "have heard" {N}.
32. More literally, "*an* instrument *of* choosing", that is, of God's choice. On this word, see "choosing" in Rom 11:5.
33. Or, "vessel, implement, utensil, tool". On this word, see "vessel" in 1 Thes 4:4.
34. Same word as in v 13. GK *4012*.
35. See Col 1:24.
36. Some manuscripts omit this word {N}.
37. Saul does not receive the Spirit through the other apostles, but through a divinely sent messenger.

A. Act 5:42, announce the good news B. 1 Cor 14:39, forbid C. Mk 1:8 D. Mt 14:28 E. 2 Cor 13:11 F. Eph 6:9, threatening G. 2 Thes 3:17 H. Lk 21:28 J. Lk 2:13 K. Rev 7:1, land L. 2 Tim 3:12 M. Mt 16:21 N. Act 10:3 O. Lk 18:33, rise up P. Mt 6:2 Q. Lk 10:30, laid on R. Act 22:13, look up S. 3 Jn 11, evil T. 1 Pet 1:16, holy U. Rev 6:8 V. 1 Pet 1:17 W. Mt 8:17 X. Mk 3:14, send out Y. Lk 2:26, see Z. Act 2:4

Acts 9:18		426	Verse

        1D. And immediately[A] *something* like scales[1] fell from his eyes   18
        2D. And he saw-again[2], and having arisen[B], was baptized[3]
        3D. And having taken food[C], he strengthened[D]   19

    3B. Now he[4] came-to-be with the disciples in Damascus *for* some days

        1C. And immediately he was proclaiming[E] Jesus[5] in the synagogues— that this *One* is the Son *of* God   20

            1D. And all the *ones* hearing were astonished[F], and were saying, "Is not this the *one* having destroyed[G] in Jerusalem the *ones* calling-upon[H] this name?[6] And he had come here for this— that he might bring them bound[7] to the chief priests!"   21

        2C. And Saul was becoming more strong[8]. And he was confounding[9] the[10] Jews dwelling in Damascus, proving that this *One* is the Christ   22
        3C. And when considerable days[11] were being fulfilled[12], the Jews plotted[13] to kill him. *But their plot[J] was known *by* Saul   23-24

            1D. And they were even[14] closely-watching[K] the gates both *by* day and *by* night so that they might kill him
            2D. But his[15] disciples, having taken *him by* night, let him down through the wall[16], having lowered[17] *him* in *a* large-basket[L]   25

    4B. And having arrived in Jerusalem, he[18] was trying[M] to join the disciples.[19] And they all were fearing him, not believing that he was[20] *a* disciple[N]   26

        1C. But Barnabas[21], having taken-hold-of[O] *him*, brought him to the apostles,[22] and related[P] *to* them   27

            1D. How he saw the Lord on the road, and that He spoke *to* him[23]
            2D. And how in Damascus he spoke-boldly[24] in the name *of* Jesus

        2C. And he was with them,[25] going in and going out in Jerusalem, speaking-boldly[26] in the name *of* the Lord[27]   28
        3C. And he was speaking and debating[Q] with the Hellenists[R], but the *ones* were attempting[28] to kill him   29
        4C. But the brothers, having learned[S] *it*,[29] brought him down to Caesarea[30], and sent him away to Tarsus[31]   30

    5B. So indeed[32] the church[33] throughout all Judea and Galilee and Samaria was having peace, while being built-up[T]. And it was being multiplied[U] while walking[V] *in* the fear *of* the Lord and *in* the comfort[34] *of* the Holy Spirit   31

12A. Now it came about *that* Peter, while going through all *the* regions[35], came down also to the saints[W] dwelling-in[X] Lydda[36]   32

    1B. And he found there *a* certain man, Aeneas *by* name, who had been paralyzed[37], lying down on *a* cot for eight years[38]   33

        1C. And Peter said *to* him, "Aeneas, Jesus Christ[39] heals[Y] you. Arise[B] and make[Z] your bed *for* yourself"[40]   34
        2C. And immediately he arose[B]

1. Used only here. GK *3318*. This word was used of "scales" of a fish, "flakes" of skin, "shells" of an egg, "bark" of a tree, "husks" and "skins" of fruits and vegetables, "flakes" of snow, etc. Something physical which produced the blindness fell off.
2. Or, "received sight". Same word as "looked up" in 22:13. Some manuscripts add, "at once" {N}.
3. Presumably, by Ananias, 22:16.
4. Some manuscripts say "Saul" {K}.
5. Some manuscripts say "the Christ" {K}.
6. The grammar indicates a "yes" answer is expected.
7. This is a participle, "having been bound".
8. On the word "become strong", see 2 Tim 2:1.
9. Or, "stirring up, throwing into confusion". Same word as in 2:6. Elsewhere only as "stir up" in 21:27, 31; and "confused" in 19:32. GK *5177*.
10. Some manuscripts omit this word {C}.
11. Saul was there for three years (Gal 1:18), though how much of this was in Arabia is not stated.
12. Or, "completed". Same word as in 7:23, 30. On this word, see "filled" in Eph 5:18. Compare Act 2:1.
13. Same word as in Mt 26:4. Related to "plot" in v 24. On this word, see "counseled" in Jn 18:14.
14. Or, "also". Some manuscripts omit this word {K}.
15. Some manuscripts say "But the disciples, having taken him..." {N}.
16. That is, the city wall, bypassing the gates. 2 Cor 11:32-33 adds that it was through a window, and that this plot enlisted the aid of the local authorities.
17. Same word as in 2 Cor 11:33; Act 27:17.
18. Some manuscripts say "Saul" {K}.
19. Saul came to see Peter, Gal 1:18.
20. More literally, "is", as the Greek typically phrases it.
21. That is, the one last mentioned in 4:36.
22. Specifically, Peter and James, Gal 1:19.
23. Or, "and that he spoke *to* Him". Or, "and what thing He spoke *to* him".
24. Same word as in v 28, and four other times of Paul in Acts. On this word, see Eph 6:20.
25. Saul was there for fifteen days, Gal 1:18.
26. Some manuscripts say "and speaking-boldly" {K}.
27. Some manuscripts add "Jesus" {K}.
28. Or, "undertaking, setting their hand to". The root word is "hand". On this word, see "undertook" in Lk 1:1.
29. In addition, Saul received a vision from the Lord, 22:17-21.
30. That is, the sea port, 8:40.
31. This is the capital city in Cilicia, and Paul's hometown, 9:11. Elsewhere only in 11:25; 22:3. GK *5433*. Related word in 9:11; 21:39.
32. The conversion of Saul, ending his overt persecution of the churches, resulted in an outward peace with the Jews. They apparently gave up on the frontal-assault method of stopping the Way.
33. Some manuscripts have this plural, "churches... were having peace. And they were being multiplied..." {A}.
34. Or, "encouragement". On this word, see "encouragement" in Act 4:36.
35. Or, "*districts, places*". This word is supplied from 20:2 (Macedonia); Mt 2:22 (Galilee), 16:13 (Caesarea), etc. The grammar does not agree with "*cities*" or "*churches*".
36. This was a town west of Jerusalem on a road to the coast. Elsewhere only in v 35, 38. GK *3375*.
37. This is a participle, "who was having been paralyzed".
38. Or, "from eight years *old*".
39. Some manuscripts say "Jesus the Christ" {N}.
40. That is, arise and do now for yourself what you have not been able to do for many years.

A. Mt 13:5 B. Lk 18:33, rise up C. Mt 24:45 D. Lk 22:43 E. 2 Tim 4:2 F. Mk 2:12 G. Gal 1:13 H. 1 Pet 1:17 J. Act 23:30 K. Lk 6:7 L. Mt 15:37 M. Heb 2:18, tempted N. Lk 6:40 O. Lk 20:20 P. Lk 8:39 Q. Mk 8:11 R. Act 11:20 S. Col 1:6, understood T. 1 Cor 14:4, edify U. Act 7:17 V. Mt 28:19, gone W. 1 Pet 1:16, holy X. Eph 3:17, dwell Y. Mt 8:8 Z. Mk 14:15, spread

Acts 9:35	428	Verse

        3C. And all the *ones* dwelling-in Lydda and Sharon[1] saw him— who[2] [then] turned to the Lord   35

  2B. Now in Joppa[3], there was *a* certain disciple, Tabitha *by* name (which being interpreted[4] means   36
"Dorcas[5]"). This *one* was full[A] *of* good[B] works and acts-of-almsgiving[6] which she was doing

        1C. And it came about in those days *that* having become sick[C], she died. And having washed[D] *her*,   37
they laid her in *an* upper-room[E]

        2C. Now Lydda being near Joppa, the disciples— having heard that Peter was[7] in it[8]— sent-out[F]   38
two men to him urging[G], "Do not delay to come to us"[9]

        3C. And having arisen, Peter went with them— whom,[10] having arrived, they brought up into the   39
upper room

            1D. And all the widows stood near him, weeping[H], and showing[J] *him* tunics[K] and garments—
all-that Dorcas was making while being with them

            2D. And Peter— having put everyone outside, and having put *down his* knees— prayed. And   40
having turned to the body, he said, "Tabitha, rise-up[L]"

            3D. And the *one* opened her eyes! And having seen Peter, she sat up

            4D. And having given her *his* hand, he raised her up[L]   41

            5D. And having called the saints and the widows, he presented[M] her alive

        4C. And it became known[N] throughout all Joppa, and many put-faith[11] upon the Lord   42

        5C. And it came about *that he* stayed considerable[12] days in Joppa with *a* certain Simon, *a* tanner[13]   43

  3B. Now *there was a* certain man in Caesarea[14], Cornelius *by* name— *a* centurion[O] from *the* cohort[P]   10:1
being called "Italian"[15], °*a* devout[16] *one,* and *one* fearing[Q] God with all his household, doing many   2
acts-of-almsgiving[17] *to* the [Jewish] people, and praying *to* God continually[R]

        1C. He saw[18] in *a* vision[19] clearly[20], as-if[S] *it* were around[21] *the* ninth hour *of* the day, *an* angel *of*   3
God having come-in to[22] him, and having said *to* him, "Cornelius!"

            1D. And the *one*— having looked-intently[T] *at* him, and having become terrified[23]— said,   4
"What is it, sir[24]?"

            2D. And he said *to* him, "Your prayers and your acts-of-almsgiving went up for *a* memorial[25]
before God. °And now, send men to Joppa, and send-for[U] *a* certain[26] Simon who is called   5
Peter. °This *one* is lodging[27] with *a* certain Simon, *a* tanner, whose house is beside *the* sea"[28]   6

        2C. And when the angel speaking *to* him[29] departed, having called two of *his* household-servants[V]   7
and *a* devout[30] soldier[W] *from* the *ones* attaching-themselves[31] *to* him, °and having described[X]   8
everything *to* them, he sent them forth to Joppa[32]

        3C. Now *on* the next day, while those[33] *ones* were journeying and drawing-near[Y] *to* the city, Peter   9
went up on the housetop[Z] around *the* sixth[34] hour to pray

            1D. And he became hungry and was wanting to eat[AA]. And while they *were* preparing[BB] *it, a*   10
trance[35] came[36] upon him

                1E. And he sees the heaven having been opened, and *a* certain object[CC] like *a* large sheet[37]   11
coming down[38], being let down[39] *by* four corners[DD] on the ground[EE]— °in which were   12
all[40] the four-footed-animals[41] and reptiles *of* the earth[42], and birds *of* the heaven

                2E. And *a* voice came to him, "Having arisen, Peter, slaughter[43] and eat[44]!"   13

1. This is the coastal plain area from Joppa to Caesarea. Used only here. GK *4926*.
2. This word is plural, referring to "all the ones".
3. This town is on the coast, about 10 miles or 16 kilometers further west from Lydda. Both towns are in the area Philip evangelized in 8:40.
4. Or, "translated", from Aramaic to Greek in this case. On this word, see 1 Cor 12:30.
5. Dorcas means "gazelle". She was known by both names, "Dorcas" in v 39, and "Tabitha" in v 40, as Peter was known by both Cephas and Peter. Note the similar statement in Jn 1:42.
6. On this word, see "almsgiving" in Mt 6:2. Acts of charity for the poor.
7. More literally, "is", as the Greek typically phrases it.
8. That is, Lydda.
9. That is, hurry to us. Some manuscripts say "urging *that he* not delay to come to them" {K}.
10. That is, Peter.
11. On "put faith upon", see Rom 4:5.
12. Or, "many". Same word as in 9:23. GK *2653*.
13. That is, a leather worker, one who prepared animal hides for various uses. Elsewhere only in 10:6, 32. GK *1114*.
14. On this word, see 8:40. Cornelius was serving at the Roman headquarters in Israel.
15. That is, the Italian cohort, made up of Romans. This may mean Cornelius was a native Italian (Roman), and may have been a volunteer. Used only here. GK *2713*.
16. Or, "godly, reverent, pious". Elsewhere only in v 7, and as "godly" in 2 Pet 2:9. GK *2356*. Related to "godliness" in 1 Tim 2:2.
17. Same word as in 9:36, and as 10:4, 31.
18. In the Greek, v 1-3 is all one sentence, "Now *a* certain man in Caesarea, Cornelius... saw in *a* vision...".
19. Or, "sight". Same word as in 9:10, 12; 10:17, 19; 11:5; 12:9; 16:9, 10; 18:9. Elsewhere only as "sight" in Mt 17:9; Act 7:31. GK *3969*. It refers to the thing seen, not the state of the one seeing. Related to the verb "appeared" in Lk 1:11; 22:43; 24:34; Act 7:2, 30; 13:31, etc; and to "vision" in Rev 9:17, and in 2 Cor 12:1. The root word is "to see". In Act 7:30, the angel "appeared" in the bush, and in the next verse Moses marvels at the "vision, sight". In 16:9, both words are used, "a vision appeared". In Act 10:10, 17 and 11:5, it occurs in a trance. "Vision" is the Greek word *orama*, from which we get "pan-orama", a full view or vision.
20. Or, "plainly, openly, distinctly". Elsewhere only as "openly" in Mk 1:45; Jn 7:10. GK *5747*. Related to "evident" in Rom 1:19.
21. Or, "clearly, about around *the*". This is the Greek word order of the verse. Luke may be emphasizing the clarity of the vision. The sight of the angel was as clear as if it were about 3 P.M. (broad daylight) inside the house (11:13). Others note that in v 30, Cornelius says the vision was at 3 P.M., and suggest that this is the meaning here, "about around 3 P.M.". Luke says "about the sixth hour" in Lk 23:44, and "around the sixth hour" in Act 10:9, but "about around" is found only here. Some manuscripts omit "around", making it "about *the* ninth hour" {N}.
22. On the idiom, "come-in to", see 16:40.
23. Or, "afraid". On this word, see Lk 24:37.
24. Or, "lord", as in Rev 7:14. Or, in the presence of this angel sent from God, Cornelius could be answering God directly, not the angel, in which case he is saying "What is it, Lord". On this word, see "Master" in Mt 8:2.
25. On this word, see Mt 26:13, where what the woman did was a memorial for her. Here, what Cornelius did was a memorial for him before God, a thing for him to be remembered-by before God. And God "remembered" (v 31) him and brought Peter to him for his salvation, 11:14.
26. Some manuscripts omit this word {B}.
27. Or, "staying as a guest". Same word as in 10:18, 32; 21:16. Elsewhere only as "give lodging" in Act 10:23; "entertained" (as guests, or showed hospitality to guests) in Act 28:7; Heb 13:2; "be strange" in Act 17:20; and "think strange" in 1 Pet 4:4, 16. GK *3826*. Related to "lodging" in Act 28:23; "host" in Rom 16:23; "received strangers" in 1 Tim 5:10; and "hospitality" in Heb 13:2. Thus, using this word group, to "strangers" the "host" "shows hospitality" and "provides lodging".
28. Some manuscripts add "This *one* will tell you what you must do" {N}.
29. Some manuscripts say "Cornelius" {K}.
30. Same word as in v 2.
31. Or, "devoting themselves" to Cornelius, by their choice. Not those "attached to" his regiment, but those who "attached themselves to" him, who were personally loyal to him. In other words, fellow God-fearers. Same word as in 8:13. On this word, see "devoting themselves to" in 2:42.
32. This is a distance of about 30 miles or 50 kilometers.
33. Some manuscripts say "while they *were* journeying..." {N}.
34. That is, noon.
35. Same word as in 11:5 (where it is paired with "vision"); 22:17. On this word, see "astonishment" in Mk 5:42.
36. Some manuscripts say "fell" {N}.
37. Elsewhere only in 11:5. GK *3855*. Related to "linen cloth" in Jn 19:40.
38. Some manuscripts add "to him" {N}.
39. Some manuscripts say "having been bound and being let down..." {C}. There are other variations.
40. That is, all types.
41. Or, "quadrupeds". Elsewhere only in 11:6; Rom 1:23. GK *5488*.
42. Some manuscripts say "four-footed animals *of* the earth and wild beasts and reptiles, and birds..." {B}.
43. Or, "kill". This word is used of slaughtering for food, as in Mt 22:4; Lk 15:23, 27, 30; Act 11:7; and for a sacrifice. Elsewhere only as "sacrifice" in Mk 14:12; Lk 22:7; 1 Cor 5:7; 10:20; "offer sacrifice" in Act 14:13, 18; and "kill" in Jn 10:10. GK *2604*. Related to "sacrifice" in Heb 9:26.
44. Same word as in v 14; 11:7. It is the common word for "eat", used 158 times. GK *2266*.

A. Mt 14:20   B. 1 Tim 5:10b   C. 2 Tim 4:20   D. 2 Pet 2:22   E. Act 1:13   F. Mk 3:14   G. Rom 12:8, exhorting   H. Jn 11:33   J. Act 18:28   K. Mt 5:40   L. Lk 18:33   M. Rom 12:1   N. Rom 1:19   O. Mt 8:5   P. Mt 27:27   Q. Eph 5:33, respecting   R. 2 Thes 3:16   S. Rom 6:13   T. Lk 4:20   U. Act 11:13   V. Rom 14:4   W. Mt 28:12   X. Jn 1:18, expound   Y. Lk 21:28   Z. Lk 5:19   AA. Heb 6:4, taste   BB. 2 Cor 9:3   CC. 1 Thes 4:4, vessel   DD. Col 1:18, beginning   EE. Rev 7:1, land

    3E. But Peter said, "By no means, Lord, because I never ate anything defiled¹ and² unclean" 14
    4E. And *a* voice again *came* to him for *a* second *time*, "*The things* which God made-clean³, don't **you** be making-defiled⁴" 15
    5E. And this⁵ took place three-times⁶, and immediately⁷ the object was taken-up^A into heaven 16

   2D. Now while Peter was being greatly-perplexed^B within himself *as to* what the vision^C which he saw might mean^D, behold⁸— the men having been sent-forth^E by Cornelius, having asked-repeatedly⁹ *as to* the house *of* Simon, stood at the gate. ˚And having called, they were inquiring^F, "Is Simon,¹⁰ the *one* being called Peter, lodging^G here¹¹?" 17, 18
   3D. And while Peter *was* pondering¹² about the vision, the Spirit said *to* him¹³, "Behold— three¹⁴ men *are* seeking^H you. ˚But¹⁵ having arisen, go down and proceed with them not doubting¹⁶ at all, because **I** have sent them forth" 19, 20
   4D. And Peter, having gone down to the men¹⁷, said, "Behold— **I** am *the one* whom you are seeking^H. What *is* the reason^J for which you are-here^K?" 21
   5D. And the *ones* said, "Cornelius— *a* centurion, *a* righteous^L man, and *one* fearing^M God, and *one* being attested^N by the whole nation *of* the Jews— was directed¹⁸ by *a* holy angel to summon^O you to his house, and to listen-to words^P from you" 22

  4C. Then having invited them in, he gave-*them*-lodging^G. And *on* the next day, having arisen, he¹⁹ went forth with them. And some²⁰ *of* the brothers from Joppa went with him 23
  5C. And *on* the next day, he²¹ entered into Caesarea. And Cornelius was expecting^Q them, having called together his relatives and close^R friends 24

   1D. And when Peter's entering *the* house came about,²² Cornelius— having met^S him, having fallen at *his* feet— paid-homage²³ 25
   2D. But Peter raised him, saying, "Stand up. **I** myself also am *a* man^T" 26
   3D. And while conversing-with²⁴ him, he went in and finds many having come-together 27
   4D. And he said to them, "**You** know how it is unlawful²⁵ *for a* Jewish man to be joining²⁶ or coming-to²⁷ *a* foreigner²⁸. And-*yet* God showed me *that I should* be calling **no** person defiled²⁹ or unclean. ˚Therefore, having been sent-for^O, I indeed came without-objection. So I ask, *for* what reason^U did you send-for^O me?" 28, 29
   5D. And Cornelius said, "Four days ago at this hour,³⁰ I was praying³¹ in my house *at* the ninth³² *hour*, and behold— *a* man stood before me in shining clothing³³ 30

    1E. And he says, 'Cornelius, your prayer was heard, and your acts-of-almsgiving were remembered³⁴ before God. ˚Therefore send to Joppa, and summon³⁵ Simon, who is called Peter. This *one* is lodging in *the* house *of* Simon, *a* tanner, beside *the* sea'³⁶ 31, 32
    2E. "Therefore I sent to you at-once^V, and **you** did well³⁷, having come 33
    3E. "So now **we** are all here before God to hear all the *things* having been commanded^W you by the Lord³⁸"

   6D. And Peter, having opened *his* mouth, said, "I understand³⁹, in accordance with [God's] truth,⁴⁰ that God is not *a* respecter-of-persons⁴¹, ˚but in every nation, the *one* fearing^M Him and working^X righteousness⁴² is acceptable⁴³ *to* Him 34, 35

    1E. "*As to* the message⁴⁴ which⁴⁵ He sent-forth^E *to* the sons^Y *of* Israel, announcing-the-good-news-of⁴⁶ peace⁴⁷ through⁴⁸ Jesus Christ— this *One* is Lord^Z *of* all⁴⁹ 36

1. That is, profane, ritually unholy. On this word, see Heb 10:29. The related verb is in v 15.
2. Some manuscripts say "or" {K}.
3. Or, "declared-clean, treated-as-clean". If God told Peter to eat it, then it is clean. Peter is not to correct God on this matter. The OT laws on clean and unclean animals pass away with the old covenant, Heb 8:13. Peter gets the message, at least in part, as seen in v 28. Same word as 11:9 and Mk 7:19. On this word, see "cleansed" in Heb 9:22.
4. Or, "declaring-defiled, treating-as-defiled". Note the tenses. God has already made these things clean. Do not be making them defiled again. The grammar implies "Stop making them defiled". On this word, see Mk 7:15.
5. That is, this conversation. Then the object is taken up.
6. This is an idiom, literally "for three-times". It is elsewhere only in 11:10. The word "three-times" is GK *5565*.
7. Some manuscripts say "again"; others omit this word {B}.
8. Some manuscripts say "and behold" {N}.
9. Or, "asked continually". Literally, they "questioned through" to the house by inquiring of one person after another until they found it. Used only here. GK *1452*.
10. Or, "inquiring whether Simon... is lodging here."
11. Elsewhere only in Lk 24:41; Jn 4:15, 16; Act 16:28; 17:6; 25:17, 24. GK *1924*.
12. Or, "reflecting, thinking". Used only here. GK *1445*. Related to the word in Mt 1:20.
13. Some manuscripts omit "to him" {C}.
14. Some manuscripts omit this word {B}.
15. That is, in contrast to what your conscience will tell you, to what you think is proper.
16. Or, "hesitating, wavering, disputing with yourself". Note 11:2-3, where others do this very thing. On this word, see Jam 1:6. The reason Peter would doubt that it was wise or proper to go with them is stated in v 28.
17. Some manuscripts add "having been sent from Cornelius to him" {N}.
18. Or, "given a divine message". On this word, see "revealed" in Lk 2:26.
19. Some manuscripts say "Peter" {K}.
20. That is, six of them, 11:12.
21. Some manuscripts say "they" {C}.
22. Or, And when it came about "*that* Peter entered" or "*that* Peter should enter". The point of the unusual grammar is that Cornelius meets him immediately at his entry, whether outside or inside. He meets him at the door of the house, or the gate of the court (like 12:13), and then in v 27 they enter the room where the people are.
23. On this word, see "worship" in Mt 14:33.
24. Used only here. GK *5326*. Related to "converse" in 24:26.
25. Or, "forbidden". That is, according to the rabbis, according to their customs. On this word, see 1 Pet 4:3.
26. Or, "associating *with*, keeping company *with*". This is equivalent to "ate with" in 11:3. On this word, see 1 Cor 6:16.
27. That is, coming to his home. Equivalent to "went in" in 11:3.
28. That is, a Gentile, a non-Jew, one from another tribe (than Abraham's). Used only here. GK *260*. The root word is "tribe".
29. In pondering what the vision might mean (v 17), in the light of the events that followed in v 19-22, Peter made a correct application to the Gentile people the Spirit was preparing him to see. Same word as in v 14.
30. This is an idiom, literally, "From *the* fourth day until this hour". The Greek thinks of it from the past forward, "from the fourth day". In English, we count it from the present backward, "four days ago".
31. Some manuscripts say "From *the* fourth day I was fasting until this hour, and praying in my house..." {B}.
32. That is, at my 3 o'clock prayers.
33. On "shining clothing", see Lk 23:11.
34. Or, "kept in mind, not forgotten". On this word, see Lk 1:54. Related to "memorial" in v 4.
35. Elsewhere only in 7:14; 20:17; 24:25. GK *3558*.
36. Some manuscripts add, "who, having arrived, will speak *to* you" {B}.
37. Or, "acted commendably", as in Mt 12:12; Lk 6:27. That is, you did a good thing by having come. Same idiom as in Mk 7:37; 1 Cor 7:37, 38; Phil 4:14; Jam 2:8, 19; 2 Pet 1:19; 3 Jn 6. This word is the adverb of "good", and means "well", "commendably" (in Mt 12:12; Lk 6:27; Gal 4:17), "rightly" (as in Mk 7:6; Jn 4:17), "nicely" (in Mt 7:9). Used 37 times. GK *2822*. Related to "good" in 1 Tim 5:10a.
38. Some manuscripts say "by God" {C}.
39. Or, "grasp, comprehend". On this word, see "overcome" in Jn 1:5.
40. On this phrase "in accordance with truth", see Lk 4:25.
41. Used only here. GK *4720*. Related to the word in Jam 2:1.
42. These are the two things said about Cornelius in v 2. In other words, even non-Jews fearing and obeying the true God are welcome to Him. They do not have to become Jews first. This is a revolutionary idea to Peter, a Jewish Christian, (note 11:3). Compare Jn 9:31. Peter upholds this principle in chapter 15.
43. Or, "welcome". On this word, see Lk 4:19.
44. Same word as in v 44. The grammar of v 36-38 is complex. Other arrangements are possible. This is the Greek word order. Some think Peter uses similar grammar as in 2:22, "As to Jesus...". Others render it "You know the message", taking the verb "you know" to govern "the message" and "the matter". Others link this with v 34-35, "acceptable *to* Him, [which is] the message which He sent...". There are other views. Consult the commentaries.
45. Some manuscripts omit this word {C}, making it possible to render it "He sent forth the message *to* the...".
46. This word modifies "He", "He sent forth... announcing", not "message". God sent the "message", and He is announcing "peace", from which it is clear that the message concerns this peace.
47. That is, salvation, peace with God. God announced, purchased, and dispenses this peace through Jesus.
48. Some think this word goes with "announcing". He sent, "announcing through Jesus Christ" the good news of peace. Others think it goes with peace, "peace through Jesus Christ". Both are true.
49. Some see this phrase as giving the scope of the message. As to the message sent forth to Israel that Jesus is the source of peace with God— this Jesus is Lord of all, both Jews and Gentiles. He is the judge and the source of forgiveness for all, v 42-43. Others see this as a parenthesis, Peter exalting Jesus after his first mention of Him.

A. Act 1:2 B. Lk 9:7 C. Act 10:3 D. Mt 26:26, is E. Mk 3:14, send out F. Act 23:34, learned G. Act 10:6, lodging H. Phil 2:21 charge J. Jn 18:38, charge K. Rev 17:8, be present L. Rom 1:17 M. Eph 5:33, respecting N. Act 6:3 O. Act 11:13, send for P. Rom 10:17 Q. Lk 3:15, waiting in expectation R. Tit 3:14, necessary S. Act 20:22 T. Mt 4:4, mankind U. 1 Cor 12:8, word V. Mk 6:25 W. Act 17:26, appointed X. Mt 26:10 Y. Gal 3:7 Z. Mt 8:2, master

	2E.	"**You** know¹ the matter² having taken place throughout all Judea, beginning from³ Galilee after the baptism^A which John proclaimed^B, *as to* Jesus from Nazareth⁴—	37 38
		1F. "How God anointed^C Him *with the* Holy Spirit and *with* power^D	
		2F. "Who went about doing-good⁵ and healing^E all the *ones* being oppressed⁶ by the devil, because God was with Him	
		1G. "And we *are* witnesses^F *of* everything which He did both in the country *of* the Jews and in Jerusalem	39
		3F. "Whom indeed⁷ they killed^G, having hung⁸ *Him* on *a* cross^H	
	3E.	"God raised^J this *One* on the third day, and granted^K *that* He become visible⁹—	40
		1F. "Not *to* all the people	41
		2F. "But *to* witnesses^F having been chosen-beforehand¹⁰ by God— *to* us, who ate with and drank with Him after He rose-up^L from *the* dead	
	4E.	"And He¹¹ commanded^M us to proclaim^B *to* the people, and to solemnly-warn¹², that this *One*¹³ is the *One* having been designated¹⁴ by God *as* judge¹⁵ *of the* living and *the* dead	42
	5E.	"All the prophets testify^N concerning this *One*¹⁶, *that* everyone believing^O in Him receives forgiveness^P *of* sins through His name"	43
7D.	While Peter *was* still speaking these words, the Holy Spirit fell¹⁷ upon all the *ones* hearing the message¹⁸		44
	1E.	And the believers of *the* circumcision¹⁹— all-who came with Peter— were astonished²⁰ that the gift^Q *of* the²¹ Holy Spirit had²² been poured-out²³ also on the Gentiles!	45
		1F. For they were hearing them speaking *in* tongues²⁴ and magnifying²⁵ God	46
	2E.	Then Peter responded, *"No one is able to forbid²⁶ the water *so that* these *may* not be baptized^R, *is he*?²⁷— who received the Holy Spirit as also we *did*	47
		1F. And he commanded²⁸ *that* they be baptized in the name *of* Jesus Christ²⁹	48
8D.	Then they asked him to stay^S some days		
4B.	Now the apostles and the brothers being throughout Judea heard that the Gentiles also accepted^T the word *of* God³⁰		11:1
	1C.	But when Peter went up to Jerusalem, the *ones* of *the* circumcision³¹ were disputing³² with him, *saying that "You went in to men having uncircumcision,³³ and you ate with them"	2 3
	2C.	But having begun³⁴, Peter was explaining³⁵ *it* to them in-order^U, saying	4
		1D. "I was in *the* city *of* Joppa praying. And in *a* trance^V, I saw *a* vision^W— *a* certain object^X like *a* large sheet coming down, being let down *by* four corners from heaven. And it came to me, *into which having looked-intently^Y, I was observing^Z	5 6

1. Peter gives this group the gospel by first reviewing what they already knew, the historical course of the life of Christ, v 37-39. Then he adds to this that God raised Him, made Him judge of all, and grants forgiveness through Him, v 40-43.
2. Or, "thing, message". This "matter" is summed up in v 38-39. Some render this "the message having come-to-be [proclaimed or spread] throughout all Judea". It is not the same word as "message" in v 36, though it can also mean this. On this word, see "word" in Rom 10:17.
3. In the Greek, the grammatical connection of this phrase "beginning from... proclaimed" to what precedes is unusual, and is simplified in some manuscripts {B}. On the idiom "beginning from", see Mt 20:8.
4. In this rendering, "you know" governs both the "matter" and the person, "Jesus". Others combine "Jesus from Nazareth" with what follows, "how God anointed Him— Jesus from Nazareth— *with*...", a Hebrew way of speaking, which is smoothed out by dropping "Him". This phrase "Jesus from Nazareth", is elsewhere only in Mt 21:11; Jn 1:45. Compare Lk 24:19-20.
5. Or, "working good". Used only here. GK *2308*. Related to "good deed" in 4:9.
6. Or, "exploited, dominated". Elsewhere only in Jam 2:6. GK *2872*.
7. Or, "also". Some manuscripts omit this word {K}.
8. Same word as in this phrase in 5:30 and Gal 3:13. Elsewhere only in Mt 18:6; 22:40; Lk 23:39; Act 28:4. GK *3203*.
9. The phrase "become visible" is also in Rom 10:20.
10. Or, "appointed beforehand". Used only here. GK *4742*. Related to "appointed" in 14:23.
11. That is, Jesus, the raised One.
12. Or, "solemnly testify". On this word, see "solemnly charge" in 1 Tim 5:21.
13. Some manuscripts say "**He**" instead of "this *One*" {N}.
14. Or, "appointed, declared, ordained". On this word, see Rom 1:4.
15. As Jesus said in Jn 5:22, 27, etc. As Paul says in 2 Tim 4:1. As Peter says in 1 Pet 4:5.
16. Or, "testify *to* this".
17. Same word as in 8:16. There, for the Samaritans' benefit, Peter, a Jew, had to lay his hands on them. Here, for the Jewish Christians' benefit, as seen in 11:15-18, the Spirit falls on these Gentiles without Peter's intervention. God used both methods to produce the one result, unity through equality in Christ, 1 Cor 12:13. Compare the case in 19:1.
18. Or, "word". Same word as "message" in v 36. On this word, see "word" in 1 Cor 12:8.
19. That is, the six Jewish Christians with Peter from Joppa (10:23; 11:12), as Luke specifies next.
20. On this word, see Mk 2:12. These Jewish Christians did not expect the Gentile believers to be accepted on equal terms.
21. That is, the gift given by the Spirit, a gift which they all heard, as explained in v 46.
22. More literally, "has", as the Greek typically phrases it.
23. Same word as in 2:17.
24. Peter and the Jewish Christians with him recognize this as "identical" to the Acts 2 experience, 11:15, 17. On "tongues", see 1 Cor 12:10.
25. On this word, see "enlarge" in 2 Cor 10:15. Related to "great" in Act 2:11. Because these Jewish Christians understood the languages in which these Gentile believers were saying these things, they knew it was same gift given to them on Pentecost, 11:15.
26. Or, "withhold". To do so is to forbid God, 11:17 (same word).
27. The grammar indicates that a "no" answer is expected. If these Gentiles received the Spirit like we Jews did, who is able to refuse them baptism? Note that here water baptism follows the falling of Spirit, the opposite of 8:16.
28. Same word as in v 33.
29. Some manuscripts say "the Lord" instead of "Jesus Christ" {B}.
30. Same statement as in 8:14, where the apostles heard the Samaritans accepted the Word of God. Both groups have become Christians without becoming Jews.
31. Since all these in Jerusalem were Jews, some think this refers to a party within the community of believers, the group which later demands that Gentiles be circumcised and keep the Law, 15:5. Here, they are forced to recognize that God saved these Gentiles, v 18. But later in chapter 15, they attempt to dictate how they must live their lives. Others think that Luke means "the Jewish Christians" in general, as in 10:45.
32. Same word as "doubting" in 10:20, which is disputing with oneself. These people are doing the very thing the Spirit told Peter not to do.
33. Though Cornelius was a devout worshiper (10:1), he was in a state of uncircumcision.
34. Some supply "[from the beginning]", based on "in order" later in the verse; others, "[to speak]" or "[to answer]".
35. Or, "setting out, setting forth". Same word as in 18:26; 28:23. Elsewhere only as "exposed" in 7:21. GK *1758*.

A. Mk 1:4   B. 2 Tim 4:2   C. Lk 4:18   D. Mk 5:30   E. Mt 8:8   F. Act 1:8   G. Mt 2:16   H. 1 Pet 2:24   J. Mt 28:6, arose   K. Eph 1:22, give
L. Lk 18:33   M. 1 Tim 1:3   N. Jn 1:7   O. Jn 3:36   P. Col 1:14   Q. Rom 5:15   R. Mk 1:8   S. Rom 11:22, continue   T. Mt 10:40, welcome
U. Lk 1:3   V. Act 10:10   W. Act 10:3   X. 1 Thes 4:4, vessel   Y. Lk 4:20   Z. Heb 10:24, consider

	1E. "And I saw the four-footed-animals *of* the earth, and the wild-beasts, and the reptiles, and the birds *of* the heaven	
	2E. "And I also heard *a* voice saying *to* me, 'Having arisen, Peter, slaughter[A] and eat!'	7
	3E. "But I said, 'By no means, Lord, because *a* defiled or unclean *thing* never[1] entered into my mouth'	8
	4E. "But *a* voice responded[2] for *a* second *time* from heaven, '*The things* which God made-clean[B], don't **you** be making-defiled'	9
	5E. "And this took place three times, and everything was pulled-up[3] again into heaven	10
2D.	"And behold— three men immediately stood at the house in which we were[4] *staying*, having been sent forth from Caesarea to me	11
	1E. "And the Spirit told me to go-with them, having made no distinction[5]	12
	2E. "And these six brothers also went with me	
3D.	"And we entered into the house *of* the man	
	1E. "And he reported[C] *to* us how he saw the[6] angel having stood in his house, and having said, 'Send-forth[7] to Joppa, and send-for[8] Simon, the *one* being called[9] Peter, who will speak words[10] to you by which you will be saved[D]— you and all your household[E]'	13 14
	2E. "And at my beginning to speak,[11] the Holy Spirit fell[12] upon them just as also upon us at *the* beginning[13]	15
	3E. "And I remembered[F] the word[G] *of* the Lord, how He was saying, '**John**[14] baptized *with* water— but **you** will be baptized with *the* Holy Spirit!'[15]	16
	4E. "Therefore if God gave the **identical**[16] **gift**[17] *to* them as also *to* us— having[18] put faith upon[19] the Lord Jesus Christ— who was **I** *to be* able to forbid[20] God?"	17
3C.	And having heard these *things*, they were quiet[21]. And they glorified[22] God, saying, "Then God granted[H] the repentance[23] leading-to life[J] *to* the Gentiles[24] also!"	18
13A. Now indeed the *ones* having been dispersed[25] because of the affliction[K] having taken place over Stephen went as far as Phoenicia[26] and Cyprus[27] and Antioch[28], speaking the word *to* no one except Jews only. But there were some of them— Cyprian and Cyrenian[29] men— who, having come to Antioch, were speaking also[30] to the Hellenists[31], announcing-as-good-news[L] the Lord Jesus		19 20
1B.	And *the* hand *of the* Lord was with them. And *a* large number, having believed, turned[M] to the Lord	21
2B.	And the word[N] about them was heard in the ears *of* the church existing[32] in Jerusalem. And they sent out Barnabas to go[33] to Antioch— who, having arrived and having seen the grace[O] *of* God, rejoiced[P]	22 23
	1C. And he was encouraging[34] everyone to be continuing-in[35] the Lord *with* purpose[36] *of* heart,[37] because he was *a* good[Q] man, and full[R] *of the* Holy Spirit and *of* faith	24
	2C. And *a* considerable crowd was added[S] *to* the Lord	
3B.	And he[38] went forth to Tarsus[39] to search-for[40] Saul. And having found *him*, he brought *him* to Antioch. And it came about	25-26
	1C. *For them*[41] *that*[42] *for a* whole year *they* were gathered-together[43] in the church and taught *a* considerable crowd	
	2C. And *that* the disciples *were* first called Christians[T] in Antioch	
4B.	And during these days,[44] prophets[U] came down from Jerusalem to Antioch	27

1. Some manuscripts say "because anything defiled or unclean never" {K}. The added word, "anything", is the same word as in 10:14.
2. Some manuscripts add "*to* me" {N}.
3. Elsewhere only in Lk 14:5. GK *413*.
4. Some manuscripts say "I was" {C}.
5. That is, between you and those Gentiles. "Made a distinction" is the same word as "doubt" in 10:20, but with different grammar. Some manuscripts have the same grammar here, "not doubting at all". Others have a different tense of this word, meaning "making no distinction" {C}. In all these cases, "no" and "not at all" is the same Greek word, GK *3594*.
6. Some manuscripts omit this word {C}, so that it says "*an* angel".
7. Same word as in 10:8, 17, 20; 11:11. On this word, see "sent out" in Mk 3:14. Some manuscripts add "men" {K}.
8. Same word as in 10:5, 29; 11:13; 20:1; 24:24, 26. Elsewhere only as "summon" in 10:22; 25:3. GK *3569*.
9. Same word as in this phrase in 10:5, 18, 32. On this word, see "call upon" in 1 Pet 1:17.
10. Same word as 10:22, 44. On this word, see Rom 10:17.
11. Peter had not even begun to apply the message to his hearers when God intervened in 10:44. It had to be this way, because Peter did not properly understand how to apply it to Gentiles! God begins to reveal this in this incident.
12. Same word as in 10:44.
13. Because it was identical to the experience in Acts 2, God's acceptance of these Gentiles was undeniable.
14. The grammar emphasizes the contrast between the two halves of this sentence.
15. Same sentence as in 1:5. Jesus said He would baptize them with the Spirit, and He did so here, with no assistance from Peter. This can only mean that He has accepted these Gentile believers on an equal basis with the Jews at Pentecost. By "you", Jesus must have been including both.
16. Or, "equal, same". On this word, see "equal" in Phil 2:6.
17. Same word as in 2:38; 8:20; 10:45; its only other uses in Acts. On this word, see Rom 5:15.
18. This phrase applies to both groups in what precedes, "[we both] having put faith upon...".
19. On "put faith upon", see Rom 4:5.
20. Or, "prevent, hinder, try to stop". Same word as in 10:47. On this word, see 1 Cor 14:39. All of Peter's actions with regard to these Gentiles were in direct response to God Himself, objectively proven by the fact that God gave them the identical gift.
21. That is, with reference to their complaint, 11:2-3. On this word, see 1 Thes 4:11.
22. Some manuscripts say "were glorifying" {N}.
23. On this word, see 2 Cor 7:10. Compare 5:31.
24. The Jewish believers knew the message was for the world. But that salvation was to come to the Gentiles apart from Judaism, with all the implications that this has, was a new thought for them. They were assuming salvation would be proclaimed to the world as part of and through a true, spiritual Judaism; that Judaism would reign and all people would become Jews as part of finding life in Christ; that Israel's culture would gloriously become world culture.
25. On this word, see 8:1, to which event Luke is referring.
26. On this region, see 21:2.
27. On this island, see 13:4.
28. This is a city north of Israel; the capital of the Roman province of Syria, mentioned also in 11:20, 22, 26, 27; 13:1; 14:26; 15:22, 23, 30, 35; 18:22; Gal 2:11. GK *522*. On another Antioch, see 13:14.
29. That is, men from the island of Cyprus (4:36, 13:4), and the city of Cyrene (2:10, 6:9).
30. Some manuscripts omit this word {K}.
31. In its only other uses in 6:1 and 9:29, this word meant foreign-born, Greek-speaking Jews, like the Cyprian and Cyrenian men speaking the gospel here. Here, it must mean "Greeks" in the sense of "Gentiles", in contrast to the "Jews only" in v 19. GK *1821*. The conversion of Greek-speaking Jews would not have aroused interest in Jerusalem. Some manuscripts say "Greeks" {C}, a word related to "Hellenist" which is found in Gal 3:28.
32. Or, "being". Same word as in 13:1, but different grammar. Some manuscripts omit this word {N}.
33. Some manuscripts omit "to go" {C}.
34. Or, "exhorting". Same word as in 14:22. This is the verb related to the meaning of "Barnabas", as explained by 4:36.
35. Or, "remaining in, staying with, abiding with". Same word as in Act 13:43; 1 Tim 5:5. Elsewhere only as "remain with" in Mt 15:32; Mk 8:2; and "stay on" in Act 18:18; 1 Tim 1:3. GK *4693*.
36. Or, "resolve, plan". That is, with a resolved, planned devotion and resolution of heart. Same word as in 2 Tim 3:10; Act 27:13. Used of God's "purpose" in Rom 8:28.
37. Or, "was encouraging everyone with purpose of heart to be...". In other words, the phrase "*with* purpose *of* heart" could be describing Barnabas's encouraging, or these believers' continuing in the Lord. In the Greek word order, it stands between the two.
38. Some manuscripts say "Barnabas" {K}.
39. On this city, see 9:30.
40. Elsewhere only in Lk 2:44, 45. GK *349*.
41. Some manuscripts make this word the subject, "And it came about that they *for a* whole year were..." {K}.
42. This is the Greek word order of this sentence. On this phrase, "and it came about that", see Lk 5:1. This word is used this way only here in Acts. Others think this word is not part of the construction found in Lk 5:1, but means "And it came about *for* them *that for* indeed *a* whole year". Some manuscripts omit this word, so that it says "And it came about... *that for a* whole year" {K}.
43. That is, Barnabas and Saul were brought together for a joint ministry in the church. Others think Luke means they "were brought-in by the church", that is, received hospitably, as this word is used in Mt 25:35. Others think he means the disciples "were gathered together" in the church, and Barnabas and Saul "taught" them, thus implying a different subject for each verb. Others simplify it as "they were gathered together with the church".
44. That is, the year just mentioned. Or, it may be a more general reference to the time of growth in Antioch.

A. Act 10:13   B. Act 10:15   C. 1 Jn 1:3, announcing   D. Lk 19:10   E. Mk 3:20, house   F. Lk 1:54   G. Rom 10:17   H. Eph 1:22, give   J. Rom 8:10   K. Rev 7:14   L. Act 5:42   M. Jam 5:19, turns back   N. 1 Cor 12:8   O. Eph 2:8   P. 2 Cor 13:11   Q. 1 Tim 5:10b   R. Mt 14:20   S. Lk 17:5, increase   T. 1 Pet 4:16   U. 1 Cor 12:28

	1C. And having stood up, one of them, Agabus *by* name, signified[1] through the Spirit *that* there would-certainly[2] be *a* great famine[A] over the whole world[3]— which took place in-the-time-of[B] Claudius[4]	28
	2C. And as any *of* the disciples was prospering[5], each *of* them determined[C] to send *money* for *a* ministry[6] *to* the brothers[D] dwelling in Judea— *which they also did, having sent *it* forth to the elders[7] by *the* hand *of* Barnabas and Saul[8]	29 30
5B.	And about that time,[9] Herod[10] the king put hands[11] on some *of* the *ones* from the church to mistreat[E] *them*	12:1
	1C. And he killed James[12], the brother *of* John, *with a* sword	2
	2C. And having seen that it was[13] pleasing[14] *to* the Jews, he proceeded to arrest[F] Peter also (now the days *of* the *Feast of* Unleavened-Bread[G] were *taking place*)— *whom indeed having seized[H], he put into prison[J]	3 4
	1D. Having handed *him* over *to* four squads[15] of soldiers[K] to guard[L] him	
	2D. Intending[M] to bring him up[N] *to* the people after the Passover[16] [Feast]	
	3C. So indeed Peter was being kept[O] in the prison. And prayer was fervently[17] being made[18] by the church to God for him	5
	4C. And when Herod was about to bring him forth[19], *on* that night Peter was sleeping between two soldiers, having been bound[P] *with* two chains[Q]. And guards[R] in front of the door were keeping-watch-over[O] the prison[J]	6
	1D. And behold— *an* angel *of the* Lord stood near, and light[20] shined[S] in the cell[21]	7
	2D. And having struck the side *of* Peter, he woke him, saying, "Arise quickly". And his chains[Q] fell off of *his* hands	
	3D. And the angel said to him, "Gird-*yourself*[22] and tie-on[T] your sandals". And he did so	8
	4D. And he says *to* him, "Put-on your cloak and be following me". *And having gone forth, he was following[23]	9
	1E. And he did not know[U] that the *thing* taking place by-means-of[24] the angel was[25] real[V], but he was thinking *that he was* seeing *a* vision[W]	
	2E. And having gone through *a* first guard-post[26] and *a* second, they came to the iron gate leading into the city, which by-itself[X] was opened *for* them	10
	3E. And having gone out, they went ahead one lane[27], and immediately the angel departed from him	
	5C. And Peter, having become within himself,[28] said, "Now I know truly[Y] that the Lord sent-out[Z] His angel and rescued[AA] me from *the* hand *of* Herod, and *from* all the expectation[29] *of* the people *of* the Jews". *And having become-aware[30], he went to the house *of* Mary, the mother *of* John (the *one* being called Mark), where there were many assembled-together[31] and praying	11 12
	1D. And he[32] having knocked-on the door[BB] *of* the gate[CC], *a* servant-girl[DD] went to *it* to answer[33]— Rhoda *by* name	13
	1E. And having recognized[EE] the voice *of* Peter, because of *her* joy she did not open the gate, but having run in, she reported[FF] *that* Peter was[34] standing in front of the gate	14
	2E. But the *ones* said to her, "You are mad[35]"	15
	3E. But the *one* was insisting *that it was* holding so[36]	
	4E. But the *ones* were saying, "It is his angel[GG]"	

1. Some manuscripts say "was signifying" {A}. On this word, see Rev 1:1.
2. More literally, "will certainly", as the Greek typically phrases it. On this word, see 24:15.
3. On this word, see Heb 2:5. Luke may be referring to Judea, or to the Roman Empire as in Lk 2:1.
4. Some manuscripts add "Caesar" {K}. That is, the Roman Emperor. See 18:2 on him.
5. Or, "was well off, having plenty, thriving". Literally, "going well" financially. Used only here. GK *2344*. Related to "prosperity" in Act 19:25.
6. Or, "service". On this word, see 1 Cor 12:5.
7. On this word, see 1 Tim 5:17. This is the first mention of them in Acts.
8. Some think Luke means Barnabas and Saul left Antioch before Herod's death in chapter 12, and returned after it in 12:25, placing the famine in A.D. 43-44. Others think he is summarizing here what occurs in 12:25, meaning they leave and return some time after Herod's death. In this case, the famine could have been in A.D. 47-48. It is also possible that multiple trips were made, to which Luke refers here in summary fashion.
9. Luke may mean the time of the famine, when Barnabas and Saul were in Jerusalem between 11:30 and 12:25. Or, this may be a more general reference to this period of time. This phrase "about that time", is also in 19:23; and is similar to the phrase in Rom 5:6; 9:9.
10. That is, Herod Agrippa I, the grandson of Herod the Great (see Mt 2:1), the son of Aristobulus. Caligula (Roman Emperor from A.D. 37-41) gave him the territory of Philip (see Lk 3:1) in A.D. 37, and the territory of Antipas (see Mt 14:1) in A.D. 39. Claudius (see Act 11:28) gave him Judea (which had been under Roman prefects like Pilate since A.D. 6, see Mt 2:22) in A.D. 41. This gave Agrippa I a kingdom as large as Herod the Great. He was king of Israel until his death in A.D. 44, which is described in v 23. Agrippa I was the first king since Herod the Great, and the last king of Israel. Upon his death, Judea was put under the rule of Roman procurators until the revolt in A.D. 66.
11. Used 177 times. GK *5931*.
12. That is, the apostle. He is often linked with Peter and John. See Lk 6:14 on him.
13. More literally, "is", as the Greek typically phrases it.
14. Or, "*a pleasing thing*". On this word, see Jn 8:29.
15. Or, "quaternions". Used only here. GK *5482*. That is, a squad of four Roman soldiers, two inside chained to the prisoner and two outside, working a three hour shift (one squad for each watch of the night). This was the usual Roman custom.
16. That is, for his execution. On this word, see Jn 18:28.
17. On this word, see 1 Pet 1:22. Some manuscripts say "fervent prayer was being made" {N}.
18. Or, "taking place". GK *1181*.
19. Or, "bring him forward, bring him before *them*". On this word, see "going ahead" in 2 Jn 9. Some manuscripts say "bring him to *them*" {N}.
20. Or, "*a* light". Did it radiate from this angel? The source of the light is not given.
21. Or, "room, quarters". That is, the dwelling-place or room inside the prison, where Peter was. Used only here. GK *3862*.
22. That is, put on and fasten your belt. The belt was worn over the tunic (undergarment) and under the cloak (outer garment, robe). Elsewhere only in Jn 21:18. GK *2439*. Related to "belt" in Rev 1:13; "gird" in Eph 6:14; "gird up" in 1 Pet 1:13; "tie around" in Jn 13:5; "undergird" in Act 27:17.
23. Some manuscripts add "him" {K}.
24. Or, "with, through". GK *1328*.
25. More literally, "is", as the Greek typically phrases it.
26. Or, "prison". This word may refer to a ward of the prison (same word as in 16:24, an inner "prison"), or to a guard post with its guard. Same word as "prison" in v 4, 5, 6, 17. On this word, see "prison" in 5:22. Related to "guard" in v 6, 19; 5:23.
27. Or, "alley, narrow street". Luke may mean "crossed the street"; or, that Peter and the angel went down the street to the first lane. On this word, see Mt 6:2.
28. That is, having collected himself, and seen that it was "real", v 9. Luke uses a similar phrase in Lk 15:17.
29. Or, "anticipation". On this word, see Lk 21:26. That is, from all that these Jews expected would happen. They expected to see Peter killed like James.
30. Or, "having realized *it*". That is, aware of where he was. Elsewhere only in 14:6. GK *5328*.
31. This is a participle, "having been assembled together". Elsewhere only in 19:25. GK *5255*. Related word in Lk 24:33.
32. Some manuscripts say "Peter" {K}.
33. That is, to listen to who is there and respond accordingly. Used only here in this sense. On this word, see "obey" in 6:7.
34. More literally, "is", as the Greek typically phrases it.
35. Or, "out of your mind". On this word, see 1 Cor 14:23.
36. That is, that it was true. The facts were holding true in the way this girl spoke them. This idiom is elsewhere only in 7:1; 17:11; 24:9.

A. Lk 21:11 B. Lk 3:2 C. Rom 1:4, designated D. Act 16:40 E. 1 Pet 3:13, do evil F. Lk 22:54 G. Mk 14:12 H. Jn 11:57 J. Act 5:22
K. Mt 28:12 L. Jn 12:25, keep M. Jam 1:18, willed N. Mt 4:1, led up O. 1 Jn 5:18, keeping P. 1 Cor 7:27 Q. Act 28:20 R. Act 5:23
S. 2 Cor 4:6 T. Eph 6:15, sandaled U. 1 Jn 2:29 V. Jn 6:55, true W. Act 10:3 X. Mk 4:28 Y. Mt 14:33 Z. Gal 4:4, sent forth AA. Gal 1:4
BB. Col 4:3 CC. Mt 26:71 DD. Jn 18:17 EE. Col 1:6, understood FF. 1 Jn 1:3, announcing GG. 1 Tim 3:16, messenger

2D. But Peter was continuing-on¹ knocking. And having opened, they saw him and were astonished^A   16

     1E. And having motioned *to* them *with his* hand to be silent^B, he related^C *to* them² how the Lord led him out of the prison   17
     2E. And he said, "Report^D these *things to* James³ and the brothers"
     3E. And having gone out, he proceeded to another place

6C. Now having become day, there was no small⁴ disturbance⁵ among the soldiers *as to* what then became *of*⁶ Peter   18
7C. And Herod, having searched-for^E him and not having found *him,* having examined^F the guards, ordered^G *that they* be led away.⁷ And having gone down from Judea to Caesarea⁸, he was spending-time⁹ there   19

     1D. Now he¹⁰ was being very-angry *with the* Tyrians and Sidonians¹¹   20
     2D. And they were coming to him with-one-accord^H. And having won-over¹² Blastus, the *one* over the bedroom¹³ *of* the king, they were asking-*for* peace, because of their country being provided-for¹⁴ from the royal¹⁵ *land*
     3D. And *on an* appointed day, Herod— having put on *the* royal clothing, and¹⁶ having sat on the judgment-seat^J— was giving-a-public-address¹⁷ to them   21

         1E. And the public-assembly^K was calling-out¹⁸, "*The* voice *of a* god and not *of a* man!"   22
         2E. And at once *an* angel *of the* Lord struck him because¹⁹ he did not give the glory *to* God   23
         3E. And having become eaten-by-worms²⁰, he expired²¹

6B. But the word *of* God²² was growing^L and being multiplied^M   24
7B. And Barnabas and Saul returned, having fulfilled^N the ministry²³ to²⁴ Jerusalem, having²⁵ taken along John²⁶ with *them* (the *one* having been called Mark)   25

14A. Now there were prophets²⁷ and teachers at Antioch^O in²⁸ the church existing²⁹ *there*— Barnabas and Simeon (the *one* being called Niger³⁰) and Lucius the Cyrenian^P, and Manaen (*one* brought-up-with³¹ Herod the tetrarch³²) and Saul.³³ °And while they *were* ministering³⁴ *to* the Lord and fasting^Q, the Holy Spirit said,³⁵ "Separate^R now³⁶ Barnabas^S and Saul *for* Me, for the work which I have called them to³⁷". Then, having fasted and prayed and laid^T *their* hands³⁸ on them, they sent *them* away³⁹   13:1   2   3

    1B. So indeed, having been sent-out⁴⁰ by the Holy Spirit, **they**⁴¹ went down to Seleucia⁴², and from there sailed-away to Cyprus⁴³   4

       1C. And having come-to-be in Salamis⁴⁴, they were proclaiming^U the word^V *of* God in the synagogues *of* the Jews. And they also were having John *as an* assistant⁴⁵   5
       2C. And having gone through the whole⁴⁶ island as far as Paphos⁴⁷, they found *a* certain man *who* was *a* magician⁴⁸, *a* Jewish false-prophet^W *for* whom *the* name was Bar-Jesus⁴⁹— °who was with the proconsul⁵⁰, Sergius Paulus, *an* intelligent⁵¹ man   6   7

         1D. This *one*,⁵² having summoned^X Barnabas and Saul, sought^E to hear the word *of* God

1. Same idiom as in Jn 8:7. On this word, see "continue" in Rom 11:22.
2. Some manuscripts omit "*to* them" {C}.
3. That is, the brother of the Lord, the leader of the Jerusalem church. See Mt 13:55 on him.
4. That is, a large commotion. This figure of speech, called "litotes" (expressing something by using the negative of its opposite, like saying "not bad" instead of "great"; "not many" instead of "a few"), occurs also in 1:5; 14:28; 15:2; 17:4, 12; 19:11, 23, 24; 20:12; 21:39; 26:19, 26; 27:20; 28:2, and is a mark of Luke's style. This word means "small, little, short, brief, few", with the specific nuance coming from the context. Used 40 times. GK *3900*.
5. Or, "commotion". Elsewhere only in 19:23. GK *5431*. Related to "disturb" in Gal 1:7.
6. Or, "what then happened *with reference to*". Same idiom as in Jn 21:21, "What *of* this *one*?"
7. That is, to execution, the Roman custom.
8. That is, to the Roman capital of Judea on the coast. See 8:40.
9. Same word as in Jn 3:22; Act 15:35. Elsewhere only as "spend" followed by a time indicator, Act 14:3, 28; 16:12; 20:6; 25:6, 14. GK *1417*.
10. Some manuscripts say "Herod" {K}.
11. That is, ones living in Tyre and Sidon. Note the threefold description of this area in 21:2.
12. Or, "convinced, persuaded", perhaps with a bribe. Same word as in Act 14:19, and as "win approval of" in Gal 1:10. On this word, see "persuade" in 1 Jn 3:19.
13. That is, the chamberlain, the one in charge of the king's sleeping quarters. A trusted attendant. Used only here. GK *3131*.
14. Or, "providing for *itself*". Or, "being fed, feeding *itself*". That is, these port cities were economically dependent on Herod. Their food came from Herod's land. Perhaps they were having some commercial dispute. Their cities were not part of Herod's kingdom, but of the province of Syria. On this word, see "feed" in Lk 23:29.
15. Elsewhere only in v 21; Jn 4:46, 49; Jam 2:8. GK *997*. That is, King Herod's land.
16. Some manuscripts omit this word {C}.
17. Or, a public oration. Used only here. GK *1319*. Related to "public assembly" next, and "public" in 16:37.
18. Elsewhere only in Lk 23:21; Act 21:34; 22:24. GK *2215*.
19. Or, "in return for". On this idiom, see 2 Thes 2:10.
20. Used only here. Related to "eating" in Mt 6:19.
21. That is, Herod died. On this word, see 5:5. Josephus, who also speaks of this, adds that he died five days later.
22. Some manuscripts say "*of the* Lord" {N}.
23. Same word as in 11:29. That is, the delivery of money to Jerusalem mentioned in 11:30.
24. Or, "in". This could be rendered "returned to Jerusalem, having fulfilled the ministry..." (the Greek word order), but this does not fit the context. It would be odd to say they took John-Mark to his own city (v 12), and it is clear that by 13:2 they have "returned" to Antioch. Some manuscripts say "from" {C}, so that it says "returned from Jerusalem, having fulfilled...".
25. Some manuscripts say "and having... " {K}.
26. John Mark is the cousin of Barnabas, Col 4:10. He is first met in 12:12 at his mother's house. Here he comes to Antioch, from which he goes out with Paul and Barnabas (13:5), and then departs from them and returns to Jerusalem in 13:13. He surfaces again in 15:37. See also 1 Pet 5:13.
27. On this word, see 1 Cor 12:28. Some manuscripts add a word meaning "some, certain", {N}, so that it says "certain prophets", or, "some prophets".
28. Or, "throughout, in relation to". Same word as "throughout" in 9:31, 42; 10:37; 11:1. GK *2848*.
29. Or, "the existing church", meaning "the local church". Same idiom as in 5:17.
30. Simeon's second name is a Latin name, meaning "black". Used only here. GK *3769*.
31. Or, "*a foster brother, childhood companion of*". This word was used of children raised in the same home who were not related. If Manaen was about the same age as Herod, he would be 65-70 years old. Used only here. GK *5343*.
32. On this word, see Lk 3:19. That is, Herod Antipas (Mt 14:1), who was exiled in A.D. 39.
33. The Greek groups the first three names and the last two names, but the reason is unclear. Saul was mentioned in 7:58; 8:1, 3; 9:1, 4, 8, 11, 17, 22, 24; 11:25, 30; 12:25.
34. Or, "serving". On this word, see Rom 15:27. This word was used of those doing "priestly service" in the temple, and of those "serving" in public office. Luke could mean "*to*" the Lord, that is, praying or worshiping. Or, he could mean "*for*" the Lord, that is, prophesying or teaching.
35. Presumably, through one of the prophets.
36. This word implies urgency. On this word, see "indeed" in Mt 13:23.
37. Or, "summoned them". On the word "call to", see 2:39. In English we prefer to say "to which I have called them".
38. On laying on of hands, see Heb 6:2.
39. Or, "they let *them* go, dismissed *them*". Same word as in 15:30, 33. On this word, see "sends away" in Mt 5:31.
40. Elsewhere only as "sent away" in 17:10. GK *1734*.
41. Some manuscripts say "these *ones*" {N}.
42. This is the port city near Antioch. Used only here. GK *4942*.
43. This is the native country of Barnabas, 4:36. Elsewhere only in 11:19; 15:39; 21:3; 27:4. GK *3251*. Related to "Cyprian" in 4:36.
44. Salamis is a city on the east end of the island.
45. Or, "helper". On this word, see "attendant" in 1 Cor 4:1. That is, Mark, 12:25.
46. Some manuscripts omit this word {K}.
47. Paphos is a city on the west end of the island. It was the Roman seat of government.
48. Or, "*a magus*", the singular form of "magi". On this word, see "magi" in Mt 2:1. Related to "practice magic" in Act 8:9.
49. Or, "Bar-Joshua". GK *979*. "Bar" means "son of" in Hebrew. Paul calls him "son *of the* devil" in v 10.
50. That is, the governor of a Roman province under the control of the Roman senate. Elsewhere only in v 8, 12; 18:12; 19:38. GK *478*.
51. Or, "understanding". On this word, see 1 Cor 1:19.
52. That is, the proconsul.

A. Mk 2:12 B. 1 Cor 14:34 C. Lk 8:39 D. 1 Jn 1:3, announcing E. Phil 4:17, seek for F. 1 Cor 2:14 G. Mt 14:28 H. Act 1:14 J. Rom 14:10 K. Act 19:30 L. Jn 3:30 M. Act 7:17 N. Eph 5:18, filled O. Act 11:19 P. Act 6:9 Q. Mt 6:16 R. Rom 1:1 S. Act 4:36 T. Lk 10:30, laid on U. Phil 1:18 V. 1 Cor 12:8 W. Rev 16:13 X. Act 2:39, call to

2D. But the magician Elymas¹ (for so his name is translated²) was opposing^A them, seeking^B to turn away^C the proconsul from the faith — 8

3D. But Saul (the *one* also *called* Paul³), having been filled^D *with the* Holy Spirit, having looked-intently^E at him, ˚said— — 9, 10

    1E. "O son *of the* devil⁴ full *of* all deceit^F and all villainy⁵, enemy *of* all righteousness— will you not cease^G perverting⁶ the straight^H ways *of* the Lord?

    2E. "And now, behold— *the* hand *of the* Lord *is* upon⁷ you, and you shall be blind, not seeing the sun for *a* time" — 11

4D. And at-once^J, mistiness⁸ and darkness fell upon him. And going around, he was seeking^B *ones*-leading-by-the-hand⁹

5D. Then the proconsul— having seen the *thing* having taken place— believed, being astounded^K at¹⁰ the teaching^L *of* the Lord — 12

2B. And having put-to-sea^M from Paphos, the *ones* around Paul¹¹ came to Perga *of* Pamphylia¹². But John, having departed¹³ from them, returned to Jerusalem. ˚But **they**, having gone through¹⁴ from Perga, arrived at Pisidian¹⁵ Antioch. And having entered into the synagogue *on* the day *of* the Sabbath, they sat-*down* — 13, 14

    1C. And after the reading *of* the Law and the Prophets, the synagogue-officials^N sent forth *a message* to them, saying, "Men, brothers, if there is any word^O *of* exhortation¹⁶ among you for the people, speak" — 15

    2C. And Paul— having stood up, and having motioned *with his* hand, said — 16

        1D. "Men^P, Israelites, and the *ones* fearing^Q God— listen

            1E. "The God *of* this people Israel chose^R our fathers — 17

            2E. "And He lifted-up¹⁷ the people during the stay^S in *the* land *of* Egypt, and with *an* uplifted^T arm, led them out of it

                1F. "And *for* about *a* forty year period, He put-up-with¹⁸ them in the wilderness^U — 18

                2F. "And having brought-down¹⁹ seven²⁰ nations in *the* land *of* Canaan, He gave *them*²¹ their land as-an-inheritance²² ˚about *in*²³ [a total of] four-hundred and fifty years²⁴ — 19, 20

            3E. "And after these *things,* He gave *them* judges until Samuel the prophet

            4E. "And from there they asked-*for a* king. And God gave them Saul— *the* son *of* Kish, *a* man from *the* tribe *of* Benjamin— *for* forty years — 21

            5E. "And having removed^V him, He raised-up^W David *for* them, for *a* king— *concerning* whom²⁵ also having testified^X, He said, 'I found David the *son of* Jesse, *a* man in-accordance-with²⁶ My heart, who will do all My desires²⁷' — 22

            6E. "From the seed^Y *of* **this** one, in accordance with *the* promise^Z, God brought²⁸ *a* Savior^AA *for*²⁹ Israel, Jesus— — 23

                1F. "John having publicly-proclaimed³⁰ *a* baptism^BB *of* repentance^CC *for* all the people *of* Israel before *the* presence³¹ *of* His coming³² — 24

            7E. "And as John was completing^DD *his* course^EE, he was saying, 'What³³ do you suppose^FF *that* I am? **I** am not *the* One. But behold— He is coming after me, *of* Whom I am not worthy^GG to untie^HH the sandal^JJ *of His* feet' — 25

1. This is not a translation of "Bar-Jesus", nor is it an otherwise known Greek word. GK *1829*. Thus, Luke's meaning is unclear to us. Some think he is translating "magician". Luke knows what "Bar-" means, having correctly "translated" (same word as next) it in 4:36. Consult the commentaries.
2. Elsewhere only in Mt 1:23; Mk 5:41; 15:22, 34; Jn 1:38, 41; Act 4:36. GK *3493*.
3. He is called Paul from this point forward in Acts.
4. That is, one originating from him, or belonging to him.
5. Or, "fraud, unscrupulousness". Used only here. GK *4816*. Related to the word in 18:14.
6. Or, "making crooked". Same word as "turn away" in v 8. On this word, see Phil 2:15.
7. That is, in a negative sense, "against". GK *2093*.
8. This man's eyes clouded up and all became darkness for him. Used only here. GK *944*.
9. Or, "hand-leaders, guides". Used only here. GK *5933*. The related verb is used of Paul in 9:8.
10. This is the Greek word order. It could also be rendered "taken place, being astounded— **put faith** upon the teaching *of* the Lord", on which compare Lk 24:25.
11. That is, the ones around Paul as their leader.
12. Perga is a city in the region of Pamphylia, which at this time was part of the Roman province of Lycia, but shortly prior to this time was a province itself. Paul returns here in 14:25, and to its port city, Attalia.
13. Or, "gone away, left, withdrawn". Some render it more strongly negative, "deserted, abandoned". Elsewhere only in Mt 7:23; Lk 9:39. GK *713*. John-Mark departed from Barnabas and Paul once they reached Perga, 15:38. The reason for his departure is not stated. Consult the commentaries for the various suggestions.
14. These two had to "go through" the Taurus mountain range. They are going inland (north) from Perga.
15. That is, the Antioch near Pisidia (it was north of its border, in the region of Phrygia, not in the region of Pisidia) as opposed to the Antioch in Syria, from which they first left, 13:1. Thus it is the Antioch (GK *522*) in the region of Phrygia and in the Roman province of Galatia. The region of Pisidia lies between this Antioch and the province of Pamphylia, as implied in 14:21, 24. This Antioch is mentioned also in 14:19, 21; 2 Tim 3:11. It was called Pisidian Antioch because there is another Antioch in Phrygia. Used only here. GK *4408*.
16. Or, "encouragement". This is a polite invitation to speak, if any among them desired to do so, in accordance with Jewish synagogue custom. The writer of Hebrews calls his book "a word of exhortation" (13:22), the only other use of this phrase. On this word, see "encouragement" in Act 4:36.
17. Or, "exalted, raised high". On this word, see Jn 8:28. Related to "uplifted" later in the verse.
18. Or, "endured, bore with". Used only here. GK *5574*. Some manuscripts use a word meaning "carried, bore, cared for" {C}, the word in Deut 1:31 (where the same variation occurs). If correct, this word, which varies by one letter, would also be used only here in the NT (GK *5578*).
19. Same word as in Lk 1:52. On this word, see "tearing down" in 2 Cor 10:4.
20. These nations are mentioned in Deut 7:1; Josh 3:10; 24:11.
21. Some manuscripts include this word {B}.
22. This word, "to give as an inheritance" is used only here. GK *2883*. This occurs in Josh 11:23; 21:43-45.
23. The grammar here, "about *in*" is not the same as "*for* about" in v 18, and is not used elsewhere. In both cases, "about" is GK *6055*.
24. Paul seems to mean that Israel received the land as their inheritance about 450 years after they left it for Egypt— 400 years in Egypt (v 17, Act 7:6), plus 40 in the desert (v 18), plus the time of Joshua's conquest (5 years by Josh 14:6, 10). In some manuscripts, this phrase comes later in the verse {C}, "And after these *things* He gave them judges about *for* 450 years". Consult the commentaries.
25. This word is singular, referring to David.
26. Or, "in agreement with, in harmony with". Paul gives his explanation of this in the next phrase. GK *2848*.
27. Or, "wants, wishes, purposes". Though used 62 times, it is plural only here and as "wants" in Eph 2:3. Elsewhere it is rendered "will". On this word, see Jn 7:17. It refers to the multiple expressions of God's will as David's life progressed. Paul combines Ps 89:20, 1 Sam 13:14, and his own words into a summary quotation giving God's view of David.
28. The key point of Paul's history review in v 17-22 is that **God** did these things. He took the initiative and acted for His people whom He chose. And so it is with the Savior. Some manuscripts say "raised up *for*" {B}.
29. Or, "*to*".
30. Or, "proclaimed-beforehand". Used only here. GK *4619*. Related to "proclaim" in 2 Tim 4:2.
31. On the phrase "before the presence", see "ahead of His presence" in Lk 9:52.
32. Or, "entering", meaning before the presence of Jesus' entering on the scene in Israel. Many simplify this to "before His coming". Same word as "coming" in Mal 3:2. On this word, see "entrance" in 1 Thes 1:9.
33. Some manuscripts say "Who" {B}. Or, this may be rendered "**I** am not what you suppose *that* **I** am".

A. Eph 6:13, resist B. Phil 2:21 C. Phil 2:15, pervert D. Act 2:4 E. Lk 4:20 F. Mt 26:4 G. 1 Cor 13:8 H. Act 8:21 J. Mt 21:19 K. Mt 7:28 L. 1 Cor 14:6 M. Act 20:13 N. Act 18:8 O. 1 Cor 12:8 P. 1 Tim 2:12 Q. Eph 5:33, respecting R. 1 Cor 1:27 S. 1 Pet 1:17 T. Lk 16:15, highly valued U. Mt 3:1 V. Act 19:26, turn away W. Mt 28:6, arose X. Jn 1:7 Y. Heb 11:11 Z. 1 Jn 2:25 AA. Lk 1:47 BB. Mk 1:4 CC. 2 Cor 7:10 DD. Eph 5:18, filled EE. 2 Tim 4:7 FF. Act 25:18 GG. Rev 16:6 HH. Mt 5:19, break JJ. Mt 10:10

Acts 13:26	442	Verse

    2D. "Men[A], brothers[B], sons[C] *of the* family *of* Abraham, and the *ones* among you fearing[D] God— the message[E] *of* this salvation[1] was sent-out[F] ***to* us**[2]   26

        1E. "For the *ones* dwelling in Jerusalem and their rulers[G], not having known[3] this *One*[4] and the voices *of* the prophets being read every Sabbath— having condemned[H] *Him*, fulfilled[5] *them*   27

            1F. "And having found no charge[6] *worthy of* death, they asked Pilate[J] *that* He be executed[K]   28

            2F. "And when they fulfilled[7] all the *things* having been written about Him, having taken *Him* down from the cross[L], they[8] laid *Him* in *a* tomb   29

        2E. "But God raised[M] Him from *the* dead—*Who appeared[N] for many days *to* the *ones* having come up with Him from Galilee to Jerusalem, who now[9] are His witnesses[O] to the people   30-31

        3E. "And **we** are announcing-as-good-news-to[P] you the promise[Q] having been made to the fathers—*that God has fulfilled[10] **this** *promise for* us their children[11]   32 / 33

            1F. "Having raised-up[12] Jesus, as it has also been written in the second Psalm— '**You** are My Son. Today **I** have fathered[R] You' [Ps 2:7]

        4E. "And that[13] He raised Him up from *the* dead *as One* no longer going to return[S] to decay, He has spoken in this manner [in Isa 55:3]— that 'I will give You[14] the holy[15], trustworthy[16] *things of* David'. *Therefore also in another *place* it says, 'You[17] will not give[18] Your holy *One* to see[19] decay' [Ps 16:10]   34 / 35

            1F. "For **David**[20], having served[21] the purpose[22] *of* God *in his* own generation,[23] fell asleep, and was put-with[24] his fathers, and saw decay[25]—*but He Whom God raised did not see decay   36 / 37

    3D. "Therefore let it be known[T] *to* you, men, brothers, that   38

        1E. "Through this *One*[26] forgiveness[U] *of* sins is being proclaimed[V] *to* you
        2E. "And[27] from all *things from* which you could not be declared-righteous[W] by *the* Law *of* Moses—*by[28] this *One* everyone believing is declared-righteous   39

    4D. "Therefore be watching-out[X] *that* the *thing* having been spoken in the Prophets [in Hab 1:5] may not come upon *you*—   40

        1E. 'Look, scoffers, and marvel[Y], and perish[29]. Because **I** am working *a* work in your days— *a* work which you will never believe if someone tells you in detail[30]' "   41

  3C. And while they[31] *were* going out, they[32] were begging[Z] *that* these words *might* be spoken *to* them on the next Sabbath. *And the gathering[33] having been released[34], many *of* the Jews and *of* the worshiping[AA] proselytes[BB] followed Paul and Barnabas— who, speaking to them, were persuading[CC] them to continue-in[DD] the grace *of* God   42 / 43

  4C. Now *on* the coming Sabbath, almost the whole city was gathered together to hear the word *of* the Lord[35]   44

    1D. But the Jews, having seen the crowds, were filled[EE] *with* jealousy[FF]. And they were contradicting[36] the *things* being spoken by Paul, blaspheming[37]   45

1. That is, this salvation brought by the Savior mentioned in v 23.
2. That is, us Jews. It was sent out by God through the Savior, not through the Jewish leaders, as seen next. His witnesses (v 31), and we (v 32), are announcing it. Some manuscripts say "you" {B}.
3. Or, "being ignorant of ". On this word, see Rom 10:3.
4. Or, "this [message of salvation]" just mentioned.
5. On this word, see "filled" in Eph 5:18.
6. The only charge was that Jesus said He was the Son of God, which He in fact was, but the Jews would not listen. On this word, see Jn 18:38. Paul uses "charge *worthy of* death" of himself in 28:18. "Worthy of death" is in 23:29; 25:11, 25; 26:31; etc.
7. Or, "finished, accomplished". On this word, see "finish" in Rev 10:7.
8. Joseph and Nicodemus, two of the rulers, members of the Sanhedrin, did so.
9. Some manuscripts omit this word {C}.
10. This is a third word for this (compare v 27, 29). Used only here. GK *1740*. Related to the word in v 27.
11. It is also possible to take "us" with what follows, "*for* their children, having raised up Jesus *for* us". Some manuscripts say "*for* our children, having..."; others, "*for* their children, having..." {C}.
12. Some think Paul is referring here to the bringing of the Savior to Israel (v 23), His entrance into ministry (v 24), as this word is used of Him in 3:22. It is not the same word as "raise up" David in 13:22, but the same idea. Others think Paul is referring to His resurrection, as this word is used in v 34, where he adds "from the dead". On this word, see Lk 18:33.
13. That is, "And *as to the fact* that".
14. That is, the Messiah.
15. The promises and decrees God made regarding David will be given to the Messiah, who will permanently fulfill them. Therefore, He cannot die as David did. Therefore Ps 16:10 says He will not experience decay in the grave, as David did. Same word as in v 35. On this word, see Heb 7:26.
16. Or, "faithful, dependable, reliable, sure". On this word, see "faithful" in Col 1:2.
17. That is, God.
18. That is, permit.
19. That is, experience.
20. Paul uses grammar that emphasizes the contrast between the two halves of this sentence, between David and Christ.
21. Or, "helped, rendered service". Elsewhere only in 20:34; 24:23. GK *5676*. Related to "assistant" in v 5.
22. Or, "plan". On this word, see "counsel" in Eph 1:11.
23. Or, "having served *his* own generation *in* the purpose *of* God".
24. Or, "added to". On this word, see "increase" in Lk 17:5.
25. Same word as in v 34, 35, 37, and in 2:27 (where Peter makes this same argument).
26. That is, through the agency of this One whom God brought (v 23), who sent us out to announce it (v 32).
27. Some manuscripts omit this word {C}.
28. Or, "in", so that it says "everyone believing in this *One* is declared-righteous". That is, by means of this One, the Savior. This "by" is in contrast with "by" (same word, GK *1877*) the Law earlier. Not the same word as "through" in v 38 (GK *1328*).
29. Or, "disappear, be destroyed". On this word, see "disfigure" in Mt 6:16.
30. This word, "tell in detail" is elsewhere only as "describe in detail" in 15:3. GK *1687*. Related to "relate" in Lk 8:39.
31. Some think this refers to Paul and Barnabas; others, to the Jews. Some manuscripts say "while the Jews *were* going out from the synagogue" {A}.
32. Some think this refers to the ones worshiping there, who follow in the next verse. Others think it refers to the Gentile worshipers in particular. Some manuscripts say "the Gentiles" {B}.
33. Or, "the synagogue, congregation, meeting". This word is used of the place, the people meeting there, and the meeting held there. "Synagogue" is transliterated from the Greek, and means "gathering". Same word as in Jam 2:2. Elsewhere this word is rendered "synagogue" 54 times. GK *5252*. Related to "gather together" in v 44.
34. Or, "broken up, brought to an end, dismissed". On this word, see "break" in Mt 5:19.
35. Some manuscripts say "the word *of* God" {C}.
36. Or, "speaking against". On this word, see Rom 10:21.
37. Some manuscripts say "contradicting and blaspheming" {B}. On this word, see 1 Tim 6:1.

A. 1 Tim 2:12 B. Act 16:40 C. Gal 3:7 D. Eph 5:33, respecting E. 1 Cor 12:8, word F. Gal 4:4, sent forth G. Rev 1:5 H. Mt 7:1, judge J. Lk 3:1 K. Lk 23:32 L. 1 Pet 2:24 M. Mt 28:6, arose N. Lk 2:26, see O. Act 1:8 P. Act 5:42 Q. 1 Jn 2:25 R. 1 Jn 2:29, born S. 2 Pet 2:21, turn back T. Rom 1:19 U. Col 1:14 V. Phil 1:18 W. Rom 3:24 X. Rev 1:11, see Y. Rev 17:8 Z. Rom 12:8, exhorting AA. Act 13:50 BB. Mt 23:15 CC. 1 Jn 3:19 DD. Act 11:23 EE. Act 2:4 FF. 2 Cor 11:2

Acts 13:46	444	Verse

    2D. And Paul and Barnabas, having spoken-boldly[1], said, "It was necessary[A] *that* the word *of* God be spoken ***to you*** first. Since you are rejecting[2] it, and judging[B] yourselves not worthy[C] *of* eternal life, behold— we are turning to the Gentiles   46

        1E. "For thus the Lord has commanded[D] us [in Isa 49:6]— 'I have placed you for *a light*[3] *to the* Gentiles, *that* you *may* be *a light* for salvation[E] as far as *the* last[4] *place of* the earth' "   47

    3D. And the Gentiles, having heard *it*, were rejoicing[F] and glorifying[G] the word *of* the Lord[5]. And all who had been appointed[6] to[7] eternal life, believed[H]   48

  5C. And the word *of* the Lord was being carried[8] through the whole region[9]   49
  6C. But the Jews incited the prominent worshiping[10] women and the leading[11] *men of* the city, and aroused[12] *a* persecution[J] against Paul and Barnabas, and drove them out[K] from their districts[L]   50
  7C. But the *ones,* having shaken-out[13] the dust *from their* feet against them, went to Iconium[14]   51
  8C. And the disciples were being filled[M] *with* joy and *with the* Holy Spirit   52

3B. Now it came about in Iconium *that* according to the same *plan*[15], they entered into the synagogue *of* the Jews and spoke in this manner, so that *a* large number *of* both Jews and Greeks believed[H]   14:1

  1C. But the Jews having disobeyed[16] aroused[N] and embittered[17] the souls[O] *of* the Gentiles against the brothers[P]   2
  2C. So indeed they spent *a* considerable time speaking-boldly[18] for[19] the Lord, *Who was* testifying[20] to the word *of* His grace, granting[21] *that* signs and wonders[Q] be taking place by their hands   3
  3C. And the multitude *of* the city was divided[22]— indeed some were with the Jews; and others, with the apostles   4
  4C. But when *an* attempt[23] came about *by* both the Gentiles and Jews together with their rulers to mistreat[R] and to stone them—   5

    1D. Having become-aware[S], they fled[24] to the cities *of* Lycaonia[25]— Lystra and Derbe, and the surrounding-region[T]. *And there they were announcing-the-good-news[U]   6 / 7

4B. And in Lystra, *a* certain man powerless[26] in the feet was sitting— *a* lame[27] *one* from his mother's womb[V], who never walked   8

  1C. This *one* heard Paul speaking— who, having looked-intently[W] *at* him, and having seen that he had[28] faith *that he might* be restored[29], *said *with a* loud voice, "Stand up straight[X] on your feet"   9 / 10
  2C. And he leaped[30] and was walking
  3C. And the crowds, having seen what Paul did, raised their voice, saying in Lycaonian, "The gods came down to us, having become-like[31] men[Y]!"   11

    1D. And they were calling Barnabas "Zeus[32]", and Paul "Hermes[33]", since **he** was the *one* leading[Z] the speaking[AA]   12
    2D. And the priest *of the* temple *of* Zeus being before[34] the city, having brought bulls and garlands to the gates,[35] was intending[36] to offer-sacrifice[BB] with the crowds   13

  4C. But the apostles[37], Barnabas and Paul— having heard-*of it,* having torn[38] their garments— leaped-out[39] into the crowd, crying-out[CC] *and saying, "Men, why are you doing these *things*? **We** also are men[Y] of-like-nature[DD] *to* you, announcing-the-good-news[U] to turn[EE] you[40] from these worthless[41] *things* to *the* living God—   14 / 15

1. Or, "speaking boldly" concurrently with the verb "said". On this word, see Eph 6:20.
2. Or, "pushing it aside". Same word as in 7:27, 39. On this word, see Rom 11:1.
3. That is, to be a light. This was said of the Messiah in Lk 2:32.
4. Same phrase as in 1:8, "as far as *the* last *place of* the earth".
5. Some manuscripts say "the word *of* God"; others, just "God" {C}.
6. Or, "assigned, stationed, arrayed, arranged". This is a participle, "were having been appointed". On this word, see "established" in Rom 13:1. Some think Luke means "predestined by God to believe". Others think he means "providentially arranged for eternal life" that day— ripe fruit ready to be harvested by Paul.
7. Or, "for". GK *1650*.
8. Or, "spread". Same word as in Mk 11:16. GK *1422*.
9. That is, the region of Phrygia, which is part of the Roman province of Galatia.
10. Same word as in v 43. It is used of Gentile God-fearers who worshiped God in the synagogue with the Jews, but did not obligate themselves to keep the whole Law as the Jews did. Elsewhere only in Mt 15:9; Mk 7:7; Act 16:14; 17:4, 17; 18:7, 13; 19:27. GK *4936*. Related to "worship" in Rom 1:25. Some manuscripts say "worshiping and prominent" {N}.
11. Or, "first, chief, foremost". The Jews incited the people of prominence against these disturbers of the peace. Same word as in Mk 6:21; Lk 19:47; Act 17:4; 25:2. On this word, see "first" in 1 Cor 15:3.
12. Or, "raised up, awakened", and figuratively, "stirred up, excited". Elsewhere only in 14:2. GK *2074*. The root word is "to raise".
13. Elsewhere only in Mt 10:14; Mk 6:11; Act 18:6. GK *1759*. Related to "shake off" in Lk 9:5.
14. This is the easternmost city in the region of Phrygia. GK *2658*.
15. Or, "in accordance with the same *thing*". Compare 17:2. This phrase is elsewhere only in 1 Cor 12:8, "according to the same" Spirit. The same phrase (except plural) is in Lk 6:23, "in the same *way*". Some render it "together" here (like the phrase in 2:47), "*that* they entered together into...".
16. Or, "refused to believe". The ones who disobeyed did what follows. They disobeyed the Son, Jn 3:36; the truth, Rom 2:8; the word, 1 Pet 2:8; the gospel of God, 1 Pet 4:17. On this word, see Rom 11:30. Some manuscripts say "the disobeying Jews" {N}.
17. Literally, "made evil". The Jews caused these Gentiles to think evil of the believers. They turned them against them. On this word, see "do evil" in 1 Pet 3:13.
18. Same word as in 13:46.
19. Or, "on the basis of, for the purposes of". GK *2093*.
20. Or, "bearing witness". The grammar indicates it is the Lord testifying. Thus, both spoke— Paul and Barnabas in words, the Lord in signs and wonders; they with the message, He with the confirmation. Compare 5:32. On this word, see Jn 1:7.
21. This explains how the Lord gave His testimony. The signs and wonders confirmed their word, as in Heb 2:3-4. On this word, see "give" in Eph 1:22. Some manuscripts say "and granting" {N}.
22. Or, "split". On this word, see "torn" in Mt 27:51. Related to "division" in 1 Cor 1:10.
23. Or, "start, onset, impulse, violent attack". Elsewhere only as "impulse" in Jam 3:4. GK *3995*. Related to "rushed" in 7:57.
24. Or, "fled for refuge". On this word, see Heb 6:18.
25. Lycaonia is the district, Lystra and Derbe are cities in that district. This is still part of the Roman province of Galatia. Used only here. GK *3377*. Related word in v 11.
26. Or, "impotent". Same word as "not-strong" in Rom 15:1.
27. Some manuscripts add "being" {K}, "being *a* lame *one*".
28. More literally, "has", as the Greek typically phrases it.
29. Or, "saved". On this word, see Jam 5:15.
30. Same word as in 3:8, when Peter healed such a one.
31. Same word as used of Jesus in Heb 2:17, on which see Mt 13:24.
32. This is the Greek name of the chief god, the god of the sky, enthroned on Olympus, known as "Jupiter" by the Romans. Used only here and in v 13. GK *2416*.
33. This is the Greek name for the son of Zeus, who was the messenger of the gods, known as "Mercury" by the Romans. Thus Paul is seen as the spokesman for Barnabas (Zeus). Used only here, and as someone's name in Rom 16:14. GK *2258*.
34. Or, "in front of, ahead of". The temple was located outside on the road before one reached the city. GK *4574*.
35. Luke may mean the gates of the city, of the temple, or of the house where Paul's team was staying.
36. Or, "wishing, wanting". On this word, see "willing" in Jn 7:17.
37. Only here and in v 4 are Barnabas and Paul called apostles in Acts. They were "sent out" by the Holy Spirit, 13:4. All other uses of this word in Acts refer to the twelve. On this word, see 1 Cor 12:28.
38. Same word as used of the high priest's action in Mt 26:65. On this word, see Lk 8:29.
39. Or, "sprang out, bounded out, jumped out, rushed out". Used only here. GK *1737*. Barnabas and Paul sprang from being in front of the crowd and about to be worshiped, to being in the crowd as fellow humans. Their action matched their words. Related to "jump up" in Mk 10:50, and "rush in" in Act 16:29. Some manuscripts say "leaped into" {K}, using the same word with a different prefix.
40. Or, "announcing-the-good-news *that* you *should* turn...", or, "announcing-the-good-news-to you to turn *you*...".
41. Or, "futile, pointless". On this word, see "futile" in 1 Cor 15:17.

A. Tit 3:14 B. Mt 7:1 C. Rev 16:6 D. Mk 10:3 E. Lk 19:9 F. 2 Cor 13:11 G. Rom 8:30 H. Jn 3:36 J. Mk 10:30 K. Jn 12:31, cast out L. Mk 10:1 M. Eph 5:18 N. Act 13:50 O. Jam 5:20 P. Act 16:40 Q. 2 Thes 2:9 R. 1 Thes 2:2 S. Act 12:12 T. Mk 1:28 U. Act 5:42 V. Lk 1:15 W. Lk 4:20 X. Heb 12:13 Y. Mt 4:4, mankind Z. Heb 13:7 AA. 1 Cor 12:8, word BB. Act 10:13, slaughter CC. Mt 8:29 DD. Jam 5:17 EE. Jam 5:19, turns back

	1D. "Who made the heaven and the earth and the sea and all the *things* in them	16
	2D. "Who allowed[A] all the nations to be going their ways in the generations having gone-by, °and yet did not leave Himself without-witness[1]—	17
	1E. "Doing-good[B]	
	2E. "Giving you[2] rains from heaven and fruitful[3] seasons	
	3E. "Filling[C] your[4] hearts *with* food[D] and gladness[5]"	
5C.	And saying these *things*, with-difficulty[E] they restrained[6] the crowds, *that they might* not offer-sacrifice[F] *to* them	18
6C.	But Jews came-over from Antioch and Iconium. And having won-over[7] the crowds, and having stoned[8] Paul, they were dragging[G] *him* outside *of* the city, thinking[9] *that* he was[10] dead	19
7C.	But the disciples having surrounded[H] him— having stood-up[J], he entered into the city	20
5B. And *on* the next day he went forth with Barnabas to Derbe. °And having announced-the-good-news-to[K] that city, and having made many disciples[11]—	21
	1C. They returned[L] to Lystra, and to Iconium, and to Antioch	
	1D. Strengthening[12] the souls[M] *of* the disciples	22
	2D. Encouraging[13] *them* to continue-in[14] the faith, and that "It-is-necessary[15] *that* we enter into the kingdom[N] *of* God through many afflictions[O]"	
	2C. And having appointed[P] elders[Q] *for* them in each church[16], having prayed with fastings[R], they commended[17] them *to* the Lord in Whom they had believed	23
6B. And having gone through Pisidia, they came to Pamphylia. °And having spoken the word[18] in Perga[19], they went down to Attalia[20]. °And from there they sailed-away to Antioch[21]— from where they had been handed-over[22] *to* the grace *of* God for the work which they completed[23]	24-25, 26
	1C. And having arrived, and having gathered together the church, they were reporting[24] all that God did with them, and that He opened *a* door *of* faith *to* the Gentiles	27
15A. Now they were spending[S] not *a* little time[25] with the disciples.[26] °And certain *ones* having come down[27] from Judea were teaching the brothers that "Unless you are circumcised[T] *by* the custom[28] *of* Moses, you cannot be saved[U]". °And[29] no small dispute[30] and debate[31] *by* Paul and Barnabas with them having taken place, they[32] appointed[33] Paul and Barnabas and some others of them to go up to the apostles and elders[Q] in Jerusalem concerning this issue[34]	28-15:1, 2
	1B. So indeed the *ones*, having been sent-forward[V] by the church, were going through both Phoenicia and Samaria, describing-in-detail[35] the conversion[36] *of* the Gentiles. And they were producing[37] great joy *in* all the brothers[W]	3
	2B. And having arrived in Jerusalem, they were welcomed[38] by the church and the apostles and the elders[Q]. And they reported[X] all-that God did with them	4
	3B. But some *of* the *ones* from the sect[Y] *of* the Pharisees having believed[39] stood-up-out-of[40] *the assembly*, saying that "It-is-necessary[41] to circumcise them and to command[Z] *them* to keep[AA] the Law *of* Moses"	5
	4B. And the apostles and the elders were gathered together to see[BB] about this matter[CC]. °And much debate[DD] having taken place, Peter, having stood up, said to them	6-7
	1C. "Men, brothers[W], **you** know that from *the* old[42] days God made-a-choice[EE] among you[43], *that* by my mouth the Gentiles *should* hear the message[CC] *of* the good-news[FF] and believe	

1. Or, "witnessless, without testimony". Used only here. GK *282*. God's works bear testimony to Him.
2. Some manuscripts say "us" {K}.
3. Or, "fruitbearing". Used only here. GK *2845*. Related to "bear fruit" in Rom 7:4.
4. Some manuscripts say "our" {K}.
5. Or, "cheerfulness". On this word, see 2:28.
6. Or, "brought to rest". Elsewhere only as "rest" in Heb 4:4, 10; and "give rest" in Heb 4:8. GK *2924*.
7. Or, "persuaded, convinced". Same word as in 12:20.
8. Paul mentions this in 2 Cor 11:25.
9. Or, "supposing". This word refers to holding an opinion. The opinion may be correct (as in Act 16:13), but usually is not correct. Same word as in Mt 5:17; 20:10; Lk 2:44; Act 7:25; 8:20; 17:29; 1 Cor 7:26, 36. Elsewhere only as "suppose" in Mt 10:34; Lk 3:23; Act 16:13, 27; 21:29; 1 Tim 6:5. GK *3787*.
10. Or, "had died". More literally, "is dead" or "has died", as the Greek typically phrases it.
11. The verb "made disciples" is the same word as in Mt 28:19.
12. Or, "Confirming". Elsewhere only in 15:32, 41; 18:23. GK *2185*. Related to "establish" in 1 Thes 3:2.
13. Or, "exhorting". Same word as in 11:23; 15:32; 20:1, 2. On this word, see "exhorting" in Rom 12:8.
14. Or, "remain in, be true to". On this word, see Gal 3:10. Related to the word in 11:23; 13:43.
15. Or, "We must enter". On this idiom, see "must" in Mt 16:21.
16. Or, "according to church, in every church, church by church". Same idiom as "house by house" in Act 2:46; "in each city" in Tit 1:5.
17. Or, "entrusted, committed, deposited". More literally, "placed beside". On this word, see "put before" in 17:3.
18. Some manuscripts add "*of* the Lord"; others, "*of* God" {B}.
19. If Paul and Barnabas did not do so in 13:13 when they arrived, they did so now.
20. This city was the main seaport of Pamphylia, the city of Perga being up-river about 7 miles or 11 kilometers.
21. That is, in Syria, probably first arriving at the same port from which they left in 13:4, Seleucia.
22. Or, "delivered, committed, entrusted". This is a participle, "they were having been handed over". Luke is referring to 13:2-4. Same word as in 15:26, 40; as "committing" in 1 Pet 2:23; and as when Judas "handed over" Jesus (see Mt 26:21 on it).
23. Paul and Barnabas completed what the Spirit sent them out from Antioch to do, 13:4. On this word, see "filled" in Eph 5:18.
24. On this word, see "declare" in Jn 16:13. Some manuscripts say "reported" {K}.
25. That is, a long time. On this idiom, see "no small" in 12:18. Some manuscripts add "there" {K}.
26. Some think it was during this time in Syrian Antioch that Paul wrote Galatians to the churches in Pisidian Antioch, Iconium, Lystra, and Derbe visited in 13:14-14:23 (the South Galatia theory). Others think it was written from Corinth (in Act 18:5) or Ephesus (in Act 19:10) or Corinth (in Act 20:3)— some to the churches just mentioned; others, to unnamed churches that Paul visited in Act 16:6 or 18:23 (the North Galatia theory).
27. That is, to Antioch, where Paul and Barnabas were staying, 14:28.
28. In other words, Gentiles had to become Jews before they could be Christians. On this word, see Lk 1:9.
29. Some manuscripts say "Therefore" {N}.
30. Or, "dissension, discord, uprising". On this word, see 23:7. On "no small", see 12:18.
31. Or, "controversy". Same word as in v 7. On this word, see "controversy" in 1 Tim 6:4.
32. That is, the brothers (v 1); the church in Antioch (v 3).
33. Or, "assigned". Same word as in 13:48.
34. Or, "controversial question". Elsewhere only in 18:15; 23:29; 25:19; 26:3. GK *2427*. Related to "debate" earlier.
35. On this word, see "tell in detail" in 13:41.
36. Or, "turning". Used only here. GK *2189*. Related to "turning" in v 19.
37. Or, "making, bringing about". On this word, see "does" in Rev 13:13.
38. Or, "accepted, received". On this word, see "accept" in Mk 4:20.
39. That is, some believers who were formerly Pharisees.
40. Same word as "stood up" in v 7, with the prefix "out of" added. These men stood up in distinction from the rest, and made the following statement. On this word, see "raised up from" in Mk 12:19.
41. On this idiom, see "must" in Mt 16:21.
42. Or "ancient", relative to the church. That is, in the beginning days of the church. Peter is referring to the events in Acts 10, now some ten years in the past. Note Mt 16:19. The extension of salvation to the Gentiles originated in the early days through me by God's choice. This now is a continuation of what God did then. Same word as in 21:16; 2 Cor 5:17. Elsewhere only as "ancient" in Mt 5:21, 33; Lk 9:8, 19; Act 15:21; 2 Pet 2:5; Rev 12:9; 20:2. GK *792*.
43. Some manuscripts say "us" {N}.

A. 1 Cor 10:13 B. 1 Tim 6:18, working good C. Rom 15:24 D. Mt 24:25 E. 1 Pet 4:18 F. Act 10:13, slaughter G. Rev 12:4, sweeps away H. Jn 10:24 J. Lk 18:33, rise up K. Act 5:42 L. 2 Pet 2:21, turn back M. Jam 5:20 N. Mt 3:2 O. Rev 7:14 P. 2 Cor 8:19 Q. 1 Tim 5:17 R. 2 Cor 11:27 S. Act 12:19, spending time T. Lk 2:21 U. Lk 19:10 V. Rom 15:24 W. Act 16:40 X. Jn 16:13, declare Y. 1 Cor 11:19, faction Z. 1 Tim 1:3 AA. 1 Jn 5:18 BB. Lk 2:26 CC. 1 Cor 12:8, word DD. 1 Tim 6:4, controversy EE. 1 Cor 1:27, chose FF. 1 Cor 15:1

2C. "And God, the heart-knower[1], testified[2]— having given the Holy Spirit *to* them, just as also *to* us. *And He made no distinction[3] between both us and them, having cleansed[A] their hearts *by* faith	8 9
3C. "Therefore why are you now testing[4] God— *by* laying *a* yoke[5] on[6] the neck *of* the disciples which neither our fathers nor **we** were able[7] to bear[B]? *Rather, we believe *that* we are saved[C] through the grace[D] *of* the Lord Jesus[8] in accordance with the way[9] those also *are saved*"	10 11

5B. And the whole assembly[E] was silent[F]. And they were listening-to Barnabas and Paul describing[10] all the signs and wonders[G] that God did[11] through them among the Gentiles — 12

6B. And after they[12] *were* silent, James[13] responded, saying, "Men[H], brothers, listen-to me— 13

    1C. "Simeon[14] described how God first visited[15] to take *a* people *for* His name from *the* Gentiles — 14
    2C. "And the words *of* the prophets agree[J] *with* this, just as it has been written [in Amos 9:11-12]— 15

        1D. 'After these *things* I will return, and I will rebuild[16] the fallen[17] tent *of* David. And I will rebuild its *things* having been torn-down[18]. And I will restore[K] it *so that the rest[19] *of* mankind[L] may seek-out[M] the Lord— even all the Gentiles upon whom My name has been called-upon[N] them[20]', says *the* Lord doing[O] these[21] *things* *known[22] from *the past* age[23]' — 16, 17, 18

    3C. "Therefore **I** judge[P] *that* we not be troubling[24] the *ones* from the Gentiles turning[Q] to God, *but *that we* write to them *that they should* be abstaining[25] *from* the contaminated[26] *things of* idols, and sexual-immorality[27], and the strangled *thing*[28], and blood[29] — 19-20

        1D. "For[30] from ancient[R] generations, Moses has the *ones* proclaiming[S] him in each city— being read in the synagogues every Sabbath" — 21

7B. Then it seemed[T] *good to* the apostles and the elders, along with the whole church, *that* having chosen[31] men from-*among* them, *they should* send *them* to Antioch with Paul and Barnabas— Judas (the *one* being called[32] Barsabbas) and Silas[33], leading[34] men among the brothers — 22

    1C. Having written by their[35] hand— 23

        1D. "The apostles and the elders, *your* brothers[36]— *to* the brothers from *the* Gentiles[37] throughout Antioch and Syria and Cilicia[38], greetings[U]
        2D. "Because we heard that some having gone out[39] from us disturbed[V] you *with* words[W], unsettling[40] your souls[41]— *to* whom we did not give-orders— *it seemed[T] *good to* us — 24, 25

            1E. "Having become of-one-accord[X]
            2E. "Having chosen men[42]
            3E. "*That we should* send *them* to you, with our beloved[Y] Barnabas and Paul—

                1F. "Men[43] having handed-over[44] their lives[Z] for the name *of* our Lord Jesus Christ — 26

        3D. "Therefore we have sent-forth[AA] Judas and Silas— they also *will be* declaring[BB] the same *things* by *spoken* word[W] — 27
        4D. "For it seemed[T] *good to* the Holy Spirit and *to* us to be laying-on[CC] you no greater burden[DD] except these essentials[45]— *that you be abstaining *from* foods-sacrificed-to-idols[EE], and blood, and strangled *things*[46], and sexual immorality — 28, 29

            1E. "Keeping[FF] yourselves from which *things*, you will do well[GG]

1. Elsewhere only in 1:24. GK *2841*.
2. That is, God testified that these Gentiles were truly and fully saved, just like we Jews, when He gave them the Spirit.
3. This word, "make a distinction", is the same word as in 11:12.
4. Or, "tempting, putting to the test". If God is put to the test by these former Pharisees (v 5), He will respond to them with disciplinary judgment, because they are rejecting the testimony He Himself has clearly given. On this word, see "tempt" in Heb 2:18.
5. Using the same word, Paul calls it a "yoke" of slavery in Gal 5:1. It is not Christ's easy "yoke", Mt 11:30.
6. This word "lay on" is the same word as in v 28; Mt 23:4. On this word, see Lk 10:30.
7. Or, "were strong-*enough*, had strength". In addition to rejecting God's own testimony, these former Pharisees are trying to impose a Law on others which they themselves could not keep (as Paul also says in Gal 6:13). On this word, see "can do" in Gal 5:6.
8. Some manuscripts add "Christ" {N}.
9. On this idiom, "in accordance with the way", see 27:25.
10. Same word as in v 14; 21:19. On this word, see "expound" in Jn 1:18. Related to "describe in detail" in v 3.
11. The signs and wonders confirm that God was with these two, and their message.
12. That is, Barnabas and Paul.
13. That is, the brother of Jesus, writer of James, and head of the Jerusalem church. See Mt 13:55 on him.
14. That is, Peter, v 7. This is the Aramaic form of "Simon", as in 2 Pet 1:1. See Lk 6:14. GK *5208*.
15. Same word as in v 36. James is referring to Cornelius in Acts 10.
16. Or, "build again". Used only in this verse, twice. GK *488*. Related to "build, build up, edify" (see "edify" in 1 Cor 14:4).
17. This is a participle, "having fallen", that is, "the tent *of* David having fallen".
18. Or, "dug down, razed to the ground, utterly destroyed". Elsewhere only in Rom 11:3, of altars. GK *2940*. The root word is "to dig".
19. Or, "the remaining *ones*". That is, those other than the Jews. Used only here. GK *2905*.
20. Or, "named upon them", as an act of ownership. That is, on whom God has placed His name. A Hebrew way of speaking. Same idiom as in Jam 2:7, "the good name having been called upon you". In both cases, "called" is the word "called upon" in 1 Pet 1:17.
21. Some manuscripts say "all these *things*. All His works are known *to* God from *the past* age" {B}.
22. On this adjective, see Rom 1:19.
23. On this phrase, "from the *past* age", see Lk 1:70.
24. Or, "annoying, causing difficulties for". Used only here. GK *4214*. Related to the word in Lk 6:18.
25. Same word as in 1 Thes 4:3. The following list is repeated in v 29 and in 21:25.
26. Or, "polluted, defiled". That is, the things defiled by their association with idol worship, specified in v 29 to mean eating "foods sacrificed to idols". Used only here. GK *246*. The related verb "defiled" is used in Dan 1:8; Mal 1:7, 12.
27. Some think James is specifically referring to the sexual immorality associated with idol worship; others, to all sexual immorality; others, to the spiritual adultery consisting of pagan worship of any kind. Some manuscripts omit "and sexual immorality", resulting in a threefold prohibition {A}. On this word, see 1 Cor 5:1. Some think this is the only moral issue, the other three being matters of Jewish dietary laws (falling under 1 Cor 10:23-33). Others think all four are moral issues associated with idol worship (falling under 1 Cor 10:14-22). There are other views.
28. That is, from eating the meat of strangled animals, because the blood remained in it. This command regarding eating blood goes back to Noah's time in Gen 9:4; and is repeated in the Law of Moses, Lev 17:10-14. Elsewhere only in v 29; 21:25. GK *4465*.
29. Some think James means contact with or eating/drinking blood. Others think he is referring to murder.
30. Some think this gives the reason for these restrictions. It is not to be saved, v 9, 11. It is so as not to offend the Jews in every city who still preach Moses. It is so as not to unnecessarily hinder the progress of the gospel with them, as in 1 Cor 9:20. Others think it gives the reason for not troubling the Gentiles, v 19. Moses already has his advocates.
31. Same word as in v 25. On this word, see 1 Cor 1:27.
32. Some manuscripts say "named" {K}.
33. See v 40 on him.
34. That is, men who were leading, leaders. On this word, see Heb 13:7.
35. That is, the apostles and elders. Note 16:4.
36. Some manuscripts say "and the brothers" {B}. On this word, see 16:40.
37. Notice that the Jewish believers do not say "Gentile brothers". They think of them as "ones from the Gentiles turning to God", v 19. They consider them brothers, and no longer part of the Gentiles (pagans), in keeping with v 14. Compare 21:25 and 1 Cor 12:2. This word means "Gentiles , nations". It sometimes refers to "non-Jews" (including Christians, as in Gal 2:12; Eph 3:1), and other times to "unbelievers, pagans", from God's point of view. Used 162 times. GK *1620*.
38. Antioch (see 11:19) is the capital of Syria. Syria and Cilicia are neighboring provinces, north of Galilee.
39. These men claimed authority they did not possess, and taught a message not propounded by the apostles or the church in Jerusalem. Some manuscripts omit "having gone out" {C}.
40. Or, "breaking up, dismantling, tearing down". Used only here. GK *412*.
41. Some manuscripts add "saying to be circumcised and keep the Law" {A}.
42. Some manuscripts say "*that* having chosen men, *we should* send..." {C}, as in v 22.
43. This phrase refers back specifically to Barnabas and Paul.
44. Or, "committed, delivered". Same word as in 14:26; 15:40. In proclaiming the gospel, these two handed over their lives to the will of God, leaving to Him the outcome of the persecutions they encountered.
45. Or, "necessities". Used only here. GK *2055*. Related to "necessity" in 1 Cor 7:26.
46. Some manuscripts have this singular as in v 20 and 21:25, "*the* strangled *thing*" {B}.

A. Heb 9:22 B. Mt 8:17, carry C. Lk 19:10 D. Eph 2:8 E. Act 6:2, multitude F. 1 Cor 14:34 G. 2 Thes 2:9 H. 1 Tim 2:12 J. Mt 18:19 K. Heb 12:12, straighten up L. Mt 4:4 M. Heb 11:6 N. 1 Pet 1:17 O. Rev 13:13 P. Mt 7:1 Q. Jam 5:19, turns back R. Act 15:7, old S. 2 Tim 4:2 T. Lk 19:11, thinking U. 2 Cor 13:11, rejoice V. Gal 1:7 W. 1 Cor 12:8 X. Act 1:14 Y. Mt 3:17 Z. Jam 5:20, soul AA. Mk 3:14, send out BB. 1 Jn 1:3, announcing CC. Lk 10:30 DD. 1 Thes 2:7, weight EE. 1 Cor 8:1 FF. Lk 2:51 GG. Mt 25:21

	5D. "Farewell[1]"	
8B.	So indeed the *ones*, having been sent-away[A], went down to Antioch. And having gathered together the multitude, they delivered the letter	30
	1C. And having read *it*, they rejoiced[B] over the encouragement[2]	31
	2C. Both Judas and Silas, also[3] themselves being prophets[C], encouraged[4] and strengthened[5] the brothers[D] with *a* long[6] message[E]	32
	3C. And having done time *there*, they were sent-away[A] with *greetings of* peace[7] from the brothers to the *ones* having sent them out[8]	33 34[9]
16A.	Now Paul and Barnabas were spending-time[F] in Antioch, teaching[G] and announcing-as-good-news[H] the word[E] *of* the Lord, along with many others also. °And after some days, Paul said to Barnabas, "Having returned[J], let us now[10] visit[K] the[11] brothers in every city in which we proclaimed[L] the word *of* the Lord *to see* how they are having[12] *things*"	35 36
	1B. And Barnabas was wanting[13] to also take along John with *them*, the *one* being called Mark	37
	1C. But Paul was considering-it-fitting[14] *that they* not be taking-along-with[15] *them* this *one* having withdrawn[16] from them since[17] Pamphylia[18], and not having gone with them to the work[M]	38
	2C. And *a* disagreement[19] took-place[20], so that they were separated[21] from one another	39
	3C. And Barnabas, having taken along Mark, sailed-off[N] to Cyprus[22]	
	2B. And Paul, having chosen[23] Silas[24], went forth, having been handed-over[25] *to* the grace *of* the Lord[26] by the brothers. °And he was going through Syria and Cilicia[27], strengthening[O] the churches[P]. °And he came also[28] to Derbe, and to Lystra	40 41 16:1
	1C. And behold, *a* certain disciple[Q] was there— Timothy[29] *by* name, *the* son *of a* believing[30] Jewish woman[31], but *of a* Greek father[32]— °who was being attested[Q] by the brothers in Lystra and Iconium	2
	2C. Paul wanted[R] this *one* to go forth with him. And having taken *him*, he circumcised[S] him because of the Jews being in those places,[33] for they all knew that his father was[34] *a* Greek	3
	3C. And as they were proceeding through the cities, they were delivering[35] *to* them the decrees[36] to be keeping[37] having been determined[38] by the apostles and elders in Jerusalem	4
	4C. So indeed the churches were being made-firm[39] *in* the faith, and were abounding[40] *in* number daily	5

1. Or, "Be well, Keep well". This is a command often used to close letters, but used only here in the NT. GK *4874*.
2. Or, "exhortation, comfort". On this word, see 4:36. Related to "encouraged" in v 32.
3. Some think Luke means in addition to those in Antioch, 13:1; others, in addition to Barnabas and Paul; others, in addition to being "leading men" in Jerusalem (v 22) sent to deliver the letter.
4. Or, "exhorted". Same word as in 11:23; 14:22. On this word, see "exhort" in Rom 12:8.
5. On this word, see 14:22. Same word as in v 41.
6. Or, "great", meaning "great" in quantity (long, lengthy) or in quality. This rendering assumes Luke is referring to the single occasion when the letter was delivered by these men, v 31. If he is referring to multiple occasions during their stay (v 33), then this would be rendered "much speaking", as it is in 20:2. Same word as "great" in Heb 5:11. On this word, see "many" in Mt 13:52.
7. "Peace to you" is a common greeting. This word is used 92 times, of peace from God, peace with God, and peace between people and governments. GK *1645*.
8. Some manuscripts say "from the brothers to the apostles" {K}.
9. Some manuscripts add as v 34, "But it seemed *good* to Silas to remain there" {A}, to prepare for v 40. Whether Silas remained, or returned to Jerusalem and was later summoned by Paul in v 40, is not known.
10. Or, "indeed". On this word, see "indeed" in Mt 13:23.
11. Some manuscripts say "our" {K}.
12. That is, to see how the believers are doing. On this idiom, compare "being ill" in Mk 1:32.
13. Some manuscripts have a related word meaning "determined, decided, resolved" {K}.
14. Same word as in 28:22. On this word, see "consider worthy" in 2 Thes 1:11.
15. Same word as in v 37; 12:25. Elsewhere only in Gal 2:1. GK *5221*. Related to "take along" in v 39.
16. Or, "departed". Some give it a stronger sense here, "abandoned, deserted". On this word, see "depart" in 1 Tim 4:1. Not related to "departed" in 13:13. Paul thought it was not "fitting" because since Perga (13:13), Mark had not worked with them. The reason he left them is not given. Some think these words imply that Paul felt Mark deserted them, and was a quitter; that he left them for reasons that reflect poorly on his character at that time. Barnabas wanted to work with his cousin (see 12:25). Mark later served with Peter, wrote the Gospel, and served with Paul, 1 Pet 5:13; 2 Tim 4:11.
17. Or, "from". This may mean that Mark had not worked with Barnabas and Paul at all since then, even in Antioch, 15:35; or, it may refer only to the work to which he now wants to return.
18. Luke is referring to 13:13.
19. Or, "a provoking, stirring up, an irritation, exasperation, aggravation". On this word, see "provoking" in Heb 10:24. Here, it is a provoking to disagreement. In Hebrews, it is a provoking to love.
20. Or, "arose, occurred". GK *1181*. The difference of opinion was not resolvable. Both men were strongly committed to their positions, and the subsequent history of the three of them proved both were right. Sometimes, as with living cells, division is multiplication, because the divided parties spread life, not a cancer of bitterness.
21. Or, "parted, split". That is, a disagreement arose, with the result that they were separated from one another by it. On this word, see "split" in Rev 6:14.
22. This was the native country of Barnabas, and the first place he went with Paul and John-Mark (13:4-5). Instead of the two of them revisiting "every city" (15:36), Barnabas and Mark take those in Cyprus which all three of them had visited (13:5-12), and Paul takes those in Pamphylia and Galatia which only he and Barnabas had visited (13:13-14:24).
23. Or, "selected", literally, "called upon". Elsewhere only as "called" in Jn 5:2. GK *2141*. The root word is "to say".
24. He is called "Silvanus" in 1 Thes 1:1. Elsewhere only in 15:22, 27, 32; 16:19, 25, 29; 17:4, 10, 14, 15; 18:5. GK *4976*.
25. On this word and phrase, see 14:26.
26. Some manuscripts say "*of* God" {B}.
27. This time, Paul went directly by land, instead of by sea. Thus, Derbe is reached first.
28. Some manuscripts omit this word {C}.
29. See 1 Tim 1:2 on him.
30. Some manuscripts say "*a certain believing...*" {K}.
31. Her name was Eunice, 2 Tim 1:5. Timothy's grandmother was named Lois.
32. That is, non-Jewish, an unbeliever. His name is not given here or in 2 Timothy.
33. That is, so that Timothy's ministry among the unbelieving Jews in the synagogues would not be hindered.
34. Some think the tense of this word implies Timothy's father was now dead.
35. Or, "passing on", "handing down" (as in 6:14). Related to the word in 15:30 (GK *2113*). Same word as in Rom 6:17; 1 Cor 11:2; 15:3; 2 Pet 2:21; Jude 3, on which see "hand over" in Mt 26:21. Related to "tradition" in 1 Cor 11:2.
36. Or, "decisions, commands". On this word, see Eph 2:15.
37. Or, "to be keeping the decrees having been...", "*that they should* be keeping the decrees having been...", the Greek word order. On this word, see Jn 12:25.
38. Or, "decided". Same word as in 21:25, and as "judge" in 15:19. Same word as in 3:13; 25:25; 27:1. On this word, see "judge" in Mt 7:1.
39. Or, "made-solid, made-strong; were being strengthened, were becoming firm". Elsewhere only as "made strong" in 3:7, 16. GK *5105*. Related to "firm" in 2 Tim 2:19, "firmness" in Col 2:5.
40. Or, "overflowing". On this word, see 2 Cor 8:2.

A. Mt 5:31 B. 2 Cor 13:11 C. 1 Cor 12:28 D. Act 16:40 E. 1 Cor 12:8, word F. Act 12:19 G. Rom 12:7 H. Act 5:42 J. Jam 5:19, turns back K. Heb 2:6, look after L. Phil 1:18 M. Mt 26:10 N. Act 20:6 O. Act 14:22 P. Rev 22:16 Q. Act 6:3 R. Jn 7:17, willing S. Lk 2:21

3B. And they went[1] through the Phrygian and Galatian[2] region, having been forbidden[3] by the Holy Spirit to speak the word in Asia.[4] *And[5] having come opposite[6] Mysia,[7] they were trying to proceed into Bithynia[8], and the Spirit *of* Jesus[9] did not allow[A] them. *And having passed-by[10] Mysia, they came down to Troas[11] 6
7
8

    1C. And *a* vision[B] appeared[C] *to* Paul during the night— *a* certain Macedonian[12] man[13] was standing, and appealing-to[D] him, and saying, "Having crossed[14] to Macedonia, help[E] us" 9

    2C. And when he saw the vision, immediately we[15] sought[F] to go forth to Macedonia, concluding[16] that God[17] had[18] called[19] us to announce-the-good-news-to[G] them 10

4B. And[20] having put-to-sea from Troas, we ran-a-straight-course[21] to Samothrace[22], and *on* the following *day* to Neapolis[23]. *And from there *we went* to Philippi, which is *a* city *of the* first[24] district[H] *of* Macedonia, *a* colony[25]. And we were spending some days in this city 11
12

    1C. And *on* the day *of* the Sabbath, we went outside the gate[26] beside *a* river where we were supposing[J] that there was *a* place *of* prayer[27]. And having sat-*down*, we were speaking *to* the women[28] having come together 13

        1D. And a certain woman worshiping[K] God— Lydia *by* name, *a* purple-fabric-dealer[29] *from* the city *of* Thyatira— was listening, whose heart the Lord opened to pay-attention-to[L] the *things* being spoken by Paul 14

        2D. And when she and her household[M] were baptized, she urged[D] us, saying, "If you have judged[N] me to be *a* believer[30] *in* the Lord, *then* having entered into my house, be staying[O] *with me*" 15

        3D. And she prevailed-upon[31] us

    2C. And it came about while we *were* going to the *place of* prayer, *that a* certain servant-girl[P] having *a* soothsaying[32] spirit met us, who was bringing-about[Q] *a* large profit[33] *to* her masters telling-fortunes[34] 16

        1D. This *one*, while closely-following[R] Paul and us[35], was crying-out[S], saying, "These men are slaves[T] *of* the Most-High[36] God, who are proclaiming[U] *to* you[37] *a* way[38] *of* salvation[V]" 17

        2D. And she was doing this for many days 18

    3C. And Paul— having been greatly-annoyed[39], and having turned *to* the spirit— said, "I command[W] you in *the* name *of* Jesus Christ to depart from her!" And it went out *at* the very hour[40]

    4C. And her masters— having seen that their hope *of* profit went-out[41], having taken-hold-of[X] Paul and Silas— dragged[42] *them* into the marketplace[43] before the rulers[Y] 19

        1D. And having brought them to the magistrates[44], they said, "These men are throwing our city into confusion[45], being Jews. *And they are proclaiming[U] customs[Z] which it is not lawful[AA] *for* us to be accepting[BB], nor to be doing,[46] being[47] Romans" 20
21

    5C. And the crowd rose up together against them. And the magistrates, having torn-off their[48] garments, were giving-orders[CC] to beat *them* with rods[49]. *And having laid many blows on[50] them, they threw *them* into prison, having commanded[W] the jailer to keep them securely[51] 22
23

1. Some manuscripts say "Now having gone through..." {N}.
2. By "the Phrygian and Galatian region" (referring to one region), Luke would mean the region of Galatia inhabited by Phrygians, which includes the cities of Iconium and Pisidian Antioch. Others render the first as a noun (as in 18:23), so that it says "Phrygia and *the* Galatian region". In this case, Phrygia is the region extending from Iconium and Antioch northward toward Bithynia, and the Galatian region is the province east of Phrygia. Some think that the unnamed cities of North Galatia referred to in the latter case were the recipients of Galatians (see 14:28).
3. Or, "prevented... from speaking". On this word, see 1 Cor 14:39.
4. That is, to continue west from Antioch into the region of Asia, bounded by the regions of Mysia to the north and Phrygia on the east. Later, Paul spends two years in Asia (19:10, 26), based in Ephesus. The seven churches of Rev 2-3 are in Asia.
5. Some manuscripts omit this word {K}.
6. Or, "along, upon, toward, to, down to, over against". GK *2848*.
7. This indicates Paul and Silas turned north (perhaps at Antioch, or at Lystra) instead of continuing west. They end up in northern Phrygia at the latitude of Mysia. The region of Mysia, like part of the region of Phrygia, was part of the Roman province of Asia. The city names are not given. GK *3695*.
8. This is the Roman province north of Asia, and east of the region of Mysia. Instead, Paul and Silas turned west.
9. This phrase "the Spirit *of* Jesus" occurs only here. Some manuscripts say "the Spirit"; others, "the Spirit *of the* Lord" {A}.
10. That is, in terms of ministry. GK *4216*.
11. Troas was a key city on the Aegean Sea (in present day Turkey, like all the cities and regions mentioned in 16:1, 6-8). This city is in the region of Mysia, in the Roman province of Asia. It was a Roman colony.
12. Macedonia is the Roman province across the Aegean Sea from Troas, part of present day Greece.
13. Some think that this man was Luke, who joins Paul in v 10.
14. That is, having crossed the Aegean Sea. On this word, see Heb 11:29.
15. This is the first "we" by which Luke includes himself in Paul's group. Some think Luke joined Paul at this point. "They" came to Troas (v 8), and "we" went to Macedonia (v 10).
16. Or, "bringing together, uniting" the vision with the call. GK *5204*.
17. Some manuscripts say "the Lord" {B}.
18. More literally, "has", as the Greek typically phrases it.
19. Or, "summoned". On this word, see "call to" in 2:39.
20. Some manuscripts say "Therefore" {B}.
21. Elsewhere only in 21:1. GK *2312*. This is a sailing term made from "straight" and "course" (2 Tim 4:7).
22. This is an island in the Aegean Sea, west and north of Troas, almost halfway to Neapolis. GK *4903*.
23. The city of Philippi is about 10 miles or 16 kilometers inland from its port city, Neapolis. GK *3735*.
24. This is a conjectural reading accepted by the UBS committee, and is not found in any Greek manuscript {D}. It is offered because Philippi was not "the" first (chief, leading) city of Macedonia, and because the Romans divided Macedonia into four "districts". Thessalonica was "the" chief city of Macedonia. Amphipolis (17:1) was "the" leading city of the district in which Philippi was located. Others consider this conjecture unnecessary, accepting the reading of the Greek manuscripts, "which is *a* leading city *of* the district...". There are other views. On this word, see 1 Cor 15:13.
25. That is, Philippi was a Roman colony in the province of Macedonia. Used only here. GK *3149*.
26. That is, the gate of the city. Some manuscripts say "city" {K}.
27. Some manuscripts say "*a place* where prayer was the custom" {C}, that is, where group prayer was customarily made. There were apparently not enough Jews (ten men were required) in this Roman colony to have a synagogue.
28. Perhaps Euodia and Syntyche (Phil 4:2) were among these women.
29. Or, "a seller of purple cloth". Thyatira was famous for its purple dyes. It is in the province of Asia. GK *4527*.
30. Or, "faithful *to*, trustworthy *in*". On this word, see "faithful" in Col 1:2.
31. Or, "forced" us, using social force or pressure. Elsewhere only as "strongly urge" in Lk 24:29. GK *4128*.
32. Or, "divination". Used only here. GK *4780*. Not related to the word at the end of the verse. Some manuscripts say "*a spirit of* soothsaying" {N}.
33. Or, "business". Same word as in v 19, and as "business" in 19:24.
34. Or, "acting as a seer, giving oracles, divining". Used only here. GK *3446*.
35. This is the last plural of this "we" section. The next is in 20:5, again in Philippi. Luke does not specifically include himself in the ones beaten and imprisoned next.
36. The hearers may have taken this to mean the highest of the gods they worshiped, not the one and only true God. Or, perhaps they understood it as a reference to the Jewish God. On this word, see "highest" in Mt 21:9.
37. Some manuscripts say "us" {B}.
38. The hearers probably took this to mean one among many ways to salvation, not the only way.
39. Paul was probably annoyed at the place this person was assuming for herself, as well as at her words. No kind of validation from her would be accepted by Paul. On this word, see "greatly disturbed" in 4:2.
40. On this phrase "*at* the very hour", see Lk 2:38.
41. Same word as "depart" and "went out" in v 18. GK *2002*.
42. Same word as 21:30; Jam 2:6. On this word, see "draw" in Jn 6:44.
43. That is, the public square where the rulers and courts were also found. Same word as in 17:17. Used 11 times. GK *59*.
44. That is, the Roman governors of the colony. There were two of them. Used in this sense also in v 22, 35, 36, 38. On this word, see "captain" in 5:26.
45. This word, "throw into confusion, agitate" is used only here. GK *1752*. Related to "disturb" in Gal 1:7.
46. Note 17:7, for example.
47. This word (GK *1639*) is not the same word as in v 20 (GK *5639*).
48. That is, the garments of Paul and Silas. The magistrates probably ordered it done, as in 18:16.
49. The word "beat with rods" is elsewhere only in 2 Cor 11:25. GK *4810*. It was a Roman method of punishment, carried out by the "officers" in v 35. Related to "rod" in 1 Cor 4:21; and "officer" in Act 16:35.
50. Luke uses this idiom "having laid on blows" also in Lk 10:30. "Blows" is the same word as "wounds" in v 33.
51. Same word as in Mk 14:44. Elsewhere only as "with-certainty" in Act 2:36. GK *857*. Related to "certainty" in Act 21:34.

A. 1 Cor 10:13 B. Act 10:3 C. Lk 2:26, see D. Rom 12:8, exhorting E. Rev 12:16 F. Phil 2:21 G. Act 5:42 H. Col 1:12, part J. Act 14:19, think K. Act 13:50 L. 1 Tim 3:8 M. Mk 3:20, house N. Mt 7:1 O. Jn 15:4, abide P. Jn 18:17 Q. Act 17:31, grant R. Lk 23:55 S. Mt 8:29 T. Rom 6:17 U. Phil 1:18 V. Lk 19:9 W. 1 Tim 3:3 X. Lk 20:20 Y. Rev 1:5 Z. Lk 9:2 AA. 1 Cor 6:12 BB. Mk 4:20 CC. Mt 14:28, order

1D. Who, having received such *a* command[A], threw them into the inner prison[B], and secured[1] their feet to the wood[2]   24

6C. And about midnight, Paul and Silas were singing-praise-to[3] God while praying. And the prisoners were listening-to[4] them. °And suddenly *a* great earthquake took place, so that the foundations *of* the jailhouse[5] were shaken[C]   25, 26

1D. And at-once[D] all the doors were opened, and the bonds[6] *of* everyone were unfastened[7]
2D. And the jailer— having become awakened, and having seen the doors *of* the prison having been opened, having drawn[E] *his* sword— was about to kill himself, supposing[F] *that* the prisoners[G] had[8] escaped[H]   27
3D. But Paul called-out *with a* loud voice, saying, "Do no harm[J] *to* yourself, for we are all here"   28
4D. And having asked-*for* lights, he rushed-in. And having become trembling[K], he fell before Paul and Silas. °And having brought them outside, he said, "Sirs[L], what must[M] I do in order that I may be saved[N]?"   29, 30

1E. And the *ones* said, "Put faith upon[9] the Lord Jesus[10], and you will be saved— you and your household". °And they spoke the word *of* the Lord[11] *to* him, along with[12] all the *ones* in his house[13]   31, 32

5D. And having taken them at that hour *of* the night, he washed[O] off *their* wounds   33
6D. And he was baptized[P] at-once[D]— he and all his *household*
7D. And having led them up to *his* house, he set *a* table[14] before *them*, and rejoiced-greatly[Q]— having believed *in* God with-*his*-whole-household[15]   34

7C. And having become day, the magistrates sent forth *their* officers[16], saying, "Release[R] those men"   35

1D. And the jailer reported[S] these words[17] to Paul, that "The magistrates have sent forth in order that you may be released. Now therefore having come out, proceed in peace"   36
2D. But Paul said to them, "Having beaten[T] us *in* public[18]— uncondemned[19] men being Romans[20]— they threw *us* into prison. And now they are throwing us out secretly[U]? No indeed[V]! But having come themselves, let them lead us out!"   37
3D. And the officers reported[S] these words *to* the magistrates   38
4D. And having heard that they were[21] Romans, they became afraid. °And having come, they appealed-to[W] them.[22] And having led *them* out, they were asking *them* to depart from the city   39

8C. And having gone forth from the prison, they went-in to[23] Lydia. And having seen the brothers[24], they encouraged[W] *them*, and went forth   40

5B. Now having traveled-through[X] Amphipolis and Apollonia, they came to Thessalonica,[25] where there was *a* synagogue *of* the Jews   17:1

1C. And in accordance with the *thing* having become-a-custom[26] *with* Paul, he went-in to them. And on three Sabbaths he reasoned[27] *with* them from the Scriptures, °opening[28] *them,* and putting-before[29] them   2, 3

1D. That the Christ had-to[30] suffer[Y] and rise-up[Z] from *the* dead
2D. And that "This *One* is the Christ— the Jesus[31] Whom **I** am proclaiming[AA] *to* you"

2C. And some of them were persuaded[BB] and were allotted-to[32] Paul and Silas— both *a* large number *of* the worshiping[33] Greeks, and not *a* few[34] *of* the leading[35] women[36]   4

1. Or, "made secure". Elsewhere only as "make secure" in Mt 27:64, 65, 66, of Christ's tomb. GK *856*. Related to "securely" in v 23.
2. Or, "beam, log, post", with chains. Or, "in the stocks". This word is used of anything made of wood. The precise method of securing Paul and Silas is not specified by this word. On this word, see "cross" in 1 Pet 2:24.
3. Same word as in Heb 2:12. Elsewhere only as "sing a hymn" in Mt 26:30; Mk 14:26. GK *5630*. Related to "hymn" in Eph 5:19.
4. Or, "overhearing". Used only here. GK *2053*.
5. On this word, see 5:21. Related to "bonds" next; to "prisoner" in v 25, 27; to "jailer" in v 23, 27, 36.
6. Or, "bindings, fetters". On this word, see "imprisonment" in Phil 1:7.
7. Or, "loosened, let go". On this word, see "let go" in Heb 13:5.
8. More literally, "have", as the Greek typically phrases it.
9. On "put faith upon", see Rom 4:5.
10. Some manuscripts add "Christ" {N}.
11. Some manuscripts say "*of* God" {B}.
12. Some manuscripts say "*to* him and *to* all the *ones* in his house" {K}.
13. That is, his family and servants.
14. That is, a table of food.
15. Or, this may be punctuated "rejoiced greatly with *his* whole household— having believed in God", the Greek word order. Used only here. GK *4109*.
16. Or, "lictors, rod-bearers". That is, the authorities who reported to the city magistrates and executed their commands. Elsewhere only in v 38. GK *4812*. Related to "beat with rods" in v 22.
17. Some manuscripts say "the words" {C}.
18. Elsewhere only in 5:18; 18:28; 20:20. GK *1323*. Related to the word in 12:21.
19. That is, without a trial. It was illegal to do this to a Roman citizen. On this word, see 22:25.
20. That is, Roman citizens. Paul was born a citizen, 22:28. Silas was also apparently a Roman citizen.
21. More literally, "are", as the Greek typically phrases it.
22. That is, not to take legal action against them, but to excuse their crime.
23. That is, went-in to her house, or went-in to her presence. This idiom, "to come or go in to" a person, is elsewhere only in Mk 6:25; 15:43; Lk 1:28; Act 10:3; 11:3; 17:2; Rev 3:20. The verb "went in" is the common verb meaning "enter, go in, come in", used 194 times. GK *1656*.
24. That is, the fellow believers, Lydia included, as "brothers" (plural) is sometimes used in the NT. To address a mixed group, "brothers" was used ("sisters" always refers to females). This word means physical brothers (males), but is also used figuratively of fellow family members in a broader sense. The reader can discern from the context whether the reference of the plural is to physical brothers, fellow-members of Abraham's family (male, or male and female Israelites), or fellow-members of God's spiritual family (male, or male and female fellow-believers). Reflecting modern sentiments, when the plural is used figuratively with reference to both men and women, some prefer to make this explicit by rendering this word "brothers and sisters". Used 343 times. GK *81*. Compare "sister" in 1 Cor 9:5.
25. These are three cities in Macedonia, Berea in v 10 being another.
26. Compare 14:1. Same idiom as in Lk 4:16.
27. Or, "discussed, spoke, held a discussion, conversed" to try to convince. Same word as in v 17; 18:4, 19; 19:8, 9. Elsewhere only as "speaking" in Act 20:7, 9; 24:25; Heb 12:5; Jude 9; and "argue" in Mk 9:34; Act 24:12. GK *1363*.
28. Or, "explaining". Same word as in Lk 24:32. Elsewhere only in Mk 7:34; Lk 2:23; 24:31, 45; Act 7:56; 16:14. GK *1380*.
29. Or, "setting before, demonstrating, pointing out". Same word as in Mt 13:24, 31. Elsewhere only as "set before" in Mk 6:41; 8:6, 7; Lk 9:16; 10:8; 11:6; Act 16:34; 1 Cor 10:27; "entrust" in Lk 12:48; 1 Pet 4:19; "commend" in Lk 23:46; Act 14:23; 20:32; and "deposit" in 1 Tim 1:18; 2 Tim 2:2. GK *4192*. Related to "deposit" in 1 Tim 6:20.
30. Or, "That it was necessary *for* the Christ to suffer". On this idiom, see "must" in Mt 16:21.
31. Some manuscripts say "This *One* is the Christ Jesus Whom..."; others, "This *One* is Christ Jesus Whom..."; others, "This *One* is Jesus Christ Whom..." {C}.
32. Or, "were attached to, assigned to". That is, by God. A similar concept is found in 1 Pet 5:3. Others state this from the human point of view ("joined themselves to, attached themselves to") rather than God's point of view. Used only here. GK *4677*. Related to "lot" in 1 Pet 5:3; and "allotted" in Eph 1:11.
33. On this word, see 13:50. Some manuscripts say "*of* the *ones* worshiping and Greeks" {B}.
34. On this idiom, see "no small" in 12:18.
35. Same word as 13:50.
36. Or, "*of the* wives *of* the leading *men*".

A. 1 Tim 1:5 B. Act 5:22 C. Act 17:13 D. Mt 21:19 E. Mk 14:47 F. Act 14:19, think G. Eph 3:1 H. Rom 2:3 J. 3 Jn 11, evil K. Heb 12:21
L. Mt 8:2, master M. Mt 16:21 N. Lk 19:10 O. 2 Pet 2:22 P. Mk 1:8 Q. Lk 10:21 R. Mt 5:31, sends away S. 1 Jn 1:3, announcing T. Jn 18:23
U. Mt 1:19 V. Mt 27:23 W. Rom 12:8, exhorting X. Lk 8:1 Y. Gal 3:4 Z. Lk 18:33 AA. Phil 1:18 BB. 1 Jn 3:19

	3C. But the Jews[1]— having become-jealous[A], and having taking along some evil[B] men *from* the marketplace,[2] and having formed-a-crowd— were throwing the city into-a-commotion[3]	5
	1D. And having suddenly-come-upon[C] the house *of* Jason, they were seeking[D] them[4] to bring *them* forth to the public-assembly[E]	
	2D. But not having found them, they were dragging[F] Jason and some brothers before the city-authorities[5], shouting[G] that	6
	1E. "The *ones* having upset[H] the world[J]— these *ones* are also present[K] here, whom Jason has received[6]	7
	2E. "And these *ones* all are acting contrary to the decrees[L] *of* Caesar[M], saying *that* Jesus is another[7] **king**"	
	3D. And they stirred-up[8] the crowd and the city-authorities hearing these *things*	8
	4D. And having received the bond[9] from Jason and the others, they released[N] them	9
6B.	And the brothers immediately[O] sent-away[P] both Paul and Silas during *the* night to Berea— who, having arrived, were going into the synagogue *of* the Jews	10
	1C. Now these *ones* were more-noble[10] *than* the *ones* in Thessalonica— who[11] received[Q] the word with all eagerness[R], examining[S] the Scriptures daily *to see* if these *things* might hold so[12]	11
	2C. So indeed many of them believed— and not *a* few *of* the prominent[13] Greek women and men	12
	3C. But when the Jews from Thessalonica came-to-know[T] that the word *of* God was proclaimed[U] by Paul in Berea also, they came there also, shaking[14] and stirring-up[15] the crowds	13
	4C. And at that time the brothers immediately[O] sent Paul away, *that he might* go as-far-as[16] to the sea. And both Silas and Timothy remained[V] there	14
7B.	Now the *ones* conducting[17] Paul brought *him* as far as Athens[18]. And having received *a* command[W] for Silas and Timothy that they should come to him as soon as *they could*, they were going away [to them]. And while Paul *was* waiting-for[X] them[19] in Athens, his spirit was being provoked[20] within him while observing[Y] the city being full-of-idols	15 16
	1C. So indeed he was reasoning[Z] in the synagogue *with* the Jews and the *ones* worshiping[21], and in the marketplace every day with the *ones* happening-to-be-there	17
	2C. And some *of* the Epicurean[22] and Stoic[23] philosophers[24] also[25] were conversing[26] *with* him	18
	1D. And some were saying, "What would this scavenger[27] be intending[AA] to say?"	
	2D. And others, "He seems to be *a* proclaimer *of* strange[28] deities[29]"— because he was announcing-the-good-news[BB] *as to* Jesus and the resurrection	
	3C. And having taken-hold-of[CC] him, they brought *him* to the Areopagus[30], saying, "Can we know what this new teaching[DD] being spoken by you *is*? For you are bringing-in[EE] some *things* being strange[31] to our ears. So we want to know what these *things* mean[32]"	19 20
	1D. Now all Athenians and the strangers residing[FF] *there* were finding-an-opportunity[33] for nothing other than to say something or to hear something newer	21
	4C. And Paul, having been stood in *the* midst *of* the Areopagus, said—	22
	1D. "Men[GG], Athenians, I see how you *are* very-religious[34] in all *respects*	

1. Some manuscripts say "But the Jews not being persuaded— having..." {N}, where "not being persuaded" is related to "persuaded" in v 4, and which could also be rendered "But the disobeying Jews...", similar to 14:2.
2. That is, idle people hanging around the marketplace.
3. On the word "throw into a commotion", see Mt 9:23.
4. That is, Paul and Silas.
5. Or, "politarchs". This is the title for the five or six member city council in Thessalonica. Elsewhere only in v 8. GK *4485*.
6. That is, "received as guests". On this word, see Lk 10:38.
7. This word means another of a different kind. On this word, see "different" in 1 Cor 12:9.
8. Or, "agitated, troubled, disturbed". Same word as in v 13. On this word, see "disturb" in Gal 1:7.
9. Or, "the sufficient-amount-of [money]". The city authorities got a pledge from Jason and the others that they would send Paul away, and took a large enough bond to ensure that they did so. Because of this quick and effective expulsion, whereby Paul was "orphaned" (1 Thes 2:17) from them, we have Paul's two letters to the Thessalonians. On this word, see "sufficient" in 2 Cor 3:5.
10. Or, "more-noble-minded, more-open-minded", referring to their spiritual "nobility". The Bereans were open to examining the Scripture on the matter. On this word, see "well-born" in 1 Cor 1:26.
11. This refers back to "these" Bereans.
12. That is, might be true. On this phrase "to hold so", see 12:15.
13. Same word as in 13:50; Mk 15:43. GK *2363*.
14. Or, "agitating, causing to move". Same word as in 2 Thes 2:2; and as Act 2:25; 4:31; 16:26. Used 15 times. GK *4888*.
15. Same word as in v 8. Some manuscripts omit "and stirring up" {B}.
16. Some manuscripts have a word that can make this mean "as-if " to the sea or toward the sea {N}. Some think the Bereans took Paul by boat to Athens; others, that they pretended to be going by sea, but went by land, throwing off their pursuers.
17. That is, the ones "put in charge" of Paul's safe journey. On this word, see "put in charge" in 6:3.
18. The city of Athens is in the Roman province of Achaia.
19. Timothy, at least, did join Paul there, and was then sent back to Thessalonica, 1 Thes 3:1.
20. Or, "stimulated". Whatever emotion was provoked— righteous anger, grief, compassion, love— Paul was clearly provoked to action, as seen by what follows. On this word, see 1 Cor 13:5.
21. On this word, see 13:50. That is, the God-fearing Gentiles.
22. This is a pleasure seeking; eat, drink, and be merry philosophy. Used only here. GK *2134*.
23. This is a philosophy of self-mastery, rationalism, self-sufficiency, austerity, and duty. Used only here. GK *5121*.
24. Used only here. GK *5815*. Related to "philosophy" in Col 2:8.
25. Some manuscripts omit this word {K}.
26. Or, "pondering, debating, disputing". Literally, they were "throwing [words] together" with Paul in a friendly manner, in accordance with the custom of these philosophers. GK *5202*.
27. Or, "babbler". This word was used of birds and people hanging around the marketplace picking up and living off of scraps falling from loads of merchandise. The word literally means "picking up seeds" (the root word is "seed", GK *5065*), and some render it "seed-picker". The philosophers are ridiculing Paul as one picking up scraps of truth from others and passing them on as his own without full understanding. Note that Paul uses phrases and quotations from both philosophies in his speech in v 22-31. "Scavenger" places emphasis on the random gathering of these tidbits of truth; "babbler, chatterer", on the unsophisticated proclamation of them. Used only here. GK *5066*.
28. Related to "being strange" in v 20. Same word as in Heb 13:9.
29. Or, "gods, divinities", as these Greeks used this word. In its other 62 uses in the NT, it is rendered "demons", as Jews and Christians use the word. GK *1228*. Note 1 Cor 10:20. Related to "demon-possessed" in Mt 8:16.
30. Transliterated from the Greek, this word means "hill of Ares" (the Greek god of war, for whom the Roman name was "Mars"). This was used to refer to the hill itself, and to the city's governing council that met there, before whom Paul was taken. One of its members is named in v 34. Elsewhere only in v 22. GK *740*. Related to the word in v 34.
31. Note the polite nuance. The philosophers do not brand Paul's teachings as "strange things", reflecting a conclusion about them. They call them things presently "being strange" to them, about which they want to know more. Same word as "think strange" in 1 Pet 4:4.
32. More literally, "what these *things* intend to be", an idiom elsewhere only in 2:12. Same word as "intending" in v 18. On this word, see "willing" in Jn 7:17.
33. Or, "having leisure, spending the time, finding the time". This is how the Athenians spent their leisure time. Elsewhere only in Mk 6:31; 1 Cor 16:12. GK *2320*. Related to "favorable opportunity" in Mt 26:16; and "opportune" in Mk 6:21.
34. Used only here. GK *1273*. This word is used to mean both "superstitious" and "religious". Related to "deities" in v 18, and "religion" in 25:19.

A. 2 Cor 11:2, jealous for   B. Act 25:18   C. Lk 21:34   D. Phil 2:21   E. Act 19:30   F. Act 8:3, dragging away   G. Mt 3:3   H. Gal 5:12   J. Heb 2:5
K. Rev 17:8   L. Eph 2:15   M. Lk 3:1   N. Mt 5:31, sends away   O. Mt 13:5   P. Act 13:4, sent out   Q. Mt 10:40, welcome   R. 2 Cor 8:19
S. 1 Cor 2:14   T. Lk 1:34, know   U. Phil 1:18   V. Jam 1:12, endure   W. Mk 12:28, commandment   X. Heb 11:10   Y. Lk 10:18, seeing   Z. Act 17:2
AA. Jn 7:17, willing   BB. Act 5:42   CC. Lk 20:20   DD. 1 Cor 14:6   EE. Mt 6:13, bring   FF. Act 2:10   GG. 1 Tim 2:12

	1E. "For while going-about and looking-carefully-at¹ your objects-of-worship^A, I also found *an* altar in which it had been inscribed, 'To *a* not-known² god'	23
	2E. "Therefore what³ you are worshiping⁴ while not-knowing⁵, this **I** am proclaiming^B *to* you	
2D.	"God, the *One* having made the world and all the *things* in it—	24
	1E. "This *One*, being Lord *of* heaven and earth, does not dwell^C in temples^D made-by-*human*-hands⁶	
	2E. "Nor is He served^E by human^F hands, [as if] being-in-need *of* something⁷— He Himself giving life and breath and all *things to* all *people*	25
3D.	"And He made from one *man*⁸ every nation^G *of* mankind⁹	26
	1E. "*That they should* dwell^C upon all *the* face *of* the earth— having determined^H *the* times¹⁰ having been appointed¹¹ *for them*, and the boundaries¹² *of* their dwelling-places¹³	
	2E. "*That they should* seek God¹⁴— if perhaps¹⁵ indeed they might grope-for¹⁶ Him and find *Him,* though indeed *He* being not far from each one *of* us	27
	1F. "For in Him we live and move and exist¹⁷, as also some *of* your^J poets have said¹⁸— 'For we are indeed the *One's* offspring¹⁹'	28
4D.	"Being then offspring *of* God, we ought not to think^K *that* the divine^L *being* is like gold or silver or stone— *a* work²⁰ *of* human^M craft²¹ and thought²²	29
5D.	"So indeed, having overlooked²³ the times *of* ignorance²⁴, God, *as to* the present *things*²⁵, is commanding^N people^M *that* everyone everywhere *should* repent^O	30
	1E. "Because He set²⁶ *a* day on which He is going to judge^P the world^Q in righteousness by *a* Man Whom He designated^H, having granted²⁷ *a* proof²⁸ *to* everyone— having raised Him up^R from *the* dead"	31
5C.	Now having heard-*of a* resurrection^S *of the* dead, some were scoffing²⁹, but others said, "We will indeed again hear you concerning this"³⁰	32
6C.	So Paul went out of their midst	33
7C.	And some men having joined^T him believed^U, among whom also *were*	34
	1D. Dionysius the Areopagite³¹	
	2D. And *a* woman— Damaris *by* name	
	3D. And others with them	
8B.	After these *things,* having departed from Athens, he³² went to Corinth³³	18:1
1C.	And having found *a* certain Jew— Aquila³⁴ *by* name, *a* Pontian³⁵ *by* nationality^V, having recently come from Italy because Claudius³⁶ *had* ordered^W all the Jews to depart from Rome³⁷— and Priscilla³⁸ his wife, he went to them	2
	1D. And because of being the same-trade, he was staying^X with them and working— for they were tent-makers³⁹ *by* trade^Y	3

1. Or, "examining, looking at again and again, considering". Elsewhere only in Heb 13:7. GK *355*.
2. Or, "unknown". Used only here. GK *58*. It is rendered this way to show its relationship to "not-knowing" next.
3. Some manuscripts say "whom..., this *One*..." {N}.
4. Or, "reverencing, showing devotion to". On this word, see "reverence" in 1 Tim 5:4.
5. Or, "being un-knowing". On this word, see "being ignorant of" in Rom 10:3. Related to "not-known", and to "ignorance" in v 30.
6. Same word as in Mk 14:58; Act 7:48; Heb 9:11, 24. Elsewhere only as "done by *human* hands" in Eph 2:11. GK *5935*. The negative of this word is in Mk 14:58.
7. Or, "someone". God does not need the offerings and sacrifices of humans.
8. Some manuscripts say "blood" {B}, so that it says "from one blood".
9. Or, "every race *of* men", "*the* whole race *of* mankind". On this word, see Mt 4:4.
10. That is, the periods of ascendancy, as in the "times" of the Gentiles (Lk 21:24).
11. Or, "commanded, prescribed, fixed, assigned". Elsewhere only as "commanded" in Mt 1:24; 8:4; Mk 1:44; Lk 5:14; Act 10:33, 48. GK *4705*. Some manuscripts say "preappointed" {K}, a related word.
12. Or, "limits". Used only here. GK *3999*.
13. Or, "habitations, settlements, colonies". That is, the limits of each nation's borders. Used only here. GK *3000*. Related to "dwell" earlier in the verse.
14. Some manuscripts say "the Lord" {A}.
15. On "if perhaps", see 8:22. Paul is expressing a hope, yet an uncertainty, about whether they would do so.
16. Or, "feel about for". On this word, see "touch" in Lk 24:39.
17. Or, "are". This is the simple verb "to be", which sometimes is used in the sense of "to exist", on which see Rev 22:14.
18. Paul quotes from Aratus (270 B.C. He was from Paul's country, Cilicia), or from Cleanthes (220 B.C.). Both were Stoics.
19. Or, "family, people". On this word, see "kind" in 1 Cor 12:28.
20. Or, "*a* carved-work, *an* engraved-work" or the "work" of some other craft. This noun refers to the thing made, stamped, engraved, carved, etc. Elsewhere only of the "mark" of the beast (see Rev 13:16). GK *5916*.
21. Whether that craft is stone-cutting, wood-carving, metal-working, etc. Same word as in Rev 18:22. Elsewhere only as "trade" in Act 18:3. GK *5492*. Related to "craftsman" in 19:24.
22. Or, "reflection". On this word, see Heb 4:12. Note the objection to this idea in 19:26.
23. Or, "disregarded, looked beyond". Used only here. GK *5666*.
24. Same word as Peter used in 3:17. On this word, see Eph 4:18. Related to "not knowing" in v 23.
25. That is, as to the present circumstances. Elsewhere only as "*as to* the *things* now" in 4:29; 5:38; 20:32; 27:22. "Now" is GK *3814*.
26. Or, "appointed, fixed, established, caused to stand". GK *2705*.
27. Or, "shown, presented, offered, brought about". Same word as in Lk 7:4; Act 22:2; Col 4:1; 1 Tim 6:17. Elsewhere only as "show" in Act 28:2; Tit 2:7; "offer" in Lk 6:29; "bring about" in Act 16:16; 19:24; and "cause" in Mt 26:10; Mk 14:6; Lk 11:7; 18:5; Gal 6:17; 1 Tim 1:4. GK *4218*.
28. Or, "pledge, assurance". Or, "faith", as this word normally means, "having granted [an opportunity for] faith *to* all"— a thought similar to "a door of faith" in 14:27. Used only here in this sense. On this word, see "faith" in Eph 2:8.
29. Used only here. GK *5949*. Related to the word in 2:13.
30. Some think this was a sincere statement; others, a polite way of putting Paul off for the indefinite future.
31. That is, a member of the council that just heard Paul. Used only here. GK *741*.
32. Some manuscripts say "Paul" {B}.
33. This city was a Roman colony, and the capital of the Roman province of Achaia (Greece).
34. On this man, see Rom 16:3.
35. That is, from Pontus, a region east of Bithynia and Galatia, mentioned also in 2:9; 1 Pet 1:1. Used only here. GK *4507*.
36. Claudius was the Roman Emperor from A.D. 41-54. He is also mentioned in 11:28. GK *3087*.
37. Some think this is referring to an event in A.D. 49, when Claudius expelled the Jews for riots that occurred at the instigation of "Chrestus" (according to Suetonius, by which name some think he means "Christos", Christ).
38. Aquila and Priscilla are mentioned again in v 18, 26. She is called "Prisca" by Paul, on which see Rom 16:3.
39. Used only here. GK *5010*.

A. 2 Thes 2:4 B. Phil 1:18 C. Eph 3:17 D. Rev 11:1 E. Mt 8:7, cure F. 1 Cor 10:13, common to humanity G. Act 15:23, Gentiles H. Rom 1:4, designated J. Eph 1:15 K. Act 14:19 L. 2 Pet 1:4 M. Mt 4:4, mankind N. 1 Tim 1:3 O. Act 26:20 P. Mt 7:1 Q. Heb 2:5 R. Lk 18:33, rise up S. Act 24:15 T. Act 5:13 U. Jn 3:36 V. 1 Cor 12:28, kind W. 1 Cor 7:17, directing X. Jn 15:4, abide Y. Act 17:29, craft

2C. And he was reasoning^A in the synagogue every Sabbath, and persuading^B Jews and Greeks. 4
But when both Silas[1] and Timothy came down from Macedonia,[2] Paul was occupying-*himself*[3] 5
with the word[4], solemnly-testifying^C *to* the Jews *that* the Christ is Jesus[5]

    1D. But while they *were* opposing[6] and blaspheming^D, he said to them, having shaken-out^E 6
his garments, "Your blood *be* upon your head, I *am* clean^F. From now *on* I will go to the
Gentiles"
    2D. And having passed on from there, he entered into *the* house *of a* certain *one* worshiping^G 7
God—Titius[7] Justus *by* name— whose house was bordering[8] *on* the synagogue

  3C. And Crispus[9], the synagogue-official[10], believed *in* the Lord with his whole household. And 8
many *of* the Corinthians hearing were believing and being baptized
  4C. And the Lord said *to* Paul during *the* night through *a* vision^H 9

    1D. "Do not be afraid[11], but be speaking, and do not be silent^J—

      1E. "Because **I** am with you, and no one will set-upon[12] you to harm^K you 10
      2E. "Because there is *a* large people *for* Me in this city"

    2D. And he sat *for a* year and six months,[13] teaching the word *of* God among them 11

  5C. Now while Gallio[14] *was* being proconsul[15] *of* Achaia^L, the Jews with-one-accord^M rose-up- 12
against[16] Paul and brought him before the judgment-seat[17], *saying that "This *one* is 13
persuading[18] people to worship^G God **contrary to the law**"[19]

    1D. And Paul being about to open *his* mouth, Gallio said to the Jews 14

      1E. "**If**[20] it were some crime[21] or evil villainy[22], O Jews, I would have borne-with[23] you
in accordance with reason^N—*but since it is issues[24] about talk[25] and names[26] and 15
your^O Law, see *to it* yourselves. **I** am not willing^P to be *a* judge *of* these *things*"

    2D. And he drove them away from the judgment-seat 16
    3D. And having all[27] taken-hold-of^Q Sosthenes[28], the synagogue-official, they were striking^R 17
him in front of the judgment seat
    4D. And none *of* these *things*[29] was-a-concern^S *to* Gallio

9B. And Paul, having stayed-on^T considerable^U days longer, having said-good-bye^V *to* the brothers[30], 18
was sailing-off to Syria[31]— and Priscilla and Aquila with him— having sheared[32] *his* head in
Cenchrea[33], for he had *a* vow[34]

  1C. And they[35] came to Ephesus[36]. And those[37] *ones* he left-behind^W there[38] 19
  2C. And he himself, having entered into the synagogue, reasoned^A *with* the Jews. *And while they 20
were asking *him* to stay for more time, he did not consent[39]. *But having said-goodbye^V, and 21
having said,[40] "I will return[41] again to you, God willing^X", he put-to-sea from Ephesus
  3C. And having come down to Caesarea^Y, having gone up and greeted^Z the church[42], he went down 22
to Antioch[43]

17A. And having done some time *there*,[44] he went forth,[45] going successively[46] through the Galatian region 23
and Phrygia[47], strengthening^AA all the disciples

1. This is the last mention of Silas in Acts. See 15:40 on him.
2. At this point, Paul wrote 1 Thessalonians (1 Thes 3:6). Some think he also wrote Galatians sometime during this stay at Corinth (see 14:28).
3. Or, "was being occupied *with*, confined *to*". That is, Paul was working full time at it. On this word, see "control" in 2 Cor 5:14.
4. Some manuscripts say "Spirit", so that it says "Paul was compelled *by* the Spirit" {B}.
5. This is the Greek word order. Or, "that Jesus is the Christ". Same phrase and word order as in v 28.
6. Or, "resisting". On this word, see Rom 13:2.
7. Some manuscripts say "Titus"; others omit this word {C}.
8. Or, "was next door *to*, adjoining, adjacent *to*". This is a participle. Used only here. GK *5327*.
9. Crispus is mentioned elsewhere only in 1 Cor 1:14. He was one of the few Paul baptized in Corinth. GK *3214*.
10. Or, "synagogue-leader". Elsewhere only in Mk 5:35, 36, 38; Lk 8:49; 13:14; Act 18:17; and plural in Mk 5:22; Act 13:15. GK *801*.
11. The grammar implies "Stop being afraid".
12. That is, attack. Same word, but different grammar, as "laid on" blows in 16:23. On this word, see "laid on" in Lk 10:30.
13. That is, Paul sat as teacher. During this time, between v 11 and v 18, while Silas and Timothy were still with him (2 Thes 1:1), he wrote 2 Thessalonians.
14. Junius Gallio was the Roman proconsul (governor) of Achaia in A.D. 51-52. He was the brother of Seneca, the philosopher. Elsewhere only in v 14, 17. GK *1136*.
15. Some think Luke means that after the 18 months, shortly after Gallio became proconsul, the Jews rose up against him. On this word, see 13:7.
16. Or, "came down upon". Used only here. GK *2987*.
17. That is, the one of Gallio. He is the highest authority in the province. Same word as in v 16, 17. On this word, see Rom 14:10.
18. Or, with a more negative overtone, "inducing". Used only here. GK *400*.
19. That is, the Roman law shielding Judaism. Gallio rejects this, seeing it as an issue regarding Jewish Law.
20. The grammar means "if it were (but it is not) some crime". Gallio uses grammar that emphasizes the contrast between the two halves of this sentence.
21. Same word as in 24:20. Elsewhere only as "wrongs" in Rev 18:5. GK *93*.
22. Used only here. GK *4815*. Related to the word in 13:10.
23. The grammar indicates Gallio has already made up his mind. On this word, see 2 Cor 11:4.
24. That is, since Paul's offense concerns issues about talk, etc. The grammar means "If, as is the case (in Gallio's opinion)"; that is, "since". Some manuscripts have this word singular, "*an* issue" {N}. On this word, see 15:2.
25. As opposed to deed. Or, "language", or a "word, message". The word is singular. On this word, see "word" in 1 Cor 12:8.
26. Perhaps Gallio means like whether "Jesus" is also "Christ".
27. Some think Luke means Gallio's men drove out Paul and the Jews, and beat Sosthenes in front of Gallio; others, that the Corinthian bystanders beat this Jewish leader. Some manuscripts add "Greeks" {B}, so that it says "all the Greeks having taken hold...". Others think that his fellow Jews beat Sosthenes for having bungled the case.
28. This Sosthenes may also have become a believer, 1 Cor 1:1.
29. Luke may mean the matters raised by the Jews; or, the actions taken toward Sosthenes; or both. Gallio was not concerned about the Jews' request or Paul and the Christians in general, or about Sosthenes in particular.
30. Or, this may be punctuated "... longer *with* the brothers, having said good bye, was sailing-off...".
31. That is, Paul's final destination was Antioch in Syria, from where he began this journey.
32. Or, "cut off [the hair of]". On this word, see 1 Cor 11:6.
33. This is the eastern port city of Corinth, facing Syria and Israel. On this word, see Rom 16:1.
34. Or, a "prayer". Same word as in 21:23. Elsewhere only as "prayer" in Jam 5:15. GK *2376*. As a result of an answered prayer or vow, probably regarding his just completed work in Corinth, Paul cut off his hair. This was a Jewish custom. Related to "pray" in Rom 9:3.
35. Some manuscripts say "he" {B}.
36. This was the capital city of the Roman province of Asia, on the Aegean coast of modern Turkey. Used 16 times. GK *2387*.
37. That is, Priscilla and Aquila.
38. That is, in Ephesus, in preparation for the planned return mentioned next. Paul has chosen Ephesus as his next center of ministry, and leaves these two companions from Corinth to prepare. He seems to have planned this in Corinth, and taken these two with him from there (v 18) for this purpose. Same word as in 21:4.
39. This word is used of nodding in agreement. Used only here. GK *2153*. Related to "nod" in Jn 13:24.
40. Some manuscripts say "But he said goodbye, having said" {K}.
41. Some manuscripts say "said, 'I must by all means make the coming feast in Jerusalem. I will return...'" {A}.
42. Some think Luke means the Jerusalem church, because the verbs "go up" and "go down" are commonly used with reference to Jerusalem.
43. Here Paul completed his second missionary journey from Antioch, to which this church committed him in 15:40. Whether or not Silas also returned is not stated (he is last mentioned in v 5). On this journey, at the Lord's direction (v 9), Paul changed from journeying from city to city, to staying in one city as a center of ministry for an extended period of time (over 18 months, v 11). Paul repeats this latter strategy next in Ephesus, staying over two years.
44. That is, in Antioch.
45. Note that the church at Antioch is not mentioned this time. Paul is returning to his new base of operations in Ephesus/Asia, which he has already chosen and prepared.
46. Or, "in order". On this word, see "successive" in Lk 8:1.
47. Or, "the Galatian and Phrygian region". Paul again travels by land from Antioch, as in 15:41-16:6. Some think the churches of Derbe, Lystra, Iconium, and Pisidian Antioch are again in view here; others, unnamed churches in North Galatia and Phrygia. Some think Luke is referring to two regions; others, to a single region, as in 16:6. Elsewhere only in 2:10; 16:6. GK *5867*.

A. Act 17:2 B. 1 Jn 3:19 C. 1 Tim 5:21, solemnly charge D. 1 Tim 6:1 E. Act 13:51 F. Tit 1:15 G. Act 13:50 H. Act 10:3 J. Mk 4:39, be still K. 1 Pet 3:13, do evil L. Act 19:21 M. Act 14:1 N. 1 Cor 12:8, word O. Eph 1:15 P. Jam 1:18 Q. Lk 20:20 R. Lk 6:29 S. 1 Cor 7:21 T. Act 11:23, continue in U. 2 Cor 3:5, sufficient V. 2 Cor 2:13 W. Act 6:2 X. Jn 7:17 Y. Act 8:40 Z. Mk 15:18 AA. Act 14:22

1B.	Now *a* certain Jew—Apollos[1] by name, *an* Alexandrian[2] *by* nationality[A], *an* eloquent[3] man— came[B] to Ephesus, being powerful[4] in the Scriptures	24
	1C. This *one* had been instructed[5] *as to* the way *of* the Lord[6]. And boiling[7] *in* spirit[8], he was speaking and teaching accurately[C] the *things* concerning Jesus[9], knowing-about[10] only the baptism[D] *of* John[11]	25
	2C. And this *one* began to speak-boldly[E] in the synagogue	26
	3C. And having heard him, Priscilla and Aquila[12] took him aside and explained[F] the way *of* God[13] *to* him more-accurately[14]	
	4C. And he wanting[G] to go to Achaia— the brothers, having urged *him* forward[15], wrote *to* the disciples to welcome[H] him[16]	27
	1D. Who[17], having arrived,[18] greatly helped the *ones* having believed through grace[19]. °For he was vigorously[20] refuting the Jews *in* public[J], showing[21] through the Scriptures *that* the Christ is Jesus	28
2B.	And it came about during Apollos's[22] being in Corinth *that* Paul, having gone through the upper regions[23], came down[24] to Ephesus[25] and found some disciples[26]	19:1
	1C. And[27] he said to them, "Did you receive *the* Holy Spirit, having believed[28]?"	2
	1D. And the *ones* said[29] to him, "But we did not even hear if *the* Holy Spirit is *given*[30]"	
	2D. And he said[31], "Into what then were you baptized?"	3
	3D. And the *ones* said, "Into John's baptism[D]"	
	4D. And Paul said, "John baptized[K] *a* baptism *of* repentance[L], saying *to* the people that they should believe in the *One* coming after him, that is, in Jesus[32]"	4
	5D. And having heard *it*, they were baptized *in*[33] the name *of* the Lord Jesus. °And Paul having laid[M] *his* hands on them, the Holy Spirit came upon[34] them, and they were speaking *in* tongues[35] and prophesying[N]	5-6
	6D. And all the men were [totaling] about twelve	7
	2C. And having entered into the synagogue,[36] he was speaking-boldly[E] for three months, reasoning and persuading[37] *as to* the[38] *things* concerning the kingdom[O] *of* God	8
	3C. But when some were becoming-hardened[39], and were disobeying[40], speaking-evil-of[41] the Way[42] before the assembly[43]— having departed[44] from them, he separated[P] the disciples, reasoning[Q] daily in the school[45] *of* Tyrannus[46]	9
	4C. And this took place for two years,[47] so that all the *ones* dwelling-in[R] Asia[S] heard the word[T] *of* the Lord[48]— both Jews and Greeks	10

1. Apollos is mentioned elsewhere only in 19:1; 1 Cor 1:12; 3:4, 5, 6, 22; 4:6; 16:12; and perhaps in Tit 3:13. GK *663*.
2. That is, Apollos was from the city of Alexandria in Egypt.
3. Or, "learned, educated". Skilled in words and knowledge. Used only here. GK *3360*.
4. Or, "strong, mighty". On this word, see Lk 24:19.
5. This is a participle, "was having been instructed". On this word, see Gal 6:6.
6. That is, Jesus, as Luke says next.
7. Elsewhere only in Rom 12:11, in this same phrase. GK *2417*. Related to "hot" in Rev 3:15.
8. Or, "*in the* Spirit". Some think Luke means being fervent and zealous, having burning zeal; others, motivated by the Holy Spirit.
9. Some manuscripts say "concerning the Lord" {A}.
10. Or, "knowing, being acquainted with, understanding". Same word as in 19:15; 24:10; 26:26. Elsewhere only as "know" in Act 10:28; 15:7; 19:25; 20:18; 22:19; Heb 11:8; Jam 4:14; Jude 10; and "understand" in Mk 14:68; 1 Tim 6:4. GK *2179*. Related to "master" in Lk 5:5; and "knowledgeable" in Jam 3:13.
11. Apollos is a partially instructed Christian, perhaps having been taught by disciples of John the Baptist. What exactly he knew and taught about Jesus is not stated, but it was "accurate" as far as it went. Perhaps his deficiency is seen in those described next in 19:2-6.
12. Paul left these two in Ephesus in v 19. Some manuscripts say "Aquila and Priscilla" {N}.
13. Some manuscripts omit "*of* God" {C}.
14. Same word as "accurately" in v 25, on which see Mt 2:8.
15. Or, "urged *him* on, inclined *him* forward", and thus "encouraged" Apollos to go. Used only here. GK *4730*.
16. In 2 Cor 3:1, Paul reminds the Corinthians that he needed no such letter.
17. That is, Apollos.
18. That is, in the Roman province of Achaia (v 27); specifically, the city of Corinth (19:1), where Paul had just been in 18:1-18, and laid a foundation (1 Cor 3:6-10) for over 18 months (Act 18:11).
19. This is the Greek word order. Some think Luke is describing Apollos who "helped... through grace"; others, the Achaians who "believed through grace".
20. Or, "forcefully". On this word, see Lk 23:10.
21. Or, "demonstrating, proving". Elsewhere only in Mt 16:1; 22:19; 24:1; Lk 17:14; Act 9:39; Heb 6:17. GK *2109*.
22. In 18:24-19:1, Luke takes pains to show how Paul and Apollos related to Ephesus and Corinth (Paul came first to both places), and one another (Apollos received instruction from disciples of Paul). That this was an issue with some in Corinth is clear from 1 Corinthians 1-4, which was written in Act 19:10.
23. Since Ephesus was on the coast, most of Asia between Ephesus and Phrygia (18:23) was upper country in relation to that city. On this word, see "part" in Rom 11:25.
24. Some manuscripts omit this word {C}.
25. This was the capital and chief city of Asia, where Paul was forbidden to go in 16:6. He stopped here briefly in 18:19-21, planning to return. Now he spends over two years here, 19:10. Apollos had just left here, 18:24-27.
26. Some think these are Christian disciples in a similar spiritual condition as Apollos in 18:25; others, disciples of John the Baptist. Some think Luke is implying they were fruit from Apollos's ministry before he met Priscilla and Aquila in 18:26. In any case, Luke's purpose in recording this event may be to demonstrate the apostolic authority of Paul, through whom these receive the Spirit just as it took place through Peter in Act 2, 8, 10, for reasons that are clear from 1 and 2 Corinthians. God gives the Spirit through Paul to ones like Apollos. There are other views of Luke's purpose. There are also differences of opinion as to why only these four occurrences of the giving of the Spirit are recorded in Acts, and the theological inferences to be drawn from this fact and from the events themselves.
27. Some manuscripts say "Ephesus. And having found some disciples, he said..." {N}.
28. Some take this participle to mean "when you believed"; others, "after you believed".
29. Some manuscripts include this word {K}.
30. This word is supplied as in Jn 7:39. Or, "hear whether there is *yet a* Holy Spirit", "hear whether there is *a* Holy Spirit". These disciples were ignorant of the coming and presence of the Spirit, and of the fulfillment of John's teaching, Mt 3:11. As John's disciples, they would have been anticipating the baptism with the Spirit that he taught.
31. Some manuscripts add "to them" {N}.
32. Some manuscripts say "Christ Jesus" {N}.
33. Or, "into". See Mk 1:9 on "baptize in".
34. The Spirit "coming upon" a person occurs elsewhere only in Mt 3:16, of Jesus. A related word is used of the Spirit "coming-upon" a person only in Lk 1:35 (Mary) and Act 1:8 (the apostles). Using different words, the Spirit "fell upon" them in Act 8:16; 10:44; 11:15; and was "poured out upon" them in Act 2:17; 10:45; Tit 3:6.
35. On this word, compare Act 2:4, 11; 10:46; 1 Cor 12:10. First Corinthians was written during Act 19:10.
36. That is, the synagogue Paul said he would return to in 18:21.
37. Same two words as in 18:4, "reasoning and persuading".
38. Some manuscripts omit this word {C}, so that it says "persuading *them* concerning the kingdom *of* God".
39. Or, "were hardening-*themselves*". On this word, see Rom 9:18.
40. Same word as in 14:2.
41. Or, "reviling, insulting". Elsewhere only in Mt 15:4; Mk 7:10; 9:39. GK *2800*.
42. On this name, see 9:2. Same word as in v 23.
43. Or, "crowd, multitude". That is, in the synagogue, v 8. On this word, see "multitude" in 6:2.
44. Or, "withdrawn". On this word, see 1 Tim 4:1.
45. That is, the school building. Used only here. GK *5391*.
46. Whether Tyrannus was the main teacher using the building, or the owner of the building, is not clear. The nature of the school is also not known. Consult the commentaries on the suggestions. Some manuscripts say "*a* certain Tyrannus"; others, "*a* certain Tyrannus, from *the* fifth hour until *the* tenth" {B}, that is, from 11 A.M. to 4 P.M.
47. During this time, Paul wrote 1 Corinthians. Some think he also wrote Galatians (see 14:28).
48. That Luke does not mean that all the Asians heard from Paul personally is clear from Col 1:7 and 2:1, for Colossae is a city in Asia. It was reached by Paul and those who went out from this base in Ephesus. The seven churches mentioned in Revelation may have been started during this time in Asia. Some manuscripts add "Jesus" {K}.

A. 1 Cor 12:28, kind B. Act 26:7, attain C. Mt 2:8 D. Mk 1:4 E. Eph 6:20 F. Act 11:4 G. Jam 1:18, willed H. Act 2:41 J. Act 16:37 K. Mk 1:8 L. 2 Cor 7:10 M. Lk 10:30, laid on N. 1 Cor 14:1 O. Mt 3:2 P. Rom 1:1 Q. Act 17:2 R. Eph 3:17 S. Act 6:9 T. 1 Cor 12:8

| Acts 19:11 | 464 | Verse |

1D. And God was doing not the ordinary¹ miracles^A by the hands *of* Paul—*so that 11-12 handkerchiefs^B or aprons² *were* even being carried-forth³ from his skin⁴ to the *ones* being sick, and the diseases^C *were* being released⁵ from them, and the evil spirits *were* going out⁶

2D. And even⁷ some *of* the Jewish exorcists⁸ going-around^D attempted⁹ to name^E the name *of* 13 the Lord Jesus over the *ones* having the evil spirits, saying, "I¹⁰ make you swear¹¹ *by* the Jesus Whom Paul is proclaiming^F"

    1E. Now there were seven sons *of a* certain Sceva¹², *a* Jewish chief priest, doing this 14

    2E. But having responded, the evil spirit said *to* them, "I know **Jesus**¹³ and know-about¹⁴ 15 Paul— but who are **you**?"

    3E. And the man in whom was the evil spirit— having leaped on them, having subdued¹⁵ 16 all¹⁶ *of them*— prevailed¹⁷ against them, so that *they* fled^G out of that house naked^H and having been wounded^J

    4E. And this became known^K *to* all the *ones* dwelling-in Ephesus— both Jews and 17 Greeks. And fear fell upon them all

3D. And the name *of* the Lord Jesus was being magnified¹⁸

4D. And many *of* the *ones* having believed were coming, confessing-out¹⁹ and declaring²⁰ 18 their [evil] practices^L

5D. And many *of* the *ones* having practiced^M sorceries²¹, having brought-together *their* 19 books²², were burning *them* up in the presence of everyone. And they calculated-up²³ the prices^N *of* them, and found *it to be* fifty thousand silver-coins²⁴

6D. Thus in accordance with *the* might²⁵ *of* the Lord,²⁶ the word²⁷ was growing^O and prevailing 20

18A. Now when these²⁸ *things* were completed^P, Paul put²⁹ in *his* spirit³⁰ *that*, having gone through Macedonia 21 and Achaia³¹, *he should* be going to Jerusalem, having said that "After I come-to-be there, I must^Q also see Rome"³²

    1B. And having sent-out^R two *of* the *ones* ministering^S *with* him to Macedonia³³— Timothy and 22 Erastus— he himself held-on³⁴ in Asia³⁵ *for a* time

    2B. Now about that time, no small disturbance³⁶ took place concerning the Way 23

        1C. For *a* certain Demetrius *by* name, *a* silversmith making silver shrines³⁷ *of* Artemis³⁸, was 24 bringing-about³⁹ no small business⁴⁰ *for* the craftsmen⁴¹—*whom having assembled-together⁴², 25 and the workers⁴³ with respect to such *things,* he said

1. Literally, miracles "not having happened" before. Another understatement (see "no small" in 12:18). That is, unusual, extraordinary miracles, because they took place without Paul's personal presence. This idiom is elsewhere only in 28:2. GK *5593*.
2. That is, aprons such as a worker would wear. Whether these were items belonging to Paul that were repeatedly carried back and forth, or items belonging to the sick brought to Paul, is not stated. Used only here. GK *4980*.
3. Or, "carried away, brought, taken". On this word, see 1 Cor 16:3.
4. Used only here. GK *5999*.
5. Or, "were being ridded, were leaving". Luke speaks from the perspective of the disease (it was removed), rather than the person (he was cured, healed). Elsewhere only in Lk 12:58; Heb 2:15. GK *557*.
6. Some manuscripts add "from them" {K}.
7. Or, "also, indeed". Luke is showing how powerful and well-known Paul's ministry came to be in Ephesus.
8. That is, ones who cast out demons with magical formulas and oaths. They used the sentence given next as part of their incantation. Used only here. GK *2020*. Related to "make swear" next.
9. Or, "undertook, took in hand". See "undertook" in Lk 1:1 on it.
10. Some manuscripts say "We" {N}.
11. Or, "put you under oath, adjure you". This seems to be intended to force the demon to leave rather than swear allegiance to Christ. Elsewhere only in Mk 5:7. GK *3991*. Related to "exorcists" earlier in the verse; "put under oath" in Mt 26:63; "adjure" in 1 Thes 5:27; and "oath" in Jam 5:12.
12. This was the man's name.
13. The grammar emphasizes the contrast between the two halves of this sentence (represented by the bold and the dash). Some manuscripts omit this, in which case "Jesus" would not be bolded, and the dash would be replaced by a comma {C}.
14. Or, "know, am acquainted with". This is a different word for "know", but no difference in meaning may be intended. These two words are not used together elsewhere in the NT. GK *1182, 2179*.
15. Or, "mastered, overpowered". On this word, see "lord over" in 1 Pet 5:3.
16. Or, "both", if only two were present or active participants in this case. Luke may mean both speakers were attacked while the other five fled. On this word, see 23:8. Some manuscripts say "them" {N}.
17. Or, "was strong, mighty, powerful, won out". Same word as in v 20; Rev 12:8. On this word, see "can do" in Gal 5:6.
18. Or, "made great". On this word, see "enlarge" in 2 Cor 10:15.
19. Or, "confessing-openly". Luke may mean "confessing-out *Jesus*", confessing their allegiance to Jesus, as this word is used in Rom 14:11; Phil 2:11. Or, he may mean "confessing-out... their practices", as this word is used in Mk 1:5; Jam 5:16. On this word, see Jam 5:16.
20. Or, "announcing, disclosing". On this word, see Jn 16:13.
21. Or, "magic things, inquiring things". That is, making inquiries of the spirits. GK *4319*.
22. That is, their books or scrolls containing the spells and incantations. On this word, see Mt 1:1.
23. Or, "counted up". Used only here. GK *5248*. Related to "calculate" in Rev 13:18.
24. Probably the Greek drachma (Lk 15:8), which is equivalent to a denarius (Mt 20:2). This is a considerable sum of money. Literally, "five ten-thousands". On this word, see "money" in Mt 25:27.
25. Or, "according to, based on" His might. Some render this phrase as an adverb, "mightily", "So the word *of* the Lord was growing mightily". On this word, see Eph 6:10.
26. This is the Greek word order. Or, "Thus in accordance with *His* might, the word *of* the Lord was growing...". In the former case, the grammar is unusual, but like "in accordance with *the* working of Satan" in 2 Thes 2:9; and like Act 22:3; Rom 16:26; Tit 1:3. In the latter case, the word order of "the word *of* the Lord" would be unique to this verse in the Greek Bible, placing emphasis on "*of* the Lord". However, some manuscripts say "the word *of* the Lord" (as eight times elsewhere in Acts) or, "the word *of* God" (as eleven times elsewhere in Acts) using the normal Greek word order {B}.
27. "The word" is used like this also in 4:4; 6:4; 8:4; 11:19; 14:25; 16:6; 17:11; 18:5. Compare 6:7; 12:24.
28. That is, Paul's ministry in Ephesus, 19:1-20— when his mission to Asia through Ephesus was finished.
29. This word means "put, place, lay" in various senses. Used 100 times. GK *5502*.
30. That is, Paul resolved or established or purposed in his spirit. Or, he "resolved in the Spirit". This phrase is used only here, but it is similar to "put in the heart" in Lk 1:66; 21:14; Act 5:4; all of which all use the same word "put". Compare 20:3, 22.
31. That is, Greece (20:2), the Roman province where Corinth and Athens are located. Elsewhere only in 18:12, 27; Rom 15:26; 1 Cor 16:15; 2 Cor 1:1; 9:2; 11:10; 1 Thes 1:7, 8. GK *938*. Paul will pass through here to strengthen the disciples, and to gather the collection he will take to Jerusalem.
32. Rather than proceeding directly to Rome, Paul envisions a journey to Jerusalem first with an offering by the Gentile churches (see 20:4), and then to Rome (and Spain, Rom 15:28). The rest of the book of Acts is occupied with the journey defined here, which ends where, but not how, Paul envisioned.
33. This trip is mentioned in 1 Cor 4:17; 16:10.
34. Or, "stayed, waited, paused". On this word, see "fix attention on" in 1 Tim 4:16.
35. That is, in Ephesus.
36. Or, "commotion". Same word and phrase as in 12:18. That is, a large disturbance.
37. Or, "temples", that is, miniature replicas of their world-famous temple. On this word, see "temple" in Rev 11:1.
38. This is Artemis of the Ephesians, a many-breasted goddess of fertility whose temple in Ephesus was considered one of the wonders of the world. Some distinguish this Artemis from the Greek goddess Artemis, who was also known as the Roman goddess Diana. Others link the three together. GK *783*.
39. Same word as in 16:16. On this word, see "grant" in 17:31.
40. Same word as in v 25, and as "profit" in 16:16, 19. On this word, see "practice" in Eph 4:19.
41. Same word as in v 38. On this word, see "designer" in Heb 11:10. Related to "craft" in 17:29.
42. The grammar indicates that Demetrius assembled the craftsmen and workers. On this word, see 12:12.
43. Some think Luke means the ones working for the silver craftsmen; others, the workers from related trades who would be affected along with the silver workers, such as ones who made these shrines out of terra cotta.

A. 1 Cor 12:10 B. Jn 11:44, face cloth C. Mt 8:17 D. 1 Tim 5:13 E. 2 Tim 2:19 F. 2 Tim 4:2 G. Rom 2:3, escape H. Jam 2:15 J. Lk 20:12 K. Rom 1:19 L. Mt 16:27 M. Rom 2:1 N. 1 Tim 5:17, honor O. Jn 3:30 P. Eph 5:18, filled Q. Mt 16:21 R. Mk 3:14 S. 1 Pet 4:10

1D. "Men, you know that prosperity¹ *for* us² is from this business^A

2D. "And you are seeing and hearing that this Paul— having persuaded³ *people* not only *from* Ephesus, but *from* almost all Asia— turned-away⁴ *a* considerable crowd, saying that the *gods* being made⁵ with hands are not gods⁶   26

3D. "But not only is-there-a-danger^B *for* us *that* **this** part⁷ *may* come into disrepute⁸, but also   27

    1E. *"That* the temple⁹ *of* the great goddess Artemis *may* be counted^C for nothing

    2E. "And *that she* whom all Asia and the world^D worships^E *may* even be about to be torn-down¹⁰ *from* her majesty^F"

2C. And having heard *it*, and having become full^G *of* rage^H, they were crying-out^J, saying, "Great   28
is Artemis *of the* Ephesians!"

    1D. And the city¹¹ was filled^K *with* confusion¹². And they rushed^L with-one-accord^M into the   29
theater, having seized^N Gaius and Aristarchus¹³— Macedonian fellow-travelers^O *of* Paul

    2D. And while Paul *was* wanting^P to enter into the public-assembly¹⁴, the disciples were not   30
letting^Q him

    3D. And even some *of* the Asian-officials¹⁵— being friends *with* him, having sent to him—   31
were urging^R *him* not to give himself to the theater

3C. Then indeed, other *ones* were crying-out^J another thing.¹⁶ For the assembly was confused¹⁷,   32
and the majority did not know for **what** reason they had come together

4C. And *some* from the crowd gave-instructions-to¹⁸ Alexander— the Jews having put him forward^S   33

    1D. And Alexander, having waved *his* hand, was intending¹⁹ to speak-a-defense^T *to* the public-assembly

    2D. But having recognized^U that he was²⁰ *a* Jew, one voice came²¹ from everyone— crying-   34
out^J for about two hours, "Great *is* Artemis *of the* Ephesians!"

5C. And the town-mayor²², having calmed the crowd, says, "Men, Ephesians, who indeed^V is there   35
of mankind^W who does not know the city *of the* Ephesians *as* being temple-keeper²³ *of* the great²⁴ Artemis, and *of the image* fallen-from-heaven²⁵?

    1D. "These *things* then being undeniable²⁶, you must²⁷ *continue*-being calmed²⁸ and doing   36
nothing reckless— °for you brought *here* these men *being* neither temple-robbers²⁹ nor   37
ones blaspheming³⁰ our³¹ goddess

    2D. "So indeed if Demetrius and the craftsmen with him have *a* complaint³² against anyone,   38
courts³³ are being led,³⁴ and there are proconsuls³⁵. Let them bring-a-charge³⁶ *against* one another

    3D. "Now if you are seeking-for^X anything further³⁷, it will be settled in the lawful³⁸   39
assembly^Y. °For indeed we are in-danger-of^B being charged^Z *with a* riot³⁹ because of   40
today— *there* being no cause⁴⁰ *for it*— in relation to which we will not⁴¹ be able to render^AA *an* account⁴² for this gathering⁴³"

6C. And⁴⁴ having said these *things*, he dismissed^BB the assembly^Y

1. Used only here. GK *2345*. Related to "prospering" in 11:29.
2. Some manuscripts say "our prosperity" {K}.
3. Or, "won over", as in 12:20; or more negatively, "induced". On this word, see 1 Jn 3:19.
4. Or, "removed". Paul removed them from the purview of our business. Elsewhere only as "removed" in Lk 16:4; Act 13:22; 1 Cor 13:2; and "transferred" in Col 1:13. GK *3496*.
5. Or, "coming into being". GK *1181*.
6. That is, the physical idols are not gods, nor are the spiritual beings they purport to represent.
7. That is, their personal interest, their job or trade of shrine-making, their line of work. To this Demetrius next adds a religious motive, the interest of their goddess. The crowd (v 28) responds (at least on the surface) to this latter threat, and the town mayor answers the latter issue in v 35-36. How many times religion is used to protect personal and commercial interests! On this word, see Rom 11:25.
8. Or, "discredit, refutation". Used only here. GK *591*. Related to "expose" in Eph 5:11.
9. Except here, this word is always used of the Jewish temple in Jerusalem, 70 times. GK *2639*. The root word is "holy". See also the unrelated word in Rev 11:1.
10. Or, "thrown down, brought down". On this word, see 2 Cor 10:4, words Paul wrote not long after this (in Act 20:2).
11. Some manuscripts say "the whole city" {N}.
12. Or, "tumult, uproar". Used only here. GK *5180*.
13. Aristarchus was from Thessalonica, and is mentioned also in 20:4; 27:2; Col 4:10; Phm 24. Note 2 Cor 8:18-19.
14. Or, "populace, crowd". Elsewhere only in 12:22; 17:5; 19:33. GK *1322*. Related word in 12:21.
15. Or, "Asiarchs", high officials of the province of Asia who were elected by the cities. Used only here. GK *825*.
16. That is, something different than Demetrius, v 24-27. Perhaps it was something anti-Jewish, causing the Jews to seek to defend themselves in v 33. Christianity was considered to be a sect of Judaism at this time. This literally renders the words of this idiom, which may be more fully phrased "some were crying out one thing; others, another". There is a similar idiom in 21:34.
17. This is a participle, "having been confused". That is, the assembly was in a state of confusion. Related to "confusion" in v 29. On this word, see "confound" in 9:22.
18. Or, "advised" (as this word is used in 1 Cor 2:16, "instruct"). That is, the crowd told Alexander to speak up, or what to say. Or, "concluded, inferred" (as it is used in Act 16:10) that Alexander was the reason. GK *5204*. Some manuscripts have a related word meaning that "they brought forward Alexander from the crowd" {B}. Alexander may be a Jew put forward by the Jews to defend Judaism and distinguish it from Christianity on the advice of some in the crowd. Some take the variant reading to mean he was a Jewish Christian brought forward by the Jews as the local culprit in this matter (like Jason in 17:6).
19. Or, "wanting, wishing". On this word, see "willing" in Jn 7:17.
20. More literally, "is", as the Greek typically phrases it.
21. Or, "came about, arose". GK *1181*.
22. Or, "town-clerk, town-secretary". This man was the chief executive of the city. He answered to the proconsul. GK *1208*.
23. Or, "temple guardian". Used only here. GK *3753*.
24. Some manuscripts add "goddess" {K}, as in v 27.
25. The Ephesians taught that the statue of Artemis fell from heaven. Note how this proves Paul's point reflected in v 26. Even they felt the need to claim a heavenly origin for their idol! Used only here. GK *1479*.
26. In spite of the fears of Demetrius (v 27), nothing has changed these facts, so stay calm. Used only here. GK *394*. Related to "without objection" in 10:29.
27. Same word as in Mt 16:21, with different grammar.
28. Or, "restrained, quiet". More literally, "it is being necessary *that* you be having been calmed". That is, it continues to be necessary that you remain being calmed. Though cumbersome in English, the Greek tenses and participles are quite vivid. Elsewhere only in v 35. GK *2948*.
29. Or, "sacrilegious *ones*", ones who commit acts of sacrilege. Used only here. GK *2645*. Related word in Rom 2:22.
30. Thus, Gaius and Aristarchus (v 29) have committed no crime. On this word, see 1 Tim 6:1.
31. Some manuscripts say "your" {B}.
32. Or, "matter". On this word, see "word" in 1 Cor 12:8.
33. Elsewhere only as "marketplace" in 17:5. GK *61*.
34. That is, they are in session. Legal recourse is available through the local courts in the marketplaces.
35. On this word, see 13:7. Recourse through the Roman governor is also available. There was only one proconsul at a time for a province. The mayor is referring to the entire category, using an abstract plural.
36. Same word as in v 40, "being charged". On this word, see Rom 8:33.
37. Or, "more, in addition". That is, anything beyond what can be settled in a private court action, anything requiring a lawful town meeting. Used only here. GK *4304*. Some manuscripts say "anything concerning other *matters*" {B}.
38. This assembly was not lawful. On this word, see "within the law" in 1 Cor 9:21.
39. This is the real concern of the leaders in v 31, and this man. Their city-state status itself— but more realistically, the job of this very official— would be endangered if it fell into mayhem and mob violence. Rome would not tolerate it. On this word, see "dispute" in 23:7.
40. Or, "source". No guilty person or crime can be pointed to as a cause for it. On this word, see "guilt" in Lk 23:4.
41. That is, in relation to which charge of rioting we will not be able to defend ourselves. Some manuscripts omit this word {C}, so that it reads "today— *there* being no cause in relation to which we will be able to render *an* account for this gathering". In either case, the point is that their conduct was not justifiable.
42. This phrase "render *an* account" is elsewhere only in Mt 12:36; Lk 16:2; Heb 13:17; 1 Pet 4:5. Compare Rom 14:12. On this word, see "word" in 1 Cor 12:8.
43. That is, "*disorderly* gathering", based on the context. On this word, see 23:12.
44. English translations number this as verse 41.

A. Act 19:24 B. 1 Cor 15:30, are in danger C. Rom 3:28, consider D. Heb 2:5 E. Act 13:50 F. Lk 9:43 G. Mt 14:20 H. Rev 16:19, fury J. Mt 8:29 K. Act 2:4 L. Act 7:57 M. Act 1:14 N. Lk 8:29 O. 2 Cor 8:19 P. Jam 1:18, willed Q. 1 Cor 10:13, allow R. Rom 12:8, exhorting S. Lk 21:30, put forth T. Lk 21:14 U. Col 1:6, understood V. Mt 27:23 W. Mt 4:4 X. Phil 4:17 Y. Rev 22:16, church Z. Rom 8:33, bring a charge AA. Mt 16:27 BB. Mt 5:31, sends away

3B.	And after the uproar[A] ceased[B], Paul— having sent for the disciples and having encouraged[1] *them*, having said-farewell[C]— went forth to proceed[2] to Macedonia.[3] °And having gone through those regions,[4] and having encouraged them *with* much speaking[5], he came to Greece[6]	20:1 2
4B.	And having done three months *there*, a plot[D] having been made[7] *against* him by the Jews while *he was* about to put-to-sea[E] for Syria— he became *of a* mind[8] *that he should* be returning[F] through Macedonia[9]	3
	1C. And Sopater, *son of* Pyrrhus[10], *a* Berean[11] was accompanying him[12]; and Aristarchus[13] and Secundus *of the* Thessalonians; and Gaius, *a* Derbean[14]; and Timothy[15]; and Tychicus[16] and Trophimus[17], Asians[18]	4
	2C. But these, having gone ahead,[19] were awaiting[G] us[20] in Troas	5
5B.	And **we** sailed-off[21] from Philippi after the days *of* the *Feast of* Unleavened-Bread[H], and came to them at Troas within five days, where we spent[J] seven days	6
	1C. And on the first *day of* the week, we[22] having been gathered together to break bread[23], Paul was speaking[K] *to* them, being about to go away *on* the next day. And he was extending the message[L] until midnight[24]. °And there were many lamps[M] in the upper-room[N] where we[25] had been gathered-together[26]	7 8
	2C. And *a* certain young-man[O], Eutychus *by* name, sitting on the window [sill], *was* being carried-away[27] *by a* deep[P] sleep[Q] while Paul *was* speaking further[28]. Having been carried-away by the sleep, he fell down from the third floor, and was picked-up dead[R]	9
	3C. But having gone down, Paul fell upon him, and having embraced[29] *him*, said, "Do not be thrown-into-a-commotion[30], for his life[S] is in him!"	10
	4C. And having gone up, and having broken[T] the bread and eaten[31], and having conversed[U] for *a* considerable *time*, until daybreak[32], in this manner he departed	11
	5C. And they brought[33] the boy [along] alive[34]. And they were not moderately[35] comforted[36]	12
6B.	And **we**[37], having gone ahead to the ship, put-to-sea[38] for Assos, intending[V] from there to pick-up[W] Paul. For thus having arranged[39] *it*, **he** was intending[V] to go-on-foot[40]. °And as he was meeting[41] us in Assos, having picked him up, we came to Mitylene[42]. °And having sailed-away[43] from there *on* the following[44] *day*, we arrived opposite[45] Chios[46]. And *on* another *day* we crossed-over[47] to Samos. And[48] *on* the next[49] *day*, we came to Miletus[50]	13 14 15
	1C. For Paul had determined[51] to sail-by Ephesus so that it might not happen *to* him *that he* lose-time[52] in Asia. For he was hurrying to be in Jerusalem— if it might be possible *for* him— the day *of* Pentecost[53]	16
	2C. But having sent from Miletus to Ephesus, he summoned[X] the elders[54] *of* the church	17
	3C. And when they came to him, he said *to* them—	18

1. Or, "exhorted". Same word as in v 2, on which see "exhort" in Rom 12:8. Some manuscripts say "disciples, having said farewell" {K}.
2. Paul is departing according to his plan in 19:21. The uproar did not force him to leave.
3. Along the way, Paul stopped in Troas, 2 Cor 2:12-13.
4. On this trip, Paul met Titus (2 Cor 7:5-7) and wrote 2 Corinthians.
5. Same phrase as "long message" in 15:32. Here Luke is referring to multiple messages and locations.
6. Greece is the more popular term for the Roman province of Achaia (see 19:21). Specifically, Paul came to the city of Corinth. During the three months here, he wrote Romans (having set his sights on Rome in 19:21), and perhaps Galatians (see 14:28). Used only here. GK *1817*.
7. Or, "having arisen". GK *1181*.
8. Or, "purpose, intention, judgment, decision, opinion". Some paraphrase this phrase as "he decided". On this word, see "purpose" in 1 Cor 1:10.
9. That is, to go by land from Corinth back up to Philippi (v 6), and then sail from its port city, Neapolis.
10. Some manuscripts omit "*son of* Pyrrhus" {B}.
11. That is, from the city of Berea, 17:10.
12. Some manuscripts add "until Asia" {B}.
13. See 19:29 on him.
14. That is, from Derbe in Galatia. The Gaius in 19:29 was from Macedonia.
15. Timothy was from Lystra in Galatia, 16:1.
16. Mentioned elsewhere only in Eph 6:21; Col 4:7; 2 Tim 4:12; Tit 3:12. GK *5608*.
17. Trophimus is from Ephesus (21:29), in the province of Asia.
18. These are the delegates carrying the offering from the churches of Macedonia, Galatia and Asia to the poor believers in Jerusalem, mentioned in 1 Cor 16:1-4, 2 Cor 8-9, and Rom 15:26. This collection is not directly mentioned in Acts (see 21:18). Note that there is no Corinthian (Achaian) mentioned, but Paul refers to their gift in Rom 15:26. Perhaps they entrusted their gift to one of these men, or to Paul himself. Perhaps Luke, who also now travels with Paul to Jerusalem (see v 5), was the delegate from Philippi.
19. The group went by sea as planned (v 3) to Troas, while Paul and Luke went by land to Philippi, and then by sea to Troas.
20. Luke reappears. The last "us" was also in Philippi in 16:17. He may have been there since then. Some think he lived there. The accounts that follow are far more detailed, reflecting Luke's eyewitness status.
21. Or, "sailed out". Elsewhere only in 15:39; 18:18. GK *1739*. Related to "sail away" in v 15; "sail" in 21:3.
22. Some manuscripts say "the disciples" {K}.
23. Some think Luke means to eat a meal; others, the Lord's Supper; others both. Same word as in v 11. Some think they ate dinner early in the evening, and the Lord's Supper in v 11. See 2:46 on this.
24. Some think Luke means midnight Saturday night (as we call it), based on the Jewish day which began at sunset; others, midnight Sunday night (as we call it), based on the Greek day which began at sunrise.
25. Some manuscripts say "they" {N}.
26. This is a participle, where "we were having been gathered-together".
27. Or, "overwhelmed, overcome". Same word as later in the verse. GK *2965*.
28. Or, "to *the* more". On this idiom, see 2 Tim 2:16.
29. That is, put his arms around him. Used only here. GK *5227*.
30. That is, such as was normally done for the dead. The grammar implies the people had started mourning Eutychus, and should stop doing it. On this word, see Mt 9:23, where this was happening.
31. The subject of all this is singular, referring to Paul. Luke may mean that Paul himself now ate, having delayed it due to his speaking to these people. Same word as in 23:14.
32. Or, "daylight, dawn". Used only here. GK *879*.
33. Luke may mean the group brought Eutychus along as they walked with Paul toward the ship. Or, he may mean they brought him "[home]" after the meeting.
34. Or, "living". This is a participle. On this word, see "came to life" in Rev 20:4.
35. Or, "measurably, within measure". Used only here. GK *3585*. Related to "measure" in Jn 3:34.
36. Another of Luke's wonderful understatements (litotes, see 12:18). The people were comforted beyond measure.
37. That is, Luke and the others. Paul walks to Assos, a city about 20 miles or 32 kilometers south of Troas.
38. Used in this sense also in Lk 8:22; Act 13:13; 16:11; 18:21; 20:3; 21:1, 2; 27:2, 4, 12, 21; 28:10, 11. On this word, see "led up" in Mt 4:1.
39. Or, "directed, commanded". See "directing" in 1 Cor 7:17 on it.
40. Or, "go by land" (versus sea), not necessarily meaning on foot. Used only here. GK *4269*.
41. That is, in the process of meeting us. While we expect Luke to say "when he met us" (and many render it such), this is not what he says. The grammar seems to imply that Luke and the others arrived first and met Paul as he was proceeding to meet them in Assos (as opposed to Paul arriving first at Assos, and meeting them at the dock).
42. This city is on the Aegean island of Lesbos, south of Assos. GK *3639*.
43. Elsewhere only in 13:4; 14:26; 27:1. GK *676*. Related to "sail off" in v 6; "sail by" in v 16; "sail" in 21:3.
44. Or, "... there, *on* the following *day* we arrived...". Elsewhere only in 7:26; 16:11; 21:18; 23:11. GK *2079*.
45. Luke probably means they anchored off shore at Chios. Used only here. GK *513*.
46. Chios and Samos are islands still further south.
47. Or, "came near, approached". Luke does not say whether they stopped there. Used only here. GK *4125*.
48. Some manuscripts say "And having stayed at Trogyllium, *on* the next-day..." {B}. Trogyllium may refer to a city on the mainland, opposite from Samos, or to the strait between it and Samos.
49. On this idiom, see Lk 13:33. Luke uses three different expressions to refer to "the next day" in this verse, a fourth in v 7, and a fifth in 21:1.
50. This city is on the coast of the province of Asia, about 30 miles or 48 kilometers south of Ephesus. The ship may have been in this port for seven days, as in Troas (v 6), and in Tyre (21:4). GK *3626*.
51. Or, "judged, decided". This decision seems to have been made in Troas in v 13, when Paul chose this ship. On this word, see "judge" in Mt 7:1.
52. Or, "waste time, spend time". Used only here. GK *5990*. Related to "spend time" in 12:19.
53. On Pentecost, see 2:1. To do so, Paul had about forty-three days from Philippi in v 6.
54. On this word, see 1 Tim 5:17. Paul calls them "overseers" in v 28.

A. Mk 5:38, commotion   B. 1 Cor 13:8   C. Mk 15:18, greet   D. Act 23:30   E. Act 20:13   F. 2 Pet 2:21, turn back   G. Jn 15:4, abide   H. Mk 14:12
J. Act 12:19, spend time   K. Act 17:2, reasoned   L. 1 Cor 12:8, word   M. Mt 25:1   N. Act 1:13   O. Act 7:58   P. Lk 24:1   Q. Jn 11:13, slumber
R. Mt 8:22   S. Jam 5:20, soul   T. Act 2:46   U. Act 24:26   V. Mk 10:32, going to   W. Act 1:2, taken up   X. Act 10:32

1D. "**You** know, from *the* first day from which I set-foot¹ in Asia²—

    1E. "How I **was**³ with you the whole time—˚serving⁴ the Lord with all humblemindedness⁵, and tears⁶, and trials^A (the *ones* having happened^B *to* me by the plots^C *of* the Jews)   19

    2E. "How⁷ I in no way drew-back⁸ *from* the *things* being profitable⁹ *so as* not to declare^D *them to* you and teach you *in* public^E and from house-to-house—˚while¹⁰ solemnly-testifying¹¹ both *to* Jews and *to* Greeks *as to* the repentance^F toward God and faith^G in our Lord Jesus¹²   20 / 21

2D. "And now, behold— having been bound¹³ *in my* spirit,¹⁴ **I** am going to Jerusalem   22

    1E. "Not knowing the *things that* will meet¹⁵ me in it—˚except that the Holy Spirit is solemnly-warning me¹⁶ in each city¹⁷, saying that imprisonment^H and afflictions^J are awaiting^K me   23

    2E. "But I am making *my* life^L *of* no account¹⁸ *as to* value *to* myself,¹⁹ so-as^M to finish^N my course²⁰ and the ministry²¹ which I received from the Lord Jesus— to solemnly-testify *to* the good-news^O *about* the grace *of* God   24

3D. "And now, behold— **I** know that **you all,** among whom I went-about proclaiming^P the kingdom²², will no longer see my face²³   25

    1E. "Therefore, I am bearing-witness^Q *to* you on this very day²⁴ that I am clean²⁵ *of* the blood *of* everyone. ˚For I did not draw back *so as* not to declare²⁶ the whole purpose²⁷ *of* God *to* you   26 / 27

    2E. "Take heed to²⁸ yourselves,²⁹ and *to* all the flock^R among which the Holy Spirit placed³⁰ **you** *as* overseers^S— to shepherd³¹ the church *of* God³² which He obtained³³ with³⁴ *His* own³⁵ blood³⁶   28

        1F. "**I** know³⁷ that after my departure savage wolves will come in among you, not sparing^T the flock   29

        2F. "And men will rise-up^U from you yourselves, speaking *things* having been perverted^V, *that they might* be drawing-away^W the disciples after them   30

        3F. "Therefore keep-watching^X, remembering³⁸ that night and day *for* three years I did not cease^Y admonishing^Z each one *of you* with tears^AA   31

4D. "And *as to* the *things* now,³⁹ I commend⁴⁰ you *to* God⁴¹, and *to* the word *of* His grace being⁴² able to build *you* up and to give *you* the inheritance^BB among all the *ones* having been sanctified⁴³   32

5D. "I coveted^CC *the* silver or gold or clothing *of* no one. ˚**You**⁴⁴ know that **these hands** served⁴⁵ my *own* needs, and the *people* being with me. ˚In all *respects,* I showed^DD you that laboring in this manner, it-is-necessary⁴⁶ to help⁴⁷ the *ones* being weak and remember the words *of* the Lord Jesus—   33-34 / 35

    1E. That He Himself said,⁴⁸ 'It is more blessed^EE to be giving than to be receiving' "

4C. And having said these *things*, having put-*down* his knees with them all, he prayed⁴⁹   36

5C. And there was much weeping^FF *from* everyone. And having fallen upon the neck *of* Paul, they were kissing^GG him, ˚suffering-pain^HH especially over the statement^JJ which he had spoken— that they were⁵⁰ no longer going see his face   37 / 38

6C. And they were accompanying^KK him to the ship

1. More literally, "went on [the ground]". On this word, see 21:4.
2. Paul was in Ephesus briefly in 18:19-21, then in 19:1-41 for about three years, v 31.
3. Or, "became, proved to be". GK *1181*. That is, how Paul conducted himself with the Ephesians, how he behaved with them, his manner of life with them.
4. Or, "serving-as-a-slave *to*". On, this word, see "are slaves" in Rom 6:6.
5. On this word, see Phil 2:3. Same phrase as in Eph 4:2.
6. Elsewhere only in v 31; Lk 7:38, 44; 2 Cor 2:4; 2 Tim 1:4; Heb 5:7; 12:17; Rev 7:17; 21:4. GK *1232*. Note Phil 3:18. Some manuscripts say "many tears" {K}.
7. Or, "That". GK *6055*. Not the same word as in the previous statement (GK *4802*).
8. Or, "shrank, withdrew". Paul's trials did not cause him to keep silent about the truth. Same word as in v 27. Elsewhere only in Gal 2:12; Heb 10:38. GK *5713*. Related to "drawing back" in Heb 10:39.
9. Or, "beneficial, advantageous, helpful". That is, the whole purpose of God, v 27. On this word, see "beneficial" in 1 Cor 6:12.
10. Paul did not draw back from teaching the Ephesians as believers, while also solemnly testifying to unbelievers.
11. On this word, see "solemnly charge" in 1 Tim 5:21. Same word as in v 24, and as "solemnly warn" in v 23.
12. Some manuscripts add "Christ" {B}.
13. Or, "tied". Same word as in 21:11, 13, 33; 24:27; Col 4:3. On this word, see 1 Cor 7:27.
14. Or, "*by* the Spirit". Verse 22-23 contrasts the Spirit's warnings with Paul's own spirit's determination (formed in submission to God). Paul has an inward constraint to go there, knowing nothing of the outcome except the affliction the Spirit says is coming. The Spirit is warning him, not binding him. Because of his determination to proceed with the plan of 19:21, we have Romans, Ephesians, Philippians, Colossians, Philemon, Luke and Acts.
15. Or, "encounter, befall, happen *to*". Elsewhere only in Lk 9:37; 22:10; Act 10:25; Heb 7:1, 10. GK *5267*.
16. Some manuscripts omit this word {K}.
17. Or, "city by city, in every city, according to city".
18. That is, continuing to live is not a factor when Paul counts the things of value to him— only finishing his course. His determination is not influenced by the certainty of affliction awaiting him, which is a measure of how sure he was that he was following the course God intended for him.
19. Some manuscripts say "But I make *an* account *of* none *of* these *things*, nor do I hold my life *as* precious *to* myself " {N}, in which, "precious" is the same word as "value" (see "precious" in 2 Pet 1:4).
20. Same word as in 2 Tim 4:7, where Paul has done so. Some manuscripts add "with joy" {N}.
21. On this word, see 1 Cor 12:5. Paul defines his ministry next, as "to solemnly testify...".
22. Some manuscripts add "*of* God" {N}. On this word, see Mt 3:2.
23. This is because Paul plans to go from Jerusalem directly to Rome (19:21), and beyond.
24. This is an idiom, "on the today day", on which see Rom 11:8.
25. Or, "pure". Same statement as in 18:6. On this word, see Tit 1:15.
26. Same words and grammar as in "drew back *so as* not to declare" in v 20. On this word, see Jn 16:13.
27. Or, "plan, counsel". On this word, see "counsel" in Eph 1:11. Romans is a sample of Paul's teaching on this.
28. Some manuscripts say "Therefore take heed to..." {K}.
29. On "take heed to yourselves", see Lk 12:1.
30. Or, "put, set, appointed, established, made". On this word, see "put" in 19:21.
31. Same word as in 1 Pet 5:2. On this word, see Rev 19:15. Related to "flock".
32. Some manuscripts say "*of the* Lord" {C}. "Church *of the* Lord" is not found elsewhere in the NT. "Church *of* God" is in 1 Cor 1:2; 10:32; 11:16, 22; 15:9; 2 Cor 1:1; Gal 1:13; 1 Thes 2:14; 2 Thes 1:4; 1 Tim 3:5, 15. Some think an early copyist unconsciously changed it to the more familiar "church of God". Others think an early copyist may have been troubled over ascribing blood to God, and substituted the easier "Lord".
33. Or, "acquired, gained for Himself". On this word, see 1 Tim 3:13.
34. Or, "through, by, via". GK *1328*.
35. This word is used 114 times. GK *2625*.
36. Some render this phrase in the usual, natural fashion, "*His* own blood" (calling Christ "God"), as in the only other places "*His* own" is used with this grammar, Jn 1:41, *"his* own brother"; Jn 5:43, "*his* own name"; Jn 7:18, *"his* own glory"; and Act 1:25, "*his* own place". Others, thinking for various reasons that Paul could not intend to refer to the blood of God, render this "the blood *of His* own *Son*". The grammar can have this meaning, and the word "own" standing alone is used this way in Act 4:23, *"their* own *people*"; Act 24:23, "*his* own *people*"; and 1 Tim 5:8, "*his* own *relatives*". Some manuscripts have different grammar (which is identical to that in Heb 9:12 and 13:12) that allows only the first possibility {A}.
37. Some manuscripts say "For I know this— that..." {N}.
38. That is, keeping in mind. Same word as in v 35. On this word, see Jn 16:21.
39. That is, as to your present circumstances. On this phrase, see "as to the present *things*" in 17:30. Some manuscripts add "brothers" {K}.
40. Same word as in 14:23.
41. Some manuscripts say "*to the* Lord" {B}.
42. The phrase that follows modifies "word". Or, "*to* God and *to* the word *of* His grace, *to* the *One* being able...". In this case, God and His word are grouped together, and a second reference to God begins here.
43. Or, "set apart *to* God, made holy". On this word, see Heb 10:29.
44. Some manuscripts say "And **you**..." {K}, which some render, "Yes, **you**...".
45. Or, "assisted, helped". On this word, see 13:36.
46. Or, "*You* must help, *one* must help". On this idiom, see "must" in Mt 16:21.
47. On this word, see 1 Tim 6:2. That is, take a part corresponding to the need of the weak. Related to "helps" in 1 Cor 12:28.
48. This is not recorded in the Gospels. It is one of the things mentioned in Jn 21:25.
49. This is the Greek word order. Or, "knees, he prayed with them all".
50. More literally, "are", as the Greek typically phrases it.

A. Jam 1:2 B. Act 21:35 C. Act 23:30 D. Jn 16:13 E. Act 16:37 F. 2 Cor 7:10 G. Eph 2:8 H. Phil 1:7 J. Rev 7:14 K. Jn 15:4, abide L. Jam 5:20, soul M. Lk 9:52 N. Heb 2:10, perfect O. 1 Cor 15:1 P. 2 Tim 4:2 Q. 1 Thes 2:12, testify R. 1 Pet 5:2 S. Phil 1:1 T. Rom 11:21 U. Lk 18:33 V. Phil 2:15 W. Act 21:1, withdraw X. 1 Thes 5:6 Y. 1 Cor 13:8 Z. Col 1:28 AA. Act 20:19 BB. Eph 1:14 CC. Gal 5:17, desire DD. Mt 3:7 EE. Lk 6:20 FF. Mt 8:12 GG. Mt 26:49 HH. Lk 2:48 JJ. 1 Cor 12:8, word KK. Rom 15:24, sent forward

| Acts 21:1 | 472 | Verse |

7B. And when it came about *that* having withdrawn[1] from them we put-to-sea[A], having run-a-straight-course[B], we came to Cos,[2] and *on* the next[3] *day* to Rhodes, and from there to Patara[4]. °And having found *a* ship crossing-over to Phoenicia[5], having boarded[C], we put-to-sea. °And having sighted[D] Cyprus, and having left it behind on the left, we were sailing to Syria. And we came down to Tyre, for there the ship was unloading *its* cargo[E]   21:1 / 2 / 3

    1C. And having found[F] the[6] disciples, we stayed there[G] seven days— who were telling Paul through the Spirit not to be setting-foot[7] in Jerusalem   4

    2C. But when it came about *that* we finished[H] the days,[8] having gone out, we were proceeding— everyone accompanying[J] us, with wives and children, as far as outside the city   5

        1D. And having put *down our* knees on the beach, having prayed,[9] °we said-farewell to one another   6

        2D. And we went-up into the ship, and those *ones* returned to *their* own *things*[10]

8B. And **we**, having completed[11] the voyage from Tyre, arrived in Ptolemais[12]. And having greeted[K] the brothers, we stayed with them one day. °And having gone-out[13] *on* the next day, we[14] came to Caesarea[15]. And having entered into the house *of* Philip the evangelist[16] (being *one* of the seven[17]), we stayed with him °(and this *one* had[18] four virgin[L] daughters prophesying[19]!)   7 / 8 / 9

    1C. And while *we were* staying-on[M] *for* more[20] days, *a* certain prophet[N] from Judea, Agabus[21] *by* name, came down. °And having come to us, and having taken Paul's belt[O], having bound[P] his *own* feet and hands, he said   10 / 11

        1D. "These *things* says the Holy Spirit— 'In this manner the Jews in Jerusalem will bind[P] the man whose belt[O] this is, and hand *him* over[Q] into *the* hands *of the* Gentiles' "

    2C. And when we heard these *things*, both we and the local-residents[22] were begging[R] *that* he not be going up to Jerusalem   12

    3C. Then[23] Paul responded, "What are you doing, weeping[S] and breaking my heart? For **I** am ready[24] not only to be bound[P], but even to die in Jerusalem for the name *of* the Lord Jesus"   13

    4C. And he not being persuaded[T], we were quiet[25], having said, "Let the Lord's will be done[U]"   14

9B. And after these[26] days, having made-preparations[27], we were going up to Jerusalem. °And *some of* the disciples from Caesarea also came with us, bringing *us to* Mnason[28]— *a* certain Cyprian, *an* old[29] disciple, with whom we might lodge[V]. °And we having come-to-be in Jerusalem, the brothers welcomed[W] us gladly   15-16 / 17

    1C. And *on* the following *day,* Paul was going in with us[30] to James[X], and all the elders[Y] were present   18

        1D. And having greeted[K] them, he was describing[31] individually[32] each *of the things* which God did among the Gentiles through his ministry[Z]   19

        2D. And the *ones,* having heard *it,* were glorifying[AA] God[33]. And they said *to* him, "You see, brother, how many myriads[34] *of* the *ones* having believed there are among the Jews![35]   20

            1E. "And they are all zealots[36] *for* the Law

            2E. "And they were informed[37] about you— that you are teaching all the Jews throughout the nations[38] **apostasy**[BB] from Moses, saying *that* they *should* not be circumcising *their* children, nor walking[CC] in *their* customs[DD]   21

            3E. "What, then, is *to be* done? They[39] will surely[EE] hear that you have come. °Therefore do this[40] which we tell you—   22-23

1. Or, "having been parted, drawn away". Same word as in Mt 26:51; Lk 22:41. Elsewhere only as "draw away" in Act 20:30. GK *685*.
2. Cos and Rhodes are islands further south from Miletus. At this point the ship makes the turn eastward toward Judea. GK *3271*.
3. Same word as in Lk 9:37; Act 25:17; 27:18. Elsewhere only as "afterwards" in Lk 7:11 (different grammar). GK *2009*.
4. This city is on the coast of the Roman province of Lycia. GK *4249*.
5. This is the coastal region where the cities of Tyre and Sidon are found, and is part of the Roman province of Syria. Note that Luke uses all three names here, Syria, Phoenicia, Tyre. Elsewhere only in 11:19; 15:3. GK *5834*. Paul's group changed to a ship making a direct run to Tyre, a journey of about three to five days.
6. There has probably been a church here since 11:19. Note 15:3. Some manuscripts omit this word {K}.
7. Same word as in 20:18; 25:1. More literally, "going upon [the ground]". Elsewhere only as "boarded" (gotten on) in Act 21:2; 27:2; and "mounted" (gotten on) in Mt 21:5. GK *2094*. Some manuscripts say "go up to Jerusalem" {K}.
8. That is, the days permitted to the group based on the ship's departure date.
9. Some manuscripts say "beach, we prayed. And having said farewell to one another, we went up..." {K}.
10. On this phrase "to *their* own *things*", see Jn 19:27.
11. Or, "continued". Some think Luke means that they finished the entire voyage by ship in Ptolemais, and that they next went by land to Caesarea; others, that they finished the voyage from Tyre in Ptolemais, then continued on by sea to Caesarea. Used only here. GK *1382*.
12. This coastal city is between Tyre and Caesarea, about 30 miles or 48 kilometers from Caesarea. GK *4767*.
13. Same word as in v 5. It could mean out to the ship as in v 5, or out on foot to Caesarea.
14. Some manuscripts say "we, the *ones* around Paul, came...". Others say "the *ones* around Paul came" {A}.
15. On this seaport, see 8:40.
16. On this word, see Eph 4:11. On Philip, see Act 6:5. He was last mentioned in this town, 8:40.
17. That is, one of the seven chosen in 6:5. Same idea as "the twelve".
18. This is an idiom, literally, "And there were *for* this *one*...".
19. Luke tells us a remarkable fact about this family. On this word, see 1 Cor 14:1.
20. Perhaps Luke means more than at first intended.
21. Agabus predicted the famine in 11:28.
22. Or, "the ones belonging to that place". Note Luke's perspective. Used only here. GK *1954*.
23. Some manuscripts say "Then Paul responded and said...". Others take "then" (meaning "at that time") with the previous verse, "Jerusalem at that time. And Paul responded...". Others say "And Paul responded" {B}.
24. This is an idiom, literally "I am holding *myself* ready", on which see 1 Pet 4:5.
25. Same word as in 11:18.
26. That is, the days spent in Caesarea, v 10.
27. Or, "having packed up, gotten ready" for the journey. It may imply "having packed up" the horses. Used only here. GK *2171*.
28. Some render this "bringing Mnason *with them*".
29. That is, one from the early days of the church. Same word as in 15:7.
30. Luke does not tell us whether this group of "us" (presumably including those in 20:4) delivered the collection at this time (he never mentions this collection in Acts. Paul may refer to it in 24:17). This is the last "we" of the section that began in 20:5, where Luke includes himself. He is physically separated from Paul in v 26-27 (as a non-Jew, and then by the imprisonment). Luke reappears in 27:1.
31. Same word as in 15:12.
32. This is an idiom, on which see Eph 5:33.
33. Some manuscripts say "the Lord" {N}.
34. Or, "ten thousands". Used as a literal number in Act 19:19 (50,000 is five 10,000's) and Rev 9:16. Elsewhere only as "myriads", a large number of uncounted thousands in Lk 12:1; Heb 12:22; Jude 14; Rev 5:11. GK *3689*. Related to "ten thousand" in Mt 18:24, and 1 Cor 4:15;14:19.
35. That is, how many myriads of believers there are among the Jews. Some manuscripts say "myriads *of* Jews there are *of* the *ones* having believed" {N}, which means the same thing..
36. But these believing Jews are not the ones in v 27. On this word, see 1 Cor 14:12.
37. Same word as in v 24. On this word, see "instructed" in Gal 6:6.
38. That is, the Jews in the dispersion. The objection raised by the Jewish believers is not to teaching the Gentiles in this way, but to teaching Jewish believers to abandon the Law of Moses. On this word, see "Gentiles" in 15:23.
39. Some manuscripts say "The multitude must surely come together. For they will hear..." {B}. The believers must assemble and discuss Paul and this matter.
40. This plan is aimed at correcting the false information given to the Jewish Christians (v 20) about Paul.

A. Act 20:13 B. Act 16:11 C. Act 21:4, setting foot D. Lk 19:11, appear E. Rev 18:11 F. Lk 2:16 G. Lk 9:27, here H. 2 Tim 3:17, equipped J. Rom 15:24, sent forward K. Mk 15:18 L. Rev 14:4 M. Rom 11:22, continue N. 1 Cor 12:28 O. Rev 1:13 P. 1 Cor 7:27 Q. Mt 26:21, hand over R. Rom 12:8, exhorting S. Jn 11:33 T. 1 Jn 3:19 U. Mt 6:10 V. Act 10:6 W. Act 2:41 X. Mt 13:55 Y. 1 Tim 5:17 Z. 1 Cor 12:5 AA. Rom 8:30 BB. 2 Thes 2:3 CC. Heb 13:9 DD. Lk 1:9 EE. 1 Cor 9:10

		1F.	"There are four men *with* us having *a* vow¹ upon themselves²	
		2F.	"Having taken along these *men*, be purified³ together-with them. And spend⁴ *money* for them, so that they will shave^A the head	24
		3F.	"And everyone will know⁵ that there is nothing *true of the things* which they have been informed about you, but even you yourself are walking-in-line⁶, keeping^B the Law	
	4E.		"But concerning the Gentiles having believed— **we** wrote-to⁷ *them,* having determined⁸ that they⁹ should guard-themselves¹⁰ *as to* food-sacrificed-to-an-idol and blood and *the* strangled *thing* and sexual immorality"	25
2C.	Then Paul— having taken along the men *on* the next¹¹ *day*, having been purified together-with them— was going into the temple, giving-notice *as to* the completion *of* the days *of* purification, until which *time* the offering¹² was offered^C for each one *of* them¹³			26
3C.	But as the seven days were about to be completed^D, the Jews from Asia,¹⁴ having seen him in the temple, were stirring-up¹⁵ the whole crowd			27
	1D.		And they put *their* hands on him, crying-out^E, "Men^F, Israelites, help^G! This is the man teaching everyone everywhere against *our* people and the Law and this place. And furthermore, he also brought Greeks into the temple, and has defiled^H this holy place"	28
		1E.	For they had previously-seen¹⁶ Trophimus¹⁷ the Ephesian in the city with him, whom they were supposing^J that Paul brought into the temple^K	29
	2D.		And the whole city was set-in-motion¹⁸, and *a* running-together¹⁹ *of* the people took place	30
	3D.		And having taken-hold-of^L Paul, they were dragging²⁰ him outside *of* the temple. And immediately^M the doors were shut^N	
4C.	And while *they were* seeking^O to kill him, *a* report went up *to* the commander²¹ *of* the [Roman] cohort^P that all Jerusalem was²² stirred-up— who at-once^Q, having taken along soldiers and centurions²³, ran down upon them			31 32
	1D.		And the *ones*, having seen the commander and the soldiers, ceased^R striking^S Paul	
	2D.		Then having drawn-near^T, the commander took-hold-of^L him	33
		1E.	And he ordered^U *that he* be bound *with* two chains^V	
		2E.	And he was inquiring^W *as to* who he might be and what he has done²⁴. But other *ones* in the crowd were calling-out^X another thing²⁵	34
	3D.		And he not being able to know the certainty²⁶ *of it* because of the uproar^Y— he ordered^U *that* he be brought into the barracks^Z	
	4D.		But when he²⁷ came-to-be on the stairs, it happened²⁸ *that* he was carried by the soldiers because of the violence^AA *of* the crowd— for the multitude *of* the people were following, crying-out^E, "Take him away"	35 36
5C.	And being about to be brought into the barracks, Paul says *to* the commander, "Is it permissible^BB *for* me to say something to you²⁹?"			37
	1D.		And the *one* said, "You know Greek? Then are **you** not the Egyptian— the *one* before these days having caused-an-upset³⁰ and led out into the wilderness the four-thousand men *of* the Assassins³¹?"	38

1. On this word, see 18:18. Upon completion of their vow, these four would cut their hair, as Paul did in 18:18.
2. For details on this vow, see Num 6.
3. Same word as in v 26. On this word, see 1 Jn 3:3.
4. That is, pay their expenses, showing your support for them. This was perceived as a good deed for a Jew, an act of charity. Elsewhere only in Mk 5:26; Lk 15:14; 2 Cor 12:15; Jam 4:3. GK *1251*. Related to "cost" in Lk 14:28.
5. Some manuscripts instead say "... in order that they will shave the head and all may know..." {K}.
6. That is, that Paul has not abandoned his Jewish heritage. On this word, see Gal 5:25.
7. Same word as in 15:20, where this occurred. In other words, the Jewish believers are not saying Gentiles should perform the Jewish customs Paul was being asked to do in v 24. On this word, see Heb 13:22. Some manuscripts say "we sent [a letter], having..." {C}.
8. Same word as 16:4.
9. Some manuscripts say "they *should* keep no such *thing*, except *that* they *should* guard..." {B}.
10. Or, "be on guard against", and so "avoid". Same word as in Lk 12:15; 2 Pet 3:17. Same word as "keeping" in 16:4 and 21:24, with different grammar. On this word, see "keep" in Jn 12:25. Not related to "abstain" in 15:29. On the four items, see 15:20, 29.
11. On this idiom, "*on* the next *day*", see Lk 13:33.
12. Elsewhere only in 24:17; Rom 15:16; Eph 5:2; Heb 10:5, 8, 10, 14, 18. GK *4714*. Related to "offer" next.
13. That is, Paul was going in repeatedly until the offerings for all five of them were completed.
14. This plan (v 23-24) would have worked with the local Jewish Christians. But when these Jews from Asia (Ephesus) recognized Paul and Trophimus (v 29), they aroused the Jerusalem Jews, and the believers could do nothing.
15. Same word as in v 31. On this word, see "confound" in 9:22.
16. This is a participle, "they were having previously seen".
17. Trophimus came with Paul in 20:4. He is mentioned elsewhere only in 2 Tim 4:20, as left sick at Miletus. GK *5576*.
18. Or, "aroused". On this word, see "move" in Rev 2:5.
19. Used only here. GK *5282*. The related verb is in 3:11.
20. Same word as in 16:19.
21. His name was Claudius Lysias, 23:26. This word means a military commander of 1000 men, similar to a modern major or colonel. In the Roman army, this person was known as a "tribune", and commanded a cohort of about 600 men plus support staff. Centurions reported to him. He was in charge of Jerusalem in the absence of the procurator (governor). He reported to the procurator, who for Lysias was Felix, 23:24. Felix was in Caesarea at this time. Used in this sense in Mk 6:21; Jn 18:12; Act 21:31, 32, 33, 37; 22:24, 26, 27, 28, 29; 23:10, 15, 17, 18, 19, 22; 24:22; 25:23. Elsewhere only in Rev 6:15; 19:18. GK *5941*.
22. More literally, "is", as the Greek typically phrases it.
23. These were commanders of 100 men. On this word, see Mt 8:5.
24. This is a participle, what "he is having done".
25. That is, than the one speaking. This is the literal rendering of this idiom. It may be more fully phrased as "some in the crowd were calling out one thing; others, another". This idiom is similar to the one in 19:32.
26. Same word as in 22:30, and as "certain" in 25:26, where Festus still struggles with it. Elsewhere only as "secure" in Heb 6:19; and "safe" in Phil 3:1. GK *855*. Related to "securely" in Act 16:23; "make secure" in 16:24; and "certainty" in Lk 1:4.
27. That is, Paul. Paul is carried off by the soldiers.
28. Elsewhere only in Mk 10:32; Lk 24:14; Act 3:10; 20:19; 1 Cor 10:11; 1 Pet 4:12; 2 Pet 2:22. GK *5201*.
29. Some manuscripts say "to speak to you" {N}.
30. Or, "caused a rebellion, revolt". On this word, see "upset" in Gal 5:12.
31. Or, "Sicarii". This was the name of a radical Jewish nationalist group that used assassination against their political opponents. The word means "dagger", and is used only here. Josephus speaks of them and of this Egyptian. Used only here. GK *4974*.

A. 1 Cor 11:5 B. Jn 12:25 C. Heb 5:7 D. Mk 13:4, accomplished E. Mt 8:29 F. 1 Tim 2:12 G. Rev 12:16 H. Mk 7:15 J. Act 14:19, think
K. Act 19:27 L. Lk 20:20 M. Mt 13:5 N. Jn 20:19, locked O. Phil 2:21 P. Mt 27:27 Q. Mk 6:25 R. 1 Cor 13:8 S. Lk 6:29 T. Lk 21:28
U. Mt 14:28 V. Act 28:20 W. Act 23:34, learn X. Act 12:22 Y. Mk 5:38, commotion Z. Rev 20:9, camp AA. Act 5:26 BB. 1 Cor 6:12, lawful

| Acts 21:39 | 476 | Verse |

    2D. And Paul said, "**I**[1] am *a* Jewish man from-Tarsus *of* Cilicia[2], *a* citizen[A] *of* no insignificant[3] city— and I beg[B] you, permit[C] me to speak to the people"   39

    6C. And he having permitted[C] *it,* Paul, standing on the stairs, motioned *with his* hand *to* the people. And *a* great silence having come about, he addressed *them in* the Hebrew[4] language[D], saying—   40

        1D. "Men[E], brothers[F], and fathers, hear my defense[G] to you now"   22:1

            1E. And having heard that he was addressing them *in* the Hebrew language[D], they granted[H] more quietness[J]   2

        2D. And he says, *"**I** am[5] *a* Jewish man   3

            1E. "Having been born in Tarsus *of* Cilicia, but having been brought-up in this city[6]
            2E. "Having been trained[K] at the feet *of* Gamaliel[7] in accordance with *the* strictness[8] the Law *of my* ancestor[9]
            3E. "Being *a* zealot[L] *for* God just as[10] **you** all are today—*who persecuted[M] this Way[11] to the point *of* death, binding[12] and handing-over[N] both men and women to prisons,   4
as indeed the high priest testifies[O] *concerning* me, and the whole Council-of-elders[P]   5

                1F. "From whom also having received letters to the brothers[F], I was proceeding[13] to Damascus *to* bring[14] bound[15] to Jerusalem even the *ones* being there, in order that they might be punished[16]

        3D. "But it came about *in* my proceeding and drawing-near[Q] *to* Damascus about mid-day[R],   6
that suddenly[S] *a* great light from heaven flashed[17] around me. *And I fell to the ground[18],   7
and heard *a* voice saying *to* me, 'Saul, Saul, why are you persecuting[M] Me?'

            1E. "And **I** answered, 'Who are You, sir?'[19]   8
            2E. "And He said to me, '**I** am Jesus the Nazarene[T], Whom **you** are persecuting'
            3E. "And the *ones* being with me saw **the light**[20]— but did not hear[21] the voice *of* the *One* speaking *to* me   9
            4E. "And I said, 'What shall I do, Lord?'   10
            5E. "And the Lord said to me, 'Having arisen, proceed into Damascus. And there it will be told you concerning everything which has been assigned[22] *to* you to do'
            6E. "But since I was not seeing because of the glory *of* that light, I came into Damascus being hand-led[U] by the *ones* being with me   11

        4D. "And *a* certain Ananias— *a* reverent[V] man in-relation-to[23] the Law, being attested[W] by all   12
the Jews dwelling[X] there[24], *having come to me, and having stood near— said *to* me,   13
'Brother Saul, see again'

            1E. "And **I** looked-up[25] at him *at* the very hour[26]
            2E. "And the *one* said—   14

                1F. 'The God *of* our fathers appointed[27] you

                    1G. 'To know[Y] His will[28]
                    2G. 'And to see[Z] the Righteous *One*[29] and hear *a* voice from His mouth
                    3G. 'Because you will be *a* witness[AA] *for* Him to all people *of the things* which you have seen and *which* you heard   15

1. Paul uses grammar that implies he will make a second statement, which is the request in the second half of this sentence. He links together his answer and his request.
2. Tarsus was the capital city in the Roman province of Cilicia.
3. On this idiom, see "no small" in 12:18.
4. That is, the spoken language of the Hebrews at that time, which modern linguists call Aramaic. Elsewhere only in 22:2; 26:14. GK *1579*. Related to the word in 6:1; and in Jn 19:20.
5. Some manuscripts have the same grammar as in 21:39, which indicates that additional statements about himself will follow {N}.
6. That is, Jerusalem.
7. Gamaliel was a famous and respected rabbi, mentioned elsewhere only in 5:34. GK *1137*.
8. Or, "exactness, precision, minuteness, accurateness". Used only here. GK *205*. Related to "strictest" in 26:5, and to "accurately" in Mt 2:8.
9. That is, the Law passed down from my father. Paul was a son of Pharisees, 23:6. On this word, see 24:14.
10. Paul also was a zealot acting "not in accordance with knowledge" (Rom 10:2) at that time in his life.
11. On this term, see 9:2.
12. This word is used with "chains and shackles" in Lk 8:29. On this word, see "bind-up" in Mt 23:4.
13. Paul was an official, authorized agent of the Sanhedrin in this matter, from whom he was proceeding.
14. On the grammar of this word, see "*to* do" in 24:17.
15. This is a participle, "having been bound". On this word, see 1 Cor 7:27. Not related to the word in v 4.
16. Elsewhere only in 26:11, where the purpose is stated— to force these believers to blaspheme Jesus. GK *5512*. Related to "punishment" in Heb 10:29.
17. Same word as in 9:3, but here "around" is also expressed separately.
18. This word refers to the "bottom" of anything. Used only here. GK *1611*.
19. See 9:5 on this question. "Sir" is the same word as "Lord" in v 10.
20. Paul uses grammar that emphasizes the contrast between the two halves of this sentence. Some manuscripts add "and became terrified" {B}.
21. Both "hear" and "voice" are the same words as in 9:7 (the grammar is different, but this in itself requires no difference in meaning). "Hear" is the common word meaning "hear, hear of, listen to", used 428 times. GK *201*. In this context, "hear" means "understand", as it does in Mk 4:33; 1 Cor 14:2. In 9:7, the others heard the sound, but saw no one. Here, they saw the light, but did not understand the voice. Both taken together give the full picture. Compare Jn 12:29.
22. Or, "appointed". On this word, see "established" in Rom 13:1.
23. Or, "with reference to, according to" the requirements of the Law. GK *2848*.
24. Some manuscripts say "dwelling in Damascus" {B}.
25. Same word as "see again" earlier, and in 9:12, 17. It means "to receive sight, see again", and simply "to look up". Here it combines both ideas, Paul saw again and looked up at Ananias. Used 25 times. GK *329*.
26. On this phrase, see Lk 2:38.
27. Or, "selected, chose, took into *His* hand, prepared *for Himself*". Elsewhere only in 3:20; 26:16. GK *4741*. The root word is "hand".
28. That is, His "whole purpose" 20:27. On this word, see Jn 7:17.
29. That is, Jesus.

A. Heb 8:11, fellow citizen   B. 2 Cor 8:4   C. 1 Tim 2:12   D. Act 2:6   E. 1 Tim 2:12   F. Act 16:40   G. 1 Pet 3:15   H. Act 17:31   J. 1 Tim 2:11   K. 1 Cor 11:32, disciplined   L. 1 Cor 14:12   M. 2 Tim 3:12   N. Mt 26:21   O. Jn 1:7   P. 1 Tim 4:14   Q. Lk 21:28   R. Act 8:26, south   S. Lk 2:13   T. Mt 2:23   U. Act 9:8   V. Lk 2:25   W. Act 6:3   X. Eph 3:17   Y. Lk 1:34   Z. Lk 2:26   AA. Act 1:8

Acts 22:16	478	Verse

      2F. 'And now, why are you delaying? Having arisen, be baptized[A], and wash-away[B] your sins, having called-upon[C] His name[1]' — 16

  5D. "And it came about *at* my having returned to Jerusalem, and while I *was* praying in the temple, *that* I came-to-be in *a* trance[D], °and saw Him saying *to* me, 'Hurry[E], and go out from Jerusalem quickly[F], because they will not accept[G] your testimony[H] about Me' — 17, 18

      1E. "And **I** said, 'Lord, they themselves know that throughout the synagogues[2] **I** was imprisoning and beating[J] the *ones* putting-faith upon[3] You. °And when the blood *of* Stephen Your witness[4] was being shed[K], I myself also was standing-near and giving-approval[5] and guarding[L] the garments *of* the *ones* killing him'[6] — 19, 20

      2E. "And He said to me, 'Be going, because **I** will send you out[M], far away to *the* Gentiles'" — 21

7C. And they were listening-to him up to this statement[N]. And they raised their voice, saying, "Take away such *a one* from the earth, for it was not proper[7] *that* he *continue*-living[8]" — 22

8C. And while they *were* shouting[9] and throwing-off *their* cloaks and throwing dust into the air, the commander ordered *that* he be brought into the barracks— having said *that* he *should* be interrogated[10] with whips[11], in order that he might learn[O] for what reason they were calling-out[12] *against* him in this manner — 23, 24

  1D. But when they stretched him out *with* the straps[13], Paul said to the centurion[P] standing *there*, "Is it lawful[Q] *for* you to whip *a* man *who* is *a* Roman and uncondemned[14]?" — 25

  2D. And having heard *it*, the centurion, having gone to the commander, reported[R], saying, "What[15] are you about to do? For this man is *a* Roman" — 26

  3D. And having gone to *him*, the commander said *to* him, "Tell me, are **you** *a* Roman?" — 27

      1E. And the *one* said, "Yes"

      2E. And the commander responded, "**I** acquired[S] this citizenship[T] *with a* large sum [of money]" — 28

      3E. And Paul said, "But **I** indeed have been born[16] *one*"

  4D. So the *ones* being about to interrogate him **immediately** withdrew[U] from him — 29

  5D. And the commander also became afraid, having learned[O] that he was[17] *a* Roman, and because he had bound[18] him

9C. And *on* the next day, wanting to know the certainty[V] *as to* why he was[19] being accused[W] by the Jews, he released[20] him, and ordered the chief priests and the whole Sanhedrin to come together. And having brought Paul down, he stood *him* before them — 30

  1D. And Paul, having looked-intently[X] *at* the Sanhedrin, said, "Men, brothers, **I** have conducted-myself[21] *with* all good conscience[22] *before* God up to this day" — 23:1

      1E. And the high priest Ananias[23] commanded[Y] the *ones* standing near him to strike[Z] his mouth[24] — 2

      2E. Then Paul said to him, "God is going to **strike** you— whitewashed[25] wall! Do **You** indeed sit *there* judging[AA] me according to the Law, and violating-the-Law[26], order[BB] *that* I be struck[Z]?" — 3

      3E. And the *ones* standing near said, "Are you reviling[CC] the high priest *of* God?" — 4

      4E. And Paul said, "I did not know[DD], brothers, that he was[27] high priest.[28] For it has been written [in Ex 22:28] that 'You shall not speak badly[29] *of a* ruler[EE] *of* your people'" — 5

1. Some manuscripts say "the name *of the* Lord" {K}.
2. Or, "synagogue by synagogue, according to the synagogues". Compare 26:11 where "all" is added.
3. On "put faith upon", see Rom 4:5.
4. Or, "martyr". On this word, see Rev 2:13.
5. Same word as in 8:1. Some manuscripts add "*to* his killing" {N}, as in 8:1.
6. Paul offers this as evidence that he is the most qualified one to reach those in Jerusalem.
7. Or, "fitting". Elsewhere only in Rom 1:28. GK *2763*.
8. This idiom means "he ought to have been killed long ago", "he should not have been permitted to live this long", "his death is long overdue" (as opposed to "he should be killed right now"). Compare 25:24.
9. Elsewhere only in Mt 12:19; Lk 4:41; Jn 11:43; 12:13; 18:40; 19:6, 12, 15. GK *3198*. Related to "clamor" in Act 23:9, and "cry out' in Mt 8:29.
10. Or, "examined". Elsewhere only in v 29. GK *458*. Related to "search out" in Mt 10:11.
11. On this word, see "scourge" in Mk 3:10. Related to the verb in v 25.
12. Same word as in 21:34.
13. Or, "*for* the straps", that is, for the whips. This word refers to a leather thong or strap, and could refer either to that with which the soldiers secured Paul, or to the leather straps in the whip. Elsewhere only of the "strap" of a sandal in Mk 1:7; Lk 3:16; Jn 1:27. GK *2666*.
14. Without a Roman judgment against Paul, the answer is no. Elsewhere only in 16:37. GK *185*.
15. Some manuscripts say "Watch what you are about to do" {A}.
16. This means that Paul's father or a previous ancestor had somehow become a citizen. For some theories, consult the commentaries. On this word, see 1 Jn 2:29.
17. More literally, "is", as the Greek typically phrases it.
18. This is a participle, "he was having bound". The commander's treatment of Paul broke the Roman law.
19. More literally, "is", as the Greek typically phrases it.
20. Or, "unbound him". Some manuscripts add "from the bonds" {N}.

Paul's case now became one with regard to Jewish law rather than Roman law. The commander would have to decide what to do with Paul after hearing the Sanhedrin's charges against him, and would keep him in protective custody until that time. As it turns out, Paul remains in this status until the end of the book. If the Jews charged and convicted Paul of desecrating the temple by bringing in a Gentile (21:28-29), the commander would execute him in accordance with Jewish law regarding the temple, even though he was a Roman citizen (but by sword, not in a disgraceful way like crucifixion). On this word, see "break" in Mt 5:19.
21. Or, "conducted-*my*-citizenship". On this word, see Phil 1:27.
22. Elsewhere only in 24:16; Rom 2:15; 9:1; 13:5; 1 Cor 8:7, 10, 12; 10:25, 27, 28, 29; 2 Cor 1:12; 4:2; 5:11; 1 Tim 1:5, 19; 3:9; 4:2; 2 Tim 1:3; Tit 1:15; Heb 9:9, 14; 10:22; 13:18; 1 Pet 3:16, 21; and as "consciousness" in Heb 10:2; 1 Pet 2:19. GK *5287*. It means "consciousness", and, "moral consciousness, conscience". The root words mean "to know together with, to have co-knowledge", so the conscience is the moral knowledge that we have together with the action itself.
23. Ananias is mentioned elsewhere only in 24:1. He was high priest from A.D. 47-58. GK *393*.
24. Whether or not Paul was struck is not stated. Paul either interrupts the command, or responds after it is done.
25. This is a participle, wall "having been whitewashed". On this word, see Mt 23:27.
26. Or, "breaking-the-Law, acting-contrary-to-the-Law". This is a participle. Used only here. GK *4174*. Related to "law-violation" in 2 Pet 2:16.
27. More literally, "is", as the Greek typically phrases it.
28. On the suggestions as to why Paul did not know this, consult the commentaries. Some think this was an informal inquiry by the Roman commander held in the Roman fortress.
29. Or, "evil-ly", referring to the name Paul called Ananias in v 3. GK *2809*. Related to "evil" in v 9.

A. Mk 1:8   B. 1 Cor 6:11   C. 1 Pet 1:17   D. Act 10:10   E. 2 Pet 3:12, hasten   F. Rev 1:1   G. Mk 4:20   H. Jn 1:7   J. Jn 18:23   K. Mt 26:28, poured out   L. Jn 12:25, keep   M. Gal 4:4, sent forth   N. 1 Cor 12:8, word   O. Col 1:6, understood   P. Mt 8:5   Q. 1 Cor 6:12   R. 1 Jn 1:3, announcing   S. 1 Thes 4:4   T. Eph 2:12   U. 1 Tim 4:1, depart   V. Act 21:34   W. Jn 5:45   X. Lk 4:20   Y. Lk 8:25   Z. Lk 6:29   AA. Mt 7:1   BB. Mt 14:28   CC. 1 Cor 4:12   DD. 1 Jn 2:29   EE. Rev 1:5

| Acts 23:6 | 480 | Verse |

    2D. And Paul, having known that the one part *of them* was¹ *of* Sadducees and the other *of*   6
Pharisees, was crying-out^A in the Sanhedrin, "Men, brothers, **I** am *a* Pharisee, *a* son *of*
Pharisees². **I**³ am being judged^B concerning *the* hope⁴ and⁵ resurrection *of the* dead"

        1E. And he having said this, *a* dispute⁶ *between* the Pharisees and Sadducees took place,   7
and the assembly^C was divided⁷

            1F. For **Sadducees**⁸ say *that* there is not *a* resurrection, nor *an* angel, nor *a* spirit—   8
but Pharisees confess^D all⁹ *three*

        2E. And *a* great clamor¹⁰ took place   9
        3E. And having stood up, some¹¹ *of* the scribes *of* the Pharisees' part¹² were battling¹³,
saying, "We are finding no evil¹⁴ in this man. And *what* if *a* spirit did speak *to* him,
or *an* angel¹⁵?"

    3D. And while *a* great dispute *was* taking place, the commander^E— having feared that¹⁶ Paul   10
might be torn-to-pieces¹⁷ by them— ordered^F the troop¹⁸, having gone down, to snatch¹⁹
him out of *the* midst^G *of* them, and bring *him* to the barracks^H

10C. And *on* the following night,²⁰ the Lord, having stood near him, said, "Take-courage²¹. For as   11
you solemnly-testified^J in Jerusalem *as to* the *things* concerning Me, so you must^K also testify^L
in Rome"

11C. And having become day,²² the Jews²³, having held *a* gathering²⁴, bound themselves under-a-   12
curse²⁵, saying *that they would* neither eat nor drink until which *time* they killed Paul

    1D. Now there were more *than* forty having made this sworn-pact²⁶—˙who, having gone to   13-14
the chief priests and the elders, said, "*With a* curse²⁷, we bound ourselves under-a-curse²⁸
to eat²⁹ nothing until which *time* we kill Paul

        1E. "Now therefore, **you,** along with the Sanhedrin, notify the commander³⁰ so that he   15
may bring him down to you³¹, as-*though you are* intending^M to determine³² the *things*
concerning him more accurately³³
        2E. "And **we** are prepared^N *that* we might kill him before he draws-near^O"

    2D. But the son *of* the sister *of* Paul— having heard-*of* the ambush³⁴, having come and entered   16
into the barracks— reported^P it *to* Paul
    3D. And Paul, having summoned^Q one *of* the centurions, said, "Lead this young-man^R away   17
to the commander, for he has something to report^P *to* him"
    4D. So indeed the *one*, having taken him along, led *him* to the commander. And he says, "Paul   18
the prisoner^S, having summoned^Q me, asked *that I* lead this young man to you— he
having something to tell you"
    5D. And the commander— having taken-hold-of^T his hand, and having withdrawn^U privately^V—   19
was asking, "What is it that you have to report^P *to* me?"

        1E. And he said that "The Jews agreed^W to ask you so that tomorrow you might bring   20
Paul down to the Sanhedrin, as-*though* intending^M to inquire^X something more
accurately concerning him
        2E. "So don't **you** be persuaded^Y *by* them. For more *than* forty men from-*among* them   21
are lying-in-wait-for^Z him who bound themselves under-a-curse neither to eat nor
drink until which *time* they kill him
        3E. "And now they are prepared^N, waiting-for^AA the promise³⁵ from you"

1. More literally, "is", as the Greek typically phrases it.
2. Some manuscripts have this singular, "*of a* Pharisee" {N}.
3. In some manuscripts, the word that makes this bold is omitted {C}.
4. Compare 24:21; and 24:15; 26:6, 7; 28:20. On "hope", see Col 1:5.
5. That is, our hope for the dead and the resurrection of the dead, stating in abbreviated form the same concept from two viewpoints. It could also be rendered "*our* hope— even *the* resurrection...". It is a dual statement of a single concept, which some simplify into one phrase, "the hope of the resurrection...". Note Paul's statement of it in 24:21.
6. Or, "dissension, discord, uprising". Same word as in 15:2; 23:10; 24:5; and as "riot" in Act 19:40; and "rebellion" in Mk 15:7; Lk 23:19, 25. The root word is "to stand", the sense in these uses being "to take a stand against" to various degrees. Elsewhere only in a different sense as "standing" in Heb 9:8. GK *5087.*
7. Same word as in 14:4.
8. Luke uses grammar that emphasizes the contrast between the two halves of this sentence.
9. Or, "both", if "nor *an* angel nor spirit" is viewed as one thing. Note v 9. This word means "both" if referring to two things, or "all" if more than two. Same word as in 19:16. Elsewhere only as "both" in Mt 9:17; 13:30; 15:14; Lk 1:6, 7; 5:7; 6:39; 7:42; Act 8:38; Eph 2:14, 16, 18. GK *317.*
10. Or, "shouting, outcry". A shouting match. On this word, see "outcry" in Heb 5:7. Related to the verb "shouting" in 22:23.
11. Some manuscripts omit "some of" {N}.
12. Same word as in v 6, where the two parts are defined.
13. That is, verbally. Or, "fighting, contending, arguing vehemently". Used only here. GK *1372.* Related to "battle" in 2 Tim 2:24.
14. Or, nothing "bad, wicked, wrong". The Jews found plenty to disagree with, but nothing evil. On this word, see 3 Jn 11. They support Paul with regard to the principles included in his stand which they agree with, but not with regard to the Christian details of his stand.
15. Some manuscripts say "and if *a* spirit did speak *to* him, or *an* angel, let us not fight against God" {N}.
16. On this idiom, see 5:26.
17. Elsewhere only of chains being "torn apart" in Mk 5:4. GK *1400.*
18. Or, "squad, detachment, band of soldiers". Same word as in v 27, where it is also singular. It is plural in Mt 22:7; Lk 23:11; Rev 9:16. Elsewhere only as "armies" in Rev 19:14, 19. GK *5128.* Related to "soldier" in Mt 28:12.
19. Or, "seize, take by force". On this word, see "snatch away" in 2 Cor 12:2.
20. That is, that night (as we call it), the night following the day mentioned in 22:30.
21. Elsewhere only in Mt 9:2, 22; 14:27; Mk 6:50; 10:49; Jn 16:33; all this same command. GK *2510.* Related to the noun "courage" in 28:15, expressed separately with the verb "to take". Some manuscripts add "Paul" {N}.
22. Note how parallel the flow of phrases is in v 11 and 12. The Lord makes a promise or oath to Paul for the purpose of life, and the Jews make an oath to God for the purpose of death (note Jn 16:2).
23. Some manuscripts say "some *of the* Jews" {B}.
24. This noun means a collection, aggregate, gathering of things. It is used of a "swarm" of bees, a "flock" of birds, so that perhaps "having formed *a* band [of conspirators]" says it here. In both NT occurrences, it is used of a gathering of people— in Act 19:40, a "*disorderly*" gathering"; here, a "*seditious*" gathering". GK *5371.* The evil nature of the gathering as a conspiracy comes from the context. The related verb is "gather" in Mt 17:22. Thus, they "held a gathering", at which they "bound themselves under a curse", resulting in a "sworn pact and alliance", v 13.
25. On this word, "to bind-under-a-curse", see "curse" in Mk 14:71. Same word as in v 14, 21. The oath these men took was, "May God curse us if we eat or drink before we kill Paul". They enlist the Jewish authorities in this pact in v 14.
26. Or, "having formed this conspiracy". This word means "conspiracy, a body of men leagued by an oath". Used only here. GK *5350.* The root word is "to swear with an oath", the word in Jam 5:12. It is a "swearing together" by a group, a "sworn alliance" (emphasizing the forty men), and a "sworn pact" (emphasizing the oath taken). Both ideas are included here.
27. On this word, see "accursed" in Rom 9:3.
28. The Greek reflected here, repeating the noun and verb of the same word, is a literal rendition of a Hebrew way of speaking. It means "we bound ourselves under a solemn curse".
29. Or, "taste". Elsewhere in Acts only in 10:10; 20:11. On this word, see "taste" in Heb 6:4. Not the same word as in v 12 and 21 (see Act 10:13).
30. That is, notify him officially. Luke does not state whether all the Sanhedrin were to be told of this plot. The conspirators may have approached the Sadducee faction and excluded the Pharisee faction. These leaders try this again two years later, in 25:3.
31. Some manuscripts add "tomorrow" {N}, as in v 20.
32. Or, "discern, distinguish". Same word as 24:22.
33. The commander had already said that he desired this, 22:30. On this word, see Mt 2:8.
34. Elsewhere only in 25:3. GK *1909.* Related to "lying in wait for" in v 21.
35. That is, the promise that the commander will bring Paul down to them at a certain time. On this word, see 1 Jn 2:25.

A. Mt 8:29 B. Mt 7:1 C. Act 6:2, multitude D. 1 Tim 6:12 E. Act 21:31 F. Mt 14:28 G. 2 Thes 2:7 H. Rev 20:9, camp J. 1 Tim 5:21, solemnly charge K. Mt 16:21 L. Jn 1:7 M. Mk 10:32, going to N. Mk 14:15 O. Lk 21:28 P. 1 Jn 1:3, announcing Q. Act 2:39, call to R. Act 7:58 S. Eph 3:1 T. Lk 20:20 U. Mt 4:12, went back V. Mt 14:13 W. Lk 22:5 X. Act 23:34, learn Y. 1 Jn 3:19 Z. Lk 11:54 AA. Act 24:15

6D.	Then indeed the commander sent away the young-man, having commanded^A *him* to tell no one "that you revealed¹ these *things* to me". ˚And having summoned^B *a* certain² two *of* the centurions^C, he said	22 23
1E.	"Prepare^D two-hundred soldiers and seventy horsemen³ and two-hundred spearmen⁴, so that they may proceed to Caesarea⁵ at *the* third hour⁶ *of* the night"	
2E.	And *that they should* provide^E mounts^F, in order that having put-on Paul, they might bring *him* safely through^G to Felix⁷ the governor, ˚*he* having written *a* letter^H having this form^J—	24 25
1F.	"Claudius Lysias⁸, *to* the most-excellent⁹ governor Felix, greetings^K	26
2F.	"I rescued^L this man having been seized^M by the Jews and being about to be killed by them, having come-suddenly-upon^N *them* with the troop¹⁰— having learned^O that he was¹¹ *a* Roman¹²	27
3F.	"And wanting to know the reason for which they were accusing^P him, I brought *him* down to their Sanhedrin— ˚whom¹³ I found being accused^P about issues¹⁴ *of* their Law, but having no accusation¹⁵ worthy^Q *of* death or imprisonment^R	28 29
4F.	"And *a* plot¹⁶ having been disclosed¹⁷ *to* me *that* would¹⁸ be against the man¹⁹, I sent *him* to you at once, having also ordered²⁰ *his* accusers to speak the *things* against him before you²¹"	30
10B.	So indeed the soldiers, in accordance with the *thing* having been commanded^S them, having picked-up^T Paul, brought *him* during *the* night to Antipatris²². ˚And *on* the next day, they²³ returned to the barracks, having let²⁴ the horsemen depart with him— ˚who²⁵, having entered into Caesarea, and having delivered the letter *to* the governor, presented^E Paul *to* him also	31 32 33
1C.	And²⁶ having read *it*, and having asked from what province he was²⁷, and having learned²⁸ that *he was* from Cilicia, ˚he said, "I will give you a hearing²⁹ whenever your accusers also arrive"— having ordered³⁰ *that* he be guarded^U in the Praetorium³¹ *of* Herod	34 35
2C.	And after five days, the high priest Ananias^V came down with some elders³² and *an* attorney³³, *a* certain Tertullus— who³⁴ brought-charges against Paul *to* the governor	24:1
1D.	And he³⁵ having been called, Tertullus began to accuse^W *him*, saying—	2
1E.	"Attaining^X much³⁶ peace through you— and reforms³⁷ taking place *for* this nation through your foresight^Y ˚both³⁸ in every way and everywhere— we welcome³⁹ *it*, most-excellent^Z Felix^AA, with all thankfulness^BB	3
2E.	"But in order that I may not hinder⁴⁰ you further^CC, I beg you to hear us briefly, *by* your kindness⁴¹	4
1F.	"For having found this man *to be*	5
1G.	"*A* plague⁴²	
2G.	"And setting-in-motion⁴³ disputes⁴⁴ *among* all the Jews throughout the world^DD	
3G.	"And *a* ringleader⁴⁵ *of* the sect^EE *of* the Nazarenes⁴⁶	
4G.	"Who even tried to profane⁴⁷ the temple	6
2F.	"Whom also we seized^FF—⁴⁸	7⁴⁹
3F.	"From whom you yourself, having examined^GG *him*, will be able to learn^HH about all these *things of* which **we** are accusing^W him	8

1. Or, "gave notice of ". Same word as "notify" in v 15. GK *1872*.
2. The commander hand-picked two men to do this. Some manuscripts omit this word {C}.
3. Or, "cavalrymen". Elsewhere only in v 32. GK *2689*. Related to "cavalry" in Rev 9:16. The root word is "horse".
4. Or, "slingers, bowmen". The precise meaning of this military term is not certain. The root word is "right", perhaps implying a weapon taken in or used by the right hand. The shield was taken in the left hand. Used only here. GK *1287*.
5. That is, the Roman capital of Judea on the coast, 65 miles or 100 kilometers from Jerusalem. See 8:40.
6. That is, 9 P.M. More literally, "from *the* third hour". Beginning from 9 P.M., the troop would be proceeding there.
7. After the death of King Herod Agrippa I in A.D. 44 (Act 12:1), the Roman Emperor Claudius (Act 18:2) put Judea under the rule of Roman procurators (similar to the prefects like Pontius Pilate). Felix was the fourth procurator of Judea, serving from A.D. 52-59. He is mentioned in chapter 23-24, and in 25:14. GK *5772*.
8. This is the name of the Roman "commander" in view since 21:31, and elsewhere only in 24:22. GK *3385*.
9. Same word as in 24:3; 26:25. On this word, see Lk 1:3.
10. Same word as in v 10.
11. More literally, "is", as the Greek typically phrases it.
12. Lysias reverses the order of events, providing himself with the higher motive (rescuing a Roman), rather his real initial motive (maintaining order, doing his duty). He omits the messy (and now irrelevant) details. Some punctuate this with what follows, "troop. Having learned that he is a Roman, and wanting to know... him, I brought...".
13. That is, Paul.
14. Or, "controversial questions". On this word, see 15:2.
15. Or, "charge". Elsewhere only in 25:16. GK *1598*. Related to "accuse" just used twice.
16. Elsewhere only in 9:24; 20:3, 19. GK *2101*.
17. On this word, see "showed" in Lk 20:37.
18. More literally, "will", as the Greek typically phrases it.
19. Some manuscripts add "from them". Others say "*that* will certainly be against the man by the Jews" {B}.
20. Lysias gave this order on the next day, after this letter was sent, but before Felix read it. Same word as "commanded" in v 22.
21. Some manuscripts add "Farewell" {B}.
22. This is a city about 40 miles or 60 kilometers from Jerusalem. Used only here. GK *526*.
23. That is, the walking soldiers. The horsemen continued on from Antipatris to Caesarea with Paul.
24. That is, the centurions in charge of the mission permitted it. Luke abbreviates.
25. That is, the horsemen.
26. Some manuscripts add "the governor" {K}.
27. More literally, "is", as the Greek typically phrases it.
28. Or, "learned-by-inquiry". Elsewhere only as "inquire" in Mt 2:4; Lk 15:26; 18:36; Jn 4:52; 13:24; Act 4:7; 10:18; 21:33; 23:20; and "ask" in Act 10:29; 23:19. GK *4785*.
29. This verb "give-a-hearing", a legal term, is used only here. GK *1358*. Or, "I will hear you fully".
30. Some manuscripts say "... arrive". And he ordered..." {K}.
31. On this word, see Phil 1:13. It was built in Caesarea by Herod the Great.
32. Some manuscripts say "the elders" {N}.
33. Or, "advocate, speaker". That is, a lawyer (in the Roman sense) who could skillfully argue their case. Some think he was a Hellenistic Jew; others, a hired Roman. Used only here. GK *4842*.
34. This word is plural, and refers back to the whole group.
35. That is, Paul.
36. Or, "long". Either "much" in quality or quantity. Tertullus begins with exaggerated flattery.
37. Used only here. GK *1480*. Some manuscripts say "prosperity" {N}. Related to "reformation" in Heb 9:10.
38. This is the Greek word order. Tertullus is exaggerating Felix's accomplishments. Or, "foresight— we welcome *it* both *in* every way and everywhere". In this case, he is exaggerating the Jews' submission to Felix.
39. Or, "accept, acknowledge, approve". On this word, see Act 2:41. The Jews welcome the peace and reforms.
40. Or, "delay, detain, cut in on, weary". On this word, see Gal 5:7.
41. Or, "graciousness, reasonableness, fairness, tolerance". Elsewhere only in 2 Cor 10:1. GK *2116*. Related to "kindness" in Phil 4:5.
42. Or, "*a* pestilent *one*, *a* diseased *one*, *a* pest, *a* troublesome *one*". That is, a public menace, a (spiritually) diseased person who is a threat to society. Elsewhere only in Lk 21:11, of literal plagues. GK *3369*.
43. Or, "arousing, agitating". Same word as in 21:30.
44. Or, more strongly, "riots". Some manuscripts have this word singular {N}, meaning "dissension". Same word as in 23:7.
45. In a more favorable context, this word would mean "leader, chief ". Used only here. GK *4756*.
46. Used in this way only here. On this word, see Mt 2:23.
47. Tertullus is referring to 21:28-29. On this word, see Mt 12:5.
48. Having raised the hammer of accusation, Tertullus stops, and hands it to Felix, instead of slamming it down himself in conclusion. Fiery demands would surely backfire. This is especially true in view of the weakness of the accusations— "a pest"?; "disputes"?; "tried to"? These are Jewish religious complaints, not violations of Roman law. Lysias was correct, 23:29. It appears the Jews are hoping for a favorable response based on political considerations and good relations, not evidence. They want a favor (25:3), not Roman justice. The Romans often went along with them in this fashion with regard to Jewish people and issues (as in the case of Jesus), but they would not do so with regard to a Roman.
49. Some manuscripts add as v 6b-8a, "And we wanted to judge *him* according to our Law. But having arrived, Lysias the commander led *him* away from our hands with much violence, having commanded his accusers to come before you" {B}. This addition also makes "from whom" in v 8 refer to Lysias rather than Paul.

A. 1 Tim 1:3 B. Act 2:39, call to C. Mt 8:5 D. Mk 14:15 E. Rom 12:1, present F. 1 Cor 15:39, livestock G. Act 27:43, bring safely through H. 2 Thes 3:17 J. 1 Pet 5:3, pattern K. 2 Cor 13:11, rejoice L. Gal 1:4 M. Lk 2:21, conceived N. Lk 21:34 O. Phil 4:11 P. Act 26:2 Q. Rev 16:6 R. Phil 1:7 S. 1 Cor 7:17, directing T. Act 1:2, taken up U. Jn 12:25, keep V. Act 23:2 W. Jn 5:45 X. Lk 20:35 Y. Rom 13:14, provision Z. Lk 1:3 AA. Act 23:24 BB. 1 Tim 4:3, thanksgiving CC. 2 Tim 2:16 DD. Heb 2:5 EE. 1 Cor 11:19, faction FF. Heb 4:14, hold on to GG. 1 Cor 2:14 HH. Col 1:6, understood

	2D. And the Jews also joined-in-the-attack[1], asserting[A] *that* these *things* hold so[2]	9
	3D. And Paul responded, the governor[B] having nodded[C] *to* him to speak	10
	1E. "Knowing-about[D] you being *a* judge[3] *to* this nation for many years,[4] I cheerfully[5] speak-a-defense[E] *as to* the *things* concerning myself—*you being able to learn[6] that	11
	1F. "It is not more than twelve days[7] since[F] I went up to Jerusalem *to* worship[8]	
	2F. "And neither in the temple did they find me arguing[9] with anyone, or causing *an* onset[10] *of a* crowd— nor in the synagogues, nor throughout the city!	12
	3F. "Nor are they able to prove[11] *to* you *the things* concerning which they now are accusing[G] me	13
	2E. "But I confess[12] this *to* you— that according to the Way[13] which they call *a* sect[14], thus I am worshiping[15] the God *of my* ancestor[16]	14
	1F. "Believing all the *things* in accordance with the Law, and the *things* having been written in the Prophets	
	2F. "Having *a* hope[H] in God which these *ones* themselves also are waiting-for[17]— that there will-certainly[18] be *a* resurrection[19] *of* both righteous *ones* and unrighteous *ones*	15
	3F. "In this[20] indeed **I** am striving[21] to have *a* blameless[J] conscience[K] toward God and people continually[L]	16
	3E. "Now after many years,[22] I came *to* do[23] acts-of-almsgiving[24] for my nation, and offerings[25], *during which they found me in the temple, having been purified[26]— not with *a* crowd, nor with *a* commotion[27]	17 18
	4E. "But *there were* some Jews from Asia— who[28] ought-to-have[29] been present[30] before you and accusing[G] *me*, if they have something against me	19
	5E. "Or let these *ones* themselves[31] say what crime[M] they found[32]— I having stood before the Sanhedrin	20
	1F. "Other-than concerning this one shout[N] which I cried-out[O] while standing among them[33]— that '**I** am being judged[P] before you today concerning *the* resurrection *of the* dead' "	21
	4D. And Felix[34] adjourned[35] them	22
	1E. Knowing[36] more-accurately[Q] the *things* concerning the Way	
	2E. Having said, "Whenever Lysias[37] the commander comes down, I will determine[38] the *things* concerning you[39] *people*"	
	3E. Having given-orders[R] *to* the centurion	23
	1F. *That* he[40] be kept[S] [in custody]	
	2F. And *that he* have *a* relaxation[41] [of custody]	
	3F. And *that they* forbid[42] none *of* his own *people* to serve[43] him	
	3C. And after some days, Felix— having arrived with Drusilla[44] *his* own[45] wife, *she* being *a* Jew— sent for Paul, and listened-to him concerning faith in Christ Jesus[46]	24

1. Or, "joined in setting upon" him. Used only here. GK *5298*. Related to "set upon" in 18:10. Some manuscripts say "agreed" {N}, using the word found in 23:20.
2. That is, that they are true. On this idiom, see 12:15.
3. That is, one administering justice. GK *3216*. Related word in Mt 7:1.
4. Felix had been the Roman procurator for about five years at this point, with two years remaining until he was replaced by Festus, v 27. See 23:24 on Felix. Paul had been out of the country for over seven years, except for the brief visit in 18:22. But he knew of Felix.
5. Used only here. GK *2315*. Related to "cheerful" in 27:36. Some manuscripts say "more-cheerfully" {N}.
6. Or, "fully know, find out". Same word as in v 8. Thus the Jews point Felix to Paul, who points him to other witnesses. Both express their confidence that Felix can find the facts through his own investigation. On this word, see "understood" in Col 1:6.
7. This is an idiom, literally, "there are no more *than* twelve days *for* me since...". The Greek counts from the past forward. We count from the present backward, and would say "No more than twelve days ago, I went...". Some think Paul is counting from his arrival in Jerusalem in 21:17 to his leaving it in 23:23; others, to his arrival in Caesarea in 23:33. There are other views.
8. Or, "*to* worship in Jerusalem". On this word, see Mt 14:33. On the grammar of it, see "*to* do" in v 17.
9. Or, "holding a discussion, speaking". That is, trying to convince anyone of anything. On this word, see "reasoned" in 17:2.
10. Or, "*a* stoppage, beginning". Paul did nothing to cause a crowd to stop and gather. Some manuscripts say "disturbance" {N}. Elsewhere only as "pressure" in 2 Cor 11:28. GK *2180*. Related to "suddenly come upon" in Lk 21:34.
11. This word means "to place beside, present, offer". Used only here in this sense. The Jews cannot place witnesses and evidence beside their assertions to prove them. On this word, see "present" in Rom 12:1.
12. Or, "acknowledge, admit, declare". On this word, see 1 Tim 6:12.
13. See 9:2 on this term.
14. Same word as in v 5.
15. Or, "serving". On this word, see Heb 12:28.
16. Or, "father". Paul is linking himself and the Way to historic Judaism, which had the protection of Roman law. Elsewhere only in 22:3 (of Law), and 28:17 (of customs). GK *4262*.
17. Or, "accepting". Same word as in Mk 15:23; Lk 2:25, 38; 12:36; 23:51; Act 23:21; Tit 2:13; Jude 21. Elsewhere only as "accept" in Heb 10:34; 11:35; "welcome" in Lk 15:2; and "receive" in Rom 16:2; Phil 2:29. GK *4657*.
18. This word with this grammar is elsewhere only in 11:28; 27:10. This word is in a similar idiom in Mt 24:6.
19. Same word as in Lk 14:14; 20:27; Jn 5:29; 11:24, 25; Act 2:31; 4:2; 17:18; 24:15; 1 Cor 15:12; Heb 6:2; 11:35; Phil 3:10; 2 Tim 2:18; Rev 20:5. Also used of the resurrection of Christ, Act 1:22; Rom 1:4; Phil 3:10; 1 Pet 1:3. Also used of a spiritual resurrection to new life in Christ, Rom 6:5. Used 42 times. GK *414*. The related verb is "rise up" in Lk 18:33. Some manuscripts add "*of the* dead" {N}.
20. That is, in his worship, v 14-15. Some manuscripts say "And in this **I** am striving..." {K}.
21. Or, "endeavoring, practicing, training, doing *my* best, making *it* a practice". Used only here. GK *828*.
22. Paul has been gone from Israel since 18:22, about five years. See v 11.
23. This is a future participle, used to express purpose. This idiom occurs elsewhere only in Mt 27:49 ("*to* save"); Act 8:27 ("*to* worship"); Act 22:5 ("*to* bring"); and Act 24:11 ("*to* worship").
24. That is, acts of charity (with the gifts sent by the Gentile churches. See Rom 15:26). On this word, see "almsgiving" in Mt 6:2.
25. On this word, see 21:26. Paul may be referring to the offerings associated with Pentecost (20:16), viewing the gifts of the Gentiles as a firstfruit offering.
26. Same word as in 21:24, 26. That is, in obedience to its laws, not in violation of them.
27. Same word as "uproar" in 21:34.
28. Paul stops abruptly, and calls for his absent eyewitness accusers to specify the charges against him. Why should he state it for them by finishing the sentence with "who accused me of defiling the temple".
29. On this idiom, see "should have" in Mt 25:27.
30. Or, "been here". That is, to have been and continue to be present. The word "ought-to-have" looks back to the beginning of this event in v 1. This word (more literally, "be present") refers to the presence of these accusers which still continues to be necessary at the moment Paul is speaking. The idea is that if they had done what they "ought to have" done, they would "be present" now. English is unable to reflect both verbs, so some render it as "ought to have been present"; others, as "ought to be present".
31. That is, the high priest and those with him (v 1), who were not eyewitnesses of anything.
32. Some manuscripts add "in me" {B}.
33. The following statement caused a great dispute and split between the Pharisees and Sadducees in 23:6— to which Lysias will attest, and about which the Romans have absolutely no interest. Thus the Jews can produce no witnesses against Paul, while Paul can produce Lysias himself to prove it was a purely religious dispute. Paul's case is strong.
34. Some manuscripts say "And having heard these *things,* Felix..." {N}.
35. Or, "deferred, postponed". Used only here. GK *327*.
36. Some think Luke means "*Although* knowing...", and therefore being without excuse for not releasing him.
37. That is, the Jerusalem commander who rescued Paul, 23:26.
38. Or, "decide". Felix will investigate through to a judicial decision. He says this in keeping with their confidence in him to "learn" the facts, v 8, 11 (a related word). Though he surely saw Lysias many times in the following two years, he did not decide the case. He had nothing to gain by deciding it. His motive is made plain in v 26. Elsewhere only in 23:15. GK *1336*. Related to "decision" in 25:21.
39. This word is plural, referring to all of them. To reflect this, "people" is added.
40. Some manuscripts say "Paul" {K}.
41. Or, "loosening, abatement". That is, a measure of freedom within his confinement, in deference to Paul's Roman citizenship. On this word, see "rest" in 2 Cor 8:13.
42. Or, "hinder, prevent, restrain, try to stop" from serving Paul. On this word, see 1 Cor 14:39.
43. On this word, see 13:36. Some manuscripts add "or come to" {N}.
44. Drusilla was the sister of Agrippa II and Bernice (25:13). Their father was Agrippa I (12:1). GK *1537*.
45. Some manuscripts omit this word; others say "his wife" {N}.
46. Some manuscripts omit this word {B}.

A. Act 25:19 B. Mt 27:2 C. Jn 13:24 D. Act 18:25 E. Lk 21:14 F. Rev 16:18 G. Jn 5:45 H. Col 1:5 J. 1 Cor 10:32 K. Act 23:1 L. 2 Thes 3:16 M. Act 18:14 N. Mk 1:26, voice O. Mt 8:29 P. Mt 7:1 Q. Mt 2:8 R. 1 Cor 7:17, directing S. 1 Jn 5:18

1D.	But while he *was* speaking[A] about righteousness[B], self-control[C] and the coming judgment[D], Felix— having become afraid[E], responded, "*As to* the present,[1] go. And having received *an* opportunity[2], I will summon[F] you"—	25
1E.	At the same time also hoping that money[G] would[3] be given *to* him by Paul.[4] Therefore indeed, sending for him very-frequently[H], he was conversing[5] *with* him	26
4C.	Now two years having been fulfilled,[6] Felix[J] received *a* successor— Porcius Festus[7]. And wishing[K] to gain[8] favor[9] *with* the Jews, Felix left Paul bound[10]. °So Festus, having set-foot[11] *in* the province, went up after three days to Jerusalem from Caesarea	27 / 25:1
1D.	And the chief priests[12] and the leading[13] *ones of the* Jews brought-charges *to* him against Paul. And they were appealing-to[L] him, °asking-*for a* favor[M] against him[14], so that he might summon[N] him to Jerusalem— while making *an* ambush[O] to kill him along the way	2 / 3
2D.	Then indeed Festus responded *that* Paul *was* being kept[P] in Caesarea, and *that he* himself *was* about to be proceeding-out [of Jerusalem] shortly[15]	4
1E.	"So", he says, "the powerful[Q] *ones* among you having gone-down-with *me*— if[16] there is something out-of-place[17] in[18] the man, let them be accusing[R] him *there*"	5
3D.	And having spent[S] days among them (not more[19] *than* eight or ten), having come down to Caesarea, having sat on the judgment-seat[T] *on* the next day, he ordered *that* Paul be brought	6
1E.	And he[20] having arrived, the Jews having come down from Jerusalem stood around him, bringing many and weighty[21] charges[22] against *him*, which they were not able[23] to prove[24]—	7
1F.	Paul speaking-in-defense[U] *that* "Neither against the Law *of* the Jews, nor against the temple, nor against Caesar, did I sin[25] anything"	8
2E.	But Festus, wishing[K] to gain[26] favor[M] *with* the Jews, having responded *to* Paul, said, "Are you willing[K], having gone up to Jerusalem, to be judged[V] there before[27] me concerning these *things*?"	9
3E.	And Paul said, "I am standing *here* before the judgment-seat[T] *of* Caesar, where I ought-to[28] be judged[V]	10
1F.	"I did *the* Jews no wrong, as **you** also are knowing very well	
2F.	"So[29] **if**[30] I am doing wrong[31] and have committed something worthy *of* death, I am not refusing[W] to die[32]— but if *the things of* which these *ones* are accusing[R] me are nothing, no one is able[33] to freely-give[34] me *to* them	11
3F.	"I appeal-to[X] Caesar"[35]	
4E.	Then Festus, having talked-with[36] *his* council[Y], responded, "You have appealed-to[X] Caesar— you will go before Caesar"	12
5C.	Now some days having passed, Agrippa[37] the king and Bernice[38] arrived[39] in Caesarea, having greeted[40] Festus	13
1D.	And while they were spending[S] more days there, Festus laid-before[41] the king the *things* concerning Paul, saying	14

1. This is an idiom, literally, "*As* holding the now", used only here.
2. Or, "*an* opportune time, *a* convenient time". GK *2789*.
3. More literally, "will", as the Greek typically phrases it.
4. Some manuscripts add "so that he might release him" {N}. It is a perfect solution for Felix. He honors Paul's Roman citizenship by not punishing him; he does not infuriate the Jews by releasing him; and he opens up the possibility of making a personal (though illegal) gain off the whole affair.
5. Elsewhere only in Lk 24:14, 15; Act 20:11. GK *3917*.
6. Or, "completed, filled up". Probably during this period, A.D. 57-59, Luke gathered the information to write the Gospel of Luke and much of Acts. Perhaps he even wrote Luke and started Acts. While present in Palestine, he was able to talk with the eyewitnesses. Same word as in 7:23, 30; 9:23. On this word, see "filled" in Eph 5:18.
7. Festus was the fifth procurator of Judea since the death of King Agrippa I (in Acts 12), appointed by the Emperor Nero, and serving from A.D. 59-62. Upon his death, the high priest had James (the leader of the Jerusalem church, Act 15:13) killed, an illegal act that cost him his position. Festus is mentioned in chapter 25 and 26. GK *5776*.
8. This word means "to lay down, deposit, lay up in store". Elsewhere only in 25:9. GK *2960*. Luke could mean "lay up a store of favor with the Jews" (gain favor), or "lay down a favor for the Jews" (grant a favor). Having been recalled to Rome regarding another incident, Felix wanted no further problems following him there, as might have happened had he released Paul.
9. Or, "gratitude". Same word as in 25:3, 9. On this word, see "grace" in Eph 2:8. Some manuscripts have this word plural {N}.
10. This is a participle, "having been bound". That is, in custody at Caesarea.
11. On this word, see 21:4. More literally, "having gone upon [the ground]".
12. Some manuscripts say the "high priest" {N}.
13. Same word as in 13:50.
14. That is, Paul.
15. Festus answers based on his schedule. He is not staying in Jerusalem long enough to summon Paul. So instead, the Jews should go to Caesarea with him, and he will deal with it right away. On this idiom, see "quickly" in Rev 1:1.
16. Or, "since", as Festus supposes there is, 25:18. The grammar means "assuming that there is something...", granting their position for now. Paul must have done evil, or the Jews would not want him so badly, and Felix would not have kept him in custody. Festus learns more in 25:19.
17. Or, "wrong". On this word, see 2 Thes 3:2. Some manuscripts say instead "this" {N}, so that it says "if there is anything in the case of this man".
18. Or, "in the case of". GK *1877*.
19. Some manuscripts say "(more than ten)" {N}.
20. That is, Paul.
21. Or, "serious". Same word as in Mt 23:23; 2 Cor 10:10. Elsewhere only as "heavy" in Mt 23:4; "burdensome" in 1 Jn 5:3; and "savage" in Act 20:29. GK *987*. Related to "weight" in 1 Thes 2:6.
22. Or, "complaints". Used only here. GK *166*. Related to "charge" in v 18, 27; 28:18
23. Or, "having the power". On this word, see "can do" in Gal 5:6.
24. Or, "attest, show". Same word as "attest" in 2:22. The Jews could not "show, display" evidence to "attest, prove" their charges. On this word, see "display" in 2 Thes 2:4.
25. This word means "do wrong, commit an offense, fail a requirement, miss the mark". Used 43 times. GK *279*. Related to the noun "sin" in Jn 8:46.
26. Or, "grant". On this word, see 24:27.
27. That is, with me as the judge. Same word and grammar as in v 10; twice in 25:26; 26:2. Here, some think Festus means "in my presence", with the Sanhedrin as judge. Same word (but different grammar) as "before" Caesar in v 12. GK *2093*.
28. Or, "should". More literally, "where it is necessary *that* I" be judged. The root word is "it is binding". This idiom refers to what should or ought to happen by necessity, the compulsion being based on what is fitting or proper or required by the circumstances. Here, as Festus knows, the necessity lies in the circumstances of the case and Paul's Roman citizenship. Same idiom as in v 24; 26:9; Lk 12:12; 13:14; Rom 8:26; 12:3; 1 Cor 8:2; Col 4:4; 1 Thes 4:1; 2 Thes 3:7; Tit 1:11; etc. GK *1256*. Same word as in the idiom "must" in Mt 16:21; and "should have" in Mt 25:27.
29. Some manuscripts say "For" {K}.
30. Paul uses grammar that emphasizes the contrast between the two halves of this sentence.
31. That is, under Roman law, the only other possibility.
32. That is, if the Romans had a case against Paul, they would have executed him. The fact that they have not done so is not because Paul refused! He is being held for political, not legal purposes. Festus knows this, but his reason for his proposal is not justice (v 9). So Paul takes it out of his hands by appealing to Caesar.
33. That is, under Roman law.
34. Or, "grant, give as a favor, graciously give", without cause. Same word as in v 16. On this word, see 1 Cor 2:12.
35. In this case, to Nero, Emperor from A.D. 54-68. This was the right of every Roman citizen in a capital case. This is repeated in v 12, 21, 25; 26:32; 28:19. If Paul could not reach Rome as a free man, he would go as a prisoner. On "Caesar", see Lk 3:1.
36. Elsewhere only in Mt 17:3; Mk 9:4; Lk 4:36; 9:30; 22:4. GK *5196*.
37. That is, Agrippa II, son of Herod Agrippa I (Act 12:1), great-grandson of Herod the Great (Mt 2:1). His Roman name was Marcus Julius Agrippa. The Emperor Claudius (18:2) made him King of Chalcis, and later made him tetrarch of the areas once ruled by Lysanias and Philip (Lk 3:1). The Emperor Nero gave him more territory in A.D. 54. He was given authority to appoint the high priests in Jerusalem, though he did not rule Judea. His capital was in Caesarea Philippi (Mt 16:13), which he renamed "Neronias". He ruled until about A.D. 100.
38. Bernice was the sister of Agrippa II and Drusilla (24:24). She was the daughter of Agrippa I (12:1). She is mentioned also in v 23; 26:30. GK *1022*.
39. Presumably from his capital in Caesarea Philippi.
40. Or, "greeting". On this word, see Mk 15:18. The tense of this verb means "having greeted [upon arrival]", or "greeting [at the time of arrival]". Some manuscripts say "*to* greet" {N}, expressing the purpose of their visit using the same grammar as "*to* do" in 24:17.
41. That is, laid before Agrippa for his consideration. Elsewhere only in Gal 2:2. GK *423*.

A. Act 17:2, reasoned B. Rom 1:17 C. 2 Pet 1:6 D. Jn 9:39 E. Lk 24:37, terrified F. Act 10:32 G. Mk 10:23, wealth H. Lk 5:33 J. Act 23:24 K. Jn 7:17, willing L. Rom 12:8, exhorting M. Eph 2:8, grace N. Act 11:13, send for O. Act 23:16 P. 1 Jn 5:18 Q. Lk 24:19 R. Jn 5:45 S. Act 12:19, spend time T. Rom 14:10 U. Lk 21:14 V. Mt 7:1 W. Heb 12:25 X. 1 Pet 1:17, call upon Y. Mk 15:1, consultation

	1E. "*A* certain man has been left-behind[1] by Felix *as a* prisoner[A], concerning whom— I having come-to-be in Jerusalem[2]— the chief priests and the elders *of* the Jews brought-charges, asking-*for a* sentence-of-condemnation[3] against him		15
	1F. "To whom I responded that it is not *a* custom[B] *with* Romans to freely-give[4] any person[5] before the *one* being accused[C] should have *his* accusers face-to-face, and should receive *a* place[6] *for a* defense[7] concerning the accusation[D]		16
	2E. "So they[8] having come-with *me* here[9]— *I* having made no delay[10], having sat on the judgment-seat[E] *on* the next *day*— I ordered[F] *that* the man be brought		17
	1F. "Concerning whom[11], the accusers having stood were bringing no charge[G] *of the evil*[12] *things* which *I* was supposing[13], but were having certain issues[14] with him		18 19
	1G. "Concerning *their* own religion[15]		
	2G. "And concerning *a* certain Jesus having died, whom Paul was asserting[16] to be alive		
	3E. "And *I*, being perplexed[H] *as to* the investigation[J] concerning these *things*,[17] was saying whether he might be willing[K] to go to Jerusalem, and there be judged[L] concerning these *things*		20
	4E. "But Paul having appealed[M] *that* he be kept for the decision *of* the Emperor[N], I ordered[O] *that* he *continue*-being-kept[18] [in custody] until which *time* I might send him up[19] to Caesar"		21
	5E. And Agrippa *says* to Festus, "I myself also was wanting[K] to hear the man"[20]		22
	6E. "Tomorrow", he says, "you will hear him"		
2D.	So *on* the next day, Agrippa and Bernice having come with great pageantry[21], and having entered into the auditorium[22] with both commanders[23] and prominent[24] men *of* the city[25], and Festus having given-orders[O]— Paul was brought		23
3D.	And Festus says, "King Agrippa, and all the men being present-with us— you see this *one* concerning whom the whole assembly[26] *of* the Jews appealed[27] *to* me, both in Jerusalem and here, shouting[P] *that* he ought not to[28] live any longer		24
	1E. "But *I* found-out[29] *that* he had[30] committed nothing worthy[Q] *of* death		25
	2E. "And this *one* himself having appealed-to[M] the Emperor, I determined[L] to send *him*— concerning whom, I do not have something certain[31] to write *to my* lord[32]		26
	3E. "Therefore I brought him before you, and especially before you King Agrippa, so that the examination[33] having taken place, I may have something I may write[34]		
	1F. "For it seems unreasonable[R] *to* me, while sending *a* prisoner[A], not also to signify[S] the charges[G] against him"		27
4D.	And Agrippa said to Paul, "It is permitted[T] *to* you to speak concerning[35] yourself"		26:1
5D.	Then Paul, having stretched-out[U] *his* hand, was speaking-a-defense[36]—		

1. This is a participle, "is having been left behind". Same word as "left" in 24:27. On this word, see 6:2.
2. That is, when I was in Jerusalem.
3. Or, "*a* judgment against". Used only here. GK *2869*. Related to "condemn" in Lk 6:37. Some manuscripts say "penalty" {N}, the word in 2 Thes 1:9.
4. Festus uses Paul's word, v 11.
5. That is, any Roman person, any Roman citizen. Some manuscripts add "to destruction" {N}.
6. That is, a place in the process, an opportunity. On this word, see Eph 4:27.
7. On this word, see 1 Pet 3:15. Related to "speak in defense" in v 8.
8. Some manuscripts omit this word {C}.
9. Or, "having come-together here". GK *5302*.
10. Or, "postponement". Used only here. GK *332*. Related to "adjourn" in 24:22.
11. Or, "Around whom", as in v 7. GK *4309*.
12. This word means "evil, wicked, bad". Some render it more specifically here from the Roman point of view, as "crimes". Used 78 times. GK *4505*. Related to "evilness" in Mt 22:18. Some manuscripts omit this word, so that it reads "no charge *of* which *things* I was supposing" {C}.
13. Or, "suspecting". Same word as in 13:25. Elsewhere only as "suspecting" in 27:27. GK *5706*. Related to "suspicion" in 1 Tim 6:4.
14. Same word as used by Lysias in his letter, 23:29.
15. Used only here. GK *1272*. Related to "very religious" in 17:22; and "deity" in 17:18.
16. Or, "claiming". Same word as in 24:9. Elsewhere only "claiming" in Rom 1:22. GK *5763*.
17. This motive is valid, but another motive was behind it at the time (v 9), which Paul thwarted.
18. With different grammar, the same word "kept" is used in two different senses in this verse. On this word, see 1 Jn 5:18.
19. Some manuscripts omit this word {N}.
20. Or, "I myself also *would* wish to hear". Rendering it as "was wanting" means it was Agrippa's actual desire in the past, either implying he already knew of Paul (similar to Herod in Lk 23:8), or meaning "I was [just now] wanting" while Festus was speaking (as in Gal 4:20). Rendering it as "*would*" wish makes it a present request. In any case, he is making an indirect, politely phrased request, less direct than saying "I want to hear him".
21. Or, "pomp". Used only here. GK *5752*.
22. Or, "audience room". Used only here. GK *211*. Related to "hearer" in Rom 2:13.
23. Or, "tribunes". On this word, see 21:31. That is, men like Lysias, though he is not said to have been there. There were five cohorts in Caesarea, each led by a tribune.
24. This is an idiom, more literally, "the men *of* the city with-respect-to prominence". Used only here. GK *2029*.
25. That is, Caesarea.
26. Or, "throng, crowd, mass, number, multitude". That is, the whole group of leaders Festus spoke with. On this word, see "multitude" in 6:2.
27. Or, "petitioned". On this word, see "intercede" in Rom 8:34.
28. On "ought to", see 25:10.
29. More literally, he "laid hold of *the fact*". On this word, see "overcome" in Jn 1:5. Some manuscripts say "But having comprehended" {N}, combining this point with point 2E.
30. More literally, "has", as the Greek typically phrases it.
31. Same word as "certainty" in in 21:34. The Romans in Judea end exactly where Lysias began, seeking this certainty.
32. That is, to the Emperor. Same word as "master" in Mt 8:2.
33. Or, "investigation". Used only here. GK *374*. Related to "examine" in 24:8.
34. Some manuscripts say "something to write" {N}.
35. Some manuscripts say "for" {N}, meaning "on behalf of ".
36. Same word as in v 2. On this word, see Lk 21:14.

A. Eph 3:1 B. Lk 1:9 C. Jn 5:45 D. Act 23:29 E. Rom 14:10 F. Mt 14:28 G. Jn 18:38 H. 2 Cor 4:8 J. 1 Tim 6:4, controversy K. Jam 1:18, willed L. Mt 7:1, judge M. 1 Pet 1:17, call upon N. Act 27:1, imperial O. Mt 14:28, order P. Mt 3:3 Q. Rev 16:6 R. Jude 10, unreasoning S. Rev 1:1 T. 1 Tim 2:12 U. Act 27:30

| Acts 26:2 | 490 | Verse |

1E. "King Agrippa, I regard¹ myself fortunate²— being about to speak-a-defense before you today concerning everything *of* which I am being accused³ by *the* Jews   2

    1F. "Especially⁴ you being *an* expert⁵ *of* all *of* both the customs^A and issues^B in relation to *the* Jews   3
    2F. "Therefore I beg⁶ *that you* listen-to me patiently

2E. "Indeed then, all the⁷ Jews know my manner-of-life from youth— *it* having taken place from *the* first⁸ in my nation⁹ and in Jerusalem, *they* knowing me beforehand¹⁰ from-the-beginning¹¹ if they are willing^C to testify^D— that¹² I lived *as a* Pharisee in accordance with the strictest¹³ sect^E *of* our religion^F   4, 5

    1F. "And now I am standing *here* being judged^G for *the* hope^H *of* the promise^J having been made by God to our fathers¹⁴— *to which our twelve tribes are hoping to attain¹⁵, while worshiping^K night and day¹⁶ with fervency¹⁷!   6, 7

        1G. "Concerning which hope, I am being accused by *the* Jews, King¹⁸
        2G. "Why is it being judged^G unbelievable¹⁹ among you²⁰ *people* if God raises^L *the* dead?   8

3E. "So indeed²¹, I thought^M to myself *that I* ought-to^N do many *things* contrary²² to the name *of* Jesus the Nazarene^O— *which indeed I did in Jerusalem   9, 10

    1F. "And I both locked-up²³ many *of* the saints^P in prisons, having received the authority^Q from the chief priests, and— while they *were* being killed²⁴— cast my vote²⁵ against *them*
    2F. "And while punishing^R them often throughout all the synagogues²⁶, I was compelling²⁷ *them* to blaspheme²⁸   11

4E. "And being exceedingly²⁹ enraged *at* them, I was persecuting^S them as far as even to the outside³⁰ cities— *during which, while proceeding to Damascus with authority^Q and *a* commission³¹ *from* the chief priests, *in the* middle *of the* day along the road, King, I saw *a* **light** from heaven beyond the brightness *of* the sun, having shined-around³² me and the *ones* going with me   12, 13

    1F. "And we all having fallen down to the ground, I heard *a* voice saying to me³³ *in* the Hebrew language^T, 'Saul, Saul, why are you persecuting^S Me? *It is* hard^U *for* you to kick against *the* goads³⁴'   14
    2F. "And I said, 'Who are You, sir?'³⁵   15
    3F. "And the Lord said³⁶, 'I am Jesus Whom **you** are persecuting. *But arise and stand on your feet. For I appeared^V *to* you for this— to appoint^W you *as a* servant^X, and *a* witness^Y   16

        1G. 'Both *of* which *things* you saw^V *as to* Me³⁷
        2G. 'And *of* which *things* I shall be seen^V *by* you³⁸ *while rescuing³⁹ you from the [Jewish] people, and from the Gentiles— to whom **I** am⁴⁰ sending you forth^Z *to open their eyes   17, 18

            1H. '*That they may* turn^AA from darkness to light, and *from* the authority^Q *of* Satan to God

1. The grammar implies "I have regarded and continue to regard". That is, I am in a state of regarding myself fortunate. On this word, see Jam 1:2.
2. Or, "blessed". On this word, see "blessed" in Lk 6:20.
3. Same word as in v 7, and in 23:28, 29. Related to "accusation" in 23:29. On this word, see "bring a charge" in Rom 8:33.
4. Or this may be punctuated, "You being especially expert *in* all...".
5. Or, "knowledgeable *one*". Used only here. GK *1195*. Related to "know".
6. Some manuscripts add "you" {N}, so that it says "I beg you to listen...".
7. Some manuscripts omit this word {C}.
8. Or, "beginning". That is, from when Paul came to Jerusalem to be brought up at the feet of Gamaliel, 22:3. On this word, see "beginning" in Col 1:18.
9. That is, Israel, as Paul uses "my nation" elsewhere in 24:17; 28:19. Some think he means Cilicia.
10. Or, "previously-knowing me". That is, before this incident. On this word, see "foreknew" in Rom 8:29.
11. That is, from the beginning of my life in Jerusalem. On this word, see "again" in Jn 3:3. Luke uses "from *the* first" (v 4) and "from-the-beginning" together also in Lk 1:2-3.
12. This is Paul's description of his "manner of life" (v 4), which all the Jews know about him.
13. Or, "most accurate, most precise, most exact". Used only here. GK *207*. Related to "strictness" in 22:3, and "accurately" in Mt 2:8.
14. That is, the hope of resurrection life with God. It is the historic hope of Israel, of Abraham (Heb 11:16).
15. Or, "come to, arrive at, reach". It is the current hope of Israel to attain to this promise. Same word as in 27:12; Eph 4:13; Phil 3:11. Elsewhere only as "come" in Act 16:1; 18:19, 24; 28:13; 1 Cor 10:11; "arrive" in Act 20:15; 21:7; 25:13; and "reach" in 1 Cor 14:36. GK *2918*.
16. That is, continually. On this phrase, see Rev 7:15.
17. Or, "earnestness". Used only here. GK *1755*. The root word is "stretch out". Related to "fervently" in 1 Pet 1:22; and "fervent" in 1 Pet 4:8.
18. Some manuscripts add "Agrippa" {N}.
19. Or, "not believable, incredible". Used elsewhere 22 times meaning "unbeliever" or "unbelieving". GK *603*.
20. This word is plural. To reflect this, "people" is added. Some think that Paul means his current audience; others, you Jews. Compare 17:32; 23:8.
21. Paul resumes from v 5. So as a Pharisee, "I thought....". Having summarized the key issue in v 6-8, he now returns to the beginning to give the details.
22. Or, "opposed, hostile". Same adjective as in 28:17; 27:4. Paul uses this word of the Jews in 1 Thes 2:15.
23. Elsewhere only in Lk 3:20. GK *2881*.
24. That is, in mob actions, as happened to Stephen (7:58; 8:1), not in legal executions through Rome. On this word, see Mt 2:16.
25. Literally, "pebble", used to cast a vote. That is, as the authorized representative of the chief priests. On this word, see "pebble" in Rev 2:17.
26. On this phrase, compare 22:19.
27. The grammar may mean "*trying to* compel", or, "*repeatedly* compelling". On this word, see Gal 6:12.
28. That is, to deny or curse (1 Cor 12:3) Jesus, if Paul is still viewing his past, and the "blasphemy" in particular, from his present Christian standpoint (note "saints" in v 10). Some think he is referring to blasphemy from the Jewish point of view as a Pharisee persecuting Christians at that time in his life, in which case blasphemy would mean confessing Jesus as the Messiah (compare Mt 26:65). On this word, see 1Tim 6:1.
29. Or, "beyond measure, very, even more". Paul could mean he was enraged "beyond measure". Or, he could mean he was enraged "even more", the persecuting in Jerusalem increasing rather than decreasing his passion. Elsewhere only as "even more" in Mt 27:23; Mk 10:26; 15:14. GK *4360*.
30. That is, outside Jerusalem or Judea.
31. Or, "full power" to act. Used only here. GK *2207*. Related to "steward" in Lk 8:3.
32. Elsewhere only in Lk 2:9. GK *4334*.
33. Some manuscripts say "speaking to me and saying..." {N}.
34. This is a proverbial saying of that day, based on an ox kicking back against the rod or goad used by the ploughman to goad him on. It is hard to resist the divine force pricking your heart. Paul speaks to what only Saul knew. On this word, see "stinger" in 1 Cor 15:56.
35. On this question, see 9:5.
36. Some manuscripts say "And the *One* said" {N}.
37. Some manuscripts omit "*as to* Me" {C}.
38. Or, "I shall appear *to* you". That is, in later visions and revelations which Paul will see.
39. Same word as in 23:27. On this word, see Gal 1:4.
40. Some manuscripts add "now" {K}.

A. Lk 1:9 B. Act 15:2 C. Jn 7:17 D. Jn 1:7 E. 1 Cor 11:19, faction F. Jam 1:26 G. Mt 7:1 H. Col 1:5 J. 1 Jn 2:25 K. Heb 12:28 L. Mt 28:6, arose M. Lk 19:11 N. Act 25:10 O. Mt 2:23 P. 1 Pet 1:16, holy Q. Rev 6:8 R. Act 22:5 S. 2 Tim 3:12 T. Act 2:6 U. Jn 6:60 V. Lk 2:26, see W. Act 22:14 X. 1 Cor 4:1, attendant Y. Act 1:8 Z. Mk 3:14, send out AA. Jam 5:19, turns back

            2H. '*That* they *may* receive forgiveness^A *of* sins, and *a* share^B among the *ones* having been sanctified¹ *by* faith in Me'

    5E. "Hence, King Agrippa, I did not become² disobedient³ *to* the heavenly vision^C, but was declaring^D   19
                                                                                                              20

        1F. "*To* the *ones* both in Damascus first and *in* Jerusalem, and *throughout* all the country *of* Judea
        2F. "And *to* the Gentiles
        3F. "*That they should* repent⁴ and turn^E to God, doing works^F worthy^G *of* repentance^H

    6E. "For these reasons, Jews, having seized^J me while being⁵ in the temple, were trying to murder^K *me*   21
    7E. "Therefore, having obtained^L help⁶ from God, I stand to this day,⁷ bearing-witness^M *to* both small and great, saying nothing outside *of the things* which both the Prophets and Moses spoke *about things* going to⁸ take place—   22

        1F. "Whether⁹ the Christ *is* subject-to-suffering¹⁰   23
        2F. "Whether He first¹¹ from¹² *a* resurrection *from the* dead is going to proclaim^N light both¹³ *to* the [Jewish] people and *to* the Gentiles^O"

6D. And while he *was* speaking these *things* in *his* defense, Festus says *in a* loud voice, "You are mad¹⁴, Paul. Great learning¹⁵ is turning **you** to madness¹⁶"   24

    1E. But Paul¹⁷ says, "I am not mad, most-excellent^P Festus, but I am declaring¹⁸ words *of* truth^Q and *of* sound-mindedness^R   25

        1F. "For the king knows about these *things*¹⁹— to whom indeed I am speaking while speaking-openly²⁰. For I am in no way persuaded^S *that* any²¹ *of* these *things* escape-notice-of^T him, for this has not been done²² in *a* corner^U   26
        2F. "King Agrippa, do you believe the Prophets? I know that you believe"   27

7D. And Agrippa *says* to Paul, "In *a* short *time*,²³ are you persuading^S me *so as* to make²⁴ me *a* Christian^V?"   28

    1E. And Paul *says*, "I would pray^W *to* God *that* both in *a* short *time* and in *a* long *time*,²⁵ not only you, but also all the *ones* hearing me today, *might* become such *ones* of-what-sort²⁶ **I** also am²⁷— except for these bonds²⁸"   29

8D. And²⁹ the king stood up, and the governor; and Bernice and the *ones* sitting with them   30

    1E. And having gone-away³⁰, they were speaking to one another, saying that "This man is in no way doing anything³¹ worthy^G *of* death or imprisonment"   31
    2E. And Agrippa said *to* Festus, "This man could have been released^X if he had not appealed-to Caesar"   32

11B. And when it was determined^Y *that* we³² *should* sail-away to Italy³³, they were handing-over^Z both Paul and some other prisoners *to a* centurion^AA *of the* Imperial³⁴ cohort^BB, Julius *by* name   27:1

    1C. And having boarded *an* Adramyttian³⁵ ship being about to sail to the places along [the coast of] Asia,³⁶ we put-to-sea— Aristarchus³⁷, *a* Macedonian *of* Thessalonica, being with us   2

1. Or, "made holy, set apart *to God*". On this word, see Heb 10:29.
2. Or, "prove to be". GK *1181*.
3. That is, Paul became totally obedient. On this idiom, see "no small" in 12:18.
4. Elsewhere only in Mt 3:2; 4:17; 11:20, 21; 12:41; Mk 1:15; 6:12; Lk 10:13; 11:32; 13:3, 5; 15:7, 10; 16:30; 17:3, 4; Act 2:38; 3:19; 8:22; 17:30; 2 Cor 12:21; Rev 2:5, 16, 21, 22; 3:3, 19; 9:20, 21; 16:9, 11. GK *3566*. Related to "repentance" next.
5. Some manuscripts omit "while being" {C}.
6. This word was used of the help or aid received from an ally. Used only here. GK *2135*. The related noun (not in the NT) is "ally".
7. Or, this may be punctuated "help from God to this day, I stand *here* testifying".
8. More literally, "*of things* going to".
9. Or, "If ". Paul presents these two issues as questions to be considered based on Scripture. These are the two main subjects Paul reasons about with the Jews— whether the Scriptures teach these two things— and are the same two subjects Jesus mentions in Lk 24:46. For simplicity, others render this word "that", making these two statements. Same idiom as in 4:19; 5:8; Mk 15:44; Jn 9:25; 1 Cor 7:16; etc. GK *1623*.
10. That is, whether the Scriptures teach that the Messiah can suffer, is capable of suffering. He does suffer, as Isa 53 shows. Note Act 3:18. First comes the suffering, then the glory, 1 Pet 1:11. Used only here. GK *4078*. Related to "sufferings" in Phil 3:10.
11. Paul may mean first before others, "whether He *the* first *One* from...", a thought similar to firstfruits of the dead in 1 Cor 15:20. Or he may mean first before glory, "whether He first" (before He comes as the King in glory, incapable of suffering) "from *a* resurrection *from the* dead" (implying also His suffering and death) is going to proclaim...". Death could not hold Jesus, 13:35. From it, He proclaims the light of salvation.
12. Or, "by, by means of ". Same phrase as "by *the* resurrection *from the* dead" in Rom 1:4.
13. Some manuscripts omit this word {K}. Paul is referring to Isa 49:6.
14. Or, "raving, out of your mind". Same word as in v 25. On this word, see 1 Cor 14:23.
15. Or, "Much learning". On this word, see "writings" in Jn 7:15.
16. Used only here. GK *3444*. Related to "mad" earlier. The Greek is *mania*, from which our word comes.
17. Some manuscripts say "But the *one* says" {K}.
18. Or, "speaking out, uttering". On this word, see "uttering" in 2:4.
19. Not firsthand, by report. Agrippa was born in A.D. 28, and lived in Rome until about A.D. 50.
20. Or, "speaking boldly, speaking freely". On this word, see "speak boldly" in Eph 6:20.
21. Some manuscripts omit this word {C}, so that it may be rendered either "For I am not persuaded *that* any *of* these *things*", *or* "For I am persuaded *that* none *of* these *things*".
22. This is a participle, "is not having been done". This is another understatement (litotes), on which see 12:18. It was done right out in the open, for all to see.
23. Or, "with *a* little *effort*, in *a* little *while*, with *a* brief *speech*". Some paraphrase this here as "almost". Whichever is chosen, v 29 is to be rendered the same way. Some take this as a question, "In [such] *a* short *time*", do you think you can persuade me?; others, as a statement, "In *a* short *time* [longer]" you are going to persuade me. In either case, Agrippa is evading a direct answer. He does not want to say "No, I do not believe the Prophets", nor does he want to say he believes them and be drawn into the discussion about what they teach (v 23). He saw exactly where Paul was leading with his question, and refused to go there. There are other views. Consult the commentaries.
24. Some manuscripts instead say "become" {A}, as in v 29, so that it says, "persuading me to become *a* Christian".
25. Or, "with *a* little *effort* and *a* great *effort*", or "with *a* brief *speech* and *a* long *speech*".
26. This word is elsewhere only in 1 Cor 3:13; Gal 2:6; 1 Thes 1:9; Jam 1:24. GK *3961*.
27. That is, Christians, to use Agrippa's word from v 28.
28. Or, "this imprisonment". Same word as "imprisonment" in v 31. On this word, see "imprisonment" in Phil 1:7. Paul is probably not implying that he was physically restrained at the time, but is speaking of his continuing custody there. Consult the commentaries.
29. Some manuscripts say "And he having said these *things*, the king..." {N}.
30. Or, "withdrawn, retired". On this word, see "went back" in Mt 4:12.
31. Some manuscripts omit this word {C}, so that it says "This man is doing nothing worthy...". Compare 23:29; 25:25.
32. Luke returns as a participant from here until the end of the book. He was last heard from in 21:18.
33. That is, when the arrangements had been made and the time to leave arrived.
34. Or, "Augustan". That is, a cohort performing duties for the Emperor. Elsewhere only as "Emperor" in 25:21, 25. GK *4935*.
35. That is, a ship from the seaport town of Adramyttium in the region of Mysia, near the town of Troas. GK *101*.
36. That is, from Caesarea, along to places on the coast of the province of Asia; along modern-day Turkey.
37. On this man, see 19:29. Both he and Luke came with Paul from Troas to Jerusalem, and apparently remained in Israel during Paul's two-year confinement. They now set off with him to Rome.

A. Col 1:14   B. Col 1:12   C. 2 Cor 12:1   D. 1 Jn 1:3, announcing   E. Jam 5:19, turns back   F. Mt 26:10   G. Rev 16:6   H. 2 Cor 7:10   J. Lk 2:21, conceived   K. Act 5:30   L. Lk 20:35, attain   M. Jn 1:7, testify   N. Phil 1:18   O. Act 15:23   P. Lk 1:3   Q. Jn 4:23   R. 1 Tim 2:9   S. 1 Jn 3:19   T. 2 Pet 3:5   U. Mk 12:10   V. 1 Pet 4:16   W. Rom 9:3   X. Mt 5:31, sends away   Y. Mt 7:1, judge   Z. Mt 26:21   AA. Mt 8:5   BB. Mt 27:27

2C. And *on* another[1] *day* we put in at Sidon[2]   3

    1D. And Julius, having treated[A] Paul humanely[3], permitted[B] *him* to obtain care[4], having gone to *his* friends

3C. And from there, having put-to-sea[C], we sailed-under-*the-shelter-of*[5] Cyprus, because of the   4
    winds being contrary.[6] ⁕And having sailed-through the open-sea[D] along Cilicia[7] and   5
    Pamphylia[8], we came down to Myra *of* Lycia[9]

    1D. And there the centurion, having found *an* Alexandrian ship[10] sailing to Italy, put us on   6
    board in it

4C. And in many days[11], sailing-slowly and with-difficulty[E], having come-to-be off Cnidus[12]— the   7
    wind not permitting us to go farther[13]— we sailed-under-*the-shelter-of* Crete[14] off Salmone[15].
    And sailing-along[16] it[17] with-difficulty[E], we came to *a* certain place being called Fair Havens[18],   8
    near *to* which was *the* city Lasea[19]

5C. And *a* considerable time having passed,[20] and the voyage being already dangerous[21] because   9
    even the Fast[22] *had* passed-by already[23]—

    1D. Paul was advising[F], ⁕saying *to* them, "Men, I perceive[G] that the voyage will-certainly[24] be   10
    with damage[25] and great loss[H]— not only *of* the cargo[J] and the ship, but also *of* our lives[K]"
    2D. But the centurion was being persuaded[L] more *by* the helmsman[M] and the captain[26] than   11
    by the *things* being said by Paul
    3D. And the harbor being unsuitable for wintering, the majority made *a* plan[27] to put-to-sea[C]   12
    from there[28]— if somehow they might be able to spend-the-winter having attained[N] to
    Phoenix[29], *a* harbor *of* Crete looking toward[30] *the* southwest and toward *the* northwest

6C. Now *a* south-*wind*[31] having blown-moderately— having supposed[O] *that they* had[32] taken-hold-   13
    of[P] *their* purpose[33], having lifted *anchor*, they were sailing-along very-near Crete. ⁕But after not   14
    much *time*, *a* violent[34] wind rushed[35] down *from* it[36]— the *one* being called the "Northeaster"[37]

    1D. And the ship having been seized[38] and not being able to face-into[39] the wind, we were   15
    being carried-along[Q], having given *ourselves* up *to it*

        1E. And having run-under-*the-shelter-of a* certain small-island being called Cauda[40], 16
        we were able with-difficulty[E] to come-to-be in-control[41] *of* the [ship's] boat[42]—
        having lifted which, they were using supports[43], undergirding[44] the ship   17
        2E. And fearing that[45] they might run-aground[46] at Syrtis[47], having lowered[48] the gear[49],
        in this manner they were being carried-along[Q]

1. That is, on the next day. Same expression as in 20:15.
2. This is a town about 69 miles or 111 kilometers north of Caesarea, in the region of Phoenicia. GK *4972*.
3. Or, "kindly". That is, with a love for a fellow human, with human decency. Used only here. GK *5793*. Related to "humaneness" in 28:2.
4. Or, "attention". Whether Luke means medical care, personal refreshment, or spiritual fellowship is not stated. Used only here. GK *2149*. Related to "take care of " in Lk 10:34. This does not imply Paul was unaccompanied by a guard.
5. Or, "sailed under *the lee of*". Elsewhere only in v 7. GK *5709*. The "lee" is the side of a ship or island sheltered from the wind.
6. Because the wind was contrary (that is, from the west) they could not sail the straighter course to the south of Cyprus, the one Paul took in 21:3. They had to take the the coastal route to the north so as to take advantage of the westerly currents there and the more favorable winds coming off the land. This advantage continues until Cnidus (v 7).
7. That is, the next Roman province west of Syria. On this word, see 6:9.
8. The next region west of Cilicia. GK *4103*.
9. That is, the town of Myra (GK *3688*) in the province of Lycia (GK *3379*), the next coastal area. It may have taken 15 days to reach Myra.
10. It was a grain ship carrying wheat (v 38); and 276 people (v 37). It was part of the grain fleet sailing from Alexandria in Egypt to Rome.
11. The trip from Myra to Cnidus, which would have taken one day with favorable winds, took many difficult days due to the contrary (northwest) winds.
12. This is a town on the coast of the next province, Asia, on the southwest extremity of modern Turkey. GK *3118*.
13. That is, farther west and north toward Italy. This verb, "permit to go farther", is used only here. GK *4661*.
14. They turned south and sailed over 100 miles or 160 kilometers to the island of Crete. At Salmone, they turned west and sailed along Crete's south coast, under the shelter of the island.
15. This is a town on the east end of the island of Crete. GK *4892*.
16. Or, "coasting along". Elsewhere only in v 13. GK *4162*.
17. That is, the south side of Crete.
18. Or, "Beautiful Harbors". This was the farthest point on Crete a ship fighting a northwest wind could reach, due to the geography of the island. This proper name as such is GK *2816*. "Havens" is the word "harbor", figuratively meaning "haven, retreat, refuge", and is elsewhere only as "harbor" in v 12. GK *3348*.
19. The city of Lasea is roughly in the middle of the island.
20. Luke may mean since the beginning of the voyage (perhaps a month and a half), or while waiting at Fair Havens for the winds to change.
21. Or, "prone to fall, prone to be tripped up". Used only here. GK *2195*. The root word is "to trip up, cause to fall".
22. That is, the fast on the Day of Atonement at the end of September or early October, the only fast commanded by the Law of Moses. The Mediterranean was considered unsafe for travel between mid-September and mid-November, when sailing ceased for the winter. Some think the Day of Atonement referred to here was October 5, A.D. 59.
23. Or, "by this time, now". On this word, see Mt 24:32.
24. Paul had been shipwrecked three times prior to this, 2 Cor 11:25. He draws this conclusion based on experience. On this word, see 24:15.
25. Or, "disaster, hardship, injury". Same word as in v 21. On this word, see "insult" in 2 Cor 12:10.
26. Or, the owner who acted as captain of the ship. Used only here. GK *3729*. The captain was probably an independent contractor working for the state, hauling grain from Egypt to Rome.
27. Or, "laid *a* plan, laid-*down* counsel, gave counsel". On the word "plan", see "counsel" in Eph 1:11.
28. Some manuscripts add "also" {K}, as at their previous stops, v 7-8.
29. This is a town about 38 miles or 61 kilometers further west on the south side of Crete. GK *5837*.
30. That is, looking toward the winds blowing in from these directions, meaning that the harbor faced west.
31. That is, a wind from the south, which would blow them west to Phoenix in a few hours.
32. More literally, "have", as the Greek typically phrases it.
33. Or, "plan, design". Same word as in 11:23.
34. Or, "tempestuous, typhonic". It is literally a wind "pertaining to a typhoon, hurricane, whirlwind". Used only here. GK *5607*.
35. More literally, "threw". On this word, see "throw" in Rev 2:22.
36. That is, from Crete, blowing down off of the island, driving them away from the coast.
37. Or, "Euraquilo", spelled in some manuscripts "Euroclydon" {B}, blowing from the northeast. Used only here. GK *2350*.
38. That is, seized suddenly and violently by the wind and carried away by it. On this word, see Lk 8:29.
39. This word means "to look in the eye, to look eye-to-eye to, face against". Used only here. GK *535*.
40. Some manuscripts spell this "Clauda" {B}. It is about 30 miles or 50 kilometers south of Phoenix, Crete. GK *3007*.
41. Or, "in command". Used only here. GK *4331*.
42. Or, "skiff, light boat", the small boat towed behind the ship, used to go to and from shore. It would have taken on a lot of water during this storm. Elsewhere only in v 30, 32. GK *5002*.
43. Or, "helps". Some think Luke is referring to ropes or cables which ancient ships carried for such an emergency. They were run under the hull and secured on deck to help hold the ship together. The straining caused by the heavy mast as the ship was tossed in the sea would spread the planks of the hull, causing the ship to founder and sink. Elsewhere only as "help" in Heb 4:16. GK *1069*. Related to "help" in Rev 12:16.
44. Used only here. GK *5690*. The root word is "gird" in 12:8.
45. On this idiom, see 5:26.
46. Literally, "fall off" the sea on to the land. Same word as in v 26, 29. On this word, see "fall from" in Gal 5:4.
47. That is, the Gulf of Sidra, off the coast of modern Libya, a place of shallow and shifting sands. If the sailors let the wind drive the ship in its path, they feared this northeast wind (if it blew long enough) would push them straight into the coastline of Africa, resulting in the certain loss of the ship. So they chose to turn to the wind, and be driven into the open sea. With storm sail set, they would have pointed the ship as much northward (away from Africa) as the ship could bear. This would drive them west. As the Northeaster abated, they could turn further north to Italy. GK *5358*.
48. Or, "let down". Same word as in v 30. Elsewhere only in Mk 2:4; Lk 5:4, 5; Act 9:25; 2 Cor 11:33. GK *5899*.
49. Or, "thing, equipment". This is a very general word. Some think Luke is referring to a lowering of the main sail. Others think he means a floating sea anchor to help control or slow the ship. On this word, see "vessel" in 1 Thes 4:4.

A. 1 Cor 7:21, make use of   B. 1 Tim 2:12   C. Act 20:13   D. Mt 18:6, deep part   E. 1 Pet 4:18   F. Act 27:22   G. Lk 10:18, seeing   H. Phil 3:7
J. Gal 6:5, load   K. Jam 5:20, soul   L. 1 Jn 3:19   M. Rev 18:17   N. Act 26:7   O. Lk 19:11, thinking   P. Heb 4:14, hold on to   Q. 2 Pet 1:17, carried

2D. And we being violently storm-tossed¹, *on the next* day they were doing *a* jettison² — 18
3D. And *on the third* day they³ threw-off^A the equipment⁴ *of* the ship with-*their*-own-hands — 19
4D. And neither sun nor stars appearing^B for many days,⁵ and no small⁶ storm lying-upon⁷ *us*, finally all hope *that* we *might* be saved^C was being taken-away⁸. °And⁹ much¹⁰ abstinence-from-food¹¹ being present,¹² at that time Paul, having stood in their midst^D, said — 20, 21

    1E. "O men, having obeyed¹³ me, *you* indeed should-have^E not put-to-sea^F from Crete and gained¹⁴ this damage and loss¹⁵
    2E. "And *as to* the *things* now, I advise¹⁶ *that* you cheer-up¹⁷. For there will be no loss^G *of* life^H from-*among* you, only *of* the ship — 22

        1F. "For *an* **angel** stood-before¹⁸ me *on* this night¹⁹ *from* the God Whose I²⁰ am, Whom also I serve²¹, °saying, 'Do not be afraid, Paul. You must^J stand-before^K Caesar. And behold— God has granted²² you all the *ones* sailing with you' — 23, 24
        2F. "Therefore, cheer up, men. For I believe God that it shall happen²³ in this manner— in accordance with the way²⁴ it has been spoken *to* me — 25
        3F. "But we must^J run-aground^L on *a* certain island" — 26

7C. Now when *the* fourteenth night came, while we *were* being driven-about²⁵ in the Adriatic-sea²⁶, during *the* middle *of* the night, the sailors were suspecting²⁷ *that* some land *was* approaching²⁸ them — 27

    1D. And having taken-soundings²⁹, they found *it to be* twenty fathoms³⁰ — 28
    2D. And having set *a* short interval³¹, and again having taken-soundings, they found *it to be* fifteen fathoms
    3D. And fearing that³² we might run-aground^L somewhere against rocky places, having thrown-off³³ four anchors from *the* stern³⁴, they were praying^M *that* day *might* come — 29
    4D. And while the sailors *were* seeking^N to flee^O from the ship, and *had* lowered the [ship's] boat to the sea *on a* pretense³⁵ as-*though* intending^P to stretch-out³⁶ anchors from *the* bow— — 30

        1E. Paul said *to* the centurion and the soldiers, "Unless these *ones* remain^Q in the ship, **you** cannot be saved^C" — 31
        2E. Then³⁷ the soldiers cut-off^R the ropes^S *of* the [ship's] boat, and let it fall-away³⁸ — 32

    5D. And until which *time* day was about to come, Paul was urging³⁹ everyone to receive⁴⁰ food^T, saying, "While waiting-in-expectation⁴¹ *for a* fourteenth day today, you are continuing without-food⁴², having taken^U nothing. °Therefore I urge you to receive food^T. For this is for your preservation⁴³. For *a* hair from the head *of* none *of* you will be lost⁴⁴" — 33, 34

        1E. And having said these *things*, and having taken^V bread, he gave-thanks^W *to* God in the presence of everyone. And having broken^X *it*, he began to eat — 35
        2E. And everyone having become cheerful⁴⁵, **they** also were taking^U food^T — 36
        3E. Now we, all the souls^H in the ship⁴⁶, were two-hundred seventy six⁴⁷ — 37

1. Used only here. GK *5928*. Related to "storm" in v 20.
2. Or, "*a throwing out*". Used only here. GK *1678*. The sailors were throwing off excess or unnecessary things in order to lighten the ship, as they do again in v 19 and v 38.
3. Some manuscripts say "we" {N}.
4. Related to "gear" in v 17. Luke could mean the "gear, tackle, rigging, furnishings". Used only here. GK *5006*. Whatever it was, it belonged to the ship, and the crew itself threw it overboard.
5. This would make it impossible for the sailors to determine their position.
6. On "no small", see 12:18.
7. Or, "pressing upon". On this word, see "press upon" in Lk 23:23.
8. Or, "removed". The worsening condition of the ship, and the growing weariness of the sailors, were also key factors. Same word as in 2 Cor 3:16; Heb 10:11. Elsewhere only as "cast off " in 27:40; 28:13. GK *4311*.
9. Or, "And there being much abstinence-from-food", or, "And much abstinence-from-food existing".
10. This could mean a "long" abstinence, or a "great, serious, severe" one.
11. Or, "lack of appetite, not-eating". Not related to "fasting". Used only here. GK *826*. Related to "without food" in v 33.
12. Luke seems to be implying that the lack of eating was the visible expression of the desperate situation and loss of hope, v 20. Note that Paul does not address the eating, but the fear, telling them twice to "cheer up", v 22, 25. By the fourteenth night (perhaps several days later), still having not eaten, but hope returning, Paul gets them to eat, v 33-38.
13. This word means "to obey one in authority". Elsewhere only of obeying God (Act 5:29, 32), and authorities (Tit 3:1, "be obedient"). Paul is not saying "I told you so". He is saying that he is the authority that should be listened to, to prepare for what he will say in v 23. And the others do listen to Paul after this, v 31, 36. GK *4272*.
14. Or, "incurred". This word means "to gain, profit, win". On this word, see Mk 8:36. It also can mean "to avoid or spare oneself " a loss, thereby "gaining" the loss. This would be rendered here, "Crete, and spared-yourselves this damage and loss".
15. These are the same two words Paul used in v 10.
16. Or, "recommend, urge publicly". Elsewhere only in v 9. GK *4147*. Note that in v 9, Paul's recommendation was his opinion, and was only half right. Here his words are based on revelation from God, and prove to be true.
17. Or, "be of good spirit, be cheerful". Same word as in v 25. Elsewhere only as "be cheerful" in Jam 5:13. GK *2313*. Related to "cheerful" in v 36, and to "cheerfully" in 24:10. Paul's "good cheer" is reminiscent of his singing praises in jail in 16:25.
18. Or, "stood by, beside, near". Same word as in the next verse. On this word, see "present" in Rom 12:1.
19. Assuming this conversation took place in the daytime, Paul means the night previous to the day on which he is now speaking. For a Jew, the day began at sundown. So what we would call "last night", he calls "this night", the night of this day. If the conversation took place at night before sunrise, then he means "earlier on this night still in progress".
20. In some manuscripts, the word that makes this bold (emphasized) is omitted {C}.

21. Or, "worship". On this word, see "worship" in Heb 12:28.
22. Or, "freely given". On this word, see "freely give" in 1 Cor 2:12.
23. Or, "be". On this word, see Mt 16:22.
24. This idiom, "in accordance with the way", is elsewhere only in 15:11. It is similar to "the way" in Mt 23:37; Lk 13:34; Act 1:11; 7:28; 2 Tim 3:8. The word "way" is used 13 times. GK *5573*.
25. Or, "carried different ways, cast about, carried through". GK *1422*.
26. That is, the sea between Crete and Greece, and Malta and Italy, as people of that day defined it. Used only here. GK *102*.
27. Or, "supposing". On this word, see "supposing" in 25:18. Some think the sailors heard waves breaking on the point of Koura on the island of Malta.
28. This is from the sailor's perspective. We would say "that they were approaching some land".
29. Or, "having heaved the lead". That is, having dropped a weighted line to the bottom. Used only in this verse. GK *1075*.
30. A fathom is the length of a man's outstretched arms, about six feet, or 1.8 meters. A sailor "measured" the distance to the bottom as he pulled up the weighted line. Used only in this verse. GK *3976*.
31. That is, an interval of time, which would allow an interval of distance. Based on the geography, some think Luke means about thirty minutes. Or, "having separated *a short distance*, having stood apart *a little*". On this word, "set an interval", see "separated" in Lk 24:51.
32. On this idiom, see 5:26.
33. Same word as in v 19. On this word, see "throw forth" in Mt 9:36.
34. That is, the rear of the ship, holding the ship in place pointing in to shore, waiting for daylight so they could see to navigate, praying that the anchors would hold until then. To do this, they would probably have raised the rudders (v 40).
35. That is, a falsely alleged motive. On this word, see Phil 1:18. Some think the sailors were intending to deceive the captain, and that a passenger, or Paul himself, overheard their plan.
36. Same word as in 4:30; 26:1. Used 16 times. GK *1753*.
37. Paul's prediction now coming to pass, the soldiers obey him as if he were the captain! In addition, the soldiers would surely regard it to be in their own self-interest to keep the sailors on board.
38. Or, "run aground", as in v 17, 26, 29. Luke does not mean "fall down" into the water, for it was already in the water. He means to presently "fall away, drift away" from the ship, or to ultimately "run aground".
39. Or, "encouraging, exhorting". Same word as in v 34. On this word, see "exhort" in Heb 12:8.
40. Or, "share in, receive a share of ". Same word as in v 34. On this word, see "share in" in Heb 12:10.
41. That is, for the storm to lift. On this word, see Lk 3:15. Same word as in 28:6.
42. Used only here. GK *827*. Related to "abstinence from food" in v 21.
43. Or, "deliverance". On this word, see "salvation" in Lk 19:9.
44. Or, "will perish". On this word, see "perish" in 1 Cor 1:18. Some manuscripts say "fall" {N}.
45. Or, "in good spirits". Used only here. GK *2314*. Related to "cheer up" in v 22.
46. Used as "ship" 22 times, and as a fishing "boat" 45 times. GK *4450*.
47. This is not a large number for that day. Josephus shipwrecked on a ship carrying 600 people. Some manuscripts say "about seventy six" {B}.

A. Mt 9:36, thrown forth B. Tit 2:11 C. Lk 19:10 D. 2 Thes 2:7 E. Mt 25:27 F. Act 20:13 G. Rom 11:15, rejection H. Jam 5:20, soul
J. Mt 16:21 K. Rom 12:1, present L. Gal 5:4, fell from M. Rom 9:3 N. Phil 2:21 O. 1 Cor 6:18 P. Mk 10:32, going to Q. Jn 15:4, abide
R. Gal 5:12 S. Jn 2:15 T. Mt 24:45 U. Rom 14:1, accept V. Rom 7:8 W. Mt 26:27 X. Act 2:46

Acts 27:38	498	Verse

      6D. And having been satisfied[A] *with* food, they were lightening[1] the ship— throwing-out[B] the wheat into the sea   38

  8C. And when it became day, they were not recognizing[C] the land. But they were looking-closely-at[D] *a* certain bay[2] having *a* beach, to which they were deliberating[3] whether[4] they might be able to drive-out[5] the ship   39

      1D. And having cast-off[6] the anchors, they were leaving *them* in the sea. At the same time, having unfastened[E] the ropes *of* the rudders[7], and having raised the sail[8] *to* the blowing [wind], they were holding[9] [course] for the beach   40

      2D. But having fallen-into[10] *a* place between-seas[11], they grounded[12] the vessel[13]   41

          1E. And the **bow**[14], having become stuck[15], remained immovable— but the stern was being broken-up[16] by the force[17] *of* the waves[18]

      3D. Now *the* plan[F] *of* the soldiers came-to-be that they should kill the prisoners, *that* none should escape, having swum-away   42

      4D. But the centurion, wanting[G] to bring Paul safely through[19], forbid[20] them *from their* intention[21]. And he ordered[H]   43

          1E. The *ones* being able to swim, having jumped-overboard[22] first, to go away to the land

          2E. And the rest *to follow*— some upon planks, and others on some *of* the *things* from the ship   44

      5D. And so it happened *that* everyone was brought-safely-through to the land

  9C. And having been brought-safely-through, then we[23] learned[24] that the island was[25] called Malta[26]   28:1

      1D. And the natives[27] were showing[J] us not the ordinary[28] humaneness[29]. For having lit *a* fire, they welcomed[K] us all because of the rain having set-upon[30] *us* and because of the cold   2

      2D. And Paul having gathered[L] *a* certain[31] quantity[32] *of* dry-sticks, and having put *them* on the fire— *a* viper having come-out[33] because of the heat fastened-on his hand   3

          1E. And when the natives saw the beast[M] hanging[N] from his hand, they were saying to one another, "Surely[O] this man is *a* murderer whom, having been brought-safely-through from the sea, Justice[34] did not allow[P] to live"   4

          2E. Then indeed the *one*, having shaken-off[Q] the beast into the fire, suffered[R] no harm   5

          3E. And the *ones* were expecting[S] *that* he *was* about to be swelling-up, or suddenly be falling down dead   6

          4E. But while they for *a* long *time were* waiting-in-expectation[S] and observing nothing out-of-place[T] happening to him— having changed *their* minds[35], they were saying *that* he was[36] *a* god

      3D. Now in the *areas* around that place were lands *belonging to* the leading[37] *official of* the island, Publius *by* name— who, having welcomed[U] us, entertained[38] *us* courteously[39] *for* three days   7

          1E. And it came about *that* the father *of* Publius *was* lying-down, being gripped[V] *with* fevers[40] and dysentery[41], to whom having gone in and having prayed, having laid[W] *his* hands on him, Paul healed[X] him   8

1. That is, so the sailors could get the ship as close to shore as possible before it hit ground. Used only here. GK *3185*.
2. Today, this bay on Malta is called St. Paul's Bay.
3. Or, "deciding, planning". On this word, see "plan" in Jn 11:53. Some manuscripts have a different tense, meaning "deliberated, decided, planned" {K}.
4. Or, "were planning (if they could) to drive out the vessel".
5. Elsewhere only in 7:45. GK *2034*.
6. Or, "removed". That is, the sailors threw off the ropes to the four anchors in v 29. On this word, see "take away" in v 20.
7. Or, "steering paddles". Greek ships had two oar-like paddles to steer the ship. Some think Luke means the sailors unlashed these rudders from their raised position, so that they could again steer the ship. Elsewhere only in Jam 3:4. GK *4382*.
8. That is, the foresail, near the bow. Used only here. GK *784*.
9. On this word, see "hold down" in Rom 1:18.
10. Or, "encountered". On this word, see Jam 1:2.
11. That is, a reef or sandbar, an underwater point of land with deeper sea on both sides. The ship did not make it all the way to shore, as they had hoped. So they had to swim. Used only here. GK *1458*.
12. Or, "ran aground, brought to shore, beached". Used only here. GK *2131*.
13. Or, "large ship". Used only here. GK *3730*. Compare "ship" in v 37.
14. That is, the front of th ship. Luke uses grammar that emphasizes the linkage between the two halves of this sentence.
15. Or, "jammed, fixed, planted". Used only here. GK *2242*.
16. Or, "broken to pieces, broken down". On this word, see "break" in Mt 5:19.
17. Or, "violence". On this word, see "violence" in 5:26.
18. Some manuscripts omit "*of* the waves" {C}.
19. This word, "to bring safely through, to save, to rescue" is also in v 44; 28:1, 4; 23:24; 1 Pet 3:20. Elsewhere only as "restore" in Mt 14:36; Lk 7:3. GK *1407*.
20. Or, "prevented, stopped". On this word, see 1 Cor 14:39.
21. Or, "purpose, will". On this word, see "will" in 1 Pet 4:3.
22. More literally, "thrown [themselves] from [the ship]". Used only here. GK *681*.
23. Some manuscripts say "they" {K}.
24. Or, "recognized", as this same word is used in 27:39.
25. More literally, "is", as the Greek typically phrases it.
26. This means the storm blew them about 476 miles or 762 kilometers west from Crete, about half the distance from Israel to Italy. Malta is about 50 miles or 80 kilometers south of Sicily. The Greek is "Melita". Used only here. GK *3514*.
27. Or, "barbarians". That is, the local non-Greek-speaking people on this Roman island. They were civilized people, but "foreigners" from Luke's Greek point of view. On this word, see "barbarian" in Col 3:11.
28. Literally, not a kindness "having happened", the same idiom as in 19:11. Another of Luke's understatements (see 12:18). That is, a love-of-mankind out of the ordinary, unusual, extraordinary. GK *5593*.
29. Or, "love-for-mankind, philanthropy, kindness". On this word, see "love for mankind" in Tit 3:4. Related to the word in 27:3.
30. Or, "having set in, having stood upon" them. That is, now pouring upon them. On this word, see "suddenly come upon" in Lk 21:34.
31. Some manuscripts omit this word {K}.
32. That is, an arm-load of sticks.
33. Some manuscripts say "come out through [the sticks]" {N}.
34. That is, the goddess of justice, justice personified as a deity; or, justice as an abstract concept. GK *1472*.
35. Or, "changed sides, turned about". Used only here. GK *3554*.
36. More literally, "is", as the Greek typically phrases it.
37. Or, "chief *man*". While this could simply mean "the leading *man*" of the island (as the plural of this word is used in 13:50; 25:2; 28:17; etc.), it has been found in inscriptions on Malta as an official title. The first man of Malta. Some think it is a title used of the highest Roman official on the island. Others think it is a title used with reference to a non-Roman office. On this word, see "first" in 1 Cor 15:3.
38. Or, "received *us* as guests, gave *us* lodging". Same word as in Heb 13:2. On this word, see "lodging" in Act 10:6.
39. Or, "kindly, in a friendly manner". Used only here. GK *5819*.
40. That is, recurring attacks of fever. Elsewhere only in Mt 8:15; Mk 1:31; Lk 4:38, 39; Jn 4:52. GK *4790*. The root word is "fire". Related to "sick with fever" in Mk 1:30.
41. Our English word comes from this Greek word, *dusenterion*. Used only here. GK *1548*.

A. 1 Cor 4:8   B. Jn 12:31, cast out   C. Col 1:6, understood   D. Heb 10:24, consider   E. Heb 13:5, let go   F. Eph 1:11, counsel   G. Jam 1:18, willed   H. Mt 14:28   J. Act 17:31, grant   K. Rom 14:1, accept   L. Mt 17:22   M. Rev 13:1   N. Act 10:39   O. 1 Cor 9:10   P. 1 Cor 10:13   Q. Lk 9:5   R. Gal 3:4   S. Lk 3:15, waiting in expectation   T. 2 Thes 3:2   U. Heb 11:17, receive   V. Mt 4:24   W. Lk 10:30, laid on   X. Mt 8:8

	2E. And this having taken place, the others on the island having infirmities[A] were also coming to *him* and being cured[B]—*who also honored[C] us *with* many honors[D], and *at our* putting-to-sea[E], provided[1] the *things* for *our* needs[2]	9 10

10C. And after three months,[3] we put-to-sea[E] in *a* ship having spent the winter at the island[4]— *an* Alexandrian[5] *one* marked[6] *with the* Twin-brothers[7]   11

    1D. And having put-in at Syracuse[8], we stayed[F] three days—*from which, having cast-off[9], we came[G] to Rhegium[10]   12-13

    2D. And after one day, *a* south *wind* having come up, we came[H] on the second day to Puteoli[11]— where, having found brothers, we were invited[J] to stay[F] with them *for* seven days[12]   14

11C. And so we came[13] to Rome. *And from there the brothers[K], having heard the *things* concerning us, came[14] as far as *the* Forum *of* Appius[15] and *the* Three Taverns[16] to meet[17] us— whom having seen, Paul, having given-thanks[L] *to* God, took[M] courage[18]   15

12B. And when we entered into Rome, it was permitted[N] *to* Paul[19] to stay[O] by himself,[20] with the soldier guarding[P] him   16

    1C. And it came about after three days *that* he[21] called-together the *ones* being leading[Q] *ones of* the Jews   17

        1D. And they having come together, he was saying to them

            1E. "**I**— men[R], brothers[K]— having done nothing contrary *to our* people or *our* ancestors[22]' customs[S], was handed-over[T] *as a* prisoner[U] from Jerusalem into the hands *of* the Romans

                1F. "Who, having examined[23] me, were wanting[V] to release[W] me because of *there* being no charge[24] *worthy of* death in connection with me   18

                2F. "But the Jews speaking-against[25] *it*, I was compelled[X] to appeal-to[Y] Caesar[26]— not as-*though* having anything to accuse[Z] my nation   19

            2E. "For this reason therefore, I called-for[27] you, to see and speak to *you*. For I am wearing[AA] this chain[28] for the sake of the hope[29] *of* Israel"   20

        2D. And the *ones* said to him   21

            1E. "**We** neither received letters from Judea concerning you, nor did any *of* the brothers having arrived report[BB] or speak anything evil[CC] concerning you

            2E. "And we consider-*it*-fitting[DD] *that we* hear from you *the things* which you think[EE]. For indeed concerning this sect[30], it is known[FF] *to* us that it is being spoken-against[GG] everywhere"   22

    2C. And having appointed[HH] *a* day *for* him, more came to him at *his* lodging[31]— *to* whom he was explaining[JJ] *it* from early-in-the-morning[KK] until evening, solemnly-testifying[LL] *as* to the kingdom[MM] *of* God, and persuading[NN] them concerning Jesus from both the Law *of* Moses and the Prophets   23

1. Same word as "laid on" in v 8. Paul laid hands on them; they "laid on" us the things we needed. Or, "put on [the ship]". On this word, see "laid on" in Lk 10:30.
2. Some manuscripts have this word singular {N}, "need".
3. That is, some time in February.
4. It would have been in the port of Valetta.
5. Being from Alexandria, Egypt, it may also have been part of the grain fleet.
6. Or, taking this adjective as a noun, "*with the* Twin-brothers mark". This word refers to the emblem, sign, ensign, insignia of a ship. Some think Luke is referring to a carved figurehead. Others think he means an emblem painted on each side of the prow. Used only here. GK *4185*.
7. Or, "Dioscuri". That is, the Greek gods Castor and Pollux, twin sons of Zeus and Leda. They were the patron gods of sailors. Used only here. GK *1483*.
8. This is the chief city of Sicily, on the east side of the island, about 80 miles or 128 kilometers north or Malta. GK *5352*.
9. Same word as in 27:40. Presumably, Luke is referring to the ropes securing them. Some manuscripts say "having gone around" {C}, which may mean "by tacking".
10. This town is on the toe of Italy, across the strait of Messina from Sicily, about 70 miles or 112 kilometers further. GK *4836*.
11. This was a major port on the west side of Italy, a journey of about 182 miles or 290 kilometers. GK *4541*.
12. Presumably this was allowed by Julius the centurion (as in 27:3), while he was attending other business. He had to make arrangements for their 130 mile or 210 kilometer journey by road to Rome. This does not imply that Paul was unguarded during this week.
13. Or, "went". Luke could be looking back, "in this manner— with such a voyage— we came to Rome". Or he could be looking forward, "in this manner— using the road from Puteoli to Rome— we went to Rome".
14. Some manuscripts say "came out" {N}.
15. Some came for a meeting here, 39 miles or 63 kilometers south of Rome.
16. Or, "Three Inns". Some came for a meeting here, 30 miles or 49 kilometers south of Rome.
17. This is an idiom, literally "for *a* meeting" with us. On this word, see Mt 25:6.
18. This noun is used only here. GK *2511*. Related to the verb in 23:11. Paul had written them the book of Romans (in Act 20:2), about three years earlier, and now takes courage from their concern for him.
19. Some manuscripts say "Rome, the centurion handed over the prisoners *to* the captain of the guard. But it was permitted..." {A}.
20. That is, in his own lodging (v 23), or rented quarters (v 30), rather than in prison.
21. Some manuscripts say "Paul" {K}.
22. That is, the customs passed down from our forefathers. On this word, see 24:14. It is plural here.
23. Same word as in 24:8.
24. Same word as in 25:18, 27. Same phrase, "charge *worthy of* death", as in 13:28.
25. Or, "objecting, opposing". Same word as in v 22. On this word, see "contradict" in Rom 10:21.
26. On this, see 25:11.
27. Or, "called you alongside *me*, called you to *me*". Or, "appealed to you to see and speak to *me*". On this word, see "exhorting" in Rom 12:8.
28. Elsewhere only in Mk 5:3, 4; Lk 8:29; Act 12:6, 7; 21:33; Eph 6:20; 2 Tim 1:16; Rev 20:1. GK *268*. Whether or not Paul has been chained since 22:29 (opinions differ), now the Romans thus maintain control of him in his quarters.
29. Same word as in 23:6; 24:15; 26:6, 7. Broadly, this refers to the fulfillment of God's promises in Jesus the Messiah. On this word, see Col 1:5.
30. That is, Christians. On this word, see "faction" in 1 Cor 11:19.
31. Elsewhere only in Phm 22. GK *3825*. Related to "entertained" in 28:7.

A. Mt 8:17, weakness B. Mt 8:7 C. 1 Tim 5:3 D. 1 Tim 5:17 E. Act 20:13 F. Rom 11:22, continue G. Act 26:7, attain H. Mk 16:2 J. Rom 12:8, exhorting K. Act 16:40 L. Mt 26:27 M. Rom 7:8 N. 1 Tim 2:12, permit O. Jn 15:4, abide P. Jn 12:25, keep Q. 1 Cor 15:3, first R. 1 Tim 2:12 S. Lk 1:9 T. Mt 26:21 U. Eph 3:1 V. Jam 1:18, willed W. Mt 5:31, sends away X. Gal 6:12 Y. 1 Pet 1:17, call upon Z. Jn 5:45 AA. Heb 5:2, surrounded BB. 1 Jn 1:3, announcing CC. Act 25:18 DD. Act 15:38 EE. Rom 8:5 FF. Rom 1:19 GG. Rom 10:21, contradict HH. Rom 13:1, established JJ. Act 11:4 KK. Mk 13:35 LL. 1 Tim 5:21, solemnly charge MM. Mt 3:2 NN. 1 Jn 3:19

	1D. And some were being persuaded[A] *by* the *things* being said, but others were not-believing[1]	24
	2D. And being not-in-agreement[2] with one another, they were departing[3]— Paul having spoken one statement[B], that	25
	1E. "The Holy Spirit spoke **rightly**[C] through Isaiah the prophet [in Isa 6:9-10] to your[4] fathers,* saying, 'Go to this people and say— [5]	26
	1F. '*In* hearing, you will hear and by no means understand. And while seeing, you will see and by no means perceive. *For the heart *of* this people became dull, and they hardly heard *with their* ears, and they closed their eyes	27
	1G. 'That they might not ever see *with their* eyes, and hear *with their* ears, and understand *in their* heart, and turn-back, and I shall heal them'[6]	
	2E. "Therefore let it be known[D] *to* you that this[7] salvation[E] *of* God was sent-forth[F] ***to the Gentiles. They*** also will hear *it*[8]"	28
		29[9]
	3C. And he[10] stayed[G] two whole years[11] in *his* own rented-*quarters*[12]. And he was welcoming[H] all the *ones* coming-in to him—*proclaiming[J] the kingdom *of* God, and teaching[K] the *things* concerning the Lord Jesus Christ with all boldness[13], without-hindrance[14]	30
		31

1. Or, "refusing to believe". On this word, see "are faithless" in 2 Tim 2:13.
2. Or, "being at variance, not being harmonious". Used only here. GK *851*. Related to "agreement" in 1 Cor 7:5, and "agree" in Mt 18:19.
3. Used only here with this grammar. These Jews were "releasing *themselves*, letting *themselves* go, dismissing *themselves*". On this word, see "sends away" in Mt 5:31.
4. Some manuscripts say "our" {B}.
5. See Mt 13:14-15 on the following quotation (through v 27), which is exactly the same there.
6. Paul places the blame on these Jews for not entering the process that results in spiritual healing— see and hear, understand, turn back, be healed. They shut their hearts, not wanting to hear it. Compare Jn 12:40.
7. Some manuscripts say "the" {K}.
8. Or, "And **they** will listen".
9. Some manuscripts add as v 29, "And he having spoken these *things*, the Jews departed, having *a* great dispute among themselves" {A}.
10. Some manuscripts say "Paul" {K}.
11. Thus closing the book of Acts some time in A.D. 62. Some think Paul's case was then dismissed, the Jews having failed to prosecute it; others, that it was heard and he won. Some think that during this two-year period in Rome, Paul wrote Ephesians, Philippians (note Phil 1:13; 4:22), Colossians, and Philemon (which are accordingly called the Prison Epistles). Others think these letters were written during an imprisonment in Ephesus during Acts 19; others, in Caesarea during the two years there, Act 24:27. After Acts 28, some think that Paul was released and traveled again, during which time he wrote 1 Timothy and Titus. Then he was imprisoned again in Rome, during which he wrote 2 Timothy. Then he was beheaded. There are other views.
12. Or, "at his own expense", in Roman government quarters. Used only here. GK *3637*. Related to "hire, pay wages".
13. Or, "confidence, openness, freedom-of-speech". This phrase, "with all boldness" is also in 4:29; Phil 1:20. On this word, see "confidence" in Heb 4:16.
14. Or, "unforbidden". Used only here. GK *219*. Related to "forbid" in 1 Cor 14:39. In the providence of God, this arrangement allowed Paul to reach Rome while being protected from the Jews by the Roman government!

A. 1 Jn 3:19 B. Rom 10:17, word C. Act 10:33, well D. Rom 1:19 E. Lk 2:30 F. Mk 3:14, send out G. Gal 3:10, continue in H. Act 2:41 J. 2 Tim 4:2 K. Rom 12:7

Overview | **Romans**

Introduction — 1:1-17

1A. The wrath of God is revealed against all ungodliness of people holding down the truth — 1:18

    1B. Because the thing known of God is evident in them, for God made it evident to them — 1:19-20
    2B. Because having known God, they did not glorify Him as God, but became futile in thinking — 1:21

        1C. They became foolish and exchanged God for an idol. God handed them to impurity — 1:22-24
        2C. Who exchanged the truth of God for the lie. God handed them to dishonor — 1:25-27
        3C. And as they did not approve of God, God handed them over to a disapproved mind — 1:28-32

    3B. Therefore you are without excuse, O human— everyone judging — 2:1

        1C. For in what you judge others, you condemn yourself, because you do the same things — 2:1-2
        2C. But are you thinking this, O human, that you will escape the judgment of God? — 2:3
        3C. Or are you disregarding His goodness, not knowing its purpose is your repentance? — 2:4
        4C. But by your unrepentance, you are storing up wrath for yourself on the day of wrath — 2:5-8

    4B. There will be affliction and distress upon every human doing evil— the Jew and the Greek — 2:9-10

        1C. For there is no respect of persons with God — 2:11
        2C. For all who sinned will be judged, whether without the Law or through the Law — 2:12-13

            1D. For the Gentiles will be judged by the things of the Law written on their hearts — 2:14-16
            2D. But if you are a Jew and rely upon the Law, do you obey it? You transgress it. Circumcision will be of no profit to transgressors of the Law — 2:17-29

    5B. What then is the advantage of the Jew? Much in every way. God keeps His promises — 3:1-8
    6B. Therefore what? Are we better than they? No. All are under sin, accountable to God — 3:9-20

2A. But now apart from law, the righteousness of God has been revealed — 3:21

    1B. And it is the righteousness of God through faith in Jesus Christ to all the ones believing — 3:22

        1C. For there is no distinction— all have sinned, and are declared righteous as a gift through the redemption in Christ, whom God set forth as the satisfaction of His wrath — 3:22-26
        2C. Therefore where is the boasting? It was shut out by faith. God is God of all by faith — 3:27-31
        3C. Abraham also believed God, and it was credited for righteousness. This was apart from circumcision and Law, so that he might become the father of all believers — 4:1-25

    2B. Therefore, we have peace with God, and access by faith into this grace in which we stand. And we boast in the hope of the glory of God, a hope which does not put to shame — 5:1-11
    3B. Because of this, just as sin and death entered the world through one man, so also the gift of righteousness and life came through one Man. Grace now reigns over sin and death — 5:12-21
    4B. Therefore should we be continuing in sin that grace might increase? No, we died to sin — 6:1-2

        1C. Or do you not know that we were baptized into His death? — 6:3
        2C. We were buried with Him that we might be raised with Him to newness of life — 6:4-11

Romans

Overview

3C. Therefore do not let sin reign in your body, for you are not under the Law, but grace	6:12-14
5B. Therefore should we commit a sin because we are not under the Law but under grace? No	6:15
1C. Do you not know you are slaves to whom you obey? You were slave of sin, but you obeyed the teaching from the heart and were set free. Present yourself to God	6:16-23
2C. Or do you not know that the Law lords over a person only while he lives? You have died to the Law, and now serve in the newness of the Spirit. But the Law did not cause my sin or death. The sin in me used the Law to kill me	7:1-25
6B. Therefore, there is now no condemnation for the ones in Christ. For the law of the Spirit of life in Christ Jesus set you free from the law of sin and death	8:1-2
1C. For what the Law could not do, God did through His own Son for us walking in accordance with the Spirit. For you are not in the flesh, but in the Spirit	8:3-9
2C. And if Christ is in you, the body is dead, but the Spirit is life	8:10
3C. And if the Spirit is in You, God will give life to your mortal bodies through the Spirit	8:11
4C. So then, brothers, we are debtors not to the flesh. For if by the Spirit you are putting to death the practices of the body, you will live—	8:12-14
1D. For all who are being led by the Spirit of God— these are sons of God	8:14-16
2D. And if we are children, we are heirs— heirs of God and fellow heirs with Christ	8:17
1E. For the sufferings of the present are not worthy to the glory to be revealed	8:18
2E. For creation is awaiting the revelation of the sons of God, to also be set free in the glory of the children of God, and is groaning and suffering-birthpains	8:19-22
3E. And we ourselves are groaning while awaiting our adoption, for we were saved in hope of this glory we do not see. And the Spirit helps us	8:23-27
3D. And we know all things are working together for good for the ones loving God	8:28-30
7B. Therefore, what shall we say to these things? If God is for us, who can be against us?	8:31-39
3A. I am telling the truth. There is great grief for me and unceasing pain in my heart over Israel	9:1-2
1B. For I would pray that I might be accursed from Christ on behalf of my kinsmen, the Israelites	9:3-5
2B. But it is not such as that the word of God has failed	9:6
1C. For all these ones from Israel are not Israel, nor children of promise. God chooses	9:6-13
2C. Therefore is God unrighteous? No. He has mercy and He hardens whom He wants	9:14-18
3C. Therefore why does He still find fault? He is the Creator, carrying out His purposes	9:19-29
3B. Therefore, what shall we say?	9:30
1C. That Gentiles, the ones not pursuing righteousness, took hold of it by faith	9:30
2C. But Israel, pursuing the Law of righteousness, did not attain it, but stumbled on Christ	9:31-33
4B. Brothers, I pray for their salvation, but their zeal is not in accordance with knowledge	10:1-2

	Overview	**Romans**

        1C. For being ignorant of God's righteousness, they did not subject themselves to it   10:3

            1D. For Christ is the end of the Law for righteousness for everyone believing   10:4
            2D. For Moses says the one having done the Law will live. But salvation is by faith   10:5-10
            3D. For Scripture says everyone putting faith in Him will be saved— obeying the report   10:11-17
                announced. But they did not all obey the report, as Isaiah said

        2C. But I say— it is not that they did not hear. The word went out   10:18
        3C. But I say— it is not that they did not know. Moses and the prophets told them   10:19-21

    5B. Therefore did God reject His people? No. The remnant was saved, the rest hardened   11:1-10
    6B. Therefore did they stumble in order to fall? No   11:11

        1C. By their trespass, salvation came to the Gentiles. How much more their fullness   11:11-12
        2C. And I glorify my ministry to the Gentiles that I might provoke them to jealousy   11:13-15
        3C. But if the root is holy, so are the branches. God can regraft them into their tree   11:16-24
        4C. For a partial hardening has happened to Israel until the fullness of Gentiles comes in   11:25-32

    7B. O the depths of God's wisdom and knowledge. To Him be the glory forever, amen   11:33-36

4A. Therefore I urge you to present your bodies as a sacrifice to God as your spiritual worship   12:1

    1B. And do not be conformed to this age, but be transformed by the renewing of your mind   12:2
    2B. For I say to all of you by the grace given to me— be thinking accurately about yourself and   12:3-21
        your place in the body; love one another, be diligent, bless your enemies, be humble
    3B. Let every soul be subject to superior authorities   13:1-7
    4B. Owe nothing to anyone except to love one another. Love is the fulfillment of the Law   13:8-10
    5B. And do this knowing the time. Lay aside darkness and put on the weapons of light   13:11-14
    6B. Now be accepting the one being weak in faith, but not for disputes about opinions   14:1

        1C. One has faith to eat, another not. Do not treat with contempt or judge one another   14:2-4
        2C. One judges a day above another. Let each be assured in his own mind. We live for the   14:5-12
            Lord. We will all stand before His judgment seat and give an account for ourselves
        3C. Therefore judge this— not to place a cause of stumbling or falling for your brother   14:13-15
        4C. Therefore do not let your good thing be blasphemed   14:16-18
        5C. So then, let us pursue the things of peace and edification   14:19-15:6
        6C. Therefore be accepting one another, as Christ accepted you, for the glory of God   15:7-12

    7B. Now may the God of hope fill you with joy and peace in believing   15:13

5A. Paul explains why he wrote, his commission by God, his present and future plans   15:14-33

Conclusion   16:1-27

| Romans 1:1 | 508 | Verse |

A. Paul, *a* slave[A] *of* Christ Jesus[1], *a* called[2] apostle[B], having been separated[3] for *the* good-news[C] *of* God   1

     1. Which He promised-beforehand[D] through His prophets in *the* Holy Scriptures[4]   2
     2. Concerning His Son—   3

         a. The *One* having come from *the* seed[E] *of* David according-to[5] *the* flesh
         b. The *One* having been designated[6] *as the* Son *of* God with[7] power according to *the* Spirit[8]   4
            of holiness[9] by[10] *the* resurrection *from the* dead
         c. Jesus Christ our Lord
         d. Through Whom we[11] received grace[F] and apostleship[12] for[13] *the* obedience *of* faith[14] among   5
            all the Gentiles[15] for the sake of His name—* among whom **you** also are called[16] *ones of*   6
            Jesus Christ

B. *To* all the *ones* being in Rome[17], beloved[G] *ones of* God, called saints[18]   7
C. Grace *to* you and peace from God our Father and *the* Lord Jesus Christ
D. First[19], I am giving-thanks[H] *to* my God through Jesus Christ for you all, because your faith is being   8
    proclaimed[J] in the whole world[K]

     1. For God is my witness[L]— Whom I am serving[M] in my spirit in[20] the good-news[C] *of* His Son—   9
        how unceasingly[21] I am making mention *of* you *always[22] in my prayers, asking[23] if somehow   10
        now at last I shall be prospered[24] in the will *of* God to come to you

         a. For I am yearning[N] to see you in order that I may impart[25] some spiritual[O] gift[26] *to* you, so   11
            that you *may* be established[27]. *And this is *that I may* be encouraged-together-with *you*   12
            among you— through each other's faith,[28] both yours and mine

E. And I do not want you to be-unaware[P], brothers[Q], that often I planned[29] to come to you— and was   13
    prevented[R] until now— in order that I might have some fruit among you also, as indeed among the
    other Gentiles

     1. I am *a* debtor[30] both *to* Greeks and barbarians,[31] both *to* wise and foolish[S]   14
     2. So for my part,[32] *I am* eager[33] also to announce-the-good-news[T] *to* you, the *ones* in Rome   15
     3. For I am not ashamed-of [34] the good-news[35], for it is *the* power[U] *of* God for[36] salvation[V] *to*   16
        everyone believing[37]— both *to the* Jew first, and *to the* Greek

         a. For *the* righteousness[38] *of* God[39] is revealed[W] in it from faith to faith,[40] just as it has been   17
            written [in Hab 2:4], "But the righteous[41] *one* shall live by faith"[42]

1. That is, a slave belonging to Christ Jesus. Some manuscripts say "Jesus Christ" {B}.
2. Or, "called *to be an* apostle". This adjective is also in v 6, 7. Paul uses it again of himself only in 1 Cor 1:1. On this word, see Rom 8:28. It was God who appointed Paul, not Paul himself, and not other humans.
3. That is, "set apart, appointed" for this purpose. Same word as in Gal 1:15, where Paul says it was from his mother's womb, and in Act 13:2. Elsewhere only in Mt 13:49; 25:32; Lk 6:22; Act 19:9; 2 Cor 6:17; Gal 2:12. GK *928*.
4. Or, "Sacred Writings". This phrase is used only here. On "Scriptures" see 2 Pet 3:16. Compare 2 Tim 3:15.
5. Or, "with respect to, in relation to". Same word as in v 4. GK *2848*. Same phrase as in 4:1; 9:3, 5.
6. Or, "declared, appointed, defined, determined, ordained, marked out as being". Same word as in Act 10:42; 17:31; Heb 4:7. Elsewhere only as "determine" in Lk 22:22; Act 2:23; 11:29; 17:26. GK *3988*. The related noun means "boundaries, borders".
7. Or, "in, by means of". Some think Paul means "designated... with power", in a mighty way, mightily, powerfully, by the resurrection; others, "God's Son with power", as opposed to His days of humiliation.
8. Or, "spirit". Some think Paul means the human spirit of Jesus, characterized by holiness, as opposed to His flesh in v 3; others, His divine nature as opposed to His human nature in v 3; others, the Holy Spirit, so that the contrast is between what His human descent shows Him to be, and what His resurrection by the Spirit shows Him to be. There are other views.
9. Elsewhere only in 2 Cor 7:1; 1 Thes 3:13. GK *43*. Related to "holiness" in Heb 12:14.
10. Or, "since, from the time of", as in Mk 10:20; Jn 9:1; or, "because of", as in 2 Cor 13:4; Rev 16:10. GK *1666*.
11. Some think Paul means "I"; others, "we apostles".
12. Or, "*the* office of apostle". Elsewhere only in Act 1:25; 1 Cor 9:2; Gal 2:8. GK *692*. Related to "apostle" in v 1.
13. That is, "to bring about". Compare Gal 2:7-9; Eph 3:8-9.
14. On "obedience *of* faith", see 16:26.
15. Or, "nations". On this word, see Act 15:23.
16. Same word as in v 1. Some think Paul means "called *ones belonging to*" Jesus; others, "*ones* called *to be*" His; others, "called *by*" Him.
17. Having set his sights on Rome in Act 19:21, having come to Corinth for the winter, Paul writes this book in Act 20:3 to prepare his way to Rome after returning to Jerusalem with the gift of the churches for the poor, Rom 15:25-29. He arrives in Rome three years later in Act 28, as a prisoner.
18. Or, "called *ones*, holy *ones*", making three parallel adjectives— beloved, called, and holy ones. On "called saints", see 1 Cor 1:2.
19. Paul details his prayers in view of his personal desires. He uses grammar that may imply a second point (perhaps regarding his plans in view of his mission, v 13, in which case he continues with "and", rather than "then" as in Heb 7:2 and Jam 3:17, or "second"). Or, this grammar may mean "first" in the sense of "above all", expecting no second point. Same grammar as in 3:2, 1 Cor 11:18.
20. Or, "in connection with". That is, in connection with the good news about or proceeding from His Son. GK *1877*.
21. Elsewhere only in 1 Thes 1:2; 2:13; 5:17. GK *90*. A related word is used in 2 Tim 1:3.
22. Or, "making mention *of* you, always in my prayers asking...".
23. That is, asking to come to you, as I know is His will for me, if perhaps He will arrange it now.
24. Or, "succeed, get along well, do well". Elsewhere only in 1 Cor 16:2; 3 Jn 2. GK *2338*.
25. Or, "give a share of". On this word, see "giving" in 12:8.
26. On the word "gift", see 1 Cor 1:7. These two words are used together only here. That is, some grace gift pertaining to the Spirit.
27. Same word as in 16:25. On this word, see 1 Thes 3:2.
28. That is, the faith in God that is active in both the Romans and Paul. More literally, "through the faith in one another".
29. Or, "set before myself, purposed". On this word, see "set forth" in 3:25.
30. Elsewhere only in Mt 6:12; 18:24; Lk 13:4; Rom 8:12; 15:27; Gal 5:3. GK *4050*. I owe them the gospel.
31. This is like saying "to the civilized (in Greco-Roman terms) and the uncivilized". On "barbarian", see Col 3:11.
32. This is an idiom, literally, So "*as to* the *thing* according to me". The idea is, "as far as it depends on me". Used only here in this sense. Used in the plural as "the *things* concerning me" (meaning "*my* circumstances") in Eph 6:21; Phil 1:12; Col 4:7; and in Act 24:22; 25:14.
33. Or, "So the eagerness on my part *is* also to announce". On this word, see "willing" in Mt 26:41. Related to "eagerly" in 1 Pet 5:2, and "eagerness" in 2 Cor 8:19.
34. Elsewhere only in Mk 8:38; Lk 9:26; Rom 6:21; 2 Tim 1:8, 12, 16; Heb 2:11; 11:16. GK *2049*. Related to "shame" in Heb 12:2; "put to shame" in 1 Jn 2:28; and "shameful" in Tit 1:11.
35. Some manuscripts add "*of* Christ" {N}.
36. That is, resulting in, leading to. GK *1650*.
37. Or, "exercising faith". On this word, see Jn 3:36. Same root word as "faith" in the next verse.
38. This word means "righteousness, rightness, justice", either from God's viewpoint, or people's viewpoint, depending on the context. Used 92 times. GK *1466*. Related to "declare righteous" in 3:24.
39. Some think Paul means righteousness "from God", the righteous status we have from God; others, "belonging to God", God's righteousness, a God kind of righteousness into which we enter by faith. There are other views.
40. Some think Paul means a righteousness "starting from faith and leading to a life of faith"; others, "beginning with faith and ending with faith"; others, "revealed from the faith of one to the faith of another". There are other views. On "faith", see Eph 2:8.
41. This word means "righteous, right, just", either from God's viewpoint, or people's viewpoint, depending on the context. Used 79 times. GK *1465*. Related to "declare righteous" in 3:24.
42. Or, "But the *one* righteous by faith shall live", the Greek word order.

A. Rom 6:17 B. 1 Cor 12:28 C. 1 Cor 15:1 D. 2 Cor 9:5, previously promised E. Heb 11:11 F. Eph 2:8 G. Mt 3:17 H. Mt 26:27 J. Phil 1:18 K. 1 Jn 2:15 L. Act 1:8 M. Heb 12:28, worship N. 1 Pet 2:2 O. 1 Cor 14:1 P. Rom 10:3, being ignorant Q. Act 16:40 R. 1 Cor 14:39, forbid S. Tit 3:3 T. Act 5:42 U. Mk 5:30 V. Lk 19:9 W. 2 Thes 2:3

| Romans 1:18 | 510 | Verse |

1A. For[1] *the* wrath[2] *of* God is revealed[3] from heaven against all ungodliness[4] and unrighteousness[5] *of* people[A] holding-down[6] the truth in[7] unrighteousness 18

    1B. Because[8] the *thing* known[9] *of* God[10] is evident[11] in them[12], for God made *it* evident[13] *to* them 19

        1C. For His invisible *things*— both His eternal[B] power[C] and divine-nature[14]— are clearly-seen[15], being understood[16] since *the* creation *of the* world *in* the *things* made, so that they are[17] without-excuse[D] 20

    2B. Because[18] having known[19] God, they did not glorify[E] *Him* as God or give-thanks[F], but became-futile[20] in their thoughts[21], and their senseless[22] heart was darkened[23] 21

        1C. While claiming to be wise, they became-foolish[24], *and exchanged[25] the glory *of* the immortal[26] God for *a* likeness[G]— *an* image[27] *of a* mortal[H] person[A], and *of* birds and *of* four-footed-animals and *of* reptiles[28] 22-23

            1D. Therefore God handed them over[29] in the desires[J] *of* their hearts to impurity[K] 24

                1E. *So that* their bodies[30] are[31] dishonored[L] among them

        2C. Who[32] exchanged[33] the truth[M] *of* God[34] for the lie[35], and worshiped[36] and served[N] the creation[37] rather than the *One* having created[O]— Who is blessed[P] forever[Q], amen 25

1. That is, "Now" or "You see,". Paul now begins his lengthy exposition of the revelation of God's righteousness (v 17), and its implications. He uses this word to assert his first point. GK *1142*.
2. That is, God's anger directed at sin. All humans are children of wrath (Eph 2:3; Rom 9:22), whose sin will bring God's wrath (Jn 3:36; Eph 5:6; Col 3:6; Heb 3:11), which is coming (Mt 3:7; Rom 2:5; Rev 6:17; 11:18; 14:10; 19:15), but from which believers are delivered (Rom 5:9; 1 Thes 1:10; 5:9). On this word, see Rev 16:19.
3. The wrath is revealed now in God's "handing over" people to their life choices, with all the consequences in this life. This only begins what also will be revealed in the future, when they will "pay the penalty" in the next life, 2 Thes 1:9. On this word, see 2 Thes 2:3.
4. Or, "impiety, godlessness, profaneness". Lack of reverence toward God. Elsewhere only in 11:26; 2 Tim 2:26; Tit 2:12; Jude 15, 18. GK *813*.
5. Or, "wrongdoing, iniquity, violation of what God considers right". This word is also used with reference to human standards of right and justice. Same word as in 1:29; 2:8; 3:5; 6:13; 9:14. Used 25 times. GK *94*. Related to "wronged" in Act 7:24, and "declare righteous" in Rom 3:24.
6. Or, "suppressing, holding back". People hold down what truth they know in their desire to live as they please. This word means "to hold down, suppress; to hold back, restrain; to hold on to, retain, hold fast". Elsewhere only as "hold on to" in Lk 8:15; 1 Cor 7:30; 11:2; 2 Cor 6:10; 1 Thes 5:21; Heb 3:6, 14; 10:23; "hold on" in 1 Cor 15:2; "hold" in Lk 14:9; Act 27:40; Rom 7:6; "hold back" in Lk 4:42; Phm 13; "restrain" in 2 Thes 2:6, 7. GK *2988*.
7. That is "in connection with, in the sphere of ". Or, "by, by means of ". GK *1877*.
8. Paul explains their "holding down", and God's wrath on it, in v 19-32. These people are acting contrary to the truth God has revealed about Himself, resulting in God's judgment. Paul continues this theme in a different way in 2:1.
9. Same adjective as in Jn 18:15, 16; Act 1:19; 2:14; 4:10, 16; 9:42; 13:38; 15:18; 19:17; 28:22, 28. Elsewhere only as "acquaintance" (a "known" one) in Lk 2:44; 23:49. GK *1196*.
10. That is, about God. Some think Paul means "what may be known, the knowable"; others, "what is known, the known". What is the known thing? It is God's existence, and the things mentioned next in v 20.
11. Or, "known, clear, visible, plainly seen". Same adjective as in Act 4:16; 1 Cor 3:13; 14:25; Gal 5:19; 1 Tim 4:15; 1 Jn 3:10. Elsewhere only as "visible" in Lk 8:17; Rom 2:28; Phil 1:13; "visibility" in Mt 4:22; Lk 8:17; and "known" in Mt 12:16; Mk 3:12; 6:14; Act 7:13; 1 Cor 11:19. GK *5745*. Related to "made evident" next.
12. Or, "among them". Some think Paul means God's existence is evident "in their minds" as evidenced by the universal drive of all humans to worship something greater than themselves. Others think he means God made it evident "among them", that is, in creation (v 20).
13. Or, "made known, made clear". Related to the word earlier in the verse. On this verb, see "made evident" in 1 Jn 2:19.
14. Or, "divineness, divinity", as seen in His attributes and actions. Used only here. GK *2522*.
15. Or, "distinctly seen, perceived". Used only here. GK *2775*. The invisible is perceived with the mind through the visible creation.
16. Or, "perceived, comprehended". See "think" in Eph 3:20 on this word.
17. Or, "so that they *might* be without excuse". This indicates either the actual result or the intended purpose of God's action in v 19. The people in v 18 are without excuse because God revealed enough about Himself in creation to make them accountable (3:19).
18. Rather than the next step in explaining v 18, others connect this with v 20 as the reason why people are without excuse (making it point 1D.). Same word as in v 19, and elsewhere in Romans only in 3:20; 8:7. Used 23 times, meaning "therefore, because". GK *1484*.
19. That is, as a result of God's revelation in creation. What people knew, they turned away from.
20. Or, "worthless". People directed their thoughts to worthless, futile, pointless things. When they stand before God, they will see just how futile they were. Used only here. GK *3471*. Related to "futile" in 1 Cor 15:17.
21. Or, "reasonings, opinions". On this word, see Jam 2:4.
22. Or, "foolish", from God's point of view. Same word as in v 31. On this word, see "without understanding" in 10:19.
23. Used 5 times. GK *5029*. Related to "darkness" in Jn 3:19.
24. Or, "were made foolish". Same word as "made foolish" in 1 Cor 1:20. GK *3701*.
25. Elsewhere only as "changed" in Act 6:14; 1 Cor 15:51, 52; Gal 4:20; Heb 1:12. GK *248*. Related to "exchange" in v 25. Same word as in Ps 106:20, "they exchanged their glory for the image of an ox", and reflecting that grammar.
26. Elsewhere of God only in 1 Tim 1:17. It is the word "mortal" (used next) with a negative prefix. On this word, see "undecayable" in 1 Cor 15:52.
27. Rendered this way, this phrase explains "likeness". More literally, "for *a* likeness *of an* image". Others think Paul means "for *a* copy *of a* figure" of a mortal, etc. On this word, see Col 1:15.
28. Here, people begin to worship God in the form of an idol, representing the infinite glory of their immortal Creator as an object of their own creation in the likeness of one of His creations.
29. Or, "delivered them". Same word as in v 26, 28. Compare Eph 4:19. God "handed over" Israel in Act 7:42. On this word, see Mt 26:21. Some manuscripts say "also handed over" {N}.
30. Some think the subject is an implied "*they*"; others, "their bodies". See the next note. The grammar permits either.
31. Some think Paul means "with the result that" this happens. Others think it expresses their purpose, "*so that they might* dishonor their bodies" or "*so that* their bodies *might* be dishonored", that is, so that they might carry out their impure desires in their bodies. Others think it defines impurity, "impurity— the dishonoring *as to* their bodies among themselves".
32. This word resumes the subject of v 22-23. Same word as in v 32. Others think v 25-27 is subordinate to v 24 (so that v 24 is 2C., v 25 is 1D., and v 26 is 2D.). There are other views.
33. Elsewhere only in v 26. GK *3563*. Same root word and grammar as "exchanged" in v 23.
34. Some think Paul means "the Truth", that is, God; others, "the truth that God revealed about Himself ".
35. Or, "for falsehood". On this word, see "falsehood" in Rev 14:5. The lie of false religion.
36. Or, "venerated". Used only here. Related to "object of worship" in 2 Thes 2:4, and "worshiping" in Act 13:50.
37. Or, "creature". Here, people worship creation as their god, rather than God as their Creator, trading truth for lies. Some think Paul is describing progressive steps away from God; others, different aspects of the same thing as in v 22-23. On this word, see 8:39

A. Mt 4:4, mankind B. Jude 6 C. Mk 5:30 D. Rom 2:1 E. Rom 8:30 F. Mt 26:7 G. Phil 2:7 H. 1 Cor 15:53, decayable J. Gal 5:16 K. 1 Thes 2:3 L. Act 5:41 M. Jn 4:23 N. Heb 12:28, worship O. Eph 2:15 P. Rom 9:5 Q. Rev 20:10

| Romans 1:26 | 512 | Verse |

    1D. For this reason God handed them over to passions[1] *of* dishonor[2]   26

        1E. For both their females[A] exchanged the natural[B] [sexual] function for[3] the *one contrary to nature*[C]

        2E. And likewise also the males[D], having left[4] the natural [sexual] function *of* the female, were inflamed[5] by their craving[6] for one another   27

            1F. Males with males committing[7] the indecent-act[8], and receiving-back[E] in themselves the return[9] which was due[10] their error[11]

    3C. And as they did not approve[12] to have God in *their* knowledge   28

        1D. God handed them over to *a* disapproved[13] mind, to do the *things* not being proper[F]

            1E. Having been filled[G] *with* all unrighteousness, evilness[14], greed[H], badness[J]   29
            2E. Full[K] *of* envy[L], murder[M], strife[N], deceit[O], malice[15]
            3E. Whisperers[16], *slanderers[17], God-haters[18], violent[P], arrogant[Q], boasters, inventors *of* evils[19], disobedient *to* parents, *senseless[R], unfaithful[20], unaffectionate[21], unmerciful   30 / 31
            4E. Who, having known[S] the regulation[22] *of* God— that the *ones* practicing[T] such *things* are worthy[U] *of* death— not only are doing them, but are also giving-approval[23] *to* the *ones* practicing *them*   32

  3B. Therefore you are without-excuse[24], O human[V]— everyone judging[25]   2:1

    1C. For in what you[26] are judging the other *person*, you are condemning[W] yourself— for you, the *one* judging, are practicing[27] the same *things*!

        1D. And we know that the judgment[X] *of* God is according to truth[28] upon the *ones* practicing such *things*   2

    2C. But are you thinking[29] this, O human— the *one* judging the *ones* practicing such *things,* and doing them [yourself]— that **you** will escape[30] the judgment[X] *of* God?   3

    3C. Or are you disregarding[31] the riches *of* His goodness[32] and forbearance[Y] and patience[Z], not knowing that the good[33] *thing of* God is leading[34] you to repentance[35]?   4

    4C. But in-accordance-with[36] your hardness[37] and *your* unrepentant[38] heart, you are storing-up[39] wrath *for* yourself on *the* day *of* wrath and *the* revelation[AA] *of the* righteous-judgment[40] *of* God—   5

        1D. Who will render[41] *to* each *one* according to his works[42]—   6

1. Elsewhere only in Col 3:5; 1 Thes 4:5. GK *4079*. Related word in Rom 7:5.
2. Paul may mean "*characterized by* dishonor", that is, "dishonorable passions"; or, "*leading to* [further] dishonor"; or, "*proceeding from* [the] dishonor" God gave them up to in v 24. On this word, see 2 Tim 2:20. Related to "dishonored" in v 24.
3. This word (GK *1650*) is a different word for "for" than in the phrase "exchanged... for" in v 23 and 25 (GK *1877*).
4. Or, more strongly, based on this context, "abandoned". On this word, see "forgive" in Mt 6:12.
5. Or, "set on fire" with burning desire. Used only here. GK *1706*. Related to "burn".
6. Or, "lusting, desiring, longing". Used only here. GK *3979*. Related to "aspire to" in 1 Tim 6:10.
7. Or, "carrying out". On this word, see "work out" in Phil 2:12.
8. Or, "the shame, indecency, shameful deed". Some give this a more abstract sense by rendering it plural in English. Elsewhere only as "shame" in Rev 16:15. GK *859*. Related to "private parts" in 1 Cor 12:23; and "behave dishonorably" in 1 Cor 7:36.
9. Or, "recompense, requital", the thing deserved. The root words mean "the wage corresponding to". Elsewhere only in 2 Cor 6:13. Here the context implies a negative sense, "penalty"; there, a positive sense, "reward". GK *521*.
10. Or, "was necessary *for,* had to be *for*". On this word, see "must" in Mt 16:21.
11. Or, "deception, delusion". On this word, see 1 Thes 2:3. Some think Paul means that such people receive in their own persons the consequences of their homosexual behavior; others, that this behavior is the penalty they receive for their error of rejecting God, v 25.
12. On this word, see 12:2. People disapprove of God for themselves, and others (v 32).
13. Note the play on the root word. They did not "approve-after-testing", so their mind was "disapproved-after-testing". On this word, see 1 Cor 9:27.
14. On this word, see Mt 22:18. Some manuscripts add "sexual immorality" before this word; others have this and the next two words in different order {C}.
15. Or, "*an* evil disposition, maliciousness", a desiring to harm others. Used only here. GK *2799*. Related to "badness" earlier.
16. Or, "gossips, slanderers". Used only here. GK *6031*. Related to "whisperings" in 2 Cor 12:20.
17. Used only here. GK *2897*. Related to "speak against" in 1 Pet 3:16.
18. Or, "God-hated". Used only here. GK *2539*. Some combine these as "slandering whisperers, God-hated violent *ones*, arrogant boasters".
19. Paul may mean "evil things", "evil things to do", "ways of doing evil". On this word, see 3 Jn 11. Related to "malice".
20. Or, "undutiful". That is, unfaithful in the sense of "not faithful to their promises". Used only here. GK *853*.
21. Or, "without natural affection, affectionless, without good feelings for others". Elsewhere only in 2 Tim 3:3. GK *845*. Some manuscripts add "unreconcilable" {A}, which is also found in 2 Tim 3:3.
22. Or, "ordinance, righteous decree". Same word as in Lk 1:6; Heb 9:1, 10. Elsewhere only as "requirement" in Rom 2:26, 8:4; "righteous acts" (the keeping of God's requirements) in Rom 5:18; Rev 15:4; 19:8; and "verdict of righteousness" (the final result) in Rom 5:16. GK *1468*. Related to "righteousness" in v 17.
23. Or, "well-pleased-with, agreeing-with, giving consent *to*". These people promote anti-God behavior. Same word as in Lk 11:48; Act 8:1; 22:20. Elsewhere only as "consent" in 1 Cor 7:12, 13. GK *5306*. Not related to "approved" in v 28, but to "well pleased" in Mt 17:5.
24. Elsewhere only in 1:20. GK *406*. Notice Paul changes from addressing "they" to "you".
25. That is, exercising judgment, applying God's Law to others. Paul speaks here to all who know the right thing, as evidenced by judging, but who do not do it. Note Jam 4:17. The point of correspondence between those in chapter 1 and those here is 1:21— they do not act in accordance with what they know. Their knowledge renders them without excuse with regard to their sin. Some think Paul is referring here to the broad case of the moral person in general; others, to the specific case of the Jew, without explicitly naming him until v 17. On this word, see Mt 7:1.
26. Or, "For while you...".
27. Used five times in 1:32-2:3. It means "to do, practice, act, commit". Used 39 times. GK *4556*. Related word in Mt 16:27.
28. This is the Greek word order. Some think Paul means that God's "judgment is truly upon" such people; others, that His "judgment based on truth is upon" them (not based on their pretensions).
29. Or, "counting, calculating". On this word, see "consider" in 3:28. Is this how you count it out? Do you calculate that you will escape? Do you add it up in such a way that you will be exempt even though you do the same things?
30. Same word as in Heb 2:3; 12:25; and Lk 21:36; Act 16:27; 2 Cor 11:33; 1 Thes 5:3. Elsewhere only as "flee out" in Act 19:16. GK *1767*.
31. Or, "caring nothing for, scoffing at, treating as unworthy of notice, looking down on, scorning". Since you continue to do the things you know are wrong, you must either think you are exempt, or you must simply be unconcerned about it, scorning God's goodness by not taking to heart its purpose. Same word as in Mt 6:24; Lk 16:13; 1 Tim 6:2; Heb 12:2. Elsewhere only as "look down on" in Mt 18:10; 1 Tim 4:12; "treat with contempt" in 1 Cor 11:22; and "despise" in 2 Pet 2:10. GK *2969*. Related to "scoffer" in Act 13:41.
32. Or, "kindness". On this word, see 3:12. Kindness is goodness in action, shown to another.
33. Or, "kind". Related to the word earlier in the verse. Same word as Lk 6:35. On this word, see 1 Pet 2:3.
34. Or, "is *trying to* lead".
35. That is, a change of mind resulting in a change of action. On this word, see 2 Cor 7:10.
36. Or, "based on, because of ". GK *2848*.
37. Or, "stubbornness". This noun is used only here. GK *5018*. Related to "harden" in 9:18. In Mk 16:14, it is combined with the word "heart" to mean "hardness-of-heart".
38. This one is unrepentant because he continues to do the same things, v 3. Used only here. GK *295*. Related to "repentance" in v 4.
39. Or, "treasuring up". On this word, see 1 Cor 16:2.
40. Or, "just verdict". This compound word is used only here. GK *1464*.
41. Or, "give back, repay, pay back". On this word, see Mt 16:27. Compare Jn 5:29; 2 Cor 11:15; 2 Tim 4:8, 14; Rev 2:23; 20:12, 13.
42. See Rev 20:12 on this phrase. Faith without works is dead, Jam 2:14-26.

A. Mt 19:4 B. 2 Pet 2:12, creatures of instinct C. Eph 2:3 D. Mt 19:4 E. Lk 16:25, receive F. Act 22:22 G. Eph 5:18 H. Eph 4:19 J. 1 Pet 2:1 K. Rom 15:14 L. Mk 15:10 M. Act 9:1 N. 1 Cor 1:11, quarrels O. Mt 26:4 P. 1 Tim 1:13 Q. Jam 4:6 R. Rom 10:19, without understanding S. Col 1:6, understood T. Rom 2:1 U. Rev 16:6 V. Mt 4:4, mankind W. 1 Cor 11:32 X. Jn 9:39 Y. Rom 3:26 Z. Heb 6:12 AA. 2 Thes 1:7

	1E. *To the*[1] *ones* seeking glory and honor and immortality[A] in accordance with endurance[B] in good work[2]— *He will render*[3] eternal life	7
	2E. But[4] *to the ones* indeed disobeying[C] the truth, and obeying[D] unrighteousness out of selfish-interest[5]— *there will be* wrath[E] and fury[F]	8
4B. *There will be* affliction[6] and distress[G] upon every soul[H] *of* the person[7] committing[8] evil— both *of the* Jew first, and *of the* Greek. °But *there will be* glory and honor and peace *to* everyone working[J] good— both *to the* Jew first, and *to the* Greek		9
		10
	1C. For there is no respect-of-persons[9] with God	11
	2C. For all who sinned without-Law will also perish[K] without-Law[10]. And all who sinned under[11] *the* Law will be judged[L] by *the* Law. °For not the hearers[12] *of* law[13] *are* righteous before God, but the doers[14] *of* law will be declared-righteous[M]	12
		13
	1D. For whenever Gentiles, the *ones* not having *the* Law[N], are doing *by* nature[15] the *things of* the Law, these *ones* not having *the* Law are *a* law *to* themselves,[16] °who are demonstrating[17] the work[O] *of* the Law[18] written[19] in their hearts—	14
		15
	1E. Their conscience[P] bearing co-witness[20]	
	2E. And *their* thoughts[21] accusing[Q] or even defending[R] between one another[22]	
	3E. On *the* day when God judges[23] the hidden[24] *things of* people[S] according to my good-news[25], through Christ Jesus[26]	16
	2D. But[27] if[28] **you** call-*yourself*[29] *a* Jew, and rely upon *the* Law, and boast[T] in God, °and know *His* will, and approve[U] the *things* mattering[30]— being instructed[V] out of the Law—°and are confident[31] *as to* yourself *that you* are *a* guide *of* blind *ones*, *a* light *of* the *ones* in darkness,°*a* corrector[32] *of* foolish[W] *ones*, *a* teacher *of* children[X], *one* having the embodiment[33] *of* knowledge and truth in the Law	17-18
		19
		20
	1E. Then[34]— the *one* teaching another, are you not teaching yourself ?[35]	21
	1F. The *one* proclaiming[Y] not to steal, do you steal?	
	2F. The *one* saying not to commit-adultery[Z], do you commit-adultery?	22

1. Paul uses grammar that links together point 1E. and 2E. as a two-part statement.
2. That is, work that is good from God's perspective. Some paraphrase this "doing good". This phrase "good work" is elsewhere only in Act 9:36; Rom 13:3; 2 Cor 9:8; Eph 2:10; Phil 1:6; Col 1:10; 2 Thes 2:17; 1 Tim 2:10; 5:10; 2 Tim 2:21; 3:17; Tit 1:16; 3:1. On "good" see 1 Tim 5:10b. On "work", see Mt 26:10. See also "good works" in Tit 2:14, which uses a different word for "good".
3. The grammar links "eternal life" to the subject of "will render" in v 6. God Himself will personally render or give back eternal life, v 7. Wrath will result, v 8.
4. Note that Paul places the "you" group in this category. They are storing up this wrath (v 5).
5. Or, "self-seeking, self-ambition". On this word, see Jam 3:14.
6. Notice the change from addressing "they" (1:19-32), or "you" (2:1-8), to the universal principle. Others place 2:9-16 under v 6, placing v 9 as 3E., v 10 as 4E., v 11 as 2D., and v 12-13 as 3D. Then v 17 becomes 4B. On this word, see Rev 7:14.
7. Or, "man, human". This word is singular. Grammatically, "the person committing evil" describes "soul" ("committing" modifies "person", not "soul"). That is, every soul belonging to the class defined as "the person committing evil", every individual in this category, both from the Jew class and the Greek class. Paul means the same thing as if he had said "everyone committing" (using the grammar from v 10, "everyone working"), but states it here in a more explicit manner. This phrase is found only here, and may be contrasted with "souls *of* people" in Rev 18:13, where both words are plural; and "every conscience (singular) of mankind (plural)" in 2 Cor 4:2. On this word, see "mankind" in Mt 4:4.
8. Or, "producing". Same word as in 1:27. Same root word as "working" in 2:10.
9. That is, neither Gentile nor Jewish persons. God has a single standard. On this word, see Jam 2:1.
10. This is the case of the "Greek" in v 9. How they sin "without the Law" of Moses, yet not "without law" from God, is explained in v 14-16. Used only in this verse. GK *492*. Related to "without *the* Law" in 1 Cor 9:21.
11. Or, "in", meaning "in the sphere of, in the domain of". Used in this sense also in 3:19; 7:23; Lk 23:40; Tit 1:6, and perhaps Jn 3:21. GK *1877*. This is the case of the "Jew" in v 9.
12. Elsewhere only in Jam 1:22, 23, 25. GK *212*. Related to "auditorium" in Act 25:23.
13. It is lowercase here because this statement applies to both groups in v 12. "Law" means one thing for the Gentiles, as explained next, and another for the Jews. Used 64 times in Romans. On this word, see 7:21.
14. Same word as in Jam 1:22, 23, 25; 4:11. Next Paul shows how neither Gentiles nor Jews are "doers" of what they know. Both are "under sin" (3:9), violators of God's Laws (written in one case in their hearts; in the other case, in the Law of Moses), and are therefore subject to God's impartial judgment in accordance with their works. GK *4475*.
15. That is, by their natural-born moral abilities, "instinctively". Others render this "having no Law by nature, are doing". That is, by birth, they are ones living apart from the Law, as in v 27. On this word, see Eph 2:3.
16. Where the Gentile's own standards coincide with God's Law, at those points they become a law to him.
17. Or, "showing, proving", in their actions. On this word, see Eph 2:7.
18. That is, their actions demonstrate that some of the requirements of God's Law are written on their hearts, as part of their own internal standard of conduct. By these requirements, they can be judged.
19. The grammar indicates that this adjective modifies "work", not "Law". Used only here. GK *1209*.
20. Their conscience bears witness with their actions to these requirements written in their hearts. It renders judgment on their actions based on these internal standards. Elsewhere only as "bearing witness with" in this same phrase in 9:1, and in 8:16. GK *5210*.
21. Or, "reflections". On this word, see "considerations" in 2 Cor 10:4.
22. The thoughts are a third witness to the requirements written on the heart, as these Gentiles apply them. Some think "one another" refers to the thoughts themselves, as they alternately accuse or defend one's action between themselves; others think it refers to the interaction with other people, as they accuse or defend their actions to one another.
23. The present tense "judges" is given a future sense by the reference to that "day". Some manuscripts say "shall judge" {N}. Some think Paul means that such people judge their actions now, and that God will also judge them on that day, using their own standards that coincide with His Law, as witnessed by their actions, conscience, and thoughts. On this basis they will be condemned because they are not "doers" of their own moral principles, v 13; 3:20. Others connect this verse to v 12 or 13, so that Paul says "will be judged" (v 12) or "will be declared righteous (v 13)... on *the* day when God judges", making a parenthesis of what comes between.
24. Or, "the secrets". On this word, see 1 Cor 4:5.
25. That is, the good news I proclaim. Compare 2 Thes 1:8. God's judgment is certain. The good news is about eternal life in Christ for all who believe. On this word, see 1 Cor 15:1.
26. Some manuscripts say "Jesus Christ" {C}.
27. Neither are the Jews "doers". They have "sinned under the Law" (v 12), and are subject to impartial judgment by God through the Law. Paul does not need to explain the "how" as with the Gentile. He only needs to apply the Law to them. They have it, and boast in their knowledge, but they do not obey it. Others group 2:1-16 together and start a new point (4B.) here, so that v 17 begins the specific application to the Jew of the general principles of 2:1-16.
28. That is, "assuming that". Instead of "But if", some manuscripts say "Behold!" {N}.
29. Or, "are named, bear the name, name *yourself*". Used only here. GK *2226*. The root word is "name".
30. On this phrase, see Phil 1:10.
31. Or, "are sure, convinced". On this word, see "persuade" in 1 Jn 3:19.
32. Or, "trainer, discipliner, instructor". On this word, see "discipliner" in Heb 12:9.
33. Or, "form, shape". Elsewhere only as "form" in 2 Tim 3:5. GK *3673*.
34. This concludes the "if" in v 17. "But if v 17-20 is true of you, then...".
35. These examples of being "judged through the Law" (v 12) are enough to prove Paul's point.

A. 1 Cor 15:42, undecayability B. Jam 1:3 C. Rom 11:30 D. 1 Jn 3:19, persuade E. Rev 16:19 F. Rev 16:19 G. 2 Cor 6:4 H. Jam 5:20 J. Phil 2:12, work out K. 1 Cor 1:18 L. Mt 7:1 M. Rom 3:24 N. Rom 7:21 O. Mt 26:10 P. Act 23:1 Q. Jn 5:45 R. Mt 21:14, speak a defense S. Mt 4:4, mankind T. 2 Cor 11:16 U. Rom 12:2 V. Gal 6:6 W. 2 Cor 11:16 X. 1 Cor 3:1, infant Y. 2 Tim 4:2 Z. Mt 5:32

      3F. The *one* detesting[1] idols, do you rob-temples[2]?

    2E. You who are boasting in *the* Law are dishonoring[3] God through transgression[A] *of* the Law[4]   23

      1F. For "the name *of* God is being blasphemed[B] among the Gentiles because of you", just as it has been written [in Isa 52:5]   24

    3E. For[5] **circumcision**[6] profits[7] if you practice[C] *the* Law[8]— but if you are *a* transgressor[D] *of the* Law, your circumcision has become uncircumcision[9]   25

      1F. So if the uncircumcised[10] *one* keeps the requirements[11] *of* the Law, will not his uncircumcision be counted[E] for circumcision?[12]   26

      2F. And the uncircumcised *one* by nature[13] who is fulfilling[F] the Law will judge[G] you, the transgressor[D] *of the* Law with *the* letter[14] and circumcision[H]   27

      3F. For the *Jew* in the visible[15] *thing* is **not** *a* Jew, nor *is* the *circumcision* in the visible *thing* in *the* flesh circumcision   28

      4F. But the *Jew* in the hidden[J] *thing is a* Jew, and circumcision *is of the* heart, by *the* Spirit not *the* letter[16]— whose praise[K] *is* not from people[L], but from God   29

5B. What then *is* the advantage *of* the Jew? Or what *is* the profit[17] *of* circumcision? *Much in every way. For[18] first— that they were entrusted[M] the oracles[19] *of* God!   3:1-2

  1C. What[20] indeed[21] if some were faithless[22]?   3

    1D. Their faithlessness[23] will not nullify[24] the faithfulness[N] *of* God, *will it*?[25]

      1E. May it never be[26]! But let God be [seen to be] true[O] and every person[L] *a* liar[27], just as it has been written [in Ps 51:4]— "So that You might be declared-righteous[28] in Your words, and prevail[P] in Your being judged[29]"   4

  2C. But if our unrighteousness demonstrates[30] *the* righteousness *of* God, what shall we say?   5

    1D. God, the *One* inflicting[Q] the wrath[R], is not unrighteous[S], *is He*?[31] (I am speaking in accordance with human[L] thinking[32])

      1E. May it never be! Otherwise how will God judge[G] the world?   6

  3C. But[33] if the truth[T] *of* God abounded[U] in my lie[34] to His glory   7

    1D. Why am **I** also still being judged[G] as *a* sinner?[35]

      1E. Indeed, *why* not *say* "Let us do evil *things* that good *things* may come?", as we are blasphemed[36], and as some affirm us to say— whose[37] condemnation[V] is just[38]   8

6B. Therefore what? Are we[39] better[40] [than they]? Not at-all[41]   9

  1C. For we already-charged[42] *that* both Jews and Greeks are all under sin[43], *just as it has been written—   10

1. Or, "abhorring". Elsewhere only as "be abominable" in Rev 21:8. GK *1009*. Related to "abomination" in Rev 17:4, and "detestable" in Tit 1:16.
2. Or, "commit sacrilege". Used only here. GK *2644*. The related noun is in Act 19:37, where it is clear that this was a problem in that day. The exact details of this behavior are uncertain to us. Some take this literally. Others take it to mean "profit from idol temples". It is related to "rob" in 2 Cor 11:8. Others think Paul means "rob God of what is due Him", including the offerings commanded by God for the support of His temple. Others take it in the general sense of "commit sacrilege" in various ways.
3. Same word as in 1:24, of the Gentiles. On this word, see Act 5:41.
4. Or, this may be a question, "Law— are you dishonoring...?".
5. Paul uses this word to assert his next point. It may be rendered "Now" or "Indeed". GK *1142*. You who call yourselves Jews and break God's Law are dishonoring God. And circumcision will not protect you.
6. Paul uses grammar that emphasizes the contrast between the two halves of this sentence.
7. Or, "benefits, helps, is of use or value". Same word as in Mt 16:26; 27:24; Mk 8:36; Lk 9:25; Jn 6:63; 12:19; 1 Cor 13:3; 14:6; Gal 5:2; Heb 4:2; 13:9. Elsewhere only as "benefit" in Mt 15:5; Mk 5:26; 7:11. GK *6067*. Related to "profit" in 3:1; "profitable" in 2 Tim 3:16; and "unprofitableness" in Heb 7:18.
8. What was done to a Jewish male when he was eight days old is only of value if he obeys God's Law. Doers will be declared righteous, not circumcised ones.
9. The rite has become worthless. This rite was given by God as a sign of the covenant with Abraham (Gen 17:9-14), but by itself is of no value. Righteousness is what is needed to be accepted by God.
10. Paul uses the same word in two senses. Here it refers to "uncircumcised" people, as also in v 27; 3:30; 4:9; Gal 2:7; Eph 2:11; Col 3:11. In v 25 and 26, it refers to a state of "uncircumcision", as elsewhere only in Act 11:3; Rom 4:10, 11, 12; 1 Cor 7:18, 19; Gal 5:6; 6:15; Col 2:13. In both cases, this word is sometimes used as another way of saying "Gentile", "non-Jew", as here. GK *213*.
11. Paul is not saying this is possible. He is saying that considering the matter in this way proves that it is obedience, not circumcision, that makes the difference. On this word, see "regulation" in 1:32.
12. The grammar indicates a "yes" answer is expected.
13. Or, this may be a question, "And will the uncircumcised... judge?", or "and will [not] the uncircumcised... judge?". Same word as in v 14.
14. That is, the Law, the written code. Same word as in v 29. On this word, see "writings" in Jn 7:15.
15. That is, the outward, open and public things like dress, rituals, culture, etc. On this word, see "evident" in 1:19.
16. Or, "in *the* spirit, not *the* letter". On "*the* letter", compare 2:27; 7:6; 2 Cor 3:6.
17. Or, "usefulness, utility, gain, benefit". Elsewhere only as "advantage" in Jude 16. GK *6066*. Related to "profit" in 2:25.
18. Some manuscripts omit this word {C}, so that it just says "First...", as in 1:8. Paul's grammar may imply there are other reasons (more are listed in 9:4); but he chooses not to list more here. Or, Paul may mean "first" in the sense of "above all". See 1:8.
19. That is, the sacred writings, the Holy Scriptures. On this word, see Heb 5:12.
20. Paul is either answering Jewish objections to what he has said, or false inferences drawn from what he has said by "some", v 8. He gives three true inferences (1C., 2C., 3C.), states the false conclusions drawn from them (level D), and refutes the false conclusions (level E).
21. Or, "What then? If some...". On this word, see Mt 27:23. Or, "For what if...".
22. Or, "did not believe, were unfaithful", with reference to the oracles God entrusted them to them as Jews, the OT. "Were faithless", "faithlessness", and "faithfulness" (and also the word "entrusted") are from the same root word, and they are rendered this way to show this connection. On this word, see 2 Tim 2:13.
23. Or, "unbelief". On this word, see "unbelief" in 1 Tim 1:13.
24. If some Jews (the majority of Israel) did not believe, will this nullify God's faithfulness with regard to the oracles He entrusted to them? On this word, see "done away with" in 6:6.
25. The grammar indicates a "no" answer is expected to this question, and the one in v 5.
26. Or, "happen, take place, come about". GK *1181*.
27. God will not abandon His promises. Though every human is found to be a liar, He will be found faithful to His word. Elsewhere only in Jn 8:44, 55; 1 Tim 1:10; Tit 1:12; 1 Jn 1:10; 2:4, 22; 4:20; 5:10. GK *6026*.
28. Or, "vindicated". When it comes to being faithful to His promises, God will be pronounced righteous by all. On this word, see 3:24.
29. Or, "in Your judging", that is, when You judge. On this word, see Mt 7:1.
30. Or, "exhibits, shows". On this word, see 5:8. If our sin provides a contrast against which God's righteousness may be exhibited, then what? "Our unrighteousness" refers to Israel, the "some who were faithless" in v 3.
31. Is it unfair for God to punish Israel, since their sin serves to prove His righteousness and faithfulness?
32. Or, "in accordance with mankind". That is, with human logic and perspective; the way a human might look at it.
33. Some manuscripts say "For" {B}.
34. Or, "falsehood". Used only here. GK *6025*. Related to "liar" in v 4.
35. Why is an individual Jew held accountable if his sin magnifies God's glory? Paul answers by showing the absurd conclusion.
36. Or, "spoken against, slandered". On this word, see 1 Tim 6:1.
37. That is, the slanderers who blaspheme Paul or affirm him to say this. Neither they nor Paul taught this. Or, more generally, ones who would say such a thing.
38. Or, "deserved, right". Elsewhere only in Heb 2:2. GK *1899*.
39. Some think Paul is referring to the Jews; others, to Christians.
40. This word means "to be before, to be first, to excel", so Paul could mean "are we better" than they, or "are we ahead". Do we have an advantage? Others take it as passive, "are we excelled?" Are they better than we? Do they have an advantage over us? The word also means "to hold something in front" for protection, so Paul could mean "are we excused", "are we shielded" by Judaism or circumcision, "do we excuse ourselves". Used only here. GK *4604*.
41. Or, "surely not". Some think Paul means "Not in every way". On this word, see "surely" in 1 Cor 9:10.
42. Or, "previously charged". Paul is referring to 1:18-2:29. Used only here. GK *4577*.
43. And therefore "children of wrath", Eph 2:3.

A. Rom 5:14   B. 1 Tim 6:1   C. Rom 2:1   D. Jam 2:9   E. Rom 3:28, consider   F. Rev 10:7, finished   G. Mt 7:1   H. Eph 2:11   J. 1 Cor 4:5
K. 1 Cor 4:5   L. Mt 4:4, mankind   M. Jn 3:36, believe   N. Eph 2:8, faith   O. Jn 6:55   P. Rev 2:7, overcome   Q. Jude 9, bring   R. Rev 16:19
S. 1 Cor 6:9, wrong-doers   T. Jn 4:23   U. 2 Cor 8:2   V. Jn 9:39, judgment

1D. "There is not *a* righteous^A *one*, not even one. °There is no *one* understanding^B. There is no *one* seeking-out^C God. °They all turned-away^D, together they became useless¹. There is no *one* doing goodness². There is not³ as-many-as⁴ one" [Ps 14:1-3] 11, 12

2D. "Their throat *is an* opened⁵ grave. With their tongues^E they were deceiving" [Ps 5:9] 13

3D. "*The* poison *of* asps *is* under their lips" [Ps 140:3]

4D. "Whose mouth is full^F *of* cursing⁶ and bitterness^G" [Ps 10:7] 14

5D. "Their feet *are* swift to shed^H blood. °Destruction and misery *are* in their ways. °And they did not know *the* way *of* peace" [Isa 59:7-8] 15-17

6D. "There is no fear^J *of* God before their eyes" [Ps 36:1] 18

2C. And we know that whatever the Law says, it speaks *to the ones* under⁷ the Law— in order that every mouth may be stopped⁸, and the whole world may become accountable⁹ *to* God 19

3C. Because by *the* works *of* law¹⁰ no flesh will be¹¹ declared-righteous^K in His sight. For through law *comes the* knowledge *of* sin 20

2A. But now apart from law¹², *the* righteousness^L *of* God¹³ has been revealed¹⁴, being attested^M by the Law and the Prophets 21

1B. And *it is the* righteousness^L *of* God through faith¹⁵ *in* Jesus Christ for all¹⁶ *the ones* believing^N 22

1C. For there is no distinction—°for all sinned^O and are coming-short-of¹⁷ the glory¹⁸ *of* God, °being¹⁹ declared-righteous²⁰ as-a-gift²¹ *by* His grace^P through the redemption²² in²³ Christ Jesus 23-24

1D. Whom God set-forth²⁴ *as* that-which-satisfies²⁵ [His wrath] 25

1E. Through faith

2E. In²⁶ His blood²⁷

3E. For²⁸ *the* demonstration²⁹ *of* His righteousness^L, because of the passing-by³⁰ *of the* sins having previously-taken-place³¹ °in³² the forbearance³³ *of* God 26

1. Or, "unprofitable, worthless". Used only here. GK *946*. Related to "unprofitable" in Mt 25:30.
2. Or, "kindness, generosity". Same word as in 2:4. Elsewhere only as "kindness" in Rom 11:22; 2 Cor 6:6; Gal 5:22 (where it is distinguished from "goodness"); Eph 2:7; Col 3:12; Tit 3:4. GK *5983*. Related to "good" in 1 Pet 2:3, and "show kindness" in 1 Cor 13:4.
3. Some manuscripts omit the words "There is not" {C}.
4. Or, "up to" one. There is not a single individual. GK *2401*.
5. This is a participle, a grave "having been opened".
6. That is, prayer for evil to come upon someone, calling down evil upon someone. Used only here. GK *725*. Related words in Jn 7:49; Gal 3:10; Rom 12:14.
7. Same word as in 2:12. What Paul said in v 10-18 certainly applies to Jews! They are not exempt.
8. Or, "shut, closed, blocked". Elsewhere only in 2 Cor 11:10; Heb 11:33. GK *5852*. If God's people are not excepted, no one is.
9. Or, "answerable, liable, subject to". Used only here. GK *5688*.
10. Placed here, this explains and concludes this section in universal terms, "law" applying in a different sense (as in 2:13) to both Jews and Greeks (v 9). Others make this point 1D., explaining and concluding the case of the Jew only. In this case, this would be rendered "*of the* Law" here and later in the verse.
11. This is an idiom, literally, "all flesh will not be". On "no flesh", see Mt 24:22. By works of law, whether the Law of Moses or the laws of conscience (2:15), all flesh (every human) earns wrath (1:18), and death (6:23).
12. That is, law of any kind. Or, "*the* Law" of Moses.
13. The contrast of the two kinds of righteousness is seen clearly in Phil 3:9. It is God's righteousness apart from my obedience to any kind of rule or law, received as a free gift by faith.
14. Same word as in 16:26; Col 1:26; 2 Tim 1:10; Tit 1:3. On this word, see "made evident" in 1 Jn 2:19.
15. Instead of giving the human point of view, some think this is from Christ's point of view, "through *the* faithfulness *of* Jesus Christ" to the work He was sent to do, leaving the human side to the next phrase ("the *ones* believing"). On this word, see Eph 2:8.
16. Or, "to all". Some manuscripts say "to all and on all" {B}.
17. Using this same word, Hebrews exhorts us not to come short of the promise in 4:1, or the grace of God in 12:15. On this word, see "be in need" in Lk 15:14.
18. Some think this means "of rendering to God the glory due Him"; others, "of reflecting the glorious character of God originally given to mankind", God's image; others, "of the glory or praise now given by God"; others, "of the future heavenly glory God will give".
19. Some think Paul means there is no distinction, for all sinned and all are declared righteous in the same way. Others take "For... God" as a parenthesis, so that he means "... for all the *ones* believing (for there... God), being declared righteous".
20. Or, "justified". Same word as in Rom 2:13; 3:4, 20, 26, 28, 30; 4:2, 5; 5:1, 9; 6:7; 8:30, 33; and Mt 12:37; Lk 16:15; 18:14; Act 13:38, 39; 1 Cor 6:11; Gal 2:16, 17; 3:8, 11, 24; 5:4; 1 Tim 3:16; Tit 3:7; Jam 2:21, 24, 25. Elsewhere only as "vindicate" in Mt 11:19; Lk 7:29, 35; 10:29, and "declare right" in 1 Cor 4:4. GK *1467*. Related to the two words in 1:17, and "unrighteousness" in 1:18.
21. Or, "freely". On this word, see "without a reason" in Gal 2:21.
22. Or, "deliverance, release". It is the "release" based on payment of a ransom, used of what Christ did on the cross in 1 Cor 1:30; Eph 1:7; Col 1:14; Heb 9:15; and for what He will do in the future in Lk 21:28; Rom 8:23; Eph 1:14; 4:30. Elsewhere only in Heb 11:35. GK *667*. Related to "ransom" in Mt 20:28 and 1 Tim 2:6; "redeem" in 1 Pet 1:18; "redemption" in Heb 9:12; and "deliverer" in Act 7:35.
23. Or, "in connection with, by, by means of". GK *1877*.
24. Or, "presented, publicly displayed". Elsewhere only as "purposed" (that is, set forth to oneself) in Eph 1:9, and "planned" in Rom 1:13. GK *4729*. Related to "presentation" in Mk 2:26. On this concept, compare Act 2:23; Rev 13:8.
25. Or, "that which propitiates; the means-of-satisfaction; the satisfying-sacrifice", the effect of which is to satisfy God's wrath and obtain His mercy (its focus is on God). Some think it means "that which expiates, covers, cleanses" our sin, the effect of which is to remove our sin and guilt (its focus is on our sin). "Propitiation" is the removal or satisfaction of wrath. Stated from the human perspective, it is the means of gaining His mercy. Jesus is the sacrifice that removes or satisfies the wrath against sin (1:18) that Paul has just proven is upon all flesh (1:18-3:20). As a result, God is "merciful" (the related word in Heb 8:12). Elsewhere only as "mercy seat" in Heb 9:5, the place where the propitiation was made. GK *2663*. Related to "satisfaction" in 1 Jn 2:2, and "make-an-offering-for-satisfaction" in Heb 2:17. We could never satisfy God's wrath against sin. He set forth His own Son as the satisfaction for His own wrath for the reason stated at the end of v 26.
26. Or, "By". GK *1877*.
27. On this word, see 1 Jn 1:7. Some think Paul means "through faith in His blood"; others, that the propitiation is both "through faith" and "in His blood". In other words, the faith is in Christ, the propitiation is in His blood.
28. That is, to prove His righteousness with regard to His passing by all the sins of the past. GK *1650*.
29. Or, "showing, proof". Same word as in v 26; 2 Cor 8:24. Elsewhere only as "sign" in Phil 1:28. GK *1893*. Related to "demonstrate" in Eph 2:7; and "evidence" in 2 Thes 1:5.
30. Or, "leaving unpunished". This word is used of debts or obligations, and also means the "remission, forgiveness" of debts. Used only here. GK *4217*.
31. Or, "happened-beforehand". That is, before Christ died for them. Used only here. GK *4588*. God "passed over" them in anticipation of the Cross. Compare Act 17:30.
32. That is, in connection with. God passed them by in connection with His forbearance.
33. Or, "holding back, delay of punishment, clemency". Elsewhere only in 2:4. GK *496*.

A. Rom 1:17   B. Mt 13:13   C. Heb 11:6   D. Rom 16:17   E. 1 Cor 12:10   F. Rev 4:6   G. Act 8:23   H. Act 2:17, pour out   J. Eph 5:21   K. Rom 3:24
L. Rom 1:17   M. Act 6:3   N. Jn 3:36   O. Act 25:8   P. Eph 2:8

	4E. For¹ the demonstration² *of* His righteousness^A at the present time, so that He *might be³* righteous^B and declaring-righteous^C the *one* of faith⁴ *in* Jesus	
2C.	Where then *is* the boasting?⁵ It was shut-out⁶. Through what kind of law⁷? *Of* works? No, but through *a* law *of* faith	27
	1D. For⁸ we consider⁹ *a* person to be declared-righteous *by* faith apart from works^D *of the* Law	28
	1E. Or *is He* the God *of* Jews only¹⁰? *Is He* not also *the* God *of* Gentiles? Yes, *of* Gentiles also, since¹¹ *there is* one God— Who will declare-righteous^C *the* circumcised by faith, and *the* uncircumcised through the *same* faith¹²	29 30
	2D. Do we then nullify^E *the* Law through the faith?¹³	31
	1E. May it never be! On the contrary, we establish¹⁴ *the* Law	
3C.	What then shall we say *that* Abraham, our forefather¹⁵ according-to¹⁶ *the* flesh, has found?¹⁷ For if Abraham was declared-righteous by works, he has *a* boast¹⁸— but not before God¹⁹	4:1 2
	1D. For²⁰ what does the Scripture say?— "And Abraham believed^F God, and it was credited²¹ *to* him for righteousness^A" [Gen 15:6]	3
	1E. Now *to* the *one* working^G, the wages²² are not credited *to him* based-on²³ grace^H, but based on debt²⁴	4
	2E. But *to* the *one* not working, but putting-faith²⁵ upon the *One* declaring the ungodly²⁶ righteous²⁷— his faith^J is credited for righteousness	5
	3E. Just as David also says [in Ps 32:1-2] *as to* the blessedness^K *of* the person^L *to* whom God credits righteousness apart from works^D—	6
	1F. "Blessed^M *are the ones* whose lawless-*deeds*²⁸ were forgiven^N, and whose sins were covered	7
	2F. "Blessed^M *is the* man whose²⁹ sin *the* Lord will never^O count^P"	8
	2D. So *is* this blessedness³⁰ upon the circumcised³¹, or upon the uncircumcised^Q also? For³² we say, "Faith was credited *to* Abraham for righteousness". How then was it credited— *to one* being in circumcision^R, or in uncircumcision^Q?	9 10
	1E. Not in circumcision, but in uncircumcision!	
	2E. And he received *the* sign^S *of* circumcision— *a* seal³³ *of* the righteousness^A *of* faith³⁴ *while* in uncircumcision— so that he *might* be³⁵	11
	1F. *The* father *of* all the *ones* believing^F through uncircumcision— so that righteousness^A *might* be credited^P also³⁶ *to* them	
	2F. And *the* father *of the* circumcised^R—	12
	1G. *To* the *ones* not of circumcision only³⁷	
	2G. But indeed *to* the *ones* walking-in-line³⁸ in the footsteps *of* the faith *of* our father Abraham *while he was* in uncircumcision³⁹	

1. Or, "For the purpose of, with a view to". GK *4639*. Not the same word as "For" in the previous phrase, but having the same general meaning.
2. That is, to prove His righteousness with regard to His present declaring-righteous through faith in Jesus. Instead of making the two "demonstration" statements parallel as here, some think this one explains the "passing by", "because of the passing by *of* the sins having previously taken place in the forbearance of God with a view to the demonstration *of* His righteousness at the present time". Then the following phrase "So that He *might* be righteous..." becomes the 4E. point.
3. Or, "so that He is", depending on whether Paul is referring to the purpose or the result of the demonstration. That is, that God might be righteous, based on the propitiation, and be seen to be righteous, based on the demonstration.
4. Same phrase as "the *ones* of faith" in Gal 3:7, 9. That is, the one who "lives by faith", Rom 1:17. Compare the phrase in 4:14.
5. Since there is no distinction between Jew and Gentile (v 22), and since it is not by our works, there can be no boasting. Boasting comes from a perceived distinction between people, a basis for feeling superior over another. On this word, see 2 Cor 7:4.
6. Or, "excluded". On this word, see Gal 4:17.
7. Some think Paul means this in the sense of "principle, system", both times in this verse; others, as "God's Law", not through a Law wrongly understood as of works, but a Law rightly understood as leading to faith, 9:31-32. On this word, see 7:21.
8. Some manuscripts say "Therefore" {B}.
9. Or, "think, count, conclude". This word means "count, calculate, compute; credit, account, put to the account; take into account; consider, evaluate, estimate, regard, think, be of the opinion". Same word as in Jn 11:50; Rom 8:18, 36; 14:14; 1 Cor 4:1; 2 Cor 10:2, 7, 11; Phil 3:13; 4:8; Heb 11:19. Elsewhere only as "count" in Lk 22:37; Act 19:27; Rom 2:26; 4:8; 6:11; 9:8; 1 Cor 13:5, 11; 2 Cor 3:5; 5:19; 2 Tim 4:16; 1 Pet 5:12; "credit" in Rom 4:3, 4, 5, 6, 9, 10, 11, 22, 23, 24; 2 Cor 12:6; Gal 3:6; Jam 2:23; and "think" in Rom 2:3; 2 Cor 11:5. GK *3357*.
10. Or, "alone". This would be the conclusion if we were saved through a Jewish Law of works.
11. Or, "if as is the case". On this word, see 8:9.
12. Or, "that faith". Paul means "the faith" just mentioned, to show which, "same" is added.
13. A natural question since Paul just nullified the Law as an item of boasting, national pride and making distinctions between people. No, the fact that God sent His Son to satisfy the justice of the Law establishes its place forever as His standard for righteousness.
14. Or, "confirm, make stand". Used in this sense also in 10:3. GK *2705*.
15. Used only here. GK *4635*. Some manuscripts say "father" {B}.
16. Or, "with respect to, in relation to". GK *2848*.
17. That is, did the Jew's physical forefather find righteousness by faith or by works? Or, "has found according to the flesh?", that is, by his works. Some manuscripts omit "has found" {N}, so that it says "... say *as to* Abraham, our forefather according to *the* flesh?"
18. That is, a matter or ground for boasting, something to boast about. On this noun, see Phil 1:26.
19. Some think this means Abraham could boast to others, but not to God, because he would simply have done what was required; others, that he does not have such a boast at all.
20. Some think Paul uses this word to assert his first point, in response to v 1. It can be rendered "Now" or "Well". What has he found? Well, what does the Scripture say? GK *1142*. Others think this is in response to v 2. Abraham has no boast before God, for what does the Scripture say? In either case, the Genesis quote is the answer, and the first main point in the lesson from Abraham.
21. Same word as "consider" in 3:28. It occurs 11 times in this chapter as "credit" and "count".
22. Or, "pay, reward". On this word, see "recompense" in Rev 22:12.
23. Or, "according to, in keeping with". GK *2848*. Same word as in v 16.
24. That is, as something owed based on the work. A wage is not based on the grace of the giver, but on the debt to the worker. Elsewhere only in Mt 6:12. GK *4052*.
25. Or, "believing", as it is rendered in v 3. This verb is normally translated "believe". It means "to believe, put faith in" and is related to the noun "faith". It is used with the preposition "upon" elsewhere only in Rom 4:24; Mt 27:42; Act 9:42; 11:17; 16:31; 22:19; and with different grammar in Rom 9:33; 10:11; Lk 24:25; 1 Tim 1:16; 1 Pet 2:6. All of these are rendered "put faith upon" to distinguish them. Compare Jn 3:15. On this word, see Jn 3:36.
26. Same word as in 5:6. On this word, see Jude 15.
27. This striking phrase is the heart of the gospel and Paul's message here. God declares the ungodly righteous by faith— not the godly, the obedient, the one who keeps the Law, who deserves it, who earns it, but the ungodly.
28. Or, "lawlessnesses". This word is plural only here and Heb 10:17. On this word, see 1 Jn 3:4.
29. Some manuscripts say "*to* whom" {N}, so that it says "*to* whom *the* Lord will never count sin".
30. Same word as in v 6.
31. Continuing the lesson to be learned from Abraham, does one have to be a Jew to receive this blessing?
32. Since the word "blessedness" comes from the reference to David in v 6, Paul first explains that he is speaking again with reference to Abraham in Gen 15.
33. Same word as in 1 Cor 9:2; 2 Tim 2:19; Rev 5:1; 8:1; 9:4. GK *5382*. Related to the verb in Eph 1:13.
34. Or, "*by* faith"; or, "*his* faith righteousness". The seal of his righteousness in Gen 15 came at least 14 years later in Gen 17.
35. Or, "so that he is", indicating either the purpose of receiving it, or the result of receiving it.
36. Here Paul is referring to the Gentiles with faith like Abraham's. Some manuscripts omit this word {C}.
37. That is, those with circumcision but without Abraham's faith.
38. That is, "*to* the *circumcised ones* walking in line". On this word, see Gal 5:25.
39. In other words, true Jews, 2:28-29; 9:8. Abraham is not the spiritual father of his descendants who are merely circumcised (though he is their physical father), but only of those with both his circumcision and his faith.

A. Rom 1:17 B. Rom 1:17 C. Rom 3:24 D. Mt 26:10 E. Rom 6:6, done away with F. Jn 3:36 G. Mt 26:10 H. Eph 2:8 J. Eph 2:8 K. Gal 4:15 L. Mt 4:4, mankind M. Lk 6:20 N. Mt 6:12 O. Gal 5:16 P. Rom 3:28, consider Q. Rom 2:26, uncircumcised R. Eph 2:1, circumcised S. 2 Thes 2:9

	3D.	For[1] the promise[A] *to* Abraham or *to* his seed[2] *that* he *should* be the inheritor[B] *of the* world[3] *was* not through[4] *the* Law[5], but through *the* righteousness *of* faith[6]	13
		1E. For if the *ones* of *the* Law[7] *are* inheritors— faith has been made-empty[8], and the promise has been nullified[9]	14
		2E. For the Law brings-about[C] wrath.[10] But[11] where there is no Law, neither *is there* transgression[12]	15
		3E. For this reason[13] *it*[14] *is* by faith[D], in order that *it may be* based on grace[E], so that the promise *might* be firm[15] *to* all the seed[F]— not *to the seed* of the Law only,[16] but also *to* the *seed* of *the* faith *of* Abraham[17]	16

        1F. Who is *the* father *of* us all—

            1G. Just as it has been written [in Gen 17:5], that "I have made you *a* father *of* many nations"   17

            2G. Before God[18] Whom he believed— the *One* giving-life-to[G] the dead, and calling[H] the *things* not being as[19] being

        2F. Who believed contrary-to[20] hope[J], upon hope, so that he *might* become[21] *the* father *of* many nations in accordance with the *thing* having been spoken [in Gen 15:5]— "So shall your seed[F] be"   18

            1G. And[22] not having weakened[K] *in* faith, he considered[23] his *own* body already[24] having become impotent[25]— being about *a* hundred years *old*— and the deadness[L] *of* the womb[M] *of* Sarah   19

            2G. But he did not waver[26] *in* unbelief[N] with reference to the promise *of* God, but became-strong[27] *in* faith   20

                1H. Having given glory *to* God

                2H. And having been fully-convinced[28] that what He had promised, He was[29] able also to do   21

        3F. Therefore indeed[30] it was credited[O] *to* him for righteousness   22

        4F. And[31] it was not written for his sake only that it was credited *to* him, but also for our sake *to* whom it is going-to[P] be credited— the *ones* putting-faith upon[32] the *One* having raised[Q] Jesus our Lord from *the* dead   23-24

            1G. Who was handed-over[33] for[34] our trespasses[R] and was raised[35] for our justification[36]   25

1. Paul uses this word to assert his next point in the lesson to be learned from Abraham. It may be rendered "Indeed" or "Moreover". GK *1142*. Since Abraham is the father of all believers, v 11-12, on what basis is the promised inheritance granted to him and to his seed? Paul points out that it was not made dependent on obedience to God's Law, but was freely given based on the righteousness resulting from faith.
2. That is, his believing offspring, his spiritual descendants, those of whom he is the father, v 11-12, 16, who are fellow-heirs with Christ, 8:17. Same word as in v 16, 18. GK *5065*. Some think Paul specifically means Christ alone, as in Gal 3:16.
3. Compare Gen 22:17-18.
4. Or, "via, by means of". GK *1328*. Same word as in 3:20, 22, 25, 27, 30, 31.
5. Or, "law". Note that Paul has combined the case of Abraham and his seed. Viewing it from Abraham's historical point of view, before the Law was given, some think Paul means "law" in general, or "a legal system" of obedience. Viewing it from the point of view of the "seed", which is the case Paul expands upon in v 14-16, others think he means God's Law, and more specifically, "works of the Law" (3:28) as taught by the Jews in Paul's day. The promise was not received by Abraham or his seed through any kind of works-righteousness, but through a faith-righteousness. These two views of "Law" occur also in v 14 and 15, but in v 16 it is agreed that Paul is referring to the Law of Moses, God's Law.
6. Or, "faith righteousness". That is, the kind of righteousness that is granted through faith. Note that in what follows, Paul does not develop the historical argument with regard to Abraham (as he does in Gal 3:17), but shows that Law and Promise are incompatible with regard to salvation.
7. That is, ones relying upon their obedience to God's Law, hoping to be accepted by God through obedience to His Law. Paul says this is the heart of Israel's error in 9:31-32; 10:3. Compare "the *one* of faith" in 3:36.
8. Or, "voided". That is, made empty of any value or place. On this word, see "emptied" in Phil 2:7.
9. The promise of a free gift is nullified, since such people would then need to obey in order to attain it. The path of promise would be a dead end. More abstractly, even if perfect obedience were attained, the reward would be earned; the inheritance would not be God's gift based on His promise. Promise and Law are mutually exclusive. On this word, see "done away with" in 6:6.
10. In addition to nullifying the path of promise, the path of Law also brings its own consequences. Because we cannot keep it, God's Law produces a result opposite of what "the ones of the Law" are hoping. It only makes us aware of our sin (3:20), condemns us for our failure to perform, and causes us to desire a Savior (Gal 3:24). It is powerless to give life, and was not given for this purpose.
11. Some manuscripts say "For" {B}.
12. Or, "violation". There is no law to violate connected with the promise of a gift, so there can be no transgression or wrath either. Promise, inheritance, gift, and grace are one reality; Law, obedience, transgression, and wrath is a different reality. On this word, see 5:14.
13. Some think this looks back to the negative side in v 14-15. Because Law nullifies the promise and brings only wrath to those under it, not the promised blessing, it is by faith. Others think it points forward to the positive side that follows, "For this reason *it is* by faith— that *it may be* based...".
14. That is, the promise, the inheritance, righteousness, salvation.
15. Or, "secure, certain, sure". On this word, see 2 Pet 1:10. It is firm because it is based on grace, not works.
16. That is, to believing Jews like Paul himself, those following Moses' Law and Abraham's faith.
17. That is, to believing Gentiles, those following Abraham's faith alone.
18. Abraham is the spiritual father before God of all believers; the father of the faith relationship with God.
19. Or, "as-*if*". Some take these words to mean "calling [into] being the things not being" in an act of creation, as seen in the birth of Isaac, v 19. Others think "the *things* not being" are the things God has planned and promised, but which do not yet exist. God calls or names them "as if" they already existed, as when He called Abraham a "father of many nations" when he had no child, v 17. GK *6055*.
20. Or, "against, beyond". That is, contrary to all that human hope could offer, upon the hope God promised.
21. Paul may mean Abraham believed for this purpose, so that he might become what God promised. Or, "so that he became", meaning that he believed, with the result that he in fact became the father of nations.
22. Paul details the scope and endurance of Abraham's faith.
23. Abraham considered it, but did not waver. Some manuscripts say "He did not consider" it {C}, meaning that his faith was so strong he did not even consider it. On this word, see Heb 10:24.
24. Or, "by this time, now". On this word, see Mt 24:32. Some manuscripts omit this word {C}.
25. Or, "become dead, as good as dead, lifeless", dead from the point of view of procreation. Same word as in Heb 11:12. Elsewhere only with different grammar as "put to death" in Col 3:5. GK *3739*. Related to "deadness" next.
26. Or, "doubt". On this word, see "doubting" in Jam 1:6.
27. Or, "was strengthened" *by* faith. On this word, see 2 Tim 2:1.
28. Same word as in 14:5.
29. More literally, "has promised, He is able", as the Greek typically phrases the tenses.
30. Some manuscripts omit this word {C}.
31. For the final time in v 13-25, Paul links Abraham and his seed.
32. On "put faith upon", see 4:5.
33. This same word is used of the action of Judas (Mt 26:48); the Jews (Mt 27:2; Jn 18:35; Act 3:13); Pilate (Jn 19:16); Jesus (Jn 19:30; Gal 2:20; Eph 5:25); and God (Rom 8:32). On this word, see Mt 26:21.
34. Or, "because of, for the sake of". This word is used twice in this verse, and twice in v 23-24 as "for [his] sake". If both occurrences in v 25 are to be taken in the same sense, some think both look backward ("because we had sinned, because we had been justified"); others, forward ("for the sake of atoning for our sin, for the sake of demonstrating our justification"). Others think Paul means "because of our trespasses" and "for the sake of our justification". GK *1328*.
35. Or, "arose". Same word as in v 24.
36. On this word, see "*a* declaring-righteous" in 5:18. Related to "declare righteous" in 5:1.

A. 1 Jn 2:25   B. Rom 8:17, heir   C. Phil 2:12, work out   D. Eph 2:8   E. Eph 2:8   F. Heb 11:11   G. Jn 5:21   H. Rom 8:30   J. Col 1:5
K. 2 Tim 4:20, sick   L. 2 Cor 4:10, dying   M. Lk 2:23   N. 1 Tim 1:13   O. Rom 4:3   P. Mk 10:32   Q. Mt 28:6, arose   R. Mt 6:14

Romans 5:1   524   Verse

2B. Therefore, having been declared-righteous[A] by faith, we have[1] peace with God through our Lord   5:1
Jesus Christ, *through Whom also we have[2] the access[3] *by* faith[4] into this grace[5] in which we stand   2

     1C. And we are boasting[6] over[7] *the* hope[B] *of* the glory *of* God
     2C. And not only *this*,[8] but we also are boasting in the afflictions[C]— knowing that the affliction is   3
producing[D] endurance[E], *and the endurance *is producing* approvedness[9], and the approvedness   4
is producing hope[B]

         1D. And the hope does not put-to-shame[10], because the love *of* God[11] has been poured-out[F]   5
in our hearts[G] through *the* Holy Spirit having been given *to* us

            1E. For while we *were* still being weak[H], yet[12] at *the* right-time[13], **Christ** died for   6
ungodly[J] *ones*

                1F. For one will rarely[14] die for *a* righteous[K] *person*   7
                2F. For[15] perhaps someone may even dare[L] to die for the good[16] *person*
                3F. But God demonstrates[17] His *own* love[M] for us, because while we *were* still   8
being sinners, Christ died for us

            2E. Therefore *by* much more, having now been declared-righteous[A] by His blood[N], we   9
shall be saved[O] from the wrath[18] through Him

                1F. For if while being enemies,[19] we were reconciled[20] *to* God through the death   10
of His Son
                2F. *By* much more, having been reconciled, we shall be saved[O] by His life[P]

     3C. And not only *this*,[21] but *we are* also boasting[22] in God through our Lord Jesus Christ, through   11
Whom we now received the reconciliation[23]

3B. Because of this,[24] just as through one man[Q] sin entered into the world, and death through the sin,   12
and so[25] death went-through[26] to all people[Q], because[27] all sinned— [28]

     1C. For until *the* Law,[29] sin was in *the* world— but sin is not charged-to-the-account[30], *there* being   13
no law[31]
     2C. Nevertheless death reigned[R] from Adam until Moses— even over the *ones* not having sinned   14
in the likeness[32] *of* the transgression[33] *of* Adam, who is *a* pattern[34] *of* the *One* coming

         1D. But not as *is* the trespass[35], so also *is* the *grace*-gift[36]—   15

            1E. For if *by* the trespass *of* the one *man,* the many[37] died[38]

                1F. *By* much more, the grace *of* God and the gift[39] by *the* grace *of* the one man
Jesus Christ abounded[S] for the many

         2D. And not as *what resulted* through one *man* having sinned, *is* the given-gift[40]—   16

1. Some manuscripts say "let us have" {A}, that is, "let us be having, enjoying", as this word is used in Act 9:31.
2. That is, we have come-to-have it. The grammar implies that we came-to-have it in the past, and continue to have it now. Some try to communicate the sense of this by paraphrasing it "we have obtained".
3. Or, "introduction, approach, admission", as into a king's presence. Elsewhere only in Eph 2:18; 3:12. GK *4643*. Related to "bring to" in 1 Pet 3:18.
4. Some manuscripts omit "*by* faith" {C}.
5. That is, this state of grace.
6. Or, "let us boast", here and in v 3, if "let us have" is adopted earlier. Same word as in v 3, 11. We boast in God's gift to us, God's accomplishment. On this word, see 2 Cor 11:16. Related to "boasting" in 3:27.
7. Or, "on, on the basis of, in, in reference to". GK *2093*. Not the same word as "in" in v 3, 11.
8. We not only boast in the hope, we boast in the affliction that produces the hope.
9. This word means the approved quality of a thing having been tested. On this word, see 2 Cor 2:9.
10. Or, "dishonor, disgrace, humiliate, disappoint". Hope would put us to shame if it never became reality, 1 Cor 15:14. Same word as in 9:33; 10:11; and Lk 13:17; 1 Cor 1:27; 2 Cor 7:14; 9:4; 1 Pet 2:6; 3:16. Elsewhere only as "shame" in 1 Cor 11:4, 5; and "humiliate" in 1 Cor 11:22. GK *2875*. Related word in 1 Jn 2:28.
11. That is, God's love for us.
12. Some manuscripts omit this word; others omit the previous "still" {C}. It is the same word, "yet, still".
13. That is, God's time. See Gal 4:4; Eph 1:10; Tit 1:3. GK *2789*.
14. Or, "hardly, scarcely". On this word, see "with difficulty" in 1 Pet 4:18.
15. Others render this word "Though, Yet" here, so that this qualifies the first case, rather than standing as a second case. GK *1142*.
16. Some think Paul is contrasting a righteous person (whom we respect) with the good person (whom we love). On this word, see 1 Tim 5:10b.
17. Or, "shows, exhibits, commends". Same word as in 3:5; 2 Cor 7:11; Gal 2:18. Elsewhere only as "commend" (see 2 Cor 3:1); and with different grammar, "stand with" in Lk 9:32, and "have existence" (see 2 Pet 3:5). GK *5319*.
18. That is, God's wrath against sin (1:18), which is coming (2:5). On this word, see Rev 16:19.
19. We were on course to receive His wrath, 1:18; 2:8, 9.
20. Elsewhere only in 2 Cor 5:18, 19, 20; and in 1 Cor 7:11. GK *2904*. Related to "reconcile" in Col 1:20; "reconcile" in Act 7:26; "reconcile" in Mt 5:24; and "reconciliation" in Rom 5:11.
21. Others make this point 3E. ("not only [shall we be saved]..."), or 3F. ("not only [reconciled and saved]...").
22. Same word as in v 2.
23. Elsewhere only in 11:15; 2 Cor 5:18, 19. GK *2903*. Related word in v 10.
24. That is, because we now received the reconciliation as a gift by grace through the sacrifice of Jesus Christ, resulting in righteousness, peace with God, and eternal life. Paul now puts this in broad perspective, comparing Christ's one act bringing life to Adam's one act bringing death, and the former reign of sin to the present reign of grace. His death brought global changes even more far-reaching than Adam's sin. Grace now reigns in the world, resulting in eternal life for all who receive the gift of righteousness.
25. Or, "in this manner". That is, through one man. Compare 1 Cor 15:22. Some render this "even so", eliminating the break at the end of the verse. On this word, see Jn 3:16.
26. Or, "spread, came through". Used by Paul also in 1 Cor 10:1; 16:5; 2 Cor 1:16. Used 43 times. GK *1451*.
27. On this idiom, see "for which" in Phil 3:12.
28. Note that Paul breaks off his thought. He picks it up again in verse 18, and gives the "so also". His basic point is that both Adam and Christ performed one act that affected all their progeny. But before he can make this point, he must explain how Adam's act affected his whole race. So next he explains the meaning of "all sinned".
29. That is, the period of time between Adam and Moses, v 14.
30. Used only here. GK *1824*. Related to "charge to my account" in Phm 18.
31. That is, since there was no law. See 4:15. With no requirement, there can be no accountability.
32. Adam violated a requirement of God. People living between Adam and Moses had no such requirements or violations. Yet they died. On this word, see Phil 2:7.
33. Or, "violation". This word refers to the violation of a law or command. With no law from God, there can be no violation of His law. Thus Paul does not mean "all sinned" in v 12 in the sense of "violated God's command". In v 13-14 Paul is proving that death is not the result of each person's individual sins, but in some sense, is a consequence upon all humanity resulting from Adam's sin, "the trespass of the one man", v 15, 17. Consult the commentaries. Having proven this, he can now compare and contrast the universal consequences of Adam's act and Christ's. Elsewhere only in 2:23; 4:15; Gal 3:19; 1 Tim 2:14; Heb 2:2; 9:15. GK *4126*. Related to "transgressor" in 2:25, 27; Jam 2:9; and "transgress" in Mt 15:2, 3.
34. Or, "model". Same word as in 1 Pet 5:3. But Adam is not a pattern not in all respects. Before Paul returns to where he left off in v 12 to explain how these two are similar (just as... so also), he first explains how they are not similar.
35. Or, "false step". Related to "fall". Same word as in v 16, 17, 18, 20. On this word, see Mt 6:14.
36. That is, the gift is not like the trespass. The contrast is between the sin which takes away life, and the gift which abounds in life. Same word as in v 16b. On this word, see "gift" in 1 Cor 1:7. Related to "grace", this word is emphasizing its "freeness". Not related to "gift" next.
37. When referring to Adam, "the many" and "all" means all his progeny, mankind. They died (v 12, 15) and were condemned (16, 18, 19). When referring to Christ, these words mean all His progeny, those "receiving" the gift (v 17), the verdict of righteousness (v 16, 18, 19).
38. That is, if by the sin of Adam, His entire progeny fell under the reign of death.
39. Same word as in v 17, the "gift" of righteousness. Elsewhere only in Jn 4:10; Act 2:38; 8:20; 10:45; 11:17; 2 Cor 9:15; Eph 3:7; 4:7; Heb 6:4; all of God's gifts. GK *1561*. Related to the verb "to give", this word emphasizes its "givenness".
40. That is, the gift given is not like the result of Adam's act. On this word, which is related to "gift" in v 15, see "gift-given" in Jam 1:17. This word emphasizes the gift as the result of an act of giving.

A. Rom 3:24 B. Col 1:5 C. Rev 7:14 D. Phil 2:12, work out E. Jam 1:3 F. Act 2:17 G. Rev 2:23 H. 1 Thes 5:14 J. Jude 15 K. Rom 1:17
L. 2 Cor 11:21 M. 1 Jn 4:16 N. 1 Jn 1:7 O. Lk 19:10 P. Rom 8:10 Q. Mt 4:4, mankind R. Rev 19:6 S. 2 Cor 8:2

	1E.	For **the judgment**[1] *is* from one *trespass*[2], resulting-in[3] *a* verdict-of-condemnation[4]— but the *grace*-gift *is* from many trespasses,[5] resulting in *a* verdict-of-righteous[6]	
	2E.	For if *by* the trespass *of* the one *man,* death reigned[A] through the one—	17
		1F. *By* much more, the *ones* receiving the abundance[B] *of* the grace[C] and *of* the gift *of* righteousness[7] will reign in life[D] through the One, Jesus Christ[8]	
3C.	So then,[9] as *it was* through one trespass[10] resulting-in a verdict-of-condemnation for all people[E], so also *it was* through one righteous-act[11] resulting-in *a* declaring-righteous[12] *issuing in* life[13] for all people[E]		18
	1D.	For just as through the disobedience[14] *of* the one man, the many were made[15] sinners	19
	2D.	So also through the obedience[F] *of* the One, the many will be made righteous *ones*	
4C.	And *the* Law[16] came-in-beside[17] that the trespass might increase[G]. But where sin increased, grace super-abounded[18], *in order that		20 21
	1D.	Just as sin reigned[A] in death	
	2D.	So also grace might reign through righteousness[H] resulting-in eternal life through Jesus Christ our Lord	
4B.	Therefore, what shall we say? Should[19] we be continuing[J] *in* sin in order that grace might increase?[20] May it never be! How shall we who died *to* sin still live in it?		6:1 2
1C.	Or do you not know that all we[21] who were baptized[K] into[22] Christ Jesus[23] were baptized into His death?		3
2C.	Therefore we were buried-with Him through baptism[L] into death, in order that just as Christ arose[24] from *the* dead through the glory *of* the Father, so also **we** might walk[M] in newness[N] *of* life		4
	1D.	For if we have become united-with[25] *Him in* the likeness[O] *of* His death, certainly we shall be also *in the likeness of His* resurrection[P]	5
		1E. Knowing[26] this— that our old[Q] person[27] was crucified-with[28] *Him* in order that the body[R] *of* sin[29] might be done-away-with[30], *so that* we no longer are-slaves[31] *to* sin	6
			1F. For the *one* having died has been declared-righteous[S] from sin[32]	7
		2E. And if we died with Christ, we believe that we shall also live-with[T] Him, *knowing that Christ— having arisen[33] from *the* dead— dies no more. Death lords-over[U] Him no longer	8-9
			1F. For *the death* that He died,[34] He died *to* sin once-for-all[35]. But *the life* that He is living, He is living *to* God	10
			2F. So also you, be counting[V] yourselves to be[36] **dead**[37] *to* sin— but living *to* God in Christ Jesus[38]	11

1. Paul uses grammar that emphasizes the contrast between the two halves of this sentence; between the judgment and the grace-gift. On this word, see Jn 9:39.
2. This is supplied from what follows. Or, "*man having sinned*" from what precedes. The contrast is between judgment as the deserved response of God to one sin, and the gift as the undeserved response of God to many sins.
3. Used twice in this verse, this word means "to, into, for, toward, resulting in, leading to, for the purpose of ". It is also in 5:18, 21; and as "leading to" in 6:16, 19, 22; 8:15. Used 1767 times. GK *1650*.
4. Same word as in v 18, and as "condemnation" in 8:1.
5. For judgment, the starting point was one sin. For the gift, the starting point was many sins.
6. Or, "justification". Used in this sense only here. Same word as "righteous-act" in v 18.
7. That is, "*consisting of* righteousness".
8. The sin of Adam brought a reign of death to all people. The gift brings a reign in life to all who receive it.
9. Paul turns now to the positive sense in which Adam is a pattern of Christ (v 14), which is also returning to what he began to say in verse 12. The first half of this verse restates v 12 using words from v 15-17. Then the "so also" is given.
10. Some render this "*the* trespass *of* one", and later, "*the* righteous act *of* One".
11. Same word as in Rev 15:4; 19:8. It is rendered "righteous act" to correspond to "one trespass" preceding and "obedience" in v 19. Others render it "verdict of righteous [upon Christ]", as it is used in v 16. On this word, see "regulation" in 1:32. Related to "declare righteous" in 3:24, "declaring righteous" here, "righteous" in v 19, and "righteousness" in v 17, 21.
12. Or, "justification". Elsewhere only as "justification" in 4:25. GK *1470*. Related to "declare righteous" in 3:24.
13. Literally, "*of* life". Or, "*resulting in* life, *characterized by* life". Paul could have added such a word earlier, "verdict-of-condemnation *issuing in* death".
14. Or, "refusal-to-listen". On this word, see 2 Cor 10:6.
15. Or, "constituted, caused to become". Same word as later in the verse. On this word, see "put in charge" in Act 6:3.
16. Paul now puts Law and grace into this broad perspective. The reign of grace resulting in righteousness and eternal life in contrast to the reign of sin through the Law resulting in death is the subject to which he turns in chapters 6-8.
17. This is the same root word as "entered" in 5:12, with the prefix "beside" added. Sin "came into the world", Law "came in beside". Elsewhere only in a negative sense as "sneaked in" in Gal 2:4. GK *4209*.
18. Elsewhere only in 2 Cor 7:4. GK *5668*. Related to the word in Mk 7:37, and in 1 Thes 5:13.
19. Some manuscripts say "Shall..." {N}.
20. A natural question. If salvation is all by grace, and we stand in grace at peace with God (5:1), and where sin increased grace abounded (5:21), then does it matter how we live after we are saved? After all, the worse sinner I am, the more God's grace and mercy will be magnified.
21. A similar construction occurs in Gal 3:27, "all you who were baptized".
22. On "baptize into", see Mk 1:9. On "baptize", see Mk 1:8.
23. Some manuscripts say "Jesus Christ" {K}.
24. Or, "was raised". On this word, see Mt 28:6.
25. Or, "united-with" the likeness; "united-together", "grown-together" *in* the likeness. This adjective is used only here. GK *5242*. Related to "grow with" in Lk 8:7. The word may imply a uniting together into a living union, as in a graft.
26. This word (see Lk 1:34) is not the same word as "knowing" in v 9 (see 1 Jn 2:29).
27. Paul uses this metaphor also in Eph 4:22; Col 3:9. Some think he means "the former self", the one "in Adam" before we became new creations "in Christ", 2 Cor 5:17. There are other views.
28. Same word as in Gal 2:19. Elsewhere only of the two thieves in Mt 27:44; Mk 15:32; Jn 19:32. GK *5365*.
29. Some think Paul means "the *physical* body *characterized by* sin", our sinful body; others, "the body *belonging to* sin", sin's body; others, "the mass *of* sin", consisting of sin; others, "the sinful self"; others, the "old person".
30. This word basically means "to work down to nothing", "to make barren, useless, inoperative, null", and therefore "powerless, ineffective", with English renderings depending on the context. Same word as in 1 Cor 6:13; Gal 3:17; 2 Thes 2:8; Heb 2:14. Elsewhere only as "bring to nothing" in 1 Cor 1:28; 2:6; "abolish" in 1 Cor 15:24, 26; Gal 5:11; Eph 2:15; 2 Tim 1:10; "nullify" in Rom 3:3, 31; 4:14; "set aside" in 1 Cor 13:8, 10, 11; "use up" (waste, exhaust, make barren) in Lk 13:7; "pass away" in 2 Cor 3:7, 11, 13, 14; "release" in Rom 7:2, 6; "alienate" in Gal 5:4. GK *2934*.
31. Or, "are serving as slaves". This word means "to be a slave to, to serve as slave to". Some think Paul means "*so that* we are no longer slaves *to* sin", expressing the result of the death (as this grammar is used in 7:3); others, "*that* we *might* no longer be serving as slaves *to* sin", expressing the purpose of the death. Both are true. Same word as in Jn 8:33; Gal 4:8, 9, 25; Tit 3:3. Elsewhere only as "serve" in Mt 6:24; Lk 16:13; Act 20:19; Rom 7:6, 25; 9:12; 12:11; 14:18; 16:18; Gal 5:13; Eph 6:7; Phil 2:22; Col 3:24; 1 Thes 1:9; 1 Tim 6:2; "serve as slaves" in Act 7:7; and "slaving" in Lk 15:29. GK *1526*. Related to "slave" in 6:17; "slavery" in 8:15; "enslaved" in 6:18; and "enslave" in 2 Cor 11:20. A key word group.
32. We are no longer slaves of sin because having died with Christ, we have been declared righteous, and therefore are freed from it.
33. Or, "been raised". Same word as in v 4.
34. More literally, "For what He died... what He is living", or "For *that* which He died... *that* which He is living".
35. Or, "one time". On this word, see Heb 7:27.
36. Some manuscripts omit "to be" {C}.
37. Paul uses grammar that emphasizes the contrast between the two halves of this sentence.
38. Some manuscripts add "our Lord" {A}. Some manuscripts say "Jesus Christ" {K}.

A. Rev 19:6 B. 2 Cor 8:2 C. Eph 2:8 D. Rom 8:10 E. Mt 4:4, mankind F. Rom 16:26 G. 2 Cor 8:15 H. Rom 1:17 J. Rom 11:22 K. Mk 1:8 L. Mk 1:4 M. Heb 13:9 N. Rom 7:6 O. Phil 2:7 P. Act 24:15 Q. Mk 2:21 R. Eph 1:23 S. Rom 3:24 T. 2 Cor 7:3, live together U. Rom 7:1 V. Rom 3:28, consider

	3C. Therefore do not let sin be reigning[1] in your mortal[A] body so that *you are* obeying[B] its desires[2], nor be presenting[3] your body-parts[4] *to* sin *as* instruments[5] *of* unrighteousness[C]	12 13
	1D. But present yourselves *to* God as-if[6] being alive[7] from *the* dead[8], and your body-parts *to* God *as* instruments *of* righteousness	
	2D. For sin shall not lord-over[D] you— for you are not under *the* Law[9], but under grace	14
5B.	Therefore, what? Should we sin[10] because we are not under *the* Law but under grace? May it never be!	15
	1C. Do you not know that *to* whom you are presenting yourselves *as* slaves for obedience[E], you are slaves *to* whom you are obeying[B]— whether *slaves of* sin, leading-to[11] death, or *slaves of* obedience, leading-to righteousness?	16
	1D. But thanks[F] *be to* God that you were slaves[12] *of* sin, but you obeyed[B] from *the* heart *the* form[13] *of* teaching[G] to which you were delivered[H]	17
	2D. And having been set-free[14] from sin, you were enslaved[15] *to* righteousness *(I am speaking in human[16] terms because of the weakness[J] of* your flesh[17])	18-19
	3D. For just as you presented your body-parts *as* slaves *to* impurity[K] and lawlessness[L] leading-to lawlessness, so now present your body-parts *as* slaves *to* righteousness leading to holiness[18]	
	1E. For when you were slaves *of* sin, you were free[M] *to* righteousness.[19] *So what fruit[N] were you having at that time? Things* over[20] which you are now ashamed[O]!	20-21
	1F. For the outcome[P] *of* those *things is* death	
	2E. But now having been set-free from sin and enslaved *to* God, you are having your fruit[N] leading-to[21] holiness[Q]	22
	1F. And the outcome[P] *is* eternal life	
	3E. For the wages[22] *of* sin *is* death, but the gift[R] *of* God *is* eternal life in Christ Jesus[23] our Lord	23
	2C. Or do you not know,[24] brothers[S] (for I am speaking *to ones* knowing *the* Law[25]), that the Law lords-over[26] the person for as much time as he lives?	7:1
	1D. For the married[27] woman has been bound[T] *by the* Law *to* the living husband. But if the husband dies, she has been released[28] from the law *of* the husband	2
	1E. So then, while the husband *is* living, she will be called[29] *an* adulteress[U] if she comes[30] *to a* different[V] husband	3
	2E. But if the husband dies, she is free[M] from the law, *so that* she is not *an* adulteress, having come *to a* different[V] husband	
	2D. So-then[31] my brothers, **you** also were put-to-death[32] *with reference to* the Law[33] through the body *of* Christ,[34] so that you *might* come[35] *to a* different[V] *One— to* the *One* having arisen[36] from *the* dead— in order that we might bear-fruit[37] *for* God[38]	4

1. This word is used in Romans of death reigning, 5:14, 17; of sin reigning, 5:21; 6:12; and of grace reigning, 5:17, 21. On this word, see Rev 19:6.
2. On this word, see Gal 5:16. Some manuscripts say "so that *you* obey it"; others, "so that *you* obey it in its desires" {B}.
3. Or, "providing, offering, putting at the disposal of ". Same word as later in the verse (note the change of tense), and in v 16, 19, and 12:1, "present your bodies as a living sacrifice". On this word, see 12:1.
4. Or, "parts, members" of your body. Same word as in 6:19; 7:5, 23. On this word, see Col 3:5.
5. Or, "tools, equipment, weapons". On this word, see "weapons" in 13:12.
6. Or, "as though". This is Paul's only use of this word. Made of two words "as" and "if ". Elsewhere only as "as if " in Mt 3:16; Mk 9:26; Lk 24:11; Act 2:3; 10:3; Heb 1:12; "like" in Mt 9:36; Lk 22:44; Act 6:15; and "about" in Mt 14:21; Lk 3:23; 9:14, 28; 22:41; 22:59; 23:44; Act 1:15; 2:41; 19:7. GK *6059*.
7. Or, "living". Same word as "live" in v 2, 10, 11. On this word, see "came to life" in Rev 20:4.
8. That is, "as if " presently possessing resurrection life like Jesus (v 4), or "as" being alive from the spiritually dead.
9. That is, the Law that came in beside, 5:20. The escape from the lordship of sin is explained by the release from the Law that occurred when we died to it. Under the Law, sin did in fact lord over them. Note 1 Cor 15:56. Paul explains this in chapter 7.
10. That is, should we commit a sin, as opposed to continuing to live in sin, v 1.
11. Or, "for, resulting in". Same word as in the next phrase, in v 19, 22, and as "resulting in" in 5:16.
12. Same noun as in Rom 1:1; 6:16, 17, 19, 20; 1 Cor 7:21, 22, 23; 12:13; 2 Cor 4:5; Gal 1:10; 3:28; 4:1, 7; Eph 6:5, 6, 8; Phil 1:1; 2:7; Col 3:11, 22; 4:1, 12; 1 Tim 6:1; 2 Tim 2:24; Tit 1:1; 2:9; Phm 16; Jam 1:1; 1 Pet 2:16; 2 Pet 1:1; 2:19; Jude 1; plus 89 times in the Gospels, Acts, Revelation (see Rev 1:1). GK *1528*. The feminine form is in Lk 1:38. Related to "fellow slaves" in Rev 19:10; "are slaves" in 6:6.
13. Or, "pattern". On this word, see "pattern" in 1 Pet 5:3.
14. Same word as in v 22. On this word, see 8:2.
15. Or, "made slaves". Elsewhere only in 6:22; Act 7:6; 1 Cor 7:15; 9:19; Gal 4:3; Tit 2:3; 2 Pet 2:19. GK *1530*. Related to "are slaves" in 6:6.
16. That is, in referring to our status as slavery to righteousness, in using the slavery analogy. On this word, see "common to humanity" in 1 Cor 10:13.
17. Some think Paul is referring to their understanding. Compare Heb 5:14.
18. Or, "sanctification". Same word as in v 22.
19. Since you were not slaves to two masters, you were slaves to sin and free with regard to righteousness.
20. Punctuated this way, this gives the answer to the previous question. Others punctuate it "at that time, over which *things* you are now ashamed?", in which case the implied answer is "none".
21. Same word as in v 19 and v 16.
22. Or, "rations". A military word. The pay earned from sin. Same word as in Lk 3:14. Elsewhere only as "rations" in 1 Cor 9:7; 2 Cor 11:8. GK *4072*.
23. Some manuscripts say "Jesus Christ" {K}.
24. Paul now takes up the other part of 6:14-15, that we are not under the Law.
25. Some think Paul means the Law of Moses; others, the general principle of law and legal justice. On this word, see 7:21.
26. Or, "rules, is master of, is lord over". This is the verb related to the word "lord". It is used in Romans of death (6:9), sin (6:14), and Law (7:1), which no longer "lord over" us; and of Christ (14:9), who "is Lord" over us. Same word as in Lk 22:25; 2 Cor 1:24. Elsewhere only as "being lords" in 1 Tim 6:15. GK *3259*. Related to "lord over" in 1 Pet 5:3.
27. This word is made of the word "man" with the prefix "under", and means "under a man, subject to a man". Used only here. GK *5635*. Not related to the words "marry" or "wedding, marriage" (Mt 22:11).
28. Same word as in v 6.
29. Or, "she will bear the name". Same word as in Act 11:26. The Law names her as such. On this word, see "revealed" in Lk 2:26.
30. Or, "comes-to-be *with*". GK *1181*. Same word as in v 3b, 4.
31. Now Paul applies to us the principle of v 1, illustrated by v 2-3, that death ends the authority of the Law.
32. Or, "were made dead *to* the Law". It is passive only here, 8:36; 2 Cor 6:9; 1 Pet 3:18. Elsewhere only in Mt 10:21; 26:59; 27:1; Mk 13:12; 14:55; Lk 21:16; Rom 8:13. GK *2506*. It is the verb related to the word "death" (see 2 Cor 11:23).
33. That is, God's Law as the basis of a relationship with Him, His terms and conditions of which we must be "doers" to be saved (if this were possible). For the Jews, the Law of Moses is the written expression of this, the "letter", and is foremost in Paul's mind here. For the Gentiles, some of the things of God's Law are written on their hearts, 2:15. Thus, it is the Law we must be "released" from if we are to be saved, the Law that will judge and condemn us before God if we must face it. We did not die to man's civil law or all law in general, but to God's Law as the standard of righteousness for acceptance by Him. Christ did not need to die to release us from our subjective legalism, however we might impose it upon ourselves in God's name, but from God's objective legal requirements. On this word, see 7:21.
34. Our "old person" was crucified with Christ (6:6), and buried with Him (6:4).
35. Same word as used in both illustrations of v 3. It is not the normal word for "marry", but that is the idea in v 3-4. GK *1181*.
36. Or, "been raised". On this word, see "arose" in Mt 28:6.
37. Same word as in v 5. Elsewhere only in Mt 13:23; Mk 4:20, 28; Lk 8:15; Col 1:6, 10. GK *2844*. Related to "fruitful" in Act 14:17.
38. Some think the metaphor is that Christ (the husband) bears fruit through us (His bride), for the glory of God, similar to Jn 15:8, 16; others think there is a change of metaphor here, from marriage to an agricultural metaphor as in Jn 15, vine and fruit.

A. 2 Cor 5:4 B. Act 6:7 C. Rom 1:18 D. Rom 7:1 E. Rom 16:26 F. Eph 2:8, grace G. 1 Cor 14:6 H. Act 16:4 J. Mt 8:17 K. 1 Thes 2:3 L. 1 Jn 3:4 M. Mt 17:26 N. Mt 7:16 O. Rom 1:16 P. Rom 10:4, end Q. Heb 12:14 R. 1 Cor 1:7 S. Act 16:40 T. 1 Cor 7:27 U. Jam 4:4, adulterous V. 1 Cor 12:9

	1E. For when we were in the flesh,¹ the passions² *of* sins³ which⁴ *were* through the Law⁵ were at-work⁶ in our body-parts⁷, so as to bear-fruit^A *for* death	5
	2E. But now⁸ we were released⁹ from the Law— having died¹⁰ *to that* by which¹¹ we were being held¹²— so that we *are* serving¹³ in newness¹⁴ *of the* Spirit¹⁵ and not *in* oldness *of the* letter¹⁶	6
3D.	Therefore, what shall we say? *Is* the Law sin?¹⁷ May it never be! On-the-contrary¹⁸, I¹⁹ *would* not *have* known²⁰ **sin** except through *the* Law	7
	1E. For indeed I *would* not *have* known²¹ coveting²² if the Law were not saying [in Ex 20:17], "You shall not covet"²³	
	1F. But sin, having taken²⁴ *an* opportunity²⁵ through the commandment²⁶, produced^B every [kind of] coveting²⁷ in me	8
	1G. For apart-from²⁸ *the* Law, sin *is* dead²⁹	
	2E. And **I** was once³⁰ alive³¹ apart from *the* Law	9
	1F. But the commandment^C having come, sin became-alive³², *and **I** died³³	10
	2F. And the commandment for life^D— this was found *in* me *to be* for³⁴ death	
	1G. For sin, having taken *an* opportunity through the commandment, deceived³⁵ me, and through it, killed³⁶ me	11
	3E. So-then **the Law**³⁷ *is* holy^E, and the commandment *is* holy and righteous^F and good^G—	12
4D.	Therefore did the good *thing* become death *for* me?³⁸ May it never be! On the contrary, *it was* sin, in order that it might become-visible³⁹ *as* sin while producing⁴⁰ death *in* me⁴¹ through the good *thing,* in order that sin^H might become extremely⁴² sinful^J through the commandment	13

1. That is, before we were Christians, new creations, in the Spirit, crucified with Him.
2. Used in this sense elsewhere only in Gal 5:24. On this word, see "sufferings" in Phil 3:10. Related word in Rom 1:26.
3. Some think Paul means "the sinful passions"; others, "the passions *belonging to* the sins"; others, "the passions *leading to* sins", along the lines of Jam 1:14.
4. The grammar indicates this refers to "the passions".
5. That is, they were increased through the Law, 5:20. Paul explains this next in v 7-8.
6. Or, "in operation, working". On this word, see "works" in 1 Cor 12:11.
7. Same word as in 6:13.
8. Paul is contrasting the present to the past (v 5), our condition before and after we died with Christ.
9. Or, "discharged, disengaged". Used in this sense also in v 2. On this word, see "done away with" in 6:6.
10. The KJV says "being dead", a conjectural reading with no manuscript support.
11. More literally, "died in-connection-with *the thing by* which we were being held". Some think Paul is referring to the Law. Others render it "died in-the-sphere-of what we were being held", referring to the state of slavery in which we were held, but from which we are now freed to "serve in newness...".
12. Or, "held down". On this word, see "holding down" in 1:18. Related to the word in Gal 5:1.
13. That is, "with the result that we are serving as slaves" to our new Master. On this word, see "are slaves" in 6:6.
14. Elsewhere only in 6:4, "newness" of life. GK *2786*.
15. Or, "spirit".
16. That is, the written code of Law, the Law of Moses (God's only written code), as in 2:27, 29; 2 Cor 3:6.
17. A natural question since Paul just said that the passions of sins were through the Law, v 5. Is God's Law the problem? Is it His Law that makes me a sinner? No, the Law is not sin, but it defined a standard against which sin rebelled, causing my death.
18. This same word follows "May it never be" elsewhere only in 3:31; 7:13; 11:11. GK *247*.
19. Some think Paul is referring to his own personal history; others, that he is speaking vividly; others, that he is speaking as a representative of Jews, or of mankind before the Law, or of Adam before the fall.
20. Or, "come to know". Or, "I did not know...". On this word, see Lk 1:34. That is, Paul would not have known of sin's presence in him as sin (1E.), and its power to kill him in relation to God (2E.). Apart from God's Law, we consider sin to be merely "your opinion" or "my mistakes or bad choices". God's Law defines sin as God Himself views it, and will view it on judgment day. When we understand His standards, we come to know that sin is in us, and is killing us.
21. Or, "known about, had knowledge of ". Or, "I was not knowing...".
22. Or, "[evil] desire". This is the normal word for "desire", used in both a positive and negative sense. When we desire what is not ours, this word can be translated "covet" as here. On this word, see "desire" in Gal 5:16. See Gal 5:17 for the verb, which is also used here.
23. The Law saying not to do it made Paul aware he was doing it.
24. Or, "received". Same word as in v 11. This is the common verb "take, receive" used 258 times. GK *3284*.
25. Or, "occasion, starting point, base of operations". Elsewhere only in v 11; 2 Cor 5:12; 11:2; Gal 5:13; 1 Tim 5:14. GK *929*. Notice the parallelism with verse 11. Sin made the commandment its base of operations.
26. Or, this phrase may go with "produced", "opportunity, produced... in me through the commandment", like v 13.
27. Once aware that it was forbidden, sin increased it. Sin stimulated coveting in rebellion to the Law. This explains how the passions of sins are "through the Law", v 5.
28. Or, "without *a* law". Note 4:15. Sin is lawlessness, 1 Jn 3:4. Sin against God requires a law from God to rebel against, a line to cross. In a more abstract sense, violation requires a rule to violate.
29. This is stated as a general principle. Sin is present, but inactive until it has a law to transgress. God's Law is the power of sin, 1 Cor 15:56. Or, "*was* dead", stating it as the historical experience of Paul.
30. Or, "formerly". Some think Paul is referring to his childhood, when he was unaware of the Law; others, to his self-righteous, complacent ignorance before the Law became real to him, like the ruler in Lk 18:21, "I kept all these things". He thought he was alive, as all do, until the Law did its work in him and he came to understand God's requirements. Others think Paul is referring to mankind before the Law was given; others, to Adam before the command. On this word, see "ever" in Gal 2:6.
31. Or, "living". Same word as in 6:13. Related to "became alive" in the next phrase.
32. Or, "sprang to life, came back to life". GK *348*. Elsewhere only as "became alive again" in Lk 15:24.
33. Used 111 times. GK *633*.
34. That is, it was "for the purpose of " life, but it "resulted in" death, both being the same word (see "resulting in" in 5:16 on it). This verse is true because it is God's command, God's standard.
35. Or, "completely deceived". Or, "opportunity, deceived me through the commandment". Same word as in 16:18; 1 Cor 3:18; 2 Cor 11:3; 2 Thes 2:3. Elsewhere only as "completely deceived" in 1 Tim 2:14. GK *1987*. It is a strengthened form of the word "deceive" in 1 Tim 2:14.
36. Used 74 times. GK *650*.
37. Paul's grammar implies there is a correlating statement, which is left unsaid, something like "But I am dead in sin". The bold word and the dash attempt to reflect this nuance in English.
38. A natural question, since Paul just said the Law resulted in death for him, v 10. Is God's Law responsible for my death? Is my condemnation to death the fault of God's requirements? This is the subject of v 13-25.
39. Or, "appear, be revealed". On this word, see "shine" in Phil 2:15.
40. On this word, used also in v 8, 15, 17, 18, 20, see "work out" in Phil 2:12.
41. Paul uses himself as the example to show that sin is the killer, not God's Law.
42. Or, "supremely, utterly, extraordinarily, exceedingly, beyond measure". On this phrase, see "beyond measure" in 1 Cor 12:31. The extremity of the consequence, death, demonstrates the extremity of the cause, sin. Otherwise, sin is merely opinion.

A. Rom 7:4 B. Phil 2:12, work out C. Mk 12:28 D. Rom 8:10 E. 1 Pet 1:16 F. Rom 1:17 G. 1 Tim 5:10b H. Jn 8:46 J. Mt 9:10, sinner

1E. For[1] we know that the Law is spiritual.[2] But **I** am[3] made-of-flesh[4], having been sold[5] under sin[6] 14

    1F. For I do not understand[7] what I am producing[8] 15

        1G. For I am not practicing[A] this which I am wanting[9]. But I am doing[B] this which I am hating[C]

    2F. But if I am doing this which I am not wanting, I am agreeing-with[10] the Law[11]— that *it is* good[D] 16

    3F. And now **I** am[12] no longer producing it, but the sin dwelling[E] in me[13] *is* 17

2E. For I know that **good**[14] does not dwell[E] in me, that is, in my flesh[15] 18

    1F. For the wanting is present[16] *in* me, but the producing the good[17] *is* not[18]

        1G. For I am not doing *the* good[F] which I am wanting. But I am practicing[A] this evil which I am not wanting 19

    2F. But if I am doing this which **I**[19] am not wanting, **I** am no longer producing it, but the sin dwelling in me[20] *is* 20

3E. I find then the law[21] *in* me, the *one* wanting to do the good[D], that the evil[22] is present *in* me 21

1. Paul explains how the Law as the objective yardstick demonstrates how extremely sinful sin is.
2. That is, the Law is spiritual in origin, coming from God (as this word is used in 1 Cor 10:3), and therefore "good", v 16. But Paul is enslaved to sin, as he explains next.
3. Note that Paul changes to the present tense in v 14-25, the significance of which is the subject of no small debate. The purpose of these verses is to explain how sin is responsible for his death, not the Law (v 13), thus defending God's Law from the charge of causing the death of those to whom it was given. Some think Paul is reflecting on his experience under the Law of Moses as a devout Pharisee who wanted to keep God's Law and earn acceptance by Him, but could not keep it. His sin produced spiritual death, a state which continued until he was saved, and died to the demands of the Law, v 6. Others think he is reflecting on his experience as a Christian rightly seeking to live in holy obedience to the laws of conscience, as led by the Spirit. He is reflecting upon law as a principle, broadly conceived, in its present place in his life, to prove what was also true under the Law of Moses, exonerating God's Law. He is unable to obey, his sin grieving the Spirit, and he lives in this state of struggle until his physical death, when he is separated from his sinful flesh. Others think it is the experience of a Christian wrongly trying to live up to rules and obligations in a desire to please God. Such a person is unable to do so, his violations producing human guilt. He continues in this state until he gives it up and walks in the Spirit, as in chapter 8. Others think that the experience described here accurately illustrates all three of these views, using differing definitions of law, sin, and death, because Paul is talking about the experience of anyone who tries to live under law as a rule of life. There are other views. Consult the commentaries.
4. On this word, see 1 Cor 3:1. Related to "fleshly" in 1 Cor 3:3, a word which some manuscripts have here {N}. Some think Paul means "carnal, fleshly", partially controlled by the flesh. Others think he means "human, of Adam's race", and therefore not good, but in bondage to sin, "in the flesh" (7:5).
5. Elsewhere only in Mt 13:46; 18:25; 26:9; Mk 14:5; Jn 12:5; Act 2:45; 4:34; 5:4. GK *4405*.
6. Same phrase as "under sin" in 3:9. Some think Paul would not say this of a Christian as described in 6:2, 6-7, 12-14, 17-18, 21-22; 7:4-6. It was our time "in the flesh" (v 5) that was dominated by sin, prior to our "release" from the Law (v 6). Others think it is an appropriate description of the sin that remains in our flesh, which by the leading of the Spirit we are striving to put to death (8:13).
7. Or, "know, acknowledge, recognize". On this word, see Lk 1:34. Paul does not acknowledge such an action as representing his true desires, or understand how to control it. He does not approve of it.
8. To use Paul's example in v 8, "I do not understand this coveting I am producing". It is not what he wants. On this word, see v 2.
9. Or, "wishing, desiring, willing". Same word as in v 16, 18, 19, 20, 21. On this word, see "willing" in Jn 7:17.
10. Or, "concurring with". Used only here, this word is made of "with" and "to say". Paul is speaking along with the Law, saying what it says, saying its demand is good; but he is not doing it. GK *5238*.
11. This proves v 14a. The Law is not the problem. Paul agrees with the Law that the action is wrong, and does not want to do it.
12. Sin enslaves Paul in spite of his own desire to obey God, and in spite of his agreement with what God is requiring of him. When God says not to do it, he agrees and does not want to do it, but sin produces it in him anyway. Thus it is sin, not God's Law, that causes his death. The sin in him is against him and against God! How extremely sinful it truly is!
13. This proves v 14b. Paul is "under sin", under its domination. The sin is using the command to produce in him actions which he hates and does not desire (v 8), yielding death (v 11). Sin is the problem, not the Law.
14. The emphasis of v 14-17 was "The Law is good, I cannot stop doing what I hate". The emphasis of v 18-20 is "I am not good, I cannot do the good I want to do". The inner good necessary to be accepted by God is not in him. On this word, see 1 Tim 5:10b.
15. That is, the flesh "sold under sin", v 14.
16. Or, "ready, at hand". Elsewhere only in v 21. GK *4154*.
17. Paul uses two different words for "good" here. "Good" (inner moral goodness) does not dwell in Paul, for though he wants it, he cannot produce the "good" (outer, visible moral goodness, 1 Tim 5:10a) corresponding to it. Both words are used of the Law, v 12, 13, 16. It is good in both senses.
18. Some manuscripts say, "but the producing the good I do not find" {B}.
19. Some manuscripts do not have the word making this emphatic (bolded) {C}.
20. This proves v 18. Good does not dwell in Paul, but sin. Good is not in him producing good, but sin is in him producing sin, and overcoming his good desires to obey God's good Law. Thus the sin in him causes his death.
21. Some think Paul means "the principle", referring to the law of sin, v 23. Others render it, "I find then *as to* the Law [of God], *in* me...". This word is used 194 times, 74 of which are in Romans. Used of God's Law, the Law of Moses, a system of law, an individual law, a principle, the first five books of the OT, the entire OT. GK *3795*. See also the note on 7:4.
22. Notice the progression. The Law is good, v 14-17; Paul is not good, v 18-20; the evil is in him, v 21-25.

A. Rom 2:1   B. Rev 13:13   C. Rom 9:13   D. 1 Tim 5:10a   E. Rom 8:11   F. 1 Tim 5:10b

	1F. For I am rejoicing-with[1] the Law *of* God according-to[2] the inner[3] person.[4]	22
	But I am seeing *a* different[A] law in my body-parts[5] waging-war-against[6] the law *of* my mind[7], and taking me captive[8] under[9] the law *of* sin existing[10] in my body-parts	23
	1G. I *am a* wretched[11] person[B]! Who will deliver[12] me from this body *of* death[13]?	24
	2G. But thanks[14] *be to* God through Jesus Christ our Lord!	25
	2F. So then,[15] **I** myself am serving[C] *the* Law *of* God *with* **the mind**[16]— but *the* law *of* sin *with* the flesh	
6B.	Therefore,[17] *there is* now[18] no condemnation[19] *for* the *ones* in Christ Jesus.[20] *For[21] the law[22] *of* the Spirit *of* life[23] in Christ Jesus[24] set you[25] free[26] from the law *of* sin and death	8:1-2
	1C. For[27] the *thing* impossible[28] *for* the Law[29], in that it was weak[D] through the flesh,[30] God *did*. Having sent[E] His *own* Son in *the* likeness[F] *of* sinful flesh[31], and for[32] sin, He condemned[G] sin in the flesh,[33] *in order that the requirement[34] *of* the Law might be fulfilled[H] in us[35]—	3
		4

1. Or, "taking pleasure with, delighting in". Used only here. Made of "with" and the word "pleasure" in Lk 8:14. Some think this could not be said of an unbeliever, whose fleshly mind is "hostile" to God, 8:7. Others think it is what would be said by those in 2:17-20 and 10:2, who think they are "alive", 7:9. GK *5310*.
2. Or, "with-respect-to *my* inner person". GK *2848*.
3. Same phrase as in 2 Cor 4:16; Eph 3:16. Compare the phrase in 1 Pet 3:4. Elsewhere only as "inside" in Mt 26:58; Mk 14:54; 15:16; Jn 20:26; Act 5:23; 1 Cor 5:12. GK *2276*.
4. This is seen in Paul's "wanting", v 15, 18, 21. Paul calls this his "mind" in v 23, 25. It is precisely here that the great deception of sin occurs. We think that because we know what is right, and intend to do it, that it is enough. It is when the commandment of God "comes" to us in its full meaning that we die (v 9), and see our captivity to sin and death, and cry out to God as in v 24.
5. Same word as in v 5.
6. Or, "fighting against". Used only here. GK *529*. Related to "fight" in 1 Tim 1:18.
7. That is, Paul's "wanting" to obey, v 15, 18, 21; the inner person, v 22. This word means "mind, intellect, understanding, way of thinking". Same word as in Lk 24:45; Rom 1:28; 7:25; 11:34; 12:2; 14:5; 1 Cor 1:10; 2:16; 14:14, 15, 19; Eph 4:17, 23; Col 2:18; 1 Tim 6:5; 2 Tim 3:8; Tit 1:15; Rev 17:9. Elsewhere only as "understanding" in Phil 4:7; 2 Thes 2:2; Rev 13:18. GK *3808*.
8. Or, "making me prisoner". On "taking captive", see 2 Cor 10:5.
9. Or, "in the sphere of, in the domain of ". Same word as "under" Law in 2:12.
10. Or, "being". It is the common verb "to be". GK *1639*.
11. Or, "miserable". Elsewhere only in Rev 3:17. GK *5417*. Related to the verb in Jam 4:9, "be miserable". Some think such a statement would not be made by the pious Pharisee who thinks he is "alive" (v 9), but by the believer truly struggling with sin. Others think this is what that Pharisee said in v 9 when the commandment came to him and "he died", and is not how Paul would speak of himself as a Christian.
12. Or, "rescue". On this word, see Col 1:13. Some think Paul is crying out for salvation; others, for resurrection.
13. Or, "the body *of* this death". That is, "this body" characterized by death. Or, the body characterized by "this death". Note 6:6.
14. Compare 1 Cor 15:57. Some manuscripts say instead "I thank God through Jesus..."; others, "The grace *of* God through Jesus...", where "grace" is the same word as "thanks" {B}.
15. Some think Paul states this as the condition in which the believer now remains until his physical death. Such a person struggles with sin as he puts to death the practices of the body by the Spirit, 8:13. Others think Paul states this as the dead end for all who would seek to be accepted by God through works of the Law, through obedience. Such a person knows what to do and so is without excuse (2:1), but he cannot do it (3:19), because sin enslaves him. He needs to be saved by grace (3:24), and then to live under grace in the newness of the Spirit (6:15, 7:6), not under the Law.
16. That is, his "wanting", v 15, 18, 21; the inner person, v 22. Paul uses grammar that emphasizes the contrast between the two halves of this sentence.
17. This "therefore" continues on in Paul's main argument, building further upon it. He turns now from correcting false inferences drawn from salvation by grace (chapters 6-7), to again teaching true ones.
18. Some think Paul means "now in becoming a Christian", in our salvation; others, "now in our life as Christians", as we live it out in the Spirit as ones who are saved. Thus some think this follows logically from 7:4-6, in contrast to the pre-Christian state described in 7:14-25, and in answer to the question of 7:24. Others think it logically continues from chapter 7, now describing the Christian life from the Spirit's point of view.
19. Those "in Christ" are completely beyond the scope of condemnation, because they have already died in Christ and are now living in Christ (Gal 2:20). They will be disciplined here as God's children (Heb 12:6); they will face reward and loss there (Rom 14:11; 1 Cor 3:15); but there is no condemnation. They battle with sin from victor's ground. Elsewhere only as "verdict of condemnation" in 5:16, 18. GK *2890*. Related to "condemned" in v 3. The opposite of "justification".
20. These have died in Christ to the Law (7:4), from which condemnation comes. All others continue to be subject to law, and will be judged and condemned by law, 2:12. Some manuscripts add "not walking according to the flesh"; others, "not walking according to *the* flesh but *the* Spirit" {A}, from v 4.
21. This explains why there is now no condemnation for those in Christ. We have been set free.
22. That is, the operative power, the controlling principle, as in 7:21, 23, 25, and later in this verse. GK *3795*.
23. That is, the life-giving Spirit, the Spirit who is life (v 10), the One by and in whom we now live and will live.
24. Or, "For the law *of* the Spirit *of* life set you free in Christ Jesus...".
25. This word is singular. Paul makes it personal. Some manuscripts say "me" {B}.
26. This word "to set free" is the same word as in 6:18, 22. Elsewhere only in Jn 8:32, 36; Rom 8:21; Gal 5:1. GK *1802*. Related to "freedom" in Gal 5:13; and "free" in Mt 17:26.
27. This explains how such ones were set free.
28. That is, to conquer the death-producing power of sin, to give life. Note Gal 3:21. On this word, see Heb 6:4.
29. More literally, "*of* the Law, *from* the Law".
30. The flesh used the Law to produce death, chapter 7. We could not keep the Law, and the Law could not empower us to do so. It only condemned us, 7:10.
31. More literally, "*of the* flesh *of* sin", the flesh characterized by sin (GK *281*). It was in the "likeness" of sinful flesh because the Son's flesh was not sinful. Note that Paul does not say "in the likeness of flesh" or "in sinful flesh". On "flesh", see Col 2:23.
32. Or, "concerning sin". Some think Paul means "[as an offering] for sin", as in Heb 10:6, 8; 13:11 and the OT; others, "for" sin in the broadest sense, to deal with sin in all its aspects. GK *4309*.
33. Or, "in *His* flesh", "the" flesh just mentioned. Some think Paul means "in His body on the cross"; others, "in the flesh which He shares with us", the very flesh through which sin dominated us.
34. Or, "regulation", as in 1:32 (where it is singular, as it is here). This word views the entire Law as a single requirement. Some take this in a legal sense, the requirement for perfect holiness. This describes our salvation, and is fulfilled in all who die with Him and now live in the Spirit. Others take it in a practical sense, the requirement for living a holy life in keeping with God's will, of loving God and neighbor. This describes our life after becoming Christians, and is fulfilled in us as we live it out in the Spirit.
35. Thus in v 1-4, some think Paul means that there is no condemnation for us because when we became Christians, we passed from the controlling power of sin leading to death to that of the Spirit of life, because God condemned sin in His Son in order that the per-

A. 1 Cor 12:9   B. Mt 4:4, mankind   C. Rom 6:6, are slaves   D. 2 Tim 4:20, sick   E. Jn 20:21   F. Phil 2:7   G. 1 Cor 11:32   H. Eph 5:18, filled

1D. The[1] *ones* walking[A] not in-accordance-with[2] *the* flesh[B], but in accordance with *the* Spirit

    1E. For[3] the *ones* being[4] in accordance with *the* flesh are thinking[5] the *things of* the flesh, but the *ones being* in accordance with *the* Spirit, the *things of* the Spirit   5

        1F. For[6] the way-of-thinking[7] *of* the flesh *is* death, but the way-of-thinking *of* the Spirit *is* life and peace   6

            1G. Because[8] the way-of-thinking *of* the flesh *is* hostility[9] toward God. For it is not subject[10] *to* the Law *of* God, for it is not even able[11]   7

    2E. And[12] the *ones* being in *the* flesh are not[13] able to please[14] God. *But **you** are not in *the* flesh, but in *the* Spirit— since[15] *the* Spirit *of* God is dwelling[C] in you   8-9

        1F. But if anyone does not have *the* Spirit *of* Christ, this *one* is not *of* Him[16]

2C. And[17] if Christ *is* in you, **the body**[18] *is* dead[19] because of sin— but the Spirit *is* life[20] because of righteousness[21]   10

3C. And[22] if the Spirit *of* the *One* having raised[D] Jesus from *the* dead is dwelling[23] in you, the *One* having raised Christ from *the* dead will also give-life-to[E] your mortal[F] bodies through[24] His Spirit dwelling[G] in you   11

4C. So then, brothers[H], we are debtors[25]— not *to* the flesh, *that we should* be living[26] in accordance with *the* flesh.[27] *For[28] if[29] you are living in accordance with *the* flesh, you are going-to[J] die[30]. But if *by the* Spirit[31] you are putting-to-death[K] the practices[L] *of* the body[M], you will live[32]—   12 13

    1D. For[33] all who are being led[34] *by the* Spirit *of* God— these are sons *of* God[35]   14

1. Verses 4b-9 identify the "us" in whom this is true (by their lifestyle, thinking pattern, and spiritual capability), and explain why it is so. Paul defines the "us" as not being in one class, but being in the other. The "us" are all those "in Christ Jesus" (v 1), "in the Spirit" (v 9). God fulfills this requirement "in us" walking with His Spirit, as opposed to those who are not in Christ. Paul is not saying "in those of us" Christians (a subgroup of "us") who walk in the Spirit, as opposed to those Christians who do not walk in the Spirit. What God did in v 3-4a, He did for all who are in Christ. The exhortation comes in v 12.

fect holiness required by the Law might be fulfilled in us, the ones having received Christ's righteousness by faith (3:22) and now living in the Spirit. Others think he means that there is no condemnation for us because now that we are Christians, we live under the controlling power of the Spirit of life, not of sin leading to death, because God condemned sin in His Son in order that the moral holiness required by God's Law might be fulfilled in our daily lives as we live in the Spirit. Others think these two are not separable, and that both are in view, as in v 10.

2. Or, "in conformity with, in harmony with, based on". This word occurs four times in v 4-5. GK *2848*.
3. This explains why this freedom is not true of the ones walking in accordance with the flesh. Their thinking is limited to the realm of the flesh. They set their minds on this realm. They are natural (1 Cor 2:14), not spiritual.
4. Or, "existing, living". Another way of saying "walking", v 4. Same word as in v 8, and as "you are" in v 9. GK *1639*.
5. Or "setting their minds on, being intent on". This is the focus of the hearts and minds of such ones. Elsewhere only in Mt 16:23; Mk 8:33; Act 28:22; Rom 11:20; 12:3, 16; 14:6; 15:5; 1 Cor 13:11; 2 Cor 13:11; Gal 5:10; Phil 1:7; 2:2, 5; 3:15, 19; 4:2, 10; Col 3:2. GK *5858*. The word also means "to be minded or disposed". Related to "way of thinking" in v 6; and "understanding" in Eph 1:8.
6. This explains why this freedom cannot be true of ones thinking the things of the flesh. The content and outlook of this thinking that occupies their mind constitutes death in relation to God. It is death, and it leads to death.
7. Or, "the mind-set, the mind, the thinking". Used three times in v 6-7. Elsewhere only as "mind" in v 27. GK *5859*. Related to "thinking" in v 5, this is the content of that thinking, what is thought.
8. This explains why the way of thinking of the flesh is death.
9. Same word as in Jam 4:4. On this word, see Eph 2:14. Related to "enemy". Note 1 Cor 2:14.
10. Or, "does not subject *itself*, is not in submission to, is not subordinate to". On this word, see Eph 5:21.
11. As Paul explained in chapter 7. It is dominated by sin.
12. Others place verse 8 as 2G., the second reason that way of thinking is death. Then verse 9 becomes point 2E., "But **you** are not...".
13. Note that v 5 defines this group by what they are doing, v 8 by what they are not able to do.
14. On this word, see 1 Thes 2:4. Related to the word in Heb 11:6. It is impossible to please God without faith.
15. Or, "if as is the case, if indeed". Same word as in Rom 3:30; 8:17; 2 Thes 1:6. Elsewhere only as "ifindeed" in 1 Cor 8:5; 15:15. GK *1642*.
16. That is, does not belong to Him. Such a person is not a Christian. All those "in Christ" have the Spirit. Compare Jude 19.
17. Note that Paul is no longer explaining "walking not in the flesh" of v 4. He is giving another aspect of the freedom of v 2. The emphasis of v 3-9 was freedom from "sin", the cause of death. Now he turns to "death" itself.
18. Paul uses grammar that emphasizes the contrast between the two halves of this sentence.
19. That is, our physical body is dead and will die. This is the only aspect of death that remains for us.
20. The Spirit is life in us now, true life, the life of God. We are set free from spiritual death. Same word as in v 6. It means "life" in all 135 of its uses. GK *2437*. Here, some take "spirit" to be the human spirit as opposed to the body, and so must render this "alive", "but the spirit *is* alive". In this case also, Paul means that the life of God is now in us. The related verb is "came to life" in Rev 20:4.
21. Some think Paul means "God's righteousness" in us by faith; others, our growing righteousness, the fruit of the Spirit living in us; others think these cannot be separated, and that he means both.
22. Not only is His Spirit life in us now, He will set our bodies free from physical death on that day.
23. Or, "living". Used of the Spirit also in v 9 and 1 Cor 3:16. Elsewhere only in Rom 7:17, 18, 20; 1 Cor 7:12, 13; 1 Tim 6:16. GK *3861*. Related to the word later in this verse.
24. Or, "by means of". Some manuscripts say "because of" {B}.
25. Not to that which enslaved us to death, but to God who set us free into life. On this word, see 1:14.
26. That is, with the result that we should be living according to the flesh. This is the realm of condemnation and death.
27. Note that Paul does not continue on with this thought as an exhortation, "We are debtors to live according to the Spirit". Instead, he continues the teaching begun in v 11 about resurrection life, picking it up with "You will live" at the end of v 13. He takes up exhortation in detail in 12:1.
28. The reason we have this debt is the outcome of each path. The path of the flesh ends in a death after earthly life, but the Spirit's path continues in a life after physical death. We are debtors to God, for we live, and we will live!
29. That is, "assuming it is true that". Same grammar as "if" in v 9b, 10, 11, 13b.
30. Or, "you are destined to die, you will die". Same idiom as in 4:24; Mt 17:22; Jn 11:51; Act 26:22; Rev 1:19.
31. Or, "spirit", the human spirit empowered by the Holy Spirit.
32. The "will live" points to the "life" of v 11, the future redemption, and our inheritance with Christ.
33. This gives the reason for "will live". If you are living by the Spirit, you "will live" with God, "for" this means you "are" one of His children.
34. This is related to being "in the Spirit" and "walking in the Spirit", of which "putting to death the practices of the body" is one part. This is the broad category of which that is one specific part. Every Christian is led by the Spirit to become more like their Father, to bear the family resemblance. In part, this leading is how the Spirit bears witness, v 16. Compare 1 Jn 3:9. On this word, see Lk 4:1.
35. Note that "children" is used in v 17. That is, family members. We are called "sons of God" elsewhere only in Mt 5:9; Lk 20:36; Rom 8:19; 9:26; Gal 3:26. Paul means "sons" versus "slaves", with all the status, security and privilege associated with the one as opposed to the other. On "sons", see Gal 3:7. Compare "children of God" in Jn 1:12.

A. Heb 13:9   B. Col 2:23   C. Rom 8:11   D. Mt 28:6, arose   E. Jn 5:21   F. 2 Cor 5:4   G. Col 3:16   H. Act 16:40   J. Mk 10:32   K. Rom 7:4   L. Mt 16:27   M. Eph 1:23

	1E. For[1] you did not receive *a* spirit[2] *of* slavery[3] again[4] leading-to[5] fear[A]. But you received *a* Spirit[6] *of* adoption[7], by Whom we are crying-out[B] "Abba[C]! Father!"	15
	2E. The Spirit Himself bears-witness-with[D] our spirit[8] that we are children[E] *of* God	16
2D.	And[9] if *we are* children, *we are* heirs[10] also. *We are* **heirs**[11] *of* God[12]— and fellow-heirs[13] *of* Christ,[14] since[15] we are suffering-with[16] *Him* in order that we may also be glorified-with[17] *Him*	17
	1E. For[18] I consider[F] that the sufferings[G] *of* the present time *are* **not worthy**[H] to the glory[19] destined[20] to be revealed[21] to[22] us	18
	2E. For[23] the eager-expectation[J] *of* the creation[24] is awaiting[25] the revelation[K] *of* the sons *of* God	19
	1F. For[26] the creation was subjected[27] to futility[28]— not willingly[29], but because of the *One* having subjected *it*— in hope[30] *that[31] the creation itself also will be set-free[32] from the slavery[L] *of* decay[33] into the freedom[M] *of* the glory[34] *of* the children[E] *of* God	20 21
	2F. For[35] we know that the whole creation is groaning-together[36] and suffering-birthpains-together[37] until the present	22
	3E. And[38] not only *creation*, but also ourselves having[39] the firstfruit[N] *of* the Spirit[40], **we** ourselves also are groaning[41] within ourselves while eagerly-awaiting adoption[42]— the redemption[O] *of* our body	23
	1F. For[43] we were saved[P] *in* hope[44]	24
	1G. But hope being seen is not hope, for who hopes-for[Q] what he sees?[45]	
	2G. But since[46] we hope-for what we do not see, we are eagerly-awaiting *it* with endurance[47]	25

1. This gives the reason or proof that they are "sons", family members.
2. That is, a spirit or disposition characteristic of slavery, a slave kind of spirit, tending toward fear. Or, "Spirit", a Holy Spirit of slavery (since there is no such thing). See "Spirit" next.
3. Or, "servility". Elsewhere only in 8:21; Gal 4:24; 5:1; Heb 2:15. GK *1525*. Related to "are slaves" in 6:6.
4. That is, such as we had when we were slaves of sin and death. Some think Paul means "receive... again"; others, "leading to fear again". We have been freed from fear, not returned to it, Heb 2:15; 1 Jn 4:18.
5. Same word as "resulting in" in 5:16.
6. Or, "spirit". Others take both occurrences as "spirit"; others take both as "Spirit".
7. On this word, see Gal 4:5. The Spirit leads us as family members of God, not as slaves. We call on God as our daddy (abba) in an intimate relationship, as Jesus did, Mk 14:36; Gal 4:6.
8. That is, our spirit crying out to our Father in v 15. We cry out "My Father"; He bears witness "My child".
9. This is the consequence of sonship. You "will live" for you are "sons", and childship implies heirship.
10. Or, "inheritors", ones designated to inherit. Same word as in Mt 21:38; Mk 12:7; Lk 20:14; Gal 3:29; 4:1, 7; Tit 3:7; Heb 6:17. Elsewhere only as "inheritor" in Rom 4:13, 14; Heb 1:2; 11:7; Jam 2:5. GK *3101*. Related to "inherit" in Gal 4:30, and "inheritance" in Eph 1:14.
11. Paul uses grammar that closely links the two halves of this sentence; heirs and fellow-heirs.
12. That is, ones God has designated to inherit from Him.
13. Or, "co-heirs". Elsewhere only in Eph 3:6; Heb 11:9; 1 Pet 3:7. GK *5169*.
14. That is, we are God's heirs and Christ's fellow heirs.
15. Same word as in v 9. The suffering always comes before the glory, 8:18; Phil 3:10; Heb 2:9; 1 Pet 1:11; 4:13.
16. Some think Paul is referring to sufferings because we are Christians, as in v 17; others, to all the sufferings we continue to endure— Christian and human— even though we are His children and heirs. Elsewhere only in 1 Cor 12:26. GK *5224*.
17. Used only here. GK *5280*. Related to "glorified" in v 30.
18. Paul uses this word to assert his first point. It may be rendered "Now" or "Indeed". Likewise in v 19. GK *1142*. Some think this affirms the greatness of our inheritance. Being heirs of God, the glory will be so great that the sufferings we endure now are not worthy of comparison. Others think Paul is offering comfort in view of the sufferings. They are nothing by comparison.
19. That is, to be compared to the glory. Compare 2 Cor 4:17.
20. This is a participle, the glory "being destined, being about to be". This word and grammar is elsewhere only in Gal 3:23; Rev 1:19; and as "about to" in Rev 3:16; 12:4. Same word as "going to" in Rom 8:13, but different grammar. On this word, see "going to" in Mk 10:32.
21. This word is used three times in Romans. Wrath is revealed (1:18); but glory will be revealed (8:18), because the righteousness of God is revealed (1:17). Compare Gal 3:23, where they awaited the faith. We await the glory. On this word, see 2 Thes 2:3.
22. Or, "for, in". GK *1650*.
23. Or, "Indeed". Some think this again confirms the greatness of the coming glory. It is so great, all creation will share in it. Others think it confirms the certainty of it. All creation is awaiting this impending glory, by the design of God.
24. Paul is personifying the physical creation. That is, "all nature". Angels and humans are not in view here. Consult the commentaries. On this word, see v 39.
25. Or, "eagerly-awaiting". Same word as in 1 Pet 3:20. Elsewhere only as "eagerly-await" in Rom 8:23, 25; 1 Cor 1:7; Gal 5:5; Phil 3:20; Heb 9:28. GK *587*.
26. Verses 20-21 give the reason creation eagerly awaits our revelation in glory. God gave it this hope.
27. That is, by God, in Gen 3:7-19. Creation shared the penalty of the Fall.
28. Or, "purposelessness, pointlessness". Elsewhere only in Eph 4:17; 2 Pet 2:18. GK *3470*. Related to "futile" in 1 Cor 15:17.
29. Or, "of its own will", still personifying creation. It was because of the Fall. Elsewhere only as "of my own will" in 1 Cor 9:17. GK *1776*. Related word in 1 Pet 5:2.
30. Or, "on hope, on the basis of hope". That is, "in the hope granted to it that". The hope is on the part of the creation, and results in its "eager expectation" in v 19. Some link this with v 19, "awaiting... in hope", making "For the creation... subjected *it*" a parenthesis. Grammatically, the hope (in the sense of "expectation") could be ascribed to God, "on the basis of the expectation that the creation itself", which would make this the only place "hope" is used with God as the subject in the Bible. On this word, see Col 1:5.
31. Or, "because", so that it says "...in hope, because the creation...".
32. On this word, see v 2. Related to "freedom" next.
33. That is, consisting of decay, or belonging to decay, or characterized by decay. On this word, see 1 Cor 15:42.
34. Some think Paul means the freedom characterized by glory, the glorious freedom; others, the freedom belonging to the glory.
35. This verse confirms that creation has this eager expectation (v 19) by reference to a generally accepted fact. The fact is known by observation; the linkage to the Fall and redemption of mankind, by God's Word.
36. Used only here. GK *5367*. Related to the word in v 23 and the word in v 26.
37. That is, for the birth of the new age. Used only here. GK *5349*. Related words in 1 Thes 5:3 and Gal 4:19.
38. Our own eager expectation, led by the Spirit in us as the firstfruit of the glory, confirms creation's eager expectation (v 19) as a second witness. Both are "awaiting" the glory to come while "groaning" in "hope". Note the repetition of these three words.
39. Some think that Paul means "since we have"; others, "even though we have".
40. Some think Paul means the initial foretaste of the Spirit, of which the fullness then will be the harvest. Others think he means "the firstfruit *which is* the Spirit", the Spirit now being the first "installment" of the fullness of all the blessings that God will bestow on us then, the firstfruit of the state of glory.
41. Related to the word in v 22. On this word, see Jam 5:9.
42. Same word as in v 15.
43. As with v 20, this gives the reason for the waiting and groaning. God saved us in hope.
44. Or, "*by* hope". That is, the hope of the redemption of our body, and living forever in glory with God.
45. Some manuscripts say "For why indeed is he hoping-for what someone sees?" {B}.
46. Or, "if", as is the case.
47. Endurance is called for because of our suffering, v 17. On this word, see Jam 1:3.

A. Eph 5:21 B. Mt 8:29 C. Mk 14:36 D. Rom 2:15, bearing co-witness E. 1 Jn 3:1 F. Rom 3:28 G. Phil 3:10 H. Rev 16:6 J. Phil 1:20
K. 2 Thes 1:7 L. Rom 8:15 M. Gal 5:13 N. 1 Cor 15:20 O. Rom 3:24 P. Lk 19:10 Q. Jn 5:45, put hope

2F. And similarly[1] also[2] the Spirit helps[3] our weakness[4]	26
1G. For we do not know what we should pray[A] as *we* ought-to,[5] but the Spirit Himself intercedes-for[6] *us*[7] with[8] inexpressible[9] groanings[10]	
2G. And the *One* searching[B] *our* hearts[11] knows[12] what the mind[13] *of* the Spirit *is,* because[14] He is interceding[15] for *the* saints[C] in accordance with God[16]	27
3D. And[17] we know that all *things* are working-together[18] for good[D] *for* the *ones* loving[E] God, the *ones* being called[19] *ones* according to His purpose[20]	28
1E. Because whom He foreknew[21], He also predestined[22] *to be* similar-to-the-form[23] *of* the image[24] *of* His Son, so that He *might* be firstborn[25] among many brothers[F]	29
2E. And whom He predestined, these He also called[26]	30
3E. And whom He called, these He also declared-righteous[G]	
4E. And whom He declared righteous, these He also glorified[27]	
7B. Therefore, what shall we say to these *things*? If[28] God *is* for us, who *is* against us?	31
1C. He Who indeed did not spare[H] *His* own Son, but handed Him over[J] for us all, how will He not also[29] with Him freely-give[30] us all *things*?	32

1. Or, "likewise, in like manner". Some think Paul means "with groaning". The groaning of the "firstfruit" in us is added as a second witness to our own, His not being a groaning for the glory to come, but similar to it, a groaning to help us as we await that glory. Others think he means "as hope sustains us while we endure (v 24), similarly the Spirit helps us". Others connect this to v 25, "Since we hope for what we do not see, we await it with endurance, and the Spirit helps us with our weakness as we wait", giving our side and God's side of the matter. Elsewhere only in Mt 20:5; 21:30, 36; 25:17; Mk 12:21; 14:31; Lk 13:5; 20:31; 22:20; 1 Cor 11:25; 1 Tim 2:9; 3:8, 11; 5:25; Tit 2:3, 6. GK *6058*.
2. Or, "indeed, even".
3. Or, "takes a share of " the load. Elsewhere only in Lk 10:40. GK *5269*. Related to the gift of "helps" in 1 Cor 12:28.
4. Some think Paul means all our weakness, to which we respond with prayer, groaning, waiting, and endurance, the prayer itself being one part of it. Others think he specifically means our weakness in praying. Some manuscripts say "weaknesses" {N}. On this word, see Mt 8:17.
5. More literally, we do not know "the what we should pray according as it is necessary [to pray]". That is, what we should pray as is necessary to pray in view of our situation. We do not know the right thing to ask with regard to the situation we are praying about. Paul is an example, 2 Cor 12:8-9. On "ought to", see Act 25:10.
6. Or, "intercedes on behalf of ". Used only here. GK *5659*. Related to the word in v 27.
7. Some manuscripts express this word {A}.
8. Or, "in".
9. This word can mean "unspoken, wordless", or, "unspeakable, inexpressible, too deep for words". Used only here. GK *227*. Related to the word "dumb, mute" in Mk 7:37; 9:17, 25.
10. Some think these are the Spirit's groanings. He intercedes with His unspoken/unspeakable (in human words) groanings to God, this being Paul's metaphorical way of describing the communication between the Father and the Spirit, like the groanings of creation, v 22. Or, the Spirit intercedes in our hearts with His groaning, prompting us to pray as needed. Others think these are our groanings. The Spirit intercedes by carrying our unspoken/unspeakable (because we do not know what to ask) groanings to God, and some include here our groanings spoken in tongues. Elsewhere only in Act 7:34. GK *5099*. Related to the words in v 22 and v 23.
11. That is, as we "groan within ourselves" (v 23), not knowing what to ask (v 26). Note the word in Act 1:24.
12. Some think Paul means "knows" in the sense of "approves of, recognizes with approval, honors, takes interest in", as this word is used in 1 Thes 5:12; others, "knows" in the simple sense.
13. That is, the content of the thinking. On this word, see "way of thinking" in 8:6. The Father, who searches our hearts to know what we are thinking, also knows (and honors) what the Spirit is interceding on our behalf. Or, the Father who searches our hearts knows (and honors) what the Spirit is prompting there.
14. That is, God knows (and honors) the Spirit's way of thinking in our situation, because the Spirit intercedes according to God's will. Or, "that", God knows the purpose and content of the Spirit's mind.
15. On this word, see 8:34, where Christ intercedes for us.
16. That is, the Spirit intercedes in accordance with God's will, asking what we could not, due to our not knowing.
17. Instead of the closing climax of this section, others make this 3F., another source of help to us. Others render this word "But", seeing this as a contrast to the groaning.
18. Or, "cooperating, helping, assisting, joining in working, contributing". Elsewhere only as "work with" in Mk 16:20; 2 Cor 6:1; Jam 2:22; and "help" in 1 Cor 16:16. GK *5300*. Related to "fellow worker" in 16:3. Some render it "that He works all *things* together for good"; others, "that *in* all *things,* He joins in working for good *for* the *ones* loving God". Some manuscripts add "God" as the subject {B}.
19. That is, the people who are called ones of God. This adjective is elsewhere only in 1:1, 6, 7; Mt 22:14; 1 Cor 1:1, 2, 24; Jude 1; Rev 17:14. GK *3105*. Related to "called" in v 30; and "calling" in 2 Pet 1:10.
20. This same word is used of God's purpose in Rom 9:11; Eph 1:11; 3:11; 2 Tim 1:9; and of human purpose in Act 11:23; 27:13; 2 Tim 3:10. Literally, the word refers to something "set before, put before" yourself; that is, a plan, purpose, design, resolve. Elsewhere only as "presentation", the bread of presentation physically "set before" God in the temple, in Mt 12:4; Mk 2:26; Lk 6:4; Heb 9:2. GK *4606*. The related verb is "purposed" in Eph 1:9.
21. Or, "knew beforehand, had advance knowledge of ". Some think this refers to God's advance knowledge of something in the person. Others think "knew" in this word has the sense of "had regard for, loved, took interest in" (similar to Gen 18:19; Jer 1:5; Amos 3:2; etc.), and therefore "chose beforehand". Same word as in 11:2; 1 Pet 1:20. Elsewhere only as "know beforehand" in Act 26:5; 2 Pet 3:17. GK *4589*. Related to "foreknowledge" in 1 Pet 1:2.
22. This word also means "to decide beforehand, to predetermine, to preappoint, to predesignate, to preset". Elsewhere only in Act 4:28; Rom 8:30; 1 Cor 2:7; Eph 1:5, 11. GK *4633*. Related to "designated" in 1:4, and "separated" in 1:1. Compare the unrelated words, "prepared beforehand" in Rom 9:23, and "appointed" in Act 13:48.
23. Or, "like-the-appearance". On this adjective, see Phil 3:21, "similar-in-form" to the body of His glory. We shall be "like" Him, says 1 Jn 3:2, using a different word. Some think Paul is referring here to that which will take place on that day; others, to that which begins to occur at salvation and is completed on that day. Compare 1 Cor 15:49; 2 Cor 3:18.
24. Or, "likeness". On this word, see Col 1:15.
25. That is, the preeminent One, first in rank, the supreme One. On this word, see Col 1:15.
26. Or, "summoned". Same word as in Mt 9:13; Rom 9:12, 24; 1 Cor 1:9; 7:17; Gal 1:6, 15; 5:8, 13; Eph 4:1, 4; Col 3:15; 1 Thes 2:12; 4:7; 5:24; 2 Thes 2:14; 1 Tim 6:12; 2 Tim 1:9; Heb 9:15; 11:8; 1 Pet 1:15; 2:9, 21; 3:9; 5:10; 2 Pet 1:3; Rev 19:9. This word also means "call" in the sense of "name" (as in Mt 1:21); or "invite" (as in Mt 22:3; Lk 14:7; Jn 2:2; 1 Cor 10:27). Used 148 times. GK *2813*. Related to "called" in v 28.
27. Paul puts this in the past tense, as something already certain, already done. This word, used 61 times, is not used elsewhere of God glorifying us, but note v 17. GK *1519*. "Glory" (GK *1518*) is used of us in Rom 8:18, 21; Jn 17:22; 1 Cor 2:7; 2 Cor 4:17; Phil 3:21; Col 1:27; 3:4; 1 Thes 2:12; 2 Tim 2:10; Heb 2:10; 1 Pet 1:7; 5:1, 4, 10.
28. Or, "since". That is, if, as is the case. GK *1623*.
29. This is the Greek word order. Some think Paul means "also with Him"; others, "also freely-give".
30. Or, "graciously grant". On this word, see 1 Cor 2:12. Related to the word "grace".

A. 1 Tim 2:8 B. 1 Cor 2:10 C. 1 Pet 1:16, holy D. 1 Tim 5:10b E. Jn 21:15, devotedly love F. Act 16:40 G. Rom 3:24 H. Rom 11:21 J. Mt 26:21, hand over

	2C. Who will bring-a-charge[1] against *the* chosen[2] *ones of* God? God[3] *is* the *One* declaring-righteous[A]!	33
	3C. Who *is* the *one who* will condemn?[4] Christ Jesus[5] *is* the *One* having died, but more, having been raised[6], Who also is at *the* right hand *of* God, Who also intercedes[7] for us!	34
	4C. What[8] shall separate[B] us from the love[C] *of* Christ[9]?	35
	1D. Affliction[D], or distress[E], or persecution[F], or famine, or nakedness[G], or danger[10], or sword?	
	1E. Just as it has been written [in Ps 44:22] that "For your sake we are being put-to-death[H] the whole day. We were considered[J] as sheep *for* slaughter[K]"	36
	2D. But in all these *things* we overwhelmingly-conquer[11] through the *One* having loved[L] us	37
	5C. For I am convinced[M] that neither death nor life, nor angels nor rulers[12], nor *things* present[13] nor *things* coming[14], nor powers[15], °nor height nor depth, nor any other creation[16] will be able to separate[B] us from the love[C] *of* God in Christ Jesus our Lord	38 39
3A. I am[17] telling *the* truth in Christ, I am not lying,[18] my conscience[N] bearing-witness-with[19] me in *the* Holy Spirit—°that there is great grief[O] *in* me, and unceasing[P] pain[Q] *in* my heart	9:1 2
	1B. For I *would* pray[20] *that* I myself *might* be **accursed**[21] from Christ for the sake of my brothers,[22] my kinsmen[R] according to *the* flesh, °who are Israelites	3 4
	1C. *Of* whom[23] *is* the adoption[24], and the glory[25], and the covenants[26], and the Law-giving, and the [temple] service[27], and the promises[S]	
	2C. *Of* whom *are* the fathers[28]	5
	3C. And from whom *is* the Christ according-to[29] *the* flesh, the *One* being[30]	
	1D. Over all	
	2D. God	
	3D. Blessed[31] forever[T], amen	
	2B. But *it is* not such as that the word[32] *of* God has failed[33]	6
	1C. For not all these *ones* from Israel *are* Israel.[34] °Nor *are they* all children[35] because they are seed[36] *of* Abraham	7
	1D. But[37], "In Isaac *a* seed[38] will be called[U] *for* you" [Gen 21:12]	

1. Same word as in Act 19:38. Elsewhere only as "charge" in Act 19:40; and "accuse" in Act 23:28, 29; 26:2, 7. GK *1592*.
2. Or, "elect, selected". Elsewhere only in Mt 22:14; 24:22, 24, 31; Mk 13:20, 22, 27; Lk 18:7; 23:35; Rom 16:13; Col 3:12; 1 Tim 5:21; 2 Tim 2:10; Tit 1:1; 1 Pet 1:1; 2:4, 6, 9; 2 Jn 1:1, 13; Rev 17:14. GK *1723*. Related to the verb in 1 Cor 1:27, and "choosing" in Rom 11:5. An unrelated word for "choose" is used in 2 Thes 2:13.
3. Others make this 1D., followed by the question "Who is the one condemning?". Then "Christ Jesus... for us" becomes 2D., followed by the question "Who shall separate us from the love of Christ?".
4. Or, "Who is the *one* condemning?" The difference between the future and present is an accent mark. On this word, see 1 Cor 11:32.
5. Some manuscripts omit this word {C}.
6. Or, "having arisen". On this word, see "arose" in Mt 28:6.
7. Or, "petitions, appeals". Same word as in 8:27; Heb 7:25. Elsewhere only as "appeal" in Act 25:24; Rom 11:2. GK *1961*. Related to the word in 8:26, and to the noun "intercessions" in 1 Tim 2:1.
8. Or, "Who". Same word as "who" in v 33, 34; "what" in 3:1; 11:15. It is used both ways. GK *5515*.
9. That is, "Christ's love" for us.
10. Elsewhere only in 2 Cor 11:26, where several are mentioned. GK *3074*. Related word in 1 Cor 15:30.
11. Or, "we are completely victorious". Used only here. GK *5664*. The root word is "overcome" in Rev 2:7.
12. Paul may mean human rulers, or angelic rulers, or both. On this word, see "beginning" in Col 1:18.
13. This is a participle, the things "having come, being present". On this word, see Heb 9:9.
14. Or, "*things* going to *be*". Same word as in 1 Cor 3:22. On this word, see "going to" in Mk 10:32.
15. Some manuscripts have "nor powers" after "nor rulers" {A}. On "powers", see Act 8:10.
16. Or, "creature, created *thing*". Same word as in 1:20, 25; 8:19, 20, 21, 22; Mk 10:6; 13:19; 16:15; 2 Cor 5:17; Gal 6:15; Col 1:15, 23; Heb 4:13; 9:11; 2 Pet 3:4; Rev 3:14. Elsewhere only as "institution" in 1 Pet 2:13. GK *3232*. Related to "create" in Eph 2:15.
17. Paul turns now to address the critical question, "If God is doing this, why has Israel not believed?".
18. Paul makes this statement also in 2 Cor 11:31; Gal 1:20; 1 Tim 2:7.
19. On this word, see "bearing co-witness" in 2:15. Paul's conscience is a second witness to what he is affirming.
20. Or, "wish" (pray in a non-religious sense). Some think Paul means "I *would* pray" but can't, because it is not possible; others, "I *could almost* pray" but don't, because it is not possible. Or, this could be rendered "I was wishing", which would mean Paul did at one time wish this could be true, similar to Moses in Ex 32:32. At one time, Paul thought he was the perfect person to reach his people, Act 22:19-20. Perhaps this thought burst from his heart when he realized that such would not be the case. With the same grammar, Paul wishes for something impossible in Gal 4:20 also. Elsewhere only in Act 26:29; 27:29; 2 Cor 13:7, 9; Jam 5:16; 3 Jn 2. GK *2377*. Related to "vow" in Act 18:18, and "praying" in 1 Tim 2:8.
21. This is a noun, *anathema*. That is, cursed by God, devoted to destruction. Same word as in 1 Cor 12:3; 16:22; Gal 1:8, 9. Elsewhere only as "*a* curse" in Act 23:14. GK *353*. On the related verb "to curse, to bind with an oath under threat of a curse", see Mk 14:71.
22. That is, that they might be saved, 10:1.
23. That is, "*To* whom *belong*".
24. On this word, see Gal 4:5. Used only here with reference to Israelites.
25. That is, the glory of God, in all its manifestations in their history.
26. On this word, see Heb 8:6. Some manuscripts say "covenant" {B}.
27. Paul may also have in mind services in the home and synagogue. On this word, see "worship" in 12:1.
28. That is, Abraham, Isaac and Jacob, as in 11:28; 15:8.
29. Or, "with respect to", as to His human ancestry. Same phrase as in 1:3.
30. Or, "the *One* Who is". The three descriptions that follow all refer to this participle. The Christ is "the *One* Who is" these three things. This could be rendered "the *One* being over all, blessed God forever" or "the *One* being God over all, blessed forever". The exact Greek is "the *One* being over all God blessed forever". The key is that grammatically, "the *One* being", "God", and "blessed" are all referring to "the Christ", just as in 2 Cor 11:31 "the *One* being blessed forever" (same words as here) refers back to "Father". Some, for theological reasons which they think outweigh the grammar and context, do not think Paul could have called Christ God here. Based on this, this view makes this a doxology to the Father, having a grammar occurring only here in the Greek Bible. It may be rendered as "... flesh. *May* the *One* being God over all *be* blessed forever", or, "... flesh, the *One* being over all. *May God be* blessed forever". Consult the commentaries on these and other views.
31. Or, "spoken well of, praised". This is an adjective. It is a description, not an action (like "blessed by God"). When used in a doxology in Greek or Hebrew (as it is in Lk 1:68; 2 Cor 1:3; Eph 1:3; 1 Pet 1:3), the word order is always "Blessed *be* God", not "God *be* blessed". Elsewhere only in Mk 14:61; Rom 1:25; 2 Cor 11:31. GK *2329*. The related verb is in Lk 6:28.
32. That is, the promises made to Abraham and his descendants, to Israel.
33. Or, "fallen". On this word, see "fall from" in Gal 5:4. The nation's rejection of Christ is not God's failure.
34. Not all the physical descendants of Jacob (Israel) making up the nation of Israel are spiritual Israel. God's word did not fail, for not all of Abraham's Israel is God's Israel, nor are they all God's children because they are Abraham's children. God's "Israel" in this sense is not the ethnic nation of physical descendants, nor the geopolitical nation in Judea, nor the religious nation living under the Law of Moses, but the spiritual nation of those receiving God's promises by faith, the physical-spiritual "seed" of Abraham in whom God continues to fulfill His promises to Abraham. Stated positively, God's word is fulfilled in all those among physical Israel who are His children, whom Paul later calls "the remnant... according to the choosing of grace" in 11:5.
35. That is, children of God, v 8. God's children will also walk in line with Abraham's faith (4:12), circumcised in heart (2:28-29).
36. That is, physical descendants. On this word, see Heb 11:11.
37. Isaac and Ishmael prove that not all Abraham's physical children are his God-promised "seed" in whom the promises would be fulfilled.
38. That is, a line of descendants fulfilling God's promises to Abraham.

A. Rom 3:24 B. Mt 19:6 C. 1 Jn 4:16 D. Rev 7:14 E. 2 Cor 6:4 F. Mk 10:30 G. 2 Cor 11:27 H. Rom 7:4 J. Rom 3:28 K. Act 8:32 L. Jn 21:15, devotedly love M. 1 Jn 3:19, persuade N. Act 23:1 O. 2 Cor 7:10 P. 2 Tim 1:3 Q. 1 Tim 6:10 R. Rom 16:7 S. 1 Jn 2:25 T. Rev 20:10 U. Rom 8:30

	1E. That is,[1] these children *of* the flesh[2] *are* not children *of* God, but the children *of* the promise[3] are counted[A] for seed[4]	8
	1F. For[5] the word *of* promise *is* this— "I will come at this time, and there will be *a* son *to* Sarah" [Gen 18:10]	9
2D.	And not only[6] *this,* but *there is* also Rebekah having bed[7] from one *man*— Isaac our father	10
	1E. For *the twins* having not yet been born[B], nor having done anything good or bad— in order that[8] the purpose[9] *of* God according to *His* choosing[10] might continue[11], not[12] of works[13] but of the *One* calling[C]— it was said *to* her [in Gen 25:23] that "the older will serve[D] the younger[14]"	11 12
	1F. Just[15] as it has been written [in Mal 1:2-3], "I loved[16] Jacob, but I hated[17] Esau"	13
2C. Therefore[18] what shall we say? *There is* not unrighteousness[E] with God, *is there*?[19] May it never be!		14
	1D. For He says *to* Moses [in Ex 33:19], "I will have-mercy-on[F] whomever I have-mercy, and I will have-compassion-on whomever I have compassion"	15
	1E. So then, *mercy is* not *of* the[20] *one* wanting[G], nor *of* the *one* running, but *of* the *One* having-mercy[F]— God[21]	16
	2D. For the Scripture says *to* Pharaoh [in Ex 9:16] that "I raised you up[22] for this very *purpose*— so that I might demonstrate[H] My power[23] in you, and so that My name might be proclaimed in all the earth"	17
	1E. So then, He has-mercy-on[F] whom He wants[G], and He hardens[24] whom He wants[G]	18
3C. Therefore[25] you will say *to* me, "Why then[26] does He still find-fault[27]? For who has resisted[28] His will[29]?"		19
	1D. O human[J], on the contrary, who are **you**, the *one* answering-back[K] *to* God? The *thing* formed will not say *to* the *one* having formed[30] *it,* "Why did you make me like-this?", *will it*?[31]	20
	2D. Or does not the potter have **authority**[32] *of* the clay to make from the same lump one vessel[L] for honor[M], and another for dishonor[33]?	21

1. Paul generalizes from Isaac and Ishmael to "children" of flesh and promise. Some think he is referring to Ishmael and Abraham's other children and their descendants, versus Isaac and the subsequent children of promise. Others think he is also referring to the case under discussion, unbelieving Israel versus believing Israel, the remnant.
2. This category of children are not children of God. The next category of children are the children of God.
3. That is, belonging to the promise, originating in the promise, proceeding from the promise. The promises to Abraham will be fulfilled in children resulting from the promise, not children independent of the promise.
4. Or, "counted as seed". That is, by God, for His purposes.
5. The generalization of v 8 is proved by the specific case of Isaac. He was born as the result of God's word of promise, and so he was counted as the "seed" promised to Abraham.
6. Jacob and Esau prove that God did not choose Abraham's promised "seed" based on their personal merit. God chose between the twins fathered by His "child of promise", Isaac, before they were born.
7. That is, having conceived. See Heb 13:4 on "bed".
8. This clause is moved forward in the Greek word order for emphasis, and could all be bolded. Paul means it was said to Rebekah before the children were born "that 'the older will serve the younger', in order that the purpose... continue". This is why it was said then.
9. Same word as in 8:28. What purpose is in view here? All agree it includes God's purpose of creating a nation based on His promise, and of defining a line to the One who would fulfill His promise, and of fulfilling His promises to Abraham. In addition, some think Paul is including God's purpose of saving individuals here; others, that personal salvation is not in view here, only national purposes. The answer influences what inferences may be drawn from v 11-13, on which, consult the commentaries. In either case, however, the example of Isaac and Jacob does at least illustrate the process of salvation which "continues" in all believers. We too were chosen before we were born (Eph 1:4), apart from our merit, and called according to His purpose (Rom 8:28), to become spiritual seed of Abraham (Gal 3:29).
10. Or, "election, selection". Or, "in relation to choosing, in choosing, based on choosing, [carried out] in accordance with [His] choosing". On this word, see 11:5.
11. Or, "remain, stay, abide". On this word, see "abide" in Jn 15:4. Some render it "stand" in the sense of "abide" only here. The grammar indicates Paul means "be continuing". God's purpose "continues" with Jacob as in the case of Isaac. God also chose Isaac before he was born, without reference to his works, and promised he would be the "seed", and "called" him.
12. Some think Paul means "the purpose... not of works...", others, "continue [being] not of works...". In either case, the purpose of God, accomplished through His choosing, carried out not on the basis of works but His call, continues in the case of Jacob, because it was said to Rebekah in advance of the birth or actions of her twins that "the older will serve the younger".
13. Or, "by works, from works". That is, not based on works, but based on the God who calls. Same phrase as in Eph 2:9, and "by works" in v 32; 11:6; Tit 3:5; etc.
14. More literally, "the greater will serve the lesser", but here used in the sense of age. In Gen 25:23, this refers to these two as individuals who would become heads of nations, "two nations, two peoples" in your womb. On "older", see "greater" in Mt 11:11. This word is elsewhere only as "lesser" in Jn 2:10; Heb 7:7; and "fewer" in 1 Tim 5:9. GK *1781*.
15. Some think this quotation explains the positive basis of God's choice, which was given negatively in v 12. Others think is restates God's choice of Jacob in different terms. Others think it proves God's choice by means of their subsequent history.
16. Israel (Jacob's nation) and Edom (Esau's nation) are the subject of Mal 1:2-5. On this word, see "*devotedly* love" in Jn 21:15.
17. Some think this means "hated" in the sense of "loved less"; others, "rejected" for God's purposes. Used 40 times. GK *3631*.
18. That is, because being "children of God" is based on God's choosing and calling, not on their works or merit.
19. A "no" answer is expected to this question. Is it unjust for God to choose one over the other? Paul's answer is that it is not unjust, because mercy is God's choice to make. God gives gifts of mercy as He chooses, as He thinks best and right. He owes it to no one. He hardens whom He chooses, as He thinks best for His purposes.
20. That is, is not in response to, dependent on.
21. God is not unrighteous because it is not a matter of justice or debt for the One showing mercy, nor of the desire, effort, or merit of the one seeking mercy. It is a matter of grace, undeserved kindness. Gift-giving is the prerogative of the giver, carried out for reasons important to the giver. God cannot be faulted for blessing Isaac and Jacob.
22. Some think this means "I spared you from the last plagues"; others, "I placed you on the stage of history". GK *1995*.
23. Both God's power to save (Israel) and to punish (Egypt) were demonstrated, His mercy and His wrath.
24. God's choice to harden instead of show mercy is also His to make. God is not unrighteous to harden because all punishment for sin is earned and deserved, just as all mercy is undeserved. This hardening was seen in the case of the Gentiles in 1:24, 26, 28. Paul will say later that God hardened those in Israel whom He did not choose, 11:7-8. Elsewhere only in Act 19:9; Heb 3:8, 13, 15; 4:7. GK *5020.* But see Exodus 7:13, 22; 8:15, 19, 32; 9:7, 12, 34, 35; 10:1, 20, 27; 11:10; 14:8; Deut 2:30; 1 Sam 6:6; 2 Chron 36:13; 2 Cor 3:14. Related to "hardness" in Rom 2:5. Another word is used in Rom 11:7.
25. That is, since God has mercy on or hardens whomever He wills.
26. Some manuscripts omit this word {C}.
27. Elsewhere only in Heb 8:8, of God finding fault with Israel. GK *3522*. Related to "faultfinders" in Jude 16.
28. Or, "opposed, stood against". On this word, see Eph 6:13. If God has mercy or hardens as He chooses, how can people be held accountable since they are unable to stand against His will in either direction? Paul's answer is that the creature cannot complain to the Creator, apart from whom he would not exist; that the Creator has the right to do as He chooses; and that God intends to demonstrate both His wrath and His mercy in mankind, v 22-24.
29. Or, "intention, purpose". On this word, see 1 Pet 4:3.
30. Or, "molded, made". Elsewhere only in 1 Tim 2:13, of Adam and Eve. GK *4421*. Related to the noun earlier.
31. The grammar indicates a "no" answer is expected.
32. Or, "power, freedom" to act. On this word, see Rev 6:8. See Prov 16:4.
33. The grammar indicates a "yes" answer is expected. On this word, see 2 Tim 2:20. On the potter, compare Isa 29:16; 45:9; Jer 18:6.

A. Rom 3:28, consider B. 1 Jn 2:29 C. Rom 8:30 D. Rom 6:6, are slaves E. Rom 1:18 F. Rom 12:8, showing mercy G. Jn 7:17, willing H. Eph 2:7 J. Mt 4:4, mankind K. Lk 14:6 L. 1 Thes 4:4 M. 1 Tim 5:17

| Romans 9:22 | 546 | Verse |

      3D. But *what*[1] if God, wanting[2] to demonstrate[3] *His* wrath and to make-known[A] His power—   22

          1E. Bore[4] with much patience[5] vessels[B] *of* wrath[6] having been prepared[7] for destruction[C]
          2E. And[8] *did so* in order that He might make-known[9] the riches[D] *of* His glory upon   23
vessels *of* mercy[E] which He prepared-beforehand[10] for glory— °even us whom[11] He   24
called[F] not only from *the* Jews, but also from *the* Gentiles?

              1F. As[12] He says also in Hosea—   25

                  1G. "I will call[F] 'Not My people[G]', 'My people'; and 'Not having been loved'[13],
'Having been loved' " [Hos 2:23]
                  2G. "And it shall be in the place where it was said *to* them 'you *are* not My   26
people[G]', there[14] they will be called[F] sons[15] *of the* living God" [Hos 1:10]

              2F. But[16] Isaiah cries-out[H] concerning Israel—   27

                  1G. "If the number[J] *of* the sons[17] *of* Israel should be like the sand *of* the sea,
the remnant[18] will be saved[K]. °For *the* Lord will accomplish[19] *His* word[20]   28
upon the earth, completing[21] and cutting-short[22]" [in Isa 10:22-23]
                  2G. And just as Isaiah said-before[L] [in Isa 1:9], "Unless *the* Lord *of* Sabaoth[M]   29
had left-behind[N] *a* seed[23] *for* us, we would have become like Sodom, and
we would have been likened[24] as Gomorrah"

  3B. Therefore,[25] what shall we say?   30

      1C. That Gentiles, the *ones* not pursuing[O] righteousness[P], took-hold-of[26] righteousness— but *a*
righteousness by faith
      2C. But Israel, pursuing *the* Law[Q] *of* righteousness, did not attain[27] to *that* Law[28]. °For what reason?   31-32

          1D. Because *they pursued it* not by faith, but as-*if it was* by works[29]
          2D. They[30] stumbled[R] *on* the Stone[S] *of* stumbling[31], °just as it has been written [in Isa 28:16],   33
"Behold— I am laying in Zion[T] *a* Stone *of* stumbling and *a* Rock[U] *of* falling[32]. And the
one[33] putting-faith[34] upon Him will not be put-to-shame[V]"

  4B. Brothers[W], my heart's **desire**[35] and petition[X] to God for them[36] *is* for *their* salvation[Y]. °For I testify[Z]   10:1-2
concerning them that they have *a* zeal[AA] *for* God— but not in-accordance-with[37] knowledge[BB]

      1C. For being-ignorant-of[38] the righteousness *of* God[39], and seeking[CC] to establish[40] *their* own   3
righteousness[41], they did not subject[42] *themselves* to the righteousness *of* God

1. Same grammar as in Act 23:9, and similar to Jn 6:62. Or, this may be a statement, "But if God... bore with much patience vessels of wrath... destruction, *it is* indeed in order that He might make known...".
2. Or, "wishing, willing, intending". Some think Paul means "*because of* wanting"; others, "*although* wanting". Same word as in v 18.
3. Same word as in v 17, of Pharaoh. Related to "demonstration" in 3:25.
4. Or, "Carried, Endured, Put up with". The idea is "carried the load consisting of such vessels". Same word as in Heb 12:20; 13:13. On this word, see "carried" in 2 Pet 1:17.
5. Same word as in 2:4, where it is for repentance.
6. Like Pharaoh. Compare Eph 2:3; 5:6; Jn 3:36; Rom 2:5, 8; 5:9. On this word, see Rev 16:19.
7. In what sense are these people prepared? Perhaps in the sense that as clay vessels they are "hardened" in their choices, 11:7-10. Who prepared them? Perhaps God (as in 9:18; 11:7-8; Jn 12:37-40); or perhaps Paul means the people themselves did (this word could be translated "having prepared *themselves*"); or, that Satan did. This word means to "put in order, prepare, equip, furnish, complete, restore". Same word as in Mt 4:21; 21:16; Mk 1:19; Heb 10:5; 11:3; 13:21. Elsewhere only as "made complete" in 1 Cor 1:10; "complete" in 1 Thes 3:10; "restore" in 2 Cor 13:11; Gal 6:1; 1 Pet 5:10; and "fully trained" in Lk 6:40. GK *2936.* Related to "restoration" in 2 Cor 13:9, and "equipping" in Eph 4:12.
8. Or, "even in order that...". Some manuscripts omit "and" {A}. In any case, Paul means "bore... in order that".
9. Same word as in 16:26; Eph 1:9; 3:3, 5, 10; Col 1:27. On this word, see "know" in Phil 1:22.
10. Note that God "endured, bore" the one, but He actively "prepared beforehand" the other, as Paul said in 8:28-30. On this word, see Eph 2:10. Not related to "prepare" in v 22.
11. Or, "us whom He also called...", or, "whom He also called, *even* us, not only...".
12. Here Paul proves that the Gentiles would be called to salvation. God will turn to people for the most part outside of Judea.
13. In Hos 1:6, 9, "Not my people" and "Not having been loved" are the names given to two of Hosea's children by God. On this word, see "*devotedly* love" in Jn 21:15.
14. Or, "in that place". Used 105 times. GK *1695.*
15. That is, family members, with reference to both sexes. See 8:14 on "sons of God".
16. Here Paul proves that only a remnant of Israel would be saved.
17. That is, the physical descendants of Jacob. On "sons", see Gal 3:7.
18. That is, God's remnant, the spiritual children of Abraham who follow his faith, 4:12. Used only here. GK *5698.* Related to the word in 11:5, the remnant according to the choosing of grace; and to "left" in 11:3.
19. Or, "do, execute, perform, carry out". On this word, see "does" in Rev 13:13.
20. Some give this a more specific meaning here, "sentence, work"; others a more general one, "matter". On this word, see 1 Cor 12:8.
21. On this word, see "accomplished" in Mk 13:4. Paul may mean "completing [the judgment]", or "carrying out [His word]", or "closing [the account]" with finality.
22. This word "cut short, shorten, limit, cut off, cut down" is used only here. GK *5335.* Some think Paul means "cutting short [the nation]", that is, cutting it down to the remnant. Others think he means "cutting short [the time]", that is, quickly. Paul is quoting the Septuagint, from which some manuscripts add additional words {A}, as seen in the KJV. The KJV, translating "word" as "work", interpretively renders this verse as "For He will finish the work, and cut it short in righteousness: because a short work will the Lord make upon the earth."
23. The seed, or descendants, is the remnant. On this word, see Heb 11:11.
24. Or, "compared". That is, we would have been used as an illustration of desolation, like Gomorrah. On this word, see "become like" in Mt 13:24.
25. This concludes what precedes, and leads to what follows. God did not fail them (v 6), they failed God.
26. Or, "seized, took possession of". On this word, see "overcome" in Jn 1:5.
27. Or, "reach, arrive at". On this word, see "came" in 1 Thes 2:16.
28. That is, they pursued the Law demanding righteousness, or containing God's righteousness, for the purpose of attaining righteousness through obedience to it. But they did not attain to its standard. Some manuscripts add "*of* righteousness" {N}.
29. Some manuscripts add "*of* law" {B}.
30. Some manuscripts say "For they..." {K}.
31. This phrase refers to a stone one accidentally strikes against and stumbles over. On this word, see "opportunity for stumbling" in 14:13. Related to the verb earlier.
32. This phrase refers to a rock deliberately placed as part of a trap, a cause of being caught, trapped, offended. Same word and phrase as in 1 Pet 2:8. On this word, see "cause of falling" in 11:9. Same word as "offense" in Gal 5:11.
33. Some manuscripts say "And everyone putting faith..." {A}.
34. On "put faith upon", see 4:5.
35. Or, "good-pleasure, good will". Same word as in 2 Thes 1:11. On this word, see "good pleasure" in Eph 1:5. Paul's grammar implies there is a correlating statement, which is left unsaid— something like "But they are not willing", which is explained in v 3.
36. Some manuscripts say "Israel" {A}.
37. Or, "based on". GK *2848.*
38. Or, "not knowing". Same word as in 1 Tim 1:13, where Paul confesses his own ignorance leading to unbelief, and Heb 5:2; 2 Pet 2:12. It also means "to be unaware, to not understand". Used 22 times. GK *51.* Related to "ignorance" in Heb 9:7, and in Act 3:17.
39. Or, "God's righteousness". That is, *from* God, or *belonging to* God. Same phrase as in 1:17; 3:21.
40. Same word as in 3:31.
41. Some manuscripts omit this word {C}. Or, "seeking to make *their* own righteousness stand".
42. Or, "they were not subjected, made subject". On this word, see Eph 5:21.

A. Rom 9:23 B. 1 Thes 4:4 C. 2 Pet 2:1 D. 1 Tim 6:17 E. Mt 9:13 F. Rom 8:30 G. Rev 21:3 H. Mt 8:29 J. Rev 13:17 K. Lk 19:10 L. Jude 17, spoken beforehand M. Jam 5:4 N. 2 Cor 4:9, forsake O. 1 Cor 14:1 P. Rom 1:18 Q. Rom 7:21 R. Rom 14:21 S. Mk 16:3 T. Jn 12:15 U. Mt 7:24, bed-rock V. Rom 5:5 W. Act 16:40 X. 1 Tim 2:1 Y. Lk 19:9 Z. Jn 1:7 AA. 2 Cor 11:2, jealousy BB. Col 1:9 CC. Phil 2:21

1D.	For[1] Christ *is the* end[2] *of the* Law[3] for[4] righteousness[A] *for* everyone believing[B]	4
2D.	For[5] Moses writes[6] [in Lev 18:5] *as to* the righteousness of the[7] Law that "The person[C] having done them will live by them".[8] *But the righteousness of[9] faith speaks as follows—	5 6

    1E. "Do not say in your heart[10]

        1F. "Who will go up into heaven?"— that is, to bring Christ down[11]

        2F. Or "who will go down into the abyss[D]?"— that is, to bring Christ up from *the* dead[12]   7

    2E. But what does it[13] say? "The word is near[E] you, in your mouth and in your heart"— that is, the word *of* faith[14] which we are proclaiming[F], *that[15]   8
    9

        1F. If you confess[16] with your mouth Jesus *as* Lord[17]

        2F. And you believe[B] in your heart that God raised[G] Him from *the* dead

        3F. You will be saved[H]

            1G. For it[18] is believed *with the* heart, resulting-in[19] righteousness[A]   10

            2G. And it is confessed *with the* mouth, resulting in salvation[J]

3D. For[20] the Scripture says [in Isa 28:16], "everyone putting-faith[21] upon Him will not be put-to-shame[K]"   11

    1E. For[22] there is no distinction *between* both Jew and Greek— for the same Lord *is* Lord *of* all, being rich[L] toward all the *ones* calling-upon[M] Him   12

    2E. For "everyone who calls-upon[M] the name *of the* Lord will be saved[H]" [Joel 2:32]   13

    3E. How then[23] may they[24] call-upon[M] *the One* in Whom they did not believe[B]? And how may they believe *the One* Whom[25] they did not hear? And how may they hear without *one* proclaiming[F]? *And how may they proclaim if they are not sent-forth[N]?—   14
    15

        1F. Just as[26] it has been written [in Isa 52:7]— "How beautiful *are* the feet *of* the *ones* announcing-good-news-of[O] good[27] *things*!"

        2F. But they[28] did not all obey[29] the good-news[P]. For[30] Isaiah says [in Isa 53:1], "Lord, who put-faith-*in*[31] our report?"[32]   16

1. Paul uses this word to assert his first point. GK *1142*. This summarizes the heart of Israel's ignorance and their wrong approach to God— the relationship between Christ, Law, righteousness, faith, and works.
2. Or, "completion, fulfillment, termination, goal, conclusion, outcome". Some think Paul means Christ is the "fulfillment" of the Law, because He fulfilled its demands for us, 8:4; others, that Christ is the "termination" of the Law as a way of righteousness, because in Him a righteousness apart from law has been revealed, 3:21; others, that Christ is the "goal" to which the Law was leading, the Law being our instructor to lead us to Christ, Gal 3:23-24. This word is used 40 times. Same word as "end" in Mt 10:22; Mk 3:26; 13:7; Lk 1:33; Jn 13:1; 1 Cor 1:8; 10:11; 15:24; 2 Cor 3:13; Phil 3:19; Heb 6:11; Rev 21:6; "fulfillment" in Lk 22:37; "goal" in 1 Tim 1:5; "outcome" in Mt 26:58; Rom 6:21; 1 Pet 1:9; 4:17. GK *5465*. Related to "finish" in Rev 10:7.
3. Some think Paul means the Law of Moses; others, the principle of law in relation to God. See 7:4 on this.
4. Or, "for the purpose of, leading to, resulting in, with a view to" righteousness for everyone. Some think Paul means "for purposes of righteousness, *for* everyone"; others, "so that there may be righteousness *for* everyone". On this word, see "resulting in" in 5:16.
5. Using this word to assert his next point, Paul details the content of Israel's ignorance. They were ignorant about the saving value of their law-righteousness, which they sought to establish. Moses implies it cannot save them because the Law requires perfect obedience in order to attain life. By contrast, God's saving righteousness, to which they did not subject themselves, comes to those who believe and confess Jesus. There are other views on the flow of thought in v 3-5. Consult the commentaries.
6. Some manuscripts say "For Moses writes that the person having done the righteousness from the Law will live by it" {N}, where "it" refers to "righteousness".
7. Some manuscripts omit this word {C}.
8. Under Law, the doing is the prerequisite of the living. Only doers will be justified, 2:13.
9. Or, "from, by". Same word as in v 5, "of " the Law. GK *1666*.
10. Paul uses phrases from Deut 30:11-14 to help describe God's saving process, explaining its current application of each. Notice the parallelism with v 9. In v 6-7 Paul gives two questions based on unbelief, representing what the righteousness by faith does not say. In v 9 he gives two statements corresponding to these two questions, representing what the righteousness by faith does say.
11. The righteousness by faith does not say "who is going to bring down the Messiah from heaven", because He has already come. Rather, it confesses Jesus as Lord (v 9), as the Messiah come down from heaven.
12. The righteousness by faith does not say "Who is going to bring Jesus back from the dead", because He has already been raised. Rather it believes that God has raised Him from the dead (v 9).
13. That is, what does the righteousness by faith say?
14. That is, the message "about faith", or "producing faith", or "calling for faith". The message is in v 9.
15. Rendered "that", the words that follow in v 9-10 detail the content of "the word of faith which we are proclaiming". Or, "because", explaining why the righteousness of faith says it is near, or why it is near you in your mouth and heart.
16. Same word as in v 10 and Mt 10:32, "If you confess me before men, I will confess you...". On this word, see 1 Tim 6:12. But "confessing Him" is not just saying words, as seen in Tit 1:16, where the same word is used.
17. Or, "Lord Jesus". Some manuscripts say "confess the word with your mouth, that Jesus *is* Lord" {N}.
18. That is, "the word of faith which we proclaim" (v 8). Note that the two verbs in this verse are passive.
18. On this word, see 5:16.
20. Asserting his next point, Paul proves that the Jews were ignorant of the true basis of salvation. The Scripture says it is faith. Others think v 11-13 are given in proof of v 10, and start a new point with v 14. There are other views of the connection and flow of v 11-18. Consult the commentaries.
21. On this phrase, "putting-faith upon", see 4:5. Same word as in v 16 (but different grammar), and as "believe" in v 4, 9, 10, 14.
22. Paul uses this word to assert his point that "everyone" means "everyone", Jews and Gentiles. GK *1142*.
23. Now Paul works out the logical implications of the Scriptures just quoted, tracing back step by step from everyone calling upon the Lord in faith to the sending forth of the messengers. The preceding Scriptures imply that the response of faith is made to a message proclaimed to everyone by ones sent forth from God. Compare Act 26:23.
24. That is, "everyone" (v 13), "Jew and Greek" (v 12). Israel's ignorance is about God's way for everyone, including themselves. Paul carries out his argument in the universal terms of the prophets, which he is applying to the case of Israel in particular.
25. The people hear Jesus in the message brought, the "report" (v 16, 17). Some render this "*of* Whom", meaning either "*from* Whom" or "*about* Whom".
26. Paul quotes Isaiah to prove that the last two steps have been done, initiating the process. God has done His part. The messengers (the apostles being the foundation) have indeed been sent forth by God to proclaim the message so that all may hear, believe, call upon Him and be saved.
27. On this word, see 1 Tim 5:10b. Some manuscripts say "... announcing-good-news-of peace, the *ones* announcing-good-news-of good *things*" {N}, the repeated word "announce-good-news" being rendered as "preach the gospel" and "bring glad tidings" in the KJV.
28. That is, all who heard the proclamation of the good news. Paul continues the universal language, which he is applying to Israel in particular.
29. Related to "hear" in v 14; and to the "obedience" of faith in 16:26, which is in view here. On this word, see Act 6:7.
30. Isaiah also predicted the rejection of God's message by Israel— further proof of their ignorance (v 3). This too is a universal principle, a reality that takes place everywhere the good news is proclaimed, a predicted response to God's message.
31. Or, "believed". Same word as in v 11. It is rendered this way to show its connection to "faith" in v 17, the same root word.
32. In Isaiah 53, the rejected "report" is about the suffering Messiah. Jn 12:38 also refers to this verse to explain the unbelief of Israel.

A. Rom 1:17   B. Jn 3:36   C. Mt 4:4, mankind   D. Rev 9:1   E. Lk 21:30   F. 2 Tim 4:2   G. Mt 28:6, arose   H. Lk 19:10   J. Lk 19:9   K. Rom 5:5
L. 1 Tim 6:18   M. 1 Pet 1:17   N. Mk 3:14, send out   O. Act 5:42   P. 1 Cor 15:1

Romans 10:17	550	Verse

        3F. So[1] the faith[2] *comes* from *a* report-hearing[3], and the report-hearing through *a* word[4] *about* Christ[5]   17

    2C. But[6] I say— *it is* not *that* they did not hear[7], *is it*?[8]   18

        1D. On the contrary— "Their voice went-out[9] into all the earth, and their words to the ends[A] *of* the world[B]" [Ps 19:4]

    3C. But I say— *it is* not *that* Israel did not know[10], *is it*?[11]   19

        1D. First Moses says [in Deut 32:21], "**I** will provoke you to jealousy[12] over *what is* not *a* nation. I will provoke you to anger[13] over *a* nation without-understanding[14]"
        2D. And Isaiah is very-bold and says [in Isa 65:1], "I was found by the *ones* not seeking[C] Me. I became visible[15] *to* the *ones* not asking-for[D] Me"   20
        3D. But with-regard-to[16] Israel He says [in Isa 65:2], "I held-out[17] My hands the whole day toward *a* disobeying[18] and contradicting[19] people"   21

5B. Therefore I say, God did not reject[20] His people, *did He*? May it never be!   11:1

    1C. For[21] **I** also am *an* Israelite, from *the* seed[E] *of* Abraham, *the* tribe[F] *of* Benjamin
    2C. God did not reject His people whom He foreknew[22]   2

        1D. Or do you not know what the Scripture says in-connection-with[23] Elijah [in 1 Kings 19:14], how he appeals[24] *to* God against Israel?[25]— *"Lord, they killed Your prophets, they tore-down[26] Your altars, and **I** alone[G] was left, and they are seeking[C] my life[H]"   3
        2D. But what does the divine-response[27] say *to* him [in 1 Kings 19:18]?— "I left-remaining[28] *for* Myself seven-thousand[29] men[30] who did not bow *a* knee *to* Baal[31]"   4
        3D. In this manner then, there has come-to-be *a* remnant[32] also at the present time, according-to[33] *the* choosing[34] *of* grace[J]   5

            1E. And if *it*[35] *is by* grace, *it is* no longer by works. Otherwise the grace becomes grace no longer[36]   6

    3C. Therefore what? This[37] which Israel is seeking-for[K], it did not obtain[L]. But the chosen[38] obtained *it,* and the rest[M] were hardened[39], *just as it has been written—   7
                                                                                                8

1. Here Paul summarizes the process he has deduced from the Scriptures he quoted above. This is what Scripture teaches as to how a person comes to be saved. Faith in the hearer comes in response to a report about Christ, and this report comes through a message proclaimed by one sent (or, a word directly from Christ in such a message). By this faith, we call upon Him and are saved. This is God's way, not works of the Law. About this Israel was ignorant.
2. That is, the faith to call upon His name and be saved.
3. Or, "*a hearing, a* report". This word means both "hearing" (the act of hearing) and "report" (the message heard). It is the same word as "report" in v 16, and is related to "hear" in v 18, and is rendered this way to show the connection to both. In addition, "hearing" means both "listening to, hearing" the words (as Israel did in v 18), and "obeying" what is heard (as they did not do in v 16). Here, Paul is referring to an obedient-hearing of the report of the good news. This word focuses on the receptor's response. On this word, see "hearing" in Heb 4:2.
4. Or, "message". That is, "the word of faith we proclaim" (v 8); the "words" of v 18 (same word in all three places). The "word" is the report sent by God (v 16); the good news (v 15); the proclamation brought by the ones sent (v 15). This word focuses on the proclaimer's message. It means "that which is said, a speech, saying, word, statement, discourse, message", and more generally, "matter, thing". It is used 68 times, by Paul only in Rom 10:8, 17, 18; 2 Cor 12:4; 13:1; Eph 5:26; 6:17. GK *4839*.
5. Or, "*from* Christ", sent through His messengers. Some manuscripts say "God" {A}.
6. Moving on from describing the content of Israel's ignorance, Paul now addresses their culpability for it. It is not that they did not hear or know. Their rejection of the message and the Prophets was willful.
7. That is, listen to it, have an opportunity to hear it. Israel did hear (listen to) the report proclaimed, but they failed to hear (obey) it.
8. This idiom (also found in v 19; 1 Cor 9:4-5; 11:22), is a double negative, literally, "They did not not hear, *did they*?", the grammar expecting a "no" answer, "No, they heard". In other words, Israel did not fail to hear, did they? Is their problem that they did not hear Jesus and the gospel proclaimed? Does this explain their ignorance and failure to subject themselves to God, v 3? No, they did hear. Israel cannot claim they did not hear the report, for the messengers took it to the world.
9. It went out, but it has not arrived everywhere yet.
10. Or, "understand". That is, know its meaning. Israel's ignorance and failure (v 3), is not because they did not know the meaning of the message about Christ being proclaimed. It was a willful rejection of the message and the OT prophecies regarding its meaning for the world and for them. They should have known better, based on the OT given to them by God, and are solely responsible for their actions. They are without excuse. On this word, see Lk 1:34.
11. Same idiom as in v 18, literally, "Israel did not not know, *did they*?", expecting a "no" answer. Israel did not fail to know. God told them from the beginning, when He first spoke to Moses, that He would go to the Gentiles and Israel would not believe.
12. The word "provoke to jealousy" is the same word as in 11:11, 14, where this is explained.
13. On this word, "provoke to anger", see Eph 6:4.
14. Or, "foolish, senseless". Same word as in Mt 15:16; Mk 7:18. Elsewhere only as "senseless" in Rom 1:21, 31. GK *852*. The nation that knows God, and has His Word, and is trained in spiritual matters, will be angered by ones with no such expertise.
15. That is, known. Elsewhere only in Act 10:40, of Christ becoming visible after His resurrection. GK *1871*.
16. As this word is used in Lk 19:9; Heb 1:8. Or, "against", as it is used in Lk 20:19. GK *4639*.
17. This verb "to hold out, stretch out" in an imploring, begging, pleading gesture, is used only here. GK *1736*.
18. Not related to "obey" in v 16, this word means "refusing to believe". On this word, see 11:30.
19. Or, "speaking against, opposing". Same word as in Act 13:45; Tit 1:9; 2:9. Elsewhere only as "speak against" in Lk 2:34 (where Jesus was appointed as a sign to be spoken against); 21:15; Jn 19:12; Act 4:14; 28:19, 22; and "deny" in Lk 20:27. GK *515*.
20. Or, "push away, push aside". This word is used by Paul of Israel's rejection of the gospel in Act 13:46. Same word as in Rom 11:2; Act 7:27, 39, of Israel rejecting Moses. Elsewhere only as "push aside" in 1 Tim 1:19. GK *723*.
21. Some take this as the motive for the denial; others, as part of the answer, "I myself am proof ".
22. Same word as in 8:29. Some think Paul is referring to the remnant (v 5); others, to "His people Israel" as a whole, of which the "remnant" now believes, and the "rest" were hardened, but hopefully will believe (v 11-31).
23. Or, "in the case of, in [the place about]". GK *1877*.
24. Or, "intercedes, petitions". On this word, see "intercede" in 8:34.
25. Some manuscripts say "Israel?— saying, 'Lord...'" {N}.
26. On this word, see Act 15:16. Some manuscripts say "and they tore-down" {K}.
27. Or, "the communication *from God*". Used only here. GK *5977*. Related to "revealed" in Lk 2:26.
28. Or, "left behind". Same word as in Heb 4:1. On this word, see "left behind" in Act 6:2.
29. Some think this is symbolic of "the full, complete number", as a multiple of seven.
30. This word means "males". The number of women and children is unstated. On this word, see 1 Tim 2:12.
31. The Jews substituted the word "shame" for "Baal", and this is reflected in Paul's grammar here. Used only here. GK *955*.
32. Used only here. GK *3307*. Related to the word in 9:27; "left" in 11:3; and "left remaining" in 11:4. This proves Israel's rejection was not a complete rejection.
33. Or, "in accordance with, based on". GK *2848*.
34. Or, "election, selection". Same word as in v 28; 9:11. Elsewhere only as "chosen" in 11:7; Act 9:15; and "election" in 1 Thes 1:4; 2 Pet 1:10. GK *1724*. See 8:33 for related words.
35. That is, the choosing.
36. Some manuscripts add "But if *it is* of works, it is no longer grace, otherwise the work is no longer work" {A}.
37. That is, righteousness, life. Israel sought it through obedience to the Law, not faith, 9:31-32; 10:3.
38. Literally, "the choosing, election", as in v 5. This abstract term refers to the whole group of those chosen.
39. Elsewhere only in Mk 6:52; 8:17; Jn 12:40; 2 Cor 3:14. GK *4800*. Another word is used in Rom 9:18. Related to "hardness" in 11:25. For another example of God doing this, see 2 Thes 2:11-12.

A. Heb 6:16   B. Heb 2:5   C. Phil 2:21   D. Lk 9:18, questioned   E. Heb 11:11   F. Rev 1:7   G. Jam 2:24   H. Jam 5:20, soul   J. Eph 2:8   K. Phil 4:17   L. Heb 11:33   M. 2 Pet 3:16, other

1D. "God gave them *a* spirit *of* stupor [Isa 29:10]— eyes *that they may* not see and ears *that they may* not hear— until this very day¹" [Deut 29:4]

2D. And David says [in Ps 69:22-23], "Let their table become² *a* snare³, and *a* trap⁴, and *a* cause-of-falling⁵, and *a* retribution⁶ *to* them. °Let their eyes be darkened^A *that they may* not see. And bend their back⁷ continually⁸" — 9, 10

6B. Therefore I say, they did not stumble⁹ in order that they might fall¹⁰, *did they*? May it never be! — 11

1C. On-the-contrary¹¹, *by* their trespass¹², salvation^B *came to* the Gentiles^C, so as to provoke them¹³ to jealousy¹⁴

1D. But if their trespass *is* riches^D *for the* world^E, and their defeat¹⁵ *is* riches *for the* Gentiles, how much more *will* their fullness¹⁶ *be*! — 12

2C. And¹⁷ I am speaking *to* **you** the Gentiles. So indeed¹⁸ to the extent¹⁹ **I** am *an* apostle^F *of the* Gentiles I glorify²⁰ my ministry^G—°if somehow²¹ I might provoke my flesh²² to jealousy and save^H some of them — 13, 14

1D. For if their rejection²³ *is* reconciliation²⁴ *for the* world, what *will their* acceptance²⁵ *be* if not life²⁶ from *the* dead? — 15

3C. But²⁷ if the firstfruit^J *is* holy, the lump *is* also.²⁸ And if the root²⁹ *is* holy, the branches *are* also — 16

1D. Now if some *of* the branches were broken-off³⁰ and **you**³¹, being *a* wild-olive-tree, were grafted-in³² among them³³ and became *a* co-partner³⁴ *of* the root, *of*³⁵ the fatness³⁶ *of* the olive tree, °do not be vaunting³⁷ *over* the branches³⁸ — 17, 18

1E. But if you vaunt, [remember] **you** are not carrying^K the root, but the root you

2E. You will say then, "Branches were broken off in order that **I** might be grafted-in" — 19

1. This is an idiom, literally, "until the today day". Elsewhere only in 2 Cor 3:14; Mt 28:15; Act 20:26.
2. More literally, "come-to-be for *a* snare, and for *a* trap, and for *a* cause of falling, and for *a* retribution...", reflecting a Hebrew way of speaking.
3. Or, "trap". Elsewhere only in Lk 21:35; 1 Tim 3:7; 6:9; 2 Tim 2:26. GK *4075*. The verb is in Mt 22:15.
4. Or, "net". A wild game trap. Used only here. GK *2560*. Related to the word for "wild animal".
5. This word means "the trip-stick" that causes the trap to spring and the prey to fall, then a "trap" set for a prey or an enemy, then a "cause of falling, a cause of being trapped or captured, a cause of offense". See also 14:13. Same word as in Mt 13:41; 16:23; 18:7; Lk 17:1; Rom 14:13; 16:17; 1 Jn 2:10; Rev 2:14. Elsewhere only as "falling" in the phrase "Rock of falling" in Rom 9:33; 1 Pet 2:8; and "offense" in 1 Cor 1:23; Gal 5:11. The Cross is a cause of falling for many. GK *4998*. On the related verb, "cause to fall", see 1 Cor 8:13.
6. Or, "pay back". Elsewhere only as "repayment" in Lk 14:12. GK *501*. Related to "payback" in Col 3:24; "repay" in 2 Thes 1:6.
7. David may mean "in bondage or slavery", "in fear or grief ", or, "under their burden".
8. Or "always, through all". On this phrase, see 2 Thes 3:16.
9. On this word, see 2 Pet 1:10. Not related to "stumble" in Rom 14:21.
10. Or, "so that (GK *2671*) they fell". Note that both the stumbling and falling are from God's viewpoint. Unbelieving Israel would not admit to either. Paul may mean "for the purpose of falling" permanently. A permanent fall was not God's purpose, was it? Or, he may mean "with the result that they have fallen". In this case, some think he means "They did not stumble with this permanent result, did they?"; others, "A permanent fall was not the only result, was it?"; others, "A fall with the possibility of getting up was not the only result, was it?". Same word as in v 22; 14:4. Used 90 times. GK *4406*. Compare Mt 21:42-44; Heb 4:11.
11. On this word and construction, see 7:7.
12. Or, "false step". Some think this is a reference to the "stumbling" of v 11, and means Israel's stepping in the wrong direction, causing them to stumble. In this case, Paul is denying that they fell permanently. Others think this refers to the related verb "fall" in v 11, and render it "fall". In this case, he is giving the other reason for their fall (whether permanent or not permanent). Same word as in v 12, and 5:15.
13. That is, Israel.
14. This word, "provoke to jealousy, make jealous", is elsewhere only in Rom 10:19; 11:14; 1 Cor 10:22. GK *4143*.
15. Or, "failure". If Israel's fall brought the spiritual wealth of the gospel to the world, what will happen when Israel believes? Elsewhere only in 1 Cor 6:7. GK *2488*. The related verb is in 2 Pet 2:20. Some take this to mean "diminishing" in order to have an opposite to "fullness" ("fulfilling") in the next phrase.
16. Some think Paul means the completion or fulfilling of Israel's full number, as in v 25, where the same word is used. Others think he means the "fullness" of their obedience to God's will, their "fulfilling" of God's command, in contrast to their trespass; others, their fullness of salvation. On this word, see Col 1:19.
17. Some manuscripts say "For" {N}.
18. Some manuscripts omit "So indeed " {N}.
19. Or, "as long as, as far as, inasmuch as". Paul could mean "inasmuch as" I am an apostle (as this phrase is used in Mt 25:40, 45); or, "as far as" I am able to reach, even to you in Rome; or, "as long as" I am alive in this ministry (as it is used in Mt 9:15; 2 Pet 1:13). This phrase occurs elsewhere only with the addition of the word "time" in the phrase "as much time" in Rom 7:1; 1 Cor 7:39; Gal 4:1.
20. That is, I magnify, honor, publicize it, so Israel will see what God is doing among the Gentiles, be provoked to jealousy, and return to God.
21. Or, "if perhaps". This is a modestly stated hope that he might be part of God's plan in this matter. On this idiom, see Phil 3:11.
22. That is, my fellow Israelites, as in 9:3.
23. Or, "throwing off, being cast away", by God. Elsewhere only as "loss" in Act 27:22. GK *613*. Related to "throw off, away" in Mk 10:50; Heb 10:35; and to "rejected" in 1 Tim 4:4. Not related to "reject" in v 1.
24. On this word, see Rom 5:11. Some think Paul is referring to the objective reconciliation of the world to God in the death of Christ; others, to the subjective reconciliation of individuals in the world upon conversion.
25. Or, "reception", by God, v 25-26. Used only here. GK *4691*. Related to "accept" in 14:1.
26. Some think Paul means the physical resurrection at the return of Messiah. Others think he means spiritual life (as in 6:13, "alive from the dead"), and refers to an unprecedented future spiritual awakening that is worldwide in scope. Others think he means a present life, "what *is their* acceptance if not" spiritual life for them as well.
27. Paul now turns from their failure, which serves the Gentiles, to their remaining potential for salvation.
28. Firstfruit refers to the first part of the lump of dough offered to God. Some think Paul is referring to Abraham, or "the fathers" (v 28). If they are holy, then the whole lump is holy, that is, Israel. Others think this metaphor has a different meaning than the next one. It refers to Jewish Christians, the firstfruit of believers in the church. If they are holy, then so is the lump from which they came. They sanctify (set apart) the unbelieving Israel lump (similar to 1 Cor 7:14).
29. The root is Abraham or the "fathers" (v 28); the branches, Israelites.
30. That is, if unbelieving branches were broken off. Physical Israel was pruned from spiritual Israel, 9:6-13. Compare Jn 15:2.
31. In v 17-24, "you" is singular, referring to a single Gentile as a representative. In v 25, "you" is plural again.
32. Paul is illustrating what God in fact did spiritually, using the concept of grafting. Whether or not an olive grower would graft wild stock to domestic stock is irrelevant to the physical process of grafting, and to Paul's point.
33. Paul is referring to Gentile Christians being grafted in to the root of Abrahamic faith (Gal 3:29), among the other branches on that tree, including Jewish Christians.
34. Or, "joint-sharer, co-participant". On this word, see Phil 1:7.
35. Some manuscripts say "*of* the root and *of* the fatness..." {B}.
36. Or, "richness, wealth". That is, the life of the tree. Some think Paul means "*of* the fat root *of* the olive tree"; others, "*of* the root— [that is,] *of* the fatness *of* the olive tree". Used only here. GK *4404*.
37. Used twice here; elsewhere only in Jam 2:13; 3:14. GK *2878*. It means "to vaunt *over*, to boast *over*, gloat *over*", to boastfully call attention to your triumph. Used of gladiators vaunting over their defeated foes.
38. Paul may be referring to the unbelieving branches, or to all of them, to even the Jewishness of Jewish Christians (the Gentile Christians perhaps continuing in the church any former anti-Jewish sentiments they may have had). This word is GK *3080*. Used 11 times.

A. Rom 1:21 B. Lk 19:9 C. Act 15:23 D. 1 Tim 6:17 E. 1 Jn 2:15 F. 1 Cor 12:28 G. 1 Cor 12:5 H. Lk 19:10 J. 1 Cor 15:20 K. Mt 8:17

	3E. Well *said*! They were broken off *by their* unbelief[A], and **you** stand *by your* faith[B]. Do not be thinking[C] lofty[1] *things*, but be fearing[2]—	20
	1F. For if God did not spare the branches in accordance with nature[3], perhaps[4] neither will He spare[5] you	21
	2D. Therefore behold *the* kindness[6] and severity[7] *of* God—	22
	1E. Severity upon the *ones* **having fallen**[8]— but *the* kindness *of* God[9] upon you, if you continue[10] *in His* kindness. Otherwise **you** also will be cut off	
	2E. But those *ones* also— if they do not continue *in* unbelief[A]— will be grafted-in. For God is able to graft them in again	23
	1F. For if **you** were cut off from the wild-olive-tree according to nature[11] and were grafted-in contrary to nature[12] into *a* cultivated-olive-tree, how much more will these, the *ones* in accordance with nature, be grafted-in *their* own olive tree!	24
4C.	For I do not want you to be unaware[D], brothers[E], *as to* this mystery[13]— in order that you not be wise[F] among[14] yourselves— that *a* hardness[15] in part[16] has happened *to* Israel until[17] the fullness[18] *of* the Gentiles comes in	25
	1D. And so[19] all Israel[20] will be saved[G], just as it has been written—	26
	1E. "The *One* delivering[H] will come[21] from Zion[J], He will turn-away[K] ungodliness[22] from Jacob[23]. *And this *is* the covenant[L] from Me *with* them, when I take-away[M] their sins" [Isa 59:20-21]	27
	2D. In relation to **the good-news**[24] *they*[25] *are* enemies[26] [of God] for your sake[27]— but in relation to the choosing[28] *of* God they are beloved[N] *ones* [of God] for the sake of the fathers[29]	28
	1E. For the gifts[O] and the calling[P] *of* God *are* without-regret[30]	29

1. That is, do not think proud thoughts. This same phrase occurs in 12:16. On this word, see "highly-*valued* " in Lk 16:15. Some manuscripts combine "think" and "lofty, high" into one word, "do not be high-minded" {N}, the word in 1 Tim 6:17.
2. Some think Paul means "be reverencing God, be in awe of God"; others, "be afraid of unbelief ".
3. That is, the natural branches. Same word as in 2:27; 11:24; Gal 2:15. On this word, see Eph 2:3.
4. Or, "[fear] that He will somehow not spare you". This phrase "perhaps, somehow" is also in 2 Cor 11:3; 12:20; Gal 4:11. Elsewhere only as "not somehow" in 1 Cor 8:9; 9:27; 2 Cor 2:7; 9:4; Gal 2:2; 1 Thes 3:5. GK *4803*. Some manuscripts omit it {C}.
5. Elsewhere only in Act 20:29; Rom 8:32; 1 Cor 7:28; 2 Cor 1:23; 12:6; 13:2; 2 Pet 2:4, 5. GK *5767*. Related to "sparingly" in 2 Cor 9:6.
6. Or, "goodness". On this word, see "goodness" in Rom 3:12.
7. Used only in this verse. GK *704*. Related to "severely" in 2 Cor 13:10.
8. A permanent fall was denied in v 11. The fall is not yet permanent, as seen in v 23. Paul uses grammar that emphasizes the contrast between the two halves of this sentence.
9. Some manuscripts omit "*of* God" {N}.
10. Compare Heb 3:6, 14. Same word as in v 23; Col 1:23, and in Rom 6:1; 1 Tim 4:16. Elsewhere only as "continue-on" in Jn 8:7; Act 12:16; "stay" in Act 10:48; 21:4; 28:12, 14; 1 Cor 16:7; Gal 1:18; "stay-on" in Act 21:10; 1 Cor 16:8; "remain" in Phil 1:24. GK *2152*.
11. Some think Paul means "according to your nature as a Gentile"; others, "the wild olive tree by its nature".
12. Some think Paul means "contrary to your nature", not your native tree; others, "contrary to normal practice". On this word, see Eph 2:3.
13. This word is used of truth hidden in the past, but now revealed by God; something known only by God's revelation. Some think the mystery is that "all" Israel will be saved in this way after the fullness of the Gentiles comes in; others, that all Israel will be saved in this way from Paul's day "until" Christ's return, implying their continued existence until then. Elsewhere only in Rom 16:25; 1 Cor 2:1, 7; 4:1; 13:2; 14:2; 15:51; Eph 1:9; 3:3, 4, 9; 5:32; 6:19; Col 1:26, 27; 2:2; 4:3; 2 Thes 2:7; 1 Tim 3:9, 16; and in Mt 13:11; Mk 4:11; Lk 8:10; Rev 1:20; 10:7; 17:5, 7. GK *3696*.
14. This phrase "among yourselves" is also in 12:16. Some manuscripts say "in yourselves" {C}.
15. Elsewhere only in Mk 3:5; Eph 4:18. GK *4801*. Related to "hardened" in 11:7.
16. That is, to part of Israel, "some" of the branches, v 17. This idiom "partial, in part" is used elsewhere only in Rom 15:15, 24; 2 Cor 1:14; 2:5. This word, meaning "part, share" in various senses, is used 42 times. GK *3538*. This idiom is related to "in part" in 1 Cor 12:27.
17. It is temporary, "until", as in Luke 21:24, "until the times of the Gentiles be fulfilled". Some think Paul means that the hardness in part ends then, and the fullness of Israel's response comes; others, that the hardness in part continues until then, when Christ returns, implying nothing about a national conversion at that time. GK *948*.
18. Same word as in v 12. That is, the "sum total, full number", or, the "completion".
19. Or, "And in this manner", "And thus". That is, with the fullness of the Gentiles coming in, and the moving of Israel to jealousy (v 11), so that they believe (v 23), and are regrafted into their tree (v 24).
20. Some think Paul means the nation of Israel as a whole (not every individual), ending the temporary "hardness in part" (v 25), resulting in "fullness" (v 12). It is "Israel" of v 25; and of 11:2, 7; 10:19, 21; 9:6 (first mention), 27, 31; Israel in contrast to the remnant. The emphasis is on "all" versus "in part". This is the answer to v 11. They have not fallen forever, God is able to do it (v 23). The remnant is saved for now, the fullness then. Just as the generation at Christ's first coming was hardened, so the generation at His second coming will be saved. Paul hoped this would be one and the same generation (that is, his generation), just as we hope it will be ours. Others do not think this is an end-time prophecy, but a description of how the Jewish remnant will be saved along with the fullness of Gentiles until Christ returns. "Israel" is not the "Israel" of v 25, but of 9:6 (second mention). "All Israel" means all true, spiritual Israel, the remnant in contrast with Israel (9:27). The emphasis is on "so" (in this manner). Thus, in this manner, alongside the continuing hardness in part, moved to jealousy, all the Jews who are to believe will believe; all the remnant will believe, all the elect Jews will be saved.
21. Some think Paul is referring to Christ's first coming; others, to His second coming.
22. This word is plural, "[acts of] ungodliness, impieties, lackings of reverence". On this word, see 1:18.
23. That is, Israel.
24. Paul uses grammar that emphasizes the contrast between the two halves of this sentence. On this word, see 1 Cor 15:1.
25. Some think Paul is referring to the remnant of as yet unsaved Jews in both halves of this verse, "choosing" having the same reference as in v 5, 7; others, to the nation as a whole ("Israel" of v 25, "His people" of v 1), not the remnant.
26. Some think Paul specifically means they are enemies of the progress of the gospel in the world, as described in 1 Thes 2:15-16.
27. Such ones are treated as enemies by God. They are rejected (v 15), so that you might be saved, summarizing v 11-15.
28. Or, "election". Same word as in 11:5. In relation to their choosing as His people.
29. That is, Abraham, Isaac and Jacob. For the sake of God's gifts and promises to them, and His calling of them, they are beloved.
30. Or, "unregretted, unchanged". The Lord does not regret His promises to Israel. He keeps them, 3:4. Elsewhere only as "unregretted" in 2 Cor 7:10. GK *294*. Related to "regret" in Mt 21:29.

A. 1 Tim 1:13   B. Eph 2:8   C. Rom 8:5   D. Rom 10:3, being ignorant of   E. Act 16:40   F. Mt 7:24   G. Lk 19:10   H. Col 1:13   J. Jn 12:15   K. Heb 12:25, turn away from   L. Heb 8:6   M. Mk 14:47, took off   N. Mt 3:17   O. 1 Cor 1:7   P. 2 Pet 1:10

Romans 11:30	556	Verse

        3D. For just as **you** once[1] disobeyed[2] God, but now were shown-mercy[A] in[3] the disobedience[4]   30
of these *Jews*,* so also these *Jews* now disobeyed *in* the mercy[B] belonging to you,[5] in   31
order that **they** also now[6] may be shown-mercy[7]

        1E. For God confined[C] all in disobedience in order that He may show-mercy[A] to all   32

  7B. O *the* depth *of* riches[D], both[8] *of the* wisdom and *the* knowledge *of* God! How unsearchable[9] *are* His   33
judgments[E] and untraceable[10] His ways!

        1C. "For who knew *the* mind[F] *of the* Lord? Or who became His counselor?" [Isa 40:13]   34
        2C. "Or who previously-gave[11] *to* Him and it will be repaid[G] *to* him?" [Job 41:11]   35
        3C. Because all *things are* from Him and through Him and for Him   36
        4C. *To* Him *be* the glory forever[H], amen

4A. Therefore, I urge[J] you, brothers[K], by the compassions[12] *of* God, to present[13] your bodies *as a* sacrifice[L]—   12:1
living, holy[M], pleasing[N] *to* God— *as* your spiritual[14] worship[15]

  1B. And do not be conformed[16] to this age[17], but be transformed[18] by the renewing[19] *of your*[20] mind[F], so   2
that you *may* be approving[21] what *is* the good[O] and pleasing[22] and perfect[P] will[Q] *of* God[23]
  2B. For[24] I say *to* everyone being among you through the grace having been given *to* me[25]   3

        1C. Not to be thinking-highly[26] *of yourself* beyond what *you* ought-to[27] think[R]
        2C. But to be thinking[R] so as to be sound-minded[28], as God apportioned[29] *to* each *a* measure[30] *of* faith[S]

            1D. For[31] just as we have many body-parts[T] in one body, and all the body-parts do not have   4
the same function[U], *in this manner we the many are one body in Christ, and individually[V]   5
body-parts *of* one another

1. Or, "formerly". On this word, see "ever" in Gal 2:6.
2. This word means "to disobey, be disobedient; to refuse to obey, comply". Elsewhere only in 2:8; 10:21; 11:31; 15:31; and in Jn 3:36; Act 14:2; 19:9; Heb 3:18; 11:31; 1 Pet 2:8; 3:1, 20; 4:17. GK 578. Related to "disobedience" in this verse, and to "disobedient" in Lk 1:17. Based on the context here, where the "obedience of faith" (16:26) is in view, some prefer to render these words "did not believe" and "unbelief", though they are not related to the word for "believe" itself.
3. Or, "*by*". Paul may mean "because of", "as a result of", "through". It is the same thought as v 11.
4. Elsewhere only in v 32; Eph 2:2; 5:6; Col 3:6; Heb 4:6, 11. GK 577. Related to "disobey" earlier.
5. This is the Greek word order of v 30-31. Some think the phrase, "*in the mercy belonging to you*" is placed forward in the Greek word order for emphasis, and belongs with the next phrase, providing a parallelism of phrases in v 30-31. Thus, it would be rendered "... disobeyed, in order that **they** also now may receive mercy *in the mercy belonging to you*".
6. Some manuscripts omit this word {C}.
7. The Gentiles received mercy in connection with Israel's disobedience. Israel receives mercy in the Gentile's mercy (not obedience).
8. Or, "riches, and *of...*", so that "riches" stands by itself, perhaps referring to riches of grace and mercy.
9. Used only here. GK 451. Related to "search" in 1 Cor 2:10.
10. Or, "inscrutable, incomprehensible". Elsewhere only in Eph 3:8. GK 453. His paths cannot be traced out.
11. Or, "gave beforehand, gave in advance". Used only here. GK 4594.
12. Or, "[acts of] compassion". Elsewhere only in 2 Cor 1:3; Phil 2:1; Col 3:12; Heb 10:28. GK 3880. The related verb "to have compassion" is used only in Rom 9:15, where it is distinguished from "mercy". Related to "compassionate" in Jam 5:11.
13. This word is used outside the Greek Bible to mean "offer" a sacrifice, and some think the context points to this meaning here. Or, Paul may mean it in the same way he used this word in 6:13, 16, 19. Present your bodies for God's use. Same word as in Lk 2:22; Act 1:3; 9:41; 23:33; 2 Cor 4:14; 11:2; Eph 5:27; Col 1:22, 28; 2 Tim 2:15. It also means "be present, be here; stand (near, by, before)", etc. Used 41 times. GK 4225.
14. Or, "reasonable, thoughtful". This is not the normal word for "spiritual". It is "word, reason" with a suffix meaning "pertaining to". Here it means pertaining to reason, or to the real ("spiritual") nature of things. The Gospel does not call for mindless ritual, but service pertaining to what is reasonable and rational in view of the compassions of God, and therefore "in spirit and truth". Elsewhere only as "of-the-word" in 1 Pet 2:2, the milk "pertaining to the word". GK 3358.
15. Or, "service". This word is used of the service of divine worship in the temple as prescribed by God. We offer ourselves in "spiritual worship", Heb 12:28; 13:15; 1 Pet 2:5; or in "reasonable service" appropriate to what God has done for us. Elsewhere only as "service" in Jn 16:2; Rom 9:4; Heb 9:1, 6. GK 3301. Related word in Heb 12:28.
16. Or, "molded". The grammar implies "Stop being conformed, do not continue to be conformed". Elsewhere only in 1 Pet 1:14. GK 5372. Some manuscripts say "And not to be conformed..., but to be transformed" {N}, making v 1-2 one sentence.
17. Or, "world". GK 172.
18. Or, "metamorphosed, changed in form". The grammar implies, "Continue to be transformed". Same word as in 2 Cor 3:18, as we behold His glory. Elsewhere only as "transfigured" in Mt 17:2; Mk 9:2. GK 3565. Related to "formed" in Gal 4:19.
19. Or, "renewal". On this word, see Tit 3:5.
20. Some manuscripts include this word {N}.
21. Or, "so that you approve", depending on whether Paul is referring to the purpose or the result. This word means "to test, examine, assay (a metal), prove by testing" and "to approve after testing". The NIV combines both meanings here "test and approve". A renewed mind allows us to approve the right things— "what is pleasing to the Lord", Eph 5:10; "the things mattering", Phil 1:10. Same word as in Rom 1:28; 2:18; 14:22; 1 Cor 16:3; 1 Thes 2:4. Elsewhere only as "test" in Lk 12:56; 14:19; 1 Cor 3:13; 1 Thes 2:4; 5:21; 1 Tim 3:10; 1 Pet 1:7; 1 Jn 4:1; "examine" in 1 Cor 11:28; and "prove" in 2 Cor 8:8, 22; 13:5; Gal 6:4. GK 1507. Related to "trial" in Heb 3:9; "approvedness" in 2 Cor 2:9; "approved" in 2 Tim 2:15; "testing" in Jam 1:3; "disapproved" in 1 Cor 9:27; and "rejected" in Heb 12:17.
22. Same word as in v 1.
23. Or, "approve what *is* the will *of* God— the *thing* good and pleasing and perfect".
24. Paul uses this word to assert his next point. GK 1142. It may be rendered "Moreover".
25. Paul is probably referring to his gift as an apostle of Jesus Christ. Compare Eph 4:7.
26. Used only here. GK 5672. Paul uses the root word "think" three times in this verse.
27. Or, "must think", in accordance with the facts. On this idiom, see Act 25:10.
28. Or, "be sensible, be serious, be in control, be moderate, be in one's senses, be in a right mind". Sound-minded thinking focuses on our spiritual endowments from God. We are to measure ourselves against God's gift to us, not against one another (2 Cor 10:12), and not against the world's standards (slave or free, rich or poor, male or female; human merit, achievement; personal opinion). "What has God given me to invest for Him, and how am I doing with it?" are sound-minded questions, not "Am I better than you?" Elsewhere only in Mk 5:15; Lk 8:35; 2 Cor 5:13; Tit 2:6; 1 Pet 4:7. GK 5404. On this word group, see 1 Tim 3:2.
29. Or, "divided, distributed". God divided the portions. On this word, see 1 Cor 7:17.
30. That is, "a quantity, a measured portion" of faith appropriate to the gifts God gives to each person in v 6. Paul is not referring to saving faith, nor to the gift of faith (1 Cor 12:9). God has given us gifts to serve Him and His people, and the faith to exercise them. We are to measure ourselves against our own use of our own faith and gifts, just as God will do on that day (Rom 14:10-12). Same word as in Eph 4:7. On this word, see Jn 3:34.
31. Paul further explains this sound-minded thinking about ourselves, using the illustration of the human body.

A. Rom 12:8 B. Mt 9:13 C. Gal 3:22 D. 1 Tim 6:17 E. Jn 9:39 F. Rom 7:23 G. 2 Thes 1:6 H. Rev 20:10 J. Rom 12:8, exhorting K. Act 16:40 L. Heb 9:26 M. 1 Pet 1:16 N. Eph 5:10 O. 1 Tim 5:10b P. 1 Cor 13:10, complete Q. Jn 7:17 R. Rom 8:5 S. Eph 2:8 T. Col 3:5 U. Mt 16:27, practice V. Eph 5:33

	2D. And having different[A] *grace*-gifts[1] according-to[2] the grace having been given[3] *to* us, *exercise them accordingly*[4]—	6
	1E. Whether prophecy[B], in accordance with the proportion[5] *of your*[6] faith[7]	
	2E. Or service[8], in-the-sphere-of[9] *your* service[10]	7
	3E. Or the *one* teaching[11], in the sphere of *your* teaching[12]	
	4E. Or the *one* exhorting[13], in the sphere of *your* exhortation[14]	8
	5E. The *one* giving[15], with[16] generosity[17]	
	6E. The *one* leading[18], with diligence[C]	
	7E. The *one* showing-mercy[19], with cheerfulness[20]	
3C.	*I say to let your*[21] love *be* sincere[22], while abhorring the evil, clinging[23] *to* the good[D]	9
4C.	*To be* affectionate[24] to one another *in* brotherly-love[E], preferring[25] one another *in* honor[F]	10
5C.	*To* not *be* hesitant[26] *in* diligence[C]	11
6C.	*To be* boiling[27] *in* spirit, serving[G] the Lord, rejoicing[H] *in* hope, enduring[J] *in* affliction[K], devoting-yourselves[L] *to* prayer, sharing[28] *in* the needs[M] *of* the saints[N], pursuing[O] hospitality[P]	12 / 13
7C.	Be blessing[Q] the *ones* persecuting you[29]— be blessing and not cursing[30]	14

1. On this word, see "gift" in 1 Cor 1:7. It is rendered this way to show its relationship to "grace" next.
2. Or, "based on". GK *2848*.
3. Compare Eph 4:7.
4. Some think Paul transitions from explanation to exhortation here, intending the reader to supply the commands needed, whether a single command is added as here, or a separate one is added to each gift. Others think this continues from v 5, explaining the second half of v 4 and the individual apportionment of v 3. It would be rendered "one another, and *are* having different grace-gifts... given *to* us—whether..."; would add no commands; and would have no commas dividing each of the seven following phrases.
5. Or, "the right relationship *to,* agreement *with*". Used only here. GK *381*.
6. Or, "the faith *given*". This is the word "the", and each of the first four gifts has it. It is taken here to mean "the faith given to you". Others think Paul means "the faith" in a different sense, as explained next.
7. Some think Paul means the personal "measure of faith" given in v 3. He may be referring to the faith that allows this person to hear the revelation from God. "Prophesy in correspondence to the faith-received revelation from God, saying nothing more, nothing less". Or he may mean "Exercise your prophetic ministry as widely as your God-given faith permits". Others think Paul means the objective content of "the faith" (as in Jude 3), "prophesy according to the right relationship to the faith delivered to us". Other prophets would discern this, as in 1 Cor 14:29.
8. Or, "ministry". This word is used regarding food preparation (Lk 10:40), apostleship (Act 1:25), the Word (Act 6:4), giving (Act 11:29; 2 Cor 9:1), missions (Act 12:25), the work of service (Eph 4:12), etc. On this word, see "ministries" in 1 Cor 12:5. The related verb is in 1 Pet 4:10, 11, where "serving" and "speaking" summarize all the gifts. It is also related to "deacons" in Phil 1:1. Some think Paul means service to the poor, sick, and suffering; others, deacon-ministry; others, all kinds of practical service.
9. Or, "in, in connection with, with, by". This word is also used in the next five phrases, but is rendered "with" in the last three. GK *1877*.
10. Or, "the service *given*". The same noun is used twice. Both the gift, and the sphere or realm in which it is used are from God. In this case, the gift of "service" for one means distributing food; for another, running the nursery, etc. Use your gift of serving in the ministry God gives you. Look to Him for both. Compare 1 Cor 12:4-6.
11. This verb is used 97 times. GK *1438*. Related to "teacher" in 1 Cor 12:28.
12. Or, "the teaching *given*". On this noun, see 1 Tim 5:17.
13. Or, "encouraging". This word means "to appeal to" in Rom 15:30; 2 Cor 5:20; 10:1; "beg" in Mt 8:34; 14:36; Act 13:42; 21:12; "exhort" in 1 Cor 1:10; Eph 4:1; Phil 4:2; 1 Thes 4:1; Tit 1:9; 2:15; "urge" in Act 16:15; 27:33; Rom 12:1; 16:17; 1 Tim 2:1; "encourage" in Act 15:32; Col 4:8; 1 Thes 4:18; "comfort" in Mt 2:18; 5:4; Act 20:12; 2 Cor 1:4; 7:6; 2 Thes 2:17. Used 109 times. In some verses, more than one of these senses is appropriate. GK *4151*.
14. Or, "encouragement, comfort". Related to the previous verb, and to "helper" in Jn 14:16. Like teaching, this takes place on a personal and group basis, formal and informal, on various subjects. On this word, see "encouragement" in Act 4:36.
15. Or, "giving a share of " one's things. Same word as in Lk 3:11; Eph 4:28. Elsewhere only as "impart" to spiritual needs in Rom 1:11; 1 Thes 2:8. GK *3556*. Paul is referring to giving proceeding from God-given faith, not human philanthropy.
16. Paul changes from referring to the sphere in which the gift is used, to the manner in which it is used, using the same Greek word.
17. Or, "simplicity, sincerity". Same word as in 2 Cor 8:2; 9:11, 13. Elsewhere only as "simplicity" in 2 Cor 1:12; and "sincerity" in 2 Cor 11:3; Eph 6:5; Col 3:22. Here, some think Paul means with "simplicity", without any self-seeking motive, respect of persons, hidden purposes; others, with "sincere concern"; others, with "generosity". Related to "generously" in Jam 1:5, and to "single" in Mt 6:22. GK *605*.
18. Or, "managing, ruling, directing, being at the head, taking the lead, standing before, presiding over". Used of elders. Same word as in 1 Thes 5:12; 1 Tim 3:4, 5, 12; 5:17. Elsewhere only as "take the lead" in Tit 3:8, 14. GK *4613*. Related to "benefactor" in 16:2. Some think this refers to leading in all kinds of Christian works; others, to elders.
19. This word is used of Jesus meeting physical needs for healing in Mt 9:27; of forgiving debt, Mt 18:33; and of God "having mercy on" us, Rom 9:15, 18; 11:30-32. Used 29 times. GK *1796*. Related to "almsgiving" in Mt 6:2. Related to "mercy" in Mt 9:13, which is used of what the Good Samaritan did, Lk 10:37. God desires it, Mt 9:13, 23:23. Related to "merciful" in Mt 5:7. Some think this refers to caring for the sick, aged, dying, and needy based on faith-driven motives, not human philanthropy.
20. Used only here. GK *2660*. Related to "cheerful" in 2 Cor 9:7.
21. What follows is clearly a series of exhortations, so most make them all commands. Here, they are given as Paul wrote them. Since he has given no clear indication that he has changed subjects, they are listed as a continuation of what he wants to "say to everyone being among you", v 3. "Love" here is a noun, "affectionate" is an adjective.
22. Or, "genuine, without hypocrisy, unhypocritical". It is the negative of the word "hypocrisy" in Gal 2:13. Elsewhere only in 2 Cor 6:6; 1 Tim 1:5; 2 Tim 1:5; Jam 3:17; 1 Pet 1:22. GK *537*.
23. Or, "joining *oneself to,* associating *with*". On this word, see "join" in 1 Cor 6:16.
24. Or, "warmly devoted, tenderly loving, dearly loving". Used of love between family members. Used only here. GK *5816*.
25. Paul may mean "leading the way for one another in honor", or "being first to honor one another", or "esteeming one another more highly in honor". Used only here. GK *4605*. Related to "regarding" in Phil 2:3.
26. This adjective is elsewhere only as "lazy" in Mt 25:26, and "troublesome" in Phil 3:1. GK *3891*. Related to "to delay" in Act 9:38.
27. This participle is used of Apollos in Act 18:25. Or, "boiling *in the* Spirit".
28. Same word as in Gal 6:6 (with teachers); Phil 4:15 ("partnered" with Paul); Rom 15:27 (in spiritual things). On this word, see 2 Jn 11.
29. Some manuscripts omit this word {C}. "Persecute" is the same word as "pursue" in v 13.
30. Or, "calling a curse upon". Same two words as in "Bless those cursing you" in Lk 6:28. Elsewhere only in Mt 25:41; Mk 11:21; Jam 3:9. GK *2933*. Related to the noun "curse" in Gal 3:10.

A. Heb 8:6, more excellent B. 1 Cor 12:10 C. 2 Cor 8:16, earnestness D. 1 Tim 5:10b E. Heb 13:1 F. 1 Tim 5:17 G. Rom 6:6, are slaves H. 2 Cor 13:11 J. Jam 1:12 K. Rev 7:14 L. Act 2:42 M. Tit 3:14 N. 1 Pet 1:16, holy O. 1 Cor 14:1 P. Heb 13:2 Q. Lk 6:28

	8C. *I say* to rejoice^A with rejoicing *ones,* to weep^B with weeping *ones*	15
	9C. *To be* thinking^C the same *thing*¹ toward one another, not thinking^C lofty² *things*, but being carried-along-with³ the lowly⁴. Do not be wise⁵ among yourselves⁶	16
	10C. *To be* giving-back^D evil for evil^E *to* no one	17
	11C. *To be* providing-for⁷ good^F *things* in the sight of all people^G, °living-in-peace⁸ with all people if possible— *as far as* from you⁹	18
	12C. *To* not *be* avenging^H yourselves, beloved^J, but give *a* place¹⁰ *to* the wrath^K *of God.* For it has been written—	19
	1D. "Vengeance¹¹ *is for* Me, **I** will repay^L, says *the* Lord" [Deut 32:35]	
	2D. "But¹² if your enemy is hungry, feed^M him. If he is thirsty, give-a-drink *to* him. For doing this, you will heap coals *of* fire¹³ upon his head" [Prov 25:21-22]	20
	13C. Do not be overcome^N by evil,¹⁴ but be overcoming evil with good^O	21
3B.	Let every soul^P be subject¹⁵ *to* superior¹⁶ authorities^Q	13:1
	1C. For there is no authority^Q except by¹⁷ God. And the existing^R *ones*¹⁸ are established¹⁹ by God. So then the *one* opposing²⁰ the authority has resisted²¹ the ordinance²² *of* God. And the *ones* having resisted will receive judgment²³ *on* themselves	2
	1D. For²⁴ the rulers^S are not *a* fear^T *to* good^O work, but *to* evil²⁵	3
	2D. Now do you want to not be fearing the authority? Be doing good^O, and you will have praise^U from him²⁶— °for he is God's servant^V *to* you for good^O	4
	3D. But if you are doing evil^E, be fearing! For he does not bear²⁷ the sword²⁸ in-vain²⁹— for he is God's servant^V, *an* avenger³⁰ for wrath³¹ *on* the *one* practicing^W evil^E	
	2C. Therefore *it is a* necessity^X to be subject— not only because of the wrath, but also because of the conscience³²	5
	3C. For because of this³³ also you pay^Y tributes³⁴. For they are ministers³⁵ *of* God devoting-themselves^Z to this very *thing*³⁶	6
	4C. Give-back³⁷ *to* all *authorities* the *things* owed³⁸— the tribute *to* the *one* owed the tribute, the tax³⁹ *to* the *one* owed the tax, the fear⁴⁰ *to* the *one* owed the fear, the honor^AA *to* the *one* owed the honor	7

1. Paul uses this same phrase in Rom 15:5; 2 Cor 13:11; Phil 2:2; 4:2. The same idea is in 1 Cor 1:10.
2. Or, "high, proud". Same phrase as in 11:20.
3. Or, "being accommodating to; associating with". That is, give up lofty thinking about yourself and allow yourself to be carried along with the lowly. Elsewhere only as "carried away by" in the sense of "led astray" in Gal 2:13; 2 Pet 3:17. GK *5270*.
4. Or, "humble". Some take the grammar to mean "lowly *things*". Be carried along with the lowly things of life, the humble tasks. Be accommodated to humble things. Others take it to mean "lowly *people*". Be associating with the lowly people. Both are true, and fitting contrasts with "thinking lofty things". On this word, see Jam 1:9.
5. This word (on which see Mt 7:24) is the same root word as "thinking" just used twice.
6. Same words as in Rom 11:25. The Corinthians did this, 1 Cor 4:10; 2 Cor 11:19 (same word for "wise").
7. Or, "planning for, taking thought for". On this word, see 2 Cor 8:21. Related to "provision" in 13:14.
8. Or, "being at peace". Elsewhere only in Mk 9:50; 2 Cor 13:11; 1 Thes 5:13. GK *1644*.
9. This is an idiom, "the from you *part*". That is, to the extent your part reaches.
10. On the phrase "give *a* place", see Eph 4:27.
11. On this word, see "punishment" in 2 Thes 1:8. Related to "avenge" earlier, and to "avenger" in 13:4.
12. Some manuscripts say "Therefore" {N}.
13. Paul is referring to the burning of shame for their behavior that will be caused by returning good for evil.
14. That is, the evil done to you. Do not be controlled and directed by it, but take the lead yourself with good.
15. Or, "submit *himself*". On this word, see Eph 5:21. Same general command as in Tit 3:1; 1 Pet 2:13.
16. That is, governmental authorities. This is a participle, to authorities "being superior". Same word as in 1 Pet 2:13. On this word, see "surpassing" in Phil 2:3. Related to "superiority" in 1 Tim 2:2.
17. Even Pharaoh, 9:17. Some manuscripts say "from" {N}.
18. Some manuscripts say "authorities" {N}.
19. Or, "put in place, stationed, arranged, arrayed, appointed, assigned". This is a participle, they "are having been established", they stand established by God. Elsewhere only as "ordered" in Mt 28:16; "placed" in Lk 7:8; "appoint" in Act 13:48; 15:2; 28:23; 1 Cor 16:15; and "assign" in Act 22:10. GK *5435*.
20. Or, "resisting", but not the same word as follows. It means "to establish, arrange, set oneself in array against". The root word is "establish" in v 1. Elsewhere only in Act 18:6; Jam 4:6; 5:6; 1 Pet 5:5. GK *530*.
21. Or, "stood against". On this word, see Eph 6:13.
22. Or, "decree, direction", that which is ordered or commanded. The authority of government is God's decree. Paul is commanding subordination to the authority of government, however that is expressed in your nation. In some nations, this includes active involvement in government. In other nations, citizens have no input. Elsewhere only as "directions" in Act 7:53. GK *1408*. Related to "edict" in Heb 11:23, and to the verb "to direct" in 1 Cor 7:17.
23. That is, from God whose ordinance was resisted. Secondarily, from the authorities, if you are caught. On this word, see Jn 9:39.
24. Paul explains and applies God's ordinance regarding government in general, dealing here with none of the exceptions.
25. That is, civil evil, crime, criminal wrong. Same word as in v 4. On this word, see 3 Jn 11. Some manuscripts have these words plural {N}, so that it says "to good works, but *to* evil *ones*".
26. Or, "it". That is, the authority mentioned earlier in this verse. Praise for good is the general rule. But Paul also was persecuted for good— for being a Christian. He does not address this here. Note 1 Pet 3:13-14; 4:13-16.
27. Or, "wear". On this word, see 1 Cor 15:49.
28. Governments have God's authority to punish evil to the fullest extent— including death. A government may choose not to punish evil with death, but this does not change the fact that it has this authority from God, and serves as His servant when carrying it out. Whether or not a government should choose not to use the sword is not addressed here.
29. That is, for no reason. On this word, see Col 2:18.
30. Elsewhere only in 1 Thes 4:6. GK *1690*. Related to "avenging" and "vengeance" in 12:19.
31. That is, for the purpose of carrying out God's wrath, as His servant. On this word, see Rev 16:19.
32. On this word, see Act 23:1. We are to submit out of fear of God's wrath expressed through His servant (government), and because of our conscience toward God based on His will. In general, these two are in agreement. But in exceptional cases, which Paul does not speak to here, the latter must always be preeminent. If government requires us to disobey God, then we must obey God and suffer the consequences, like Peter (Act 5:28-29) and Daniel (Dan 6). Early Christians suffered death rather than deny Christ.
33. Some think Paul means because such authorities are serving God's purposes (v 1-5); others, because of wrath and conscience (v 5).
34. Same word as in v 7. Tributes were paid by foreigners to a ruling state, such as that paid by Israel to Rome. Elsewhere only in Lk 20:22; 23:2. GK *5843*.
35. Or, "public servants", as when we say prime minister or defense minister, etc. Note that Paul is talking here about the Roman government that ruled the world from the city to which this letter is addressed, a foreign power that conquered and subjugated his nation and took away their freedom and right of self-government. Yet Paul says the Romans are "servants of God". This word was was used of priests in the OT. Elsewhere only in Rom 15:16 (of Paul); Phil 2:25 (of Epaphroditus); Heb 1:7 (of angels); and Heb 8:2 (of Jesus). GK *3313*. Related to the verb in 15:27.
36. Some think Paul means serving the public good, and God's purposes (v 1-4); others, collecting the taxes.
37. Some manuscripts say "Therefore give..." {K}. On this word, see "render" in Mt 16:27.
38. Or, "due". This noun is rendered "owed" to show its relation to "owing" in v 8. On this word, see "due" in 1 Cor 7:3.
39. This refers to taxes, duties, tolls, etc. paid to your own country. Here the local government is addressed. Same word as in Mt 17:25. GK *5465*.
40. Or, "respect". On this word, see Eph 5:21.

A. 2 Cor 13:11 B. Jn 11:33 C. Rom 8:5 D. Mt 16:27, render E. 3 Jn 11 F. 1 Tim 5:10a G. Mt 4:4, mankind H. 2 Cor 10:6, punish J. Mt 3:17 K. Rev 16:19 L. 2 Thes 1:6 M. 1 Cor 13:3, dole out N. Rev 2:7 O. 1 Tim 5:10b P. Jam 5:20 Q. Rev 6:8 R. Mt 26:26, is S. Rev 1:5 T. Eph 5:21 U. 1 Cor 4:5 V. 1 Cor 3:5 W. Rom 2:1 X. 1 Cor 7:26 Y. Rev 10:7, finished Z. Act 2:42 AA. 1 Tim 5:17

4B. Be owing[1] nothing *to* anyone except to be loving one another. For the *one* loving the other[2] has fulfilled[A] *the* Law   8

    1C. For the *saying* "You shall not commit-adultery[B], you shall not murder[C], you shall not steal[3], you shall not covet[D]" [Ex 20:13-17], and if *there is* any other commandment[E], is summed-up[F] in this saying[G]— in the[4] "You shall love your neighbor[H] as[5] yourself" [Lev 19:18]   9
    2C. Love does not work[J] harm[6] *to* the neighbor. Therefore love *is the* fulfillment[7] *of the* Law   10

5B. And *do* this,[8] knowing the time, that *it is* already *the* hour *for* you[9] to arise[10] from sleep[K]   11

    1C. For now our salvation[L] *is* nearer than when we believed
    2C. The night is advanced[M], and the day has drawn-near[N]   12
    3C. Therefore let us lay-aside[11] the works *of* the darkness, and let us put-on the weapons[12] *of* the light. °Let us walk properly[13] as in[14] *the* day   13

        1D. Not *in* revelries[15] and drunkenness[16], not *in* beds[17] and sensualities[O], not *in* strife[P] and jealousy[Q]
        2D. But put-on[18] the Lord Jesus Christ, and do not be making provision[19] *for* the flesh— for *its* desires[R]   14

6B. Now be accepting[20] the *one* being weak[21] *in* the faith[22]— [but] not for disputes[23] *about* opinions[24]   14:1

    1C. One has faith to eat all *things,* but the *one* being weak[S] eats vegetables[25]   2

        1D. Let not the *one* eating be treating-with-contempt[26] the *one* not eating   3
        2D. And let not the *one* not eating be judging[T] the *one* eating— for God accepted him. °Who are **you**, the *one* judging[27] *a* household-servant[28] belonging-to-another[U]?   4

            1E. *To his* own master[V] he stands or falls
            2E. And he will stand[29], for the Lord[30] is able to make him stand

    2C. For[31] one judges[T] *a* day beyond *a* day[32], but another judges every day *alike*. Let each *one* be fully-convinced[33] in *his* own mind[W]   5

        1D. The *one* thinking[34] *as to* the day, is thinking *for the* Lord[35]   6
        2D. And the *one* eating, is eating *for the* Lord— for he gives-thanks[X] *to* God
        3D. And the *one* not eating, is not eating *for the* Lord— and he gives-thanks[X] *to* God[36]
        4D. For[37] none *of* us[38] lives *for* himself, and none dies *for* himself. °For if we live, we live *for* the Lord; and if we die, we die *for* the Lord. Therefore[39] if we live and if we die, we are the Lord's   7-8

            1E. For Christ died and came-to-life[40] for this— that He might be-Lord[Y] both *of* dead and living *ones*   9

        5D. But[41] why are **you** judging[T] your brother? Or why also are **you** treating your brother with contempt?   10

1. Related to the word in v 7. The "owing" and the "loving" here refer to the same group of people. Thus, Paul is referring to our personal relations with individuals. Paul's main point here is that love is a debt we always owe to all, which he shows by contrast to debts we can pay off. He is not giving an absolute rule, "Never borrow anything from your neighbor". Paul means "Keep all your balances (monetary and otherwise) with other people clear or paid up as agreed— except love, which is never clear or paid up". On this word, see "ought" in 1 Jn 4:11.
2. That is, the other person, in the broadest of terms. Same word as "other" commandment in v 9. GK *2283*.
3. Some manuscripts add "you shall not bear false witness" {B}.
4. Some manuscripts omit "in the" {C}, which introduces the quotation.
5. Or, "like". See Mt 19:19.
6. Or, "evil", civil or personal. On this word, see "evil" in 3 Jn 11.
7. Or, "fulfilling". On this word, see "fullness" in Col 1:19.
8. Paul is probably referring to all of chapters 12-13 to this point. This is a motive for all of it.
9. Some manuscripts say "us" {B}.
10. Or, "be raised, be awakened". On this word, see "arose" in Mt 28:6.
11. Or, "put aside, put away", like a garment. Same word as in Act 7:58; Eph 4:22, 25; Col 3:8; Heb 12:1; Jam 1:21; 1 Pet 2:1. Elsewhere only as "put away" in Mt 14:3. GK *700*. Some manuscripts say "let us throw off " {A}.
12. Or, "tools, instruments". Same word as in Jn 18:3; 2 Cor 6:7; 10:4. Elsewhere only as "instruments" in Rom 6:13. GK *3960*. Related to "arm yourselves" in 1 Pet 4:1, and "full armor" in Eph 6:11.
13. Or, "decently, with propriety". Elsewhere only in 1 Cor 14:40; 1 Thes 4:12. GK *2361*.
14. Or, "during". Some think Paul means the daytime, as in broad daylight; others, as in the future day with Jesus, when He comes; others, as in the present daylight of the gospel. GK *1877*.
15. This word is used of wild parties with drunken antics and debauchery of all kinds. Elsewhere only in Gal 5:21; 1 Pet 4:3. GK *3269*.
16. This word is plural, and may mean "episodes of drunkenness, drinking bouts". Elsewhere only in Lk 21:34; Gal 5:21. GK *3494*. Related word in Jn 2:10.
17. That is, sex, and in this context, illicit sex, orgies. Same word as in 9:10. On this word, see Heb 13:4.
18. Or, "dress in, wear, clothe-*yourself*-in", like a garment. Same word as in v 12; Mt 6:25; 27:31; Mk 6:9; 15:20; Lk 8:27; 12:22; 15:22; 24:49; Act 12:21; 1 Cor 15:53, 54; Gal 3:27; Eph 4:24; 6:11, 14; Col 3:10, 12; 1 Thes 5:8. Elsewhere only as "dress in" in Mt 22:11; Mk 1:6; Rev 1:13; 15:6; 19:14. GK *1907*.
19. Or, "foresight, forethought, plan". Elsewhere only as "foresight" in Act 24:2. GK *4630*. Related to "providing for" in 12:17.
20. Same word as in v 3; 15:7; and as "welcome" in Act 28:2. It also means "take, take aside". Used 12 times. GK *4689*.
21. Such a person is not fully aware of the implications of their faith for their behavior, and is carrying over things from their former way of life— observing days, rituals, rules about foods, etc. Some think the weaker brother here is the Jewish Christian who was unable to leave his former traditions completely behind. This person would "judge" the Gentile Christian for not following these traditions, and the Gentile Christian would "treat him with contempt" for his opinions. That the Jewish Christians were the ones not being accepted may be the reason Paul concludes as he does in 15:7-12. But we do not know the precise circumstances. There are other views. Consult the commentaries. In any case, neither person is saying their course must be followed to be saved, as in Act 15:1. GK *820*.
22. Or, "*in* faith". The faith of these people is weak in that it does not allow them to accept or enjoy their full freedom in Christ.
23. This word means "discernments, judgments", and negatively, the "disputes, quarrels" that result from this behavior. On this word, see "discernment" in 1 Cor 12:10. Related to "dispute" in Act 11:2.
24. Or, "reasonings, thoughts, doubts". On this word, see "thoughts" in Jam 2:4. That is, for the purpose of correcting the weaker one's opinions about matters of Christian living by disputing with that person based on your knowledge.
25. An occasion of eating may be in view here, such as a banquet attended by both groups of believers. The weak person's faith or beliefs lead them to conclude that God does not want them to eat the meat, perhaps out of fear of defilement. This person feels the meat has a negative spiritual significance and must be avoided. The strong person's faith leads them to put no significance in the matter. Paul addresses both, the strong first.
26. Or, "despising, disregarding". Same word as in v 10. Used of the Pharisee in Lk 18:9. On this word, see 1 Thes 5:20.
27. Paul continues addressing the one "judging". The two are addressed again using the same two verbs in v 10.
28. Or, "slave", generally. Same word as in Lk 16:13; Act 10:7. Elsewhere only as "servants" in 1 Pet 2:18. GK *3860*. Related to "house".
29. Or, "he will be caused to stand, made to stand". Same word as "make stand" next. On this word, see "standing" in Mk 13:14.
30. Or, "Master". Same word as "master" earlier in the verse. On this word, see "master" in Mt 8:2. Some manuscripts say "God" {A}.
31. Paul uses this word to assert his next point. It may be rendered "Moreover". GK *1142*. Some manuscripts omit this word {C}.
32. This person feels one day has a positive spiritual significance beyond "ordinary" days, and must be observed as such. Perhaps Paul is referring to the Sabbath, or some other "holy" day on the Jewish calendar. Compare Gal 4:10; Col 2:16.
33. Each should follow the course proceeding from their own faith in Christ. On this word, see "fulfill" in Lk 1:1.
34. On this word, see Rom 8:5. This person thinks of the day in a special way, and honors it more highly, out of a desire to worship God more deeply. He or she is "intent on" honoring the day in a special way. This is the weak one.
35. Some manuscripts add "and the *one* not thinking *of* the day, does not think *for the* Lord" {N}.
36. In other words, both are making their choices for the right reasons. Both are living for the Lord.
37. Paul generalizes from his illustrations in v 6. We Christians are all living for the Lord, in life and death.
38. That is, none of us Christians— weak or strong.
39. Therefore the point is that we all are the Lord's— in all of life's choices, and in death. He is our Lord.
40. Or, "lived, became alive". On this word, see Rev 20:4. This refers to Christ's resurrection. Some manuscripts say "died and rose"; others, "also died and rose and lived" {A}.
41. That is, if we are all the Lord's in life and death (v 9), then why do **you** judge one another?

A. Eph 5:18, filled   B. Mt 5:32   C. Jam 4:2   D. Gal 5:17, desire   E. Mk 12:28   F. Eph 1:10   G. 1 Cor 12:8, word   H. Act 7:27   J. Mt 26:10   K. Jn 11:13, slumber   L. Lk 19:9   M. 2 Tim 2:16   N. Lk 21:28   O. 2 Pet 2:2   P. 1 Cor 1:11, quarrels   Q. 2 Cor 11:2   R. Gal 5:16   S. 2 Tim 4:20, sick   T. Mt 7:1   U. Heb 11:34, foreigner   V. Mt 8:2   W. Rom 7:23   X. Mt 26:27   Y. Rom 7:1, lord over

	1E. For we will all stand before the judgment-seat[1] *of* God[2]. °For it has been written [in Isa 45:23] "*As* **I** live", says *the* Lord, "every knee will bow ***to*** **Me**. And every tongue will confess-out[3] *to* God"	11
	2E. So then,[4] each *of* us will give[A] *an* account[B] for himself *to* God[5]	12
3C. Therefore let us no longer be judging one another. But rather judge[6] this—		13
	1D. Not to be placing[C] *an* opportunity-for-stumbling[7] or *a* cause-of-falling[8] *for* the brother[D]	
	1E. I know[9] and am convinced[E] in *the* Lord Jesus that nothing[10] *is* defiled[11] in itself[12], except *to* the *one* considering[F] anything to be defiled— *to* that *one* it is defiled[13]	14
	2D. For[14] if your brother is grieved[15] because of food[G], you are no longer walking[H] according-to[16] love	15
	3D. Do not be destroying[J] *with*[17] your food[G] that *one* for whom Christ died	
4C. Therefore do not be letting your[18] good[19] *thing* be blasphemed[20]		16
	1D. For the kingdom[K] *of* God is not eating[L] and drinking[M], but righteousness and peace and joy[21] in *the* Holy Spirit	17
	2D. For the *one* serving[22] Christ in this[23] *is* pleasing[N] *to* God and approved[24] *by* people	18
5C. So then, let us be pursuing[25] the *things of* peace[26] and the *things of* edification[27] for one another		19
	1D. Do not be tearing-down[O] the work[28] *of* God for the sake of food[G]	20
	1E. **All *things***[29] *are* clean[30]— but *it is* evil[P] *for* the person[Q] eating[R] *with* an opportunity-for-stumbling[31]	
	2E. *It is* good[S] not to eat[R] meats, nor to drink wine[32], nor *to do anything* by which your brother stumbles[33]	21
	2D. *The* faith[34] which[35] **you** have, be having for[36] yourself in the sight of God	22
	1E. Blessed[T] *is* the *one* not judging[U] himself in[37] what he is approving[38]	

1. Or, "the tribunal". Same word as in 2 Cor 5:10; of Pilate in Mt 27:19; Jn 19:13; of Herod in Act 12:21; of Gallio in Act 18:12, 16, 17; and of Festus in Act 25:6, 10, 17. Elsewhere only as "step" in Act 7:5. GK *1037*.
2. Some manuscripts say "Christ" {B}.
3. Or, "praise", as in 15:9. Same word and idea as in Phil 2:11. On this word, see Jam 5:16.
4. Some manuscripts say "Therefore" {C} instead of "So then".
5. Some manuscripts omit "to God" {C}.
6. That is, in the sense of "determine, decide, resolve". What follows to v 15 is directed at the strong person. Same word as earlier in the verse. On this word, see Mt 7:1.
7. Or, "an occasion to take offense; an occasion to stumble *into sin*". Same word as in 14:20; 1 Cor 8:9. Elsewhere only as "stumbling" in Rom 9:32, 33; 1 Pet 2:8. GK *4682*. Related to "stumble" in Rom 14:21, and the word in 2 Cor 6:3.
8. On this word, see 11:9. The difference is that the "opportunity for stumbling" may cause an accidental fall, an unintentional result. The "cause of falling" is intentional, a consciously chosen thing. In this case, the strong person deliberately proceeds with behavior he knows is objectionable to the weak person, perhaps even in defiance of him. Jesus said it is better to die than to do this, Mt 18:6.
9. Before Paul continues exhorting the strong, he firmly acknowledges his agreement with their position. As to knowledge, they are correct. But there is another way of viewing it besides "in itself", as he goes on to explain.
10. That is, nothing in the category of things under discussion here.
11. Or, "common, impure, ritually defiled" as opposed to "holy". Compare Mk 7:15. On this word, see Heb 10:29.
12. That is, by means of being what it is. Even in the OT, pig was not unclean because it was pig. All things God created are good. It was unclean to the Jews because God said so. Now God says all things are clean.
13. Regardless of what it is in itself and to God, it is defiled to a person who thinks it to be such; it is defiled to their conscience. They make it defiled for themselves, in spite of what God says. The strong person's judgment of their opinions will not help them grow out of it. It may harden them in their weakness, or cause division. Loving acceptance may give them the chance.
14. Some manuscripts say "But" {K}.
15. Or, "distressed, caused pain, caused sorrow". This is not godly sorrow (2 Cor 7:8-11), but self-destructive sorrow. Such people follow the behavior of the strong, without the support of their conscience, apart from their own faith, and afterward suffer under their conscience, and are hindered in their growth and walk with God. On this word, see 2 Cor 7:9.
16. Or, "in accordance with, in harmony with, based on". GK *2848*.
17. Or, "*for*".
18. Some think Paul means "you strong ones"; others, all of you, strong and weak. This word is plural.
19. Some think Paul means your food, your freedom in Christ; others, your salvation; others, the gospel. On this word, see 1 Tim 5:10b.
20. Or, "spoken against". Some think Paul means by outsiders; others, by the weak ones. Thus some think this is addressed to the strong—"Do not let your exercise of freedom cause it to be spoken against by your weaker brother" (as mere self-indulgence, for example). Others think Paul is speaking to both the strong and the weak—"Do not let the gospel (or your salvation) be blasphemed by the unbelievers because of your selfish disputing over your opinions about these matters". On this word, see 1 Tim 6:1.
21. Some think these three things refer to our relationship with God. It is the subjective experience of these three things from God that the strong can take from the weak. Others think they refer to our relationship with one another.
22. That is, serving as a slave to Christ. On this word, see "are slaves" in 6:6.
23. Some think Paul means "in this righteousness, peace, and joy in the Holy Spirit which the kingdom of God is really about"; others, "in this Spirit"; others, "in this way" (foregoing your rights for others). Some manuscripts say "in these *things*" {N}.
24. On this adjective, see 2 Tim 2:15. This is as opposed to being blasphemed, v 16. Related to the word in v 22.
25. On this word, see 1 Cor 14:1. Some manuscripts say "we are pursuing" {D}.
26. That is, belonging to or leading to peace... and edification.
27. Or, "building up". Same word as in 15:2; 1 Cor 14:3, 5, 12, 26; 2 Cor 12:19; Eph 4:29. Elsewhere only as "building up" in 2 Cor 10:8; 13:10; Eph 4:12, 16; and as a "building" in Mt 24:1; Mk 13:1, 2; 1 Cor 3:9; 2 Cor 5:1; Eph 2:21. GK *3869*. Related to "edify" in 1 Cor 14:4.
28. Some think Paul means God's work in the church; others, the work God is doing in the weak one.
29. Paul uses grammar that emphasizes the contrast between the two halves of this sentence.
30. This phrase is similar to 1 Cor 6:12, "All things are lawful".
31. Some think Paul means for the strong person whose eating is accompanied with an opportunity for others to stumble; others, for the weak person who eats in violation of his conscience. Same word as in v 13. Related to "stumbles" in v 21.
32. Some think this refers to an additional limitation the weak placed on themselves; others think Paul is generalizing the issue (similar to 1 Cor 10:31), without necessarily implying this was really an issue for them.
33. Or, "takes offense". Same word as in Jn 11:9, 10; Rom 9:32; 1 Pet 2:8. Elsewhere only as "strikes against" in Mt 4:6; 7:27; Lk 4:11. GK *4684*. Some manuscripts add "or is caused to fall or is made weak" {B}. Related to the word in v 13.
34. Paul is referring to the faith to eat all things (v 2), the faith of the strong person.
35. Some manuscripts omit this word {C}, so that it means either "The faith you have" or "Do you have faith?"
36. Or, "in the interest of, in relation to". GK *2848*.
37. Or, "by". GK *1877*.
38. On this word, see 12:2. Some take this to mean "Blessed is the strong person who does not judge himself over these things like the weak one does"; others, "Blessed is the strong person who does not approve the wrong things, bringing judgment on himself".

A. Eph 1:22　B. Act 19:40　C. Act 19:21, put　D. Act 16:40　E. 1 Jn 3:19, persuade　F. Rom 3:28　G. Mk 7:19　H. Heb 13:9　J. 1 Cor 1:18, perish　K. Mt 3:2　L. Mt 6:19　M. Col 2:16　N. Eph 5:10　O. Mt 24:2　P. 3 Jn 11　Q. Mt 4:4, mankind　R. Act 10:13　S. 1 Tim 5:10a　T. Lk 6:20　U. Mt 7:1

| Romans 14:23 | 566 | Verse |

        2E. But the *one* doubting[1] has been condemned[A] if he eats, because *it was* not from faith.   23
And everything[2] which *is* not from faith[3] is sin[4]

        3E. But **we**— the strong[5] *ones*— ought[6] to be carrying[7] the weaknesses[8] *of* the *ones* not-   15:1
strong[9], and not to be pleasing[B] ourselves[10]

    3D. Let each *of* us be pleasing[B] his neighbor[C] for good[D], toward [his] edification[E]   2

        1E. For even Christ did not please[B] Himself, but just as it has been written [in Ps 69:9],   3
"The reproaches[F] *of* the *ones* reproaching[G] You fell upon Me"

            1F. For all that was written-before[H] was written for our instruction[J], in order that   4
we might have hope through endurance[K] and through[11] the encouragement[L] *of*
the Scriptures

        4D. Now may the God *of* endurance[K] and encouragement[L] grant you to be thinking the same[12]   5
thing among one another according to Christ Jesus[13], *in order that with-one-accord[M]   6
you may with one mouth be glorifying[N] the God and Father *of* our Lord Jesus Christ

  6C. Therefore, be accepting[14] one-another[15], just as Christ also accepted you[16]— for[17] *the* glory *of* God   7

    1D. For[18] I say *that* Christ[19] has become[20] *a* servant[21] *of the* circumcised[22] on behalf of *the*   8
truth *of* God—

        1E. So that *He might* confirm[O] the promises[P] *of* the fathers[23]
        2E. And[24] the Gentiles *might* glorify[N] God for *His* mercy, just as it has been written—   9

            1F. "For this reason I will praise[25] You among *the* Gentiles, and I will sing-praise[Q]
to Your name" [Ps 18:49]
            2F. And again he says, "Celebrate[R], Gentiles, with His people" [Deut 32:43]   10
            3F. And again, "All Gentiles, be praising[26] the Lord, and let all the peoples praise[27]   11
Him" [Ps 117:1]
            4F. And again Isaiah says, "There will be the root[S] of Jesse, even the *One* rising-up[28]   12
to rule[29] *the* Gentiles. *The* Gentiles will put-*their*-hope[T] upon Him" [Isa 11:10]

  7B. Now may the God *of* hope[30] fill[U] you *with* all joy and peace in believing, so that you *may* be   13
abounding[V] in hope by *the* power *of the* Holy Spirit

5A. Now I am convinced[W], my brothers— even I myself concerning you— that you yourselves also are full[31]   14
of goodness, having been filled[U] *with* all knowledge, being able also to admonish[X] one another

  1B. But I wrote more-boldly[32] *to* you[33]— in part[34] as reminding you again— because of the grace having   15
been given *to* me by God *so that I *might* be *a* minister[Y] *of* Christ Jesus[35] to the Gentiles   16

    1C. Performing-priestly-service-for[36] the good-news[Z] *of* God in order that the offering[37] *of* the
Gentiles[AA] might become acceptable[38], having been sanctified[39] by *the* Holy Spirit

  2B. I then have *this* boasting[40] in Christ Jesus[41] *as to* the *things* pertaining to God. *For I will not dare[BB]   17-18
to speak anything *of things* which Christ did not accomplish[42] through me *in* word and deed for[43]
the obedience[44] *of* the Gentiles

1. This refers to the weak person, the one not having "the faith which you have" regarding the matter. On this word, see Jam 1:6.
2. Some think Paul means "everything in regard to issues like this"; others, "everything, period", so that he is giving the broad general principle (like Heb 11:6) which includes the matters in this context.
3. Some think Paul means "proceeding from Christian faith", so that he is giving the general principle that all actions outside of Christian faith are sin, of which the actions here are one example. Others think he is referring to the faith guiding our conscience, so that he is giving the broad principle that everything done in violation of our conscience is sin, including the things here. Others think he means the faith that permits us to exercise our freedom in these matters, as "faith" is used in v 1, 2, 22, 23, so that he means everything done while doubting whether Christ permits it is sin.
4. Some manuscripts have 16:25-27 here {A}. See 16:25.
5. Or, "powerful, able". That is, the spiritually strong. The strong would agree completely with 14:22-23. This is the point Paul also wants them to see, the one that breaks the deadlock, the one they were not seeing. 14:23 is not just "their problem". GK *1543*.
6. Same word as "owing" in 13:8. This is a debt we owe.
7. Or, "bearing, bearing with". The strong are not to just tolerate the weak, but to carry, support and help them. Same word as in Gal 6:2, "carry one another's burdens". Paul himself approaches life this way, 1 Cor 10:31-33. On this word, see Mt 8:17.
8. Used only here. GK *821*. Related to "weak" in 14:1, 2; and "weakness" in Mt 8:17.
9. Or, "powerless, not able". Same word as "strong" earlier, with a negative prefix. This is a broader term, including, but not limited to the "weak" ones of 14:1. Same word as "powerless" in Act 14:8. On this word, see "impossible" in Heb 6:4.
10. That is, pleasing ourselves without regard to the impact of our behavior on others.
11. Some manuscripts omit this word {N}.
12. Paul is not praying the Romans will agree about the foods and days, but about their treatment of one another, eliminating the judging and the treating with contempt mentioned in 14:3. On "think the same *thing*", see 12:16.
13. Paul may mean "according to His will"; or, "in accordance with His example and commands"; or "in relation to Christ Jesus". "According to" is GK *2848*.
14. This is Paul's conclusion of this discussion. He repeats the same word he began with in 14:1.
15. Same word as 14:13, 19. GK *253*.
16. Some manuscripts say "us" {A}.
17. Some think Paul means "accept one another... for..."; others, "accepted you for..."; others, both.
18. Some think these verses imply that the Jewish Christians were the weak ones not being accepted. Others think both groups may have been composed of former Jews and Gentiles. Some manuscripts say "Now" {K}.
19. Some manuscripts say "Jesus Christ" {K}.
20. Some manuscripts say "became" {N}.
21. Or, "minister". Related to the verb Jesus used of Himself in Mt 20:28. On this word, see 1 Cor 3:5.
22. That is, the Jews. On this word, see Eph 2:11.
23. That is, the promises belonging to Abraham, Isaac and Jacob.
24. Others take this as a second thing Paul says, "For I say *that* Christ has become...; but *that* the Gentiles glorify".
25. On this word, see "confess out" in Jam 5:16. Not related to the word in v 11.
26. Elsewhere only in Lk 2:13, 20; 19:37; Act 2:47; 3:8, 9; Rev 19:5. GK *140*. Related words in Heb 13:15; Mt 21:16.
27. Or, "commend, approve, compliment". This word is different but related to "praising" earlier in this verse. Elsewhere only in Lk 16:8; 1 Cor 11:2; 17, 22. GK *2046*. Related to the word in 1 Cor 4:5. Some manuscripts say "and all peoples, praise Him" {N}.
28. Or, "standing up". On this word, see Lk 18:33.
29. Or, "be ruler *of*". Same word as in Mk 10:42. Elsewhere it is used 84 times meaning "to begin". GK *806*. Related to "ruler" in Rev 1:5, and "beginning in Col 1:18.
30. That is, the One granting us hope, the source of hope, as in "God of endurance" (v 5) and "God of peace" (v 33).
31. Elsewhere only in Mt 23:28; Jn 19:29; 21:11; Rom 1:29; Jam 3:8, 17; 2 Pet 2:14. GK *3550*. Not related to "filled" next.
32. Or, "more daringly". That is, more boldly than the Romans may have expected. Or, "very boldly". Used only here. GK *5529*. Related to "dare" in v 18.
33. Some manuscripts add "brothers" {N}.
34. This is the Greek position of "in part". Some take it with what follows, as here. Paul wrote partially to remind the Romans and partially for the reason he states in v 23-24. Others take this with what precedes. He "wrote more boldly in part", that is, in some parts of the book, such as chapter 14. On "in part", see 11:25.
35. Some manuscripts say "Jesus Christ" {K}.
36. Or, "serving as priest for". Used only here. GK *2646*. Paul applies the word describing the work of priests who offered sacrifices in the temple to his work in connection with the gospel. He is doing temple duties in God's spiritual temple. Related to "priesthood" (Heb 7:11), "priest", "temple", "temple duties" (1 Cor 9:13). Not related to "minister" earlier.
37. On this word, see Act 21:26. That is, in order that the offering to God consisting of the Gentiles may become acceptable to Him. In calling them an offering, some think Paul is thinking of Isa 66:20, where the same concept occurs. Some think Paul means the Gentiles are his own offering; others, that they offer themselves to God.
38. Or, "welcome". Same word as in 15:31; 2 Cor 8:12; 1 Pet 2:5. Elsewhere only as "very acceptable" in 2 Cor 6:2. GK *2347*. Related to "acceptable" in Lk 4:19.
39. Or, "made holy, set apart [to God]". On this word, see Heb 10:29. This word refers back to "offering".
40. That is, this act of boasting by Paul just written in v 16, as to his God-given ministry for Christ. On this noun, see 2 Cor 7:4. His boasting is in Christ Jesus, who made him a minister to the Gentiles and is working through him. Or, "*my* boasting". Literally "the boasting" just given, but some manuscripts omit "the" {C}.
41. Some manuscripts say "Jesus Christ" {K}.
42. On this word, see "work out" in Phil 2:12. Stated positively, it would be "For I will dare only to speak of what Christ accomplished through me".
43. Or, "for the purpose of, leading to, resulting in". On this word, see "resulting in" in 5:16.
44. That is, the obeying of what they hear. On this word, see 16:26.

A. 1 Cor 11:32 B. 1 Thes 2:4 C. Act 7:27 D. 1 Tim 5:10b E. Rom 14:19 F. Heb 10:33 G. 1 Pet 4:14 H. Gal 3:1, portray J. 1 Tim 5:17, teaching K. Jam 1:3 L. Act 4:36 M. Act 1:14 N. Rom 8:30 O. 1 Cor 0:6 P. 1 Jn 2:25 Q. Eph 5:19, make melody R. Rev 12:12 S. Rev 22:16 T. Jn 5:45 U. Eph 5:18 V. 2 Cor 8:2 W. 1 Jn 3:19, persuade X. Col 1:28 Y. Rom 13:6 Z. 1 Cor 15:1 AA. Act 15:23 BB. 2 Cor 11:21

Romans 15:19	568	Verse

      1C. By[1] *the* power *of* signs and wonders[2]   19
      2C. B*y the* power *of the* Spirit *of* God[3]

  3B. So-that[4] from Jerusalem and around as far as Illyricum,[5] I have completed[6] the good-news[A] *of* Christ, and *was* thus[7] being ambitious[8] to be announcing-the-good-news[B] where Christ was not named[9], in order that I might not be building[C] upon *a* foundation[D] belonging-to-another[E]   20

      1C. But just as it has been written [in Isa 52:15], "*Ones to* whom it was not declared[F] concerning Him will see[G], and they who have not heard will understand[10]"   21

  4B. Therefore indeed I was hindered[H] *as to* many *things*[11] *from* coming to you. •But now no longer having *a* place[J] in these regions, and having *a* yearning[12] for many years *that I should* come to you• whenever I am proceeding into Spain— [13]   22-23
                                                                                                                                                  24

      1C. For[14] I hope, while proceeding-through[K], to see you and to be sent-forward[15] there by you, if I may first be filled[16] in part[17] *with* your *company*
      2C. But now I am proceeding to Jerusalem, serving[18] the saints[L]   25

          1D. For Macedonia and Achaia[19] were well-pleased[20] to make *a* certain contribution[21] for the poor[M] *among* the saints in Jerusalem   26
          2D. For they were well-pleased, and[22] they are their debtors[23]   27

              1E. For if the Gentiles shared[24] *in* their spiritual[N] *things*, they are indebted[O] also to minister[25] *to* them in fleshly[26] *things*

      3C. Having then completed[P] this, and having sealed[27] this fruit[Q] *to* them, I will go through you into Spain   28
      4C. And I know that while coming to you, I will come in *the* fullness[R] *of the* blessing[S] *of* Christ[28]   29

  5B. Now I appeal-to[T] you, brothers[29], through our Lord Jesus Christ, and through the love *of* the Spirit[30], to struggle-with[31] me in *your* prayers to God for me—   30

      1C. That I may be delivered[32] from the *ones* disobeying[U] in Judea   31
      2C. And *that* my service[33] for Jerusalem may prove-to-be[34] acceptable[V] *to* the saints[L]
      3C. In order that having come in joy to you by *the* will[W] *of* God[35], I may rest-up-with[36] you   32

  6B. Now the God *of* peace *be* with you all, amen[37]   33

  A. Now I commend[38] *to* you our sister Phoebe— *she* being also[39] *a* servant[40] *of* the church in Cenchrea[41]—•in order that you may receive[X] her in *the* Lord worthily[Y] *of* the saints[L], and may stand-by[42] her in whatever matter[Z] she may be having-need *of* you. For she herself indeed became[43] *a* benefactor[44] *of* many, and *of* me myself   16:1 / 2

1. That is, "accomplish... by".
2. That is, the signs of the apostle, 2 Cor 12:12. On "signs and wonders", see 2 Thes 2:9.
3. Some manuscripts omit "*of* God"; others say "*the* Holy Spirit" {C}.
4. This resumes from v 17 (2B.), summarizing the extent of his God-given ministry.
5. In modern terms, from Israel up and around the Mediterranean to north of Greece in the area of the Balkans.
6. Or, "fulfilled". Paul has "completed [the announcing of] the good news *about* Christ". "Fully preached" paraphrases this. Same word as in Act 13:25; 14:26; and as "fulfill" in Col 1:25. He finished his pioneering ministry in these areas, leaving them for others to build upon. He finished what he was to do. On this word, see "filled" in Eph 5:18.
7. Some take this as looking back, "And thus engaged in this work". Others take this word ("thus, so, in this manner, as follows") as referring to what follows, and begin a new sentence with v 20, "And in this manner *I was* being ambitious— to announce...". On this word, see "so" in Jn 3:16. Some manuscripts say "Christ. And thus I am ambitious..." {N}.
8. Or, "aspiring, making it my ambition, pursuing as my ambition". Elsewhere only in 2 Cor 5:9; 1 Thes 4:11. GK *5818*.
9. That is, called upon in faith, acknowledged, confessed. On this word, see 2 Tim 2:19.
10. Same word as in Mt 13:13.
11. Or, "many *times*".
12. Used only here. GK *2163*. Related to "yearn for" in 1 Pet 2:2.
13. Paul does not complete this sentence. He takes the subject up again in v 28. Some manuscripts do complete it, adding "I will come to you" {A}.
14. Paul explains how the Romans fit in to his yearning for Spain, and his plan to get there.
15. Same word as in Act 15:3; 1 Cor 16:6, 11; 2 Cor 1:16; Tit 3:13; 3 Jn 6. Elsewhere only as "accompany" in Act 20:38; 21:5. GK *4636*.
16. Or, "filled full". That is, may have my fill of your company; may enjoy your company to my satisfaction. Elsewhere only in Lk 1:53; 6:25; Jn 6:12; Act 14:17. GK *1855*.
17. Paul may mean "in part" compared to the fullness of a longer visit; or "for a while". Same idiom as in v 15.
18. Or, "ministering *to*". Not related to "minister" in v 16 or v 27, but to "service" in v 31. On this word, see "ministering" in 1 Pet 4:10 (GK *1354*). Paul calls it a "ministry to the saints" in 2 Cor 8:4 (same word as "service" in v 31).
19. On these examples, see the note on 1 Cor 16:1.
20. On this word, see Mt 17:5. It was their pleasure to do so.
21. Or, "fellowship". That is, a tangible sign of partnership. This contribution is referred to in 2 Cor 8-9; 1 Cor 16:1-4; Act 24:17. Related to the word "shared" in v 27. Same word as in 2 Cor 9:13. On this word, see "fellowship" in 1 Cor 1:9.

22. Or, "indeed".
23. On this word, see 1:14. Related to "indebted" in v 27.
24. On this word, see 2 Jn 11. Related to "contribution" in v 26.
25. Or, "serve". This word is used of priestly service in the temple, and of public service. This is the "priestly service" of the Gentiles. Elsewhere only in Act 13:2; Heb 10:11. GK *3310*. Related to "minister" in Rom 13:6; "service" in 2 Cor 9:12; and "ministering" in Heb 1:14.
26. Or, "material". Same word and concept as in 1 Cor 9:11. On this word, see 1 Cor 3:3.
27. That is, secured and certified in accordance with its intention, v 31b. Some put the emphasis on securing its complete and honest delivery; others, on certifying and ensuring its proper significance in relation to Jewish and Gentile Christians, as Paul envisioned it. Paul seems to have seen it as symbolic of the love and unity of both parts of the church, and seems to have viewed it as part of his mission as an apostle. On this word, see Eph 1:13.
28. Some manuscripts say "blessing *of* the gospel *of* Christ" {A}.
29. Some manuscripts omit this word {C}.
30. Some think Paul means the love originating in the Spirit, proceeding from the Spirit to us, produced in us by the Spirit. Others think he means "the Spirit's love" for us.
31. Or, "fight along with". Used only here. GK *5253*. Related to "struggle" in 1 Tim 4:10. This word indicates Paul is asking for earnestness and effort on the Romans' part.
32. Or, "rescued". On this word, see Col 1:13.
33. Or, "ministry". On this word, see "ministry" in 1 Cor 12:5. Some manuscripts say "gift-bearing" {A}.
34. Or, "come-to-be, become, be". GK *1181*.
35. Some manuscripts say "Jesus Christ"; others, "Christ Jesus"; others, "*the* Lord Jesus". Others say "in order that I may come in joy to you through *the* will *of* God and may rest up *with* you" {C}.
36. Used only here. GK *5265*. Related to "refresh" in Phm 7.
37. Some manuscripts include 16:25-27 here {A}. See 16:25.
38. Same word as in 2 Cor 3:1. Paul is introducing Phoebe to the Romans, she probably being the one who delivered this letter.
39. Or, "indeed". Some manuscripts omit this word {C}. Same word as "indeed" in v 2. GK *2779*.
40. Or, Paul may mean "deaconess". Same word as "deacon" in Phil 1:1. Compare 1 Tim 3:11.
41. This is the eastern seaport of Corinth, facing toward Ephesus and Jerusalem. Elsewhere only in Act 18:18. GK *3020*.
42. Or, "help, aid". Same word as in 2 Tim 4:17, and as "provide" in Act 23:24. It is the word "stand near, stand by" used in a figurative sense, just as in English. On this word, see "present" in 12:1.
43. Or, "was, proved to be". GK *1181*.
44. Or, "patron, protector, helper". Used only here. GK *4706*. Related to "lead" in 12:8.

A. 1 Cor 15:1　B. Act 5:42　C. 1 Cor 14:4, edify　D. 1 Tim 6:19　E. Heb 11:34, foreigners　F. Jn 16:13　G. Lk 2:26　H. Gal 5:7　J. Eph 4:27　K. Lk 13:22, journeying through　L. 1 Pet 1:16, holy　M. Gal 4:9　N. 1 Cor 14:1　O. Rom 13:8, owing　P. 2 Cor 7:1, perfecting　Q. Mt 7:16　R. Col 1:19　S. 2 Cor 9:5　T. Rom 12:8, exhorting　U. Rom 11:30　V. Rom 15:16　W. Jn 7:17　X. Act 24:15, wait for　Y. 3 Jn 6　Z. Mt 18:19

B. Greet[A] Prisca[1] and Aquila[2]— my fellow-workers[3] in Christ Jesus, who risked[4] their *own* neck[5] for my life, *to* whom not only am **I** giving-thanks[B], but also all the churches *of* the Gentiles— and the church at their house[6]

1. Greet Epaenetus, my beloved[C], who is *the* firstfruit[7] *of* Asia[8] for Christ
2. Greet Mary, who labored-at[D] many *things* for you[9]
3. Greet Andronicus and Junias[10], my kinsmen[11] and my fellow-captives[12], who are notable[13] among[14] the apostles[E], who also were[15] in Christ before me
4. Greet Ampliatus, my beloved[C] in *the* Lord
5. Greet Urbanus, our fellow-worker[F] in Christ, and Stachys my beloved[C]
6. Greet Apelles, the approved[G] *one* in Christ
7. Greet the *ones* from the *ones*[16] *of* Aristobulus
8. Greet Herodion, my kinsman
9. Greet the *ones* from the *ones of* Narcissus, the *ones* being in *the* Lord
10. Greet Tryphaena and Tryphosa,[17] the *ones* laboring[D] in *the* Lord
11. Greet Persis[18] the beloved[C], who labored-at[D] many *things* in *the* Lord
12. Greet Rufus[19], the chosen[20] *one* in *the* Lord, and his mother and mine
13. Greet Asyncritus, Phlegon, Hermes[21], Patrobas, Hermas and the brothers with them
14. Greet Philologus and Julia[22], Nereus and his sister, and Olympas, and all the saints with them
15. Greet one another with *a* holy kiss[23]

C. All[24] the churches *of* Christ greet[A] you

D. Now I urge[H] you, brothers[J], to be watching-out-for[25] the *ones* producing[K] the dissensions[26] and the causes-of-falling[L] contrary to the teaching which **you** learned[M], and be turning-away[27] from them

1. For such *ones* are not serving[N] our Lord Christ[28], but their *own* stomach[29]. And by smooth-talk and flattery[30], they deceive[31] the hearts *of* the guileless[32] *ones*
2. For your obedience[O] reached[33] to all. Therefore I am rejoicing[P] over you. But I want you to be wise with-reference-to[34] the good[Q], and innocent[35] with-reference-to the evil[R]
3. And the God *of* peace will crush[36] Satan under your feet shortly[S]
4. The grace *of* our Lord Jesus[37] *be* with you[38]

E. Timothy my fellow-worker[F] greets[39] you, and *so do* Lucius[40] and Jason[41] and Sosipater[42], my kinsmen

1. **I**, Tertius, greet[A] you— the *one* having written the letter in *the* Lord[43]
2. Gaius, the host[44] *of* me and *of* the whole church, greets you
3. Erastus, the steward[45] *of* the city, greets you, and *so does* Quartus, *our* brother

24[46]

1. Paul always calls her Prisca (Rom 16:3; 1 Cor 16:19; 2 Tim 4:19). Luke always calls her Priscilla (Act 18:2, 18, 26), a diminutive, more familiar form of Prisca, like saying Debbie instead of Deborah. Some manuscripts say "Priscilla" here {N}. She is mentioned before her husband in four of the six references. GK *4571*.
2. Aquila is mentioned in Act 18:2, 18, 26 as a Jewish man whom Paul met in Corinth, and in 1 Cor 16:19; 2 Tim 4:19. GK *217*.
3. Elsewhere only in Rom 16:9, 21; 1 Cor 3:9; 2 Cor 1:24; 8:23; Phil 2:25; 4:3; Col 4:11; 1 Thes 3:2; Phm 1:1, 24; 3 Jn 8. GK *5301*.
4. Or, "put down, laid down". They put down their neck on the block, stuck out their neck. Elsewhere only as "pointing out" in 1 Tim 4:6. GK *5719*.
5. The circumstances are unknown to us, but Paul is apparently referring to a life-threatening situation for them. Used 7 times. GK *5549*.
6. Churches in that day met in homes, Act 2:46; 1 Cor 16:19; Col 4:15; Phm 2.
7. On this word, see 1 Cor 15:20. Compare 1 Cor 16:15.
8. That is, the Roman province of Asia, of which Ephesus was a key city. Some manuscripts say "Achaia" {N}.
9. Some manuscripts say "us" {N}.
10. This is a male name. Some manuscripts have it as a female name, "Junia" {A}. Originally, Paul's letter had no accents. When they were added in later manuscripts, some accented this as a male name (as two co-workers, like those in v 21; perhaps brothers), others as a female name (as perhaps a husband and wife, or brother and sister, as with "Julia" in v 15). Used only here. GK *2687*.
11. That is, fellow Jews, fellow countrymen. Same word as in v 11, 21; 9:3. Elsewhere only as "relatives" in Mk 6:4; Lk 1:58; 2:44; 14:12; 21:16; Jn 18:26; Act 10:24. GK *5150*.
12. Paul may mean they once shared an imprisonment with him; or, that they too were once jailed for Christ, without implying it was at the same time or place as any of his many imprisonments prior to this letter (2 Cor 6:5; 11:23). We do not know the details. Elsewhere only in Col 4:10; Phm 23. GK *5257*. Related to "take captive" in 2 Cor 10:5; and "captives" in Lk 4:18. Not related to "prisoner" in Eph 3:1.
13. Or, "famous, distinguished, outstanding, prominent". Elsewhere only as "notorious" in Mt 27:16, of Barabbas. GK *2168*.
14. Some think Paul means well known "as apostles", meaning they were apostles in the wider sense of the word; others, well known "to the apostles" (the twelve), their imprisonment having taken place in Judea (where they were believers before Paul).
15. The grammar means "have been and are in Christ". GK *1181*.
16. Paul could mean "the relatives", "the servants", "the household members". He probably means "Greet the believers (as he further defines it after this same phrase in v 11) from the members of the Aristobulus household".
17. These are names of two women, perhaps sisters. Some think they were twins because of the similarity of their names, which mean "Delicate" and "Dainty".
18. This is a woman.
19. Some think this may be the one mentioned in Mk 15:21. On why, consult the commentaries. It was a very common name for a slave. It means "red".
20. On this word, see 8:33. Some take it here to mean "choice, distinguished", since all Christians are "chosen"; others, "chosen by God". Compare "brother" in v 23.
21. Some manuscripts reverse the position of "Hermes" and "Hermas" {K}.
22. Perhaps she was the wife or sister of Philologus.
23. Elsewhere only in 1 Cor 16:20; 2 Cor 13:12; 1 Thes 5:26; 1 Pet 5:14; and in Lk 7:45; 22:48. Men kissed men, women kissed women. It was a form of greeting. GK *5799*.
24. Perhaps Paul is referring to the representatives with him, Act 20:4. This book was written in Act 20:3. Some manuscripts omit this word {K}.
25. Or, "watching". On this word, see "looking for" in 2 Cor 4:18.
26. Elsewhere only in Gal 5:20. GK *1496*. The root words mean "a standing in two".
27. Or, "avoiding, turning aside". Elsewhere only in 3:12; 1 Pet 3:11. GK *1712*.
28. Some manuscripts say "Lord Jesus Christ" {K}.
29. Same word as in Phil 3:19. Such people are self-serving, and serve the desires of this life. On this word, see "womb" in Lk 1:15.
30. Or, "good-sounding argument, false eloquence, praise". Paul may mean their good speech about you (praise, flattery); or, their good-sounding but false speech regarding what they are teaching. On this word, see "blessing" in 2 Cor 9:5.
31. Or, "completely deceive". On this word, see 7:11.
32. Or, "innocent, unsuspecting". Elsewhere only as "innocent" in Heb 7:26, of Christ. GK *179*.
33. That is, the report of it reached to all. Used only here. GK *919*.
34. Or, "for the purpose of", as also later in this sentence. GK *1650*.
35. Or, "pure". Elsewhere only in Mt 10:16; Phil 2:15. GK *193*. Compare Mt 10:16; 1 Cor 14:20.
36. Paul is alluding to Gen 3:15, and repeats the promise of final victory. On this word, see "bruised" in Mt 12:20.
37. Some manuscripts add "Christ". Some manuscripts have this benediction, "The grace...with you", in verse 24 instead of here. Others have it after verse 27, concluding the letter {A}.
38. Some manuscripts add "amen" {K}.
39. Some manuscripts have this plural {N}, so that it says "... worker, and Lucius... kinsmen, greet you".
40. Some think this is Luke (Phm 24). Elsewhere only in Act 13:1. GK *3372*.
41. Some think this is the Jason of Act 17:5-9.
42. Some think this is the "Sopater" of Act 20:4.
43. This is the Greek word order. Or, "greet you in the Lord, the *one* having written the letter". Tertius wrote this book of Romans down for Paul, or copied it from what Paul wrote.
44. Paul is apparently staying with Gaius in Corinth as he writes this letter. This may be the Gaius in 1 Cor 1:14. Elsewhere only as "stranger" Mt 25:35, 38, 43, 44; 27:7; Act 17:21; Eph 2:12, 19; Heb 11:13; 3 Jn 5; and "strange" in Act 17:18; Heb 13:9; 1 Pet 4:12. GK *3828*. Related to "lodge" in Act 10:6.
45. Or, "manager, administrator". Some suggest a more specific meaning here, such as "treasurer". On this word, see 1 Pet 4:10.
46. Some manuscripts have a benediction like v 20b here as v 24 ("The grace *of* our Lord Jesus Christ *be* with you all. Amen") instead of as v 20b {A}. See the note on v 20b.

A. Mk 15:18   B. Mt 26:27   C. Mt 3:17   D. Mt 11:28, being weary   E. 1 Cor 12:28   F. Rom 16:3   G. 2 Tim 2:15   H. Rom 12:8, exhorting   J. Act 16:40   K. Rev 13:13, does   L. Rom 11:9   M. Phil 4:11   N. Rom 6:6, are slaves   O. Rom 16:26   P. 2 Cor 13:11   Q. 1 Tim 5:10b   R. 3 Jn 11   S. Rev 1:1, quickly

F. Now[1] *to the* One being able to establish[2] you 25

    1. In-accordance-with[3] my good-news[A] and the proclamation[B] *of* Jesus Christ[4]

        a. [Which is] in-accordance-with[5] *the* revelation[C] *of the* mystery[6]

            1. Having been kept-silent[D] *for* eternal[E] times[7]
            2. But having now been revealed[8]   26
            3. And having been made-known[9]

                a. Through *the* prophetic[F] Scriptures[10]
                b. According to *the* command[11] *of* the eternal[E] God
                c. For *the* obedience[12] *of* faith[13]
                d. To all the nations[14]

    2. *To the* only wise God through Jesus Christ, *to* Whom[15] *be* the glory forever[16], amen   27

1. This doxology (v 25-27) appears in different places in the manuscripts {C}. Some manuscripts have it here, omitting v 24. Some manuscripts have it both here and after 14:23, omitting 16:24. Some have it after 14:23 and end the letter with 16:24. Some do not have it at all, ending the letter with 16:24. One has it after 15:33 and ends the letter with 16:23. Several theories have been suggested to account for these variances, on which consult the commentaries.
2. Same word as in 1:11. On this word, see 1 Thes 3:2.
3. Or, "Based on, In relation to". GK *2848*. That is, "establish you in accordance with...".
4. That is, about Jesus Christ. This proclamation is given in its greatest detail in this book.
5. This is explaining the "good news" and "proclamation". They are in harmony with the mystery God kept hidden, but now revealed. Others make this point 2., further explaining "establish" (in which case, "[which is]" is omitted).
6. On this word, see 11:25. This mystery is defined by the next three phrases.
7. On this phrase, "eternal times", see 2 Tim 1:9.
8. Same word as in 3:21.
9. These two verbs— revealed, made known— also occur together in Col 1:26, 27.
10. Compare 1:2.
11. Or, "order". Same word as in 1 Cor 7:6, 25; 2 Cor 8:8; 1 Tim 1:1; Tit 1:3. Elsewhere only as "authority" in Tit 2:15. GK *2198*. The related verb is in Lk 8:25.
12. This word is used with reference to Christ in 2 Cor 10:5, and the truth in 1 Pet 1:22. Elsewhere only in Rom 1:5; 5:19; 6:16; 15:18; 16:19; 2 Cor 7:15; 10:6; Phm 21; Heb 5:8; 1 Pet 1:2, 14. GK *5633*. Related to "obey" in "obey the faith" in Act 6:7; "not obey the good news" in Rom 10:16; 2 Thes 1:8; and "obeying Him" in Heb 5:9. Related to "obedient" in 2 Cor 2:9.
13. Some think Paul means the obedience "which consists of faith"; others, "which comes from faith"; others, the "faith kind of obedience"; others, the obedience "to the faith". Same phrase as in 1:5. Thus he opens and closes the book with this thought. On "faith", see Eph 2:8.
14. Or, "Gentiles". On this word, see "Gentiles" in Act 15:23.
15. Some think this refers to "God"; others, to "Jesus Christ". Some manuscripts omit "to Whom" {N}, so that it says "*To the* only wise God, through Jesus Christ, *be* the glory forever, amen".
16. On this idiom, "into the ages", see Rev 20:10. Some manuscripts say "forever and ever" {A}.

A. 1 Cor 15:1 B. 1 Cor 1:21 C. 2 Thes 1:7 D. 1 Cor 14:34, be silent E. Mt 25:46 F. 2 Pet 1:19

1 Corinthians   Overview

Introduction	1:1-9
1A. I exhort you brothers, that you all speak the same thing, and that there not be divisions among you	1:10
1B. For I hear that there are quarrels among you, divisions over Paul, Apollos, Cephas, Christ	1:11-12
2B. Has Christ been divided? Was Paul crucified for you? Were you baptized in Paul's name?	1:13
1C. I give thanks I baptized none of you	1:14-16
2C. For He did not send me to baptize, but to speak the gospel without wisdom of speech	1:17
1D. For the speech of the cross is foolishness to the world, but God's power to us	1:18
2D. For God said He would destroy the wisdom of the wise. He did so in saving us	1:19-31
3C. And I having come to you, I did not proclaim God's mystery with human wisdom	2:1-5
4C. Yet we are speaking wisdom to the mature, but a wisdom not of this age or its rulers	2:6
1D. Rather we speak God's wisdom— the hidden wisdom predestined for our glory	2:7-9
2D. And God revealed it to us through the Spirit. We speak it in Spirit-taught words	2:10-13
3D. But a natural person does not accept the things of the Spirit of God	2:14
4D. But the spiritual person examines all things	2:15-16
5C. And I, brothers, was not able to speak to you then as to spiritual ones. I gave you milk	3:1-2
6C. But even still you are fleshly, walking like mankind, saying I am of Paul, Apollos	3:3-4
3B. Therefore what is Apollos and Paul?— Servants through whom you believed	3:5
1C. I planted, Apollos watered, but God was causing the growth. We are not anything	3:6-7
2C. Apollos and I are one, for we are co-workers of God. You are His farm, His building	3:8-17
3C. Let no one deceive himself. The wisdom of this world is foolishness with God	3:18-20
4C. So then, let no one be boasting in people. All things are yours	3:21-23
5C. Let a person consider us as attendants of Christ, and stewards of the mysteries of God	4:1-5
4B. I applied these things to Apollos and me that you may learn not to be puffed up about men	4:6-21
2A. Sexual immorality is being heard of among you. Remove the immoral person from among you	5:1-13
3A. Does any one of you dare to take your cases before the unrighteous judges and not the saints?	6:1-11
4A. Flee sexual immorality. Your body is for the Lord, a part of Christ, and a temple of the Spirit	6:12-20
5A. Now concerning the things which you wrote	7:1
1B. Concerning marriage issues	7:1-24
2B. Concerning virgins, and the remarriage of widows	7:25-40
3B. Concerning the eating of foods sacrificed to idols	8:1
1C. We know that we all have knowledge. Knowledge puffs up, but love builds up	8:1-3
2C. Therefore we know that an idol is nothing, and that there in only one God	8:4-6
3C. But all do not know this. Some eat by the custom of the idol, staining their conscience	8:7
4C. But food will not bring us near to God. We lose or gain nothing by it	8:8

	5C. But watch out that this right of yours does not somehow cause the weak to stumble	8:9-12
	6C. If meat causes my brother to stumble, I will never eat it again. Follow my example. I freely give up any right so as not to hinder the gospel, but advance it	8:13-9:23
	7C. Run so as to lay hold of the prize, and so as not to become disapproved. Remember Israel. They are examples to us. Take heed, and flee from idolatry	9:24-10:22
	8C. All things are lawful, but not all is beneficial. Be seeking the good of the other	10:23-30
	9C. Therefore do all to the glory of God. Become blameless to all, imitators of me	10:31-11:1
4B. Head coverings for women when prophesying		11:2-16
5B. Proper conduct at the Lord's Supper		11:17-34
6B. Concerning spiritual gifts		12:1
	1C. You were led away to the speechless idols. Know then how the Spirit leads	12:2-3
	2C. Now there are differences of gifts, ministries, and things-worked, given by the one God	12:4-6
	3C. And the manifestation of the Spirit is given to each for our benefit, as He wills	12:7-11
	4C. For just as the human body has many body-parts but is one body, so also is Christ	12:12
	1D. For with one Spirit we were all baptized into one body	12:13
	2D. For the body is not one body-part, but many, all placed by God	12:14-19
	3D. And there are many body-parts, but one body, blended together by God	12:20-26
	4D. And you are the body of Christ and its body-parts. Be zealous for the greater gifts	12:27-31
	5C. And I show you a way still beyond measure— love. Be pursuing love	12:31-14:1
	6C. Now be zealous for spiritual gifts, but even more that you might be prophesying	14:1
	1D. For one speaking in a tongue speaks to God, edifying himself, not the church	14:2-5
	2D. Now the one prophesying is greater, unless the tongues are interpreted to edify	14:5-12
	3D. Therefore, let the one speaking in tongues pray to interpret. Otherwise, those hearing will not know what is said, or be edified	14:13-19
	4D. Brothers, do not be children in your understanding. Be mature. The tongues are for the unbelievers, the prophecy is for the believers	14:20-25
	5D. What then is to be done, brothers? In church, do all things for edification	14:26-38
	6D. So then my brothers, be zealous to prophesy, do not forbid tongues, be orderly	14:39-40
7B. Now I make known the good news which I announced to you, through which you are saved		15:1-2
	1C. I delivered to you that Christ died, and was raised, appearing to many	15:3-11
	2C. How is it some are saying there is no resurrection? If He is not raised, all is empty	15:12-19
	3C. But He has been raised, the firstfruit. For as in Adam all die, in Christ all are raised	15:20-34
	4C. How are they raised? Like a seed sown. The natural is sown, the spiritual raised	15:35-49
	5C. Behold— We will not all sleep, but we will all be changed, death conquered	15:50-57
	6C. So then brothers, abound in the work of the Lord. Your labor is not empty	15:58
8B. Concerning the collection for the poor in Jerusalem		16:1-11
9B. Concerning Apollos		16:12
Conclusion		16:13-24

		Verse
1 Corinthians 1:1	576	

> A. Paul, *a* called apostle *of* Christ Jesus[1] *by the* will *of* God, and Sosthenes[2] *our* brother   1
> B. *To* the church *of* God being in Corinth,[3] *to* ones having been sanctified[4] in Christ Jesus, called[5] saints[6]   2
>
>> 1. With[7] all the *ones* calling-upon[A] the name *of* our Lord Jesus Christ in every place, their *Lord* and ours[8]
>
> C. Grace *to* you and peace from God our Father and *the* Lord Jesus Christ   3
> D. I am giving-thanks[B] *to* my[9] God always for you for the grace[C] *of* God having been given *to* you in Christ Jesus[10]—   4
>
>> 1. Because[11] you were enriched[12] in everything in[13] Him— in all speech[14] and all knowledge, °even as the testimony[D] *of* Christ[15] was confirmed[16] in you[17]   5-6
>>
>>> a. So that[18] you *are* not lacking[E] in any gift[19] while eagerly-awaiting[F] the revelation[G] *of* our Lord Jesus Christ   7
>>> b. Who[20] also will confirm you until *the* end[21], *so as to* be blameless[22] on the day *of* our Lord Jesus Christ[23]   8
>>
>> 2. God *is* faithful,[24] through Whom you were called[H] into *the* fellowship[25] *of* His Son, Jesus Christ our Lord   9

1A. Now I exhort[J] you, brothers[K], by the name *of* our Lord Jesus Christ, that you all be speaking the same thing[26], *and that* there not be divisions[27] among you, but[28] *that* you be made-complete[29] in the same mind[30] and in the same purpose[31]   10

> 1B. For it was made-clear[L] *to* me concerning you, my brothers, by the *ones of* Chloe,[32] that there are quarrels[33] among you. °Now I mean[M] this— that each *of* you is saying "I am *of* Paul", and "I *of* Apollos[34]", and "I *of* Cephas[35]", and "I *of* Christ"   11, 12
> 2B. Has[36] Christ been divided[N]? Paul was not crucified[O] for you, *was he*?[37] Or were you baptized[P] in[38] the name *of* Paul?   13
>
>> 1C. I give-thanks[B] *to* God[39] that I baptized none *of* you, except Crispus[40] and Gaius[41], °so that no one may say that you were baptized[42] in my name!   14-15
>>
>>> 1D. Now I baptized also the household[Q] *of* Stephanas[43]. As *to the* rest[44], I do not know if I baptized any other   16
>>
>> 2C. For Christ did not send me forth[R] to be baptizing, but to be announcing-the-good-news[S]— not in wisdom[T] *of* speech,[45] in order that the cross[U] *of* Christ may not be made-empty[46]   17

1. Some manuscripts say "Jesus Christ" {B}. On "called apostle", see Rom 1:1.
2. Perhaps this man is the one in Act 18:17, the leader of the synagogue in Corinth beaten in Paul's place, if he subsequently became a Christian. Otherwise, he is unknown to us. GK *5398*.
3. Paul spent over 18 months in Corinth in Act 18:1-18, and writes this letter in Act 19:10.
4. Or, "made holy, set apart [to God]". On this word, see Heb 10:29.
5. Same word and grammar as in "called" apostle, v 1. "Called" is an adjective. On this word, see Rom 8:28. Some think Paul means "saints because called"; others, "called to be saints".
6. Or, "holy *ones*". On this word, see "holy" in 1 Pet 1:16. "Sanctified" and "saints" are the verb and adjective of the same word. It means "holy, dedicated to God, separated from the world and set apart to God's service". Same phrase as in Rom 1:7.
7. Some think Paul means "to the church... with all", expanding the addressees of this letter to all Christians; others, "called saints with all", linking the Corinthians to the larger body of Christ.
8. Or, "their *place* and ours".
9. Some manuscripts omit this word {A}.
10. Some manuscripts say "Jesus Christ" {K}.
11. Or, "That". GK *4022*. In any case, Paul is detailing the grace given.
12. Or, "made rich". Elsewhere only in 2 Cor 6:10; 9:11. GK *4457*. Related to "riches, wealth".
13. Or, "in connection with, by". GK *1877*.
14. Or, "word, doctrine, speaking". Same words as the gift in 12:8, the "word" of "knowledge". Some think Paul means "in all your speech", in every form of speaking and knowing, including all supernatural gifts of speaking and knowledge; others, "in all our speech", "in all doctrine and knowledge" we spoke to you.
15. That is, "*about* Christ"; Paul's message, the gospel.
16. Or, "established, strengthened, made firm". Same word as in v 8; Mk 16:20; Rom 15:8; Heb 2:3. Elsewhere only as "establish" in 2 Cor 1:21; Col 2:7; Heb 13:9. GK *1011*. Related to "firm" in 2 Pet 1:10, and "confirmation" in Phil 1:7.
17. Or, "among you". Some think Paul means "confirmed among you" by the miraculous gifts which Paul displayed, Rom 15:19; 2 Cor 12:12; Heb 2:3; others, "confirmed in you" by the Corinthians' display of Christian character and acceptance of truth in the heart, and by their gifts of the Spirit such as prophecy and tongues. Others see no reference to gifts at all. The Corinthians were enriched "in the doctrine and knowledge of Jesus Christ even as the testimony about Christ was established in your hearts".
18. Or, "With the result that". Some think Paul means "given... so that"; others, "enriched... so that"; others, "confirmed... so that".
19. That is, any gift (in the broadest sense) given by God's grace, v 4. Same word as in Rom 1:11; 6:23; 11:29; 1 Cor 7:7; 12:4, 9, 28, 30, 31; 2 Cor 1:11; 1 Tim 4:14; 2 Tim 1:6. Elsewhere only as "*grace-gift*" in Rom 5:15, 16; 12:6; 1 Pet 4:10. GK *5922*. Related to "grace" in Eph 2:8.
20. Some think Paul is referring to Christ in v 6, 7; others, to God in v 4 (making this point 2.).
21. This phrase, "until the end", is elsewhere only in 2 Cor 1:13. On related phrases, see Mt 10:22.
22. On this word, see Tit 1:6. There is similar grammar in 1 Thes 3:13 and Phil 3:21.
23. Some manuscripts omit this word {C}.
24. Note the past tense in v 5-6, present tense in v 7, future tense in v 8. God is faithful in all three senses.
25. This word means "sharing, partnership, communion, participation, contribution". The Greek word is *koinonia*. Same word as in Act 2:42; 2 Cor 6:14; 13:13; Gal 2:9; Phil 2:1; Phm 6; 1 Jn 1:3, 6, 7. Elsewhere only as "sharing" in 1 Cor 10:16; Heb 13:16; "partnership" in 2 Cor 8:4; Phil 1:5; 3:10; and "contribution" (a physical sharing) in Rom 15:26; 2 Cor 9:13. GK *3126*. Related to "share" in 2 Jn 11; "sharer" in 2 Pet 1:4; "sharing" in 1 Tim 6:18; "common" in Jude 3.
26. This phrase "speak the same *thing*" is used only here. See Rom 12:16 on "think the same *thing*".
27. Or, "splits, tears". The Greek is *schisma*, from which our word "schism" comes. Same word as in Jn 7:43; 9:16; 10:19; 1 Cor 11:18; 12:25. Elsewhere only as "tear" in Mt 9:16; Mk 2:21. GK *5388*. Note 11:18-19 on divisions. Related to "torn" in Mt 27:51.
28. The first two phrases speak of external consensus or unity, the next two of the internal from which it proceeds.
29. Or, "mended, put in order, restored". This is a participle, be "having been made complete". On this word, see "prepared" in Rom 9:22.
30. Or, "understanding". On this word, see Rom 7:23.
31. Or, "intention, judgment". That is, the judgments and purposes resulting from the understanding or mind in the previous phrase. Same word as in Rev 17:13, 17. Elsewhere only as "mind" in Act 20:3; "opinion" in 1 Cor 7:25, 40; 2 Cor 8:10; and "consent" in Phm 14. GK *1191*.
32. Paul may mean "family members" or "slaves" of this household. These people may have been sent by Chloe to Paul, or this may simply define their household. Chloe may have lived in Corinth, or in Ephesus (from which Paul was writing this book in Act 19:10). She is mentioned only here. GK *5951*.
33. Same word as in Tit 3:9. Elsewhere only as "strife" in Rom 1:29; 13:13; 1 Cor 3:3; 2 Cor 12:20; Gal 5:20; Phil 1:15; 1 Tim 6:4. GK *2251*. It means "quarrels" when plural; "strife" when singular. These quarrels led to "divisions" (v 10), which are described next.
34. Act 18:24-19:1 seems to have been included specifically to show the relationship of Paul to Apollos, and both to Corinth.
35. That is, Peter. The Corinthians formed parties, as they did with their philosophers. The opinions and reasonings of these four groups has been inferred and described in several ways. Consult the commentaries. On "Cephas", see Gal 1:18.
36. Some take this as an exclamation, "Christ has been divided!".
37. The grammar of this question expects a "no" answer.
38. On "baptized in", see Mk 1:9.
39. Some manuscripts omit "*to God*" {C}.
40. Crispus is the former synagogue leader mentioned in Act 18:8.
41. Paul stayed with Gaius when he later came to Corinth, Rom 16:23.
42. Some manuscripts say "that I baptized" {N}.
43. Stephanas was the firstfruit of Achaia, who came to visit Paul in Ephesus, 16:15, 17. GK *5107*.
44. Or, "remainder". On this word, see "other" in 2 Pet 3:16.
45. Paul could mean the content of the speech (as in v 18); or, the manner of speaking (as in 2:1, 4). Same word as in v 5.
46. That is, emptied of what God gave it. On this word, see "emptied" in Phil 2:7. Note 1 Cor 2:5.

A. 1 Pet 1:17 B. Mt 26:27 C. Eph 2:8 D. Act 4:33 E. Lk 15:14, be in need F. Rom 8:19, awaiting G. 2 Thes 1:7 H. Rom 8:30 J. Rom 12:8 K. Act 16:40 L. 1 Cor 3:13 M. Jn 12:49, say N. 1 Cor 7:17, apportioned O. Mt 27:35 P. Mk 1:8 Q. Mk 3:20, house R. Mk 3:14, send out S. Act 5:42 T. 1 Cor 12:8 U. Mt 10:38

    1D. For[1] the speech[2] *of* the cross is foolishness[A] *to the* ones **perishing**[3]— but is *the* power[B] *of* God *to* us being saved[C]   18

    2D. For[4] it has been written [in Isa 29:14], "I will destroy[5] the wisdom *of* the wise *ones,* and I will set-aside[D] the intelligence[E] *of* the intelligent[6] *ones*". °Where *is the* wise one? Where *is the* scribe[7]? Where *is the* debater[8] *of* this age? Did not God make-foolish[9] the wisdom *of* the[10] world?   19, 20

        1E. For[11] since, in the wisdom *of* God, the world through[12] its wisdom did not know[13] God,[14] God was well-pleased[F] through the foolishness[A] *of* the proclamation[15] to save[C] the *ones* believing[G]   21

            1F. Because indeed Jews are asking-*for*[H] signs[16] and Greeks are seeking[J] wisdom, but **we** are proclaiming[17] Christ crucified[18]—   22, 23

                1G. *To* Jews— *an* offense[19]
                2G. And *to* Gentiles[20]— foolishness
                3G. But *to* the called[K] *ones* themselves, both Jews and Greeks— Christ *the* power *of* God and *the* wisdom *of* God   24
                4G. Because the foolish[L] *thing of* God[21] is wiser *than* humans[M], and the weak[N] *thing of* God *is* stronger *than* humans   25

        2E. For look-*at*[22] your calling[O], brothers— that *there are* not many wise according-to[23] *the* flesh,[24] not many powerful[25], not many well-born[26]   26

            1F. But God chose[27] the foolish[L] *things of* the world in order that He might be putting the wise *ones* to shame[P]   27
            2F. And God chose the weak[N] *things of* the world in order that He might be putting the strong *things* to shame
            3F. And God chose the low-born[28] *things of* the world, and the *things* having been treated-with-contempt[29]— the *things* not being[30], in order that He might bring-to-nothing[31] the *things* being[32]   28
            4F. So that no flesh may boast[33] in the sight of God[34]   29
            5F. But by Him **you** are in Christ Jesus, Who became wisdom *to* us from God— both[35] righteousness and holiness[36], and redemption[37]— °in order that, just as it has been written [in Jer 9:24], "Let the *one* boasting be boasting in *the* Lord"   30, 31

  3C. And **I**, having come to you, brothers, did not come[38] in accordance with superiority[39] *of* speech or *of* wisdom while proclaiming[40] *to* you the mystery[41] *of* God   2:1

    1D. For I determined[Q] not to know anything among you except Jesus Christ— and this *One* having been crucified   2
    2D. And **I** was[42] with you in weakness[R], and in fear[S], and in much trembling[43]   3
    3D. And my speech[44] and my proclamation[45] *was* not in persuasive words[46] *of* wisdom, but in demonstration[47] *of the* Spirit and power[B], °in order that your faith might not be in *the* wisdom *of* humans[M], but in *the* power *of* God   4, 5

1. For what follows is what the message of the cross is, by God's definition. To announce it with human wisdom is to empty it of its power to accomplish one or both of these God-intended purposes.
2. Or, the "message, word". Same word as in v 17. That is, the content of the message— Christ crucified, v 23.
3. Such people are on this path. Paul uses grammar that emphasizes the contrast between the two halves of this sentence. This word is used 90 times of "perishing, being destroyed, lost, ruined" in both an earthly and eternal sense. Elsewhere by Paul only in Rom 2:12; 1 Cor 10:10; 15:18; 2 Cor 2:15; 4:3, 9; 2 Thes 2:10; and as "destroy" in Rom 14:15; 1 Cor 1:19; 8:11; 10:9. GK *660*. Related to "destruction" in 2 Pet 2:1.
4. For it is God's plan and intention to show through the gospel the foolishness of human wisdom.
5. Same word as "perishing" in v 18, with different grammar.
6. Or this may be rendered "insight *of* the insightful, cleverness *of* the clever, understanding *of* the understanding". Elsewhere only in Mt 11:25; Lk 10:21; Act 13:7. GK *5305*.
7. That is, the scholar, the expert in the Law. GK *1208*.
8. Or, "disputer". Used only here. GK *5186*. Related to "controversies" in 1 Tim 6:4; "issue" in Act 15:2; and "debate" in Mk 8:11.
9. In the gospel, God acted in deliberate contradiction to human wisdom as a judgment on it. He made it foolish by saving through that foolish proclamation (v 21-25), and by saving ones the world considers foolish (v 26-31).
10. Some manuscripts say "this" world {N}. The grammar indicates a "yes" answer is expected.
11. The first half of this verse tells why God made it foolish, the second half how He did it.
12. Or, "by, by means of", as also later in the verse. GK *1328*.
13. Or, "come to know". On this word, see Lk 1:34.
14. Human wisdom did not lead the world to God (as they think), but away from Him (as He declares). Paul expands this in v 22-24.
15. Or, "proclaimed message". That is, the foolishness belonging to the proclamation (from the world's point of view), to the content of the message, to "Christ crucified", v 23. Elsewhere only in Mt 12:41; Mk 16 (short ending); Lk 11:32; Rom 16:25; 1 Cor 2:4; 15:14; 2 Tim 4:17; Tit 1:3. GK *3060*. The related verb is in v 23. Note that this "foolishness" is later called God's wisdom, 2:7. Thus God was well pleased to save the ones believing by His wisdom, not the world's wisdom. On God's view of the world's opinion, see 3:19.
16. Some manuscripts say "*a* sign" {K}.
17. This word means "proclaim as a herald". On this word, see 2 Tim 4:2. Related to "proclamation" in v 21, but not to "proclaim" in 2:1.
18. Or, "*a* crucified Messiah". This is a participle, "having been crucified".
19. Or, a "trap". On this word, see "cause of falling" in Rom 11:9.
20. Some manuscripts say "Greeks" {N}.
21. That is, the message, the proclamation (v 21) of Christ crucified (v 23), proceeding from God.
22. Or, this may be a statement, not a command, "For you see your calling...". On this word, see "see" in Rev 1:11.
23. Or, "with respect to, in relation to" human standards or natural gifts. GK *2848*.
24. Or, "that not many *are* wise... flesh", or, "that not many wise... flesh *are called*". Likewise for the next two phrases.
25. Or, "mighty, strong". Same word as in Act 25:5. Used of Apollos in Act 18:24. On this word, see Lk 24:19.
26. Or, "noble". Elsewhere only in Lk 19:12 (physical nobility); Act 17:11 (spiritual nobility). GK *2302*.
27. Or, "called out, picked out, selected". Same word as in v 28; Mk 13:20; Lk 6:13; 9:35; 10:42; 14:7; Jn 6:70; 13:18; 15:16, 19; Act 1:2, 24; 6:5; 13:17; 15:22, 25; Eph 1:4; Jam 2:5. Elsewhere only as "made a choice" in Act 15:7. GK *1721*. Related to "chosen" in Rom 8:33.
28. Or, "base, not-noble, not-well-born", answering to the word "well-born" in v 26. Ones of no family. Used only here. GK *38*.
29. Or, "despised". On this word, see 1 Thes 5:20.
30. Some manuscripts say "... treated with contempt, and the *things* not being" {B}. That is, the things not "being, existing" as anything at all in the eyes of the world.
31. Same word as in 2:6.
32. That is, God chose things thought to be worthless, nothing, to void things thought to be of value, important.
33. More literally, "so that all flesh may not boast". On "no flesh", see Mt 24:22. On "boast", see 2 Cor 11:16.
34. Some manuscripts say "His", {N}, so that it says "in His sight".
35. Paul closely links these two terms. Some think there are three parallel concepts, "wisdom..., both righteousness and holiness, and redemption". Others think the last three terms explain "wisdom". Others think the last three terms stand for and detail the unexpressed "power of God" (note v 24).
36. Or, "sanctification". On this word, see Heb 12:14.
37. Some think Paul means our initial redemption at salvation, and that it is placed last for emphasis; others, that it refers to our final redemption. On this word, see Rom 3:24.
38. That is, in Act 18:1.
39. Or, "preeminence, excellence". On this word, see 1 Tim 2:2.
40. This word means to proclaim as a messenger. See Phil 1:18 on it. Compare the word in 1 Cor 1:23.
41. That is, the gospel. See v 7 on this word. Some manuscripts say "testimony" {B}, as in 1:6.
42. Or, "came-to-be-with, came to". GK *1181*.
43. This is the opposite of human self-confidence, because Paul's power had to come from God. On this word, see Phil 2:12. Compare 2 Cor 2:14-3:6; 1 Thes 2:1-12.
44. Some take this word as in 2:1, referring to Paul's manner of speaking; others, as in 1:18, referring to the content of his speaking; others, as a general reference to his speaking.
45. Same word as in 1:21. Some think Paul means the content, the message; others, the act of proclamation; others, the form of the message.
46. Some manuscripts omit "words", either leaving it implied, "the persuasive *words of* wisdom", or meaning "the persuasion *of* wisdom". Other manuscripts say "persuasive words *of* human wisdom" {C}.
47. Or, "proof, display". Some think Paul means "*from* the Spirit and power". His words were spoken "in connection with the demonstration or proof in their hearts proceeding from or given by the Spirit and God's power", rather than in connection with persuasive words proceeding from human wisdom. Others think Paul means his words were spoken "in connection with proof that the Spirit and power were in him". Compare 1 Thes 1:5. Some think miracle working, or miraculous gifts are included here. Used only here. GK *618*. Related to "display" in 4:9.

A. 1 Cor 2:14 B. Mk 5:30 C. Lk 19:10 D. Gal 2:21 E. Eph 3:4, understanding F. Mt 17:5 G. Jn 3:36 H. 1 Jn 5:14, request J. Phil 2:21
K. Rom 8:28 L. Tit 3:9 M. Mt 4:4, mankind N. 1 Thes 5:14 O. 2 Pet 1:10 P. Rom 5:5, put to shame Q. Mt 7:1, judge R. Mt 8:17 S. Eph 5:21

4C. Yet we are speaking wisdom^A among the mature¹, but *a* wisdom not *of* this age, nor *of* the rulers^B *of* this age— the *ones* being brought-to-nothing²   6

    1D. Rather³ we are speaking God's wisdom in *a* mystery⁴— the *wisdom* having been hidden⁵   7

        1E. Which God predestined^C before the ages for our glory
        2E. Which none *of* the rulers *of* this age has understood^D. For if they had understood, they would not have crucified the Lord *of* glory   8
        3E. But⁶ *it is* just as it has been written—   9

            1F. "*Things* which *an* eye did not see, and *an* ear did not hear, and *which* did not come-up⁷ on *the* heart *of a* human— which⁸ God prepared^E *for* the *ones* loving^F Him"⁹

    2D. And¹⁰ God revealed^G *it*¹¹ **to us** through the¹² Spirit   10

        1E. For the Spirit searches¹³ all *things,* even the deep^H *things of* God

            1F. For who *among* people^J knows^K the *things of* the person except the spirit *of* the person within him? In this manner also, no one has known^D the *things of* God except the Spirit *of* God   11

        2E. And **we** did not receive the spirit *of* the world¹⁴, but the Spirit from God, in order that we might know^K the *things* having been freely-given¹⁵ *to* us by God—   12

            1F. *Things* which we also are speaking— not in words taught^L *by* human wisdom,¹⁶ but in *words* taught *by the* Spirit¹⁷, combining¹⁸ spiritual^M *things with* spiritual *words*   13

    3D. But *a* natural¹⁹ person^J does not accept²⁰ the *things of* the Spirit *of* God   14

        1E. For they are foolishness²¹ *to* him
        2E. And he is not able to understand^D, because they are spiritually examined²²

    4D. But the spiritual²³ *person* examines all²⁴ *things,* yet he himself is examined by no one²⁵   15

        1E. For "who knew^D *the* mind^N *of the* Lord, who will instruct Him?" [Isa 40:13], and **we** have *the* mind^N *of* Christ²⁶   16

5C. And **I**, brothers, was not able to speak *to* you as *to* spiritual^M *ones*, but as *to ones* made-of-flesh²⁷, as *to* infants²⁸ in Christ. ⁎I gave you milk to drink, not²⁹ food^O, for you were not yet able   3:1   2
6C. But not-even³⁰ still³¹ now are you able, ⁎for you are³² still fleshly³³   3

    1D. For where *there is* jealousy^P and strife³⁴ among you, are you not fleshly and walking^Q in accordance with human^J *thinking*³⁵?
    2D. For whenever one says, "I am *of* Paul", and another "I *am of* Apollos", are you not [mere] humans³⁶?   4

1. Or, "complete, perfect". Some think Paul means the "spiritual ones" (2:15; 3:1), as opposed to "infants" (3:1). Others think he means "Christians" as opposed to "natural ones" (2:14). On this word, see "complete" in 1 Cor 13:10.
2. Same word as in 1:28. Or, "done away with, nullified". On this word, see "done away with" in Rom 6:6.
3. Same word as "But" in v 4, 5, 9, 12, 13. GK *247*.
4. Some think Paul means "speaking... in a mystery"; others, "God's wisdom [contained] in *a* mystery". "Mystery" refers to something hidden in the past, but now revealed by God, that is, the gospel. It is defined in v 7-13; Rom 16:25-26; Eph 3:3-7; Col 1:26-28. On this word, see Rom 11:25.
5. This verb modifies "wisdom", not "mystery". Elsewhere only in Eph 3:9; Col 1:26; Lk 10:21. GK *648*. Related to the words in Mk 4:22; Jn 8:59; 1 Cor 4:5.
6. That is, "But *this wisdom is*", or *"But we are speaking"* (in both cases, referring back to v 7). Paul is continuing the contrast with what "this age" (v 6) thinks, as exemplified in its rulers (v 6, 8). This could also be placed as point 2D. Others take this as a direct contrast to the rulers and their action described in v 8, making this point 1F. "But *it happened* just as...".
7. Or, "arise". Same phrase as in Act 7:23; Lk 24:38. GK *326*.
8. Instead of "which", some manuscripts say "all that" {N}.
9. Some think Paul is paraphrasing Isa 64:4; others, summarizing several passages. Consult the commentaries. God's mystery or hidden wisdom contains things which are not human in origin and not known by humans, but which He planned from eternity, kept hidden until Christ, and revealed in the gospel, v 10-13.
10. Or, "But, Now". Some manuscripts say "For" {B}.
11. That is, the "hidden wisdom" in the "mystery" (v 7), containing things "predestined" (v 8) and "prepared" (v 9), but unimagined by humans (v 9). Or, "*them*", the prepared things (v 9), contained in the hidden wisdom (v 7).
12. Some manuscripts say "His Spirit" {N}.
13. Or, "inquires, investigates, examines". Elsewhere only in Jn 5:39; 7:52; Rom 8:27; 1 Pet 1:11; Rev 2:23. GK *2236*.
14. Some think Paul means "Satan"; others, the spirit of human wisdom in general.
15. Or, "granted", given as a gift or favor without cause. Same word as in Act 25:11, 16; Rom 8:32; Gal 3:18; and as "grant" in Lk 7:21; Act 3:14; 27:24; Phil 1:29; 2:9; Phm 22. Elsewhere only as "forgive" twelve times (see Lk 7:42). GK *5919*. This is the verb related to the word "grace" in Eph 2:8.
16. Or, "not in taught words *of* human wisdom".
17. Some manuscripts say "Holy Spirit" {N}.
18. This word means "combine, compare, explain". Some think Paul means that spiritual truths or thoughts of God (v 10-11) are combined with the spiritual words given by the Holy Spirit. Others think he means "explaining spiritual *things* to spiritual *people*". It is used of Joseph "interpreting" the dream in Gen 40:8. There are other views. Elsewhere only as "compare" in 2 Cor 10:12. GK *5173*.
19. This word means "pertaining to the soul", a soul-person, a person limited to the human soul's abilities and perspectives, a non-Christian, the human animal. Jude 19 adds "not having the Spirit". Jam 3:15 combines "earthly, natural, demonic". Elsewhere only in 1 Cor 15:44, 46, of the natural, physical body. GK *6035*.
20. Or, "receive, welcome". On this word, see "welcome" in Mt 10:40.
21. Same word as in 1:18, 21, 23. Elsewhere only in 3:19. GK *3702*. Related to "foolish" in Tit 3:9, and the verb in 1:20 and Rom 1:22.
22. Or, "investigated, questioned, discerned". This word is used of arriving at the truth through questioning and investigation, as in a judicial hearing. The natural person does not have the spiritual ability to properly examine spiritual things or people. Elsewhere only in 2:15; 4:3, 4; 9:3; 10:25, 27; 14:24; and in Lk 23:14; Act 4:9; 12:19; 17:11; 24:8; 28:18. GK *373*. Related to "examination" in Act 25:26.
23. This word means "pertaining to the Spirit", a Spirit-person, a person under the direction of the Holy Spirit. Used in this sense only in 3:1; 14:37; and Gal 6:1. On this word, see 14:1.
24. Some manuscripts can be understood to say "examines everyone, yet..." {C}.
25. That is, no one without the Spirit; no natural person.
26. The spiritual person has the mind of Christ and examines things using God's wisdom. Some manuscripts say "*of the* Lord" {B}.
27. Or, "fleshy *ones*". That is, ones like non-believers in their thinking, ones upon whom the Spirit has made very little impact as yet since they had just become believers. Paul is not faulting such people. He regards them as infants. Same word as in Rom 7:14; 2 Cor 3:3. Elsewhere only as "fleshy" in Heb 7:16. GK *4921*. Some manuscripts say "fleshly" {N}, using the related word in v 3.
28. Or, "children, immature *ones*, child-like *ones*, minors (not yet of age)". Same word as in Heb 5:13. Elsewhere only as "child" in Mt 11:25; 21:16; Lk 10:21; Rom 2:20; 1 Cor 13:11; Gal 4:1, 3; Eph 4:14; and "child-like" in 1 Thes 2:7. GK *3758*. Related to "be child-like" in 14:20.
29. Some manuscripts say "and not" {K}.
30. Some manuscripts say "neither" {K}.
31. Some manuscripts omit this word {A}.
32. The contrast is between what the Corinthians "were" (v 1-2), which was appropriate at the time, and what they "are" now, which is no longer appropriate at all.
33. Or, "carnal". This word means "pertaining to the flesh", flesh-people; here, Christians still living like non-Christians; people with the Spirit, living by the flesh. Paul is faulting the Corinthians here. This sense occurs in 2 Cor 1:12; 1 Pet 2:11. Elsewhere only in the sense of "material, physical" in Rom 15:27; 1 Cor 9:11; 2 Cor 10:4. GK *4920*. Related to "made of flesh" in v 1.
34. On this word, see "quarrels" in 1:11. Some manuscripts add "and divisions" {B}.
35. Or, "in accordance with mankind". That is, with human logic, goals, ways of viewing things. The grammar indicates a "yes" answer is expected to this question, and the next one.
36. And so Paul returns full circle to where he began in 1:12-13. Some manuscripts say "fleshly" {N}, as in v 3.

A. 1 Cor 12:8   B. Rev 1:5   C. Rom 8:29   D. Lk 1:34, know   E. Mk 14:15   F. Jn 21:15, devotedly love   G. 2 Thes 2:3   H. 2 Cor 8:2   J. Mt 4:4, mankind   K. 1 Jn 2:29   L. Jn 6:45   M. 1 Cor 14:1   N. Rom 7:23   O. Mk 7:19   P. 2 Cor 11:2   Q. Heb 13:9

3B. Therefore, what[1] is Apollos? And what is Paul?— servants[2] through whom you believed, even as the Lord gave[A] to each[3] one

    1C. I planted, Apollos watered, but God was causing-growth[B]

        1D. So then neither is the *one* planting anything, nor the *one* watering, but God causing the growth

    2C. And the *one* planting and the *one* watering are one[4], but each will receive *his* own reward[C] according to *his* own labor[5]. °For we are God's fellow-workers[6]; you are God's farm, God's building[D]

        1D. I laid[7] *a* foundation[E] according-to[8] the grace *of* God having been given *to* me as *a* wise master-builder[9], and another is building-upon[F] it
        2D. But let each *one* be watching-out[10] how he builds-upon[F] it

            1E. For no one can lay[G] another **foundation**[11] other than the *one which* is laid[12], which is Jesus Christ
            2E. And if one builds[F] gold, silver, precious stones, wood, hay, straw upon the[13] foundation[E], °each *one's* work will become evident[H]

                1F. For the day[14] will make *it* clear[15], because it is revealed[J] by fire. And the fire itself[16] will test[17] what-sort[K] each *one's* work is

                    1G. If one's work which he built-upon[F] *it* shall remain[18], he will receive *a* reward[C]
                    2G. If one's work shall be burned-up, he will suffer-loss[19]. But he himself will be saved[L], yet so as through fire

        3D. Do you not know that you are God's temple[20], and the Spirit *of* God is dwelling[M] in you[21]? If anyone ruins[22] the temple *of* God, God will ruin this[23] *one*. For the temple *of* God is holy[N]— which[24] **you** are!

    3C. Let no one be deceiving[O] himself. If anyone among you thinks[P] *that he* is wise in this age, let him become foolish, in order that he may become wise. °For the wisdom *of* this world is foolishness with God

        1D. For it has been written [in Job 5:13], "*He is* the *One* catching the wise in their craftiness[25]"
        2D. And again [in Ps 94:11], "*The* Lord knows the thoughts[26] *of* the wise, that they are futile[27]"

    4C. So then, let no one be boasting[Q] in people[R]

        1D. For all *things* are yours—°whether Paul or Apollos or Cephas or *the* world or life or death or *things* present or *things* coming[28]— all *things* are yours
        2D. And you *are* Christ's, and Christ *is* God's

    5C. Let *a* person be considering[29] us in-this-manner— as attendants[30] *of* Christ, and stewards[31] *of the* mysteries[S] *of* God

        1D. Here[32], furthermore[T], it is sought[U] in[33] stewards that one be found faithful[34]

1. Both here and in the next phrase, some manuscripts say "who" instead of "what" {N}. Some manuscripts reverse the names, Paul first, then Apollos {A}.
2. Or, "ministers", not faction leaders. The root word means "to serve". It is used in the NT of Christ, household servants, ministers/servants of Christ, deacons, and government authorities. Same word as Mt 20:26; 22:13; 23:11; Mk 9:35; 10:43; Jn 2:5, 9; 12:26; Rom 13:4; 15:8; 16:1; 2 Cor 6:4; 11:23; Col 1:7; 1 Tim 4:6. Elsewhere only as "minister" in 2 Cor 3:6; 11:15; Gal 2:17; Eph 3:7; 6:21; Col 1:23, 25; 4:7; and "deacon" in Phil 1:1; 1 Tim 3:8, 12. GK *1356*. Related to "ministry" in 1 Cor 12:5. Some manuscripts say "Paul, other than servants..." {N}, "other than" also being found in 2 Cor 1:13.
3. That is, to Paul and Apollos.
4. Or, "one *thing*", that is, in one category. This is detailed in v 9. Paul and Apollos are God's fellow workers.
5. Or, "toil, work". Same word as in 15:58; 1 Thes 1:3; Rev 2:2; 14:13. It also means "troubles" (see Lk 18:5). Used 18 times. GK *3160*. Related to "being weary" in Mt 11:28.
6. Paul may mean "Apollos and I are co-workers serving God"; or, "we are co-workers with God".
7. Some manuscripts say "I have laid" {N}. That is, in Corinth.
8. Or, "based on". GK *2848*.
9. Or, "architect". Used only here. GK *802*. The Greek is *architekton*, from which we get our English word.
10. Or, "beware". On this word, see "see" in Rev 1:11.
11. Same word as in v 10, 12; Rom 15:20; Eph 2:20.
12. Or, "than the *one* lying *there*". This is a participle. That is, the one laid by God and Paul in Corinth (v 10), and more broadly than Corinth, by God at the cross (Gal 1:6-7). This part of the building is done. GK *3023*. Not related to "lay" earlier.
13. Some manuscripts say "this" {N}.
14. That is, the day of judgment. See Rom 14:10; 2 Cor 5:10.
15. Or, "make *it* evident, reveal *it*, show *it*". "Make clear" is the same word as in 1 Cor 1:11; Col 1:8; Heb 9:8; 2 Pet 1:14. Elsewhere only as "indicate" in Heb 12:27; 1 Pet 1:11. GK *1317*. Related to "evident" in Gal 3:11.
16. Or, "it", so that it says "And of what sort each *one's* work is, the fire will test it". Some manuscripts omit this word {C}.
17. Or, "prove, examine by testing". On this word, see "approve" in Rom 12:2.
18. Some manuscripts say "remains" {N}, the difference being an accent mark.
19. Or, "forfeit" (the reward). Same word as in 2 Cor 7:9; Phil 3:8. Elsewhere only as "forfeit" in Mt 16:26; Mk 8:36; Lk 9:25. GK *2423*. Related to "loss" in Phil 3:7.
20. Same word as in Eph 2:21; 1 Cor 6:19; 2 Cor 6:16. The concept is also in 1 Pet 2:5; 4:17; Rom 8:9; etc.
21. This word is plural. "You (collectively) are the temple, and the Spirit dwells in you (collectively)". Compare 6:19, where each Corinthian is individually a temple of God.
22. Or, "corrupts, destroys, spoils". Elsewhere only as "corrupt" in 15:33; 2 Cor 7:2; 11:3; Eph 4:22; Rev 19:2; and "destroy" in 2 Pet 2:12; Jude 10. GK *5780*.
23. Some manuscripts say "will ruin him" {N}.
24. Some think Paul is referring back to "holy"; others, to "temple". The temple, considered as a spiritual building of living stones in which God lives— you all are that temple.
25. Or, "trickery, cunning". Elsewhere only in Lk 20:23; 2 Cor 4:2; 11:3; Eph 4:14. GK *4111*. Related to "crafty" in 2 Cor 12:16.
26. Or, "reasonings, opinions". On this word, see Jam 2:4.
27. Or, "worthless", in terms of knowing God. On this word, see 1 Cor 15:17. Compare Act 14:15; 1 Pet 1:18.
28. On this phrase, "*things* present or *things* coming", see Rom 8:38.
29. Or, "counting, estimating, regarding". On this word, see Rom 3:28.
30. Or, "assistants, servants, underlings, helpers", such as of a king, a court, a temple, a doctor, or some other superior. Same word as in Lk 4:20. Elsewhere only as "servant" in Lk 1:2; Jn 18:36; Act 26:16; "assistant" in Act 13:5; "officer" of the court in Mt 5:25; and "officer" of the temple (see Jn 18:12). GK *5677*. Related to "serve" in Act 13:36.
31. Or, "household managers, administrators". On this word, see 1 Pet 4:10.
32. Paul may mean "here on earth" or "here in this matter". GK *6045*.
33. That is, "in the case of ". GK *1877*.
34. Or, "trustworthy, dependable". Same word as in Mt 24:45; 25:21, 23; 2 Tim 2:2. On this word, see Col 1:2.

A. Eph 1:22 B. Jn 3:30, grow C. Rev 22:12, recompense D. Rom 14:19, edification E. 1 Tim 6:19 F. Jude 20, building up G. Act 19:21, put H. Rom 1:19 J. 2 Thes 2:3 K. Act 26:29 L. Lk 19:10 M. Rom 8:11 N. 1 Pet 1:16 O. Rom 7:11 P. Lk 19:11 Q. 2 Cor 11:16 R. Mt 4:4, mankind S. Rom 11:25 T. 2 Pet 3:16, other U. Phil 2:21

	2D. Now *to* me, it is *a* very small *thing*¹ that I should be examined² by you, or by *a* human^A day^B *of judgment*	3
	3D. But I do not even examine myself!	
	1E. For I am conscious^C of nothing *against* myself, but I have not been declared-right³ by this	4
	2E. But the *One* examining me is *the* Lord	
	4D. So then do not be judging⁴ anything before *the* time^D, until the Lord comes	5
	1E. Who will both⁵ illuminate^E the hidden⁶ *things of* the darkness,⁷ and reveal^F the motives⁸ *of* the hearts	
	2E. And at-that-time^G the praise⁹ will come *to* each *one* from God	
4B.	Now brothers^H, I applied¹⁰ these *things* to myself and Apollos for your sakes, in order that in us you might learn^J the *saying* "*Do* not go¹¹ beyond *the things* which have been written"— in order that you might not be puffed-up¹², one on behalf of the one against the other¹³	6
	1C. For who discerns¹⁴ you *to be* superior?	7
	2C. And what do you have that you did not receive? But if indeed you received *it*, why do you boast as-*though* not having received *it*?	
	3C. You are already satisfied¹⁵! You already became-rich^K! You became-kings¹⁶ without us! And o-that indeed you became-kings, in order that **we** also might reign with you. °For¹⁷ I think^L God displayed¹⁸ us the apostles *as* last,¹⁹ like *ones* condemned-to-death— because	8 9
	1D. We were made²⁰ *a* spectacle²¹ *to* the world^M— both *to* angels and *to* people	
	1E. We *are* foolish *ones* for the sake of Christ, but you *are* wise *ones* in Christ	10
	2E. We *are* weak *ones*, but you *are* strong *ones*	
	3E. You *are* distinguished^N *ones*, but we *are* dishonored^O *ones*	
	4E. Until the present hour indeed we hunger, and thirst, and are naked²², and are beaten²³, and live-transiently²⁴, °and labor^P— working^Q *with our* own hands	11 12
	5E. While being reviled²⁵, we bless^R; while being persecuted^S, we endure^T; while being slandered, we conciliate²⁶	13
	2D. We were made like *the* sweepings²⁷ *of* the world^M, *the* scum²⁸ *of* all *things*, up to now	
	4C. I am writing these *things* not shaming^U you, but admonishing²⁹ *you* as my beloved^V children^W	14
	1D. For if you should have ten-thousand tutors^X in Christ, yet *you do* not *have* many fathers	15
	2D. For **I** fathered^Y you in Christ Jesus through the good-news^Z. °Therefore I exhort^AA you— be³⁰ imitators^BB *of* me	16
	3D. For this reason I sent Timothy *to* you³¹	17
	1E. Who is my beloved^V and faithful^CC child^W in *the* Lord	
	2E. Who will remind you *as to* my ways in Christ Jesus³², just as I am teaching everywhere in every church	
	4D. Now some were puffed-up as-*if* I *were* not coming to you. °But I will come to you soon, if the Lord wills^DD	18-19

1. More literally, "it is for *a* very small *thing*". That is, "it means very little" to me.
2. That is, as to his faithfulness, his execution of his stewardship. On this word, see 2:14. Same word as in v 4.
3. That is, right before God, faithful, innocent, worthy of reward and praise (v 5). My self-judgment as to my faithfulness— good or bad— lacks God's perspective, so I do not judge myself. The fact that I am ignorant of a fault will not relieve me of responsibility for it, and loss (3:15). On this word, see "declared righteous" in Rom 3:24.
4. The grammar implies "stop judging", or, "do not make a habit of judging".
5. Or, "also".
6. Same word as in 14:25; Mk 4:22; Lk 8:17; Rom 2:16, 29; 2 Cor 4:2; 1 Pet 3:4. Elsewhere only as "secret" in Mt 6:4, 6; 10:26; Lk 12:2; Jn 7:4, 10, 18:20. GK *3220.* Related to the verb "hidden" in Jn 8:59.
7. That is, the things the darkness hides, the unseen things. God will reveal the whole picture.
8. Or, "counsels, purposes, plans". On this word, see "counsel" in Eph 1:11.
9. Or, "approval, commendation". Elsewhere only in Rom 2:29; 13:3; 2 Cor 8:18; Eph 1:6, 12, 14; Phil 1:11; 4:8; 1 Pet 1:7; 2:14. GK *2047.* Related to the verb in Rom 15:11.
10. Or, "transformed, adapted, changed". Used in a rhetorical sense only here. I transformed my teaching into an exposition concerning myself and Apollos. On this word, see "transform" in Phil 3:21.
11. The verb is not expressed. Some manuscripts say "To not think beyond..." {N}.
12. That is, puffed up with pride. Same word as in v 18, 19. Elsewhere only in 1 Cor 5:2; 8:1; 13:4; Col 2:18. GK *5881.*
13. That is, for example, one on behalf of Paul against Apollos.
14. Or, "distinguishes, differentiates". Same word as in 6:5; 14:29. On this word, see "doubting" in Jam 1:6. The related noun occurs in 12:10, "discernments" of spirits. We are puffed up with pride and divide into parties because we think we are superior. We are right and they are wrong. Paul asks, "Who distinguishes you as superior to someone else?", "Who regards you as superior?". Others translate "Who makes you to differ?", that is, who among you makes you superior?
15. Or, "filled". Or, "You already have enough, have all *you* want, have *your* fill". This is a participle, you are already "having been satisfied". Note the sarcasm in these 3 phrases, and how they build to a climax. Elsewhere only in Act 27:38. GK *3170.*
16. Or, "reigned" as kings, as this word is used later in the verse. On this word, see "reign" in Rev 19:6.
17. I wish we reigned with you, for our state as apostles is quite the opposite.
18. Or, "exhibited". On this word, see 2 Thes 2:4.
19. That is, last in status, regarded as low as men condemned to die. God put us on display as the lowest in rank of all people, looking up to your exalted position! Paul enlarges this in verses 10-13.
20. Or, "We became" here and in v 13 (2D.). GK *1181.*
21. Or, a "show, theater". Elsewhere only as "theater" in Act 19:29, 31. The Greek is *theatron.* GK *2519.* Related to "make a spectacle" in Heb 10:33.
22. Or, "poorly clothed". That is, without proper clothing. Used only here. GK *1217.* Related to "naked" in Jam 2:15, and "nakedness" in 2 Cor 11:27.
23. This word means "to strike with the fist". Elsewhere only in Mt 26:67; Mk 14:65; 2 Cor 12:7; 1 Pet 2:20. GK *3139.*
24. Or, "are unsettled, unstable, vagabonds, drifters, homeless; wandering from place to place". That is, the apostles are always moving from place to place, without a permanent home. It is a negative word. It is hard to find a single English word for this that does not add its own connotations. Used only here. GK *841.* Not related to "home", but to "unsteady, unstable".
25. Or "slandered, insulted, spoken to abusively, reproached". Elsewhere only in Jn 9:28; Act 23:4; 1 Pet 2:23. GK *3366.* Related to "a reviling" in 1 Pet 3:9; and "reviler" in 1 Cor 5:11.
26. Or, "encourage, appeal, exhort, comfort". On this word, see "exhorting" in Rom 12:8.
27. Or, "rinsings, filth, trash", that which is cleaned out when something is cleaned. Used only here. GK *4326.* The root word is "clean".
28. Or, "dregs, scrapings, offscouring", that which is wiped off or scraped out. Used only here. GK *4370.* The related verb means "to wipe around".
29. On this word, see Col 1:28. Some manuscripts say "I am admonishing" {C}.
30. Or, "become". GK *1181.*
31. However, the letter would arrive first, 16:10.
32. Some manuscripts omit this word {C}.

A. 1 Cor 10:13, common to humanity B. 2 Pet 3:8 C. Act 5:2, shared the knowledge D. Mt 8:29 E. Heb 6:4, enlighten F. 1 Jn 2:19, make evident G. Mt 24:9, then H. Act 16:40 J. Phil 4:11 K. 1 Tim 6:18, be rich L. Lk 19:11 M. 1 Jn 2:15 N. Lk 7:25, glorious O. 1 Cor 12:23, more without honor P. Mt 11:28, being weary Q. Mt 26:10 R. Lk 6:28 S. 2 Tim 3:12 T. 2 Cor 11:4, bear with U. Lk 18:2, have regard for V. Mt 3:17 W. 1 Jn 3:1 X. Gal 3:24 Y. 1 Jn 2:29, born Z. 1 Cor 15:1 AA. Rom 12:8 BB. Eph 5:1 CC. Col 1:2 DD. Jn 7:17

	1E.	And I shall come-to-know[A] not the talk[1] *of* the *ones* having been puffed-up[B], but the power[C]. °For the kingdom[D] *of* God *is* not in[2] talk, but in power	20
	2E.	What do you want? Should I come to you with *a* rod[3], or with love and *a* spirit *of* gentleness[E]?	21

2A. Sexual-immorality[4] is **actually**[5] being heard-*of* among you— and such sexual immorality which *is* not even[6] among the Gentiles, that someone has[7] *the* wife *of his* father[8]   5:1

    1B. And **you** are puffed-up[9], and did not mourn[F] instead, in order that the *one* having done[G] this deed[H] might be taken out of your midst[10]   2

    2B. For indeed **I**, being[11] absent[J] *in* the body but present[K] *in* the[12] spirit, have already judged[13]— as-*though* being present[14]— the *one* having thus committed[L] this *thing*   3

        1C. In the name *of* our Lord Jesus[15]   4
        2C. You and my spirit having been gathered-together[M]
        3C. With[16] the power[C] *of* our Lord Jesus
        4C. *You are* to hand-over[17] such *a one to* Satan for *the* destruction[18] *of his* flesh[19], in order that *his* spirit may be saved[N] on the day *of* the Lord[20]   5

    3B. Your boast[21] *is* not good. Do you not know that *a* little leaven[22] leavens the whole lump[23]? °Clean-out[24] the old leaven, in order that you may be *a* new lump, just as you are unleavened[O]   6-7

        1C. For indeed, our Passover [Lamb] was sacrificed[25]— Christ
        2C. So then let us celebrate-the-feast[26] not with old leaven,[27] nor with *the* leaven *of* badness[28] and evilness[P], but with *the* unleavened[O] *loaves of* purity[29] and truth[Q]   8

    4B. I wrote[30] you in the letter[31] not to associate-with[32] sexually-immoral[33] *ones*—°not[34] at-all[35] *meaning* with the sexually-immoral *ones of* this world, or *with* the greedy and[36] swindlers[37], or *with* idolaters, because then you *would* have to go out of the world!   9-10

        1C. But now[38] I wrote[39] *to* you not to associate-with *them* if anyone being named *a* brother[R] should be *a* sexually-immoral *one,* or *a* greedy *one,* or *an* idolater, or *a* reviler[40], or *a* drunkard[41], or *a* swindler[S]— not even to eat with such *a one*   11
        2C. For what do I have to do with[42] judging[43] the *ones* outside[44]?   12
        3C. Are **you** not judging the *ones* inside?[45]
        4C. But God judges[46] the *ones* outside   13

    5B. Remove[47] the evil[T] *one* from-*among* you yourselves[48]

3A. Does any one *of* you, having *a* matter[U] against the other, **dare**[V] to go-to-court[49] before the unrighteous[W] *ones*, and not before the saints[X]?   6:1

1. Or, "speech, word". On this word, see "word" in 12:8.
2. Or, "in the sphere of". GK *1877*.
3. That is, a rod used to give whippings, as happened to Paul in Act 16:22. Same word as in Heb 9:4; Rev 2:27; 12:5; 19:15. Elsewhere only as "staff" in Mt 10:10; Mk 6:8; Lk 9:3; Heb 11:21; Rev 11:1; and "scepter" in Heb 1:8. GK *4811*. Related to "beat with rods" in Act 16:22.
4. This word, rendered "fornication" by the KJV, refers to illicit sex in general, to sexual intercourse outside of the marriage relationship. It is also used metaphorically of spiritual unfaithfulness to God. Elsewhere only in Mt 5:32; 15:19; 19:9; Mk 7:21; Jn 8:41; Act 15:20, 29; 21:25; 1 Cor 6:13, 18; 7:2; 2 Cor 12:21; Gal 5:19; Eph 5:3; Col 3:5; 1 Thes 4:3; Rev 2:21; 9:21; 14:8; 17:2, 4; 18:3; 19:2. GK *4518*. The Greek is *porneia*. Related to the noun in 5:9; the verb in 6:18; and "prostitute" in 6:15.
5. Same word as in 6:7. Elsewhere only following "not" as "at all" in Mt 5:34; 1 Cor 15:39. GK *3914*.
6. Some manuscripts add "named" {N}.
7. That is, as his wife or cohabiting sexual partner. Same word as in 7:2, and Mt 14:4, where Herod "has" his brother's wife. It is the common verb "to have", used 708 times. GK *2400*.
8. That is, his step mother. Evidently this woman was not a Christian, since Paul does not address her case (note v 12).
9. This is a participle, you are "having been puffed up". Same word as in 4:6.
10. Some take this as a question, "And you are puffed up, and did not rather mourn...?" On this word, see 2 Thes 2:7.
11. Some manuscripts say "as being absent" {N}.
12. That is, "*my* spirit". Note v 4.
13. Or, "determined". Some think Paul means "I have judged... the *one* having"; others, "I have determined... *as to* the *one* having". This is the Greek order of phrases in v 3-5. On this word, see Mt 7:1.
14. That is, in body. On this word, see Rev 17:8.
15. Some manuscripts add "Christ"; others say "the Lord Jesus" {C}. Some take this phrase with "gathered together"; others, with "hand over"; others, with both. Paul placed it first for emphasis.
16. This word means "together with, along with, accompanied by", not "by means of". GK *5250*. Some take this with "gathered-together"; others, with "hand over".
17. Or, "deliver". Used for handing over prisoners to the authorities. Same phrase as in 1 Tim 1:20. Compare Mt 18:15-20; 2 Thes 3:14-15. Some think this refers to a special apostolic power, as seen in Act 5:1-11 and 13:9-11; others, to putting him out of the church, as in v 13; Mt 18:17. On this word, see Mt 26:21.
18. Same word as in 1 Thes 5:3; 2 Thes 1:9. Elsewhere only as "ruin" in 1 Tim 6:9. GK *3897*. Related to "utterly-destroyed" in Act 3:23; and to "destroyer" in 1 Cor 10:10.
19. Some think Paul means the sinful flesh, the fleshly lusts; others, the physical body, that is, for suffering and death; others, both.
20. Some manuscripts add "Jesus"; others add "Jesus Christ"; others say "our Lord Jesus Christ" {B}.
21. That is, the matter about which you are boasting; the content of your boast. On this word, see Phil 1:26.
22. Some think Paul is referring to the evil this man represents; others, to the evil man himself; others, to the Corinthians' boasting concerning their tolerance of him. In any case, the evil referred to will permeate like leaven, and change the whole church for the worse. Clean it out! On this word, and the verb next, see Mt 13:33.
23. That is, lump of dough.
24. Some manuscripts say "Therefore, clean-out" {N}.
25. On this word, see "slaughter" in Act 10:13 Some manuscripts add "for us" {N}.
26. Used only here. GK *2037*. Related to "feast" in Jn 13:29.
27. As part of the Jewish Passover, all leaven is removed from the house and unleavened bread is eaten as a reminder of the haste with which the Israelites left Egypt. Paul applies this to the Corinthians' spiritual lives.
28. Or, "malice". That is, moral or interpersonal badness. On this word, see 1 Pet 2:1.
29. Or, "sincerity". On this word, see 2 Cor 1:12.
30. Or, "I did write". On this word, see 1 Jn 2:12.
31. Some think Paul means a previous letter, which we do not have. Others think he is referring to this letter, to what is implied in v 2, 5.
32. Or, "mingle together, mix with, keep company". Elsewhere only in 5:11; 2 Thes 3:14. GK *5264*. The root word is "mix".
33. Or, "fornicators". Elsewhere only in 5:10, 11; 6:9; Eph 5:5; 1 Tim 1:10; Heb 12:16; 13:4; Rev 21:8; 22:15. GK *4521*. Related word in 5:1.
34. Some manuscripts add prior to "not" the word "indeed" {N}, rendered "yet" in the KJV.
35. Or, "surely not *meaning*". On this word, see "surely" in 9:10.
36. Some manuscripts say "or" {N}.
37. Or, "robbers, plunderers". Same word as in v 11; 6:10. On this word, see "ravenous" in Mt 7:15. Related to "plundering" in Heb 10:34, and "snatch away" in 2 Cor 12:2.
38. Or, "But as it is", making a logical connection to what was previously written, rather than a temporal connection. This idiom "but now" is used both ways. Same idiom as in 7:14; 12:20; 14:6. "Now" is GK *3814*.
39. Or, "I did write". That is, here in this letter, and clarified here. Same word and grammar as in v 9.
40. Elsewhere only in 6:10. GK *3368*. The related verb is in 4:12.
41. Elsewhere only in 6:10. GK *3500*. Related to "get drunk" in Jn 2:10.
42. On this phrase, see Jn 2:4.
43. Some manuscripts add "also" {N}. On this word, see Mt 7:1.
44. That is, the ones outside the church, non-Christians.
45. The grammar indicates a "yes" answer is expected. We are to judge ones inside the church who are living like non-Christians.
46. Or, "God will judge". The difference is an accent mark.
47. Or, "Take out, Purge, Expel, Put away". Used only here. GK *1976*. The root word is "take". Paul is echoing the phrase in Deut 17:7; 19:19; 22:21, 24; 24:7; where this same word is used. Some manuscripts begin this sentence with "And" {N}, which is rendered "Therefore" by the KJV.
48. This phrase "you yourselves" is elsewhere only in 7:35; 11:13; and Mk 6:31; Act 20:30.
49. Or, "to be judged". This word normally means "to judge", as in 5:12, 13; 6:2, 3. But it is also a legal term meaning "to take to court, to sue, to be judged in court", as here and v 6. Same word as "sue" in Mt 5:40. On this word, see "judge" in Mt 7:1.

A. Lk 1:34, know B. 1 Cor 4:6 C. Mk 5:30 D. Mt 3:2 E. Eph 4:2 F. Jam 4:9 G. Rom 2:1, practicing H. Mt 26:10, work J. 2 Cor 13:10 K. Rev 17:8 L. Phil 2:12, work out M. Mt 25:35, brought in N. Lk 19:10 O. Mk 14:12, unleavened bread P. Mt 22:18 Q. Jn 4:23 R. Act 16:40 S. Mt 7:15, ravenous T. Act 25:18 U. Mt 18:19 V. 2 Cor 11:21 W. 1 Cor 6:9, wrongdoers X. 1 Pet 1:16, holy

1B. Or[1] do you not know that the saints will judge[A] the world? And if the world is judged by you, are you unworthy *of the* smallest cases[2]? •Do you not know that we will judge angels?[3] *Shall I* not-indeed[4] *mention things*-pertaining-to-*this*-life[5]?   2, 3

  2B. So indeed, if you have cases[6] pertaining-to-*this*-life, are you seating[7] these [as judges]— the *ones* having been of-no-account[8] in the church? •I say *this* to your shame[9]   4, 5

    1C. So is there[10] not among you anyone wise who[11] will be able to discern[12] between his brother[B] *and this brother*— •but[13] brother is going-to-court[14] against brother, and this before unbelievers[C]?   6

  3B. So indeed[15], it is **already**[D] actually[16] *a* defeat[17] *for* you[18] that you have lawsuits[E] with each other   7

    1C. Why[19] not rather be wronged[F]? Why not rather be defrauded[20]?
    2C. But **you** are wronging and defrauding— and this [your own] brothers![21]   8

      1D. Or do you not know that wrongdoers[22] will not inherit[G] God's kingdom[H]?   9

        1E. Do not be deceived[J]. Neither sexually-immoral[K] *ones,* nor idolaters, nor adulterers, nor homo-erotic-partners[23], nor homosexuals[24], •nor thieves, nor greedy *ones*— not[25] drunkards, not revilers, not swindlers[26]— will inherit[G] *the* kingdom *of* God   10

        2E. And some *of you* were these *things*. But you washed-*them*-away[27], but you were sanctified[28], but you were declared-righteous[L] in the name *of the* Lord Jesus Christ[29] and in the Spirit *of* our God   11

4A. "All *things* are lawful[30] *to* me", but not all *things* are beneficial[31]. "All *things* are lawful *to* me", but **I** will not be mastered[32] by any   12

  1B. Foods *are for* the stomach[M], and the stomach *for* foods[33]. But God will do-away-with[34] both this and these   13

  2B. But the body[35] *is* not *for* sexual-immorality[N], but *for* the Lord, and the Lord *is for* the body. •And God both raised[O] the Lord, and will raise us up[36] by His power   14

  3B. Do you not know that your bodies are body-parts[37] *of* Christ? Therefore, having taken-away the body-parts *of* Christ, shall I make *them* body-parts *of a* prostitute[38]? May it never be!   15

1. Some manuscripts omit this word {N}.
2. Or, "courts, tribunals", as in Jam 2:6. Used of courts, and the cases heard there. Elsewhere only in v 4. GK *3215*.
3. The grammar of this question expects a "yes" answer.
4. This word implies a question expecting a "no" answer, "No, don't mention them". Used only here. GK *3615*. Others rephrase this as "How much more the things pertaining to this life!"
5. Same word as in v 4. On this word, see "pertaining to life" in Lk 21:34.
6. Or, "courts". Same word as in v 2.
7. Some take this as a command, "seat these... church!"; others as an exclamation, "you seat these... church!"; others, as a question. On this word, see "sat-*down*" in Rev 20:4.
8. Or, "disregarded, despised, disdained". As a command, Paul means "seat the least one in the church as judge rather than go to unbelievers!" As a statement or a question, he is referring to the seating of unbelievers (v 6) as judges over them by going to their courts. On this word, see "treat with contempt" in 1 Thes 5:20.
9. That is, to cause them to be ashamed. Elsewhere only in 15:34, where this sentence also refers to what precedes. GK *1959*. Related to the verb in 4:14, where Paul says he is not writing what precedes to shame them.
10. Some render this "[Is it] so [that] there is not".
11. Some manuscripts say "So is there not among you *a* wise *one*, not even one who..." {N}.
12. Or, "make a discernment, evaluation, decision". Same word as in 4:7.
13. Some take this phrase as part of the previous question; others, as a separate sentence, either as an exclamation, or as a question.
14. Same word as in v 1.
15. Same phrase, "so indeed", as in v 4. Paul moves from where to try the case, to the fact that such lawsuits exist at all. Both sides already lost before God before the case is even heard! Some manuscripts omit "so" {C}.
16. Same word as in 5:1.
17. Or, "failure". On this word, see Rom 11:12.
18. Some manuscripts say "among you" {K}.
19. More literally, "For what reason are you not rather being...", both times in this verse. GK *1328*.
20. Or, "robbed, deprived", as Christ taught, Mt 5:38-42. The party pressing the lawsuit has been defeated because he did not follow Christ in this matter. It is better to be wronged and defrauded than to have a lawsuit with a brother, even though you are in the right. Same word as in Mk 10:19; 1 Cor 6:8. Elsewhere only as "fraudulently withhold" in Jam 5:4; "deprive" in 1 Cor 7:5; and "rob" in 1 Tim 6:5. GK *691*.
21. Though Paul could mean that the party filing the lawsuit was in the wrong and trying to defraud his brother through it, perhaps he is turning to the other party, the one committing the wrong. This party has been defeated by the sin itself. Paul addresses this party in v 9-11.
22. Or, "unrighteous *ones*", as in v 1. Same root word as "wrong" in v 7 and 8 (see Act 7:24), and rendered this way to show the connection. Used 12 times. GK *96*.
23. Or, "catamites". This word was used of men and boys who gave themselves to be kept and used homosexually by older men. Thankfully, modern English has no commonly used word for this practice. GK *3434*.
24. That is, an adult male who engages in sex with another male. Made of two words "male-bed". "To have bed" means to have intercourse, as in Rom 9:10. Elsewhere only in 1 Tim 1:10. GK *780*.
25. Paul changes from "nor" to "not". Perhaps this is stylistic, or perhaps he highlights these because they describe the issues in Corinth resulting in their lawsuits. Some manuscripts continue to say "nor" in these three cases {N}.
26. Same word as in 5:10, 11. On "reviler" and "drunkard", see 5:11.
27. Or, "you washed away *your sins*, you washed *yourselves*". It is not passive, as in "you were washed". Some think Paul is referring to when the Corinthians believed and were baptized. Elsewhere only in Act 22:16, "wash away your sins". GK *666*. Related to "washing" in Eph 5:26.
28. Or, "made holy, set apart [to God]". On this word, see Heb 10:29.
29. Some manuscripts omit this word {C}.
30. Or, "permitted, authorized, right, proper" before God. This phrase is used twice here and in 10:23. Paul probably made this statement to them with reference to the external things formerly commanded to him as a Jew, especially food restrictions (a subject found both here and in 10:23). The Corinthians appear to have misapplied this to the area of sexual behavior, which Paul now corrects. Paul appears to be quoting it as their slogan. Same word as in Mt 12:2, 4, 10, 12; 14:4; 19:3; 20:15; 22:17; 27:6; Mk 2:24, 26; 3:4; 6:18; 10:2; 12:14; Lk 6:2, 4, 9; 14:3; 20:22; Jn 5:10; and with regard to Roman law in Jn 18:31; Act 16:21; 22:25. Elsewhere only as "is permitted" in 2 Cor 12:4; "is permissible" in Act 21:37; and "is proper" in Act 2:29. GK *2003*.
31. Or, "useful, profitable, expedient, advantageous, helpful" (brought together for good). Same word as in 10:23; 2 Cor 8:10; 12:1; and as "benefit" in 1 Cor 12:7; Heb 12:10. Elsewhere only as "be profitable" in Act 20:20; "be better" (see Mt 18:6); "be expedient" in Mt 19:10; and "bring together" in Act 19:19. GK *5237*. Related to "benefit" in 1 Cor 7:35.
32. Or, "be under the authority or power of". Elsewhere only as "have authority" in Lk 22:25; 1 Cor 7:4. GK *2027*. Related to "authority" in Rev 6:8.
33. Some think Paul is again quoting the Corinthians' slogan, which they were applying to sexual matters. "It's only natural", and has no moral or eternal consequence. Others think this is Paul's statement, affirming that this is the purpose for which God created foods, and thus "All things are lawful" is correctly applied to them. They have no other significance, and no place in the next life.
34. Or, "bring to nothing, nullify". God will abolish both the stomach and the foods. On this word, see Rom 6:6.
35. The case of the body is different. It was not made for sex, but for the Lord. And it will not be done away with, but transformed (Phil 3:21), resurrected. It has a permanent place in the next life.
36. Some manuscripts say "raised us up"; others, "raises us up" {B}. "Raise up" (GK *1995*) is related to "raise" earlier.
37. Or, "limbs, members of the body". On this word, see Col 3:5.
38. Or, "whore". Elsewhere only in Mt 21:31, 32; Lk 15:30; 1 Cor 6:16; Heb 11:31; Jam 2:25; Rev 17:1, 5, 15, 16; 19:2. GK *4520*. Related to the "sexual immorality" word group in 5:1; 5:9; 6:18.

A. Mt 7:1   B. Act 16:40   C. Mt 17:17, unbelieving   D. Mt 24:32   E. Jn 9:39, judgment   F. Act 7:24   G. Gal 4:30   H. Mt 3:2   J. Jam 5:19, err   K. 1 Cor 5:9   L. Rom 3:34   M. Lk 1:15, womb   N. 1 Cor 5:1   O. Mt 28:6, arose

| 1 Corinthians 6:16 | 590 | Verse |

    1C. Or¹ do you not know that the *one* joining² *himself to a* prostitute is one body *with her*? For He says [in Gen 2:24] "the two will be³ one flesh"   16

    2C. But the *one* joining *himself to* the Lord is one spirit *with Him*   17

    3C. Be fleeing⁴ sexual immorality   18

4B. Every sin which *a* person^A may do is outside the body.⁵ But the *one* committing-sexual-immorality⁶ is sinning against *his* own body

    1C. Or do you not know that your body is *the* temple *of* the Holy Spirit in you, Whom you have from God?   19

    2C. And you are not your *own*⁷, °for you were bought^B *with a* price^C   20

    3C. Therefore glorify^D God in your body⁸

5A. Now concerning *the things* which you wrote⁹   7:1

    1B. *It is* good¹⁰ *for a* man^A not to touch¹¹ *a* woman

        1C. But because of sexual-immoralities^E, let each *man* have¹² his *own* wife, and let each *woman* have *her* own husband   2

            1D. Let the husband give-back^F *to his* wife *her* due¹³, and likewise also the wife *to her* husband   3

            2D. The wife does not have-authority¹⁴ *over her* own body, but the husband *does*. And likewise also the husband does not have-authority *over his* own body, but the wife *does*   4

            3D. Do not be depriving^G one another— except perhaps by agreement¹⁵, for *a* time, in order that you may devote-yourselves¹⁶ *to* prayer¹⁷ and [then] be¹⁸ together¹⁹ again— in order that Satan may not tempt^H you because of your lack-of-self-control²⁰   5

        2C. But I am saying this²¹ by way of concession, not by way of command^J. °And²² I wish^K *that* all people^A were as indeed myself²³   6-7

            1D. But each has *his* own gift²⁴ from God— one in this manner, and another in this manner

        3C. And I say *to* the unmarried²⁵ and the widows— *it is* good *for* them if they remain^L as I also *am*   8

            1D. But if they do not have-self-control²⁶, let them marry²⁷. For it is better^M to marry than to be burning²⁸   9

        4C. But *to the ones* having married I command^N— not I, but the Lord²⁹—   10

            1D. *That a* wife not be separated³⁰ from *her* husband. °But if indeed she is separated, let her remain^L unmarried, or let her be reconciled^O *to her* husband   11

            2D. And *that a* husband not leave³¹ *his* wife

        5C. But *to* the rest³² I say, not the Lord³³—   12

            1D. If any brother has *an* unbelieving^P wife, and this *one* consents³⁴ to dwell^Q with him, let him not leave her. °And if any woman has *an* unbelieving husband, and this *one* consents to dwell with her, let her not leave *her* husband³⁵   13

1. Some manuscripts omit this word {C}.
2. This word means "join, unite, cling to, glue together". It is used of a husband and wife in Mt 19:5; of a believer and the Lord in 1 Cor 6:17; of joining or associating with others in Lk 15:15; Act 5:13; 8:29; 9:26; 10:28; 17:34. Elsewhere only as "cling" in Lk 10:11; Rom 12:9; and in the idiom "reached" in Rev 18:5. GK *3140*. Related word in Mk 10:7.
3. Literally, "be for one flesh", a Hebrew way of speaking.
4. Same word as in 10:14 (idolatry); 1 Tim 6:11 (love of money); 2 Tim 2:22 (youthful desires). Used 29 times. GK *5771*.
5. All sin proceeds from the heart outwardly (Mt 15:18-20) against the Lord (like idolatry), and usually also against another person (like theft). With sexual immorality, sin is in addition against one's own body. Some do not think Paul intends to imply that *only* immorality is against the body. It is also true of drugs, drunkenness, gluttony, etc. Others think Paul means sexual sin is different from all other sin, and suggest various senses in which this might be true.
6. Or, "engaging in illicit sex, fornicating". This verb is related to the words in 5:1, 9; 6:15. Elsewhere only in 10:8; Rev 2:14, 20; 17:2; 18:3, 9. GK *4519*.
7. More literally, "You are not your own's" or "You are not *of* yourself". That is, you do not belong to yourself. To those who would say "I can do what I want, because it is my body", Paul says, Not so!
8. Some manuscripts add "and in your spirit, which are God's" {A}.
9. Some manuscripts add "*to* me" {N}. The Corinthians wrote to Paul about several issues, and he now begins to answer their questions. Some think their questions are behind each B. point through 16:1, and perhaps even the question about Apollos in 16:12. Six of the nine B. points that follow begin with "Now concerning", a phrase Paul uses elsewhere only twice (1 Thes 4:9; 5:1). Others think the lack of "Now concerning" at 11:2 (and the comment in 11:18, and other factors) indicates that Paul returns there to writing proactively (as in chapters 1-6) about issues he heard about from other sources (perhaps the three men mentioned in 16:17). In this case, the B. points beginning at 11:2 would become A. points. Then again, perhaps chapters 11-16 are a mixture of Paul's issues and their questions. In any case, the understanding of each separate section in chapters 7-16 is unaffected by this question. Lacking an explicit indication from Paul that he has finished with their letter, the TransLine continues at the B. level for the rest of the book.
10. Or, "commendable, praiseworthy, advantageous, noble, desirable". Same word as in v 8, 26. On this word, see 1 Tim 5:10a.
11. Or, "to take hold of, cling to, have contact with". That is, it is good not to marry. Used 39 times, mostly of touching to heal. Used only here with reference to marriage and sexual contact. It also means "light" a lamp or fire. GK *721*.
12. Or, "be having". That is, marry, and have sexually, as this word is used in 5:1. In order to avoid sexual immorality, let these God-created needs be fulfilled in one another.
13. That is, give back what is owed to one another. The physical is in view here, but it is true in all ways. Some manuscripts say "the kindness being due *her*" {N}. Elsewhere only as "owed" in Rom 13:7; and "debt" in Mt 18:32. GK *4051*. The related verb is "ought" in 1 Jn 4:11.
14. Or, "have the right". That is, the authority to refuse or deprive the other of sexual relations. On this word, see "mastered" in 6:12. Related to "right" in 8:9.
15. Used only here. GK *5247*. Related to "harmony" in 2 Cor 6:15.
16. This word means "to have time *for*, have leisure *for*", have free time to devote to something, and then "give your time *to*, devote yourself *to*". Elsewhere only as "unoccupied" in Mt 12:44. GK *5390*.
17. Some manuscripts say "for fasting and prayer" {A}.
18. On this word, see "is" in Mt 26:26. Some manuscripts say "come" {N}.
19. On "together", see "at the same *place*" in Act 2:47.
20. Or, "lack of power over yourself". Elsewhere only in Mt 23:25 as "self-indulgence". GK *202*. Related to "without-self-control" in 2 Tim 3:3.
21. Some think Paul is referring to v 2, to marry; others, to v 5, the making of such agreements.
22. Some manuscripts say "For" {B}.
23. That is, single and pure. Paul prefers the single life for reasons he explains in verses 32-35.
24. Both marriage and singleness are a gift from God. On this word, see 1:7.
25. Used of men and women. Elsewhere only in v 11, 32, 34. GK *23*.
26. Elsewhere only as "exercises-self-control" in 1 Cor 9:25, of the self-control of athletes. GK *1603*. Related to the word in v 5, and to words in Tit 1:8 and 2 Pet 1:6.
27. Same word as in v 10, 28, 33, 34, 36, 39. Used 28 times. GK *1138*. Related to "give in marriage" in v 38, and "wedding" in Mt 22:11.
28. That is, with sexual desire. On this word, see 2 Cor 11:29, where Paul uses it of burning with anger or concern.
29. See the Lord's command in Mt 5:31-32; 19:1-12; Mk 10:1-12; Lk 16:18.
30. Whether by separating herself, or by being sent away by the husband. The command applies to both cases. On this word, see Mt 19:6.
31. Or, "abandon, divorce". Used only in v 11, 12, 13 in this sense. On this subject, see Mt 5:31. Same word as Rev 2:4, "left" your first love. This word is used 143 times in the NT, mostly as "to leave, permit, allow" and "to forgive" (see Mt 6:12). GK *918*.
32. As seen by what follows, Paul means those in marriages where one partner became a believer. On this word, see "other" in 2 Pet 3:16.
33. That is, Jesus did not address this issue while on earth. Paul has no command from the Lord. Note v 25.
34. Or, "approves". On this word, see "give approval" in Rom 1:32.
35. Some manuscripts say "leave him" {N}.

A. Mt 4:4, mankind B. Rev 5:9 C. 1 Tim 5:17, honor D. Rom 8:30 E. 1 Cor 5:1 F. Mt 16:27, render G. 1 Cor 6:7, defraud H. Heb 2:18 J. Rom 16:26 K. Jn 7:17, willing L. Jn 15:4, abide M. Heb 1:4 N. 1 Tim 1:3 O. Rom 5:10 P. Mt 17:17 Q. Rom 8:11

	1E. For the unbelieving husband has been sanctified¹ by *his* wife. And the unbelieving wife has been sanctified by the brother²	14
	2E. Otherwise then your children are unclean, but now³ they are holy⁴	
2D.	But if the unbelieving *one* separates^A, let *such a one*⁵ separate. The brother or the sister has not been enslaved^B by such *things*⁶, but God has called^C you⁷ in peace	15
	1E. For⁸ how do you know, wife, whether you will save^D *your* husband? Or how do you know, husband, whether you will save *your* wife?	16
	2E. Except⁹ *that* as the Lord¹⁰ apportioned¹¹ to each *one,* as God has called^C each *one,* in this manner let him be walking^E. And thus I am directing¹² in all the churches	17
	1F. Was anyone called^C having been circumcised^F? Let him not conceal¹³ *it*. Has anyone been called¹⁴ in uncircumcision^G? Let him not be circumcised	18
	1G. Circumcision^H is nothing, and uncircumcision is nothing, but *the* keeping *of the* commandments^J *of* God	19
	2G. Each in the calling^K *in* which he was called^C— in this let him remain^L	20
	2F. Were you called *as a* slave^M? Do not let it be *a* concern¹⁵ to you. But if also¹⁶ you are able to become free^N, rather make-use-of^O *the opportunity*¹⁷	21
	1G. For the *one* having been called^C in *the* Lord *as a* slave^M is *a* freedperson *of the* Lord. Likewise¹⁸ the *one* having been called *as a* free^N *one* is *a* slave *of* Christ	22
	2G. You were bought *with a* price¹⁹— do not become slaves *of* people²⁰	23
	3G. Each in what he was called^C, brothers— in this let him remain^L with God	24
2B.	Now concerning virgins²¹, I do not have *a* command^P *from the* Lord, but I am giving *an* opinion²² as *one* having been shown-mercy^Q by *the* Lord to be trustworthy^R	25

1. Or, "consecrated, made holy". On this word, see Heb 10:29. Though the marriage is not "in the Lord" (v 39), the marriage and family have been made holy by the presence of the believer. Such a person is consecrated as a husband or wife, not as an individual before God. Rather than being "defiled" by the unbeliever, who is probably an idolater, the believer "sets apart, consecrates" the unbeliever, and the children.
2. Some manuscripts say "husband" {A}. Paul means the "believing husband".
3. Or, "but as it is". On this idiom, see 5:11
4. On this word, see 1 Pet 1:16. Related to "sanctified" earlier.
5. This command refers back to "the unbelieving *one*", whether the husband or the wife. The subject is rendered "such a one" here instead of "him" (as normal, with reference to both genders) to more clearly bring this out. Paul makes the universal reference he implies here explicit in the next sentence.
6. Or, "in such *matters*", or relationships. Or, "by such *ones*" who have departed, the unbelievers. You are "free" (v 39) from that partner to live in peace, not still bound to the deserter and living in turmoil. The "hardness of heart" (Mt 19:8) of the deserter has destroyed the marriage. Move on with the Lord in peace.
7. Some manuscripts say "us" {B}.
8. Note the difference. Stay together because of the positive impact you as a believer will have regardless of whether or not your partner comes to Christ, v 14. But if the unbeliever leaves, let the marriage go and move on, because you do not know if such a one will ever come to Christ and return to the marriage. Thus Paul gives the reason for accepting the dissolution of the marriage caused by the unbelieving partner. Some connect this verse with v 12-13, so that Paul is giving a further reason to stay together. In this case, v 15 becomes point 1F., a parenthesis, and this verse becomes 3E.
9. Having said that the believer is "not enslaved" to human relationships in v 15, Paul now contrasts this statement with the broader view. This is the general principle of Christian living extending beyond marriage to all of life, of which the case in v 15 is an exception. In general, focus on serving Christ in whatever place or status in life He called you, rather than trying to change or escape from your obligations or situation. Allow Him to bring about change from within, through you. Some smooth this idiom as "but, only, however, nevertheless". It normally means "except, unless, if not". In any case, it indicates a contrast with what precedes.
10. Some manuscripts say "God" here, and "the Lord" in the next phrase, reversing them {N}.
11. Or, "divided, distributed, assigned". Some manuscripts say "has apportioned" {N}. Same word as in Rom 12:3, of spiritual gifts, and in 2 Cor 10:13. Elsewhere only as "divided" in Mt 12:25, 26; Mk 3:24, 25, 26; 6:41; Lk 12:13; 1 Cor 1:13; 7:34; Heb 7:2. GK *3532*.
12. Or, "commanding, ordering, giving orders". Same word as in Lk 8:55; Act 7:44; 1 Cor 9:14; 16:1; Tit 1:5. Elsewhere only as "give directions *to*" in Mt 11:1; "order" in Act 18:2; "give orders *to*" in Act 24:23; "set in order" in 1 Cor 11:34; "arrange" in Act 20:13; and "command" in Lk 3:13; 17:9, 10; Act 23:31; Gal 3:19. GK *1411*.
13. Or "pretend he is uncircumcised, mask *it*". Let the Jewish Christians not seek to undo their Jewish heritage. Used only here. GK *2177*. This is a medical term meaning "to pull over the foreskin", used metaphorically here.
14. Some manuscripts say "Was anyone called" {N}, as in the first sentence.
15. Same word as in Mt 22:16; Mk 12:14; Jn 10:13; 12:6; Act 18:17; 1 Cor 9:9; 1 Pet 5:7. Elsewhere only as "care" in Mk 4:38; Lk 10:40. GK *3508*.
16. Or, "even, indeed". The grammar means "Assuming that you are able to become free". This word adds one of three nuances to the condition, so that it means assuming that "also", or "even", or "indeed". "If also" is in 2 Cor 11:15. "If even", meaning "even though", is in Mk 14:29; Lk 11:8; 18:4; 2 Cor 4:16; 5:16; 7:8, 12; 11:6; 12:11; Phil 2:17 ("if even"); Col 2:5; Heb 6:9. "If indeed" is in Lk 11:18; 1 Cor 4:7; 2 Cor 4:3. A related idiom is used in Phil 3:12; 1 Pet 3:14.
17. All three nuances mentioned in the note above are advocated here, since Paul does not state what it is these slaves are to make use of. Some think he means "Assuming that you also (while not being concerned about it, but serving where the Lord called you) are able to become free, rather make use of *this opportunity*", making this a parenthetical softening of "not a concern". Others think he means "Assuming that you indeed are able to become free, rather make use of *your new freedom*", so that in this verse he addresses both slave and free, as in v 18 he addressed both circumcised and uncircumcised. Others think he means "Assuming you even are able to become free, rather make use of *your present state*", heightening the exhortation to serve Christ now. Do not wait until you are free to serve Him.
18. Some manuscripts say "Likewise also" {N}.
19. Same sentence as in 6:20.
20. Some think Paul means "do not sell yourself as a slave". Others think he means "do not become slaves of the opinions of others regarding your status as slave or free", including this with v 22 in the parallel to v 19.
21. That is, unmarried females usually, but sometimes males (as in English). Here, some think Paul means females, as in the other uses of this word in this context (v 28, 34, 36, 37, 38. In these cases, the grammar is clear. Here in v 25, it is not specific). Others think he means both, because what follows is specifically applied to both, v 26-28, 32-34. In any case, what should they and their families do about past commitments to arranged marriages, or about future marriages? Marriages were arranged by the parents, and commitments were made between families and individuals. Should they cancel or honor them? Should their child go ahead and marry? For example, what should two people in the status of Joseph and Mary do, Mt 1:18-19. During this status, which could last a year, the still virgin couple continued to live with their respective parents, but they were considered to be man and wife, based on the commitments made by the families. On this word, see Rev 14:4.
22. Or, "judgment". Same word as in v 40. On this word, see "purpose" in 1:10.

A. Mt 19:6   B. Rom 6:18   C. Rom 8:30   D. Lk 19:10   E. Heb 13:9   F. Lk 2:21   G. Rom 2:26, uncircumcised   H. Eph 2:11, circumcised
J. Mk 12:28   K. 2 Pet 1:10   L. Jn 15:4, abide   M. Rom 6:17   N. Mt 17:26   O. 1 Cor 7:31   P. Rom 16:26   Q. Rom 12:8   R. Col 1:2, faithful

1C. I think^A then *that* this¹ is good^B because of the present² necessity³, that *it is* good^B *for a* person^C to be^D so⁴   26

    1D. Have you been bound⁵ *to a* woman⁶? Do not be seeking^E *a* release⁷   27
    2D. Have you been released⁸ from *a* woman? Do not be seeking *a* wife
    3D. But even if you⁹ marry, you did not sin. And if the¹⁰ virgin marries, she did not sin   28

       1E. But such *ones* will have affliction^F *in* the flesh, and **I** am sparing^G you¹¹

2C. And this I say, brothers^H— the time¹² is shortened¹³, so that **henceforth**   29

    1D. Even the *ones* having wives should be^D as-*though* not having
    2D. And the *ones* weeping^J as-*though* not weeping   30
    3D. And the *ones* rejoicing^K as-*though* not rejoicing
    4D. And the *ones* buying^L as-*though* not holding-on-to¹⁴
    5D. And the *ones* making-use-of¹⁵ the world as-*though* not making-full-use-of¹⁶ *it*   31
    6D. For the form¹⁷ *of* this world is passing away

3C. Now I want you to be free-from-concern¹⁸   32

    1D. The unmarried^M man is concerned-about^N the *things of* the Lord— how he may please^O the Lord

       1E. But the *man* having married is concerned-*about* the *things of* the world— how he   33
          may please his wife,° and he has been divided¹⁹   34

    2D. And the unmarried^M woman²⁰, and the virgin, is concerned-*about* the *things of* the Lord— that she may be holy^P both *in* the body and *in* the spirit

       1E. But the *woman* having married is concerned-*about* the *things of* the world— how she may please *her* husband

4C. Now I am saying this²¹ for the benefit²² *of* you yourselves— not that I may throw *a* noose²³ on   35
you, but toward good-order²⁴ and devotion²⁵ *to* the Lord, undistractedly²⁶

    1D. But if one²⁷ thinks *that* he is behaving-dishonorably²⁸ toward his virgin *daughter*²⁹— if   36
       she is beyond-the-bloom-of-youth³⁰, and it ought^Q to be³¹ so,³² let him³³ do what he wants.
       He is not sinning. Let them marry
    2D. But he who   37

       1E. Stands steadfast^R in his heart,³⁴ not having *a* necessity³⁵

1. That is, the status of being a virgin and unmarried mentioned in v 25.
2. This is a participle, "having come, being present". On this word, see Heb 9:9.
3. Or, "constraint, pressure, compulsion", and then a "distress, calamity" caused by external necessities or forces. Paul's advice is given in view of some unusual circumstance, perhaps a persecution or a famine. Same word as in Mt 18:7; Lk 14:18; Rom 13:5; 1 Cor 7:37; 9:16; Heb 7:12, 27; 9:16, 23; Jude 3. Elsewhere only as "compulsion" in 2 Cor 9:7; Phm 14; "constraint" in 2 Cor 6:4; 12:10; and "distress" in Lk 21:23; 1 Thes 3:7. GK *340*.
4. More literally, "that the being so *is* good *for a* person". Some think Paul means "the being a virgin, unmarried" (v 25), this phrase clarifying and emphasizing the previous one. Others think he means "that *it is* good *for a* person to be as-follows" (as this word is used in Mt 1:18; Rom 10:6; Rev 9:17; etc. GK *4048*). Others take this to mean "to be as he is", so that it is broad enough to include the unmarried and married in what follows.
5. Some think Paul is referring to the agreements or arrangements for marriage previously made by their families. This view renders the next word "woman". Others think he means bound in marriage, as this word is used in 7:39; Rom 7:2. This view renders the next word "wife". Used 43 times as "bind, tie". GK *1313*.
6. Used three times in this verse, this word means either "woman" or "wife", based on the context. It is used 215 times in the NT. GK *1222*.
7. Or, "*an* unbinding, untying, *a* loosing". That is, a release from a pledge or obligation. Some think Paul means "Do not seek a release from your commitment to marry. Do not break your commitments"; others, "Do not seek a a divorce", as in v 10-11. Used only here. GK *3386*. Related to the next word.
8. Or, "unbound, untied, loosed". Used 42 times in the NT, but only here with regard to a man-woman relationship. Those who take the first view of the previous word give this related word the same meaning, "released" from a commitment to marry. Those who take the previous word to mean "divorce" give this word a different meaning, such as "freed from the marriage bond" by any circumstance; or, more broadly, "unmarried" (including those never married). On this word, see "break" in Mt 5:19.
9. If you take the next step and marry, you have not sinned. Paul states this for both parties. "You" is the male.
10. Some manuscripts say "*a virgin*" {N}.
11. That is, Paul is trying to spare the young couples from the problems they will have caused by the "present necessity" (v 26).
12. That is, the time remaining in one's life to serve Christ before one dies, or He comes.
13. Or, "drawn in, compressed". This is a participle, "is having been shortened", is in a state of shortness. Elsewhere only as "wrapped up" in Act 5:6, of a dead body. GK *5366*.
14. Or, "retaining". Compare 2 Cor 6:10. On this word, see "hold down" in Rom 1:18.
15. Or, "using". Same word as in 7:21; 9:12, 15. Elsewhere only as "use" in Act 27:17; 2 Cor 3:12; 1 Tim 1:8; 5:23; "act" in 2 Cor 1:17; 13:10; and "treat" in Act 27:3. GK *5968*. Related to "make full use" next.
16. This verse speaks of an internal separation from this world that is reflected in actions. Same word as in 9:18, where Paul does this. Some give this word a negative flavor, "abuse".
17. On this word, see "outward appearance" in Phil 2:7. The present form of this world is passing away.
18. Or, "without a care". Elsewhere only in Mt 28:14. GK *291*.
19. Paul is not saying marriage is bad. But in view of the "present necessity", it may be unwise. Some manuscripts say "and he has been divided. And the unmarried woman and the unmarried virgin...". Others say "and the woman has been divided. And the unmarried virgin...". Others say "The wife and the unmarried virgin have also been divided. She is concerned..." {D}.
20. That is, the widow (v 39-40), the abandoned or divorced (v 15).
21. That is, that the unmarried should remain so.
22. Or, "profit, advantage". Elsewhere only in 10:33. GK *5239*. Related to "beneficial" in 6:12.
23. Or, "a slip knot", a rope used as a lasso, a snare, or a restraint, a halter. A choke chain. That is, not to try to restrain or control you. Used only here. GK *1105*.
24. Or, "what is proper, appropriate, decent, becoming, presentable". The word means "of good form, elegant, graceful". Same word as "presentable" in 12:24. GK *2363*. Related to "properly" in 14:40.
25. Or, "service, constant waiting upon, attending to". Used only here. GK *2339*. Related to "serve" in 9:13.
26. Used only here. GK *597*. This adverb is related to "distracted" in Lk 10:40.
27. In v 36-38, some think Paul is addressing the father of a daughter of marriageable age; others, a groom betrothed or engaged to a girl. Consult the commentaries on these and other views.
28. Or, "improperly, disgracefully, indecently", the opposite of "good order" in v 35. Such would be the father's position if he acted against his daughter's will and needs (v 7, 9) and did not permit her to wed (it was his decision to make in that day). He would be dishonoring himself, and placing her in danger of temptation and disgrace. Those who think Paul is referring to the groom take this to mean "if the man is unable to control his passions". Elsewhere only in 13:5. GK *858*.
29. Those who think this refers to the groom supply "*fiancee*".
30. That is, of marriageable age, past full physical development. Those who think Paul is referring to the groom think he means "if she is beyond her prime", that is, getting old; or, "if he is of strong passions" and needs to marry her. Used only here. GK *5644*.
31. Or, "become". GK *1181*.
32. That is, if the marriage is right and ought to take place, all things considered; if the father feels it is his duty to permit his daughter to marry, all things considered.
33. That is, the father making this decision. In the other view, this refers to the groom.
34. That is, believing it is best for his daughter to remain single as Paul said, in spite of the cultural pressure against this decision. In this case, the father is certain that this is the honorable choice in his daughter's case, all things considered. In the other view, this refers to the groom's resolve to remain single.
35. Or, "constraint, obligation, compulsion". Same word as in v 26. Outside forces, including his daughter's desires and needs, are not compelling the father to do otherwise. Nothing is compelling him to act against his best judgment. In the other view, this means that the groom's sexual passions are not forcing him to marry.

A. Act 14:19   B. 1 Tim 5:10a   C. Mt 4:4, mankind   D. Mt 26:26, is   E. Phil 2:21   F. Rev 7:14   G. Rom 11:21   H. Act 16:40   J. Jn 11:33   K. 2 Cor 13:11   L. Rev 5:9   M. 1 Cor 7:8   N. Mt 6:25, be anxious   O. 1 Thes 2:4   P. 1 Pet 1:16   Q. 1 Jn 4:11   R. Col 1:23

　　　　2E. And has authority¹ concerning² *his* own will
　　　　3E. And has determinedᴬ this in *his* own heart— to keep³ *his* virgin *daughter*
　　　　4E. He will do well⁴

　　　3D. So then, both the *one* giving his virgin *daughter*⁵ in marriage is doing well, and⁶ the *one* not giving-in-marriage⁷ will do⁸ betterᴮ　　　38

　5C. *A* wife has been bound⁹ for as much time as her husband lives　　　39

　　　1D. But if *her* husband falls-asleep¹⁰, she is freeᶜ to be married *to* whom she wishesᴰ— only in *the* Lord
　　　2D. But she is happier¹¹ if she remainsᴱ thus¹², according to my opinionᶠ— and **I** also think that *I* have *the* Spirit *of* God　　　40

3B. Now concerning the foods-sacrificed-to-idols¹³　　　8:1

　1C. We know that we all have knowledge¹⁴

　　　1D. Knowledge puffs-upᴳ, but love builds-upᴴ
　　　2D. If¹⁵ anyone thinksᴶ *that he* has come-to-know¹⁶ anything, he did not-yet know¹⁷ as *he* ought-to¹⁸ know.¹⁹ *But if one loves*ᴷ God, this *one* has been known by Him²⁰　　　2　3

　2C. Therefore concerning the eating *of* the foods-sacrificed-to-idols— we knowᴸ that *an* idol *is* nothing²¹ in *the* world, and that *there is* no²² God except one　　　4

　　　1D. For even if-indeed²³ there are *ones* being calledᴹ gods, whether in heaven or on earth— as-indeed there are many gods and many lords²⁴— *yet for* us *there is*　　　5　6

　　　　1E. One God the Father, from Whom *are* all *things*. And we *are*²⁵ for Him
　　　　2E. And one Lord Jesus Christ, through Whom *are* all *things*. And we *are* through Him

　3C. But *this* knowledge *is* not in all *people*　　　7

　　　1D. But some, *by* the accustomed-habit²⁶ *of* the idol until now, eat *this food* as food-sacrificed-to-an-idol.²⁷ And their conscienceᴺ, being weakᴼ, is stained²⁸

　4C. But foodᴾ will not bring us²⁹ near³⁰ to God— neither³¹ if we do not eat are we lacking³², nor if we eat are we abounding³³　　　8

1. Or, "power, freedom to act". That is, the father has the freedom and resources to do what he wants to do. Nothing is preventing him from doing as he thinks best. For example, a father who was a slave would not have this authority. In the other view, this means that the groom has power over his own passions, a positive restatement of the previous phrase. On this word, see Rev 6:8.
2. Or, "in relation to, with regard to". GK *4309*.
3. That is, to keep her as she is, unmarried; to keep his daughter in his household and support her so that she can serve the Lord undistractedly, v 35. Those who think Paul is referring to the groom think he means "to keep his virgin fiancee in that status" or "to keep his virgin fiancee a virgin", implying either "to not marry her" or "to delay marrying her".
4. That is, he will be doing a good or commendable thing. On this idiom, see Act 10:33. Some manuscripts say "he does well" {K}.
5. Some manuscripts omit "his virgin *daughter*" {N}.
6. Some manuscripts say "but" {K}.
7. Used twice in this verse, this word (GK *1139*) is elsewhere only in Mt 22:30; 24:38; Mk 12:25; Lk 17:27; 20:35; all in the phrase "marry and give-in-marriage", where the word "marry" is the word in 1 Cor 7: 9. Here, those who think Paul is referring to the groom in v 36-38 take this word to mean the same thing as "marry" in 7:9. Related word in Lk 20:34. Some manuscripts say "give out in marriage" both times in this verse {N}, the word also being a variant for this word in Mt 22:30; 24:38; Lk 17:27; 20:35.
8. Some manuscripts say "does" {K}.
9. Same word as in v 27. Some manuscripts add "*by the* Law" {N}.
10. That is, dies. Same word as 15:6, 18, 20, 51. On this word, see 1 Thes 4:13.
11. Or, "more blessed, more fortunate". On this word, see "blessed" in Lk 6:20.
12. That is, single, so that she can serve undistractedly, v 35. However, outside of this "present necessity" (v 26), Paul advises younger widows to remarry, 1 Tim 5:11-15.
13. That is, the eating of meat or foods that had been previously offered as a sacrifice to an idol. Part was burned on the altar to the deity, part was eaten at a meal in the idol's temple, and part was sold in the meat market. As unbelievers, it was the Corinthians' custom to buy and eat this meat (v 7), but now they have become concerned about it in view of their commitment to Christ. Elsewhere only in Act 15:29; 21:25; 1 Cor 8:4, 7, 10; 10:19; Rev 2:14, 20. GK *1628*.
14. Some think Paul is referring to a claim the Corinthians made about themselves in their letter to him. He corrects the spirit of it, in light of the fact of v 7.
15. Some manuscripts say "And if " {N}.
16. Or, "has known". Same word as "know" and "known" next, on which see "know" in Lk 1:34. Some manuscripts say "knows" {N}.
17. Some manuscripts say "he has not yet known" {K}. Some manuscripts add "anything" {N}, so that it says "not yet know anything".
18. Or, "as it is necessary". On this idiom, see Act 25:10.
19. The knowledge we all have (v 1) is at best a partial (13:9), dim reflection (13:12). It never fully attains.
20. That is, assuming that you love God, you are known by God, because the love you have is from God, 1 Jn 4:7. Love defines our relationship to God and His family, not knowledge. Knowledge proves nothing, for even the demons know Him (Jam 2:19). Love shows that a relationship has been established.
21. Or, "that *there is* no idol", that is, no genuine representation of any god.
22. Some manuscripts add "other" {N}.
23. That is, even if there are many called gods, as is the case, yet for us there is one God. On this word, see "since" in Rom 8:9.
24. Paul later calls them "demons", 10:20.
25. Or, "*exist, live*". Same idea in the second statement in this verse.
26. Or, "custom, habitual use, the being accustomed to a thing". Same word as "custom" in 11:16. Some manuscripts instead have the word used later in the verse, "conscience, consciousness" {A}.
27. Such people eat the food as if the "sacrifice", the "eating", and the "idol" still carried their old meanings. They have not yet escaped the former mental associations.
28. Or, "dirtied, soiled, defiled". Elsewhere only in Rev 3:4; 14:4. GK *3662*. Related to "stain" in 2 Cor 7:1. Such people have a dirty conscience because they suspect (incorrectly) that eating these idol-sacrifices is an offense to God.
29. That is, us having knowledge, whose choices are the focus of the entire discussion in chapters 8-10. Paul is correcting a false estimation of the spiritual significance of eating or not eating that the strong might hold, and even proclaim to the weak— that they gain spiritually by exercising this freedom, or lose by restricting it. Verse 8 is also true for the weak ones in v 7, but it does not address their case. They would say the opposite of v 8— that they are better not to eat, and worse if they eat.
30. Or, "present us". This word, "bring near", is the same word as "present" in Rom 12:1. Some manuscripts say "does not bring near" {N}. Some think Paul means "present us to our advantage, bring us near", based on the context. When food is spiritually considered, we lack no advantage if we do not eat, and we gain none if we do eat. But the word itself is neutral, and others prefer a neutral meaning here, "present". When food is physically considered, it does not "present" us to God for either reward or judgment. It has neither a positive nor a negative effect on us before God. Compare Rom 14:17.
31. Note the precision of Paul's statement. He does not say "eating or not eating is neither good nor bad". He says not eating causes no lack, eating no gain. This is true for both strong and weak; both directly for themselves, and indirectly for themselves through its effect on others. However, not eating can bring reward, and eating can bring loss. This is true for the weak (directly, as seen in v 7, 10-11) and the strong (indirectly, the loss being seen in v 9, 12, the gain beginning in v 13). Note that it is this side of things, the indirect effects of the behavior of the strong on others and on themselves, that Paul turns to and develops beginning in 8:9. Some manuscripts say "For neither" {N}.
32. Or, "are we in need". That is, before God. On this word, see "be in need" in Lk 15:14.
33. Some manuscripts invert the order of these two clauses, putting "if we eat... abounding" first {N}. On this word, see 2 Cor 8:2.

A. Mt 7:1, judge B. Heb 1:4 C. Mt 17:26 D. Jn 7:17, willing E. Jn 15:4, abide F. 1 Cor 7:25 G. 1 Cor 4:6 H. 1 Cor 14:4, edify J. Lk 19:11 K. Jn 21:15, devotedly love L. 1 Jn 2:29 M. Jn 12:49, say N. Act 23:1 O. 1 Thes 5:14 P. Mk 7:19

5C. But be watching-out[A] *that* this right[1] *of* yours does not somehow become *an* opportunity-for-stumbling[2] *to* the weak[3] *ones*   9

    1D. For if someone sees you— the *one* having knowledge[4]— reclining[5] [to eat] in *an* idol-temple, will not his conscience[B], being weak[C], be built-up[6] so as to eat the foods-sacrificed-to-idols?   10

        1E. For[7] the *one* being weak[8] is being destroyed[9] by your knowledge— the brother[D] for the sake of whom Christ died!   11

        2E. And in this manner sinning[E] against the brothers and striking[10] their conscience[B] while being weak[F], you are sinning against Christ   12

6C. For-this-very-reason[11], if food[G] causes my brother to fall, I will never eat meats, ever[12]— in-order-that[13] I may not cause my brother to fall[14]   13

    1D. Am I[15] not free[16]? Am I not *an* apostle[H]? Have I not seen Jesus[17] our Lord? Are **you** not my work[J] in *the* Lord?[18]   9:1

        1E. If *to* others I am not *an* apostle, yet indeed I am *to* you. For **you** are the seal[K] *of* my apostleship[L] in *the* Lord— *this[19] is my defense[M] *to* the *ones* examining[N] me!   2   3

    2D. We do not fail[20] to have *the* right to eat and drink, *do we*?[21] *We do not fail to have *the* right to take along *a* sister[22] who is *a* wife[23], *do we*?— as also the other apostles, and the brothers[24] *of* the Lord, and Cephas[25]. *Or[26] I alone and Barnabas[O]— do not we have *the* right not to be working?[27]   4-5   6

        1E. Who ever serves-as-a-soldier[P] *with* his own rations[Q]? Who plants *a* vineyard and does not eat the fruit[R] *of* it? Or who shepherds[S] *a* flock and does not eat of the milk *of* the flock?   7

        2E. I am not speaking these *things* according to [mere] human[T] thinking[28], *am I*? Or does not the Law also say these *things*?[29] *For in the Law *of* Moses it has been written [in Deut 25:4], "You shall not muzzle *a* threshing ox"   8   9

            1F. God is not concerned[U] about the oxen, *is He*?[30]
            2F. Or is He surely[31] speaking for our sake?
            3F. Indeed[32] it was written for our sake— because[33] the *one* plowing ought[V] to plow on the basis of hope[W], and the *one* threshing *to* thresh on the basis of hope *that he might* partake[34]   10

        3E. If **we** sowed[X] spiritual[Y] *things* to you, *is it a* great *thing* if **we** shall reap fleshly[35] *things from* you?   11

        4E. If others partake of *this* right *over* you[36], *should* we not more?   12

1. Or, "authority, power", the "right" to eat this food. Same word as in 9:4, 5, 6, 12, 18; Jn 1:12; 2 Thes 3:9; Heb 13:10; Rev 22:14. Elsewhere only as "authority", 91 times (see Rev 6:8). Knowledge brings a power, a freedom to act. But do not allow your actions to cause unintended harm to those who do not have your knowledge. Freedom is bounded by love of God and our neighbor.
2. On this word, see Rom 14:13. It refers to an accidental cause of someone else stumbling or taking a misstep.
3. The weak here are those with a weak conscience (v 7), who follow the strong believer's example and then have a dirty conscience about it. Their knowledge of God's truth is not sufficient to support their acting this way. On this word, see 1 Thes 5:14. Some manuscripts say "the *ones* being weak" {K}.
4. Note Paul does not say "the strong one". Whether this person is "strong" will depend on how he or she uses their knowledge.
5. People in that day laid down to eat. Though not the subject here, later Paul addresses the question of whether the stronger brother should be doing this at all, 10:14-22. There he says it is wrong to do so.
6. Or, "established, strengthened". The grammar indicates a "yes" answer is expected. Same word as in 8:1.
7. Some manuscripts say "And"; others, "Therefore" {N}.
8. Some manuscripts say "the brother being weak" {K}.
9. Or, "ruined". On this word, see "perish" in 1:18. Some manuscripts say "will perish" {N}.
10. Or, "assaulting", and thus "wounding". On this word, see Lk 6:29.
11. That is, to not be a cause of stumbling (v 9), and thus sin against Christ (v 12). Elsewhere only in 10:14. GK *1478*.
12. On this idiom, "never... ever", see Jn 4:14.
13. Or, "so that I will not cause". GK *2671*.
14. Note that this is a negative reason for doing this— so that others are not caught in a trap that hinders them from further spiritual growth or damages their spiritual life. Such causes of falling will come (Mt 18:7), but Paul acts so as not to unnecessarily become one by his own personal choices. The positive reason is given in 9:24. This word means "cause to fall, be caught, be trapped; to take offense; to give offense". Jesus said it is better to die than to do this, Mt 18:6. Same word as in Mt 5:29, 30; 13:21; 18:6, 8, 9; 24:10; 26:31, 33; Mk 4:17; 9:42, 43, 45, 47; 14:27, 29; Lk 17:2; Jn 16:1; 2 Cor 11:29. Elsewhere only as "take offense" in Mt 11:6; 13:57; 15:12; Mk 6:3; Lk 7:23; and "offend" in Mt 17:27; Jn 6:61. GK *4997*. On the related noun, see Rom 11:9.
15. Paul now uses himself (in foregoing his right to financial support) as an example of choosing not to use one's rights for the good of the progress of the gospel, so as to justify the bold statement in 8:13.
16. That is, Paul's behavioral decisions are not based on the opinions of others. He is free to eat meat. The choice to not do so is his free choice, made not because someone disapproves of the meat, but because he is seeking something greater than meat. He returns to this in v 19. On this word, see Mt 17:26. Some manuscripts reverse these two questions, putting "apostle" first {N}.
17. Some manuscripts add "Christ" {K}.
18. Paul's point in saying this is to prove that he has certain rights because of his status, calling, and work. Specifically, he has certain rights over the Corinthians, because he is an apostle to them, one being the right to financial support, which he proves in v 4-12. Note that v 1-14 are aimed at proving he has the right which he gives up in v 12, 15.
19. Some think this is a parenthetical comment regarding the defense of Paul's apostleship, a matter he does not discuss further here. In this case, "this" looks back to "you are the seal". Others think he means his defense regarding the strong statement in 8:13; that is, regarding his call to place a voluntary restriction on our "rights" for the good of other believers. In this case, "this" looks forward to what follows, and verse 2 is parenthetical. This sentence would begin point 2D., "This is my defense *to* the *ones* examining me—".
20. Note that Paul's first argument (v 4-12), is negative. Surely we are not excluded from this right, are we? His conclusion in v 12 is that he did not make use of this right from which he was not excluded. Compare v 13-14.
21. That is, to eat and drink from you, at your expense, to sustain ourselves through our work in the Lord. On the grammar of this and the next question, see Rom 10:18. More literally, "we do not not have the right..., *do we*?" or *"It is* not *that* we do not have the right, *is it*?" You would not say Barnabas and I do not have the right, would you? We are not excluded from the rights all others have, are we? The grammar expects a "no" answer.
22. That is, a fellow believer, a spiritual sister, as also in Mt 12:50; Rom 16:1; 1 Cor 7:15. Used also of physical sisters, as in Lk 10:39. Used 26 times. GK *80*. Compare "brother" in Act 16:40.
23. The grammar expects a "no" answer. Barnabas and I have the right to take with us on our journeys a wife who is a believer at the church's expense. On this idiom, see "*a* man *who was*" in Lk 24:19.
24. On the brothers and sisters of the Lord, see Mt 13:55-56.
25. That is, Peter. On this name, see Gal 1:18.
26. The first two questions say "If all others have this right, we are not excluded, are we?" Now Paul says the reverse, "Even if all others are excluded from this right over you, do not we alone have it?"
27. That is, not to work outside the ministry— at tentmaking— to support ourselves in our ministry to you. The grammar implies "Surely we have the right not to work, do we not?", and expects a "yes" answer.
28. Or, "according to mankind". That is, based merely on the authority of the human illustrations just given. The grammar expects a "no" answer. Paul is speaking in accordance with God's Law.
29. The grammar expects a "yes" answer.
30. More literally, "It is not *a* concern *to* God *about* the oxen, *is it*?" Not muzzling the ox allowed it to eat the grain while it was threshing it. The grammar expects a "no" answer. That is, God is not concerned about how the animal is fed. The law was given for the Israelites' benefit, to teach them a lesson. The ox would be fed with or without this law. Whether it is before, during, or after threshing is not the real concern of God.
31. Or, "certainly, by all means". Same word as in Lk 4:23; Act 21:22; 28:4; and as "by all means" in 1 Cor 9:22. Elsewhere only with a negative as "not at all" (surely not) in Rom 3:9; 1 Cor 5:10; 16:12. GK *4122*.
32. Or, "For". Paul uses this word to assert his answer. GK *1142*.
33. Or, "that", so that it says "[meaning] that the *one* plowing...".
34. Same word as in v 12, on which see Heb 2:14. Some manuscripts say instead "hope, and the *one* threshing in hope *ought* to partake of his hope" {N}.
35. Or, "material". Similar statement in Rom 15:27. On this word, see 1 Cor 3:3. Paul commands this in Gal 6:6.
36. That is, the right to financial support in view in this section.

A. Rev 1:11, see   B. Act 23:1   C. 1 Thes 5:14   D. Act 16:40   E. Act 25:8   F. 2 Tim 4:20, sick   G. Mk 7:19   H. 1 Cor 12:28   J. Mt 26:10
K. Rom 4:11   L. Rom 1:5   M. 1 Pet 3:15   N. 1 Cor 2:14   O. Act 4:36   P. 1 Tim 1:18, fight   Q. Rom 6:23, wages   R. Mt 7:16   S. Rev 19:15
T. Mt 4:4, mankind   U. 1 Cor 7:21   V. 1 Jn 4:11   W. Col 1:5   X. 2 Cor 9:6   Y. 1 Cor 14:1

3D. Nevertheless,¹ we did not make-use-of^A this right^B. But we are bearing² all *things*, in-order-that³ we might not give any hindrance⁴ *to* the good-news^C *of* Christ

4D. Do⁵ you not know that the *ones* working^D the temple-*duties*⁶ eat the *things*⁷ from the temple, *that* the *ones* serving *at* the altar divide-a-share *with* the altar? *So also the Lord directed⁸ the *ones* proclaiming^E the good-news^C to be living^F from the good-news 13 14

5D. But **I** have not made-use-of any *of* these *things*⁹ 15

    1E. And I did not write these *things* in order that it might become so in my case¹⁰, for it would be better^G *for* me to die rather than¹¹— no one shall empty^H my boast¹²!

        1F. For¹³ if I am announcing-the-good-news¹⁴, it is not *a* boast *for* me 16

            1G. For¹⁵ *a* necessity¹⁶ is lying-upon¹⁷ me
            2G. For woe is *to* me if I do not announce-the-good-news

        2F. For¹⁸ if I am practicing^J this¹⁹ of-*my*-own-will²⁰, I have *a* reward²¹; but if not-of-*my*-own-will, I have been entrusted^K *a* stewardship²² 17

        3F. What then is **my** reward?²³ That while announcing-the-good-news, I might place^L the good-news²⁴ free-of-charge²⁵, so as not to make-full-use-of²⁶ my right^B in²⁷ the good-news²⁸ 18

6D. For²⁹ while being free³⁰ from all *people*, I enslaved^M myself *to* all in order that I might gain^N the more 19

    1E. Indeed I became 20

        1F. *To* the Jews as *a* Jew, in order that I might gain Jews
        2F. *To* the *ones* under *the* Law³¹, as under *the* Law— not being myself under *the* Law³²— in order that I might gain the *ones* under *the* Law
        3F. *To* the *ones* without-*the*-Law³³, as without-*the*-Law— not being without-*the*-law *of* God³⁴, but within-*the*-law³⁵ *of* Christ— in order that I might gain the *ones* without-*the*-Law 21

    2E. I became weak^O *to* the weak,³⁶ in order that I might gain the weak³⁷ 22
    3E. I have become all *things to* all *people*,³⁸ in order that I might by all means save^P some

1. Having proven that he cannot be denied this right, this is Paul's conclusion. He chose not to exercise this right, so as not to hinder the gospel. The Corinthians also should forego rights that no one would ever deny are theirs, for the sake the the weaker brother, and the gospel.
2. Or, "enduring". On this word, see 13:7, "love bears all things".
3. Or, "so that we will not give". GK *2671*.
4. Used only here. GK *1600*. Related to "hindered" in Gal 5:7.
5. Now Paul makes his point even stronger. Having said that he did not make use of a right from which he was not excluded, he now says he did not and will not make use of the right which he was specifically commanded by the Lord, v 13-18
6. Or, "sacred *services* or *things*". On this word, see "sacred" in 2 Tim 3:15. Related to "temple", "priest".
7. Some manuscripts omit "the *things*" {C}, so that it says "eat from the temple". The Jewish priests ate portions of some sacrifices.
8. On this word, see 7:17. See Mt 10:10; Lk 10:7 on the command.
9. Even though Jesus commanded it. So also you should forego rights given to you in Scripture by God— rights based on knowledge of the truth— for the weaker brother, based on love.
10. Or, "in me, in connection with me". GK *1877*.
11. This idiom occurs ten other times, six meaning "rather than", four meaning "more than". Paul breaks off this thought, and with emotion, gives an exclamation. Some manuscripts say "rather than that anyone should make my boast empty" {B}.
12. That is, the thing Paul boasts about. No one will empty his boast of its content. Paul did he not make use of his right to financial support, and this sacrifice of his right is a personal matter of boasting for him which he would rather die than give up. On this word, also in v 16, see Phil 1:26.
13. Paul would lose his matter of boasting if he accepted their financial support, for he cannot boast *that* he announces the gospel, only in *how* he does so sacrificially. Broadly stated, there is no boast in receiving my due, in utilizing my rights, while doing my duty. The boast is in not doing so while doing my duty.
14. That is, "If I carry out my ministry", "If I fulfill what Jesus called me to do". On this word, see Act 5:42.
15. Paul has no boast because he has no choice in the matter. It is not optional. He must preach the gospel.
16. Or, "*a* constraint, *a* compulsion". On this word, see 7:26.
17. Or, "is laid upon, is imposed upon, is pressing upon". On this word, see "pressing upon" in Lk 23:23. Jesus stopped Paul on the road and assigned (Act 22:10) him this task. It is his duty and obligation to his Master. It is his destiny. It is not a freely chosen act of service. He must do it, or suffer woe. Of course, it is also his joy and passion.
18. Paul distinguishes between two scenarios of "announcing the gospel". Only one has reward for him.
19. That is, announcing the gospel.
20. On this word, see "willingly" in Rom 8:20. The related word is used next (GK *220*). They may also be rendered "willingly... unwillingly, voluntarily... not voluntarily". The idea here is "by my own choice".
21. Or, "recompense, wage, compensation". Some think Paul means that if he by his own choice had taken up this ministry of announcing the gospel, he would have the reward due him for it (whether a reward by God; or financial support from those he serves; or a reward from the task itself). But this is not the case for him. It was a necessity, a stewardship, laid on him. In this case, this point would be 3G., another reason it is not a boast for him. He does not have this ministry in reward mode, but in stewardship mode. Others think he means that if he performs his assigned ministry in a way that in addition reflects his own willing devotion— as he is doing by not accepting support— then he has a reward from God. In this case, he is positively stating the means by which he can have a reward for his work. There are other views of this and the flow of v 15-18. Consult the commentaries. On this word, see "recompense" in Rev 22:12.
22. That is, a position of management responsibility. Paul uses the word "stewardship" of his ministry again in Eph 3:2; Col 1:25. On this word, see Eph 1:10. A steward was a slave assigned a management task by his master. The task was the master's choice and assignment, not the steward's. The steward's task was to be faithful, 1 Cor 4:2. He had no boast in doing what he was obligated to do, Lk 17:10. Paul means that if he did not take up this ministry by his own choice or add an element to it of his own choice (depending on the meaning of the first phrase), he nevertheless must still perform it, for it is a task, a necessity, a responsibility laid upon him as a steward.
23. That is, for announcing the gospel, carrying out my assigned ministry (v 16), since it is not in the doing of it.
24. Some manuscripts add "*of* Christ" {N}.
25. Or, "without charge". Used only here. GK *78*. Related to "cost" in Lk 14:28 (GK *1252*).
26. Elsewhere only in 7:31. GK *2974*. Related to "make use of " in v 12, 15.
27. Or, "in connection with". GK *1877*.
28. Paul's reward for doing his duty is to accept no human reward or wage, even though it is his right to receive it. His reward is to sacrifice it, to share Christ's sufferings, Phil 3:10. This is a reward to Paul because by carrying out his ministry this way— and doing so purely out of devotion, not any kind of obligation to anyone— he earns the opportunity to boast in how he did what was laid upon him to do, a boast he will not allow them to make empty. So also you, by choosing to give up your rights for the weaker brother, you can earn the ability to boast in your choices.
29. Concluding his justification of his bold statement in 8:13, Paul now expands beyond the pay illustration to a general principle. He does all things for the sake of the gospel, and so should the Corinthians.
30. Paul again emphasizes this point made in 9:1. He makes his sacrifices freely, by choice, not obligation or law. Same word as in 9:1.
31. This is a broader group than "Jews", including proselytes and God-fearers. On this word, see Rom 7:21.
32. Note Gal 2:19-20. Some manuscripts omit "not being myself under the Law" {A}.
33. That is, living outside the Law. This refers to Gentiles, as opposed to those living under the Law, v 20. The same word is used four times in this verse. Elsewhere only as "lawless" in Lk 22:37; Act 2:23; 2 Thes 2:8; 1 Tim 1:9; 2 Pet 2:8. GK *491*.
34. Some manuscripts say "*to* God", and "*to* Christ" next {N}.
35. This word means "within the law, legal, under the law, lawful, subject to the law". Elsewhere only as "lawful" in Act 19:39. GK *1937*.
36. Some manuscripts say "I became *to* the weak *ones* as weak" {N}.
37. This is what Paul said in 8:13, and it is the goal of this exhortation to the Corinthians.
38. Paul gives up all personal liberties and rights for the progress of the gospel among all people.

A. 1 Cor 7:31 B. 1 Cor 8:9 C. 1 Cor 15:1 D. Mt 26:10 E. Phil 1:18 F. Rev 20:4, came to life G. 1 Tim 5:10a, good H. Phil 2:7 J. Rom 2:1 K. Jn 3:36, believe L. Act 19:21, put M. Rom 6:18 N. Mk 8:36 O. 1 Thes 5:14 P. Lk 19:10

4E. And I am doing all[1] *things* for the sake of the good-news[A], in order that I might become *a* co-partner[2] *of* it 23

7C. Do you not know[3] that the *ones* running[B] in *a* race[C] **all**[4] run— but one receives the prize[5]? Be running in this manner[6]— that you may take-hold-of[D] *the prize*[7] 24

1D. And everyone competing[8] exercises-self-control[E] *as to* all *things.* So **those**[9] do it in order that they might receive *a* decayable[F] crown[G]— but we *an* undecayable[H] *one* 25

2D. So-indeed[10] **I** run in this manner, as not aimlessly[11]. I box in this manner, as not beating[J] *the* air. °But I bruise[12] my body and make *it my* slave[13], *that* having proclaimed[K] *to* others, I myself should not somehow become disapproved[14] 26
27

1E. For[15] I do not want you to be unaware[L] brothers, that our fathers were all under the cloud,[16] and all went through the sea,° and all were baptized[17] into Moses in the cloud and in the sea,° and all ate the same spiritual[18] food,° and all drank the same spiritual drink[19] 10:1
2
3-4

1F. For they were drinking from *a* spiritual[20] rock following *them.* And the rock was Christ[21]

2E. But God was not well-pleased[M] with the majority *of* them, for they were strewn[22] in the wilderness[N] 5

3E. Now these *things* took place *as* our examples[O], so that we *might* not be desirers[23] *of* evil *things,* as those also desired[P] 6

1F. And do not be[24] idolaters, as some *of* them, as-indeed it has been written [in Ex 32:6], "The people sat-*down* to eat and drink, and stood up to play" 7

2F. And let us not be committing-sexual-immorality[Q], as some *of* them committed sexual immorality, and twenty three[25] thousand fell *in* one day [Num 25:1-9] 8

3F. And let us not be putting Christ[26] to the test[27], as some *of* them[28] tested[R], and were being destroyed by the serpents[S] [Num 21:5-6] 9

4F. And do not be grumbling[T], like some *of* them grumbled, and perished[29] by the destroyer[30] [Num 16:41-49] 10

5F. Now these[31] *things* were happening *to* those *ones* as-an-example. And it was written for our admonition[U], on whom the ends[32] *of* the ages have come[33] 11

4E. So then[34] let the *one* thinking[35] *that he* stands be watching-out[V] *that* he may not fall[36] 12

1F. *A* temptation[37] has not seized[38] you except *what is* common-to-humanity[39] 13

2F. And God *is* faithful[W], Who will not allow[40] you to be tempted[41] beyond what you are able, but also with the temptation will make[X] *the* way-out, *that you may* be able to endure[42]

5E. For-this-very-reason[43], my beloved[Y], be fleeing[Z] from idolatry[44] 14

1. Some manuscripts say "this" instead of "all *things*" {N}.
2. That is, one assisting in the advance of it. On this word, see Phil 1:7.
3. Paul just said in 8:13-9:23 that the Corinthians should limit their freedom so that they do not cause their brother to stumble or hinder the gospel— that is, for the good of others. Now he says they should do this so that they might lay hold of their own personal reward, and not lose any reward they already have— that is, for their own good.
4. Paul uses grammar that emphasizes the contrast between the two halves of this sentence.
5. Elsewhere only in Phil 3:14, the goal Paul aims at. GK *1092*. See also Heb 12:1-2.
6. Some think this looks back. Run like the athlete who wins the prize in order that you might lay hold of your prize; run like a winner. Others think it looks forward. Run in such a way that you lay hold of the prize; run to win.
7. That is, that you may earn it, and keep it.
8. Or, "striving, contending [for a prize]". On this word, see "struggle" in 1 Tim 4:10.
9. Paul uses grammar that emphasizes the contrast between the two halves of this sentence.
10. This word, "well then, hence, therefore, so indeed" is elsewhere only in Heb 13:13; and as "well then" in Lk 20:25. GK *5523*.
11. Or, "uncertainly, unknowingly"— like eating without any thought of the impact on others. Used only here. GK *85*. Related to "uncertain" in 1 Cor 14:8; and "uncertainly" in 1 Tim 6:17.
12. Or, "give a black eye to, beat black and blue, treat severely". On this word, see "wear out" in Lk 18:5.
13. Or, "subjugate *it*". Used only here. GK *1524*.
14. Or, "rejected after testing, disqualified" for the prize, "failing to meet the test". Elsewhere only in Rom 1:28; 2 Cor 13:5, 6, 7; 2 Tim 3:8; Tit 1:16; Heb 6:8. GK *99*. See the positive word, "approved" in 2 Tim 2:15. That is, that I may receive and keep my reward. The idea is that Paul does not want to run the race and then be disqualified and forfeit the prize due to some rule violation. In context, the danger for the Corinthians is that they might run the race and seem to win a reward based on their knowledge and effort, but then lose the reward because of the harm they caused their fellow believers through lack of love in matters such as eating meat offered to idols, or in falling into idolatry (10:14).
15. A fall into disapproval is not theoretical. It happened to Israel. God disciplines those who do not obey him. Paul is the positive example, Israel the negative. Israel did not exercise self-control and run for the prize as Paul did.
16. See Ex 13:21.
17. On this word, see Mk 1:8. Some manuscripts say "baptized themselves", "had themselves baptized" {C}.
18. Same word as twice in v 4. On this word, see 14:1. That is, the physical manna they ate was spiritual in origin, coming to the Israelites from God.
19. That is, the water they drank was spiritual in origin, because it was provided by God, as described next.
20. Note that this word is here applied to the source of the water, not the water itself as previously. Paul could mean that the physical rock following them (based on Jewish tradition) was spiritual in origin; that is, from the realm of God. Or, he may be referring to the nature of the rock. It was a spiritual, supernatural, invisible rock; that is, Christ Himself.
21. Some think Paul is agreeing with a Jewish tradition that a physical rock giving water followed the Israelites, and is identifying that rock as Christ. Others think he is saying Christ was the source of water following them, not any physical rock, correcting the tradition. Compare Ex 17:6; Num 20:8.
22. Or, "spread out, strewn about". That is, killed and left. Used only here. GK *2954*. Same word as in Num 14:16 (killed, slaughtered). All but two were "disapproved", v 27.
23. Or, "*ones who* desire". This noun is used only here. GK *2122*. Related to "desired" next.
24. Or, "be becoming". GK *1181*.
25. Num 25:9 says 24,000. Paul gives a correct, approximate number.
26. Some manuscripts say "the Lord"; others, "God" {B}.
27. On "put to the test", see Mt 4:7. Related to "tested" next.
28. Some manuscripts add "also" {K}.
29. Same word as "being destroyed" in v 9, with different grammar. On this word, see 1:18.
30. Used only here. GK *3904*. Related to the verb in Heb 11:28. Not related to "perished" earlier.
31. That is, the consequences of sin just described. Some manuscripts say "all these *things*" {B}.
32. On this word, see Rom 10:4. Related to "conclusion" in Heb 9:26.
33. Or, "arrived, reached". The preceding ages ended in Christ. Christ begins a new age. On this word, see "attain" in Act 26:7.
34. Now Paul applies these examples to the Corinthians.
35. Such a person supposes he stands based on his knowledge, but he may be falling into sin, as Israel did. On this word, see Lk 19:11.
36. That is, fall into sin and "become disapproved" (9:27), and lose one's reward. Same word as in v 8, on which see Rom 11:11.
37. Or, "trial, testing". The testing or temptation in this context is in regard to meat offered to idols— with reference to both loving the weaker brother and idolatry, as seen next. Some think v 13 is an encouragement, "You need not fall. Your temptations are not unique, and do not exceed your strength. God will show you the way out". Others think it is a warning, "You have only had common human temptations up to now. Worse is coming, but God will help you". On this word, see "trials" in Jam 1:2.
38. Or, "taken". This common word meaning "to take, to receive" is used 258 times. GK *3284*.
39. Or, "human". Elsewhere only as "human" in Act 17:25; Rom 6:19; 1 Cor 2:13; 4:3; Jam 3:7; 1 Pet 2:13. GK *474*.
40. Same word as in Mt 24:43; Lk 4:41; 22:51; Act 14:16; 16:7; 28:4. Elsewhere only as "let" in Act 19:30; 23:32; 27:32; "leave" in Act 27:40; and "let alone" in Lk 4:34. GK *1572*.
41. Related to "temptation" in v 12, 13. On this word, see Heb 2:18.
42. Or, "bear up under". Same word as in 2 Tim 3:11, of persecution. Elsewhere only as "bear up" in 1 Pet 2:19, of unjust treatment. GK *5722*.
43. That is, that you may not fall while thinking you stand, v 12. Same word as 8:13.
44. Paul now applies this to eating in idols' temples, an issue mentioned but not addressed in 8:10. Your knowledge in which you stand will cause you to fall if you think you can do this and not arouse the jealousy of God.

A. 1 Cor 15:1 B. 2 Thes 3:1 C. Rev 14:20, stade D. Jn 1:5, overcome E. 1 Cor 7:9, have self control F. 1 Cor 15:53 G. Rev 4:4 H. 1 Cor 15:52 J. Jn 18:23 K. 2 Tim 4:2 L. Rom 10:3, being ignorant of M. Mt 17:5 N. Mt 3:1 O. 1 Pet 5:3, pattern P. Gal 5:17 Q. 1 Cor 6:18 R. Heb 2:18, tempted S. Rev 19:9 T. Lk 5:30 U. Eph 6:4 V. Rev 1:11, see W. Col 1:2 X. Rev Rev 13:13, does Y. Mt 3:17 Z. 1 Cor 6:18

1F. I speak as *to* wise[1] *ones,* **you** judge[2] what I say—	15
1G. The cup *of* blessing[3] which we bless[A]— is it not *a* sharing[4] *of* the blood[B] *of* Christ? The bread which we break—is it not *a* sharing *of* the body *of* Christ?	16
1H. Because *there is* one bread, we the many are one body[5]— for we all partake[C] from the one bread	17
2G. Look-at[D] Israel according to *the* flesh[6]— are not the *ones* eating the sacrifices[E] sharers[7] *of* the altar?	18
2F. Therefore what am I saying? That food-sacrificed-to-an-idol[F] is anything, or that *an* idol is anything?[8]	19
1G. On the contrary, that *the things* which they[9] are sacrificing[G], they are sacrificing *to* demons[10], and not *to* God[11]. And I do not want you to be[12] sharers *of* the demons	20
2G. You cannot[13] drink *the* Lord's cup and *the* demons' cup. You cannot partake[C] *of the* Lord's table and *the* demons' table	21
3G. Or do we provoke the Lord to jealousy[14]? We are not stronger *than* He, *are we*?[15]	22
8C. All *things* are lawful,[16] but not all *things* are beneficial.[17] All *things* are lawful, but not all *things* build-up[18]. °Let no one be seeking[H] his *own thing*, but[19] the *thing of* the other[20]	23 24
1D. Be eating anything being sold in *the* meat-market, examining[21] nothing for the sake of conscience.[22] °For "The earth and the fullness[23] *of* it *are* the Lord's" [Ps 24:1]	25 26
2D. If one *of* the unbelievers invites[J] you,[24] and you want to go, eat anything being set-before[K] you, examining nothing for the sake of conscience[L]. °But if one[25] should say *to* you "This is offered-in-sacrifice[26]", do not eat[27]— for the sake of that *one* having disclosed[28] *it,* and the conscience[29]	27 28
1E. Now *the* conscience I mean *is* not the *one of* oneself,[30] but the *one of* the other[31]	29
1F. For[32] why[33] is my freedom[M] being judged[34] by another's conscience? °If[35] **I** am partaking[C] *with* thanks[36], why am I being blasphemed[N] for *that* which **I** am giving-thanks[O]?	30
9C. Therefore,[37] whether you are eating or drinking or doing anything, be doing all for *the* glory *of* God	31
1D. Be[38] blameless[39] both *to* Jews and Greeks, and *to* the church *of* God	32
1E. Just as **I** also am pleasing[P] all *people* as *to* all *things*, not seeking[H] the benefit[Q] *of* myself, but the *benefit of* the many— in order that they might be saved[R]	33
2D. Be imitators[S] *of* me, just as I also *am of* Christ	11:1
4B. Now I praise[T] you[40] because[41] you have remembered[42] me *as to* everything, and you are holding-on-to[U] the traditions[43], just as I delivered[V] *to* you. °And[44] I want you to know[W] that Christ is the head[X] *of* every man[45], and the husband[46] *is* the head *of a* wife[47], and God *is* the head *of* Christ[48]	2 3

1. Or, "sensible". On this word, see Mt 7:24.
2. This is a command.
3. That is, "the cup of blessing", as it was called in the Passover meal, which we bless with regard to the Lord's Supper, as Jesus did on that night. On this word, see 2 Cor 9:5.
4. Or, "communion, partnership". On this word, see "fellowship" in 1:9. Related to "sharer" in v 18, 20.
5. Partaking of the one bread makes us sharers of Christ, and makes us one with all the others who do so. Paul's point is that the same is true in the idol temple. Others render this, "Because we the many are one body, one bread".
6. That is, the physical nation of Israel worshiping in the temple of Jerusalem.
7. Or, "partners, fellowshipers". Same word as in v 20. Related to "sharing" in v 16. On this word, see 2 Pet 1:4.
8. These are the same two points of "knowledge" that Paul began with in 8:4 and 8:8. Some manuscripts reverse them, putting "that *an* idol is anything" first {K}.
9. Some manuscripts say "the Gentiles" {C}.
10. The Gentiles used this word to mean "deities" (as in Act 17:18), but the Jews and Christians used it to mean "demons". Used 63 times. GK *1228*. Related to "demon possessed" in Mt 8:16.
11. Or, "and *to a* no god". Paul may be quoting Deut 32:17.
12. Or, "be becoming". GK *1181*.
13. That is, without provoking God to jealousy (v 22), and bringing His judgment upon you (v 7, 11).
14. On the word "provoke to jealousy", see Rom 11:11. Paul may be referring to Deut 32:21.
15. The grammar expects a "no" answer.
16. Same phrase as in 6:12. Now Paul returns to the matter of eating foods sacrificed to idols begun in 8:1. Both here and in the next sentence, some manuscripts add "*to* me" {N}, as in 6:12. Paul may again be quoting the Corinthians' slogan here.
17. As just seen, some things harm other believers, some things disqualify from reward, some things bring God's discipline upon us.
18. Or, "edify". Same word as 8:1, 10. On this word, see "edify" in 14:4.
19. Some manuscripts add "each" {N}, as in Phil 2:4.
20. This is beneficial to both you and the other. It is the guiding principle in this whole matter, and is applied in detail next. Compare Phil 2:3-4.
21. On this word, see 2:14. Make no investigation or inquiry in any way about where the meat came from.
22. Some think Paul means "examining nothing with questions your conscience might propose"; others, "examining nothing, making no inquiries, so as not to trouble your conscience".
23. That is, everything filling it. On this word, see Col 1:19.
24. That is, to his home, not to the idol's temple, as Paul said in v 14-22.
25. Paul is apparently referring to a weaker brother who is a fellow guest at that meal.
26. Used only here. GK *2638*. Some manuscripts say "food-sacrificed-to-idols", the word in 8:1.
27. The grammar implies "stop eating".
28. That is, for his good (v 24), out of love for him (as discussed in 8:1-9:23). On this word, see "showed" in Lk 20:37.
29. That is, for not harming his conscience, 8:12. Some manuscripts add the quotation from v 26, "For the earth and the fullness *of* it *are* the Lord's" {A}. Paul does not mean the conscience of the one he is exhorting, as he did in v 25 and 27, so he clarifies this next.
30. Because your conscience is not harmed by it. The food is not an issue for you, the strong one.
31. That is, the one who disclosed it, v 28.
32. Some think Paul is defending the stronger one, so as to balance love's sacrifice with the freedom in Christ. His or her freedom exercised in good conscience is not limited by the judgment of another's conscience. If the strong one partakes with thanksgiving, others have no right to blaspheme him. He has the right to eat. But in this case, do not eat, out of love for the weaker one. This choice is based on love, not on any guilt in the strong one's conscience caused by the other person, and not by any submission to his viewpoint. Others think Paul is exhorting the strong one, as in Rom 14:16. Do not eat, for why should you give an occasion for your freely chosen behavior to come under condemnation? Why conduct yourself in a way that what you receive with thanksgiving, others blaspheme you for? Do not do so.
33. Or, "for what purpose". Not the same word as in v 30. On this word, see Mt 27:46.
34. Or, "condemned". On this word, see Mt 7:1.
35. Some manuscripts say "But if " or "For if " {K}.
36. This word also means "grace", hence we speak of "saying grace". GK *5921*. Related to "give thanks" next.
37. Paul concludes with the broadest possible expression of the principle he has been teaching since 8:1.
38. Or, "Be becoming". GK *1181*. Same word as in 11:1.
39. Or, "without an opportunity for stumbling, without offense". Elsewhere only in Phil 1:10; Act 24:16. GK *718*. It is the negative of the word "opportunity for stumbling" in 8:9.
40. Some manuscripts add "brothers" {N}.
41. Or, "that". GK *4022*.
42. Or, "kept me in mind" as to all my teachings and your questions. On this word, see Lk 1:54.
43. Or, "what is handed down, delivered". Used in this sense in 2 Thes 2:15; 3:6. Elsewhere only in Mt 15:2, 3, 6; Mk 7:3, 5, 8, 9, 13; Gal 1:14; Col 2:8. GK *4142*. Related to "delivered" next.
44. Or, "But, Now". Same word as "now" in v 2, and "but" in v 17. GK *1254*. "And" or "Now" would mean this continues with the questions about which the Corinthians have kept Paul in mind, as seen in their writing to him about them, 7:1. "But" would mean this begins an issue about which they had not kept Paul in mind, or had not held on to his teaching, about which he now writes to correct them. In this case, some think Paul is continuing to respond to their questions; others, that he now moves on to an issue about which he heard from other sources (as perhaps in the next issue, v 18). See 7:1.
45. Same word as "husband" next. It means either "man" or "husband", based on the context. Used 216 times. GK *467*.
46. Or, "and the man *is the* head of *his* wife". Or, "the man is *the* head *of a* woman", when the two are considered as a pair.
47. This word means either "woman" or "wife", depending on the context. It is used 215 times. GK *1222*.
48. This is the general spiritual principle. Paul now applies this principle to a question from the Corinthians specific to their culture, "Should women continue to wear veils while praying or prophesying". It was their custom to do so (v 16), and Paul argues to continue it.

A. Lk 6:28 B. 1 Jn 1:7 C. Heb 2:14 D. Rev 1:11, see E. Heb 9:26 F. 1 Cor 8:1 G. Act 10:13, slaughter H. Phil 2:21 J. Rom 8:30, called K. Act 17:3, put before L. Act 23:1 M. Gal 5:13 N. 1 Tim 6:1 O. Mt 26:27 P. 1 Thes 2:4 Q. 1 Cor 7:35 R. Lk 19:10 S. Eph 5:1 T. Rom 15:11 U. Rom 1:18, hold down V. Act 16:4 W. 1 Jn 2:29 X. Mk 12:10

1C.	Every man praying[A] or prophesying[B] while having *a covering* down *over his* head is shaming[1] his head[2]. °And every woman praying or prophesying[3] *with* the head unveiled[4] is shaming her head[5]	4 5
1D.	For[6] she is one and the same *with the one* having been shaved[7]	
1E.	For if *a* woman is not veiling-*herself*[8], let her also[9] have-*herself*-sheared[10]	6
2E.	But if *it is* shameful[11] *for a* woman to have-*herself*-sheared or shaved, let her be veiling-*herself*	
2D.	For *a* **man**[12] ought[C] not to be veiling the head, being *the* image[D] and glory[E] *of* God— but the woman is *the* glory *of* man[13]	7
1E.	For man is not from woman, but woman from man[14]	8
2E.	For indeed man was not created[F] for the sake of the woman, but woman for the sake of the man[15]	9
3E.	For this reason,[16] the woman ought[C] to be having authority[17] on *her* head because of the angels[18]	10
4E.	Nevertheless[19] *there is* neither woman without man, nor[20] man without woman in *the* Lord. °For just as the woman *is* from the man, so also the man *is* through the woman. And all *things are* from God	11 12
2C.	Judge[G] among[21] you yourselves[22]— is it fitting[23] *that an* unveiled woman *should* pray[A] *to* God?	13
3C.	Does not even nature[24] itself teach[H] you that if *a* **man**[25] has long hair, it is *a* dishonor[J] *to* him— but if *a* woman has long hair, it is *a* glory[E] *to* her? Because[26] the long hair has been given *to* her[27] for[28] *a* covering[29]	14 15
4C.	But if anyone seems[30] to be contentious, **we** do not have such *a* custom[31], nor *do* the churches *of* God	16

1. Or, "dishonoring". On this word, see "put to shame" in Rom 5:5.
2. Some think Paul means Christ; others, the man's physical head; others, both. The reason is given in v 7.
3. Some think Paul is implying that this praying and prophesying took place "in church" for both the man and the woman; others, elsewhere for the woman, based on 14:34.
4. Or, "uncovered, without a head covering". Elsewhere only in v 13. GK *184*. Related to "veil" in v 6.
5. Some think Paul means the woman's husband, v 3; others, her physical head, v 6; others, both. When she is praying or prophesying, a woman should wear a veil in order to honor her husband and marriage and herself, not shame them. Her spiritual equality is to be exercised in subordination to her marriage relationship, so as not to bring unnecessary shame on them or on Christ from her society— as this is expressed in her culture.
6. The woman shames her head because she identifies herself with the ones her society considers shamed, and thus brings unnecessary insult upon the gospel from her society. It was improper in that society to not wear a veil.
7. Some think Paul is referring to adulteresses, who were shaved in Israel. Others think he is referring to women who try to look like men. Elsewhere only in v 6 and Act 21:24, shaving men's heads for a vow. GK *3834*.
8. Or, "covering". Used twice here, and elsewhere only in v 7. GK *2877*. Related to "unveiled" in v 5.
9. If you are going this far in violating proper decorum, then why not go all the way and cut off your hair!
10. Elsewhere only in Act 18:18, of Paul keeping his vow; and in Act 8:32, of sheep. GK *3025*.
11. It was shameful in the culture of that day, but in other cultures the length of a woman's hair is not a matter of decency or shame. There is nothing to be gained for Christ by violating one's societal standards of decency. Much can be unnecessarily lost. On this word, see Tit 1:11.
12. Paul uses grammar that emphasizes the contrast between the two halves of this sentence.
13. Some think Paul is implying something the man is that the woman is not. Adam reflects God's image in a way Eve does not, because he is in the position of rule and authority. However, perhaps Paul is instead stating something the woman is that the man is not. Adam is the human counterpart of God's attributes, created from Him to reflect His glory. He ought to reflect that glory, not veil it. Eve, in addition to reflecting God's image and glory like Adam (including the dominion they were given as a pair, Gen 1:26-28), also reflects the glory of Adam, being created from him as his counterpart, v 8-9. The aspects of her that are a counterpart to the man are related specifically to her as his mate, to the marriage relationship. In a special way, her spirit and body "corresponds" to him, making them a pair. Since the glory of her "mateness" is for him and no other, honoring it is honoring him, herself, and their marriage. She should honor it in whatever way is appropriate in her culture— in the case here, by veiling the head.
14. That is, Eve, the first woman, was made from Adam (Gen 2:21-22), rather than from dust.
15. Paul is referring to Gen 2:18-24, where Eve was made from Adam to be a mate suitable to him. Paul is not saying that Genesis means the woman was created to serve the man as his slave, but that she was created to complete him, to be his mate, to be the second half of the pair, as Adam observed among the animals he named.
16. That is, because the woman was created from man and for man (v 8-9); because she is the glory of man (v 7), the completion of man as his mate.
17. Some think Paul means a veil as a "*symbol of* authority", symbolizing the husband's authority and the wife's freedom to act within it. It symbolizes that she is exercising her spiritual freedom to pray and prophesy within the chain of relationships as established by God. Since she is her husband's mate, she should wear a veil while praying or prophesying. Others think Paul means she ought to have "control over" her head so as not to bring shame upon herself and others, as this same phrase means in Rev 11:6; 14:18; 20:6. On this word, see Rev 6:8. Some manuscripts say "*a veil*" {A}.
18. Or, "messengers". Some think Paul is referring to the angels present during worship. Note 4:9. Others think he is referring to the human messengers, the preachers present during worship. There are other views. On this word, see "messengers" in 1 Tim 3:16.
19. The creation of woman from man and for man is the order of the first creation, our existence as humans on earth. This order does not exist in the new creation, where there is no male or female in the Lord, Gal 3:28. But at the present, we live and have responsibilities in both spheres. Balancing the woman's freedom "in the Lord", with what was "fitting" (v 13) by their cultural standards, and would not bring unnecessary insult and shame to Christ, is Paul's goal in this whole section.
20. Some manuscripts put the "man without woman" phrase first {K}.
21. Or, "within". GK *1877*.
22. Paul asks them to use their common sense in this matter. On "you yourselves", see 5:13.
23. Or, "proper, suitable, seemly, becoming". Same word as in Mt 3:15; 1 Tim 2:10; Tit 2:1; Heb 2:10; 7:26. Elsewhere only as "proper" in Eph 5:3. GK *4560*. Our "judgment" as to what is "fitting" differs by culture. For example, if Christian women in Western cultures were made to wear veils, it would not be judged "fitting" at all, but would bring the very insults and shame upon the church that Paul is trying to avoid here. Compare 14:34, where the same issue arises.
24. The grammar expects a "yes" answer to this question. By "nature", some think Paul means the physical makeup of man and woman, women in general having a richer endowment of hair. Others think he means the natural disposition and preferences of men and women in this matter, as reflected in the customs regarding hair. Note that his point is not about how long one's hair should be, or what our customs regarding hair should be, but that woman's natural covering of hair honors her in a special way when she is not wearing a veil, and as such, shows that a veil is also honorable. On this word, see Eph 2:3.
25. Paul uses grammar that emphasizes the contrast between the two halves of this sentence.
26. Or, "That", making this a second question. GK *4022*.
27. Some manuscripts omit "to her" {C}.
28. Or, "corresponding to, answering to". GK *505*.
29. Elsewhere only as "cloak" in Heb 1:12. GK *4316*.
30. Or, "thinks, presumes". That is, seems to you, or thinks in himself. On this word, see "thinking" in Lk 19:11.
31. That is, if you want to debate this, we have no other custom. All our women wear the veil. This is the habit we are accustomed to in the churches. Elsewhere only in Jn 18:39, and as "accustomed habit" in 1 Cor 8:7. GK *5311*. Some think Paul means "we have no custom of fighting about these things".

A. 1 Tim 2:8   B. 1 Cor 14:1   C. 1 Jn 4:11   D. Col 1:15   E. 2 Pet 2:10   F. Eph 2:15   G. Mt 7:1   H. Rom 12:7   J. 2 Tim 2:20

5B. But while commanding^A this, I do not praise¹   17

   1C. Because you are coming-together not for the better^B, but for the worse

      1D. For first², while you *are* coming-together in church³, I am hearing⁴ *that there* are divisions^C among you. And *a certain part*⁵ *of it* I believe^D—   18

         1E. For there indeed have-to⁶ be factions⁷ among you, in order that the approved⁸ *ones* may also⁹ become known^E among you¹⁰   19

      2D. So¹¹ while you *are* coming-together¹² at the same *place*¹³, it is not *that you may* eat *the* Lord's^F Supper! *For at the eating^G, each *one* is taking *his* own dinner¹⁴ before *others*¹⁵. And one is hungry, and another is drunk¹⁶   20 21

         1E. You do not indeed^H fail to have houses for eating and drinking, *do you*?¹⁷   22
         2E. Or are you treating the church *of* God with contempt¹⁸, and humiliating^J the *ones* not having¹⁹?

      3D. What should I say *to* you? Shall I praise^K you? In this²⁰ I do not praise

   2C. For **I** received^L from the Lord what I also handed-over²¹ *to* you—   23

      1D. That the Lord Jesus, in the night *on* which He was being handed-over, took bread. *And having given-thanks^M, He broke^N it, and said "This²² is²³ My body, the *one being given*²⁴ for you. Be doing this for My remembrance²⁵"   24

      2D. Similarly also the cup after the dining²⁶, saying, "This cup is the new^O covenant^P in My blood^Q. Be doing this, as-often-as²⁷ you drink *it*, for My remembrance"   25

      3D. For as-often-as you eat this bread and drink the²⁸ cup, you are proclaiming^R the death *of* the Lord, until which *time* He comes   26

   3C. So then, whoever eats the²⁹ bread or³⁰ drinks the cup *of* the Lord unworthily³¹ shall be guilty³² *of* the body and the blood *of* the Lord. *But let *a* person^S examine³³ himself, and in this manner let him eat of³⁴ the bread and drink of the cup   27 28

      1D. For the *one* eating and drinking³⁵ while not rightly-judging³⁶ the body³⁷, is eating and drinking judgment³⁸ *on* himself. *For this reason many among you *are* weak^T and sick^U, and many³⁹ sleep^V   29 30

1. As Paul did in 11:2. Same word as in v 2, 22.
2. Paul uses grammar that may imply a second issue is to be named (as perhaps in v 20); or, he means "first" in the sense of "above all". Same grammar as in Rom 1:8.
3. Or, "*an* assembly, *a* congregation". That is, a gathering of people, often in a home. On this word, see Rev 22:16.
4. Perhaps Paul heard it from the same people as in 1:11, or those in 16:17. This may mean the Corinthians did not ask Paul about this issue; or, that in addition to their question about the Lord's Supper, Paul had heard this news about them.
5. Or, "And some part I believe". That is, "in part". Same idiom as in Act 5:2, and elsewhere only as "any part" in Lk 11:36.
6. Or, "must". Or, "it is necessary *that* there be...". On this idiom, see "must" in Mt 16:21.
7. This word means "a choice, a chosen opinion, a taking of sides". Same word as in Gal 5:20. Then it means the "school, sect, or party" professing that opinion— as in the "sect" of Sadducees in Act 5:17; Pharisees in Act 15:5; 26:5; Nazarenes in Act 24:5; the Way in Act 24:14; Christians in Act 28:22. Then, if rejected, this opinion becomes a "heresy", as this word is elsewhere only used in 2 Pet 2:1. Our word "heresy" is from this word. GK *146*. These groups should not be built around personalities, 1 Cor 1:10. But Christianity itself was seen as a sect or faction of Judaism— and this was necessary in order to separate out the approved ones, Christians. Related to "chose" in Mt 12:18; and "divisive" in Tit 3:10.
8. This adjective means "approved after testing". See 2 Tim 2:15 on it.
9. Or, "indeed". Some manuscripts omit this word {C}.
10. Choices between good and bad, right and wrong exist in order to separate the approved from the disapproved.
11. Or, "Then, Therefore". This is either a second problem, or a specific manifestation of the first problem.
12. Same word as in 11:17, 18, 33, 34; 14:23, 26. GK *5302*.
13. On this idiom, "at the same *place*", see Act 2:47.
14. Same word as "Supper" preceding. On this word, see Lk 14:12. Related to "dining" in v 25.
15. That is, they are not waiting for one another and eating together, v 33. They are eating independently. Paul is referring to the "love-feast" or common meal associated with the Lord's Supper at that time.
16. They are not sharing food. Some take to the point of excess, others do not get enough. Note v 33. Elsewhere only in Mt 24:49; Act 2:15; 1 Thes 5:7; Rev 17:6. GK *3501*. Related to "get drunk" in Jn 2:10.
17. The grammar expects a "no" answer. Same grammar as in 9:4. More literally, "you do not indeed not have houses..., *do you*?".
18. Or, "looking down on" the church. On this word, "treat with contempt", see "disregard" in Rom 2:4.
19. That is, the poor, the have-nots who are going hungry at your dinner, v 21.
20. Some punctuate this "Shall I praise you in this? I do not praise".
21. Or, "delivered, handed down". Same word as later in v 23; and as "delivered" in 11:2; 15:3; etc. On this word, see Mt 26:21.
22. Some manuscripts say "Take, eat, this..." {A}.
23. On this word, see Mt 26:26.
24. The verb "being given" is supplied from Lk 22:19. Some manuscripts here say "being broken" {A}, using the same word as "broke" earlier in this verse, a word used 14 times in the NT, always of breaking bread (see Act 2:46 on it).
25. Or, "reminder, calling to memory". Same word as in 11:25; Lk 22:19 (by Jesus of the Lord's Supper). Elsewhere only as "reminder" in Heb 10:3, in the sacrifices there was a "reminder" of sin year by year. GK *390*.
26. That is, the eating of dinner. Same word as in Lk 22:20. Elsewhere only as "have dinner" in Lk 17:8; Rev 3:20. GK *1268*. Related to "dinner" in v 21.
27. Or, "as many times as". That is, as often as you drink this cup, not as often as you drink anything. Jesus gives no indication of how often it should be done. Elsewhere only in 11:26; Rev 11:6, "as often as they desire". GK *4006*.
28. Some manuscripts say "this" {N}.
29. Some manuscripts say "this" {N}.
30. Some manuscripts say "and" {K}.
31. That is, in a manner unworthy of the Lord— by being in sin during the very act of remembering His sacrifice for sin! In the Corinthians case, Paul is referring to the way in which they were conducting themselves while partaking of the Lord's Supper, as described in v 18-22— their actions and attitudes toward it and one another. Used only here. GK *397*. Related to "unworthy" in 6:2.
32. Or, "liable *for*, answerable *for*". Same word as in Mk 3:29; Jam 2:10. Elsewhere only as "liable *to*" in Mt 5:21, 22; and "subject *to*" in Mt 26:66; Mk 14:64; Heb 2:15. GK *1944*. Such people are rendered "guilty" by their unworthy conduct with regard to the Lord's Supper, and therefore "liable" to the Lord's discipline for their actions, v 32.
33. Or, "test, approve". Same word as "prove" in 2 Cor 13:5. On this word, see "approve" in Rom 12:2.
34. Or, "from". Same preposition used with "drink" next. GK *1666*.
35. Some manuscripts add "unworthily" {A}, as in v 27.
36. Or "discerning, distinguishing". By "body", some think Paul means "the Lord's Supper as a remembrance of His body and blood on the cross". Thus some think Paul means "Not distinguishing the Lord's Supper from all other meals", treating the bread and wine as common. That is, not properly reverencing or hallowing the remembrance of the Lord, and therefore the Lord Himself. Others think he means "Not appreciating the true nature and full meaning of the Lord's Supper, the Lord's body given for you", failing to see what these elements mean in themselves and for your behavior. That is, they are partaking of this remembrance without applying it to themselves, without seeing the ways in which His sacrifice for us requires that we be holy and sacrifice ourselves for our fellow believers. By "body", others think Paul means "the church, the body of believers". Thus he means "while not appreciating the true meaning of the body of Christ with whom you are celebrating this remembrance", failing to properly honor one another and join together as one body in the remembrance of the Lord. Same word as in v 31, and related to "judgment" next. It is rendered this way to show these connections. On this word, see "doubting" in Jam 1:6.
37. Some manuscripts say "the body *of* the Lord" {A}. In the Greek word order, the phrase "while not rightly-judging the body" is at the end of the sentence, after "himself".
38. That is, discipline, as Paul says in v 32. See Heb 12:7-11. Sickness and death are examples of this discipline. On this word, see Jn 9:39.
39. This is a different word than earlier, perhaps meant to convey "many-*others*". GK *2653*.

A. 1 Tim 1:3 B. Heb 1:4 C. 1 Cor 1:10 D. Jn 3:36 E. Rom 1:19, evident F. Rev 1:10 G. Act 10:13 H. Mt 27:23 J. Rom 5:5, put to shame K. Rom 15:11 L. Lk 17:34, taken M. Mt 26:27 N. Act 2:46 O. Heb 8:13 P. Heb 8:6 Q. 1 Jn 1:7 R. Phil 1:18 S. Mt 4:4, mankind T. 1 Thes 5:14 U. Mk 16:18 V. 1 Thes 4:13, falling asleep

| 1 Corinthians 11:31 | 610 | Verse |

        1E. But[1] if we were rightly-judging ourselves, we would not be being judged[2]   31

        2E. But while being judged, we are being disciplined[3] by the Lord, in-order-that[4] we might not be condemned[5] with the world   32

    4C. So then my brothers, while coming-together so as to eat, be waiting-for[A] one another. *If[6] one is hungry, let him eat at home, in-order-that[7] you might not come-together for[8] judgment   33-34

    5C. And I will set-in-order[B] the remaining[C] *things* whenever I come

 6B. Now concerning the spiritual[D] *gifts*[9], brothers, I do not want you to be unaware[E]   12:1

    1C. You know that when[10] you were Gentiles[11], *you were* being led-away[12] to the speechless[13] idols, however[14] you were being led. *Therefore I make-known[F] *to* you that   2

                                                                                             3

        1D. No one speaking by *the* Spirit *of* God is saying "Jesus *is* accursed[15]"

        2D. And no one is able to say "Jesus *is* Lord"[16] except by *the* Holy Spirit[17]

    2C. Now there are differences[18] *of* gifts[19], but the same Spirit. *And there are differences *of* ministries[20], and the same Lord. *And there are differences *of things*-worked[21], but[22] the same God working[23] all *things* in all *persons*   4-5

                                                                                             6

    3C. And the manifestation[24] *of* the Spirit is given *to* each *one* for *our* benefit[25]   7

        1D. For *to* one, *a* word[26] *of* wisdom[27] is given through the Spirit   8

        2D. And *to* another, *a* word *of* knowledge[28] according-to[29] the same Spirit

        3D. *To*[30] *a* different[31] one, faith[32] by the same Spirit   9

        4D. And *to* another, gifts *of* healings[33] by the one[34] Spirit

1. Some manuscripts say "For" {N}.
2. That is, be experiencing judgment as described in v 30. Same word as next, on which see Mt 7:1.
3. Or, "corrected, trained, instructed, educated". We are disciplined as God's children, not condemned with unbelievers. Same word as in Lk 23:16, 22; 2 Cor 6:9; Heb 12:6, 7, 10; Rev 3:19. Used of parents disciplining their children, and government disciplining (with whippings, floggings) its wayward subjects. Here, discipline by God with sickness and death is in view. Elsewhere only as "correct" in 2 Tim 2:25; and "train" in Act 7:22; 22:3; 1 Tim 1:20; Tit 2:12. GK *4084*. Related to "training" in 2 Tim 3:16.
4. Or, "so that we will not", depending on whether Paul is referring to the purpose or the result of the discipline. GK *2671*.
5. That is, "judged against", pronounced judgment upon. Used 18 times. GK *2891*. Same root word as "judge rightly", "judgment", and "judge". Thus the same root word is used six times in v 29-32.
6. Some manuscripts say "And if " {N}.
7. Or, "so that you will not". GK *2671*.
8. Or, "resulting in, leading to". On this word, see "resulting in" in Rom 5:16.
9. Some supply "*gifts*" here, based on 12:4, 31; others, "*manifestations*" from v 7, in light of v 2-3; others, "*people*", as in 14:37. Both words "spiritual" and "gift" are used together only in Rom 1:11.
10. Compare Act 15:23. Some manuscripts omit this word {N}, so that it says "... that you were Gentiles being led away...".
11. That is, pagans, non-believers. On this word, see Act 15:23.
12. The Corinthians were led away to the idols by outside forces. Not so now. Paul wants them to understand, to not be unaware of how the Spirit is working among them and through them. GK *552*.
13. The idols neither spoke, nor did they lead you to speak! Not so with the Spirit, whose influence is known to you, and is discernable by its results. On this word, see "meaningless" in 14:10.
14. Or, "whenever", as in 11:34; Rom 15:24; Phil 2:23. This idiom is elsewhere only as "as if " in 2 Cor 10:9.
15. Or, "Jesus *be* cursed". The word is *anathema*. It means "the object of a curse". On this word, see Rom 9:3.
16. That is, from the heart, not simply mouthing the words. Compare Jn 6:44; Rom 10:9.
17. Paul gives no historical context to verse 3. Many theories about what may lie behind this verse have been proposed. Consult the commentaries. In any case, Paul begins his discussion of spiritual things by distinguishing the ministry of the Spirit from what the Corinthians experienced from their speechless idols.
18. Or, "divisions, varieties, allotments, distributions". Used only in v 4-6. GK *1348*. The related verb is "distributing" in v 11.
19. This emphasizes the source. They are gifts of grace freely given without merit in the receiver. Same word as in v 9, 28, 30, 31. On this word, see 1:7.
20. Or, "services", ways of serving, spheres of serving. This emphasizes the purpose— to serve others. Same word as in Act 1:17, 25; 6:1, 4; 11:29; 12:25; 20:24; 21:19; Rom 11:13; 1 Cor 16:15; 2 Cor 3:7, 8, 9; 4:1; 5:18; 6:3; 8:4; 9:1, 12, 13; 11:8; Eph 4:12; Col 4:17; 2 Tim 4:5. Elsewhere only as "service" in Lk 10:40; Rom 12:7; 15:31; 1 Tim 1:12; 2 Tim 4:11; Heb 1:14; Rev 2:19. GK *1355*. Related to "servant" in 3:5; and "ministering" in 1 Pet 4:10.
21. Or, "effects, products, results, what is worked" in us. This emphasizes the result which is produced in and through us by God. That is, there are different manifestations or results of God's working in us, different "activities, operations, workings" of God in us, different things He accomplishes in and through us. This Greek word is formed like "gift" in v 4. As God's giving results in a "thing given" (a gift), so His working (v 6) results in a "thing worked" (a work, though this English word is ambiguous). Thus "teaching" is a gift, a service, and a spiritual work of God in and through the teacher. Elsewhere only in v 10. GK *1920*.
22. Some manuscripts say "and" {N}.
23. On this word, see "works" in v 11. Related to "*things*-worked".
24. Or, "open disclosure, public revelation". Gifts are public disclosures of the Spirit in us. Some think Paul means gifts are our means of exhibiting the Spirit; others, His means of exhibiting Himself. Elsewhere only as "open disclosure" in 2 Cor 4:2. GK *5748*. Related to "evident" in Rom 1:19; and "make evident" in 1 Jn 2:19.
25. Or, "profit". This is an idiom, "with a view to the *thing* being beneficial". Same word as "beneficial" in 6:12. Compare the similar phrase in Heb 12:10.
26. This common word, *logos*, used 330 times, means "word, speech, talk, saying, statement, message, reason, account, matter". GK *3364*.
27. This word, *sophia*, is used 51 times, in 1 Cor only in 1:17, 19, 20, 21, 22, 24, 30; 2:1, 4, 5, 6, 7, 13; 3:19; 12:8. Some think Paul is using the word as he did in 2:6-13, where the wisdom we speak (2:6) is the Spirit's revelation (2:10) about God's mystery, Christ (2:7), spoken in words taught by the Spirit (2:13). Others define it as a "wise saying" revealed by the Spirit for a specific circumstance (such as when on trial, Lk 21:15). Others define it more generally, as an appropriate speaking of God's wisdom to a specific circumstance, "wise counsel". GK *5053*.
28. Elsewhere only in Lk 1:77; 11:52; Rom 2:20; 11:33; 15:14; 1 Cor 1:5; 8:1, 7, 10, 11; 13:2, 8; 14:6; 2 Cor 2:14; 4:6; 6:6; 8:7; 10:5; 11:6; Eph 3:19; Phil 3:8; Col 2:3; 1 Tim 6:20; 1 Pet 3:7; 2 Pet 1:5, 6; 3:18. GK *1194*. Some define it as knowledge of the revealed word of God. Others define it as a revelation of unknown facts, such as when Jesus knew the woman had five husbands, Jn 4:18, 29.
29. Or, "based on, by way of ". GK *2848*.
30. Some manuscripts say "And *to*..." {N}.
31. In verses 8-10, "another" can mean "another of the same kind" (GK *257*, used 155 times, also as "other"). "Different" can mean "another of a different kind" (GK *2283*, used 98 times, mainly as "another, other"). The change of terms may be stylistic, or Paul may be intending to divide the gifts into three groupings. If the latter, there are different opinions as to what the meaning of these three groupings might be. Consult the commentaries.
32. Used in 1 Cor only in 2:5; 12:9; 13:2, 13; 15:14, 17; 16:13. Most define it based on 13:2, faith so as to move mountains. Faith to perform works of faith, 2 Thes 1:11. On this word, see Eph 2:8.
33. That is, the effecting of healings as seen in Act 3:6; 4:30; 5:15-16; 8:7; 9:34; 10:38; 28:8-9. Elsewhere only in 12:28, 30. GK *2611*. Note Lk 9:1, 6; 10:8-9. Related to "heal" in Mt 8:8. See also "cure" in Mt 8:7.
34. Some manuscripts say "by the same Spirit" {A}.

A. Heb 11:10   B. 1 Cor 7:17, directing   C. 2 Pet 3:16, other   D. 1 Cor 14:1   E. Rom 10:3, being ignorant of   F. Phil 1:22, know

5D. And *to* another, *things*-worked[1] *by* miracles[2]   10
6D. And[3] *to* another, prophecy[4]
7D. And[5] *to* another, discernments[6] *of* spirits
8D. To[7] *a* different *one*, kinds[A] *of* tongues[8]
9D. And *to* another, interpretation[9] *of* tongues
10D. But the one and the same Spirit works[10] all these *things*, distributing[11] *to* each *one* individually[12], just as He wills[13]   11

4C. For just as the [human] body is one [body] and has many body-parts[14], and all the body-parts *of* the [human] body[15], being many, are one body, so also *is* Christ[16]   12

    1D. For indeed[17] with[18] one Spirit, **we** all[19] were baptized[20] into one body[21]— whether Jews or Greeks, whether slaves or free. And we all were given one Spirit to drink[22]   13
    2D. For indeed the body is not one body-part, but many[23]   14

        1E. If the foot should say, "Because I am not *a* hand, I am not *a part* of the body", it is not for this *reason* not *a part* of the body. °And if the ear should say, "Because I am not *an* eye, I am not *a part* of the body", it is not for this *reason* not *a part* of the body   15 / 16
        2E. If the whole body *were an* eye, where *would* the hearing *be*? If *the* whole *were an* ear, where *would* the smelling *be*?   17
        3E. But now[24], God placed[B] the body-parts— each one *of* them— in the body, just as He wanted[C]   18
        4E. And if all were one body-part, where *would* the body *be*?   19

    3D. But now,[25] *there are* **many**[26] body-parts— but one body[27]   20

        1E. And the eye cannot say *to* the hand, "I do not have need[D] *of* you". Or again the head *to* the feet, "I do not have need *of* you"   21
        2E. On the contrary, much rather the body-parts *of* the body seeming[E] to be weaker[F] are necessary[G]. °And *the things of* the body which we are thinking[E] to be more-without-honor[28], *on* these we are putting-on more honor[29]   22 / 23

1. Or, "products, effects, workings *of His* powers; effects *which are* miraculous, *consisting of* miracles; workings *by Him of* miracles". That is, miraculous things God does by the working of His powers. On this word, see v 6. This does not refer to a human ability to produce a miracle (note Act 3:12; 4:30), but to the miraculous result itself, produced by God. To another, God gives miracles (compare v 28, where this gift is simply "miracles"). The related verb (in v 11) is used with "miracles" in Gal 3:5, of God "working miracles".
2. Or "powers". That is, supernatural effects of the powers of God other than healing (though healings were also miracles). For example, execution, Act 5:9; raising the dead, Act 9:40; blinding, Act 13:11. Same word as in Mt 7:22; 11:20, 21, 23; 13:54, 58; Mk 6:2, 5; 9:39; Lk 10:13; 19:37; Act 2:22; 8:13; 19:11; 1 Cor 12:28, 29; 2 Cor 12:12; Gal 3:5; Heb 2:4. Same word as "power" in Lk 5:17; 6:19; 8:46; 9:1; Act 1:8; 3:12; 4:33; Rom 15:19; 1 Cor 2:4; 2 Thes 2:9; etc. On this word, see "power" in Mk 5:30.
3. Some manuscripts omit this word {C}.
4. That is, the output of a prophet when he or she prophesies. Prophets (noun, 12:28, 29; 14:29, 32, 37, see 12:28) prophesy (verb, 11:4, 5; 13:9; 14:1, 3, 4, 5, 24, 31, 39, see 14:1) prophecies (noun, 12:10; 13:2, 8; 14:6, 22). Elsewhere only in Mt 13:14; Rom 12:6; 1 Thes 5:20; 1 Tim 1:18; 4:14; 2 Pet 1:20, 21; Rev 1:3; 11:6; 19:10; 22:7, 10, 18, 19. GK *4735*. Prophets are the direct mouthpiece of God, Lk 1:70. Compare Mt 26:68; Mk 14:65; Lk 2:36; 7:39; Jn 4:18, 19; 11:51; Act 2:17, 30; 11:28; 21:9-11; 1 Cor 14:30; Eph 3:5; 2 Pet 1:21; Rev 1:3; 22:18. Some define this gift as speaking revelation from God confirmed by supernatural knowledge of past, present, or future events. Others define it as speaking revelation from God, but without the supernatural confirmation aspect. Others define it as "speaking for God, preaching, forthtelling", defining it based on its results in the hearer (14:3, 31) rather than its source.
5. Some manuscripts omit this word {C}.
6. Or "judgments, distinguishings". Same word as in Heb 5:14. Elsewhere only as "disputes" in Rom 14:1. GK *1360*. The related verb is in 14:29. It is the gift of distinguishing the source of a spirit or message or act, as in 14:29; 1 Jn 4:1-3. Act 16:16-18 may be an example. 1 Cor 14:29 may indicate that prophets also had this gift. Some think it is based on revelation.
7. Some manuscripts say "And *to...*" {N}.
8. That is, "languages". For two views of this gift, see 14:2. "Tongues" (plural) may refer to this gift in Mk 16:17; Act 2:3, 4; 10:46; 19:6; 1 Cor 12:10, 28, 30; 13:1, 8; 14:5, 6, 18, 22, 23, 39; and "tongue" (singular) in 1 Cor 14:2, 4, 9, 13, 14, 19, 26, 27. "New tongues" is in Mk 16:17; "other tongues" is in Act 2:4. Related to "other-tongues" in 1 Cor 14:21. Elsewhere only of the organ itself in Mk 7:33; Lk 16:24; Rev 16:10; of languages in Act 2:11; of peoples grouped by language in Rev 5:9; 7:9; 10:11; 11:9; 13:7; 14:6; 17:15; of humans beings in Rom 14:11; Phil 2:11; and of speech in Mk 7:35; Lk 1:64; Act 2:26; Rom 3:13; Jam 1:26; 3:5, 6, 8; 1 Pet 3:10; 1 Jn 3:18. GK *1185*.
9. Or, "translation". Used only here and 14:26. GK *2255*. Related to "translated" in Jn 1:42; "translated" in Act 13:8; "interpreter" in 1 Cor 14:28; and "interpret" in 1 Cor 12:30.
10. Or, "effects, produces". Same word as in v 6; and in Gal 2:8; 3:5; 5:6; Eph 1:11, 20; Phil 2:13; Jam 5:16. Elsewhere only as "at work" in Mt 14:2; Mk 6:14; Rom 7:5; 2 Cor 1:6; 4:12; Eph 2:2; 3:20; Col 1:29; 1 Thes 2:13; 2 Thes 2:7. GK *1919*. Related to "working" in Phil 3:21; "*things*-worked" in 1 Cor 12:6; and "effective" in Heb 4:12. The root word is "work" in Mt 26:10.
11. Or, "dividing". Elsewhere only in Lk 15:12. GK *1349*. Related to "differences" in v 4.
12. Or, "*to each one his* own". On this word, see "own" in Act 20:28.
13. Or, "wants, wishes". On this word, see Jam 1:18.
14. Or, "members, parts". On this word, see Col 3:5. Used 13 times in this chapter.
15. Some manuscripts say "the one body" {N}.
16. Having detailed diversity (v 7-10) and unity (v 11), Paul now illustrates both in the human body. Each phrase of v 12 is discussed next. The "one body" (1D), with "many members" (2D), is "one body" (3D). "So also Christ" (4D).
17. This phrase "For indeed" is also in v 14; 5:7; 11:9; 14:8; and as "For even" in 8:5. It occurs 39 times.
18. Or, "in, by". Paul could mean "by" the Spirit, that the Spirit baptized us into one body. Or he could mean that Jesus baptized us into one body "by means of, in, with" the Spirit. Elsewhere, Jesus is always the baptizer "in, with" the Spirit. On "with, in, by" the Spirit, see Mk 1:8. GK *1877*.
19. Unity is the point here. To make the body metaphor work, Paul must prove believers are all parts of "one body".
20. This word is used regarding the Spirit only here, and when contrasting John's baptism "in" or "with" water to Jesus' baptism "in" or "with" the Spirit. On this word, see Mk 1:8.
21. That is, the body of Christ. The baptism makes us "one body", and the gifts make us "many members".
22. Some see this as a different metaphor with the same point, unity. Our unity is produced through a Spirit baptism, through a drink of living water. We are given the Spirit to drink either by the Father (as in Jn 14:16, 26); or by Jesus (as in Jn 15:26; 16:7). Others see this as something distinct from the baptism. Consult the commentaries. The verb "give to drink" is GK *4540*. Some manuscripts add "into", so that it says "And we were all made to drink into one Spirit" {N}.
23. Now Paul shows that the differences in the body are necessary and intentional. We should not devalue ourselves because we are not some other part we admire. Those who consider themselves lesser members than others are still essential members of the body, and are needed by the body as God placed them.
24. Or, "But as it is". On this idiom, see 5:11.
25. In contrast to his previous point (v 14), Paul gives another side of the illustration.
26. Paul uses grammar that emphasizes the contrast between the two halves of this sentence.
27. The diverse members still form one body, each part mutually dependent on the other. Those who consider themselves more honorable members are dependent on the lesser members of the body.
28. Elsewhere only as "without honor" in Mt 13:57; Mk 6:4; and "dishonored" in 1 Cor 4:10. GK *872*. Here it is a comparative, "more dishonored", that is, "less honored, less honorable". Related to "dishonor" in Act 5:41.
29. Perhaps like putting on a gold ring or shoes or a cloak. The verb "put on" is used of a robe in Mt 27:28.

A. 1 Cor 12:28 B. Act 19:21, put C. Jn 7:17, willing D. Tit 3:14 E. Lk 19:11, thinking F. 1 Thes 5:14 G. Tit 3:14

	1F. Indeed our private[1] *parts* have more presentability[2], °but our presentable *parts* have no need[3]	24
	3E. But God blended-together[4] the body, having given more honor[A] to the *body-part* lacking[B], °in order that there should not be division[C] in the body, but *that* the body-parts should be having the same concern[5] for one another	25
	4E. And if one body-part is suffering[D], all the body-parts are suffering-with[E] *it*. If one[6] body-part is being glorified[F], all the body-parts are rejoicing-with *it*	26
4D.	And **you** are *the* body *of* Christ, and body-parts in part[7]	27
	1E. And God placed[G] some[8] in the church *as* first, apostles[9]; second, prophets[10]; third, teachers[11]; then miracles[12]; then gifts[H] *of* healings[J], helps[13], administrations[14], kinds[15] *of* tongues[K]	28
	2E. All *are* not apostles, *are they*?[16] All *are* not prophets, *are they*? All *are* not teachers, *are they*? All *do* not *do* miracles, *do they*[17]? °All do not have gifts *of* healings, *do they*? All do not speak *in* tongues,[18] *do they*? All do not interpret[19], *do they*?	29 30
	3E. But be zealous-for[20] the greater[21] gifts[22]	31
5C. And[23] I show[L] you *a* way[24] still[25] beyond measure[26]		
	1D. If I speak *in* the tongues[K] *of* humans[M] and *of* angels[27], but I do not have love[N]— I have become *a* sounding[28] brass [gong] or *a* clanging cymbal	13:1
	1E. And if I have prophecy[O] and know[29] all mysteries[P] and all knowledge[Q], and if I have all faith so as to remove[R] mountains, but I do not have love— I am nothing	2

1. That is, our reproductive organs, our "shameful" parts (related to "indecent" in Rom 1:27), or our "un-honored, dishonorable, unbecoming" parts (related to "behave dishonorably" in 1 Cor 7:36). Used only here. GK *860*.
2. Or, "decorum, decency, propriety". That is, because we put more honor on such parts by covering them with clothing. Our presentable members have no need of this. Used only here. GK *2362*. A related word follows.
3. Some manuscripts add "*of* honor" {N}.
4. Or, "united, mixed together, combined, composed". Elsewhere only as "united" in Heb 4:2. GK *5166*. Related to "mix" in Rev 14:10.
5. The equality of honor comes from the mutual dependence. On this word, "be having concern", see "be anxious for" in Mt 6:25.
6. Some manuscripts omit this word {C}, so it says "if *a* body part...".
7. Some think Paul means "body parts [of it] in part", meaning the Corinthians are only part of Christ's body, which is worldwide; others, "body-parts in [your assigned] part"; others, "body parts viewed as individual parts of the whole", that is, "individually". Perhaps Paul means "you are a partial body-part", meaning for example, not "the eye", but "the eye in part". This phrase "in part" is elsewhere only in 13:9, 10, 12; and is similar to "in part" in Rom 11:25.
8. Paul starts to say "some *as* apostles, others *as* prophets" (as in Eph 4:11), but then combines this with "first... second" in order to rank the gifts.
9. Or, "sent ones, official representatives, messengers". Jesus chose the twelve and gave them this name, Lk 6:13. They and Paul were personally sent by Christ to the world as eyewitnesses of Christ (Act 1:21-22), with miraculous powers, (Act 2:43; 8:18; 2 Cor 12:12; Heb 2:4). Other than of the Twelve and Paul, this word is used of Jesus in Heb 3:1; perhaps of James in Gal 1:19; of Barnabas and Saul, sent by the Holy Spirit in Act 14:14; of "missionaries, delegates, representatives" sent by churches in 2 Cor 8:23; Phil 2:25, and perhaps Rom 16:7; and of "messengers" in general in Jn 13:16. Used four times of "false apostles", who claim this authority. Some define this gift narrowly, as those Jesus Himself chose and sent as His eyewitnesses. Others define it broadly as "missionary, church planter". GK *693*. Used 80 times.
10. Used 144 times, in this sense perhaps in Lk 11:49; Act 11:27; 13:1; 15:32; 21:10; 1 Cor 14:29, 32, 37; Eph 2:20; 3:5; 4:11; Rev 18:20; 22:6, 9. Elsewhere only of Christians, John the Baptist, Jesus, the Cretan prophet (Tit 1:12), and in Revelation. GK *4737*. The feminine word is used of Anna (Lk 2:36), and in Rev 2:20. See the related words in 1 Cor 12:10; 14:1; 2 Pet 1:19.
11. Used 59 times, in this sense as in Act 13:1; Eph 4:11; 1 Tim 2:7; 2 Tim 1:11; Heb 5:12; Jam 3:1. Elsewhere only of Jesus, John the Baptist, teachers of Israel, false teachers. GK *1437*. Apollos is a good one, Act 18:24-28. Related words in Rom 12:7; 1 Cor 14:6.
12. Or, "powers". Same word as in 12:10.
13. This means "helpful deeds, assistance, aid, support". Used only here. GK *516*. Related to the word in 1 Tim 6:2; and in Rom 8:26. The root words imply "take a part corresponding to the need".
14. Or, "governing, leadership, management". Used only here. GK *3236*. A related word meaning "pilot of a ship, helmsman" is in Rev 18:17.
15. Same word as in Mt 13:47; Mk 9:29; 1 Cor 12:10; 14:10. Elsewhere only as "offspring" in Act 17:28, 29; Rev 22:16; "family" in Act 4:6; 7:13; 13:26; 1 Pet 2:9; "nation" in Act 7:19; 2 Cor 11:26; Gal 1:14; Phil 3:5; and "nationality" in Mk 7:26; Act 4:36; 18:2, 24. GK *1169*. It is plural only in 1 Corinthians.
16. The grammar of all these questions expects a "no" answer.
17. Or, "All *are* not [workers of] miracles, *are they*", "All *do* not *have* [the gift of] miracles, *do they*". See 12:10.
18. Some think Paul means "in the church, officially" as opposed to "in the closet, privately".
19. Same word as in 14:5, 13, 27. Elsewhere only as "translate" in Act 9:36; and of "interpreting" Scripture in Lk 24:27. GK *1450*. On this word group, see 12:10.
20. Same word as in 14:1.
21. Verse 28 is the only place Paul ranks the gifts, other than prophecy and tongues in chapter 14. Some manuscripts say "better" {N}, the word in 7:9, 38; 11:17; Heb 1:4.
22. The Spirit distributes the gifts as He desires, v 11, 18. But since we do not know the works He has prepared for us (Eph 2:10), we should seek to lay hold of all that for which we were laid hold (Phil 3:12). We should aim high, desiring that God produce the greatest possible results through us, so that we can be of maximum value to the body. Do not all seek to have the same gift, because all do not have it. But seek to have the greater gifts. Some think Paul means to seek to have the greater gifts expressed in your local church; others, seek to have them personally.
23. Having completed his primary explanation of gifts, Paul now describes their needed balance, love.
24. Or, "path". Some think the "way" is love; others, gifts exercised with love. On this word, see Lk 3:4.
25. This word means "still, yet, as yet"; and "furthermore" (as in Lk 14:26; Act 2:26; 21:28; Heb 11:36), "longer, more". "Still" is used with a phrase like this only in Lk 1:15; Jn 11:30; Rom 5:6; Rev 12:8. Paul may mean it in the second sense, "and furthermore, I show you a way beyond measure". Used 93 times. GK *2285*.
26. This idiom is rendered "extremely" in Rom 7:13; 2 Cor 1:8; 4:17; Gal 1:13. The word itself means "excess", as elsewhere only in 2 Cor 4:7; 12:7. The Greek word is *huperbole,* from which we get "hyperbole", meaning "excessive or exaggerated speech". While some gifts are "greater" than others, love is beyond measure, and outside the ranking of gifts. It is in a still unmeasured category— as infinite as the character of God, and operative in every member of the body of Christ (whereas no gift is possessed by all believers). Some render this phrase as a comparative here, love is a "more excellent" path than gifts; others as a superlative, "most excellent" ("excellent" comes from the context, where it is "beyond measure" in the direction of good). Related to "surpassing" in 2 Cor 9:14. GK *5651*.
27. Some think this is a hyperbole, "even *of* angels, [if that were possible]", giving the maximum, unattainable height of expression of the gift, as in v 2-3. The Greek word order is "If *in* the tongues *of* humans I speak, even [or 'and'; the word means both] *of* angels". Others think Paul is referring to something truly possible and attainable.
28. That is, a brass making its sound. Used only here. GK *2490*.
29. Some think Paul is referring to an additional gift or gifts; others, to the extent of the gift of prophecy— if God is giving me revelations to speak to the point that I know all His mysteries and knowledge.

A. 1 Tim 5:17 B. Lk 15:14, be in need C. 1 Cor 1:10 D. Gal 3:4 E. Rom 8:17 F. Rom 8:30 G. 1 Cor 12:18 H. 1 Cor 1:7 J. 1 Cor 12:9
K. 1 Cor 12:10 L. 1 Tim 6:15 M. Mt 4:4, mankind N. 1 Jn 4:16 O. 1 Cor 12:10 P. Rom 11:25 Q. 1 Cor 12:8 R. Act 19:26, turn away

		Verse
2E.	And if I dole-out[1] all my possessions[2], and if I hand-over[3] my body so that I may boast[4], but I do not have love^A— I am profited^B nothing	3
2D.	Love^A is patient[5]. Love shows-kindness[6]	4
1E.	Love[7] does not envy[8], does not brag, is not puffed-up^C, *does not behave-dishonorably[9], does not seek[10] its *own things*, is not provoked[11], does not count[12] the bad[13], *does not rejoice^D over unrighteousness^E, but rejoices-with the truth^F, *bears[14] all *things*, believes^G all *things*, hopes^H all *things*, endures[15] all *things*	5 6 7
3D.	Love never fails[16]. But if *there are* prophecies^J, they will be set-aside[17]. If *there are* tongues^K, they will cease[18]. If *there is* knowledge^L, it will be set-aside	8
1E.	For we know^M in part^N, and we prophesy^O in part—*but when the complete[19] *thing* comes, the[20] *thing* in part will be set-aside	9-10
2E.	When I was *a* child^P, I was speaking like *a* child, thinking[21] like *a* child, counting[22] like *a* child[23]— when[24] I have become[25] *a* man, I have set-aside the *things of* the child	11
3E.	For now we are seeing through[26] *a* mirror, in *an* enigma[27]— but then face to face	12
4E.	Now I know in part— but then I will know-fully[28], just as I also was fully-known	
4D.	But now[29] these three are remaining^Q— faith^R, hope^S, love^A. But love *is the* greater[30] *of* these	13
5D.	Be pursuing[31] love	14:1

1. Or, "give away" piece by piece. This word was used of "feeding" a child by putting little bits in the mouth. That is, if I dole out all my possessions piece by piece to poor ones. Elsewhere only as "feed" in Rom 12:20. GK *6039*. Related to "piece of bread" in Jn 13:26.
2. Or, "belongings". This is a participle, on which see Heb 10:34.
3. Or, "deliver". Paul may mean deliver his body into slavery to help others or feed the poor; or, as a martyr. On this word, see 11:23.
4. Compare 9:16. On this word, see 2 Cor 11:16. Some manuscripts say "that I may be burned", perhaps as in Daniel 3, or as a martyr {C}.
5. Or, "has patience, waits patiently". Same verb as in Mt 18:26, 29; Lk 18:7; 1 Thes 5:14; Jam 5:7, 8; 2 Pet 3:9. Elsewhere only as "wait patiently" in Heb 6:15. GK *3428*. Related to "patience" in Heb 6:12. The root words mean "is long to anger, is keeping anger far away".
6. This verb is used only here. GK *5980*. Related to "goodness" in Rom 3:12; and "good" in 1 Pet 2:3. Kindness is goodness in action.
7. It is also possible to punctuate by grouping the first two, "Love waits patiently, shows kindness, love does not envy, love does not brag"; or, the second two, "Love waits patiently, love shows kindness, does not envy, love does not brag". Some manuscripts omit the third "love" {C}.
8. Or, "does not behave jealously" in a negative sense. On this word, see "jealous-for" in 2 Cor 11:2.
9. On "behave dishonorably", see 7:36.
10. Same word as 10:24, 33; Phil 2:21.
11. That is, to anger. Or, "irritated". Elsewhere only in Act 17:16. GK *4236*. Related to "provoking" in Heb 10:24.
12. Or, "account, calculate, consider". Some think Paul means "take account of it"; others, "count it against", hold a grudge, be resentful; others, "impute it" to others. On this word, see "consider" in Rom 3:28.
13. Or, "wrong". Some think Paul means the wrong suffered; others, the wrong done. On this word, see "evil" in 3 Jn 11.
14. Or, "endures, covers, shelters, protects". Elsewhere only in 9:12; 1 Thes 3:1, 5. GK *5095*. The root word means "roof" (Mt 8:8).
15. Or, "perseveres". On this word, see Jam 1:12.
16. Or, "falls, falls *down*". Used in this sense also in Lk 16:17. On this word, see "fall" in Rom 11:11. Related word in Rom 9:6.
17. Or, "made idle, done away with". Same word as in v 10, 11. On this word, see "done away with" in Rom 6:6.
18. Or, "leave off, stop, come to an end". Some think tongues cease before the "complete thing" comes and "sets aside" the other gifts, v 10. Others think they cease when "the complete thing" comes. Same word as in Lk 5:4; 8:24; 11:1; Act 5:42; 6:13; 13:10; 20:1, 31; 21:32; Eph 1:16; Col 1:9; Heb 10:2; 1 Pet 4:1. Elsewhere only as "stop" in 1 Pet 3:10. GK *4264*.
19. Or, "perfect, mature, finished, having attained its end or purpose". Some think "the complete thing" is the completed revelation of the NT. Once complete, the gifts of revelation and confirmation (including prophecy and knowledge) ceased or continued in a non-revelatory sense. Others think it refers to the fullness that comes when Christ returns. We shall then be like Him, 1 Jn 3:2. The body will be "mature", Eph 4:13 (same word). The partial will be completed and prophecy and knowledge will no longer be needed. There are other views. Same word as in Jam 1:4. Elsewhere only as "perfect" in Mt 5:48; 19:21; Rom 12:2; Heb 9:11; Jam 1:17, 25; 3:2; 1 Jn 4:18; and "mature" in 1 Cor 2:6; 14:20; Eph 4:13; Phil 3:15; Col 1:28; 4:12; Heb 5:14. GK *5455*. Related to "to perfect" in Heb 2:10.
20. Some manuscripts say "then the" {N}.
21. On this word, see Rom 8:5. I set my mind on things as a child does.
22. Or, "calculating, evaluating". Same word as in v 5. A narrower term, focusing on intellectual reasoning.
23. That is, with partial understanding. Prophecy, tongues, and knowledge belong to the period of childhood. They will appear as childish when the complete comes. Not wrong; just partial, incomplete, rudimentary.
24. Some manuscripts say "But when" {N}.
25. This word "have become" is the same word and form as 9:22; 13:1; 2 Cor 12:11. GK *1181*. As it is characteristic of adults to have done so now, so it will be of us then. Paul is comparing the state of childhood with the state of adulthood. As an adult, I have put away childish things and am going on in the things of adulthood.
26. Or, "by means of, with". GK *1328*.
27. That is, in a form that is imperfectly seen, indistinctly reflected, hence "dimly, unclearly, indirectly". Used of sayings that were "riddles". Ancient mirrors were made of polished metal, and produced an imperfect reflection. Our present vision of God is like a reflection in a primitive mirror. But then, we will see His face, Rev 22:4. Used only here. GK *141*.
28. On this word, used twice in this verse, see "understood" in Col 1:6.
29. Paul says "these three", as a group, are remaining, love being the greater. Some think he means "But as it is, these three remain forever, in contrast to the gifts, which cease when Jesus comes". This means faith and hope must take on a new meaning after He comes, since as we know them now, faith becomes sight and hope is fulfilled. What this new meaning might be is differently explained. Others think Paul means "But at the present, these three virtues remain, along with gifts, but superior to them. But love is superior to them all". Faith and hope are added because they are our present connection to "then" in v 8-13. These three are remaining as more fundamental, more important, and more powerful than gifts. Love is superior "beyond measure" (12:31), because God is love. Love is as infinite and as eternal as He is. All these other things are expressions of His love, and His love gives meaning to them. Pursue love, and all these three will grow, and gifts will have value, v 1-3. There are other views. Consult the commentaries.
30. Though the form of this word is "greater", some think the sense of it here is "greatest".
31. Or, "running after, seeking after". Same word as in Rom 12:13; 14:19; 1 Thes 5:15; 1 Tim 6:11; 2 Tim 2:22; Heb 12:14; 1 Pet 3:11; "press on" in Phil 3:12, 14; and "persecute" in 2 Tim 3:12. Used 45 times. GK *1503*. Others link this with what follows, "Pursue love and be zealous-for...".

A. 1 Jn 4:16   B. Rom 2:25   C. 1 Cor 4:6   D. 2 Cor 13:11   E. Rom 1:18   F. Jn 4:23   G. Jn 3:36   H. Jn 5:45, put hope   J. 1 Cor 12:10   K. 1 Cor 12:10
L. 1 Cor 12:8   M. Lk 1:34   N. 1 Cor 12:27   O. 1 Cor 14:1   P. 1 Cor 3:1, infant   Q. Jn 15:4, abide   R. Eph 2:8   S. Col 1:5

6C. Now be zealous-for¹ the spiritual² *gifts*, but even-more³ that you might be prophesying⁴

    1D. For⁵ the *one* speaking^A in⁶ *a* tongue⁷ is not speaking *to* people^B, but *to* God⁸— for no one hears⁹, but he speaks mysteries¹⁰ *with his* spirit¹¹. *But the *one* prophesying is speaking edification^C and exhortation^D and consolation¹² *to* people   2 / 3

        1E. The *one* speaking *in a* tongue is edifying¹³ himself.¹⁴ But the *one* prophesying is edifying *the* church^E   4

        2E. And I wish¹⁵ *that* you all *were* speaking *in* tongues, but even-more¹⁶ that you might be prophesying   5

    2D. Now¹⁷ the *one* prophesying *is* greater¹⁸ than *one* speaking *in* tongues— unless¹⁹ he interprets²⁰ in order that the church may receive edification^C

        1E. But now²¹, brothers^F, if I come to you speaking *in* tongues²²   6

            1F. What will I profit²³ you, unless I speak *to* you either by²⁴ *a* revelation^G or by knowledge^H or by *a* prophecy^J or by *a* teaching²⁵?

        2E. Likewise²⁶ the lifeless *things* giving *a* sound^K— whether *a* flute or harp   7

            1F. If it does not give *a* distinction *in* the tones, how will the *thing* being fluted or the *thing* being harped be known^L?

                1G. For indeed, if *a* trumpet gives *an* uncertain^M sound^K, who will prepare^N himself for battle^O?   8

            2F. So also you²⁷ with the tongue²⁸— if you do not give *a* clear word²⁹, how will the *thing* being spoken be known? For you will be speaking into *the* air!   9

1. Now Paul returns to where he left off in 12:31. Same word as in 12:31; 14:39. Related to "zealots" in 14:12. On this word, see "jealous for" in 2 Cor 11:2.
2. This word means "pertaining to the spirit". Elsewhere only in Rom 1:11; 7:14; 15:27; 1 Cor 2:13, 15; 3:1; 9:11; 10:3, 4; 12:1; 14:37; 15:44, 46; Gal 6:1; Eph 1:3; 5:19; 6:12; Col 1:9; 3:16; 1 Pet 2:5. GK *4461*. The root word is "spirit".
3. Or, "still more". Used 81 times, it means "more", or in a contrast, "rather, instead". GK *3437*. Some render it "especially" here. Same word as in v 5.
4. This verb is elsewhere only in 11:4, 5; 13:9; 14:3, 4, 5, 24, 31, 39; and in Mt 7:22; 11:13; 15:7; 26:68; Mk 7:6; 14:65; Lk 1:67; 22:64; Jn 11:51; Act 2:17, 18; 19:6; 21:9; 1 Pet 1:10; Jude 14; Rev 10:11; 11:3. GK *4736*. Related words in 1 Cor 12:10; 28; 2 Pet 1:19.
5. Seek to prophesy, for tongues has no edification value to the church— unless accompanied by the interpretation. Paul's focus in chapter 14 is specifically on defining the value and place of tongues in the public assembly of the local church.
6. Or, "*with*". When "speaking" is connected to "tongues" it is always with the same grammatical construction, which implies either "in" or "with" tongues. Only in 14:19 is the actual preposition with the same meaning used (GK *1877*).
7. What was occurring in Corinth is different from what occurred in Acts 2. In Acts, the speaking was in public and was understood by the native speakers of the language present. In 1 Cor 14, the speaking was in church and was not understood unless accompanied by the gift of interpretation. Based on this some think that there are two different gifts of tongues; others that the one gift was used in two ways. Thus, some think Paul is not referring here to the gift seen in Acts 2, but to a different gift, a personal prayer language understood only by God. In Corinth they were using this gift in church. Since no one understood, the result was confusion. Others think he is referring to the same gift seen in Acts 2. In Corinth they were using it for worship in church with no native speakers present who could interpret and no one with the spiritual gift of interpretation. Since no one understood, the result was confusion. See 12:10 on "tongue".
8. That is, the speaker addresses his speech to God (speaking, praying, singing, blessing), whereas prophets address their speech to people for edification. The one speaking in a tongue is not focused on people and edification.
9. That is, hears with understanding. Some take this to mean no one except a native speaker as in Acts 2, or an interpreter as in v 5. The speaker does not address people in general because they do not understand. Others think Paul means no human understands because it is a personal prayer language addressed to God. The speaker does not address any human being, because none understands and none is intended to understand. Same word as in Act 22:9.
10. That is, truths yet to be explained. They need interpretation (v 5), to be understood. Prophecy speaks truths immediately understood. On this word, see Rom 11:25.
11. Paul may be emphasizing the source of the mysteries spoken, "*in the Holy* Spirit" (as in 12:2); or that they are spoken "*with his* spirit", apart from his mind (as in 14:14, 15); or that they are spoken "*with his* spiritual *gift*" (as this same word is used in 14:12). All are true, of course. He clearly does not mean "silently", "*in his* spirit".
12. Or, "comfort, encouragement". Used only here. GK *4171*. Related to "encourage" in 1 Thes 5:14.
13. Or, "building up, strengthening, establishing". Same word as in v 17, and as "build up" in Act 9:31; 20:32; 1 Cor 8:1, 10; 10:23; 1 Thes 5:11. Used 40 times. GK *3868*. Related to "edification" in v 3, 5, 12, 26 (on which see Rom 14:19), and "builder" in Act 4:11.
14. This is not because the speaker understands, but because God is speaking through him. All gifts edify the person using them, but with tongues alone is it possible for this to be the only benefit that takes place. Some think this personal benefit is God's intended use of this gift, a personal prayer language for self-edification. Others think the gift was given to be used with unbelievers as described in v 21-22, and that the personal benefit is a by-product, as with all other gifts.
15. Or, "want". Some think Paul wishes this "in theory", knowing that neither is possible (as he said in 12:11, 18, 30), just as in 7:7 he "wished" (same word and grammar) all to be single like him even though each has his own gift from God. Others think Paul truly "wants" all to do both— to develop a personal prayer language, and to focus on edifying others by proclaiming the truth. On this word, see "willing" in Jn 7:17.
16. Same exact phrase as in v 1. Or, "rather", if Paul is making a contrast with tongues.
17. Or, "But, And". Some manuscripts say "For" {K}.
18. That is, in this person's ability to edify the church, not personally. Paul wants edification to be the focus.
19. Literally, "except unless", an idiom elsewhere only in 15:2; 1 Tim 5:19. It means "with this exception, unless...".
20. Sometimes the tongue-speaker also had the gift of interpretation; other times not, v 13, 28. The interpretation is equal to prophecy in edification value. For this reason, Paul allows both to contribute to the church, 14:27, 29. His focus is on edification. On this word, see 12:30.
21. Or, "But as it is". As in 5:11 and 12:20, Paul is beginning a point in his argument in contrast to what he previously said. But now, in contrast to the case with interpretation, what can tongues alone profit you? His intent in v 6-12 is to prove that tongues alone has no edification value to others, so the Corinthians should be seeking to edify through the greater gifts (12:31).
22. Some think Paul means "actually speaking in tongues in your presence"; others, "as one with this gift, as a tongues-speaker". See the next note.
23. Some think Paul means that only if his tongue is interpreted can its content, which could be one of these four things, profit the hearers. Others, that since his tongue cannot profit the hearers, if Paul is to do so he must instead use one of these other four gifts. Same word as in 13:3. On this word, see Rom 2:25.
24. Or, "with, in", four times in this verse. GK *1877*. Some manuscripts omit the fourth "by", so that it says, "by *a* prophecy or *a* teaching" {C}.
25. This noun is used 30 times. GK *1439*. Related to "teacher" in 12:28.
26. Or, "yet", meaning "*There are* lifeless *things* giving *a* sound, whether *a* flute or harp, **yet** if it does not give *a* distinction...". GK *3940*.
27. Paul applies the lesson of the flute and harp to the Corinthians.
28. This is the Greek word order. Or, "So also you— if you do not give *a* clear word with the tongue". Some think Paul is referring to normal speaking, articulating words; others, to the interpretation of the gift.
29. Or, "give intelligible speech". The speaker must give a word that is understandable by the hearer.

A. Jn 12:49 B. Mt 4:4, mankind C. Rom 14:19 D. Act 4:36, encouragement E. Rev 22:16 F. Act 16:40 G. 2 Thes 1:7 H. 1 Cor 12:8 J. 1 Cor 12:10 K. Mk 1:26, voice L. Lk 1:34 M. Lk 11:44, unmarked N. 2 Cor 9:3 O. Rev 12:7, war

3E. There are perhaps¹ so-many kinds^A *of spoken* sounds² in *the* world, and none³ *is* meaningless⁴   10

    1F. If then I do not know the force⁵ *of* the *spoken* sound, I will be *a* barbarian⁶ *to* the *one* speaking, and the *one* speaking *a* barbarian with me   11

4E. So also you⁷— since you are zealots⁸ *for* spiritual⁹ *gifts*, be seeking¹⁰ that you may abound^B for the edification^C *of* the church   12

3D. Therefore¹¹ let the *one* speaking *in a* tongue pray¹² in order that he might interpret^D   13

    1E. For¹³ if I am praying^E *in a* tongue, my spirit¹⁴ is praying, but my mind¹⁵ is unfruitful¹⁶   14
    2E. What then is *to be done*¹⁷? I will pray *with* the spirit, and¹⁸ I will also pray *with* the mind. I will sing-praise^F *with* the spirit, and I will also sing-praise *with* the mind   15
    3E. Otherwise¹⁹, if you are blessing²⁰ *with*²¹ *your* spirit²² [only], how will the *one* filling^G the place²³ *of* the uninstructed²⁴ say the "Amen" at your thanksgiving^H, since he does not know what you are saying?   16

        1F. For **you**²⁵ are giving-thanks^J well^K— but the other *person* is not being edified^L   17

    4E. I give-thanks^J *to* God²⁶ I speak *in* tongues more *than* all *of* you. *But in church*,²⁷ I want^M to speak five words *with* my mind in order that I might also instruct^N others, *rather* than ten-thousand words^O *in a* tongue   18-19

4D. Brothers, do not be children^P *in your* understanding²⁸. But be childlike²⁹ *in* evilness^Q, and be mature³⁰ *in your* understanding   20

    1E. It has been written in the Law [in Isa 28:11-12] that "I will speak *to* this people³¹ by *people of* other-tongues³², and by *the* lips *of* others.³³ And not even in this manner will they listen-to Me, says *the* Lord"³⁴   21

1. This word is an idiom meaning here "If it should happen [that they can be counted]", which some smooth into "who knows" how many, or, "maybe" so many, or, "doubtless" so many. This idiom is elsewhere only in 15:37. GK *5593*.
2. This is a common word used of a "sound" or "voice", and the same word as "sound" in v 7, 8. Here and in v 11, it has the sense of "language" or "speech", the spoken sounds of humans.
3. Some manuscripts say "none *of* them" {N}.
4. Paul has a play on words here. There are many kinds of "voices" but none is "voiceless", many kinds of "speech", but none is "speechless". It means "speechless" in the sense of "unable to communicate" here; and is used in the sense of "incapable of speaking" in 1 Cor 12:2; 2 Pet 2:16. Elsewhere only as "silent" in Act 8:32. GK *936*.
5. That is, the meaning. This is from the hearer's viewpoint; v 9 is from the speaker's viewpoint. On this word, see "power" in Mk 5:30.
6. Or, "foreigner". That is, unable to communicate in a common language. On this word, see Col 3:11.
7. Having proved his point— that tongues alone does not edify— Paul now gives the conclusion for the Corinthians. Note that he does not state the conclusion as might be expected, "So do not speak in tongues in church without interpretation", but as a positive, "so seek to edify the church", which excludes speaking tongues in church without interpretation.
8. Or, "zealous *ones,* enthusiasts, zealous admirers". This noun is elsewhere only in Lk 6:15; Act 1:13; 21:20; 22:3; Gal 1:14; Tit 2:14; 1 Pet 3:13. GK *2421*. Related to verb "be zealous for" in v 1.
9. Or, "spirits". Same word as in Holy "Spirit". Used here (and perhaps in 14:2, 14, 15, 16, 32; Eph 1:17; 2 Thes 2:2; 2 Tim 1:7; Rev 22:6) in the sense of "spiritual *manifestation*" or "spiritual *gift*". GK *4460*. Related to "spiritual" in 14:1.
10. Or, "striving for, trying to obtain". Same word as in 10:24, 33; 13:5; Col 3:1. On this word, see Phil 2:21.
11. Now Paul draws the positive conclusion from v 5 and v 12.
12. Some think Paul means the one desiring to speak in a tongue should first pray in his native language for the gift of interpretation, so that his tongue can edify. Others think he means the one speaking in a tongue should pray in this tongue for the purpose of interpreting it, so that the interpretation may edify the body.
13. Some manuscripts omit this word {C}.
14. Or, "spiritual *gift*", as in v 12. Paul may mean my "human spirit", or my "spiritual gift" of tongues. See v 2.
15. Or, "understanding, intellect". Same word as in v 15 (twice), 19. On this word, see Rom 7:23.
16. Or, "barren, unproductive". Same word as in Mt 13:22; Mk 4:19; Eph 5:11; Tit 3:14; 2 Pet 1:8. Elsewhere only as "fruitless" in Jude 12. GK *182*. My mind produces nothing for edification. What I pray is a mystery to me (v 2), and bears no fruit in others.
17. What is the tongue-speaker personally to do? What is the conclusion of the matter for the individual? Same idiom as in v 26, and in Act 21:22.
18. Or, "but". Same word as in the next sentence. Some think Paul means "I will pray with one or the other separately". I will abound for edification by praying privately in tongues "with my spirit" for myself, and praying publicly "with my mind" (in the common language) for the church. Others think he means "I will pray with both sequentially". I will abound for edification of the church by praying in my tongue "with my spirit" and then praying also the interpretation "with my mind". Others think he means "I will pray with both at the same time", meaning in his normal language.
19. If you do not follow the course in v 15, this is what will result.
20. On this word, see Lk 6:28. Some manuscripts say "shall bless" {N}.
21. Some manuscripts omit this word, leaving it implied {C}.
22. Or, "spiritual *gift*", as in v 12. Equivalent to v 14, "praying [a blessing] in a tongue".
23. Some think Paul means "the status"; others, "the physical location", the seats, the room. On this word, see Eph 4:27.
24. Or "untrained, unskilled; a layman, outsider, uninformed *one, one* not versed in a thing". Same word as in 14:23, 24. Elsewhere only as "untrained" in Act 4:13; 2 Cor 11:6. GK *2626*. This person is defined in this verse as one who "does not know what you are saying". He is not versed on the significance of the gift of tongues, and he does not understand the tongue you just spoke in.
25. Paul uses grammar that emphasizes the contrast between the two halves of this sentence.
26. Some manuscripts say "my God" {N}. Note that Paul's purpose here is to confirm by his own example what he taught in v 15 and illustrated in v 16-17, that is, do not use tongues without interpretation in the church.
27. Where then did Paul speak in tongues? Some think outside the church, to unbelievers, in accordance with v 22, Acts. Others think privately in a personal prayer language for personal edification, v 4, 28.
28. Or, "thinking, thoughts". That is, regarding tongues. The grammar may imply "stop being children". Used only here, twice. GK *5856*. Related to "thinking" in 13:11.
29. Or, "be infants, babies, children". This verb is used only here. GK *3757*. Related to "infant" in 3:1. Not related to "children" earlier.
30. Or, "complete, perfect". Same word as "complete" in 13:10. Compare Rom 16:19.
31. That is, Israel. "This people" (singular) is elsewhere only in Mt 13:15; 15:8; Mk 7:6; Lk 21:23; Act 13:17; 28:26, 27. On "people", see Rev 21:3.
32. Or, "different-tongues", the languages of others. This word is a combination of "other" (different) and "tongues", the two words found separately in Act 2:4. Used only here. GK *2280*.
33. That is, by people speaking foreign languages. This verse describes exactly what happened in Acts 2. Some think this indicates that "tongues" in 1 Cor 14 is the same as that seen in Acts 2. Others agree that this verse describes what happened in Acts 2, but think that 1 Cor 14 also describes a different gift, a personal prayer language. Some manuscripts say "by other lips" {N}. "Others" is the same word as in the compound word preceding.
34. In Isaiah 28, it was a sign of judgment on Israel through the Assyrian conqueror. If Israel will not listen to the prophets, God will speak to them through foreigners as punishment for their unbelief.

A. 1 Cor 12:28   B. 2 Cor 8:2   C. Rom 14:19   D. 1 Cor 12:30   E. 1 Tim 2:8   F. Eph 5:19, make melody   G. 1 Thes 2:16, fill up   H. 1 Tim 4:3
J. Mt 26:27   K. Act 10:33   L. 1 Cor 14:4   M. Jn 7:17, willing   N. Gal 6:6   O. 1 Cor 12:8   P. 1 Jn 2:14   Q. 1 Pet 2:1, badness

2E. So then¹ the tongues are for *a* sign²— not *for* the *ones* believing^A, but *for* the unbelievers.³ But the prophecy *is* not *for* the unbelievers^B, but *for* the *ones* believing⁴   22

    1F. Therefore, if the whole church comes-together at the same *place*⁵, and they all speak *in* tongues,⁶ and uninstructed⁷ *ones* or unbelievers come-in, will they not say that you are mad⁸?   23

    2F. But if they all prophesy, and some unbeliever or⁹ *an* uninstructed *one* comes in, he is convicted¹⁰ by all. He is examined^C by all. °The¹¹ hidden^D *things of* his heart become evident¹². And thus, having fallen on *his* face, he will give-worship^E *to* God, declaring^F that God is really^G among you   24   25

5D. What then is *to be done*¹³, brothers^H? Whenever you come-together, each¹⁴ *one* has *a* psalm^J, has *a* teaching^K, has *a* revelation¹⁵, has *a* tongue^L, has *an* interpretation^M. Let all *things* be done^N for edification^O   26

    1E. If anyone speaks *in a* tongue, *let it be done* by two or *at* the most three, and in turn, and let one¹⁶ *person* interpret^P   27

        1F. But if there is no interpreter¹⁷, let him be silent^Q in church. And let him speak **to himself** and *to* God¹⁸   28

    2E. And let two or three prophets speak, and let the others¹⁹ discern²⁰. °But if *a prophecy* is revealed^R *to* another being seated, let the first be silent²¹   29-30

        1F. For you can all prophesy individually²², in order that all may learn^S, and all may be exhorted²³   31

        2F. And *the* spirits²⁴ *of* prophets are subject^T *to* prophets²⁵   32

        3F. For God is not *the God of* disorder²⁶, but *of* peace   33

    3E. As²⁷ in all the churches²⁸ *of* the saints, °let the women²⁹ be silent³⁰ in the churches.³¹ For it is not permitted³² *for* them to speak³³   34

        1F. But let them be subject^T, just as the Law also says³⁴

1. This is Paul's application of the OT quotation, the mature thinking he wants the Corinthians to have.
2. Some think it is a sign of God's presence in the one speaking, as in Acts 2, a sign that God was speaking to the hearers. It was responded to based on the state of the hearer's heart. Some believed, some rejected, as seen in Acts 2. Israel was supposed to speak for God. Instead, God now speaks to Israel through foreign languages. In Acts 2, the tongues sign created the opportunity to say "Repent and be saved, or face judgment". Others think it was a sign of judgment on Israel, as in Isaiah.
3. That is, tongues are for use outside of the church setting, as seen in Acts. In the church setting, without interpretation, this gift is ineffective for all but the speaker, v 3, 23. The believers may be "instructed" about it, but still do not understand it.
4. When used in the church setting, prophecy is effective for all, even any unbelievers present, v 24-25. It is not "for a sign", but for the things mentioned in v 3, 31.
5. Same phrase as in 11:20.
6. That is, without interpretation. Paul is referring to the fact of its occurrence, not the manner (for example, in a disorderly manner). Since it is not for believers (v 22), that is, not for the church setting, what follows will be the result.
7. Same word as in v 16, 24. Note that "uninstructed" and "unbeliever" are plural here, singular in v 24.
8. Or, "raving, out of your mind. Since no one understands, they conclude you are mad. The grammar indicates a "yes" answer is expected. This word was used of being "mad" with rage, bloodlust, a god, wine, love, joy, etc. Used of mad dogs. Elsewhere only in Jn 10:20 (of Jesus); Act 12:15 (of a girl); Act 26:24, 25 (of Paul). GK *3419*. Related to "madness" in Act 26:24.
9. Both will understand what is said and neither needs instruction on the significance of the gift of prophecy. Since it is for believers, that is, the church setting, it will have a positive effect in that environment upon all present.
10. Or, "exposed, rebuked". On this word, see "expose" in Eph 5:11. All the prophets speak to this person's heart.
11. Some manuscripts say "And thus, the hidden..." {N}.
12. Or, "known". On this word, see Rom 1:19.
13. What is the church to do? What is the conclusion of the matter for the church? Same phrase as v 15.
14. Some manuscripts say "each *of* you" {N}. Each has what God has given him, these being examples.
15. On this word, see 2 Thes 1:7. Some manuscripts reverse this, putting "tongue" here, and "revelation" next {K}.
16. This is the number "one". Paul could mean that one person is to interpret for all three speaking in tongues; or, that one person interprets per speaker. GK *1651*.
17. Note that the speaker must know in advance that his tongue can be interpreted, or he is not to speak out loud. Used only here. GK *1449*. See also 12:10.
18. Some think Paul means "speak silently to himself and God", so as to exercise his gift without causing confusion in the church. Others think he means "speak privately, somewhere else, out loud, to himself and God". In either case, the speaker is to use the gift God gave him, not abandon it. But he is to use it properly, v 40.
19. That is, "the others of the same kind", meaning the other prophets. Same with "another" later in the verse.
20. This is the verb related to "discernment" (12:10) of spirits. Prophets seem to be among those having this gift. That is, discern whether God is the source of the prophecy. On this word, see "doubt" in Jam 1:6.
21. The grammar means "keep silent". Some think Paul means "immediately". God would not give a revelation to both at the same time, v 33. Others think he means "before the second one speaks. Do not speak at the same time".
22. Or, "one by one". On this idiom, see Eph 5:33.
23. Or, "encouraged". On this word, see Rom 12:8.
24. Same word as in v 12. Paul could mean "the human spirits" or "the spiritual gifts".
25. The prophets and the tongue-speakers (as seen in v 28) are not in a state of uncontrollable ecstasy, possessed by the gods as in the Corinthians' former pagan religions. There is a shared control by the Spirit and the prophet.
26. Or, "unruliness, commotions". On this word, see Jam 3:16. God is not the source.
27. Or, "As in all the churches, let the wives *of* the saints be silent in the churches", that is, Christian wives. Or, "but *of* peace, as in all the churches *of* the saints. Let the wives...". Some manuscripts have v 34-35 after v 40 {B}.
28. As in 11:16 with veils, Paul appeals to the general practice or custom of the churches with which he was associated. Some think it is going beyond what is said to teach that these customs apply to every church in every culture. The principle must be applied in each culture so that the intended result is achieved, that is, to conduct ourselves in church honorably and without bringing unnecessary shame on the gospel. Others think it is going beyond what is said to view these as culturally specific applications, and that veils and silence should be observed in all churches. Others accept the first position with regard to veils, and the second position with regard to women.
29. Or, "wives". "Wives" are mainly in view here, based on v 35. Some manuscripts say "your" women {N}. On this word, see 1 Tim 2:11.
30. Same word used of tongue-speakers and prophets, v 28, 30. They were instructed to be silent regarding expressing their gift. Same word as in Lk 18:39; Act 12:17; 15:12, 13. Elsewhere only as "keep silent" in Lk 9:36; Rom 16:25; and "become silent" in Lk 20:26. GK *4967*.
31. Some think that women prayed and prophesied in the church like the men, the women being veiled, the men bare-headed (subordinating this verse to 11:4-5). Aside from such participation led by the Spirit, they are to remain quiet. General talking and asking questions are in view here, v 35. Others think that women prayed and prophesied elsewhere (subordinating 11:4-5 to this verse), and that Paul is forbidding all speaking in church by women.
32. Or, "allowed". On this word, see 1 Tim 2:12.
33. Or, "talk". Some think Paul means to speak out of order, as with the tongue-speakers and prophets. His point with all three groups is "properly and in order" (v 40), not "shamefully and out of order". Others take this absolutely. On this word, see Jn 12:49.
34. Note Paul's explanation in 11:8-9 and 1 Tim 2:13-14. It is part of God's created order before the Fall (Gen 2:18), and part of His curse after the Fall (Gen 3:16). Compare Eph 5:23-24.

A. Jn 3:36   B. Mt 17:17, unbelieving   C. 1 Cor 2:14   D. 1 Cor 4:5   E. Mt 14:33   F. 1 Jn 1:3, announcing   G. Jn 8:36   H. Act 16:40   J. Eph 5:19
K. 1 Cor 14:6   L. 1 Cor 12:10   M. 1 Cor 12:10   N. Mt 6:10   O. Rom 14:19   P. 1 Cor 12:30   Q. 1 Cor 14:34   R. 2 Thes 2:3   S. Phil 4:11   T. Eph 5:21

2F. And if they want to learn^A anything, let them question^B *their* own husbands at home. For it is shameful¹ *for a* woman² to speak in church	35
4E. Or³ did the word *of* God go-forth from you? Or did it reach^C to you only?	36
5E. If anyone thinks^D *that he* is *a* prophet or *a* spiritual^E *person*, let him acknowledge⁴ *the things* which I am writing *to* you— that they are *a* commandment⁵ *of the* **Lord**	37
1F. But if anyone does not-know *this*, he is not-known⁶	38
6D. So then my⁷ brothers, be zealous-for^F the prophesying. And do not be forbidding⁸ the speaking *in* tongues. °But let all *things* be done^G properly^H, and in accordance with order	39 40
7B. Now I make-known^J *to* you, brothers, the good-news⁹ which I announced-as-good-news¹⁰ *to* you, which you also received^K, in which you also stand, °through which you also are being saved^L— if¹¹ you are holding-on¹² *in* that¹³ message^M I announced-as-good-news *to* you, unless¹⁴ you believed^N in-vain¹⁵	15:1 2
1C. For I delivered^O *to* you among *the* first¹⁶ *things* what I also received^K—	3
1D. That Christ died for our sins in accordance with the Scriptures^P	
2D. And that He was buried	4
3D. And that He has been raised^Q *on* the third day in accordance with the Scriptures	
4D. And that He appeared^R *to* Cephas¹⁷, then *to* the twelve¹⁸	5
1E. After that He appeared *to* over five-hundred brothers at-one-time^S, of whom the majority are remaining^T until now.¹⁹ But some fell-asleep^U	6
2E. After that He appeared *to* James²⁰, then *to* all the apostles	7
3E. And last *of* all, as-if-indeed²¹ *to* the untimely-born²² *one*, He appeared *to* me also	8
1F. For **I** am the least *of* the apostles— who am not fit^V to be called^W *an* apostle, because I persecuted^X the church *of* God	9
2F. But *by the* grace^Y *of* God I am what I am	10
3F. And His grace toward me did not become²³ empty²⁴. But I labored even more *than* them all²⁵— yet not I, but the grace *of* God with me	
5D. So whether *it was* I or those, thus we are proclaiming^Z, and thus you believed^N	11
2C. But if Christ is being proclaimed²⁶ that He has been raised^Q from *the* dead, how *is it* some are saying among you that there is no resurrection^AA *of* dead *ones*?²⁷	12
1D. Now if there is no resurrection *of* dead *ones,* neither has Christ been raised. °And if Christ has not been raised	13-14
1E. Then our proclamation^BB *is* also²⁸ **empty**^CC	
2E. Your²⁹ faith *is* also **empty**	
3E. And we are even found *to be* false-witnesses^DD *of* God³⁰, because we testified^EE against³¹ God that He did raise Christ— Whom He did not raise if-indeed³² then dead *ones* are not raised	15

1. Same word as in 11:6. A woman shames herself and her church in the eyes of her society. Paul's goal is to avoid bringing unnecessary shame on the church. On this word, see Tit 1:11.
2. Some manuscripts say "women" {K}.
3. Some think this is said specifically in regard to women, making this point 3F. Others think is applies to all the directions for public worship given in v 26-35.
4. Or, "recognize". On this word, see "understood" in Col 1:6.
5. On this word, see Mk 12:28. Some manuscripts say "that they are commandments..." {N}.
6. Or, "not-recognize... not-recognized". If someone does not recognize this, he or she is not recognized as a prophet or spiritual person. The same word is repeated. Some manuscripts have this as a command, "let him be not-known" {B}. On this word, see "being ignorant of" in Rom 10:3.
7. Some manuscripts omit this word {C}.
8. Or, "preventing, hindering, trying to stop". "Forbidding" is verbally "hindering". Same word as in Mt 19:14; Mk 9:38, 39; 10:14; Lk 9:49, 50; 18:16; 23:2; Act 10:47; 11:17; 16:6; 24:23; 27:43; 1 Thes 2:16; 1 Tim 4:3; 3 Jn 10. Elsewhere only as "hinder" in Lk 11:52; "prevent" in Act 8:36; Rom 1:13; Heb 7:23; "withhold" in Lk 6:29; and "restrain" in 2 Pet 2:16. GK 3266. Related to "prevent" in Mt 3:14; and "without hindrance" in Act 28:31.
9. Or, "gospel", the good news about Jesus Christ, the good news from God. Same word as in Mt 4:2; 24:14; 26:13; Mk 1:1, 14, 15; 16:15; Act 15:7; 20:24; Rom 1:1, 16; 2 Cor 4:3; Gal 1:6; 2:2, 7; Eph 1:13; 3:6; Phil 1:5, 7; Col 1:5; 1 Thes 2:4; 2 Thes 1:8; 2 Tim 1:8, 10; 1 Pet 4:17; Rev 14:6. Used 76 times. GK 2295.
10. In this verse Paul uses the noun and the verb of the same word, as also in Gal 1:11. On this verb, see Act 5:42.
11. The grammar means "assuming that you are holding on".
12. The unique grammar here indicates Paul is speaking of what we hold on "in" or "with". Elsewhere, with different grammar, this word means "hold on to", as in 7:30; 11:2. On this word, see "hold down" in Rom 1:18.
13. Or, "which", but not the word used elsewhere in v 1-2 (GK 4005). The uncertainty arises because of this issue of the resurrection addressed in this chapter. If the Corinthians do not believe Jesus was raised, they are not saved. GK 5515.
14. The Corinthians would have believed in vain if there is no resurrection, v 17. On this idiom, see 14:5.
15. That is, to no purpose. On this word, see Col 2:18.
16. That is, the most important things. This word means "first, foremost, leading". Used 155 times. GK 4755 and 4756.
17. That is, Peter. On this name, see Gal 1:18.
18. This may be a title, not a count, as in Lk 24:33. Judas was gone at this point, but they are still called "the twelve", as in Jn 20:24. They are called "the eleven" in Mt 28:16; Mk 16:14; Lk 24:9, 33. Or, if Paul is using this term in the revised sense of Act 1:26 and 6:12 (note also Act 2:14), then Matthias is the twelfth.
19. This letter was written in about A.D. 55, in Act 19:10, about 25 years after the death of Christ.
20. That is, the brother of the Lord. See Mt 13:55 on him.
21. Or, "as it were". Used only here. GK 6062. It is "as if" because Paul was not in fact born "late" in God's plan, but was separated from his mother's womb, Gal 1:15.
22. Or, "abnormally born". This word means "miscarriage, abortion, forced birth, untimely birth". Perhaps Paul refers to himself as a "forced birth". Before the normal course of events led to his spiritual birth, Christ intercepted him on the road and "forced" his birth. Or perhaps he intends a general sense, "one not born in a normal way". Or perhaps he means, "an apostle born after the normal time", after Christ ascended. Used only here. GK 1765.
23. Or, "prove to be". Same word as in Act 26:19. GK 1181.
24. Or, "without result". Same word as in v 14, 58.
25. Paul may mean "than all of them together"; or, "than any one of them".
26. That is, by all these witnesses in v 5-8, and others. Assuming that Christ's body was raised as all these witnesses are proclaiming, how can resurrection be impossible?
27. These people were not saying that there is no heaven and hell, but that our bodies will not be resurrected. We will be spirits. Some philosophers taught that the body was evil, part of this world. Note the response in Act 17:32.
28. If Christ's resurrection is not an objective, historical reality, then Christianity is worthless, and the worst deception ever foisted upon the world. Apart from His resurrection, none of it is believable or worth believing. If He was raised, then nothing other than what Jesus and His apostolic witnesses said about God is believable or worth believing. There is no middle ground for Paul. Some manuscripts omit this word {C}.
29. Some manuscripts say "Our" {B}.
30. That is, concerning God.
31. That is, against or in contradiction to the truth of God. Or, "by God", under oath, as this word is used in Heb 6:13, 16. That is, we claimed God's authority for our message. GK 2848.
32. That is, "if we assume it is true that the dead are not raised", as is the case under this false teaching. On this idiom, see "since" in Rom 8:9.

A. Phil 4:11 B. Lk 9:18 C. Act 26:7, attain D. Lk 19:11 E. 1 Cor 14:1 F. 1 Cor 14:1 G. Mt 6:10 H. Rom 13:13 J. Phil 1:22, know K. Lk 17:34, taken L. Lk 19:10 M. 1 Cor 12:8, word N. Jn 3:36 O. Act 16:4 P. 2 Pet 3:16 Q. Mt 28:6, arose R. Lk 2:26, see S. Heb 7:27, once for all T. Jn 15:4, abide U. 1 Thes 4:13 V. 2 Cor 3:5, sufficient W. Rom 8:30 X. 2 Tim 3:12 Y. Eph 2:8 Z. 2 Tim 4:2 AA. Act 24:15 BB. 1 Cor 1:21 CC. 1 Thes 2:1 DD. Mt 26:60 EE. Jn 1:7

2D. For if dead *ones* are not raised, neither has Christ been raised. °And if Christ has not been raised   16-17

    1E. Your faith *is* futile¹. You are **still** in your sins
    2E. Then also the *ones* having fallen-asleep² in Christ³ perished⁴   18

3D. If we are *ones* having hoped⁵ in Christ **in this life**^A **only**, we are more pitiable⁶ *than* all people^B   19

3C. But now, Christ has been raised from *the* dead— *the* firstfruit⁷ *of* the *ones* having fallen-asleep   20

  1D. For since death *came* through *a* man, *the* resurrection^C *of* dead *ones* also *came* through *a* man   21
  2D. For just as in⁸ Adam all die, so also in Christ all⁹ will be given-life¹⁰. °But each in *his* own order¹¹—   22-23

    1E. Christ *the* firstfruit
    2E. After-that¹² the *ones of* Christ¹³ at His coming¹⁴
    3E. Then¹⁵ *comes* the end^D— when He hands-over¹⁶ the kingdom^E *to* His God and Father, when He¹⁷ has abolished¹⁸ all rule¹⁹ and all authority^F and power^G   24

      1F. For He²⁰ must^H reign^J until which *time* He²¹ has put^K all the enemies under His feet   25
      2F. Death^L, *the* last enemy, is abolished²²— °for "He²³ subjected^M **all *things*** under His²⁴ feet" [Ps 8:6]   26-27

        1G. But when He says²⁵ that "**All *things*** have been subjected", *it is* clear^N that this is except the *One* having subjected all *things* to Him²⁶
        2G. But when all *things* **are subjected** *to* Him²⁷, then the Son Himself also²⁸ will be subjected *to* the *One*²⁹ having subjected all *things* to Him, in³⁰ order that God may be all *things* in all³¹   28

3D. Otherwise³², what will the *ones* being baptized^O for³³ the dead^P do?³⁴ If dead *ones* are not raised at-all^Q, why indeed are they baptized for them³⁵?   29
4D. Why indeed³⁶ are **we** in danger³⁷ every hour?   30

    1E. I die daily³⁸— by³⁹ your boasting⁴⁰, brothers⁴¹, which I have in Christ Jesus our Lord   31
    2E. If in accordance with human^B *thinking*⁴² I fought-wild-animals⁴³ at Ephesus, what *is* the profit⁴⁴ *to* me?   32

1. Or, "useless, pointless, to no end, worthless". Same word as in 3:20; 1 Pet 1:18. Elsewhere only as "worthless" in Act 14:15; Tit 3:9; Jam 1:26. GK *3469*. Related to "become futile" in Rom 1:21; "futility" in Rom 8:20; "in vain" (futilely) in Mt 15:9; "worthless-talkers" in Tit 1:10; and "worthless-talk" in 1 Tim 1:6.
2. That is, having died. On this word, see 1 Thes 4:13.
3. That is, as Christians.
4. Or, "were lost". That is, died in their sins. On this word, see 1 Cor 1:18.
5. Or, the two verbs may be combined as "If we have hoped". Or, "If we are **only** *ones* having hoped in Christ **in this life**".
6. That is, more deserving of pity. On this adjective, see Rev 3:17.
7. Or, "first portion". Jesus is the first, the representative of what is to come. Elsewhere only in Rom 8:23; 11:16; 16:5; 1 Cor 15:23; 16:15; 2 Thes 2:13; Jam 1:18; Rev 14:4. GK *569*. Some manuscripts say "dead. He became *the* firstfruit..." {N}.
8. That is, in the sphere of, in connection with. GK *1877*.
9. This is the Greek word order. Some punctuate it "as all in Adam die, so also all in Christ...". That is, all humanity dies, all believers will be raised. Unbelievers will be raised also, but they are not "in Christ", and are not in view here. Others punctuate it "as all die in Adam, so also all will be given life in Christ". In this case, Paul is referring to the universal resurrection of all humanity, some to life, others to judgment, as in Jn 5:29; Act 24:15.
10. Or, "made alive". Same word as in v 36, 45, on which see Jn 5:21.
11. Or, "group". This word means a "class, division, group, rank", and is used of a "detachment, division" of troops. It also means the "arrangement, turn". Used only here. GK *5413*.
12. Or, "Then, Next in order". Same word as in v 6, 7. Same word as "then" in 12:28; 15:46; 1 Thes 4:17. Used 16 times. GK *2083*.
13. That is, belonging to Christ.
14. That is, both those dead, and those still living, 1 Thes 4:16-17. On this word, see 2 Thes 2:8.
15. Or, "Next". It implies nothing as to the length of time between the coming of Jesus and the end; only that they are sequential events. P-M (see the note on Rev 20:1) thinks there is an interval of 1000 years between them; A-M thinks there is no significant interval between them. The end comes immediately after Christ returns. Same word as in v 5, 7; Mt 4:28; 1 Tim 2:13. Used 15 times. GK *1663*.
16. Or, "delivers". Some manuscripts have this word in the same tense as the verbs following {N}, so that the three of them would be rendered "hands over... abolishes... puts". On this word, see Mt 26:21.
17. Some think this refers to the Son, and what He does before He hands over the kingdom, this phrase continuing the subject of "He hands over" earlier, which also continues in "He must reign" in v 25. Reading forward from v 24 to 25, one would naturally assume there is no change in subject. Others think this verb refers back to "the God and Father", and is referring to what the Father will do prior to when Christ hands it over. Since the One subjecting all things under His feet is the Father in v 26-28, Paul may intend us to read that fact back into v 24-25.
18. Paul changes tense, indicating that the rule, authority, and power are "abolished" (and the enemies are "put", v 25) before Christ "hands over" the kingdom. P-M thinks the abolishing, reigning, and putting down of enemies, including death last, takes place during the interval (that is, the millennium) between His coming and the end (when He hands over the kingdom). A-M thinks the reigning is taking place now, and the abolishing and putting down take place immediately after His coming, just before He hands over the kingdom. There is no interval between these final events. On this word, see "done away with" in Rom 6:6.
19. Paul may mean this in an abstract sense, the very principle and position of these things apart from God, as well as the beings holding those positions, human or angelic. Or he may mean it in a personal sense, "every ruler and every authority and power", the enemy beings themselves. Same word as "rulers" in Rom 8:38.
20. That is, the Son.
21. Some think Paul means the Father, as in v 27; Ps 110:1; Ps 8:6; others, the Son.
22. Or, "done away with, nullified". Same word as in v 24. Once all are raised, death no longer has any meaning. Compare Rev 20:14.
23. That is, the Father.
24. That is, the Son.
25. Some think Paul means "when God says in Psalm 8:6"; others, "when God says at the end" (note the change to "have been subjected").
26. That is, "except the Father who subjected all things to the Son", v 28. He remains the Father. Compare 11:3.
27. That is, the Son.
28. Some manuscripts omit this word {C}.
29. That is, the Father.
30. Some think Paul means "will be subjected... in order that..."; others, "the *One* having subjected... in order that".
31. This same phrase, "all *things* in all", is used of Christ in Eph 1:23.
32. That is, "Otherwise, if v 20-28 is not the case, then what?".
33. This may mean "on behalf of ", "for the sake of ", "because of ", or "with reference to". GK *5642*.
34. What Paul means here is uncertain. Note that v 29 is in the third person— the ones, they, them— and that v 30 has an emphatic "**we**". Some think this indicates Paul is talking about what some other people do. Some think he is sarcastically referring to some pagan practice of proxy baptism familiar to the Corinthians. However, no such practice is known at this time from other sources. Others think it was "because of " the dead, because of the influence of their lives, or to be with them. Consult the commentaries.
35. Some manuscripts say "for the dead" {N}.
36. Or, "Why also", or "And why". Same phrase as "why indeed" in v 29.
37. Or, "in peril, at risk". Elsewhere only in Lk 8:23; Act 19:27, 40. GK *3073*. The related noun is in Rom 8:35.
38. That is, I face death daily. Note 2 Cor 4:11.
39. Used only here. GK *3755*. This word was used in strong affirmations or solemn oaths, like "by Zeus, by God". Paul means, I swear this is true "by the boasting I do concerning you".
40. On this word, see 2 Cor 7:4. It refers to the act of boasting.
41. Some manuscripts omit this word {C}.
42. Or, "in accordance with mankind". That is, for human motives and goals, with no promise of a resurrection.
43. It was unlawful to throw a Roman citizen such as Paul to the animals in the amphitheater, so this was either an unofficial mob action, or Paul is using this term with reference to his human enemies, or it is a figure of speech. It is not mentioned in Acts or in 2 Cor 11:23-29. He may mean "If I even went so far as to do this, what is the profit if the dead are not raised?" Used only here. GK *2562*.
44. Or, "advantage, help, use, good, benefit". Elsewhere only in Jam 2:14, 16. GK *4055*.

A. Rom 8:10   B. Mt 4:4, mankind   C. Act 24:15   D. Mk 13:7   E. Mt 3:2   F. Rev 6:8   G. Mk 5:30   H. Mt 16:21   J. Rev 19:6   K. Act 19:21   L. 2 Cor 11:23   M. Eph 5:21   N. Gal 3:11, evident   O. Mk 1:8   P. Mt 8:22   Q. 1 Cor 5:1, actually

3E. If dead *ones* are not raised, "Let us eat and drink, for tomorrow we die"[1] [Isa 22:13]

5D. Do not be deceived[A]— bad[B] companionships[2] corrupt[C] good[D] habits[3]. °Sober-up[4] righteously[5] and do not be sinning,[6] for some have *an* ignorance[7] *of* God. I speak to your shame[8]   33-34

4C. But someone will say, "How are the dead raised[E]? And *with* what kind of body do they come?"   35

    1D. Foolish[F] *one*! What **you** sow is not given-life[9] unless it dies   36
    2D. And *as to* what you sow— you do not sow the body *which* will come, but *a* bare[G] seed[10], perhaps[11] *of* wheat or *of* some *of* the rest[H]. °And God gives it *a* body just as He willed[J]— indeed, *to* each *of* the seeds *its* own body[12]   37, 38

        1E. Not all flesh[K] *is* the same flesh. But *there is* one[13] *of* humans[L], and another flesh *of* livestock[14], and another flesh *of* birds, and another *of* fish[15]   39
        2E. And *there are* heavenly[M] bodies[16] and earthly[N] bodies. But the glory[O] *of* the heavenly *is* one *kind*, and the *glory of* the earthly *is* different[P]   40
        3E. *There is* one glory *of the* sun, and another glory *of the* moon, and another glory *of the* stars. For star differs[Q] *from* star in glory[O]   41

    3D. So also *is* the resurrection *of* the dead   42

        1E. It is sown in decay[17], it is raised in undecayability[18]
        2E. It is sown in dishonor[R], it is raised in glory[O]   43
        3E. It is sown in weakness[S], it is raised in power[T]
        4E. It is sown *a* natural[19] body, it is raised *a* spiritual[U] body   44

    4D. If[20] there is[21] *a* natural body, there is also *a* spiritual *body*

        1E. So also it has been written [in Gen 2:7], "The first man, Adam, became *a* living soul[22]". The Last Adam[23] *became a* life-giving[24] spirit   45

    5D. But the spiritual *body is* not first— but the natural *body*, then the spiritual   46

        1E. The first man *was* from earth, made-of-dust[25]. The second[26] Man *is* from heaven[27]   47
        2E. Such as *was* the *one* made-of-dust— such *ones* also *are* the *ones* made-of-dust.[28] And such as *is* the heavenly[M] *One*— such *ones* also *are* the heavenly *ones*   48
        3E. And just as we bore the image[29] *of* the *one* made of dust, we shall also bear[30] the image *of* the heavenly *One*   49

5C. Now I say this, brothers— that flesh and blood[31] are not able to inherit[V] *the* kingdom[W] *of* God, nor does decay inherit undecayability[32]   50

    1D. Behold, I tell you *a* mystery[33]— we will not **all** fall-asleep[X]. But we will **all** be changed[34]— in *a* moment[35], in *the* blink[36] *of an* eye, at the last trumpet[37]   51, 52

        1E. For it will trumpet, and the dead will be raised[E] undecayable[38], and **we**[39] will be changed
        2E. For this decayable[40] *body* must[Y] put-on[41] undecayability, and this mortal[Z] *body must* put on immortality[42]   53

1. Because our claim to speak God's good news is clearly false.
2. Or, "associations". This word refers to those one habitually converses with, shares company with. Used only here. GK 3918. Related to "converse" in Act 24:26. Paul is referring to those influencing the "some" in v 12. He may be quoting a proverb current in his day.
3. Or, "customs, character". Used only here. GK 2456.
4. Used only here. GK 1729. "Wake up from a drunken stupor, come to your senses". Related to "sober" in 1 Pet 1:13.
5. Or, "rightly". Same word as in 1 Thes 2:10; Tit 2:12; 1 Pet 2:23. Elsewhere only as "justly" in Lk 23:41. GK 1469. Related to "righteous", "righteousness", and "declare righteous" (see Rom 3:24).
6. The grammar implies "stop sinning".
7. Elsewhere only in 1 Pet 2:15. GK 57. Related word in Rom 10:3.
8. On this word, see 6:5. That is, to cause you to be ashamed.
9. Same word as in v 22. That is, a new life, a new form.
10. That is, an individual grain. On this word, see Mt 13:31
11. This is an idiom, "if it should turn out to be so, if it should happen". Same idiom as in 14:10. GK 5593.
12. These bodies God gives take many forms and have many degrees of glory, as can be seen by the following examples. If this is so now, God will do so also then. He will give us new bodies in connection with this body, but with a new glory and dimension. There are different forms of existence and glory for the same type of thing— flesh, stars, etc.— even in the natural world. So the human body can also exist in a different form with a different glory.
13. Some manuscripts add "flesh" {K}
14. This word is used of animals kept as property— horses, donkeys, cattle, sheep, etc. Elsewhere only as "mount" in Lk 10:34; Act 23:24; and "cattle" in Rev 18:13. GK 3229. Related to "property" in Mt 19:22.
15. Some manuscripts reverse "fish" and "birds" {K}.
16. Some think Paul is referring to angelic bodies versus human bodies next; others, to celestial bodies, as in v 41. On this word, see Eph 1:23.
17. Or, "corruption, ruin, destruction". Same word as in v 50; Rom 8:21; Gal 6:8. Elsewhere only as "destruction" in 2 Pet 2:12; "corruption" in 2 Pet 1:4; 2:19; and "perishing" in Col 2:22. GK 5785. "Decay" comes from the verb which means "to corrupt, destroy, ruin, spoil", on which see "ruin" in 3:17. Related also to "decayable" in v 53, and "undecayability" next.
18. Or, "incorruptibility". Same word as in v 50, 53, 54. Elsewhere only as "immortality" in Rom 2:7; Eph 6:24; 2 Tim 1:10. GK 914. Related to "undecayable" in v 52.
19. That is, material, physical. On this word, see 2:14.
20. Some manuscripts omit this word {K}.
21. Or, "exists". GK 1639.
22. This word is related to "natural" in verse 44. Literally, "came to be for a living soul... for a life-giving spirit", a literal translation of a Hebrew way of speaking. On this word, see Jam 5:20.
23. That is, Christ. Adam means "man" in Hebrew. Christ is the last progenitor, the last head of a race.
24. That is, one giving resurrection life, creating spiritual bodies. Same word as "given life" in v 22.
25. Elsewhere only in v 48, 49. GK 5954.
26. This word corresponds with v 46. First the natural man, second the spiritual Man.
27. Paul is speaking as to their origin and nature. The second Man is from heaven, the spiritual realm, though He took a body in common with Adam's race. He will return from heaven to give us our new bodies, v 22-23. Some manuscripts say "the Lord from heaven" {A}.
28. That is, as to the composition and nature of the body, Adam's family takes after him, Christ's after Him.
29. Or, "likeness". On this word, see Col 1:15.
30. Used twice in this verse, and in Rom 13:4. Elsewhere only of "wearing" clothes in Mt 11:8; Jn 19:5; Jam 2:3. GK 5841. Some manuscripts say "let us also bear" {B}.
31. That is, our mortal human bodies, characterized by decay.
32. On "decay" and "undecayability", see v 42.
33. On this word, see Rom 11:25. That is, a truth formerly hidden, but now revealed.
34. Same word as in v 52. On this word, see "exchanged" in Rom 1:23.
35. This word means "indivisible, not cut-able". An indivisible unit of time. Used only here. GK 875.
36. Or, a "twinkle", which is a "wink". This noun is used of various rapid events, depending on what word it is associated with— "in the throw of a spear", "in the rush of a wind", "in the quivering of a harp", "in the twinkling of a star", "in the flapping of a wing", etc. Used only here. GK 4846.
37. Compare Mt 24:31; 1 Thes 4:16.
38. Or, "imperishable, not subject to decay, incorruptible". Same word as in 9:25; 1 Pet 1:4. Elsewhere only as "imperishable" in Mk 16 (short ending); 1 Pet 1:23; 3:4; and "immortal" in Rom 1:23; 1 Tim 1:17. GK 915. Related to the two words in v 53, and to the two words in v 42.
39. Some think Paul means "we all" (as in v 51), all Christians. Others, we who are living, who did not "fall asleep" (v 51; 1 Thes 4:15-17).
40. Or, "perishable, corruptible". Elsewhere only as "decayable" in 1 Cor 9:25; 15:54; "perishable" in 1 Pet 1:18, 23; and "mortal" in Rom 1:23. GK 5778. Related to "ruin" in 3:17; and "decay" in 15:42.
41. Or, "wear, dress in", like a garment. Used four times in v 53-54. On this word, see Rom 13:14.
42. Or, "un-dying, deathlessness". Elsewhere only in v 54; 1 Tim 6:16. GK 114. Related to "mortal" preceding. The root word is "death".

A. Jam 5:19, err   B. 3 Jn 11, evil   C. 1 Cor 3:17, ruin   D. 1 Pet 2:3   E. Mt 28:6, arose   F. 2 Cor 11:16   G. Jam 2:15, naked   H. 2 Pet 3:16, other   J. Jn 7:17   K. Col 2:23   L. Mt 4:4, mankind   M. Eph 3:10   N. Phil 2:10   O. 2 Pet 2:10   P. 1 Cor 12:9   Q. Phil 1:10, mattering   R. 2 Tim 2:20   S. Mt 8:17   T. Mk 5:30   U. 1 Cor 14:1   V. Gal 4:30   W. Mt 3:2   X. 1 Thes 4:13   Y. Mt 16:21   Z. 2 Cor 5:4

2D. And when this decayable *body* puts-on undecayability, and this mortal *body* puts on immortality, then the saying having been written will come-about[1]—	54
1E. "Death[A] was swallowed-up[B] in victory[C]" [Isa 25:8]	
3D. "Death, where *is* **your** victory? Death[2], where is **your** stinger[3]?" [Hos 13:14]	55
1E. Now the stinger[4] *of* death *is* sin, and the power[D] *of* sin *is* the Law[5]. °But thanks[E] *be* to God, the *One* giving us the victory[6] through our Lord Jesus Christ	56-57
6C. So then my beloved[F] brothers[G], be[7] steadfast[H], immovable[8], always abounding[J] in the work *of* the Lord, knowing that your labor[K] is not empty[9] in *the* Lord	58
8B. Now concerning the collection[10] for the saints[L], just as I directed[11] *in* the churches *of* Galatia, so **you** do also	16:1
1C. Every first *day of the* week,[12] let each *of* you put-aside[13] beside himself[14], storing-up[15] whatever thing[16] he may be prospered[M]	2
1D. In-order-that[17] when I come, collections might not be taking place at-that-time[N]	
2C. And when I arrive, whomever you approve[O], I will send these *ones* with letters[18] to carry-forth[19] your grace-*gift*[P] to Jerusalem. °And if it is fitting[20] *that* I also go, they will go with me	3 4
3C. Now[21] I will come to you whenever I go through Macedonia,[22] for I am going through Macedonia[23]	5
1D. And perhaps[24] I will continue[Q] with you, or even spend-the-winter, in order that **you** may send me forward[R] wherever I may go	6
2D. For I do not want to see you now in passing, for[25] I am hoping to stay[S] with you *for* some time, if the Lord permits[26]	7
3D. But I will stay-on[S] in Ephesus[27] until Pentecost, °for *a* great and effective[28] door has opened *to* me, and *there are* many opposing[T]	8-9
4C. But if Timothy comes,[29] see that he may come-to-be with you fearlessly.[30] For he is working[U] the work[V] *of the* Lord as I also	10
1D. Therefore let no one treat him with contempt[31]	11
2D. And send him forward[R] in peace in order that he may come to me, for I am waiting-for[W] him with the brothers[32]	
9B. Now[33] concerning Apollos[34] *our* brother, I strongly urged[X] him that he come to you with the brothers[35]	12
1C. And it was not at all *his* will[Y] that he come now, but he will come whenever he finds-an-opportunity[Z]	

1. Or, "take place, happen, come to pass". GK *1181*.
2. Some manuscripts say "Hades", as does the Septuagint.
3. Some manuscripts have "stinger" in the previous phrase and "victory" in this one {B}.
4. That is, the part that does harm, that injects the poison. As the scorpion delivers its poison through its stinger, so death does through sin. Sin is what brings separation from God in death, the bitterest of poisons. Apart from sin, death is powerless. Same word as in v 55; Rev 9:10. Elsewhere only as "goad" in Act 26:14. GK *3034*.
5. The Law of God establishes the line to cross, the rule to break—and the penalty for doing so.
6. Elsewhere only in v 54, 55; Mt 12:20. GK *3777*. Related to the word in 1 Jn 5:4, and to "overcome" in Rev 2:7.
7. Or, "become". GK *1181*.
8. Used only here. GK *293*. Related to "moved away" in Col 1:23.
9. Or, "in vain". Same word as in v 10, 14.
10. That is, the collection Paul was raising from the Gentile churches for the poor Christians in Jerusalem. See 2 Cor 8-9 for more. Here Paul gives the Galatians as an example for the Corinthians (he wrote this book in Act 19:10). Later, he gives the Macedonians as examples for them in 2 Cor 8, and reports that he had given the Corinthians as examples for the Macedonians in 2 Cor 9:2 (written in Act 20:2). And later, he reports the contribution given by the Corinthians and Macedonians to the Romans in Rom 15:26 (written in Act 20:3). Elsewhere only in v 2. GK *3356*.
11. Perhaps Paul did this on the trip mentioned in Act 18:23. On this word, see 7:17.
12. That is, Sunday by Sunday.
13. Or, "lay *away*, put *down*". On this word, see "put" in Act 19:21.
14. That is, at home.
15. Or, "treasuring up". Same word as in Lk 12:21; Rom 2:5; 2 Cor 12:14; Jam 5:3; 2 Pet 3:7. Elsewhere only as "treasure up" in Mt 6:19, 20, where it is used with the related noun "treasure". GK *2564*. Note Mt 19:21.
16. On the phrase "whatever thing", see Col 3:17.
17. Or, "So that... collections will not...". GK *2671*.
18. These approved people would be official representatives. Some are named in Act 20:4. This may also be punctuated "... you approve with letters, I will send these *ones*...". In one case, the Corinthians give each person they approve a letter of authorization; in the other case, Paul gives them letters of introduction to those to whom he would be sending them in Judea and Jerusalem.
19. Or, "bring, take away". Same word as in Act 19:12. Elsewhere only as "carry away" in Lk 16:22; Rev 17:3; 21:10; and "take away" in Mk 15:1. GK *708*. The root word is "bring, carry".
20. Or, "worthy". Paul may mean that if the amount collected made it appropriate for him to go, he would do so; or, that if it is fitting for him to go at that time, in view of other circumstances, he would go. Later, in Act 19:21, while still in Ephesus, after writing this letter, Paul decided he would go to Jerusalem. He did go, leaving from Corinth in Act 20:3. There are no Corinthians in the list of those who went with him in Act 20:4, for reasons unknown. On this word, see "worthy" in Rev 16:6.
21. Paul gives the Corinthians more details about when he plans to come there to finalize and send the collection, and the reasons for this plan. If v 12 is not taken as the final question in the Corinthians' letter to Paul, then the conclusion of the letter begins here instead of in v 13. See v 12.
22. This took place in Act 20:1-2.
23. This represents a change in plans already communicated to them. See 2 Cor 1:16.
24. Or, "it may be that". This idiom, more literally "having turned out *that way*", is used only here. It is the same word as in the idiom in 15:37, with different grammar.
25. Some manuscripts say "but" {N}.
26. Paul stayed 3 months (Act 20:3), during which he wrote Romans. On this word, see 1 Tim 2:12.
27. Paul is writing this letter from Ephesus.
28. Or, "active". On this word, see Heb 4:12.
29. Paul sent Timothy ahead to Macedonia in Act 19:22, and from there to Corinth, 1 Cor 4:17. Whether or not Timothy made it there is not known. Note 2 Cor 1:1.
30. Paul was probably concerned about Timothy's age, since he writes to Timothy eight to ten years later and says "Let no one look down on your youth", 1 Tim 4:12.
31. On this word, see "treat with contempt" in 1 Thes 5:20.
32. Some think Paul means "the brothers with him"; others, "the brothers with me".
33. Or, "And". This is the last occurrence of "Now concerning", and a question about the return of Apollos, whom the Corinthians loved, can easily be imagined as part of their letter to Paul (see 7:1). Or, if this is not in response to their letter, it may be rendered "And concerning". In this case Paul is updating them about Apollos, as he just did regarding Timothy. In this view the conclusion of the book begins at v 5, making the update on Paul point A., the command about Timothy (v 10) point B., the update on Apollos point C., and then continuing with point D. in v 13.
34. See Act 18:24 on Apollos.
35. Some think Paul means the brothers with Paul, perhaps those in v 17; others, the brothers with Apollos.

A. 2 Cor 11:23 B. Heb 11:29 C. 1 Cor 15:57 D. Mk 5:30 E. Eph 2:8, grace F. Mt 3:17 G. Act 16:40 H. Col 1:23 J. 2 Cor 8:2 K. 1 Cor 3:8 L. 1 Pet 1:16, holy M. Rom 1:10 N. Mt 24:9, then O. Rom 12:2 P. Eph 2:8, grace Q. Jam 1:25 R. Rom 15:24, sent forward S. Rom 11:22, continue T. Phil 1:28 U. Mt 26:10 V. Mt 26:10 W. Heb 11:10 X. Rom 12:8, exhorting Y. Jn 7:17 Z. Act 17:21

A.	Keep-watching^A, be standing-*firm*¹ in the faith, be acting-like-men², be growing-strong³, °let all your *things* be done^B in love	13-14
B.	And I exhort^C you, brothers— you know the household^D *of* Stephanas⁴, that it is *the* firstfruit^E *of* Achaia⁵, and they appointed⁶ themselves for ministry^F *to* the saints^G—°that **you** also be subject⁷ *to* such *ones,* and *to* everyone helping⁸ and laboring^H	15 16
C.	Now I am rejoicing^J over the coming⁹ *of* Stephanas and Fortunatus and Achaicus, because these *ones* filled-up^K your lack¹⁰. °For they refreshed^L my spirit and yours.¹¹ Therefore be acknowledging¹² such *ones*	17 18
D.	The churches *of* Asia¹³ greet^M you. Aquila and Prisca¹⁴ greet you earnestly^N in *the* Lord, along with the church at their house. °All the brothers greet you	19 20
E.	Greet one another with *a* holy kiss^O	
F.	The greeting *of* Paul *by* my *own* hand¹⁵—	21
	1. If anyone does not love¹⁶ the Lord¹⁷, let him be accursed¹⁸	22
	2. Marana tha¹⁹	
	3. The grace^P *of* the²⁰ Lord Jesus²¹ *be* with you	23
	4. My love²² *be* with you all in Christ Jesus²³	24

1. This word is also in Gal 5:1; Phil 1:27; 4:1; 1 Thes 3:8; 2 Thes 2:15. Elsewhere only as "stand" in Mk 3:31; 11:25; Jn 8:44; Rom 14:4. GK *5112*.
2. Or, "be manly, be courageous". Used only here. GK *437*. This is the word "man" made into a verb.
3. Or, "be strengthened". On this word, see "be strengthened" in Eph 3:16.
4. Paul baptized this household, 1:16.
5. On this word, see Act 19:21. This is the Roman province in which Corinth is located.
6. Or, "stationed, arranged, established". On this word, see "established" in Rom 13:1.
7. Related to "appointed" earlier. Station yourselves under such ones. On this word, see Eph 5:21.
8. Or, "working with *us*". On this word, see "work together" in Rom 8:28.
9. That is, to Ephesus, where Paul was.
10. That is, your physical lack, your absence. Both "your lack by me", "your lack of me". These men made up for your absence, filling the gap between us. They probably brought letters and information to Paul, and he may be sending this letter back with them. Others think Paul means "your lack [of service]", as in Phil 2:30. The grammar of "your lack" here is different from the other occurrences of this word. Some manuscripts have the same grammar {N}. On this word, see Phil 2:30.
11. Paul may mean that sending these men refreshed your spirit when you sent them. Sending them set you at ease, and with their arrival here, you can take comfort. Or, that these men refreshed your spirit upon their return to Corinth with this letter (it will be past tense when the Corinthians read this letter).
12. On this word, see "understood" in Col 1:6. Fully recognize them.
13. Ephesus, the city from which Paul is writing, is in the Roman province of Asia.
14. Some manuscripts say "Priscilla" {N}. See Rom 16:3 on these two. Paul had found them in Corinth, Act 18:1-2. They went with Paul to Ephesus, Act 18:18-19, where they met and helped Apollos, Act 18:24-26.
15. This is the same phrase as in Col 4:18; 2 Thes 3:17. Similar to Phm 19. This may indicate Paul had been dictating to a secretary until here.
16. Same word as *affectionately*-love in Jn 21:15. Elsewhere by Paul only in Tit 3:15. It is related to "kiss" in v 20.
17. Some manuscripts add "Jesus Christ" {K}.
18. The word is the word *anathema*, on which see Rom 9:3.
19. This is a transliterated Aramaic phrase, either marana tha, "Lord, come!", or maran atha, "The Lord has come". Used only here. GK *3448*. Like "Amen", "Hosanna", and other terms, it crossed over to Greek— and English— without translation.
20. Some manuscripts say "our" {K}.
21. Some manuscripts add "Christ" {N}.
22. This is the word *agape,* the word in chapter 13. On this word, see 1 Jn 4:16.
23. Some manuscripts add "amen" {B}.

A. 1 Thes 5:6   B. Mt 6:10   C. Rom 12:8   D. Mk 3:25, house   E. 1 Cor 15:20   F. 1 Cor 12:5   G. 1 Pet 1:16, holy   H. Mt 11:28, being weary
J. 2 Cor 13:11   K. 1 Thes 2:16   L. Phm 7   M. Mk 15:18   N. Mt 13:52, many   O. Rom 16:16   P. Eph 2:8

2 Corinthians

Overview

Introduction	1:1-2
1A. Blessed be God who comforts us in all our affliction so that we may be able to comfort others	1:3-11
2A. Our conscience boasts that we conducted ourselves with you in simplicity and purity from God	1:12
1B. For we are writing no other thing than what you read or indeed, understand	1:13
2B. And I hope you will understand that we are your boast, even as you are ours	1:13-14
3B. And in this confidence, I was intending to come to you first, on the way to Macedonia	1:15-16
4B. Therefore, while intending this, did I act with lightness? I changed plans to spare you	1:17-2:11
5B. Now having come to Troas, I had no rest at not finding Titus. I went to Macedonia	2:12-13
6B. But thanks be to God who leads us, and makes the aroma of Christ evident through us	2:14
1C. Because we are the fragrance of Christ— of death to some, of life to others	2:15-16
2C. For we are not like those peddling the Word. We are speaking in Christ before God	2:17
3C. Are we commending ourselves? You are our letter of recommendation from Christ	3:1-3
4C. And we have such a confidence through Christ toward God	3:4
1D. Not that we are sufficient from ourselves to count anything as out of ourselves	3:5
2D. But our sufficiency is from God, who made us ministers of a new covenant	3:6
3D. And this ministry comes with a permanent glory surpassing the old covenant	3:7-11
4D. Therefore we use much boldness, reflecting the glory, not veiling it like Moses	3:12-18
5C. For this reason, having this ministry even as we received mercy, we do not lose heart	4:1
1D. But we renounced hidden motives. If the truth is veiled, it is so in the perishing	4:2-6
2D. But we have this treasure in clay vessels. Death is at work in us, life in you	4:7-12
3D. But we believe, therefore we speak, knowing God will raise us with Jesus	4:13-15
4D. Therefore we do not lose heart, but we are renewed daily by hope	4:16-5:8
5D. Therefore we are ambitious to please God, for we must all appear before Him	5:9-11
7B. Now we have been made known to God, and I hope also in your consciences	5:11
1C. We are not commending ourselves, but giving you an opportunity to boast in us	5:12
2C. For it we lost our senses, it is for God! If we are sound minded, it is for you!	5:13
3C. For Christ's love controls us— He died for all, and we live for Him as new creations	5:14-17
4C. And all things are from God— the One who reconciled us and gave us this ministry	5:18-19
5C. Therefore we are ambassadors for Christ, since God is appealing through us	5:20
1D. We are begging on behalf of Christ— Be reconciled to God!	5:20-6:2
2D. In nothing giving an opportunity for stumbling, so the ministry is not faulted	6:3
3D. But in everything commending ourselves as God's servants	6:4-10
8B. Our mouth and heart have opened wide to you, Corinthians. You open wide also. Do not become mis-yoked to unbelievers. Make room for us. I do not condemn you	6:11-7:4
9B. I have been filled with comfort by the news of you brought by Titus	7:4-16
3A. Now we make known to you the grace of God granted in the churches of Macedonia—	8:1

Overview		**2 Corinthians**

1B. That their abundance of joy and deep poverty abounded into their generosity — 8:2-6
2B. But just as you abound in everything, be abounding also in this grace. Complete the doing — 8:7-15
3B. I am sending Titus and two brothers to you so that you may be prepared when I come — 8:16-9:5
4B. Now this I say— the one sowing sparingly will reap sparingly. God will help you — 9:6-14
5B. Thanks be to God for His indescribable gift — 9:15

4A. Now I beg to not have to be bold toward some considering us as walking according to the flesh — 10:1-2

    1B. For we do not wage war according to the flesh, but with God's weapons — 10:3-6
    2B. You are looking at things according to appearance — 10:7

        1C. If anyone is confident in himself that he is Christ's, we are also — 10:7
        2C. For if I boast about our authority which the Lord gave us, I will not be put to shame — 10:8-11
        3C. For we do not dare to compare ourselves with those who commend themselves — 10:12
        4C. And we will not boast unmeasurable things, but based on the standard God gave us — 10:13-16
        5C. But let the one boasting boast in the Lord, for the one He commends is approved — 10:17-18

    3B. O that you would bear with me in a little bit of foolishness, yet keep bearing with me — 11:1

        1C. For I am jealous for you. I fear for you that your minds are being corrupted — 11:2-3
        2C. For if one comes to you with another Jesus, spirit or gospel, you bear with them nicely! — 11:4
        3C. For I in no way come short of the superlative apostles— except for my self-support — 11:5-15

    4B. Again I say, receive me even if as foolish, in order that I also may boast a little bit — 11:16

        1C. What I am speaking is not according to the Lord, but as in foolishness — 11:17
        2C. Since many are boasting according to the flesh, I also will boast— in my weaknesses — 11:18-33
        3C. It is necessary to boast, so I will go on to visions and revelations of the Lord — 12:1-10

    5B. I have become foolish— you compelled me! I ought to be being commended by you! — 12:11

        1C. For I in no way come short of the superlative apostles— the signs prove it — 12:11-12
        2C. For in what were you worse off than the others, except that I was not your burden — 12:13-18

    6B. All this time are you thinking we are defending ourselves? We are speaking before God — 12:19

        1C. For I fear that having come, we may not find each other such as we would want — 12:20-21
        2C. This is the third time I am coming to you — 13:1

            1D. Every word shall be established based on the mouth of two and three witnesses — 13:1
            2D. If I come I will not spare you, since you are seeking proof of Christ in me. Prove yourselves! We pray you not do anything bad, for your sakes, not mine — 13:2-9

        3C. I am writing these things while absent so I may not have to act severely when I come — 13:10

Conclusion — 13:11-14

A.	Paul, *an* apostle[A] *of* Christ Jesus[1] by *the* will *of* God, and Timothy[2] *our* brother	1
B.	*To* the church *of* God being in Corinth,[3] together-with all the saints[B] being in all Achaia[4]	
C.	Grace *to* you and peace from God our Father and *the* Lord Jesus Christ	2

1A. Blessed[C] *be* the God and Father *of* our Lord Jesus Christ, the Father *of* compassions[5] and God *of* all comfort[6], *the *One* comforting[D] us concerning[7] all our affliction[E] so that we *might* be able to comfort the ones in[8] every affliction with the comfort *by* which we ourselves are being comforted by God — 3, 4

    1B. Because just as the sufferings[F] *of* Christ[9] are abounding[G] in us, so our comfort also is abounding through Christ — 5

        1C. And if we are being afflicted[H]— *it is* for the sake of your comfort and salvation[10] — 6

        2C. If we are being comforted— *it is* for the sake of your comfort, the *comfort* being at-work[11] in *your* endurance[J] *of* the same sufferings which **we** also are suffering[K]

            1D. And our hope for you *is* firm[12], knowing that as you are sharers[L] *of* the sufferings, so also *of* the comfort — 7

    2B. For we do not want you to be unaware[M], brothers[N], with-reference-to[13] our affliction[E] having taken place in Asia,[14] that we were burdened[15] extremely[O] beyond *our* power[16], so that we despaired[17] even *of* living[18] — 8

        1C. But **we** had[19] the sentence *of* death in ourselves in order that we should not be trusting[20] in ourselves, but in God, the *One* raising the dead — 9

            1D. Who delivered us from so great *a* death[21], and will deliver[22] *us* — 10

            2D. In Whom we have put *our* hope that He will indeed[23] still[24] deliver *us*—*you also joining-in-helping[25] *in your* prayer for us — 11

                1E. In-order-that[26] thanks might be given[P] on our[27] behalf by many faces[28] *as to* the gift[29] *granted* to us through many *prayers*[30]

2A. For[31] our boasting[32] is this— the testimony[Q] *of* our conscience[33] that[34] we conducted-*ourselves*[R] in the world, and especially toward you, in simplicity[35] and purity[36] *from* God[37], and[38] not in fleshly[S] wisdom, but in *the* grace *of* God — 12

    1B. For we are writing no other *things* to you other than *the things* which you read or indeed understand[39] — 13

    2B. And I hope that you will understand until *the* end[40]—*just as you also did understand us in part[41]— that[42] we are your boast[43], even as you also *are* ours, on the day *of* our[44] Lord Jesus — 14

1. Some manuscripts say "Jesus Christ" {K}.
2. Paul is now with Timothy, whom he had sent to Macedonia and Corinth (in Act 19:22; 1 Cor 4:17), and had written to the Corinthians about in 1 Cor 16:10-11. Whether Timothy ever reached Corinth is not mentioned. He is mentioned again in this book only in v 19. See 1 Tim 1:2 on Timothy.
3. This letter was written in Act 20:2, before Paul's three-month stay in Corinth in Act 20:2-3.
4. This is the Roman province in which the city of Corinth was located (see Act 19:21). It is also called "Greece" in Act 20:2.
5. Or, "acts of compassion, mercy". That is, the Father characterized by compassions; or, the Father who is the source of the compassions we experience. On this word, see Rom 12:1.
6. Or, "encouragement". That is, the God who is the source of all comfort, of every kind of comfort. Paul uses this word and its related verb 10 times in v 3-7. On this word, see "encouragement" in Act 4:36.
7. Or, "in reference to, for, upon, over". GK *2093*. Same word as "in" in 7:4; 1 Thes 3:7.
8. Or, "within, in the sphere of, under". GK *1877*.
9. On this subject, see Phil 1:29; 3:10; Col 1:24; 1 Pet 4:13; Jn 15:20; Rom 8:17; Heb 13:13; etc. Paul could mean the sufferings we experience because we are Christians; or, the suffering Christ experiences when His people are made to suffer (Act 9:4). Or, he could mean both, the sufferings of Christ which He shares with His people.
10. Some manuscripts omit "and salvation... your comfort", which resulted in other variations {A}.
11. Or, "in operation". On this word, see "works" in 1 Cor 12:11.
12. Or, "sure, secure", like an anchor. On this word, see 2 Pet 1:10.
13. Or, "concerning, about". GK *5642*.
14. That is, where Paul intended to remain in 1 Cor 16:8-9. This happened during Acts 19, after Paul wrote 1 Corinthians, and may be foreshadowed by "many opposing" in 1 Cor 16:9. We do not know to what Paul refers, but the Corinthians did, perhaps through Titus. Some think it was a persecution; others, a sickness. Some manuscripts add "*to* us" {N}, so it says "having happened *to* us in Asia".
15. Or, "weighed down". Same word as 5:4; 1 Tim 5:16. Elsewhere only as "weighed down" in Mt 26:43; Lk 9:32; 21:34. GK *976*. Related to the word in 1 Thes 2:9.
16. Some take this as a single description of Paul's internal distress, "burdened... beyond our power"; others, as two descriptions, "burdened extremely" externally, and "beyond our power" internally.
17. Or, "were utterly at a loss, were in great perplexity, were utterly perplexed". On this word, see "utterly perplexed" in 4:8.
18. Or, "even *that we should* live". That is, they could not see how they would survive the danger facing them. GK *2409*.
19. Or, "have". The grammar implies it continues to be true.
20. Or, "having confidence, putting confidence, relying". Same word as in Mt 27:43; Lk 11:22. On this word, see "persuade" in 1 Jn 3:19.
21. That is, "*a* [peril] *of* death", as in 11:23. Paul considered himself dead. Some manuscripts say "so many deaths" {B}.
22. Some manuscripts say "and delivers *us*"; others omit this phrase {B}. On this word, see Col 1:13.
23. Or, "even, also". GK *2779*.
24. That is, in the future. Instead of "hope that... still", some manuscripts say "hope. And He will still deliver *us*" {C}.
25. Paul may mean "joining with me"; "joining together with one another"; or, "joining with others". Used only here. GK *5348*.
26. Or, "So that thanks will be given...". GK *2671*.
27. Some manuscripts say "your" {B}.
28. Or, "persons". That is, persons viewed as faces looking up to God in prayer. On this word, see "presence" in Lk 9:52.
29. That is, the gift of future deliverance from the peril of death.
30. Or, "*people*", people praying.
31. Paul uses this word to assert his first main point, as in Rom 1:18. GK *1142*. Paul is under attack, and he is writing 2 Corinthians to vindicate himself and his apostleship, and to expose his detractors. But he begins with his answer, without first detailing the questions being raised about him. Thus we feel as if we are jumping into the middle of their conversation here, and we must infer what was being said about Paul from the responses he gives. He begins by boasting that he behaved with simplicity and purity, and then proves it by recounting the reasons for his decisions, and sharing his inner thoughts regarding his ministry, 1:12-7:4. In chapters 10-13, Paul takes on his detractors more directly. This book is a deeply personal and introspective look into the heart of Paul. Acts is the outside view; this is the inside view.
32. Our boasting or glorying is our conscience giving its testimony as to our behavior toward you, not our boasting as to our strengths or accomplishments. To understand this statement, compare Rom 9:1. Here Paul does not begin with an "I" statement, such as "I am the apostle who brought you the gospel and the ones attacking me are wrong for the following reasons", that is, with a direct boast about his ministry and a rebuke of them. Instead he says his boasting is his conscience bearing witness, almost as if it were a third party. On this word, see 7:4.
33. That is, the testimony proceeding from our conscience. On this word, see Act 23:1.
34. What follows in this verse is the "testimony" that our "conscience" is "boasting".
35. Or, "frankness". On this word, see "generosity" in Rom 12:8. Some manuscripts say "holiness" {B}.
36. Or, "sincerity". Paul is referring to the purity of his motives, which come from God, thus, his "sincerity". Elsewhere only in 1 Cor 5:8 and 2 Cor 2:17. GK *1636*. Related to "pure" in Phil 1:10.
37. Literally "*of* God". That is, God-given, derived from God. Others render this "godly"; others, "god-like"; others, "*before* God". Some take this with both of the preceding words; others, only with "purity".
38. Some manuscripts omit this word {C}.
39. Paul's simplicity and purity of motive is reflected in his writing. There is no hidden meaning or motive. Perhaps some were accusing him of this by saying, "there is a hidden meaning in Paul's words"; or, "he does not mean what he says".
40. Some think Paul means "fully, completely" in contrast with the Corinthians' past partial understanding; others, "until the end of your lives" or "until the end of the world" (as in 1 Cor 1:8). On this word, see Rom 10:4. Some manuscripts say "even until *the* end" {K}.
41. Paul may mean "some of you understood us" or "you understood us partially". On this idiom, see Rom 11:25.
42. Some think Paul means "you will understand...that"; others, "you did understand... that". In either case, it is clear that Paul knows he does not enjoy the unqualified favor of all in Corinth.
43. That is, the content of your boast. On this word, see Phil 1:26.
44. Some manuscripts omit this word {C}, so that it says "the day *of* the Lord Jesus".

A. 1 Cor 12:28   B. 1 Pet 1:16, holy   C. Rom 9:5   D. Rom 12:8, exhorting   E. Rev 7:14   F. Phil 3:10   G. 2 Cor 8:2   H. 2 Cor 4:8   J. Jam 1:3   K. Gal 3:4
L. 2 Pet 1:4   M. Rom 10:3, ignorant of   N. Act 16:40   O. 1 Cor 12:31, beyond measure   P. Mt 26:27, given thanks   Q. Act 4:33   R. Eph 2:3   S. 1 Cor 3:3

3B. And *in* this confidence[1], I was intending[A] first[2] to come to you in order that you might have *a* second[3] benefit[4], *and[5] to go through you to Macedonia, and from Macedonia to come again to you, and to be sent-forward[6] by you to Judea[7] 15 16

4B. Therefore,[8] while intending[A] this, I did not then act *with* lightness[9], *did I*? Or do I plan[10] *the things* which I plan according-to[11] *the* flesh— so that there is with me the yes, yes, and the no, no?[12] 17

    1C. But *as* God *is* faithful,[13] our message[B] to you is[14] not yes and no[15] 18

        1D. For God's Son Jesus Christ, the *One* having been proclaimed[C] among you by us— by me and Silvanus[16] and Timothy— did not become[17] yes and no, but has become[18] yes in Him[19] 19

            1E. For as many as *there are* promises[D] *of* God— in Him *is* the yes[20]! 20
            2E. Therefore also through Him[21] *is* [spoken] the amen[22] *to* God for *His* glory[23], through us[24]

    2C. And the *One* establishing[25] us with you for[26] Christ and having anointed[E] us[27] *is* God[28]—*the *One* also having sealed[F] us, and having given the pledge[29] *of* the Spirit in our hearts 21-22

1. Paul may be referring to his self-confidence (v 12), the confidence of a clear conscience and pure motives. Or, he may mean his confidence in their mutual relationship, v 14. It is clear from v 15-17 that his change of plans regarding his next visit to Corinth had become an issue with some in Corinth, and was used to cast him in a bad light. Here Paul recounts his original plan, the plan he changed in 1 Cor 16:3-6. Elsewhere only in 2 Cor 3:4; 8:22; 10:2; Eph 3:12; Phil 3:4. GK *4301.*
2. Or, "formerly". This is the position of this word in the Greek word order. Some think Paul means "to come to you first", on the way to Macedonia. Others think he means "I was intending formerly", referring to the plan he changed. Same word as in Gal 4:13; Heb 7:27. Elsewhere only as "former" in Eph 4:22; Heb 10:32; 1 Pet 1:14; and "formerly" in Jn 6:62; 7:50; 9:8, 1 Tim 1:13; Heb 4:6. GK *4728.*
3. Paul may mean "second" because this would be his second visit to them, making the visit described next (upon his return from Macedonia) his third visit. See "again" in 2:1. Or, "second" may refer to the return visit described next. I was coming to you first so that you might have a second visit when I return from Macedonia. The word does not mean "dual, double, twice", but this gives the sense of it here for this view. Used 37 times, all rendered "second". GK *1311.*
4. Or "grace, kindness, favor". Some think Paul is referring to his upcoming visit with the Corinthians as a benefit of God's grace to them (compare Rom 1:11; 15:29); others, as a personal act of kindness toward them. Some manuscripts say "joy" {B}. On "have a benefit", see "have gratitude" in Lk 17:9.
5. Or, "indeed, even", defining the two benefits.
6. Same word as in Rom 15:24 of the Romans sending Paul forward into Spain.
7. This original plan led Paul to Corinth first— clockwise from Ephesus to Corinth to Macedonia, then back to Corinth, and then to Jerusalem. Paul changed this plan when he wrote 1 Cor 16:3-6. His new plan was to go to Corinth last— counterclockwise from Ephesus through Macedonia to Corinth, stay for the winter, and then go to Jerusalem. This was his actual course, as seen in 2 Cor 2:12-13; Act 20:1-3. Before he came to Corinth, somewhere in Macedonia, Titus (coming from Corinth, 2 Cor 7:5-6) met him, and Paul wrote this letter (in Act 20:2). Not long after this letter, he arrived in Corinth and stayed three months, and then changed his plans again about the trip to Jerusalem, Act 20:3.
8. In these words, Paul is apparently referring to accusations made against him. Some saw his change in plans as evidence that he was not a divinely directed apostle, but made and changed his plans as a mere man.
9. That is, did I make my plans lightly?. Was I vacillating, fickle? The grammar indicates a "no" answer is expected. Used only here. GK *1786.* Related to the word in 4:17.
10. Or, "decide, resolve". On this word, see Jn 11:53. Related to "intending" in v 15, 17.
11. Or, "based on" human desires. GK *2848.*
12. That is, are my plans based on human uncertainty? If so, the next question could be "Is your message, the gospel, also uncertain?" Paul's answer begins in v 18 with an answer to this broader question, and moves to the specific question in v 23.
13. Some think this is an oath, like Rom 14:11 (which has the same grammar). Same idiom as in 2 Cor 11:10. Others render it "But God *is* faithful in-that our message...". There is a similar idiom in Gal 1:20. On "faithful", see Col 1:2.
14. Some manuscripts say "was" {N}.
15. There is no wavering or uncertainty in the message we brought. It is as firm as God's Son's accomplishment.
16. That is, Silas. See 1 Thes 1:1 on Silvanus.
17. Or, "did not prove to be... but has proven to be"; or, "was not... but has been (and continues to be)". GK *1181.*
18. Some think the subject of both occurrences of this verb is the Son, "the Son did not become yes and no, but He has become yes in connection with the Father"; others think the subject changes, "for the Son did not prove to be yes and no among you, but the message has proven to be yes in Christ"; others think the subject of both verbs is "the message" (the Son the three of us proclaimed among you), "the message did not prove to be uncertain, but has proven to be yes in Christ".
19. Some think Paul means "Our message is not 'maybe' (uncertain or vacillating), for the Son of God Himself did not become a 'maybe', but has become the 'yes' in connection with God and His promises". Paul is affirming the certainty of the message by the Son's connection with God. Others think he means "Our message is not uncertain, for the Son did not prove Himself to be uncertain among you, but the message has proven to be a 'yes' in Christ in your own experience of Him". He is affirming the certainty of the message by its result among them.
20. That is, Christ is the fulfillment, the confirmation, the affirmation of all the promises of God.
21. Instead of "Therefore also through Him", some manuscripts say "And in Him" {N}.
22. That is, the amen of response to God's message, and acceptance of it.
23. This is the Greek word order. Or, "for glory **to God**".
24. Or, "by us". Some think Paul means "through us messengers". Through Christ, the amen is spoken by all who accept this message brought to them through us. Others think he means "by us Christians". Through Him, the amen is spoken by us all, in response to God's message. Others think he means "by us messengers". Through Him, the amen is spoken by us messengers as we bring the message to you.
25. That is, establishing us together in the faith. The faithful God is the One doing this for both us who are bringing the message, and you who are receiving it. On this word, see "confirm" in 1 Cor 1:6.
26. This word is used in Rom 16:5; Phm 6; 1 Pet 1:11. Or, "in Christ", as in Act 24:24; Gal 2:16. This idiom is elsewhere only in different senses, six times. This is not Paul's normal phrase for "in Christ". GK *1650.*
27. Some think the "us" in this and the next two phrases carries forward the "us" in the first phrase, and so refers to Paul and his companions as ones specially anointed (commissioned) by God to bring the message to the Corinthians. Others think the "us" carries forward the "us with you" in the first phrase, and so refers to what is true of all Christians. In this case, some think Paul means anointed to reign with Christ (note Rom 5:17); others, anointed with the Spirit.
28. This is the Greek word order of this phrase, "the *One* establishing... and having anointed *is* God".
29. This word means "earnest money, down payment, first installment, deposit", a partial payment of an obligation, pledging that the remainder is forthcoming. Elsewhere only in 5:5 and Eph 1:14. GK *775.*

A. Jam 1:18, willed B. 1 Cor 12:8, word C. 2 Tim 4:2 D. 1 Jn 2:25 E. Lk 4:18 F. Eph 1:13

| 2 Corinthians 1:23 | 640 | Verse |

    3C. And **I** call-upon[A] God *as* witness[B] for my soul[C] that sparing[D] you[1] I no longer came[2] to Corinth— *not that we are lording-over[E] your faith, but we are fellow-workers[F] *of* your joy[3]. For you stand *in your* faith[4]   23
24

        1D. For[5] I determined[G] this *for* myself— not to come to you again[6] in grief[H]   2:1

           1E. For if **I** grieve[J] you, who indeed *is* the *one* cheering[K] me except the *one* being grieved by me?   2

        2D. And I wrote this very *thing*[7] in order that having come, I should not have grief[H] from *the ones of* whom I ought-to-have[8] rejoicing[L]— having confidence[9] in you all that my joy is *the joy of* you all   3

           1E. For I wrote *to* you through many tears[10], out of much affliction[M] and anguish[N] *of* heart— not that you might be grieved[J], but that you might know[O] **the love**[P] which I have especially[11] for you   4

               1F. But[12] if anyone has caused-grief,[13] he has grieved not me, but in part[14] (that I not be *a* burden[15]), you all   5
               2F. This[16] punishment by the majority[17] *is* sufficient[18] *for* such *a* one   6

                   1G. So that on-the-contrary[19], instead you *should* forgive[Q] and comfort[20] *him*, *that* such *a* one should not somehow be swallowed-up[R] *by* more grief[H]   7
                   2G. Therefore I urge you to confirm[21] *your* love for him   8

           2E. For I also wrote for this *purpose*— that I might know[22] your approvedness[23], whether you are obedient[24] in all *things*   9

               1F. And[25] *to* whom you are forgiving[Q] anything, I also   10

                   1G. For indeed what **I** have forgiven, if I have forgiven anything,[26] *is* for your sakes in *the* presence *of* Christ, *in order that we may not be exploited[27] by Satan. For we are not unaware[S] *as to* his schemes[28]   11

5B. Now[29] having come to Troas[30] for the good-news[T] *of* Christ— and *a* door having been opened *for* me by *the* Lord— *I had no rest[31] in my spirit *at* my not finding Titus[32] my brother. But having said-goodbye[33] *to* them, I went forth to Macedonia[34]   12
13
6B. But thanks[U] *be* to God, the *One* always leading us in triumph[35] in Christ and making the aroma[36] *of* the knowledge *of* Him[37] known[38] through us in every place   14

1. Sparing them grief was Paul's motive for changing his plans, which he explains in 2:1-11. An incident had occurred causing grief in the church with which the Corinthians had to deal, v 5-7. Paul's presence would have increased the grief.
2. That is, came "first", according to his original plan, v 15-16. Paul is on the way there now.
3. The aim of Paul and his co-workers is to bring the the joy of salvation to the Corinthians.
4. Or, "*by your* faith"; "*in* the faith"; "*by* faith".
5. Instead of "For", some manuscripts have a word meaning "Now, But, And" {C}.
6. Some think Paul means "come again". He did not want this planned second visit to be one of grief, so he aborted it. Others think he means "again in grief", implying there was a former "sorrowful visit" not recorded in Acts, and thus making the aborted visit mentioned here his third planned visit. For more, see 12:14; 13:1; 1:15. The Greek word order is "not again in grief to you to come".
7. That is, his change of plans, 1:23. Some manuscripts add "*to* you" {N}. Some think Paul wrote of this change in 1 Cor 16:5-7. Others think he is referring to some other letter, now lost. Others think he is referring to chapters 10-13, sent as a separate letter before chapters 1-9, but combined in Corinth into the form we have it. This theory is based on the internal content and tone of the two sections. It has no support in the ancient manuscripts we presently have. There are other views. Compare the notes on v 4; 7:8, 12.
8. On this idiom, see "should have" in Mt 25:27. Same grammar as in Act 24:19.
9. That is, having confidence that the Corinthians share Paul's joy in the gospel of Christ and would therefore respond to the directions in his letter and correct the problem.
10. Some think the tears were over the divisions and immorality in 1 Cor 1-6. Others think this description is too strong to refer to 1 Cor 1-6, and that Paul must be referring to some other letter. On this word, see Act 20:19.
11. Same word as in 1:12. Paul's love for the Corinthians is seen in his speaking the truth to them about their behavior. GK *4359*.
12. Paul pauses to comment on the case about which he wrote to them in order to avoid coming to them again in grief, v 1.
13. Some think Paul is referring to the man living with his father's wife, delivered to Satan in 1 Cor 5; others, to the ringleader of opposition to Paul's apostolic authority in Corinth (see chapters 10-13). There are other theories. Compare 7:12.
14. Same idiom as in Rom 11:25. Some think Paul means the man who sinned is only "partially" responsible for the Corinthians' grief. The Corinthians' actions, Paul's letter, and the "punishment" (v 6) they carried out also caused grief in the church. Others think that he grieved them "to some degree"; others, that he grieved "some of them".
15. Or, "weigh heavily". Some think Paul means "that I not exaggerate, put too severely" the extent of the grief; others "that I not be a burden to him", by blaming him for all the grief; others, "that I not be a burden to you all" by detailing your responsibility in the matter. On this word, see 1 Thes 2:9.
16. Paul may mean "This grief-causing punishment"; or, "This punishment of which Titus has now informed me".
17. Some think this implies a minority who preferred a more lenient approach; others, a harsher approach.
18. Or, "enough, adequate". Same word as in 3:5. It was sufficient because it led to repentance. Some think Paul is referring to a punishment such as that in 1 Cor 5:5, 13.
19. Some think Paul means on the contrary to the minority view, which sought a harsher, continued punishment; others, on the contrary to continuing the punishment (without reference to a minority view). Elsewhere only in Gal 2:7; 1 Pet 3:9. GK *5539*.
20. Or, "encourage". On this word, see "exhort" in Rom 12:8.
21. That is, to publicly affirm, reaffirm. Elsewhere only as "ratify" in Gal 3:15. GK *3263*.
22. Or, "come to know". On this word, see Lk 1:34.
23. This word means "the approved quality of a thing having been tested, the approval that comes after testing". Same word as in 9:13; Rom 5:4; Phil 2:22. Elsewhere only as the "test" in 2 Cor 8:2; and its result, the "proof" in 2 Cor 13:3. GK *1509*. On this word group, see "approve" in Rom 12:2.
24. And now I know it. You were obedient. Elsewhere only in Act 7:39; Phil 2:8. GK *5675*. Related to "obedience" in Rom 16:26.
25. And in view of your approved handling of the matter, I am following you in forgiving whoever needs it— whether the one in v 5-6, or any other involved in this incident. The matter is closed.
26. Some manuscripts say "For if indeed I have forgiven anything *to* whom I have forgiven *it, it is* for... " {N}.
27. Or, "cheated, defrauded, taken advantage of". On this word, see 1 Thes 4:6.
28. Or, "thoughts". On this word, see "minds" in 3:14.
29. Moving on from discussing his aborted plans, Paul summarizes his travels before he met Titus returning with news from Corinth.
30. Paul was there in Act 16:8. The trip here in v 12-13 was in Act 20:2.
31. Or, "refreshment, relief". Same word as in 7:5, on which, see 8:13.
32. A door was opened, but since Paul could not find Titus, he felt he had to go to Macedonia seeking him so as to find out about how things went at Corinth and put his spirit at rest.
33. Or, "having taken leave, bid farewell". Elsewhere only in Mk 6:46; Lk 9:61; 14:33; Act 18:18, 21. GK *698*.
34. After a lengthy reflection on his ministry and motivation, in 7:5 Paul completes this description of his travels, giving his thoughts after he found Titus and heard the report from Corinth.
35. Or, "triumphing over us, causing us to triumph". Elsewhere only as "triumph over" in Col 2:15. GK *2581*. Note the change to the present tense. Paul moves from his past change of itinerary to a lengthy reflection on his present ministry (2:14-6:10), occasioned by the positive report of Titus concerning the Corinthians, 7:5-7. It is a remarkable look into the heart of Paul. Because he returns to the meeting of Titus in 7:5, some call this an extended digression. Others think the heart revealed here is the main thing he wanted to communicate to them. It is mature thinking, Phil 3:15. Though I had no rest in my spirit, nevertheless God is leading me in triumph. His triumph does not depend on whether I understand what He is doing or what I am feeling— or on whether those to whom I speak choose life or death. He leads me in His victory.
36. Or, "smell, odor". Elsewhere only in v 16; Jn 12:3; Eph 5:2; Phil 4:18. GK *4011*.
37. That is, the aroma consisting of our knowledge about Christ (or, God).
38. Or, "making evident, making manifest, revealing". On this word, see "made evident" in 1 Jn 2:19.

A. 1 Pet 1:17   B. Act 1:8   C. Jam 5:20   D. Rom 11:21   E. Rom 7:1   F. Rom 16:3   G. Mt 7:1, judge   H. 2 Cor 7:10   J. 2 Cor 7:9   K. Rev 12:12, celebrate   L. 2 Cor 13:11   M. Rev 7:14   N. Lk 21:25   O. Lk 1:34   P. 1 Jn 4:16   Q. Lk 7:42   R. Heb 11:29   S. 1 Thes 5:8   T. 1 Cor 15:1   U. Eph 2:8, grace

1C. Because we are *the* fragrance[1] *of* Christ *for* God[2] among the *ones* being saved[A], and among the 15
ones perishing[B]— *to* **the ones**[3] *an* aroma from death to death,[4] but *to* the others *an* aroma 16
from life to life.[5] And who *is* sufficient[6] for these *things*?

2C. For[7] we are not like the many[8] peddling[9] the word *of* God. But as from purity[10], but as from 17
God, we are speaking in Christ before God

3C. Are we beginning to commend[11] ourselves again? Or we do not have-need *of* letters[C] *of* 3:1
recommendation[12] to you or from[13] you, like some, *do we*? *You** are our letter— 2

    1D. *It* having been inscribed[14] in our hearts[15]
    2D. *It* being known[D] and being read by all people[E]
    3D. *You* being made-known[16] that you are *a* letter *from*[17] Christ 3

        1E. Having been served[F] by us
        2E. Having been inscribed

            1F. Not *with* ink, but *with the* Spirit *of the* living God
            2F. Not in tablets made-of-stone, but in tablets *which are* hearts[G] made-of-flesh[18]

4C. And we have such *a* confidence[19] through Christ toward God[20] 4

    1D. Not that we are sufficient[21] from ourselves[22] to count[H] anything as out of ourselves 5
    2D. But our sufficiency[23] *is* from God, *Who indeed made us sufficient[24] *as* ministers[25] *of a* 6
new[J] covenant[K]— not[26] *of the* letter[27] but *of the* Spirit[28]. For the letter kills,[29] but the Spirit
gives-life[L]
    3D. And if the ministry[M] *of* death having been engraved[30] in letters *on* stones came in glory 7
(so that the sons[31] *of* Israel could not look-intently[N] at the face *of* Moses, because of the
glory *of* his face[32]— the *glory* passing-away[33]), *how shall the ministry *of* the Spirit not 8
be more in glory!

        1E. For if *in* the ministry[34] *of* condemnation[O] *there was* glory, *by* much more the ministry 9
of righteousness[P] is abounding[Q] *in* glory

            1F. For indeed the [ministry of the letter][35] having been glorified[36] has not been 10
glorified in this respect— because of the surpassing[R] glory

        2E. For if the [ministry of the letter] passing-away *was* with glory, *by* much more the 11
[ministry of the Spirit] remaining[S] *is* in glory

    4D. Therefore, having such *a* hope,[37] we are using great boldness[T], *and *are* not like Moses[38] 12-13

1. Or, "good smell", as in the "fragrance of a rose". Elsewhere only in Eph 5:2; Phil 4:18. GK *2380*.
2. Or, "*to* God". Paul may mean that to God, we smell like Christ among those we minister, "to God" being added to show His approval of us. Or he may mean "for God", for the purposes of His triumph.
3. Paul uses grammar that emphasizes the contrast between this group and the next.
4. Some think Paul means "from Christ's death to their death". Such people see Jesus as dead, and only smell His death on Paul, leading to their own eternal death. Others think he means they consider the message of Christ to originate and result in death.
5. Some think Paul means "from Christ's life to their life". Paul has the aroma of resurrection life to these people, leading them to eternal life. Others think he means they consider the message we bring as originating in life, and resulting in life.
6. Same word as in 3:5. Who is equal to the task? Some think Paul leaves the question unanswered here, but means "No one is humanly sufficient. Our sufficiency is from God", as he says in 3:5-6. Others think that the question implies a choice, "Us, or those speaking against us?", and that v 17 is the answer, "We are, for we are not like them...".
7. Some think this answers the previous question; others, that it is the next point in his argument, stating v 15 in comparative terms. The many influencing you change the message to make it more appealing. We speak it as God intended it, recognizing that the dual effect produced is His plan, 1 Cor 1:18-19.
8. Some manuscripts say "others" {B}.
9. Or, "hawking, being hucksters of ". We are not selling it for personal gain, retailing it, being a merchant of it. This word comes to mean "adulterate", since it includes the idea of using all the tricks of the trade to make the product more sellable. Thus here it refers to both wrong motives and wrong methods. Used only here. GK *2836*.
10. Same word as in 1:12. This gives the internal source of Paul's words, pure motives. The next phrase gives its external source, God.
11. Or, "exhibit, show, present". Are we proclaiming our own competence? Paul pauses to answer a false conclusion that could be drawn from 2:14-17, and perhaps was made about him by his opponents. God Himself commended us when He saved you! Same word as in 2 Cor 4:2; 5:12; 6:4; 10:12, 18; 12:11; Rom 16:1. On this word, see "demonstrate" in Rom 5:8.
12. That is, to prove that we are who we say we are, that we are God's authorized representatives. Apollos (Act 18:27) and Phoebe (Rom 16:1) received such letters. The grammar expects a "no" answer.
13. Some manuscripts say "or *letters of* recommendation from you" {N}.
14. Or, "written in, recorded". Same word as in v 3. Elsewhere only as "recorded" in Lk 10:20. GK *1582*.
15. Christ wrote you as the letter we carry in our hearts, not in our pockets. Some manuscripts say "your hearts" {A}.
16. When people read "it", the letter about you inscribed in our hearts, what follows is what is made known about you. Same word as in 2:14. Not related to the word earlier.
17. Or, "*about*". Some think Paul means "from Christ to others", written by Christ; others, "about Christ to others".
18. This is the Greek word order. Or, "but in tablets made of flesh—in hearts". On the idiom "tablets *which are* hearts", see "*a man who was a* prophet" in Lk 24:19. On this word, see 1 Cor 3:1.
19. That is, as described in 2:14-3:3, confidence that God is leading us in His triumph, and that we are the fragrance of Christ among you, and that we speak in Christ from God to you, and that you are our credentials from Christ. On this word, see 1:15.
20. Next Paul further explains the source of this confidence. It is not based on self-sufficiency (v 5), but on sufficiency God granted us for the ministry in which He placed us (v 6), and on the glory inherent to this ministry itself (v 7-11). Therefore we use boldness reflecting this confidence and glory (v 12-18).
21. Or, "competent, fit, adequate, enough, worthy". Same word as in 2:6, 16; Mt 28:12; as "fit" in 1 Cor 15:9; Mt 3:11; 8:8; as "competent" in 2 Tim 2:2; and as "enough" in Mk 15:15. It often means "considerable, many". Used 39 times. GK *2653*. Related to "sufficiency" and "made sufficient" in v 6.
22. That is, from our own resources and abilities.
23. Or, "qualification, fitness". Used only here. GK *2654*.
24. On "made sufficient", see "qualified" in Col 1:12.
25. Or, "servants". On this word, see "servants" in 1 Cor 3:5. Related to "served" in v 3, and "ministry" in v 7, 8, 9.
26. Some think Paul means "ministers... not *of the* letter..."; others, "new covenant *which is* not *of the* letter...".
27. On this word, see Rom 2:27, 29.
28. Or, "spirit". Not of the Law (in the sense described in v 7), but of the Spirit. Or, not of a code in letters, but of true righteousness in the spirit, "written on the heart" (Heb 8:10); a circumcision of the heart (Rom 2:29). Some think Paul means "spirit" in each case down through v 18.
29. The Law brings the death sentence, Rom 6:23; 7:10-11. It is a ministry of death. The "killing" and "giving life" are amplified in v 9.
30. Or, "carved, chiseled". This word modifies "ministry", not "letters". Others render this "ministry *of* death in letters, having been engraved *on* stones", the Greek word order. In this case, Paul is describing two characteristics, in letters (versus in the Spirit), engraved in stone (versus hearts). Used only here. GK *1963*.
31. That is, descendants. On this word, see Gal 3:7.
32. The Israelites were afraid to come near Moses, Ex 34:29-30. God's glory made Moses' face shine temporarily.
33. Or, "being done away". Same word as in v 11, 13, 14. On this word, see "done away with" in Rom 6:6.
34. Some manuscripts say "For if the ministry *of* condemnation *has* glory" {B}.
35. Both here and in v 11 and 13, the Greek says "the *thing*", leaving the reader to supply the reference from the context. To make Paul's point clearer, the fuller phrase has been supplied in brackets.
36. The ministry of the letter was glorified in the face of Moses, and in other ways. Yet it has no glory at all compared to the surpassing glory of the ministry of the Spirit. It does not lack glory in itself, but its glory pales by comparison.
37. Some think Paul means the hope which characterizes this ministry, the hope of an "abounding" (v 9) and "remaining" (v 11) glory. By "hope" he does not mean "wish", but "expectation". Others think "hope" is equivalent to "confidence" in v 4, and make this point 5C., a resumption of his main argument.
38. Based on the confidence (v 4), which issues from this hope, we use much boldness, in keeping with the glory of the ministry God has given us as His sufficient servants of the new covenant. We are not like Moses, who hid his fading glory. We reflect a growing glory. The flow and meaning of v 12-18 is difficult. Consult the commentaries.

A. Lk 19:10 B. 1 Cor 1:18 C. 2 Thes 3:17 D. Lk 1:34 E. Mt 4:4, mankind F. 1 Pet 4:10, ministering G. Rev 2:23 H. Rom 3:28, consider J. Heb 8:13
K. Heb 8:6 L. Jn 5:21 M. 1 Cor 12:5 N. Lk 4:20 O. 2 Cor 7:3 P. Rom 1:17 Q. 2 Cor 8:2 R. 2 Cor 9:14 S. Jn 15:4, abide T. Heb 4:16, confidence

1E.	He was putting^A *a* veil^B on his face so that the sons^C *of* Israel *might* not look-intently[1] at the end[2] *of* the [face of glory][3] passing-away[4]	
	1F. But[5] their minds[6] were hardened[7], for until this very day[8] the same veil[9] remains^D on the reading *of* the old^E covenant[10]— *it* not being unveiled[11] because[12] it passes-away[13] in Christ	14
	2F. Indeed[14], until today whenever Moses is being read, *a* veil lies^F on their heart	15
	3F. But whenever[15] it[16] turns to *the* Lord[17], the veil is taken-away[18]	16
	1G. Now the Lord is the Spirit,[19] and where the Spirit *of the* Lord *is, there is* freedom[20]!	17
2E.	But[21] **we** all *with a* face having been unveiled^G, while reflecting the glory *of the* Lord as a mirror[22], are being transformed[23] *into* the same image^H from glory to glory,[24] just-as[25] from *the* Lord, *the* Spirit[26]	18
5C. For this reason,[27] having this ministry even-as[28] we received-mercy[29], we do not lose-heart[30]		4:1
1D. But we renounced[31] the hidden^J *things of* shame[32]		2
1E. Not walking^K in craftiness[33], nor handling-deceitfully[34] the word *of* God		

1. Same word as in v 7.
2. Or, "cessation, termination, finish, goal". On this word, see Rom 10:4.
3. As in v 7. Others supply "[ministry of the letter]" as in v 11 (which is then explained in various ways); and there are other views.
4. Ex 34:34-35 says Moses repeatedly would remove the veil before God, then speak unveiled before the people, and then veil his face until he went before God again. From the point of view of Paul's application of this event here, after Moses proclaimed the words of the old covenant with the effect of God's glory shining from his face for all to see, he veiled his face so they would not focus on the imminent cessation of this fading glory. The fading glory symbolized the temporary nature of that covenant.
5. Paul draws an application from Moses for Israel.
6. Or, "thoughts". Same word as in 4:4; 11:3; Phil 4:7. Elsewhere only as "thoughts" in 2 Cor 10:5; and "schemes" in 2 Cor 2:11. GK 3784. Related to "think" in Eph 3:20.
7. But the Israelites were hardened to the spiritual meaning of this fading glory, and did not understand that the temporary glory of Moses pointed to the temporary glory of the covenant he brought. This means they were hardened to the true nature and meaning of the old covenant itself, which is seen in the fact that a veil still remains on their understanding of it whenever they read it, until this very day. On this word, see Rom 11:7.
8. On this phrase, "until this very day", see Rom 11:8. Some manuscripts say "until this day" {N}.
9. It is the "same veil" in that, like the one on Moses, it hides the temporary glory. But unlike the one on Moses, this veil is on the hearts of the ones looking (here, reading), not on the thing seen (here, the old covenant). Elsewhere only in v 13, 15, 16. GK 2820. The related verb is in 4:3.
10. This is the only place where the old covenant is called such. Compare Heb 8:13. On this word, see Heb 8:6.
11. That is, the veil not being removed. Elsewhere only in v 18. GK 365.
12. Or, "that", "it not being unveiled [that is, revealed] to them that it [the old covenant] passes away in Christ".
13. Or, "is done away". The same word as in v 7, 11, 13.
14. Paul repeats this to make clear that the veil is not on the Law, but on their hearts. Same word as "But" beginning v 14. GK 247.
15. Or, "at the time when". Elsewhere only in v 15. GK 2471.
16. Or, "he". Some think Paul is referring to such a veiled heart (v 15) or hardened mind (v 14) as just mentioned. This may be simplified by supplying "*a person, a Jew, a heart, one*". Others render it "he", referring to "Moses" as the type of the person turning to the Lord. When Moses returned to the presence of God, he first removed the veil, Ex 34:34. As with Moses physically, so today spiritually. The veil is removed when one turns to the Lord. There are other views.
17. Some think Paul means "God", as in the physical case of Moses in Ex 34:34; others, "Christ", as in the spiritual case today, as defined by v 14b.
18. On this word, see Act 27:20.
19. Some think this is intended to link the "Lord" in view in v 16 (that is, in the reference to Ex 34) to the Spirit today. As Moses physically turned to the Lord speaking then, we must spiritually turn to the Spirit speaking now. Others think Paul means "Christ is the Spirit", continuing the link of "Lord" back to "in Christ" in v 14b. That is, Christ is the Spirit of the Lord (as used in the OT) in our experience of God. Christ is the Spirit in the same sense as "I and the Father are one" and "The one having seen Me has seen the Father" (Jn 10:30; 14:9).
20. That is, freedom from the ministry of death (v 7), and all it entails (Rom 8:2); freedom as full members of God's family (Rom 8:15, Gal 5:1). Some manuscripts say "there *is* freedom", meaning, "in-that-place *there is* freedom" {N}. On this word, see Gal 5:13.
21. Or, "And". Now Paul gives the application of Moses for us, the other side of the comparison begun in v 13. "We are not like Moses. He was... But we are...". Others think Paul has dropped the link to v 13, and that this links to v 17. "There is freedom! And we all..." (giving a spiritual sense in which we are like Moses, not unlike him, in contrast to hardened Israel).
22. Or, "looking at the glory *of the* Lord as in a mirror". Moses veiled his face to hide the temporary physical glory produced in him by God's glory, v 13. All we Christians with unveiled face boldly "reflect" the growing spiritual glory of the Lord being produced in us. Others link this to v 17 as point 2G. Moses took off the veil to look at the glory, and to reflect it to the people. We also with unveiled face, "looking at" (or, "reflecting") the glory, are spiritually transformed. This word, "reflecting as a mirror", is used only here. GK 3002.
23. On this word, see Rom 12:2. Our "reflection" of the glory is growing in intensity as we are transformed by the Lord, the Spirit. Or, while we are "looking at" the glory, we are being transformed by it.
24. Some think Paul means not from glory to fading to glory to fading, like Moses. But from glory leading to more glory, continually. Others think he means "from *His* glory to *our* glory".
25. Or, "as". That is, just as would be expected. Same word as "like" in v 13. Used 13 times. GK 2749.
26. Or, "*the* Lord *who is the* Spirit", as stated in v 17. Others think Paul means "*the* Lord Spirit", "*the* Spirit *who is* Lord", similar to "the Lord God"; others, "*the* Lord *of the* Spirit", the Lord who sends the Spirit. There are other views. Consult the commentaries.
27. That is, because we have such a confidence (3:4), having been made sufficient for this ministry by God (3:6), and are serving in the glory of this ministry with boldness. Others make this point 5D., the conclusion of the previous section, and start the new point in 4:7.
28. Or, "just as". That is, from the Lord, as a gift of His grace. This phrase is added to explain the true nature of this ministry. It is something received as a gift of grace, just like salvation. Therefore we do not lose heart in it. It is part of His triumph, not our personal achievement for Him. We are discovering the greatness of His gift, not creating it. GK 2777.
29. On this word, see "showing mercy" in Rom 12:8.
30. Or, "grow weary". Same word as in v 16; Lk 18:1; Eph 3:13. Elsewhere only as "grow weary" in Gal 6:9; 2 Thes 3:13. GK 1591.
31. Or, "disowned". Without this renouncing, we would be losing heart. Used only here. GK 584.
32. That is, the secret things proceeding from shameful motives (such as pleasing people, Gal 1:10); or resulting in shame when they are known; or the secret things that shame leads one to hide. In v 2-6, Paul is speaking to the internal cause of losing heart. Our failure to attain hidden motives or goals of self-interest causes us to lose heart. Paul renounces them, and simply speaks the truth, leaving the results to God. Therefore he does not lose heart when the majority reject him, v 3. God's plan is twofold, 2:16. On this word, see Heb 12:2.
33. Or, "trickery". That is, using any means to gain our ends. On this word, see 1 Cor 3:19.
34. Or, "adulterating, counterfeiting, falsifying". Used only here. GK 1516. Related to "deceit" in Mt 26:4.

A. Act 19:21   B. 2 Cor 2:14   C. Gal 3:7   D. Jn 15:4, abide   E. Mk 2:21   F. Mt 3:10   G. 2 Cor 3:14   H. Col 1:15   J. 1 Cor 4:5   K. Heb 13:9

  2E. But *by* the open-disclosure¹ *of* the truth, commending² ourselves to every conscience^A *of* mankind³ in the sight of God

  3E. And if indeed⁴ our good-news^B is veiled⁵, it is veiled in⁶ the *ones* perishing^C   3

    1F. In whose case the god *of* this age blinded the minds^D *of* the unbelievers^E so that *they might* not see⁷ the illumination⁸ *of* the good-news^B *of* the glory *of* Christ— Who is *the* image^F *of* God   4

  4E. For we are not proclaiming^G ourselves, but Jesus Christ⁹ *as* Lord, and ourselves *as* your slaves^H for the sake of Jesus¹⁰   5

    1F. Because God, the *One* having said "Light will shine¹¹ out of darkness", *is* He Who shined in our hearts for¹² *the* illumination *of* the¹³ knowledge *of* the glory *of* God in *the* face *of* Jesus¹⁴ Christ   6

2D. But¹⁵ we have this treasure¹⁶ in vessels made-of-clay, in order that the excess¹⁷ *of* the power^J may be God's and not from us   7

  1E. In every *way*   8

    1F. Being afflicted¹⁸, but not restrained¹⁹
    2F. Being perplexed²⁰, but not utterly-perplexed²¹
    3F. Being persecuted^K, but not forsaken²²   9
    4F. Being struck down, but not perishing^C

  2E. At-all-times^L carrying-around in *our* body the dying²³ *of* Jesus²⁴, in order that the life *of* Jesus may also be made-evident²⁵ in our body   10

    1F. For **we** the *ones* living are always being handed-over^M to death for the sake of Jesus, in order that the life *of* Jesus may also be made-evident in our mortal^N flesh   11

  3E. So then, death²⁶ is at-work²⁷ in us, but life in you   12

3D. But²⁸ having the same spirit²⁹ *of* faith in accordance with the *thing* having been written [in Ps 116:10], "I believed^O, therefore³⁰ I spoke"— **we** also believe, therefore we also speak   13

  1E. Knowing that the *One* having raised^P the Lord³¹ Jesus will also raise us with³² Jesus, and will present^Q *us* with you   14

    1F. For all³³ *things are* for your sakes— in order that grace^R, having increased^S through the more *people*, may cause thanksgiving^T to abound^U to the glory *of* God   15

4D. Therefore we do not lose-heart^V. But even though³⁴ our outer person^W is being destroyed³⁵, nevertheless our³⁶ inner *person* is being renewed³⁷ day *in* and day *out*   16

  1E. For the momentary lightness³⁸ *of* our affliction^X is producing^Y *for* us *an* eternal^Z weight^AA *of* glory extremely beyond measure³⁹, °while we *are* not looking-for⁴⁰ the *things* being seen, but the *things* not being seen   17
                                      18

1. Or, "manifestation". On this word, see "manifestation" in 1 Cor 12:7.
2. Or, "presenting, showing, recommending". That is, presenting ourselves positively. On this word, see 3:1. This word does not mean "gaining their approval, causing them to approve of us". Some think Paul means that in the sight of God, he recommends himself for the approval of every kind of human conscience by means of an open disclosure of the truth, not by means of any secret crafty subterfuge. As to the response, some approve, others reject and persecute him. Others think he means that he presents himself to their conscience in such a way that it approves of his sincere and honest approach, even if outwardly they reject and persecute him.
3. Or, "people". In this phrase, "conscience" is singular and "mankind" is plural, "every *individual* conscience of *all* people". Compare "every soul *of the* person" in Rom 2:9.
4. Or, "And even if". On this idiom, see "if also" in 1 Cor 7:21.
5. This is a participle, "is having been veiled". Likewise in the next phrase. Assuming that the open disclosure of the truth of the gospel is indeed veiled in the hearer, it is not because of the messenger. On this word, see "covers" in 1 Pet 4:8. Related to "veil" in 3:14.
6. That is, "in the case of", as next. GK *1877*.
7. Or, "so that the illumination.... *might* not shine forth *on them*". Some manuscripts add "*on* them" {N}. Used only here. GK *878*. Related to "daybreak" in Act 20:11.
8. Elsewhere only in v 6. GK *5895*. Related to "light" in v 6.
9. Some manuscripts say "Christ Jesus" {N}.
10. Some manuscripts say "your slaves through Jesus" {B}.
11. Elsewhere only in Mt 5:15, 16; 17:2; Lk 17:24; Act 12:7. GK *3290*. Paul is referring to Gen 1:3. Some manuscripts say "... having told light to shine..." {N}.
12. God shined in our hearts to create in us the illumination for others to see, consisting of the knowledge of the glory of God as seen in the person of Christ. We give out the illumination to which those perishing are blinded, v 4.
13. That is, "*consisting of* the" or "*produced by* the", as in v 4.
14. Some manuscripts omit this word; others say "Christ Jesus" {C}.
15. Paul now turns to the external causes of losing heart, suffering and persecution.
16. That is, the gospel (v 4), the knowledge of His glory (v 6), which we proclaim in this ministry we received. On this word, see Mt 12:35.
17. Same word as in 12:7. Paul may mean the excess of quantity, "abundance"; or, the excess of quality, "excellence".
18. Or, "pressed, oppressed, distressed, squeezed". Same word as in 1:6; 7:5; 1 Thes 3:4; 2 Thes 1:6, 7; 1 Tim 5:10; Heb 11:37. Elsewhere only as "constricted" in Mt 7:14; and "pressing" in Mk 3:9. GK *2567*. Related to "affliction" in Rev 7:14.
19. Or, "confined, distressed, cramped, restricted". Elsewhere only in 6:12. GK *5102*. Related to "distresses" in 6:4.
20. Or, "uncertain, at a loss". Elsewhere only in Mk 6:20; Lk 24:4; Jn 13:22; Act 25:20; Gal 4:20. GK *679*. Related to "perplexity" in Lk 21:25; and "greatly perplexed" in Lk 9:7.
21. Or, "despairing". Elsewhere only as "despaired" in 1:8. GK *1989*. Related to the previous word. Or, "at a loss, but not utterly at a loss".
22. Or, "abandoned, deserted, left behind". Same word as in Mt 27:46; Mk 15:34; Heb 10:25; 13:5. Elsewhere only as "abandon" in Act 2:27, 31; "desert" in 2 Tim 4:10, 16; and "leave behind" in Rom 9:29. GK *1593*.
23. Or, "the putting to death". Or the result, "the death, deadness". Elsewhere only as "deadness" in Rom 4:19. GK *3740*.
24. Some think Paul means "the dying that we do for Jesus", "the peril of death we experience for Jesus"; others, "the putting to death done to Jesus in us", the attack upon Him in and through us; others, "the Jesus kind of dying", by violent persecution. Some manuscripts say "*of* the Lord Jesus" {K}.
25. Or, "made known, revealed, made visible". Same word as in v 11. On this word, see 1 Jn 2:19.
26. Some think Paul means "physical death is at work in us, spiritual life in you". Others think he means "our physical dying is at work in us, our spiritual life in you". That is, the dying of Jesus we carry works bodily death in us; the life of Jesus we thus make evident works life in you.
27. Or, "working, being worked". On this verb, see "works" in 1 Cor 12:11.
28. The answer to external causes of losing heart is an eternal perspective, knowing God will raise us. Having this perspective, we press on in spite of the dangers.
29. Or, "Spirit". Some think Paul means the disposition of faith the psalmist had; others, the Spirit producing faith.
30. Some manuscripts add "and" {N}, "and therefore...".
31. Some manuscripts omit "the Lord" {B}.
32. Some manuscripts say "by" {N}.
33. That is, all our work and suffering.
34. That is, "Accepting that our outer person even is being destroyed...". On this idiom, see "if also" in 1 Cor 7:21.
35. Or, "ruined, spoiled, consumed, wasted". Same word as in Lk 12:33; Rev 8:9; 11:18. Elsewhere only as "corrupted" in 1 Tim 6:5. GK *1425*. The related noun is used of the "decay" of the grave in Act 2:27.
36. Some manuscripts omit this word {N}, so that it says "the inner...".
37. We are renewed by looking forward to our eternal glory (v 17), and our eternal body (5:1). Elsewhere only in Col 3:10. GK *363*. Related to "renewing" in Tit 3:5; and "renew" in Heb 6:6.
38. Elsewhere only as "light" in Mt 11:30. GK *1787*. Related to "lightness" in 1:17.
39. This phrase "extremely beyond measure" contains the same root word repeated with two different prepositions, "excessively beyond excess", "extremely beyond the extreme", "immeasurably beyond measure". On this word, see "beyond measure" in 1 Cor 12:31. Some take this phrase with "weight"; others, with "producing".
40. Or, "looking at, looking out for, looking to, watching for". Elsewhere only as "watch" in Phil 3:17; "look out for" in Gal 6:1; Phil 2:4; "watch out" in Lk 11:35; "watch out for" in Rom 16:17. GK *5023*. Related to "goal" in Phil 3:14.

A. Act 23:1 B. 1 Cor 15:1 C. 1 Cor 1:18 D. 2 Cor 3:14 E. Mt 17:17, unbelieving F. Col 1:15 G. 2 Tim 4:2 H. Rom 6:17 J. Mk 5:30 K. 2 Tim 3:12 L. 1 Thes 5:16, always M. Mt 26:21 N. 2 Cor 5:4 O. Jn 3:36 P. Mt 28:6, arose Q. Rom 12:1 R. Eph 2:8 S. 2 Cor 8:15 T. 1 Tim 4:3 U. 2 Cor 8:2 V. 2 Cor 4:1 W. Mt 4:4, mankind X. Rev 7:14 Y. Phil 2:12, work out Z. Mt 25:46 AA. 1 Thes 2:7

| 2 Corinthians 5:1 | 648 | Verse |

   1F. For the *things* being seen *are* temporary^A, but the *things* not being seen *are* eternal^B

  2E. For we know that if our earthly^C house^D— *our* tent¹— is torn-down², we have *a* building³ from God, *a* house not-made-by-*human*-hands^E, eternal, in the heavens 5:1

   1F. For indeed in this *tent* we are groaning^F, yearning^G to put-on-over⁴ *ourselves* our dwelling⁵ from heaven—*inasmuch as we,⁶ having taken-off⁷ *this tent*, shall not be found naked⁸ 2 3

    1G. For⁹ indeed we, the *ones* being in the tent¹⁰, are groaning^F, being burdened¹¹— because we do not want to take-off *our earthly tent*, but to put on *our heavenly dwelling* over *it*, in order that the mortal¹² may be swallowed-up¹³ by the life 4

   2F. And the *One* having made^H us for this very *thing*¹⁴ *is* God, the *One* having¹⁵ given us *His* pledge^J— the Spirit¹⁶ 5

   3F. So while always being confident¹⁷, and knowing that while being-at-home in the body, we are away-from-home¹⁸, from the Lord *(for we walk by faith, not by appearance¹⁹)—*yet we are confident,²⁰ and prefer²¹ rather²² 6 7 8

    1G. To get-away-from-home— out of the body
    2G. And to get-at-home— with the Lord

 5D. Therefore we indeed²³ are ambitious²⁴ to be pleasing²⁵ *to* Him— whether being at-home or being away-from-home²⁶ 9

  1E. For we all must^K appear²⁷ before the judgment-seat^L *of* Christ in order that each *one* might receive-back²⁸ the *things done* in²⁹ the body, in-accordance-with³⁰ *the things* which he practiced^M— whether good^N or bad³¹ 10

  2E. Therefore knowing^O the fear^P *of* the Lord,³² we are persuading³³ people³⁴ 11

7B. Now³⁵ we have been made known³⁶ *to* God. And I hope *that we* also have been made known³⁷ in your consciences³⁸

1. Or, "our earthly house *which is our* tent". Literally, "our earthly house *of* the tent". That is, our physical body. Same grammar as v 5, "the pledge— the Spirit". Note our temporary earthly "tent" vs. our eternal "building". Elsewhere only in v 4. GK *5011*.
2. Or, "taken down, put down". That is, if we die. On this word, see Mt 24:2.
3. Some think Paul is referring to our resurrection body, skipping over the time between death and the Second Coming when we receive it (compare 1 Cor 15:53); others, to heaven itself, or a house or "place to stay" (Jn 14:2) that our soul enters upon death until the resurrection. There are other views.
4. Used of putting on an outer garment over another garment. Used only here and in v 4. GK *2086*. Related to "put on" in 1 Cor 15:53. Related to "outer garment" in Jn 21:7. There Peter was "naked" (same word as in 2 Cor 5:3), so he put his outer garment on over. Here Paul is referring to putting on our new body over our present one. Some think he is referring to "being changed" (1 Cor 15:52) at Christ's coming; others, to our putting it on at our death.
5. On this word, see Jude 6. Related to "house".
6. Or, "if indeed we" in the sense of "since indeed we".
7. Same word as in v 4. Elsewhere only as "strip" in Mt 27:28; Lk 10:30; and "strip off" in Mt 27:31; Mk 15:20. GK *1694*. Some manuscripts say "having put-on *the heavenly dwelling*" {C}, using the same word as in 1 Cor 15:53, and related to "put on over" in v 2.
8. There are many views on this clause. Consult the commentaries. One view is that Paul means "since having shed our old body (or, 'put on' our new one if the variant is accepted), we shall not in fact be found disembodied". This is the reverse of v 1. Having torn down this tent, we will have a building, v 1. Having put on the new (which means shedding the old), we will not be without a body, v 2. On this word, see Jam 2:15.
9. The purpose of this verse is to explain that the "yearning" in v 2 is not a desire to die— for we do not want to take off this tent— but a desire to live, to put on our new body, to be swallowed up by life.
10. That is, physically alive on earth. Same word as in v 1.
11. On this word, see 1:8. We are burdened because we do not want to put off the body (to die), but we yearn to put on the new spiritual body. We are pulled in both directions, as Paul expresses in Phil 1:21-24. We want to be "changed", 1 Cor 15:51-53. Others think Paul means we are burdened because we do not want to be without a body.
12. Same word as in 1 Cor 15:53, 54, this mortal body putting on immortality. Elsewhere only in Rom 6:12; 8:11; 2 Cor 4:11. GK *2570*. It means "subject to death". The root word is "to die".
13. Same word as in 1 Cor 15:54. On this word, see Heb 11:29.
14. That is, the receiving of an immortal body.
15. Some manuscripts add next "also" {N}.
16. Or, "the pledge *which is* the Spirit". Literally, "the pledge *of* the Spirit".
17. That is, in the present life we live by faith. This is a positive way of saying "not lose heart". Same word as in v 8; 7:16; Heb 13:6. Elsewhere only as "bold" in 2 Cor 10:1, 2. GK *2509*. It means "to be bold, confident, courageous".
18. The same root word is used with different prefixes— to be at home, to be away from home; living at home, living abroad. Both are used only in 5:6, 8, 9. GK *1685* and *1897*. The second word is related to "go on a journey" in Mt 21:33. Note that Paul reverses the reference of these two words in v 8.
19. Or, "outward-appearance, what is seen, sight". Some take this to mean "not by what we physically see in this world"; others, "not by a physical seeing of the heavenly realities". Same word as in Lk 9:29. Elsewhere only as "form" in Lk 3:22; Jn 5:37; 1 Thes 5:22. GK *1626*.
20. That is, in the future that awaits us when we die.
21. On this word, see "well pleased" in Mt 17:5. Not related to "pleasing" in v 9.
22. What follows probably anticipates Christ's return, but may refer to Paul's death, as in Phil 1:23.
23. Or, "also". We do not lose heart, looking to the next life, 4:16. We indeed are ambitious (the opposite of losing heart), looking to the rest of this life, to be pleasing to God both here and when we stand before Him. Others make this 4F., we prefer to be with Him, therefore we also are ambitious to be pleasing to Him.
24. Or, "we make it our aim". On this word, see Rom 15:20.
25. On this adjective, see Eph 5:10. We want God to be pleased with us, whether here or there.
26. That is, in the body or out of the body; or, with the Lord or away from the Lord. Both mean the same thing, whether here now, or standing before Him as described next.
27. Or, "be made known, be revealed". Same word as "reveal" in 1 Cor 4:5. On this word, see "made evident" in 1 Jn 2:19.
28. Or, "receive in full, get for oneself, get, obtain, receive in recompense". That is, receive back what is due. This word was used of receiving a wage, recompense, or reward. Same word as in Mt 25:27; Eph 6:8; Col 3:25; Heb 11:19. Elsewhere only as "receive" in Heb 10:36; 11:39; 1 Pet 1:9; 5:4; and with different grammar, "bring" in Lk 7:37. GK *3152*.
29. That is, while in this life, "during the time of" the body. Or, "by means of, through, with". GK *1328*.
30. Same word as in Lk 12:47. GK *4639*.
31. On this word, see Jam 3:16. Some manuscripts have a different word meaning "evil, wicked, bad" {N}.
32. That is, the reverence for the Lord and the desire to please Him that this fact (v 10) elicits in us.
33. Some render this "we are *trying to* persuade". On this word, see 1 Jn 3:19.
34. Some think Paul means he persuades people that he is pleasing God in his work and motives; others, that he persuades them so as to please God regarding what God called him to do, that is, to preach the gospel, 5:20-21.
35. Or, "But, And". Having openly reflected before God and the Corinthians upon himself and his ministry (2:14-5:11), Paul now turns back to them, and states the facts about his motives and responsibilities as an apostle more directly to their need. As in 3:1, he again begins by denying a motive of self-commendation. Others punctuate this "persuade people, but we have...", continuing that point. This view thinks Paul persuades people about his motives and intentions, but that God knows his motives are true, and he hopes the Corinthians know this as well.
36. Same word as "appear" in v 10. It is a play on words, moving from what will be then, to what is now. We have already been made known to God in every way— our work, motives, conduct, all the things discussed in 2:14-5:11.
37. This is the purpose of Paul's writing. To make sure this hope is realized, he now speaks plainly and explicitly.
38. On this word, see Act 23:1. It is plural only here.

A. Mt 13:21 B. Mt 25:46 C. Phil 2:10 D. Mk 3:25 E. Mk 14:58 F. Jam 5:9 G. 1 Pet 2:2 H. Phil 2:12, work out J. 2 Cor 1:22 K. Mt 16:21 L. Rom 14:10 M. Rom 2:1 N. 1 Tim 5:10b O. 1 Jn 2:29 P. Eph 5:21

1C.	We¹ are not again commending^A ourselves *to* you, but *are* giving you *an* opportunity² *for a* boast³ about us, in order that you may have *an answer* for the *ones* boasting^B in appearance⁴ and not in heart^C	12
2C.	For⁵ if we lost-*our*-senses⁶, *it is for* God! If we are sound-minded⁷, *it is for* you!	13
3C.	For⁸ the love^D *of* Christ⁹ controls¹⁰ us, *we* having determined¹¹ this—	14
1D.	That¹² One¹³ died for all, therefore all¹⁴ died. *And He died for all so that the *ones* living¹⁵ might no longer be living *for* themselves, but *for* the *One* having died and been raised¹⁶ for them¹⁷	15
1E.	So then¹⁸ from now *on*, **we** regard¹⁹ no one based-on²⁰ *the* flesh²¹	16
1F.	Even though²² we have known²³ Christ based on *the* flesh,²⁴ nevertheless now we no longer are knowing *Him thus*	
2E.	So then if anyone *is* in Christ, *he is a* new creation²⁵. The old *things* passed-away. Behold— new *things* have come-into-being²⁶	17
4C.	And all *things*²⁷ *are* from God, the *One* having reconciled²⁸ us²⁹ *to* Himself through Christ³⁰, and having given us the ministry^E *of* reconciliation³¹—	18
1D.	How that³² God was in Christ³³ reconciling³⁴ *the* world *to* Himself—³⁵	19
1E.	Not counting^F their trespasses^G *against* them	
2E.	And having placed^H the message^J *of* reconciliation in us	
5C.	Therefore,³⁶ we are ambassadors³⁷ on behalf of Christ, since³⁸ God *is* appealing³⁹ through us	20

1. This is our motive for speaking about ourselves as we do. Some manuscripts say "For we" {N}.
2. Or, "starting point". On this word, see Rom 7:8.
3. That is, to have a matter to boast about. On this word, see Phil 1:26.
4. That is, in what humans see and respect, not in what God sees, as in v 16.
5. That is, "And I hope (v 11)... For...".
6. Paul is referring to what his opponents said about him— that he is mad with fanaticism. This was said of Jesus in Mk 3:21 (same word), and of Paul in Act 26:24 (different word).
7. Paul is referring to what he says about himself. Compare Act 26:25, where a related word is used. On this word, see Rom 12:3.
8. This is our motive for conducting ourselves as we do.
9. Paul could mean our love for Christ, but probably means His love for us, as expressed in v 14-15.
10. Or, "compels". This word means "to hold in, enclose (Lk 8:45), confine (Lk 19:43), hold (in custody, Lk 22:63); to hold shut (Act 7:57); to hold attention on, be occupied with (Act 18:5), be absorbed in; to be held under the positive control of, gripped (Phil 1:23), governed, ruled, overcome; to be held under the negative control of, gripped (Mt 4:24; Lk 4:38; 8:37; Act 28:8), afflicted, distressed"; and elsewhere only as "held" (Lk 12:50). GK *5309*. The root word is "to hold". Here, some think Paul means Christ's love "controls, governs, directs" us. Others extend this to mean "drives, compels, urges us on".
11. Or, "having made this judgment". On this word, see "judge" in Mt 7:1.
12. Some manuscripts add "if" {N}, so that it says "That if One died for all, then all died".
13. This is the number "one". That is, that one Man died for all.
14. Some think Paul means all the world, as in v 19. Note 1 Jn 2:2. Others think he means all believers.
15. Some think Paul means living in Christ, v 17; others, alive in this world (making this group the same as "all" in v 14, 19).
16. Or, "having arisen". On this word, see "arose" in Mt 28:6.
17. Or, "having died for them, and having been raised".
18. That is, since all died, and the ones living are living for Him. Same in v 17.
19. Or, "know". This word means "to know", here in the sense of "to regard, recognize, take interest in, value". Same word as "know" in 1 Thes 5:12, on which see 1 Jn 2:29.
20. Or, "in accordance with, according to, in relation to". GK *2848*.
21. We no longer relate to people based on human distinctions or what they are in the flesh. As ones dead and living in Christ, the world is in a new position for us. We regard people only in relation to the One who died for them— either as needing Him, or as living for Him.
22. Even the way we regard Christ has changed. On this idiom, see "if also" in 1 Cor 7:21. Regardless of the fact that we have known Christ in this manner, we no longer do.
23. On this word, used twice in this verse, see Lk 1:34.
24. This phrase "based on the flesh" has the same meaning as in the first part of the verse, "based on human viewpoints and distinctions". Paul may have personally known Jesus while He was on earth, but that is not what he is saying here. He is saying that he regarded Him from a fleshly perspective, a human point of view, based on His human status as a Galilean. On what this verse might imply about Paul, consult the commentaries.
25. Or, "creature". Same phrase as in Gal 6:15. As ones who have died (v 14), believers are new creations, living a new life for Him.
26. Or, "come, come about, come to pass". Same word as in Jn 1:3. Some manuscripts say "all *things* have become new" {A}, where "become" is the same word as "come into being". GK *1181*.
27. Paul continues his thoughts about himself and his ministry. The love of Christ controls us. And God, who reconciled us and gave us this ministry, is the source of all things in it (compare 2:14-16). The "us, we" has the same reference throughout all of point 7B. Paul is speaking of himself and his fellow workers, as models for all believers. Others place this as point 3E., further describing the life of all God's new creations. The "us" in v 18a (and some think, 18b and 19) refers directly to all believers. In this case, Paul returns to his main line of thought in v 20.
28. On this word, see Rom 5:10. Same word as in v 19, 20.
29. Paul states with reference to himself and his fellow workers what is objectively true of the whole world, and subjectively true of all believers. See note 7.
30. Some manuscripts say "Jesus Christ" {K}.
31. God gave us (and you, in your various ways) the ministry of bringing this message of reconciliation to the world. So we take them the message and beg, v 20. Same word as in v 19. On this word, see Rom 5:11.
32. On "how that" see 11:21. Paul is giving God's statement of the matter.
33. This is the Greek word order. Some take this to mean "God was in Christ, reconciling", making two doctrinal points; others, "God was reconciling in Christ", making one point. Consult the commentaries.
34. Reconciliation has both an objective sense (which was finished on the cross for all the world), and a subjective sense (each individual's acceptance of it by faith). The former is done forever, the latter continues as the message of reconciliation is taken to the world. In Christ's ministry on earth, God accomplished the former and began the latter.
35. The following two phrases explain how God "was reconciling"— by "not counting" (which continues from the cross forward, forever), and by "having placed" (which is finished). He placed this message in the apostles and witnesses of Christ, and through them, in all believers. It has been delivered once for all, Jude 3).
36. Having given us this ministry (v 18) and message (v 19), God made us His ambassadors.
37. This verb is elsewhere only in Eph 6:20. GK *4563*. Related to "delegation" in Lk 14:32; 19:14.
38. This is the word "as" in the sense of "seeing that, since, because". Same word as in 2 Pet 1:3. Generally, it is rendered this way when it is giving a true relation; and as "as-*though*, as-*if*" when it is giving a false or theoretical relation, as in Act 23:15, 20; 27:30; 28:19; 1 Cor 4:18; 1 Pet 4:12. Here, Paul means we are His ambassadors because God is in fact appealing through the message He placed in us (v 19), just as a president does through a message sent to another country. GK *6055*.
39. On this word, see "exhorting" in Rom 12:8. The combination "appeal... beg" is also in 2 Cor 8:4; 10:1-2.

A. 2 Cor 3:1   B. 2 Cor 11:16   C. Rev 2:23   D. 1 Jn 4:16   E. 1 Cor 12:5   F. Rom 3:28, consider   G. Mt 6:14   H. Act 19:21, put   J. 1 Cor 12:8, word

1D. We are begging¹ on behalf of Christ— "Be reconciled^A to God! °He² made^B the *One* not having known^C sin *to be* sin³ for us, in order that **we** might become *the* righteousness^D *of* God in Him". °And working-with *Him*⁴, we also are appealing^E *that* **you**⁵ not receive the grace *of* God in vain⁶ 21

6:1

    1E. For⁷ He says [in Isa 49:8], "I heard you *at the* acceptable^F time. And I helped^G you on *the* day *of* salvation^H". Behold— now *is the* very-acceptable⁸ time. Behold— now *is the* day *of* salvation 2

2D. In⁹ nothing¹⁰ giving^J **any** opportunity-for-stumbling¹¹, in order that the ministry^K may not be faulted^L 3
3D. But in everything, as God's servants^M, commending^N ourselves 4

    1E. In great endurance^O— in¹² afflictions^P, in constraints^Q, in distresses¹³; °in beatings^R, in prisons^S, in disturbances¹⁴; in labors^T, in watchings¹⁵, in fastings^U 5
    2E. In purity^V, in knowledge, in patience^W, in kindness^X; in *a* holy spirit¹⁶, in sincere¹⁷ love, °in *the* word *of* truth¹⁸, in *the* power *of* God 6

7

    3E. Through¹⁹ the weapons²⁰ *of* righteousness²¹ *for* the right *hand* and *the* left²²; through²³ glory and dishonor^Y, through evil-report and good-report²⁴ 8
    4E. As deceivers^Z and true^AA *ones*, °as being not-known^BB and being fully-known^CC; as dying and behold we live, as being disciplined²⁵ and not being put-to-death^DD; as being grieved^EE but always rejoicing^FF; as poor^GG but enriching^HH many, as having nothing and holding-on-to²⁶ all *things* 9

10

8B. Our mouth²⁷ has opened to you, Corinthians, our heart has been opened-wide. °You are not restrained²⁸ in us, but you are restrained in your *own* deep-feelings^JJ. °Now *as* the same return²⁹— I speak as *to my* children^KK— **you** also open-wide³⁰ 11-12

13

    1C. Do not be *ones* being mis-yoked³¹ *to* unbelievers³² 14

        1D. For what partnership³³ *is there for* righteousness and lawlessness^LL? Or³⁴ what fellowship^MM *is there for* light with darkness?
        2D. And what *is the* harmony³⁵ *of* Christ with Beliar³⁶? Or what share³⁷ *is there for a* believer with *an* unbeliever? 15
        3D. And what agreement³⁸ *is there for the* temple *of* God with idols 16
        4D. For **we**³⁹ are *the* temple *of the* living God, just as God said [in Lev 26:12], that "I will dwell^NN in them, and I will walk-among *them,* and I will be their God, and **they** will be My people"
        5D. Therefore, "Come out of their midst and be separated⁴⁰", says *the* Lord, "and do not touch^OO *an* unclean *thing*⁴¹" [Isa 52:11] 17

            1E. "And **I** will take you in⁴² °and be *a* father⁴³ *to* you 18
            2E. "And **you** will be sons and daughters *to* me", says *the* Lord Almighty^PP

        6D. Therefore, having **these** promises, beloved^QQ, let us cleanse^RR ourselves from every stain⁴⁴ *of* flesh and spirit, perfecting⁴⁵ holiness^SS in *the* fear *of* God 7:1

2C. Make-room-for^TT us— we wronged^UU no one, we corrupted⁴⁶ no one, we exploited⁴⁷ no one. I am not speaking⁴⁸ for *your* condemnation⁴⁹ 2

3

1. Or, "pleading". On this word, see 8:4.
2. Some manuscripts say "For He..." {K}.
3. That is, in terms of God's relation to it, as with "righteousness" next. He who never knew sin was made our sin, that we who never knew righteousness might become God's righteousness in Him.
4. Some think Paul means "*you*". On "working-with", see Jn 8:46.
5. In 5:21, "Be reconciled" is general, applying to all. Here, Paul specifically applies it to the Corinthians.
6. Or, "for no purpose, without result". On this word, see "empty" in 1 Thes 2:1. Note 6:14-7:1. Some think this will be the result if the Corinthians turn away and follow the ones in 5:12, or the false apostles in 11:13. Compare 13:5; Gal 3:4; 4:11; 5:4; 1 Cor 15:2. Others think Paul is referring to a fruitless and rewardless life before God.
7. This verse applies both to the specific case (v 1), and the general case (5:21).
8. Related to "acceptable" earlier. On this word, see "acceptable" in Rom 15:16.
9. In this arrangement, verses 3 and 4 describe the manner of their "begging" (5:20) in their general ministry as apostles. Others take them as describing the manner of their specific "appealing" (6:1) to the Corinthians.
10. That is, except Christ Himself, who is the "stone of stumbling", Rom 9:33. Note 1 Cor 10:32; Rom 14:13.
11. Used only here. GK *4683*. Related to the word in Rom 14:13.
12. The first three refer to general trials, the second three to specific ones.
13. Or, "difficulties". Elsewhere only in Rom 2:9; 8:35; 2 Cor 12:10. GK *5103*. Related to "restrained" in 4:8.
14. Same word as in Lk 21:9. That is, mob actions, as seen in Acts. On this word, see "disorder" in Jam 3:16.
15. Or, "sleepless nights". Elsewhere only in 11:27. GK *71*. Related to "keep alert" in Eph 6:18. Perhaps Paul means due to ministry, prayer, making tents, traveling, etc.
16. Or, "*the* Holy Spirit". That is, a spirit that is holy, as in 1 Cor 7:34. Compare 2 Cor 7:1.
17. Or, "genuine, without hypocrisy". On this word, see Rom 12:9.
18. Some think Paul means "truthful speech"; others, the message characterized by truth, the gospel, as in Col 1:5; others, the declaration of the truth.
19. Or, "With, By", that is, by means of. Same word as "through" next, though used in a different sense there. GK *1328*.
20. Same word as in 10:4, on which see Rom 13:12.
21. That is, weapons proceeding from, or belonging to, or supplied by, or used for righteousness.
22. Some think Paul means "fully armed for any fight from any direction". Others think he means offensive weapons for the right hand (a sword), defensive weapons for the left (a shield), in keeping with the soldier of that day.
23. That is, by way of, with, amid.
24. Or, "slander and praise, ill-repute and good-repute". They are related, opposite words. Both are used only here. GK *1556* (related to "slander" in 1 Cor 4:13) and GK *2367* (related to "commendable" in Phil 4:8).
25. Compare Ps 118:18. On this word, see 1 Cor 11:32.
26. Compare 1 Cor 7:30. On this word, see "holding down" in Rom 1:18.
27. Used 78 times. GK *5125*.
28. Or, "cramped, distressed". Same word as in 4:8. There is no restraint of love in us toward you Corinthians, no cramping of space for you in our hearts. But you are restrained in your hearts toward us, you have a small cramped space for us there.
29. Or, "recompense, requital". Or, "Now *give* the same return". That is, as the same recompense due me (love from one's children) which was due you (love from one's father), open wide your hearts to me. Repay my open heart of fatherly love toward you with your open heart of love for me as my spiritual children. This involves both a turning from those misleading them, 6:14-7:1, and a turning to Paul, 7:2. On this word, see Rom 1:27.
30. That is, your hearts, as in v 11. Same word as in v 11. Elsewhere only as "widen" in Mt 23:5. GK *4425*.
31. This word means "yoked to a different species of animal", like a donkey and an ox (Deut 22:10). Paul is broadly referring to various kinds of relationships. Used only here. GK *2282*.
32. As in 6:1, Paul pointedly addresses the Corinthians about a key problem. This was one source of their mistaken attitudes toward Paul, and their less than wide-open feelings toward him.
33. Used only here. GK *3580*. Related to "companions" (partners) in Lk 5:7.
34. Some manuscripts say "And" {K}.
35. Or, "agreement", a blending of voices, a shared interest. Used only here. GK *5245*. Related to "agreement" in 1 Cor 7:5; "music" in Lk 15:25; and "agree" in Mt 18:19.
36. This is a transliterated Hebrew word meaning "worthlessness". It is a name of Satan. Used only here. GK *1016*. Some manuscripts say "Belial" {K}.
37. Or, "portion". On this word, see "part" in Col 1:12.
38. This word is used of a decision agreed upon by vote, a mutual decision. Used only here. GK *5161*. Related to "consented" in Lk 23:51.
39. Some manuscripts say "**you**" {B}.
40. Or, "set apart". On this word, see Rom 1:1.
41. Or, "*person*", as perhaps indicated by the context here (v 14), on which compare Act 10:28; 1 Cor 7:14.
42. This word, "take in, welcome in, receive in", is used only here. GK *1654*. Related to "welcome" in Mt 10:40.
43. More literally, "be for *a* father... be for sons", a Hebrew way of speaking.
44. Or, "defilement". Used only here. GK *3663*. Related to "stain" in 1 Cor 8:7.
45. Or, "completing, finishing, accomplishing, bringing about, bringing to its end, bringing to completeness". Same word as in Gal 3:3; Phil 1:6. Elsewhere only as "complete" in Rom 15:28; 2 Cor 8:6, 11; Heb 8:5; and "accomplish" in Heb 9:6; 1 Pet 5:9. GK *2200*. Related to "finished" in Rev 10:7, and "perfect" in Heb 2:10.
46. Or, "destroyed, ruined". On this word, see "ruin" in 1 Cor 3:17.
47. Or, "defrauded". On this word, see 1 Thes 4:6.
48. Paul may be referring to the defense he just made for himself in v 2. Or, he may be referring more broadly to his defense so far in the letter.
49. That is, to condemn you. Elsewhere only in 3:9. GK *2892*.

A. Rom 5:10 B. Rev 13:13, does C. Lk 1:34 D. Rom 1:17 E. Rom 12:8, exhorting F. Lk 4:19 G. Rev 12:16 H. Lk 19:9 J. Eph 1:22 K. 1 Cor 12:5 L. 2 Cor 8:20 M. 1 Cor 3:5 N. 2 Cor 3:1 O. Jam 1:3 P. Rev 7:14 Q. 1 Cor 7:26, necessity R. Rev 13:3, wound S. Act 5:22 T. 1 Cor 3:8 U. 2 Cor 11:27 V. 2 Cor 11:3 W. Heb 6:12 X. Rom 3:12, goodness Y. 2 Tim 2:20 Z. 1 Tim 4:1, deceitful AA. Jn 6:55 BB. Rom 10:3, ignorant of CC. Col 1:6, understood DD. Rom 7:4 EE. 2 Cor 7:9 FF. 2 Cor 13:11 GG. Gal 4:9 HH. 1 Cor 1:5 JJ. Phil 1:8 KK. 1 Jn 3:1 LL. 1 Jn 3:4 MM. 1 Cor 9:1 NN. Col 3:16 OO. 1 Cor 7:1 PP. Rev 1:8 QQ. Mt 3:17 RR. Heb 9:22 SS. Rom 1:4 TT. 2 Pet 3:9 UU. Act 7:24

		Verse
1D. For I have said-before[A] that you are in our hearts so as to die-together[1] and to live-together[2]		
2D. *There is* great confidence[B] *in* me toward you		4
3D. *There is* much boasting[3] *by* me about you		

9B. I have been filled[C] *with* comfort[D]. I am super-abounding[E] *with* joy in all our affliction[F]

    1C. For indeed we having come to Macedonia,[4] our flesh[5] had no rest[G], but *we were* being afflicted[H]   5
in every *way*— battles[6] outside, fears[J] inside

    2C. But the *One* comforting[K] the downcast[7], God, comforted us by the coming *of* Titus— and not   6-7
only by his coming, but also by the comfort[D] *with* which he was comforted over you while
reporting[L] *to* us your yearning[M], your mourning, your zeal[N] for me, so that I rejoiced[O] more

        1D. Because even though[8] I grieved[P] you by the letter[9], I do not regret[Q] *it*   8

        2D. Even though[10] I was regretting *it* (for[11] I see that that letter grieved you, even though[12] for
an hour), now I am rejoicing[O]— not that you were grieved, but that you were grieved[13]   9
into repentance[R]

            1E. For you were grieved in-accordance-with[14] God, in order that you might suffer-loss[S]
in nothing by us

                1F. For the grief[15] in accordance with God works[T] unregretted[16] repentance[17]   10
leading-to[18] salvation[U]

                2F. But the grief *of* the world produces[V] death

            2E. For behold this very *thing,* the being grieved[P] in accordance with God, how much   11
earnestness[19] it produced[V] *in* you— even *a* defense[20], even indignation[21], even fear[22],
even yearning[23], even zeal[24], even punishment[25]. In everything you demonstrated[W]
yourselves to be pure[X] *in* the matter[Y]

            3E. So even though[26] I wrote *to* you [causing grief], *it was*   12

                1F. Not[27] for the sake of the *one* having done wrong[28]
                2F. Nor for the sake of the *one* having been wronged[29]
                3F. But for the sake of making your earnestness[Z] for us[30] evident[AA] to you in the
sight of God
                4F. For this reason,[31] we have been comforted[K]   13

    3C. But[32] in addition to our comfort[D], we rejoiced[O] even more abundantly over the joy *of* Titus,
because his spirit has been refreshed[BB] by you all

        1D. Because if I have boasted[CC] anything *to* him about you, I was not put-to-shame[DD]. But as   14
we spoke all *things to* you in truth, so also our boasting before Titus proved-to-be *the* truth
        2D. And his deep-feelings[EE] are especially for you, while remembering the obedience[FF] *of*   15
you all— how you received[GG] him with fear and trembling[33]

    4C. I[34] am rejoicing[O] because in everything I am confident[HH] in you   16

3A. Now we make known *to* you, brothers, the grace *of* God having been granted[35] in the churches *of*   8:1
Macedonia[36]—

    1B. That in *a* great test[37] of affliction[F], their abundance[38] *of* joy and their down deep[39] poverty[40]   2
abounded[41] into the riches *of* their generosity[JJ]

1. Elsewhere only as "die with" in Mk 14:31; 2 Tim 2:11. GK *5271*.
2. Or, "so as to die-with *you* and to live-with *you*". Others render it "so that *you* died with *us* and live with *us*". Some explain the fact that "die" is first by taking Paul to mean "die in Christ, live our Christian lives". Elsewhere only as "live with" in Rom 6:8 and 2 Tim 2:11, where "dies" also comes first. GK *5182*.
3. This noun refers to the act of boasting. Elsewhere only in Rom 3:27; 15:17; 1 Cor 15:31; 2 Cor 1:12; 7:14; 8:24; 11:10, 17; 1 Thes 2:19; Jam 4:16. GK *3018*. See Phil 1:26 on "boast" and 2 Cor 11:16 on the verb, "to boast". The "boast" word group is used 59 times in the NT, almost half in this book, all but 4 by Paul.
4. That is, when we came into Macedonia. Paul resumes where he left off in 2:13. "Rest" also occurs in 2:13.
5. Note that in 2:13 Paul said "spirit".
6. Or, "fights, conflicts". That is, with spiritual enemies. On this word, see 2 Tim 2:23.
7. Or, "depressed, lowly, humble". On this word, see "lowly" in Jam 1:9.
8. More literally, "Because if I even caused you grief...". That is, "assuming that I even caused you grief...". The same idiom occurs twice more in this verse, and in v 12. On this idiom, see "if also" in 1 Cor 7:21.
9. On this letter, see 2:3.
10. More literally, "If I even was regretting it", assuming that I even was regretting it.
11. Some manuscripts omit this word. In addition, others have a participle, "seeing that the letter..." {C}.
12. More literally, "If even for *an* hour", assuming that it was even for a short time.
13. This word means "to grieve, cause grief, sorrow, pain, distress". Same word as in Mt 14:9; 17:23; 18:31; 19:22; 26:22, 37; Mk 10:22; 14:19; Jn 16:20; 21:17; Rom 14:15; 2 Cor 2:2, 4, 5; 6:10; 7:8, 9, 11; Eph 4:30; 1Thes 4:13; 1 Pet 1:6. Elsewhere only as "cause grief" in 2 Cor 2:5. GK *3382*. Related to "grief" in v 10.
14. Or, "according to [the will of] God". Likewise in v 10, 11.
15. Or, "sorrow, pain, distress". Same word as in Lk 22:45; Jn 16:6, 20, 21, 22; Rom 9:2; 2 Cor 2:1, 3, 7; 7:10; 9:7; Phil 2:27; Heb 12:11. Elsewhere only as "sorrows" in 1 Pet 2:19. GK *3383*.
16. Others render this "repentance for unregretted salvation", a salvation that will never be regretted. On this word, see "without regret" in Rom 11:29.
17. Worldly (human) sorrow is simply regret over a loss or failure. Repentance is a change of mind leading to a change of behavior. Elsewhere only in Mt 3:8, 11; Mk 1:4; Lk 3:3, 8; 5:32; 15:7; 24:47; Act 5:31; 11:18; 13:24; 19:4; 20:21; 26:20; Rom 2:4; 2 Cor 7:9; 2 Tim 2:25; Heb 6:1, 6; 12:17; 2 Pet 3:9. GK *3567*. The related verb is in Act 26:20.
18. Or, "for". On this word, see "resulting in" in Rom 5:16.
19. That is, earnestness to obey God, to do what is right before Him in response to that grief. On this word, see 8:16. Same word as in v 12.
20. That is, a verbal defense in a good sense, perhaps of their loyalty to God and Paul. On this word, see 1 Pet 3:15.
21. That is, anger toward the wrongs committed among them. Used only here. GK *25*. Related to the word in Mt 20:24.
22. Paul may mean fear of God; of Paul coming with a rod, 1 Cor 4:21; or of Titus, v 15. On this word, see Eph 5:21.
23. Some think Paul means a yearning for Paul, as in v 7; a yearning for him to come. Elsewhere only in v 7. GK *2161*. Related word in 1 Pet 2:2.
24. Some think Paul means zeal to carry out Paul's instructions; a zeal for Paul (v 7), for God, and for their church. On this word, see "jealousy" in 11:2.
25. Paul is referring to the man in 2:5-6. On this word, see 2 Thes 1:8. The related verb is in 10:6.
26. More literally, "If I even wrote *to* you [causing grief]", accepting that I even did this.
27. That is, not primarily, not mainly. Same idiom as in 3:10. In comparison to the main reason, it was not for this reason.
28. This statement leads some to think that the person in view here and in 2:4-8, 11 could not be the man described in 1 Cor 5. Would Paul make a statement like this about a person like that? Others think Paul is simply stating that his primary purpose was to affect the church, not the man. Otherwise he would have written to him directly.
29. Some think Paul means the father in 1 Cor 5:1; others, Paul himself (see 2:5). Same word as in the previous phrase, and as 7:2.
30. The phrase "earnestness for" is also in 8:16. Compare "zeal for" in 7:7, which uses a different word. Some manuscripts say "our earnestness for you" {N}.
31. That is, because this was our intention, we were comforted by your response.
32. Some manuscripts connect this clause with the previous one, and say "your" instead of "our", so that it says "For this reason we have been comforted in your comfort. And we rejoiced even more abundantly..." {N}.
33. On "fear and trembling", see Phil 2:12.
34. Some manuscripts say "Therefore I..." {K}.
35. Or, "given". Paul is referring to the grace seen in the joy and generosity he mentions next in v 2. On this word, see "give" in Eph 1:22.
36. That is, where Paul was laboring at the time he was writing this letter, 7:5. The churches we know about in Macedonia are those at Philippi, Thessalonica, and Berea (Act 16:12-17:14).
37. Or, "trial". Related to "proving", v 8. On this word, see "approvedness" in 2:9. That is, a testing characterized by affliction that "proved" their genuineness as Christians. Compare 1 Thes 1:6, 2:14.
38. Or, "surplus". Elsewhere only in Rom 5:17; 2 Cor 10:15; Jam 1:21. GK *4353*. Related to "abounded" later in the verse.
39. Same word as in Lk 5:4; 1 Cor 2:10. Elsewhere only as "depth" in Mt 13:5; Mk 4:5; Rom 8:39; 11:33; Eph 3:18. GK *958*. The related verb is in Lk 6:48.
40. That is, extreme poverty. Same word as in v 9.
41. This word means "to abound, exceed, overflow, surpass, be in excess, be more than enough, be leftover". Same word as in Mt 5:20; Mk 12:44; Lk 12:15; 15:17; 21:4; Act 16:5; Rom 3:7; 5:15; 15:13; 1 Cor 8:8; 14:12; 15:58; 2 Cor 1:5; 3:9; 4:15; 8:7; 9:8, 12; Phil 1:9, 26; 4:12, 18; Col 2:7; 1 Thes 3:12; 4:1, 10. Elsewhere only as "cause to abound" in Mt 13:12; 25:29; 2 Cor 9:8; Eph 1:8; and "leftover" in Mt 14:20; 15:37; Lk 9:17; Jn 6:12, 13. GK *4355*. Related to "abundance" in v 2 and in v 14.

A. Jude 17, spoken beforehand B. Heb 4:16 C. Eph 5:18 D. Act 4:36, encouragement E. Rom 5:20 F. Rev 7:14 G. 2 Cor 8:13 H. 2 Cor 4:8 J. Eph 5:21 K. Rom 12:8, exhorting L. Jn 16:13, declare M. 2 Cor 7:11 N. 2 Cor 11:2, jealousy O. 2 Cor 13:11 P. 2 Cor 7:9 Q. Mt 21:29 R. 2 Cor 7:10 S. 1 Cor 3:15 T. Mt 26:10 U. Lk 19:9 V. Phil 2:12, work out W. Rom 5:8 X. 1 Pet 3:2 Y. Mt 18:19 Z. 2 Cor 8:16 AA. 1 Jn 2:19, made evident BB. Phm 7 CC. 2 Cor 11:16 DD. Rom 5:5 EE. Phil 1:8 FF. Rom 16:26 GG. Mt 10:40, welcome HH. 2 Cor 5:6 JJ. Rom 12:8

1C. Because I testify[A] *that they gave*   3

    1D. In accordance with *their* ability[1], and beyond *their* ability
    2D. Of-*their*-own-accord[2]
    3D. With *a* great appeal[B] begging[3] *from* us[4] the favor[5] and the partnership[6] *of this* ministry[C]   4
        to the saints[D]
    4D. And not as we hoped[7], but they gave **themselves** first[8] *to* the Lord and *to* us by *the* will   5
        of God

2C. So that[9] we urged[10] Titus that just as he previously-began[11], so also he should complete[12] this   6
    grace[13] with reference to you also

2B. But just as you are abounding[E] in everything— *in* faith and speech[F] and knowledge[G] and all   7
earnestness[H], and *in* the love from us in you[14]— *I urge* that you also be abounding in this grace[J]

    1C. I am not speaking by way of command[K], but *am* proving[15] through the earnestness[H] *of* others   8
    the genuineness[16] *of* your love also

        1D. For you know the grace[17] *of* our Lord Jesus Christ— that for your[18] sakes He became-poor[19]   9
        while being rich[20], in order that **you** might become-rich[L] *by* the poverty[21] *of* that One

    2C. And I am giving *an* opinion[M] in this *matter*, for this[22] is beneficial[N] *for* you, who began-   10
    beforehand[23] from last year not only the doing, but the wanting[O] *to do*
    3C. But now indeed complete[24] the doing, so that just as *was* the eagerness[25] *of* the wanting[O], so   11
    also *may be* the completing out of *what you* have

        1D. For if the eagerness is there, *it is* acceptable[26] to whatever degree *a person* may have, not   12
        to-the-degree[27] he does not have[28]
        2D. For *it is* not in order that *there may be* rest[29] *for* others, affliction[30] *for* you, but out of   13
        equality[31]—* at the present time your abundance[32] *being* for the need[P] *of* those *ones,* in   14
        order that the abundance *of* those *ones* also may come-to-be for your need[33], so that there
        may be equality

            1E. Just as it has been written [in Ex 16:18], "The *one gathering* much did not increase[34],   15
            and the *one gathering* little did not have-less"

3B. Now thanks[J] *be* to God, the *One* having given[35] the same earnestness[36] for you in the heart *of* Titus   16

    1C. Because he welcomed[Q] **the urging**[37]— but being more earnest[38], went-out[39] to you of-*his*-   17
    own-accord[R]!

1. Or, "power, strength, capability". Same word as next. On this word, see "power" in Mk 5:30.
2. Or, "voluntarily, by *their* own choice". Elsewhere only in v 17. GK *882*.
3. This shows the degree of the Macedonians' initiative in the matter. Same two root words as in 2 Cor 5:20 and 10:1-2, "appealing... begging". Used together only in these three places. The word "beg" also means "to ask, pray", and is used 22 times. GK *1289*.
4. Some manuscripts add "*that* we accept" {N}, which changes the following to "the grace-*gift* and the partnership".
5. Or, "grace". The Macedonians begged Paul for the "grace" (favor, v 4) to share in this "grace" (v 6, 7, 19) to the saints, by the "grace" (v 1) of God, remembering the "grace" (v 9) of Jesus, giving "grace" (thanks, v 16) to God. How Paul richly uses this word in this chapter! Yet he does not use the related word "gift" (1 Cor 1:7) at all, nor does he use the normal verb "to give" in relation to their offering. On this word, see "grace" in Eph 2:8.
6. Or, "participation". On this word, see "fellowship" in 1 Cor 1:9.
7. Or, "expected". The Macedonians went far beyond what Paul expected— giving themselves, not just their money. On this word, see "put hope" in Jn 5:45.
8. Some think Paul means "first" in order; others, "first" in importance; others, both. The giving by the Macedonians followed their dedication of themselves to the Lord and to Paul. It was a fruit of this broader and deeper dedication of themselves to the service of Christ. It was not simply a gracious act of charity.
9. Paul's appeal to Titus to complete the collection in Corinth springs from the Macedonians' example of giving (8:1-5), to whom Paul had used the Achaians (Corinthians) as an example of being prepared to give (9:2).
10. Or, "appealed to". Related to "appeal" in v 4, and "urging" in v 17, where Titus responds to this. On this word, see "exhorting" in Rom 12:8.
11. That is, in the implementation of 1 Cor 16:1-4, before Titus returned to Paul in 2 Cor 7:6. Same word as "began beforehand" in v 10.
12. Same word as in v 11.
13. Or, "grace-*gift*, [act of] grace". On this word, see Eph 2:8. Paul calls this a "collection" (1 Cor 16:1); a "contribution" or, "sharing, fellowship" (2 Cor 9:13; Rom 15:26); a "grace *gift*" (1 Cor 16:3; 2 Cor 8:19); a "ministry, service" (2 Cor 9:1); a "blessing" (2 Cor 9:5); a "priestly service" (2 Cor 9:12).
14. Some manuscripts say "from you in us" {C}.
15. Or, "testing, proving by test". Same word as "prove" in v 22. On this word, see "approve" in Rom 12:2. Paul will "prove" the extent of the Corinthians' love using the earnestness of the Macedonians as the standard of comparison.
16. Or, the "legitimacy". The root idea is "legitimate birth". Elsewhere only as "genuine" in Phil 4:3; 1 Tim 1:2; Tit 1:4. GK *1188*. Related to "genuinely" in Phil 2:20.
17. Or, "grace *gift*", "[act of] grace". Same word as in v 6.
18. Some manuscripts say "our" {B}.
19. Used only here. GK *4776*.
20. Compare Phil 2:6. When the Son became a man, He left His glory (Jn 17:5) and became impoverished by comparison. On this adjective, see 1 Tim 6:17.
21. Elsewhere only in 8:2; Rev 2:9. GK *4775*. Related to "became poor" in this verse, and to "poor" in Gal 4:9.
22. Some think Paul means "giving my opinion" (rather than a command); others, the Corinthians' participation in this collection.
23. Some think Paul means the Corinthians began before the Macedonians got involved; others, before Paul had asked them. Their "wanting" may have led to a question to Paul as to how they could become involved, which he answered in 1 Cor 16:1-4. Elsewhere only as "previously-began" in v 6. GK *4599*.
24. Or, "bring to completion". Same word as later in the verse. On this word, see "perfecting" in 7:1.
25. Same word as in v 12, 19.
26. That is, a gift, the concrete expression of the eagerness, is acceptable. On this word, see Rom 15:16.
27. Or, "to the extent, insofar as". Same word as earlier in the verse and as 1 Pet 4:13. Elsewhere only as "as" Rom 8:26. GK *2771*.
28. Compare 1 Cor 16:2. The Macedonians gave more, 2 Cor 8:3.
29. Or, "relief, relaxation, abatement". Same word as in 2 Cor 2:13; 7:5; 2 Thes 1:7. Elsewhere only as "relaxation" in Act 24:23. GK *457*.
30. Or, "pressure, distress, trouble", because you gave too much. On this word, see Rev 7:14. Some manuscripts say "and affliction" {N}.
31. Or, "fairness, equity". Same word as in v 14. Elsewhere only as "fairness" in Col 4:1. GK *2699*.
32. Same word as in Mt 12:34; Lk 6:45. Elsewhere only as "leftovers" in Mk 8:8. GK *4354*. Related to the words in v 2.
33. Some think Paul means "so they can help you materially someday when you need it"; others, "so they can help you with your spiritual needs, based on the mutual relationship established", as in 9:14 (in prayer); Rom 15:27; 1 Cor 9:11; Phil 4:17 (fruit).
34. Elsewhere only in Rom 5:20; 6:1; 2 Cor 4:15; Phil 4:17; 1 Thes 3:12; 2 Thes 1:3; 2 Pet 1:8. GK *4429*. This word is often combined with "abound", to which it leads. In Ex 16, the Israelites gathered the same amount of manna for each person, so none had an excess or a shortage. The sense here is "did not increase [beyond his need]... have less [than his need]".
35. Or, "granted". Same word as in 8:1. Some manuscripts say "the God giving..." {N}.
36. Or, "diligence, eagerness". That is, the same kind as Paul's. Same word as in 7:11, 12; 8:7, 8. Elsewhere only as "diligence" in Rom 12:8, 11; Heb 6:11; 2 Pet 1:5; "effort" in Jude 3; and "haste" in Mk 6:25; Lk 1:39. GK *5082*. Related to the word in v 17.
37. Or, "appeal". Paul uses grammar that emphasizes the contrast between the two halves of this sentence, between the external urging of Paul and the internal choice of Titus. This word is related to "urge" in v 6, and refers to that verse. Same word as "appeal" in v 4.
38. Or, "more diligent, eager". Titus apparently already intended to return, or to suggest to Paul that he return, and so welcomed Paul's appeal. His earnestness was more than just a response to Paul's urging. He went out to them again with this letter. Elsewhere only as "diligent" twice in v 22. GK *5080*. Related to "earnestness" in v 16; "diligently" in Tit 3:13; and "be diligent" in Eph 4:3.
39. That is, along with this letter, and with the brothers mentioned next. Titus "went out", and Paul "sent" the next two with him, from the Corinthians' perspective, when they read this letter. Paul could also have said, "he is going out".

A. Jn 1:7 B. Act 4:36, encouragement C. 1 Cor 12:5 D. 1 Pet 1:16, holy E. 2 Cor 8:2 F. 1 Cor 12:8, word G. 1 Cor 12:8 H. 2 Cor 8:16 J. Eph 2:8, grace K. Rom 16:26 L. 1 Tim 6:18 M. 1 Cor 1:10, purpose N. 1 Cor 6:12 O. Jn 7:17, willing P. Phil 2:30, lack Q. Mt 10:40 R. 2 Cor 8:3

2C.	And we sent with him the brother[1] whose praise[A] in[2] the good-news[3] *is* through all the churches	18
	1D. And not only *this,* but *who was* also appointed[4] by the churches[5] *to be* our fellow-traveler[6] with[7] this grace-*gift*[B] being ministered[C] by us	19
	1E. For[8] the glory *of* the Lord Himself[9]; and *to show* our[10] eagerness[11]	
	2D. Avoiding[12] this— *that* anyone should fault[13] us in this abundance[14] being ministered[C] by us	20
	1E. For we are providing-for[15] good[D] *things*— not only in the sight of *the* Lord, but also in the sight of people[E]	21
3C.	And we sent with them our brother whom we often proved[16] in many *things as* being diligent[17], but now *is* much more diligent *with* great confidence[F] in you	22
4C.	If *any* ask[18] about Titus— *he is* my partner[G] and fellow-worker[H] for you; if *as to* our brothers[19]— they are delegates[20] *of* the churches, *a* glory *of* Christ[21]	23
5C.	Therefore, *be* demonstrating[22] to them, to[23] *the* face[24] *of* the churches, the demonstration[25] *of* your love and our boasting[J] about you	24
	1D. For indeed, it is superfluous *for* me to write *to* you concerning *the* ministry[26] to the saints[27]	9:1
	1E. For I know your eagerness[K], which I am boasting about you *to the* Macedonians— that "Achaia has been prepared [to give] since last year". And your zeal[L] stirred-up[M] the majority	2
	2D. But I sent the brothers in order that our boast about you might not be made-empty[N] in this respect— in order that, just as I was saying,[28] you may be prepared[29]	3
	1E. *That* we should not somehow be put-to-shame[O] (that I[30] not say you) in this confidence[31] if Macedonians come with me and find you unprepared[32]	4
	2E. Therefore I regarded[P] *it* necessary[Q] to urge[R] the brothers that they go-ahead to you and prepare-beforehand your previously-promised[33] blessing[34]— *that* this *may* be ready[S] thus as *a* blessing and not as greediness[35]	5
4B.	Now this *I say*[36]— the *one* sowing[37] sparingly[38] will also reap sparingly. And the *one* sowing for[39] blessings will also reap for blessings. °Each *should give* just as he has chosen-beforehand[40] *in his* heart— not out of grief[41], or out of compulsion[42]	6 7
	1C. For God loves *a* cheerful[43] giver	

1. Note 12:18. It is not known to whom Paul is referring. Perhaps it is one of those mentioned in Act 20:4.
2. Or, "in connection with". GK *1877*.
3. That is, who is praised by all the churches in connection with his work in spreading the gospel. On this word, see 1 Cor 15:1.
4. Or, "chosen, elected". More literally, "but also having been appointed". This man was chosen by the churches to accompany their gift. Note 1 Cor 16:3. This word means "to stretch out the hand, to vote by raising the hand", and simply "to appoint". Elsewhere only in Act 14:23. GK *5936*. Related to "chosen beforehand" in Act 10:41.
5. Which churches? If 9:4 implies that they were not Macedonians, perhaps here Paul means those of Asia (Act 20:4).
6. Elsewhere only in Act 19:29, where it is used of Gaius and Aristarchus. GK *5292*.
7. That is, "together with". Some manuscripts say "in" {N}.
8. Some take this with "appointed", expressing the purpose of the churches; others, with "ministered", expressing the purpose of Paul.
9. Some manuscripts omit this word; others say "For the same glory *of the* Lord" {C}.
10. Some manuscripts say "your" {K}.
11. Or, "willingness, readiness". That is, our eagerness to help the believers in Jerusalem. Elsewhere only in 8:11, 12; 9:2; Act 17:11. GK *4608*. Related to words in 1 Pet 5:2; and in Rom 1:15.
12. Or, "Keeping away from". That is, "we sent with him... avoiding". On this word, see "keep away" in 2 Thes 3:6.
13. Or, "find fault with, blame, criticize, censure". Elsewhere only in 6:3. GK *3699*. Related to "blemish" (a physical fault) in 2 Pet 2:13.
14. That is, this bountiful gift. Used only here. GK *103*.
15. Or, "taking thought for, exercising foresight for". Elsewhere only in Rom 12:17; 1 Tim 5:8. GK *4629*. Related to "provision" in Rom 13:14. Some manuscripts say "... by us, while providing-for..." {N}.
16. Or, "proved by testing". Same word as in v 8.
17. Same word as later in the verse, and as "more earnest" in v 17. A person begins a work with eagerness and earnest zeal. A person is proven to have diligence as the work is carried out and completed.
18. Paul is giving a written commendation of these people, the kind mentioned in 3:1. Titus represents Paul.
19. That is, the one in v 18 and the one in v 22.
20. Or, "official representatives, apostles". The brothers represent the churches. On this word, see "apostle" in 1 Cor 12:28.
21. This is a second description of these brothers, parallel with "delegates". Paul may mean Christ's glory, a glory proceeding from Christ, or a glory to Christ. It does not modify "churches".
22. Or, "giving proof of, showing". Some manuscripts have this as a command {N}, so that it says "Therefore, demonstrate... the demonstration of your love". That is, through your reception of these brothers and your assembling of your gift with their help. On this word, see Eph 2:7.
23. Some manuscripts say "and to" {K}.
24. Or, "presence". This is the literal rendering of this idiom, which means "before the churches". These men represent the face or presence of their churches witnessing what the Corinthians do. Whatever the Corinthians do, they do before these men and the churches they represent. On this word, see "presence" in Lk 9:52.
25. Or, "sign, proof, evidence". On this word, see Rom 3:25. Related to "demonstrating" earlier.
26. Or, "service". On this word, see 1 Cor 12:5.
27. Same phrase as 8:4, "the ministry to the saints". That is, to write regarding the details of this ministry to the poor in Jerusalem and your need to be part of it. The Corinthians already knew this. There is no need to be promoting this ministry. Note that our limited knowledge of the details of this ministry come from elsewhere, Rom 15:26; 1 Cor 16:1-4.
28. That is, to the Macedonians, v 2. Paul was saying that "they have been prepared", v 2. Now he wants to make sure that they are really prepared.
29. Or, "ready". This is a participle, "you may be having been prepared", that is, that you may stand prepared. Same word as in v 2. Elsewhere only in Act 10:10; 1 Cor 14:8. GK *4186*. Related to "preparation" in Jn 19:31.
30. That is, to say nothing of you. The Corinthians would bear the greater shame if they failed to complete what they began. Some manuscripts say "we" {B}.
31. Or, "project, undertaking". On this word, see "assurance" in Heb 11:1. Some give this a subjective meaning, "this confidence I have in you on the basis of which I boasted about you". Paul's boast would be made empty (v 3) if his confidence in them proved false. Others give it an objective meaning, "lest we be put to shame in this project we are organizing for the benefit of Jerusalem and the church". Some manuscripts add "*of* boasting" {B}, as in 11:17.
32. Used only here. GK *564*. Related to the word in v 3.
33. This is a participle, "your blessing having been previously promised". Some think Paul means "promised by you"; others, "promised by me" to the Macedonians, as in v 2. Elsewhere only as "promised beforehand" in Rom 1:2. GK *4600*.
34. That is, your blessing for the poor in Jerusalem, the gift you promised to give as a blessing to them. Same word as four times in v 5-6, and as in Rom 15:29; 1 Cor 10:16; Gal 3:14; Eph 1:3; Heb 6:7; 12:17; Jam 3:10; 1 Pet 3:9; Rev 5:12, 13; 7:12. Elsewhere only as "flattery" in Rom 16:18. GK *2330*. The related verb is in Lk 6:28.
35. That is, as an exhibit of your blessing upon the Jerusalem church, and not of your greediness in withholding what you promised. On this word, see "greed" in Eph 4:19.
36. Or, "Now *as to* this *giving*", or, "*demonstration*", or "*gift*".
37. Used 52 times. GK *5062*. Related to "seed" in Heb 11:11.
38. Used only in this verse. GK *5768*. Related to "spare" in Rom 11:21.
39. That is, "for the purpose of", or "on the basis of". GK *2093*. "Blessings" is the same word as in v 5. Some take the phrase in an adverbial sense, "sow blessingly", that is, bountifully, generously.
40. Or, "has preferred, chosen for himself, deliberately purposed". Used only here. GK *4576*. The root word is "choose" in 2 Thes 2:13. Some manuscripts say "chooses beforehand" {N}.
41. That is, from a heart grieving or pained over the loss of the money given, from a grudging heart. On this word, see 7:10. Related to the word in Deut 15:10.
42. Or, "necessity". On this word, see "necessity" in 1 Cor 7:26.
43. Or, "happy, merry, glad". Used only here. GK *2659*. Related to "cheerfulness" in Rom 12:8.

A. 1 Cor 4:5 B. 2 Cor 8:6, grace C. 1 Pet 4:10 D. 1 Tim 5:10a E. Mt 4:4, mankind F. 2 Cor 1:15 G. 2 Pet 1:4, sharer H. Rom 16:3 J. 2 Cor 7:4 K. 2 Cor 8:19 L. 2 Cor 11:2, jealousy M. Col 3:21, provoke N. Phil 2:7 O. Rom 5:5 P. Jam 1:2 Q. Tit 3:14 R. Rom 12:8, exhorting S. Mk 14:15, prepared

2C.	And God is able to cause all grace to abound[A] to you in order that in everything, always having all sufficiency[1], you may be abounding for every[2] good work	8
	1D. Just as[3] it has been written [in Ps 112:9], "He scattered[B], he gave *to* the needy[4] *ones*, his righteousness[C] remains[D] forever[E]"	9
3C.	And the *One* supplying[5] seed[6] *to* the *one* sowing, and bread for eating[7], will supply[8] and multiply[F] your seed[9], and will grow[10] the fruits[11] of[12] your righteousness. *In everything[13], *you will*[14] be enriched[G] for all[15] generosity[16]—	10 11
	1D. Which[17] through us is *going to*[18] produce[H] thanksgiving[J] *to* God, *because the ministry[19] *of* this service[20] is not only *going to be* filling-up[21] the needs[K] *of* the saints[L], but also abounding[A] through many thanksgivings[J] *to* God!	12
	1E. Through[22] the approvedness[23] *of* this ministry, *they will be*[24] glorifying[M] God for the obedience[25] *of* your confession[26] to[27] the good-news[N] *of* Christ, and *the* generosity[28] *of* the contribution[29] for them and for all[30]	13

1. Or, "self-sufficiency". Made of two words "self " and "to be enough, sufficient, content" (used in 12:9). It is freedom from circumstances based on contentment before God resulting in a self-sufficiency in Him which enables a generosity toward others. Elsewhere only as "contentment" in 1 Tim 6:6. GK *894*.
2. There is a five-fold repetition of the root word "all, every" here, "**every** grace to abound to you in order that in **every**thing, at **every** time having **every** sufficiency, you may abound for **every** good work".
3. Some think Paul means "God is able... just as", meaning God scatters and gives to the poor through His people abounding in good work, v 8. Others think he means "that you may be abounding... just as", meaning the human giver scatters and gives, and his righteousness, seen in his acts of generosity, will be remembered and rewarded here and hereafter (or, will continue as long as he lives).
4. That is, the working poor. Used only here. GK *4288*. Related to the word in Lk 21:2. Compare the unrelated word "poor" in Gal 4:9.
5. Or, "providing, furnishing, giving, granting". Elsewhere only in Gal 3:5; Col 2:19; 2 Pet 1:5, 11. GK *2220*. Related to the word in Eph 4:16. Some manuscripts have this as a prayer, "Now may the *One* supplying... supply and multiply... and grow..." {N}.
6. That is, physical seed to grow bread. Same word as later in the verse. Used 6 times. GK *5078*. Some manuscripts have a different word here {N}, GK *5065* (the word related to "sowing" in v 6).
7. Or, "food". Some take "bread for eating" with what follows, so that it says "will both supply bread for eating and multiply your seed". On this word, see Mt 6:19.
8. Or, "provide". As God does in the physical realm with seed and its product (bread), so He will do in the spiritual realm with the seed you sow and its product (fruits of righteousness). Same root word as "supplying" earlier in the verse. Elsewhere only in 1 Pet 4:11. GK *5961*.
9. Some think Paul means the resources sown for His kingdom. God will supply and multiply what you sow, the crop of seed you sow, the seed you scatter. Others think he means the resources able to be sown, the store of resources from which one can sow for Him. He will supply and multiply your ability to sow.
10. Or, "cause to grow, increase". Same word as "causing growth" in in 1 Cor 3:6, 7. On this word, see Jn 3:30.
11. Or, "products". On this word, see Mt 26:29.
12. Some think Paul means "fruits *consisting of* righteousness" in your life. The seed you sow in His kingdom grows a crop of righteousness in you. Others think he means "fruits *proceeding from* your [act of] righteousness". From the seed you sow He will grow a harvest of blessings for you, in this life and the next; or, a harvest of blessings for others, taking whatever full-grown form He produces.
13. Some think Paul is referring to the financial ability to be generous; others, to the inward spiritual qualities that would lead one to be generous; others, to both, and the opportunities to express them.
14. Or, "righteousness—*you* being enriched in everything". The grammar is unusual. Some supply the "will be" time relation from the previous verbs, so that this restates v 10 for the specific case in view. Others render this as a participle giving the circumstance in which "your" sowing and growing takes place ("*you* being enriched by God"), continuing the general principle of v 10. Others link this to v 8, making all of v 9 and 10 a parenthesis, "that having all sufficiency, you may be abounding... being enriched".
15. Some think Paul means "every kind of "; others, "every occasion of, every opportunity for".
16. Same word as in 8:2 and 9:13. Others think Paul means "simplicity, singleness of mind" to serve God, the broad category of which generosity is one specific manifestation. On this word, see Rom 12:8.
17. That is, their generosity or singleness, as realized in the specific case in view.
18. The present tense verbs are given a future sense by the context, since the Corinthians' generous participation in this collection is still future, and it is the completion of this endeavor which results in the "producing" because of the "filling up" and "abounding" (v 12), and the "glorifying" God for the Corinthians (v 13). Thus this phrase means "which through our delivery of it will produce thanksgiving by those receiving it".
19. Same word as in Act 11:29 and 12:25, of another delivery of monetary relief. On this word, see 1 Cor 12:5.
20. That is, "the ministry *consisting of* this service". This word means "public service", and in this context, public service for God (for the believing public). It was also used of "priestly service", and some think Paul has this nuance in mind here. Same word as in Lk 1:23; Phil 2:17, 30. Elsewhere only as "ministry" in Heb 8:6; 9:21. GK *3311*. Paul is referring to the Corinthians' ministry in performing this service by giving the money. Related to the verb "minister" in Rom 15:27, which refers to this collection.
21. Or, "supplying, replenishing, fill by adding to". Elsewhere only as "supplied" in 11:9. GK *4650*. Not related to the two words rendered "supply" in v 10.
22. Or, "By", Occasioned by. This verse explains why the believers in Jerusalem will give thanks, v 12. GK *1328*.
23. On this word, see 2:9. It means the approved quality of a thing having been tested. Some think Paul means "the approved nature of this ministry", which is in keeping with the Christian standard of love. Others think he means "the approved quality of your character which this ministry demonstrates", the "proof which this ministry provides as to your obedience and generosity". Compare the opposite case in Jam 2:14-16.
24. This sentence has the same unusual grammar as in v 11. The future sense is supplied from the context. Or, "*They* glorifying God through the approvedness...". "They" refers to the saints abounding with thanksgivings in v 12.
25. Or "submission, compliance". On this word, see "submission" in 1 Tim 2:11.
26. Some think Paul means the Corinthians' obedience to Christ "proceeding from" (motivated by) their confession of Christ; others, their obedience "to" their confession of Christ. Others change the word order to "the obedience to the good news *of* Christ *which characterizes* your confession". This word means "confession, public declaration, acknowledgment". Elsewhere only in 1 Tim 6:12, 13; Heb 3:1; 4:14; 10:23. GK *3934*. Related to "confess" in 1 Tim 6:12.
27. Or, "with reference to". GK *1650*.
28. Or, "sincerity, singlemindedness". Same word as in v 11.
29. Or, "sharing, fellowship". Some take this phrase in its narrower sense, "the generosity *of your* contribution for them and for all"; others in its broader sense, "the sincerity *of your* fellowship toward them and toward all". Same word as in Rom 15:26 (as is "for"), referring to this gift. On this word, see "fellowship" in 1 Cor 1:9.
30. That is, your contribution intended for the physical relief of the Jerusalem believers and for the spiritual benefit of all believers through the good will Paul hopes will result from this act.

A. 2 Cor 8:2 B. Jn 16:32 C. Rom 1:17 D. Jn 15:4, abide E. Rev 20:10 F. Act 7:17 G. 1 Cor 1:5 H. Phil 2:12, work out J. 1 Tim 4:3 K. Phil 2:30, lack L. 1 Pet 1:16, holy M. Rom 8:30 N. 1 Cor 15:1

        1F. While they also *are* yearning-for¹ you *in* prayer for you, because of the surpassing² grace^A *of* God upon you   14

5B. Thanks^A *be to* God for His indescribable³ gift⁴   15

4A. Now **I**, Paul, myself, am appealing-to^B you⁵ by the gentleness^C and kindness^D *of* Christ, I who **face-to-face**⁶ *am* lowly^E among you— but while absent^F am-bold^G toward you! °And I am begging⁷ *that I may* not [have to] be bold⁸ while present, *with* the confidence⁹ *with* which I am considering^H to dare¹⁰ [to act]¹¹ against some considering us as walking^J in accordance with *the* flesh¹²   10:1   2

    1B. For [though] walking in *the* flesh, we are not waging-war¹³ in accordance with *the* flesh. °For the weapons^K *of* our warfare^L *are* not fleshly¹⁴, but powerful^M *in* God¹⁵ for *the* tearing-down¹⁶ *of* fortresses. *We are*¹⁷   3-4

        1C. Tearing-down¹⁸ considerations¹⁹, °and every height²⁰ being raised-up^N against the knowledge *of* God   5

        2C. And taking-captive²¹ every thought²² to the obedience^O *of* Christ²³

        3C. And being ready²⁴ to punish²⁵ all disobedience²⁶, when your obedience is fulfilled²⁷   6

    2B. You are looking *at things* according to appearance²⁸   7

        1C. If someone²⁹ is confident^P *in* himself³⁰ *that he* is Christ's³¹, let him consider^H this again in himself— that just as he *is* Christ's, so also *are* we³²

        2C. For³³ if I should boast anything³⁴ more³⁵ about our authority^Q, which the Lord gave³⁶ for building-up^R and not for tearing you down, I shall not be put-to-shame^S—   8

            1D. In order that I may not seem as-*if I* would [merely] frighten you by *my* letters³⁷!   9

                1E. Because³⁸, "The **letters**"³⁹, he⁴⁰ says, "*are* weighty^T and strong^U— but the presence *of his* body *is* weak^V, and *his* speaking^W *is* treated-with-contempt⁴¹"   10

1. Or, "longing for, desiring". On this word, see 1 Pet 2:2.
2. Elsewhere only in 3:10; Eph 1:19; 2:7; 3:19. GK *5650*.
3. Used only here. GK *442*. Related to "tell in detail" in Act 13:41.
4. Some think Paul is referring to the grace of God (v 8) which will enable the Corinthians to abound for this contribution, in which case this would be point 4C. Others think he means the great result of this contribution just described, the unity and good-will it will bring about between Jewish and Gentile believers. In this case, this would be point 2D. In both these views, Paul is thanking God in advance for the gift he anticipates God will give in relation to this endeavor. Others think he is referring to God's gift of His Son, the grand model for all our giving, as he closes the subject. On this word, see Rom 5:15.
5. In chapters 10-13, Paul is answering some opponents in Corinth who were saying that he was not truly an apostle, like the others. He was simply a human leader, with no more authority than any other traveling preacher. Paul wants to correct them, to prove his authority, to expose his detractors, but he is very reluctant to openly defend himself (12:19). The result is a very personal and emotional struggle by Paul with how much to say and how to say it. His opponents were probably the Judaizers (11:22), whom he calls false apostles, deceitful workers (11:13). Some think that having finished his basically positive words to the Corinthians, Paul now turns to pointedly address them about those among them who were speaking against him. Others think chapters 10-13 was a separate letter (see 2:3), suggesting several scenarios.
6. Or, "in relation to *my* presence". Same idiom as in Act 25:16. Paul is quoting his detractors here. Apparently some detractors were attempting to discredit Paul by saying "He talks big when he is not here!" Compare v 10-11. Paul uses grammar that emphasizes the contrast between this phrase and the next.
7. The third and final use of this word in 2 Corinthians, and the third combination of it with "appeal". See 8:4.
8. Paul wants to be bold in speech now so that he does not have to be bold in action ("act severely", 13:10) when he comes. He prefers to remain "lowly among you". On "be bold" here and in v 1, see "be confident" in 5:6.
9. On this word, see 1:15. Paul's confidence was in the spiritual weapons God had granted him to use in this spiritual war (10:4), and in the authority granted him by God (10:8). Note 13:2, he will not spare them.
10. Or, "to be bold", "to be courageous" against. On this word, see 11:21.
11. This is supplied from 13:10.
12. That is, with mere human authority and power. These detractors questioned Paul's motives, and the authority of his ministry.
13. Or, "fighting". On this word, see "fight" in 1 Tim 1:18. Related to "warfare" in v 4; and "soldier" in Mt 28:12.
14. That is, pertaining to the flesh, physical. On this word, see 1 Cor 3:3.
15. Or, "*for* God". Or, "*by* God", meaning "divinely powerful".
16. Or, "destruction, demolition". This noun is elsewhere only in v 8; 13:10. GK *2746*. The related verb is next.
17. The next three phrases refer to what Paul is doing with his powerful weapons. It is a military metaphor. When a rebellious city was conquered, first the walls and defenses were torn down and breached, then the people taken captive, and the offenders punished.
18. Or, "pulling down, destroying, demolishing". Same verb as in Lk 12:18; Act 19:27. Elsewhere only as "bring down" in Lk 1:52; Act 13:19; and "take down" in Mk 15:36, 46; Lk 23:53; Act 13:29. GK *2747*.
19. Or, "reflections, thoughts, reasonings, calculations". Elsewhere only as "thoughts" in Rom 2:15. GK *3361*. Same root word as "considering" in v 2, and rendered this way to show the connection.
20. Or, "elevation, barrier", raised up for defense against an attacker. Every obstacle of pride. Elsewhere only in Rom 8:39. GK *5739*.
21. Or, "taking prisoner, captivating". Elsewhere only in Lk 21:24; Rom 7:23; 2 Tim 3:6. GK *170*. Related to "captive" in Eph 4:8.
22. Or, "mind". On this word, see "minds" in 3:14.
23. That is, into the fortress of obedience to Christ (continuing the military metaphor).
24. This idiom is literally "holding *in* readiness". Related idiom in 12:14.
25. Or, "avenge". Elsewhere only as "avenge" in Lk 18:3, 5; Rom 12:19; Rev 6:10; 19:2. GK *1688*. The related noun is in 7:11.
26. Or, "every refusal-to-listen". Elsewhere only in Rom 5:19; Heb 2:2. GK *4157*. Related to "ignore" in Mk 5:36.
27. Or, "made full". After the full obedience of the majority, Paul will punish the disobedient, the "some" in v 2, the ministers of Satan in 11:15 and the Corinthians who follow them. Note 13:2.
28. This is a difficult sentence. The verb can be a statement, "you are looking"; a command, "look at"; or a question, "are you looking?". The "looking" could be at things "according to appearance"; "in *your* presence"; or "before *your* face" (similar to Gal 3:1, "before the eyes"). In any case, all imply the same thing— Look deeper! Same word as in 5:12, on which see "presence" in Lk 9:52.
29. Or, "anyone". That is, one of the "some considering" in v 2; such a one as mentioned in v 10-11.
30. In other words, in his own mind.
31. Some think Paul means "belongs to Christ"; others, more specifically, "is Christ's *servant*" or minister.
32. Some manuscripts add "Christ's" {K}.
33. Paul uses this word to assert his next point, as also in v 12. GK *1142*.
34. This word occurs with the verb "boast" elsewhere only as "anything" in 7:14, and "bit" in 11:16. GK *5516*.
35. Or, "further, more abundant, greater". That is, more than claiming to be Christ's servant, v 7. GK *4358*. Same two words as in Lk 12:4, not having "anything more" to do.
36. Some manuscripts add "us" {N}.
37. That is, as these detractors say about Paul. Paul is sarcastically answering the assertion of his opponents (v 10). He will not be put to shame because his actions when he is present will match his words, proving that he was not merely trying to frighten them through his letters. Some smooth this out by saying "*I say this* (v 8) in order that I may not...".
38. Paul pauses to explain why he mentions his letters.
39. Paul uses grammar that emphasizes the contrast between the two halves of this sentence.
40. That is, the opponent alluded to in verse 2. Paul may be referring to their leader, or he may mean "one says" in a general sense. Perhaps this was these opponents' response to what Paul said in 1 Cor 5:3-5. Some manuscripts say "they say" {N}.
41. Or, "despised, disdained". This is a participle, "having been treated with contempt". Compare Act 17:32. Note the passive, "others disdain his speech". Yet see Gal 4:14, same word. On this word, see 1 Thes 5:20.

A. Eph 2:8, grace B. Rom 12:8, exhorting C. Eph 4:2 D. Act 24:4 E. Jam 1:9 F. 2 Cor 13:10 G. 2 Cor 5:6, being confident H. Rom 3:28 J. Heb 13:9 K. Rom 13:12 L. 1 Tim 1:18, fight M. Lk 24:19 N. 2 Cor 11:20, lifts up O. Rom 16:26 P. 1 Jn 3:19, persuade Q. Rev 6:8 R. Rom 14:19, edification S. 1 Jn 2:28 T. Act 25:7 U. Rev 18:8 V. 1 Thes 5:14 W. 1 Cor 12:8, word

2E. Let such *a one* consider[A] this— that such as we are *in* word[B] by letters while absent[C], such *ones we are* also *in* deed[D] while present[E]!   11

3C. For we do not dare to class[1] or compare[F] ourselves *with* some *of* the *ones* commending[2] themselves[3]   12

    1D. But **they**— measuring themselves by themselves, and comparing themselves *with* themselves— do not understand[4]

4C. And **we** will not boast[G] in unmeasured[5] *things*, but in-relation-to[6] the measure[H] *of* the standard[7] which God apportioned[J] *to* us *as a* measure[H]— to reach as far as even you[8]   13

    1D. For we are not— as-*if* not reaching to you— overextending ourselves.[9] For we arrived[10] even as far as you in connection with the good-news[K] *of* Christ!—   14

        1E. Not boasting in unmeasured *things*, in labors[L] belonging-to-others[11]   15
        2E. But having *the* hope[M], while your faith *is* growing[N], *that we might* be enlarged[12] in[13] you in relation to our standard *of measure*, for *an* abundance[14]—

            1F. *That we might* announce-the-good-news[O] in the *regions* beyond you   16
            2F. Not *that we might* boast[G] in the prepared[15] *things* in *the* standard *of measure* belonging-to-another

5C. But "let the *one* boasting[G] be boasting in *the* Lord" [Jer 9:24]. For not that *one* commending[P] himself is approved[16], but *the one* whom the Lord commends   17-18

3B. O-that you *would* bear-with me[17] *as to a* little bit[18] *of* foolishness[19]— but indeed, keep-bearing-with[20] me!   11:1

    1C. For I am jealous-for[21] you *with a* jealousy[22] *of* God[23]   2

        1D. For I betrothed[24] you *to* one husband, *that I might* present[Q] *you as a* pure[R] virgin[S] *to* Christ
        2D. But I am fearing that[25] as the serpent deceived[T] Eve by his craftiness[U], your[26] minds[27] should somehow be corrupted[28] from sincerity[29] and purity[30] for[31] Christ   3

    2C. For indeed if the *one* coming proclaims[V] another[W] Jesus whom we did not proclaim, or you receive[X] *a* different[Y] spirit[32] which you did not receive[33], or *a* different good-news[K] which you did not accept[Z]— you bear-with[34] *him* nicely[35]!   4

    3C. For I think[AA] *that I* have in no way come-short-of[36] the superlative[37] apostles. But even though[38] *I am* untrained[39] in speech[40], nevertheless *I am* not *in* knowledge. But in every *way* we made this[41] evident[42] in all *things*[43] to you   5-6

1. Used only here. GK *1605*. There is a play on words with the next word (GK *5173*). Both are from the root word "judge". The idea is, we do not "judge ourselves to be in" their class, or "judge ourselves with" them as the standard. Paul's sarcasm is evident here.
2. Same word as v 18.
3. If Paul did boast, it would not be in his accomplishments as compared to the accomplishments of others.
4. That is, understand that self-commendation means nothing. The reality is in v 18. In the light of an absolute standard of measure, our self-commendation means nothing. Some people commend themselves for their sin! On this word, see Mt 13:13.
5. Or, "*things* beyond measure, *things* without measure". Elsewhere only in v 15. GK *296*.
6. Or, "in accordance with, based on". GK *2848*.
7. Or, "rule, norm, sphere, province". That is, "*consisting of* the standard". This word refers to the criteria of measure, the standard or measuring rod by which God measures Paul's work. God's standard of measure for Paul is a length or extent of service reaching to Corinth and beyond. This word can also figuratively refer to the thing measured by the standard. In this case, it would refer to the measured-out "territory" of Paul's ministry, the "province" or "sphere" of work God allotted to him. Same word as in v 15, 16. Elsewhere only in Gal 6:16. GK *2834*.
8. If Paul did boast, it would be in his own accomplishments as measured by what God gave him to do.
9. That is, in our boasting to you about what God has done through us. It is Paul's opponents who are overextending.
10. Or, "arrived-first". On this word, see "came" in 1 Thes 2:16.
11. As his opponents did. Since they built on another's foundation, their own contribution could not be measured. On this word, see "foreigners" in Heb 11:34.
12. Or, "magnified, made large". Elsewhere only as "lengthen" in Mt 23:5; and "magnify" in Lk 1:47, 58; Act 5:13; 10:46; 19:17; Phil 1:20. GK *3486*.
13. Or, "among, by". That is, that in your growth, we might be enlarged beyond you, farther out into the sphere of measure given to us by God (which extends to Rome). A few months later, Paul wrote Romans from Corinth. GK *1877*.
14. This is explained by what follows. Paul's hope as a pioneer is to produce the greatest geographical abundance of believers possible within his sphere, not to retrace the steps of others. On this word, see 8:2.
15. Or, "the ready *things*", the things someone else has already gotten ready, the "labors of others" (v 15). On this word, see Mk 14:15.
16. On this word, see 2 Tim 2:15. Paul has the Corinthians themselves as God's commendation of him, 3:2.
17. Or, this may be taken with what follows, "bear with my little bit *of* foolishness".
18. Or, "something". The same word as "anything" in 10:8. "Little bit" is also in 11:16.
19. Paul considers boasting about himself to be foolishness, 11:16, 17, 21; 12:11; and not beneficial, 12:1.
20. Instead of a command (like those in v 16), this may be a statement, "you are bearing with me". On this word, see v 4.
21. Or, "zealous-for", I am zealous for you with a zeal of God. Same word as "jealous" in Jam 4:2; "become-jealous" in Act 17:5; and "jealous-of" in Act 7:9. Elsewhere only as "zealous-for" in 1 Cor 12:31; 14:1, 39; "zealously-seek" in Gal 4:17, 18; and "envy" in 1 Cor 13:4. GK *2420*. Related to the next word; and to "zealot" in 1 Cor 14:12.
22. Or, "zeal". Same word as in Act 5:17; 13:45; Rom 13:13; 1 Cor 3:3; 2 Cor 12:20; Gal 5:20; Jam 3:14, 16. Elsewhere only as "zeal" in Jn 2:17; Rom 10:2; 2 Cor 7:7, 11; 9:2; Phil 3:6; Heb 10:27. GK *2419*.
23. Some think Paul means "a God-kind of jealousy, godly jealousy"; others, a jealousy "*from* God".
24. Or, "promised in marriage". Like a bride's father, Paul promised the Corinthians to Christ. Used only here. GK *764*.
25. See Act 5:26 on this idiom.
26. Some manuscripts say "so your..." {N}.
27. Or, "thoughts", as in 10:5. On this word, see 3:14.
28. Or, "ruined, spoiled". On this word, see "ruin" in 1 Cor 3:17.
29. Or, "simplicity". On this word, see "generosity" in Rom 12:8.
30. Some manuscripts omit "and purity" {C}. Elsewhere only in 6:6. GK *55*. Related to "pure" in 1 Pet 3:2.
31. Or, "with regard to, towards, in". GK *1650*.
32. Paul may mean "Spirit"; or something like a spirit of slavery to laws (Gal 5:1) versus a spirit of freedom (2 Cor 3:17).
33. That is, when we proclaimed the gospel to you.
34. Or, "endure, put up with". Same word as in 11:1, 19, 20; and Mt 17:17; Mk 9:19; Lk 9:41; Act 18:14; Eph 4:2; Col 3:13; 2 Thes 1:4; 2 Tim 4:3; Heb 13:22. Elsewhere only as "endure" in 1 Cor 4:12. GK *462*. Some manuscripts have different grammar (like v 1), meaning "you *would* bear with" {N}.
35. Or, "well". Same word as in Mk 7:9, where it is also used sarcastically. Some think this is a second reason to bear with Paul, v 1. You bear with him, so keep bearing with me! Others make this 1E., a sarcastic rebuke of them, continued in v 5-6. Consult the commentaries. On this word, see "well" in Act 10:33.
36. Or, "come behind, been inferior to, been less than". Same word as in 12:11, and as "in need" in v 9.
37. Elsewhere only in 12:11. GK *5663*. Some think Paul is referring to the chief apostles— Peter, James and John. Bear with me (v 1), for I am not inferior to the most-eminent apostles, as seen in the signs I do (12:11-12). Like them, I am someone to whom you should listen. Others think Paul is referring to the "false apostles" (v 13), sarcastically calling them "[these] super apostles", and saying, listen to me, for I am certainly not their inferior. "Superlative" is intended to be a neutral translation, the tone of voice making it clear. "Super" and "most-eminent" are renderings that represent the two views.
38. More literally, "If I even am untrained", assuming that I even am untrained. On this idiom, see "if also" 1 Cor 7:21.
39. Or, "*a* layman". On this word, see "uninstructed" in 1 Cor 14:16. Paul was not a trained Greek orator.
40. In the one view, Paul means this in comparison to the "super apostles". In other words, this as an exception to "in no way". In the other view, he means this in comparison to his opponents who were saying this about him, not the most-eminent apostles. On this word, see "word" in 1 Cor 12:8.
41. Some manuscripts say "ourselves" {N}.
42. Or, "known". This is a participle, "*we are ones* having made evident". Some manuscripts say "*we were made evident*" {N}, that is, "*we are ones* having been made evident". On this word, see 1 Jn 2:19.
43. Or, "among all *people*" instead of "in all *things*".

A. Rom 3:28 B. 1 Cor 12:8 C. 2 Cor 13:10 D. Mt 26:10, work E. Rev 17:8 F. 1 Cor 2:13, combine G. 2 Cor 11:16 H. Jn 3:34 J. 1 Cor 7:17 K. 1 Cor 15:1 L. 1 Cor 3:8 M. Col 1:5 N. Jn 3:30 O. Act 5:42 P. 2 Cor 3:1 Q. Rom 12:1 R. 1 Pet 3:2 S. Rev 14:4 T. Rom 7:11 U. 1 Cor 3:19 V. 2 Tim 4:2 W. 1 Cor 12:9 X. Rom 7:8, taken Y. 1 Cor 12:9 Z. Mt 10:40, welcome AA. Rom 3:28, consider

1D. Or¹ did I commit^A *a* sin [by] humbling^B myself² in order that **you** might be exalted^C— because I freely³ announced-as-good-news *to* you the good-news⁴ *of* God? 7

    1E. I robbed⁵ other churches— having taken rations⁶ *from them* for your ministry⁷! 8
    2E. And while being present with you and having been in-need⁸, I did not burden^D anyone— for the brothers having come from Macedonia supplied^E my need⁹ 9
    3E. And in every *way* I kept^F and will keep myself unburdensome *to* you
    4E. *As the* truth *of* Christ is in me¹⁰, this boasting^G will not be stopped^H for me in the regions *of* Achaia!¹¹ ˚For what reason? 10
        11

        1F. Because I do not love you? God knows *I do*
        2F. But what I am doing, I indeed will do— in order that I may cut-off^J the opportunity^K *of* the *ones* wanting *an* opportunity that¹² they might be found^L *to be* just as also we in what they are boasting 12

            1G. For such *ones are* false-apostles, deceitful workers, transforming¹³ *themselves* into apostles *of* Christ 13

                1H. And no wonder, for Satan himself transforms *himself* into *an* angel *of* light 14
                2H. Therefore, *it is* no great *thing* if also his ministers^M are disguising¹⁴ *themselves* as ministers *of* righteousness— whose end^N shall be according to their works¹⁵ 15

4B. Again I say, let no one think^O me to be foolish¹⁶. Otherwise indeed¹⁷, receive me even if as foolish, in order that **I** also may boast¹⁸ *a* little bit^P! 16

    1C. In this confidence¹⁹ *of* boasting^G, what I am speaking, I am not speaking according-to²⁰ *the* Lord, but as in foolishness²¹ 17
    2C. Since many are boasting according-to²² *the* flesh, **I** also will boast! 18

        1D. For with-pleasure²³ you bear-with the unwise²⁴, being wise 19

            1E. For you bear-with²⁵ *it* 20

                1F. If anyone enslaves²⁶ you
                2F. If anyone devours²⁷ *you*
                3F. If anyone takes²⁸ *you*
                4F. If anyone lifts-up²⁹ *himself*
                5F. If anyone beats^Q you in *the* face³⁰

        2D. I speak in-accordance-with³¹ *my* dishonor³²— how that³³ **we** have been weak³⁴! 21
        3D. But³⁵ in whatever anyone may dare *to boast*— I am speaking in foolishness— **I** also dare³⁶
        4D. Are they Hebrews? I also. Are they Israelites? I also. Are they seed^R *of* Abraham? I also 22

1. Paul brings up one way in which his opponents might have seen him to be inferior.
2. That is, by making tents in order to pay his own expenses. More sarcasm. Paul's opponents saw this as degrading. In the Greco-Roman culture, good teachers and philosophers charged for their teaching, and earned a living from it. So Paul's opponents took the fact that he did not do so as an indication that he was, or thought himself to be, inferior. "Humbling... exalted" could also be translated "Lowering... lifted up". The same two words are used in Mt 23:12; Lk 14:11; 18:14; Jam 4:10; 1 Pet 5:6. See also Phil 2:8-9.
3. Or, "as a gift, without payment". Paul did not allow the Corinthians to support him. This was not because he could not charge, but because he chose not to do so. He did not want to be seen as just earning a living like a philosopher, nor the gospel to be seen as just another teaching. On this word, see "without reason" in Gal 2:21.
4. Paul uses the verb and noun of the same word. See Gal 1:11.
5. Or, "took booty from, stripped off spoils, plundered, sacked". Used only here. GK *5195*. It is figurative for accepting financial support. More sarcasm. I sinned by not accepting money from you (v 7), and I robbed others to make it possible!
6. Or, "wages". That is, money to live on. On this word, see "wages" in Rom 6:23.
7. That is, for my ministry to you. Paul allowed the Philippians to support him after he left them, Phil 4:15-16. On this word, see 1 Cor 12:5.
8. On this word, see Lk 15:14. Same word as "come short" in v 5.
9. Or, "lack, shortage". On this word, see "lack" in Phil 2:30. Same root word as "in need" earlier.
10. Same type of oath as in 1:18. Or, "It is the truth *of* Christ in me that this...".
11. See 1 Cor 9:1-27, especially v 15 where Paul says he would rather die than give up this boast.
12. Or, "opportunity to be found". GK *2671*. This phrase defines the content of the opportunity the opponents wanted. They want the opportunity to be recognized as equal to Paul, to be found by people to be just like him. To attain this, they want Paul to accept pay just like they do. Paul cuts off their opportunity to be seen as his equal by refusing this right, thus striking at their money motive. There are other views of this clause. Consult the commentaries.
13. That is, outwardly. On this word, see Phil 3:21.
14. Same word as "transform" in v 13, 14, but here followed by "as". These people transform themselves to hide their true motives and intent; that is, they disguise themselves.
15. See Rev 20:12 on this.
16. Same word as in Lk 11:40; 12:20; Rom 2:20; 1 Cor 15:36; 2 Cor 12:6, 11; Eph 5:17; 1 Pet 2:15. Elsewhere only as "unwise" in v 19. GK *933*.
17. This idiom, "otherwise indeed", is literally, "But if [this is] not indeed [the case]". This idiom is elsewhere only in Mt 6:1; 9:17; Lk 5:36, 37; 10:6; 13:9; 14:32. Related to the idiom "otherwise" in Jn 14:2.
18. Elsewhere only in 2 Cor 5:12; 7:14; 9:2; 10:8, 13, 15, 16, 17; 11:12, 16, 18, 30; 12: 1, 5, 6, 9; and Rom 2:17, 23; 5:2, 3, 11; 1 Cor 1:29, 31; 3:21; 4:7; 13:3; Gal 6:13, 14; Eph 2:9; Phil 3:3; Jam 1:9; 4:16. GK *3016*. See 7:4 on the related noun.
19. Some give this word a subjective meaning here, "in this confidence I have about my status as God's apostle, about which I am boasting". Others give it an objective sense, "in this subject of boasting" forced upon Paul by his opponents; or "in this undertaking of boasting" Paul is about to begin in order to give the true foundation for understanding him and these opponents. On this word, see "assurance" in Heb 11:1.
20. Or, "in keeping with, in harmony with" how the Lord would speak. Or, "for, in relation to". GK *2848*.
21. Same word as in v 1, 21. Elsewhere only in Mk 7:22. GK *932*. Related to "foolish" in v 16.
22. Or, "based on, in keeping with" human standards. GK *2848*.
23. Or, "gladly". On this word, see Mk 6:20.
24. Or, "foolish". It is the same word as "foolish" in v 16, but here there is a play on words— "with the unwise, being wise", or, "with the senseless, being sensible". More sarcasm.
25. On this word, used here and in v 19, see v 4.
26. Or, "reduces you to slavery or bondage". In v 20 Paul is describing how his opponents treated the Corinthians, and yet were still accepted. Elsewhere only in Gal 2:4. GK *2871*. Related to "are slaves" in Rom 6:6.
27. Some think this refers to financial exploitation. Compare Mk 12:40; Rom 16:18; Phil 3:19. On this word, see Mk 12:40.
28. That is, take advantage of you. Same word as v 8, having "taken" support from other churches, and as 12:16. This is the common word meaning "take, receive", used 258 times in the NT. GK *3284*.
29. Or, "lifts *his hand*" in a threat; "raises *his voice*" in anger (as in Act 22:22); lifts himself up into positions of authority; lifts himself up in pride and presumption. Same word as in Lk 24:50; Jn 6:5, 13:18; 17:1; Act 1:9; 1 Tim 2:8. Used 19 times. GK *2048*.
30. Paul may mean this literally, as in Jn 18:22; Act 23:2. Or it may be a figurative reference to insulting, dishonoring treatment.
31. Or, "in relation to, with regard to; according to, based on; to, for the purpose of ". GK *2848*.
32. Or, "disgrace". You bear with the unwise (v 19), so bear with my dishonor, my weakness (as my opponents regard it). Others think Paul means "I speak to my dishonor", that is, I admit to my "dishonor" my "weakness" by comparison with them in this matter of boasting in the flesh. In either case, he is being sarcastic. On this word, see 2 Tim 2:20.
33. These two words, "how that" occur together elsewhere only in 5:19 and 2 Thes 2:2. They indicate that Paul is referring to something someone else said. Note 10:10.
34. More sarcasm. As they say, we have been weak by comparison to them in these matters. This is to my "dishonor"! On this word, see "sick" in 2 Tim 4:20. Some manuscripts say "we were weak" {B}.
35. But in spite of my "weakness" in this matter, I will now boast also.
36. This word means to be daring, to have the courage to do something, to venture or be bold to do something. Same word as in 10:2, 12. Paul is reluctant to boast about himself (10:8), he thinks it to be foolish (11:17), yet he dares to do it (11:21) because he is compelled to do so by his opponents (12:11). Elsewhere only in Mt 22:46; Mk 12:34; 15:43; Lk 20:40; Jn 21:12; Act 5:13; 7:32; Rom 5:7; 15:18; 1 Cor 6:1; Phil 1:14; Jude 9. GK *5528*.

A. Rev 13:13, does   B. Phil 4:12   C. Jn 8:28, lifted up   D. 2 Cor 12:13   E. 2 Cor 9:12, filling up   F. 1 Jn 5:18   G. 2 Cor 7:4   H. Rom 3:19   J. Lk 13:7, cut down   K. Rom 7:8   L. 2 Pet 3:10   M. 1 Cor 3:5, servants   N. Rom 10:4   O. Lk 19:11   P. 2 Cor 11:1   Q. Jn 18:23   R. Heb 11:11

5D.	Are they servants^A *of* Christ? I speak being distraught[1]— I more	23
	1E. In far-more labors^B, in far-more prisons,[2] in many-more[3] beatings^C, in deaths[4] often	
	1F. By Jews five-times I received forty *lashes* less one.[5] °Three-times I was beaten-with-rods[6]. Once I was stoned.[7] Three-times I was shipwrecked.[8] I have done *a* night-and-day[9] in the deep[10]	24-25
	2E. *On* journeys often— *in* dangers^D *from* rivers, *in* dangers *from* robbers^E, *in* dangers from *my* nation[11], *in* dangers from Gentiles^F, *in* dangers in *the* city, *in* dangers in *the* wilderness, *in* dangers at sea, *in* dangers among false-brothers	26
	3E. *In* labor^B and hardship, in watchings[12] often, in hunger and thirst, in fastings[13] often, in cold and nakedness[14]	27
	4E. Apart from the external[15] *things, there is* the daily pressure[16] *on* me, the concern^G *for* all the churches— °Who is weak^H, and I am not weak? Who is caused-to-fall^J, and **I** do not burn[17]?	28 29
	5E. If it-is-necessary[18] to boast, I will boast the *things of* my weakness^K! °The God and Father *of the*[19] Lord Jesus[20], the *One* being blessed[21] forever^L, knows that am not lying[22]	30-31
	6E. In Damascus, the ethnarch[23] *of* Aretas[24] the king was guarding^M the city *of the* Damascenes to seize[25] me. °And I was lowered[26] in *a* basket through *a* window through the wall and escaped^N his hands	32 33
3C.	It-is-necessary[27] to boast. *It is* not **beneficial**[28]— but I will come to visions[29] and revelations^O *from the* Lord	12:1
	1D. I know^P *a* man in Christ[30], fourteen years ago[31]	2
	1E. Whether in *the* body, I do not know, or outside *of* the body, I do not know. God knows	
	2E. *That* such *a* one *was* snatched-away[32] to *the* third heaven[33]	
	2D. And I know such *a* man[34]	3
	1E. Whether in *the* body or apart from the body, I do not know. God knows	
	2E. That he was snatched away into paradise[35], and heard unspeakable[36] words which *are* not permitted[37] *for a* man[38] to speak	4
	3D. I will boast^Q on behalf of such *a* one. But I will not boast on behalf of myself, except in the[39] weaknesses^K	5
	1E. For if I should desire^R to boast, I will not be foolish^S, for I will be speaking *the* truth^T	6
	2E. But I am sparing^U *you, that* no one might credit^V to me beyond what he sees *as to* me, or hears *as to* something[40] from me	

1. Or, "deranged, beside myself, mad, irrational". Clearly Paul was very reluctant to boast these things. He has said something like this four times now, v 16, 17, 21, 23. Used only here. GK *4196*. Related to "madness", 2 Pet 2:16.
2. Some manuscripts reverse this phrase and the next one, {N}, so that "in many-more beatings" comes first.
3. Paul could mean "many more in quantity" or "much greater in severity". Used only here. GK *5649*. Related to "surpassing" in 9:14.
4. Though used 120 times, this is the only place where this word is plural. "In death situations many times". GK *2505*.
5. The Law allowed a maximum of 40 lashes, Deut 25:3. To protect against a miscount, the Jews gave 39.
6. Once was in Act 16:22, the only other occurrence of this word. This was a Roman punishment.
7. This was at Lystra, recorded in Act 14:19.
8. This is not counting the one that came later in Act 27. The three here are unknown to us.
9. This is one word, a "night-day", a full day. Used only here. GK *3819*.
10. Presumably, floating on debris after one of the shipwrecks. The incident is unknown to us. Used only here. GK *1113*.
11. Or, "people, kind". That is, fellow Israelites. On this word, see "kind" in 1 Cor 12:28.
12. Or, "sleepless nights". Perhaps, "alerts". On this word, see 6:5.
13. That is, voluntary skipping of meals for spiritual purposes, as opposed to involuntary "hunger and thirst" previously. Elsewhere only in 6:5; Lk 2:37; Act 14:23; 27:9 (its only singular use). GK *3763*. The verb is in Mt 6:16.
14. Elsewhere only in Rom 8:35; Rev 3:18. GK *1219*. Related to "naked" in 1 Cor 4:11.
15. Or, "the *things* besides" these things just mentioned, meaning that apart from the other things of this nature that I have not included here, there is the daily pressure. Elsewhere only as "except for" in Mt 5:32; Act 26:29. GK *4211*. Related to "outside" in 12:2.
16. Or, "onset, care, attention, oversight, stoppage, hindrance". On this word, see "onset" in Act 24:12. Some think this is an independent phrase, referring to the pressure of people coming to Paul, or people attacking him, etc. Others think the next clause explains this one.
17. That is, burn with concern or anger. Elsewhere only as "burning" with passion in 1 Cor 7:9; "flaming" in Eph 6:16; "set on fire" in 2 Pet 3:12; and "refined" in Rev 1:15; 3:18. GK *4792*. The root word is "fire".
18. Or, "*I must, I* have to". On this idiom, see "must" in Mt 16:21.
19. Some manuscripts say "our" {K}.
20. Some manuscripts add "Christ" {K}.
21. Or, "the *One who* is blessed". "Blessed" is an adjective, not part of the verb. The grammar indicates this phrase refers to "the God and Father", not to "Lord Jesus". On this word, see Rom 9:5.
22. Some think Paul means "in what I am boasting here in v 22-33"; others think it refers to the preceding boasts; others, to the next boast in v 32-33.
23. That is, governor. Used only here. GK *1617*. Some think Paul adds this because his opponents were distorting the incident against him, saying he ran away. Paul states the facts.
24. Aretas IV was king of Nabatea, a territory east of Damascus, from 9 B.C. to A.D. 40. He was the father-in-law of Herod Antipas (Mt 14:1). Herod divorced his daughter to marry Herodias, and Aretas went to war with him. Used only here. GK *745*.
25. On this word, see Jn 11:57. Some manuscripts say "wishing to seize" {B}.
26. Same word as in Act 9:25 where this incident is recorded. On this word, see Act 27:17.
27. Same idiom as in 11:30. Some manuscripts instead have the word meaning "indeed, certainly, surely" here (see "indeed" in Mt 13:23 on it) {A}, so that it says "*It is* surely not beneficial to boast, but...".
28. Or, "profitable, advantageous". It does not benefit Paul, and exposes him to the charge of self-commendation. Perhaps for this reason, Paul puts what follows in the third person. It gives him some verbal distance from what he relates. Paul uses grammar that emphasizes the contrast between the two halves of this sentence. This is a participle, "being beneficial". Same word as in 1 Cor 6:12. Some manuscripts instead say, "*It is* not beneficial *for* me, but..." {A}.
29. Elsewhere only in Lk 1:22; 24:23; Act 26:19. GK *3965*. Related to "appear" in Act 1:3; and "vision" in Act 10:3 and Rev 9:17.
30. That is, a Christian man.
31. This is an idiom, "before fourteen years".
32. Or, "caught up, seized, taken, carried off by force". This is a participle, was "having been snatched away". Same word as in v 4, and Mt 11:12; 12:29; 13:19; Act 8:39. Elsewhere only as "snatch up" in 1 Thes 4:17 (the rapture); Rev 12:5; "snatch" in Jn 10:12, 28, 29; Act 23:10; Jude 23; and "take away by force" in Jn 6:15. GK *773*. Related to "seized" in Lk 8:29; and "plundering" in Heb 10:34.
33. Some think the first heaven is the "sky" (where the birds fly, as this word is used in Mt 6:26; 16:3; Rev 11:6), the second is space (where the sun, moon, and stars are, as in Mt 5:18; Rev 14:7; 21:1), the third is God's presence (as in Eph 6:9; Phil 3:20; Heb 8:1). Used 273 times. GK *4041*.
34. Some think v 3-4 describes the same event as v 2; others, the second stage of that event; others, a separate event.
35. Some think this is the same thing as the third heaven; others, something different. Elsewhere only in Lk 23:43; Rev 2:7. GK *4137*.
36. This word has two senses— unspeakable because it is beyond human ability, or, not to be spoken because it is too holy. Probably the latter meaning is intended here, in view of the next phrase. Not related to "speak" which follows. Used only here. GK *777*.
37. This is a participle, "being permitted". On this word, see "lawful" in 1 Cor 6:12.
38. Paul seems to mean "man" in the sense of "mortal". Whatever it was, it was for Paul, no one else.
39. Some manuscripts say "my" {N}.
40. Some manuscripts omit this word {C}, so that it says "hears from me".

A. 1 Cor 3:5   B. 2 Thes 3:8   C. Rev 13:3, wound   D. Rom 8:35   E. Mt 21:13   F. Act 15:23   G. 1 Pet 5:7, anxiety   H. 2 Tim 4:20, sick   J. 1 Cor 8:13   K. Mt 8:17   L. Rev 20:10   M. Gal 3:23, kept in custody   N. Rom 2:3   O. 2 Thes 1:7   P. 1 Jn 2:29   Q. 2 Cor 11:16   R. Jn 7:17, willing   S. 2 Cor 11:16   T. Jn 4:23   U. Rom 11:21   V. Rom 3:28, consider

	4D. And¹ *for* the excess² *of* the revelations^A— for-this-reason³, in order that I⁴ might not be exalted⁵, *a* thorn⁶ *in*⁷ the flesh was given *to* me, *a* messenger^B *of* Satan to⁸ beat⁹ me, in order that I might not be exalted¹⁰	7
	1E. I appealed-to^C the Lord about this three-times, that it¹¹ might depart^D from me	8
	2E. And He has said *to* me— "My grace^E is sufficient¹² *for* you. For *My*¹³ power^F is perfected¹⁴ in weakness¹⁵"	9
	3E. Therefore most-gladly¹⁶ I will rather¹⁷ boast in my weaknesses, in order that the power *of* Christ may dwell¹⁸ upon me	
	4E. For this reason I am well-pleased^G with weaknesses, with insults¹⁹, with constraints^H, with persecutions^J and²⁰ distresses^K for the sake of Christ. For whenever I am weak, at that time I am powerful²¹	10
5B. I have become foolish²²— **you** compelled^L me! For **I** ought to be being commended^M by you!		11
	1C. For I in no way came-short-of^N the superlative²³ apostles, even though²⁴ I am nothing—	
	1D. The **signs**²⁵ *of* the apostle^O were produced²⁶ among you in²⁷ all endurance^P *in* both signs and wonders, and miracles²⁸	12
	2C. For what is it *as to* which you were worse-off²⁹ than the other churches?	13
	1D. Except that **I** myself did not burden³⁰ you— forgive^Q me this wrong-doing³¹!	
	2D. Behold— this³² *is the* third³³ *time* I am ready³⁴ to come to you, and I will not be *a* burden³⁵	14
	1E. For I am not seeking^R your *things*, but you	
	2E. For the children ought not to be storing-up³⁶ *for* the parents, but the parents *for* the children	
	3E. But **I** will most gladly spend^S and be expended³⁷ for your souls^T— though³⁸ while loving you more, I am loved less!³⁹	15
	3D. But let it be— **I** did not weigh you down⁴⁰, but being crafty⁴¹, I took you *by* deceit⁴²!	16
	1E. *As to* anyone *of* whom I have sent-out^U to you— I did not exploit⁴³ you through him, did I?	17
	2E. I urged⁴⁴ Titus *to go*, and I sent the brother with *him*.⁴⁵ Titus did not exploit you, *did he*?⁴⁶ Did we not walk^V *in* the same spirit? *In* the same footsteps?⁴⁷	18

1. In this rendering, "And... revelations" is connected with what follows. Others connect it with v 5, "except in the weaknesses... and *in* the... revelations". Others link it to v 6, "credit to me beyond what... me, and [credit to me] *by means of* the excessive greatness *of* the revelations [I have received]".
2. Paul may mean the excess of quality, "excellence"; or, the excess of quantity, "abundance". Same word as in 4:7. On this word, see "beyond measure" in 1 Cor 12:31.
3. This is the Greek word order. Some manuscripts omit this word {C}, so that it says "And in order that I might not be exalted *for the excess of the revelations*, ...", the phrase "for... revelations" being moved forward in the Greek word order for emphasis. Other arrangements of this unusual grammar have been suggested. Consult the commentaries.
4. Here it becomes clear that v 2-6 refer to Paul himself.
5. Or, "that I may not exalt *myself*". Elsewhere only in 2 Thes 2:4, of the Antichrist. GK *5643*.
6. Used of any pointed piece of wood. Used only here. GK *5022*.
7. Or, "*for*". For suggestions on what this thorn was, a centuries-old debate, consult the commentaries. Note Gal 4:15.
8. Or, "in order that it might"; or, "in order that he might". GK *2671*.
9. Or, "strike". On this word, see 1 Cor 4:11.
10. Some manuscripts omit this second occurrence of "in order that I may not be exalted" {B}.
11. Or, "he", the messenger, instead of "it", the thorn. Perhaps if Paul was thinking of the thorn, he would have said "be taken away" to match "was given" in v 7. If so, then "he" would be correct here. But on "depart", compare Mk 1:42 and Act 19:12.
12. Or, "is enough, is adequate". Elsewhere only as "is enough" in Mt 25:9; Jn 6:7; 14:8; and "be content" in Lk 3:14; 1 Tim 6:8; Heb 13:5; 3 Jn 10. GK *758*. Related to "sufficient" in Mt 6:34.
13. Some manuscripts include this word {A}.
14. Or, "brought to completion". On this word, see "finished" in Rev 10:7.
15. God's power is "brought to completion, consummation" in weakness. This statement is a key to understanding what God is doing in this world. Jesus Himself is the prime example of this. The greatness of God's power is seen in the weakness of the means He uses to accomplish His works. Thus, His greatest victory is found in the worst human defeat imaginable— the rejection, betrayal, and execution of the Son of God. On this word, see Mt 8:17.
16. Or, "with-the-greatest-pleasure". Same word as in v 15. On this word, see "with pleasure" in Mk 6:20.
17. Paul may mean "rather than ask God to remove the weaknesses"; or, "rather than anything else".
18. Or, "spread a tent" over me, "take up quarters" in me. Used only here. GK *2172*. Related to "dwell" in Rev 7:15, and "tent" in 2 Cor 5:1.
19. Or, "violent mistreatment, outrages" committed against a person. Elsewhere only as "damage" in Act 27:10, 21. GK *5615*. Related to "mistreat" in 1 Thes 2:2.
20. Some manuscripts say "with" {N}.
21. Or, "strong, mighty". Related to "power" in v 9, and rendered this way to show the relationship. Same word as in 10:4, and as "strong" in 13:9. On this word, see Lk 24:19.
22. Same word as in 11:16. Some manuscripts add "while boasting" {N}.
23. Same phrase as in 11:5. See there on the two views of this.
24. More literally, "If I even am nothing", assuming that I even am nothing. On this idiom, see "if also" in 1 Cor 7:21.
25. Or, "the signs indeed"; that is, "the *true* signs". Others take the grammar to mean "the signs *of* the **apostle**" ("the apostle indeed"); that is, "the *true* apostle". In either case, Paul means the signs that distinguish an apostle sent by Christ Himself (versus a church) as His apostle, that place one in or out of that elite group. Paul is in, those troubling the Corinthians are out. Others think the grammar implies a statement corresponding to this sentence which is left unsaid, "But you took no notice".
26. Or, "accomplished, worked, done". That is, by Christ, through Paul. Those taking "superlative" to mean "chief" take Paul to mean "just like they would have done". Those taking it sarcastically to mean "super" take him to mean "which those troubling you are unable to do, lacking the power". Same word as "accomplish" in Rom 15:18. On this word, see "work out" in Phil 2:12.
27. That is, "in the sphere of, in connection with". GK *1877*. The signs were done in connection with Paul's enduring of such trials as he just described (not in great glory). Both are part of his ministry.
28. On this word, see 1 Cor 12:10. Compare Rom 15:19; Gal 3:5. On "wonder", see 2 Thes 2:9. The same 3 words are in Heb 2:4.
29. Or, "inferior, less". Used only here. GK *2273*. Related to "less" in v 15, not to "come short" in v 11.
30. Same word and thought as in 11:9. Elsewhere only in v 14. GK *2915*.
31. On this word, see "unrighteousness" in Rom 1:18.
32. Some manuscripts omit this word {N}, so that it says "*a third time*".
33. The first visit was in Acts 18, prior to writing 1 Corinthians. Some think there was a second "sorrowful visit" not mentioned in Acts (based on 2 Cor 2:1; 12:14; 13:1), making this proposed visit after 2 Corinthians the third. Others think Paul means this is the third planned visit, the third time he was "ready to come". The second planned visit never occurred because Paul changed his plans, 2:1. Note how he says this in 13:1. See also 13:2 and 1:15.
34. This is an idiom, "I am holding *myself* ready", on which see 1 Pet 4:5.
35. Some manuscripts say "I will not burden you" {K}.
36. Same word as 1 Cor 16:2.
37. Or, "spent out, exhausted". Related to "spend". Used only here. GK *1682*.
38. Some manuscripts say "even though" {B}.
39. Or, this may be a question, "am I loved less?". Some manuscripts say "...souls. If I love you more, am I loved less?" {C}.
40. This word, "weigh down" is used only here. GK *2851*. Not related to "burden" in v 13, 14, but the same idea. Related to "burden-on" in 2 Thes 2:9, and to "very weighed down" in Mk 14:40.
41. Perhaps Paul's opponents accused him of this. Used only here. GK *4112*. Related to "craftiness" in 11:3.
42. More sarcasm. Let this be your assertion— It was not you, Paul, it was the people you sent who did it! On this word, see Mt 26:4.
43. On this word, see 1 Thes 4:6. The grammar expects a "no" answer to this question.
44. Same word as in 8:6; 9:5.
45. Paul may mean he appealed to Titus to go on this trip, carrying this letter. That is, the trip described in 8:6, 16-23. In this case, he means "[to go back to you]". "Sent" is from the Corinthians' point of view upon receipt of this letter, as in 8:17. Or, Paul may be referring to the previous trip from which Titus returned in 7:6. In this case, he means "[to go to you last time]".
46. The grammar expects a "no" answer.
47. The grammar expects a "yes" answer for these last two questions.

A. 2 Thes 1:7 B. 1 Tim 3:16 C. Rom 12:8, exhorting D. 1 Tim 4:1 E. Eph 2:8 F. Mk 5:30 G. Mt 17:5 H. 2 Cor 6:4 J. Mk 10:30 K. 2 Cor 6:4
L. Gal 6:12 M. 2 Cor 3:1 N. 2 Cor 11:5 O. 1 Cor 12:28 P. Jam 1:3 Q. Lk 7:42 R. Phil 2:21 S. Act 21:24 T. Jam 5:20 U. Mk 3:14 V. Heb 13:9

6B. All-this-time¹ are you thinking^A that we are defending-*ourselves*² to you?³ We are speaking before God in Christ— and *speaking* all *things*, beloved^B, for the sake of your edification^C   19

  1C. For I am fearing that⁴ having come, I may somehow find you *to be* not such as I want⁵, and **I** may be found *by* you *to be* such as you do not want⁶—   20

    1D. That⁴ somehow *there may be* strife^D, jealousy⁷, rages⁸, selfish-interests^E, slanders, whisperings⁹, puffings¹⁰ [with pride], disorders¹¹

    2D. That⁴ I having come again,¹² my God should humble¹³ me before¹⁴ you, and I should mourn¹⁵ many *of* the *ones* having previously-sinned¹⁶ and not having repented^F over¹⁷ the impurity^G and sexual-immorality^H and sensuality^J which they practiced^K   21

  2C. This *is the* third¹⁸ *time* I am coming to you   13:1

    1D. Every word shall be established^L based-on¹⁹ *the* mouth *of* two and three witnesses^M

    2D. I have said-before^N and I am saying-beforehand^N, as being-present^O the second²⁰ *time* and being-absent^P now,²¹ *to* the *ones* having previously-sinned²² and *to* all the rest^Q—   2

      1E. That if I come again I will not spare²³ *you*— •since you are seeking^R *a* proof²⁴ *of* Christ speaking in me, Who is not weak^S toward you, but is strong in you   3

        1F. For indeed²⁵ He was crucified because-of²⁶ weakness^T, but He lives because-of *the* power^U *of* God   4

        2F. For indeed **we**²⁷ are²⁸ weak in²⁹ Him, but we will live with Him because of *the* power *of* God toward you³⁰

      2E. Test³¹ **yourselves** *to see* if you are in the faith! Prove³² **yourselves**!   5

        1F. Or do you not know³³ yourselves, that Jesus Christ *is* in you?— unless indeed you are disapproved³⁴

        2F. But I hope that you will come-to-know³⁵ that **we** are not disapproved   6

      3E. And we are³⁶ praying to God *that* you *may* not do anything bad³⁷   7

        1F. Not in order that **we** may appear^V approved³⁸

        2F. But in order that **you** may be doing the good^W, and **we** may be as disapproved³⁹

          1G. For we cannot *do* anything against the truth, but [only] for the truth⁴⁰   8

          2G. For we are rejoicing^X whenever **we** are weak^S but **you** are strong⁴¹   9

      4E. This⁴² also we are praying— your restoration⁴³

  3C. For this reason I am writing these *things* while absent⁴⁴— in order that while being-present^O, I may not act⁴⁵ severely⁴⁶ according-to⁴⁷ the authority^Y which the Lord gave me for building-up^C and not for tearing-down^Z   10

1. Instead of "All this time", some manuscripts say "Again" {A}.
2. On this word, see "speak a defense" in Lk 21:14.
3. This could also be a statement, "All this time, you are thinking...".
4. See Act 5:26 on this idiom.
5. That is, fighting and bickering as described next, or living in immorality, as described in v 21.
6. That is, as a disciplinarian, handing out punishment from God (13:2), to people over whom he publicly mourns, 12:21.
7. On this word, see 11:2. Some manuscripts have these first two words as plural (like those that follow), "quarrels, jealousies" {N}.
8. Or, "fits of rage, outbursts of anger". It is plural only here and Gal 5:20. On this word, see "fury" in Rev 16:19.
9. Or, "gossipings, slanderings". Used only here. GK *6030*. Related word in Rom 1:29.
10. Or, "conceits, [acts of] pride". Used only here. GK *5883*. Related to "puffed up" in 1 Cor 4:6.
11. Or, "disturbances". On this word, see Jam 3:16.
12. Some think Paul means "having come, my God should **again** humble me before you", "again" being moved forward in the Greek word order for emphasis.
13. To have to face and deal with such sin among them would be a humbling, mournful experience. On this word, see Phil 4:12.
14. Or, "to, with regard to". GK *4639*.
15. That is, in the process of "not sparing" them, 13:2. On this word, see Jam 4:9.
16. That is, previous to being exhorted by Paul in person or by letter. In others words, ones having been taught and warned who still did not repent. Some think Paul specifically means "previous to my second visit"; others, "previous to receiving my exhortations in 1 Corinthians". Elsewhere only in 13:2. GK *4579*.
17. Or, "in relation to, at, concerning". GK *2093*.
18. Note how Paul says this in 12:14, and the views of it there. Some think this clarifies 12:14, pointing to a third actual visit; others think 12:14 clarifies this, meaning Paul is referring to a third intended visit.
19. Or, "on the basis of ". Same phrase as in Mt 18:16; Deut 19:15.
20. Some think Paul means "as when I was present the second time", confirming that a second visit occurred (the sorrowful visit of 2:1. See 12:14). Others think he means "as though now being present in the spirit the second time, and being absent in the body", as these words are used in 1 Cor 5:3, the first time Paul had to act in this way. Some manuscripts add "I write" {N}, so that it says "...second *time*, and I write being absent now..." {N}.
21. This is the Greek word order. Some think these two phrases go with the previous two verbs— "I have said before, as being present the second *time*, and I am saying beforehand, being absent now..." (dropping the second "and"). Others think both go with the last verb, "I am saying beforehand— as being present the second *time*, and being absent now".
22. Same word as in 12:21.
23. Paul delayed coming in order to spare (1:23, same word) the Corinthians, but will not spare them when he arrives. Paul struck a man with temporary blindness in Act 13:11, and handed over offending believers to Satan in 1 Cor 5:5; 1 Tim 1:20. Here, he does not state explicitly what he has in mind. On this word, see Rom 11:21.
24. Or, "test", as in 8:2. On this word, see "approvedness" in 2:9. Same root word as "prove" in v 5; "disapproved" in v 5, 6, 7; and "approved" in v 7.
25. Some manuscripts say "For indeed although" {N}.
26. Or, "from, out of ". The source of the crucifixion of Jesus was "weakness"— either our weakness (sin) or His weakness (His human body, His humiliation as a man). But He lives because of (same word) the power of God, as we will (same word). GK *1666*.
27. That is, Paul himself is weak in his relations with the Corinthians, in the eyes of his detractors (in one sense), and in fact (in another sense, 4:7-12; 12:9-10).
28. Some manuscripts say "**we** also are" {K}.
29. Some manuscripts say "with" {A}.
30. That is, toward you and through us. Some manuscripts omit "toward you" {A}.
31. You are seeking a proof in me, v 3? I say test yourselves! On this word, see "tempted" in Heb 2:18.
32. Or, "Examine", as in 1 Cor 11:28. See if you are genuine. On this word, see "approve" in Rom 12:2.
33. Or, "recognize, understand". On this word, see "understood" in Col 1:6.
34. Or, "failing the test". Same word as in v 6, 7. On this word, see 1 Cor 9:27.
35. Or, "know, understand, recognize". On this word, see Lk 1:34. Related to "know" in v 5.
36. Some manuscripts say "I am" {N}.
37. Or, "wrong, evil, harmful". That is, such as the things in 12:20-21, things harmful to the truth and yourselves. Paul would prefer not to find this, and not to have to exercise his authority in punishing them. On this word, see "evil" in 3 Jn 11.
38. That is, because you obeyed our commands and submitted to us. On this word, see 2 Tim 2:15.
39. That is, because we did not exercise our disciplinary power, thus "proving" ourselves before you (v 3), because your good response eliminated the occasion for us to use this power.
40. That is, we pray as in v 7 because we could never desire otherwise. It would be against the truth for us to desire that you would continue in evil so that we could exercise our power against you.
41. Or, "powerful, mighty". That is, when we appear to be weak because you are strong and we are not required to use our power. On this word, see "powerful" in Lk 24:19. Related to the word in v 3.
42. Some manuscripts say "And this..." {K}.
43. Or, "completion, maturation". Used only here. GK *2937*. The related verb is used in verse 11.
44. Elsewhere only in 1 Cor 5:3; 2 Cor 10:1, 11; 13:2; Phil 1:27; Col 2:5. GK *582*.
45. Same word as in 1:17.
46. Or, "sharply, harshly". Elsewhere only in Tit 1:13. GK *705*. Related to "severity" in Rom 11:22.
47. Or, "based on, in keeping with". GK *2848*.

A. Lk 19:11 B. Mt 3:17 C. Rom 14:19, edification D. 1 Cor 1:11, quarrels E. Jam 3:14 F. Act 26:20 G. 1 Thes 2:3 H. 1 Cor 5:1 J. 2 Pet 2:2 K. Rom 2:1 L. Mk 13:14, standing M. Act 1:8 N. Jude 17, spoken beforehand O. Rev 17:8 P. 2 Cor 13:10 Q. 2 Pet 3:16, other R. Phil 2:21 S. 2 Tim 4:20, sick T. Mt 8:17 U. Mk 5:30 V. Phil 2:15, shine W. 1 Tim 5:10a X. 2 Cor 13:11 Y. Rev 6:8 Z. 2 Cor 10:4

A. Finally, brothers^A, be rejoicing¹, be restored², be exhorted³, be thinking the same *thing*,⁴ be living-in-peace^B. And the God *of* love and peace will be with you   11
B. Greet^C one another with *a* holy kiss^D   12
C. All⁵ the saints^E greet you
D. The⁶ grace^F *of* the Lord Jesus Christ and the love^G *of* God⁷ and the fellowship^H *of* the Holy Spirit⁸ *be* with you all⁹   13

1. Or, "farewell". Same word as in v 9; Lk 1:14; 10:20; Act 5:41; 15:31; Rom 12:15; Phil 1:18; 3:1; 4:4; Col 1:24; 1 Pet 4:13: Rev 19:7. It means "greetings, hail" only in Mt 26:49; 27:29; 28:9; Mk 15:18; Lk 1:28; Jn 19:3; and with different grammar, in Act 15:23; 23:26; Jam 1:1; 2 Jn 10, 11. Paul uses it 29 times, all as "rejoice" except perhaps here. It is not used elsewhere in the NT to mean "farewell" (but it has this meaning), nor in a conclusion to a book as here. Here then, some think "farewell" best suits this context; others, "rejoice". Used 74 times. GK *5897*. Related to "joy" in Lk 24:52.
2. Or, "made complete, put in order". Related to the word in v 9. Same word as in Gal 6:1, on which see "prepared" in Rom 9:22.
3. Or, "be encouraged, comforted". On this word, see Rom 12:8.
4. On this phrase, see Rom 12:16.
5. Verses 12-13 are numbered here as they are in the Greek versions. In English versions, this sentence is verse 13.
6. In English versions, this sentence is verse 14.
7. That is, the grace proceeding from or bestowed by Christ, the love originating from or produced by God.
8. Some think Paul means the fellowship among believers produced by the Holy Spirit; others, the fellowship of believers with the Holy Spirit.
9. Some manuscripts add "Amen" {N}.

A. Act 16:40 B. Rom 12:18 C. Mk 15:18 D. Rom 16:16 E. 1 Pet 1:16, holy F. Eph 2:8 G. 1 Jn 4:16 H. 1 Cor 1:9

Overview   # Galatians

Introduction	1:1-5
1A. I am marveling that you are so quickly turning away to a different gospel	1:6-7
1B. But even if we should, or anyone is announcing a contrary gospel, let him be accursed	1:8-10
2B. For I make known to you that I did not receive my gospel from humans, but by revelation	1:11-12
1C. For you heard of my former conduct in Judaism as a persecutor of the church	1:13-14
2C. But when God revealed His Son in me, I did not consult with humans	1:15-2:10
3C. And I rebuked Cephas for violating the principles of the gospel with the Gentiles	2:11-21
2A. O foolish Galatians, who bewitched you?	3:1
1B. Did you receive the Spirit by works or faith? Will you now perfect yourselves with the flesh?	3:2-5
2B. Know then that the ones of faith are the sons of Abraham	3:6-7
1C. The Scripture said all the Gentiles will be blessed in Abraham	3:8
2C. So then, the ones of faith are blessed with Abraham. Those of the Law are under a curse, and are not declared righteous. Christ redeemed us from the curse of the Law	3:9-14
3C. Brothers, the promises to Abraham were not nullified by the Law which came later	3:15-18
4C. Why then the law? It was added because of the transgressions, until Christ came	3:19-20
5C. Is the Law against the promises? No. It was our tutor leading to Christ. We are now not under a tutor, for we are sons of God, seed of Abraham, and heirs of the promise	3:21-29
3B. Now I say, when we were minors we were slaves to the elemental things. But when God sent His Son, He adopted you as sons and heirs. Why are you turning back to slavery?	4:1-11
4B. I beg you, become as I. Have I become your enemy for speaking the truth to you?	4:12-20
5B. Tell me, do you not hear the Law? They are of the slave woman, we are of the free woman	4:21-31
3A. Christ set us free for freedom. Therefore stand firm, and do not again be held in a yoke of slavery	5:1
1B. Behold— I say to you that if you receive circumcision, Christ will profit you nothing	5:2
2B. And I testify again that if you receive circumcision, you are a debtor to the whole law	5:3
3B. You who are trying to be justified by law were separated from Christ and grace	5:4-6
4B. You were running well, who hindered you? He will bear his judgment	5:7-10
5B. But I, brothers, if I am still proclaiming circumcision, why am I being persecuted?	5:11
6B. O-that the ones upsetting you would cut themselves off!	5:12
4A. For you were called for freedom, only do not use the freedom for an opportunity for the flesh	5:13
1B. But be serving one another through love. The whole Law is fulfilled in this	5:13-15
2B. And I say— be walking by the Spirit and you will never fulfill the desire of the flesh	5:16-25
3B. Let us not become conceited, challenging one another. Restore those who have fallen	5:26-6:5
4B. And let the one being instructed share all good things with the ones instructing	6:6
5B. We reap what we sow. Let us not grow weary while doing good. We will reap	6:7-10
Conclusion	6:11-18

Galatians 1:1	678	Verse

    A. Paul— *an* apostle not from humans[A] nor through *a* human, but through Jesus Christ and God *the* Father,   1
the *One* having raised[B] Him from *the* dead—*and all the brothers with me   2
    B. *To* the churches *of* Galatia[1]
    C. Grace *to* you and peace from God our[2] Father and *the* Lord Jesus Christ—*the *One* having given[C]   3-4
Himself for our sins so that He might rescue[3] us out of the present[4] evil age, according-to[5] the will
of our God and Father,* *to* Whom *be* the glory forever and ever[D], amen   5

1A. I am marveling[E] that you are so quickly[6] turning-away[7] from the *One* having called[F] you by *the* grace[G]   6
    of Christ[8], to *a* different[9] good-news[H]—*which is not another[10] [good news], except[11] there are some   7
    disturbing[12] you, and intending[13] to change[14] the good-news *of* Christ

    1B. But even if we or *an* angel from heaven should announce-a-good-news[J] *to* you[15] other-than[16] what   8
we announced-as-good-news[J] *to* you, let him be accursed[17]. *As we have said-before[18], I am also   9
now saying again— if anyone is[19] announcing-a-good-news-to[J] you other-than what you received,
let him be accursed

        1C. For am I now[20] *trying to* win-approval-of[21] humans[A], or God?   10
        2C. Or am I seeking[K] to please[L] humans? If[22] I were still[23] *seeking to* please humans, I would not
be *a* slave[M] *of* Christ

    2B. For[24] I make-known[N] *to* you, brothers[O], *as to* the good-news[H] having been announced-as-good-   11
news[25] by me, that it is not according to *a* human[26]. *For **I** neither received[27] it from *a* human[A], nor   12
was I taught *it*, but *I received it* through *a* revelation[28] *of* Jesus Christ

        1C. For you heard-*of* my former conduct[29] in Judaism   13

            1D. That I was persecuting[P] the church *of* God extremely[Q], and destroying[30] it
            2D. And I was advancing[R] in Judaism beyond many contemporaries[31] in my nation[S], being far   14
more *a* zealot[T] *for* the traditions[U] *of* my fathers[32]

        2C. But when God[33]— the *One* having separated[34] me from my mother's womb[35], and having   15
called[F] *me* through His grace[G]— was well-pleased[V] *to reveal[W] His Son in[36] me in order that   16
I might be announcing Him as good news among the Gentiles

            1D. I did not immediately[X] communicate[37] *with* flesh and blood,*nor did I go up to Jerusalem   17
to the apostles before me, but I went away to Arabia[38], and returned[Y] back[Z] to Damascus[39]
            2D. Then after three years I went up to Jerusalem to visit[40] Cephas[41]   18

                1E. And I stayed[AA] with him fifteen days
                2E. But I did not see another *of* the apostles[BB] except James[42], the brother *of* the Lord   19
                3E. Now *the things* which I am writing *to* you, behold— *I affirm* in the sight of God that[43]   20
I am not lying[CC]

            3D. Then I went into the regions *of* Syria and Cilicia[44]   21

                1E. And I was not-known[45] by face *to* the churches *of* Judea in Christ   22
                2E. But they were only hearing that "the *one* once persecuting[P] us is now announcing-   23
as-good-news[J] the faith[DD] which he was once destroying[EE]"
                3E. And they were glorifying[FF] God in[46] me   24

1. On the churches referred to, and when this book was written, see Act 14:28.
2. Some manuscripts say "God *the* Father and our Lord Jesus Christ" {B}.
3. Or, "deliver, take out, set free". Same word as in Act 7:10, 34; 12:11; 23:27; 26:17. Elsewhere only as "tear out" in Mt 5:29; 18:9. GK *1975*.
4. This is a participle, "having come, being present". On this word, see Heb 9:9.
5. Or, "in accordance with, based on, in keeping with". GK *2848*.
6. Or, "soon, hastily". Some think Paul means quickly with reference to his last visit; others, to their conversion; others, to the appearance of these false teachers. Same word as in Lk 14:21; 16:6; Jn 11:31; 13:27; 2 Thes 2:2; 2 Tim 4:9; Heb 13:23. Elsewhere only as "soon" in Act 17:15; 1 Cor 4:19; Phil 2:19, 24; Heb 13:19; "hastily" in 1 Tim 5:22; and "faster" in Jn 20:4. GK *5441*. Related word in Rev 1:1.
7. Or, "deserting, changing position, transferring yourself, taking yourselves away". On this word, see "removed" in Heb 11:5.
8. Some manuscripts omit "*of* Christ" {C}.
9. This word means "another of a different kind". Compare 2 Cor 11:4. On this word, see 1 Cor 12:9.
10. This word means "another of the same kind". It is not good news at all, but bondage, slavery to works of the Law. On this word, see 1 Cor 12:9.
11. Some think Paul means "I am marveling... except", providing Paul's explanation of why this is happening "so quickly"; others, "not another [good news], except" some are proclaiming it as such.
12. Or, "stirring up, troubling, throwing into confusion, agitating". Same word as in 5:10; Mt 2:3; Act 15:24; 1 Pet 3:14. Elsewhere only as "troubled" in Lk 24:38; Jn 11:33; 12:27; 13:21; 14:1, 27; "frightened" in Mt 14:26; Mk 6:50; Lk 1:12; and "stir up" in Jn 5:7; Act 17:8, 13. GK *5429*. Related to "disturbance" in Act 12:18.
13. Or, "wanting, wishing, desiring". On this word, see "willing" in Jn 7:17.
14. Or, "to alter, turn around". Elsewhere only in Act 2:20, of changing the sun to darkness. GK *3570*.
15. Some manuscripts omit "*to* you" {C}.
16. Or, "against, contrary to, rather than". GK *4123*.
17. This is the word *anathema*. On this word, see Rom 9:3.
18. Some think Paul is referring to the previous verse; others, to when he was present with these Galatians. On this word, see "spoken beforehand" in Jude 17.
19. Note the grammar. Verse 8 refers to what might happen in the future, "In the unlikely event that I or an angel should be saying it". Verse 9 refers to what is happening now, "Assuming that someone is in fact saying it".
20. That is, in saying v 8-9. Apparently Paul's opponents accused him of being a people-pleaser (a Gentile-pleaser), that is, of reshaping the gospel to appeal to Gentiles by dropping any requirement for circumcision.
21. Or, "persuade, convince"; or, "win over", as in Act 12:20. Paul states it as a challenge to them. On this word, see "persuade" in 1 Jn 3:19.
22. Some manuscripts say "For if..." {N}.
23. That is, as Paul did as a Pharisee; and as these false-teachers are now doing by trying to retain circumcision, 6:12-13.
24. Paul uses this word to assert his next point. GK *1142*. Some manuscripts say "But" {C}.
25. Paul uses both the verb and the noun of the same word, as also in 1 Cor 15:1; 2 Cor 11:7; Rev 14:6. This same verb is in v 8, 9, 16, 23; 4:13, on which see Act 5:42.
26. Or, "according to mankind". Its content is neither based on nor in keeping with the teaching or authority of any human source.
27. Same word as 1 Cor 11:23; 15:3. Paul received the good news from Jesus. The Galatians received (same word) it from Paul (v 9). Paul next explains how this happened. Same word as in 1 Cor 15:1; Phil 4:9; Col 2:6; 1 Thes 2:13; 4:1; 2 Thes 3:6. On this word, see "taken" in Lk 17:34.
28. Same word as in 2:2; 1 Cor 14:26; Rom 16:25. On this word, see 2 Thes 1:7. That is, "*from* Jesus Christ".
29. Or, "way of life". On this word, see 1 Pet 1:15.
30. Or, "ravaging, pillaging". Elsewhere only in v 23, and in Act 9:21 by believers about Paul! GK *4514*.
31. Or, "people of my own age". Used only here. GK *5312*.
32. Or, "forefathers, ancestors". Or, "*for* my ancestral traditions". That is, the traditions handed down from my forefathers. Used only here. GK *4257*.
33. Some manuscripts omit "God" {C}, so that it says "But when He...".
34. That is, to Himself. Same word as in 2:12, on which see Rom 1:1.
35. That is, "from birth". On this phrase, see Lk 1:15.
36. Or, "in my case", which some take to mean "to me". GK *1877*.
37. Or, "consult, confer". This word is used of receiving counsel and of giving it. Here, it means to receive something. Elsewhere only in 2:6, where it means to impart something. GK *4651*.
38. Elsewhere only in 4:25. GK *728*. Related to "Arab" in Act 2:11.
39. The events of this verse took place during Act 9:19-23. On Damascus, see Act 9:2.
40. This word means "to visit in order to get to know someone, to make the acquaintance of ". Used only here. GK *2707*. See Act 9:26-29 on this.
41. Some manuscripts say "Peter" {N}. Peter was the name more familiar to the Galatians, as to us. Peter is Greek, Cephas is Aramaic. Except for Gal 2:7, 8, Paul always calls him Cephas. Except for Jn 1:42, the Gospels and Acts always call him Simon or Peter. Elsewhere only in 1 Cor 1:12; 3:22; 9:5; 15:5; Gal 2:9, 11, 14. GK *3064*. See Lk 6:14 on Peter.
42. Or, "apostles, only James...". See Mt 13:55 on James. On the brothers of Jesus, see Mt 13:55-56.
43. This oath is similar to the oaths in Rom 14:11; 2 Cor 1:18; 11:10. All four have this word (GK *4022*) pointing to the content of the oath, though it is left untranslated in the other places.
44. This takes place in Act 9:30. Tarsus, Paul's hometown, is in the Roman province of Cilicia.
45. Literally "I was being not-known", that is, I continued to be unknown. On this word, see "ignorant of " in Rom 10:3.
46. That is, "in connection with". GK *1877*.

A. Mt 4:4, mankind   B. Mt 28:6, arose   C. Eph 1:22   D. Rev 20:10   E. Rev 17:8   F. Rom 8:30   G. Eph 2:8   H. 1 Cor 15:1   J. Act 5:42   K. Phil 2:21   L. 1 Thes 2:4   M. Rom 6:17   N. Phil 1:22, know   O. Act 16:40   P. 2 Tim 3:12   Q. 1 Cor 12:31, beyond measure   R. 2 Tim 2:16   S. 1 Cor 12:28, kind   T. 1 Cor 14:12   U. 1 Cor 11:2   V. Mt 17:5   W. 2 Thes 2:3   X. Mt 13:5   Y. 2 Pet 2:21, turn back   Z. Mk 15:13, again   AA. Rom 11:22, continue   BB. 1 Cor 12:28   CC. Act 5:3   DD. Eph 2:8   EE. Gal 1:13   FF. Rom 8:30

| Galatians 2:1 | 680 | Verse |

 4D. Then after fourteen years I again went up to Jerusalem[1] with Barnabas[A], having also taken along Titus[B] with[C] *me*   2:1

   1E. And I went up based-on[2] *a* revelation[3], and laid-before[D] them the good-news[E] which I am proclaiming[F] among the Gentiles— but privately[4], *to* the *ones* having-the-reputation-of[5] *being something*— *that* somehow I might not be running[6], or have run, in vain[7]   2

   2E. But[8] not even[9] Titus, the *one* with me, being *a* Greek[G], was compelled[10] to be circumcised[H]. °Now[11] *this arose*[12] because of the false-brothers secretly-brought-in[13]—   3 / 4

     1F. Who sneaked-in[14] to spy-out[15] our freedom[J] which we have in Christ Jesus, in order that they might enslave[16] us

     2F. *To* whom we yielded[17] *in* submission[K] not-even for *an* hour, in order that the truth *of* the good-news[E] might continue[18] with you   5

   3E. And from the *ones* having-the-reputation-of being something[19]— of-what-sort[L] they ever[20] were makes no difference[21] *to* me; God does not receive *the* face[22] *of a* human[M]— indeed[23] *to* me[24] the *ones* having-the-reputation communicated[25] nothing. But on-the-contrary[N]   6 / 7

     1F. Having seen that I have been entrusted[O] the good-news *for* the uncircumcised[26], just as Peter *for* the circumcised[P]—

       1G. For the *One* having worked[27] *in* Peter for *an* apostleship[Q] *of* the circumcised, worked also *in* me for the Gentiles   8

     2F. And having recognized[R] the grace having been given *to* me   9

     3F. James[28] and Cephas[29] and John— the *ones* having-the-reputation-of being pillars[S]— gave *the* right *hands of* fellowship[30] *to* me and Barnabas, that we *should* go to the Gentiles and they to the circumcised

       1G. They asked only that we should be remembering[31] **the poor**— *as to* which, I also was eager[T] to do this[32] very *thing*   10

 3C. And when Cephas[33] came to Antioch[34], I opposed[35] *him* to his face— because he was condemned[36]   11

   1D. For before certain *ones* came from James, he was eating with the Gentiles   12

   2D. But when they came, he was drawing-back[U], and separating[V] himself, fearing[W] the *ones* of *the* circumcision[37]

1. Some think Paul is referring to his third visit in Act 15:1-3, the trip regarding the controversy over the gospel. Acts 15 gives the public view of it, Gal 2 the private view. Others think he means his second visit, the humanitarian trip of Act 11:29-30; 12:25. "Again" could apply to either. Paul is listing the encounters relevant to his gospel.
2. Or, "according to, in accordance with, because of ". GK *2848*.
3. Same word as in 1:12.
4. On this idiom, see Mt 14:13. Those who think Paul is describing the visit in Act 15 think this occurred in Act 15:4, before the public meeting in Act 15:6.
5. Or, "seeming [to people in general] *to be*", and thus, "being recognized *as*", "being acknowledged *as*". That is, the recognized leaders of the church of Jerusalem. On this word, compare Mk 10:42 and "seems" in Lk 22:24. Some think Paul is referring to those in Act 15:6. He is politely referring to them as the leaders of the Jerusalem church, and is not being derogatory or sarcastic, or questioning their importance. Yet he does avoid calling them anything like "the apostles before me" (1:17), or giving the impression he submitted to them in any way. Paul is addressing them as equals. Same word as in v 6, 9. GK *1506*. "Something" is taken from v 6. Paul calls them "pillars" in v 9, though a broader group may be intended in v 2, 6.
6. That is, running in my work, my proclamation of the gospel to the Gentiles. On this word, see 2 Thes 3:1.
7. Or, "for nothing, to no end or result or effect". Some render this phrase "— whether somehow I am running or have run in vain", expressing the topic to be discussed, the grammar implying that Paul expected a "no" answer. Others think Paul is expressing his personal fear or apprehension that his work might come to no effect because of the opposition of some in Jerusalem. His fear was not regarding his work or gospel, but regarding what might happen to his work if he allowed a rift to develop with those in Jerusalem over the issue of circumcision. In either case, Paul laid it before the leaders to help them see that what he was doing was from God. On this word, see "empty" in 1 Thes 2:1. Compare 1 Thes 3:5, which has similar grammar, and the same phrase "in vain".
8. As proof that the Jerusalem leaders supported Paul, the situation regarding Titus is given.
9. That is, nothing was required even in his particular case, much less in regard to my ministry in general.
10. Same word as used of the Judaizers "compelling" Gentiles to live like Jews, 2:14. On this word, see 6:12.
11. Or, "And, But".
12. Or, "*it was*". That is, this attempt to have Titus circumcised. Others supply "*he was not compelled*"; others, "*he was not circumcised*"; others "*we went up*". There are other views of the connection between v 4-5 and v 2-3. The problem is that we do not know the historical details to which Paul is alluding. Each view of the connection is based on a suggested scenario as to exactly what happened. Consult the commentaries.
13. Some think Paul is referring to what happened in Antioch in Act 15:1, and that Titus was taken to Jerusalem as a "test case". Others think he means the issue with Titus in particular arose in Jerusalem. This adjective is used only here. GK *4207*. Related to "secretly bring in" in 2 Pet 2:1.
14. Or, "slipped in", with unworthy motives. On this word, see "came in beside" in Rom 5:20.
15. Used only here. GK *2945*. Related to "spies" in Heb 11:31.
16. On this word, see 2 Cor 11:20. It has the prefix "under", "enslave us under *them*, reduce us to slavery".
17. Or, "gave way, drew back". Used only here. GK *1634*.
18. Or, "remain continually". On this word, see Lk 22:28.
19. Notice that Paul does not finish this sentence. He leaves us expecting "I received nothing", but changes to "they communicated nothing to me".
20. Or, "formerly, once". Some think Paul is referring to these leaders' past standing before Jesus when He was on earth; others, to their standing as leaders in the church in Jerusalem when this took place. Used 29 times. GK *4537*.
21. Paul took no note of the earthly status, rank, or position of these leaders. And neither does God. On this word, see "mattering" in Phil 1:10.
22. That is, God is impartial. On "receive the face", see Lk 20:21.
23. Or, "well, for". Some think Paul means it "makes no difference *to* me... for *to* me the *ones*... communicated nothing". The human position of these leaders was of no consequence in this matter to me or to God, for they added nothing to me. Others think this resumes what Paul began to say earlier, "from the *ones* having the reputation of being something... well, *to* me the *ones*...". GK *1142*.
24. In the Greek word order, "*to* me" is the first word in this clause, receiving Paul's emphasis.
25. Or, "contributed, added". Same word as in 1:16.
26. That is, the proclamation of the good news to the Gentiles. On this word, see Rom 2:26.
27. On this word, used twice in this verse, and in 3:5, see 1 Cor 12:11. The miraculous powers of Peter and Paul objectively proved that God was empowering them both.
28. That is, the brother of the Lord (see 1:19). The apostle James was dead by this time (Act 12:2).
29. Some manuscripts say "Peter" {N}. On this name, see 1:18.
30. Or, "partnership". On this word, see 1 Cor 1:9. The "right hand *of* fellowship", a reference to the acceptance of Paul and Barnabas as full partners, is found only here.
31. That is, "keeping in mind". On this word, see Jn 16:21.
32. Or, "which indeed, I was eager to do this very thing". Some smooth this phrase by leaving out this word (considering it to be redundant), "which very thing I also was eager to do". Note 1 Cor 16:1.
33. Some manuscripts say "Peter" {N}.
34. On this city, see Act 11:19.
35. Or, "resisted, stood against". I stood against him face to face. On this word, see "resist" in Eph 6:13.
36. Or, "he had been condemned", literally, "he was having been condemned". Paul may mean that some believers in Antioch had condemned Peter's behavior; or, that Peter was self-condemned by his behavior. The grammar means Peter was in a state of condemnation, he was standing condemned. Elsewhere only in 1 Jn 3:20, 21. GK *2861*.
37. Peter was fearing that the Jewish believers would accuse him of violating the Law of Moses by eating with the Gentiles. The issue here was not Gentiles keeping the Law (as in Acts 15), but Jewish Christians (like Peter) keeping the Law.

A. Act 4:36   B. Tit 1:4   C. Act 15:38, take along with   D. Act 25:14   E. 1 Cor 15:1   F. 2 Tim 4:2   G. Gal 3:28   H. Lk 2:21   J. Gal 5:13   K. 1 Tim 2:11   L. Act 26:29   M. Mt 4:4, mankind   N. 2 Cor 2:7   O. Jn 3:36, believe   P. Eph 2:11   Q. Rom 1:5   R. Lk 1:34, know   S. 1 Tim 3:15   T. Eph 4:3, diligent   U. Act 20:20   V. Rom 1:1   W. Eph 5:33, respecting

3D. And the other Jews also[1] joined-in-hypocrisy[2] *with* him, so that even Barnabas was carried-away[3] *by* their hypocrisy[4] — 13

4D. But when I saw that they were[5] not walking-straight[6] with regard to the truth *of* the good-news[A], I said *to* Cephas[7] in front of everyone— "If **you** being *a* Jew are living Gentile-ly and not Jewish-ly[8], how[9] *is it* you are compelling[B] the Gentiles to Judaize[10]?" — 14

    1E. We[11] *are* Jews *by* nature[C], and not sinners[D] from *the* Gentiles[12]. °But[13] knowing that *a* person[E] is not declared-righteous[F] by works[G] *of the* Law except[14] through faith[H] *in* Jesus Christ, even **we** believed[J] in Christ Jesus[15] — 15-16

        1F. In order that we might be declared-righteous by faith *in* Christ, and not by works *of the* Law

        2F. Because by works *of the* Law, no flesh will[16] be declared-righteous

    2E. But if[17] while seeking[K] to be declared-righteous[F] in Christ[18], we also ourselves were found *to be* sinners,[19] *is* then Christ *a* minister[L] *of* sin?[20] May it never be — 17

        1F. For if I am building[M] again these *things* which I tore-down[21], I am demonstrating[22] myself *to be a* transgressor[N] — 18

            1G. For[23] through[24] *the* Law, **I** died *to the* Law, in order that I might live *to* God — 19

                1H. I have been crucified-with[O] Christ[25]

                2H. And **I** no longer am living, but Christ is living in me[26] — 20

                3H. And what I am now[27] living in *the* flesh[28], I am living by faith[29] *in* the Son *of* God[30]— the *One* having loved[P] me, and having handed Himself over[Q] for me

1. Some manuscripts omit this word {C}.
2. Used only here. GK *5347*. Same root word as "hypocrisy" next.
3. That is, led astray. On this word, see "carried along with" in Rom 12:16.
4. Or, "insincerity". Elsewhere only in Mt 23:28; Mk 12:15; Lk 12:1; 1 Tim 4:2; 1 Pet 2:1. GK *5694*. Related to "pretend" in Lk 20:20; "hypocrite" in Mt 6:2; and "sincere" in Rom 12:9.
5. More literally, "are", as the Greek typically phrases it.
6. Or, "being straightforward, walking a straight path". Used only here. GK *3980*.
7. On this word, see 1:18. Some manuscripts say "Peter" {N}.
8. These two words, "Gentile-ly, in a Gentile manner" (GK *1619*), and "Jewish-ly, in a Jewish manner" (GK *2680*), are used only here. Paul simply turned the nouns "Gentile, Jew" into adverbs. If you as a Jew have moved from strict adherence to the Jewish laws to a partial freedom from the Law, why should Gentiles do the reverse? When Peter withdrew from eating with the Gentiles, his behavior said "you Gentiles must become like these Jews".
9. Some manuscripts say "why" {N}.
10. Or, "to live like Jews". Paul turned the word "Jew" into a verb. Used only here. GK *2678*. The Judaizers taught that the Gentile Christians had to live like Jews— following their traditions and laws, especially circumcision (Act 15:1)— to be saved.
11. Some think Paul's quotation of what he said to Peter continues to v 21. Others think v 15-21 is Paul's present explanation of that event to the Galatians. In either case, v 15-21 may summarize the discussion that followed the challenge in v 14.
12. Or, "nations". On this word, see Act 15:23.
13. Some manuscripts omit this word {C}.
14. That is, "if *he does* not *come* through faith". The idiom "if not, unless, except" is used by Paul in Rom 10:15; 11:23; 1 Cor 8:8; 9:16; 14:6, 7, 9; 15:36; 2 Thes 2:3; 2 Tim 2:5. This is stated from the Jewish point of view, as an addition to their lifetime of obedience to God. We Jews who have faithfully obeyed God's Law all our lives know that we cannot be declared righteous if we do not come to Jesus by faith. Note that this implies that once they are declared righteous by faith, the Law-keeping is no longer relevant for salvation. They stand before God just like Gentiles. Paul takes up this inference in v 17.
15. Some manuscripts say "Jesus Christ" {N}.
16. This is an idiom, literally, "all flesh will not...", on which see Mt 24:22.
17. The grammar means "assuming it is true that".
18. That is, "in union with Christ", explained by v 16 as "by faith in Christ and not by works of the Law".
19. That is, ones equivalent in status to "sinners from *the* Gentiles", v 15; ones no longer living under the Law but outside the Law, and thus to some degree in violation of the Law. Some put the emphasis on the changed status at the time of salvation; others, on the conduct in violation of the Law thereafter, like Peter eating with these Gentiles. In the explanation below, both aspects are included.
20. There are several views on the exact meaning of this verse. Consult the commentaries. One way of stating Paul's full meaning may be expressed in three points. 1. If as is the case, we "Jews by nature" (v 15), while seeking to be justified "by faith in Christ and not by works of the Law" (v 16), turned to Him in faith, 2. And if as is the case, we were therefore then and thereafter rightly found or considered by the Law of Moses to be in the same class as "sinners from the Gentiles" (v 15), and violators of the Law of Moses whenever we lived "Gentile-ly and not Jewish-ly" (v 14), 3. Then are we to say that Christ is a servant of sin for turning us from our status and lifestyle as Jews living under the Law, to the status and partial-lifestyle of Gentiles living without the Law? If the Law is still in force as our rule of life, as the Jewish Christians in Antioch were saying by their behavior, then Jesus must have been wrong to turn us away from it in general, and a promoter in particular of Peter's sin of eating with these Gentiles. To illustrate this, if Peter ate roast pig (one food forbidden by the Law) with the Gentiles, then he did in fact violate the Law of Moses. If he did so under the leading of Christ, then Christ did in fact promote the violation of the Law of Moses. Does this mean Christ is a promoter of sin? No way! Because this violation of the Law of Moses is no longer a sin, because the Law is no longer in force as a rule of life for Christians. The fact is, the one who tries to "rebuild" the Law and put it in force is the real transgressor, v 18. For "I died to the Law", ending its reign over me forever, v 19. I now live by faith, v 20.
21. Or, "destroyed, abolished, nullified". On this word, see Mt 24:2.
22. Or, "showing, exhibiting". On this word, see Rom 5:8. Christ is not a minister of sin, for if as a Christian I am rebuilding these laws as a rule of life which as a Jew I tore down to be saved by faith, then I am the transgressor, not Him. It is the rebuilding and trying to obey them in addition to faith (as Peter did when he retreated), not the tearing them down in Christ and the violating them as a consequence of faith (as Peter did when he ate with them), that now makes one a transgressor of God's Law.
23. I am now the real transgressor of the Law because it is through the working of the Law itself that I died to the Law to become alive to God. By trying to rebuild the Law after dying to it, I show myself to be a transgressor of its very intent and work. And I am setting aside the grace of God, v 21.
24. By "through the Law", some think Paul means the Law's work in punishing sin with death. Through the Law's requirements which I failed to keep, I became subject to the penalty of death. Having died with Christ, that penalty is paid. Thus I died to the Law and its demands, and to rebuild it is to transgress the verdict of the Law itself. Others think he means the Law's work in leading us, and Paul in particular, to Christ. Through the Law, I came to learn that I could not keep the Law or be righteous. Thus the Law itself taught me to abandon it and to seek Christ for salvation. Having done so, I died with Him, and thus died to the Law. To rebuilt it is to transgress what the Law itself taught me.
25. This phrase explains how "I died to the Law".
26. This phrase explains how it is Paul is now dead, yet "living to God". His pre-Christian self living under the Law is dead. Now Christ is living in him, creating life in him in a new realm. Note that Paul does not say "I am living in Christ" here, but "Christ is living in me", giving Paul a new kind of life. Paul is dead, crucified.
27. That is, as a Christian, justified by faith, with Christ living in me.
28. That is, in my continued human existence on earth.
29. Or, "in faith", in the sphere of faith, not law. I do not continue to live by the works of the Law as a way of life, in the sphere of the Law. I am crucified with Christ, dead to the Law, and living in the sphere of faith and the Spirit.
30. Instead of "Son *of* God", some manuscripts say "God and Christ" {A}.

A. 1 Cor 15:1   B. Gal 6:12   C. Eph 2:3   D. Mt 9:10   E. Mt 4:4, mankind   F. Rom 3:24   G. Mt 26:10   H. Eph 2:8   J. Jn 3:36   K. Phil 2:21
L. 1 Cor 3:5, servants   M. 1 Cor 4:4, edify   N. Jam 2:9   O. Rom 6:6   P. Jn 21:15, devotedly love   Q. Mt 26:21, hand over

	2G. I am not setting-aside[1] the grace *of* God![2] For if righteousness[A] *comes* through *the* Law, then Christ died without-a-reason[3]	21
2A. O foolish[4] Galatians, who bewitched[5] you[6], before whose eyes[7] Jesus Christ was portrayed[8] *as* crucified[9]?		3:1
1B. I want to learn[B] only this from you— did you receive the Spirit by works *of the* Law, or by *the* hearing[10] *of* faith?		2
1C. Are you so foolish? Having begun-with[11] *the* Spirit, are you now perfecting-*yourselves*[12] with *the* flesh?		3
2C. Did you suffer[13] so many *things* in-vain[14]— if indeed *it* really *was* in-vain?		4
3C. *Did* then the *One* supplying[15] you the Spirit and working[16] miracles[C] among you *do it* because-of[17] works *of the* Law, or because-of *the* hearing *of* faith?		5
2B. Just as Abraham "believed God and it was credited[18] *to* him for righteousness", *know then that the ones of faith[19]— these are *the* sons[20] *of* Abraham		6-7
1C. Now the Scripture[D], having foreseen[E] that God declares the Gentiles righteous by faith, announced-the-good-news-beforehand[21] *to* Abraham [in Gen 12:3]— that "All the Gentiles will be blessed[22] in[23] you"		8
2C. So then the *ones* of faith are being blessed[F] together-with Abraham, the *man-of*-faith[24]		9
1D. For all-who are of *the* works *of the* Law are under *a* curse[25]		10
1E. For it has been written [in Deut 27:26] that "Cursed[26] *is* everyone who is not continuing-in[27] all the *things* having been written in the book *of* the Law, *that he might* do[28] them"[29]		
2D. And that no one is declared-righteous[G] by[30] *the* Law before God *is* evident[31]—		11
1E. Because "The righteous[H] *one* will live by faith" [Hab 2:4]		
2E. But the Law is not of faith, but "The *one*[32] having done[J] these *things* shall live by them" [Lev 18:5]		12
3D. Christ redeemed[33] us from the curse *of* the Law		13
1E. Having become *a* curse for us		
1F. Because[34] it has been written [in Deut 21:23], "Cursed *is* everyone hanging[K] on *a* tree[L]"		
2E. In order that the blessing[M] *of* Abraham[35] might come[36] to the Gentiles in Christ Jesus[37]		14
3E. In order that we might receive the promise[38] *of* the Spirit[39] through faith		
3C. Brothers[N], I speak in accordance with human[O] *thinking*[40]— though *it is* [a covenant] *of a* human[O], no one sets-aside[P] or adds-conditions-to[41] *a* covenant[Q] having been ratified[42]		15
1D. Now the promises were spoken *to* Abraham and *to* his seed[R]		16

1. Or, "nullifying, rejecting, declaring invalid". Same word as in Mk 7:9; 1 Cor 1:19; Gal 3:15; 1 Tim 5:12; Heb 10:28. Elsewhere only as "reject" in Mk 6:26; Lk 7:30; 10:16; Jn 12:48; 1 Thes 4:8; Jude 8. GK *119*. Related word in Heb 7:18.
2. Some think Paul means "the grace of God in giving the Law to Israel", as Paul's opponents charged him, because he set aside the Law or "nullified" it (Rom 3:31) by preaching grace. In setting aside Law-keeping, I am not setting aside God's grace as you claim I do. Others think Paul means "the grace of God saving us", as Paul is charging his opponents, because they are setting aside the grace of God by trying to rebuild the Law as a rule of life. I am not setting aside grace to rebuild Law-keeping, as you are doing. In either case, if Law-keeping was the path to righteousness, Christ did not need to die.
3. Same word as in Jn 15:25. The word means "as a gift, freely, without payment", and then "without a reason". The root word is "gift". Elsewhere only as "freely" in Mt 10:8; 2 Cor 11:7; and "as a gift" in Rom 3:24; 2 Thes 3:8; Rev 21:6; 22:17. GK *1562*.
4. Or, "senseless". Same word as in v 3. On this word, see Tit 3:3.
5. Or, "charmed", figuratively meaning "beguiled, deceived". It was also used in the sense of "cast a spell on". Used only here. GK *1001*.
6. Some manuscripts add "to not obey the truth" {N}.
7. More literally "*to* whom, before *the* eyes".
8. Or, "placarded, posted in a public proclamation, publicly set forth or proclaimed". Used of a man "posting a proclamation" that he was no longer responsible for the debts of his son. Same word as in Jude 4. Elsewhere only as "write before" in Rom 15:4; Eph 3:3. GK *4592*. Some manuscripts add "among you" {N}.
9. This is a participle, "having been crucified".
10. Or, "report". Some think Paul means "the act of obedient hearing proceeding from or characterized by faith", that is, believing the gospel. Was it by your works, or by your believing?; others, "the report concerning faith in Christ". Was it by your works, or by the preaching of the gospel to you? Same word as in v 5; Rom 10:17. On this word, see Heb 4:2.
11. Or, "begun-in, begun-by". That is, "in the sphere of the Spirit"; or, "by means of the Spirit". Likewise with "flesh" next. Elsewhere only as "begun in" in Phil 1:6. GK *1887*.
12. Or, "completing, finishing *yourselves*". Or, "being perfected, being finished". On this word, see 2 Cor 7:1.
13. Some think Paul is referring to persecution. Others render this "Did you experience" so many benefits of the Spirit. The word is sometimes used this way outside the NT. Same word as in Mt 17:12; 27:19; Act 17:3; Phil 1:29; 1 Thes 2:14; 2 Thes 1:5; 1 Pet 2:20, 21; 4:19; Rev 2:10; etc. Used 42 times in the NT, always rendered "suffer". GK *4248*.
14. That is, to no avail. Same word as in 4:11. On this word, see Col 2:18.
15. Or, "providing". On this word, see 2 Cor 9:10.
16. Same word as in 2:8. On this word, see 1 Cor 12:11.
17. Or, "from, out of, by". That is, was the source your works or your faith? Same nuance of this word as in 2 Cor 13:4. GK *1666*.
18. On this word, see "consider" in Rom 3:28. "Credit for righteousness" is also in Rom 4:3, 5, 9, 22; Jam 2:23. Paul is quoting Gen 15:6.
19. That is, the ones originating in and living by faith, not works. Same phrase as in Rom 3:26.
20. Used 377 times, this word was used of male physical or adopted offspring; more broadly of physical or adopted "descendants, children", including males and females, as in "sons of Israel" in Rom 9:27; 2 Cor 3:7, and "sons of humans" in Mk 3:28; Eph 3:5 ; figuratively of spiritual descendants or children, as here (note that Paul changes to "seed" in 3:29), and "sons of God" in v 25; and more figuratively, of people characterized by or related to a quality, people whose identity is defined in some way by a relationship to a quality, as in "sons of disobedience" in Eph 2:2, and "sons of light" in 1 Thes 5:5. Reflecting modern sentiments, when both men and women are in view, some prefer to make this explicit by rendering this word "descendants" or "children". The explicit "sons and daughters" is found in 2 Cor 6:18; Act 2:17. GK *5626*. Compare "daughter" in Lk 13:16.
21. Used only here. GK *4603*. Related to the word in Act 5:42.
22. Elsewhere only in Act 3:25. GK *1922*. Related to the word in Lk 6:28. Same word as in Gen 12:3; 18:18; 22:18; 26:4; 28:14.
23. Or, "in connection with", as their spiritual father, Rom 4:11-12. GK *1877*.
24. Or, "the believer, the faithful". Rendered this way to show the relationship to "faith" earlier. On this word, see "faithful" in Col 1:2.
25. The curse is in the Law itself. Elsewhere only in v 13; Heb 6:8; Jam 3:10; 2 Pet 2:14. GK *2932*. The related verb is in Rom 12:14.
26. Elsewhere only in v 13. GK *2129*. Related to "curse" earlier in this verse.
27. Or, "staying in, remaining in, abiding in, being faithful to, being true to". Same word as in Act 14:22; Heb 8:9. Elsewhere only as "stay in" in Act 28:30. GK *1844*.
28. This idiom "*that he might* do", is also in Lk 2:27; Heb 10:7, 9.
29. That is, only "doers" of the Law are justified, Rom 2:12-13. And none are doers.
30. Or, "in *the* Law", in the sphere of the Law, or "under" the Law, as in Rom 2:12. GK *1877*.
31. Or, "clear, plain". Same word as in Mt 26:73. Elsewhere only as "clear" in 1 Cor 15:27. GK *1316*. Related to "make clear" in 1 Cor 3:13.
32. Some manuscripts say "The person..." {N}.
33. Same word as in 4:5. On this word, see Eph 5:16.
34. Some render this word "For" (GK *4022*). Some manuscripts have a different word, "For" {K}, the word in v 10 (GK *1142*).
35. That is, the blessing promised to him, the blessing of being declared righteous by faith, v 8.
36. Or, "come to pass for". GK *1181*.
37. Some manuscripts say "Jesus Christ" {N}.
38. On this word, see 1 Jn 2:25. Some manuscripts say "blessing" {A}, the word earlier.
39. That is, the promise consisting of the Spirit, the Holy Spirit.
40. Or, "in accordance with mankind". That is, from the human point of view, as people do about their affairs.
41. Used only here. GK *2112*. Related to "directing" in 1 Cor 7:17.
42. Paul now applies this bit of human truth to God's covenant with Abraham. The Law did not change it. On this word, see "confirm" in 2 Cor 2:8.

A. Rom 1:17 B. Phil 4:11 C. 1 Cor 12:10 D. 2 Pet 3:16 E. Act 2:31 F. Lk 6:28 G. Rom 3:24 H. Rom 1:17 J. Rev 13:13 K. Act 10:39 L. 1 Pet 2:24, cross M. 2 Cor 9:5 N. Act 16:40 O. Mt 4:4, mankind P. Gal 2:21 Q. Heb 8:6 R. Heb 11:11

	1E. He[1] does not say [in Gen 13:15] "and *to* seeds", as-*though speaking* in reference to many; but as-*though speaking* in reference to one, "and *to* your seed[2]"— who is Christ	
2D.	And this I say— the Law, having come-about after four-hundred and thirty years,[3] does not un-ratify[4] *the* covenant[A] having been previously-ratified[5] by God[6], so as to do-away-with[7] the promise	17
	1E. For if the inheritance[B] *is* of *the* Law, it is no longer of *the* promise[8]	18
	2E. But God has freely-given[9] *it* to Abraham through[10] *the* promise	
4C. Why then the Law? It was added[11] because of the transgressions[12]		19
1D.	Until which *time* the Seed should come *to* Whom[13] the promise has been made[14]	
2D.	Having been commanded[15] through angels by *the* hand *of a* mediator[16]	
	1E. Now a[17] mediator is not [a mediator] *of* [only] one [party], but God is one[18]	20
5C. *Is* the Law then against the promises *of* God[19]? May it never be! For if *a* Law being able to give-life[C] had been given, righteousness[D] really[20] would have been by *the* Law!		21
1D.	But[21] the Scripture[22] confined[23] all *things* under sin[24], in order that the promise by faith *in* Jesus Christ[25] might be given *to* the *ones* believing[E]	22
2D.	And before the faith[26] came, we were being kept-in-custody[27] under *the* Law— being confined[28] until[29] the faith[30] destined[31] to be revealed[F]	23
3D.	So then the Law has been[32] our tutor[33] leading-to[34] Christ, in order that we might be declared-righteous[G] by faith	24
4D.	But the faith[35] having come, we are no longer under *a* tutor, °for you all are sons[H] *of* God[36] through faith in Christ[37] Jesus	25-26
	1E. For all you who were baptized[38] into Christ put-on[39] Christ. °There is no Jew nor Greek[40], there is no slave[J] nor free[K], there is no male[L] and female[M]. For **you** all are one in Christ Jesus	27-28
	2E. And if[41] you *are* Christ's, then you are seed *of* Abraham— heirs[42] according-to[43] *the* promise	29
3B. Now I say[44]— for as much time as the[45] heir[N] is *a* child[46], he is no different[O] *from a* slave. Being *the* [future] owner[47] of all, °nevertheless[48] he is under guardians[P] and stewards[49] until the pre-appointed[50] day *of* the father		4:1 2

1. That is, the One who spoke the promises. Or, "it", the Scriptures.
2. That is, descendant. Paul was well aware that "seed" has a plural, collective sense, as he himself uses it in 3:29, "You (plural) are seed (singular, as here)". Here, Paul's point is that it also has a singular sense, which he applies to Christ. The promises were made to the near-term receiver (Abraham), and to the far-term fulfiller of them (Christ, v 19), for all his descendants. Same word as in v 19, on which see Heb 11:11.
3. The reference to 430 years comes from Ex 12:40, 41. Some think Paul means "after 430 years in Egypt", a period which began in Gen 46, the promises having been repeated to Abraham, Isaac, and Jacob. There are other views.
4. On this word, see "nullified" in Mt 15:6. Related to "having been previously ratified" later in the verse; and to "ratify" in v 15.
5. Used only here. GK 4623.
6. Some manuscripts add "in Christ" {A}.
7. Or, "nullify, make invalid, render inoperative". On this word, see Rom 6:6.
8. If the source of the inheritance has become the Law, then the promise no longer has any significance.
9. Or, "given as a gift". Related to "grace". On this word, see 1 Cor 2:12.
10. Or, "by means of". GK 1328.
11. It was not added to the covenant of promise, v 15. It was a distinct covenant added beside it, Rom 5:20. On this word, see "increase" in Lk 17:5.
12. Where there is no law, no requirement, there is no sin (Rom 4:15) or accountability (Rom 5:13). The Law made sin a violation, a transgression of God's requirements. The Law gave knowledge of sin (Rom 3:20). The Law taught the need for a Savior, Gal 3:23. On this word, see Rom 5:14.
13. That is, Christ, v 16. Thus the Law was in force from Moses "until" Christ came.
14. More literally, "*to* Whom it has been promised", that is, to Whom the promise was spoken, v 16.
15. Or, "ordained, set in order, arranged". On the Law and angels, compare Act 7:38, 53; Heb 2:2. On this word, see "directing" in 1 Cor 7:17. Related to "directions" in Act 7:53.
16. That is, Moses, who mediated the covenant of Law between God and the people of Israel. For the covenant of promise, God spoke directly with Abraham. On this word, see Heb 8:6.
17. That is, any mediator, a generic mediator. Literally, "the mediator", the one in general.
18. A mediator stands between two sides— for the Law, between God and Israel. The covenant of promise is superior to that of Law because God is the only party, Heb 6:13-18. There is no mediator, only God acting alone, promising something directly to Abraham. There are many interpretations of this verse. Consult the commentaries. Paul does not fully spell out his meaning here, but leaves a lot to be understood.
19. Some manuscripts omit "*of* God" {C}.
20. And in this case, the Law would have nullified the promise (v 18), and made Christ's death unnecessary (2:21). On this word, see Jn 8:36.
21. Or, "On the contrary, Rather", in contradiction to that theory. GK 247.
22. That is, God speaking in the Law, and in the promises made prior to the Law to Abraham.
23. Or, "enclosed, hemmed in, shut in on all sides". Same word as in v 23; Rom 11:32. Elsewhere only as "enclosed" in Lk 5:6. GK 5168.
24. As stated in Rom 3:9, and proved in Rom 3:10-20. "Under sin" is the same phrase as in Rom 3:9.
25. Or, "by the faithfulness *of* Jesus Christ". That is, the promise coming to us by means of faith in Jesus; or, by means of the faithfulness of Jesus to what God sent Him to do.
26. That is, the faith just mentioned, the faith in Jesus Christ, v 22. On this word, see Eph 2:8. Related to "believing" next.
27. Or, "guarded". Elsewhere only as "guard" in 2 Cor 11:32; Phil 4:7; 1 Pet 1:5. GK 5864.
28. Some manuscripts say "having been confined" {N}.
29. Or, "for, to". GK 1650.
30. That is, the one just mentioned, the faith in Jesus Christ.
31. This is a participle, "being destined, being about to be". Same word and grammar as in Rom 8:18. On this word, see "going to" in Mk 10:32.
32. Or, "become, come to be". GK 1181.
33. Or, "guardian, guide". This person was a slave who took the child to and from school, and supervised and guided his conduct. This implies that the Law is inferior and temporary, belonging to the period of childhood. The key thing the Law teaches is the knowledge of sin, and therefore the need for a Savior. Elsewhere only in v 25; 1 Cor 4:15. GK 4080.
34. Or, "until", as in v 23. On this word, see "resulting in" in Rom 5:16. GK 1650.
35. That is, the one mentioned, faith in Jesus Christ, v 22, 23.
36. That is, children of God. On "sons of God", see Rom 8:14.
37. Some think Paul means "through faith in Christ", the Greek word order; others, "sons *of* God in Christ Jesus through faith".
38. This construction is similar to Rom 6:3, except the verbs here call for "you" instead of "we". On this word, see Mk 1:8.
39. Or, "are wearing, dressed in". That is, put on like a garment. On this word see Rom 13:14.
40. That is, a non-Jew, a Gentile. It is paired with "Jew" like this 16 times. Used 25 times. GK 1818. In Christ there is no religious division of the world based on Judaism; no economic division based on slavery; no division based on gender.
41. The grammar means "Assuming you are".
42. Some manuscripts say "and heirs" {K}.
43. Or, "based on, in relation to". GK 2848.
44. Having mentioned being "sons of God" and "heirs", Paul now takes this up and applies it to the Galatians. Note that his starting point is an illustration spoken in accordance with human thinking, as in 3:15.
45. That is, the one in general, any heir.
46. That is, a minor. Same word as in v 3, on which see "infant" in 1 Cor 3:1.
47. Or, "master, lord". On this word, see "master" in Mt 8:2.
48. Or, "... *from a* slave, [though] being *the* [future] owner *of* all. But he is under...".
49. Or, "household managers". On this word, see 1 Pet 4:10.
50. Or, "fixed beforehand, pre-set, fixed in advance". Used only here. GK 4607.

A. Heb 8:6 B. Eph 1:14 C. Jn 5:21 D. Rom 1:17 E. Jn 3:36 F. 2 Thes 2:3 G. Rom 3:24 H. Gal 3:7 J. Rom 6:17 K. Mt 17:26 L. Mt 19:4 M. Mt 19:4 N. Rom 8:17 O. Phil 1:10, mattering P. Lk 8:3, steward

	1C. In this manner¹ also **we**², when we were children, were enslaved³ under the elemental⁴ *things of* the world	3
	2C. But when the fullness^A *of* time came, God sent-forth⁵ His Son—	4
	1D. Having come⁶ from *a* woman	
	2D. Having come under *the* Law ˚in order that He might redeem^B the *ones* under *the* Law	5
	3D. In order that we [all] might receive^C the adoption⁷	
	4D. And because⁸ you are sons⁹, God sent-forth the Spirit *of* His Son into our¹⁰ hearts crying-out^D, "Abba^E! Father!"	6
	3C. So then you are no longer *a* slave,¹¹ but *a* son— and if *a* son, also *an* heir^F through God¹²	7
	4C. But **at that time**¹³ not knowing^G God, you were-slaves¹⁴ to the *ones by* nature¹⁵ not being gods—˚but now having known^H God, yet rather having been known^H by God	8 9
	1D. How *is it* you are turning-back¹⁶ again to the weak^J and poor¹⁷ elemental *things to* which again you are wanting^K to be-slaves^L anew^M?	
	1E. You are observing^N days and months and seasons and years	10
	2E. I am fearing *for* you, that¹⁸ I somehow have labored in-vain^O for you	11
4B.	I beg^P you, brothers, become as I, because I also *became* as you¹⁹	12
	1C. You did me no wrong^Q. ˚And you know²⁰ that I first²¹ announced-the-good-news^R *to* you because of *a* weakness²² *of* the flesh	13
	1D. And you did not treat-with-contempt²³ nor loathe²⁴ your trial²⁵ in-connection-with my flesh, but you welcomed^S me as *an* angel²⁶ *of* God, as Christ Jesus	14
	2D. Where²⁷ then *is* your blessedness²⁸? For I testify^T *concerning* you that, if possible, you *would* have given your eyes²⁹ *to* me, having torn *them* out	15
	2C. So then, have I become your enemy while speaking-the-truth^U *to* you?	16
	3C. They are zealously-seeking^V you— not commendably³⁰, but they want to shut you out³¹ in-order-that³² you might be zealously-seeking them	17
	4C. Now³³ *it is* good to be zealously-sought in *a* commendable³⁴ *thing* at-all-times³⁵, and not only during my being present with you—˚my³⁶ children^W, *as to* whom again I am suffering-birth-pains³⁷ until which *time* Christ is formed³⁸ in you	18 19
	1D. But I was [just now] wishing³⁹ to be present⁴⁰ with you now⁴¹, and to change^X my tone⁴², because I am perplexed⁴³ with you	20
5B.	Tell me, the *ones* wanting to be under *the* Law, do you not hear *the* Law?	21
	1C. For it has been written that Abraham had two sons— one by the slave-woman^Y and one by the free^Z *woman*. ˚But the *one* by the slave-woman has been born according to *the* flesh, and the *one* by the free *woman* through⁴⁴ *the* promise	22 23

1. That is, as future heirs under guardianship while children.
2. Some think Paul means "we Jewish Christians" in v 3-5; others, "all Christians, we and you" in v 3-7. In any case, the Jew-Gentile distinction is clearly not his main point in this section. Note the change in v 6 from "you" to "our".
3. Or, "we had been enslaved". This is a participle, we "were having been enslaved". On this word, see Rom 6:18.
4. This word refers to the basic components or fundamental principles of a thing, the ABCs of a thing. Some think Paul means the rudimentary knowledge of God available in the world before Christ, the elementary forms of religion, Jewish and Gentile; others, the physical and ritual aspects of such religions in particular; others, the elemental spiritual beings associated with pagan religions. Same word as in v 9; Col 2:8, 20; and as "elements" in Heb 5:12. Elsewhere only as physical "elements" in 2 Pet 3:10, 12. GK *5122*. Related to "walk in line" in 5:25.
5. Same word as in v 6, and as "sent out" in Act 12:11; 13:26; 22:11. Used 13 times. GK *1990*. Related to "send out" in Mk 3:14.
6. Or, "come to be, come into being". Jesus "came into being" as a human, and in this sense was "born", from a woman and under the Law. The Son "came (same word) in the likeness of humans", Phil 2:7. John expresses this by saying "The Word became (same word) flesh". On this word, see 2 Pet 1:20.
7. Elsewhere only of Israel (Rom 9:4), and believers (Rom 8:15, 23; Eph 1:5). GK *5625*.
8. Some render this "that", meaning, "and as proof that". GK *4022*.
9. That is, children. On this word, see 3:7.
10. Some manuscripts say "your" {A}.
11. Referring to v 3.
12. Compare Rom 8:17. Some manuscripts say "*of* God through Christ" {A}.
13. That is, when you were a slave, not a son, v 7. Paul uses grammar that emphasizes the contrast between the two halves of this sentence; between then and now.
14. Or, "served as slaves". Same word as in v 9.
15. By nature, they were idols of stone and wood, or demons (1 Cor 10:20). On this word, see Eph 2:3.
16. The turning to Judaism and Law-keeping by the Galatians is called a turning back again to the elemental things to which they were enslaved as Gentiles. The rudimentary nature of these things is the same, though the form is different. On this word, see Jam 5:19.
17. This word means "poor, destitute, impoverished, *a* beggar". It is used of one dependent on begging for survival. These elemental things have nothing to offer. Elsewhere only in Mt 5:3; 11:5; 19:21; 26:9, 11; Mk 10:21; 12:42, 43; 14:5, 7; Lk 4:18; 6:20; 7:22; 14:13, 21; 16:20, 22; 18:22; 19:8; 21:3; Jn 12:5, 6, 8; 13:29; Rom 15:26; 2 Cor 6:10; Gal 2:10; Jam 2:2, 3, 5, 6; Rev 3:17; 13:16. GK *4777*. Related to "poverty" and "became poor" in 2 Cor 8:9. Compare the unrelated word "needy" in 2 Cor 9:9.
18. On this idiom, see Act 5:26.
19. That is, become believers living by faith, not Jewish-ly, because as as such, I became like you, living Gentile-ly.
20. Paul reminds the Galatians that they had reason to treat him poorly when he first came, but they did not do so.
21. Or, "formerly, before". On this word, see 2 Cor 1:15.
22. Or, "sickness". On this word, see Mt 8:17.
23. Or, "reject with contempt". On this word, see 1 Thes 5:20.
24. Used only here, *ekptuo* even sounds like what it means— "to spit out, to spurn". GK *1746*.
25. Or, "temptation". Paul's condition was a trial for the Galatians, or a temptation to reject him. Some manuscripts say "my trial" or "the trial" {A}. On this word, see Jam 1:2.
26. Or, "*a* messenger". On this word, see "messenger"in 1 Tim 3:16.
27. Some manuscripts say "What" {N}, so that it says "What then [happened to] your blessedness?". Used 48 times. GK *4544*.
28. That is, your feeling of a sense of blessing in my work among you. You had it then, and expressed it in your response to me. Where is it now? Elsewhere only in Rom 4:6, 9. GK *3422*. Related to "blessed" in Lk 6:20.
29. Some think Paul had some type of eye disease, and further, that this was his "thorn in the flesh", 2 Cor 12:7. However, this may simply be a hyperbole showing the extent of their devotion, as in the phrase "you would have given me the shirt off your back".
30. Or, "fitly, appropriately". On this word, see "well" in Act 10:33.
31. Or, "exclude you". Paul may mean his opponents want to position the Gentile believers as excluded from God's highest blessing— in particular, because they are uncircumcised— so that the Gentile believers must pursue them and the Jewish way of life (v 10) in order to gain or feel the acceptance and approval of God. Others think he means "exclude you from us" (ones like Paul), to isolate you from us. There are other views. Elsewhere only in Rom 3:27. GK *1710*.
32. Or, "so that you will". GK *2671*.
33. Since Paul is also zealously-seeking the Galatians, he adds this personal word (v 18-20), so they can see the difference between his motives and those of his opponents (which he spells out in 6:12-13).
34. Or, "good". It is fine to be pursued by me or anyone else, as long as the reason for it is commendable. Same word as "good" earlier in this verse, on which see 1 Tim 5:10a. Related to the word in v 17.
35. As Paul himself is doing even now, and not only when he is there with the Galatians. On this word, see "always" in 1 Thes 5:16.
36. Some start a new sentence here (making it 5C.), omitting the "But" beginning v 20. Some manuscripts say "little children" {N}.
37. Elsewhere only in v 27; Rev 12:2. GK *6048*. Related to the words in Rom 8:22 and 1 Thes 5:3.
38. That is, until you reflect Christ's image. Used only here. GK *3672*. Related to "transformed" in Rom 12:2; "conformed" in Phil 3:10; and "similar to the form" in Rom 8:29.
39. Or, "I *would* wish", if it were possible. Same grammar as in Act 25:22; Rom 9:3.
40. Same word as in v 18. Not only when I am present (v 18), but I wish I was present. On this word, see Rev 17:8.
41. On this word, see "right now" in 2 Thes 2:7.
42. That is, the tone expressed in this letter. On this word, see "voice" in Mk 1:26.
43. Or, "at a loss". On this word, see 2 Cor 4:8.
44. Or, "by means of ". One was born according to the normal course of nature; the other by virtue of the promise.

A. Col 1:19 B. Eph 5:16 C. Lk 16:25 D. Mt 8:29 E. Mk 14:36 F. Rom 8:17 G. 1 Jn 2:29 H. Lk 1:34 J. 1 Thes 5:14 K. Jn 7:17, willing L. Rom 6:6 M. Jn 3:3, again N. Lk 6:7, closely watching O. Col 2:18 P. 2 Cor 8:4 Q. Act 7:24, wronged R. Act 5:42 S. Mt 10:40 T. Jn 1:7 U. Eph 4:15 V. 2 Cor 11:2, jealous for W. 1 Jn 3:1 X. Rom 1:23, exchanged Y. Jn 18:17, servant girl Z. Mt 17:26

	2C. Which *things* are being allegorized¹, for these *women* are two covenants^A—	24
	1D. One² *is* from Mount Sinai³, bearing^B *children* for slavery^C, which is Hagar *(now⁴ Hagar is Mount Sinai in Arabia). And she⁵ corresponds⁶ *to* the present Jerusalem,⁷ for⁸ she⁹ is *a* slave¹⁰ with her children^D	25
	2D. But¹¹ the Jerusalem above is free^E— which is our¹² mother	26
	1E. For¹³ it has been written [in Isa 54:1], "Celebrate^F, barren^G *one,* the *one* not giving-birth^H. Break-forth and shout^J, the *one* not suffering-birth-pains^K. Because many more *are* the children^D *of* the desolate¹⁴ than *of* the *one* having the husband!"	27
	3D. And **you**¹⁵, brothers, are children^D *of the* promise in accordance with Isaac	28
	3C. But just as at-that-time^L the *one* having been born^B according to *the* flesh was persecuting^M the *one born* according to *the* Spirit, so also now.¹⁶ *But what does the Scripture say?	29 30
	1D. "Send-out^N the slave-woman and her son. For the son *of* the slave-woman shall by no means inherit¹⁷ with the son *of* the free *woman*" [Gen 21:10]	
	4C. Therefore, brothers, we are not children^D *of a* slave-woman, but *of* the free *woman*	31
3A.	Christ set us free¹⁸ *for* freedom¹⁹. Therefore be standing-*firm*^O, and do not again be held-in²⁰ *a* yoke²¹ *of* slavery^C	5:1
	1B. Behold— **I**, Paul, say *to* you that if you receive-circumcision²², Christ will profit^P you nothing	2
	2B. And I testify²³ again *to* every man receiving-circumcision that he is *a* debtor^Q to do the whole Law²⁴	3
	3B. You who are [trying to be] declared-righteous^R by *the* Law were alienated²⁵ from Christ. You fell-from²⁶ grace²⁷	4
	1C. For *by*²⁸ *the* Spirit, by faith²⁹, **we** are eagerly-awaiting^S *the* hope *of* righteousness	5
	2C. For in Christ Jesus neither circumcision^T nor uncircumcision^U can-do³⁰ anything, but faith working³¹ through love	6
	4B. You were running well^V. Who hindered³² you *that you should* not be persuaded³³ by the³⁴ truth? The persuasion³⁵ *is* not from the *One* calling^W you	7 8
	1C. *A* little leaven^X leavens the whole lump	9
	2C. **I** am persuaded³⁶ with reference to you in *the* Lord that you will think^Y no other *thing*	10
	3C. But the *one* disturbing^Z you will bear^AA the judgment^BB, whoever he may be	
	5B. But³⁷ **I**, brothers, if I am still proclaiming^CC circumcision^T, why am I still being persecuted^M?	11
	1C. Then³⁸ the offense³⁹ *of* the cross^DD has been abolished⁴⁰	

1. This word means to speak another meaning other than the literal meaning, "to speak figuratively, metaphorically; to interpret allegorically". Paul may mean that as written in Scripture these facts "contain an allegory" or a spiritual sense underlying the literal sense, almost like a type. Or, he may mean that he is now interpreting them in an allegorical fashion, drawing out a spiritual meaning from the literal events. Used only here. GK *251*.
2. That is, one woman representing one covenant.
3. This is where Moses received the Law. Elsewhere only in v 25; Act 7:30, 38. GK *4982*.
4. Some manuscripts say "for..."; others, "for Mount Sinai is in Arabia", omitting "Hagar" {C}. The grammar indicates that Paul means the word "Hagar" itself, or the concept of Hagar as representing a covenant, is identified with Mount Sinai. Some think Paul means that Mount Sinai was also called "Hagar" (or a word that sounds like "Hagar") in their day by the Arabians, thus supporting his identification with an etymological argument. Others think Paul is emphasizing that the Hagar-Mount Sinai-covenant concept under discussion is "in Arabia", that is, it is not in the promised land. Consult the commentaries.
5. That is, Hagar.
6. This word means "to be in the same series with", such as in the same line, rank, category, etc. Used only here. GK *5368*.
7. Hagar is allegorically the Law Covenant, and corresponds to the present physical Jerusalem, and is the mother of slaves, and a slave herself.
8. Some manuscripts say "and" {K}.
9. That is, the present Jerusalem.
10. Or, "serves as a slave". On this word, see "are slaves" in Rom 6:6.
11. Fully stated, this side of the comparison would be "The other is from the land of promise, bearing children for freedom— which is Sarah. She corresponds to the Jerusalem above. For she lives as a free woman with her children of promise". But Paul abbreviates and jumps right to the main points— she is free, and she is our mother.
12. Some manuscripts say "mother *of* us all" {A}. Sarah is allegorically the New Covenant, and corresponds to the heavenly Jerusalem, and is the free mother of free children.
13. This is given to prove that she is our mother.
14. That is, unable to bear children, referring to Sarah. On this word, see "wilderness" in Mt 3:1.
15. Some manuscripts say "**we**" {B}.
16. See Gen 21:9. The physical descendants of Abraham persecute the spiritual descendants of Abraham.
17. Elsewhere only in Mt 5:5; 19:29; 25:34; Mk 10:17; Lk 10:25; 18:18; 1 Cor 6:9, 10; 15:50; Gal 5:21; Heb 1:4, 14; 6:12; 12:17; 1 Pet 3:9; Rev 21:7. GK *3099*. Related to "heir" in Rom 8:17, and "inheritance" in Eph 1:14.
18. On "set free", see Rom 8:2. Same root word as "freedom" next.
19. That is, the freedom that belongs to us as children of the free woman, 4:31. On this word, see 5:13. Instead of "Christ... standing-*firm*", some manuscripts say "Therefore, stand-*firm in* the freedom *in* which Christ set us free" {B}.
20. Or, "caught in, entangled in, ensnared in, loaded down with, held subject to". Do not put your neck back in that yoke again. On this word, see "be hostile" in Mk 6:19.
21. Same word as in Act 15:10, "the yoke which neither we nor our fathers have been able to bear"; and 1 Tim 6:1; Mt 11:29, 30. Elsewhere only as "balance scale" in Rev 6:5. GK *2433*.
22. Using this same word, the Judaizers said "you must be circumcised to be saved", Act 15:1, 5. Paul says that if a person tries to approach God through works, Christ cannot help him; he must keep all the Law. In Col 2:11, Paul says that we are spiritually circumcised in Christ. On this word, see "circumcise" in Lk 2:21.
23. Or, "affirm, bear witness", as a witness to the truth. On this word, see 1 Thes 2:12.
24. If you proceed with works, then you must keep the whole Law to be justified. Compare Jam 2:10.
25. Same word as "released" in Rom 7:2, 6, but with a more negative meaning, "estranged, cut off, separated". Their relationship with Christ is severed. On this word, see "done away with" in Rom 6:6.
26. Or, "fell off". Same word as in 2 Pet 3:17. Elsewhere only as "fall off" in Act 12:7; Jam 1:11; 1 Pet 1:24; "fall away" in Act 27:32; "fail" in Rom 9:6; and "run aground" (fall off the sea) in Act 27:17, 26, 29. GK *1738*.
27. We either come by grace and faith, or we come by our own works of obedience. These are mutually exclusive paths. If we choose the latter, Christ cannot help us and we will not receive His grace. On this word, see Eph 2:8.
28. Or, "*in*".
29. Or, "are eagerly awaiting *the* hope *of* righteousness by faith".
30. Or, "avails; has power, strength, ability, validity for". Compare 1 Cor 7:19. Same word as in Phil 4:13; Jam 5:16. Used 28 times, mostly as "be able, be strong, be strong-*enough*". GK *2710*. Related to "strong" in Rev 18:8; and "strength" in Eph 1:19.
31. Or, "being in operation, being at work, producing an effect". On this word, see "works" in 1 Cor 12:11.
32. Or, "thwarted, cut in on". Elsewhere only in Act 24:4; Rom 15:22; 1 Thes 2:18; 1 Pet 3:7. GK *1601*. Related to "hindrance" in 1 Cor 9:12.
33. Or, "be obeying the truth". This word is related to "persuasion" next, and is the same word as in v 10. It is rendered this way to show the relationship. On this word, see 1 Jn 3:19.
34. Some manuscripts omit this word {C}.
35. Used only here. GK *4282*.
36. Or, "confident". Same word as in v 7, but different grammar.
37. Apparently some of these disturbers were saying that Paul is, or really meant to be, proclaiming circumcision. But their own behavior towards Paul proves that this is not true.
38. That is, if I were in fact proclaiming it.
39. Or, "trap, cause of falling". On this word, see "cause of falling" in Rom 11:9. The cross is the "trip-stick" in a trap set by God in Zion, Rom 9:33. Note Lk 2:34. This "trap" reveals what is in the heart. If one trips over it, he is caught in the trap. The cross is what makes the gospel offensive (1 Cor 1:23, same word), and God intends this to be so (1 Cor 1:18-25).
40. Or, "done away with, nullified". Note 6:12. On this word, see "done away with" in Rom 6:6.

A. Heb 8:6 B. 1 Jn 2:29, born C. Rom 8:15 D. 1 Jn 3:1 E. Mt 17:26 F. Rev 12:12 G. Heb 11:11 H. Lk 2:11, born J. Mt 3:3 K. Gal 4:19 L. Mt 24:9, then M. 2 Tim 3:12 N. Jn 12:31, cast out O. 1 Cor 16:13 P. Rom 2:25 Q. Rom 1:14 R. Rom 3:24 S. Rom 8:19, awaiting T. Eph 2:11, circumcised U. Rom 2:26, uncircumcised V. Act 10:33 W. Rom 8:30 X. Mt 13:33 Y. Rom 8:5 Z. Gal 1:7 AA. Mt 8:17, carry BB. Jn 9:39 CC. 2 Tim 4:2 DD. Mt 10:38

	6B.	O-that¹ the *ones* upsetting² you *would* indeed cut-*themselves*-off³!	12
4A.		For⁴ **you** were called^A for freedom⁵, brothers^B, only *do* not *use* the freedom for *an* opportunity⁶ *for* the flesh	13
	1B.	But be serving⁷ one another through love^C	
		1C. For the whole Law has been fulfilled⁸ in one saying— in the "You shall love your neighbor as⁹ yourself" [Lev 19:18]	14
		2C. But if you are biting and devouring^D one another, watch out *that* you may not be consumed¹⁰ by one another	15
	2B.	And I say— be walking^E *by the* Spirit, and you will never¹¹ fulfill¹² *the* desire¹³ *of the* flesh^F	16
		1C. For¹⁴ the flesh desires¹⁵ against the Spirit, and the Spirit against the flesh	17
		1D. For¹⁶ these are contrary¹⁷ *to* one another¹⁸ in-order-that¹⁹ you might not be doing²⁰ these *things* which you may be wanting^G	
		2C. But if you are being led²¹ *by the* Spirit, you are not under *the* Law²²	18
		3C. Now the works *of* the flesh are evident^H— which are²³ sexual-immorality^J, impurity^K, sensuality^L, °idolatry, sorcery^M, hostilities^N, strife²⁴, jealousy²⁵, rages²⁶, selfish-interests^O, dissentions^P, factions^Q, °envy²⁷, drunkenness²⁸, revelries^R, and the *things* like these	19 20 21
		1D. *As to* which *things* I tell you beforehand^S, just as I said-before^S, that the *ones* practicing^T such *things* will not inherit^U *the* kingdom^V *of* God	
		4C. But the fruit²⁹ *of* the Spirit is love^C, joy^W, peace^X, patience^Y, kindness^Z, goodness³⁰, faithfulness^AA, °gentleness^BB, self-control^CC	22 23
		1D. Against such *things* there is no law	
		5C. And the *ones of* Christ Jesus³¹ crucified³² the flesh^F, with *its* passions^DD and desires^EE	24
		6C. If we are living^FF *by the* Spirit, let us also be walking-in-line³³ *with the* Spirit	25

1. Or, "Would that". Elsewhere only in 1 Cor 4:8; 2 Cor 11:1; Rev 3:15. GK *4054*.
2. Or, "disturbing, troubling". Same word as in Act 17:6. Elsewhere only as "cause an upset" in Act 21:38. GK *415*.
3. Paul means either that they should "castrate themselves, make eunuchs of themselves" (a sarcastic response to their desire for circumcision), or "cut themselves off from the congregation". Same word as in "if your hand offends, cut it off " in Mk 9:43, 45. Elsewhere only in Jn 18:10, 26; Act 27:32. GK *644*.
4. Paul uses this word to assert his next main point. It could be rendered "Indeed". GK *1142*.
5. Or, "liberty". Same word as in Gal 2:4; 5:1; Rom 8:21; 1 Cor 10:29; 2 Cor 3:17; 1 Pet 2:16; 2 Pet 2:19. Elsewhere only as "liberty" in Jam 1:25; 2:12. GK *1800*. Related to "set free" in Gal 5:1.
6. Or, "base of operations, occasion". On this word, see Rom 7:8.
7. On this word, see "are slaves" in Rom 6:6.
8. On this word, see "filled" in Eph 5:18. Some manuscripts say "is fulfilled" {N}.
9. Or, "like". See Mt 19:19 on this command.
10. Or, "destroyed, used up, squandered". Elsewhere only in Lk 9:54, call down fire to "consume" them. GK *384*.
11. This is an emphatic negative, the strongest in Greek, meaning "never, by no means, in no way". Elsewhere in the Epistles only in Rom 4:8; 1 Cor 8:13; 1 Thes 4:15; 5:3; Heb 8:11, 12; 10:17; 13:5; 1 Pet 2:6; 2 Pet 1:10; and in Rev 2:11; 3:3, 5, 12; 9:6; 15:4; 18:7, 14, 21, 22, 23; 21:25, 27. See also Mt 5:20; Mk 13:2; Lk 9:27; Jn 8:50.
12. Or, "finish, bring to completion". On this word, see "finish" in Rev 10:7. The desire will be there enticing and drawing us away (Jam 1:14-15), but it can never conceive as long as we are fulfilling the desires of the Spirit. The two paths are mutually exclusive. As Christians, it is the ever-growing direction of our life to be walking on the Spirit's path, 1 Jn 3:9. But it is a choice, which is why Paul commands it here.
13. This word means "strong desire", both in a good and bad sense. When used of evil sexual desire, it can be rendered "lust". When used of desiring what is not ours, it can mean "coveting". It is singular here, referring to the category, a collective whole. This same word is singular also in Lk 22:15; Phil 1:23; Col 3:5; 1 Thes 2:17; 4:5; Jam 1:14, 15; 2 Pet 1:4; 1 Jn 2:16, 17; Rev 18:14; and plural in Mk 4:19; Jn 8:44; Rom 1:24; 6:12; 13:14; Gal 5:24; Eph 2:3; 4:22; 1 Tim 6:9; 2 Tim 2:22; 3:6; 4:3; Tit 2:12; 3:3; 1 Pet 1:14; 2:11; 4:2; 2 Pet 2:18; 3:3; Jude 16, 18. Elsewhere only as "coveting" in Rom 7:7, 8; and "lust" in 1 Pet 4:3; 2 Pet 2:10. GK *2123*. See the verb in v 17.
14. This verse is intended to prove the "never" of v 16. It can never happen because the Spirit is against the flesh. The two are in opposition, preventing us from carrying out the flesh's desire when we walk in the Spirit.
15. Or, "covets, lusts, longs for". See Jam 1:14-15; 1 Jn 2:16; 1 Pet 2:11; Rom 13:14; etc. Same word as in Mt 5:28; 13:17; Lk 15:16; 16:21; 17:22; 22:15; 1 Cor 10:6; 1 Tim 3:1; Heb 6:11; Jam 4:2; 1 Pet 1:12; Rev 9:6. Elsewhere only as "covet" in Act 20:33; Rom 7:7; 13:9. GK *2121*. The related noun is in v 16.
16. Some manuscripts say "And" {N}.
17. Or, "are opposed, are settled or fixed against". On this word, see "opposing" in Phil 1:28.
18. Paul is not saying that there is a battle of equals, only that they are opposing forces. They are not equal. Before Christ, the flesh was dominant, leading to death (Rom 7:5-6). Now the Spirit is dominant, leading us to conformity to Christ, Rom 8:5-14, 29; 2 Cor 3:18. The flesh has been crucified with Christ, v 24.
19. Or, "so that you will not". GK *2671*.
20. That is, be doing the "desire of the flesh" (v 16) we may want to do. More literally, "in order that whatever you might be wanting—these *things* you might not be doing". Compare 1 Jn 3:9. The Spirit prevents us from living according to the flesh. He leads us to holiness. The opposite is not true. Though we can choose to obey it, the flesh cannot prevent us from "walking by the Spirit", otherwise v 17 disproves rather than proves v 16.
21. The grammar means "assuming that you are led", that is, that you are a Christian. Same word as in Rom 8:14. All Christians are "led by the Spirit" in this verse. All Christians are "not under the Law", that is, not living in the sphere of the Law, but in the sphere of the Spirit, as Paul explained in 2:19-20 and Rom 6:14. But the Galatians were wanting to be under the Law, 4:21. On this word, see Lk 4:1.
22. Paul put this sentence here to make clear that he does not mean that the flesh should be controlled by Law. As Christians we are no longer dominated by the flesh, v 16. Nor are we under the Law as a way of life, 5:1. We are on a third course, walking in the Spirit, being led by the Spirit, growing the fruit of the Spirit. Paul had to clearly make this point because the Judaizers said "Do not fulfill the desire of the flesh, walk in line with the Law as we do". We live a new life in the Spirit (Rom 7:5-6; 8:1-4), no longer mastered by sin or Law, but grace (Rom 6:14, 15).
23. Some manuscripts add next "adultery" {N}.
24. Some manuscripts say "quarrels" {N}, the plural of this word. On this word, see "quarrels" in 1 Cor 1:11.
25. On this word, see 2 Cor 11:2. Some manuscripts have this plural {N}.
26. Or, "fits of rage, [outbursts of] anger". Same word as in 2 Cor 12:20.
27. Or, "[acts of] envy", it is plural. On this word, see Mk 15:10. The related verb is in v 26. Some manuscripts next add "murders" {C}.
28. This word is plural, and may mean "episodes of drunkenness, drinking bouts". On this word, see Rom 13:13.
29. Fruit is produced by the life of God within us, 1 Jn 3:9. It is the natural product of our spiritual life. Note that Paul says "fruit" (singular), not "fruits". The "fruit" of the Spirit is the lifestyle that the He produces, which has the following nine qualities. In v 19, the "works" (plural) are the individual acts that the flesh produces.
30. Elsewhere only in Rom 15:14; Eph 5:9; 2 Thes 1:11. GK *20*. Related to "good" in 1 Tim 5:10b.
31. That is, those who belong to Him. Some manuscripts omit "Jesus" {C}.
32. Compare Rom 6:6; Gal 2:19-20.
33. Or, "walking in order, following in line". That is, living in conformity and agreement with the Spirit. Elsewhere only in Act 21:24; Rom 4:12; Gal 6:16; Phil 3:16. GK *5123*. Related to "elemental" in 4:3.

A. Rom 8:30 B. Act 16:40 C. 1 Jn 4:16 D. Mk 12:40 E. Heb 13:9 F. Col 2:23 G. Jn 7:17, willing H. Rom 1:19 J. 1 Cor 5:1 K. 1 Thes 2:3 L. 2 Pet 2:2 M. Rev 18:23 N. Eph 2:14 O. Jam 3:14 P. Rom 16:17 Q. 1 Cor 11:19 R. Rom 13:13 S. Jude 17, spoken beforehand T. Rom 2:1 U. Gal 4:30 V. Mt 3:2 W. Lk 24:52. X. Act 15:33 Y. Heb 6:12 Z. Rom 3:12, goodness AA. Eph 2:8, faith BB. Eph 4:2 CC. 2 Pet 1:6 DD. Rom 7:5 EE. Gal 5:16 FF. Rev 20:4, came to life

3B. Let[1] us not become conceited[2] *ones*, challenging[3] one another, envying one another   26

    1C. Brothers[A], even if[4] *a* person[B] is overtaken[5] in some trespass[6]   6:1

        1D. **You** spiritual[C] *ones* be restoring[7] such *a one* in *a* spirit *of* gentleness[8], looking-out-for[D] yourself *that* **you** also not be tempted[E]
        2D. Be carrying[F] one another's burdens[9], and in this manner you will fulfill[10] the law *of* Christ[11]   2

    2C. For if anyone thinks[G] *that he* is something while being nothing, he is deceiving[12] himself   3
    3C. But let each *one* prove[13] his *own* work[H]— and then he will have the boast[14] with reference to himself alone, and not with reference to the other *person*. °For each *one* will carry[F] *his* own load[15]   4 / 5

4B. And let the *one* being instructed-in[16] the word share[J] *with* the *one* instructing in all good[K] *things*[17]   6
5B. Do not be deceived[18], God is not mocked[19]. For whatever *a* person sows[L], this he will also reap   7

    1C. Because the *one* sowing to his *own* flesh[M] will reap decay[20] from the flesh. But the *one* sowing to *the* Spirit will reap eternal life from the Spirit   8
    2C. And let us not grow-weary[21] while doing[N] good[O]. For *in His* own time[22] we not losing-heart[23] will reap   9
    3C. So then, while[24] we have opportunity[25], let us be working[P] good[K] to everyone, but especially to the family-members[26] *of* the faith[Q]   10

A. See *with* what large letters I wrote *to* you *with* my *own* hand![27]   11

    1. All who want to make-a-good-showing[28] in *the* flesh[M]— these *ones* are compelling[29] you to receive-circumcision[R] only in order that they may not be persecuted[S] *for* the cross[T] *of* Christ   12

        a. For not even the *ones* receiving-circumcision[30] themselves are keeping[U] *the* Law   13
        b. But they want you to receive-circumcision in order that they might boast[V] in your flesh[M]

    2. But *for* me, may it never be *that I should* boast[V] except in the cross[T] *of* our Lord Jesus Christ   14

        a. Through which[31] *the* world has been crucified *to* **me**, and I *to the* world
        b. For[32] neither circumcision nor uncircumcision is[33] anything, but *a* new creation[34]   15

    3. And all who[35] will walk-in-line[36] *with* this standard[37]— peace and mercy *be* upon them, and[38] upon the Israel[39] *of* God   16
    4. Henceforth[40] let no one be causing troubles[41] *for* me. For **I** bear[F] the brand-marks[42] *of* Jesus[43] on my body   17

B. *May* the grace *of* our Lord Jesus Christ *be* with your spirit, brothers. Amen   18

1. Others place this with the previous section (making it 7C.), and begin the new point with 6:1.
2. This adjective refers to ones acting based on "empty pride", "empty glory" (the root meaning of the word). It is clearly defined in 6:3. Used only here. GK *3030*. Related to "conceit" in Phil 2:3. The correct kind of glory is seen in 6:4-5.
3. Or, "provoking, calling forth (to fight)". Used only here. GK *4614*.
4. That is, even if it is an explicit case of sin, do not handle it based on the empty glory that you are superior or invincible, but with the attitude that follows.
5. Or, "detected, surprised, caught". GK *4624*.
6. Or, "false step". On this word, see Mt 6:14.
7. That is, be engaged in the process of restoration. On this word, see "prepared" in Rom 9:22.
8. On this word, see Eph 4:2. Same word as in Gal 5:23.
9. Or, "weights". On this word, see "weight" in 1 Thes 2:7.
10. Or, "fill up". Instead of "you will fulfill", some manuscripts have this word as a command, "fulfill" {C}. On this word, see "fill up" in 1 Thes 2:16.
11. That is, the command to love one another, Jn 13:34; 1 Jn 4:21.
12. Used only here. GK *5854*. It is made of the word "understanding" (in 1 Cor 14:20) and the word "deceive" (in 1 Tim 2:14). Such a person is deceived in his understanding. Related to "deceiver" in Tit 1:10.
13. Or, "test, examine, put to the test". That is, "prove by test". On this word, see "approve" in Rom 12:2.
14. That is, the content or matter of boasting, the thing to boast about. On this word, see Phil 1:26.
15. Or, "cargo, burden". With regard to the burdens of others, we should "be carrying" them, v 2. But with regard to reward, we each "will carry" our own load of "work" accomplished for Christ. We will be rewarded for our individual effort, not in relation to the work of others. Thus to think you are something because of your association with the work of another (v 3), to be conceited or envious in relation to the work of another (5:26), is self-deception (v 3). Elsewhere only as "burden" in Mt 11:30; 23:4; Lk 11:46; and "cargo" in Act 27:10. GK *5845*. Related to "burden" in Mt 11:28.
16. Or, "taught, informed, made to understand". Same word as later in the verse; and in Lk 1:4; Act 18:25; Rom 2:18; 1 Cor 14:19. Elsewhere only as "informed" in Act 21:21, 24. GK *2994*.
17. Compare 1 Cor 9:11.
18. This section is related to v 6, but extends beyond that subject into every area of life, as seen in Paul's conclusion in v 10. This is the general principle. This same phrase occurs in 1 Cor 6:9; 15:33; Jam 1:16. On this word, see "err" in Jam 5:19.
19. From the word for "nose", this word means "to turn up the nose at, to mock, to sneer at". Used only here. GK *3682*. Related word in Lk 16:14. It mocks God to think we can act contrary to His will, and be rewarded for it.
20. Or, "corruption, destruction". On this word, see 1 Cor 15:42.
21. On this word, see "lose heart" in 2 Cor 4:1. Same word as in 2 Thes 3:13.
22. Or, impersonally, "*in its* own time". On this phrase, see 1 Tim 2:6.
23. Or, "fainting, giving out, giving up, coming undone, tiring out, becoming exhausted, failing" in our souls or hearts. Same word as in Heb 12:3, 5. Elsewhere only as "become exhausted" physically in Mt 15:32; Mk 8:3. GK *1725*.
24. Or, "as". That is, "while you have the opportunity to do so in this life". There is a time for sowing and a time for reaping. Sow while you have the opportunity. Paul does not mean "when the circumstances happen to present themselves". We are to actively "take the lead in doing good works", Tit 3:8, 14. GK *6055*.
25. Or, "time, an occasion". Same word as "time" in v 9. Compare Eph 5:16. On this word, see Mt 8:29.
26. Or, "kinsmen, relatives". Elsewhere only in Eph 2:19; 1 Tim 5:8. GK *3858*.
27. Some think this means Paul wrote the whole letter; others, v 11-18 only, after an assistant wrote down the rest. Compare 1 Cor 16:21; Col 4:18; 2 Thes 3:17.
28. Or, "to make a good impression, to put on a good face". Used only here. GK *2349*. Related to "face".
29. Or, "forcing". Same word as in 2:3, 14. Elsewhere only in Mt 14:22; Mk 6:45; Lk 14:23; Act 26:11; 28:19; 2 Cor 12:11. GK *337*. Related to "compulsion" in 1 Pet 5:2; "necessary" in Tit 3:14; and "necessity" in 1 Cor 7:26.
30. Some manuscripts say "having received circumcision" {N}.
31. Or, "through Whom". Some think Paul is referring to the "cross"; others, to "Lord Jesus Christ".
32. Some manuscripts say "For in Christ Jesus, neither..." {A}.
33. Some manuscripts say "can do" {N}, as in 5:6.
34. Or, "a new creature". Same phrase as in 2 Cor 5:17. On this word, see Rom 8:39.
35. This "all who" is in contrast with those in v 12.
36. Same word as in 5:25. Some manuscripts say "who are walking in line" {N}.
37. Or, "rule, norm", referring to the principle in v 14-15. All who guide their path and live by this standard, by this measuring rod— boasting only in Christ, not in the flesh— peace on them. On this word, see 2 Cor 10:13.
38. Or, "even". "And" would mean Paul is addressing Jewish Christians separately. "Even" would mean he is addressing all Christians as "the Israel of God". GK *2779*.
39. The contrast is with "Israel according to the flesh", 1 Cor 10:18. Used 68 times. GK *2702*.
40. Or, "Finally". GK *3370*.
41. On the phrase "cause troubles", see Lk 18:5.
42. That is, the marks of ownership of a slave. Paul is referring to his scars from persecution, in contrast to those in v 12. Used only here. GK *5116*.
43. Some manuscripts say "Christ"; others, "*the* Lord Jesus"; others, "our Lord Jesus Christ" {N}.

A. Act 16:40   B. Mt 4:4, mankind   C. 1 Cor 14:1   D. 2 Cor 4:18, looking for   E. Heb 2:18   F. Mt 8:17, carry   G. Lk 19:11   H. Mt 26:10
J. 2 Jn 11   K. 1 Tim 5:10b   L. 2 Cor 9:6   M. Col 2:23   N. Rev 13:13   O. 1 Tim 5:10a   P. Mt 26:10   Q. Eph 2:8   R. Lk 2:21, circumcise
S. 2 Tim 3:12   T. Mt 10:38   U. Jn 12:25   V. 2 Cor 11:16

Ephesians

Overview

Introduction	1:1-2
1A. Blessed be the God who has blessed us with every spiritual blessing in Christ	1:3
1B. Even as He chose us in Him to be holy, having predestined us for adoption through Him	1:4-6
2B. In whom we have redemption through His blood and forgiveness according to His grace	1:7-10
3B. In whom we were allotted an inheritance, so that we might be for the praise of His glory	1:11-12
4B. In whom you were sealed with the Holy Spirit of promise, the pledge of our inheritance	1:13-14
2A. For this reason, I do not cease giving thanks for you, making mention of you in my prayers	1:15-16
1B. That God may give you a spirit of wisdom and revelation in the knowledge of Him	1:17
2B. So that you, the eyes of your heart having been enlightened, may know	1:18
1C. What is the hope of His calling	1:18
2C. What is the riches of the glory of His inheritance among the saints	1:18
3C. And what is the greatness of His power for us, the ones believing, in accordance with the working of the might of His strength	1:19
1D. Which He worked in Christ, having raised Him and seated Him at His right hand	1:20-23
2D. Indeed, you were dead in trespasses and sins. We were all children of wrath	2:1-3
3D. But God made us alive, and raised us with Him, and seated us with Him, in order to demonstrate His grace in His kindness toward us in Christ. This is His gift	2:4-10
3A. Therefore, remember	2:11
1B. That you Gentiles were excluded from God and His people— hopeless and without God	2:11-12
2B. But now you were made near by the blood of Christ, and we are one in Him	2:13-18
3B. So then, you are no longer strangers, but fellow-citizens and family-members of God	2:19-22
4B. For this reason I, Paul, a prisoner for you— if indeed you heard of my stewardship for you	3:1-13
5B. For this reason I pray that you may be strengthened and know His love	3:14-21
4A. Therefore I exhort you to walk worthily, keeping the unity of the Spirit, building up the body	4:1-16
5A. Therefore walk no longer like Gentiles, but put on the new person. Be imitators of God	4:17-5:14
6A. Therefore be walking wisely. Understand God's will. Be filled with the Spirit in all relationships	5:15-6:9
7A. Finally, become strong in the Lord. Put on the full armor in our spiritual battle	6:10-20
Conclusion	6:21-24

Ephesians 1:1	698	Verse

    A. Paul, *an* apostle[A] *of* Christ Jesus[1] by *the* will *of* God   1

    B. *To* the saints[B] being in Ephesus[2] and faithful[C] in Christ Jesus

    C. Grace *to* you and peace from God our Father and *the* Lord Jesus Christ   2

1A. Blessed[3] *be* the God and Father *of* our Lord Jesus Christ, the *One* having blessed[D] us with[4] every spiritual[E] blessing[F] in the heavenly *places*[5] in Christ   3

    1B. Even as He chose[G] us in Him before *the* foundation *of the* world[6], *that* we *might* be holy[7] and without-blemish[H] in His presence   4

        1C. In love[8] *having predestined[J] us for adoption[K] through Jesus Christ to Himself according-to[9] the good-pleasure[10] *of* His will[L]   5

            1D. For *the* praise[M] *of the* glory[N] *of* His grace[O] which He graciously-bestowed-on[11] us in the Beloved[12] *One*   6

    2B. In Whom[13] we have the redemption[P] through His blood[Q], the forgiveness[R] *of* trespasses[S], according to the riches[T] *of* His grace *which He caused-to-abound[14] to us   7   8

        1C. In[15] all wisdom[U] and understanding[16] *having made-known[V] *to* us the mystery[W] *of* His will[17] according to His good-pleasure, which He purposed[18] in Himself[19]   9

            1D. For *a* stewardship[20] *of* the fullness[21] *of* times, *that* He *might* sum-up[22] all *things* in Christ— the *things* at[23] the heavens and the *things* on the earth, in Him   10

    3B. In Whom[24] also we[25] were allotted[26] *an* inheritance   11

        1C. Having been predestined[27] according to *the* purpose[28] of *the* One working[X] all *things* in accordance with the counsel[29] *of* His will[L]

            1D. So that[30] we, the *ones*[31] having previously-hoped[32] in the Christ[33], *might* be for *the* praise[M] *of* His glory[N]   12

1. Some manuscripts say "Jesus Christ" {N}.
2. Some manuscripts omit the words "in Ephesus" {C}. For this and other reasons, some think this letter was intended for several cities (including Laodicea, Col 4:16). Paul spent over two years in Ephesus in Act 19. On the writing of this letter, see Act 28:30.
3. Or, "Blessed *is*". On this adjective, see Rom 9:5. Related to the verb and noun later in this verse.
4. Or, "by means of ". GK *1877*.
5. On "heavenly *places*", see 3:10.
6. That is, prior to creation. Compare 2 Tim 1:9. On this phrase, see 1 Pet 1:20.
7. Same word translated "saints" in v 1. On this word, see 1 Pet 1:16.
8. Or, "in love" may be taken with what precedes, "in His presence in love, having predestined...".
9. Or, "based on; in accordance with, in harmony with". Same word as in v 7, 9, 11. GK *2848*.
10. Or, "desire, good-will". Same word as in v 9; Phil 2:13. Elsewhere only as "well-pleasing" in Mt 11:26; Lk 10:21; "good-will" in Lk 2:14; Phil 1:15; and "desire" in Rom 10:1; 2 Thes 1:11. GK *2306*. Related to "well-pleased" in Mt 17:5.
11. Or, "His grace *with* which He graced us", "His favor *with* which He favored us". Paul uses a verb related to the previous word "grace". Elsewhere only as "favored" in Lk 1:28. GK *5923*. Instead of "which", some manuscripts have a phrase meaning "in which, by which, with which" {N}. This would allow this phrase to be rendered either from God's point of view, as "His grace in the sphere of which He favored us", or "with which He favored us"; or from our point of view, as "His grace in the sphere of which He made us accepted", as in the KJV. Related to "grace" in 2:8.
12. This is a participle, "the *One* having been loved", as in Col 3:12.
13. That is, Christ, v 3; Him, v 4; the Beloved One, v 6.
14. Or, "caused to overflow", and thus, "richly granted". On this word, see "abound" in 2 Cor 8:2.
15. That is, "In connection with, By means of ". GK *1877*. Or, this phrase may be taken with what precedes, "caused to abound to us in all wisdom and understanding". In addition, in both connections, some think Paul means "In all [our] wisdom and understanding" (which we possess in connection with the gospel); others, "In all [His] wisdom and understanding" (in the execution of His plan to cause His grace to abound, or in making known as He has done the mystery which He has kept silent until now, Rom 16:26; Col 1:26).
16. Or, "insight, intelligence". Elsewhere only in Lk 1:17. GK *5860*. Related to "thinking" in Rom 8:5.
17. The mystery of God's will is that He redeems everyone (Jew and Gentile) through Christ's blood. This was hidden, but is now revealed (3:5-6), and accomplished (3:11).
18. Or, "set forth, planned", so that it says "which He set forth in Him", that is, Christ. On this word, see "set forth" in Rom 3:25. Related to "purpose" in 1:11; 3:11.
19. Or, "Him", Christ.
20. Or, "*an* arrangement, mode of operation, economy, dispensation, administration, government", as it is used in 3:9; Lk 16:2; 1 Tim 1:4. Elsewhere only in the sense of "the office or sphere of responsibility of a steward", the position of management responsibility, in 3:2; Lk 16:3, 4; 1 Cor 9:17; Col 1:25. Related to "steward" in 1 Pet 4:10. Paul was the "steward" initially given the "stewardship position" (3:2) to enlighten all the Gentiles about the "mode of operation" of the mystery (3:9). Here, he means "for *an* arrangement" for providing salvation to the world. GK *3873*.
21. It is a stewardship "belonging to" the fullness of times; in other words, introduced for the fullness of times. When the "fullness (same word as here) of time" came, God sent forth His Son (Gal 4:4), and this stewardship is for His times. On this word, see Col 1:19.
22. Or, "gather together into one". Elsewhere only in Rom 13:9. GK *368*. This is God's good pleasure which He purposed.
23. This word in this phrase is found only here. GK *2093*. Elsewhere it always says "in" (GK *1877*) the heavens, as in 3:15; Col 1:16, 20; 1 Cor 8:5. Some manuscripts do say "in" here; others say "both the *things* in..." {N}.
24. That is, Christ, v 3; Him, v 10.
25. Based on what follows in v 12, some think Paul means "we Jewish Christians" here. Based on what precedes in v 3-10, others think he means "all we believers".
26. This word means "to choose by lot, to assign, to allot, to obtain by lot". Used only here. GK *3103*. The related noun means "lot, share" (see Col 1:12 on it). Some think Paul means we were "allotted, assigned an inheritance" by God, and thus "obtained an inheritance", which is mentioned in v 14, 18; Col 1:12; 1 Pet 1:4. Others think he means "allotted *to* God". That is, we were "the lot chosen by God, allotted by God to Himself ", and thus "made an inheritance" to God, as possibly meant in v 18, and as said of Israel in Deut 9:29; 32:9. We would be His inheritance in the sense that in us, He inherits the praise of His people, v 12.
27. This word modifies "we". Same word as in v 5.
28. Or, "plan, design". Same word as in 3:11. On this word, see Rom 8:28. Related to "purposed" in v 9.
29. Or, "determination, decision, intention, resolution, purpose, plan". Used of God and people. Elsewhere only as "purpose" in Lk 7:30; Act 2:23; 4:28; 13:36; 20:27; "plan" in Lk 23:51; Act 5:38; 27:12, 42; "intention" in Heb 6:17; and "motive" in 1 Cor 4:5. GK *1087*. Related to "will" in 1 Pet 4:3.
30. This is the same word translated "For" used at this same point in the other three stanzas (v 6, 10, 14b), but here it is used with the verb "to be". More literally, "For us to be for *the* praise *of* His glory, the *ones* having previously hoped in the Christ".
31. Some think Paul means "we" Jewish Christians in contrast with "you" Gentile Christians, v 13. Compare 2:14-18; 3:6. The bringing together of these two groups in Christ (which is "the mystery", 3:6) is a theme of this book. Here, Paul wants to explicitly link both groups directly to the spiritual blessings in the heavens for which he is blessing God. Others think he means "all we Christians having hoped in Christ since our conversion" in contrast with "you" the readers in particular, who also have heard and believed.
32. Or, "hoped beforehand". Used only here. GK *4598*. Some think Paul means "before the Christ came"; others, "before you Gentiles", who had no hope, 2:12.
33. Or, "in Christ". In Greek, "Christ" can have the article "the" (as it does here), and be understood either way (that is, as the name "Christ", or the title "the Christ, the Messiah").

A. 1 Cor 12:28 B. 1 Pet 1:16, holy C. Col 1:2 D. Lk 6:28 E. 1 Cor 14:1 F. 2 Cor 9:5 G. 1 Cor 1:27 H. Col 1:22 J. Rom 8:29 K. Gal 4:5 L. Jn 7:17 M. 1 Cor 4:5 N. 2 Pet 2:10 O. Eph 2:8 P. Rom 3:24 Q. 1 Jn 1:7 R. Col 1:14 S. Mt 6:14 T. 1 Tim 6:17 U. 1 Cor 12:8 V. Phil 1:22, know W. Rom 11:25 X. 1 Cor 12:11

Ephesians 1:13	700	Verse

    4B. In Whom[1] also **you**[2]— having heard the word[3] *of* truth[A], the good-news[B] *of* your salvation[C], in which[4] also having put-faith[5]— were sealed[6] *with* the Holy Spirit *of* promise[7]   13

        1C. Who[8] is *a* pledge[9] *of* our inheritance[10] until *the* [final] redemption[11] *of His* possession[12]   14

            1D. For *the* praise *of* His glory

2A. For this reason[13] **I** also— having heard-*of* your[14] faith[D] in the Lord Jesus and love[E] toward all the saints[F]—   15
do not cease[G] giving-thanks[H] for you, making mention *of you* in my prayers   16

    1B. That the God *of* our Lord Jesus Christ[15]— the Father *of* glory[16]— may give you *a* spirit[17] *of* wisdom[J] and revelation[K] in[18] *the* knowledge[L] *of* Him   17

    2B. So that you— **the eyes *of* your heart**[19] **having been enlightened**[20]— *may* know[M]   18

        1C. What is the hope *of* His calling[21]
        2C. What[22] *is* the riches *of* the glory *of* His inheritance[23] among[24] the saints[25]
        3C. And what *is* the surpassing[N] greatness *of* His power[O] toward[26] us, the *ones* believing, in-accordance-with[27] the working[P] *of* the might[Q] *of* His strength[28]   19

            1D. Which He worked[29] in Christ   20

                1E. Having raised[R] Him from *the* dead
                2E. And having seated[30] *Him* at His right *hand* in the heavenly *places*, *far above all rule[S] and authority[T] and power[O] and lordship[31] and every name being named[32]— not only in this age, but also in the *one* coming   21
                3E. And He subjected[U] all *things* under His feet   22
                4E. And He gave[33] Him *as* head over all *things* to the church—*which is His body[34], the fullness[35] *of* the One filling[V] all *things* in all[36]   23

            2D. Indeed, you *were*[37] dead[38] *in* your trespasses[W] and sins[X] *in which you formerly walked[Y]   2:1-2

                1E. In accordance with the [present] age[39] *of* this world[Z]

1. That is, Christ, v 12.
2. This is the Greek word order of v 13-14. The main sentence is "In Whom also you... were sealed *with* the Holy Spirit *of* promise... for *the* praise *of* His glory".
3. Or, "the message *of* the truth". On this word, see 1 Cor 12:8.
4. Or, "in Whom", so that this "in Whom" resumes the previous one, "salvation— in Whom also, having believed, you were sealed".
5. On the phrase "put faith in", see Jn 3:15. The punctuation in the previous note avoids this combination.
6. That is, given a mark of ownership, security, certification. Same word as in 4:30; Mt 27:66; Rom 15:28; 2 Cor 1:22; Rev 7:3, 4, 5, 8; 10:4; 20:3; 22:10. Elsewhere only as "certified" in Jn 3:33; 6:27. GK *5381*.
7. That is, characterized as the One promised. The promised Spirit.
8. That is, the Spirit. Or, "Which", the sealing.
9. On this word, see 2 Cor 1:22. The down payment is the Spirit.
10. Elsewhere only in Mt 21:38; Mk 12:7; Lk 12:13; 20:14; Act 7:5; 20:32; Gal 3:18; Eph 1:18; 5:5; Col 3:24; Heb 9:15; 11:8; 1 Pet 1:4. GK *3100*. Related to "heir" in Rom 8:17; and "inherit" in Gal 4:30.
11. Compare Rom 8:23; Eph 4:30. On this word, see Rom 3:24.
12. Or, "purchased possession, acquisition, obtaining". Some think Paul means "until *the* redemption *of us as His* possession". This word is used of Israel in the OT, and of the church in the NT, "a people for [God's] possession", 1 Pet 2:9. Others think he means "until *the* redemption, the obtaining *of our inheritance*". On this word, see "obtaining" in 1 Thes 5:9.
13. That is, because God has blessed us in this way (v 3-14), and you have responded.
14. The word "your" here is an idiom meaning "in relation to you, with respect to you". It occurs elsewhere only in Act 17:28; 18:15.
15. On this phrase, compare Rom 15:6; 2 Cor 1:3; 11:31; Eph 1:3; Col 1:3; 1 Pet 1:3; and Mt 27:46; Jn 20:17; Rev 3:2.
16. That is, characterized by glory. The glorious Father.
17. Or, "*the* Spirit". Paul could mean "*the* Spirit *giving* wisdom and revelation"; or a "spiritual *gift*" of wisdom and revelation (as this word is used in 1 Cor 14:12); or, a "disposition" based on wisdom and revelation (similar to Gal 6:1).
18. That is, "in the sphere of " or "in connection with" the knowledge of Him.
19. Some manuscripts say "understanding" {K}. Some manuscripts say "the heart" {C}.
20. Or, "illuminated". Same word as in 3:9. On this word, see Heb 6:4. The grammar is unusual (but similar to 3:18), so there are different views on exactly how this phrase connects to the context. In general, this phrase gives the result of the preceding and the basis of the following. Grammatically, Paul is putting emphasis on this phrase. May God give you a spirit of wisdom and revelation resulting in having the eyes of your heart enlightened so that you may know the spiritual truths of 1:18-2:10.
21. Some think Paul means the subjective hope which the calling works in our heart; others, the objective hope which belongs to the calling; everything to which we have been called in this life and the next. On "calling", see 2 Pet 1:10.
22. Some manuscripts say "And what" {N}.
23. Some think Paul means the glorious riches belonging to the inheritance; others, the riches belonging to the glory belonging to the inheritance; others, the riches belonging to the glorious inheritance.
24. Or, "in". Some think Paul means God's inheritance which He gives to us; that is, the spiritual blessings now (1:3-14), and the fullness which we await (1 Pet 1:4). On "inheritance among", see Act 20:32; 26:18. Others think Paul means God's own inheritance in the saints, consisting of the saints, His possession. See "allotted" in v 11 for more on this view.
25. Or, "holy *ones*", angels and believers. Compare 1 Thes 3:13.
26. Or, "for". GK *1650*.
27. Same word as "according to" in 1:5. This phrase makes a transition to what follows. What precedes is in accordance with the strength which God used to raise Christ from the [physically] dead, and to make us alive from the [spiritually] dead, 2:1-5. Some think Paul means "believing in accordance with"; others, "His power... [which is] in accordance with"; others, "the hope...the riches... the power... [which are] in accordance with"; others, "that you may know (v 18) ... in accordance with".
28. Or, "power, might". Same phrase as in 6:10. Elsewhere only in Mk 12:30, 33; Lk 10:27; 2 Thes 1:9; 1 Pet 4:11; 2 Pet 2:11; Rev 5:12; 7:12. GK *2709*. Related to "strong" in Rev 18:8.
29. On this word, see 1 Cor 12:11. Related to "working" in v 19.
30. Some manuscripts say "And He seated" {N}. Compare Ps 110:1.
31. Or, "dominion, authority", whether angelic, demonic, or human. On this word, see "authority" in 2 Pet 2:10. Similar words are used in 3:10; 6:12; Col 1:16; 2:10, 15; Rom 8:38; 1 Cor 15:24; 1 Pet 3:22.
32. That is, every ruling power by whatever name it is known. People are called "names" in Act 1:15.
33. This word means "give, grant". Used 414 times. GK *1443*.
34. Used 142 times of the physical body (dead or alive) of a human or animal, and of the "body of Christ", the church, as in Rom 12:5; 1 Cor 12:13, 27; Eph 4:4, 12, 16; 5:23, 30; Col 1:18, 24; 2:19; 3:15. GK *5393*. Related to "bodily" in Lk 3:22 and Col 2:9; and "fellow body members" in Eph 3:6.
35. Some think Paul means Christ's body is the "full number, full amount belonging to the One filling all"; others, His body is "that which is filled up by the One filling all", that is, the receptacle holding Christ's fullness; others, His body is "that which fills up the One filling all", that is, that which completes the "body" by forming the complement to the head. On this word, see Col 1:19.
36. Or, "with all". The One filling all is Christ. Some think Paul means "with all *things*", that is, filling all the universe with all His blessings or all the things that constitute it; others, "in all *ways*"; others, "in all [His people]". This same phrase "all in all" is used in 1 Cor 12:6; 15:28; and is similar to Col 3:11.
37. More literally, "you being dead", a participle. Some think Paul starts out to say "You being dead... God made alive", as in Col 2:13, but breaks off this sentence to detail the Gentile's sin, and lump Jews and Gentiles together as children of wrath. Then he starts over in v 4 and completes the thought, "We being dead... God made alive...". Others note that this is the same grammar as in Col 1:21, where no intervening thoughts occur.
38. That is, spiritually dead. Compare Col 2:13. The word is also used in this sense in 2:5; 5:14; Mt 8:22; 23:27; Jn 5:25; 1 Pet 4:6; Rev 3:1. On this word, see Mt 8:22.
39. Some think Paul means the aim or character of this age, and render this word "course". Same word as in 1:21; 2:7; 3:9. Also in Lk 16:8; Rom 12:2; 1 Cor 1:20; 2:6; 1 Tim 6:17; 2 Tim 4:10; etc. GK *172*.

A. Jn 4:23 B. 1 Cor 15:1 C. Lk 19:9 D. Eph 2:8 E. 1 Jn 4:16 F. 1 Pet 1:16, holy G. 1 Cor 13:8 H. Mt 26:27 J. 1 Cor 12:8 K. 2 Thes 1:7 L. Col 1:9 M. 1 Jn 2:29 N. 2 Cor 9:14 O. Mk 5:30 P. Phil 3:21 Q. Eph 6:10 R. Mt 28:6, arose S. Col 1:18, beginning T. Rev 6:8 U. Eph 5:21 V. Eph 5:18 W. Mt 6:14 X. Jn 8:46 Y. Heb 13:9 Z. 1 Jn 2:15

Ephesians 2:3 — 702 — Verse

      2E. In accordance with the ruler[A] *of* the authority[1] *of* the air[2], *of* the spirit[3] now being at-work[B] in the sons[C] *of* disobedience[4]

          1F. Among whom even **we**[5] all formerly[D] conducted-*ourselves*[6] in the desires[E] *of* our flesh[F], doing the wants[7] *of* the flesh and *of* the thoughts[G]   3

          2F. And we were *by* nature[8] children[H] *of* wrath[9], as also the rest[10]

   3D. But God, being rich[J] in mercy[K] because of His great love[L] *with* which He loved[M] us—   4
      even we being dead[N] *in* trespasses[O]—   5

      1E. Made-*us*-alive-with[P] Christ— *by* grace you are saved[11]
      2E. And raised-*us*-with *Him*   6
      3E. And seated-*us*-with *Him* in the heavenly-*places*[Q], in Christ Jesus
      4E. In order that He might demonstrate[12] in the coming[13] ages the surpassing[R] riches[S] *of* His grace in *His* kindness[T] toward us in Christ Jesus   7

          1F. For *by* grace[14] you are saved[15] through faith[16]   8
          2F. And this[17] *is* not from you. *It is* the gift[U] *of* God—*not of*[18] works[V], in order that no one may boast[W]   9

              1G. For we are His workmanship[19], having been created[20] in Christ Jesus for good works[21]— which God prepared-beforehand[22] in order that we might walk[X] in them   10

3A. Therefore remember[23]   11

   1B. That formerly[D] you[24], the Gentiles[Y] *in the* flesh[F], the *ones* being called "*the* uncircumcised[25]" by the[26] *one* being called "*the* circumcised[27]" (*one* done-by-*human*-hands[28] *in the* flesh)—*that you were at* that time without Christ   12

      1C. Having been excluded[29] *from* the citizenship[30] *of* Israel, and strangers[Z] *from* the covenants[AA] *of* promise[BB]
      2C. Having no hope[CC], and without-God[31] in the world

   2B. But now in Christ Jesus **you**, the *ones* formerly[D] being far-away, were made[32] near[DD] by the blood[EE] *of* Christ   13

      1C. For He Himself is our peace[FF]— the *One* having made[GG] both[33] one, and having broken-down[HH] the dividing-wall[34] *of* partition[35], the hostility[36]   14

1. Or, "power". Same word as in 1:21; 3:10; 6:12. Used of demonic authority also in Lk 22:53; Act 26:18; Col 1:13; 2:15; 1 Pet 3:22. On this word, see Rev 6:8. Some take it here in a collective sense, as the "empire".
2. Some think this means "atmosphere"; others, the same general thing as "heavenly places" in 6:12. Elsewhere only in Act 22:23; 1 Cor 9:26; 14:9; 1 Thes 4:17; Rev 9:2; 16:17. GK *113*.
3. The grammar naturally means that Satan is the ruler "*of* the authority... [and] *of* the spirit...", or "*of* the authority... [which is] the spirit...". Some think "spirit" has a collective sense here, meaning "the spirits" or "the spirit world"; others, that it means "the evil spiritual influence". Taking the grammar differently, others think Paul intends "the ruler... air" and "the spirit...disobedience" to be parallel descriptions of Satan.
4. That is, characterized by disobedience, or, belonging to disobedience as a child to a parent. Same phrase as in 5:6; Col 3:6. This disobedience results in unbelief. On this word, see Rom 11:30.
5. Some think Paul means "we Jews"; others, "we Jews and Gentiles". There is no distinction, Rom 3:22-23.
6. Or, "lived, behaved". Same word as in 2 Cor 1:12; 1 Tim 3:15; Heb 13:18; 1 Pet 1:17. Elsewhere only as "live" in Heb 10:33; 2 Pet 2:18; and "return" in Act 5:22; 15:16. GK *418*. The related noun "conduct" is in 1 Pet 1:15.
7. Or, "desires, wishes". This word is plural elsewhere only as "desires" in Act 13:22. On this word, see "will" in Jn 7:17.
8. This word means "the natural constitution or condition inherited by birth; the natural disposition or character; the natural order of things, nature, and its creatures". Here, Paul may mean "by their condition as spiritually dead humans" (v 1); or, "by their character as sinners". Elsewhere only in Rom 1:26; 2:14, 27; 11:21, 24; 1 Cor 11:14; Gal 2:15; 4:8; Jam 3:7; 2 Pet 1:4. GK *5882*.
9. That is, objects of wrath, belonging to wrath. On this word, see Rev 16:19.
10. Some think Paul means "as also the Gentiles"; others, "as also the rest who still are". On this word, see "other" in 2 Pet 3:16.
11. This is a participle, you "are having been saved", as also in v 8. On this word, see Lk 19:10.
12. Or, "display, show, give proof of, prove". Same word as in Rom 2:15; 9:17, 22; 2 Cor 8:24; 1 Tim 1:16; Tit 2:10; 3:2; Heb 6:10, 11. Elsewhere only as "show" in 2 Tim 4:14. GK *1892*. Related to "demonstration" in Rom 3:25.
13. More literally, the ages "coming-upon *us*". On this word, see "coming upon" in Lk 21:26.
14. Same word as in Jn 1:14; Rom 3:24; 4:4; 6:14; Eph 1:2, 6, 7; 3:2, 7; Heb 4:16; Jam 4:6. It also means "favor" in Lk 1:30; 2:52; Act 2:47; 24:27; 1 Pet 2:19; "thanks" in 1 Cor 10:30; 15:57; 2 Cor 8:16; 9:15; "gratitude" in Lk 17:9; "grace-*gift*" in 1 Cor 16:3; 2 Cor 8:19; "credit" in Lk 6:32; and "benefit" in 2 Cor 1:15. Used 155 times. GK *5921*. Related to "freely give" in 1 Cor 2:12; "gift" in 1 Cor 1:7; and "graciously bestow on" in Eph 1:6.
15. This is a participle, you "are having been saved". The same phrase is in v 5.
16. Used 243 times, this word means "faith, trust", and sometimes "faithfulness". It sometimes refers to the "body of faith", the thing believed. It is rendered "proof" in Act 17:31, and "pledge" in 1 Tim 5:12. GK *4411*. The related verb is "believe" in Jn 3:36.
17. Grammatically, "this" does not refer specifically to "faith" or "grace". It refers to the being "saved" (v 8), to all God has done for us as described in v 4-8, including the grace and faith.
18. Or, "out of, from, by". That is, originating in. GK *1666*.
19. Or, "creation, piece of workmanship, thing made". We are the result of God's making. Elsewhere only as "the *things* made" in Rom 1:20. GK *4473*. Not related to "works" in v 9.
20. Same word as in v 15. Related to the word in the phrase "new creation" in 2 Cor 5:17; Gal 6:15.
21. On "good works", see Rom 2:7; Tit 3:14.
22. We are not saved because of our good works, but in order that we may do them. Elsewhere only in Rom 9:23. GK *4602*. Compare Phil 2:12-13; 3:12.
23. This is the first command of the book. Paul applies all he has said about what the blessed God did for us directly to the Ephesians. From a new and personal vantage point (the Ephesians' own memory of their former status), he proclaims their changed status based on the work of Christ. Eph 2:11-22 is Paul's positive statement of the status of the Gentiles. In Galatians, Paul defended this teaching against the Judaizers. On this word, see Jn 16:21.
24. Some manuscripts say "That you— formerly Gentiles" {K}, reversing the order of the two words.
25. Or, "uncircumcision". On this word, see Rom 2:26.
26. That is, by the Jew. The Jews called the Gentiles "uncircumcised", and therefore unlike us, outsiders, excluded.
27. Or, "circumcision". This word refers to "circumcised" people, as in Rom 3:30; 15:8; Gal 2:7; Col 3:11. It also refers to a state of "circumcision", as in Rom 2:25; 1 Cor 7:19; Phil 3:3; Col 4:11; Tit 1:10. In both cases, this word is sometimes used as another way of saying "Jew", as here. In some places, like here, either is appropriate. Used 36 times. GK *4364*. Related to the verb in Lk 2:21.
28. On this word, see "made by *human* hands" in Act 17:24. Compare Col 2:11.
29. Or, "estranged, alienated". On this word, see 4:18.
30. Or, "state, body politic". That is, excluded from the condition and rights of a citizen. The Gentiles were excluded from participation in the government and worship that God established on earth in the nation of Israel. Elsewhere only in Act 22:28. GK *4486*. In v 19, using the same root word, Paul says Gentile believers are now "fellow citizens".
31. Or, "Godless *ones*". That is, without the true God. This word also means "denying God". Our word "atheist" comes from this word. Used only here. GK *117*.
32. Or, "became, came-to-be". GK *1181*.
33. That is, both groups, Jews and Gentiles, into one group, v 15. Same word as in v 16, 18. On this word, see "all" in Act 23:8.
34. Used only here. GK *3546*.
35. Or, "separation". That is, the wall dividing Jew and Gentile, and separating both from God. The wall is the Law. On this word, see "fence" in Lk 14:23.
36. Or, "hatred, enmity". Elsewhere only in v 16; Lk 23:12; Rom 8:7; Gal 5:20; Jam 4:4. GK *2397*. Related to "enemy".

A. Rev 1:5 B. 1 Cor 12:11, works C. Gal 3:7 D. Gal 2:6, ever E. Gal 5:16 F. Col 2:23 G. Lk 1:51 H. 1 Jn 3:1 J. 1 Tim 6:17 K. Mt 9:13 L. 1 Jn 4:16 M. Jn 21:15, devotedly love N. Mt 8:22 O. Mt 6:14 P. Col 2:13, made alive together Q. Eph 3:10 R. 2 Cor 9:14 S. 1 Tim 6:17 T. Rom 3:12, goodness U. Mt 5:23 V. Mt 26:10 W. 2 Cor 11:16 X. Heb 13:9 Y. Act 15:23 Z. Rom 16:23, host AA. Heb 8:6 BB. 1 Jn 2:25 CC. Col 1:5 DD. Lk 21:30 EE. 1 Jn 1:7 FF. Act 15:33 GG. Rev 13:13, does HH. Mt 5:19, break

1D. In His flesh[1] *having abolished[2] the Law *of* commandments[A] in decrees[3], in order that	15
1E. He might create[4] the two in Himself into one new[B] man[5], making peace[C]	
2E. And He might reconcile[D] both in one body[6] *to* God through the cross, having killed[E] the hostility[F] by it[7]	16
2C. And having come, He announced-as-good-news[G]	17
1D. Peace[C] *to* you, the *ones* far-away, and peace[8] *to* the *ones* near	
2D. Because[9] through Him we both have the access[10] in[11] one Spirit to the Father	18
3B. So then, you are no longer strangers[H] and foreigners[J], but you are fellow-citizens *with* the saints[K], and family-members[12] *of* God	19
1C. Having been built[L] upon the foundation[M] *of* the[13] apostles[14] and prophets[15]— Christ Jesus[16] Himself being *the* cornerstone[17]	20
1D. In Whom *the* whole building[N] being fitted-together[18] is growing[O] into *a* holy temple[P] in[19] *the* Lord	21
2D. In Whom also **you** are being built-together into *a* dwelling-place[20] *of* God in *the* Spirit[21]	22
4B. For this reason,[22] I, Paul, the prisoner[23] *of* Christ Jesus[24] for the sake of you the Gentiles—[25]	3:1
1C. If indeed you[26] heard-*of* the stewardship[27] *of* the grace *of* God having been given[28] *to* me for you— that[29] by way of revelation[Q]	2 3
1D. The mystery[30] was made-known[R] *to* me	
1E. Just as I wrote-before[31] in brief, *with reference to which you are able, while reading, to perceive[S] my understanding[32] in the mystery *of* Christ	4
2D. Which[33] *in* other generations[T] was not made-known[R] *to* the sons[U] *of* humans[V] as it was now revealed[W] *to* His holy apostles and prophets by *the* Spirit	5
3D. *That* the Gentiles are fellow-heirs[X] and fellow-body-members and fellow-partakers[Y] *of* the[34] promise[35] in Christ Jesus[36] through the good-news[Z]	6
1E. *Of* which I was made[37] *a* minister[38] according-to[39] the gift[AA] *of* the grace *of* God having been given[40] *to* me by-way-*of* the working[BB] *of* His power	7
2C. This grace[41] was given **to me**, the less-than-least *of* all saints[K], *that* I might	8
1D. Announce-as-good-news[G] *to*[42] the Gentiles the untraceable[43] riches[CC] *of* Christ	
2D. And enlighten[44] everyone[45] *to* see what *is* the stewardship[46] *of* the mystery having been hidden[DD] from the *past* ages[47] in God, the *One* having created[EE] all *things*[48]	9
3D. So that now, the multifaceted[49] wisdom[FF] *of* God might be made-known[R] *to* the rulers[GG] and the authorities[HH] in the heavenly[50] *places*	10
1E. Through the church	
2E. According-to[51] *the* purpose[JJ] *of* the ages[52], which He accomplished[53] in Christ Jesus our Lord	11

1. In this rendering, "in His flesh" has Paul's emphasis. Others also place "hostility" in this phrase, so that it says "Having abolished in His flesh the hostility, the Law". Others place "in His flesh" with what precedes, "and having broken down the dividing wall of partition, the hostility, in His flesh."
2. On this word, see "done away with" in Rom 6:6.
3. Or, "regulations, decisions, ordinances". Elsewhere only in Lk 2:1; Act 16:4; 17:7; Col 2:14. GK *1504*.
4. Elsewhere only in Mt 19:4; Mk 13:19; Rom 1:25; 1 Cor 11:9; Eph 2:10; 3:9; 4:24; Col 1:16; 3:10; 1 Tim 4:3; Rev 4:11; 10:6. GK *3231*. Related to "creation" in Rom 8:39; and "creator".
5. Some think Paul means one new kind of individual, neither Jew nor Gentile; others, one new corporate body of mankind, the body of Christ, the church. On this word, see "mankind" in Mt 4:4.
6. That is, "one [corporate] body", parallel to "one new man".
7. Or, "on it", that is, the cross. Or, "in Himself". Same word as "Himself" in v 15.
8. Compare Isa 57:19. Some manuscripts omit this word {N}.
9. Or, "That". GK *4022*.
10. Or, "introduction, admission". On this word, see Rom 5:2.
11. Or, "by". GK *1877*.
12. Or, "kinsmen". On this word, see Gal 6:10.
13. Some think Paul means the foundation "consisting of the apostles and"; others, "laid by the apostles and ". Compare 3:5.
14. That is, the twelve. On this word, see 1 Cor 12:28.
15. Some think Paul is referring to OT prophets; others, NT prophets. Same grammar as "shepherds and teachers" in 4:11. On this word, see 1 Cor 12:28.
16. Some manuscripts say "Jesus Christ" {K}.
17. Some render this "Christ Jesus being its cornerstone". Elsewhere only in 1 Pet 2:6. GK *214*. See also Mt 21:42. Compare Isa 28:16.
18. Or, "framed together, joined together". In ancient buildings, stones were "fitted together". Elsewhere only in 4:16. GK *5274*.
19. Some think Paul means "holy temple in *the* Lord"; others, "growing... in *the* Lord". That is, in connection with the Lord.
20. Thus, we Christians collectively are the spiritual temple where God dwells. Compare 1 Pet 2:5. GK *2999*.
21. Some think Paul means "being built... by *the* Spirit"; others, " being built... in spirit", in a spiritual manner, spiritually; others, a "dwelling place *for* God in *the* Spirit".
22. That is, because God has made you Gentiles a part of His family through Christ.
23. Used of Paul also in Act 23:18; 25:14, 27; 28:17; Eph 4:1; 2 Tim 1:8; Phm 1:1, 9. Elsewhere only in Mt 27:15, 16; Mk 15:6; Act 16:25, 27; Heb 10:34; 13:3. GK *1300*. Related to "imprisonment" in Phil 1:7.
24. Some manuscripts say "*of* the Lord Jesus"; others, "*of* Christ"; others, "*of* Jesus Christ" {C}.
25. Some think Paul does not finish this sentence. He starts to pray for them, then breaks off this sentence, and diverges to explain his commission. Then he returns to his prayer in v 14. Others render this, "... I, Paul *am* the prisoner", avoiding the break.
26. The grammar means "Assuming that you heard". "If indeed" is also in 4:21; 2 Cor 5:3; Gal 3:4; Col 1:23.
27. Having heard of this stewardship, the readers would understand why Paul says "for your sake" in v 1. Some think Paul means "the position of management responsibility" as apostle to the Gentiles; others, "the arrangement" in which he was a "steward" of the grace of God. On this word, see 1:10. It is the stewardship "*with reference to*" or "*characterized by*" God's grace which was given to Paul.
28. Grammatically, this word refers to grace, "the grace... having been given". Note v 7 and 8. It does not refer to "stewardship" here, "the stewardship... having been given", as it does in Col 1:25.
29. This begins Paul's description (v 3-12) of the content he assumes the readers heard about his stewardship. Some manuscripts omit this word {C}.
30. The mystery is defined in v 6. On this word, see Rom 11:25. Some manuscripts say "He made known the mystery *to* me" {N}.
31. Some think Paul is referring to what he just wrote, in 1:9-10; 2:11-22. You will be able to understand the mystery as stated in v 6 by reading what I just said. Others think he is referring to his earlier letters, or to a letter now lost.
32. Or, "insight". That is, my understanding in connection with the mystery concerning Christ. Same word as in Mk 12:33; Lk 2:47; Col 1:9; 2:2; 2 Tim 2:7. Elsewhere only as "intelligence" in 1 Cor 1:19. GK *5304*.
33. This refers to "mystery", either in v 4 or v 3.
34. Some manuscripts say "His promise" {N}
35. Some think Paul means the promise of the Spirit, as in 1:13; others, the promise of salvation, as in 2 Tim 1:1. On this word, see 1 Jn 2:25.
36. Some manuscripts omit this word {K}.
37. Or, "I became". Some manuscripts say "I became" {K}, using a different form of this word. GK *1181*.
38. Or, "servant". On this word, see "servants" in 1 Cor 3:5.
39. Or, "in accordance with, based on, by way of ". Same word as "by way of" next. GK *2848*.
40. This word goes with "grace", as in v 2. In some manuscripts it goes with "gift" {N}. These amount to nearly the same thing, "the gift *consisting of* the grace given" vs. "the gift given *consisting of the* grace".
41. That is, the grace mentioned in v 7 or v 2.
42. Some manuscripts say "among" {N}.
43. Its dimensions cannot be traced out. On this word, see Rom 11:33.
44. Same word as in 1:18.
45. Some manuscripts omit this word {C}, so that it says "And bring to light what *is* the...".
46. Or, "arrangement, mode of operation". On this word, see 1:10. Some manuscripts say "fellowship" {K}.
47. On "*past* ages", see Lk 1:70.
48. Some manuscripts add "through Jesus Christ" {N}.
49. Or, "many-sided". Used only here. GK *4497*.
50. The phrase "in the heavenly *places*" is elsewhere only in Eph 1:3, 20; 2:6; 6:12. This word is elsewhere only in Jn 3:12; 1 Cor 15:40, 48, 49; Phil 2:10; 2 Tim 4:18; Heb 3:1; 6:4; 8:5; 9:23; 11:16; 12:22. GK *2230*.
51. Or, "in accordance with, in harmony with, based on". GK *2848*.
52. Or, "*the* eternal purpose".
53. On this word, see "does" in Rev 13:13.

A. Mk 12:28 B. Heb 8:13 C. Act 15:33 D. Col 1:20 E. Rom 7:11 F. Eph 2:14 G. Act 5:42 H. Rom 16:23, host J. 1 Pet 2:11 K. 1 Pet 1:16, holy L. Jude 20, building up M. 1 Tim 6:19 N. Rom 14:19, edification O. Jn 3:30 P. Rev 11:1 Q. 2 Thes 1:7 R. Phil 1:22, know S. Eph 3:20, think T. Mt 24:34 U. Gal 3:7 V. Mt 4:4, mankind W. 2 Thes 2:3 X. Rom 8:17 Y. Eph 5:7 Z. 1 Cor 15:1 AA. Rom 5:15 BB. Phil 3:21 CC. 1 Tim 6:17 DD. 1 Cor 2:7 EE. Eph 2:15 FF. 1 Cor 12:8 GG. Col 1:18, beginning HH. Rev 6:8 JJ. Rom 8:28.

Ephesians 3:12	706	Verse

        1F. In Whom we have boldness[A] and access[1] in confidence[B], through faith *in* Him[2]   12

    3C. Therefore I ask *that you*[3] not lose-heart[C] in connection with my afflictions[D] for-your-sake[4]— which is[5] your[6] glory!   13

5B. For this reason[7] I bow my knees before the Father[8], *from Whom *the* whole[9] family[10] in *the* heavens and on earth is named[E]   14-15

    1C. *Asking* that He might grant *to* you in accordance with the riches[F] *of* His glory[G]   16

        1D. *That you* be strengthened[11] *with* power[H] through His Spirit in *your* inner person[12]
        2D. *So-that*[13] Christ *may* dwell[14] in your hearts through faith   17
        3D. *In-order-that*[15] you— **having**[16] **been rooted**[J] **and founded**[17] **in love**— might be strong-enough[18]   18

            1E. To grasp[19] together-with all the saints what *is* the width and length and height and depth[20]
            2E. And to know[21] the love *of* Christ surpassing[K] knowledge[22]   19

        4D. *In-order-that*[23] you might be filled[L] to all the fullness[M] *of* God[24]

    2C. Now *to* the *One* being able to do super-abundantly[N] beyond all *of the things* which we ask or think[25] according to the power[H] being at-work[26] in us—*to* Him *be* the glory[G] in the church and[27] in Christ Jesus for all generations forever and ever[O], amen   20 21

4A. Therefore **I**, the prisoner[P] in *the* Lord, exhort[Q] you to walk worthily[28] *of* the calling *with* which you were called[29]   4:1

    1B. With all humblemindedness[30] and gentleness[31]   2
    2B. With patience[R]
    3B. Bearing-with[S] one another in love
    4B. Being diligent[32] to keep[33] the unity[34] *of* the Spirit[35] in the bond[T] *of* peace[36]—   3

        1C. *There is*[37] one body[38] and one Spirit, just as you also[39] were called in one hope *of* your calling[40]   4

1. Same word as in 2:18.
2. Or, "through His faithfulness" to what God gave Him to do.
3. Some think Paul means "*that I* not lose heart". In addition, some think he asks "you"; others, "God".
4. Same word as in v 1 and 6:20, on which see Col 1:24.
5. That is, inasmuch as it is your glory, seeing that it is your glory, since it is your glory. Paul generalizes. My situation, my imprisonment and afflictions, is for your glory. This may be simplified to "which are your glory".
6. Some manuscripts say "our" {A}.
7. Paul now resumes where he left off in v 1. Same phrase as 3:1, which is elsewhere only in Tit 1:5.
8. Some manuscripts add "*of* our Lord Jesus Christ" {B}.
9. Or, "every". Same word and grammar as in "*the* whole" building in 2:21. GK *4246*.
10. Or, "clan, tribe, people, nation", a group whose identity is traced to a common father. Elsewhere only in Lk 2:4; Act 3:25. GK *4255*. Related to "father" preceding. There is a play on words here, "the Father, from Whom the whole father-grouping... is named". The whole family of God directly fathered by Him is in view. Others render it "every family", meaning "every father-grouping", every group based on a father. All such groupings owe their name to the Father, who ultimately (or directly, in the case of angels) is their Father-creator. Others render it more abstractly as "all fatherhood". In any case, Paul's point is to focus us on the Father, creator of the new life in us.
11. Elsewhere only as "become strong" in Lk 1:80; 2:40; and "grow strong" in 1 Cor 16:13. GK *3194*.
12. This phrase, "inner person", is elsewhere only in Rom 7:22; 2 Cor 4:16. Compare 1 Pet 3:4.
13. Instead of expressing the result, "strengthened... *so that* Christ", others see this as a second request, "might grant first, that you be strengthened, and second, that Christ might dwell". In the former case, a growing spiritual strength leads to a growing presence of Christ. In the latter case, the two requests are an impersonal and a personal way of saying the same thing.
14. Or, "settle down, have His home, reside", that is, be at home. Used mostly of dwelling or living in a place, as in Mt 2:23; 4:13; Act 1:19; 9:22, 35; 19:17; etc. Used of God in Mt 23:21; Act 7:48; 17:24; and of the fullness dwelling in Christ in Col 1:19; 2:9. Used 44 times. GK *2997*. Related to "dwelling place" in 2:22; and "dwell" in Jam 4:5.
15. Or, "That", making this point 2C., a second primary request.
16. This phrase, "having been rooted and founded in love" has Paul's emphasis (in the Greek word order, it precedes "in order that", and concludes v 17). It gives the result of what precedes and the basis for what follows. The construction is similar to 1:18. In this arrangement (compare the view in notes 13, 15 and 23) Paul means "strengthened so that Christ may dwell in your hearts, resulting in you being rooted and founded in love in order that you may be strong enough to grasp and to know the love of Christ". This foundation of love flows from Christ, and leads to Christ. It is the goal of the strength prayed for, and the foundation for reaching the fullness of God. Living out His love, we come to know its dimensions.
17. Or, "established". This word means "to lay or establish a foundation". Same word as in Mt 7:25; Col 1:23. Elsewhere only as "laid the foundation of" in Heb 1:10; and "establish" in 1 Pet 5:10. GK *2530*. Related to "foundation" in 2:20; 1 Tim 6:19.
18. Or, "be fully able". Used only here. GK *2015*. Related to "strength" in 1:19.
19. Or, "comprehend, seize, lay hold of ". On this word, see "overcome" in Jn 1:5.
20. Some think Paul is describing the dimensions of Christ's love— to grasp it mentally, and to know it experientially. Others think he is referring to "the multi-faceted wisdom of God" (3:10), seen in the mystery. There are other views. Consult the commentaries. Some manuscripts say "depth and height" {N}.
21. Paul is referring to experiential knowledge that includes, but exceeds mental knowledge. On this word, see Lk 1:34.
22. Or, "And to know Christ's knowledge-surpassing love". Some think Paul means the love surpassing what can be grasped intellectually, the love only known by personally living and experiencing it; others, the love that transcends knowledge in its greatness.
23. Or, "That", making this point 3C., a third primary request.
24. Some manuscripts say "in order that all the fullness *of* God may be filled up" {A}.
25. Or, "understand, perceive, imagine". That is, think about, think out, intend to ask. Elsewhere only as "consider" in 2 Tim 2:7; "understand" in Mt 24:15; Mk 13:14; Rom 1:20; 1 Tim 1:7; Heb 11:3; "perceive" in Mt 15:17; 16:9, 11; Mk 7:18; 8:17; Eph 3:4; and "comprehend" in Jn 12:40. GK *3783*. Related to "mind" in 2 Cor 3:14 and in Rom 7:23.
26. Or, "in operation". Same word and grammar as in 2:2; 2 Cor 1:6; Col 1:29. On this word, see "works" in 1 Cor 12:11.
27. Some manuscripts omit this word {N}.
28. That is, in a manner worthy of. On this word, see 3 Jn 6. Here Paul details this worthy walk from our perspective as part of the Lord's body of believers.
29. On "calling", see 2 Pet 1:10. On the related word "called", see Rom 8:30. The same two words are in v 4.
30. Or, "lowliness of mind". Same phrase as in Act 20:19. On this word, see Phil 2:3. The opposite of this is in Rom 12:16; Gal 6:3.
31. Or, "meekness". Elsewhere only in 1 Cor 4:21; 2 Cor 10:1; Gal 5:23; 6:1; Col 3:12; 2 Tim 2:25; Tit 3:2; Jam 1:21; 3:13; 1 Pet 3:16. GK *4559*. Related to the word in 1 Tim 6:11; and to "gentle" in 1 Pet 3:4.
32. Or, "making every effort, being eager, being earnest, hastening, doing *your* best". Same word as in 2 Tim 2:15; 4:9, 21; Tit 3:12; Heb 4:11; 2 Pet 1:10, 15; 3:14. Elsewhere only as "be eager" in Gal 2:10; 1 Thes 2:17. GK *5079*. Related to "earnest" in 2 Cor 8:17; "diligently" in Tit 3:13; and "earnestness" in 2 Cor 8:16.
33. Or, "preserve, guard, protect". On this word, see 1 Jn 5:18.
34. Or, "oneness". Elsewhere only in v 13. GK *1942*.
35. That is, the unity which the Spirit produces, the Spirit-given unity.
36. Some think Paul means "the bond *which consists of* peace"; others, "the bond *which leads to* peace", that is, love (as in Col 3:14).
37. The following defines seven points of the unity given by the Spirit, seven things all Christians share.
38. That is, the body of Christ, the church, 1:23; 5:23; Rom 12:5; 1 Cor 12:27; Col 1:24.
39. Some manuscripts omit this word {N}.
40. Compare 1:18. There is one hope belonging to our calling. On "called, calling", see v 1.

A. Heb 4:16, confidence B. 2 Cor 1:15 C. 2 Cor 4:1 D. Rev 7:14 E. 2 Tim 2:19 F. 1 Tim 6:17 G. 2 Pet 2:10 H. Mk 5:30 J. Col 2:7
K. 2 Cor 9:14 L. Eph 5:18 M. Col 1:19 N. 1 Thes 5:13 O. Rev 20:10 P. Eph 3:1 Q. Rom 12:8 R. Heb 6:12 S. 2 Cor 11:4 T. Act 8:23

	1D. One Lord, one faith¹, one baptism²	5
	2D. One God and Father *of* all³— the *One* over all and through all and in all⁴	6
2C.	And⁵ *to* each⁶ one⁷ *of* us grace^A was given according to the measure^B *of* the gift⁸ *of* Christ	7
	1D. For this reason it says [in Ps 68:18], "having ascended to on-high⁹, He led captivity captive¹⁰, He gave¹¹ gifts¹² *to* people^C"	8
	1E. Now¹³ what does the "He ascended" mean¹⁴ except that He also descended¹⁵ into¹⁶ the lower¹⁷ parts¹⁸ *of* the earth?¹⁹	9
	2E. The *One* having descended is Himself also the *One* having ascended far above all the heavens, in order that He might fill^D all *things*²⁰	10
	2D. And He Himself gave some *as* apostles^E, and others *as* prophets^F, and others *as* evangelists²¹, and others *as* shepherds²² and teachers²³	11
	1E. For²⁴ the equipping²⁵ *of* the saints^G	12
	1F. For *the* work^H *of* ministry²⁶	
	2F. For *the* building-up^J *of* the body *of* Christ	
	2E. Until we all attain²⁷	13
	1F. To the unity²⁸ *of* the faith, and *of* the knowledge²⁹ *of* the Son *of* God³⁰	
	2F. To *a* mature³¹ man	
	3F. To *the* measure^B *of the* stature^K *of* the fullness^L *of* Christ	
	3E. So that we may no longer be children^M, being tossed-about³² and carried-around *by* every wind *of* teaching^N	14
	1F. By the trickery³³ *of* people^C	

1. Some think Paul is referring to saving faith (as in Eph 2:8); others, to "the faith", the truth (as in Jude 3). Compare v 13.
2. Paul could be referring to the baptism of the Spirit by which all are placed in the body of Christ, 1 Cor 12:13; to our spiritual baptism into the death, burial and resurrection of Christ, Rom 6:4-5; Col 2:12; or to water baptism (one rite of initiation, irrespective of how it is performed). Some think he is referring to the one event of initiation, which includes all three of these.
3. For each "all" in this verse, some think Paul means "all believers", Jew and Gentile; others, "all *things*", the whole universe.
4. Some manuscripts say in "us all"; others, "you all" {A}.
5. Or, "But". Paul may mean "And", giving another point of unity. "One" is the first word in this Greek sentence, as in the phrases in v 4-6. There is unity in that each individual has received a measure of grace from Christ (Rom 12:6). Gifts are a mark of unity and diversity at the same time, 1 Cor 12. Or, Paul may mean "But", contrasting the unity in v 4-6 with the diversity seen in our gifts. He goes on to describe the giving in v 8-10; some of the gifts in v 11; and the purpose in v 12-16.
6. This word is used 82 times. GK *1667*.
7. That is, to each individual, each single one. This word is the number "one", the same word as in "one" body, spirit, etc. On this phrase, see Mt 26:22. This word is used 345 times. GK *1651*.
8. Some think that "gift" here means "spiritual gift". Thus grace was given proportionate to "the measure belonging to the spiritual gift given to each one by Christ". In other words, Christ gave differing gifts (some named in v 11) to His body, and with them grace and faith (Rom 12:3) of proportionate measure. The Spirit distributes them to each one, as He wills, 1 Cor 12:11. Others think that the gift is the grace. Grace was given according to "the measured gift of it given by Christ to each one". This grace is seen in one's spiritual gifts, opportunities, and much more. Compare Rom 12:3. On this word, see Rom 5:15.
9. That is, into heaven. On this word, see Lk 1:78. Paul quotes the psalm as a prediction that Christ would give gifts.
10. Or, "He took prisoner prisoners-of-war". The victor in battle takes prisoner his conquered foes. The verb means "to take captive, to make prisoners of war", and is used only here, GK *169*. The noun means "captivity, prisoner of war" and is elsewhere only in Rev 13:10, GK *168*. Related to "captive" in Lk 4:18; "take captive" in 2 Cor 10:5; and "fellow-captive" in Rom 16:7.
11. The Hebrew in Ps 68:18 says "received". Paul interprets or applies this to mean that Christ received them from God, and gave them to His people, who respond as in Ps 68:19. The victor takes or receives spoils, and gives them to his people. There are other views. Consult the commentaries. Some manuscripts say "and He gave..." {B}.
12. Elsewhere only in Mt 7:11; Lk 11:13; Phil 4:17. GK *1517*. Same word as in the psalm.
13. Paul draws a further conclusion about the Messiah from the psalm. The psalm implies that He also descended.
14. On this word, see "is" in Mt 26:26.
15. Some manuscripts say "He also first descended" {A}.
16. Or, "to". GK *1650*.
17. This phrase "lower parts *of* the earth" is used only here. Some manuscripts omit "parts" so that it says "to the lower *things of* the earth"

{C}. "Lower" is used only here, GK *3005*. Compare "under the earth" in Phil 2:10; Rev 5:3. Note the contrast between "lower" here, and "far above" in v 10.
18. The plural "parts" often means "regions, districts", as in Mt 2:22; 15:21; Act 2:10; 19:1; etc. The plural is used only here by Paul. On this word, see Rom 11:25.
19. Some think this refers to Christ's incarnation on earth— He descended to earth and died, then ascended to heaven leading as captive His conquered foes (sin and death and Satan) and gave gifts (the spiritual gifts of which Paul is speaking). Others think it refers to a descent into Hades after His death— He descended into the grave, into Hades, the holding place of the dead. He led those believers held captive there to heaven with Him. Then He gave gifts to His people. In either case, Paul's main point is that "He gave gifts", which he repeats in verse 11.
20. Some think Paul means "with His presence"; others, "with His working". There are other views.
21. This is from the noun "gospel" (see "good news" in 1 Cor 15:1). This person is a "gospel-izer", one who proclaims the good news of the gospel. Elsewhere only in Act 21:8 (Philip); and 2 Tim 4:5 (Timothy). GK *2296*.
22. Used of shepherds of sheep, and metaphorically of Jesus. Elsewhere only in Mt 9:36; 25:32; 26:31; Mk 6:34; 14:27; Lk 2:8, 15, 18, 20; Jn 10:2, 11, 12, 14, 16; Heb 13:20; 1 Pet 2:25. GK *4478*. Used only here in the sense of a spiritual gift and leader in the church. Only here has it been translated "pastor". The related verb, "to shepherd, to tend or feed the flock", is in 1 Pet 5:2 (where elders are to do it), and Act 20:28. Related to "flock" in 1 Pet 5:2.
23. Some think the grammar indicates that both these words— shepherds and teachers— refer to the same person in two roles, "shepherd-teachers"; others, to two people belonging to the same class (local church workers versus traveling workers like the first three) and sharing some responsibilities. Note that "apostles and prophets" has the same grammar in 2:20; 3:5.
24. Or, "With a view to". GK *4639*. Not the same word as "for" in the next two phrases (GK *1650*).
25. Or, "preparing, furnishing, training". This noun is used only here. GK *2938*. Related to the verb "prepare" in Rom 9:22, which is rendered "fully trained" in Lk 6:40.
26. Or, "service". This work is where the gifts given to each one (v 7, 16) are put into action. On this word, see 1 Cor 12:5.
27. Or, "reach, arrive at, come to". On this word, see Act 26:7.
28. Same word as in v 3.
29. Or, "full knowledge". On this word, see Col 1:9.
30. Some think Paul means the unity of the faith in, and the knowledge of, the Son of God. That is, until the faith in and knowledge of Him is the same in all believers. Others think he means the unity consisting of the Son of God's faith and knowledge as the measure, similar to the lofty goal of the third phrase.
31. Or, "finished, complete, perfect". On this word, see "complete" in 1 Cor 13:10.
32. Or, "tossed up and down, back and forth", as by waves in the sea. Used only here. GK *3115*. Related to "surge" in Jam 1:6.
33. Or, "cunning, sleight of hand". This word means "dice playing", from the word for "dice". Used only here. GK *3235*.

A. Eph 2:8 B. Jn 3:34 C. Mt 4:4, mankind D. Eph 5:18 E. 1 Cor 12:28 F. 1 Cor 12:28 G. 1 Pet 1:16, holy H. Mt 26:10 J. Rom 14:19, edification K. Mt 6:27, life span L. Col 1:19 M. 1 Cor 3:1, infant N. 1 Tim 5:17

	2F. By craftiness^A with-regard-to^1 the scheme^2 of error^3	
	4E. But *that* while speaking-the-truth^4 in love^5, we may grow^B *as to* all *things* into^6 Him Who is the head— Christ	15
	1F. From Whom the whole body	16
	1G. Being fitted-together^7 and held-together^8 by every joint^C *of* supply^9	
	2G. According to *the* working^10 in measure^D *of* each^E individual^F part^G	
	2F. Is producing^H the growth *of* the body^11	
	3F. For *the* building-up^J *of* itself in love	
5A. Therefore^12 this I say and testify^13 in *the* Lord— *that* you be walking^K no longer as indeed the Gentiles^14 are walking, in *the* futility^L *of* their mind^M		17
	1B. Being darkened^15 in *their* understanding^N, having been excluded^16 *from* the life *of* God	18
	1C. Because of the ignorance^17 being in them	
	2C. Because of the hardness^O *of* their hearts^P	
	2B. Who, having become callous^18, gave themselves over^19 to sensuality^Q for *the* practice^20 *of* every impurity^R with greed^21	19
	3B. But **you** did not learn^S Christ in this manner, ˚if indeed you heard Him, and were taught in Him, even as it is *the* truth in Jesus^22—	20-21
	1C. *That* in-relation-to^23 *your* former way-of-life^T, you lay-aside^U the old person^24 being corrupted^25 in-accordance-with^26 the desires^V *of* deception^27	22
	2C. And *that you* be being renewed^28 *in* the spirit *of* your mind^M	23
	3C. And *that you* put-on^29 the new^W person^X having been created^Y in accordance with God, in righteousness and holiness^30 *of* truth^31	24
	4B. Therefore, having laid-aside^32 the lie^33	25
	1C. Each *of you* be speaking truth^Z with his neighbor^AA, because we^34 are body-parts^BB *of* one another	
	2C. Be angry^35 and-*yet* do not be sinning. Do not let the sun go down upon your angriness^36, ˚nor give *a* place^37 *to* the devil	26-27
	3C. Let the *one* stealing be stealing no longer. But rather let him be laboring^CC, working^DD the good^EE *thing* with his own^38 hands, in order that he might have *something* to give^39 *to* the *one* having *a* need^FF	28
	4C. Let every bad^40 word not proceed^41 out of your mouth. But if *there is* something good^EE for edification^J *of* the need^FF, *speak* in order that it may give grace^GG *to* the *ones* hearing. ˚And do not grieve^HH the Holy Spirit *of* God, with Whom^42 you were sealed^JJ for *the* day *of* redemption^KK	29 30

1. Or, "with a view to, for, toward", expressing the aim of the craftiness. The KJV paraphrases here. GK *4639*.
2. Or, "scheming". Same word as in 6:11, the schemes of the devil. The planned system or method.
3. Or, "deception". On this word, see 1 Thes 2:3. Paul may mean the scheme characterized by error ("deceitful scheming"); or, leading to error; or, proceeding from error.
4. This is the verb related to "truth". Some think that here it means "adhering to the truth"; others, "living out the truth"; others, "speaking the truth of the gospel", in opposition to the error in v 14. Elsewhere only in Gal 4:16. GK *238*. Related to "truth" in Jn 4:23.
5. Some take this with what follows, "truth, in love we may grow...", with "in" meaning "in the sphere of ". Note that "in love" occurs again in v 16.
6. That is, into closer union with Him. Or, "to" Him as the goal. Or, "for" Him. GK *1650*.
7. Same word as in 2:21.
8. Same word as in Col 2:19, and as "brought together" in Col 2:2. GK *5204*.
9. Or, "support". That is, by what every joint supplies. Each Christian is a "joint" through which the life of Christ is "supplied" to the body as each joint "works" its "gift" according to the "measure" of "grace" given to it, producing the growth of the body. Elsewhere only as "provision" in Phil 1:19. GK *2221*. The related verb is used in Col 2:19.
10. Same word as in 1:19; 3:7. On this noun, see Phil 3:21.
11. The body produces the growth of the body, like every other living organism.
12. Paul further details the worthy walk of 4:1 from the perspective of a departure from our former way of life.
13. Or, "affirm", as a witness to the truth. On this word, see 1 Thes 2:12.
14. Compare Act 15:23. Some manuscripts say "the rest of the Gentiles" {N}.
15. This is a participle, "Being having been darkened", that is, being in a state of darkness. Or, "Having been darkened in their understanding, being excluded". Elsewhere only in Rev 9:2; 16:10. GK *5031*. Related to "darkness" in Jn 3:19.
16. Or "alienated, estranged". Elsewhere only in Eph 2:12; Col 1:21, also of Gentiles. GK *558*.
17. Elsewhere only in Act 3:17; 17:30; 1 Pet 1:14. GK *53*. Related to the word in Rom 10:3.
18. Or, "past feeling, dead to feeling". They are past feeling shame, morally insensitive, having no sense of right and wrong. Used only here. GK *556*.
19. This word, "gave over", is the same word as in Rom 1:24, 26, 28, of God "handing over" the Gentiles.
20. Or, "pursuit, business, working". Elsewhere only as "effort" in Lk 12:58; "business" in Act 19:24, 25; and "profit" in Act 16:16, 19. GK *2238*. The root word is "work".
21. Or, "greediness". That is, with a desire for more and more. Related to "increase" in 2 Cor 8:15. Greed is a desire for increase. Same word as in Mk 7:22; Lk 12:15; Rom 1:29; Eph 5:3; Col 3:5; 1 Thes 2:5; 2 Pet 2:3, 14. Elsewhere only as "greediness" in 2 Cor 9:5. GK *4432*. Related to "exploit" in 1 Thes 4:6.
22. This is the Greek word order. Or, "even as there is truth in Jesus"; or, "even as truth is in Jesus". Compare the phrase in v 18, "the ignorance being in them", where the grammar is clear.
23. Or, "with respect to, with regard to". GK *2848*.
24. The metaphor of the "old person" is also in Rom 6:6; Col 3:9. On this word, see "mankind" in Mt 4:4. See also 2 Cor 5:17; Gal 6:15.
25. Or, "corrupting *itself*". On this word, see "ruin" in 1 Cor 3:17.
26. Or, "based on, by way of, in the interest of, for the purposes of ". Same word as in v 24. GK *2848*.
27. Or, "deceit". Paul may mean the desires proceeding from deception, belonging to deception (deception's desires), or characterized by deception (deceptive or deceitful desires). On this word, see 2 Pet 2:13.
28. Or, "be becoming renewed, be getting yourself renewed". Used only here. GK *391*. In the parallel passage in Col 3:10, Paul uses a different word.
29. Or, "wear" like a garment. On this word, see Rom 13:14. Same word as in 6:11, 14.
30. Or, "devoutness". Elsewhere only in Lk 1:75. GK *4009*. Not related to the normal word for "holy". Related to "devoutly" in 1 Thes 2:10; and "holy" in Heb 7:26.
31. Some think Paul means "true holiness", holiness characterized by truth; others, "truth's holiness", holiness belonging to the truth. Compare "desires of deception" in v 22. In addition, some think "*of* truth" modifies "holiness" only; others, "righteousness and holiness".
32. Same word as in v 22.
33. Or, "falsehood". In this rendering, Paul is referring to the lie of their futile Gentile way of thinking and living, the falsehood about which they were darkened in their understanding. This introduces the commands given next. Or, this may only introduce the command to speak truth. In this case, point 4B. would be "Therefore", and point 1C. would be "Having laid aside falsehood, each...". On this word, see "falsehood" in Rev 14:5.
34. That is, we in the body of Christ. The whole body will suffer if you fail to speak truth.
35. This is the verb related to "anger" in v 31. This verse deals with the right kind of anger— anger against sin, evil, falsehood (v 25), not people (Mt 5:22, same word). Verse 31 deals with the wrong kind of anger. On this word, see Rev 11:18. Compare Ps 4:4.
36. This is a different word, but related to "be angry" earlier. It means the state of anger that results from provocation; the irritation, the exasperation, the angry mood. Used only here. GK *4240*. Related to "provoke to anger" in 6:4.
37. The word "place, location" is used here in the sense of "opportunity, chance", as in Act 25:16; Rom 12:19; Heb 12:17. Used 94 times. GK *5536*.
38. Some manuscripts omit this word {C}.
39. Or, "give a share of ". On this word, see Rom 12:8.
40. Or, "corrupt, worthless, rotten, unfit". On this word, see "bad" tree in Mt 7:17.
41. In English, we prefer to say "Let no bad word proceed". Same idiom as in 5:5.
42. Or, "by Whom, in Whom".

A. 1 Cor 3:19 B. Jn 3:30 C. Col 2:19 D. Jn 3:34 E. Eph 4:7 F. Eph 4:7, one G. Rom 11:25 H. Rev 13:13, does J. Rom 14:19, edification K. Heb 13:9 L. Rom 8:20 M. Rom 7:23 N. Lk 1:51, thought O. Rom 11:25 P. Rev 2:23 Q. 2 Pet 2:2 R. 1 Thes 2:3 S. Phil 4:11 T. 1 Pet 1:15, conduct U. Rom 13:12 V. Gal 5:16 W. Heb 8:13 X. Mt 4:4, mankind Y. Eph 2:15 Z. Jn 4:23 AA. Act 7:27 BB. Col 3:5 CC. Mt 11:28, being weary DD. Mt 26:10 EE. 1 Tim 5:10b FF. Tit 3:14 GG. Eph 2:8 HH. 2 Cor 7:9 JJ. Eph 1:13 KK. Rom 3:24

Ephesians 4:31	712	Verse

    5C. Let all bitterness[A] and anger[B] and wrath[C] and clamor[1] and blasphemy[D] be taken-away[2] from you, along-with all malice[3]. °And[4] be kind[5] to one another, tenderhearted[E], forgiving[F] each other just as God in Christ also forgave you[6]   31, 32

  5B. Therefore be imitators[7] *of* God, as beloved[G] children[H]   5:1

    1C. And be walking[J] in love[K], just as Christ also loved us[8], and handed Himself over[L] for us[9]— *an* offering[M] and *a* sacrifice[N] to God for *an* aroma *of* fragrance[10]   2

    2C. But[11] let sexual-immorality[O], and all impurity[P] or greed[Q], not even be named[12] among you, as is proper[R] *for* saints— °and[13] filthiness[14], and foolish-talk or coarse-joking[15], which are not fitting— but rather thanksgiving[S]   3, 4

      1D. For you know[16] this— recognizing[17] that every sexually-immoral or impure or greedy *person* (that[18] *is, an* idolater) does not have[19] *an* inheritance[T] in the kingdom[U] *of* Christ and God   5

      2D. Let no one deceive[V] you *with* empty[W] words, for because of these *things* the wrath[C] *of* God is coming upon the sons *of* disobedience[20]   6

      3D. Therefore do not be fellow-partakers[21] *with* them   7

    3C. For you were formerly darkness[X], but now *you are* light[Y] in *the* Lord   8

      1D. Be walking[J] as children[H] *of* light[22]— °for the fruit *of* the light[23] *is* in[24] all goodness[Z] and righteousness[AA] and truth[BB]— °approving what is pleasing[25] *to* the Lord   9, 10

      2D. And do not be participating[26] *in* the unfruitful[CC] works *of* darkness[X], but rather even be exposing[27] *them*   11

        1E. For[28] it is shameful[DD] even to speak the *things* being done *in* secret by them, °but[29] all *things* being exposed by the light[Y] become-visible[30]   12-13

          1F. For[31] everything becoming-visible is light[32]. Therefore he[33] says, "Awake[EE], sleeping[FF] *one*, and rise-up[GG] from the dead[HH], and Christ will shine-on[34] you"[35]   14

6A. Therefore[36] be watching[JJ] carefully[37] how[38] you walk[J]— not as unwise, but as wise, °redeeming[39] the time[40]— because the days are evil[KK]   15-16

  1B. For this reason, do not be foolish[LL] *ones*, but understand[41] what the will[MM] *of* the Lord *is*   17

  2B. And do not get-drunk[NN] *with* wine[OO]— in[42] which is wild-living[43]— but be filled[44] *with*[45] *the* Spirit   18

1. On this word, see "outcry" in Heb 5:7. There is an example of it in Act 23:9, where this word is used.
2. Or, "removed". GK *149*.
3. That is, the desire to cause harm or distress in others. On this word, see "badness" in 1 Pet 2:1.
4. Some manuscripts omit this word {C}.
5. Or, "good". On this word, see "good" in 1 Pet 2:3.
6. Some manuscripts say "us" {B}.
7. Or, "followers, emulators, mimickers". Used only here of God, as love, v 2; and light, v 9. Elsewhere only in 1 Cor 4:16; 11:1; 1 Thes 1:6; 2:14; Heb 6:12. GK *3629*. The related verb is in 2 Thes 3:7.
8. Some manuscripts say "you" {B}.
9. Some manuscripts say "you" {A}.
10. This phrase, "aroma *of* fragrance" also occurs in Phil 4:18. On both words, see 2 Cor 2:14-16.
11. Paul now forbids the opposites of God's kind of love.
12. That is, identified as part of your behavior. On this word, see 2 Tim 2:19.
13. Some manuscripts say "nor" here and next {N}, "nor filthiness, nor foolish talk, nor coarse joking".
14. Or, "indecency, obscenity, shamefulness" in word or deed. Used only here. GK *157*. Related to "filthy language" in Col 3:8.
15. Or, "vulgar wittiness". Used only here. GK *2365*.
16. Or, this may be a command, "know this". On this word, see 1 Jn 2:29.
17. Or, "knowing, understanding". Some think Paul means "you know to obey v 3-4, for you recognize that persons characterized by such things are not part of God's kingdom"; others, "you know this—recognizing [by your own experience]— that...". Others regard the repetition of "know" as similar (two different words are used here) to a Hebrew way of speaking which places emphasis on the knowing, "you know with certainty, you surely know". Others omit this word as redundant. On this word, see Lk 1:34.
18. Paul makes this connection also in Col 3:5. Some manuscripts say "who" {N}. "Idolater" is GK *1629*.
19. In English, we prefer to say "that no sexually immoral... has".
20. Same phrase as in 2:2.
21. That is, of these sins. Elsewhere only in 3:6. GK *5212*. The root word is "partakers" in Heb 3:1.
22. That is, characterized by light.
23. Some manuscripts say "Spirit" {A}.
24. Some think Paul means "in the sphere of"; others, "consisting in". GK *1877*.
25. Or, "acceptable". Elsewhere only in Rom 12:1, 2; 14:18; 2 Cor 5:9; Phil 4:18; Col 3:20; Tit 2:9; Heb 13:21. GK *2298*. Related to the words in 1 Thes 2:4 and Heb 11:5. On "approving", see Rom 12:2, where both theses words also occur.
26. Or, "having fellowship *with*". On this word, see "co-partnered" in Phil 4:14.
27. Or, "rebuking, convicting, bringing to light". That is, expose them with a rebuke. "Expose" is used here to show the connection with what follows. Same word as in v 13; and in Mt 18:15; Jn 3:20. Elsewhere only as "rebuke" in Lk 3:19; 1 Tim 5:20; 2 Tim 4:2; Tit 1:13; 2:15; Heb 12:5; Rev 3:19; "convict" in Jn 8:46; 16:8; 1 Cor 14:24; Jam 2:9; Jude 15; and "refute" in Tit 1:9. GK *1794*. Related to "rebuking" in 2 Tim 3:16.
28. This emphasizes why we should not participate in these works (v 11a). They are shameful to speak about, except in exposing them to God's light.
29. This explains why we should expose these works (v 11b).
30. Or, "are made visible". Or, "being exposed are made visible by the light". When we expose these works of darkness, they become visible to the person in God's light, visible for what they are in God's eyes. On this word, see "made evident" in 1 Jn 2:19.
31. This explains the value of making such works visible in God's light.
32. That is, as these works become visible in the light (v 13), they reflect the light, and become a light-source of God to the person. The light of God penetrates the darkness of such people by reflecting off their exposed deeds into their hearts, making it possible for them to respond to God. They either respond to this light, or run from it (compare Jn 3:19-21). There are other views on the flow and meaning of v 12-14. Consult the commentaries.
33. Or, "it says". Paul may mean that the one exposing the person's sin says this to the person. Thus the believer exposes the person's works, making them visible in God's light, which reflects into the heart. Here, the believer calls upon the person to respond to the light. Or, Paul may be quoting a written source unknown to us. Or, he may be paraphrasing from Isa 60:1. In any case, this is addressed to the spiritually dead one.
34. Or, "give light to, shine out to". Some render it figuratively, "enlighten". Used only here. GK *2213*.
35. Through the light reflecting to this one from his exposed works of darkness, someone is able to call him to rise to new life and come out into the day. Respond to the light and receive a new life, and Christ will shine on you, transforming you now and forever. Compare Rom 13:11.
36. Paul further details the worthy walk with regard to our relationships in various spheres.
37. On this adverb, see "accurately" in Mt 2:8.
38. Some manuscripts reverse the words, "how carefully" {B}.
39. Or, "buying back, buying up" the time for the Lord. That is, making the most of the time, taking advantage of every opportunity, saving your time from being lost. Same phrase as in Col 4:5. Elsewhere only in Gal 3:13; 4:5. GK *1973*. The root word is "buy".
40. Or, "opportunity, moment, occasion". Same word as "opportunity" in Gal 6:10.
41. Instead of a command, some manuscripts say "but *ones* understanding..." {N}. On this word, see Mt 13:23.
42. That is, "in connection with". GK *1877*.
43. Or, "debauchery, profligacy". Elsewhere only in Tit 1:6; 1 Pet 4:4. GK *861*. Related to the word used in Lk 15:13 of the prodigal son.
44. Same word as in Lk 2:40; Act 5:3; 13:52; Rom 1:29; 15:13, 14; 2 Cor 7:4; Eph 3:19; Phil 1:11; Col 1:9; 2 Tim 1:4. On this command, see Phil 2:2. Note the parallel passage in Col 3:16, which says "let the word of Christ dwell in you richly". This word also means "fill up, fulfill, make full, complete". Used 86 times. GK *4444*. Related to "full" in Mt 14:20, and "fullness" in Col 1:19.
45. Or, "by", meaning "be filled *with the fullness of God* by means of the Spirit".

A. Act 8:23 B. Rev 16:19, fury C. Rev 16:19 D. 1 Tim 6:4 E. 1 Pet 3:8 F. Lk 7:42 G. Mt 3:17 H. 1 Jn 3:1 J. Heb 13:9 K. 1 Jn 4:16 L. Mt 26:21, hand over M. Act 21:26 N. Heb 9:26 O. 1 Cor 5:1 P. 1 Thes 2:3 Q. Eph 4:19 R. 1 Cor 11:13, fitting S. 1 Tim 4:3 T. Eph 1:14 U. Mt 3:2 V. 1 Tim 2:14 W. 1 Thes 2:1 X. Jn 3:19 Y. Jn 1:5 Z. Gal 5:22 AA. Rom 1:17 BB. Jn 4:23 CC. 1 Cor 14:14 DD. Tit 1:11 EE. Mt 28:6, arose FF. 1 Thes 5:10 GG. Lk 18:33 HH. Mt 8:22 JJ. Rev 1:11, see KK. Act 25:18 LL. 2 Cor 11:16 MM. Jn 7:17 NN. Jn 2:10 OO. 1 Tim 5:23

1C. Speaking^A to each other with^1 psalms^2 and hymns^3 and spiritual^4 songs^5	19
2C. Singing^6 and making-melody^7 *with* your heart^B *to* the Lord	
3C. Giving-thanks^C always for all *things* in *the* name *of* our Lord Jesus Christ *to our* God and Father	20
4C. Being-subject^8 *to* one another in *the* fear^9 *of* Christ^10	21
1D. Wives^11— *to your* own husbands, as *to* the Lord	22
1E. Because *a* husband is *the* head^12 *of his* wife as also Christ *is the* head *of* the church— He^13 *being the* Savior^D *of* the body	23
1F. Nevertheless^14, as the church is subject *to* Christ, in this manner also *let* the wives *be to their*^15 husbands in everything	24
2D. Husbands, be loving^E *your* wives	25
1E. Just as Christ also loved^E the church and handed Himself over^F for her^16 *in order that* He might sanctify^17 her, having cleansed^18 her with^19 the washing^20 *of* water by^21 *the* word^22	26
1F. In order that **He** might present^23 the church *to* Himself *as* glorious^G— not having spot^H or wrinkle or any *of* such *things*, but that she might be holy^J and without-blemish^K	27
2E. In this manner,^24 husbands ought also^25 to be loving their wives as their *own* bodies. The *one* loving his wife is loving himself^26	28
1F. For^27 no one ever hated^L his *own* flesh^M, but he nourishes^N and cherishes^O it	29
1G. Just as Christ^28 also *does* the church, because we are body-parts^29 *of* His body^30	30
2F. "For^31 this *cause a* man shall leave-behind^P *his* father and mother and shall be joined^Q to his wife, and the two will be one flesh^32" [Gen 2:24]	31

1. Or, "in, by means of ". GK *1877*. Some manuscripts omit this word, leaving it implied {C}.
2. Elsewhere only in Lk 20:42; 24:44; Act 1:20; 13:33; 1 Cor 14:26; Col 3:16. GK *6011*. Our word "psalm" comes from this word.
3. Elsewhere only in Col 3:16. GK *5631*. That is, a song of praise. The related verb is "sing praise" in Act 16:25. Our word "hymn" comes from this word.
4. Some manuscripts omit this word {B}. It is present in Col 3:16. On this word, see 1 Cor 14:1.
5. Elsewhere only in Col 3:16; Rev 5:9; 14:3; 15:3. GK *6046*. Our word "ode" comes from this Greek word.
6. Elsewhere only in Col 3:16; Rev 5:9; 14:3; 15:3. GK *106*. This is the verb related to "songs" preceding.
7. Or, "singing psalms, psalming, singing praise". Elsewhere only as "sing praise" in Rom 15:9; 1 Cor 14:15; Jam 5:13. GK *6010*. This is the verb related to "psalms" preceding. Also used of "playing" the harp in the OT (as in 1 Sam 16:16, 17, 23). Paul may be referring to a distinction in the type of song, "singing-songs and singing-praises (or, psalms)"; or, to "singing and making melody (or, music)".
8. Or, "Submitting, Being subordinate, Subjecting yourselves". The root word means "to arrange, put in order" (see "establish" in Rom 13:1 on it). This word adds the prefix "under". Thus it means "to place under, to arrange under, to subordinate; to subject oneself, to submit voluntarily". This word is used of submission by Christ to the Father, 1 Cor 15:28, and His parents, Lk 2:51; of everything to Christ, 1 Cor 15:27, 28; Eph 1:22; Phil 3:21; of the church to Christ, Eph 5:24; of angels to Christ, 1 Pet 3:22; of Christians to one another, Eph 5:21; of Christians to the gospel, Rom 10:3; 2 Cor 9:13 (noun); of Christians to leaders, 1 Cor 16:16; of Christians to God, Jam 4:7; Heb 12:9; of demons to the apostles, Lk 10:17, 20; of people to government, Rom 13:1, 5; Tit 3:1; 1 Pet 2:13; of servants to masters, Tit 2:9; 1 Pet 2:18; of younger men to older, 1 Pet 5:5; of wives to husbands, Eph 5:24; 1 Cor 14:34; Col 3:18; Tit 2:5; 1 Pet 3:1, 5; 1 Tim 2:11 (noun); of children to parents, 1 Tim 3:4 (noun). Elsewhere only in Rom 8:7, 20; 1 Cor 14:32; Heb 2:5, 8. GK *5718*. Related to "submission" in 1 Tim 2:11.
9. This word often means "fear" in the sense of "fright, terror", but also in the sense of "respect, awe, reverence", as in Lk 1:65; 5:26; 7:16; Act 2:43; 9:31; Rom 3:18; 13:7; 1 Pet 1:17. Used 47 times. GK *5832*. The related verb is "respecting" in Eph 5:33.
10. Some manuscripts say "God"; others, "*the* Lord"; others, "Jesus Christ" {N}.
11. Some manuscripts say "Wives, be subject"; others, "Let wives be subject" {B}.
12. Using this same word, God is the head of Christ, 1 Cor 11:3; Christ is the head of the man, 1 Cor 11:3; the church, Eph 1:22; Col 1:18; all rule and authority, Col 2:10; and the husband is the head of the wife, 1 Cor 11:3. On this word, see Mk 12:10.
13. Some manuscripts say "and He Himself is *the* Savior..." {N}.
14. Or, "But, However". Although the husband is not the wife's savior, and therefore not her head in the same way as Christ is head of the church, she should act toward him as the church does toward Christ. Others render this word "Now, So, Even, Indeed", in which case Paul is emphasizing his point rather than giving a contrasting statement, making this point 2E. GK *247*.
15. Some manuscripts say "*their* own" {K}.
16. That is, husbands must love their wives sacrificially, sacrificing themselves for the good of their wives. They are not saviors of their wives, but they should have the Savior's self-sacrificial love toward them.
17. Or, "make holy, set apart to God". On this word, see Heb 10:29.
18. Or, "cleansing", concurrently with the sanctifying. Some think this cleansing occurs prior to the sanctifying to present her holy, initiating it, and refers to the cleansing of salvation, or to water baptism in particular. Others think this cleansing occurs concurrently with the sanctifying, describing it; or is viewed from the standpoint of its final accomplishment. In this case, it is the lifelong cleansing work of the Word associated with sanctification. On this word, see Heb 9:22.
19. Or, "*by, in*".
20. Or, "bath", the washing place. Elsewhere only in Tit 3:5. GK *3373*. Related to "wash" in 2 Pet 2:22.
21. Or, "with, in". This word means "in connection with, by means of, with the instrument of ". GK *1877*.
22. Some think Paul means "cleansed... by the word"; others, "the washing... by the word"; others, "sanctify... by the word". Some think this "word" is "the gospel", as this word is used in Rom 10:8, "the word of faith we proclaim"; others, the word of confession by the individual at baptism; others, the word of God, as this word is used in 6:17. On this word, see Rom 10:17
23. That is, as a bride to a bridegroom, as in 2 Cor 11:2. On this word, see Rom 12:1 Some manuscripts say "in order that He might present her *to* Himself *as* the glorious..." {K}.
24. That is, "just as Christ", resuming from v 25— with sacrificial love for her. Just as Christ loved **His** body the church (v 25-27), husbands ought to love their wives as **their** bodies. The spiritual is the pattern for the earthly. Paul explains this in v 29-30. Others think this looks forward to the "as", "In this manner— as a person loves his own body— husbands should love their wives".
25. Some manuscripts omit this word {C}.
26. This is because she is his body. They are one flesh. Compare 1 Cor 7:3-4. Paul proves this in v 31-32.
27. Husbands "ought" to love their wives because this is how humans normally treat their bodies (v 29), and how Christ treats His body, the church (v 30). She is your body.
28. Some manuscripts say "the Lord" {N}.
29. On this concept, see Rom 12:4-5; 1 Cor 12:12-27. On this word, see Col 3:5.
30. Some manuscripts add "of His flesh and of His bones" {A}, that is, we are created from Christ as Eve was from Adam, Gen 2:23. We, the new creation, are the bride of the Last Adam, spiritually created from Him, and for Him.
31. Paul now quotes Gen 2:24 to prove the premise of v 28, that the wife is the husband's own body (compare 1 Cor 6:16). Some think this is quoted with reference to Christ, allegorically speaking of His first or second coming, making it point 1H.
32. So the one loving his wife is loving himself, v 28. The husband is the head of the wife, and the wife is the body of the husband. They are one. More literally, "be for one flesh", a Hebrew way of speaking.

A. Jn 12:49 B. Rev 2:23 C. Mt 26:27 D. Lk 1:47 E. Jn 21:15, devotedly love F. Mt 26:21, hand over G. Lk 7:25 H. 2 Pet 2:13 J. 1 Pet 1:16 K. Col 1:22 L. Rom 9:13 M. Col 2:23 N. Eph 6:4 O. 1 Thes 2:7 P. Act 6:2 Q. Mk 10:7

| Ephesians 5:32 | 716 | Verse |

        1G. This mystery[1] is great, but **I** am speaking[2] with reference to Christ and with reference to the church   32

        3E. Nevertheless,[3] you also individually[4], let each in this manner be loving his wife as himself. And *let* the wife *see* that[5] she be respecting[6] her husband   33

    3D. Children, be obeying[A] your parents in *the* Lord[7], for this is right[B]   6:1

        1E. "Be honoring[C] your father and mother"— which is *the* first commandment[D] with *a* promise—*"in order that it may be[8] well *with* you, and you may be long-lived upon the earth[9]" [Deut 5:16]   2   3

    4D. And fathers, do not be provoking your children to anger[10], but be nourishing[11] them in *the* training[12] and admonition[13] *of the* Lord   4

    5D. Slaves[E], be obeying[A] *your* masters[F] according-to[14] *the* flesh[G] with fear and trembling[15], in *the* sincerity[H] *of* your heart, as *to* Christ   5

        1E. Not by way of eye-service[J] as people-pleasers[16], but as slaves[E] *of* Christ   6

            1F. Doing the will[K] *of* God from *the* soul[L]
            2F. Serving[17] with good-will, as *to* the Lord[18] and not *to* people[M]   7
            3F. Knowing that each *one,* if he does anything good[19], he will receive this back[N] from *the* Lord— whether slave or free   8

    6D. And masters[F], be doing the same *things* to them   9

        1E. Giving-up[20] the threatening[21]
        2E. Knowing that both their Master[F] and yours[22] is in *the* heavens. And there is no respect-of-persons[23] with Him

7A. Finally,[24] become-strong[25] in *the* Lord, and in the might[26] *of* His strength   10

  1B. Put-on[O] the full-armor[27] *of* God so-that you *may* be able to stand[28] against the schemes[29] *of* the devil   11

    1C. Because the struggle[30] *for* us[31] is not against blood and flesh[32], but against the rulers[P], against the authorities[Q], against the world-powers[33] *of* this darkness[34], against the spiritual[R] *forces*[35] *of* evilness[S] in the heavenly-*places*[T]   12

    2C. For this reason, take-up[U] the full-armor *of* God in order that you may be able to resist[36] on the evil day, and having worked[37] everything, to stand   13

  2B. Stand [firm] therefore   14

    1C. Having girded[38] your waist[V] with truth[39]
    2C. And having put-on[O] the breastplate *of* righteousness[40]

1. Some think Paul is looking back to v 31. The mystery of this human one-flesh relationship is great, but I am applying it to Christ and the church. Others think this points forward to what follows in v 32. This mystery of which I am about to speak is great, but Christ and His church have a relationship similar to the human one. Note that v 32 relates to v 31 as v 30 does to v 29. Paul is linking the human (v 29 and 31) to Christ and the church (v 30 and 32). Thus he could have said here, "Just as Christ and the church, because the church is His bride" (to put it in the same form as v 30). They are one spirit, 1 Cor 6:17. He calls this a mystery because this relationship was not previously known, but has now been revealed by God. There are other views. Consult the commentaries. On this word, see Rom 11:25.
2. Note the emphasis on "I". This is not the primary meaning of Gen 2:24, "but I" am speaking of it in this way.
3. Some think Paul is referring to v 28. Husbands "ought to love" based on the reasons given, v 28-32. "Nevertheless", Paul now emphatically commands the husbands. Each of you personally and individually are to do this. It was a revolutionary idea to the men of that day. Others think he is referring to v 32, making this point 2G. The mystery is great, nevertheless, love your wives. Or, "**I** am speaking with reference to Christ, nevertheless **you** love your wives".
4. This idiom, "individually" is more literally "according to one", "in relation to one" (that is, a single one); "according to each". Elsewhere only in Jn 21:25; Act 21:19; Rom 12:5; 1 Cor 14:31. It is related to "one by one" in Mk 14:19.
5. This Greek construction giving the content of the command also occurs in 2 Cor 8:7.
6. This word is used 95 times, mostly to mean "fear, be afraid", as in Mt 2:22; Mk 5:33; Act 5:26. It is also used of "fear" in the sense of "reverence, respect, awe", as in Mt 9:8; Act 13:26; 1 Pet 2:17. Both meanings are found in Mt 10:28. Our "respect" for God should not contain any "fear, fright", 1 Jn 4:18; Rom 8:15 (noun). Only here is this word used of a wife to her husband. 1 Pet 3:2 uses the related noun of the wife, and 1 Pet 3:6 excludes "fear, fright" there as well. GK *5828*. The related noun is "fear" in Eph 5:21.
7. That is, "obeying... in the Lord". Some manuscripts omit "in *the* Lord" {C}.
8. Or, "come-to-be, become". GK *1181*.
9. Or, "land", the land of Israel. See the note on Rev 7:1.
10. This word means "to make angry, provoke to anger". Elsewhere only in Rom 10:19. GK *4239*. Related to "angriness" in 4:26.
11. Or "nurturing, bringing up". Elsewhere only in 5:29. GK *1763*.
12. Or, "instruction, discipline". On this word, see 2 Tim 3:16.
13. Or, "warning, instruction". Elsewhere only in 1 Cor 10:11; Tit 3:10. GK *3804*. Related to "admonish" in Col 1:28.
14. Or, "with respect to, in relation to". That is, your human masters. GK *2848*.
15. On "fear and trembling", see Phil 2:12.
16. Elsewhere only in Col 3:22. GK *473*.
17. That is, serving as slaves. On this word, see "are slaves" in Rom 6:6.
18. Or, "Master". The same word is in v 5, 8, 9, 10. Perhaps it is a play on words. On this word, see "master" in Mt 8:2.
19. Compare Col 3:25. On this word, see 1 Tim 5:10b. Some manuscripts say "that whatever good *thing* each *one* does" {N}.
20. Or, "Abandoning, Deserting, Letting go". On this word, see "let go" in Heb 13:5.
21. Elsewhere only as "threat" in Act 4:29; and 9:1, where Paul was threatening Christians! GK *581*. Related word in Act 4:17.
22. Some manuscripts say "that your Master also" {K}.
23. Or, "partiality". On this word, see Jam 2:1.
24. Some manuscripts add "my brothers" {N}.
25. Or, "be strengthened" by. On this word, see 2 Tim 2:1.
26. This phrase "might *of* His strength" is also in 1:19. Compare "might *of* His glory" in Col 1:11. Same word as in Col 1:11; Act 19:20; and as "mighty deed" in Lk 1:51; and "power" in Heb 2:14. It also means "ruling power, sovereignty", and is elsewhere only rendered "dominion" in 1 Tim 6:16; 1 Pet 4:11; 5:11; Jude 25; Rev 1:6; 5:13. GK *3197*.
27. That is, complete in all its pieces. Same word as in v 13. On this word, see Lk 11:22.
28. That is, in a military sense, to stand your ground. This same word is in v 13, 14. GK *2705*.
29. Or, "methods, stratagems". Elsewhere only in 4:14. GK *3497*. Our word "method" comes from this word.
30. Or, "wrestling, conflict". The personal fight, the one-on-one battle. Used only here. GK *4097*.
31. Some manuscripts say "you" {B}.
32. On "blood and flesh", see Heb 2:14.
33. Or, "world-rulers, world forces". Used only here. GK *3179*.
34. On this word, see Jn 3:19. Some manuscripts say "*of* the darkness *of* this age" {N}.
35. Or, "*beings, hosts*". Literally, "the spiritual *ones*".
36. Or, "stand against, oppose, withstand, set oneself against". Same root word as "stand" later in this verse. Same word as in Mt 5:39, "do not resist an evil person"; Lk 21:15; Act 6:10; Rom 9:19; 13:2; and in Jam 4:7 and 1 Pet 5:9, "resist the devil". Elsewhere only as "oppose" in Act 13:8; Gal 2:11; 2 Tim 3:8; 4:15. GK *468*.
37. On this word, see "worked out" in Phil 2:12. Some think Paul means "having done, accomplished" all preparations for the battle; others, "having overcome" the enemy, having "worked him down" to the ground.
38. Or, "tied". That is, having prepared for work. People in that day tied up their garment around their waist to prepare for work. See 1 Pet 1:13 for a similar metaphor. Elsewhere only in Lk 12:35, 37; 17:8; and as "girded-with" in Rev 1:13; 15:6. GK *4322*. The root word is "gird" in Act 12:8.
39. Some think Paul means objective truth, God's truth. Others think he means truthfulness, truth-speaking, truth-telling in the broadest sense; the state of living in harmony with God's truth in deed and word, intellectually and interpersonally, 4:15, 25. On this word, see Jn 4:23.
40. Some think Paul means objective, faith-righteousness, our unassailable position in Christ. Others think he means personal rightness, character-righteousness, moral rectitude, devoutness, holy living, the state of living in harmony with God's holy character. Note 4:24; 5:9. On this word, see Rom 1:17.

A. Act 6:7 B. Rom 1:17, righteous C. 1 Tim 5:3 D. Mk 12:28 E. Rom 6:17 F. Mt 8:2 G. Col 2:23 H. Rom 12:8, generosity J. Col 3:22 K. Jn 7:17 L. Jam 5:20 M. Mt 4:4, mankind N. 2 Cor 5:10, receive back O. Rom 13:14 P. Col 1:18, beginning Q. Rev 6:8 R. 1 Cor 14:1 S. Mt 22:18 T. Eph 3:10 U. Act 1:2 V. Heb 7:5, loins

3C.	And having sandaled[1] *your* feet with *the* readiness[2] *of* the good-news[A] *of* peace[B]	15
4C.	With[3] all *these* having taken-up[C] the shield *of* faith[D], with which you will be able to quench[E] all the flaming[4] arrows *of* the evil *one*	16
5C.	And take the helmet *of* salvation[F], and the sword[5] *of* the Spirit[6]— which is *the* Word[G] *of* God	17
6C.	Praying[7] with[8] every-kind-of prayer[H] and petition[J] at every opportunity[9] in[10] *the* Spirit, and keeping-alert[11] for it[12] with all perseverance[13] and petition[J]	18

    1D. Concerning all[14] the saints[K]

    2D. And for me—   19

        1E. That *a* word[15] may be given *to* me in connection with *the* opening[16] *of* my mouth[17] with boldness[L] to make-known[M] the mystery[N] *of* the good-news[18]

            1F. For the sake of which I am-an-ambassador[O] in *a* chain[19]   20

        2E. That with it[20] I may speak-boldly[21], as I ought-to[P] speak

---

A.	Now in order that **you** also[22] may know the *things* concerning me— what I am doing— Tychicus[23] will make everything known *to* you	21
1.	The beloved[Q] brother[R] and faithful[S] minister[T] in *the* Lord, whom I sent to you for this very *reason*— in order that you may know[24] the *things* concerning us, and he may encourage[U] your hearts	22
B.	Peace[B] *be* to the brothers[R], and love[V] with faith[W] from God *the* Father and *the* Lord Jesus Christ	23
C.	Grace[X] *be* with all the *ones* loving[Y] our Lord Jesus Christ with undecayability[25]	24

1. Elsewhere only as "tie on" in Mk 6:9; Act 12:8. GK *5686*. This verb is related to "sandal" in Mt 10:10.
2. Or, "preparedness". Some think Paul means the readiness for battle proceeding from the good news that you are at peace with God; the state of being prepared to stand in God's battle, brought about in you by the gospel of peace. Others, the readiness to proclaim the good news about peace with God. Used only here. GK *2288*. Related to "ready" in Tit 3:1; 1 Pet 3:15; and to "prepared" in 2 Tim 2:21.
3. Or, "In connection with". GK *1877*. Some manuscripts say "Above" {N}, meaning, "In addition to".
4. Literally, "the arrows having been set on fire". On this word, see "burn" in 2 Cor 11:29.
5. Or, "saber, dagger". Elsewhere only in Mt 10:34; 26:47, 51, 52, 55; Mk 14:43, 47, 48; Lk 21:24; 22:36, 38, 49, 52; Jn 18:10, 11; Act 12:2; 16:27; Rom 8:35; 13:4; Heb 4:12; 11:34, 37; Rev 6:4; 13:10, 14. GK *3479*.
6. That is, the Spirit's sword, the sword belonging to the Spirit, or the sword from the Spirit.
7. That is, "Stand therefore" (v 14), "fully armed" (v 14-17), "praying".
8. Or, "by means of". GK *1328*.
9. This idiom may be rendered "at every opportunity"; or, "in every season, all the time", meaning always, at all times; or, "on every occasion" of standing in battle. Same phrase as "in every season" in Lk 21:36. On this word, see "time" in Mt 8:29.
10. That is, "in the sphere of, in connection with, in union with". GK *1877*.
11. Or, "keeping watch". Same word as in Mk 13:33; Lk 21:36. Elsewhere only as "keeping watch" in Heb 13:17. GK *70*. Related to "watchings" in 2 Cor 6:5.
12. That is, for the purpose of prayer, with a view to prayer.
13. Used only here. GK *4674*. Related to "persevere" in Heb 11:27; and "be devoted to" in Act 2:42.
14. Note the fourfold repetition of "all, every" (GK *4246*) in v 18, addressing the what, when, how, and whom of the matter.
15. That is, a word from God, a Spirit-directed and empowered word, as Jesus promised, Mt 10:20; Mk 13:11. On this word, see 1 Cor 12:8.
16. This noun is used only here. GK *489*.
17. The idiom of "opening the mouth" to speak is elsewhere only in Mt 5:2; 13:35; Act 8:32, 35; 10:34; 18:14; Rev 13:6.
18. That is, consisting of the good news. Some manuscripts omit "*of* the good news" {A}.
19. Same word used of Paul in Act 28:20, when this letter may have been written (see Act 28:30).
20. Or, "in it". This word may modify "word" (meaning "with the word given"), or "mouth". In other words, pray that God would give me what to say, and that I would boldly speak it, as I ought. Or, rather than a second request, Paul may mean "In order that in connection with it [the mystery of the good news, v 19] I may speak boldly, as I ought", making this point 2F. Grammatically, it does not refer to "chain".
21. Or, "speak freely, speak openly". This word is used of Paul in Act 9:27, 28; 13:46; 14:3; 19:8; and of Apollos in Act 18:26. Elsewhere only as "speak openly" in Act 26:26; and "be bold" in 1 Thes 2:2. GK *4245*. Related to "boldness" in v 19.
22. Paul's emphasis is on "you". Some think he means "you also, in addition to the Colossians". Compare Col 4:7. Some take this to mean that Colossians was written first.
23. See Act 20:4 on him. Compare Col 4:7-8.
24. Or, "come to know". On this word, see Lk 1:34.
25. Or, "incorruptibility, immortality". On this word, see 1 Cor 15:42. This is the Greek word order. Some join this phrase with the first word, "Grace be... Christ, with immortality". Others link it to "loving". In this case some think Paul means "loving Him in a manner that is undecayable"; with a love that is undecaying, unfading, undiminishing, not growing cold. Others give this a positive meaning, "in sincerity", since a love that does not wane is a sincere love. Others think it refers to loving Christ "in union with immortality", that is, "forever". Some manuscripts add "amen" {A}.

A. 1 Cor 15:1 B. Act 15:33 C. Act 1:2 D. Eph 2:8 E. 1 Thes 5:19 F. Lk 2:30 G. Rom 10:17 H. 1 Tim 2:1 J. 1 Tim 2:1 K. 1 Pet 1:16, holy L. Heb 4:16, confidence M. Phil 1:22, know N. Rom 11:25 O. 2 Cor 5:20 P. Act 25:10 Q. Mt 3:17 R. Act 16:40 S. Col 1:2 T. 1 Cor 3:5, servant U. Rom 12:8, exhort V. 1 Jn 4:16 W. Eph 2:8 X. Eph 2:8 Y. Jn 21:15, devotedly love

Overview   # Philippians

Introduction	1:1-2
1A. I am thanking God for you for your partnership in the gospel, and praying your love abounds	1:3-11
2A. Now I want you to know that my circumstances have come for the advancement of the good news	1:12
1B. So that my imprisonment in Christ has become visible in the whole Praetorium	1:13
2B. And so that the majority of the brothers are more daring to speak the word	1:14-18
3B. And I am rejoicing in this. But I will rejoice, for I know it will turn out for my deliverance	1:19-26
4B. Only conduct yourselves worthily, so that I may be hearing of you whether I come or not	1:27-30
5B. If then you have any encouragement, fill up my joy by being united in a love like Christ's	2:1-11
6B. So then my beloved, be working out your salvation— not as in my presence, but now much more in my absence. For God is working in you	2:12-13
7B. Be doing all things with out grumbling, that you may be blameless children, for my boast	2:14-16
8B. But if I even am poured out for you, I am rejoicing in it, and with you. Do the same	2:17-18
3A. Now I am hoping to send Timothy to you, and to come myself. But I sent Epaphroditus to you	2:19-30
4A. Finally my brothers, be rejoicing in the Lord	3:1
1B. Be watching out for the dogs. For we are the circumcision, the ones worshiping in the Spirit, and not putting confidence in flesh	3:2-4
1C. If any other person thinks he may have confidence in the flesh, I more	3:4-6
2C. But what things were gains to me, these I have regarded to be a loss for the sake of Christ	3:7
3C. I regard all things a loss, and I forfeited them for the sake of the knowledge of Christ	3:8
1D. In order that I might gain Christ and be found in Him with faith righteousness	3:9
2D. That I might know Him and His power, being conformed to His death and resurrection. Not that I have obtained it, but I press on to take hold of it	3:10-14
4C. Therefore, all who are mature— let us be thinking this	3:15-16
5C. Be imitators of me, brothers, for our citizenship is in heaven	3:17-21
6C. So then my beloved brothers, be standing firm in this manner	4:1
7C. I exhort Euodia and I exhort Syntyche to be thinking the same thing in the Lord	4:2-3
2B. Be rejoicing in the Lord always, again I will say, be rejoicing	4:4
3B. Let your kindness be known to all people	4:5
4B. Be anxious for nothing, but let your requests be made known to God	4:6-7
5B. Finally, brothers, be considering these things— the true, honorable, right, pure, lovely things	4:8
6B. Be practicing these things which you learned and received and heard and saw in me	4:9
5A. Now I rejoiced over your gift to me through Epaphroditus. My God will meet your needs	4:10-20
Conclusion	4:21-23

Philippians 1:1   722   Verse

    A. Paul and Timothy, slaves[A] *of* Christ Jesus[1]   1
    B. *To* all the saints[B] in Christ Jesus being in Philippi,[2] together-with *the* overseers[3] and deacons[4]
    C. Grace *to* you and peace from God our Father and *the* Lord Jesus Christ   2

1A. I am giving-thanks[C] *to* my God upon every remembrance[5] *of* you—*always in my every petition[D] for you   3-4
    all[6], making the petition with joy

    1B. On-the-basis-of[7] your partnership[8] for[9] the good-news[E] from the first day until the present   5
    2B. Being confident-of[F] this very *thing*— that the *One* having begun *a* good[G] work[H] in you will perfect[10]   6
        it until *the* day *of* Christ Jesus[11]

        1C. Just as it is right[J] *for* me to think[K] this[12] about[13] you all, because of my having you in *my*   7
            heart[14]— both[15] in my imprisonment[16], and in the defense[L] and confirmation[17] *of* the good-
            news— you all being my co-partners[18] *of* grace

            1D. For God *is* my witness[M] how I am yearning-for[N] you all with *the* deep-feelings[19] *of*   8
                Christ Jesus

    3B. And I am praying[O] this— that your love may be abounding[P] still more and more in[20] knowledge[Q]   9
        and all perception[21]

        1C. So that you *may* be approving[R] the *things* mattering[22]   10
        2C. In-order-that[23] you might be pure[24] and blameless[25] for[26] *the* day *of* Christ, *having been filled[S]   11
            with *the* fruit[T] *of* righteousness[U] which *comes* through Jesus Christ
        3C. To *the* glory[V] and praise[W] *of* God

2A. Now I want you to know, brothers[X], that the *things* concerning[27] me have come[Y] rather[28] for *the*   12
    advancement[29] *of* the good-news[E]

    1B. So that my imprisonment in[30] Christ became visible[31] in the whole Praetorium[32], and *to* all the rest   13
    2B. And *so that* the majority *of* the brothers[X]— being confident[33] in the Lord[34] *because-of*[35] my   14
        imprisonment— are more daring[Z] to fearlessly speak the word[36]

        1C. Some indeed *speak* because of envy[AA] and strife[BB]— but some also are proclaiming[37] Christ   15
            because of good-will[CC]

            1D. The[38] ones *speak* out of love, knowing that I am appointed[39] for *the* defense[L] *of* the   16
                good-news[E]
            2D. But the others are proclaiming[DD] Christ out of selfish-interest[EE], not purely[40], supposing[41]   17
                to raise[42] trouble[FF] *in* my imprisonment[43]

1. Some manuscripts say "Jesus Christ" {K}.
2. Paul was in Philippi in Act 16:12-40 and 20:2, 6. On the writing of this letter, see Act 28:30.
3. Or, "superintendents, guardians". The Greek is *episkopos*, from which we get "episcopal". The KJV translates this word "bishop". Elsewhere only of leaders of the church (Act 20:28; 1 Tim 3:2; Tit 1:7); and of Jesus (1 Pet 2:25). GK *2176*. These leaders were also called "elders" (Tit 1:5-7; 1 Tim 5:17). Related to "office-of-an-overseer" in 1 Tim 3:1; "exercising oversight" in 1 Pet 5:2; and "look after" in Heb 2:6.
4. Or, "servants, assistants, ministers". Our word "deacon" comes from this word, *diakonos*. Used of a leadership position only here and 1 Tim 3:8, 12; and perhaps in Rom 16:1 (of Phoebe). On this word, see "servants" in 1 Cor 3:5. Related to "serve" in 1 Tim 3:10.
5. Or, "on the basis of *my* entire remembrance".
6. This is the Greek word order. Or, "for you all" may be placed with what follows, "petition, making the petition for you all with joy".
7. Or, "For", in the sense of "Because of", as in 1 Thes 3:9. In any case, it is the reason for Paul's thanksgiving. GK *2093*.
8. Or, "fellowship, contribution, participation, sharing". Same word as in 3:10; and as "fellowship" in 2:1. On this word, see "fellowship" in 1 Cor 1:9. Related to "partnered" in 4:15; "co-partners" in 1:7; and "co-partnered" in 4:14. Some think Paul is referring to the Philippians' partnership in the advancement of the gospel in general; others, to their partnership in providing financial support to Paul in particular, 4:15; others, both.
9. That is, "with reference to, regarding, in". Same word as in 2:22.
10. Or, "complete, accomplish, finish, bring to completion". On this word, see 2 Cor 7:1.
11. Some manuscripts say "Jesus Christ" {N}.
12. That is, to have this confidence in God with reference to you, since you are in my heart as partners of grace.
13. Or, "with reference to". GK *5642*.
14. Some render this "because of your having me in *your* heart".
15. This is the Greek word order of this verse. Some think Paul means "having you in *my* heart both in... good news"; others, "You all being my co-partners *of* grace both in... good news".
16. This word means "bonds, bindings, fetters", and then "imprisonment". Same word as in Act 20:23; 23:29; 26:31; Phil 1:13, 14, 17; Col 4:18; 2 Tim 2:9; Phm 10, 13. Elsewhere only as "binding" in Mk 7:35; and "bonds" in Lk 8:29; 13:16; Act 16:26; 26:29; Heb 11:36; Jude 6. "Bond" does not specifically mean "chain", but it can refer to the more specific words like "chains and shackles", as in Lk 8:29. GK *1301*. Related to "prisoner" in Eph 3:1, and "jailer".
17. Or, "establishment". Elsewhere only in Heb 6:16. GK *1012*. Related to "confirmed" in 1 Cor 1:6.
18. Or, "fellow-sharers, co-participants". Elsewhere only in Rom 11:17; 1 Cor 9:23; Rev 1:9. GK *5171*. Related to "partnership" in v 5.
19. Or, "heart, affections". This word means "bowels, inward parts" (as in Act 1:18), and then the "deep feelings" stirring there— feelings of compassion (Col 3:12), affection, mercy (Lk 1:78), anger (not in NT), etc. It is used of the home of these feelings (often translated "heart"), and of the emotions or feelings themselves. Elsewhere only in Lk 1:78; 2 Cor 6:12; 7:15; Phil 2:1; Col 3:12; Phm 7, 12, 20; 1 Jn 3:17. GK *5073*. Related to "to have deep feelings" in Mt 9:36.
20. Some think Paul means "in the sphere of"; others, "with, by means of". GK *1877*.
21. Or, "insight, discernment". That is, every form of moral and spiritual insight. Used only here. GK *151*. Related to "perceive" in Lk 9:45; and "faculties" in Heb 5:14.
22. Or, "being worth more, more valuable, excellent, essential". Same phrase as in Rom 2:18. The word means "to differ" (as in 1 Cor 15:41; Gal 4:1); "to make a difference" (as in Gal 2:6). Here it refers to things that "differ" in that they "are better, more important, more valuable, superior, essential, excellent", or some think "right". Same word as "worth" in Mt 6:26. Used 13 times. GK *1422*. Compare Eph 5:10. On the related adjective, "different, more excellent", see Heb 8:6.
23. Or, "That", making this a second request, parallel with "that your love" in v 9. GK *2671*.
24. Purity of motive is the idea. Elsewhere only in 2 Pet 3:1. GK *1637*. Related to "purity" in 2 Cor 1:12.
25. Or, "without an opportunity for stumbling". On this word, see 1 Cor 10:32.
26. Or, "in, until". Same word as "for" in Eph 4:30; 2 Pet 2:9; 3:7. GK *1650*. Not the same word as "until" in v 6 (GK *948*).
27. That is, my circumstances. On this phrase see "for my part" in Rom 1:15.
28. Or, "more". That is, rather than what you might think. Paul's circumstances have come not to hinder, but rather to advance the gospel.
29. Or, "progress, furtherance". Same word as in 1:25. Elsewhere only as "progress" in 1 Tim 4:15. GK *4620*. Related to "advance" in 2 Tim 2:16.
30. That is, "in connection with". Others take this with what follows, so that it says "became known *to be* in Christ", the Greek word order.
31. Or, "known". On this word, see "evident" in Rom 1:19.
32. Or, "palace, governor's headquarters, governor's residence". That is, Caesar's palace or headquarters. This is a transliterated Latin word. Elsewhere only of the palace of Herod in Caesarea where Paul was held, Act 23:35; and of the Roman fortress in Jerusalem where Jesus was tried, Mt 27:27; Mk 15:16; Jn 18:28, 33; 19:9. GK *4550*.
33. Or, "having confidence, putting confidence, trusting". On this word, see "persuade" in 1 Jn 3:19.
34. The Greek word order is "brothers in *the* Lord being confident". Some render it "brothers in *the* Lord— being confident".
35. Or, "*by means of, in, for*".
36. On this word, see 1 Cor 12:8. Some manuscripts add "*of* God"; others, "*of the* Lord" {B}.
37. Or, "heralding", "proclaiming as a herald". Not the same word as v 17, 18. On this word, see 2 Tim 4:2.
38. Some manuscripts reverse the order of v 16 and v 17 {N}.
39. Or, "destined". Elsewhere in this sense only in Lk 2:34; 1 Thes 3:3. On this word, see "lying" in Mt 3:10.
40. Used only here. GK *56*. Related to "pure" in 1 Pet 3:2.
41. Or, "thinking, expecting". Elsewhere only in Jn 21:25; Jam 1:7. GK *3887*.
42. On this word, see "arose" in Mt 28:6. Some manuscripts say "to bring on" {N}.
43. The content of the message is the same (unlike Galatians), but the motive is different.

A. Rom 6:17   B. 1 Pet 1:16, holy   C. Mt 26:27   D. 1 Tim 2:1   E. 1 Cor 15:1   F. 1 Jn 3:19, persuade   G. 1 Tim 5:10b   H. Mt 26:10   J. Rom 1:17, righteous   K. Rom 8:5   L. 1 Pet 3:15   M. Act 1:8   N. 1 Pet 2:2   O. 1 Tim 2:8   P. 2 Cor 8:2   Q. Col 1:9   R. Rom 12:2   S. Eph 5:18   T. Mt 7:16   U. Rom 1:17   V. 2 Pet 2:10   W. 1 Cor 4:5   X. Act 16:40   Y. Mk 16:2   Z. 2 Cor 11:21   AA. Mk 15:10   BB. 1 Cor 1:11, quarrels   CC. Eph 1:5, good pleasure   DD. Phil 1:18   EE. Jam 3:14   FF. Rev 7:14, affliction

	2C. What indeed^A *does it matter* except that¹ *in* every way, whether *in* pretense² or *in* truth, Christ is being proclaimed³!	18
3B.	And I am rejoicing^B in this.⁴ But I also will rejoice, *for I know that this will turn-out^C *for* me for deliverance⁵	19
	1C. Through your prayer, and *the* provision⁶ *of* the Spirit *of* Jesus Christ	
	2C. According-to⁷ my eager-expectation⁸ and hope^D that I will in no way be put-to-shame^E, but *that* with all boldness^F, as always, even now Christ will be magnified⁹ in my body, whether by life or by death— *for *to* me, the living *is* Christ, and the dying¹⁰ *is* gain¹¹	20 21
	1D. Now if *it is* the living in *the* flesh^G— this *for* me *means* fruit^H *from* work^J	22
	2D. And I do not know¹² what I shall choose^K, *but¹³ I am gripped¹⁴ by the two— having the desire^L that *I might* depart¹⁵ and be with Christ, for¹⁶ *that is* better^M *by* much more	23
	3D. But the remaining^N in the flesh^G *is* more-necessary^O for your sake	24
	4D. And being confident-of^P this, I know that I will remain^Q and continue^R *with* you all for your advancement^S and joy *of* faith, *in order that your boast¹⁷ may be abounding^T in Christ Jesus in me, through my presence^U again with you	25 26
4B.	Only¹⁸ be conducting-*yourselves*¹⁹ worthily^V *of* the good-news^W *of* Christ, in order that whether having come and seen you or being absent^X, I may be hearing-*of* the *things* concerning you²⁰—	27
	1C. That you are standing-*firm*^Y in one spirit, contending-together²¹ *with* one soul^Z *for* the faith *of* the good-news, *and not being frightened²² in any way by the *ones* opposing²³ *you*— which is *a* sign²⁴ *of* destruction^AA *for* them, but *of* your salvation²⁵, and this²⁶ from God	28
	2C. Because²⁷ *to* you was granted²⁸ the *thing*²⁹ for Christ's sake— not only the believing in Him, but also the suffering^BB for His sake, *having the same struggle³⁰ such as you saw in me, and now are hearing *to be* in me	29 30
5B.	If then³¹ there is³² any encouragement³³ in³⁴ Christ, if any consolation³⁵ *of* love³⁶, if any fellowship³⁷ *of the* Spirit, if any deep-feelings^CC and compassions³⁸, *fill-up³⁹ my joy⁴⁰—	2:1 2

1. This phrase, "except that" occurs elsewhere only in Act 20:23. Some manuscripts omit "that" {N}. Others render this "What then? Only that…".
2. Or, "false motive, pretext", a falsely-alleged motive hiding the true intent. Same word as in Mk 12:40; Lk 20:47; Act 27:30. Elsewhere only as "excuse" in Jn 15:22; and "pretext" in 1 Thes 2:5. GK *4733*.
3. This word means "to proclaim, announce, declare as a messenger". Same word as in v 17; and Act 4:2; 13:5, 38; 15:36; 16:17, 21; 17:3, 13, 23; 26:23; Rom 1:8; 1 Cor 2:1; 9:14; 11:26; Col 1:28. Elsewhere only as "announce" in Act 3:24. GK *2859*. Related to "proclaimer" in Act 17:18. Compare the word in 2 Tim 4:2.
4. That is, the advancement of the gospel (v 12), through Paul (v 13), and through the brothers (v 14-18).
5. Or, "preservation". Same word as in Act 7:25. On this word, see "salvation" in Lk 19:9.
6. Or, "supply". On this word, see "supply" in Eph 4:16.
7. Or, "Based on". GK *2848*.
8. Elsewhere only in Rom 8:19. GK *638*.
9. On this word, see "enlarged" in 2 Cor 10:15.
10. Paul's grammar is referring to the moment of death, the end of this life associated with "death" earlier. One may substitute the previous nouns to which these participles refer, "life is Christ, death is gain". The reason death is gain is given in v 23.
11. Or, "advantage, profit". On this word, see 3:7.
12. That is, Paul has not yet gained knowledge of his own choice in the matter. Or, "make known" (as this word is used in its other 24 occurrences), "reveal, declare". GK *1192*. In this case, Paul means he is not revealing his own choice between these two desires that grip him, but is convinced by outside factors that he must remain, v 25.
13. Some manuscripts say "for" {K}.
14. Or, "controlled, governed". On this word, see "controls" in 2 Cor 5:14. Same word as "held" in Lk 12:50.
15. On this word, see Lk 12:36. This is a euphemism for death. Related to "departure" in 2 Tim 4:6.
16. Some manuscripts omit this word {C}.
17. That is, the matter or content of your boast. Elsewhere only in 2:16; Rom 4:2; 1 Cor 5:6; 9:15, 16; 2 Cor 1:14; 5:12; 9:3; Gal 6:4; Heb 3:6. GK *3017*. Related to "boasting" in 2 Cor 7:4.
18. That is, irrespective of "my presence again with you" (v 26), my deliverance (v 19). On this word, see "alone" in Jam 2:24.
19. Or, "conducting your citizenship, living your citizen-life, performing your duties as citizens" of heaven (see 3:20, same root word). The root word is "citizen". Elsewhere only in Act 23:1. GK *4488*. Related to "citizen" in Heb 8:11; and "citizenship" in Eph 2:12.
20. This phrase, "the *things* concerning you" also occurs in 2:19, 20. See also 2:23; Col 4:8; Eph 6:22.
21. That is, as in an athletic contest. Elsewhere only in 4:3. GK *5254*. Related to "compete" in 2 Tim 2:5.
22. Or, "scared, startled, intimidated". Used only here. GK *4769*. Used of racehorses.
23. Or, "the *ones* being hostile, contrary, in opposition, adversaries". Same word as in Lk 13:17; 21:15; 1 Cor 16:9; 2 Thes 2:4; 1 Tim 5:14. Elsewhere only as "is contrary to" in Gal 5:17; 1 Tim 1:10. GK *512*.
24. Or, "*a* proof, *a* pointing to". On this word, see "demonstration" in Rom 3:25. Related to "evidence" in 2 Thes 1:5; and "demonstrate" in Eph 2:7.
25. Some manuscripts say "but *to* you *of* salvation" {N}.
26. Grammatically, this does not directly modify "salvation" or "sign". Some think it modifies the whole idea of a sign to you of salvation. This sign, seen in your behavior, comes from God. Others think it refers to the sign and destiny it points to for both groups. Others, connecting this phrase with a dash, think it refers to the standing firm, contending, and not being frightened. This confident response to the opposition, which is a sign to all, comes to you from God.
27. That is, I urge this (v 27-28) because you share my suffering and struggle. Others link this to "And this from God", making it point 1D. This sign of salvation seen in your response to opposition is from God because it indicates He has given you the double blessing of believing in Him and suffering for Him (Act 5:41).
28. On this word, see "freely give" in 1 Cor 2:12. The root word is "grace". Compare 1 Pet 4:13.
29. This is the Greek word order. Some think this points to the twofold phrase that follows, the believing and the suffering. It may be rendered "the *following thing*". Others think it refers to the suffering only, the "believing" being added to emphasize it by contrast. It may be rendered "the *suffering*".
30. Or, "conflict, fight". On this word, see "race" in Heb 12:1. Same word as the good "fight" of faith in 1 Tim 6:12.
31. Some think the connection is "If then as ones sharing in this struggle", 1:30; others, "If then as ones walking worthily", 1:27; others, "If then while awaiting my deliverance from prison", 1:13-19.
32. Grammatically, the "if" means "assuming that it is true that". Some think Paul means "If you have any of these things for me in my imprisonment, then fill up my joy (which I already have in the gospel being preached, 1:19) to overflowing by thinking and living with the same selfless love as Christ". Others think he means "If I have a relationship with you based on any of these things, let me exhort you to fill up my joy"; others, "If these things exist in you, then put them into action by filling up my joy".
33. Or, "comfort, exhortation". On this word, see Act 4:36.
34. That is, "in the sphere of Christ", Christian encouragement.
35. Or, "comfort". Used only here. GK *4172*. Related to the word in 1 Cor 14:3; and "encourage" in 1 Thes 5:14.
36. That is, proceeding from love, originating in love. On this word, see 1 Jn 4:16.
37. Or, "partnership *of* spirit". Same word as "partnership" in 1:5.
38. Or, "*acts of* compassion". On this word, see Rom 12:1.
39. Or, "fulfill, make full, complete". Same word as in 4:18, 19. Used 86 times, but as a command only here, Eph 5:18 (which is passive, "be filled"), and Mt 23:32 ("fill up", same exact form). On this word, see "filled" in Eph 5:18.
40. Same root word as "rejoice" in 1:19. I am rejoicing, I will rejoice, so you make my rejoicing full. On this word, see Lk 24:52.

A. Mt 27:23   B. 2 Cor 13:11   C. Lk 21:13   D. Col 1:5   E. 1 Jn 2:28   F. Heb 4:16, confidence   G. Col 2:23   H. Mt 7:16   J. Mt 26:10   K. 2 Thes 2:13   L. Gal 5:16   M. Heb 1:4   N. Rom 11:22, continue   O. Tit 3:14   P. Phil 1:6   Q. Jn 15:4, abide   R. Jam 1:25   S. Phil 1:12   T. 2 Cor 8:2   U. 2 Thes 2:8, coming   V. 3 Jn 6   W. 1 Cor 15:1   X. 2 Cor 13:10   Y. 1 Cor 16:13   Z. Jam 5:20   AA. 2 Pet 2:1   BB. Gal 3:4   CC. Phil 1:8

1C. *Which is* that¹ you be thinking^A the same *thing*² while³ having the same love, *as ones* united-in-spirit⁴ while thinking^A the one *thing*⁵—

    1D. *Doing* nothing based-on⁶ selfish-interest⁷, nor based on conceit⁸, but *with* humble-mindedness⁹ regarding¹⁰ one another *as* surpassing¹¹ yourselves   3

    2D. Not each looking-out-for¹² your *own things*, but also¹³ each the *things of* others   4

2C. Be thinking¹⁴ this¹⁵ in you,¹⁶ which also *was* in Christ Jesus   5

    1D. Who, while being¹⁷ in *the* form¹⁸ *of* God, did not regard^B the being equal¹⁹ *with* God a thing-to-be-grasped²⁰, *but emptied²¹ Himself   6 / 7

        1E. Having taken *the* form *of a* slave^C

        2E. Having come²² in *the* likeness²³ *of* humans²⁴

    2D. And having been found as *a* man *in* outward-appearance²⁵, *He humbled²⁶ Himself   8

        1E. Having become obedient^D to the point *of* death— and *a* death *of a* cross^E!

    3D. Therefore God also highly-exalted Him, and granted^F Him the²⁷ name above every name, in-order-that²⁸   9 / 10

        1E. Every knee should bow at the name *of* Jesus— *of* heavenly^G *ones*, and earthly²⁹ *ones*, and *ones* under-the-earth³⁰

        2E. And every tongue should confess-out³¹ that Jesus Christ *is* Lord^H— to *the* glory *of* God the Father   11

6B. So then my beloved^J, just as you always obeyed³², be working-out³³ your salvation^K with fear^L and trembling³⁴— not as³⁵ in my presence^M only, but now much more in my absence   12

    1C. For God is the *One* working³⁶ in you³⁷ both the wanting³⁸ and the working,³⁹ for *His* good-pleasure^N   13

1. The word "that" refers to the content of Paul's joy, just as in 1:9 it refers to the content of his prayer. GK *2671*.
2. That is, that you may be likeminded, having the same mind. On this phrase, see Rom 12:16.
3. Others make these four separate items, in which case both the words "while" would be replaced by a comma.
4. Or, "harmonious, of one accord". This adjective is made of two words, "soul" and a prefix meaning "together". Used only here. GK *5249*.
5. Or, "being intent on the one *thing*". We become harmonious by all focusing our minds on one thing. Some think the one thing is self-sacrificial love, as mentioned in the previous phrase, and further described negatively and positively in v 3-4, and exemplified by Christ in v 5-8. Others think this is another way of saying "being likeminded".
6. Or, "in keeping with, in accordance with, by way of, in relation to". GK *2848*.
7. Or, "selfish-ambition". Same word as in 1:17.
8. Or, "empty glory", falsely thinking you are something. Used only here. GK *3029*. Related to "conceited" in Gal 5:26.
9. Or, "lowliness of mind, humility". This word is made of two words, "humble" and "mind". Same word as in Act 20:19; Eph 4:2; Col 3:12; 1 Pet 5:5. Elsewhere only as "humility" in Col 2:18, 23. GK *5425*. Related to "be humble" in v 8; "humbleminded" in 1 Pet 3:8; and "lowly" in Jam 1:9.
10. That is, taking the lead in thinking of one another this way. Same word as in v 6.
11. Or, "being superior, better than". Same word as in 3:8 and 4:7. Elsewhere only as "superior" in Rom 13:1; 1 Pet 2:13. GK *5660*.
12. Or, "watching, keeping eyes on". Same word as "watching" in 3:17.
13. Some manuscripts omit this word {C}.
14. Or, "setting your mind on". Same word as twice in v 2; and in 1:7; 2:2, 5; 3:15, 19; 4:2, 10. On this word, see Rom 8:5. Some manuscripts begin this sentence with "For" {B}.
15. That is, that which was just described— selfless, self-sacrificial love.
16. That is, be thinking this in your hearts and minds, or setting your hearts and minds on this.
17. Or, "existing". Or, "*although* being". Paul is describing Christ's state before He became a man. This word is an alternative word for the common verb "to be", and is used in this sense 45 times. It is also used of things "belonging" to a person in Act 4:32, 37; "being present" in a person, 2 Pet 1:8; and as an idiom, "possessions" (see Heb 10:34). GK *5639*.
18. Or, "shape, appearance". This is a clear statement that Christ existed as God before He took the "form" (v 7, same word) of a slave. Elsewhere only in Mk 16:12. GK *3671*. An angel could appear in the "form" of a human. But no finite being could ever be said to exist in the "form" of the infinite God, or to be "equal" with Him.
19. Same word as in Jn 5:18 (where Jesus was calling God His own Father, "making Himself equal with God"), and as in Mt 20:12; Lk 6:34; Rev 21:16. Elsewhere only as "identical" in Mk 14:56, 59; Act 11:17. GK *2698*.
20. Or, "a booty, a prize to be hoarded; a seizing, robbery". Used only here. GK *772*. Related to "plunder" in Heb 10:34; and "snatch away" in 2 Cor 12:2. This word means actively "a seizing, a robbery", and passively, "the thing seized, the prize, the booty, the plunder". Some think Paul means Jesus did not regard His equality as a robbery, a usurpation, as something not His by right and nature. In other words, He emptied Himself of what was truly His. Others think he means Jesus did not regard His equality as a treasure to be grasped and held on to, but emptied Himself. In any case, the point of the context is self-sacrifice of rights.
21. This word means "to empty, to make void, to make of no effect". Same word as in 1 Cor 9:15. Elsewhere only as "be made empty" in Rom 4:14; 1 Cor 1:17; 2 Cor 9:3. GK *3033*. Related to "empty" in 1 Thes 2:1. Compare Jn 1:14; 2 Cor 8:9.
22. Or, "come into being", and in this sense, "been born". On this word, see Gal 4:4.
23. Or, "outward appearance, form". Elsewhere only in Rom 1:23; 5:14; 6:5; 8:3; Rev 9:7. GK *3930*. Related to "become like" in Mt 13:24.
24. Or, "men". Same word as "man" in v 8. Paul could be referring to the "male-ness" of Jesus here also, or he could be referring more broadly to His "human-ness". This word, *anthropos*, is used both ways. On this word, see "mankind" in Mt 4:4.
25. Or, "form, shape". That is, in contrast to His true inner nature. Elsewhere only as "form" in 1 Cor 7:31. GK *5386*. Josephus used this word of a king who took off his kingly robes and put on sackcloth, taking on a humble "outward appearance".
26. Note that Jesus humbled Himself as God by becoming a man, and then humbled Himself as a man as well. On this word, see 4:12.
27. Some manuscripts say "*a* name" {B}.
28. Or, "so that every knee will bow... and every tongue will...". GK *2671*.
29. Same word as in 3:19. Elsewhere only in Jn 3:12; 1 Cor 15:40; 2 Cor 5:1; Jam 3:15. GK *2103*.
30. Used only here. GK *2973*. This word refers to the netherworld, the world of the dead. Compare Rev 5:3.
31. Or, "openly acknowledge". Some do so by choice; others will find themselves with no other choice. Some manuscripts say "and every tongue will confess-out..." {C}. Same word as Rom 14:11. On this word, see Jam 5:16.
32. That is, obeyed God. On this word, see Act 6:7. Related to "obedient" in v 8.
33. Work out in action what God put inside. Work out the things for which you have been taken hold, 3:12; the works God has created for you, Eph 2:10. Same word as in 1 Pet 4:3. Elsewhere only as "work" in Eph 6:13; "accomplish" in Rom 15:18; "produce" in Rom 5:3; 7:8, 13, 15, 17, 18, 20; 2 Cor 4:17; 7:10, 11; 9:11; 12:12; Jam 1:3; "bring about" in Rom 4:15; "commit" in Rom 1:27; 2:9; 1 Cor 5:3; and "made" in 2 Cor 5:5. GK *2981*.
34. This phrase "fear and trembling" is also in 1 Cor 2:3; 2 Cor 7:15; Eph 6:5. "Trembling" is elsewhere only in Mk 16:8, paired with "astonishment". GK *5571*. The related verb is in Mk 5:33.
35. Some manuscripts omit this word {A}. Some think "not... absence" modifies the "obeyed" phrase; others, the "working-out" phrase. In the Greek word order, it stands between the two phrases.
36. Same word as later in this verse. Related to "work-out". On this word, see 1 Cor 12:11.
37. Or, "For the *One* working in you is **God**— both to will and to work...".
38. Or, "the willing, desiring". On this word, see "willing" in Jn 7:17.
39. Some think Paul means that God is working in you "to carry out His will and work through you". Others think he means God is working in you "both *that you may* want and work"; that is, to create in you both the desire and the work. Note Eph 2:10. We must work this out in our lives with the utmost seriousness, Phil 3:13.

A. Rom 8:5 B. Jam 1:2 C. Rom 6:17 D. 2 Cor 2:9 E. Mt 10:38 F. 1 Cor 2:12, freely give G. Eph 3:10 H. Mt 8:2, master J. Mt 3:17 K. Lk 19:9 L. Eph 5:21 M. 2 Thes 2:8, coming N. Eph 1:5

7B. Be doing all *things* without grumblings[1] and arguments[2], °in-order-that[3] you may become[4] blameless[A] and innocent[5], children[B] *of* God without-blemish[C]   14-15

    1C. Amidst[D] *a* crooked[E] and perverted[6] generation[F], among whom you are shining[7] as lights[8] in *the* world, °holding-out[9] *the* word *of* life   16
    2C. For *a* boast[G] *for* me in *the* day *of* Christ, that I did not run in vain nor labor in vain[10]

  8B. But if I even[11] am being poured-out[12] upon the sacrifice[H] and service[13] *of* your faith,[14] I am rejoicing[J] [over it], and rejoicing-with you all. °And **you** also be rejoicing the same *way*, and be rejoicing-with me   17 / 18

3A. Now I am hoping[K] in *the* Lord Jesus to send Timothy *to* you soon, in order that **I** also may be cheered, having come-to-know[L] the *things* concerning you[15]   19

  1B. For I have no one likeminded, who will genuinely be concerned-*about*[16] the *things* concerning you   20

    1C. For the *ones* all are seeking[17] their *own things*, not the *things of* Jesus Christ   21
    2C. But you know his approvedness[18], because he served[M] with me for[19] the good-news[N] as *a* child[B] *with a* father   22
    3C. So indeed I am hoping to send this *one* at-once[O], whenever I see the *things* with-respect-to[20] me   23

  2B. And I am confident[P] in *the* Lord that I myself also will come soon[Q]   24
  3B. But I regarded[R] *it* necessary[S] to send to you Epaphroditus[21]— my brother and fellow-worker[T] and fellow-soldier[U] and your delegate[22] and minister[23] *of* my need[V]   25

    1C. Because he was yearning-for[W] you all,[24] and *was* being distressed[25] because you heard that he was sick[X]   26

       1D. For indeed he was sick nearly *to* death   27
       2D. But God had-mercy-on[Y] him— and not him only, but also me, in order that I should not have grief[Z] upon[26] grief

    2C. Therefore I sent him more-eagerly[AA], in order that having seen him again, you may rejoice[J], and **I** may be less-grieved   28
    3C. So receive[BB] him in *the* Lord with all joy, and be holding such *ones* precious[27], °because he drew-near[CC] to the point *of* death for the sake of the work *of* Christ[28]— having risked[29] his life[DD] in order that he might fill-up[EE] your lack[30] *of* service[FF] to me   29-30

4A. Finally, my brothers[GG], be rejoicing[J] in *the* Lord. To be writing the same[31] *things to* you *is* not troublesome[32] *for* **me**[33]— and *is* safe[HH] *for* you   3:1

  1B. Be watching-out-*for*[JJ] the dogs[KK], be watching out *for* the evil[LL] workers, be watching out *for* the mutilation[34]. °For **we** are the circumcision,[35] the *ones* worshiping[36] in the Spirit *of* God[37], and boasting[MM] in Christ Jesus, and not putting-confidence[P] in *the* flesh[NN]— °though myself having confidence[OO] even in *the* flesh   2 / 3 / 4

    1C. If any other *person* thinks *that* he may put-confidence[P] in *the* flesh, I more—

       1D. *In* circumcision *the* eighth day   5

1. Or, "complainings". Elsewhere only in Jn 7:12; Act 6:1; 1 Pet 4:9. GK *1198*. Related to "grumbler" in Jude 16; and "grumble" in Lk 5:30 and 15:2.
2. Or, "disputes". On this word, see "thoughts" in Jam 2:4.
3. Or, "so that you will become". GK *2671*.
4. Or, "be, prove to be". GK *1181*. Some manuscripts say "be" {N}.
5. Or, "pure". On this word, see Rom 16:19.
6. This is a participle, "having been perverted", or "distorted (morally), misled, turned away". Same word as in Mt 17:17; Lk 9:41; 23:2; Act 13:10; 20:30. Elsewhere only as "turn away" in Act 13:8. GK *1406*.
7. Or, "appearing, are visible". Same word as in Jn 1:5; 1 Jn 2:8; Rev 1:16; and as "appear" in Mt 6:18; 23:28. Used 31 times. GK *5743*.
8. Or, "stars, luminaries, light-givers". That is, sources of light. Note 2 Cor 3:18 and 4:6, reflecting the Lord. Elsewhere only as "brilliance" in Rev 21:11. GK *5891*.
9. Or, "holding forth, presenting; holding, holding fast; fixing attention on". Some think Paul means "lights holding forth the word"; others, "lights, since you are holding the word". On this word, see "fix attention on" in 1 Tim 4:16.
10. That is, for no result or purpose. On this word, see "empty" in 1 Thes 2:1. Paul hopes that their growth will be something he can boast about on that day, boasting that his work was fruitful, not empty.
11. After the exhortations, Paul now reflects further on his outlook stated in point 3B. This idiom means "assuming that I even am being poured out..., I am rejoicing". He is not questioning whether or not he is being poured out, but is stating his position even assuming this to be the case. On this grammar, compare Mk 14:29.
12. Or, "pouring-*myself* out". That is, as a sacrificial offering. On this word, see 2 Tim 4:6, where Paul says "I am being poured out".
13. That is, priestly service. Same word as in v 30. If my life is expended in ministry to you, I am rejoicing over it. You rejoice too, and do not be sad about it. On this word, see 2 Cor 9:12.
14. Some think Paul means "upon my sacrifice and priestly service for your faith"; others, "upon the sacrifice consisting of your faith which in priestly service I am offering to God"; others, "upon the sacrifice consisting of your faith which in priestly service you are offering to God".
15. That is, your circumstances.
16. Or, "care-*for*". On this word, see "be anxious" in Mt 6:25.
17. This common word is used 117 times. GK *2426*.
18. On this word, see 2 Cor 2:9. It means the approved quality of a thing after having been tested.
19. Same word as in 1:5.
20. Same word as "concerning" in "the *things* concerning" in 1:27, but with different grammar.
21. Epaphroditus is mentioned elsewhere only in 4:18. GK *2073*.
22. Or, "representative, sent one, messenger". Same word as in 2 Cor 8:23, on which see "apostle" in 1 Cor 12:28.
23. Related to "service" in v 30. On this word, see Rom 13:6.
24. Some manuscripts say "yearning to see you all" {C}.
25. Or, "troubled, anxious". Elsewhere only in Mt 26:37; Mk 14:33. GK *86*.
26. Or, "in addition to". Some think Paul means the grief of Epaphroditus's death on top of the grief of my imprisonment; others, the grief over his death in addition to the grief of his sickness. GK *2093*.
27. Or, "honored, respected, esteemed". Same word as in Lk 7:2; 1 Pet 2:4, 6. Elsewhere only as "distinguished" in Lk 14:8. GK *1952*.
28. Some manuscripts say "*the* Lord" {B}.
29. Or, "having exposed *his* life to danger". Used only here. GK *4129*. Some manuscripts say "having not regarded" {N}.
30. Or, "shortcoming, deficiency". Paul may mean "what your service lacked to be as complete as you would have made it had you been here to see the needs in addition to the gift you sent by Epaphroditus (4:18)". Or, he may mean "the lack *of* you *in* the service to me", the lack of your presence here to render the further service needed. Compare 1 Cor 16:17. Same word as in Lk 21:4; 1 Cor 16:17; Col 1:24; 1 Thes 3:10. Elsewhere only as "need" in 2 Cor 8:14; 9:12; 11:9. GK *5729*. Related to "be in need" in Lk 15:14.
31. Some think Paul is referring to the command to rejoice, which he already commanded the Philippians in 2:18. Others think this refers to the threefold repetition that follows; others, to some previous oral instruction; others, to the warning to stand firm against opponents already made in 1:27-28.
32. That is, it causes no reluctance or hesitation for Paul. On this word, see "hesitant" in Rom 12:11.
33. Paul uses grammar that emphasizes the contrast between this phrase and the next.
34. Paul uses three harsh names for the Judaizers, whom he also addressed in Galatians. See Gal 2:14. He harshly refers to this party as "the mutilation" rather than "the circumcision" (a related word). Used only here. GK *2961*.
35. That is, the true circumcision. We are circumcised in heart, not in the flesh. See Col 2:11; Rom 2:28-29.
36. Or, "serving". On this word, see Heb 12:28.
37. Some manuscripts say "worshiping God in the Spirit"; others, "worshiping in the Spirit" {B}.

A. Phil 3:6 B. 1 Jn 3:1 C. Col 1:22 D. 2 Thes 2:7, midst E. 1 Pet 2:18 F. Mt 24:34 G. Phil 1:26 H. Heb 9:26 J. 2 Cor 13:11 K. Jn 5:45, put hope L. Lk 1:34, know M. Rom 6:6, are slaves N. 1 Cor 15:1 O. Mk 6:25 P. 1 Jn 3:19, persuade Q. Gal 1:6, quickly R. Jam 1:2 S. Tit 3:14 T. Rom 16:3 U. Phm 2 V. Tit 3:14 W. 1 Pet 2:2 X. 2 Tim 4:20 Y. Rom 12:8, showing mercy Z. 2 Cor 7:10 AA. Tit 3:13, diligently BB. Act 24:15, wait for CC. Lk 21:28 DD. Jam 5:20, soul EE. 1 Thes 2:16 FF. 2 Cor 9:12 GG. Act 16:40 HH. Act 21:34, certainty JJ. Rev 1:11, see KK. Rev 22:15 LL. 2 Jn 11 MM. 2 Cor 11:16 NN. Col 2:23 OO. 2 Cor 1:15

      2D. From *the* nation[1] *of* Israel, *the* tribe *of* Benjamin, *a* Hebrew from Hebrews
      3D. In relation to *the* Law— *a* Pharisee
      4D. In relation to zeal— persecuting[A] the church   6
      5D. In relation to *the* righteousness[B] in *the* Law[2]— having been[3] blameless[4]

  2C. But[5] what *things* were gains[6] *to* me, these I have regarded *to be a* loss[7] for the sake of Christ   7
  3C. But more than that, I am indeed regarding[8] all *things* to be *a* loss for the sake of the surpassing[C]   8
greatness of the knowledge[D] *of* Christ Jesus my Lord, for the sake of Whom I suffered-loss-of[9] all *things* and am regarding *them as* garbage[10]

      1D. In order that I might gain[E] Christ, °and be found in Him   9

            1E. Not having my *own* righteousness from *the* Law, but the *one* through faith *in* Christ[11]— the righteousness from God on the basis of faith

      2D. *That I might* know[F] Him, and the power[G] *of* His resurrection[H], and the[12] partnership[13] *of*   10
His sufferings[14]— being conformed[15] *to* His death °if somehow[16] I might attain[17] to [the   11
power of][18] the resurrection-out[19] from *the* dead

            1E. Not that I already obtained[20] *it*[21] or have already been made-perfect[22], but I am   12
pressing-on[J] *to see* if I may indeed[23] take-hold-of[24] that for which[25] also I was taken hold of by Christ Jesus[26]
            2E. Brothers, **I** do not[27] consider[K] myself to have taken hold, but one *thing I do*—   13

                1F. Forgetting[L] **the *things* behind**[28]— and stretching-toward[29] the *things* ahead, I am pressing-on[J] toward *the* goal, for the prize[30] *of* the upward[31] calling[M] *from*   14
God[32] in Christ Jesus

  4C. Therefore, all who *are* mature[33]— let us be thinking[34] this   15

      1D. And if you are thinking anything differently[35], God will reveal[N] this also[36] *to* you
      2D. Nevertheless, to what *thinking* we attained[37], *by* the same *let us* be walking-in-line[38]   16

  5C. Be[39] fellow-imitators[40] *of* me, brothers[O], and be watching[41] the *ones* walking[P] in this manner,   17
just as you have us *as a* pattern[42]

      1D. For many walk, *as to* whom I was often saying *to* you, and now even weeping[Q] say— *they*   18
are the enemies *of* the cross *of* Christ

            1E. Whose end[R] *is* destruction[S]   19
            2E. Whose god *is their* stomach[T], and glory[U] *is* in their shame[V]
            3E. The *ones* thinking[43] the earthly[W] *things*

      2D. For our place-of-citizenship[44] is in *the* heavens, from where also we are eagerly-awaiting[X]   20
the Savior[Y]— *the* Lord Jesus Christ

            1E. Who will transform[45] the body *of* our lowliness[46] *so as to be* similar-in-form[47] *to* the   21
body *of* His glory[U], according-to[48] the working[49] *that* enables Him also[50] to subject[Z] all *things* to Himself

1. Or, "people". On this word, see "kind" in 1 Cor 12:28.
2. That is, the external adherence to Jewish rules of righteousness, not the internal righteousness before God.
3. Or, "proven to be". GK *1181*.
4. Or, "without fault or guilt". Same word as in 2:15; Lk 1:6; 1 Thes 3:13. Elsewhere only as "faultless" in Heb 8:7. GK *289*. Related word in 1 Thes 5:23.
5. Some manuscripts omit this word {C}.
6. Or, "advantages, profits, things gained". Elsewhere only in 1:21; Tit 1:11. GK *3046*. The related verb is in v 8.
7. Elsewhere only in v 8; and in Act 27:10, 21, a loss in a shipwreck. GK *2422*.
8. Or, "taking the lead in thinking". On this word, see Jam 1:2.
9. Or, "forfeited". Related to "loss" in v 7, 8. On this word, see 1 Cor 3:15. Same word as "forfeit" in Mk 8:36.
10. Or, "rubbish, dung, excrement, leavings, refuse". Used only here. GK *5032*.
11. Or, "*the* faithfulness *of* Christ" in doing what He was sent to do.
12. Some manuscripts omit this word {C}.
13. Or, "participation, sharing". On this word see 1:5. Note Col 1:24.
14. Same word as in Rom 8:18; 2 Cor 1:5, 6, 7; Col 1:24; 2 Tim 3:11; Heb 2:9, 10; 10:32; 1 Pet 1:11; 4:13; 5:1, 9. Elsewhere only as "passion" in Rom 7:5; Gal 5:24. GK *4077*. The verb is in 1:29.
15. Or, "taking on a like form or appearance". We must now take on the form of Christ's death (2 Cor 4:7-12). Only then can we know His power. 2 Cor 12:9 says "my power is perfected in weakness". Later we will take on the form of His glory (3:21; Rom 8:17). Used only here. GK *5214*. Related to "similar-in-form" in v 21.
16. Or, "if perhaps". This phrase, "if somehow" occurs elsewhere only in Act 27:12; Rom 1:10; 11:14. A modestly stated hope.
17. Or, "reach, arrive at". On this word, see Act 26:7.
18. This is supplied from v 10. Some think Paul means the spiritual power of it in this life, as in Eph 1:19-20; 2 Cor 4:10-11. Others think he is referring to the future physical resurrection.
19. This is the normal word "resurrection", with the prefix "out" added. The emphasis is upon "out" to fullness of life and power. Used only here. GK *1983*.
20. This is the common word "take, receive". Both ideas are combined here. On this word, see "taken" in Rom 7:8.
21. Some think Paul means "knowing Him" in this way, v 10; others, the knowledge of Him, v 8; others, the "prize", v 14; others, "the power of the resurrection", v 11.
22. Or, "reached the goal, come to the end" (as in Lk 13:32); "been made complete, finished". On this word, see "perfect" in Heb 2:10. Related to "mature" in v 15.
23. Or, "also". Or, this may be smoothed out as "I am pressing on that I may indeed take hold". The grammar means Paul presses on for the purpose of taking hold of it.
24. On this word, used three times in v 12-13, see "overcome" in Jn 1:5.
25. Or, "if I may indeed take hold, because I also was taken hold of by Christ Jesus". The phrase "for which" is elsewhere only as "upon which" in 4:10; Lk 11:22; Act 7:33; and as "because" in Rom 5:12; 2 Cor 5:4.
26. Some manuscripts omit this word {C}.
27. Some manuscripts say "not yet" {B}.
28. Paul uses grammar that emphasizes the contrast between this phrase and the next.
29. Used only here. GK *2085*. The root word is "stretch out" in Act 27:30.
30. On this word, see 1 Cor 9:24, run to win the prize.
31. Or, "above". Some think Paul means "for the prize *belonging to my* calling [from] above *from* God", that is, the "crown" due him for finishing his calling, the course God called him to, 2 Tim 4:7-8; others, "for the prize *belonging to my* calling [to salvation] [from] above *from* God", that is, my heavenly reward as a Christian; others, "for the prize *consisting of* the upward calling *from* God", that is, the prize of "departing and being with Christ" (1:23) at the end of his "pressing on" here. Same word as in Jn 11:41. Elsewhere only as "up" in Heb 12:15; "above" in Jn 8:23; Act 2:19; Gal 4:26; Col 3:1, 2; and "top" in Jn 2:7. GK *539*.
32. This is the Greek word order. Some think Paul means "the prize... from God"; others, "the calling from God".
33. On this word, see "complete" in 1 Cor 13:10. Same root word as "perfected" in v 12.
34. Or, "having this mind". On this word, see Rom 8:5.
35. Or, "otherwise". Used only here. GK *2284*.
36. If you are thinking something differently on this subject— and therefore less maturely than Paul— God will reveal this less mature thinking to you. Compare Jn 7:17. Nevertheless, keep walking in what you know, while pressing on.
37. Or, "arrived, reached". On this word, see "came" in 1 Thes 2:16.
38. Or, "following in order". On this word, see Gal 5:25. Live what you know. Compare Rom 14:6, 22. Some manuscripts say "by the same rule *let us* walk in line, *let us* think the same *thing*" {A}.
39. Or, "Become". GK *1181*.
40. Used only here. GK *5213*. Related to "imitator" in Eph 5:1.
41. That is, watching them as examples. On this word, see "look for" in 2 Cor 4:18.
42. Or, "example, model". On this word, see 1 Pet 5:3.
43. Or, "setting their minds on". Same word as in v 15; 4:2.
44. Or, "commonwealth, state, community". Used only here. GK *4487*. We are foreigners here, resident aliens, 1 Pet 2:11.
45. Or, "change the form of ". Same word as in 2 Cor 11:13, 14. Elsewhere only as "applied" in 1 Cor 4:6; and "disguise" in 2 Cor 11:15. GK *3571*. Related to "outward appearance" in 2:7.
46. Or, "humiliation, humble condition". On this word, see Jam 1:10.
47. Or, "like-in-appearance". This adjective is elsewhere only in Rom 8:29. GK *5215*. Related to "conform" in 3:10. The root word is "form" in 2:6-7, where Christ in the "form" of God took on the "form" of a slave. We will be "like" Jesus, says 1 Jn 3:2, using a different word.
48. Or, "based on, by way of ". GK *2848*.
49. Or, "operation, action". Elsewhere only in Eph 1:19; 3:7; 4:16; Col 1:29; 2:12; 2 Thes 2:9, 11. GK *1918*. Related to "works" in 1 Cor 12:11; and "effective" in Heb 4:12.
50. Or, "the working *that results in* Him being able also...", "the working [He works] *so that* He is able also...".

A. 2 Tim 3:12 B. Rom 1:17 C. Phil 2:3 D. 1 Cor 12:8 E. Mk 8:36 F. Lk 1:34 G. Mk 5:30 H. Act 24:15 J. 1 Cor 14:1, pursue K. Rom 3:28 L. Heb 13:2 M. 2 Pet 1:10 N. 2 Thes 2:3 O. Act 16:40 P. Heb 13:9 Q. Jn 11:33 R. Rom 10:4 S. 2 Pet 2:1 T. Lk 1:15, womb U. 2 Pet 2:10 V. Heb 12:2 W. Phil 2:10 X. Rom 8:19, awaiting Y. Lk 1:47 Z. Eph 5:21

	6C. So then, my beloved^A and yearned-for brothers^B, my joy and crown^C, be standing-*firm*^D in this manner in *the* Lord, beloved	4:1
	7C. I exhort^E Euodia and I exhort Syntyche to be thinking the same[1] *thing* in *the* Lord. °Yes[2], I ask you also, genuine^F comrade[3]—	2-3
	1D. Be helping[4] these *women* who contended-together[5] *with* me in connection with the good-news^G, along-with both Clement and the rest^H *of* my fellow-workers^J, whose names *are* in *the* book *of* life[6]	
2B. Be rejoicing[7] in *the* Lord always, again I will say, be rejoicing		4
3B. Let your kindness[8] be known *to* all people. The Lord *is* near[9]		5
4B. Be anxious-*about*^K nothing, but in everything— *by* prayer^L and petition^M with thanksgivings^N— let your requests^O be made-known^P to God		6
	1C. And the peace^Q *of* God surpassing^R all understanding^S will guard[10] your hearts and your minds[11] in Christ Jesus	7
5B. Finally, brothers, be considering^T these *things*— whatever *things* are true^U, whatever *things are* honorable^V, whatever *things are* right^W, whatever *things are* pure^X, whatever *things are* lovely, whatever *things are* commendable[12], if *there is* any virtue[13], and if *there is* any praise^Y		8
6B. Be practicing[14] these *things* which you indeed learned^Z, and received^AA, and heard, and saw in me, and the God *of* peace will be with you		9
5A. Now I rejoiced in *the* Lord greatly that now at last you revived[15] *your* thinking about[16] me— upon which[17] indeed you were thinking, but you were lacking-opportunity		10
1B. Not that I speak in relation to *a* need^BB		11
	1C. For **I** learned[18] to be content[19] in *the things in* which I am[20]	
	1D. I indeed know-*how*^CC to be humbled[21]	12
	2D. I also know-*how* to abound^DD	
	2C. In anything and in all *things,* I have learned-the-secret[22]—	
	1D. Both to be filled-to-satisfaction[23] and to be hungry	
	2D. Both to abound and to be in-need[24]	
	3C. I can-do[25] all *things* by-means-of[26] the[27] *One* strengthening[28] me	13
2B. Nevertheless, you did well[29] having co-partnered[30] *in* my affliction^EE		14
	1C. And **you** also know, Philippians, that in *the* beginning *of* the good-news^G when I departed from Macedonia,[31] no church partnered[32] *with* me in *the* matter^FF *of* giving^GG and receiving except you alone. °Because even[33] in Thessalonica you sent *to* me both once and twice[34] for *my* need^HH	15 16
	1D. Not that I am seeking-for[35] the gift^JJ, but I am seeking-for the fruit^KK increasing^LL to your account^FF	17

Philippians 4:1   732   Verse

1. Same phrase as in 2:2. Between exhortations to all his readers, Paul addresses these two women directly, individually, and publicly. The details are not given. He may be addressing them regarding the big issue just discussed. In this case, he means they each should be thinking the same thing as Paul on this matter, the same "mature thinking" he has just outlined. Perhaps they were hanging on to the things of Judaism and not pressing on like Paul. Or, he may mean they should be thinking the same thing as each other, be like-minded. In this case, Paul would be referring to some personal disagreement with no relation to the context here, and this would be point 2B. It would be an aside, somewhat like 1 Tim 5:23.
2. Some manuscripts say "And" {K}.
3. This word means "paired or yoked together", and is used of a wife or a "yoke-fellow". Used only here. GK *5187*. The identity of this man is unknown to us. Some take this word as a name "Syzygus", though this name is not known elsewhere in Greek.
4. Used only here by Paul. Elsewhere in this sense only in Lk 5:7. "Be taking hold with them". On this word, see "concerned" in Lk 2:21.
5. That is, they fought in the battle alongside Paul. On this word, see 1:27.
6. On the "book of life", see Rev 3:5.
7. Here Paul returns to where he started in 3:1.
8. Or, "gentleness, graciousness, reasonableness, fairness". Elsewhere only as "kind" in 1 Tim 3:3; Tit 3:2; Jam 3:17; 1 Pet 2:18. GK *2117*. Related to "kindness" in Act 24:4. Note "gentleness and kindness" in 2 Cor 10:1.
9. Some place this sentence with the next point. The motivation it provides fits in both places. "Near" can mean physically "close by" (as in Eph 2:13, 17; Act 1:12), or close in time (as in Rom 13:11; Rev 1:3). On this word, see Lk 21:30.
10. Or, "protect, keep". On this word, see "kept in custody" in Gal 3:23.
11. Or, "thoughts". On this word, see 2 Cor 3:14.
12. Or, "praiseworthy, attractive, favorable". Used only here. GK *2368*. Related to "good report" in 2 Cor 6:8.
13. Or, "moral excellence". On this word, see 2 Pet 1:3.
14. Or, "doing, accomplishing; be engaged in, carrying out". Note that v 8 is what to think; v 9 is what to do. On this word, see Rom 2:1.
15. Or, "caused to bloom or blossom again". Used only here. GK *352*.
16. Or, "with reference to, concerning, for". GK *5642*. "Thinking about" is the same phrase as in 1:7. On "thinking", see 2:5.
17. Or, "upon whom". That is, upon the thing about me, upon my circumstance. On this phrase, see "for which" in 3:12.
18. Same word as in v 9. This is the common verb "to learn", whether from instruction, inquiry, or experience. Used 25 times. GK *3443*.
19. Or, "independent, self-sufficient" in the Lord. Used only here. GK *895*. Related to "sufficiency" in 2 Cor 9:8.
20. That is, in whatever my circumstances are at the time.
21. Or, "made low". Like Jesus, same word as 2:8. Same word as in Mt 18:4; 23:12; Lk 14:11; 18:14; 2 Cor 11:7; 12:21; Jam 4:10; 1 Pet 5:6. Elsewhere only as "made low" in Lk 3:5. GK *5427*. Related to "lowly" in Jam 1:9.
22. Or, "I have been instructed, I have been initiated". Used only here. GK *3679*. Paul may mean that he has "learned the secret [of how to be content in]", or "been instructed [in how to be content in]" both being filled and hungering. The secret is v 13. Or, he may mean that he "has been instructed", or "learned the secret [which is]" both to be filled and to hunger. The secret is being both filled and hungry at the same time— filled with food, hungry for the Lord; abounding in the Lord, in need of things. This would be similar to "having nothing yet holding on to all things", 2 Cor 6:10; "abundance of joy and down deep poverty", 2 Cor 8:2; "when I am weak, then I am powerful", 2 Cor 12:10; "a slave, but the Lord's freedperson", 1 Cor 7:22; "the lowly boasting in his height, the rich in his lowliness", Jam 1:9. The secret Paul learned was to look at life in both dimensions at the same time in any and all circumstances.
23. Or, "to be satisfied, to eat one's fill". Same word as in Mt 5:6; 14:20; 15:33, 37; Mk 6:42; 7:27; 8:4, 8; Lk 6:21; 9:17; 15:16; 16:21; Jn 6:26; Rev 19:21. Elsewhere only as "filled" in Jam 2:16. GK *5963*.
24. Or, "come short, lack". On this word, see Lk 15:14. Same root word as "need" in v 11, and "lack" in 2:30.
25. Or, "am strong-*enough for*". GK *2710*. Same word as in Gal 5:6.
26. Or, "in, in union with". GK *1877*.
27. Some manuscripts say "Christ strengthening me" {A}.
28. Or, "making me strong". On this word, see "become strong" in 2 Tim 2:1.
29. Or, "acted commendably". On this idiom, see Act 10:33.
30. Or, "participated, shared-together". Elsewhere only as "participate" in Eph 5:11; Rev 18:4. GK *5170*. Related to "co-partner" in 1:7, and "shared" in 4:15.
31. That is, on Paul's first journey to Achaia, when he left Macedonia for Athens in Act 17:14.
32. Or, "shared". That is, only the Philippians helped Paul financially to reach others. He did not accept support from those he ministered to, including the Philippians when he was there. They sent money to him to help him reach those in Thessalonica. On this word, see "share" in 2 Jn 11. Related to "co-partnered" in v 14; and to "partnership" in 1:5.
33. That is, even in the beginning, before I even left Macedonia; even in Thessalonica, before I went to Berea. Paul left them for Thessalonica in Act 17:1, went to Berea in Act 17:10, then left Macedonia in Act 17:14.
34. That is, once and again, more than once, several times. Same phrase as 1 Thes 2:18.
35. Same word as in Mt 12:39; 16:4; Lk 4:42; Act 19:39; Rom 11:7; Heb 11:14; 13:14. Elsewhere only as "seek after" in Mt 6:32; Lk 12:30; "search for" in Act 12:19; and "seek" in Act 13:7. GK *2118*. The root word is "seek" in 2:21.

A. Mt 3:17 B. Act 16:40 C. Rev 4:4 D. 1 Cor 16:13 E. Rom 12:8 F. 2 Cor 8:8, genuineness G. 1 Cor 15:1 H. 2 Pet 3:16, other J. Rom 16:3 K. Mt 6:25 L. 1 Tim 2:1 M. 1 Tim 2:1 N. 1 Tim 4:3 O. 1 Jn 5:15 P. Phil 1:22, know Q. Act 15:33 R. Phil 2:3 S. Rom 7:23, mind T. Rom 3:28 U. Jn 6:55 V. 1 Tim 3:8 W. Rom 1:17, righteous X. 1 Pet 3:2 Y. 1 Cor 4:5 Z. Phil 4:11 AA. Lk 17:34, taken BB. Mk 12:44 CC. 1 Jn 2:29, know DD. 2 Cor 8:2 EE. Rev 7:14 FF. 1 Cor 12:8, word GG. Jam 1:17, gift giving HH. Tit 3:14 JJ. Eph 4:8 KK. Mt 7:16 LL. 2 Cor 8:15

3B.	And I am receiving everything in full[1], and I am abounding[A]. I have been filled-up[2], having received[B] from Epaphroditus[C] the *things* from you— *an* aroma *of* fragrance[3], *an* acceptable[D] sacrifice[E], pleasing[F] *to* God	18
4B.	And my God will fill-up[4] every need[G] *of* yours according-to[5] His riches[H] in glory[J] in Christ Jesus	19
5B.	Now *to* our God and Father *be* the glory[J] forever and ever[K], amen	20

A.	Greet[L] every saint[M] in[6] Christ Jesus	21
B.	The brothers[N] with me greet you. *All the saints greet you, but especially the *ones* from Caesar's household[7]	22
C.	The grace[O] *of* the[8] Lord Jesus Christ *be* with your spirit[9]	23

1. That is, I am acknowledging receipt in full as to everything. As an accounting term, this word means "to receive in full". Same word as Mt 6:2, 5, 16; Lk 6:24; Phm 15. GK *600*.
2. Or, "I have become full". Same word as in v 2:2; 4:19.
3. Same phrase as in Eph 5:2.
4. Some manuscripts say "And may my God fill up" {B}, making it a prayer.
5. Or, "based on, in accordance with, in harmony with". GK *2848*.
6. Some think Paul means "Greet... in Christ"; others, "saint in Christ".
7. These people had the closest contact with Paul. Nero was emperor at this time. On this word, see "house" in Mk 3:25.
8. Some manuscripts say "our" {K}.
9. Some manuscripts say "with you all" {N}. Some add "amen" {A}.

A. 2 Cor 8:2   B. Mt 10:40, welcome   C. Phil 2:25   D. Lk 4:19   E. Heb 9:26   F. Eph 5:10   G. Tit 3:14   H. 1 Tim 6:17   J. 2 Pet 2:10   K. Rev 20:10   L. Mk 15:18   M. 1 Pet 1:16, holy   N. Act 16:40   O. Eph 2:8

Overview		**Colossians**

Introduction	1:1-2
1A. We are giving thanks to God always while praying for you	1:3
1B. Having heard of your faith in Christ, and the love you have for all the saints	1:4-8
2B. We pray you may be filled with the knowledge of His will, that you may walk worthily	1:9-10
1C. Bearing fruit in every good work and growing in the knowledge of God	1:10
2C. Being empowered with all power toward total endurance and patience	1:11
3C. Giving thanks to the Father who delivered us into the kingdom of His Son	1:12-13
1D. In whom we have the redemption, the forgiveness of sins	1:14
2D. Who is the image of the invisible God, the firstborn of all creation	1:15-18
3D. Who is the beginning, the firstborn from the dead, He reconciled you through Him	1:18-23
2A. Now I am rejoicing in my sufferings for you and His church, and in your firmness of faith	1:24-2:5
3A. As then you received Christ, be walking in Him, rooted, built and established in the faith	2:6-7
1B. Watch out no one takes you captive by human thinking not in accordance with Christ because	2:8
1C. In Him dwells all the fullness of the Deity in bodily form	2:9
2C. And in Him you are complete	2:10
3C. In whom also you were circumcised, having been buried with Him in baptism, in which you also were raised with Him. Indeed, He made you alive with Him	2:11-15
2B. Therefore let no one judge you in eating and Sabbaths, shadows of coming things	2:16-17
3B. Let no one decide against you based on man-made religion, not holding on to Christ	2:18-19
4B. If you died with Christ, why submit to decrees according to the teachings of humans?	2:20-23
5B. If then you were raised with Christ, be seeking the things above. You died, so put to death the sins of the flesh. Lay aside the things of the old person, and put on the new	3:1-11
4A. Therefore as chosen ones of God, holy and having been loved—	3:12
1B. Put on deep feelings of compassion, and love, forgiving one another	3:12-14
2B. And let the peace of Christ be arbitrating in your hearts	3:15
3B. And be thankful	3:15
4B. Let the word of Christ be dwelling in you richly, with all wisdom and gratitude	3:16
5B. And everything, whatever you may do in word or deed, do all in the name of Jesus	3:17
•B. Follow my commands regarding wives, husbands, children, fathers, slaves, masters	3:18-4:1
12B. Be devoting yourself to prayer, keeping watch in it, praying also for us	4:2-4
13B. Be walking with wisdom toward outsiders, redeeming the time	4:5-6
Conclusion	4:7-18

Colossians 1:1 738 Verse

A. Paul, *an* apostle^A *of* Christ Jesus¹ by *the* will *of* God, and Timothy *our* brother   1
B. *To* the saints² and faithful³ brothers^B in Christ in Colossae⁴   2
C. Grace *to* you and peace from God our Father⁵

1A. We are giving-thanks^C *to* God *the* Father⁶ *of* our Lord Jesus Christ always⁷ while praying for you   3

  1B. Having heard-*of* your faith^D in Christ Jesus, and the love^E which you have for all the saints °because   4-5
    of⁸ the hope⁹ being reserved¹⁰ *for* you in the heavens—

    1C. Which¹¹ you previously-heard-*of* in the word^F *of* the truth— the good-news^G °coming^H to you   6

      1D. Just as also in all the world it¹² is bearing-fruit^J and growing¹³
      2D. Just as *it is doing* also in¹⁴ you since¹⁵ the day you heard and understood¹⁶ the grace *of* God
      in truth¹⁷, °just as¹⁸ you¹⁹ learned^K *it* from Epaphras²⁰, our beloved^L fellow-slave^M, who is   7

        1E. *A* faithful servant²¹ *of* Christ on your²² behalf
        2E. The *one* also having made-clear^N *to* us your love in *the* Spirit   8

  2B. For this reason²³ **we** also, since the day we heard, do not cease^O praying for you, and asking that   9
    you may be filled^P *with* the knowledge²⁴ *of* His will in all spiritual^Q wisdom^R and understanding²⁵—
    so that you may walk^S worthily^T *of* the Lord, toward total pleasing²⁶ [of Him]   10

    1C. Bearing-fruit^J in every good^U work and growing in²⁷ the knowledge *of* God
    2C. Being empowered²⁸ with all power^V according-to²⁹ the might^W *of* His glory³⁰, toward total³¹   11
    endurance^X and patience^Y
    3C. With joy³² °giving-thanks^C *to* the Father having qualified³³ you³⁴ for *your* part³⁵ *of* the share³⁶   12
    of the saints in the light³⁷—°Who delivered³⁸ us out of the authority³⁹ *of* darkness^Z and   13
    transferred^AA *us* into the kingdom^BB *of* the Son *of* His love⁴⁰

      1D. In Whom we have the redemption⁴¹, the forgiveness⁴² *of* sins   14

1. Some manuscripts say "Jesus Christ" {K}.
2. Or, "holy". On this word, see "holy" in 1 Pet 1:16.
3. Used 67 times, this adjective means "faithful, believing", and sometimes, "believer"; and "trustworthy" (see 1 Tim 1:15). GK *4412*. The related verb is "believe" in Jn 3:36.
4. Paul did not minister in this city in the province of Asia (2:1). It was probably reached by his associate Epaphras (v 7) during Paul's ministry in Ephesus in Act 19:10. On the writing of this letter, see Act 28:30.
5. Some manuscripts add "and the Lord Jesus Christ"; others, "and Jesus Christ our Lord" {A}.
6. Some manuscripts say "to *the* God and Father..." {C}.
7. Some think Paul means "giving thanks always", as in 1 Cor 1:4; 1 Thes 1:2; 2 Thes 1:3. Others think Paul means "praying always", as in v 9. In the Greek, as in the English, "always" stands between the two phrases.
8. Some think Paul means the Colossians have this love because of the hope, as the fruit of the hope. The Christian life is faith working through love (Gal 5:6), energized by hope. Others think he is referring back to both faith and love. Others think he means "we are giving thanks... because of".
9. Same word as in v 23, 27; Act 23:6; Rom 5:2; 8:24; 1 Cor 13:13; 2 Cor 1:7; Eph 1:18; 2:12; Phil 1:20; 1 Tim 1:1; Tit 1:2; 2:13; Heb 6:11; 1 Jn 3:3. Used 53 times. GK *1828*. The related verb is in Jn 5:45.
10. Or "laid away". Same word as in 2 Tim 4:8. Elsewhere only as "laying away" in Lk 19:20; and "destined" in Heb 9:27. GK *641*.
11. This word refers back to the "hope".
12. That is, the good news. Some manuscripts add "and" {N}, so that it says "coming to you just as also in all the world. And it is bearing fruit...".
13. On this word, see Jn 3:30. Same word as in v 10. Some manuscripts omit "and growing" {N}.
14. Or, "among". GK *1877*.
15. This is an idiom, literally, "from which *day*". Same phrase as in v 9. See Rev 16:18 on it.
16. Or, "fully understood, knew, fully knew, recognized, acknowledged". Used elsewhere by Paul only as "understand" in 2 Cor 1:13, 14; "know" in Rom 1:32; 2 Cor 13:5; 1 Tim 4:3; "fully know" in 1 Cor 13:12; 2 Cor 6:9; and "acknowledge" in 1 Cor 14:37; 16:18. Used elsewhere 32 times, mostly as "know, recognize, learn". GK *2105*. The related noun is "knowledge" in v 9.
17. Paul may mean "in reality, truly". Or he may mean "in its true form" vs. the false teaching there. On this word, see Jn 4:23.
18. Paul ties the Colossians' faith directly to Epaphras. Paul is showing them that what they heard from Epaphras is the truth of the gospel, the same gospel that is bearing fruit in all the world. It was faithfully delivered by Epaphras. The false teaching they are now hearing, and which he addresses in this book, did not come from Epaphras.
19. Some manuscripts add "also" {N}.
20. Epaphras is also mentioned in 4:12, and Phm 23. Paul takes pains here to establish his reliability. GK *2071*.
21. Or, "minister". On this word, see 1 Cor 3:5.
22. Some manuscripts say "our" {B}.
23. That is, having heard of their growing faith and love, v 4. Compare Col 1:4, 9 with Eph 1:15-17.
24. Or, "full knowledge, recognition, understanding, acknowledgment". Same word as in Rom 1:28; 3:20; 10:2; Eph 1:17; 4:13; Phil 1:9; Col 1:10; 3:10; 1 Tim 2:4; 2 Tim 2:25; 3:7; Tit 1:1; Phm 6; Heb 10:26; 2 Pet 1:2, 3, 8; 2:20. Elsewhere only as "full knowledge" in Col 2:2. GK *2106*. The related verb is "understand" in v 6.
25. Or, "in all wisdom and spiritual understanding". On this word see Eph 3:4.
26. Or, "for all pleasing", every kind of pleasing, pleasing in every respect. This construction occurs elsewhere only in v 11 and in 2 Cor 9:11, "for all generosity". "Pleasing" is used only here. GK *742*. Related to the word in 1 Thes 2:4, and in Eph 5:10.
27. Or, "*by*".
28. Or, "strengthened" with all strength. Elsewhere only as "strengthened" in Heb 11:34. GK *1540*. Related to "power" next, and the word in 2 Tim 2:1.
29. Or, "based on, in accordance with". GK *2848*.
30. That is, belonging to His glory; or, characterized by His glory, His glorious might. On this word, see 2 Pet 2:10.
31. Or, "all". On this phrase, see "total pleasing" in v 10.
32. This is the Greek word order. Some take "with joy" with what precedes, so that it says "... and patience with joy, giving thanks...".
33. Or, "made fit, competent, adequate, sufficient". Elsewhere only as "made sufficient" in 2 Cor 3:6. GK *2655*. Some manuscripts say "called" {B}.
34. Some manuscripts say "us" {B}.
35. Or, "portion, share", that which results from a division. Same word as in Lk 10:42; Act 8:21. Elsewhere only as "share" in 2 Cor 6:15; and "district" in Act 16:12. GK *3535*. "Part" and "share" are used together also in Act 8:21, "you have no part nor share in this matter".
36. Or, "portion, allotment", that which is assigned by lot. Here, the context gives it the idea of "inheritance", the share we inherit from our Father. Same word as in Act 1:17; 8:21; 26:18. Elsewhere only of casting "lots" in Mt 27:35; Mk 15:24; Lk 23:34; Jn 19:24; Act 1:26; and of an assigned "lot" of people in 1 Pet 5:3. GK *3102*. Related to "allotted" in Eph 1:11; "allotted to" in Act 17:4.
37. Some think Paul means "qualified you... by the light" (the gospel); others, "the share... in the *kingdom of* the light"; others, "*of* the saints *who are* in the light", that is, in heaven, in the presence of God; others, "*of* the holy *ones* [angels] *who are* in the light".
38. Or, "rescued, saved". Elsewhere only in Mt 6:13; 27:43; Lk 1:74; Rom 7:24; 11:26; 15:31; 2 Cor 1:10; 1 Thes 1:10; 2 Thes 3:2; 2 Tim 3:11; 4:17, 18; 2 Pet 2:7, 9. GK *4861*.
39. Or, "jurisdiction, dominion, power". On this word, see Rev 6:8.
40. That is, the Son who is the object of His love, His beloved Son. Compare 3:12. Same word as in v 4.
41. On this word, see Rom 3:24. Some manuscripts add "through His blood" {A}, as in Eph 1:7.
42. Or, "release, pardon, cancellation". Same word as in Mt 26:28; Mk 1:4; 3:29; Lk 1:77; 3:3; 24:47; Act 2:38; 5:31; 10:43; 13:38; 26:18; Eph 1:7; Heb 9:22; 10:18. Elsewhere only as "release" in Lk 4:18. GK *912*. The related verb also means "let go, abandon, send away".

A. 1 Cor 12:28 B. Act 16:40 C. Mt 26:27 D. Eph 2:8 E. 1 Jn 4:16 F. 1 Cor 12:8 G. 1 Cor 15:1 H. Rev 17:8, be present J. Rom 7:4
K. Phil 4:11 L. Mt 3:17 M. Rev 19:10 N. 1 Cor 3:13 O. 1 Cor 13:8 P. Eph 5:18 Q. 1 Cor 14:1 R. 1 Cor 12:8 S. Heb 13:9 T. 3 Jn 6
U. 1 Tim 5:10b V. Mk 5:30 W. Eph 6:10 X. Jam 1:3 Y. Heb 6:12 Z. Jn 3:19 AA. Act 19:26, turn away BB. Mt 3:2

| Colossians 1:15 | 740 | Verse |

  2D. Who is *the* image[1] *of* the invisible God, *the* firstborn[2] *of* all creation[A]   15

    1E. Because all *things* were created[B] by[3] Him   16

      1F. In the heavens, and on the earth
      2F. The visible *things,* and the invisible *things*— whether thrones[C], or lordships[4], or rulers[D], or authorities[E]
      3F. All *things* have been created through[5] Him, and for Him

    2E. And He Himself is before[6] all *things*   17
    3E. And all *things* have existence[7] in Him
    4E. And He Himself is the head *of* the body, the church[8]   18

  3D. Who is *the* beginning[9], *the* firstborn from the dead, in order that He Himself might come-to-be[10] holding-first-place[11] in all *things*

    1E. Because *the Father* was well-pleased[F]   19

      1F. *That* all the fullness[12] *should* dwell[G] in Him
      2F. And *that He should* reconcile[13] all *things* through Him to Himself, having made-peace through the blood[H] *of* His cross[J]   20

        1G. Through Him[14]— whether the *things* on the earth, or the *things* in the heavens

    2E. Indeed[15] you *were* formerly being excluded[16], and enemies[17] *in* the mind[K], in evil[L] works. But now He reconciled[18] *you* in the body *of* His flesh[19] through *His* death— *that He might* present[M] you holy and without-blemish[20] and blameless[N] in His presence   21, 22

      1F. If indeed you continue[O] *in* the faith— having been founded[P], and steadfast[21], and not being moved-away from the hope *of* the good-news[Q] which you heard   23

        1G. The *one* having been proclaimed[R] in all creation under heaven
        2G. *Of* which **I,** Paul, became *a* minister[22]

2A. Now I[23] am rejoicing[S] in *my* sufferings[T] for your sake[24], and in my flesh[U] I am filling-up-in-turn[25] the *things* lacking[V] *from*[26] the afflictions[W] *of* Christ[27], for the sake of His body, which is the church   24

  1B. *Of* which **I** became *a* minister[X] according-to[28] the stewardship[29] *of* God having been given *to* me for you, *that* I might fulfill[30] the word *of* God— the mystery[31] having been hidden[Y] from the *past* ages[32] and from the *past* generations   25, 26

    1C. But now it was revealed[Z] *to* His saints, *to* whom God willed[33] to make-known[34] what *is* the riches *of* the glory *of* this mystery among the Gentiles   27
    2C. Which[35] is Christ in you, the hope *of* glory

      1D. Whom **we** are proclaiming[AA]— admonishing[36] every person[BB], and teaching every person with all wisdom, in order that we may present[M] every person mature[37] in Christ[38]   28

        1E. For which[39] I also am laboring, struggling[40] according to His working[41] being at-work[42] in me with power   29

1. Or, "likeness, form". Used in the NT of the portrait imprinted on a coin in Mt 22:20; Mk 12:16; Lk 20:24; of idols (false images of God) in Rom 1:23; of the image of the beast in Rev 13:14, 15; 14:9, 11; 15:2; 16:2; 19:20; 20:4; of the image of Christ to which we will be shaped in Rom 8:29; 1 Cor 15:49; 2 Cor 3:18; Col 3:10; of the image of God in which mankind was created in 1 Cor 11:7; of the image of Adam which we share in 1 Cor 15:49; of Christ as the image of God in 2 Cor 4:4; Col 1:15; and elsewhere only of the reality of which the Law was a shadow in Heb 10:1. GK *1635*. Jesus is the likeness of the invisible God imprinted in human flesh; "the exact representation of His essence", Heb 1:3; the "form" of God in outward appearance as a man, Phil 2:6-8; the "Word" in flesh, Jn 1:14.
2. That is, God's firstborn (and "only born", Jn 1:18) human Son, the preeminent one, first in rank; the one having firstborn status and rights. When Jesus became a man, He became part of His creation, but not just any part. He is first over all, the preeminent One over all creation and created beings, Phil 2:9-11. Paul gives four reasons for this in verse 16-18. This word is used of Christ also in 1:18; Lk 2:7; Rom 8:29; Heb 1:6; Rev 1:5. Elsewhere only in Heb 11:28; 12:23. GK *4758*. Note Ps 89:27.
3. Or, "in" Him. GK *1877*.
4. On these four "invisible things", compare Eph 1:21. On this word, see "authority" in 2 Pet 2:10.
5. Or, "by" Him, "in connection with" Him. GK *1328*.
6. That is, the Son existed before any created thing existed.
7. Or, "hold together". The Son is the cause of the continued existence of the universe. On this word, see 2 Pet 3:5.
8. That is, the new creation.
9. Or, "ruler". This word means "beginning" in various senses in Mt 19:4, 8; 24:8, 21; Mk 1:1; 10:6; 13:8, 19; Jn 1:1, 2; 2:11; 6:64; 8:25, 44; 15:27; 16:4; Act 11:15; Phil 4:15; Heb 1:10; 2:3; 3:14; 5:12; 6:1; 7:3; 2 Pet 3:4; 1 Jn 1:1; 2:7, 13, 14, 24; 3:8, 11; 2 Jn 5, 6; Rev 3:14; 21:6, 13; "first" in Lk 1:2; 26:4; and "corner" in Act 10:11; 11:5 (the beginning of the sheet). Elsewhere only as "rulers" in Lk 12:11; Rom 8:38; Eph 3:10; 6:12; Col 1:16; 2:15; Tit 3:1; and "rule" in the sense of "power, dominion", in Lk 20:20; 1 Cor 15:24; Eph 1:21; Col 2:10; and in the sense of "domain" (sphere of authority) in Jude 6. GK *794*. Jesus is the firstfruit of the resurrection (1 Cor 15:20-23), the beginning of the new creation, the founder of a new humanity, the first cause of all creation (Rev 3:14), the ruler of all. A related word is used of Jesus in Rev 1:5, the "ruler" of the kings of the earth. On the related verb, which usually means "begin", see "rule" in Rom 15:12.
10. Or, "be". GK *1181*.
11. Or, "being first, being preeminent, being first in rank". Used only here. GK *4750*. This is the verb related to the word "first".
12. That is, the fullness of God, as in 2:9. Others render this "because all the fullness *of God* was well pleased to dwell in Him". Same word as in 2:9; Mt 9:16; Mk 2:21; Jn 1:16; Rom 11:12, 25; 15:29; 1 Cor 10:26; Gal 4:4; Eph 1:10, 23; 3:19; 4:13. Elsewhere only as "fillings" in Mk 6:43; 8:20; and "fulfillment" in Rom 13:10. GK *4445*.
13. Elsewhere only in v 22 and Eph 2:16. GK *639*. See the related word in Rom 5:10.
14. Some manuscripts omit "through Him" {C}. This phrase expands "reconcile all *things* through Him".
15. Paul applies this reconciliation directly to the Colossians.
16. Or, "alienated, estranged", that is, from God. The Colossians were living in this condition. On this word, see Eph 4:18.
17. Some think Paul means "regarded as enemies" by God, Rom 5:10; others, "living as enemies, hostile to God".
18. Some think Paul means God reconciled; others, Christ. Some manuscripts say "you were reconciled" {C}.
19. That is, His fleshly body.
20. Or, "without defect, blameless". Elsewhere only in Eph 1:4; 5:27; Phil 2:15; Heb 9:14; 1 Pet 1:19; Jude 24; Rev 14:5. GK *320*.
21. Or, "firm". Elsewhere only in 1 Cor 7:37; 15:58. GK *1612*. Related to "support" in 1 Tim 3:15.
22. Or, "servant". Same word as in v 25.
23. Some manuscripts instead say "I who now..." {K}, connecting this more closely with the preceding phrase.
24. Same preposition ("for the sake of") as in similar statements in Eph 3:1, 13; 6:20; Phil 1:29; Col 2:1; 2 Thes 1:5. GK *5642*.
25. Or, "filling-up-on-my-part", or simply "filling up". That is, filling up my part of what is lacking from Christ's afflictions. Used only here. GK *499*. Related to "filled" in Eph 5:18.
26. Same grammar as in 1 Thes 3:10. That is, lacking from the afflictions of Christ remaining to be accomplished.
27. Christ continues to suffer and be humiliated by people until He returns in glory. He suffers when the people in His body the church suffer (note Act 9:4). In this sense, the measure of His afflictions is not yet full. Compare Act 14:22; 2 Cor 1:5. Thus in Paul's own bodily sufferings, he is enduring afflictions which Christ is also enduring. This continues even today, until they are "filled up". Peter says we are to rejoice to the degree that we share in the sufferings of Christ, 1 Pet 4:13. There are other views. Consult the commentaries.
28. Or, "based on, by way of". Same word as in v 29. GK *2848*.
29. That is, the position of management responsibility. On this word, see Eph 1:10.
30. Or, "complete". Paul's stewardship was to fulfill the word of God by proclaiming the mystery hidden in the past, but now revealed through him; that is, by taking the gospel to the Gentiles, Eph 3:8, 9. Same word as "complete" in Rom 15:19.
31. The word of God in view is specified here as the mystery hidden but now revealed. On this word, see Rom 11:25.
32. On "from the *past* ages", see Lk 1:70.
33. Or, "desired, wanted, wished". On this word, see Jn 7:17.
34. The verbs "revealed" and "make known" also occur in Rom 16:26. On this word, see "know" in Phil 1:22.
35. That is, the hidden mystery (v 26) which was now revealed (v 27), which Paul now defines. Compare Eph 3:2-11.
36. Or, "warning, advising, instructing". Elsewhere only in Act 20:31; Rom 15:14; 1 Cor 4:14; Col 3:16; 1 Thes 5:12, 14; 2 Thes 3:15. GK *3805*. Related to "admonition" in Eph 6:4.
37. Or, "complete, finished, full-grown, perfect". On this word, see "complete" in 1 Cor 13:10.
38. Some manuscripts add "Jesus" {N}.
39. That is, "To which end".
40. Or, "striving, fighting". On this word, see 1 Tim 4:10.
41. Same noun as in 2:12. On this word, see Phil 3:21. Related to the verb "at work" which follows.
42. Or, "in operation". Same grammar as in 2 Cor 1:6; Eph 3:20. On this word, see "works" in 1 Cor 12:11.

A. Rom 8:39 B. Eph 2:15 C. Rev 20:11 D. Col 1:18, beginning E. Rev 6:8 F. Mt 17:5 G. Eph 3:17 H. 1 Jn 1:7 J. Mt 10:38 K. Lk 1:51, thoughts L. Act 25:18 M. Rom 12:1 N. Tit 1:6 O. Rom 11:22 P. Eph 3:17 Q. 1 Cor 15:1 R. 2 Tim 4:2 S. 2 Cor 13:11 T. Phil 3:10 U. Col 2:23 V. Phil 2:30 W. Rev 7:14 X. 1 Cor 3:5, servant Y. 1 Cor 2:7 Z. 1 Jn 2:19, made evident AA. Phil 1:18 BB. Mt 4:4, mankind

	2B. For[1] I want you to know how great *a* struggle[A] I am having for your sake, and the *ones* in Laodicea, and all-who have not seen my face in *the* flesh[2], °in order that their hearts might be encouraged[3]—	2:1 2
	1C. *They* having been brought-together[4] in love, and[5] for[6] all *the* riches[B] *of* the full-assurance[C] *of* understanding[7], for[8] *the* full-knowledge[9] *of* the mystery[D] *of* God— Christ[10]	
	1D. In Whom[11] are all the treasures[E] *of* wisdom[F] and knowledge[G], hidden-away[12]	3
	3B. I[13] am saying this[14] in order that no one may be deluding[H] you with persuasive-argument[15]	4
	1C. For even though[16] I am absent *in* the flesh, nevertheless I am with you *in* the spirit, rejoicing[J] and seeing your order[17] and the firmness[18] *of* your faith in Christ	5
3A.	As then you received[K] Christ Jesus the Lord[19], be walking[L] in Him—°having been rooted[20], and being built-up[M] in Him, and being established[21] *in* the faith[22] just as you were taught, abounding[N] in thanksgiving[23]	6-7
	1B. Be watching-out[O] *that* there will not be anyone taking you captive[24] through philosophy[25] and empty[P] deception[26], according-to[27] the tradition[Q] *of* humans[R], according to the elemental[28] *things of* the world, and not according to Christ	8
	1C. Because in Him dwells[S] all the fullness[T] *of* the Deity[29] bodily[30]	9
	2C. And in Him you are complete[31], Who is the head *of* all rule[32] and authority[U]	10
	3C. In Whom you also were circumcised[V] *with a* circumcision[W] not-done-by-*human*-hands[X], in the taking-off[33] *of* the body[34] *of* the flesh[Y] *in*[35] the circumcision *of* Christ—°having been buried-with Him in baptism[Z]	11 12
	1D. In which[36] you also were raised-with *Him* through faith *in* the working[AA] *of* God, the *One* having raised Him from *the* dead	

1. Paul expands on his reference to his "sufferings" (1:24) and his "struggle" (1:29) for the Colossians' sake.
2. This may imply that Paul did not know most of them.
3. Paul may specifically mean this in reference to the false teaching disturbing them. On this word, see "exhorting" in Rom 12:8.
4. Or, "united, joined, knit together". Same word as "held together" in Eph 4:16; Col 2:19. Or, "instructed", as in 1 Cor 2:16; Act 19:33. GK 5204. This word refers back to the "they" in "their hearts"; that is, to the people, rather than specifically to the "hearts".
5. That is, brought together in the sphere of love, and for the purpose of having what follows, thus giving two aspects of God's aim in bringing these people together. Others link this to "encouraged", putting "having been brought together in love" in a parenthesis, thus giving two aspects to Paul's purpose— their encouragement in love, and their knowledge of Christ.
6. That is, that these people might have or attain to what follows; for the purpose of or toward the goal of sharing in what follows. On this word, see "resulting in" in Rom 5:16.
7. Same word as in 1:9, on which see Eph 3:4 (where it is also linked to the mystery of Christ).
8. Same word as in the previous phrase. Some think it has the same meaning here, this phrase explaining or expanding the previous one, in parallel to it. Others think here it means "leading to, resulting in". In this case, the previous fullness of understanding (the means) leads to or results in what follows (the end).
9. On this noun, see "knowledge" in 1:9. It is rendered "full knowledge" here because Paul has just said "full assurance". He uses the related word "knowledge" in v 3.
10. Some manuscripts say the mystery "of God"; others, "of God, which is Christ"; others, "of God the Father of Christ"; others, "of the God and Father of Christ"; others, "of the God and Father and of Christ" {B}.
11. Or, "In which", referring to "mystery". The sense is the same, because the mystery is Christ.
12. This is the Greek word order. On this adjective, see Mk 4:22. Some link this with the verb, "in Whom all the treasures... are hidden-away"; others with the noun, "in Whom are all the hidden treasures of...". Others leave it here as a second fact. In this case, the treasures are in Christ, and they are hidden-away, as treasures usually are. They are not lying on the surface. One must look beyond any initial impression of a crucified one. They are hidden away as treasures to be discovered. Some take "hidden away" in the sense of "stored up, treasured up".
13. Some manuscripts say "And I" {N}.
14. Some think Paul is looking back to 2:1-3, or 1:24-2:3, or even 1:9-2:3. He may mean he is saying this which he wants them to know (v 1) about himself and his ministry (1:24-2:3), so no one will be deluded about him, as happened in Corinth. This explains why he has included these personal words about himself. Or he may be referring to his words about Christ (1:24-2:13), so no one will be deluded by false teaching, about which he speaks in detail beginning in v 6. Others think this is looking forward to what Paul begins to say in v 6, and begin the next main point (3A.) here.
15. Or, "plausible, probable, credible argument". Used only here. GK 4391.
16. Literally, "For if I even am...". This idiom means, "accepting that I even am absent, nevertheless...". See "if also" in 1 Cor 7:21 on it.
17. Same word as in 1 Cor 14:40, properly and in "order". GK 5423.
18. Used only here. GK 5106. Related to "firm" in 2 Tim 2:19; and "made firm" in Act 16:5.
19. Or, "Christ Jesus as Lord".
20. Elsewhere only in Eph 3:17. GK 4845. Related to "root" in Lk 8:13; Heb 12:15.
21. Note that Paul uses three words different from 1:23 (rooted, built up, established), but with the same idea. On this word, see "confirm" in 1 Cor 1:6.
22. Or, "in your faith". On this word, see Eph 2:8.
23. On this word, see 1 Tim 4:3. Some manuscripts say abounding "in it [the faith] with thanksgiving"; others "in Him with thanksgiving" {B}.
24. Or, "carrying you off as booty or plunder" from the truth to the slavery of error. Used only here. GK 5194.
25. The Greek word is *philosophia*, meaning "love of wisdom". Used only here. GK 5814. Related word in Act 17:18. Paul is referring to the human pursuit of wisdom apart from God's revelation.
26. On this word, see 2 Pet 2:13.
27. Or, "based on, by way of, in harmony with, in accordance with". Used three times in this verse. GK 2848.
28. Same word as in v 20. On this word, see Gal 4:3.
29. Or, "the divine nature". Used only here. GK 2540. This is an abstract noun for "God", related to "God". All the fullness of the divine essence dwells in Christ, not just a certain divine quality. This is a clear statement of Christ's deity.
30. That is, "in bodily form", in His incarnate body. Or, more abstractly, "in concrete reality" versus in mere appearance. This word is an adverb related to "body" (see Eph 1:23). Used only here. GK 5395.
31. This is a participle, you "are having been made complete" or "full". You stand full and complete. On this word, see "filled" in Eph 5:18. Related to "fullness" in v 9.
32. Or, "every ruler". On this word, see "beginning" in 1:18.
33. Or, "removal, stripping off *as of clothes*". It is called the "body" of (sinful) flesh in contrast to the physical foreskin removed by human hands. In this view, this phrase further describes our spiritual circumcision. Others take "the body of flesh" to refer to Christ's flesh, and this whole phrase ("the taking off... circumcision *of* Christ") as a symbolic reference to His violent death. Consult the commentaries. Used only here. GK 589. Related to "stripped" in v 15.
34. Compare Rom 6:6. On this word, see Eph 1:23. Some manuscripts say "body *of* the sins *of* the flesh" {N}.
35. Or, "by". Paul may mean "in the circumcision that belongs to Christ", that is, spiritual circumcision in contrast to that in the flesh by hands. Or he may mean "by the circumcision performed by Christ" spiritually, on our heart. In either case, he goes on to say it is the spiritual circumcision that corresponds to our being buried with Him in baptism.
36. Or, "In Whom", in which case some link this to v 12 as point 1D., "buried-with Him... in Whom you also were raised-together"; and others make it point 4C., parallel to the "In Whom you also" phrase in v 11.

A. Heb 12:1, race B. 1 Tim 6:17 C. 1 Thes 1:5, fullness of conviction D. Rom 11:25 E. Mt 12:35 F. 1 Cor 12:8 G. 1 Cor 12:8 H. Jam 1:22 J. 2 Cor 13:11 K. Lk 17:34, taken L. Heb 13:9 M. Jude 20 N. 2 Cor 8:2 O. Rev 1:11, see P. 1 Thes 2:1 Q. 1 Cor 11:2 R. Mt 4:4, mankind S. Eph 3:17 T. Col 1:19 U. Rev 6:8 V. Lk 2:21 W. Eph 2:11, circumcised X. Mk 14:58 Y. Col 2:23 Z. Heb 6:2, cleansing AA. Phil 3:21

Colossians 2:13	744	Verse

    2D. Indeed, you[1] being dead[A] in the trespasses[B] and the uncircumcision[C] *of* your flesh[D]— He[2] made you[3] alive-together[4] with Him   13

        1E. Having forgiven[E] us[5] all the trespasses

        2E. Having wiped-out[6] the written-document[7] against us *with its* decrees[8], which was opposed[9] *to* us— indeed, He has taken it out of the middle[10], having nailed[11] it *to* the cross[F]!   14

            1F. Having stripped[12] the rulers and the authorities, He exposed[13] *them* in public[G], having triumphed-over[H] them in Him[14]!   15

2B. Therefore let no one judge[J] you in eating and[15] in drinking[16], or in respect to *a* feast[17] or new-moon[18] or Sabbath   16

    1C. Which are *a* shadow *of* the coming[K] *things*, but the body[19] *is* Christ's[20]   17

3B. Let no one decide-against[21] you *who-is*[22]   18

    1C. Delighting[23] in humility[24] and worship[25] *of* angels[26]
    2C. Dwelling-upon[27] *things* which he has seen[28]
    3C. Being puffed-up[L] in-vain[29] by the mind[M] *of* his flesh[30]
    4C. And not holding-on-to[31] the head— from Whom the whole body, being supplied[32] and held-together[N] by the joints[33] and ligaments[34], is growing[O] the growth *of* God[35]   19

1. This is the same point Paul makes in Eph 2:1, 4. Note also Col 1:21-22.
2. Some think Paul means "God", from v 12; others, "Christ", rendering "with Him" next as "with Himself".
3. Some manuscripts omit this word. Others say "us" {B}.
4. The verb "make alive together" is elsewhere only as "make alive with" in Eph 2:5 (where "with" is not separately expressed, as it is here). GK *5188*.
5. Some manuscripts say "you" {A}.
6. Or, "blotted out, smeared out, rubbed out, erased", and therefore "cancelled, removed". Same word as in Act 3:19; Rev 3:5. Elsewhere only as "wipe away" in Rev 7:17; 21:4. GK *1981*.
7. This word means "hand-written document", and was often used of a certificate of debt. Some think Paul is referring to the Law, as in Eph 2:15; others, to a formal written document containing the charges against us, backed up by the decrees of the Law. There are other views. Used only here. GK *5934*.
8. Some take this with what follows, "against us, which *by its* decrees was opposed *to* us"; others, with what precedes, "*with its* decrees against us"; others, as "written document... *with its* decrees". On this word, see Eph 2:15. The related verb is in 2:20.
9. Or, "set against, hostile, contrary". This adjective is elsewhere only as "adversary" in Heb 10:27. GK *5641*.
10. That is, out from between us and God. On this word, see "midst" in 2 Thes 2:7.
11. Used only here. GK *4669*. Related to "nail" in Jn 20:25.
12. This word means "take off of, strip off of, strip away from". Some think Paul means God "stripped off their power", or "disarmed" these rulers; others, that Jesus "stripped them away from Himself" in their attempt to conquer Him. Elsewhere only as "stripped off" in 3:9. GK *588*. Related to "taking off" in v 11; and to "taken off" in 2 Cor 5:3.
13. Or, "publicly disgraced". Same word as in Mt 1:19, of Joseph not wanting to "publicly-expose" Mary.
14. Or, "in it", "by it", the cross, v 14. Instead of the cross being a public stripping of the clothes, exposure, and disgraceful death for Christ (as crucifixions were considered to be), it was in fact a stripping off of the power and authority of these rulers, and a public exposure of their end, as proven by His resurrection.
15. Some manuscripts say "or" {N}.
16. Or, "food and drink", as these same two nouns are used in Jn 6:55. Same two words as in Rom 14:17. Paul is referring to ritual observances regarding eating, aesthetic dietary rules, lists of approved and disapproved foods, etc. Used only in the three places noted here. GK *4530*.
17. Or, "festival". Used of Jewish feasts. On this word, see Jn 13:29. Religious festivals and pilgrimages.
18. Compare Num 10:10; 28:11; 1 Sam 20:5, 18; Ps 81:3. Used only here. GK *3741*. Note the progression from yearly or periodic festivals, to monthly celebrations, to weekly observances. All three of these terms are used in 1 Chron 23:31; 2 Chron 2:4; 31:3; Neh 10:34; Hos 2:11; etc.
19. Or, in a figurative sense, the "substance", the "reality". The OT rituals are shadowy pointers to the coming of the future realities in Christ. Said in reverse, Christ is the body that casts the shadows contained in the rituals of the Law. He is the reality. On this word, see Eph 1:23.
20. Or, "*belongs to* Christ".
21. Or, "umpire against you, declare you the loser, disqualify you from winning the prize, rob you of the prize". This is a word from the games. Used only here. GK *2857*. Related to "arbitrate" in 3:15, which is the same root word without the prefix "against". Related to "prize" in 1 Cor 9:24.
22. Or, "*by*".
23. Or, "Desiring *to do so* in connection with humility...". This word is used in the sense of "delight" also in Mk 12:38 and Lk 20:46, of scribes "delighting" in walking around in robes; perhaps in Mt 27:43; and in 1 Sam 18:22; 2 Sam 15:26; Ps 22:8; 111:2; etc. On this word, see "willing" in Jn 7:17.
24. Some think Paul means "*false* humility", or what some regard as humility; others, "*aesthetic* humility", aesthetic behavior which these teachers termed "humility". Same word as in v 23. On this word, see "humblemindedness" in Phil 2:3.
25. Or, "veneration". This word refers to the external observances of religious worship. On this word, see "religion" in Jam 1:26.
26. Or, "angel's worship", a mystical worship of God with the angels.
27. This word means "to step into" or "stand on". Paul could mean "dwelling upon", "entering into", "taking a stand on", "delving into", "intruding into", "entering at length upon". Such people focus on their visions. Some think Paul means "*things* which he has seen while entering-in" a mystical or heavenly experience. Used only here. GK *1836*. Some manuscripts say "*things* he has not seen" {B}, the difference lying in whether he has seen *false* visions, or has not seen *true* visions.
28. Thus, some think these are Paul's descriptions of these false teachers. Others think Paul is quoting their terminology. In this case, this could be rendered "Delighting in 'humility' and 'angel's worship', *things* which he has seen while 'entering in'".
29. This word can mean "without cause, without result, without purpose". Elsewhere only in Rom 13:4; 1 Cor 15:2; Gal 3:4; 4:11. GK *1632*.
30. That is, the mind characterized by his flesh, controlled by his flesh. Such people are following a self-created religion, not the true God.
31. Or, "holding tight, holding firm, keeping hold of". On this word, see Heb 4:14.
32. Or, "supported". On this word, see 2 Cor 9:10.
33. Or, "ligaments". Elsewhere only in Eph 4:16. GK *913*.
34. Or, "fasteners". On this word, see "bond" in Act 8:23.
35. That is, the growth which God produces. Compare 1 Cor 3:6.

A. Mt 8:22 B. Mt 6:14 C. Rom 2:26, uncircumcised D. Col 2:23 E. Lk 7:42 F. Mt 10:38 G. Heb 4:16, confidence H. 2 Cor 2:14, lead in triumph
J. Mt 7:1 K. Mk 10:32, going to L. 1 Cor 4:6 M. Rom 7:23 N. Eph 4:16 O. Jn 3:30

| Colossians 2:20 | 746 | Verse |

4B. If you[1] died with Christ from[2] the elemental[3] *things of* the world, why, as-*though* living in *the* world, do you submit-to-decrees[4]—*"do not handle, nor taste[5], nor touch"* (*things* which[6] are all for[7] perishing[8] *in* the use[9]!)— according-to[10] the commandments[11] and teachings[A] *of* humans[B]? 20
21-22

   1C. Which[12] are indeed having the talk[13] *of* wisdom[C] in-connection-with[14] will-worship[15], and humility[D], and[16] harsh-treatment[17] *of the* body[E]— not in connection with any [real] value[18] against[19] *the* indulgence[20] *of the*[21] flesh[22] 23

5B. If then[23] you were raised-with Christ, be seeking[F] the *things* above[G] where Christ is, sitting at *the* right *hand of* God. *Be thinking[24] the *things* above[G], not the *things* upon the earth 3:1
2

   1C. For you died, and your life has been hidden[25] with Christ in God. *When Christ appears[26]— your[27] life— then **you** also will appear with Him in glory[H] 3-4

   2C. Therefore, put-to-death[J] *your* body-part[28] *things* on earth— sexual-immorality[K], impurity[L], passion[29], evil[M] desire[N], and greed[O]— which is idolatry 5

     1D. Because of which *things* the wrath[P] *of* God is coming upon the sons[Q] *of* disobedience[30] 6
     2D. In[31] which *things* **you** also formerly walked[R], when you were living in these *things* 7
     3D. But now **you** also[32], lay-aside[S] all *these things*— wrath[P], anger[T], malice[33], blasphemy[U], filthy-language[34] from your mouth; *do not be lying to one another 8
9

        1E. Having stripped-off[35] the old[V] person[B] with his practices[W]
        2E. And having put-on[X] the new[Y] *person* being renewed[Z] to[36] knowledge[37] in-accordance-with[38] *the* image[AA] *of the* One having created[BB] him 10

1. Some manuscripts say "Therefore, if you..." {N}.
2. Or, "away-from". Your burial in Christ was a burial away from these things; a separation from these things. GK *608*.
3. Same word as in v 8.
4. Used only here. GK *1505*. Related to "decree" in 2:14.
5. Or, "eat". On this word, see Heb 6:4.
6. Grammatically, this begins a new phrase describing the things forbidden by the previous commands. It is Paul's judgment about the objects of their prohibitions. Others render this as sarcasm, "(*things which are all leading-to* [spiritual] *ruin by the consumption of them, according to the commandments and teachings of humans!*)".
7. That is, for the purpose of, destined for, intended for. On this word, see "resulting in" in Rom 5:16. Or, "leading to".
8. Or, "destruction, ruin". On this noun, see "decay" in 1 Cor 15:42.
9. Or, "using up, consumption". Paul shows the folly of these false-teachers' decrees by giving God's view of any foods they might forbid. Their decrees concern things like foods, which are all designed by God to be destroyed by their consumption and consumed in their use— things which have no spiritual or eternal value! Paul does not bother to specifically refute any of their other decrees. He just gives this one example. Compare Mt 15:17-18 and 1 Tim 4:3-4. Used only here. GK *712*.
10. Or, "based on". Same word as in v 8.
11. Elsewhere only in Mt 15:9; Mk 7:7; where Jesus also refers to these words from Isa 29:13. GK *1945*.
12. This refers to the decrees according to the commandments and teachings of humans, v 21-22.
13. Or, "word, report, reputation". But such teachings do not have the reality. They result in a self-discipline and an adherence to rules that have no value with God, that "will not bring us near to God", 1 Cor 8:8. On this word, see "word" in 1 Cor 12:8.
14. Or, "in the sphere of ". GK *1877*.
15. Or, "self-imposed, self-made worship", do-it-yourself religion, worshiping the dictates of your own will. Used only here. GK *1615*. This word may have been coined by Paul. The worship of such people is based on the self-disciplined adherence to their self-created rules, based on their self-created beliefs.
16. Some manuscripts omit this word {C}, so that it says "and humility *with* harsh treatment *of the* body".
17. Or, "harshness, severity". Used only here. GK *910*. The root word is "to spare" in Rom 11:21; this word means "unsparing". Paul is referring to self-denying asceticism as an act of the will, based on the teachings of humans.
18. Same word as "price" in 1 Cor 6:20; 7:23; and "precious-value" in 1 Pet 2:7. On this word, see "honor" in 1 Tim 5:17.
19. Or, "for"; or "*leading* to" as in Jn 11:4. This word could imply to "restrain" or to "promote". Either meaning is possible here. GK *4639*.
20. Or, "gratification". This word means "fullness, being filled up". It is used in a positive sense, "filled to satisfaction", and in a negative sense, "over-fullness, satiety, indulgence". Either meaning is possible here. Used only here. GK *4447*.
21. Flesh may mean "body" or "human nature", as in Mt 19:5; Rom 1:3; 2 Cor 4:11; 7:5; 12:7; Gal 2:20; Eph 2:11; 5:29; Phil 1:22, 24; Col 1:22, 24; 2:1, 5; 1 Tim 3:16; etc. Or it may mean "sinful nature" or "old man", as in Rom 7:5; 8:3-13; 13:14; Gal 5:13; Eph 2:3; 2 Pet 2:10, etc. Either meaning is possible here. Used 147 times. GK *4922*.
22. That is, religious asceticism regarding foods and festivals and other outward things has no ability to restrain sensual indulgence. Compare Mt 15:17-20. Self-discipline is of value against the sins of the flesh and is taught by Jesus (Mt 5:29) and Paul (1 Cor 9:27; 1 Tim 4:7). What Paul is rejecting as having only the talk of wisdom is self-discipline with regard to human rules. Others think Paul makes two separate statements here, "with no value" (the rules have no real value) and "for *the* indulgence *of their* flesh" (they teach these things for their own gratification, indulging the puffed up mind of their flesh, v 18). Another view translates it "not *in* any honor for satisfaction *of* the flesh". That is, they harshly deny the body, giving no honor to satisfying the legitimate physical needs of the body. There are other views.
23. Paul now turns from the false and wrong path to the true one. A focus on the things above, on Christ and our life with Him, leads us to put to death the sinful indulgence of the flesh on earth— the very things adherence to man-made religion and rituals have no value against, 2:23.
24. Or, "setting your mind on". Same word as in Phil 2:5. On this word, see Rom 8:5.
25. That is, hidden safely away, like a treasure. On this word, see Jn 8:59.
26. Or, "is revealed". Same word as later in the verse. On this word, see "made evident" in 1 Jn 2:19.
27. Some manuscripts say "our" {B}.
28. Or, "members, limbs". That is, the things carried out or accomplished by the "parts" of the body, defined by what follows; not the physical parts themselves, but the sinful uses to which the body is "presented" (Rom 6:13, 19). In other words, "the old person with his practices", v 9. Same word as in Rom 6:13, 19; and Mt 5:29, 30; Rom 7:5, 23; Jam 3:5, 6; 4:1. Elsewhere only in the context of the body of Christ in Rom 12:4, 5; 1 Cor 6:15; 12:12-27 (13 times); Eph 4:25; 5:30. GK *3517*.
29. Or, "lustfulness". On this word, see Rom 1:26.
30. On this phrase, see Eph 2:2. Some manuscripts omit "upon the sons *of* disobedience" {C}.
31. This same preposition is used in the phrase beginning and ending this verse, "In which *things*... in these *things*". It means "in, among". So Paul could also mean "In which [sins] you walked while living among these [sons of disobedience]"; or, "Among whom you walked while living in these [sins]". GK *1877*.
32. In v 7, the Colossians' conduct had been "also" with the disobedient ones. Now, it is "also" with believers.
33. That is, the desire to cause pain and distress in others. On this word, see "badness" in 1 Pet 2:1.
34. Or, "shameful language, dirty talk, obscene speech". Used only here. GK *155*. Related to "filthiness" in Eph 5:4. The root word is "shame" in Heb 12:2.
35. Same word as "stripped" in 2:15.
36. Or, "for, toward". GK *1650*. Not "in the sphere of ".
37. Or, "full knowledge, true knowledge". On this word, see 1:9.
38. Some think Paul means "*a* knowledge in accordance with"; others, "renewed... in accordance with". Compare Eph 4:23. Same word as in Eph 4:22, 24. GK *2848*.

A. 1 Tim 5:17   B. Mt 4:4, mankind   C. 1 Cor 12:8   D. Col 2:18   E. Eph 1:23   F. Phil 2:21   G. Phil 3:14, upward   H. 2 Pet 2:10   J. Rom 4:19, impotent   K. 1 Cor 5:1   L. 1 Thes 2:3   M. 3 Jn 11   N. Gal 5:16   O. Eph 4:19   P. Rev 16:19   Q. Gal 3:7   R. Heb 13:9   S. Rom 13:12   T. Rev 16:19, fury   U. 1 Tim 6:4   V. Mk 2:21   W. Mt 16:27   X. Rom 13:14   Y. Mk 2:22   Z. 2 Cor 4:16   AA. Col 1:15   BB. Eph 2:15

| Colossians 3:11 | 748 | Verse |

        1F. Where there is no Greek and Jew, circumcised and uncircumcised, barbarian[1], Scythian[2], slave[A], free[B]   11

        2F. But Christ *is* all *things* and in all *persons*

4A. Therefore, as chosen[3] *ones of* God, holy[4] and having been loved[5]—   12

  1B. Put-on[6] deep-feelings[7] *of* compassion[C], kindness[D], humblemindedness[E], gentleness[F], patience[G]

    1C. Bearing-with[H] one another, and forgiving[J] each other— if anyone has *a* complaint against anyone   13

      1D. Just as indeed the Lord[8] forgave you, so also you *forgive*

    2C. And over[9] all these *things*, *put on* love[K], which is *the* bond[L] *of* perfection[10]   14

  2B. And let the peace[M] *of* Christ[11] be arbitrating[12] in your hearts— into which[13] indeed you were called[N] in one body   15

  3B. And be thankful

  4B. Let the word[O] *of* Christ[14] be dwelling[15] in you richly   16

    1C. With all wisdom,[16] teaching[P] and admonishing[Q] each other *with* psalms[R], hymns[S], spiritual[T] songs[17]

    2C. With gratitude[18], singing[U] with[19] your hearts *to* God[20]

  5B. And everything— whatever thing[21] you may do in word[O] or in deed[V]— *do* all *things* in *the* name *of the* Lord Jesus, giving-thanks[W] *to* God *the* Father[22] through Him   17

  6B. Wives, be subject[23] *to your* husbands[24], as it is fitting[X] in *the* Lord   18

  7B. Husbands, be loving[Y] *your* wives, and do not be bitter[25] toward them   19

  8B. Children[Z], be obeying[AA] *your* parents in all *things*, for this is pleasing[BB] in *the* Lord   20

  9B. Fathers, do not be provoking[26] your children, in order that they may not be discouraged[27]   21

  10B. Slaves[A], be obeying[AA] *your* masters according-to[28] *the* flesh[CC] in all *things*, not with eye-service[29], as people-pleasers[DD], but in sincerity[EE] *of* heart, fearing[FF] the Lord[30]   22

    1C. Whatever you do,[31] be working from *the* soul[GG], as *for* the Lord and not *for* people[HH]— knowing that from *the* Lord you will receive[JJ] the payback[32] *of* the inheritance[33]. You are serving[34] the Lord Christ!   23, 24

    2C. For[35] the *one* doing-wrong[36] will receive-back[37] what he did-wrong, and there is no respect-of-persons[KK]   25

  11B. Masters[LL], be granting[MM] *to your* slaves[A] the just[38] *thing*, and fairness[39], knowing that **you** also have *a* Master[LL] in heaven   4:1

  12B. Be devoting-yourselves[NN] *to* prayer, keeping-watch[40] in it with thanksgiving[OO], *praying at the same time also for us—   2-3

    1C. That God may open *to* us *a* door[41] *for* the word[O] *that we may* speak the mystery[PP] *of* Christ because of which I also have been bound[42]

    2C. That[43] I may make it clear[44], as I ought-to[45] speak   4

  13B. Be walking[QQ] with wisdom[RR] toward the *ones* outside, redeeming[SS] the time[46]   5

    1C. Your speech[O] always *being* with grace[TT], having been seasoned[UU] *with* salt *that you may* know how you ought-to[45] answer each one   6

1. That is, a non-Greek-speaking, uncivilized person, from the Roman and Greek perspective. Our word "barbarian" comes from this word. Plato divided the world into two groups, "Greeks and barbarians", just as the Jews divided it into "Jew and Gentile". The Romans included themselves with the Greeks, but the Greeks considered the Romans to be barbarians! Same word as in Rom 1:14; 1 Cor 14:11. Elsewhere only as "natives" in Act 28:2, 4. GK *975*. It could be translated "foreigner", but there is a certain amount of arrogance in the term.
2. Scythians were legendary for their fierceness, savagery, and brutality. They came from the East 600 years before Christ and brutalized Palestine. Their name lived on in memory, and referred to the feared, savage enemy from the East. In Christ, these are meaningless distinctions. Used only here. GK *5033*.
3. Or, "elect, selected". On this word, see Rom 8:33.
4. Or, "saints". On this word, see 1 Pet 1:16.
5. Paul uses the participle here, as in 1 Thes 1:4; 2 Thes 2:13. Some render this "beloved" here, as in Eph 1:6. On this word, see "*devotedly-*love" in Jn 21:15. Paul uses the related adjective "beloved" in Col 1:7; 4:7, 9, 14; and the noun "*of* His love" in 1:13.
6. Or, "Wear". That is, put on like a garment. Same word as in v 10. On this word, see Rom 13:14.
7. Or, "*a* heart". On this word, see Phil 1:8.
8. Some manuscripts instead say "Christ"; others, "God" {C}.
9. Or, "upon, in addition to". That is, like a final cloak put on over everything. GK *2093*.
10. Some think Paul means "the bond characterized by perfection, the perfect bond" for the church; others, "the bond binding together the virtues of v 12-13 in perfection. On this word, see "maturity" in Heb 6:1.
11. That is, the peace Christ gives, Jn 14:27. Some manuscripts say "God" {N}.
12. Or, "deciding, umpiring, judging, ruling". Let this peace sit as governor, administrator, in your hearts. Used only here. GK *1093*. Related to "decide against" in 2:18.
13. That is, the peace of Christ.
14. Some manuscripts say "God" {A}.
15. Elsewhere only of God (2 Cor 6:16); the Spirit (Rom 8:11; 2 Tim 1:14); and faith (2 Tim 1:5). GK *1940*.
16. Some take this phrase with the preceding one, "dwell within you richly in all wisdom".
17. This is the Greek word order. Some take "*with* psalms... songs" with the next phrase, "with gratitude, singing *with* psalms... songs in your hearts". On this word, see Eph 5:19. Some manuscripts say "psalms and hymns and spiritual songs" {N}, as in Eph 5:19.
18. Same word as in Lk 17:9.
19. Or, "in". This is the Greek word order. Or, "with gratitude in your hearts, singing *to* God".
20. Some manuscripts say "*to the* Lord" {A}, as in Eph 5:19.
21. Not the same grammar as in v 23, which does not have this word. The phrase "whatever thing" is elsewhere only in Mk 6:23; 1 Cor 16:2; and is nearly the same as the phrase in Lk 10:35; Jn 2:5; 14:13; 15:16. It is usually simplified to "whatever". It is similar to "what thing" in Jn 8:25. This word is GK *5516*.
22. Some manuscripts say "*to our* God and Father" {B}.
23. On this word, see Eph 5:21. Note that Col 3:18-4:1 parallels Eph 5:21-6:9.
24. Some manuscripts say "*your* own husbands" {N}, as in Eph 5:22.
25. Or, "be embittered". Elsewhere only as "make bitter" in Rev 8:11; 10:9, 10. GK *4393*. Related to "bitterness" in Act 8:23; "bitter" in Jam 3:14; and "bitterly" in Lk 22:62.
26. Or, "stirring up, arousing, irritating". Elsewhere only as "stir up" in 2 Cor 9:2, in a good sense. GK *2241*. Some manuscripts have the same word as in Eph 6:4, "provoke to anger" {B}, which is not related to this word.
27. Or, "disheartened, dispirited, despondent". Used only here. GK *126*.
28. Or, "with respect to, in relation to". GK *2848*. That is, your human masters.
29. That is, serving only when your master is watching. Elsewhere only in Eph 6:6. GK *4056*.
30. Some manuscripts say "fearing God" {N}.
31. Some manuscripts say "And everything— whatever thing you may do" {N}, as in v 17.
32. Or, "reward". Used only here. GK *502*. Related to "retribution" in Rom 11:9, and "repay" in 2 Thes 1:6.
33. That is, consisting of the inheritance. On this word, see Eph 1:14.
34. Or, "You are *a* slave *to* the Lord Christ". On this word, see "are slaves" in Rom 6:6. This could also be translated as a command, "Be serving the Lord Christ". Both renderings make good sense. Some manuscripts say "For you are serving" {N}.
35. Some manuscripts say "But" {K}.
36. Some think Paul is referring to the master; others, to the slave; others, to both. Compare Eph 6:8. On this word, see Act 7:24.
37. On this word, see 2 Cor 5:10. "You will reap what you sow" is the idea, Gal 6:8.
38. Or, "right, righteous". On this word, see "righteous" in Rom 1:17.
39. Or, "equity, equality". On this word, see "equality" in 2 Cor 8:13.
40. Or, "staying alert". On this word, see 1 Thes 5:6.
41. Same concept as in 1 Cor 16:9; 2 Cor 2:12; and perhaps Rev 3:8. This word means "door, gate, entrance". Used 39 times. GK *2598*. Related to "doorkeeper" in Jn 18:17.
42. On this word, see 1 Cor 7:27. Related to "imprisonment" in v 18.
43. Or, rather than a second request, this may be point 1D., "In order that I might make it clear...". In this case, Paul means "In order that by means of this open door, I might be able to make it clear". Without an open door, he could not make it clear and speak it as he would like to speak it.
44. Or, "make it known, reveal it". On this word, see "made evident" in 1 Jn 2:19.
45. Or, "should". On this idiom, see Act 25:10.
46. Same phrase as in Eph 5:16.

A. Rom 6:17 B. Mt 17:26 C. Rom 12:1 D. Rom 3:12, goodness E. Phil 2:3 F. Eph 4:2 G. Heb 6:12 H. 2 Cor 11:4 J. Lk 7:42 K. 1 Jn 4:16 L. Act 8:23 M. Act 15:33 N. Rom 8:30 O. 1 Cor 12:8 P. Rom 12:7 Q. Col 1:28 R. Eph 5:19 S. Eph 5:19 T. 1 Cor 14:1 U. Eph 5:19 V. Mt 26:10, work W. Mt 26:27 X. Phm 8 Y. Jn 21:15, devotedly love Z. 1 Jn 3:1 AA. Act 6:7 BB. Eph 5:10 CC. Col 2:23 DD. Eph 6:6 EE. Rom 12:8, generosity FF. Eph 5:33, respecting GG. Jam 5:20 HH. Mt 4:4, mankind JJ. Lk 16:25 KK. Jam 2:1 LL. Mt 8:2 MM. Act 17:31 NN. Act 2:42 OO. 1 Tim 4:3 PP. Rom 11:25 QQ. Heb 13:9 RR. 1 Cor 12:8 SS. Eph 5:16 TT. Eph 2:8 UU. Mk 9:50

A. All the *things* concerning me Tychicus[1] will make-known[A] *to* you   7

    1. The beloved[B] brother, and faithful[C] minister[D], and fellow-slave[E] in *the* Lord,˚whom I sent to   8
you for this very *reason*—

        a. In order that you may know[2] the *things* concerning us[3], and he may encourage[4] your hearts

    2. Together-with Onesimus[5], the faithful[C] and beloved[B] brother, who is from-*among* you   9
    3. They will make all the *things* here known *to* you

B. Aristarchus[F], my fellow-captive[G], greets[H] you, and *so does* Mark[J], the cousin *of* Barnabas[K],   10
concerning whom you received commands[6] (if he comes to you, welcome[L] him),˚and Jesus, the *one*   11
being called[M] Justus—

    1. The *ones* being from *the* circumcision[7]— these alone[8]!
    2. Fellow-workers[N] for the kingdom[O] *of* God, who proved-to-be[9] *a* comfort[10] *to* me

C. Epaphras[P] greets you— the *one* from-*among* you,[11] *a* slave[Q] *of* Christ Jesus[12] always struggling[13] for   12
you in *his* prayers, in-order-that[14] you might stand[15] mature[16] and having been fully-assured[17] in all
the will *of* God

    1. For I testify[R] *concerning* him that he has great pain[18] for you, and the *ones* in Laodicea, and the   13
ones in Hierapolis[19]

D. Luke[S], the beloved[B] physician, greets you, and Demas[T]   14
E. Greet the brothers[U] in Laodicea, and Nymphas[20], and the church at her house   15
F. And when *this* letter[V] is read among you, cause that[21] it also be read in the church *of the* Laodiceans,   16
and that **you** also read the *letter* from Laodicea[22]
G. And say *to* Archippus[W]— "See-to[X] the ministry[Y] which you received[Z] in *the* Lord, in order that you   17
may be fulfilling[AA] it"
H. The greeting *of* Paul *by* my *own* hand— remember[23] my imprisonment[24]. Grace *be* with you[25]   18

1. See Act 20:4 on him. Compare Eph 6:21-22.
2. Or, "come to know". On this word, see Lk 1:34.
3. Compare Eph 6:22. Some manuscripts say "that he may know the *things* concerning you" {B}.
4. Same word as in Eph 6:22.
5. This is the man about whom the book of Philemon was written. He and Tychicus probably carried this letter to the Colossians.
6. Same word as in Lk 15:29; Jn 11:57; Act 17:15. On this word, see "commandment" in Mk 12:28.
7. That is, Jewish Christians, as this word is used in Act 10:45; Gal 2:7, 8, etc. On this word, see "circumcised" in Eph 2:11.
8. That is, these only of that class— the circumcision, Jews. These were the only fellow Jews serving with Paul at this time. This is the Greek word order, which reflects Paul's broken heart over the rejection of Christ by his people, Rom 9:1-2.
9. Or, "were, became". GK *1181*.
10. Or, "consolation, assuagement". Used only here. GK *4219*.
11. That is, a resident of Colossae. Same phrase as in v 9.
12. Some manuscripts omit this word {C}.
13. Or, "striving, fighting". On this word, see 1 Tim 4:10.
14. Or, "that", giving the content of the prayers of Epaphras instead of the purpose of them. GK *2671*.
15. Or, "be caused to stand". GK *2705*.
16. Or, "complete". Same word as in 1:28.
17. On this word, see "fulfilled" in Lk 1:1. Related to "full assurance" in 2:2. Some manuscripts instead say "and having been completed" {N}, a related word.
18. That is, Epaphras knows the ache that results from serious toil and struggle on their behalf. Elsewhere only in Rev 16:10, 11; 21:4. This word also means the "toil, exertion" that produces the pain. GK *4506*. Compare Rom 9:2. Some manuscripts say "zeal"; others, "labor" {N}.
19. These two cities were near Colossae.
20. This is a woman. Some manuscripts have this as a man, and the church at "his house"; others say "and their house" {C}. Used only here. GK *3809*.
21. The idiom "cause that" is also in Jn 11:37; Rev 13:15. GK *2671*.
22. Some think this is a reference to the book of Ephesians (see Eph 1:1); others, to some letter unknown to us.
23. That is, keep in mind. Do not forget it before the Lord. On this word, see Jn 16:21.
24. Or, "bonds". On this word, see Phil 1:7.
25. This word is plural. Some manuscripts add "amen" {A}.

A. Phil 1:22, know B. Mt 3:17 C. Col 1:2 D. 1 Cor 3:5, servants E. Rev 19:10 F. Act 19:29 G. Rom 16:7 H. Mk 15:18 J. 1 Pet 5:13 K. Act 4:36 L. Mt 10:40 M. Jn 12:49, say N. Rom 16:3 O. Mt 3:2 P. Col 1:7 Q. Rom 6:17 R. Jn 1:7 S. Phm 24 T. 2 Tim 4:10 U. Act 16:40 V. 2 Thes 3:17 W. Phm 2 X. Rev 1:11 Y. 1 Cor 12:5 Z. Lk 17:34, taken AA. Eph 5:18, filled

1 Thessalonians

Overview

Introduction	1:1
1A. We are giving thanks to God always for you all	1:2
1B. Unceasingly remembering your work of faith, labor of love, and endurance of hope	1:3
2B. Knowing, brothers, your election, because	1:4
1C. Our good news came to you in power, and in the Spirit, and in great conviction	1:5
2C. And you became imitators of us and the Lord, accepting the word in much affliction	1:6-10
2A. For you yourselves know our entrance to you, brothers— that it has not been empty	2:1
1B. But we spoke the good news to you while conducting ourselves in a blameless manner	2:2-12
2B. And for this reason we are giving thanks unceasingly— because you accepted the message from us as the word of God. For you became imitators of the churches of Judea	2:13-16
3A. And we, brothers, were very eager to see you again, and Satan hindered us	2:17-18
1B. For who is our hope or joy or crown of boasting? Is it not even you?	2:19-20
2B. Therefore, bearing it no longer, we sent Timothy to encourage you and know your faith	3:1-5
3B. And Timothy having just now returned with good news about you, we were encouraged	3:6-10
4B. Now may God direct our way to you and cause you to abound in love	3:11-13
4A. Finally brothers, we ask that as you received from us how to walk, that you be abounding more in it	4:1-2
1B. For this is the will of God— your holiness, that you be abstaining from sexual immorality	4:3-8
2B. But concerning brotherly love, you have no need that anyone write, for you are God-taught	4:9-12
5A. And we do not want you to be unaware, brothers, concerning the ones falling asleep	4:13
1B. For if we believe Jesus arose, God will bring with Him the ones having fallen asleep	4:14-18
2B. But concerning the times and seasons, you have no need to be written, for you know it	5:1-11
6A. And we ask you, brothers, to be esteeming those who labor among you superabundantly in love	5:12-13
7A. Now we exhort you, brothers	5:14
1B. Admonish the disorderly, encourage the fainthearted, hold on to the weak, be patient to all	5:14
2B. See that no one returns evil for evil to anyone, but be pursuing the good	5:15
3B. Rejoice always, pray unceasingly, give thanks in everything. For this is the will of God	5:16-18
4B. Do not quench the Spirit, do not treat prophecies with contempt, but be testing all things	5:19-21
5B. Be holding on to the good, be abstaining from every form of evil	5:21-22
Conclusion	5:23-28

		Verse

    A. Paul and Silvanus[1] and Timothy   1
    B. *To* the church *of the* Thessalonians[2] in God *the* Father and *the* Lord Jesus Christ
    C. Grace *to* you and peace[3]

1A. We are giving-thanks[A] *to* God always for you all, making mention *of you*[4] in our prayers   2

    1B. Unceasingly[5] °remembering your work[B] *of* faith[6], and labor[C] *of* love[D], and endurance[E] *of* hope[F] *in* our Lord[7] Jesus Christ, before[8] our God and Father   3
    2B. Knowing, brothers having been loved[G] by God, your election[9], °because[10]—   4-5

        1C. Our good-news[H] did not come to you in word[J] only, but also in power[K], and in *the* Holy Spirit, and with great fullness-of-conviction[11]— just as you know what-kind-of *men* we proved-to-be[12] among you for your sake
        2C. And **you** became imitators[13] *of* us and *of the* Lord, having accepted[L] the word[J] in much affliction[M] with *the* joy *of the* Holy Spirit, °so that you became *an* example[14] *to* all the *ones* believing[N] in Macedonia and in Achaia   6   7

            1D. For from you the word[J] *of* the Lord has sounded-forth[15]— not only in Macedonia and in[16] Achaia, but[17] in every place your faith toward God has gone-out[18]— so that we *are* having no need[O] to speak anything!   8

                1E. For they themselves[19] are reporting[P] about us *as to* what-sort-of[Q] entrance[20] we had with you, and how you turned[R] to God from idols[S]   9

                    1F. To be serving[21] *the* living and true[T] God
                    2F. And to be awaiting His Son from the heavens, Whom He raised[U] from the dead— Jesus, the *One* delivering[V] us from the coming wrath[22]   10

2A. For[23] you yourselves[24] know our entrance to you, brothers[W]— that it has not been[25] empty[26]   2:1

    1B. But[27] having previously-suffered and been mistreated[28] in Philippi[29], as you know,[30] we were bold[X] in our God to speak the good-news[H] *of* God[31] to you in *a* great conflict[32]   2

        1C. For[33] our exhortation[34] *is* not from error[35], nor from impurity[36], nor in deceit[37]. °But just as we have been approved[Y] by God to be entrusted-*with*[N] the good-news[H], so we speak— not as pleasing[38] people[Z], but God, the *One* testing[39] our hearts   3-4

1. Silvanus is mentioned elsewhere only in 2 Cor 1:19; 2 Thes 1:1; 1 Pet 5:12. GK *4977.* He is called "Silas" in Acts (see Act 15:40). He was a prophet, and Paul's companion when they came to Thessalonica.
2. Paul was at this city in the Roman province of Macedonia in Act 17:1-10, and wrote this letter in Act 18:5, when Timothy returned to him (1 Thes 3:6).
3. Some manuscripts add "from God our Father and *the* Lord Jesus Christ" {A}.
4. Some manuscripts include "*of* you" {N}.
5. Some take this with what precedes, "making mention... unceasingly". On this word, see Rom 1:9.
6. That is, work proceeding from faith, or belonging to faith (faith's work), or characterized by faith. Likewise with labor and endurance.
7. Some think Paul means "hope *in* our Lord"; others, "faith, love, hope *in* our Lord".
8. This is the Greek word order of this verse. Some think Paul means "remembering... before our God"; others, that the work, labor and endurance are "before our God".
9. Or, "selection, choosing". On this word, see "choosing" in Rom 11:5. Some take "by God" with this phrase, "loved, your election by God".
10. Or, "that". Some think Paul means knowing "how God chose you before the foundation of the world, because..."; others, "how God chose you when we were with you— that...".
11. Or, "fullness of certainty, fullness of assurance" on our part, as ones "fully-convinced" (the related verb in Rom 14:5). This is the opposite of "in word only". The word "great" is separately expressed here. The root word is "full". Elsewhere only as "full-assurance" in Col 2:2; Heb 6:11; 10:22. GK *4443.*
12. Or, "became, were". This same word is used in a further statement about Paul's behavior in 2:7. On this word, see "comes" in 2 Pet 1:20.
13. The sense in which Paul means this is described next, and repeated in 2:14— you believed and suffered. On this word, see Eph 5:1.
14. Or, "pattern". On this word, see "pattern" in 1 Pet 5:3. Some manuscripts have it plural {N}.
15. Used only here. GK *2010.* Related to "sounding" brass in 1 Cor 13:1; and trumpet "blast" in Heb 12:19.
16. Some manuscripts omit this word {C}.
17. Some manuscripts say "but also" {N}.
18. Some punctuate the verse "... place. Your faith toward God has gone out, so that..."; others, "...sounded forth. Your faith toward God has gone out not only in Macedonia and Achaia, but in every place so that...".
19. This is in contrast to "we" in the last phrase of v 8.
20. Or, "entering, coming". Some think this word refers to the manner of Paul's "coming" to the them. Paul described his "entrance" in v 5, and does so again in detail in 2:1-12. Others think it refers to the kind of "reception" the Thessalonians gave him. Same word as in 2:1; 2 Pet 1:11. Elsewhere only as "coming" in Act 13:24; and "entering" in Heb 10:19. GK *1658.*
21. On this word, see "are slaves" in Rom 6:6. Note the opposite in Gal 4:8.
22. Note 5:9. On the wrath of God, see Rom 1:18.
23. In 2:1-12, Paul turns from proving the election of these Thessalonians based on their genuine response to his ministry, to a vindication of the motive and manner of his ministry to them. He has alluded to this in 1:5, "what kind" of men, and 1:9, "what sort" of entrance. 2:1-12 expounds on his ministry ("what sort of entrance" in 1:9a), and 2:13-16 expounds on their reception of it ("how you turned to God" in 1:9b). Many think Paul's purpose in giving this detailed vindication of his ministry was to defend against false charges made against him by the Jews, charges that can be seen behind his statements.
24. Paul may mean that while "we" know the truth about you (v 4), "you yourselves" know the truth about us and our ministry to you. Others think he means "they themselves" (1:9) report about our entrance, but "you yourselves" know about it. Others think he means "you yourselves" versus others in general, and those opposing in particular.
25. Or, "become, proved to be". The grammar implies "has not and still is not". These same two words are used also in 3:5 ("prove to be in vain") and 1 Cor 15:10 ("become empty"). GK *1181.*
26. Or, "in vain, futile; without result, effect, or content". Some think that here Paul means empty of content, purpose, earnestness on his part; others, empty of results or effect in the Thessalonians, v 13-14. Same word as in Lk 1:53; 1 Cor 15:10, 14, 58; Eph 5:6; Col 2:8; Jam 2:20. Elsewhere only as "in vain" in 2 Cor 6:1; Gal 2:2; Phil 2:16; 1 Thes 3:5; "futile" in Act 4:25; and "empty-*handed*" in Mk 12:3; Lk 20:10, 11. GK *3031.*
27. Some manuscripts say "But even" {K}.
28. Or, "insulted, treated in an arrogant manner". Same word as in Mt 22:6; Lk 18:32; Act 14:5. Elsewhere only as "insult" in Lk 11:45. GK *5614.* Related to "insult" in 2 Cor 12:10; and "violent" in 1 Tim 1:13.
29. This occurred in Act 16:9-40. From Philippi Paul went to Thessalonica, Act 17:1. Both are in Macedonia.
30. They may have treated Paul's wounds, like the jailer in Act 16:33.
31. That is, the "good news *from* God". It was not empty, but full of the boldly spoken good news from God.
32. Or, "struggle". Some think Paul is referring to an external "conflict, fight, opposition"; others, to his internal "struggle, strain, exertion (like an athlete)". On this word, see "race" in Heb 12:1.
33. Paul explains why he did this even amid such opposition. He brings God's message by God's commission.
34. Or, "appeal, urging". On this word, see "encouragement" in Act 4:36.
35. Or, "deception, delusion, a going astray, a wandering". The exhortation is not from error or false doctrine, but truth. Same word as in Rom 1:27; Eph 4:14; 2 Thes 2:11; Jam 5:20; 2 Pet 2:18; 3:17; 1 Jn 4:6; Jude 11. Elsewhere only as "deception" in Mt 27:64. GK *4415.* Related to "deceitful" in 1 Tim 4:1.
36. The exhortation does not originate in impure desire, but holiness. This word is usually used of sexual impurity, as in 4:7, and some give it this meaning here. The religious worship of their day was rooted in sexual impurity. Others give this word a more general meaning, including greed and glory-seeking from v 5-6. Elsewhere only in Mt 23:27; Rom 1:24; 6:19; 2 Cor 12:21; Gal 5:19; Eph 4:19; 5:3; Col 3:5. GK *174.*
37. The exhortation is not given in connection with deceitful methods, including flattery (v 5), but in simple sincerity. On this word, see Mt 26:4.
38. Elsewhere only in Mt 14:6; Mk 6:22; Act 6:5; Rom 8:8; 15:1, 2, 3; 1 Cor 7:32, 33, 34; 10:33; Gal 1:10; 1 Thes 2:15; 4:1; 2 Tim 2:4. GK *743.* Related to the words in Jn 8:29; Col 1:10; Eph 5:10.
39. Or, "proving by test, examining". Same word as "approved" earlier.

A. Mt 26:27 B. Mt 26:10 C. 1 Cor 3:8 D. 1 Jn 4:16 E. Jam 1:3 F. Col 1:5 G. Jn 21:15, devotedly love H. 1 Cor 15:1 J. 1 Cor 12:8 K. Mk 5:30 L. Mt 10:40, welcome M. Rev 7:14 N. Jn 3:36, believe O. Tit 3:14 P. 1 Jn 1:3, announcing Q. Act 26:29 R. Jam 5:19, turns back S. 1 Jn 5:21 T. Jn 7:28 U. Mt 28:6, arose V. Col 1:13 W. Act 16:40 X. Eph 6:20, speak boldly Y. Rom 12:2 Z. Mt 4:4, mankind

	1D. For neither did we at-any-time[A] come with *a* word[1] *of* flattery, as you know	5
	1E. Nor with *a* pretext[B] *for* greed[C]— God *is* witness[D] 2E. Nor seeking[E] glory[F] from people[G]— neither from you, nor from others, *[although] being able to be with weight[2] as apostles *of* Christ	6-7
	2D. But we proved-to-be child-like[3] in your midst[H]	
	3D. As when *a* nurse[4] cherishes[5] her children[J], *in this manner longing-affectionately[6] *for* you, we were well-pleased[K] to impart[L] to you not only the good-news[M] *of* God, but also our *own* lives[7], because you became beloved[N] *ones to* us	8
	2C. For you remember, brothers, our labor[O] and hardship— working[8] *by* night and *by* day[9] so-as not to be *a* burden-on[10] any *of* you, we proclaimed[P] to you the good-news[M] *of* God	9
	3C. You and God *are* witnesses[D] how devoutly[11] and righteously[Q] and blamelessly[R] we were *with*[12] you, the *ones* believing— *just-as you know how each one *of* you, as *a* father his *own* children	10 11
	1D. *We were*[13] exhorting[S] you[14] and encouraging[T] and testifying[15] so-that[16] you *might* walk[U] worthily[V] *of* God, the *One* calling[17] you into His *own* kingdom[W] and glory	12
	2B. And[18] for this reason[19] **we** are indeed[20] giving-thanks[X] *to* God unceasingly[Y]— because[21] having received[Z] *the* word *of* God heard[22] from us, you accepted[AA] not *the* word *of* humans[G], but— as it truly[BB] is— *the* word *of* God, which also is at-work[23] in you, the *ones* believing	13
	1C. For **you** became imitators[CC], brothers, *of* the churches *of* God existing[DD] in Judea in Christ Jesus, because **you** also suffered[EE] the same *things* by *your* own countrymen as they also by the Jews—	14

	1D. The *ones* also[24] having killed[FF] **the Lord** Jesus and the prophets[25]
	  2D. And having driven us out[26]
	  3D. And not being pleasing[GG] *to* God
	  4D. And *being* contrary[27] *to* all people[G]— *forbidding[28] us to speak *to* the Gentiles in order that they might be saved[HH]
	  5D. So that *they* fill-up[29] *the measure of* their sins always. But the wrath[30] came[31] upon them to the uttermost[32]
		15
		
		16

3A.	And **we**, brothers— having been orphaned[33] from you for *a* season[JJ] *of an* hour[34] in face, not *in* heart— were more eager[35] with great desire[KK] to see your face. *Because[36] we wanted[37] to come to you— **I**[38], Paul, both once and twice[39]— and Satan hindered[LL] us	17 18

1. Or, "speech", that is, "flattering speech", speech characterized by flattery. "Flattery" is used only here, GK *3135*.
2. This word means "weight or burden". Some think Paul means "weight of influence, dignity, authority". Others think Paul is referring to the weight or burden of financial support, as in v 9. Same word as in 2 Cor 4:17. Elsewhere only as "burden" in Mt 20:12; Act 15:28; Gal 6:2; Rev 2:24. GK *983*. Related to "burden-on" in 2:9.
3. Or, "children, minors, innocent *ones*". That is, as opposed to "with weight", relating to you based on our authority. It is the word "child, baby" used in a metaphorical sense, "innocent *ones*", without adult self-confidence, as in 1 Cor 2:3. On this word, see "infant" in 1 Cor 3:1. The related verb is in 1 Cor 14:20. Some manuscripts say "gentle" {B}, making a single metaphor, "gentle in your midst, as when *a* nurse cherishes her children. In this manner..." (on "gentle", see "kind" in 2 Tim 2:24).
4. Or, "feeder". This word refers to one who feeds or rears a child, including the mother. Paul may be referring to himself as the mother, as he does in Gal 4:19, or simply as the nurse of the children put in his care. Used only here. GK *5577*. Related to "feed" in Lk 23:29.
5. Or, "gives warmth to, warms in one's bosom". Elsewhere only in Eph 5:29. GK *2499*. The root word is "warm".
6. Used only here. GK *3916*. This word was found on a gravestone of parents "longing" for their dead child.
7. Or, "souls". Some think Paul means "to expend our own lives for you". We poured out our lives for you. Others think he means "to impart our own souls to you", joining souls with you in love. On this word, see "soul" in Jam 5:20.
8. Same word as in 2 Thes 3:8. On this word, see Mt 26:10. Some manuscripts add "for" {N}, so that it says "hardship. For working...".
9. On "*by* night and *by* day", see Rev 7:15.
10. Or, "be burdensome, put a weight on, weigh heavily on". That is, put a financial burden on you. Elsewhere only in 2 Thes 3:8; 2 Cor 2:5. GK *2096*. Related to "weight" in v 7; and "burdened" in 2 Cor 1:8.
11. Used only here. GK *4010*. Related to "holy" in Heb 7:26.
12. Or, "*to, toward, for*".
13. This is supplied from v 10. Others suggest "how *we dealt with* each one *of* you as... children, exhorting..."; others change it to "how... we exhorted, and encouraged..". There are other views.
14. This is the Greek word order of verse 11-12. Some smooth it out by omitting this word, "how *we were* exhorting and encouraging and imploring each one *of* you as *a* father his *own* children, so that...".
15. Or, "affirming", as witnesses to the truth. Same word as in Gal 5:3; Eph 4:17. Elsewhere only as "bear witness" in Act 20:26; 26:22. GK *3458*. Related to "witness" in v 10, on which see Act 1:8.
16. This clause gives the purpose of these actions. Or, "that you walk", giving the content of the exhorting, encouraging and testifying. The idiom is literally "for you to walk".
17. Some manuscripts say "having called" {B}. See Rom 8:30 on "called".
18. Some manuscripts omit this word {N}.
19. This looks forward to the "because" phrase next. Others think it looks backward, "Because we spoke the gospel of God to you in this way and for this purpose", v 2-12; or, "because God is the One calling you into His kingdom", v 12. In this case, Paul says "And for this reason, **we** are indeed giving thanks *to* God unceasingly that having received...".
20. Or, "also", along with you.
21. Or, "that", so that it says "giving thanks unceasingly that...", giving the content of the thanksgiving.
22. Or, "having received from us *the* word heard *from* God". This idiom is literally, "received *the* word *of* hearing from us *of* God", that is, the word or message consisting of what was heard from us, which is from God. On this noun, see "hearing" in Heb 4:2.
23. Or, "in operation". Same word as Eph 3:20; and "working" in Phil 2:13. On this word, see "works" in 1 Cor 12:11.
24. Or, "both", so that it says "the *ones* having killed both the Lord Jesus and the prophets".
25. As Jesus said, Mt 23:31, 37; Lk 11:47-51. As Stephen said, Act 7:52. Some manuscripts say "*their* own prophets" {A}.
26. The word "drove out" is the word "persecuted" with the prefix "out" added. Used only here. GK *1691*.
27. Or, "hostile, opposite, opposed". Same word as in Mt 14:24; Mk 6:48; Act 26:9; 27:4; 28:17; Tit 2:8. Elsewhere only as "opposite" in Mk 15:39. GK *1885*.
28. Or, "hindering, preventing". On this word, see 1 Cor 14:39.
29. The Jews fill the measure of their sins fuller at all times. Compare Gen 15:16. Others think Paul is expressing the purpose of God, "so that *they might* fill up". Compare Mt 23:34-35. Same word as in 1 Cor 16:17; Phil 2:30. Elsewhere only as "fulfill" in Mt 13:14; Gal 6:2; and "filling" in 1 Cor 14:16. GK *405*. Related word in Mt 23:32.
30. Some think Paul means the wrath of God appropriate to Israel's sin (Rom 1:18). The kingdom was taken from them (Mt 21:43; 23:38); the truth hidden from them (Lk 19:42); their hearts hardened by God (Rom 11:7). Others think he means the end-time wrath of the Messiah, the "coming wrath" (1 Thes 1:10; 5:9), beginning with their hardening, but looking forward to the destruction of Jerusalem and the wrath associated with the Second Coming. On this word, see Rev 16:19. Some manuscripts add "*of* God" {A}.
31. Same word as Mt 12:28; Lk 11:20. Elsewhere only as "attain" in Rom 9:31; Phil 3:16; "arrive" in 2 Cor 10:14; and "precede" in 1 Thes 4:15. GK *5777*. Some manuscripts say "has come" {N}.
32. This phrase means "to the end, to the full extent, to the completion", as to the content of it. Or, "to the end, at last, finally, continually", as to the time of it. Elsewhere only as "to the end" in Mt 10:22; 24:13; Mk 13:13; Jn 13:1; and "continually" in Lk 18:5. Here, Paul could mean "fully", in its full manifestation, to the extreme. Or he could mean "at last, finally". On this word, see "end" in Rom 10:4.
33. Or, "made orphans". The idea is that Paul was unwillingly and abruptly separated from those he loved, as seen in Act 17:5-10. Used only here. GK *682*. Related to the word in Jam 1:27.
34. That is, for a short time.
35. Or, we "made more effort". On this word, see "being diligent" in Eph 4:3.
36. Or, "For, Therefore". Paul's desire to see the Thessalonians was increased by Satan's prevention of it (compare 3:5). On this word, see Rom 1:21.
37. Or, "intended, desired". On this word, see "willing" in Jn 7:17.
38. Paul uses grammar that emphasizes this word. He may be clarifying the editorial "we" in "we wanted" as referring to himself; or if that "we" includes Silvanus and Timothy, he means "especially me".
39. That is, repeatedly. Same phrase as in Phil 4:16.

A. Gal 2:6, ever   B. Phil 1:18, pretense   C. Eph 4:19   D. Act 1:8   E. Phil 2:21   F. 2 Pet 2:10   G. Mt 4:4, mankind   H. 2 Thes 2:7   J. 1 Jn 3:1   K. Mt 17:5   L. Rom 12:8, give   M. 1 Cor 15:1   N. Mt 3:17   O. 2 Thes 3:8   P. 2 Tim 4:2   Q. 1 Cor 15:34   R. 1 Thes 5:23   S. Rom 12:8   T. 1 Thes 5:14   U. Heb 13:9   V. 3 Jn 6   W. Mt 3:2   X. Mt 26:27   Y. Rom 1:9   Z. Lk 17:34, taken   AA. Mt 10:40, welcome   BB. Mt 14:33   CC. Eph 5:1   DD. Mt 26:26, is   EE. Gal 3:4   FF. Rom 7:11   GG. 1 Thes 2:4   HH. Lk 19:10   JJ. Mt 8:29, time   KK. Gal 5:16   LL. Gal 5:7

1B.	For what¹ *is* our hope^A, or joy^B, or crown^C *of* boasting^D— or *is it* not indeed you— before our Lord Jesus² at His coming^E? °For **you** are our glory and joy	19 20
2B.	Therefore, bearing³ *it* no longer, we preferred⁴ to be left-behind^F in Athens⁵ alone⁶, °and we sent Timothy, our brother and *a* fellow-worker⁷ *of* God in⁸ the good-news^G *of* Christ	3:1-2
1C.	So that he might establish⁹ you and encourage^H you¹⁰ concerning your faith, °*that* no one *might* be disturbed¹¹ by these afflictions¹²	3
1D.	For you yourselves know that we are appointed¹³ for this	
2D.	For even when we were with you, we were telling you beforehand^J that we were¹⁴ going to be afflicted^K, just as indeed it happened, and *just as* you know	4
3D.	For this reason¹⁵, and I bearing *it* no longer, I sent *Timothy* so as to know^L your faith— *that* the *one* tempting^M had not somehow tempted¹⁶ you and our labor proved-to-be¹⁷ in vain¹⁸	5
3B.	And Timothy having just-now^N come to us¹⁹ from you, and having announced-the-good-news^O *to* us *as to* your faith and love, and that you have *a* good^P remembrance *of* us always,²⁰ yearning^Q to see us just as we also you— °because of this we were encouraged^H, brothers^R, over you in all our distress²¹ and affliction²², through your faith^S	6 7
1C.	Because now we live!— if **you** are standing-*firm*^T in *the* Lord	8
2C.	For what thanksgiving^U can we return²³ *to* God for you for all the joy^B *with* which we are rejoicing²⁴ because of you before our God?—	9
1D.	Praying super-abundantly^V *by* night and *by* day that *we may* see your face, and complete^W the *things* lacking^X *from* your faith^S	10
4B.	Now may our God and Father Himself and our Lord Jesus²⁵ direct^Y our way to you	11
1C.	And may the Lord cause you to increase^Z and abound^AA *in* love for one another and for everyone (just as we also for you), °so that He may establish^BB your hearts *so as to be* blameless²⁶ in holiness^CC before our God and Father at the coming^E *of* our Lord Jesus²⁷ with all His holy *ones*²⁸. Amen²⁹	12 13
4A.	Finally then, brothers^R, we ask^DD you, and exhort³⁰ in *the* Lord Jesus that³¹ just as you received^EE from us how you ought-to^FF be walking^GG and pleasing^HH God (just as you also are walking³²), that you be abounding^AA more. °For you know what commands^JJ we gave *to* you through the Lord Jesus	4:1 2
1B.	For this is *the* will^KK *of* God— your holiness³³	3
1C.	*That* you be abstaining³⁴ from sexual-immorality³⁵	
2C.	*That* each *of* you know-how^LL to acquire³⁶ control *of* his *own* vessel³⁷ in holiness and honor^MM, °not in *the* passion^NN *of* desire³⁸ as indeed the Gentiles not knowing^LL God	4 5
3C.	*That*³⁹ no *one* overstep⁴⁰ and exploit⁴¹ his brother⁴² in the matter⁴³	6
4C.	Because *the* Lord *is the* avenger^OO concerning all these *things*, just as we also told you before, and solemnly-warned^PP	
1D.	For God did not call^QQ us for⁴⁴ impurity^RR, but in holiness	7
2D.	So-therefore⁴⁵ the *one* rejecting^SS is not rejecting *a* human^TT, but God, the *One* also⁴⁶ giving⁴⁷ His Holy Spirit to you⁴⁸	8

1. Or, "who". This word is used both ways. GK *5515*.
2. Some manuscripts add "Christ" {K}.
3. Or, "enduring". That is, when Paul could no longer bear the separation. Same word as in v 5. On this word, see 1 Cor 13:7.
4. Or, "were well pleased, were delighted". On this word, see "well pleased" in Mt 17:5.
5. This is recorded in Act 17:15-18:1.
6. This word is plural, going with "we". Some think it is an editorial "we", referring to Paul alone. On this word, see Jam 2:24.
7. On this word, see Rom 16:3. Instead of "fellow-worker", some manuscripts have a word meaning "servant" or "minister". Others have both words, "minister and fellow-worker". Others say "and minister *of* God and our fellow-worker..." {B}.
8. Or, "in connection with". GK *1877*.
9. Or, "stabilize, support, fix, set, confirm, strengthen". Same word as in v 13; Lk 22:32; Rom 1:11; 16:25; 2 Thes 2:17; 3:3; Jam 5:8; 2 Pet 1:12; Rev 3:2. Elsewhere only as "set" in Lk 9:51; "fixed" in Lk 16:26; "support" in 1 Pet 5:10. GK *5114*. Related to "steadfastness" in 2 Pet 3:17.
10. Some manuscripts include this word {N}.
11. Or, "shaken, moved". Used only here. GK *4883*. Some think Paul means "deceived". The root word means "to shake".
12. Paul was concerned about the Thessalonians' reaction to the persecution they all experienced. On this word, see Rev 7:14.
13. Or, "destined". Same word as in Phil 1:16. Paul was destined to proclaim the gospel to the Gentiles. The flip side of this destiny was suffering and persecution at the hands of his countrymen.
14. More literally, "are", as the Greek typically phrases it.
15. That is, to explain the afflictions, v 3.
16. More literally, "did tempt... prove to be", as the Greek typically phrases it.
17. Or, "become". Same word as in 1:5.
18. That is, without lasting result. Same word as "empty" in 2:1.
19. As recorded in Act 18:5. This was the occasion for writing this letter.
20. Or, "and that you have *a* good remembrance *of* us, always yearning to see us".
21. Or, "constraint". On this word, see "necessity" in 1 Cor 7:26.
22. On this word, see Rev 7:14. Some manuscripts say "affliction and distress" {K}.
23. Or, "repay, give back". On this word, see "repay" in 2 Thes 1:6.
24. This is the verb related to "joy", so Paul is saying "for all the joy with which we are-joyful...". On this word, see 2 Cor 13:11.
25. Some manuscripts add "Christ" {K}.
26. Same grammar as in 1 Cor 1:8.
27. Some manuscripts add "Christ" {K}.
28. Some think Paul means redeemed ones, "saints", as seen in 4:14; others, "angels", as seen in 2 Thes 1:7; Mk 8:38; others, both. On this word, see 1 Pet 1:16.
29. Some manuscripts omit this word {C}.
30. Or, "urge". Same word as in v 10. On this word, see Rom 12:8.
31. Some manuscripts omit this word {N}, so that it says "Lord Jesus— just as you received...".
32. Some manuscripts omit "just as you also are walking" {A}.
33. Or, "sanctification". Used of the process and the result of growing in the holiness of God. Same word as in v 4, 7. On this word, see Heb 12:14.
34. Or, "keeping away, avoiding, holding back, holding off, holding away from". Same word as in Act 15:20, 29; 1 Thes 5:22; 1 Tim 4:3; 1 Pet 2:11; and as "be distant" in Mt 15:8. GK *600*.
35. This word refers to sexual immorality of all kinds, before marriage (1 Cor 7:2), and during marriage (Mt 5:32). On this word, see 1 Cor 5:1.
36. Or, "get, obtain, procure, gain". Same word as in Mt 10:9; Act 1:18; 8:20; 22:28. Elsewhere only as "get" in Lk 18:12; and "gain" in Lk 21:19. GK *3227*. Related to "property" (the thing acquired) in Mt 19:22; and "owner" in Act 4:34.
37. Since the earliest times, opinion has been divided over whether Paul uses "vessel" here to refer to "body" (as in 2 Cor 4:7), or "wife" (as in 1 Pet 3:7). Thus he may mean "to acquire his own wife" in holiness, referring to premarital purity and to pursuing marriage in order to avoid immorality (1 Cor 7:2-5). This is a Hebrew way of speaking, as seen in Ruth 4:10. "Each of you" would then be limited to "all the unmarried". Or Paul may mean "to acquire *mastery of* his own body", "each of you" then meaning "all of you". This is a very general word, also meaning "container, instrument, object, thing, gear". Used 23 times. GK *5007*.
38. That is, the passion proceeding from desire, or belonging to desire. On this word, see Gal 5:16..
39. There is a grammatical difference in this statement versus the previous two. Some think it means this is the conclusion or summary. Others think it indicates a new subject, business relations. God's will is your holiness— in sexual matters, and now in business matters. Others think it gives the purpose of the previous two commands, "*So that* no *one may* overstep...".
40. Or, "go beyond, transgress". Used only here. GK *5648*.
41. Or, "take advantage of, cheat, defraud". Elsewhere only in 2 Cor 2:11; 7:2; 12:17, 18. GK *4430*. Related to "greed" in Eph 4:19. The idea is, "take advantage of someone for our own selfish purposes, self-seeking fraud".
42. That is, his fellow believer, whether male or female. On this word, Act 16:40.
43. Some think Paul means "the matter of sexual purity under discussion", taking the verbs in a figurative sense. Others think he means business matters, taking the verbs in a literal sense. On this word, see Mt 18:19.
44. That is, "for the purpose of". Same word as in Eph 2:10, "for" good works. GK *2093*.
45. Or, "Therefore for that very reason". On this word, see Heb 12:1.
46. Some manuscripts omit this word {C}.
47. Some manuscripts say "having given" {N}.
48. Some manuscripts say "us" {N}.

A. Col 1:5 B. Lk 24:52 C. Rev 4:4 D. 2 Cor 7:4 E. 2 Thes 2:8 F. Act 6:2 G. 1 Cor 15:1 H. Rom 12:8, exhorting J. Jude 17, spoken beforehand
K. 2 Cor 4:8 L. Lk 1:34 M. Heb 2:18 N. 2 Thes 2:7, right now O. Act 5:42 P. 1 Tim 5:10b Q. 1 Pet 2:2 R. Act 16:40 S. Eph 2:8 T. 1 Cor 16:13
U. 1 Tim 4:3 V. 1 Thes 5:13 W. Rom 9:22, prepare X. Phil 2:30 Y. Lk 1:79 Z. 2 Cor 8:15 AA. 2 Cor 8:2 BB. 1 Thes 3:3 CC. Rom 1:4
DD. Jn 17:9, pray EE. Lk 17:34, taken FF. Act 25:10 GG. Heb 13:9 HH. 1 Thes 2:4 JJ. 1 Tim 1:5 KK. Jn 7:17 LL. 1 Jn 2:29, know
MM. 1 Tim 5:17 NN. Rom 1:26 OO. Rom 13:4 PP. 1 Tim 5:21, solemnly charge QQ. Rom 8:30 RR. 1 Thes 2:3 SS. Gal 2:21, set aside
TT. Mt 4:4, mankind

2B. But concerning brotherly-love[1], you have no need[A] *that anyone should* be writing *to* you 9

    1C. For **you** yourselves are God-taught[2] so-that[3] *you might* be loving[B] one another
    2C. For indeed you are doing it toward all the brothers[C] in all Macedonia 10
    3C. But we exhort[D] you, brothers, to be abounding[E] more, ⁕and to be ambitious[4] to be quiet[5], and to 11
        be doing *your* own *things*[6] and working *with* your own[7] hands, just as we commanded[F] you

        1D. In order that you may walk[G] properly[H] toward the *ones* outside, and may have need[A] 12
            of nothing[8]

5A. And we[9] do not want you to be unaware[J], brothers[C], concerning the *ones* falling-asleep[10], in-order-that[11] 13
you may not grieve[K] as indeed[12] the others[L]— the *ones* not having *a* hope[M]

    1B. For if we believe that Jesus died and rose-up[N], so also[13] God will bring with Him the *ones* having 14
    fallen asleep through[14] Jesus

        1C. For we say this *to* you by *the* word[O] *of the* Lord, that **we**— the *ones* living, the *ones* remaining[15] 15
        until the coming[16] *of* the Lord— will in-no-way[17] precede[P] the *ones* having fallen asleep

            1D. Because[18] the Lord Himself will descend from heaven with *a* shouted-command[19], with 16
                a voice *of an* archangel[20], and with *a* trumpet[21] *of* God
            2D. And the dead in Christ will rise-up[N] first
            3D. Then **we**— the *ones* living, the *ones* remaining— will be snatched-up[22] together[23] with 17
                them in *the* clouds[24] to meet[25] the Lord in *the* air[Q]
            4D. And so we shall always be with *the* Lord

        2C. So then, be encouraging[26] one another with these words 18

    2B. But concerning the times[R] and the seasons[27], brothers, you have no need[A] *that anything should* be 5:1
    written *to* you

        1C. For you yourselves accurately[S] know that *the* day *of the* Lord[28] comes in this manner— like *a* 2
        thief[29] in *the* night

            1D. When[30] they are saying "peace and security[T]", then unexpected[31] destruction[U] suddenly- 3
                comes-upon[32] them, just as[33] the birth-pain[34] *on* the *one* having *a child* in *the* womb[35].
                And they will by no means escape[V]

        2C. But **you**, brothers, are not in darkness[W], so that the day should overtake[X] you like *a* thief[36] 4

            1D. For[37] **you** all are sons[Y] *of* light[38], and sons *of* day. We are not *of* night, nor *of* darkness 5

        3C. So then, let us not be sleeping[Z] like the others[L], but let us be keeping-watch[39] and being sober[AA] 6

            1D. For the *ones* sleeping[Z], are sleeping[Z] *at* night. And the *ones* getting-drunk[BB], are-drunk[CC] 7
                at night
            2D. But let **us**, being *of the* day, be sober[AA] 8

                1E. Having put on *a* breastplate *of* faith[DD] and love[EE]
                2E. And *a* helmet[40]— *the* hope[M] *of* salvation[FF]

1. That is, love expressed toward your Christian brothers and sisters. On this word, see Heb 13:1.
2. Or, "taught-by-God". This adjective is used only here. GK *2531*. God is love, and as He abides in us, He teaches us to be like Himself.
3. That is, toward the end or goal that you be loving one another. God Himself teaches you to this end. Others think Paul means "so that *you are* loving one another", giving the result of God's teaching.
4. Or, "and to make it *your* ambition to be quiet". On this word, see Rom 15:20.
5. Or, "to lead a quiet life". Same word as in Lk 14:4; Act 11:18; 21:14. Elsewhere only as "rest" in Lk 23:56, describing Sabbath behavior. GK *2483*. Related to "quietness" in 1 Tim 2:11; and "quiet" in 1 Pet 3:4.
6. That is, tending to your own affairs. On this phrase, see Jn 19:27.
7. Some manuscripts omit this word {C}.
8. Or, "no one". GK *3594*.
9. Some manuscripts say "I" {N}.
10. Or, "sleeping". That is, dead; or, ones dying from time to time. Same word as in v 14, 15. Not the same word as in 5:6, 7. This word is used as a euphemism for "death" also in Mt 27:52; Jn 11:11; Act 7:60; 13:36; 1 Cor 7:39; 11:30; 15:6, 18, 20, 51; 2 Pet 3:4. Used 18 times. GK *3121*. Some manuscripts say "having fallen asleep" {N}.
11. Or, "so that" you will not grieve. GK *2671*.
12. Christians do not grieve over the eternal loss of the dead one, as do those without hope. Both grieve over the temporal, earthly loss of a loved one.
13. Or, "in this manner also". For clarity, some add next *"we believe that"*.
14. Or, "by means of Jesus". In the Greek word order, "through Jesus" stands between "falling asleep" and "will bring". Some think Paul means "through Jesus (by His agency) God will bring with Him the *ones*..."; others, "the *ones* having fallen asleep through Jesus", which some think means "having fallen asleep into the presence of God through what Jesus has done", having entered into rest through Jesus. "In Jesus" is a paraphrase representing this view. From this rest Jesus will bring them with Him. GK *1328*.
15. Or, "the *ones* being left-behind". Used only here and v 17. GK *4335*. The root word means "to leave". Paul is referring to those remaining alive at that time, those who have not yet fallen asleep. We, like Paul, hope we are in this group.
16. Same word as in 2:19; 3:13; 5:23. On this word, see 2 Thes 2:8.
17. Or, "never". This is an emphatic negative, on which see "never" in Gal 5:16.
18. Or, "That", a second thing Paul says to you by the word of the Lord, v 15.
19. Or, "signal-call, word of command, command". Used only here. GK *3026*. Related to "order" in Mt 14:28.
20. That is, a ruling or chief angel. On this word, see Jude 9.
21. That is, a trumpet sound. Elsewhere only in Mt 24:31; 1 Cor 14:8; 15:52; Heb 12:19; Rev 1:10; 4:1; 8:2, 6, 13; 9:14. GK *4894*.
22. Our word "rapture" comes from the Latin translation of this word. The timing of this event in relation to the coming of Christ is a subject of debate. On this word, see "snatched away" in 2 Cor 12:2.
23. Or, "at the same time". Same word as in Mt 13:29; 20:1; Rom 3:12; 1 Thes 5:10. Elsewhere only as "at the same time" in Act 24:26; 27:40; Col 4:3; 1 Tim 5:13; Phm 22. GK *275*. The resurrection of the Christian dead and the living Christians are consecutive events ("first"... "then"), which occur at the same time, so that we will all meet Jesus together in the air. See also 1 Cor 15:51-52.
24. Some think Paul means "in *the* clouds", as the place where the returning believers are; others, "in clouds" or "on clouds", by means of clouds, enveloped in clouds, into the clouds. GK *1877*.
25. This is an idiom, literally "for *a* meeting *of* the Lord". On this, see Mt 25:6.
26. Or, "comforting". Same word as in 5:11. On this word, see "exhorting" in Rom 12:8.
27. On this word, see "time" in Mt 8:29. The phrase "the times or the seasons" is also in Act 1:7.
28. This phrase, "day of the Lord", occurs in the NT only in Act 2:20; 1 Cor 1:8; 5:5; 2 Cor 1:14; 2 Thes 2:2; 2 Pet 3:10. Related "day" phrases that refer to end-time events occur in Mt 7:22; 10:15; 12:36; 24:36; Mk 13:32; Lk 17:24, 30; Jn 6:39; 11:24; 12:48; Rom 2:5, 16; 1 Cor 3:13; Eph 4:30; Phil 1:6, 10; 2:16; 2 Thes 1:10; 2 Tim 1:12, 18; 4:8; 2 Pet 2:9; 3:7, 12; 1 Jn 4:17; Jude 6; Rev 6:17; 16:14; etc.
29. That is, unexpected and unwelcome. Same word as in Mt 24:43; Lk 12:39; 2 Pet 3:10; Rev 3:3; 16:15. Used 16 times. GK *3095*.
30. Some manuscripts say "For when" {N}.
31. Or, "sudden, unforeseen". Same word as in Lk 21:34, which brings out another aspect of this for Christians. This adjective modifies "destruction". It is a destruction which may be described as "unexpected, sudden, unforeseen" by such people. When their expectation is for peace and safety, it comes upon them. It is not sudden in the sense of "instantaneous", but in its onset. Many prefer to render this as an adverb, "suddenly, with unexpectedness".
32. On this word, see Lk 21:34. It is used here in the sense of "come upon suddenly or by surprise, spring upon".
33. Some think the main point of comparison is the "sudden unexpectedness" with which both begin. While the mother goes on as normal, the birthpains suddenly begin. Other think the main point is that both start small and relentlessly build to an inevitable conclusion. Other secondary nuances of the analogy have also been suggested.
34. Elsewhere only in Mt 24:8; Mk 13:8; and in as "pains" in Act 2:24. GK *6047*. Related words in Gal 4:19 and Rom 8:22.
35. The phrase "having *a child* in *the* womb" is also in Mt 1:18, 23; 24:19; Mk 13:17; Lk 21:23; Rev 12:2. Same word as in Lk 1:31. Elsewhere only as "glutton" in Tit 1:12, one living for their belly. GK *1143*.
36. That day will not, or should not (Lk 21:34-36; Mt 24:42-25:13; etc.) come unexpectedly to Christians, because we are watching for it.
37. Some manuscripts omit this word {K}.
38. That is, belonging to the light. Same phrase as in Lk 16:8. Compare Eph 5:9.
39. Or, "staying alert, keeping awake". Elsewhere only in v 10; and in Mt 24:42, 43; 25:13; 26:38, 40, 41; Mk 13:34, 35, 37; 14:34, 37, 38; Lk 12:37; Act 20:31; 1 Cor 16:13; Col 4:2; 1 Pet 5:8; Rev 3:2, 3; 16:15. GK *1213*.
40. Compare the breastplate and helmet in Eph 6:14, 17.

A. Tit 3:14   B. Jn 21:15, devotedly love   C. Act 16:40   D. Rom 12:8   E. 2 Cor 8:2   F. 1 Tim 1:3   G. Heb 13:9   H. Rom 13:13   J. Rom 10:3, ignorant of   K. 2 Cor 7:9   L. 2 Pet 3:16   M. Col 1:5   N. Lk 18:33   O. 1 Cor 12:8   P. 1 Thes 2:16, came   Q. Eph 2:2   R. 2 Tim 1:9   S. Mt 2:8   T. Lk 1:4, certainty   U. 1 Cor 5:5   V. Rom 2:3   W. Jn 3:19   X. Jn 1:5, overcome   Y. Gal 3:7   Z. 1 Thes 5:10   AA. 1 Pet 1:13   BB. Jn 2:10   CC. 1 Cor 11:21   DD. Eph 2:8   EE. 1 Jn 4:16   FF. Lk 19:9

	3D. Because God did not appoint[1] us for wrath,[2] but for *the* obtaining[3] of salvation[A] through our Lord Jesus Christ—	9
	1E. The *One* having died for us in order that whether we are keeping-watch[B] or sleeping[4], we may live together[C] with Him	10
	4C. Therefore be encouraging[D] one another, and building-up[E] one the other[5], just as you are also doing	11

6A. And we ask[F] you, brothers, to know[6] the *ones* laboring[G] among you, and leading[H] you in *the* Lord, and admonishing[J] you, °and to be esteeming[7] them super-abundantly[8] in love because of their work. Be living-in-peace[K] among yourselves 12
  13
7A. Now we exhort[D] you, brothers— 14

    1B. Be admonishing[J] the disorderly[9] *ones*, be encouraging[10] the fainthearted *ones*, be holding-on-to[11] the weak[12] *ones*, be patient[L] with everyone
    2B. See *that* no one gives-back[13] evil[M] for evil *to* anyone, but always be pursuing[N] the good[O], both[14] for one another and for everyone 15
    3B. Be rejoicing[P] always[15], °be praying[Q] unceasingly[16], °be giving-thanks[R] in everything. For this *is the* will[S] *of* God in Christ Jesus for you 16-18
    4B. Do not be quenching[17] the Spirit,[18] °do not be treating prophecies[T] with contempt[19], °but[20] be testing[21] all *things* 19-21
    5B. Be holding-on-to[22] the good[23], °be abstaining[U] from every form[24] *of* evil 22

    A. Now may the God *of* peace Himself sanctify[25] you wholly[26]. And may your whole[27] spirit and soul[V] and body[28] be preserved[29] blamelessly[30] at the coming[W] *of* our Lord Jesus Christ 23

        1. Faithful[X] *is* the *One* calling[Y] you, Who also will do *it* 24

    B. Brothers, be praying also[31] for us 25
    C. Greet[Z] all the brothers with *a* holy kiss[AA] 26
    D. I adjure[32] you *by* the Lord *that this* letter be read *to* all the brothers[33] 27
    E. The grace *of* our Lord Jesus Christ *be* with you[34] 28

1. Or, "make, destine". Same word as in Jn 15:16; Act 1:7; 1 Tim 1:12; 2:7; 2 Tim 1:11; Heb 1:2; 1 Pet 2:8. On this word, see "put" in Act 19:21.
2. Some think Paul is referring in particular to the wrath of the tribulation as described in Revelation. Others think he is referring in general to the opposite of salvation, the destiny of the unbelievers. Compare 1:10.
3. Or, "possession". Same word as in 2 Thes 2:14. Elsewhere only as "possession" in Eph 1:14; 1 Pet 2:9; and "preserving" in Heb 10:39. GK *4348*. Related to "obtain" in 1 Tim 3:13.
4. Same word as in 5:6, 7. Not related to "fallen asleep" in 4:13, 14, 15. Some think Paul means whether we are physically alive (living, remaining, 4:15) and therefore "keeping watch", or dead (fallen asleep, 4:15). Others think he means "sleep" in the same sense as in v 6, where believers are commanded not to do it. Believers sleeping in an unprepared state, similar to the unbelievers, will be overtaken by the event, but saved nevertheless. Used 22 times. GK *2761*. Compare Lk 21:34-36.
5. This is an idiom, literally, "one the one". These two words are the numeral "one". On "one", see Eph 4:7.
6. That is, in the sense of "to stand in close relationship with, to recognize, respect". On this word, see 1 Jn 2:29.
7. Or, "regarding, considering". On this word, see "regard" in Jam 1:2. It is a play on words, because this word also means "to lead, rule", as in Heb 13:7. Take the lead in thinking of your leaders superabundantly in love.
8. Or, "immeasurably, surpassingly, beyond all measure". Elsewhere only in Eph 3:20; 1 Thes 3:10. GK *5655*. Related word in Rom 5:20.
9. Used only here. GK *864*. Related words are used in 2 Thes 3:6, 7.
10. Or, "consoling". Same word as in 2:12. Elsewhere only as "console" in Jn 11:19, 31. GK *4170*. Related to "consolation" in 1 Cor 14:3; Phil 2:1.
11. Or, "clinging to, being devoted to, helping, supporting". Do not abandon the weak. Same word as in Tit 1:9. Elsewhere only as "be devoted to" in Mt 6:24; Lk 16:13. GK *504*.
12. Or, "sick". The context seems to point to spiritual weakness. The word is used of both physical (as in Act 5:15, 16) and spiritual (as in 1 Cor 8:7; 9:22) sickness or weakness. Used 26 times. GK *822*. Related to "weakness" in Mt 8:17.
13. Same word as in Rom 12:17; 1 Pet 3:9. On this word, see "render" in Mt 16:27.
14. Some manuscripts omit this word {C}.
15. Or, "at all times". Used 41 times, 27 being by Paul. GK *4121*.
16. Same word as in 1:2; 2:13. On this word, see Rom 1:9.
17. Or, "stifling, suppressing, extinguishing". Same word as in Mt 12:20; Mk 9:48; Eph 6:16; Heb 11:34. Elsewhere only as "go out" in Mt 25:8. GK *4931*.
18. That is, in all His gifts, manifestations, and promptings.
19. This word "treat with contempt" also means "disdain, despise, reject with contempt". Same word as in Lk 18:9; 23:11; Act 4:11; Rom 14:3, 10; 1 Cor 1:28; 16:11; 2 Cor 10:10; Gal 4:14. Elsewhere only as "be of no account" in 1 Cor 6:4. GK *2024*. Related word in Mk 9:12.
20. Some manuscripts omit this word {N}.
21. Or, "proving by testing". On this word, see "approve" in Rom 12:2. Compare 1 Jn 4:1; 1 Cor 14:29.
22. Some take these two phrases with what precedes, "but be testing all *things*, holding on to the good, abstaining from every form *of* evil", so that they refer specifically to the spiritual manifestations. Others pair them as separate exhortations, with a broad reference, similar to Phil 4:8. On this word, see "hold down" in Rom 1:18.
23. That is, that which is commendable, beautiful, praiseworthy. On this word, see 1 Tim 5:10a.
24. Or, "outward appearance". This word also means "species, kind, class, sort", and some prefer this meaning here. On this word, see "appearance" in 2 Cor 5:7.
25. Or, "make you holy, set you apart [to Himself]". On this word, see Heb 10:29.
26. Or, "through and through, in every way, altogether". Used only here. GK *3911*. This adjective is made of two words, "whole" and "complete". May God "make you holy through and through", in every aspect of your life.
27. This adjective is related to "wholly". It is made of two words, "whole" and "parts", meaning "complete in all its parts, entire, complete"; and thus, "intact, sound, undamaged". Elsewhere only in Jam 1:4, where it is explained as "lacking in nothing". GK *3908*. Related to "wholeness" in Act 3:16. Here, some think Paul means "whole", and modifies the nouns, "whole spirit and soul and body". Others think he means "complete, sound", and link it to the verb "be preserved **complete**", or sound. In this case, the Greek word order would indicate that this word is emphatic.
28. This threefold division occurs only here. "Soul and spirit" is in Heb 4:12; "soul and body" in Mt 10:28; "heart and soul and mind" in Mt 22:37; and "spirit and body" in Jam 2:26. "Soul" is our immaterial part that relates to this earth. "Spirit" is our immaterial part that relates to God. Some think we have three parts. Others think we have two parts, with the immaterial part being viewed from two different viewpoints.
29. Or, "kept, guarded, protected". On this word, see "keeping" in 1 Jn 5:18.
30. That is, in such a way as to incur no blame on yourself. This adverb is elsewhere only in 2:10. GK *290*. Related to "blameless" in Phil 3:6.
31. Some manuscripts omit this word {C}.
32. That is, I make you swear, I put you under oath by the Lord, that it will be done; I command you as if under oath. Used only here. GK *1941*. Related to "make swear" in Act 19:13, and some manuscripts have that word here {N}. Related to "oath" in Jam 5:12; and "put under oath" in Mt 26:63.
33. Some manuscripts say "holy brothers" {A}.
34. Some manuscripts add "amen" {A}.

A. Lk 19:9 B. 1 Thes 5:6 C. 1 Thes 4:17 D. Rom 12:8, exhorting E. 1 Cor 14:4, edify F. Jn 17:9, pray G. Mt 11:28, being weary H. Rom 12:8 J. Col 1:28 K. Rom 12:18 L. 1 Cor 13:4 M. 3 Jn 11 N. 1 Cor 14:1 O. 1 Tim 5:10b P. 2 Cor 13:11 Q. 1 Tim 2:8 R. Mt 26:27 S. Jn 7:17 T. 1 Cor 12:10 U. 1 Thes 4:3 V. Jam 5:20 W. 2 Thes 2:8 X. Col 1:2 Y. Rom 8:30 Z. Mk 15:18 AA. Rom 16:16

Overview		# 2 Thessalonians

Introduction	1:1-2
1A. We ought to be giving thanks always concerning you, brothers, just as it is fitting	1:3
1B. Because your faith is growing, and your love toward one another is increasing	1:3-4
1C. Which is evidence of the righteous judgment of God that you will be considered worthy of the kingdom for the sake of which you are suffering	1:5-10
2C. For which also we pray always concerning you, in order that God may consider you worthy of the calling and fulfill every desire of goodness and work of faith with power	1:11-12
2A. Now we ask you, brothers, not to alarmed as though the day of the Lord is present	2:1-2
1B. Let no one deceive you. The apostasy must come first, and the man of lawlessness	2:3-5
2B. And you know what is restraining him now. Jesus will kill him when He comes	2:6-12
3A. But we ought to be giving thanks always concerning you, brothers loved by the Lord	2:13
1B. Because God chose you to be the firstfruit for salvation, to which He also called you	2:13-14
2B. So then, brothers, be standing firm, and be holding on to the traditions you were taught	2:15
3B. And may our Lord Jesus and God our Father comfort your hearts and establish you	2:16-17
4A. Finally brothers, be praying for us. And may the Lord direct you into His love and endurance	3:1-5
5A. Now we command you, brothers, to be keeping away from every brother walking disorderly	3:6-16
Conclusion	3:17-18

	A. Paul and Silvanus[A] and Timothy	1
	B. *To* the church *of the* Thessalonians[1] in God our Father and *the* Lord Jesus Christ	
	C. Grace *to* you and peace from God our[2] Father and *the* Lord Jesus Christ	2
1A.	We ought[B] to be giving-thanks[C] *to* God always for you brothers, just as it is fitting[D]	3
	1B. Because your faith is growing-abundantly, and the love *of* each one *of* you all toward one another is increasing[E]—*so that we ourselves *are* boasting in you among the churches *of* God with reference to your endurance[F] and faith[G] in all your persecutions[H] and afflictions[J] which you are bearing-with[K]	4
	1C. *Which is* evidence[3] *of* the righteous[L] judgment[4] *of* God that[5] you *will* be considered-worthy[6] *of* the kingdom[M] *of* God for the sake of which you also[7] are suffering[N]	5
	1D. Since[8] *it will be a* righteous[L] *thing* with[9] God to repay[10] affliction[11] *to the ones* afflicting[O] you, *and *to give* you, *the ones* being afflicted[O], rest[12] along with us	6 7
	1E. At the revelation[13] *of* the Lord Jesus from heaven with angels *of* His power[14] *in flaming[15] fire[16]	8
	1F. Giving punishment[17] *to the ones* not knowing[P] God, and[18] *the ones* not obeying[Q] the good-news[R] *of* our Lord Jesus[19]	
	1G. Who will pay *the* penalty[20]— eternal[S] destruction[21] from[22] *the* presence[T] *of* the Lord, and from the glory[U] *of* His strength[23]	9
	2F. When[24] He comes to be glorified[25] in His saints[V], and marveled-at[26] among[27] all *the ones* having believed[28]— because our testimony[W] to you was believed— on that day[29]	10
	2C. For which[30] also[31] we are praying always for you, in order that[32] our God may consider you worthy[33] *of* the calling[34], and may fulfill[X] every desire[35] *of* goodness[36] and work[Y] *of* faith[37] with [His] power[Z]	11
	1D. So that the name *of* our Lord Jesus[38] may be glorified in you[39] and you in Him, according-to[40] the grace *of* our God and *the* Lord Jesus Christ	12

1. This letter was written in Act 18:11.
2. Some manuscripts omit this word {C}, so that it says "God *the* Father".
3. Or, "*a plain indication, a* proof ". The evidence is the Thessalonians' growing faith, love, and endurance amidst their afflictions. Used only here. GK *1891*. Related to "demonstrate" in Eph 2:7, and "sign" in a similar statement in Phil 1:28.
4. Some think Paul is referring to God's present judgment of the Thessalonians as seen in their trials, His evidence-producing testing of them now. Others think he is referring to the future judgment God will make about them, His considering them worthy on that future day; others, to the present judgment He makes about them, His present considering them worthy, which will also be experienced by them on that future day. Their behavior now (the "fruit" in their lives) is evidence that His judgment of them (and their persecutors) will be (or is and will be) righteous. On this word, see Jn 3:19.
5. This idiom is literally "for you to be considered worthy". Some think it gives the purpose of the testing or evidence, or of God's future judgment of the Thessalonians ("... God, so that you *may* be considered worthy"); others, the result of His judgment of them ("... God, so that you *will* be [or, are] considered worthy"); others, the content of His judgment about them ("... God that you *will* be [or, are] considered worthy").
6. Elsewhere only in Lk 20:35; Act 5:41. GK *2921*. Related to the word in v 11.
7. Or, "indeed". Some think Paul means "also", along with us (note v 7).
8. Or, "If as is the case". On this word, see Rom 8:9.
9. Or, "before, in the sight of ". GK *4123*.
10. Or, "return, give back, requite". Same word as in Rom 12:19 and Heb 10:30, "vengeance is mine, I will repay"; and in Lk 14:14; Rom 11:35. Elsewhere only as "return" in 1 Thes 3:9. GK *500*. Related to "payback" in Col 3:24; and "retribution" in Rom 11:9.
11. The "affliction" is the punishment of v 8-9. Same word as in v 4.
12. Or, "relief, refreshment". On this word, see 2 Cor 8:13. The "rest" is the kingdom of God of v 5. It will be rest, relief from their suffering.
13. Or, "disclosure". That is, the second coming of Christ. Same word as in Rom 2:5; 8:19; 1 Cor 1:7; 1 Pet 1:7, 13; 4:13. Elsewhere only of truth revealed by God in Lk 2:32; Rom 16:25; 1 Cor 14:6, 26; 2 Cor 12:1, 7; Gal 1:12; 2:2; Eph 1:17; 3:3; Rev 1:1. GK *637*. See the related verb in 2:3.
14. That is, angels in possession of God's power. Or, "His angels *of* power", or, "His powerful angels".
15. Elsewhere only as "flame" in Lk 16:24; Act 7:30; Heb 1:7; Rev 1:14; 2:18; 19:12. GK *5825*.
16. More literally, "in *a* fire *of* flame", a fire characterized by flame, an expression found only here. Some manuscripts say "in *a* flame *of* fire" {N}, a flame belonging to a fire (as in the other uses of the word "flame").
17. Or, "vengeance". Grammatically, "the Lord Jesus" is the subject of this word. Same word as in 2 Cor 7:11; 1 Pet 2:14. Elsewhere only as "vengeance" in Lk 18:7, 8; 21:22; Act 7:24; and in Rom 12:19 and Heb 10:30, "Vengeance is mine". GK *1689*. Related to "punish" in 2 Cor 10:6; and "avenger" in Rom 13:4.
18. Or, "even". Some think the two groups named here refer to Gentiles and Jews; others, that this is another description of the first group.
19. Some manuscripts add "Christ" {K}.
20. Or, "punishment". Same word as in Jude 7. Related to the word "punishment" in v 8.
21. Same word as in 1 Thes 5:3. On this word, see 1 Cor 5:5.
22. Some think Paul means "away from"— such ones will be separated "away from" His presence. Others think he means "proceeding from"— the penalty proceeds from the Lord. Others think he means "because of ". GK *608*.
23. That is, the glory originating in or emanating from His strength. On this word, see Eph 1:19.
24. Returning to Jesus as the subject, Paul concludes his description of what will take place at His "revelation". Others make this point 2G., "who will pay the penalty... when He comes to be glorified".
25. Elsewhere only in v 12. GK *1901*. Related to the word in Rom 8:30.
26. Or, "admired, wondered at". On this word, see "caused to marvel" in Rev 17:8.
27. Both "among" here and "in" earlier in the verse are the same word, and can be translated "in, by, among". GK *1877*.
28. Some manuscripts say "the *ones* believing" {N}.
29. This is the Greek word order. Some render this "believed— because our testimony to you in connection with that day was believed".
30. Or, "To which *end*". In this rendering Paul is referring to v 3-4, their faith and love; or to v 5, their worthiness ("I am praying that you continue to grow in faith and love [or, worthiness], in order that God may indeed consider you worthy now, and fulfill your efforts for Him"). Others think he is referring to v 5-10, their participation in the blessed event of that day, their salvation, making this point 2D. ("I am praying that you will be among those receiving His rest and glorifying the Lord on that day, specifically, that even now God might consider you worthy"). Others think this is a general reference to that future day, making this point 3F. ("Aiming at which blessed day for us all, I am praying that God might even now consider you worthy"). Others think this refers to their believing in v 10, making this point 1G. ("I am praying that you believe our testimony, in order that God..."). Consult the commentaries.
31. Or, "indeed". Some think Paul means in addition to giving thanks for it, v 3.
32. Paul may be giving the purpose of his prayer ("in order that"), or the content of it ("that"). GK *2671*.
33. This word "consider worthy, deserving, fitting" is related to the word in v 5. Same word as in Lk 7:7; 1 Tim 5:17; Heb 3:3; 10:29. Elsewhere only as "consider fitting" in Act 15:38; 28:22. GK *546*. Related to "worthy" in Rev 16:6; and "worthily" in 3 Jn 6.
34. On this word, see 2 Pet 1:10. Related to "called" in 2:14.
35. Or, "good pleasure". On this word, see "good pleasure" in Eph 1:5.
36. Some think Paul means your "every desire *for* goodness"; others, "all *the* good pleasure *of* [God's] goodness" (that is, His will for you). On this word, see Gal 5:22.
37. That is, works proceeding from faith, or characterized by faith. Compare 1 Thes 1:3; Gal 5:6.
38. Some manuscripts add "Christ" {N}.
39. Some think Paul means glorified now, in your goodness and works fulfilled with power; others, on that day, v 10.
40. Or, "based on, in accordance with". GK *2848*.

A. 1 Thes 1:1 B. 1 Jn 4:11 C. Mt 26:27 D. Rev 16:6, worthy E. 2 Cor 8:15 F. Jam 1:3 G. Eph 2:8 H. Mk 10:30 J. Rev 7:14 K. 2 Cor 11:4 L. Rom 1:17 M. Mt 3:2 N. Gal 3:4 O. 2 Cor 4:8 P. 1 Jn 2:29 Q. Act 6:7 R. 1 Cor 15:1 S. Mt 25:46 T. Lk 9:52 U. 2 Pet 2:10 V. 1 Pet 1:16, holy W. Act 4:33 X. Eph 5:18, filled Y. Mt 26:10 Z. Mk 5:30

| 2 Thessalonians 2:1 | 768 | Verse |

2A. Now we ask[A] you, brothers[B], concerning the coming[C] of our Lord Jesus Christ and our gathering-together[1] to Him,* that you not be quickly[D] shaken[E] from *your* understanding[F] nor alarmed[2]— neither by *a* spirit[3], nor by *a* word[G], nor by *a* letter[4] as-*if* through us[5], how that[6] the day *of* the Lord[7] is present[8]   2:1
  2

   1B. Let no one deceive[H] you in any way, because *it will not be present*[9] unless the apostasy[10] comes first,[11] and the man[J] *of* lawlessness[12] is revealed[13]—   3

      1C. The son[K] *of* destruction[14]
      2C. The *one* opposing[15] and exalting[L] *himself* over[16] everything being called[M] god or *an* object-of-worship[17], so that he sits-*down*[18] in the temple[N] *of* God[19], displaying[20] himself, that he is god   4
      3C. Do you not remember[O] that while still being with you I was telling[M] you these *things*?   5

   2B. And you know the *thing* restraining[21] **now**, so that he *might* be revealed[P] in his *own* time[22]   6

      1C. For the mystery[23] *of* lawlessness[Q] is already at-work[24]— only *there is* the *one* restraining[25] right-now[26] until he comes[27] out of *the* midst[28]   7
      2C. And then the lawless[R] *one* will be revealed[P]   8

         1D. Whom the Lord Jesus[29] will kill[30] *with* the breath *of* His mouth, and do-away-with[31] *by* the appearance[32] *of* His coming[33]
         2D. Whose[34] coming is in accordance with *the* working[S] *of* Satan[T]   9

            1E. With all power[U] and signs[35] and wonders[36] *of* falsehood[37]

1. Or, "assembling, meeting". Elsewhere only in Heb 10:25. GK *2191*. The related verb is used in Mt 24:31 and Mk 13:27 of gathering together Christ's elect at the end. See 1 Thes 4:15-17.
2. Or, "frightened, troubled". Elsewhere only in Mt 24:6 and Mk 13:7, "do not be alarmed, it is not yet the end". GK *2583*.
3. Or, a "spiritual *gift* or *manifestation*", such as a prophecy (see 1 Cor 14:12 on this use of this word).
4. Compare "word" and "letter" in 2:15 and 3:14.
5. Some think "as if through us" applies to all three; others, to the last two; others, to the letter only.
6. On "how that", see 2 Cor 11:21. This phrase indicates Paul is quoting what someone else said.
7. On "the day of the Lord", see 1 Thes 5:2. Some manuscripts say "day *of* Christ" {N}.
8. Or, "has come, is here". On this word, see Heb 9:9.
9. This is supplied from the end of v 2. Others supply "*it will not come*".
10. Or, "abandonment, rebellion, falling away". Elsewhere only in Act 21:21. GK *686*. Related to "depart", 1 Tim 4:1. Some have identified this with a first-century religious or political event; others, with such an event in history. Others think Paul is referring to a religious apostasy future to him, and still future to us.
11. Some think Paul means that these two things— the apostasy and the man of lawlessness— must occur before the day of the Lord comes. Others think he means they are among the first events of the day of the Lord.
12. On this word, see 1 Jn 3:4. Some manuscripts say the "man *of* sin" {B}. Some think this refers to a first-century person like Nero; others, to various other people in history. Others think it is not a man, but a personification of evil. Others think this is a man yet to be revealed, the still future Antichrist.
13. Or, "disclosed, made known". Elsewhere only in Mt 10:26; 11:25, 27; 16:17; Lk 2:35; 10:21, 22; 12:2; 17:30; Jn 12:38; Rom 1:17, 18; 8:18; 1 Cor 2:10; 3:13; 14:30; Gal 1:16; 3:23; Eph 3:5; Phil 3:15; 2 Thes 2:6, 8; 1 Pet 1:5, 12; 5:1. GK *636*. The noun is in 1:7. This word means "revealed" in the sense of "uncovered, unveiled". Compare "made evident" in 1 Jn 2:19.
14. This phrase is used of Judas in Jn 17:12. That is, belonging to, destined to destruction. On this word, see 2 Pet 2:1.
15. Or, "setting himself against, being contrary to". On this word, see Phil 1:28.
16. Or, "above, against". GK *2093*.
17. Or, "object of veneration". Elsewhere only in Act 17:23, of idols. GK *4934*. Related to "worship" in Act 13:50, and Rom 1:25.
18. Or, "takes *his* seat". This man sits in authority. On this word, see Rev 20:4. Some manuscripts add "as God" {A}.
19. The phrase "temple of God" is used of the Jewish temple; of Christians as the temple of God; and of the heavenly temple. Some think Paul means the Jewish temple (Mt 24:15), and that it will be rebuilt prior to the tribulation. Others think it is an abstract term for the visible church on earth. This man demands worship. There are other views.
20. Or, "showing, attesting, exhibiting, proving". Same word as in 1 Cor 4:9. Elsewhere only as "attest" in Act 2:22; and "prove" in Act 25:7. GK *617*. Related to "demonstration" in 1 Cor 2:4.
21. Same word as in v 7. On this word, see "hold down" in Rom 1:18.
22. Some think the restrainer is the Holy Spirit, making this "the *One* restraining". Others think this refers to some agent of God restraining evil, such as government, or the church (the body of Christ). Others think it is God's action of binding Satan; or granting dominance to the Gentiles, Lk 21:24; or waiting for the gospel to be proclaimed to the world, Mt 24:14. There are many other views.
23. That is, the time belonging to him. Compare "your hour" in Lk 22:53. Compare the similar phrase in 1 Tim 2:6.
24. On this word, see Rom 11:25. The mystery of rebellion against God and the laws of God is now working.
25. Or, "in operation, working". On this word, see "works" in 1 Cor 12:11.
26. Paul changes from the "thing" restraining, to the "one" restraining. Some think this points to the identity of the restrainer as the Holy Spirit, since the neuter word "spirit" refers to the person of the Spirit. Others think it refers to the personal head of a government system. There are other views.
27. Or, "at this moment". Used by Paul only as "now" in 1 Cor 4:13; 8:7; 13:12; 15:6; 16:7; Gal 1:9, 10; 4:20; "present" in 1 Cor 4:11; and "just now" in 1 Thes 3:6. On this word, see "now" in Rev 12:10.
28. Or, " becomes, comes to be". GK *1181*. This is a common word used 669 times, but rendered "taken" only here (NIV). The word itself implies nothing as to whether he "comes out" on his own initiative, or is forced out by another. It simply means "until he is no longer in the middle". Some find the nuance "taken out, removed" in the context. On this word, see "comes" in 2 Pet 1:20.
29. Or, "out *of the* middle, from among". This phrase is elsewhere only in Mt 13:49; Act 17:33; 23:10; 1 Cor 5:2; 2 Cor 6:17; Col 2:14. The restrainer stands between Satan and his plan for world domination. This restraining activity will cease. This word, "midst, middle, amidst", is used 58 times. GK *3545*.
30. Some manuscripts omit this word {C}.
31. On this word, see Mt 2:16. Some manuscripts say "consume" {N}, the word in Lk 9:54.
32. Or, "bring to an end". On this word, see Rom 6:6.
33. Elsewhere only in 1 Tim 6:14; 2 Tim 1:10; 4:1, 8; Tit 2:13. GK *2211*. Related to ""appeared" in Tit 2:11.
34. Or, "presence". The Greek word is *parousia*. Used of Christ's return in Mt 24:3, 27, 37, 39; 1 Cor 15:23; 1 Thes 2:19; 3:13; 4:15; 5:23; 2 Thes 2:1; Jam 5:7, 8; 2 Pet 1:16; 3:4, 12; 1 Jn 2:28. Elsewhere only in 1 Cor 16:17; 2 Cor 7:6, 7; 2 Thes 2:9; and as "presence" in 2 Cor 10:10; Phil 1:26; 2:12. GK *4242*. The related verb is "be present" in Rev 17:8.
35. That is, the lawless one. "Coming" is the same word as in v 8.
36. Same word as in Mt 24:24; Rev 13:13, 14; 16:14; 19:20; and Mt 26:48; Mk 13:4; 16:17, 20; Lk 11:30; 21:25; Jn 2:18; 20:30; Rom 4:11; 2 Thes 3:17; Rev 12:1. Used 77 times. GK *4956*.
37. The word "wonders" is always plural, and always appears with "signs". Elsewhere only in Mt 24:24; Mk 13:22; Jn 4:48; Act 2:19, 22, 43; 4:30; 5:12; 6:8; 7:36; 14:3; 15:12; Rom 15:19; 2 Cor 12:12; Heb 2:4. GK *5469*.
38. Some think this applies to all three; others to the last two; others, to wonders only. In addition, some think it means they are false, counterfeit; others, that their purpose is falsehood; others, that they proceed from falsehood. On this word, see Rev 14:5.

A. Jn 17:9, pray   B. Act 16:40   C. 2 Thes 2:8   D. Gal 1:6   E. Act 17:13   F. Rom 7:23, mind   G. 1 Cor 12:8   H. Rom 7:11   J. Mt 4:4, mankind   K. Gal 3:7   L. 2 Cor 12:7   M. Jn 12:49, say   N. Rev 11:1   O. Jn 16:21   P. 2 Thes 2:3   Q. 1 Jn 3:4   R. 1 Cor 9:21, without the law   S. Phil 3:21   T. Rev 12:9   U. Mk 5:30

	2E.	And with every deception[A] *of* unrighteousness[1] *for* the[2] ones perishing[B]— because[3] they did not receive[4] the love[C] *of* the truth[D] so that they *might* be saved[E]	10
		1F. And for this reason, God sends[5] them *a* working[6] *of* error[7] so that they *will* believe[F] the falsehood[8], *in order that all the ones not having believed[F] *in* the truth[D], but having taken-pleasure[9] *in* unrighteousness, may be condemned[G]	11 12
3A.	But[10] **we** ought[H] to be giving-thanks[J] *to* God always for you, brothers having been loved[K] by *the* Lord	13
	1B.	Because God chose[11] you *to be the* firstfruit[12] for salvation[L] in[13] *the* holiness[14] *of the* Spirit[15] and faith[16] *in the* truth[D]	
		1C. To which also[17] He called[M] you through[18] our good-news[N]	14
		2C. For *the* obtaining[19] *of the* glory *of* our Lord Jesus Christ	
	2B.	So then, brothers[O], be standing-*firm*[P], and be holding-on-to[Q] the traditions[20] which you were taught[R]— whether by word[S] [of mouth], or by our letter[T]	15
	3B.	And may our Lord Jesus Christ Himself and God our Father[21]— the *One* having loved[K] us, and having given *us* eternal[U] comfort[22] and good[V] hope[W] by grace[23]—*comfort[X] your hearts, and establish[Y] *you* in every good[V] work[Z] and word[24]	16 17
4A.	Finally, brothers, be praying for us	3:1
	1B.	That the word[S] *of* the Lord may run[25] and be glorified[AA], just as also with you	
	2B.	And that we may be delivered[BB] from out-of-place[26] and evil[CC] people[DD]	2
		1C. For faith[27] *is* not *possessed by* everyone[28]	
		2C. But the Lord is faithful[EE]— Who will establish[Y] you, and protect[FF] *you* from the evil one[29]	3
		1D. And we are confident[GG] in *the* Lord concerning you, that *the things* which we are commanding[30], you also[31] are doing and will do	4
		2D. And may the Lord direct[HH] your hearts into the love[C] *of* God[32], and into the endurance[33] *of* Christ	5
5A.	Now we command[JJ] you, brothers, in *the* name *of* our[34] Lord Jesus Christ, *that* you be keeping-away[35] from every brother walking[KK] disorderly[36], and not according to the tradition[LL] which they[37] received[MM] from us	6
	1B.	For you yourselves know how *you* ought-to[NN] be imitating[38] us	7
		1C. Because we were not disorderly[39] among you	
		2C. Nor did we eat bread as-a-gift[40] from anyone, but *were* working[OO] with labor[PP] and hardship[41] by night and by day[42] so-as not to be *a* burden-on[QQ] any *of* you—	8
		1D. Not because we do not have *the* right[43]	9
		2D. But in order that we might give ourselves *as a* pattern[44] *to* you, so that *you may* be imitating[RR] us	
	2B.	For even when we were with you, we commanded[JJ] this *to* you— that "if anyone does not want[SS] to work[45], neither let him eat"	10

1. Some think Paul means deception leading to unrighteousness; others, proceeding from unrighteousness; others, characterized by unrighteousness, unrighteous deception. On this word, see Rom 1:18.
2. Some manuscripts say "in the *ones* perishing" {N}.
3. Or, "in return for". This idiom is elsewhere only in Lk 1:20; 12:3; 19:44; Act 12:23.
4. Or, "accept". On this word, see "welcome" in Mt 10:40.
5. Some manuscripts say "will send" {N}.
6. Same word as in v 9. Same root word as "at work" in v 7.
7. Or, "deception". Some think Paul means a working leading to error; others, a working characterized by error or deception, a delusion. On this word, see 1 Thes 2:3.
8. Or, "lie". Same word as in v 9. At the first coming, God polarized Israel with the truth about the Christ, Rom 11:7-10. At the Second Coming, He polarizes the entire world with the lie about the Antichrist.
9. Or, "delighted *in*, been well-pleased *with*". These people did not "desire" (related word) goodness, 1:11. On this word, see "well-pleased" in Mt 17:5.
10. That is, in contrast to such people as in v 10-12; or, in contrast to this concern about you being shaken, 2:1-2.
11. Elsewhere only in Phil 1:22; Heb 11:25. GK *145*. See also the unrelated word "chosen" in Rom 8:33.
12. On this word, see 1 Cor 15:20. Some manuscripts say "from *the* beginning" instead of "*to be the* firstfruit" {B}. On the phrase "from *the* beginning", see Mt 19:4. The Thessalonians were the first of many more to come.
13. Or, "by means of, through, in the sphere of, in connection with". GK *1877*.
14. Or, "sanctification". On this word, see Heb 12:14.
15. Or, "*of your* spirit". Paul could mean the holiness produced by the Spirit, or the holiness characterizing your spirit.
16. Or, "belief". More literally, "faith *of the* truth", faith or belief whose object is the truth. On this noun, see Eph 2:8. Related to "believed" in v 12.
17. Some manuscripts omit this word {C}.
18. Or, "by means of". GK *1328*.
19. Or, "*a* possession". That is, "for our obtaining of His glory"; or, "for our becoming a possession of His glory". On this word, see 1 Thes 5:9.
20. Same word as in 3:6. On this word, see 1 Cor 11:2.
21. Some manuscripts say "our God and Father" {N}.
22. On this word, see "encouragement" in Act 4:36. Paul uses the related verb next.
23. That is, "having given us... by grace".
24. Same word as in v 15. Some manuscripts say "word and work" {N}.
25. That is, run speedily ahead, without obstacle or delay. Used only here of the Word "running". Elsewhere only of people running (18 times), and once of horses running. GK *5556*.
26. Or, "unnatural, strange, improper, wrong". That is, out of place morally, spiritually, socially, religiously, legally. Paul is referring to those who attacked him. Elsewhere only in Lk 23:41; Act 25:5; 28:6. GK *876*. The root word is "place" in Eph 4:27.
27. Or, "the faith". On this word, see Eph 2:8.
28. Or, "faith *does* not *belong to* everyone". Literally, "the faith *is* not *of* everyone". "Faith" is the subject of the Greek sentence. In English, we prefer to say "for not everyone has faith".
29. Or, "from evil". Same word as in v 2.
30. On this word, see 1 Tim 1:3. Some manuscripts add "you" {N}.
31. Some manuscripts omit this word {C}.
32. Some think Paul means love for God; others, love from God.
33. Some think Paul means endurance for Christ; others, the endurance that comes from Christ; others, the endurance exemplified by Christ. On this word, see Jam 1:3.
34. Some manuscripts omit this word {C}, so that it says "in the name *of* the Lord...".
35. Or, "avoiding, standing aloof". Elsewhere only as "avoiding" in 2 Cor 8:20. GK *5097*.
36. Or, in an "out of order, out of ranks, undisciplined, idle, lazy" manner. Elsewhere only in v 11. GK *865*. The related verb is in v 7.
37. Some manuscripts say "you"; others, "he" {B}.
38. Or, "emulating, following, mimicking". Elsewhere only in v 9; Heb 13:7; 3 Jn 11. GK *3628*. Related to "imitator" in Eph 5:1.
39. Or, "leading an undisciplined, disorderly life". Used only here. GK *863*. Related to the word in v 6; and the word in 1 Thes 5:14.
40. Or, "freely, without payment". Paul did not accept support from the Thessalonians when he was in Thessalonica. On this word, see "without a reason" in Gal 2:21.
41. Elsewhere only in 2 Cor 11:27; 1 Thes 2:9; all in combination with "labor". GK *3677*.
42. On this phrase, see Rev 7:15. Some manuscripts say "night and day", that is, continually {N}.
43. Or, "authority". On this word, see 1 Cor 8:9. On this "right", compare 1 Cor 9:1-18.
44. Or, "example, model". On this word, see 1 Pet 5:3.
45. This verse makes clear the nature of the "disorderly" behavior in view in v 6. Same word as in v 8.

A. 2 Pet 2:13 B. 1 Cor 1:18 C. 1 Jn 4:16 D. Jn 4:23 E. Lk 19:10 F. Jn 3:36 G. Mt 7:1, judge H. 1 Jn 4:11 J. Mt 26:27 K. Jn 21:15, devotedly love L. Lk 19:9 M. Rom 8:30 N. 1 Cor 15:1 O. Act 16:40 P. 1 Cor 16:13 Q. Heb 4:14 R. Rom 12:7 S. 1 Cor 12:8 T. 2 Thes 3:17 U. Mt 25:46 V. 1 Tim 5:10b W. Col 1:5 X. Rom 12:8, exhorting Y. 1 Thes 3:2 Z. Mt 26:10 AA. Rom 8:30 BB. Col 1:13 CC. Act 25:18 DD. Mt 4:4, mankind EE. Col 1:2 FF. Jn 12:25, keep GG. 1 Jn 3:19, persuade HH. Lk 1:79 JJ. 1 Tim 1:3 KK. Heb 13:9 LL. 2 Thes 2:15 MM. Lk 17:34, taken NN. Act 25:10 OO. Mt 26:10 PP. 1 Cor 3:8 QQ. 1 Thes 2:9 RR. 2 Thes 3:7 SS. Jn 7:17, willing

3B.	For we are hearing *of* some among you walking[A] disorderly[B], not working[C] at all, but being-busybodies[1]	11
1C.	Now *to* such *ones* we command[D] and exhort[E] in[2] *the* Lord Jesus Christ— that while working[C] with quietness[F], they eat their *own* bread	12
2C.	But **you**, brothers, do not grow-weary[3] while doing-good[4]. °And if anyone does not obey[G] our word[H] through *this* letter[J]	13-14
1D.	Be taking-note-of[5] this *one*— to not[6] be associating-with[K] him, in order that he may be ashamed[7]	
2D.	And do not be regarding[L] him as *an* enemy, but be admonishing[M] him as *a* brother[N]	15
3C.	And may the Lord *of* peace Himself give you peace continually[8] in every way[9]. The Lord *be* with you all	16

A.	The greeting *of* Paul *by* my *own* hand, which is *a* sign[O] in every letter[10]. I write in this manner	17
B.	The grace *of* our Lord Jesus Christ *be* with you all[11]	18

1. Or, "working around, puttering around, doing unnecessary things, meddling". Used only here. GK *4318*. Note Paul's play on the root word "work", "not working, but working around". Related to "busybodies" in 1 Tim 5:13.
2. Some manuscripts say "through our Lord Jesus Christ" {N}.
3. That is, in your souls. Same word as in Gal 6:9.
4. Or, "while doing right". Used only here. GK *2818*. It is made up of the verb "to do" and the word "good", two words found separately in the phrase "do good" in Gal 6:9; Jam 4:17; etc. It is related to "good works" in Tit 2:14.
5. Or, "marking". Used only here. GK *4957*.
6. Some manuscripts say "this *one*, and do not associate..." {N}.
7. Or, "turned on himself". On this word, see "have regard for" in Lk 18:2.
8. Or, "through all". This phrase occurs elsewhere only in Mt 18:10; Mk 5:5; Lk 24:53; Act 2:25; 10:2; 24:16; Rom 11:10; Heb 9:6; 13:15.
9. Some manuscripts say "place" {A}.
10. Our word "epistle" comes from this Greek word. Same word as in Act 15:30; 23:25; Rom 16:22; 2 Cor 3:1; 10:10; Col 4:16; 2 Thes 2:2; 2 Pet 3:16. Used 24 times. GK *2186*. The related verb "to write a letter" is in Heb 13:22 as "wrote to".
11. Some manuscripts add "amen" {A}.

A. Heb 13:9 B. 2 Thes 3:6 C. Mt 26:10 D. 1 Tim 1:3 E. Rom 12:8 F. 1 Tim 2:11 G. Act 6:7 H. 1 Cor 12:8 J. 2 Thes 3: 17 K. 1 Cor 5:9 L. Jam 1:2 M. Col 1:28 N. Act 16:40 O. 2 Thes 2:9

Overview		# 1 Timothy

Introduction		1:1-2
1A.	Just as I urged you to stay on in Ephesus while I was proceeding to Macedonia, do so	1:3
	1B. In order to command certain ones not to teach or pay attention to different doctrines or myths	1:4
	2B. And the goal of your command is love— from a pure heart, good conscience, sincere faith	1:5-11
2A.	I have gratitude for the One having strengthened me, having put me into service by His grace	1:12-17
3A.	I am depositing this instruction with you, Timothy, in accordance with prophecies about you	1:18
	1B. In order that by them you may fight the good fight, having faith and a good conscience	1:19-20
	2B. First of all then, I urge that prayers be made for all people by the men in every place	2:1-8
	3B. Similarly, I urge that women adorn themselves fittingly. Let them be learning in quietness	2:9-15
	4B. Overseers must be above reproach, meeting godly character qualifications	3:1-7
	5B. Deacons similarly must be honorable, faithful people	3:8-13
4A.	I am writing these things to you hoping to come to you soon, but in case I am slow	3:14
	1B. In order that you may know how to behave in the church, the pillar and support of the truth	3:15
	2B. And the mystery of godliness is confessedly great	3:16
	1C. He was revealed, declared righteous, seen, proclaimed, believed, taken up in glory	3:16
	2C. But the Spirit explicitly says that in later times, some will depart from the faith	4:1-5
	3C. While pointing out these things to the brothers, you will be a good servant of Jesus	4:6-7
	3B. But be training yourself for godliness	4:7
	1C. For godliness is profitable for all things, having promise for this life and the next	4:8-11
	2C. Let no one be looking down on your youth, but become a pattern in speech, conduct, love	4:12
	3C. Until I come, be paying attention to reading, exhortation, teaching, your gift, and yourself	4:13-16
	4B. Be appealing to older men as fathers, younger men as brothers, women as mothers and sisters	5:1-2
	5B. Be honoring real widows. Families have first responsibility. Put qualified widows on the list	5:3-16
	6B. Let elders having led well be considered worthy of double honor. Rebuke the ones sinning	5:17-25
	7B. Let all who are slaves be regarding their masters as worthy of all honor	6:1-2
5A.	Be teaching and exhorting these things	6:2
	1B. If anyone teaches differently, he is conceited, and diseased about controversies and riches	6:3-10
	2B. But you, O man of God, flee these things and pursue godly virtues. Fight the good fight	6:11-12
	3B. I command you in the sight of God and Jesus to keep the commandment until He comes	6:13-16
	4B. Command the rich ones to be rich in good works, that they may take hold of real life	6:17-19
	5B. O Timothy, guard the deposit, turning aside from empty chatterings of false knowledge	6:20-21

		Verse
A.	Paul, *an* apostle[A] *of* Christ Jesus[1] according to *the* command[B] *of* God our Savior[C] and Christ Jesus[2] our hope[D]	1
B.	*To* Timothy,[3] genuine[4] child[E] in *the* faith[F]	2
C.	Grace[G], mercy[H], peace[J] from God *the* Father[5] and Christ Jesus[6] our Lord	

1A. Just as I urged[K] you to stay-on[L] in Ephesus while *I was* proceeding to Macedonia,[7] *do so*   3

    1B. In order that you might command[8] certain *ones* not to be teaching-different-*doctrines*[9], *nor to be paying-attention-to[M] myths[10] and endless genealogies[11]   4

        1C. Which cause[N] speculations[12] rather than *a* stewardship[13] *of* God, *which is* by[14] faith

    2B. And the goal[15] *of your* command[16] is love[17]— from *a* pure[O] heart, and *a* good[P] conscience[Q], and *a* sincere[18] faith[F]   5

        1C. Having departed[19] *from* which[20], some turned-aside[21] into worthless-talk[22]   6

            1D. Wanting[R] to be Law-teachers[23]   7
            2D. Not understanding[S] either *the things* which they are saying, or about[24] what *things* they are speaking-confidently[25]

        2C. Now we know that the Law *is* good[26] if one is using it lawfully, *knowing this— that law is not laid-down[27] *for a* righteous[28] *one* but *for*   8-9

            1D. Lawless[T] *ones* and rebellious[U] *ones*
            2D. Ungodly[V] *ones* and sinful[W] *ones*
            3D. Unholy *ones* and profane[29] *ones*
            4D. Father-thrashers and mother-thrashers[30]
            5D. Man-slayers[31], *sexually-immoral[X] *ones*, homosexuals[Y], slave-traders[32], liars, perjurers[33]   10
            6D. And if any other *thing* is contrary[34] *to* healthy[35] teaching[Z] *according-to[36] the good-news[AA] *of* the glory *of* the blessed[BB] God which[37] **I** was entrusted[CC]   11

1. Some manuscripts say "Jesus Christ" {K}.
2. Some manuscripts say "*the* Lord Jesus Christ" {K}.
3. First mentioned in Act 16:1-3, Timothy served with Paul from then on. He was with Paul during his imprisonment, Phm 1. Paul mentions him in all of his letters except Galatians, Ephesians, and Titus. These men had a long and deep friendship and a partnership in the gospel. Paul calls him "my fellow worker", Rom 16:21; "my beloved and faithful child in the Lord", 1 Cor 4:17; one of "kindred spirit", and "proven worth", Phil 2:19-23. Used 24 times. GK *5510*.
4. Or, "true-born, legitimate". On this word, see "genuineness" in 2 Cor 8:8. A related word is used of Timothy in Phil 2:20.
5. Some manuscripts say "God our Father" {N}.
6. Some manuscripts say "Jesus Christ" {K}.
7. Some think this took place after Paul was released from Roman custody (see Act 28:30). He probably told Timothy not to meet him in Macedonia, but to stay on the job in Ephesus. Now he writes to encourage and help Timothy in his work.
8. Or, "give orders, instruct, direct", announce what must be done. Same word as in 4:11; 5:7; 6:13, 17; and 1 Cor 7:10; 11:17; 1 Thes 4:11; 2 Thes 3:4, 6, 10, 12; and as "instruct" in Mt 10:5; and "order" in Mk 8:6; Lk 9:21; Act 1:4. Used 32 times. GK *4133*. The related noun is in v 5.
9. Or, "teaching error, teaching other *than the truth,* giving divergent teachings". Elsewhere only in 6:3. GK *2281*.
10. Or, "fables, tales, legends". Elsewhere only in 1 Tim 4:7; 2 Tim 4:4; Tit 1:14; 2 Pet 1:16. GK *3680*.
11. Both were of Jewish origin. Elsewhere only in Tit 3:9. GK *1157*. Related to "trace a genealogy" in Heb 7:6.
12. Or, "questionings". Used only here. GK *1700*. Related to "seek out" in Heb 11:6. Here, the questionings are not seeking out God, but useless things like genealogies, which do not aid faith, and may even harm it (see 6:4-5). Related to "controversies" in 6:4, which some manuscripts have here {B}.
13. Or, "arrangement, mode of operation". On this word, see Eph 1:10. Some manuscripts instead say "edification *from* God" {N}.
14. Or, "in the sphere of, in connection with". That is, by faith in what God has revealed, not human speculation. The grammar indicates this modifies "stewardship". GK *1877*.
15. Or, "end, aim". On this word, see "end" in Rom 10:4.
16. Or, "instruction, order". Same word as in Act 5:28; 16:24; 1 Thes 4:2. Elsewhere only as "instruction" in 1 Tim 1:18. GK *4132*. Related to the word in v 3.
17. The grammar indicates that the goal is love proceeding from the following three sources, not just any love.
18. Or, "genuine, without hypocrisy". On this word, see Rom 12:9.
19. Or, "missed the mark, deviated". Elsewhere only as "miss the mark" in 6:21; 2 Tim 2:18. GK *846*. Or, "*From* which, having departed, some turned aside". Same construction as in 1:19; 6:10, 21.
20. This word is plural, referring to the clean heart, good conscience and sincere faith.
21. Or, "turned away". Same word as in 5:15; 6:20; 2 Tim 4:4. Elsewhere only as "dislocated" in Heb 12:13. GK *1762*.
22. Or, "futile, useless, pointless, vain talk". Used only here. GK *3467*. Related to "futile" in 1 Cor 15:17; and "worthless talkers" in Tit 1:10.
23. Elsewhere only in Lk 5:17; Act 5:34 (of Gamaliel). GK *3791*.
24. Such people do not understand the subject matter, nor how their words relate to it.
25. Or, "confidently asserting, insisting". Elsewhere only in Tit 3:8. GK *1331*.
26. That is, outwardly good, pleasing, useful, advantageous. On this word, see 5:10a. There is no "if" to its inner goodness (Rom 7:12).
27. Or, "set in place, given; does not exist". On this word, see "lying" in Mt 3:10.
28. The Law is for the instruction and punishment of Law-breakers, not for those who are righteous by faith in Christ. These people have missed the mark on this and are still attempting to teach and live by the rule of law instead of love. On this word, see Rom 1:17.
29. Or, "worldly, godless, irreligious". That is, one who lives by material, earthly values, without regard for spiritual things. Elsewhere only in 4:7; 6:20; 2 Tim 2:16; Heb 12:16. GK *1013*. Related to "profane" in Mt 12:5.
30. Both words are used only here, and have as their root word the word "thresh" in 5:18. Paul could mean "*ones* treading-on-parents" or "thrashing" or "abusing" them in the broadest sense— physically, verbally, financially, emotionally, socially, etc. In this case, "thrashing" is the opposite of "honoring" them. Or, the meaning could be restricted to physical abuse, "assaulting, thrashing", as the root verb is used in the Greek OT in Judg 8:7 (thrash, NASB), 16 (disciplined, NASB). The Law is for "parent-strikers", "parent-bashers". Or, he could mean "crushing" to the point of death, "parent-killers". Paul is figuratively referring to the violation of the fifth commandment, the only question being the scope of the violation he has in mind. GK *4260* and *3618*.
31. That is, murderers. The word "slayer" is related to the word in the sixth commandment, "You shall not murder", on which see Jam 4:2. Used only here. GK *439*. With regard to women, this word meant "husband-killers". Compare the unrelated word "murderer" in 1 Jn 3:15.
32. Or, "man-stealers, kidnappers". Used of one who kidnaps people to sell them. Used only here. GK *435*.
33. Or, "oath-breakers". Used only here. GK *2156*. Related to "break oath" in Mt 5:33.
34. Or, "opposes". On this word, see "oppose" in Phil 1:28.
35. Or, "sound, correct". This is a participle, "teaching being healthy". Used of "teaching" in 1 Tim 1:10; 2 Tim 4:3; Tit 1:9; 2:1; of "words" in 1 Tim 6:3; 2 Tim 1:13; of "faith" in Tit 1:13; 2:2. Elsewhere only in Lk 5:31; 7:10; 15:27; 3 Jn 2. GK *5617*. Related to "healthy" in Mt 12:13.
36. Or, "based on, in accordance with". Some instead link this phrase with v 8, "using it lawfully... in accordance with"; or, with v 9, "knowing this... in accordance with". GK *2848*.
37. This word modifies "good news".

A. 1 Cor 12:28 B. Rom 16:26 C. Lk 1:47 D. Col 1:5 E. 1 Jn 3:1 F. Eph 2:8 G. Eph 2:8 H. Mt 9:13 J. Act 15:33 K. Rom 12:8, exhort L. Act 11:23, continuing in M. 1 Tim 3:8 N. Act 17:31, grant O. Tit 1:15, clean P. 1 Tim 5:10b Q. Act 23:1 R. Jn 7:17, willing S. Eph 3:20, think T. 1 Cor 9:21, without the law U. Tit 1:6 V. Jude 15 W. Mt 9:10, sinner X. 1 Cor 5:9 Y. 1 Cor 6:9 Z. 1 Tim 5:17 AA. 1 Cor 15:1 BB. Lk 6:20 CC. Jn 3:36, believe

2A.	I have gratitude¹ *to* Christ Jesus our Lord, the *One* having strengthened^A me, because He regarded^B me trustworthy², having appointed³ *me* for service⁴—*I formerly^C being⁵ a* blasphemous⁶ *one*, *and a* persecutor, *and a* violent⁷ *one*!	12 13
1B.	But I was shown-mercy^D because being ignorant^E, I acted^F in unbelief⁸. *And the grace *of* our Lord overflowed, along with *the* faith and love *which are* in⁹ Christ Jesus	14
2B.	The saying^G *is* trustworthy¹⁰ and worthy^H *of* full¹¹ acceptance— that Christ Jesus came into the world to save^J sinners^K, *of* whom **I** am foremost¹²	15
3B.	But for this reason I was shown-mercy^D— in order that in me, *the* foremost, Christ Jesus¹³ might demonstrate¹⁴ all patience^L, for *a* pattern¹⁵ *for* the *ones* going to put-faith upon¹⁶ Him for eternal life	16
4B.	Now *to* the King *of* the ages¹⁷, *to the* immortal^M invisible only¹⁸ God, *be* honor and glory forever and ever^N, amen	17
3A.	I am depositing¹⁹ this instruction²⁰ *with* you, *my* child^O Timothy, in accordance with the preceding²¹ prophecies^P about you	18
1B.	In order that by them²² you may fight²³ the good fight²⁴, *having faith and *a* good^Q conscience^R	19
1C.	Having pushed-aside²⁵ which²⁶, some suffered-shipwreck²⁷ with respect to the faith²⁸	
1D.	*Of* whom are Hymenaeus²⁹ and Alexander, whom I handed-over^S *to* Satan³⁰ in order that they may be trained³¹ not to blaspheme³²	20
2B.	First *of* all then, I urge^T *that* petitions³³, prayers³⁴, intercessions³⁵, thanksgivings^U be made	2:1
1C.	For all people^V	
2C.	For kings and all the *ones* being in *a place of* superiority³⁶, in order that we may spend³⁷ *a* tranquil and quiet³⁸ life^W in all godliness³⁹ and dignity^X	2
3C.	This⁴⁰ *is* good^Y, and acceptable⁴¹ in the sight of our Savior^Z God, *Who desires⁴² all⁴³ people^V to be saved^J, and to come to *the* knowledge^AA *of the* truth	3-4

1. Sparked by "entrusted" in v 11, how natural it is for Paul to think back with gratitude for his own ministry just before he begins to "deposit" his instructions on ministry with Timothy. On "have gratitude", see Lk 17:9. Some manuscripts say "And I have gratitude" {N}.
2. Or, "faithful". That is, a faithful or trustworthy one who would fulfill the ministry to which God was appointing him. Same word as in v 15.
3. Or, "having put" into service. Same word as in 2:7; 2 Tim 1:11; 1 Thes 5:9; Jn 15:16; Act 1:7; Heb 1:2. On this word, see "put" in Act 19:21.
4. Or, "ministry". On this word, see "ministries" in 1 Cor 12:5.
5. Some manuscripts say "service— the *one* formerly being..." {N}.
6. That is, one who slandered or spoke against God and His people. Elsewhere only in Act 6:11; 2 Tim 3:2; 2 Pet 2:11. GK *1061*. Related to "blasphemy" in 6:4; and "to blaspheme" in 6:1.
7. Or, "insolent". Elsewhere only in Rom 1:30. GK *5616*. Note 1 Cor 15:9. Related to "insult" in 2 Cor 12:10; and "mistreat" in 1 Thes 2:2.
8. Same word as in Mt 13:58; Mk 6:6; 9:24; 16:14; Rom 4:20; 11:20, 23; Heb 3:12, 19. Elsewhere only as "faithlessness" in Rom 3:3. GK *602*.
9. The grammar indicates this modifies "faith and love".
10. Or, "faithful". Same word as in 3:1; 4:9; 2 Tim 2:11; Tit 3:8; Rev 21:5; 22:6. On this word, see "faithful" in Col 1:2.
11. Or, "complete, total, entire, all". Acceptance without reservation. This common word is normally rendered "all, every". GK *4246*.
12. Or, "chief, first, *the* leading *one*". Compare 1 Cor 15:9; Eph 3:8. Yet Paul also says 2 Cor 12:11. On this word, see "first" in 1 Cor 15:3.
13. Some manuscripts say "Jesus Christ" {N}.
14. Or, "show, display, give proof of ". On this word, see Eph 2:7.
15. Or, "sketch, outline". Elsewhere only in 2 Tim 1:13. GK *5721*. Related to "pattern" in 1 Pet 5:3.
16. On "put faith upon", see Rom 4:5.
17. Or, "the King *of* eternity, the eternal King". GK *172*. Compare the similar "age" phrases in 1 Cor 10:11; Eph 3:11; Heb 9:26.
18. Some manuscripts add "wise" {N}, the only wise God.
19. Or, "placing before, entrusting, committing, setting before". Same word as in 2 Tim 2:2. On this word, see "put before" in Act 17:3. Related to "deposit" in 6:20.
20. Or, "command". That is, the following set of instructions, directives, commands, regarding men, women, elders and deacons, which Paul wants to "deposit" with Timothy "in order that by them he may fight the good fight". This makes v 18-20 the beginning of the next section. Others think Paul is referring back to v 3 or v 5, the "command" to turn the Ephesians from pursuing bad teaching to the goal of love. Others think the command is "that you fight the good fight". In both these cases, v 18-20 is viewed as the conclusion of what precedes, a new main point beginning in 2:1. Compare 3:14. Same word as "command" in v 5. Related to the word in Mt 10:5, where Jesus "instructed" them.
21. On this word, see "going ahead" in 2 Jn 9. That is, the prophecies preceding Timothy's ministry, having to do with what God would do through him. Compare 4:14.
22. Paul may mean "by following the contents of this instruction", the "instruction" now being viewed as individual "instructions". Or he may mean "in the sphere of the prophecies, in connection with the prophecies"; that in living out the prophecies, you may fight the good fight with the help of this instruction.
23. This word means "fight in war, serve as soldier". It is the same root word as the words for soldier, army, warfare, captain. Elsewhere only as "serve as a soldier" in Lk 3:14; 1 Cor 9:7; 2 Tim 2:4; and "wage war" in 2 Cor 10:3; Jam 4:1; 1 Pet 2:11. GK *5129*.
24. Same root word as the previous verb. Or, "War the good warfare". Elsewhere only as "warfare" in 2 Cor 10:4. GK *5127*.
25. Or, "rejected". On this word, see "reject" in Rom 11:1. Or, "which having pushed aside, some suffered shipwreck". Same construction as in 1:6.
26. This is singular, and refers to the "good conscience".
27. Or, "were shipwrecked". Elsewhere only in 2 Cor 11:25. GK *3728*.
28. Or, "*their* faith". Paul may mean these men ran "the Christian faith, the truth" into the rocks as they ignored their conscience. Or, having ignored their conscience, they ran their personal faith aground, suffering a disaster.
29. Some think this is the same person as in 2 Tim 2:17. Some think Alexander is the one in Act 19:33, or the one in 2 Tim 4:14. Others reject both of these conjectures. GK *5628*.
30. This same phrase occurs in 1 Cor 5:5.
31. Or, "disciplined". On this word, see "disciplined" in 1 Cor 11:32.
32. On this word, see 6:1. Perhaps Paul means "speak against the word of God", as in 6:1; Tit 2:5.
33. Or, "prayer requests". The root word is "ask", and this word refers to "what is asked". Same word as in Rom 10:1; Eph 6:18; Phil 1:4; 4:6; 1 Tim 5:5; Heb 5:7. Elsewhere only as "prayer" in Lk 1:13; 2:37; 5:33; 2 Cor 1:11; 9:14; Phil 1:19; 2 Tim 1:3; Jam 5:16; 1 Pet 3:12. GK *1255*.
34. This is a general term for "prayer". Elsewhere only in Mt 21:13, 22; Mk 9:29; 11:17; Lk 6:12; 19:46; 22:45; Act 1:14; 2:42; 3:1; 6:4; 10:4, 31; 12:5; 16:13, 16; Rom 1:10; 12:12; 15:30; 1 Cor 7:5; Eph 1:16; 6:18; Phil 4:6; Col 4:2, 12; 1 Thes 1:2; 1 Tim 5:5; Phm 4, 22; Jam 5:17; 1 Pet 3:7; 4:7; Rev 5:8; 8:3, 4. GK *4666*. The related verb is in 1 Tim 2:8.
35. Or, "petitions". Elsewhere only as "prayer" in 4:5. GK *1950*. Related to "intercede" in Rom 8:34.
36. Elsewhere only in 1 Cor 2:1. GK *5667*. Related to "superior" in Rom 13:1.
37. Or, "lead, pass, live". Elsewhere only in Tit 3:3. GK *1341*.
38. On this word, see 1 Pet 3:4. Related to "quietness" in v 11.
39. Or, "devotion, reverence, piety". Elsewhere only in 3:16; 4:7, 8; 6:3, 5, 6, 11; 2 Tim 3:5; Tit 1:1; and in Act 3:12; 2 Pet 1:3, 6, 7; 3:11. GK *2354*. Related to "reverence" in 5:4; "godly" in 2 Tim 3:12; and "devout" in Act 10:2.
40. That is, such prayer. Some manuscripts say "For this..." {N}.
41. Or, "pleasing". Or, this may be punctuated "good and acceptable" to God. Elsewhere only in 5:4. GK *621*. Related to "welcome" in Act 2:41; and "acceptance" in 1 Tim 1:15.
42. This word is used 208 times, meaning "wish, want, will, desire". On this word, see "willing" in Jn 7:17. Compare 1 Tim 4:10; 2 Pet 3:9 (different word); 1 Jn 2:2.
43. Some think Paul means "every individual"; others, "all kinds of people". Compare 4:10.

A. 2 Tim 2:1, become strong B. Jam 1:2 C. 2 Cor 1:15, first D. Rom 12:8 E. Rom 10:3 F. Rom 13:13, does G. 1 Cor 12:8, word H. Rev 16:6 J. Lk 19:10 K. Mt 9:10 L. Heb 6:12 M. 1 Cor 15:52, undecayable N. Rev 20:10 O. 1 Jn 3:1 P. 1 Cor 12:10 Q. 1 Tim 5:10b R. Act 23:1 S. Mt 26:21 T. Rom 12:8, exhorting U. 1 Tim 4:3 V. Mt 4:4, mankind W. 1 Jn 2:16, life X. 1 Tim 3:4 Y. 1 Tim 5:10a Z. Tit 1:3 AA. Col 1:9

| 1 Timothy 2:5 | 780 | Verse |

        1D. For *there is* one God, and one mediator[A] *of* God and people[B]— *the* man[B] Christ Jesus   5

            1E. The *One* having given Himself *as a* ransom[1] for all   6
            2E. The testimony[C] *given in His* own[2] times

                1F. For which **I** was appointed[D] *a* proclaimer[E] and *an* apostle[F]— I am telling *the* truth[3]; I am not lying— *a* teacher[G] *of the* Gentiles in[4] faith and truth[5]   7

    4C. So I want the men[H] in every place to be praying[6], lifting-up[J] holy[K] hands without anger[L] and argument[7]   8

3B. Similarly also[8], *I urge that* women be adorning[9] themselves in well-ordered[10] apparel[11], with[12] modesty[13] and sound-mindedness[14]   9

    1C. Not in braided *hair* and[15] gold, or pearls, or very-expensive[M] clothing
    2C. But through[16] good[17] works[N], which is fitting[18] *for* women professing[19] godliness[20]   10
    3C. Let *a* woman[21] be learning[O] in quietness[22] with all submission[23]   11

        1D. And I do not permit[24] *a* woman to teach[25], nor to have-authority-over[26] *a* man[27], but to be in quietness   12

            1E. For Adam was formed[P] first, then Eve   13
            2E. And Adam was not deceived[28], but the woman, having been completely-deceived[29], has come-to-be[30] in transgression[31]   14

        2D. But she[32] will be saved[33] by The Childbearing[34], if they[35] continue[36] in faith and love and holiness[37] with sound-mindedness[Q]   15

4B. The saying *is* trustworthy[R]— if anyone aspires-to[S] *the* office-of-overseer[38], he desires[T] *a* good[U] work[N]   3:1

    1C. Therefore the overseer[V] must[W] be above-reproach[39]   2

        1D. *A* man *of* one woman[40]

1. Used only here. GK *519*. Same root word as "redemption". On this word group, see Rom 3:24.
2. Or, impersonally, "*in its* own times", "*at the* proper times". Same phrase as in 6:15; Tit 1:3; and Gal 6:9 (singular). Some think Paul means "given in God's own times"; others "given in the gospel's own times"; others, "given at the proper times to all people". Consult the commentaries. On "own", see Act 20:28. On the testimony, compare 1 Jn 5:9-12.
3. Some manuscripts add "in Christ" {A}. That is, when I say that God appointed me an apostle.
4. Or, "in connection with". GK *1877*.
5. Compare Tit 1:1, the faith of the chosen ones and the knowledge of the truth.
6. Used 85 times. GK *4667*. Related to "prayer" in 2:1.
7. On this word, see "thoughts" in Jam 2:4. Some manuscripts have it plural {N}.
8. Some manuscripts omit this word {C}.
9. Or, "putting in order, arranging, decorating". Same word as in Mt 23:29; Lk 21:5; Tit 2:10; 1 Pet 3:5; Rev 21:2, 19. Elsewhere only as "put in order" in Mt 12:44; 25:7; Lk 11:25. GK *3175*. Related to "adornment" in 1 Pet 3:3.
10. Or, "modest, respectable" in the sense of "appropriate, balanced". Elsewhere only as "respectable" in 3:2. GK *3177*. This is the same root word as "adorning" earlier. The phrase could be translated, "to put themselves in order in well-ordered apparel". It is modesty with reference to what is respectable and honorable in one's culture.
11. Or, "clothing, deportment, attire". Used only here. GK *2950*.
12. That is, along with. GK *3552*.
13. Or, "a sense of shame, bashfulness, respect, regard for others". Used only here. GK *133*.
14. Or, "good sense, moderation, discretion, self-control". Elsewhere only in v 15; Act 26:25. GK *5408*. On this word group, see 3:2.
15. Some manuscripts say "or" {N}.
16. Or, "by means of, with". GK *1328*. Adorn yourself through your good works, not through your wardrobe. The Greek word order is "But, which is fitting... godliness, through good works".
17. That is, works characterized by inner moral goodness, fittingly reflecting that of the women. On this word, see 5:10b.
18. Or, "proper, suitable". On this word, see 1 Cor 11:13.
19. Or, "promising". Elsewhere in this sense only in 6:21. Elsewhere 13 times meaning "to promise". GK *2040*.
20. Or, "reverence, worship of God, piety". Used only here. GK *2537*. Related to "God-fearing" in Jn 9:31; and "godliness" in 1 Tim 2:2.
21. This word means "woman" or "wife", based on the context. Used 215 times. It occurs also in 2:9, 10, 12, 14; 3:2, 11, 12; 5:9. The Greek is *gune* from which we get "gyne-cology". GK *1222*.
22. Elsewhere only in v 12; Act 22:2; 2 Thes 3:12. GK *2484*. Related to "quiet" in v 2; and " be quiet" in 1 Thes 4:11.
23. Same word as in 3:4; Gal 2:5. Elsewhere only as "obedience" in 2 Cor 9:13. GK *5717*. Related to "be subject" in Eph 5:21.
24. Or, "allow". Same word as in 1 Cor 14:34; and as Mt 8:21; 19:8; Jn 19:38; Act 21:40; 26:1; Heb 6:3. Used 18 times. GK *2205*.
25. Since women teach younger women (Tit 2:4) and prophesy (1 Cor 11:5), Paul cannot mean this absolutely. Some note "man" in the next phrase and think women are not to teach men. Others note the context and think women are not to teach in the public worship services. Just how far this exclusion might extend is debated. Others apply the underlying principle— women are not to teach outside the authority relationships God has created, meaning here the authority granted them by the elders. Others think the issue is similar to "veils" in 1 Cor 11:1-16; and the "kiss" in Rom 16:16. See also 1 Cor 14:34-35. On this word, see Rom 12:7.
26. Or, "domineer, play the master, lord it over, be ruler over, have power over, dictate to, give orders to". Used only here. GK *883*. The main idea is "to have independent rule over". The related noun means "master, ruler, autocrat, self-doer".
27. Or, "husband", translated based on the context. Used 216 times. It occurs also in 2:8; 3:2, 12; 5:9. GK *467*.
28. Or, "misled". Elsewhere only in Eph 5:6; Jam 1:26. GK *572*. Related to "deception" in 2 Pet 2:13. This is the word used by Eve in Gen 3:13.
29. Same word as "deceived" in 2 Cor 11:3, of Eve. It is a strengthened form of the word "deceived" just used, which some manuscripts have here {N}.
30. Or, "has come" into. GK *1181*.
31. Adam came-to-be in transgression by deliberate choice; Eve, by deception. On this word, see Rom 5:14.
32. That is, the woman referred to in verse 11. Others think Paul is referring to Eve, making this verse point 1F.
33. This word means "to save, preserve, keep safe". It is related to "savior" and "salvation". It must refer to spiritual salvation here because "continuing in faith" has no impact on physical preservation through childbearing. On this word, see Lk 19:10.
34. Or, "through *her* childbearing". Used only here. GK *5450*. The related verb is in 5:14. Women will be saved through Christ's birth if they (the women) continue. Though the woman is to be submissive, she is saved directly and independently through Christ, just like the man, Gal 3:26-29. Perhaps Paul refers to the Savior in this unusual way to emphasize the unique role wives played in the human descent of Jesus from Eve to Mary, as promised in Gen 3:15. Others think Paul means the woman will be saved through (meaning "while living in") her allotted sphere as childbearer, if they (the women) continue. Thus man will be saved in his "toil", woman in her "childbearing", Gen 3:16-17.
35. That is, the women, the class represented by "she" earlier in the verse. Some think Paul means the husband and wife of v 12-14. They will both be saved in the same way, if they continue.
36. Or, "remain, abide". On this word, see "abide" in Jn 15:4.
37. Or, "sanctification". On this word, see Heb 12:14.
38. Same word as "office" in Act 1:20. Elsewhere only as "visitation" in Lk 19:44; 1 Pet 2:12. GK *2175*. Related to "overseer" in v 2.
39. Or, "without blame, beyond criticism, unable to be laid hold of or attacked, irreproachable". Elsewhere only in 5:7; 6:14. GK *455*.
40. Or, "husband *of* one wife". See 2:11, 12 on these two words. This phrase also occurs in 3:12; Tit 1:6. See 5:9 for the reverse, "woman *of* one man". "Man *of* one woman" points to character. "Husband *of* one wife" points to marital status. One can meet one of these and fail the other. Paul is not referring to polygamy (5:9 would then refer to polyandry, which was not an issue). Some think Paul means elders must be married, and married only once. Since this would exclude

A. Heb 8:6   B. Mt 4:4, mankind   C. Act 4:33   D. 1 Tim 1:12   E. 2 Tim 1:11   F. 1 Cor 12:28   G. 1 Cor 12:28   H. 1 Tim 2:12   J. 2 Cor 11:20   K. Heb 7:26   L. Rev 16:19, wrath   M. 1 Pet 3:4, very precious   N. Mt 26:10   O. Phil 4:11   P. Rom 9:20   Q. 1 Tim 2:9   R. Col 1:2, faithful   S. 1 Tim 6:10   T. Gal 5:17   U. 1 Tim 5:10a   V. Phil 1:1   W. Mt 16:21

2D. Sober[1], sound-minded[2], respectable[3]
3D. Hospitable[A]
4D. Skillful-at-teaching[4]
5D. Not *a* drunken[5] *one*, not *a* brawler[6], but kind[B], non-quarrelsome[7] — 3
6D. Not-a-money-lover[8]
7D. Leading[9] *his* own household[C] well[10], having children[11] in submission[D], with all dignity[12] — 4

    1E. But if one does not know-*how*[E] to lead *his* own household, how will he take-care-of[13] *a* church *of* God? — 5

8D. Not *a* new-convert[14], in order that, he may not fall into *the* judgment[15] *of* the devil[F], having become conceited[16] — 6

2C. And *he* must[G] also have *a* good[H] testimony[J] from the *ones* outside,[17] in order that he may not fall into reproach[K], and *a* snare[L] *of* the devil — 7

5B. Deacons[M] similarly *must be* — 8

  1C. Honorable[18], not double-tongued[19], not paying-attention-to[20] much wine[N], not fond-of-shameful-gain[O], *holding[P] the mystery[Q] *of* the faith with *a* clean[R] conscience[S] — 9
  2C. And let these also first be tested[21], then let them be serving[22], being blameless[23] — 10
  3C. Women[24] *deacons* similarly *must be* honorable, not slanderous[25], sober[T], faithful[U] in all *things*[26] — 11
  4C. Let deacons be men *of* one woman, leading[V] *their* children and *their* own households well — 12
  5C. For the *ones* having served well obtain[27] *for* themselves *a* good[H] standing[28], and great confidence[29] in *their* faith in[30] Christ Jesus — 13

4A. I am writing these[31] *things to* you hoping[W] to come to you quickly[X], *but in-case I am slow[32] — 14-15

  1B. In order that you may know how *you* ought-to[33] conduct-*yourself*[34] in *the* household[35] *of* God— which is *the* church *of the* living God, *the* pillar[36] and support[37] *of* the truth[Y]

men who remained single or who remarried as Paul advised (1 Cor 7:7-8, 15, 39), others make exceptions for widowers, single men, men divorced before they were Christians, etc. Where to draw the line is debated. Others think Paul means "not divorced". Others think he means they must be sexually loyal to their wife, excluding men who sought sexual satisfaction from others, making this the only direct reference to sexual purity in the list. This was a major issue in the early church (Eph 5:3-8; 1 Cor 6:12-20; 1 Thes 4:3-6, etc.), and is so today.

1. Or, "Temperate". That is, "serious, sober in judgment", as the related verb is used in 1 Pet 1:13. Elsewhere only in 3:11; Tit 2:2. GK *3767*. The word also means physically sober, not drunk, which Paul addresses in v 3.
2. Or, "prudent, discreet, self-controlled, moderate, temperate". Elsewhere only in Tit 1:8; 2:2, 5. GK *5409*. Related to "sound-mindedness" in 2:9; "be sound-minded" in Rom 12:3; "sound-mind" in 2 Tim 1:7; "sound-mindedly" in Tit 2:12; and "train" (make sound-minded) in Tit 2:4.
3. Or, "honorable", or "well-ordered" (as this word is used in 2:9).
4. Elsewhere only in 2 Tim 2:24. GK *1434*. Related to "teacher". This is the only "ability" (or, "gift") in the list. Compare Tit 1:9.
5. Or, "one who is quarrelsome due to his wine". Elsewhere only in Tit 1:7. GK *4232*. Related Greek words mean "drunken violence or frolic", "to mistreat like a drunken man", "to play drunken tricks", "to behave badly due to wine". The elder must not be one with a reputation for drunken behavior and exhibitions.
6. Or, a "striker, bully, belligerent *one*"; figuratively, "quarrelsome, combative". Elsewhere only in Tit 1:7. GK *4438*. Related to "wound" in Rev 13:3; and "strike" in Rev 8:12. Some manuscripts add after this "not fond of shameful gain" {N}, the word in v 8.
7. Or, "disinclined to fight, not a fighter, peaceable". Elsewhere only in Tit 3:2. GK *285*.
8. Elsewhere only as "without love of money" in Heb 13:5. GK *921*. Related to "love of money" in 6:10.
9. Or, "Directing, Ruling, Managing". Same word as in v 5, 12; 5:17. On this word, see Rom 12:8.
10. Or, "commendably". Same word as in v 12, 13; 5:17. On this word, see Act 10:33.
11. Some think this implies that the elder must have children. Others think it applies only if he has children. On this word, see 1 Jn 3:1.
12. Or, "seriousness, respect-worthiness, reverence". Some think Paul means the elder must direct his house and children with all dignity. Others think he means the children must have the dignity or respectfulness. Same word as in 2:2. Elsewhere only in Tit 2:7. GK *4949*. Related to "honorable" in v 8. Note Tit 1:6 on the elder's children.
13. Elsewhere only in Lk 10:34, 35, of the good Samaritan. GK *2150*. Related to "care" in Act 27:3; and "carefully" in Lk 15:8. This word also means "to have charge of, to have the management of".
14. Or, "novice, newly planted *one*". The Greek word is *neophutos* from which we get "neophyte". Used only here. GK *3745*.
15. Some think Paul means "the kind of judgment made by the devil", that is, accusing the believers, a judgmental spirit. Others think he means "the condemnation pronounced by God upon the devil". On this word, see Jn 9:39.
16. Or, "clouded with pride". On this word, see 6:4.
17. That is, outside the church. Compare Col 4:5; 1 Thes 4:12.
18. Or, "Worthy of respect, Dignified, Noble". Elsewhere only in v 11; Tit 2:2; Phil 4:8. GK *4948*. Related to "dignity" in 1 Tim 3:4.
19. Or, "insincere". More literally, "double-worded", saying one thing and meaning another, or one thing to some and another to others. Used only here. GK *1474*.
20. Or, "giving heed to, devoting *themselves* to", and therefore "being addicted to". In Tit 2:3 Paul uses the word "enslaved" in this phrase. Same word as in 1:4; 4:1, 13; Tit 1:14; Act 8:6, 10, 11; 16:14; Heb 2:1; 2 Pet 1:19; and as "take heed to" in Lk 12:1; and "beware of" in Mt 10:17. Used 24 times. GK *4668*.
21. Or, "approved, approved by testing". On this word, see "approve" in Rom 12:2.
22. Or, "be serving as deacons, be deacons". Related to "deacon". Same word as in v 13. On this word, see "ministering" in 1 Pet 4:10.
23. Or, "unaccused". That is, "being [found] blameless". On this word see Tit 1:6.
24. Or, "Wives". On this word, see "woman" in 2:11. Some think Paul means "Women *deacons*"; others, "*Their* wives", the wives of the deacons. Compare Rom 16:1.
25. Same word as in 2 Tim 3:3; Tit 2:3. Elsewhere it is the word "devil" ("slanderer") 34 times, as in v 7. GK *1333*.
26. For example, the things listed in 5:10.
27. Or, "gain possession of, acquire, gain". Same word as in Act 20:28. Elsewhere only as "preserve" in Lk 17:33. GK *4347*. Related to "obtaining" in 1 Thes 5:9.
28. Or, "step, rank, grade, degree". Used only here. GK *957*. Some think Paul means before God; others, before people.
29. Or, "boldness". On this word, see Heb 4:16.
30. Or, "in *the* faith *which is* in".
31. That is, the following exhortations. This is the second part of Paul's "deposit" with Timothy, 1:18. Others think this looks back to 2:1-3:13, making this the conclusion of that section. In this case, the next main section begins in 4:1.
32. More literally, "if I should be slow, if I delay". That is, if for any reason Paul chooses to proceed slowly, to slow his travel. It is not passive ("am delayed"). Elsewhere only in 2 Pet 3:9. GK *1094*. Related to "slow" in Lk 24:25; Jam 1:19; and "slowness" in 2 Pet 3:9.
33. Or, "how *one* ought to conduct *oneself*". On this idiom, see Act 25:10.
34. Or, "live, behave". On this word, see Eph 2:3.
35. That is, in God's family— yourself, the old, the young, the widows, the elders, the slaves, the rich— the church. Or, in God's "house", the spiritual temple of which Christ is the cornerstone and high priest. On this word, see "house" in Mk 3:20.
36. Elsewhere only in Gal 2:9; Rev 3:12; 10:1. GK *5146*.
37. Or, "foundation, mainstay". Used only here. GK *1613*. Related to "steadfast" in Col 1:23. Some take these words with what follows, "The mystery *of* godliness is *the* pillar and support *of* the truth and confessedly great".

A. Tit 1:8 B. Phil 4:5, kindness C. Mk 3:20, house D. 1 Tim 2:11 E. 1 Jn 2:29, know F. Rev 12:9 G. Mt 16:21 H. 1 Tim 5:10a J. Jn 1:7 K. Heb 10:33 L. Rom 11:9 M. Phil 1:1 N. 1 Tim 5:23 O. Tit 1:7 P. 1 Jn 1:8, have Q. Rom 11:25 R. Tit 1:15 S. Act 23:1 T. 1 Tim 3:2 U. Col 1:2 V. 1 Tim 3:4 W. Jn 5:45, put hope X. Rev 1:1 Y. Jn 4:23

2B. And the mystery^A *of* godliness¹ is confessedly² great— 16

    1C. Who³

        1D. Was revealed⁴ in *the* flesh^B, was declared-righteous⁵ in *the* spirit⁶
        2D. Was seen⁷ *by* messengers⁸, was proclaimed^C among *the* nations⁹
        3D. Was believed^D in *the* world, was taken-up¹⁰ in glory^E

    2C. But the Spirit explicitly says that in later times, some will depart¹¹ *from* the faith, paying-attention-to^F deceitful¹² spirits and teachings *of* demons^G 4:1

        1D. By means of *the* hypocrisy^H *of* liars¹³ having been seared¹⁴ *as to their* own conscience^J— 2

            1E. Forbidding^K to marry^L 3
            2E. *Commanding* to abstain^M *from* foods^N which God created^O for *a* receiving¹⁵ with thanksgiving¹⁶ *by* the *ones who are* believers¹⁷ and¹⁸ know¹⁹ the truth

                1F. Because every creature^P *of* God *is* good^Q 4
                2F. And nothing being received^R with thanksgiving *is to be* rejected²⁰, for it is sanctified²¹ by *the* word^S *of* God and prayer²² 5

    3C. While pointing-out^T these²³ *things* to the brothers^U, you will be *a* good^Q servant²⁴ *of* Christ Jesus²⁵, while being nourished²⁶ *in* the words^S *of* the faith^V and the good^Q teaching^W which you have closely-followed^X. But be declining²⁷ the profane²⁸ and old-womanish²⁹ myths^Y 6 / 7

3B. But be training³⁰ yourself for godliness^Z

    1C. For bodily³¹ training³² is profitable^AA for *a* little³³, but godliness is profitable for all *things*— having promise *for* the present life and the *one* coming. The saying *is* trustworthy and worthy *of* full^BB acceptance 8 / 9

        1D. For we are laboring^CC and struggling³⁴ for this,³⁵ because we have put *our* hope^DD upon *the* living God, Who is *the* Savior^EE *of* all people^FF— especially *of* believers³⁶ 10
        2D. Be commanding^GG and teaching^HH these *things* 11

1. Having mentioned the "truth", Paul now reflects on this truth and Timothy's responsibility to it. On this word, see 2:2.
2. Or, "undeniably, indisputably, by common confession". This adverb is used only here. GK *3935*. Related to "confess" in 6:12.
3. That is, Christ. Some manuscripts say "Which" (referring to "mystery"); others, "God" {A}.
4. Or, "Appeared, Was made known, Was made visible". On this word, see "made evident" in 1 Jn 2:19.
5. Or, "vindicated, proved righteous". On this word, see Rom 3:24. We are "declared righteous" by grace. Jesus received this verdict because He was in fact perfect.
6. Some think Paul means "in *His human* spirit", as a man; others, "by *the Holy* Spirit"; others, "in *His divine* spirit", as the God-man. In any case, this is the divine verdict on Christ's life, on the person who "was revealed in the flesh". He is internally righteous and perfect, not merely externally (as the Pharisees conceived of it, Phil 3:6)
7. Or, "appeared *to*", as this word is used in 1 Cor 15:5-8. Some think Paul means "during His whole life"; others, "after His resurrection"; others, "in heaven after His ascension". On this word, see "see" in Lk 2:26.
8. Or, "angels". That is, by the apostles and others who then proclaimed Him. This word is rendered "messenger" in Mt 11:10; Mk 1:2; Lk 7:24, 27; 9:52; 2 Cor 12:7; Jam 2:25. It is indeed a great mystery that God chose to reveal Himself in such a way. Note Act 10:41; 13:31. Or, "angels", as in its other 168 uses. GK *34*. In this case, some think Paul means that the Word was seen by angels in human form, but by contrast, His message of salvation was proclaimed to humans by human witnesses. Others arrange the six statements in groups of three, so that Jesus was seen by angels in heaven after His ascension, as the climax of the first group of three. There are other views of the connection with "angels". Note that most render this "angels".
9. Or, "Gentiles". This is one of the two parts of Paul's message in Act 26:23, and the commission in Lk 24:47. On this word, see "Gentiles" in Act 15:23.
10. Same word as in Mk 16:19 and Act 1:2, 11, 22, when Jesus ascended.
11. Or, "withdraw". The root words mean "to stand away from". The context can give it a more negative meaning, "desert, revolt, apostatize", as here. Same word as in Lk 2:37; 4:13; 8:13; 13:27; Act 12:10; 19:9; 2 Cor 12:8; 2 Tim 2:19; Heb 3:12. Elsewhere only as "withdraw" in Act 15:38; 22:29; and "draw away" in Act 5:37, 38. GK *923*. Related to "apostasy" in 2 Thes 2:3.
12. Or, "deceiving". Elsewhere only as "deceiver" in Mt 27:63; 2 Cor 6:8; 2 Jn 7. GK *4418*. Related to "error" in 1 Thes 2:3.
13. Or, "false speakers". People will pay attention to spirits and teachings of demons which are proclaimed to them by means of human liars. Used only here. GK *6016*.
14. Or, "branded with a red hot iron", from the word for "branding iron". Used only here. GK *3013*.
15. Or, "sharing". Used only here. GK *3562*. Related to "share-in" in Heb 12:10.
16. Or, "gratitude, thankfulness". Used 15 times. GK *2374*. Related to "give thanks" in Mt 26:27.
17. Or, "believing". On this adjective, see "faithful" in Col 1:2.
18. The grammar is unusual, and elsewhere only in 5:5; Tit 1:15; and Jn 10:12. Paul combines an adjective and a participle in a twofold description of a single group of people. Literally, "*by* the believers and *ones who* know (or, "*ones having known*") the truth", two descriptions of a Christian. Here it is simplified in English to avoid giving the false impression that Paul is speaking of two different groups. Others simplify this further to "the ones who believe and know".
19. Or, "understand, acknowledge". The grammar of this participle means "having come to know in the past, and continuing to know". Rendered "know", the emphasis is on the continuing state of knowing, corresponding to "believers". Rendered "and *ones* having known the truth", the emphasis is on the completed action in past time, in contrast to these false teachers. On this word, see "understood" in Col 1:6.
20. Or, "thrown off, thrown away", as worthless. Used only here. GK *612*. Related to "throw away" in Heb 10:35; and "rejection" in Rom 11:15.
21. Or, "made holy, consecrated". On this word, see Heb 10:29.
22. Or, "intercession" (as in 2:1). Rather than any food making a believer unholy, it is the believer who makes the food holy. Anything one can thank God for is permissible to eat.
23. That is, 3:16-4:5, regarding truth, those deceiving others to depart from it, and correcting their false teachings.
24. Or, "minister". On this word, see 1 Cor 3:5.
25. Some manuscripts say "Jesus Christ" {K}.
26. Or, "brought up, nurtured, reared, trained". As Timothy is teaching things like 3:16-4:5, the true and false about Christ, these words will serve his hearers and nourish Timothy himself. Used only here. GK *1957*. Related to "feed" in Lk 23:29.
27. Or, "refusing". Same word as in 5:11; Tit 3:10. On this word, see "refuse" in Heb 12:25.
28. Used in two other commands like this one, 1 Tim 6:20; 2 Tim 2:16. On this word, see 1 Tim 1:9.
29. That is, belonging to or characteristic of old women. Used only here. GK *1212*. The root word is "old woman".
30. Or, "exercising". On this word, see Heb 5:14. Related to "training" in v 8.
31. That is, pertaining to the body. On this word, see Lk 3:22.
32. Some think Paul means physical training, gymnastic training. Others think he means "Christian asceticism". Used only here. GK *1215*. Related to the word in Heb 5:14.
33. Paul may mean "to a small degree"; or, "for a little while". On this word, see "small" in Act 12:18.
34. Or, "competing, fighting, striving". Same word as in Col 1:29; 4:12. Elsewhere only as "strive" in Lk 13:24; "fight" in Jn 18:36; 1 Tim 6:12; 2 Tim 4:7; and "compete" in 1 Cor 9:25. GK *76*. It is an athletic term, used in "run, train, exercise" in v 7, 8. Related to the noun "race" in Heb 12:1; "struggle with" in Rom 15:30; "contend" in Jude 3; and "agony" in Lk 22:44. Some manuscripts say "suffering reproach" instead of "struggling" {C}.
35. That is, to experience God's promise for this life and the one coming.
36. What God did for the world (2 Cor 5:19), is effective only for those who believe (Jn 1:11-12, 3:16).

A. Rom 11:25 B. Col 2:23 C. 2 Tim 4:2 D. Jn 3:36 E. 2 Pet 2:10 F. 1 Tim 3:8 G. 1 Cor 10:20 H. Gal 2:13 J. Act 23:1 K. 1 Cor 14:39 L. 1 Cor 7:9 M. 1 Thes 4:3 N. Mk 7:19 O. Eph 2:15 P. Rom 8:39, creation Q. 1 Tim 5:10a R. Rom 7:8, taken S. 1 Cor 12:8 T. Rom 16:4, risked U. Act 16:40 V. Eph 2:8 W. 1 Tim 5:17 X. Mk 16:17, accompany Y. 1 Tim 1:4 Z. 1 Tim 2:2 AA. 2 Tim 3:16 BB. 1 Tim 1:15 CC. Mt 11:28, being weary DD. Jn 5:45, put hope EE. Lk 1:47 FF. Mt 4:4, mankind GG. 1 Tim 1:3 HH. Rom 12:7

2C. Let no one be-looking-down-on[1] your youth,[2] but be[A] a pattern[B] *for* the believers in speech[C], in conduct[D], in love[3], in faith[E], in purity	12
3C. Until I come,[4] be paying-attention-to[F] the reading[5], the exhortation[G], the teaching[H]	13
1D. Do not be careless[6] of the gift[J] in you,[7] which was given *to* you through[8] a prophecy[K], with[9] *the* laying-on[10] *of* the hands *of* the council-of-elders[11]	14
2D. Be taking-care-with[12] these *things,* be[13] in these *things,* in order that your progress[L] may be evident[M] to everyone	15
3D. Be fixing-*your*-attention-on[14] yourself and *your* teaching[H]. Be continuing[N] *in* them. For while doing this, you will save[O] both yourself and the *ones* hearing you	16
4B. Do not sharply-rebuke[15] *an* older[16] *man,* but be appealing-to[17] *him* as *a* father	5:1
1C. Younger *men* as brothers	
2C. Older *women* as mothers	2
3C. Younger *women* as sisters in all purity	
5B. Be honoring[18] widows[19]— the real[20] widows	3
1C. Now if any widow has children or grandchildren, let them first learn[P] to reverence[21] *their* own household[Q], and to give-back[R] *a* return[22] *to their* ancestors[23]. For this is acceptable[24] in the sight of God	4
1D. But the *one who is a* real widow and[25] has been left-alone[26] has put *her* hope[S] upon God,[27] and continues-in[T] petitions[U] and prayers *by* night and *by* day	5
1E. But the *one* living-indulgently[28] is-dead while living	6
2D. And be commanding[V] these[29] *things* in order that they may be above-reproach[W]	7
3D. But if anyone does not provide-for[30] *his* own *relatives,* and especially family-members[31], he has denied[X] the faith[Y], and he is worse *than an* unbeliever[32]	8
2C. Let *a* widow be put-on-the-list[33]	9
1D. Having become not fewer *than* sixty years *old*	
2D. *A* woman *of* one man[34]	
3D. Being attested[35] by good[36] works[37]—	10
1E. If she brought-up-children	
2E. If she received-strangers[38]	
3E. If she washed *the* feet *of* saints[39]	
4E. If she aided[Z] *ones* being afflicted[AA]	
5E. If she followed-after[BB] every good[40] work	

1. Or, "treating with contempt". On this word, see "disregard" in Rom 2:4.
2. Timothy was 28-32 years old at this time. Train yourself to be a pattern for others, so that such "looking down on you" does not become the characteristic way you are viewed.
3. Some manuscripts say "in love, in spirit, in faith" {N}.
4. Or, "While I am coming".
5. The context implies the public reading of Scripture, and Timothy's exhortation and teaching from it. Elsewhere only in Act 13:15; 2 Cor 3:14. GK *342*.
6. Or, "neglect, be unconcerned about". On this word, see "neglect" in Heb 2:3.
7. Paul says this again in 2 Tim 1:6, in different words. He may be referring to Timothy's gift of evangelist (2 Tim 4:5), or to his sphere of ministry.
8. Or, "by". GK *1328*.
9. Or, "along with". GK *3552*.
10. On laying on of hands, see Heb 6:2. On the prophecy, compare 1:18. Timothy's gift and ministry were given to him by means of a prophecy made about him, along with the blessing of the council of elders.
11. Elsewhere only of Israel's council of elders in Lk 22:66; Act 22:5. GK *4564*.
12. Or, "practicing, thinking about, meditating on". Used of "practicing" with a bow. Elsewhere only in a negative sense, "plot" in Act 4:25. GK *3509*. The root word means "care, concern". The word in v 14 is the same root word with a negative prefix, "to not take care, be careless".
13. This is the simple verb "to be", perhaps implying here, "be spending your time in these things". GK *1639*.
14. Or, "holding attention on, focusing attention on, paying attention to". Same word as in Lk 14:7 Act 3:5. Elsewhere only as "hold on" (stay) in Act 19:22; and "hold out" in Phil 2:16. GK *2091*. The root word is "to hold".
15. Or, "severely rebuke". Used only here. GK *2159*. The root word is "strike" (GK *4448*).
16. Elsewhere in this sense only in 5:2; Lk 15:25; Jn 8:9; Act 2:17; and possibly 1 Pet 5:5; 2 Jn 1; 3 Jn 1. It usually means "elder". On this word, see "elder" in 1 Tim 5:17.
17. Or, "urging". On this word, see "exhorting" in Rom 12:8.
18. All widows deserve honor, but "real widows" are singled out for special honor, shown by what follows in v 4-8 and v 16 to be referring to financial aid or support by the church. Same word as in Mk 7:6; Jn 5:23; Eph 6:2; 1 Pet 2:17; and as "priced" in Mt 27:9. Used 21 times. GK *5506*. Related to "honor" in 1 Tim 5:17, and "precious" in 2 Pet 1:4.
19. Used 26 times. GK *5939*.
20. Same word as in 5:5, 16; 6:19. On this word, see "really" in Jn 8:36. That is, widows dependent on God alone, in contrast with widows who have relatives, are of marriageable age, or whose character and deeds have not demonstrated a dependence on God and His family members.
21. Or, "show devotion, respect, godliness". Elsewhere only as "worship" in Act 17:23. GK *2355*. Related to "godliness" in 2:2. The children should show piety toward the widow in their household by supporting her.
22. Or, "recompense, repayment". Used only here. GK *304*.
23. In this context, Paul means their living mother or grandmother. Elsewhere only in 2 Tim 1:3. GK *4591*.
24. Or, "pleasing". On this word, see 2:3. Some manuscripts say "good and acceptable" {N}.
25. Same unusual grammar as in 4:3, joining an adjective and a participle in a twofold description of this woman. Literally, "the real widow and *one* having been left alone". Here, the second phrase explains what Paul means by "real" from the church's perspective. She is left alone in two senses— by husband, and by relatives.
26. Or, "made alone". Used only here. GK *3670*. This is a participle, literally, "having been left alone".
27. And therefore she deserves the loving assistance of God's family.
28. Or, "living for pleasure, living riotously". Elsewhere only in Jam 5:5. GK *5059*. This widow is physically alive, but spiritually dead.
29. Some think this refers only to v 5-6, so that "they" next refers to the widows, making this point 2E. Others think Paul is referring to v 3-6, the duties of children and widows in the church.
30. Or, "think of beforehand, have regard for". Planning is included. On this word, see 2 Cor 8:21.
31. Or, "kinsmen, relatives". On this word see Gal 6:10.
32. That is, because an unbeliever makes no claim to godliness, or to being a child of the God who is love.
33. Or, "enrolled, enlisted". Used only here. GK *2899*. The historical detail behind this is uncertain. Some think this refers to a list of widows financially supported by the church. Thus, these are the requirements to be supported, expanding on v 5. Others think this refers to a list of official widow-deaconesses serving the church. Thus all "real" widows in the church should be honored as charity, v 3-8. Widows "on the list" then have these further qualifications because they are servants of the church, v 9-15.
34. Or, "wife *of* one husband" This is the same phrase as in 3:2 except for the reversal of gender. The same question must be faced as in 3:2. If Paul means married only once, then the very widows who follow his command to remarry in v 14 would thereby exclude themselves later in life.
35. Or, "borne witness". On this word, see Act 6:3.
36. This word means "good" in the sense of outwardly good, beautiful, fine, commendable, praiseworthy, pleasing. Same word as in Mt 7:17; 13:8; Mk 9:50; Jn 10:32; Rom 7:18; 1 Cor 7:26; 1 Tim 2:3; 3:1, 7, 13; 6:12; Tit 3:14; "beautiful" stones in Lk 21:5; "fine" pearls in Mt 13:45; "commendable" in Gal 4:18. Used 100 times. GK *2819*.
37. What follows are examples of good works, of sources to attest the widow's character, not a list of qualifications. For example, Paul probably does not mean to exclude childless widows. But if she had children, they could attest to her character.
38. Or, "showed hospitality to strangers, welcomed strangers". Used only here. GK *3827*. Made of two words, "to receive, accept" and "strangers". Note Mt 25:35, "I was a stranger and you invited me in". Related to "lodge" in Act 10:6; and "reception" in Lk 5:29.
39. Footwashing was an act of hospitality in ancient culture, normally performed by the servants. Jesus did this in Jn 13:3-17.
40. This word means "good" in the sense of meeting a high standard of worth or value; possessing intrinsic goodness; useful, beneficial; inner goodness; morally right. Same word as in Mt 5:45; 7:17;

A. Rev 2:10 B. 1 Pet 5:3 C. 1 Cor 12:8, word D. 1 Pet 1:15 E. Eph 2:8 F. 1 Tim 3:8 G. Act 4:36, encouragement H. 1 Tim 5:17 J. 1 Cor 1:7
K. 1 Cor 12:10 L. Phil 1:12, advancement M. Rom 1:19 N. Rom 11:22 O. Lk 19:10 P. Phil 4:11 Q. Mk 3:20, house R. Mt 16:27, render
S. Jn 5:45, put hope T. Act 11:23 U. 1 Tim 2:1 V. 1 Tim 1:3 W. 1 Tim 3:2 X. 2 Tim 2:12 Y. Eph 2:8 Z. 1 Tim 5:16 AA. 2 Cor 4:8 BB. Mk 16:20

3C. But be declining[1] younger[2] widows — 11

    1D. For when they grow-sensual[3] *against* Christ, they want to marry—*having condemnation[4] [upon themselves] because[5] they set-aside[6] *their* first pledge[7] — 12

    2D. And at the same time also they are learning[A] *to be* idle[8], while going-around[9] the houses — 13

    3D. And not only idle, but also babblers[10] and busybodies[11]— speaking the *things* not being proper[12]

    4D. Therefore, I want[B] younger *widows* — 14

        1E. To marry
        2E. To bear-children
        3E. To manage-the-house[13]
        4E. To give *to the one* opposing[C] no opportunity[14] for the sake of reviling[15]
        5E. For some already turned-aside[D] after[16] Satan — 15

    4C. If any believing-*woman*[17] has widows,[18] let her be aiding[19] them, and let the church not be burdened[E], in order that it may aid the real widows — 16

6B. Let the elders[20] having led[21] well[22] be considered-worthy[F] *of* double[23] honor[24] — 17

    1C. Especially[25] the *ones* laboring[G] in word[H] and teaching[26]

        1D. For the Scripture[J] says [in Deut 25:4]— "You shall not muzzle[K] *a* threshing ox" — 18
        2D. And "The worker[27] *is* worthy[L] *of* his wages[28]"

    2C. Do not be accepting[M] *an* accusation[N] against *an* elder unless[29] on the basis of two or three witnesses[30] — 19

        1D. Be rebuking[31] the *ones* sinning[32] in the presence of all,[33] in order that the rest[O] also may have fear[P] — 20

    3C. I solemnly-charge[34] *you* in the sight of God and Christ Jesus[35] and the chosen[Q] angels— that you keep[R] these[36] *things* without pre-judgment[37], doing nothing according-to[38] partiality[39] — 21

1. Or, "refusing". Same word as in 4:7. Paul probably means "decline to put them on the list", not "decline to honor them". A young "real" widow with several young children would be among the most needy of the church, 1 Jn 3:17.
2. Some take this to mean "younger than sixty", v 9. Others think Paul means "young widows" such as would bear children, v 14.
3. That is, they desire the pleasures of marriage, material and sexual. Young widows desire children and a home of their own. This desire leads them into pursuing marriage rather than the service to which they pledged themselves. Used only here. GK *2952*. Related to "luxury" in Rev 18:3; and "live luxuriously" in Rev 18:7, 9. In Revelation, it is sinful sensuality/luxury versus the commands of God; here, it is a normal desire for marriage versus their pledge to serve Christ as a widow.
4. Or, "judgment [against them]". Paul could mean condemnation by God; by others; by herself; or all of these. Same word as "judgment" in 1 Cor 11:29; Gal 5:10, on which see Jn 9:39.
5. Or, "that", "having *the* condemnation that they set aside *their* first pledge".
6. Or, "nullified, invalidated, rejected". On this word, see Gal 2:21.
7. Or, "faith, conviction". That is, such widows fall under incrimination for leaving their work of faith, for setting aside their former pledge to serve Christ in this way. On this word, see "faith" in Eph 2:8.
8. Or, "lazy, unproductive". On this word, see "useless" in Jam 2:20.
9. Or, "wandering around". These women are going, but doing nothing. Elsewhere only in Act 19:13; Heb 11:37. GK *4320*.
10. Or, "silly, trifling, nonsense talkers; prattlers". Used only here. GK *5827*. Related to "talking nonsense" in 3 Jn 10.
11. GK *4319*. Related to the word in 2 Thes 3:11.
12. More literally, "not being necessary", based on what is fitting or proper. On this idiom, see "ought to" in Act 25:10.
13. Or, "be master of the house". Used only here. GK *3866*. Related to "house-master" in Mt 20:1; and "master" in Jude 4.
14. Or, "occasion, base of operations". On this word, see Rom 7:8.
15. Or, "insult, abuse". That is, of the church, or of the Lord. On this word, see 1 Pet 3:9
16. Or, "behind". That is, "[to follow] after". GK *3958*.
17. Some manuscripts say " believing-*man* or believing-*woman*" {B}.
18. Some think Paul means "[younger] widows" in need of support. Others think he means "[non-family] widows" in her household, such as servants or friends. Others think he means "[family-member] widows", repeating v 8 explicitly for this case.
19. Or, "helping, assisting, supplying". Used twice in this verse and elsewhere only in v 10. GK *2064*.
20. That is, the church leaders with leadership responsibility, especially teaching. Called "overseers" in 3:2. "Elders" is used of the Jewish leaders 30 times; of the church leaders in Act 11:30; 14:23; 15:2, 4, 6, 22, 23; 16:4; 20:17; 21:18; 1 Tim 5:17, 19; Tit 1:5; Jam 5:14; 1 Pet 5:1; and possibly 1 Pet 5:5; 2 Jn 1; 3 Jn 1; twelve times of the 24 elders in Revelation; five times meaning "older" (see 1 Tim 5:1); and once meaning "Old Testament saints" in Heb 11:2. GK *4565*. Related to "council of elders" in 1 Tim 4:14. See also "overseer" in Phil 1:1.
21. Or, "directed, ruled, been at the head". Same word as in 3:4, 5, 12. On this word, see Rom 12:8.
22. Or, "commendably". That is, measured by God-blessed results and effectiveness, not good intentions. Same word as in 3:4.
23. Or, "twofold, twice as much". Elsewhere only in Mt 23:15; Rev 18:6. GK *1487*. Some think Paul means twice as much as someone else, perhaps widows, deacons, other elders, or the average congregation member. Others think he means the honor of financial support in addition to the respect due this man as an elder. Enable such an elder to serve more, perhaps full time, in view of his proven performance and God's blessing on his ministry.
24. Or, "esteem, value, price, honorarium". All elders are honored as such, based on their position. Some are worthy of additional honor based on their good performance in the task of "ruling". What is this honor? Compensation or double the esteem? The word "honor" can mean either. It means "price" in Mt 27:6; 1 Cor 6:20; 7:23; "value" in Col 2:23; and "honor" in 1 Tim 6:1; Heb 3:3. Used 41 times. GK *5507*. The related verb is used in 5:3 referring to the financial support of widows. Since Paul's justification for this in v 18 concerns the payment of wages, the second or double honor in his mind seems to be financial support from the church.
25. The ability to teach is a qualification to be an elder (3:2; Tit 1:9), so all elders teach and lead in varying degrees. But the elders excelling ("leading well") in word and teaching are "especially" worthy of double honor, as compared with elders excelling in other forms of leadership and oversight.
26. Paul could mean "*the* Word and teaching", or, "speech and teaching". The word "teaching" usually means "that which is taught, doctrine" as in 1:10; 4:1, 6; Eph 4:14; 2 Tim 4:3; but also means "the act of teaching", as in 4:13. Same word as in Mt 15:9; Mk 7:7; Rom 12:7; Col 2:22; 1 Tim 4:16; 6:1, 3; 2 Tim 3:10, 16; Tit 1:9; 2:1, 7, 10. Elsewhere only as "instruction" in Rom 15:4. GK *1436*. Related to "teacher".
27. Same word as in 2 Tim 2:15, where Paul also refers to laboring in the "Word of truth". Used 16 times. GK *2239*. Related to "work" in Mt 26:10.
28. Paul is quoting Jesus (Lk 10:7).
29. Literally "except unless", meaning "with this exception, unless...". On this idiom, see 1 Cor 14:5.
30. Compare Mt 18:15-17. This is based on Deut 19:15.
31. Or, "exposing, convicting". On this word, see "expose" in Eph 5:11.
32. That is, the elders shown to be sinning based on the process in v 19.
33. Some think Paul means all the other elders; others, the whole church.
34. Same word as in 2 Tim 4:1. That is, testify in the form of a command. Elsewhere only as "solemnly-testify" in Act 2:40; 8:25; 18:5; 20:21, 24; 23:11; 28:23; Heb 2:6; and "solemnly-warn" in Lk 16:28; Act 10:42; 20:23; 1 Thes 4:6; 2 Tim 2:14. GK *1371*. Related to "testify" in Jn 1:7; and in 1 Thes 2:12.
35. Some manuscripts say "the Lord Jesus Christ" {N}.
36. Some think Paul means these matters of pay and discipline, v 17-20; others, strictly the matters about discipline (v 19-20), making this point 2D.
37. Or, "judgment beforehand, advance judgment". Used only here. GK *4622*. Do not begin with the answer.
38. Or, "based on, by way of ". GK *2848*.
39. Or, "bias, partisanship, inclination (toward someone)". Used only here. GK *4680*. Related to "join up" in Act 5:36.

A. Phil 4:11 B. Jam 1:18, willed C. Phil 1:28 D. 1 Tim 1:6 E. 2 Cor 1:8 F. 2 Thes 1:11 G. Mt 11:28, being weary H. 1 Cor 12:8 J. 2 Pet 3:16 K. Mk 4:39, silenced L. Rev 16:6 M. Mk 4:20 N. Tit 1:6 O. 2 Pet 3:16, other P. Eph 5:21 Q. Rom 8:33 R. Jn 12:25

4C. Be laying hands¹ on no one hastily², nor sharing^A *in the* sins belonging-to-others³	22
1D. Be keeping^B yourself pure⁴	
1E. No longer be-a-water-drinker⁵, but be using^C *a* little wine⁶ for the sake of *your* stomach and your frequent^D sicknesses⁷	23
2D. The sins *of* some people are clear-beforehand⁸, going ahead-of^E *them* to judgment,⁹ but indeed *for* some they follow-after^F	24
3D. Similarly also the good^G works *are* clear-beforehand, and the *ones* having *it* otherwise¹⁰ are not able to be hidden¹¹	25
7B. Let all-who are under *a* yoke^H *as* slaves^J be regarding^K *their* own masters¹² *as* worthy^L *of* all honor^M, in order that the name *of* God and the teaching^N may not be blasphemed¹³	6:1
1C. And let the *ones* having believing^O masters not be disregarding^P *them* because they are brothers^Q, but let them be serving^R *them* more¹⁴, because the *ones* being helped¹⁵ *by* the good-work¹⁶ are believers^O and beloved^S *ones*	2
5A. Be teaching^T and exhorting^U these *things*	
1B. If anyone teaches-different-*doctrines*^V, and does not come-to¹⁷ healthy¹⁸ words— the *ones of* our Lord Jesus Christ— and *to* the teaching^W in accordance with godliness^X, ˚he has become conceited¹⁹, understanding^Y nothing, but being diseased²⁰ with respect to controversies²¹ and word-battles²²	3 4
1C. Out of which comes envy^Z, strife^AA, blasphemies²³, evil^BB suspicions, ˚constant-frictions²⁴ *from* people²⁵ having been corrupted^CC *as to* the mind^DD, and having been robbed²⁶ *of* the truth while supposing^EE *that* godliness^X is *a* means-of-gain²⁷	5
1D. Now godliness^X with contentment²⁸ **is** *a* means of great gain	6
1E. For we brought-in nothing to the world	7
2E. *It is* clear²⁹ that neither can we bring-out³⁰ anything	
3E. But having sustenance³¹ and coverings³², *with* these *things* we shall be content³³	8
2D. But the *ones* wanting^FF to be-rich^GG fall into temptation^HH, and *a* snare³⁴, and many foolish^JJ and harmful desires^KK which plunge³⁵ people into ruin^LL and destruction^MM	9
1E. For the love-of-money³⁶ is *a* root³⁷ *of* all evils³⁸— aspiring-to³⁹ which, some were led-astray⁴⁰ from the faith, and pierced themselves *with* many pains⁴¹	10
2B. But **you,** O man *of* God, be fleeing^NN these⁴² *things,* and be pursuing^OO righteousness^PP, godliness^X, faith, love, endurance^QQ, gentleness	11

1. On this concept, see Heb 6:2. Some think this refers strictly to the commissioning of new elders; others, to any new "leaders"; others, strictly to the restoring of elders who repented from sin, v 20.
2. Or, "quickly". On this word, see "quickly" in Gal 1:6.
3. If Timothy appoints a man unqualified by sin or restores one too quickly, he shares in his sin as an elder. On this word, see "foreigners" in Heb 11:34.
4. That is, from the sins of others. On this word, see 1 Pet 3:2.
5. That is, one who exclusively drinks water. Used only here. GK *5621*. The grammar implies "stop being a water drinker". Some think this is strictly a personal remark for Timothy, brought to Paul's mind by his exhortation to purity. Others think Paul includes this personal remark also to make clear that he is not referring to any kind of ascetic abstinence when he says "keep yourself pure".
6. That is, fermented grape juice. There is another word for unfermented grape juice (not used in the NT), but the word here can be used in this sense when "new" is added (as in Mt 9:17). Same word as in Lk 1:15; 10:34; Jn 2:10; Rom 14:21; Eph 5:18; 1 Tim 3:8. Used 34 times. GK *3885*. Related to "drunkenness" in 1 Pet 4:3.
7. Or, "weaknesses, ailments". On this word, see "weakness" in Mt 8:17.
8. Or, "known beforehand", or simply "clear, evident, obvious". Same word as in v 25. Elsewhere only as "clear" in Heb 7:14. GK *4593*.
9. The sins of these people are known by others, and are already awaiting them at judgment. Others' sins will not be known until that judgment. This is certainly true of God's future judgment. In this context, some think Paul means "your judgment", regarding their qualifications for laying on of hands, v 22. Act on what is known. For some, their sins are not discovered until later— whether after their appointment, or at the judgment seat, 1 Cor 4:5.
10. That is, not clear beforehand. The good deeds of a person are also obvious to all, and those not obvious cannot remain hidden upon examination. Good character is verifiable. Make your decision based on openly known character, good and bad, specifically looking also for good works not openly known. Used only here. GK *261*.
11. Or, "kept secret". On this word, see Jn 8:59.
12. On this word, used also in v 2, see Jude 4.
13. Or, "slandered, insulted, spoken against", with reference to people, angels or God. Elsewhere only in Mt 9:3; 26:65; 27:39; Mk 2:7; 3:28, 29; 15:29; Lk 12:10; 22:65; 23:39; Jn 10:36; Act 13:45; 18:6; 19:37; 26:11; Rom 2:24; 3:8; 14:16; 1 Cor 10:30; 1 Tim 1:20; Tit 2:5; 3:2; Jam 2:7; 1 Pet 4:4; 2 Pet 2:2, 10, 12; Jude 8, 10; Rev 13:6; 16:9, 11, 21. GK *1059*. Related word in 6:4, and in 1:13.
14. Or, "but rather let them be serving *them*, because".
15. Or, "benefitting, receiving benefit". Elsewhere only in Lk 1:54; Act 20:35. GK *514*. Related to "helps" in 1 Cor 12:28.
16. Or, "good-service". Elsewhere only as "good deed" in Act 4:9. GK *2307*. The root word is "work". Related to "doing good" in Act 10:38.
17. That is, in the sense of "agree with, come to agreement with, approach consensus with". Used only here in this sense. On this word, see "approach" in Heb 10:22.
18. This is a participle, "words being healthy". On this word, see 1:10.
19. Or, "clouded with pride". Such a person has elevated himself above this godly teaching instead of submitting himself to it. Same word as in 3:6. Elsewhere only in 2 Tim 3:4. GK *5605*. Physically, this word means "shrouded in smoke".
20. Or, "sick, ailing". Used only here. GK *3796*. Related to "disease" in Mt 8:17.
21. Same word as in 2 Tim 2:23; Tit 3:9. Elsewhere only as "debate" in Jn 3:25; Act 15:2, 7; and "investigation" in Act 25:20. GK *2428*. Related to "speculations" in 1:4; "debater" in 1 Cor 1:20; and "issue" (controversial question) in Act 15:2.
22. Used only here. GK *3363*. Related word in 2 Tim 2:14.
23. That is, "evil-speaking, slander, insult" against God or others. Elsewhere only in Mt 12:31; 15:19; 26:65; Mk 3:28; 7:22; 14:64; Lk 5:21; Jn 10:33; Eph 4:31; Col 3:8; Jude 9; Rev 2:9; 13:1, 5, 6; 17:3. GK *1060*. Related words in 1:13; 6:1.
24. Or, "constant-wranglings". Used only here. GK *1384*. Some manuscripts say "useless wranglings" {K}.
25. The rest of this verse refers to "people", on which see "mankind" in Mt 4:4.
26. Or, "deprived". On this word, see "defrauded" in 1 Cor 6:7.
27. Such people pursue these matters for personal gain. They seek to establish and enhance themselves by promoting a "new" teaching. Elsewhere only in v 6. GK *4516*. Some manuscripts add after this "from such *things* withdraw yourself" {A}.
28. Or, "sufficiency, enough-ness". On this word, see "sufficiency" in 2 Cor 9:8. Related to "content" in Phil 4:11.
29. Or, "Because neither can we bring out anything". Some manuscripts include this word, saying "*It is* clear that..."; others say, "*It is* true that..." {A}. Consult the commentaries for other views.
30. Paul uses the same root word with two different prefixes— "bring in" and "bring out"; "carry in, carry out". GK *1662, 1766*.
31. Or, "foods, means of subsistence". This word is plural. Used only here. GK *1418*. Related to "food" in Mt 24:45.
32. This word is used of both clothing and shelter. Some think it refers only to clothing here. Used only here. GK *5004*.
33. Or, "satisfied". On this word, see "sufficient" in 2 Cor 12:9. Related to "contentment" in v 6.
34. Same word as in 3:7. On this word, see Rom 11:9.
35. Elsewhere only as "sink" in Lk 5:7. GK *1112*.
36. Used only here. GK *5794*. Related to "money-lovers" in 2 Tim 3:2; and to the word in 1 Tim 3:3.
37. Or, "*the* root *of* all [kinds of] evil". On this word, see Heb 12:15.
38. Or, "bad *things*", moral, societal, criminal, spiritual, and otherwise. On this word, see "evil" in 3 Jn 11.
39. Or, "reaching out for, striving for, stretching toward". Or, "which aspiring to, some were led astray". Same construction as in 1:6. Same word as in 3:1. Elsewhere only in Heb 11:16. GK *3977*.
40. Or, "wandered away, went astray". Elsewhere only in Mk 13:22. GK *675*.
41. Elsewhere only in Rom 9:2. GK *3850*. Related to "suffer pain" in Lk 2:48.
42. Some think Paul means the different doctrines, controversies and word battles of v 3-4 that lead to all the problems in v 5, which flow from love of money. Others think he specifically means the love of money in v 9-10.

A. 2 Jn 11 B. 1 Jn 5:18 C. 1 Cor 7:31, make use of D. Lk 5:33 E. 2 Jn 9 F. Mk 16:20 G. 1 Tim 5:10a H. Gal 5:1 J. Rom 6:17 K. Jam 1:2 L. Rev 16:6 M. 1 Tim 5:17 N. 1 Tim 5:17 O. Col 1:2, faithful P. Rom 2:4 Q. Act 16:40 R. Rom 6:6, are slaves S. Mt 3:17 T. Rom 12:7 U. Rom 12:8 V. 1 Tim 1:3 W. 1 Tim 5:17 X. 1 Tim 2:2 Y. Act 18:25, know about Z. Mk 15:10 AA. 1 Cor 1:11, quarrels BB. Act 25:18 CC. 2 Cor 4:16, destroyed DD. Rom 7:23 EE. Act 14:19, think FF. Jam 1:18, willed GG. 1 Tim 6:18 HH. Jam 1:2, trials JJ. Tit 3:3 KK. Gal 5:16 LL. 1 Cor 5:5, destruction MM. 2 Pet 2:1 NN. 1 Cor 6:18 OO. 1 Cor 14:1 PP. Rom 1:17 QQ. Jam 1:3

	1C. Be fighting[1] the good[A] fight[B] *of* faith	12
	2C. Take-hold-of[2] eternal life, into which you were called[3], and confessed[4] the good[A] confession[5] in the presence of many witnesses[C]	
3B.	I command[6] you[7] in the sight of God, the *One* giving-life-to[8] all *things*, and Christ Jesus, the *One* having testified[D] the good[A] confession before[9] Pontius Pilate[E]—°*that* you keep[F] the commandment[10]	13
		14
	unspotted[G], above-reproach[11], until the appearance[H] *of* our Lord Jesus Christ	
	1C. Which *in His* own[12] times, the blessed[J] and only[K] Ruler[13] will show[14]—	15
	1D. The King *of* the *ones* being-kings[15] and Lord *of* the *ones* being-lords[16]	
	2D. The only[K] *One* having immortality[L], dwelling[M] *in* unapproachable light	16
	3D. Whom none *of* mankind[17] saw, nor is able to see	
	4D. *To* Whom *be* honor[N] and eternal dominion[O], amen	
4B.	Be commanding[18] the *ones* rich[19] in the present age	17
	1C. Not to be-high-minded	
	2C. Nor to have put-hope[P] on *the* uncertainty *of* riches[20], but upon[21] God[22], the *One* richly granting[Q] us all *things* for enjoyment[23]	
	3C. To be working-good[24]	18
	4C. To be-rich[25] in good[26] works[R]	
	5C. To be generous, sharing[27] *ones*, °treasuring-up *for* themselves *a* good[A] foundation[28] for the future[29]	19
	6C. In order that they may take-hold-of[S] real[30] life[T]	
5B.	O Timothy, guard[U] the deposit[31], turning-aside-*from*[V] the profane[W] empty-chatterings[32] and opposing-arguments[33] *of* the falsely-named[34] "knowledge[X]"—°professing[35] which, some missed-the-mark[36] with respect to the faith. Grace *be* with you[37]	20
		21

1. On this word, see "struggling" in 4:10. Same words as in 2 Tim 4:7, where Paul did so.
2. Same word as in v 19. On this word, see Lk 20:20.
3. On this word, see Rom 8:30. Some manuscripts say "also called" {N}.
4. Or, "declared, publicly acknowledged, admitted, agreed about". Same word as in Mt 10:32; Lk 12:8; Jn 1:20; 9:22; 12:42; Act 23:8; 24:14; Rom 10:9, 10; Tit 1:16; Heb 11:13; Jn 1:9; 2:23; 4:2, 3, 15; 2 Jn 7; Rev 3:5. Elsewhere only as "declare" in Mt 7:23; 14:7; Act 7:17; and "praising" in Heb 13:15. GK *3933*. Related to "confession" next; and to "confess-out" in Jam 5:16.
5. Same word as in v 13. On this word, see 2 Cor 9:13.
6. Same word as in v 17; 1:3.
7. Some manuscripts omit this word {C}.
8. Or, "making alive". Elsewhere only as "keep alive" in Lk 17:33; Act 7:19. GK *2441*. Some manuscripts have a related word {N}, on which see Jn 5:21.
9. Or, "in the time of ". GK *2093*.
10. Some think Paul means the commandment of v 11-12; others, the whole book; others, the commandment of Jesus to love one another, Jn 13:34; others, all the obligations of the gospel. Note that he does not say "this" commandment, though some think this is what he means. This word is used only here in this letter. On this word, see Mk 12:28. Not related to "command" earlier.
11. On this word, see 3:2. The grammar indicates these two adjectives modify "commandment".
12. On this phrase, see 2:6.
13. On this word, see "court official" in Act 8:27.
14. That is, reveal, make known. Same word as in Rev 4:1; Jn 14:8, 9; 20:20. Used 33 times, all rendered "show". GK *1259*.
15. Or, "the *ones* reigning" as kings. This is the verb related to "king". On this word, see "reign" in Rev 19:6. Compare Rev 19:16.
16. Or, "the *ones* ruling or lording" as lords or masters. On this verb, see "lord over" in Rom 7:1.
17. On this idiom, see Mk 11:2.
18. After his solemn command (v 13-14), Paul returns to the previous subject, just as he did in 5:22. Same word as in v 13.
19. Same word as in Mt 19:23; 27:57; Lk 6:24; 16:1; 2 Cor 8:8; Eph 2:4; Jam 1:10; 2:5; Rev 2:9. Used 28 times. GK *4454*. Related to "riches" next, and "be rich" in v 18.
20. Or, "wealth". Same word as in Mt 13:22; Rom 11:33; Eph 3:8; Heb 11:26; Jam 5:2. Used 22 times. GK *4458*.
21. Some manuscripts say "in" {N}.
22. Some manuscripts say "the living God" {A}.
23. Or, "pleasure". Elsewhere only in Heb 11:25. GK *656*.
24. That is, to do things having or proceeding from inner goodness. Related to "good" in 5:10b. This verb is related to "works" next, and is rendered this way to show this. Elsewhere only as "do good" in Act 14:17. GK *14*.
25. This verb is also in v 9; Lk 12:21; 2 Cor 8:9. Used 12 times. GK 4456. Related to "rich" and "riches" in v 17.
26. Or, "commendable, praiseworthy, noble". On this word, see 5:10a.
27. That is, characterized by sharing. Used only here. GK *3127*. Related to "fellowship" in 1 Cor 1:9.
28. Elsewhere only in Lk 6:48, 49; 14:29; Rom 15:20; 1 Cor 3:10, 11, 12; Eph 2:20; 2 Tim 2:19; Heb 6:1; 11:10; Rev 21:14, 19. GK *2529*. Related to "founded" in Eph 3:17.
29. This is a participle, "the *thing* coming". Same idiom as "in the future" in Lk 13:9.
30. Some manuscripts say "eternal life" {A}. On this word, see 5:3.
31. This word means "that which is entrusted to another". Some think Paul is referring to the deposit he made in Timothy in this whole book, 1:18; others, to the gift or ministry God deposited in Timothy; others, to the gospel itself. Elsewhere only in 2 Tim 1:12,14. GK *4146*. The related verb is in 1:18.
32. Elsewhere only in 2 Tim 2:16. GK *3032*. The root word is "empty" in 1 Thes 2:1.
33. Or, "objections, contradictions". Used only here. GK *509*. Related to "oppose" in 2 Tim 2:25.
34. The Greek word is *pseudonumos*, from which comes our word "pseudonym". Used only here. GK *6024*.
35. Or, "promising". On this word, see 2:10. Or, "which professing, some missed the mark". Same construction as in 1:6.
36. On this word, see "departed" in 1:6.
37. This word is plural. Some manuscripts have it singular {A}. Some add "amen" {A}.

A. 1 Tim 5:10a B. Heb 12:1, race C. Act 1:8 D. Jn 1:7 E. Lk 3:1 F. 1 Jn 5:18 G. 2 Pet 3:14 H. 2 Thes 2:8 J. Lk 6:20 K. Jam 2:24, alone L. 1 Cor 15:53 M. Rom 8:11 N. 1 Tim 5:17 O. Eph 6:10, might P. Jn 5:45 Q. Act 17:31 R. Mt 26:10 S. Lk 20:20 T. Rom 8:10 U. Jn 12:25, keep V. 1 Tim 1:6 W. 1 Tim 1:9 X. 1 Cor 12:8

Overview		# 2 Timothy

Introduction — 1:1-2

1A. I have gratitude to God as I have unceasing remembrance concerning you in my prayers, for which reason I am reminding you to rekindle the gift of God in you — 1:3-7

2A. Therefore, do not be ashamed of the testimony of our Lord, nor of me His prisoner — 1:8

    1B. But suffer hardship with me for the gospel according to the power of God who called us — 1:8-12
    2B. Be holding the pattern of healthy words which you heard from me. Guard the good deposit — 1:13-14
    3B. You know that all the ones in Asia turned away from me — 1:15
    4B. Onesiphorus was not ashamed of my chain, but found me in Rome and refreshed me — 1:16-18

3A. Therefore you, my child, become strong in the grace in Christ Jesus — 2:1

    1B. And the things you heard from me, deposit these with faithful people who can teach others — 2:2
    2B. Suffer hardship with me like a good soldier of Christ Jesus — 2:3-7
    3B. Remember Jesus Christ, for whose gospel I suffer hardship that others may obtain salvation — 2:8-14
    4B. Be diligent to present yourself approved to God, an unashamed worker of the word of truth — 2:15

        1C. But be shunning profane empty chatterings, and be a vessel for honor in God's house — 2:16-21
        2C. And be fleeing youthful desires, and pursuing righteousness, faith, love and peace — 2:22
        3C. And be declining foolish controversies. Be kind to all, gently correcting them if possible — 2:23-26

    5B. But know this— that the last days will be difficult. Be turning away from the corrupted ones — 3:1-9

4A. Now you closely followed my teaching, way of life, persecutions and sufferings for the gospel — 3:10-11

    1B. Such persecutions I endured! And the Lord delivered me out of them all — 3:11
    2B. And indeed, all the ones desiring to live godly in Christ Jesus will be persecuted — 3:12
    3B. But evil people and impostors will get worse, deceiving and being deceived — 3:13
    4B. But you, be continuing in the things which you learned and were convinced of, knowing that from babyhood you have known the God-breathed Scriptures which make wise for salvation — 3:14-17

5A. I solemnly charge you in the sight of God and Christ— Proclaim the word, rebuke, warn, exhort — 4:1-2

    1B. For there will be a time when they will not bear with healthy teaching — 4:3-4
    2B. But you, be sober, suffer hardship, do the work of an evangelist, fulfill your ministry — 4:5
    3B. For I am being poured out, and the time of my departure has stood near — 4:6-8

Conclusion — 4:9-22

2 Timothy 1:1	796	Verse

    A. Paul, *an* apostle[A] *of* Christ Jesus   1

        1. By *the* will[B] *of* God
        2. In-relation-to[1] *the* promise *of* life in Christ Jesus

    B. *To* Timothy,[2] beloved[C] child[D]   2
    C. Grace, mercy, peace from God *the* Father and Christ Jesus our Lord

1A. I have gratitude[3] *to* God— Whom I serve[4] from *my* ancestors[5] with *a* clean[E] conscience[F]— as I have   3
unceasing[6] remembrance concerning you in my prayers *by* night and *by* day

    1B. Yearning[G] to see you, having remembered[7] your tears[H], in order that I may be filled[J] *with* joy   4
    2B. Having received *a* reminder[8] *of* the sincere[9] faith in you, which first dwelt[K] in your grandmother   5
    Lois and your mother Eunice[10], and I am convinced[L] that *it is* also in you

        1C. For which reason I am reminding you to be rekindling[11] the gift[M] *of* God which is in you   6
        through the laying-on[12] *of* my hands

            1D. For God did not give us *a* spirit[13] *of* fearfulness[14], but *of* power, and love, and *a* sound- mind[15]   7

2A. Therefore,[16] do not be ashamed-of[17] the testimony[N] *of* our Lord,[18] nor me His prisoner[O]   8

    1B. But suffer-hardship-with[19] *me for* the good-news[P], according-to[20] *the* power[Q] *of* God—*the* One   9
    having saved[R] us, and having called[S] *us with a* holy calling[21]

        1C. Not according-to[22] our works[T], but according to *His* own purpose[U] and grace[V] having been
        given *to* us in Christ Jesus before eternal[W] times[23], *but now having been revealed[24] through   10
        the appearance[25] *of* our Savior[X] Christ Jesus[26]—

            1D. Having **abolished**[27] death— and brought-to-light[28] life[Y] and immortality[Z] through the
            good-news[P], *for which **I** was appointed[AA] *a* proclaimer[29] and apostle[A] and teacher[30]   11

                1E. For which reason[31] I also am suffering[BB] these *things*, but I am not ashamed   12

                    1F. For I know *in* Whom I have believed, and I am convinced[L] that He is able to
                    guard[CC] my deposit[32] until[33] that day

    2B. Be holding[DD] *the* pattern[34] *of* healthy[35] words which you heard from me in[36] *the* faith and love *which*   13
    are in Christ Jesus. *Guard[CC] the good[EE] deposit[37] through *the* Holy Spirit dwelling[K] in us   14
    3B. You know[38] this— that all the *ones* in Asia[39] turned-away-from[FF] me, *among* whom are Phygelus   15
    and Hermogenes
    4B. May the Lord grant[GG] mercy[HH] *to* the household[JJ] *of* Onesiphorus[40], because he often refreshed[41] me,   16
    and he was not ashamed-of[KK] my chain[LL]

        1C. But having come-to-be in Rome, he sought[MM] me diligently[42] and found *me*. *May the Lord   17-18
        grant[GG] him to find mercy[HH] from *the* Lord on that day
        2C. And **you** know very-well how many *things* he ministered[43] in Ephesus

1. Or, more specifically, "for, in the interest of" the proclamation of this promise; or "based on" the promise. GK *2848*.
2. On the writing of this letter, see Act 28:30.
3. On "have gratitude", see Lk 17:9.
4. Or, "worship". On this word, see "worship" in Heb 12:28.
5. Or, "forefathers". That is, as Paul's ancestors did. On this word, see 1 Tim 5:4.
6. Elsewhere only in Rom 9:2. GK *89*. Related to "unceasingly" in Rom 1:9.
7. Or, "recalled". On this word, see Lk 1:54. Related to "remembrance" in v 3; "reminder" in v 5; and "reminding" in v 6.
8. Paul does not say what this reminder was. Perhaps a letter or some news reminded Paul of Timothy's faith. Or, he may mean "having called to mind", without reference to an external reminder. Elsewhere only in 2 Pet 1:13; 3:1. GK *5704*. Related to "remind" in Jn 14:26, and to the word in v 6.
9. Or, "genuine, without hypocrisy". On this word, see Rom 12:9.
10. Timothy's mother is referred to in Act 16:1.
11. Or, "be fanning to a flame, kindling, keeping in full flame". Some take this to mean "restart what has died down in your life"; others, "keep your gift burning full flame". Used only here. GK *351*.
12. Compare the similar statement in 1 Tim 4:14. On the laying on of hands, see Heb 6:2.
13. Or, "Spirit"; or, "a spiritual *gift*", referring to v 6, as this word is used in 1 Cor 14:12.
14. Or, "timidity, cowardice" in a bad sense. That is, characterized by fearfulness. This word refers to the fear to act, as opposed to the fear in response to circumstances. It is fear resulting from a lack of moral courage. See the related word "afraid" in Mk 4:40. Some think Paul is thinking of Timothy as one who was being fearful or timid. Others think he is thinking of himself as one who was not being fearful amidst his circumstances. Used only here. GK *1261*.
15. Or, "self-discipline, self-control, moderation, prudence". Used only here. GK *5406*. See the related words in 1 Tim 3:2.
16. Paul begins his reminding, which he introduced in v 6 as the purpose of this letter.
17. Same word as in v 12, 16. The grammar means "do not become ashamed", not "stop being ashamed". Do not start feeling shame because of my imprisonment, like those in v 15. On this word, see Rom 1:16.
18. That is, the testimony about our Lord; the gospel Paul proclaimed; the healthy words (v 13).
19. Elsewhere only in 2:3. GK *5155*. The same word without the prefix "with" occurs in 2:9; 4:5.
20. Or, "based on, by way of". GK *2848*.
21. Or, "*to a* holy calling". On this word, see 2 Pet 1:10.
22. Same word as in v 8. Used twice here.
23. That is, before time began in eternity past. "Eternal times" is also in Rom 16:25; Tit 1:2. Compare Eph 1:4. The word "times" is GK *5989*, and is used 54 times.
24. On this word, see "made evident" in 1 Jn 2:19. Same word as in Tit 1:3; Rom 16:26.
25. Same word as in 4:1, 8. On this word, see 2 Thes 2:8.
26. Some manuscripts say "Jesus Christ" {N}.
27. Or, "done away with, rendered powerless". On this word, see "done away with" in Rom 6:6. Same word as in 1 Cor 15:26. Paul uses grammar here that emphasizes the contrast between the two halves of this sentence.
28. Or, "having illuminated, having lit up, shined the light on". On this word, see "enlightened" in Heb 6:4.
29. Or, "herald". Elsewhere only in 1 Tim 2:7; 2 Pet 2:5. GK *3061*. Related to "proclaim" in 2 Tim 4:2.
30. Note that Paul uses the same three words in 1 Tim 2:7. Some manuscripts add "*of the* Gentiles" {B}.
31. That is, because I was appointed proclaimer, apostle and teacher of the gospel of Christ.
32. Same word as in v 14. Some think Paul means "what Christ has deposited or entrusted with me"; that is, the gospel or Paul's ministry or gifts, as in v 14; 1 Tim 6:20. Others think he means "what I have deposited or entrusted with Christ"; that is, his reward or soul or life. On this word, see 1 Tim 6:20. Related to the word in 2:2.
33. Or, "for". GK *1650*.
34. Or, "model, outline, sketch". On this word, see 1 Tim 1:16.
35. This is a participle, "of words being healthy". On this phrase, see 1 Tim 1:10.
36. Or, "in connection with". This is the Greek word order. Some think Paul means "Be holding... in *the* faith and love"; others, "which you heard from me in *the* faith and love".
37. Paul may be referring to the "healthy words" in v 13 (note 2:2); or, to the "gift *of* God" in v 6; or, to both.
38. This is one reason or basis for these exhortations. The response of others to Paul's imprisonment is fresh in his mind. Some turned away from Paul after his arrest. One sought him out and refreshed him.
39. Or, "all the *ones* in connection with Asia". Asia is the Roman province of which Ephesus was the capital. Paul probably means that all the witnesses to his work in Asia who could have come to his aid at his trial in Rome failed to do so. He may be implying that they never came to Rome, or that having come to Rome for this purpose, they deserted him and went home. Compare 4:16.
40. This man is mentioned elsewhere only in 4:19. GK *3947*. Some think Paul's words imply that he was now dead.
41. Used only here. GK *434*. Related to "refreshing" in Act 3:20.
42. Some manuscripts say "more-diligently" {N}. On this word, see Tit 3:13.
43. On this word, see 1 Pet 4:10. Some manuscripts add "*to me*" {N}.

A. 1 Cor 12:28 B. Jn 7:17 C. Mt 3:17 D. 1 Jn 3:1 E. Tit 1:15 F. Act 23:1 G. 1 Pet 2:2 H. Act 20:19 J. Eph 5:18 K. Col 3:16 L. 1 Jn 3:19, persuade M. 1 Cor 1:7 N. Act 4:33 O. Eph 3:1 P. 1 Cor 15:1 Q. Mk 5:30 R. Lk 19:10 S. Rom 8:30 T. Mt 26:10 U. Rom 8:28 V. Eph 2:8 W. Mt 25:46 X. Lk 1:47 Y. Rom 8:10 Z. 1 Cor 15:42, undecayability AA. 1 Thes 5:9 BB. Gal 3:4 CC. Jn 12:25, keep DD. 1 Jn 1:8, have EE. 1 Tim 5:10a FF. Heb 12:25 GG. Eph 1:22, give HH. Mt 9:13 JJ. Mk 3:20, house KK. 2 Tim 1:8 LL. Act 28:20 MM. Phil 2:21

3A. Therefore **you**, my child^A, become-strong¹ in² the grace in Christ Jesus	2:1
1B. And *the things* which you heard from me through³ many witnesses^B, these *things* deposit⁴ *with* faithful^C people^D who will be competent⁵ to teach^E others also	2
2B. Suffer-hardship⁶ with *me* like *a* good^F soldier^G *of* Christ Jesus⁷	3
1C. No one while serving-as-a-soldier^H entangles⁸ *himself in* the affairs *of* life^J, in order that he may please^K *the one* having enlisted⁹ *him*	4
2C. And also if one competes [in athletic contests], he is not crowned unless he competes lawfully¹⁰	5
3C. The laboring^L farmer must¹¹ *be* first to receive-a-share¹² *of* the fruits¹³	6
4C. Be considering^M what I am saying, for the Lord will¹⁴ give you understanding^N in everything	7
3B. Be remembering¹⁵ Jesus Christ having been raised¹⁶ from *the* dead, from *the* seed^O *of* David, according to my good-news^P—* in connection with which I am suffering-hardship^Q to the point of imprisonment¹⁷ like *a* criminal¹⁸	8 9
1C. Nevertheless the Word *of* God has not been bound¹⁹	
2C. For this reason,²⁰ I am enduring^R all *things* for the sake of the chosen^S *ones*, in order that **they** also may obtain²¹ salvation^T in Christ Jesus with eternal glory	10
1D. The saying²² *is* trustworthy^C, for	11
1E. If we died-with^U *Him*, we will also live-with^V *Him*	
2E. If we are enduring^R, we will also reign-with *Him*	12
3E. If we shall deny²³ *Him*, that *One* also will deny²⁴ us	
4E. If we are faithless²⁵, that *One* remains^W faithful²⁶, for²⁷ He cannot deny Himself	13
2D. Be reminding^X *them* of these *things*,²⁸ solemnly-warning^Y in the sight of God²⁹ not to battle-about-words³⁰	14
1E. For³¹ nothing useful³²	
2E. To³³ *the* overthrow³⁴ *of* the *ones* hearing	
4B. Be diligent³⁵ to present^Z yourself approved³⁶ *to* God, *a* worker^AA not-needing-to-be-ashamed³⁷, cutting-straight³⁸ the word *of* truth³⁹	15
1C. But be shunning⁴⁰ the profane⁴¹ empty-chatterings^BB	16
1D. For they⁴² will advance⁴³ further⁴⁴ in ungodliness^CC	

1. Or, "be strengthened, be strong". Same word as in Act 9:22; Rom 4:20; Eph 6:10. Elsewhere only as "strengthen" in Phil 4:13; 1 Tim 1:12; 2 Tim 4:17. GK *1904*.
2. Or, "by". GK *1877*.
3. Some think Paul means "with many witnesses" present (as he says in 1 Tim 6:12, with a different word). Others think he means "through many witnesses" attesting to his words. GK *1328*.
4. Or, "entrust". On this word, see 1 Tim 1:18. Related to "deposit" in 2 Tim 1:12, 14.
5. Or, "fit, sufficient, worthy, adequate". On this word, see "sufficient" in 2 Cor 3:5.
6. Some manuscripts say "**You** therefore, suffer hardship... " {N}. On "suffer hardship with", see 1:8.
7. Some manuscripts say "Jesus Christ" {K}.
8. Elsewhere only in 2 Pet 2:20. GK *1861*. Related to "braiding" in 1 Pet 3:3. The root word is "woven" in Mt 27:29 (GK *4428*).
9. This verb, "to enlist soldiers, to gather an army" is used only here. GK *5133*. Related to "soldier" and "serve as a soldier".
10. That is, according to the rules. For Timothy the athlete, the rules demand suffering hardship.
11. Or, "has to". More literally, "It is necessary *that* the laboring farmer *be* first". On this idiom, see Mt 16:21. Or, "ought-to, should", on which see Act 25:10.
12. Or, "to share in". On this word, see "share in" in Heb 12:10.
13. Some think the fruits are "rewards", as if Paul said the laboring farmer (as opposed to the idle one) "will" be first to partake of the reward for his work. Others think Paul means this farmer must or ought to be first to practice what he preaches, to partake of the faith and love and endurance amidst trials he labors to produce in others. One fruit of preaching the gospel is hardship, suffering, even persecution, 3:12. Timothy, the Christian farmer, must be first to partake of this, as Paul did to the point of imprisonment (v 9). There are other views.
14. Some manuscripts say "I am saying. For may the Lord give" {N}, making it a prayer.
15. That is, be keeping in mind. On this word, see Jn 16:21.
16. Or, "having arisen". On this word, see "arose" in Mt 28:6.
17. Or, "bonds". On this word, see Phil 1:7. Not the same word as "chain" in 1:16.
18. This word is used of thieves, murderers, traitors, criminals in the eyes of the law or the government. Paul was regarded as a criminal. Elsewhere only of the two thieves in Lk 23:32, 33, 39. GK *2806*.
19. That is, imprisoned. On this word, see 1 Cor 7:27. Related to "imprisonment" earlier.
20. Or, "Because of this". Some think this refers backward, "Because the Word of God is not bound, I am enduring... in order that"; others, forward, "For this reason I am enduring— in order that **they** also...".
21. Or, "gain, find". On this word, see "attain" in Lk 20:35.
22. Some think Paul is looking back to "that they may obtain salvation in Christ". Others think he is referring to what follows in v 11-13. This phrase occurs in 1 Tim 1:15; 3:1; 4:9; Tit 3:8; but only in 1 Tim 4:9 is it also followed by "for".
23. Some manuscripts say "if we are denying" {N}.
24. Same word as in v 13; and in Mt 10:33; Act 3:13; 4:16; 1 Tim 5:8; 2 Tim 3:5; Tit 1:16; 2 Pet 2:1; 1 Jn 2:22; etc. Used 33 times. Used of Peter in Mt 26:70, 72, and the other Gospels. GK *766*.
25. Or, "without faith, unfaithful". Same word as in Rom 3:3. Elsewhere only as "not believe" in Mk 16:11, 16; Lk 24:11, 41; Act 28:24; 1 Pet 2:7. GK *601*. Related to "unbelief " in 1 Tim 1:13. Some think Paul means "if we are unbelieving". Others think he means "if we prove unfaithful in a trial", as Peter did.
26. Some think Paul means "He remains faithful to us, He will uphold us", as He did Peter, Phil 1:6. Others think he means "He will remain faithful to Himself, He will be holy and just, He will punish or deny us", Heb 2:3. Compare Mk 8:38. Same word as in v 2.
27. Some manuscripts omit this word {N}.
28. That is, v 11-13. Some begin the next main point (4B.) here.
29. Some manuscripts say "the Lord" {B}.
30. Used only here. GK *3362*. The related noun is in 1 Tim 6:4.
31. That is, for no useful purpose, goal, end, or result. The kind of battles in view serve no useful purpose, and have no useful result even if won. Some battles must be fought, Act 15:2; Tit 1:11, etc.
32. Or, "good, beneficial, profitable". Used only here. GK *5978*.
33. Paul may mean "tending toward" or "resulting in". This is the same preposition as "for" in the preceding phrase, but with different grammar. GK *2093*.
34. Or, "ruin, destruction". Elsewhere only in 2 Pet 2:6. GK *2953*. Our word "catastrophe" comes from this Greek word. Related to "overturn" in Mt 21:12.
35. Or, "Be eager, Make every effort". On this word, see Eph 4:3.
36. Or, "genuine, approved by testing". Elsewhere only in Rom 14:18; 16:10; 1 Cor 11:19; 2 Cor 10:18; 13:7; Jam 1:12. GK *1511*. See Rom 12:2 for related words.
37. Or, "not having a cause for shame". Used only here. GK *454*. Related to the verb "ashamed" in 1:8.
38. Used only here, this word is made of the words "to cut" and "straight". It is a rare word, found elsewhere only in Prov 3:6; 11:5. If it has the same sense here, it means "cutting a straight path for the word of truth", as one would cut a path for a road, avoiding detours such as empty chatter (v 16), youthful desires (v 22), and foolish controversies (v 23). Others think the metaphor is agricultural here since "worker" often means "farm laborer"— "plowing straight rows for the word". Others think the metaphor is of a stonecutter "cutting straight" the word. Others take "straight" in the sense of "right", and translate "rightly dividing" or "accurately handling". The sense is clear, though the precise metaphor is not certain. GK *3982*.
39. Some think Paul is referring to the gospel, the word given to and through the apostles; others to the OT Scriptures, from which Apollos showed that the Christ is Jesus (Act 18:28) and Paul showed that the Christ must suffer and be raised (Act 26:22-23).
40. Or, "avoiding, going around". Same word as in Tit 3:9. GK *4325*.
41. On this word, see 1 Tim 1:9. This same phrase occurs in 1 Tim 6:20.
42. That is, the ones speaking profane, empty chatterings.
43. Or, "progress, cut forward". Elsewhere only in 3:9, 13; and Lk 2:52; Rom 13:12; Gal 1:14. GK *4621*. Related to "advancement" in Phil 1:12.
44. Or, "to more". This phrase is elsewhere only in 3:9; Act 4:17; 20:9; 24:4. Note "to the worse" in 3:13.

A. 1 Jn 3:1 B. Act 1:8 C. Col 1:2, faithful D. Mt 4:4, mankind E. Rom 12:7 F. 1 Tim 5:10a G. Mt 28:12 H. 1 Tim 1:18, fight J. 1 Jn 2:16 K. 1 Thes 2:4 L. Mt 11:28, being weary M. Eph 3:20, think N. Eph 3:4 O. Heb 11:11 P. 1 Cor 15:1 Q. Jam 5:13 R. Jam 1:12 S. Rom 8:33 T. Lk 19:9 U. 2 Cor 7:3, die together V. 2 Cor 7:3, live together W. Jn 15:4, abide X. Jn 14:26 Y. 1 Tim 5:21, solemnly charge Z. Rom 12:1 AA. 1 Tim 5:18 BB. 1 Tim 6:20 CC. Rom 1:18

2 Timothy 2:17	800	Verse

      2D. And their talk[1] will have *a* spreading[2] like gangrene   17

           1E. *Of* whom are Hymenaeus and Philetus— *who missed-the-mark*[A] with regard to the truth[B], saying *that* the[3] resurrection[C] has already[D] taken place   18

           2E. And they are overturning[4] the faith[E] *of* some

           3E. Nevertheless, the firm[5] foundation[F] *of* God stands, having this seal[6]—   19

                  1F. "*The* Lord knows[G] the *ones* being His"

                  2F. And "Let everyone naming[7] the name[8] *of the* Lord[9] depart[H] from unrighteousness"

      3D. Now in *a* large house there are not only golden and silver vessels[J], but also wooden and made-of-clay— even some for honor[K], and others for dishonor[10]. *If then one cleanses*[11] *himself from these*[12] *things, he will be a vessel*[J] *for honor*[K]   20 / 21

           1E. Having been sanctified[13]

           2E. Useful[L] *to* the Master[14]

           3E. Having been prepared[M] for every good[N] work

  2C. And be fleeing[O] the youthful desires[15], and be pursuing[P] righteousness, faith, love, peace, with[16] the *ones* calling-upon[Q] the Lord from *a* pure[R] heart   22

  3C. And be declining[S] the foolish[T] and ignorant[17] controversies[18], knowing that they breed[19] battles[20]   23

      1D. And *a* slave[U] *of the* Lord must[V] not battle[21], but *must* be kind[22] to everyone, skillful-at-teaching[W], forbearing[23], *correcting*[24] the *ones* opposing with gentleness[X]   24 / 25

           1E. If perhaps God may grant[Y] them repentance[Z] leading-to[AA] *the* knowledge[BB] *of the* truth, *and they may return-to-their-senses*[25] from the snare[CC] *of* the devil   26

                  1F. Having been caught[26] by him, for the will *of that*[27] one

5B. But know this— that during *the* last days[28] difficult[29] times will be present[30]   3:1

  1C. For the people[DD] will be   2

      1D. Self-lovers[31], money-lovers[32]

      2D. Boasters, arrogant[EE], blasphemous[FF], disobedient[GG] *to* parents

      3D. Ungrateful[HH], unholy, unaffectionate[33], unreconcilable[34], slanderous[JJ], without-self-control[35], untamed[36], not-lovers-of-good[37], traitors[38], reckless   3 / 4

      4D. Having become conceited[KK]

      5D. Pleasure-lovers rather than God-lovers

      6D. Holding[LL] *a* form[MM] *of* godliness[NN], but having denied[OO] the power[PP] *of* it   5

  2C. Indeed, be turning-away-from these *ones*

      1D. For from these are the *ones* creeping[39] into the houses and taking-captive[40] little-women[41]   6

           1E. Having been heaped *with* sins

           2E. Being led[QQ] *by* various[RR] desires[SS]

           3E. Always learning[TT] and never being able to come to *the* knowledge[BB] *of the* truth[B]   7

1. Or, "word, message". That is, the talk of the ones speaking such chatterings. On this word, see "word" in 1 Cor 12:8.
2. Elsewhere only as "pasture" in Jn 10:9. GK *3786*. This noun is used of sheep spreading out in a pasture. It is also a medical term for a spreading skin ulcer.
3. Some manuscripts say "*the* resurrection..." {C}.
4. Or, "upsetting, overthrowing". Elsewhere only in Jn 2:15, Jesus "overturned" the money tables; Tit 1:11. GK *426*.
5. Or, "solid". Some think the firm foundation is the truth of the gospel. Others think it is the church in Ephesus (where Timothy is), or the church as a whole, as in 1 Tim 3:15. Same word as in 1 Pet 5:9. Elsewhere only as "solid" in Heb 5:12, 14. GK *5104*. Related to "be made firm" in Act 16:5; and "firmness" in Col 2:5.
6. The seal has two parts, one from God's point of view and one from the human point of view. On this word, see Rom 4:11.
7. This verb is elsewhere only in Mk 3:14; Lk 6:13, 14; Act 19:13; Rom 15:20; 1 Cor 5:11; Eph 1:21; 3:15; 5:3. GK *3951*. The related noun is next.
8. Used 231 times. GK *3950*.
9. Some manuscripts say "*of* Christ" {K}.
10. Some think Paul means some are honored house members (true believers), others are dishonored (false believers and false teachers). The latter are thrown out of the house. We can be for honor if we separate ourselves from them. Others think he means some teachers serve honorable purposes; others serve dishonorable or common purposes, like a clay pot for washing dishes. Every house has both. We can be useful for honorable purposes if we cleanse ourselves from "these things". Elsewhere only in Rom 1:26; 9:21; 1 Cor 11:14; 15:43; 2 Cor 6:8; 11:21. GK *871*. Related word in Act 5:41.
11. Or, "cleans-out". Elsewhere only as "clean out" in 1 Cor 5:7. GK *1705*. Same word as "clean" in Jn 15:2, with the prefix "out".
12. Some think Paul means from the profane, empty chatterings. If we cleanse ourselves of the worthless talk which Paul addresses often in 1, 2 Timothy, and Titus, we can be useful to the Master for honorable things. Otherwise, we can only be of common use. Others think "these things" refers to the other vessels, the ones made of wood or earth. We must cleanse ourselves of these dishonorable teachers, like those of v 18, to be a vessel for honor.
13. Or, "set apart, made holy". On this word, see Heb 10:29.
14. On this word, see Jude 4. Some manuscripts say "and useful *to* the Master" {N}.
15. This word means "strong desire", in both a good and a bad sense. Other passages use "desire" to refer to the desire for sex (1 Thes 4:5); for wealth (1 Tim 6:9); for "new" teaching (2 Tim 4:3); for other desires of the flesh (Gal 5:16-21). On this word, see Gal 5:16.
16. Or, "along with". Some punctuate this "pursue... peace, along with"; others, "pursue... love, [and] peace with the ones...". GK *3552*.
17. Or, "uneducated, uninstructed, untrained, uninformed". Used only here. GK *553*. Related to "train" in Tit 2:12.
18. Or, "debates". On this word, see 1 Tim 6:4.
19. Or, "father, produce". On this word, see "born" in 1 Jn 2:29.
20. Or, "fights, conflicts, quarrels". Elsewhere only in 2 Cor 7:5; Tit 3:9; Jam 4:1. GK *3480*.
21. Same word as in Jam 4:2. Elsewhere only as "fight" in Jn 6:52; Act 7:26. GK *3481*. There is an example of this in Act 23:9, using a related word. The related noun is in v 23. Related to "word-battles" in 1 Tim 6:4.
22. Or, "gentle, soothing, calming". Used only here. GK *2473*. Note Paul's approach in 1 Thes 2:7, where some manuscripts have this word.
23. That is, bearing evil without resentment, able to endure evil. Used only here. GK *452*.
24. Or, "teaching, training, disciplining". On this word, see "disciplined" in 1 Cor 11:32. Related to "training" in 3:16.
25. Or, "become sober again, come to *their* senses again". Used only here. GK *392*. Related to "be sober" in 1 Pet 1:13.
26. Or, "captured alive". Elsewhere only in Lk 5:10, of the disciples "catching" men. GK *2436*. The root word is "alive".
27. Some think Paul means "caught by the devil for his will"; others, "caught by the Lord's bondservant for God's will"; others, "snare of the devil— having been caught by the devil— for God's will".
28. On this phrase, note Heb 1:2.
29. Or, "hard, hard to bear, troublesome, hard to deal with, dangerous". Elsewhere only as "violent" in Mt 8:28. GK *5901*.
30. Or, "be at hand, be here, have come". On this word, see Heb 9:9. Same word as in 2 Thes 2:2.
31. Used only here. GK *5796*.
32. Elsewhere only in Lk 16:14. GK *5795*. Related word in 1 Tim 6:10.
33. On this word, see Rom 1:31. That is, "without natural affection" of parents and children.
34. Or, "implacable, unforgiving". The root word means "truce". That is, unwilling to make a truce, to negotiate a solution, to be reconciled. Used only here. GK *836*.
35. Or, "powerless". Without power over oneself. Without moral power. Used only here. GK *203*. Related word in 1 Cor 7:5.
36. Or, "savage, brutal". Used only here. GK *466*.
37. Or, "without love of good". Used only here. GK *920*. It is the negative of the word in Tit 1:8.
38. On this word, see "betrayer" in Act 7:52.
39. Or, "slipping, pressing". Used only here. GK *1905*.
40. Or, "taking prisoner", figuratively. On this word, see 2 Cor 10:5.
41. This is a diminutive of the word "woman", formed like "little-daughter" in Mk 5:23; "little-boy" in Jn 6:9; etc. Here, the sense of it is determined by the context. Some think it has a sense derogatory of the women described by the next three phrases, such as "*weak*-women, *silly*-women, *foolish*-women, *gullible*-women". Others think it is derogatory of the creepers, who prey on and captivate "*helpless*-women, *vulnerable*-women". Used only here. GK *1220*. Grammatically, the next three phrases refer to the "women", not to the ones creeping in.

A. 1 Tim 1:6, departed B. Jn 4:23 C. Act 24:15 D. Mt 24:32 E. Eph 2:8 F. 1 Tim 6:19 G. Lk 1:34 H. 1 Tim 4:1 J. 1 Thes 4:4 K. 1 Tim 5:17 L. Phm 11 M. Mk 14:15 N. 1 Tim 5:10b O. 1 Cor 6:18 P. 1 Cor 14:1 Q. 1 Pet 1:17 R. Tit 1:15, clean S. Heb 12:25, refuse T. Tit 3:9 U. Rom 6:17 V. Mt 16:21 W. 1 Tim 3:2 X. Eph 4:2 Y. Eph 1:22, give Z. 2 Cor 7:10 AA. Rom 5:16, resulting in BB. Col 1:9 CC. Rom 11:9 DD. Mt 4:4, mankind EE. Jam 4:6 FF. 1 Tim 6:13 GG. Lk 1:17 HH. Lk 6:35 JJ. 1 Tim 3:11 KK. 1 Tim 6:4 LL. 1 Jn 1:8, have MM. Rom 2:20, embodiment NN. 1 Tim 2:2 OO. 2 Tim 2:12 PP. Mk 5:30 QQ. Lk 4:1 RR. 1 Pet 4:10, diversified SS. Gal 5:16 TT. Phil 4:11

	2D. And the way^A Jannes and Jambres^1 opposed^B Moses, in this manner these also oppose^B the truth— people^C having been corrupted *as to* the mind^D, disapproved^2 with respect to the faith	8
	1E. But they will not advance^E further, for their folly^F will be very-evident *to* everyone, as also the *folly of* those *two* came-to-be^3	9
4A. Now **you** closely-followed^4 my teaching^G, way-of-life, purpose^H, faith^J, patience^K, love^L, endurance^M, persecutions^5, sufferings^N— such as happened *to* me at Antioch, at Iconium, at Lystra^6	10 11
	1B. Such persecutions I endured^O! And the Lord delivered^P me out of *them* all	
	2B. And indeed all the *ones* wanting^7 to live godly^8 in Christ Jesus will be persecuted^9	12
	3B. But evil^Q people^C and impostors^10 will advance^E to the worse— deceiving^R and being deceived	13
	4B. But **you**, be continuing^11 in *the things* which you learned^S and were convinced-of	14
	1C. Knowing from whom^12 you learned, ˚and that^13 from babyhood^14 you *have* known^15 the sacred^16 writings^17 being able to make you wise for salvation^T, through faith in Christ Jesus	15
	1D. All Scripture^18 *is* God-breathed^19, and profitable^20 for teaching^21, for rebuking^22, for correcting^23, for training^24 in righteousness	16
	1E. In order that the person^C *of* God may be complete^25, having been equipped^26 for every good^U work	17
5A. I solemnly-charge^27 *you* in the sight of God, and Christ Jesus^28, the *One* going-to^V judge^W *the* living and *the* dead^29, and^30 *by* His appearance^31 and His kingdom^X— ˚proclaim^32 the Word^Y. Stand-at^33 *it* in-season^34, out-of-season^35. Rebuke^36, warn^37, exhort^38 with all patience^Z and instruction^AA	4:1 2
	1B. For there will be *a* time when they will not bear-with^BB healthy^39 teaching^CC	3
	1C. But while itching^40 *with respect to* the hearing^41, they will heap-up^42 teachers *for* themselves in accordance with *their* own desires^DD	
	2C. And they will turn the hearing away^EE **from the truth**^43— and be turned-aside^FF to myths^GG	4
	2B. But **you**, be sober^HH in all *things*, suffer-hardship^44, do *the* work^JJ *of an* evangelist^45, fulfill^46 your ministry^KK	5

1. According to Jewish tradition, these were the names of Pharaoh's magicians who opposed Moses in Ex 7:11, 22; 8:7, 18; 9:11. These names are mentioned only here in the Bible. They opposed Moses by substituting a counterfeit (a human/demon-generated "miracle") and a teaching that "explained" Moses. GK *2612, 2614*.
2. That is, rejected after testing. On this word, see 1 Cor 9:27. It is the negative of "approved" in 2:15.
3. Or, "proved to be". GK *1181*.
4. On this word, see "accompany" in Mk 16:17. Some manuscripts say "have closely followed" {N}, as in 1 Tim 4:6.
5. On this word, see Mk 10:30. The related verb is in the next verse.
6. Paul is referring to the events in Act 13:50-14:20, when he first came to these three cities. Timothy was found by Paul in Lystra on his second trip in Act 16:1-3. Timothy may have been an eyewitness of some of these events.
7. Or, "intending, desiring, wishing". On this word, see "willing" in Jn 7:17.
8. Or, "in a godly manner". Elsewhere only in Tit 2:12. GK *2357*. Related to "godliness" in 1 Tim 2:2.
9. Same word as Mt 5:10-12, 44; 10:23; Lk 21:12; Jn 15:20; Act 9:4; 22:4; Rom 12:14; 1 Cor 15:9. See "pursue" in 1 Cor 14:1 on it.
10. Used only here, this word meant "one who howls enchantments; magicians, sorcerers, wizards". But it came to be used of "swindlers, deceivers, cheaters" in general. One who fools people. GK *1200*.
11. Or, "abiding, remaining". On this word, see "abide" in Jn 15:4.
12. This word is plural, and includes Timothy's mother and grandmother (1:5), and Paul, and perhaps others. Some manuscripts have it singular {B}, referring to Paul.
13. Or, "learned— because indeed from babyhood...".
14. Or, from "*a baby, an* infant". That is, from your earliest memory. On this word, see "baby" in Lk 1:41.
15. Literally, "you are knowing" from then until now. The Greek looks forward from the past. In English, we look backward from the present, "you have known".
16. Or, "holy". Same word as in Mark's short ending. Elsewhere only as "temple-*duties*" in 1 Cor 9:13. GK *2641*. Related to "temple".
17. The Scriptures (a different word, v 16) are called "sacred writings" only here. On this word, see Jn 7:15.
18. Or, "Every Scripture", that is, every book or passage. Or, "All God-breathed Scripture *is* also profitable...". On this word, see 2 Pet 3:16.
19. Or, "God-inspired, inspired by God", the method being described in 2 Pet 1:21. This word is made of two words, "God" and "to breathe, exhale". Used only here. GK *2535*. This word is constructed like "God-taught" in 1 Thes 4:9.
20. Or, "useful, valuable, beneficial". Elsewhere only in 1 Tim 4:8; Tit 3:8. GK *6068*. The related verb is in Rom 2:25.
21. Same word as in 3:10; 4:3. On this word, see 1 Tim 5:17.
22. That is, the refuting, exposing, rebuking, or conviction of sin or error. Used only here. GK *1791*. Related to "rebuke" in 2 Pet 2:16; "conviction" in Heb 11:1; and the verb in 2 Tim 4:2.
23. Or, "improving, amending, restoring, reforming". Used only here.

24. Or, "discipline, instruction, education". Same word as in Eph 6:4. Elsewhere only as "discipline" in Heb 12:5, 7, 8, 11. GK *4082*. Related to "discipline" in 2 Cor 11:32.
25. Or, "perfect in its kind, fitted to its purpose, capable, proficient". Used only here. GK *787*.
26. Or, "furnished, completed, finished". Elsewhere only as "finished" in Act 21:5. GK *1992*. Related to "prepared" in Rom 9:22.
27. On this word, see 1 Tim 5:21. Some manuscripts say "Therefore I solemnly charge" {N}.
28. Some manuscripts say "and *of* the Lord Jesus Christ" {K}.
29. That is, the ones alive at His coming, and the ones dead. Compare Act 10:42; 1 Pet 4:5.
30. Instead of "and", some manuscripts say "at" {B}, so that it says, "at His appearing and His kingdom".
31. Same word as in v 8; 1:10.
32. Or, "announce, make known, herald". This word means "to proclaim as a herald" (compare the word in Phil 1:18). Used 61 times, as in Mt 4:23; 10:7, 27; 24:14; 26:13; Mk 1:45; 5:20; 6:12; 7:36; 16:15; Lk 4:18, 19; Act 8:5; 9:20; 10:42; Rom 10:14; 1 Cor 1:23; 2 Cor 4:5; 11:4; Gal 2:2; 5:11; Phil 1:15; Col 1:23; 1 Thes 2:9; 1 Tim 3:16; 1 Pet 3:19; Rev 5:2. GK *3062*. Related to "proclaimer" in 1:11; and "proclamation" in 1 Cor 1:21.
33. Or, "Stand by, Stand upon", and therefore "Attend to *it*, Be ready". Same word as "stood near" in v 6.
34. Or, "in a favorable opportunity, opportune-ly, conveniently". Elsewhere only as "conveniently" in Mk 14:11. GK *2323*. Related to "opportune" in Mk 6:21.
35. This is related to the previous word. Used only here. GK *178*.
36. Or, "Convict, Convince, Refute, Expose". Related to the word in 3:16. On this word, see "expose" in Eph 5:11.
37. Or, "rebuke, censure, reprove". Used only here by Paul. Same word as in Mt 12:16; and as "rebuke" in Mt 8:26; 16:22; Mk 8:33; 10:48; Lk 4:41; 9:55; 17:3; 18:15; 19:39; 23:40; Jude 9. Used 29 times. GK *2203*. Related to "punishment" in 2 Cor 2:6.
38. Or, "encourage". On this word, see Rom 12:8.
39. Or, "sound doctrine". This is a participle, "teaching being healthy". On this word and phrase, see 1 Tim 1:10.
40. Or, "while being tickled". Used only here. GK *3117*.
41. Or, "the ear". It is singular. Same word as in v 4. On this word, see Heb 4:2.
42. Or, "accumulate". Used only here. GK *2197*. Related to "heaped" in 3:6.
43. Paul uses grammar that emphasizes the contrast between the two halves of this sentence; from truth, to myths.
44. Same word as in 2:9. On this word, see Jam 5:13. Related word in 2 Tim 1:8.
45. Or, "proclaimer of the gospel". On this word, see Eph 4:11.
46. Or, "accomplish, bring to completion". This is the same word Paul uses of his own ministry in v 17. On this word, see Lk 1:1.

A. Act 27:25 B. Eph 6:13, resist C. Mt 4:4, mankind D. Rom 7:23 E. 2 Tim 2:16 F. Lk 6:11, rage G. 1 Tim 5:17 H. Rom 8:28 J. Eph 2:8 K. Heb 6:12 L. 1 Jn 4:16 M. Jam 1:3 N. Phil 3:10 O. 1 Cor 10:13 P. Col 1:13 Q. Act 25:18 R. Jam 5:19, err S. Phil 4:11 T. Lk 19:9 U. 1 Tim 5:10b V. Mk 10:32 W. Mt 7:1 X. Mt 3:2 Y. 1 Cor 12:8 Z. Heb 6:12 AA. 1 Cor 14:6, teaching BB. 2 Cor 11:4 CC. 1 Tim 5:17 DD. Gal 5:16 EE. Heb 12:25, turn away from FF. 1 Tim 1:6 GG. 1 Tim 1:4 HH. 1 Pet 1:13 JJ. Mt 26:10 KK. 1 Cor 12:5

2 Timothy 4:6	804	Verse

    3B. For **I** am already being poured-out[1], and the time *of* my departure[2] has stood-near[3]   6

        1C. I have fought[4] the good fight. I have finished[A] the course[5]. I have kept[B] the faith[6]   7

        2C. Henceforth, the crown[C] *of* righteousness[7] is reserved[8] *for* me, which the Lord, the righteous judge, will render[D] *to* me on that day— and not only *to* me, but also *to* all the *ones* having loved[E] His appearance[F]   8

  A. Be diligent[9] to come to me quickly[G]   9

    1. For Demas[10] deserted[11] me, having loved[E] the present age[12], and went to Thessalonica   10
    2. Crescens *has gone* to Galatia, Titus to Dalmatia[13]
    3. Luke[H] only is with me   11
    4. Having picked-up[J] Mark[K], bring *him* with yourself, for he is useful[L] *to* me for service[M]
    5. And I sent-forth[N] Tychicus[O] to Ephesus   12
    6. While coming, bring the cloak[14] which I left-behind[P] in Troas with Carpus, and the books[15]— especially the parchments[16]   13

  B. Alexander the coppersmith[17] showed[18] many evil[Q] *things against* me. The Lord will render[19] *to* him according to his works[20], *as to whom, **you** also be guarding[R] *yourself*, for he greatly opposed[21] our words[S]   14, 15

  C. At my first defense[22], no one was present[23] *with* me, but they all deserted[T] me. May it not be counted[U] *against* them   16

    1. But the Lord stood-by[V] me and strengthened[W] me, in order that through me the proclamation[X] might be fulfilled[24], and all the Gentiles might hear[25]   17
    2. And I was delivered[Y] out of *a* lion's mouth[26]
    3. The[27] Lord will deliver[Y] me from every evil[Z] work[AA], and He will save[28] *me* into His heavenly[BB] kingdom[CC]— *to* Whom *be* the glory forever and ever[DD], amen   18

  D. Greet Prisca[EE] and Aquila, and the household[FF] *of* Onesiphorus[GG]   19
  E. Erastus[29] remained[HH] in Corinth, but I left-behind[30] Trophimus[JJ] sick[31] in Miletus[32]   20
  F. Be diligent to come before winter   21
  G. Eubulus greets you, and [so do] Pudens, and Linus, and Claudia[33], and all the brothers[KK]
  H. The Lord[34] *be* with your[35] spirit. Grace *be* with you[36]   22

1. Or, "poured out as a sacrifice on the altar, poured out as a drink offering, offered up". Elsewhere only in Phil 2:17, also of Paul. GK *5064*. This word is used in the OT of pouring a drink offering of wine at the foot of the altar, Num 28:7; Ex 29:40.
2. Or, "loosing up, breaking up". That is, Paul's death. Used only here. GK *385*. This word was used of soldiers "breaking" camp, of a ship weighing anchor. The related verb is in Phil 1:23.
3. Or, "has stood by, is imminent, is impending". On this word, see "suddenly come upon" in Lk 21:34.
4. On this word, see "struggle" in 1 Tim 4:10. Compare this same phrase in 1 Tim 6:12.
5. Or, "racecourse". Elsewhere only in Act 13:25; 20:24. GK *1536*. Related to the verb "to run".
6. Some think Paul means "I have been loyal to the faith"; others, "I have preserved the gospel entrusted to me".
7. That is, consisting of or belonging to righteousness. On this word, see Rom 1:17.
8. Or, "laid away". On this word, see Col 1:5.
9. Or, "Make haste, Make every effort". Same word as in v 21. On this word, see Eph 4:3.
10. Demas is mentioned elsewhere only in Col 4:14 and Phm 24. GK *1318*.
11. Or, "abandoned". Same word as in v 16. On this word, see "forsaken" in 2 Cor 4:9.
12. Or, "world". Same word as Rom 12:2; 1 Cor 1:20; 2:6; 2 Cor 4:4; Gal 1:4; Eph 1:21; 1 Tim 6:17; Tit 2:12; etc. GK *172*.
13. This is the district north and west of Macedonia, directly across the sea from Italy; the southern part of Illyricum (Rom 15:19). Used only here. GK *1237*.
14. This refers to a heavy outer coat. Used only here. GK *5742*.
15. Or, "scrolls", usually made from papyrus. Our word "Bible" comes from this word. On this word, see "scroll" in Rev 5:1.
16. That is, scrolls made from animal skins, which were more expensive than papyrus scrolls. Used only here. GK *3521*.
17. Or, "blacksmith, metalworker". The root word is the word meaning "copper, brass, bronze" (GK *5910*). But this word was also used of "metalworkers" in general, so "coppersmith" may be too specific. Used only here. GK *5906*.
18. Or, "displayed, declared, demonstrated, exhibited, informed, charged". On this word, see "demonstrate" in Eph 2:7. Some think this took place at Paul's trial, where Alexander "informed against" Paul; others think it was more personal, perhaps physical harm. Some suggest this is the same Alexander as in 1 Tim 1:20, or the one in Act 19:33.
19. Same word as in v 8. On this word, see Mt 16:27. Some manuscripts say "May the Lord render..." {N}, making it a prayer.
20. On this phrase, see Rev 20:12.
21. On this word, see "resist" in Eph 6:13. Some manuscripts say "he has greatly opposed" {N}.
22. At the preliminary hearing, Paul was abandoned. On this word, see 1 Pet 3:15.
23. Or, "stood by, came alongside, approached". No one supported Paul, or testified on his behalf. GK *4134*.
24. Same word as in 4:5.
25. This completed Paul's mission. He knew that he was to take the gospel all the way to the top of the Roman Empire, Act 23:11; 27:23-24. Having done this, he now says "I have finished the course", v 7.
26. Some think this is a general reference, meaning "great danger". Paul was not immediately executed. Others think it is a specific reference to his accuser, or to the magistrate, or to Satan. If there was insufficient evidence, Paul would be bound over to a later trial. At the final trial he was condemned and executed. This is why he asks Timothy twice to make every effort to come quickly, before winter, v 9, 21.
27. Some manuscripts say "And the Lord..." {N}.
28. Or, "preserve, deliver". On this word, see Lk 19:10.
29. Some think this is the man mentioned in Act 19:22, and perhaps the one mentioned in Rom 16:23. GK *2235*.
30. Same word as in v 13. On this word, see Jude 6.
31. That is, "being sick, ailing". Same word as in Mt 10:8; Phil 2:26; and "weak" in Rom 14:1; 1 Cor 8:11. Used 33 times. GK *820*. Related to "weakness" in Mt 8:17.
32. On this town, see Act 20:15. It is near this man's hometown of Ephesus.
33. This is a woman's name.
34. Some manuscripts say "The Lord Jesus Christ"; others, "The Lord Jesus" {B}.
35. This is singular.
36. This word is plural, as in 1 Tim 6:21. Some manuscripts have it singular. Some add "amen" {A}.

A. Rev 10:7 B. 1 Jn 5:18 C. Rev 4:4 D. Mt 16:27 E. Jn 21:15, devotedly love F. 2 Thes 2:8 G. Gal 1:6 H. Phm 24 J. Act 1:2, taken up K. 1 Pet 5:13 L. Phm 11 M. 1 Cor 12:5, ministries N. Mk 3:14, send out O. Act 20:4 P. Jude 6 Q. 3 Jn 11 R. Jn 12:25, keep S. 1 Cor 12:8 T. 2 Tim 4:10 U. Rom 3:28, consider V. Rom 12:1, present W. 2 Tim 2:1, become strong X. 1 Cor 1:21 Y. Col 1:13 Z. Act 25:18 AA. Mt 26:10 BB. Eph 3:10 CC. Mt 3:2 DD. Rev 20:10 EE. Rom 16:3 FF. Mk 3:20, house GG. 2 Tim 1:16 HH. Jn 15:4, abide JJ. Act 21:29 KK. Act 16:40

Overview		# Titus

Introduction — 1:1-4

1A. I left you on Crete in order that you might set straight the things lacking, and appoint elders in each city as I directed you— if one is blameless, a man of one woman, having believing children — 1:5-6

    1B. For the overseer must be blameless, as God's steward — 1:7-9
    2B. For there are many rebellious ones and deceivers whom it is necessary to silence — 1:10-16

2A. But you be speaking the things which are fitting for healthy teaching — 2:1

    1B. That old men be sober, honorable, sound-minded, healthy in faith, love and endurance — 2:2
    2B. That old women be reverent, not slanderous or drunks, teachers of the young women — 2:3-5
    3B. Be exhorting younger men to be sound minded, following your example — 2:6-8
    4B. Be exhorting slaves to be subject to their masters that they may adorn the teaching of our Savior — 2:9-10
    5B. For the grace of God appeared bringing salvation for all people, instructing us how to live — 2:11-14
    6B. Be speaking these things, and be exhorting and be rebuking with all authority — 2:15

3A. Be reminding them to be subject to rulers, ready for good works, not quarrelsome but gentle to all — 3:1-2

    1B. For we also were once foolish, disobedient, being deceived and slaves to various desires — 3:3
    2B. But when the kindness and love-for-mankind of our Savior God appeared, He saved us — 3:4-8
    3B. And concerning these things I want you to be speaking confidently. These are good for people — 3:8
    4B. But be shunning foolish controversies, genealogies, quarrels, and battles about the Law — 3:9
    5B. Be declining a divisive person, knowing that such a one is perverted and self-condemned — 3:10-11

Conclusion — 3:12-15

A. Paul, *a* slave^A *of* God, and *an* apostle^B *of* Jesus Christ 1

    1. In-relation-to[1] *the* faith *of the* chosen^C *ones of* God, and *the* knowledge^D *of the* truth *which is* in-accordance-with[2] godliness^E
    2. On-the-basis-of[3] *the* hope^F *of* eternal life, which the non-lying[4] God promised before eternal times[5] 2

        a. But He revealed[6] His word^G *in His* own times[7]— in *the* proclamation^H which **I** was entrusted-with[J] according-to[8] *the* command^K *of* our Savior^L God[9] 3

B. *To* Titus[10], genuine[11] child^M according-to[12] *a* common[13] faith 4
C. Grace and peace[14] from God *the* Father and Christ Jesus[15] our Savior

1A. For this reason I left you behind^N in Crete, in order that you might set-straight[16] the *things* lacking[17], and appoint[18] elders[19] in each city[20] as **I** directed^O you— *if one is blameless[21], a man of* one woman,[22] having believing^P children^M *who are* not under[23] *an* accusation[24] *of* wild-living[25] or rebellious[26] *ones* 5 6

  1B. For the overseer[27] must^Q be blameless, as God's steward[28] 7

    1C. Not self-willed[29], not quick-tempered, not *a* drunken^R one, not *a* brawler^S, not fond-of-shameful-gain[30]
    2C. But hospitable[31], *a* lover-of-good[32], sound-minded[33], just[34], holy^T, self-controlled[35] 8
    3C. Holding-on-to[36] the faithful^P word^G in accordance with the teaching[37], so that he may be able both to exhort[38] with[39] healthy[40] teaching and refute[41] the *ones* contradicting[42] 9

  2B. For there are indeed[43] many rebellious^U *ones,* worthless-talkers[44], and deceivers[45]— especially the *ones* from the circumcision^V— *whom it-is-necessary[46] to silence[47] 10 11

    1C. Who are overturning^W whole households^X, teaching *things* which *they* ought not to[48] *teach* for the sake of shameful[49] gain[50]

      1D. One of them, their own prophet[51], said "Cretans *are* always liars, evil^Y beasts^Z, lazy^AA gluttons^BB" 12
      2D. This testimony^CC is true[52] 13

    2C. For which reason, be rebuking^DD them severely^EE in order that they may be healthy^FF in the faith, *not paying-attention-to^GG Jewish myths^HH and commandments^JJ *of* people^KK turning-away-from^LL the truth 14

      1D. All *things are* clean[53] *to* the clean. But *to* the *ones* having been defiled[54] and *who are* unbelieving[55], nothing *is* clean[56] 15

1. Or, more specifically, "For, In the interest of; In accordance with, In harmony with". Some think Paul means his apostleship is "in harmony with" the faith of the chosen, because their faith is in harmony with God's truth. Others think he means his apostleship is "in the interest of, toward the furtherance of" their faith. GK *2848*.
2. Same word as "in relation to" earlier. Some think Paul means "in accordance with" godliness; others, "furthering" or "leading to" godliness.
3. Or, "For, Upon, In, In reference to". Some think Paul means "apostle... on the basis of (or resting on) this hope". He was sent out based on this hope for the faith and knowledge of the chosen ones. Others think this is a further description of the faith and knowledge, "*the* faith... and knowledge... *which are* based on (or resting on) this hope", making this point a. GK *2093*.
4. That is, truthful. Paul refers to God in this way because of the Cretans' well-known problem with lying. See v 12. Used only here. GK *950*.
5. On "eternal times", see 2 Tim 1:9. Before the beginning of time.
6. Same word as in 2 Tim 1:10.
7. On "*in His* own times", see 1 Tim 2:6.
8. Or, "based on". GK *2848*.
9. The phrase "our Savior God" is also in 1 Tim 2:3; Tit 2:10; 3:4.
10. Titus is mentioned elsewhere only in 2 Cor 2:13; 7:6, 13, 14; 8:6, 16, 23; 12:18; Gal 2:1, 3; 2 Tim 4:10. GK *5519*. On the writing of this letter, see Act 28:30.
11. Same word as in 1 Tim 1:2. The idea is "legitimately born".
12. Or, "in relation to, in the interest of, based on". GK *2848*.
13. Or, "shared". Same word as in Jude 3.
14. Some manuscripts say "Grace, mercy, peace from..." {A}.
15. Some manuscripts say "and *the* Lord Jesus Christ" {N}.
16. Or, "correct, set in order". Used only here. GK *2114*. The root word is "straight". Related to "correcting" in 2 Tim 3:16.
17. Or, "falling short". That is, the things left to be done. Same word as in 3:13. On this word, see Jam 1:5.
18. Or, "put in charge". On this word, see "put in charge" in Act 6:3.
19. That is, church leaders. On this word, see 1 Tim 5:17.
20. Or, "city by city", more literally, "according to city". Compare Act 14:23.
21. Or, "unaccused" of doing anything wrong, "not having been called in" on any charge. Elsewhere only in v 7; 1 Tim 3:10; 1 Cor 1:8; Col 1:22. GK *441*.
22. Or, "husband *of* one wife". On this phrase, see 1 Tim 3:2.
23. Or, "in the sphere of". Same word as in Rom 2:12. This phrase describes the children. This requirement is positively stated in 1 Tim 3:4.
24. Or, "charge". On the reason for this requirement, see 1 Tim 3:5. Elsewhere only in 1 Tim 5:19; Jn 18:29. GK *2990*. Related to "accuse" in Jn 5:45.
25. On this word, see Eph 5:18. This is the opposite of "filled with the Spirit".
26. Same word as in v 10; 1 Tim 1:9. Elsewhere only as "not subject" in Heb 2:8. GK *538*. This word also describes the children.
27. Note that "elder" and "overseer" are used here with reference to the same person. On this word, see Phil 1:1.
28. Or, "household manager, administrator". On this word, see 1 Pet 4:10.
29. Or, "stubborn, arrogant, self-pleasing, obstinate". Elsewhere only in 2 Pet 2:10. GK *881*.
30. Or, "fond of dishonorable, disgraceful, dishonest gain; avaricious". Elsewhere only in 1 Tim 3:8. GK *153*. Related to "greedily" in 1 Pet 5:2. This word is made up of the two words which are used separately in v 11— "shameful" and "gains".
31. That is, a lover of strangers. Elsewhere only in 1 Tim 3:2; 1 Pet 4:9. GK *5811*. Related to "hospitality" in Heb 13:2.
32. Or, "good-loving". Used only here. GK *5787*.
33. Same word as in 2:2, 5. On this word, see 1 Tim 3:2.
34. That is, law-abiding, observant of right, upright, right with God and their fellow man. On this word, see "righteous" in Rom 1:17.
35. Used only here. GK *1604*. On the related words, see 1 Cor 7:9.
36. Or, "Being devoted to". On this word, see 1 Thes 5:14.
37. That is, the apostolic teaching or doctrine he had received.
38. Same word as in 2:6, 15. On this word, see Rom 12:8.
39. Or, "in, by, by means of". GK *1877*.
40. This is a participle, "teaching being healthy". On this word, see 1 Tim 1:10.
41. Or, "correct, rebuke". Same word as "rebuke" in v 13; 2:15. On this word, see "expose" in Eph 5:11.
42. Or, "opposing, talking back, speaking against". Same word as in 2:9. On this word, see Rom 10:21.
43. Some manuscripts omit this word, {C}.
44. That is, ones talking of worthless, futile, vain, pointless things. Used only here. GK *3468*. Related word in 1 Tim 1:6.
45. This word means ones who deceive the understanding. Used only here. GK *5855*. Related word in Gal 6:3.
46. Or, "whom one must silence". On this idiom, see "must" in Mt 16:21.
47. Or, "muzzle, bridle, gag, stop the mouth". Used only here. GK *2187*. The root word is "mouth".
48. On "ought to", see Act 25:10.
49. Or, "disgraceful". Elsewhere only in 1 Cor 11:6; 14:35; Eph 5:12. GK *156*. Related to "shame" in Heb 12:2, and "put to shame" in 1 Jn 2:28.
50. Or, "advantage, profit". On this word, see Phil 3:7.
51. Paul quotes Epimenides, a Cretan poet/philosopher born in 659 B.C.
52. The Cretans' conduct was proverbial. Their name "Cretan" was turned into a verb which meant "to lie like a Cretan". For example, they claimed to have the temple of Zeus on their island, one of their more famous lies. Note "non-lying" in 1:2.
53. This (v 15-16) is a "severe rebuke". Or, "pure". Same word as in Jn 13:10; 15:3; Act 18:6; Rom 14:20; 1 Tim 3:9; 2 Tim 1:3 Rev 15:6; and as "pure" in Mt 5:8; 1 Tim 1:5; 2 Tim 2:22; Jam 1:27; 1 Pet 1:22. Used 27 times. GK *2754*. Related to "cleansed" in Heb 9:22.
54. Or, "stained, polluted". That is, morally corrupted. Elsewhere only in Jn 18:28; Heb 12:15; Jude 8. GK *3620*. Related to "defilement" in 2 Pet 2:10.
55. Or, "unbelievers". On this adjective, see Mt 17:17. Paul joins a participle and an adjective in a twofold description of these people, "the having been defiled and unbelieving *ones*". On this unusual grammar, see 1 Tim 4:3.
56. That is, all external things are ritually clean to those spiritually clean on the inside, that is, saved. But to those defiled on the inside, nothing on the outside is truly clean. Thus, to the saved, all foods

A. Rom 6:17 B. 1 Cor 12:28 C. Rom 8:33 D. Col 1:9 E. 1 Tim 2:2 F. Col 1:5 G. 1 Cor 12:8 H. 1 Cor 1:21 J. Jn 3:36, believe K. Rom 16:26 L. Lk 1:47 M. 1 Jn 3:1 N. Jude 6, left behind O. 1 Cor 7:17 P. Col 1:2, faithful Q. Mt 16:21 R. 1 Tim 3:3 S. 1 Tim 3:3 T. Heb 7:26 U. Tit 1:6 V. Eph 2:11, circumcised W. 2 Tim 2:18 X. Mk 3:20, house Y. 3 Jn 11 Z. Rev 13:1 AA. Jam 2:20, useless BB. 1 Thes 5:3, womb CC. Jn 1:7 DD. Eph 5:11, expose EE. 2 Cor 13:10 FF. 1 Tim 1:10 GG. 1 Tim 3:8 HH. 1 Tim 1:4 JJ. Mk 12:28 KK. Mt 4:4, mankind LL. Heb 12:25

1E. But both their mind[A] and conscience[B] have been defiled[C]
2E. They are confessing[1] to know God, but *by their* works[D] they are denying[E] *Him* 16

    1F. Being detestable[2], and disobedient[F], and disapproved[3] for every good[G] work

2A. But **you** be speaking[H] *the things* which are fitting[4] *for* healthy[J] teaching[5]— 2:1

  1B. *That* old-men[6] be sober[K], honorable[L], sound-minded[M] 2

    1C. Being healthy[J] *in* faith[N], *in* love[O], *in* endurance[P]

  2B. *That* old-women[7] similarly *be* reverent[8] in behavior, not slanderous[Q], not having been enslaved[R] *to* much wine[S], teachers-of-good[9] 3

    1C. In order that they may train[10] the young *women* to be 4

      1D. Husband-lovers, children-lovers[11]
      2D. Sound-minded[M], pure[T], working-at-home[12], good[G] 5
      3D. While being subject[U] to *their* own husbands
      4D. In order that the word[V] *of* God may not be blasphemed[W]

  3B. Be exhorting[X] the younger[13] *men* similarly to be sound-minded[14] °with-respect-to[15] all *things*, while showing[16] yourself *as a* pattern[17] *of* good[Y] works 6-7

    1C. In *your* teaching *showing* uncorruptness[18], dignity[19], °healthy[Z] uncondemnable[20] speech[V] 8
    2C. In order that the *one from the* contrary[21] *side* may be ashamed[22], having nothing bad[AA] to say about us[23]

  4B. *Be exhorting* slaves[BB] to be subject[U] *to their* own masters[CC] in all[24] *things* 9

    1C. To be pleasing[DD], not contradicting[EE], °not pilfering[FF], but demonstrating[25] all good[G] faith[26] 10
    2C. In order that they may adorn[27] the teaching *of* our Savior[GG] God in all *things*

  5B. For the grace[HH] *of* God appeared[28] bringing-salvation[29] *for* all people[30], °training[JJ] us that 11-12

    1C. Having denied[E] ungodliness[KK] and worldly[31] desires[LL]
    2C. We should live sound-mindedly[32] and righteously[MM] and godly[NN] in the present age, °while waiting-for[OO] the blessed[PP] hope[QQ] and appearance[RR] *of* the glory *of* our great God and Savior[33] Jesus Christ[34] 13

      1D. Who gave Himself for us in order that He might redeem[SS] us from all lawlessness[TT], and might cleanse[UU] for Himself *a* special[35] people— zealots[VV] *for* good[36] works 14

  6B. Be speaking[H] these *things,* and be exhorting[X], and be rebuking[37] with all authority[38]. Let no one be disregarding[39] you 15

are clean because they are not under any law or requirement regarding foods, 1 Tim 4:4-5. But to unbelievers, even the dietary "laws" they do obey do not bring them purity because they themselves are defiled, not the foods.
1. Same word as in Rom 10:9-10. On this word, see 1 Tim 6:12.
2. Used only here. GK *1008*. Related to "abomination" in Rev 17:4.
3. Or, "rejected, disqualified, failing to meet the test". On this word, see 1 Cor 9:27.
4. Or, "proper". On this word, see 1 Cor 11:13.
5. Same phrase as in 1:9.
6. Or, "aged men". This term refers to what we would call "middle-aged" and "senior" men, the older generations who are to be an example to the younger one. Elsewhere only in Lk 1:18; Phm 9 (of Paul in his fifties). GK *4566*. Related to "elder" in 1:5, which is the comparative form, "older, elder".
7. Same word as "old men" (v 2), except feminine in form. Used only here. GK *4567*.
8. Or, "like a holy person, like a priestess". Used only here. GK *2640*. Related to "priest, temple".
9. Or, "teaching-what-is-good". Used only here. GK *2815*.
10. Or, "advise, urge". The idea is "train the mind, make sound-minded, bring good sense". Used only here. GK *5405*. Same root word as "sound-minded" in 2:2, 5; "sound-mindedly" in 2:12; and "to be sound-minded" in 2:6.
11. Or, "Husband-loving, children-loving". Both are used only here. GK *5791* and *5817*.
12. This rare word is used only here. The emphasis is on "working", so as not to be idle busybodies, 1 Tim 5:13. GK *3877*. Some manuscripts have another word meaning "watching the home, housekeeping" and "mistress of the house" {N}.
13. Same word as "young" in v 4, except this is masculine and comparative in form, "younger". "Young" is found only in Tit 2:4; "younger" is in Lk 15:12, 13; 22:26; Jn 21:18; Act 5:6; 1 Tim 5:1, 2, 11, 14; Tit 2:6; 1 Pet 5:5. On this word, see "new" in Mk 2:22.
14. Or, "be sensible, serious". On this verb, see Rom 12:3. See 1 Tim 3:2 for related words.
15. Others take this phrase with what follows, "... sound-minded, while with respect to all *things* showing...".
16. Or, "presenting, offering". Same word as "offering" in Lk 6:29, and "showing" in Act 28:2. On this word, see "grant" in Act 17:31.
17. Or, "example". On this word, see 1 Pet 5:3. Paul did this in Phil 3:17; 2 Thes 3:9; etc.
18. Or, "lack of corruption; soundness, purity". Used only here. GK *917*. Related to "undecayable" in 1 Cor 15:52.
19. Or, "seriousness". On this word, see 1 Tim 3:4. Some manuscripts add next "incorruptibility" {N}.
20. That is, not blameworthy, beyond reproach. Used only here. GK *183*. It is the negative of the word "condemn" in Gal 2:11.
21. Or, "opposite". Or, "the *one* contrary, the opponent". Used by Paul of doing things "contrary to the name of Jesus" in Act 26:9, and "nothing contrary to our people" in Act 28:17. On this word, see 1 Thes 2:15.
22. Or, "may be turned on himself". On this word, see "have regard for" in Lk 18:2.
23. Some manuscripts say "you" {N}.
24. This is the Greek word order. Some take this phrase with what follows, "to be pleasing in all *things*".
25. Or, "showing". Same word as in 3:2. On this word, see Eph 2:7. Not the same word as "showing" in Tit 2:7.
26. Or, "fidelity, faithfulness". That is, genuine faithfulness, not eye-service, Eph 6:6. Act in good faith. On this word, see Eph 2:8.
27. Or, "decorate, make attractive". On this word, see 1 Tim 2:9.
28. Or, "showed itself, made an appearance". Paul is referring to the first coming of Christ. Same word as in 3:4; Act 27:20. Elsewhere only as "shine upon" in Lk 1:79. GK *2210*. Related to "appearance" in v 13.
29. Or, "the grace of God *bringing* salvation appeared *for* all people...". Used only here. GK *5403*. Related to "salvation" in Lk 2:30 and 19:9.
30. Paul may mean "all humanity". Grace appeared providing the opportunity for salvation to all, 1 Tim 2:4. Or he may mean "all kinds" of people. Note the context (v 1-10) is men and women, young and old, slave and master.
31. That is, pertaining to this world. On this word, see "earthly" in Heb 9:1.
32. Or, "sensibly, moderately, prudently". Used only here. GK *5407*. See related words in 1 Tim 3:2.
33. Some think Paul is calling Jesus our "great God and Savior". Others render this "*of* the glory *of* the great God and our Savior", referring to the Father and the Son. Consult the commentaries. Compare 2 Pet 1:1.
34. Some manuscripts say "Christ Jesus" {N}.
35. Or, "chosen". Used only here. GK *4342*. Used in the OT of Israel as "a special (or peculiar) people (or a people for God's own possession, a treasured possession) above all nations" in Ex 19:5; Deut 7:6; 14:2; 26:18.
36. Or, "beautiful, commendable, praiseworthy, outwardly good". GK *2819*. This "good works" is elsewhere only in Mt 5:16; 26:10; Mk 14:6; Jn 10:32, 33; 1 Tim 3:1; 5:10a, 25; 6:18; Tit 2:7; 3:8, 14; Heb 10:24; 1 Pet 2:12. See also the "good works" phrase in Rom 2:7. Compare Jam 2:14-26.
37. Same word as in 1:13; 2 Tim 4:2. On this word, see "expose" in Eph 5:11.
38. Or, "command", as this word is used in 1:3.
39. Used only here. GK *4368*. Related to "look down on" in 1 Tim 4:11.

A. Rom 7:23 B. Act 23:1 C. Tit 1:15 D. Mt 26:10 E. 2 Tim 2:12 F. Lk 1:17 G. 1 Tim 5:10b H. Jn 12:49 J. 1 Tim 1:10 K. 1 Tim 3:2 L. 1 Tim 3:8 M. 1 Tim 3:2 N. Eph 2:8 O. 1 Jn 4:16 P. Jam 1:3 Q. 1 Tim 3:11 R. Rom 6:18 S. 1 Tim 5:23 T. 1 Pet 3:2 U. Eph 5:21 V. 1 Cor 12:8, word W. 1 Tim 6:1 X. Rom 12:8 Y. 1 Tim 5:10a Z. Mt 12:13 AA. Jam 3:16 BB. Rom 6:17 CC. Jude 4 DD. Eph 5:10 EE. Rom 10:21 FF. Act 5:21, kept back GG. Tit 1:3 HH. Eph 2:8 JJ. 1 Cor 11:32, disciplined KK. Rom 1:18 LL. Gal 5:16 MM. 1 Cor 15:34 NN. 2 Tim 3:12 OO. Act 24:15 PP. Lk 6:20 QQ. Col 5:5 RR. 2 Thes 2:8 SS. 1 Pet 1:18 TT. 1 Jn 3:4 UU. Heb 9:22 VV. 1 Cor 14:12

3A. Be reminding^A them to be subject^B *to* rulers^C, *to* authorities;¹ to be obedient²; to be ready^D for every good^E work; *to blaspheme^F no one; to be non-quarrelsome^G, kind^H, demonstrating^J all gentleness³ toward all people^K

   1B. For **we** also were once foolish⁴, disobedient^L, being deceived^M, being-slaves⁵ *to* various desires^N and pleasures^O, spending^P *life* in malice⁶ and envy^Q, detested⁷, hating^R one another

   2B. But when the kindness^S and love-for-mankind⁸ *of* our Savior^T God appeared^U, ***He saved**^V **us**⁹

      1C. Not by works^W which **we** did in [our] righteousness
      2C. But according-to¹⁰ His mercy^X, through *a* washing¹¹ *of* regeneration¹² and *a* renewing¹³ *of the* Holy Spirit

         1D. Whom He richly poured-out^Y upon us through Jesus Christ our Savior^T

      3C. In order that having been declared-righteous^Z by the grace^AA *of* that *One*, we might become heirs^BB according-to¹⁴ *the* hope^CC *of* eternal life¹⁵
      4C. The saying^DD *is* trustworthy^EE

   3B. And concerning these *things,* I want you to be speaking-confidently^FF, in order that the *ones* having believed *in* God may be careful¹⁶ to take-the-lead¹⁷ *in* good^GG works^W. These *things* are good^GG and profitable^HH *for* people^K
   4B. But be shunning¹⁸ foolish¹⁹ controversies^JJ, and genealogies^KK, and quarrels^LL, and battles^MM pertaining-to-the-Law. For they are unprofitable^NN and worthless²⁰
   5B. Be declining²¹ *a* divisive²² person^K after *a* first and second admonition^OO, *knowing that such *a one* has been perverted²³ and is sinning, being self-condemned

---

A. When I send Artemas or Tychicus^PP to you, be diligent^QQ to come to me in Nicopolis²⁴, for I have determined^RR to spend-the-winter there
B. Diligently²⁵ send-forward²⁶ Zenas the lawyer²⁷ and Apollos, in order that nothing may be lacking^SS *for* them
C. And let our *people* also be learning to take-the-lead *in* good^GG works for necessary²⁸ needs²⁹, in order that they may not be unfruitful^TT
D. All the *ones* with me greet you
E. Greet the *ones* loving³⁰ us in *the* faith
F. Grace *be* with you all³¹

Verse

3:1
2

3

4-5

6

7
8

9

10-11

12

13

14

15

1. Or, "to be subject to rulers; to obey authorities". The Greek word order is "... them *to* rulers, *to* authorities, to be subject, to be obedient". Some manuscripts say "to be subject *to* rulers and authorities, to be obedient" {B}.
2. This word means "to obey one in authority". On this word, see "obey" in Act 27:21.
3. Same two words as in 2 Cor 10:1, "the gentleness and kindness of Christ". On this word, see Eph 4:2.
4. Or, "senseless, without understanding". Elsewhere only in Lk 24:25; Rom 1:14; Gal 3:1, 3; 1 Tim 6:9. GK *485*.
5. Or, "serving as slaves". On this word, see "are slaves" in Rom 6:6.
6. That is, the desire to cause pain or distress in others. On this word, see "badness" in 1 Pet 2:1.
7. Or, "loathed, hated; detestable, loathsome; hateful". Used only here. GK *5144*. Not related to the next word.
8. Elsewhere only as "humaneness" in Act 28:2. GK *5792*. The Greek is *philanthropia*. Related to "humanely" in Act 27:3.
9. In the Greek word order, "He saved us" is after "mercy", giving it Paul's emphasis.
10. Or, "based on, by way of". GK *2848*.
11. On this word, see Eph 5:26. Some think Paul means the washing leading to regeneration; that is, water baptism, the Christian rite of initiation. Others think he means the spiritual washing proceeding from regeneration; that is, the cleansing of our sin that occurs at the new birth.
12. Or, "rebirth". Elsewhere only in Mt 19:28 of the future Messianic age. GK *4098*.
13. Or, "renewal". That is, the renewing to a new life proceeding from the Spirit. God saved us through the "bath" of a rebirth (Jn 3:3), and the "renewing" to a new life being performed by the Holy Spirit. Elsewhere only in Rom 12:2. GK *364*. Related to the verbs in 2 Cor 4:16 and Heb 6:6.
14. Or, "with respect to, in accordance with, based on". GK *2848*.
15. This is the Greek word order. Some think Paul means "heirs *of* eternal life in accordance with [our present] hope"; others, "heirs, in accordance with [our present] hope *of* eternal life".
16. Or, "give thought, be intent, be concerned". Used only here. GK *5863*. Related to "think" in Rom 8:5.
17. Or, "put *themselves* at the head, busy oneself *with*". Same word as in v 14. On this word, see "leading" in Rom 12:8.
18. Same word as in 2 Tim 2:16.
19. Or, "stupid, silly". Same word as in Mt 7:26; 23:17; 25:2, 3, 8; 1 Cor 1:25, 27; 3:18; 4:10; 2 Tim 2:23. Elsewhere only as "fool" in Mt 5:22. GK *3704*. Related to "foolishness" in 1 Cor 2:14.
20. Or, "useless, futile, pointless". On this word, see "futile" in 1 Cor 15:17.
21. Or, "refusing" and therefore "rejecting, avoiding". Refuse to talk or have anything to do with a divisive person. Warn him, but do not debate with him. If he fails to respond, refuse his company. Same word as in 1 Tim 4:7; 5:11; 2 Tim 2:23. On this word, see "refuse" in Heb 12:25.
22. Or, "factious". Used only here. GK *148*. Related to "faction" in 1 Cor 11:19.
23. Or, "turned aside, turned-from [the right path]". Used only here. GK *1750*.
24. Some think this is the city in western Greece. There are other cities by this name. Used only here. GK *3776*.
25. Or, "With haste, Urgently". Same word as in 2 Tim 1:17. Elsewhere only as "eagerly" in Phil 2:28; and "earnestly" in Lk 7:4. GK *5081*. Related to "earnestness" in 2 Cor 8:16.
26. Or, "accompany". On this word, see Rom 15:24.
27. That is, the expert in Roman law (probably). On this word, see "Law-expert" in Lk 7:30.
28. Or, "indispensable, pressing, required". For example, needs such as helping with whatever Zenas and Apollos may be lacking for their journey. Same word as in Act 13:46; 1 Cor 12:22; 2 Cor 9:5; Phil 1:24; 2:25; Heb 8:3. Elsewhere only as "close" in Act 10:24. GK *338*. Related to "compel" in Gal 6:12.
29. Used 49 times. GK *5970*.
30. Paul uses this word only one other time, 1 Cor 16:22. On this word, see "*affectionately* love" in Jn 21:15.
31. Some manuscripts add "amen" {A}.

A. Jn 14:26 B. Eph 5:21 C. Col 1:18, beginning D. Mk 14:15, prepared E. 1 Tim 5:10b F. 1 Tim 6:1 G. 1 Tim 3:3 H. Phil 4:5, kindness J. Eph 2:7 K. Mt 4:4, mankind L. Lk 1:17 M. Jam 5:19, err N. Gal 5:16 O. Lk 8:14 P. 1 Tim 2:2 Q. Mk 15:10 R. Rom 9:13 S. Rom 3:12, goodness T. Tit 1:3 U. Tit 2:11 V. Lk 19:10 W. Mt 26:10 X. Mt 9:13 Y. Act 2:17 Z. Rom 3:24 AA. Eph 2:8 BB. Rom 8:17 CC. Col 1:5 DD. 1 Cor 12:8, word EE. Col 1:2, faithful FF. 1 Tim 1:7 GG. 1 Tim 5:10a HH. 2 Tim 3:16 JJ. 1 Tim 6:4 KK. 1 Tim 1:4 LL. 1 Cor 1:11 MM. 2 Tim 2:23 NN. Heb 7:18, unprofitableness OO. Eph 6:4 PP. Act 20:4 QQ. Eph 4:3 RR. Mt 7:1, judge SS. Jam 1:5 TT. 1 Cor 14:14

Overview		Philemon
Introduction		1-3
1A. I am giving thanks to my God always		4
1B. Making mention of you in my prayers so the fellowship of your faith may become effective		4-6
2B. For I had much joy in your love, because the saints have been refreshed through you		7
2A. Therefore, although having boldness to command you, I rather am appealing to you for Onesimus		8-10
1B. Whom I fathered in my imprisonment		10
2B. The one formerly useless to you, but now useful both to you and to me		11
3B. Whom I sent back to you		12
4B. Whom I was wishing to hold back with myself, but not without your consent.		13-16
3A. Therefore, if you hold me as a partner, accept him as me. If he owes you anything, I will repay		17-19
4A. Yes, brother, may I profit from you in the Lord. Refresh my deep feelings in Christ		20
Conclusion		21-25

		Verse
	A. Paul, *a* prisoner[A] *of* Christ Jesus[1], and Timothy *our* brother	1:1
	B. *To* Philemon,[2] our beloved[B] *one* and fellow-worker[C]	
	1. And *to* Apphia *our* sister[3]	2
	2. And *to* Archippus[4] our fellow-soldier[5]	
	3. And *to* the church at your house	
	C. Grace *to* you and peace from God our Father and *the* Lord Jesus Christ	3
1A.	I am giving-thanks[D] *to* my God always[6]	4
	1B. Making mention *of* you in my prayers °while hearing-*of* your love[E] and faith[7] which you have toward the Lord Jesus and for all the saints[F]	5
	1C. So that[8] the fellowship[9] *of* your faith[G] may become[10] effective[11] by[12] *the* knowledge[H] *of* every good[J] *thing*[13] in us[14] for[15] Christ	6
	2B. For I had[16] much joy[K] and encouragement[L] in[17] your love, because the deep-feelings[M] *of* the saints have been refreshed[18] through you, brother	7
2A.	Therefore, [although] having much boldness[N] in Christ to be commanding[O] you *to do* the fitting[19] *thing*, for the sake of love I am rather appealing[P]— being such *a one* as[20] Paul, *an* old-man[21], and now also *a* prisoner[A] *of* Christ Jesus[22]—°I am appealing to you concerning my child[Q] Onesimus[23]	8 9 10
	1B. Whom I fathered[R] in *my* imprisonment[S]	
	2B. The *one* formerly useless[24] *to* you, but now useful[25] both[26] *to* you and *to* me	11
	3B. Whom I sent-back[T] *to* you— him[27], that is, my *own* deep feelings[28]!	12
	4B. Whom **I** was wishing[U] to hold-back[V] with myself, in order that on behalf of you, he might be serving[W] me in *my* imprisonment[29] *for* the good-news[X]	13
	1C. But without your consent[Y], I wanted[Z] to do nothing, in order that your good[30] *deed* should not be as-*if* based-on[31] compulsion[32], but based-on willingness[33]	14
	2C. For[34] perhaps for this reason he was separated[35] for *an* hour— in order that you might receive him in full[36] forever	15
	1D. No longer as *a* slave[AA], but beyond *a* slave— *a* beloved[B] brother[BB]	16
	1E. Especially *to* me	
	2E. But how much more *to* you— both in *the* flesh[CC], and in *the* Lord![37]	
3A.	Therefore if you hold me *as a* partner[DD], accept[EE] him as me[38]. °And if *as to* anything[39] he wronged[40] you or owes[FF] *you*, charge this *to* my account[41]. °**I**, Paul, wrote *it with* my *own* hand— **I** will repay[42]	17-18 19
	1B. In order that I may not be saying *to* you that you indeed owe[43] yourself *to* me[44]	

1. Some manuscripts say "Jesus Christ" {K}.
2. Philemon is not mentioned elsewhere. Apphia is probably his wife.
3. Some manuscripts say "And *to* the beloved Apphia" {A}.
4. This man is also mentioned in Col 4:17. He was a leader in the church at Philemon's house in Colossae. Some think he was also a relative of Philemon— perhaps his son, or a friend of the family.
5. Elsewhere only in Phil 2:25. GK *5369*.
6. In the Greek word order, this word stands here. Some take it with "I am giving thanks"; others with "making mention". The same issue arises in Col 1:3.
7. Or, "faithfulness". Only here does Paul say "love and faith" instead of "faith and love". This is the Greek word order. Some think both "love and faith" are toward the Lord and for the saints, viewing faith toward the Lord as "spiritual" faith, and faith toward the saints as "practical" faith in action, or as faithfulness. Others regroup these phrases as "love for all the saints" and "faith toward the Lord Jesus", as Paul says in Col 1:4; Eph 1:15.
8. What follows is the content and goal of Paul's prayer for Philemon.
9. Or, "contribution, participation, partnership, sharing". Some think Paul means "that the partnership of your faith with ours (or, the faith which you share in common with us) may be the source of effective service in you". Others think he means "that the contribution or sharing of your faith toward the needs of others may become effective", both toward spiritual and material needs. Others think he means "that the fellowship or participation that others have in your faith may become effective in them". On this word, see 1 Cor 1:9.
10. Or, "prove to be". GK *1181*.
11. Or, "active". On this word, see Heb 4:12.
12. Or, "in". Some think this gives the means by which the faith becomes effective; others, the sphere in which it is to become effective. GK *1877*.
13. Some manuscripts say "every good work" {N}.
14. That is, us Christians. Some manuscripts say "in you" (plural) {B}, that is, "in you" or "among you" there.
15. Or, "in". Some think Paul means "become effective... for Christ"; others, "every good thing... for Christ"; others, "in us for Christ". Some manuscripts say "Christ Jesus" {N}. GK *1650*.
16. Some manuscripts say "For we have" {N}.
17. Or, "on the basis of, in reference to". GK *2093*.
18. Or, "revived, given rest". Same word as in v 20; 1 Cor 16:18; 2 Cor 7:13. Elsewhere only as "give rest" in Mt 11:28; and "rest" in Mt 26:45; Mk 6:31; 14:41; Lk 12:19; 1 Pet 4:14; Rev 6:11; 14:13. GK *399*. Related to "rest" in Mt 12:43.
19. Or, "proper, right". This is a participle, "the *thing* being fitting". Elsewhere only in Eph 5:4; Col 3:18. GK *465*.
20. Some start a new sentence here. "... being such *a* one [as prefers to appeal rather than command]. As Paul— *an* old man, and now also *a* prisoner *of* Christ Jesus— I am appealing to you". Others take this whole phrase with what follows, "... rather appealing. Being such *a* one as... I am appealing to you".
21. Paul was in his fifties. On this word, see Tit 2:2. Some think Paul means "ambassador", as the related verb means in Eph 6:20.
22. Some manuscripts say "Jesus Christ" {K}.
23. This man was a runaway slave belonging to Philemon. He is mentioned elsewhere only in Col 4:9. GK *3946*.
24. This is a play on words because his name, Onesimus, means "useful". Used only here. GK *947*. Related to "unprofitable" in Mt 25:30.
25. Elsewhere only in 2 Tim 2:21; 4:11. GK *2378*.
26. Some manuscripts omit this word {C}.
27. This is the Greek word order of this verse. That is, not just him, but my own deep feelings as well; him— nay, my own deep feelings! Some manuscripts say for verse 12, "I sent him, that is, my *own* deep feelings, back *to* you"; others, "I sent *him* back. Now **you** receive him, that is, my *own* deep feelings" {B}. There are other variations.
28. Onesimus represents Paul's deep feelings, which he sent back to Philemon hoping that Philemon would refresh them (v 20), as he had others (v 7). Same word as in v 7.
29. Paul abandoned this wish and sent Onesimus back.
30. Some think Paul is referring to Philemon's theoretical good deed toward Paul had Paul kept Onesimus for service. Others think he is referring to Philemon's future "goodness" in general, however he might choose to display it. Paul is not directly asking or expecting him to sent Onesimus back. He simply did not want any goodness by Philemon to be forced. On this word, see 1 Tim 5:10b.
31. Or, "according to, by way of". GK *2848*.
32. Or, "force, necessity". That is, because you were forced to approve of it because I kept him here. On this word see "necessity" in 1 Cor 7:26. Related to "by compulsion" in 1 Pet 5:2.
33. Or, "voluntary choice". That is, "not as if by force, but by voluntary choice", "not as if forcibly, but voluntarily". Used only here. GK *1730*. On related words, see 1 Pet 5:2.
34. This is a second reason Paul did not keep Onesimus. Perhaps what follows is God's purpose for them in all this.
35. Notice Paul does not say "ran away, fled". He makes no mention of the culpability of either slave or master.
36. That is, receive in full and close the account. On the word "receive in full", see Phil 4:18.
37. That is, a slave in the flesh, a brother in the Lord.
38. This is the content of Paul's appeal. That is, receive Onesimus back with joy and thankfulness, as if I myself came back to you; not with punishment.
39. Some think Paul means "assuming that he is indebted to you for the loss associated with his running away, or for secondary losses resulting from it". Had Onesimus stolen things when he left, Paul would have explicitly addressed it here. Others think Paul is implying that Onesimus stole from Philemon.
40. Or, "harmed". On this word, see Act 7:24.
41. Charge my child's debt to his father. This word, "charge to the account", is used only here. GK *1823*. Related word in Rom 5:13.
42. Or, "make compensation, pay the damages, repay the debt". Used only here. GK *702*.
43. Or, "still-owe". Used only here. GK *4695*.
44. In other words, I am personally guaranteeing what Onesimus owes you. Accept him based on our partnership and my personal guarantee, so that I will not be forced to remind you of your even greater debt to me as a reason for doing what I ask. Paul had apparently led Philemon to Christ.

A. Eph 3:1 B. Mt 3:17 C. Rom 16:3 D. Mt 26:27 E. 1 Jn 4:16 F. 1 Pet 1:16, holy G. Eph 2:8 H. Col 1:9 J. 1 Tim 5:10b K. Lk 24:52 L. Act 4:36 M. Phil 1:8 N. Heb 4:16, confidence O. Lk 8:25 P. Rom 12:8, exhorting Q. 1 Jn 3:1 R. 1 Jn 2:29, born S. Phil 1:7 T. Lk 23:7, send up U. Jam 1:18, willed V. Rom 1:18, hold down W. 1 Pet 4:10, ministering X. 1 Cor 15:1 Y. 1 Cor 1:10, purpose Z. Jn 7:17, willing AA. Rom 6:17 BB. Act 16:40 CC. Col 2:23 DD. 2 Pet 1:4, sharer EE. Rom 14:1 FF. 1 Jn 4:11, ought

4A. Yes, brother, may¹ **I** profit² *from* you in *the* Lord. Refresh³ my deep-feelings^A in Christ 20

   A. I wrote *to* you having confidence^B *in* your obedience⁴, knowing that you will do even beyond⁵ *the* 21
      things which I am saying
   B. And at the same time also, prepare^C lodging⁶ *for* me. For I hope^D that through your prayers, I shall 22
      be granted^E *to* you
   C. Epaphras^F, my fellow-captive^G in Christ Jesus, greets^H you, °*as do* Mark^J, Aristarchus^K, Demas^L, 23-24
      Luke⁷, my fellow-workers^M
   D. The grace *of* the⁸ Lord Jesus Christ *be* with your⁹ spirit 25

1. Having appealed for the sake of Onesimus, Paul now appeals for his own sake. Note Paul's emphasis on "I". He phrases this as a personal wish (the grammar is similar to a prayer request), thus presenting it to Philemon as a polite request.
2. Or, "may I be favored *by* you, may I benefit *from* you". That is, may I have the profit of joy and thankfulness which I will gain when you accept him as me. Used only here. GK *3949*.
3. Same word as in v 7.
4. Some think Paul means obedience to God; others, to Paul. On this word, see Rom 16:26.
5. Paul leaves it to Philemon to be generous. This could be taken to mean, "show him even more kindness", or, "send him back to me", or, "set him free". Paul does not directly ask.
6. On this word, see Act 28:23, which may have been the "lodging" from which Paul wrote this letter.
7. Luke is mentioned elsewhere by name only in Col 4:14; 2 Tim 4:11. The writer of Luke and Acts. Some think he is the "Lucius" in Rom 16:21. GK *3371*.
8. Some manuscripts say "our" Lord {B}.
9. This word is plural. Some manuscripts add "amen" {A}.

A. Phil 1:8 B. 1 Jn 3:19, persuade C. Mk 14:15 D. Jn 5:45, put hope E. 1 Cor 2:12, freely give F. Col 1:7 G. Rom 16:7 H. Mk 15:18 J. 1 Pet 5:13 K. Act 19:29 L. 2 Tim 4:10 M. Rom 16:3

Hebrews

Overview

1A. God, having spoken long ago by the prophets, spoke to us in these latter days by a Son — 1:1-2

    1B. Who— being the radiance of His glory and the exact representation of His essence, and upholding all things by His word— having made purification of sins, sat down on high — 1:3

        1C. Having become better than the angels, as the Son, Ruler, Creator they worship — 1:4-14

    2B. For this reason, we must pay attention to what we have heard, that we may not drift away — 2:1-4
    3B. For God did not subject to angels the coming world— but we see Jesus crowned with glory and honor because of the suffering of death — 2:5-9
    4B. For it was fitting for God to perfect the Author of our salvation through sufferings. He partook of humanity that by His death He might free us, and be our merciful High Priest — 2:10-18
    5B. Hence, brothers, consider Jesus as faithful to God. He is worthy of more glory than Moses — 3:1-6
    6B. Therefore, "Today, do not harden your hearts against God as Israel did in the wilderness" — 3:7-11

        1C. Watch that there will never be an evil heart of unbelief in you in departing from God — 3:12-19
        2C. Let us fear lest any of you should seem to have come short of entering His rest — 4:1-10
        3C. Let us be diligent to enter that rest. For the word of God is living and effective — 4:11-13

2A. Therefore having a great High Priest— Jesus, the Son of God— let us be holding on to the confession — 4:14

    1B. For we have One tempted like us, without sin. So let us be approaching to receive grace — 4:15-16
    2B. For every human priest is appointed on behalf of people to offer gifts and sacrifices for sin — 5:1-4
    3B. So also, Christ was appointed by God and learned obedience through His suffering — 5:5-8
    4B. And having been perfected, He became the cause of eternal salvation to all obeying Him, having been designated by God as High Priest according to the order of Melchizedek — 5:9-10

        1C. Concerning whom, our message is great and hard to explain to you — 5:11

            1D. For although you ought to be teachers, you again need to be taught the milk — 5:12-14
            2D. Therefore let us be carried on to maturity, not again laying the foundation — 6:1-2
            3D. And this we will do if God permits. For it is impossible to renew to repentance those having fallen aside, crucifying Him again and publicly disgracing Him — 6:3-8
            4D. But concerning you, we are convinced of better things, of your salvation. But we desire you to be imitators of those who inherit the promises through faith — 6:9-20

        2C. For this Melchizedek remains a priest perpetually, greater than Abraham and Levi — 7:1-10
        3C. Now indeed, what need was there for another priesthood? It indicates a setting aside of the old one, and a bringing in of a better hope through which we draw near to God — 7:11-19
        4C. And His priesthood has God's oath-swearing, so Jesus guarantees a better covenant — 7:20-22
        5C. And unlike Levitical priests, He remains forever. Hence He can save completely — 7:23-25
        6C. For such a High Priest was fitting for us— having offered Himself once for all — 7:26-28

    5B. The main point is— we have such a High Priest, minister in the true tabernacle built by God — 8:1-2

        1C. For a high priest is appointed to offer sacrifices. Jesus must also have something to offer — 8:3
        2C. Now indeed, if He were on earth He would not be a priest according to the Law — 8:4-5

	3C. But He has obtained a more excellent ministry as mediator of a better covenant enacted on better promises	8:6
	1D. For if that first covenant was faultless, God would not have made a second	8:7-13
	2D. Now indeed, the first covenant had its ministry, which is unable to perfect us	9:1-10
	3D. But Christ as High Priest entered the heavenly tabernacle once for all through His own blood, having obtained eternal redemption	9:11-14
	4D. And for this reason He is mediator of a new covenant, so that we may receive the promise of the eternal inheritance, a death having occurred for redemption	9:15-28
	5D. For the Law is never able to perfect us through the yearly sacrifice. Therefore Jesus came and God did so through the offering of His body once for all	10:1-10
	6D. And every priest has stood, daily offering sacrifices unable to take away sins. But Jesus offered one sacrifice for all time and sat down, having perfected us	10:11-14
	7D. And the Spirit also testifies to us, for there is no longer an offering for sin	10:15-18
	6B. Therefore brothers, having confidence to enter by His blood and a great High Priest	10:19-21
	1C. Let us be approaching with a true heart in full assurance of faith	10:22
	2C. Let us be holding on to the confession of our hope without wavering	10:23
	3C. And let us be considering one another for the provoking to love and good works	10:24-25
	4C. For if we disregard Jesus, no sacrifice for sin remains, only fearful judgment	10:26-31
3A. Now remember the former days when you endured a great struggle of sufferings		10:32-33
	1B. For indeed you accepted your plundering with joy. Do not throw away your confidence	10:34-35
	2B. For you have need of endurance by faith, in order that you may receive the promise	10:36-39
	3B. Now faith is the assurance of the things being hoped. For in this the elders were attested. They lived by faith, and died not receiving the promise, looking away to the reward	11:1-40
	4B. So therefore, let us run our race with endurance, looking to Jesus who endured the cross	12:1-2
	1C. For consider the One having endured such opposition, that you may not lose heart	12:3-4
	2C. And have you forgotten the Lord's discipline? You are enduring discipline as sons	12:5-11
	3C. Therefore, straighten up your feeble knees. And be making straight paths for your feet	12:12-13
	1D. Be pursuing peace and the holiness without which no one will see the Lord. For you have approached Mount Zion. Be watching out that you do not refuse Him	12:14-29
	2D. Let brotherly love continue	13:1
	3D. Do not be forgetting hospitality	13:2
	4D. Remember the prisoners, the ones being mistreated	13:3
	5D. Let marriage be honored by all	13:4
	6D. Let character be without the love of money	13:5-6
	7D. Remember the ones leading you	13:7-8
	8D. Do not be carried away by strange teachings. We have a spiritual altar	13:9-16
	9D. Be obeying the ones leading you	13:17
	10D. Be praying for us	13:18-19
	5B. Now may the God of peace prepare you in every good thing so that you may do His will	13:20-21
Conclusion		13:22-25

| Hebrews 1:1 | 822 | Verse |

1A. God, having spoken long-ago[A] in-many-portions[1] and in-many-ways[2] to the fathers by the prophets[B], *spoke to us at *the* last[3] *of* these days by[4] *a* Son[5], Whom He appointed[C] inheritor[6] *of* all *things,* through Whom also He made the worlds[7] 1-2

    1B. Who— being *the* radiance[8] *of* His glory and exact-representation[9] *of* His essence[10], and upholding[11] all *things by* the word[D] *of* His power[12]— having made purification[E] *of* sins[13], sat-*down* at *the* right hand *of* the Majesty[14] on high[15] 3

        1C. Having become so-much better[16] *than* the angels, *by*-as-much-as[17] He has inherited[F] *a* more-excellent[G] name than they 4

            1D. For *to* which *of* the angels did He ever say, "**You** are my Son. Today[18] **I** have fathered[H] you"? [Ps 2:7]; and again, "**I** will be[19] *a* father *to* Him, and **He** will be *a* son *to* Me"? [1 Chron 17:13] 5

            2D. And again[20], when He brings the Firstborn[J] into the world[21] He says [in Deut 32:43], "And let all *the* angels *of* God give-worship[22] *to* Him" 6

            3D. And with regard to **the angels**[23] He says [in Ps 104:4], "The *One* making His angels winds, and His ministers[K] *a* flame[L] *of* fire"—*but with regard to the Son *He says* 7 8

                1E. "Your throne[M], God,[24] *is* forever and ever[N]. And the scepter[O] *of* straightness[25] *is the* scepter *of* Your[26] kingdom. *You loved[P] righteousness and hated lawlessness[27]. For this reason, God[28], your God anointed[Q] You *with the* oil[R] *of* gladness[S] beyond Your companions[29]" [Ps 45:6-7] 9

                2E. And, "**You**[30], Lord, laid-the-foundation-of[T] the earth at *the* beginnings. And the heavens are works *of* Your hands. *They** will perish[U], but **You** continue[31]. Indeed they will all become-old[V] like *a* garment, *and You will roll them up[W] as-if *a* cloak[32]. They will indeed be changed[33] like *a* garment[34]. But **You** are the same, and Your years will not end[35]" [Ps 102:25-27] 10 11 12

            4D. And with regard to which *of* the angels has He ever said "Be sitting on My right *side* until I put Your enemies *as a* footstool *of* Your feet"? [Ps 110:1] *Are they not all ministering[36] spirits being sent-forth[X] for service[Y] for the sake of the *ones* going to inherit[F] salvation[37]? 13 14

    2B. For this reason,[38] we must[Z] pay more attention to[AA] the *things* having been heard,[39] that we may not-ever[40] drift-away[41] 2:1

        1C. For[42] if the word[BB] having been spoken through angels[43] proved-to-be[44] firm[45], and every transgression[CC] and disobedience[46] received *a* just[DD] penalty[47], *how shall **we** escape[EE], having neglected[48] **so great** *a* salvation[FF]?— which 2 3

1. Or, "many parts, many shares". God's revelation came piece by piece, over the centuries. Used only here. GK *4495*.
2. Or, "many manners, methods". In types, symbolic actions, dreams, visions, etc. Used only here. GK *4502*.
3. Or, "end". "Last" is singular, "days" is plural. Same phrase as in Num 24:14; Jer 23:20; 49:39; Dan 10:14. A similar phrase with "last" plural is in Gen 49:1; Deut 8:16; Josh 24:27; Jer 30:24; Ezek 38:16; Dan 2:28, 29, 45; Hos 3:5; Mic 4:1. Some think the writer means "in these last days", the days which have now begun with the appearance of the Messiah, Messiah's days. Compare Heb 9:26. Others think he means "at the last of these days to which I just referred", the OT age in which the fathers and the prophets lived. Same word as in "at the last of times" in 1 Pet 1:20; "in the last time" in 1 Pet 1:5; Jude 18; "the last days" in Act 2:17; 2 Tim 3:1; Jam 5:3; 2 Pet 3:3; "the last day" in Jn 6:39; 40, 44, 54; 11:24; 12:48; and "the last hour" in 1 Jn 2:18. Used 52 times. GK *2274*.
4. Or, "in". Same word as just used with "prophets". GK *1877*.
5. Or, "by *His* Son". That is, by One whose essential quality is that He is God's Son (as in 3:6; 5:8; 7:28), not merely a prophet.
6. On this word, see "heir" in Rom 8:17. Compare Ps 2:8.
7. Or, "the ages", the universe of time and space. Some think this means the visible and invisible worlds. Same word as in 11:3; and as "age" in 6:5; 9:26; Act 15:18; Rom 12:2; 1 Cor 10:11; 2 Cor 4:4; Eph 1:21; 1 Tim 6:17. GK *172*.
8. Or, "reflection". God is light. Jesus is the brilliance or reflection of that light beaming forth. Used only here. GK *575*.
9. Or, "exact imprint". As the imprint matches the die, so Christ matches God in the very "essence" of His being. Used only here. GK *5917*.
10. Or, "substance, actual being, reality". Whatever the essence of the Father is, the Son is also, as is true of all fathers and sons. Compare Jn 5:18; Col 2:9; Jn 12:45; 14:9. On this word, see "assurance" in 11:1.
11. Or, "carrying, bearing". Compare Col 1:17. On this word, see "carried" in 2 Pet 1:17.
12. That is, Christ's word characterized by power, His powerful word.
13. Some manuscripts add "through Himself" {B}. Some manuscripts say "our sins" {N}.
14. Or, "Greatness". Elsewhere only in 8:1; Jude 25. GK *3488*.
15. Or, "in high [places]", that is, heaven. GK *5734*. Related to "on-high" in Lk 1:78; and "highest" in Mt 21:9.
16. This is a key word in Hebrews, found also in 6:9; 7:7, 19, 22; 8:6; 9:23; 10:34; 11:16, 35, 40; 12:24. Used 19 times. GK *3202*.
17. Or, "to the degree that". These two words "so much... *by* as much as" occur together also in 10:25. A similar phrase occurs in Heb 7:20, 22; Rev 18:7. Jesus is better to the degree that His name, Son, is better.
18. Some think "today" refers to Christ's birth or incarnation, Lk 1:35; others, His baptism, Lk 3:22; others, His resurrection, Act 13:33; others, His exaltation to His throne, Heb 1:3, 8. Used 41 times. GK *4958*.
19. More literally, "be for *a* father... be for *a* son", a Hebrew way of speaking. This quote is also in 2 Sam 7:14.
20. Or, "And when again He brings...", the Greek word order. Some take this as introducing another point, the word order being changed to separate it from the preceding point; others, as meaning "And when God again brings", referring to the Second Coming.
21. Some think the writer means the earthly world at Christ's first coming; others, at His second coming; others, the "invisible world" of His Father when Christ was enthroned at His right hand. On this word, see 2:5.
22. On this word, see Mt 14:33. The Septuagint is being quoted.
23. The writer uses grammar that emphasizes the contrast between the two halves of this sentence; between the angels and the Son.
24. The Son is addressed as "God" here, as with "Lord" in v 10. The writer is comparing angels who serve God, to the Son who rules eternally from the throne of God as the Son of God. Some render this "God *is* Your throne forever...".
25. That is, moral straightness, uprightness. The Son's rule will be characterized by moral straightness. Used only here. GK *2319*. Related to "straight" in Act 8:21.
26. Some manuscripts say "His" {B}.
27. Some manuscripts say "unrighteousness", {N} ("iniquity" in KJV).
28. Some think the Son is being addressed as God again; others, that it is referring twice to God as the anointer, as might be paraphrased "the God who is Your God anointed You".
29. Some think this refers to angels; others, to humans; others, to believers, to all the Son's brothers (2:12) who rule with Him.
30. That is, the Son, who is addressed as "Lord" next. The writer compares the created angels to the eternal Son of God who created the universe and will end it.
31. Or, "remain continually". On this word, see Lk 22:28.
32. Or, "mantle", an outer covering "thrown around" the body, a robe. On this word, see "covering" in 1 Cor 11:15.
33. Or, "exchanged", as in Rom 1:23.
34. Some manuscripts omit the words "like a garment" {B}.
35. Or, "come to an end". On this word, see "fail" in Lk 16:9.
36. This adjective is related to "ministers" in v 7; and "ministry" in 8:6. Used only here. GK *3312*.
37. Here, salvation is viewed in its future sense, as yet to be inherited in its fullness, for which we await the Son (9:28).
38. That is, because God spoke by His Son (1:2), and because of who He is (1:3-14). Because the Son sat down on the highest seat of power (1:3), having made purification for our sins (1:3), as the Son of God (1:5), worshiped by angels (1:6), as the eternal ruler over what He created (1:8-12), awaiting the subjection of His enemies (1:13), we must pay attention to Him. His glory requires it.
39. We must pay more attention to what God said and did through His Son, and spoke about Him in the OT, so as to understand and obey. After justifying this statement in v 2-4, such paying attention begins in v 5.
40. Or, "that not at any time, that not perhaps". Same word as "not ever" in 3:12; and "at any time" in 4:1. GK *3607*.
41. Or, "float by, glide by, slip away", as in a boat floating by its anchorage. Used only here. GK *4184*.
42. This explains why we must pay attention.
43. That is, the Law of Moses, Act 7:38, 53; Gal 3:19.
44. Or, "was". GK *1181*.
45. Or, "sure, steadfast". On this word, see 2 Pet 1:10.
46. Or, "refusal to hear". On this word, see 2 Cor 10:6.
47. This word means "wages given back", whether a "penalty" as here, or a "reward" as it is elsewhere only used in 10:35; 11:26. GK *3632*.
48. Elsewhere only as "pay no concern" in Mt 22:5; "be careless" in 1 Tim 4:14; and "not care for" in Heb 8:9. GK *288*.

A. Jude 4, formerly B. 1 Cor 12:28 C. 1 Thes 5:9 D. Rom 10:17 E. 2 Pet 1:9 F. Gal 4:30 G. Heb 8:6 H. 1 Jn 5:18 J. Col 1:15 K. Rom 13:6 L. 2 Thes 1:8, flaming M. Rev 20:11 N. Rev 20:10 O. 1 Cor 4:21, rod P. Jn 21:15, devotedly love Q. Lk 4:18 R. Jam 5:14 S. Jude 24 T. Eph 3:17, founded U. 1 Cor 1:18 V. Heb 8:13, made old W. Rev 6:14, roll up X. Mk 3:14, send out Y. 1 Cor 12:5, ministries Z. Mt 16:21 AA. 1 Tim 3:8, pay attention to BB. 1 Cor 12:8 CC. Rom 5:14 DD. Rom 3:8 EE. Rom 2:3 FF. Lk 19:9

1D. Having begun to be spoken[1] by the Lord[2]
2D. Was confirmed[3] to[4] us by the *ones* having heard—*God testifying-with both signs and 4
wonders,[5] and various miracles[A], and distributions[6] *of the* Holy Spirit, according to His[7] will

3B. For[8] He did not subject[B] ***to* angels**[9] the coming[10] world[11] concerning which we are speaking[12] 5

1C. But[13] one solemnly-testified[C] somewhere saying, "What is man[14] that You remember[15] him, or 6
the son *of* man[16] that You look-after[17] him? *You made him lower than angels[18] *for* a little *while*[19]. 7
You crowned him *with* glory and honor[20]. *You subjected[B] all *things* under his feet" [Ps 8:4-6] 8

1D. For[21] in the subjecting[B] all *things to* him[22], He left **nothing** not-subject[23] *to* him
2D. But[24] now we do not yet see all *things* having been subjected[B] ***to* him**[25]
3D. But we[26] see the *One* having been made lower than angels[27] *for* a little *while*— Jesus[28]— 9
having been crowned *with* glory and honor because-of[29] the suffering[D] *of* the death

1E. So-that[30] *by the* grace[E] *of* God[31] He might taste death[32] for everyone

1. This is an idiom, literally, "having received *a* beginning to be spoken". What the Lord began, He continued through the apostles.
2. This salvation was not spoken through angels (v 2), but through God's Son Himself, and borne witness by God Himself.
3. Related to "firm" in v 2. On this word, see 1 Cor 1:6.
4. Or, "for" us. GK *1650*.
5. On "signs and wonders", see 2 Thes 2:9. "Signs, wonders, miracles" is also in Act 2:22; 2 Cor 12:12.
6. Some think this refers to gifts or manifestations given by the Spirit; others, to distributions consisting of the Spirit, given by God. Elsewhere only as "division" in 4:12. GK *3536*. Compare Gal 3:5; Jn 3:34; 1 Cor 12:11; Act 5:32.
7. Some think the writer means "God's" will, taking this with all three phrases, or the last only; others, the "Spirit's" will, taking this with the last phrase only.
8. The writer now continues his description of the Son, paying more attention to the relationship between His glory and His death. Here, he explains that His glory as Ruler in the coming world was obtained through His death. It is as a man, because of His death, that He has been crowned with this glory and honor. There are other views on the flow. Consult the commentaries.
9. The rulership of the coming world was not promised to angels.
10. Same word as in 6:5 (coming age); 13:14 (coming city); 10:1 (coming good things). On this word, see "going to" in Mk 10:32.
11. Or, "inhabited earth". Some think the writer means Messiah's kingdom, inaugurated by Christ, presently ruled by Him, and to be fully manifested in His future reign of glory. It was "coming" from the OT or the divine decree point of view. It is the world of salvation, present and future, the same thing as "so great a salvation", v 3. Others think he means the world after Christ comes again, the future fullness, and that it is "coming" from the Christian's point of view. It is the salvation we are "going to inherit", 1:14. Compare 6:5; 9:28; 10:37. Elsewhere only in Mt 24:14; Lk 2:1; 4:5; 21:26; Act 11:28; 17:6, 31; 19:27; 24:5; Rom 10:18; Heb 1:6; Rev 3:10; 12:9; 16:14. This word refers to the earth as an inhabited place, to its inhabitants, and sometimes to the "world" from the Roman point of view (the Roman world). GK *3876*. Related to "house".
12. Some think the writer is referring back to 1:14 (inherit salvation), and 2:3. Others think he means speaking "in the subject at hand", including what follows; others, more generally, "in this book".
13. The writer quotes Ps 8 to prove the coming world is not subjected to angels.
14. Or, "mankind, humanity". That is, Adam's race. On this word, see "mankind" in Mt 4:4.
15. That is, keep him in mind, for his benefit. On this word, see Lk 1:54.
16. Or, "*the* Son *of* Man". Some think this means what it means in the psalm. It is a Hebrew parallelism, and means the same thing as "man" earlier, "humanity, or the offspring of humanity". Thus the writer means "not to angels. But it is as someone said, to man". Others think the writer is applying this to Jesus, and means "the Son of Man", and that each "him" that follows down through v 8 also refers to Christ. Thus he means "not to angels. But it is as someone said of man with reference to the Messiah who would fulfill it". In either case, Adam failed, but Christ fulfilled this. The difference between the two views is that the first thinks the writer quotes the psalm here and makes this application to Christ in v 9; the second applies it to Him all the way through, resulting in a different understanding of point 3C. On "*a* son *of* man", see Jn 5:27.
17. Or, "visit, care for". Same word as in Mt 25:36, 43; Jam 1:27. Elsewhere only as "visit" in Lk 1:68, 78; 7:16; Act 7:23; 15:14, 36; and as "look-for" in Act 6:3. GK *2170*. The root word is "to look".
18. This quote is from the Septuagint, which says "angels". The Hebrew has a word here meaning "God" or "gods, heavenly beings", which the Septuagint took in the latter sense and rendered "angels".
19. Or, "*a* little bit lower than angels". In the one case, it is "*a* little bit lower (in physical status, being mortal)"; in the other case, it is "lower (in status) for a little *while*" (where "a" is the word rendered "bit". GK *5516*), expressing the temporary nature of this status. The same phrase is in v 9, and is elsewhere only in Jn 6:7, "*a* little bit". The word "little" is elsewhere only meaning "*a* little *while*" in Act 5:34; "*a* short *time*" in Lk 22:58; "short" in Act 27:28; and "*a* few" in Heb 13:22. GK *1099*.
20. Some manuscripts add "And You set him over the works *of* Your hands" {B}, from the psalm.
21. Here, the writer draws out his point from the psalm. God did not subject the coming world to angels (v 5), for this psalm says all things are subjected to man (or, Jesus), leaving nothing not subject to him, including the coming world.
22. Some manuscripts omit the words "*to* him" {C}.
23. Or, "independent, rebellious". On this word, see "rebellious" in Tit 1:6. Related to "subjecting" earlier.
24. But this subjection is not yet seen in this world.
25. If the writer means "son of man" (mankind) in v 6, then this means that even though God made man to be crowned with rulership, it is not yet true of him because of sin. But we do see it is true of Jesus (v 9), who became a man to fulfill this, and has been crowned with this glory and honor. The coming world is subject to Him, and we will reign with Him. He contrasts its present lack of fulfillment in man (v 8), with its present fulfillment in Jesus (v 9). If he means "Son of Man" (Jesus) in v 6, then this means that we do not yet see it fulfilled in Jesus. He is on the throne while His enemies are being subdued (1:13), but we will not see all things subject to Him until He returns. But we do see Him crowned with glory and honor by God (v 9), fulfilling that part of the psalm. He contrasts the present lack of fulfillment in Jesus (His enemies are not yet subdued) with the partial fulfillment we do see, the glory and honor (v 9).
26. We, represented by the eyewitnesses, saw this at Christ's resurrection and ascension (1:3), and see it now.
27. That is, having been made a man, Phil 2:7.
28. Note how the writer puts "Jesus" in a similar emphatic position in 3:1; 4:14; 6:20; 12:2.
29. Or, "for the sake of". In this rendering, this phrase gives the reason for Christ's crowning with glory. Others render this "But we see Jesus— the *One* having been made lower... for the sake of the suffering *of* the death— having been crowned...", this phrase giving the reason for His incarnation. There are other views.
30. Some think this phrase gives the purpose of the death just mentioned; others, of the being made lower; others, of everything in v 9, Christ's incarnation, suffering, death, and glorification.
31. Some manuscripts instead say "so that apart from God" {A}, meaning either "apart from His divine nature", or that He tasted death "for all, apart from God" (like 1 Cor 15:27), or that God forsook Him on the cross, Mk 15:34.
32. The phrase "taste death" occurs also in Mt 16:28; Mk 9:1; Lk 9:27; Jn 8:52. On "taste", see Heb 6:4.

A. 1 Cor 12:10   B. Eph 5:21   C. 1 Tim 5:21, solemnly charge   D. Phil 3:10   E. Eph 2:8

Hebrews 2:10 826 Verse

4B. For[1] it was fitting[2] *for* Him for-the-sake-of Whom *are* all *things* and through Whom *are* all *things, that in* bringing[3] many sons[A] to glory[B], *He should* perfect[4] the Author[5] *of* their salvation[C] through sufferings[D]   10

    1C. For both the *One*[6] making-holy[7] and the *ones* being made holy *are* all from one *Father*[8]   11

        1D. For which reason He is not ashamed[E] to be calling[F] them **brothers**[G], ˚saying—   12

            1E. "I will declare[H] Your name *to* My brothers. I will sing-praise[J] to you in *the* midst *of the* congregation[K]" [Ps 22:22]
            2E. And again [in Isa 8:17], "**I** will be trusting[9] in Him"[10]   13
            3E. And again [in Isa 8:18], "Behold— I and the children[L] whom God gave *to* Me"

    2C. Therefore, since the children[L] have shared[M] *of* blood and flesh[11], He Himself also similarly[12] partook[13] *of* the same *things*   14

        1D. In order that through death

            1E. He might do-away-with[14] the *one* having the power[N] *of* death— that is, the devil[O]
            2E. And He might release[15] these— all-who *by the* fear[P] *of* death were subject-to[16] slavery[Q] through all *their* living[17]   15

        2D. For He surely does not take-hold-of[18] angels, but He takes hold of *the* seed[R] *of* Abraham[19]   16

    3C. Hence[20], He had-to[21] become-like[S] *His* brothers in all *things*[22] in order that He might become **a merciful** and faithful[23] High Priest[24] *in* the *things* pertaining to God, so as to make-an-offering-for-satisfaction[25] [of God's wrath] *as* to the sins *of* the people[T]   17

        1D. For having Himself been tempted[26] in what[27] He has suffered,[28] He is able to help[U] the *ones* being tempted   18

5B. Hence[29] holy brothers[G], partakers[30] *of a* heavenly[V] calling[W], consider[31] the Apostle[32] and High Priest *of* our confession[33]— Jesus[34]— ˚*as* being faithful[35] *to* the *One* having appointed[36] Him, as also *was* Moses in[37] His whole[38] house[39]   3:1

    2

1. Now the writer explains why Jesus left His heavenly glory to become a man and die.
2. Or, "suitable, proper". Same word as in 7:26. On this word, see 1 Cor 11:13.
3. Or, "leading". Some render this "having brought", referring to those brought prior to Christ in the OT age. Others render it "bringing", so that the "bringing to glory" occurs at the same time as the "perfecting" of the Author, and includes all believers. That is, "when He brought", coincident in time with when "He perfected". It cannot mean "while in the process of bringing". Others take this with "Author", "... *are* all *things*, to perfect through sufferings the Author *of* their salvation having brought many sons to glory". On this word, see "led" in Lk 4:1.
4. Or, "complete, finish, bring to its goal". God brought His human Son to proven moral perfection as a man and fully qualified Him to be mankind's Savior and High Priest. In 5:8, Jesus "learned obedience" through suffering. "Perfected" is used again of Him in 5:9. Same word as in 7:19, 28; 9:9; 10:1, 14; 11:40; 12:23; Jn 17:23; Jam 2:22; 1 Jn 2:5; 4:12, 17, 18. Elsewhere only as "make perfect" in Phil 3:12; "finish" in Act 20:24; "complete" in Lk 2:43; "come to the end" in Lk 13:32; and "accomplish" in Jn 4:34; 5:36; 17:4; 19:28. GK *5457*. Related to "complete" in 1 Cor 13:10; "perfection" in Heb 7:11; "perfecter" in Heb 12:2; "finish" in Rev 10:7.
5. Or, "Prince, Pioneer, Leader, Originator, Founder, Captain". The root word is "to begin", so this word basically means "the beginner, the starter" in various senses. Elsewhere only in 12:2; Act 3:15; and as "leader" in Act 5:31. GK *795*.
6. Jesus and those He makes holy all call God "Father".
7. Or, "sanctifying". On this word, see "sanctified" in 10:29.
8. Some think "*Father*" is implied; others, "*ancestor*", Adam, as in Act 17:26; others, "*ancestor*", Abraham; others, "*nature*", blood and flesh, as in v 14.
9. Or, "putting confidence, relying". On this word, see "persuade" in 1 Jn 3:19.
10. The Messiah shares our trust in the Father.
11. This order of words is elsewhere only in Eph 6:12. Some rearrange it as "flesh and blood". The phrase "flesh and blood" is only in Mt 16:17; 1 Cor 15:50; Gal 1:16. Some think "blood and flesh" puts the emphasis on us as mortal, with life derived from our parents. Some manuscripts say "flesh and blood" {K}.
12. That is, by being "born of a woman", Gal 4:4. Used only here. GK *4181*.
13. Or, "shared in", but not related to the word earlier. Elsewhere only in 5:13; 7:13; and 1 Cor 9:10, 12; 10:17, 21, 30. GK *3576*. Related to "partaker" in 3:1.
14. Or, "render powerless". On this word, see Rom 6:6.
15. Or, "free". On this word, see Act 19:12.
16. Or, "held in, caught in". On this word, see "guilty" in 1 Cor 11:27.
17. That is, during their entire lifetime.
18. That is, with a view of helping. Same word as in 8:9, where God "took hold of" Israel's hand to lead them from Egypt, freeing them from slavery. Here, Jesus takes hold of slaves of sin to free them, v 15. On this word, see Lk 20:20.
19. That is, the "many sons" of v 10; Abraham's spiritual descendants by faith, Gal 3:29; Rom 4:11-12.
20. Here the writer draws the conclusion of v 10-16— Jesus was obligated to become a man, suffer and die. It had to be this way to fulfill the Father's will. This word is used also in 3:1; 7:25; 8:3; 9:18; and as "from which" in 11:19. Used 15 times. GK *3854*.
21. Or, "He was obligated to". Same word as "obligated" in 5:3, 12. On this word, see "ought" in 1 Jn 4:11. Only here is it used of what Christ was obligated to do. He was obligated by the Father's will, by what the Father thought "fitting" (v 10).
22. That is, in blood and flesh, suffering, death, living in obedience to God, being tempted. Compare 4:15; 5:7-8; 7:26.
23. Some think the writer means "faithful" to God (as this word is used in 3:2) as High Priest; others, "trustworthy" to believers, as well as merciful. On this word, see Col 1:2.
24. The subject of Jesus as our High Priest is taken up in detail in the second division of the book, beginning at 4:14.
25. Or, "make propitiation, propitiate, satisfy". That is, to make a sacrificial offering to satisfy God's wrath against sin, to gain His mercy. He offered Himself, 7:27, 9:26. God's response to this is to be "merciful", the related word in 8:12. Elsewhere only as "be merciful" in Lk 18:13. Some think it means "to expiate", on which see Rom 3:25. GK *2661*. See Rom 3:25 on this word group.
26. Or, "tested". Same word as in Mt 4:1, 3; Mk 1:13; Lk 4:2; 1 Cor 7:5; 10:13; Gal 6:1; 1 Thes 3:5; Heb 4:15; Jam 1:13, 14. Elsewhere only as "test" in Mt 16:1; 19:3; 22:18, 35; Mk 8:11; 10:2; 12:15; Lk 11:16; Jn 6:6; 8:6; Act 5:9; 15:10; 1 Cor 10:9; 2 Cor 13:5; Heb 3:9; 11:17; Rev 2:2, 10; 3:10; and "try" in Act 9:26; 16:7; 24:6. GK *4279*. Related to "trial, temptation, test", on which see "trial" in Jam 1:2.
27. Or, "in that, because".
28. Or, "For having been tempted in what He Himself has suffered".
29. This gives the conclusion and application of the foregoing. Some start a new A. point here.
30. Or, "partners, sharers". That is, sharers in God's call to the world to come. Same word as in 3:14; 6:4; 12:8. Elsewhere only as "companions" in Heb 1:9; Lk 5:7. GK *3581*. Related to "partook" in 2:14; and "partnership" in 2 Cor 6:14.
31. Or, "contemplate, think carefully about". Same word as in 10:24. This is a similar idea to "pay more attention" in 2:1.
32. This word is used of Jesus only here. He was "sent forth" from God with an authoritative message. On this word, see 1 Cor 12:28.
33. Some think the writer means "Whom we confess"; others, "belonging to our objective confession of faith". Same word as in 4:14.
34. Some manuscripts say "Christ Jesus" {K}. The writer is placing emphasis on "Jesus" (see 2:9).
35. Jesus did not die an unfortunate death. He was faithful to the task God appointed Him, just like Moses. On this word, see Col 1:2.
36. Or, "made Him *such*". Same word as in Mk 3:14, 16. On this word, see "does" in Rev 13:13.
37. Some connect this to Moses; others, to Jesus, placing a comma after Moses. This is the Greek word order.
38. Some manuscripts omit this word {C}.
39. That is, God's household, the nation of Israel. God said this about Moses in Num 12:7.

A. Gal 3:7 B. 2 Pet 2:10 C. Lk 19:9 D. Phil 3:10 E. Rom 1:16 F. Rom 8:30 G. Act 16:40 H. 1 Jn 1:3, announcing J. Act 16:25 K. Rev 22:16, church L. 1 Jn 2:14 M. 2 Jn 11 N. Eph 6:10, might O. Rev 12:9 P. Eph 5:21 Q. Rom 8:15 R. Heb 11:11 S. Mt 13:24 T. Rev 21:3 U. Rev 12:16 V. Eph 3:10 W. 2 Pet 1:10

| Hebrews 3:3 | 828 | Verse |

    1C. For this *One* has been considered-worthy[A] *of* **more** glory[B] than Moses— to the degree that[1] the *One*[2] having built[C] *the house*[3] has more honor[D] *than* the house   3

        1D. For every house is built[C] by someone, but[4] the *One*[5] having built[C] all *things is* God   4
        2D. And[6] **Moses**[7] *was* faithful[E] in His[8] whole house as *a* servant[9], for *a* testimony[10] *of* the *things which* will be spoken[11]—˚but Christ *was faithful* as *a* Son over His house   5 / 6

            1E. Whose house **we** are, if-indeed[12] we hold-on-to[13] *our* confidence[F] and *our* boast[14] *of* the hope[15]

6B. Therefore, just as the Holy Spirit says[16] [in Ps 95:7-11], "Today, if you hear His voice,˚do not harden[G] your hearts[H] as in the rebellion during the day *of* testing[17] in the wilderness[J], ˚where your fathers tested[18] *Me* with *a* trial[19] and saw My works ˚*for* forty years. Therefore I was-angry[20] with this[21] generation[K] and said, 'They are always going-astray[L] *in* the heart, and **they** did not know My ways'. ˚As I swore[M] in My wrath[N], they will *never*[22] enter into My rest[23]"   7-8 / 9 / 10 / 11

    1C. Be watching-out[O], brothers, so that there will not-ever[P] be in any *of* you *an* evil[Q] heart *of* unbelief[R] in departing[24] from *the* living God. ˚But be exhorting[S] yourselves[25] each day[26], as long as it is called "Today", in order that none of you may be hardened[G] *by the* deceitfulness[27] *of* sin   12 / 13

        1D. For we have become[28] partakers[29] *of* Christ[30] if-indeed[31] we hold-on-to[T] the beginning[U] *of our* assurance[32] firm[V] until *the* end[33]—˚in *that it* is said[34] [in Ps 95:7-8], "Today, if you hear His voice, do not harden[G] your hearts as in the rebellion"   14 / 15

            1E. For who[35] having heard[36] rebelled[37]? But *was it* not all the *ones* having come out of Egypt through Moses?[38]   16
            2E. And *with* whom was He angry *for* forty years? *Was it* not *with* the *ones* having sinned, whose corpses fell in the wilderness[J]?   17
            3E. And *to* whom did He swear[M] *that they* will not enter[39] into His rest, except *to* the *ones* having disobeyed[W]?   18
            4E. And we see that they were not able to enter because of unbelief[R]   19

1. Or, "by as much as". Same phrase as in 7:20.
2. Or "*one*". Some take this as a general maxim giving the magnitude of Christ's glory by comparison; others, as meaning that Christ is the builder of the house of which Moses was a part.
3. The Greek simply says "it", "he has more honor *than* the house, the *One* having built it". Since English is dependent on word order, we need to express "the house" at this point in the sentence.
4. Or, "and".
5. Some think this refers to the Father, who is working through the Son (1:2) to build all things. Others think this refers to the Son, thus naming Him as God, the builder of the house (v 3). In either case, the writer is referring to the exalted role of Christ versus Moses.
6. Both Moses and Christ were faithful (v 2) to the responsibilities God gave them in the building of His house (v 5-6)— but Moses as a "servant" "in" God's house, Christ as "Son" "over" God's house.
7. The writer uses grammar that emphasizes the contrast between the two halves of this sentence; between Moses and Christ.
8. Or, "his". Some think the writer means "God's" house in v 2, 5, and 6; God's house as it existed under Moses (its OT form), and as it exists under Christ (its NT form). Others think he means Moses' house (Israel) here, and Christ's house (the church) in v 6.
9. Or, "assistant", a freely serving assistant (not a slave). The writer is not depreciating Moses, but is respectfully using the word God used of him in Num 12:7, "My servant Moses". Used only here. GK *2544*.
10. Or, "for evidence". On "for *a* testimony", see Mk 1:44.
11. Some think the writer means the things later (after Moses) to be spoken about Christ. Moses foreshadowed in word and type, and became a testimony to the things spoken later about Christ, many of which are detailed in this book. Moses was faithful as "a shadow of the coming good things", 10:1. Others think he is referring to Num 12:8, and Moses' work at that time in history. Moses was faithful to testify of all the things which God would later speak to him on the mountain.
12. Same word as in v 14; 6:3. Some manuscripts instead say "if we hold on to..." {C}.
13. Same word as in v 14; 10:23. It is also used in this sense in Lk 8:15, describing the good soil, which holds on to the word they hear with endurance. On this word, see "hold down" in Rom 1:18.
14. That is, the content of our boast, consisting of that for which we hope. On this word, see Phil 1:26.
15. Some manuscripts add "firm until the end" {B} as in v 14.
16. The writer concludes the first main section of the book by quoting from Ps 95, and then expounding and applying it in 3:12-4:13. "So do not be like that generation in Moses' day. Enter into the rest that they never did". There are other views on the flow. Consult the commentaries.
17. Or, "trial, temptation". On this word, see "trials" in Jam 1:2. Related to "tested" next.
18. Or, "tempted". On this word, see "tempted" in 2:18.
19. Or, "by way of *a* proving, a putting to the test". Used only here. GK *1508*. Related to "approved" in Rom 12:2. Not related to "testing" or "tested". Some manuscripts say "fathers tested *Me*, proved Me, and saw" {N}, using the verb in Rom 12:2.
20. Elsewhere only in v 17. GK *4696*.
21. Some manuscripts say "that" {N}.
22. Literally, "If they will enter into My rest". This is the conclusion of a Hebrew oath, "May [?] happen to me if they will enter into My rest". See Ruth 1:17 for an example. The same idiom is in 4:3, 5; Mk 8:12.
23. In Moses' day, this meant the promised land (Num 14:28-30; Deut 12:9), the physical inheritance, an earthly picture of our spiritual rest and inheritance, which we enter when we cease from our works as God did (4:10), by faith. Because the psalmist says it is still available in his day, the writer argues in 4:3, 10 that it refers to a spiritual rest with God that has existed from the seventh day. Elsewhere only in 3:18; 4:1, 3, 5, 10, 11; Act 7:49. GK *2923*. The verb is in 4:4, 8, 10.
24. Or, "withdrawing, falling away, deserting". On this word, see 1 Tim 4:1. Related to "apostasy" in 2 Thes 2:3. Jesus used this word in the parable of the sower (Lk 8:13) of those who believe for a while and then "depart". The warnings throughout Hebrews address this group, exhorting them to "hold on to the word with endurance" (Lk 8:15).
25. Or, "one another".
26. This is an idiom, literally "according to each day". It is stronger than "daily" in 7:27 and 10:11, a similar phrase.
27. Or, "deception". On this word, see "deception" in 2 Pet 2:13.
28. The grammar of this word means "we have become and continue to be". On this word, see "comes" in 2 Pet 1:20.
29. On this word, see 3:1.
30. Some think the writer means "*with* Christ"; others, "*in* Christ".
31. Same words, "if-indeed we hold-on-to", as in v 6.
32. Or, "*of* the reality". On this word, see 11:1. Some give this a subjective sense, our initial "assurance" in Christ; the "confidence" we had since the beginning; our confident "frame of mind" described in v 6. Others give it an objective sense, "the reality" of God we experienced at the beginning; the "objective hope" in which we boasted and had confidence in v 6.
33. On "until *the* end", see 6:11.
34. More literally, "in the being said", meaning either "in light of what is said", or, "while it is being said". This idiom is similar to 8:13. We must hold on until the end because the psalm says that as long as it is "today" we must not harden our hearts. We need endurance, 10:36. Others connect this to v 13, treating v 14 as a parenthesis, "hardened by the deceitfulness of sin... while it is being said...". Others start a new sentence here, making this point 2D., and render "For" in v 16 as "indeed", so that it says "In that it is said, 'Today... rebellion', who indeed, having heard, rebelled?"
35. Some render this word "some", and take both parts of this verse as statements, not questions. GK *5515*.
36. The danger of unbelief is not abstract. Israel heard the message, but failed to enter due to unbelief.
37. Or, "provoked *Him*, embittered *Him*". Used only here. GK *4176*. Related to "be bitter" in Col 3:19; and "rebellion" in Heb 3:8, 15.
38. The grammar expects a "yes" answer to this and the next question.
39. All males over 20 years old at the time of the Exodus, except for Joshua and Caleb, failed to enter the promised land, Num 14:29-30.

A. 2 Thes 1:11 B. 2 Pet 2:10 C. Heb 9:2, prepare D. 1 Tim 5:17 E. Col 1:2 F. Heb 4:16 G. Rom 9:18 H. Rev 2:23 J. Mt 3:1 K. Mt 24:34 L. Jam 5:19, err M. Jam 5:12 N. Rev 16:19 O. Rev 1:11, see P. Heb 2:1 Q. Act 25:18 R. 1 Tim 1:13 S. Rom 12:8 T. Heb 3:6 U. Col 1:18 V. 2 Pet 1:10 W. Rom 11:30

2C. Therefore, let us fear[A] that[1] at any time while *a* promise to enter into His rest[B] *is* left-remaining[2] [open], any of you should seem[C] to have come-short[3]—*for indeed, we have had-good-news-announced[4], just as those[5] also

    1D. But the word[D] *of* hearing[6] did not profit[E] those *ones, they* not having been united[7] *in* faith[F] *with* the *ones* having heard[8]

        1E. For we, the *ones* having believed[G], enter into the[9] rest[10]
        2E. Just as He has said, "As I swore in My wrath, they shall *never* enter into My rest" [Ps 95:11]

    2D. And-yet[11], *His* works[H] have been done[12] since *the* foundation[J] *of the* world

        1E. For[13] He has spoken somewhere about the seventh *day* as follows— "And God rested[K] on the seventh day from all His works[H]" [Gen 2:2]
        2E. And[14] in this [Ps 95:11] again, "They shall *never* enter into My rest[B]"

    3D. Since[15] then it remains[16] *that* some *may* enter into it, and the *ones* formerly[L] having had-good-news-announced[M] *to them* did not enter because of disobedience[N], *He again designates[17] a certain day— "Today"— saying by David[18] after so much time just as it has been said-before[O], "Today, if you hear His voice, do not harden[P] your hearts" [Ps 95:7-8]

        1E. For if Joshua had given them rest, He[19] would not be speaking after these *things* about **another** day[20]

    4D. Therefore *a* Sabbath-rest[21] remains *for* the people[Q] *of* God

        1E. For the *one* having entered into His rest, also himself rested from his works,[22] just as God *did* from *His* own

3C. Therefore,[23] let us be diligent[24] to enter into that[25] rest, in order that no one may fall[26] in[27] the same example[R] *of* disobedience[N]

    1D. For the word[28] *of* God *is* living[S] and effective[29]

        1E. And sharper than any double-edged sword[T]
        2E. And piercing as-far-as *the* division[U] *of* soul[V] and spirit, and joints and marrows
        3E. And able-to-judge *the* thoughts[30] and intentions[31] *of the* heart

    2D. And there is no creation[32] hidden[33] in His sight, but all *things are* naked[W] and having been laid-open[34] *to* His eyes *to* Whom the account[35] *will be given by* us

1. This construction expresses fear that a negative result may occur. It is similar to Act 5:26.
2. Related to "remain" in v 6, 9. The writer proves this rest has been open since the seventh day in v 3-10. On this word, see "left behind" in Act 6:2.
3. Or, "missed, failed to reach" it. That is, that any individual among you should come short of entering like Israel did, due to unbelief (3:19), an evil heart of unbelief (3:12), deception by sin (3:13); that any should come short of receiving the promise due to a lack of genuine faith. Stated positively, let us be diligent that every person among you may enter, v 11. Same word as in 12:15 and Rom 3:23. On this word, see "be in need" in Lk 15:14.
4. That is, the word God spoke about His Son (1:2), to which we must pay attention (2:1). Our "good news" was spoken by the Lord and "confirmed to us by the *ones* having heard" (2:3). Israel's came through Moses. It is the promise of "rest". This is a participle, "we are *ones* having had good news announced". Same word as in v 6.
5. The writer compares those to whom he is writing (compare 2:3) with the generation in Moses' day who fell in unbelief (3:15-19).
6. That is, the message they heard, the subjective hearing. Or, "the message *of* the report", the objective message. This word means the ear, the faculty of hearing, the act of hearing or listening, and the message heard (the report, rumor, fame, account, news etc.). Same word as in Mt 13:14; Lk 7:1; Act 28:26; 1 Cor 12:17; Gal 3:2, 5; 2 Tim 4:3, 4; Heb 5:11; 2 Pet 2:8. Elsewhere only as "report" in Jn 12:38 and Rom 10:16 ("who has believed our report"); Mt 4:24; 14:1; Mk 1:28; and as "rumor" in Mt 24:6; Mk 13:7; "report-hearing" in Rom 10:17; "ear" in Mk 7:35; Act 17:20; 1 Cor 12:17; and "heard" in 1 Thes 2:13. GK *198*.
7. It did not profit Moses' generation because they refused to unite in faith with the ones hearing God's promise in faith (Moses, Joshua, Caleb). These three believed God's promise, and so believed they could and would enter, in spite of the obstacles. The others did not believe God, and so doubted they could defeat the enemies. The application is that in the same way, the gospel will not profit you if you do not unite in faith with those believing God. On this word, see "blended together" in 1 Cor 12:24.
8. "Those ones" were not united in faith with "the ones who heard" in faith. Same word as in 2:3. Some manuscripts say "the word of hearing" was not united with "faith"— "but the word *of* hearing, not having been united *with* faith *in* the *ones* having heard, did not profit those *ones*" {B}. The point is the same in either case— they did not have faith in God.
9. Some manuscripts omit this word {C}.
10. Then as now, we enter by faith. We are excluded by unbelief.
11. The writer calls to the attention of the reader that God entered His rest on the seventh day. This proves that the concept of "rest" in Ps 95 is not limited to the promised land in Moses' day, but refers to something existing since the seventh day of creation. Elsewhere only in Act 14:17. GK *2792*. Related to "although" in Jn 4:2.
12. This is a participle, "*are* having been done". GK *1181*.
13. Genesis is quoted to prove when God's rest began.
14. The psalm is quoted again to prove that the rest was already existing when those in Moses' time failed to enter it.
15. Having proven that the "rest" has existed since creation, the writer now proves that it still remains open (v 1). It remains open as long as it is called "Today" (note the phrase in 3:13).
16. God's promise will not go unfulfilled. On this word, which is also in v 9, see "left behind" in Jude 6.
17. Or, "declares, fixes, determines, appoints". That is, in Psalm 95. On this word, see Rom 1:4.
18. Or, "in David", that is, in the Psalms.
19. That is, God, speaking by David in this psalm.
20. The "rest" cannot be the physical rest in the promised land under Joshua, otherwise David's psalm would not have offered it "Today". It refers to a spiritual rest, a sharing in the rest God entered on the seventh day.
21. Used only here. GK *4878*.
22. Some think the writer means "having entered salvation by faith", resting from works. Others think he means "having died and entered the presence of God", resting from our works on earth. There are other views.
23. Having made two negative applications of Ps 95, the writer now makes a positive one. Thus his applications are "Do not actively fall away", 3:12; "Do not passively come short", 4:1; and "Be diligent to enter". Some make this point 5D., and start a new point with v 12, making it 7B. or 3C.
24. Or, "make every effort". On this word, see Eph 4:3.
25. That is, the rest mentioned in v 1, proven to exist in v 3-10.
26. That is, perish. Same word as in 3:17, on which see Rom 11:11.
27. Or, "by". That is, by following the same example. GK *1877*.
28. That is, God's spoken and written word; His word Israel disobeyed; His word now proclaimed to us; His word of examination when we stand before Him; this word from the Psalms that is speaking to the heart.
29. Or, "active, at-work, operative", accomplishing His will, Isa 55:11. Elsewhere only in 1 Cor 16:9; Phm 6. GK *1921*. Related to "working" in Phil 3:21.
30. Or, "reflections". Elsewhere only in Mt 9:4; 12:25; Act 17:29. GK *1927*. Related to "pondered" in Mt 1:20.
31. Or, "designs, resolutions, insights". The point is that God will be able to discern genuine faith from dead faith and unbelief. He will flay open the heart and reveal truth of the matter for every person, separating action from motive, 1 Cor 4:5. Elsewhere only in 1 Pet 4:1. GK *1936*.
32. Or, "creature". On this word, see Rom 8:39.
33. Or, "unseen, invisible, unnoticed". Used only here. GK *905*. Related to "disfigure" in Mt 6:16.
34. Or, "exposed, laid bare". This word means "to take by the throat, to bend back the neck (to slit the throat), to expose for the kill". Thus, all things are naked and exposed for God's judgment. Used only here. GK *5548*. The root word is "neck".
35. Same word as in 13:17; Mt 12:36; Lk 16:2; Act 19:40; 1 Pet 4:5. More literally, "to Whom *is* the account *for* us", to Whom our account must be given. On this word, see "word" in 1 Cor 12:8.

A. Eph 5:33, respecting B. Heb 3:11 C. Lk 19:11, thinking D. 1 Cor 12:8 E. Rom 2:25 F. Eph 2:8 G. Jn 3:36 H. Mt 26:10 J. Heb 9:26 K. Act 14:18, restrained L. 2 Cor 1:15, first M. Act 5:42 N. Rom 11:30 O. Jude 17, spoken beforehand P. Rom 9:18 Q. Rev 21:3 R. Jn 13:15 S. Rev 20:4, came to life T. Eph 6:17 U. Heb 2:4, distribution V. Jam 5:20 W. Jam 2:15

| Hebrews 4:14 | 832 | Verse |

2A. Therefore,¹ having *a* great High Priest² having gone through the heavens³— Jesus, the Son *of* God⁴— let us be holding-on-to⁵ the confession⁶   14

  1B. For we do not have *a* high priest not being able to sympathize-with our weaknesses^A, but *One* having been tempted⁷ in all *things*⁸ in accordance with *our* likeness⁹, without¹⁰ sin   15

    1C. So let us be approaching^B the throne^C *of* grace^D with confidence¹¹, in order that we may receive mercy^E and find grace for well-timed¹² help¹³   16

  2B. For every high priest being taken^F from-*among* men^G is appointed¹⁴ for¹⁵ people^G *in* the *things* pertaining to God, in order that he might offer^H both gifts^J and sacrifices^K for sins   5:1

    1C. Being able to deal-gently *with* the *ones* being ignorant^L and going-astray^M, since he himself is also surrounded¹⁶ *with* weakness^A   2

      1D. And because of it¹⁷, he is obligated^N to be offering^H *sacrifices* for sins— just as for the people^O, so also for himself   3

    2C. And one does not take^F the honor^P *to* himself, but *receives it* being called^Q by God, just as also Aaron   4

  3B. So also¹⁸, Christ did not glorify^R Himself to become High Priest   5

    1C. But the *One* having said to Him [in Ps 2:7] "**You** are My Son. Today¹⁹ **I** have fathered^S You" did, *just as also in another *place* He says, "You *are a* priest forever^T according to the order *of* Melchizedek" [Ps 110:4]   6
    2C. Who, in the days *of* His flesh²⁰   7

      1D. Having offered²¹ both petitions^U and supplications²² with *a* strong outcry²³ and tears^V to the *One* being able to save^W Him from²⁴ death, and having been heard because of *His* reverence²⁵
      2D. Although²⁶ being *a* Son²⁷   8
      3D. Learned^X obedience^Y from *the things* which He suffered²⁸

  4B. And having been perfected²⁹, He became *the* cause³⁰ *of* eternal^Z salvation^AA *to* all the *ones* obeying³¹ Him, *having been designated³² by God *as* High Priest according to the order *of* Melchizedek   9 / 10

    1C. Concerning whom³³ our message-*to-speak*³⁴ is great³⁵ and hard-to-interpret³⁶ *so as* to speak, since you have become sluggish³⁷ *in* the hearing³⁸   11

      1D. For indeed, [although] being obligated^N to be teachers because of the time,³⁹ you again have *a* need^BB *that* someone be teaching^CC you the elements⁴⁰ *of* the beginning^DD *concerning* the oracles⁴¹ *of* God. And you have become *ones* having⁴² *a* need^BB *of* milk and⁴³ not *of* solid^EE food⁴⁴   12

        1E. For everyone partaking^FF *of* milk *is* inexperienced⁴⁵ *in* the word^GG *of* righteousness⁴⁶, for he is *an* infant^HH   13

1. Verses 14-16 are a transition to the next major section of the book. Some place it as the end of the first section. Note the similarities to the transition to 3A. in 10:32-35.
2. First mentioned in 2:17, this term looks forward to the second major section of the book, which concerns Jesus as our great High Priest, and the implications of this for us, and for the priestly system established under the Law of Moses.
3. That is, back to His throne, 1:3. Compare 7:26; Eph 4:10.
4. This term looks backward, to the ground covered in the first main section of the book.
5. Or, "keeping hold of, grasping firmly on to, taking hold of ". Used 47 times, it also means "seize, arrest, hold back, hold fast". Same word as in Mk 7:3; Col 2:19; 2 Thes 2:15; Rev 2:13, 15, 25; and as "take hold of " in Heb 6:18. GK *3195*.
6. Same word as in 10:23; 3:1. On this word, see 2 Cor 9:13.
7. Or, "tested". On this word, see 2:18.
8. Or, "in all *respects*". Same phrase as in 2:17; Col 3:20, 22; Act 17:22.
9. Elsewhere only in 7:15. GK *3928*. Related to "become like" in 2:17.
10. Or, "apart from". The writer may mean "without any sin on His part", or, that Jesus was tempted in all things "apart from sin"— He was not tempted by His own sin like we are, because He had no sin. On this word, see Jam 2:18.
11. Or, "boldness, freedom of speech". Same word as in Act 2:29; 2 Cor 7:4; 1 Tim 3:13; Heb 3:6; 10:19, 35; 1 Jn 2:28; 3:21; 4:17; 5:14. Elsewhere only as "boldness" in Act 4:13, 29, 31; 28:31; 2 Cor 3:12; Eph 3:12; 6:19; Phil 1:20; Phm 8; "openness" in Mk 8:32; Jn 7:13; "public" in Jn 7:4, 26; 11:54; 18:20; Col 2:15; and "plainness" in Jn 10:24; 11:14; 16:25, 29. GK *4244*. Related to "speak boldly" in Eph 6:20.
12. Or, "strategic, opportune, seasonable". On this word, see "opportune" in Mk 6:21.
13. On this word, see "support" in Act 27:17. Related to the word in Rev 12:16.
14. Same word as in 7:28; 8:3. GK *2770*. On this word, see "put in charge" in Act 6:3.
15. Or, "for the sake of, on behalf of ". GK *5642*.
16. Or, "beset, clothed". Same word as in 12:1, the witnesses "surrounding" us. Elsewhere only as "lie around" in Mk 9:42; Lk 17:2; and "wear" in Act 28:20. GK *4329*.
17. That is, his weakness. Some manuscripts say "this" {N}.
18. Christ fulfills these two characteristics of a high priest. He too was appointed by God; and He too is qualified to minister to the people based on His life experience. Yet His qualifications are of a different order than theirs.
19. On this quotation, see 1:5.
20. Or, "in His days *of* the flesh". That is, during His life on earth.
21. Or, "brought to *Him*". Same word as in v 1, 3. Also in 8:3, 4; 9:7, 9, 14, 25, 28;10:1, 2, 8, 11, 12; 11:4, 17. Used 47 times. GK *4712*.
22. Or, "pleas, pleadings". Used only here. GK *2656*. This word also means the olive branch brought by the pleader coming to plead. On "petition", see 1 Tim 2:1.
23. Or, "shout, cry". Elsewhere only as "shout" in Mt 25:6; Lk 1:42; "clamor" in Act 23:9; Eph 4:31; and "crying" in Rev 21:4. GK *3199*. Related to "shout" in Act 22:23, and "cry out" in Mt 8:29.
24. Or, "out of ". Some take this to mean "from dying"; others, "from the peril of death"; others, "out of death" through resurrection. Note that it is not said here what Jesus prayed for or when, only to whom He prayed and that He was heard, and that in the process, He learned obedience. Some think that this is referring to Gethsemane, Luke 22:41-44; others, that it has a wider reference. GK *1666*.
25. Or, "piety, godly fear, devotion". Elsewhere only in 12:28, where we are to exercise it. GK *2325*. Related to "reverent" in 11:7 and Lk 2:25. The root words mean "to take hold well" with reference to the commands of God.
26. Some take this phrase with what precedes (praying and being heard... although); others, with what follows (learned obedience, although). The main sentence is "Who... learned obedience".
27. That is, one whose essential quality is that He is God's Son. Compare 1:2.
28. Jesus learned obedience to the Father's will from undeserved suffering, not from personal sin like the high priests of 5:2. Same concept as in 2:10. "Suffered" in v 8 (see Gal 3:4 on it) is the verb related to "sufferings" in 2:10. Compare Phil 2:8.
29. That is, by sufferings. On this word, see 2:10.
30. Or, "source, grounds". On this word, see "guilt" in Lk 23:4.
31. Compare Rom 16:26. On this word, see Act 6:7.
32. Or, "called, addressed, named". Used only here. GK *4641*.
33. That is, Melchizedek, 5:10; 7:1. Or, "which", referring to Christ as High Priest, the main subject in 7:1-10:18.
34. Or, "word, message, discourse". It is rendered this way to show its relationship to the related word "speak" later. More literally, "concerning whom the message *for* us *is* great and hard-to-interpret to speak". On this word, see "word" in 1 Cor 12:8.
35. Same word as "long" in Act 15:32. It can mean great in quantity ("lengthy"), or in quality.
36. That is, difficult for me to explain to you, to put in words you will understand, given your spiritual condition. Used only here. GK *1549*. The root word is "translate" in 7:2.
37. Or, "lazy, dull". Elsewhere only in 6:12. GK *3821*.
38. Or, "ears". Same word as in 4:2, and related to "obedience" in 5:8.
39. That is, enough time has passed in your Christian life so that you ought to be teachers, not babes.
40. Or, "the fundamentals, the basics, the ABCs of a thing". On this word see "elemental" in Gal 4:3. These things are named in 6:1-2, and are next called "milk". Some manuscripts say "need *that someone* be teaching you what *are* the elements..." {C}. The difference is an accent mark.
41. Or, "sayings, declarations, pronouncements". Thus the whole phrase means "the basics consisting of the first things taught regarding the oracles of God". Elsewhere only in Act 7:38; Rom 3:2; 1 Pet 4:11. GK *3359*. Related to "word" in 1 Cor 12:8.
42. That is, continuing to have.
43. Some manuscripts omit this word {C}.
44. In this context, solid food refers to the teaching about Christ as High Priest. On this word, see Mt 24:45.
45. Or, "unaccustomed, unacquainted with". This is versus "trained" in the next verse. Used only here. GK *586*.
46. That is, characterized by, or leading to, or about righteousness.

A. Mt 8:17 B. Heb 10:22 C. Rev 20:11 D. Eph 2:8 E. Mt 9:13 F. Rom 7:8 G. Mt 4:4, mankind H. Heb 5:7 J. Mt 5:23 K. Heb 9:26
L. Rom 10:3 M. Jam 5:19, err N. Heb 2:17, had to O. Rev 21:3 P. 1 Tim 5:17 Q. Rom 8:30 R. Rom 8:30 S. 1 Jn 5:18 T. Rev 20:10
U. 1 Tim 2:1 V. Act 20:19 W. Lk 19:10 X. Phil 4:11 Y. Rom 16:25 Z. Mt 25:46 AA. Lk 19:9 BB. Tit 3:14 CC. Rom 12:7 DD. Col 1:18
EE. 2 Tim 2:19, firm FF. Heb 2:14 GG. 1 Cor 12:8 HH. 1 Cor 3:1

Hebrews 5:14	834	Verse

  2E. But the solid food is *for the* mature¹— the *ones* because of habit² having *their* faculties³ trained⁴ for discernment⁵ *of* both good^A and evil^B   14

 2D. Therefore, having left the message⁶ *of* the beginning⁷ *concerning* Christ, let us be carried-along⁸ to maturity⁹   6:1

  1E. Not again laying-down *a* foundation^C *of* repentance^D from dead^E works¹⁰ and faith^F toward God¹¹, *of* instruction^G *about* cleansings¹² and laying-on¹³ *of* hands, and *about the* resurrection^H *of the* dead^E and eternal^J judgment^K   2

 3D. And this we will do¹⁴ if-indeed¹⁵ God permits^L   3

  1E. For *it is* impossible¹⁶ **to renew**¹⁷ **again to repentance**^D the *ones*   4

   1F. Having once¹⁸ been enlightened¹⁹ and²⁰ having tasted²¹ the heavenly^M gift^N
   2F. And having been made²² partakers²³ *of* the Holy Spirit
   3F. And having tasted *the* good^A word^O *of* God and *the* powers²⁴ *of the* coming age   5
   4F. And having fallen-away²⁵— crucifying-again²⁶ *for* themselves the Son *of* God, and publicly-disgracing²⁷ *Him*   6

  2E. For land having drunk the rain coming often upon it, and producing^P *a* plant²⁸ useful^Q *to* those for whose sake it is also farmed, receives²⁹ *a* blessing^R from God   7
  3E. But *land* bringing-forth thorns^S and thistles *is* disapproved³⁰ and near^T *a* curse³¹, whose end³² *is* for burning   8

 4D. But concerning you, beloved³³, we are **convinced-of**^U better^V *things*, and *things* having salvation^W— even though we are speaking in this manner   9

  1E. For God *is* not unjust^X *so as* to forget^Y your work^Z and the love³⁴ which you demonstrated³⁵ for His name, having served³⁶ the saints^AA and [still] serving   10

1. That is, the full-grown, the adult. On this word, see "complete" in 1 Cor 13:10.
2. Or "practice, constant use". Used only here. GK *2011*. It refers to a state or condition of body or mind, to something one "has", sometimes as the result of practice. The root word is "to have". The immature are inexperienced in the word. The mature, by the habit which they have of using it, have trained their moral faculties.
3. Or, the "senses" or "abilities to perceive or discern" morally. Used only here. GK *152*. Related to "perception" in Phil 1:9.
4. Or, "exercised". This is a participle, "having *their* faculties having been trained". Elsewhere only in 12:11; 1 Tim 4:7; 2 Pet 2:14, "trained in greed". GK *1214*. Related to "training" in 1 Tim 4:8.
5. Or, "distinguishing". On this word, see 1 Cor 12:10.
6. Or, the "word, doctrine". On this word, see "word" in 1 Cor 12:8.
7. Same word as in 5:12. That is, the message consisting of the first things taught about Christ. Some think this means "the basic teaching about Jesus as the promised Messiah"; others, the foundational things mentioned next. On this word, see Col 1:18.
8. Or, "brought, moved, borne along, driven". Same word as in Act 27:15, 17. On this word, see "carried" in 2 Pet 1:17.
9. Or, "perfection, completeness". Elsewhere only as "perfection" in Col 3:14. GK *5456*. Related to "perfect" in 2:10; and "mature" in 5:14.
10. Same phrase as in 9:14. Works without faith are dead, just as faith without works is dead (Jam 2:26). Thus some think the writer means "faithless works, works devoid of life", Jewish rituals and works of the law performed apart from faith. Others think he means more generally "works leading to or producing death"; that is, sinful works.
11. Or, "faith upon God". This phrase is used only here. It is related to "put faith upon" in Rom 4:5.
12. Or, "washings, baptisms". Same word as in 9:10 and Mk 7:4, where it is also plural. Elsewhere only as singular in Col 2:12, buried with Him in "baptism". GK *968*. Related to the usual word "baptism" in Mk 1:4, which is never plural. The word "baptize" means "cleanse" in Mk 7:4. Some think the writer means teachings regarding the Christian view of Jewish cleansings, certainly a foundational item for the Hebrew believers. All six items here refer to their Jewish foundation, from which they must move on to Christian maturity. If he means "baptisms", some think he means Jewish washings/baths (and perhaps John's baptism and pagan baptisms) versus Christian baptism; others, that the plural stands for the singular, and simply means Christian "baptism". There are other views.
13. This noun is elsewhere only in Act 8:18; 1 Tim 4:14; 2 Tim 1:6. GK *2120*. The related verb (see Lk 10:30) is used in this sense twelve times to heal, as in Mt 9:18; Mk 16:18; Lk 4:40; Act 28:8; twice to pray a blessing (Mt 19:13, 15); three times to commission leaders (Act 6:6; 13:3; 1 Tim 5:22); and four times to bestow the Spirit (Act 8:17, 19; 9:17; 19:6).
14. That is, carry you on to maturity, v 1. Some manuscripts say "And let us do this" {A}.
15. Elsewhere only in 3:6, 14. GK *1570*.
16. Compare 10:29. Same phrase as in 6:18; 10:4; 11:6. Same word as in Mt 19:26; Mk 10:27; Lk 18:27; Rom 8:3. Elsewhere only as "powerless" in Act 14:8; and "not strong" in Rom 15:1. GK *105*.
17. Or, "restore". In the Greek word order, "it is impossible" is the first word in v 4, "to renew again to repentance" is in v 6 (preceding "crucifying"), placing emphasis on it. Used only here. GK *362*. On the related words "renewal" and "renew", see Tit 3:5.
18. That is, one time, not "formerly". This is in contrast with "again" crucify and "again" (a second time) repent. Some link this only with "enlightened"; others, with all four verbs, enlightened, tasted, made, tasted. It is used eight times in Hebrews. On this word, see "once for all" in Jude 3.
19. Or, "illuminated, lit up, given light". Some think this refers to their initial turning to Jesus, and their baptism. Compare 10:26, "having received the knowledge of the truth". Same word as in 10:32; Eph 1:18; 3:9. Elsewhere only as "illuminate" in 1 Cor 4:5; Rev 18:1; 21:23; "give light" in Lk 11:36; Jn 1:9; Rev 22:5; and "bring to light" in 2 Tim 1:10. GK *5894*.
20. This is not the same word as the "and" beginning the next three phrases. It is the same word as in the middle of v 5. For this reason, these two items are grouped together, like the two in v 5. However, it may also be rendered "enlightened— both having tasted... and having been made...", the latter two phrases explaining "enlightened".
21. This word is used both in the sense of "experienced" and of "partaken". It is used of a spiritual "tasting" in Heb 6:4, 5; 1 Pet 2:3; of "tasting" death (see Heb 2:9); and elsewhere only of "eating" (Act 10:10; 20:11; 23:14) or "tasting" (Mt 27:34; Lk 14:24; Jn 2:9; Col 2:21) food. GK *1174*. Some think the "gift" is salvation or forgiveness. Others think it is Christ (Jn 4:10); others, the Lord's Supper.
22. Or, "having come-to-be, become, been". GK *1181*.
23. Or, "partners, sharers". On this word, see 3:1. Note 10:32-34. This could mean sharers in the Spirit's person, gifts, or work.
24. Or, "miracles", as in 2:4.
25. Or, "fallen aside". Used only here. GK *4178*. Related to "trespass" in Mt 6:14. The root word is "fall" in 3:17; 4:11.
26. Or, "re-crucifying". This phrase defines the sense in which such ones have fallen away— publicly turning away and denouncing Jesus— and the reason they cannot be renewed to repentance. Thus, it means "*since they are* crucifying-again". This is the word "crucifying" with the prefix "again". Used only here. GK *416*.
27. Or, "making an example of, holding up for contempt, making a show of, putting to shame". Used only here. GK *4136*. The noun (not used in the NT) means "a precedent, an example, a proof from example, a lesson, a warning". The picture here is of one who publicly renounces Christ, rejoining the group crying "Crucify Him".
28. Or, "grass", any kind of small green plant. Used only here. GK *1083*. Our word "botany" comes from this word.
29. Or, "receives a share of ". Such ones can be led on to maturity, by God's blessing. The writer's grammar may mean "receives a share of blessing", or, "receives blessings". On this word, see "share in" in 12:10.
30. Or, "rejected, failing to meet the test". On this word, see 1 Cor 9:27.
31. That is, is facing a curse, near to being cursed. On this word, see Gal 3:10.
32. Or, "outcome". This kind of land has only one destiny. The writer is referring to judgment, as in 10:29. On this word, see Rom 10:4.
33. Used only here in this book. On this word, see Mt 3:17.
34. Some manuscripts say "labor *of* love" {N}.
35. Or, "showed". Same word as in v 11. On this word, see Eph 2:7.
36. Note 10:32-34. On this word, see "ministering" in 1 Pet 4:10.

A. 1 Tim 5:10a B. 3 Jn 11 C. 1 Tim 6:19 D. 2 Cor 7:10 E. Mt 8:22 F. Eph 2:8 G. 1 Cor 14:6, teaching H. Act 24:15 J. Mt 25:46 K. Jn 9:39 L. 1 Tim 2:12 M. Eph 3:10 N. Rom 5:15 O. Rom 10:17 P. Lk 2:11, born Q. Lk 9:62, fit R. 2 Cor 9:5 S. Lk 6:44 T. Lk 21:30 U. 1 Jn 3:19, persuade V. Heb 1:4 W. Lk 19:9 X. 1 Cor 6:9, wrong-doers Y. Heb 13:2 Z. Mt 26:10 AA. 1 Pet 1:16, holy

	2E. But we desire[A] *that* each *of* you be demonstrating the **same** diligence[1] toward the full-assurance[2] *of* hope[B] until *the* end[3], *in order that you may not be sluggish[4], but imitators[C] *of* the *ones* inheriting[D] the promises[E] through faith and patience[5]	11 12
	1F. For God, having promised[6] to Abraham, swore[7] by Himself— since He had by no one greater to swear—*saying [in Gen 22:17], "Surely while blessing[F] I will bless you, and while multiplying[G] I will multiply[8] you". *And so, having waited-patiently[9], he obtained[H] the promise	13 14 15
	1G. For people[10] swear by the greater *one*. And *for* them the oath[J] for confirmation[K] *is the* end[11] *of* every dispute[L]	16
	2G. By which *custom* God, intending[M] even more to show[N] the unchangeableness *of* His intention[12] *to* the heirs[O] *of* the promise, guaranteed[13] *with an oath*	17
	1H. In order that by two unchangeable things[14] in which *it is* impossible[P] *for* God to lie, we— the *ones* having fled[15] to take-hold-of[Q] the hope being set-before[16] *us*— may have strong encouragement[17]	18
	1I. Which *hope* we have as *an* anchor *of* the soul[R], both secure[18] and firm[S] and entering into the inner *side of* the curtain[19], *where *a* forerunner for us went in— Jesus—	19 20
	1J. Having become High Priest forever[T] according to the order *of* Melchizedek	
2C. For this Melchizedek[20]—		7:1
	1D. King *of* Salem, priest *of* the Most-High[U] God, **remains**[21] *a priest perpetually*[22]—	
	1E. The *one* having met[V] Abraham returning[W] from the defeat[23] *of* the kings and having blessed[F] him, *to whom also Abraham divided[X] *a* tenth[24] from everything[25], *who is*	2
	1F. First, being translated[Y]— king *of* righteousness[26]	
	2F. And then also, king *of* Salem— which is king *of* peace[27]	
	3F. Fatherless, motherless, genealogy-less, having neither *a* beginning[Z] *of* days nor *an* end[AA] *of* life,[28] but having been made-like[29] the Son *of* God	3
	2D. Now observe[BB] how great this *one is to* whom indeed[30] Abraham the patriarch[31] gave *a* tenth from the choicest-spoils[32]	4
	1E. Indeed, **the *ones***[33] from the sons *of* Levi receiving the priestly-office[34] have *a* commandment[CC] to be collecting-a-tenth-from[35] the people[DD] according to the Law[36]— that is, *from* their brothers[EE], even though *their brothers* have come-out[37] of the loins[38] *of* Abraham—	5

1. On this word, see "earnestness" in 2 Cor 8:16. Related to "diligent" in Heb 4:11.
2. On this word, see 10:22. On this verse, compare 10:36.
3. That is, the end of life, or Christ's return. This phrase "until *the* end" is also in Rev 2:26, and is similar to the phrase in Heb 3:14. On related phrases, see Mt 10:22.
4. Same word as in 5:11.
5. That is, ones like Abraham next, and those in chapter 11. Elsewhere only in Rom 2:4; 9:22; 2 Cor 6:6; Gal 5:22; Eph 4:2; Col 1:11; 3:12; 1 Tim 1:16; 2 Tim 3:10; 4:2; Jam 5:10; 1 Pet 3:20; 2 Pet 3:15. GK *3429*. The related verb is in v 15.
6. Some think this means when God promised, He swore at the same time, in Gen 22; others, having previously promised since Gen 12, He swore in Gen 22. The grammar permits either.
7. On this word, see Jam 5:12. It is used seven times in Hebrews.
8. This is a literal translation of a Hebrew way of speaking, meaning, I will surely bless, I will surely multiply.
9. On this word, see "is patient" in 1 Cor 13:4. Some think this refers to the 25 years between the promise and the birth of Isaac.
10. Some manuscripts add "indeed" {N}.
11. Or, "conclusion". Elsewhere only in Mt 12:42; Lk 11:31; Rom 10:18. GK *4306*.
12. Or, "will, purpose". On this word, see "counsel" in Eph 1:11. Related to the previous verb. It could also be rendered "purposing... His purpose", "willing... His will", "determining... His determination".
13. Or, "interposed, mediated, pledged Himself as surety". Used only here. GK *3541*. Related to "mediator" in 8:6.
14. That is, the promise and the oath.
15. Or, "fled for refuge, taken refuge". Or, this may be punctuated "we, the *ones* having fled for refuge, may have strong encouragement to take hold...". Elsewhere only in Act 14:6. GK *2966*. Used of fleeing to a city of refuge in Deut 4:42; 19:5; Josh 20:9. The picture is that we have fled from sin to a city of refuge in order to lay hold of the hope of life, eternal life.
16. That is, by God. Or, "lying before". On this word, see 12:1.
17. That is, encouragement to wait patiently (like Abraham) in order to obtain the promises. On this word, see Act 4:36.
18. Or, "certain, safe, firm". On this word, see "certainty" in Act 21:34.
19. That is, into the true Holy of Holies. On this word, see 9:3.
20. This is the fourth mention of Melchizedek, 5:6, 10; 6:20. Chapter 7 is exposition of the meaning of this person. Here the writer draws his points from Gen 14:17-20. In v 14 he takes up Ps 110, the only other place Melchizedek is mentioned. GK *3519*.
21. Or, "continues, abides". In the Greek word order, v 1-3 is one long sentence with the subject ("this Melchizedek") coming first, and this phrase held until the very end (after "Son of God"), for emphasis. The writer returns to this point in v 23-25. On this word, see "abide" in Jn 15:4.
22. Or, "continually" and in this sense, "for all time, forever". On this idiom, see "for all time" in 10:12.
23. Used only here. GK *3158*. Same word as in Gen 14:17.
24. Same word as in v 4, 8, 9. Elsewhere only in Jn 1:39; Rev 11:13; 21:20. GK *1281*. The related verbs are in v 5 and v 6.
25. That is, from all the spoils.
26. This is the translation of the Hebrew name Melchizedek.
27. The translation of the Hebrew word for "Salem" is "peace".
28. That is, none of these are recorded in the OT. Melchizedek is made to appear in Scripture as a prefiguration of Christ.
29. Or, "made to resemble, copied from". Used only here. GK *926*. Related to "likeness" in 4:15; and "become like" in 2:17. Jesus "became like" His brothers (2:17). Melchizedek was "copied from" the Son of God. Note that the writer does not say made like "Jesus", who had a mother and a genealogy, but "the Son of God", who does not.
30. Some manuscripts omit this word {C}.
31. This word means the head or beginning or ruler of a family or tribe. Elsewhere only in Act 2:29; 7:8, 9. GK *4256*. The root word is "father".
32. This word literally means "the top of the heap"; and regarding the harvest it meant "firstfruits". Used only here. GK *215*.
33. The writer uses grammar that emphasizes the contrast between the two halves of this statement, between "the ones" and "the one" in v 6.
34. Elsewhere only in Lk 1:9. GK *2632*. Related to "priesthood" in v 11.
35. Elsewhere only as "to give a tenth of" in Mt 23:23; Lk 11:42; 18:12. GK *620*. Related to "tenth" in v 4; and to the verb in v 6. "Tithe" is an Old English word meaning "tenth".
36. See Num 18:21-26. The Levites received it for their service as priests, but did not receive a portion of the land.
37. The point is that the Levitical priests had a commandment authorizing them to collect a tenth, even though collecting it from their own brothers. Melchizedek had no commandment, yet collected it from Abraham, to whom he was no relation! Melchizedek is greater than Abraham, and by extension, the Levitical priests. This is a participle modifying "brothers", "even though having come out".
38. Or, "reproductive organs, groin". Same word as in v 10; and Act 2:30, where Jesus is a fruit of David's loins. It is a Hebrew way of speaking, as in Gen 35:11; 2 Chron 6:9; etc. We would say "although they were descendants of Abraham". This word also means the "waist", where one ties a belt or ties up his garments to prepare for work. Elsewhere only as "waist" in Mt 3:4; Mk 1:6; Lk 12:35; Eph 6:14; 1 Pet 1:13. GK *4019*.

A. Gal 5:17 B. Col 1:5 C. Eph 5:1 D. Gal 4:30 E. 1 Jn 2:25 F. Lk 6:28 G. Act 7:17 H. Heb 11:33 J. Jam 5:12 K. Phil 1:7 L. Heb 12:3, opposition M. Jam 1:18, willed N. Act 18:28 O. Rom 8:17 P. Heb 6:4 Q. Heb 4:14, hold on to R. Jam 5:20 S. 2 Pet 1:10 T. Rev 20:10 U. Mt 21:9, highest V. Act 20:22 W. 2 Pet 2:21, turn back X. 1 Cor 7:17, apportioned Y. Jn 1:42 Z. Col 1:18 AA. Rom 10:4 BB. Lk 10:18, seeing CC. Mk 12:28 DD. Rev 21:3 EE. Act 16:40

1F.	Yet the *one* not tracing-*his*-genealogy¹ from them has collected-a-tenth² *from* Abraham, and has blessed^A the *one* having the promises! °And apart from all dispute³, the lesser *one* is blessed^A by the better⁴ *one*	6 7
2E.	And **here**⁵, dying^B men⁶ receive^C the tenths—	8
1F.	Yet there, *it is* being attested^D that he⁷ is living!	
3E.	And so to speak,⁸ through Abraham, even Levi— the *one* receiving^C *the* tenths⁹— has paid-a-tenth. °For he was still in the loins^E *of his* father when Melchizedek met^F him¹⁰	9 10
3C. Now indeed,¹¹ if perfection¹² had been through the Levitical priesthood¹³— for the [Jewish] people^G have received-the-Law on the basis of it¹⁴— what further^H need^J *would there have been that* another priest *should* arise^K according to the order *of* Melchizedek, and not be named^L according to the order *of* Aaron?¹⁵	11
1D.	For¹⁶ the priesthood being changed¹⁷, of necessity¹⁸ there is¹⁹ also *a* change²⁰ *of* law	12
1E.	For²¹ *the One* about Whom these²² *things* are spoken has partaken²³ *of* another tribe^M from which no one has attended-to²⁴ the altar^N	13
1F.	For *it is* clear^O that our Lord has risen²⁵ from Judah— for which tribe Moses spoke nothing concerning priests²⁶	14
2E.	And it is still^H even-more very-clear²⁷ if Another²⁸ Priest arises^K in accordance with the likeness^P *of* Melchizedek, °Who has become *such* not based-on²⁹ *the* law *of a* fleshy³⁰ commandment^Q, but based on *the* power^R *of an* indestructible³¹ life^S!	15 16
1F.	For it is attested³² that "You *are a* priest forever^T according to the order *of* Melchizedek" [Ps 110:4]	17
2D.	For³³ *a* **setting-aside**³⁴ *of the* preceding^U commandment^Q takes place,³⁵ because of its weakness^V and unprofitableness³⁶ °(for the Law perfected^W nothing)—	18 19
1E.	And *a* bringing-in³⁷ *of a* better^X hope, through which we draw-near^Y *to* God	

1. Or, "naming *his* genealogy, being genealogized". This is the verb related to "genealogy" in 1 Tim 1:4. Used only here. GK *1156.*
2. Same word as in v 5, but without the prefix "from", which is implied. Elsewhere only as "paid *a* tenth" in v 9. GK *1282.* Melchizedek took a tenth from Abraham and blessed him. Therefore he is the greater of the two.
3. Or, "without any argument". On this word, see "opposition" in 12:3.
4. This is a key word in Hebrews. On this word, see 1:4.
5. The writer uses grammar that emphasizes the contrast between the two halves of this sentence.
6. That is, priests from the sons of Levi.
7. That is, Melchizedek. He "remains a priest perpetually", v 2-3. His death is not recorded.
8. This is an idiom, literally, "And so as to say *a* word". It was used to limit a startling statement. Used only here. GK *2229.*
9. That is, the tenths from the people according to the Law, v 5.
10. That is, Levi was represented by Abraham when Abraham gave the tenth to Melchizedek, v 2. The point is that Levi, representing the entire Aaronic priesthood under the Law of Moses, is therefore shown to be inferior to Melchizedek.
11. This phrase "Now indeed, Now, So, Then" resumes the argument. It occurs also in 8:4 and 9:1. Each time, it introduces a comparison between the Levitical system and the priesthood/ministry of Christ. Here, having proven the personal superiority of Melchizedek to Abraham (v 6-7), and therefore to Levi (v 9-10), the writer now demonstrates the superiority of this priesthood predicted in Ps 110 to the Levitical priesthood. He does this by drawing inferences from three aspects of Ps 110. First, from the new order, v 11. Then from "swore", v 20. Then from "forever", v 23.
12. Or, "completeness", the attainment of everything required before God. Later the writer will say the yearly sacrifice proves this was not attained, 10:1-2. Elsewhere only as "fulfillment" in Lk 1:45. GK *5459.* Related to "perfect" in 2:10.
13. Elsewhere only in v 12, 24. GK *2648.*
14. That is, the priesthood. The Law rests upon the priesthood, which administers it. Thus the writer means "If the priesthood— and the Law they ministered to the people— had perfected them".
15. Though Melchizedek was mentioned in Genesis, the new priestly order is mentioned in Ps 110, long after the establishment of Aaron's priesthood. This implies that the Levitical priesthood and law was imperfect and temporary. The new will replace the old, and do what it could not do. If this were not so, if the Levitical system was God's final plan leading to perfection, what need would there be for the new one? Thus the very existence of this statement in Ps 110 proves that the Levitical system, like Levi, is inferior, and that something better was coming.
16. Since the Psalm proves that there is a change in priesthood, the writer now extends this by stating and proving (in v 13-17) the necessary corollary, that there is a change of law. He shifts from discussing the priesthood to the law. By proving the corollary, he further proves the main point of v 11. Others think this verse is parenthetical (making it part of 3C.), and that v 13 and v 15 (which would become 1D. and 2D.) are proving that a change in priesthood has in fact taken place, replacing the inferior Levitical one. Consult the commentaries.
17. On this word, see "removed" in 11:5.
18. Same word as in 7:27; 9:16, 23. On this word, see 1 Cor 7:26.
19. Or, "takes place, occurs". GK *1181.*
20. Or, "changeover". On this word, see "removal" in 11:5. Related to "changed" earlier.
21. The historical fact that Jesus, as the Priest of Ps 110, is from Judah (in fulfillment of Gen 49:10) in violation of the Law of Moses, proves that He also brings a change of law.
22. That is, Ps 110:4.
23. Same word as in 2:14, where Jesus "partook" of blood and flesh.
24. That is, served as priest. Only the sons of Levi can be priests under the Law of Moses. On this word, see "pay attention to" in 1 Tim 3:8.
25. Or, "sprung up". Elsewhere only of the sun rising in Mt 5:45; 13:6; Mk 4:6; 16:2; Jam 1:11; the clouds in Lk 12:54; a light in Mt 4:16; and the morning star in 2 Pet 1:19. GK *422.*
26. Some manuscripts say "priesthood" {N}.
27. The writer piles up the words here. It is even more clear that a change of law must occur since not only is Jesus of a different tribe than the priests, but human lineage is not even a qualification! It is not based on the lineage of Melchizedek at all (he has none), but on his continuing to "live" forever. Used only here. GK *2867.* Related to "clear" in v 14.
28. Or, "Different". The word means, "another of a different kind". Same word as in v 11 and 13. On this word, see "different" in 1 Cor 12:9.
29. Or, "according to". GK *2848.*
30. Or, "made of flesh". That is, the laws regarding the priest's physical descent. On this word, see "made of flesh" in 1 Cor 3:1.
31. Used only here. GK *186.* This is another way of saying "a priest forever" as in v 17.
32. Or, "witnessed, testified". On this word, see Act 6:3. Some manuscripts say "He attests" {N}.
33. The writer now concludes by plainly stating the meaning of "a change of law" in v 12, and thus the meaning of Ps 110. Ps 110 predicts a new Priest in a new priesthood, which requires a new Law. This means Jesus brings a setting aside of the Law and the Levitical system, which was not able to perfect (v 11), as He brings in better hope.
34. Or, "annulment, abolishment, abrogation". The new High Priest brings an end to the old system. The writer uses grammar that emphasizes the contrast between the two halves of this sentence; between the setting aside and the bringing in. Elsewhere only in 9:26, of sin. GK *120.* Related to the verb "set aside" in 10:28.
35. The setting aside takes place in the establishment of the new priesthood, in fulfillment of the psalm.
36. Or, "uselessness". The Law could not save those approaching, v 25; 10:1-4. Elsewhere only as "unprofitable" in Tit 3:9. GK *543.* Related to "profit" in Rom 2:25.
37. Or, "introduction". Used only here. GK *2081.* The root word is "bring-in".

A. Lk 6:28 B. Rom 7:10 C. Rom 7:8, taken D. Act 6:3 E. Heb 7:5 F. Heb 7:1 G. Rev 21:3 H. 1 Cor 12:31, still J. Tit 3:14 K. Lk 18:33, rise up L. Jn 12:49, say M. Rev 1:7 N. Rev 8:3 O. 1 Tim 5:24, clear beforehand P. Heb 4:15 Q. Mk 12:28 R. Mk 5:30 S. Rom 8:10 T. Rev 20:10 U. 2 Jn 9, going ahead V. 1 Thes 5:14 W. Heb 2:10 X. Heb 1:4 Y. Lk 21:28

4C.	And¹ to the degree that *it was* not without² *an* oath-swearing³ (for **the ones**⁴ have become⁵ priests without *an* oath-swearing—*but the *One* with *an* oath-swearing, through the *One*⁶ saying to Him [in Ps 110:4], *"The* Lord swore^A and He will not change-*His*-mind^B, You *are a* priest forever⁷")—	20 21
	1D. To that degree⁸ also⁹ **Jesus** has become *the* guarantee¹⁰ *of a* better^C covenant^D	22
5C.	And¹¹ **the many**¹² have been¹³ [Levitical] priests because of *their* being prevented^E from continuing¹⁴ *by* death—	23
	1D. But the *One*, because of His remaining^F forever^G, has *a* permanent¹⁵ priesthood	24
	2D. Hence also, He is able to save^H completely¹⁶ the *ones* coming-to^J God through Him, always living so as to intercede^K for them	25
6C.	For¹⁷ such *a* High Priest was indeed fitting¹⁸ *for* us— holy¹⁹, innocent^L, undefiled^M, having been separated²⁰ from sinners, and having become higher *than* the heavens	26
	1D. Who does not have *the* daily necessity²¹— as indeed the high priests— to be offering^N sacrifices^O first for *His* own sins, then the *sins of* the people^P	27
	1E. For He did this²² once-for-all²³, having offered^N Himself	
	2D. For the Law appoints²⁴ men having weakness^Q *as* high priests, but the word^R *of* the oath-swearing after the Law²⁵ *appoints a* Son having been perfected^S forever^G	28
5B. Now *the* main-point²⁶ in the *things* being said *is*— we have such *a* High Priest, Who sat-*down* at *the* right *hand of* the throne^T *of* the Majesty^U in the heavens,*Minister^V *of* the Holies²⁷, indeed²⁸ *of* the true²⁹ tabernacle³⁰, which the Lord pitched³¹, not³² *a* human^W		8:1 2
	1C. For every high priest is appointed that *he might* be offering^X both gifts^Y and sacrifices^O. Hence it is³³ necessary^Z *that* this *One* also have something which He may offer³⁴	3
	2C. Now indeed,³⁵ if He were on earth He would not even be *a* priest— *there* being the *ones* offering³⁶ the gifts according-to³⁷ *the* Law	4
	1D. Who are serving^AA *a* copy^BB and *a* shadow *of* the heavenly^CC *things*— just as Moses has been warned³⁸, being about to complete³⁹ the tabernacle	5
	1E. For "See", He says [in Ex 25:40], *"that* you make everything according to the pattern^DD having been shown *to* you on the mountain"	
	3C. But He has now obtained^EE *a* **more-excellent**⁴⁰ ministry⁴¹, *by* as much as He is indeed *the* mediator⁴² *of a* **better**^C covenant⁴³, which has been enacted on better promises⁴⁴!	6
	1D. For if that first *covenant* had been faultless⁴⁵, no place would have been sought^FF *for a* second	7

1. Continuing the exposition of Ps 110, the writer now draws an inference from "swore".
2. Or, stated positively, to the degree that Jesus became High Priest by the oath of God Himself... to that degree He is the guarantee of a better covenant.
3. This noun is elsewhere only in v 21, 28. GK *3993*. Related to "oath" in 6:16.
4. The writer uses grammar that emphasizes the contrast between the two halves of this sentence; between the ones (the Levitical priests) and the One (Christ).
5. This is a participle, "are having become". The Levitical priests have become and continue to be priests apart from an oath-swearing. GK *1181*.
6. That is, the Father.
7. Some manuscripts add "according to the order of Melchizedek" {A}.
8. This construction "to the degree that... to that degree" (or, "by as much as... by so much") is used only here. Similar to Rev 18:7. Related to the construction in 1:4; 10:25. The first component ("to the degree") is also used in 3:3; 9:27 ("just as").
9. Some manuscripts omit this word {C}.
10. Or, "pledge, security". Used only here. GK *1583*.
11. Continuing the exposition of Ps 110, the writer now draws an inference from "forever".
12. Or, "the more", more than one. Many were needed in succession, since they died. The writer uses grammar that emphasizes the contrast between the two halves of this sentence; between the many and the One.
13. Many have been and continue to be priests, because of death. This is a participle, "are having been". GK *1181*.
14. That is, from continuing as priests. On this word, see Jam 1:25.
15. Or, "unchangeable", not passing over to another. Used only here. GK *563*.
16. Or, "wholly, fully". This is a phrase, "to the full". Some think the writer means complete as to duration, that is, "forever". Others think he means complete as contrasted to the Law, which perfects nothing, v 19. Elsewhere only in Lk 13:11. GK *4117*.
17. Now the writer summarizes and concludes this point, and hints at the next one in v 27.
18. Same word as in 2:10.
19. Or, "devout". That is, holy in character, pleasing to God, pure. Elsewhere only in Act 2:27; 13:34, 35; 1 Tim 2:8; Tit 1:8; Rev 15:4; 16:5. GK *4008*. Related to "holiness" in Eph 4:24; "devoutly" in 1 Thes 2:10; and "unholy" in 1 Tim 1:9; 2 Tim 3:2.
20. On this word, see Mt 19:6. Some think the writer means separated in character, taking this with what precedes. Jesus lived without sin. Others think he means separated physically, "to the heavens", taking it with what follows.
21. Jesus intercedes for us daily, but does not have the necessity when He does so to offer a sacrifice for Himself first, as the high priests do when they make their offering on the Day of Atonement. On this word, see 1 Cor 7:26.
22. That is, made an offering for the sins of all people. Compare 2:17.
23. Same word as in Rom 6:10; Heb 9:12; 10:10. Elsewhere only as "at one time" in 1 Cor 15:6. GK *2384*. Related word in Jude 3.
24. Same word as in 8:3, on which see 5:1.
25. That is, the oath contained in the Ps 110 passage, which was written after the Law.
26. Or, "the chief point, the summary, the sum of the matter". At this point, the writer turns from Christ's person as High Priest in the order of Melchizedek, to His work as High Priest. Elsewhere only in Act 22:28 of a "sum" of money. GK *3049*. Related to "head".
27. Or, "Holy *Places*". This sense occurs only in Hebrews— of the heavenly Holy Place in 8:2; 9:12; 10:19; of the whole earthly Holy Place, the Tabernacle in 9:1; of and its two parts, the outer Holy Place, 9:2; and the inner Holy of Holies, 9:3, 24, 25; 13:11; and in 9:8. "Holy Place" occurs in Mt 24:15; Act 6:13; 21:28, but in these cases the Greek word "Place" is expressed. Normally this word is translated "holy" (as in "Holy" Spirit), or "saints" ("holy" ones). On this word, see 1 Pet 1:16.
28. Or, "and". GK *2779*.
29. Or, "genuine", the one in heaven, not the copy on earth. Same word as in 9:24. On this word, see Jn 7:28.
30. Same word as in 8:5; 9:2, 3, 6, 8, 11, 21; 13:10. It means "tent, dwelling place". The "tent" which served as the Lord's dwelling place in the OT, later reproduced in the temple, is called the "tabernacle". On this word, see "dwelling" in Lk 9:33.
31. Or, "set up, erected". This is the verb used of pitching a tent. Used only here. GK *4381*.
32. Some manuscripts say "and not" {N}.
33. Or, "*was*". Some take this as a general statement of principle, like the first half of the verse, and supply *is*. Others think it refers specifically to the cross, and supply *was*.
34. Compare 5:1-2. Since Jesus was appointed High Priest in the order of Melchizedek, this means that He must have something to offer to God on behalf of people. He offered Himself, 7:27.
35. See 7:11 on this phrase. This begins a comparison that is completed in v 6. Some manuscripts say "For indeed" {N}.
36. Some manuscripts say "*there* being priests offering" {N}.
37. Or, "based on, in accordance with, in harmony with". That is, as the Law required. GK *2848*.
38. Or, "divinely instructed". On this word, see "revealed" in Lk 2:26.
39. That is, to make or build it. On this word, see "perfecting" in 2 Cor 7:1.
40. Same word as in 1:4. Elsewhere only as "different" in 9:10; Rom 12:6. GK *1427*. Related to "mattering" in Phil 1:10.
41. Or, "priestly service". On this word, see "service" in 2 Cor 9:12. Related to "minister" in v 2.
42. This word is used only of Moses in Gal 3:19-20; and of Christ in 1 Tim 2:5; Heb 8:6; 9:15; 12:24. GK *3542*.
43. Same word as in 7:22; 8:8, 9, 10; 9:4, 15, 20; 10:16, 29; 12:24; 13:20; and in Mt 26:28; Mk 14:24; Lk 1:72; 22:20; Act 3:25; 7:8; Rom 9:4; 11:27; 1 Cor 11:25; 2 Cor 3:6, 14; Gal 3:15, 17; 4:24; Eph 2:12; Rev 11:19. Elsewhere only as "will" in Heb 9:16, 17. GK *1347*. The related verb is in v 10.
44. The writer is referring to the new covenant quoted next, and to the promises in v 10-12.
45. On this word, see "blameless" in Phil 3:6. Related to "finding fault with" in v 8.

A. Jam 5:12 B. Mt 21:29, regret C. Heb 1:4 D. Heb 8:6 E. 1 Cor 14:39, forbid F. Jn 15:4, abide G. Rev 20:10 H. Lk 19:10 J. Heb 10:22, approach K. Rom 8:34 L. Rom 16:18, guileless M. Heb 13:4 N. Heb 9:28, bear O. Heb 9:26 P. Rev 21:3 Q. Mt 8:17 R. 1 Cor 12:8 S. Heb 2:10 T. Rev 20:11 U. Heb 1:3 V. Rom 13:6 W. Mt 4:4, mankind X. Heb 5:7 Y. Mt 5:23 Z. Tit 3:14 AA. Heb 12:28, worship BB. Jn 13:15, example CC. Eph 3:10 DD. 1 Pet 5:3 EE. Lk 20:35, attain FF. Phil 2:21

1E. For, finding-fault-with[1] them, He says [in Jer 31:31-34], "Behold— days are coming, says *the* Lord, and I will consummate[2] *a* new covenant[A] for the house[B] *of* Israel and for the house *of* Judah   8

    1F. "Not in accordance with the covenant which I made *with* their fathers on *the* day I took-hold-of[3] their hand to lead them out of *the* land *of* Egypt   9

        1G. "Because **they** did not continue[C] in My covenant, and **I** did not-care-for[D] them, says *the* Lord

    2F. "Because this *is* the covenant which I will covenant[4] *with* the house *of* Israel after those days, says *the* Lord—   10

        1G. "Giving[E] My laws into their mind[5], I will also write them upon their heart
        2G. "And I will be God[6] *to* them and **they** will be *a* people[F] *to* Me
        3G. "And they will by no means each teach[G] his *fellow*-citizen[7] and each his brother[H], saying, 'Know[8] the Lord', because they all will know[J] Me from *the* small[9] *one* up to their great *one*   11
        4G. "Because I will be merciful[10] *to* their wrong-doings[11], and I will never remember[12] their sins[13] again"   12

2E. In *that* He says[14] "New[15]", He has made the first old[16]   13
3E. And the *thing* becoming old and growing-aged[17] *is* near disappearance

2D. Now indeed,[18] the first *covenant* also[19] had regulations[K] *of* service[20] and the earthly[21] Holy Place[22]   9:1

    1E. For the first tabernacle[23] was prepared[24]— in which *were* both the lampstand[L] and the table, and the Presentation[25] *of* the bread— which is called[M] *the* Holies[26]. °And behind the second curtain[27] *was the* tabernacle being called *the* Holies *of* Holies[28], °having   2
        3
        4

        1F. *A* golden altar-of-incense[29]
        2F. And the ark[30] *of* the covenant[A] having been covered[N] on-all-sides *with* gold

            1G. In which[31] *was a* golden jar having the manna[32], and the rod[O] *of* Aaron[33] having budded[P], and the tablets *of* the covenant[34]
            2G. And above it *were the* cherubim[35] *of* glory[Q] overshadowing[36] the mercy-seat[37]   5

        3F. Concerning which *things* there is not *time* now to be speaking in detail[38]

    2E. And these *things* thus having been prepared   6

        1F. The priests accomplishing[R] the services[S] are continually[39] going into **the first**[40] tabernacle—°but into the second only the high priest *goes* once *a* year, not without blood   7

1. Or, "blaming" them. On this word, see Rom 9:19. The problem was with "them", not with the covenant. Some manuscripts say "For finding fault, He says to them..." {B}.
2. Or, "accomplish, complete, execute". On this word, see "accomplished" in Mk 13:4.
3. This is a participle, more literally, "on the day of my having taken hold of their hand". On this word, see Lk 20:20.
4. The verb and noun of the same word are used. Same word as in Act 3:25; Heb 10:16. Elsewhere only as "made the will" in Heb 9:16, 17; and as "confer" in Lk 22:29. GK 1416. On the noun, see 8:6.
5. On this word, see "thought" in Lk 1:51. The Septuagint is being quoted here. In 10:16, this is changed to "upon their heart... upon their mind".
6. Same construction as in 1:5. It is a Hebrew way of speaking. More literally, "I will be for God to them, and they will be for a people to Me".
7. Elsewhere only as "citizen" in Lk 15:15; 19:14; Act 21:39. GK 4489. Some manuscripts say "neighbor" {A}.
8. Or, "Come to know". On this word, see Lk 1:34.
9. Or, "little". That is, insignificant. Some think the sense of these words here is "least, greatest". Same phrase as in Act 8:10. Some manuscripts say "their small one" {N}.
10. Or, "propitious, gracious". Elsewhere only in Mt 16:22. GK 2664. Related to "make an offering for satisfaction" in 2:17.
11. This word is normally translated "unrighteousness" (see Rom 1:18). It is plural only here. Related to "wronged" in Act 7:24.
12. Or, "call to mind, keep in mind". That is, I will forget them. Same word as in Lk 1:54.
13. Some manuscripts add "and their lawless-deeds" {N}, as in 10:17.
14. The writer summarizes his point from Jeremiah. Literally, "In the saying". Same idiom as in 3:15, except there it is passive.
15. This word is used of the new covenant also in Lk 22:20; 1 Cor 11:25; 2 Cor 3:6; Heb 8:8; 9:15. It means new in the sense of "fresh, recent, unused" versus "stale, worn out, obsolete". Compare 12:24. Same word as in Mk 2:21; 14:25; Jn 13:34. Used 42 times. GK 2785.
16. That is, made it obsolete. He replaced the old with the new. This word "made old" is elsewhere only in 1:11 and Lk 12:33 in the sense of "worn out"; and as "becoming old" here in this verse, with different grammar. GK 4096. Related to "old" in Mk 2:21, which is used of the "old" covenant in 2 Cor 3:14.
17. That is, old in years. On this word, see "become old" in Jn 21:18.
18. Having quoted the new covenant of which Christ is the minister, the writer now begins a comparison of the two ministries. First he describes and comments on the old, 9:1-10. Then he turns to the new, 9:11. On this phrase, see 7:11.
19. Or, "even". The writer may mean that both the second (8:10-12) and the first covenant have divinely ordained content. Or, he may be referring to this as the next matter regarding the first covenant which he will discuss and compare. Some manuscripts omit this word {C}.
20. Or, "worship". That is, the service of divine worship as prescribed by God. Same word as in v 6. On this word, see "worship" in Rom 12:1.
21. Or, "worldly", that is, "pertaining to this world". Elsewhere only as "worldly" in Tit 2:12. GK 3176. The root word is "world".
22. On this term, see "Holies" in 8:2. This is the only place where the singular is used of the Holy Place in Hebrews. Here it refers to the whole thing.
23. That is, the first "room" of the two-room tabernacle tent, the part the priests entered, v 6. Same word as in 8:2.
24. Or, "built, erected, made ready, furnished". Same word as in 9:6; 11:7; 1 Pet 3:20. Elsewhere only as "build" in 3:3, 4; and "make ready" in Mt 11:10; Mk 1:2; Lk 1:17; 7:27. GK 2941.
25. Or, "setting before". On this word, see Mk 2:26.
26. That is, the Holy Place. The word is plural, not singular as in v 1. On this word, see 8:2. For the detail on all this, see Ex 24-27.
27. Or, "veil". Elsewhere only of the curtain that was torn when Christ died in Mt 27:51; Mk 15:38; Lk 23:45; and in a different sense in Heb 6:19; 10:20. The first veil kept the people (except the priests) out of the Holy Place. The second veil kept the priests (except the high priest once a year) out of the Holy of Holies. GK 2925.
28. That is, the Holy of Holies. The Septuagint uses both phrases to refer to the Most Holy Place, "Holies of Holies", and "Holy of Holies". It is the second room, where only the high priest entered, v 7. On this word, see 8:2.
29. Or, "censer". See Ex 30:1-10 regarding the altar of incense, which was outside the veil, but associated with the Holy of Holies on the Day of Atonement, Ex 30:10. Note that the writer says "having", as opposed to "in which" (as with the lampstand, v 2, and the jar, v 4). Some think he means "having" in the sense of "associated with" (as in 6:9), for the altar and the ark. For other views, consult the commentaries. See Lev 16:12-13 for the censer used inside the veil on the Day of Atonement. It was not kept inside the veil, but taken in once a year. Used only here. GK 2593. Related words in Lk 1:9, 11.
30. Or, "box, chest". That is, the gold-covered box containing God's covenant written on stone. The ark of the covenant in heaven is in Rev 11:19. Elsewhere only of Noah's ark (boat) in Mt 24:38; Lk 17:27; Heb 11:7; 1 Pet 3:20. GK 3066.
31. That is, the ark.
32. See Ex 16:32-34. It was placed "before the Testimony" at the time of Moses. This jar of manna is not mentioned elsewhere in Scripture. On "manna", see Rev 2:17.
33. The rod was placed "before the Testimony" at the time of Moses (Num 17:1-11), and is not mentioned again in the OT.
34. See Ex 25:16; 31:18; Deut 10:5. 1 Kings 8:9 says that at that time, only the tablets were inside the ark. The other items were probably lost in 1 Sam 4:10-11. The ark itself was destroyed or taken in 2 Kings 25:8-10.
35. That is, winged creatures. This is a transliterated Hebrew word, from Ex 25:18-22. There were two cherubs, made of gold. Used only here. GK 5938. Same word as in Gen 3:24; 1 Sam 4:4; 2 Sam 22:11; 1 King 6:23-35; Ezek 10:1-20, etc. They are called "living creatures" (the word in Rev 4:6) in Ezek 10:15, 20.
36. Or, "shadowing down upon". Used only here. GK 2944.
37. Or, "the place of propitiation" where the blood of the sacrifice was offered to satisfy the justice of God. It was on top of the ark. Used of the place and the offering. Same word as in Ex 25:17, 21-22; Lev 16:14-16. On this word, see "that which satisfies" in Rom 3:25.
38. More literally, "according to part", or "part by part".
39. Or, "through all times", meaning all through the year as opposed to once per year for the high priest. On this idiom, see 2 Thes 3:16.
40. The writer uses grammar that emphasizes the contrast between the two halves of this sentence.

A. Heb 8:6 B. Mk 3:20 C. Gal 3:10 D. Heb 2:3, neglected E. Eph 1:22 F. Rev 21:3 G. Rom 12:7 H. Act 16:40 J. 1 Jn 2:29 K. Rom 1:32 L. Rev 1:12 M. Jn 12:49, say N. Lk 22:64 O. 1 Cor 4:21 P. Mt 13:26 Q. 2 Pet 2:10 R. 2 Cor 7:1, perfecting S. Rom 12:1, worship

1G. Which he offers^A for himself and the ignorances¹ of the people^B

    2F. The Holy Spirit making this clear^C— *that* the way *of* the Holies² has not yet been made-known³ while the first tabernacle⁴ *was*⁵ still having^D *a* standing⁶   8

        1G. Which⁷ *is*⁸ *a* symbol⁹ for the present¹⁰ time, according to which¹¹ both gifts and sacrifices are¹² offered^A   9

            1H. Not being able to perfect^E the *one* worshiping^F in relation to *the* conscience^G
            2H. *Being* only— in-addition-to¹³ foods^H and drinks and different^J cleansings¹⁴— regulations¹⁵ *of* flesh¹⁶ being imposed¹⁷ until *the* time *of* reformation¹⁸   10

3D. But Christ, having arrived¹⁹ as High Priest *of* the good^K *things* having come²⁰, **entered²¹ once-for-all^L into the Holies^M**   11

    1E. Through the greater and more-perfect²² tabernacle²³ not made-by-*human*-hands^N— that is, not *of* this creation^O
    2E. And not through²⁴ *the* blood *of* goats and calves, but through *His* own blood²⁵   12
    3E. Having obtained²⁶ eternal^P redemption²⁷

        1F. *For* if the blood *of* goats and bulls²⁸ and *the* ashes *of a* heifer²⁹ sprinkling^Q the *ones* having been defiled^R sanctifies³⁰ for the cleansing³¹ *of* the flesh   13
        2F. *By* how much more will the blood *of* Christ, Who through *the* eternal^P Spirit³² offered^A Himself without-blemish^S *to* God, cleanse^T our³³ conscience^G from dead works³⁴, so that *we may* worship³⁵ *the* living God!   14

1. That is, sins of ignorance. See Num 15:27-31. Used only here. GK *52*. Related to the word in Rom 10:3.
2. On this word, see 8:2. That is, the way into the Holies. Some think the writer means the earthly "Holy of Holies", the second tabernacle in v 7, as this word is used in v 3, 25; 13:11; others, the true, heavenly Holy Place, as this word is used in v 12; 8:2; 10:19.
3. Or, "revealed". No one had open access, or confident entrance (10:19). The people were excluded; the priests restricted. On this word, see "made evident" in 1 Jn 2:19.
4. This meant the "outer" room of the tabernacle in v 2 and 6, the only other places this phrase occurs. Some think it means this here also. As long as the outer tabernacle had a standing before God, the way in was not revealed. Others think the writer now means first in time, the human-built earthly tabernacle as a whole, the sanctuary of the first covenant, including the current temple (note 13:10). As long as the tabernacle and temple had a standing before God, the way in was not revealed. Thus some think the contrast is between the physical Holy Place and Holy of Holies; others, the physical outer Holy Place and the heavenly one; others, the earthly sanctuary as a whole, and the heavenly one. These views differ on the physical reference of the words, but the symbolic meaning is the same for them all. As long as the Levitical system was in place, the way-in to the presence of God was not revealed.
5. Or, "*is*". Whichever tense is supplied, it ceased having a standing before God when Christ died and the veil was torn. Though it continued to physically stand for a time, the way-in to the true Holies had then been made known.
6. Some think the writer means "physically standing, existing"; others, "having a standing, status, appointed place" in the divine order. Before Christ died, both views come to the same thing.
7. This refers to the "first tabernacle" in v 8. Thus some think the writer means "which outer Holy Place"; others, "which earthly OT tabernacle and temple". Both views include the worship that took place there, and the separation from the presence of God implied.
8. Or, "*was*".
9. Or, "analogy, illustration". This is the word "parable", but it is not used here of a story with a spiritual point, as in the Gospels. Here it is used of a real, existing thing with a symbolic meaning. The first tabernacle, with its sacrifices and regulations that cannot perfect, is symbolic of the fact that access to God has not been gained thereby. Compare 10:1-3. Same word as in 11:19. On this word, see "parable" in Mt 13:3.
10. This is a participle, "having come, being present". Some think this "*was a* symbol" for Israel, "for the [then] present" OT times before the "reformation" (v 10), a symbol of the fact that the Levitical system could not gain them free access to God; others, that it "*is a* symbol" for us, "for the [now] present" NT times after the "reformation" (v 10), a symbol pointing to the better reality Christ brought (v 11-12). Elsewhere only in Rom 8:38; 1 Cor 3:22; 7:26; Gal 1:4; 2 Thes 2:2; 2 Tim 3:1. GK *1931*.
11. Some manuscripts say "throughout which", referring to the "present time" {N}.
12. This present tense is from the point of view of the symbol, which refers to when the tabernacle still had a standing. Thus this could be rendered "were offered". However, it could also indicate that the sacrifices were still going on in the temple, dating this letter before the temple's destruction in A.D. 70.
13. Or, "on top of, in the matter of ". Same word as in 2 Cor 7:13. GK *2093*. In this rendering, gifts and sacrifices for sin are things in addition to the three things mentioned next, all five being in the category of "regulations of flesh". Others render this "*Relating* only to foods and drinks...". In this case, the gifts and sacrifices had no value to cleanse sin, only to cleanse in matters relating to "regulations of flesh" like foods, drinks, and different cleansings. There are other views.
14. Or, "washings, baptisms". See Mk 7:4. On this word, see Heb 6:2.
15. Some manuscripts say "and regulations..." {A}. Same word as in v 1. On this word, see Rom 1:32.
16. That is, for the flesh. The symbol can best be understood by comparing v 13-14. The symbol (v 9) is that the first tabernacle concerned gifts and sacrifices unable to bring internal, heart cleansing, but only an external, transitory, ritual purification of the flesh. The Levitical regulations for gifts, sacrifices, foods, drinks, and cleansings did not clear the conscience. Thus they could never open the way to God. They brought a cleansing of the flesh, but not life. On this word, see Col 2:23.
17. Or, "laid upon" them. On this word, see "pressing upon" in Lk 23:23.
18. Used only here. GK *1481*. Related to "reform" in Act 24:2. The root word is "make straight".
19. Or, "having appeared, having come". That is, in heaven. Related to "come" next. GK *4134*.
20. GK *1181*. Using a different word (the one in 10:1), some manuscripts say "*of* the coming good *things*" {B}.
21. In the Greek word order, "entered... Holies" is in v 12, just before "having obtained...". It is held until then for emphasis.
22. On this word, see "complete" in 1 Cor 13:10. The comparative form, "more perfect", is used only here.
23. Some think the writer means passing "through" the heavenly tabernacle, which is described in 9:24 as "heaven itself "; others, "by means of " His resurrection body, as the word "through" is used twice in v 12. There are other views.
24. Or, "with, by means of ". GK *1328*.
25. Christ offers His own blood as the sacrifice. He is both Priest and Lamb. On this word, see 1 Jn 1:7.
26. Or, "Obtaining" at the time He entered. GK *2351*. Same word as "find" in 4:16; Mt 11:29. On this word, see "found" in 2 Pet 3:10.
27. Elsewhere only in Lk 1:68; 2:38. GK *3391*. See the related word in Rom 3:24.
28. Some manuscripts say "bulls and goats" {K}, as in 10:4. On the Day of Atonement, the goat was offered for the people, the bull for the high priest.
29. See Num 19:1-22. The ashes were mixed with water and sprinkled on the defiled one.
30. Or, "consecrates". On this word, see 10:29.
31. Or, "purity, cleanness". Used only here. GK *2755*. Related to "cleanse" in v 14.
32. Or, "*His* eternal spirit". Some manuscripts say "*the* Holy Spirit" {A}.
33. Some manuscripts say "your" {C}.
34. On "dead works", see 6:1.
35. Or, "serve". On this word, see 12:28.

A. Heb 5:7 B. Rev 21:3 C. 1 Cor 3:13, make clear D. 1 Jn 1:8 E. Heb 2:10 F. Heb 12:28 G. Act 23:1 H. Mk 7:19 J. Heb 8:6, more excellent K. 1 Tim 5:10b L. Heb 7:27 M. Heb 8:2 N. Act 17:24 O. Rom 8:39 P. Mt 25:46 Q. Heb 10:22 R. Mk 7:15 S. Col 1:22 T. Heb 9:22

4D. And for this reason¹ He is *the* mediator^A *of a* new^B covenant^C, so that the *ones* having been called^D may receive the promise^E *of* the eternal inheritance^F— *a* death having taken-place² for *the* redemption^G *from* the transgressions^H committed under³ the first covenant⁴   15

  1E. For where *there is a* will⁵, *it is a* necessity^J *that the* death *of* the *one* having made-the-will⁶ be brought-forth⁷   16

    1F. For *a* will over dead *ones is* firm^K, since it does not ever have [legal] power⁸ when the *one* having made-the-will is living   17

  2E. Hence, not even the first *covenant* has been inaugurated⁹ without blood¹⁰   18

    1F. For every commandment^L having been spoken *to* all the people^M by Moses according-to¹¹ the Law—   19

      1G. Having taken the blood *of* the calves and the goats¹² along with water and scarlet wool and hyssop, he sprinkled^N both the book itself and all the people, saying "This *is* the blood *of* the covenant which God commanded^O to you" [Ex 24:8]   20

      2G. And¹³ he likewise sprinkled^N *with* the blood both the tabernacle^P and all the objects^Q *of* the ministry^R   21

  3E. Indeed according-to¹⁴ the Law almost¹⁵ everything is cleansed¹⁶ with blood, and forgiveness^S does not take-place¹⁷ apart-from^T blood-shedding¹⁸   22

  4E. Therefore *it was a* necessity^J *that* **the copies**¹⁹ *of the things* in the heavens be cleansed *with* these²⁰ *things*— but the heavenly^U *things* themselves *with* better^V sacrifices^W than these   23

    1F. For Christ did not enter into *the* Holies²¹ made-by-*human*-hands^X— copies²² *of* the true^Y *things*   24

      1G. But into heaven itself, now to appear²³ *in* the presence *of* God for us

    2F. Nor *did He enter* in order that He might offer^Z Himself often— as indeed the high priest enters into the Holies yearly with *the* blood belonging-to-another^AA— otherwise He *would* had-to-have²⁴ suffered²⁵ often since *the* foundation *of the* world²⁶   25, 26

      1G. But now He has appeared²⁷ once-for-all²⁸ at *the* conclusion²⁹ *of the* ages for *the* setting-aside^BB *of* sin by the sacrifice³⁰ *of* Himself³¹

    3F. And³² just as³³ it is destined³⁴ *for* people^CC to die once^DD and after this *comes the* judgment^EE   27

      1G. So also Christ³⁵, having been offered^Z once^DD so as to bear³⁶ *the* sins *of* many, will appear³⁷   28

        1H. For *a* second *time*
        2H. Without *reference to* sin³⁸
        3H. *To* the *ones* eagerly-awaiting^FF Him
        4H. For salvation^GG

1. That is, because Christ entered the Holies having obtained redemption by the offering of Himself, v 11-14.
2. That is, Christ's. He is now the mediator of our eternal inheritance. But He is also the one who died so that we could receive the inheritance. His blood redeemed us from sin, and it ratifies the covenant.
3. That is, "at the time of", before Christ. GK *2093*.
4. The sacrificial system only "covered" sins, it did not remove them. It never could, 10:4. Jesus did.
5. On this word, see "covenant" in 8:6. The same Greek word is used in both senses in this context, a "covenant" in v 15, 20; and a "will" in v 16, 17. The writer gives a human illustration, a will, which is a special kind of covenant. The will promising an inheritance cannot be enforced until the death of the one making it. In the same way, the new covenant could not be put in force and we could not receive the promise of the eternal inheritance until a death occurred— the death of our Substitute. A death is required.
6. The verb and noun of the same word are used here, and in v 17. On this verb, see "covenant" in 8:10.
7. One must "bring forth, present, produce" evidence that the maker of the will has died. On this word, see "carried" in 2 Pet 1:17.
8. On this word, "have power", see "can do" in Gal 5:6.
9. Or, "ratified, dedicated". Elsewhere only in 10:20. GK *1590*. Moses and Christ inaugurated covenants with blood.
10. Blood was required for the ratification of the covenant, although the blood of a substitute, not of the one having made it.
11. Or, "based on, in harmony with, with respect to". GK *2848*.
12. Some manuscripts omit "and the goats" {C}.
13. This happened at a later time. Some of the details in v 19-21 are not specifically mentioned in Exodus.
14. Or, "based on". GK *2848*.
15. Or, "nearly". Elsewhere only in Act 13:44; 19:26. GK *5385*.
16. Or, "purified". Same word as in v 14, 23; 10:2; Act 15:9; 2 Cor 7:1; Eph 5:26; Tit 2:14; 1 Jn 1:7, 9. Used of "cleansing" lepers (as in Mt 8:2); and foods (Mk 7:19). Used 31 times. GK *2751*. Related to "purification" in 2 Pet 1:9; "cleansing" in Heb 9:13; and "clean" in Tit 1:15.
17. Or, "come about, come to pass, happen". Or, "and there is no forgiveness". On this word, see "comes" in 2 Pet 1:20.
18. Or, "blood-pouring" on the altar. This noun is formed from "blood" and "to pour out". Used only here. GK *136*.
19. The writer uses grammar that emphasizes the contrast between the two halves of this sentence; between the copies and the heavenly things themselves. Same word as in 8:5. All the earthly things were "copies and shadows" of the heavenly. On this word, see "example" in Jn 13:15.
20. That is, the things mentioned in v 18-22, the application of the sprinkled blood of sacrificed animals.
21. That is, the "Holy of Holies", as in v 25. Christ's action as High Priest is in view. Others think the writer means the earthly Holy Place as a whole. On this word, see 8:2.
22. That is, a "copy, imprint, antitype" corresponding to an original, example, type. On this word, see "corresponding-thing" in 1 Pet 3:21. Related to "pattern" in 8:5. Not related to "copies" in 9:23.
23. Or, "to become visible". Same word as in Mt 27:53. GK *1872*.
24. Or, "*would* have-had to suffer". On "had-to-have", see "should have" in Mt 25:27.
25. If Christ had to offer Himself often because His offering of Himself had only temporary strength, He would have to be born, suffer, and die over and over again since the world began.
26. This phrase, "since *the* foundation *of the* world", occurs elsewhere only in Mt 13:35; 25:34; Lk 11:50; Heb 4:3; Rev 13:8; 17:8. On "before the... world", see 1 Pet 1:20. "Foundation" is GK *2856*.
27. Or, "has been made known, revealed". On this word, see "made evident" in 1 Jn 2:19.
28. Or, "once", one time. On this word see Jude 3.
29. Or, "end, consummation, close, completion". The past ages before Christ were all brought to a consummation or conclusion in Him. On this word, see Mt 24:3. Note the plural "ages" here.
30. This word refers to sacrificial offerings made to God. Used of animal sacrifices in Mt 9:13; Lk 2:24; 1 Cor 10:18; Heb 5:1; 9:9. Used of spiritual sacrifices in Rom 12:1; Phil 4:18; Heb 13:15, 16; 1 Pet 2:5. Used 28 times. GK *2602*. Related to "slaughter" in Act 10:13; and "altar" in Rev 8:3.
31. Or, "through His sacrifice".
32. The writer now turns from Christ's entering the true Holy of Holies to His return from it with salvation for His people.
33. Or, "to the degree that, by as much as, according as". Just as there are two steps for us, so for Him. Just as one follows the other for people, so one will follow the other for Christ. As certain as judgment follows death for us, so certain is His second appearance for us. On this phrase, see "degree" in 7:22.
34. Or, "reserved, laid away". It is reserved as something certain. On this word, see "reserved" in Col 1:5.
35. For Christ's side of the comparison begun in v 27, the writer does not merely say He died and was favorably judged by God. He gives the deeper significance of each event, in keeping with the previous context. Christ's death was as an offering to bear sin. And since this offering was accepted (favorably judged), He will appear again for salvation to those awaiting Him. Behind the latter point is the similar case of the high priest on the Day of Atonement. Just as his coming out of the earthly Holies signified that God had accepted the sacrifice and temporarily covered sin, so Christ's return signifies that God has accepted His sacrifice and granted a permanent salvation. Just as the people eagerly awaited the high priest, so we eagerly await Jesus.
36. Or, "take up, take upon *Himself*". This phrase is related to Isa 53:12. Same word as in 1 Pet 2:24. Jesus took these sins upon Himself for us. Elsewhere only as "offer" (in the sense of "bring up, carry up" to God) in Heb 7:27; 13:15; Jam 2:21; 1 Pet 2:5; "bring up" in Mt 17:1; Mk 9:2; and "carry up" in Lk 24:51. GK *429*.
37. Or, "be seen". On this word, see "see" in Lk 2:26. Thus, the writer uses three different words in the same sense in v 24, 26, 28.
38. Or, "apart from sin". When Christ is seen again by those awaiting Him, it will be with the inheritance, v 15.

A. Heb 8:6 B. Heb 8:13 C. Heb 8:6 D. Rom 8:30 E. 1 Jn 2:25 F. Eph 1:14 G. Rom 3:24 H. Rom 5:14 J. 1 Cor 7:26 K. 2 Pet 1:10 L. Mk 12:28 M. Rev 21:1 N. Heb 10:22 O. Mk 10:3 P. Heb 8:2 Q. 1 Thes 4:4, vessel R. 2 Cor 9:12, service S. Col 1:14 T. Jam 2:18, without U. Eph 3:10 V. Heb 1:4 W. Heb 9:26 X. Act 17:24 Y. Jn 7:28 Z. Heb 5:7 AA. Heb 11:34, foreigners BB. Heb 7:18 CC. Mt 4:4, mankind DD. Jude 3, once for all EE. Jn 3:19 FF. Rom 8:19, awaiting GG. Lk 19:9

5D.	For the Law— having *a* shadow *of* the coming good[A] *things*, not the very image[1] *of* the things— is never able to perfect[B] the *ones* approaching[C] yearly *with* the same sacrifices[D] which they offer[E] perpetually[2]	10:1
	1E. Otherwise would they not have ceased[F] being offered[3]— because of the *ones* worshiping[G] no longer having *a* consciousness[H] *of* sins, having been cleansed[J] once-for-all[K]?	2
	2E. But in them[4] *there is a* yearly reminder[5] *of* sins. ˚For *it is* impossible[L] *for the* blood *of* bulls and goats to take-away[M] sins	3-4
	3E. Therefore, while entering into the world, He says[6] [in Ps 40:6-8], "You did not desire[N] sacrifice[D] and offering[O], but You prepared[P] *a* body *for* Me[7]. ˚You were not well-pleased[Q] *with* whole-burnt-offerings[R] and *offerings* for sin". ˚Then I said, Behold, I have come[8]— in *the* roll *of a* book[9] it has been written about Me—*that I might* do Your will[S], God".	5 6 7
	1F. Saying above that "You did not desire nor were You well-pleased *with* sacrifices[10] and offerings and whole-burnt-offerings and *offerings* for sin"— which are being offered[E] according-to[11] *the* Law![12]	8
	2F. Then He has said, "Behold, I have come *that I might* do Your will[13]" —	9
	1G. He does-away-with[14] the first in-order-that[15] He might establish[16] the second[17]	
	2G. By which will[S] we have been made-holy[18] through the offering[O] *of* the body *of* Jesus Christ once-for-all[T]	10
6D.	And **every priest**[19] stands ministering[U] daily, and offering[E] often the same sacrifices[D] which are never able to take-away[V] sins—	11
	1E. But this *One,* having offered[E] **one** sacrifice[D] for sins for all time[20], sat-*down* at *the* right hand *of* God, ˚henceforth waiting[W] until His enemies are put *as a* footstool *of* His feet	12 13
	1F. For *by* one offering[O] He has perfected[B] for all time the *ones* being made-holy[X]	14
7D.	And the Holy Spirit also testifies[Y] *to* us—	15
	1E. For after the *statement* [in Jer 31:33] having said, ˚"This *is* the covenant which I will covenant with them after those days, says *the* Lord— while giving My laws upon their hearts, I will also write them upon their mind[21]"	16
	2E. *Then He says*[22] "And I will never remember[23] their sins and their lawless-*deeds*[24] again"	17
	3E. Now where *there is* forgiveness[25] *of* these *things, there is* no longer *an* offering[O] for sin[26]!	18
6B.	Therefore,[27] brothers[Z], having confidence[AA] for the entering[28] *of* the Holies[29] by the blood[BB] *of* Jesus— ˚which fresh[30] and living[31] way[32] He inaugurated[CC] *for* us through[33] the curtain[34], that is, His flesh[35]— ˚and *having a* great Priest over the house[DD] *of* God	19 20 21
1C.	Let us be approaching[36] *God* with *a* true[EE] heart[FF] in full-assurance[37] *of* faith[GG]—	22

1. Or, "likeness, form". That is, it is a shadow, not the true likeness, the reality. On this word, see Col 1:15.
2. Or, "continually". That is, year after year for as long as the temple stands, and in this sense, "forever". Same idiom as in 7:3, and as "for all time" in 10:12. Some connect this to "perfect", as it is in v 14, "is never able to perfect for all time the *ones* approaching year by year *with* the same sacrifices which they offer".
3. The grammar indicates a "yes" answer is expected. This may imply the temple was still in use.
4. That is, in the sacrifices. The yearly sacrifices themselves are not a cure for sin, but a reminder that sin is still present. They do not open the way to God. Rather, they are a reminder that the way is not open.
5. On this word, see "remembrance" in 1 Cor 11:24 (the bread and cup).
6. The writer quotes the psalm in v 5-7, and applies the quote in v 8-10.
7. The Septuagint is being quoted, which says "you prepared a body for me". The Hebrew says "you opened my ears".
8. Same word as in v 9; 10:37. On this word, see "am here" in Jn 8:42.
9. That is, in the scrolls of the Old Testament, in the "book-roll", "book's scroll". I have come to take the body You prepared for Me and offer it as the sacrifice You desired, as it is written in Your book, the OT. On this word, see "scroll" in Rev 5:1.
10. Some manuscripts have these two words singular, "sacrifice and offering" {N}, as in v 5.
11. Or, "based on, in keeping with". GK *2848*.
12. The sacrifices offered under the Mosaic Law, and offered correctly under the terms of the Law, were not pleasing to God. They were not sufficient. They were a temporary covering of sin until the perfect sacrifice came.
13. Some manuscripts add "God" {N}, as in v 7.
14. Or, "abolishes, kills". On this word, see "kill" in Mt 2:16. When used of laws, it meant "to abolish". When used of wills, it meant "to revoke".
15. Or, more simply, "first to establish the second". GK *2671*.
16. Or, "make stand". GK *2705*.
17. God takes away the Levitical system of animal sacrifices (v 8), to establish His will (v 9a).
18. Same word as in v 14. Note the change of tenses, "have been" here, "are being" in v 14. This is a participle, we "are having been made holy". On this word, see "sanctify" in 10:29.
19. The writer uses grammar that emphasizes the contrast between the two halves of this statement; between what every priest does vs. this One in v 12. Some manuscripts say "high priest" {A}.
20. Same idiom as in v 14. Elsewhere only as "perpetually" in 7:3; 10:1. GK *1457*. This word means "uninterrupted, continuous, unbroken, unceasing, carried through for the whole span, perpetual", and in this sense, "for all time, forever". The root word is "carry through". The priests "offer" sacrifices continually and perpetually, because they have no lasting value, 10:1. Jesus "offered" one sacrifice which is continually and perpetually effective, which "carries through" in effectiveness for the whole span of existence, so He sat down. Some think this goes with what follows, He "sat down for all time", demonstrating that His priestly work of offering a sacrifice was done.
21. Some manuscripts have this word plural {N}.
22. A glance at the full quotation in 8:10-12 makes clear that the writer skips all the words between "write them..." and here. For this reason, and because this statement is the one he speaks of in v 18, many add something like "Then He says" here, and some manuscripts include it {N}. Others break the quotation at "days", and use "says *the* Lord" to make the separation, so that it says "having said, 'This is... after those days', *the* Lord says, 'While giving My laws... mind. And I will never remember... again' ".
23. The grammar of the verb "I will remember" differs slightly from 8:12, which quotes the Septuagint precisely.
24. Or, "lawlessnesses". On this word, see "lawlessness" in 1 Jn 3:4.
25. Or, "release, pardon". Same word as in 9:22. On this word, see Col 1:14.
26. No further sacrifice is needed because sin has been removed forever.
27. The writer closes the second section of the book with exhortations, just as he did the first section, 3:7-4:13. Note the similarity to 4:14-16. There he introduces Jesus as High Priest, here he applies it. Some think this closing section extends to v 39, making v 26 point 7B. (a warning), and v 32 point 8B. (a comfort, softening the warning, as 6:9-12 did for its warning). Then 11:1 becomes point 3A. Others begin the final section of the book here, making this point 3A. (see the note on 10:32).
28. That is, confidence to use the entrance, boldness and freedom to enter. On this word, see "entrance" in 1 Thes 1:9.
29. That is, the heavenly Holy Place. On this word, see 8:2.
30. Or, "new, recent". Used only here. GK *4710*. This word also meant "freshly slaughtered". Related to "recently" in Act 18:2.
31. Some think the writer means "leading to life"; others, "alive and abiding forever"; others, that it is living because the way is Jesus Himself.
32. This is related to "entering" earlier, which is a "way-in". Here it is the "way" into the Holies.
33. Or, "with, by means of". GK *1328*.
34. Or, "veil". On this word, see 9:3.
35. Some think the writer means the "way... that is, His flesh", so that Christ's body on the cross is the way through the curtain into the Holies for us. Others think he means "the curtain, that is, His flesh", so that Christ inaugurated the way "through" in the sense of "by means of" the curtain on His true identity, His flesh. Others think He inaugurated the way "through" the curtain into the Holies, "by means of" His flesh, applying the word "through" in a different sense to "flesh". In any case, His body on the cross is a curtain to unbelievers, a way in for believers. On this word, see Col 2:23.
36. That is, approaching God on His throne of grace in the Holies, using the way Jesus inaugurated. Same word and exhortation as in 4:16. Same word as in 10:1. It means "come to, go to, approach". Used 86 times. GK *4665*.
37. Same word as in 6:11. On this word, see "fullness of conviction" in 1 Thes 1:5.

A. 1 Tim 5:10b B. Heb 2:10 C. Heb 10:22 D. Heb 9:26 E. Heb 5:7 F. 1 Cor 13:8 G. Heb 12:28 H. Act 23:1, conscience J. Heb 9:22 K. Jude 3 L. Heb 6:4 M. Mk 14:47, took off N. Jn 7:17, willing O. Act 21:26 P. Rom 9:22 Q. Mt 17:5 R. Mk 12:33 S. Jn 7:17 T. Heb 7:27 U. Rom 15:27 V. Act 27:20 W. Heb 11:10, wait for X. Heb 10:29, sanctified Y. Jn 1:7 Z. Act 16:40 AA. Heb 4:16 BB. 1 Jn 1:7 CC. Heb 9:18 DD. Mk 3:20 EE. Jn 7:28 FF. Rev 2:23 GG. Eph 2:8

	1D.	Having *our* hearts sprinkled[1] from *an* evil[A] conscience[B]	
	2D.	And having *our* body[C] washed[2] *with* clean[D] water	
2C.		Let us be holding-on-to[E] the confession[3] *of our* hope[4] without-wavering[5]. For the *One* having promised *is* faithful[F]	23
3C.		And let us be considering[6] one another for *the* provoking[7] *of* love[G] and good[H] works[8]	24
	1D.	Not forsaking[J] the gathering-together[9] *of* ourselves, as *is a* habit[K] *with* some, but exhorting[10] one another, and so-much more *by*-as-much-as[11] you see the day drawing-near[L]	25
4C.		For while[12] we *are* willfully[13] sinning[14] after the receiving *of* the knowledge[M] *of* the truth, *a* sacrifice[N] no longer remains[O] for sins, but some fearful[P] expectation[15] *of* judgment[Q] and *a* zeal[R] *of* fire[16] going to consume[S] the adversaries[T]	26 27
	1D.	Anyone having set-aside[17] *the* Law *of* Moses dies without compassions[18] upon *the* testimony *of* two or three witnesses[U]	28
	2D.	*For* how much worse punishment[19] do you think[V] he will be considered-worthy[W]— the *one*	29
		1E. Having trampled-underfoot[20] the Son *of* God	
		2E. And having regarded[X] *as* defiled[21] the blood *of* the covenant by which[22] he was sanctified[23]	
		3E. And having insulted[24] the Spirit *of* grace?[25]	
	3D.	For we know the *One* having said [in Deut 32:35], "Vengeance[Y] *is for* Me, **I** will repay[26]", and again [in Deut 32:36], *"The* Lord will judge[Z] His people"	30
	4D.	*It is a* fearful[P] *thing* to fall into *the* hands *of the* living God	31
3A.		Now[27] remember the former days during which, having been enlightened[28], you endured[29] *a* great struggle[30] *of* sufferings[AA]— on this *hand* being made-a-spectacle[31] *by* both reproaches[32] and afflictions[BB], and on this[33] *hand* having become partners[CC] *of the ones* living[34] in this manner[35]	32 33

1. As the priests sprinkled animal blood on bodies and things to cleanse them, so Christ sprinkled His blood on our hearts. Same idea as in 9:13-14. Elsewhere only in 9:13, 19, 21. GK *4822*. The related noun is in 12:24.
2. As the high priest was to bathe before entering the Holy of Holies (Lev 16:4), so we have been spiritually bathed so as to enter the heavenly Holies with Jesus. Some think the writer is referring to baptism; others, to what baptism represents. On this word, see 2 Pet 2:22. Related to the word in Eph 5:26. Compare Ezek 36:25-26.
3. Same word as in 4:14. That is, the hope we confess.
4. On "hope", compare 3:6; 6:11, 18, 19; 7:19. Some manuscripts say "faith" {K}, but no Greek manuscripts.
5. Or, "unbending, unswerving". Used only here. GK *195*.
6. That is, thinking carefully about, fixing your spiritual eyes upon. Same word as in 3:1 where the writer exhorted his readers to consider Jesus; and Mt 7:3; Lk 6:41; 12:24, 27; Rom 4:19; Jam 1:23, 24. Elsewhere only as "look closely (at)" in Act 7:31, 32; 27:39; "observe" in Act 11:6; and "perceive" in Lk 20:23. GK *2917*.
7. Or, "inciting, stirring up". Elsewhere only as "disagreement" in Act 15:39. GK *4237*. The related verb is in 1 Cor 13:5, "Love is not provoked". This is a graphic word to use here.
8. On "good works", see Tit 2:14.
9. On this word, see 2 Thes 2:1. It is related to "synagogue".
10. Or, "encouraging". Same word as in 3:13; 13:22. On this word, see Rom 12:8.
11. Or, "so much more to the degree that...". This phrase "so much... by as much as", occurs elsewhere only in 1:4.
12. This participle "while sinning" may be rendered as a conditional statement, "For *if* we continue-sinning".
13. Or, "voluntarily, by our own choice, willingly, deliberately". On this word, see "willingly" in 1 Pet 5:2.
14. The nature of the sinning in view is seen in v 28-29— rejection of Christ and His sacrifice. If we turn away from Christ and His final once-for-all sacrifice of Himself, what other sacrifice can be offered for sins? None. On this word, see Act 25:8.
15. Or, "waiting-for, looking-for, reception". Used only here. GK *1693*. Related to "wait for" in 11:10. All that remains is to look for and wait to receive judgment from an avenging God. Better to repent!
16. That is, avenging zeal. The writer is alluding to Isa 26:11. Compare 2 Thes 1:7-9.
17. Or, "rejected". On this word, see Gal 2:21.
18. Or, "*acts of* compassion". On this word, see Rom 12:1.
19. This word means "vengeance, retribution" for one who has been wronged, the wrong being described next. Used only here. GK *5513*. Related to "punish" in Act 22:5.
20. Same word as in Mt 5:13; Lk 8:5. Elsewhere only as "trample" in Mt 7:6; Lk 12:1. GK *2922*.
21. Or, "common". Same word as in Mk 7:2, 5; Act 10:14, 28; 11:8; Rom 14:14; Rev 21:27. Elsewhere only as "common" (in the sense of "shared") in Act 2:44; 4:32; Tit 1:4; Jude 3. GK *3123*. Related to "defile" in Mk 7:15; and "share" in 2 Jn 11. Thus the writer could mean "unclean, defiled" vs. "holy"; or, "common", no different than any other blood.
22. This word modifies "blood".
23. Or, "set apart *to God*, consecrated, made holy, hallowed, treated as holy". This word means to make holy or treat as holy in both a moral and a ritual sense. Same word as in Mt 23:17, 19; Act 20:32; 26:18; Rom 15:16; 1 Cor 1:2; 6:11; 7:14; Eph 5:26; 1 Thes 5:23; 1 Tim 4:5; 2 Tim 2:21; Heb 9:13. Elsewhere only as "treat as holy" in Mt 6:9; Lk 11:2; "set apart" in Jn 10:36; 17:17, 19; 1 Pet 3:15; and "make holy" in Heb 2:11; 10:10, 14; 13:12; Rev 22:11. GK *39*. Related to "holiness" in Heb 12:14 and Rom 1:4. The root word is "holy" (set apart to God) in 1 Pet 1:16.
24. Or, "arrogantly treated". Used only here. GK *1964*. Related to "mistreat" in 1 Thes 2:2.
25. Instead of a question, some take this as a statement, or an exclamation.
26. On this word, see 2 Thes 1:6. Some manuscripts add, "says the Lord" {N}.
27. Or, "But, And". The third section is an exhortation to endurance by faith. Note the similarities of the transition here in v 32-35 to the one in 4:14-16. There is a command (4:14, 10:32), followed by a reason (4:15, 10:34), followed by a quick application/conclusion (4:16, 10:35), then the main exposition begins (5:1, 10:36). As with that section, the writer first introduces the subject (in 4:14-16, High Priest; here, endurance by faith), then follows with the exposition of the subject (5:1-10:18; here, 10:36-11:40), then concludes with exhortations. Those who start point 3A. in 10:19 would then make this 5B. (a softening of the warning in 10:26, similar to 6:9-12), and would then make 11:1 point 6B. Others think 10:19-39 closes the second section of the book, and make 11:1 point 3A. (see 10:19). There are other views. These different views arise because there is clearly a change of subject matter, but neither 10:32 nor 11:1 have the language of a clear, explicit lead point. 10:32 makes a gentle opening, leading into the subject from their own past endurance of suffering; 11:1 makes an abrupt lead point. 10:19 is an excellent lead point, but does not seem to carry all the weight of chapter 11. Strictly as exhortations, 10:39 could connect with 12:1, omitting 11:1-40. Chapter 11 is closely connected to 10:32-39 and to chapter 12. No view is without its problems, but the one taken here may more simply allow the words themselves to carry the thought. Be aware, however, that most commentaries take one of the other views.
28. Or, "given light, illuminated". On this word, see 6:4.
29. On this verb, "to endure", which is also in 12:2, 3, 7, see Jam 1:12. "Endurance" occurs in 10:36, 12:1.
30. Or, "contest". Used only here. GK *124*. Related to "compete" in 2 Tim 2:5. Our word "athletics" comes from this word.
31. Or, "made a show; being publicly exposed *to*". Used only here. GK *2518*. Related word in 1 Cor 4:9.
32. Or, "insults, disgraces". Elsewhere only in 11:26; 13:13; Rom 15:3; 1 Tim 3:7. GK *3944*. Related to the verb in 1 Pet 4:14; and the word in Lk 1:25.
33. The idiom "on this *hand*... on this *hand*" may be referring to different occasions "sometimes... sometimes", or to different groups among them "in part... in part".
34. That is, being treated in this way. This word could be rendered here the ones "being turned upside down, reversed, turned back, overturned" in this way. On this word, see "conducted-*ourselves*" in Eph 2:3. Some manuscripts have the word in Jn 2:15 {N}, of tables "overturned".
35. That is, amid reproach and affliction for Christ.

A. Act 25:18 B. Act 23:1 C. Eph 1:23 D. Tit 1:15 E. Heb 3:6 F. Col 1:2 G. 1 Jn 4:16 H. 1 Tim 5:10a J. 2 Cor 4:9 K. Lk 1:9, custom L. Lk 21:28 M. Col 1:9 N. Heb 9:26 O. Jude 6, left behind P. Heb 12:21 Q. Jn 3:19 R. 2 Cor 11:2, jealousy S. Act 10:13, eat T. Col 2:14, opposed U. Act 1:8 V. Lk 19:11 W. 2 Thes 1:11 X. Jam 1:2 Y. 2 Thes 1:8, punishment Z. Mt 7:1 AA. Phil 3:10 BB. Rev 7:14 CC. 2 Pet 1:4, sharers

| Hebrews 10:34 | 852 | Verse |

1B. For indeed you sympathized-with the prisoners[1], and you accepted[2] with joy the plundering[3] *of* your possessions[4], knowing *that you*-yourselves[5] have *a* better[A] and abiding[B] possession[6] 34

    1C. So do not throw-away your confidence[7], which has *a* great reward[C] 35

2B. For[8] you have need[D] *of* endurance[9], in order that having done the will *of* God,[10] you might receive[E] the promise[F] 36

    1C. For yet *in a* very little *while*,[11] "the One coming[G] will come[H] and will not delay. °But My[12] righteous[J] *one* will live by faith[K]. And if he draws-back[13], My soul[L] is not well-pleased[14] with him" [Hab 2:3-4] 37-38

    2C. But **we** are not *of a* drawing-back[15] resulting-in[M] destruction[N], but *of a* faith[K] resulting in *the* preserving[O] *of the* soul[L] 39

3B. Now[16] faith[K] is *the* assurance[17] *of*[18] *things* being hoped-for[P], *the* conviction[19] *of* things not being seen[20]. °For[21] in this[22] the elders[23] were attested[24] 11:1
      2

    1C. *By* faith[25] we understand[26] *that* the worlds[27] have been prepared[Q] *by the* word[28] *of* God, so that the *thing* being seen *has*[29] not[30] come-into-being[31] from *things* being visible[32] 3

    2C. *By* faith Abel offered[R] *to* God *a* greater sacrifice[S] than Cain,[33] through which[34] he was attested to be righteous— God testifying[35] about his gifts[T]. And through it, [although] having died, he is still speaking[36] 4

1. Instead of "the prisoners", some manuscripts say "*the* bonds"; others, "my bonds" {B}, a related word.
2. Same word as in 11:35. On this word, see "wait for" in Act 24:15.
3. Or, "robbery, seizing". Elsewhere only in Mt 23:25 and Lk 11:39, where Jesus accused the Pharisees of it. GK *771*.
4. Or, "belongings, property". This is a participle, "the *things* belonging, being present" to one, "being at one's disposal, being at hand". Used is this sense only in Mt 19:21; 24:47; 25:14; Lk 8:3; 11:21; 12:15, 33, 44; 14:33; 16:1; 19:8; 1 Cor 13:3. Same word as "belonging" in Act 4:32, 37. Elsewhere only as "is" (see "being" in Phil 2:6). The related noun is used next in this verse.
5. Some manuscripts say "knowing *that you* have *for* yourselves *a* better..."; others, "knowing in yourselves *that you* have *a* better" {A}.
6. On this noun, see Act 2:45. Some manuscripts add "in heaven" {N}.
7. Hold on to it (3:6) with endurance. On this word, see 4:16.
8. That is, remember when you endured (v 32), for you have need of endurance (v 36).
9. Same word as in 12:1. Endurance by faith is what links together chapters 10-12. On this word, see Jam 1:3. Related to "endure" in v 32.
10. God's will is that we live by faith, as the writer goes on to say in v 38, loosely quoting Hab 2:3-4 from the Septuagint.
11. More literally, "For yet *in* how how little *time*". This idiom, "how how little", is also in Isa 26:20. The word "how" is repeated for emphasis. It may be rendered "how how", "how very", or simply "very" (GK *4012*).
12. Some manuscripts omit this word {B}, so that it says "But *the* righteous *one* will live...".
13. Or, "shrinks back, withdraws". On this word, see Act 20:20. Related to the word in v 39.
14. Or, "takes no pleasure" in him. On this word, see Mt 17:5.
15. That is, we are not characterized by a drawing back in unbelief, but by a going on in faith. Used only here. GK *5714*. Related to the word in v 38.
16. Now the writer takes up and proves by example that God's people have always endured by faith (10:36-39).
17. The root word means that which "stands under". Outside the NT, this word is used of the "reality, essence" of God behind the physical universe; the "title-deed" guaranteeing ownership of a property; the "resolution, determination" of the soldier seen in battle; the "foundation" supporting the building; the "plan, purpose" behind an endeavor, etc. Thus, its meaning in Heb 1:3 ("essence") is clear and common. In all its other NT uses ("confidence" in 2 Cor 9:4; 11:17; and "assurance" in Heb 3:14; 11:1), it is debated whether it refers to the subjective reality in the person, the frame of mind serving as the ground or basis of action; or to an objective reality outside the person on which action is based. Thus, here some think faith is the subjective "assurance" we have about what hope sees in the future; the "firm confidence" in these hoped-for things that forms the basis of our actions in keeping with them. So for example, faith is the inner assurance God gives us that Jesus will return, which results in our living in anticipation of that event. Others think faith is God's gift in us which gives a present "substance" or "objective reality" to the things hoped-for, making them real things to us. So, faith makes the return of Christ an objectively real thing to us, to which we respond with confidence and appropriate action. Others think this means faith is the objective "title deed" guaranteeing for us the hoped-for things. In any case, the key thing in this portion of Hebrews is that the readers need endurance (10:36), and faith is the basis of it, which the writer now proves with examples. By a faith seeing Him who is unseen and looking to the reward, Moses left Egypt. By a faith having seen the promises from afar, Abraham lived as a pilgrim, awaiting a heavenly country. The writer exhorts the readers to respond similarly in 12:1-2— not to have faith, but to live by faith with endurance. GK *5712*.
18. That is, *"about, regarding"*.
19. This phrase reinforces the first phrase in whichever sense is adopted there. Thus subjectively, faith is the inner "conviction, certainty", "the being convinced" about things not seen. So for example, faith is the conviction that heaven exists. Objectively, faith is the "proof, evidence", "the thing convincing" and bringing conviction about things not seen. So faith provides the proof that heaven exists. Used only here. GK *1793*. The related verb is "expose" in Eph 5:11. In summary, faith is our inner confidence and certainty about these things, leading to action; or, faith is what makes these things real and proves them to us, leading us to place our confidence in them and act in accordance with them.
20. By this phrase, the writer includes present and past unseen realities with the future realities "hoped-for". One or the other of these two statements about faith can be substituted for "by faith" in chapter 11. By conviction of things not seen, Noah built the ark; by assurance of things hoped for, Moses refused to be called...; etc.
21. 11:1 is what God means by faith, for in this He attested those of old. In this kind of faith in His promise they endured, doing His will, 10:36-38.
22. That is, in faith (11:1); living by faith (10:38); enduring by faith while awaiting God's promises (10:36).
23. That is, the OT saints described in chapter 11. Similar to "the fathers" in 1:1. On this word, see 1 Tim 5:17.
24. Or, "borne witness", by God in His word. Same word as in v 4, 5, and 39. On this word, see Act 6:3.
25. The enumeration begins in Genesis 1, and continues with "by faith" examples through Joshua 6 (Rahab, v 31).
26. Or, "perceive". On this word, see "think" in Eph 3:20.
27. Same word as in 1:2.
28. That is, by His commands in Genesis 1, like "Let there be light".
29. Some manuscripts say "the *things* being seen *have*" {N}.
30. More literally, "*has* come-into-being not from *things* being visible". Some render this, "*has* come from *things* not being visible". Some think the "not visible things" are "words of God". Others think the phase means "from nothing".
31. Or, "come, been made". Same word as in Jn 1:3.
32. The eternal invisible One made the visible things. When the chain of cause and effect is followed back to the beginning, the first material effect proceeds from an invisible cause, from a different reality. On this word, see "shine" in Phil 2:15.
33. See Gen 4:4-5.
34. As with "it" later in the verse, this refers either to "faith", or to Abel's "sacrifice", the expression of his faith.
35. Or, "bearing witness". Same word as "attested" in v 2.
36. Some think Abel speaks to the importance of faith to please God; others to the importance of blood sacrifice. Others think the writer is referring to Gen 4:10— Abel's blood is still crying out from the ground for God's vengeance upon those who kill God's righteous ones. Compare Heb 12:24.

A. Heb 1:4 B. Jn 15:4 C. Heb 2:2, penalty D. Tit 3:14 E. 2 Cor 5:10, receive back F. 1 Jn 2:25 G. Mk 16:2 H. Jn 8:42, am here J. Rom 1:17
K. Eph 2:8 L. Jam 5:20 M. Rom 5:16 N. 2 Pet 2:1 O. 1 Thes 5:9, obtaining P. Jn 5:45, put hope Q. Rom 9:22 R. Heb 5:7 S. Heb 9:26 T. Mt 5:23

3C. *By* faith Enoch was removed[1], *so as* not to see[A] death— "And he was not found because God removed him" [Gen 5:24]   5

    1D. For[2] before the removal[3], he has been attested[4] to have pleased[5] God
    2D. And without faith *it is* impossible[B] to please *Him*. For the *one* coming-to[C] God must[D] **believe**[6] that He is, and He becomes *the* rewarder *to* the *ones* seeking Him out[7]   6

4C. *By* faith Noah, having been warned[8] about the *things* not yet being seen, having been reverent[9], prepared[E] *the* ark[F] for *the* salvation[10] *of* his household[G]   7

    1D. Through which[11] he condemned[H] the world and became *an* inheritor[J] *of* the righteousness[K] according-to[12] faith

5C. *By* faith Abraham, being called[L], obeyed[13] to go out to *a* place which he was going-to[M] receive for *an* inheritance[N]. And he went out not knowing[O] where he was[14] going   8

    1D. *By* faith he stayed[15] in *the* land *of* the promise[P] as *a* land belonging-to-another[16], having dwelled[Q] in tents[R] with Isaac and Jacob— the fellow-heirs[S] *of* the same promise   9

        1E. For he was waiting-for[17] the city having foundations[T]— *of* which[18] God *is* designer[19] and maker[20]   10

    2D. *By* faith— and Sarah herself *being* barren[21]— he[22] received power[U] for *the* foundation[23] *of a* seed[24] even beyond *the* time *of* mature-age[25], since he regarded[V] the *One* having promised *to be* faithful[W]   11

        1E. Therefore indeed from one *man*— and *he* having become impotent[26] *as to* these[27] *things*— were born[28] *seed* as the stars *of* heaven *in* number, and countless as the sand by the shore *of* the sea   12

    3D. In accordance with faith, these[29] all died not having received[X] the promises, but having seen them from a distance[30], and having greeted[31] *them*, and having confessed[Y] that they are strangers[Z] and pilgrims[32] on the earth   13

        1E. For the *ones* saying such *things* are making-clear[33] that they are seeking-for[AA] *a* homeland[34]   14
        2E. And *if*[35] they had been remembering[36] that *homeland* from which they came out, they would have had opportunity[BB] to return—*but as-it-is*[37], they are aspiring-to[CC] *a* better[DD] *homeland*, that is, *a* heavenly[EE] *one*   15, 16
        3E. Therefore God is not ashamed-of[FF] them, to be called[GG] their God.[38] For He prepared[HH] *a* city *for* them

6C. *By* faith Abraham has offered[JJ] Isaac while being tested[KK]. And the *one* having received[39] the promises was offering *his* only-born[40], *with-regard-to whom[41] it was said [in Gen 21:12] that "In Isaac *a* seed[42] will be called[LL] *for* you"   17, 18

1. Or, "transferred, changed, put in another place". Elsewhere only as "changed" in Heb 7:12; Jude 4; "transferred" in Act 7:16; and with different grammar, "turn away" in Gal 1:6. GK *3572*.
2. None of Enoch's acts of faith are known to us, but his faith is proved by the fact that God was pleased with him.
3. Or, "the change, changeover, transformation". Same word as in 12:27. Elsewhere only as "change" in 7:12. GK *3557*. Related to "removed" earlier.
4. The grammar implies Enoch has been and continues to be attested.
5. This word is quoted from the Septuagint. The Hebrew says "he walked with God". Elsewhere only in v 6; 13:16. GK *2297*. Related to "pleasing" in Eph 5:10; and "pleasingly" in Heb 12:28.
6. This word is related to "faith" earlier. On this word, see Jn 3:36.
7. Or, "searching for Him". This word, "to seek out", is also in Act 15:17; Rom 3:11; 1 Pet 1:10. Elsewhere only as "seek for" in Heb 12:17; and "require" in Lk 11:50, 51. GK *1699*.
8. Or, "divinely-instructed". Same word as in 8:5.
9. That is, fearing God. Used only here. GK *2326*. Related to "reverence" in 5:7.
10. Or, "deliverance", physical salvation. On this word, see Lk 19:9.
11. This could refer to "faith", or the "ark" constructed by faith. Noah believed God, the world did not.
12. Or, "based on, by way of". GK *2848*.
13. This is the Greek word order. Some render it "called to go out..., obeyed". On this word, see Act 6:7. Related to the "obedience" of faith in Rom 16:26.
14. More literally, "is", as the Greek typically phrases it.
15. Or, "lived as a foreigner, stranger". Elsewhere only in Lk 24:18. GK *4228*. Related to "stay" in 1 Pet 1:17; and "foreigner" in 1 Pet 2:11.
16. That is, as if the land were not his, as a stranger or foreigner in it, looking for another land, v 10. On this word, see "foreigners" in 11:34.
17. Elsewhere only in Act 17:16; 1 Cor 11:33; 16:11; Jam 5:7; and as "waiting" in Heb 10:13. GK *1683*.
18. This modifies "city", not "foundations".
19. Or, "craftsman, tradesman, artisan". Elsewhere only as "craftsman" in Act 19:24, 38; Rev 18:22. GK *5493*. Related to "craft" in Act 17:29.
20. Used only here, this word means "builder, maker, creator; builder of public works". GK *1321*.
21. This phrase shows the extent of Abraham's faith. His faith was in spite of "his own body having become lifeless... and the deadness of Sarah's womb", Rom 4:19. The latter was the greater— she was barren and post-menopausal, Gen 18:11. Some manuscripts omit this word {C}. Elsewhere only in Lk 1:7, 36; 23:29; Gal 4:27. GK *5096*.
22. Or, "by faith also, barren Sarah herself received power for *the* foundation *of* a seed even beyond *the* time *of* maturity, since she regarded...". Some manuscripts make this rendering explicit by adding "gave birth" {N}, so that it says "... seed and gave birth beyond *the* time...". Whether the subject of "received" is Abraham or Sarah has been debated from early times. In Genesis, the promise, the faith in it, and the seed that was founded were Abraham's. Some suggest the grammar was misconstrued by early copyists, and that the writer simply meant "By faith he also, *with* barren Sarah herself, received". Consult the commentaries.
23. Or, "beginning", but not "conception". Abraham received power to begin the seed (posterity) God promised when God empowered him to father a child through Sarah. If "seed" is taken in the sense of "sperm", then this word means "depositing, sowing, laying down". It is used in Greek of the male part of procreation, depositing seed in the female, not of the female conceiving. Elsewhere only in the phrase, "foundation of the world" (see 9:26). GK *2856*.
24. The writer either means "the deposit of seed (sperm)", or, "the foundation or beginning of a seed (a posterity)". With Sarah as the subject, some render this "power in connection with *his* deposit *of* a seed". The Greek is *sperma* from which we get "sperm", meaning "descendants, posterity" (as in 2:16; 11:18) and "seeds" of plants (as in Mt 13:24). It has the meaning of "sperm" also, but not in the NT, unless here. Used 43 times. GK *5065*. Related to "sow" in 2 Cor 9:6.
25. Or, "the season *of* age". That is, beyond the childbearing time of life for both of them, Rom 4:19. On this word, see "life span" in Mt 6:27.
26. Or, "dead, lifeless". Same word as in Rom 4:19.
27. That is, his powers of procreation.
28. Or, "fathered". On this word, see 1 Jn 2:29. Some manuscripts say "came" {N}.
29. This refers to those mentioned in v 8-12, Abraham, Isaac, Jacob, and Sarah.
30. Some manuscripts add "and having been convinced" {N}, so that it says, "a distance, and having been convinced *of them*, and having greeted...".
31. This is the word used in the greetings at the end of the NT letters, as in 13:24. On this word, see Mk 15:18.
32. Or, "temporary residents, sojourners". On this word, see 1 Pet 1:1. This is referring to Gen 23:4.
33. Or, "making known, revealing". GK *1872*.
34. Or, "a fatherland, a land of one's fathers". Same word as in Jn 4:44. Elsewhere only as "hometown" in Mt 13:54, 57; Mk 6:1, 4; Lk 4:23, 24. GK *4258*. They did not look to this earth as their homeland, but to heaven, v 16. They dwelt in tents, awaiting the city God would build for them, v 9-10. They were enduring by faith, awaiting the promise— the point of this chapter.
35. The writer uses grammar that emphasizes the contrast between the two halves of this statement.
36. That is, if they had in mind their former homeland when they said they were strangers and pilgrims, they could have returned at any time. But they meant it with reference to their heavenly homeland.
37. Or, "but now", in a logical sense. On this idiom, see 1 Cor 5:11.
38. That is, to be called "the God of Abraham, Isaac and Jacob", as God called Himself in Ex 3:15.
39. Elsewhere only as "welcome" in Act 28:7. GK *346*.
40. On this word, see Jn 1:18. Isaac was the only child of promise, and the only child through Sarah.
41. That is, Isaac. Or, "to whom", that is, Abraham.
42. That is, descendants.

A. Mt 13:17, experience B. Heb 6:4 C. Heb 10:22, approach D. Mt 16:21 E. Heb 9:2 F. Heb 9:4 G. Mk 3:20, house H. 1 Cor 11:32 J. Rom 8:17 K. Rom 1:17 L. Rom 8:30 M. Mk 10:32 N. Eph 1:14 O. Act 18:25, know about P. 1 Jn 2:25 Q. Eph 3:17 R. Lk 9:33, dwelling S. Rom 8:17 T. 1 Tim 6:19 U. Mk 5:30 V. Jam 1:2 W. Col 1:2 X. Rom 7:8, taken Y. 1 Tim 6:12 Z. Rom 16:23, host AA. Phil 4:17 BB. Mt 8:29, time CC. 1 Tim 6:10 DD. Heb 1:4 EE. Eph 3:10 FF. Rom 1:16 GG. 1 Pet 1:17, call upon HH. Mk 14:15 JJ. Heb 5:7 KK. Heb 2:18, tempted LL. Rom 8:30

1D. Having considered¹ that God *was* able to raise^A *him* even from *the* dead, from-which² he also received him back³ in *a* symbol⁴ — 19

7C. *By* faith Isaac blessed^B Jacob and Esau even concerning coming *things* — 20
8C. *By* faith Jacob, while dying, blessed^B each *of* the sons *of* Joseph, and "worshiped^C [leaning] on the top^D *of* his staff⁵" [Gen 47:31] — 21
9C. *By* faith Joseph, while coming-to-an-end⁶, mentioned⁷ concerning the departure⁸ *of* the sons *of* Israel, and gave-commands^E concerning his bones⁹ — 22
10C. *By* faith Moses, having been born^F, was hidden^G *for* three months by his parents, because they saw the child^H *was* beautiful¹⁰ and did not fear^J the edict¹¹ *of* the king — 23
11C. *By* faith Moses, having become great¹² — 24

    1D. Refused to be called^K son *of* Pharaoh's daughter

        1E. Having chosen^L rather to be mistreated-with¹³ the people^M *of* God than to be having *a* temporary^N enjoyment^O *of* sin — 25
        2E. Having¹⁴ regarded^P the reproach^Q *of* the Christ¹⁵ to be greater riches^R *than* the treasures^S *of* Egypt¹⁶ — 26
        3E. For he was looking-away¹⁷ to the reward¹⁸

    2D. *By* faith he left¹⁹ Egypt, not having feared²⁰ the fury^T *of* the king. For he persevered²¹ as seeing²² the invisible *One* — 27
    3D. *By* faith he has performed²³ the Passover^U and the sprinkling²⁴ *of* the blood in order that the *one* destroying²⁵ the firstborns^V might not touch them — 28

12C. *By* faith they crossed²⁶ the Red²⁷ Sea as through dry^W land— *of* which having taken *the* test²⁸, the Egyptians were swallowed-up²⁹ — 29
13C. *By* faith the walls *of* Jericho fell, having been encircled^X for seven days — 30
14C. *By* faith Rahab the prostitute^Y did not perish-with the *ones* having disobeyed^Z, having welcomed^AA the spies with peace — 31
15C. And what more may I say? — 32

    1D. For time will fail me while telling about Gideon³⁰, Barak, Samson, Jephthah, both David and Samuel, and the prophets,* who through faith — 33

        1E. Conquered kingdoms, worked^BB righteousness³¹, obtained³² promises
        2E. Stopped^CC *the* mouths *of* lions,* quenched^DD *the* power^EE *of* fire, escaped^FF *the* edges³³ *of* the sword — 34
        3E. Were strengthened^GG from weakness^HH, became mighty^JJ in battle^KK, put-to-flight armies^LL *of* foreigners³⁴

    2D. Women received^MM their dead by resurrection^NN— but others were tortured, not accepting^OO redemption³⁵, in order that they might obtain^PP *a* better resurrection^NN — 35

        1E. And others received^MM *a* trial³⁶ *of* mockings and whippings³⁷, and furthermore *of* bonds³⁸ and prison^QQ — 36
        2E. They were stoned, they were sawn-in-two³⁹, they died by murder^RR *of* the sword — 37
        3E. They went-around in sheepskins, in skins-of-goats

1. Or, "calculated, accounted". On this word, see Rom 3:28. Abraham had the promise, and the command to offer Isaac. He obeyed, trusting based on the promise that God would work it out— by raising Isaac from the dead if necessary.
2. That is, from the dead. Or, "dead. Hence, ...", making this point 2D. In this case the writer means "Hence, by his faith, he received him back". On this word, see "hence" in 2:17.
3. On this word, "received back", see 2 Cor 5:10.
4. Or, "analogy, illustration". Same word as in 9:9. Some think the writer means "in an illustration of the Father and Christ". Others think he means "in a figure of speech, so to speak".
5. The Septuagint is being quoted. The Hebrew says "bed". Originally, only the Hebrew consonants were written, the vowels being supplied verbally. The difference between "bed" and "staff" is which vowels are supplied.
6. Or, "while dying", but a different word than verse 21. This is a euphemism for death. This is the same word used in the Septuagint in Gen 50:26. On this word, see Mk 9:48.
7. The word implies that Joseph "called to mind and spoke of" this. On this word, see Jn 16:21.
8. Or, "exodus". That is, from Egypt. On this word, see Lk 9:31. The Greek word is *exodos*.
9. At the Exodus, Joseph's bones were taken along (Ex 13:19), and buried in Shechem (Josh 24:32).
10. On this word, see Act 7:20, where it is also used of Moses. Same word as in Ex 2:2.
11. Or, "command, decree". Used only here. GK *1409*.
12. Same word as in Ex 2:11. Related to "older" in Rom 9:12. This could mean "great" in stature versus babyhood in v 23, that is, "grown up". Or, it could mean great in status in Egypt, versus the plight of the Jews. This common word means "great", with the specific sense of it determined by its context: "large, long, high, loud, old, intense, important, profound". Used 194 times. GK *3489*.
13. Used only here. GK *5156*. Related to the word in v 37.
14. Or, this could be point 1F., giving the reason for Moses' choice in v 25.
15. Some think the writer means the reproach Moses experienced for the sake of the Christ, God's Anointed One; others, the reproach resting upon, belonging to the Christ Himself, as in 13:13.
16. Some manuscripts say "in Egypt" {K}.
17. Or, "looking intently, focusing attention on". Used only here. GK *611*.
18. Related to "rewarder" in v 6. On this word, see "penalty" in 2:2.
19. Or, "left behind". On this word, see "left behind" in Act 6:2.
20. Moses fled Egypt for Midian because he was afraid Pharaoh would kill him, Ex 2:14-15. Some think this is the reference here, so that verse 28 follows in chronological order, explaining his fear in various ways. Others think this verse is referring to the second time Moses left Egypt, the Exodus, and all the events associated with it from the ten plagues to the drowning of the army. "Not fearing the wrath of the king" is an appropriate description of Moses in this period, especially regarding his personal confrontations of Pharaoh during the plagues, which were before the Passover.
21. Or, "endured, persisted, was steadfast". Used only here. GK *2846*. Related to "perseverance" in Eph 6:18.
22. Some think the writer means "as though he saw"; others, "in as much as he saw, as one who saw".
23. Having made reference to the entire event of leaving Egypt, the writer now speaks of one crucial and enduring aspect of it. The grammar implies that Moses kept or performed it, and that it continues to be performed (it is established). On this word see "does" in Rev 13:13.
24. Or, "pouring". Used only here. GK *4717*. This is referring to Ex 12:7, 22.
25. This term, "the *one* destroying", is quoted from Ex 12:23. Used only here. GK *3905*. Related to "destroyer" in 1 Cor 10:10.
26. Or, "went through, stepped across". Elsewhere only in Lk 16:26; Act 16:9. GK *1329*.
27. The Septuagint is being quoted, Ex 13:18. The Hebrew says, "the sea of reeds". Elsewhere only in Act 7:36. GK *2261*.
28. Or, "attempt". This idiom means "having taken *the* test, having taken *an* attempt, having received *the* trial". This word is elsewhere only as "trial" in v 36. GK *4278*. Related to "trial" in Jam 1:2.
29. Same word as in 1 Cor 15:54; 2 Cor 2:7; 5:4; Rev 12:16; and "swallow" in Mt 23:24. Elsewhere only as "devour" in 1 Pet 5:8. Based on the word "to drink", this word means "to drink down". GK *2927*.
30. Some manuscripts place an "and" between each name {N}. The first four names are from Judges 4-16.
31. Or, "justice", as in 2 Sam 8:15. On this word, see Rom 1:17.
32. Or, "attained". Elsewhere only in Rom 11:7; Heb 6:15; Jam 4:2. GK *2209*.
33. This is an idiom, literally, "mouths". That is, the two edges of a double-edged sword. Same word as "mouths" of lions earlier. On this word, see "mouth" in 2 Cor 6:11.
34. Or, "strangers, *ones* belonging to others". Elsewhere only as "belonging to another" in Lk 16:12; Act 7:6; Rom 14:4; 15:20; 2 Cor 10:15, 16; 1 Tim 5:22; Heb 9:25; 11:9; and "stranger" in Mt 17:25, 26; Jn 10:5. GK *259*.
35. Or, "deliverance, release". On this word, see Rom 3:24.
36. On this idiom, see "test" in v 29.
37. Or, "scourgings". This is the word for a "whip", as in Act 22:24. On this word, see "scourge" in Mk 3:10.
38. Or, "bindings". On this word, see "imprisonment" in Phil 1:7. Not related to "prison" next.
39. Used only here. GK *4569*. Either before or after "sawn in two", some manuscripts add "they were tested" (or, "tempted") {C}, the word in 2:18. Some think the word "test, tempt" is a copyist's misspelling of some other word like "burned" or "pierced", etc.

A. Mt 28:6, arose B. Lk 6:28 C. Mt 14:33 D. Mt 24:31, end E. Mk 10:3, command F. 1 Jn 2:29 G. Jn 8:59 H. 1 Jn 2:14 J. Eph 5:33, respecting K. Jn 12:49, say L. 2 Thes 2:13 M. Rev 21:3 N. Mt 13:21 O. 1 Tim 6:17 P. Jam 1:2 Q. Heb 10:33 R. 1 Tim 6:17 S. Mt 12:35 T. Rev 16:19 U. Jn 18:28 V. Col 1:15 W. Mk 3:3, withered X. Jn 10:24, surrounded Y. 1 Cor 6:15 Z. Rom 11:30 AA. Mt 10:40 BB. Mt 26:10 CC. Rom 3:19 DD. 1 Thes 5:19 EE. Mk 5:30 FF. 1 Cor 6:18, flee GG. Col 1:11, empowered HH. Mt 8:17 JJ. Rev 18:8, strong KK. Rev 12:7, war LL. Rev 20:9, camp MM. Rom 7:8, taken NN. Act 24:15 OO. Act 24:15, wait for PP. Lk 20:35, attain QQ. Act 5:22 RR. Act 9:1

        1F. Being in-need^A, being afflicted^B, being mistreated¹—*of whom the world was   38
            not worthy^C
        2F. Wandering^D in desolate-places and mountains and caves and openings *of* the earth

16C. And these all, having been attested^E through *their* faith, did not receive^F the promise^G—*God   39-40
having provided² something better^H for us, in order that they should not be perfected³ apart from us

4B. So-therefore⁴ we also— having **so large** *a* cloud *of* witnesses⁵ surrounding^J us, having laid-aside^K   12:1
every weight⁶ and the easily-entangling⁷ sin— let us be running^L the race⁸ being set-before⁹ us with
endurance¹⁰, *while looking-away¹¹ toward the author^M and perfecter¹² *of* the faith¹³— Jesus— Who   2
endured¹⁴ *a* cross for¹⁵ the joy being set-before Him, having disregarded¹⁶ *the* shame¹⁷, and has sat-
down at *the* right *hand of* the throne^N *of* God

  1C. For consider¹⁸ the *One* having endured **such** opposition¹⁹ by sinners against Himself²⁰, in order   3
     that you may not be weary^O *in* your souls^P, losing-heart²¹—

    1D. You²² did not yet resist to the point *of* blood while struggling against sin!²³   4

  2C. And have you²⁴ completely-forgotten²⁵ the exhortation^Q which speaks²⁶ *to* you as sons^R?—   5
     "My son, do not be thinking-lightly²⁷ *of* the discipline²⁸ *of the* Lord, nor losing-heart while
     being rebuked^S by Him. *For *the one* whom *the* Lord loves^T He disciplines²⁹, and He whips³⁰   6
     every son whom He accepts^U" [Prov 3:11-12]

    1D. You³¹ are enduring [your trials] for discipline³². God is dealing^V *with* you as *with* sons   7

       1E. For what son *is there* whom *his* father does not discipline?
       2E. But if you are without discipline, *of* which all have become partakers³³, then you   8
          are illegitimate³⁴ *children* and not sons

    2D. Furthermore, we had **fathers *of* our flesh**³⁵ *as* discipliners³⁶ and were respecting^W *them*—   9
     but³⁷ shall we not much more be subject^X *to* the Father *of* [our] spirits³⁸ and live?

       1E. For **the *ones***³⁹ were disciplining *us* for *a* few days according to the *thing* seeming^Y   10
          good to them— but the *One* does so for *our* benefit⁴⁰, so that *we may* share-in⁴¹ His
          holiness

    3D. And all discipline **for the present**⁴² does not seem^Y to be *a thing of* joy, but *of* grief^Z— but   11
     later it yields⁴³ the peaceful⁴⁴ fruit^AA *of* righteousness *to* the *ones* having been trained^BB by it

1. Or, "caused to suffer, tormented, maltreated". Elsewhere only in 13:3. GK *2807*. Related to the word in 11:25.
2. Or, "foreseen". Used only here. GK *4587*.
3. Or, "completed, finished". On this word, see 2:10.
4. This word indicates a strong inference. "Therefore for that very reason". Elsewhere only in 1 Thes 4:8. GK *5521*. The writer now applies the lesson learned from "the elders" in 11:1-40, returning to the exhortation of 10:36-39.
5. That is, the witnesses just cited in chapter 11, witnesses of endurance by faith while awaiting the promises.
6. Or, "bulk, mass". Here, it refers to a burden that impedes or hinders the progress of the runner. Used only here. GK *3839*.
7. This word is not found elsewhere in Greek. The precise shade of meaning is not certain. Others suggest "easily ensnaring or encircling or besetting or clinging". Whatever the shade, the writer clearly means we should lay aside the sin which hinders us from running the race. GK *2342*. One early manuscript says "easily distracting" {A}.
8. Or, "contest". Elsewhere only as "struggle" in Phil 1:30; Col 2:1; "conflict" in 1 Thes 2:2; and "fight" in 1 Tim 6:12; 2 Tim 4:7. GK *74*. Related to "struggle" in 1 Tim 4:10; "struggling" in Heb 12:4; "contend" in Jude 3; and "conquered" in Heb 11:33.
9. Or, "being laid before", by God. Or, "setting before, lying before". Same word as in v 2; 6:18. Elsewhere only as "is present" in 2 Cor 8:12; and "set forth" in Jude 7. GK *4618*. The root word is "lying" in Mt 3:10.
10. Same word as in 10:36. This is a key Christian virtue.
11. That is, fixing our eyes on Jesus. Run the race while focusing intently on the finish line, Jesus Christ. Elsewhere only as "see" in Phil 2:23. GK *927*.
12. Or, "finisher, consummator, completer". Used only here. GK *5460*. Related to "perfect" in 2:10.
13. Or, "*of* faith", or, "*of our* faith".
14. Same word as in 10:32 and 12:3, 7. On this word, see Jam 1:12.
15. That is, to obtain His joy, for the sake of His "race", His "finish line", His purpose for coming, His completing of what the Father sent Him to do, His victory, the purchase of redemption. Then Christ returned to His place of glory and sat down. Others render this "instead of the joy", meaning Christ turned away from potential human joys to the cross; or, from His actual heavenly joys as the Son to the work God gave Him to do on earth. GK *505*.
16. Or, "cared nothing for". On this word, see Rom 2:4. Christ looked to the joy and turned away from the shame.
17. Or, "humiliation, disgrace". Elsewhere only in Lk 14:9; 2 Cor 4:2; Phil 3:19; Jude 13; Rev 3:18. GK *158*. Related to "be ashamed" in Rom 1:16; and "put to shame" in 1 Jn 2:28.
18. Or, "count up, calculate in comparison, compare". Used only here. GK *382*. Related to "consider" in 11:19.
19. Or, "dispute, hostility, rebellion, contradiction". Elsewhere only as "dispute" in 6:16; 7:7; and "rebellion" in Jude 11. GK *517*. Related to "speak against" in Lk 2:34, where Jesus is a sign to be opposed.
20. Some manuscripts say "themselves" {C}. In this case, the idea would be like Num 16:38, meaning sinners against their own selves, sinners at the cost of their own lives.
21. Or, "giving out, giving up, fainting". This is the Greek word order. Some take "*in* your souls" with this word, "be weary, fainting *in* your souls". Same word as in v 5. On this word, see Gal 6:9.
22. Some start a new point here, connecting v 4 with v 5 in point 2C., "You did not yet resist... and you have forgotten".
23. In other words, the suffering you must endure does not yet compare to His suffering. Some think "blood" continues the athletic metaphor of the race; others, that it refers specifically to martyrdom.
24. Or, this may be a statement, "And you have...".
25. This word means "to forget utterly or completely or altogether". If the readers thought they should be exempt from suffering for their faith, they must have forgotten Prov 3:11-12, and they must have failed to "consider" the Son, v 3. Used only here. GK *1720*.
26. Or, "reasons". On this word, see "reasoned" in Act 17:2.
27. Or, "making light of, making little of ". Used only here. GK *3902*.
28. Or, "instruction, training, correction, corporal punishment". Often used regarding child-rearing. Same word as in v 7, 8, 11. On this word, see "training" in 2 Tim 3:16. The related verb is in v 6.
29. Same word as in v 7, 10. On this word, see 1 Cor 11:32.
30. Or "scourges". Here, this word refers to the father's corporal punishment for purposes of loving correction. Elsewhere only in Mt 10:17; 23:34; and of the scourging of Jesus, God's Son, in Mt 20:19; Mk 10:34; Lk 18:33; Jn 19:1. GK *3463*. Related to "whippings" in 11:36; and "whip" in Act 22:25.
31. The writer now applies this OT quote to his readers. Others render this as a command, "Be enduring [your trials] for discipline". Some manuscripts say "If you endure discipline, God is dealing..." {N}.
32. That is, for training as children in righteousness and holiness. As we endure, we grow and mature. Compare Jam 1:3-4; Rom 5:3-4.
33. Or, "sharers". On this word, see 3:1.
34. Or, "born out of wedlock", and so not family members, not having a father to train them, not heirs. Used only here. GK *3785*.
35. That is, human fathers. The writer uses grammar that emphasizes the contrast between the two halves of this statement. On this word, see Col 2:23.
36. Or, "correctors, trainers". Related to "discipline" in v 5 and 6. Elsewhere only as "corrector" in Rom 2:20. GK *4083*.
37. Some manuscripts omit this word {C}.
38. Some think the writer means "of *our* spirits", in contrast to the first part of the verse; others, "of *all* spirits", including human spirits, a more general title for God. The grammar expects a "yes" answer to this question.
39. The writer uses grammar that emphasizes the contrast between the two halves of this statement.
40. This is an idiom, "for the *thing* being beneficial" for us, from God's viewpoint. 1 Cor 12:7 has a similar phrase.
41. Or, "receive a share of, partake of ". Same word as in Act 2:46. Elsewhere only as "receive" in Heb 6:7; Act 24:25; 27:33, 34; and "receive a share" in 2 Tim 2:6. GK *3561*. Related to "receiving" in 1 Tim 4:3.
42. The writer uses grammar that emphasizes the contrast between the two halves of this statement. This is a participle, "the *time* being present".
43. Or, "gives back, pays back". Same word as in Rev 22:2. On this word, see "render" in Mt 16:27.
44. Elsewhere only in Jam 3:17. GK *1646*.

A. Lk 15:14 B. 2 Cor 4:8 C. Rev 16:6 D. Jam 5:19, err E. Heb 11:2 F. 2 Cor 5:10, receive back G. 1 Jn 2:25 H. Heb 1:4 J. Heb 5:2 K. Rom 13:12 L. 2 Thes 3:1 M. Heb 2:10 N. Rev 20:11 O. Jam 5:15, being ill P. Jam 5:20 Q. Act 4:36, encouragement R. Gal 3:7 S. Eph 5:11, exposing T. Jn 21:15, devotedly love U. Mk 4:20 V. Heb 5:7, offer W. Lk 18:2, have regard for X. Eph 5:21 Y. Lk 19:11, thinking Z. 2 Cor 7:10 AA. Mt 7:16 BB. Heb 5:14

3C. Therefore straighten-up[1] the hands having been slackened[2] and the knees having been made-feeble[3]. *And be making straight[4] paths *for* your feet, in order that the lame[5] *part* may not be dislocated[6] but rather may be healed[A] — 12, 13

    1D. Be pursuing[B] peace[C] with[7] all *people*, and the holiness[8] without which[9] no one will see the Lord — 14

        1E. While exercising-oversight[10] — 15

            1F. *That* someone[11] *may* not *be* coming-short[12] of the grace[D] *of* God
            2F. *That* some root[13] *of* bitterness[E] growing[14] up may not be causing-trouble[F], and many be defiled[15] by it[16]
            3F. *That* someone *may* not *be* some sexually-immoral[17] or profane[18] like Esau, who sold[19] his *own* firstborn-rights[20] for one meal[21] — 16

                1G. For[22] you know that indeed afterward,[23] while wanting[G] to inherit[H] the blessing[J], he was rejected[24]— for he did not find *a* place[K] *of* repentance[25]— even-though having sought-for[L] it[26] with tears[M] — 17

        2E. For you have not come-to *a* mountain[27] being touched[28] — 18

            1F. And *a* fire having been burning[29]
            2F. And darkness[30]
            3F. And gloom[31]
            4F. And *a* storm[32]
            5F. And *a* blast[33] *of a* trumpet — 19
            6F. And *a* sound[34] *of* words[N]— *of* which, the *ones* having heard begged[O] *that a* word[P] not be added[Q] *to* them[35]

                1G. For they were not bearing[R] the *thing* being commanded— "If even *a* wild-animal[S] should touch the mountain, it shall be stoned[36]" [Ex 19:12-13] — 20

            7F. And so fearful[37] was the *thing* appearing[38], Moses said "I am terrified[39] and trembling[40]" — 21

        3E. But you have come to Mount Zion[41] — 22

            1F. And *the* city *of the* living God, *the* heavenly[T] Jerusalem[42]
            2F. And *the* myriads[U] *of* angels, *a* festive-gathering[43]
            3F. And *the* church[44] *of the* firstborn[45] *ones* having been registered[46] in *the* heavens — 23

1. Or, "set straight, restore, make erect". Elsewhere only as "make straight" in Lk 13:13; and "restore" in Act 15:16. GK 494. This word is made of two words, "up" and "make straight". Related to "straight" in the next verse.
2. Or, "relaxed at the side, neglected, weakened". Elsewhere only in Lk 11:42. GK 4223.
3. Or, "made lame, disabled, paralyzed". Elsewhere only as "paralyzed" in Lk 5:18, 24; Act 8:7; 9:33. GK 4168. Related to "paralytic" in Mt 4:24. These two phrases are similar to Isa 35:3.
4. This adjective is elsewhere only in Act 14:10. GK 3981.
5. Used 14 times. GK 6000.
6. Or, "turned out *of joint*". Used only here in a medical sense. On this word, see "turned aside" in 1 Tim 1:6.
7. Some think the writer means to pursue being at peace "with" all people, as this word is used with the related verb in Rom 12:18. While enduring your trials, as in 10:32-34, pursue both peace with your persecutors and holiness with God. Others think he means peace "with" all believers, so as not to harm the cause of Christ, as in Rom 14:19. Others think he means to pursue peace (salvation) "together with, along with" all people, the subject that follows. GK 3552.
8. Or, "sanctification, dedication *to God*, consecration *to God*". This word is used of the process of becoming holy, "holy-making, sanctification", and of the result of that process, "holiness". Holy means "set apart or dedicated to God". Same word as in Rom 6:19, 22; 1 Cor 1:30; 1 Thes 4:3, 4, 7; 2 Thes 2:13; 1 Tim 2:15. Elsewhere only as "sanctification" in 1 Pet 1:2. GK 40. Related to "holy, holy *ones*, saints" (see 1 Pet 1:16); "sanctify, make holy" (see 10:29); and the words in Heb 12:10 and Rom 1:4.
9. This last phrase begins a warning that extends to v 29.
10. Or, "seeing to *it*, watching over". Pursue it yourself, and watch over others. On this word, see 1 Pet 5:2.
11. The writer uses "some" as the subject of all three statements, in a way difficult to reproduce in English. GK 5516.
12. Same word as in 4:1.
13. That is, a root characterized by bitterness, a bitter root. The writer is referring to a person. See Deut 29:18; Act 8:23. This word is used of plant roots in Mt 3:10; 13:6; etc; and of the "cause, origin" in 1 Tim 6:10. Used 17 times. GK 4844. Related to "rooted" in Col 2:7.
14. Or, "coming, springing". On this word, see Lk 8:6.
15. Or, "stained, polluted". On this word, see Tit 1:15.
16. That is, the root of bitterness. Some manuscripts say "this" {N}.
17. On this word, see 1 Cor 5:9. Some think the writer means Esau was spiritually adulterous. Others take it as a literal description of Esau (in keeping with Jewish traditions). Others place a comma here, so that only "profane" refers to Esau.
18. On this word, see 1 Tim 1:9. It denotes a man of the world, material, lacking reverence or spirituality.
19. Used in this sense also in Act 5:8, 7:9. See Gen 25:29-34. On this word, see "render" in Mt 16:27.
20. That is, the status and inheritance rights of the firstborn son. Used only here. GK 4757. Related to "firstborn" in Col 1:15.
21. Or, "eating", one act of eating. Or, "who gave back his *own* firstborn rights in exchange for one eating". On this word, see "eating" in Mt 6:19.
22. This is intended to explain why we should not live a profane life like Esau.
23. That is, later on when Isaac was blessing his two sons, Jacob and Esau, Gen 27:30-40.
24. This word means "rejected as the result of a test; rejected as unfit, unqualified, unworthy". Some think it is God who rejected Esau. Isaac wanted to bless him (Gen 27:4), and thought he was doing so. Others think the writer means that Isaac rejected Esau in that he refused to withdraw his blessing of Jacob. Elsewhere only of Christ rejected by people in Mt 21:42; Mk 8:31; 12:10; Lk 9:22; 17:25; 20:17; 1 Pet 2:4, 7. GK 627. Related to "approve" in Rom 12:2.
25. Or, "change of mind". On this word, see 2 Cor 7:10. Some think Esau found no place for a "change of mind" by Isaac. Others think Esau could not repent of his profane lifestyle that had now resulted in his rejection. In this case, compare Heb 6:4-6. Others think Esau did repent, but his repentance could not now change the situation. In any case, do not be like Esau, for having turned away, even when he later wanted the blessing, he could not have it.
26. That is, the blessing. Some think the writer is referring to "repentance", and punctuate this verse "rejected. For he did not find *a* place *of* repentance, although...".
27. Some manuscripts include this word {B}. It is stated in v 20.
28. That is, the physical, earthly Mount Sinai in Ex 19 as opposed to a spiritual heavenly Mount Zion in v 22. On this word, see Lk 24:39.
29. Some render this "For you have not come to a fire being touched and having been burning", that is, to a physical (or palpable) and burning fire. See Deut 4:11; 5:22. On this word, see Mt 5:15.
30. Used only here. GK 1190. Same word as in Ex 14:20; 20:21; Deut 4:11; 5:22.
31. Some manuscripts say "darkness" {N}, so that it says "... burning, and *to* gloom, and *to* darkness, and...". On this word, see 2 Pet 2:4.
32. Used only here. GK 2590. Same word as in Deut 4:11; 5:22.
33. Or, "sound". On this word, see "news" in Lk 4:37.
34. On this word, see "voice" in Mk 1:26. This phrase, "sound *of* words", comes from Deut 4:12.
35. This is referring to Ex 20:19. When the Israelites heard the sound of God's words, they begged that God not speak to them.
36. Some manuscripts add "or shot *with an* arrow" {N}, from Ex 19:13.
37. Elsewhere only in 10:27, 31. GK 5829. Related to "terrified" next.
38. That is, the sight that he saw. This verb is used only here. GK 5751.
39. Elsewhere only in Mk 9:6, at the transfiguration. GK 1769.
40. This seems to be the writer's summary statement regarding the events in Exodus, not a direct quote. Note Deut 9:19; Ex 3:6; 19:16, 19. Same word as in Act 7:32, which is also of Moses. Elsewhere only in Act 16:29. GK 1958.
41. This refers to the heavenly Mount Zion, as seen in what follows. On this word, see Jn 12:15.
42. That is, the city Abraham (11:10) and we (13:14) look for.
43. Or, "a public festival, general assembly". Used only here. GK 4108. Used of an assembly of a whole nation for a public feast. Some punctuate so that this begins point 3F., "*The* general-assembly and church...".
44. Or, "assembly". Some think these are OT believers; others, NT believers; others, all believers. On this word, see Rev 22:16.
45. That is, firstborn as to privileges, inheritance. On this word, see Col 1:15.
46. Or, "enrolled, listed". We are on the census of heaven. On this word, see Lk 2:1.

A. Mt 8:8 B. 1 Cor 14:1 C. Act 15:33 D. Eph 2:8 E. Act 8:23 F. Lk 6:18, being troubled G. Jn 7:17, willing H. Gal 4:30 J. 2 Cor 9:5 K. Eph 4:27 L. Heb 11:6, seeking out M. Act 20:19 N. Rom 10:17 O. Heb 12:25, refuse P. 1 Cor 12:8 Q. Lk 17:5, increase R. 2 Pet 1:17, carry S. Rev 13:1, beast T. Eph 3:10 U. Act 21:20

4F.	And *the* Judge, God *of* all[1]	
5F.	And *the* spirits *of* righteous[A] *ones* having been perfected[2]	
6F.	And *the* mediator[B] *of the* new[3] covenant[C], Jesus	24
7F.	And *the* blood[D] *of* sprinkling[4] speaking better[5] than Abel[6]	

    4E. Be watching-out[7] *that* you not refuse[8] the *One* speaking   25

        1F. For if those did not escape[9], having refused the *One* warning[10] on earth[11], much more we *will not escape*— the *ones* turning-away-from[12] the *One warning* from *the* heavens[13]

            1G. Whose voice shook[E] the earth at that time[14]   26
            2G. But now He has promised, saying [in Hag 2:6]— "**I will shake**[15] once[16] more not only the earth, but also the heaven"

                1H. And the *phrase* "once more" indicates[17] the[18] removal[19] *of the things* being shaken[E]— as *of things* having been made— so that the *things* not being shaken[E] may continue[20]   27

        2F. Therefore while receiving[F] *an* unshakable kingdom[G], let us have gratitude[21], through which we may worship[22] God pleasingly[23], with reverence[H] and awe[24].   28
        For indeed our God *is a* consuming fire[25]   29

2D. Let[26] brotherly-love[27] continue[J]   13:1
3D. Do not be forgetting[28] hospitality[29]   2

    1E. For through this some having entertained[30] angels did not know[31] *it*

4D. Remember[32]   3

    1E. The prisoners[K] as-*though* having been imprisoned-with[33] *them*
    2E. The *ones* being mistreated[L]— as-*though* also yourselves being in *their* body[34]

5D. *Let* marriage[M] *be* honored[35] by all[36], and the bed[37] undefiled[38]   4

    1E. For[39] God will judge[N] *the* sexually-immoral-*ones*[40] and adulterers[41]

6D. *Let* character[42] *be* without-love-of-money[43], being content[44] *with* the present *things*[45]   5

    1E. For He Himself has said [in Deut 31:6], "I will never[46] let you go[47], nor will I by any means forsake[48] you"

1. This is the Greek word order and normal way of translating. It also fits the pattern of 1F., 2F., and 6F. Others render it "*to God, the judge of* all".
2. That is, the OT believers mentioned in 11:40. On this word, see 2:10. The writer says "spirits" because they still await the resurrection. His point is that all those righteous ones from Jewish history are with Jesus.
3. Used only here with "covenant". This word means "new" in the sense of "young" as opposed to "aged". See Mk 2:22 on it. A different word for "new" is used in 8:13.
4. See 9:19-28 on this. On this word, see 1 Pet 1:2. The related verb is in 10:22.
5. On this word, see 1:4. Some manuscripts have this plural, "better *things*" {N}.
6. Abel's blood called out for vengeance. Christ's blood speaks forgiveness.
7. Same word and form of exhortation as in 3:12.
8. Or, "decline, reject, shun, beg off ". Same word as "begged" in verse 19. Same word as later in this verse; and in Act 25:11. Elsewhere only as "decline" in 1 Tim 4:7; 5:11; 2 Tim 2:23; Tit 3:10; "excuse" in Lk 14:18, 19; and "request" in Mk 15:6. GK *4148*.
9. Same word as in 2:3.
10. That is, God, v 19. This word refers to a divine warning. Same word as in 8:5.
11. That is, on Mount Sinai, but phrased more broadly here to contrast with heaven next.
12. Same word as in Mt 5:42; Lk 23:14; Act 3:26; Rom 11:26; 2 Tim 1:15; 4:4; Tit 1:14. Elsewhere only as "return" in Mt 26:52. GK *695*.
13. As God revealed Himself to Israel at Mt Sinai through Moses, so now He is revealing Himself to the world from heaven through Jesus and the Holy Spirit. In both cases, the one turning away from what God reveals will suffer the consequences. And God's warning is clear, He will judge the world through Jesus, Jn 5:21-27; Acts 10:42; 17:31. We who turn away will not escape. Next, the writer proves this. When God keeps His promise to shake all creation (v 26), only those not being shaken will remain (v 27), those part of His kingdom (v 28). The others will be "removed".
14. See Ex 19:18.
15. On this word, see Mt 21:10. Some manuscripts say "I am shaking" {N}, in a prophetic sense.
16. Or, "one-time more, yet one-time, still one-time". That is, one more time. On this word, see "once for all" in Jude 3.
17. Or, "makes clear, reveals, shows". On this word, see "make clear" in 1 Cor 3:13.
18. Some manuscripts omit this word {C}, so that it says "*a* removal".
19. Or, "change". On this word, see 11:5.
20. Or, "remain". Some think the writer means that the visible manifestation of God's kingdom (the temple and OT economy begun at Sinai) will be removed and His unshakable kingdom established. Others think he is referring to the end-time, when Christ returns. On this word, see "abide" in Jn 15:4.
21. On "have gratitude", see Lk 17:9.
22. Or, "serve". This may also be rendered "through which let us worship". This word refers to giving religious service or worship to God. Same word as in 9:9, 14; 10:2; and Act 7:7, 42; 24:14; 26:7; Phil 3:3. Elsewhere only as "serve" in 8:5; 13:10; and Mt 4:10; Lk 1:74; 2:37; 4:8; Act 27:23; Rom 1:9, 25; 2 Tim 1:3; Rev 7:15; 22:3. GK *3302*. Related to "worship" in Rom 12:1.
23. Or, "acceptably", to God. Used only here. GK *2299*. Related to the verb "to please" in 11:5.
24. Or, "fear". Used only here. GK *1290*.
25. This is alluding to Deut 4:24.
26. Just as the writer broadened his exhortation from our relationship to God to our relationship with others in 10:24, so he does here in what follows. He broadens out from the pursuit of holiness and God (12:14-29) to commands regarding our personal relationships.
27. That is, the love of fellow Christians. Made of the word "brother" and "love". Elsewhere only in Rom 12:10; 1 Thes 4:9; 1 Pet 1:22; 2 Pet 1:7. GK *5789*. Related word in 1 Pet 3:8.
28. Or, figuratively, "be neglecting, overlooking". Elsewhere only in 6:10; 13:16; and Mt 16:5; Mk 8:14; Lk 12:6; Phil 3:13; Jam 1:24. GK *2140*. Related to "forgetful" in Jam 1:25.
29. Or, "love of strangers". Elsewhere only in Rom 12:13. GK *5810*. Related to "hospitable" in Tit 1:8.
30. Or, "lodged, received as guests". Same word as in Act 28:7. On this word, see "lodging" in Act 10:6.
31. Or, "were unaware [of it]". This is referring to Abraham in Gen 18-19. On this word, see "escape notice" in 2 Pet 3:5.
32. That is, in the sense of "keep in mind, do not forget". Same word as in 2:6; 8:12. Related to the word in v 7.
33. Or, "bound with". Used only here. GK *5279*. Related to "imprisonment" in Phil 1:7.
34. That is, as though you yourself were suffering their mistreatment, walking in their shoes. Or, "as also yourselves being in *a* body", exposed to the same potential for mistreatment. In this case, the word "as-*though*" has a different sense here than in the previous phrase.
35. Or, "respected". Same word as in Act 5:34. Some take this as a statement, "Marriage *is* honored among all". The verb must be supplied. Note that this is in a list of nine other commands, and that v 5 has the same grammar. On this word, see "precious" in 2 Pet 1:4.
36. Or, "among all" or "in all *things*", in every respect.
37. That is, the marriage bed, sexual relations. Elsewhere only in Lk 11:7; Rom 9:10; 13:13. GK *3130*. Related to "bedroom" in Act 12:20. The root word is "lying" in Mt 3:10.
38. Or, "unstained, unsoiled". Same word used of Jesus in 7:26. Elsewhere only in Jam 1:27; 1 Pet 1:4. GK *299*.
39. Some manuscripts say "But" {N}.
40. That is, those not honoring marriage, but pursuing sex outside of marriage. On this word, see 1 Cor 5:9.
41. That is, those defiling the marriage bed by committing adultery.
42. Or, "way *of life*, manner *of living*". Used only here in this sense. On this word, see "way" in Act 27:25.
43. On this word, see "not a money lover" in 1 Tim 3:3.
44. Or, "satisfied". On this word, see "sufficient" in 2 Cor 12:9.
45. This is a participle, "the *things* being present". That is, with what you have now.
46. Or, "by no means", as in the next phrase. This is an emphatic negative, on which see Gal 5:16.
47. Or, "turn you loose, give you up". Elsewhere only as "unfasten" in Act 16:26; 27:40; and "give up" in Eph 6:9. GK *479*.
48. Or, "desert, abandon". On this word, see 2 Cor 4:9.

A. Rom 1:17   B. Heb 8:6   C. Heb 8:6   D. 1 Jn 1:7   E. Act 17:13   F. Lk 17:34, taken   G. Mt 3:2   H. Heb 5:7   J. Jn 15:4, abide   K. Eph 3:1   L. Heb 11:37   M. Mt 22:11, wedding   N. Mt 7:1

2E.	So that while being confident[A] we say, "*The* Lord *is a* helper *for* me and[1] I will not fear[B]. What[2] will *a* human[C] do *to* me?" [Ps 118:6]	6
7D.	Remember[3] the *ones* leading[4] you, who spoke the word *of* God *to* you, whose faith[5] be imitating[D] while looking-carefully-at[E] the result[6] *of their* way-of-life[7]	7
1E.	Jesus Christ *is* the same yesterday and today and forever[8]	8
8D.	Do not be carried-away[9] *by* various[10] and strange[11] teachings[F]	9
1E.	For *it is* good[G] *for* the heart to be established[12] *by* grace[H], not *by* foods[13] in-connection-with[14] which the *ones* walking[15] were not profited[J]	
2E.	We[16] have *an* altar[17] from which the *ones* serving[18] *in* the tabernacle[K] have no right[19] to eat[20]	10
1F.	For[21] *of* animals[L] *from* which the blood is brought into the Holies[22] by the high priest for sin— the bodies *of* these are burned-up outside *of* the camp[M]	11
2F.	Therefore[23] Jesus also— in order that He might make the people holy[24] with *His* own blood[N]— suffered[O] outside *of* the gate[25]	12
3F.	So-indeed[26], let us go-out[27] to Him outside *of* the camp, bearing[P] His reproach[Q].	13
	For here[28] we do not have *an* abiding[R] city, but we are seeking-for[29] the *one* coming[30]	14

1. Some manuscripts omit this word {C}.
2. Others punctuate this, "and I will not fear what *a* human will do *to me*".
3. That is, keep in mind. This word is used with reference to past (Lk 17:32) and current (Gal 2:10; Col 4:18; 1 Thes 1:3) things. On this word, see Jn 16:21.
4. Or, "ruling". Because of the past tense of "spoke", and the word "result", some think the writer is referring to leaders who had died. Remember and imitate the example of their life. In this case, the time relation of this word is taken from "spoke", so that he means "Remember the *ones who were* leading you". Others think he is referring to "the *ones who are* leading you", meaning the same thing as in 1 Thes 5:12-13. Thus, this command is complementary to v 17. This verse focuses on their teaching and example, v 17 on their leadership. Same word as v 17, 24; Lk 22:26; Act 14:12; 15:22; and as "ruling" in Mt 2:6; Act 7:10. On this word, see "regard" in Jam 1:2. GK *2451*. Related to "being governor" in Lk 2:2.
5. Or, "faithfulness". On this word, see Eph 2:8.
6. Or, "end, outcome". GK *1676*.
7. Or, "behavior, conduct". On this word, see "conduct" in 1 Pet 1:15.
8. Jesus will produce the same outcome in your lives that He did in theirs. Others take this with v 9, Jesus is the same, so do not follow strange teachings. On "forever", see Rev 20:10.
9. Or, "taken away". On this word, see "remove" in Lk 22:42. Some manuscripts say "carried around" {N}.
10. Or, "diversified", as in 1 Pet 4:10. This word also means "intricate, riddling, ambiguous, cunning", and this more negative meaning may be intended here.
11. Or, "foreign". On this word, see "host" in Rom 16:23.
12. Or, "strengthened, confirmed". On this word, see "confirmed" in 1 Cor 1:6.
13. That is, to be established by grace, not by what we eat or do not eat; by spiritual means, not physical; by spiritual worship, not physical; by teachings such as those in Hebrews, not teachings about foods. The Jews gained no spiritual benefit from the physical foods. The writer does not make his point any more specific, so there are several views regarding what the more specific nature of these teachings may have been. Consult the commentaries. Same word as 9:10; 1 Tim 4:3. On this word, see Mk 7:19.
14. Or, "by means of". GK *1877*.
15. This word means to physically "walk" (Mt 4:18; 9:5); "walk around" (Mk 5:42; 12:38); and to figuratively walk in the sense of "live, behave, conduct one's daily life" (as in Rom 6:4; 8:4; 13:13, 14, 15; 2 Cor 5:7; Gal 5:16; 1 Jn 1:6). Used 95 times. GK *4344*. Some manuscripts say "having walked" {N}.
16. Verses 10-14 are rich with OT allusions and possible inferences. Consult the commentaries. The writer is giving the basis for his statement that it is good to be established by grace not foods, and drawing an application from it for his readers.
17. That is, a spiritual altar or place of sacrifice and worship. The writer does not make this any more specific, and says nothing more about it. Because of this, there are several views on what more specific meaning might be found here. Some think the altar is the cross; others, Jesus; others, the true altar in heaven (8:2; 9:11); others, the Lord's Supper. Note that the general meaning alone is sufficient for the writer's own actual conclusion in v 15. Through Jesus, let us offer up spiritual sacrifices of praise on our spiritual altar of worship to God. On this word, see Rev 8:3.
18. Or, "worshiping", as in 12:28. That is, the Jewish priests, representing all the people in the Levitical system.
19. Or, "authority". The reason they have no right is explained in v 11-12. On this word, see 1 Cor 8:9.
20. To "eat from the altar" means to eat the meat of the sacrificial animal leftover after the blood was offered. In the Law, God gave the priests the right to eat this meat. Thus, the one bringing the sacrifice gained a spiritual benefit. The priests gained a physical benefit from the altar— the food. But they gained no spiritual benefit from eating it, v 9. We have an altar from which no such physical benefit can be gained. The writer explains why next. Some think he is implying that we spiritually eat from our altar and the Jews do not; others think he is not implying that anyone eats from it. Note that he says nothing more about "eating", and makes no application of this to the Lord's Supper. This is probably because he has in mind the Day of Atonement, as seen in v 11, and no "eating" took place from that sacrifice.
21. In the Law, the priests were commanded to burn the body of the sacrifices on the Day of Atonement outside the camp, Lev 16:27. There was nothing left to eat. They had no right to this meat from their altar. Note that the writer's point is not where the animals died (it was in the temple), but that their bodies were burned outside the camp and not eaten.
22. That is, the Holy of Holies. On this word, see 8:2.
23. First the writer applies this to Jesus. Jesus offered His own blood in the heavenly temple. But He is similar to the Day of Atonement sacrifices in that He suffered "outside the camp".
24. On this word, "make holy", see "sanctify" in 10:29.
25. Looking backward to v 9, the implication of this is that there is nothing to eat. The body is gone. There is no eating associated with His sacrifice. We are established by the grace that comes through His sacrifice, not by any physical connection to His sacrifice, or any kind of association with foods or eating. We have a spiritual altar. So do not be carried away by teachings linking physical eating to any spiritual benefits. The physical did not profit the priests spiritually, and will not profit you. Looking forward to v 13, the writer takes another step. He drops the "not eaten" aspect and applies the "outside the camp" aspect in a way with much broader implications than foods alone. GK *4783*.
26. Now the writer applies this to his readers. On this word, see 1 Cor 9:26.
27. The readers must go out to Jesus where He was sacrificed for sin, and identify themselves with Him there, and bear the reproach He bears as a result of being that sacrifice. Worship there is spiritual, not physical. Some think this is also implying that they must leave the Levitical, Jewish system. There are other views. Consult the commentaries.
28. That is, in this world, this age.
29. Same word used of Abraham in 11:14. On this word, see Phil 4:17.
30. That is, the city coming, the heavenly Jerusalem, 12:22.

A. 2 Cor 5:6 B. Eph 5:33, respecting C. Mt 4:4, mankind D. 2 Thes 3:7 E. Act 17:23 F. 1 Cor 14:6 G. 1 Tim 5:10a H. Eph 2:8 J. Rom 2:25 K. Heb 8:2 L. Rev 4:6, living creatures M. Rev 20:9 N. 1 Jn 1:7 O. Gal 3:4 P. 2 Pet 1:17, carried Q. Heb 10:33 R. Jn 15:4

3E.	Therefore¹ through Him let us be continually^A offering^B *a* sacrifice^C *of* praise² *to* God— that is, *the* fruit^D *of* lips praising³ His name. °And do not be forgetting^E good-doing⁴ and sharing⁵. For *with* such⁶ sacrifices God is pleased⁷	15 16
9D.	Be obeying⁸ the *ones* leading^F you and be yielding⁹, for **they** are keeping-watch^G for your souls^H as *ones who* will render *an* account^J—	17
1E.	In order that they may be doing this¹⁰	
1F.	With joy	
2F.	And not while groaning^K, for this *would be* unprofitable¹¹ *for* you	
10D.	Be praying^L for us	18
1E.	For we are persuaded^M that we have *a* good^N conscience^O, wanting to conduct-ourselves^P well¹² in all *things*¹³	
2E.	And I especially appeal-to^Q *you* to do this in order that I may be restored^R *to* you sooner	19
5B.	Now may the God *of* peace— the *One* having brought-up^S from *the* dead the Great Shepherd^T *of* the sheep in-connection-with¹⁴ *the* blood^U *of the* eternal^V covenant^W, our Lord Jesus—	20
1C.	Prepare¹⁵ you in every good¹⁶ *thing* so that *you may* do His will	21
2C.	While doing^X *in* us¹⁷ the pleasing^Y *thing* in His sight through Jesus Christ	
3C.	*To* Whom¹⁸ *be* the glory forever and ever¹⁹, amen	

A.	Now I exhort^Q you, brothers^Z, bear-with²⁰ the word^AA *of* exhortation^BB. For indeed I wrote-to²¹ you with *a* few²² *words*	22
B.	Take-notice-of²³ our brother Timothy having been released²⁴, with whom if he comes quicker²⁵, I will see you	23
C.	Greet^CC all the *ones* leading^F you and all the saints^DD	24
D.	The *ones* from Italy greet you²⁶	
E.	Grace *be* with you all²⁷	25

1. It is good to be established by grace, not foods. We have a spiritual altar outside of the Levitical system, not one with physical associations with foods like the one in the camp. Therefore let us offer up spiritual sacrifices through Him. Some manuscripts omit this word {C}.
2. That is, consisting of praise. Peter likewise refers to "spiritual sacrifices" in a spiritual temple, 1 Pet 2:5. Used only here. GK 139. The related verb is in Rom 15:11. Not related to "praising" next.
3. Or, "confessing His name". This phrase is used only here in the Greek Bible. It means "giving praise/thanks to His name" or "confessing/acknowledging His name". It has the same grammar as used with the related word in Mt 11:25 ("I praise You"), and in the OT as "give thanks" to the Lord or to His name (Ps 7:17; 18:49; 44:8; 45:17; 52:9; 54:6; 92:1; 99:3; 106:47; 122:4; 140:13; 142:7), and "confess" Your name (1 King 8:33, 35). On this word, see "confessed" in 1 Tim 6:12.
4. This noun is used only here. GK 2343.
5. On this noun, see "fellowship" in 1 Cor 1:9.
6. Note that expressions of love for God and neighbor are combined as spiritual sacrifices pleasing to Him.
7. This is in direct contrast to animal sacrifices, which were not well-pleasing (10:5-7, an unrelated word). On this word, see 11:5.
8. Or, "Be persuaded by". On this word, see "persuade" in 1 Jn 3:19.
9. Or, "giving way, deferring, withdrawing". Used only here. GK 5640.
10. That is, leading and keeping watch over you.
11. Used only here. GK 269. This is a compound word indicating that it would not release the intended result for you.
12. Or, "rightly, honorably". Same root word as "good" earlier. This could be rendered "commendable conscience... conduct ourselves commendably". On this word, see Act 10:33.
13. Or, "in all *respects*, among all *people*".
14. Or, "in, by, with, by means of". GK 1877.
15. Or, "Equip, Furnish, Complete". On this word, see Rom 9:22.
16. On this word, see 1 Tim 5:10b. Some manuscripts say "in every good work" {A}.
17. Some manuscripts say "you" {A}.
18. This may be referring to "God", the main subject of the sentence. Or, it may be referring to "Jesus Christ", the nearest possibility, making this point 1D.
19. On this idiom, see Rev 20:10. Some manuscripts just say "forever" {C}.
20. Same word as 2 Tim 4:3, of bearing with healthy teaching. On this word, see 2 Cor 11:4.
21. Or, "sent in a letter to". Elsewhere only in Act 15:20; 21:25. GK *2182*. This is the verb related to "letter" in 2 Thes 3:17.
22. The writer may mean he wrote briefly, compared to what he might have said about the subject. Or, this may be an understatement, meaning he wrote at length. On this word, see "little" in 2:7.
23. Or, this may be a statement, not a command, "You know of ". On this word, see "know" in Lk 1:34. It is used in this sense only here.
24. Or, "having departed", as in Act 28:25. Some think the writer means "having been released" from prison; others, "having departed" on a journey. On this word, see "sends away" in Mt 5:31.
25. Same word as "sooner" in v 19. The writer could mean more quickly than Timothy's progress so far would indicate; or, sooner than he himself plans to depart. But we know nothing of the circumstances. Or, simply "quickly, soon", dropping the comparative aspect. On this word, see Jn 13:27.
26. Some take this to mean this letter is being written to Italy, and the ones that are with the writer from Italy send their greetings back; others, that it is being written from Italy, and the ones there join the writer in greeting the readers.
27. Some manuscripts add "Amen" {A}.

A. 2 Thes 3:16 B. Heb 9:28, bear C. Heb 9:26 D. Mt 7:16 E. Heb 13:2 F. Heb 13:7 G. Eph 6:18, keep alert H. Jam 5:20 J. Act 19:40 K. Jam 5:9 L. 1 Tim 2:8 M. 1 Jn 3:19 N. 1 Tim 5:10a O. Act 23:1 P. Eph 2:3 Q. Rom 12:8, exhorting R. Mk 8:25 S. Mt 4:1, led up T. Eph 4:11 U. 1 Jn 1:7 V. Mt 25:46 W. Heb 8:6 X. Rev 13:13 Y. Eph 5:10 Z. Act 16:40 AA. 1 Cor 12:8 BB. Act 4:36, encouragement CC. Mk 15:18 DD. 1 Pet 1:16, holy

Overview		**James**

Introduction	1:1
1A. Regard it all joy, my brothers, when you fall into various trials, knowing endurance is produced	1:2-3
1B. And let endurance be having its complete work, that you may be complete, lacking nothing	1:4
2B. And if anyone is lacking wisdom, let him ask from God and it will be given to him	1:5-8
3B. And let the lowly brother be boasting in his height, and the rich one in his lowliness	1:9-11
4B. Blessed is the man who endures the trial, because he will receive the crown of life	1:12
5B. Let no one say God is tempting him to do evil, for God tempts no one. Do not be deceived	1:13-16
2A. My beloved brothers, every good giving and perfect gift comes down from the Father of lights	1:16-17
1B. He brought us into being by the word of truth to be a kind of firstfruit of His creatures	1:18
2B. You know this, but be slow into anger. For anger does not work the righteousness of God	1:19-20
3B. Therefore receive with gentleness the implanted word being able to save your souls	1:21
4B. But be doers of the word, not hearers only, deluding yourselves with worthless religion	1:22-27
3A. My brothers, do not be holding your faith with respect of persons	2:1-13
4A. My brothers, what is the profit if someone claims to have faith, but does not have works?	2:14
1B. If one is lacking and you give words only, what is the profit? So faith is dead by itself	2:15-17
2B. But "You have faith, I have works". Faith without works is mere belief, like demons	2:18-19
3B. But do you want to know it is useless? Look at Abraham and Rahab	2:20-25
4B. For just as the body without spirit is dead, so also faith without works is dead	2:26
5A. Do not become many teachers, my brothers, knowing that we will receive a greater judgment	3:1-2
1B. If one does not stumble in speech, he is a perfect man, for the tongue is small but powerful	3:2-6
2B. The tongue is the world of unrighteousness, staining the whole body, setting our life on fire	3:6-10
3B. My brothers these things ought not to be so. The tree is known by its fruit	3:10-12
4B. Who is wise among you? Let him show it in his works done in the gentleness of wisdom	3:13
1C. But if you have selfish interest in your heart, do not lie against the truth. This is not wisdom from above. This produces disorder and every bad thing	3:14-18
2C. From what source are fights among you? Are they not from your pleasures?	4:1-3
3C. Adulterous ones, do you not know that friendship with the world is hostility toward God?	4:4-5
4C. But He gives greater grace. Therefore submit to God, draw near, mourn, be humbled	4:6-10
5B. Do not speak against one another, brothers. There is one Judge, but who are you?	4:11-12
6A. Come now, ones making plans apart from God. You boast in your pretensions. This is evil	4:13-17
7A. Come now, rich ones, weep over your miseries coming upon you.	5:1-6
8A. Therefore be patient, brothers, until the coming of the Lord. Do not be groaning. Do not be swearing an oath. Be praying. Be singing praise. Pray for the sick. Turn back ones wandering	5:7-20

	A. James,[1] *a* slave[A] *of* God and *the* Lord Jesus Christ	1
	B. *To* the twelve tribes[B] in the dispersion[2]	
	C. Greetings[C]	
1A.	Regard[3] *it* all joy[4], my brothers[D], whenever you fall-into[5] various[E] trials[6], °knowing that the testing[7] *of* your faith is producing[F] endurance[8]	2-3
	1B. And let endurance[9] be having *its* complete[10] work[11], in order that you may be complete and whole[G], lacking in nothing	4
	2B. And if any *of* you is lacking[12] wisdom[H], let him be asking from the God giving generously[13] *to* all and not reproaching[14], and it will be given *to* him	5
	1C. But let him be asking in faith[J], not doubting[15] at all, for the *one* doubting is like *a* surge[16] *of the* sea being blown-by-wind and tossed	6
	1D. For let that person[K] not be supposing[L] that he will receive anything from the Lord— *a* double-minded[17] man, unstable[M] in all his ways	7 8
	3B. And let the lowly[18] brother be boasting[N] in his height,°and the rich[O] *one* in his lowliness[19]	9-10
	1C. Because he will pass-away like *a* flower *of* grass[20]	
	1D. For the sun rose[P] with the burning-heat[21] and dried-up[Q] the grass, and its flower fell-off[R], and the beauty *of* its appearance[S] perished[T]	11
	2D. In this manner also the rich *one* will fade-away[22] in his pursuits[23]	
	4B. Blessed[24] *is the* man[U] who endures[25] *the* trial[26], because having become[27] approved[28], he will receive the crown[V] *of* life[29] which He[30] promised *to* the *ones* loving[W] Him	12
	5B. Let no one being tempted[31] be saying that "I am being tempted by[32] God"	13
	1C. For God is not-tempted[33] *by* evils[X], and He Himself tempts no one,°but each *one* is tempted by *his* own desire[34] while being drawn-away[35] and enticed[36]	14

1. Some think this is the half-brother of Jesus, leader of the church in Jerusalem. See Mt 13:55 on him. There are other views. Consult the commentaries.
2. On this word, see 1 Pet 1:1. Some think James is addressing Jewish Christians dispersed outside of Judea; others, that he is referring metaphorically to the true people of God.
3. Or, "Deem, Consider, Think", take the lead in thinking, lead out in thinking. Same word as in Act 26:2; 2 Cor 9:5; Phil 2:3, 6, 25; 3:7, 8; 2 Thes 3:15; 1 Tim 1:12; 6:1; Heb 10:29; 11:11, 26; 2 Pet 1:13; 2:13; 3:9, 15. Elsewhere only as "esteem" in 1 Thes 5:13; and "leading" (see Heb 13:7). GK *2451*.
4. The Hebrews did this, Heb 10:34 (same word). Related to "rejoice" in the similar statements in Act 5:41; Col 1:24; 1 Pet 4:13.
5. Or, "encounter". Elsewhere only in Lk 10:30, "fell into robbers"; Act 27:41. GK *4346*.
6. Or, "testings, temptations". Same word as in Lk 22:28; Act 20:19; Gal 4:14; Jam 1:12; 1 Pet 1:6; 4:12; 2 Pet 2:9. Elsewhere only as "testing" in Lk 8:13; Heb 3:8; Rev 3:10; and "temptation" in Mt 6:13; 26:41; Mk 14:38; Lk 4:13; 11:4; 22:40, 46; 1 Cor 10:13; 1 Tim 6:9. GK *4280*. The related verb is "tempted" in v 13.
7. Some think James means "the process-of-testing, the proving-by-test"; others, "the means-of-testing", so that he means "knowing that this means-of-testing your faith"; others, "the genuineness", the result-of-testing, the being-proven-genuine, as this word is used in 1 Pet 1:7, its only other occurrence. GK *1510*. On the related words, see "approve" in Rom 12:2. Not related to "trials".
8. Or, "perseverance, steadfastness, patience, fortitude". Same word as in Rom 5:3, 4. Elsewhere only in Lk 8:15; 21:19; Rom 2:7; 8:25; 15:4, 5; 2 Cor 1:6; 6:4; 12:12; Col 1:11; 1 Thes 1:3; 2 Thes 1:4; 3:5; 1 Tim 6:11; 2 Tim 3:10; Tit 2:2; Heb 10:36; 12:1; Jam 1:4; 5:11; 2 Pet 1:6; Rev 1:9; 2:2, 3, 19; 3:10; 13:10; 14:12. GK *5705*. On the verb, see Jam 1:12. This is a key Christian virtue.
9. Note how James uses words in pairs here— endurance, complete, lacking, ask, give, doubt, lowly, tempt, desire, sin, etc. The pairs link the flow of thought. This is a characteristic of his style.
10. Or, "perfect, finished". Same word as later in the verse. On this word, see 1 Cor 13:10. The related verb is used of Christ perfected by sufferings in Heb 2:10; 5:9.
11. That is, let endurance produce its complete work in you. Let it finish its work, attain its end, complete its job. Its end is proven character. Compare Rom 5:3-5. On this word, see Mt 26:10.
12. Or, "falling short". That is, lacking wisdom to handle the trial. Elsewhere only in 1:4; 2:15; and Lk 18:22; Tit 1:5; 3:13. GK *3309*.
13. Or, "simply, openly, without reservation, sincerely". Used only here. GK *607*. Related to "generosity" in Rom 12:8.
14. Or, "reprimanding, scolding". God does not scold us when we ask for wisdom. On this word, see 1 Pet 4:14.
15. In this sense, this word means "to be divided in the mind, to waver, to dispute with oneself". Same phrase as in Act 10:20. Same word as in Mt 21:21; Mk 11:23; Rom 14:23; Jude 22; and as "waver" in Rom 4:20. Elsewhere only as "to dispute" in Act 11:2; Jude 9; "to make distinctions" in Act 11:12; 15:9; Jam 2:4; "to discern" in Mt 16:3; 1 Cor 4:7; 6:5; 14:29; and "to rightly judge" in 1 Cor 11:29, 31. GK *1359*. Related to "discernment" in 1 Cor 12:10. The doubter is called "double-minded" in v 8. This indicates that the doubting in view is not uncertainty about how God might choose to answer, but the kind proceeding from dual commitments, part to God and part to self or the world. Doubters are not single-hearted in their asking.
16. Or, "wave, billow". The sense is defined by the rest of the verse. Doubters are driven by outside circumstances, not internal faith. They are unstable and inconsistent in their faith. Elsewhere only in Lk 8:24. GK *3114*. Related to "tossed about" in Eph 4:14.
17. Elsewhere only in 4:8. GK *1500*.
18. Or, "poor, humble", whether regarding the spirit, or the material circumstances (as here). Same word as in Lk 1:52; Rom 12:16; 2 Cor 10:1. Elsewhere only as "humble" in Jam 4:6; Mt 11:29; 1 Pet 5:5; and "downcast" in 2 Cor 7:6. GK *5424*. Related to "humblemindedness" in Phil 2:3; "lowliness" in Jam 1:10; "humbleminded" in 1 Pet 3:8; and "be humble" in Phil 4:12.
19. Or, "humiliation". In other words, focus on your spiritual realities, not your material circumstances. This perspective is essential for joy and endurance, and is exemplified in Heb 10:32-34. The poor focus on their spiritual wealth; the rich on the lowly path to true wealth. Some think James is not referring to the rich one here as a Christian brother, but in contrast to the poor Christian brother. In this case, he is sarcastically telling the rich one to boast in what will be his source of humiliation at the judgment. Same word as in Lk 1:48; Phil 3:21. Elsewhere only as "humiliation" in Act 8:33. GK *5428*.
20. The poor will also pass away (4:14), but the rich need the reminder not to focus on this life. Rich people's glory is only temporary. True riches, or poverty, awaits when they give an account of their use of God's gifts to them. Compare 1 Tim 6:17-19.
21. Elsewhere only in Mt 20:12; Lk 12:55. GK *3014*.
22. Or, "wither, die off, waste away". Used only here. GK *3447*.
23. Or, "journeys, goings, undertakings, ways". Elsewhere only as "journey" in Lk 13:22. GK *4512*.
24. On this adjective, see Lk 6:20.
25. This is the verb related to "endurance" in v 3. Same word as in Mt 10:22; 24:13; Mk 13:13; Rom 12:12; 1 Cor 13:7; 2 Tim 2:10, 12; Heb 10:32; 12:2, 3, 7; Jam 5:11; 1 Pet 2:20. Elsewhere only as "stay" in Act 17:14; and "stay behind" in Lk 2:43. GK *5702*.
26. Or, "temptation". Same word as in v 2.
27. Or, "proved to be, been". GK *1181*.
28. On this adjective, see 2 Tim 2:15.
29. That is, consisting of life.
30. Some manuscripts say "the Lord"; others, "God" {A}.
31. Or, "tested". Same root word as "trial" in v 2, 12. God may bring a test to strengthen our faith and endurance, but James clarifies that God never tempts us to do evil. That comes from within. On this word, see Heb 2:18.
32. Or, "from". That is, that it is coming from God, that He is the source of the temptation.
33. Or, "untempted". God cannot be tempted. He can be "tested, tried", as in Heb 3:9-10. Used only here. GK *585*.
34. This is the Greek word order of this sentence. It could also be rendered "but each *one* is tempted while being drawn away and enticed by his own desire". Our own desire for the bait makes it a temptation. On this word, see Gal 5:16.
35. Or, "dragged away, pulled out". Used only here. GK *1999*. Related to "draw" in Jn 6:44.
36. Or, "lured, baited, entrapped". Elsewhere only in 2 Pet 2:14, 18. GK *1284*.

A. Rom 6:17 B. Rev 1:7 C. 2 Cor 13:11, rejoice D. Act 16:40 E. 1 Pet 4:10, diversified F. Phil 2:12, work out G. 1 Thes 5:23 H. 1 Cor 12:8 J. Eph 2:8 K. Mt 4:4, mankind L. Phil 1:17 M. Jam 3:8, restless N. 2 Cor 11:16 O. 1 Tim 6:17 P. Heb 7:14 Q. Mk 3:1, became withered R. Gal 5:4, fell from S. Lk 9:52, presence T. 1 Cor 1:18 U. 1 Tim 2:12 V. Rev 4:4 W. Jn 21:15, devotedly love X. 3 Jn 11

	1D. Then the desire[A], having conceived[B], gives-birth[C] to sin	15
	2D. And the sin, having been fully-formed[1], brings-forth[2] death	
	3D. Do not be deceived[3]!	16
2A.	My[4] beloved[D] brothers[E], *every good[F] gift-giving[5] and every perfect[6] gift-given[7] is from-above[G], coming down from the Father *of* lights[8], with Whom there is no variation[9] or shadow[10] *of* turning[11]	17
	1B. Having willed[12] it, He brought us into being[13] *by the* word[H] *of* truth[J] so that we *might* be *a* kind-of firstfruit[14] *of* His creatures	18
	2B. You know[15] *this*[16], my beloved brothers[17], but let every person[K] be quick[L] to listen, slow to speak, slow into anger[M]	19
	1C. For[18] *the* anger *of a* man[N] does not produce[19] *the* righteousness *of* God[20]	20
	3B. Therefore having laid-aside[O] all filthiness[21] and abundance[22] *of* badness[23], receive[24] with gentleness[25] the implanted[26] word[H] being able to save[P] your souls[Q]	21
	4B. But[27] be[28] doers[R] *of the* word[H] and not hearers[S] only, deluding[29] yourselves	22

1. Or, "having been brought to completion, having run its course". On this word, see "performing" in Lk 13:32.
2. Or, "gives birth to", but not the same word as preceding. Elsewhere only as "brought into being" in v 18. GK *652*.
3. Ending this section with a command like this is not found elsewhere in James, but it is not ungrammatical. Standing alone, it is an even stronger point. On this word, see "err" in 5:19.
4. The flow of thought in v 16-22 is not certain. There is clearly a change of subject in the second half of the chapter, but where to make the break is not clear. The clues are conflicting, and require a choosing between two traits of James's style, and a deviation from his style. In this rendering, the deviation is letting "Do not be deceived" stand alone, ending that point. This allows the new main point to begin with a "My brothers" as normal for James (and exactly like 2:1; 5:19), and yields a simple, natural flow to v 22. Many others keep "Do not be deceived, my beloved brothers" together as normal, joining it to "every good gift..." as point 2C. In this case James means not to be deceived about temptation because temptation does not come from God, but rather good gifts come from above— thus giving a negative and a positive argument for this. This means the new main point (2A.) begins in v 19 with "Know this.... But...", which is the deviation from normal this view must accept (see v 19), along with a less simple flow to v 22. There are other views. Consult the commentaries.
5. Or, "*act of* giving". Elsewhere only as "giving" in Phil 4:15. GK *1521*. It is a gift considered as an act of giving by the giver.
6. Same word as "complete" in v 4.
7. Elsewhere only as "given-gift" in Rom 5:16. GK *1564*. It is a gift considered as the result of the act of giving in the previous word, which is related to this one. The gift of salvation is the greatest of the good and perfect gifts from above.
8. That is, the creator of the heavenly bodies— sun, moon and stars. The word "light" is plural elsewhere only in Act 16:29. See Jn 1:5 on it.
9. Or, "change". Used only here. GK *4164*. God does not change like His creation. His relationship to us does not change.
10. This refers to a "shadow from" something, as light shines upon it. Used only here. GK *684*.
11. James may mean a shadow characterized by turning, a "turning shadow" (like "forgetful hearer" in v 25), like the shadow turns on a sundial as the sun moves. Or, a shadow caused by turning. God's changing creation does not cause any change of perspective in Him. Used only here. GK *5572*. Some manuscripts say "variation *of a* turning shadow" {B}.
12. Or, "wanted, desired, intended, wished". Used 37 times, mostly of the wants and intentions of people. Used of God only as "willing" in Mt 11:27; Lk 10:22; 22:42; 1 Cor 12:11; "intending" in Heb 6:17; and "wishing" in 2 Pet 3:9. GK *1089*. Related to "counsel" in Eph 1:11.
13. Or, "He gave us birth", that is, spiritual birth, through the gospel. Same word as "brings-forth" in v 15.
14. That is, the sacred part, the part consecrated to God. Some think James is referring to these early believers as the firstfruit of the church, like 2 Thes 2:13; others, to all believers as a firstfruit of the coming change in the universe, Rom 8:20-21. On this word, see 1 Cor 15:20.
15. Or, "understand". This same word and form is elsewhere only in Eph 5:5; Heb 12:17. James uses a different form of this word in the question in 4:4; and an unrelated word for "know" in the clear command in 5:20. Some render this as a command, "Know *this*"; others, as a statement. Some manuscripts say "So then my beloved brothers, let every person be quick..." {B}, a reading also linking v 19 to v 17-18. On this word, see 1 Jn 2:29.
16. Some think James is referring to what precedes. You know or are to know that the gift of salvation comes down from God, who brought us forth by the word of truth. Exhortations to actions in keeping with this gift then follow next. Note the repetition of "word" in v 18, 21, 22, and the "receive" in v 21 following the giving in v 17-18. Others, beginning the new point (2A.) here, take this as a command to know what follows. James commands his readers to know a command, which he then begins with "but" or "and". "Know this— and let every person be quick to listen...". To explain the "but, and" that follows (which this view omits in translation), it is suggested that James is quoting a well-known proverb (to the readers) from an unknown source (to us), and that he retains this word from that source. Some then regard v 19b-21 as a kind of introduction or transition to what James commands us to know in v 22.
17. A command precedes "brothers" in 1:2, 16; 2:5; 3:1; 4:11; 5:7, 9, 10; and follows it in 2:1; 5:12, 19. "Brothers" is connected with a question in 2:14; 3:12; and a statement in 3:10. Only here is it followed by "but". "My beloved brothers" is also in 1:16; 2:5.
18. James makes clear that the "anger" is his point. Do not receive the word of truth in anger, but in gentleness. His point is true in the broadest sense, but some think he has in mind the over-aggressive zeal so often displayed by the Jews in Acts. Do not receive your salvation with the same kind of anger-driven fanaticism displayed by the Jews— anger, clamor, hatred of those opposing, violence; the fights and battles of Jam 4:1. This will not bring about God's result.
19. Or, "work, accomplish, bring about". On this word, see Mt 26:10.
20. Some think James means the righteousness God requires; others, the righteousness God is working.
21. That is, moral dirt or contamination. Used only here. GK *4864*. Related to "filthy" in 2:2; Rev 22:11; and "dirt" in 1 Pet 3:21.
22. On this word, see 2 Cor 8:2. Some think James means the abundance of badness overflowing from the heart; others, the remainder, residue, leftovers of badness. There are other views.
23. Or, "evilness", moral badness. On this word, see 1 Pet 2:1.
24. Or, "accept". On this word, see "welcome" in Mt 10:40.
25. This is in contrast with "anger" in v 20. Same word as in 3:13. Used of Christ in 2 Cor 10:1. On this word, see Eph 4:2. James himself displayed this gentleness in handling the problem in Acts 15, and was a victim of such anger (see the note on Act 24:27).
26. That is, the word of the gospel implanted within you. Used only here. GK *1875*. This is probably a reference to the parable of the sower who sows the gospel seed, Lk 8:5-15.
27. This may be thought of as the opposite extreme of the angry fanaticism in v 19-21, if that is what James has in mind there. Do not receive the word with anger or badness. But neither receive it in word only. To receive it in word only as a mere hearer is to delude yourself that you even have the gift.
28. Or, "prove to be, become". GK *1181*.
29. Or, "deceiving, defrauding" by false reasoning. Elsewhere only in Col 2:4. GK *4165*. Mere hearers are deluding themselves by thinking they are saved. That kind of faith cannot save a person, 2:14. It is worthless, 1:26.

A. Gal 5:16 B. Lk 2:21 C. Lk 2:11, born D. Mt 3:17 E. Act 16:40 F. 1 Tim 5:10b G. Jn 3:3, again H. 1 Cor 12:8 I. Jn 4:23 J. Mt 4:4, mankind L. Rev 22:7, quickly M. Rev 16:19, wrath N. 1 Tim 2:12 O. Rom 13:12 P. Lk 19:10 Q. Jam 5:20 R. Rom 2:13 S. Rom 2:13

	1C. Because if anyone is *a* hearer *of the* word and not *a* doer	23
	1D. This *one* is like *a* man^A considering^1 the face *of* his birth^2 in *a* mirror. °For he considered himself, and he has gone-away, and he immediately^B forgot^C what-sort^D *of man* he was^3	24
	2C. But the *one* having looked^E into *the* perfect^4 law *of* liberty^5, and having continued^6— not having become *a* forgetful hearer^7, but *a* doer *of* work—	25
	1D. This *one* will be blessed^8 in his doing^9	
	3C. If anyone^10 thinks^F *that he* is religious^11 while not bridling^12 his tongue, but deceiving^G his heart, the religion^13 *of* this *one is* worthless^14. °This is pure^H and undefiled^J religion before *our* God and Father—	26 27
	1D. To be looking-after^K orphans^15 and widows in their affliction^L 2D. To be keeping^M oneself unspotted^N by the world^O	
3A. My brothers, do not be holding^16 the faith *of* our Lord^17 Jesus Christ *of* glory^18 with respect-of-persons^19		2:1
1B. For if *a* gold-ringed man^A in shining^P clothing enters into your gathering^20, and *a* poor^Q man in filthy^R clothing also enters		2
	1C. And you look-upon^21 the *one* wearing^S the shining clothing, and say^22 "**You** be sitting here, well^23" 2C. And you say *to* the poor *man*, "**You** stand there, or be sitting^24 under^25 my footstool" 3C. Did you not make-distinctions^26 among yourselves, and become judges *with* evil^T thoughts^27?	3 4
2B. Listen, my beloved brothers—		5
	1C. Did^28 not God choose^U the poor^Q in the world^29 to be rich^V in^30 faith, and inheritors^W *of* the kingdom^X which He promised *to* the *ones* loving Him? °But **you** dishonored^Y the poor *man* 2C. Do not the rich^V oppress^Z you and themselves drag^31 you into courts^AA? °Do not **they** blaspheme^BB the good^CC name having been called^32 upon you? 3C. If indeed^33 you are fulfilling^DD *the* royal law^34 according to the Scripture [in Lev 19:18], "You shall love your neighbor as^35 yourself", you are doing well^36. °But if you are showing-respect-of-persons^37, you are working^38 *a* sin, being convicted^39 by the Law as transgressors^40	6 7 8 9
	1D. For whoever keeps^M the whole Law but stumbles^EE in one *thing*, has become guilty^FF *of* all	10
	1E. For the *One* having said "Do not commit-adultery^GG", also said "Do not murder^HH" 2E. Now if you do not commit-adultery, but you murder, you have become *a* transgressor *of the* Law	11
	4C. So speak and so do, as *ones* going to be judged^JJ by *the* law *of* liberty^41	12
	1D. For judgment^KK *will be* merciless *to* the *one* not having done^42 mercy^43 2D. Mercy^44 vaunts^45 *over* judgment	13

1. Or, "looking closely at". On this word, see Heb 10:24.
2. Or, "existence, origin". That is, his natural, physical face. On this word, see "existence" in 3:6.
3. This man saw his face reflected, but took no action. It had no permanent effect on him. He heard the facts about himself and salvation, and may even intellectually believe them (2:14), but he did not obey the gospel (Rom 10:16).
4. Or, "complete", as in v 4. Some think James means "perfect" because it is able to give life, which the Law could not do. Others think he means "complete", brought to completion in Christ, Mt 5:17. There are other views.
5. Or, "freedom". That is, leading to liberty. Same phrase as in 2:12. On this word, see "freedom" in Gal 5:13. James is referring to the gospel, the "word of truth" (v 18), the "implanted word" (v 21).
6. Elsewhere only in 1 Cor 16:6; Phil 1:25; Heb 7:23. GK *4169*.
7. More literally, "*a hearer of* forgetfulness". James means a hearer characterized by forgetfulness; next, a doer characterized by work.
8. Same adjective as in v 12.
9. That is, in what he is doing. This is another word pair. Related to the word "doer". Used only here. GK *4474*.
10. Some manuscripts add "among you" {N}.
11. This word refers to one who keeps religious observances, the externals of religion. Used only here. GK *2580*.
12. Or, "restraining, controlling". On this word, see 3:2. This verse illustrates "hearers"; the following, "doers".
13. Or, "worship, religious service". Same root word as "religious" earlier. Same word as in v 27; Act 26:5. Elsewhere only as "worship" in Col 2:18. GK *2579*.
14. Or, "futile, pointless". On this word, see "futile" in 1 Cor 15:17.
15. Elsewhere only in Jn 14:18. GK *4003*. The Greek is *orphanos,* from which we get "orphan". The related verb is in 1 Thes 2:17.
16. Or, "you are not holding... respect of persons, *are you*?", expecting a "no" answer. On this word, see "have" in 1 Jn 1:8.
17. Some think James means the faith "*in* our Lord"; others, "*originated by* our Lord" (the objective faith, Jude 3).
18. This is the Greek word order of this phrase. Some think James means "our glorious Lord Jesus Christ" (our Lord characterized by glory); others, "our Lord Jesus Christ, [the Lord] *of* glory"; others "our Lord Jesus Christ, the Glory [of God]"; others, "*our Lord Jesus Christ from* glory" (heaven).
19. Or, "partiality, favoritism, acceptance of faces". This word is based on a Hebrew way of speaking, "to receive the face", which is in Lk 20:21; Gal 2:6. Elsewhere only in Rom 2:11; Eph 6:9; Col 3:25. GK *4721*. The related verb is in v 9. Related words occur in Act 10:34 and in 1 Pet 1:17.
20. Or, "synagogue, congregation, meeting". Used elsewhere only of the Jewish synagogue. It means "gathering", and is used of the place, the congregation who meets there, and the meeting. On this word, see Act 13:43. Related to "gather together" in Heb 10:25. James may be referring to the "church assembly" of these Jewish Christians, using their familiar term "synagogue". James uses the word "church" in 5:14.
21. That is, look with favor upon. Elsewhere only in Lk 1:48; 9:38. GK *2098*.
22. Some manuscripts add "*to him*" {N}.
23. Or, "beautifully, splendidly, appropriately". Sit here in a good seat. On this word, see Act 10:33.
24. Some manuscripts say "**You** stand or be sitting there under...", others, "**You** stand there or be sitting here under..." {B}.
25. That is, "at". Same word as in Ex 19:17, "at" the foot of the mountain. "Under" its shadow. GK *5679*.
26. Or, "waver" from the truth. On this word, see "doubting" in 1:6. The grammar expects a "yes" answer.
27. Or, "reasonings, thinking". More literally, "judges *of* evil thoughts", judges characterized by evil thoughts. Same word as in Mt 15:19; Mk 7:21; Lk 2:35; Rom 1:12; 1 Cor 3:20. Elsewhere only as "reasoning" in Lk 5:22; 6:8; 9:47; "opinion" in Rom 14:1; "argument" in Lk 9:46; Phil 2:14; 1 Tim 2:8; and "doubt" in Lk 24:38. GK *1369*. Related to "reason" in Lk 5:21.
28. Both this question and the next one expect a "yes" answer.
29. Some manuscripts say "*of* this world" {N}. Compare 1 Cor 1:26-29.
30. That is, in the sphere of, in connection with. GK *1877*.
31. Same word as in Act 16:19, where this happened to Paul.
32. Or, "named" upon. Same idiom as in Act 15:17. That is, the good name your Owner has given you, "Christian". Related to the word in Lk 2:21.
33. Or, "If however, If truly".
34. That is, the law of love , quoted next. "Royal" is related to "king, kingdom". Some think it is royal in that it originated with the King; others, in that it is the king of laws relating to our conduct toward one another; others, in that it is the law of His kingdom. There are other views. On "royal", see Act 12:20.
35. Or, "like". On this command, see Mt 19:19.
36. That is, you are acting commendably, rightly; doing a good thing. On this idiom, see Act 10:33.
37. Used only here. GK *4719*. Related to the word in v 1.
38. Same word as "produce" in 1:20.
39. Or, "exposed, rebuked". On this word, see "exposing" in Eph 5:11.
40. That is, violators of the Law. Elsewhere only in v 11; Rom 2:25, 27; Gal 2:18. GK *4127*. Related to "transgression" in Rom 5:14. You have violated the royal law just quoted.
41. On "law of liberty", see 1:25.
42. This is another word pair. "Do" in the previous verse is the same word. That is, "shown mercy", as this idiom is rendered in Lk 1:72.
43. As Jesus often said, Mt 5:7; 6:14-15; 7:1-2; 9:13; 18:33-35; 25:41-46.
44. Some manuscripts say "And mercy..." {N}.
45. Or, "boasts over". On this word, see Rom 11:18. Mercy triumphs and exults over judgment like a defeated foe.

A. 1 Tim 2:12 B. Mt 13:5 C. Heb 13:2 D. Act 26:29 E. Lk 24:12, stooped to look F. Lk 19:11 G. 1 Tim 2:14 H. Tit 1:15, clean J. Heb 13:4 K. Heb 2:6 L. Rev 7:14 M. 1 Jn 5:18 N. 2 Pet 3:14 O. 1 Jn 2:15 P. Rev 22:1 Q. Gal 4:9 R. Rev 22:11 S. 1 Cor 15:49, bear T. Act 25:18 U. 1 Cor 1:27 V. 1 Tim 6:17 W. Rom 8:17, heir X. Mt 3:2 Y. Act 5:41 Z. Act 10:38 AA. 1 Cor 6:32, case BB. 1 Tim 6:1 CC. 1 Tim 5:10a DD. Rev 10:7, finished EE. 2 Pet 1:10 FF. 1 Cor 11:27 GG. Mt 5:32 HH. Jam 4:2 JJ. Mt 7:1 KK. Jn 3:19

4A. What *is* the profit[A], my brothers[B], if someone claims[1] to have faith[C], but does not have works[2]? The faith[3] is not able to save[D] him, *is it*?   14

  1B. If brother or sister are naked[4] and lacking[E] daily food[F], °and one of you says *to* them "Go in peace, be warmed and filled[5]", but you do not give them the necessities *of* the body, what *is* the profit[6]?   15-16

    1C. In this manner also, faith, if it does not have works, is dead[G] by[7] itself   17

  2B. But[8] someone[9] will say "**You** have faith, and **I** have works"   18

    1C. Show[H] me your faith without[10] the[11] works,[12] and **I** will show you the[13] faith by my works
    2C. **You** believe[J] that God is one[14]? You do well[15]. Even the demons[K] believe[16] and shudder!   19

  3B. But do you want to know[17], O empty[18] person[L], that faith without works is useless[19]?   20

    1C. Abraham our father— was he not declared-righteous[M] by works[20], having offered[N] Isaac his son on the altar?[21]   21

      1D. Do you see[22] that faith was working-with[O] his works, and the faith was perfected[23] by the works? °And the Scripture was fulfilled[P], the *one* [in Gen 15:6] saying[24] "And Abraham believed[J] God, and it was credited[Q] *to* him for righteousness". And he was called[R] *a* friend[S] *of* God   22   23

      2D. Do you *all*[25] see[26] that *a* person[L] is declared-righteous[M] by works, and not by faith alone[27]?   24

    2C. And likewise also Rahab the prostitute[T]— was she not declared-righteous[M] by works, having received[28] the messengers[U], and having sent-*them*-out[V] *by a* different[W] way?   25

  4B. For just as the body without spirit[29] is dead[G], so also faith without works is dead   26

1. Or, "says *that he* has". Such a person says he has true faith, but only has the demons' kind of faith, v 19. On this word see "say" in Jn 12:49.
2. Or, "actions, deeds". James is referring to works as the fruit of faith, not as the means of salvation. The discussion that follows is not about whether faith saves, but about the kind of faith that saves— living faith (which shows itself or "is perfected" in our daily actions and choices) versus dead faith (which is merely having correct beliefs, an intellectual faith or allegiance that has no effect on behavior). On this subject, see Mt 7:21; Jn 15:2; Rom 2:7; Eph 2:10; Rev 20:12. On this word, see Mt 26:10.
3. Or, "*That* faith". That is, "the" faith without works just mentioned. The grammar expects a "no" answer.
4. That is, without adequate clothing, poorly clothed. Based on the context, this word can also mean "unclothed, wearing undergarments only, bare naked". Same word as in Mt 25:36, 38, 43, 44; Mk 14:51, 52; Jn 21:7; Act 19:16; 2 Cor 5:3; Heb 4:13; Rev 3:17; 16:15; 17:16. Elsewhere only as "bare" in 1 Cor 15:37. GK *1218*. The related verb is in 1 Cor 4:11.
5. That is, by someone else. Or, "warm *yourselves* and fill *yourselves*". That is, take care of it yourself. On this word, see "filled to satisfaction" in Phil 4:12.
6. Words without corresponding actions are of no value. Same word as in v 14.
7. This is the Greek word order. Some move this phrase forward, "faith by itself"; others add a verb here, "is dead, *being* by itself". As to this phrase, some think it means "by itself", that is, alone; others, "in accordance with itself, in harmony with itself". That is, it is outwardly dead in accordance with its inner nature. GK *2848*.
8. Some think James means "But in objection to your argument, James"; others, "But in contradiction of your claim in v 14 to have faith, O man". This phrase "But someone will say" is elsewhere only in 1 Cor 15:35.
9. Exactly who this is and what he says is not easy to see. Some think James puts his argument in the mouth of this third party. "You have faith [alone], and I [like James] have [faith with] works. Show me...". The response is also part of the quotation, which extends to the end of v 18 or v 19. It is as if James said "And someone like me will say 'You claim to have faith, and I have works. Show me...'". Others think this is an objector asserting that both are correct. "You have faith [alone], and I [like James] have [faith with] works". Both are acceptable to God. God has called some to have faith with works and some to have faith alone. It is as if James said "But someone like you will say, 'One has faith and another has works'". James defeats this logic by addressing the one claiming a faith without works. There are other views. Consult the commentaries. It comes down to which unusual phraseology is more acceptable— to say "But someone will say", not referring to an objection but to your own next argument; or to say "You... I" here, when you mean "One... another". In either case, the main point (v 18b-19) is the same, and is clear and powerful.
10. Or, "apart from". Same word as in v 20, 26. Used 41 times. GK *6006*.
11. Or, "*your*". Some manuscripts say "your" {N}.
12. The only way one could do this would be to point to his beliefs, which James answers next in 2C.
13. Or, "*my*". Some manuscripts say "my" {N}.
14. Or, this may be a statement. Compare Deut 6:4. Some manuscripts say, "There is one God" {B}.
15. On this phrase, see Act 10:33.
16. Even demons have that kind of faith. "Believe" and "faith" are the same root word. Intellectual agreement to and confession of correct theological doctrines alone is not the saving kind of faith. Compare Tit 1:16.
17. Or, "But are you willing to recognize", or "acknowledge". On this word, see Lk 1:34.
18. That is, empty of understanding, senseless. On this word, see 1 Thes 2:1.
19. Or, "inactive, unproductive, idle". Literally, "not-working", a play on words. Same root word as "works". This word is also used of land "lying fallow"; of men "unemployed, idle". Same word as in Mt 12:36; 2 Pet 1:8. Elsewhere only as "idle" in Mt 20:3, 6; 1 Tim 5:13; and "lazy" in Tit 1:12. GK *734*. Some manuscripts say "dead" {B}.
20. James means "faith with works", the subject under discussion. We are saved "not of works" (Eph 2:9), but "for good works" (Eph 2:10). James is dwelling on the works side of it whereas Paul focuses on the faith side. God declared Abraham righteous by faith in Gen 15:6, and Paul emphasizes this point in Rom 4:1-5. James is referring to Abraham's faith as "perfected" or "completed" (v 22) by his works in the offering of Isaac in Gen 22. For James, Abraham's actions in Gen 22 demonstrate that the faith he had in Gen 15 was genuine, saving faith.
21. The grammar expects a "yes" answer.
22. Or, "notice". The "you" refers to the empty person. Or, this may be a statement, "You see...". On this word, see Rev 1:11.
23. Or, "completed, brought to its goal, fulfilled". Related to "complete" in 1:4. On this word, see Heb 2:10. Living faith reaches its living completion in the corresponding actions flowing from it like fruit from the vine. Dead faith, faith alone, is not "fulfilled" by corresponding actions flowing from it, Rev 3:2.
24. When God declared Abraham righteous by faith in Gen 15:6, it was a prediction of Abraham's future behavior. His future works in Gen 22 were contained in his faith in Gen 15. His faith "continued", becoming a "doer of work", 1:25.
25. "You" here is plural. James turns from addressing the empty person in v 22, to addressing us all, as he applies the case of Abraham.
26. Or, "perceive". Or, this may be a statement, "You see...". On this word, see Lk 2:26. Not related to the word in v 22. Some manuscripts begin this sentence with "So-indeed" {N}, using the word found in 1 Cor 9:26.
27. Or, "only". "Faith alone" is the faith of "hearers only" and of demons. It is defective faith, dead faith. "Faith with works" for James (that is, living faith with works after salvation) is equivalent to "faith" for Paul (examine the notes on Rom 2:7 and Tit 2:14 to see his emphasis on "good works"). Just as the vine bears its fruit, so living faith bears works. Works are not added on to living faith any more than apples are added on to trees. The life within flows out by nature. "Faith apart from works of the Law" for Paul (that is, faith apart from works done before salvation to earn salvation) is a subject not addressed by James. Same word as "only" in 1:22. Used 114 times as GK *3667, 3668*.
28. That is, "received into her house". On this word, see Lk 10:38.
29. Or, "breath". GK *4460*.

A. 1 Cor 15:32 B. Act 16:40 C. Eph 2:8 D. Lk 19:10 E. Jam 1:5 F. Mt 24:45 G. Mt 8:22 H. 1 Tim 6:15 J. Jn 3:36 K. 1 Cor 10:20 L. Mt 4:4, mankind M. Rom 3:24 N. Heb 9:28, bear O. Rom 8:28, working together P. Eph 5:18, filled Q. Rom 4:3 R. Rom 8:30 S. Lk 14:10 T. 1 Cor 6:15 U. 1 Tim 3:16 V. Jn 12:31, cast out W. 1 Cor 12:9

5A. Do not become¹ many² teachers³, my brothers⁴, knowing that we⁵ will receive *a* greater judgment⁶. 3:1
For we all⁷ stumble many⁸ *ways* 2

   1B. If one does not stumble⁹ in speech^A, this *one is a* perfect¹⁰ man, able to bridle¹¹ also the whole body¹²

      1C. Now if¹³ we put bridles¹⁴ into the mouths *of* horses so-that¹⁵ they obey^B us, we also guide their whole body. °Behold also ships being so large and being driven^C by hard^D winds— they are guided by *a* very small rudder^E where the impulse^F *of* the *one* steering wants^G 3 4

         1D. So also the tongue is *a* small body-part^H, and boastfully-declares¹⁶ great *things* 5

      2C. Behold how-small *a* fire kindles^J how-great¹⁷ *a* forest

         1D. And the tongue *is a* fire¹⁸ 6

   2B. The¹⁹ tongue^K is made²⁰ the world²¹ *of* unrighteousness^L among our body-parts^H— the *thing* staining^M the whole body, and setting-on-fire²² the course²³ *of our* existence²⁴, and being set-on-fire by Gehenna²⁵

      1C. For every nature *of* both wild-animals^N and birds, *of* both reptiles and sea-creatures, is tamed^O, and has been tamed *by* the human^P nature²⁶ 7

      2C. But none *of* mankind²⁷ is able to tame the tongue— *a* restless²⁸ evil^Q, full^R *of* death-bringing poison 8

      3C. With it we bless^S the Lord²⁹ and Father, and with it we curse^T the people^U having been made in accordance with *the* likeness *of* God— °*a* blessing^V and *a* curse^W come out of the same mouth 9 10

   3B. My brothers, these *things* ought³⁰ not to be so. °The spring^X does not gush out of the same opening the sweet and the bitter, *does it*?³¹ °*A* fig tree is not able, my brothers, to make^Y olives, or *a* grapevine figs, *is it*? Neither³² *is* salty water *able* to make^Y sweet³³ *water* 11 12

   4B. Who³⁴ *is* wise and knowledgeable³⁵ among you?³⁶ Let him show^Z from *his* good^AA conduct^BB his works^CC *done* in *the* gentleness³⁷ *of* wisdom³⁸ 13

1. Or, "be". The grammar may mean "Stop becoming, Stop being", or, "Do not engage in the process of becoming". Same word and grammar as in 1 Cor 14:20, "Do not be children"; Rom 12:16, "Do not be wise"; 1 Cor 7:23, "Do not become slaves"; Eph 5:17, "Do not be foolish", etc.; and as Jam 1:22, "Be doers". GK *1181*.
2. Some take this with the command, "Do not many *of you* become teachers", that is, not many of you should become teachers; others, with the noun, "Do not become many teachers", that is, a multitude of teachers.
3. Some think James means official church teachers; others, unofficial teachers in a broad sense. Compare Act 15:24; Rom 2:19-20; 1 Tim 1:6-7; Tit 1:11; and 1 Cor 14:1; Heb 5:12.
4. These words on speech are directed to "my brothers", to everyone. James exhorts his readers to think twice about becoming teachers because of the serious effects of the tongue. In what follows, he details the power of the uncontrolled tongue, and exhorts those causing divisions and arguments based on self-interest and earthly wisdom. Spiritually unqualified teachers, or even unbelieving teachers, were certainly one source of this. On this word, see Act 16:40.
5. That is, we teachers.
6. This is because teachers have greater knowledge, Lk 12:47, 48. To whom much is given, much is required.
7. That is, all of us, including the teachers.
8. Or, "many *times*, often, greatly". On this word, see Mt 13:52.
9. This is another word pair. On this word, see 2 Pet 1:10.
10. Same word as "complete" in 1:4.
11. This word means "to lead or guide as with a bridle, to restrain, to hold in check". It means "to bridle" in the sense of "to control". Elsewhere only in 1:26. GK *5902*. It is made of two words, "bit or bridle" (the word in v 3) and "to lead".
12. This is because to do so, one would have to have control of his heart, for the mouth speaks what is in the heart, Mt 12:34; 15:18.
13. Instead of "Now if", some manuscripts say "Look, we put" {C}.
14. This word can mean "bit" or "bridle", but James seems to have the whole bridle in view here, including the reins. The bit goes into the mouth of the horse, and the rider "guides" the horse with the reins. Another word pair. Elsewhere only in Rev 14:20. GK *5903*.
15. Or, "that they *might* obey us".
16. This word, "to declare boastfully, to boast, loudly declare" is used only here. GK *902*. The small part— the bridle, rudder, tongue— has a great effect on the whole horse, ship, body.
17. Literally, "what-sized fire kindles what-sized forest". The same word is used twice, another word pair. It means "how great" or "how small" depending on the context. Elsewhere only in Col 2:1. GK *2462*.
18. The tongue causes negative effects on us and on those around us all out of proportion to its size, or our intentions.
19. Others punctuate this, "fire, the world *of* unrighteousness. The tongue is set among our body parts *as the thing* staining...". Some manuscripts say "So the tongue..." {N}.
20. Or, "constituted, set". It is made such by sin in our hearts, Mt 15:19. Or, "makes *itself*, renders *itself*". This word with this grammar is elsewhere only in Jam 4:4, ("makes *himself*") and Rom 5:19 (twice). On this word, see "put in charge" in Act 6:3.
21. That is, the sphere in which unrighteousness works; or, a world characterized by unrighteousness, an unrighteous world.
22. Used only in this verse. GK *5824*. Related to "flaming" in 2 Thes 1:8.
23. Used only here. GK *5580*. Used of a running course. The root word is "run". Or it may be a different word meaning "wheel, circle".
24. Or, "birth, origin". Elsewhere only as "birth" in 1:23; Mt 1:18; Lk 1:14; and "genealogy" in Mt 1:1. GK *1161*. That is, the course of our lives from birth to death.
25. Or, "hell". On this word, see Mt 5:22. Used only here outside the Gospels.
26. Same word as earlier in the verse. In both cases, James may mean it in the sense of "natural disposition", or in the sense of "kind, species". On this word, see Eph 2:3.
27. On this phrase, see Mk 11:2.
28. Or, "unstable". Elsewhere only as "unstable" in 1:8. GK *190*. Related to "disorder" in 3:16. Some manuscripts say "unruly" {B}, that is, uncontrollable.
29. Some manuscripts say "God" {A}.
30. Or, "must". Our tongue ought not to be the world of unrighteousness in our life, setting on fire our course of life, giving forth blessings and cursings from the same opening. It is true for mankind in general, but not for those born from above, speaking the wisdom from above, led by the Spirit. Control of the tongue is a characteristic of the doer of the word, 1:26. Used only here. GK *5973*.
31. The grammar expects a "no" answer to this question and the next. The tree is known by its fruit. The fruit reveals the heart.
32. Some manuscripts say "Thus no spring *is able* to make salty water and sweet *water*" {B}.
33. Elsewhere only in v 11; Rev 10:9, 10. GK *1184*.
34. Now James applies this to ones causing problems among his readers. What follows applies to teachers, but is written broadly so as to also include their hearers and followers, those influenced by the teachers, who reflect the same kind of negative behavior. Because of the breadth of the application that develops, some begin a new A. point here; others at 4:1; others, at 4:4.
35. Or, "expert, well-instructed, skilled, learned, acquainted with a thing". Used only here. GK *2184*. Related to "know-about" in Act 18:25; and "master" in Lk 5:5.
36. Who claims the wisdom and knowledge to become a teacher, or to be one? It is ones claiming to have knowledge and using it to direct or correct others who are causing the problems among them. James now begins to examine their fruit. What does that which comes from you say about the source of your wisdom? God is not producing the jealousy and disorder (3:14-16), or the fights and quarrels (4:1-3). These come from you, from your own worldly self-interests (4:1-5). You need to submit to God, cleanse yourselves, humble yourselves, 4:7. Note the change of tone. James does not call them "brothers", but "adulterous ones, sinners". He calls them to repent.
37. Same word as in 1:21.
38. Wise teachers are not seen in their claims, boasts or knowledge, but in their own actions and in the actions they produce in their listeners. A tree is known by its fruit. The fruit reveals the source of the wisdom.

A. 1 Cor 12:8 B. 1 Jn 3:19, persuade C. Lk 8:29 D. Jn 6:60 E. Act 27:40 F. Act 14:5, attempt G. Jam 1:18, willed H. Col 3:5 J. Lk 12:49 K. 1 Cor 12:10 L. Rom 1:18 M. Jude 23 N. Rev 13:1, beast O. Mk 5:4, subdue P. 1 Cor 10:13, common to humanity Q. 3 Jn 11 R. Rom 15:14 S. Lk 6:28 T. Rom 12:14 U. Mt 4:4, mankind V. 2 Cor 9:5 W. Gal 3:10 X. Jn 4:6 Y. Rev 13:13, does Z. 1 Tim 6:15 AA. 1 Tim 5:10a BB. 1 Pet 1:15 CC. Mt 26:10

1C.	But if you have bitter jealousy[A] and selfish-interest[1] in your heart[2], do not be vaunting[3] and lying[B] against the truth[C]	14
	1D. This wisdom[D] is not coming down from-above[E], but *is* earthly[F], natural[G], demonic	15
	1E. For where jealousy and selfish-interest *are,* in-that-place[4] *there is* disorder[5] and every bad[6] thing[7]	16
	2D. But the wisdom from-above[E] is first pure[H], then peaceful[J], kind[K], yielding[8], full[L] *of* mercy[M] and good[N] fruits[O], impartial[9], sincere[10]	17
	1E. And *the* fruit[O] *of* righteousness[11] is sown[P] in peace[Q] by[12] the *ones* making[R] peace[Q]	18
2C.	From-what-source[13] *are* fights[14] and from-what-source[15] *are* battles[16] among you? *Are they* not from-here[S]— from your pleasures[17] waging-war[18] in your body-parts[19]?	4:1
	1D. You desire[T] and do not have— you murder[20]	2
	2D. And you are jealous[21] and are not able to obtain[U]— you battle[V] and fight[W]	
	3D. You[22] do not have because of your not asking[X]	
	4D. You ask and do not receive because you ask badly[23], in order that you may spend[Y] *it* in connection with your pleasures[Z]	3
3C.	Adulterous[24] *ones*, do you not know that friendship *with* the world[AA] is hostility[BB] *toward* God? Therefore, whoever wants[CC] to be *a* friend[DD] *of* the world makes-*himself*[25] *an* enemy[26] *of* God	4
	1D. Or do you think that the Scripture speaks[27] vainly[28]?	5
	2D. He yearns[EE] jealously[29] for[30] the spirit[31] which He made-to-dwell[32] in us!	
4C.	But He gives greater grace. Therefore it says [in Prov 3:34], "God opposes[FF] *the* arrogant[33], but gives grace *to the* humble[34]"	6
	1D. Therefore, submit[GG] *to* God, but[35] resist[HH] the devil and he will flee[JJ] from you	7
	2D. Draw-near[KK] *to* God, and He will draw-near *to* you	8
	3D. Cleanse[LL] your hands, sinners, and purify[MM] your hearts, double-minded[36] *ones*	
	4D. Be miserable[37] and mourn[38] and weep[39]. Let your laughter be turned into mourning[40], and *your* joy into dejection[41]	9
	5D. Humble-*yourselves*[42] in the presence of *the* Lord, and He will exalt[NN] you	10
5B.	Do[43] not be speaking-against[OO] one another, brothers. The *one* speaking-against *a* brother or[44] judging his brother is speaking-against *the* Law[45] and judging[46] *the* Law	11
	1C. But if you are judging *the* Law, you are not *a* doer[PP] *of the* Law, but *a* judge	
	2C. There is one Lawgiver and Judge[47]— the *One* being able to save[QQ] and to destroy[48]	12
	3C. But[49] who are **you**, the *one* judging *your* neighbor[50]?	
6A.	Come now, the *ones* saying "Today or tomorrow we will travel to such-and-such city, and we will do[R] *a* year there, and we will do-business[RR] and make-a-gain[SS]"—	13

1. Or, "selfish ambition, party spirit". Elsewhere only in 3:16; Rom 2:8; 2 Cor 12:20; Gal 5:20; Phil 1:17; 2:3. GK *2249*.
2. Your heart is known by what it produces. These things produce disorder and worthless things, v 16. Some manuscripts have this word plural {N}.
3. That is, in your abilities as a teacher, claiming to be "wise and knowledgeable". Same word as in 2:13.
4. Same word as "there" in 2:3; 4:13. On this word, see Rom 9:26.
5. Or, "unsteadiness, disturbance, instability". Same word as in 1 Cor 14:33; 2 Cor 12:20. Elsewhere only as "disturbance" in Lk 21:9; 2 Cor 6:5. GK *189*. Used of a lack of order, confusion; and a breech of order, disturbance.
6. Or, "worthless, evil". Elsewhere only in Jn 3:20; 5:29; Rom 9:11; 2 Cor 5:10; Tit 2:8. GK *5765*.
7. Or, "matter". On this word, see "matter" in Mt 18:19.
8. Or, "compliant, obedient, ready to obey, reasonable". Used only here. GK *2340*.
9. Or, "not making distinctions, not divisive, non-judgmental", or "unhesitating, unwavering, undivided". Used only here. GK *88*. Related to "doubt" in 1:6.
10. Or, "genuine, without hypocrisy". On this word, see Rom 12:9. Some manuscripts say "and sincere" {N}.
11. That is, the fruit consisting of righteousness, or produced by righteousness. James may mean the "fruit" in our life consisting of righteousness is sown as a seed in the lives of others in peace, not quarreling, and in connection with our desire to bring about peace in their lives. Or, he may mean the "harvest of fruit" in others produced by righteousness from above in them is sown in peace by ones seeking to bring peace. On this word, see Rom 1:17.
12. Or, "*for*".
13. That is, are they "from above", or from some other source?
14. Or, "wars, conflicts". On this word, see "war" in Rev 12:7. The related verb is in v 2.
15. Some manuscripts omit "from what source" {N}. GK *4470*.
16. On this word, see 2 Tim 2:23. The related verb is in v 2.
17. Same word as in v 3. On this word, see Lk 8:14.
18. Or, "serving as soldiers". On this word, see "fight" in 1 Tim 1:18.
19. Same word as in 3:5, 6. On this word, see Col 3:5. The grammar indicates a "yes" answer is expected.
20. In this context, the battles, fights and murder seem to be primarily verbal, not physical (although these words are true even of the physical). If so, this may refer to "character assassination" to achieve some end one desires. Used elsewhere 11 times of physical murder, as in the sixth commandment, Jam 2:11. GK *5839*. Related to "murder" in Act 9:1, and "murderer" in Act 7:52.
21. Or, "you envy". Some combine this with "murder", grouping the phrases "you desire and do not have. You murder and envy and cannot obtain. You battle and fight". On this word, see 2 Cor 11:2.
22. Some manuscripts say "And you"; others, "But you" {N}.
23. Or, "wrongly", with evil motives or purposes. GK *2809*.
24. Or, "Adulteresses". James is referring to spiritual adultery, as Jesus did using this same word as in Mt 12:39; 16:4; Mk 8:38. Elsewhere only as "adulteress" in Rom 7:3; 2 Pet 2:14. GK *3655*. Some manuscripts say "Adulterers and adulteresses" {A}.
25. Same word as "is made" in 3:6.
26. Same root word as "hostility". This is another word pair.
27. Some think this means that what follows is a quotation from the OT. If so, it is not known to us, or it is a loose paraphrase of the sense of Scripture. Others think it refers to the quote in v 6. Others do not think it introduces a quotation, but simply means "Does Scripture speak vainly about spiritual adultery and God's response to it?"
28. Or, "to no purpose, in an empty manner". Used only here. GK *3036*. Related to "empty" in 2:20.
29. And God will respond accordingly to your spiritual adultery. This is an idiom, more literally, "to jealousy", "in accordance with jealousy". On this word, see "envy" in Mk 15:10.
30. On this word, "yearn for", see 1 Pet 2:2.
31. Or, "Spirit". Others render this sentence, "The Spirit which He caused-to-dwell in us yearns jealously for *us*" (grammatically, "spirit" can be the subject or the object of "yearn for"). In either case, God is yearning for us. Others render it, "The spirit which He caused-to-dwell in us yearns enviously". In this case, James is referring to the human yearning for evil, or for its own selfish desires.
32. Or, "caused to dwell". Used only here. GK *3001*. Some manuscripts say "which dwelt in us" {B}, meaning "which made His dwelling is us".
33. Or, "proud, haughty". Elsewhere only in Lk 1:51; Rom 1:30; 2 Tim 3:2; 1 Pet 5:5. GK *5662*. Related to "arrogance" in Mk 7:22.
34. On this word, see "lowly" in 1:9. The related verb is in 4:10.
35. Some manuscripts omit this word {N}.
36. Same word as in 1:8.
37. Or, "Lament". Used only here. GK *5415*. Related to "miseries" in 5:1; and "wretched" in Rom 7:24.
38. Same word as in Mt 5:4; Lk 6:25. Elsewhere only in Mt 9:15; Mk 16:10; 1 Cor 5:2; 2 Cor 12:21; Rev 18:11, 15, 19. GK *4291*.
39. Jesus said, Blessed are those who "mourn" (Mt 5:4), or "weep" (Lk 6:21, 25), using these same two words. On this word, see Jn 11:33.
40. Related to the verb earlier. Elsewhere only in Rev 18:7, 8; 21:4. GK *4292*.
41. Or, "gloominess, depression", a casting of the eyes downward. Used only here. GK *2993*.
42. Or, "Be humbled". On this word, see Phil 4:12.
43. Rather than concluding the section on speech with an application to the "brothers" (versus the adulterous ones who need to repent), others make this point 6A.
44. Some manuscripts say "and" {N}.
45. That is, because the Law says to love your neighbor, to which James alludes in v 12. It forbids slander. In speaking against a brother, you are contradicting the Law.
46. That is, administering it as a judge, passing judgment by means of the Law, judging with respect to the Law. Same word as earlier, but used in a different sense. On this word, see Mt 7:1.
47. Some manuscripts omit "and Judge" {N}.
48. Compare Mt 10:28. On this word, see "perish" in 1 Cor 1:18.
49. Some manuscripts omit this word {N}.
50. On this word see Act 7:27. Some manuscripts say "the other" {N}.

A. 2 Cor 11:2 B. Act 5:3, lie to C. Jn 4:23 D. 1 Cor 12:8 E. Jn 3:3, again F. Phil 2:10 G. 1 Cor 2:14 H. 1 Pet 3:2 J. Heb 12:11 K. Phil 4:5, kindness L. Rom 15:14 M. Mt 9:13 N. 1 Tim 5:10b O. Mt 7:16 P. 2 Cor 9:6 Q. Act 15:33 R. Rev 13:13, does S. Rev 22:2, on this side T. Gal 5:17 U. Heb 11:33 V. 2 Tim 2:24 W. Rev 2:16 X. 1 Jn 5:14, request Y. Act 21:24 Z. Lk 8:14 AA. 1 Jn 2:15 BB. Eph 2:14 CC. Jam 1:18, willed DD. Lk 14:10 EE. 1 Pet 2:2 FF. Rom 13:2 GG. Eph 5:21, be subject HH. Eph 6:13 JJ. 1 Cor 6:18 KK. Lk 21:28 LL. Heb 9:22 MM. 1 Jn 3:3 NN. Jn 8:28, lifted up OO. 1 Pet 3:16 PP. Rom 2:13 QQ. Lk 19:10 RR. 2 Pet 2:3, exploit SS. Mk 8:36, gain

	1B. Who do not know^A the^1 *thing of* tomorrow! What^2 *is* your life^B? For you^3 are *a* vapor appearing^C for *a* little *while,* then indeed disappearing^D	14
	2B. Instead^4 of you saying, "If the Lord wills^E, we indeed^5 will live, and we will do this or that"	15
	3B. But as-it-is^6, you are boasting^F in your pretensions^7. All such boasting^G is evil^H	16
	4B. Therefore, *to one* knowing^J to be doing good^8 and not doing *it, to* him it is *a* sin	17
7A.	Come now, rich^K ones, weep^L while wailing over your miseries coming-upon^M *you*	5:1
	1B. Your riches^N have rotted and your garments^O have become moth-eaten. ˙Your gold and silver have become corroded^9. And their corrosion will be for *a* testimony^10 against you, and will eat^P your flesh^Q like fire. You stored-up^11 in *the* last days!	2-3
	2B. Behold— the wages^R *of* the workers having mowed your fields, the *wages* having been fraudulently-withheld^12 by you, cry-out^S. And the outcries^13 *of* the *ones* having reaped have entered into the ears *of the* Lord *of* Sabaoth^14	4
	3B. You lived-in-luxury^15 upon the earth, and you lived-indulgently^16. You fattened^T your hearts in^17 *a* day *of* slaughter^U	5
	4B. You condemned^V, you murdered^W the righteous^18. He does not oppose^19 you!	6
8A.	Therefore^20 be patient^21, brothers^X, until the coming^Y *of the* Lord	7
	1B. Behold— the farmer^Z waits-for^AA the precious^BB fruit^CC *of the* land, being-patient with it until it receives *the* early and late rain^22. ˙**You** also be-patient. Establish^DD your hearts, because the coming^Y *of the* Lord has drawn-near^EE	8
	2B. Do not be groaning^23 against one another, brothers, in order that you may not be judged^24. Behold— the Judge stands in front of the doors	9
	3B. Take *as an* example^FF *of* suffering-hardship^25 and patience^GG, brothers^26, the prophets who spoke in the name *of the* Lord. ˙Behold— we consider-blessed^HH the *ones* having endured^27	10 11
	1C. You heard *of* the endurance^JJ *of* Job, and you saw the outcome^28 *from the* Lord— that the Lord is large-hearted^29 and compassionate^30	
	4B. And^31 above all^32, my brothers, do not be swearing^33— neither *by* heaven nor *by* earth nor *by* any other oath^34. But let your yes be yes and *your* no *be* no, in order that you may not fall under judgment^KK	12
	5B. Is anyone among you suffering-hardship^35? Let him be praying^LL	13
	6B. Is anyone cheerful^MM? Let him be singing-praise^NN	
	7B. Is anyone among you sick^OO? Let him summon^PP the elders^QQ *of the* church, and let them pray^LL over him, having anointed^36 him^37 *with* oil^38 in the name *of the* Lord	14
	1C. And the prayer^RR *of* faith^39 will restore^40 the *one* being ill^41, and the Lord will raise^SS him	15
	2C. And if he has committed^42 sins,^43 it^44 will be forgiven^TT him	

1. That is, what will happen tomorrow. Some manuscripts omit this word {B}, so that it says, "Who do not know *of* tomorrow what your life *will be*. For...".
2. On this word, see "what kind of " in Mt 21:23. Some manuscripts say "For what..." {B}.
3. Some manuscripts omit "For". Others say "it is" instead of "you are" {C}.
4. The flow is "Come now the ones saying... instead of you saying...".
5. Or, "both".
6. Or, "But now", in a logical sense. On this idiom, see 1 Cor 5:11.
7. Or, "prideful boastings". Same word as "boastful-pride" in 1 Jn 2:16. Not related to "boasting" earlier.
8. This is a general rule, in this context referring to being humble before the Lord and seeking His will in a matter, and not boasting in our arrogant pretensions. On this word, see 1 Tim 5:10a.
9. Or, "tarnished". Used only here. GK *2995*. Related to "corrosion" next (GK *2675*), another word pair.
10. Or, "evidence, proof ". On "for *a* testimony", see Mk 1:44.
11. Or, "treasured up". This is the verb related to "treasure". But it is not the treasure the rich thought they were storing up! James could mean they stored up "treasure", or "wrath", or "witnesses" or "miseries". On this word, see 1 Cor 16:2.
12. On this word, see "defrauded" in 1 Cor 6:7. Some manuscripts say "withheld" {A}.
13. Used only here. GK *1068*. The related verb is in Lk 18:7, where God brings about justice for His elect who "cry out" to Him. Compare Deut 24:14-15. Not related to "cry out" earlier.
14. This is a Hebrew word transliterated into Greek. It means "hosts" or "armies". Elsewhere only in Rom 9:29. GK *4877*.
15. Used only here. GK *5587*. Related to "luxury" in Lk 7:25; and "reveling" in 2 Pet 2:13.
16. Or, "lived for pleasure". On this word, see 1Tim 5:6.
17. Or, "in connection with", referring to the Second Coming. Some manuscripts say "as in" {N}.
18. Or, "the righteous *one*". James probably means "the righteous" in a collective sense, as a class. It is God's righteous ones, including the laborers just mentioned. Some think James is referring to Jesus in particular, "the righteous *One*".
19. Or, "resist". Same word as in 4:6. On this word, see Rom 13:2.
20. Beyond being a concluding series of short exhortations, some group 5:7-20 in various ways. Here, they are grouped as the final exhortations to those awaiting His coming. Consult the commentaries for other suggestions.
21. Or, "wait patiently". Same word as in v 7, 8. On this word, see 1 Cor 13:4. Related to "patience" in v 10.
22. Some manuscripts include the word "rain" {B}. That is, the autumn and spring rains.
23. Or, "grumbling, complaining". Same word as in Rom 8:23; 2 Cor 5:2, 4; Heb 13:17. Elsewhere only as "sigh" in Mk 7:34. GK *5100*. Related to "groaning" in Rom 8:26.
24. On this word, see Mt 7:1. Some manuscripts say "condemned" {K}.
25. This noun, "suffering hardship", is used only here. GK *2801*. The related verb is in v 13.
26. Some manuscripts say "my brothers" {N}.
27. Same word as in 1:12. Heb 11 details many of these people, with the same lesson.
28. Or, "end, result, conclusion". On this word, see "end" in Rom 10:4.
29. Or, "very affectionate, very merciful, very sympathetic". Used only here. GK *4499*. Made of two words, "large, great" and "deep feelings" (see Phil 1:8).
30. Elsewhere only in Lk 6:36. GK *3881*. Related to "compassions" in Rom 12:1.
31. Or, "But, Now".
32. Same phrase as in 1 Pet 4:8. Some think James means "especially"; others, "before everything *else*", do this first; others, that he says this because he is repeating what the Lord Himself said.
33. That is, swearing an oath to guarantee your word, such as "I swear by heaven I will do this". Some think oaths in everyday conversation are in view. Compare the Lord's words in Mt 5:34-37. To understand the scope of this command, other verses must be considered alongside it. For example, note Heb 6:16. God swore in Heb 6:13. The angel swore in Rev 10:6. Paul swore, 1 Cor 15:31; 2 Cor 1:23; Gal 1:20; and called God as a witness, Phil 1:8. Jesus was put under oath in Mt 26:63, and Paul put his readers under oath in 1 Thes 5:27. Same word as in Mt 23:20, 21, 22; Lk 1:73; Act 2:30; Heb 3:11, 18; 4:3; 6:13, 16; 7:21; Rev 10:6. Elsewhere only as "swear-with-an-oath" in Mt 5:34, 36; 26:74; Mk 6:23; 14:71; and "swear-an-oath" in Mt 23:16, 18. GK *3923*.
34. Elsewhere only in Mt 5:33; 14:7, 9; 26:72; Mk 6:26; Heb 6:16; and of God in Lk 1:73; Act 2:30; Heb 6:17. GK *3992*. Related to "oath-swearing" in Heb 7:20; and "adjure" in 1 Thes 5:27.
35. Or, "suffering misfortune, bearing hardship". Elsewhere only in 2 Tim 2:9; 4:5. GK *2802*. Related to the word in v 10; and the word in 2 Tim 1:8.
36. Or, "rubbed, smeared". Elsewhere only of the sick in Mk 6:13; of the head while fasting in Mt 6:17; of the feet of Jesus in Lk 7:38, 46; Jn 11:2; 12:3; and of the dead body of Jesus in Mk 16:1. GK *230*. Some see this as medicinal here, as in Lk 10:34, which uses a different verb. Others see it as symbolic of the Spirit, as perhaps in Mk 6:13. There are other views.
37. Some manuscripts omit this word {C}.
38. Or, "olive oil". Same word as in Mk 6:13; Lk 10:34. Used 11 times. GK *1778*. Related to "olives" in 3:12.
39. That is, the prayer characterized by faith, or proceeding from faith. Compare 1:6.
40. This word normally means "save" in a spiritual sense, as in 1:21; 2:14; 4:12. It is used with the sense of "save from disease, make well, restore, heal" only in Mt 9:21, 22; Mk 5:23, 28, 34; 6:56; 10:52; Lk 8:36, 48, 50; 17:19; 18:42; Jn 11:12; Act 4:9; 14:9. On this word, see "save" in Lk 19:10.
41. Or, "weary, sick". Elsewhere only as "weary" in Heb 12:3. GK *2827*. This is a different word than 5:14.
42. This is a participle, if he "is having committed". That is, if he is in a state of having committed sins, causing his sickness.
43. Some sickness is caused by sin, Jn 5:14; 1 Cor 11:30.
44. That is, this committing of sins.

A. Act 18:25, know about B. Rom 8:10 C. Phil 2:15, shine D. Mt 6:16, disfigure E. Jn 7:17, willing F. 2 Cor 11:16 G. 2 Cor 7:4 H. Act 25:18 J. 1 Jn 2:29 K. 1 Tim 6:17 L. Jn 11:33 M. Lk 21:26 N. 1 Tim 6:17 O. 1 Pet 3:3 P. Act 10:13 Q. Col 2:23 R. Rev 22:12, recompense S. Mt 8:29 T. Lk 23:29, feed U. Act 8:32 V. Lk 6:37 W. Jam 4:2 X. Act 16:40 Y. 2 Thes 2:8 Z. Jn 15:1 AA. Heb 11:10 BB. 2 Pet 1:4 CC. Mt 7:16 DD. 1 Thes 3:2 EE. Lk 21:28 FF. Jn 13:15 GG. Heb 6:12 HH. Lk 1:48 JJ. Jam 1:3 KK. Jn 3:19 LL. 1 Tim 2:8 MM. Act 27:22, cheer up NN. Eph 5:19, make melody OO. 2 Tim 4:20 PP. Act 2:39, call to QQ. 1 Tim 5:17 RR. Act 18:18, vow SS. Mt 28:6, arose TT. Mt 6:12

3C. Therefore[1] be confessing-out[2] *your* sins *to* one another, and be praying[A] for one another so that you may be healed[B]   16

4C. *A* prayer[3] *of a* righteous[C] *person* can-do[4] much while working[5]

   1D. Elijah was *a* person[D] of-like-nature[6] *to* us, and he prayed[E] *with* prayer[7] *that it* not rain. And it did not rain upon the land *for* three years and six months   17
   2D. And he prayed[E] again, and the heaven[F] gave rain, and the earth produced[G] its fruit[H]   18

8B. My[8] brothers[J], if anyone among you errs[9] from the truth[K] and someone turns him back[10], *let him[11] know[L] that the *one* having turned-back *a* sinner[M] from *the* error[12] *of* his way will save[N] his[13] soul[14] from death, and will cover[O] *a* multitude[P] *of* sins   19-20

1. Some manuscripts omit this word {N}. That is, because of the link between sin and sickness.
2. Or, "acknowledging openly, admitting". This is the word "confess" (see 1 Tim 6:12) with the prefix "out" added. Same word as in Mt 3:6; Mk 1:5; Act 19:18; Rom 14:11; Phil 2:11. It also means "acknowledge" in the positive sense of "praise" in Mt 11:25; Lk 10:21; Rom 15:9. Elsewhere only as "consent" in Lk 22:6. GK 2018.
3. Or, "petition, prayer request". Note 1 Pet 3:12. On this word, see "petition" in 1 Tim 2:1.
4. Same word as in Phil 4:13, "I can do all things".
5. Or, "at work". This word modifies "prayer", and comes last in the sentence, as seen in this rendering. Some think James means "[in its] working, operating". That is, in the result the prayer produces while it is working, such as stopping the rain. Others think he means "while [it is] working, while at work" (that is, while the prayer is being answered by God, which for Elijah extended for three and one half years); others, "while being worked, put in operation [by the one praying]" (that is, while the person is praying); others, "while being worked, energized [by the Spirit]" (that is, while the Spirit is energizing the prayer, working it in him); others, "the working prayer, the effective prayer" (that is, the prayer that works, the prayer that God answers). In any case, it does not mean "the strong prayer, the earnest prayer", as if its working was dependent on how strongly the person prays. On this word, see "works" in 1 Cor 12:11.
6. Elsewhere only in Act 14:15. GK *3926*.
7. The idiom "prayed with prayer" is a Hebrew way of speaking, meaning "He prayed earnestly". On this word, see 1 Tim 2:1.
8. Some manuscripts omit this word {N}.
9. Or, "wanders, goes astray, is led astray". Same word as "deceive" in Gal 6:7; 2 Tim 3:13; 1 Jn 1:8; "mislead" in Rev 2:20; "go astray" in Heb 3:10; 1 Pet 2:25; "wander" in Heb 11:38; "be mistaken" in Mk 12:24, 27. Used 39 times. GK *4414*. Related to "error" in v 20 (another word pair), and rendered this way to reflect this.
10. This verb "turn back" is also in v 20. It means "to turn" in Act 9:35, 40; 15:19; 1 Thes 1:9; "turn back" in Lk 1:16, 17; 22:32; Gal 4:9; "turn around" in Mk 5:30; 8:33; Jn 21:20; and "return" in Lk 17:4; Act 15:36; 1 Pet 2:25; 2 Pet 2:22. Used 36 times. GK *2188*. Related to "conversion" in Act 15:3.
11. That is, the one who turns him back. Some manuscripts say "you know that" {B}.
12. Or, "wandering". On this word see 1 Thes 2:3.
13. That is, the wandering sinner's soul (or life). Some manuscripts say "will save *a* soul from death itself"; others, "will save *a* soul from death" {C}.
14. Or, "life". Compare 1 Cor 11:30. This word sometimes has the sense of "person". Same word as in Mt 10:28; 11:29; 12:18; 26:38; Mk 12:30; Lk 2:35; Act 2:27; 41, 43; 7:14; 27:37; Rom 2:9; 1 Cor 15:45; Col 3:23; 1 Thes 5:23; Heb 4:12; 13:17; 1 Pet 1:9; 2:11; Rev 6:9; 18:13, 20:4. Elsewhere as "life", as in Mt 2:20; 6:25; 10:39; 16:26; Mk 10:45; Lk 12:20; 14:26; Jn 10:15; 13:37; Act 15:26; 1 Thes 2:8; 1 Jn 3:16; Rev 12:11. Used 103 times. GK *6034*.

A. Rom 9:3 B. Mt 8:8 C. Rom 1:17 D. Mt 4:4, mankind E. 1 Tim 2:8 F. 2 Cor 12:2 G. Mt 13:26, budded H. Mt 7:16 J. Act 16:40 K. Jn 4:23 L. Lk 1:34 M. Mt 9:10 N. Lk 19:10 O. 1 Pet 4:8 P. Act 6:2

Overview	**1 Peter**

Introduction	1:1-2
1A. Blessed be God, the One having caused us to be born again according to His great mercy	1:3
1B. To a living hope through the resurrection of Jesus Christ from the dead	1:3
2B. To an undecayable, undefiled, unfading inheritance reserved in heaven for you	1:4-5
3B. In which you are rejoicing greatly, though right now having been grieved by various trials	1:6-12
2A. Therefore—	1:13
1B. Put your hope completely on the grace being brought to you at the revelation of Jesus Christ	1:13
2B. Be holy in all your conduct, just as He is holy	1:14-16
3B. Conduct the time of your stay with fear, knowing you were redeemed with His blood	1:17-21
4B. Love one another from a pure heart, having been born again through the living word of God	1:22-25
5B. Yearn like babies for the milk of the Word. Coming to the Living Stone, you are living stones being built as a spiritual house for a holy priesthood. You are a people to report His virtues	2:1-10
6B. Beloved, I exhort you as foreigners and pilgrims to be abstaining from fleshly desires	2:11-12
7B. Be subject to every human institution for the Lord's sake	2:13-15
8B. As free ones— honor everyone. Be loving the brotherhood, fearing God, honoring the king	2:16-17
1C. Servants, being subject to your masters. For you were called to suffer like Christ	2:18-25
2C. Likewise wives, being subject to your own husbands	3:1-6
3C. Husbands likewise, showing honor to the feminine one as to a fellow heir	3:7
4C. And finally, everyone— being likeminded, sympathetic, brother-loving, tenderhearted, humbleminded, not giving back evil for evil, but blessing them	3:8-12
3A. And who will do you evil for doing good? But though you might be suffering, you are blessed!	3:13-14
1B. But do not fear their fear, nor be disturbed, but set apart Christ as Lord in your hearts	3:14
1C. Being ready always for a defense to everyone asking a reason for the hope in you	3:15-16
2C. Having a good conscience in order that the ones maligning you may be put to shame	3:16-17
2B. Because Christ also suffered for sins, in order that He might bring you to God	3:18-22
3B. Therefore, Christ having suffered, you also arm yourselves with the same intention	4:1-7
4B. Therefore be sound-minded, sober in prayer, loving, hospitable, ministering your gift	4:7-11
5B. Beloved, do not think your fiery trials to be strange, but be rejoicing to share His sufferings!	4:12-18
6B. So then, let the ones suffering according to the will of God be entrusting their souls in good-doing to a faithful Creator	4:19
1C. Therefore I exhort the elders— Shepherd the flock of God among you by example	5:1-4
2C. Likewise, younger men—Be subject to the elders	5:5
3C. And everyone— Clothe yourselves with humblemindedness. Be sober. Resist the devil. And the God of all grace will restore and establish you. To Him be the dominion	5:5-11
Conclusion	5:12-14

A. Peter, *an* apostle[A] *of* Jesus Christ — 1
B. *To the* chosen[1] pilgrims[2] *of the* dispersion[3] *of* Pontus, Galatia, Cappadocia, Asia, and Bythinia[4]

    1. According-to[5] *the* foreknowledge[6] *of* God *the* Father — 2
    2. In[7] *the* sanctification[8] *of the* Spirit
    3. For[9] obedience[10], and *the* sprinkling[11] *of the* blood[B] *of* Jesus Christ

C. May grace[C] and peace be multiplied[D] *to* you

1A. Blessed[E] *be* the God and Father *of* our Lord Jesus Christ, the *One* having caused us to be born-again[12] — 3
according to His great mercy[F]

    1B. To *a* living hope[G] through[13] *the* resurrection[H] *of* Jesus Christ from *the* dead
    2B. To *an* undecayable[14] and undefiled[J] and unfading[15] inheritance[K] having been reserved[16] in *the* — 4
    heavens for you—

        1C. The *ones* being guarded[L] by *the* power *of* God through faith for[17] *a* salvation[M] ready[N] to be — 5
        revealed[O] in *the* last[P] time

    3B. In which[18] you are rejoicing-greatly[Q], [although] right-now *for a* little *while,* if it is necessary[19], having — 6
    been grieved[R] by various trials[S] *in order that the* genuineness[20] *of* your faith— *being* more-valuable[T] — 7
    than gold (*which is* perishing[U]), though being tested[21] by fire— may be found resulting-in praise[V] and
    glory[W] and honor[X] at *the* revelation[Y] *of* Jesus Christ

        1C. Whom not having seen[22], you are loving[Z] — 8
        2C. In Whom— [although] now not seeing *Him,* but believing[AA]— you are rejoicing-greatly[Q] *with*
        inexpressible[23] and glorified[24] joy *while receiving*[25] the outcome[26] *of* your faith, *the* salvation[M] — 9
        of your souls[BB]

            1D. Concerning which salvation prophets[27] sought-out[28] and searched-out[29]— the *ones* having — 10
            prophesied[CC] about the grace[C] for[30] you—

                1E. Searching[31] for what *person* or what manner of time[32] the Spirit *of* Christ in them was — 11
                indicating[DD], while predicting[33] the sufferings[EE] for Christ and the glories[W] after these
                2E. *To* whom it was revealed[O] that they were ministering[FF] them[34] not *for* themselves, — 12
                but *for* you[35]

                    1F. Which *things* now were declared[GG] *to* you through the *ones* having announced-
                    the-good-news-to[HH] you by[36] *the* Holy Spirit having been sent-forth[JJ] from heaven
                    2F. Into which *things* angels desire[KK] to look[LL]

2A. Therefore[37]— — 13

    1B. Having girded-up[38] the waist[39] *of* your minds[MM], being sober[40]— put-*your*-hope[41] completely[42] upon
    the grace[C] being brought *to* you at *the* revelation[Y] *of* Jesus Christ
    2B. As children[NN] *of* obedience,[43] not being conformed[44] *to* the former desires[OO] in-connection-with — 14
    your ignorance[PP], *but in accordance with the holy *One* having called[QQ] you— be holy yourselves — 15
    also in all *your* conduct[45]

        1C. Because[46] it has been written that[47] "You shall be holy, because **I** am holy[48]" [Lev 19:2] — 16

1. Same word as in 2:9. On this word, see Rom 8:33.
2. Or, "temporary residents, ones staying in a strange place, sojourners". Same word as in 2:11, where it is paired with "foreigner". Elsewhere only in Heb 11:13, where it is paired with "stranger". GK *4215*.
3. Elsewhere only in Jam 1:1 and Jn 7:35, referring to the dispersion of the Jews from Israel. Some take it in this sense here and think Peter is writing to Jewish Christians. Others think he is writing primarily to Gentile Christians (based on 1:14, 18; 2:10; 4:3-4; etc.) and means it in a general sense, emphasizing that they are pilgrims. Related to "dispersed" in Act 8:1, of the Christians dispersed as a result of the persecution in Jerusalem. GK *1402*.
4. These are all Roman provinces in what is now known as Turkey.
5. Or, "Based on, In accordance with, By way of". Same word as in v 3. GK *2848*.
6. Or, "advance knowledge, pre-determination". The Greek word is *prognosis*, from which our English word comes. Elsewhere only in Act 2:23. GK *4590*. Related to "foreknown" in v 20.
7. Or, "By, In the sphere of, In connection with". GK *1877*.
8. Or, "holiness, holy-making". On this word, see "holiness" in Heb 12:14.
9. Or, "Resulting in". We are chosen "for" obedience. It is the result that occurs because we are chosen, Eph 2:10. On this word, see "resulting in" in Rom 5:16. Same word as "resulting in" in v 7.
10. Same word as in v 14, 22. On this word, see Rom 16:26.
11. This term is from the Jewish sacrificial system. Elsewhere only in Heb 12:24. GK *4823*. Related to the verb in Heb 10:22.
12. Or, "having given us new birth, having regenerated us, having fathered us again". Elsewhere only in 1:23. GK *335*. The root word (without the prefix "again") is also used of God "fathering" us (see "born" in 1 Jn 2:29).
13. Some make "through... dead" point 2B., modifying "born again".
14. Or, "imperishable". On this word, see 1 Cor 15:52.
15. It will not wither and fade and waste away. Used only here. GK *278*. Related to the word in 5:4, and to "fade away" in Jam 1:11.
16. Or, "kept, protected, held". On this word, see 2 Pet 2:17.
17. Or, "until". GK *1650*.
18. Some think Peter is referring to all of v 3-5; others render it "In Whom", referring to the Father or the Son in v 3; others, "During which", referring to "last time" in v 5. It does not directly modify salvation, faith, inheritance, resurrection, or hope alone.
19. Not all Peter's readers were suffering. More literally, "if it is being necessary". Some manuscripts omit "it is" {C}, so that it says "if being necessary". Note the similar phrase in 3:17, which explains this phrase. On this word, see "must" in Mt 16:21.
20. That is, "genuineness" as proved by testing. On this word, see "testing" in Jam 1:3. Related to "tested" later in the verse. Endurance through the trial proves the genuineness of the faith, Jam 1:12.
21. Genuine faith is more precious than "tested and approved" gold. What fire is to gold, trials are to faith. On this word, see "approved" in Rom 12:2.
22. Some manuscripts say "known" {A}.
23. Or, "untellable, unspeakable". Used only here. GK *443*. Related to "tell" in Act 23:22 (GK *1718*).
24. This is a participle, "having been glorified", full of glory from above. Same word as in 2:12; 4:11; 4:16. On this word, see Rom 8:30.
25. Or, "obtaining". Same word as in 5:4. On this word, see "receive back" in 2 Cor 5:10.
26. Or, "goal, end". On this word, see "end" in Rom 10:4.
27. Compare Mt 13:17. On this word, see 1 Cor 12:28.
28. On this word, see Heb 11:6. The root word is "seek".
29. Or, "carefully inquired". Used only here. GK *2001*.
30. Or, "the grace *that would come* to you".
31. On this word, see 1 Cor 2:10. Related to "searched out" above.
32. Or, "what *time* or what manner of time", meaning what date or what age. On this word, see Mt 8:29.
33. Or, "bearing witness beforehand, testifying in advance". This word modifies "Spirit". Used only here. GK *4626*.
34. That is, the prophecies.
35. Some manuscripts say "us" {N}.
36. Some manuscripts omit this word, leaving it implied {C}.
37. This word for "Therefore, For this reason" is only used here in this book. It begins a series of exhortations to us as people born again to a living hope. Used 53 times in the NT. GK *1475*.
38. Or, "Having tied up". This metaphor means "having prepared for mental action or work, having pulled yourselves together". To prepare to work, people in the ancient world pulled up their long robes and belted them at the waist. We might similarly say, "Having rolled up the sleeves of your mind". Used only here. GK *350*. The root word is "gird" in Act 12:8.
39. More literally, "waists (plural) *of* your (plural) mind (singular), as often in Greek. On this word, see "loins" Heb 7:5.
40. Or, "well-balanced, self-controlled, clear-headed". Elsewhere only in 1 Thes 5:6, 8; 2 Tim 4:5; 1 Pet 4:7; 5:8. GK *3768*. Related word in 1 Tim 3:2.
41. On the verb "put hope", see Jn 5:45. Related to "hope" in 1:3, 21; 3:15. Used only here as a command.
42. Or, "fully, totally, perfectly". Used only here. GK *5458*. Related to "complete" in 1 Cor 13:10.
43. That is, children characterized by obedience, obedient children.
44. Or, "conforming *yourselves*". On this word, see Rom 12:2.
45. Or, "way-of-life, behavior". Same word as in 2:12; 3:1, 2, 16; Gal 1:13; 1 Tim 4:12; Jam 3:13; 2 Pet 2:7. Elsewhere only as "way-of-life" in Eph 4:22; Heb 13:7; 1 Pet 1:18; and "behaviors" in 2 Pet 3:11. GK *419*. The related verb is in v 17.
46. This word is used three times by Peter, each introducing an OT quote, 1:16, 24; 2:6. On this word, see Rom 1:21.
47. Some manuscripts omit this word {C}, which serves to introduce the quotation. Some manuscripts omit "am", leaving it implied {C}.
48. This adjective means "dedicated to God" It is also used of the "Holy" Spirit, and as "saints" (holy ones). Used 233 times. GK *41*. The related verb is "sanctify" (make holy) in Heb 10:29.

A. 1 Cor 12:28 B. 1 Jn 1:7 C. Eph 2:8 D. Act 7:17 E. Rom 9:5 F. Mt 9:13 G. Col 1:5 H. Act 24:15 J. Heb 13:4 K. Eph 1:14 L. Gal 3:23, kept in custody M. Lk 19:9 N. Mk 14:15, prepared O. 2 Thes 2:3 P. Heb 1:2 Q. Lk 10:21 R. 2 Cor 7:9 S. Jam 1:2 T. Mt 13:46 U. 1 Cor 1:18 V. 1 Cor 4:5 W. 2 Pet 2:10 X. 1 Tim 5:17 Y. 2 Thes 1:7 Z. Jn 21:15, devotedly love AA. Jn 3:36 BB. Jam 5:20 CC. 1 Cor 14:1 DD. 1 Cor 3:13, make clear EE. Phil 3:10 FF. 1 Pet 4:10 GG. Jn 16:13 HH. Act 5:42 JJ. Mk 3:14, send out KK. Gal 5:17 LL. Lk 24:12, stoop to look MM. Lk 1:51, thoughts NN. 1 Jn 3:1 OO. Gal 5:16 PP. Eph 4:18 QQ. Rom 8:30

| 1 Peter 1:17 | 890 | Verse |

   3B. And if you are calling-upon[1] *as* Father the *One* judging[A] without-respect-of-persons[2] according to the work[3] *of* each *person*— conduct[4] the time *of* your stay[5] with fear[6]   17

      1C. Knowing that you were redeemed[7] from your futile[8] way-of-life[B] handed-down-from-your-fathers   18

          1D. Not *with* perishable[C] *things*— silver or gold
          2D. But *with the* precious[D] blood[E] *of* Christ, as *of a* lamb without-blemish[F] and without-spot[G]   19

              1E. Having been **foreknown**[9] before *the* foundation[H] *of the* world[10]— but having appeared[11] at *the* last[J] *of* times for your sake   20

                  1F. The believers[12] through Him in God— the *One* having raised[K] Him from *the* dead and having given Him glory— so that your faith and hope are in God   21

   4B. Having purified[L] your souls[M] in[13] obedience[N] *of* the truth[14] for *a* sincere[15] brotherly-love[16]— love[O] one another fervently[17] from *a* pure[P] heart[18]   22

      1C. Having been born-again[Q] not from perishable[C] seed but imperishable[19], through *the* living and abiding[20] word[R] *of* God   23

          1D. Because, "All flesh[S] *is* like grass, and all its[21] glory like *a* flower *of* grass. The grass was dried-up[T], and the flower fell-off[U]. *But the* word[V] *of the* Lord abides[W] forever[X]" [Isa 40:6-8]— and this is the word[V] having been announced-as-good-news[Y] to you   24   25

   5B. Having then laid-aside[Z] all badness[22], and all deceit[23] and hypocrisies[24] and jealousies[AA], and all slanders— *yearn[25] like newborn babies[BB] for the deceitless[26] milk of-the-Word[27]   2:1   2

      1C. In order that by it you may grow[CC] in[28] [your] salvation[29]
      2C. If[30] you tasted[31] that the Lord *is* good[32]   3

          1D. Coming to Whom *as the* living Stone[33] having been rejected[DD] **by people**[34]— but chosen[EE], precious[35] with God   4

              1E. You yourselves also, as living stones, are being built[36] *as a* spiritual[FF] house[GG], for[37] *a* holy priesthood, to offer[HH] spiritual[FF] sacrifices[38] acceptable[JJ] *to* God through Jesus Christ   5

                  1F. Because it is contained[39] in Scripture, "Behold, I am laying *a* Stone in Zion— *a* chosen[EE], precious[40] Cornerstone[KK]. And the *one* putting-faith[41] upon Him will never be put-to-shame[LL]" [Isa 28:16]   6
                  2F. The *precious*-value[42] then *is for* you, the *ones* believing[43]   7
                  3F. But *for ones* not-believing[44]— "*The* Stone[MM] which the *ones* building rejected[DD], this became[45] *the* head *of the* corner[46]" [Ps 118:22], *and "a Stone of* stumbling[NN] and *a* Rock[OO] *of* falling[47]" [Isa 8:14]   8

                      1G. Who stumble[PP] while disobeying[48] the word[R]— to which[49] indeed they were appointed[50]

1. Same word as in Act 2:21; 9:14, 21; 22:16; Rom 10:12, 13, 14; 1 Cor 1:2; 2 Tim 2:22. Used 30 times, also as "call". GK *2126*.
2. Or, "impartially". Used only here. GK *719*. Related to "respect of persons" in Jam 2:1.
3. On this phrase, see Rev 20:12.
4. On this verb, see Eph 2:3. The related noun is in v 15.
5. Or, "sojourn, stay as foreigners". That is, your stay on earth. Elsewhere only in Act 13:17. GK *4229*. The related verb is in Heb 11:9.
6. That is, fear of God, reverence. On this word, see Eph 5:21.
7. Elsewhere only in Lk 24:21; Tit 2:14. GK *3390*. On this word group, see Rom 3:24.
8. Or, "useless, worthless, pointless", in terms of knowing God. On this word, see 1 Cor 15:17.
9. Peter uses grammar that emphasizes the contrast between the two halves of this sentence. On this word, see Rom 8:29. Related to the word in 1:2.
10. This phrase "before... world" is elsewhere only in Jn 17:24; Eph 1:4. On "since the foundation of the world", see Heb 9:26.
11. Or, "having been made known, revealed". Same word as in 5:4. On this word, see "made evident" in 1 Jn 2:19.
12. That is, the ones who through Jesus are believers in God. Some manuscripts say "The *ones* believing"; others, "The *ones* having believed" {N}. On this word, see "faithful" in Col 1:2.
13. Or, "by". GK *1877*.
14. That is, to the truth. Compare Rom 16:26. Some manuscripts add "through the Spirit" {A}.
15. Or, "unhypocritical". On this word, see Rom 12:9.
16. On this word, see Heb 13:1. The word "love" in the command next is not related.
17. Or, "earnestly, intensely". Elsewhere only in Lk 22:44; Act 12:5. GK *1757*. Related to "fervent" in 1 Pet 4:8. The root word is "stretch out".
18. Some manuscripts say "from *the* heart" {C}.
19. Same word as "undecayable" in v 4.
20. Some manuscripts add "forever" {N}, so that it says "through *the* Word *of* God, living and abiding forever". On this word, see Jn 15:4.
21. Some manuscripts say "and all *the* glory *of* man *is* like" {N}.
22. This word is used of circumstantial badness or misfortune in Mt 6:34, "trouble". It is also used of moral badness in general, "evilness, wickedness, depravity". It is "evilness" in Act 8:22; 1 Cor 14:20; 1 Pet 2:16; and "badness" in Rom 1:29; 1 Cor 5:8; Jam 1:21; 1 Pet 2:1. However, some of these may fall into the next meaning. Elsewhere only of interpersonal badness, "malice, ill-will", the desire to cause pain or distress to another through words and actions. It is "malice" in Eph 4:31; Col 3:8; Tit 3:3. GK *2798*. Related to "evil" in 3 Jn 11.
23. On this word, see Mt 26:4. Same word as in 2:22; 3:10.
24. Or, "insincerities". Same root word as "sincere" in 1:22, without the negative prefix. On this word, see Gal 2:13.
25. This word, "yearn for, long for", is also in 2 Cor 9:14; Phil 1:8; 2:26; Jam 4:5. Elsewhere only as "yearn" in Rom 1:11; 2 Cor 5:2; 1 Thes 3:6; 2 Tim 1:4. GK *2160*. Related to "yearning" in 2 Cor 7:11; "yearned-for" in Phil 4:1; and "yearning" in Rom 15:23.
26. Or, "pure, unadulterated". Used only here. GK *100*. Same root word as "deceit" in v 1, with a negative prefix added.
27. Or, milk "pertaining-to-the-Word". Or, "spiritual" milk, milk pertaining to the real, spiritual nature of things. On this word, see "spiritual" in Rom 12:1. It is related to "word" in 1 Cor 12:8, and "oracle" in Heb 5:12. Peter uses the normal word for "spiritual" in 2:5.
28. Or, "in relation to, with reference to, into, to". *GK 1650*.
29. Some manuscripts omit "in [your] salvation" {N}.
30. Some manuscripts say "If indeed" {B}, using the word "since" in Rom 8:9.
31. Peter is alluding to Ps 34:8. The grammar implies "assuming that you tasted", that you have partaken of Him. If you tasted, drink the milk and grow. If not (a point not addressed here), by all means partake. On this word, see Heb 6:4.
32. Or, "kind". That is, actively good. Same word as in Lk 5:39; 6:35; Rom 2:4; 1 Cor 15:33. Elsewhere only as "kind" in Eph 4:32; and "easy" in Mt 11:30. GK *5982*. Related to "goodness" in Rom 3:12; and "show kindness" in 1 Cor 13:4.
33. Having completed the baby/milk/growth metaphor, Peter abruptly changes metaphors in order to continue to describe other aspects of our new spiritual reality. Just as 1:10-12 added on a block of teaching to that section, so he adds on some teaching here. We are babies feeding on the Word, living stones in a spiritual temple, priests offering spiritual sacrifices in that temple, a chosen family, etc.
34. Peter uses grammar that emphasizes the contrast between the two halves of this sentence. On this word, see "mankind" in Mt 4:4.
35. These last two words come from the quotation of Isa 28:16 in v 6.
36. Or, "are building *yourselves*". Some take this as a command, "be built, let yourselves be built, build *yourselves*". On this word, see "edify" in 1 Cor 14:4.
37. Some manuscripts omit this word {N}.
38. Praise, doing good, and sharing are examples, Heb 13:15-16. On this word, see Heb 9:26.
39. Or, "it stands, it says". Used only here in this sense. GK *4321*.
40. On this word, see Phil 2:29. Related to the word in 1:19.
41. On "putting faith upon", see Rom 4:5.
42. This word is related to "precious" in v 6, and is rendered this way to show this. The "value, benefit" of this Cornerstone is for you who believe. On this word, see "honor" in 1 Tim 5:17.
43. For believers, Christ is the cornerstone of a new building. For unbelievers, He is a stone of stumbling. On this word, see Jn 3:36.
44. On this word, see "are faithless" in 2 Tim 2:13. Some manuscripts say "disobeying" {N}, using the word in v 8.
45. This is an idiom, literally, "came-to-be for", reflecting a Hebrew way of speaking.
46. On this phrase, see Mk 12:10.
47. That is, a rock causing a fall. On this word and phrase, see Rom 9:33.
48. Some think Peter means "who stumble [because they are] being disobedient *to* the word"; others render this "who stumble *at* the word [by] being disobedient". On this word, see Rom 11:30.
49. Some think Peter means they were appointed to stumble on Christ as a result of their disobedience to the Word. Compare Rom 11:7-10. Others think he means they were appointed to be disobedient.
50. Or, "destined". Same word as in 1 Thes 5:9.

A. Mt 7:1 B. 1 Pet 1:15, conduct C. 1 Cor 15:53, decayable D. 2 Pet 1:4 E. 1 Jn 1:7 F. Col 1:22 G. 2 Pet 3:14, unspotted H. Heb 11:11 J. Heb 1:2 K. Mt 28:6, arose L. 1 Jn 3:3 M. Jam 5:20 N. Rom 16:26 O. Jn 21:15, devotedly love P. Tit 1:15, clean Q. 1 Pet 1:3 R. 1 Cor 12:8 S. Act 2:17 T. Mk 3:1, become withered U. Gal 5:4, fell from V. Rom 10:17 W. Jn 15:4 X. Rev 20:10 Y. Act 5:42 Z. Rom 13:12 AA. Mk 15:10, envy BB. Lk 1:41 CC. Jn 3:30 DD. Heb 12:17 EE. Rom 8:33 FF. 1 Cor 14:1 GG. Mk 3:20 HH. Heb 9:28, bear JJ. Rom 15:16 KK. Eph 2:20 LL. Rom 5:5 MM. Mk 16:3 NN. Rom 14:13, opportunity for stumbling OO. Mt 7:24, bedrock PP. Rom 14:21

2E.	And you *are a* chosen^A family^1, *a* royal priesthood, *a* holy nation, *a* people^B for *His* possession^2— so that you may report^3 the virtues^4 *of* the *One* having called^C you out of darkness into His marvelous^D light	9
	1F. Who once *were* not *a* people^B, but now *are the* people *of* God^5; the *ones* not having received-mercy^E, but now having received-mercy	10
6B.	Beloved^6, I exhort^F you as foreigners^7 and pilgrims^8 to be abstaining^G *from* fleshly^H desires^J which wage-war^9 against the soul^K, °holding your conduct^L good^10 among the Gentiles	11 12
	1C. In order that in what they are speaking-against^M you as evil-doers^11, they may by observing^N *your* good works glorify^O God on *the* day *of* visitation^12	
7B.	Be subject^13 *to* every human^P institution^14 for the Lord's sake^15— whether *to a* king as being superior^16, or *to* governors^Q as being sent by him^17 for *the* punishment^R *of* evil-doers and praise^S *of* good-doers^18	13 14
	1C. Because thus^19 is the will *of* God, *that* while doing-good^T, *you* may be silencing^20 the ignorance^U *of* foolish^V people^W	15
8B.	As^21 free^22 *ones*— and not having the freedom^X as *a* covering^23 *of* evilness^24, but as slaves^Y *of* God— honor^25 everyone. Be loving^Z the brotherhood^26, be fearing^AA God, be honoring^BB the king^27	16 17
	1C. Servants^28, being subject^CC *to your* masters^DD with all fear^29— not only *to* the good^EE and kind^FF *ones*, but also *to* the crooked^30 *ones*	18
	1D. For this *finds* favor^31— if, for the sake of *a* consciousness^32 *of* God, one bears-up^33 while suffering^GG sorrows^34 unjustly	19
	1E. For what-kind-of^HH credit^35 *is it* if while sinning and being beaten^JJ, you will endure^36? 2E. But if while doing-good^T and suffering^GG you will endure, this *finds* favor with God	20
	2D. For you were called^C to this^37	21
	1E. Because Christ also suffered^38 for you^39, leaving-behind *a* pattern^40 *for* you, in order that you might follow-after^KK His footsteps	
	1F. Who "did not commit^LL sin, nor was deceit^MM found in His mouth" [Isa 53:9] 2F. Who^41—	22 23
	1G. While being reviled^42, was not reviling-in-return 2G. While suffering^GG, was not threatening^NN, but was committing^43 *Himself*^44 *to* the *One* judging^OO righteously^PP	
	3F. Who Himself bore^45 our sins in His body on the cross^46 in order that we, having died^47 *to* sins, might live *for* righteousness^QQ	24

1. Or, "race, people, nation". That is, Abraham's spiritual family, Gal 3:29. On this word, see "kind" in 1 Cor 12:28.
2. In using these descriptions, Peter is alluding to Ex 19:5-6; Isa 43:20-21, etc. On "possession", see Eph 1:14.
3. Or, "send out, proclaim". Elsewhere only in Mark's short ending. GK *1972*.
4. Or, "moral excellencies". On this word, see 2 Pet 1:3. Some render this "praises" here, or "miracles" (manifestations of His divine power).
5. Peter is alluding to Hosea 1:6-10; 2:23, as Paul does in Rom 9:25.
6. Peter continues with his exhortations regarding Christian living. Others make this a new A. point. Same word as in 4:12.
7. Or, "resident aliens". Elsewhere only in Act 7:6, 29; Eph 2:19. GK *4230*. Related to "stay" in 1:17.
8. On this word, see 1:1. The concept of "foreigners and pilgrims" flows from v 9. We are God's nation, residing temporarily among earthly nations.
9. Or, "serve as soldier". On this word, see "fight" in 1 Tim 1:18.
10. Or, "commendable, praiseworthy, outwardly good". On this word, see 1 Tim 5:10a. Same word as later in the verse.
11. Or, "criminals". Christians were rebels against the Emperor for failing to worship him. Because they were regarded as criminals, they were punished by the State; that is, they suffered for Christ, 4:16. Elsewhere only in v 14; 4:15. GK *2804*. Related to "do evil" in 3:17.
12. Same word as in Lk 19:44. Some think Peter means the day of God's judgment; others the day of human judgment; others, the day when God visits them with the opportunity for salvation. In Lk 19:44, Christ's ministry was the day of visitation for Israel, which they rejected. On this phrase, note Isa 10:3. On this word, see "office of overseer" in 1 Tim 3:1.
13. Same word as in 2:18; 3:1; 5, 22; 5:5. On this word, see Eph 5:21.
14. Or, "creation, created thing". Used only here in this sense. On this word, see "creation" in Rom 8:39.
15. Those who are citizens of God's nation must still know how to behave regarding human institutions. Peter's answer is to live in such a manner that this is a non-issue. Such an understanding as follows in 2:13-3:12 is crucial to avoiding trials (1:6) based on the unnecessary violation of societal norms.
16. Same word as in Rom 13:1.
17. Some think Peter is referring to "the king"; others think he means "Him", the Lord, as in Rom 13:1-4.
18. Used only here. GK *18*. Related to the word in v 15, 20.
19. Some think this refers to what precedes, being good-doers; others, to what follows, silencing them through good-doing.
20. Or, "muzzling". On this word, see Mk 4:39.
21. Some make this point 2C., "As free *ones*... God", some making it a command, "[Live] as free *ones*". Then "Honor everyone... king" becomes point 3C., and "Servants" point 4C. This allows "being subject" in v 18 to be linked with "be subject" in v 13, rather than with "honor everyone" in v 17, as here.
22. We are all free in Christ, servants of no human, but slaves of God, equal before Him. There are no human distinctions, Gal 3:28. But we live in two realms. In the earthly human realm, we choose as free ones to submit to the human responsibilities under which we live. We do this so as not to bring unnecessary attacks upon us as Christians, so that we can peacefully pursue Christ's spiritual goals, which are independent of these human relationships. We serve Him in a spiritual kingdom that transcends human society, but lives within its bounds for the sake of expediency. On this word, see Mt 17:26.
23. Used only here. GK *2127*. Related to "veil" in 2 Cor 3:13-16; and "cover" in 1 Pet 4:8; and in Rom 4:7. Compare Gal 5:13.
24. Or, "badness", as in 2:1. Same word as the "evil" in "evil-doer" in v 12, 14.
25. The grammar of the next three commands is different.
26. That is, the community of believers. Elsewhere only in 5:9. GK *82*.
27. These are general commands for everyone. Peter next details "honor everyone" for specific groups.
28. Or, "Slaves". That is, honor everyone— servants, being subject. Peter continues with his commands, using different grammar. On this word, see "household-servant" in Rom 14:4.
29. That is, "with all respect", or "in all fear [of God]". On this word, see Eph 5:21.
30. Or, "dishonest, unscrupulous". Elsewhere only in Lk 3:5; Act 2:40; Phil 2:15. GK *5021*. That is, dishonest or crooked toward you, as seen in v 19.
31. That is, with God, v 20. Same word as in Lk 1:30; 2:52; Act 7:46. On this word, see "grace" in Eph 2:8. Some manuscripts add "with God" {B}.
32. Or, "conscience *toward* God". Some manuscripts say "for the sake of *a* good conscience" {B}. On this word, see "conscience" in Act 23:1.
33. On this word, see "endure" in 1 Cor 10:13.
34. This word is plural only here. On this word, see "grief" in 2 Cor 7:10.
35. Or, "fame, glory". Used only here. GK *3094*.
36. Or, "remain under". On this word, see Jam 1:12.
37. That is, to bear up under unjust suffering for Christ.
38. On this word, see Gal 3:4. Some manuscripts say "died" {A}.
39. Some manuscripts say "for us, ... pattern *for* us" {A}.
40. Or, "model". Used of a tracing or sketch. Jesus left behind a pattern for us to fill in with our own lives, an exemplar for us to copy. Used only here. GK *5681*.
41. This verse is referring to Isa 53:7.
42. On this word, see 1 Cor 4:12. Related to "revile in return" next, which is used only here (GK *518*). Related word in 3:9.
43. Or, "delivering". On this word, see "hand over" in Mt 26:21.
44. Some think Peter means "*Himself*", as in Lk 23:46; others, "*them*", as in Lk 23:34; others, "*it*", meaning "His cause" or "His unjust suffering".
45. On this word, see Heb 9:28. Same word as in Isa 53:11, 12.
46. Or, "tree, wood". This is not the normal word for "cross" (place of crucifixion), which Peter never uses (though he does use "crucify"). This word means "cut wood, timber, tree", and was used of anything made of wood, like "beam, post, bench, stocks, gallows, stake, cross", etc. It is used to refer to the "cross" also in Act 5:30; 10:39; 13:29; and as "tree" in Gal 3:13. Elsewhere it means "tree" (of life) in Rev 2:7; 22:2, 14, 19; "wood" in Lk 23:31; Act 16:24; 1 Cor 3:12; Rev 18:12; and "club" in Mt 26:47, 55; Mk 14:43, 48; Lk 22:52. GK *3833*.
47. Or, "being dead". This word means "die" in the sense of "depart from, be removed from". Used only here. GK *614*.

A. Rom 8:33 B. Rev 21:3 C. Rom 8:30 D. Jn 9:30, marvel E. Rom 12:8, show mercy F. Rom 12:8 G. 1 Thes 4:3 H. 1 Cor 3:3 J. Gal 5:16 K. Jam 5:20 L. 1 Pet 1:15 M. 1 Pet 3:16 N. 1 Pet 3:2 O. Rom 8:30 P. 1 Cor 10:13, common to mankind Q. Mt 27:2 R. 2 Thes 1:8 S. 1 Cor 4:5 T. Lk 6:33 U. 1 Cor 15:34 V. 2 Cor 11:16 W. Mt 4:4, mankind X. Gal 5:13 Y. Rom 6:17 Z. Jn 21:15, devotedly love AA. Eph 5:33, respecting BB. 1 Tim 5:3 CC. Eph 5:21 DD. Jude 4 EE. 1 Tim 5:10b FF. Phil 4:5, kindness GG. Gal 3:4 HH. Mt 21:23 JJ. 1 Cor 4:11 KK. Mk 16:20 LL. Rev 13:13, does MM. 1 Pet 2:1 NN. Act 4:17 OO. Mt 7:1 PP. 1 Cor 15:34 QQ. Rom 1:17

    4F. *By* Whose bruise[1] you were healed[A]

  2E. For you were going-astray[B] like sheep,[2] but now you returned[C] to the Shepherd[3] and   25
    Overseer[4] *of* your souls[D]

2C. Likewise wives, being subject[5] *to your* own husbands— in order that even if any are disobeying[6]   3:1
  the word[E], they may be gained[7] without *a* word[E] by the conduct[F] *of their* wives, ⸰having   2
  observed[8] your pure[9] conduct[F] with fear[10]

  1D. *Of* whom, let *what is observed* be[11]   3

    1E. Not the outside adornment[12] *consisting of a* braiding *of* hair, and *a* wearing *of* gold
     things or *a* putting-on *of* garments[13]
    2E. But the hidden[G] person[H] *of* the heart in[14] the imperishable[J] *adorning consisting of* the   4
     gentle[15] and quiet[16] spirit, which is very-precious[17] in the sight of God

  2D. For in this manner formerly also the holy wives putting-hope[K] in God were adorning[L]   5
    themselves— being subject *to their* own husbands

    1E. As Sarah obeyed[M] Abraham, calling[N] him lord[18], *of* whom[19] you became[20] children[O]   6
     while[21] doing-good[22] and not fearing[P] any terror[23]

3C. Husbands likewise, living-with[24] *them* according-to[25] knowledge[26], showing[27] honor[28] *to* the   7
  feminine[29] *one*

  1D. As[30] *to* the weaker[31] vessel[32]
  2D. As indeed[33] *to your*[34] fellow-heirs[35] *of the* grace *of* life[36]
  3D. So that your[37] prayers[Q] *may* not be hindered[R]

1. Or, "welt, wound". Used only here. GK *3698*. Same word as in Isa 53:5.
2. Peter is referring to Isa 53:6.
3. On this word, see Eph 4:11. Used of Christ also in Heb 13:20; Jn 10:2. The related verb is in 1 Pet 5:2.
4. Used only here of Christ, but four times of the church leaders. On this word, see Phil 1:1. Related to "exercising oversight" in 1 Pet 5:2.
5. That is, proceeding from 2:17, "honor everyone— wives, being subject". On this word, see Eph 5:21.
6. On this word, see Rom 11:30. Compare 2:8; 4:17; Rom 2:8; Jn 3:36.
7. Same word as in Mt 18:15; 1 Cor 9:19-22. On this word, see Mk 8:36.
8. Or, "watched". Elsewhere only in 2:12. GK *2227*. Related to "eyewitness" in 2 Pet 1:16.
9. Elsewhere only in 2 Cor 7:11; 11:2; Phil 4:8; 1 Tim 5:22; Tit 2:5; Jam 3:17; 1 Jn 3:3. GK *54*. Related to "purity" in 2 Cor 11:3; "purely" in Phil 1:17; "purity" in 1 Tim 4:12; 5:2; and "purify" in 1 Jn 3:3.
10. That is, your pure behavior carried out respectfully, or in the fear of God. "With fear" goes with "your conduct", not with "observing". Same word as in 1:17; 2:18; 3:16. On this word, see Eph 5:21. The related verb is used of the wife in Eph 5:33 ("respecting").
11. Peter simply says "let it be". Others supply "their adornment" from what follows, "let *their adornment* be".
12. Used only here in this sense. On this word, see "world" in 1 Jn 2:15. Our word "cosmetic" comes from this Greek word, *kosmos*. Related to "adorning" in v 5.
13. Or, "clothing, apparel". It is also used more specifically of outer clothing, "cloak, robe". Used 60 times. GK *2668*.
14. That is, dressed in, as this word is used in Jam 2:2. GK *1877*.
15. Or, "meek". Elsewhere only in Mt 5:5; 11:29; 21:5. GK *4558*. Related to the words in 1 Tim 6:11 and Eph 4:2. A review of the usage of this word group makes clear that this is a key Christian virtue, not just a female virtue.
16. Elsewhere only in 1 Tim 2:2. GK *2485*. Related to "be quiet" in 1 Thes 4:11.
17. Or, "highly valuable". Same word as in Mk 14:3. Elsewhere only as "very expensive" in 1 Tim 2:9. GK *4500*.
18. Or, "sir", referring to Gen 18:12. Sarah treated Abraham with respect, in his terms. On this word, see "master" in Mt 8:2.
19. That is, of Sarah.
20. Or, "were made, came-to-be". GK *1181*.
21. As to the nuance implied by these two participles (doing good, fearing), some think Peter means "*by* doing good"; others, "*as long as you are* doing good" or "*if you are* doing good"; others, "*since you are* doing good" or "*as ones* doing good". It could be rendered "*of* whom you doing good and not fearing any terror became children".
22. That is, doing good as wives. Same word as 2:20, doing good as servants. On this word, see Lk 6:33.
23. Or, "intimidation (from outside), fright (from within)". Compare 4:19. Such women fear no consequence stemming from their doing what is right, but entrust themselves to God. Used only here. GK *4766*. Related to "frighten" in Lk 21:9.
24. Or, "dwelling with". That is, proceeding from 2:17, "honor everyone— husbands...". Used only here. GK *5324*. The root word is "house".
25. Or, "in accordance with, in harmony with, based on". GK *2848*.
26. Some think Peter means Christian knowledge, the knowledge that a wife is God's creation, equal in Christ, as opposed to what the pagan world thought of her. Others take this more generally, "in an understanding way", "knowledgeably", with consideration. On this word, see 1 Cor 12:8.
27. Or, "assigning, portioning out, according". Used only here. GK *671*.
28. On this noun, see 1 Tim 5:17. Related to the verb in 2:17.
29. This word means "belonging to the woman, womanly". Used only here. GK *1221*. Some take it as an abstract equivalent to "female, wife, woman". This adjective has the same relationship to "woman" as "royal" (2:9) does to "king"; as "earthly" (2 Cor 5:1) does to "earth"; as "divine" (2 Pet 1:4) does to "God". It is rendered in the OT as the "manner of women" in Gen 18:22; "woman's" clothing in Deut 22:5; the "women's" court in Est 2:11; and the "woman's" (that is, the queen's) crown in Est 2:17. Peter means husbands must show their wives honor not simply as a wife (a male perspective), but as feminine. That is, honor her in relation to her God-created feminine nature, her value and contribution as a woman, the characteristics belonging to her as a woman. Honor her in her terms.
30. In the Greek word order, "as *to the* weaker vessel, *to* the feminine *one*" precedes "showing". Some take both phrases with "living with", as "living with *them* according to knowledge, as *with a* weaker vessel, the feminine *one*", or "living with the female according to knowledge, as *with a* weaker vessel". Others take both with "showing", as here. It is also possible to split them, "living with *them* according to knowledge, as *with a* weaker vessel, showing honor *to* the feminine *one*".
31. That is, "lacking power" relative to the male vessel. The woman is weaker physically, which has resulted in her being weaker societally in ways that vary by culture, time, and the intervention of law. The word is used of Paul vs. others, 1 Cor 9:22; of weaker Christians, 1 Cor 8:9; of Christians with less prominent gifts, 1 Cor 12:22; of Christians vs. the world, 1 Cor 1:27. On this word, see 1 Thes 5:14.
32. This word is used of Paul in Act 9:15 ("instrument"); of ministers in 2 Tim 2:21; of people as vessels of wrath or mercy in Rom 9:21-23; of the human body in 2 Cor 4:7. The term "vessel" puts the emphasis on the woman as a creation of God, as opposed to using a word that views her from the husband's point of view, such as "partner, helper". On this word, see 1 Thes 4:4.
33. Or, "also".
34. Some manuscripts say "As indeed *being their* fellow heirs..." {B}.
35. Regardless of the woman's relative weakness to the male, however manifested in any particular culture, spiritually before God she is equal, a fellow-heir of God's promises. Christian husbands must treat their wives as such. On this word, see Rom 8:17.
36. That is, the grace-gift of spiritual life, which all Christians equally possess. On "grace", see Eph 2:8.
37. Some think Peter means the husband's prayers; others, their prayers together.

A. Mt 8:8 B. Jam 5:19, err C. Jam 5:19, turns back D. Jam 5:20 E. 1 Cor 12:8 F. 1 Pet 1:15 G. 1 Cor 4:5 H. Mt 4:4, mankind J. 1 Pet 1:4, undecayable K. Jn 5:45 L. 1 Tim 2:9 M. Act 6:7 N. Rom 8:30 O. 1 Jn 3:1 P. Eph 5:33, respecting Q. 1 Tim 2:1 R. Gal 5:7

| 1 Peter 3:8 | 896 | Verse |

    4C. And finally, everyone¹— *being* likeminded², sympathetic, brother-loving³, tender-hearted⁴, humbleminded⁵, ˚not giving-back^A evil^B for evil or reviling⁶ for reviling, but on the contrary, blessing^C *them*   8 / 9

        1D. Because⁷ you were called^D to this⁸, in order that you might inherit^E *a* blessing^F. ˚For "the *one* desiring⁹ to love life and see good^G days—   10

            1E. "Let him stop^H *his* tongue from evil^B, and *stop his* lips *that they* not speak deceit^J
            2E. "And let him turn-away^K from evil^B, and let him do good^G   11
            3E. "Let him seek^L peace, and let him pursue^M it
            4E. "Because *the* eyes *of the* Lord *are* upon *the* righteous^N, and His ears *are* open to their prayer^O. But *the* face *of the* Lord *is* against *ones* doing evil^B *things*" [Ps 34:12-16]   12

3A. And who *is the one who* will do you evil¹⁰ if you become zealots¹¹ *for* good^G? ˚But even though you might be suffering¹² for the sake of righteousness, *you are* blessed¹³ *ones*!   13-14

    1B. But do not fear their fear,¹⁴ nor be disturbed¹⁵, ˚but set Christ¹⁶ apart¹⁷ *as* Lord^P in your hearts   15

        1C. *Being* ready¹⁸ always for *a* defense¹⁹ *to* everyone asking you *a* reason²⁰ for the hope^Q in you, but with gentleness²¹ and fear²²   16
        2C. Having *a* good^G conscience^R in order that in what you are spoken-against²³, the *ones* maligning²⁴ your good^G conduct^S in Christ may be put-to-shame^T

            1D. For *it is* better to be suffering^U while doing-good^V, if the will *of* God should [so] will^W *it*, than while doing-evil^X   17

    2B. Because²⁵ Christ also suffered²⁶ once-for-all²⁷ for sins— *a* righteous^N One for unrighteous *ones*— in order that He might bring you²⁸ to God   18

        1C. Having been **put-to-death**²⁹ *in the* flesh^Y— but made-alive³⁰ *by the* Spirit³¹

            1D. By Whom³² also³³ having gone, He proclaimed³⁴ *to* the spirits³⁵ in prison³⁶— ˚*ones* having disobeyed^Z formerly when the patience^AA *of* God was waiting³⁷ in *the* days *of* Noah while *an* ark^BB *was* being prepared^CC   19-20

                1E. In which³⁸ *a* few— that is, eight³⁹ souls— were brought-safely⁴⁰ through *the* water⁴¹
                2E. Which⁴² also *as to* you⁴³ *a* corresponding-thing⁴⁴ now saves^DD— baptism^EE   21

1. That is, proceeding from 2:17, "honor everyone— everyone...". Peter continues his commands, changing the grammar once again.
2. Or, "harmonious". Used only here. GK *3939*.
3. Or, "brother-lovers". That is, loving fellow Christians. Used only here. GK *5790*. Related to "brotherly love" in Heb 13:1.
4. Or, "good-hearted". Elsewhere only in Eph 4:32. GK *2359*. It is made of "good" and "deep feelings" in Phil 1:8.
5. Used only here. GK *5426*. Related to "humblemindedness" in Phil 2:3. Some manuscripts say "courteous" {A}.
6. Or, "insult, abuse". Elsewhere only 1 Tim 5:14. GK *3367*. Related to "reviled" in 2:23.
7. Some manuscripts say "Knowing that" {N}.
8. Some think this refers back to "blessing *them*"; others, forward to "inherit *a* blessing".
9. Or, "wanting, intending". On this word, see "willing" in Jn 7:17.
10. Or, "harm; mistreat you". Related to "evil *things*" in v 12, and rendered this way to show this. Elsewhere only as "mistreat" in Act 7:6, 19; 12:1; "harm" in Act 18:10; and "embitter" in Act 14:2. GK *2808*.
11. Or, "zealous". On this word, see 1 Cor 14:12.
12. Or, "if you even should suffer... *you would be* blessed ones". Regardless of the possibility that you might suffer for righteousness, you are blessed ones. Such suffering does not indicate God's displeasure with you, but His blessing. Compare Act 5:41.
13. Or, "fortunate". On this word, see Lk 6:20.
14. Peter may mean the fear such people generate, their intimidation. Or, he may mean do not fear what they fear.
15. On this word, see Gal 1:7. Peter is paraphrasing from Isa 8:12-13.
16. Some manuscripts say "set apart the Lord God in your hearts" {A}.
17. Or, "regard holy *the* Lord Christ", "hallow Christ *as* Lord". On this word, "set apart", see "sanctify" in Heb 10:29.
18. Same word as in 1:5. On this word, see "prepared" in Mk 14:15.
19. That is, to speak a defense. Elsewhere only in Act 22:1; 25:16; 1 Cor 9:3; 2 Cor 7:11; Phil 1:7, 16 (Paul's job!); 2 Tim 4:16. GK *665*. The related verb is in Lk 21:14.
20. Or, "word, speech, message, statement, account". On this word, see "word" in 1 Cor 12:8.
21. On this word, see Eph 4:2. Related to "gentle" in 3:4.
22. Some think this means "respect"; others the fear of God. On this word, see Eph 5:21.
23. Or, "slandered, spoken evil of". Elsewhere only in 2:12; Jam 4:11. GK *2895*. Related to "slanders" in 2:1; and "slanderer" in Rom 1:30. Some manuscripts say "in what they speak against you as evildoers" {A}.
24. Or, "speaking spitefully of, insulting, verbally abusing". Elsewhere only as "mistreating" in Lk 6:28. GK *2092*.
25. As in 2:21, Peter now gives Christ as our example to follow when suffering, making it explicit in 4:1. Here he adds a focus on His glory after suffering to the fact of His suffering.
26. We must set Christ apart (v 15), because He also suffered (v 18). Some manuscripts say "died" {B}. Same word as in v 14, 17; 4:1.
27. Or, "once", one time. On this word, see Jude 3.
28. Some manuscripts say "us" {C}.
29. Peter uses grammar that emphasizes the contrast between the two halves of this sentence. On this word, see Rom 7:4.
30. Or, "given life". On this word, see "give life to" in Jn 5:21.
31. Some think Peter means "*in* [His human] spirit" in contrast to His flesh; others, "*in the sphere of the* spirit"; others, "*by* [the Holy] Spirit". The spirit is not "made alive", but remains alive after death. But Jesus could be said to be made alive as a human spirit in the realm of the spirit, that is, to have entered the realm of the spirit in His human spirit, like all others who die. "Made alive" naturally refers to His resurrection, for the body must be "made alive".
32. Or, "In which". Some think Peter means "in His spirit" after He died; others, "in the state of being dead in the flesh and alive in (by) the spirit"; others, "by means of the Holy Spirit".
33. Or, "even", meaning "He even proclaimed"
34. Or, "made a proclamation". Some think Jesus proclaimed the gospel to the people; others, His victory over sin and Satan to either the people or the angels. There are other views on these verses, and all views raise unanswered questions. Consult the commentaries. Peter seems to be describing a sequence of events. Christ was put to death, made alive, went to the prison, proclaimed. His main point is not *what* He proclaimed, but *that* He proclaimed, and then went into heaven to the right hand of God, v 22. On this word, see 2 Tim 4:2.
35. It is clear that the spirits are in prison, and that their disobedience occurred during the days of Noah as explained in v 20. Some think these are the spirits of people who died in the flood. Others think they are angels who sinned during the time of Noah, as possibly referred to in 2 Pet 2:4; Jude 6; Gen 6:1-4. "Spirits" is used both ways, as seen in Heb 1:14; 12:23.
36. Some think this refers to Hades (see Rev 1:18), and is referred to in 2 Pet 2:4. On this word, see Act 5:22.
37. That is, as described in Gen 6:3. On this word, see Rom 8:19.
38. That is, the ark.
39. Compare Gen 7:13. On "souls", see Jam 5:20.
40. On this word, "to bring safely through", see Act 27:43. Here, the preposition "through" is repeated. Related to "saves" next.
41. Or, "brought-safely-through by means of *the* water".
42. This is the Greek word order of "which... baptism". Some think this refers back to the "water", making this point 1F. As Noah was saved by means of the water, so also you by means of the water of baptism. Others think it refers to the event, to Noah being "brought safely through the water". Just as God brought Noah safely through the water (representing death) to a new physical life, so also Christ brings you through the water of baptism (representing death) to a new spiritual life. There are other views.
43. Some manuscripts say "us" {N}.
44. This word is used of the "antitype, echo, reflection, copy" of the "pattern" (on which see 5:3). Thus in Heb 9:24, Moses' tabernacle is a "copy" of the heavenly pattern (Act 7:44). If taken this way here, baptism would be a copy of the flood, the reality, which is not likely. It is also used outside the NT in the opposite sense, of the fulfillment, the finished product made from a discarded pattern. Some take it this way here, "which also *as a* fulfillment, baptism now saves you". Others take it in a broader sense, meaning "corresponding to", without any formal type-antitype meaning, "which also, corresponding to baptism, now saves you". Others think Peter means baptism and the flood are both reflections of the spiritual reality of death to sin and new life in Him, "which also *as a* copy, baptism now saves you". Elsewhere only as "copy" in Heb 9:24. GK *531*. Some manuscripts simplify the grammar to "corresponding *to* which, baptism now saves you" {A}.

A. Mt 16:27, render B. 3 Jn 11 C. Lk 6:28 D. Rom 8:30 E. Gal 4:30 F. 2 Cor 9:5 G. 1 Tim 5:10b H. 1 Cor 13:8, cease J. Mt 26:4 K. Rom 16:17 L. Phil 2:21 M. 1 Cor 14:1 N. Rom 1:17 O. 1 Tim 2:1, petition P. Mt 8:2, master Q. Col 1:5 R. Act 23:1 S. 1 Pet 1:15 T. Rom 5:5 U. Gal 3:4 V. Lk 6:33 W. Jn 7:17 X. Mk 3:4, do harm Y. Col 2:23 Z. Rom 11:30 AA. Heb 6:12 BB. Heb 9:4 CC. Heb 9:2 DD. Lk 19:10 EE. Mk 1:4

1 Peter 3:22 898 Verse

        1F. Not¹ *a* putting-off² *of* dirt *from the* flesh^A
        2F. But *an* appeal³ to God *for*⁴ *a* good conscience^B
        3F. Through *the* resurrection⁵ *of* Jesus Christ—˚Who is at *the* right hand *of* God   22

            1G. Having gone⁶ into heaven
            2G. Angels and authorities and powers^C having been subjected^D *to* Him

3B. Therefore, Christ having suffered⁷ *in the* flesh^A, **you** also arm-*yourselves*⁸ *with* the same intention⁹   4:1

    1C. Because¹⁰ the *one* having suffered *in the* flesh has ceased¹¹ *from* sin,˚ so as to live¹² the   2
        remaining time in *the* flesh^A no longer *for*¹³ *the* desires^E *of* humans^F, but *for the* will^G *of* God
    2C. For the time¹⁴ having passed¹⁵ *is* enough^H *for you* to have worked-out^J the will¹⁶ *of* the Gentiles,   3
        having walked¹⁷ in sensualities^K, lusts¹⁸, drunkenness¹⁹, revelries^L, drinking-parties²⁰ and
        unlawful²¹ idolatries

        1D. In connection with which²², they are thinking-*it*-strange²³ *that* you *are* not running-with^M   4
            them into the same excess²⁴ *of* wild-living^N, while *they* continue blaspheming²⁵

            1E. Who shall render^O *an* account^P *to* the *One* being ready²⁶ to judge^Q *the* living and   5
                the dead²⁷

    3C. For to this²⁸ *end* it²⁹ was announced-as-good-news³⁰ even *to the* dead³¹—   6

        1D. That they might **be judged**³² according-to³³ people³⁴ *in the* flesh³⁵— but be living according
            to God³⁶ *in the* spirit³⁷

    4C. And³⁸ the end^R *of* all *things* has drawn-near^S   7

4B. Therefore be sound-minded^T, and be sober^U in³⁹ *your* prayers^V

1. Peter makes sure we understand that he is not saying that baptism itself, a ceremony, the water, saves us.
2. Or, "removal". Elsewhere only in 2 Pet 1:14. GK *629*.
3. Or, "request, question". Used only here. GK *2090*. Related to "to question" in Lk 9:18. Or, "pledge, answer", rendered either as "*the* pledge *to keep a* good conscience toward God", or "*the* pledge to God *from a* good conscience". In any case, Peter is talking about the spiritual commitment to God that took place at the ceremony.
4. Or, "*from, of*".
5. Thus, Peter says that both being born again (1:3), and being saved (3:21), are through the resurrection of Jesus.
6. Same word as in v 19.
7. Same word as in 3:18. Some manuscripts add "for us"; others, "for you" {A}.
8. Or, "prepare, equip *yourselves*". Used only here. GK *3959*. It is a military term. Related to "fully armed", "full armor" in Lk 11:21-22; and "weapons" in Rom 13:12. Other related words outside the NT mean "arm for war", "armament", "heavily armed", "bear arms", "army", etc.
9. Or, "thought, insight, way of thinking". That is, the intention to "suffer for righteousness" (3:13), like Christ (3:18). On this word, see Heb 4:12, "intentions" of the heart.
10. Some think "Because... sin" refers to Christ, and then "so as to live... God" continues on from "arm *yourselves*". Others think it refers to Christians, continuing on from the command. There are other views. Consult the commentaries.
11. Or, "stopped". That is, because the one having suffered for righteousness is one who has ceased living for the sinful desires the world lives for, and is living for the will of God. Such people have taken a stand for righteousness and suffered as a result. They have committed themselves to live for the will of God, whatever the cost. Same word as "stop" in 3:10.
12. Some think this gives the purpose and goal of the ceasing; others, the result, "so that *he* lives". Used only here. GK *1051*.
13. Or, "*in, by*", as also later in the verse.
14. On this word, see 2 Tim 1:9. Some manuscripts add "*of* life" {N}.
15. Some manuscripts add "*for* us" {N}.
16. Or, "purpose". Same word as in Rom 9:19. Elsewhere only as "intention" in Act 27:43. GK *1088*. That is, to be doing what the unbelievers choose to do.
17. Or, "proceeded, lived". Some manuscripts say "walking" {N}. The grammar indicates that this verb refers to the unexpressed subjects (it is plural) of "worked out" (that is, to Peter's readers), not to "Gentiles". "*For you*" is added earlier to reflect this. On this word, see "gone" in Mt 28:19.
18. Same word as "desires" in v 2.
19. This word is plural, "[episodes of] drunkenness". Used only here. GK *3886*. Related to "wine" in 1 Tim 5:23.
20. Used only here. GK *4542*. The root word is "drink".
21. Or, "forbidden, lawless". That is, contrary to the Law of God. Elsewhere only in Act 10:28. GK *116*.
22. That is, the "sensualities... idolatries".
23. Or, "are surprised". Same word as in 4:12, and as "being strange" in Act 17:20. On this word, see "lodging" in Act 10:6.
24. Or, "flood, pouring-out". Used only here. GK *431*.
25. The grammar indicates that this is a further description of "they" who are "thinking it strange". "*They continue*" is added to reflect this. In addition, Peter may mean blaspheming "you", or "God", or both. On this word, see 1 Tim 6:1.
26. Literally, "holding *Himself* ready", an idiom elsewhere only in Act 21:13; 2 Cor 12:14; and similar to 2 Cor 10:6. GK *2290*.
27. Compare Act 10:42; 2 Tim 4:1.
28. Or, "For this *purpose*". Same phrase as "to this" in 2:21; 3:9; "for this" in Mk 1:38; Act 26:16; Rom 14:9; 2 Cor 2:9; 1 Tim 4:10.
29. Or, "*Christ*", taking the subject from v 1.
30. Used 54 times in the NT, this verb is passive elsewhere only in Mt 11:5; Lk 7:22; 16:16; Gal 1:11; Heb 4:2, 6; 1 Pet 1:25. Only here in 1 Pet 4:6 is it used with no subject expressed (unless "Christ" is the subject). On this word, see Act 5:42.
31. Same word as in v 5. Some think Peter means spiritually dead ones, as described in v 3. Thus he uses "dead" in two senses, like Jesus did in Mt 8:22, "Let the [spiritually] dead bury the [physically] dead". It "was announced" to formerly dead ones like you (Eph 2:1) so that like Christ, they might suffer the judgment of people in the flesh, but live according to God in the spirit. This positive reason is added to the negative one in v 3 as a reason to so arm yourselves. Others think Peter means the gospel was announced to the physically dead, like the "spirits in prison" in 3:19. Others think he means it was announced to departed Christians while they were still alive, so that after their physical death at the hands of people they might live like God in spirit. In these last two views, this would become point 1F., explaining "judge the dead". On this word, see Mt 8:22.
32. Peter uses grammar that emphasizes the contrast between the two halves of this sentence.
33. Or, "in accordance with, by way of, in keeping with". GK *2848*.
34. That is, in accordance with human standards and verdicts. Once people become Christians, they are called to suffer for doing good as Christ did, as He gave us the example (2:21), as He warned (Jn 15:18-21), as Paul also stated (2 Tim 3:12). The suffering is limited to this life, as with Christ. The world judges them on earth even to the point of physical death. But they live both now and forever in the spirit for God. On this word, see "mankind" in Mt 4:4.
35. That is, "*in the sphere of the* flesh", our human existence on earth. Same word as in v 1, 2.
36. That is, in accordance with God's standards, verdict, will. "According to God" is also in 5:2, and elsewhere only in Rom 8:27; 2 Cor 7:9, 10, 11; Eph 4:24. Those who think verse 6 is referring to physically dead people take this to mean "according to the likeness or nature of God". Such people were judged in accordance with all mankind's human fleshly nature, and now after death they live in accordance with God's spiritual nature.
37. Or, "Spirit". Since our "spirit" lives in the realm of the "Spirit", it is difficult to separate these two ideas. That is, "*in the sphere of the* spirit".
38. Peter gives a further motive to arm yourselves to suffer, 4:1. James makes the same connection in 5:8-11. Others place this in point 4B. as a motive for what follows, in which case this word would be rendered "Now". As with "The Lord is near" in Phil 4:5, it fits in both places.
39. Or, "for, for the purpose of". GK *1650*.

A. Col 2:23   B. Act 23:1   C. Eph 1:21   D. Eph 5:21   E. Gal 5:16   F. Mt 4:4, mankind   G. Jn 7:17   H. Mt 6:34, sufficient   J. Phil 2:12
K. 2 Pet 2:2   L. Rom 13:13   M. Act 3:11, run together   N. Eph 5:18   O. Mt 16:27   P. Act 19:40   Q. Mt 7:1   R. Mk 13:7   S. Lk 21:28
T. Rom 12:3   U. 1 Pet 1:13   V. 1 Tim 2:1

1 Peter 4:8	900 Verse

    1C. Above all, having fervent[1] love[A] for each other— because love covers[2] *a* multitude *of* sins   8
    2C. *Being* hospitable[3] to one another without grumbling[4]   9
    3C. As each[5] received *a* grace-gift[6], ministering[7] it to each other as good stewards[8] *of the*   10
           diversified[9] grace[B] *of* God—

        1D. If anyone speaks[C], as *speaking* oracles[10] *of* God   11
        2D. If anyone serves[11], as *serving* by strength[D] which God supplies[E]

    4C. In order that God may be glorified[F] in all *things* through Jesus Christ

        1D. *To* Whom[12] is the glory[G] and the dominion[H] forever and ever[J], amen

5B. Beloved[K], do not be thinking-strange[13] the fiery[14] *suffering* among you coming *upon* you for *a* trial[15],   12
    as-*though a* strange[L] *thing were* happening[M] *to* you

    1C. But be rejoicing[16] to-the-degree[N] you are sharing[17] in the sufferings[O] *of* Christ, in order that   13
        you may also rejoice while being overjoyed[18] at the revelation[P] *of* His glory[G]!

        1D. If you are being reproached[19] in[20] *the* name *of* Christ, *you are* blessed[21] *ones*— because   14
            the Spirit *of* glory[22] and *of* God[23] is resting[Q] upon you[24]

            1E. For let none *of* you be suffering[R] as *a* murderer[S] or thief or evil-doer[T], or as *a* meddler[25]   15
            2E. But if *one suffers* as *a* Christian[26]— let him not be ashamed[U], but let him be glorifying[F]   16
                God in this name[27]

    2C. Because *it is* time[V] *that* the judgment[W] begin from the household[28] *of* God. But if *it begins* first   17
        from us, what *will be* the outcome[29] *of* the *ones* disobeying[30] the good-news[X] *of* God?

        1D. "And if the righteous[Y] *one* is saved[Z] with-difficulty[31], where will the ungodly[AA] and sinner[BB]   18
            appear[32]?" [Prov 11:31]

6B. So then, let indeed the *ones* suffering[R] according to the will *of* God be entrusting[CC] their souls[DD] in   19
    good-doing[33] *to a* faithful[34] Creator

    1C. Therefore[35] I exhort[EE] the elders[36] among you— *I* the fellow-elder[37] and witness[FF] *of* the   5:1
        sufferings[O] *of* Christ, the sharer[38] also *of* the glory[G] going-to[39] be revealed[GG]— *shepherd[40] the   2
        flock[41] *of* God among you, exercising-oversight[42]

        1D. Not by-compulsion[43], but willingly[44], according to God[45]
        2D. Nor greedily[46], but eagerly[47]

1. Or, "earnest, intense". Used only here. GK *1756*. Related to "fervently" in 1:22; and "fervency" in Act 26:7.
2. Or, "veils, conceals, hides". Same word as in Jam 5:20; Mt 8:24; 10:26; Lk 8:16; 23:30. Elsewhere only as "veil" in 2 Cor 4:3. GK *2821*. Related to "covering" in 2:16. Some manuscripts say "will cover" {N}. Peter may be quoting Prov 10:12.
3. On this word, see Tit 1:8. It is a qualification for elders.
4. Some manuscripts have this noun plural {N}. On this word, see Phil 2:14.
5. In the Greek, "each" is singular, and "ministering" is plural. Peter thus individualizes the case for every person. This kind of grammar occurs also in Mt 18:35; Jn 7:53; Act 2:6, 8; Heb 8:11; Rev 5:8; 20:13.
6. This word is rendered this way to show its relationship to "grace" following. This is the word used for spiritual gifts by Paul. Some think these are in view here. Others think all God's gifts to us are in view. Peter groups them in two categories, speaking and serving. On this word, see "gift" in 1 Cor 1:7.
7. Or, "serving". This word means "to serve, help, attend to, take care of" in any sense. Same word as in Mt 4:11; Mk 1:13; Act 19:22; 2 Cor 8:19, 20; 2 Tim 1:18; 1 Pet 1:12. Elsewhere only as "serve" in Mt 8:15; 20:28; 25:44; 27:55; Mk 1:31; 10:45; 15:41; Lk 4:39; 8:3; 10:40; 12:37; 17:8; 22:26, 27; Jn 12:2, 26; Act 6:2; Rom 15:25; 2 Cor 3:3; 1 Tim 3:10, 13; Phm 13; Heb 6:10; 1 Pet 4:11. GK *1354*. Related to "servant" in 1 Cor 3:5; "ministry" in 1 Cor 12:5.
8. Or, "managers, household administrators". Elsewhere only in Lk 12:42; 16:1, 3, 8; Rom 16:23; 1 Cor 4:1, 2; Gal 4:2; Tit 1:7. GK *3874*. Related to "stewardship" in Eph 1:10.
9. Or, "multi-colored, variegated, manifold". Same word as "various" in 1:6, and 8 other times. GK *4476*.
10. Or, "sayings, declarations, pronouncements". On this word, see Heb 5:12.
11. Same word as "ministering" in v 10.
12. Some think this refers to "Jesus Christ", the nearest choice; others, to "God", the main subject of the sentence.
13. Or, "be being surprised at". Same word as in v 4. Related to "strange" later in this verse.
14. Elsewhere only as "burning" in Rev 18:9, 18. GK *4796*. Here it is used figuratively to mean "painful" or "intense".
15. Or, "test". On this word, see Jam 1:2. Compare Rev 2:10.
16. This is the same counsel given in Jam 1:2, "Regard it all joy". "Joy" is the same root word as "rejoice". On this word, see 2 Cor 13:11.
17. Or, "taking a share". On this word, see 2 Jn 11. Compare Col 1:24.
18. On this word, see "rejoice greatly" in Lk 10:21. "Rejoice" and "be overjoyed" are also used together in Mt 5:12.
19. This word means "to heap insults on, revile" and "to reprimand, scold, express displeasure at blameworthy behavior". Elsewhere only in Mt 5:11; 11:20; 27:44; Mk 15:32; 16:14; Lk 6:22; Rom 15:3; Jam 1:5. GK *3943*. The related noun is in Heb 10:33.
20. Or, "in connection with". GK *1877*.
21. Or, "fortunate". Same word as in 3:14.
22. Some manuscripts add "and power" {A}.
23. Or, "the [presence] *of* glory and the Spirit *of* God", or, "the [name] *of* glory and the Spirit *of* God".
24. Some manuscripts add "He is blasphemed according to them, and He is glorified according to you" {A}.
25. Or, "busybody". Related to "exercise oversight" in 5:2, this is one who looks upon the affairs of others. Used only here. GK *258*.
26. That is, suffers unjustly because he or she is a Christian. Elsewhere only in Act 11:26; 26:28. GK *5985*.
27. That is, "Christian". Some manuscripts say "matter" {N}.
28. Or, "family, house". It begins in the persecutions you are facing and will face. On this word, see "house" in Mk 3:20.
29. Same word as in 1:9.
30. Same word as in 3:1.
31. If Christians suffer such fiery trials on earth, what awaits the unbeliever? What will happen to those who ignore or reject Jesus Christ? Same word as in Act 14:18; 27:7, 8, 16. Elsewhere only as "rarely" in Rom 5:7. GK *3660*.
32. Or, "make an appearance, show themselves". On this word, see "shine" in Phil 2:15.
33. This is a noun, used only here. GK *17*. Related to "good-doer" in 2:14; and the verb in 2:15, 20; 3:6, 17.
34. On this word, see Col 1:2. Some manuscripts say "as *to a* faithful Creator" {K}.
35. In view of the sufferings, I exhort you elders to provide oversight. Some manuscripts omit this word {N}.
36. That is, the church leaders. On this word, see 1 Tim 5:17.
37. Used only here. GK *5236*. Related to "elder". Compare 2 Jn 1; 3 Jn 1.
38. Some think Peter is referring back the glory he shared in at the transfiguration. He has already shared in what will be revealed. Others think he is referring to the future glory he will share with his fellow elders, to which he refers again in v 4. On this word, see 2 Pet 1:4.
39. Or, "being about to, destined to". On this word, see Mk 10:32.
40. Same word as in Jn 21:16; Act 20:28. On this word, see Rev 19:15. "Shepherd", "sheep", and "flock" are related words.
41. Elsewhere only in Lk 12:32; Act 20:28, 29; 1 Pet 5:3. GK *4480*. Related word in Jn 10:16.
42. This is the verb related to "overseer" (see Phil 1:1), the other name for this church leader. It means "to care for, look upon, visit, oversee, examine, watch over". Elsewhere only in Heb 12:15. GK *2174*. The root word is "to look upon". Some manuscripts omit this word {C}. Related to "meddler" in 4:15.
43. Or, "not by necessity". Not by force, by obligation. Not draftees, reluctantly serving. Used only here. GK *339*. Related to "compel" in Gal 6:12; and "compulsion" in Phm 14 (a good example of this).
44. That is, voluntarily, by choice. Elsewhere only as "willfully" in Heb 10:26. GK *1731*. Related to "willingness" in Phm 14; and "willingly" in Rom 8:20.
45. That is, according to the will of God, as God would have you to do. Some manuscripts omit this phrase {C}.
46. Or, "with fondness for dishonest gain". Used only here. GK *154*. A related word is used as a qualification for elders in Tit 1:7, and for deacons in 1 Tim 3:8. Not serving like a hireling, for pay.
47. Or, "willingly", but not related to the previous word. Used only here. GK *4610*. Related to "eager" in Rom 1:15; and "eagerness" in 2 Cor 8:19.

A. 1 Jn 4:16   B. Eph 2:8   C. Jn 12:49   D. Eph 1:19   E. 2 Cor 9:10   F. Rom 8:30   G. 2 Pet 2:10   H. Eph 6:10, might   J. Rev 20:10   K. Mt 3:17   L. Rom 16:23, host   M. Act 21:35   N. 2 Cor 8:12   O. Phil 3:10   P. 2 Thes 1:7   Q. Phm 7, refreshed   R. 1 Pet 4:1   S. Act 7:52   T. 1 Pet 2:12   U. 1 Jn 2:28, put to shame   V. Mt 8:29   W. Jn 9:39   X. 1 Cor 15:1   Y. Rom 1:17   Z. Lk 19:10   AA. Jude 15   BB. Mt 9:10   CC. Act 17:3, put before   DD. Jam 5:20   EE. Rom 12:8   FF. Act 1:8   GG. 2 Thes 2:3

	3D. Nor as lording-over¹ *your* lots², but being³ patterns⁴ *for* the flock	3
	4D. And the Chief-shepherd having appeared^A, you will receive⁵ the unfading⁶ crown^B *of* glory⁷	4
2C.	Likewise, younger^C *men*— be subject^D *to the* elders⁸	5
3C.	And everyone⁹—	

    1D. Clothe-*yourselves*-with¹⁰ humblemindedness^E *toward* one another

        1E. Because "God opposes¹¹ *the* arrogant¹², but He gives grace^F *to the* humble^G" [Prov 3:34]
        2E. Therefore humble^H *yourselves* under the mighty hand *of* God in order that He may exalt^J you at *the* proper-time¹³   6

            1F. Having cast¹⁴ all your anxiety¹⁵ upon Him, because He is concerned¹⁶ about you   7

    2D. Be sober^K, keep-watch^L. Your adversary¹⁷ *the* devil^M is walking-around like *a* roaring lion, seeking^N someone to devour¹⁸   8

        1E. Whom resist¹⁹, firm²⁰ *in* the faith²¹, knowing *that* the same *kinds of* sufferings^O *are* being accomplished²² *by* your brotherhood^P *in* the world   9

    3D. And the God *of* all grace^F, the *One* having called^Q you²³ into His eternal^R glory^S in Christ Jesus²⁴— *you* having suffered^T *a* little²⁵— will²⁶ Himself restore²⁷, support²⁸, strengthen²⁹, establish³⁰ *you*. *To Him be*³¹ the dominion³² forever³³, amen   10
                                                                                                                                   11

A. I wrote *to* you   12

    1. Through Silvanus³⁴, the faithful^U brother^V, as³⁵ I count^W *him*
    2. With *a* few³⁶ words
    3. Exhorting^X and bearing-witness *that* this³⁷ is *the* true^Y grace^F *of* God— in which, stand³⁸ [firm]

B. She³⁹ in Babylon⁴⁰ chosen-with⁴¹ *you* greets^Z you. Also Mark⁴², my son   13
C. Greet one another with *a* kiss⁴³ *of* love^AA   14
D. Peace^BB *to* you, *to* all the *ones* in Christ⁴⁴

1. Or, "domineering, ruling over". Their leadership is not directive, telling, but doing, serving. It is not "executive" leadership, but "servant" leadership. Elsewhere only in Mt 20:25; Mk 10:42; and as "subdue" in Act 19:16. GK *2894*. Related to the word in Rom 7:1.
2. That is, the ones allotted-to (the related verb in Act 17:4) your charge by God; your sphere of authority; those for whom you are responsible. Note Heb 13:17. On this word, see "share" in Col 1:12.
3. Or, "proving to be, becoming". GK *1181*.
4. This word means "imprints (of a stamp), copies, figures, models, examples". Elders are to be the model or pattern or example of what it means to be a Christian. Same word as in Act 7:44; Rom 5:14; Phil 3:17; 2 Thes 3:9; 1 Tim 4:12; Tit 2:7; Heb 8:5. Elsewhere only as "example" in 1 Cor 10:6; 1 Thes 1:7; "mark" in Jn 20:25; "image" in Act 7:43; "form" in Act 23:25; Rom 6:17. GK *5596*. Related to "strike" in Lk 6:29.
5. Same word as in 1:9.
6. Used only here. GK *277*. Related to "unfading" in 1:4.
7. That is, consisting of, belonging to, or characterized by glory.
8. Or, "*to your* elders". Some think Peter means older men in general; others, the church leaders just mentioned.
9. Some manuscripts say, "And everyone, being subject *to* one another, clothe *yourselves* with humblemindedness" {N}.
10. This word is used of tying on a garment, such as an apron. Used only here. GK *1599*.
11. Or, "resists". On this word, see Rom 13:2.
12. Or "proud, haughty". On this word, see Jam 4:6.
13. On this word, see "time" in Mt 8:29. Some manuscripts say "at the time *of* visitation" {A}, adding the word used in 2:12.
14. Or, "thrown". Elsewhere only in Lk 19:35, of "casting" their garments on the donkey for Jesus. GK *2166*.
15. Or, "care, concern, worry". Same word as in Mt 13:22; Mk 4:19; Lk 8:14; 21:34. Elsewhere only as "concern" in 2 Cor 11:28. GK *3533*. Related to "be anxious" in Mt 6:25.
16. This idiom is more literally "because it is *a* concern *to* Him about you". On this word, see 1 Cor 7:21.
17. Or, "enemy, opponent, accuser". Elsewhere only in Mt 5:25; Lk 12:58; 18:3. GK *508*. Some manuscripts say "because your adversary..." {N}.
18. Persecutions seem to be in view, "sufferings" (v 9). Some manuscripts say "seeking whom he may devour"; others, "seeking to devour" {C}. On this word, see "swallow up" in Heb 11:29.
19. Resist the devil. Same word as in Jam 4:7.
20. On this adjective, see 2 Tim 2:19.
21. Or, "in *your* faith". On this word, see Eph 2:8.
22. Or "completed". This word also means "paid" as in paying a debt, "knowing *that* the same *debt of* sufferings *is being* paid *by* your brotherhood". On this word, see "perfecting" in 2 Cor 7:1.
23. Some manuscripts say "us" {A}.
24. Some manuscripts omit this word {C}.
25. This can mean after having suffered a short time (as in 1:6); or a small quantity (as in Lk 5:3; and "few" here in v 12); or to a small degree (as in Lk 7:47b). On this word, see "small" in Act 12:18. This is the Greek word order of this verse. Others place this clause first in the sentence, in order to make the sentence smoother, "And [after] having suffered a little, the God *of* all grace... will Himself ".
26. Some manuscripts say "may the God *of* all grace... Himself restore..." {B}, making it a prayer.
27. Or, "complete, prepare, equip". On this word, see "prepare" in Rom 9:22.
28. Or, "establish, fix, set". On this word, see "establish" in 1 Thes 3:2.
29. Or, "make strong". Used only here. GK *4964*. With a negative prefix, the root word means "to be weak, sick" (see "sick" in 2 Tim 4:20 on it), and is used often in the NT.
30. Or, "found". That is, establish your foundation, set you on a firm foundation. On this word, see "founded" in Eph 3:17.
31. Or, "*is*", as it is expressed in 4:11.
32. Some manuscripts say "the glory and the dominion" {B}, as in 4:11.
33. Some manuscripts say "forever and ever" {A}. On this idiom, see Rev 20:10.
34. On Silvanus, see 1 Thes 1:1. Some think this means Silvanus wrote this book down for Peter; others, that he delivered the book to the readers; others, that he did both both.
35. Others take this with what follows, "As I account *it*, through *a* few words".
36. That is, briefly. Same word as "little" in v 10. Not the same word as the similar statement in Heb 13:22.
37. That is, this which Peter has written and taught in this letter.
38. Instead of a command, some manuscripts say "in which you stand" {N}. GK *2705*.
39. Some think Peter is referring to his wife; others, to the church in Babylon. Compare 2 Jn 1, 13. Some manuscripts add "church" {A}.
40. Some think Peter means literal Babylon (in present-day Iraq). Others think he is referring to Rome. GK *956*.
41. This adjective is used only here. GK *5293*. It is the word "chosen" in 1:1 combined with "with".
42. According to early Christian writers, after Mark left Paul and went with Barnabas (Act 15:37-39) his cousin (Col 4:10), he became Peter's interpreter and wrote the Gospel of Mark under his direction. He also assisted Paul again, as seen in 2 Tim 4:11; Phm 24. See Act 12:25. GK *3453*.
43. On this word, see Rom 16:16. Some manuscripts say "with *a* holy kiss" {A}.
44. Some manuscripts add "Jesus" {A}. Some add "amen" {A}.

A. 1 Jn 2:19, made evident B. Rev 4:4 C. Tit 2:6 D. Eph 5:21 E. Phil 2:3 F. Eph 2:8 G. Jam 1:9, lowly H. Phil 4:12 J. Jn 8:28, lifted up
K. 1 Pet 1:13 L. 1 Thes 5:6 M. Rev 12:9 N. Phil 2:21 O. Phil 3:10 P. 1 Pet 2:17 Q. Rom 8:30 R. Mt 25:46 S. 2 Pet 2:10 T. 1 Pet 4:1
U. Col 1:2 V. Act 16:40 W. Rom 3:28, consider X. Rom 12:8 Y. Jn 6:55 Z. Mk 15:18 AA. 1 Jn 4:16 BB. Act 15:33

Overview	**2 Peter**

Introduction	1:1-2
1A. Since His divine power has granted us all things for life and godliness by His own glory and virtue	1:3
1B. Through which qualities He has granted us the promises through which we share in His nature	1:4
2B. And indeed for this very reason you having applied all diligence	1:5
3B. Supply virtue, knowledge, self control, endurance, godliness, brotherly love and love	1:5-7
4B. For these qualities make you neither useless nor unfruitful in the knowledge of Christ	1:8
5B. For the one in whom these qualities are not present is blind, having forgotten his purification	1:9
6B. Therefore brothers, be more diligent to be making your calling and election firm	1:10-11
2A. Therefore, I will always remind you about these things, even though you have known the truth	1:12
1B. And I regard it right to be arousing you with a reminder as long as I am in this bodily tent	1:13-14
2B. And I will be diligent that after my departure you may be able to remember these things	1:15
3B. For we made known to you the power and coming of our Lord Jesus as eyewitnesses	1:16-18
4B. And we have the prophetic word more firm, to which you are doing well to pay attention	1:19-21
5B. But there will also be false teachers among you who will bring in destructive heresies	2:1
1C. And many will follow their sensualities, because of whom the truth will be blasphemed	2:2
2C. And in greed they will exploit you with fabricated words	2:3
3C. For whom the judgment is not idle, for God will judge them and protect the godly	2:3-10
4C. Daring, self-willed ones— they blaspheme dignities. But they will be destroyed	2:10-13
5C. They are spots and blemishes, reveling in their deceptions, trained in greed	2:13-14
6C. Children of a curse— they went astray in the way of Balaam	2:14-16
7C. They are waterless springs, for whom the gloom of darkness has been reserved	2:17-22
3A. Beloved, I am writing this to arouse you to remember the words of the prophets and apostles	3:1-2
1B. Knowing this first— that mockers will come denying the coming of the day of the Lord	3:3-7
2B. But do not let it escape your notice, beloved, that one day with God is like a thousand years	3:8
1C. The Lord is not slow about the promise, but is patient, not wishing any to perish	3:9
2C. But the day of the Lord will come like a thief, so what kind of people should you be?	3:10-12
3C. But in accordance with His promise, we are looking for a new heavens and new earth	3:13
3B. Therefore beloved, while looking for these things, be diligent to be found unspotted	3:14-16
4B. You therefore, beloved, knowing this beforehand	3:17
1C. Be guarding yourselves in order that you may not fall from your own steadfastness	3:17
2C. And be growing in the grace and knowledge of our Lord and Savior Jesus Christ	3:18

	A. Simeon[1] Peter, *a* slave[A] and apostle[B] *of* Jesus Christ	1
	B. *To* the *ones* having received[2] *an* equally-precious[3] faith[4] *with* us[5] by-means-of[6] *the* righteousness[7] *of* our God[8] and Savior[C] Jesus Christ[9]	
	C. May grace and peace be multiplied[D] *to* you in[10] *the* knowledge[E] *of* God[11] and Jesus[12] our Lord	2
1A.	Since[13] His[14] divine[F] power[G] has granted[15] us **all *things*** pertaining-to life[H] and godliness[J] through the knowledge[E] *of* the One[16] having called[K] us by[17] *His* own[18] glory[L] and virtue[19]	3
	1B. Through which *qualities*[20] He has granted us the precious[21] and greatest *things*-promised[22] in order that through these[23] you might become sharers[24] *of the* divine[25] nature[26]	4
	1C. Having escaped-from[M] the corruption[27] in the world by[28] *evil* desire[N]	
	2B. And indeed *for* this very *reason*[29] *you* having applied[30] all diligence[31]	5
	3B. In[32] your faith, supply[33] virtue[34]	
	1C. And in *your* virtue, knowledge[O]	
	2C. And in *your* knowledge, self-control[35]	6
	3C. And in *your* self-control, endurance[P]	
	4C. And in *your* endurance, godliness[36]	
	5C. And in *your* godliness, brotherly-love[37]	7
	6C. And in *your* brotherly-love, love[38]	
	4B. For these *qualities* being-present[39] *in* you and increasing[Q] make[40] *you* neither[41] useless[42] nor unfruitful[43] in the knowledge[E] *of* our Lord Jesus Christ	8
	5B. For *the one in* whom these *qualities* are not present[R] is blind, being shortsighted[44], having forgotten[45] the purification[46] *of* his former[S] sins	9

1. This word reflects the Aramaic form of "Simon". See Lk 6:14. Some manuscripts say "Simon" {B}.
2. This word means to receive something by divine will, or to obtain something through the casting of lots. It is a graphic word to use here. It points to God as the sovereign giver, and to us as receiving without effort on our part. Same word as in Act 1:17. Elsewhere only as "obtained by lot" in Lk 1:9; and "cast lots" in Jn 19:24. GK *3275*.
3. Some think Peter means equal in value, worth; others, equal in honor and privilege. Used only here. GK *2700*.
4. That is, saving faith. On this word, see Eph 2:8.
5. Some think Peter means "us apostles"; others, "you Gentile Christians with us Jewish Christians".
6. Or, "in, in connection with, by, through". GK *1877*.
7. Some think Peter is referring to the gift of righteousness given to us, "equally precious... by means of the gift given"; others, to the character quality of God, "equally precious... by means of the righteous character of God who gave it to us". Others link this to "faith", "faith *with* us in connection with *the* righteousness *of* our God".
8. Some think Peter means "*belonging to* our God"; others, "*from* our God".
9. Some think Peter is calling Jesus "our God and Savior". It is the exact same grammatical construction as "our Lord and Savior Jesus Christ" in 1:11; 2:20; 3:18. Others render it "our God and *the* Savior Jesus Christ". The issue is whether Peter is using "God" here as a proper name as in v 2 (making this two persons), or as a title like "Lord" (making this two titles or descriptions of one person). The same question arises in Tit 2:13.
10. Or, "by means of ", as in v 1.
11. Some think Peter means "*about* God"; others, "*from* God".
12. Some manuscripts say "Christ Jesus"; others, "Jesus Christ" {A}.
13. This is the word "as" in the sense of "since, seeing that, because" (see 2 Cor 5:20). Verses 3-7 are all one sentence, the main Greek sentence being more literally, "Because of His divine power having granted... and indeed *you* having applied all diligence, supply virtue".
14. As to the reference of "His", "the *One*" having called, and "He" has granted (v 4), some think Peter means the Father, the Son, the Father; others, Jesus in all three cases; others, the Son, the Father, the Father.
15. Or, "bestowed, given as a gift". Elsewhere only in v 4; Mk 15:45. GK *1563*. This is a participle, "Because of His divine power having granted". Related to "gift" in Rom 5:15; Mt 5:23.
16. Some think Peter means "*from* the *One*"; others, "*about* the *One*".
17. Or, "*to*". Some think Peter means "having called us *by*"; others, "having granted us... *by*".
18. Some manuscripts omit this word and add "through" {B}, so that it says "called us through glory and virtue".
19. Or, "moral excellence, excellence of character". Elsewhere only in v 5; Phil 4:8; 1 Pet 2:9. GK *746*.
20. That is, through His glory and virtue. Others think Peter means "which *things*", referring to the "all things" in v 3.
21. Same word as in 1 Pet 1:19. Used 13 times. GK *5508*. Related to "equally precious" in v 1; "honoring" in 1 Tim 5:3; and "preciousness" in Rev 18:19.
22. Peter means that God has granted us what He had promised (forgiveness, life, the Spirit, etc.), not that He has made new promises to us. Elsewhere only as "promise" in 3:13. GK *2041*.
23. That is, "these things promised". Others think Peter means "these qualities" again, the glory and virtue.
24. Or, "partners". Same word as in 1 Cor 10:18, 20; 2 Cor 1:7; 1 Pet 5:1. Elsewhere only as "partner" in Mt 23:30; Lk 5:10; 2 Cor 8:23; Phm 17; Heb 10:33. GK *3128*. Related to "fellowship" in 1 Cor 1:9.
25. Elsewhere only in v 3; Act 17:29. GK *2521*. Related to the word in Rom 1:20; and to "God".
26. That is, His moral characteristics and qualities. Only here is this word used of God. On this word, see Eph 2:3. We do not become gods, like Him in substance. We become His children, like our Father in character qualities.
27. Same word as in 2:19.
28. Or, "by means of, in connection with". GK *1877*. Or, "the corruption in desire in the world". Some manuscripts say "the *evil* desire and corruption in the world"; others, "the desire *of* corruption in the world" {B}.
29. Or, "And indeed *as to* this very *thing*". That is, because God has granted all this for the purpose stated. The idiom "this very" is elsewhere only in Rom 9:17; 13:6; 2 Cor 2:3; 5:5; 7:11; Gal 2:10; Eph 6:22; Phil 1:6; Col 4:8.
30. Or, "brought in beside *it*". Used only here. GK *4210*.
31. On this word, see "earnestness" in 2 Cor 8:16. Related to the verb in v 10.
32. Or, "In connection with, In the sphere of ". This same word is in each phrase through v 7. GK *1877*.
33. Or, "provide, furnish". Same word as in v 11. On this word, see 2 Cor 9:10.
34. Same word as in v 3.
35. Elsewhere only in Act 24:25; Gal 5:23. GK *1602*. Related to the word in 1 Cor 7:9; and in Tit 1:8.
36. Same word as in v 3; 3:11. On this word, see 1 Tim 2:2.
37. That is, love of fellow Christians. On this word, see Heb 13:1. Note 1 Jn 4:20.
38. This is the Greek word *agape*. It is the God kind of love, volitional love, love by choice. On this word, see 1 Jn 4:16.
39. Or, "existing". On this word, see "being" in Phil 2:6.
40. Or, "render", or, "put-*you*-in-a-state-of-being...". On this word, see "put in charge" in Act 6:3.
41. Peter means that this will make you very useful and fruitful. This figure of speech is called a litotes, on which see Act 12:18.
42. Or, "idle, unproductive". On this word, see Jam 2:20, faith without works is "useless".
43. This is the same word Jesus used in Mt 13:22. On this word, see 1 Cor 14:14.
44. Or, "nearsighted". Such people are so focused on the earthly that they are blind to the spiritual consequences of being a "hearer only", Jam 1:22. Used only here. GK *3697*. Our word "myopia" comes from this Greek word. This person does not see the distant reality.
45. This is an idiom, literally, "having received forgetfulness *of* ". Such people put it out of their mind. This is the reason for their blindness. "Forgetfulness" is used only here. GK *3330*.
46. Same word as in Lk 2:22; Jn 2:6; 3:25; Heb 1:3. Elsewhere only as "cleansing" in Mt 1:44; Lk 5:14. GK *2752*. Related to "cleanse" in Heb 9:22.

A. Rom 6:17 B. 1 Cor 12:28 C. Lk 1:47 D. Act 7:17 E. Col 1:9 F. 2 Pet 1:4 G. Mk 5:30 H. Rom 8:10 J. 1 Tim 2:2 K. Rom 8:30 L. 2 Pet 2:10 M. 2 Pet 2:18 N. Gal 5:16 O. 1 Cor 12:8 P. Jam 1:3 Q. 2 Cor 8:15 R. Rev 17:8 S. Jude 4, formerly

	6B. Therefore brothers^A, be **more** diligent¹ to be making² your calling³ and election⁴ firm⁵	10
	1C. For while doing^B these *things*, you will by no means ever^C stumble⁶	
	2C. For in this manner the entrance⁷ into the eternal^D kingdom^E *of* our Lord and Savior Jesus Christ will be richly supplied⁸ *to* you	11
2A.	Therefore, I will-certainly⁹ always be reminding^F you about these *things,* even though *you are ones* knowing^G and¹⁰ having been established^H in *the* truth being present¹¹ *with you*	12
	1B. And I regard^J *it* right^K to be arousing¹² you with *a* reminder for as long as I am in this [bodily] tent¹³	13
	1C. Knowing^G that the putting-off^L *of* my [bodily] tent is imminent¹⁴, just as indeed our Lord Jesus Christ made-clear¹⁵ *to* me	14
	2B. And I will also be diligent *that* at-any-time¹⁶ after my departure¹⁷, you *may* have *the ability* to produce^B the memory¹⁸ *of* these *things*	15
	3B. For we made-known^M *to* you the power^N and coming¹⁹ *of* our Lord Jesus Christ	16
	1C. Not having followed-after²⁰ cleverly-devised²¹ myths^O, but having been made²² eyewitnesses *of* the majesty²³ *of* that *One*	
	1D. For *He* having received from God *the* Father *the* honor^P and glory^Q *of* such²⁴ *a* voice²⁵ having been carried²⁶ *to* Him by the Majestic²⁷ Glory^Q—	17
	1E. "This is My Son, My Beloved^R, in Whom **I** was²⁸ well-pleased^S"	
	2D. We²⁹ ourselves also heard this voice having been carried out of heaven, being with Him on the holy mountain	18
	4B. And we have the prophetic³⁰ word^T *as* more-firm³¹, *to* which you are doing well³² *to* be paying-attention^U as *to a* lamp^V shining^W in *a* dismal³³ place until which *time the* day dawns and *the* morning-star³⁴ rises^X in your hearts³⁵	19
	1C. Knowing^Y this first³⁶— that no prophecy³⁷ *of* Scripture comes³⁸ *from* one's own³⁹ interpretation⁴⁰	20
	1D. For no prophecy was ever carried⁴¹ *by the* will *of a* human^Z	21
	2D. But people⁴² being carried by *the* Holy Spirit spoke from God	

1. Or, "eager; take more pains, make every effort". Same word as in 1:15; 3:14. On this word, see Eph 4:3.
2. Same word as "doing" next. Some manuscripts say "... diligent in order that through your good works you may make..." {A}.
3. Elsewhere only in Rom 11:29; 1 Cor 1:26; 7:20; Eph 1:18; 4:1, 4; Phil 3:14; 2 Thes 1:11; 2 Tim 1:9; Heb 3:1. GK *3104*. Related to "called" in Rom 8:28.
4. Or, "choosing, selection". On this word, see "choosing" in Rom 11:5.
5. Or, "secure, sure, steadfast, reliable". Elsewhere only in v 19; Rom 4:16; 2 Cor 1:7; Heb 2:2; 3:14; 6:19; 9:17. GK *1010*. Related to "confirm" in 1 Cor 1:6.
6. Elsewhere only in Rom 11:11; Jam 2:10; 3:2. GK *4760*. Related to "from stumbling" in Jude 24.
7. Or, "entering, entry". On this word, see 1 Thes 1:9.
8. Same word as in v 5.
9. Or, "I must", "I **will**". On this word, see Mt 24:6. Some manuscripts say "I will not be negligent to always be reminding" {N}, using the word "neglect" in Heb 2:3.
10. Peter uses two participles here. In English, we prefer to say "even though you know and have been established".
11. Same word as in v 9. On this word, see Rev 17:8.
12. The phrase "arousing with a reminder" is also in 3:1.
13. Or, "dwelling place". Same word as in v 14. Elsewhere only as "dwelling place" in Act 7:46. GK *5013*. Using a related word, Paul also refers to our present body as a "tent" in 2 Cor 5:1. Related to "dwelt" in Jn 1:14. This term points to the temporary nature of our present body.
14. Or, "coming soon, quick, swift". Some think Peter means "soon"; others, "swift", that is, sudden and violent. For this reason he is writing now. Elsewhere only as "swift" in 2:1. GK *5442*.
15. Peter may be referring to what John later recorded in Jn 21:18-19; or, to a more recent revelation. On this word, see 1 Cor 3:13.
16. Or, "I will also be diligent at all times *that*...". Used only here. GK *1668*.
17. That is, his death. On this word, see Lk 9:31.
18. Or, "to make the remembrance". Used only here. GK *3647*. Some think Peter is referring to the writing of the Gospel of Mark, which Mark is said to have done under Peter's direction.
19. Some think Peter is referring to Christ's first coming, of which the apostles were eyewitnesses. Others think he is referring to His second coming, of which they were eyewitnesses to a foretaste— the Transfiguration. On this word, see 2 Thes 2:8.
20. Or, "followed out, pursued, complied with". Elsewhere only in 2:2, 15. GK *1979*.
21. This is a participle, myths "having been cleverly devised". GK *5054*.
22. Or, "having been, having come-to-be". GK *1181*.
23. On this word, see Lk 9:43. Related to "Majestic" next; and "majesty" in Heb 1:3.
24. Or, a voice "such-as-this". Used only here. GK *5524*.
25. Or, "utterance". Same word as in v 18; 2:16. On this word, see Mk 1:26. This may refer to the voice (such a unique voice), or to the content spoken (an utterance such as this). In either case, the content is given next.
26. Or, "carried along, borne along, brought forth". This same word is used four times in v 17, 18, 21. It generally means "to bear, carry, bring". Used 66 times. GK *5770*.
27. Or, "Magnificent". Used only here. GK *3485*.
28. On "I was well pleased", see Mt 17:5. Some manuscripts say, "This is My beloved Son" {B}, as in Matthew.
29. That is, Peter James and John, Mt 17:1-8. Note the connection, "For He having received it (v 17)... we ourselves heard it".
30. That is, the word written by the prophets— in particular, about the Messiah. Elsewhere only in Rom 16:26. GK *4738*. Related word in 1 Cor 12:28.
31. Same word as in 1:10. Some think Peter means "And we [all] have the more firm prophetic word". That is, we have the OT prophecies, which are an even stronger witness than our eyewitness account of the voice from heaven. Go to the Scriptures! Others think he means "And we [apostles] have the prophetic word [made] more firm", that is, more certain as to its meaning. Peter has the God-intended meaning of the Messianic prophecies more firm because he was an eyewitness of their fulfillment in Christ, of which the Transfiguration of v 17-18 is one example.
32. That is, you are doing a good thing, acting commendably, by paying attention. On this idiom, see Act 10:33.
33. Or, "squalid, dark". That is, morally dark. Used only here. GK *903*.
34. Or, "light-bearer". Used only here. GK *5892*. Not the same word as "morning star" (two words) in Rev 2:28; 22:16, but the same idea.
35. Some think Peter means until Christ returns, when we shall be like Him, 1 Jn 3:2. Others think he means until you are mature Christians as described in v 5-8, until your faith is perfected in love.
36. That is, of first importance. Same phrase as in 3:3.
37. On this word, see 1 Cor 12:10. More literally, "every prophecy *of* Scripture does not come".
38. Same word as "came" in 2:1; "become" in 1:4; "made" in 1:16. GK *1181*. Used 669 times, it means "to become", mostly in the sense of "come to be, come into being, originate, arise, be made", or in the sense of "come about, happen, take place". Peter could be referring to a prophecy's origin— "no prophecy [as written] comes into being *from* [the prophet's] own interpretation" of events. God is the author, v 21; Jer 23:16; Ezek 13:3. Or, he could be referring to its fulfillment— "no prophecy [as fulfilled] comes to pass *from* [one's] own interpretation" of it. Fulfillment originates with the Author, v 21. To understand the Messianic prophecies like Isa 53, the key is how God fulfilled them, not how a human interprets them. Thus Peter had the prophetic word more firm (v 19), because he heard and saw firsthand God's fulfillment of it. Or he could be referring to a prophecy's interpretation— "no prophecy comes [to be understood] *from* personal interpretation", because God is the author, v 21. A Spirit-filled guide (like Jesus, Lk 24:27, 45; or we apostles who have it more firm, v 19) is needed to "open" the OT Scriptures. False teachers bring in heresies, 2:1. The untaught "twist" the Scripture, 3:16.
39. Or, "personal, private". Same word as in 1:3; 2:16, 22; 3:3, 16, 17. On this word, see Act 20:28.
40. Or, "explanation". Used only here. GK *2146*. The related verb is "explained" in Mk 4:34.
41. That is, "carried" out of heaven, as this word is used in v 18; or, "brought" to the prophet, as it is used in 2:11. Same word as later in this verse; and as "carried along" in Heb 6:1. See v 17 on it.
42. Same word as "human". Some manuscripts say "holy people" {A}.

A. Act 16:40 B. Rev 13:13 C. Gal 2:6 D. Mt 25:46 E. Mt 3:2 F. Jn 14:26 G. 1 Jn 2:29 H. 1 Thes 3:2 J. Jam 1:2 K. Rom 1:17, righteous L. 1 Pet 3:21 M. Phil 1:22, know N. Mk 5:30 O. 1 Tim 1:4 P. 1 Tim 5:17 Q. 2 Pet 2:10 R. Mt 3:17 S. Mt 17:5 T. 1 Cor 12:8 U. 1 Tim 3:8 V. Lk 11:34 W. Phil 2:15 X. Heb 7:14 Y. Lk 1:34 Z. Mt 4:4, mankind

5B. But false-prophets^A also came¹ among the people^B, as there will also be false-teachers among you who will secretly-bring-in² heresies^C of destruction³— even denying^D the Master^E having bought^F them⁴, bringing swift⁵ destruction upon themselves 2:1

    1C. And many will follow-after^G their sensualities⁶, because of whom the way of the truth^H will be blasphemed^J 2

    2C. And in greed^K they will exploit⁷ you with fabricated⁸ words^L 3

    3C. For whom the judgment^M from-long-ago^N is not idle⁹, and their destruction^O is not asleep

        1D. For if 4

            1E. God did not spare^P angels having sinned, but handed-them-over¹⁰ to¹¹ chains¹² of gloom¹³, having cast-them-into-hell¹⁴

                1F. Being reserved¹⁵ for¹⁶ judgment^Q

            2E. And He did not spare the ancient^R world^S, but He protected^T the eighth¹⁷ one, Noah, a proclaimer^U of righteousness 5

                1F. Having brought a flood¹⁸ upon the world^S of ungodly^V ones

            3E. And He condemned^W the cities of Sodom and Gomorrah, having reduced-them-to-ashes by an overthrow¹⁹ 6

                1F. Having made^X them an example^Y of things coming to ungodly²⁰ ones

            4E. And He delivered^Z Lot, a righteous one being oppressed²¹ by the conduct^{AA} of the lawless²² ones in connection with sensuality^{BB} 7

                1F. For by sight²³ and hearing²⁴, the righteous one dwelling among them day after day²⁵ was tormenting^{CC} his righteous soul^{DD} with their lawless²⁶ works^{EE} 8

        2D. Then the Lord knows-how^{FF} 9

            1E. To deliver²⁷ godly^{GG} ones from a trial²⁸

            2E. And to reserve unrighteous^{HH} ones for the day of judgment²⁹, while being punished³⁰

                1F. And especially the ones proceeding after the flesh^{JJ} in a lust³¹ for defilement³², and despising³³ authority³⁴ 10

    4C. Daring³⁵, self-willed^{KK} ones— they do not tremble^{LL} while blaspheming^{MM} glories³⁶, *where³⁷ angels being greater³⁸ in strength and power do not bring a blasphemous^{NN} judgment^Q against them³⁹ from the Lord⁴⁰ 11

1. Or, "came-to-be, arose, were". GK *1181*. Prophecy "comes" from God (1:20), but false prophets also "came", same word.
2. Or, "secretly introduce". Used only here. GK *4206*. The related adjective is in Gal 2:4.
3. That is, heresies characterized by destruction, destructive heresies; or, heresies leading to destruction. Same word as later in the verse, as in v 3; 3:7, 16; and as in Mt 7:13; Jn 17:12; Act 8:20; Rom 9:22; Phil 1:28; 3:19; 2 Thes 2:3; 1 Tim 6:9; Heb 10:39; Rev 17:8, 11. Elsewhere only as "waste" in Mt 26:8; Mk 14:4. GK *724*. Related to "perish" in 1 Cor 1:18.
4. Compare 1 Jn 2:2.
5. Same word as "imminent" in 1:14.
6. Or, "lustful indulgences, debaucheries, indecent conduct, outrageous sexual behavior". Same word as in 2:7, 18; Jude 4. Elsewhere only in Mk 7:22; Rom 13:13; 2 Cor 12:21; Gal 5:19; Eph 4:19; 1 Pet 4:3. GK *816*. Some manuscripts say "destructions" {K}, the same word as in v 1, 3, rendered here "pernicious ways" in the KJV.
7. Or, "buy and sell, trade in, make merchandise of". Elsewhere only as "do business" in Jam 4:13. GK *1864*.
8. Or, "formed, made, made-up". The Greek word is *plastos* from which we get "plastic". Used only here. GK *4422*. The related verb, "to form, mold, make", is in Rom 9:20.
9. That is, it is prepared. Used only here. GK *733*. Related to "useless" in Jam 2:20.
10. Or, "delivered *them*". On this word, see Mt 26:21.
11. Or, "*with, in*".
12. Used only here. GK *4937*. Some manuscripts say "pits" {C}, using GK *4987*.
13. Or "blackness", used of the gloom of the netherworld. Elsewhere only in v 17; Jude 6, 13; Heb 12:18. GK *2432*.
14. This verb is used only here. GK *5434*. Or, "cast into Tartarus", the Greek term for the place of punishment, similar to the Jewish term "Gehenna". Note Jude 6; 1 Pet 3:19.
15. Same word as in v 17.
16. Or, "until". GK *1650*. Same word as in v 9; 3:7; Jude 6.
17. This is an idiom meaning the eighth along with seven others. Compare Gen 7:13; 1 Pet 3:20.
18. Elsewhere only in Mt 24:38, 39; Lk 17:27. GK *2886*. The Greek is *kataklusmos*, from which we get "cataclysm".
19. On this word, see 2 Tim 2:14. Same word as in Gen 19:29. Some manuscripts omit this word "*by an* overthrow" {C}.
20. Some manuscripts have the verbal form of this word here (there is one letter difference), resulting in the translation "having made *an* example *of the ones* intending to live ungodly" {C}. Both words are in Jude 15.
21. This word means "to be worn out by toil or suffering". Elsewhere only in Act 7:24. GK *2930*.
22. That is, ones who rebel against law, who live unlawfully, who live contrary to what is "set down". Not related to the word in v 8. Elsewhere only in 3:17. GK *118*. The root word is "place, set".
23. Or, "a seeing", what one sees. That is, by what he saw. This noun is used only here. GK *1062*.
24. Or, "report", what one hears. On this noun, see Heb 4:2.
25. This is the Greek word order. Some think Peter means "dwelling day after day"; others, "tormenting day after day".
26. Or, "contrary to law". The root word is "law". Same word as in 1 Tim 1:9. GK *491*.
27. Or, "rescue". Same word as in v 7.
28. Or, "test, temptation". On this word, see Jam 1:2. Some manuscripts have this word plural {N}.
29. This phrase "day *of* judgment" occurs also in 3:7; Mt 10:15; 11:22, 24; 12:36; 1 Jn 4:17; Jude 6. Same word as in v 4.
30. Elsewhere only in Act 4:21. GK *3134*. Related to "punishment" in Mt 25:46.
31. Or, "desire". On this word, see "desire" in Gal 5:16.
32. Or, "with *a* defiled desire", a desire characterized by defilement. Peter is referring to the incident of v 6-8, described in Gen 19:4-5, the pursuit of homosexual intercourse. Used only here. GK *3622*. A related word is in v 20, and the verb is used in Jude 8.
33. Or, "scorning, disregarding". On this word, see "disregard" in Rom 2:4.
34. Or, "lordship, dominion". Same word as in Jude 8. Elsewhere only as "lordship" in Eph 1:21; Col 1:16. GK *3262*. The root word is "lord". Some think Peter means "authority" in general; others, the "lordship" of Christ (2:1, denying the Master); others, the rule of angels (Col 1:16); others, the authority of church leaders.
35. Or, "Bold". Used only here. GK *5532*. On the related verb, which is used in Jude 9, see 2 Cor 11:21.
36. Or, "dignities, majesties". Same word as in Jude 8. Some think Peter means human dignities; others, angelic dignities. Some think Jude 8-9 explains this. It is plural elsewhere only in 1 Pet 1:11. This word is used 166 times meaning "glory" is various senses. GK *1518*. Related to "glorified" in Rom 8:30.
37. Some take this to mean "in the place where, in the situation in which"; others, "whereas". GK *3963*.
38. Some think Peter means "greater than the daring ones"; others, "greater than the glories".
39. Some think Peter means the glories; others, the daring ones. Thus some think angels who are greater than these daring ones do not blaspheme the daring ones; others, that angels greater than the glories blasphemed by the daring ones do not blaspheme these glories.
40. Some manuscripts say "before the Lord"; others omit "from the Lord" {C}.

A. Rev 16:13 B. Rev 21:3 C. 1 Cor 11:19, factions D. 2 Tim 2:12 E. Jude 4 F. Rev 5:9 G. 2 Pet 1:16 H. Jn 4:23 J. 1 Tim 6:1 K. Eph 4:19 L. 1 Cor 12:8 M. Jn 9:39 N. 2 Pet 3:5 O. 2 Pet 2:1 P. Rom 11:21 Q. Jn 3:19 R. Act 15:7, old S. 1 Jn 2:15 T. Jn 12:25, keep U. 2 Tim 1:11 V. Jude 15 W. 1 Cor 11:32 X. Act 19:21, put Y. Jn 13:15 Z. Col 1:13 AA. 1 Pet 1:15 BB. 2 Pet 2:2 CC. Rev 14:10 DD. Jam 5:20 EE. Mt 26:10 FF. 1 Jn 2:29, know GG. Act 10:2, devout HH. 1 Cor 6:9, wrong-doers JJ. Col 2:23 KK. Tit 1:7 LL. Mk 5:33 MM. 1 Tim 6:1 NN. 1 Tim 1:13

1D. But these *ones are*¹ like unreasoning^A animals^B having been born^C *as creatures*-of-instinct² for capture and destruction^D. While blaspheming^E in³ *things* which they are ignorant^F, they will also be destroyed⁴ in their⁵ destruction⁶, *being wronged^G *as the* wages *of* wrong-doing⁷   12

  13

5C. *They are* spots⁸ and blemishes *who are* regarding⁹ the reveling¹⁰ during *the* day *to be a* pleasure^H

    1D. Reveling¹¹ in their deceptions¹² while feasting-with¹³ you
    2D. Having eyes full^J *of an* adulteress¹⁴ and restless¹⁵ *of* sin   14
    3D. Enticing¹⁶ unstable¹⁷ souls^K
    4D. Having *a* heart trained¹⁸ *in* greed¹⁹

6C. Children^L *of a* curse²⁰— *they went-astray^M, leaving-behind^N *the* straight^O way, having followed-after^P the way *of* Balaam the *son of* Bosor²¹, who loved^Q *the* wages *of* wrong-doing²²   15

    1D. But he had *a* rebuke *of his* own law-violation²³— *a* speechless^R donkey having uttered^S in *the* voice *of a* human^T restrained^U the madness *of* the prophet^V   16

7C. These *ones* are waterless²⁴ springs^W, and mists²⁵ being driven^X by *a* storm²⁶— *for* whom the gloom²⁷ *of* the darkness^Y has been reserved²⁸   17

    1D. For while uttering²⁹ pompous³⁰ *words of* futility³¹, they entice³² by³³ *the* desires³⁴ *of the* flesh^Z, *by* sensualities³⁵, *the ones* barely³⁶ escaping-from³⁷ *the ones* living^AA in error^BB   18

        1E. Promising them freedom³⁸, themselves being slaves^CC *of* corruption³⁹   19

            1F. For *by* what one has been defeated^DD, *by* this he has been enslaved^EE

1. Others do not add this word, making v 12-13 all one sentence, "But these ones, like... ignorant, will also be destroyed".
2. Or, "creatures-of-nature". This is the Greek word order. Some punctuate it "... animals, creatures-of-instinct, born for..."; others, "unreasoning natural animals", making a single description. This word means "natural, belonging to nature, pertaining to the natural order of things". Some think Peter means "as ones living in the manner pertaining to the natural world", that is, in a purely physical and instinctual manner. They live like animals led by their physical appetites to their destruction. Others think he means "as ones belonging only to the natural order", that is, as only physical creatures of nature, devoid of a spirit. They are like part of the animal kingdom, and share their fate. Elsewhere only as "natural" in Rom 1:26, 27. GK *5879*. Related to the word in Jude 10.
3. That is, "in connection with, in the sphere of ". GK *1877*.
4. Same word as in Jude 10. This is the sense in which they are like the animals. Related to "destruction".
5. Some think Peter means "the animals' destruction", they will share their fate; others, "their *own* destruction", the destruction belonging to them as people; others think it is a Hebrew way of speaking meaning, "they will surely be destroyed"; others give it a different sense, "destroyed in their corruption".
6. Same word as earlier in the verse, and as "corruption" in v 19.
7. Or, "unrighteousness", as in Act 1:18. That is, "*for* wrong-doing". Or, "being harmed *as the* wages *of* harm, being defrauded *as the* wages *of* fraud". The same phrase ,"wages *of* wrong", is in v 15, and some think the same meaning must be given in both places. Others do not, and render this "harm" here, and "wrong" or "unrighteousness" there. Same word as in 2 Cor 12:13; Heb 8:12. Some manuscripts say "receiving *the* wages *of* wrong" {B}.
8. Or, "stains". Some place the points from here through v 16 at the "E." level, as examples of their wrong-doing. Elsewhere only in Eph 5:27. GK *5070*. Related to the word in Jude 12. "Spots and blemishes" is the opposite of Jesus, whom Peter says is "without-blemish and without-spot" in 1 Pet 1:19 (same words with a negative prefix). In 2 Pet 3:14, Peter exhorts us to be unspotted and unblemished.
9. "Regarding" is a participle, like those in the D. points that follow. In the Greek word order, "regarding... pleasure" comes first in this sentence. Some take it with the preceding point (1D.), and then take "*They are* spots and blemishes" as beginning the new sentence.
10. This noun is elsewhere only as "luxury" in Lk 7:25. GK *5588*. Related to the verb that follows.
11. This verb is used only here. GK *1960*. Related to "live in luxury" in Jam 5:5.
12. Or, "deceits". Same word as in Eph 4:22; Col 2:8; 2 Thes 2:10. Elsewhere only as "deceitfulness" in Mt 13:22; Mk 4:19; Heb 3:13. GK *573*. The related verb is "deceive" in 1 Tim 2:14. Some manuscripts say "love feasts" {B}, as in Jude 12.
13. Elsewhere only in Jude 12. GK *5307*.
14. That is, eyes full of desire for an adulterous woman, a woman with whom to commit adultery. On this word, see "adulterous" in Jam 4:4. Some manuscripts say "adultery" {A}.
15. Or, "unceasing, not resting" *from* sin. This modifies "eyes". Peter could mean eyes "restless to continue sinning", or eyes "never resting from their sinning". Used only here. GK *188*. Related to "rest" in Heb 3:11, which has no negative prefix.
16. Or, "Luring, Entrapping, Baiting". Same word as in v 18. On this word, see Jam 1:14.
17. Elsewhere only in 3:16. GK *844*.
18. Or, "exercised". This is a participle, "having been trained". On this word, see Heb 5:14.
19. Or, "*for* greed, *from* greed, *by* greed". On this word, see Eph 4:19. Some manuscripts have this plural, "greedy *things*" {K}.
20. That is, children characterized by a curse, or under a curse; or, "accursed children". On this word, see Gal 3:10.
21. Some manuscripts say "Beor" {A}, the spelling in the Septuagint. Consult the commentaries on the theories regarding this spelling. GK *1082*. On Balaam, see Num 22-24, 31.
22. Or, "reward *of* unrighteousness", "the pay *of* wrong-doing". Same phrase as in v 13. Compare Jude 11.
23. Or, "law-breaking". That is, lawlessness, evil-doing. Used only here. GK *4175*. Related to "violate the law" in Act 23:3. The root word is "law".
24. Same word as in Jude 12. GK *536*.
25. Some manuscripts say "... springs, clouds being..." {N}.
26. Or, "gust, gale, whirlwind". Elsewhere only in Mk 4:37 and Lk 8:23 as a "storm" of wind. GK *3278*. Some think Peter means that they are "waterless", never providing rain, as in Jude 12; others, that they drift along obscuring the truth; others, that they are unstable and fleeting.
27. On this word, see 2:4. This phrase *"for* whom... reserved" is also in Jude 13.
28. Or, "kept". Same word as in 1 Pet 1:4; 2 Pet 2:4, 9; 3:7; Jude 13; and as "kept" in Jude 6. On this word, see "keeping" in 1 Jn 5:18. Some manuscripts add "forever" {N}.
29. Same word used of the donkey in v 16. Elsewhere only as "speak" in Act 4:18. GK *5779*. Related to the word in Act 2:4.
30. Or, "excessive in size, overgrown, swollen, bombastic". Elsewhere only in Jude 16. GK *5665*.
31. Or, "uselessness, worthlessness". On this word, see Rom 8:20.
32. Same word as in v 14.
33. Or, "with". Such teachers use the desires of the flesh and sensualities as the means to entice those barely escaping.
34. Or, "lusts". On this word, see Gal 5:16.
35. Or, "*the* sensual desires *of the* flesh", or "*the* desires *of the* flesh *for* sensualities". On this word, see 2:2.
36. That is, the ones just beginning to turn from the world to God. Used only here, this word could mean "to a small extent", or, "for a short time". GK *3903*. Some manuscripts say "actually" {A}, on which see "really" in Jn 8:36.
37. Some manuscripts say "having escaped-from" {N}. Elsewhere only in 1:4; 2:20. GK *709*.
38. That is, freedom from the Law, from holy standards. Peter calls them "lawless" in 3:17. Some people taught that salvation is of the spirit, and it does not matter what one does with the body. Perhaps something like this is in view here. On this word, see Gal 5:13.
39. That is, moral corruption. On this word, see "decay" in 1 Cor 15:42.

A. Jude 10   B. Rev 4:6, living creatures   C. 1 Jn 2:29   D. 1 Cor 15:42, decay   E. 1 Tim 6:1   F. Rom 10:3   G. Act 7:24   H. Lk 8:14   J. Rom 15:14   K. Jam 5:20   L. 1 Jn 3:1   M. Jam 5:19, err   N. Act 6:2   O. Act 8:21   P. 2 Pet 1:16   Q. Jn 21:15, devotedly love   R. 1 Cor 14:10   S. 2 Pet 2:18   T. Mt 4:4, mankind   U. 1 Cor 14:39, forbid   V. 1 Cor 12:28   W. Jn 4:6   X. Lk 8:29   Y. Jn 3:19   Z. Col 2:23   AA. Eph 2:3, conducted ourselves   BB. 1 Thes 2:3   CC. Rom 6:17   DD. 2 Pet 2:20   EE. Rom 6:18

2 Peter 2:20	914	Verse

        2D. For¹ if— having escaped-from^A the defilements *of* the world by *the* knowledge^B *of* our² Lord and Savior Jesus Christ, and again having been entangled^C *by* these *things*— they are defeated³   20

            1E. *Then* the last *state* has become worse⁴ *for* them *than* the first

                1F. For it *would* be better^D *for* them not to have known^E the way *of* righteousness than having known^E, to turn-back⁵ from the holy^F commandment^G having been delivered⁶ *to* them   21

            2E. The⁷ *thing* of the true^H proverb^J has happened^K *to* them—   22

                1F. "*The* dog having returned⁸ to *its* own vomit"⁹
                2F. And, "*The* sow having washed¹⁰ *herself returns* to *a* wallowing *of the* mire"

3A. Beloved^L, I am now^M writing this second letter *to* you, in which¹¹ *letters* I am arousing¹² your pure^N mind^O with *a* reminder¹³ *to remember¹⁴ the words^P having been spoken-beforehand^Q by the holy^F prophets, and the commandment^G *of* the Lord and Savior *from* your apostles¹⁵   3:1   2

    1B. Knowing^R this first— that mockers¹⁶ will come with mocking¹⁷ in *the* last^S days   3

        1C. Proceeding in accordance with their own desires¹⁸
        2C. And saying, "Where is the promise^T *of* His coming¹⁹? For since²⁰ the fathers fell-asleep^U, everything is continuing^V in-this-manner²¹ from *the* beginning^W *of* creation^X"   4
        3C. For this escapes-notice-of²² those *who are* willing²³—   5

            1D. That *by* the word^Y *of* God there were heavens from-long-ago²⁴, and *an* earth having existence²⁵ out of water and by water

                1E. Through which²⁶ the world²⁷ at that time was destroyed²⁸, having been flooded²⁹ *with* water   6

                2D. And *by* the same word the present heavens and earth have been stored-up³⁰ *for* fire, being reserved³¹ for *the* day *of the* judgment^Z and destruction³² *of* ungodly^AA people^BB   7

    2B. But do not let this one *thing* be escaping your notice, beloved^L— that one day³³ with *the* Lord *is* like³⁴ *a* thousand years³⁵, and *a* thousand years *is* like one day   8

        1C. *The* Lord is not being slow^CC *about* the promise³⁶ as some regard^DD slowness, but He is being patient^EE toward you³⁷, not wishing³⁸ any to perish³⁹, but all to make-room⁴⁰ for repentance^FF   9
        2C. But *the* day *of the* Lord⁴¹ will come^GG like *a* thief⁴²— during which the heavens will pass-away with-a-roar, and *the* elements⁴³ will be destroyed^HH while burning⁴⁴, and *the* earth and the works^JJ in it will be found⁴⁵   10

            1D. All these *things* thus⁴⁶ being destroyed^HH, what-kind-of^KK *people* ought you⁴⁷ to⁴⁸ be in holy^F behaviors⁴⁹ and *acts of* godliness⁵⁰, *looking-for^LL and hastening⁵¹ the coming^MM *of* the day *of* God⁵²   11   12

                1E. Because of which *the* heavens will be destroyed^HH, being set-on-fire^NN, and *the* elements are melted⁵³ while burning

1. Some think this refers to the false teachers, continuing the subject of v 17, and of "entice" and "promising". Others think this refers to the victims mentioned in v 18b-19. Others think this is a general principle referring to all.
2. Some manuscripts omit this word {C}, making it "the Lord" or "*our* Lord".
3. Or, "overcome, beaten, worsted". Elsewhere only in v 19. GK *2487*. Related to "defeat" in Rom 11:12.
4. Same phrase as in Mt 12:45; Lk 11:26.
5. Or, "return", as this word is used in its other 34 occurrences. GK *5715*. Related to the word in v 22.
6. Same word as in Jude 3. On this word, see Act 16:4.
7. Some manuscripts say "And the" {N}.
8. Or, "having turned". On this word, see "turns back" in Jam 5:19. Related to "turn back" in v 21.
9. Compare Prov 26:11.
10. Or, "bathed". Like the sow, these people washed themselves in "the knowledge of our Lord and Savior" (v 20) and "the way of righteousness" (v 21), but then returned to what they always were all along. The outward washing did not change what they were on the inside. Same word as in Act 9:37; 16:33; Heb 10:22. Elsewhere only as "bathed" in Jn 13:10. GK *3374*.
11. This word is plural. Some think Peter is referring to 1 Peter; others, to some other letter.
12. Or, "awakening, stirring up". Same word as in 1:13. On this word, see Jn 6:18.
13. Same word as in 1:13. On this word, see 2 Tim 1:5.
14. Or, "keep in mind". That is, to not forget. Same word as in Jude 17.
15. Some manuscripts say "... commandment *of* us, the apostles *of* the Lord and Savior" {N}.
16. Elsewhere only in Jude 18. GK *1851*. Related to the noun "mocking" next, and to the verb in Lk 23:11.
17. Or, "in mockery". Some manuscripts omit "with mocking" {N}. Used only here. GK *1848*.
18. Same phrase as in Jude 16, 18. On this word, see Gal 5:16.
19. That is, the fulfillment of this promise to come. On this word, see 2 Thes 2:8.
20. This is an idiom, "from which *day*", on which see Rev 16:18.
21. That is, as it is now. Things now are as they have been since creation. The predictions changed nothing.
22. Or, "is unnoticed-by". Same word as in v 8; Mk 7:24; Lk 8:47; Act 26:26. Elsewhere only as "not-know" in Heb 13:2. GK *3291*.
23. These people willingly ignore this. They are willfully ignorant. Peter adds this word to make clear that he does not mean that it accidentally escaped their notice. More literally, "them being willing". On this word, see Jn 7:17.
24. Elsewhere only in 2:3. GK *1732*.
25. Same word as in Col 1:17. This participle is not passive, "having been made, formed, compacted". It means "having existed, stood-together, continued, endured, held together". GK *5319*.
26. This is plural, referring to the water and the word of God (note v 7, "the same word"). There are other views.
27. Same word as in 2:5. On this word, see 1 Jn 2:15.
28. Or, "perished". Same word as "perish" in v 9. On this word, see "perish" in 1 Cor 1:18. Related to "destruction" in v 7.
29. This is the verb related to the word in 2:5. Used only here. GK *2885*.
30. On this word, see 1 Cor 16:2. This is a participle, they "are having been stored up"; they are in this state.
31. Same word as in 2:17.
32. Related to "destroyed" in v 6. On this word, see 2:1.
33. This is the common word for "day", used 389 times. GK *2465*.
34. Or, "as". GK *6055*. This is a comparison, not a formula. Same word as "as" in v 9; and "like" in v 10.
35. Peter is alluding to Ps 90:4.
36. Or, "*The* Lord *of* the promise is not being slow".
37. Some manuscripts say "toward us"; others, "patient for your sake" {A}.
38. Or, "wanting, willing". For the uses of this word regarding God, see "willed" in Jam 1:18. Compare 1 Tim 2:4.
39. Same word as in Jn 3:16; 1 Cor 1:18.
40. Or, "give way, have room; go forward to, progress to, come to, reach". Same word as in 2 Cor 7:2. Elsewhere only as "have room" in Mk 2:2; Jn 2:6; 21:25; "give way" in Mt 19:11, 12; "advance" in Mt 15:17; Jn 8:37. GK *6003*.
41. On this phrase, "day of the Lord", see 1 Thes 5:2.
42. That is, suddenly, unexpectedly, disastrously. On coming like a thief, see 1 Thes 5:2. Some manuscripts add "at night" {N}.
43. Same word as in v 12. On this word, see "elemental" in Gal 4:3.
44. Or, "being consumed by heat, being burned up". Elsewhere only in v 12. GK *3012*.
45. Or, "discovered", that is, found out. The reading is uncertain. Some manuscripts say "will not be found" (compare Rev 16:20; 20:11); others, "will be found being destroyed"; others, "will be burned up"; others, "will disappear" {D}. Some suggest it may be a question, "and will the earth... be found?". Same word as in v 14. Elsewhere by Peter only in 1 Pet 1:7; 2:22. Used 176 times in the NT. GK *2351*.
46. Or, "in this manner". Some manuscripts instead say "therefore" {B}.
47. Some manuscripts say "we" {C}.
48. On "ought to", see Act 25:10.
49. This is the only place this word is plural. On this word, see "conduct" in 1 Pet 1:15.
50. This is the only place this word is plural, to show which, *acts of* is added. On this word, see 1Tim 2:2.
51. Or, "hurrying, promoting zealously, advancing, seeking eagerly". This is to be a subject of prayer (Mt 6:10) and action (Mt 24:14). Elsewhere only as "to hurry" in Lk 2:16; 19:5, 6; Act 20:16; 22:18. GK *5067*.
52. A "day of God" is also mentioned in Rev 16:14.
53. Used only here. GK *5494*. Some manuscripts say "will melt" {N}.

A. 2 Pet 2:18 B. Col 1:9 C. 2 Tim 2:4 D. Heb 1:4 E. Col 1:6, understood F. 1 Pet 1:16 G. Mk 12:28 H. Jn 6:55 J. Jn 10:6, figure of speech K. Act 21:35 L. Mt 3:17 M. Mt 24:32, already N. Phil 1:10 O. Lk 1:51, thoughts P. Rom 10:17 Q. Jude 17 R. Lk 1:34 S. Heb 1:2 T. 1 Jn 2:25 U. 1 Thes 4:13 V. Lk 22:28 W. Col 1:18 X. Rom 8:39 Y. 1 Cor 12:8 Z. Jn 3:19 AA. Jude 15 BB. Mt 4:4, mankind CC. 1 Tim 3:15 DD. Jam 1:2 EE. 1 Cor 13:4 FF. 2 Cor 7:10 GG. Jn 8:84, am here HH. Mt 5:19, break JJ. Mt 26:10 KK. 1 Jn 3:1 LL. Lk 3:15, waiting in expectation MM. 2 Thes 2:8 NN. 2 Cor 11:29, burn

3C. But in accordance with His promise^A, we are looking-for^B new^C heavens and *a* new earth in which[1] righteousness dwells[2] 13

3B. Therefore beloved^D, while looking-for^B these *things* 14

    1C. Be diligent[3] to be found unspotted[4] and unblemished[5] *by* Him,[6] in peace^E
    2C. And be regarding^F the patience^G *of* our Lord *to be* salvation^H 15

        1D. Just as also our beloved^D brother^J Paul wrote *to* you[7] according-to[8] the wisdom^K having been given *to* him—° as also *he writes* in all *his* letters, speaking in them concerning these *things* 16

            1E. In which *letters* are some *things* hard-to-understand[9] which the untaught[10] and unstable[11] twist[12]— as also the other[13] Scriptures[14]— to their own destruction^L

4B. **You** therefore, beloved^D, knowing-*this*-beforehand^M 17

    1C. Be guarding[15] *yourselves* in order that you may not fall-from^N *your* own steadfastness[16], having been carried-away-by[17] the error^O *of* the lawless^P ones
    2C. And be growing^Q in *the* grace^R and knowledge^S *of* our Lord and Savior^T Jesus Christ 18

        1D. *To* Him *be* the glory^U both now, and to *the* day *of* eternity[18]. Amen[19]

1. This is plural, referring to the new heavens and earth.
2. That is, has its home, settles down. On this word, see Eph 3:17.
3. Same word as in 1:10.
4. Or, "spotless, without stain, pure". Same word as in 1 Tim 6:14; Jam 1:27. Elsewhere only as "without spot" in 1 Pet 1:19. GK *834*.
5. Or, "blameless, defectless". These two words are the opposites of 2:13. Used only here. GK *318*. Related to "without-blemish" in 1 Pet 1:19.
6. Or, "*in* Him". Some punctuate this "to be found *by* Him in peace, unspotted and unblemished".
7. As to which specific letter Peter might have in mind, consult the commentaries.
8. Or, "based on, by way of ". GK *2848*.
9. Used only here. GK *1554*.
10. Or, "unlearned, ignorant". Used only here. GK *276*.
11. Same word as in 2:14, which refers to the ones the false teachers try to entice.
12. Or, "distort, wrench, dislocate, torture, torment". Given the nature of the false teaching in chapter 2, Peter is probably referring to Paul's teaching on salvation by faith apart from works of the Law. The false teachers changed grace into sensuality, Jude 4. Used only here. GK *5137*. Used of "stretching" on a rack, "torturing".
13. Or, "the rest of, the remaining". This word does not mean "other of a different kind", but the others remaining in the category under discussion, the rest. Used 55 times. GK *3370*.
14. Peter is putting Paul's writings on the same level as the other Scriptures (the OT), or in the same category (as books read in the church services). Compare v 2. The word "Scriptures" (or, "Writings") is used 50 times in the NT, always referring to the Old Testament. GK *1210*. It is related to the verb "it is written" (GK *1211*).
15. Same word as "protected" in 2:5, its only other use by Peter. On this word, see "keep" in Jn 12:25.
16. Or, "firmness, fixedness, establishment". Used only here. GK *5113*. Related to "establish" in 1:12.
17. Or, "led away by, carried along with". That is, led astray. On this verb, see "carried along with" in Rom 12:16.
18. The phrase "day *of* eternity" is used only here. This is an idiom, literally "to *the* day *of the* age". GK *172*.
19. Some manuscripts omit the word {C}.

A. 2 Pet 1:4, things promised   B. Lk 3:15, waiting in expectation   C. Heb 8:13   D. Mt 3:17   E. Act 15:33   F. Jam 1:2   G. Heb 6:12   H. Lk 19:9   J. Act 16:40   K. 1 Cor 12:8   L. 2 Pet 2:1   M. Rom 8:29, foreknew   N. Gal 5:4   O. 1 Thes 2:3   P. 2 Pet 2:7   Q. Jn 3:30   R. Eph 2:8   S. 1 Cor 12:8   T. Lk 1:47   U. 2 Pet 2:10

1 John

Overview

1A. What we witnessed concerning the word of life, we announce. And we write that our joy may be full	1:1-4
2A. And this is the message we have heard from Him and are declaring to you—	1:5

    1B. God is light. If we are walking in the light, we have fellowship, and He cleanses us from sin — 1:5-10
    2B. My little children, I am writing that you may not sin. By this we know we are in Him — 2:1-6
    3B. Beloved, I am not writing a new command to you, but an old one— the message you heard — 2:7
    4B. Yet I am writing a new command, because the darkness is passing and the Light is shining — 2:8-11
    5B. I am writing to you because your sins are forgiven, you know Him, you overcame Satan — 2:12-13
    6B. I wrote to you because you know the Father, the Word of God is abiding in you — 2:14
    7B. Do not be loving the world, nor the things in it. It is not from Him, and it is passing away — 2:15-17

3A. Children, it is the last hour — 2:18

    1B. And many antichrists have arisen. They went out from us, but they were not of us — 2:18-19
    2B. And you have an Anointing from the Holy One, and you all have knowledge. Let what you heard from the beginning be abiding in you. As His Anointing is teaching you, be abiding in it — 2:20-27
    3B. And now little children, abide in Him, that if He appears, we may have confidence before Him — 2:28

        1C. You know everyone doing righteousness has been born from Him. Little children, do not be deceived. By this the children of God and the children of the devil are evident — 2:29-3:10
        2C. Everyone not doing righteousness is not from God— and the one not loving. Little children, let us be loving in deed and truth. By this we will persuade our heart before Him — 3:10-24

    4B. Beloved, do not believe every spirit, but be testing them, because many false prophets went out — 4:1-6

4A. Beloved, let us be loving one another — 4:7

    1B. Because the love is from God — 4:7-8
    2B. By this the love of God was made known among us— He sent His Son that we might live — 4:9-10
    3B. Beloved, if God loved us in this manner, we also ought to be loving one another — 4:11

        1C. No one has ever seen God; if we are loving one another, God is abiding in us — 4:12-16
        2C. God is love; the one abiding in the love is abiding in God, and God is abiding in him — 4:16-19
        3C. If someone claims to love God and is hating his brother, he is a liar — 4:20
        4C. And we have His command— that the one loving God should be loving his brother also — 4:21

    4B. Everyone believing that Jesus is the Christ has been born from God, and is loving God's children — 5:1

        1C. By this we know we love His children— when we love God and do His commandments — 5:2

            1D. For this is the love of God— that we be keeping His commandments — 5:3
            2D. Because everything born of God is victorious over the world. Faith is the victory — 5:4
            3D. And who is victorious if not the one believing that Jesus is the Son of God! — 5:5-12

        2C. I wrote these things to you who believe that you may know that you have eternal life — 5:13
        3C. And this is the confidence we have before Him— He hears us, He keeps us from sinning, we are of God, His Son gave us understanding to know the true One, we are in the true One — 5:14-21

1 John 1:1	920	Verse

1A. *That*-which[1] was from *the* beginning[2], *that* which we[3] have heard, *that* which we have seen[A] *with* our eyes, *that* which we looked-*at*[B] and our hands touched[C], concerning the word[4] *of* life[5]—   1

    1B. *Indeed*[6] life[7] was made-known[8]! And we have seen[9], and are testifying[10], and are announcing *to* you the eternal[D] life[11] which was with the Father, and was made-known[12] *to* us!   2

    2B. *That*-which[13] we have seen and heard we are announcing[14] also[15] *to* you so that **you** also may have fellowship[16] with us   3

        1C. And indeed our fellowship *is* with the Father, and with His Son Jesus Christ

    3B. And **we** are writing these *things*[17] in order that our[18] joy[E] may be full[19]   4

2A. And this is the message[20] which we have heard from Him and are declaring[21] *to* you—   5

    1B. That God is light[F], and there is not any darkness[G] in Him

        1C. If we claim[H] that we have fellowship with Him and we are walking[J] in the darkness[K], we are lying, and not doing[L] the truth[22]   6

        2C. But if we are walking in the light[23] as **He** is in the light, we have fellowship with one another, and the blood[24] *of* Jesus[25] His Son cleanses[26] us from all sin   7

            1D. If we claim that we do not have[27] sin,[28] we are deceiving[M] ourselves, and the truth[29] is not in us   8

            2D. If we are confessing[30] our sins, He is faithful[N] and righteous[31] *to*[32] forgive[O] us the sins, and cleanse us from all unrighteousness[P]   9

                1E. If we claim that we have not sinned,[33] we are making[L] Him *a* liar, and His word[Q] is not in us   10

    2B. My[34] little-children[35], I am writing these[36] *things* to you in order that you may not sin. And if anyone sins,[37] we have *an* advocate[38] with the Father— Jesus Christ *the* Righteous[R]   2:1

        1C. And He Himself is *the* satisfaction[39] for our sins— and not for ours only, but also for the whole world's[40]   2

1. Or, "What". Some think this refers to the person of Christ; others, to the message of life He brought; others, to both.
2. Some think John means "What was from the beginning of the ministry of Christ", as in Jn 15:27; 16:4; others, "What was God's plan from the beginning of creation", as in Jn 1:1; Gen 1:1. There are other views. On this word, see Col 1:18.
3. Some think this refers to the apostles; others to John himself (a literary plural). There are other views.
4. Or, "message". Some think John means "concerning the Word" (the person, as in Jn 1:1); others, "concerning the message", which includes all aspects of Christ's person and work. On this word, see 1 Cor 12:8.
5. Some think John means Who or which "*gives* life"; others, Who or which "*is* life"; others, which is "*about* life"; others, "*about* the Life" (Jesus). "Life" is elsewhere in 1 Jn only in 1:2; 2:25; 3:14, 15; 5:11, 12, 13, 16, 20. On this word, see Rom 8:10.
6. Or, "And". Same word as in v 3. Before John completes the thought that he is declaring his eyewitness testimony, he leaps ahead to exclaim the result produced by the Christ he personally witnessed— eternal life was made known! This could routinely have been stated if v 3 and v 2 were reversed, "That which was from the beginning... concerning the word of life (v 1), we are announcing also to you in order that you may have fellowship with us. And indeed our fellowship is with... Christ (v 3). Indeed life was made known! And we have seen, and are testifying, and are announcing to you the eternal life... made known to us (v 2)". However, John moves this forward for emphasis. Verse 2 is parenthetic to v 1 and 3, but it is an emphatic thought, not a parenthetic one. GK *2779*.
7. Or, "the Life", "*this* life" (the one just mentioned).
8. Or, "appeared, was revealed, was manifested". Some think this is a personal reference to Jesus, who "appeared"; others, to the eternal life that was "made known" in Him. This verb is used both ways. On this word, see "made evident" in 2:19.
9. In this rendering, this verb is referring forward to "eternal life", as do the next two verbs. Others think this verb refers back to "life", and thus render it "we have seen *it*".
10. Or, "bearing witness, attesting". Same word used for the Baptist in Jn 1:7, 8, 15, 32, 34.
11. Or, "Life". Some think this is a reference to the incarnate Christ; others, to eternal life, as in Jn 17:2, 3.
12. Or, "appeared". Same word as earlier in the verse.
13. This resumes from v 1, after the emphatic placement of v 2.
14. Or, "reporting, declaring". Same word as in v 2. Used 45 times. GK *550*. Related to "declare" in v 5.
15. Some manuscripts omit this word {N}.
16. Or, "partnership, communion". Same word as in v 3, 6, 7. On this word, see 1 Cor 1:9.
17. Some think John is referring to this letter as a whole; others, to v 1-3 in particular. There are other views. Some manuscripts say, "And we are writing these *things to* you" {B}.
18. Some manuscripts say "your" {A}. John could mean "our" in the sense of "my", or, "yours and mine".
19. Or, "complete". John's joy is made full by hearing of his children walking in the truth, 3 Jn 4. He writes to help accomplish this. This is a participle, "may be having been made full". On this phrase, see Jn 16:24.
20. Elsewhere only in 3:11. GK *32*. Related to "declaring" later in this verse.
21. Or, "reporting, proclaiming". On this word, see Jn 16:13. Related to "announcing" in v 2, 3.
22. On "doing the truth", compare "doing sin" in Jn 8:34.
23. As children of the God who is light, we are children of light walking toward the light, Jn 3:21; 8:12; 12:35, 36, 46; Rom 13:12; Eph 5:8; 1 Thes 5:5; 1 Pet 2:9; 1 Jn 2:8. This is our pattern of life.
24. Elsewhere of Christ's blood only in Mt 26:28; 27:4, 6, 24, 25; Mk 14:24; Lk 22:20, 44; Jn 6:53, 54, 55, 56; 19:34; Act 5:28; 20:28; Rom 3:25; 5:9; 1 Cor 10:16; 11:25, 27; Eph 1:7; 2:13; Col 1:20; Heb 9:12, 14; 10:19, 29; 12:24; 13:12, 20; 1 Pet 1:2, 19; 1 Jn 5:6, 8; Rev 1:5; 5:9; 7:14; 12:11; 19:13. Used 97 times. GK *135*. Jesus is the sacrificial offering, the spotless Lamb of God whose blood is offered in our place as a satisfaction (see 2:2), reconciling us to God. See Rom 3:23-25.
25. Some manuscripts add "Christ" {N}.
26. Or, "purifies". Same word as in v 9, on which see Heb 9:22.
27. This is the common word "have, hold", used 708 times. GK *2400*.
28. On "have sin", compare Jn 9:41; 15:22, 24; 19:11. Some think John means we claim we have no guilt, no need for cleansing, no need for a Savior; others, no sin nature or inclination to sin.
29. Some think John means "God's truth, objective reality"; others, the gospel. Same word as in v 6, on which see Jn 4:23.
30. Or, "admitting, agreeing about". On this word, see 1 Tim 6:12.
31. Or, "just, right". God is righteous to forgive because of 2:2. On this word, see Rom 1:17.
32. More literally, "that He might forgive"; that is, to carry out His purpose to forgive us. GK *2671*.
33. That is, that we have not personally committed a sin in the past.
34. Others make this point 2E., John's answer to 1:10 (similar in function to 1:7 and 1:9, though different in form). Then 2:3 continues on as point 2B. The precise flow of thought of this book is difficult to be certain of in places because there are so many repetitions and possible connections of thought, word, and phrase. Though it has the easiest Greek, this is the hardest book in the NT to follow the connections of thought. Yet the message of the book is clear and powerful, because it is found in John's boldly absolute sentences and brief paragraphs, and is not dependent on how the book as a whole is arranged. Consult the commentaries for other suggestions on how to arrange the book.
35. Jesus used this word of the disciples in Jn 13:33. Elsewhere only in 1 Jn 2:12, 28; 3:7, 18; 4:4; 5:21. GK *5448*. Related to "children" in 3:1. Not related to "children" in 2:14.
36. Some think John is referring to 1:5-10 or 1:5-2:17, the things regarding sin and walking in the light; others, to the whole letter.
37. That is, commits a sin, an act of sin. As in 1:6-7 and 8-9, John joins both sides of the coin, the not sinning and the sinning. John addresses living in sin as a pattern of life in 3:9.
38. Only here is this word used of Jesus— our "Advocate, Defender, Intercessor". On this word, see "Helper" in Jn 14:16.
39. Or, "propitiation", the means of removing God's wrath. Elsewhere only in 4:10. GK *2662*. See Rom 3:25 on this word group.
40. Or, "*those of* the whole world". Jesus paid the price for all. Compare Jn 3:16; 12:47; Rom 5:18; 1 Tim 4:10; 1 Jn 4:14.

A. Lk 2:26 B. 1 Jn 4:14 C. Lk 24:39 D. Mt 25:46 E. Lk 24:52 F. Jn 1:5 G. Jn 1:5 H. Jn 12:49, say J. Heb 13:9 K. Jn 3:19 L. Rev 13:13 M. Jam 5:19, err N. Col 1:2 O. Mt 6:12 P. Rom 1:18 Q. 1 Cor 12:8 R. Rom 1:17

2C.	And by this¹ we know^A that we have come-to-know² Him³— if we are keeping^B His commandments⁴	3
	1D. The *one* claiming^C that "I have come-to-know Him" and not keeping^B His commandments^D is *a* liar, and the truth⁵ is not in this *one*	4
	2D. But whoever is keeping^B **His** word^E, truly^F the love^G *of* God⁶ has been perfected⁷ in this *one*	5
	3C. By this⁸ we know^A that we are in Him—*the *one* claiming to be abiding^H in Him ought^J just as that *One* walked^K also himself thus⁹ to be walking	6
3B.	Beloved¹⁰, I am not writing *a* new^L commandment¹¹ *to* you, but *an* old¹² commandment which you had from *the* beginning¹³. The old commandment is the word¹⁴ which you heard¹⁵	7
4B.	Yet-again¹⁶ I am writing *a* new^L commandment *to* you, which¹⁷ is true¹⁸ in Him and in you, because¹⁹ the darkness²⁰ is passing-away²¹ and the true²² Light²³ is already shining²⁴	8
	1C. The²⁵ *one* claiming^C to be in the light and hating^M his brother²⁶ is in the darkness until now²⁷	9
	1D. The *one* loving^N his brother is abiding^H in the light, and there is no cause-of-falling^O in him²⁸	10
	2D. But the *one* hating his brother is in the darkness, and is walking^K in the darkness, and does not know^P where he is going because the darkness blinded his eyes	11
5B.	I am writing²⁹ *to* you, little-children³⁰, because³¹ *your* sins have been forgiven^Q you for-the-sake-of³² His name	12
	1C. I am writing *to* you, fathers, because you have known^A the *One* from *the* beginning³³	13
	2C. I am writing *to* you, young-men³⁴, because you have overcome³⁵ the evil^R *one*	

1. "By this" is a key phrase in 1 John, occurring 12 times. John wants us to know how to know spiritual truth. Compare 2:3, 5; 3:10, 16, 19, 24; 4:2, 9, 13, 17; 5:2; and Jn 13:35; 15:8; 16:30.
2. Or, "have known". On this word, see Lk 1:34.
3. Those who make this point 2B. (see the note on "My" in v 1) link this to "God" in 1:5, rather than "Jesus" in 2:2.
4. We cannot claim to know Jesus if we do not do what He says. Jesus said so, Mt 7:21-23; Lk 6:46.
5. That is, God's truth is not at work in him.
6. Some think John means God's love in us, as in 4:12. This person does know God because God's love is in him. Others think he means our love for God, as in 5:3. This person's love for God has been brought to completion in true knowledge of Him.
7. Or, "brought to completion, reached its goal". Here this comes by keeping His word; in 4:12, by loving one another. On this word, see Heb 2:10.
8. In this arrangement, the "by this we know" statements (2C. and 3C.) are paralleled. "This" points forward to what follows, and, "in Him" points to "abiding in Him". Others think "this" refers back to "keeping His word" or "love perfected" in v 5. In this case, "By this..." would be part of point 2D. Then "The *one* claiming..." would be point 3D., paralleling v 4.
9. Some manuscripts omit this word {C}, leaving "... ought also himself to be walking just as that *One* walked".
10. On this word, see Mt 3:17. Some manuscripts say instead "Brothers" {N}.
11. Some think John means "in what I just said" (do not sin, v 1; keep His commandments, v 3; walk as He walked, v 6); others, "in what I am about to say" about loving your brother (v 9-11). He may mean both, "in what I am writing you here in 1:5-2:17", or in this book.
12. Some think John means it is old in that it was contained in the Law of Moses; others, that it is old from John's point of view. That is, it was spoken by Jesus Himself. Both "keep my commands" (2:3-6; Jn 14:15, 21, 23, 24) and "love one another" (2:9-11; Jn 13:34; 15:12) are commands of Jesus. Others think he means it is "old" from the readers' point of view. That is, it is a command they have had since they first became Christians. On this word, see Mk 2:21.
13. That is, from when you first heard, from the beginning of your Christian life. On this word, see Col 1:18.
14. Or, "message". That is, His word (v 5), the gospel. This "old word" contained all the thoughts in this book. John merely expands on certain aspects of it. "I am not writing some new thing to you, but what you already know". On this word, see 1 Cor 12:8.
15. Some manuscripts add "from *the* beginning" {N}.
16. Or, "On the other hand". Most think the new command is implied in v 9-11, "love one another". Compare 3:11; 2 Jn 5, 6. It is new in that it is Christ's new command (Jn 13:34) which John's readers newly received at salvation. Yet perhaps John simply means that he is writing all of this to them as a new command. He is commanding them anew with a fresh statement of the old command. The old command is the word you heard from the beginning, the new command is the word he is writing here. Both include righteousness and love. On this word, see "again" un Mk 15:13.
17. The grammar indicates this does not refer to "new" or "commandment". Some think it refers to the whole concept, to "what I am writing"; others, to the newness of it, "*the newness of* which". There are other views.
18. Or, "genuine, real". Some think John means the content of the command is "truly seen, genuinely present" in Him and them, though to a different degree; others, that the newness is truly seen in Him (as the giver of it) and you (as the ones now doing it). There are other views. Used elsewhere by John in 2:27; Jn 3:33 ("truthful"); 4:18; 5:31, 32; 6:55; 7:18; 8:13, 14, 17, 26; 10:41; 19:35; 21:24; 3 Jn 12. On this word, see Jn 6:55.
19. Some think John is explaining why it is new, because it is from Christ, the true light; others, why it is true in Him and in you, because His light is already shining in you; others, why he is writing it, as in v 12-14.
20. That is, spiritual darkness. Same word as in 1:5; 2:9, 11. On this word, see Jn 1:5. Related to the word in 1:6.
21. Same word as in v 17; 1 Cor 7:31. GK *4135*.
22. Related to "true" earlier. Used elsewhere by John in 5:20; Jn 1:9; 4:23, 37; 6:32; 7:28; 8:16; 15:1; 17:3; 19:35; Rev 3:7, 14; 6:10; 15:3; 16:7; 19:2, 9, 11; 21:5; 22:6. On this word, see Jn 7:28.
23. Some think John means Jesus, as in Jn 1:9; others, God's truth, His word, the gospel. There are other views.
24. The true light is dispelling the darkness. On this word, see Phil 2:15.
25. This is the statement, or the continuation of the statement, of what is not new but old, yet is new.
26. That is, fellow believer. On this word, see Act 16:40.
27. Such a person has been, and continues to be in the darkness, in spite of whatever may be claimed.
28. Or, "it". Some think John means there is nothing "in him", the loving brother, to cause his brother to fall; others, to cause himself to fall. Others think he means there is nothing "in it", the light, to cause him to fall.
29. John continues to explain his writing of this section or the whole book. Others think that v 12-14 strictly point forward to the writing of the command in v 15. Same word as in 1:4; 2:1, 7, 8, 13, 14. Used 191 times. GK *1211*.
30. Some think "little children, fathers, young men" each refer to all Christians, from three viewpoints; others, that "little children" refers to everyone (as elsewhere in the letter, see 2:1), and that John then divides everyone into two groups, "young men" and "fathers"; others, that John is referring to three groups of Christians. In the last two views, some think the groups represent stages of spiritual growth; others, tenure as a Christian; others, physical age. On this word, see v 1.
31. Some render this word "that", and likewise in the next five statements, giving the content of John's writing rather than the reason for it.
32. Or, "because of ". GK *1328*.
33. Some think John is referring to the Father; others, the Son. Some think he means from the beginning of time or creation (as in Jn 1:1); others, from the beginning of His ministry.
34. As to physical age, this word refers to those in the physical prime of life, about 24-40 years old. Used 11 times. GK *3734*. Related to the word in Act 7:58.
35. Or, "conquered". On this word, see Rev 2:7.

A. Lk 1:34 B. 1 Jn 5:18 C. Jn 12:49, say D. Mk 12:28 E. 1 Cor 12:8 F. Mt 14:33 G. 1 Jn 4:16 H. Jn 15:4 J. 1 Jn 4:11 K. Heb 13:9 L. Heb 8:13 M. Rom 9:13 N. Jn 21:15, devotedly love O. Rom 11:9 P. 1 Jn 2:29 Q. Mt 6:12 R. Act 25:18

1 John 2:14	924	Verse

      6B. I wrote[1] *to* you, children[2], because you have known[A] the Father   14

           1C. I wrote *to* you, fathers, because you have known the *One* from *the* beginning[B]
           2C. I wrote *to* you, young-men, because you are strong[C] *ones,* and the word[D] *of* God is abiding[E] in you, and you have overcome[F] the evil[G] *one*

      7B. Do not be loving[3] the world,[4] nor the *things* in the world[5]   15

           1C. If anyone is loving the world, the love[H] *of* the Father[6] is not in him

                 1D. Because everything in the world— the desire[7] *of* the flesh[8], and the desire *of* the eyes, and the boastful-pride[9] *of* life[10]— is not from the Father, but is from the world   16

           2C. And the world is passing-away,[11] and its desire. But the *one* doing the will *of* God abides[E] forever[J]   17

3A. Children[K], it is *the* last[L] hour[12]   18

      1B. And just as you heard that *the* Antichrist[13] is coming, even now many antichrists have arisen[14]— from which we know that it is *the* last hour[15]

           1C. They went out from us, but they were not of[16] us   19

                 1D. For if they had been of us, they would have remained[E] with us
                 2D. But *they went out* in order that they might be made-evident[17] that they all are not[18] of us

      2B. And **you** have *an* Anointing[19] from the Holy *One*[20], and you all have-knowledge[21]   20

           1C. I did not write[22] *to* you because you do not know the truth, but because you know it[23], and that[24] every lie is not from the truth[25]   21

                 1D. Who is the[26] liar if not the *one* denying[M] that Jesus is the Christ? This *one* is the antichrist, the *one* denying the Father and the Son   22

                      1E. Everyone denying the Son does also-not have the Father   23
                      2E. The[27] *one* confessing[28] the Son also has the Father

                 2D. Let[29] what **you heard**[30] from *the* beginning[B] be abiding[E] in you   24

                      1E. If what you heard **from *the* beginning** abides in you, **you** also will abide in the Son and in the Father
                      2E. And this is the promise[31] which He Himself promised[32] *to* us[33]— eternal life   25

                 3D. I wrote these *things to* you concerning the *ones* deceiving[N] you   26

           2C. And the Anointing which **you** received[34] from Him is abiding[E] in you. And you have no need[O] that anyone should be teaching[P] you,[35] but   27

1. Some think "wrote" refers to a former letter; others, that "writing" is from John's point of view, "wrote" is from the readers' point of view; others, that "wrote" refers to what is already written, "writing" to the whole letter; others, that "wrote" refers to the letter as complete, "writing" as in process; others, that the change of tense is merely stylistic. Perhaps John means "I am writing this with a view to your future", because of the present status you have already attained in Christ, and "I wrote it on the basis of your past", for the same reason. In other words, I am writing hoping to build upon your present status, I wrote based on it. In this case, the change of tense gives a different sense to "because". Some manuscripts say here "I am writing" {A}, causing the KJV and other English translations since then to include this sentence in v 13 as the third group.
2. Same word as in v 18, its only other use in this book. Used 52 times. GK *4086*. Not related to "little children" in v 12.
3. The grammar can mean "Stop loving", or, "Do not be in the habit of loving". On this word, see "devotedly love" in Jn 21:15.
4. This is the first command of this book. John concludes this section with a specific or focused application of what he meant in v 1 when he said "that you may not sin". The message is "God is light" (1:5), John is writing that you may not sin (2:1), so do not love the world.
5. John is not referring to the people in the world (as this word is used in Jn 3:16; 1 Jn 4:14), but to the world system, the world ruled by Satan (as in 1 Jn 5:19); to human existence, desires, and purposes apart from God. This word, *kosmos*, is used 186 times. GK *3180*. It is used of the physical "world, universe"; of humanity, the people of the world; and of the world order and system of human existence. It means "adornment" in 1 Pet 3:3. The related verb means "to adorn" (see 1 Tim 2:9), "put in order".
6. Some think John means "our love for the Father". One cannot love the world and the Father, Jam 4:4. Others think he means "the Father's love in us", as in 4:16. If one loves the world, God's love is not dwelling in him. Some manuscripts say "*of* God" {N}.
7. On this word, see Gal 5:16. It should not be narrowed to sexual desires here, but taken broadly.
8. That is, belonging to or proceeding from the flesh, the eyes, life. On this word, see Col 2:23.
9. Or, "arrogance, pretension". Elsewhere only as "pretension" in Jam 4:16. GK *224*. Related to "boaster" in Rom 1:30; 2 Tim 3:2.
10. Or, "means of life, goods, property, livelihood, mode of life, manner of living", the externals of life. It is pride flowing from the things one has, the externals of the way one lives, the living one enjoys. Same word as in Lk 8:14; 1 Tim 2:2; 2 Tim 2:4. Elsewhere only as "goods" in 1 Jn 3:17; "property" in Lk 15:12, 30; and "living" in Mk 12:44; Lk 8:43; 21:4. GK *1050*. Related to "live" in 1 Pet 4:2; "manner of life" in Act 26:4; and "pertaining to life" in Lk 21:34.
11. Some think John means this in the same sense in which the darkness is passing away in 2:8 (same word). It is being supplanted. Others think he means it is transitory. Others think he is emphasizing that it will be done away with when Christ returns. It is not just transitory, it is contradictory to His interests. It will be judged.
12. A "last hour" is mentioned only here. The KJV renders this "time", which gives the sense of it here. Same word as in Jn 4:21, 23; 5:25, 28; 16:2, 32; Rom 13:11; Rev 3:10; 9:15. On this word, see Lk 2:38.
13. Elsewhere only in 1 Jn 2:18; 22; 4:3; 2 Jn 7. GK *532*. Some manuscripts say "the Antichrist" {B}. Paul calls him the "man of lawlessness" in 2 Thes 2:3. See there for the views on the meaning of this.
14. Or, "come-to-be, come". GK *1181*. Not the same word as "is coming" earlier in the verse.
15. The last or final hour (period of time) extends from the predicted appearance of antichrists until Christ returns.
16. Or, "from". That is, part of us, belonging to us, originating with us.
17. Or, be "made known, revealed, shown, made visible". This word means "revealed" in the sense of "made visible, made open" (compare "revealed" in 2 Thes 2:3). Same word as in Rom 1:19; 2 Cor 4:10, 11; 7:12; 11:6. Elsewhere only as "make known" in Jn 7:4; 2 Cor 2:14; 3:3; 5:11; Heb 9:8; 1 Jn 1:2; 4:9; "reveal" in Jn 1:31; 2:11; 17:6; Rom 3:21; 16:26; 1 Cor 4:5; Col 1:26; 1 Tim 3:16; 2 Tim 1:10; Tit 1:3; Rev 3:18; 15:4; "manifest" in Jn 21:1, 14; "make visible" in Mk 4:22; Jn 9:3; "become visible" in Jn 3:21; Eph 5:13, 14; "make clear" in Col 4:4; "appear" in Mk 16:12, 14; 2 Cor 5:10; Col 3:4; Heb 9:26; 1 Pet 1:20; 5:4; 1 Jn 2:28; 3:2, 5, 8. GK *5746*. Related to "evident" in Rom 1:19; "clearly" in Act 10:3; and "manifestation" in 1 Cor 12:7.
18. That is, that none of them are from us. Others render it "made evident, because they are not all of us". That is, not all the people in church are part of us (compare the parable of the wheat and the darnel in Mt 13:24-43).
19. Some think John means the Holy Spirit, the Helper (Jn 14:26), who teaches us all things; others, the Word of God, as in v 14, an anointing of truth. Elsewhere only in v 27, where John expands on this. GK *5984*. The related verb is in Lk 4:18.
20. That is, Christ, as in Lk 4:34; Jn 6:69; Act 3:14.
21. Or, "you all know *the truth*", supplying "truth" from v 21. John is emphasizing the fact of knowing here, not the content of what is known. Because of this fact, which is true because they have the Anointing, they can discern the truth with regard to the content of knowledge proposed by these deceivers. John expands on this next, in v 21-26. Some manuscripts say, "and you know all *things*" {B}. On this word, see "know" in 2:29a.
22. That is, in this matter, v 18-27.
23. That is, you know the truth about Jesus.
24. Or, "because", depending on whether this is another reason John wrote, or another thing they know.
25. Or, in smoother English, "no lie is from the truth". It does not originate in or belong to the truth. On this word, see Jn 4:23.
26. In keeping with English idiom, some render this "a".
27. Some manuscripts omit this sentence {N}.
28. Or, "declaring". Same word as in 4:15. On this word, see 1 Tim 6:12.
29. Or, "You— let what you heard...". Some manuscripts say "Therefore let" {N}.
30. That is, the truth, v 21.
31. This noun is used 52 times, but only here by John. GK *2039*.
32. This verb is used 15 times, but only here by John. GK *2040*.
33. Some manuscripts say "you" {A}.
34. Or, "And you— the Anointing which you received...".
35. That is, you do not need human wisdom or "new" teachings. The Spirit will teach you, Jn 14:26; 16:12-15.

A. Lk 1:34 B. Col 1:18 C. Rev 18:8 D. 1 Cor 12:8 E. Jn 15:4, abide F. Rev 2:7 G. Act 25:18 H. 1 Jn 4:16 J. Rev 20:10 K. 1 Jn 2:14
L. Heb 1:2 M. 2 Tim 2:12 N. Jam 5:19, err O. Tit 3:14 P. Rom 12:7

1 John 2:28

          1D. As **His**[1] Anointing[A] is teaching[B] you about all *things,* and is true[2] and is not *a* lie
          2D. And just as it[3] taught you
          3D. Be abiding[4] in it[5]

  3B. And[6] now, little-children[C], be abiding[7] in Him, so that if[8] He appears[9], we may have confidence[10], and not be put-to-shame[11] by[12] Him at His coming[D]   28

     1C. If you know[13] that He[14] is righteous[E], you know[15] that everyone also[16] doing[F] righteousness[17] has been born[18] from[19] Him[20]   29

          1D. See what-kind-of[21] love[G] the Father has given *to* us— that we should be called[22] children[23] *of* God! And we are![24]   3:1

              1E. For this reason[25] the world does not know[H] us, because it did not know Him[26]

          2D. Beloved[J], we are **now** children *of* God, and what we will be has not yet appeared[27]. We[28] know[K] that if He appears[29], we will be like[L] Him, because we will see Him just as He is   2
          3D. And everyone having this hope[M] in[30] Him is purifying[31] himself, just as that *One* is pure[N]   3

              1E. Everyone doing[F] sin[32] also is doing lawlessness. Indeed sin is lawlessness[33]. °And you know[K] that that *One* appeared in order that He might take-away[34] sins[35]   4-5
              2E. And there is no sin in Him[36]

                  1F. Everyone abiding[O] in Him is not sinning[37]   6
                  2F. Everyone sinning has not seen Him, nor known[H] Him

          4D. Little-children[38], let no one be deceiving[P] you—   7

              1E. The *one* doing[F] righteousness is righteous[E], just as that *One* is righteous[E]
              2E. The *one* doing[F] sin is of the devil, because the devil is sinning[39] from *the* beginning   8
              3E. The Son *of* God appeared for this— that He might destroy[Q] the works[R] *of* the devil[40]

1. Some manuscripts say "the same" {N}, "As the same Anointing...".
2. Some think John means that the Anointing is real, genuine; others, that the teaching is true. Same word as in 2:8.
3. Or, "He". Some think John means "just as His Anointing is teaching you now, and it taught you from the beginning"; others, just as His Anointing is teaching you now, and He (Jesus) taught you during His earthly ministry".
4. Or, this may be a statement, "you are abiding". Some manuscripts say "you will abide" {N}.
5. Or, "Him". Some think John means "in it", the teaching about all things (as in v 24); others, "in Him", Christ (as in v 28), the subject of the teaching.
6. Some make v 28 the conclusion of the previous section, and begin the new section at 2:29 or 3:1.
7. John turns from abiding in Christ's truth as taught by His Anointing, to abiding in His character— righteousness (2:29-3:9), and love (3:10-24). Thus 2:29-3:24 defines what John means here by "abide in Him". This section expands on what John briefly stated earlier, when he said the one walking as He walked (in righteousness, 2:6, and love, 2:10) is abiding in the light. On this word, see Jn 15:4.
8. That is, if Jesus appears now. It is the timing that is uncertain. Some manuscripts say "when" {N}.
9. Or, "is revealed", referring to His second coming, as in 3:2; Col 3:4; 1 Pet 5:4. On this word, see "made evident" in v 19.
10. Or, "boldness". Same word as in 3:21; 4:17; and 5:14. On this word, see Heb 4:16.
11. Or, "disgraced, ashamed". Same word as in 2 Cor 10:8; Phil 1:20. Elsewhere only as "ashamed" in Lk 16:3; 1 Pet 4:16. GK *159*. Related to "be ashamed" in Rom 1:16.
12. John is referring to the objective result of Christ's judgment, 2 Cor 5:10. Or, "from, away from, because of", so that it says "shrink in shame from Him". In this case, John is continuing the reference to our subjective state at that time, giving the opposite of "confidence". An objective putting to shame would produce a subjective shrinking in shame, so John may have had both in mind. Compare Mk 8:38. GK *608*.
13. Or, "recognize, understand". Not the same word as next, but they are often used interchangeably. Used 318 times. GK *3857*.
14. Some take both "He" and "Him" in this verse to refer to Jesus; others, to the Father. Others take "He" as Jesus and "Him" as the Father— if you know that Jesus (the One having been fathered by God, 5:18) is righteous, you know that everyone doing righteousness like Jesus has also been fathered by God, because of the family resemblance.
15. Or, "understand". Or, this could be a command, "Know that...". On this word, see Lk 1:34.
16. Some manuscripts omit this word {N}.
17. Same phrase as in 3:7, 10. Compare "doing sin" in Jn 8:34.
18. Or, "fathered by". God is our Father when we are born again. Same word as in 3:9; 4:7; 5:1, 4, 18; Jn 1:13; and Jn 3:3-8, "born" again. This is the old word "begat" used in genealogies. It is used of the man "fathering, becoming the father of, begetting", as in Mt 1:2-16; 1 Cor 4:15; Phm 10; of the woman "bearing", as in Lk 1:13; 23:29; Jn 16:21; and of the child as "born, being begotten, being fathered", as here. Used 97 times. On its use with reference to Christ, see 5:18. GK *1164*. Related word in 1 Pet 1:3.
19. Or, "of", "fathered by". Same word as "by" in Mt 1:18. GK *1666*.
20. John explains this concept next, connecting our being born as God's children to our living like Jesus in righteousness. We do righteousness because we are born from Him. Therefore we are like Him now, and will also be like Him when He comes.
21. Or, "what sort of". Same word as in Mt 8:27; Lk 1:29; 7:39; 2 Pet 3:11. Elsewhere only as "what" in Mk 13:1. GK *4534*. Based on the context here, John means "how great, how wonderful".
22. That is, by God Himself!
23. Same word as in 1 Jn 3:2, 10; 5:2; 2 Jn 1, 4, 13; 3 Jn 4; and Jn 1:12; Rom 8:16, 17, 21; Eph 2:3; 5:1, 8; Phil 2:15. Used 99 times. GK *5451*. Related to "little children" in 2:1.
24. Some manuscripts omit "And we are" {A}.
25. Some think this looks back, "because we are His children"; others, forward, "because it did not know Him".
26. Some think John means the Father, as Jesus taught in Jn 15:21; 16:2-3; others, Jesus, as in Jn 1:10.
27. Or, "been made known, been revealed". On this word, see "made evident" in 2:19. More literally, "did not yet appear" or "was not yet revealed". In English idiom, we prefer to say "has not". Some render this verse "Beloved, we are now children of God, and He has not yet appeared. We know what we will be, because if He appears, we will be like Him...".
28. Some manuscripts say "But we know" {N}.
29. Or, "is revealed". Same word as earlier in the verse, v 5, and v 8.
30. That is, "[fixed] on Him".
31. That is, doing righteousness, 2:29. As God's children looking forward to the fullness of what we shall be, we strive now to be holy as He is holy. We strive to become like our Father. Those living this way will have confidence when He comes, 2:28. Same word as in Jam 4:8; 1 Pet 1:22. Elsewhere only in Jn 11:55; Act 21:24, 26; 24:18. GK *49*. Related to "pure" in 1 Pet 3:2; and "purification" in Act 21:26 (GK *50*).
32. On "doing sin", see Jn 8:34.
33. That is, rebellion against law. Same word as in Mt 7:23; 13:41; 23:28; 24:12; Rom 6:19; 2 Cor 6:14; 2 Thes 2:3, 7; Tit 2:14; Heb 1:9. Elsewhere only in the plural, as "lawless-*deeds*" in Rom 4:7; Heb 10:17. GK *490*.
34. Same word as in Jn 1:29, "takes away the sins of the world". Some manuscripts say "our sins" {A}. GK *149*.
35. Doing sin is contradictory to Christ's mission. How can you have your hope in Him (v 3) who came to take away sins, and be doing sin?
36. More literally, "And sin is not in Him".
37. Or, "continuing to sin". That is, continuing in sin as a pattern of life. See v 9. The same word is used of the devil in v 8. There are other views. Consult the commentaries.
38. On this word, see 2:1. Some manuscripts say "children"{N}, using the word in 2:14.
39. Or, "is *continuing to* sin since the beginning". In English idiom, we say "has been sinning". John is not making an historical statement about the devil (he "has sinned"), but is describing his habitual course of action (he "is sinning") from the beginning.
40. Compare Jn 8:41. On this word, see Rev 12:9.

A. 1 Jn 2:20 B. Rom 12:7 C. 1 Jn 2:1 D. 2 Thes 2:8 E. Rom 1:17 F. Rev 13:13 G. 1 Jn 4:16 H. Lk 1:34 J. Mt 3:17 K. 1 Jn 2:29 L. Rev 1:13, resembling M. Col 1:5 N. 1 Pet 3:2 O. Jn 15:4 P. Jam 5:19, err Q. Mt 5:19, break R. Mt 26:10

        4E. Everyone having been born[1] from God is not doing[A] sin— because His seed[2] is   9
            abiding[B] in him, and he is not able[3] to be sinning,[4] because he has been born from God
        5E. By this, the children[C] *of* God and the children *of* the devil are evident[5]   10

  2C. Everyone not[6] doing[A] righteousness[D] is not from God[7]— and[8] *the one* not loving[E] his brother[9]

    1D. Because this is the message[10] which you heard from *the* beginning[11]— that we should be   11
        loving[E] one another

        1E. Not as Cain. He was of the evil[F] *one,* and he slew[12] his brother   12

            1F. And for what reason did he slay him? Because his works[G] were evil[F], but the
                ones of his brother *were* righteous[H]

                1G. And[13] do not be marveling[14], brothers[15], if the world hates[J] you!   13

    2D. **We** know[K] that we have passed from death into life[16], because we are loving[E] the brothers   14

        1E. *The one* not loving[17] is abiding[B] in death[18]
        2E. Everyone hating[J] his brother is *a* murderer[19]. And you know[K] that every murderer   15
            does not have[20] eternal life abiding[B] in him

    3D. By this we have come-to-know[21] love[L]— because that *One* laid-*down* His life[22] for us.   16
        And **we** ought[M] to lay-*down* our lives[N] for the brothers[O]

        1E. But whoever has the goods[23] *of* the world[P], and sees[24] his brother having *a* need[Q],   17
            and shuts[R] his deep-feelings[S] from him, how is the love[L] *of* God[25] abiding in him[26]?

    4D. Little children,[27] let us not be loving[E] *with* word[T] nor tongue[U], but in deed[G] and truth[V].   18
        And[28] by this, we will know[29] that we are of the truth[30], and we will persuade[31] our heart[32]   19
        before Him[33]

        1E. Because[34] if our heart **is condemning**[35] us, *we know* that God is greater[36] *than* our   20
            hearts, and He knows[W] all *things*
        2E. Beloved[X], if **our**[37] **heart** is not condemning *us*[38], we have confidence[39] before God.   21
            And[40] whatever we are asking, we are receiving from Him, because we are keeping[Y]   22
            His commandments[Z], and doing[A] the pleasing[41] *things* in His sight

            1F. And this is His commandment[Z]— that we believe[AA] *in* the name *of* His Son Jesus   23
                Christ, and *that* we be loving[E] one another, just as He gave us *the* commandment[42]
            2F. And *the one* keeping[Y] His commandments is abiding[B] in Him, and He in him[43]   24
            3F. And by this we know[W] that He is abiding in us— from the Spirit[44] Whom He
                gave *to* us

  4B. Beloved[X], do not be believing[AA] every spirit,[45] but be testing[46] the spirits *to see* if they are from   4:1
    God, because many false-prophets[BB] have gone out into the world

1. Or, "fathered". The same word occurs later in this verse. On this word, see 2:29.
2. We have been fathered by God. His life implanted in us changes us from within just as the life flowing in the vine produces fruit. If His life is in us, we cannot continue living contrary to His nature. If we have His life we will be growing in accordance with that life, as all living things do. In this view, His "seed" is the divine nature (2 Pet 1:4). Others think the seed is the Holy Spirit; others, His word; others, Christians ("because His offspring is abiding in Him").
3. Or, "he cannot". This word means "can, is able, is capable, has the power or ability to". Used 210 times. GK *1538*. Related to "power" in Mk 5:30; "powerful" in Lk 24:19; and "empower" in Col 1:11.
4. John does not mean that God's children never sin, as he made clear in 1:8-10, but that they cannot continue to live in sin as a pattern of life. Same concept as in v 6. The children of God and the devil are seen in their pattern of life. This is similar to 1:6-7. God's children are walking in the light, not walking in the darkness. They are living like their Father. By this we can tell the difference, v 10. There are other views. Consult the commentaries.
5. Or, "known, manifest, clear". On this word, see Rom 1:19. Related to the verb in 1 Jn 2:19.
6. Note that what John stated positively in 2:29, he states negatively here. Others join this to point 5E., and start the new point here with v 11.
7. That is, belonging to God, born from God, originating in God.
8. With this, John makes a transition from righteousness to love as the character quality of abiding in Christ (2:28). He begins with a negative statement instead of a positive one (as in 2:29).
9. That is, his fellow Christian. On this word, see Act 16:40.
10. On this word, see 1:5.
11. That is, the beginning of your Christian life.
12. Same word as "slay" next. Elsewhere only in Rev 5:6, 9, 12; 6:4, 9; 13:3, 8; 18:24. GK *5377*. Related to "slaughter" in Act 8:32.
13. Some manuscripts omit this word {C}.
14. The grammar implies "stop marveling". This incident should cause us to expect the world to hate us, as Jesus Himself said in Jn 15:19-20. Righteous living before God brings hate from the world. Compare 2 Tim 3:12. On this word, see Rev 17:8.
15. Some manuscripts say "my brothers" {N}.
16. This phrase was used by Jesus in Jn 5:24.
17. Some manuscripts add "his brother"; others, "the brother" {A}.
18. This is such a person's natural state. He remains in death and darkness, Jn 12:46; 1 Jn 2:9.
19. As Jesus taught in Mt 5:21-26. Literally, a "person-killer", like Cain. Elsewhere only in Jn 8:44. GK *475*.
20. In English, we prefer to say "no murderer has". Compare Rev 21:8.
21. Or, "have known". On this word, see Lk 1:34.
22. This phrase was used by Jesus in Jn 10:11, 15, 17; 15:13.
23. Or, "means, livelihood, living, what it takes to live". On this word, see "life" in in 2:16.
24. Or, "observes, looks at, perceives". Used only here in this book. On this word, see Lk 10:18.
25. Some think John means "love for God" as in 4:20; others, "God's love", as with eternal life in v 15; others, the God-kind of love.
26. As James said, Jam 2:15-17. God's love is not in him.
27. Some manuscripts say "My little children" {N}.
28. Some manuscripts omit this word {C}.
29. Some manuscripts say "we know" {A}.
30. That is, that we belong to the truth, and originate in it.
31. Or, "convince". This word can also mean "conciliate, pacify, set at ease, assure", and some prefer this nuance here. By loving in deed and truth, we will have confidence and not be ashamed if He appears, 2:28. With differing grammar, this word means "convince, persuade, win over, put confidence, have confidence, trust, obey". Used 52 times. GK *4275*.
32. Some think John is referring to our conscience (a word John never uses). On this word, see Rev 2:23.
33. Both now, and when He comes, 2:28.
34. Instead of "because if... that", some punctuate the Greek words so that they mean "whatever thing" (the same idiom as in Col 3:17). In this case, John means "we will persuade our heart before Him— whatever thing our heart is condemning— because God is greater...". Others render this verse "Because if our heart is condemning *us*, because God is greater", the second "because" resuming the first. Since it is redundant, it is omitted in translation, as in the KJV. There are other views.
35. Or, "blaming, laying a charge against, passing judgment on, convicting". We persuade our heart that we are from or of the truth, that we are God's children, in spite of that for which our heart is still condemning us. Same word as in v 21, on which see Gal 2:11.
36. We persuade ourselves by our love in action, because it proves we are His. We know He sees more than what our hearts are saying. He sees our pattern of life as His children. God's love working in us and through us gives us confidence when our hearts point us to a failure. In addition, as ones walking in the light, we respond to what our heart is saying, 1:9. For the one walking in the light, the fact that God knows us absolutely is a source of comfort and assurance, because the light exposes our works, Jn 3:21. There are other views. Consult the commentaries.
37. Some manuscripts omit this word {C}, leaving it implied.
38. Some manuscripts include this pronoun {B}.
39. Or, "boldness". Same word as in 2:28, and pointing back to that verse. Doing righteousness (3:1-9) and loving the brothers (3:10-24) gives us this confidence, because it proves our mutual relationship (v 24) is genuine.
40. This verse gives one aspect of that confidence. Compare 5:14-15.
41. On this adjective, see Jn 8:29.
42. That is, in Jn 15:12.
43. This explains why this person's requests are answered, Jn 15:7.
44. That is, the Spirit promised in Jn 14:16-17, 23-26; 15:26; 16:13-15.
45. That is, as a spirit presents itself in the teachings of a human being. John now gives a warning regarding the "antichrists" mentioned in 2:18-19.
46. Or, "examining, putting to the test, proving by testing". On this word, see "approve" in Rom 12:2.

A. Rev 13:13 B. Jn 15:4 C. 1 Jn 3:1 D. Rom 1:17 E. Jn 21:15, devotedly love F. Act 25:18 G. Mt 26:10, work H. Rom 1:17 J. Rom 9:13 K. 1 Jn 2:29 L. 1 Jn 4:16 M. 1 Jn 4:11 N. Jam 5:20, soul O. Act 16:40 P. 1 Jn 2:15 Q. Tit 3:14 R. Jn 20:19, locked S. Phil 1:8 T. 1 Cor 12:8 U. 1 Cor 12:10 V. Jn 4:23 W. Lk 1:34 X. Mt 3:17 Y. 1 Jn 5:18 Z. Mk 12:28 AA. Jn 3:36 BB. Rev 16:13

1 John 4:2   930   Verse

    1C. By this you know[1] the Spirit *of* God[2]—   2

        1D. Every spirit[3] that is confessing[A] Jesus Christ *as* having come[4] in *the* flesh[B] is from God
        2D. And every spirit that is not confessing Jesus[5] is not from God   3

            1E. And this is the *spirit of* the Antichrist[C]— which, you have heard that it is coming, and now it is already in the world

    2C. **You** are from God,[6] little children, and you have overcome[D] them[7]. Because greater is the *One*[8] in you than the *one* in the world[9]   4
    3C. **They**[10] are from the world.[11] For this reason they are speaking from the world, and the world is listening-to them   5
    4C. **We**[12] are from God. The *one* knowing[E] God is listening-to[13] us. He who is not from God is not listening-to us. From this[14], we know[E] the Spirit[15] *of* truth[16] and the spirit *of* error[17]   6

4A. Beloved[F], let us be loving[G] one another   7

    1B. Because the love[18] is from God! And everyone loving has been born[19] from God, and knows[E] God

        1C. The *one* not loving did not know[E] God, because God is love[20]   8

    2B. By this[21] God's love[22] was made-known[23] among[24] us— that God has sent-forth[25] His only-born[26] Son into the world in order that we might live[H] through Him   9

        1C. In this is love[27]— not that **we** have loved[28] God, but that **He** loved us, and sent-forth His Son *to be the* satisfaction[29] for our sins   10

    3B. Beloved[F], if God loved[G] us in-this-manner[30], **we** also ought[31] to be loving[G] one another[32]   11

        1C. No one has ever seen[33] God; if we are loving one another,[34] God is abiding[J] in us, and His love[35] has been perfected[36] in us   12

            1D. By this we know[E] that we are abiding in Him, and He in us— because He has given *to* us of His Spirit[37]   13
            2D. And **we** have seen[38], and are testifying[39] that the Father has sent-forth the Son *to be* Savior[K] *of* the world[L]. °Whoever confesses[40] that Jesus is the Son *of* God,[41] God is abiding in him, and he in God   14 / 15
            3D. And **we**[42] have come-to-know[43] and have believed[44] the love which God has in[45] us   16

1. Or, "recognize". Or, this may be a command, "By this, know...". This word is used twice in v 6. On this word, see Lk 1:34.
2. Or, "the spirit *from* God", maintaining the same sense as in "every spirit" in v 1 and next.
3. That is, as presented in a human being.
4. Or, "Jesus *as* Christ having come", or, "Jesus Christ having come in the flesh". Compare 2:22; 5:1; 2 Jn 7; Rom 10:9. That is, confess the person we know as Jesus Christ (including all that He is and did) as having come from the Father in genuine human flesh. All this is summed up in the next verse in one word, "Jesus".
5. Some manuscripts add "*as* having come in *the* flesh" {A}.
6. That is, you belong to Him, and originate in Him, being born from Him.
7. That is, the false prophets (v 1) who are not confessing Jesus (v 3).
8. That is, the God you are from, whom we know abides in us from the Spirit He gave us, 3:24. He leads us to hear Him and His messengers, instead of continuing to hear the world. By this we know He abides in us.
9. That is, the evil one, 5:19.
10. That is, the false prophets, v 1.
11. That is, they belong to the world which is passing away, and originate in it.
12. Some think John means "We apostles"; others, "We Christian apostles and teachers"; others, "We Christians", the same group as "you" in v 4.
13. That is, listening and obeying.
14. Some think this refers to v 6a, the second test; others, to all of v 1-6, to both tests. John usually says "by (GK *1877*) this", as in v 2. This is the only place in this book he says "from (GK *1666*) this".
15. Or, "spirit", in the same sense as "every spirit" in v 1-3.
16. John may mean "belonging to the truth", or, "speaking truth". Likewise with "error" next.
17. Or, "deception". On this word, see 1 Thes 2:3. Related to "deceive" in 1:8; 2:26; 3:7.
18. Or, "*this* love"; or, "love". Some think John means the love just mentioned; because the Christian love we express to one another comes from God. Others think he means "love" in an abstract sense.
19. Or, "fathered". This love indicates we have a living relationship with God. Christian love flows from our being born from God, and our growing knowledge of God. On this word, see 2:29.
20. The one not loving in this manner could not have known the One who is love.
21. This is how we came to know this love— by what God did for us.
22. Or, "the love *of* God".
23. Same word as in 1:2.
24. Or, "in connection with us", or, "in us", in the new life He has given us. GK *1877*.
25. Same word as in Jn 5:36, 38; 6:29; 7:29; 8:42; 11:42; 17:3, 8, 18, 21; 20:21; 1 Jn 4:10, 14; etc. On this word, see "send out" in Mk 3:14.
26. Or, "one and only, unique, only begotten". On this word, see Jn 1:18.
27. God's love defines what love really is. True love is defined not by what we do, by how we conceive of it, by our devotion, but by what God has done in sending His Son. Compare 3:16.
28. Some manuscripts say "**we** loved" {B}.
29. Or, "propitiation". On this word, see 2:2.
30. Or, "if God so loved us", that is, loved us to such an extent. On this word, see Jn 3:16.
31. This word is used to express an obligation or debt. Same word as in Jn 13:14; Rom 15:1; Eph 5:28; 2 Thes 1:3; 1 Jn 2:6; 3:16; 3 Jn 8. It also means "have to" in Heb 2:17; "obligated" in Lk 17:10; Heb 5:3, 12; "indebted" in Lk 11:4; and "owe" in Mt 18:28; Rom 13:8; Phm 18. Used 35 times. GK *4053*. Related to "debtors" in Rom 1:14; "due" in 1 Cor 7:3; and "debt" in Rom 4:4.
32. We expect John to say "loving God", as he does in v 20, 21. Fully stated, this should be "we ought to be loving God. And if we love God, we ought to be loving one another (His children)". What explains this jump? What justifies drawing this command to love one another from God's love for us? Four answers follow.
33. First, we cannot see God, but we do see His children. If we are loving them, then God is abiding in us. Thus the jump in v 11 is from what we cannot see to what we can see in ourselves. The love we express to one another demonstrates not only that we love God, but that He is abiding in us and loving through us. The command is justified because such love demonstrates that God is dwelling in us.
34. That is, with the love from God (v 7), made known to us in His Son (v 9).
35. Literally, "the love *of* Him". Some think John means "His love for us"; others, "our love for Him"; others, both, the love that characterizes Him which we express to one another.
36. Or, "brought to completion, brought to its goal, brought to full development". This is a participle, meaning it "is having been perfected", it stands perfected. Same word as in v 17, 18; and in 2:5, where keeping His word is the subject. On this word, see Heb 2:10.
37. Or, "from His Spirit". Love does not and cannot stand alone as a witness that God is abiding in us. The love in view here is inseparably linked to two other witnesses. The Spirit is the second witness.
38. Our confession of Christ is the third witness. Some think the emphatic "we" here refers to John and the eyewitnesses. Our confession of Jesus (v 15) is then in response to their eyewitness testimony. Others think the "we" refers to all Christians. We all see and confess Him, using "see" in the sense of Spirit-directed sight. Same word as in v 12 and 1:1; Jn 1:14, 32; 11:45. Used 22 times, all rendered "see" except Lk 7:24; Jn 4:35, "look-*at*". GK *2517*.
39. Both "seen and "testifying" are the same words as in 1:1-2.
40. The grammar indicates that an act of confession is in view. On this word, see 1 Tim 6:12.
41. Note how John links together Christ's person (Son of God) and His work (Savior of the world).
42. John's and each Christian's personal testimony is now added to the previous three witnesses.
43. Or, "have known". Same word as in 2:3, 4; 3:16.
44. Some manuscripts say "and believe" {N}.
45. Some think John means "in connection with us", as seen in the cross; others, "in us", abiding in us, as "has in" is used in 5:10 and in 3:15. We know He is abiding in us because we have personally experienced His love in us.

A. 1 Tim 6:12 B. Col 2:23 C. 1 Jn 2:18 D. Rev 2:7 E. Lk 1:34 F. Mt 3:17 G. Jn 21:15, devotedly love H. Rev 20:4, came to life J. Jn 15:4 K. Lk 1:47 L. 1 Jn 2:15

    2C. God is love¹; and the *one* abiding^A in the love² is abiding in God, and God is abiding³ in him

        1D. By this,⁴ the love⁵ has been perfected⁶ with⁷ us in-order-that⁸ we may have confidence⁹   17
on the day *of* judgment^B, because¹⁰ just as that *One* is, **we** also are,¹¹ in this world

            1E. Fear¹² is not in¹³ love¹⁴— rather, perfect¹⁵ love throws¹⁶ fear out¹⁷, because fear has¹⁸   18
punishment¹⁹— and the *one* fearing has not been perfected in love
            2E. **We**²⁰ are loving²¹ because **He** first loved us   19

    3C. If²² someone claims^C that "I love God" and is hating^D his brother^E, he is *a* liar. For the *one* not   20
loving^F his brother whom he has seen, cannot²³ be loving^F God Whom he has not seen
    4C. And we have this commandment^G from Him— that the *one* loving^F God should be loving his   21
brother also

4B. Everyone believing^H that Jesus is the Christ has been born²⁴ from God. And everyone loving^F the   5:1
One having fathered²⁵ is loving also²⁶ the *one* having been born²⁷ from Him

    1C. By this we know^J that we are loving^F the children²⁸ *of* God— when²⁹ we are loving God and   2
doing³⁰ His commandments³¹

        1D. For this is the love *of* God³²— that we be keeping^K His commandments³³   3

            1E. And His commandments are not burdensome³⁴

1. Now John moves from what we cannot see (v 12) to what we do know. Thus the jump in v 11 is from what we do know about God to what we can see in ourselves. We know that God is love because of v 9. Loving one another demonstrates that we are in a mutual abiding relationship with Him. The command is justified because such love demonstrates a personal relationship with God. This is the word *agape*. Same word as in Mt 24:12; Jn 13:35; 15:10; Rom 5:5; 8:35; 13:10; 15:30; 1 Cor 13:4; 2 Cor 5:14; Gal 5:6; Eph 3:17; Phil 1:9; 1 Thes 5:13; 1 Tim 1:5; Heb 10:24; 2 Pet 1:7; 1 Jn 2:15; 3:16; 5:3; Jude 21. Used 116 times. GK *27*. Related to "*devotedly-love*" in Jn 21:15.
2. Or, "*this* love"; or, "love". That is, the love just mentioned; the love that God is, and inspires in us.
3. Some manuscripts omit this word {N}.
4. Some think this refers to the preceding verse, "By this mutual abiding", as here, NIV, NASB. By means of this mutual abiding, this love has been brought to its goal with us, that we may have confidence. Others think this refers to the next clause, "In this the love has been perfected with us— that we have confidence", as in NKJV, NRSV. This love is brought to its goal in our confidence regarding the day of judgment, in the casting out of fear. There are other views.
5. That is, the love just mentioned, God's love in which we are abiding, v 16. Some place the emphasis on its being God's love; others, on our abiding in it, on its being our love; others on both, on the mutual relationship of love.
6. Same word as in v 12.
7. Some link this to the noun as "the love with us", taking this to mean "our love". Most take it with the verb, "perfected with us". In this case, some think John means "together with us", with our cooperation, in company with us; others, "among us", in our mutual love as Christians. Used elsewhere in this book only of fellowship "with" in 1:3, 6, 7; and remaining "with" in 2:19. Used also in 2 Jn 2, 3, "will be with us". GK *3552*.
8. Or, "so that we will have confidence". GK *2671*.
9. Same word as in 2:28. God's love has been perfected with us now, in our behavior, because we love as He does. This results in confidence before Him both now and regarding that future day, as John also said in 3:18-21.
10. This explains why we have this confidence. On this word, see Eph 5:21.
11. Some think John means "because just as Jesus is abiding in the Father's love, we also are abiding in it", reflecting what Jesus said in Jn 15:9-10. Others think he means "because we are like Jesus in character". If he specifically means "because just as Jesus is loving, we are loving", then v 19 explains this phrase. There are other views.
12. This explains with a negative argument why such love produces confidence. The love that comes to us as God's gift and is perfected in a mutual abiding relationship brings no fear with it. Quite the opposite.
13. This reflects the Greek word order and grammar. In English, we prefer to say "There is no fear in love", where "in" means "in connection with, in the sphere of, within". GK *1877*.
14. More literally "the love", as also later in the verse. John could mean specifically the love under discussion here in v 16-17, "Fear is not in *this* love". Or he could be making his specific point by referring here to a universal truth about love.
15. Or, "complete, fully developed". Related to the verb "perfected" in v 12, 17, 18. On this word, see "complete" in 1 Cor 13:10.
16. Or, "puts, casts, drives". On this word, see Rev 2:22.
17. Fear is part of a relationship based on performance, with punishment for failure. A mutual relationship of love not based on performance eliminates all fear.
18. Some think John means fear has to do with punishment; others, that fear brings or contains punishment by anticipating it.
19. Elsewhere only in Mt 25:46. GK *3136*. The related verb is in 2 Pet 2:9.
20. This explains with a positive argument why such love produces confidence. Our love is a result of the relationship, not a cause of it. It is the visible result of our relationship with the invisible God.
21. Both God and others are in view. Some manuscripts add "God"; others, "Him" {A}.
22. John now makes the same point from the negative side. The failure to love the brother who is seen demonstrates that no relationship with the loving God exists, no matter what is claimed. The command to love one another is justified by the fact that no other course is possible for those who know Him. If God's love is not flowing through us to others, then we have no relationship with Him.
23. Some manuscripts say "how can he..." {A}, as in 3:17. John gives the rhetorical question in 3:17; the categorical denial here.
24. Or, "fathered". Same word as later in the verse, and as "fathered" next. On this word, see 2:29.
25. There is a change in the grammar of this word here, reflected in the change from "born" to "fathered".
26. Some manuscripts omit this word {C}.
27. That is, "everyone loving the [God] having fathered [us] is loving also the [brother] having been born from Him". Or, "... having been fathered from Him".
28. This refers back to "the *one* having been born from Him" in v 1.
29. That is, when the loving the children is occurring together with the loving God and obeying.
30. On this word, see Rev 13:13. Some manuscripts say, "keeping" {B}.
31. We know we are loving our brothers, God's children, with love from God (4:7) when our love is part of our full family relationship with God and them. Human affection, friendship, and philanthropy alone are not "the love which God has in us". For John, loving the brothers cannot be separated from, and does not exist apart from the three other aspects of the family relationship— loving God, keeping His commandments, believing in His Son. For John, these four things exist together, or not at all. He has already said we cannot claim to love God and leave out one of the other three. Here he is saying we cannot claim to love the brothers and leave out one of the other three. In v 2-5, John binds together the four concepts, along with faith, being born from God, and victory over the world, into one inseparable unit.
32. That is, love for God.
33. Since these commandments include "believe in His Son" and "love one another" (3:23), the four ideas are linked together again.
34. Or, "heavy". Compare Mt 11:30. Same word as "heavy" in Mt 23:4, of the load imposed by the Pharisees. On this word, see "weighty" in Act 25:7.

A. Jn 15:4   B. Jn 3:19   C. Jn 12:49, says   D. Rom 9:13   E. Act 16:40   F. Jn 21:15, devotedly love   G. Mk 12:28   H. Jn 3:36   J. Lk 1:34   K. 1 Jn 5:18

	2D. Because everything¹ having been born^A from God is being-victorious-over² the world³	4
	1E. And this is the victory⁴ having been-victorious-over⁵ the world— our faith^B!	
	3D. And⁶ who is the *one* being-victorious-over the world if not the *one* believing⁷ that Jesus is the Son *of* God!	5
	1E. This *One*⁸ is the *One* having come⁹ by¹⁰ water and blood¹¹— Jesus Christ (not in¹² the water only,¹³ but in the water and in¹⁴ the blood). And the Spirit is the *One* testifying¹⁵— because¹⁶ the Spirit is the truth^C	6
	2E. Because¹⁷ the *ones* testifying are three¹⁸—*the Spirit and the water and the blood¹⁹— and the three are for the one²⁰ *thing*. *If we receive^D the testimony *of* humans²¹, the testimony *of* God is greater!	7-8 9
	3E. Because²² this is the testimony *of* God— that²³ He has testified about His Son	
	1F. The *one* believing^E in the Son *of* God has the testimony in himself	10
	2F. The *one* not believing^E God²⁴ has made Him *a* liar, because he has not believed in the testimony which God has testified about His Son²⁵	
	4E. And this is the testimony²⁶— that God gave us eternal^F life^G, and this life is in His Son	11
	1F. The *one* having the Son has the life	12
	2F. The *one* not having the Son *of* God does not have the life	
2C.	I wrote these²⁷ *things* to you, the *ones* believing in the name *of* the Son *of* God, in order that you may know^H that you have eternal **life**²⁸	13
3C.	And this is the confidence²⁹ which we have before Him—	14
	1D. That if we request³⁰ anything according to His will,³¹ He hears us. *And if we know that He hears us— whatever we request— we know that we have the requests³² which we have requested from Him	15

1. John is stating a universal principle in the broadest generic terms. Whatever is born of God overcomes. He uses this idiom also in Jn 3:6; 6:37, 39; 17:2, 7, 24; 1 Jn 2:16.
2. Or, "overcoming". On this word, see "overcoming" in Rev 2:7. It is related to "victory" in this verse, and is rendered this way to show the relationship.
3. Those who love God will keep His commandments because they are born from God, and as His children, are overcoming the world and the sin in it. Love and obedience are inseparable; being victorious is inevitable.
4. That is, the means of victory or overcoming, the power that overcomes. The Greek word is *nike*. Used only here. GK *3772*. Related to the preceding verb; and "victory" in 1 Cor 15:57.
5. Or, "having overcome". Some think John is referring to the victory that took place when we were born again. Others give it a present sense, "*that* overcomes", referring to the victory occurring at the same time as our "keeping His commands". There are other views.
6. John further defines the victorious one. Note the opposite question in 2:22. Some manuscripts omit this word {C}.
7. Or, "having faith". Related to "faith" in v 4. On this word, see Jn 3:36.
8. That is, Jesus the Son of God. Who is the one overcoming if not the one believing Jesus is the Son of God, because Jesus has a threefold divine witness to His identity.
9. That is, the One who came. This word points to His historical coming from God as Messiah and Savior. This "coming" corresponds to the "sending forth" in 4:10.
10. That is, "by means of, through". GK *1328*.
11. The water and blood are two of the three witnesses testifying to Jesus the Son of God, the Spirit being the third, v 7. Some think they refer to His baptism (which was accompanied by His Father's witness, "This is My beloved Son"), and His death (which was a real death, and was accompanied by the witness of the resurrection). Others think they refer to His birth (note Jn 3:5), where He came in real flesh, and His dying a real death. Others think they refer to the "blood and water" that came from His side on the cross, proving the reality of His death, Jn 19:34. On "blood", see 1:7. There are other views. Consult the commentaries. Some manuscripts add "and Spirit" {A}.
12. Some think John means "in connection with"; others, "by, by means of "; others, "with, accompanied with". Some think no difference of meaning is intended between "by" earlier and "in" here, rendering all four "by". GK *1877*.
13. Some were apparently teaching Jesus came in water only, which John denies here. The precise nature of this false teaching is uncertain, but it clearly involved some kind of denial of the death of Jesus the Son of God. Some think it involves the nature of the person Who died; others, the significance of His death. A denial that God truly took on human flesh and died would be in keeping with the emphasis in 4:2; 2 Jn 7. Some think John is refuting a heresy at that time which accepted that Jesus was God's Messiah who began His mission at His baptism, but denied His death had any significance, the divine Christ having left the human Jesus in Gethsemane. There are other views. Consult the commentaries.
14. Note that earlier John referred to the water and blood as if they were a single concept, "by water and blood". Here and in v 7 he refers to each one independently. Some think the unified concept refers to His life or ministry as a whole, the individuality to the separate historical events that begin and end it. There are other views.
15. Or, "bearing witness". This verb is in v 6, 7, 9, 10. The related noun "testimony" is used 6 times in v 9-11. See Jn 1:7 on both.
16. The Spirit is presently adding His testimony to the two historical witnesses because the Spirit is the truth. It is His nature and His ministry to testify to the truth about Jesus. Compare Jn 15:26; 16:13.
17. Here John gives the significance of these three witnesses to his point. They are three divine witnesses to Jesus. Who is the one overcoming (v 5), if not the one believing the three divine witnesses?
18. Some manuscripts add at this point, three "in heaven— The Father, the Word and the Holy Spirit, and these three are one. And the *ones* giving testimony on the earth are three"— the Spirit..... {A}.
19. Some give the water and blood a different meaning here than in v 6. Several symbolic meanings are suggested. Others think they mean the same thing in both places.
20. That is, the three witnesses are in agreement. They testify to one and the same thing, in keeping with Deut 19:15.
21. That is, if the testimony of human witnesses is accepted as sufficient evidence for a matter, how much more the testimony of divine witnesses! John appeals to our general human practice of believing three witnesses. On this word, see "mankind" in Mt 4:4.
22. Here John emphasizes the finality of this testimony. God's testimony is that He has spoken on this matter. The one believing Jesus is the Son of God is overcoming because He is believing what God said.
23. Same construction and meaning as in v 11, 14. Compare 2:25; 3:11, 23; 5:4. Some manuscripts say "which" {N}, so that it says "Because this is the testimony *of* God which He...".
24. Some manuscripts say "the Son" {A}.
25. God said, "This is My beloved Son", Mt 3:17; 2 Pet 1:16-18. To not believe this is to call Him a liar. Note the reverse in Jn 3:33, and the similar statement in Jn 3:18.
26. Now John states the content of the testimony God has given. His testimony is regarding both the person of Jesus (He is God's Son) and the mission of Jesus (God gave us eternal life in Him). Thus the one believing Jesus is the Son of God overcomes the world because there is a threefold witness to His identity, because God Himself has testified concerning His Son, and because God's testimony is that He gave us eternal life in His Son.
27. That is, the things regarding loving God, loving one another, being born from God, keeping His commands, and believing in His Son concerning whom God has testified and in whom is eternal life. This is the conclusion of chapter 5. Others give this a narrower focus as point 5E., concluding v 5-12 only; others, a broader focus as point 5A., concluding the whole book.
28. Some manuscripts add "and that you may believe in the name *of* the Son *of* God" {N}. Compare John 20:31.
29. That is, what we know with confidence, picking up from v 13. Same word as in 2:28.
30. This word means "ask, ask for, request". Used four times in v 14-16. Used 70 times. GK *160*. Related to the noun in v 15.
31. As Jesus did in Lk 22:42. Compare 3:22.
32. Elsewhere only in Lk 23:24; Phil 4:6. GK *161*.

A. 1 Jn 2:29   B. Eph 2:8   C. Jn 4:23   D. Rom 7:8, taken   E. Jn 3:36   F. Mt 25:46   G. Rom 8:10   H. 1 Jn 2:29

	1E. If anyone sees[1] his brother[2] sinning[A] *a* sin[B] not *leading*[3] to death[4], he shall request, and He[5] will give him life[6]— *for* the *ones* sinning *a sin* not *leading* to death	16
	2E. There is *a* sin *leading* to death.[7] I am not saying that he should pray[8] about that	
	3E. All unrighteousness[C] is sin, and there is sin not *leading* to death	17
2D.	We know[D] that everyone having been born[9] from God is not sinning[10]	18
	1E. But the *One* having been fathered[11] from God is keeping[12] him[13]	
	2E. And the evil[E] *one* is not touching[14] him	
3D.	We know[D] that we are from God, and the whole world[F] lies[G] in[15] the evil[E] *one*	19
4D.	And we know[D] that the Son *of* God has come[H], and has given us understanding[J] in order that we might know[16] the true[17] *One*	20
5D.	And we are in[18] the true *One*, in His Son Jesus Christ	
	1E. This[19] *One* is the true God and eternal life	
	2E. Little-children[K], guard[20] yourselves from idols[21]	21

1. That is, observes an outward sinful action about which one might pray that God would forgive— such as Peter denying the Lord; the people crucifying Christ (Lk 23:34); stoning Stephen (Act 7:60); hating a brother (1 Jn 3:15); not meeting the physical need of a brother (3:17); loving the world (2:15); sinning (3:6); etc. John moves from prayer in general (v 14-15) to prayer for a brother in need in particular. On this word, see Lk 2:26.
2. Some think John means a professing Christian; others, a genuine Christian; others, a non-Christian, "a neighbor". The question arises due to the uncertainty regarding the meaning of "death" and "life" later.
3. Same idiom as a "sickness *leading* to death" in Jn 11:4.
4. Some think John means "spiritual, eternal death"; others, "physical death", as in 1 Cor 11:30.
5. Some think John means God. We request, God gives. Others think he means the one requesting, "he will give...", as in Jam 5:20.
6. Some think John means physical life; others, spiritual vitality and fellowship; others, salvation.
7. What is this sin? The answer depends on whether John is referring to physical death or spiritual, eternal death. If the former, it could be any sin leading to this level of discipline from God, as in Act 5:5, 10; 1 Cor 11:30. If the latter, some think it is the same thing as the blasphemy of the Spirit in Mk 3:30. Some define it as the sin of apostasy. The ones in 1 Jn 2:19, 22 who went out from us teaching lies about Jesus are an example. Others define it as knowing and deliberate rejection of Christ, as in Heb 6:4-6; 10:26-29. There are other views. Consult the commentaries.
8. Or, "ask, question". Used only here in 1 John. On this word, see Jn 17:9. Some think it is synonymous with "request" in v 16. Others think that it implies "that he should not question God on this". In any case, this sin is different than the one in v 16, and is not a matter for us to ask about. This is the Father's matter, which He will deal with based on His own will.
9. Same word as "fathered" next. These same two renderings also occur together in v 1.
10. As John said in 3:9.
11. Or, "born". Same word as "born" earlier in the verse, but there is a change of grammar here. Some think John means Jesus. This word is used of Jesus in the sense of being "born" in Mt 2:1, 4; Lk 1:35; Jn 18:37; and in the sense of being "fathered" by God in Mt 1:20; Act 13:33; Heb 1:5; 5:5. Others render it "the *one* having been born from God keeps himself " from sin, referring to the Christian. On this word, see "born" in 2:29.
12. Same word as in Jn 17:11, 12, 15; and 1 Jn 2:3, 4, 5; 3:22, 24; 5:3. It means "keep" in the sense of "guarding" (Mt 27:54); "keeping watch over" (Act 12:6); "preserve" (1 Thes 5:23); "reserve" (see 2 Pet 2:17); and "obey, observe". Used 70 times. GK *5498*. Related to "jail" (the place of keeping) in Act 5:18.
13. Some manuscripts say "himself " {B}, in keeping with the latter of the two views on "fathered" in note 11.
14. That is, to bring him harm. On this word, see 1 Cor 7:1.
15. Or, "in the sphere of, in the domain of, in union with". Some extend this to mean "in the power of, under the authority of ". GK *1877*.
16. Some render this "so that we know", giving the result rather than the purpose, a rendering further supported by some manuscripts {N}. On this word, see Lk 1:34.
17. That is, the real, genuine God. Used three times in this verse. Same word as the "true" God in Jn 17:3; 1 Thes 1:9; and as the "true" Light in 1 Jn 2:8. On this word, see Jn 7:28. Some manuscripts say "the true God" {A}.
18. Same word as "in" in v 19. We originate from God (v 19), and live in union with Him.
19. Grammatically this could refer to "Jesus Christ", or "the true *One*". Some think it would be redundant to say that the true One is the true God. John says here what he also says in Jn 1:1. Others think John repeats his reference to the Father to add emphasis to it and to prepare for his command regarding idols.
20. Or, "keep, protect". Used only here in 1 John. On this word, see "keep" in Jn 12:25. Not related to "keep"in v 18.
21. Or, "images". Some think John means literal idols, false gods, and the worship associated with them; others, anything that takes the place of God in one's life, including false teachings (2:22-23; 4:3) and improper desires (2:15). Compare Col 3:5; Eph 5:5. There are other views. Elsewhere only in Act 7:41; 15:20; Rom 2:22; 1 Cor 8:4, 7; 10:19; 12:2; 2 Cor 6:16; 1 Thes 1:9; Rev 9:20. GK *1631*. Some manuscripts add "amen" {A}.

A. Act 25:8 B. Jn 8:46 C. Rom 1:18 D. 1 Jn 2:29 E. Act 25:18 F. 1 Jn 2:15 G. Mt 3:10 H. Jn 8:42, am here J. Lk 1:51, thoughts K. 1 Jn 2:1

Overview	**2 John**
Introduction	1-3
1A. I rejoiced greatly that I have found some of your children walking in the truth	4
2A. And now I ask you, lady, that we be loving one another	5
1B. And this is love— that we be walking according to His commandments	6
2B. This is the commandment, just as you heard from the beginning, that you should be walking in it	6
3B. Because many deceivers went out into the world— the ones not confessing Christ	7
4B. Be watching yourselves in order that you may receive a full reward. Do not receive anyone who does not bring the teaching of Christ	8-11
Conclusion	12-13

	A. The elder[1]	1
	B. *To the* chosen[2] lady[3], and *to* her children[4]	
	1. Whom[5] **I** love[A] in truth[6]— and not only I, but also all[7] the *ones* having known[B] the truth[C]— because of the truth abiding[D] in us	2
	a. And it will be with us forever[E]	
	b. Grace, mercy, peace from God *the* Father, and from Jesus[8] Christ— the Son *of* the Father— will be with us[9] in truth and love	3
1A.	I rejoiced[F] greatly that I have found *some* of your children walking[G] in *the* truth[10], just as we received commandment[11] from the Father	4
2A.	And now I ask you, lady— not as-*if* writing[12] you *a* new[H] commandment, but *the one* which we had from *the* beginning[I]— that we be loving[13] one another	5
	1B. And this is love[K]— that we be walking according to His commandments	6
	2B. This is the commandment, just as[14] you[15] heard from *the* beginning, that you should be walking in it[16]	
	3B. Because many deceivers[L] went-out[17] into the world— the *ones* not confessing[18] Jesus Christ *as* coming in *the* flesh[19]	7
	1C. This is the deceiver and the antichrist[M]	
	4B. Be watching[N] yourselves,[20] in order that you[21] may not lose[22] *the things* which we[23] accomplished[24], but may receive[O] *a* full[P] reward[25]	8
	1C. Everyone going-ahead[26] and not abiding[D] in the teaching[Q] *of* Christ[27] does not have God	9
	2C. The *one* abiding in the teaching[28]— this *one* has both the Father and the Son	
	3C. If anyone comes to you[29] and does not bring this teaching,[30] do not receive[31] him into *the* house, and do not speak greetings[32] *to* him	10
	1D. For the *one* speaking greetings *to* him shares[33] *in* his evil[R] works[S]	11

	A. Having many *things* to write *to* you[34], I did not want *to do so* with papyrus-*paper*[35] and black-*ink*[36]. But I hope to come-to-be[37] with you and to speak mouth to mouth[38], in order that our[39] joy may be full[40]	12
	B. The children *of* your chosen sister greet[T] you[41]	13

1. This word is used in the sense of "older" (see 1 Tim 5:1); and "church leader" (see 1 Tim 5:17). Peter also referred to himself as an "elder" in 1 Pet 5:1. John could intend either meaning here. The same opening occurs in 3 Jn 1.
2. Same word as in v 13. On this word, see Rom 8:33.
3. Some think this is an individual, turning one or the other of these words into a person's name— "the chosen Kuria" (a known proper name), or the "lady Electa". Others think John is referring to a local congregation, and he is writing from another "sister" congregation, v 13. Elsewhere only in v 5. GK *3257*. This is the feminine form of the word "lord, master, sir" (see "master" in Mt 8:2).
4. John could be referring to a lady and her biological children; a lady and her spiritual children (possibly a church meeting in her home); or a church and its congregation. On this word, see 1 Jn 3:1.
5. This word is plural, referring to the lady and her children.
6. Or, "in *the* truth", "in connection with *the* truth". GK *1877*.
7. Paul made a similar statement about Prisca and Aquila in Rom 16:4.
8. Some manuscripts say "from *the* Lord Jesus Christ" {A}.
9. Some manuscripts say "you" {N}.
10. Or, "in truth". Same phrase as in 3 Jn 3.
11. Same word as in v 5, 6. Used 14 times in 1 John. The command we received is to believe in Jesus and love one another, 1 Jn 3:23. On this word, see Mk 12:28.
12. Some manuscripts say "I am writing" {N}, rendered "I wrote" by some.
13. Just as in 1 John, love, keeping His commandments (v 6), and confessing Christ (v 7-11) are inseparably linked.
14. Some manuscripts say "that just as..." {N}.
15. This word is plural, as is the next "you" in this verse. John turns from the lady to address them all.
16. Some think John means "love", the main subject in view; others, "commandment", the nearest choice; others, "truth" (v 4).
17. Same word as in 1 Jn 2:19; 4:1. Some manuscripts say "entered" {N}.
18. Same word as in 1 Jn 2:23; 4:3. On this word, see 1 Tim 6:12.
19. That is, that Jesus truly became a man to become the satisfaction for sin. See 1 Jn 2:2; 4:2. On this word, see Col 2:23.
20. This exhortation is addressed to them all. All the pronouns and verbs in v 8 and v 10 are plural.
21. Some manuscripts say "we" {A}.
22. Or, "ruin, destroy, waste". Same word as in Jn 6:12, 39; 12:25; 18:9; etc. On this word, see "perish" in 1 Cor 1:18.
23. Some manuscripts say, "you" {B}. Thus the manuscripts present three variations, "we may not lose *the things* which we accomplished"; "you may not lose *the things* which you accomplished"; and "you may not lose *the things* which we accomplished".
24. Same word as in 3 Jn 5.
25. Or, "compensation". Paul also focused on this goal using the same word, 1 Cor 3:8, 14; 9:17,18. See also Col 3:24; 2 Tim 4:8. On this word, see "recompense" in Rev 22:12.
26. Or, "leading forth, going before, advancing". Perhaps the deceivers used this word of their teaching— it is going ahead to a more advanced doctrine than that taught by the apostles. Same word as in Mt 2:9; 14:22; 21:9, 31; 26:32; 28:7; Mk 6:45; 10:32; 11:9; 14:28; 16:7; 1 Tim 5:24. Elsewhere only as "precede" in Lk 18:39; 1 Tim 1:18; Heb 7:18; "bring forth" in Act 12:6; 17:5; "bring before" in Act 25:26; and "bring" in Act 16:30. GK *4575*. The root word is "bring, lead". Some manuscripts say "transgressing" {N}.
27. This could mean "the teaching *about* Christ"; or, "Christ's teaching".
28. Some manuscripts add "*of* Christ" {A}.
29. Some think John is referring to a false teacher coming to the church. An itinerant teacher/prophet who claims to speak for God but who denies Christ comes seeking to address the church meeting in your home. He comes "to you" (plural), the chosen lady and her children, v 1. The following verbs are plural. Others think that in addition, this is also an individual responsibility.
30. That is, this teaching about Christ.
31. Or, "take". That is, do not extend your hospitality to him, as you would to fellow Christians. On this word, see "taken" in Rom 7:8.
32. This word is used both of the initial greetings (the welcome) and the final greetings (the farewell), and John could have either in mind here. Either official or private greetings may be in view. On this word, see "rejoice" in 2 Cor 13:11. Not the same word as in v 13.
33. Or, "takes part with, participates in, takes a share with, partners with". Elsewhere only in Rom 12:13; 15:27; Gal 6:6; 1 Tim 5:22; Heb 2:14; 1 Pet 4:13; and as "partnered" in Phil 4:15. GK *3125*. Related to "fellowship" in 1 Cor 1:9; and "sharer" in 2 Pet 1:4; and "common" in Jude 3.
34. This word is plural both times in this verse.
35. That is, a leaf of paper made from the separated layers of the papyrus plant. Used only here. GK *5925*.
36. On this word, see 3 Jn 13, where John says "black and reed".
37. Or, "be". Same phrase as in 1 Cor 16:10. GK *1181*.
38. We would say, "face to face" (as Paul does in 1 Cor 13:12). This same phrase occurs in 3 Jn 14.
39. Some manuscripts say "your" {B}.
40. This is a participle, "may be having been made full". Same idiom as in Jn 16:24.
41. This word is singular, referring to the lady. Some manuscripts add "Amen" {A}.

A. Jn 21:15, devotedly love   B. Lk 1:34   C. Jn 4:23   D. Jn 15:4   E. Rev 20:10   F. 2 Cor 13:11   G. Heb 13:9   H. Heb 8:13   J. Col 1:18   K. 1 Jn 4:16   L. 1 Tim 4:1, deceitful   M. 1 Jn 2:18   N. Rev 1:11, see   O. Lk 16:25   P. Mt 14:20   Q. 1 Cor 14:6   R. Act 25:18   S. Mt 26:10   T. Mk 15:18

Overview		3 John
Introduction		1
1A. Beloved, I pray that you may prosper and be healthy— just as your soul is prospering		2-4
2A. Beloved, you are doing a faithful thing for the brothers, whom you will do well to send forward		5-8
3A. I wrote something to the church, but Diotrephes is not accepting us		9-10
4A. Beloved, do not be imitating the evil, but the good		11
5A. For Demetrius, he has been attested by all, by the truth, and we also are testifying		12
Conclusion		13-15

A. The elder[1]   1
B. *To* the beloved[A] Gaius[2], whom **I** love[B] in truth[3]

1A. Beloved, I pray[C] *that* with respect to all[4] *things* you *may* prosper[5] and be healthy[6], just as your soul[D] is   2
   prospering

   1B. For I rejoiced greatly[7] while brothers *were* coming and testifying[E] *concerning* your truth[8]— how[9]   3
       you are walking[F] in *the* truth[10]
   2B. I have no joy[11] greater *than* these[12] *things*— that I may be hearing-*of* my children[G] walking in the truth   4

2A. Beloved[A], you are doing *a* faithful[13] *thing*— whatever you may accomplish[14]— for the brothers[H] (and this,   5
    for strangers[15]!)

   1B. Who testified[E] *concerning* your love[16] before *the* church   6
   2B. *As to* whom you will do well[17], having sent-*them*-forward[18] worthily[19] *of* God

       1C. For they went out for[20] the Name[21], taking[J] nothing from the Gentiles[22]   7
       2C. Therefore **we** ought[K] to be supporting[23] such *ones*, in order that we may be[24] fellow-workers[25]   8
           for[26] the truth[L]

3A. I wrote something[27] *to* the church,[28] but Diotrephes, the *one* loving-to-be-first[29] *among* them, is not   9
    accepting[30] us. °For this reason, if I come, I will call-to-mind[31] his deeds[M] which he is doing[N]—   10

   1B. Talking-nonsense-about[32] us *with* malicious[33] words[O]
   2B. And not being content[34] with these *things*, neither is he himself accepting the brothers
   3B. And he is forbidding[35] and putting-out[36] of the church the *ones* wanting[P] *to do so*

4A. Beloved[A], do not be imitating[Q] the evil[37], but the good[R]   11

   1B. The *one* doing-good[S] is from God
   2B. The[38] *one* doing-evil[39] has not seen[40] God

5A. *With regard to* Demetrius[41]— he has been attested[42] by everyone, and by the truth[L] itself   12

   1B. And **we**[43] also are testifying[E], and you know that our testimony[T] is true[U]

A. I had many *things* to write *to* you, but I do not wish[V] to write *to* you with black-ink[44] and reed-pen[45].   13
   But I hope[W] to see you at-once[X], and we will speak mouth to mouth   14
B. Peace *to* you   15[46]
C. The friends[Y] greet[Z] you
D. Greet the friends by name

1. On this word, see 2 Jn 1.
2. Nothing is known of this man. This name is used elsewhere of three individuals, Act 19:29; 20:4; Rom 16:23 and 1 Cor 1:4. GK *1127*.
3. Or, "in *the* truth". Same phrase as in 2 Jn 1.
4. In the Greek word order, "with respect to all *things*" comes first, before "I pray". Some take it with both verbs following; others, with "prosper" only, "*that* you *may* prosper with respect to all *things*, and be healthy".
5. Or, "succeed, go well". Same word as later in the verse. On this word, see Rom 1:10.
6. Or, "well, sound". Used of physical health and of doctrinal health or sound doctrine. On this word, see 1 Tim 1:10. May your life and health prosper as your soul prospers spiritually.
7. Same phrase as in 2 Jn 4.
8. That is, the truth characterizing your life. The same idiom is used in v 6 regarding Gaius's love.
9. Same word as in Act 15:14, in a similar context. Or, "just as, even as". GK *2777*.
10. Or, "in truth". Same phrase as in 2 Jn 4.
11. Some manuscripts say, "grace, favor" {A}, meaning no greater favor from God.
12. Some manuscripts have this word singular, "this" {N}.
13. That is, a thing characterized by faith. On this word, see Col 1:2.
14. Or, "work, carry out, perform". Same word as 2 Jn 8. John is referring to showing hospitality to these brothers, and assisting them on their way. On this word, see "work" in Mt 26:10.
15. That is, for brothers who are strangers to you! It was remarkable then as it is now. Compare 1 Cor 6:6, 8. On this word, see "host" in Rom 16:23. Some manuscripts say "and for strangers" {N}.
16. That is, the love characterizing Gaius's life.
17. That is, you will do a good thing by doing this. On this idiom, see Act 10:33.
18. That is, when you help them to continue their journey. On this word, see Rom 15:24.
19. Paul makes a similar plea on behalf of Phoebe in Rom 16:2, using this same word. Elsewhere only in Eph 4:1; Phil 1:27; Col 1:10; 1 Thes 2:12. GK *547*. The related verb is in 2 Thes 1:11.
20. Or, "for the sake of, on behalf of". GK *5642*.
21. Or, "*His* name". That is, the Lord Jesus Christ, Son of God.
22. Or, "nationals, foreigners, pagans, non-believers". That is, the ones to whom these brothers were sent. Elsewhere only in Mt 5:47; 6:7; 18:17. GK *1618*. Related to the normal word for "Gentiles" in Act 15:23. Paul followed the same principle, 1 Cor 9:1-18. Our word "ethnic" comes from this word *ethnikos*.
23. This word means "to take up from below, to take up by getting under, to bear up", and in this sense, "to support". It is related to the word "taking" in v 7. We are to "take up" those missionaries who "take" nothing from the Gentiles. On this word, see "assume" in Lk 7:43. Some manuscripts say "to receive" {N}.
24. Or, "prove-to-be, become". GK *1181*.
25. Or, "co-workers". On this word, see Rom 16:3. When we support those who go, we share in their work.
26. Or, "*with, in*". John may mean co-workers "with them" in spreading the truth; or, co-workers "with the truth".
27. Some manuscripts omit this word. Others say, "I would have written *to* the church" {B}. Some think John is referring to 2 John; others, to a letter we do not have.
28. Perhaps it was a letter of recommendation for "the brothers". If so, Diotrephes ignored it and refused to accept them.
29. Or, "loving to have preeminence". Used only here. GK *5812*.
30. Or, "receiving, welcoming". That is, Diotrephes does not accept John's authority alongside of his own. Elsewhere only in v 10. GK *2110*. In his desire to maintain his position or power, Diotrephes put himself above the apostle John, rejecting his written message and even rejecting those who accepted it, v 10.
31. Or, "remember". I will call his deeds to the attention of him and the church. On this word, see "remind" in Jn 14:26.
32. Or, more formally, "bringing unjustified charges against". Used only here. GK *5826*. Related to "babblers" in 1 Tim 5:13.
33. Or, "evil, bad". On this word, see Act 25:18.
34. Or, "satisfied". On this word, see "sufficient" in 2 Cor 12:9.
35. Or, "hindering, preventing, trying to stop". On this word, see 1 Cor 14:39.
36. Or, "throwing out, sending out, expelling, driving out". Same word as "throw out" in Jn 9:34, 35. On this word, see "cast out" in Jn 12:31.
37. This word is used of "bad" in the sense of "harm, injury", moral "evil", and social "wrong, evil, crime". Used 50 times. GK *2805*. Related to "badness" in 1 Pet 2:1; and "do evil" in 1 Pet 3:13.
38. Some manuscripts say "But the..." {N}.
39. Related to "evil" earlier. On this word, see "do harm" in Mk 3:4.
40. Same word as in 1 Jn 3:6. On this word, see Lk 2:26.
41. This grammar is used only here with the following verb. Most simplify this to "Demetrius has been attested". John gives a strong recommendation for Demetrius. Perhaps he was one rejected by Diotrephes. Or, perhaps he was the bearer of this letter.
42. Or, "borne witness". On this word, see Act 6:3. Same word as "testifying" next, with different grammar.
43. John is referring to himself.
44. Same word as in 2 Jn 12; and "ink" in 2 Cor 3:3. Elsewhere only as "black" in Mt 5:36; Rev 6:5, 12. GK *3506*.
45. That is, a reed writing instrument. Used only here in this sense. Note that 2 Jn 12 says "paper and black". On this word, see "stick" in Mk 15:36.
46. In English versions, this verse is part of verse 14.

A. Mt 3:17 B. Jn 21:15, devotedly love C. Rom 9:3 D. Jam 5:20 E. Jn 1:7 F. Heb 13:9 G. 1 Jn 3:1 H. Act 16:40 J. Rom 7:8 K. 1 Jn 4:11
L. Jn 4:23 M. Mt 26:10, work N. Rev 13:13 O. 1 Cor 12:8 P. Jam 1:18, willed Q. 2 Thes 3:7 R. 1 Tim 5:10b S. Lk 6:33 T. Jn 1:7
U. Jn 6:55 V. Jn 7:17, willing W. Jn 5:45, put hope X. Mt 13:5, immediately Y. Lk 14:10 Z. Mk 15:18

Overview		**Jude**

Introduction	1-2
1A. Beloved, I had the necessity to write exhorting you to be contending for the faith delivered once for all. For certain ungodly ones sneaked in changing grace into sensuality	3-4
2A. Now I want to remind you that God judges unbelief and immorality	5-7
3A. Yet these dreaming ones defile the flesh, reject authority, and blaspheme glories. Woe to them	8-11
4A. These ones are spots, waterless clouds, fruitless trees, wild waves, wandering stars. But Enoch prophesied their judgment	12-15
5A. These ones are grumblers, faultfinders, proceeding according to their own desires. But you, beloved, remember that the apostles said mockers would come	16-18
6A. These ones are the ones causing divisions— natural ones, not having the Spirit. But you, beloved keep yourselves in the love of God	19-23
7A. Now to Him who is able to keep you from stumbling, God our Savior, be glory forever	24-25

A. Jude,[1] *a* slave[A] *of* Jesus Christ, and brother *of* James[2]   1
B. *To* the called[B] *ones* having been loved[3] by[4] God *the* Father, and having been kept[5] *by*[6] Jesus Christ
C. May mercy and peace and love be multiplied[C] *to* you   2

1A. Beloved[D], while making[E] every effort[F] to be writing *to* you concerning our common[7] salvation[G], I had   3
the necessity[H] to write *to* you exhorting[J] *you* to be contending[8] *for* the faith[9] having been delivered[K] once-for-all[10] *to* the saints[L]

     1B. For certain persons[M] sneaked-in[11]— the *ones* formerly[12] having been portrayed[13] for this[14] judgment[N],   4
ungodly[15] *ones*

         1C. Changing[16] the grace[O] *of* our God into sensuality[P]
         2C. And denying[17] our only Master[18] and Lord[Q], Jesus Christ

2A. Now[19] I want to remind[R] you— you[20] knowing[21] all[22] *things*—   5

     1B. That the Lord[23], having once[24] saved[25] *the* people[S] out of *the* land *of* Egypt, afterwards[26] destroyed[T] the *ones* not having believed[U]
     2B. And He has kept[27] angels— the *ones* not having kept their *own* domain[28], but having left-behind[29]   6
their own dwelling[30]— *in* eternal[31] bonds[32] under gloom[33], for *the* judgment[V] *of the* great day
     3B. As[34] Sodom and Gomorrah and the cities[35] around them *in* like manner[36] *to* these[37]— having   7
indulged-in-sexual-immorality[38], and having gone after other[39] flesh— are set-forth[W] *as an* example, undergoing *the* penalty[40] *of* eternal[X] fire

3A. Yet in the same way also, these dreaming[41] *ones* are defiling[42] *the* flesh[Y], and rejecting[Z] authority[43], and   8
blaspheming[AA] glories[44]

1. Or, "Judah, Judas". This is the younger brother of James, and half-brother of Jesus. See Mt 13:55 on him.
2. That is, the leader of the church in Jerusalem, on whom, see Mt 13:55.
3. On this word, see "*devotedly* love" in Jn 21:15. Some manuscripts say "sanctified" {A}.
4. Or, "in". GK *1877*.
5. Or, "protected, guarded". On this word, see 1 Jn 5:18.
6. Or, "*for, in*".
7. Or, "shared". Same word as in Act 2:44; 4:32; Tit 1:4. GK *3123*. Related to "share" in 2 Jn 11.
8. Or, "fighting, struggling". Such behavior is seen in this letter. Used only here. GK *2043*. Related to "race" in Heb 12:1. Compare Phil 1:27 (an unrelated word).
9. That is, the body of doctrine, the "apostles' teaching" about Christ, Act 2:42.
10. Or, "once, one time". Jesus delivered it one time only, but some are creeping in trying to change it. Same word as in Heb 9:26; 10:2; 1 Pet 3:18. Elsewhere only as "once" in 2 Cor 11:25; Phil 4:16; 1 Thes 2:18; Heb 6:4; 9:7, 27, 28; 12:26, 27; Jude 5. GK *562*. Related word in Heb 7:27.
11. Or, "crept in, came in by the side". Used only here. GK *4208*.
12. Or, "long ago, already, all this time". Elsewhere only as "long ago" (centuries ago) in Mt 11:21; Lk 10:13; Heb 1:1; "already" (hours ago) in Mk 15:44; "former" (your lifetime prior to Christ) in 2 Pet 1:9; and as "all this time" (in this letter) in 2 Cor 12:19. GK *4093*. Related to "old".
13. Or, "written-of-beforehand". On this word, see Gal 3:1. Some think Jude means portrayed in 2 Pet 2-3. Note v 18. Others, in Paul's letters; others, in the book of Enoch mentioned in v 14-15; others, in the OT.
14. To what is Jude referring? Some think he means the sneaking in as false teachers; others, the judgment described in the remainder of the letter; others, the judgment contained in the faith once delivered, v 3. Others think the judgment described in 2 Pet 2:3 was in his mind.
15. This is the Greek word order. Or, this may be punctuated "the ungodly *ones* formerly having been...". Same word as in v 15
16. Or, "altering" or more negatively, "perverting". On this word, see "removed" in Heb 11:5.
17. Same word as in 2 Tim 3:5; Tit 1:16; 2 Pet 2:1; 1 Jn 2:22, 23. On this word, see 2 Tim 2:12.
18. Or, "owner, sovereign lord, absolute ruler". Used of God or Christ in Lk 2:29; Act 4:24; 2 Tim 2:21; 2 Pet 2:1; Rev 6:10. Elsewhere only of human masters in 1 Tim 6:1, 2; Tit 2:9; 1 Pet 2:18. GK *1305*. Some manuscripts say "denying the only Sovereign-Lord God, and our Lord Jesus Christ {A}.
19. Some manuscripts say "Therefore" {N}.
20. Some manuscripts omit this word {C}, so that it says "remind you knowing all *things*".
21. Some think Jude means "*although* you *are* knowing"; others, "*since* you *are* knowing".
22. Instead of "all *things*", some manuscripts say "this" {D}.
23. Instead of "the Lord", some manuscripts say "Jesus"; others, "God" {D}.
24. That is, one time. Same word as "once for all" in v 3. Some manuscripts have this word in the previous phrase, "you *are* knowing all *things* once for all" {D}.
25. Or, "delivered, rescued". On this word, see Lk 19:10.
26. Or, "subsequently, next, secondly". The root word is "second" in 2 Cor 1:15.
27. Or, "reserved". Compare 2 Pet 2:4; 1 Pet 3:19. Same word as "reserved" in v 13.
28. Or, "rule", their sphere or position of rule or authority. This word often means "beginning" in various senses. Some think Jude means that these angels did not keep their "beginning", the state in which God created them. They rebelled. Others think he is referring to the place or position of rulership assigned to them by God. On this word, see "beginning" in Col 1:18.
29. Or, "abandoned". Same word as in 2 Tim 4:13, 20; Tit 1:5. Elsewhere only as "remain" in Heb 4:6, 9; 10:26. GK *657*.
30. Or, "home, dwelling place, abode, habitation". Some think this means these angels came down from heaven to earth, and are the sons of God in Gen 6:2. Elsewhere only in 2 Cor 5:2. GK *3863*.
31. Elsewhere only in Rom 1:20. GK *132*.
32. Or, "bindings". On this word, see "imprisonment" in Phil 1:7.
33. Same word as in v 13. On this word, see 2 Pet 2:4.
34. Or, "*Just* as". By this word Jude moves on to a third example. Note the tenses, "destroyed" (v 5), "has kept" (v 6), "are set forth" (v 7). These cities stand as an example, still visible to all who go to see. On this word, see "as" in Mt 19:19.
35. That is, Admah and Zeboiim, Deut 29:23.
36. Some think Jude means "in like manner... having indulged", implying the angels in v 6 also went after "other" flesh. The similarity is in the sin. Others think he means "in like manner... are set forth", meaning all three illustrations in v 5-7 are examples of the punishment of sin, as in 2 Pet 2:6. The similarity is in their fate. There are other views.
37. This is the Greek word order of this verse. Some think Jude means "These angels" (v 6) who also sinned this way; others, "these Israelites and angels" (v 5-6) who were also judged by God. There are other views.
38. Used only here. GK *1745*. Related to the verb in 1 Cor 6:18, "to commit sexual immorality". It is the word "go-a-whoring, play the harlot" in Gen 38:24; Ex 34:16; Lev 19:29; 21:9; Num 25:1; etc.
39. Or, "different". These two phrases modify "Sodom and Gomorrah", and refer to the homosexual intercourse recorded in their case, Gen 19:4-5. Those who think Jude means that this also describes the sin of angels find this in Gen 6:2, where the sons of God (taken to mean angels) took wives ("other flesh") from among humans. In this view, Jude 6; 2 Pet 2:4, 10; and 1 Pet 3:19 all refer to this event in Gen 6. On this word, see "different" in 1 Cor 12:9.
40. Or, "punishment". Same word as in 2 Thes 1:9. Elsewhere only as "justice" in Act 28:4. GK *1472*.
41. These false teachers support their teachings with pretended prophetic revelations, visions they have in dreams. Elsewhere only in Act 2:17. GK *1965*.
42. Same word as in Tit 1:15. Related to the words in 2 Pet 2:10, 20.
43. Or, "lordship, dominion". Same word as in 2 Pet 2:10, and same views as to the meaning.
44. Same word as in 2 Pet 2:10, and same views as to the meaning.

A. Rom 6:17   B. Rom 8:28   C. Act 7:17   D. Mt 3:17   E. Rev 13:13, does   F. 2 Cor 8:16, earnestness   G. Lk 19:9   H. 1 Cor 7:26   J. Rom 12:8   K. Act 16:4   L. 1 Pet 1:16, holy   M. Mt 4:4, mankind   N. Jn 9:39   O. Eph 2:8   P. 2 Pet 2:2   Q. Mt 8:2, master   R. Jn 14:26   S. Rev 21:3   T. 1 Cor 1:18, perish   U. Jn 3:36   V. Jn 3:19   W. Heb 12:1, set before   X. Mt 25:46   Y. Col 2:23   Z. Gal 2:21, set aside   AA. 1 Tim 6:1

1B. Now Michael[A] the archangel[1]— when he was speaking[2] concerning the body *of* Moses while disputing[B] *with* the devil— did not dare[C] to bring[3] *a* judgment[D] *of* blasphemy[E], but said, "May *the* Lord rebuke[F] you"[4]   9

2B. But these *ones* —   10

    1C. Whatever *things* they do not understand[G], they blaspheme[H]

    2C. And whatever *things* they know instinctually[5] like unreasoning[6] animals, by these they are being destroyed[7]

3B. Woe[8] *to* them, because   11

    1C. They went *in the* way *of* Cain[9]

    2C. And they poured-forth[10] *in the* error[J] *of* Balaam[11], *for* wages[K]

    3C. And they perished[12] *in the* rebellion[L] *of* Korah[13]

4A. These *ones* are the *ones who* are   12

    1B. Spots[14] in your love-*feasts*[15], feasting-with[M] you fearlessly[16], tending[17] themselves

    2B. Waterless clouds being carried-along by winds

    3B. Fruitless[N] autumn trees having died twice,[18] having been uprooted

    4B. Wild waves *of the* sea foaming-up[19] their shames[O]   13

    5B. Wandering stars[P] *for* whom the gloom *of* darkness has been reserved[20] forever[Q]

    6B. But indeed Enoch, *the* seventh[21] from Adam, prophesied[R] *with regard to* these *ones*— saying[22]   14

        1C. "Behold— *the* Lord came with His holy myriads[23] *to execute[S] judgment[T] against all, and to convict[24] every soul[25]   15

            1D. "Concerning all their works[U] *of* ungodliness[26] which they did-godlessly[27]

            2D. "And concerning all the harsh[V] *things* which ungodly[28] sinners spoke against Him"

5A. These *ones* are grumblers[29], faultfinders, proceeding in accordance with their *own* desires[W]. And their mouth speaks pompous[X] *words*, marveling-at[30] faces for the sake of advantage[Y]   16

    1B. But you beloved[Z], remember[31] the words[AA] having been spoken-beforehand[32] by the apostles[BB] *of* our Lord Jesus Christ—   17

        1C. That they were saying *to* you that[33] "In *the* last[CC] time there will be mockers proceeding in accordance with their *own* desires[W] *of* ungodliness[34]"   18

6A. These *ones* are the *ones* causing-divisions[35]— natural[DD] *ones*, not having *the* Spirit   19

    1B. But you beloved[Z], while building-up[36] yourselves *on*[37] your most holy faith, while praying[EE] *in*[38] *the* Holy Spirit—*keep[FF] yourselves in *the* love[GG] *of* God[39], while waiting-for[HH] the mercy *of* our Lord Jesus Christ for eternal life   20 / 21

        1C. And be having-mercy-on[40] some doubting[41] *ones*   22

        2C. And be saving[JJ] others, snatching[42] *them* out of *the* fire   23

        3C. And be having-mercy-on[43] others with fear[KK], hating even the tunic[44] having been stained[45] by the flesh[46]

1. Elsewhere only in 1 Thes 4:16. GK *791*. Made of two words, "angel", and a word meaning "beginning, first, preeminent, chief, ruler" (see "beginning" in Col 1:18). Thus it means, "the ruler of angels" or "the chief angel".
2. Or, "reasoning". On this word, see "reasoned" in Act 17:2.
3. Or, "pronounce, bring a charge against, assail, inflict". Michael did not dare to charge the devil with blasphemy, speaking against God. He left the pronouncing of that judgment to God. Note 2 Pet 2:11. Elsewhere only as "inflict" in Rom 3:5. GK *2214*.
4. This incident is contained in a Jewish tradition outside the OT. Even angels superior to us do not blaspheme others, even when such ones are wrong. It may or may not imply that the "glories" in v 8 are angels.
5. Or, "naturally". Used only here. GK *5880*. Related to the word in 2 Pet 2:12; and "nature" in Eph 2:3.
6. Same word as in 2 Pet 2:12. Elsewhere only as "unreasonable" in Act 25:27. GK *263*.
7. Same word as in 2 Pet 2:12. On this word, see "ruin" in 1 Cor 3:17.
8. Others begin a new A. point here, and make the leading points the responses instead of the "these ones" statements. In this case, the "A." points are 4A. "Woe"; 5A. "And Enoch also", v 14; 6A. "But you", v 17; and 7A. "But you", v 20. There are other views.
9. Compare Gen 4:3-8; 1 Jn 3:12. Jude may mean "murdering people's souls", or "hating the righteous".
10. That is, they "poured *themselves* into, gave *themselves* to, rushed into". Used only here in this sense. On this word, see "poured out" in Act 2:17.
11. This is the same example used in 2 Pet 2:15. Elsewhere only in Rev 2:14. GK *962*. On the sin of Balaam, see Rev 2:14.
12. Or, "lost *themselves*, were destroyed". On this word, see 1 Cor 1:18.
13. See Num 16:3, 13, 28. Korah was rebelling against God's chosen leader.
14. Or, "Stains". They mar you with their presence. Or, "Reefs, Hidden rocks". They are a hidden danger, deceiving those they feast with. Used only here. GK *5069*. Related to "stained" in v 23; and "spots" in 2 Pet 2:13.
15. Used only here in this sense. Only here is it plural. On this word, see "love" in 1 Jn 4:16.
16. This is the Greek word order. Some place this word with the next phrase, "tending themselves without-fear".
17. Or, "shepherding, pasturing, feeding". On this word, see "shepherd" in Rev 19:15.
18. They died twice because they are fruitless and uprooted. They are dead in sin and cut off from the source of life, Christ.
19. That is, casting up to the surface like foam on waves. Used only here. GK *2072*. Related to "foam at the mouth" in Mk 9:18.
20. Same phrase as in 2 Pet 2:17, "for whom... reserved".
21. That is, based on the record in Genesis 5. Noah was the tenth.
22. Jude is quoting from the book of Enoch, a Jewish book not part of the Old Testament.
23. Or, holy "ten thousands". On this word, see Act 21:20.
24. Or, "rebuke, expose". On this word, see "expose" in Eph 5:11.
25. On this word, see Jam 5:20. Instead of "every soul", some manuscripts say "all the ungodly"; others, "all the ungodly *among* them" {N}.
26. That is, works characterized by ungodliness, and thus, ungodly works. On this word, see Rom 1:18.
27. Used only here. GK *814*. This is the verb related to the previous word, "ungodliness". It means "to live in an ungodly manner".
28. Same word as in v 4, and related to the two words in the previous phrase. Elsewhere only in 2 Pet 2:5, 6; 3:7; and Rom 4:5; 5:6; 1 Tim 1:9; 1 Pet 4:18. GK *815*.
29. Or "complainers". Used only here. GK *1199*. Related to "grumbling" in Phil 2:14; and "to grumble" in Lk 5:30.
30. Or, "admiring, being amazed at". That is, flattering people. This is a Hebrew idiom. On this word, see "caused to marvel" in Rev 17:8.
31. That is, keep in mind, do not forget. Same word as in 2 Pet 3:2. On this word, see Lk 1:54.
32. Same word as in 2 Pet 3:2; Act 1:16. It also means "said before" and "told beforehand". Used 15 times. GK *4625*.
33. Some manuscripts omit this word {C}. It introduces the quotation, which appears to be of 2 Pet 3:3.
34. That is, desires characterized by ungodliness, and thus, ungodly desires. This word is plural to modify "desires". Same word as in v 15.
35. Or, "dividing, marking off boundaries, making separations". Used only here. GK *626*. Some manuscripts add "themselves" {A}, so that it says "separating themselves".
36. Same word as in Col 2:7. Elsewhere only as "build upon" in 1 Cor 3:10, 12, 14; Eph 2:20. GK *2224*.
37. Or, "*in, by*". Jude may mean "*by* the faith", the body of doctrine, as in v 3; or "*in* your faith", with the process described in 2 Pet 1:5-7.
38. Or, "by, in the sphere of, in connection with". GK *1877*. Compare Eph 6:18.
39. Note v 1. Jude may mean "God's love" for you, as in Jn 15:10; or, "your love for God".
40. Or, "pitying, showing mercy to". Elsewhere only in v 23; Rom 9:16. GK *1790*. Some manuscripts say instead "And be refuting some disputing *ones*" {C}.
41. Or, "disputing" (as in v 9), "wavering". Some manuscripts have this word as part of the subject— and be having mercy on some, "while making a difference" (or, "making a distinction") {C}.
42. Or, "catching up, seizing". On this word, see 2 Cor 12:2.
43. Some manuscripts omit this phrase, combining the second and third group: "And be saving some, snatching *them* out of *the* fire with fear, hating even the garment...". {C}.
44. Or, "shirt". That is, the undergarment worn next to the skin. On this word, see Mt 5:40.
45. Or, "spotted". Elsewhere only in Jam 3:6. GK *5071*. Related to "spot" in 2 Pet 2:13, and in Jude 12.
46. Though the sense of v 22-23 is clear, the exact words Jude wrote are not. To summarize, some manuscripts read as here, with some substituting the word "refute" for "have mercy on" in v 22. One says "And be having mercy on some doubting *ones;* be saving *them*, snatching *them* out of *the* fire. And be having mercy on others with fear". Some say "And be refuting some disputing *ones*. And be saving others, snatching *them* out of *the* fire with fear". Some say "And be having mercy on some, making a difference. And with fear be saving others, snatching *them* out of *the* fire". One recently discovered very old manuscript says "Snatch some out of *the* fire. And be having mercy on doubting *ones* with fear" {C}.

A. Rev 12:7 B. Jam 1:6, doubting C. 2 Cor 11:21 D. Jn 3:19 E. 1 Tim 6:4 F. 2 Tim 4:2, warn G. 1 Jn 2:29, know H. 1 Tim 6:1 J. 1 Thes 2:3
K. Rev 22:12, recompense L. Heb 12:3, opposition M. 2 Pet 2:13 N. 1 Cor 14:14, unfruitful O. Heb 12:2 P. Rev 6:13 Q. Rev 20:10
R. 1 Cor 14:1 S. Jn 5:27 T. Jn 3:19 U. Mt 26:10 V. Jn 6:60, hard W. Gal 5:16 X. 2 Pet 2:18 Y. Rom 3:1, profit Z. Mt 3:17 AA. Rom 10:17
BB. 1 Cor 12:28 CC. Heb 1:2 DD. 1 Cor 2:14 EE. 1 Tim 2:8 FF. 1 Jn 5:18 GG. 1 Jn 4:16 HH. Act 24:15 JJ. Lk 19:10 KK. Eph 5:21

7A. Now *to* the *One* being able to keep[1] you from-stumbling[2], and to make *you* stand in the presence *of* His   24
glory[A] without-blemish[3], with gladness[4]

   1B. *To the* only God[5] our Savior[B]   25
   2B. Through Jesus Christ our Lord
   3B. *Be* glory[A], majesty[C], dominion[D], and authority[E] before every age[6], and now, and for all ages[7], amen

1. Or, "guard, protect". Same word as "guard" in 2 Pet 3:17. On this word, see Jn 12:25.
2. Or, "not-stumbling". Used only here. GK *720*. Related to the word in 2 Pet 1:10.
3. Or, "blameless". On this word, see Col 1:22.
4. Or, "exultation, great joy". Elsewhere only in Lk 1:14, 44; Act 2:46; Heb 1:9. GK *21*. Related to "greatly rejoice" in Lk 10:21.
5. Some manuscripts add "wise" {A}, so that it says "*To the* only wise God", as in Rom 16:27.
6. Or, "before all time". Some manuscripts say "*to the* only God our Savior *be* glory and majesty, dominion and authority, both now and forever, amen" {N}.
7. Or, "and forever" (see Rev 20:10).

A. 2 Pet 2:10 B. Lk 1:47 C. Heb 1:3 D. Eph 6:10, might E. Rev 6:8

Overview	**Revelation**

Introduction	1:1-8
1A. I, John, was on the island of Patmos because of the word of God and the testimony of Jesus	1:9
1B. I heard a voice saying, Write in a book what you see, and send it to the seven churches	1:10-12
2B. And having turned, I saw One like a son of man standing amidst seven golden lampstands	1:13-16
3B. And when I saw Him, I fell as dead. And He laid His right hand upon me, saying	1:17
1C. Do not fear. I am the First and the Last. I have the keys of death and Hades	1:18
2C. Write the things which you saw, which are, and which are destined to take place	1:19
3C. The seven stars are the angels of the seven churches. The lampstands are the churches	1:20
4C. To Ephesus, write— Remember, and repent, and do the first works	2:1-7
5C. To Smyrna, write— Do not fear what you are about to suffer. Be faithful until death	2:8-11
6C. To Pergamum, write— Repent of the teaching of the Nicolaitans	2:12-17
7C. To Thyatira, write— Repent of tolerating Jezebel. Hold on until I come	2:18-29
8C. To Sardis, write— You are dead. Remember what you heard, keep it, and repent	3:1-6
9C. To Philadelphia, write— I have given you an open door, hold on to your crown	3:7-13
10C. To Laodicea, write— You are lukewarm. Be zealous and repent. Open the door	3:14-22
2A. After these things, the first voice said, Come up here to heaven, and I will show the things which must take place after these things. Immediately I came-to-be in the Spirit	4:1-2
1B. And behold— a throne, One sitting upon the throne, 24 elders and 4 living creatures	4:2-11
2B. And I saw on the right hand of the One upon the throne a scroll sealed-down with seven seals	5:1
1C. And I saw an angel saying, Who is worthy to open the scroll? No one was able	5:2-3
2C. And I wept. One of the elders says, Do not weep. The Lion of Judah will open it	5:4-5
3C. And I saw a Lamb, and He came and took it from the One sitting upon the throne	5:6-7
4C. And when He took the scroll, every created thing in heaven and earth worshiped Him	5:8-14
5C. And I saw when the Lamb opened the first seal— a white horse with one conquering	6:1-2
6C. And when He opened the second seal— a fire-red horse with one removing peace	6:3-4
7C. And when He opened the third seal— a black horse with one setting famine prices	6:5-6
8C. And when He opened the fourth seal— a pale-green horse with Death and Hades	6:7-8
9C. And when He opened the fifth seal— martyrs under the altar crying for vengeance	6:9-11
10C. And when He opened the sixth seal— an earthquake, the sky darkened, all hide	6:12-17
11C. After this I saw four angels restrained from harming the land, sea, and trees, until another angel sealed 144,000 slaves of God on their foreheads	7:1-8
12C. After these things I saw a multitude in heaven, coming out of the great affliction	7:9-17
13C. And when He opened the seventh seal— silence in heaven for half an hour	8:1
3B. And I saw the seven angels who stand before God, and seven trumpets were given to them	8:2
1C. And another angel filled a censer with fire from the altar and threw it to the earth	8:3-5
2C. And the first angel trumpeted— hail and fire with blood burn a third of vegetation	8:6-7
3C. And the second angel trumpeted— a third of sea life and ships are destroyed	8:8-9
4C. And the third angel trumpeted— a third of rivers and springs are made bitter	8:10-11
5C. And the fourth angel trumpeted— a third of sun, moon, and stars darkened	8:12
6C. And I saw and I heard an eagle say, Woe because of the 3 remaining trumpets	8:13

Revelation

        7C. And the fifth angel trumpeted— locusts torment for 5 months. The first woe passed   9:1-12
        8C. And the sixth angel trumpeted—   9:13

            1D. And I heard a voice tell the sixth angel to release the four angels at the Euphrates to lead an army of 200,000,000 to kill a third of mankind. The rest did not repent   9:13-21
            2D. And I saw another angel holding a little scroll stand on land and sea and swear that when the seventh angel is about to trumpet, the mystery of God was finished   10:1-7
            3D. And the angel said to eat the little scroll. It was sweet and bitter. Prophesy again   10:8-11
            4D. And a rod was given to me to measure the temple. The two witnesses described   11:1-13
            5D. The second woe passed away. Behold, the third woe is coming quickly   11:14

        9C. And the seventh angel trumpeted   11:15

            1D. And loud voices were saying, The kingdom of the world became His kingdom   11:15
            2D. And the 24 elders worshiped God saying, The time came to judge and reward   11:16-18

    4B. And the temple of God in heaven was opened, and the ark of His covenant appeared   11:19

        1C. And a great sign appeared in heaven— a woman with Child, in torment to give birth   12:1-2
        2C. And another sign appeared in heaven—   12:3

            1D. And behold— a great fire-red dragon with seven heads and ten horns   12:3-4
            2D. And the dragon stood in front of the woman to devour her child. She gave birth to a Son, Who was caught up to His throne. She fled, nourished for 1260 days   12:4-6
            3D. And there was a war in heaven. The dragon was thrown to earth— woe   12:7-12
            4D. And the dragon pursued the woman, but she was protected by God   12:13-16
            5D. And the dragon was enraged at the woman, and went to make war with her seed   12:17-18
            6D. And I saw a beast coming up out of the sea. The dragon gave him his power. The world worshiped him, and he made war with the saints and overcame them   13:1-10
            7D. And I saw another beast come up out of the land. And he made all the world worship the first beast, performing great signs and deceiving the whole world   13:11-18
            8D. And I saw the Lamb standing on Mt Zion with the 144,000 singing a new song   14:1-5
            9D. And I saw three angels proclaiming an eternal gospel, judgment and a warning   14:6-13
            10D. And I saw one on a white cloud told to reap the harvest of the earth, and another angel was told to gather the grapes into the winepress of God's fury   14:14-20

        3C. And I saw another sign in heaven, great and marvelous—   15:1

            1D. Seven angels with seven plagues— the last, because the fury of God was finished   15:1
            2D. And I saw the victors from the beast standing on a sea of glass, singing to God   15:2-4

    5B. After these things I saw, and the temple of the tabernacle of testimony in heaven was opened   15:5

        1C. And the 7 angels came out of the temple and were given 7 bowls of God's wrath   15:6-16:1
        2C. And the first poured his bowl into the land— a sore on the beast's followers   16:2
        3C. And the second poured his bowl into the sea— all sea life died   16:3
        4C. And the third poured his bowl into the rivers and springs— they became blood   16:4-7
        5C. And the fourth poured his bowl on the sun— it scorches people   16:8-9

6C. And the fifth poured his bowl on the throne of the beast— his kingdom is darkened	16:10-11
7C. And the sixth poured his bowl on the Euphrates— it is dried up and three demons gathered the kings of the earth at Har-magedon for the great day of God Almighty	16:12-16
8C. And the seventh angel poured his bowl on the air— It is done! A great earthquake takes place. Babylon the Great receives the wrath of God. Hail falls	16:17-21
9C. And one of the seven angels takes me to see the judgment of the great prostitute	17:1-2
1D. And I saw a woman sitting on a beast, drunk with the blood of the saints	17:3-6
2D. And I wondered greatly. The angel tells me the mystery of the woman and beast	17:6-18
3D. After these things I saw an angel come and say, Babylon the Great fell, it fell	18:1-3
4D. And I heard a voice say, Come out of her, and call for judgment. Earth laments	18:4-20
5D. And a strong angel threw a millstone into the sea and pronounced her judgment	18:21-24
10C. After these things I heard a great multitude in heaven rejoice over her downfall	19:1-4
11C. And a voice came from the throne, saying, Give praise to our God, all his slaves	19:5
12C. And I heard a great multitude like the sound of many waters and strong thunders	19:6
1D. Saying, Hallelujah, He reigns. Rejoice, because the wedding of the Lamb came	19:6-7
2D. And authority was given to her to clothe herself with shining clean fine linen	19:8
3D. And he says to me, Write— blessed are those called to the wedding of the Lamb	19:9
13C. And he says to me, These words are true, of God. And I fell to worship him	19:9-10
6B. And I saw heaven having been opened	19:11
1C. And behold— a white horse with Christ riding it, and His armies following Him	19:11-16
2C. And I saw an angel call the birds to eat the flesh of the armies of the beast	19:17-18
3C. And I saw the beast and the kings and their armies gathered against Christ. The beast was seized, and thrown with the false prophet into the lake of fire. The rest were killed	19:19-21
4C. And I saw an angel coming down with the key of the abyss, and a great chain. He seized the dragon and bound him, and threw him into the abyss for 1000 years	20:1-3
5C. And I saw thrones, and the souls who did not worship the beast. And they came to life and reigned 1000 years. Then Satan will be released, and will deceive the nations. Then the devil was thrown into the lake of fire where the beast and the false prophet are	20:4-10
7B. And I saw a great white throne, and the One sitting on it, from Whom heaven and earth fled. The dead were judged. Those not written in the book of life were thrown into the lake of fire	20:11-15
8B. And I saw a new heaven and earth, for the first passed away	21:1
1C. And I saw the new Jerusalem. God dwells with mankind, and makes all things new	21:2-8
2C. And one of the seven angels showed me the new Jerusalem where we shall reign	21:9-22:5
3A. And he said to me, These words are trustworthy and true. Blessed is the one obeying this book	22:6-7
4A. And I, John, am the one hearing these things. I fell to worship him. He said, Worship God	22:8-9
5A. And He says to me, Do not seal up the words of the prophecy of this book. I am coming quickly and My recompense is with me. Let the one thirsting come. Do not add to the words of this book	22:10-20
Conclusion	22:21

A. *The* revelation[1] *of* Jesus Christ[2]   1

    1. Which God gave Him to show[A] His slaves[3] *the things* which must[B] take-place[4] quickly[5]
    2. And He signified[6], having sent-forth[7] through His angel *to* His slave John—

        a. Who testified-to[C] the word[D] *of* God and[8] the testimony[9] *of* Jesus Christ— *to* all[10] that he saw   2

    3. Blessed[E] *is* the *one* reading, and the *ones* hearing the words[D] *of this* prophecy[11] and keeping[12]   3
       the *things* having been written in it, for the time *is* near[13]

B. John—   4

    1. *To* the seven[14] churches in Asia[15], grace *to* you and peace

        a. From the *One Who* is and *Who* was and *Who* is coming[16]
        b. And from the seven Spirits[17] that *are* before His throne[F]
        c. And from Jesus Christ—   5

           1. The Faithful[G] Witness[18]
           2. The Firstborn[19] *of* the dead
           3. And the Ruler[20] *of* the kings *of* the earth

    2. *To* the *One* loving[21] us and having released[22] us from our sins by His blood[H]—*and He made us   6
       a kingdom[23], priests *to* His God and Father— *to* Him *be* the glory and the dominion forever and
       ever[24], amen

        a. Behold[25]— He is coming with the clouds[26]   7

           1. And every eye will see Him— even[27] they who pierced[28] Him
           2. And all the tribes[29] *of* the earth[30] will beat-their-breasts[31] over Him

        b. Yes! Amen!

1. Or, "disclosure, unveiling, uncovering". Used only here in this book, and the related verb is not used in this book. On this word, see 2 Thes 1:7. The interpretation of this book, especially chapters 4-20, depends on what it is one thinks is being revealed. The book is interpreted in light of this decision. In general, there are three approaches to this question today, each with several variations in the details, and each often held in some combination with one of the others. **The Past View** (or the Preterist View) thinks Jesus is revealing the destruction of Jerusalem in A.D. 70, or that combined with the judgment of the Roman Empire. All the details are interpreted in this light. Thus, the prophecies have been fulfilled. The book is not giving a chronological sequence of events, but repeated symbols of that historical judgment and the victory of the early church over the enemies persecuting it. **The Spiritual View** (or the Idealist, Symbolic, Allegorical View) thinks Jesus is revealing timeless spiritual principles regarding the victory of the kingdom of God over the forces of evil. These principles are fulfilled repeatedly throughout the church age. Thus, the prophecies are being fulfilled. The book is not giving a sequence of events, nor events that have a single fulfillment in history, but a picture of what will repeatedly occur in history until the end. Every generation expects to see and does see the principles symbolized in this book fulfilled in the persecutions, triumphs, and judgments of its own day. **The Future View** thinks Jesus is revealing what will take place at the end of the age, just before He returns. Thus, the prophecies are yet to be fulfilled. The book gives a sequence of actual events that will occur at that time. Every generation since the first hopes He will come immediately, and looks for possible precursors of the fulfillment of the book. As each Jewish generation anticipated the Messiah, and young maidens dreamed of being the one to give Him birth, so the church anticipates His return, and considers how this prophecy might be fulfilled in its day, and prepares itself (1 Jn 3:3). These three approaches are also taken to the other prophetic passages in the NT, such as Mt 24. The reader should consult commentaries holding the various views in order to understand in context how those views handle the book and the details. The TransLine can only highlight the views, and "this view thinks" does not mean all adherents of that view hold that position. Most issues noted should be considered to imply the statement "There are other views. Consult the commentaries".
2. Some think John means "the revelation *given by* Jesus Christ"; others, "the revelation *about* Jesus Christ".
3. That is, believers. Same word as in 2:20; 6:15; 7:3; 10:7; 11:18; 13:16; 15:3; 19:2, 5, 18; 22:3, 6. On this word, see Rom 6:17.
4. Or, "come to pass, happen". GK *1181*. This phrase, "to show... quickly", is also in 22:6. See also 1:19; 4:1.
5. This idiom means "with quickness, speed, haste, swiftness", and thus "quickly, at once, without delay, speedily, shortly, soon". Some think John means quickly in the sense of "soon, imminently", whether by our clock (the Past View), or by God's clock (the Future View); others, in the sense of "rapidly, swiftly, without delay" once these events begin. Same word as in 22:6; Lk 18:8; Act 12:7; 22:18; 1 Tim 3:14. Elsewhere only as "shortly" in Act 25:4; Rom 16:20. GK *5443*. Related to "quickly" in Rev 22:7 and Gal 1:6.
6. Or, "showed by signs, signaled, indicated, made known". Elsewhere only in Jn 12:33; 18:32; 21:19; Act 11:28; 25:27. GK *4955*. This is the verb related to the word "sign".
7. Same word as in 22:6. On this word, see "send out" in Mk 3:14.
8. Or, "even"; that is, the word given by God, even (more specifically), the testimony of Jesus Christ.
9. The angel "testified to... the testimony", or, he "bore witness to... the witness" (the declaration) of Jesus. Some think John means "the testimony *given by* Jesus"; others, "the testimony *about* Jesus". On this word, see Jn 1:7.
10. Some manuscripts add "and" {K}, "and *to* all".
11. Same word as in 11:6; 19:10; 22:7, 10, 18, 19. On this word, see 1 Cor 12:10.
12. That is, the one reading the book aloud in public, and the ones hearing and keeping it. On this word, see 1 Jn 5:18.
13. Same phrase as in 22:10. "Near" is also in Mt 24:32, 33; Rom 13:11; Phil 4:5. On this word, see Lk 21:30.
14. This number is used 55 times in Revelation, 33 times elsewhere in the NT. GK *2231*.
15. That is, the Roman province of Asia, present-day western Turkey.
16. That is, the Father. Same phrase as in v 8; 4:8. Similar phrase in 11:17; 16:5.
17. Or, "spirits". "Seven spirits" also occurs in 3:1; 4:5 (as seven lamps, as in Zech 4:2); and 5:6 (as seven eyes, as in Zech 4:10). Some think John means the Holy Spirit, the sevenfold fullness of the Spirit of God, the imagery coming from Zech 4:1-10; Isa 11:2. Others think these are angels (as in 1 Tim 5:21; Lk 9:26), or some other spirit beings.
18. These words may be rendered as a single description, as in 3:14; or, separately, "the Witness, the Faithful *One*", as in 2:13.
19. Same phrase as in Col 1:18. On this word, see Col 1:15. That is, the preeminent one, first in rank.
20. Used only here of Christ. Elsewhere of human rulers, officials, or princes, and of the ruler of demons. Used 37 times. GK *807*. Related to "beginning" in Col 1:18. Both "firstborn" and "ruler" were used with reference to the Messiah in Ps 89:27.
21. Some manuscripts say "having loved" {N}. On this word, see "devotedly love" in Jn 21:15.
22. Or, "loosed, freed". Same word as in 9:14, 15; 20:3, 7. On this word, see "break" in Mt 5:19. Some manuscripts say "washed" {A}.
23. On this word, see Mt 3:2. Some manuscripts say "...us kings and priests *to*..." {N}.
24. On this idiom, see 20:10. Some manuscripts omit "and ever" {C}.
25. This verse gives the theme of the book. Some think it refers to Christ's second coming; the Past View thinks it refers to His coming in judgment in A.D. 70 using the Roman army.
26. Compare Mt 24:30; 26:64; 1 Thes 4:17; and Dan 7:13. The Past View thinks these are not literal clouds, but a symbol of Christ's power and judgment, as in Ps 18:9; Isa 19:1; etc.
27. Or "and".
28. On this word, see Jn 19:37, where John is quoting Zech 12:10.
29. Same statement as in Mt 24:30. Same word as in Rev 5:9; 7:9; 11:9; 13:7; 14:6. Used of the tribes of Israel in 5:5; 7:4-8; 21:12. Used 31 times. GK *5876*.
30. Or, "land". The Past View thinks this refers to Israel in A.D. 70.
31. Or, "strike *themselves,* beat *themselves,* mourn greatly". Same word as in Mt 11:17; 24:30; Lk 8:52; 23:27; Rev 18:9. Elsewhere only with different grammar as "cut" in Mt 21:8; Mk 11:8. GK *3164*. Related to "lamentation" in Act 8:2. Some think John means these people will do this "in repentance" (as in Zech 12:10). Others, "in despair" (as in Rev 6:16; 18:9).

A. Rev 4:1 B. Mt 16:21 C. Jn 1:7 D. 1 Cor 12:8 E. Lk 6:20 F. Rev 20:11 G. Col 1:2 H. 1 Jn 1:7

Revelation 1:8 — 960 — Verse

    C. "**I am**[1] the Alpha and the Omega[2]", says the Lord God[3], "the *One Who* is and *Who* was and *Who* is coming, the Almighty[4]"   8

1A. **I, John, your**[5] brother and co-partner[A] in the affliction[6] and kingdom[7] and endurance[B] in[8] Jesus[9], came-to-be on the island being called Patmos[10] because of the word *of* God and[11] the testimony[12] *of* Jesus[13]   9

    1B. I came-to-be[14] in *the* Spirit[15] on the Lord's[16] day, and I heard behind me *a* loud voice[C] like [the sound] *of a* trumpet[17], *saying   10 / 11

        1C. "Write[18] in *a* book[D] what you see[19], and send *it to* the seven churches[20]— to Ephesus, and to Smyrna, and to Pergamum, and to Thyatira, and to Sardis, and to Philadelphia, and to Laodicea"

        2C. And I turned[E] to see the voice which was speaking[21] with me   12

    2B. And having turned, I saw seven golden lampstands[22]. *And in *the* midst *of* the lampstands[23] *I saw* One resembling[24] *a* son *of* man[25] having been dressed-in[26] *a* robe reaching-to-the-feet, and having been girded-with[F] *a* golden belt[27] at the breasts[28]   13

        1C. And His head and hair *were* white[G] like white wool, like snow[29]   14

        2C. And His eyes *were* like *a* flame[H] *of* fire

        3C. And His feet *were* resembling brass[30], like *something* having been refined[31] in *a* furnace   15

        4C. And His voice[C] *was* like *the* sound[C] *of* many waters[32]

        5C. And *He was* holding[J] seven stars in His right hand[33]   16

        6C. And *a* sharp double-edged sword[K] *was* coming-out[34] of His mouth

        7C. And His face[35] *was* like the sun shines[L] in its power[36]

    3B. And when I saw Him, I fell at His feet as-*though* dead. And He placed His right *hand* upon me, saying[37]   17

        1C. "Do not be fearing[M]. **I** am the First and the Last,[38] *and the *One* living[N]. And I became dead[O], and behold— I am living[N] forever and ever[39]. And I have the keys[40] *of* death and Hades[41]   18

1. God is personally guaranteeing the prophecy of v 7, and of the book as a whole.
2. These are the first and last letters of the Greek alphabet. This phrase is also in 21:6 (of the Father); and 22:13 (of Jesus). Some manuscripts add "*the* beginning and *the* end" {A}, which explains it. GK *270* and *6042.*
3. Some manuscripts omit this word {K}.
4. Same word as in 4:8; 11:17; 15:3; 16:7, 14; 19:6, 15; 21:22. Elsewhere only in 2 Cor 6:18. GK *4120.*
5. Some manuscripts add a word meaning "both, also" {K}, so that it says "I, John, both your brother...".
6. On this word, see 7:14. The Past View (see 1:1) thinks John means the "tribulation" of A.D. 70, which is the tribulation described in this book. Others think he means the affliction we all face as Christians, as in Jn 16:33; Act 14:22.
7. On this word, see Mt 3:2. Some manuscripts say "affliction, and in the kingdom and endurance" {N}.
8. Or, "in connection with". GK *1877.*
9. Some manuscripts add "Christ" either before or after "Jesus" {N}.
10. John was exiled to this island in the Aegean Sea during the reign of the Roman Emperor Domitian (A.D. 81-96), and some think it was during this period that this book was written. Others think it was written prior to A.D. 70. Used only here. GK *4253.*
11. Or, "even". See this same phrase in 1:2.
12. Some manuscripts say "and because of the testimony..." {N}. On "the testimony *of* Jesus", see 19:10.
13. By these two phrases, some think John means he was on Patmos "in order to receive this revelation given by Jesus"; others, "because I was preaching the gospel there"; others, that he was exiled there "because of preaching about these things". Some manuscripts add "Christ" {N}.
14. Or, "was, became". Same word as in v 9; 4:2. GK *1181.*
15. Or, "spirit". This phrase, "in *the* Spirit", is also in 4:2; 17:3; 21:10. John may mean "in a trance" (Act 10:10; 22:17); or, "outside the body" (2 Cor 12:2). Or he may mean "in *the* Spirit", that is, under the power of the Spirit.
16. That is, the day belonging to the Lord. Some think John means Sunday. Others think he means the future "day of-the-Lord" to which John went in this vision (though this is not the usual expression for this). Elsewhere only in 1 Cor 11:20. GK *3258.*
17. Some think this is the voice of an angel. Compare v 2; 4:1. The person amidst the lampstands has a different voice, v 15. Others think both descriptions are of the voice of the One amidst the lampstands.
18. Some manuscripts say "**I** am the Alpha and the Omega, the First and the Last, and write..." {N}.
19. Used 132 times meaning "see, look (at), watch". GK *1063.*
20. Some manuscripts add "in Asia" {K}.
21. Some manuscripts say "spoke" {N}.
22. That is, stands on which lamps were placed or hung. Not candlesticks. Used 12 times. GK *3393.*
23. Some manuscripts say "seven lampstands" {N}.
24. Or, "like, similar to". This word occurs with this grammar elsewhere only in 14:14, in this same phrase. John uses this word elsewhere only as "like" in Jn 8:55; 9:9; 1 Jn 3:2; Rev 9:7, 10, 19; 13:4, 11; 18:18; and as "resembling" in Rev 1:15; 2:18; 4:3, 6, 7; 9:7; 11:1; 13:2; 14:14; 21:11, 18. Used 45 times. GK *3927.* Related to "likeness" in 9:7.
25. Or, "*the* Son *of* Man". Some think John is implying that the One before him is the person described by this phrase in Dan 7:13; others, that this is simply a description functioning like the one in Dan 7:13, and meaning "like a human". As in Dan 7:13, He is like a human in appearance, but others factors (there, the coming on the clouds, etc.; here, the items noted next) indicate this One is no mere human. In either case, this person is later identified as the Son of God, Rev 2:18. The same person is described in 19:11-16. On this phrase, "*a* son *of* man", see Jn 5:27.
26. Some think this clothing is symbolic of Jesus being High Priest; others, more generally, of His dignity and high rank. Compare Dan 10:5-6. Same word as in 15:6 and 19:14. On this word, see "put on" in Rom 13:14.
27. Elsewhere only in Mt 3:4; 10:9; Mk 1:6; 6:8; Act 21:11; Rev 15:6. GK *2438.* Related to "gird" in this verse, and in Act 12:8.
28. This is a mark of dignity, not a belt at the waist as normal. Elsewhere only in Lk 11:27; 23:29. GK *3466.* Similar to the seven angels with the seven bowls in 15:6 (which uses the word "chest").
29. Elsewhere only in Mt 28:3, also of the appearance of Jesus. GK *5946.* Compare Dan 7:9.
30. Or, "metal". It is not known what specific metal John is referring to. The root word means "copper, brass, bronze" (GK *5910*), but also "metal" in general. Compare Dan 10:6. Elsewhere only in 2:18. GK *5909.*
31. Or, "fired, made fiery hot". Same word as in 3:18. This word means "to burn, to make fiery hot, to set on fire". It is the verb related to "fire". Some think John means "gleaming brass, as refined in a furnace". Others think he means "glowing brass, as made red-hot in a furnace". The grammar links this word to "something" in the furnace. In some manuscripts, it is linked to "brass", as "brass, like *brass* having been refined...". In others, it is linked to "feet"— "His feet... as though having been made fiery hot..." {C}. On this word, see "burn" in 2 Cor 11:29.
32. On "many waters", see 14:2.
33. Some think this is symbolic of Christ's power and authority over the churches; others, of His protection.
34. Or, "proceeding, going out". Same word as in 4:5; 9:17, 18; 11:5; 19:15. Used 33 times. GK *1744.* Note 2:12, 16; Isa 11:4; 2 Thes 2:8.
35. Or, "outward appearance". Note Dan 10:6. Same word as in Jn 11:44. Elsewhere only as "appearance" in Jn 7:24. GK *4071.*
36. That is, his face shined as bright as the noon-day sun, like the sun at its full strength. Compare Mt 17:2. On this word, see Mk 5:30.
37. Some manuscripts add "*to* me" {K}, though no Greek manuscripts.
38. This phrase "first and last" is elsewhere only in 1:17; 2:8; 22:13; all of Jesus. Compare Isa 41:4; 44:6; 48:12.
39. On this idiom see 20:10. Some manuscripts add "Amen" {N}.
40. Keys are symbolic of authority over something.
41. This phrase "death and Hades" is elsewhere only in 20:13, 14. "Hades", meaning "unseen", is where the dead go; the place of the dead. Elsewhere only in Mt 11:23; 16:18; Lk 10:15; 16:23; Act 2:27, 31; Rev 6:8. GK *87.*

A. Phil 1:7   B. Jam 1:3   C. Rev 4:5, voices   D. Rev 5:1, scroll   E. Jam 5:19, turns back   F. Eph 6:14   G. Jn 4:35   H. 2 Thes 1:8, flaming   J. 1 Jn 1:8, have   K. Rev 2:16   L. Phil 2:15   M. Eph 5:33, respecting   N. Rev 20:4, came to life   O. Mt 8:22

2C.	"Therefore¹ write *the things* which you saw, and² *the things* which are, and *the things* which are destined³ to take place after these *things*	19
3C.	*"As to* the mystery^A *of* the seven stars which you saw upon⁴ My right *hand*, and the seven golden lampstands— the seven stars are angels⁵ *of* the seven churches, and the seven lampstands⁶ are seven churches	20
4C.	"*To* the angel *of* the church in Ephesus⁷, write— These *things* says the *One* holding-on-to⁸ the seven stars in His right *hand*, the *One* walking in *the* midst^B *of* the seven golden lampstands	2:1

      1D. "I know your works^C and⁹ labor and your endurance^D   2

          1E. "And that you cannot bear-with^E evil^F *ones*¹⁰
          2E. "And you tested^G the *ones* calling themselves apostles^H (and they are not) and you found them *to be* false
          3E. "And you have endurance¹¹, and bore-up¹² for the sake of My name, and have not become-weary¹³   3

      2D. "But I have against you that you left¹⁴ your first¹⁵ love¹⁶   4
      3D. "Therefore, be remembering¹⁷ from where you have fallen, and repent^J, and do^K the first works^C   5

          1E. "Otherwise¹⁸, I am coming *to* you¹⁹. And I will move²⁰ your lampstand^L from its place unless you repent
          2E. "But this you have— that you hate^M the works^C *of* the Nicolaitans²¹, which **I** also hate   6

      4D. "Let *the one* having *an* ear hear what the Spirit is saying *to* the churches²²   7
      5D. "*To* the *one* overcoming²³, I will give him *authority*²⁴ to eat from the tree *of* life²⁵ which is in²⁶ the paradise^N *of* God²⁷

  5C. "And *to* the angel *of* the church in Smyrna, write— These *things* says the First and the Last Who became dead and came-to-life²⁸   8

      1D. "I know your affliction²⁹, and³⁰ poverty³¹ (but you are rich^O), and the blasphemy³² by the *ones* saying *that* they are Jews³³ (and they are not), but *are a* synagogue *of* Satan   9
      2D. "Do not be fearing³⁴ at all³⁵ *the things* which you are about to suffer^P   10

          1E. "Behold— the devil is going to throw *some* of you into prison^Q so that you may be tested³⁶. And you will have affliction^R *for* ten days³⁷
          2E. "Be³⁸ faithful^S until³⁹ death, and I will give you the crown^T *of* life⁴⁰

      3D. "Let *the one* having *an* ear hear what the Spirit is saying *to* the churches   11
      4D. "*The one* overcoming will never be harmed^U by the second death⁴¹

1. Some manuscripts omit this word {N}.
2. Or, "even". This verse gives an outline of the book. Some think Jesus means the things which you saw (chapter 1), which are (chapters 2-3), which are destined to take place (chapters 4-22). Others think He means the things which you saw, even the things which are (Chapter 1-3), and the things destined to take place (chapters 4-22). Others think it refers to the whole book, the things which you saw (chapters 1-22), even the things which are and the things destined after. Others think Jesus means the things you saw and what they are (chapter 1), and the things going to happen after these (chapters 2-22).
3. Or, "about to". Used with this grammar elsewhere only as "about to" in 3:16; 12:4; and "destined to" in Rom 8:18; Gal 3:23. Compare Rev 1:1; 4:1; 22:6. On this word, see "going to" in Mk 10:32.
4. That is, on His open palm or in contact with His hand. Note that in 1:16, John said "in His hand". GK *2093*.
5. Or, "messengers". Some think Jesus means "angel", as elsewhere in the book. Perhaps they are a kind of guardian angel. He addresses the angel as if it were the church. Others think He means a human messenger (as the word is used in Mt 11:10; Lk 7:24; 9:52; Jam 2:25; etc.), either a representative sent to John, or the chief teacher or overseer. Compare 2:20. Others think He is simply personifying the churches themselves. On this word, see "messengers" in 1 Tim 3:16.
6. Some manuscripts add "which you saw" {N}.
7. The seven churches were actual first-century churches. In addition, they represent churches existing at all times until Christ returns, and by application, the individuals in them. In addition, some holding the Future View (see 1:1) think they are symbolic of periods of church history.
8. Or, "holding firm, keeping hold of". Same word as in 2:13, 14, 15, 25; 3:11, on which see Heb 4:14. Not the same word as in 1:16.
9. Or, "even", so that it says "your works— even your labor and endurance". The same issue arises in 2:9, 19. Some manuscripts add "your" {N}, so that it says "your labor and your endurance" {N}.
10. Some think these are the same evil ones described again next and in v 6; others take this more generally here.
11. Same word as in v 2.
12. Same word as "bear-with" in v 2.
13. Same root word as "labor" in v 2. Thus, this is the third repetition from v 2. On this word, see Mt 11:28.
14. Or, "left behind, abandoned, let go". Some think Jesus means the believers have fallen into a cold orthodoxy; others, that He is referring to ones among the new generation who were not yet believers, who had not yet "overcome" (v 7), although they adhered to orthodox doctrine (v 6). Same word as "neglected" in Mt 23:23. On this word, see "forgive" in Mt 6:12.
15. Some think Jesus means the fervency of love you had when you were first saved; others, the love your church had at the first, among the first generation of Christians, the former generation.
16. Some place the emphasis of these words on the inward devotion to Christ (their love for Him has diminished); others, on the outward expression of that devotion in acts of love (they have become lazy in loving others). On this word, see 1 Jn 4:16.
17. Or, "keeping in mind". On this word, see Jn 16:21.
18. This is an idiom, literally, "But if [you do] not", on which see Jn 14:2.
19. Some manuscripts add "quickly" {N}, as in 2:16; 3:11. Some think Jesus is referring to a special coming in judgment; others, to the Second Coming, that is, "Otherwise when I come, I am coming to you for judgment". On "coming", see Mk 16:2.
20. Or, "arouse, shake, remove". Some think Jesus will move their lampstand from a place of blessing to a place of discipline. He will hit it like an earthquake, shaking it down to the foundation, arousing them to action. Others think He means that He will move it away, remove it, from being a church. Same word as in 6:14; Mt 23:4; Act 17:28. Elsewhere only as "shake" in Mt 27:39; Mk 15:29; and "set in motion" in Act 21:30; 24:5. Our word "kinetic" comes from this word. GK *3075*. A related word is in Col 1:23.
21. That is, the followers Nicholas. Elsewhere only in v 15. GK *3774*. Their views are described in v 14.
22. Note the plural. In each letter, both this and the overcomer statement are addressed to all the churches.
23. Or, "conquering, prevailing, vanquishing, being victorious". Same word as in Lk 11:22; Jn 16:33; Rom 12:21; 1 Jn 2:13, 14; 4:4; Rev 2:11, 17, 26; 3:5, 12, 21; 5:5; 11:7; 12:11; 13:7; 15:2; 17:14; 21:7. Elsewhere only as "conquer" in Rev 6:2; "be victorious over" in 1 Jn 5:4, 5; and "prevail" in Rom 3:4. GK *3771*. Related to "victory" in 1 Jn 5:4; and in 1 Cor 15:57.
24. Or, "*the right*" (same Greek word). Compare 22:14. This word is expressed in 6:8; 9:3.
25. The tree of life is also mentioned in 22:2, 14, 19. The next word ("which") modifies "tree". On "tree", see "cross" in 1 Pet 2:24.
26. Some manuscripts say "in *the* midst *of* the paradise..." {N}.
27. Some manuscripts say "My God" {A}, as in 3:2, 12.
28. This description comes from 1:18, but note the change in tense from "am living" to "came to life" or "became alive". Jesus is referring to His death and resurrection.
29. On this word, see 7:14. Some manuscripts say "your works and affliction" {N}.
30. Or, "even", so that it says "I know your affliction— even the poverty...". Same issue as in 2:2.
31. Some think this poverty is a result of persecution by, or caused by the ones mentioned next. On this word, see 2 Cor 8:9.
32. On this word, see 1 Tim 6:4. That is, the evil-speaking against them, and God.
33. Regardless of their culture or lineage or religion, these people are not Jews because they are not following Christ.
34. The grammar implies, "Stop fearing, Do not continue fearing".
35. Some manuscripts say "Do not be fearing *the things* which..." {N}.
36. That is, that your faith might be tested. On this word, see "tempted" in Heb 2:18.
37. Or, "you will have *an* affliction *of* ten days". Some think Jesus means ten literal days; others, ten periods of time; others, a brief period of time.
38. Or, "Become faithful *ones*", "Prove-to-be faithful *ones*". GK *1181*.
39. Or, "as far as, to the extent of". This does not mean that the Smyrnans will all actually be martyred. Same phrase as in 12:11; Act 22:4. Same word as in 2:25, 26. GK *948*.
40. Some think Jesus means the crown consisting of life, as in Jam 1:12. Your persecutors will think you are defeated, but I will give the victor's crown to you. Others think Jesus means a special martyr's crown, should they be martyred.
41. The second death is also mentioned in 20:6, 14; 21:8.

A. Rom 11:25 B. 2 Thes 2:7 C. Mt 26:10 D. Jam 1:3 E. Mt 8:17, carry F. 3 Jn 11 G. Heb 2:18, tempted H. 1 Cor 12:28 J. Act 26:20 K. Rev 13:13 L. Rev 1:13 M. Rom 9:13 N. 2 Cor 12:4 O. 1 Tim 6:17 P. Gal 3:4 Q. Act 5:22 R. Rev 7:14 S. Col 1:2 T. Rev 4:4 U. Act 7:24, wronged

6C. "And *to* the angel *of* the church in Pergamum, write— These *things* says the *One* having the sharp double-edged sword[A]   12

    1D. "I know where[1] you dwell[B]— where Satan's throne[2] *is*   13

        1E. And you are holding-on-to[3] My name[4]
        2E. And you did not deny[C] My faith[5]— even during the days *of* Antipas[6], My witness[7], My[8] faithful[D] *one*, who was killed among you where Satan dwells[B]

    2D. "But I have *a* few *things* against you   14

        1E. "Because you have there *ones* holding-on-to the teaching[E] *of* Balaam, who was teaching[F] Balak to put *a* cause-of-falling[9] before the sons[G] *of* Israel

            1F. "To eat foods-sacrificed-to-idols[10]
            2F. "And to commit-sexual-immorality[11]

        2E. "So **you** also have *ones* holding-on-to the teaching[E] *of* the Nicolaitans likewise[12]   15

    3D. "Therefore[13] repent[14]   16

        1E. "Otherwise[15], I am coming[H] *to* you quickly[16]. And I will fight[17] against them[18] with the sword[19] *of* My mouth

    4D. "Let the *one* having *an* ear hear what the Spirit is saying *to* the churches   17
    5D. "*To* the *one* overcoming[J]—

        1E. "I will give him[20] *some of* the hidden[21] manna[22]
        2E. "And I will give him *a* white pebble[23]. And having been written upon the pebble *is a* new name which no one knows except the *one*[24] receiving *it*

7C. "And *to* the angel *of* the church in Thyatira, write— These *things* says the Son *of* God, the *One* having His[25] eyes like *a* flame *of* fire, and His feet resembling brass[K]   18

    1D. "I know[L] your works[M] and[26] love[N] and faith[27] and service[28] and your endurance[O]. And your last works *are* greater[29] *than* the first   19
    2D. "But I have[30] against you that you are tolerating[31] the woman[32] Jezebel[33]— the *one* calling[34] herself *a* prophet[35]   20

        1E. "And she is teaching[36] and misleading[P] My slaves[Q] to commit-sexual-immorality, and to eat foods-sacrificed-to-idols
        2E. "And I gave her time in order that she might repent[R]. And she is not willing[S] to repent from her sexual-immorality[37]   21

1. Some manuscripts say "your works, and where..." {N}.
2. Some think Jesus is referring to the fact that this city was a major center for emperor worship; others, that it had an altar to Zeus; others, that it was the seat of worship for Asklepius, a serpent god. There are other views.
3. Same word as in v 14, 15, and 2:1.
4. Jesus may mean this in the sense of refusing to say "Lord Caesar".
5. Some think Jesus means "your faith in Me". Others, "My gospel", the objective content of the faith.
6. Some manuscripts say "days *in* which Antipas *was* My witness..." {N}. Nothing is known about this man with certainty beyond what is here. Consult the commentaries for the various speculations.
7. This word came to be used of one who witnessed to the point of death, a "martyr". Some give it this meaning here, and in 17:6; Act 22:20. On this word, see Act 1:8.
8. Some manuscripts omit this word {N}, so that it says "My faithful witness".
9. On this word, see Rom 11:9. Jesus is referring specifically to the two activities mentioned next. These two issues are mentioned in Num 25:1-2; 31:15-16, and they were also the problem here in Pergamum.
10. On this word, see 1 Cor 8:1. Same word as in v 20. Jesus is referring to eating at pagan feasts and temples, sharing socially in their worship events. Compare 1 Cor 10:14-22.
11. On this word, see 1 Cor 6:18. Same word as in v 20. These same two issues are prohibited in Act 15:29. Some think sexual sin was a problem in Pergamum; others, that in their case it refers to spiritual adultery. Sexual activity was part of pagan worship.
12. This is the Greek word order. The relationship of "so...also...likewise" is difficult. Some think Jesus means "So (following a false teacher) you also (like Israel) have ones holding on to the teaching of the Nicolaitans [to do] likewise (to continue their pagan practices of idolatry and immorality)". Others think, "So (in a manner similar to the Balaamites) you also (in addition to the Balaamites, as a second group) have ones likewise (teaching these two pagan practices) holding on to...". The first view sees the Nicolaitans as illustrated by Balaam, the second view sees two separate groups with teachings that are similar at least with regard to these immorality and idolatry issues. There are other views. Some manuscripts say "which *thing* I hate" {N}, in place of "likewise".
13. Some manuscripts omit this word {N}.
14. That is, repent of tolerating these people, or else I will come to "you" (singular, referring to the church) and make war with "them". On this word, see Act 26:20.
15. On this word, see 2:5.
16. Or, "soon". On this word, see 22:7.
17. Or, "wage war, battle". Same word as in 12:7; Jam 4:2. Elsewhere only as "wage war" in 13:4; 17:14; 19:11. GK *4482*. Related to "war" in 12:7.
18. By "them", some think Jesus means "the Nicolaitans"; others, "those holding on to their teaching"; others, the church.
19. This sword is mentioned also in 1:16; 2:12; 19:15, 21. Elsewhere only in 6:8; Lk 2:35. GK *4855*. Some think Jesus is referring to a special coming in judgment; others, to the Second Coming, as in 2:5.
20. Some manuscripts add "to eat" {N}.
21. This is a participle, "having been hidden". On this word, see Jn 8:59.
22. Manna was the name Israel gave to the perishable daily bread from heaven given them by God for forty years in the wilderness, Ex 16:4-36. Some was saved in a jar and placed before the ark, Ex 16:34. Some think Jesus is referring to this jar of manna, "hidden" in the sanctuary. Others think He means "spiritual food" nourishing eternal life. Symbolically, manna is the heavenly God-given sustenance of eternal life (like the "fruit" of the tree of life or the "water" of the river of life) hidden from mankind since the garden of Eden. There is a sense in which Christ Himself is this "bread of life", Jn 6. "Manna" is elsewhere only in Jn 6:31, 49; Heb 9:4. GK *3445*.
23. Elsewhere only as "vote" in Act 26:10. GK *6029*. Some think Jesus is referring to the stones used to cast a vote, a black pebble meaning "guilty", a white one meaning "acquitted"; others, to the white stone used as an "admission ticket" to a banquet; others, to a symbol of being counted as included. There are other views.
24. Or, "*One*". Some think Jesus is referring to Himself, and the new name is the one in 3:12; 19:12; others, to the recipient, and the new name is that person's own new name.
25. Some manuscripts omit this word {N}.
26. Or, "even", "your works— even your love and faith and service and endurance". Same issue as in 2:2.
27. Or, "faithfulness". On this word, see Eph 2:8.
28. On this word, see "ministries" in 1 Cor 12:5. Some manuscripts say "service and faith" {K}. Some think "service" describes "love", and "endurance" describes "faith".
29. Either greater in quantity, "more"; or, greater in quality, "superior, better".
30. Some manuscripts add "*a few things*"; others, "much" {N}, in which case, what follows would be "against you, because you...".
31. Or, "allowing, letting go on". Used in this sense also in Jn 11:48. On this word, see "forgive" in Mt 6:12.
32. Some manuscripts say "your" woman {B}, leading some to think Jesus means "your wife", and that this implies that the "angel" of the church is actually a human "messenger". On this issue, see "angel" in 1:20. On this word, see 1 Tim 2:11.
33. Jezebel was the wife of King Ahab, who led Israel into idolatry, 1 Kings 16:31; 2 Kings 9:22. Here, some think this was a literal woman in the church, this being her actual name, or a symbolic name for her; others, that it is personifying a heresy, perhaps referring again to the Nicolaitans, based on her teachings. Used only here. GK *2630*.
34. On this word, see "say" in Jn 12:39. Some manuscripts say "who calls herself" {N}.
35. This is the feminine form of "prophet" in 1 Cor 12:28, found elsewhere only in Lk 2:36. GK *4739*.
36. Some manuscripts say "prophet, to teach and mislead..." {K}.
37. Some manuscripts say, "time in order that she might repent from her sexual immorality. And she did not repent" {K}.

A. Rev 2:16 B. Eph 3:17 C. 2 Tim 2:12 D. Col 1:2 E. 1 Cor 14:6 F. Rom 12:7 G. Gal 3:7 H. Mk 16:2 J. Rev 2:7 K. Rev 1:15 L. 1 Jn 2:29 M. Mt 26:10 N. 1 Jn 4:16 O. Jam 1:3 P. Jam 5:19, err Q. Rev 1:1 R. Act 26:20 S. Jn 7:17

3D. "Behold— I am throwing[1] her into *a* bed[2], and the *ones* committing-adultery[3] with her into *a* great affliction[4], unless they repent[A] from her[5] works[B]. *And I will kill[C] her children[6] with *a* death[7]   22
23

    1E. "And all the churches will know[8] that **I** am the *One* searching[9] minds[10] and hearts[11], and I will give[D] *to* you, *to* each *one,* according to your works[12]

4D. "But I say *to* you[13], *to* the rest[E] in Thyatira— all-who are not holding[F] this teaching, who did not know[G] the deep[H] *things of* Satan (as they[14] say)—   24

    1E. "I am not putting[15] another burden[16] upon you
    2E. "However[17], hold-on-to[18] what you have[19] until whenever[20] I come   25

5D. "And the *one* overcoming[J] and[21] the *one* keeping[K] My works[22] until *the* end[23]—   26

    1E. "I will give him authority[L] over the nations. *And he will shepherd[24] them with *an* iron[25] rod like clay[26] vessels[M] are broken-to-pieces[27], *as **I** also have received from My Father   27
28
    2E. "And I will give him the morning star[28]

6D. "Let the *one* having *an* ear hear what the Spirit is saying *to* the churches   29

8C. "And *to* the angel *of* the church in Sardis, write— These *things* says the *One* having[F] the seven Spirits[29] *of* God and the seven stars   3:1

    1D. "I know[N] your works[B]— that you have *a* name[30] that you are alive[31], and you are dead[32]
    2D. "Be[33] keeping-watch[34], and establish[35] the remaining[36] *things* which were-about-to[37] die, for I have not found your works fulfilled[38] in the sight of My[39] God   2

    1E. "Therefore be remembering[40] how[41] you have received and you heard, and be keeping[K] *it*, and repent[A]   3
    2E. "Therefore if you do not keep-watch, I will come[42] like *a* thief[43]. And you will never know[G] at what hour I will come[O] upon you

    3D. "But[44] you have *a* few names[45] in Sardis who did not stain[46] their garments[P]. And they will walk[Q] with Me in white[47] *garments*, because they are worthy[R]   4
    4D. "The *one* overcoming[J] will in-this-manner[48] clothe *himself*[49] in white[S] garments[P]   5

1. Or, "putting", as in Mt 8:6. This word means "to throw, cast, put". Used 122 times. GK *965*. Some manuscripts say "I will throw" {N}.
2. Some think Jesus means "a bed" of sickness; others, a bed of judgment and death. This bed is in contrast with her bed of adultery. GK *3109*. Some manuscripts say "prison" {A}.
3. As in v 14, 20, some think Jesus means spiritual adultery; others, physical adultery. On this word, see Mt 5:32a.
4. On this word, see 7:14. Some think this refers to the great tribulation prior to the Second Coming (compare 2:5); others, to a special judgment.
5. That is, the works she teaches, models, and leads her followers to commit, v 20. Some manuscripts say "their" {A}.
6. That is, the followers of her teachings. On this word, see 1 Jn 3:1.
7. This is the normal word for "death". Some think Jesus means "pestilence" (an epidemic of disease) as in 6:8, based on Hebrew usage like Ezek 33:27; others, "I will surely kill", in imitation of a Hebrew idiom (compare Mt 15:4).
8. Or, "will come to know". On this word, see Lk 1:34.
9. Or, "investigating, examining". On this word, see 1 Cor 2:10.
10. Or, "inward parts". Used only here. GK *3752*. It also means "kidney", as in Lev 3:4, etc. Same word as in Ps 7:9; 16:7; 26:2; 73:21; 139:13; Jer 11:20; 12:2; 17:10; 20:12; Lam 3:13.
11. Used 156 times, this word refers to the seat of all aspects of a person's inner life. GK *156*. God is the "heart-knower" in Act 15:8.
12. See 20:12 on this.
13. Some manuscripts say "you and *to* the rest..." {N}.
14. Some think Jesus means as the faithful Christians sarcastically call the teachings of those following Jezebel; others, as those following her actually call their own teachings.
15. Or, "throwing", as in v 22, possibly a play on words. I have no other command for you, just hold on where you are, resisting her. Some manuscripts say "I will not put" {N}.
16. Some link this to the decree in Act 15:28, where the same word is used, and where the two issues mentioned in v 20 are forbidden. Others think Jesus means "any other weighty command". On this word, see "weight" in 1 Thes 2:7.
17. Or, "Only, But, Nevertheless, Yet". Used only here by John. On this word, see "nevertheless" in Mt 11:22.
18. Same word as in 2:1; 3:11.
19. That is, the things mentioned in v 19.
20. This word is used with "until" only here, emphasizing the indefinite time reference. Or, "until which *time*", leaving this word unexpressed. "Until" is used 49 times (GK *948*).
21. Or, "even", so that what follows explains "overcoming".
22. That is, as opposed to "her works", v 22.
23. That is, the end of one's life, or Christ's return, whichever comes first. On "until *the* end", see Heb 6:11.
24. Or, "rule". In this context, the overcomer will rule with force, crushing opposition, and leading them to their destiny. "Shepherding with an iron rod" is mentioned also in 12:5; 19:15. Compare Mt 25:32. Jesus is quoting Ps 2:9. Jesus also shepherds believers, leading them to their destiny, 7:17 (same word), but no iron rod is required. On this word, see 19:15.
25. Or, "made of iron". Elsewhere only in Act 12:10; Rev 9:9; 12:5; 19:15. GK *4971*.
26. Or, vessels "made of clay, belonging to a potter". Used only here. GK *3039*. Our word "ceramic" comes from this word.
27. In other words, the overcomer will share in the event described in Rev 19:15. Some manuscripts have this word in the future tense, creating a separate sentence, "iron rod. Like clay vessels, they will be broken to pieces, as" {N}. On this word, see "bruised" in Mt 12:20.
28. This phrase is elsewhere only in 22:16, of Christ. Some think Jesus means "Myself"; others, "the light of a new day" (meaning eternal life). Compare 2 Pet 1:19 (a different word). There are other views.
29. Or, "spirits". See 1:4 on this. The seven stars are in 1:20.
30. That is, a reputation.
31. Or, "are living", spiritually. On this word, see "came to life" in 20:4.
32. That is, spiritually. What others think about these people does not match what Jesus knows to be true. On this word, see Mt 8:22.
33. Or, "Become *ones who are* keeping watch". GK *1181*.
34. Or, "staying alert, keeping awake". On this word, see 1 Thes 5:6.
35. Or, "stabilize". On this word, see 1 Thes 3:2.
36. Or, "the other *things*, the rest". That is, the persons and things that are part of your church, whatever still has some life and is part of your living foundation. Some put the emphasis on the qualities and graces; others, on the people. Same word as in 8:13. On this word, see "other" in 2 Pet 3:16.
37. This word with this grammar is elsewhere only in Act 12:6. On this word, see "going to" in Mk 10:32. Some manuscripts say "are about to" {K}.
38. Or, "completed". This is a participle, "having been fulfilled". Same word as "completed" in 6:11; and also used of fulfilling or completing a service (Act 12:25; Col 4:17); a course (Act 13:25), a work (Act 14:26; 2 Thes 1:11); righteousness (Mt 3:15); etc. Jesus has not yet found their faith fulfilled in their actions. The works that proceed from genuine faith are not there, indicating they are about to wither and die (Lk 8:13, 14). They claim to live, but bear no fruit. Compare Tit 1:16; Jam 2:22, 26. On this word, see "filled" on Eph 5:18.
39. Some manuscripts omit this word {N}. Compare v 12; Eph 1:17.
40. That is, "be keeping in mind". Same word as in 2:5.
41. Some think Jesus means "in what way or manner"; others think He is referring to the content of what these people received and heard, as when we say "remember how I said that...". GK *4802*.
42. Same word as in the next sentence. Some manuscripts add "upon you" {N}.
43. This phrase, "like *a* thief", is also in 16:15. On this concept, see 1 Thes 5:2. Some think Jesus is referring to the Second Coming; others, to a special coming in judgment.
44. Some manuscripts omit this word, and add "even" {K}, "You have *a* few names even in Sardis...".
45. People are referred to as "names" also in 11:13; Act 1:15. Here, it is in contrast with "name" in v 1. On this word, see 2 Tim 2:19.
46. Same word as in 14:4. That is, did not soil by sin. They are "unspotted by the world", Jam 1:27. There are other views suggesting a more specific reference than this. On this word, see 1 Cor 8:7.
47. On this concept, see "white garments" in 4:4.
48. Or, "thus". That is, like those in v 4, walking with Me. Some manuscripts say "The *one* overcoming— this *one* will cloth *himself*..." {B}.
49. Compare 19:8.

A. Act 26:20 B. Mt 26:10 C. Rom 7:11 D. Eph 1:22 E. 2 Pet 3:16, other F. 1 Jn 1:8, have G. Lk 1:34 H. Lk 24:1 J. Rev 2:7 K. 1 Jn 5:18 L. Rev 6:8 M. 1 Thes 4:4 N. 1 Jn 2:29 O. Jn 8:42, am here P. 1 Pet 3:3 Q. Heb 13:9 R. Rev 16:6 S. Rev 4:4

|||||1E. And I will never¹ wipe-out² his name from the book^A *of* life³
|||||2E. And I will confess⁴ his name before My Father and before His angels

||||5D. "Let *the one* having *an* ear hear what the Spirit is saying *to* the churches |||||| 6

|9C. "And *to* the angel *of* the church in Philadelphia, write— These *things* says the Holy^B *One*, the True^C *One*, the *One* having the key *of* David⁵, the *One* opening and no one will shut⁶, and shutting^D and no one opens⁷ |||||| 7

|||1D. "I know your works⁸— |||||| 8

|||||1E. "Behold— I have given^E before you *an* opened⁹ door (which,¹⁰ no one is able to shut it)

|||2D. "Because¹¹ you have *a* little¹² power¹³, and you kept^F My word^G, and you did not deny^H My name—

|||||1E. "Behold— I am giving^E *some* from the synagogue *of* Satan, the *ones* saying *that* they are Jews (and they are not), but they are lying¹⁴ |||||| 9
|||||2E. "Behold— I will make^J them so that¹⁵

|||||||1F. "They will come^K and worship¹⁶ before your feet
|||||||2F. "And they may¹⁷ know¹⁸ that **I** loved^L you

|||3D. "Because you kept the word^G *of* My endurance¹⁹— |||||| 10

|||||1E. "**I** also will keep²⁰ you²¹ from²² the hour²³ *of* testing²⁴—

|||||||1F. "The *hour* going-to²⁵ come^M upon the whole²⁶ world²⁷, to test^N the *ones* dwelling^O upon the earth²⁸

|||||2E. "I am²⁹ coming^M quickly³⁰. Be holding-on-to^P what you have in order that no one may take your crown^Q |||||| 11

|||4D. "The *one* overcoming^R— |||||| 12

|||||1E. "I will make^J him *a* pillar³¹ in the temple³² *of* My³³ God, and he will never go outside again
|||||2E. "And I will write upon him

|||||||1F. "The name *of* My God

1. Or, "by no means". This is an emphatic negative (see Gal 5:16).
2. Or, "smear out, blot out, erase". In other words, the overcomer will live forever, he will remain. On this word, see Col 2:14. Same word as in Ex 32:32-33; Ps 69:28. Some think this implies the names of all who have lived on earth are written in the book, and Jesus will erase the non-overcomer; others do not think it implies that non-overcomers are written in the book of life and must be erased. It is a statement about what Jesus will not do to overcomers, not what He will do to non-overcomers. Others think it is a list of professing believers (ones claiming to be alive, v 1), from which their name can be erased.
3. This book is also mentioned in 13:8; 17:8; 20:12, 15; 21:27; Phil 4:3. Compare Lk 10:20; Dan 12:1.
4. Or, "declare, acknowledge". Same word as in Mt 10:32; Lk 12:8. On this word, see 1 Tim 6:12.
5. That is, the authority to open and close David's house, the Messiah's kingdom, and the city of David, the heavenly Jerusalem. Compare Isa 22:22.
6. Some manuscripts say "shuts" {N}.
7. Some manuscripts say "will open" {N}.
8. The content of these works is detailed in the two "because" statements (2D. and 3D.).
9. Some think this is a door of opportunity and service, as in 1 Cor 16:9; 2 Cor 2:12; Col 4:3. Others think Jesus means a door of salvation, of entrance into His kingdom, which no one can shut so as to keep them out, especially their Jewish adversaries in v 9. This is a participle, "having been opened", standing open. GK *487*.
10. Some manuscripts say "opened door, and no one..." {N}.
11. Or, "That". In this arrangement, their works are the reason for the action that follows in v 9, just as in v 10 and 17. This view parallels the "Because" statements. Others think this continues from "I know" after a parenthesis containing the "Behold" statement— "I know your works... that you have *a* little power...". This becomes point 2E., and verse 9 point 2D. Others think Jesus is giving the reason for having given them the opened door, making the "Behold" statement above point 2D., and this point 1E., and verse 9 point 3D. This view parallels the "Behold" statements.
12. Some think Jesus means "you have little power", meaning "hardly any". He means "you have little power, yet you kept My word". Others think He means "you have *a* little power", meaning "some, which you are using effectively".
13. Or, "strength". Some think Jesus is referring to their numbers; others, to their spiritual power, or their ability to influence the community.
14. Because you have a little power, I will exercise My power for you. Some think Jesus means He will give them some Jewish converts from among their enemies. Others think this does not mean they are converts, only that the church in Philadelphia will be exalted over them in some way. On this word, see "lie to" in Act 5:3.
15. Same grammar as in 13:12, to "make... so that they will...". Others simplify this to "make them come and worship... and know". This phrase defines the sense in which Jesus is "giving" them.
16. Or, "prostrate-themselves, pay homage". On this word, see "give worship" in 4:10. It is used with "before" elsewhere only in 15:4; Lk 4:7. As to the internal attitude behind this act, some think Jesus means "worship [Me]", indicating a conversion. Others think He means "prostrate themselves [to you]", as an act of submission.
17. The word "so that" is followed by a "will" verb and a "may" verb like this also in 22:14. Some think no distinction is intended.
18. Or, "understand, recognize". On this word, see Lk 1:34.
19. Punctuated this way, this means the message proceeding from My endurance. In this case, the endurance is Christ's. Compare 2 Thes 3:5. Others punctuate this as "My word *of* endurance", My command to endure. In this case, the endurance is ours. In the Greek word order, "My" is the last word. On this word, see Jam 1:3.
20. Or, "preserve, protect, guard". Same word as "kept" in the previous phrase. On this word, see 1 Jn 5:18.
21. Some think that this, along with the promises and warnings at this point in all seven letters (2:5, 10, 16, 22-23; 3:3, 9-11, 16-20), refers to the first-century church, but can be applied to all believers. Others think this, along with those in the other letters, refers to the Second Coming, which has been imminent to all believers since the first century, and so speaks directly to all believers until then.
22. Or, "out of, away from". "Keep from" is elsewhere only in Jn 17:15, "keep from the evil one", where it is contrasted with "take out of the world". A similar phrase, "saved from the hour", occurs in Jn 12:27. Some think Jesus means "preserve you through" the hour of testing, like Israel during the plagues of Egypt. Some holding the Future View (see 1:1) think He means "keep you from entering" the hour itself, by means of the rapture (1 Thes 4:17).
23. That is, "period". This hour is, or includes, all the judgments described later in this book. The Future View thinks this refers to the final period of tribulation before Christ returns. The Past View thinks it is the hour of judgment on Israel in A.D. 70. The Spiritual View thinks it is symbolic of the crisis point in the trials that come upon people and nations throughout history. Compare Dan 12:1; Mt 24:21; Mk 13:19; 2 Thes 2:8-10. On this word, see Lk 2:38.
24. Or "trial". On this word, see "trials" in Jam 1:2. Related to "test" later in this verse.
25. Or, "being about to". This participle modifies "hour". On this word, see Mk 10:32.
26. This word means "whole, all, entire". Used 109 times. GK *3910*.
27. This phrase "whole world" is elsewhere only in Mt 24:14; Act 11:28; Rev 12:9; 16:14. On this word, see Heb 2:5. A similar phrase using a different word for "world" is in Mt 16:26; 26:13; Rom 1:8; 1 Jn 2:2; 5:19. Some think this means this hour of testing is universal, worldwide in scope, affecting all humans. The Past View takes "world" in the sense of the civilized world, the Roman Empire, as it is used in Lk 2:1; Act 24:5.
28. Or, "land". This phrase, "the *ones* dwelling upon the earth" is elsewhere only in 6:10; 8:13; 11:10; 13:8, 14; 17:8. A similar phrase using this word is in 13:12 and 17:2. Some think it refers in particular to the unbelievers living on the earth. The Past View (see 1:1) renders it "upon the land", and takes it to refer to apostate Israel.
29. Some manuscripts say "Behold— I am..." {N}.
30. The phrase "I am coming" occurs seven times in this book (see 22:20). On "quickly", see 22:7.
31. That is, a permanent part, something firmly planted and never moving. The sense is defined by what comes next, "will never go outside again". Many ancient pillars still stand today. On this word, see 1 Tim 3:15.
32. This word is used metaphorically, like "pillar". The overcomer will be permanently in the presence of God. On this word, see Rev 11:1.
33. On "My God", see 3:2.

A. Mt 1:1 B. 1 Pet 1:16 C. Jn 7:28 D. Jn 20:19, locked E. Eph 1:22 F. 1 Jn 5:18 G. 1 Cor 12:8 H. 2 Tim 2:12 J. Rev 13:13, does K. Jn 8:42, am here L. Jn 21:15, devotedly love M. Mk 16:2 N. Heb 2:18, tempted O. Eph 3:17 P. Rev 2:1 Q. Rev 4:4 R. Rev 2:7

2F. "And the name *of* the city *of* My God, the new Jerusalem[1]— the *one* coming down out of heaven from My God
3F. "And My new name[2]

5D. "Let the *one* having *an* ear hear what the Spirit is saying *to* the churches   13

10C. "And *to* the angel *of* the church in Laodicea[3], write— These *things* says the Amen, the Faithful[A] and True[B] Witness[4], the Beginning[5] *of* the creation[C] *of* God   14

1D. "I know your works[D]— that you are neither cold nor hot.[6] O-that[E] you were cold or hot[7]   15

1E. "So because you are lukewarm and neither hot nor cold[8], I am about-to[9] spew[10] you out of My mouth[11]   16

2D. "Because you say that[12] "I am *a* rich[13] one, and I have become-rich[F], and I have *a* need[G] *for* nothing", and you do not know that **you** are the *one* wretched[14] and pitiable[15] and poor[16] and blind and naked[H]—*"I counsel[J] you to buy[K] from Me   17   18

1E. "Gold having been refined[17] by fire, in order that you may become-rich[F]
2E. "And white garments,[18] in order that you may clothe *yourself*, and the shame[L] *of* your nakedness[M] may not be revealed[19]
3E. "And eye-salve[20] to rub-in[21] your eyes, in order that you may see

3D. "**I** rebuke[N] and discipline[22] all whom I love[O]. Therefore be zealous[23], and repent[P]   19

1E. "Behold— I stand at the door.[24] And I am knocking[25]   20
2E. "If anyone hears My voice and opens[26] the door, I also[27] will come-in to[28] him. And I will have-dinner[29] with him, and he with Me

4D. "The *one* overcoming[Q]— I will give him authority[30] to sit *down* with Me on My throne, as **I** also overcame and sat *down* with My Father on His throne   21
5D. "Let the *one* having *an* ear hear what the Spirit is saying *to* the churches"   22

2A. After these *things* I saw, and behold— *there was an* opened[31] door in heaven[32], and the first voice which I heard speaking with me like [the sound] *of a* trumpet[33] saying, "Come-up here[34] and I will show[35] you *the things* which must[R] take-place[36] after these *things*". *Immediately[37] I came-to-be in *the* Spirit[38]   4:1   2

1B. And behold— *a* throne was setting[S] *there* in heaven, and *One* sitting on the throne[T]

1C. And the *One* sitting *was* resembling[39] *a* jasper[40] stone and *a* carnelian[41] *in* appearance[U]   3
2C. And *a* rainbow[42] *was* around the throne resembling *an* emerald[43] *in* appearance
3C. And around the throne *I saw* twenty four thrones[T]   4
4C. And on the thrones *I saw* twenty four elders[44] sitting— having been clothed in white[45] garments[V], and[46] golden crowns[47] on their heads
5C. And lightnings[48] and voices[49] and thunders[50] are coming-out from the throne   5
6C. And seven torches[51] *of* fire *are* burning[W] before the throne (which are the seven Spirits[52] *of* God)

1. The new Jerusalem is mentioned again in 21:2, 10.
2. Compare 19:12 and 22:4.
3. Some manuscripts say "*of* the Laodiceans" {K}.
4. Compare 1:5; 19:11. That is, to all God has revealed through Him.
5. Related to "ruler" in 1:5. On this word, see Col 1:18. Jesus may mean "Ruler of creation". Or, He may mean "the Beginning", as this word is used in Rev 21:6; 22:13 ("the Beginning and the End"), that is, the origin or first cause of creation, as in Jn 1:1-3.
6. Some think Jesus means "unbelievers or believers"; others prefer to leave it indefinite. Others think He means they are "useless, good for nothing, barren", neither cold refreshing water, nor hot medicinal water. "Hot" is related to "boiling" in Act 18:25.
7. Some think Jesus means clearly and openly in one group or the other. The hardest group to reach are the self-deceived who think they are right with God, but are not. Others think He means "of some use or value".
8. Some manuscripts say "cold nor hot" {N}, as in v 15.
9. Judgment is coming, but there is still time for v 19.
10. Or, "vomit". Used only here. GK *1840*. Not related to "spit" (Mk 7:33).
11. That is, to reject them, and separate them from Himself.
12. Some manuscripts omit this word {N}, which serves to introduce the quotation.
13. Some think Jesus means rich with spiritual riches they in fact do not have; others, rich with material riches blinding them to the true spiritual riches they do not have. On this adjective, see 1 Tim 6:17.
14. On this word, see Rom 7:24. Compare 1 Cor 4:8.
15. Or, "miserable". Elsewhere only in 1 Cor 15:19. GK *1795*.
16. Or, "destitute, beggarly, impoverished". On this word, see Gal 4:9.
17. Same word as in 1:15. That is, pure gold. Some think this refers to true spiritual riches; others, to something more specific like faith or righteousness.
18. Some think these symbolize righteousness, or purity, or holiness, as in 4:4.
19. Or, "made evident, visible". On this word, see "made evident" in 1 Jn 2:19. Some think Jesus means "at My coming". Compare 16:15; 1 Jn 2:28. Others think He is referring to a special judgment upon their church.
20. Some think this is symbolic of the word of God; others, the Holy Spirit. Used only here. GK *3141*.
21. Or, "anoint". Used only here. GK *1608*. Related to "anoint" in Lk 4:18.
22. Or, "train, correct". Same word as in Heb 12:6.
23. Used only here. GK *2418*. Related to the word in 1 Cor 14:1.
24. That is, as a friend who loves you. Some think Jesus means the door of their heart; others, the door of His return, His second coming (like Mt 24:33; Jam 5:9); others, at the door of their church, as an outsider to it.
25. Jesus is calling on them to respond. He desires entrance to their lives, and their authentic salvation.
26. What follows is dependent on their response.
27. Or, "indeed". Some manuscripts omit this word {C}.
28. Compare Jn 14:23. Jesus will come in and share in such a person's life. On "come-in to", see Act 16:40.
29. Or, "have supper, eat the main meal". Some think this illustrates the fellowship they will have once such a person opens the door. They will share spiritual food. Others think this refers to the banquet at Christ's coming in 19:9. On this word, see "dining" in 1 Cor 11:25. Related to "banquet" in Rev 19:9. Compare Lk 12:37.
30. This word is taken from 6:8, etc.
31. This is a participle, "having been opened". John did not see it open up. He saw it standing open.
32. That is, set in the sky.
33. That is, the voice in 1:10. As there, some think this is the voice of Christ; others, of an angel. Note both in 1:1-2.
34. Some who hold the Future View (see 1:1) think this symbolizes the rapture.
35. Same word as in 1:1; 17:1; 21:9, 10; 22:1, 6, 8. On this word, see 1 Tim 6:15.
36. Or, "happen, come to pass". The phrase "*the things* which must take place" is also in 1:1; 22:6. GK *1181*.
37. Some manuscripts say "And immediately" {N}.
38. Or, "spirit". On this phrase, see 1:10. Some think this is a renewal of that state following a break in time after 3:22; others, a deeper level of that state begun in 1:10.
39. The resemblance seems to be in the color. Same word as in 1:13.
40. It is uncertain what stone John is referring to. Elsewhere only in 21:11, 18, 19. GK *2618*. Some think it is a diamond, based on 21:11; others, a red or green stone. He may be referring to its translucent radiance or brilliance.
41. That is, reddish or ruby in color, like this precious stone. Elsewhere only in 21:20. GK *4917*.
42. Or, "halo, circle of radiance". Some think John means an arc; others, a full circle. Elsewhere only in 10:1. GK *2692*. Compare Ezek 1:28.
43. That is, green. Used only here. GK *5039*.
44. These elders are mentioned also in v 10; 5:5, 6, 8, 11, 14; 7:11, 13; 11:16; 14:3; 19:4. Some think they are humans; others, angels. Some think they represent the church; others, Israel and the church (as in 21:12, 14); others, all the faithful of the ages; others, all the angels. Same word as in 1 Tim 5:17.
45. Rev 3:5, 18 also mentions "white garments". "White" clothing is mentioned in 3:4; 6:11; 7:9, 13, 14; 19:14. Suggestions for the symbolic meaning of white include purity, holiness, righteousness, glory, and victory. On this word, see Rev 4:35.
46. Some manuscripts add "they had" {K}.
47. Or, "wreaths". A "golden crown" is also mentioned in 14:14. "Crown" is also in 2:10; 3:11; 4:10; 6:2; 9:7; 12:1. It is the victor's crown, not the king's crown (a diadem, 13:1). Same word as in 1 Cor 9:25; Phil 4:1; 1 Thes 2:19; 2 Tim 4:8; Jam 1:12; 1 Pet 5:4. Elsewhere only of the crown of thorns, Mt 27:29; Mk 15:17; Jn 19:2, 5. GK *5109*.
48. John may mean bolts of lightning, or flashes of lightning. Same word as in 8:5; 11:19; 16:18. Used 9 times. GK *847*.
49. Or, "sounds". Used 55 times in Rev, both of voices (like 5:2) and sounds (like 9:9; 14:2; 18:22). On this word, see Mk 1:26. Some manuscripts reverse these, so that it says "thunders and voices" {K}.
50. That is, crashes or peals of thunder. These three things also occur in 8:5; 11:19; 16:18. Used 12 times. GK *1103*.
51. Or, "lamps". Same word as in 8:10. On this word, see "lamp" in Mt 25:1.
52. Or, "spirits". On the seven Spirits, see 1:4.

A. Col 1:2 B. Jn 7:28 C. Rom 8:39 D. Mt 26:10 E. Gal 5:12 F. 1 Tim 6:18 G. Tit 3:14 H. Jam 2:15 J. Jn 18:24 K. Rev 5:9 L. Heb 12:2 M. 2 Cor 11:27 N. Eph 5:11, expose O. Jn 21:15, affectionately love P. Act 26:20 Q. Rev 2:7 R. Mt 16:21 S. Mt 3:10, lying T. Rev 20:11 U. Rev 9:17, vision V. 1 Pet 3:3 W. Mt 5:15

7C.	And before the throne[A] *is something* like[1] *a* sea of-glass[2], resembling[B] crystal[3]	6
8C.	And in *the* midst[C] *of* the throne and around the throne[4] *are* four living-creatures[5] being full[6] *of* eyes on the front and on the back	
1D.	And the first living-creature *is* resembling *a* lion. And the second living-creature *is* resembling *a* calf[7]. And the third living-creature *is* having the face like *of a* man[8]. And the fourth living-creature *is* resembling *a* flying eagle	7
2D.	And the four living-creatures, each one[9] *of* them having six wings apiece, are full *of* eyes around and inside[10]	8
3D.	And they do not have *a* rest[11] *by* day and *by* night[12], saying "Holy[D], holy, holy *is* the Lord God Almighty[13], the *One Who* was and *Who* is and *Who* is coming"	
9C.	And whenever[14] the living-creatures will give glory[E] and honor[F] and thanks[G] *to* the *One* sitting on the throne, *to* the *One* living forever and ever[H], *the twenty four elders will fall before the *One* sitting on the throne, and will give-worship[15] *to* the *One* living forever and ever, and will cast[16] their crowns before the throne, saying	9 10
1D.	"You are worthy[J], our Lord and God,[17] to receive the glory and the honor and the power[K], because **You** created[L] all *things*. And they existed[18] and were created because-of[19] Your will[M]"	11
2B.	And I saw upon[20] the right *hand of* the *One* sitting on the throne *a* scroll[21] having been written inside and on-the-back[22], having been sealed-down[23] *with* seven seals[24]	5:1
1C.	And I saw *a* strong angel proclaiming[N] with *a* loud voice, "Who *is* worthy[J] to open the scroll and to break[O] its seals?"	2
1D.	And no one in heaven nor on earth nor under the earth[25] was able to open the scroll, nor to look-*at*[26] it	3
2C.	And I was weeping[27] greatly because no one worthy[J] was found[28] to open[29] the scroll, nor to look-*at* it. *And one of the elders says *to* me, "Do not be weeping. Behold— the Lion from the tribe[P] *of* Judah, the Root *of* David, **overcame**[30] *so as* to open[31] the scroll and[32] its seven seals"	4 5
3C.	And I saw[33] in *the* midst *of* the throne and the four living-creatures, and in *the* midst *of* the elders[34]— there was *a* Lamb[35] as-*if* having been slain[36], standing	6
1D.	Having seven horns,[37] and seven eyes[38] (which are the seven[39] Spirits *of* God having been sent-forth[Q] into all the earth[40])	
2D.	And He came, and He has taken *it*[41] out of the right *hand of* the *One* sitting on the throne	7
4C.	And when He took the scroll	8
1D.	The four living-creatures and the twenty four elders fell before the Lamb— each *one*[42] holding[R] *a* harp[43] and golden bowls being full *of* incense (which are the prayers[44] *of* the saints[45]). *And they are singing[S] *a* new[T] song, saying "You are worthy[J] to take the scroll and to open its seals, because	9
1E.	"You were slain[U]	
2E.	"And You bought[46] *for* God with Your blood[V] *some* from every tribe[P] and tongue[W] and people[X] and nation[Y]	

1. Some manuscripts omit "*something* like" {N}.
2. That is, made of glass. On this word, see 15:2. Compare Ex 24:10; Ezek 1:22, 26.
3. That is, bright or clear or shining like rock-crystal. Elsewhere only in 22:1. GK *3223*. Related word in 21:11.
4. That is, on all four sides. In front and behind and the right and the left.
5. Or, "living-beings, living-ones". The root word is "living". These beings are also referred to in 4:7, 8, 9; 5:6, 8, 11, 14; 6:1, 3, 5, 6, 7; 7:11; 14:3; 15:7; 19:4. Elsewhere only meaning "animal" in Heb 13:11; 2 Pet 2:12; Jude 10. GK *2442*. Compare "cherubim" in Heb 9:5. There are many suggestions as to what their symbolic meaning might be. Some think they are angels similar to those in Ezek 10 and Isa 6. Some think they represent the animal kingdom.
6. Elsewhere only in v 8; 5:8; 15:7; 17:3 ("being full-of", reflecting different grammar), 4; 21:9; and Mt 23:25, 27; Lk 11:39; Rom 3:14. GK *1154*. Related to "fill" in Mk 4:37.
7. Elsewhere only in Lk 15:23, 27, 30, the fatted calf; and Heb 9:12, 19, the sacrificial calf. GK *3675*.
8. Or, "human". On this word, see "mankind" in Mt 4:4.
9. This is an idiom, literally "one by one *of* them". On this idiom, see "one by one" in Mk 14:19.
10. This may mean around their bodies and under their wings.
11. Or, "a stopping, a cessation from activity". Same phrase as in 14:11. On this word, see Mt 12:43. Related to the verb in 14:13.
12. That is, the living creatures repeatedly say this without stopping to sleep. It does not mean they say it over and over without pause, one sentence after another. It means they say it repeatedly, daytime and nighttime. On this phrase, see 7:15.
13. On this word see 1:8. On the next description, see 1:4.
14. The grammar indicates this is something repeatedly done. Verse 8 indicates how often.
15. Same word as in 3:9; 5:14; 7:11; 9:20; 11:1, 16; 13:4, 8, 12, 15; 14:7, 9, 11; 15:4; 16:2; 19:4, 10, 20; 20:4; 22:8, 9. On this word, see Mt 14:33.
16. Or, "throw, put". On this word see "throwing" in 2:22.
17. Some manuscripts say "You are worthy, Lord, to receive..." {N}.
18. On this word, see "is" in Mt 26:26. Some manuscripts say "they exist" {A}.
19. Or, "on account of". That is, by reason of. GK *1328*.
20. Or, "over". That is, on His open palm, or up-facing hand. Same word, but different grammar than 1:20.
21. Or, "book". Some think this scroll contains all the details of the judgments and revelations of chapters 6-22, of the plan of God. Jesus does not read the scroll, but He "signifies" (1:1) its contents in the signs and pictures that follow. Others think that chapters 6-19 represents the content of the seven seals, not the scroll itself. This means the contents of the scroll are not revealed. In this case, some suggest it is Christ's title deed to the earth; others, the book of life; others, the will assuring and detailing our inheritance; others, the sentence against Jerusalem; others, the redemptive plan of God; others, the New Covenant. This word is used 32 times meaning "book, scroll", and twice as "certificate" (see Mt 19:7). GK *1046*. Related to "book" in Mt 1:1 and "little scroll" in Rev 10:2.
22. Or, "behind". That is, a scroll written on both sides. Scrolls normally had writing only on one side— the inside as you rolled it between your two hands. This one is so full it is written on both sides.
23. Used only here. GK *2958*. Related to "sealed" in 7:3, and "seal" in chapters 5-6.
24. Some think John means the leading edge has seven seals on it, all of which must be opened before the scroll can be read. This was the common way of sealing. Others think the seals are on the rolled edge, down through the scroll, so that when a seal is opened, the contents of the scroll become known up to the next seal. On this word, see Rom 4:11.
25. That is, in the world of the dead, called Hades in 1:18. "Under the earth" is elsewhere only in v 13. It is not related to the word in Phil 2:10.
26. That is, to look at its contents. On this word, see "see" in 1:11.
27. Whatever the reason, clearly John took it personally. Some think he wept because the promise made to him in 4:1 to see the future was in danger of not being fulfilled; others, because it appeared God's purposes would not be accomplished now, but delayed. Perhaps he wept at the unworthiness of all, including himself. On this word, see Jn 11:33.
28. This is the Greek word order. John could also mean "no one was found *to be* worthy...".
29. Some manuscripts add "and read" {N}.
30. On this word, see 2:7. On the Lion of Judah, see Gen 49:9-10. On the Root of David, see 22:16; Isa 11:1-10.
31. Or, "*so that* He might open", for the purpose of opening it.
32. Some manuscripts add "to break" {N} from v 2.
33. Some manuscripts add "and behold" {N}.
34. Some think John means between the living creatures and the elders; others, at the throne, surrounded by the living creatures and elders.
35. Or, "Little-lamb". This reflects the symbolism of Isa 53:7, and of Christ's sacrificial death as the Passover lamb. Used of Christ also in Rev 5:8, 12, 13; 6:1, 16; 7:9, 10, 14, 17; 12:11; 13:8; 14:1, 4, 10; 15:3; 17:14; 19:7, 9; 21:9, 14, 22, 23, 27; 22:1, 3. Elsewhere only in Jn 21:15; Rev 13:11. GK *768*.
36. The Lamb is standing alive, even though it has the marks of having been slain. For a lamb, this would mean that its throat was cut, and it was bloodied. On this word, see 1 Jn 3:12.
37. The horns symbolize power and strength.
38. Some think this symbolizes Christ's fullness of knowledge and wisdom.
39. Some manuscripts omit this word {C}. See 1:4 on the seven Spirits.
40. Or, "eyes (which are the seven Spirits *of* God) having been sent...". Thus, some think John means "eyes... sent"; others, "Spirits... sent". Compare Zech 4:2, 10.
41. Some manuscripts say "the book" {N}.
42. Some think this applies only to the 24 elders.
43. On this word, see 15:2. Some manuscripts say "harps" {N}.
44. Some think these are prayers in general; others, prayers for justice and vindication, as in 6:10; 8:3-4.
45. Some think John means all the believers of all ages. All their unanswered prayers in this matter are remembered, and will soon be answered. Others think he means the believers on earth (or in the land) undergoing persecution during the tribulation there who are currently praying about this matter.
46. Or, "purchased". Some manuscripts add "us" {A}. Same word as in 14:3, 4; Mt 14:15; 1 Cor 6:20; 7:23; 2 Pet 2:1. Used 30 times. GK *60*. Related to "marketplace".

A. Rev 20:11 B. Rev 1:13 C. 2 Thes 2:7 D. 1 Pet 1:16 E. 2 Pet 2:10 F. 1 Tim 5:17 G. 1 Tim 4:3, thanksgiving H. Rev 20:10 J. Rev 16:6 K. Mk 5:30 L. Eph 2:15 M. Jn 7:17 N. 2 Tim 4:2 O. Mt 5:19 P. Rev 1:7 Q. Mk 3:14, send out R. 1 Jn 1:8, have S. Eph 5:19 T. Heb 8:13 U. 1 Jn 3:12 V. 1 Jn 1:7 W. 1 Cor 12:10 X. Rev 21:3 Y. Act 15:23, Gentiles

3E. "And You made them¹ *a* kingdom² and priests *to* our God	10
4E. "And they will reign³ upon⁴ the earth"	

2D. And I saw, and I heard *the* voice *of* many angels around the throne, and *of* the living-creatures, and *of* the elders— and the number *of* them was myriads^A *of* myriads, and thousands *of* thousands—˚saying *with a* loud voice   11
  12

    1E. "Worthy^B is the Lamb having been slain to receive the power^C and riches^D and wisdom^E and strength^F and honor^G and glory^H and blessing⁵"

3D. And I heard every creature which *is* in the heaven and on earth and under the earth⁶ and on⁷ the sea, and all the *things*⁸ in them, saying   13

    1E. "*To* the *One* sitting on the throne and *to* the Lamb *be* the blessing and the honor and the glory and the dominion^J forever and ever^K"

4D. And the four living-creatures were saying "amen"   14
5D. And the elders⁹ fell and worshiped¹⁰

5C. And I saw when the Lamb opened *the* first¹¹ of the seven¹² seals,¹³ and I heard one of the four living-creatures saying like *a* voice^L *of* thunder^M, "Come¹⁴"   6:1

    1D. And I saw¹⁵, and behold— *there was a* white¹⁶ horse,¹⁷ and the *one* sitting¹⁸ on it having *a* bow¹⁹   2
    2D. And *a* crown²⁰ was given *to* him
    3D. And he went out conquering^N, and²¹ in order that he might conquer^N

6C. And when He opened the second seal, I heard the second living-creature saying, "Come"   3

    1D. And another horse— *a* fire-red²² *one*— went out   4
    2D. And *to* the *one* sitting²³ on it, *authority*²⁴ was given *to* him to take the peace²⁵ from the earth, and²⁶ that they will slay²⁷ one another²⁸
    3D. And *a* great sword²⁹ was given *to* him

7C. And when He opened the third seal, I heard the third living-creature saying, "Come"   5

    1D. And I saw, and behold— *there was a* black³⁰ horse, and the *one* sitting on it holding *a* balance-scale^O in his hand
    2D. And I heard *something* like³¹ *a* voice^L in *the* midst *of* the four living-creatures, saying   6

        1E. "A quart³² *of* wheat *for a* denarius³³, and three quarts *of* barley³⁴ *for a* denarius
        2E. "And do not harm^P the olive-oil^Q and the wine"³⁵

8C. And when He opened the fourth seal, I heard *the* voice *of* the fourth living-creature saying, "Come"   7

    1D. And I saw, and behold— *there was a* pale-green³⁶ horse, and the one sitting on³⁷ it. Death *was the* name *for* him. And Hades^R was following with him   8

1. Some manuscripts say "us" {A}.
2. Compare 1:6. Some manuscripts say "kings" {N}.
3. Some manuscripts say "they are reigning"; others, "we will reign" {A}. In either case, the Past and Spiritual Views (see 1:1) think this refers to a present spiritual reign in Christ's spiritual kingdom on earth as described in 20:5; the Future View, to a future visible reign on earth, as described in 20:5. On this word, see 19:6.
4. Or, "over". GK *2093*.
5. Or, "praise". Same word as in v 13 and 7:12. Note that seven things are named. On this word, see 2 Cor 9:5.
6. Same phrase as in v 3.
7. Same word as "on" earlier in "on earth". Some manuscripts say "in" {K}. Some manuscripts say "and is on..."; others, "and which are on..." {B}. GK *2093*.
8. Or, "sea— even all the *creatures* in them— saying". That is, in all the places mentioned. Compare Ps 146:6.
9. Some manuscripts say "the twenty four elders" {K}. See 4:4.
10. On this word, see 4:10. Some manuscripts add "Him who lives forever and ever" {K}.
11. Same word as in 9:12. On this word see "one" in Eph 4:7.
12. Some manuscripts omit this word {N}.
13. Some think the seals correspond to the "beginning of birth-pains" in Mt 24:6, 7, 9. The Past View (see 1:1) thinks the seals symbolize non-sequential things regarding the tribulation for Jerusalem in A.D. 70; the Future View, sequential things regarding the end-time tribulation. Within these views, some think the seals occur prior to the tribulation, and that once the scroll is opened, the tribulation begins with the trumpets in chapter 8; others, that the tribulation begins here. The Spiritual View regards the seals as things that occur repeatedly throughout history, with the last three specifically focused on, or intensifying during, the end time.
14. Or, "Go". Some think the command is addressed to the horseman; others, to John. Some manuscripts say "Come and see" here and in v 3, 5 and 7 {B}, which would clarify that the commands are addressed to John. On this word, see Mk 16:2.
15. Some manuscripts omit "And I saw" here, in v 5, and in v 8 {B}.
16. Some think this symbolizes holiness; others, victory. On this word, see 4:4.
17. Some think the four horsemen are the unfolding of a single event— conquest leads to killing and to famine and to death. Others think they are separate events. Compare Zech 1:8; 6:1-8.
18. Some think this refers to the victorious conquest by the gospel, and the rider is Christ; others, to wars between nations, militarism. The Past View sees it as war in Israel, and the rider as the Roman general going forth to conquer Jerusalem. Some holding the Future View think the rider is the Antichrist.
19. Some think the bow symbolizes military power. Some think the fact that arrows are not mentioned is significant. Used only here. GK *5534*.
20. Some think this symbolizes victory; others, royalty. On this word, see 4:4.
21. Or, "even". This phrase explains the previous one. This rider went out conquering in order that he might be victorious. He went out vanquishing in order that he might prevail.
22. Some think this symbolizes bloodshed. Elsewhere only in 12:3. GK *4794*. Related to "fire".
23. Some think the rider represents the antichrist forces opposing the advance of the gospel by the first horse, and persecuting those spreading it. Some holding the Future View think the rider is the end-time Antichrist. Some think none of the riders are intended to be a specific person, but are personifications of the content of the seal.
24. This word is taken from v 8.
25. Some think John means "the peace" following the first seal; others, "peace" in general. Some holding the Future View think this removal of peace happens at the mid-point of the tribulation, based on Dan 9:27; others, early in the tribulation, as part of the birthpains (Mt 24:6-8). The Past View thinks John means "peace from the land" of Israel. On this word, see Act 15:33.
26. Or, "even". This phrase is explaining the previous. Note the change of subject.
27. Same word as in 5:6; 6:9.
28. Some think John is referring to war; others, to personal, criminal violence, civil disorder.
29. Or, "large knife" carried in a sheath. Some think this symbolizes great bloodshed; others, awesome killing power. Elsewhere in Revelation only in 13:10, 14. On this word, see Eph 6:17.
30. Some think this symbolizes mourning. The rider personifies famine (but not to the point of starvation).
31. Some manuscripts omit "*something* like" {N}.
32. Literally, a "choenix", a Greek dry measure used for grain, equivalent to about a quart or liter. This was the daily allowance for a slave. Used only in this verse. GK *5955*.
33. This was a worker's daily wage. In other words, a one-day supply of wheat for one person will cost the entire daily wage of a laborer. This proclamation is setting market prices during a famine. On this word, see Mt 20:2.
34. Barley was the poor people's food. It took more of it to be equal in nourishment. Used only here. GK *3208*. Related word in Jn 6:9.
35. Some think this is limiting the effect of the famine. It harms field crops, but not orchards (oil) and vineyards (wine). Others think it is indicating who will suffer. The poor (who eat the wheat and barley) will suffer, versus the rich (who will still be able to buy the luxuries of oil and wine). Whether oil and wine were considered luxuries or staples is a matter of debate.
36. Used of a "pale", unhealthy person. It is the look of death. Elsewhere only of grass as "green" in Mk 6:39; Rev 8:7; 9:4. GK *5952*.
37. Or, "over, above". Not the same word as in in v 2, 4, 5. Used 19 times. GK *2062*.

A. Act 21:20 B. Rev 16:6 C. Mk 5:30 D. 1 Tim 6:17 E. 1 Cor 12:8 F. Eph 1:19 G. 1 Tim 5:17 H. 2 Pet 2:10 J. Eph 6:10, might K. Rev 20:10 L. Rev 4:5 M. Rev 4:5 N. Rev 2:7, overcome O. Gal 5:1, yoke P. Act 7:24, wronged Q. Jam 5:14, oil R. Rev 1:18

2D. And authority[1] was given *to* them over *a* fourth *of* the earth[2]— to kill with sword[3] and with famine[A] and with pestilence[4] and by the wild-beasts[5] *of* the earth

9C. And when He opened the fifth seal, I saw under the altar[6] the souls[B] *of* the *ones* having been slain[7] because of the word[C] *of* God and[8] because of the testimony[D] which they were holding[9]

    1D. And they cried-out[E] *with a* loud voice, saying "How long[10], holy and true[F] Master[G], are You not judging[H] and avenging[11] our blood from the *ones* dwelling[J] upon the earth?"
    2D. And *a* white robe[12] was given *to* them, *to* each *one*
    3D. And it was told *to* them that[13] they shall rest[14] *a* short time[15] longer, until[16] also[17] *the number of* their fellow-slaves[K] and[18] their brothers[L] going to be killed as also they, may be completed[19]

10C. And I saw when He opened the sixth seal

    1D. And[20] *a* great earthquake[M] took place
    2D. And the sun[21] became black[N] like *a* sackcloth made-of-hair
    3D. And the whole[22] moon became like blood[O]
    4D. And the stars[23] *of* the heaven fell to the earth— as *a* fig tree being shaken[P] by *a* great wind throws[Q] its late-figs[24]
    5D. And the heaven[R] was split[25] like *a* scroll[S] being rolled-up[26]
    6D. And every mountain and island were moved[27] out of their places
    7D. And[28] the kings *of* the earth and the princes[29] and the commanders[30] and the rich[T] and the powerful[U] and every slave[V] and free[31] *one* hid[W] themselves in the caves and in the rocks *of* the mountains. And they are saying *to* the mountains and the rocks

        1E. "Fall upon us and hide[W] us from *the* face[32] *of* the *One* sitting on the throne, and from the wrath[X] *of* the Lamb, because the great day[33] *of* Their[34] wrath came[35], and who is able to stand?"

1. Or, "power, capability, freedom to act". Same word as "right" in 1 Cor 8:9. It is also used of "authorities", human and angelic. Used 102 times. GK *2026*. Related to "having authority" in Lk 22:25.
2. Or, "land". John may mean this as a geographical limit, to kill those living over a fourth of the land, or a fourth of the globe. Or, he may mean it as a numerical limit, to kill a fourth of mankind. The Past View thinks he means one fourth of Israel, a portion of the nation, prior to the final destruction.
3. Not the same word as in v 4. On this word, see 2:16.
4. That is, an epidemic of disease. This word is used in this sense only here and perhaps in 2:23; 18:8. It is the normal word "death", used earlier in this verse. On this word, see 2 Cor 11:23. These four "deaths" are also mentioned in Ezek 14:21.
5. This word was used of all kinds of wild animals, especially those hunted for game. They kill the wounded and defenseless. On this word, see "beast" in 13:1.
6. Some think John means the altar of incense, as in 8:3-5; others, an altar of sacrifice, based on their martyrdom. On this word, see 8:3.
7. John is referring to those martyred during the first four seals, which to the Future View means during the final tribulation, and to the Spiritual View means throughout history. Same word as in v 4. The persecutors, or their successors, are still on earth, v 10.
8. Or, "even", explaining the previous phrase. On the combination of "word" and "testimony", see 20:4.
9. Or, "having". Some think John means "their testimony which they had"; others, "His testimony which they held", the testimony of Jesus, 12:17; 19:10. On this word, see "have" in 1 Jn 1:8.
10. On this idiom, see Mt 17:17.
11. Same word as in 19:2. On this word, see "punish" in 2 Cor 10:6. Related to "vengeance" in Rom 12:19, "Vengeance is Mine, I will repay". How long will You withhold it? Compare Lk 18:7-8.
12. A "white robe" is also in 7:9, 13, 14; Mk 16:5. "Robe" is elsewhere only in 22:14; Mk 12:38; Lk 15:22; 20:46. GK *5124*. See "white garments" in 4:4. Some manuscripts have this plural, "white robes were given" {K}.
13. Or, "that they should rest, so that they will rest", or more simply, "to rest". GK *2671*. This grammar is like 9:4.
14. Some think this means "rest from their labors", as in 14:13. Others, "rest from crying for vengeance". On this word, see "refreshed" in Phm 7.
15. Some think this time of delay ends with the seventh trumpet, based on 10:6 (same word). The prayers begin to be answered in 8:3-5 and the trumpets. Others think it ends with this verse, and begins to be answered in the next seal. See 8:2 on the relationship of seals and trumpets. "Short time" is also in 20:3, and elsewhere only in Jn 7:33; 12:35. On "short", see "least" in Mt 11:11.
16. The judgment of this seal is vengeance for their deaths in answer to their prayers. But it is delayed.
17. Or, "until *the number of* both their fellow slaves and their brothers".
18. Or, "even", explaining "fellow slaves". Some think there is one group here, their fellow Christian martyrs; others, two groups, their "fellow slaves" who are not martyred, and their "brothers" who will also be martyred.
19. Or, "filled up, filled full". Some manuscripts say "until also their fellow-slaves... may complete [their course]" {N}, dropping the idea of a quantity filled full. On this word, see "filled" in Eph 5:18.
20. Some manuscripts say "And behold" {K}. Some take the following things as symbolic of political and national upheavals and dissolutions. Some holding the Future View (see 1:1) take them as literal end-time events. The Past View takes them as symbolic of the dissolution and destruction of Israel. Some, especially the Spiritual View, think these are general apocalyptic symbols representing catastrophic end-time events, and are not intended to represent anything more specific. Also, some think these things are the same event as described in 16:17-21; others, the beginning of what concludes there. See 8:2 on the relationship of the seals, trumpets and bowls. These descriptions are also found in the OT prophets, and in Mt 24:29.
21. Some think the sun, moon, and stars symbolize levels of governmental power and authority. Note there are seven components named here, earth, sun, moon, stars, heaven, mountain and island. It signifies completeness.
22. Some manuscripts omit this word {N}.
23. This word is also used in 1:16, 20; 2:1, 28; 3:1, 8:10, 11, 12; 9:1; 12:1, 4; 22:16. In some of these places, stars are angelic beings. Note 9:1 and 12:4. Used 24 times. GK *843*.
24. This word is used of the late figs which never ripen and fall off in a spring wind. Used only here. GK *3913*.
25. Or, "separated, parted". John may mean "split in two like a scroll sometimes splits in two when being rolled up". Or, he may mean "parted from earth, rolled up like a scroll is rolled up". Elsewhere only as "separate" in Act 15:39. GK *714*.
26. Elsewhere only in Heb 1:12, like a garment. GK *1813*.
27. On this word, see 2:5. Some think this is the same as 16:18; others, a precursor to it.
28. Note that there are seven categories of persons listed here.
29. Or, "great ones, nobles, magnates". Elsewhere only in Mk 6:21; Rev 18:23. GK *3491*.
30. On this word, see Act 21:31. Some manuscripts say "the rich and the commanders" {N}.
31. On this word, see Mt 17:26. Some manuscripts say "every free *one*" {N}.
32. Or, "presence". On this word, see "presence" in Lk 9:52.
33. Some think this "great day" is Christ's return, Mt 24:29-31. Others think it is the end-time "tribulation" or some point within it. The Past View thinks it is the destruction of Jerusalem in A.D. 70, the end of the nation of Israel. A "great day" is spoken of in 16:14; and Jn 7:37; 19:31; Act 2:20; Jude 6. Note also Joel 2:11, 31; Zeph 1:14.
34. Some manuscripts say "His" {A}.
35. The verb "came" is the same word and grammar as in 5:7; 8:3; 11:18; 14:7, 15; 17:1, 10; 18:10; 19:7. That is, it is here, it has arrived. These people are trying to hide themselves from what is happening, and what is about to happen next. This is the common word for "come, go", on which see Mk 16:2.

A. Lk 21:11 B. Jam 5:20 C. 1 Cor 12:8 D. Jn 1:7 E. Mt 8:29 F. Jn 7:28 G. Jude 4 H. Mt 7:1 J. Rev 3:10 K. Rev 19:10 L. Act 16:40 M. Rev 11:19 N. 3 Jn 13, black ink O. 1 Jn 1:7 P. Mt 21:10 Q. Rev 2:22 R. 2 Cor 12:2 S. Rev 5:1 T. 1 Tim 6:17 U. Rev 18:8, strong V. Rom 6:17 W. Jn 8:59 X. Rev 16:19

11C. After[1] this[2] I saw four angels standing at the four corners[A] *of* the earth, holding-back[B] the four winds[3] *of* the earth in order that *a* wind might not blow[4] on the land[5], nor on the sea, nor against any tree[6]   7:1

    1D. And I saw another angel coming-up from *the* rising[C] *of the* sun[7], having *a* seal[D] *of the* living God. And he cried-out[E] *with a* loud voice *to* the four angels *to* whom *authority* was given *to* them to harm[F] the land and the sea, saying   2

         3

        1E. "Do not harm[F] the land nor the sea nor the trees until we seal[8] the slaves[G] *of* our God upon their foreheads[9]"

    2D. And I heard the number[H] *of* the *ones* having been sealed, one-hundred forty four thousand,[10] having been sealed from every tribe[J] *of the* sons[K] *of* Israel[11]—   4

        1E. From[12] *the* tribe *of* Judah, twelve thousand having been sealed[13]   5
        2E. From *the* tribe *of* Reuben, twelve thousand
        3E. From *the* tribe *of* Gad, twelve thousand
        4E. From *the* tribe *of* Asher, twelve thousand   6
        5E. From *the* tribe *of* Naphtali, twelve thousand
        6E. From *the* tribe *of* Manasseh,[14] twelve thousand
        7E. From *the* tribe *of* Simeon, twelve thousand   7
        8E. From *the* tribe *of* Levi, twelve thousand
        9E. From *the* tribe *of* Issachar, twelve thousand
        10E. From *the* tribe *of* Zebulun, twelve thousand   8
        11E. From *the* tribe *of* Joseph, twelve thousand
        12E. From *the* tribe *of* Benjamin, twelve thousand having been sealed

12C. After these *things* I saw, and behold— *there was a* great multitude[15] (which, no one was able to number it) from every nation[L], and *all* [16] tribes[J] and peoples[M] and tongues[N], standing before the throne and before the Lamb, having been clothed-with white robes[17], and palm-branches[18] in their hands   9

    1D. And they are crying-out[E] *with a* loud voice, saying, "Salvation[19] *belongs to* our God sitting on the throne and *to* the Lamb"   10
    2D. And all the angels were standing around[20] the throne and the elders[21] and the four living-creatures. And they fell on their faces before the throne and gave-worship[O] *to* God, saying   11
           12

        1E. "Amen. The[22] blessing[P] and the glory and the wisdom and the thanksgiving[Q] and the honor and the power and the strength[R] *be* to our God forever and ever[S], amen"

    3D. And one of the elders responded, saying *to* me, "These *ones* having been clothed-with the white robes— who are they, and from where did they come?"   13

        1E. And I have said *to* him, "My[23] lord[T], **you** know"   14
        2E. And he said *to* me, "These[24] are the *ones* coming[25] out of the great affliction[26]. And they washed[27] their robes and made them white[28] in the blood[U] *of* the Lamb

1. Some manuscripts say "And after..." {N}.
2. Within the vision itself, some think the question of 6:17, "who is able to stand", is now answered, both for those on earth (7:1-8) and in heaven (7:9-17). Some holding the Future View think these next two scenes are in proper time sequence within the seven seals, occurring either at some point during or at the end of the tribulation; others, that they are not in time sequence, the sealing occurring before the opening of the first seal in 6:1, and the praises after the tribulation. Thus some think "after this" means "the next thing to happen"; others, "the next thing I saw". The Spiritual View thinks these two scenes describe the situation of believers on earth and in heaven during the seals; that is, during the entire church age. Some manuscripts say "these *things*" {N}.
3. These winds are not mentioned again in this book.
4. Or, "no wind might blow". Within the vision itself, some think the "blowing" looks forward to the catastrophes of the coming trumpets and bowls, the destruction yet to come. Others think the four winds refer back to the four horsemen of chapter 6. Some holding the Future View take the winds literally. The Spiritual View thinks they are symbolic of God's judgments throughout the church age.
5. Same word as "earth" earlier in the verse. This word means "earth" versus heaven (Mt 24:35; Mt 13:27; Rev 1:5; 5:6; 14:15; 16:1; 21:1); "land" versus sea (Mk 4:1; Jn 21:8; Rev 10:2); the "land" of Israel, Sodom, Egypt, etc. (Mt 2:6; Lk 4:25; 21:23; Act 7:3; 13:17); "ground" (Mt 15:35; 25:18; Jn 8:6; Act 9:4); and "soil" (Mt 13:5; Lk 13:7). Used 82 times in Revelation in the first and second senses, and the Past View thinks in the third sense in some of those places (the "land" of Israel). Used 250 times in the NT. GK *1178*.
6. Some think the sea and tree symbolize the nations and their leaders.
7. That is, from the east, from a new day. Same phrase as in 16:12.
8. A seal is a mark of ownership, security. The sealing is for protection, as seen in 9:4. Compare Ezek 9:4-11. Same word as in v 4, 5, 8; 10:4; 20:3; 22:10. On this word, see Eph 1:13.
9. This group is referred to again in 9:4; 14:1. The mark is the name of the Lamb and His Father, 14:1. Note also 3:12; 22:4. The beast also does this (13:16), and note 17:5. Some think it means they are protected from divine judgments only, not from the beast or other people (13:7, 15; 20:4); others, from death from any source; others, from demonic attack (as in 9:4). In addition, some think they are eventually martyred. Some think they are sealed to be martyred, this giving the full number of 6:11. Some holding the Future View think they are sealed in order to live and enter the earthly kingdom of 20:4.
10. Some think this number is symbolic of the totality of these people. Others think it is a literal quantity.
11. Some holding the Spiritual View or the Future View take this symbolically, as representing Christian believers, spiritual Israel, the church on earth. They are numbered to show that all are accounted for, none are lost. Others holding the Future View take it literally, as representing Jewish believers during the tribulation. The Past View sees them as representing the Jewish Christian remnant who escaped Jerusalem.
12. Or, "Out of ". Some, not all. There are several different arrangements of the names of the tribes in the Bible. The significance of John's arrangement of names here, if there is any, is not known. Consult the commentaries.
13. Some manuscripts have "having been sealed" after all twelve phrases {K}.
14. The sons of Jacob are listed in Gen 35:22-26. In Gen 48:5-22, Jacob claims Joseph's sons Ephraim and Manasseh and blesses them. Then in Gen 49, Jacob blesses all his twelve sons. Here in Rev 7:8, Dan (Jacob's son) is omitted, and Manasseh (Joseph's son) is included. Some think Dan was omitted because he fell into idolatry; others, because the Antichrist would come from his tribe.
15. This multitude is identified in v 14. On this word, see Mk 2:13.
16. John switches from the singular (nation) to the plural (tribes).
17. Or, "having put on white robes". On "white robes", see 6:11. Verse 14 says they are whitened in His blood.
18. Some think these are a symbol of rejoicing or triumph. Some think they reflect the Feast of Booths. On this word, see "palm trees" in Jn 12:13.
19. Or, "Salvation *is in* our God". Some think this means "the deliverance, the victory" from the tribulation. Others, "the salvation from sin and all its consequences", v 14. Same word as in 12:10; 19:1, on which see Lk 19:9.
20. The grammar makes clear that the angels were surrounding all three; that is, the throne, elders and four creatures.
21. Note that the 24 elders are distinct from the great multitude. This may imply that one or the other of these two groups is not the church.
22. Note that there are seven items named.
23. Some manuscripts omit this word {N}. By "lord", John means "sir", a term of respect (see "master" in Mt 8:2).
24. Those who think the "great affliction" refers to the trials of the entire church age think that this is the whole church. Those who think it is the end-time tribulation think these are all the believers who died during that event, or the martyrs only. Some think this is the same group described in v 3-8, now described in heaven. The Past View thinks this is a view of heaven given to encourage those suffering persecution in Israel.
25. Some take this to mean that this scene occurs in heaven during the great affliction, with people still coming out. Others take this to mean "those who came out", and think this scene occurs after the end of the great affliction during the millennium on earth (note v 15-16), or on the new earth (note the similarities to chapter 21), or in heaven.
26. Or, "tribulation, oppression, trouble, distress". The phrase "great affliction" also occurs in Mt 24:21; Act 7:11; Rev 2:22. The word "affliction" may also be used of an end-time event in Mt 24:9, 29; Mk 13:19, 24; 2 Thes 1:6. The Future View (see 1:1) thinks the elder is referring to the final period of wrath on unbelievers and persecution of believers at the end of the age, culminated by the return of Christ, and described in chapters 6-19 (some think it is seven years long, based on Dan 9:27). The Spiritual View thinks it is the affliction and persecution experienced by believers from the first century until Christ returns. The Past View thinks it is the time of Israel's destruction. Same word as in Rev 1:9; 2:9, 10, 22; and in Mt 13:21; Mk 4:17; Jn 16:21, 33; Act 7:10; 11:19; 14:22; 20:23; Rom 2:9; 5:3; 8:35; 12:12; 1 Cor 7:28; 2 Cor 1:4, 8; 2:4; 4:17; 6:4; 7:4; 8:2, 13; Eph 3:13; Phil 4:14; Col 1:24; 1 Thes 1:6; 3:3, 7; 2 Thes 1:4; Heb 10:33; Jam 1:27. Elsewhere only as "trouble" in Phil 1:17. GK *2568*. The related verb is in 2 Cor 4:8.
27. Same word as in 22:14. Elsewhere only in Lk 5:2. GK *4459*.
28. Or, "whitened them". On this word, "made white", see Mk 9:3.

A. Mk 12:10 B. Heb 4:14, hold on to C. Mt 2:2, east D. Rom 4:11 E. Mt 8:29 F. Act 7:24, wronged G. Rev 1:1 H. Rev 13:17 J. Rev 1:7 K. Gal 3:7 L. Act 15:23, Gentiles M. Rev 21:3 N. 1 Cor 12:10 O. Mt 14:33 P. 2 Cor 9:5 Q. 1 Tim 4:3 R. Eph 1:19 S. Rev 20:10 T. Mt 8:2, master U. 1 Jn 1:7

Revelation 7:15	980	Verse

        1F. "For this reason, they are before the throne[1] *of* God, and they are serving[2] Him *by* day and *by* night[3] in His temple[4]   15

        2F. "And the *One* sitting on the throne will dwell[5] over them. °They will not[6] hunger anymore, nor thirst anymore, nor may the sun fall upon them, nor any scorching-heat[A]   16

                1G. "Because the Lamb at[7] *the* center *of* the throne will shepherd[8] them, and guide[B] them to springs[C] *of the* waters[D] *of* life[9]   17

                2G. "And God will wipe-away[10] every tear from their eyes"

  13C. And when[11] He opened the seventh seal, *a* silence[12] took place in heaven *for* about *a* half hour   8:1

3B. And I saw[13] the seven angels who stand before God, and seven trumpets were given *to* them   2

    1C. And another angel[14] came and stood at the altar, holding *a* golden censer   3

        1D. And much incense was given *to* him so-that[15] he will give *it, with*[16] the prayers[17] *of* all[18] the saints[E], upon the golden altar[19] before the throne[F]

            1E. And the smoke *of* the incense, *with* the prayers *of* the saints, went up from *the* hand[20] *of* the angel before God   4

        2D. And the angel has taken the censer, and he filled[G] it from the fire *of* the altar and threw *it* to the earth[21]   5

        3D. And there came[22] thunders and voices and lightnings[23] and *an* earthquake[H]

    2C. And the seven angels[24] having the seven trumpets prepared[J] themselves in order that they might trumpet. °And the first[25] trumpeted, and there came hail[K] and fire[26] having been mixed with blood,[27] and it was thrown to the land[28]   6
                                                                                                                                                           7

        1D. And *a* third[29] *of* the land was burned-up, and *a* third *of* the trees[30] was burned-up, and all *the* green[31] grass was burned-up

    3C. And the second angel trumpeted, and *something* like *a* great mountain[32] burning[L] *with* fire was thrown into the sea   8

        1D. And *a* third *of* the sea[33] became blood.[34] And *a* third *of* the creatures in the sea, the *ones* having life[M], died. And *a* third *of* the ships[N] were destroyed[O]   9

    4C. And the third angel trumpeted, and *a* great star[35] fell from heaven[P], burning[L] like *a* torch[Q]. And it fell on *a* third *of* the rivers, and on the springs[C] *of* waters[D]. °And the name *of* the star is called[R] Wormwood[36]   10
  11

1. Some think this indicates these people are "in heaven", before the throne of chapters 4-5. Others think they are "on earth" because of the things that follow— day and night, the sun falling on them, etc.
2. Or, "worshiping". This word is used of serving God in the temple. Same word as in 22:3. On this word, see "worship" in Heb 12:28.
3. This phrase "*by* day and *by* night" is elsewhere only in 4:8; 12:10; 14:11; 20:10; Lk 18:7; Act 9:24. It means "both during the day and during the night". The phrase "*by* night and *by* day" is only in Mk 5:5; 1 Thes 2:9; 3:10; 2 Thes 3:8; 1 Tim 5:5; 2 Tim 1:3. A related phrase ("night and day", meaning "continually") using the same words but different grammar is in Mk 4:27; Lk 2:37; Act 20:31; 26:7.
4. Some think the elder means the temple in heaven, chapters 4-5; 11:19; others, the temple on the new earth, which is the Lord God and the Lamb, 21:22. Some holding the Future View think he means a temple on earth during the millennium of 20:4.
5. Or, "live, take up residence, encamp, pitch a tent". Elsewhere only in Jn 1:14; Rev 12:12; 13:6; 21:3. GK *5012*. This is the verb related to the word "tent". Note that here God dwells "over" them, protecting them from harm. In 21:3 He dwells "with" them. Jesus dwelt "among" us, Jn 1:14.
6. Some think this is a symbolic way of saying they will have every need met.
7. Or, "between" the throne and all the others. This idiom is elsewhere only as "between" in Mt 13:25; 1 Cor 6:5; and "in the midst" in Mk 7:31.
8. Used of Christ also in Mt 2:6; Rev 12:5; 19:15. On this word, see 19:15.
9. Same phrase as in 21:6. On this word, see Rom 8:10. Some manuscripts say "living springs *of* waters" {N}.
10. Same word as in 21:4. On this word, see "wipe out" in Col 2:14.
11. Or, "whenever". This is a different word than with the other six seals, and grammar elsewhere only in Mk 11:19. Here, it may indicate repetition, "and when in repetition of past seals He opened". Or, it may indicate an indefiniteness about the exact time the seal was opened, since only silence followed, "and whenever He opened...". GK *4020*.
12. Some think this silence signals a break in the continuity before the trumpets recapitulate the seals in greater detail. Others think this is a dramatic pause signifying the fearful nature of the terrible events to come. Elsewhere only in Act 21:40. GK *4968*.
13. This is a new heavenly scene, angels and trumpets. Some think the seventh seal, trumpet and bowl each represent the end. The first six seals, trumpets and bowls either overlap to some degree, or recapitulate the same ground in greater detail, or cover subsequent periods prior to the end. Others think the seventh seal is made up of the seven trumpets, and the seventh trumpet is made up of the seven bowls. In this case, some holding the Future View think this means they are sequential in time. Others think that this is simply a literary device, a way of "signifying" (1:1) it. In the TransLine, the trumpets begin a new point at the "B" level without regard to any of these views, simply as a subject-grouping of this heavenly scene.
14. Because the angel symbolically mediates prayers from believers to God, some think he represents Christ, our High Priest. Others think this is simply "another angel".
15. Or, "in order that he might give", or simply "to give". GK *2671*.
16. Or, "*for*". John could mean "with", either along with their prayers or along with the bowls of incense representing their prayers mentioned in 5:8. Or, he could mean "for", as representing or assisting the prayers. In this case, the incense represents the prayers, as in 5:8. In the former case, it is offered with the prayers. In either case, it symbolizes the fragrant aroma and acceptability they have to God.
17. Some think these represent the prayers for vengeance in 6:10.
18. Some think this means all saints of all time; that is, "all" who left vengeance to God, asking Him to repay according to deeds, like Paul in 2 Tim 4:14; Rom 12:19. Some holding the Future View think this means all the saints from the end-time tribulation.
19. Some think this is a different altar from the one mentioned earlier and in v 5; others think there is only one altar. Thus some think this is the altar of incense, and the other is the altar of burnt offerings. Same word as 6:9; 8:5; 9:13; 11:1; 14:18; 16:7. Used 23 times. GK *2603*. Related to "sacrifice" in Heb 9:26.
20. When the incense is poured from his hand on to the coals, smoke rises "from his hand", so to speak.
21. Or, "land". This represents God's answer, detailed in the trumpets next.
22. Or, "took place, were". GK *1181*. Same word as in v 7.
23. These are the same three things as in 4:5, coming from His throne.
24. The Future View (see 1:1) takes what follows as literal (or as symbolic of) supernatural events at the end of the age, like the plagues on Egypt. The Spiritual View treats them as symbols of God's repetitive judgments on sinful people throughout the ages. The emphasis here is that they are from God, and they are partial, aimed at repentance. The Past View takes them as symbolic of God's judgments on Israel by means of the Roman army.
25. Some manuscripts add "angel" {N}.
26. The combination of hail and fire is also in Ex 9:24. It indicates supernatural hail.
27. Some think this is symbolic of the destruction of life. Some holding the Future View think John means literal blood; others, a red rain.
28. Or, "earth". It is rendered "land" here in contrast with "sea" in v 8. On this word, see 7:1.
29. The trumpets are a warning meant to lead to repentance, 9:20. They are partial ("one third"), whereas the bowls (chapter 15) are final ("all"). Literally, it is "the third" down through v 12. The Greek thinks of it as "the third part", English as "a third". Likewise with a fourth in 6:8, a tenth in 11:13, etc. Some manuscripts omit "And *a third of* the land was burned up" {N}.
30. The land and the trees were protected in 7:3.
31. Some think this is symbolic of people and leaders and nations; others, part of a general apocalyptic symbol not expected to interpreted in detail. Some holding the Future View think think this is literal vegetation, and that John means "all the green grass on one third of the land", where it is in season perhaps; others, "all green grass worldwide". Compare 9:4.
32. Some think this symbolizes a kingdom or nation's destruction; others, a meteor; others, that it is simply an apocalyptic symbol.
33. The sea was protected in 7:3.
34. Some holding the Future View think John means "became real blood"; others, "became blood-red". Compare Ex 7:17-18. Compare Rev 6:12; 11:6; 16:3-6.
35. On this word, see 6:13. Some think John means a meteor; others, an angel (as in 1:20; 9:1); others, that this is symbolic of a great leader.
36. Or, "Bitter". This is a bitter herb, known as absinth today (which comes from this Greek word). Used only in this verse. GK *952*.

A. Rev 16:9 B. Lk 6:39 C. Jn 4:6 D. Jn 3:23 E. 1 Pet 1:16, holy F. Rev 20:11 G. Mk 4:37 H. Rev 11:19 J. Mk 14:15 K. Rev 16:21 L. Mt 5:15 M. Jam 5:20, soul N. Act 27:37 O. 2 Cor 4:16 P. 2 Cor 12:2 Q. Mt 25:1, lamp R. Jn 12:49, say

Revelation 8:12	982	Verse

  1D. And *a third of* the waters became¹ wormwood. And many *of* the people^A died from the waters, because they were made-bitter^B

 5C. And the fourth angel trumpeted, and *a third of* the sun was struck², and *a third of* the moon, and *a third of* the stars   12

  1D. So-that³ *a third of* them might be darkened^C, and the day might not shine^D *for a third of* it, and the night likewise

 6C. And⁴ I saw, and I heard one eagle⁵ flying in mid-heaven⁶, saying *with a* loud voice   13

  1D. "Woe, woe, woe *for* the *ones* dwelling upon the earth,⁷ because-of⁸ the remaining^E blasts^F *of* the trumpet *of* the three angels being about to trumpet!"

 7C. And the fifth angel trumpeted, and I saw *a* star⁹ from heaven^G having fallen to the earth. And the key *of* the shaft¹⁰ *of* the abyss¹¹ was given *to* him. °And he opened the shaft *of* the abyss   9:1   2

  1D. And smoke went-up from the shaft like *the* smoke *of a* great furnace. And the sun and the air was darkened^H by the smoke *of* the shaft
  2D. And locusts¹² came out of the smoke to the earth. And authority^J was given *to* them as the scorpions *of* the earth have authority   3

   1E. And it was told *to* them that¹³ they shall not harm^K the grass¹⁴ *of* the land, nor any green *thing*, nor any tree, but only the people^A who do not have the seal^L *of* God on *their* foreheads¹⁵   4
   2E. And *authority* was given *to* them so that they might not kill them, but so that they¹⁶ will be tormented^M *for* five months¹⁷   5
   3E. And their torment^N *was* like *the* torment *of a* scorpion when it strikes *a* person^A
   4E. And¹⁸ during those days the people^A will seek^O death, and will by no means find it. And they will desire^P to die, and death flees^Q from them   6

  3D. And the likenesses¹⁹ *of* the locusts *were* like²⁰ horses having been prepared^R for battle^S   7

   1E. And on their heads *were something* like crowns^T resembling gold
   2E. And their faces *were* like faces *of* people²¹
   3E. And they had hair like *the* hair *of* women²²   8
   4E. And their teeth were like *ones of* lions
   5E. And they had breastplates like iron breastplates   9
   6E. And the sound^F *of* their wings *was* like *the* sound^F *of* chariots^U, *of* many horses running into battle^S
   7E. And they have tails like scorpions, and stingers^V   10
   8E. And their authority^J to harm^K people^A *for* five months *is* in their tails

  4D. They have *a* king over them²³— the angel *of* the abyss.²⁴ *The* name *for* him *in* Hebrew *is* Abaddon. And in Greek he has *the* name Apollyon²⁵   11
  5D. The first woe passed-away²⁶. Behold— two woes are still coming after these *things*   12

 8C. And²⁷ the sixth angel trumpeted   13

1. This is not the same grammar as "became blood" in v 8. It is a Hebrew way of speaking, as in Jn 16:20; Act 5:36; 1 Cor 15:45; Heb 1:5; etc. Literally, "came-to-be for wormwood". Some think John means it became literal wormwood; others, "as bitter as wormwood"; others, "mixed with wormwood".
2. Or, "hit" with a blow. Used only here. GK *4448*. Related to "wound" in 13:3. This word was used of being "struck" by lightning, love, fear, misfortune. The sun, moon and stars were already mentioned in the sixth seal, 6:12. Some think this is symbolic of government and leaders; others, of the light of the truth (spiritual darkness). Some holding the Future View (see 1:1) take it literally.
3. Or, "So that... were darkened, and... did not shine". GK *2671*.
4. This breaks the trumpets into a group of four and three (three woes), as the four horsemen did for the seals.
5. Or, "vulture", as in Mt 24:28; Lk 17:37. Elsewhere only as "eagle" in Rev 4:7; 12:14. GK *108*. Some manuscripts say "angel" {N}.
6. That is, mid-air, where the birds fly, as in 19:17. Some think it is a literal eagle; others, an angel as in 14:6.
7. That is, the unbelievers, as seen in 9:4. On this phrase, see 3:10.
8. Or, "from". GK *1666*.
9. Some think this "star" is one of God's angels, perhaps the one in 20:1; others, Satan or one of his angels, taking "fallen" in a theological sense; others, some human leader. On this word, see 6:13.
10. Besides v 1-2, this word is elsewhere only as "well" in Lk 14:5; Jn 4:11, 12. GK *5853*. It refers to an opening into a deep hole in the ground. Here, an opening to those "under the earth", 5:13.
11. Elsewhere only in Lk 8:31 (where demons feared being sent here); Rom 10:7; and Rev 9:2, 11; 11:7; 17:8; 20:1, 3. GK *12*. Note 2 Pet 2:4; Jude 6. The word means "without [known] depth", and is rendered by some "bottomless".
12. Elsewhere only in v 7; Mt 3:4; Mk 1:6. GK *210*. Some think the locusts are demons. Others think they symbolize false teachings, errors, delusions, and moral corruption. Others think they symbolize human armies, the forces of evil (some holding the Past View think they represent the army of Rome against Israel). Some holding the Future View think they are literal, but special locusts. Compare Joel 2.
13. Or, it was told to them "not to harm, that they should not harm, so that they will not harm". GK *2671*.
14. Same word as in 8:7 where it was burned up. Some holding the Future View think the grass referred to here is the other 2/3 not destroyed in 8:7; others, that this indicates time has passed and the grass has grown back. Others think these are not sequential in time, or are apocalyptic symbols not intended to be interpreted at this level of detail.
15. This either implies that there are no other believers on earth except those so sealed, or that believers who were not sealed will also be tormented by this. This seal was placed on their foreheads in 7:3-4.
16. Note the change of subject.
17. Five months is the life span of ordinary locusts, May to September. Some take this literally; others, symbolically of a limited period of time.
18. This verse explains the extent of the torment. People will wish they could die from it, but they will not die from it.
19. Or, "resemblances, outward appearances". On this word, see Phil 2:7.
20. Same word as "resembling" next, and in 1:13. Related to the word earlier. Or, "the resemblances *were* resembling".
21. Or, "men". John may mean like human faces; or, like a man's face in particular (bearded?). Same word as in v 6.
22. Some think this means that they have long hair.
23. This is unlike regular locusts, Prov 30:27. Some think this is God's angel. Others, Satan's, or Satan himself.
24. Some think John means the angel who opened the abyss in 9:2; others, "the angel *from* the abyss", and in charge of these ones.
25. Both these names are used only here. Both mean "Destroyer". GK *3* and *661*.
26. Same word as in 11:14. GK *599*.
27. Some manuscripts omit this word, so that it says "two woes are still coming. After these *things*, the sixth angel trumpeted" {N}.

A. Mt 4:4, mankind B. Col 3:19 C. Rom 1:21 D. Phil 2:15 E. 2 Pet 3:16, other F. Rev 4:5, voices G. 2 Cor 12:2 H. Eph 4:18 J. Rev 6:8 K. Act 7:24, wronged L. Rev 7:2 M. Rev 14:10 N. Rev 14:11 O. Phil 2:21 P. Gal 5:17 Q. 1 Cor 6:18 R. Mk 14:15 S. Rev 12:7, war T. Rev 4:4 U. Act 8:28 V. 1 Cor 15:56

1D.	And I heard one voice from the four[1] horns *of* the golden altar[2] before God °saying *to* the sixth angel— the *one* having the trumpet— "Release[A] the four angels[3] having been bound[B] at the great river Euphrates[4]"	14
1E.	And the four angels[5] were released— the *ones* having been prepared[C] for the hour and day and month and year[6]— in order that they might kill *a* third *of* mankind[7]	15
2E.	And the number[D] *of* the troops[E] *of* cavalry[8] *was* two hundred million[9]. I[10] heard the number *of* them	16
3E.	And I saw the horses and the *ones* sitting on them in the vision[11] as follows—	17
1F.	Having[12] breastplates [the color] of-fire and of-hyacinth[13] and of-sulphur[14]	
2F.	And the heads *of* the horses *are* like heads *of* lions. And fire and smoke and sulphur[15] is coming-out[16] of their mouths[17]	
4E.	*A* third *of* mankind were killed from these three plagues[18]— by[19] the fire and the smoke and the sulphur coming-out of their mouths	18
1F.	For the authority[F] *of* the horses[20] is in their mouth and in their tails. For their tails *are* like snakes— having heads[21]— and with them they do harm[G]	19
5E.	And the rest[H] *of* mankind who were not killed by these plagues—	20
1F.	They did not-even[22] repent[J] from the works[K] *of* their hands, so-that they will not worship[L] demons and idols—	
1G.	The golden *ones* and the silver *ones* and the brass *ones* and the stone *ones* and the wooden *ones*— which are neither able to see, nor to hear, nor to walk	
2F.	And they did not repent[J] from their murders[M], nor from their sorcerer's-potions[23], nor from their sexual-immorality[N], nor from their thefts	21
2D.	And[24] I saw another[25] strong angel coming down from heaven,[26] having been clothed-with[27] *a* cloud[28]. And the rainbow[29] *was* over[30] his head, and his face *was* like the sun[31], and his feet *were* like pillars[O] *of* fire[32]	10:1
1E.	And *he was* holding[33] in his hand *an* opened[34] little-scroll[35]	2
2E.	And he placed his right foot upon the sea and the left *one* upon the land,[36] °and he cried-out[P] *with a* loud voice— as indeed *a* lion roars	3
1F.	And when he cried-out, the seven thunders[37] spoke their voices	
2F.	And when the seven thunders spoke[38], I was about to write. And I heard *a* voice from heaven saying,[39] "Seal[Q] *the things* which the seven thunders spoke, and do not write them"	4
3E.	And the angel whom I saw standing upon the sea and upon the land lifted-up his right[40] hand to heaven °and swore[41]	5 6
1F.	By the *One* living forever and ever[R]— Who created[S] the heaven and the *things* in it, and the land and the *things* in it, and[42] the sea and the *things* in it	

1. Some manuscripts omit this word {C}.
2. That is, the one in 8:3, on which the incense was burned. This may symbolize a link to the prayers offered there.
3. Some think these are good angels; others, demons. Some think they are the same ones as in 7:1.
4. Elsewhere only in 16:12. This is a 1700 mile river beginning in eastern Turkey, running southwest into northern Syria, and then turning southeast and running through central Iraq into the Persian Gulf just north of Kuwait. It is one of the borders of the land promised to Abraham, Gen 15:18. The Garden of Eden was here, Gen 2:14. It was also the eastern border of the Roman Empire. GK *2371*.
5. Though it is not stated, John seems to mean the four angels are the leaders of the horsemen mentioned next.
6. That is, for that specific moment in history.
7. That is, unbelievers (note v 20; as in 9:4). The purpose changes from tormenting (9:5), to killing. On this word, see Mt 4:4.
8. Literally, the troops "pertaining to a horse". Used only here. GK *2690*. Related to "horsemen" in Act 23:23, and "horse". These are the troops led by the four angels to kill a third of mankind. Some think these troops are angels or demons. Others think they represent human armies. The Past View thinks it is symbolic of the Roman Army, the Tenth Legion that destroyed Israel.
9. Literally, "twenty-thousand ten-thousands", that is, 20,000 times 10,000. Some take this literally; others, symbolically. On the word for 10,000, see "myriad" in Act 21:20. The word for 20,000 is used only here, GK *1490*.
10. Some manuscripts say "And I heard" {K}.
11. Same word as in Act 2:17. Elsewhere only as "appearance" in Rev 4:3. Related to "vision" in Act 10:3. GK *3970*.
12. Some think this refers to the rider and the horse; others, to the rider only.
13. This precious stone also mentioned in 21:20 is either dark blue or dark red. GK *5610*.
14. That is, yellow. Used only here. GK *2523*. John could mean the breastplates are tri-colored; or, that there are ones of each color.
15. Same word as in v 18. On this word, see 14:10. Related to "of-sulphur" preceding.
16. Same word as in 1:16.
17. John could mean all three come from each horse; or, that one plague comes from each horse.
18. On this word, see "wound" in 13:3. Some manuscripts omit this word {N}.
19. Some manuscripts repeat "by" with the next two {N}, "and by the smoke and by the sulphur".
20. Some manuscripts say "For their authority is in" {K}.
21. This phrase modifies "tails". Their tails have heads. This is the sense in which they resemble snakes.
22. Or, "not". GK *4028*. Not the same word as in v 21. Some manuscripts do have the same word as v 21 {N}.
23. This word refers to the potions, drugs, charms, and poisons used in sorcery. Used only here. GK *5760*. Related to "sorcerer" in 21:8; and "sorcery" in 18:23, the broader word (which some manuscripts have here {N}).
24. Some would place 10:1-11:14 at the "C" level in the outline, between the sixth and seventh trumpet, in a similar manner to the two points in chapter 7. In the TransLine, it is placed here because John does not begin with "After these things" (indicating a change of subject) as in chapter 7, and because John specifically closes the sixth trumpet (the second woe) in 11:14. Some think the sixth trumpet, the second woe, extends from 9:13 to 11:13. Others think it extends from 9:13 to 9:21, and that chapters 10-11 are unrelated visions, similar to the two visions in chapter 7.
25. Some think this is symbolic of Christ, due to similarities in the description; others think it is another strong angel, as in 5:2.
26. John's perspective for the visions in 10:1-11:14 is from earth. Note v 1, 4, 8, 11:12.
27. Or, "having put on *a* cloud".
28. Elsewhere in this book only in 1:7; 11:12; 14:14, 15, 16. On this word, see 14:14.
29. Some think this is an emerald rainbow like the one in 4:3. Others think it is like the well-known multi-colored rainbow.
30. Or, "upon". GK *2093*.
31. Compare 1:16; 18:1.
32. Compare 1:15.
33. Or, "having". Some manuscripts say "And he had" {N}.
34. This is a participle, "having been opened". Same word as in v 8. GK *487*.
35. Elsewhere only in v 9, 10. GK *1044*. Note also v 8. Some think this is the scroll of 5:1, which is now open. Others think its contents are chapter 11; or 11-22, the prophecies yet to be given to John. Others think it is John's commission, v 11, emphasizing the magnitude of what is coming. Others think it is the gospel, or the Word of God.
36. Some think this symbolizes that this angel's message is for the whole world; some think the land and sea symbolizes the land of Israel and the Gentile nations. Others think it symbolizes the angel's authority over the whole world.
37. Some think these are spoken by angels; others, by God.
38. Some manuscripts add "their voices" {K}, as in v 3.
39. Some think this is the voice of God; others, Christ; others, an angel. Some manuscripts add "*to* me" {K}.
40. Some manuscripts omit this word {N}.
41. Same word as in Jam 5:12. The angel raises his right hand and swears a solemn oath. Similar to Dan 12:7.
42. Some manuscripts omit "and the sea and the *things* in it" {A}.

A. Mt 5:19, break B. 1 Cor 7:27 C. Mk 14:15 D. Rev 13:17 E. Act 23:10 F. Rev 6:8 G. Act 7:24, wronged H. 2 Pet 3:16, other J. Act 26:20
K. Mt 26:10 L. Rev 4:10 M. Act 9:1 N. 1 Cor 5:1 O. 1 Tim 3:15 P. Mt 8:29 Q. Eph 1:13 R. Rev 20:10 S. Eph 2:15

2F. That there will be no more time[1] [of delay], *but during the days *of* the sound[2] *of* the seventh angel— when he is about-to[3] trumpet[4]— the mystery[5] *of* God[6] was indeed[7] finished[8] 7

    1G. As He announced-as-good-news-to[A] His slaves[B], the prophets[9]

3D. And the voice which I heard from heaven[10] *was* again speaking with me, and saying "Go, take the opened scroll[11] in the hand *of* the angel standing upon the sea and upon the land" 8

    1E. And I went to the angel, telling him to give[12] me the little-scroll[13] 9
    2E. And he says *to* me, "Take, and eat it up[14]. And it will make your stomach bitter. But in your mouth it will be sweet[C] like honey[15]"
    3E. And I took the little-scroll[16] out of the hand *of* the angel, and I ate it up. And it was like sweet honey in my mouth. And when I ate it, my stomach was made-bitter[D] 10
    4E. And they[17] say *to* me, "You must[E] prophesy[F] again[18] for[19] many peoples[G] and nations and tongues and kings"[20] 11

4D. And *a measuring*-rod[21] resembling[H] *a* staff[22] was given[23] *to* me, saying[24] 11:1

    1E. "Arise[J], and measure[25] the temple[26] *of* God,[27] and the altar[K], and the *ones* worshiping[L] in it. *And put[M] the court[N] outside *of* the temple on-the-outside[28], and do not measure it, because it was given *to* the Gentiles[29] 2
    2E. And they will trample[30] the holy city[31] *for* forty and[32] two months[33]

1. This answers the question of 6:10, "how long?". No more time will intervene. Similar to Dan 12:6-7. Some think this means "time" in an absolute sense. On this word, see 2 Tim 1:9.
2. Or, "blast" as in 8:13, the "blast" of the trumpet.
3. Or, "going to". This word and grammar, "when... about to", is elsewhere only in Mk 13:4; Lk 21:7, "the sign when these things are about to take place". On this word, see "going to" in Mk 10:32.
4. This phrase is meant to clarify the last. This could mean "when he is about to begin to trumpet", or, "when he shall trumpet". Some think it means that when he raises the trumpet to blow it, the delay will be over, God's final judgment is here. Others think he means that the delay will end with the content of the seventh trumpet. Note 16:17.
5. Same word as in 1:20; 17:5, 7. On this word, see Rom 11:25.
6. Some think this means the mystery of God carrying out His wrath toward sin; others, of God's whole purpose in human history, His plan of redemption and judgment. Note what is said after the seventh trumpet is blown, 11:15-18.
7. Or, "also".
8. Or, "completed, accomplished, fulfilled". The angel vividly states this future event as if it had already occurred, pointing to its certainty. A similar statement is made with the seventh bowl in 16:17, using a different word and tense, "It is done". Same word as in 11:7; 15:1, 8; 17:17; 20:3, 5, 7; Mt 7:28; 10:23; 11:1; 13:53; 19:1; 26:1; Lk 2:39; Jn 19:28, 30; 2 Tim 4:7. Elsewhere only as "accomplished" in Lk 12:50; "perfected" in 2 Cor 12:9; "fulfilled" in Lk 18:31; 22:37; Act 13:29; Rom 2:27; Gal 5:16; Jam 2:8; and "pay" in Mt 17:24; Rom 13:6. GK *5464*. Related to "perfect" in 2 Cor 7:1 and in Heb 2:10; "complete" in 1 Cor 13:10; and "end" in Rom 10:4.
9. Some think this means the OT prophets; others, the NT prophets; others, both. On this word, see 1 Cor 12:28.
10. That is, the voice in v 4. The focus shifts from the angel to John.
11. Some manuscripts say "little-scroll" {N}, as in v 2. On this word, see 5:1.
12. Some manuscripts have this as a command, "... him, "Give me the little scroll" {N}.
13. Some manuscripts say "scroll" {N}, as in v 8.
14. Or, "devour it, consume it". Same word as in 10:10; and "devour" in 11:5; 12:4; 20:9. On this word, see "devour" in Mk 12:40. Similar to Ezek 2:8-3:3, where eating symbolized "filling your body" with God's words.
15. Some think this means the prophecies of God's righteous wrath are sweet at first, but also bitter once pondered; others, that the gospel is sweet for believers, but includes a bitter message regarding unbelievers.
16. Some manuscripts say "scroll" {N}, as in v 8.
17. That is, the voice from heaven and the angel, v 8. Or, an indefinite "they", meaning "it was said to me". Some manuscripts say "he says" {N}, referring to the angel.
18. Some think this is referring to the prophecy of chapter 11, in which case this could be combined with the next sentence in point 4D.; others, to chapters 11-22. Some think John sat down or laid down (note 11:1, "Arise, Get up") due to his bitter stomach. In other words, "you are not finished yet, you have much more to prophesy in addition to what has been prophesied to this point. Rise and measure...".
19. Some think this means John must prophesy "for" them, prophesy things destined to occur to them (as this word is used in Jn 12:16; Rev 22:16); others, "against" them (as it is used in Lk 12:53); others, "about" them; others, "before" them. GK *2093*.
20. Similar to the phrase in 11:9; 13:7; 14:6; 17:15. "Nations" is used 3 times in Revelation before this verse, 19 times after. "Kings" is used 3 times in Revelation before this verse, 17 times after.
21. This is similar to Ezek 40:3; Zech 2:1; Rev 21:15. Same word as "rod" in 21:15, 16. On this word, see "stick" in Mk 15:36.
22. John may mean a walking stick or a shepherd's rod. On this word, see "rod" in 1 Cor 4:21.
23. By whom? The only candidate in the context is the angel of 10:9. Otherwise, John does not tell us.
24. Some manuscripts say "*to* me. And the angel stood, saying, Rise..." {A}. Some think the one speaking is the voice of the angel in 10:1, 5, 8; others, the voice from heaven in 10:4, 8.
25. John measures to identify and mark off what is God's (the temple and its worshipers). The things that do not belong to God are not measured. Some think this is symbolic of marking believers for God's protection during the wrath that falls in v 13, or in the bowls, or in the book. Some think it is the same thing as the sealing in 7:4.
26. That is, the inner sanctuary, the Holy Place and the Holy of Holies, as opposed to the rest of the temple complex included in what is mentioned in v 2. Used in Revelation only in 3:12; 7:15; 11:1, 2, 19; 14:15, 17; 15:5, 6, 8; 16:1, 17; 21:22. This word is used of the temple, the sanctuary of the temple, the body as a temple (as in 1 Cor 6:19), and the church as a temple (Eph 2:21). Used 45 times. GK *3724*. See also the unrelated word in Act 19:27.
27. Some holding the Future View think John means a future temple on earth in Jerusalem, 2 Thes 2:4; Dan 9:27; Ezek 40-48. Others think the temple, altar, worshipers and holy city all symbolize "the church", and "trampling" its persecution. Others think this refers to the temple in Jerusalem in the first century to illustrate the separation of this age.
28. That is, leave it out, omit it, exclude it, do not include it on the inside. The word "outside" is repeated twice, and the verb also includes it. More literally, "throw-out the outside court *of* the temple outside" your measurement.
29. Or, "nations". On this word, see Act 15:23.
30. Or, "tread". Same word as in Lk 21:24, where Jerusalem will be trampled until the times of the Gentiles are fulfilled. On this word, see Lk 10:19. The Past View (see 1:1) thinks this is the destruction of Jerusalem by the Romans; the Spiritual View and some holding the Future View, a symbol of the persecuted church. Others holding the Future View think it is a persecution of end-time Israel by the Gentile nations.
31. The "holy city" is mentioned in Mt 4:5; 27:53, Jerusalem; and in Rev 21:2, 10; 22:19, the New Jerusalem.
32. Some manuscripts omit this word {C}.
33. Forty-two months is also mentioned in 13:5. It is equivalent to 1260 days, 11:3; 12:6. See also 12:14, time, times, and half a time. Some take the time indicated literally; others, as symbolic (half of seven) of a limited time, the limited time of the wicked's triumph. Some think the periods are concurrent. Some holding the Future View think the two witnesses (11:3) and the protection of the woman (12:6, 14) are in the first half of the seven-year tribulation, and the beast (13:5) and this trampling of Jerusalem (11:2) are in the second half of it. Others holding the Future View think they all refer to the second half of the tribulation.

A. Act 5:42 B. Rev 1:1 C. Jam 3:12 D. Col 3:19 E. Mt 16:21 F. 1 Cor 14:1 G. Rev 21:3 H. Rev 1:13 J. Mt 28:6 K. Rev 8:3 L. Rev 4:10 M. Jn 12:31, cast out N. Mt 26:3, courtyard

	3E. "And I will give *authority to* my two witnesses,[1] and they will prophesy[2] *for* one-thousand two-hundred sixty days, having been clothed-with[3] sackcloth	3
	1F. "These are the two olive-trees[4] and the two lampstands[A] standing in the presence of the Lord[5] *of* the earth	4
	2F. "And if anyone is intending[6] to harm[B] them, fire[7] comes-out[8] of their mouth and devours[C] their enemies. Indeed,[9] if anyone should intend to harm them, in this manner he must[D] be killed	5
	3F. "These *ones* have the authority[10] to shut[E] the heaven[F] in-order-that[11] no rain may fall *for* the days *of* their prophecy[12]	6
	4F. "And they have authority over the waters[G]— to be turning them into blood[H]— and *authority* to strike the earth[13] with every plague[J], as often as they may want[K]	
	4E. "And when they finish[L] their testimony[M], the beast coming up out of the abyss[14] will make war[15] against them, and overcome[N] them, and kill them	7
	1F. "And their corpse[16] *will be* on the wide-road[O] *of* the great city which spiritually[17] is called Sodom and Egypt[18]— where also their[19] Lord was crucified[20]	8
	2F. "And *some* from[21] the peoples and tribes and tongues and nations look-at[22] their corpse *for* three and *a* half days	9
	3F. "And they do not permit[23] their corpses to be put[P] in *a* tomb[Q]	
	4F. "And the *ones* dwelling upon the earth[24] rejoice[25] over them and celebrate[R]	10
	5F. "And they will send[26] gifts[S] *to* one another, because these two prophets tormented[T] the *ones* dwelling upon the earth	
	5E. "And after the three and *a* half days, *a* breath[27] *of* life from God entered in them, and they stood on their feet	11
	1F. "And great fear[U] fell upon the *ones* seeing[V] them[28]	
	2F. "And they[29] heard *a* loud voice from heaven saying *to* them, "Come-up here". And they went-up into heaven in the cloud, and their enemies watched[V] them	12
	3F. "And at that hour *a* great earthquake[W] took place, and *a* tenth *of* the city fell	13
	4F. "And seven thousand names[30] *of* people[X] were killed in the earthquake, and the rest[Y] became terrified[Z] and gave glory[31] *to* the God *of* heaven"	
5D.	The second woe passed-away[32]. Behold— the third woe is coming quickly[33]	14
9C.	And the seventh angel trumpeted[34]	15
	1D. And there came[35] loud voices in heaven,[36] saying "The kingdom[37] *of* the world became[38] *the kingdom of* our Lord and *of* His Christ. And He will reign[AA] forever and ever[BB]"	
	2D. And the twenty four elders sitting on their thrones in the presence of God fell on their faces and gave-worship[CC] *to* God, saying "We give-thanks[DD] *to* You, Lord God Almighty[EE], the *One Who* is and *Who* was[39]	16 17
	1E. "Because You have taken[FF] Your great power[GG], and You *began to* reign[40]	
	2E. "And the nations became-angry[41]	18

1. Some holding the Future View (see 1:1) think these are Enoch and Elijah, because they did not die (Heb 11:5; 2 Kings 2:11; Mal 4:5), or Moses and Elijah, because they appeared on the mountain at the transfiguration of Christ (Mt 17:4). The Spiritual View thinks they are symbolic of the church, or its martyrs in particular. Some holding the Past View think they are literal prophets in Jerusalem during that time. On this word, see Act 1:8.
2. That is, regarding the judgment about to fall, and what people should do in light of it. On this word, see 1 Cor 14:1.
3. Or, "having put on sackcloth".
4. Compare Zech 4:3, 12-14.
5. Some manuscripts say "*of* God" {N}.
6. Or, "wanting, willing, desiring". Same word as later in the verse. On this word, see "willing" in Jn 7:17.
7. Those who identify the two witnesses as the church thinks this symbolizes the future judgment of God. Those who think they are two individuals take it literally, or as a symbol of immediate destruction caused by their pronouncement.
8. Fire going out from the mouth is also mentioned in 9:17, 18.
9. The first sentence states the fact, this one states the warning.
10. They have the same power and resources as Moses and Elijah. On this word, see 6:8.
11. Or, "so that no rain falls". GK *2671*.
12. That is, the days of their prophetic activity, the 1260 days. Note Jam 5:17. On this word, see 1 Cor 12:10.
13. Or, "land". On this word, see 7:1.
14. The beast is mentioned in this manner again in 17:8. On "beast", see 13:1. On "abyss", see 9:1.
15. Some think that "make war" implies that these are not simply two individuals, but symbolic of many witnesses; others, that one does not simply "kill" these two, v 5. This speaks of the effort required to accomplish it. On the phrase "make war", see 13:7.
16. Some think that the singular "corpse" implies they are symbolic. It is plural in v 9b. On this word, see Mk15:45.
17. Elsewhere only in 1 Cor 2:14. GK *4462*. Related to "spiritual" in 1 Cor 14:1.
18. Some think these names symbolize moral corruption, and spiritual oppression of believers.
19. Some manuscripts say "our" {N}.
20. Those who think the two witnesses are the church think John is referring to Jerusalem as symbolic of all the cities of the world, as perhaps also in 18:24. Others accept the literal reference of the words. On this word, see Mt 27:35.
21. Same phrase as in 3:9; and "*some* of " in 2:10.
22. On this word, see "see" in 1:11. Some manuscripts say "will look at" {K}.
23. On this word, see "forgive" in Mt 6:12. Some manuscripts say "will not permit" {N}.
24. Or, "land". On this phrase, see 3:10.
25. On this word, see 2 Cor 13:11. Some manuscripts say "will rejoice... and will celebrate" {N}.
26. Some manuscripts say "they send" {N}.
27. Or, "spirit". Same word as in 13:15.
28. After all, what can they do besides kill them? The fear proceeds from the witnesses' clearly unstoppable power, and their killers' impotence.
29. Some manuscripts say "I" {B}.
30. Same idiom as in 3:4.
31. Compare 6:16; 9:20. Some think this indicates a genuine repentance. Others, think it is due to terror. On this word, see 2 Pet 2:10.
32. Same word as in 9:12; and as 21:1, 4. GK *599*.
33. Or, "soon". On this word, see 22:7. That is, the seventh trumpet.
34. Some think the woeful content is seen in the seven bowls in chapter 16. Here the heavenly rejoicing is given. See the note on 8:2.
35. Same word as in 8:5 and as "become" next.
36. Note that here, John's perspective returns to heaven. Compare 10:1.
37. That is, the kingdom presently ruled by Satan, Eph 2:2; 1 Jn 5:19. On this word, see Mt 3:2. Some manuscripts have this word plural {N}.
38. Or, "was made". GK *1181*. The moment has arrived. This is stated as if it were already accomplished. Some holding the Spiritual and Past Views (see 1:1) think this is referring to Christ's present reign in His spiritual kingdom over His own subjects. Others think it refers to His future reign in full glory over everyone, including His enemies.
39. Some manuscripts add "and *Who* is coming" {B}, as in 1:4. Some think John omits it because God has now come. His coming is here. Note 16:5, where the same issue arises.
40. Or, "You reigned, became king". Same word and tense as in 19:6. God began to visibly reign over His enemies.
41. Or, "became wrathful". God asserted His rule, took control of this world, and the nations became angry and wrathful, not repentant. Elsewhere only in Mt 5:22; 18:34; 22:7; Lk 14:21; 15:28; Eph 4:26; Rev 12:17. GK *3974*. Related to "wrath" in 16:19.

A. Rev 1:12 B. Act 7:24, wronged C. Mk 12:40 D. Mt 16:21 E. Jn 20:19, locked F. 2 Cor 12:2 G. Jn 3:23 H. 1 Jn 1:7 J. Rev 13:3, wound K. Jn 7:17, willing L. Rev 10:7 M. Jn 1:7 N. Rev 2:7 O. Lk 14:21 P. Act 19:21 Q. Lk 23:53 R. Rev 12:12 S. Mt 5:23 T. Rev 14:10 U. Eph 5:21. V. Lk 10:18, seeing W. Rev 11:19 X. Mt 4:4, mankind Y. 2 Pet 3:16, other Z. Lk 24:37 AA. Rev 19:6 BB. Rev 20:10 CC. Rev 4:10 DD. Mt 26:27 EE. Rev 1:8 FF. Rom 7:8 GG. Mk 5:30

Revelation 11:19	990	Verse

      3E. "And Your wrath[1] came[2], and the time[A]

          1F. *For* the dead[3] to be judged[B]
          2F. "And to give the reward[C] *to* Your slaves[D] the prophets and the saints[E] and[4] the *ones* fearing[F] Your name— the small and the great
          3F. "And to destroy the *ones* destroying[5] the earth[6]"

4B. And the temple[G] *of* God in heaven was opened.[7] And the ark[H] *of* His covenant[8] appeared[9] in His temple. And there came lightnings and voices and thunders[10] and *an* earthquake[11] and *a* great hail   19

  1C. And *a* great sign[J] appeared in heaven—   12:1

      1D. *There was a* woman[12], having been clothed-with the sun, and the moon *was* under her feet and *a* crown[K] *of* twelve stars[13] on her head, *and having a child* in *her* womb[L]   2
      2D. And[14] she is crying-out[15]— suffering-birth-pains[M], and being-in-torment[16] to give-birth[N]

  2C. And another sign appeared in heaven—   3

      1D. And behold— *there was a* great fire-red[17] dragon[18], having seven heads and ten horns, and seven diadems[19] on his heads

          1E. And his tail sweeps-away[20] *a* third *of* the stars[21] *of* heaven[O] and threw them to the earth   4

      2D. And the dragon is standing[22] before the woman being about to give-birth[N], in order that when she gives-birth, he might devour[P] her child[Q]

          1E. And she gave-birth[N] to *a* Son, *a* male[R] *child,* Who is going to shepherd[23] all the nations with *an* iron rod   5
          2E. And her child[Q] was snatched-up[24] to God, and to His throne
          3E. And the woman fled[25] into the wilderness[26] where she has *a* place there[27] having been prepared[S] by God, in order that they might nourish[28] her there *for* one-thousand two-hundred sixty days[29]   6

      3D. And[30] there was *a* war[31] in heaven.[32] Michael[33] and his angels *were*[34] to fight[35] against the dragon   7

          1E. And the dragon and his angels fought. *And he[36] did not prevail[37], nor was *a* place[38] *for* them[39] still found in heaven   8

1. Same root word as "angry". They became angry and Your anger came; their wrath was provoked and Your wrath came. On this word, see 16:19.
2. On this word, see 6:17.
3. That is, all the dead, resulting in reward for believers, and the punishment for others described in 20:11-15. The time has arrived. The details of this are given later in the book.
4. Or, "even". This could refer to two groups, "Your slaves the prophets, and the saints, even the *ones* fearing...". Compare 10:7. Or, "Your slaves— the prophets and the saints— even the *ones* fearing...". Compare 16:6, 18:20. Others punctuate it to indicate three groups— prophets, saints and ones fearing (as perhaps in 18:24).
5. Or, "corrupting". Same word as earlier, and as in 8:9. On this word, see 2 Cor 4:16. Related to "corrupted" in 19:2.
6. Or, "land". On this word, see 7:1.
7. Some think this verse is the conclusion of the seventh trumpet (making it point 3D.), and begin the new section with 12:1 (either as point 4B. or 4D.). Some holding the Past View (see 1:1) think what follows continues to depict the destruction of Israel; others, that it moves on to describe the destruction of the Roman Empire. In the TransLine, this opening of the temple is taken as introducing the next heavenly scene, the next subject-grouping, which through three signs in heaven gives a panoramic view of history from the ark Moses copied to the end of the age. The progression of heavenly scenes at the B. level is, the seals are opened, the trumpets blow, the temple is opened here. Then the temple of the tabernacle is opened in 15:5, heaven is opened in 19:11, heaven and earth disappear in 20:11, the new heaven and earth appear in 21:1.
8. That is, the box containing the covenant. This ark is mentioned only here and Heb 9:4 in the NT. The heavenly ark symbolizes God's commitment to the covenant, and its enduring force. He keeps it in a safe and honored place. This is the heavenly ark Moses copied (Heb 8:5). The earthly ark was kept in the tabernacle (in the Holy of Holies), and the heavenly tabernacle may be the "temple" in view here (called the "tabernacle of testimony" in 15:5). Some manuscripts add "*of* the Lord" {N}. On this word, see Heb 8:6.
9. Or, "was seen". Same word as in 12:1, 3, on which see "see" in Lk 2:26.
10. These three things occurred when John entered heaven in 4:5, and prior to the trumpets in 8:5. Here some think they mark the beginning of a new scene. They occur once more at the beginning of the seventh bowl in 16:18.
11. An earthquake occurs prior to the trumpets (8:5), and the heavenly signs (11:19). A great earthquake occurs in the sixth seal (6:12), and in the sixth trumpet (11:13). The greatest earthquake occurs in the seventh bowl (16:18). Used 14 times. GK *4939*.
12. This woman is not Mary alone, as v 17 makes clear. Some think she represents believing Israel; others, the whole believing community, including Israel (which gives Jesus birth) and the church (her persecuted seed, v 17).
13. These may represent the twelve tribes of Israel. Note Gen 37:9, where Jacob is the sun, Rachel the moon. On this word, see 6:13.
14. Some manuscripts omit this word {N}, so that it says "And having *a child* in *her* womb, she is crying out".
15. On this word, see Mt 8:29. Some manuscripts say "cried out" {N}.
16. Or, "being in torture, anguish". On this word, see 14:10.
17. Same word as in 6:4. Some think this symbolizes Satan's murderous character. He kills through deception.
18. That is, Satan, 12:9; 20:2. Elsewhere only in 12:4, 7, 13, 16, 17; 13:2, 4, 11; 16:13. GK *1532*.
19. That is, king's crowns. See 13:1; Dan 7:7-8. Some think the heads, horns and crowns symbolize Satan's great power; others suggest a more specific meaning in keeping with the explanation given in 17:9-12.
20. Elsewhere only as "drag" in Jn 21:8; Act 14:19; 17:6; and "drag away" in Act 8:3. GK *5359*. It may imply an unwillingness to go.
21. Some think this refers to angels who rebelled with Satan. See "stars" in 6:13. Note that this is some time prior to the birth of the Child.
22. GK *2705*. Or, "was standing" (GK *5112*), which would be followed later by "when she gave birth".
23. On this phrase, "shepherd with an iron rod", see 2:27.
24. Or, "snatched away". Note the jump from Christ's birth to His ascension. On this word, see "snatched away" in 2 Cor 12:2.
25. The Spiritual View (see 1:1) thinks this is symbolic of the preservation of believers through the trials and persecutions of this world. The Past View thinks it refers to the flight of Christians from Israel before A.D. 70. The Future View thinks this jumps forward to the end time and a flight to safety during the tribulation, the next thing to say about her. Compare Mt 24:15-28. On this word, see 1 Cor 6:18.
26. Or, "desert". Same word as in v 14. On this word, see Mt 3:1.
27. Some manuscripts omit this word {N}.
28. Or, "provide for, feed". Who "they" are is not stated. Same word as in v 14; and as "provided for" in Act 12:20. On this word, see "feed" in Lk 23:29.
29. On this time period, see "forty and two months" in 11:2.
30. Some think this explains why the woman had to flee, and that v 6 is resumed in v 13-14.
31. Or, "battle, fight". This word may mean an extended war, or a single battle. Same word as in Mt 24:6; Mk 13:7; Lk 21:9; and in the phrase "make war", on which see 13:7. Elsewhere only as "battle" in Lk 14:31; 1 Cor 14:8; Heb 11:34; Rev 9:7, 9; 16:14; 20:8; and "fight" in Jam 4:1. GK *4483*. Related to the verb "fight" next.
32. Some think this occurred at the original fall of Satan; others, at the Cross (Lk 10:18; Jn 12:31; 16:11); others, at Christ's ascension in v 5. Some holding the Future View think it will occur before the future tribulation, or at its midpoint, Dan 9:27; 12:1, 7.
33. This angel is the guardian of Israel in Dan 10:13, 21; 12:1. Mentioned elsewhere only in Jude 9. GK *3640*.
34. This verb is supplied from the first sentence. GK *1181*.
35. The grammar is of this sentence is unusual. Supplying "were", this gives the purpose of Michael, and may imply that Michael initiated the war to force Satan out of heaven. Others think that Satan initiated it, and the task of forcing him out was given to Michael. Without supplying "were", the grammar is unclear. Consult the commentaries. On this word, see 2:16.
36. Some manuscripts say "they" {N}.
37. Or, "he was not strong-*enough,* he was not able". On this word, see "can do" in Gal 5:6.
38. That is, they lost their place in heaven. Their place is now on earth, for a short time, v 12.
39. Some manuscripts say "him" {N}.

A. Mt 8:29 B. Mt 7:1 C. Rev 22:12, recompense D. Rev 1:1 E. 1 Pet 1:16, holy F. Eph 5:33, respecting G. Rev 11:1 H. Heb 9:4
J. 2 Thes 2:9 K. Rev 4:4 L. 1 Thes 5:3 M. Gal 4:19 N. Lk 2:11, born O. 2 Cor 12:2 P. Mk 12:40 Q. 1 Jn 3:1 R. Mt 19:4 S. Mk 14:15

| Revelation 12:9 | 992 | Verse |

    2E. And the great dragon was thrown-*down*[A]— the ancient[B] serpent[1], the *one* being called[C] *the* devil[2] and Satan[3], the *one* deceiving[D] the whole world[4]— he was thrown-*down* to the earth[5]. And his angels were thrown-*down* with him   9

    3E. And I heard *a* loud voice in heaven, saying   10

        1F. "Now[6] the salvation[7] and the power[E] and the kingdom[F] *of* our God and the authority[G] *of* His Christ came[8], because the accuser[9] *of* our brothers[H] was thrown-*down*— the *one* accusing[J] them[10] before our God *by* day and *by* night[11]

            1G. "And **they**[12] overcame[13] him because-of[14] the blood[K] *of* the Lamb and because of the word[L] *of* their testimony[15]. And they did not love[16] their life until[17] death[18]   11

        2F. "For this reason— celebrate[19], heavens, and the *ones* dwelling[M] in them. Woe *for* the land[20] and the sea, because the devil went down to you   12

            1G. "Having great fury[N]
            2G. "Knowing that he has *a* short[21] time[O]"

  4D. And when[22] the dragon saw that he was thrown-*down* to the earth, he pursued[23] the woman who gave-birth to the male *Child*   13

    1E. And the two wings *of* the great eagle[P] were given *to* the woman in order that she might fly into the wilderness, into her place where she is nourished there *for a* time and times and half *of a* time[24] from *the* presence *of* the serpent   14

    2E. And the serpent threw[25] water[26] from his mouth after the woman like *a* river, in order that he might cause[Q] her *to be* swept-away-by-a-river[27]   15

    3E. And the earth helped[28] the woman. Indeed the earth opened its mouth and swallowed-up[R] the river which the dragon threw from his mouth   16

  5D. And the dragon became-angry[S] at the woman, and he went to make war[T] against the rest[U] *of* her seed[29]— the *ones* keeping[V] the commandments[W] *of* God and holding[X] the testimony[Y] *of* Jesus[30]. *And he stood[31] on the sand *of* the sea   17   18

  6D. And I saw *a* beast[32] coming-up out of the sea,[33] having ten horns and seven heads,[34] and ten diadems[35] upon his horns, and names[36] *of* blasphemy[37] on his heads   13:1

    1E. And the beast which I saw was resembling[Z] *a* leopard, and his feet *were* like *ones of a* bear, and his mouth *was* like *a* mouth *of a* lion[38]   2

    2E. And the dragon gave him his power[E] and his throne[AA] and great authority[G]

1. Or, "snake", referring to Gen 3. Satan is called this in 2 Cor 11:3; Rev 12:14, 15; 20:2. Used 14 times. GK *4058*.
2. This word means "slanderer". Used in this sense 34 times, and as "slanderous" three times (see 1 Tim 3:11). GK *1333*.
3. This is a transliteration of a Hebrew word meaning "adversary". Used 36 times. GK *4928*.
4. On this "whole world", see 3:10.
5. Note that here Satan is thrown out of heaven. In 20:3 he is thrown into the abyss. In 20:10 he is thrown into the lake of fire.
6. Or, "At this moment, At this time". Elsewhere by John only Jn 2:10; 5:17; 9:19, 25; 13:7, 19, 33, 37 ("right now"); 14:7; 16:12, 24, 31; 1 Jn 2:9; Rev 14:13. See "right now" in 2 Thes 2:7 for Paul's uses of this word. Used 36 times. GK *785*.
7. Or, "deliverance". Same word as in 7:10; 19:1, on which see Lk 19:9.
8. Or, "came about, took place, came to pass". Some think this took place at the Cross and is experienced now spiritually. Others think it is a still future event. GK *1181*.
9. Used only here. GK *2992*. Related to the verb following.
10. This is why Jesus is interceding for us, Heb 7:25.
11. On the idiom "*by* day and *by* night", see 7:15.
12. That is, the brothers, v 10. Some take the mention of "death" that follows to mean these brothers are martyrs.
13. Or, "were victorious over". On this word, see 2:7.
14. Or, "by reason of". This word is used twice in this verse. GK *1328*. Same word as in 1:9; 4:11; 6:9; 13:14; 20:4. John uses the word "by" in 1:5 (GK *1877*).
15. Some think John means "the Word of God (the gospel) to which they bore testimony". Compare "testimony *of* Jesus" in 19:10. On this word, see Jn 1:7.
16. John does not mean these believers did not love to live. Rather, they did not choose to focus and direct their love toward life on this earth, but toward life with Jesus. On this word, see "*devotedly* love" in Jn 21:15.
17. Or, "as far as, up to". Same word as in 2:10, "be faithful until death". These believers loved Jesus more than their life, until they died, as Jesus directed in Jn 12:25.
18. This could refer to a martyr's death; or, more broadly, to the end of their lives, however they died.
19. Or, "be glad, be cheered, make merry, enjoy yourself". It is used of festive rejoicing and celebration with others. Same word as 11:10; 18:20; and as Lk 15:23, 24, 29, 32; Act 7:41; Rom 15:10; Gal 4:27. Elsewhere only as "enjoy oneself" (without a specific object of celebration) in Lk 12:19; 16:19; and as "cheer" in Act 2:26; 2 Cor 2:2. GK *2370*. Related to "gladness" (the joy of celebration) in Act 2:28.
20. Or, "earth". On this word, see 7:1.
21. Same word as in 17:10.
22. Some think that this verse picks up from v 6, with v 14 repeating v 6, and resuming from that point. The same views of the timing of v 6 are found here.
23. Or, "persecuted", but v 14 may indicate he could not catch her. This word is used both ways, as "pursue" in 1 Cor 14:1; and as "persecute" in 2 Tim 3:12. GK *1503*.
24. This time notation is equivalent to 1260 days in v 6, which is three and one half years. It is found elsewhere only in Dan 7:25; 12:7. On this time notation, see "forty and two months" in 11:2.
25. This is the common word "throw, cast", used 122 times. Not related to "spew" in 3:16, or "spit" in Mk 7:33. Same word as "thrown-*down*" in v 9.
26. Some think this is symbolic of an army or some overwhelming force; others think it could be literal; others take it as a flood of false teachings in contrast to the water of life.
27. Or, "river-borne". This adjective is used only here. GK *4533*. Related to "river" earlier.
28. Or, "gave aid *to*, came to the aid *of*". Elsewhere only in Mt 15:25; Mk 9:2, 24; Act 16:9; 21:28; 2 Cor 6:2; Heb 2:18. GK *1070*. Related to "help" in Heb 4:16; and "helper" in Heb 13:6.
29. That is, her spiritual descendants, Gal 3:29. The sign moves from the Child, to the woman, to her children. John clearly means Christians, but some think he means Gentile Christians as distinct from the Jewish mother church; others, Jewish Christians; others, the 144,000; others, all Christians. On this word, see Heb 11:11.
30. A similar phrase occurs in 14:12. This could mean "the testimony *given by* Jesus", or, "the testimony *concerning* Jesus". In either case, it is the gospel. Some manuscripts add "Christ" {K}.
31. Some manuscripts say "And I stood" {B}, referring to John in 13:1.
32. The word "beast" means "wild animal". Same word as in 11:7; 13:2, 3, 4, 11, 12, 14, 15, 17, 18; 14:9, 11; 15:2; 16:2, 10, 13; 17:3, 7, 8, 11, 12, 13, 16, 17; 19:19, 20; 20:4, 10. Daniel's four beasts also came out of the sea, Dan 7:3. Some think the beast is the Roman Empire (and its heads, the emperors); others, a symbol of anti-Christian government throughout history; others, the final world empire; others, the end-time Antichrist. Many hold a combination of these views. Elsewhere only as "wild beast" in Mk 1:13; Act 11:6; Rev 6:8; 18:2; "beast" in Act 28:4 and 5 (a snake); Tit 1:12; and "wild animal" in Heb 12:20; Jam 3:7. GK *2563*.
33. Some think the sea is symbolic of "nations", as in 17:15; Dan 7:17; others, of the abyss, Rev 11:7. Others take it literally.
34. The dragon has seven heads and ten horns, 12:3; the beast has ten horns and seven heads, his mirror image. The beast and the seven heads (kings) and ten horns (kings) are explained in 17:7-18. Daniel's fourth beast also had ten horns, Dan 7:7. Some manuscripts say "seven heads and ten horns" {K}.
35. Elsewhere only of the dragon's seven diadems in 12:3; and Christ's "many" in 19:12. GK *1343*. A diadem is a king's crown, as opposed to the victor's crown or wreath mentioned in 4:4. Here only are they on the horns, not the heads, which is why there are ten instead of seven. They are on the horns to indicate that the horns are kings, 17:12.
36. Some manuscripts say "*a* name" {C}. John seems to mean one name on each head, as with the diadems on the horns. Both "names" and "name" could mean a different name on each, or the same name on each.
37. That is, names characterized by blasphemy, blasphemous names. On this word, see 1 Tim 6:4.
38. The lion, the bear, and the leopard were the first three beasts in Daniel's vision, Dan 7:4-6.

A. Rev 2:22, throw B. Act 15:7, old C. Rom 8:30 D. Jam 5:19, err E. Mk 5:30 F. Mt 3:2 G. Rev 6:8 H. Act 16:40 J. Jn 5:45 K. 1 Jn 1:7 L. 1 Cor 12:8 M. Rev 7:15 N. Rev 16:19 O. Mt 8:29 P. Rev 8:13 Q. Rev 13:13, does R. Heb 11:29 S. Rev 11:18 T. Rev 13:7 U. 2 Pet 3:16, other V. 1 Jn 5:18 W. Mk 12:28 X. 1 Jn 1:8, have Y. Jn 1:7 Z. Rev 1:13 AA. Rev 20:11

3E.	And *I saw* one of his heads as-*if* having been slain[1] to[2] death. And his wound[3] *of* death[4] was cured[5]	3
4E.	And the whole earth was caused-to-marvel[6] [while following] after the beast	
	1F. And they gave-worship[7] *to* the dragon, because he gave the authority[A] *to* the beast	4
	2F. And they gave worship *to* the beast saying, "Who *is* like the beast, and who can wage-war[8] against him?"	
5E.	And *a* mouth was given *to* him speaking great *things*[9] and[10] blasphemies[B]. And authority[A] to act[11] *for* forty and[12] two months was given *to* him	5
	1F. And he opened his mouth for blasphemies[B] against God— to blaspheme[C]	6
	1G. His name	
	2G. And His dwelling[13]— the *ones* dwelling[14] in heaven	
	2F. And *authority*[15] was given *to* him to make war[16] against the saints[D], and to overcome[17] them	7
	3F. And authority was given *to* him over every tribe and people[18] and tongue and nation	
6E.	And all the *ones* dwelling upon the earth[19] will worship[E] him— *each* whose name[20] has not been written in the book *of* life[21] *of* the Lamb having been slain[F] since *the* foundation *of the* world[22]	8
	1F. If anyone has *an* ear, let him hear[23]—	9
	1G. If anyone *is* for captivity[24], he is going into captivity	10
	2G. If anyone *is* to be killed[25] with *a* sword, he *is* to be killed with *a* sword	
	3G. Here[26] is the endurance[G] and the faith[27] *of* the saints[28]	
7D.	And I saw another beast[29] coming-up out of the land[30]. And he had two horns like *a* lamb. And he was speaking like *a* dragon	11
	1E. And he exercises all the authority[A] *of* the first beast in his presence	12
	2E. And he makes the earth and the *ones* dwelling[H] in it so that[31] they will worship[E] the first beast[32] whose[33] wound *of* death was cured	
	3E. And he does[34] great signs,[35] so that he even makes fire to come-down out of heaven[36] to the earth in the presence of *the* people[J]	13

1. This is the same phrase used of the Lamb in 5:6, "as-*if* having been slain" (compare 13:8). This head has the marks of death.
2. Or, "resulting in, leading to". GK *1650*.
3. This word means "blow, stroke", and its result, the "wound, bruise, beating". Same word as in v 12, 14 (from a sword); Act 16:33. It is rendered "blow" in Lk 10:30 (with fists); 12:48; Act 16:23 (with rods); and "beating" in 2 Cor 6:5; 11:23. Elsewhere only as a "plague, calamity" inflicted on the world by God in Rev 9:18, 20; 11:6; 15:1, 6, 8; 16:9, 21; 18:4, 8; 21:9; 22:18. GK *4435*. Related to "strike" in Rev 8:12.
4. That is, characterized by death, the death wound.
5. Same word as in v 12. Compare v 14. On this word, see Mt 8:7. Some think John means the head (itself called the beast in v 12, 14) came to life in another form (perhaps the eighth, 17:11); others, that head itself was healed. Compare 17:8-11. Some think this refers to an end-time revived Roman Empire; others, to the ruler himself, who will rise to power based on a mock resurrection; others, to the repeatedly revived pagan state throughout history. The Past View links it to Nero or some other Roman Emperor. Many hold a combination of these views.
6. Same word as in 17:8.
7. On this word, see 4:10. Same word as in v 8, 12, 15.
8. Or, "fight, battle". Same word as in 17:14; 19:11. On this word, see "fight" in 2:16.
9. Note the similarity to Dan 7:8, 11, 20, 25.
10. Or, "even".
11. Some manuscripts say "to make war" {N} as in v 7, where "make" is the same word as "act" here (on which see "does" in v 13).
12. Some manuscripts omit this word {C}. On this time notation, see 11:2. Compare Dan 7:25.
13. Or, "tent, tabernacle". That is, God's place of dwelling. Same word as in 21:3. On this word, see Lk 9:33.
14. This is the verb related to the word just used. This phrase explains the first. The "dwelling" of God in view is not heaven, but His people living there; not His house, but His household. Compare 12:12. Some think John is referring to angels, the ones who threw Satan out. Others, to God's people. On this word, see 7:15. Some manuscripts say "And the *ones* dwelling", making this a third thing the beast blasphemes. Other manuscripts combine both phrases into one, "His dwelling in heaven" {B}.
15. Some manuscripts include this word; others omit the whole sentence, "And... overcome them" {A}.
16. Or, "do battle", two words in Greek. The phrase "make war" is elsewhere only in 11:7; 12:17; 19:19. This noun "war" is the same word as in 12:7; and is related to the verb "wage war" in 13:4.
17. Or, "conquer". On this word, see 2:7. Note Dan 7:21, 23.
18. Some manuscripts omit "and people" {N}. This implies worldwide power. On this phrase, compare 5:9; 7:9; 11:9; 14:6.
19. On this phrase, see 3:10.
20. Literally, "And they will worship Him— all the *ones* (plural) dwelling upon the earth *of* whom (singular) his name has not been written...". The Greek jumps from the plural to the individual case. This grammar (without the jump from plural to singular) occurs again with "whose" in v 12. Some manuscripts have it all plural, all "*of* whom their names have not been written" {N}.
21. On this book, see 3:5.
22. This is where this phrase is found in the Greek word order of this verse. Some think John means "the Lamb slain since the foundation...."; others, "written in the book... since the foundation", as in 17:8. On this phrase, "since *the* foundation *of the* world", see Heb 9:26.
23. What follows is spoken to those who do not worship the beast, and means "Do not worship the beast, whatever the cost. Your earthly destiny, whether captivity or death, is in God's hands".
24. Or, "If anyone *is* [destined to go] into captivity...". Some manuscripts say "If anyone leads into captivity, he is going into captivity" {B}. The word "captivity" means "prisoner of war". On this word, see Eph 4:8.
25. Some manuscripts say "If anyone kills with the sword, he must be killed with the sword" {B}. In the case of the variant readings for these two sentences, some think this is warning believers (the "anyone") not to retaliate against the beast; others, encouraging believers that their persecutors (the "anyone") will suffer retribution.
26. Or, "At this point, On this occasion". At this point, endurance and faith are needed. There are four "Here is" statements, Rev 13:10, 18; 14:12; 17:9. GK *6045*.
27. Or, "faithfulness". On this word, see Eph 2:8.
28. The saints will endure in their faith. They will go into captivity or be put to death rather than worship the beast. They will endure even to the point of death, 12:11. Compare 14:12.
29. Some think this is a system of false religion; others, a person. He is called the "false prophet" in 16:13; 19:20; 20:10. Some identify him with someone in history; others think he is the end-time assistant of the first beast.
30. This is versus the sea in v 1. Or, "earth". On this word, see 7:1. This beast has a different origin. The symbolism of "sea" versus "land" is explained in various ways. For example, the nations versus Israel; a foreigner versus someone from Asia (where the seven churches are); a demonic being from the abyss (11:7) versus a human; from outside the political system versus from within it, etc.
31. Same grammar as in 3:9, "make... so that they will". Similar to 13:15, 16, to "cause... that they should".
32. Note that v 3 says one of his heads had this wound. Some think this change has significance; others think it is the normal way of speaking, "one of the heads" being the location of the beast's wound.
33. Same grammar as with "whose" in v 8; 20:8. Literally, the "beast *of* whom his wound *of* death was cured". See v 3.
34. In v 12-16, "exercise", "make", "do", and "cause" are the same Greek word. It is used eight times in these verses. It also means "accomplish, produce, commit, act, perform, appoint". Used 568 times. GK *4472*.
35. These "great signs" are also mentioned in Mt 24:24; 2 Thes 2:9-10. Some think they are fake miracles, tricks; others, genuine ones. It depends on the extent of the authority granted to this beast by God. (Compare 2 Thes 2:11). There is nothing in this context indicating they are fake. Their purpose is deception, and this is enhanced if their content is real. On "signs", see 2 Thes 2:9.
36. That is, the sky. God sent fire from heaven on Sodom (Lk 17:29; Gen 19:24); on Egypt (Ex 9:23); on David's sacrifice (1 Chron 21:26); and on Solomon's sacrifice (2 Chron 7:1). Satan did it in Job 1:16. Elijah called it down (1 King 18:36-38; 2 King 1:10, 12, 14); and the disciples wanted to (Lk 9:54). God will do it again in Rev 20:9. On this word, see 2 Cor 12:2.

A. Rev 6:8   B. 1 Tim 6:4   C. 1 Tim 6:1   D. 1 Pet 1:16, holy   E. Rev 4:10   F. 1 Jn 3:12   G. Jam 1:3   H. Eph 3:17   J. Mt 4:4, mankind

Revelation 13:14

    4E. And he deceives[1] the *ones* dwelling upon the earth[2] because-of[3] the signs[A] which it was given him to do in the presence of the beast—   14

        1F. Telling the *ones* dwelling upon the earth to make *an* image *to* the beast[4] who has the wound *of* the sword[B] and lived[5]

    5E. And *authority* was given *to* him to give breath[6] *to* the image *of* the beast, in order that the image *of* the beast might even[7] speak and cause[8] that all-who do not give-worship[C] *to* the image *of* the beast should be killed[D]   15

    6E. And he causes everyone— the small and the great, and the rich[E] and the poor[F], and the free[G] and the slaves[H]—   16

        1F. That they[9] should give them[10] *a* mark[11] on their right hand or on their forehead

        2F. And[12] that no one should be able to buy or to sell except the *one* having the mark— the[13] name *of* the beast or the number[14] *of* his name   17

            1G. Here[15] is wisdom[J]. Let the *one* having understanding[K] calculate[16] the number[17] *of* the beast, for it is *the* number *of a* man[18]   18

            2G. And his number *is* six-hundred sixty six[19]

8D. And I saw, and behold— the[20] Lamb *was* standing on Mount Zion[21], and with Him one-hundred forty four thousand[22] having His name and[23] the name *of* His Father having been written on their foreheads[24]   14:1

    1E. And I heard *a* sound[L] from heaven like *a* sound *of* many waters[25], and like *a* sound *of* loud thunder. And the sound which I heard *was* like *that of* harpists harping with their harps. *And they[26] are singing[M] something like[27] *a* new[N] song[O] before the throne, and before the four living-creatures[P] and the elders[Q]   2, 3

    2E. And no one was able to learn[R] the song except the one-hundred forty four thousand, the *ones* having been bought[28] from the earth[29]

        1F. These are *ones* who were[30] not stained[31] with women, for they are virgins[32]   4

        2F. These *are*[33] the *ones* following the Lamb wherever He goes

        3F. These were bought from mankind[S] *to be the* firstfruit[34] *to* God and *to* the Lamb

        4F. And falsehood[35] was not found in their mouth   5

        5F. They[36] are without-blemish[37]

1. Same word as in 19:20, which is referring to 13:14-17. Compare Mt 24:24; Rev 12:9. On this word, see "err" in Jam 5:19.
2. On this phrase, see 3:10.
3. That is, by reason of, as in 12:11.
4. This image is mentioned again in v 15; 14:9, 11; 15:2; 16:2; 19:20; 20:4. On "image", see Col 1:15.
5. Or, "came to life, became alive". The beast had a mortal wound, but "was cured" (v 3, 12), and so "lived". On this word, see "came to life" in 20:4. Compare 17:11.
6. This word means "breath, spirit". Same word as "breath" of life in 11:11, and some think John means that here, genuine life. Others think he means an appearance of life. It depends on the extent of the authority granted to this beast by God. The KJV says "life" here, which is an interpretation following the first view.
7. Or, "both".
8. John may mean that the speaking image causes this to happen. Or, "might both speak and act, in order that all who...". On the idiom "cause that", see Col 4:16. Some manuscripts omit "that", so that it says "cause all who" {C}.
9. Who is specified by "they" is not defined. John probably means "the authorities" who do such things.
10. Some manuscripts say "receive *on* them" {N}.
11. The mark of the beast is mentioned also in v 17; 14:9, 11; 16:2; 19:20; 20:4. It is evidence of submission. It mimics God's mark on the 144,000 in 7:3; 14:1. Some think it is a literal, physical mark; others think it is symbolic. GK *5916*.
12. Some manuscripts omit this word, {A}, so that it says "... forehead, in order that no one...".
13. This defines what the mark is. Some manuscripts say "the mark or the name..." {N}.
14. Same word as 7:4; 9:16; 13:18; 15:2. Used 18 times. GK *750*.
15. At this point, wisdom is needed. Compare 13:10.
16. Elsewhere only in Lk 14:28. It means "to calculate with pebbles". Related to "pebble" in 2:17. The letters of the alphabet had numeric equivalents. So the letters of a person's name could be added up, the name of the beast adding up to 666. John does not give the language in which the adding is to be done. Should it be equivalent Greek letters, the language of this book, or Hebrew letters, the language of the OT (note both in 9:11)? Or should it be in the native language of the beast's name? John gives no indication that it is anything other than the language of his readers. GK *6028*.
17. Compare 15:2.
18. Or, "for it is *a* number *of* man", that is, a human number, as humans normally count. Compare 21:17. On this word, see "mankind" in Mt 4:4.
19. Some manuscripts say "six-hundred sixteen" {A}, perhaps being changed to agree with "Nero Caesar". When calculated using Hebrew characters, the Latin form of "Nero Caesar" is equivalent to 616, the Greek form to 666. Some think this number is symbolic; others, a literal reference to someone in history, like Nero; others, a literal reference to the future Antichrist. There are other views. Some holding the Future View (see 1:1) think it cannot be understood until the beast arrives and the actual number of the mark is assigned. His number (the actual mark, which could be his name, initials, title, or an acronym) at that time will equal 666 when rendered in Greek. Thus John would not mean the beast can be known in advance by calculating his name, but that when v 16-17 occur, his name will calculate to 666.
20. Some manuscripts omit this word {A}, so that it says "Behold—*there was a* Lamb standing".
21. Some think John means the literal mountain at Jerusalem, meaning this group is still living on earth. Others think this is symbolic of heaven, or of the New Jerusalem, meaning this group is with Christ in heaven. On this word, see Jn 12:15.
22. Some think this is the same group as in chapter 7. Those sealed there all arrive safely here (whether still on earth, or in heaven). Others think this represents a different, special group.
23. Some manuscripts omit "name and" {K}, so that it says "having His Father's name".
24. Some think this is the seal mentioned in 7:3-8; 9:4.
25. This phrase "many waters" occurs also in 1:15; 17:1; 19:6; and Jn 3:23. On the plural "waters", see Jn 3:23.
26. "They" sing before the four creatures and 24 elders, who themselves sang a new song with harps back in 5:8-10. Some think "they" are not identified, and that only the 144,000 could learn this song from them. In this case, some think "they" are angels; others, the redeemed. Others think "they" are the 144,000, meaning they are in heaven.
27. Some manuscripts omit this word, so that it simply says "singing *a* new song" {C} as in 5:9.
28. Same word as in v 4. On this word, see 5:9.
29. Some think "from the earth" implies they are in heaven; others, that they are holy, as explained in v 4-5.
30. That is, prior to this gathering on Mount Zion, v 1.
31. Or, "soiled, defiled". That is, they never committed sexual immorality, the proof of which is that they have never even been with a woman; they are virgins. Same word as in 3:4. On this word, see 1 Cor 8:7.
32. Same word used of Mary in Mt 1:23; Lk 1:27; the ten virgins in Mt 25:1, 7, 11; and Philip's daughters in Act 21:9. Elsewhere only in 1 Cor 7:25, 28, 34, 36, 37, 38; 2 Cor 11:2. GK *4221*. Related to "virginity" in Lk 2:36. Some think this is symbolic of spiritual faithfulness; others, of moral purity, taking this word to mean "morally chaste" rather than "unmarried", as it is sometimes used outside the NT. Some holding the Future View take this description literally, thinking that this will be a time of distress like 1 Cor 7:26, leading these men not to marry.
33. Or, "*were*". Which word to supply here is unclear because the previous sentence is present tense and the next is past tense. John is referring to their obedience. Some think he means "these were the ones following Him prior to this gathering on Mount Zion"; others, "these are the ones following Him now, and in the future". Some think they followed Him to earth; others, on earth.
34. That is, the first part of what is to come, the part offered to God. Some think John means they are the first part of a larger group to follow; others, simply the part offered to God, without implying there are more to follow. On this word, see 1 Cor 15:20.
35. Or, "lie, deceit". Some think John means falsehood in general; others, the falsehood proclaimed by the beast in particular. Same word as in 21:27; 22:15; 2 Thes 2:9, 11. Elsewhere only as "lie" in Jn 8:44; Rom 1:25; Eph 4:25; 1 Jn 2:21, 27. GK *6022*.
36. Some manuscripts say "For they..." {N}.
37. On this word, see Col 1:22. Some manuscripts add "before the throne *of* God" {K}.

A. 2 Thes 2:9   B. Eph 6:17   C. Rev 4:10   D. Rom 7:11   E. 1 Tim 6:17   F. Gal 4:9   G. Mt 17:26   H. Rom 6:17   J. 1 Cor 12:8   K. Rom 7:23, mind   L. Rev 4:5, voices   M. Eph 5:19   N. Heb 8:13   O. Eph 5:19   P. Rev 4:6   Q. Rev 4:4   R. Phil 4:11   S. Mt 4:4

| Revelation 14:6 | 998 | Verse |

9D. And I saw another[1] angel flying in mid-heaven[2], having eternal[A] good-news[3] to announce-as-good-news[4] to[5] the *ones* sitting[6] on the earth— indeed, to every nation and tribe and tongue and people[B]   6

    1E. Saying with *a* loud voice "Fear[C] God and give Him glory[D], because the hour *of* His judgment[E] came[7]. And give-worship[F] to the *One* having made the heaven and the land[8] and sea[9] and springs[G] *of* waters"   7

    2E. And another angel, *a* second[10], followed, saying "Babylon the great fell, it fell[11]— she who has given-a-drink-*to* all the nations from the wine[H] *of* the passion[12] *of* her sexual-immorality[J]"   8

    3E. And another angel, *a* third, followed them, saying with *a* loud voice, "If anyone worships[F] the beast and his image and receives *a* mark on his forehead or on his hand   9

        1F. "He himself will also drink from the wine *of* the fury *of* God[13] having been mixed undiluted in the cup *of* His wrath[K]. And he will be tormented[14] with fire and sulphur[15] in the presence of holy angels[16], and in the presence of the Lamb   10

            1G. "And the smoke *of* their torment[17] goes up forever and ever[18]   11
            2G. "And they do not have *a* rest[L] by day and by night[19]— the *ones* worshiping the beast and his image, and if anyone receives the mark *of* his name

        2F. Here[20] is the endurance[M] *of* the saints[21]— the *ones* keeping[N] the commandments[O] *of* God and the faith *of* Jesus[22]   12

    4E. And I heard *a* voice from heaven saying[23], "Write— 'Blessed[24] *are* the dead dying in *the* Lord from-now-on[25]! Yes[26], says the Spirit, so that[27] they will rest[28] from their labors[P], for[29] their works[Q] are following with them"   13

10D. And I saw and behold—   14

    1E. *There was a* white cloud[30], and *one* sitting on the cloud resembling *a* son *of* man[31], having *a* golden crown[32] upon his head and *a* sharp sickle[R] in his hand

        1F. And another[33] angel came out of the temple,[34] crying-out[S] with *a* loud voice *to* the *one* sitting on the cloud,[35] "Send[T] your sickle and reap, because the[36] hour to reap came[37], because the harvest[U] *of* the earth was dried-up[38]"   15

        2F. And the *one* sitting on the cloud cast[V] his sickle over[39] the earth, and the earth was reaped[40]   16

    2E. And another angel came out of the temple in heaven, he also having *a* sharp sickle[R]   17

        1F. And another angel came-out[41] from the altar[42]— the *one* having authority[W] over the fire.[43] And he called-out[44] with *a* loud voice *to* the *one* having the sharp sickle, saying, "Send[T] your sharp sickle and gather[X] the clusters[45] *from* the grapevine *of* the earth, because its grapes[Y] became ripe"   18

        2F. And the angel cast[V] his sickle into the earth, and gathered[X] the grapevine *of* the earth, and threw[V] *it* into the great winepress[Z] *of* the fury *of* God   19

1. There are several views on what "another" refers to. The last angel mentioned was in 12:7, or perhaps 14:2. John may mean "another like I saw before" in 8:13. He may mean "another in addition to all I have already seen". "Another angel" also occurs in 7:2; 8:3; 10:1; 14:8, 9, 15, 17, 18; and 18:1. Some manuscripts omit this word {B}.
2. That is, in the sky. Same word as in 8:13. On this word, see 19:17.
3. Some think the content of this good news is in v 7, a proclamation of the consummation of God's purpose, a warning and call for repentance. Others think this good news is in addition to the warning of v 7, and refers to the gospel of salvation. On this word, see 1 Cor 15:1.
4. John uses the noun and verb of the same word, as in Gal 1:11.
5. Or, "across, upon, over, for". This is the only place in the NT where this preposition is used following this verb. GK *2093*. Some manuscripts omit it {N}, so that it says "to announce-as-good-news-to the *ones* sitting".
6. Same word rendered "sit" throughout this book, 33 times. Same word as in Mt 4:16; Lk 1:79; 21:35. Used 91 times. GK *2764*. Some manuscripts say "dwelling" {N}.
7. The future judgment is here, it has come. It has begun. On this word, see 6:17.
8. Or, "earth". On this word, see 7:1.
9. Some manuscripts say "the sea" {N}.
10. Some manuscripts omit this word {B}.
11. This is a further announcement of the judgment that came, v 7. The same pronouncement occurs in 18:2, where this fall is described in more detail. We would say "has fallen". On "Babylon the great", see 16:19. Some manuscripts say "Babylon fell, it fell, that great city, because she has given..." {K}.
12. Or, "fury". Same phrase as in 18:3. On this word, see "fury" in 16:19. Some think this means "fury" here also, the wine of the fury of God (as in v 10) that belongs to her sexual immorality.
13. The "wine of the fury of God" is also mentioned in 14:19; 16:19; 19:15. There is a play on words with the "wine of the passion" in v 8, for these are the exact same words. If you drink her wine, you will drink His wine also.
14. Or, "tortured". Elsewhere only in 9:5; 11:10; 12:2; 20:10; and Mt 8:6, 29; 14:24; Mk 5:7; 6:48; Lk 8:28; 2 Pet 2:8. GK *989*. Related to "torment" in v 11; Lk 16:23; and "tormentor" in Mt 18:34.
15. Or, "brimstone". Elsewhere only in Lk 17:29; Rev 9:17, 18; 19:20; 20:10; 21:8. GK *2520*.
16. Some manuscripts say "the holy angels" {N}.
17. Or, "torture, pain, anguish". Elsewhere only in 9:5; 18:7, 10, 15. GK *990*. A similar statement is made in 19:3.
18. This is an idiom, "into ages *of* ages", not the normal "into the ages *of* the ages". The grammar here is unique. See 20:10.
19. This phrase "they do not have a rest by day... night" is the same one used of the four living creatures in 4:8.
20. Or, "At this point". The saints do not worship the beast or receive his mark. They endure to the death. Compare 13:10. Some think this is John's comment; others, a continuation of the angel's proclamation.
21. On this word, see "holy" in 1 Pet 1:16. Some manuscripts say "saints. Here *are* the *ones*..." {N}.
22. Some think this means "the faith Jesus gave"; others, the faith of which He is the object, their faith in Him. On "faith", see Eph 2:8.
23. Some manuscripts add "*to* me" {N}.
24. Or, "Fortunate". On this word, see Lk 6:20.
25. Or, "henceforth, from this time". This is the Greek word order. Some think this means "Blessed... from now on"; others, "dying... from now on". "From now on" means "under the domination of the beast". Note that 20:4 again refers to this group. The fact that these martyrs are blessed does not mean other believers not martyred are not blessed. On this phrase, "from now *on*", see Mt 26:64.
26. Some manuscripts omit this word {A}.
27. Or, "in order that they may rest". That is, "they are dying in the Lord so that they will rest". Those who choose to live "in the beast" (so to speak) will not have the rest they think they are gaining, v 11.
28. This is the verb related to "rest" in v 11. On this word, see "refreshed" in Phm 7.
29. Some manuscripts say "And" {N}.
30. A "white cloud" and "one sitting on a cloud" is mentioned only here in v 14-16. Compare 10:1. "Clouds" are mentioned in 10:1; Mt 17:5; 24:30; 26:64; Act 1:9; 1 Thes 4:17. Used 25 times. GK *3749*. Compare Dan 7:13.
31. Some think this is referring to Christ; others, to an angel who looked like a human. See 1:13 on this phrase.
32. On this word, see 4:4. It is the victor's crown. A "golden crown" is also worn by the 24 elders, its only other occurrence in this book. Christ wears many "diadems" in 19:12, the king's crown. Some think this pictures Christ at His return. Others think it is an angel He sends to reap the earth at the end of the age.
33. Some think this indicates the one on the white cloud was an angel. Others think it refers to the angels in v 6, 8, and 9. Note the issue with this word in v 6.
34. That is, the temple opened in 11:19. This is the first angel to come out.
35. Some think the fact that an angel tells the one on the cloud what to do indicates that the one on the cloud is an angel. Others think this merely pictures the command to begin the final harvest as coming directly from the Father.
36. Some manuscripts say "your" {N}, which may also be rendered "because the hour came *for* you to reap".
37. That is, it is here, it has come.
38. Or, "became dried up". The grain has become dry, and thus ripe for harvest. Same word as in 16:12; Jn 15:6. On this word, see "withered" in Mk 3:1.
39. Or, "upon, to, across". GK *2093*.
40. Jesus said an angel performs this task, Mt 13:39; Mt 24:31. Some think this grain harvest refers to the gathering of believers at the end of the age (some think it is the rapture), and the grape harvest in v 19 refers to the gathering of unbelievers for judgment. Others think both pictures refer to unbelievers. The Past View sees this as referring to the final judgment on Jerusalem.
41. Some manuscripts omit this word {C}, leaving it implied.
42. John probably means the altar in 8:3, linking this to the prayers of the saints.
43. Perhaps this is the angel of 8:3-5.
44. Or, "he voiced with a loud voice". John uses the verb and noun of the same word. This is the only use of this verb in Revelation. On this phrase, see Mk 1:26.
45. Used only here. GK *1084*.

A. Mt 25:46 B. Rev 5:9 C. Eph 5:33, respecting D. 2 Pet 2:10 E. Jn 3:19 F. Rev 4:10 G. Jn 4:6 H. 1 Tim 5:23 J. 1 Cor 5:1 K. Rev 16:19 L. Mt 12:43 M. Jam 1:3 N. 1 Jn 5:18 O. Mk 12:28 P. 1 Cor 3:8 Q. Mt 26:10 R. Mk 4:29 S. Mt 8:29 T. Jn 20:21 U. Mk 4:29 V. Rev 2:22, throw W. Rev 6:8 X. Lk 6:44 Y. Lk 6:44 Z. Rev 19:15

| Revelation 14:20 | 1000 | Verse |

        3F. And the winepress was trodden[1] outside the city.[2] And blood came out of the winepress up to the bridles[A] *of* the horses, one-thousand six-hundred stades[3] away[4]   20

3C. And I saw another sign[B] in heaven,[5] great and marvelous[6]—   15:1

    1D. Seven angels having seven plagues[7]— the last, because the fury[C] *of* God was finished[8] in them
    2D. And I saw *something* like *a* sea of-glass[9] having been mixed *with* fire,[10] and the *ones* overcoming[11] from the beast and from his image[12] and from the number *of* his name[13] standing upon the sea of-glass, holding harps *of* God[14]   2

        1E. And they are singing[D] the song[E] *of* Moses[15] the slave[F] *of* God, and the song[16] *of* the Lamb, saying   3

            1F. "Your works[G] *are* great and marvelous, Lord God Almighty[H]
            2F. "Your ways *are* righteous[J] and true[K], King *of* the nations[17]
            3F. "Who will never[L] come-to-fear[18], Lord, and glorify[M] Your name?   4

                1G. "Because *You* alone *are* holy[19]
                2G. "Because all the nations will come and worship[20] before You
                3G. "Because Your righteous-acts[21] were revealed[N]"

5B. And after these *things*[22] I saw[23], and the temple[O] *of* the tabernacle[P] *of* testimony[24] in heaven[25] was opened[26]   5

    1C. And the seven angels having the seven plagues[27] came out of the temple, having been dressed-in clean[Q] shining[R] linen[28] and having been girded-with[29] golden belts around the chests[S]   6

        1D. And one of the four living-creatures gave *to* the seven angels seven golden bowls[30] being full[T] *of* the fury[C] *of* God, the *One* living forever and ever[U]   7
        2D. And the temple was filled[V] *with* smoke from the glory[W] *of* God, and from His power[X]. And no one was able to enter into the temple until the seven plagues *of* the seven angels were finished[Y]   8
        3D. And I heard *a* loud voice[31] from the temple saying *to* the seven angels, "Go and pour-out[Z] the seven[32] bowls *of* the fury[33] *of* God into the earth"   16:1

1. Same word as in 19:15.
2. Some think this refers to Jerusalem; others think it is symbolic.
3. That is, about 184 miles or 296 kilometers. A Roman stade is 607 feet or 185 meters. The Greek measure varied from 607 to 738 feet. Some think this is a literal distance. John may mean up to this height at the winepress, and flowing away to this distance. It is symbolic of the complete judgment of the whole earth. In addition to this, some take it literally. Same word as in Mt 14:24; Lk 24:13; Jn 6:19; 11:18; Rev 21:16. In addition to "stade" as a measure of distance, it also means "stadium" and the "race" held there. Elsewhere only as "race" in 1 Cor 9:24. GK *5084*.
4. This word is used as a measure also in Jn 11:18; 21:8. GK *608*.
5. This is the third sign John sees in heaven, linking it to what precedes, yet it is a precursor to the seven bowls that follow. Some put it with what follows and start the next main point (5B.) here. The sign is judgment for those on earth, and rejoicing for those who overcame the beast.
6. This phrase "great and marvelous" is elsewhere only in v 3. On "marvelous", see "marvel" in Jn 9:30.
7. These angels appear in advance, just as the beast did in 11:7, and Babylon the great in 14:8. All the players for what follows are now introduced. On this word, see "wound" in 13:3.
8. John sees this here as a sign. In v 5, it is carried out in detail. John refers to it here as if it were already accomplished, as in 10:7. On this word, see 10:7.
9. Or, "made-of-glass". Used twice in this verse, and elsewhere only in 4:6, before the throne. GK *5612*.
10. Some think the sea of fire symbolizes the persecution on earth the overcomers passed through; others, the judgment about to fall on the earth in the coming bowls, like the Red Sea that drown the Egyptians after Israel passed through.
11. Or, "coming off victorious from", "conquerors from". The beast overcame these overcomers on earth (13:7), but they overcame him before God through their death. Some think John is referring to martyrs; others, to all the believers. On this word, see 2:7.
12. Some manuscripts add "and from his mark" {N}.
13. That is, the mark of the beast, 13:17.
14. John may mean "harps for worshipping God", "harps given by God", or "harps belonging to God". This is the third mention of "harps", 5:8; 14:2. Elsewhere only in 1 Cor 14:7. GK *3067*. Some manuscripts say "the harps *of* God" {N}.
15. It is not the same song, but a song like the one Moses sang. Some think John means a song of victory and deliverance after "overcoming" Egypt, as in Ex 15. Others think he means a song like the song at the end of Moses' life in Deut 32. In addition, some think John means a song sung by Moses; others, a song about Moses.
16. Some think this is a second song; others think there is only one song of victory. In addition, some think John means a song sung by Christ after He "overcame" the world, Rev 5:5; Jn 16:33; others, a song about Christ.
17. On this word, see "Gentiles" in Act 15:23. Some manuscripts say "ages"; others, "saints" {B}.
18. Or, "fear". Many do not fear and glorify, but all will do so. Some manuscripts say "come-to-fear You, Lord" {N}. Compare Jer 10:7. On this word, see "respecting" in Eph 5:33.
19. That is, holy in character. On this word, see Heb 7:26.
20. Or, "prostrate-*themselves*". Every knee will bow. On this word, see 4:10.
21. Same word as in 19:8.
22. The phrase "after these *things*" is also in 4:1; 7:9; 9:12; 18:1; 19:1; 20:3. It is singular in 7:1.
23. Some manuscripts add "and behold" {N}.
24. Or, the "tent *of* witness", the tent containing the witness, because the ark containing the covenant is there. That is, the temple containing or consisting of the tabernacle which contained the testimony in the ark. On this tabernacle in heaven, note Heb 8:2, 5; 9:11. The earthly copy of the tabernacle (or, tent) of testimony is mentioned in Act 7:44; Ex 38:21; Num 1:50, 53; 9:15; 10:11; 17:7; etc. On earth, the ark of the covenant was kept in the Holy of Holies, which was the inmost part of the tabernacle of testimony. The mobile "tabernacle" (tent) was used in the wilderness, and was replaced by the "temple" in Jerusalem under Solomon.
25. Some think John means the same temple opened in 11:19 to see the ark is reopened here to let the seven angels out (implying it had been closed again in 11:19). Others think John means the larger "temple" was opened in 11:19, exposing the ark inside its own smaller, inner, "temple consisting of the tabernacle of testimony", which is opened here, allowing the angels to come out. Others think John intends us to apply the pattern of the earthly tabernacle, where the ark was found in the inmost part of it. This would mean that the heavenly temple is being opened from the inside out. From God's presence, His heavenly throne-room, the heavenly temple is opened in 11:19; that is, what is here called the "tabernacle of testimony", the tabernacle inside which the heavenly ark is seen (11:19). Here, the way into the larger "temple" containing this tabernacle is opened, from which the angels come out. Then in 19:11, heaven is opened (that is, the outer doors of the heavenly temple are opened, so to speak) and Christ comes out of the heavenly temple to earth.
26. This scene resumes from 11:19 after the three signs in heaven given in 12:1-15:4. Some think the seven bowls are the seventh trumpet and third woe. Others think they recapitulate the bowls and trumpets. Without regard to any of these views, point 5B. presents the next heavenly scene. See 11:19 on the progression of heavenly scenes.
27. This phrase "the seven angels having the seven plagues" refers back to v 1 where they were seen as such in the sign. Here in this event, the actual unfolding of what was seen in v 1, they have not yet received the seven bowls full of the seven plagues. This occurs next in v 7.
28. Some manuscripts say "stone" {B}.
29. Same word for "girded-with" and for "golden belts" as in 1:13.
30. The word "bowls" is only used with reference to these judgments, and in 5:8, of "golden bowls" holding the prayers of the saints. This may be a deliberate link to those prayers. GK *5786*.
31. Since no one could enter the temple, this seems to be the voice of God.
32. Some manuscripts omit this word {N}.
33. Some think these are end-time judgments. Some holding the Spiritual View (see 1:1) think they are symbolic of the final judgment that falls on every individual in this life who fails to heed the partial judgments (the trumpets) aimed at producing repentance. Some holding the Past View think these represent the final judgment upon Israel and Jerusalem in A.D. 70; others, on the Roman Empire.

A. Jam 3:3 B. 2 Thes 2:9 C. Rev 16:19 D. Eph 5:19 E. Eph 5:19 F. Rom 6:17 G. Mt 26:10 H. Rev 1:8 J. Rom 1:17 K. Jn 7:28 L. Gal 5:16 M. Rom 8:30 N. 1 Jn 2:19, made evident O. Rev 11:1 P. Heb 8:2 Q. Tit 1:15 R. Rev 22:1 S. Jn 13:25 T. Rev 4:6 U. Rev 20:10 V. Mk 4:37 W. 2 Pet 2:10 X. Mk 5:30 Y. Rev 10:7 Z. Act 2:17

2C. And the first went and poured out his bowl into¹ the land²— and *a* bad³ and evil⁴ sore⁵ came upon the people^A having the mark *of* the beast and the *ones* giving worship *to* his image⁶

3C. And the second⁷ poured out his bowl into the sea⁸— and it became blood^B like *of a* dead *man*.⁹ And every soul^C *of* life¹⁰ died— the *things* in the sea

4C. And the third¹¹ poured-out^D his bowl into the rivers and the springs^E *of* waters¹²— and it¹³ became blood

    1D. And I heard the angel *of* the waters¹⁴ saying, "You are righteous¹⁵— the *One Who* is and *Who* was¹⁶, the holy¹⁷ *One*— because You judged^F these *things*

        1E. "Because they shed^D *the* blood *of* saints^G and prophets^H, and You have given¹⁸ them blood to drink. They¹⁹ are worthy²⁰ *of it*"

    2D. And I heard *a voice*²¹ *from* the altar saying, "Yes, Lord God Almighty^J, Your judgments^K *are* true^L and righteous^M"

5C. And the fourth²² poured out his bowl upon the sun— and *authority* was given *to* it²³ to scorch²⁴ the people²⁵ with fire

    1D. And the people^A were scorched *with a* great scorching-heat²⁶
    2D. And they blasphemed²⁷ the name *of* God, the *One* having the authority^N over these plagues
    3D. And they did not repent^O so as to give Him glory^P

6C. And the fifth²⁸ poured out his bowl upon the throne *of* the beast²⁹— and his kingdom became darkened³⁰

    1D. And they were biting³¹ their tongues because-of³² the pain^Q
    2D. And they blasphemed the God *of* heaven because of their pains, and because of their sores³³
    3D. And they did not repent^O from their works^R

7C. And the sixth³⁴ poured out his bowl upon the great river Euphrates³⁵— and its water was dried-up^S, in order that the way might be prepared^T *for* the kings from *the* rising *of the* sun³⁶

    1D. And I saw three unclean spirits like frogs *come* out of the mouth *of* the dragon, and out of the mouth *of* the beast, and out of the mouth *of* the false-prophet³⁷

        1E. For they are spirits *of* demons³⁸ doing signs,³⁹ which go out to the kings *of* the whole world⁴⁰ to gather them together⁴¹ for the battle⁴² *of* the great day *of* God⁴³ Almighty^J

    2D. "Behold— I am coming like *a* thief.⁴⁴ Blessed^U *is* the *one* keeping-watch⁴⁵, and keeping^V his garments⁴⁶ in order that he not be walking-around^W naked^X and they see his shame^Y"
    3D. And they⁴⁷ gathered them together to the⁴⁸ place being called^Z Har-Magedon⁴⁹ *in* Hebrew

8C. And the seventh⁵⁰ poured out his bowl upon the air^AA— and *a* loud voice came out of the temple⁵¹ from the throne saying, "It is done⁵²"

    1D. And there came lightnings and voices and thunders⁵³

1. Some manuscripts say "upon" {N}.
2. This stands versus the "sea" next. Same word as "earth" in v 1. On this word, see 7:1. Some take the descriptions that follow literally; others, think they are apocalyptic symbols not intended to be interpreted in detail.
3. Or, "harmful", as in Act 16:28; 28:5. On this word, see "evil" in 3 Jn 11.
4. On this word, see Act 25:18. Others render these two general words more graphically in various ways. Compare the versions.
5. Those with the beast's mark now receive God's mark.
6. John either means that these are the only people left on earth, or that the believers are protected from the bowl judgments as Israel was protected from the plagues on Egypt.
7. Some manuscripts add "angel" {N}.
8. Some take this literally; other think it symbolizes the nations.
9. Some think John means coagulated blood.
10. This is a Hebrew way of speaking based on Gen 1:21, meaning "every living creature". John clarifies it as "in the sea". On this word, see Rom 8:10.
11. Some manuscripts add "angel" {N}.
12. Some think this symbolizes the sources of life; others take it literally.
13. That is, the water. Or, "they". Some manuscripts say "they became" {B}, that is, the rivers and springs.
14. John may mean the third angel in the previous verse, or, some other angel.
15. Or, "just". Some manuscripts say "You are righteous, Lord— " {K}.
16. Some manuscripts say "and *Who* is coming" instead of "the holy One" {K}. Compare 11:17; 1:4.
17. Same word as in 15:4.
18. Some manuscripts say "You gave" {C}.
19. Some manuscripts say "For they..." {N}.
20. Or, "deserving, fit". Same word used of the saints in 3:4, and in 4:11; 5:2, 4, 9, 12; Mt 3:8; Jn 1:27; Act 13:46; 23:29. Used 41 times. GK *545*. Related to "consider worthy" in 2 Thes 1:11.
21. Some manuscripts say "another" {K}, so that it says "I heard another *from* the altar".
22. Some manuscripts add "angel" {N}.
23. Or, "him". It may refer to the sun, or to the angel.
24. Elsewhere only in v 9; Mt 13:6; Mk 4:6. GK *3009*.
25. That is, the unbelievers, as seen by their response in v 9. Some think the sun symbolizes political leaders, and that this therefore symbolizes political oppression. Others take it literally.
26. Elsewhere only in 7:16. GK *3008*. Related to "scorch" in v 8.
27. Same word as in v 11, 21. On this word, see 1 Tim 6:1.
28. Some manuscripts add "angel" {N}.
29. That is, the throne given him by the dragon, 13:2; the seat of his power.
30. This is a participle, it "became having been darkened". It was rendered dark. Some think this is a physical darkness (as in Egypt) upon the seat of spiritual darkness. Others think it is a moral or spiritual darkness. Others think it refers to internal strife and disorder within his kingdom. On this word, see Eph 4:18.
31. Used only here. GK *3460*.
32. Or, "from". Same word as in v 11, 21. GK *1666*.
33. Same word as in v 2. Some think this means that they still have the sores from the first bowl. GK *1814*.
34. Some manuscripts add "angel" {N}.
35. This river was mentioned in 9:14, the sixth trumpet. Some think this symbolizes the removal of all barriers in preparation for the last battle. Others take it literally. Babylon (v 19) is on the Euphrates, about 50 miles or 80 kilometers south of Baghdad.
36. That is, from the east; or, from the new day. Same phrase as in 7:2. Some think these kings are separate from the kings of the whole earth, v 14; others, that they are part of that group. Some think this is referring to Christ's army which will destroy the kings gathered in v 14. Compare the sixth trumpet, 9:14. Others think this refers to human kings of eastern empires who battle the kings of western empires (the Roman Empire, the beast's empire) gathered in v 14 in a final human conflict. Others think these kings from the east come to join forces with the kings of the west against Israel.
37. That is, the second beast, 13:11. One unclean spirit comes from each of them. Same word as in 19:20; 20:10. Used 11 times. GK *6021*.
38. That is, demon spirits, spirits which are demons.
39. Some render this "false prophet (for they are spirits *of* demons doing signs) which go out to the kings...", making it all one sentence.
40. On "whole world", see 3:10. Some think these kings are the kings mentioned in 17:12-14. Some manuscripts say "to the kings *of* the earth and *of* the whole world" {K}.
41. This word "gather together" is used of a gathering for battle in 16:14, 16; 19:19; and 20:8. On this word, see "brought in" in Mt 25:35.
42. Some think John means the battle against the Lamb, 17:14; 19:19. On this word, see "war" in 12:7.
43. The "day of God" is also mentioned in 2 Pet 3:12.
44. On coming "like a thief", see 3:3. This is either the angel speaking the words of Christ, or Christ Himself speaking. A similar interjection occurs in 22:7. This is directly addressed to all readers of this book.
45. Or, "staying alert". Same word as in Mt 24:42; 1 Thes 5:6.
46. The symbol is of one who is sleeping, and who is overcome by such a sudden and overwhelming catastrophe that he has to flee without getting dressed. Keep watch, and keep your garments ready. It symbolizes spiritual readiness. The garments may symbolize righteousness, as in 3:4-5, 18.
47. Or, "he". This could mean "he" the angel; "He", God; or "they", the spirits. Some manuscripts have different grammar that only means "they" {N}.
48. Some manuscripts omit "the" {N}, so that it says "*a* place".
49. This is a transliterated Hebrew word, sometimes spelled "Armagedon". Its meaning and location are uncertain. Consult the commentaries for the theories. "Har" means "mountain, hill". This is the only place this name occurs in the Bible. GK *762*.
50. Some manuscripts add "angel" {N}.
51. Some manuscripts say "temple *of* heaven" {A}. Compare the name in 15:5.
52. Or, "It has happened, taken place, come to pass". Same word as in 21:6; Mt 6:10. GK *1181*. It is spoken as if it were already completed. Once poured, it is finished, though the content of it must now take place. Compare 10:7, "it was finished".
53. Compare 4:5; 8:5; 11:19; where these same three things occur.

A. Mt 4:4, mankind B. 1 Jn 1:7 C. Jam 5:20 D. Act 2:17, pour out E. Rev 8:10 F. Mt 7:1 G. 1 Pet 1:16, holy H. 1 Cor 12:28 J. Rev 1:8 K. Jn 3:19 L. Jn 7:28 M. Rom 1:17 N. Rev 6:8 O. Act 26:20 P. 2 Pet 2:10 Q. Col 4:13 R. Mt 26:10 S. Mk 3:1, become withered T. Mk 14:15 U. Rev 22:14 V. 1 Jn 5:18 W. Heb 13:9, walking X. Jam 2:15 Y. Rom 1:27, indecent act Z. Rom 8:20 AA. Eph 2:2

2D. And *a* great earthquake[1] took place such as did not take place since[2] *a* human[3] came-to-be[4] upon the earth— so-large *an* earthquake, so great

3D. And the great city[5] came-to-be in three parts[6]   19

4D. And the cities *of* the nations fell

5D. And Babylon[7] the great was remembered[8] in the presence *of* God— to give her the cup[9] *of* the wine *of* the fury[10] *of* His wrath[11]

6D. And every island fled[A], and *the* mountains were not found[12]   20

7D. And great hail[13] weighing about *a* talent[14] comes down from heaven upon the people. And the people[B] blasphemed[C] God because of the plague[D] *of* the hail, because its plague is extremely great[15]   21

9C. And one of the seven angels having the seven bowls came and spoke with me, saying[16], "Come, I will show[17] you the judgment[E] *of* the great prostitute[18] sitting on many waters[19], *with whom the kings *of* the earth[20] committed-sexual-immorality[21], and the *ones* dwelling-in the earth[22] got-drunk[F] from the wine *of* her sexual-immorality[23]"   17:1   2

    1D. And he carried me away in *the* Spirit[24] to *a* wilderness[G]. And I saw *a* woman sitting on[25] *a* scarlet beast[26] being-full-of[H] names *of* blasphemy[27] having seven heads and ten horns   3

        1E. And the woman had been clothed-with[28] purple and scarlet, and gilded[29] *with* gold, and *with* precious stone and pearls,[30] having   4

            1F. *A* golden cup in her hand being-full[H] *of* abominations[31] and[32] the impure *things of* her sexual-immorality[33]

            2F. And *a* name having been written upon her forehead, *a* mystery[34]— "Babylon the Great, the mother *of* the prostitutes and *of* the abominations *of* the earth"   5

        2E. And I saw the woman being-drunk[J] from the blood *of* the saints[K], and[35] from the blood *of* the witnesses[L] *of* Jesus   6

    2D. And having seen her, I wondered *with* great wonder.[36] *And the angel said *to* me, "For what reason do you wonder? I will tell you the mystery *of* the woman, and *of* the beast carrying[M] her— the *one* having the seven heads and the ten horns   7

        1E. "The beast[N] which you saw was and is not[37] and is going to come-up out of the abyss[38]. And he goes[39] to destruction[40]   8

1. See 11:19 on the earthquakes in this book.
2. This idiom is literally "from which *time*" here and in Lk 13:7; 24:21; and with different grammar, "from which *hour*" in Lk 7:45; and "from which *day*" in Act 24:11; Col 1:6, 9; 2 Pet 3:4.
3. Or, "mankind". On this word, see "mankind" in Mt 4:4. Some manuscripts have this plural, "people, mankind" {N}.
4. Or, "came into being", as in Jn 1:3. That is, since Adam. GK *1181*.
5. Some think this refers to Jerusalem, as in 11:8; others, to Babylon, as in 17:18; 18:10, 16, 18, 19, 21.
6. Some take this symbolically. Others think John means the great city was physically split into three parts. On this word, see Rom 11:25.
7. Babylon is mentioned also in 14:8; 17:5; 18:2, 10, 21. Some holding the Past View (see 1:1) think Babylon is Jerusalem in A.D. 70 (note 18:24); others, Rome, the Roman Empire persecuting believers after A.D. 70. The Spiritual View thinks Babylon refers to Rome in John's day as a symbol of the the anti-Christian world system which exists throughout this age, and of the final intense manifestation of it in the end time. The Future View thinks Babylon represents the end-time anti-Christian world system as a whole (political, economic, religious), or the end-time apostate religious system under the Antichrist in particular, or the literal city in which these powers are centered (either a literal Babylon on the Euphrates, or Rome). GK *956*. Same word as in 1 Pet 5:13.
8. That is, "kept in mind" (not forgotten) as in Lk 1:54, or, "recalled to mind, brought to mind".
9. This cup was also mentioned in 14:10. Compare 18:6.
10. Similar phrase as in 19:15. Same word as in Lk 4:28; Rom 2:8; Heb 11:27; Rev 12:12; 14:10, 19; 15:1, 7; 16:1. This is the anger or wrath that boils over from the heart. Elsewhere only as "rage" in Act 19:28; 2 Cor 12:20; Gal 5:20; Eph 4:31; Col 3:8; and as "passion" in Rev 14:8; 18:3. GK *2596*. Related word in Mt 2:16.
11. This is detailed in chapters 17-18. Same word as in Mt 3:7; Lk 3:7; 21:23; Jn 3:36; Rom 1:18; 2:5, 8; 3:5; 4:15; 5:9; 9:22; 12:19; 13:4, 5; Eph 2:3; 4:31; 5:6; Col 3:6, 8; 1 Thes 1:10; 2:16; 5:9; Heb 3:11; 4:3; Rev 6:16, 17; 11:18; 14:10; 19:15. Elsewhere only as "anger" in Mk 3:5; 1 Tim 2:8; Jam 1:19, 20. GK *3973*. This is the anger or wrath or settled indignation proceeding from one's nature or disposition. This word overlaps in meaning with "fury". On the related verb, see "become angry" in 11:18.
12. Compare this to 6:14. Some think this is symbolic of nations and kingdoms; others take it literally. On this word, see 2 Pet 3:10.
13. Elsewhere only in 8:7; 11:19. GK *5898*.
14. That is, about 58-94 pounds or 26-43 kilograms, depending on the system of measurement, which varied by time and place. This word, "weighing a talent", is used only here. GK *5418*.
15. This implies it is not yet the end. They are still alive, cursing God, as after the fourth and fifth bowl. The coming of Christ brings the end, 19:19.
16. Some manuscripts add "to me" {N}.
17. Same word as in 4:1.
18. That is, of Babylon, 16:19. Same word as in 17:5, 15, 16; 19:2, on which see 1 Cor 6:15. The prostitute represents a "great city", 17:18; 18:16.
19. This is explained in v 15. The prostitute also sits on the beast, v 3. On the phrase "many waters", see 14:2.
20. Or, "land", in the Past View. The phrase "kings of the earth" is also in 1:5; 6:15; 17:18; 18:3, 9; 19:19; 21:24.
21. Some holding the Future View think this is symbolic of spiritual and religious prostitution, of end-time false and apostate religion under the Antichrist, which has political (v 9, 18), religious (v 6) and economic (18:3, 11-19) aspects to it. She spiritually prostituted herself, the kings joined with her in it, and the world became drunk on it. She is an integral part of the world system. Others holding the Future and Spiritual Views think this immorality describes the anti-Christian world system as a whole. See 16:19.
22. Or, "inhabiting". On this phrase, see 3:10. The grammar is different here. The Past View renders this word "land" (see 7:1).
23. A similar phrase occurs in 14:8; 18:3. The same root word occurs three times. The great whore went-whoring with the kings and the world became drunk from her whoredom; the great immoral one engaged-in-immorality with the kings and the world became drunk from her immorality. On this word group, see 1 Cor 5:1.
24. Or, "in spirit". Same phrase as in 21:10. On this phrase, see 1:10.
25. Some think this symbolizes that the prostitute is supported by the political power of the beast (until v 16).
26. The names, heads, and horns link this beast to the beast in 13:1, and prepare for the explanation that follows in v 8-14.
27. That is, blasphemous names. On this word, see 1 Tim 6:4.
28. Or, "had put on purple...". This is a participle, she "was having been clothed". Same with "gilded".
29. That is, adorned, covered. Elsewhere only in 18:16. GK *5998*. Related to "gold" next.
30. The same five adornments are mentioned again in 18:16. It all speaks of luxury.
31. Or, "detestable, loathsome *things*". Elsewhere only in Mt 24:15; Mk 13:14; Lk 16:15; Rev 17:5; 21:27. This word is used of things connected with idolatry, of things spiritually detestable to God and His people. GK *1007*. Related to "detestable" in Tit 1:16; and "detesting" in Rom 2:22.
32. Or, "even", defining it. This could be a second description of what is filling the cup. Or, this could be a second thing she is "having", making this point 2F.
33. Some manuscripts say "*of* the sexual immorality *of* the earth" {B}.
34. Some think this word is part of her name, "Mystery Babylon the Great". Some think it means that the name "Babylon" is to be interpreted mystically, meaning Rome or Jerusalem. Others think it means her meaning is not known apart from the revelation of God, and that the mystery is explained next. On this word, see Rom 11:25.
35. Or, "even".
36. Or, "I marveled *with* great marvel", "I was amazed *with* great amazement". That is, I wondered greatly what it meant. "Wondered" is the same word as in Mk 15:44, and as "caused to marvel" in v 8.
37. Some holding the Future View (see 1:1) think the angel is referring to the future ruler's death-blow in 13:3, from which he recovers, which is the occasion of his coming out of the abyss and rising to power. The Spiritual View thinks this refers to the continual rising and falling of empires until Christ returns, the final one being described as the "eighth" in v 11.
38. Same phrase as in 11:7. Compare 13:1. On "abyss", see 9:1. Note how the angel says this at the end of the verse, "will be present".
39. Some manuscripts say "abyss, and to go..." {B}.
40. This is spoken of in 19:20. Same word as in v 11. On this word, see 2 Pet 2:1.

A. 1 Cor 6:18   B. Mt 4:4, mankind   C. 1 Tim 6:1   D. Rev 13:3, wound   E. Jn 9:39   F. Jn 2:10   G. Mt 3:1   H. Rev 4:6   J. 1 Cor 11:21
K. 1 Pet 1:16, holy   L. Act 1:8   M. Mt 8:17   N. Rev 13:1

	1F. "And the *ones* dwelling upon the earth¹ whose name² has not been written on³ the book *of* life^A since *the* foundation *of the* world⁴ will be caused-to-marvel⁵ while seeing the beast— because he was and is not and will be present⁶	
2E.	"Here⁷ *is* the mind⁸ having wisdom^B— The seven heads are seven mountains⁹ where the woman sits¹⁰ on them, and they are seven kings¹¹	9
	1F. "The five fell, the one is¹²	10
	2F. "The other did not yet come^C. And when he comes^C, he must^D remain^E *a* short¹³ *time*	
	3F. "And the beast which was and is not, is himself also *an* eighth.¹⁴ And he is from¹⁵ the seven. And he goes to destruction¹⁶	11
3E.	"And the ten horns which you saw are ten kings¹⁷ who did not-yet¹⁸ receive *a* kingdom^F, but they receive authority^G as kings with the beast *for* one hour¹⁹	12
	1F. "These have one purpose²⁰, and they give their power and authority *to* the beast	13
	2F. "These will wage-war^H against the Lamb. And the Lamb will overcome^J them— because He is Lord *of* lords and King *of* kings, and²¹ the *ones* with Him *are* called^K *ones* and chosen^L *ones* and faithful^M *ones*"	14
4E.	And he says *to* me, "The waters which you saw where the prostitute sits, are peoples^N and multitudes^O and nations and tongues	15
5E.	"And the ten horns which you saw, and²² the beast— these will hate^P the prostitute²³ and they will make her desolated²⁴ and naked^Q, and they will eat her flesh²⁵, and they will burn her up²⁶ with fire	16
	1F. "For God gave^R *it* into their hearts to do His purpose²⁷, and to do one purpose,²⁸ and to give their kingdom *to* the beast— until the words^S *of* God will be finished²⁹	17
6E.	"And the woman whom you saw is the great city³⁰ having *a* kingdom^F over the kings *of* the earth"	18
3D.	After³¹ these *things* I saw another angel coming down from heaven³², having great authority^G. And the earth was illuminated^T by his glory^U. *And he cried-out³³ with *a* strong voice, saying	18:1 2
	1E. "Babylon³⁴ the great fell, it fell! And it became *a* dwelling-place *of* demons^V, and *a* prison³⁵ *of* every unclean spirit, and *a* prison *of* every unclean bird, and *a* prison *of* every unclean and hated³⁶ wild-beast³⁷	
	1F. "Because all the nations have drunk³⁸ from the wine *of* the passion³⁹ *of* her sexual-immorality^W	3
	2F. "And the kings *of* the earth committed-sexual-immorality^X with her⁴⁰	
	3F. "And the merchants *of* the earth became-rich^Y by the power^Z *of* her luxury"	
4D.	And I heard another voice from heaven,⁴¹ saying	4
	1E. "Come out of her, my people^AA, so-that⁴² you will not participate⁴³ *in* her sins, and so that you will not receive of her plagues^BB	

1. On this phrase, see 3:10.
2. This is the same grammar as with "whose" in 13:8, the ones "*of* whom the name has not been written...".
3. Here it says written "on", as in 3:12; 14:1; 17:5. GK *2093*. It says written "in" in 13:8; 20:12; 21:27; 22:18, 19. GK *1877*.
4. On the phrase "since the foundation of the world", see Heb 9:26.
5. Or, "be astonished, amazed". Same word and grammar as in 13:3. Same word as "wondered" in v 6, 7; Mk 15:44; Lk 1:21. Elsewhere as "marvel" 37 times. GK *2513*. Related to "marvelous" in 15:1.
6. Or, "will come, will be here". Some manuscripts say "is present" {N}. Only here is it future tense. Same word as in Lk 13:1; 1 Cor 5:3; 2 Cor 10:2. Used 24 times. GK *4205*. Related to "coming" in 2 Thes 2:8. The reading "and yet is" in the KJV is based on a printing error in the Greek text of Erasmus (see the Introduction on him).
7. Or, "At this point", a mind having wisdom is needed. Similar to the statement in 13:18. Some take this phrase, "Here is the mind having wisdom", with the previous verse.
8. Same word as "understanding" in 13:18. On this word, see "mind" in Rom 7:23.
9. Some think this is geographical, and points to Rome, which is known as the city on seven hills. Others think it is political, and points to kingdoms headed by the kings mentioned next. Note that the seven heads/mountains/kings belong to the beast. The woman sits on the seven heads/mountains (v 9), on the beast (v 3), on the many waters (v 1, 15). This is the common word for "mountain, mount, hill", used 63 times. GK *4001*.
10. Note how this is explained in v 18. Some think this means the woman is an empire; others, that she controls or guides the kings in their empires.
11. The seven heads of the beast represent seven kings, and the beast himself is an eighth king, v 11.
12. Some think the seven kings/kingdoms represent seven world kingdoms, five prior to John (such as Egypt, Assyria, Babylon, Persia and Greece); one at John's time (Rome "is" when John wrote); and one yet to come (symbolizing all anti-God governments until the end; or, the final empire at the end). Compare Dan 7. Others think they symbolize the fullness of the Roman empire, which itself is a symbol of the anti-God world system that exists in various forms until Christ returns. Others identify the kings as seven specific Roman Emperors. Some manuscripts say "and the one is" {K}.
13. Or, "*a little while*". Same word as in 12:12. Elsewhere as a time designation only in Act 26:28, 29; and as "little" in Act 14:28; Jam 4:14; 1 Pet 1:6; 5:10 (perhaps). On this word, see "small" in Act 12:18.
14. The Future and Spiritual Views (see 1:1) think the eighth is the final world kingdom and/or world ruler (the Antichrist).
15. Some think the angel means this king is "*one* of the seven", that is, the seventh after his mortal wound is healed; others, that this kingdom is "out of the seven", meaning it comes from them, but is distinct from them, as the final embodiment of them.
16. The eighth does not "fall". He goes to destruction. Some think this means the eighth is destroyed by Christ in 19:20.
17. Daniel's fourth beast also had ten horns representing ten kings, Dan 7:7, 24. Note that these "ten kings" help destroy Babylon (v 16-17), and that the "kings of the earth" weep over this (18:9). Some think the ten kings symbolize all the nations under the power of the Antichrist, or the fullness of his political power. Some holding the Future View think they represent a ten-nation confederacy serving the Antichrist.
18. Instead of "not yet", some manuscripts say "not" {N}.
19. That is, a short period of time. This hour ends when the Lamb overcomes them, v 14. On this word, see Lk 2:38.
20. That is, to advance the kingdom of the beast. Same word as in v 17.
21. This last phrase may be rendered as part of the subject, "And the Lamb and the called and chosen and faithful *ones* with Him will overcome them".
22. Some manuscripts say "on" {K}.
23. The beast turns against Babylon, the prostitute riding on his back, and destroys her. The kings of the earth in league with her, and the merchants, and the sailors, mourn her destruction in 18:9-20. Thus the beast destroys Babylon, carrying out God's will, and Christ destroys the beast when He returns. Some think the beast does this at the point at which he demands worship of himself. He destroys all religion and sets himself up as god, 2 Thes 2:4.
24. This is a participle, make her "having been made desolate", they will render her desolate. On this word, see "desolated" in 18:17. Some holding the Past View (see 1:1) think the beast is Rome and the woman is Jerusalem, and the ten kings are the governors of Rome's ten provinces.
25. This word is plural, "*pieces of* her flesh", in keeping with how wild beasts devour an animal. Same grammar as in 19:18, 21. They devour the prostitute's wealth and resources, and burn her carcass.
26. This word, "burn up", is the same word as in 8:7; 18:8. GK *2876*.
27. On this word, used in v 13 and twice in this verse, see 1 Cor 1:10.
28. That is, to unite together to do God's purpose.
29. Or, "completed, fulfilled". That is, until all God's prophetic words come to pass. On this word, see 10:7.
30. On "the great city", see 16:19. Some think this refers to the woman in terms of the capital city where her power is located. She is the city, and the system of power over the kings of the earth proceeding from the city. Some think the city is Rome; others, Jerusalem; others, literal Babylon; others, an end-time city. Others do not think it is a physical city, but a system of anti-Christian deception.
31. Some manuscripts say "And after..." {N}.
32. Note that John's perspective continues to be from earth, the wilderness, 17:3.
33. On this word, see Mt 8:29. Some manuscripts add "mightily" {K}.
34. On Babylon, see 16:19. This same exclamation is in 14:8.
35. Same word as in 2:10; 20:7. On this word, see Act 5:22.
36. This is a participle, "having been hated". On this word, see Rom 9:13.
37. Some manuscripts omit the last "prison" statement, so that it says "and *a* prison *of* every unclean and hated bird" {C}. There are other variations in the order of the three "prison" statements and the word "hated". On this word, see "beast" in 13:1.
38. Some manuscripts say "fallen" {D}, so that it says "the nations have fallen because of the wine...".
39. See the same phrase in 14:8.
40. Similar phrase in 17:2; 18:9.
41. Some think this is the voice of an angel; others, of Christ. Note that John's perspective is still from earth.
42. Or, "so that you might not", and likewise later in the verse. GK *2671*.
43. On this word, see "co-partnered" in Phil 4:14.

A. Rev 3:5 B. 1 Cor 12:8 C. Mk 16:2 D. Mt 16:21 E. Jn 15:4, abide F. Mt 3:2 G. Rev 6:8 H. Rev 13:4 J. Rev 2:7 K. Rom 8:28 L. Rom 8:33 M. Col 1:2 N. Rev 5:9 O. Mk 2:13 P. Rom 9:13 Q. Jam 2:15 R. Eph 1:22 S. 1 Cor 12:8 T. Heb 6:4, enlightened U. 2 Pet 2:10 V. 1 Cor 10:20 W. 1 Cor 5:1 X. 1 Cor 6:18 Y. 1 Tim 6:18 Z. Mk 5:30 AA. Rev 21:3 BB. Rev 13:3, wound

1F.	"Because her sins reached[1] as far as heaven, and God remembered[2] her wrongs[A]	5
2E.	"Render[3] *to* her as indeed she herself rendered[4], and double[5] the doubles[6] in accordance with her works[B]	6
1F.	"Mix double *for* her in the cup *in* which she mixed	
2F.	"To the degree she glorified[C] herself and she lived-luxuriously[7], to that degree[8] give her torment[9] and mourning[D]	7
3E.	"Because[10] she says in her heart that[11] 'I sit *as* queen and I am not *a* widow, and I will never see[E] mourning[D]', *for this reason her plagues will come in one day— death[12] and mourning[D] and famine[F]— and she will be burned-up[13] with fire	8
1F.	"Because the Lord God, the *One* having judged[14] her, *is* strong[15]	
4E.	"And the kings *of* the earth having committed-sexual-immorality with her and lived-luxuriously will weep[G] and beat-their-breasts[16] over her when they see the smoke *of* her burning[H], *while standing at *a* distance because of the fear[J] *of* her torment[K], saying	9 10
1F.	'Woe, woe, the great city, Babylon, the strong[17] city— because your judgment[L] came *in* one hour[M]'	
5E.	"And the merchants *of* the earth weep[G] and mourn[18] over her	11
1F.	"Because no one buys their cargo[19] anymore—*cargo	12
1G.	"*Of* gold and *of* silver and *of* precious[N] stone[O] and *of* pearls[P]	
2G.	"And *of* fine-linen[Q] and *of* purple and *of* silk and *of* scarlet	
3G.	"And everything made-of-citron[20] wood, and every object[R] made-of-ivory[21], and every object from very-precious[N] wood[22] and brass and iron and marble	
4G.	"And cinnamon and spice[23] and incense and perfume[S] and frankincense[T]	13
5G.	"And wine[U] and olive-oil[V] and fine-flour and wheat[W] and cattle[X] and sheep	
6G.	"And *of* horses and *of* carriages[24]	
7G.	"And *of* bodies[25]— even[26] souls[Y] *of* people[Z]	
2F.	"And[27] the fruit[28] *of* the desire[AA] *of* your soul[29] departed from you— indeed all the rich[30] *things* and shining[BB] *things* perished[31] from you, and *people*[32] will never find[CC] them anymore	14
3F.	"The merchants[33] *of* these *things*— the *ones* having become-rich[DD] from her— will stand at *a* distance because of the fear *of* her torment, weeping and mourning, *saying[34]	15 16
1G.	'Woe, woe, the great city— the *one* having been clothed-with fine-linen[Q] and purple and scarlet, and having been gilded[EE] with gold, and *with* precious[N] stone[O] and pearl[P]—*because so much wealth[FF] was desolated[35] *in* one hour!'	17

1. This word means "to join, glue, unite, cling". The idea of the idiom is that Babylon's sins "cling-together [in a mass reaching or heaping] as far as heaven". Some think this is an allusion to the tower of Babel in Gen 11:4. On this word, see "join" in 1 Cor 6:16.
2. Or, "kept in mind". Used of God only here. On this word, see Jn 16:21. Compare the related word in Lk 1:54.
3. Or, "Give back". Some think this is addressed to God's agents for Babylon's destruction, the beast and ten kings in 17:16-17. Others think it is a prayer to God by the voice in v 4, symbolic of the prayers of the saints. On this word, see Mt 16:27.
4. Some manuscripts add "*to you*" {N}.
5. This verb is used only here. GK *1488*. Some manuscripts add "*to her*" {N}.
6. That is, give her back double for the things she has doubled to others. On "doubles", which occurs again in the next sentence, see 1 Tim 5:17.
7. Or, "live sensually", in a material and sexual sense. Elsewhere only in v 9. GK *5139*. Related to "luxury" in v 3.
8. This construction "to the degree... to that degree" is similar to that found in Heb 7:20, 22.
9. Same word as in v 10, 15. On this word, see 14:11.
10. Some take this as the reason for what precedes, making it point 3F., and then begin point 3E. with "For this reason".
11. Some manuscripts omit this word {K}, which serves to introduce the quotation.
12. Or, "pestilence", as in 6:8.
13. Same word as in 17:16, to which this seems to refer.
14. On this word, see Mt 7:1. Some manuscripts say "the *One* judging" {K}.
15. Or, "mighty, powerful". Used 29 times. GK *2708*. Related to "strength" in Eph 1:19; and "can do" in Gal 5:6.
16. Same word as in 1:7, over Christ.
17. Same word as in v 8.
18. Some manuscripts say "will weep and mourn" {N}.
19. Or, "freight". The merchants weep for their own financial loss, not because they care about Babylon. Elsewhere only in v 12; Act 21:3. GK *1203*.
20. This is a decorative wood from N. Africa. Used only here. GK *2591*.
21. Used only here. GK *1804*. This word is part of an "ivory" word group based on the word from which we get "elephant".
22. On this word, see "cross" in 1 Pet 2:24. Some manuscripts say "stone" {A}.
23. Some manuscripts omit "and spice" {N}.
24. This refers to a four-wheeled carriage or wagon. Used only here. GK *4832*. Not the same word as a "chariot" in 9:9.
25. That is, slaves; human livestock; treated as commodities like horses and wagons. On this word, see Eph 1:23.
26. Or, "and", "And *of* bodies. And souls *of* people". There is a difference of grammar here. "Bodies" has the same grammar as the items in 1G., 2G, and 6G.; "souls" as the items in 3G, 4G, and 5G. "And" might indicate two different groups are in view, or that the people are being viewed from two different angles (the merchants' vs. God's). "Even" would mean this is the climax to the list.
27. Here the voice from heaven (v 4) addresses Babylon directly.
28. Or, "ripe fruit". Used only here. GK *3967*. The plums of your soul's desire.
29. That is, the fruit your soul desired, the fruit you hoped to gain, the prosperity and wealth you desired.
30. This word means "shining, sleek, fat, oily (anointed with oil)". The things of luxury. Used only here. GK *3353*.
31. On this word, see 1 Cor 1:18. Some manuscripts say "departed" {N}, as earlier in the verse.
32. Some manuscripts say "you" {N}.
33. After the lengthy description of v 12-14, the voice from heaven (v 4) resumes and completes the merchants' response.
34. Some manuscripts say "and saying" {N}.
35. Same word as in v 19; 17:16. Elsewhere only in Mt 12:25; Lk 11:17. GK *2246*.

A. Act 18:14, crime B. Mt 26:10 C. Rom 8:30 D. Jam 4:9 E. Mt 13:17, experience F. Lk 21:11 G. Jn 11:33 H. 1 Pet 4:12, fiery J. Eph 5:21 K. Rev 14:11 L. Jn 3:19 M. Lk 2:38 N. 2 Pet 1:4 O. Mk 16:3 P. Mt 13:45 Q. Rev 19:8 R. 1 Thes 4:4, vessel S. Mt 26:7 T. Mt 2:11 U. 1 Tim 5:23 V. Jam 5:14, oil W. Mk 4:28, grain X. 1 Cor 15:39, livestock Y. Jam 5:20 Z. Mt 4:4, mankind AA. Gal 5:16 BB. Rev 22:1 CC. 2 Pet 3:10 DD. 1 Tim 6:18 EE. Rev 17:4 FF. 1 Tim 6:17, riches

6E.	"And every helmsman¹ and everyone sailing to *a* place² and sailors and all-who work^A the sea stood at *a* distance, °and were crying-out^B while seeing the smoke *of* her burning, saying 'What city *is* like³ the great city?' °And they threw dirt on their heads⁴ and were crying-out, weeping^C and mourning^D, saying	18 19

    1F. 'Woe, woe, the great city by which all the *ones* having ships at sea became-rich^E because-of⁵ her preciousness⁶— because she was desolated^F *in* one hour!'

  7E. "Celebrate⁷ over her, heaven and saints and⁸ apostles⁹ and prophets, because God judged^G your judgment¹⁰ from her"   20

5D. And one strong angel picked-up *a* stone^H like *a* large millstone¹¹, and threw^J *it* into the sea, saying   21

  1E. "In this manner, Babylon the great city will be thrown-*down*^J *with* violence¹² and never found again

    1F. "And *a* sound *of* harpists and musicians and flute-players and trumpeters will never be heard in you again   22
    2F. "And every craftsman^K *of* every craft^L will never be found in you again
    3F. "And *a* sound *of a* mill¹³ will never be heard in you again
    4F. "And *a* light *of a* lamp^M will never shine^N in you again   23
    5F. "And *a* sound¹⁴ *of a* bridegroom and bride will never be heard in you again

  2E. "Because your merchants were the princes^O *of* the earth
  3E. "Because all the nations were deceived^P by your sorcery¹⁵, °and in her *the* blood *of* prophets and saints was found, even¹⁶ *of* all the *ones* having been slain^Q upon the earth"   24

10C. After¹⁷ these *things* I heard *something* like¹⁸ *a* loud voice *of a* great multitude¹⁹ in heaven²⁰ *of* *ones* saying   19:1

  1D. "Hallelujah²¹— the salvation^R and the glory²² and the power *of* our²³ God!²⁴

    1E. "Because His judgments^S *are* true and righteous   2
    2E. "Because He judged^G the great prostitute^T who corrupted²⁵ the earth with her sexual-immorality²⁶, and He avenged²⁷ the blood²⁸ *of* His slaves^U from her hand"

  2D. And *a* second *time* they have said, "Hallelujah! And her smoke goes up²⁹ forever and ever^V"   3
  3D. And the twenty four elders and the four living-creatures fell and gave-worship^W *to* God, the *One* sitting on the throne, saying "Amen. Hallelujah!"   4

11C. And³⁰ *a* voice³¹ came out from the throne, saying "Give-praise^X *to* our God, all His slaves³², and³³ the *ones* fearing^Y Him— the³⁴ small and the great³⁵"   5
12C. And I heard *something* like *the* voice³⁶ *of a* great multitude³⁷ and like *the* sound *of* many waters³⁸ and like *the* sound *of* strong thunders   6

  1D. Saying, "Hallelujah! Because *the* Lord our³⁹ God, the Almighty^Z, *began to* reign⁴⁰. °Let us rejoice^AA and be overjoyed^BB, and give⁴¹ the glory *to* Him, because the wedding⁴² *of* the Lamb came⁴³, and His wife⁴⁴ prepared^CC herself"   7

1. Or, "pilot" of the ship. Elsewhere only in Act 27:11, which also mentions the captain or owner-captain. GK *3237*.
2. Instead of "to *a* place", some manuscripts say "on the sea"; others, "on the river"; others, "on the ships" {B}.
3. Same word as in the similar question in 13:4. On this word, see "resembling" in 1:13.
4. This is a symbol of grief.
5. Or, "from, by, out of ". GK *1666*.
6. Or, "costliness". That is, Babylon's precious things. Used only here. GK *5509*. Related to "precious" in 17:4; 18:12, 16; 21:11, 19; 2 Pet 1:4.
7. Here the voice from heaven (v 4) directly addresses the believers again (as in v 4). On this word, see 12:12. Compare 11:10.
8. Some manuscripts omit this word {N}, so that it says "heaven and holy apostles and", where "saints" is the same word as "holy".
9. Some think this refers to the twelve; others take it in the broader sense. On this word, see 1 Cor 12:28.
10. God exacted your verdict or sentence from Babylon. By "your judgment", some think the verdict Babylon exacted from believers is meant (as in Mt 7:2); others, the verdict believers wanted God to exact from Babylon; others, a judgment favorable to believers (judgment was passed in favor of the saints, as in Dan 7:22). Same word as in 17:1. On this word, see Jn 9:39.
11. That is, the large one turned by a donkey, as in Mk 9:42. Used only here. GK *3684*.
12. That is, with the rush of a sudden attack. Used only here. GK *3996*. Related to "rush" in Act 7:57.
13. That is, the small one turned by two women, as in Mt 24:41.
14. Or, "voice". Same word as used twice in v 22, on which see "voices" in 4:5. "Sound" refers to all the sounds associated with a wedding.
15. Elsewhere only in Gal 5:20. GK *5758*. Related to the word in 9:21.
16. Or, "and".
17. Some manuscripts say "And after..." {N}. Note that John's perspective changes from the wilderness (17:3-18:24) back to heaven, where he last was in 17:1-2. The angel of 17:1 returns John to heaven (so to speak), and may remain with him until 19:10. Here, John hears heaven's response to what he has been shown in chapters 17-18.
18. Some manuscripts omit "*something* like" {N}.
19. A "great multitude" is mentioned also in v 6 and in 7:9. Some think this is a group of angels (as in 5:11), and that redeemed ones are called to join in v 5; others, that this group is made up of redeemed ones (as in 7:9).
20. Note that the trumpets were followed by loud voices in heaven and the 24 elders praising God in 11:15-18, the last time either was heard. Some think this is that same multitude.
21. This is a transliterated Hebrew word meaning "Praise the Lord". Elsewhere only in v 3, 4, 6. GK *252*.
22. Some manuscripts add "and the honor" {N}.
23. Some manuscripts say "the Lord our God" {K}.
24. The grammar here is not the same as in "*be to*" our God in 1:6; 5:13; 12; Rom 11:36; 16:27; Gal 1:5; Eph 3:21; Phil 4:20; 1 Tim 1:17; 2 Tim 4:18; Heb 13:21; 2 Pet 3:18; Jude 25. It is the same as Rev 12:10, and "came" or "came to pass" could be added here also. It may also be rendered, "*is of* our God", meaning either "*is from* our God" or "*belongs to* our God" (as in 7:10).
25. Or, "was corrupting". On this word, see "ruin" in 1 Cor 3:17. Related to "destroying" in 11:18.
26. Compare 14:8; 17:2; 18:3.
27. Same word as in 6:10.
28. This blood is mentioned in 17:6; 18:24.
29. Same expression as in 14:11.
30. Some think this looks forward, and that v 6-7 is spoken in response to this command. The multitude just gave praise to God for the judgment of Babylon (looking back), and now the command is given to praise Him for the new day that has arrived (looking forward). Others think this concludes the praise of the previous section, and make this point 4D. Verse 6 then begins a new point (11C.) that is unrelated to this command, but is a second thing John "heard", parallel with the first thing he heard in v 1.
31. This is apparently the voice of one of the angels at the throne. Jesus never says "our God". He says "My God", and "My God and your God", Jn 20:17.
32. His slaves include angels and humans, as seen in v 10. On this word, see 1:1.
33. Or, "even", making both phrases refer to humans. With "and", "all His slaves" may be all-inclusive, and this phrase may refer to humans in particular. Some manuscripts omit this word {C}, so that it says "all His slaves fearing Him".
34. Some manuscripts say "both the small..." {K}.
35. This phrase appears also in 11:18; 13:16; 19:18; and as "great and small" in 20:12. It is always used of humans. Compare Act 8:10; 26:22; Heb 8:11.
36. On this word, see 4:5. Same word as "sound" later.
37. Some think this is in response to the command in v 5, and therefore is a group of redeemed ones. In this case, "His wife" (v 7) is the name of this group. Others think these are angels singing about redeemed ones, His wife. Others think this multitude includes angels and humans.
38. On "many waters", see 14:2, which also has "loud thunder".
39. Some manuscripts omit this word {C}.
40. Or, the Lord "reigned", or "became king". Same word and tense as in 11:17. Same word as in 5:10; 11:15; 20:4, 6; 22:5; Lk 1:33; Rom 5:14, 17, 21; 6:12; 1 Cor 15:25. Elsewhere only as "be king" in Mt 2:22; Lk 19:14, 27; 1 Tim 6:15; and "become king" in 1 Cor 4:8. GK *996*. Related to "king" and "kingdom".
41. Some manuscripts say "... and be overjoyed. And we will give the glory..." {C}.
42. Or, "wedding-celebration". This wedding of the Lamb is mentioned only here. Same word as in v 9. It pictures the permanent and complete union of Christ and His people. On this word, see Mt 22:11.
43. That is, it is here, it has arrived, as this word is used in 14:7 and 6:17. Some think this wedding is the Second Coming itself, and the banquet pictures an eternal celebration with Christ. Some holding the Future View think the wedding takes place in heaven after the rapture, before Christ's return in v 11, and the banquet takes place after His return.
44. Same word as in 21:9, where it occurs along with the word "bride". Some think this represents the redeemed of all time, 21:12, 14. Some holding the Future View think it represents the redeemed of the church from Pentecost to the rapture. On this word, see 1 Cor 11:3.

A. Mt 26:10 B. Mt 8:29 C. Jn 11:33 D. Jam 4:9 E. 1 Tim 6:18 F. Rev 18:17 G. Mt 7:1 H. Mk 16:3 J. Rev 2:22, throw K. Heb 11:10, designer L. Act 17:29 M. Lk 11:34 N. Phil 2:15 O. Rev 6:15 P. Jam 5:19, err Q. 1 Jn 3:12 R. Lk 19:9 S. Jn 3:19 T. Rev 17:1 U. Rev 1:1 V. Rev 20:10 W. Rev 4:10 X. Rom 15:11, praise Y. Eph 5:33, respecting Z. Rev 1:8 AA. 2 Cor 13:11 BB. Lk 10:21, rejoice greatly CC. Mk 14:15

2D. And[1] *authority*[2] was given *to* her to[3] clothe *herself* with shining[A] clean[4] fine-linen[5]. For the fine-linen is the righteous-acts[6] *of* the saints[B]   8

3D. And he[7] says *to* me, "Write— 'Blessed[C] *are* the *ones* having been called[8] to the banquet[9] *of* the wedding *of* the Lamb' "   9

13C. And he says *to* me, "These[10] words are true[D] *ones of* God[11]". *And I fell in front of his feet to give-worship[12] *to* him   10

1D. And he says *to* me "See[E] *that you* not *do it*.[13] I am *a* fellow-slave[14] *of* you and your brothers[F]— the *ones* holding[G] the testimony[H] *of* Jesus.[15] Give worship *to* God. For the testimony *of* Jesus is the spirit[16] *of* prophecy'"

6B. And I saw heaven[17] having been opened[18]   11

1C. And behold— *there was a* white[19] horse, and the *One* sitting on it being called[20] Faithful[K] and True[21]

1D. And He judges[L] and wages-war[M] in righteousness[N]
2D. And His eyes *are* like[22] *a* flame *of* fire, and upon His head *are* many diadems[23]   12

1E. He has[24] *a* name having been written which no one knows except Himself
2E. And *He* has[25] clothed *Himself* with *a* garment having been dipped[26] *in* blood   13

3D. And His name has been called[O]— The Word *of* God[27]
4D. And the armies[P] in heaven[28] were following Him on white horses, *the riders* having been dressed-in white clean[Q] fine-linen[R]   14
5D. And *a* sharp sword comes out *of* His mouth,[29] in order that He may strike the nations with it   15
6D. And He Himself will shepherd[30] them with *an* iron rod[31]
7D. And He Himself treads[32] the winepress[33] *of* the wine *of* the fury[S] *of* the wrath[T] *of* God Almighty[U]
8D. And He has *a* name having been written on the garment and[34] on His thigh— "King *of* kings, and Lord *of* lords"[35]   16

1. Some place all of v 8 in the quotation preceding; others, only the first sentence, making the "For..." statement the words of John. Others think none of v 8 is part of the song just quoted.
2. The word "authority" is supplied from 6:8, as throughout this book.
3. Or, "that she might". GK *2671*.
4. Same word as in v 14. Some manuscripts say "shining and clean" {N}.
5. This is her wedding dress. Used twice in this verse, and in v 14. Elsewhere only in 18:12, 16. GK *1115*. Related to the word in Lk 16:19.
6. Same word as in 15:4. Their works follow with them, 14:13. Some think John means God's "verdicts *of* justification" pronounced upon the saints. On this word, see "regulation" in Rom 1:32.
7. Some think this is the angel who has been guiding John since 17:1. This occurs again in 22:8 with another such angel. Others think it is the voice of the one in v 5, who is now with him in person.
8. Or, "summoned, invited". Elsewhere, John only uses this word to mean "named", as in v 11, 13. On this word, see Rom 8:30. Some think these guests are also the bride, just as Christ is the lamb and the shepherd. Some holding the Future View think the guests and the bride are different groups.
9. Or, "dinner, supper". Same word as in v 17. On this word, see "dinner" in Lk 14:12. Compare Mt 26:29; Lk 13:29. The wedding banquet typically began after the wedding and lasted several days.
10. Some think this applies to v 9; others, to all this angel has been part of since 17:1.
11. Some manuscripts say "are the true *words of* God" {N}.
12. Or, "pay homage". On this word, see 4:10. John may have thought the angel was God Himself speaking to him, or he may have wished to pay homage to the angel as to a superior. In any case, the angel corrects him.
13. Same idiom as in 22:9. Similar to Mt 8:4; Mk 1:44; and the positive command in Heb 8:5. In Mt 8:4, a second verb is stated, "See *that* you tell". Here, the verb "you do" is to be supplied by the reader. In English, using the same verb of seeing, we might say "watch it" or "look out" or "see here", all meaning "do not do that".
14. Same word as in 6:11; 22:9. Elsewhere only in Mt 18:28, 29, 31, 33; 24:29; Col 1:7; 4:7. GK *5281*.
15. Some think this means the testimony "*given by* Jesus"; others, "*about* Jesus". Later in this verse, it means "*given by* Jesus". Same phrase as in 1:2, 9; 12:17; 20:4. Compare 6:9; 12:11.
16. That is, the testimony given by Jesus is the inspiration (breath) of prophecy, this one and all others. What the angel is speaking is Christ's testimony, not the angel's. Prophecy has its source in the testimony given by Jesus, borne by the Spirit. So worship Him, not the angel who delivered it. The testimony given by Jesus is the content of what the Spirit inspires the prophets to speak.
17. This is the only place John sees heaven opened. This is the next step in the progression of heavenly scenes (see 11:19 and 15:5). Everything so far has pointed forward to Christ's return, but stopped short of personalizing it. This is the climax to which all has pointed. Some think what follows describes His second coming to earth at the end of the age. Some holding the Past View think it describes His spiritual conquest of the nations by His army (Christians) with the gospel (the sword from His mouth, the Word of God).
18. Same word as in 4:1 (a door); 5:2 (the seals); 11:19; 15:5 (the temple). It is opened so Jesus and His army can come to earth. Same word as in Jn 1:51; Act 10:11. GK *487*.
19. Some think white symbolizes victory here. See 4:4.
20. Some manuscripts omit this word {C}, so that it says "the *One* sitting upon it *is* faithful and true".
21. Compare 3:14. Same word as in v 9.
22. Some manuscripts omit this word {C}. Same description as in 1:14; 2:18.
23. On this word, see 13:1. It is a king's crown.
24. This is a participle, "*He is* having". This refers to the person (Jesus) as the subject, not to the diadems, and not specifically to His head. John does not say where this name is written.
25. Or, "And *He* has been clothed-with *a* garment...". This is a participle, "*He is* having clothed *himself*". A form of the verb "to be" has been supplied to each of the four descriptions in v 12-13.
26. Some think the blood is Christ's own (from the cross). Others think it is the blood of His martyrs, those slain for Him. Others think John is referring to the blood of His enemies already killed. Elsewhere only in Lk 16:24; Jn 13:26. GK *970*. Related to "baptism" in Mk 1:4. Some manuscripts say "sprinkled" {B}.
27. Some think John is referring to Jn 1:1, 14.
28. Some think this army is made up of angels, 2 Thes 1:7; others, of the redeemed, Rev 17:14; others, of both.
29. Same words as in 1:16. Some think this means that whatever Jesus speaks happens. Jesus needs no physical weapon to kill His enemies, v 21. Compare 2 Thes 2:8. Some holding the Past View (see 1:1) think this symbolizes the gospel, by which He conquers them.
30. That is, "rule", a sense also in 2:27; 12:5 (see 2:27). The usual sense is "tend to, care for, protect, guide". Elsewhere only in Mt 2:6; Lk 17:7; Jn 21:16; Act 20:28; 1 Cor 9:7; 1 Pet 5:2; Rev 2:27; 7:17; 12:5; and as "tending" in Jude 12. GK *4477*. Related to the noun "shepherd" in Eph 4:11; and "flock" in 1 Pet 5:2.
31. Overcomers will be with Jesus, 2:27. Same words as in 12:5. Jesus will crush all opposition, breaking them like pottery, 2:27. He will herd this flock to its destiny in a way that permits no opposition or deviation.
32. Same word as in 14:20, where this press is also mentioned. On this word, see "trample" in Lk 10:19.
33. Jesus treads the winepress from which comes the wine of wrath that they must drink, 14:10; 16:19. This is truly the "wrath of the Lamb", 6:16. The suffering Savior is also the executor of God's wrath, 2 Thes 1:7-8.
34. Or, "even", meaning on the portion of the garment that covered His thigh.
35. The phrase "King of kings and Lord of lords" is also in 17:14; and in a different form, in 1 Tim 6:15.

A. Rev 22:1 B. 1 Pet 1:16, holy C. Rev 22:14 D. Jn 7:28 E. Lk 2:26 F. Act 16:40 G. 1 Jn 1:8, have H. Jn 1:7 J. 1 Cor 12:10 K. Col 1:2 L. Mt 7:1 M. Rev 13:4 N. Rom 1:17 O. Rom 8:30 P. Act 23:10, troop Q. Tit 1:15 R. Rev 19:8 S. Rev 16:19 T. Rev 16:19 U. Rev 1:8

Revelation 19:17	1014	Verse

2C. And I saw one angel standing in the sun, and he cried-out[A] with *a* loud voice, saying *to* all the birds flying in mid-heaven[1]   17

    1D. "Come, be gathered-together[B] for the great[2] banquet[C] *of* God, *in order that you may eat the* flesh[3] *of* kings, and *the* flesh[D] *of* commanders[4], and *the* flesh *of* powerful[E] *ones,* and *the* flesh *of* horses and *of* the *ones* sitting on them, and *the* flesh *of* everyone— both[5] free and slaves, both[6] small and great"   18

3C. And I saw the beast and the kings *of* the earth and their armies[F] having been gathered-together[7] to make war[8] against the *One* sitting on the horse, and against His army[F]   19

    1D. And the beast was seized[G], and with him the false-prophet[H] having done the signs[J] in his presence[9], by which he deceived[K] the *ones* having received the mark[L] *of* the beast, and the *ones* giving-worship[M] *to* his image[N]   20

        1E. While living[10], the two were thrown into the lake *of* fire[11] burning[O] with sulphur[12]

    2D. And the rest[P] were killed with the sword *of* the *One* sitting on the horse, the *sword* having come-out[13] of His mouth   21
    3D. And all the birds were filled-to-satisfaction[Q] from their flesh

4C. And I saw[14] *an* angel coming down from heaven, having the key *of* the abyss[15], and *a* great chain[R] on his hand. *And he seized[S] the dragon— the ancient serpent, who is *the* devil and Satan[16]— and bound[T] him *for a* thousand years[17]   20:1, 2

    1D. And he threw him into the abyss, and shut[U] and sealed[V] *it* over him[18]— in order that he might not deceive[K] the nations[19] anymore until the thousand years are finished[20]. After[21] these *things* he must[W] be released[22] *for a* short time[23]   3

5C. And[24] I saw thrones[X]— and they[25] sat-*down*[26] on them, and judgment[27] was given *to* them— and the souls[28] *of* the *ones* having been beheaded[29] because of the testimony[Y] *of* Jesus and[30] because of the word[Z] *of* God, and[31] they who did not worship the beast nor his image, and did not receive the mark upon the forehead and upon their hand   4

1. That is, in the sky. Elsewhere only in 8:13; 14:6. GK *3547*.
2. Some manuscripts say "the banquet *of* the great God" {N}.
3. This word is plural all five times in this verse, and in v 21. It could be rendered "eat pieces-of-flesh *of* kings", etc. See 17:16.
4. Same word as in 6:15, where a similar sentence occurs.
5. Some manuscripts omit this word {K}, making one expression "free and slave— both small and great".
6. A different method of saying "both... and" is used here. It can also be rendered "and small and great".
7. Same word as in 16:14 and 19:17.
8. Or, "make the war, do the battle", meaning the one previously mentioned, the one in 16:14, 16 (Har-Magedon) and 17:14. This is the only time "the" is included in the phrase "make war" (on which see 13:7), and some manuscripts omit it {N}.
9. Compare 13:14.
10. Or, "alive". Their final sentence is immediately executed.
11. That is, the lake characterized by fire, the fiery lake. It is also mentioned in 20:10, 14, 15; 21:8. It is the second death, 20:14; 21:8.
12. On this word, see 14:10.
13. Or, "gone out". GK *2002*. Not related to the word in v 15; 1:16.
14. Some think 19:11-22:5 proceeds in chronological order, meaning that this binding for a thousand years follows Christ's return. Since His coming precedes the 1000 years (the millennium), this view is called "pre-millennialism" (P-M). It believes there will be a literal 1000-year kingdom on earth after His second coming. The final judgment of 20:11 follows this millennium. Others think 20:1-10 is not in chronological order, but gives another symbolic overview of this present age (being similar in placement to the visions between the sixth and seventh seals, and trumpets; or, this point being placed as 7B.). Just as chapter 12 returns to the beginning, so does chapter 20. In one view, Satan is bound at Christ's death, believers live and reign in heaven with Him in this present age. The 1000 years is symbolic of this whole age between His two comings. The battle of 20:8 is the same battle as 19:19. The judgment of 20:11 follows immediately after His return in 19:11. This view is called "a-millennialism" (A-M), because it believes there is no literal 1000-year kingdom on earth after His second coming. In another view, 20:1-10 depicts the end of the present church age. It will be a 1000-year period (whether literal or symbolic in length) that will be a golden age brought about by the conversion of the nations to Christ through the church (symbolized by the binding of Satan, either at Christ's death, or still in the future). Satan will lead a rebellion at the end of it, and then Christ will return. This view is called "post-millennialism" (PST), because it believes Christ returns after this millennium. There are variations of each of these three views.
15. On this word, see 9:1. Some think this is that same angel.
16. These four names are also in 12:9. A-M thinks this indicates that this binding began then, when Satan was thrown out of heaven.
17. This "1000 years", known as the millennium (a Latin word meaning 1000 years), is mentioned only in 20:2, 3, 4, 5, 6, 7.
18. P-M views this as a confinement from all activity on earth; A-M and PST as a restriction, a restraint on Satan's activities at the national level, so that he is prevented from prematurely bringing about the battle in v 8, and from stopping the gospel, Mt 24:14.
19. P-M thinks believers survive His coming and repopulate the earth. From the succeeding generations, nations and unbelievers arise. A-M and PST think these are nations of this present world.
20. Or, "completed, fulfilled". Same word as in v 5, 7, on which see 10:7.
21. Some manuscripts say "And after..." {N}.
22. Same word as in 20:7, and 9:14.
23. This is described in v 7. On "short time", see 6:11. Not the same words as 12:12.
24. This is the Greek word order of this verse.
25. Some think John is referring back to Christ and the redeemed in 19:14, 19, and that the souls that follow are a sub-group of this larger group. Others think he is anticipating those he speaks of next. He saw thrones and souls who did not worship the beast. And the souls came to life or lived and sat on the thrones and reigned with Him 1000 years. Other passages speak about those who reign with Christ, apostles (Mt 19:28); the saints (1 Cor 6:2; Dan 7:27); the overcomers (Rev 3:21); etc. Some think these other passages apply here; others, to the new city in chapter 21.
26. Or, "sat". Same word as in 3:21; and in Mt 19:28; 20:21; 25:31; 26:36; Act 2:3; Heb 1:3; 8:1. Used 46 times. GK *2767*.
27. That is, authority to judge as ones sitting on the thrones, and the work of judgment. On this word, see Jn 9:39.
28. Same word as in 6:9.
29. That is, executed. Used only here. GK *4284*. The root word is "axe". These were martyrs for Jesus.
30. The combination of "testimony of Jesus" and "word of God" is elsewhere only in 1:2, 9; 6:9.
31. Or, "even". There is a change of grammar here. Some think this gives further details about the souls who were beheaded, "even they who"; others, that it details a separate group of ones not executed, but who did not worship the beast.

A. Mt 8:29 B. Mt 25:35, brought in C. Rev 19:9 D. Col 2:23 E. Rev 18:8, strong F. Act 23:10, troop G. Jn 11:57 H. Rev 16:13 J. 2 Thes 2:9 K. Jam 5:19, err L. Rev 13:16 M. Rev 4:10 N. Rev 13:14 O. Mt 5:15 P. 2 Pet 3:16, other Q. Phil 4:12 R. Act 28:20 S. Heb 4:14, hold on to T. 1 Cor 7:27 U. Jn 20:19, locked V. Eph 1:13 W. Mt 16:21 X. Rev 20:11 Y. Jn 1:7 Z. 1 Cor 12:8

1D. And they[1] came-to-life[2] and reigned[3] with Christ *for a*[4] thousand years. °The[5] rest[6] *of* the dead did not come-to-life[7] until the thousand years were finished[A]. This *is* the first[8] resurrection[9]   5

    1E. Blessed[B] and holy[C] *is* the *one* having *a* part[D] in the first resurrection   6
    2E. The second death[10] does not have authority[E] over these, but they will be priests *of* God and *of* Christ, and will reign[F] with Him *for* the[11] thousand years

2D. And when the thousand years are finished[12], Satan will be released[G] from his prison[H]. °And he will go out to deceive[13] the nations in the four corners[J] *of* the earth— Gog and Magog[14]— to gather them together for the battle[15], whose number[16] *is* like the sand *of* the sea   7-8

    1E. And they went-up over the breadth[17] *of* the earth, and surrounded[18] the camp[19] *of* the saints[C] and[20] the city having been loved[21]   9
    2E. And fire came down from heaven[22] and devoured[K] them
    3E. And the devil, the *one* deceiving them, was thrown into the lake *of* fire[23] and sulphur— where both[24] the beast and the false prophet *are*[25]   10
    4E. And they will be tormented[L] *by* day and *by* night[26] forever and ever[27]

7B. And I saw *a* great white throne[28], and the *One* sitting on it— from Whose presence the earth fled[29], and the heaven, and *a* place was not found *for* them   11

    1C. And I saw the dead[30]— the great and the small[31]— standing before the throne[32]   12
    2C. And books[33] were opened. And another book was opened, which is *the book of* life[34]

        1D. And the dead were judged[M] from the *things* having been written in the books— according-to[35] their works
        2D. And the sea gave the dead in it, and death and Hades[36] gave the dead in them, and they were judged[M]— each *one*— according to their works   13

1. That is, the souls. Some think this means the martyrs and victors over the beast only. Others think these people represent all the saints, all the overcomers.
2. Or, "lived, became alive". Same word and tense as elsewhere only in v 5; 2:8; Rom 14:9; and as "became alive" in Lk 15:32; and "lived" in Rev 13:14; Act 26:5. Same word as "living, alive" in Lk 20:38; Jn 5:25; 11:25. This is the common word for "live, be alive", used 140 times. GK *2409*. Related to "life" in Rom 8:10. It is generally agreed that this word must mean the same thing in v 4 and v 5. These souls "live" in a sense in which the rest of the dead do not live. P-M thinks John means their bodies were resurrected and they reigned with Christ on earth in the 1000-year kingdom, where the OT promises are literally fulfilled on earth. The rest were not resurrected until later. This view thinks there is more than one phase to the resurrection. A-M thinks he means their souls "lived and reigned" with Christ in heaven and/or on earth (beginning at salvation) during this age. They enjoyed true life with God. The OT promises are spiritually fulfilled in the church, or forfeited due to unbelief. The rest did not live and reign with Christ during this time. Their souls did not enjoy life with God. This condition of existing as souls continues for both groups until the 1000 years (the church age) are finished, when both are resurrected and go on to their separate futures. This view thinks there is one resurrection for all at the end of the age. PST thinks this describes the future victory of the church during the millennium.
3. Same word as in v 6. A-M and PST place the thrones and reigning in heaven and/or spiritually on earth; P-M, on earth.
4. Some manuscripts say "the" {N}, as in v 3, 5, 6, 7. "The" means the one previously mentioned in v 2.
5. Some manuscripts say "And the rest..." {N}.
6. Some think this means all except the actual martyrs. Other believers and all non-believers await the end of the 1000 years. Others think it refers to the non-believers only. Same word as in 19:21.
7. Erasmus (see the Introduction) introduced a reading not found in any Greek manuscript, "live again". It was included in the KJV.
8. First implies at least a second, though no "second resurrection" is specifically mentioned as such. P-M thinks first/second refers to the physical resurrection of different groups. The first resurrection is of believers here, and the second is of unbelievers at v 12. A-M thinks first/second applies to two different kinds of resurrection for the same group. The first is the coming to life with Him in heaven after physical death or the spiritual coming to life at salvation (in either case, it is the life that the rest of the dead do not have); the second is the physical resurrection of the body.
9. Used only here and v 6 in this book. Used of physical resurrection, and of a spiritual resurrection to new life in Christ, Rom 6:5. On this word, see Act 24:15.
10. On the second death, see 2:11. It is the lake of fire, v 14.
11. Some manuscripts omit this word, {C}, so it says "*a* thousand years".
12. Same word as in v 3, 5.
13. A-M and PST think this is the deception mentioned in 16:14, before Christ returns. P-M thinks it is at the end of the future millennium which begins after Christ returns. Same word as in v 3, 10.
14. The precise meaning of these terms is uncertain. They are mentioned in Ezek 38-39 (see 38:2). Here, they refer to God's enemies among the nations in the four corners of the earth. Both are used only here in the NT. GK *1223*, *3408*.
15. Or, "war". On this word, see "war" in 12:7. A-M and PST think this is the battle of 19:19; P-M thinks it is a battle 1000 years after the one in 19:19.
16. Same grammar as in 13:12. Literally, "*of* whom their number *is* like...".
17. Or, "width". Elsewhere only as "width" in 21:16; Eph 3:18. GK *4424*.
18. Or, "encircled". Used only here. GK *3238*. Related word in Jn 10:24.
19. John may mean this in a general sense, as in Heb 13:11, 13. Or he may mean it in a military sense, the "army" or "battle line" (as in Heb 11:34), or the army "encampment, barracks" (as in Act 23:10, etc). Used 10 times. GK *4213*. Related to "throw up" in Lk 19:43.
20. Or, "even".
21. Or, "the Beloved city". Same word and grammar as in Col 3:12. Some think John means "the church"; others, "Jerusalem".
22. Some manuscripts say "from God out of heaven" {A}, as in 3:12; 21:2, 10. On "fire from heaven", see 13:13.
23. On this lake, see 19:20.
24. Or, "also". Some manuscripts omit this word {N}.
25. P-M thinks this reflects the sequential relationship between 19:20 and 20:10. They are separated by 1000 years. A-M and PST think this symbolic picture (20:1-10) ends at the same time as 19:11-21, so that 19:20 and 20:10 are talking about sequential events at the same time in history, Christ's return.
26. On this phrase, see 7:15.
27. This is an idiom, literally "into the ages *of* the ages". Same phrase as 1:6, 18; 4:9, 10; 5:13; 7:12; 10:6; 11:15; 15:7; 19:3; 22:5. A slightly different phrase is found only in 14:11. This word (GK *172*) is found in the idiom "forever" ("into the ages") and "forever and ever" ("into the ages *of* the ages") over 50 times. It is also rendered "age" and "world" (see Heb 1:2). It is used 122 times. Related to "eternal" in Mt 25:46.
28. This is the next step in the progression of heavenly scenes (see 11:19). Heaven and earth flee from the presence of the One sitting on the throne (they are described in 21:1 as having "passed away"). Used 47 times in this book, and 15 other times in the NT. GK *2585*. A-M and PST think this is the next chronological event after the return of Christ, and indicates that the visions in 20:1-10 are giving another view of the present age. P-M thinks this chronologically follows the 1000 years just described.
29. Same word as in 16:20, as is "found".
30. Some think this refers to the whole human race; others, to unbelievers only. A-M and PST think this is the last (and only) judgment, Mt 25:31-46; Rom 14:10; 2 Cor 5:10. P-M thinks it is the final phase of judgment, and refers to "the rest" of v 5, and all unbelievers.
31. Some manuscripts reverse these {K}, so that it says "the small and the great". On this phrase, see 19:5.
32. Instead of "the throne", some manuscripts say "God" {K}.
33. That is, books of deeds or works. Compare Dan 7:10; Mal 3:16; Mt 12:37.
34. Some think this implies the redeemed are present; others, that if the unbelievers are not found in this book, sentence is passed upon them in accordance with their works. On this book, see 3:5.
35. Or, "based on, in accordance with, in keeping with". GK *2848*. This phrase "according to works" is also in Rom 2:6; 2 Cor 11:15; 2 Tim 1:9; 4:14; 1 Pet 1:17; Rev 2:23; 18:6; 20:13. Works are the fruit by which the tree is known. They do not produce life, they evidence life.
36. On "death and Hades", see 1:18.

A. Rev 10:7 B. Rev 22:14 C. 1 Pet 1:16, holy D. Rom 11:25 E. Rev 6:8 F. Rev 19:6 G. Rev 20:3 H. Act 5:22 J. Mk 12:10 K. Mk 12:40 L. Rev 14:10 M. Mt 7:1

| Revelation 20:14 | 1018 | Verse |

    3C. And death and Hades were thrown into the lake *of* fire.[1] This is the second death[2]— the lake *of* fire[3]   14

    4C. And if anyone was not found having been written in the book *of* life, he was thrown into the lake *of* fire   15

8B. And I saw *a* new[A] heaven and *a* new earth, for the first heaven and the first earth passed-away[4]. And there is no longer *a* sea[5]   21:1

    1C. And I[6] saw the holy city— *the* new[A] Jerusalem— coming down out of heaven from God, having been prepared[B] like *a* bride having been adorned[C] *for* her husband   2

        1D. And I heard *a* loud voice from the throne[7], saying "Behold— the dwelling[8] *of* God *is* with mankind[D]   3

            1E. "And He will dwell[E] with them

            2E. "And they themselves will be His peoples[9]

            3E. "And God Himself with them will be their God[10]

            4E. "And He will wipe-away every tear[F] from their eyes[11]   4

            5E. "And there will no longer be death[G], nor will there be mourning[H] nor crying[J] nor pain[K] any longer, because[12] the first[L] *things* passed away"

        2D. And the *One* sitting on the throne said, "Behold— I am making all *things* new[A]"   5

        3D. And he[13] says[14], "Write, because these words are trustworthy[15] and true[M]"

        4D. And He said *to* me, "They[16] are done[17]   6

            1E. "I am the Alpha and the Omega,[18] the Beginning[N] and the End[O]

            2E. "*To* the *one* thirsting, **I** will give from the spring[19] *of* the water *of* life as-a-gift[20]. The *one* overcoming[P] will inherit[Q] these[21] *things*, and I will be God *to* him and **he** will be *a* son[R] *to* Me   7

            3E. "But *for* the cowardly[22] *ones*, and unbelieving[23] *ones*, and *ones* having been abominable[24], and murderers[S], and sexually-immoral[T] *ones*, and sorcerers[25], and idolaters, and all the liars[26]— their part[27] *will be* in the lake burning *with* fire and sulphur, which is the second death"   8

    2C. And one of the seven angels having the seven bowls being-full[U] *of* the seven last plagues came[28] and spoke with me, saying "Come, I will show[29] you the bride[30], the wife *of* the Lamb"   9

        1D. And he carried me away in *the* Spirit[31] to *a* great and high mountain, and showed[V] me the holy city Jerusalem,[32] coming down out of heaven from God   10

            1E. Having the glory[W] *of* God, the[33] brilliance[X] *of* it resembling[Y] *a* very-precious[Z] stone[AA] like *a* jasper[BB] stone, shining-like-crystal[34]   11

            2E. Having *a* great and high wall[35]   12

            3E. Having twelve gates, and twelve angels at the gates, and names having been inscribed— which are the names[36] *of* the twelve tribes[CC] *of* the sons[R] *of* Israel

                1F. Three gates from *the* east, and three gates from *the* north, and three gates from *the* south, and three gates from *the* west   13

1. Since there are no longer any "dead", death itself is vanquished. On this lake, see 19:20.
2. The saints experience the first, but not the second death, 2:11. Some think the first death is our physical death. Some holding the A-M view think the first death is our spiritual death to sin.
3. Some manuscripts omit "the lake *of* fire" {K}.
4. This is the final scene, a new heaven and earth. Some think "passed away", along with "fled" and "not found" in 20:11, refers to the complete disappearance and re-creation of this earth; others, to a renovation of it. Compare 2 Pet 3:10-13. Same word as in v 4.
5. Some think John means there is no sea on the new earth. Others think this looks backward to the passing away of the old sea, along with old earth and heaven.
6. Some manuscripts say "I, John" {K}.
7. Some manuscripts say "heaven" {N}.
8. Or, "tent, tabernacle". Same word as in 13:6. The related verb is next.
9. Or, "people". This word is plural here. Used 142 times, the plural is found elsewhere only in Lk 2:31; Act 4:25, 27; Rom 15:11; Rev 7:9; 10:11; 11:9; 17:15. GK *3295*. Some manuscripts have this word singular {B}. Here, it may mean "His people" (His group of people, as in the "people" of Israel, as perhaps in Act 4:27), or "His peoples" (people groups). Elsewhere this phrase, "they will be His people", uses the singular word, 2 Cor 6:16; Heb 8:10. The singular is found in Rev 5:9; 13:7; 14:6; 18:4.
10. Some manuscripts omit "their God" {C}, so that it says "and God Himself will be with them".
11. Same phrase in 7:17.
12. Some manuscripts omit this word {C}, so that it says "any longer—the first *things* passed away".
13. Or, "He says". Note the change of tense. Some think this indicates that this is the angel speaking. This angel also commanded John to write in 19:9; and a voice from heaven told him to write in 14:13. Others think the One on the throne continues to speak.
14. Some manuscripts say "said" {K}. Some manuscripts add "*to* me" {N}.
15. Or, "faithful". Same word as in 22:6; 1 Tim 1:15. Some manuscripts reverse the two {K}, so that it says "true and trustworthy". On this word, see "faithful" in Col 1:2.
16. That is, "all *things*" in v 5.
17. Or, "have taken place, come to pass, happened". These things stand as done. Same word as in 16:17, where it is singular. Some manuscripts have it singular here {N}. Not the same word as "finished" in 10:7. God speaks of these future events as if they have already happened. On this word, see Mt 6:10.
18. On "Alpha and Omega", see 1:8. This is the guarantee that they will come to pass.
19. Mentioned also in 7:17. On this word, see Jn 4:6.
20. Or, "freely". Same word as in 22:17.
21. Some manuscripts say "all these *things*" {K}.
22. Or, "fearful, timid", afraid to act. On this word, see "afraid" in Mk 4:40. This is referring to those who denied Christ under persecution, who did not endure to death (2:10), who "drew back" (Heb 10:39) out of fear.
23. Or, "unfaithful, faithless". On this word, see Mt 17:17.
24. Or, "detestable, vile, abhorrent". On this word, see "detesting" in Rom 2:22. Related to "abomination" in 17:4.
25. Elsewhere only in 22:15. GK *5761*. Related to the word in 9:21.
26. And who is a liar? See 1 Jn 2:4, 22; 5:10.
27. Or, "share". That is, their inheritance or place. Same word as Mt 24:51; Rev 20:6; 22:19. On this word, see Rom 11:25.
28. Some manuscripts add "*to* me" {K}.
29. Same language as in 17:1-3. This is one of those angels, linking this, and all the visions of chapters 19-22, to the scene of the bowl judgments. John is again given a guided tour to show him more detail about what has just been said.
30. Same word as in 18:23; 21:2; 22:17. GK *3811*. "Wife" is the same word as in 19:7. That is, the angel will show John the destiny of the bride, the place where she will be.
31. Or, "in spirit". Same phrase as in 17:3; 1:10.
32. The angel gives a general tour of the city in v 11-27. Compare 22:1. Some manuscripts say "the great and holy city Jerusalem" {N}.
33. Some manuscripts say "and the..." {N}.
34. Or, "being-clear-like-crystal". This verb is used only here. GK *3222*. Related to "crystal" in 22:1.
35. This symbolizes the security of the inhabitants living inside, and the exclusion of those not permitted to enter, 21:27; 22:15.
36. Some manuscripts omit "the names" {C}.

A. Heb 8:13 B. Mk 14:15 C. 1 Tim 2:9 D. Mt 4:4 E. Rev 7:15 F. Act 20:19 G. 2 Cor 11:23 H. Jam 4:9 J. Heb 5:7, outcry K. Col 4:13 L. 1 Cor 15:3 M. Jn 7:28 N. Col 1:18 O. Rom 10:4 P. Rev 2:7 Q. Gal 4:30 R. Gal 3:7 S. Act 7:52 T. 1 Cor 5:9 U. Rev 4:6 V. Rev 4:1 W. 2 Pet 2:10 X. Phil 2:15, lights Y. Rev 1:13 Z. 2 Pet 1:4 AA. Mk 16:3 BB. Rev 4:3 CC. Rev 1:7

	4E. And the wall *of* the city has[1] twelve foundations[A], and on them *are the* twelve[2] names *of* the twelve apostles[B] *of* the Lamb	14
	5E. And the *one* speaking with me had *a* golden measuring[3] rod[C], in order that he might measure the city and its gates and its wall	15
	1F. And the city lies square— indeed its length *is* as much as also[4] the width	16
	2F. And he measured the city *with* the rod— a-matter-of twelve thousand stades[5]. Its length and width and height are equal[D]	
	3F. And he measured its wall— *a* hundred forty four cubits[6] (*a* human's[E] measure, which is *an* angel's [also])[7]	17
	6E. And the material[8] *of* its wall *is* jasper, and the city *is* pure gold resembling pure[9] glass	18
	7E. The[10] foundations[A] *of* the wall *of* the city have been adorned[11] *with* every precious[F] stone[G]	19
	1F. The first foundation *is* jasper[12]; the second, sapphire; the third, chalcedony; the fourth, emerald[13]; *the fifth, sardonyx; the sixth, carnelian[14]; the seventh, chrysolite; the eighth, beryl; the ninth, topaz; the tenth, chrysoprase; the eleventh, hyacinth[15]; the twelfth, amethyst	20
	8E. And the twelve gates *are* twelve pearls[H]— individually, each one *of* the gates was from one pearl	21
	9E. And the wide-road[I] *of* the city *is* pure gold, like transparent glass	
	10E. And I did not see *a* temple[K] in it, for its temple *is* the Lord God Almighty[L] and the Lamb[16]	22
	11E. And the city has no need[M] *of* the sun nor the moon, in order that they might shine[17] *on* it. For the glory[N] *of* God illuminated[O] it, and its lamp[P] *is* the Lamb	23
	12E. And the nations[18] will[19] walk[Q] by its light	24
	13E. And the kings *of* the earth bring their glory[N] into it. *And its gates will never be shut[R] *by* day[20]— for night will not exist[S] there	25
	1F. And they will bring the glory[N] and the honor[T] *of* the nations into it	26
	2F. And every defiled[U] *thing*, and the *one* doing abomination[21] and falsehood[V], will never enter into it— but only the *ones* having been written in the Lamb's book *of* life[22]	27
2D. And[23] he showed[W] me *a* river[24] *of* the water *of* life, shining[25] like crystal[X], proceeding out from the throne *of* God and *of* the Lamb, *in* the middle *of* its wide-road[26]	22:1 2
	1E. And on this *side* and on that *side*[27] *of* the river *is a* tree *of* life[28] producing[Y] twelve fruits[Z], yielding[AA] its fruit[Z] every month[29]. And the leaves *of* the tree *are* for the service[30] *of* the nations[31]	
	2E. And there will[32] no longer be any accursed[33] *thing*	3
	3E. And the throne *of* God and *of* the Lamb will be in it	
	4E. And His slaves[BB] will serve[34] Him, *and see His face[35]	4
	1F. And His name *will be* on their foreheads	
	2F. And[36] there will be no more night.[37] And they do[38] not have *a* need[M] *of* the light *of a* lamp and *the* light *of the* sun, because the Lord God will give-light[39] upon them	5

1. This is a participle, "*is* having".
2. Some manuscripts omit this word {K}.
3. Same word as "measure" in v 17. On this word, see "measure" in Jn 3:34. Some manuscripts omit this word {N}.
4. Some manuscripts omit this word {C}.
5. On this measure of distance, see 14:20. Here it is equivalent to about 1380 miles or 2220 kilometers.
6. A cubit is the length of a forearm from the elbow to the tip of the middle finger, about 18 inches or .46 meters. The word means "forearm". So either the height or the width of the wall was about 216 feet or 66 meters. Elsewhere only in Mt 6:27; Lk 12:25; Jn 21:8. GK *4388*.
7. John could mean that the angel's forearm was the same measure, or that the angel was using mankind's measure. In any case, John wants us to know he is using standard measuring terms.
8. The meaning of this word is uncertain. John may mean "the material of which the wall was made". Or, "the material built into the wall", an inlay or a trim or coping. Used only here. GK *1908*. One of the foundations is also adorned with jasper, v 19.
9. This is the same word just used with gold. John may mean "clear", which he clearly says in v 21. Or he may mean "clean, without impurity, bright". On this word, see "clean" in Tit 1:15.
10. Some manuscripts say "And the..." {N}.
11. Same word as in v 2. It is a participle, "*are* having been adorned".
12. On this word, see 4:3. The next two gems are mentioned only here.
13. Used only here. GK *5040*. Related to the word in 4:3, of the rainbow around the throne.
14. The previous gem is mentioned only here, but see 4:3 on this one.
15. The previous four gems are mentioned only here, as is the next. This one is related to the word in 9:17. GK *5611*.
16. God is worshiped in person, face to face, not in a separate or special place.
17. The sun and moon are not needed for this purpose. On this word, see Phil 2:15.
18. The identity of these nations is uncertain. Perhaps the peoples (21:3) of the redeemed live outside of the city, as well as inside it. John does not explicitly say where the people live. From this verse it is clear that there are people outside the city, and from v 26, that they come and go. From 22:3 it is clear that His people serve Him in the city. Beyond this, nothing is stated. Some manuscripts add "*of* the *ones* saved" {K}.
19. Note that as John closes this part of the tour, he changes from present tense physical description to statements of knowledge using the future tense. Compare 22:3.
20. That is, shut during the daytime, in anticipation of the darkness of night, because there will be no night.
21. On this word, see 17:4. Related to the word in 21:8.
22. On this book, see 3:5.
23. Now the angel turns from the city-tour point of view to things of special importance to believers.
24. Some manuscripts say "the pure river" {N}.
25. Or, "bright, brilliant, radiant". Some think John means "clear", the light shining through it. Same word as in Lk 23:11; Act 10:30; Jam 2:2, 3; Rev 15:6; 18:14; 19:8. Elsewhere only as "bright" in Rev 22:16. GK *3287*. Related to "shine" in 2 Cor 4:6; "brightness" in Act 26:13; and "radiantly" in Lk 16:19.
26. On this word, see Lk 14:21. Some make this phrase the beginning of the next sentence, "In the middle...".
27. This is an idiom, literally, "from here (the near side on which he stood) and from there (the far side)", pointing to both with the hands. Compare the perspective in Jn 19:18. "From here" is GK *1949*, used 10 times. "From there" is GK *1696*, used 37 times.
28. On "tree of life", see 2:7.
29. Some think this tree yields all twelve fruits every month. Others, a different fruit each month. The description in v 2 is similar to Ezek 47:7-12. This is more literally, "according to each month". Compare the similar idiom "each day" in Heb 3:13.
30. Or, "cure, treatment, care, healing". This word was used of "service, care, attendance upon" parents, children, masters, the sick, the gods, animals, plants, buildings, graves, etc. Elsewhere only as "cure" in Lk 9:11; and "body of servants" (the ones performing the service) in Lk 12:42. GK *2542*. Related to "servant" in Heb 3:5; and "cure" in Mt 8:7. Here, John may mean the "curing, healing" of the nations; or, he may be referring to service of some other kind. It is rendered in this neutral way to reflect both possibilities.
31. John could mean "*by* the nations"; or, "*for* the nations".
32. Note that as in 21:24, John shifts to the future tense as he closes this part of the tour.
33. Or, "cursed". That is, a thing under a curse. Used only here. GK *2873*. Related to "curse" in Mt 26:74.
34. Or, "worship". On this word, see "worship" in Heb 12:28. Not related to "service" in v 2.
35. As Jesus promised in Mt 5:8. Note Heb 12:14.
36. Note that this is stated in 21:23-25 from the point of view of the city and those living outside it. Here it is stated again from the point of view of His slaves living in the city.
37. Instead of "be no more night", some manuscripts say "be no night there" {N}.
38. Some manuscripts say "will" {N}.
39. Same word as "illuminated" in 21:23. On this word, see "enlightened" in Heb 6:4.

A. 1 Tim 6:19 B. 1 Cor 12:28 C. Mk 15:36, stick D. Phil 2:6 E. Mt 4:4, mankind F. 2 Pet 1:4 G. Mk 16:3 H. Mt 13:45 J. Lk 14:21 K. Rev 11:1 L. Rev 1:8 M. Tit 3:14 N. 2 Pet 2:10 O. Heb 6:4, enlightened P. Lk 11:34 Q. Heb 13:9 R. Jn 20:19, locked S. Mt 26:26, is T. 1 Tim 5:17 U. Heb 10:29 V. Rev 14:5 W. Rev 4:1 X. Rev 4:6 Y. Rev 13:13, does Z. Mt 7:16 AA. Mt 16:27, render BB. Rev 1:1

Revelation 22:6   1022   Verse

        3F. And they will reign[1] forever and ever[A]

3A. And he[2] said *to* me, "These words[B] *are* trustworthy and true.[3] And the Lord, the God *of* the spirits[4] *of* the prophets, sent-forth His angel[5] to show His slaves *the things* which must take place quickly[6]   6

    1B. "And[7] behold— I[8] am coming quickly.[9] Blessed[C] *is* the *one* keeping[D] the words[B] *of* the prophecy *of* this book[10]"   7

4A. And I, John,[11] *am* the *one* hearing and seeing[12] these *things*. And when I heard and saw, I fell to worship[13] in front of the feet *of* the angel[14] showing me these *things*   8

    1B. And he says *to* me, "See *that you* not do it.[15] I[16] am *a* fellow-slave[E] *of* you and *of* your brothers[F] the prophets, and *of* the *ones* keeping[D] the words[B] *of* this book. Give-worship *to* God"   9

5A. And He[17] says *to* me, "Do not seal[G] the words *of* the prophecy *of* this book, for the time is near[18]   10

    1B. "Let the *one* doing-unrighteousness[19] still do-unrighteousness. And let the filthy[20] *one* still be-filthy. And let the righteous[H] *one* still do[J] righteousness[21]. And let the holy[K] *one* still be made-holy[22]   11
    2B. "Behold[23]— I am coming quickly. And My recompense[24] *is* with Me— to render[25] to each *one* as his work[L] is[26]. "I *am* the Alpha and the Omega,[27] the First and the Last,[28] the Beginning[M] and the End[29]   12
                                                                                                                13

        1C. "Blessed[30] *are* the *ones* washing[N] their robes[31] so that   14

            1D. "Their right[32] over the tree *of* life will exist[33]
            2D. "And they may enter into the city *by* the gates[34]

        2C. "Outside[35] *are* the dogs[36] and the sorcerers[O], and the sexually-immoral[P] *ones*, and the murderers[Q], and the idolaters, and everyone loving[R] and doing[J] falsehood[37]   15

    3B. "**I**, Jesus, sent My angel to testify[S] these *things* to you[38] for[39] the churches[40]. **I** am the Root[41] and the Offspring[42] *of* David, the bright Morning Star[43]   16

        1C. "And[44] the Spirit and the bride[45] say, "Come"   17
        2C. "And let the *one* hearing say, "Come"[46]
        3C. "And let the *one* thirsting, come[47]

1. Same word as in 20:4, where they reign 1000 years. On this word, see 19:6.
2. This seems to be the angel who has been with John since 21:9 (21:9, 10, 15, 16, 17; 22:1), whom John falls to worship in v 8.
3. This was also said in 21:5.
4. The angel could mean the prophets' human spirit; or, their spiritual gift or manifestation (as this word is used in 1 Cor 14:12). In other words, the God who gives prophecies to the prophets sent His angel to reveal these things. Some manuscripts say "the God *of* the holy prophets" {N}.
5. That is, the one speaking here. Compare 1:1. Note how many similarities there are between v 6-7 and 1:1-3.
6. This entire phrase "to show... quickly" is exactly the same as in 1:1. This is the conclusion of the whole book, and restates the purpose of it.
7. Some manuscripts omit this word {N}.
8. Some think Christ is speaking here, interjecting this statement. Others think the angel of v 6 is still speaking, reporting what Christ said, which is what he was sent to do. Compare 16:15 and 22:10, 12.
9. Or, "soon". Same word as in Rev 2:16; 3:11; 11:14; 22:12, 20; Mt 5:25; 28:7, 8; Lk 15:22; Jn 11:29. Elsewhere only as "soon" in Mk 9:39; and "quick" in Jam 1:19. GK *5444*. Related to "quickly" in v 6.
10. A similar blessing was given in 1:3. This is the first time the completed book is referred to since 1:3.
11. This is the second "I, John" of the book, the other being in 1:9. "John" is also in 1:1, 4.
12. Same word as in 1:11. Some manuscripts say "seeing and hearing" {N}.
13. Same word as in 19:10, where John fell to worship another of the seven angels having the bowls. See there on the meaning. If the angel stated the words in v 7 on behalf of the One who sent him (v 6), John's confusion is understandable.
14. That is, the angel in v 6.
15. Same phrase as in 19:10.
16. Some manuscripts say "For I am..." {K}.
17. Or, "he". Some think that the speaker is still the angel of v 9, reporting the words of Christ, carrying out his assigned task, as explained in v 16. Others think Christ Himself is now speaking, based on what follows, giving His conclusion to the book. As with 22:7, the result is the same either way. These are the words of Christ, either directly spoken or reported by another. This issue regarding the speaker recurs until v 20.
18. This same phrase, "the time is near", is in 1:3.
19. Or, "doing wrong". Related to "righteousness" later, and rendered this way to show this. On this word, see "wronged" in Act 7:24.
20. That is, moral filth, the opposite of "holy" later in the verse. Elsewhere only in Jam 2:2. GK *4865*. Related to the verb next; "filthiness" in Jam 1:21; and "dirt" in 1 Pet 3:21.
21. On this word, see Rom 1:17. Some manuscripts say "be righteous" {N}.
22. In other words, do what you are going to do. Make your choices in life. I will render back to you accordingly, v 12. This is a serious warning to follow Christ. On this word, see "sanctify" in Heb 10:29.
23. Some manuscripts say "And behold..." {N}.
24. This word means "wages, pay". When positive, it is "a reward"; when negative, "a penalty, punishment". In this case, Jesus returns with both reward and punishment for the two groups in the previous verse, based on their work, as described in v 14-15. Used 29 times. GK *3635*.
25. Or, "give back", whether a reward or punishment. Same word as 18:6; Mt 16:27. GK *625*.
26. Some manuscripts say "shall be" {N}.
27. Christ says this here, whereas in 1:8 it is the Father. It is God's guarantee that what He is saying will occur.
28. On this phrase, see 1:17. Used three times of Jesus.
29. This phrase was used of the Father in 21:6. On this word, see Rom 10:4. Some manuscripts reverse these phrases, so that it says "the Beginning and the End, the First and the Last" {N}.
30. This is the seventh beatitude in Revelation. See 1:3; 14:13; 16:15; 19:9; 20:6; 22:7, 14. On this word, see Lk 6:20.
31. That is, "in the blood of the Lamb", as in 7:14, which uses this same phrase. Instead of "washing their robes", some manuscripts say "doing His commandments" {A}.
32. Or, "authority". Same word as in 1 Cor 8:9. This is the same phrase as "authority over" in 2:26; 6:8; 11:6; 13:7; 14:18; 16:9. The same concept occurs in 2:7.
33. Or, "be". GK *1639*. In other words, in order that they will have the right to eat from the tree of life. This right exists for those who have washed their robes in His blood. Same word as in 4:11; 21:25; Mt 6:30; Lk 12:28; 23:12; Act 17:28; Rom 13:1. On this word, see "is" in Mt 26:26. On "tree of life", see v 2.
34. Only those written in the Lamb's book can enter, 21:27.
35. Some manuscripts say "For outside..." {K}.
36. That is, the morally impure. Elsewhere only in Mt 7:6; Lk 16:21; Phil 3:2; 2 Pet 2:22. GK *3264*.
37. Or, "*a* lie". On this word, see 14:5.
38. This word is plural. Jesus, through the angel He sent, through John (1:1), is testifying to us all.
39. Some manuscripts say "in" {N}.
40. This word means "church, congregation, assembly". Used 114 times. GK *1711*.
41. Same statement as in 5:5. Jesus is called the Root of Jesse in Rom 15:12. Some think this means the root originating with David, springing up from David, which grew to become the Messiah, Isa 11:1; others, the ancestor (referring to His pre-existence as God) from which David grew. On this word, see Heb 12:15.
42. Or, "Descendant". Used only here of Christ. On this word, see "kind" in 1 Cor 12:28.
43. The morning star is mentioned in 2:28. On this word, see 6:13. Same word as His "star" in Mt 2:2. There is a different word in 2 Pet 1:19. Some manuscripts say "the Bright and Morning Star" {K}. Jesus is the precursor of the new day, visible before sunrise. He is visible now, prior to the new day He brings at His return.
44. Some think Jesus is still speaking, quoting two others witnesses who say "Come". Others think John or the angel is speaking.
45. That is, His church. They are saying "Come, Lord Jesus", or, "Come to Jesus" (addressing unbelievers).
46. He is exhorting those hearing this book read either to invite others to Christ, or to say "Come, Lord Jesus".
47. Here, He clearly means "come to Christ, come to the city, come to the living water".

A. Rev 20:10 B. 1 Cor 12:8 C. Rev 22:14 D. Rev 1:3 E. Rev 19:10 F. Act 16:40 G. Eph 1:13 H. Rom 1:17 J. Rev 13:13 K. 1 Pet 1:16 L. Mt 26:10 M. Col 1:18 N. Rev 7:14 O. Rev 21:8 P. 1 Cor 5:9 Q. Act 7:52 R. Jn 21:15, affectionately love S. Jn 1:7

| Revelation 22:18 | 1024 | Verse |

    4C. "Let[1] the *one* wanting[2], take[3] *the* water *of* life as-a-gift[4]

 4B. "**I** testify[5] *to* everyone hearing the words *of* the prophecy *of* this book[6]—   18

    1C. "If anyone adds[A] to them,[7] God will add[8] to him the plagues[B] having been written in this book
    2C. "And if anyone takes-away[C] from the words *of* the book *of* this prophecy, God will take[C] his part[9]   19
        away-from[10] the tree[11] *of* life[12], and out-from the holy city— the *ones* having been written in this book

 5B. "The *One*[13] testifying these *things* says, "Yes, I am coming[14] quickly"   20

Amen.[15] Come,[16] Lord Jesus. °The grace *of* the Lord Jesus[17] *be* with all[18]   21

1. Some manuscripts say "And let..." {K}.
2. Or, "wishing, desiring, being willing". On this word, see "willing" in Jn 7:17.
3. Or, "receive". On this word, see Rom 7:8.
4. Or, "freely, without payment". Same word as in 21:6. On this word, see "without a reason" in Gal 2:21.
5. Note that "I" is emphatic, as in v 16. Some think this is John speaking, since it is he who "testifies" (1:2). Others think Christ continues to speak. Others think the angel He sent to "testify" (v 16) is speaking. Some manuscripts say "For I testify" {K}.
6. The book opens with a blessing on those who read, hear, and keep it, 1:3. It ends with this curse on any who would change its message.
7. That is, to the words of this book, Revelation. Some think this is addressed to the copiers of the book, the scribes; others, to the readers who might change or ignore the application of the book; others, to teachers or prophets who might want to add other revelations to it, or delete or dilute part of it.
8. That is, apply to such a person's case in particular.
9. Or, "share". Same word as in 20:6; 21:8, on which see Rom 11:25.
10. John uses two different prepositions here, which are rendered "away from" (GK *608*) and "out from" (GK *1666*) to display this.
11. Some manuscripts say "book" {K}. When Erasmus (see the Introduction) printed his Greek NT, the last six verses of Revelation were missing from the single Greek manuscript he had. So he translated them into Greek from the Latin Vulgate. When his Greek text was later used by the authors of the King James Version in 1611, "book" was included. In this case, as with some of the other variants marked {K}, the reading is not found in any Greek manuscript.
12. On this tree, see 2:7.
13. Some think this is the One in v 16, 18, "I, Jesus"; others, the angel He sent to testify, v 16.
14. This is the seventh occurrence of "I am coming". See 2:5, 16; 3:11; 16:15; 22:7, 12, 20.
15. This is John's conclusion to the book.
16. Some manuscripts say "Yes, come..." {N}.
17. Some manuscripts say "our Lord Jesus Christ" {A}.
18. Some manuscripts say "with you all"; others, "with the saints"; others, "with all the saints" {B}. Some manuscripts add "amen" {B}.

A. Lk 10:30, laid on B. Rev 13:3, wound C. Mk 14:47, took off

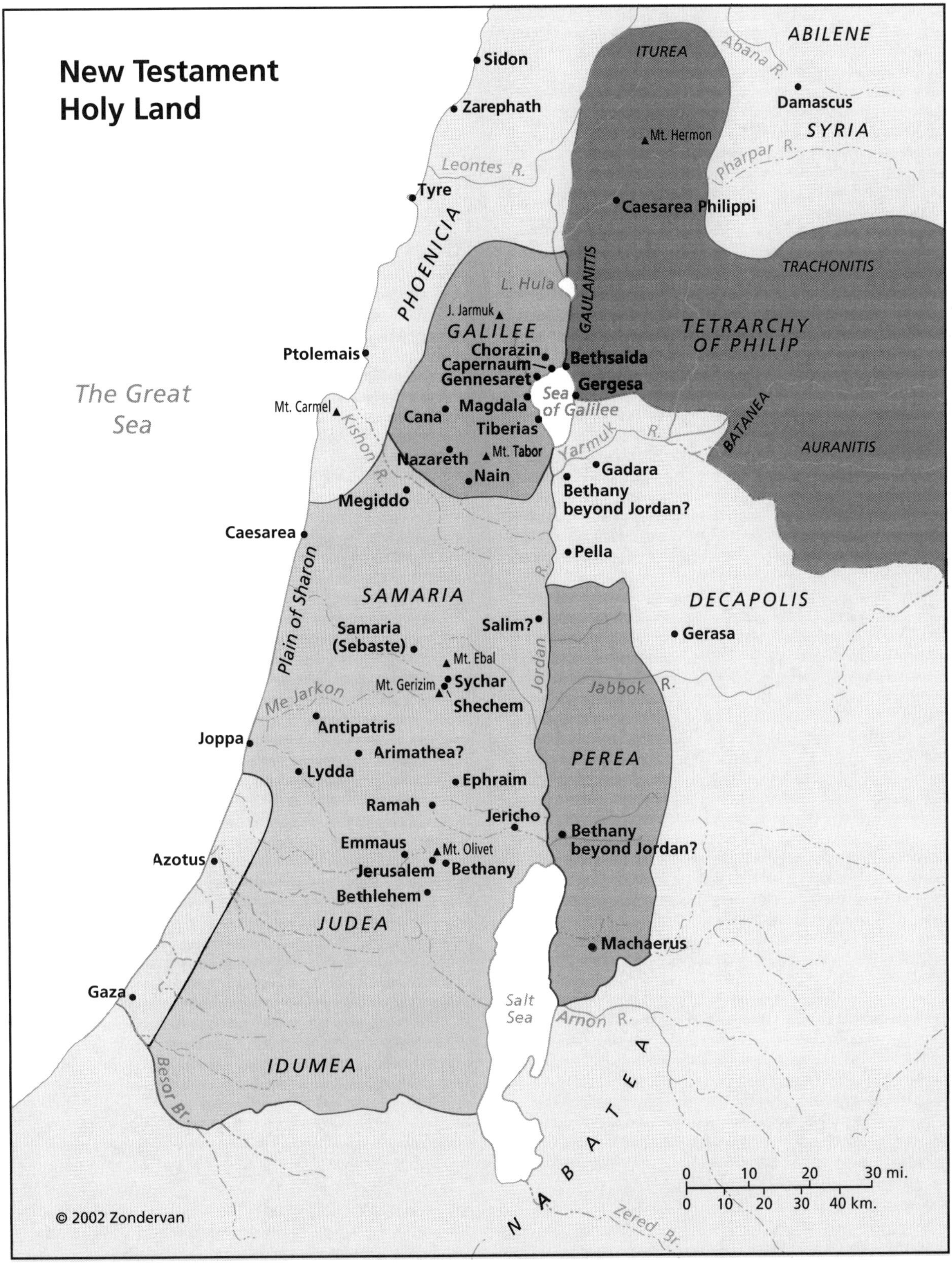
New Testament
Holy Land
Sidon
Zarephath
Tyre
Leontes R.
PHOENICIA
ITUREA
ABILENE
Abana R.
Damascus
SYRIA
Mt. Hermon
Pharpar R.
Caesarea Philippi
TRACHONITIS
GAULANITIS
L. Hula
J. Jarmuk
GALILEE
TETRARCHY
OF PHILIP
Ptolemais
Chorazin
Capernaum
Gennesaret
Bethsaida
Gergesa
The Great
Sea
Mt. Carmel
Kishon R.
Cana
Magdala
Tiberias
Sea
of Galilee
Yarmuk R.
BATANEA
AURANITIS
Nazareth
Mt. Tabor
Nain
Gadara
Megiddo
Bethany
beyond Jordan?
Caesarea
Pella
Plain of Sharon
SAMARIA
Jordan R.
DECAPOLIS
Salim?
Gerasa
Samaria
(Sebaste)
Mt. Ebal
Mt. Gerizim
Sychar
Shechem
Me Jarkon
Jabbok R.
Antipatris
Joppa
Arimathea?
PEREA
Lydda
Ephraim
Ramah
Jericho
Bethany
beyond Jordan?
Emmaus
Mt. Olivet
Azotus
Jerusalem
Bethany
Bethlehem
JUDEA
Machaerus
Gaza
Salt
Sea
Arnon R.
IDUMEA
Besor Br.
NABATEA
Zered Br.
0 10 20 30 mi.
0 10 20 30 40 km.
© 2002 Zondervan

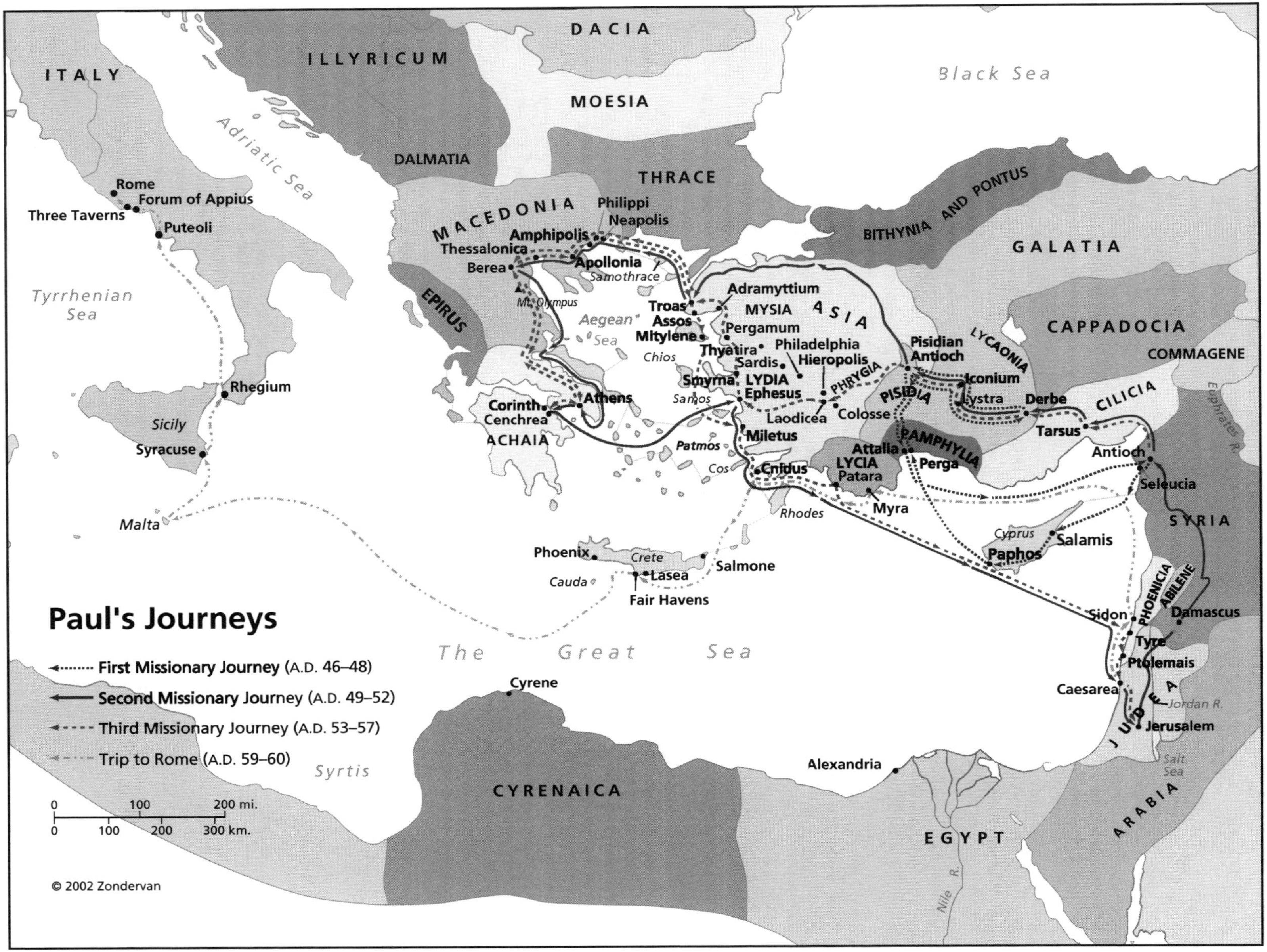
Paul's Journeys
First Missionary Journey (A.D. 46–48)
Second Missionary Journey (A.D. 49–52)
Third Missionary Journey (A.D. 53–57)
Trip to Rome (A.D. 59–60)
0 100 200 mi.
0 100 200 300 km.
© 2002 Zondervan
ITALY
ILLYRICUM
DACIA
MOESIA
DALMATIA
THRACE
MACEDONIA
EPIRUS
ACHAIA
BITHYNIA AND PONTUS
GALATIA
CAPPADOCIA
COMMAGENE
ASIA
MYSIA
LYDIA
PHRYGIA
PISIDIA
LYCAONIA
PAMPHYLIA
LYCIA
CILICIA
SYRIA
PHOENICIA
ABILENE
JUDEA
ARABIA
EGYPT
CYRENAICA
Black Sea
Adriatic Sea
Tyrrhenian Sea
Aegean Sea
The Great Sea
Syrtis
Euphrates R.
Jordan R.
Nile R.
Salt Sea
Rome
Forum of Appius
Three Taverns
Puteoli
Rhegium
Sicily
Syracuse
Malta
Philippi
Neapolis
Amphipolis
Thessalonica
Apollonia
Berea
Samothrace
Mt. Olympus
Corinth
Cenchrea
Athens
Troas
Assos
Mitylene
Chios
Samos
Patmos
Cos
Rhodes
Adramyttium
Pergamum
Thyatira
Sardis
Philadelphia
Hieropolis
Smyrna
Ephesus
Laodicea
Colosse
Miletus
Cnidus
Patara
Myra
Attalia
Perga
Pisidian Antioch
Iconium
Lystra
Derbe
Tarsus
Antioch
Seleucia
Cyprus
Salamis
Paphos
Crete
Phoenix
Cauda
Lasea
Fair Havens
Salmone
Sidon
Tyre
Ptolemais
Caesarea
Damascus
Jerusalem
Alexandria
Cyrene

We want to hear from you. Please send your comments about this book to us in care of the address below. Thank you.

ZONDERVAN™

GRAND RAPIDS, MICHIGAN 49530 USA
WWW.ZONDERVAN.COM